Jona

April 8, 2007

Happy Easter.

Mom

Can I play
in the gym.

BEST.
EMU

Boys BIBLE

THE ULTIMATE MANUAL

Boys
BIBLE
THE ULTIMATE MANUAL

NEW INTERNATIONAL VERSION

GENERAL EDITOR

RICK OSBORNE

zonderkidz

The children's group of Zondervan

www.zonderkidz.com

Requests for information should be addressed to:
Grand Rapids, Michigan 49530

The Holy Bible, New International Version®
Copyright © 1973, 1978, 1984 by International Bible Society

2:52 Boys' Bible
Copyright © 2002 by Zondervan
All rights reserved

Published by Zondervan
Grand Rapids, Michigan 49530

Library of Congress Catalog Card Number 2002103715

07 08 09 10 • 10 9 8 7

You will be pleased to know that a portion of the purchase price of your new NIV® Bible has been provided to International Bible Society to help spread the gospel of Jesus Christ around the world!

Table of Contents

NIV Preface

THE NEW INTERNATIONAL VERSION is a completely new translation of the Holy Bible made by over a hundred scholars working directly from the best available Hebrew, Aramaic and Greek texts. It had its beginning in 1965 when, after several years of exploratory study by committees from the Christian Reformed Church and the National Association of Evangelicals, a group of scholars met at Palos Heights, Illinois, and concurred in the need for a new translation of the Bible in contemporary English. This group, though not made up of official church representatives, was transdenominational. Its conclusion was endorsed by a large number of leaders from many denominations who met in Chicago in 1966.

Responsibility for the new version was delegated by the Palos Heights group to a self-governing body of fifteen, the Committee on Bible Translation, composed for the most part of biblical scholars from colleges, universities and seminaries. In 1967 the New York Bible Society (now the International Bible Society) generously undertook the financial sponsorship of the project—a sponsorship that made it possible to enlist the help of many distinguished scholars. The fact that participants from the United States, Great Britain, Canada, Australia and New Zealand worked together gave the project its inter-national scope. That they were from many denominations—including Anglican, Assemblies of God, Baptist, Brethren, Christian Reformed, Church of Christ, Evangelical Free, Lutheran, Mennonite, Methodist, Nazarene, Presbyterian, Wesleyan and other churches—helped to safeguard the translation from sectarian bias.

How it was made helps to give the New International Version its distinctiveness. The translation of each book was assigned to a team of scholars. Next, one of the Intermediate Editorial Committees revised the initial translation, with constant reference to the Hebrew, Aramaic or Greek. Their work then went to one of the General Editorial Committees, which checked it in detail and made another thorough revision. This revision in turn was carefully reviewed by the Committee on Bible Translation, which made further changes and then released the final version for publication. In this way the entire Bible underwent three revisions, during each of which the translation was examined for its faithfulness to the original languages and for its English style.

All this involved many thousands of hours of research and discussion regarding the meaning of the texts and the precise way of putting them into English. It may well be that no other translation has been made by a more thorough process of review and revision from committee to committee than this one.

From the beginning of the project, the Committee on Bible Translation held to certain goals for the New International Version: that it would be an accurate translation and one that would have clarity and literary quality and so prove suitable for public and private reading, teaching, preaching, memorizing and liturgical use. The Committee also sought to preserve some measure of continuity with the long tradition of translating the Scriptures into English.

In working toward these goals, the translators were united in their commitment to the authority and infallibility of the Bible as God's Word in written form. They believe that it contains the divine answer to the deepest needs of humanity, that it sheds unique light on our path in a dark world, and that it sets forth the way to our eternal well-being.

The first concern of the translators has been the accuracy of the translation and its fidelity to the thought of the biblical writers. They have weighed the significance of the lexical and grammatical details of the Hebrew, Aramaic and Greek texts. At the same time, they have striven for more than a word-for-word translation. Because thought patterns and syntax differ from language to language, faithful communication of the meaning of the writers of the Bible demands frequent modifications in sentence structure and constant regard for the contextual meanings of words.

A sensitive feeling for style does not always accompany scholarship. Accordingly the Committee on Bible Translation submitted the developing version to a number of stylistic consultants. Two of them read every book of both Old and New Testaments twice—once before and once after the last major revision—and made invaluable suggestions. Samples of the translation were tested for clarity and ease of reading by various kinds of people—young and old, highly educated and less well educated, ministers and laymen.

Concern for clear and natural English—that the New International Version should be idiomatic but not idiosyncratic, contemporary but not dated—motivated the translators and consultants. At the same time, they tried to reflect the differing styles of the biblical writers. In view of the international use of English, the translators sought to avoid obvious Americanisms on the one hand and obvious Anglicisms on the other. A British edition reflects the comparatively few differences of significant idiom and of spelling.

As for the traditional pronouns "thou," "thee" and "thine" in reference to the Deity, the translators judged that to use these archaisms (along with the old verb forms such as "doest," "wouldest" and "hadst") would violate accuracy in translation. Neither Hebrew, Aramaic nor Greek uses special pronouns for the persons of the Godhead. A present-day translation is not enhanced by forms that in the time of the King James Version were used in everyday speech, whether referring to God or man.

For the Old Testament the standard Hebrew text, the Masoretic Text as published in the latest editions of *Biblia Hebraica*, was used throughout. The Dead Sea Scrolls contain material bearing on an earlier stage of the Hebrew text. They were consulted, as were the Samaritan Pentateuch and the ancient scribal traditions relating to textual changes. Sometimes a variant Hebrew reading in the margin of the Masoretic Text was followed instead of the text itself. Such instances, being variants within the Masoretic tradition, are not specified by footnotes. In rare cases, words in the consonantal text were divided differently from the way they appear in the Masoretic Text. Footnotes indicate this. The translators also consulted the more important early versions—the Septuagint; Aquila, Symmachus and Theodotion; the Vulgate; the Syriac Peshitta; the Targums; and for the Psalms the *Juxta Hebraica* of Jerome. Readings from these versions were occasionally followed where the Masoretic Text seemed doubtful and where accepted principles of textual criticism showed that one or more of these textual witnesses appeared to provide the correct reading. Such instances are footnoted. Sometimes vowel letters and vowel signs did not, in the judgment of the translators, represent the correct vowels for the original consonantal text. Accordingly some words were read with a different set of vowels. These instances are usually not indicated by footnotes.

The Greek text used in translating the New Testament was an eclectic one. No other piece of ancient literature has such an abundance of manuscript witnesses as does the New Testament. Where existing manuscripts differ, the translators made their choice of readings according to accepted principles of New Testament textual criticism. Footnotes call attention to places where there was uncertainty about what the original text was. The best current printed texts of the Greek New Testament were used.

There is a sense in which the work of translation is never wholly finished. This applies to all great literature and uniquely so to the Bible. In 1973 the New Testament in the New International Version was published. Since then, suggestions for corrections and revisions have been received from various sources. The Committee on Bible Translation carefully considered the suggestions and adopted a number of them. These were incorporated in the first printing of the entire Bible in 1978. Additional revisions were made by the Committee on Bible Translation in 1983 and appear in printings after that date.

As in other ancient documents, the precise meaning of the biblical texts is sometimes uncertain. This is more often the case with the Hebrew and Aramaic texts than with the Greek text. Although archaeological and linguistic discoveries in this century aid in understanding difficult passages, some uncertainties remain. The more significant of these have been called to the reader's attention in the footnotes.

In regard to the divine name *YHWH*, commonly referred to as the *Tetragrammaton*, the translators adopted the device used in most English versions of rendering that name as "Lord" in capital letters to distinguish it from *Adonai*, another Hebrew word rendered "Lord," for which small letters are used. Wherever the two names stand together in the Old Testament as a compound name of God, they are rendered "Sovereign Lord."

Because for most readers today the phrases "the Lord of hosts" and "God of hosts" have little meaning, this version renders them "the Lord Almighty" and "God Almighty." These renderings convey the sense of the Hebrew, namely, "he who is sovereign over all the 'hosts' (powers) in heaven and on earth, especially over the 'hosts' (armies) of Israel." For readers unacquainted with Hebrew this does not make clear the distinction between *Sabaoth* ("hosts" or "Almighty") and *Shaddai* (which can also be translated "Almighty"), but the latter occurs infrequently and is always footnoted. When *Adonai* and *YHWH Sabaoth* occur together, they are rendered "the Lord, the LORD Almighty."

As for other proper nouns, the familiar spellings of the King James Version are generally retained. Names traditionally spelled with "ch," except where it is final, are usually spelled in this translation with "k" or "c," since the biblical languages do not have the sound that "ch" frequently indicates in English—for example, in *chant*. For well-known names such as Zechariah, however, the traditional spelling has been retained. Variation in the spelling of names in the original languages has usually not been indicated. Where a person or place has two or more different names in the Hebrew, Aramaic or Greek texts, the more familiar one has generally been used, with footnotes where needed.

To achieve clarity the translators sometimes supplied words not in the original texts but required by the context. If there was uncertainty about such material, it is enclosed in brackets. Also for the sake of clarity or style, nouns, including some proper nouns, are sometimes substituted for pronouns, and vice versa. And though the Hebrew writers often shifted back and forth between first, second and third personal pronouns without change of antecedent, this translation often makes them uniform, in accordance with English style and without the use of footnotes.

Poetical passages are printed as poetry, that is, with indentation of lines and with separate stanzas. These are generally designed to reflect the structure of Hebrew poetry. This poetry is normally characterized by parallelism in balanced lines. Most of the poetry in the Bible is in the Old Testament, and scholars differ regarding the scansion of Hebrew lines. The translators determined the stanza divisions for the most part by analysis of the subject matter. The stanzas therefore serve as poetic paragraphs.

As an aid to the reader, italicized sectional headings are inserted in most of the books. They are not to be regarded as part of the NIV text, are not for oral reading, and are not intended to dictate the interpretation of the sections they head.

The footnotes in this version are of several kinds, most of which need no explanation. Those giving alternative translations begin with "Or" and generally introduce the alternative with the last word preceding it in the text, except when it is a single-word alternative; in poetry quoted in a footnote a slant mark indicates a line division. Footnotes introduced by "Or" do not have uniform significance. In some cases two possible translations were considered to have about equal validity. In other cases, though the translators were convinced that the translation in the text was correct, they judged that another interpretation was possible and of sufficient importance to be represented in a footnote.

In the New Testament, footnotes that refer to uncertainty regarding the original text are introduced by "Some manuscripts" or similar expressions. In the Old Testament, evidence for the reading chosen is given first and evidence for the alternative is added after a semicolon (for example: Septuagint; Hebrew father). In such notes the term "Hebrew" refers to the Masoretic Text.

It should be noted that minerals, flora and fauna, architectural details, articles of clothing and jewelry, musical instruments and other articles cannot always be identified with precision. Also measures of capacity in the biblical period are particularly uncertain (see the table of weights and measures following the text).

Like all translations of the Bible, made as they are by imperfect man, this one undoubtedly falls short of its goals. Yet we are grateful to God for the extent to which he has enabled us to realize these goals and for the strength he has given us and our colleagues to complete our task. We offer this version of the Bible to him in whose name and for whose glory it has been made. We pray that it will lead many into a better understanding of the Holy Scriptures and a fuller knowledge of Jesus Christ the incarnate Word, of whom the Scriptures so faithfully testify.

The Committee on Bible Translation

June 1978
(Revised Aug 1983)

Names of the translators and editors may be secured from the International Bible Society translation sponsors of the New International Version, 1820 Jet Stream Drive, Colorado Springs, Colorado 08921-3696 U.S.A.

OLD TESTAMENT

GENESIS

Who wrote this book?

There is some debate about who wrote Genesis. However, many scholars believe Moses wrote it.

Why was this book written?

Genesis tells how God created the universe and human beings. It also covers the special promises God made to Abraham.

What do we learn about God in this book?

God created all things. He loves people, but he will punish sin. God promises, however, to save people who trust him.

What people are important in this book?

Important people in this book are Adam and Eve, Noah, Abraham and Sarah, Isaac and Rebekah, Jacob and Rachel, and Joseph.

When did this happen?

No one knows when the creation or the flood occurred. Abraham was born about 2150 B.C. His great-grandson Joseph died about 1800 B.C.

Where did this happen?

Genesis 1–11 happened in Mesopotamia. Genesis 12–36 took place in Canaan, which is also called the promised land or Palestine. The rest of Genesis took place in Egypt.

What are some of the stories in this book?

God creates the universe	Genesis 1
God creates Adam and Eve	Genesis 2
Adam and Eve sin	Genesis 3
Noah builds an ark	Genesis 6
God sends a flood to punish sin	Genesis 7–8
God gives promises to Abraham	Genesis 12
Abraham prays for a city	Genesis 18
Jacob steals Esau's blessing	Genesis 27
Jacob's name is changed	Genesis 32
Joseph's brothers sell him into slavery	Genesis 37
Joseph becomes a ruler	Genesis 39–41

The Beginning

In the beginning God created the heavens and the earth. ²Now the earth was[a] formless and empty, darkness was over the surface of the deep, and the Spirit of God was hovering over the waters.

³And God said, "Let there be light," and there was light. ⁴God saw that the light was good, and he separated the light from the darkness. ⁵God called the light "day," and the darkness he called "night." And there was evening, and there was morning—the first day.

⁶And God said, "Let there be an expanse between the waters to separate water from water." ⁷So God made the expanse and separated the water under the expanse from the water above it. And it was so. ⁸God called the expanse "sky." And there was evening, and there was morning—the second day.

⁹And God said, "Let the water under the sky be gathered to one place, and let dry ground appear." And it was so. ¹⁰God called the dry ground "land," and the gathered waters he called "seas." And God saw that it was good.

¹¹Then God said, "Let the land produce vegetation: seed-bearing plants and trees on the land that bear fruit with seed in it, according to their various kinds." And it was so. ¹²The land produced vegetation: plants bearing seed according to their kinds and trees bearing fruit with seed in it according to their kinds. And God saw that it was good. ¹³And there was evening, and there was morning—the third day.

¹⁴And God said, "Let there be lights in the expanse of the sky to separate the day from the night, and let them serve as signs to mark seasons and days and years, ¹⁵and let them be lights in the expanse of the sky to give light on the earth." And it was

[a] 2 Or possibly *became*

GET SMARTER

Saving the Best 'til Last

READ GENESIS 1:1–27

Have you ever wondered why God waited until the last day to make humans? Were we less important than the trees and the fleas? Were we just a last minute idea? Not by a long shot! God was saving the best 'til last. In verse 26, God says, "Let us make man in our image ... and let them rule ... over all the earth." Because we're made in God's image, we have a super special place in creation. The rest of the world is here for us to enjoy. Hey! How much better does it get? But it's not all a free ride. God gave us strong bodies for a reason. He made us physical beings, put us here on a cool planet, but then made us responsible for looking after it. That responsibility begins with our bodies—keeping them healthy and strong—and includes caring for our families, backyards, cities and countries.

Your next reading is on page 4.

so. ¹⁶God made two great lights—the greater light to govern the day and the lesser light to govern the night. He also made the stars. ¹⁷God set them in the expanse of the sky to give light on the earth, ¹⁸to govern the day and the night, and to separate light from darkness. And God saw that it was good. ¹⁹And there was evening, and there was morning—the fourth day.

²⁰And God said, "Let the water teem with living creatures, and let birds fly above the earth across the expanse of the sky." ²¹So God created the great creatures of the sea and every living and moving thing with which the water teems, according to their kinds, and every winged bird according to its kind. And God saw that it was good. ²²God blessed them and said, "Be fruitful and increase in number and fill the water in the seas, and let the birds increase on the earth." ²³And there was evening, and there was morning—the fifth day.

²⁴And God said, "Let the land produce living creatures according to their kinds: livestock, creatures that move along the ground, and wild animals, each according to its kind." And it was so. ²⁵God made the wild animals according to their kinds, the livestock according to their kinds, and all the creatures that move along the ground according to their kinds. And God saw that it was good.

²⁶Then God said, "Let us make man in our image, in our likeness, and let them rule over the fish of the sea and the birds of the air, over the livestock, over all the earth, ^a and over all the creatures that move along the ground."

²⁷So God created man in his own image,
in the image of God he created him;
male and female he created them.

²⁸God blessed them and said to them, "Be fruitful and increase in number; fill the earth and subdue it. Rule over the fish of the sea and the birds of the air and over every living creature that moves on the ground."

²⁹Then God said, "I give you every seed-bearing plant on the face of the whole earth and every tree that has fruit with seed in it. They will be yours for food. ³⁰And to all the beasts of the earth and all the birds of the air and all the creatures that move on the ground—everything that has the breath of life in it—I give every green plant for food." And it was so.

³¹God saw all that he had made, and it was very good. And there was evening, and there was morning—the sixth day.

^a 26 Hebrew; Syriac *all the wild animals*

Get a Load of This...

God made sea monsters (see Genesis 1:21), and some people believe they may still be alive! In 1977, a Japanese fishing ship netted what looked like a dead plesiosaur—an ocean-going dinosaur thought to be long extinct—off the New Zealand coast. The creature was 32 feet long and weighed 4,000 pounds.

2 Thus the heavens and the earth were completed in all their vast array.

²By the seventh day God had finished the work he had been doing; so on the seventh day he rested*a* from all his work. ³And God blessed the seventh day and made it holy, because on it he rested from all the work of creating that he had done.

Adam and Eve

⁴This is the account of the heavens and the earth when they were created.

When the LORD God made the earth and the heavens— ⁵and no shrub of the field had yet appeared on the earth*b* and no plant of the field had yet sprung up, for the LORD God had not sent rain on the earth*b* and there was no man to work the ground, ⁶but streams*c* came up from the earth and watered the whole surface of the ground— ⁷the LORD God formed the man*d* from the dust of the ground and breathed into his nostrils the breath of life, and the man became a living being.

⁸Now the LORD God had planted a garden in the east, in Eden; and there he put the man he had formed. ⁹And the LORD God made all kinds of trees grow out of the ground—trees that were pleasing to the eye and good for food. In the middle of the garden were the tree of life and the tree of the knowledge of good and evil.

¹⁰A river watering the garden flowed from Eden; from there it was separated into four headwaters. ¹¹The name of the first is the Pishon; it winds through the entire land of Havilah, where there is gold. ¹²(The gold of that land is good; aromatic resin*e* and onyx are also there.) ¹³The name of the second river is the Gihon; it winds through the entire land of Cush.*f* ¹⁴The name of the third river is the Tigris; it runs along the east side of Asshur. And the fourth river is the Euphrates.

---

a 2 Or *ceased*; also in verse 3   *b 5* Or *land*; also in verse 6
c 6 Or *mist*   *d 7* The Hebrew for *man (adam)* sounds like and may be related to the Hebrew for *ground (adamah)*; it is also the name *Adam* (see Gen. 2:20).   *e 12* Or *good; pearls*
f 13 Possibly southeast Mesopotamia

What Cool Is All About

READ GENESIS 2:4–25

Some guys think the way to be cool is to be on their own, utterly independent, doing their own thing. Well, would you really like to live *alone* in a tree fort in the middle of a swamp for ten years? God said, "It is not good for the man to be alone" (verse 18). God wasn't just saying that Adam needed a wife. Adam also needed a family and friends. He needed other people. As humans, we are created to be with other people and live in relationship with them. Just like zebras like living with other zebras, people need other people. But don't forget that every relationship is a two-way street: Other people love us and care for us, and we need to love and look out for them. Bottom line: Being cooler doesn't mean being a one-man show, it means living in relationship with others.

Your next reading is on page 6.

GET COOLER

¹⁵The LORD God took the man and put him in the Garden of Eden to work it and take care of it. ¹⁶And the LORD God commanded the man, "You are free to eat from any tree in the garden; ¹⁷but you must not eat from the tree of the knowledge of good and evil, for when you eat of it you will surely die."

¹⁸The LORD God said, "It is not good for the man to be alone. I will make a helper suitable for him."

¹⁹Now the LORD God had formed out of the ground all the beasts of the field and all the birds of the air. He brought them to the man to see what he would name them; and whatever the man called each living creature, that was its name. ²⁰So the man gave names to all the livestock, the birds of the air and all the beasts of the field.

But for Adam*ᵃ* no suitable helper was found. ²¹So the LORD God caused the man to fall into a deep sleep; and while he was sleeping, he took one of the man's ribs*ᵇ* and closed up the place with flesh. ²²Then the LORD God made a woman from the rib*ᶜ* he had taken out of the man, and he brought her to the man.

²³The man said,

"This is now bone of my bones
   and flesh of my flesh;
she shall be called 'woman,*ᵈ*'
   for she was taken out of man."

²⁴For this reason a man will leave his father and mother and be united to his wife, and they will become one flesh.

²⁵The man and his wife were both naked, and they felt no shame.

The Fall of Man

Now the serpent was more crafty than any of the wild animals the LORD God had made. He said to the woman, "Did God really say, 'You

ᵃ 20 Or the man   ᵇ 21 Or took part of the man's side
ᶜ 22 Or part   ᵈ 23 The Hebrew for woman sounds like the Hebrew for man.

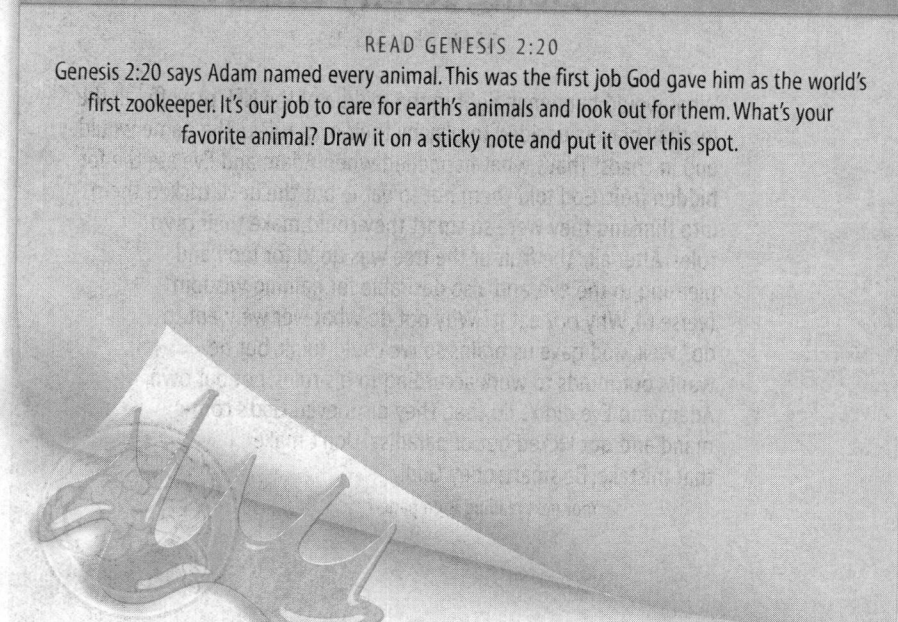

Make It Stick

READ GENESIS 2:20

Genesis 2:20 says Adam named every animal. This was the first job God gave him as the world's first zookeeper. It's our job to care for earth's animals and look out for them. What's your favorite animal? Draw it on a sticky note and put it over this spot.

must not eat from any tree in the garden'?"

2The woman said to the serpent, "We
may eat fruit from the trees in the garden,
3but God did say, 'You must not eat fruit
from the tree that is in the middle of the
garden, and you must not touch it, or you
will die.' "

4"You will not surely die," the serpent
said to the woman. 5"For God knows that
when you eat of it your eyes will be
opened, and you will be like God, knowing good and evil."

6When the woman saw that the fruit of
the tree was good for food and pleasing
to the eye, and also desirable for gaining
wisdom, she took some and ate it. She
also gave some to her husband, who was
with her, and he ate it. 7Then the eyes of
both of them were opened, and they realized they were naked; so they sewed fig
leaves together and made coverings for
themselves.

8Then the man and his wife heard the
sound of the LORD God as he was walking
in the garden in the cool of the day, and
they hid from the LORD God among the
trees of the garden. 9But the LORD God
called to the man, "Where are you?"

10He answered, "I heard you in the garden, and I was afraid because I was naked; so I hid."

11And he said, "Who told you that you
were naked? Have you eaten from the
tree that I commanded you not to eat
from?"

12The man said, "The woman you put
here with me—she gave me some fruit
from the tree, and I ate it."

13Then the LORD God said to the woman, "What is this you have done?"

The woman said, "The serpent deceived
me, and I ate."

14So the LORD God said to the serpent,
"Because you have done this,

"Cursed are you above all the livestock
    and all the wild animals!
You will crawl on your belly
    and you will eat dust
    all the days of your life.
15And I will put enmity
    between you and the woman,

Being Really Smart

READ GENESIS 3:1–7

GET SMARTER

What would happen if, right in the middle of the NFL playoffs, all the
football players decided to play by their own rules? The game would
end in chaos! That's what happened when Adam and Eve ate the forbidden fruit. God told them not to eat it, but the devil tricked them
into thinking they were so smart they could make their *own*
rules. After all, "the fruit of the tree was good for food and
pleasing to the eye, and also desirable for gaining wisdom"
(verse 6). Why *not* eat it? Why not do whatever we want to
do? Well, God gave us brains so we could think, but he
wants our minds to work according to his rules, not our own.
Adam and Eve didn't do that. They disobeyed God's command and got kicked out of paradise. Don't make
that mistake. Be smart; obey God!

Your next reading is on page 7.

and between your offspring[a] and
  hers;
he will crush[b] your head,
  and you will strike his heel."

[16]To the woman he said,

"I will greatly increase your pains in
    childbearing;
  with pain you will give birth to
    children.
Your desire will be for your husband,
  and he will rule over you."

[17]To Adam he said, "Because you listened to your wife and ate from the tree
about which I commanded you, 'You
must not eat of it,'

"Cursed is the ground because of you;
  through painful toil you will eat of it
    all the days of your life.
[18]It will produce thorns and thistles for
    you,

and you will eat the plants of the
    field.
[19]By the sweat of your brow
  you will eat your food
until you return to the ground,
  since from it you were taken;
for dust you are
  and to dust you will return."

[20]Adam[c] named his wife Eve,[d] because
she would become the mother of all the
living.
[21]The LORD God made garments of skin
for Adam and his wife and clothed them.
[22]And the LORD God said, "The man has
now become like one of us, knowing
good and evil. He must not be allowed to
reach out his hand and take also from the
tree of life and eat, and live forever." [23]So
the LORD God banished him from the Gar-

[a] 15 Or seed   [b] 15 Or strike   [c] 20 Or The man
[d] 20 Eve probably means living.

Getting Tight With God

READ GENESIS 3:8–24

Talk about potential! When God first created humans, they had direct
access to him, as easy as picking up a walkie-talkie. Adam and Eve
walked and talked with God face-to-face every day. God created people in his image and had a close, loving relationship with them. In
fact, God's original design for human beings was that they would
never even die. But one day Adam and Eve disobeyed God big-time
and their relationship with God was broken. Then when "the
man and his wife heard the sound of the LORD God as he was
walking . . . they hid . . . among the trees of the garden" (verse
8). Adam and Eve and their descendants—everyone living
today—were separated from God by sin and would have to
die. But God *knew* this would happen, and through Jesus,
made a way to bring us back. Now we can have a relationship with God as our Father, with him caring, loving and
guiding us—just like things were originally meant
to be. And now, when we die, we can live forever
with God in heaven. Isn't that great?

Your next reading is on page 9.

den of Eden to work the ground from which he had been taken. ²⁴After he drove the man out, he placed on the east side*a* of the Garden of Eden cherubim and a flaming sword flashing back and forth to guard the way to the tree of life.

Cain and Abel

4 Adam*b* lay with his wife Eve, and she became pregnant and gave birth to Cain.*c* She said, "With the help of the LORD I have brought forth*d* a man." ²Later she gave birth to his brother Abel.

Now Abel kept flocks, and Cain worked the soil. ³In the course of time Cain brought some of the fruits of the soil as an offering to the LORD. ⁴But Abel brought fat portions from some of the firstborn of his flock. The LORD looked with favor on Abel and his offering, ⁵but on Cain and his offering he did not look with favor. So Cain was very angry, and his face was downcast.

⁶Then the LORD said to Cain, "Why are

a 24 Or *placed in front*   *b 1* Or *The man*   *c 1 Cain* sounds like the Hebrew for *brought forth or acquired.* *d 1* Or *have acquired*

Make It Stick

_____

_____

_____

_____

_____

_____

_____

READ GENESIS 4:8

Cain and Abel didn't get along, and siblings have been fighting ever since. God wants us to learn how to love others and get along with them by learning how to love our brothers and sisters and get along with them. We don't always do that though, do we? Write down two or three things you fight with your brother or sister about.

you angry? Why is your face downcast? [7]If you do what is right, will you not be accepted? But if you do not do what is right, sin is crouching at your door; it desires to have you, but you must master it."

[8]Now Cain said to his brother Abel, "Let's go out to the field."[a] And while they were in the field, Cain attacked his brother Abel and killed him.

[9]Then the LORD said to Cain, "Where is your brother Abel?"

"I don't know," he replied. "Am I my brother's keeper?"

[10]The LORD said, "What have you done? Listen! Your brother's blood cries out to me from the ground. [11]Now you are under a curse and driven from the ground, which opened its mouth to receive your brother's blood from your hand. [12]When you work the ground, it will no longer yield its crops for you. You will be a restless wanderer on the earth."

[13]Cain said to the LORD, "My punishment is more than I can bear. [14]Today you are driving me from the land, and I will be hidden from your presence; I will be a restless wanderer on the earth, and whoever finds me will kill me."

[15]But the LORD said to him, "Not so[b]; if anyone kills Cain, he will suffer vengeance seven times over." Then the LORD put a mark on Cain so that no one who found him would kill him. [16]So Cain went out from the LORD's presence and lived in the land of Nod,[c] east of Eden.

[17]Cain lay with his wife, and she became pregnant and gave birth to Enoch. Cain was then building a city, and he named it after his son Enoch. [18]To Enoch was born Irad, and Irad was the father of Mehujael, and Mehujael was the father of Methushael, and Methushael was the father of Lamech.

[19]Lamech married two women, one named Adah and the other Zillah. [20]Adah gave birth to Jabal; he was the father of those who live in tents and raise livestock. [21]His brother's name was Jubal; he was the father of all who play the harp and

[a] 8 Samaritan Pentateuch, Septuagint, Vulgate and Syriac; Masoretic Text does not have "Let's go out to the field."
[b] 15 Septuagint, Vulgate and Syriac; Hebrew Very well
[c] 16 Nod means wandering (see verses 12 and 14).

Restless Wanderer

READ GENESIS 4:1–16

After Cain killed Abel, God condemned Cain to be a "restless wanderer on the earth." Cain felt so sorry for himself he drew back from God, saying "Today you are driving me from the land, and I will be hidden from your presence" (verse 14). But God never said he was going to leave Cain. It was Cain's guilt that made *him* withdraw from God. He was like a boy who got upset, took his ball and headed home. When we sin, we become separated not only from God, but from other people. Our sin doesn't make God go away, but it creates a barrier between us that can only be removed by forgiveness. If you're feeling down because of something you've done, don't give up like Cain did. Ask God for forgiveness and apologize to the people you've wronged.

Your next reading is on page 12.

Gross!

Genesis 6:4 says that when the "sons of God" married the "daughters of men," they had children who were giants, called the Nephilim (see Numbers 13:31–33). Some people think these "sons of God" were fallen angels (demons) marrying women. Weird, huh? Other people say they were godly sons of Seth marrying sinful daughters of Cain.

flute. 22Zillah also had a son, Tubal-Cain, who forged all kinds of tools out of[a] bronze and iron. Tubal-Cain's sister was Naamah.

23Lamech said to his wives,

"Adah and Zillah, listen to me;
　wives of Lamech, hear my words.
I have killed[b] a man for wounding me,
　a young man for injuring me.
24If Cain is avenged seven times,
　then Lamech seventy-seven times."

25Adam lay with his wife again, and she gave birth to a son and named him Seth,[c] saying, "God has granted me another child in place of Abel, since Cain killed him." 26Seth also had a son, and he named him Enosh.

At that time men began to call on[d] the name of the LORD.

From Adam to Noah

5 This is the written account of Adam's line.

When God created man, he made him in the likeness of God. 2He created them male and female and blessed them. And when they were created, he called them "man.[e]"

3When Adam had lived 130 years, he had a son in his own likeness, in his own image; and he named him Seth. 4After Seth was born, Adam lived 800 years and had other sons and daughters. 5Altogether, Adam lived 930 years, and then he died.

6When Seth had lived 105 years, he became the father[f] of Enosh. 7And after he became the father of Enosh, Seth lived 807 years and had other sons and daughters. 8Altogether, Seth lived 912 years, and then he died.

9When Enosh had lived 90 years, he became the father of Kenan. 10And after he became the father of Kenan, Enosh lived 815 years and had other sons and daughters. 11Altogether, Enosh lived 905 years, and then he died.

12When Kenan had lived 70 years, he became the father of Mahalalel. 13And after he became the father of Mahalalel, Kenan lived 840 years and had other sons and daughters. 14Altogether, Kenan lived 910 years, and then he died.

15When Mahalalel had lived 65 years, he became the father of Jared. 16And after he became the father of Jared, Mahalalel lived 830 years and had other sons and daughters. 17Altogether, Mahalalel lived 895 years, and then he died.

18When Jared had lived 162 years, he became the father of Enoch. 19And after he became the father of Enoch, Jared lived 800 years and had other sons and

a 22 Or *who instructed all who work in means granted.* *d 26* Or *to proclaim* *b 23* Or *I will kill* *c 25* *Seth* probably means granted. *d 26* Or *to proclaim* *e 2* Hebrew *adam* *f 6* *Father* may mean *ancestor;* also in verses 7–26.

daughters. ²⁰Altogether, Jared lived 962 years, and then he died.

²¹When Enoch had lived 65 years, he became the father of Methuselah. ²²And after he became the father of Methuselah, Enoch walked with God 300 years and had other sons and daughters. ²³Altogether, Enoch lived 365 years. ²⁴Enoch walked with God; then he was no more, because God took him away.

²⁵When Methuselah had lived 187 years, he became the father of Lamech. ²⁶And after he became the father of Lamech, Methuselah lived 782 years and had other sons and daughters. ²⁷Altogether, Methuselah lived 969 years, and then he died.

²⁸When Lamech had lived 182 years, he had a son. ²⁹He named him Noah[a] and said, "He will comfort us in the labor and painful toil of our hands caused by the ground the LORD has cursed." ³⁰After Noah was born, Lamech lived 595 years and had other sons and daughters. ³¹Al-together, Lamech lived 777 years, and then he died.

³²After Noah was 500 years old, he became the father of Shem, Ham and Japheth.

The Flood

6 When men began to increase in number on the earth and daughters were born to them, ²the sons of God saw that the daughters of men were beautiful, and they married any of them they chose. ³Then the LORD said, "My Spirit will not contend with[b] man forever, for he is mortal[c]; his days will be a hundred and twenty years."

⁴The Nephilim were on the earth in those days—and also afterward—when the sons of God went to the daughters of men and had children by them. They were the heroes of old, men of renown.

⁵The LORD saw how great man's wick-

^a 29 Noah sounds like the Hebrew for comfort.   ^b 3 Or My spirit will not remain in   ^c 3 Or corrupt

Make It Stick

Some people believe dinosaurs and people lived together after the story of creation in Genesis, and were wiped out in Noah's Flood. Other people think dinosaurs lived long before God created people and that they became toast when a giant meteorite hit the Earth. We know one thing for sure: God created everything, including dinosaurs. Draw your favorite one here on a sticky note.

edness on the earth had become, and that every inclination of the thoughts of his heart was only evil all the time. ⁶The LORD was grieved that he had made man on the earth, and his heart was filled with pain. ⁷So the LORD said, "I will wipe mankind, whom I have created, from the face of the earth—men and animals, and creatures that move along the ground, and birds of the air—for I am grieved that I have made them." ⁸But Noah found favor in the eyes of the LORD.

⁹This is the account of Noah.

Noah was a righteous man, blameless among the people of his time, and he walked with God. ¹⁰Noah had three sons: Shem, Ham and Japheth.

¹¹Now the earth was corrupt in God's sight and was full of violence. ¹²God saw how corrupt the earth had become, for all the people on earth had corrupted their ways. ¹³So God said to Noah, "I am going to put an end to all people, for the earth is filled with violence because of them. I am surely going to destroy both them and the earth. ¹⁴So make yourself an ark of cypress*a* wood; make rooms in it and coat it with pitch inside and out. ¹⁵This is how you are to build it: The ark is to be 450 feet long, 75 feet wide and 45 feet high.*b* ¹⁶Make a roof for it and finish*c* the ark to within 18 inches*d* of the top. Put a door in the side of the ark and make lower, middle and upper decks. ¹⁷I am going to bring floodwaters on the earth to destroy all life under the heavens, every creature that has the breath of life in it. Everything on earth will perish. ¹⁸But I will establish my covenant with you, and you will enter the ark—you and your sons and your wife and your sons' wives with you. ¹⁹You are to bring into the ark two of all living creatures, male and female, to keep them alive with you. ²⁰Two of every kind of bird, of every kind of animal and of every kind of creature that moves along the ground will come to you to be kept alive. ²¹You

a 14 The meaning of the Hebrew for this word is uncertain.
b 15 Hebrew *300 cubits long, 50 cubits wide and 30 cubits high* (about 140 meters long, 23 meters wide and 13.5 meters high)   *c 16* Or *Make an opening for light by finishing*   *d 16* Hebrew *a cubit* (about 0.5 meter)

Hammer-swinging Hero

READ GENESIS 6:6—7:10

It didn't take long after Adam and Eve for sin to completely ruin God's beautiful creation. Soon, "every inclination of the thoughts of [people's] heart was only evil all the time" (Genesis 6:5). That's why God decided to destroy them all and start over. "But Noah found favor in the eyes of the LORD" (verse 8). What made Noah different? He *trusted* and *obeyed* God. He proved this when God asked him to build the ark. Even though his neighbors thought he was nuts, Noah kept on hammering. And when the rains came and the rest of the world went belly up, Noah's trust and obedience helped his family survive. The point here is that God rewards those who trust and obey him. You don't have to be perfect. You just need to make obeying God your highest priority.

Your next reading is on page 15.

are to take every kind of food that is to be eaten and store it away as food for you and for them."

22 Noah did everything just as God commanded him.

7 The LORD then said to Noah, "Go into the ark, you and your whole family, because I have found you righteous in this generation. 2 Take with you seven[a] of every kind of clean animal, a male and its mate, and two of every kind of unclean animal, a male and its mate, 3 and also seven of every kind of bird, male and female, to keep their various kinds alive throughout the earth. 4 Seven days from now I will send rain on the earth for forty days and forty nights, and I will wipe from the face of the earth every living creature I have made."

5 And Noah did all that the LORD commanded him.

6 Noah was six hundred years old when the floodwaters came on the earth. 7 And Noah and his sons and his wife and his sons' wives entered the ark to escape the waters of the flood. 8 Pairs of clean and unclean animals, of birds and of all creatures that move along the ground, 9 male and female, came to Noah and entered the ark, as God had commanded Noah. 10 And after the seven days the floodwaters came on the earth.

11 In the six hundredth year of Noah's life, on the seventeenth day of the second month—on that day all the springs of the great deep burst forth, and the floodgates of the heavens were opened. 12 And rain fell on the earth forty days and forty nights.

13 On that very day Noah and his sons, Shem, Ham and Japheth, together with his wife and the wives of his three sons, entered the ark. 14 They had with them every wild animal according to its kind, all livestock according to their kinds, every creature that moves along the ground according to its kind and every bird according to its kind, everything with wings. 15 Pairs of all creatures that have the breath of life in them came to Noah and entered the ark. 16 The animals going in were male and female of every living thing, as God had commanded Noah. Then the LORD shut him in.

17 For forty days the flood kept coming on the earth, and as the waters increased they lifted the ark high above the earth. 18 The waters rose and increased greatly on the earth, and the ark floated on the surface of the water. 19 They rose greatly on the earth, and all the high mountains under the entire heavens were covered. 20 The waters rose and covered the mountains to a depth of more than twenty feet.[b,c] 21 Every living thing that moved on the earth perished—birds, livestock, wild animals, all the creatures that swarm over the earth, and all mankind. 22 Everything on dry land that had the breath of life in its nostrils died. 23 Every living thing on the face of the earth was wiped out; men and animals and the creatures that move along the ground and the birds of the air were wiped from the earth. Only Noah was left, and those with him in the ark.

[a] 2 Or seven pairs; also in verse 3   [b] 20 Hebrew fifteen cubits (about 6.9 meters)   [c] 20 Or rose more than twenty feet, and the mountains were covered

Get a Load of This...

In Genesis 6:15, God gave exact dimensions for the ark: 450 feet long, 75 feet wide and 45 feet tall—twice as long as a Boeing 747! Noah's ark was the largest ship ever built until 1858 when the *Great Eastern* was constructed. It was 669 feet long.

Gross!

Comparing Genesis 7:11 with Genesis 8:13–14, we find out that the people and the animals were in the ark for just over a year. During that time, animals produce *a lot* of manure. Imagine the stink! Noah was probably more than ready to open the window when he finally did. Any idea how he got rid of all that poop?

24The waters flooded the earth for a hundred and fifty days.

But God remembered Noah and all the wild animals and the livestock that were with him in the ark, and he sent a wind over the earth, and the waters receded. 2Now the springs of the deep and the floodgates of the heavens had been closed, and the rain had stopped falling from the sky. 3The water receded steadily from the earth. At the end of the hundred and fifty days the water had gone down, 4and on the seventeenth day of the seventh month the ark came to rest on the mountains of Ararat. 5The waters continued to recede until the tenth month, and on the first day of the tenth month the tops of the mountains became visible.

6After forty days Noah opened the window he had made in the ark 7and sent out a raven, and it kept flying back and forth until the water had dried up from the earth. 8Then he sent out a dove to see if the water had receded from the surface of the ground. 9But the dove could find no place to set its feet because there was water over all the surface of the earth; so it returned to Noah in the ark. He reached out his hand and took the dove and brought it back to himself in the ark. 10He waited seven more days and again sent out the dove from the ark. 11When the dove returned to him in the evening, there in its beak was a freshly plucked olive leaf! Then Noah knew that the water had receded from the earth. 12He waited seven more days and sent the dove out again, but this time it did not return to him.

13By the first day of the first month of Noah's six hundred and first year, the water had dried up from the earth. Noah then removed the covering from the ark and saw that the surface of the ground was dry. 14By the twenty-seventh day of the second month the earth was completely dry.

15Then God said to Noah, 16"Come out of the ark, you and your wife and your sons and their wives. 17Bring out every kind of living creature that is with you—the birds, the animals, and all the creatures that move along the ground—so they can multiply on the earth and be fruitful and increase in number upon it."

18So Noah came out, together with his sons and his wife and his sons' wives. 19All the animals and all the creatures that move along the ground and all the birds—everything that moves on the earth—came out of the ark, one kind after another.

20Then Noah built an altar to the LORD and, taking some of all the clean animals and clean birds, he sacrificed burnt offerings on it. 21The LORD smelled the pleasing aroma and said in his heart: "Never again will I curse the ground because of man, even though*a* every inclination of his heart is evil from childhood. And never again will I destroy all living creatures, as I have done.

a 21 Or man, for

22 "As long as the earth endures,
  seedtime and harvest,
  cold and heat,
  summer and winter,
  day and night
  will never cease."

God's Covenant With Noah

9 Then God blessed Noah and his sons, saying to them, "Be fruitful and increase in number and fill the earth. 2The fear and dread of you will fall upon all the beasts of the earth and all the birds of the air, upon every creature that moves along the ground, and upon all the fish of the sea; they are given into your hands. 3Everything that lives and moves will be food for you. Just as I gave you the green plants, I now give you everything.

4"But you must not eat meat that has its lifeblood still in it. 5And for your lifeblood I will surely demand an accounting. I will demand an accounting from every animal. And from each man, too, I will demand an accounting for the life of his fellow man.

6 "Whoever sheds the blood of man,
  by man shall his blood be shed;
  for in the image of God
  has God made man.

7As for you, be fruitful and increase in number; multiply on the earth and increase upon it."

8Then God said to Noah and to his sons with him: 9"I now establish my covenant with you and with your descendants after you 10and with every living creature that was with you—the birds, the livestock and all the wild animals, all those that came out of the ark with you—every living creature on earth. 11I establish my covenant with you: Never again will all life be cut off by the waters of a flood; never again will there be a flood to destroy the earth."

12And God said, "This is the sign of the covenant I am making between me and you and every living creature with you, a covenant for all generations to come: 13I have set my rainbow in the clouds, and it will be the sign of the covenant between me and the earth. 14Whenever I bring clouds over the earth and the rainbow ap-

GET SMARTER

Waiting and Watching

READ GENESIS 7:11—8:12

Ever sit out most of a game on the bench? Did it drive you crazy? Think about Noah. After 150 days of flooding, he had to sit tight for another 150 days while the water went down. Then he had to wait *another* 40 days before sending out a dove to look for dry land. Nothing. He waited seven more days and sent it out again. It came back with a leaf. Noah waited seven *more* days before sending it out again. When it didn't return, Noah knew it was safe to go out. Talk about being *patient*. Noah waited for direction from God before he did a thing. But he didn't just sit around. He kept busy and sought God so he would be ready when the time came to move out. If you do the same, you'll be ready to jump into action when God calls.

Your next reading is on page 17.

Get a Load of This...

The rainbow is God's promise never again to destroy his creatures with a flood (Genesis 9:8–13). It's his "signature in the sky." Did you know every rainbow is actually a complete circle? The full circle can't be seen from the ground, only from an airplane.

pears in the clouds, ¹⁵I will remember my covenant between me and you and all living creatures of every kind. Never again will the waters become a flood to destroy all life. ¹⁶Whenever the rainbow appears in the clouds, I will see it and remember the everlasting covenant between God and all living creatures of every kind on the earth."

¹⁷So God said to Noah, "This is the sign of the covenant I have established between me and all life on the earth."

The Sons of Noah

¹⁸The sons of Noah who came out of the ark were Shem, Ham and Japheth. (Ham was the father of Canaan.) ¹⁹These were the three sons of Noah, and from them came the people who were scattered over the earth.

²⁰Noah, a man of the soil, proceeded[a] to plant a vineyard. ²¹When he drank some of its wine, he became drunk and lay uncovered inside his tent. ²²Ham, the father of Canaan, saw his father's nakedness and told his two brothers outside. ²³But Shem and Japheth took a garment and laid it across their shoulders; then they walked in backward and covered their father's nakedness. Their faces were turned the other way so that they would not see their father's nakedness.

²⁴When Noah awoke from his wine and found out what his youngest son had done to him, ²⁵he said,

"Cursed be Canaan!
    The lowest of slaves
    will he be to his brothers."

²⁶He also said,

"Blessed be the LORD, the God of Shem!
    May Canaan be the slave of Shem.[b]
²⁷May God extend the territory of Japheth[c];
    may Japheth live in the tents of Shem,
    and may Canaan be his[d] slave."

²⁸After the flood Noah lived 350 years. ²⁹Altogether, Noah lived 950 years, and then he died.

The Table of Nations

This is the account of Shem, Ham and Japheth, Noah's sons, who themselves had sons after the flood.

The Japhethites

²The sons[e] of Japheth:
    Gomer, Magog, Madai, Javan, Tubal, Meshech and Tiras.
³The sons of Gomer:
    Ashkenaz, Riphath and Togarmah.

---

[a] 20 Or soil, was the first   [b] 26 Or be his slave   [c] 27 Japheth sounds like the Hebrew for extend.   [d] 27 Or their   [e] 2 Sons may mean descendants or successors or nations; also in verses 3, 4, 6, 7, 20–23, 29 and 31.

⁴The sons of Javan:
Elishah, Tarshish, the Kittim and the Rodanim.ᵃ ⁵(From these the maritime peoples spread out into their territories by their clans within their nations, each with its own language.)

The Hamites

⁶The sons of Ham:
Cush, Mizraim,ᵇ Put and Canaan.
⁷The sons of Cush:
Seba, Havilah, Sabtah, Raamah and Sabteca.
The sons of Raamah:
Sheba and Dedan.

⁸Cush was the fatherᶜ of Nimrod, who grew to be a mighty warrior on the earth. ⁹He was a mighty hunter before the LORD; that is why it is said, "Like Nimrod, a mighty hunter before the LORD." ¹⁰The first centers of his kingdom were Babylon, Erech, Akkad and Calneh, inᵈ Shinar.ᵉ

¹¹From that land he went to Assyria, where he built Nineveh, Rehoboth Ir,ᶠ Calah ¹²and Resen, which is between Nineveh and Calah; that is the great city.

¹³Mizraim was the father of
the Ludites, Anamites, Lehabites, Naphtuhites, ¹⁴Pathrusites, Casluhites (from whom the Philistines came) and Caphtorites.
¹⁵Canaan was the father of
Sidon his firstborn,ᵍ and of the Hittites, ¹⁶Jebusites, Amorites, Girgashites, ¹⁷Hivites, Arkites, Sinites, ¹⁸Arvadites, Zemarites and Hamathites.

Later the Canaanite clans scattered ¹⁹and

ᵃ 4 Some manuscripts of the Masoretic Text and Samaritan Pentateuch (see also Septuagint and 1 Chron. 1:7); most manuscripts of the Masoretic Text Dodanim   ᵇ 6 That is, Egypt; also in verse 13   ᶜ 8 Father may mean ancestor or predecessor or founder; also in verses 13, 15, 24 and 26.
ᵈ 10 Or Erech and Akkad—all of them in   ᵉ 10 That is, Babylonia   ᶠ 11 Or Nineveh with its city squares
ᵍ 15 Or of the Sidonians, the foremost

Get a Load of This...

Read the roll call in Genesis 10. Phew! Ever wonder why the Bible lists so many names? It's partly because God wants us to know he cares about each individual he created. The longest list of names is in 1 Chronicles 1–9.

the borders of Canaan reached from Sidon toward Gerar as far as Gaza, and then toward Sodom, Gomorrah, Admah and Zeboiim, as far as Lasha. ²⁰These are the sons of Ham by their clans and languages, in their territories and nations.

The Semites

²¹Sons were also born to Shem, whose older brother was ᵃ Japheth; Shem was the ancestor of all the sons of Eber.

²²The sons of Shem:

Elam, Asshur, Arphaxad, Lud and Aram.

²³The sons of Aram:

Uz, Hul, Gether and Meshech. ᵇ

²⁴Arphaxad was the father of ᶜ Shelah,

and Shelah the father of Eber.

²⁵Two sons were born to Eber:

One was named Peleg, ᵈ because in his time the earth was divided; his brother was named Joktan.

²⁶Joktan was the father of

Almodad, Sheleph, Hazarmaveth, Jerah, ²⁷Hadoram, Uzal, Diklah, ²⁸Obal, Abimael, Sheba, ²⁹Ophir, Havilah and Jobab. All these were sons of Joktan.

³⁰The region where they lived stretched from Mesha toward Sephar, in the eastern hill country. ³¹These are the sons of Shem by their clans and languages, in their territories and nations.

³²These are the clans of Noah's sons, according to their lines of descent, within their nations. From these the nations spread out over the earth after the flood.

The Tower of Babel

Now the whole world had one language and a common speech. ²As men moved eastward, ᵉ they found a plain in Shinar ᶠ and settled there. ³They said to each other, "Come, let's make bricks and bake them thoroughly." They used brick instead of stone, and tar for mortar. ⁴Then they said, "Come, let us build ourselves a city, with a tower that reaches to the heavens, so that we may make a name for ourselves and not be scattered over the face of the whole earth."

⁵But the LORD came down to see the city and the tower that the men were building. ⁶The LORD said, "If as one people speaking the same language they have begun to do this, then nothing they plan to do will be impossible for them. ⁷Come, let us go down and confuse their language so they will not understand each other."

⁸So the LORD scattered them from there over all the

ᵃ 21 Or Shem, the older brother of   ᵇ 23 See Septuagint and 1 Chron. 1:17; Hebrew Mash   ᶜ 24 Hebrew; Septuagint father of Cainan, and Cainan was the father of   ᵈ 25 Peleg means division.   ᵉ 2 Or from the east; or in the east   ᶠ 2 That is, Babylonia

earth, and they stopped building the city.
⁹That is why it was called Babel*ª*—because there the LORD confused the language of the whole world. From there the LORD scattered them over the face of the whole earth.

From Shem to Abram

¹⁰This is the account of Shem.

Two years after the flood, when Shem was 100 years old, he became the father*ᵇ* of Arphaxad. ¹¹And after he became the father of Arphaxad, Shem lived 500 years and had other sons and daughters.

¹²When Arphaxad had lived 35 years, he became the father of Shelah. ¹³And after he became the father of Shelah, Arphaxad lived 403 years and had other sons and daughters.*ᶜ*

¹⁴When Shelah had lived 30 years, he became the father of Eber. ¹⁵And after he became the father of Eber, Shelah lived 403 years and had other sons and daughters.

¹⁶When Eber had lived 34 years, he became the father of Peleg. ¹⁷And after he

became the father of Peleg, Eber lived 430 years and had other sons and daughters.

¹⁸When Peleg had lived 30 years, he became the father of Reu. ¹⁹And after he became the father of Reu, Peleg lived 209 years and had other sons and daughters.

²⁰When Reu had lived 32 years, he became the father of Serug. ²¹And after he became the father of Serug, Reu lived 207 years and had other sons and daughters.

²²When Serug had lived 30 years, he became the father of Nahor. ²³And after he became the father of Nahor, Serug lived 200 years and had other sons and daughters.

²⁴When Nahor had lived 29 years, he became the father of Terah. ²⁵And after

ª 9 That is, Babylon; *Babel* sounds like the Hebrew for confused.   *ᵇ 10* *Father* may mean *ancestor;* also in verses 11–25.   *ᶜ 12,13* Hebrew; Septuagint (see also Luke 3:35, 36 and note at Gen. 10:24) *35 years, he became the father of Cainan. ¹³And after he became the father of Cainan, Arphaxad lived 430 years and had other sons and daughters, and then he died. When Cainan had lived 130 years, he became the father of Shelah. And after he became the father of Shelah, Cainan lived 330 years and had other sons and daughters*

Building Big

READ GENESIS 11:1–9

God was *not* impressed when he saw the tower of Babel. Its builders weren't building it for God or to help other people. Ego and pride were their big motivators. They said, "Let us build ourselves . . . a tower . . . so that we may make a name for ourselves" (verse 4). God stopped them by confusing and scattering them. He wasn't against people building towers. God applauds when human beings put out a lot of effort and strive for excellence. He thinks it's great when they build big things to help others. The tallest office building in the world is 1,489 feet tall— much taller than the tower of Babel—but did God stop people from building it? No. Why not? Because they were just trying to build a place to do business. The people in Babel had all the wrong motives. When you build, build big, but build for the right reasons.

Your next reading is on page 21.

he became the father of Terah, Nahor lived 119 years and had other sons and daughters. 26After Terah had lived 70 years, he became the father of Abram, Nahor and Haran.

27This is the account of Terah.

Terah became the father of Abram, Nahor and Haran. And Haran became the father of Lot. 28While his father Terah was still alive, Haran died in Ur of the Chaldeans, in the land of his birth. 29Abram and Nahor both married. The name of Abram's wife was Sarai, and the name of Nahor's wife was Milcah; she was the daughter of Haran, the father of both Milcah and Iscah. 30Now Sarai was barren; she had no children.

31Terah took his son Abram, his grandson Lot son of Haran, and his daughter-in-law Sarai, the wife of his son Abram, and together they set out from Ur of the Chaldeans to go to Canaan. But when they came to Haran, they settled there.

32Terah lived 205 years, and he died in Haran.

The Call of Abram

12 The LORD had said to Abram, "Leave your country, your people and your father's household and go to the land I will show you.

2"I will make you into a great nation
    and I will bless you;
I will make your name great,
    and you will be a blessing.
3I will bless those who bless you,
    and whoever curses you I will curse;
and all peoples on earth
    will be blessed through you."

4So Abram left, as the LORD had told him; and Lot went with him. Abram was seventy-five years old when he set out from Haran. 5He took his wife Sarai, his nephew Lot, all the possessions they had accumulated and the people they had acquired in Haran, and they set out for the land of Canaan, and they arrived there.

6Abram traveled through the land as far as the site of the great tree of Moreh at Shechem. At that time the Canaanites were in the land. 7The LORD appeared to Abram and said, "To your offspringª I will give this land." So he built an altar there to the LORD, who had appeared to him.

8From there he went on toward the hills east of Bethel and pitched his tent, with Bethel on the west and Ai on the east. There he built an altar to the LORD and called on the name of the LORD. 9Then Abram set out and continued toward the Negev.

Abram in Egypt

10Now there was a famine in the land, and Abram went down to Egypt to live there for a while because

_____
ª 7 Or seed

the famine was severe. ¹¹As he was about to enter Egypt, he said to his wife Sarai, "I know what a beautiful woman you are. ¹²When the Egyptians see you, they will say, 'This is his wife.' Then they will kill me but will let you live. ¹³Say you are my sister, so that I will be treated well for your sake and my life will be spared because of you."

¹⁴When Abram came to Egypt, the Egyptians saw that she was a very beautiful woman. ¹⁵And when Pharaoh's officials saw her, they praised her to Pharaoh, and she was taken into his palace. ¹⁶He treated Abram well for her sake, and Abram acquired sheep and cattle, male and female donkeys, menservants and maidservants, and camels.

¹⁷But the LORD inflicted serious diseases on Pharaoh and his household because of Abram's wife Sarai. ¹⁸So Pharaoh summoned Abram. "What have you done to me?" he said. "Why didn't you tell me she was your wife? ¹⁹Why did you say, 'She is my sister,' so that I took her to be my wife? Now then, here is your wife. Take her and go!" ²⁰Then Pharaoh gave orders about Abram to his men, and they sent him on his way, with his wife and everything he had.

Abram and Lot Separate

So Abram went up from Egypt to the Negev, with his wife and everything he had, and Lot went with him. ²Abram had become very wealthy in livestock and in silver and gold.

³From the Negev he went from place to place until he came to Bethel, to the place between Bethel and Ai where his tent had been earlier ⁴and where he had first built an altar. There Abram called on the name of the LORD.

⁵Now Lot, who was moving about with Abram, also had flocks and herds and tents. ⁶But the land could not support them while they stayed together, for their possessions were so great that they were not able to stay together. ⁷And quarreling arose between Abram's herdsmen and the herdsmen of Lot. The Canaanites and

The Ripple Effect
READ GENESIS 12:1–9

Ever toss rocks into a pond to see them splash? You've probably noticed that each splash creates ripples that quickly spread way out across the water's surface. Our lives are like rocks thrown in the water. The "splash" we make creates ripples that affect the lives of others, either for good or for bad. God knew about this "ripple effect" when he told Abraham, "All peoples on earth will be blessed through you" (verse 3). Because Abraham obeyed God, his life made a huge cannonball of a splash—ripples went completely around the planet and blessed hundreds of millions of people. God could use Abraham's life that way because Abraham had a close relationship with God. If you make God the center of your life and obey what he tells you, you too can have a positive ripple effect on people around you.

Your next reading is on page 23.

Perizzites were also living in the land at that time.

⁸So Abram said to Lot, "Let's not have any quarreling between you and me, or between your herdsmen and mine, for we are brothers. ⁹Is not the whole land before you? Let's part company. If you go to the left, I'll go to the right; if you go to the right, I'll go to the left."

¹⁰Lot looked up and saw that the whole plain of the Jordan was well watered, like the garden of the LORD, like the land of Egypt, toward Zoar. (This was before the LORD destroyed Sodom and Gomorrah.) ¹¹So Lot chose for himself the whole plain of the Jordan and set out toward the east. The two men parted company: ¹²Abram lived in the land of Canaan, while Lot lived among the cities of the plain and pitched his tents near Sodom. ¹³Now the men of Sodom were wicked and were sinning greatly against the LORD.

¹⁴The LORD said to Abram after Lot had parted from him, "Lift up your eyes from where you are and look north and south, east and west. ¹⁵All the land that you see I will give to you and your offspring ᵃ forever. ¹⁶I will make your offspring like the dust of the earth, so that if anyone could count the dust, then your offspring could be counted. ¹⁷Go, walk through the length and breadth of the land, for I am giving it to you."

¹⁸So Abram moved his tents and went to live near the great trees of Mamre at Hebron, where he built an altar to the LORD.

Abram Rescues Lot

14 At this time Amraphel king of Shinar,ᵇ Arioch king of Ellasar, Kedorlaomer king of Elam and Tidal king of Goiim ²went to war against Bera king of Sodom, Birsha king of Gomorrah, Shinab king of Admah, Shemeber king of Zeboiim, and the king of Bela

ᵃ 15 Or *seed*; also in verse 16　　ᵇ 1 That is, Babylonia; also in verse 9

Make It Stick

READ GENESIS 13:9

Abraham had a "you first" attitude while Lot was only looking out for number one. Write these words on a sticky note: "You, Us, Me." When you go to make a decision, think about how you can put the other person first, the two of you second and yourself third.

(that is, Zoar). ³All these latter kings joined forces in the Valley of Siddim (the Salt Sea[a]). ⁴For twelve years they had been subject to Kedorlaomer, but in the thirteenth year they rebelled.

⁵In the fourteenth year, Kedorlaomer and the kings allied with him went out and defeated the Rephaites in Ashteroth Karnaim, the Zuzites in Ham, the Emites in Shaveh Kiriathaim ⁶and the Horites in the hill country of Seir, as far as El Paran near the desert. ⁷Then they turned back and went to En Mishpat (that is, Kadesh), and they conquered the whole territory of the Amalekites, as well as the Amorites who were living in Hazazon Tamar.

⁸Then the king of Sodom, the king of Gomorrah, the king of Admah, the king of Zeboiim and the king of Bela (that is, Zoar) marched out and drew up their battle lines in the Valley of Siddim ⁹against Kedorlaomer king of Elam, Tidal king of Goiim, Amraphel king of Shinar and Arioch king of Ellasar—four kings against five. ¹⁰Now the Valley of Siddim was full of tar pits, and when the kings of Sodom and Gomorrah fled, some of the men fell into them and the rest fled to the hills. ¹¹The four kings seized all the goods of Sodom and Gomorrah and all their food; then they went away. ¹²They also carried off Abram's nephew Lot and his possessions, since he was living in Sodom.

¹³One who had escaped came and reported this to Abram the Hebrew. Now Abram was living near the great trees of Mamre the Amorite, a brother[b] of Eshcol and Aner, all of whom were allied with Abram. ¹⁴When Abram heard that his relative had been taken captive, he called out the 318 trained men born in his household and went in pursuit as far as Dan. ¹⁵During the night Abram divided his men to attack them and he routed them, pursuing them as far as Hobah, north of Damascus. ¹⁶He recovered all the goods and brought back his relative Lot

---

[a] 3 That is, the Dead Sea   [b] 13 Or a relative; or an ally

---

GET STRONGER

God Gives Abraham Raw Courage

READ GENESIS 14

When four powerful kings and their armies swooped down on the land, scooped up people and goods and left their cities up in smoke, Abraham and his small army of shepherds counter-attacked. They fought so fiercely that they conquered four enemy armies. This battle was personal. The kings had captured Abraham's nephew, Lot. Abraham *had* to rescue Lot. Where did he get such power? He knew that God was with him. His faith gave him courage, and his raw courage gave him the strength that helped him win the battle. When you have a problem or trouble, trust God for courage to face your problem and do what's right. Giving you courage is one way that God makes you strong. When Abraham came riding home with Lot, the good king of Salem told him, "Blessed be God Most High, who delivered your enemies into your hand" (verse 20).

Your next reading is on page 27.

Check out Genesis 15:1.
Imagine having to kill, cut up and burn an animal every time you wanted to worship God! Yuck! *Don't* try this one at home! God used to require blood sacrifices to pay for people's sins, but since Jesus shed his blood for us, animal sacrifices are no longer necessary (Hebrews 9:13–15).

and his possessions, together with the women and the other people.

¹⁷After Abram returned from defeating Kedorlaomer and the kings allied with him, the king of Sodom came out to meet him in the Valley of Shaveh (that is, the King's Valley).

¹⁸Then Melchizedek king of Salem*ᵃ* brought out bread and wine. He was priest of God Most High, ¹⁹and he blessed Abram, saying,

"Blessed be Abram by God Most High,
     Creatorᵇ of heaven and earth.
²⁰And blessed beᶜ God Most High,
     who delivered your enemies into your hand."

Then Abram gave him a tenth of everything.

²¹The king of Sodom said to Abram, "Give me the people and keep the goods for yourself."

²²But Abram said to the king of Sodom, "I have raised my hand to the LORD, God Most High, Creator of heaven and earth, and have taken an oath ²³that I will accept nothing belonging to you, not even a thread or the thong of a sandal, so that you will never be able to say, 'I made Abram rich.' ²⁴I will accept nothing but what my men have eaten and the share that belongs to the men who went with me—to Aner, Eshcol and Mamre. Let them have their share."

God's Covenant With Abram

15 After this, the word of the LORD came to Abram in a vision:

"Do not be afraid, Abram.
I am your shield,ᵈ
your very great reward.ᵉ"

²But Abram said, "O Sovereign LORD, what can you give me since I remain childless and the one who will inheritᶠ my estate is Eliezer of Damascus?" ³And Abram said, "You have given me no children; so a servant in my household will be my heir."

⁴Then the word of the LORD came to him: "This man will not be your heir, but a son coming from your own body will be your heir." ⁵He took him outside and said, "Look up at the heavens and count the stars—if indeed you can count them." Then he said to him, "So shall your offspring be."

⁶Abram believed the LORD, and he credited it to him as righteousness.

⁷He also said to him, "I am the LORD, who brought you out of Ur of the Chaldeans to give you this land to take possession of it."

⁸But Abram said, "O Sovereign LORD, how can I know that I will gain possession of it?"

⁹So the LORD said to him, "Bring me a heifer, a goat

ᵃ *18* That is, Jerusalem   ᵇ *19* Or *Possessor*; also in verse 22   ᶜ *20* Or *And praise be to*   ᵈ *1* Or *sovereign*   ᵉ *1* Or *shield; / your reward will be very great*   ᶠ *2* The meaning of the Hebrew for this phrase is uncertain.

and a ram, each three years old, along with a dove and a young pigeon."

¹⁰Abram brought all these to him, cut them in two and arranged the halves opposite each other; the birds, however, he did not cut in half. ¹¹Then birds of prey came down on the carcasses, but Abram drove them away.

¹²As the sun was setting, Abram fell into a deep sleep, and a thick and dreadful darkness came over him. ¹³Then the LORD said to him, "Know for certain that your descendants will be strangers in a country not their own, and they will be enslaved and mistreated four hundred years. ¹⁴But I will punish the nation they serve as slaves, and afterward they will come out with great possessions. ¹⁵You, however, will go to your fathers in peace and be buried at a good old age. ¹⁶In the fourth generation your descendants will come back here, for the sin of the Amorites has not yet reached its full measure."

¹⁷When the sun had set and darkness had fallen, a smoking firepot with a blazing torch appeared and passed between the pieces. ¹⁸On that day the LORD made a covenant with Abram and said, "To your

Make It Stick

_____

_____

_____

_____

_____

_____

_____

READ GENESIS
15:10–21

When people made blood sacrifices, they often made a covenant—a promise to God. How about making a "commit, then spit" covenant? Take a sticky note, write a short commitment (promise) to God on it, smear some saliva on it, then stick it here. But let it dry first!

descendants I give this land, from the river[a] of Egypt to the great river, the Euphrates— 19the land of the Kenites, Kenizzites, Kadmonites, 20Hittites, Perizzites, Rephaites, 21Amorites, Canaanites, Girgashites and Jebusites."

Hagar and Ishmael

16 Now Sarai, Abram's wife, had borne him no children. But she had an Egyptian maidservant named Hagar; 2so she said to Abram, "The LORD has kept me from having children. Go, sleep with my maidservant; perhaps I can build a family through her."

Abram agreed to what Sarai said. 3So after Abram had been living in Canaan ten years, Sarai his wife took her Egyptian maidservant Hagar and gave her to her husband to be his wife. 4He slept with Hagar, and she conceived.

When she knew she was pregnant, she began to despise her mistress. 5Then Sarai said to Abram, "You are responsible for the wrong I am suffering. I put my servant in your arms, and now that she knows she is pregnant, she despises me. May the LORD judge between you and me."

6"Your servant is in your hands," Abram said. "Do with her whatever you think best." Then Sarai mistreated Hagar; so she fled from her.

7The angel of the LORD found Hagar near a spring in the desert; it was the spring that is beside the road to Shur. 8And he said, "Hagar, servant of Sarai, where have you come from, and where are you going?"

"I'm running away from my mistress Sarai," she answered.

9Then the angel of the LORD told her, "Go back to your mistress and submit to her." 10The angel added, "I will so increase your descendants that they will be too numerous to count."

11The angel of the LORD also said to her:

"You are now with child
    and you will have a son.
You shall name him Ishmael,[b]
    for the LORD has heard of your misery.
12He will be a wild donkey of a man;
    his hand will be against everyone
    and everyone's hand will be against him,
and he will live in hostility
    toward[c] all his brothers."

13She gave this name to the LORD who spoke to her: "You are the God who sees me," for she said, "I have now seen[d] the One who sees me." 14That is why the well was called Beer Lahai Roi[e]; it is still there, between Kadesh and Bered.

15So Hagar bore Abram a son, and Abram gave the name Ishmael to the son she had borne. 16Abram was eighty-six years old when Hagar bore him Ishmael.

The Covenant of Circumcision

17 When Abram was ninety-nine years old, the LORD appeared to him and said, "I am God Almighty[f]; walk before me and be blameless. 2I will confirm my covenant between me and you and will greatly increase your numbers."

3Abram fell facedown, and God said to him, 4"As for me, this is my covenant with you: You will be the father of many nations. 5No longer will you be called Abram[g]; your name will be Abraham,[h] for I have made you a father of many nations. 6I will make you very fruitful; I will make nations of you, and kings will come from you. 7I will establish my covenant as an everlasting covenant between me and you and your descendants after you for the generations to come, to be your God and the God of your descendants after you. 8The whole land of Canaan, where you are now an alien, I will give as an everlasting possession to you and your descendants after you; and I will be their God."

9Then God said to Abraham, "As for you, you must keep my covenant, you and your descendants after you for the generations to come. 10This is my covenant with you and your descendants after you, the covenant you are to keep: Every male among you shall be circumcised. 11You are to undergo circumcision, and it will be the sign of the covenant between me and you. 12For the generations to come every male among you who is eight days old must be circumcised, including those born in your household or bought with money from a foreigner—those who are not your offspring. 13Whether born in your household or bought with your

---

money, they must be circumcised. My covenant in your flesh is to be an everlasting covenant. ¹⁴Any uncircumcised male, who has not been circumcised in the flesh, will be cut off from his people; he has broken my covenant."

¹⁵God also said to Abraham, "As for Sarai your wife, you are no longer to call her Sarai; her name will be Sarah. ¹⁶I will bless her and will surely give you a son by her. I will bless her so that she will be the mother of nations; kings of peoples will come from her."

¹⁷Abraham fell facedown; he laughed and said to himself, "Will a son be born to a man a hundred years old? Will Sarah bear a child at the age of ninety?" ¹⁸And Abraham said to God, "If only Ishmael might live under your blessing!"

¹⁹Then God said, "Yes, but your wife Sarah will bear you a son, and you will call him Isaac.ᵃ I will establish my covenant with him as an everlasting covenant for his descendants after him. ²⁰And as for Ishmael, I have heard you: I will surely bless him; I will make him fruitful and will greatly increase his numbers. He will be the father of twelve rulers, and I will make him into a great nation. ²¹But my covenant I will establish with Isaac, whom Sarah will bear to you by this time next year." ²²When he had finished speaking with Abraham, God went up from him.

²³On that very day Abraham took his son Ishmael and all those born in his household or bought with his money, every male in his household, and circumcised them, as God told him. ²⁴Abraham was ninety-nine years old when he was circumcised, ²⁵and his son Ishmael was thirteen; ²⁶Abraham and his son Ishmael were both circumcised on that same day. ²⁷And every male in Abraham's household, including those born in his household or bought from a foreigner, was circumcised with him.

ᵃ 19 *Isaac* means *he laughs.*

This May Hurt

READ GENESIS 17:1–12

Few words make guys squirm as much as "circumcision." No wonder! Being circumcised means having the foreskin (loose skin at the tip of your penis) cut off. Ouch! That hurts!—Especially if you have it done as a teen or adult. Thankfully, most circumcisions are done on infants. But when God first had Abraham start the practice, he was 99 years old! (Pass the painkillers, please!) God didn't ask Abraham to do this just so he could watch him grit his teeth. It symbolized an important, personal and total agreement between them. "You are to undergo circumcision, and it will be the sign of the covenant between me and you" (verse 11). Circumcision is no longer required for believers (Galatians 6:15). Today it doesn't matter whether you're circumcised or not, because you can have a new covenant in Jesus that makes a change in your heart, not a change in your body.

Your next reading is on page 28.

The Three Visitors

18 The LORD appeared to Abraham near the great trees of Mamre while he was sitting at the entrance to his tent in the heat of the day. ²Abraham looked up and saw three men standing nearby. When he saw them, he hurried from the entrance of his tent to meet them and bowed low to the ground.

³He said, "If I have found favor in your eyes, my lord,ᵃ do not pass your servant by. ⁴Let a little water be brought, and then you may all wash your feet and rest under this tree. ⁵Let me get you something to eat, so you can be refreshed and then go on your way—now that you have come to your servant."

"Very well," they answered, "do as you say."

⁶So Abraham hurried into the tent to Sarah. "Quick," he said, "get three seahsᵇ of fine flour and knead it and bake some bread."

⁷Then he ran to the herd and selected a choice, tender calf and gave it to a servant, who hurried to prepare it. ⁸He then brought some curds and milk and the calf that had been prepared, and set these before them. While they ate, he stood near them under a tree.

⁹"Where is your wife Sarah?" they asked him.

"There, in the tent," he said.

¹⁰Then the LORDᶜ said, "I will surely return to you about this time next year, and Sarah your wife will have a son."

Now Sarah was listening at the entrance to the tent, which was behind him. ¹¹Abraham and Sarah were already old and well advanced in years, and Sarah was past the age of childbearing. ¹²So Sarah laughed to herself as she thought, "After I am worn out and my masterᵈ is old, will I now have this pleasure?"

¹³Then the LORD said to Abraham, "Why did Sarah laugh and say, 'Will I really have a child, now that I am old?' ¹⁴Is anything too hard for the LORD? I will return to you

---

a 3 Or *O Lord*   *b 6* That is, probably about 20 quarts (about 22 liters)   *c 10* Hebrew *Then he*   *d 12* Or *husband*

Hey! I'm Not Joking!

READ GENESIS 18:1–15

When God said Sarah would have a child, she burst out laughing. How was that possible? She was pushing ninety, and Abraham was about to celebrate the big 1-0-0. When God broke the news to Abraham, he laughed so hard he fell face first on the ground (Genesis 17:17). But God asked, "Is anything too hard for the LORD?" (Genesis 18:14). Sure enough, a year later Sarah gave birth to Isaac. Abraham and Sarah's mistake was forgetting that God can do the impossible. You've probably made that mistake too, thinking, "No way God can do this because . . ." or "I'm too young" or "I don't have enough money." You may not see how God can change the situation you're in, but God is not limited like humans are. He can do anything. So have faith and give God some elbow room to do miracles.

Your next reading is on page 32.

at the appointed time next year and Sarah will have a son."

15Sarah was afraid, so she lied and said, "I did not laugh."

But he said, "Yes, you did laugh."

Abraham Pleads for Sodom

16When the men got up to leave, they looked down toward Sodom, and Abraham walked along with them to see them on their way. 17Then the LORD said, "Shall I hide from Abraham what I am about to do? 18Abraham will surely become a great and powerful nation, and all nations on earth will be blessed through him. 19For I have chosen him, so that he will direct his children and his household after him to keep the way of the LORD by doing what is right and just, so that the LORD will bring about for Abraham what he has promised him."

20Then the LORD said, "The outcry against Sodom and Gomorrah is so great and their sin so grievous 21that I will go down and see if what they have done is as bad as the outcry that has reached me. If not, I will know."

22The men turned away and went toward Sodom, but Abraham remained standing before the LORD.a 23Then Abraham approached him and said: "Will you sweep away the righteous with the wicked? 24What if there are fifty righteous people in the city? Will you really sweep it away and not spareb the place for the sake of the fifty righteous people in it? 25Far be it from you to do such a thing— to kill the righteous with the wicked, treating the righteous and the wicked alike. Far be it from you! Will not the Judgec of all the earth do right?"

26The LORD said, "If I find fifty righteous people in the city of Sodom, I will spare the whole place for their sake."

27Then Abraham spoke up again: "Now that I have been so bold as to speak to the Lord, though I am nothing but dust and ashes, 28what if the number of the righteous is five less than fifty? Will you destroy the whole city because of five people?"

"If I find forty-five there," he said, "I will not destroy it."

29Once again he spoke to him, "What if only forty are found there?"

He said, "For the sake of forty, I will not do it."

30Then he said, "May the Lord not be angry, but let me speak. What if only thirty can be found there?"

He answered, "I will not do it if I find thirty there."

31Abraham said, "Now that I have been so bold as to speak to the Lord, what if only twenty can be found there?"

He said, "For the sake of twenty, I will not destroy it."

32Then he said, "May the Lord not be angry, but let me speak just once more. What if only ten can be found there?"

He answered, "For the sake of ten, I will not destroy it."

33When the LORD had finished speaking with Abraham, he left, and Abraham returned home.

Sodom and Gomorrah Destroyed

19 The two angels arrived at Sodom in the evening, and Lot was sitting in the gateway of the city. When he saw them, he got up to meet them and bowed down with his face to the ground. 2"My lords," he said, "please turn aside to your servant's house. You can wash your feet and spend the night and then go on your way early in the morning."

"No," they answered, "we will spend the night in the square."

3But he insisted so strongly that they did go with him and entered his house. He prepared a meal for them, baking bread without yeast, and they ate. 4Before they had gone to bed, all the men from every part of the city of Sodom—both young and old—surrounded the house. 5They called to Lot, "Where are the men who came to you tonight? Bring them out to us so that we can have sex with them."

6Lot went outside to meet them and shut the door behind him 7and said, "No, my friends. Don't do this wicked thing. 8Look, I have two daughters who have never slept with a man. Let me bring them out to you, and you can do what you like with them. But don't do anything to these men, for they have come under the protection of my roof."

9"Get out of our way," they replied. And they said, "This fellow came here as an alien, and now he wants to play the

---

a 22 Masoretic Text; an ancient Hebrew scribal tradition but the LORD remained standing before Abraham
b 24 Or forgive; also in verse 26   c 25 Or Ruler

Most people picture angels with wings, like the *cherubim* in Genesis 3:24. But not all angels have wings. When Lot met some angels in Genesis 19, they looked like normal men. No wonder Hebrews 13:2 tells us that some people have shown kindness to angels without knowing it!

judge! We'll treat you worse than them." They kept bringing pressure on Lot and moved forward to break down the door.

¹⁰But the men inside reached out and pulled Lot back into the house and shut the door. ¹¹Then they struck the men who were at the door of the house, young and old, with blindness so that they could not find the door. ¹²The two men said to Lot, "Do you have anyone else here—sons-in-law, sons or daughters, or anyone else in the city who belongs to you? Get them out of here, ¹³because we are going to destroy this place. The outcry to the LORD against its people is so great that he has sent us to destroy it."

¹⁴So Lot went out and spoke to his sons-in-law, who were pledged to marry*ᵃ* his daughters. He said, "Hurry and get out of this place, because the LORD is about to destroy the city!" But his sons-in-law thought he was joking.

¹⁵With the coming of dawn, the angels urged Lot, saying, "Hurry! Take your wife and your two daughters who are here, or you will be swept away when the city is punished."

¹⁶When he hesitated, the men grasped his hand and the hands of his wife and of his two daughters and led them safely out of the city, for the LORD was merciful to them. ¹⁷As soon as they had brought them out, one of them said, "Flee for your lives! Don't look back, and don't stop anywhere in the plain! Flee to the mountains or you will be swept away!"

¹⁸But Lot said to them, "No, my lords,*ᵇ* please! ¹⁹Your*ᶜ* servant has found favor in your*ᶜ* eyes, and you*ᶜ* have shown great kindness to me in sparing my life. But I can't flee to the mountains; this disaster will overtake me, and I'll die. ²⁰Look, here is a town near enough to run to, and it is small. Let me flee to it—it is very small, isn't it? Then my life will be spared."

²¹He said to him, "Very well, I will grant this request too; I will not overthrow the town you speak of. ²²But flee there quickly, because I cannot do anything until you reach it." (That is why the town was called Zoar.*ᵈ*)

²³By the time Lot reached Zoar, the sun had risen over the land. ²⁴Then the LORD rained down burning sulfur on Sodom and Gomorrah—from the LORD out of the heavens. ²⁵Thus he overthrew those cities and the entire plain, including all those living in the cities—and also the vegetation in the land. ²⁶But Lot's wife looked back, and she became a pillar of salt.

²⁷Early the next morning Abraham got up and returned to the place where he had stood before the LORD. ²⁸He looked down toward Sodom and Gomorrah, toward all the land of the plain, and he saw dense smoke rising from the land, like smoke from a furnace.

²⁹So when God destroyed the cities of the plain, he remembered Abraham, and he brought Lot out of the

ᵃ 14 Or *were married to*   *ᵇ 18* Or *No, Lord;* or *No, my lord*   *ᶜ 19* The Hebrew is singular.   *ᵈ 22 Zoar* means *small.*

catastrophe that overthrew the cities where Lot had lived.

Lot and His Daughters

³⁰Lot and his two daughters left Zoar and settled in the mountains, for he was afraid to stay in Zoar. He and his two daughters lived in a cave. ³¹One day the older daughter said to the younger, "Our father is old, and there is no man around here to lie with us, as is the custom all over the earth. ³²Let's get our father to drink wine and then lie with him and preserve our family line through our father."

³³That night they got their father to drink wine, and the older daughter went in and lay with him. He was not aware of it when she lay down or when she got up.

³⁴The next day the older daughter said to the younger, "Last night I lay with my father. Let's get him to drink wine again tonight, and you go in and lie with him so we can preserve our family line through our father." ³⁵So they got their father to drink wine that night also, and the younger daughter went and lay with him. Again he was not aware of it when she lay down or when she got up.

³⁶So both of Lot's daughters became pregnant by their father. ³⁷The older daughter had a son, and she named him Moab*ᵃ*; he is the father of the Moabites of today. ³⁸The younger daughter also had a son, and she named him Ben-Ammi*ᵇ*; he is the father of the Ammonites of today.

Abraham and Abimelech

20 Now Abraham moved on from there into the region of the Negev and lived between Kadesh and Shur. For a while he stayed in Gerar, ²and there Abraham said of his wife Sarah, "She is my sister." Then Abimelech king of Gerar sent for Sarah and took her.

³But God came to Abimelech in a

ᵃ 37 Moab sounds like the Hebrew for *from father.*
ᵇ 38 Ben-Ammi means *son of my people.*

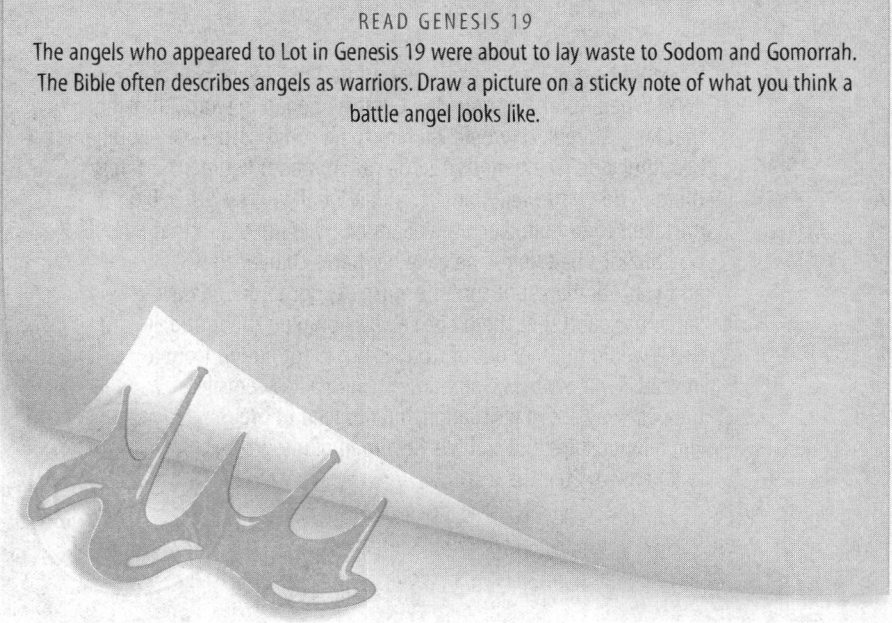

Make It Stick

READ GENESIS 19

The angels who appeared to Lot in Genesis 19 were about to lay waste to Sodom and Gomorrah. The Bible often describes angels as warriors. Draw a picture on a sticky note of what you think a battle angel looks like.

dream one night and said to him, "You are as good as dead because of the woman you have taken; she is a married woman."

⁴Now Abimelech had not gone near her, so he said, "Lord, will you destroy an innocent nation? ⁵Did he not say to me, 'She is my sister,' and didn't she also say, 'He is my brother'? I have done this with a clear conscience and clean hands."

⁶Then God said to him in the dream, "Yes, I know you did this with a clear conscience, and so I have kept you from sinning against me. That is why I did not let you touch her. ⁷Now return the man's wife, for he is a prophet, and he will pray for you and you will live. But if you do not return her, you may be sure that you and all yours will die."

⁸Early the next morning Abimelech summoned all his officials, and when he told them all that had happened, they were very much afraid. ⁹Then Abimelech called Abraham in and said, "What have you done to us? How have I wronged you that you have brought such great guilt upon me and my kingdom? You have done things to me that should not be done." ¹⁰And Abimelech asked Abraham, "What was your reason for doing this?"

¹¹Abraham replied, "I said to myself, 'There is surely no fear of God in this place, and they will kill me because of my wife.' ¹²Besides, she really is my sister, the daughter of my father though not of my mother; and she became my wife. ¹³And when God had me wander from my father's household, I said to her, 'This is how you can show your love to me: Everywhere we go, say of me, "He is my brother."' "

¹⁴Then Abimelech brought sheep and cattle and male and female slaves and gave them to Abraham, and he returned Sarah his wife to him. ¹⁵And Abimelech said, "My land is before you; live wherever you like."

¹⁶To Sarah he said, "I am giving your brother a thousand shekels^a of silver. This is to cover the offense against you before all who are with you; you are completely vindicated."

^{a} 16 That is, about 25 pounds (about 11.5 kilograms)

Little Lies, Big Trouble

READ GENESIS 20

When you get in trouble, are you tempted to lie your way out? Don't do it! When Abraham arrived in Gerar, he began to worry, thinking that King Abimelech would kill him so he could grab Sarah, Abraham's beautiful wife (see Genesis 12:10–13). Abraham figured the safest thing to do was to tell Abimelech that Sarah was his sister. Big mistake. When Abimelech took Sarah, God warned him that he was buzzard bait unless he gave her back. Abimelech was angry at Abraham, but since he wasn't eager to die, he gave Sarah back and sent them both away. Abraham thought a little lie would get him out of trouble, but it got him *in* trouble instead. Same with us: Sometimes telling a lie seems like the best way out of a situation, but lies lead to broken relationships and trouble. Be a man of integrity and always tell the truth.

Your next reading is on page 34.

GET SMARTER

17Then Abraham prayed to God, and God healed Abimelech, his wife and his slave girls so they could have children again, 18for the LORD had closed up every womb in Abimelech's household because of Abraham's wife Sarah.

The Birth of Isaac

21 Now the LORD was gracious to Sarah as he had said, and the LORD did for Sarah what he had promised. 2Sarah became pregnant and bore a son to Abraham in his old age, at the very time God had promised him. 3Abraham gave the name Isaac*a* to the son Sarah bore him. 4When his son Isaac was eight days old, Abraham circumcised him, as God commanded him. 5Abraham was a hundred years old when his son Isaac was born to him.

6Sarah said, "God has brought me laughter, and everyone who hears about this will laugh with me." 7And she added, "Who would have said to Abraham that Sarah would nurse children? Yet I have borne him a son in his old age."

Hagar and Ishmael Sent Away

8The child grew and was weaned, and on the day Isaac was weaned Abraham held a great feast. 9But Sarah saw that the son whom Hagar the Egyptian had borne to Abraham was mocking, 10and she said to Abraham, "Get rid of that slave woman and her son, for that slave woman's son will never share in the inheritance with my son Isaac."

11The matter distressed Abraham greatly because it concerned his son. 12But God said to him, "Do not be so distressed about the boy and your maidservant. Listen to whatever Sarah tells you, because it is through Isaac that your offspring*b* will be reckoned. 13I will make the son of the maidservant into a nation also, because he is your offspring."

a 3 Isaac means he laughs.   *b 12 Or seed*

Make It Stick

READ IN GENESIS 20

Truth is always your best defense (Proverbs 13:6). If you tell the truth, you never have to worry about someone finding you out, because you'll have nothing to hide. Write "Truth is my best defense" on a sticky note and press it down here.

¹⁴Early the next morning Abraham took some food and a skin of water and gave them to Hagar. He set them on her shoulders and then sent her off with the boy. She went on her way and wandered in the desert of Beersheba.

¹⁵When the water in the skin was gone, she put the boy under one of the bushes. ¹⁶Then she went off and sat down nearby, about a bowshot away, for she thought, "I cannot watch the boy die." And as she sat there nearby, she*ª* began to sob.

¹⁷God heard the boy crying, and the angel of God called to Hagar from heaven and said to her, "What is the matter, Hagar? Do not be afraid; God has heard the boy crying as he lies there. ¹⁸Lift the boy up and take him by the hand, for I will make him into a great nation."

¹⁹Then God opened her eyes and she saw a well of water. So she went and filled the skin with water and gave the boy a drink.

²⁰God was with the boy as he grew up. He lived in the desert and became an archer. ²¹While he was living in the Desert of Paran, his mother got a wife for him from Egypt.

The Treaty at Beersheba

²²At that time Abimelech and Phicol the commander of his forces said to Abraham, "God is with you in everything you do. ²³Now swear to me here before God that you will not deal falsely with me or my children or my descendants. Show to me and the country where you are living as an alien the same kindness I have shown to you."

²⁴Abraham said, "I swear it."

²⁵Then Abraham complained to Abimelech about a well of water that Abimelech's servants had seized. ²⁶But Abimelech said, "I don't know who has done this. You did not tell me, and I heard about it only today."

²⁷So Abraham brought sheep and cattle and gave them to Abimelech, and the two men made a treaty. ²⁸Abraham set apart seven ewe lambs from the flock, ²⁹and Abimelech asked Abraham, "What

ª 16 Hebrew; Septuagint the child

Watching Out for Ishmael

READ GENESIS 21:8–21

Hagar was a single parent, and it must have been difficult for Ishmael to grow up without a father, just as it's difficult for boys in single-parent homes today. But God was Ishmael's heavenly Father, and God didn't forget about him. He promised to make Ishmael into a great nation. Verse 20 tells us "God was with the boy as he grew up." If you or one of your friends are in that situation, God won't forget you either. When fathers and mothers go separate ways, as Abraham and Hagar did, it's difficult for the kids to deal with. But God is watching out for you and will never stop loving you. You can look to God as your Father even more if your natural father isn't with you. He'll see you through life no matter how tough things get.

Your next reading is on page 35.

is the meaning of these seven ewe lambs you have set apart by themselves?"

30He replied, "Accept these seven lambs from my hand as a witness that I dug this well."

31So that place was called Beersheba,a because the two men swore an oath there.

32After the treaty had been made at Beersheba, Abimelech and Phicol the commander of his forces returned to the land of the Philistines. 33Abraham planted a tamarisk tree in Beersheba, and there he called upon the name of the LORD, the Eternal God. 34And Abraham stayed in the land of the Philistines for a long time.

Abraham Tested

 Some time later God tested Abraham. He said to him, "Abraham!"

"Here I am," he replied.

2Then God said, "Take your son, your only son, Isaac, whom you love, and go to the region of Moriah. Sacrifice him there as a burnt offering on one of the mountains I will tell you about."

3Early the next morning Abraham got up and saddled his donkey. He took with him two of his servants and his son Isaac. When he had cut enough wood for the burnt offering, he set out for the place God had told him about. 4On the third day Abraham looked up and saw the place in the distance. 5He said to his servants, "Stay here with the donkey while I and the boy go over there. We will worship and then we will come back to you."

6Abraham took the wood for the burnt offering and placed it on his son Isaac, and he himself carried the fire and the knife. As the two of them went on together, 7Isaac spoke up and said to his father Abraham, "Father?"

a 31 Beersheba can mean well of seven or well of the oath.

The Camping Trip

READ GENESIS 22:1–19

Put yourself in Abraham's sandals: After 99 years, God finally gives you and your wife the son he had promised, then asks you to kill him as a sacrifice. But when Abraham had Isaac on the altar, God stopped him and said, "Now I know that you fear God, because you have not withheld from me your son, your only son " (verse 12). Imagine Isaac's relief! God didn't really want Abraham to kill Isaac; he just wanted to make sure Abraham was willing to obey him. This whole story may seem . . . well, a bit strange, but it was a great picture of how God would later sacrifice Jesus, his own Son, to save us all from our sins (see John 3:16 on page 1376). This story also shows that adults need to obey God. Sometimes you may think you can't wait to grow up so you can do whatever you want. That's not the way it works. Everyone has to obey the authorities, and God. Might as well start learning now. If you get in the habit of obeying adults and authorities now, then when you're an adult, it'll be easier to obey God when he calls you to do tough things.

Your next reading is on page 37.

"Yes, my son?" Abraham replied.

"The fire and wood are here," Isaac said, "but where is the lamb for the burnt offering?"

⁸Abraham answered, "God himself will provide the lamb for the burnt offering, my son." And the two of them went on together.

⁹When they reached the place God had told him about, Abraham built an altar there and arranged the wood on it. He bound his son Isaac and laid him on the altar, on top of the wood. ¹⁰Then he reached out his hand and took the knife to slay his son. ¹¹But the angel of the LORD called out to him from heaven, "Abraham! Abraham!"

"Here I am," he replied.

¹²"Do not lay a hand on the boy," he said. "Do not do anything to him. Now I know that you fear God, because you have not withheld from me your son, your only son."

¹³Abraham looked up and there in a thicket he saw a ram*a* caught by its horns. He went over and took the ram and sacrificed it as a burnt offering instead of his son. ¹⁴So Abraham called that place The LORD Will Provide. And to this day it is said, "On the mountain of the LORD it will be provided."

¹⁵The angel of the LORD called to Abraham from heaven a second time ¹⁶and said, "I swear by myself, declares the LORD, that because you have done this and have not withheld your son, your only son, ¹⁷I will surely bless you and make your descendants as numerous as the stars in the sky and as the sand on the seashore. Your descendants will take possession of the cities of their enemies, ¹⁸and through your offspring*b* all nations on earth will be blessed, because you have obeyed me."

¹⁹Then Abraham returned to his servants, and they set off together for Beersheba. And Abraham stayed in Beersheba.

Nahor's Sons

²⁰Some time later Abraham was told, "Milcah is also a mother; she has borne sons to your brother Nahor: ²¹Uz the firstborn, Buz his brother, Kemuel (the father of Aram), ²²Kesed, Hazo, Pildash, Jidlaph and Bethuel." ²³Bethuel became the father of Rebekah. Milcah bore these eight sons to Abraham's brother Nahor. ²⁴His concubine, whose name was Reumah, also had sons: Tebah, Gaham, Tahash and Maacah.

The Death of Sarah

23 Sarah lived to be a hundred and twenty-seven years old. ²She died at Kiriath Arba (that is, Hebron) in the land of Canaan, and Abraham went to mourn for Sarah and to weep over her.

³Then Abraham rose from beside his dead wife and spoke to the Hittites.*c* He said, ⁴"I am an alien and a stranger among you. Sell me some property for a burial site here so I can bury my dead."

⁵The Hittites replied to Abraham, ⁶"Sir, listen to us. You are a mighty prince among us. Bury your dead in the choicest of our tombs. None of us will refuse you his tomb for burying your dead."

⁷Then Abraham rose and bowed down before the people of the land, the Hittites. ⁸He said to them, "If you are willing to let me bury my dead, then listen to me and intercede with Ephron son of Zohar on my behalf ⁹so he will sell me the cave of Machpelah, which belongs to him and is at the end of his field. Ask him to sell it to me for the full price as a burial site among you."

¹⁰Ephron the Hittite was sitting among his people and he replied to Abraham in the hearing of all the Hittites who had come to the gate of his city. ¹¹"No, my lord," he said. "Listen to me; I give*d* you the field, and I give*d* you the cave that is in it. I give*d* it to you in the presence of my people. Bury your dead."

¹²Again Abraham bowed down before the people of the land ¹³and he said to Ephron in their hearing, "Listen to me, if you will. I will pay the price of the field. Accept it from me so I can bury my dead there."

¹⁴Ephron answered Abraham, ¹⁵"Listen to me, my lord; the land is worth four hundred shekels*e* of silver, but what is that between me and you? Bury your dead."

¹⁶Abraham agreed to Ephron's terms and weighed out for him the price he had

---

a 13 Many manuscripts of the Masoretic Text, Samaritan Pentateuch, Septuagint and Syriac; most manuscripts of the Masoretic Text *a ram behind* him,   *b 18* Or *seed*
c 3 Or *the sons of Heth*; also in verses 5, 7, 10, 16, 18 and 20
d 11 Or *sell*   *e 15* That is, about 10 pounds (about 4.5 kilograms)

named in the hearing of the Hittites: four hundred shekels of silver, according to the weight current among the merchants.

¹⁷So Ephron's field in Machpelah near Mamre—both the field and the cave in it, and all the trees within the borders of the field—was deeded ¹⁸to Abraham as his property in the presence of all the Hittites who had come to the gate of the city. ¹⁹Afterward Abraham buried his wife Sarah in the cave in the field of Machpelah near Mamre (which is at Hebron) in the land of Canaan. ²⁰So the field and the cave in it were deeded to Abraham by the Hittites as a burial site.

Isaac and Rebekah

24 Abraham was now old and well advanced in years, and the LORD had blessed him in every way. ²He said to the chief*a* servant in his household, the one in charge of all that he had, "Put your hand under my thigh. ³I want you to swear by the LORD, the God of heaven and the God of earth, that you will not get a wife for my son from the daughters of the Canaanites, among whom I am living, ⁴but will go to my country and my own relatives and get a wife for my son Isaac."

⁵The servant asked him, "What if the woman is unwilling to come back with me to this land? Shall I then take your son back to the country you came from?"

⁶"Make sure that you do not take my son back there," Abraham said. ⁷"The LORD, the God of heaven, who brought me out of my father's household and my native land and who spoke to me and promised me on oath, saying, 'To your offspring*b* I will give this land'—he will send his angel before you so that you can get a wife for my son from there. ⁸If the woman is unwilling to come back with you, then you will be released from this oath of mine. Only do not take my son back there." ⁹So the servant put his hand under the thigh of his master Abraham and swore an oath to him concerning this matter.

¹⁰Then the servant took ten of his mas-

a 2 Or *oldest* *b 7* Or *seed*

God Is Out Front

READ GENESIS 24:1–21

Trusting God for little things—like finding enough flies to feed your pet lizard—doesn't seem difficult; so why is it so hard to trust God for big things? If he can do *anything*, why worry more about the big things than the little things? To God, there's no difference. Abraham's servant knew how to trust God for big things. When he went to find Isaac a wife, he was really on the spot! So he put it in God's hands and prayed, "O LORD ... give me success today" (verse 12). He knew God would go ahead of him, and God did just that. God is still way out front today. He has a plan for your life, and he'll help you get the right education, find the right job and marry the right girl. Like Abraham's servant, you just need to pray and trust God to lead you.

Your next reading is on page 40.

ter's camels and left, taking with him all kinds of good things from his master. He set out for Aram Naharaim[a] and made his way to the town of Nahor. 11He had the camels kneel down near the well outside the town; it was toward evening, the time the women go out to draw water.

12Then he prayed, "O LORD, God of my master Abraham, give me success today, and show kindness to my master Abraham. 13See, I am standing beside this spring, and the daughters of the townspeople are coming out to draw water. 14May it be that when I say to a girl, 'Please let down your jar that I may have a drink,' and she says, 'Drink, and I'll water your camels too'—let her be the one you have chosen for your servant Isaac. By this I will know that you have shown kindness to my master."

15Before he had finished praying, Rebekah came out with her jar on her shoulder. She was the daughter of Bethuel son of Milcah, who was the wife of Abraham's brother Nahor. 16The girl was very beautiful, a virgin; no man had ever lain with her. She went down to the spring, filled her jar and came up again.

17The servant hurried to meet her and said, "Please give me a little water from your jar."

18"Drink, my lord," she said, and quickly lowered the jar to her hands and gave him a drink.

19After she had given him a drink, she said, "I'll draw water for your camels too, until they have finished drinking." 20So she quickly emptied her jar into the trough, ran back to the well to draw more water, and drew enough for all his camels. 21Without saying a word, the man watched her closely to learn whether or not the LORD had made his journey successful.

22When the camels had finished drinking, the man took out a gold nose ring weighing a beka[b] and two gold bracelets weighing ten shekels.[c] 23Then he asked, "Whose daughter are you? Please tell me, is there room in your father's house for us to spend the night?"

24She answered him, "I am the daughter of Bethuel, the son that Milcah bore to Nahor." 25And she added, "We have plenty of straw and fodder, as well as room for you to spend the night."

26Then the man bowed down and worshiped the LORD, 27saying, "Praise be to the LORD, the God of my master Abraham, who has not abandoned his kindness and faithfulness to my master. As for me, the LORD has led me on the journey to the house of my master's relatives."

28The girl ran and told her mother's household about these things. 29Now Rebekah had a brother named Laban, and he hurried out to the man at the spring. 30As soon as he had seen the nose ring, and the bracelets on his sister's arms, and had heard Rebekah tell what the man said to her, he went out to the man and found him standing by the camels near the spring. 31"Come, you who are blessed by the LORD," he said. "Why are you standing out here? I have prepared the house and a place for the camels."

32So the man went to the house, and the camels were unloaded. Straw and fodder were brought for the camels, and water for him and his men to wash their feet. 33Then food was set before him, but he said, "I will not eat until I have told you what I have to say."

"Then tell us," ⌊Laban⌋ said.

34So he said, "I am Abraham's servant. 35The LORD has blessed my master abundantly, and he has become wealthy. He has given him sheep and cattle, silver and gold, menservants and maidservants, and camels and donkeys. 36My master's wife Sarah has borne him a son in her[d] old age, and he has given him everything he owns. 37And my master made me swear an oath, and said, 'You must not get a wife for my son from the daughters of the Canaanites, in whose land I live, 38but go to my father's family and to my own clan, and get a wife for my son.'

39"Then I asked my master, 'What if the woman will not come back with me?'

40"He replied, 'The LORD, before whom I have walked, will send his angel with you and make your journey a success, so that you can get a wife for my son from my own clan and from my father's family. 41Then, when you go to my clan, you will be released from my oath even if they refuse to give her to you—you will be released from my oath.'

42"When I came to the spring today, I said, 'O LORD, God of my master Abraham,

---

a 10 That is, Northwest Mesopotamia   *b 22* That is, about 1/5 ounce (about 5.5 grams)   *c 22* That is, about 4 ounces (about 110 grams)   *d 36* Or *his* if you will, please grant success to the journey on which I have come. ⁴³See, I am standing beside this spring; if a maiden comes out to draw water and I say to her, "Please let me drink a little water from your jar," ⁴⁴and if she says to me, "Drink, and I'll draw water for your camels too," let her be the one the LORD has chosen for my master's son.'

⁴⁵"Before I finished praying in my heart, Rebekah came out, with her jar on her shoulder. She went down to the spring and drew water, and I said to her, 'Please give me a drink.'

⁴⁶"She quickly lowered her jar from her shoulder and said, 'Drink, and I'll water your camels too.' So I drank, and she watered the camels also.

⁴⁷"I asked her, 'Whose daughter are you?'

"She said, 'The daughter of Bethuel son of Nahor, whom Milcah bore to him.'

"Then I put the ring in her nose and the bracelets on her arms, ⁴⁸and I bowed down and worshiped the LORD. I praised the LORD, the God of my master Abraham, who had led me on the right road to get the granddaughter of my master's brother for his son. ⁴⁹Now if you will show kindness and faithfulness to my master, tell me; and if not, tell me, so I may know which way to turn."

⁵⁰Laban and Bethuel answered, "This is from the LORD; we can say nothing to you one way or the other. ⁵¹Here is Rebekah; take her and go, and let her become the wife of your master's son, as the LORD has directed."

⁵²When Abraham's servant heard what they said, he bowed down to the ground before the LORD. ⁵³Then the servant brought out gold and silver jewelry and articles of clothing and gave them to Rebekah; he also gave costly gifts to her brother and to her mother. ⁵⁴Then he and the men who were with him ate and drank and spent the night there.

When they got up the next morning, he said, "Send me on my way to my master."

⁵⁵But her brother and her mother replied, "Let the girl remain with us ten days or so; then youᵃ may go."

⁵⁶But he said to them, "Do not detain me, now that the LORD has granted success to my journey. Send me on my way so I may go to my master."

⁵⁷Then they said, "Let's call the girl and ask her about it." ⁵⁸So they called Rebekah and asked her, "Will you go with this man?"

"I will go," she said.

⁵⁹So they sent their sister Rebekah on her way, along with her nurse and Abraham's servant and his men. ⁶⁰And they blessed Rebekah and said to her,

"Our sister, may you increase
   to thousands upon thousands;
may your offspring possess
   the gates of their enemies."

⁶¹Then Rebekah and her maids got ready and mount-

ᵃ 55 Or she

Gross!

When Rebekah drew water for the camels (Genesis 24:20), she was in for a lot of work! The amount of water camels can glug down would cause most other animals to explode. A large camel can drink as much as 21 gallons of water in ten minutes. Camels are also fantastic spitters! And riding their humps might make you hurl. Aren't camels wonderfully disgusting?

ed their camels and went back with the man. So the servant took Rebekah and left.

62Now Isaac had come from Beer Lahai Roi, for he was living in the Negev. 63He went out to the field one evening to meditate,a and as he looked up, he saw camels approaching. 64Rebekah also looked up and saw Isaac. She got down from her camel 65and asked the servant, "Who is that man in the field coming to meet us?"

"He is my master," the servant answered. So she took her veil and covered herself.

66Then the servant told Isaac all he had done. 67Isaac brought her into the tent of his mother Sarah, and he married Rebekah. So she became his wife, and he loved her; and Isaac was comforted after his mother's death.

The Death of Abraham

25 Abraham tookb another wife, whose name was Keturah. 2She bore him Zimran, Jokshan, Medan, Midian, Ishbak and Shuah. 3Jokshan was the father of Sheba and Dedan; the descendants of Dedan were the Asshurites, the Letushites and the Leummites. 4The sons of Midian were Ephah, Epher, Hanoch, Abida and Eldaah. All these were descendants of Keturah.

5Abraham left everything he owned to Isaac. 6But while he was still living, he gave gifts to the sons of his concubines and sent them away from his son Isaac to the land of the east.

7Altogether, Abraham lived a hundred and seventy-five years. 8Then Abraham breathed his last and died at a good old age, an old man and full of years; and he was gathered to his people. 9His sons Isaac and Ishmael buried him in the cave of Machpelah near Mamre, in the field of Ephron son of Zohar the Hittite, 10the field Abraham had bought from the Hittites.c There Abraham was buried with his wife Sarah. 11After Abraham's death, God blessed his son Isaac, who then lived near Beer Lahai Roi.

a 63 The meaning of the Hebrew for this word is uncertain.
b 1 Or had taken   c 10 Or the sons of Heth

You Be the Best "You"

READ GENESIS 25:19–34

Jacob and Esau were twins, but they were as different as night and day. Esau was red, hairy and muscular; Jacob was . . . well, let's just say if he was a kid today, he'd be a computer geek. As they got older, "Esau became a skillful hunter, a man of the open country, while Jacob was a quiet man, staying among the tents" (verse 27). These differences didn't make one brother better than the other. They simply had different skills. Jacob wasn't a macho outdoorsman like Esau, but Esau wasn't nearly the cook or camp manager Jacob was. All of us have different strengths and come in different shapes and sizes, too. These differences don't make us better or worse than others. So rather than compare yourself with others, work to discover your own unique strengths. Ask God to help you be the best "you" that you can be.

Your next reading is on page 42.

GET COOLER

Ishmael's Sons

¹²This is the account of Abraham's son Ishmael, whom Sarah's maidservant, Hagar the Egyptian, bore to Abraham.

¹³These are the names of the sons of Ishmael, listed in the order of their birth: Nebaioth the firstborn of Ishmael, Kedar, Adbeel, Mibsam, ¹⁴Mishma, Dumah, Massa, ¹⁵Hadad, Tema, Jetur, Naphish and Kedemah. ¹⁶These were the sons of Ishmael, and these are the names of the twelve tribal rulers according to their settlements and camps. ¹⁷Altogether, Ishmael lived a hundred and thirty-seven years. He breathed his last and died, and he was gathered to his people. ¹⁸His descendants settled in the area from Havilah to Shur, near the border of Egypt, as you go toward Asshur. And they lived in hostility toward*a* all their brothers.

Jacob and Esau

¹⁹This is the account of Abraham's son Isaac.

Abraham became the father of Isaac, ²⁰and Isaac was forty years old when he married Rebekah daughter of Bethuel the Aramean from Paddan Aram*b* and sister of Laban the Aramean.

²¹Isaac prayed to the LORD on behalf of his wife, because she was barren. The LORD answered his prayer, and his wife Rebekah became pregnant. ²²The babies jostled each other within her, and she said, "Why is this happening to me?" So she went to inquire of the LORD.

²³The LORD said to her,

"Two nations are in your womb,
    and two peoples from within you will be
        separated;
one people will be stronger than the other,
    and the older will serve the younger."

²⁴When the time came for her to give birth, there were twin boys in her womb. ²⁵The first to come out was red, and his whole body was like a hairy garment; so they named him Esau.*c* ²⁶After this, his brother came out, with his hand grasping Esau's heel; so he was named Jacob.*d* Isaac was sixty years old when Rebekah gave birth to them.

²⁷The boys grew up, and Esau became a skillful hunter, a man of the open country, while Jacob was a quiet man, staying among the tents. ²⁸Isaac, who had a taste for wild game, loved Esau, but Rebekah loved Jacob.

²⁹Once when Jacob was cooking some stew, Esau came in from the open country, famished. ³⁰He said to Jacob, "Quick, let me have some of that red stew! I'm famished!" (That is why he was also called Edom.*e*)

³¹Jacob replied, "First sell me your birthright."

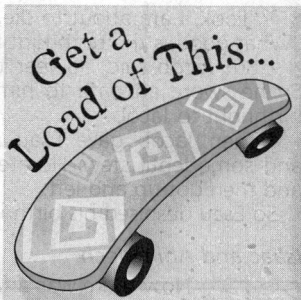

Get a Load of This...

If Jacob and Esau were twins, why didn't they look alike? Because they were fraternal twins—they each developed from a separate egg. If they had developed from the same egg, they would have been identical. One in every 40 people born is a twin.

---

a 18 Or *lived to the east of*   *b 20* That is, Northwest Mesopotamia   *c 25 Esau* may mean *hairy*; he was also called Edom, which means *red.*   *d 26 Jacob* means *he grasps the heel* (figuratively, *he deceives*).   *e 30 Edom* means *red.*

³²"Look, I am about to die," Esau said. "What good is the birthright to me?"

³³But Jacob said, "Swear to me first." So he swore an oath to him, selling his birthright to Jacob.

³⁴Then Jacob gave Esau some bread and some lentil stew. He ate and drank, and then got up and left.

So Esau despised his birthright.

Isaac and Abimelech

Now there was a famine in the land—besides the earlier famine of Abraham's time—and Isaac went to Abimelech king of the Philistines in Gerar. ²The LORD appeared to Isaac and said, "Do not go down to Egypt; live in the land where I tell you to live. ³Stay in this land for a while, and I will be with you and will bless you. For to you and your descendants I will give all these lands and will confirm the oath I swore to your father Abraham. ⁴I will make your descendants as numerous as the stars in the sky and will give them all these lands, and through your offspring*ᵃ* all nations on earth will be blessed, ⁵because Abraham obeyed me and kept my requirements, my commands, my decrees and my laws." ⁶So Isaac stayed in Gerar.

⁷When the men of that place asked him about his wife, he said, "She is my sister," because he was afraid to say, "She is my wife." He thought, "The men of this place might kill me on account of Rebekah, because she is beautiful."

⁸When Isaac had been there a long time, Abimelech king of the Philistines looked down from a window and saw Isaac caressing his wife Rebekah. ⁹So Abimelech summoned Isaac and said, "She is really your wife! Why did you say, 'She is my sister'?"

Isaac answered him, "Because I thought I might lose my life on account of her."

¹⁰Then Abimelech said, "What is this you have done to us? One of the men might well have slept with your wife, and you would have brought guilt upon us."

¹¹So Abimelech gave orders to all the

ᵃ 4 Or seed

A House Divided

READ GENESIS 25:27–28; 27:6–36

If your mom lets you get away with stuff and your dad doesn't (or the other way around), it can be tempting to hide things from one parent, or play them against each other to get what you want. This is *not* how a family should work. That's what happened in Isaac and Rebekah's family and it caused them nothing but trouble. "Isaac . . . loved Esau, but Rebekah loved Jacob" (Genesis 25:28). This favoritism led Rebekah and Jacob to deceive Isaac and rip off Esau. Family members should not keep secrets from each other, and certainly they shouldn't cheat one another to get what they want. Every family member should love and look out for every other family member. As a man, you will one day be responsible to help your own family get along, so learn to treat every member of your family with love now.

Your next reading is on page 50.

people: "Anyone who molests this man or his wife shall surely be put to death."

12 Isaac planted crops in that land and the same year reaped a hundredfold, because the LORD blessed him. 13 The man became rich, and his wealth continued to grow until he became very wealthy. 14 He had so many flocks and herds and servants that the Philistines envied him. 15 So all the wells that his father's servants had dug in the time of his father Abraham, the Philistines stopped up, filling them with earth.

16 Then Abimelech said to Isaac, "Move away from us; you have become too powerful for us."

17 So Isaac moved away from there and encamped in the Valley of Gerar and settled there. 18 Isaac reopened the wells that had been dug in the time of his father Abraham, which the Philistines had stopped up after Abraham died, and he gave them the same names his father had given them.

19 Isaac's servants dug in the valley and discovered a well of fresh water there. 20 But the herdsmen of Gerar quarreled with Isaac's herdsmen and said, "The water is ours!" So he named the well Esek,a because they disputed with him. 21 Then they dug another well, but they quarreled over that one also; so he named it Sitnah.b 22 He moved on from there and dug another well, and no one quarreled over it. He named it Rehoboth,c saying, "Now the LORD has given us room and we will flourish in the land."

23 From there he went up to Beersheba. 24 That night the LORD appeared to him and said, "I am the God of your father Abraham. Do not be afraid, for I am with you; I will bless you and will increase the number of your descendants for the sake of my servant Abraham."

25 Isaac built an altar there and called on the name of the LORD. There he pitched his tent, and there his servants dug a well.

26 Meanwhile, Abimelech had come to him from Gerar, with Ahuzzath his personal adviser and Phicol the commander of his forces. 27 Isaac asked them, "Why have you come to me, since you were hostile to me and sent me away?"

28 They answered, "We saw clearly that the LORD was with you; so we said, 'There ought to be a sworn agreement between us'—between us and you. Let us make a treaty with you 29 that you will do us no harm, just as we did not molest you but always treated you well and sent you away in peace. And now you are blessed by the LORD."

30 Isaac then made a feast for them, and they ate and drank. 31 Early the next morning the men swore an oath to each other. Then Isaac sent them on their way, and they left him in peace.

32 That day Isaac's servants came and told him about the well they had dug. They said, "We've found water!" 33 He called it Shibah,d and to this day the name of the town has been Beersheba.e

34 When Esau was forty years old, he married Judith daughter of Beeri the Hittite, and also Basemath daughter of Elon the Hittite. 35 They were a source of grief to Isaac and Rebekah.

Jacob Gets Isaac's Blessing

27 When Isaac was old and his eyes were so weak that he could no longer see, he called for Esau his older son and said to him, "My son."

"Here I am," he answered.

2 Isaac said, "I am now an old man and don't know the day of my death. 3 Now then, get your weapons—your quiver and bow—and go out to the open country to hunt some wild game for me. 4 Prepare me the kind of tasty food I like and bring it to me to eat, so that I may give you my blessing before I die."

5 Now Rebekah was listening as Isaac spoke to his son Esau. When Esau left for the open country to hunt game and bring it back, 6 Rebekah said to her son Jacob, "Look, I overheard your father say to your brother Esau, 7 'Bring me some game and prepare me some tasty food to eat, so that I may give you my blessing in the presence of the LORD before I die.' 8 Now, my son, listen carefully and do what I tell you: 9 Go out to the flock and bring me two choice young goats, so I can prepare some tasty food for your father, just the way he likes it. 10 Then take it to your father to eat, so that he may give you his blessing before he dies."

11 Jacob said to Rebekah his mother,

---

a 20 Esek means dispute.   b 21 Sitnah means opposition.
c 22 Rehoboth means room.   d 33 Shibah can mean oath or seven.   e 33 Beersheba can mean well of the oath or well of seven.

"But my brother Esau is a hairy man, and I'm a man with smooth skin. ¹²What if my father touches me? I would appear to be tricking him and would bring down a curse on myself rather than a blessing."

¹³His mother said to him, "My son, let the curse fall on me. Just do what I say; go and get them for me."

¹⁴So he went and got them and brought them to his mother, and she prepared some tasty food, just the way his father liked it. ¹⁵Then Rebekah took the best clothes of Esau her older son, which she had in the house, and put them on her younger son Jacob. ¹⁶She also covered his hands and the smooth part of his neck with the goatskins. ¹⁷Then she handed to her son Jacob the tasty food and the bread she had made.

¹⁸He went to his father and said, "My father."

"Yes, my son," he answered. "Who is it?"

¹⁹Jacob said to his father, "I am Esau your firstborn. I have done as you told me. Please sit up and eat some of my game so that you may give me your blessing."

²⁰Isaac asked his son, "How did you find it so quickly, my son?"

"The LORD your God gave me success," he replied.

²¹Then Isaac said to Jacob, "Come near so I can touch you, my son, to know whether you really are my son Esau or not."

²²Jacob went close to his father Isaac, who touched him and said, "The voice is the voice of Jacob, but the hands are the hands of Esau." ²³He did not recognize him, for his hands were hairy like those of his brother Esau; so he blessed him. ²⁴"Are you really my son Esau?" he asked.

"I am," he replied.

²⁵Then he said, "My son, bring me some of your game to eat, so that I may give you my blessing."

Jacob brought it to him and he ate; and he brought some wine and he drank. ²⁶Then his father Isaac said to him, "Come here, my son, and kiss me."

²⁷So he went to him and kissed him. When Isaac caught the smell of his clothes, he blessed him and said,

"Ah, the smell of my son
  is like the smell of a field
  that the LORD has blessed.
²⁸May God give you of heaven's dew

and of earth's richness—
  an abundance of grain and new
    wine.
²⁹May nations serve you
  and peoples bow down to you.
Be lord over your brothers,
  and may the sons of your mother
    bow down to you.
May those who curse you be cursed
  and those who bless you be blessed."

³⁰After Isaac finished blessing him and Jacob had scarcely left his father's presence, his brother Esau came in from hunting. ³¹He too prepared some tasty food and brought it to his father. Then he said to him, "My father, sit up and eat some of my game, so that you may give me your blessing."

³²His father Isaac asked him, "Who are you?"

"I am your son," he answered, "your firstborn, Esau."

³³Isaac trembled violently and said, "Who was it, then, that hunted game and brought it to me? I ate it just before you came and I blessed him—and indeed he will be blessed!"

³⁴When Esau heard his father's words, he burst out with a loud and bitter cry and said to his father, "Bless me—me too, my father!"

³⁵But he said, "Your brother came deceitfully and took your blessing."

³⁶Esau said, "Isn't he rightly named Jacob[a]? He has deceived me these two times: He took my birthright, and now he's taken my blessing!" Then he asked, "Haven't you reserved any blessing for me?"

³⁷Isaac answered Esau, "I have made him lord over you and have made all his relatives his servants, and I have sustained him with grain and new wine. So what can I possibly do for you, my son?"

³⁸Esau said to his father, "Do you have only one blessing, my father? Bless me too, my father!" Then Esau wept aloud.

³⁹His father Isaac answered him,

"Your dwelling will be
  away from the earth's richness,
  away from the dew of heaven above.
⁴⁰You will live by the sword
  and you will serve your brother.

---

[a] 36 Jacob means he grasps the heel (figuratively, he deceives).

But when you grow restless,
   you will throw his yoke
   from off your neck."

Jacob Flees to Laban

41Esau held a grudge against Jacob because of the blessing his father had given him. He said to himself, "The days of mourning for my father are near; then I will kill my brother Jacob."

42When Rebekah was told what her older son Esau had said, she sent for her younger son Jacob and said to him, "Your brother Esau is consoling himself with the thought of killing you. 43Now then, my son, do what I say: Flee at once to my brother Laban in Haran. 44Stay with him for a while until your brother's fury subsides. 45When your brother is no longer angry with you and forgets what you did to him, I'll send word for you to come back from there. Why should I lose both of you in one day?"

46Then Rebekah said to Isaac, "I'm disgusted with living because of these Hittite women. If Jacob takes a wife from among the women of this land, from Hittite women like these, my life will not be worth living."

28 So Isaac called for Jacob and blesseda him and commanded him: "Do not marry a Canaanite woman. 2Go at once to Paddan Aram,b to the house of your mother's father Bethuel. Take a wife for yourself there, from among the daughters of Laban, your mother's brother. 3May God Almightyc bless you and make you fruitful and increase your numbers until you become a community of peoples. 4May he give you and your descendants the blessing given to Abraham, so that you may take possession of the land where you now live as an alien, the land God gave to Abraham." 5Then Isaac sent Jacob on his way, and he went to Paddan Aram, to Laban son of Bethuel the Aramean, the brother of Rebekah, who was the mother of Jacob and Esau.

6Now Esau learned that Isaac had blessed Jacob and had sent him to Paddan Aram to take a wife from there, and that when he blessed him he commanded him, "Do not marry a Canaanite woman," 7and that Jacob had obeyed his father and mother and had gone to Paddan Aram. 8Esau then realized how displeasing the Canaanite women were to his father Isaac; 9so he went to Ishmael and married Mahalath, the sister of Nebaioth and daughter of Ishmael son of Abraham, in addition to the wives he already had.

Jacob's Dream at Bethel

10Jacob left Beersheba and set out for Haran. 11When he reached a certain place, he stopped for the night because the sun had set. Taking one of the stones there, he put it under his head and lay down to sleep. 12He had a dream in which he saw a stairwayd resting on the earth, with its top reaching to heaven, and the angels of God were ascending and descending on it. 13There above ite stood the Lord, and he said: "I am the Lord, the God of your father Abraham and the God of Isaac. I will give you and your descendants the land on which you are lying. 14Your descendants will be like the dust of the earth, and you will spread out to the west and to the east, to the north and to the south. All peoples on earth will be blessed through you and your offspring. 15I am with you and will watch over you wherever you go, and I will bring you back to this land. I will not leave you until I have done what I have promised you."

16When Jacob awoke from his sleep, he thought, "Surely the Lord is in this place, and I was not aware of it." 17He was afraid and said, "How awesome is this place! This is none other than the house of God; this is the gate of heaven."

18Early the next morning Jacob took the stone he had placed under his head and set it up as a pillar and poured oil on top of it. 19He called that place Bethel,f though the city used to be called Luz.

20Then Jacob made a vow, saying, "If God will be with me and will watch over me on this journey I am taking and will give me food to eat and clothes to wear 21so that I return safely to my father's house, then the Lordg will be my God 22andh this stone that I have set up as a pillar will be God's house, and of all that you give me I will give you a tenth."

a 1 Or greeted   b 2 That is, Northwest Mesopotamia; also in verses 5, 6 and 7   c 3 Hebrew El-Shaddai
d 12 Or ladder   e 13 Or There beside him   f 19 Bethel means house of God.   g 20,21 Or Since God . . . father's house, the Lord   h 21,22 Or house, and the Lord will be my God, 22then

Jacob Arrives in Paddan Aram

29 Then Jacob continued on his journey and came to the land of the eastern peoples. ²There he saw a well in the field, with three flocks of sheep lying near it because the flocks were watered from that well. The stone over the mouth of the well was large. ³When all the flocks were gathered there, the shepherds would roll the stone away from the well's mouth and water the sheep. Then they would return the stone to its place over the mouth of the well.

⁴Jacob asked the shepherds, "My brothers, where are you from?"

"We're from Haran," they replied.

⁵He said to them, "Do you know Laban, Nahor's grandson?"

"Yes, we know him," they answered.

⁶Then Jacob asked them, "Is he well?"

"Yes, he is," they said, "and here comes his daughter Rachel with the sheep."

⁷"Look," he said, "the sun is still high; it is not time for the flocks to be gathered. Water the sheep and take them back to pasture."

⁸"We can't," they replied, "until all the

Make It Stick

READ GENESIS 28:10–15

You'd have to have rocks in your head to use a rock for a pillow like Jacob did. But what a dream he had! Imagine what the special effects would be if this was a high-budget movie. Write down (or draw) what you think it looked like.

flocks are gathered and the stone has been rolled away from the mouth of the well. Then we will water the sheep."

9While he was still talking with them, Rachel came with her father's sheep, for she was a shepherdess. 10When Jacob saw Rachel daughter of Laban, his mother's brother, and Laban's sheep, he went over and rolled the stone away from the mouth of the well and watered his uncle's sheep. 11Then Jacob kissed Rachel and began to weep aloud. 12He had told Rachel that he was a relative of her father and a son of Rebekah. So she ran and told her father.

13As soon as Laban heard the news about Jacob, his sister's son, he hurried to meet him. He embraced him and kissed him and brought him to his home, and there Jacob told him all these things. 14Then Laban said to him, "You are my own flesh and blood."

Jacob Marries Leah and Rachel

After Jacob had stayed with him for a whole month, 15Laban said to him, "Just because you are a relative of mine, should you work for me for nothing? Tell me what your wages should be."

16Now Laban had two daughters; the name of the older was Leah, and the name of the younger was Rachel. 17Leah had weaka eyes, but Rachel was lovely in form, and beautiful. 18Jacob was in love with Rachel and said, "I'll work for you seven years in return for your younger daughter Rachel."

19Laban said, "It's better that I give her to you than to some other man. Stay here with me." 20So Jacob served seven years to get Rachel, but they seemed like only a few days to him because of his love for her.

21Then Jacob said to Laban, "Give me my wife. My time is completed, and I want to lie with her."

22So Laban brought together all the people of the place and gave a feast. 23But when evening came, he took his daughter Leah and gave her to Jacob, and Jacob lay with her. 24And Laban gave his servant girl Zilpah to his daughter as her maidservant.

25When morning came, there was Leah! So Jacob said to Laban, "What is this you have done to me? I served you for Rachel, didn't I? Why have you deceived me?"

26Laban replied, "It is not our custom here to give the younger daughter in marriage before the older one. 27Finish this daughter's bridal week; then we will give you the younger one also, in return for another seven years of work."

28And Jacob did so. He finished the week with Leah, and then Laban gave him his daughter Rachel to be his wife. 29Laban gave his servant girl Bilhah to his daughter Rachel as her maidservant. 30Jacob lay with Rachel also, and he loved Rachel more than Leah. And he worked for Laban another seven years.

Jacob's Children

31When the LORD saw that Leah was not loved, he opened her womb, but Rachel was barren. 32Leah became pregnant and gave birth to a son. She named him Reuben,b for she said, "It is because the LORD has seen my misery. Surely my husband will love me now."

33She conceived again, and when she gave birth to a son she said, "Because the LORD heard that I am not loved, he gave me this one too." So she named him Simeon.c

34Again she conceived, and when she gave birth to a son she said, "Now at last my husband will become attached to me, because I have borne him three sons." So he was named Levi.d

35She conceived again, and when she gave birth to a son she said, "This time I will praise the LORD." So she named him Judah.e Then she stopped having children.

30 When Rachel saw that she was not bearing Jacob any children, she became jealous of her sister. So she said to Jacob, "Give me children, or I'll die!"

2Jacob became angry with her and said, "Am I in the place of God, who has kept you from having children?"

3Then she said, "Here is Bilhah, my maidservant. Sleep with her so that she can bear children for me and that through her I too can build a family."

4So she gave him her servant Bilhah as a wife. Jacob slept with her, 5and she became pregnant and bore him a son. 6Then Rachel said, "God has vindicated me; he

---

a 17 Or delicate   b 32 Reuben sounds like the Hebrew for he has seen my misery; the name means see, a son.
c 33 Simeon probably means one who hears.   d 34 Levi sounds like and may be derived from the Hebrew for attached.   e 35 Judah sounds like and may be derived from the Hebrew for praise.

Get a Load of This...

In 1996, a sheep named Dolly was the result of scientists' attempts to make a perfect sheep through genetic engineering. While it may appear that Jacob's method worked because of human superstition, in reality his method worked because of God's intervention and blessing (Genesis 31:9).

has listened to my plea and given me a son." Because of this she named him Dan.[a]

7Rachel's servant Bilhah conceived again and bore Jacob a second son. 8Then Rachel said, "I have had a great struggle with my sister, and I have won." So she named him Naphtali.[b]

9When Leah saw that she had stopped having children, she took her maidservant Zilpah and gave her to Jacob as a wife. 10Leah's servant Zilpah bore Jacob a son. 11Then Leah said, "What good fortune!"[c] So she named him Gad.[d]

12Leah's servant Zilpah bore Jacob a second son. 13Then Leah said, "How happy I am! The women will call me happy." So she named him Asher.[e]

14During wheat harvest, Reuben went out into the fields and found some mandrake plants, which he brought to his mother Leah. Rachel said to Leah, "Please give me some of your son's mandrakes."

15But she said to her, "Wasn't it enough that you took away my husband? Will you take my son's mandrakes too?"

"Very well," Rachel said, "he can sleep with you tonight in return for your son's mandrakes."

16So when Jacob came in from the fields that evening, Leah went out to meet him. "You must sleep with me," she said. "I have hired you with my son's mandrakes." So he slept with her that night.

17God listened to Leah, and she became pregnant and bore Jacob a fifth son. 18Then Leah said, "God has rewarded me for giving my maidservant to my husband." So she named him Issachar.[f]

19Leah conceived again and bore Jacob a sixth son. 20Then Leah said, "God has presented me with a precious gift. This time my husband will treat me with honor, because I have borne him six sons." So she named him Zebulun.[g]

21Some time later she gave birth to a daughter and named her Dinah.

22Then God remembered Rachel; he listened to her and opened her womb. 23She became pregnant and gave birth to a son and said, "God has taken away my disgrace." 24She named him Joseph,[h] and said, "May the LORD add to me another son."

Jacob's Flocks Increase

25After Rachel gave birth to Joseph, Jacob said to Laban, "Send me on my way so I can go back to my own homeland. 26Give me my wives and children, for whom I have served you, and I will be on my way. You know how much work I've done for you."

27But Laban said to him, "If I have found favor in your eyes, please stay. I have learned by divination that[i] the

---

[a] 6 *Dan* here means *he has vindicated.*　　[b] 8 *Naphtali* means *my struggle.*
[c] 11 Or *"A troop is coming!"*　　[d] 11 *Gad* can mean *good fortune* or *a troop.*
[e] 13 *Asher* means *happy.*　　[f] 18 *Issachar* sounds like the Hebrew for *reward.*
[g] 20 *Zebulun* probably means *honor.*　　[h] 24 *Joseph* means *may he add.*
[i] 27 Or possibly *have become rich and*

Lord has blessed me because of you."
28He added, "Name your wages, and I will pay them."

29Jacob said to him, "You know how I have worked for you and how your livestock has fared under my care. 30The little you had before I came has increased greatly, and the Lord has blessed you wherever I have been. But now, when may I do something for my own household?"

31"What shall I give you?" he asked.

"Don't give me anything," Jacob replied. "But if you will do this one thing for me, I will go on tending your flocks and watching over them: 32Let me go through all your flocks today and remove from them every speckled or spotted sheep, every dark-colored lamb and every spotted or speckled goat. They will be my wages. 33And my honesty will testify for me in the future, whenever you check on the wages you have paid me. Any goat in my possession that is not speckled or spotted, or any lamb that is not dark-colored, will be considered stolen."

34"Agreed," said Laban. "Let it be as you have said." 35That same day he removed all the male goats that were streaked or spotted, and all the speckled or spotted female goats (all that had white on them) and all the dark-colored lambs, and he placed them in the care of his sons. 36Then he put a three-day journey between himself and Jacob, while Jacob continued to tend the rest of Laban's flocks.

37Jacob, however, took fresh-cut branches from poplar, almond and plane trees and made white stripes on them by peeling the bark and exposing the white inner wood of the branches. 38Then he placed the peeled branches in all the watering troughs, so that they would be directly in front of the flocks when they came to drink. When the flocks were in heat and came to drink, 39they mated in front of the branches. And they bore young that were streaked or speckled or spotted. 40Jacob set apart the young of the flock by themselves, but made the rest face the streaked and dark-colored animals that belonged to Laban. Thus he made separate flocks for himself and did not put them with Laban's animals. 41Whenever the stronger females were in heat, Jacob would place the branches in the troughs in front of the animals so they would mate near the branches, 42but if the animals were weak, he would not place them there. So the weak animals went to Laban and the strong ones to Jacob. 43In this way the man grew exceedingly prosperous and came to own large flocks, and maidservants and menservants, and camels and donkeys.

Jacob Flees From Laban

31 Jacob heard that Laban's sons were saying, "Jacob has taken everything our father owned and has gained all this wealth from what belonged to our father." 2And Jacob noticed that Laban's attitude toward him was not what it had been.

3Then the Lord said to Jacob, "Go back to the land of your fathers and to your relatives, and I will be with you."

4So Jacob sent word to Rachel and Leah to come out to the fields where his flocks were. 5He said to them, "I see that your father's attitude toward me is not what it was before, but the God of my father has been with me. 6You know that I've worked for your father with all my strength, 7yet your father has cheated me by changing my wages ten times. However, God has not allowed him to harm me. 8If he said, 'The speckled ones will be your wages,' then all the flocks gave birth to speckled young; and if he said, 'The streaked ones will be your wages,' then all the flocks bore streaked young. 9So God has taken away your father's livestock and has given them to me.

10"In breeding season I once had a dream in which I looked up and saw that the male goats mating with the flock were streaked, speckled or spotted. 11The angel of God said to me in the dream, 'Jacob.' I answered, 'Here I am.' 12And he said, 'Look up and see that all the male goats mating with the flock are streaked, speckled or spotted, for I have seen all that Laban has been doing to you. 13I am the God of Bethel, where you anointed a pillar and where you made a vow to me. Now leave this land at once and go back to your native land.' "

14Then Rachel and Leah replied, "Do we still have any share in the inheritance of our father's estate? 15Does he not regard us as foreigners? Not only has he sold us, but he has used up what was paid for us. 16Surely all the wealth that God took away from our father belongs to us and our children. So do whatever God has told you."

[17]Then Jacob put his children and his wives on camels, [18]and he drove all his livestock ahead of him, along with all the goods he had accumulated in Paddan Aram,[a] to go to his father Isaac in the land of Canaan.

[19]When Laban had gone to shear his sheep, Rachel stole her father's household gods. [20]Moreover, Jacob deceived Laban the Aramean by not telling him he was running away. [21]So he fled with all he had, and crossing the River,[b] he headed for the hill country of Gilead.

Laban Pursues Jacob

[22]On the third day Laban was told that Jacob had fled. [23]Taking his relatives with him, he pursued Jacob for seven days and caught up with him in the hill country of Gilead. [24]Then God came to Laban the Aramean in a dream at night and said to him, "Be careful not to say anything to Jacob, either good or bad."

[25]Jacob had pitched his tent in the hill country of Gilead when Laban overtook him, and Laban and his relatives camped there too. [26]Then Laban said to Jacob, "What have you done? You've deceived me, and you've carried off my daughters like captives in war. [27]Why did you run off secretly and deceive me? Why didn't you tell me, so I could send you away with joy and singing to the music of tambourines and harps? [28]You didn't even let me kiss my grandchildren and my daughters good-by. You have done a foolish thing. [29]I have the power to harm you; but last night the God of your father said to me, 'Be careful not to say anything to Jacob, either good or bad.' [30]Now you have gone off because you longed to return to your father's house. But why did you steal my gods?"

[31]Jacob answered Laban, "I was afraid, because I thought you would take your daughters away from me by force. [32]But if you find anyone who has your gods, he shall not live. In the presence of our rela-

---

[a] 18 That is, Northwest Mesopotamia   [b] 21 That is, the Euphrates

---

Shoplifter Steals Gods

READ GENESIS 31

It might seem strange to think of bowing down to a statue as if it were a god. However, many people in Bible times did exactly that. But what good could come from praying to a god that could be stolen away like Laban's were? When they were missing, Laban was frantic. "Now Rachel had taken the household gods and ... was sitting on them. Laban searched through everything in the tent but found nothing" (verse 34). What a laugh! Laban's gods couldn't even protect them*selves*, never mind him! They couldn't even complain about being sat on. Worshiping idols is not only wrong, it just doesn't add up. God commanded us not to worship idols (Exodus 20:3–6) because he didn't want us to waste time relying on something that can't fix our problems. Instead we should rely on him, the One true God who can do anything.

Your next reading is on page 53.

tives, see for yourself whether there is anything of yours here with me; and if so, take it." Now Jacob did not know that Rachel had stolen the gods.

33 So Laban went into Jacob's tent and into Leah's tent and into the tent of the two maidservants, but he found nothing. After he came out of Leah's tent, he entered Rachel's tent. 34 Now Rachel had taken the household gods and put them inside her camel's saddle and was sitting on them. Laban searched through everything in the tent but found nothing.

35 Rachel said to her father, "Don't be angry, my lord, that I cannot stand up in your presence; I'm having my period." So he searched but could not find the household gods.

36 Jacob was angry and took Laban to task. "What is my crime?" he asked Laban. "What sin have I committed that you hunt me down? 37 Now that you have searched through all my goods, what have you found that belongs to your household? Put it here in front of your relatives and mine, and let them judge between the two of us.

38 "I have been with you for twenty years now. Your sheep and goats have not miscarried, nor have I eaten rams from your flocks. 39 I did not bring you animals torn by wild beasts; I bore the loss myself. And you demanded payment from me for whatever was stolen by day or night. 40 This was my situation: The heat consumed me in the daytime and the cold at night, and sleep fled from my eyes. 41 It was like this for the twenty years I was in your household. I worked for you fourteen years for your two daughters and six years for your flocks, and you changed my wages ten times. 42 If the God of my father, the God of Abraham and the Fear of Isaac, had not been with me, you would surely have sent me away empty-handed. But God has seen my hardship and the toil of my hands, and last night he rebuked you."

Make It Stick

READ GENESIS 31:19

God made an important rule against the worship of other gods. Turn to Exodus 20:3 on page 110 and write the rule down on your sticky note. Then stick the note here. Can you think of some false "gods" in your life, things that distract you from God?

43Laban answered Jacob, "The women are my daughters, the children are my children, and the flocks are my flocks. All you see is mine. Yet what can I do today about these daughters of mine, or about the children they have borne? 44Come now, let's make a covenant, you and I, and let it serve as a witness between us."

45So Jacob took a stone and set it up as a pillar. 46He said to his relatives, "Gather some stones." So they took stones and piled them in a heap, and they ate there by the heap. 47Laban called it Jegar Sahadutha,a and Jacob called it Galeed.b

48Laban said, "This heap is a witness between you and me today." That is why it was called Galeed. 49It was also called Mizpah,c because he said, "May the LORD keep watch between you and me when we are away from each other. 50If you mistreat my daughters or if you take any wives besides my daughters, even though no one is with us, remember that God is a witness between you and me."

51Laban also said to Jacob, "Here is this heap, and here is this pillar I have set up between you and me. 52This heap is a witness, and this pillar is a witness, that I will not go past this heap to your side to harm you and that you will not go past this heap and pillar to my side to harm me. 53May the God of Abraham and the God of Nahor, the God of their father, judge between us."

So Jacob took an oath in the name of the Fear of his father Isaac. 54He offered a sacrifice there in the hill country and invited his relatives to a meal. After they had eaten, they spent the night there.

55Early the next morning Laban kissed his grandchildren and his daughters and blessed them. Then he left and returned home.

Jacob Prepares to Meet Esau

32 Jacob also went on his way, and the angels of God met him. 2When Jacob saw them, he said, "This is the camp of God!" So he named that place Mahanaim.d

3Jacob sent messengers ahead of him to his brother Esau in the land of Seir, the country of Edom. 4He instructed them: "This is what you are to say to my master Esau: 'Your servant Jacob says, I have been staying with Laban and have remained there till now. 5I have cattle and donkeys, sheep and goats, menservants and maidservants. Now I am sending this message to my lord, that I may find favor in your eyes.' "

6When the messengers returned to Jacob, they said, "We went to your brother Esau, and now he is coming to meet you, and four hundred men are with him."

7In great fear and distress Jacob divided the people who were with him into two groups,e and the flocks and herds and camels as well. 8He thought, "If Esau comes and attacks one group,f the groupf that is left may escape."

9Then Jacob prayed, "O God of my father Abraham, God of my father Isaac, O LORD, who said to me, 'Go back to your country and your relatives, and I will make you prosper,' 10I am unworthy of all the kindness and faithfulness you have shown your servant. I had only my staff when I crossed this Jordan, but now I have become two groups. 11Save me, I pray, from the hand of my brother Esau, for I am afraid he will come and attack me, and also the mothers with their children. 12But you have said, 'I will surely make you prosper and will make your descendants like the sand of the sea, which cannot be counted.' "

13He spent the night there, and from what he had with him he selected a gift for his brother Esau: 14two hundred female goats and twenty male goats, two hundred ewes and twenty rams, 15thirty female camels with their young, forty cows and ten bulls, and twenty female donkeys and ten male donkeys. 16He put them in the care of his servants, each herd by itself, and said to his servants, "Go ahead of me, and keep some space between the herds."

17He instructed the one in the lead: "When my brother Esau meets you and asks, 'To whom do you belong, and where are you going, and who owns all these animals in front of you?' 18then you are to say, 'They belong to your servant Jacob. They are a gift sent to my lord Esau, and he is coming behind us.' "

19He also instructed the second, the third and all the others who followed the herds: "You are to say the same thing to

a 47 The Aramaic Jegar Sahadutha means witness heap.
b 47 The Hebrew Galeed means witness heap.
c 49 Mizpah means watchtower.   d 2 Mahanaim means two camps.   e 7 Or camps; also in verse 10   f 8 Or camp

Esau when you meet him. 20And be sure to say, 'Your servant Jacob is coming behind us.' " For he thought, "I will pacify him with these gifts I am sending on ahead; later, when I see him, perhaps he will receive me." 21So Jacob's gifts went on ahead of him, but he himself spent the night in the camp.

Jacob Wrestles With God

22That night Jacob got up and took his two wives, his two maidservants and his eleven sons and crossed the ford of the Jabbok. 23After he had sent them across the stream, he sent over all his possessions. 24So Jacob was left alone, and a man wrestled with him till daybreak. 25When the man saw that he could not overpower him, he touched the socket of Jacob's hip so that his hip was wrenched as he wrestled with the man. 26Then the man said, "Let me go, for it is daybreak."

But Jacob replied, "I will not let you go unless you bless me."

27The man asked him, "What is your name?"

"Jacob," he answered.

28Then the man said, "Your name will no longer be Jacob, but Israel,a because you have struggled with God and with men and have overcome."

29Jacob said, "Please tell me your name."

But he replied, "Why do you ask my name?" Then he blessed him there.

30So Jacob called the place Peniel,b saying, "It is because I saw God face to face, and yet my life was spared."

31The sun rose above him as he passed Peniel,c and he was limping because of his hip. 32Therefore to this day the Israelites do not eat the tendon attached to the socket of the hip, because the socket of Jacob's hip was touched near the tendon.

a 28 *Israel* means *he struggles with God.*   b 30 *Peniel* means *face of God.*   c 31 Hebrew *Penuel,* a variant of *Peniel*

All-night Wrestling Match

READ GENESIS 32:1–12; 22–32

To win a wrestling match, you need physical strength. You also need speed and skill. But more than anything you need determination. Professional athletes agree that being completely sold on succeeding is the key to winning. Jacob had this sort of determination when he wrestled with God. Jacob's name was even changed to Israel, which means "he struggles with God." By now, after many years as a shepherd, Jacob was a strong, outdoors type of guy. Still . . . wrestling all night? Talk about determination! Not to mention lots of sweat and maybe even blood. We need to continually seek God like Jacob, like someone in a wrestling match who refuses to give up. The next time you see a wrestling match, think of how you need to be determined to know God.

Your next reading is on page 55.

Jacob Meets Esau

33 Jacob looked up and there was Esau, coming with his four hundred men; so he divided the children among Leah, Rachel and the two maidservants. ²He put the maidservants and their children in front, Leah and her children next, and Rachel and Joseph in the rear. ³He himself went on ahead and bowed down to the ground seven times as he approached his brother.

⁴But Esau ran to meet Jacob and embraced him; he threw his arms around his neck and kissed him. And they wept. ⁵Then Esau looked up and saw the women and children. "Who are these with you?" he asked.

Jacob answered, "They are the children God has graciously given your servant."

⁶Then the maidservants and their children approached and bowed down. ⁷Next, Leah and her children came and bowed down. Last of all came Joseph and Rachel, and they too bowed down.

⁸Esau asked, "What do you mean by all these droves I met?"

"To find favor in your eyes, my lord," he said.

⁹But Esau said, "I already have plenty, my brother. Keep what you have for yourself."

¹⁰"No, please!" said Jacob. "If I have found favor in your eyes, accept this gift from me. For to see your face is like seeing the face of God, now that you have received me favorably. ¹¹Please accept the present that was brought to you, for God has been gracious to me and I have all I need." And because Jacob insisted, Esau accepted it.

¹²Then Esau said, "Let us be on our way; I'll accompany you."

¹³But Jacob said to him, "My lord knows that the children are tender and that I must care for the ewes and cows that are nursing their young. If they are driven hard just one day, all the animals will die. ¹⁴So let my lord go on ahead of his servant, while I move along slowly at the pace of the droves before me and that of the children, until I come to my lord in Seir."

¹⁵Esau said, "Then let me leave some of my men with you."

"But why do that?" Jacob asked. "Just let me find favor in the eyes of my lord."

¹⁶So that day Esau started on his way back to Seir. ¹⁷Jacob, however, went to Succoth, where he built a place for himself and made shelters for his livestock. That is why the place is called Succoth.ᵃ

¹⁸After Jacob came from Paddan Aram,ᵇ he arrived safely at theᶜ city of Shechem in Canaan and camped within sight of the city. ¹⁹For a hundred pieces of silver,ᵈ he bought from the sons of Hamor, the father of Shechem, the plot of ground where he pitched his tent.

ᵃ 17 Succoth means shelters.   ᵇ 18 That is, Northwest Mesopotamia
ᶜ 18 Or arrived at Shalem, a   ᵈ 19 Hebrew hundred kesitahs; a kesitah was a unit of money of unknown weight and value.

²⁰There he set up an altar and called it El Elohe Israel.ᵃ

Dinah and the Shechemites

34 Now Dinah, the daughter Leah had borne to Jacob, went out to visit the women of the land. ²When Shechem son of Hamor the Hivite, the ruler of that area, saw her, he took her and violated her. ³His heart was drawn to Dinah daughter of Jacob, and he loved the girl and spoke tenderly to her. ⁴And Shechem said to his father Hamor, "Get me this girl as my wife."

⁵When Jacob heard that his daughter Dinah had been defiled, his sons were in the fields with his livestock; so he kept quiet about it until they came home.

⁶Then Shechem's father Hamor went out to talk with Jacob. ⁷Now Jacob's sons had come in from the fields as soon as they heard what had happened. They were filled with grief and fury, because Shechem had done a disgraceful thing inᵇ Israel by lying with Jacob's daughter—a thing that should not be done.

⁸But Hamor said to them, "My son Shechem has his heart set on your daughter. Please give her to him as his wife. ⁹Intermarry with us; give us your daughters and take our daughters for yourselves. ¹⁰You can settle among us; the land is open to you. Live in it, tradeᶜ in it, and acquire property in it."

¹¹Then Shechem said to Dinah's father and brothers, "Let me find favor in your eyes, and I will give you whatever you ask. ¹²Make the price for the bride and the gift I am to bring as great as you like, and I'll pay whatever you ask me. Only give me the girl as my wife."

¹³Because their sister Dinah had been defiled, Jacob's sons replied deceitfully as they spoke to Shechem and his father Hamor. ¹⁴They said to them, "We can't do such a thing; we can't give our sister to a man who is not circumcised. That would be a disgrace to us. ¹⁵We will give our consent to you on one condition only: that you become like us by circumcising all your males. ¹⁶Then we will give you our

---

ᵃ 20 *El Elohe Israel* can mean *God, the God of Israel* or *mighty is the God of Israel.*   ᵇ 7 Or *against*   ᶜ 10 Or *move about freely*; also in verse 21

Making Things Right

READ GENESIS 33:1–11

People often joke that the last words any man wants to say are, "I was wrong." But that's exactly what a real man needs to do. Jacob knew that he had wronged Esau and that he had to make things right. Esau also reacted the right way, by forgiving Jacob. "Esau ran to meet Jacob and embraced him; he threw his arms around his neck and kissed him. And they wept" (verse 4). When you do something wrong to someone, you need to ask for forgiveness, just like Jacob needed to—though bowing down seven times is optional. You also need to freely forgive those who have wronged you. This is a cornerstone for how our family, church and society should work. Everyone makes mistakes, so when you don't forgive each other, things fall apart. That's why real men are always willing to say, "I'm sorry."

Your next reading is on page 60.

daughters and take your daughters for ourselves. We'll settle among you and become one people with you. 17But if you will not agree to be circumcised, we'll take our sister^a and go."

18Their proposal seemed good to Hamor and his son Shechem. 19The young man, who was the most honored of all his father's household, lost no time in doing what they said, because he was delighted with Jacob's daughter. 20So Hamor and his son Shechem went to the gate of their city to speak to their fellow townsmen. 21"These men are friendly toward us," they said. "Let them live in our land and trade in it; the land has plenty of room for them. We can marry their daughters and they can marry ours. 22But the men will consent to live with us as one people only on the condition that our males be circumcised, as they themselves are. 23Won't their livestock, their property and all their other animals become ours? So let us give

our consent to them, and they will settle among us."

24All the men who went out of the city gate agreed with Hamor and his son Shechem, and every male in the city was circumcised.

25Three days later, while all of them were still in pain, two of Jacob's sons, Simeon and Levi, Dinah's brothers, took their swords and attacked the unsuspecting city, killing every male. 26They put Hamor and his son Shechem to the sword and took Dinah from Shechem's house and left. 27The sons of Jacob came upon the dead bodies and looted the city where^b their sister had been defiled. 28They seized their flocks and herds and donkeys and everything else of theirs in the city and out in the fields. 29They carried off all their wealth and all their women and children, taking as plunder everything in the houses.

^a 17 Hebrew *daughter*   ^b 27 Or *because*

Make It Stick

READ GENESIS 33:9

Jacob and Esau had fought over the family birthright and their father's possessions. But God blessed them both apart from their father's goods. Whether your parents are rich or poor doesn't matter, because God is your real provider, not your parents. Write, "God is my provider" on a sticky note and place it here.

³⁰Then Jacob said to Simeon and Levi, "You have brought trouble on me by making me a stench to the Canaanites and Perizzites, the people living in this land. We are few in number, and if they join forces against me and attack me, I and my household will be destroyed."

³¹But they replied, "Should he have treated our sister like a prostitute?"

Jacob Returns to Bethel

35 Then God said to Jacob, "Go up to Bethel and settle there, and build an altar there to God, who appeared to you when you were fleeing from your brother Esau."

²So Jacob said to his household and to all who were with him, "Get rid of the foreign gods you have with you, and purify yourselves and change your clothes. ³Then come, let us go up to Bethel, where I will build an altar to God, who answered me in the day of my distress and who has been with me wherever I have gone." ⁴So they gave Jacob all the foreign gods they had and the rings in their ears, and Jacob buried them under the oak at Shechem. ⁵Then they set out, and the terror of God fell upon the towns all around them so that no one pursued them.

⁶Jacob and all the people with him came to Luz (that is, Bethel) in the land of Canaan. ⁷There he built an altar, and he called the place El Bethel,ᵃ because it was there that God revealed himself to him when he was fleeing from his brother.

⁸Now Deborah, Rebekah's nurse, died and was buried under the oak below Bethel. So it was named Allon Bacuth.ᵇ

⁹After Jacob returned from Paddan Aram,ᶜ God appeared to him again and blessed him. ¹⁰God said to him, "Your name is Jacob,ᵈ but you will no longer be called Jacob; your name will be Israel.ᵉ" So he named him Israel.

¹¹And God said to him, "I am God Almighty ᶠ; be fruitful and increase in number. A nation and a community of nations will come from you, and kings will come from your body. ¹²The land I gave to Abraham and Isaac I also give to you, and I will give this land to your descendants after you." ¹³Then God went up from him at the place where he had talked with him.

¹⁴Jacob set up a stone pillar at the place where God had talked with him, and he poured out a drink offering on it; he also poured oil on it. ¹⁵Jacob called the place where God had talked with him Bethel. ᵍ

The Deaths of Rachel and Isaac

¹⁶Then they moved on from Bethel. While they were still some distance from Ephrath, Rachel began to give birth and had great difficulty. ¹⁷And as she was having great difficulty in childbirth, the midwife said to her, "Don't be afraid, for you have another son." ¹⁸As she breathed her last—for she was dying—she named her son Ben-Oni.ʰ But his father named him Benjamin.ⁱ

¹⁹So Rachel died and was buried on the way to Ephrath (that is, Bethlehem). ²⁰Over her tomb Jacob set up a pillar, and to this day that pillar marks Rachel's tomb.

²¹Israel moved on again and pitched his tent beyond Migdal Eder. ²²While Israel was living in that region, Reuben went in and slept with his father's concubine Bilhah, and Israel heard of it.

Jacob had twelve sons:
²³The sons of Leah:
    Reuben the firstborn of Jacob,
    Simeon, Levi, Judah, Issachar and
    Zebulun.
²⁴The sons of Rachel:
    Joseph and Benjamin.
²⁵The sons of Rachel's maidservant Bilhah:
    Dan and Naphtali.
²⁶The sons of Leah's maidservant Zilpah:
    Gad and Asher.
These were the sons of Jacob, who were born to him in Paddan Aram.

²⁷Jacob came home to his father Isaac in Mamre, near Kiriath Arba (that is, Hebron), where Abraham and Isaac had stayed. ²⁸Isaac lived a hundred and eighty years. ²⁹Then he breathed his last and died and was gathered to his people, old and full of years. And his sons Esau and Jacob buried him.

ᵃ 7 El Bethel means God of Bethel.   ᵇ 8 Allon Bacuth means oak of weeping.   ᶜ 9 That is, Northwest Mesopotamia; also in verse 26   ᵈ 10 Jacob means he grasps the heel (figuratively, he deceives).   ᵉ 10 Israel means he struggles with God.   ᶠ 11 Hebrew El-Shaddai   ᵍ 15 Bethel means house of God.   ʰ 18 Ben-Oni means son of my trouble.   ⁱ 18 Benjamin means son of my right hand.

Esau's Descendants

36

This is the account of Esau (that is, Edom).

²Esau took his wives from the women of Canaan: Adah daughter of Elon the Hittite, and Oholibamah daughter of Anah and granddaughter of Zibeon the Hivite— ³also Basemath daughter of Ishmael and sister of Nebaioth.

⁴Adah bore Eliphaz to Esau, Basemath bore Reuel, ⁵and Oholibamah bore Jeush, Jalam and Korah. These were the sons of Esau, who were born to him in Canaan.

⁶Esau took his wives and sons and daughters and all the members of his household, as well as his livestock and all his other animals and all the goods he had acquired in Canaan, and moved to a land some distance from his brother Jacob. ⁷Their possessions were too great for them to remain together; the land where they were staying could not support them both because of their livestock. ⁸So Esau (that is, Edom) settled in the hill country of Seir.

⁹This is the account of Esau the father of the Edomites in the hill country of Seir.

¹⁰These are the names of Esau's sons:
Eliphaz, the son of Esau's wife Adah, and Reuel, the son of Esau's wife Basemath.
¹¹The sons of Eliphaz:
Teman, Omar, Zepho, Gatam and Kenaz.
¹²Esau's son Eliphaz also had a concubine named Timna, who bore him Amalek. These were grandsons of Esau's wife Adah.
¹³The sons of Reuel:
Nahath, Zerah, Shammah and Mizzah. These were grandsons of Esau's wife Basemath.
¹⁴The sons of Esau's wife Oholibamah daughter of Anah and granddaughter of Zibeon, whom she bore to Esau:
Jeush, Jalam and Korah.

¹⁵These were the chiefs among Esau's descendants:
The sons of Eliphaz the firstborn of Esau:
Chiefs Teman, Omar, Zepho, Kenaz, ¹⁶Korah,ᵃ Gatam and Amalek. These were the chiefs descended from Eliphaz in Edom; they were grandsons of Adah.
¹⁷The sons of Esau's son Reuel:
Chiefs Nahath, Zerah, Shammah and Mizzah. These were the chiefs descended from Reuel in Edom; they were grandsons of Esau's wife Basemath.
¹⁸The sons of Esau's wife Oholibamah:
Chiefs Jeush, Jalam and Korah. These were the chiefs descended from Esau's wife Oholibamah daughter of Anah.

¹⁹These were the sons of Esau (that is, Edom), and these were their chiefs.

²⁰These were the sons of Seir the Horite, who were living in the region:
Lotan, Shobal, Zibeon, Anah, ²¹Dishon, Ezer and Dishan. These sons of Seir in Edom were Horite chiefs.
²²The sons of Lotan:
Hori and Homam.ᵇ Timna was Lotan's sister.
²³The sons of Shobal:
Alvan, Manahath, Ebal, Shepho and Onam.
²⁴The sons of Zibeon:
Aiah and Anah. This is the Anah who discovered the hot springsᶜ in the desert while he was grazing the donkeys of his father Zibeon.
²⁵The children of Anah:
Dishon and Oholibamah daughter of Anah.
²⁶The sons of Dishonᵈ:
Hemdan, Eshban, Ithran and Keran.
²⁷The sons of Ezer:
Bilhan, Zaavan and Akan.
²⁸The sons of Dishan:
Uz and Aran.
²⁹These were the Horite chiefs:
Lotan, Shobal, Zibeon, Anah, ³⁰Dishon, Ezer and Dishan. These were the Horite chiefs, according to their divisions, in the land of Seir.

ᵃ 16 Masoretic Text; Samaritan Pentateuch (see also Gen. 36:11 and 1 Chron. 1:36) does not have Korah.   ᵇ 22 Hebrew Hemam, a variant of Homam (see 1 Chron. 1:39)   ᶜ 24 Vulgate; Syriac discovered water; the meaning of the Hebrew for this word is uncertain.   ᵈ 26 Hebrew Dishan, a variant of Dishon

The Rulers of Edom

31These were the kings who reigned in Edom before any Israelite king reigned*a*: 32Bela son of Beor became king of Edom. His city was named Dinhabah.

33When Bela died, Jobab son of Zerah from Bozrah succeeded him as king.

34When Jobab died, Husham from the land of the Temanites succeeded him as king.

35When Husham died, Hadad son of Bedad, who defeated Midian in the country of Moab, succeeded him as king. His city was named Avith.

36When Hadad died, Samlah from Masrekah succeeded him as king.

37When Samlah died, Shaul from Rehoboth on the river*b* succeeded him as king.

38When Shaul died, Baal-Hanan son of Acbor succeeded him as king.

39When Baal-Hanan son of Acbor died, Hadad*c* succeeded him as king. His city was named Pau, and his wife's name was Mehetabel daughter of Matred, the daughter of Me-Zahab.

40These were the chiefs descended from Esau, by name, according to their clans and regions:

Timna, Alvah, Jetheth, 41Oholibamah, Elah, Pinon, 42Kenaz, Teman, Mibzar, 43Magdiel and Iram. These were the chiefs of Edom, according to their settlements in the land they occupied.

This was Esau the father of the Edomites.

Joseph's Dreams

37 Jacob lived in the land where his father had stayed, the land of Canaan.

2This is the account of Jacob.

Joseph, a young man of seventeen, was tending the flocks with his brothers, the sons of Bilhah and the sons of Zilpah, his father's wives, and he brought their father a bad report about them.

3Now Israel loved Joseph more than any of his other sons, because he had been born to him in his old age; and he made a richly ornamented*d* robe for him. 4When his brothers saw that their father loved him more than any of them, they hated him and could not speak a kind word to him.

5Joseph had a dream, and when he told it to his brothers, they hated him all the more. 6He said to them, "Listen to this dream I had: 7We were binding sheaves of grain out in the field when suddenly my sheaf rose and stood upright, while your sheaves gathered around mine and bowed down to it."

8His brothers said to him, "Do you intend to reign over us? Will you actually rule us?" And they hated him all the more because of his dream and what he had said.

9Then he had another dream, and he told it to his brothers. "Listen," he said, "I had another dream, and this time the sun and moon and eleven stars were bowing down to me."

10When he told his father as well as his brothers, his father rebuked him and said, "What is this dream you had? Will your mother and I and your brothers actually come and bow down to the ground before you?" 11His brothers were jealous of him, but his father kept the matter in mind.

Joseph Sold by His Brothers

12Now his brothers had gone to graze their father's flocks near Shechem, 13and Israel said to Joseph, "As you know, your brothers are grazing the flocks near Shechem. Come, I am going to send you to them."

"Very well," he replied.

14So he said to him, "Go and see if all is well with your brothers and with the flocks, and bring word back to me." Then he sent him off from the Valley of Hebron.

When Joseph arrived at Shechem, 15a man found him wandering around in the fields and asked him, "What are you looking for?"

16He replied, "I'm looking for my brothers. Can you tell me where they are grazing their flocks?"

17"They have moved on from here," the

a 31 Or *before an Israelite king reigned over them*
b 37 Possibly the Euphrates   *c 39* Many manuscripts of the Masoretic Text, Samaritan Pentateuch and Syriac (see also 1 Chron. 1:50); most manuscripts of the Masoretic Text *Hadar*
d 3 The meaning of the Hebrew for *richly ornamented* is uncertain; also in verses 23 and 32.

Joseph

READ GENESIS 37–50

GET DEEPER When Joseph was a teenager, he had two dreams about how his brothers, and even his parents, would bow down to him. Joseph didn't have the maturity to handle these revelations. Instead of humbling himself before God and keeping his dreams to himself, he told his brothers—who were jealous of him already—about the dreams. But as he got older, Joseph learned that God was in control. He knew that only God could interpret Pharaoh's dream. "'I cannot do it,' Joseph replied to Pharaoh, 'but God will give Pharaoh the answer he desires'" (Genesis 41:15–16).

GET COOLER Joseph was very self-centered as a teenager. He enjoyed being his father's favorite son, and he lorded it over his brothers. His father even made him a special coat to remind everyone how special his son was, and Joseph wore it proudly. "Now Israel loved Joseph more than any of his other sons . . . and he made a richly ornamented robe for him" (Genesis 37:3). But when Joseph was sold into slavery, he learned what it was like to have other people lord it over *him*. Talk about a wake-up call! This experience taught him that life wasn't all about being a leader or great, but that it was about serving others. He realized that he had suffered in order to become a blessing to others.

GET STRONGER As the favorite son, Joseph had life pretty easy. He didn't do as much of the hard labor that his older brothers did. But years of slavery and prison changed all that. And even though he was a handsome man, he had to overcome sexual temptation and learn to control his body. He knew his body belonged to God.

GET SMARTER It's difficult to become wise when you're stuck on yourself like Joseph used to be. But suffering changed him. By learning to rely on God, Joseph was able to focus his mind and achieve incredible results. He began by applying his mind to running Potiphar's household and was eventually put in charge of everything. The same thing happened in prison. And eventually Joseph's God-given abilities earned him the highest position in Egypt. "Then Pharaoh said to Joseph . . . 'There is no one so discerning and wise as you . . . I hereby put you in charge of the whole land of Egypt'" (Genesis 41:39–41).

Your next reading is on page 65.

man answered. "I heard them say, 'Let's go to Dothan.' "

So Joseph went after his brothers and found them near Dothan. ¹⁸But they saw him in the distance, and before he reached them, they plotted to kill him.

¹⁹"Here comes that dreamer!" they said to each other. ²⁰"Come now, let's kill him and throw him into one of these cisterns and say that a ferocious animal devoured him. Then we'll see what comes of his dreams."

²¹When Reuben heard this, he tried to rescue him from their hands. "Let's not take his life," he said. ²²"Don't shed any blood. Throw him into this cistern here in the desert, but don't lay a hand on him." Reuben said this to rescue him from them and take him back to his father.

²³So when Joseph came to his brothers, they stripped him of his robe—the richly ornamented robe he was wearing— ²⁴and they took him and threw him into the cistern. Now the cistern was empty; there was no water in it.

²⁵As they sat down to eat their meal, they looked up and saw a caravan of Ishmaelites coming from Gilead. Their camels were loaded with spices, balm and myrrh, and they were on their way to take them down to Egypt.

²⁶Judah said to his brothers, "What will we gain if we kill our brother and cover up his blood? ²⁷Come, let's sell him to the Ishmaelites and not lay our hands on him; after all, he is our brother, our own flesh and blood." His brothers agreed.

²⁸So when the Midianite merchants came by, his brothers pulled Joseph up out of the cistern and sold him for twenty shekels^a of silver to the Ishmaelites, who took him to Egypt.

²⁹When Reuben returned to the cistern and saw that Joseph was not there, he tore his clothes. ³⁰He went back to his brothers and said, "The boy isn't there! Where can I turn now?"

³¹Then they got Joseph's robe, slaughtered a goat and dipped the robe in the blood. ³²They took the ornamented robe back to their father and said, "We found this. Examine it to see whether it is your son's robe."

³³He recognized it and said, "It is my son's robe! Some ferocious animal has devoured him. Joseph has surely been torn to pieces."

³⁴Then Jacob tore his clothes, put on sackcloth and mourned for his son many days. ³⁵All his sons and daughters came to comfort him, but he refused to be comforted. "No," he said, "in mourning will I go down to the grave^b to my son." So his father wept for him.

³⁶Meanwhile, the Midianites^c sold Joseph in Egypt to Potiphar, one of Pharaoh's officials, the captain of the guard.

Get a Load of This...

Hieroglyphics are symbols used in the earliest Egyptian writing. Scientists weren't able to decipher Egyptian hieroglyphics until 1822. The key to the puzzle was the Rosetta Stone, accidentally discovered by Napoleon's soldiers in Egypt. It was a piece of rock with a message written in hieroglyphics and Greek.

---

^a 28 That is, about 8 ounces (about 0.2 kilogram)   ^b 35 Hebrew *Sheol*
^c 36 Samaritan Pentateuch, Septuagint, Vulgate and Syriac (see also verse 28); Masoretic Text *Medanites*

Judah and Tamar

38 At that time, Judah left his brothers and went down to stay with a man of Adullam named Hirah. ²There Judah met the daughter of a Canaanite man named Shua. He married her and lay with her; ³she became pregnant and gave birth to a son, who was named Er. ⁴She conceived again and gave birth to a son and named him Onan. ⁵She gave birth to still another son and named him Shelah. It was at Kezib that she gave birth to him.

⁶Judah got a wife for Er, his firstborn, and her name was Tamar. ⁷But Er, Judah's firstborn, was wicked in the LORD's sight; so the LORD put him to death.

⁸Then Judah said to Onan, "Lie with your brother's wife and fulfill your duty to her as a brother-in-law to produce offspring for your brother." ⁹But Onan knew that the offspring would not be his; so whenever he lay with his brother's wife, he spilled his semen on the ground to keep from producing offspring for his brother. ¹⁰What he did was wicked in the LORD's sight; so he put him to death also.

¹¹Judah then said to his daughter-in-law Tamar, "Live as a widow in your father's house until my son Shelah grows up." For he thought, "He may die too, just like his brothers." So Tamar went to live in her father's house.

¹²After a long time Judah's wife, the daughter of Shua, died. When Judah had recovered from his grief, he went up to Timnah, to the men who were shearing his sheep, and his friend Hirah the Adullamite went with him.

¹³When Tamar was told, "Your father-in-law is on his way to Timnah to shear his sheep," ¹⁴she took off her widow's clothes, covered herself with a veil to disguise herself, and then sat down at the entrance to Enaim, which is on the road to Timnah. For she saw that, though Shelah had now grown up, she had not been given to him as his wife.

¹⁵When Judah saw her, he thought she was a prostitute, for she had covered her face. ¹⁶Not realizing that she was his daughter-in-law, he went over to her by the roadside and said, "Come now, let me sleep with you."

"And what will you give me to sleep with you?" she asked.

¹⁷"I'll send you a young goat from my flock," he said.

"Will you give me something as a pledge until you send it?" she asked.

¹⁸He said, "What pledge should I give you?"

"Your seal and its cord, and the staff in your hand," she answered. So he gave them to her and slept with her, and she became pregnant by him. ¹⁹After she left, she took off her veil and put on her widow's clothes again.

²⁰Meanwhile Judah sent the young goat by his friend the Adullamite in order to get his pledge back from the woman, but he did not find her. ²¹He asked the men who lived there, "Where is the shrine prostitute who was beside the road at Enaim?"

"There hasn't been any shrine prostitute here," they said.

²²So he went back to Judah and said, "I didn't find her. Besides, the men who lived there said, 'There hasn't been any shrine prostitute here.' "

²³Then Judah said, "Let her keep what she has, or we will become a laughingstock. After all, I did send her this young goat, but you didn't find her."

²⁴About three months later Judah was told, "Your daughter-in-law Tamar is guilty of prostitution, and as a result she is now pregnant."

Judah said, "Bring her out and have her burned to death!"

²⁵As she was being brought out, she sent a message to her father-in-law. "I am pregnant by the man who owns these," she said. And she added, "See if you recognize whose seal and cord and staff these are."

²⁶Judah recognized them and said, "She is more righteous than I, since I wouldn't give her to my son Shelah." And he did not sleep with her again.

²⁷When the time came for her to give birth, there were twin boys in her womb. ²⁸As she was giving birth, one of them put out his hand; so the midwife took a scarlet thread and tied it on his wrist and said, "This one came out first." ²⁹But when he drew back his hand, his brother came out, and she said, "So this is how you have broken out!" And he was named Perez.ᵃ ³⁰Then his brother, who

---

ᵃ 29 Perez means breaking out.

had the scarlet thread on his wrist, came out and he was given the name Zerah.[a]

Joseph and Potiphar's Wife

39 Now Joseph had been taken down to Egypt. Potiphar, an Egyptian who was one of Pharaoh's officials, the captain of the guard, bought him from the Ishmaelites who had taken him there.

²The Lord was with Joseph and he prospered, and he lived in the house of his Egyptian master. ³When his master saw that the Lord was with him and that the Lord gave him success in everything he did, ⁴Joseph found favor in his eyes and became his attendant. Potiphar put him in charge of his household, and he entrusted to his care everything he owned. ⁵From the time he put him in charge of his household and of all that he owned, the Lord blessed the household of the Egyptian because of Joseph. The blessing of the Lord was on everything Potiphar had, both in the house and in the field. ⁶So he left in Joseph's care everything he had; with Joseph in charge, he did not concern himself with anything except the food he ate.

Now Joseph was well-built and handsome, ⁷and after a while his master's wife took notice of Joseph and said, "Come to bed with me!"

⁸But he refused. "With me in charge," he told her, "my master does not concern himself with anything in the house; everything he owns he has entrusted to my care. ⁹No one is greater in this house than I am. My master has withheld nothing from me except you, because you are his wife. How then could I do such a wicked thing and sin against God?" ¹⁰And though she spoke to Joseph day after day, he refused to go to bed with her or even be with her.

¹¹One day he went into the house to attend to his duties, and none of the household servants was inside. ¹²She caught him by his cloak and said, "Come to bed with me!" But he left his cloak in her hand and ran out of the house.

¹³When she saw that he had left his cloak in her hand and had run out of the house, ¹⁴she called her household servants. "Look," she said to them, "this Hebrew has been brought to us to make sport of us! He came in here to sleep with me, but I screamed. ¹⁵When he heard me scream for help, he left his cloak beside me and ran out of the house."

¹⁶She kept his cloak beside her until his master came home. ¹⁷Then she told him this story: "That Hebrew slave you brought us came to me to make sport of me. ¹⁸But as soon as I screamed for help, he left his cloak beside me and ran out of the house."

¹⁹When his master heard the story his wife told him, saying, "This is how your slave treated me," he burned with anger. ²⁰Joseph's master took him and put him in

---

[a] *30 Zerah* can mean *scarlet* or *brightness*.

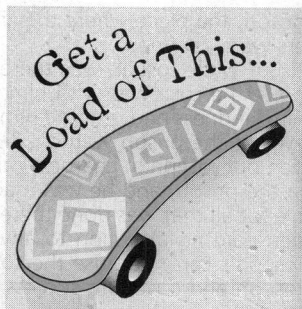

Get a Load of This...

Want a simple recipe for becoming a leader? Look at Joseph in Genesis 39:1–4, 20–23. He was faithful in the little things and was soon given more. Eventually, everything in the prison was under his care. Work hard, serve others and trust God, and you'll have learned how to lead.

prison, the place where the king's prisoners were confined.

But while Joseph was there in the prison, 21the LORD was with him; he showed him kindness and granted him favor in the eyes of the prison warden. 22So the warden put Joseph in charge of all those held in the prison, and he was made responsible for all that was done there. 23The warden paid no attention to anything under Joseph's care, because the LORD was with Joseph and gave him success in whatever he did.

The Cupbearer and the Baker

40 Some time later, the cupbearer and the baker of the king of Egypt offended their master, the king of Egypt. 2Pharaoh was angry with his two officials, the chief cupbearer and the chief baker, 3and put them in custody in the house of the captain of the guard, in the same prison where Joseph was confined. 4The captain of the guard assigned them to Joseph, and he attended them.

After they had been in custody for some time, 5each of the two men—the cupbearer and the baker of the king of Egypt, who were being held in prison—had a dream the same night, and each dream had a meaning of its own.

6When Joseph came to them the next morning, he saw that they were dejected. 7So he asked Pharaoh's officials who were in custody with him in his master's house, "Why are your faces so sad today?"

8"We both had dreams," they answered, "but there is no one to interpret them."

Then Joseph said to them, "Do not interpretations belong to God? Tell me your dreams."

9So the chief cupbearer told Joseph his dream. He said to him, "In my dream I saw a vine in front of me, 10and on the vine were three branches. As soon as it budded, it blossomed, and its clusters ripened into grapes. 11Pharaoh's cup was in my hand, and I took the grapes, squeezed them into Pharaoh's cup and put the cup in his hand."

12"This is what it means," Joseph said to him. "The three branches are three days. 13Within three days Pharaoh will lift up your head and restore you to your position, and you will put Pharaoh's cup in his hand, just as you used to do when you were his cupbearer. 14But when all goes well with you, remember me and show me kindness; mention me to Pharaoh and get me out of this prison. 15For I was forcibly carried off from the land of the Hebrews, and even here I have done nothing to deserve being put in a dungeon."

16When the chief baker saw that Joseph had given a favorable interpretation, he said to Joseph, "I too had a dream: On my head were three baskets of bread.a 17In the top basket were all kinds of baked goods for Pharaoh, but the birds were eating them out of the basket on my head."

18"This is what it means," Joseph said. "The three baskets are three days. 19Within three days Pharaoh will lift off your head and hang you on a tree.b And the birds will eat away your flesh."

20Now the third day was Pharaoh's birthday, and he gave a feast for all his officials. He lifted up the heads of the chief cupbearer and the chief baker in the presence of his officials: 21He restored the chief cupbearer to his position, so that he once again put the cup into Pharaoh's hand, 22but he hangedc the chief baker, just as Joseph had said to them in his interpretation.

23The chief cupbearer, however, did not remember Joseph; he forgot him.

Pharaoh's Dreams

41 When two full years had passed, Pharaoh had a dream: He was standing by the Nile, 2when out of the river there came up seven cows, sleek and fat, and they grazed among the reeds. 3After them, seven other cows, ugly and gaunt, came up out of the Nile and stood beside those on the riverbank. 4And the cows that were ugly and gaunt ate up the seven sleek, fat cows. Then Pharaoh woke up.

5He fell asleep again and had a second dream: Seven heads of grain, healthy and good, were growing on a single stalk. 6After them, seven other heads of grain sprouted—thin and scorched by the east wind. 7The thin heads of grain swallowed up the seven healthy, full heads. Then Pharaoh woke up; it had been a dream.

8In the morning his mind was troubled,

---

a 16 Or three wicker baskets   b 19 Or and impale you on a pole   c 22 Or impaled so he sent for all the magicians and wise men of Egypt. Pharaoh told them his dreams, but no one could interpret them for him.

⁹Then the chief cupbearer said to Pharaoh, "Today I am reminded of my shortcomings. ¹⁰Pharaoh was once angry with his servants, and he imprisoned me and the chief baker in the house of the captain of the guard. ¹¹Each of us had a dream the same night, and each dream had a meaning of its own. ¹²Now a young Hebrew was there with us, a servant of the captain of the guard. We told him our dreams, and he interpreted them for us, giving each man the interpretation of his dream. ¹³And things turned out exactly as he interpreted them to us: I was restored to my position, and the other man was hanged.ª"

¹⁴So Pharaoh sent for Joseph, and he was quickly brought from the dungeon. When he had shaved and changed his clothes, he came before Pharaoh.

¹⁵Pharaoh said to Joseph, "I had a dream, and no one can interpret it. But I have heard it said of you that when you hear a dream you can interpret it."

¹⁶"I cannot do it," Joseph replied to Pharaoh, "but God will give Pharaoh the answer he desires."

¹⁷Then Pharaoh said to Joseph, "In my dream I was standing on the bank of the Nile, ¹⁸when out of the river there came up seven cows, fat and sleek, and they grazed among the reeds. ¹⁹After them, seven other cows came up—scrawny and very ugly and lean. I had never seen such ugly cows in all the land of Egypt. ²⁰The lean, ugly cows ate up the seven fat cows that came up first. ²¹But even after they ate them, no one could tell that they had done so; they looked just as ugly as before. Then I woke up.

²²"In my dreams I also saw seven heads of grain, full and good, growing on a single stalk. ²³After them, seven other heads sprouted—withered and thin and scorched by the east wind. ²⁴The thin heads of grain swallowed up the seven good heads. I told this to the magicians, but none could explain it to me."

²⁵Then Joseph said to Pharaoh, "The

ª 13 Or impaled

Out on His Own
READ GENESIS 41:14–40

Joseph had it good growing up, receiving special treatment as his father's favorite son. But when he was sold into slavery, he left his comfortable life behind. His rough experiences forced Joseph to rely completely on God for the first time in his life. Now he had no one looking out for him. He *had* to depend on God. When Joseph was called to interpret Pharaoh's dream, he didn't know what it meant, but he knew God did. "'I cannot do it,' Joseph replied to Pharaoh, 'but God will give Pharaoh the answer he desires'" (Genesis 41:16). We all need to come to a place like Joseph where we completely rely on God. We don't need to leave our families like he did—we can still receive their love and support—but we *do* need to realize that God is in control and rely on him.

Your next reading is on page 67.

Get a Load of This...

Check out Genesis 41:48–49. Joseph stored up grain in preparation for the coming famine. In the ancient world, grain was often stored underground in huge pits. Managing and protecting these storehouses was such an important job that the sons of kings fought over who got to do it!

dreams of Pharaoh are one and the same. God has revealed to Pharaoh what he is about to do. ²⁶The seven good cows are seven years, and the seven good heads of grain are seven years; it is one and the same dream. ²⁷The seven lean, ugly cows that came up afterward are seven years, and so are the seven worthless heads of grain scorched by the east wind: They are seven years of famine.

²⁸"It is just as I said to Pharaoh: God has shown Pharaoh what he is about to do. ²⁹Seven years of great abundance are coming throughout the land of Egypt, ³⁰but seven years of famine will follow them. Then all the abundance in Egypt will be forgotten, and the famine will ravage the land. ³¹The abundance in the land will not be remembered, because the famine that follows it will be so severe. ³²The reason the dream was given to Pharaoh in two forms is that the matter has been firmly decided by God, and God will do it soon.

³³"And now let Pharaoh look for a discerning and wise man and put him in charge of the land of Egypt. ³⁴Let Pharaoh appoint commissioners over the land to take a fifth of the harvest of Egypt during the seven years of abundance. ³⁵They should collect all the food of these good years that are coming and store up the grain under the authority of Pharaoh, to be kept in the cities for food. ³⁶This food should be held in reserve for the country, to be used during the seven years of famine that will come upon Egypt, so that the country may not be ruined by the famine."

³⁷The plan seemed good to Pharaoh and to all his officials. ³⁸So Pharaoh asked them, "Can we find anyone like this man, one in whom is the spirit of God*a*?"

³⁹Then Pharaoh said to Joseph, "Since God has made all this known to you, there is no one so discerning and wise as you. ⁴⁰You shall be in charge of my palace, and all my people are to submit to your orders. Only with respect to the throne will I be greater than you."

Joseph in Charge of Egypt

⁴¹So Pharaoh said to Joseph, "I hereby put you in charge of the whole land of Egypt." ⁴²Then Pharaoh took his signet ring from his finger and put it on Joseph's finger. He dressed him in robes of fine linen and put a gold chain around his neck. ⁴³He had him ride in a chariot as his second-in-command,*b* and men shouted before him, "Make way*c*!" Thus he put him in charge of the whole land of Egypt.

⁴⁴Then Pharaoh said to Joseph, "I am Pharaoh, but without your word no one will lift hand or foot in all Egypt." ⁴⁵Pharaoh gave Joseph the name Zaphenath-Paneah and gave him Asenath daughter of Potiphera, priest of On,*d* to be his wife. And Joseph went throughout the land of Egypt.

⁴⁶Joseph was thirty years old when he entered the

a 38 Or *of the gods*   *b 43* Or *in the chariot of his second-in-command; or in his second chariot*   *c 43* Or *Bow down*   *d 45* That is, Heliopolis; also in verse 50 service of Pharaoh king of Egypt. And Joseph went out from Pharaoh's presence and traveled throughout Egypt. ⁴⁷During the seven years of abundance the land produced plentifully. ⁴⁸Joseph collected all the food produced in those seven years of abundance in Egypt and stored it in the cities. In each city he put the food grown in the fields surrounding it. ⁴⁹Joseph stored up huge quantities of grain, like the sand of the sea; it was so much that he stopped keeping records because it was beyond measure.

⁵⁰Before the years of famine came, two sons were born to Joseph by Asenath daughter of Potiphera, priest of On. ⁵¹Joseph named his firstborn Manasseh*ᵃ* and said, "It is because God has made me forget all my trouble and all my father's household." ⁵²The second son he named Ephraim*ᵇ* and said, "It is because God has made me fruitful in the land of my suffering."

⁵³The seven years of abundance in Egypt came to an end, ⁵⁴and the seven years of famine began, just as Joseph had said. There was famine in all the other lands, but in the whole land of Egypt there was food. ⁵⁵When all Egypt began to feel the famine, the people cried to Pharaoh for food. Then Pharaoh told all the Egyptians, "Go to Joseph and do what he tells you."

⁵⁶When the famine had spread over the whole country, Joseph opened the storehouses and sold grain to the Egyptians, for the famine was severe throughout Egypt. ⁵⁷And all the countries came to Egypt to buy grain from Joseph, because the famine was severe in all the world.

Joseph's Brothers Go to Egypt

42 When Jacob learned that there was grain in Egypt, he said to his sons, "Why do you just keep looking at each other?" ²He continued, "I have heard that there is grain in Egypt. Go down there and buy some for us, so that we may live and not die."

³Then ten of Joseph's brothers went

ᵃ 51 Manasseh sounds like and may be derived from the Hebrew for forget. ᵇ 52 Ephraim sounds like the Hebrew for twice fruitful.

Preparing for the Big Day

READ GENESIS 41:41–57

It takes loads of preparation and letting God guide you, to get yourself ready for a career. At first glance, it looks like Joseph became the second most powerful ruler of the world overnight. But Pharaoh wouldn't hand over control of his kingdom to just anyone. Joseph had spent many hard years in Potiphar's house and in prison learning what it took to be a leader so when it came time to do what God wanted, he was ready. A successful career won't just fall in your lap either. As a young man, you need to think about which direction you'd like to go and the education and training it takes to get there. Try out different things. See where your interests are. Then, when the time comes to step out, you'll be ready, just like Joseph was.

Your next reading is on page 69.

Get a Load of This...

Most prisons in the ancient world were cruel, dirty places—not a whole lot more than pits in the ground where prisoners survived on bread and water. Blech! Egyptian prisons, like the one Joseph's brother was sent to, could have been in the houses of military officers—not nearly as bad as prisons in other places.

down to buy grain from Egypt. ⁴But Jacob did not send Benjamin, Joseph's brother, with the others, because he was afraid that harm might come to him. ⁵So Israel's sons were among those who went to buy grain, for the famine was in the land of Canaan also.

⁶Now Joseph was the governor of the land, the one who sold grain to all its people. So when Joseph's brothers arrived, they bowed down to him with their faces to the ground. ⁷As soon as Joseph saw his brothers, he recognized them, but he pretended to be a stranger and spoke harshly to them. "Where do you come from?" he asked.

"From the land of Canaan," they replied, "to buy food."

⁸Although Joseph recognized his brothers, they did not recognize him. ⁹Then he remembered his dreams about them and said to them, "You are spies! You have come to see where our land is unprotected."

¹⁰"No, my lord," they answered. "Your servants have come to buy food. ¹¹We are all the sons of one man. Your servants are honest men, not spies."

¹²"No!" he said to them. "You have come to see where our land is unprotected."

¹³But they replied, "Your servants were twelve brothers, the sons of one man, who lives in the land of Canaan. The youngest is now with our father, and one is no more."

¹⁴Joseph said to them, "It is just as I told you: You are spies! ¹⁵And this is how you will be tested: As surely as Pharaoh lives, you will not leave this place unless your youngest brother comes here. ¹⁶Send one of your number to get your brother; the rest of you will be kept in prison, so that your words may be tested to see if you are telling the truth. If you are not, then as surely as Pharaoh lives, you are spies!" ¹⁷And he put them all in custody for three days.

¹⁸On the third day, Joseph said to them, "Do this and you will live, for I fear God: ¹⁹If you are honest men, let one of your brothers stay here in prison, while the rest of you go and take grain back for your starving households. ²⁰But you must bring your youngest brother to me, so that your words may be verified and that you may not die." This they proceeded to do.

²¹They said to one another, "Surely we are being punished because of our brother. We saw how distressed he was when he pleaded with us for his life, but we would not listen; that's why this distress has come upon us."

²²Reuben replied, "Didn't I tell you not to sin against the boy? But you wouldn't listen! Now we must give an accounting for his blood." ²³They did not realize that Joseph could understand them, since he was using an interpreter.

²⁴He turned away from them and began to weep, but then turned back and spoke to them again. He had Simeon taken from them and bound before their eyes.

²⁵Joseph gave orders to fill their bags with grain, to put each man's silver back in his sack, and to give them

provisions for their journey. After this was done for them, ²⁶they loaded their grain on their donkeys and left.

²⁷At the place where they stopped for the night one of them opened his sack to get feed for his donkey, and he saw his silver in the mouth of his sack. ²⁸"My silver has been returned," he said to his brothers. "Here it is in my sack."

Their hearts sank and they turned to each other trembling and said, "What is this that God has done to us?"

²⁹When they came to their father Jacob in the land of Canaan, they told him all that had happened to them. They said, ³⁰"The man who is lord over the land spoke harshly to us and treated us as though we were spying on the land. ³¹But we said to him, 'We are honest men; we are not spies. ³²We were twelve brothers, sons of one father. One is no more, and the youngest is now with our father in Canaan.'

³³"Then the man who is lord over the land said to us, 'This is how I will know whether you are honest men: Leave one of your brothers here with me, and take food for your starving households and go. ³⁴But bring your youngest brother to me so I will know that you are not spies but honest men. Then I will give your brother back to you, and you can trade*a* in the land.'"

³⁵As they were emptying their sacks, there in each man's sack was his pouch of silver! When they and their father saw the money pouches, they were frightened. ³⁶Their father Jacob said to them, "You have deprived me of my children. Joseph is no more and Simeon is no more, and now you want to take Benjamin. Everything is against me!"

³⁷Then Reuben said to his father, "You may put both of my sons to death if I do not bring him back to you. Entrust him to my care, and I will bring him back."

³⁸But Jacob said, "My son will not go down there with you; his brother is dead and he is the only one left. If harm comes to him on the journey you are taking, you will bring my gray head down to the grave*b* in sorrow."

a 34 Or *move about freely*   *b 38* Hebrew *Sheol*

I've Changed!—Honest!

READ GENESIS 42:1–8; 45:1–14

When Joseph's brothers came to Egypt, he tested them to see if they had truly repented and changed. They had broken his trust in the past, and they needed to rebuild it. That's why "he pretended to be a stranger and spoke harshly to them" (Genesis 42:7). Trust is difficult to rebuild once it is broken. If you go to the mall with a friend and he shoplifts, if he later says he's sorry, forgive him, sure, but you don't have to walk into the same store with him next week. It's the same thing when you blow it: Your parents need you to prove yourself in that area before they trust you again. They forgive you, but they want to be sure you won't do it again. Until then, they may put you on a "shorter leash." If you've truly changed, your actions will show it and they'll soon trust you again.

Your next reading is on page 73.

The Second Journey to Egypt

43 Now the famine was still severe in the land. 2So when they had eaten all the grain they had brought from Egypt, their father said to them, "Go back and buy us a little more food."

3But Judah said to him, "The man warned us solemnly, 'You will not see my face again unless your brother is with you.' 4If you will send our brother along with us, we will go down and buy food for you. 5But if you will not send him, we will not go down, because the man said to us, 'You will not see my face again unless your brother is with you.' "

6Israel asked, "Why did you bring this trouble on me by telling the man you had another brother?"

7They replied, "The man questioned us closely about ourselves and our family. 'Is your father still living?' he asked us. 'Do you have another brother?' We simply answered his questions. How were we to know he would say, 'Bring your brother down here'?"

8Then Judah said to Israel his father, "Send the boy along with me and we will go at once, so that we and you and our children may live and not die. 9I myself will guarantee his safety; you can hold me personally responsible for him. If I do not bring him back to you and set him here before you, I will bear the blame before you all my life. 10As it is, if we had not delayed, we could have gone and returned twice."

11Then their father Israel said to them, "If it must be, then do this: Put some of the best products of the land in your bags and take them down to the man as a gift—a little balm and a little honey, some spices and myrrh, some pistachio nuts and almonds. 12Take double the amount of silver with you, for you must return the silver that was put back into the mouths of your sacks. Perhaps it was a mistake. 13Take your brother also and go back to the man at once. 14And may God Almighty*a* grant you mercy before the man so that he will let your other brother and Benjamin come back with you. As for me, if I am bereaved, I am bereaved."

15So the men took the gifts and double the amount of silver, and Benjamin also. They hurried down to Egypt and present-

ed themselves to Joseph. 16When Joseph saw Benjamin with them, he said to the steward of his house, "Take these men to my house, slaughter an animal and prepare dinner; they are to eat with me at noon."

17The man did as Joseph told him and took the men to Joseph's house. 18Now the men were frightened when they were taken to his house. They thought, "We were brought here because of the silver that was put back into our sacks the first time. He wants to attack us and overpower us and seize us as slaves and take our donkeys."

19So they went up to Joseph's steward and spoke to him at the entrance to the house. 20"Please, sir," they said, "we came down here the first time to buy food. 21But at the place where we stopped for the night we opened our sacks and each of us found his silver—the exact weight— in the mouth of his sack. So we have brought it back with us. 22We have also brought additional silver with us to buy food. We don't know who put our silver in our sacks."

23"It's all right," he said. "Don't be afraid. Your God, the God of your father, has given you treasure in your sacks; I received your silver." Then he brought Simeon out to them.

24The steward took the men into Joseph's house, gave them water to wash their feet and provided fodder for their donkeys. 25They prepared their gifts for Joseph's arrival at noon, because they had heard that they were to eat there.

26When Joseph came home, they presented to him the gifts they had brought into the house, and they bowed down before him to the ground. 27He asked them how they were, and then he said, "How is your aged father you told me about? Is he still living?"

28They replied, "Your servant our father is still alive and well." And they bowed low to pay him honor.

29As he looked about and saw his brother Benjamin, his own mother's son, he asked, "Is this your youngest brother, the one you told me about?" And he said, "God be gracious to you, my son." 30Deeply moved at the sight of his brother, Joseph hurried out and looked for a

a 14 Hebrew *El-Shaddai*

place to weep. He went into his private room and wept there.

³¹After he had washed his face, he came out and, controlling himself, said, "Serve the food."

³²They served him by himself, the brothers by themselves, and the Egyptians who ate with him by themselves, because Egyptians could not eat with Hebrews, for that is detestable to Egyptians. ³³The men had been seated before him in the order of their ages, from the firstborn to the youngest; and they looked at each other in astonishment. ³⁴When portions were served to them from Joseph's table, Benjamin's portion was five times as much as anyone else's. So they feasted and drank freely with him.

A Silver Cup in a Sack

44 Now Joseph gave these instructions to the steward of his house: "Fill the men's sacks with as much food as they can carry, and put each man's silver in the mouth of his sack. ²Then put my cup, the silver one, in the mouth of the youngest one's sack, along with the silver for his grain." And he did as Joseph said.

³As morning dawned, the men were sent on their way with their donkeys. ⁴They had not gone far from the city when Joseph said to his steward, "Go after those men at once, and when you catch up with them, say to them, 'Why have you repaid good with evil? ⁵Isn't this the cup my master drinks from and also uses for divination? This is a wicked thing you have done.' "

⁶When he caught up with them, he repeated these words to them. ⁷But they said to him, "Why does my lord say such things? Far be it from your servants to do anything like that! ⁸We even brought back to you from the land of Canaan the silver we found inside the mouths of our sacks. So why would we steal silver or gold from your master's house? ⁹If any of your servants is found to have it, he will die; and the rest of us will become my lord's slaves."

¹⁰"Very well, then," he said, "let it be as you say. Whoever is found to have it will become my slave; the rest of you will be free from blame."

¹¹Each of them quickly lowered his sack to the ground and opened it. ¹²Then the steward proceeded to search, beginning with the oldest and ending with the youngest. And the cup was found in Benjamin's sack. ¹³At this, they tore their clothes. Then they all loaded their donkeys and returned to the city.

¹⁴Joseph was still in the house when Judah and his brothers came in, and they threw themselves to the ground before him. ¹⁵Joseph said to them, "What is this you have done? Don't you know that a man like me can find things out by divination?"

¹⁶"What can we say to my lord?" Judah replied. "What can we say? How can we prove our innocence? God has uncovered your servants' guilt. We are now my lord's slaves—we ourselves and the one who was found to have the cup."

¹⁷But Joseph said, "Far be it from me to do such a thing! Only the man who was found to have the cup will become my slave. The rest of you, go back to your father in peace."

¹⁸Then Judah went up to him and said: "Please, my lord, let your servant speak a word to my lord. Do not be angry with your servant, though you are equal to Pharaoh himself. ¹⁹My lord asked his servants, 'Do you have a father or a brother?' ²⁰And we answered, 'We have an aged father, and there is a young son born to him in his old age. His brother is dead, and he is the only one of his mother's sons left, and his father loves him.'

²¹"Then you said to your servants, 'Bring him down to me so I can see him for myself.' ²²And we said to my lord, 'The boy cannot leave his father; if he leaves him, his father will die.' ²³But you told your servants, 'Unless your youngest brother comes down with you, you will not see my face again.' ²⁴When we went back to your servant my father, we told him what my lord had said.

²⁵"Then our father said, 'Go back and buy a little more food.' ²⁶But we said, 'We cannot go down. Only if our youngest brother is with us will we go. We cannot see the man's face unless our youngest brother is with us.'

²⁷"Your servant my father said to us, 'You know that my wife bore me two sons. ²⁸One of them went away from me, and I said, "He has surely been torn to pieces." And I have not seen him since. ²⁹If you take this one from me too and

harm comes to him, you will bring my gray head down to the grave[a] in misery.'

30"So now, if the boy is not with us when I go back to your servant my father and if my father, whose life is closely bound up with the boy's life, 31sees that the boy isn't there, he will die. Your servants will bring the gray head of our father down to the grave in sorrow. 32Your servant guaranteed the boy's safety to my father. I said, 'If I do not bring him back to you, I will bear the blame before you, my father, all my life!'

33"Now then, please let your servant remain here as my lord's slave in place of the boy, and let the boy return with his brothers. 34How can I go back to my father if the boy is not with me? No! Do not let me see the misery that would come upon my father."

Joseph Makes Himself Known

45 Then Joseph could no longer control himself before all his attendants, and he cried out, "Have everyone leave my presence!" So there was no one with Joseph when he made himself known to his brothers. 2And he wept so loudly that the Egyptians heard him, and Pharaoh's household heard about it.

3Joseph said to his brothers, "I am Joseph! Is my father still living?" But his brothers were not able to answer him, because they were terrified at his presence.

4Then Joseph said to his brothers, "Come close to me." When they had done so, he said, "I am your brother Joseph, the one you sold into Egypt! 5And now, do not be distressed and do not be angry with yourselves for selling me here, because it was to save lives that God sent me ahead of you. 6For two years now there has been famine in the land, and for the next five years there will not be plowing and reaping. 7But God sent me ahead of you to preserve for you a remnant on earth and to save your lives by a great deliverance.[b]

8"So then, it was not you who sent me here, but God. He made me father to Pharaoh, lord of his entire household and ruler of all Egypt. 9Now hurry back to my father and say to him, 'This is what your son Joseph says: God has made me lord of all Egypt. Come down to me; don't delay. 10You shall live in the region of Goshen

and be near me—you, your children and grandchildren, your flocks and herds, and all you have. 11I will provide for you there, because five years of famine are still to come. Otherwise you and your household and all who belong to you will become destitute.'

12"You can see for yourselves, and so can my brother Benjamin, that it is really I who am speaking to you. 13Tell my father about all the honor accorded me in Egypt and about everything you have seen. And bring my father down here quickly."

14Then he threw his arms around his brother Benjamin and wept, and Benjamin embraced him, weeping. 15And he kissed all his brothers and wept over them. Afterward his brothers talked with him.

16When the news reached Pharaoh's palace that Joseph's brothers had come, Pharaoh and all his officials were pleased. 17Pharaoh said to Joseph, "Tell your brothers, 'Do this: Load your animals and return to the land of Canaan, 18and bring your father and your families back to me. I will give you the best of the land of Egypt and you can enjoy the fat of the land.'

19"You are also directed to tell them, 'Do this: Take some carts from Egypt for your children and your wives, and get your father and come. 20Never mind about your belongings, because the best of all Egypt will be yours.' "

21So the sons of Israel did this. Joseph gave them carts, as Pharaoh had commanded, and he also gave them provisions for their journey. 22To each of them he gave new clothing, but to Benjamin he gave three hundred shekels[c] of silver and five sets of clothes. 23And this is what he sent to his father: ten donkeys loaded with the best things of Egypt, and ten female donkeys loaded with grain and bread and other provisions for his journey. 24Then he sent his brothers away, and as they were leaving he said to them, "Don't quarrel on the way!"

25So they went up out of Egypt and came to their father Jacob in the land of Canaan. 26They told him, "Joseph is still alive! In fact, he is ruler of all Egypt." Jacob was stunned; he did not believe

a 29 Hebrew Sheol; also in verse 31   b 7 Or save you as a great band of survivors   c 22 That is, about 7 1/2 pounds (about 3.5 kilograms) them. ²⁷But when they told him everything Joseph had said to them, and when he saw the carts Joseph had sent to carry him back, the spirit of their father Jacob revived. ²⁸And Israel said, "I'm convinced! My son Joseph is still alive. I will go and see him before I die."

Jacob Goes to Egypt

So Israel set out with all that was his, and when he reached Beersheba, he offered sacrifices to the God of his father Isaac.

²And God spoke to Israel in a vision at night and said, "Jacob! Jacob!"

"Here I am," he replied.

³"I am God, the God of your father," he said. "Do not be afraid to go down to Egypt, for I will make you into a great nation there. ⁴I will go down to Egypt with you, and I will surely bring you back again. And Joseph's own hand will close your eyes."

⁵Then Jacob left Beersheba, and Israel's sons took their father Jacob and their children and their wives in the carts that Pharaoh had sent to transport him. ⁶They also took with them their livestock and the possessions they had acquired in Canaan, and Jacob and all his offspring went to Egypt. ⁷He took with him to Egypt his sons and grandsons and his daughters and granddaughters—all his offspring.

⁸These are the names of the sons of Israel (Jacob and his descendants) who went to Egypt:

Reuben the firstborn of Jacob.
⁹The sons of Reuben:
Hanoch, Pallu, Hezron and Carmi.
¹⁰The sons of Simeon:
Jemuel, Jamin, Ohad, Jakin, Zohar and Shaul the son of a Canaanite woman.
¹¹The sons of Levi:
Gershon, Kohath and Merari.
¹²The sons of Judah:
Er, Onan, Shelah, Perez and Zerah (but Er and Onan had died in the land of Canaan).
The sons of Perez:
Hezron and Hamul.
¹³The sons of Issachar:

Don't Beat Yourself Up

READ GENESIS 45:14–24; 46:1–4; 50:15–21

The saying "forgive and forget" doesn't just apply to others, it also applies to forgiving yourself. Joseph forgave his brothers for selling him into slavery. But they hadn't forgiven themselves. This made them suspect Joseph hadn't really forgiven them either. They said, "What if Joseph holds a grudge against us and pays us back for all the wrongs we did to him?" (Genesis 50:15). This suspicion drove a wedge of fear between Joseph's brothers and Joseph. They should have believed him when he expressed his forgiveness, put the past behind them and started over. Sometimes we act like Joseph's brothers. Others may forgive us, but we're still kicking ourselves for our past mistakes and just can't forgive ourselves. God urges us to "love others as we love ourselves." That means he wants us to love ourselves and forgive ourselves.

Your next reading is on page 81.

Tola, Puah,[a] Jashub[b] and Shimron.
14 The sons of Zebulun:
    Sered, Elon and Jahleel.

15 These were the sons Leah bore to Jacob in Paddan Aram,[c] besides his daughter Dinah. These sons and daughters of his were thirty-three in all.

16 The sons of Gad:
    Zephon,[d] Haggi, Shuni, Ezbon, Eri, Arodi and Areli.
17 The sons of Asher:
    Imnah, Ishvah, Ishvi and Beriah.
    Their sister was Serah.
    The sons of Beriah:
      Heber and Malkiel.

18 These were the children born to Jacob by Zilpah, whom Laban had given to his daughter Leah—sixteen in all.

19 The sons of Jacob's wife Rachel:
    Joseph and Benjamin. 20 In Egypt, Manasseh and Ephraim were born to Joseph by Asenath daughter of Potiphera, priest of On.[e]
21 The sons of Benjamin:
    Bela, Beker, Ashbel, Gera, Naaman, Ehi, Rosh, Muppim, Huppim and Ard.

22 These were the sons of Rachel who were born to Jacob—fourteen in all.

23 The son of Dan:
    Hushim.
24 The sons of Naphtali:
    Jahziel, Guni, Jezer and Shillem.

25 These were the sons born to Jacob by Bilhah, whom Laban had given to his daughter Rachel—seven in all.

26 All those who went to Egypt with Jacob—those who were his direct descendants, not counting his sons' wives—numbered sixty-six persons. 27 With the two sons[f] who had been born to Joseph in Egypt, the members of Jacob's family, which went to Egypt, were seventy[g] in all.

28 Now Jacob sent Judah ahead of him to Joseph to get directions to Goshen. When they arrived in the region of Goshen, 29 Joseph had his chariot made ready and went to Goshen to meet his father Israel. As soon as Joseph appeared before him, he threw his arms around his father[h] and wept for a long time.

30 Israel said to Joseph, "Now I am ready to die, since I have seen for myself that you are still alive."

31 Then Joseph said to his brothers and to his father's household, "I will go up and speak to Pharaoh and will say to him, 'My brothers and my father's household, who were living in the land of Canaan, have come to me. 32 The men are shepherds; they tend livestock, and they have brought along their flocks and herds and everything they own.' 33 When Pharaoh calls you in and asks, 'What is your occupation?' 34 you should answer, 'Your servants have tended livestock from our boyhood on, just as our fathers did.' Then you will be allowed to settle in the region of Goshen, for all shepherds are detestable to the Egyptians."

47 Joseph went and told Pharaoh, "My father and brothers, with their flocks and herds and everything they own, have come from the land of Canaan and are now in Goshen." 2 He chose five of his brothers and presented them before Pharaoh.

3 Pharaoh asked the brothers, "What is your occupation?"

"Your servants are shepherds," they replied to Pharaoh, "just as our fathers were." 4 They also said to him, "We have come to live here awhile, because the famine is severe in Canaan and your servants' flocks have no pasture. So now, please let your servants settle in Goshen."

5 Pharaoh said to Joseph, "Your father and your brothers have come to you, 6 and the land of Egypt is before you; settle your father and your brothers in the best part of the land. Let them live in Goshen. And if you know of any among them with special ability, put them in charge of my own livestock."

7 Then Joseph brought his father Jacob in and presented him before Pharaoh. After Jacob blessed[i] Pharaoh, 8 Pharaoh asked him, "How old are you?"

9 And Jacob said to Pharaoh, "The years of my pilgrimage are a hundred and thirty. My years have been few and difficult, and they do not equal the years of the pilgrim-

a 13 Samaritan Pentateuch and Syriac (see also 1 Chron. 7:1); Masoretic Text Puvah   b 13 Samaritan Pentateuch and some Septuagint manuscripts (see also Num. 26:24 and 1 Chron. 7:1); Masoretic Text Iob   c 15 That is, Northwest Mesopotamia   d 16 Samaritan Pentateuch and Septuagint (see also Num. 26:15); Masoretic Text Ziphion   e 20 That is, Heliopolis   f 27 Hebrew; Septuagint the nine children g 27 Hebrew (see also Exodus 1:5 and footnote); Septuagint (see also Acts 7:14) seventy-five   h 29 Hebrew around him i 7 Or greeted age of my fathers." [10]Then Jacob blessed[a] Pharaoh and went out from his presence.

[11]So Joseph settled his father and his brothers in Egypt and gave them property in the best part of the land, the district of Rameses, as Pharaoh directed. [12]Joseph also provided his father and his brothers and all his father's household with food, according to the number of their children.

Joseph and the Famine

[13]There was no food, however, in the whole region because the famine was severe; both Egypt and Canaan wasted away because of the famine. [14]Joseph collected all the money that was to be found in Egypt and Canaan in payment for the grain they were buying, and he brought it to Pharaoh's palace. [15]When the money of the people of Egypt and Canaan was gone, all Egypt came to Joseph and said, "Give us food. Why should we die before your eyes? Our money is used up."

[16]"Then bring your livestock," said Joseph. "I will sell you food in exchange for your livestock, since your money is gone." [17]So they brought their livestock to Joseph, and he gave them food in exchange for their horses, their sheep and goats, their cattle and donkeys. And he brought them through that year with food in exchange for all their livestock.

[18]When that year was over, they came to him the following year and said, "We cannot hide from our lord the fact that since our money is gone and our livestock belongs to you, there is nothing left for our lord except our bodies and our land. [19]Why should we perish before your eyes—we and our land as well? Buy us and our land in exchange for food, and we with our land will be in bondage to Pharaoh. Give us seed so that we may live and not die, and that the land may not become desolate."

[20]So Joseph bought all the land in Egypt for Pharaoh. The Egyptians, one and all, sold their fields, because the famine was too severe for them. The land became Pharaoh's, [21]and Joseph reduced the people to servitude,[b] from one end of Egypt to the other. [22]However, he did not buy the land of the priests, because they received a regular allotment from Pharaoh and had food enough from the allotment Pharaoh gave them. That is why they did not sell their land.

[23]Joseph said to the people, "Now that I have bought you and your land today for Pharaoh, here is seed for you so you can plant the ground. [24]But when the crop comes in, give a fifth of it to Pharaoh. The other four-fifths you may keep as seed for the fields and as food for yourselves and your households and your children."

[25]"You have saved our lives," they said. "May we find favor in the eyes of our lord; we will be in bondage to Pharaoh."

[26]So Joseph established it as a law concerning land in Egypt—still in force today—that a fifth of the produce belongs to Pharaoh. It was only the land of the priests that did not become Pharaoh's.

[27]Now the Israelites settled in Egypt in the region of Goshen. They acquired property there and were fruitful and increased greatly in number.

[28]Jacob lived in Egypt seventeen years, and the years of his life were a hundred and forty-seven. [29]When the time drew near for Israel to die, he called for his son Joseph and said to him, "If I have found favor in your eyes, put your hand under my thigh and promise that you will show me kindness and faithfulness. Do not bury me in Egypt, [30]but when I rest with my fathers, carry me out of Egypt and bury me where they are buried."

"I will do as you say," he said.

[31]"Swear to me," he said. Then Joseph swore to him, and Israel worshiped as he leaned on the top of his staff.[c]

Manasseh and Ephraim

48 Some time later Joseph was told, "Your father is ill." So he took his two sons Manasseh and Ephraim along with him. [2]When Jacob was told, "Your son Joseph has come to you," Israel rallied his strength and sat up on the bed.

[3]Jacob said to Joseph, "God Almighty[d] appeared to me at Luz in the land of Canaan, and there he blessed me [4]and said to me, 'I am going to make you fruitful and will increase your numbers. I will make you a community of peoples, and I will give this land as an everlasting possession to your descendants after you.'

[5]"Now then, your two sons born to you

---

[a] 10 Or *said farewell to*   [b] 21 Samaritan Pentateuch and Septuagint (see also Vulgate); Masoretic Text *and he moved the people into the cities*   [c] 31 Or *Israel bowed down at the head of his bed*   [d] 3 Hebrew *El-Shaddai*

Get a Load of This...

When someone sneezes and you say, "Bless you," did you realize you were wishing God's favor upon them? That's what blessing someone meant during Bible times—like when Jacob blessed Joseph's two sons (Genesis 48:9). Remember that the next time someone sneezes!

in Egypt before I came to you here will be reckoned as mine; Ephraim and Manasseh will be mine, just as Reuben and Simeon are mine. [6]Any children born to you after them will be yours; in the territory they inherit they will be reckoned under the names of their brothers. [7]As I was returning from Paddan,[a] to my sorrow Rachel died in the land of Canaan while we were still on the way, a little distance from Ephrath. So I buried her there beside the road to Ephrath" (that is, Bethlehem).

[8]When Israel saw the sons of Joseph, he asked, "Who are these?"

[9]"They are the sons God has given me here," Joseph said to his father.

Then Israel said, "Bring them to me so I may bless them."

[10]Now Israel's eyes were failing because of old age, and he could hardly see. So Joseph brought his sons close to him, and his father kissed them and embraced them.

[11]Israel said to Joseph, "I never expected to see your face again, and now God has allowed me to see your children too."

[12]Then Joseph removed them from Israel's knees and bowed down with his face to the ground. [13]And Joseph took both of them, Ephraim on his right toward Israel's left hand and Manasseh on his left toward Israel's right hand, and brought them close to him. [14]But Israel reached out his right hand and put it on Ephraim's head, though he was the younger, and crossing his arms, he put his left hand on Manasseh's head, even though Manasseh was the firstborn.

[15]Then he blessed Joseph and said,

"May the God before whom my fathers
　　Abraham and Isaac walked,
the God who has been my shepherd
　　all my life to this day,
[16]the Angel who has delivered me from all harm
　　—may he bless these boys.
May they be called by my name
　　and the names of my fathers Abraham and Isaac,
and may they increase greatly
　　upon the earth."

[17]When Joseph saw his father placing his right hand on Ephraim's head he was displeased; so he took hold of his father's hand to move it from Ephraim's head to Manasseh's head. [18]Joseph said to him, "No, my father, this one is the firstborn; put your right hand on his head."

[19]But his father refused and said, "I know, my son, I know. He too will become a people, and he too will become great. Nevertheless, his younger brother will be greater than he, and his descendants will become a group of nations." [20]He blessed them that day and said,

"In your[b] name will Israel pronounce this blessing:
　'May God make you like Ephraim and
　　Manasseh.' "

---

[a] 7 That is, Northwest Mesopotamia   [b] 20 The Hebrew is singular.

So he put Ephraim ahead of Manasseh.

21Then Israel said to Joseph, "I am about to die, but God will be with you[a] and take you[a] back to the land of your[a] fathers. 22And to you, as one who is over your brothers, I give the ridge of land[b] I took from the Amorites with my sword and my bow."

Jacob Blesses His Sons

49 Then Jacob called for his sons and said: "Gather around so I can tell you what will happen to you in days to come.

2 "Assemble and listen, sons of Jacob;
   listen to your father Israel.

3 "Reuben, you are my firstborn,
   my might, the first sign of my strength,
   excelling in honor, excelling in power.
4 Turbulent as the waters, you will no longer excel,
   for you went up onto your father's bed,
   onto my couch and defiled it.

5 "Simeon and Levi are brothers—
   their swords[c] are weapons of violence.
6 Let me not enter their council,
   let me not join their assembly,
   for they have killed men in their anger
   and hamstrung oxen as they pleased.
7 Cursed be their anger, so fierce,
   and their fury, so cruel!
   I will scatter them in Jacob
   and disperse them in Israel.

8 "Judah,[d] your brothers will praise you;
   your hand will be on the neck of your enemies;
   your father's sons will bow down to you.
9 You are a lion's cub, O Judah;
   you return from the prey, my son.
   Like a lion he crouches and lies down,
   like a lioness—who dares to rouse him?
10 The scepter will not depart from Judah,
   nor the ruler's staff from between his feet,
   until he comes to whom it belongs[e]
   and the obedience of the nations is his.
11 He will tether his donkey to a vine,
   his colt to the choicest branch;
   he will wash his garments in wine,
   his robes in the blood of grapes.
12 His eyes will be darker than wine,
   his teeth whiter than milk.[f]

13 "Zebulun will live by the seashore
   and become a haven for ships;
   his border will extend toward Sidon.

14 "Issachar is a rawboned[g] donkey
   lying down between two saddlebags.[h]
15 When he sees how good is his resting place
   and how pleasant is his land,
   he will bend his shoulder to the burden
   and submit to forced labor.

16 "Dan[i] will provide justice for his people
   as one of the tribes of Israel.
17 Dan will be a serpent by the roadside,
   a viper along the path,
   that bites the horse's heels
   so that its rider tumbles backward.

18 "I look for your deliverance, O LORD.

19 "Gad[j] will be attacked by a band of raiders,
   but he will attack them at their heels.

20 "Asher's food will be rich;
   he will provide delicacies fit for a king.

21 "Naphtali is a doe set free
   that bears beautiful fawns.[k]

22 "Joseph is a fruitful vine,
   a fruitful vine near a spring,
   whose branches climb over a wall.[l]
23 With bitterness archers attacked him;
   they shot at him with hostility.
24 But his bow remained steady,
   his strong arms stayed[m] limber,
   because of the hand of the Mighty One of Jacob,
   because of the Shepherd, the Rock of Israel,
25 because of your father's God, who helps you,

a 21 The Hebrew is plural.   b 22 Or And to you I give one portion more than to your brothers—the portion
c 5 The meaning of the Hebrew for this word is uncertain.
d 8 Judah sounds like and may be derived from the Hebrew for praise.   e 10 Or until Shiloh comes; or until he comes to whom tribute belongs   f 12 Or will be dull from wine, / his teeth white from milk   g 14 Or strong   h 14 Or campfires
i 16 Dan here means he provides justice.   j 19 Gad can mean attack and band of raiders.   k 21 Or free; / he utters beautiful words   l 22 Or Joseph is a wild colt, / a wild colt near a spring, / a wild donkey on a terraced hill
m 23,24 Or archers will attack . . . will shoot . . . will remain . . . will stay

Get a Load of This...

Joseph asked his family, once he was dead, to carry his old, dusty bones back to Canaan (Genesis 50:25). Rattle, rattle, clunk, rattle. Why did he bother? It was a sign that Joseph trusted God to one day bring his people out of Egypt and return them to the Promised Land.

because of the Almighty,[a] who blesses you
with blessings of the heavens above,
blessings of the deep that lies below,
blessings of the breast and womb.
26 Your father's blessings are greater
than the blessings of the ancient mountains,
than[b] the bounty of the age-old hills.
Let all these rest on the head of Joseph,
on the brow of the prince among[c] his brothers.

27 "Benjamin is a ravenous wolf;
in the morning he devours the prey,
in the evening he divides the plunder."

28 All these are the twelve tribes of Israel, and this is what their father said to them when he blessed them, giving each the blessing appropriate to him.

The Death of Jacob

29 Then he gave them these instructions: "I am about to be gathered to my people. Bury me with my fathers in the cave in the field of Ephron the Hittite, 30 the cave in the field of Machpelah, near Mamre in Canaan, which Abraham bought as a burial place from Ephron the Hittite, along with the field. 31 There Abraham and his wife Sarah were buried, there Isaac and his wife Rebekah were buried, and there I buried Leah. 32 The field and the cave in it were bought from the Hittites.[d]"

33 When Jacob had finished giving instructions to his sons, he drew his feet up into the bed, breathed his last and was gathered to his people.

50 Joseph threw himself upon his father and wept over him and kissed him. 2 Then Joseph directed the physicians in his service to embalm his father Israel. So the physicians embalmed him, 3 taking a full forty days, for that was the time required for embalming. And the Egyptians mourned for him seventy days.

4 When the days of mourning had passed, Joseph said to Pharaoh's court, "If I have found favor in your eyes, speak to Pharaoh for me. Tell him, 5 'My father made me swear an oath and said, "I am about to die; bury me in the tomb I dug for myself in the land of Canaan." Now let me go up and bury my father; then I will return.' "

6 Pharaoh said, "Go up and bury your father, as he made you swear to do."

7 So Joseph went up to bury his father. All Pharaoh's officials accompanied him—the dignitaries of his court and all the dignitaries of Egypt— 8 besides all the members of Joseph's household and his brothers and those belonging to his father's household. Only their children and their flocks and herds were left in Goshen. 9 Chariots and horsemen[e] also went up with him. It was a very large company.

10 When they reached the threshing floor of Atad,

near the Jordan, they lamented loudly and bitterly; and there Joseph observed a seven-day period of mourning for his father. [11]When the Canaanites who lived there saw the mourning at the threshing floor of Atad, they said, "The Egyptians are holding a solemn ceremony of mourning." That is why that place near the Jordan is called Abel Mizraim.[a]

[12]So Jacob's sons did as he had commanded them: [13]They carried him to the land of Canaan and buried him in the cave in the field of Machpelah, near Mamre, which Abraham had bought as a burial place from Ephron the Hittite, along with the field. [14]After burying his father, Joseph returned to Egypt, together with his brothers and all the others who had gone with him to bury his father.

Joseph Reassures His Brothers

[15]When Joseph's brothers saw that their father was dead, they said, "What if Joseph holds a grudge against us and pays us back for all the wrongs we did to him?" [16]So they sent word to Joseph, saying, "Your father left these instructions before he died: [17]'This is what you are to say to Joseph: I ask you to forgive your brothers the sins and the wrongs they committed in treating you so badly.' Now please forgive the sins of the servants of the God of your father." When their message came to him, Joseph wept.

[18]His brothers then came and threw themselves down before him. "We are your slaves," they said.

[19]But Joseph said to them, "Don't be afraid. Am I in the place of God? [20]You intended to harm me, but God intended it for good to accomplish what is now being done, the saving of many lives. [21]So then, don't be afraid. I will provide for you and your children." And he reassured them and spoke kindly to them.

The Death of Joseph

[22]Joseph stayed in Egypt, along with all his father's family. He lived a hundred and ten years [23]and saw the third generation of Ephraim's children. Also the children of Makir son of Manasseh were placed at birth on Joseph's knees.[b]

[24]Then Joseph said to his brothers, "I am about to die. But God will surely come to your aid and take you up out of this land to the land he promised on oath to Abraham, Isaac and Jacob." [25]And Joseph made the sons of Israel swear an oath and said, "God will surely come to your aid, and then you must carry my bones up from this place."

[26]So Joseph died at the age of a hundred and ten. And after they embalmed him, he was placed in a coffin in Egypt.

Gross!

Joseph was *embalmed* (Genesis 50:26). Embalming was how the Egyptians prepared bodies for burial. They removed all internal organs except the heart. Some experts believe the brain was pulled out through the nose using a hook! Then the body was filled with spices and wrapped in bandages soaked with oil.

---

[a] 11 *Abel Mizraim* means *mourning of the Egyptians.*   [b] 23 That is, were counted as his

EXODUS

Who wrote this book?
Moses.

Why was this book written?
Exodus shows how God used his power to rescue the Israelites from slavery.

What happens in this book?
God brings ten terrible plagues on Egypt. He forces Pharaoh to let God's people go.
God gives the Israelites the Ten Commandments and other laws by which to live.

What do we learn about God in this book?
God uses his power to rescue helpless people. God expects his people to live moral and righteous lives.

What people are important in this book?
The important people in this book are Moses and Aaron.

When did this happen?
The Israelites left Egypt about 1446 B.C. The Law was given at Sinai shortly afterward.

Where did this happen?
Exodus 1–12 took place in Egypt. Most other events took place at Mount Sinai.

What are some of the stories in this book?
Baby Moses	Exodus 2
A burning bush	Exodus 3
The ten plagues	Exodus 7–11
The Passover	Exodus 12
Crossing the Red Sea	Exodus 14
The Ten Commandments	Exodus 20
Building the tabernacle	Exodus 25–27
The golden calf	Exodus 32

The Israelites Oppressed

1 These are the names of the sons of Israel who went to Egypt with Jacob, each with his family: ²Reuben, Simeon, Levi and Judah; ³Issachar, Zebulun and Benjamin; ⁴Dan and Naphtali; Gad and Asher. ⁵The descendants of Jacob numbered seventy*a* in all; Joseph was already in Egypt.

⁶Now Joseph and all his brothers and all that generation died, ⁷but the Israelites were fruitful and multiplied greatly and became exceedingly numerous, so that the land was filled with them.

⁸Then a new king, who did not know about Joseph, came to power in Egypt. ⁹"Look," he said to his people, "the Israelites have become much too numerous for us. ¹⁰Come, we must deal shrewdly with them or they will become even more numerous and, if war breaks out, will join our enemies, fight against us and leave the country."

¹¹So they put slave masters over them to oppress them with forced labor, and they built Pithom and Rameses as store cities for Pharaoh. ¹²But the more they were oppressed, the more they multiplied and spread; so the Egyptians came to dread the Israelites ¹³and worked them ruthlessly. ¹⁴They made their lives bitter with hard labor in brick and mortar and with all kinds of work in the fields; in all their hard labor the Egyptians used them ruthlessly.

¹⁵The king of Egypt said to the Hebrew midwives, whose names were Shiphrah and Puah, ¹⁶"When you help the Hebrew women in childbirth and observe them on the delivery stool, if it is a boy, kill him; but if it is a girl, let her live." ¹⁷The midwives, however, feared God and did not do what the king of Egypt had told them to do; they let the boys live. ¹⁸Then the king of Egypt summoned the midwives and asked

a 5 Masoretic Text (see also Gen. 46:27); Dead Sea Scrolls and Septuagint (see also Acts 7:14 and note at Gen. 46:27) *seventy-five*

GET STRONGER

A Real Man

READ EXODUS 1:8—2:10

Pharaoh felt threatened by how fast the Hebrew population was growing. Women called midwives helped Hebrew women deliver their babies, so Pharaoh ordered them, "If it's a boy, kill him!" (Exodus 1:16). Why did he single out the boys? Because he knew that boys would grow up to be strong men who might fight against him. God made men strong and gave them an instinct to fight for their families. As Nehemiah 4:14 says, "Fight for your ... sons and your daughters, your wives and your homes." This doesn't mean that a "real man" is some GI Joe commando with a blazing machine gun. In God's book, a real man is someone who stands up and fights for what he knows is right. Physical strength is great, but it's more important to have godly character and courage.

Your next reading is on page 82.

them, "Why have you done this? Why have you let the boys live?"

¹⁹The midwives answered Pharaoh, "Hebrew women are not like Egyptian women; they are vigorous and give birth before the midwives arrive."

²⁰So God was kind to the midwives and the people increased and became even more numerous. ²¹And because the midwives feared God, he gave them families of their own.

²²Then Pharaoh gave this order to all his people: "Every boy that is born^a you must throw into the Nile, but let every girl live."

The Birth of Moses

Now a man of the house of Levi married a Levite woman, ²and she became pregnant and gave birth to a son. When she saw that he was a fine child, she hid him for three months. ³But when she could hide him no longer, she got a papyrus basket for him and coated it with tar and pitch. Then she placed the child in it and put it among the reeds along the bank of the Nile. ⁴His sister stood at a distance to see what would happen to him.

⁵Then Pharaoh's daughter went down to the Nile to bathe, and her attendants were walking along the river bank. She saw the basket among the reeds and sent her slave girl to get it. ⁶She opened it and saw the baby. He was crying, and she felt sorry for him. "This is one of the Hebrew babies," she said.

⁷Then his sister asked Pharaoh's daughter, "Shall I go and get one of the Hebrew women to nurse the baby for you?"

⁸"Yes, go," she answered. And the girl went and got the baby's mother. ⁹Pharaoh's daughter said to her, "Take this baby and nurse him for me, and I will pay you." So the woman took the baby and nursed him. ¹⁰When the child grew older, she took him to Pharaoh's daughter and he became her son. She named him Moses,^b saying, "I drew him out of the water."

^a 22 Masoretic Text; Samaritan Pentateuch, Septuagint and Targums *born to the Hebrews*   ^b 10 *Moses* sounds like the Hebrew for *draw out*.

GET SMARTER

Moses Jumps the Gun

READ EXODUS 2:11–25

Moses had so much patience he could put up with more than two million people wailing and complaining at once. Ho! Now *that* is patience! He wasn't always that way, though. In the beginning he had almost zero self-control or patience. God had promised to deliver the Hebrews from Egypt after four hundred years; and, assuming that the time had come, Moses got the idea that he was the Deliverer and needed to help God fulfill prophecy (see Acts 7:25). He was in such a hurry that he killed an Egyptian. Result? He had to run for his life. Alone. Moses had physical strength but something was clearly lacking. It just goes to prove that real strength comes from having inner strength and waiting on God. Do your pushups, sure, but do some "inner pushups" as well. Work on your self-control and patience "muscles."

Your next reading is on page 84.

Moses Flees to Midian

[11]One day, after Moses had grown up, he went out to where his own people were and watched them at their hard labor. He saw an Egyptian beating a Hebrew, one of his own people. [12]Glancing this way and that and seeing no one, he killed the Egyptian and hid him in the sand. [13]The next day he went out and saw two Hebrews fighting. He asked the one in the wrong, "Why are you hitting your fellow Hebrew?"

[14]The man said, "Who made you ruler and judge over us? Are you thinking of killing me as you killed the Egyptian?" Then Moses was afraid and thought, "What I did must have become known."

[15]When Pharaoh heard of this, he tried to kill Moses, but Moses fled from Pharaoh and went to live in Midian, where he sat down by a well. [16]Now a priest of Midian had seven daughters, and they came to draw water and fill the troughs to water their father's flock. [17]Some shepherds came along and drove them away, but Moses got up and came to their rescue and watered their flock.

[18]When the girls returned to Reuel their father, he asked them, "Why have you returned so early today?"

[19]They answered, "An Egyptian rescued us from the shepherds. He even drew water for us and watered the flock."

[20]"And where is he?" he asked his daughters. "Why did you leave him? Invite him to have something to eat."

[21]Moses agreed to stay with the man, who gave his daughter Zipporah to Moses in marriage. [22]Zipporah gave birth to a son, and Moses named him Gershom,[a] saying, "I have become an alien in a foreign land."

[23]During that long period, the king of Egypt died. The Israelites groaned in their slavery and cried out, and their cry for help because of their slavery went up to God. [24]God heard their groaning and he remembered his covenant with Abraham, with Isaac and with Jacob. [25]So God looked on the Israelites and was concerned about them.

Moses and the Burning Bush

3 Now Moses was tending the flock of Jethro his father-in-law, the priest of Midian, and he led the flock to the far side of the desert and came to Horeb, the mountain of God. [2]There the angel of the LORD appeared to him in flames of fire from within a bush. Moses saw that though the bush was on fire it did not burn up. [3]So Moses thought, "I will go over and see this strange sight—why the bush does not burn up."

[4]When the LORD saw that he had gone over to look, God called to him from within the bush, "Moses! Moses!"

And Moses said, "Here I am."

[5]"Do not come any closer," God said. "Take off your sandals, for the place where you are standing is holy

---

Get a Load of This...

When Moses saw a bush up in flames, but not burning, he was so curious he strolled over for a closer look (Exodus 3). But when a voice inside the fire said, "I am God!" Moses nearly had a heart attack and didn't want to look anymore.

---

[a] 22 *Gershom* sounds like the Hebrew for *an alien there*.

ground." ⁶Then he said, "I am the God of your father, the God of Abraham, the God of Isaac and the God of Jacob." At this, Moses hid his face, because he was afraid to look at God.

⁷The LORD said, "I have indeed seen the misery of my people in Egypt. I have heard them crying out because of their slave drivers, and I am concerned about their suffering. ⁸So I have come down to rescue them from the hand of the Egyptians and to bring them up out of that land into a good and spacious land, a land flowing with milk and honey—the home of the Canaanites, Hittites, Amorites, Perizzites, Hivites and Jebusites. ⁹And now the cry of the Israelites has reached me, and I have seen the way the Egyptians are oppressing them. ¹⁰So now, go. I am sending you to Pharaoh to bring my people the Israelites out of Egypt."

¹¹But Moses said to God, "Who am I, that I should go to Pharaoh and bring the Israelites out of Egypt?"

¹²And God said, "I will be with you. And this will be the sign to you that it is I who have sent you: When you have brought the people out of Egypt, you[a] will worship God on this mountain."

¹³Moses said to God, "Suppose I go to the Israelites and say to them, 'The God of your fathers has sent me to you,' and they ask me, 'What is his name?' Then what shall I tell them?"

¹⁴God said to Moses, "I AM WHO I AM.[b] This is what you are to say to the Israelites: 'I AM has sent me to you.' "

¹⁵God also said to Moses, "Say to the Israelites, 'The LORD,[c] the God of your fathers—the God of Abraham, the God of Isaac and the God of Jacob—has sent me to you.' This is my name forever, the name by which I am to be remembered from generation to generation.

¹⁶"Go, assemble the elders of Israel and say to them, 'The LORD, the God of your fathers—the God of Abraham, Isaac and Jacob—appeared to me and said: I have watched over you and have seen what has been done to you in Egypt. ¹⁷And I have promised to bring you up out of your mis-

[a] 12 The Hebrew is plural.   [b] 14 Or I WILL BE WHAT I WILL BE   [c] 15 The Hebrew for LORD sounds like and may be derived from the Hebrew for I AM in verse 14.

Excuses, Excuses!

READ EXODUS 3:1–15; 4:10–17

When God told Moses to deliver the Hebrews from Egypt, Moses argued with God. Not cool. He tried every excuse except "my back hurts" to get out of doing it. When Moses argued that Pharaoh would never listen to him, God said, "Now go. I will help you" (Exodus 4:12). Moses did go and God did help him. We tell ourselves, "Man, what could puny little me ever do for God?" But when God created each of us, he gave us the gifts and abilities we would need to do the job he wanted us to do. It's not cool to argue with God and say we can't do a job. When we do that, we're arguing against the way God made us. Remember, even if a job *is* huge, God's promise to Moses is also for us: "I will help you."

Your next reading is on page 89.

ery in Egypt into the land of the Canaanites, Hittites, Amorites, Perizzites, Hivites and Jebusites—a land flowing with milk and honey.'

18"The elders of Israel will listen to you. Then you and the elders are to go to the king of Egypt and say to him, 'The LORD, the God of the Hebrews, has met with us. Let us take a three-day journey into the desert to offer sacrifices to the LORD our God.' 19But I know that the king of Egypt will not let you go unless a mighty hand compels him. 20So I will stretch out my hand and strike the Egyptians with all the wonders that I will perform among them. After that, he will let you go.

21"And I will make the Egyptians favorably disposed toward this people, so that when you leave you will not go empty-handed. 22Every woman is to ask her neighbor and any woman living in her house for articles of silver and gold and for clothing, which you will put on your sons and daughters. And so you will plunder the Egyptians."

Signs for Moses

4 Moses answered, "What if they do not believe me or listen to me and say, 'The LORD did not appear to you'?"

2Then the LORD said to him, "What is that in your hand?"

"A staff," he replied.

3The LORD said, "Throw it on the ground."

Moses threw it on the ground and it became a snake, and he ran from it. 4Then the LORD said to him, "Reach out your hand and take it by the tail." So Moses reached out and took hold of the snake and it turned back into a staff in his hand. 5"This," said the LORD, "is so that they may believe that the LORD, the God of their fathers—the God of Abraham, the God of Isaac and the God of Jacob—has appeared to you."

6Then the LORD said, "Put your hand inside your cloak." So Moses put his hand into his cloak, and when he took it out, it was leprous,a like snow.

7"Now put it back into your cloak," he said. So Moses put his hand back into his cloak, and when he took it out, it was restored, like the rest of his flesh.

8Then the LORD said, "If they do not believe you or pay attention to the first mi-

raculous sign, they may believe the second. 9But if they do not believe these two signs or listen to you, take some water from the Nile and pour it on the dry ground. The water you take from the river will become blood on the ground."

10Moses said to the LORD, "O Lord, I have never been eloquent, neither in the past nor since you have spoken to your servant. I am slow of speech and tongue."

11The LORD said to him, "Who gave man his mouth? Who makes him deaf or mute? Who gives him sight or makes him blind? Is it not I, the LORD? 12Now go; I will help you speak and will teach you what to say."

13But Moses said, "O Lord, please send someone else to do it."

14Then the LORD's anger burned against Moses and he said, "What about your brother, Aaron the Levite? I know he can speak well. He is already on his way to meet you, and his heart will be glad when he sees you. 15You shall speak to him and put words in his mouth; I will help both of you speak and will teach you what to do. 16He will speak to the people for you, and it will be as if he were your mouth and as if you were God to him. 17But take this staff in your hand so you can perform miraculous signs with it."

Moses Returns to Egypt

18Then Moses went back to Jethro his father-in-law and said to him, "Let me go back to my own people in Egypt to see if any of them are still alive."

Jethro said, "Go, and I wish you well."

19Now the LORD had said to Moses in Midian, "Go back to Egypt, for all the men who wanted to kill you are dead." 20So Moses took his wife and sons, put them on a donkey and started back to Egypt. And he took the staff of God in his hand. 21The LORD said to Moses, "When you return to Egypt, see that you perform before Pharaoh all the wonders I have given you the power to do. But I will harden his heart so that he will not let the people go. 22Then say to Pharaoh, 'This is what the LORD says: Israel is my firstborn son, 23and I told you, "Let my son go, so he may worship me." But you refused to let him go; so I will kill your firstborn son.' "

a 6 The Hebrew word was used for various diseases affecting the skin—not necessarily leprosy.

Get a Load of This...

In ancient Egypt, pyramids and palaces were made from blocks of stone. Just about everything else—homes and storehouses—were built with mud bricks. Those mud bricks got hard when they dried in the sun but they still crumbled easily. That's why straw was used to hold them together (Exodus 5:7).

²⁴At a lodging place on the way, the LORD met ⌐Moses⌐ᵃ and was about to kill him. ²⁵But Zipporah took a flint knife, cut off her son's foreskin and touched ⌐Moses'⌐ feet with it.ᵇ "Surely you are a bridegroom of blood to me," she said. ²⁶So the LORD let him alone. (At that time she said "bridegroom of blood," referring to circumcision.)

²⁷The LORD said to Aaron, "Go into the desert to meet Moses." So he met Moses at the mountain of God and kissed him. ²⁸Then Moses told Aaron everything the LORD had sent him to say, and also about all the miraculous signs he had commanded him to perform.

²⁹Moses and Aaron brought together all the elders of the Israelites, ³⁰and Aaron told them everything the LORD had said to Moses. He also performed the signs before the people, ³¹and they believed. And when they heard that the LORD was concerned about them and had seen their misery, they bowed down and worshiped.

Bricks Without Straw

5 Afterward Moses and Aaron went to Pharaoh and said, "This is what the LORD, the God of Israel, says: 'Let my people go, so that they may hold a festival to me in the desert.' "

²Pharaoh said, "Who is the LORD, that I should obey him and let Israel go? I do not know the LORD and I will not let Israel go."

³Then they said, "The God of the Hebrews has met with us. Now let us take a three-day journey into the desert to offer sacrifices to the LORD our God, or he may strike us with plagues or with the sword."

⁴But the king of Egypt said, "Moses and Aaron, why are you taking the people away from their labor? Get back to your work!" ⁵Then Pharaoh said, "Look, the people of the land are now numerous, and you are stopping them from working."

⁶That same day Pharaoh gave this order to the slave drivers and foremen in charge of the people: ⁷"You are no longer to supply the people with straw for making bricks; let them go and gather their own straw. ⁸But require them to make the same number of bricks as before; don't reduce the quota. They are lazy; that is why they are crying out, 'Let us go and sacrifice to our God.' ⁹Make the work harder for the men so that they keep working and pay no attention to lies."

¹⁰Then the slave drivers and the foremen went out and said to the people, "This is what Pharaoh says: 'I will not give you any more straw. ¹¹Go and get your own straw wherever you can find it, but your work will not be reduced at all.' " ¹²So the people scattered all over Egypt to gather stubble to use for straw. ¹³The slave drivers kept pressing them, saying, "Complete the work required of you for each day, just as when you had straw." ¹⁴The Israelite foremen appointed by Pharaoh's slave drivers were beaten and were asked, "Why didn't

---

ᵃ 24 Or ⌐Moses' son⌐; Hebrew him   ᵇ 25 Or and drew near ⌐Moses'⌐ feet you meet your quota of bricks yesterday or today, as before?"

¹⁵Then the Israelite foremen went and appealed to Pharaoh: "Why have you treated your servants this way? ¹⁶Your servants are given no straw, yet we are told, 'Make bricks!' Your servants are being beaten, but the fault is with your own people."

¹⁷Pharaoh said, "Lazy, that's what you are—lazy! That is why you keep saying, 'Let us go and sacrifice to the LORD.' ¹⁸Now get to work. You will not be given any straw, yet you must produce your full quota of bricks."

¹⁹The Israelite foremen realized they were in trouble when they were told, "You are not to reduce the number of bricks required of you for each day." ²⁰When they left Pharaoh, they found Moses and Aaron waiting to meet them, ²¹and they said, "May the LORD look upon you and judge you! You have made us a stench to Pharaoh and his officials and have put a sword in their hand to kill us."

God Promises Deliverance

²²Moses returned to the LORD and said, "O Lord, why have you brought trouble upon this people? Is this why you sent me? ²³Ever since I went to Pharaoh to speak in your name, he has brought trouble upon this people, and you have not rescued your people at all."

6 Then the LORD said to Moses, "Now you will see what I will do to Pharaoh: Because of my mighty hand he will let them go; because of my mighty hand he will drive them out of his country."

²God also said to Moses, "I am the LORD. ³I appeared to Abraham, to Isaac and to Jacob as God Almighty,ᵃ but by my name the LORDᵇ I did not make myself known to them.ᶜ ⁴I also established my covenant with them to give them the land of Canaan, where they lived as aliens. ⁵Moreover, I have heard the groaning of the Israelites, whom the Egyptians are enslaving, and I have remembered my covenant.

⁶"Therefore, say to the Israelites: 'I am the LORD, and I will bring you out from under the yoke of the Egyptians. I will free you from being slaves to them, and I will redeem you with an outstretched arm and with mighty acts of judgment. ⁷I will take you as my own people, and I will be your

God. Then you will know that I am the LORD your God, who brought you out from under the yoke of the Egyptians. ⁸And I will bring you to the land I swore with uplifted hand to give to Abraham, to Isaac and to Jacob. I will give it to you as a possession. I am the LORD.' "

⁹Moses reported this to the Israelites, but they did not listen to him because of their discouragement and cruel bondage.

¹⁰Then the LORD said to Moses, ¹¹"Go, tell Pharaoh king of Egypt to let the Israelites go out of his country."

¹²But Moses said to the LORD, "If the Israelites will not listen to me, why would Pharaoh listen to me, since I speak with faltering lipsᵈ?"

Family Record of Moses and Aaron

¹³Now the LORD spoke to Moses and Aaron about the Israelites and Pharaoh king of Egypt, and he commanded them to bring the Israelites out of Egypt.

¹⁴These were the heads of their familiesᵉ:

The sons of Reuben the firstborn son of Israel were Hanoch and Pallu, Hezron and Carmi. These were the clans of Reuben.

¹⁵The sons of Simeon were Jemuel, Jamin, Ohad, Jakin, Zohar and Shaul the son of a Canaanite woman. These were the clans of Simeon.

¹⁶These were the names of the sons of Levi according to their records: Gershon, Kohath and Merari. Levi lived 137 years.

¹⁷The sons of Gershon, by clans, were Libni and Shimei.

¹⁸The sons of Kohath were Amram, Izhar, Hebron and Uzziel. Kohath lived 133 years.

¹⁹The sons of Merari were Mahli and Mushi.

These were the clans of Levi according to their records.

²⁰Amram married his father's sister Jochebed, who bore him Aaron and Moses. Amram lived 137 years.

²¹The sons of Izhar were Korah, Nepheg and Zicri.

ᵃ3 Hebrew *El-Shaddai*   ᵇ3 See note at Exodus 3:15.
ᶜ3 Or *Almighty, and by my name the LORD did I not let myself be known to them?*   ᵈ12 Hebrew *I am uncircumcised of lips;* also in verse 30   ᵉ14 The Hebrew for *families* here and in verse 25 refers to units larger than clans.

22The sons of Uzziel were Mishael, Elzaphan and Sithri.

23Aaron married Elisheba, daughter of Amminadab and sister of Nahshon, and she bore him Nadab and Abihu, Eleazar and Ithamar.

24The sons of Korah were Assir, Elkanah and Abiasaph. These were the Korahite clans.

25Eleazar son of Aaron married one of the daughters of Putiel, and she bore him Phinehas.

These were the heads of the Levite families, clan by clan.

26It was this same Aaron and Moses to whom the LORD said, "Bring the Israelites out of Egypt by their divisions." 27They were the ones who spoke to Pharaoh king of Egypt about bringing the Israelites out of Egypt. It was the same Moses and Aaron.

Aaron to Speak for Moses

28Now when the LORD spoke to Moses in Egypt, 29he said to him, "I am the LORD. Tell Pharaoh king of Egypt everything I tell you."

30But Moses said to the LORD, "Since I speak with faltering lips, why would Pharaoh listen to me?"

7 Then the LORD said to Moses, "See, I have made you like God to Pharaoh, and your brother Aaron will be your prophet. 2You are to say everything I command you, and your brother Aaron is to tell Pharaoh to let the Israelites go out of his country. 3But I will harden Pharaoh's heart, and though I multiply my miraculous signs and wonders in Egypt, 4he will not listen to you. Then I will lay my hand on Egypt and with mighty acts of judgment I will bring out my divisions, my people the Israelites. 5And the Egyptians will know that I am the LORD when I stretch out my hand against Egypt and bring the Israelites out of it."

6Moses and Aaron did just as the LORD commanded them. 7Moses was eighty

Make It Stick

READ EXODUS 7:8–11

God helped Moses do some … well … pretty *bizarre* miracles to prove that God was with him.
If you could choose any three miracles to show people God's power, what would you choose?
Write your ideas on a sticky note.

years old and Aaron eighty-three when they spoke to Pharaoh.

Aaron's Staff Becomes a Snake

8The LORD said to Moses and Aaron, 9"When Pharaoh says to you, 'Perform a miracle,' then say to Aaron, 'Take your staff and throw it down before Pharaoh,' and it will become a snake."

10So Moses and Aaron went to Pharaoh and did just as the LORD commanded. Aaron threw his staff down in front of Pharaoh and his officials, and it became a snake. 11Pharaoh then summoned wise men and sorcerers, and the Egyptian magicians also did the same things by their secret arts: 12Each one threw down his staff and it became a snake. But Aaron's staff swallowed up their staffs. 13Yet Pharaoh's heart became hard and he would not listen to them, just as the LORD had said.

The Plague of Blood

14Then the LORD said to Moses, "Pharaoh's heart is unyielding; he refuses to let the people go. 15Go to Pharaoh in the morning as he goes out to the water. Wait on the bank of the Nile to meet him, and take in your hand the staff that was changed into a snake. 16Then say to him, 'The LORD, the God of the Hebrews, has sent me to say to you: Let my people go, so that they may worship me in the desert. But until now you have not listened. 17This is what the LORD says: By this you will know that I am the LORD: With the staff that is in my hand I will strike the water of the Nile, and it will be changed into blood. 18The fish in the Nile will die, and the river will stink; the Egyptians will not be able to drink its water.' "

19The LORD said to Moses, "Tell Aaron, 'Take your staff and stretch out your hand over the waters of Egypt—over the streams and canals, over the ponds and all the reservoirs'—and they will turn to blood. Blood will be everywhere in Egypt, even in the wooden buckets and stone jars."

20Moses and Aaron did just as the LORD had commanded. He raised his staff in the presence of Pharaoh and his officials and struck the water of the Nile, and all the water was changed into blood. 21The fish in the Nile died, and the river smelled so

---

Just Another Guy

READ EXODUS 7:14–18; 8:1–4, 16–22

God told Moses, "Go to Pharaoh and say to him, 'Let my people go'" (Exodus 8:1). You have to hand it to Moses. He had no fear of people. He marched right up and gave orders to the greatest ruler on earth. OK, so you aren't Moses and, true, you should honor and respect those in authority. But the point is this: Don't be over wowed by them. Be like the football fan who once saw a famous coach in an airport. He wanted to talk to the coach, but was sooo nervous. He finally convinced himself that the coach was just another guy and went over and talked with him. Yup! It's true! Famous people and "stars" are just people. So never feel you're less of a person than a "star." You may be a little jittery about approaching them, but remember, in God's eyes they're no better than you are.

Your next reading is on page 94.

Gross!

OK! The plague of frogs has ended! They're all *dead!* Get out the snow shovels, boys! We've got to pile them in heaps! (Exodus 8:14). *Hooeeeee!* Do they *ever* stink! OK, move ... *Squissh!* Man! Stepped on another one!

bad that the Egyptians could not drink its water. Blood was everywhere in Egypt.

22But the Egyptian magicians did the same things by their secret arts, and Pharaoh's heart became hard; he would not listen to Moses and Aaron, just as the LORD had said. 23Instead, he turned and went into his palace, and did not take even this to heart. 24And all the Egyptians dug along the Nile to get drinking water, because they could not drink the water of the river.

The Plague of Frogs

25Seven days passed after the LORD struck the Nile. 1Then the LORD said to Moses, "Go to Pharaoh and say to him, 'This is what the LORD says: Let my people go, so that they may worship me. 2If you refuse to let them go, I will plague your whole country with frogs. 3The Nile will teem with frogs. They will come up into your palace and your bedroom and onto your bed, into the houses of your officials and on your people, and into your ovens and kneading troughs. 4The frogs will go up on you and your people and all your officials.' "

5Then the LORD said to Moses, "Tell Aaron, 'Stretch out your hand with your staff over the streams and canals and ponds, and make frogs come up on the land of Egypt.' "

6So Aaron stretched out his hand over the waters of Egypt, and the frogs came up and covered the land. 7But the magicians did the same things by their secret arts; they also made frogs come up on the land of Egypt.

8Pharaoh summoned Moses and Aaron and said, "Pray to the LORD to take the frogs away from me and my people, and I will let your people go to offer sacrifices to the LORD."

9Moses said to Pharaoh, "I leave to you the honor of setting the time for me to pray for you and your officials and your people that you and your houses may be rid of the frogs, except for those that remain in the Nile."

10"Tomorrow," Pharaoh said.

Moses replied, "It will be as you say, so that you may know there is no one like the LORD our God. 11The frogs will leave you and your houses, your officials and your people; they will remain only in the Nile."

12After Moses and Aaron left Pharaoh, Moses cried out to the LORD about the frogs he had brought on Pharaoh. 13And the LORD did what Moses asked. The frogs died in the houses, in the courtyards and in the fields. 14They were piled into heaps, and the land reeked of them. 15But when Pharaoh saw that there was relief, he hardened his heart and would not listen to Moses and Aaron, just as the LORD had said.

The Plague of Gnats

16Then the LORD said to Moses, "Tell Aaron, 'Stretch out your staff and strike the dust of the ground,' and throughout the land of Egypt the dust will become gnats." 17They did this, and when Aaron stretched out his hand with the staff and struck the dust of the ground,

gnats came upon men and animals. All the dust throughout the land of Egypt became gnats. [18]But when the magicians tried to produce gnats by their secret arts, they
could not. And the gnats were on men and animals.

[19]The magicians said to Pharaoh, "This is the finger of
God." But Pharaoh's heart was hard and he would not
listen, just as the LORD had said.

The Plague of Flies

[20]Then the LORD said to Moses, "Get up early in the
morning and confront Pharaoh as he goes to the water
and say to him, 'This is what the LORD says: Let my people go, so that they may worship me. [21]If you do not let
my people go, I will send swarms of flies on you and
your officials, on your people and into your houses. The
houses of the Egyptians will be full of flies, and even the
ground where they are.

[22]" 'But on that day I will deal differently with the land
of Goshen, where my people live; no swarms of flies will
be there, so that you will know that I, the LORD, am in this
land. [23]I will make a distinction[a] between my people and
your people. This miraculous sign will occur tomorrow.' "

[24]And the LORD did this. Dense swarms of flies poured
into Pharaoh's palace and into the houses of his officials,
and throughout Egypt the land was ruined by the flies.

[25]Then Pharaoh summoned Moses and Aaron and
said, "Go, sacrifice to your God here in the land."

[26]But Moses said, "That would not be right. The sacrifices we offer the LORD our God would be detestable to
the Egyptians. And if we offer sacrifices that are detestable in their eyes, will they not stone us? [27]We must
take a three-day journey into the desert to offer sacrifices to the LORD our God, as he commands us."

[28]Pharaoh said, "I will let you go to offer sacrifices to
the LORD your God in the desert, but you must not go
very far. Now pray for me."

[29]Moses answered, "As soon as I leave you, I will pray
to the LORD, and tomorrow the flies will leave Pharaoh
and his officials and his people. Only be sure that Pharaoh does not act deceitfully again by not letting the
people go to offer sacrifices to the LORD."

[30]Then Moses left Pharaoh and prayed to the LORD,
[31]and the LORD did what Moses asked: The flies left
Pharaoh and his officials and his people; not a fly remained. [32]But this time also Pharaoh hardened his heart
and would not let the people go.

The Plague on Livestock

Then the LORD said to Moses, "Go to Pharaoh and
say to him, 'This is what the LORD, the God of the
Hebrews, says: "Let my people go, so that they
may worship me." [2]If you refuse to let them go
and continue to hold them back, [3]the hand of the LORD
will bring a terrible plague on your livestock in the
field—on your horses and donkeys and camels and on

[a] 23 Septuagint and Vulgate; Hebrew *will put a deliverance*

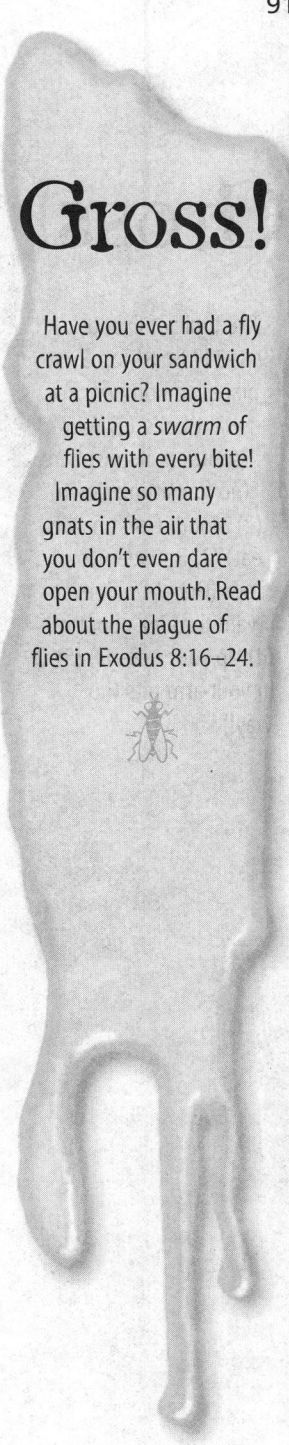

Gross!

Have you ever had a fly
crawl on your sandwich
at a picnic? Imagine
getting a *swarm* of
flies with every bite!
Imagine so many
gnats in the air that
you don't even dare
open your mouth. Read
about the plague of
flies in Exodus 8:16–24.

Gross!

The topic of Exodus 9:8–11? Boils! Top 5 places you do *not* want boils: (1) Your southern hemisphere (no fun sitting down) (2) Mouth (can't hardly eat) (3) Between your toes (Ouch! Don't even want to think about it!) (4) Up your nose (?) (5) In your arm pits (no way!)

your cattle and sheep and goats. 4But the LORD will make a distinction between the livestock of Israel and that of Egypt, so that no animal belonging to the Israelites will die.' "

5The LORD set a time and said, "Tomorrow the LORD will do this in the land." 6And the next day the LORD did it: All the livestock of the Egyptians died, but not one animal belonging to the Israelites died. 7Pharaoh sent men to investigate and found that not even one of the animals of the Israelites had died. Yet his heart was unyielding and he would not let the people go.

The Plague of Boils

8Then the LORD said to Moses and Aaron, "Take handfuls of soot from a furnace and have Moses toss it into the air in the presence of Pharaoh. 9It will become fine dust over the whole land of Egypt, and festering boils will break out on men and animals throughout the land."

10So they took soot from a furnace and stood before Pharaoh. Moses tossed it into the air, and festering boils broke out on men and animals. 11The magicians could not stand before Moses because of the boils that were on them and on all the Egyptians. 12But the LORD hardened Pharaoh's heart and he would not listen to Moses and Aaron, just as the LORD had said to Moses.

The Plague of Hail

13Then the LORD said to Moses, "Get up early in the morning, confront Pharaoh and say to him, 'This is what the LORD, the God of the Hebrews, says: Let my people go, so that they may worship me, 14or this time I will send the full force of my plagues against you and against your officials and your people, so you may know that there is no one like me in all the earth. 15For by now I could have stretched out my hand and struck you and your people with a plague that would have wiped you off the earth. 16But I have raised you up*a* for this very purpose, that I might show you my power and that my name might be proclaimed in all the earth. 17You still set yourself against my people and will not let them go. 18Therefore, at this time tomorrow I will send the worst hailstorm that has ever fallen on Egypt, from the day it was founded till now. 19Give an order now to bring your livestock and everything you have in the field to a place of shelter, because the hail will fall on every man and animal that has not been brought in and is still out in the field, and they will die.' "

20Those officials of Pharaoh who feared the word of the LORD hurried to bring their slaves and their livestock inside. 21But those who ignored the word of the LORD left their slaves and livestock in the field.

22Then the LORD said to Moses, "Stretch out your hand toward the sky so that hail will fall all over Egypt—on men and animals and on everything growing in the

a 16 Or have spared you

fields of Egypt." 23When Moses stretched out his staff toward the sky, the LORD sent thunder and hail, and lightning flashed down to the ground. So the LORD rained hail on the land of Egypt; 24hail fell and lightning flashed back and forth. It was the worst storm in all the land of Egypt since it had become a nation. 25Throughout Egypt hail struck everything in the fields—both men and animals; it beat down everything growing in the fields and stripped every tree. 26The only place it did not hail was the land of Goshen, where the Israelites were.

27Then Pharaoh summoned Moses and Aaron. "This time I have sinned," he said to them. "The LORD is in the right, and I and my people are in the wrong. 28Pray to the LORD, for we have had enough thunder and hail. I will let you go; you don't have to stay any longer."

29Moses replied, "When I have gone out of the city, I will spread out my hands in prayer to the LORD. The thunder will stop and there will be no more hail, so you may know that the earth is the LORD's. 30But I know that you and your officials still do not fear the LORD God."

31(The flax and barley were destroyed, since the barley had headed and the flax was in bloom. 32The wheat and spelt, however, were not destroyed, because they ripen later.)

33Then Moses left Pharaoh and went out of the city. He spread out his hands toward the LORD; the thunder and hail stopped, and the rain no longer poured down on the land. 34When Pharaoh saw that the rain and hail and thunder had stopped, he sinned again: He and his officials hardened their hearts. 35So Pharaoh's heart was hard and he would not let the Israelites go, just as the LORD had said through Moses.

The Plague of Locusts

10 Then the LORD said to Moses, "Go to Pharaoh, for I have hardened his heart and the hearts of his officials so that I may perform these miraculous signs of mine among them 2that you may tell your children and grandchildren how I dealt harshly with the Egyptians and how I performed my signs among them, and that you may know that I am the LORD."

3So Moses and Aaron went to Pharaoh and said to him, "This is what the LORD, the God of the Hebrews, says: 'How long will you refuse to humble yourself before me? Let my people go, so that they may worship me. 4If you refuse to let them go, I will bring locusts into your country tomorrow. 5They will cover the face of the ground so that it cannot be seen. They will devour what little you have left after the hail, including every tree that is growing in your fields. 6They will fill your houses and those of all your officials and all the Egyptians—something neither your fathers nor your forefathers have ever seen from the day they settled in this land till now.' " Then Moses turned and left Pharaoh.

7Pharaoh's officials said to him, "How long will this man be a snare to us? Let the people go, so that they

Gross!

Here's yet another plague in Exodus 9:13–26. Have you seen hailstones the size of pebbles or even golf balls? Imagine hailstones so big they knocked the brains out of cows and flattened every blade of barley in sight! That is *not* the time to run out to the corner store for a jug of milk, unless you want to be flattened into a splat.

may worship the LORD their God. Do you not yet realize that Egypt is ruined?"

⁸Then Moses and Aaron were brought back to Pharaoh. "Go, worship the LORD your God," he said. "But just who will be going?"

⁹Moses answered, "We will go with our young and old, with our sons and daughters, and with our flocks and herds, because we are to celebrate a festival to the LORD."

¹⁰Pharaoh said, "The LORD be with you—if I let you go, along with your women and children! Clearly you are bent on evil.ᵃ ¹¹No! Have only the men go; and worship the LORD, since that's what you have been asking for." Then Moses and Aaron were driven out of Pharaoh's presence.

¹²And the LORD said to Moses, "Stretch out your hand over Egypt so that locusts will swarm over the land and devour everything growing in the fields, everything left by the hail."

¹³So Moses stretched out his staff over Egypt, and the LORD made an east wind blow across the land all that day and all that night. By morning the wind had brought the locusts; ¹⁴they invaded all Egypt and settled down in every area of the country in great numbers. Never before had there been such a plague of locusts, nor will there ever be again. ¹⁵They covered all the ground until it was black. They devoured all that was left after the hail—everything growing in the fields and the fruit on the trees. Nothing green remained on tree or plant in all the land of Egypt.

¹⁶Pharaoh quickly summoned Moses and Aaron and said, "I have sinned against the LORD your God and against you. ¹⁷Now forgive my sin once more and pray to the LORD your God to take this deadly plague away from me."

¹⁸Moses then left Pharaoh and prayed to the LORD. ¹⁹And the LORD changed the wind to a very strong west wind, which caught up the locusts and carried them into the Red Sea.ᵇ Not a locust was left anywhere in Egypt. ²⁰But the LORD hardened Pharaoh's heart, and he would not let the Israelites go.

ᵃ 10 Or *Be careful, trouble is in store for you!*
ᵇ 19 Hebrew *Yam Suph*; that is, Sea of Reeds

GET SMARTER

In This Corner ... Pharaoh!

READ EXODUS 10:13–20

Ever see some bald, big-mouthed, bloody-lipped wrestling bozo practically press his nose against the TV camera as he shouts how he's going to cream so-and-so and *no way* he's ever going to back down? Well, put a tall crown on his head and you have Pharaoh, king of Egypt. He absolutely refused to back down no matter how much God battered Egypt. He refused to admit he was wrong. He came to the point where he *couldn't* listen any more; God had hardened his heart (Exodus 10:20). Take a lesson: A real man is smart enough to know when he's wrong. He admits his mistake and he backs down. The only time a real man never backs down is when he knows he's right. But when others point out that he's wrong, he admits it and he changes.

Your next reading is on page 98.

The Plague of Darkness

21Then the LORD said to Moses, "Stretch out your hand toward the sky so that darkness will spread over Egypt—darkness that can be felt." 22So Moses stretched out his hand toward the sky, and total darkness covered all Egypt for three days. 23No one could see anyone else or leave his place for three days. Yet all the Israelites had light in the places where they lived.

24Then Pharaoh summoned Moses and said, "Go, worship the LORD. Even your women and children may go with you; only leave your flocks and herds behind."

25But Moses said, "You must allow us to have sacrifices and burnt offerings to present to the LORD our God. 26Our livestock too must go with us; not a hoof is to be left behind. We have to use some of them in worshiping the LORD our God, and until we get there we will not know what we are to use to worship the LORD."

27But the LORD hardened Pharaoh's heart, and he was not willing to let them go. 28Pharaoh said to Moses, "Get out of my sight! Make sure you do not appear before me again! The day you see my face you will die."

29"Just as you say," Moses replied, "I will never appear before you again."

The Plague on the Firstborn

11 Now the LORD had said to Moses, "I will bring one more plague on Pharaoh and on Egypt. After that, he will let you go from here, and when he does, he will drive you out completely. 2Tell the people that men and women alike are to ask their neighbors for articles of silver and gold." 3(The LORD made the Egyptians favorably disposed toward the people, and Moses himself was highly regarded in Egypt by Pharaoh's officials and by the people.)

4So Moses said, "This is what the LORD says: 'About midnight I will go throughout Egypt. 5Every firstborn son in Egypt will die, from the firstborn son of Pharaoh, who sits on the throne, to the firstborn son of the slave girl, who is at her hand mill, and all the firstborn of the cattle as well. 6There will be loud wailing throughout Egypt—worse than there has ever been or ever will be again. 7But among the Israelites not a dog will bark at any man or animal.' Then you will know that the LORD makes a distinction between Egypt and Israel. 8All these officials of yours will come to me, bowing down before me and saying, 'Go, you and all the people who follow you!' After that I will leave." Then Moses, hot with anger, left Pharaoh.

9The LORD had said to Moses, "Pharaoh will refuse to listen to you—so that my wonders may be multiplied in Egypt." 10Moses and Aaron performed all these wonders before Pharaoh, but the LORD hardened Pharaoh's heart, and he would not let the Israelites go out of his country.

The Passover

12 The LORD said to Moses and Aaron in Egypt, 2"This month is to be for you the first month, the first month of your year. 3Tell the whole community of Israel that on the tenth day of this month each man is to take a lamb[a] for his family, one for each household. 4If any household is too small for a whole lamb, they must share one with their nearest neighbor, having taken into account the number of people there are. You are to determine the amount of lamb needed in accordance with what each person will eat. 5The animals you choose must be year-old males without defect, and you may take them from the sheep or the goats. 6Take care of them until the fourteenth day of the month, when all the people of the community of Israel must slaughter them at twilight. 7Then they are to take some of the blood and put it on the sides and tops of the doorframes of the houses where they eat the lambs. 8That same night they are to eat the meat roasted over the fire, along with bitter herbs, and bread made without yeast. 9Do not eat the meat raw or cooked in water, but roast it over the fire—head, legs and inner parts. 10Do not leave any of it till morning; if some is left till morning, you must burn it. 11This is how you are to eat it: with your cloak tucked into your belt, your sandals on your feet and your staff in your hand. Eat it in haste; it is the LORD's Passover.

12"On that same night I will pass through Egypt and strike down every firstborn—both men and animals—and I will

a 3 The Hebrew word can mean lamb or kid; also in verse 4.

bring judgment on all the gods of Egypt. I am the LORD. ¹³The blood will be a sign for you on the houses where you are; and when I see the blood, I will pass over you. No destructive plague will touch you when I strike Egypt.

¹⁴"This is a day you are to commemorate; for the generations to come you shall celebrate it as a festival to the LORD— a lasting ordinance. ¹⁵For seven days you are to eat bread made without yeast. On the first day remove the yeast from your houses, for whoever eats anything with yeast in it from the first day through the seventh must be cut off from Israel. ¹⁶On the first day hold a sacred assembly, and another one on the seventh day. Do no work at all on these days, except to prepare food for everyone to eat—that is all you may do.

¹⁷"Celebrate the Feast of Unleavened Bread, because it was on this very day that I brought your divisions out of Egypt. Celebrate this day as a lasting ordinance for the generations to come. ¹⁸In the first month you are to eat bread made without yeast, from the evening of the fourteenth day until the evening of the twenty-first day. ¹⁹For seven days no yeast is to be found in your houses. And whoever eats anything with yeast in it must be cut off from the community of Israel, whether he is an alien or native-born. ²⁰Eat nothing made with yeast. Wherever you live, you must eat unleavened bread."

²¹Then Moses summoned all the elders of Israel and said to them, "Go at once and select the animals for your families and slaughter the Passover lamb. ²²Take a bunch of hyssop, dip it into the blood in the basin and put some of the blood on the top and on both sides of the doorframe. Not one of you shall go out the door of his house until morning. ²³When the LORD goes through the land to strike down the Egyptians, he will see the blood on the top and sides of the doorframe and will pass over that doorway, and he

Make It Stick

READ EXODUS 12:7

God told the Israelites there was a major curfew, and to stay indoors. Why? To spoil their fun? No. When you keep God's commands, they keep you safe. Obeying your parents does the same thing. Draw a doorframe and color red blood dripping down it. Inside the frame, write one of your mom's common sense rules.

will not permit the destroyer to enter your houses and strike you down.

24"Obey these instructions as a lasting ordinance for you and your descendants. 25When you enter the land that the LORD will give you as he promised, observe this ceremony. 26And when your children ask you, 'What does this ceremony mean to you?' 27then tell them, 'It is the Passover sacrifice to the LORD, who passed over the houses of the Israelites in Egypt and spared our homes when he struck down the Egyptians.' " Then the people bowed down and worshiped. 28The Israelites did just what the LORD commanded Moses and Aaron.

29At midnight the LORD struck down all the firstborn in Egypt, from the firstborn of Pharaoh, who sat on the throne, to the firstborn of the prisoner, who was in the dungeon, and the firstborn of all the livestock as well. 30Pharaoh and all his officials and all the Egyptians got up during the night, and there was loud wailing in Egypt, for there was not a house without someone dead.

The Exodus

31During the night Pharaoh summoned Moses and Aaron and said, "Up! Leave my people, you and the Israelites! Go, worship the LORD as you have requested. 32Take your flocks and herds, as you have said, and go. And also bless me."

33The Egyptians urged the people to hurry and leave the country. "For otherwise," they said, "we will all die!" 34So the people took their dough before the yeast was added, and carried it on their shoulders in kneading troughs wrapped in clothing. 35The Israelites did as Moses instructed and asked the Egyptians for articles of silver and gold and for clothing. 36The LORD had made the Egyptians favorably disposed toward the people, and they gave them what they asked for; so they plundered the Egyptians.

37The Israelites journeyed from Rameses

Make It Stick

READ EXODUS 12:12

To show that there was no God but him, God mocked the so-called "gods" of Egypt. The sun god looked dim when God sent three days of darkness. The life-giving Nile River, which the Egyptians worshiped as a god, was filled with blood and death. The frog-god stunk when millions of frogs rotted. Draw a picture of a dead frog on a sticky note.

to Succoth. There were about six hundred thousand men on foot, besides women and children. ³⁸Many other people went up with them, as well as large droves of livestock, both flocks and herds. ³⁹With the dough they had brought from Egypt, they baked cakes of unleavened bread. The dough was without yeast because they had been driven out of Egypt and did not have time to prepare food for themselves.

⁴⁰Now the length of time the Israelite people lived in Egypt*ᵃ* was 430 years. ⁴¹At the end of the 430 years, to the very day, all the LORD's divisions left Egypt. ⁴²Because the LORD kept vigil that night to bring them out of Egypt, on this night all the Israelites are to keep vigil to honor the LORD for the generations to come.

Passover Restrictions

⁴³The LORD said to Moses and Aaron, "These are the regulations for the Passover:

"No foreigner is to eat of it. ⁴⁴Any slave you have bought may eat of it after you have circumcised him, ⁴⁵but a temporary resident and a hired worker may not eat of it.

⁴⁶"It must be eaten inside one house; take none of the meat outside the house. Do not break any of the bones. ⁴⁷The whole community of Israel must celebrate it.

⁴⁸"An alien living among you who wants to celebrate the LORD's Passover must have all the males in his household circumcised; then he may take part like one born in the land. No uncircumcised male may eat of it. ⁴⁹The same law applies to the native-born and to the alien living among you."

⁵⁰All the Israelites did just what the LORD had commanded Moses and Aaron. ⁵¹And on that very day the LORD brought the Israelites out of Egypt by their divisions.

Consecration of the Firstborn

13 The LORD said to Moses, ²"Consecrate to me every firstborn male. The first offspring of every womb among the Israelites belongs to me, whether man or animal."

ᵃ 40 Masoretic Text; Samaritan Pentateuch and Septuagint Egypt and Canaan

---

The Reason for the Season

READ EXODUS 12:12–29

God gave the Israelites very specific instructions about celebrating the Passover. He wanted them to always remember what he had done for them. God said, "This is a day you are to commemorate . . . celebrate it as a festival" (Exodus 12:14). Even today, we as Christians celebrate important days and special get-togethers. We have special church events, such as at Christmas and Easter. As we grow up, it's important not to neglect these special times with family and friends. When we gather to celebrate special days, it reminds us of what we believe. We are also strengthening each other's faith. Most of all, gathering to celebrate these days reminds us of who God is and all that he has done for us. God is the real reason behind every special season. When we get excited about special days and know why we're celebrating them, it keeps us together and keeps us strong.

Your next reading is on page 99.

³Then Moses said to the people, "Commemorate this day, the day you came out of Egypt, out of the land of slavery, because the LORD brought you out of it with a mighty hand. Eat nothing containing yeast. ⁴Today, in the month of Abib, you are leaving. ⁵When the LORD brings you into the land of the Canaanites, Hittites, Amorites, Hivites and Jebusites—the land he swore to your forefathers to give you, a land flowing with milk and honey—you are to observe this ceremony in this month: ⁶For seven days eat bread made without yeast and on the seventh day hold a festival to the LORD. ⁷Eat unleavened bread during those seven days; nothing with yeast in it is to be seen among you, nor shall any yeast be seen anywhere within your borders. ⁸On that day tell your son, 'I do this because of what the LORD did for me when I came out of Egypt.' ⁹This observance will be for you like a sign on your hand and a reminder on your forehead that the law of the LORD is to be on your lips. For the LORD brought you out of Egypt with his mighty hand. ¹⁰You must keep this ordinance at the appointed time year after year.

¹¹"After the LORD brings you into the land of the Canaanites and gives it to you, as he promised on oath to you and your forefathers, ¹²you are to give over to the LORD the first offspring of every womb. All the firstborn males of your livestock belong to the LORD. ¹³Redeem with a lamb every firstborn donkey, but if you do not redeem it, break its neck. Redeem every firstborn among your sons.

¹⁴"In days to come, when your son asks you, 'What does this mean?' say to him, 'With a mighty hand the LORD brought us out of Egypt, out of the land of slavery. ¹⁵When Pharaoh stubbornly refused to let us go, the LORD killed every firstborn in Egypt, both man and animal. This is why I sacrifice to the LORD the first male offspring of every womb and redeem each of my firstborn sons.' ¹⁶And it will be like a sign

GET STRONGER

Nation in Migration

READ EXODUS 12:31–42

When the Israelites finally left Egypt, the men's muscles were rock hard from years of slave labor; the women were also strong and "vigorous" (Exodus 1:19). They had strength in numbers, too. "There were about 600,000 men on foot, besides women and children" (Exodus 12:37). Watch out! Nation in migration! But muscles and mass didn't make them *really* strong. Without unity they would have just been a big disorganized mob. What gave them strength was having a strong leader, Moses, and all of them wanting the same thing—to serve and obey God. It's the same with your family or your church today. When you work to be in agreement, God gives you power. So for the sake of unity, be respectful of others' opinions. Remember, when you "dis" unity, you create disunity. A real man tries to unify his group, not divide it.

Your next reading is on page 101.

Get a Load of This...

Pretend you are like the Israelites in Exodus 12:35–36. You've been a slave all your life. Now you are finally free, thanks to God! But God says, "Oh yeah, one more thing: Before you go, ask the Egyptians for gold, silver and clothes. They'll give them to you." Not only are you free but you just plundered the guys who made you slaves. Sweet!

on your hand and a symbol on your forehead that the LORD brought us out of Egypt with his mighty hand."

Crossing the Sea

17When Pharaoh let the people go, God did not lead them on the road through the Philistine country, though that was shorter. For God said, "If they face war, they might change their minds and return to Egypt." 18So God led the people around by the desert road toward the Red Sea.[a] The Israelites went up out of Egypt armed for battle.

19Moses took the bones of Joseph with him because Joseph had made the sons of Israel swear an oath. He had said, "God will surely come to your aid, and then you must carry my bones up with you from this place."[b]

20After leaving Succoth they camped at Etham on the edge of the desert. 21By day the LORD went ahead of them in a pillar of cloud to guide them on their way and by night in a pillar of fire to give them light, so that they could travel by day or night. 22Neither the pillar of cloud by day nor the pillar of fire by night left its place in front of the people.

14 Then the LORD said to Moses, 2"Tell the Israelites to turn back and encamp near Pi Hahiroth, between Migdol and the sea. They are to encamp by the sea, directly opposite Baal Zephon. 3Pharaoh will think, 'The Israelites are wandering around the land in confusion, hemmed in by the desert.' 4And I will harden Pharaoh's heart, and he will pursue them. But I will gain glory for myself through Pharaoh and all his army, and the Egyptians will know that I am the LORD." So the Israelites did this.

5When the king of Egypt was told that the people had fled, Pharaoh and his officials changed their minds about them and said, "What have we done? We have let the Israelites go and have lost their services!" 6So he had his chariot made ready and took his army with him. 7He took six hundred of the best chariots, along with all the other chariots of Egypt, with officers over all of them. 8The LORD hardened the heart of Pharaoh king of Egypt, so that he pursued the Israelites, who were marching out boldly. 9The Egyptians—all Pharaoh's horses and chariots, horsemen[c] and troops—pursued the Israelites and overtook them as they camped by the sea near Pi Hahiroth, opposite Baal Zephon.

10As Pharaoh approached, the Israelites looked up, and there were the Egyptians, marching after them. They were terrified and cried out to the LORD. 11They said to Moses, "Was it because there were no graves in Egypt that you brought us to the desert to die? What have you done to us by bringing us out of Egypt? 12Didn't we say to you in Egypt, 'Leave us alone; let us serve the Egyptians'? It would have been better for us to serve the Egyptians than to die in the desert!"

a 18 Hebrew *Yam Suph*; that is, Sea of Reeds   b 19 See Gen. 50:25.
c 9 Or *charioteers*; also in verses 17, 18, 23, 26 and 28

¹³Moses answered the people, "Do not be afraid. Stand firm and you will see the deliverance the LORD will bring you today. The Egyptians you see today you will never see again. ¹⁴The LORD will fight for you; you need only to be still."

¹⁵Then the LORD said to Moses, "Why are you crying out to me? Tell the Israelites to move on. ¹⁶Raise your staff and stretch out your hand over the sea to divide the water so that the Israelites can go through the sea on dry ground. ¹⁷I will harden the hearts of the Egyptians so that they will go in after them. And I will gain glory through Pharaoh and all his army, through his chariots and his horsemen. ¹⁸The Egyptians will know that I am the LORD when I gain glory through Pharaoh, his chariots and his horsemen."

¹⁹Then the angel of God, who had been traveling in front of Israel's army, withdrew and went behind them. The pillar of cloud also moved from in front and stood behind them, ²⁰coming between the armies of Egypt and Israel. Throughout the night the cloud brought darkness to the one side and light to the other side; so neither went near the other all night long.

²¹Then Moses stretched out his hand over the sea, and all that night the LORD drove the sea back with a strong east wind and turned it into dry land. The waters were divided, ²²and the Israelites went through the sea on dry ground, with a wall of water on their right and on their left.

²³The Egyptians pursued them, and all Pharaoh's horses and chariots and horsemen followed them into the sea. ²⁴During the last watch of the night the LORD looked down from the pillar of fire and cloud at the Egyptian army and threw it into confusion. ²⁵He made the wheels of their chariots come off ᵃ so that they had difficulty driving. And the Egyptians said, "Let's get away from the Israelites! The LORD is fighting for them against Egypt."

ᵃ 25 Or He jammed the wheels of their chariots (see Samaritan Pentateuch, Septuagint and Syriac)

Muscle-flexing Time

READ EXODUS 13:18; 14:5–31

The armies of the Lord left Egypt "armed for battle" (Exodus 13:18), but they weren't invincible. The Egyptian army still had a lot more military muscle. Pharaoh sent 600 chariots—the tanks of those times—after the Israelites, and trapped them against the sea. Without God's help, the Israelites would've been fish food. So Moses told them, "Do not be afraid. Stand firm and . . . the LORD will fight for you" (Exodus 14:13–14). The Israelites obeyed. And when they just stood back and let God do his thing, he put the entire Egyptian army on rinse cycle. So take a tip and don't let fear control you. Do everything you can, sure, but then trust God to do the rest. God wants you to be strong, inside and out—convictions and muscles—but when you're in over your head, remember: God's got the most muscle, and he stands with you.

Your next reading is on page 104.

26Then the LORD said to Moses, "Stretch out your hand over the sea so that the waters may flow back over the Egyptians and their chariots and horsemen." 27Moses stretched out his hand over the sea, and at daybreak the sea went back to its place. The Egyptians were fleeing toward*a* it, and the LORD swept them into the sea. 28The water flowed back and covered the chariots and horsemen—the entire army of Pharaoh that had followed the Israelites into the sea. Not one of them survived.

29But the Israelites went through the sea on dry ground, with a wall of water on their right and on their left. 30That day the LORD saved Israel from the hands of the Egyptians, and Israel saw the Egyptians lying dead on the shore. 31And when the Israelites saw the great power the LORD displayed against the Egyptians, the people feared the LORD and put their trust in him and in Moses his servant.

The Song of Moses and Miriam

15 Then Moses and the Israelites sang this song to the LORD:

"I will sing to the LORD,
 for he is highly exalted.
The horse and its rider
 he has hurled into the sea.
2 The LORD is my strength and my song;
 he has become my salvation.
He is my God, and I will praise him,
 my father's God, and I will exalt him.
3 The LORD is a warrior;
 the LORD is his name.
4 Pharaoh's chariots and his army
 he has hurled into the sea.
The best of Pharaoh's officers
 are drowned in the Red Sea.*b*
5 The deep waters have covered them;
 they sank to the depths like a stone.
6 "Your right hand, O LORD,
 was majestic in power.
Your right hand, O LORD,
 shattered the enemy.
7 In the greatness of your majesty
 you threw down those who
  opposed you.
You unleashed your burning anger;
 it consumed them like stubble.
8 By the blast of your nostrils
 the waters piled up.

The surging waters stood firm like a
  wall;
 the deep waters congealed in the
  heart of the sea.
9 "The enemy boasted,
 'I will pursue, I will overtake them.
I will divide the spoils;
 I will gorge myself on them.
I will draw my sword
 and my hand will destroy them.'
10 But you blew with your breath,
 and the sea covered them.
They sank like lead
 in the mighty waters.

11 "Who among the gods is like you,
  O LORD?
Who is like you—
 majestic in holiness,
 awesome in glory,
 working wonders?
12 You stretched out your right hand
 and the earth swallowed them.

13 "In your unfailing love you will lead
 the people you have redeemed.
In your strength you will guide them
 to your holy dwelling.
14 The nations will hear and tremble;
 anguish will grip the people of
  Philistia.
15 The chiefs of Edom will be terrified,
 the leaders of Moab will be seized
  with trembling,
 the people*c* of Canaan will melt away;
16 terror and dread will fall upon them.
By the power of your arm
 they will be as still as a stone—
until your people pass by, O LORD,
 until the people you bought*d* pass by.
17 You will bring them in and plant them
 on the mountain of your
  inheritance—
the place, O LORD, you made for your
  dwelling,
 the sanctuary, O Lord, your hands
  established.
18 The LORD will reign
 for ever and ever."

19When Pharaoh's horses, chariots and horsemen*e* went into the sea, the LORD brought the waters of the sea back over them, but the Israelites walked through the sea on dry ground. 20Then Miriam the

---

a 27 Or *from*   *b 4* Hebrew *Yam Suph*; that is, Sea of Reeds; also in verse 22   *c 15* Or *rulers*   *d 16* Or *created*   *e 19* Or *charioteers* prophetess, Aaron's sister, took a tambourine in her hand, and all the women followed her, with tambourines and dancing. 21Miriam sang to them:

"Sing to the LORD,
  for he is highly exalted.
The horse and its rider
  he has hurled into the sea."

The Waters of Marah and Elim

22Then Moses led Israel from the Red Sea and they went into the Desert of Shur. For three days they traveled in the desert without finding water. 23When they came to Marah, they could not drink its water because it was bitter. (That is why the place is called Marah.ª) 24So the people grumbled against Moses, saying, "What are we to drink?"

25Then Moses cried out to the LORD, and the LORD showed him a piece of wood. He threw it into the water, and the water became sweet.

There the LORD made a decree and a law for them, and there he tested them. 26He said, "If you listen carefully to the voice of the LORD your God and do what is right in

ª 23 Marah means bitter.

Make It Stick

READ EXODUS 15:22–27
A man who looks to God for help, especially in times of trouble, is a good leader. What have you been grumbling about lately? Using cards (or sticky notes!), build a "grumble building" out of your complaints. Pray about them. Then knock them over (or rip them up). As easily as you did that, God can solve your problems.

his eyes, if you pay attention to his commands and keep all his decrees, I will not bring on you any of the diseases I brought on the Egyptians, for I am the LORD, who heals you."

27Then they came to Elim, where there were twelve springs and seventy palm trees, and they camped there near the water.

Manna and Quail

16 The whole Israelite community set out from Elim and came to the Desert of Sin, which is between Elim and Sinai, on the fifteenth day of the second month after they had come out of Egypt. 2In the desert the whole community grumbled against Moses and Aaron. 3The Israelites said to them, "If only we had died by the LORD's hand in Egypt! There we sat around pots of meat and ate all the food we wanted, but you have brought us out into this desert to starve this entire assembly to death."

4Then the LORD said to Moses, "I will rain down bread from heaven for you. The people are to go out each day and gather enough for that day. In this way I will test them and see whether they will follow my instructions. 5On the sixth day they are to prepare what they bring in, and that is to be twice as much as they gather on the other days."

6So Moses and Aaron said to all the Israelites, "In the evening you will know that it was the LORD who brought you out of Egypt, 7and in the morning you will see the glory of the LORD, because he has heard your grumbling against him. Who are we, that you should grumble against us?" 8Moses also said, "You will know that it was the LORD when he gives you meat to eat in the evening and all the bread you want in the morning, because he has heard your grumbling against him. Who are we? You are not grumbling against us, but against the LORD."

9Then Moses told Aaron, "Say to the entire Israelite community, 'Come before the LORD, for he has heard your grumbling.' "

10While Aaron was speaking to the whole Israelite community, they looked

GET SMARTER

Rumbling, Grumbling, Stumbling

READ EXODUS 16:1–16

Have you ever been grouchy because you were hungry or tired? Your belly starts rumbling, and then you start grumbling. No sooner does your mom step in the door but you burst out, "I need food *now*! There's *nothing* to eat!" Whoops! Bad move. You sound just like an Israelite! Instead of simply *asking* God for food, they bellyached to Moses. Now, sometimes being grumpy just means you need to take care of your body. You suffer when you don't get enough sleep or food or when you're bummed out about something. Those aren't excuses, however. Moses said, "Come before the LORD, for he has heard your grumbling" (Exodus 16:9). In other words, just ask. God knows your needs and he'll provide what you need. Next time, before the belly rumbles makes you grumble and stumble—or when you need help of any kind— ask God. He's listening.

Your next reading is on page 106.

toward the desert, and there was the glory of the LORD appearing in the cloud.

¹¹The LORD said to Moses, ¹²"I have heard the grumbling of the Israelites. Tell them, 'At twilight you will eat meat, and in the morning you will be filled with bread. Then you will know that I am the LORD your God.' "

¹³That evening quail came and covered the camp, and in the morning there was a layer of dew around the camp. ¹⁴When the dew was gone, thin flakes like frost on the ground appeared on the desert floor. ¹⁵When the Israelites saw it, they said to each other, "What is it?" For they did not know what it was.

Moses said to them, "It is the bread the LORD has given you to eat. ¹⁶This is what the LORD has commanded: 'Each one is to gather as much as he needs. Take an omer ᵃ for each person you have in your tent.' "

¹⁷The Israelites did as they were told; some gathered much, some little. ¹⁸And when they measured it by the omer, he who gathered much did not have too much, and he who gathered little did not have too little. Each one gathered as much as he needed.

¹⁹Then Moses said to them, "No one is to keep any of it until morning."

²⁰However, some of them paid no attention to Moses; they kept part of it until morning, but it was full of maggots and began to smell. So Moses was angry with them.

²¹Each morning everyone gathered as much as he needed, and when the sun grew hot, it melted away. ²²On the sixth day, they gathered twice as much—two omers ᵇ for each person—and the leaders of the community came and reported this to Moses. ²³He said to them, "This is what the LORD commanded: 'Tomorrow is to be a day of rest, a holy Sabbath to the LORD. So bake what you want to bake and boil what you want to boil. Save whatever is left and keep it until morning.' "

²⁴So they saved it until morning, as Moses commanded, and it did not stink or get maggots in it. ²⁵"Eat it today," Moses said, "because today is a Sabbath to the LORD. You will not find any of it on the ground today. ²⁶Six days you are to gather it, but on the seventh day, the Sabbath, there will not be any."

²⁷Nevertheless, some of the people went out on the seventh day to gather it, but they found none. ²⁸Then the LORD said to Moses, "How long will you ᶜ refuse to keep my commands and my instructions? ²⁹Bear in mind that the LORD has given you the Sabbath; that is why on the sixth day he gives you bread for two days. Everyone is to stay where he is on the seventh day; no one is to go out." ³⁰So the people rested on the seventh day.

³¹The people of Israel called the bread manna. ᵈ It was white like coriander seed and tasted like wafers made with honey. ³²Moses said, "This is what the LORD has commanded: 'Take an omer of manna and keep it

Get a Load of This...

Check out Exodus 16:31. Imagine eating something called *"What is it?"* (seriously, that's what *manna* means!) every meal, every day for forty years. That's what the Israelites called the honey-flavored wafers that appeared each morning in the desert. ("What's for lunch?" "What is it?" "Hey, I asked first.") "Mom, pass the ba-manna bread, please." "May I have another manna-wich?"

ᵃ16 That is, probably about 2 quarts (about 2 liters); also in verses 18, 32, 33 and 36   ᵇ22 That is, probably about 4 quarts (about 4.5 liters)   ᶜ28 The Hebrew is plural.   ᵈ31 Manna means What is it? (see verse 15).

for the generations to come, so they can see the bread I gave you to eat in the desert when I brought you out of Egypt.' "

³³So Moses said to Aaron, "Take a jar and put an omer of manna in it. Then place it before the LORD to be kept for the generations to come."

³⁴As the LORD commanded Moses, Aaron put the manna in front of the Testimony, that it might be kept. ³⁵The Israelites ate manna forty years, until they came to a land that was settled; they ate manna until they reached the border of Canaan.

³⁶(An omer is one tenth of an ephah.)

Water From the Rock

17 The whole Israelite community set out from the Desert of Sin, traveling from place to place as the LORD commanded. They camped at Rephidim, but there was no water for the people to drink. ²So they quarreled with Moses and said, "Give us water to drink."

Moses replied, "Why do you quarrel with me? Why do you put the LORD to the test?"

³But the people were thirsty for water there, and they grumbled against Moses. They said, "Why did you bring us up out of Egypt to make us and our children and livestock die of thirst?"

⁴Then Moses cried out to the LORD, "What am I to do with these people? They are almost ready to stone me."

⁵The LORD answered Moses, "Walk on ahead of the people. Take with you some of the elders of Israel and take in your hand the staff with which you struck the Nile, and go. ⁶I will stand there before you by the rock at Horeb. Strike the rock, and water will come out of it for the people to drink." So Moses did this in the sight of the elders of Israel. ⁷And he called the place Massah*a* and Meribah*b* because the Israelites quarreled and because they test-

---

a 7 Massah means *testing.*   *b 7 Meribah* means *quarreling.*

Helping Hands

READ EXODUS 17:8–16

The Israelites had to cooperate in order to defeat the Amalekites. During the battle, Moses raised up his hands while holding the "staff of God," as a symbol of the Israelites' appeal to God for help and victory. When Moses was pooped out, "Aaron and Hur held his hands up . . . so that his hands remained steady till sunset" (Exodus 17:12). Aaron and Hur supported Moses and did their part to help Israel win. Aaron could have said, "Aw, man, what's the deal with the hands?" If he had, the Amalekites would have won. Instead, he supported Moses' authority and cooperated. It's the same today: You should support your parents, teachers and other leaders, and do everything you can to help them. That includes honoring their decisions and obeying their rules. By the way, did you notice this is the first mention of a dude called Joshua? We'll see a lot of him later on. Joshua rocks! And the first time we meet him, he's obeying Moses and doing his job—leading the army.

Your next reading is on page 109.

ed the Lord saying, "Is the Lord among us or not?"

The Amalekites Defeated

8The Amalekites came and attacked the Israelites at Rephidim. 9Moses said to Joshua, "Choose some of our men and go out to fight the Amalekites. Tomorrow I will stand on top of the hill with the staff of God in my hands."

10So Joshua fought the Amalekites as Moses had ordered, and Moses, Aaron and Hur went to the top of the hill. 11As long as Moses held up his hands, the Israelites were winning, but whenever he lowered his hands, the Amalekites were winning. 12When Moses' hands grew tired, they took a stone and put it under him and he sat on it. Aaron and Hur held his hands up—one on one side, one on the other—so that his hands remained steady till sunset. 13So Joshua overcame the Amalekite army with the sword.

14Then the Lord said to Moses, "Write this on a scroll as something to be remembered and make sure that Joshua hears it, because I will completely blot out the memory of Amalek from under heaven."

15Moses built an altar and called it The Lord is my Banner. 16He said, "For hands were lifted up to the throne of the Lord. The*a* Lord will be at war against the Amalekites from generation to generation."

Jethro Visits Moses

18 Now Jethro, the priest of Midian and father-in-law of Moses, heard of everything God had done for Moses and for his people Israel, and how the Lord had brought Israel out of Egypt.

2After Moses had sent away his wife Zipporah, his father-in-law Jethro received her 3and her two sons. One son was named Gershom,*b* for Moses said, "I have become an alien in a foreign land"; 4and

---

a 16 Or *"Because a hand was against the throne of the Lord, the* *b 3* Gershom sounds like the Hebrew for *an alien there.*

Make It Stick

READ EXODUS 18

If a super-prophet like Moses listened to Jethro, you should listen to mentors, too. A mentor is a person who is there to give you advice when you need help. This person follows God closely and wants you to do the same. Write the name of a mentor you trust, and write why you respect him or her.

the other was named Eliezer,[a] for he said, "My father's God was my helper; he saved me from the sword of Pharaoh."

[5] Jethro, Moses' father-in-law, together with Moses' sons and wife, came to him in the desert, where he was camped near the mountain of God. [6] Jethro had sent word to him, "I, your father-in-law Jethro, am coming to you with your wife and her two sons."

[7] So Moses went out to meet his father-in-law and bowed down and kissed him. They greeted each other and then went into the tent. [8] Moses told his father-in-law about everything the LORD had done to Pharaoh and the Egyptians for Israel's sake and about all the hardships they had met along the way and how the LORD had saved them.

[9] Jethro was delighted to hear about all the good things the LORD had done for Israel in rescuing them from the hand of the Egyptians. [10] He said, "Praise be to the LORD, who rescued you from the hand of the Egyptians and of Pharaoh, and who rescued the people from the hand of the Egyptians. [11] Now I know that the LORD is greater than all other gods, for he did this to those who had treated Israel arrogantly." [12] Then Jethro, Moses' father-in-law, brought a burnt offering and other sacrifices to God, and Aaron came with all the elders of Israel to eat bread with Moses' father-in-law in the presence of God.

[13] The next day Moses took his seat to serve as judge for the people, and they stood around him from morning till evening. [14] When his father-in-law saw all that Moses was doing for the people, he said, "What is this you are doing for the people? Why do you alone sit as judge, while all these people stand around you from morning till evening?"

[15] Moses answered him, "Because the people come to me to seek God's will. [16] Whenever they have a dispute, it is brought to me, and I decide between the parties and inform them of God's decrees and laws."

[17] Moses' father-in-law replied, "What you are doing is not good. [18] You and these people who come to you will only wear yourselves out. The work is too heavy for you; you cannot handle it alone. [19] Listen now to me and I will give you some advice, and may God be with you. You must be the people's representative before God and bring their disputes to him. [20] Teach them the decrees and laws, and show them the way to live and the duties they are to perform. [21] But select capable men from all the people—men who fear God, trustworthy men who hate dishonest gain—and appoint them as officials over thousands, hundreds, fifties and tens. [22] Have them serve as judges for the people at all times, but have them bring every difficult case to you; the simple cases they can decide themselves. That will make your load lighter, because they will share it with you. [23] If you do this and God so commands, you will be able to stand the strain, and all these people will go home satisfied."

[24] Moses listened to his father-in-law and did everything he said. [25] He chose capable men from all Israel and made them leaders of the people, officials over thousands, hundreds, fifties and tens. [26] They served as judges for the people at all times. The difficult cases they brought to Moses, but the simple ones they decided themselves.

[27] Then Moses sent his father-in-law on his way, and Jethro returned to his own country.

At Mount Sinai

19 In the third month after the Israelites left Egypt—on the very day—they came to the Desert of Sinai. [2] After they set out from Rephidim, they entered the Desert of Sinai, and Israel camped there in the desert in front of the mountain.

[3] Then Moses went up to God, and the LORD called to him from the mountain and said, "This is what you are to say to the house of Jacob and what you are to tell the people of Israel: [4] 'You yourselves have seen what I did to Egypt, and how I carried you on eagles' wings and brought you to myself. [5] Now if you obey me fully and keep my covenant, then out of all nations you will be my treasured possession. Although the whole earth is mine, [6] you[b] will be for me a kingdom of priests and a holy nation.' These are the words you are to speak to the Israelites."

[7] So Moses went back and summoned the elders of the people and set before them all the words the LORD had com-

---

[a] 4 Eliezer means my God is helper.   [b] 5,6 Or possession, for the whole earth is mine. 6 You

manded him to speak. [8]The people all responded together, "We will do everything the LORD has said." So Moses brought their answer back to the LORD.

[9]The LORD said to Moses, "I am going to come to you in a dense cloud, so that the people will hear me speaking with you and will always put their trust in you." Then Moses told the LORD what the people had said.

[10]And the LORD said to Moses, "Go to the people and consecrate them today and tomorrow. Have them wash their clothes [11]and be ready by the third day, because on that day the LORD will come down on Mount Sinai in the sight of all the people. [12]Put limits for the people around the mountain and tell them, 'Be careful that you do not go up the mountain or touch the foot of it. Whoever touches the mountain shall surely be put to death. [13]He shall surely be stoned or shot with arrows; not a hand is to be laid on him. Whether man or animal, he shall not be permitted to live.' Only when the ram's horn sounds a long blast may they go up to the mountain."

[14]After Moses had gone down the mountain to the people, he consecrated them, and they washed their clothes. [15]Then he said to the people, "Prepare yourselves for the third day. Abstain from sexual relations."

[16]On the morning of the third day there was thunder and lightning, with a thick cloud over the mountain, and a very loud trumpet blast. Everyone in the camp trembled. [17]Then Moses led the people out of the camp to meet with God, and they stood at the foot of the mountain. [18]Mount Sinai was covered with smoke, because the LORD descended on it in fire. The smoke billowed up from it like smoke from a furnace, the whole mountain[a] trembled violently, [19]and the sound of the trumpet grew louder and louder. Then Moses spoke and the voice of God answered him.[b]

[20]The LORD descended to the top of Mount Sinai and called Moses to the top of the mountain. So Moses went up [21]and

_____

[a] 18 Most Hebrew manuscripts; a few Hebrew manuscripts and Septuagint _all the people_　　[b] 19 Or _and God answered him with thunder_

Dazzling Display of Fire and Love

READ EXODUS 19:1–25

If you've ever seen a big fireworks show, you know how awesome and huge all the colors and explosions are. Now imagine a display like that on top of a live volcano! It would be hard to know whether to be thrilled or scared, wouldn't it? "The LORD descended to the top of Mount Sinai and called Moses to the top of the mountain. So Moses went up" (Exodus 19:20). Moses went up the mountain to seek God and God gave him some important instructions. Moses wasn't afraid. He knew that no matter how big God was, God loved him. The special effects and fire didn't scare him, and God's love drew him near. Sometimes God's power frightens us. But his love is always there, too. Part of being a godly man is knowing you can always go to God and talk to him.

Your next reading is on page 110.

the Lᴏʀᴅ said to him, "Go down and warn the people so they do not force their way through to see the Lᴏʀᴅ and many of them perish. ²²Even the priests, who approach the Lᴏʀᴅ, must consecrate themselves, or the Lᴏʀᴅ will break out against them."

²³Moses said to the Lᴏʀᴅ, "The people cannot come up Mount Sinai, because you yourself warned us, 'Put limits around the mountain and set it apart as holy.' "

²⁴The Lᴏʀᴅ replied, "Go down and bring Aaron up with you. But the priests and the people must not force their way through to come up to the Lᴏʀᴅ, or he will break out against them."

²⁵So Moses went down to the people and told them.

The Ten Commandments

20 And God spoke all these words:

²"I am the Lᴏʀᴅ your God, who brought you out of Egypt, out of the land of slavery.

³ "You shall have no other gods before*ᵃ* me.

⁴ "You shall not make for yourself an idol in the form of anything in heaven above or on the earth beneath or in the waters below. ⁵You shall not bow down to them or worship them; for I, the Lᴏʀᴅ your God, am a jealous God, punishing the children for the sin of the fathers to the third and fourth generation of those who hate me, ⁶but showing love to a thousand ⌊generations⌋ of those who love me and keep my commandments.

⁷ "You shall not misuse the name of the Lᴏʀᴅ your God, for the Lᴏʀᴅ will not hold anyone guiltless who misuses his name.

⁸ "Remember the Sabbath day by keeping it holy. ⁹Six days you shall labor and do all your work, ¹⁰but the seventh day is a Sabbath to the Lᴏʀᴅ your God. On it you shall not do any work, neither you, nor your son or daugh-

---

ᵃ 3 Or *besides*

Batteries Included

READ EXODUS 20:1–8, 12–17

Ever ripped open a gift and—Wow!—It's that way cool toy you were just hoping someone would buy you! But . . . it needs special batteries and "batteries are not included." Your new toy is great, but it's dead. Major frustration. It can be like that trying to live a godly life. How do you keep all God's commandments: honor your parents, don't steal, don't lie, don't covet someone else's stuff, etc.? Great commands, but where do you get the power to consistently obey them? Hey, the answer is right in the Ten Commandments. The last six commands tell you how to love people and relate to them, but the first four are all about loving God. Love God sincerely, have a good relationship with him, and you'll have the power to love others (see also Mark 12:30–31). If obeying God's commands sometimes seems like a tough order, remember: batteries are included!

Your next reading is on page 111.

ter, nor your manservant or maidservant, nor your animals, nor the alien within your gates. ¹¹For in six days the LORD made the heavens and the earth, the sea, and all that is in them, but he rested on the seventh day. Therefore the LORD blessed the Sabbath day and made it holy.

¹² "Honor your father and your mother, so that you may live long in the land the LORD your God is giving you.

¹³ "You shall not murder.

¹⁴ "You shall not commit adultery.

¹⁵ "You shall not steal.

¹⁶ "You shall not give false testimony against your neighbor.

¹⁷ "You shall not covet your neighbor's house. You shall not covet your neighbor's wife, or his manservant or maidservant, his ox or donkey, or anything that belongs to your neighbor."

¹⁸When the people saw the thunder and lightning and heard the trumpet and saw the mountain in smoke, they trembled with fear. They stayed at a distance ¹⁹and said to Moses, "Speak to us yourself and we will listen. But do not have God speak to us or we will die."

²⁰Moses said to the people, "Do not be afraid. God has come to test you, so that the fear of God will be with you to keep you from sinning."

²¹The people remained at a distance, while Moses approached the thick darkness where God was.

Idols and Altars

²²Then the LORD said to Moses, "Tell the Israelites this: 'You have seen for yourselves that I have spoken to you from heaven: ²³Do not make any gods to be alongside me; do not make for yourselves gods of silver or gods of gold.

²⁴ 'Make an altar of earth for me and sacrifice on it your burnt offerings and fellowship offerings,ᵃ your sheep and goats and your cattle. Wherever I cause my name to be honored, I will come to you and bless

ᵃ 24 Traditionally peace offerings

Trash Can Heads

READ EXODUS 20:12–17 AGAIN!

When God said, "You shall not covet," he meant don't go crazy for something that someone else has that you want. These last six commands have a whole lot to do with attitude—our attitude toward other people, and the way we relate to them. In our society, we have chances *every day* to break God's commands. Even if we don't break them, we can see others breaking them in real life, on TV, in videos or in computer games. The Bible says, "Hate evil, love good" (Amos 5:15), so don't sit around watching things that hurt other people or destroy relationships. If you see and tolerate bad things long enough, you'll start to think they're OK. Instead, stand up to them. You wouldn't eat a rotten-banana-and-fish-head sandwich, right? If you wouldn't put garbage in your body, why put garbage in your mind?

Your next reading is on page 124.

you. 25If you make an altar of stones for me, do not build it with dressed stones, for you will defile it if you use a tool on it. 26And do not go up to my altar on steps, lest your nakedness be exposed on it.'

21 "These are the laws you are to set before them:

Hebrew Servants

2"If you buy a Hebrew servant, he is to serve you for six years. But in the seventh year, he shall go free, without paying anything. 3If he comes alone, he is to go free alone; but if he has a wife when he comes, she is to go with him. 4If his master gives him a wife and she bears him sons or daughters, the woman and her children shall belong to her master, and only the man shall go free.

5"But if the servant declares, 'I love my master and my wife and children and do not want to go free,' 6then his master must take him before the judges.*a* He shall take him to the door or the doorpost and pierce his ear with an awl. Then he will be his servant for life.

7"If a man sells his daughter as a servant, she is not to go free as menservants do. 8If she does not please the master who has selected her for himself,*b* he must let her be redeemed. He has no right to sell her to foreigners, because he has broken faith with her. 9If he selects her for his son, he must grant her the rights of a daughter. 10If he marries another woman, he must not deprive the first one of her food, clothing and marital rights. 11If he does not provide her with these three things, she is to go free, without any payment of money.

Personal Injuries

12"Anyone who strikes a man and kills him shall surely be put to death. 13However, if he does not do it intentionally, but God lets it happen, he is to flee to a place I will designate. 14But if a man schemes and kills another man deliberately, take him away from my altar and put him to death.

15"Anyone who attacks*c* his father or his mother must be put to death.

16"Anyone who kidnaps another and either sells him or still has him when he is caught must be put to death.

17"Anyone who curses his father or mother must be put to death.

18"If men quarrel and one hits the other with a stone or with his fist*d* and he does not die but is confined to bed, 19the one who struck the blow will not be held responsible if the other gets up and walks around outside with his staff; however, he must pay the injured man for the loss of his time and see that he is completely healed.

20"If a man beats his male or female slave with a rod and the slave dies as a direct result, he must be punished, 21but he is not to be punished if the slave gets up after a day or two, since the slave is his property.

22"If men who are fighting hit a pregnant woman and she gives birth prematurely*e* but there is no serious injury, the offender must be fined whatever the woman's husband demands and the court allows. 23But if there is serious injury, you are to take life for life, 24eye for eye, tooth for tooth, hand for hand, foot for foot, 25burn for burn, wound for wound, bruise for bruise.

26"If a man hits a manservant or maidservant in the eye and destroys it, he must let the servant go free to compensate for the eye. 27And if he knocks out the tooth of a manservant or maidservant, he must let the servant go free to compensate for the tooth.

28"If a bull gores a man or a woman to death, the bull must be stoned to death, and its meat must not be eaten. But the owner of the bull will not be held responsible. 29If, however, the bull has had the habit of goring and the owner has been warned but has not kept it penned up and it kills a man or woman, the bull must be stoned and the owner also must be put to death. 30However, if payment is demanded of him, he may redeem his life by paying whatever is demanded. 31This law also applies if the bull gores a son or daughter. 32If the bull gores a male or female slave, the owner must pay thirty shekels*f* of silver to the master of the slave, and the bull must be stoned.

33"If a man uncovers a pit or digs one and fails to cover it and an ox or a donkey falls into it, 34the owner of the pit must pay for the loss; he must pay its owner, and the dead animal will be his.

35"If a man's bull injures the bull of an-

---

a 6 Or before God   b 8 Or master so that he does not choose her   c 15 Or kills   d 18 Or with a tool e 22 Or she has a miscarriage   f 32 That is, about 12 ounces (about 0.3 kilogram) other and it dies, they are to sell the live one and divide both the money and the dead animal equally. 36However, if it was known that the bull had the habit of goring, yet the owner did not keep it penned up, the owner must pay, animal for animal, and the dead animal will be his.

Protection of Property

22 "If a man steals an ox or a sheep and slaughters it or sells it, he must pay back five head of cattle for the ox and four sheep for the sheep.

2"If a thief is caught breaking in and is struck so that he dies, the defender is not guilty of bloodshed; 3but if it happens[a] after sunrise, he is guilty of bloodshed.

"A thief must certainly make restitution, but if he has nothing, he must be sold to pay for his theft.

4"If the stolen animal is found alive in his possession—whether ox or donkey or sheep—he must pay back double.

5"If a man grazes his livestock in a field or vineyard and lets them stray and they graze in another man's field, he must

[a] 3 Or if he strikes him

Make It Stick

_____

_____

_____

_____

_____

_____

_____

READ EXODUS 21:12–21
No one has the right to bully or intimidate others. You don't have the right to punch or hurt others. You don't even have the right to touch or tickle someone else unless they think it's cool. Think of three ways you can encourage friends to respect others at recess and in your neighborhood and write them here.

make restitution from the best of his own field or vineyard.

⁶"If a fire breaks out and spreads into thornbushes so that it burns shocks of grain or standing grain or the whole field, the one who started the fire must make restitution.

⁷"If a man gives his neighbor silver or goods for safekeeping and they are stolen from the neighbor's house, the thief, if he is caught, must pay back double. ⁸But if the thief is not found, the owner of the house must appear before the judges*a* to determine whether he has laid his hands on the other man's property. ⁹In all cases of illegal possession of an ox, a donkey, a sheep, a garment, or any other lost property about which somebody says, 'This is mine,' both parties are to bring their cases before the judges. The one whom the judges declare*b* guilty must pay back double to his neighbor.

¹⁰"If a man gives a donkey, an ox, a sheep or any other animal to his neighbor for safekeeping and it dies or is injured or is taken away while no one is looking, ¹¹the issue between them will be settled by the taking of an oath before the Lord that the neighbor did not lay hands on the other person's property. The owner is to accept this, and no restitution is required. ¹²But if the animal was stolen from the neighbor, he must make restitution to the owner. ¹³If it was torn to pieces by a wild animal, he shall bring in the remains as evidence and he will not be required to pay for the torn animal.

¹⁴"If a man borrows an animal from his neighbor and it is injured or dies while the owner is not present, he must make restitution. ¹⁵But if the owner is with the animal, the borrower will not have to pay. If the animal was hired, the money paid for the hire covers the loss.

Social Responsibility

¹⁶"If a man seduces a virgin who is not pledged to be married and sleeps with her, he must pay the bride-price, and she shall be his wife. ¹⁷If her father absolutely refuses to give her to him, he must still pay the bride-price for virgins.

¹⁸"Do not allow a sorceress to live.

¹⁹"Anyone who has sexual relations with an animal must be put to death.

²⁰"Whoever sacrifices to any god other than the Lord must be destroyed.*c*

²¹"Do not mistreat an alien or oppress him, for you were aliens in Egypt.

²²"Do not take advantage of a widow or an orphan. ²³If you do and they cry out to me, I will certainly hear their cry. ²⁴My anger will be aroused, and I will kill you with the sword; your wives will become widows and your children fatherless.

²⁵"If you lend money to one of my people among you who is needy, do not be like a moneylender; charge him no interest.*d* ²⁶If you take your neighbor's cloak as a pledge, return it to him by sunset, ²⁷because his cloak is the only covering he has for his body. What else will he sleep in? When he cries out to me, I will hear, for I am compassionate.

²⁸"Do not blaspheme God*e* or curse the ruler of your people.

²⁹"Do not hold back offerings from your granaries or your vats.*f*

"You must give me the firstborn of your sons. ³⁰Do the same with your cattle and your sheep. Let them stay with their mothers for seven days, but give them to me on the eighth day.

³¹"You are to be my holy people. So do not eat the meat of an animal torn by wild beasts; throw it to the dogs.

Laws of Justice and Mercy

23 "Do not spread false reports. Do not help a wicked man by being a malicious witness.

²"Do not follow the crowd in doing wrong. When you give testimony in a lawsuit, do not pervert justice by siding with the crowd, ³and do not show favoritism to a poor man in his lawsuit.

⁴"If you come across your enemy's ox or donkey wandering off, be sure to take it back to him. ⁵If you see the donkey of someone who hates you fallen down under its load, do not leave it there; be sure you help him with it.

⁶"Do not deny justice to your poor people in their lawsuits. ⁷Have nothing to do with a false charge and do not put an innocent or honest person to death, for I will not acquit the guilty.

⁸"Do not accept a bribe, for a bribe

---

a 8 Or *before God*; also in verse 9   *b 9* Or *whom God declares*   *c 20* The Hebrew term refers to the irrevocable giving over of things or persons to the Lord, often by totally destroying them.   *d 25* Or *excessive interest*   *e 28* Or *Do not revile the judges*   *f 29* The meaning of the Hebrew for this phrase is uncertain.

blinds those who see and twists the words of the righteous.

9"Do not oppress an alien; you yourselves know how it feels to be aliens, because you were aliens in Egypt.

Sabbath Laws

10"For six years you are to sow your fields and harvest the crops, 11but during the seventh year let the land lie unplowed and unused. Then the poor among your people may get food from it, and the wild animals may eat what they leave. Do the same with your vineyard and your olive grove.

12"Six days do your work, but on the seventh day do not work, so that your ox and your donkey may rest and the slave born in your household, and the alien as well, may be refreshed.

13"Be careful to do everything I have said to you. Do not invoke the names of other gods; do not let them be heard on your lips.

The Three Annual Festivals

14"Three times a year you are to celebrate a festival to me.

15"Celebrate the Feast of Unleavened Bread; for seven days eat bread made without yeast, as I commanded you. Do this at the appointed time in the month of Abib, for in that month you came out of Egypt.

"No one is to appear before me empty-handed.

16"Celebrate the Feast of Harvest with the firstfruits of the crops you sow in your field.

"Celebrate the Feast of Ingathering at the end of the year, when you gather in your crops from the field.

17"Three times a year all the men are to appear before the Sovereign LORD.

18"Do not offer the blood of a sacrifice to me along with anything containing yeast.

"The fat of my festival offerings must not be kept until morning.

Make It Stick

READ EXODUS 23:2

It's fun to be in the middle of a big crowd, cheering for your favorite sports team. But when it comes to deciding between right and wrong, doing the right thing might mean standing alone. Write on a sticky note, "I will resist peer pressure."

19"Bring the best of the firstfruits of your soil to the house of the LORD your God.

"Do not cook a young goat in its mother's milk.

God's Angel to Prepare the Way

20"See, I am sending an angel ahead of you to guard you along the way and to bring you to the place I have prepared. 21Pay attention to him and listen to what he says. Do not rebel against him; he will not forgive your rebellion, since my Name is in him. 22If you listen carefully to what he says and do all that I say, I will be an enemy to your enemies and will oppose those who oppose you. 23My angel will go ahead of you and bring you into the land of the Amorites, Hittites, Perizzites, Canaanites, Hivites and Jebusites, and I will wipe them out. 24Do not bow down before their gods or worship them or follow their practices. You must demolish them and break their sacred stones to pieces. 25Worship the LORD your God, and his blessing will be on your food and water. I will take away sickness from among you, 26and none will miscarry or be barren in your land. I will give you a full life span.

27"I will send my terror ahead of you and throw into confusion every nation you encounter. I will make all your enemies turn their backs and run. 28I will send the hornet ahead of you to drive the Hivites, Canaanites and Hittites out of your way. 29But I will not drive them out in a single year, because the land would become desolate and the wild animals too numerous for you. 30Little by little I will drive them out before you, until you have increased enough to take possession of the land.

31"I will establish your borders from the Red Sea*a* to the Sea of the Philistines,*b* and from the desert to the River.*c* I will hand over to you the people who live in the land and you will drive them out before you. 32Do not make a covenant with them or with their gods. 33Do not let them live in your land, or they will cause you to sin against me, because the worship of their gods will certainly be a snare to you."

The Covenant Confirmed

24 Then he said to Moses, "Come up to the LORD, you and Aaron, Nadab and Abihu, and seventy of the elders of Israel. You are to worship at a distance, 2but Moses alone is to approach the LORD; the others must not come near. And the people may not come up with him."

3When Moses went and told the people all the LORD's words and laws, they responded with one voice, "Everything the LORD has said we will do." 4Moses then wrote down everything the LORD had said.

He got up early the next morning and built an altar at the foot of the mountain and set up twelve stone pillars representing the twelve tribes of Israel. 5Then he sent young Israelite men, and they offered burnt offerings and sacrificed young bulls as fellowship offerings*d* to the LORD. 6Moses took half of the blood and put it in bowls, and the other half he sprinkled on the altar. 7Then he took the Book of the Covenant and read it to the people. They responded, "We will do everything the LORD has said; we will obey."

8Moses then took the blood, sprinkled it on the people and said, "This is the blood of the covenant that the LORD has made with you in accordance with all these words."

9Moses and Aaron, Nadab and Abihu, and the seventy elders of Israel went up 10and saw the God of Israel. Under his feet was something like a pavement made of sapphire,*e* clear as the sky itself. 11But God did not raise his hand against these leaders of the Israelites; they saw God, and they ate and drank.

12The LORD said to Moses, "Come up to me on the mountain and stay here, and I will give you the tablets of stone, with the law and commands I have written for their instruction."

13Then Moses set out with Joshua his aide, and Moses went up on the mountain of God. 14He said to the elders, "Wait here for us until we come back to you. Aaron and Hur are with you, and anyone involved in a dispute can go to them."

15When Moses went up on the mountain, the cloud covered it, 16and the glory of the LORD settled on Mount Sinai. For six days the cloud covered the mountain, and on the seventh day the LORD called to Moses from within the cloud. 17To the Israelites the glory of the LORD looked like a consuming fire on top of the mountain. 18Then Moses entered the cloud as he

---

a 31 Hebrew *Yam Suph;* that is, Sea of Reeds   *b 31* That is, the Mediterranean   *c 31* That is, the Euphrates
d 5 Traditionally *peace offerings*   *e 10* Or *lapis lazuli*

went on up the mountain. And he stayed on the mountain forty days and forty nights.

Offerings for the Tabernacle

25 The LORD said to Moses, ²"Tell the Israelites to bring me an offering. You are to receive the offering for me from each man whose heart prompts him to give. ³These are the offerings you are to receive from them: gold, silver and bronze; ⁴blue, purple and scarlet yarn and fine linen; goat hair; ⁵ram skins dyed red and hides of sea cows *ᵃ*; acacia wood; ⁶olive oil for the light; spices for the anointing oil and for the fragrant incense; ⁷and onyx stones and other gems to be mounted on the ephod and breastpiece.

⁸"Then have them make a sanctuary for me, and I will dwell among them. ⁹Make this tabernacle and all its furnishings exactly like the pattern I will show you.

The Ark

¹⁰"Have them make a chest of acacia wood—two and a half cubits long, a cubit and a half wide, and a cubit and a half high.*ᵇ* ¹¹Overlay it with pure gold, both inside and out, and make a gold molding around it. ¹²Cast four gold rings for it and fasten them to its four feet, with two rings on one side and two rings on the other. ¹³Then make poles of acacia wood and overlay them with gold. ¹⁴Insert the poles into the rings on the sides of the chest to carry it. ¹⁵The poles are to remain in the rings of this ark; they are not to be removed. ¹⁶Then put in the ark the Testimony, which I will give you.

¹⁷"Make an atonement cover*ᶜ* of pure gold—two and a half cubits long and a cubit and a half wide.*ᵈ* ¹⁸And make two cherubim out of hammered gold at the ends of the cover. ¹⁹Make one cherub on one end and the second cherub on the other; make the cherubim of one piece with the cover, at the two ends. ²⁰The cherubim are to have their wings spread upward, overshadowing the cover with them. The cherubim are to face each other, looking toward the cover. ²¹Place the cover on top of the ark and put in the ark the Testimony, which I will give you. ²²There, above the cover between the two cherubim that are over the ark of the Testimony, I will meet with you and give you all my commands for the Israelites.

The Table

²³"Make a table of acacia wood—two cubits long, a cubit wide and a cubit and a half high.*ᵉ* ²⁴Overlay it with pure gold and make a gold molding around it. ²⁵Also make around it a rim a handbreadth*ᶠ* wide and put a gold molding on the rim. ²⁶Make four gold rings

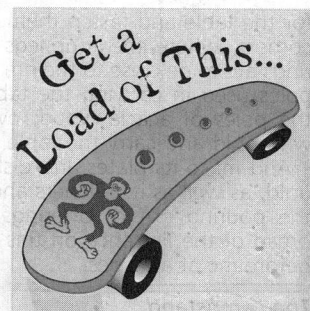

Get a Load of This...

When the Israelites carried the ark in Exodus 25:10, it was wrapped in a curtain, then the hides of sea cows, and finally in blue cloth, so no one could look directly at it.

ᵃ 5 That is, dugongs   *ᵇ 10* That is, about 3 3/4 feet (about 1.1 meters) long and 2 1/4 feet (about 0.7 meter) wide and high   *ᶜ 17* Traditionally *a mercy seat*   *ᵈ 17* That is, about 3 3/4 feet (about 1.1 meters) long and 2 1/4 feet (about 0.7 meter) wide   *ᵉ 23* That is, about 3 feet (about 0.9 meter) long and 1 1/2 feet (about 0.5 meter) wide and 2 1/4 feet (about 0.7 meter) high   *ᶠ 25* That is, about 3 inches (about 8 centimeters) for the table and fasten them to the four corners, where the four legs are. ²⁷The rings are to be close to the rim to hold the poles used in carrying the table. ²⁸Make the poles of acacia wood, overlay them with gold and carry the table with them. ²⁹And make its plates and dishes of pure gold, as well as its pitchers and bowls for the pouring out of offerings. ³⁰Put the bread of the Presence on this table to be before me at all times.

The Lampstand

³¹"Make a lampstand of pure gold and hammer it out, base and shaft; its flower-like cups, buds and blossoms shall be of one piece with it. ³²Six branches are to extend from the sides of the lampstand—three on one side and three on the other. ³³Three cups shaped like almond flowers with buds and blossoms are to be on one branch, three on the next branch, and the same for all six branches extending from the lampstand. ³⁴And on the lampstand there are to be four cups shaped like almond flowers with buds and blossoms. ³⁵One bud shall be under the first pair of branches extending from the lampstand, a second bud under the second pair, and a third bud under the third pair—six branches in all. ³⁶The buds and branches shall all be of one piece with the lampstand, hammered out of pure gold.

³⁷"Then make its seven lamps and set them up on it so that they light the space in front of it. ³⁸Its wick trimmers and trays are to be of pure gold. ³⁹A talent ᵃ of pure gold is to be used for the lampstand and all these accessories. ⁴⁰See that you make them according to the pattern shown you on the mountain.

The Tabernacle

26 "Make the tabernacle with ten curtains of finely twisted linen and blue, purple and scarlet yarn, with cherubim worked into them by a skilled craftsman. ²All the curtains are to be the same size—twenty-eight cubits long and four cubits wide.ᵇ ³Join five of the curtains together, and do the same with the other five. ⁴Make loops of blue material along the edge of the end curtain in one set, and do the same with the end curtain in the other set. ⁵Make fifty loops on one curtain and fifty loops on the end curtain of the other set, with the loops opposite each other. ⁶Then make fifty gold clasps and use them to fasten the curtains together so that the tabernacle is a unit.

⁷"Make curtains of goat hair for the tent over the tabernacle—eleven altogether. ⁸All eleven curtains are to be the same size—thirty cubits long and four cubits wide.ᶜ ⁹Join five of the curtains together into one set and the other six into another set. Fold the sixth curtain double at the front of the tent. ¹⁰Make fifty loops along the edge of the end curtain in one set and also along the edge of the end curtain in the other set. ¹¹Then make fifty bronze clasps and put them in the loops to fasten the tent together as a unit. ¹²As for the additional length of the tent curtains, the half curtain that is left over is to hang down at the rear of the tabernacle. ¹³The tent curtains will be a cubitᵈ longer on both sides; what is left will hang over the sides of the tabernacle so as to cover it. ¹⁴Make for the tent a covering of ram skins dyed red, and over that a covering of hides of sea cows.ᵉ

¹⁵"Make upright frames of acacia wood for the tabernacle. ¹⁶Each frame is to be ten cubits long and a cubit and a half wide,ᶠ ¹⁷with two projections set parallel to each other. Make all the frames of the tabernacle in this way. ¹⁸Make twenty frames for the south side of the tabernacle ¹⁹and make forty silver bases to go under them—two bases for each frame, one under each projection. ²⁰For the other side, the north side of the tabernacle, make twenty frames ²¹and forty silver bases—two under each frame. ²²Make six frames for the far end, that is, the west end of the tabernacle, ²³and make two frames for the corners at the far end. ²⁴At these two corners they must be double from the bottom all the way to the top, and fitted into a single ring; both shall be like that. ²⁵So there will be eight frames and sixteen silver bases—two under each frame.

²⁶"Also make crossbars of acacia wood: five for the frames on one side of the tabernacle, ²⁷five for those on the other side, and five for the frames on the west, at the

---

ᵃ 39 That is, about 75 pounds (about 34 kilograms)
ᵇ 2 That is, about 42 feet (about 12.5 meters) long and 6 feet (about 1.8 meters) wide   ᶜ 8 That is, about 45 feet (about 13.5 meters) long and 6 feet (about 1.8 meters) wide
ᵈ 13 That is, about 1 1/2 feet (about 0.5 meter)   ᵉ 14 That is, dugongs   ᶠ 16 That is, about 15 feet (about 4.5 meters) long and 2 1/4 feet (about 0.7 meter) wide

far end of the tabernacle. 28The center crossbar is to extend from end to end at the middle of the frames. 29Overlay the frames with gold and make gold rings to hold the crossbars. Also overlay the crossbars with gold.

30"Set up the tabernacle according to the plan shown you on the mountain.

31"Make a curtain of blue, purple and scarlet yarn and finely twisted linen, with cherubim worked into it by a skilled craftsman. 32Hang it with gold hooks on four posts of acacia wood overlaid with gold and standing on four silver bases. 33Hang the curtain from the clasps and place the ark of the Testimony behind the curtain. The curtain will separate the Holy Place from the Most Holy Place. 34Put the atonement cover on the ark of the Testimony in the Most Holy Place. 35Place the table outside the curtain on the north side of the tabernacle and put the lampstand opposite it on the south side.

36"For the entrance to the tent make a curtain of blue, purple and scarlet yarn and finely twisted linen—the work of an embroiderer. 37Make gold hooks for this curtain and five posts of acacia wood overlaid with gold. And cast five bronze bases for them.

The Altar of Burnt Offering

27 "Build an altar of acacia wood, three cubits*a* high; it is to be square, five cubits long and five cubits wide.*b* 2Make a horn at each of the four corners, so that the horns and the altar are of one piece, and overlay the altar with bronze. 3Make all its utensils of bronze—its pots to remove the ashes, and its shovels, sprinkling bowls, meat forks and firepans. 4Make a grating for it, a bronze network, and make a bronze ring at each of the four corners of the network. 5Put it under the ledge of the altar so that it is halfway up the altar. 6Make poles of acacia wood for the altar and overlay them with bronze. 7The poles are to be inserted into the rings so they will be on two sides of the altar when it is carried. 8Make the altar hollow, out of boards. It is to be made just as you were shown on the mountain.

The Courtyard

9"Make a courtyard for the tabernacle. The south side shall be a hundred cubits*c* long and is to have curtains of finely twist-ed linen, 10with twenty posts and twenty bronze bases and with silver hooks and bands on the posts. 11The north side shall also be a hundred cubits long and is to have curtains, with twenty posts and twenty bronze bases and with silver hooks and bands on the posts.

12"The west end of the courtyard shall be fifty cubits*d* wide and have curtains, with ten posts and ten bases. 13On the east end, toward the sunrise, the courtyard shall also be fifty cubits wide. 14Curtains fifteen cubits*e* long are to be on one side of the entrance, with three posts and three bases, 15and curtains fifteen cubits long are to be on the other side, with three posts and three bases.

16"For the entrance to the courtyard, provide a curtain twenty cubits*f* long, of blue, purple and scarlet yarn and finely twisted linen—the work of an embroiderer—with four posts and four bases. 17All the posts around the courtyard are to have silver bands and hooks, and bronze bases. 18The courtyard shall be a hundred cubits long and fifty cubits wide,*g* with curtains of finely twisted linen five cubits*h* high, and with bronze bases. 19All the other articles used in the service of the tabernacle, whatever their function, including all the tent pegs for it and those for the courtyard, are to be of bronze.

Oil for the Lampstand

20"Command the Israelites to bring you clear oil of pressed olives for the light so that the lamps may be kept burning. 21In the Tent of Meeting, outside the curtain that is in front of the Testimony, Aaron and his sons are to keep the lamps burning before the LORD from evening till morning. This is to be a lasting ordinance among the Israelites for the generations to come.

The Priestly Garments

28 "Have Aaron your brother brought to you from among the Israelites, along with his sons Nadab and Abihu, Eleazar

---

a 1 That is, about 4 1/2 feet (about 1.3 meters)   *b 1* That is, about 7 1/2 feet (about 2.3 meters) long and wide
c 9 That is, about 150 feet (about 46 meters); also in verse 11
d 12 That is, about 75 feet (about 23 meters); also in verse 13
e 14 That is, about 22 1/2 feet (about 6.9 meters); also in verse 15   *f 16* That is, about 30 feet (about 9 meters)
g 18 That is, about 150 feet (about 46 meters) long and 75 feet (about 23 meters) wide   *h 18* That is, about 7 1/2 feet (about 2.3 meters)

and Ithamar, so they may serve me as priests. [2]Make sacred garments for your brother Aaron, to give him dignity and honor. [3]Tell all the skilled men to whom I have given wisdom in such matters that they are to make garments for Aaron, for his consecration, so he may serve me as priest. [4]These are the garments they are to make: a breastpiece, an ephod, a robe, a woven tunic, a turban and a sash. They are to make these sacred garments for your brother Aaron and his sons, so they may serve me as priests. [5]Have them use gold, and blue, purple and scarlet yarn, and fine linen.

The Ephod

[6]"Make the ephod of gold, and of blue, purple and scarlet yarn, and of finely twisted linen—the work of a skilled craftsman. [7]It is to have two shoulder pieces attached to two of its corners, so it can be fastened. [8]Its skillfully woven waistband is to be like it—of one piece with the ephod and made with gold, and with blue, purple and scarlet yarn, and with finely twisted linen.

[9]"Take two onyx stones and engrave on them the names of the sons of Israel [10]in the order of their birth—six names on one stone and the remaining six on the other. [11]Engrave the names of the sons of Israel on the two stones the way a gem cutter engraves a seal. Then mount the stones in gold filigree settings [12]and fasten them on the shoulder pieces of the ephod as memorial stones for the sons of Israel. Aaron is to bear the names on his shoulders as a memorial before the LORD. [13]Make gold filigree settings [14]and two braided chains of pure gold, like a rope, and attach the chains to the settings.

The Breastpiece

[15]"Fashion a breastpiece for making decisions—the work of a skilled craftsman. Make it like the ephod: of gold, and of blue, purple and scarlet yarn, and of finely twisted linen. [16]It is to be square—a span[a] long and a span wide—and folded double. [17]Then mount four rows of precious stones on it. In the first row there shall be a ruby, a topaz and a beryl; [18]in the second row a turquoise, a sapphire[b] and an emerald; [19]in the third row a jacinth, an agate and an amethyst; [20]in the fourth row a chrysolite, an onyx and a jas-

per.[c] Mount them in gold filigree settings. [21]There are to be twelve stones, one for each of the names of the sons of Israel, each engraved like a seal with the name of one of the twelve tribes.

[22]"For the breastpiece make braided chains of pure gold, like a rope. [23]Make two gold rings for it and fasten them to two corners of the breastpiece. [24]Fasten the two gold chains to the rings at the corners of the breastpiece, [25]and the other ends of the chains to the two settings, attaching them to the shoulder pieces of the ephod at the front. [26]Make two gold rings and attach them to the other two corners of the breastpiece on the inside edge next to the ephod. [27]Make two more gold rings and attach them to the bottom of the shoulder pieces on the front of the ephod, close to the seam just above the waistband of the ephod. [28]The rings of the breastpiece are to be tied to the rings of the ephod with blue cord, connecting it to the waistband, so that the breastpiece will not swing out from the ephod.

[29]"Whenever Aaron enters the Holy Place, he will bear the names of the sons of Israel over his heart on the breastpiece of decision as a continuing memorial before the LORD. [30]Also put the Urim and the Thummim in the breastpiece, so they may be over Aaron's heart whenever he enters the presence of the LORD. Thus Aaron will always bear the means of making decisions for the Israelites over his heart before the LORD.

Other Priestly Garments

[31]"Make the robe of the ephod entirely of blue cloth, [32]with an opening for the head in its center. There shall be a woven edge like a collar[d] around this opening, so that it will not tear. [33]Make pomegranates of blue, purple and scarlet yarn around the hem of the robe, with gold bells between them. [34]The gold bells and the pomegranates are to alternate around the hem of the robe. [35]Aaron must wear it when he ministers. The sound of the bells will be heard when he enters the Holy Place before the LORD and when he comes out, so that he will not die.

[a] 16 That is, about 9 inches (about 22 centimeters) [b] 18 Or *lapis lazuli* [c] 20 The precise identification of some of these precious stones is uncertain. [d] 32 The meaning of the Hebrew for this word is uncertain.

³⁶"Make a plate of pure gold and engrave on it as on a seal: HOLY TO THE LORD. ³⁷Fasten a blue cord to it to attach it to the turban; it is to be on the front of the turban. ³⁸It will be on Aaron's forehead, and he will bear the guilt involved in the sacred gifts the Israelites consecrate, whatever their gifts may be. It will be on Aaron's forehead continually so that they will be acceptable to the LORD.

³⁹"Weave the tunic of fine linen and make the turban of fine linen. The sash is to be the work of an embroiderer. ⁴⁰Make tunics, sashes and headbands for Aaron's sons, to give them dignity and honor. ⁴¹After you put these clothes on your brother Aaron and his sons, anoint and ordain them. Consecrate them so they may serve me as priests.

⁴²"Make linen undergarments as a covering for the body, reaching from the waist to the thigh. ⁴³Aaron and his sons must wear them whenever they enter the Tent of Meeting or approach the altar to minister in the Holy Place, so that they will not incur guilt and die.

"This is to be a lasting ordinance for Aaron and his descendants.

Consecration of the Priests

29 "This is what you are to do to consecrate them, so they may serve me as priests: Take a young bull and two rams without defect. ²And from fine wheat flour, without yeast, make bread, and cakes mixed with oil, and wafers spread with oil. ³Put them in a basket and present them in it—along with the bull and the two rams. ⁴Then bring Aaron and his sons to the entrance to the Tent of Meeting and wash them with water. ⁵Take the garments and dress Aaron with the tunic, the robe of the ephod, the ephod itself and the breastpiece. Fasten the ephod on him by its skillfully woven waistband. ⁶Put the turban on his head and attach the sacred diadem to the turban. ⁷Take the anointing oil and anoint him by pouring it on his head. ⁸Bring his sons and dress them in tunics ⁹and put headbands on them. Then tie sashes on Aaron and his sons.^a The priesthood is theirs by a lasting ordinance. In this way you shall ordain Aaron and his sons.

¹⁰"Bring the bull to the front of the Tent of Meeting, and Aaron and his sons shall lay their hands on its head. ¹¹Slaughter it in the LORD's presence at the entrance to the Tent of Meeting. ¹²Take some of the bull's blood and put it on the horns of the altar with your finger, and pour out the rest of it at the base of the altar. ¹³Then take all the fat around the inner parts, the covering of the liver, and both kidneys with the fat on them, and burn them on the altar. ¹⁴But burn the bull's flesh and its hide and its offal outside the camp. It is a sin offering.

¹⁵"Take one of the rams, and Aaron and his sons shall lay their hands on its head. ¹⁶Slaughter it and take the blood and sprinkle it against the altar on all sides. ¹⁷Cut

^a 9 Hebrew; Septuagint on them

Get a Load of This...

Exodus 28:15–30 talks about breastplates. They were a piece of armor that soldiers wore into battle. The high priest also wore a fancy breastplate, or breastpiece. The Urim and Thummim were mysterious objects (probably stones) that somehow—no one knows exactly how—helped the high priest find out what God's will was.

the ram into pieces and wash the inner parts and the legs, putting them with the head and the other pieces. ¹⁸Then burn the entire ram on the altar. It is a burnt offering to the LORD, a pleasing aroma, an offering made to the LORD by fire.

¹⁹"Take the other ram, and Aaron and his sons shall lay their hands on its head. ²⁰Slaughter it, take some of its blood and put it on the lobes of the right ears of Aaron and his sons, on the thumbs of their right hands, and on the big toes of their right feet. Then sprinkle blood against the altar on all sides. ²¹And take some of the blood on the altar and some of the anointing oil and sprinkle it on Aaron and his garments and on his sons and their garments. Then he and his sons and their garments will be consecrated.

²²"Take from this ram the fat, the fat tail, the fat around the inner parts, the covering of the liver, both kidneys with the fat on them, and the right thigh. (This is the ram for the ordination.) ²³From the basket of bread made without yeast, which is before the LORD, take a loaf, and a cake made with oil, and a wafer. ²⁴Put all these in the hands of Aaron and his sons and wave them before the LORD as a wave offering. ²⁵Then take them from their hands and burn them on the altar along with the burnt offering for a pleasing aroma to the LORD, an offering made to the LORD by fire. ²⁶After you take the breast of the ram for Aaron's ordination, wave it before the LORD as a wave offering, and it will be your share.

²⁷"Consecrate those parts of the ordination ram that belong to Aaron and his sons: the breast that was waved and the thigh that was presented. ²⁸This is always to be the regular share from the Israelites for Aaron and his sons. It is the contribution the Israelites are to make to the LORD from their fellowship offerings.ᵃ

²⁹"Aaron's sacred garments will belong to his descendants so that they can be anointed and ordained in them. ³⁰The son who succeeds him as priest and comes to the Tent of Meeting to minister in the Holy Place is to wear them seven days.

³¹"Take the ram for the ordination and cook the meat in a sacred place. ³²At the entrance to the Tent of Meeting, Aaron and his sons are to eat the meat of the ram and the bread that is in the basket. ³³They are to eat these offerings by which

atonement was made for their ordination and consecration. But no one else may eat them, because they are sacred. ³⁴And if any of the meat of the ordination ram or any bread is left over till morning, burn it up. It must not be eaten, because it is sacred.

³⁵"Do for Aaron and his sons everything I have commanded you, taking seven days to ordain them. ³⁶Sacrifice a bull each day as a sin offering to make atonement. Purify the altar by making atonement for it, and anoint it to consecrate it. ³⁷For seven days make atonement for the altar and consecrate it. Then the altar will be most holy, and whatever touches it will be holy.

³⁸"This is what you are to offer on the altar regularly each day: two lambs a year old. ³⁹Offer one in the morning and the other at twilight. ⁴⁰With the first lamb offer a tenth of an ephahᵇ of fine flour mixed with a quarter of a hinᶜ of oil from pressed olives, and a quarter of a hin of wine as a drink offering. ⁴¹Sacrifice the other lamb at twilight with the same grain offering and its drink offering as in the morning—a pleasing aroma, an offering made to the LORD by fire.

⁴²"For the generations to come this burnt offering is to be made regularly at the entrance to the Tent of Meeting before the LORD. There I will meet you and speak to you; ⁴³there also I will meet with the Israelites, and the place will be consecrated by my glory.

⁴⁴"So I will consecrate the Tent of Meeting and the altar and will consecrate Aaron and his sons to serve me as priests. ⁴⁵Then I will dwell among the Israelites and be their God. ⁴⁶They will know that I am the LORD their God, who brought them out of Egypt so that I might dwell among them. I am the LORD their God.

The Altar of Incense

30 "Make an altar of acacia wood for burning incense. ²It is to be square, a cubit long and a cubit wide, and two cubits highᵈ—its horns of one piece with it. ³Overlay the top and all the sides and the horns with pure gold, and make a gold

---

ᵃ 28 Traditionally *peace offerings*   ᵇ 40 That is, probably about 2 quarts (about 2 liters)   ᶜ 40 That is, probably about 1 quart (about 1 liter)   ᵈ 2 That is, about 1 1/2 feet (about 0.5 meter) long and wide and about 3 feet (about 0.9 meter) high molding around it. ⁴Make two gold rings for the altar below the molding—two on opposite sides—to hold the poles used to carry it. ⁵Make the poles of acacia wood and overlay them with gold. ⁶Put the altar in front of the curtain that is before the ark of the Testimony—before the atonement cover that is over the Testimony—where I will meet with you.

⁷"Aaron must burn fragrant incense on the altar every morning when he tends the lamps. ⁸He must burn incense again when he lights the lamps at twilight so incense will burn regularly before the LORD for the generations to come. ⁹Do not offer on this altar any other incense or any burnt offering or grain offering, and do not pour a drink offering on it. ¹⁰Once a year Aaron shall make atonement on its horns. This annual atonement must be made with the blood of the atoning sin offering for the generations to come. It is most holy to the LORD."

Atonement Money

¹¹Then the LORD said to Moses, ¹²"When you take a census of the Israelites to count them, each one must pay the LORD a ransom for his life at the time he is counted. Then no plague will come on them when you number them. ¹³Each one who crosses over to those already counted is to give a half shekel,ᵃ according to the sanctuary shekel, which weighs twenty gerahs. This half shekel is an offering to the LORD. ¹⁴All who cross over, those twenty years old or more, are to give an offering to the LORD. ¹⁵The rich are not to give more than a half shekel and the poor are not to give less when you make the offering to the LORD to atone for your lives. ¹⁶Receive the atonement money from the Israelites and use it for the service of the Tent of Meeting. It will be a memorial for the Israelites before the LORD, making atonement for your lives."

Basin for Washing

¹⁷Then the LORD said to Moses, ¹⁸"Make a bronze basin, with its bronze stand, for washing. Place it between the Tent of Meeting and the altar, and put water in it. ¹⁹Aaron and his sons are to wash their hands and feet with water from it. ²⁰Whenever they enter the Tent of Meeting, they shall wash with water so that they will not die. Also, when they ap-

proach the altar to minister by presenting an offering made to the LORD by fire, ²¹they shall wash their hands and feet so that they will not die. This is to be a lasting ordinance for Aaron and his descendants for the generations to come."

Anointing Oil

²²Then the LORD said to Moses, ²³"Take the following fine spices: 500 shekelsᵇ of liquid myrrh, half as much (that is, 250 shekels) of fragrant cinnamon, 250 shekels of fragrant cane, ²⁴500 shekels of cassia—all according to the sanctuary shekel—and a hinᶜ of olive oil. ²⁵Make these into a sacred anointing oil, a fragrant blend, the work of a perfumer. It will be the sacred anointing oil. ²⁶Then use it to anoint the Tent of Meeting, the ark of the Testimony, ²⁷the table and all its articles, the lampstand and its accessories, the altar of incense, ²⁸the altar of burnt offering and all its utensils, and the basin with its stand. ²⁹You shall consecrate them so they will be most holy, and whatever touches them will be holy.

³⁰"Anoint Aaron and his sons and consecrate them so they may serve me as priests. ³¹Say to the Israelites, 'This is to be my sacred anointing oil for the generations to come. ³²Do not pour it on men's bodies and do not make any oil with the same formula. It is sacred, and you are to consider it sacred. ³³Whoever makes perfume like it and whoever puts it on anyone other than a priest must be cut off from his people.' "

Incense

³⁴Then the LORD said to Moses, "Take fragrant spices—gum resin, onycha and galbanum—and pure frankincense, all in equal amounts, ³⁵and make a fragrant blend of incense, the work of a perfumer. It is to be salted and pure and sacred. ³⁶Grind some of it to powder and place it in front of the Testimony in the Tent of Meeting, where I will meet with you. It shall be most holy to you. ³⁷Do not make any incense with this formula for yourselves; consider it holy to the LORD. ³⁸Whoever makes any like it to enjoy its fragrance must be cut off from his people."

ᵃ 13 That is, about 1/5 ounce (about 6 grams); also in verse 15   ᵇ 23 That is, about 12 1/2 pounds (about 6 kilograms)   ᶜ 24 That is, probably about 4 quarts (about 4 liters)

Bezalel and Oholiab

31 Then the LORD said to Moses, ²"See, I have chosen Bezalel son of Uri, the son of Hur, of the tribe of Judah, ³and I have filled him with the Spirit of God, with skill, ability and knowledge in all kinds of crafts— ⁴to make artistic designs for work in gold, silver and bronze, ⁵to cut and set stones, to work in wood, and to engage in all kinds of craftsmanship. ⁶Moreover, I have appointed Oholiab son of Ahisamach, of the tribe of Dan, to help him. Also I have given skill to all the craftsmen to make everything I have commanded you: ⁷the Tent of Meeting, the ark of the Testimony with the atonement cover on it, and all the other furnishings of the tent— ⁸the table and its articles, the pure gold lampstand and all its accessories, the altar of incense, ⁹the altar of burnt offering and all its utensils, the basin with its stand— ¹⁰and also the woven garments, both the sacred garments for Aaron the priest and the garments for his sons when they serve as priests, ¹¹and the anointing oil and fragrant incense for the Holy Place. They are to make them just as I commanded you."

The Sabbath

¹²Then the LORD said to Moses, ¹³"Say to the Israelites, 'You must observe my Sabbaths. This will be a sign between me and you for the generations to come, so you may know that I am the LORD, who makes you holy.ᵃ

¹⁴" 'Observe the Sabbath, because it is holy to you. Anyone who desecrates it must be put to death; whoever does any work on that day must be cut off from his people. ¹⁵For six days, work is to be done, but the seventh day is a Sabbath of rest, holy to the LORD. Whoever does any work on the Sabbath day must be put to death. ¹⁶The Israelites are to observe the Sabbath, celebrating it for the generations to come as a lasting covenant. ¹⁷It will be a sign between me and the Israelites forever, for in six days the LORD made the heavens and the earth, and on the seventh day he abstained from work and rested.' "

ᵃ 13 Or who sanctifies you; or who sets you apart as holy

Talk About Talent

READ EXODUS 31:1–11

There's no such thing as a "self-made" man. God designed each person with different talents, skills and abilities, and we need to develop these gifts. You can glorify God in lots of ways. Banging a drum as a professional musician, programming computers, designing buildings, putting out fires, and treating athletic injuries are just some of the thousands of careers where you can bring glory to God through your work. But great craftsmen don't become great overnight. They have to recognize their gifts, then work to develop or "refine" the raw talent that God has given them. This can mean lots of schooling and practice; no NBA star scores fifty points the first time he picks up a basketball. Careers should be fun. But God also gives us abilities so that we can contribute to our communities, making them better places.

Your next reading is on page 126.

[18]When the LORD finished speaking to Moses on Mount Sinai, he gave him the two tablets of the Testimony, the tablets of stone inscribed by the finger of God.

The Golden Calf

32 When the people saw that Moses was so long in coming down from the mountain, they gathered around Aaron and said, "Come, make us gods[a] who will go before us. As for this fellow Moses who brought us up out of Egypt, we don't know what has happened to him."

[2]Aaron answered them, "Take off the gold earrings that your wives, your sons and your daughters are wearing, and bring them to me." [3]So all the people took off their earrings and brought them to Aaron. [4]He took what they handed him and made it into an idol cast in the shape of a calf, fashioning it with a tool. Then they said, "These are your gods,[b] O Israel, who brought you up out of Egypt."

[5]When Aaron saw this, he built an altar in front of the calf and announced, "Tomorrow there will be a festival to the LORD." [6]So the next day the people rose early and sacrificed burnt offerings and presented fellowship offerings.[c] Afterward they sat down to eat and drink and got up to indulge in revelry.

[7]Then the LORD said to Moses, "Go down, because your people, whom you brought up out of Egypt, have become corrupt. [8]They have been quick to turn away from what I commanded them and have made themselves an idol cast in the shape of a calf. They have bowed down to it and sacrificed to it and have said, 'These are your gods, O Israel, who brought you up out of Egypt.'

[9]"I have seen these people," the LORD said to Moses, "and they are a stiff-necked people. [10]Now leave me alone so that my anger may burn against them and that I may destroy them. Then I will make you into a great nation."

[11]But Moses sought the favor of the LORD his God. "O LORD," he said, "why should your anger burn against your people, whom you brought out of Egypt with great power and a mighty hand? [12]Why should the Egyptians say, 'It was with evil intent that he brought them out, to kill them in the mountains and to wipe them off the face of the earth'? Turn from your fierce anger; relent and do not bring disaster on your people. [13]Remember your servants Abraham, Isaac and Israel, to whom you swore by your own self: 'I will make your descendants as numerous as the stars in the sky and I will give your descendants all this land I promised them, and it will be their inheritance forever.' " [14]Then the LORD relented and did not bring on his people the disaster he had threatened.

[15]Moses turned and went down the mountain with

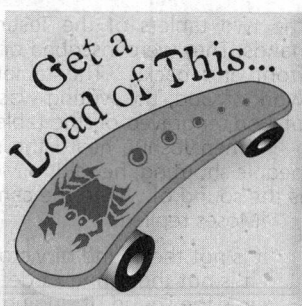

Get a Load of This...

God wrote the Ten Commandments on stone tablets with his finger, made the universe with his hands and saves everyone who believes in him by the strength of his right arm. Take a hint; don't challenge God to an arm wrestling match!

---

[a] 1 Or *a god*; also in verses 23 and 31　　[b] 4 Or *This is your god*; also in verse 8
[c] 6 Traditionally *peace offerings*

the two tablets of the Testimony in his hands. They were inscribed on both sides, front and back. ¹⁶The tablets were the work of God; the writing was the writing of God, engraved on the tablets.

¹⁷When Joshua heard the noise of the people shouting, he said to Moses, "There is the sound of war in the camp."

¹⁸Moses replied:

"It is not the sound of victory,
    it is not the sound of defeat;
    it is the sound of singing that I
        hear."

¹⁹When Moses approached the camp and saw the calf and the dancing, his anger burned and he threw the tablets out of his hands, breaking them to pieces at the foot of the mountain. ²⁰And he took the calf they had made and burned it in the fire; then he ground it to powder, scattered it on the water and made the Israelites drink it.

²¹He said to Aaron, "What did these people do to you, that you led them into such great sin?"

²²"Do not be angry, my lord," Aaron answered. "You know how prone these people are to evil. ²³They said to me, 'Make us gods who will go before us. As for this fellow Moses who brought us up out of Egypt, we don't know what has happened to him.' ²⁴So I told them, 'Whoever has any gold jewelry, take it off.' Then they gave me the gold, and I threw it into the fire, and out came this calf!"

²⁵Moses saw that the people were running wild and that Aaron had let them get out of control and so become a laughing-stock to their enemies. ²⁶So he stood at the entrance to the camp and said, "Whoever is for the LORD, come to me." And all the Levites rallied to him.

²⁷Then he said to them, "This is what the LORD, the God of Israel, says: 'Each man strap a sword to his side. Go back and forth through the camp from one end to the other, each killing his brother and friend and neighbor.' " ²⁸The Levites did as Moses commanded, and that day about three thousand of the people died. ²⁹Then Moses said, "You have been set apart to the LORD today, for you were against your

Take a Stand

READ EXODUS 32:1–24, 30–35

Sometimes a man has to stand up against a group's wrong decisions. When the Israelites pressured Aaron to build them an idol to worship, Aaron caved in and had a golden calf made. His excuse was, "They *told* me to do it." He even lied to Moses, saying he just dumped the gold jewelry into a pot in the fire, and out came the calf! (Yeah, *right*.) When the time came to fess up to what he had done, Aaron tried to play hot potato. Just like a goalie deflects a puck from the net, Aaron tried to deflect the blame onto others. Learn from Aaron's error: Don't do something just because everyone else is doing it. You can't say, "It's what everybody's doing. It's not my fault." In the end, no matter who is prodding you, you are the one who will be judged for your actions.

Your next reading is on page 127.

own sons and brothers, and he has blessed you this day."

³⁰The next day Moses said to the people, "You have committed a great sin. But now I will go up to the LORD; perhaps I can make atonement for your sin."

³¹So Moses went back to the LORD and said, "Oh, what a great sin these people have committed! They have made themselves gods of gold. ³²But now, please forgive their sin—but if not, then blot me out of the book you have written."

³³The LORD replied to Moses, "Whoever has sinned against me I will blot out of my book. ³⁴Now go, lead the people to the place I spoke of, and my angel will go before you. However, when the time comes for me to punish, I will punish them for their sin."

³⁵And the LORD struck the people with a plague because of what they did with the calf Aaron had made.

33 Then the LORD said to Moses, "Leave this place, you and the people you brought up out of Egypt, and go up to the land I promised on oath to Abraham, Isaac and Jacob, saying, 'I will give it to your descendants.' ²I will send an angel before you and drive out the Canaanites, Amorites, Hittites, Perizzites, Hivites and Jebusites. ³Go up to the land flowing with milk and honey. But I will not go with you, because you are a stiff-necked people and I might destroy you on the way."

⁴When the people heard these distressing words, they began to mourn and no one put on any ornaments. ⁵For the LORD had said to Moses, "Tell the Israelites, 'You are a stiff-necked people. If I were to go with you even for a moment, I might destroy you. Now take off your ornaments and I will decide what to do with you.' " ⁶So the Israelites stripped off their ornaments at Mount Horeb.

The Tent of Meeting

⁷Now Moses used to take a tent and pitch it outside the camp some distance away, calling it the "tent of meeting." Anyone inquiring of the LORD would go to the tent of meeting outside the camp. ⁸And whenever Moses went out to the tent, all the people rose and stood at the

God as a Close Friend
READ EXODUS 33:9–23

You might be willing to wait in line for hours to get an autograph or just a glimpse of your favorite star. Moses had the chance to be with the most famous of all. God spoke with Moses "face to face, as a man speaks with his friend" (Exodus 33:11). God also wants you to seek him with all your heart. He wants you to get to know him like a close friend. Celebrities often have to disguise themselves so their fans don't recognize them and mob them. This is where God is so much better. He is *the* greatest yet he still wants to be with each of us. He's not afraid of being mobbed! He is always there for you, not just for an autograph or a handshake, but to be your friend and have a close relationship with you. Ask God to help you to get to know him better.

Your next reading is on page 130.

entrances to their tents, watching Moses until he entered the tent. 9As Moses went into the tent, the pillar of cloud would come down and stay at the entrance, while the LORD spoke with Moses. 10Whenever the people saw the pillar of cloud standing at the entrance to the tent, they all stood and worshiped, each at the entrance to his tent. 11The LORD would speak to Moses face to face, as a man speaks with his friend. Then Moses would return to the camp, but his young aide Joshua son of Nun did not leave the tent.

Moses and the Glory of the LORD

12Moses said to the LORD, "You have been telling me, 'Lead these people,' but you have not let me know whom you will send with me. You have said, 'I know you by name and you have found favor with me.' 13If you are pleased with me, teach me your ways so I may know you and continue to find favor with you. Remember that this nation is your people."

14The LORD replied, "My Presence will go with you, and I will give you rest."

15Then Moses said to him, "If your Presence does not go with us, do not send us up from here. 16How will anyone know that you are pleased with me and with your people unless you go with us? What else will distinguish me and your people from all the other people on the face of the earth?"

17And the LORD said to Moses, "I will do the very thing you have asked, because I am pleased with you and I know you by name."

18Then Moses said, "Now show me your glory."

19And the LORD said, "I will cause all my goodness to pass in front of you, and I will proclaim my name, the LORD, in your presence. I will have mercy on whom I will have mercy, and I will have compassion on whom I will have compassion. 20But," he said, "you cannot see my face, for no one may see me and live."

21Then the LORD said, "There is a place near me where you may stand on a rock. 22When my glory passes by, I will put you in a cleft in the rock and cover you with my hand until I have passed by. 23Then I will remove my hand and you will see my back; but my face must not be seen."

The New Stone Tablets

34 The LORD said to Moses, "Chisel out two stone tablets like the first ones, and I will write on them the words that were on the first tablets, which you broke. 2Be ready in the morning, and then come up on Mount Sinai. Present yourself to me there on top of the mountain. 3No one is to come with you or be seen anywhere on the mountain; not even the flocks and herds may graze in front of the mountain."

4So Moses chiseled out two stone tablets like the first ones and went up Mount Sinai early in the morning, as the LORD had commanded him; and he carried the two stone tablets in his hands. 5Then the LORD came down in the cloud and stood there with him and proclaimed his name, the LORD. 6And he passed in front of Moses, proclaiming, "The LORD, the LORD, the compassionate and gracious God, slow to anger, abounding in love and faithfulness, 7maintaining love to thousands, and forgiving wickedness, rebellion and sin. Yet he does not leave the guilty unpunished; he punishes the children and their children for the sin of the fathers to the third and fourth generation."

8Moses bowed to the ground at once and worshiped. 9"O Lord, if I have found favor in your eyes," he said, "then let the Lord go with us. Although this is a stiff-necked people, forgive our wickedness and our sin, and take us as your inheritance."

10Then the LORD said: "I am making a covenant with you. Before all your people I will do wonders never before done in any nation in all the world. The people you live among will see how awesome is the work that I, the LORD, will do for you. 11Obey what I command you today. I will drive out before you the Amorites, Canaanites, Hittites, Perizzites, Hivites and Jebusites. 12Be careful not to make a treaty with those who live in the land where you are going, or they will be a snare among you. 13Break down their altars, smash their sacred stones and cut down their Asherah poles.a 14Do not worship any other god, for the LORD, whose name is Jealous, is a jealous God.

15"Be careful not to make a treaty with those who live in the land; for when they prostitute themselves to their gods and

a 13 That is, symbols of the goddess Asherah

sacrifice to them, they will invite you and you will eat their sacrifices. 16And when you choose some of their daughters as wives for your sons and those daughters prostitute themselves to their gods, they will lead your sons to do the same.

17"Do not make cast idols.

18"Celebrate the Feast of Unleavened Bread. For seven days eat bread made without yeast, as I commanded you. Do this at the appointed time in the month of Abib, for in that month you came out of Egypt.

19"The first offspring of every womb belongs to me, including all the firstborn males of your livestock, whether from herd or flock. 20Redeem the firstborn donkey with a lamb, but if you do not redeem it, break its neck. Redeem all your firstborn sons.

"No one is to appear before me empty-handed.

21"Six days you shall labor, but on the seventh day you shall rest; even during the plowing season and harvest you must rest.

22"Celebrate the Feast of Weeks with the firstfruits of the wheat harvest, and the Feast of Ingathering at the turn of the year.a 23Three times a year all your men are to appear before the Sovereign LORD, the God of Israel. 24I will drive out nations before you and enlarge your territory, and no one will covet your land when you go up three times each year to appear before the LORD your God.

25"Do not offer the blood of a sacrifice to me along with anything containing yeast, and do not let any of the sacrifice from the Passover Feast remain until morning.

26"Bring the best of the firstfruits of your soil to the house of the LORD your God.

"Do not cook a young goat in its mother's milk."

27Then the LORD said to Moses, "Write down these words, for in accordance with these words I have made a covenant with you and with Israel." 28Moses was there with the LORD forty days and forty nights without eating bread or drinking water. And he wrote on the tablets the words of the covenant—the Ten Commandments.

The Radiant Face of Moses

29When Moses came down from Mount Sinai with the two tablets of the Testimony in his hands, he was not aware that his face was radiant because he had spoken with the LORD. 30When Aaron and all the Israelites saw Moses, his face was radiant, and they were afraid to come near him. 31But Moses called to them; so Aaron and all the leaders of the community came back to him, and he spoke to them. 32Afterward all the Israelites came near him, and he gave them all the commands the LORD had given him on Mount Sinai.

33When Moses finished speaking to them, he put a veil over his face. 34But whenever he entered the LORD's presence to speak with him, he removed the veil until he came out. And when he came out and told the Israelites what he had been commanded, 35they saw that his face was radiant. Then Moses would put the veil back over his face until he went in to speak with the LORD.

Sabbath Regulations

35 Moses assembled the whole Israelite community and said to them, "These are the things the LORD has commanded you to do: 2For six days, work is to be done, but the seventh day shall be your holy day, a Sabbath of rest to the LORD. Whoever does any work on it must be put to death. 3Do not light a fire in any of your dwellings on the Sabbath day."

Materials for the Tabernacle

4Moses said to the whole Israelite community, "This is what the LORD has commanded: 5From what you have, take an offering for the LORD. Everyone who is willing is to bring to the LORD an offering of gold, silver and bronze; 6blue, purple and scarlet yarn and fine linen; goat hair; 7ram skins dyed red and hides of sea cowsb; acacia wood; 8olive oil for the light; spices for the anointing oil and for the fragrant incense; 9and onyx stones and other gems to be mounted on the ephod and breastpiece.

10"All who are skilled among you are to come and make everything the LORD has commanded: 11the tabernacle with its tent and its covering, clasps, frames,

a 22 That is, in the fall   b 7 That is, dugongs; also in verse 23 crossbars, posts and bases; 12the ark with its poles and the atonement cover and the curtain that shields it; 13the table with its poles and all its articles and the bread of the Presence; 14the lampstand that is for light with its accessories, lamps and oil for the light; 15the altar of incense with its poles, the anointing oil and the fragrant incense; the curtain for the doorway at the entrance to the tabernacle; 16the altar of burnt offering with its bronze grating, its poles and all its utensils; the bronze basin with its stand; 17the curtains of the courtyard with its posts and bases, and the curtain for the entrance to the courtyard; 18the tent pegs for the tabernacle and for the courtyard, and their ropes; 19the woven garments worn for ministering in the sanctuary—both the sacred garments for Aaron the priest and the garments for his sons when they serve as priests."

20Then the whole Israelite community withdrew from Moses' presence, 21and everyone who was willing and whose heart moved him came and brought an offering to the Lord for the work on the Tent of Meeting, for all its service, and for the sacred garments. 22All who were willing, men and women alike, came and brought gold jewelry of all kinds: brooches, earrings, rings and ornaments. They all presented their gold as a wave offering to the Lord. 23Everyone who had blue, purple or scarlet yarn or fine linen, or goat hair, ram skins dyed red or hides of sea cows brought them. 24Those presenting an offering of silver or bronze brought it as an offering to the Lord, and everyone who had acacia wood for any part of the work brought it. 25Every skilled woman spun with her hands and brought what she had spun—blue, purple or scarlet yarn or fine linen. 26And all the women who were willing and had the skill spun the goat hair. 27The leaders brought onyx stones and other gems to be mounted on the ephod and breastpiece. 28They also brought spices and olive oil for the light and for the anointing oil and for the fragrant incense. 29All the Israelite men and women who were willing brought to the LORD freewill offerings for all the work the LORD through Moses had commanded them to do.

Bezalel and Oholiab

30Then Moses said to the Israelites, "See, the LORD has chosen Bezalel son of Uri, the son of Hur, of the tribe of Judah, 31and he has filled him with the Spirit of God, with skill, ability and knowledge in all kinds of crafts— 32to make artistic designs for work in gold, silver and bronze, 33to cut and set stones, to work in wood and to engage in all kinds of artistic craftsmanship. 34And he has given both him and Oholiab son of Ahisamach, of the tribe of Dan, the ability to teach others. 35He has filled them with skill to do all kinds of work as craftsmen, designers, embroiderers in blue, purple and scarlet yarn and fine linen, and weavers—all of them master craftsmen and designers.

1So Bezalel, Oholiab and every skilled person to whom the LORD has given skill and ability to know how to carry out all the work of constructing the sanctuary are to do the work just as the LORD has commanded."

2Then Moses summoned Bezalel and Oholiab and every skilled person to whom the LORD had given ability and who was willing to come and do the work. 3They received from Moses all the offerings the Israelites had brought to carry out the work of constructing the sanctuary. And the people continued to bring freewill offerings morning after morning. 4So all the skilled craftsmen who were doing all the work on the sanctuary left their work 5and said to Moses, "The people are bringing more than enough for doing the work the LORD commanded to be done."

6Then Moses gave an order and they sent this word throughout the camp: "No man or woman is to make anything else as an offering for the sanctuary." And so the people were restrained from bringing

GET SMARTER.

Generous Hands

READ EXODUS 35:4–9; 36:1–7

Has your pastor ever shouted out in church, "People! Stop giving! You are giving way too much!"? The people of Israel were told just that. Moses asked them to bring an offering to the Lord to build the new worship center, and they brought so much that they had to be ordered not to bring any more. What an attitude! Too often we think about giving generously but the extra cash somehow never makes it from our wallet into the offering. The people of Israel didn't just have generous thoughts, they had generous hands. That's the kind of hand-eye coordination God likes! God loves a cheerful giver (2 Corinthians 9:7)! Great things can be accomplished in the church when we cheerfully give and think about something bigger than just spending money on ourselves. When you work hard and earn money, give generously and cheerfully to God's work.

Your next reading is on page 139.

more, 7because what they already had was more than enough to do all the work.

The Tabernacle

8All the skilled men among the workmen made the tabernacle with ten curtains of finely twisted linen and blue, purple and scarlet yarn, with cherubim worked into them by a skilled craftsman. 9All the curtains were the same size—twenty-eight cubits long and four cubits wide.a 10They joined five of the curtains together and did the same with the other five. 11Then they made loops of blue material along the edge of the end curtain in one set, and the same was done with the end curtain in the other set. 12They also made fifty loops on one curtain and fifty loops on the end curtain of the other set, with the loops opposite each other. 13Then they made fifty gold clasps and used them to fasten the two sets of curtains together so that the tabernacle was a unit.

14They made curtains of goat hair for the tent over the tabernacle—eleven altogether. 15All eleven curtains were the same size—thirty cubits long and four cubits wide.b 16They joined five of the curtains into one set and the other six into another set. 17Then they made fifty loops along the edge of the end curtain in one set and also along the edge of the end curtain in the other set. 18They made fifty bronze clasps to fasten the tent together as a unit. 19Then they made for the tent a covering of ram skins dyed red, and over that a covering of hides of sea cows.c

20They made upright frames of acacia wood for the tabernacle. 21Each frame was ten cubits long and a cubit and a half wide,d 22with two projections set parallel to each other. They made all the frames of the tabernacle in this way. 23They made twenty frames for the south side of the tabernacle 24and made forty silver bases to go under them—two bases for each frame, one under each projection. 25For the other side, the north side of the tabernacle, they made twenty frames 26and forty silver bases—two under each frame. 27They made six frames for the far end, that is, the west end of the tabernacle, 28and two frames were made for the corners of the tabernacle at the far end. 29At these two corners the frames were double from the bottom all the way to the top and fitted into a single ring; both were

made alike. 30So there were eight frames and sixteen silver bases—two under each frame.

31They also made crossbars of acacia wood: five for the frames on one side of the tabernacle, 32five for those on the other side, and five for the frames on the west, at the far end of the tabernacle. 33They made the center crossbar so that it extended from end to end at the middle of the frames. 34They overlaid the frames with gold and made gold rings to hold the crossbars. They also overlaid the crossbars with gold.

35They made the curtain of blue, purple and scarlet yarn and finely twisted linen, with cherubim worked into it by a skilled craftsman. 36They made four posts of acacia wood for it and overlaid them with gold. They made gold hooks for them and cast their four silver bases. 37For the entrance to the tent they made a curtain of blue, purple and scarlet yarn and finely twisted linen—the work of an embroiderer; 38and they made five posts with hooks for them. They overlaid the tops of the posts and their bands with gold and made their five bases of bronze.

The Ark

37 Bezalel made the ark of acacia wood—two and a half cubits long, a cubit and a half wide, and a cubit and a half high.e 2He overlaid it with pure gold, both inside and out, and made a gold molding around it. 3He cast four gold rings for it and fastened them to its four feet, with two rings on one side and two rings on the other. 4Then he made poles of acacia wood and overlaid them with gold. 5And he inserted the poles into the rings on the sides of the ark to carry it.

6He made the atonement cover of pure gold—two and a half cubits long and a cubit and a half wide.f 7Then he made two cherubim out of hammered gold at the ends of the cover. 8He made one cherub on one end and the second cherub on

---

a 9 That is, about 42 feet (about 12.5 meters) long and 6 feet (about 1.8 meters) wide   b 15 That is, about 45 feet (about 13.5 meters) long and 6 feet (about 1.8 meters) wide   c 19 That is, dugongs   d 21 That is, about 15 feet (about 4.5 meters) long and 2 1/4 feet (about 0.7 meter) wide   e 1 That is, about 3 3/4 feet (about 1.1 meters) long and 2 1/4 feet (about 0.7 meter) wide and high   f 6 That is, about 3 3/4 feet (about 1.1 meters) long and 2 1/4 feet (about 0.7 meter) wide the other; at the two ends he made them of one piece with the cover. 9The cherubim had their wings spread upward, overshadowing the cover with them. The cherubim faced each other, looking toward the cover.

The Table

10Theya made the table of acacia wood—two cubits long, a cubit wide, and a cubit and a half high.b 11Then they overlaid it with pure gold and made a gold molding around it. 12They also made around it a rim a handbreadthc wide and put a gold molding on the rim. 13They cast four gold rings for the table and fastened them to the four corners, where the four legs were. 14The rings were put close to the rim to hold the poles used in carrying the table. 15The poles for carrying the table were made of acacia wood and were overlaid with gold. 16And they made from pure gold the articles for the table—its plates and dishes and bowls and its pitchers for the pouring out of drink offerings.

The Lampstand

17They made the lampstand of pure gold and hammered it out, base and shaft; its flowerlike cups, buds and blossoms were of one piece with it. 18Six branches extended from the sides of the lampstand—three on one side and three on the other. 19Three cups shaped like almond flowers with buds and blossoms were on one branch, three on the next branch and the same for all six branches extending from the lampstand. 20And on the lampstand were four cups shaped like almond flowers with buds and blossoms. 21One bud was under the first pair of branches extending from the lampstand, a second bud under the second pair, and a third bud under the third pair—six branches in all. 22The buds and the branches were all of one piece with the lampstand, hammered out of pure gold.

23They made its seven lamps, as well as its wick trimmers and trays, of pure gold. 24They made the lampstand and all its accessories from one talentd of pure gold.

The Altar of Incense

25They made the altar of incense out of acacia wood. It was square, a cubit long and a cubit wide, and two cubits highe—its horns of one piece with it. 26They over-

laid the top and all the sides and the horns with pure gold, and made a gold molding around it. 27They made two gold rings below the molding—two on opposite sides—to hold the poles used to carry it. 28They made the poles of acacia wood and overlaid them with gold.

29They also made the sacred anointing oil and the pure, fragrant incense—the work of a perfumer.

The Altar of Burnt Offering

38 Theyf built the altar of burnt offering of acacia wood, three cubitsg high; it was square, five cubits long and five cubits wide.h 2They made a horn at each of the four corners, so that the horns and the altar were of one piece, and they overlaid the altar with bronze. 3They made all its utensils of bronze—its pots, shovels, sprinkling bowls, meat forks and firepans. 4They made a grating for the altar, a bronze network, to be under its ledge, halfway up the altar. 5They cast bronze rings to hold the poles for the four corners of the bronze grating. 6They made the poles of acacia wood and overlaid them with bronze. 7They inserted the poles into the rings so they would be on the sides of the altar for carrying it. They made it hollow, out of boards.

Basin for Washing

8They made the bronze basin and its bronze stand from the mirrors of the women who served at the entrance to the Tent of Meeting.

The Courtyard

9Next they made the courtyard. The south side was a hundred cubitsi long and had curtains of finely twisted linen, 10with twenty posts and twenty bronze bases, and with silver hooks and bands on the posts. 11The north side was also a hundred cubits long and had twenty posts

a 10 Or He; also in verses 11–29   b 10 That is, about 3 feet (about 0.9 meter) long, 1 1/2 feet (about 0.5 meter) wide, and 2 1/4 feet (about 0.7 meter) high   c 12 That is, about 3 inches (about 8 centimeters)   d 24 That is, about 75 pounds (about 34 kilograms)   e 25 That is, about 1 1/2 feet (about 0.5 meter) long and wide, and about 3 feet (about 0.9 meter) high   f 1 Or He; also in verses 2–9   g 1 That is, about 4 1/2 feet (about 1.3 meters)   h 1 That is, about 7 1/2 feet (about 2.3 meters) long and wide   i 9 That is, about 150 feet (about 46 meters)

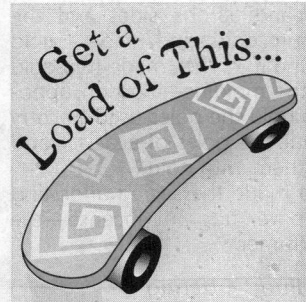

Get a Load of This...

How much Egyptian treasure was melted down and used to make the Tent of Meeting and all the things used in it? One ton of gold and almost four tons of silver and 2 ½ tons of bronze! Whoeeee! At today's market price, that would be a tent worth nearly 12 million dollars!

and twenty bronze bases, with silver hooks and bands on the posts.

¹²The west end was fifty cubits*ᵃ* wide and had curtains, with ten posts and ten bases, with silver hooks and bands on the posts. ¹³The east end, toward the sunrise, was also fifty cubits wide. ¹⁴Curtains fifteen cubits*ᵇ* long were on one side of the entrance, with three posts and three bases, ¹⁵and curtains fifteen cubits long were on the other side of the entrance to the courtyard, with three posts and three bases. ¹⁶All the curtains around the courtyard were of finely twisted linen. ¹⁷The bases for the posts were bronze. The hooks and bands on the posts were silver, and their tops were overlaid with silver; so all the posts of the courtyard had silver bands.

¹⁸The curtain for the entrance to the courtyard was of blue, purple and scarlet yarn and finely twisted linen— the work of an embroiderer. It was twenty cubits*ᶜ* long and, like the curtains of the courtyard, five cubits*ᵈ* high, ¹⁹with four posts and four bronze bases. Their hooks and bands were silver, and their tops were overlaid with silver. ²⁰All the tent pegs of the tabernacle and of the surrounding courtyard were bronze.

The Materials Used

²¹These are the amounts of the materials used for the tabernacle, the tabernacle of the Testimony, which were recorded at Moses' command by the Levites under the direction of Ithamar son of Aaron, the priest. ²²(Bezalel son of Uri, the son of Hur, of the tribe of Judah, made everything the Lᴏʀᴅ commanded Moses; ²³with him was Oholiab son of Ahisamach, of the tribe of Dan—a craftsman and designer, and an embroiderer in blue, purple and scarlet yarn and fine linen.) ²⁴The total amount of the gold from the wave offering used for all the work on the sanctuary was 29 talents and 730 shekels,*ᵉ* according to the sanctuary shekel.

²⁵The silver obtained from those of the community who were counted in the census was 100 talents and 1,775 shekels,*ᶠ* according to the sanctuary shekel— ²⁶one beka per person, that is, half a shekel,*ᵍ* according to the sanctuary shekel, from everyone who had crossed over to those counted, twenty years old or more, a total of 603,550 men. ²⁷The 100 talents*ʰ* of silver were used to cast the bases for the sanctuary and for the curtain— 100 bases from the 100 talents, one talent for each base. ²⁸They used the 1,775 shekels*ⁱ* to make the hooks for the posts, to overlay the tops of the posts, and to make their bands.

²⁹The bronze from the wave offering was 70 talents and 2,400 shekels.*ʲ* ³⁰They used it to make the bases for

ᵃ 12 That is, about 75 feet (about 23 meters)   *ᵇ 14* That is, about 22 1/2 feet (about 6.9 meters)   *ᶜ 18* That is, about 30 feet (about 9 meters)   *ᵈ 18* That is, about 7 1/2 feet (about 2.3 meters)   *ᵉ 24* The weight of the gold was a little over one ton (about 1 metric ton).   *ᶠ 25* The weight of the silver was a little over 3 3/4 tons (about 3.4 metric tons).   *ᵍ 26* That is, about 1/5 ounce (about 5.5 grams)   *ʰ 27* That is, about 3 3/4 tons (about 3.4 metric tons)   *ⁱ 28* That is, about 45 pounds (about 20 kilograms)   *ʲ 29* The weight of the bronze was about 2 1/2 tons (about 2.4 metric tons).

the entrance to the Tent of Meeting, the bronze altar with its bronze grating and all its utensils, ³¹the bases for the surrounding courtyard and those for its entrance and all the tent pegs for the tabernacle and those for the surrounding courtyard.

The Priestly Garments

39 From the blue, purple and scarlet yarn they made woven garments for ministering in the sanctuary. They also made sacred garments for Aaron, as the LORD commanded Moses.

The Ephod

²They^a made the ephod of gold, and of blue, purple and scarlet yarn, and of finely twisted linen. ³They hammered out thin sheets of gold and cut strands to be worked into the blue, purple and scarlet yarn and fine linen—the work of a skilled craftsman. ⁴They made shoulder pieces for the ephod, which were attached to two of its corners, so it could be fastened. ⁵Its skillfully woven waistband was like it—of one piece with the ephod and made with gold, and with blue, purple and scarlet yarn, and with finely twisted linen, as the LORD commanded Moses.

⁶They mounted the onyx stones in gold filigree settings and engraved them like a seal with the names of the sons of Israel. ⁷Then they fastened them on the shoulder pieces of the ephod as memorial stones for the sons of Israel, as the LORD commanded Moses.

The Breastpiece

⁸They fashioned the breastpiece—the work of a skilled craftsman. They made it like the ephod: of gold, and of blue, purple and scarlet yarn, and of finely twisted linen. ⁹It was square—a span^b long and a span wide—and folded double. ¹⁰Then they mounted four rows of precious stones on it. In the first row there was a ruby, a topaz and a beryl; ¹¹in the second row a turquoise, a sapphire^c and an emerald; ¹²in the third row a jacinth, an agate and an amethyst; ¹³in the fourth row a chrysolite, an onyx and a jasper.^d They were mounted in gold filigree settings. ¹⁴There were twelve stones, one for each of the names of the sons of Israel, each

engraved like a seal with the name of one of the twelve tribes.

¹⁵For the breastpiece they made braided chains of pure gold, like a rope. ¹⁶They made two gold filigree settings and two gold rings, and fastened the rings to two of the corners of the breastpiece. ¹⁷They fastened the two gold chains to the rings at the corners of the breastpiece, ¹⁸and the other ends of the chains to the two settings, attaching them to the shoulder pieces of the ephod at the front. ¹⁹They made two gold rings and attached them to the other two corners of the breastpiece on the inside edge next to the ephod. ²⁰Then they made two more gold rings and attached them to the bottom of the shoulder pieces on the front of the ephod, close to the seam just above the waistband of the ephod. ²¹They tied the rings of the breastpiece to the rings of the ephod with blue cord, connecting it to the waistband so that the breastpiece would not swing out from the ephod—as the LORD commanded Moses.

Other Priestly Garments

²²They made the robe of the ephod entirely of blue cloth—the work of a weaver— ²³with an opening in the center of the robe like the opening of a collar,^e and a band around this opening, so that it would not tear. ²⁴They made pomegranates of blue, purple and scarlet yarn and finely twisted linen around the hem of the robe. ²⁵And they made bells of pure gold and attached them around the hem between the pomegranates. ²⁶The bells and pomegranates alternated around the hem of the robe to be worn for ministering, as the LORD commanded Moses.

²⁷For Aaron and his sons, they made tunics of fine linen—the work of a weaver— ²⁸and the turban of fine linen, the linen headbands and the undergarments of finely twisted linen. ²⁹The sash was of finely twisted linen and blue, purple and scarlet yarn—the work of an embroiderer—as the LORD commanded Moses.

³⁰They made the plate, the sacred diadem, out of pure gold and engraved on it, like an inscription on a seal: HOLY TO THE

^a 2 Or He; also in verses 7, 8 and 22   ^b 9 That is, about 9 inches (about 22 centimeters)   ^c 11 Or lapis lazuli   ^d 13 The precise identification of some of these precious stones is uncertain.   ^e 23 The meaning of the Hebrew for this word is uncertain.

LORD. [31]Then they fastened a blue cord to it to attach it to the turban, as the LORD commanded Moses.

Moses Inspects the Tabernacle

[32]So all the work on the tabernacle, the Tent of Meeting, was completed. The Israelites did everything just as the LORD commanded Moses. [33]Then they brought the tabernacle to Moses: the tent and all its furnishings, its clasps, frames, crossbars, posts and bases; [34]the covering of ram skins dyed red, the covering of hides of sea cows[a] and the shielding curtain; [35]the ark of the Testimony with its poles and the atonement cover; [36]the table with all its articles and the bread of the Presence; [37]the pure gold lampstand with its row of lamps and all its accessories, and the oil for the light; [38]the gold altar, the anointing oil, the fragrant incense, and the curtain for the entrance to the tent; [39]the bronze altar with its bronze grating, its poles and all its utensils; the basin with its stand; [40]the curtains of the courtyard with its posts and bases, and the curtain for the entrance to the courtyard; the ropes

[a] 34 That is, dugongs

Make It Stick

_____

_____

_____

_____

_____

_____

_____

READ EXODUS 40:34

God camped with Israel because he wanted to be with them. He wants to be with you, too. He promises to never leave you or forsake you (Hebrews 13:5). Remember, God's presence is always with you. Jot down what times in your life you especially need to know that God is there with you...

and tent pegs for the courtyard; all the furnishings for the tabernacle, the Tent of Meeting; ⁴¹and the woven garments worn for ministering in the sanctuary, both the sacred garments for Aaron the priest and the garments for his sons when serving as priests.

⁴²The Israelites had done all the work just as the LORD had commanded Moses. ⁴³Moses inspected the work and saw that they had done it just as the LORD had commanded. So Moses blessed them.

Setting Up the Tabernacle

40 Then the LORD said to Moses: ²"Set up the tabernacle, the Tent of Meeting, on the first day of the first month. ³Place the ark of the Testimony in it and shield the ark with the curtain. ⁴Bring in the table and set out what belongs on it. Then bring in the lampstand and set up its lamps. ⁵Place the gold altar of incense in front of the ark of the Testimony and put the curtain at the entrance to the tabernacle.

⁶"Place the altar of burnt offering in front of the entrance to the tabernacle, the Tent of Meeting; ⁷place the basin between the Tent of Meeting and the altar and put water in it. ⁸Set up the courtyard around it and put the curtain at the entrance to the courtyard.

⁹"Take the anointing oil and anoint the tabernacle and everything in it; consecrate it and all its furnishings, and it will be holy. ¹⁰Then anoint the altar of burnt offering and all its utensils; consecrate the altar, and it will be most holy. ¹¹Anoint the basin and its stand and consecrate them.

¹²"Bring Aaron and his sons to the entrance to the Tent of Meeting and wash them with water. ¹³Then dress Aaron in the sacred garments, anoint him and consecrate him so he may serve me as priest. ¹⁴Bring his sons and dress them in tunics. ¹⁵Anoint them just as you anointed their father, so they may serve me as priests. Their anointing will be to a priesthood that will continue for all generations to come." ¹⁶Moses did everything just as the LORD commanded him.

¹⁷So the tabernacle was set up on the first day of the first month in the second year. ¹⁸When Moses set up the tabernacle, he put the bases in place, erected the frames, inserted the crossbars and set up the posts. ¹⁹Then he spread the tent over the tabernacle and put the covering over the tent, as the LORD commanded him.

²⁰He took the Testimony and placed it in the ark, attached the poles to the ark and put the atonement cover over it. ²¹Then he brought the ark into the tabernacle and hung the shielding curtain and shielded the ark of the Testimony, as the LORD commanded him.

²²Moses placed the table in the Tent of Meeting on the north side of the tabernacle outside the curtain ²³and set out the bread on it before the LORD, as the LORD commanded him.

²⁴He placed the lampstand in the Tent of Meeting opposite the table on the south side of the tabernacle ²⁵and set up the lamps before the LORD, as the LORD commanded him.

²⁶Moses placed the gold altar in the Tent of Meeting in front of the curtain ²⁷and burned fragrant incense on it, as the LORD commanded him. ²⁸Then he put up the curtain at the entrance to the tabernacle.

²⁹He set the altar of burnt offering near the entrance to the tabernacle, the Tent of Meeting, and offered on it burnt offerings and grain offerings, as the LORD commanded him.

³⁰He placed the basin between the Tent of Meeting and the altar and put water in it for washing, ³¹and Moses and Aaron and his sons used it to wash their hands and feet. ³²They washed whenever they entered the Tent of Meeting or approached the altar, as the LORD commanded Moses.

³³Then Moses set up the courtyard around the tabernacle and altar and put up the curtain at the entrance to the courtyard. And so Moses finished the work.

The Glory of the LORD

³⁴Then the cloud covered the Tent of Meeting, and the glory of the LORD filled the tabernacle. ³⁵Moses could not enter the Tent of Meeting because the cloud had settled upon it, and the glory of the LORD filled the tabernacle.

³⁶In all the travels of the Israelites, whenever the cloud lifted from above the tabernacle, they would set out; ³⁷but if the cloud did not lift, they did not set out—until the day it lifted. ³⁸So the cloud of the LORD was over the tabernacle by day, and fire was in the cloud by night, in the sight of all the house of Israel during all their travels.

LEVITICUS

Who wrote this book?
Moses.

Why was this book written?
Leviticus shows the Israelites how to worship God and live a holy life.

What happens in this book?
Moses gives the people and the priests of Israel God's instructions.

What do we learn about God in this book?
God is holy and expects his people to be holy. God accepts sacrifices and forgives people who sin.

What people are important in this book?
The important people in this book are Moses and Aaron.

When did this happen?
God's instructions were given about 1445 B.C.

Where did this happen?
The Israelites were camped at Mount Sinai when these instructions were given.

What are some of the stories in this book?
Aaron is ordained high priest   Leviticus 8
Aaron's sons disobey God   Leviticus 10
God sets special holidays   Leviticus 23

The Burnt Offering

The LORD called to Moses and spoke to him from the Tent of Meeting. He said, 2"Speak to the Israelites and say to them: 'When any of you brings an offering to the LORD, bring as your offering an animal from either the herd or the flock.

3"'If the offering is a burnt offering from the herd, he is to offer a male without defect. He must present it at the entrance to the Tent of Meeting so that it[a] will be acceptable to the LORD. 4He is to lay his hand on the head of the burnt offering, and it will be accepted on his behalf to make atonement for him. 5He is to slaughter the young bull before the LORD, and then Aaron's sons the priests shall bring the blood and sprinkle it against the altar on all sides at the entrance to the Tent of Meeting. 6He is to skin the burnt offering and cut it into pieces. 7The sons of Aaron the priest are to put fire on the altar and arrange wood on the fire. 8Then Aaron's sons the priests shall arrange the pieces, including the head and the fat, on the burning wood that is on the altar. 9He is to wash the inner parts and the legs with water, and the priest is to burn all of it on the altar. It is a burnt offering, an offering made by fire, an aroma pleasing to the LORD.

10"'If the offering is a burnt offering from the flock, from either the sheep or the goats, he is to offer a male without defect. 11He is to slaughter it at the north side of the altar before the LORD, and Aaron's sons the priests shall sprinkle its blood against the altar on all sides. 12He is to cut it into pieces, and the priest shall arrange them, including the head and the fat, on the burning wood that is on the altar. 13He is to wash the inner parts and the legs with water, and the priest is to bring all of it and burn it on the altar. It is a burnt offering, an offering made by fire, an aroma pleasing to the LORD.

14"'If the offering to the LORD is a burnt offering of birds, he is to offer a dove or a young pigeon. 15The priest shall bring it to the altar, wring off the head and burn

[a] 3 Or he

Give God Your Best

READ LEVITICUS 1:1–4, 2:1–3; 3:1–6

It's your birthday. Your uncle hands you your present, you tear the paper off and *Wow!* It's that remote control model airplane you've been really wanting! Only … it's not new. It's some kid's beat up, old plane. Man! The remote doesn't work. The propeller barely moves. "Houston, we do *not* have lift-off." How would you feel? That's how God feels with some of our gifts. When the Israelites gave offerings, Leviticus 1:3 said they should "offer a male without defect." Read that again: *"without defect."* God wants you to give him your best. That means don't just give him the parts of your life you don't want. It means when you receive money, give an offering to church first. Don't just toss God your leftover pocket change. It means have a daily prayer and Bible reading time and don't just pray on the run. Give God your best.

Your next reading is on page 145.

it on the altar; its blood shall be drained out on the side of the altar. 16He is to remove the crop with its contents[a] and throw it to the east side of the altar, where the ashes are. 17He shall tear it open by the wings, not severing it completely, and then the priest shall burn it on the wood that is on the fire on the altar. It is a burnt offering, an offering made by fire, an aroma pleasing to the LORD.

The Grain Offering

2 " 'When someone brings a grain offering to the LORD, his offering is to be of fine flour. He is to pour oil on it, put incense on it 2and take it to Aaron's sons the priests. The priest shall take a handful of the fine flour and oil, together with all the incense, and burn this as a memorial portion on the altar, an offering made by fire, an aroma pleasing to the LORD. 3The rest of the grain offering belongs to Aaron and his sons; it is a most holy part of the offerings made to the LORD by fire.

4" 'If you bring a grain offering baked in an oven, it is to consist of fine flour: cakes made without yeast and mixed with oil, or[b] wafers made without yeast and spread with oil. 5If your grain offering is prepared on a griddle, it is to be made of fine flour mixed with oil, and without yeast. 6Crumble it and pour oil on it; it is a grain offering. 7If your grain offering is cooked in a pan, it is to be made of fine flour and oil. 8Bring the grain offering made of these things to the LORD; present it to the priest, who shall take it to the altar. 9He shall take out the memorial portion from the grain offering and burn it on the altar as an offering made by fire, an aroma pleasing to the LORD. 10The rest of the grain offering belongs to Aaron and his sons; it is a most holy part of the offerings made to the LORD by fire.

11" 'Every grain offering you bring to the LORD must be made without yeast, for you are not to burn any yeast or honey in an offering made to the LORD by fire. 12You may bring them to the LORD as an offering of the firstfruits, but they are not to be offered on the altar as a pleasing aroma. 13Season all your grain offerings with salt. Do not leave the salt of the covenant of your God out of your grain offerings; add salt to all your offerings.

14" 'If you bring a grain offering of first-fruits to the LORD, offer crushed heads of new grain roasted in the fire. 15Put oil and incense on it; it is a grain offering. 16The priest shall burn the memorial portion of the crushed grain and the oil, together with all the incense, as an offering made to the LORD by fire.

The Fellowship Offering

3 " 'If someone's offering is a fellowship offering,[c] and he offers an animal from the herd, whether male or female, he is to present before the LORD an animal without defect. 2He is to lay his hand on the head of his offering and slaughter it at the entrance to the Tent of Meeting. Then Aaron's sons the priests shall sprinkle the blood against the altar on all sides. 3From the fellowship offering he is to bring a sacrifice made to the LORD by fire: all the fat that covers the inner parts or is connected to them, 4both kidneys with the fat on them near the loins, and the covering of the liver, which he will remove with the kidneys. 5Then Aaron's sons are to burn it on the altar on top of the burnt offering that is on the burning wood, as an offering made by fire, an aroma pleasing to the LORD.

6" 'If he offers an animal from the flock as a fellowship offering to the LORD, he is to offer a male or female without defect. 7If he offers a lamb, he is to present it before the LORD. 8He is to lay his hand on the head of his offering and slaughter it in front of the Tent of Meeting. Then Aaron's sons shall sprinkle its blood against the altar on all sides. 9From the fellowship offering he is to bring a sacrifice made to the LORD by fire: its fat, the entire fat tail cut off close to the backbone, all the fat that covers the inner parts or is connected to them, 10both kidneys with the fat on them near the loins, and the covering of the liver, which he will remove with the kidneys. 11The priest shall burn them on the altar as food, an offering made to the LORD by fire.

12" 'If his offering is a goat, he is to present it before the LORD. 13He is to lay his hand on its head and slaughter it in front of the Tent of Meeting. Then Aaron's sons shall sprinkle its blood against the altar on all sides. 14From what he offers he is to

---

[a] 16 Or crop and the feathers; the meaning of the Hebrew for this word is uncertain.   [b] 4 Or and   [c] 1 Traditionally peace offering; also in verses 3, 6 and 9

make this offering to the Lord by fire: all the fat that covers the inner parts or is connected to them, ¹⁵both kidneys with the fat on them near the loins, and the covering of the liver, which he will remove with the kidneys. ¹⁶The priest shall burn them on the altar as food, an offering made by fire, a pleasing aroma. All the fat is the Lord's.

¹⁷" 'This is a lasting ordinance for the generations to come, wherever you live: You must not eat any fat or any blood.' "

The Sin Offering

The Lord said to Moses, ²"Say to the Israelites: 'When anyone sins unintentionally and does what is forbidden in any of the Lord's commands—

³" 'If the anointed priest sins, bringing guilt on the people, he must bring to the Lord a young bull without defect as a sin offering for the sin he has committed. ⁴He is to present the bull at the entrance to the Tent of Meeting before the Lord. He is to lay his hand on its head and slaughter it before the Lord. ⁵Then the anointed priest shall take some of the bull's blood and carry it into the Tent of Meeting. ⁶He is to dip his finger into the blood and sprinkle some of it seven times before the Lord, in front of the curtain of the sanctuary. ⁷The priest shall then put some of the blood on the horns of the altar of fragrant incense that is before the Lord in the Tent of Meeting. The rest of the bull's blood he shall pour out at the base of the altar of burnt offering at the entrance to the Tent of Meeting. ⁸He shall remove all the fat from the bull of the sin offering—the fat that covers the inner parts or is connected to them, ⁹both kidneys with the fat on them near the loins, and the covering of the liver, which he will remove with the kidneys— ¹⁰just as the fat is removed from the ox*a* sacrificed as a fellowship offering.*b* Then the priest shall burn them on the altar of burnt offering. ¹¹But the hide of the bull and all its flesh, as well as the head and legs, the inner parts and offal— ¹²that is, all the rest of the bull—he must take outside the camp to a place ceremonially clean, where the ashes are thrown, and burn it in a wood fire on the ash heap.

¹³" 'If the whole Israelite community sins unintentionally and does what is forbidden in any of the Lord's commands, even though the community is unaware of the matter, they are guilty. ¹⁴When they become aware of the sin they committed, the assembly must bring a young bull as a sin offering and present it before the Tent of Meeting. ¹⁵The elders of the community are to lay their hands on the bull's head before the Lord, and the bull shall be slaughtered before the Lord. ¹⁶Then the anointed priest is to take some of the bull's blood into the Tent of Meeting. ¹⁷He shall dip his finger into the

Get a Load of This...

Leviticus 2:4–9 talks about the priests baking "grain offerings" for the Lord. Some were cakes, some were flour and oil "prepared on griddle" (Yum! Sounds like pancakes!), and other goodies "cooked in a pan." Sounds good so far, right? But then the priests had to deliberately burn some grain!

---

a 10 The Hebrew word can include both male and female.   *b 10* Traditionally *peace offering*; also in verses 26, 31 and 35 blood and sprinkle it before the L ORD seven times in front of the curtain. ¹⁸He is to put some of the blood on the horns of the altar that is before the L ORD in the Tent of Meeting. The rest of the blood he shall pour out at the base of the altar of burnt offering at the entrance to the Tent of Meeting. ¹⁹He shall remove all the fat from it and burn it on the altar, ²⁰and do with this bull just as he did with the bull for the sin offering. In this way the priest will make atonement for them, and they will be forgiven. ²¹Then he shall take the bull outside the camp and burn it as he burned the first bull. This is the sin offering for the community.

²²" 'When a leader sins unintentionally and does what is forbidden in any of the commands of the L ORD his God, he is guilty. ²³When he is made aware of the sin he committed, he must bring as his offering a male goat without defect. ²⁴He is to lay his hand on the goat's head and slaughter it at the place where the burnt offering is slaughtered before the L ORD. It is a sin offering. ²⁵Then the priest shall take some of the blood of the sin offering with his finger and put it on the horns of the altar of burnt offering and pour out the rest of the blood at the base of the altar. ²⁶He shall burn all the fat on the altar as he burned the fat of the fellowship offering. In this way the priest will make atonement for the man's sin, and he will be forgiven.

²⁷" 'If a member of the community sins unintentionally and does what is forbidden in any of the L ORD's commands, he is guilty. ²⁸When he is made aware of the sin he committed, he must bring as his offering for the sin he committed a female goat without defect. ²⁹He is to lay his hand on the head of the sin offering and slaughter it at the place of the burnt offering. ³⁰Then the priest is to take some of the blood with his finger and put it on the horns of the altar of burnt offering and pour out the rest of the blood at the base of the altar. ³¹He shall remove all the fat, just as the fat is removed from the fellowship offering, and the priest shall burn it on the altar as an aroma pleasing to the L ORD. In this way the priest will make atonement for him, and he will be forgiven.

³²" 'If he brings a lamb as his sin offering, he is to bring a female without de-

fect. ³³He is to lay his hand on its head and slaughter it for a sin offering at the place where the burnt offering is slaughtered. ³⁴Then the priest shall take some of the blood of the sin offering with his finger and put it on the horns of the altar of burnt offering and pour out the rest of the blood at the base of the altar. ³⁵He shall remove all the fat, just as the fat is removed from the lamb of the fellowship offering, and the priest shall burn it on the altar on top of the offerings made to the L ORD by fire. In this way the priest will make atonement for him for the sin he has committed, and he will be forgiven.

5 " 'If a person sins because he does not speak up when he hears a public charge to testify regarding something he has seen or learned about, he will be held responsible.

²" 'Or if a person touches anything ceremonially unclean—whether the carcasses of unclean wild animals or of unclean livestock or of unclean creatures that move along the ground—even though he is unaware of it, he has become unclean and is guilty.

³" 'Or if he touches human uncleanness—anything that would make him unclean—even though he is unaware of it, when he learns of it he will be guilty.

⁴" 'Or if a person thoughtlessly takes an oath to do anything, whether good or evil—in any matter one might carelessly swear about—even though he is unaware of it, in any case when he learns of it he will be guilty.

⁵" 'When anyone is guilty in any of these ways, he must confess in what way he has sinned ⁶and, as a penalty for the sin he has committed, he must bring to the L ORD a female lamb or goat from the flock as a sin offering; and the priest shall make atonement for him for his sin.

⁷" 'If he cannot afford a lamb, he is to bring two doves or two young pigeons to the L ORD as a penalty for his sin—one for a sin offering and the other for a burnt offering. ⁸He is to bring them to the priest, who shall first offer the one for the sin offering. He is to wring its head from its neck, not severing it completely, ⁹and is to sprinkle some of the blood of the sin offering against the side of the altar; the rest of the blood must be drained out at the base of the altar. It is a sin offering.

[10]The priest shall then offer the other as a burnt offering in the prescribed way and make atonement for him for the sin he has committed, and he will be forgiven.

[11]" 'If, however, he cannot afford two doves or two young pigeons, he is to bring as an offering for his sin a tenth of an ephah[a] of fine flour for a sin offering. He must not put oil or incense on it, because it is a sin offering. [12]He is to bring it to the priest, who shall take a handful of it as a memorial portion and burn it on the altar on top of the offerings made to the LORD by fire. It is a sin offering. [13]In this way the priest will make atonement for him for any of these sins he has committed, and he will be forgiven. The rest of the offering will belong to the priest, as in the case of the grain offering.' "

The Guilt Offering

[14]The LORD said to Moses: [15]"When a person commits a violation and sins unintentionally in regard to any of the LORD's holy things, he is to bring to the LORD as a penalty a ram from the flock, one without defect and of the proper value in silver, according to the sanctuary shekel.[b] It is a guilt offering. [16]He must make restitution for what he has failed to do in regard to the holy things, add a fifth of the value to that and give it all to the priest, who will make atonement for him with the ram as a guilt offering, and he will be forgiven.

[17]"If a person sins and does what is forbidden in any of the LORD's commands, even though he does not know it, he is guilty and will be held responsible. [18]He is to bring to the priest as a guilt offering a ram from the flock, one without defect and of the proper value. In this way the priest will make atonement for him for the wrong he has committed unintentionally, and he will be forgiven. [19]It is a guilt offering; he has been guilty of[c] wrongdoing against the LORD."

The LORD said to Moses: [2]"If anyone sins and is unfaithful to the LORD by deceiving his neighbor about something entrusted to him or left in his care or stolen, or if he cheats him, [3]or if he finds lost property and lies about it, or if he swears falsely, or if he commits any such sin that people may do— [4]when he thus sins and becomes guilty, he must return what he has stolen or taken by extortion, or what was entrusted to him, or the lost property he found, [5]or whatever it was he swore falsely about. He must make restitution in full, add a fifth of the value to it and give it all to the owner on the day he presents his guilt offering. [6]And as a penalty he must bring to the priest, that is, to the LORD, his guilt offering, a ram from the flock, one without defect and of the proper value. [7]In this way the priest will make atonement for him before the LORD, and he will be forgiven for any of these things he did that made him guilty."

The Burnt Offering

[8]The LORD said to Moses: [9]"Give Aaron and his sons this command: 'These are the regulations for the burnt offering: The burnt offering is to remain on the altar hearth throughout the night, till morning, and the fire must be kept burning on the altar. [10]The priest shall then put on his linen clothes, with linen undergarments next to his body, and shall remove the ashes of the burnt offering that the fire has consumed on the altar and place them beside the altar. [11]Then he is to take off these clothes and put on others, and carry the ashes outside the camp to a place that is ceremonially clean. [12]The fire on the altar must be kept burning; it must not go out. Every morning the priest is to add firewood and arrange the burnt offering on the fire and burn the fat of the fellowship offerings[d] on it. [13]The fire must be kept burning on the altar continuously; it must not go out.

The Grain Offering

[14]" 'These are the regulations for the grain offering: Aaron's sons are to bring it before the LORD, in front of the altar. [15]The priest is to take a handful of fine flour and oil, together with all the incense on the grain offering, and burn the memorial portion on the altar as an aroma pleasing to the LORD. [16]Aaron and his sons shall eat the rest of it, but it is to be eaten without yeast in a holy place; they are to eat it in the courtyard of the Tent of Meeting. [17]It must not be baked with yeast; I have given it as their share of the offerings made to me by fire. Like the sin offering and the guilt offering, it is most holy. [18]Any male

---

[a] 11 That is, probably about 2 quarts (about 2 liters)
[b] 15 That is, about 2/5 ounce (about 11.5 grams)
[c] 19 Or has made full expiation for his   [d] 12 Traditionally peace offerings

descendant of Aaron may eat it. It is his regular share of the offerings made to the LORD by fire for the generations to come. Whatever touches them will become holy.*[a]* "

[19]The LORD also said to Moses, [20]"This is the offering Aaron and his sons are to bring to the LORD on the day he[b] is anointed: a tenth of an ephah[c] of fine flour as a regular grain offering, half of it in the morning and half in the evening. [21]Prepare it with oil on a griddle; bring it well-mixed and present the grain offering broken[d] in pieces as an aroma pleasing to the LORD. [22]The son who is to succeed him as anointed priest shall prepare it. It is the LORD's regular share and is to be burned completely. [23]Every grain offering of a priest shall be burned completely; it must not be eaten."

The Sin Offering

[24]The LORD said to Moses, [25]"Say to Aaron and his sons: 'These are the regulations for the sin offering: The sin offering is to be slaughtered before the LORD in the place the burnt offering is slaughtered; it is most holy. [26]The priest who offers it shall eat it; it is to be eaten in a holy place, in the courtyard of the Tent of Meeting. [27]Whatever touches any of the flesh will become holy, and if any of the blood is spattered on a garment, you must wash it in a holy place. [28]The clay pot the meat is cooked in must be broken; but if it is cooked in a bronze pot, the pot is to be scoured and rinsed with water. [29]Any male in a priest's family may eat it; it is most holy. [30]But any sin offering whose blood is brought into the Tent of Meeting to make atonement in the Holy Place must not be eaten; it must be burned.

The Guilt Offering

7 " 'These are the regulations for the guilt offering, which is most holy: [2]The guilt offering is to be slaughtered in the place where the burnt offering is slaughtered, and its blood is to be sprinkled against the altar on all sides. [3]All its fat shall be offered: the fat tail and the fat that covers the inner parts, [4]both kidneys with the fat on them near the loins, and the covering of the liver, which is to be removed with the kidneys. [5]The priest shall burn them on the altar as an offering made to the LORD by fire. It is a

guilt offering. [6]Any male in a priest's family may eat it, but it must be eaten in a holy place; it is most holy.

[7]" 'The same law applies to both the sin offering and the guilt offering: They belong to the priest who makes atonement with them. [8]The priest who offers a burnt offering for anyone may keep its hide for himself. [9]Every grain offering baked in an oven or cooked in a pan or on a griddle belongs to the priest who offers it, [10]and every grain offering, whether mixed with oil or dry, belongs equally to all the sons of Aaron.

The Fellowship Offering

[11]" 'These are the regulations for the fellowship offering[e] a person may present to the LORD:

[12]" 'If he offers it as an expression of thankfulness, then along with this thank offering he is to offer cakes of bread made without yeast and mixed with oil, wafers made without yeast and spread with oil, and cakes of fine flour well-kneaded and mixed with oil. [13]Along with his fellowship offering of thanksgiving he is to present an offering with cakes of bread made with yeast. [14]He is to bring one of each kind as an offering, a contribution to the LORD; it belongs to the priest who sprinkles the blood of the fellowship offerings. [15]The meat of his fellowship offering of thanksgiving must be eaten on the day it is offered; he must leave none of it till morning.

[16]" 'If, however, his offering is the result of a vow or is a freewill offering, the sacrifice shall be eaten on the day he offers it, but anything left over may be eaten on the next day. [17]Any meat of the sacrifice left over till the third day must be burned up. [18]If any meat of the fellowship offering is eaten on the third day, it will not be accepted. It will not be credited to the one who offered it, for it is impure; the person who eats any of it will be held responsible.

[19]" 'Meat that touches anything ceremonially unclean must not be eaten; it must be burned up. As for other meat, anyone ceremonially clean may eat it. [20]But if anyone who is unclean eats any

---

a 18 Or *Whoever touches them must be holy*; similarly in verse 27　*b 20* Or *each*　*c 20* That is, probably about 2 quarts (about 2 liters)　*d 21* The meaning of the Hebrew for this word is uncertain.　*e 11* Traditionally *peace offering*; also in verses 13–37 meat of the fellowship offering belonging to the LORD, that person must be cut off from his people. ²¹If anyone touches something unclean—whether human uncleanness or an unclean animal or any unclean, detestable thing—and then eats any of the meat of the fellowship offering belonging to the LORD, that person must be cut off from his people.' "

Eating Fat and Blood Forbidden

²²The LORD said to Moses, ²³"Say to the Israelites: 'Do not eat any of the fat of cattle, sheep or goats. ²⁴The fat of an animal found dead or torn by wild animals may be used for any other purpose, but you must not eat it. ²⁵Anyone who eats the fat of an animal from which an offering by fire may be ᵃ made to the LORD must be cut off from his people. ²⁶And wherever you live, you must not eat the blood of any bird or animal. ²⁷If anyone eats blood, that person must be cut off from his people.' "

The Priests' Share

²⁸The LORD said to Moses, ²⁹"Say to the Israelites: 'Anyone who brings a fellowship offering to the LORD is to bring part of it as his sacrifice to the LORD. ³⁰With his own hands he is to bring the offering made to the LORD by fire; he is to bring the fat, together with the breast, and wave the breast before the LORD as a wave offering. ³¹The priest shall burn the fat on the altar, but the breast belongs to Aaron and his sons. ³²You are to give the right thigh of your fellowship offerings to the priest as a contribution. ³³The son of Aaron who offers the blood and the fat of the fellowship offering shall have the right thigh as his share. ³⁴From the fellowship offerings of the Israelites, I have taken the breast that is waved and the thigh that is presented and have given them to Aaron the priest and his sons as their regular share from the Israelites.' "

³⁵This is the portion of the offerings made to the LORD by fire that were allotted to Aaron and his sons on the day they were presented to serve the LORD as priests. ³⁶On the day they were anointed,

ᵃ 25 Or fire is

Their Regular Share

READ LEVITICUS 7:28–38

Joke: Some boys were bragging about how much money their fathers made. After they had finished, the pastor's son said, "My dad talks for twenty minutes and makes so much money that it takes four guys to bring it to him." Pastors actually *don't* get all the money in the offering baskets. But they do deserve to get *some*. Why? Because that's the way God set things up. Leviticus 7:34 says that God gave part of the Israelites' offerings to the priests "as their regular share from the Israelites." That was how things worked in the Old Testament, and though we now live in the New Testament age, God's church has some real financial needs, too. As you start to earn your own money, remember, it's a man's responsibility to support his family, to help in the community and—very importantly—to support his church.

Your next reading is on page 148.

the LORD commanded that the Israelites give this to them as their regular share for the generations to come.

37These, then, are the regulations for the burnt offering, the grain offering, the sin offering, the guilt offering, the ordination offering and the fellowship offering, 38which the LORD gave Moses on Mount Sinai on the day he commanded the Israelites to bring their offerings to the LORD, in the Desert of Sinai.

The Ordination of Aaron and His Sons

The LORD said to Moses, 2"Bring Aaron and his sons, their garments, the anointing oil, the bull for the sin offering, the two rams and the basket containing bread made without yeast, 3and gather the entire assembly at the entrance to the Tent of Meeting." 4Moses did as the LORD commanded him, and the assembly gathered at the entrance to the Tent of Meeting.

5Moses said to the assembly, "This is what the LORD has commanded to be done." 6Then Moses brought Aaron and his sons forward and washed them with water. 7He put the tunic on Aaron, tied the sash around him, clothed him with the robe and put the ephod on him. He also tied the ephod to him by its skillfully woven waistband; so it was fastened on him. 8He placed the breastpiece on him and put the Urim and Thummim in the breastpiece. 9Then he placed the turban on Aaron's head and set the gold plate, the sacred diadem, on the front of it, as the LORD commanded Moses.

10Then Moses took the anointing oil and anointed the tabernacle and everything in it, and so consecrated them. 11He sprinkled some of the oil on the altar seven times, anointing the altar and all its utensils and the basin with its stand, to consecrate them. 12He poured some of the anointing oil on Aaron's head and anointed him to consecrate him. 13Then he brought Aaron's sons forward, put tunics on them, tied sashes around them and put headbands on them, as the LORD commanded Moses.

14He then presented the bull for the sin offering, and Aaron and his sons laid their hands on its head. 15Moses slaughtered the bull and took some of the blood, and with his finger he put it on all the horns of the altar to purify the altar. He poured out the rest of the blood at the base of the altar. So he consecrated it to make atonement for it. 16Moses also took all the fat around the inner parts, the covering of the liver, and both kidneys and their fat, and burned it on the altar. 17But the bull with its hide and its flesh and its offal he burned up outside the camp, as the LORD commanded Moses.

18He then presented the ram for the burnt offering, and Aaron and his sons laid their hands on its head. 19Then Moses slaughtered the ram and sprinkled the blood against the altar on all sides. 20He cut the ram into pieces and burned the head, the pieces and the fat. 21He washed the inner parts and the legs with water and burned the whole ram on the altar as a burnt offering, a pleasing aroma, an offering made to the LORD by fire, as the LORD commanded Moses.

22He then presented the other ram, the ram for the ordination, and Aaron and his sons laid their hands on its head. 23Moses slaughtered the ram and took some of its blood and put it on the lobe of Aaron's right ear, on the thumb of his right hand and on the big toe of his right foot. 24Moses also brought Aaron's sons forward and put some of the blood on the lobes of their right ears, on the thumbs of their right hands and on the big toes of their right feet. Then he sprinkled blood against the altar on all sides. 25He took the fat, the fat tail, all the fat around the inner parts, the covering of the liver, both kidneys and their fat and the right thigh. 26Then from the basket of bread made without yeast, which was before the LORD, he took a cake of bread, and one made with oil, and a wafer; he put these on the fat portions and on the right thigh. 27He put all these in the hands of Aaron and his sons and waved them before the LORD as a wave offering. 28Then Moses took them from their hands and burned them on the altar on top of the burnt offering as an ordination offering, a pleasing aroma, an offering made to the LORD by fire. 29He also took the breast—Moses' share of the ordination ram—and waved it before the LORD as a wave offering, as the LORD commanded Moses.

30Then Moses took some of the anointing oil and some of the blood from the altar and sprinkled them on Aaron and his garments and on his sons and their garments. So he consecrated Aaron and his garments and his sons and their garments.

[31] Moses then said to Aaron and his sons, "Cook the meat at the entrance to the Tent of Meeting and eat it there with the bread from the basket of ordination offerings, as I commanded, saying,[a] 'Aaron and his sons are to eat it.' [32] Then burn up the rest of the meat and the bread. [33] Do not leave the entrance to the Tent of Meeting for seven days, until the days of your ordination are completed, for your ordination will last seven days. [34] What has been done today was commanded by the LORD to make atonement for you. [35] You must stay at the entrance to the Tent of Meeting day and night for seven days and do what the LORD requires, so you will not die; for that is what I have been commanded." [36] So Aaron and his sons did everything the LORD commanded through Moses.

The Priests Begin Their Ministry

On the eighth day Moses summoned Aaron and his sons and the elders of Israel. [2] He said to Aaron, "Take a bull calf for your sin offering and a ram for your burnt offering, both without defect, and present them before the LORD. [3] Then say to the Israelites: 'Take a male goat for a sin offering, a calf and a lamb—both a year old and without defect—for a burnt offering, [4] and an ox[b] and a ram for a fellowship offering[c] to sacrifice before the LORD, together with a grain offering mixed with oil. For today the LORD will appear to you.' "

[5] They took the things Moses commanded to the front of the Tent of Meeting, and the entire assembly came near and stood before the LORD. [6] Then Moses said, "This is what the LORD has commanded you to do, so that the glory of the LORD may appear to you."

[7] Moses said to Aaron, "Come to the altar and sacrifice your sin offering and your burnt offering and make atonement for yourself and the people; sacrifice the offering that is for the people and make atonement for them, as the LORD has commanded."

[8] So Aaron came to the altar and slaughtered the calf as a sin offering for himself. [9] His sons brought the blood to him, and he dipped his finger into the blood and put it on the horns of the altar; the rest of the blood he poured out at the base of the altar. [10] On the altar he burned the fat, the kidneys and the covering of the liver from the sin offering, as the LORD commanded Moses; [11] the flesh and the hide he burned up outside the camp.

[12] Then he slaughtered the burnt offering. His sons handed him the blood, and he sprinkled it against the altar on all sides. [13] They handed him the burnt offering piece by piece, including the head, and he burned them on the altar. [14] He washed the inner parts and the legs and burned them on top of the burnt offering on the altar.

[15] Aaron then brought the offering that was for the people. He took the goat for the people's sin offering and slaughtered it and offered it for a sin offering as he did with the first one.

[16] He brought the burnt offering and offered it in the prescribed way. [17] He also brought the grain offering, took a handful of it and burned it on the altar in addition to the morning's burnt offering.

[18] He slaughtered the ox and the ram as the fellowship offering for the people. His sons handed him the blood, and he sprinkled it against the altar on all sides. [19] But the fat portions of the ox and the ram— the fat tail, the layer of fat, the kidneys and the covering of the liver— [20] these they laid on the breasts, and then Aaron burned the fat on the altar. [21] Aaron waved the breasts and the right thigh before the LORD as a wave offering, as Moses commanded.

[22] Then Aaron lifted his hands toward the people and blessed them. And having sacrificed the sin offering, the burnt offering and the fellowship offering, he stepped down.

[23] Moses and Aaron then went into the Tent of Meeting. When they came out, they blessed the people; and the glory of the LORD appeared to all the people. [24] Fire came out from the presence of the LORD and consumed the burnt offering and the fat portions on the altar. And when all the people saw it, they shouted for joy and fell facedown.

---

[a] 31 Or I was commanded: [b] 4 The Hebrew word can include both male and female; also in verses 18 and 19.   [c] 4 Traditionally peace offering; also in verses 18 and 22

The Death of Nadab and Abihu

10 Aaron's sons Nadab and Abihu took their censers, put fire in them and added incense; and they offered unauthorized fire before the LORD, contrary to his command. ²So fire came out from the presence of the LORD and consumed them, and they died before the LORD. ³Moses then said to Aaron, "This is what the LORD spoke of when he said:

" 'Among those who approach me
   I will show myself holy;
in the sight of all the people
   I will be honored.' "

Aaron remained silent.

⁴Moses summoned Mishael and Elzaphan, sons of Aaron's uncle Uzziel, and said to them, "Come here; carry your cousins outside the camp, away from the front of the sanctuary." ⁵So they came and carried them, still in their tunics, outside the camp, as Moses ordered.

⁶Then Moses said to Aaron and his sons Eleazar and Ithamar, "Do not let your hair become unkempt,ᵃ and do not tear your clothes, or you will die and the LORD will be angry with the whole community. But your relatives, all the house of Israel, may mourn for those the LORD has destroyed by fire. ⁷Do not leave the entrance to the Tent of Meeting or you will die, because the LORD's anointing oil is on you." So they did as Moses said.

⁸Then the LORD said to Aaron, ⁹"You and your sons are not to drink wine or other fermented drink whenever you go into the Tent of Meeting, or you will die. This is a lasting ordinance for the generations to come. ¹⁰You must distinguish between the holy and the common, between the unclean and the clean, ¹¹and you must teach the Israelites all the decrees the LORD has given them through Moses."

¹²Moses said to Aaron and his remaining sons, Eleazar and Ithamar, "Take the grain offering left over from the offerings made to the LORD by fire and eat it prepared without yeast beside the altar, for it is most holy. ¹³Eat it in a holy place, be-

ᵃ 6 Or Do not uncover your heads

Playing With Fire

READ LEVITICUS 10:1–11

When "fire came out from the . . . LORD" and burned the sacrifices, all the Israelites were amazed and worshiped God (Leviticus 9:24). Yet right afterwards, Aaron's two sons, Nadab and Abihu, served God . . . "contrary to his command" (Leviticus 10:1). Hey! These guys *knew* better, yet they resisted obeying God. Didn't they take God seriously? Small surprise that once again "fire came out from the . . . LORD." Only this time it toasted *them!* Now, this was a special case of divine judgment. We're God's children and we don't have to wear asbestos suits to church. He is *not* going to send fire out of the pastor's pulpit to burn us when we blow it. But God does want us to live his way and receive his blessings. So let's not just go through the motions and play at church. Let's take our faith seriously.

Your next reading is on page 156.

cause it is your share and your sons' share of the offerings made to the LORD by fire; for so I have been commanded. 14But you and your sons and your daughters may eat the breast that was waved and the thigh that was presented. Eat them in a ceremonially clean place; they have been given to you and your children as your share of the Israelites' fellowship offerings.ᵃ 15The thigh that was presented and the breast that was waved must be brought with the fat portions of the offerings made by fire, to be waved before the LORD as a wave offering. This will be the regular share for you and your children, as the LORD has commanded."

16When Moses inquired about the goat of the sin offering and found that it had been burned up, he was angry with Eleazar and Ithamar, Aaron's remaining sons, and asked, 17"Why didn't you eat the sin offering in the sanctuary area? It is most holy; it was given to you to take away the guilt of the community by making atonement for them before the LORD. 18Since its blood was not taken into the Holy Place, you should have eaten the goat in the sanctuary area, as I commanded."

19Aaron replied to Moses, "Today they sacrificed their sin offering and their burnt offering before the LORD, but such things as this have happened to me. Would the LORD have been pleased if I had eaten the sin offering today?" 20When Moses heard this, he was satisfied.

Clean and Unclean Food

11 The LORD said to Moses and Aaron, 2"Say to the Israelites: 'Of all the animals that live on land, these are the ones you may eat: 3You may eat any animal that has a split hoof completely divided and that chews the cud.

4" 'There are some that only chew the cud or only have a split hoof, but you must not eat them. The camel, though it chews the cud, does not have a split hoof; it is ceremonially unclean for you. 5The coney,ᵇ though it chews the cud, does not have a split hoof; it is unclean for you. 6The rabbit, though it chews the cud, does not have a split hoof; it is unclean for you. 7And the pig, though it has a split hoof completely divided, does not chew the cud; it is unclean for you. 8You must not eat their meat or touch their carcasses; they are unclean for you.

9" 'Of all the creatures living in the water of the seas and the streams, you may eat any that have fins and scales. 10But all creatures in the seas or streams that do not have fins and scales—whether among all the swarming things or among all the other living creatures in the water—you are to detest. 11And since you are to detest them, you must not eat their meat and you must detest their carcasses. 12Anything living in the water that does not have fins and scales is to be detestable to you.

13" 'These are the birds you are to detest and not eat because they are detestable: the eagle, the vulture, the

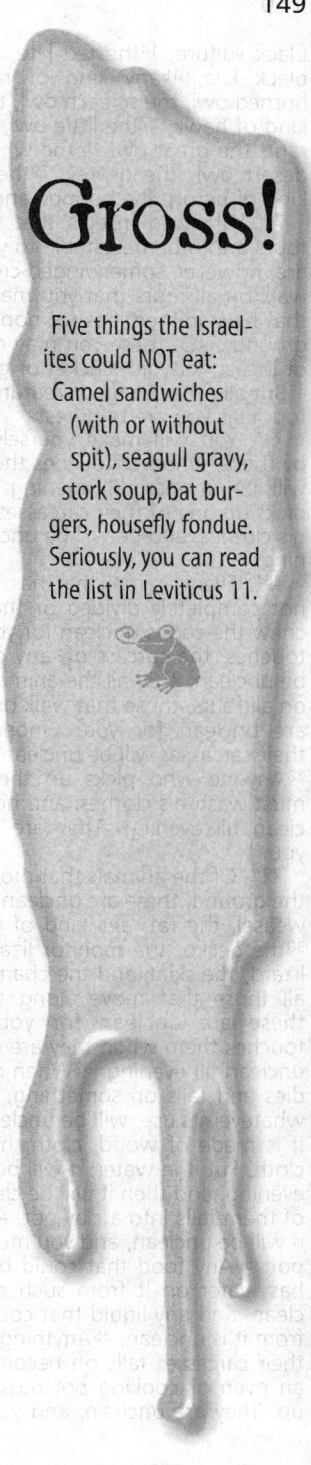

Gross!

Five things the Israelites could NOT eat: Camel sandwiches (with or without spit), seagull gravy, stork soup, bat burgers, housefly fondue. Seriously, you can read the list in Leviticus 11.

ᵃ 14 Traditionally *peace offerings*   ᵇ 5 That is, the hyrax or rock badger black vulture, [14]the red kite, any kind of black kite, [15]any kind of raven, [16]the horned owl, the screech owl, the gull, any kind of hawk, [17]the little owl, the cormorant, the great owl, [18]the white owl, the desert owl, the osprey, [19]the stork, any kind of heron, the hoopoe and the bat.[a]

[20]" 'All flying insects that walk on all fours are to be detestable to you. [21]There are, however, some winged creatures that walk on all fours that you may eat: those that have jointed legs for hopping on the ground. [22]Of these you may eat any kind of locust, katydid, cricket or grasshopper. [23]But all other winged creatures that have four legs you are to detest.

[24]" 'You will make yourselves unclean by these; whoever touches their carcasses will be unclean till evening. [25]Whoever picks up one of their carcasses must wash his clothes, and he will be unclean till evening.

[26]" 'Every animal that has a split hoof not completely divided or that does not chew the cud is unclean for you; whoever touches ∟the carcass of⌟ any of them will be unclean. [27]Of all the animals that walk on all fours, those that walk on their paws are unclean for you; whoever touches their carcasses will be unclean till evening. [28]Anyone who picks up their carcasses must wash his clothes, and he will be unclean till evening. They are unclean for you.

[29]" 'Of the animals that move about on the ground, these are unclean for you: the weasel, the rat, any kind of great lizard, [30]the gecko, the monitor lizard, the wall lizard, the skink and the chameleon. [31]Of all those that move along the ground, these are unclean for you. Whoever touches them when they are dead will be unclean till evening. [32]When one of them dies and falls on something, that article, whatever its use, will be unclean, whether it is made of wood, cloth, hide or sackcloth. Put it in water; it will be unclean till evening, and then it will be clean. [33]If one of them falls into a clay pot, everything in it will be unclean, and you must break the pot. [34]Any food that could be eaten but has water on it from such a pot is unclean, and any liquid that could be drunk from it is unclean. [35]Anything that one of their carcasses falls on becomes unclean; an oven or cooking pot must be broken up. They are unclean, and you are to re-

gard them as unclean. [36]A spring, however, or a cistern for collecting water remains clean, but anyone who touches one of these carcasses is unclean. [37]If a carcass falls on any seeds that are to be planted, they remain clean. [38]But if water has been put on the seed and a carcass falls on it, it is unclean for you.

[39]" 'If an animal that you are allowed to eat dies, anyone who touches the carcass will be unclean till evening. [40]Anyone who eats some of the carcass must wash his clothes, and he will be unclean till evening. Anyone who picks up the carcass must wash his clothes, and he will be unclean till evening.

[41]" 'Every creature that moves about on the ground is detestable; it is not to be eaten. [42]You are not to eat any creature that moves about on the ground, whether it moves on its belly or walks on all fours or on many feet; it is detestable. [43]Do not defile yourselves by any of these creatures. Do not make yourselves unclean by means of them or be made unclean by them. [44]I am the LORD your God; consecrate yourselves and be holy, because I am holy. Do not make yourselves unclean by any creature that moves about on the ground. [45]I am the LORD who brought you up out of Egypt to be your God; therefore be holy, because I am holy.

[46]" 'These are the regulations concerning animals, birds, every living thing that moves in the water and every creature that moves about on the ground. [47]You must distinguish between the unclean and the clean, between living creatures that may be eaten and those that may not be eaten.' "

Purification After Childbirth

12 The LORD said to Moses, [2]"Say to the Israelites: 'A woman who becomes pregnant and gives birth to a son will be ceremonially unclean for seven days, just as she is unclean during her monthly period. [3]On the eighth day the boy is to be circumcised. [4]Then the woman must wait thirty-three days to be purified from her bleeding. She must not touch anything sacred or go to the sanctuary until the days of her purification are over. [5]If she gives birth to a

---

[a] 19 The precise identification of some of the birds, insects and animals in this chapter is uncertain.

daughter, for two weeks the woman will be unclean, as during her period. Then she must wait sixty-six days to be purified from her bleeding.

6" 'When the days of her purification for a son or daughter are over, she is to bring to the priest at the entrance to the Tent of Meeting a year-old lamb for a burnt offering and a young pigeon or a dove for a sin offering. 7He shall offer them before the LORD to make atonement for her, and then she will be ceremonially clean from her flow of blood.

" 'These are the regulations for the woman who gives birth to a boy or a girl. 8If she cannot afford a lamb, she is to bring two doves or two young pigeons, one for a burnt offering and the other for a sin offering. In this way the priest will make atonement for her, and she will be clean.' "

Regulations About Infectious Skin Diseases

13 The LORD said to Moses and Aaron, 2"When anyone has a swelling or a rash or a bright spot on his skin that may become an infectious skin disease,a he must be brought to Aaron the priest or to one of his sonsb who is a priest. 3The priest is to examine the sore on his skin, and if the hair in the sore has turned white and the sore appears to be more than skin deep,c it is an infectious skin disease. When the priest examines him, he shall pronounce him ceremonially unclean. 4If the spot on his skin is white but does not appear to be more than skin deep and the hair in it has not turned white, the priest is to put the infected person in isolation for seven days. 5On the seventh day the priest is to examine him, and if he sees that the sore is unchanged and has not spread in the skin, he is to keep him in isolation another seven days. 6On the seventh day the priest is to examine him again, and if the sore has faded and has not spread in the skin, the priest shall pronounce him clean; it is only a rash. The man must wash his clothes, and he will be clean. 7But if the rash does spread in his skin after he has shown himself to the priest to be pronounced clean, he must appear before the priest again. 8The priest is to examine him, and if the rash has spread in the skin, he shall pro-

nounce him unclean; it is an infectious disease.

9"When anyone has an infectious skin disease, he must be brought to the priest. 10The priest is to examine him, and if there is a white swelling in the skin that has turned the hair white and if there is raw flesh in the swelling, 11it is a chronic skin disease and the priest shall pronounce him unclean. He is not to put him in isolation, because he is already unclean.

12"If the disease breaks out all over his skin and, so far as the priest can see, it covers all the skin of the infected person from head to foot, 13the priest is to examine him, and if the disease has covered his whole body, he shall pronounce that person clean. Since it has all turned white, he is clean. 14But whenever raw flesh appears on him, he will be unclean. 15When the priest sees the raw flesh, he shall pronounce him unclean. The raw flesh is unclean; he has an infectious disease. 16Should the raw flesh change and turn white, he must go to the priest. 17The priest is to examine him, and if the sores have turned white, the priest shall pronounce the infected person clean; then he will be clean.

18"When someone has a boil on his skin and it heals, 19and in the place where the boil was, a white swelling or reddish-white spot appears, he must present himself to the priest. 20The priest is to examine it, and if it appears to be more than skin deep and the hair in it has turned white, the priest shall pronounce him unclean. It is an infectious skin disease that has broken out where the boil was. 21But if, when the priest examines it, there is no white hair in it and it is not more than skin deep and has faded, then the priest is to put him in isolation for seven days. 22If it is spreading in the skin, the priest shall pronounce him unclean; it is infectious. 23But if the spot is unchanged and has not spread, it is only a scar from the boil, and the priest shall pronounce him clean.

24"When someone has a burn on his skin and a reddish-white or white spot appears in the raw flesh of the burn, 25the priest is to examine the spot, and if the

---

a 2 Traditionally *leprosy*; the Hebrew word was used for various diseases affecting the skin—not necessarily leprosy; also elsewhere in this chapter. b 2 Or *descendants* c 3 Or *be lower than the rest of the skin*; also elsewhere in this chapter hair in it has turned white, and it appears to be more than skin deep, it is an infectious disease that has broken out in the burn. The priest shall pronounce him unclean; it is an infectious skin disease. 26But if the priest examines it and there is no white hair in the spot and if it is not more than skin deep and has faded, then the priest is to put him in isolation for seven days. 27On the seventh day the priest is to examine him, and if it is spreading in the skin, the priest shall pronounce him unclean; it is an infectious skin disease. 28If, however, the spot is unchanged and has not spread in the skin but has faded, it is a swelling from the burn, and the priest shall pronounce him clean; it is only a scar from the burn.

29"If a man or woman has a sore on the head or on the chin, 30the priest is to examine the sore, and if it appears to be more than skin deep and the hair in it is yellow and thin, the priest shall pronounce that person unclean; it is an itch, an infectious disease of the head or chin. 31But if, when the priest examines this kind of sore, it does not seem to be more than skin deep and there is no black hair in it, then the priest is to put the infected person in isolation for seven days. 32On the seventh day the priest is to examine the sore, and if the itch has not spread and there is no yellow hair in it and it does not appear to be more than skin deep, 33he must be shaved except for the diseased area, and the priest is to keep him in isolation another seven days. 34On the seventh day the priest is to examine the itch, and if it has not spread in the skin and appears to be no more than skin deep, the priest shall pronounce him clean. He must wash his clothes, and he will be clean. 35But if the itch does spread in the skin after he is pronounced clean, 36the priest is to examine him, and if the itch has spread in the skin, the priest does not need to look for yellow hair; the person is unclean. 37If, however, in his judgment it is unchanged and black hair has grown in it, the itch is healed. He is clean, and the priest shall pronounce him clean.

38"When a man or woman has white spots on the skin, 39the priest is to examine them, and if the spots are dull white, it is a harmless rash that has broken out on the skin; that person is clean.

40"When a man has lost his hair and is bald, he is clean. 41If he has lost his hair from the front of his scalp and has a bald forehead, he is clean. 42But if he has a reddish-white sore on his bald head or forehead, it is an infectious disease breaking out on his head or forehead. 43The priest is to examine him, and if the swollen sore on his head or forehead is reddish-white like an infectious skin disease, 44the man is diseased and is unclean. The priest shall pronounce him unclean because of the sore on his head.

45"The person with such an infectious disease must wear torn clothes, let his hair be unkempt,a cover the lower part of his face and cry out, 'Unclean! Unclean!' 46As long as he has the infection he remains unclean. He must live alone; he must live outside the camp.

Regulations About Mildew

47"If any clothing is contaminated with mildew—any woolen or linen clothing, 48any woven or knitted material of linen or wool, any leather or anything made of leather— 49and if the contamination in the clothing, or leather, or woven or knitted material, or any leather article, is greenish or reddish, it is a spreading mildew and must be shown to the priest. 50The priest is to examine the mildew and isolate the affected article for seven days. 51On the seventh day he is to examine it, and if the mildew has spread in the clothing, or the woven or knitted material, or the leather, whatever its use, it is a destructive mildew; the article is unclean. 52He must burn up the clothing, or the woven or knitted material of wool or linen, or any leather article that has the contamination in it, because the mildew is destructive; the article must be burned up.

53"But if, when the priest examines it, the mildew has not spread in the clothing, or the woven or knitted material, or the leather article, 54he shall order that the contaminated article be washed. Then he is to isolate it for another seven days. 55After the affected article has been washed, the priest is to examine it, and if the mildew has not changed its appearance, even though it has not spread, it is unclean. Burn it with fire, whether the mildew has affected one side or the other. 56If, when the priest examines it, the mil-

a 45 Or clothes, uncover his head

dew has faded after the article has been washed, he is to tear the contaminated part out of the clothing, or the leather, or the woven or knitted material. ⁵⁷But if it reappears in the clothing, or in the woven or knitted material, or in the leather article, it is spreading, and whatever has the mildew must be burned with fire. ⁵⁸The clothing, or the woven or knitted material, or any leather article that has been washed and is rid of the mildew, must be washed again, and it will be clean."

⁵⁹These are the regulations concerning contamination by mildew in woolen or linen clothing, woven or knitted material, or any leather article, for pronouncing them clean or unclean.

Cleansing From Infectious Skin Diseases

14 The LORD said to Moses, ²"These are the regulations for the diseased person at the time of his ceremonial cleansing, when he is brought to the priest: ³The priest is to go outside the camp and examine him. If the person has been healed of his infectious skin disease,ª ⁴the priest shall order that two live clean birds and some cedar wood, scarlet yarn and hyssop be brought for the one to be cleansed. ⁵Then the priest shall order that one of the birds be killed over fresh water in a clay pot. ⁶He is then to take the live bird and dip it, together with the cedar wood, the scarlet yarn and the hyssop, into the blood of the bird that was killed over the fresh water. ⁷Seven times he shall sprinkle the one to be cleansed of the infectious disease and pronounce him clean. Then he is to release the live bird in the open fields.

⁸"The person to be cleansed must wash his clothes, shave off all his hair and bathe with water; then he will be ceremonially clean. After this he may come into the camp, but he must stay outside his tent for seven days. ⁹On the seventh day he must shave off all his hair; he must shave his head, his beard, his eyebrows and the rest of his hair. He must wash his clothes and bathe himself with water, and he will be clean.

¹⁰"On the eighth day he must bring two male lambs and one ewe lamb a year old, each without defect, along with three-tenths of an ephahᵇ of fine flour mixed with oil for a grain offering, and one logᶜ of oil. ¹¹The priest who pro-

nounces him clean shall present both the one to be cleansed and his offerings before the LORD at the entrance to the Tent of Meeting.

¹²"Then the priest is to take one of the male lambs and offer it as a guilt offering, along with the log of oil; he shall wave them before the LORD as a wave offering. ¹³He is to slaughter the lamb in the holy place where the sin offering and the burnt offering are slaughtered. Like the sin offering, the guilt offering belongs to the priest; it is most holy. ¹⁴The priest is to take some of the blood of the guilt offering and put it on the lobe of the right ear of the one to be cleansed, on the thumb of his right hand and on the big toe of his right foot. ¹⁵The priest shall then take some of the log of oil, pour it in the palm of his own left hand, ¹⁶dip his right forefinger into the oil in his palm, and with his finger sprinkle some of it before the LORD seven times. ¹⁷The priest is to put some of the oil remaining in his palm on the lobe of the right ear of the one to be cleansed, on the thumb of his right hand and on the big toe of his right foot, on top of the blood of the guilt offering. ¹⁸The rest of the oil in his palm the priest shall put on the head of the one to be cleansed and make atonement for him before the LORD.

¹⁹"Then the priest is to sacrifice the sin offering and make atonement for the one to be cleansed from his uncleanness. After that, the priest shall slaughter the burnt offering ²⁰and offer it on the altar, together with the grain offering, and make atonement for him, and he will be clean.

²¹"If, however, he is poor and cannot afford these, he must take one male lamb as a guilt offering to be waved to make atonement for him, together with a tenth of an ephahᵈ of fine flour mixed with oil for a grain offering, a log of oil, ²²and two doves or two young pigeons, which he can afford, one for a sin offering and the other for a burnt offering.

²³"On the eighth day he must bring them for his cleansing to the priest at the entrance to the Tent of Meeting, before the LORD. ²⁴The priest is to take the lamb

---

ª 3 Traditionally *leprosy*; the Hebrew word was used for various diseases affecting the skin—not necessarily leprosy; also elsewhere in this chapter.   ᵇ 10 That is, probably about 6 quarts (about 6.5 liters)   ᶜ 10 That is, probably about 2/3 pint (about 0.3 liter); also in verses 12, 15, 21 and 24   ᵈ 21 That is, probably about 2 quarts (about 2 liters) for the guilt offering, together with the log of oil, and wave them before the LORD as a wave offering. ²⁵He shall slaughter the lamb for the guilt offering and take some of its blood and put it on the lobe of the right ear of the one to be cleansed, on the thumb of his right hand and on the big toe of his right foot. ²⁶The priest is to pour some of the oil into the palm of his own left hand, ²⁷and with his right forefinger sprinkle some of the oil from his palm seven times before the LORD. ²⁸Some of the oil in his palm he is to put on the same places he put the blood of the guilt offering—on the lobe of the right ear of the one to be cleansed, on the thumb of his right hand and on the big toe of his right foot. ²⁹The rest of the oil in his palm the priest shall put on the head of the one to be cleansed, to make atonement for him before the LORD. ³⁰Then he shall sacrifice the doves or the young pigeons, which the person can afford, ³¹one^a as a sin offering and the other as a burnt offering, together with the grain offering. In this way the priest will make atonement before the LORD on behalf of the one to be cleansed."

³²These are the regulations for anyone who has an infectious skin disease and who cannot afford the regular offerings for his cleansing.

Cleansing From Mildew

³³The LORD said to Moses and Aaron, ³⁴"When you enter the land of Canaan, which I am giving you as your possession, and I put a spreading mildew in a house in that land, ³⁵the owner of the house must go and tell the priest, 'I have seen something that looks like mildew in my house.' ³⁶The priest is to order the house to be emptied before he goes in to examine the mildew, so that nothing in the house will be pronounced unclean. After this the priest is to go in and inspect the house. ³⁷He is to examine the mildew on the walls, and if it has greenish or reddish depressions that appear to be deeper than the surface of the wall, ³⁸the priest shall go out the doorway of the house and close it up for seven days. ³⁹On the seventh day the priest shall return to inspect the house. If the mildew has spread on the walls, ⁴⁰he is to order that the contaminated stones be torn out and thrown into an unclean place outside the town.

⁴¹He must have all the inside walls of the house scraped and the material that is scraped off dumped into an unclean place outside the town. ⁴²Then they are to take other stones to replace these and take new clay and plaster the house.

⁴³"If the mildew reappears in the house after the stones have been torn out and the house scraped and plastered, ⁴⁴the priest is to go and examine it and, if the mildew has spread in the house, it is a destructive mildew; the house is unclean. ⁴⁵It must be torn down—its stones, timbers and all the plaster—and taken out of the town to an unclean place.

⁴⁶"Anyone who goes into the house while it is closed up will be unclean till evening. ⁴⁷Anyone who sleeps or eats in the house must wash his clothes.

⁴⁸"But if the priest comes to examine it and the mildew has not spread after the house has been plastered, he shall pronounce the house clean, because the mildew is gone. ⁴⁹To purify the house he is to take two birds and some cedar wood, scarlet yarn and hyssop. ⁵⁰He shall kill one of the birds over fresh water in a clay pot. ⁵¹Then he is to take the cedar wood, the hyssop, the scarlet yarn and the live bird, dip them into the blood of the dead bird and the fresh water, and sprinkle the house seven times. ⁵²He shall purify the house with the bird's blood, the fresh water, the live bird, the cedar wood, the hyssop and the scarlet yarn. ⁵³Then he is to release the live bird in the open fields outside the town. In this way he will make atonement for the house, and it will be clean."

⁵⁴These are the regulations for any infectious skin disease, for an itch, ⁵⁵for mildew in clothing or in a house, ⁵⁶and for a swelling, a rash or a bright spot, ⁵⁷to determine when something is clean or unclean.

These are the regulations for infectious skin diseases and mildew.

Discharges Causing Uncleanness

The LORD said to Moses and Aaron, ²"Speak to the Israelites and say to them: 'When any man has a bodily discharge, the discharge is unclean. ³Whether it continues flowing

---

^a 31 Septuagint and Syriac; Hebrew ³¹such as the person can afford, one

from his body or is blocked, it will make him unclean. This is how his discharge will bring about uncleanness:

4 " 'Any bed the man with a discharge lies on will be unclean, and anything he sits on will be unclean. 5Anyone who touches his bed must wash his clothes and bathe with water, and he will be unclean till evening. 6Whoever sits on anything that the man with a discharge sat on must wash his clothes and bathe with water, and he will be unclean till evening.

7 " 'Whoever touches the man who has a discharge must wash his clothes and bathe with water, and he will be unclean till evening.

8 " 'If the man with the discharge spits on someone who is clean, that person must wash his clothes and bathe with water, and he will be unclean till evening.

9 " 'Everything the man sits on when riding will be unclean, 10and whoever touches any of the things that were under him will be unclean till evening; whoever picks up those things must wash his clothes and bathe with water, and he will be unclean till evening.

11 " 'Anyone the man with a discharge

Make It Stick

_____

_____

_____

_____

_____

_____

_____

READ LEVITICUS
14:37–38
Why laws about mildew? Simple. God didn't want the Israelites' houses to look like your bedroom. Write five cleanliness laws God might make about your room. Here are two for starters: "Remove half-eaten plates of food from under your bed." "Don't leave grimy socks laying around more than two days."

touches without rinsing his hands with water must wash his clothes and bathe with water, and he will be unclean till evening.

¹²" 'A clay pot that the man touches must be broken, and any wooden article is to be rinsed with water.

¹³" 'When a man is cleansed from his discharge, he is to count off seven days for his ceremonial cleansing; he must wash his clothes and bathe himself with fresh water, and he will be clean. ¹⁴On the eighth day he must take two doves or two young pigeons and come before the Lord to the entrance to the Tent of Meeting and give them to the priest. ¹⁵The priest is to sacrifice them, the one for a sin offering and the other for a burnt offering. In this way he will make atonement before the Lord for the man because of his discharge.

¹⁶" 'When a man has an emission of semen, he must bathe his whole body with water, and he will be unclean till evening. ¹⁷Any clothing or leather that has semen on it must be washed with water, and it will be unclean till evening. ¹⁸When a man lies with a woman and there is an emission of semen, both must bathe with water, and they will be unclean till evening.

¹⁹" 'When a woman has her regular flow of blood, the impurity of her monthly period will last seven days, and anyone who touches her will be unclean till evening.

²⁰" 'Anything she lies on during her period will be unclean, and anything she sits on will be unclean. ²¹Whoever touches her bed must wash his clothes and bathe with water, and he will be unclean till evening. ²²Whoever touches anything she sits on must wash his clothes and bathe with water, and he will be unclean till evening. ²³Whether it is the bed or anything she was sitting on, when anyone touches it, he will be unclean till evening.

²⁴" 'If a man lies with her and her monthly flow touches him, he will be unclean for seven days; any bed he lies on will be unclean.

²⁵" 'When a woman has a discharge of

GET STRONGER

Thou Shalt Bathe With Water

READ LEVITICUS 15:1–17

Everyone likes a person who keeps himself clean. It's no fun to be around a friend whose armpits stink, right? A long time ago, God gave Moses laws teaching people to wash their bodies. If a man had a bodily discharge he had to "bathe with water" (Leviticus 15:11). These laws made a lot of sense—and Moses didn't even have a microscope or know anything about germs! Is God ahead of the game, or *what*? So after you go to the bathroom, wash your hands in water with lots of soap. It's also a good idea to take a regular bath or shower, and to peel off your grimy, filthy clothes and hurl them to their death down the laundry chute. As you become a man, you need to learn to stay clean. It's bad for germs and good for friendships. Wash your pits and people won't run away.

Your next reading is on page 160.

blood for many days at a time other than her monthly period or has a discharge that continues beyond her period, she will be unclean as long as she has the discharge, just as in the days of her period. 26Any bed she lies on while her discharge continues will be unclean, as is her bed during her monthly period, and anything she sits on will be unclean, as during her period. 27Whoever touches them will be unclean; he must wash his clothes and bathe with water, and he will be unclean till evening.

28" 'When she is cleansed from her discharge, she must count off seven days, and after that she will be ceremonially clean. 29On the eighth day she must take two doves or two young pigeons and bring them to the priest at the entrance to the Tent of Meeting. 30The priest is to sacrifice one for a sin offering and the other for a burnt offering. In this way he will make atonement for her before the LORD for the uncleanness of her discharge.

31" 'You must keep the Israelites separate from things that make them unclean, so they will not die in their uncleanness for defiling my dwelling place,a which is among them.' "

32These are the regulations for a man with a discharge, for anyone made unclean by an emission of semen, 33for a woman in her monthly period, for a man or a woman with a discharge, and for a man who lies with a woman who is ceremonially unclean.

The Day of Atonement

16 The LORD spoke to Moses after the death of the two sons of Aaron who died when they approached the LORD. 2The LORD said to Moses: "Tell your brother Aaron not to come whenever he chooses into the Most Holy Place behind the curtain in front of the atonement cover on the ark, or else he will die, because I appear in the cloud over the atonement cover.

3"This is how Aaron is to enter the sanctuary area: with a young bull for a sin offering and a ram for a burnt offering. 4He is to put on the sacred linen tunic, with linen undergarments next to his body; he is to tie the linen sash around him and put on the linen turban. These are sacred garments; so he must bathe himself with water before he puts them

on. 5From the Israelite community he is to take two male goats for a sin offering and a ram for a burnt offering.

6"Aaron is to offer the bull for his own sin offering to make atonement for himself and his household. 7Then he is to take the two goats and present them before the LORD at the entrance to the Tent of Meeting. 8He is to cast lots for the two goats—one lot for the LORD and the other for the scapegoat.b 9Aaron shall bring the goat whose lot falls to the LORD and sacrifice it for a sin offering. 10But the goat chosen by lot as the scapegoat shall be presented alive before the LORD to be used for making atonement by sending it into the desert as a scapegoat.

11"Aaron shall bring the bull for his own sin offering to make atonement for himself and his household, and he is to slaughter the bull for his own sin offering. 12He is to take a censer full of burning coals from the altar before the LORD and two handfuls of finely ground fragrant incense and take them behind the curtain. 13He is to put the incense on the fire before the LORD, and the smoke of the incense will conceal the atonement cover above the Testimony, so that he will not die. 14He is to take some of the bull's blood and with his finger sprinkle it on the front of the atonement cover; then he shall sprinkle some of it with his finger seven times before the atonement cover.

15"He shall then slaughter the goat for the sin offering for the people and take its blood behind the curtain and do with it as he did with the bull's blood: He shall sprinkle it on the atonement cover and in front of it. 16In this way he will make atonement for the Most Holy Place because of the uncleanness and rebellion of the Israelites, whatever their sins have been. He is to do the same for the Tent of Meeting, which is among them in the midst of their uncleanness. 17No one is to be in the Tent of Meeting from the time Aaron goes in to make atonement in the Most Holy Place until he comes out, having made atonement for himself, his household and the whole community of Israel.

18"Then he shall come out to the altar that is before the LORD and make atonement for it. He shall take some of the

a 31 Or my tabernacle   b 8 That is, the goat of removal; Hebrew azazel; also in verses 10 and 26

Get a Load of This...

Check out Leviticus 16:21– 22. *Scapegoat* means "escape-goat." On the Day of Atonement, goat number one was killed. This goat did not *scape*. The priest confessed Israel's sin over goat number two, then let it *scape* into the desert. It symbolically carried "on itself all their sins."

bull's blood and some of the goat's blood and put it on all the horns of the altar. ¹⁹He shall sprinkle some of the blood on it with his finger seven times to cleanse it and to consecrate it from the uncleanness of the Israelites.

²⁰"When Aaron has finished making atonement for the Most Holy Place, the Tent of Meeting and the altar, he shall bring forward the live goat. ²¹He is to lay both hands on the head of the live goat and confess over it all the wickedness and rebellion of the Israelites—all their sins—and put them on the goat's head. He shall send the goat away into the desert in the care of a man appointed for the task. ²²The goat will carry on itself all their sins to a solitary place; and the man shall release it in the desert.

²³"Then Aaron is to go into the Tent of Meeting and take off the linen garments he put on before he entered the Most Holy Place, and he is to leave them there. ²⁴He shall bathe himself with water in a holy place and put on his regular garments. Then he shall come out and sacrifice the burnt offering for himself and the burnt offering for the people, to make atonement for himself and for the people. ²⁵He shall also burn the fat of the sin offering on the altar.

²⁶"The man who releases the goat as a scapegoat must wash his clothes and bathe himself with water; afterward he may come into the camp. ²⁷The bull and the goat for the sin offerings, whose blood was brought into the Most Holy Place to make atonement, must be taken outside the camp; their hides, flesh and offal are to be burned up. ²⁸The man who burns them must wash his clothes and bathe himself with water; afterward he may come into the camp.

²⁹"This is to be a lasting ordinance for you: On the tenth day of the seventh month you must deny yourselves[a] and not do any work—whether native-born or an alien living among you— ³⁰because on this day atonement will be made for you, to cleanse you. Then, before the LORD, you will be clean from all your sins. ³¹It is a sabbath of rest, and you must deny yourselves; it is a lasting ordinance. ³²The priest who is anointed and ordained to succeed his father as high priest is to make atonement. He is to put on the sacred linen garments ³³and make atonement for the Most Holy Place, for the Tent of Meeting and the altar, and for the priests and all the people of the community.

³⁴"This is to be a lasting ordinance for you: Atonement is to be made once a year for all the sins of the Israelites."

And it was done, as the LORD commanded Moses.

Eating Blood Forbidden

17 The LORD said to Moses, ²"Speak to Aaron and his sons and to all the Israelites and say to them: 'This is what the LORD has commanded: ³Any Israelite who sacrifices an ox,[b] a lamb or

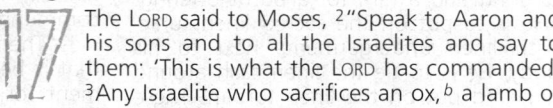

---

[a] 29 Or *must fast*; also in verse 31   [b] 3 The Hebrew word can include both male and female.

a goat in the camp or outside of it [4]instead of bringing it to the entrance to the Tent of Meeting to present it as an offering to the LORD in front of the tabernacle of the LORD—that man shall be considered guilty of bloodshed; he has shed blood and must be cut off from his people. [5]This is so the Israelites will bring to the LORD the sacrifices they are now making in the open fields. They must bring them to the priest, that is, to the LORD, at the entrance to the Tent of Meeting and sacrifice them as fellowship offerings.[a] [6]The priest is to sprinkle the blood against the altar of the LORD at the entrance to the Tent of Meeting and burn the fat as an aroma pleasing to the LORD. [7]They must no longer offer any of their sacrifices to the goat idols[b] to whom they prostitute themselves. This is to be a lasting ordinance for them and for the generations to come.'

[8]"Say to them: 'Any Israelite or any alien living among them who offers a burnt offering or sacrifice [9]and does not bring it to the entrance to the Tent of Meeting to sacrifice it to the LORD—that man must be cut off from his people.

[10]" 'Any Israelite or any alien living among them who eats any blood—I will set my face against that person who eats blood and will cut him off from his people. [11]For the life of a creature is in the blood, and I have given it to you to make atonement for yourselves on the altar; it is the blood that makes atonement for one's life. [12]Therefore I say to the Israelites, "None of you may eat blood, nor may an alien living among you eat blood."

[13]" 'Any Israelite or any alien living among you who hunts any animal or bird that may be eaten must drain out the blood and cover it with earth, [14]because the life of every creature is its blood. That is why I have said to the Israelites, "You must not eat the blood of any creature, because the life of every creature is its blood; anyone who eats it must be cut off."

[15]" 'Anyone, whether native-born or alien, who eats anything found dead or torn by wild animals must wash his clothes and bathe with water, and he will be ceremonially unclean till evening; then he will be clean. [16]But if he does not wash his clothes and bathe himself, he will be held responsible.' "

Unlawful Sexual Relations

18 The LORD said to Moses, [2]"Speak to the Israelites and say to them: 'I am the LORD your God. [3]You must not do as they do in Egypt, where you used to live, and you must not do as they do in the land of Canaan, where I am bringing you. Do not follow their practices. [4]You must obey my laws and be careful to follow my decrees. I am the LORD your God. [5]Keep my decrees and laws, for the man who obeys them will live by them. I am the LORD.

[6]" 'No one is to approach any close relative to have sexual relations. I am the LORD.

[a] 5 Traditionally *peace offerings*   [b] 7 Or *demons*

Leviticus 17:10 sounds kind of like a horror movie. Some horror movies—which we *don't* recommend you watching—show "vampires" drinking blood. God had some rules against snacking on blood. Eating blood? Yuk! How gross! A chocolate milk shake would taste better.

7 " 'Do not dishonor your father by having sexual relations with your mother. She is your mother; do not have relations with her.

8 " 'Do not have sexual relations with your father's wife; that would dishonor your father.

9 " 'Do not have sexual relations with your sister, either your father's daughter or your mother's daughter, whether she was born in the same home or elsewhere.

10 " 'Do not have sexual relations with your son's daughter or your daughter's daughter; that would dishonor you.

11 " 'Do not have sexual relations with the daughter of your father's wife, born to your father; she is your sister.

12 " 'Do not have sexual relations with your father's sister; she is your father's close relative.

13 " 'Do not have sexual relations with your mother's sister, because she is your mother's close relative.

14 " 'Do not dishonor your father's brother by approaching his wife to have sexual relations; she is your aunt.

15 " 'Do not have sexual relations with your daughter-in-law. She is your son's wife; do not have relations with her.

16 " 'Do not have sexual relations with your brother's wife; that would dishonor your brother.

17 " 'Do not have sexual relations with both a woman and her daughter. Do not have sexual relations with either her son's daughter or her daughter's daughter; they are her close relatives. That is wickedness.

18 " 'Do not take your wife's sister as a rival wife and have sexual relations with her while your wife is living.

19 " 'Do not approach a woman to have sexual relations during the uncleanness of her monthly period.

20 " 'Do not have sexual relations with your neighbor's wife and defile yourself with her.

21 " 'Do not give any of your children to

Don't Make Me Hurl!

READ LEVITICUS 18:1–24

Like some boys you may know—many Israelites had picked up some sick attitudes from living in Egypt. On top of that, they were about to move into Canaan, and the Canaanites were even worse! The Canaanites had such perverted attitudes toward sex that "the land vomited out its inhabitants" (Leviticus 18:25). So before the Israelites crossed the Jordan, God laid out some very detailed rules about sexual behavior. He made it clear what was right and what was wrong. God's sexual rules still apply today, so if you're with a crowd of boys who start talking about perverted things, or "talking trash" about women or girls, leave.

Your next reading is on page 162.

GET STRONGER

be sacrificed[a] to Molech, for you must not profane the name of your God. I am the LORD.

22" 'Do not lie with a man as one lies with a woman; that is detestable.

23" 'Do not have sexual relations with an animal and defile yourself with it. A woman must not present herself to an animal to have sexual relations with it; that is a perversion.

24" 'Do not defile yourselves in any of these ways, because this is how the nations that I am going to drive out before you became defiled. 25Even the land was defiled; so I punished it for its sin, and the land vomited out its inhabitants. 26But you must keep my decrees and my laws. The native-born and the aliens living among you must not do any of these detestable things, 27for all these things were done by the people who lived in the land before you, and the land became defiled. 28And if you defile the land, it will vomit you out as it vomited out the nations that were before you.

29" 'Everyone who does any of these detestable things—such persons must be cut off from their people. 30Keep my requirements and do not follow any of the detestable customs that were practiced before you came and do not defile yourselves with them. I am the LORD your God.' "

Various Laws

19 The LORD said to Moses, 2"Speak to the entire assembly of Israel and say to them: 'Be holy because I, the LORD your God, am holy.

3" 'Each of you must respect his mother and father, and you must observe my Sabbaths. I am the LORD your God.

4" 'Do not turn to idols or make gods of cast metal for yourselves. I am the LORD your God.

5" 'When you sacrifice a fellowship offering[b] to the LORD, sacrifice it in such a way that it will be accepted on your behalf. 6It shall be eaten on the day you sacrifice it or on the next day; anything left over until the third day must be burned up. 7If any of it is eaten on the third day, it is impure and will not be accepted. 8Whoever eats it will be held responsible because he has desecrated what is holy to the LORD; that person must be cut off from his people.

9" 'When you reap the harvest of your land, do not reap to the very edges of your field or gather the gleanings of your harvest. 10Do not go over your vineyard a second time or pick up the grapes that have fallen. Leave them for the poor and the alien. I am the LORD your God.

11" 'Do not steal.
" 'Do not lie.
" 'Do not deceive one another.

12" 'Do not swear falsely by my name and so profane the name of your God. I am the LORD.

13" 'Do not defraud your neighbor or rob him.
" 'Do not hold back the wages of a hired man overnight.

14" 'Do not curse the deaf or put a stumbling block in front of the blind, but fear your God. I am the LORD.

15" 'Do not pervert justice; do not show partiality to the poor or favoritism to the great, but judge your neighbor fairly.

16" 'Do not go about spreading slander among your people.
" 'Do not do anything that endangers your neighbor's life. I am the LORD.

17" 'Do not hate your brother in your heart. Rebuke your neighbor frankly so you will not share in his guilt.

18" 'Do not seek revenge or bear a grudge against one of your people, but love your neighbor as yourself. I am the LORD.

19" 'Keep my decrees.
" 'Do not mate different kinds of animals.
" 'Do not plant your field with two kinds of seed.
" 'Do not wear clothing woven of two kinds of material.

20" 'If a man sleeps with a woman who is a slave girl promised to another man but who has not been ransomed or given her freedom, there must be due punishment. Yet they are not to be put to death, because she had not been freed. 21The man, however, must bring a ram to the entrance to the Tent of Meeting for a guilt offering to the LORD. 22With the ram of the guilt offering the priest is to make atonement for him before the LORD for the sin he has committed, and his sin will be forgiven.

a 21 Or to be passed through the fire; b 5 Traditionally peace offering

23 " 'When you enter the land and plant any kind of fruit tree, regard its fruit as forbidden.[a] For three years you are to consider it forbidden[a]; it must not be eaten. 24In the fourth year all its fruit will be holy, an offering of praise to the LORD. 25But in the fifth year you may eat its fruit. In this way your harvest will be increased. I am the LORD your God.

26 " 'Do not eat any meat with the blood still in it.

" 'Do not practice divination or sorcery.

27 " 'Do not cut the hair at the sides of your head or clip off the edges of your beard.

28 " 'Do not cut your bodies for the dead or put tattoo marks on yourselves. I am the LORD.

29 " 'Do not degrade your daughter by making her a prostitute, or the land will turn to prostitution and be filled with wickedness.

30 " 'Observe my Sabbaths and have reverence for my sanctuary. I am the LORD.

31 " 'Do not turn to mediums or seek out spiritists, for you will be defiled by them. I am the LORD your God.

32 " 'Rise in the presence of the aged, show respect for the elderly and revere your God. I am the LORD.

33 " 'When an alien lives with you in your land, do not mistreat him. 34The alien living with you must be treated as one of your native-born. Love him as yourself, for you were aliens in Egypt. I am the LORD your God.

35 " 'Do not use dishonest standards when measuring length, weight or quantity. 36Use honest scales and honest weights, an honest ephah[b] and an honest hin.[c] I am the LORD your God, who brought you out of Egypt.

37 " 'Keep all my decrees and all my laws and follow them. I am the LORD.' "

---

[a] 23 Hebrew uncircumcised   [b] 36 An ephah was a dry measure.   [c] 36 A hin was a liquid measure.

Human Subway Walls

READ LEVITICUS 19:28

GET STRONGER

If you were given a really nice photo of yourself and your friends and wanted to put hilarious speech bubbles on it, wouldn't it be better to stick them on temporarily with sticky notes? That way you could show your friends and laugh, then remove the bubbles. Well, God was making that kind of point when he said, "Do not ... put tattoo marks on yourselves" (verse 28). He didn't want the Israelites to decorate their bodies with graffiti like subway walls. Now, whether a guy has or gets get tattoos or not doesn't change God's love for him, but for your own sake, remember that tattoos are *permanent*. A tattoo that might seem cool to you when you're young could be extremely *un-cool* when you're older. What do you do then? It's not like face-painting where you just wash the stuff off. Remember, your body is the temple of God. Be careful what you write on the walls.

Your next reading is on page 164.

Punishments for Sin

20 The LORD said to Moses, 2"Say to the Israelites: 'Any Israelite or any alien living in Israel who gives[a] any of his children to Molech must be put to death. The people of the community are to stone him. 3I will set my face against that man and I will cut him off from his people; for by giving his children to Molech, he has defiled my sanctuary and profaned my holy name. 4If the people of the community close their eyes when that man gives one of his children to Molech and they fail to put him to death, 5I will set my face against that man and his family and will cut off from their people both him and all who follow him in prostituting themselves to Molech.

6" 'I will set my face against the person who turns to mediums and spiritists to prostitute himself by following them, and I will cut him off from his people.

7" 'Consecrate yourselves and be holy, because I am the LORD your God. 8Keep my decrees and follow them. I am the LORD, who makes you holy.[b]

9" 'If anyone curses his father or mother, he must be put to death. He has cursed his father or his mother, and his blood will be on his own head.

10" 'If a man commits adultery with another man's wife—with the wife of his neighbor—both the adulterer and the adulteress must be put to death.

11" 'If a man sleeps with his father's wife, he has dishonored his father. Both the man and the woman must be put to death; their blood will be on their own heads.

12" 'If a man sleeps with his daughter-in-law, both of them must be put to death. What they have done is a perversion; their blood will be on their own heads.

13" 'If a man lies with a man as one lies

---

[a] 2 Or *sacrifices*; also in verses 3 and 4   [b] 8 Or *who sanctifies you*; or *who sets you apart as holy*

Make It Stick

READ LEVITICUS 19:32

Make a habit of standing up or saying hello when elderly people walk into the room. It's a sign of real respect. Talk to them. Don't be shy or rude, just because they seem old or forgetful! Write down three other things you could do to show respect to older people.

with a woman, both of them have done what is detestable. They must be put to death; their blood will be on their own heads.

14" 'If a man marries both a woman and her mother, it is wicked. Both he and they must be burned in the fire, so that no wickedness will be among you.

15" 'If a man has sexual relations with an animal, he must be put to death, and you must kill the animal.

16" 'If a woman approaches an animal to have sexual relations with it, kill both the woman and the animal. They must be put to death; their blood will be on their own heads.

17" 'If a man marries his sister, the daughter of either his father or his mother, and they have sexual relations, it is a disgrace. They must be cut off before the eyes of their people. He has dishonored his sister and will be held responsible.

18" 'If a man lies with a woman during her monthly period and has sexual relations with her, he has exposed the source of her flow, and she has also uncovered it. Both of them must be cut off from their people.

19" 'Do not have sexual relations with the sister of either your mother or your father, for that would dishonor a close relative; both of you would be held responsible.

20" 'If a man sleeps with his aunt, he has dishonored his uncle. They will be held responsible; they will die childless.

21" 'If a man marries his brother's wife, it is an act of impurity; he has dishonored his brother. They will be childless.

22" 'Keep all my decrees and laws and follow them, so that the land where I am bringing you to live may not vomit you out. 23You must not live according to the customs of the nations I am going to drive out before you. Because they did all these things, I abhorred them. 24But I said to you, "You will possess their land; I will give it to you as an inheritance, a land flowing with milk and honey." I am the LORD your God, who has set you apart from the nations.

25" 'You must therefore make a distinction between clean and unclean animals and between unclean and clean birds. Do not defile yourselves by any animal or bird

What Does My Future Hold?

READ LEVITICUS 20:6

GET SMARTER

Everyone wants to know what's going to happen in their future. That's normal, and God is happy when we do our best to find out his plan for our life. But reading horoscopes, visiting fortune-tellers or palm readers and phoning psychic hotlines is not very smart. For one thing, it's being disobedient to God and not trusting *him* for your future. For another, a lot of so-called "psychic" stuff is fake, so why follow the advice of someone who only wants to cheat you out of your money? On the other hand, a spirit medium might actually be in contact with spirits—*evil* spirits, that is. Why listen when evil spirits advise you how to make important decisions? Listen, you may know people who have Ouija boards or tarot cards or read horoscopes who say, "It's just fun! Lighten up!" but tell them, "No way! I'm trusting *my* future to God."

Your next reading is on page 167.

or anything that moves along the ground—those which I have set apart as unclean for you. ²⁶You are to be holy to me ᵃ because I, the LORD, am holy, and I have set you apart from the nations to be my own.

²⁷" 'A man or woman who is a medium or spiritist among you must be put to death. You are to stone them; their blood will be on their own heads.' "

Rules for Priests

21 The LORD said to Moses, "Speak to the priests, the sons of Aaron, and say to them: 'A priest must not make himself ceremonially unclean for any of his people who die, ²except for a close relative, such as his mother or father, his son or daughter, his brother, ³or an unmarried sister who is dependent on him since she has no husband—for her he may make himself unclean. ⁴He must not make himself unclean for people related to him by marriage,ᵇ and so defile himself.

⁵" 'Priests must not shave their heads or shave off the edges of their beards or cut their bodies. ⁶They must be holy to their God and must not profane the name of their God. Because they present the offerings made to the LORD by fire, the food of their God, they are to be holy.

⁷" 'They must not marry women defiled by prostitution or divorced from their husbands, because priests are holy to their God. ⁸Regard them as holy, because they offer up the food of your God. Consider them holy, because I the LORD am holy—I who make you holy.ᶜ

⁹" 'If a priest's daughter defiles herself by becoming a prostitute, she disgraces her father; she must be burned in the fire.

¹⁰" 'The high priest, the one among his brothers who has had the anointing oil poured on his head and who has been ordained to wear the priestly garments, must not let his hair become unkemptᵈ or tear his clothes. ¹¹He must not enter a place where there is a dead body. He must not make himself unclean, even for his father or mother, ¹²nor leave the sanctuary of his God or desecrate it, because he has been dedicated by the anointing oil of his God. I am the LORD.

¹³" 'The woman he marries must be a virgin. ¹⁴He must not marry a widow, a divorced woman, or a woman defiled by

prostitution, but only a virgin from his own people, ¹⁵so he will not defile his offspring among his people. I am the LORD, who makes him holy.ᵉ' "

¹⁶The LORD said to Moses, ¹⁷"Say to Aaron: 'For the generations to come none of your descendants who has a defect may come near to offer the food of his God. ¹⁸No man who has any defect may come near: no man who is blind or lame, disfigured or deformed; ¹⁹no man with a crippled foot or hand, ²⁰or who is hunchbacked or dwarfed, or who has any eye defect, or who has festering or running sores or damaged testicles. ²¹No descendant of Aaron the priest who has any defect is to come near to present the offerings made to the LORD by fire. He has a defect; he must not come near to offer the food of his God. ²²He may eat the most holy food of his God, as well as the holy food; ²³yet because of his defect, he must not go near the curtain or approach the altar, and so desecrate my sanctuary. I am the LORD, who makes them holy.ᶠ' "

²⁴So Moses told this to Aaron and his sons and to all the Israelites.

22 The LORD said to Moses, ²"Tell Aaron and his sons to treat with respect the sacred offerings the Israelites consecrate to me, so they will not profane my holy name. I am the LORD.

³"Say to them: 'For the generations to come, if any of your descendants is ceremonially unclean and yet comes near the sacred offerings that the Israelites consecrate to the LORD, that person must be cut off from my presence. I am the LORD.

⁴" 'If a descendant of Aaron has an infectious skin diseaseᵍ or a bodily discharge, he may not eat the sacred offerings until he is cleansed. He will also be unclean if he touches something defiled by a corpse or by anyone who has an emission of semen, ⁵or if he touches any crawling thing that makes him unclean, or any person who makes him unclean, whatever the uncleanness may be. ⁶The one who touches any such thing will be unclean till evening. He must not eat any

---

ᵃ 26 Or be my holy ones   ᵇ 4 Or unclean as a leader among his people   ᶜ 8 Or who sanctify you; or who set you apart as holy   ᵈ 10 Or not uncover his head   ᵉ 15 Or who sanctifies him; or who sets him apart as holy   ᶠ 23 Or who sanctifies them; or who sets them apart as holy
ᵍ 4 Traditionally leprosy; the Hebrew word was used for various diseases affecting the skin—not necessarily leprosy.

of the sacred offerings unless he has bathed himself with water. ⁷When the sun goes down, he will be clean, and after that he may eat the sacred offerings, for they are his food. ⁸He must not eat anything found dead or torn by wild animals, and so become unclean through it. I am the LORD.

⁹" 'The priests are to keep my requirements so that they do not become guilty and die for treating them with contempt. I am the LORD, who makes them holy. ᵃ

¹⁰" 'No one outside a priest's family may eat the sacred offering, nor may the guest of a priest or his hired worker eat it. ¹¹But if a priest buys a slave with money, or if a slave is born in his household, that slave may eat his food. ¹²If a priest's daughter marries anyone other than a priest, she may not eat any of the sacred contributions. ¹³But if a priest's daughter becomes a widow or is divorced, yet has no children, and she returns to live in her father's house as in her youth, she may eat of her father's food. No unauthorized person, however, may eat any of it.

¹⁴" 'If anyone eats a sacred offering by mistake, he must make restitution to the priest for the offering and add a fifth of the value to it. ¹⁵The priests must not desecrate the sacred offerings the Israelites present to the LORD ¹⁶by allowing them to eat the sacred offerings and so bring upon them guilt requiring payment. I am the LORD, who makes them holy.' "

Unacceptable Sacrifices

¹⁷The LORD said to Moses, ¹⁸"Speak to Aaron and his sons and to all the Israelites and say to them: 'If any of you—either an Israelite or an alien living in Israel—presents a gift for a burnt offering to the LORD, either to fulfill a vow or as a freewill offering, ¹⁹you must present a male without defect from the cattle, sheep or goats in order that it may be accepted on your behalf. ²⁰Do not bring anything with a defect, because it will not be accepted on your behalf. ²¹When anyone brings from the herd or flock a fellowship offeringᵇ to the LORD to fulfill a special vow or as a freewill offering, it must be without defect or blemish to be acceptable. ²²Do not offer to the LORD the blind, the injured or the maimed, or anything with warts or festering or running sores. Do not place any of these on the altar as an offering

made to the LORD by fire. ²³You may, however, present as a freewill offering an oxᶜ or a sheep that is deformed or stunted, but it will not be accepted in fulfillment of a vow. ²⁴You must not offer to the LORD an animal whose testicles are bruised, crushed, torn or cut. You must not do this in your own land, ²⁵and you must not accept such animals from the hand of a foreigner and offer them as the food of your God. They will not be accepted on your behalf, because they are deformed and have defects.' "

²⁶The LORD said to Moses, ²⁷"When a calf, a lamb or a goat is born, it is to remain with its mother for seven days. From the eighth day on, it will be acceptable as an offering made to the LORD by fire. ²⁸Do not slaughter a cow or a sheep and its young on the same day.

²⁹"When you sacrifice a thank offering to the LORD, sacrifice it in such a way that it will be accepted on your behalf. ³⁰It must be eaten that same day; leave none of it till morning. I am the LORD.

³¹"Keep my commands and follow them. I am the LORD. ³²Do not profane my holy name. I must be acknowledged as holy by the Israelites. I am the LORD, who makesᵈ you holyᵉ ³³and who brought you out of Egypt to be your God. I am the LORD."

23 The LORD said to Moses, ²"Speak to the Israelites and say to them: 'These are my appointed feasts, the appointed feasts of the LORD, which you are to proclaim as sacred assemblies.

The Sabbath

³" 'There are six days when you may work, but the seventh day is a Sabbath of rest, a day of sacred assembly. You are not to do any work; wherever you live, it is a Sabbath to the LORD.

The Passover and Unleavened Bread

⁴" 'These are the LORD's appointed feasts, the sacred assemblies you are to proclaim at their appointed times: ⁵The LORD's Passover begins at twilight on the

---

ᵃ 9 Or who sanctifies them; or who sets them apart as holy; also in verse 16   ᵇ 21 Traditionally peace offering
ᶜ 23 The Hebrew word can include both male and female.
ᵈ 32 Or made   ᵉ 32 Or who sanctifies you; or who sets you apart as holy

fourteenth day of the first month. ⁶On the fifteenth day of that month the LORD's Feast of Unleavened Bread begins; for seven days you must eat bread made without yeast. ⁷On the first day hold a sacred assembly and do no regular work. ⁸For seven days present an offering made to the LORD by fire. And on the seventh day hold a sacred assembly and do no regular work.' "

Firstfruits

⁹The LORD said to Moses, ¹⁰"Speak to the Israelites and say to them: 'When you enter the land I am going to give you and you reap its harvest, bring to the priest a sheaf of the first grain you harvest. ¹¹He is to wave the sheaf before the LORD so it will be accepted on your behalf; the priest is to wave it on the day after the Sabbath. ¹²On the day you wave the sheaf, you must sacrifice as a burnt offering to the LORD a lamb a year old without defect, ¹³together with its grain offering of two-tenths of an ephah*ᵃ* of fine flour mixed with oil—an offering made to the LORD by fire, a pleasing aroma—and its drink offering of a quarter of a hin*ᵇ* of wine.

¹⁴You must not eat any bread, or roasted or new grain, until the very day you bring this offering to your God. This is to be a lasting ordinance for the generations to come, wherever you live.

Feast of Weeks

¹⁵" 'From the day after the Sabbath, the day you brought the sheaf of the wave offering, count off seven full weeks. ¹⁶Count off fifty days up to the day after the seventh Sabbath, and then present an offering of new grain to the LORD. ¹⁷From wherever you live, bring two loaves made of two-tenths of an ephah of fine flour, baked with yeast, as a wave offering of firstfruits to the LORD. ¹⁸Present with this bread seven male lambs, each a year old and without defect, one young bull and two rams. They will be a burnt offering to the LORD, together with their grain offerings and drink offerings—an offering made by fire, an aroma pleasing to the LORD. ¹⁹Then sacrifice one male goat for a

ᵃ 13 That is, probably about 4 quarts (about 4.5 liters); also in verse 17   *ᵇ 13* That is, probably about 1 quart (about 1 liter)

Everybody Party!

READ LEVITICUS 23:1–25, 33–41

Holidays, birthdays, family picnics, victory celebrations and giant school events are lots of fun! Everyone likes a good party or celebration. The kind of parties you should pass up, however, are the parties where people go wild and disobey and dishonor God. Some people's idea of a "good time" is to sit around swearing, telling dirty jokes, and worse. But God's celebrations, feasts and parties are happy, holy times, with eating and laughing and fun. Look at God's parties listed here. God *commanded* his people to have happy times! He told the whole nation to celebrate a *one-day* Passover party, a *seven-day* flat bread party, a *one-day* food party, a *one-day* rootin' tootin' harvest party to celebrate his blessings, a *one-day* trumpets party, and a *week-long* camp-out tent party! Wow!!

Your next reading is on page 172.

sin offering and two lambs, each a year old, for a fellowship offering.[a] [20]The priest is to wave the two lambs before the LORD as a wave offering, together with the bread of the firstfruits. They are a sacred offering to the LORD for the priest. [21]On that same day you are to proclaim a sacred assembly and do no regular work. This is to be a lasting ordinance for the generations to come, wherever you live.

[22]" 'When you reap the harvest of your land, do not reap to the very edges of your field or gather the gleanings of your harvest. Leave them for the poor and the alien. I am the LORD your God.' "

Feast of Trumpets

[23]The LORD said to Moses, [24]"Say to the Israelites: 'On the first day of the seventh month you are to have a day of rest, a sacred assembly commemorated with trumpet blasts. [25]Do no regular work, but present an offering made to the LORD by fire.' "

Day of Atonement

[26]The LORD said to Moses, [27]"The tenth day of this seventh month is the Day of Atonement. Hold a sacred assembly and deny yourselves,[b] and present an offering made to the LORD by fire. [28]Do no work on that day, because it is the Day of Atonement, when atonement is made for you before the LORD your God. [29]Anyone who does not deny himself on that day must be cut off from his people. [30]I will destroy from among his people anyone who does any work on that day. [31]You shall do no work at all. This is to be a lasting ordinance for the generations to come, wherever you live. [32]It is a sabbath of rest for you, and you must deny yourselves. From the evening of the ninth day of the month until the following evening you are to observe your sabbath."

Feast of Tabernacles

[33]The LORD said to Moses, [34]"Say to the Israelites: 'On the fifteenth day of the seventh month the LORD's Feast of Tabernacles begins, and it lasts for seven days. [35]The first day is a sacred assembly; do no regular work. [36]For seven days present offerings made to the LORD by fire, and on the eighth day hold a sacred assembly and present an offering made to the LORD by fire. It is the closing assembly; do no regular work.

[37](" 'These are the LORD's appointed feasts, which you are to proclaim as sacred assemblies for bringing offerings made to the LORD by fire—the burnt offerings and grain offerings, sacrifices and drink offerings required for each day. [38]These offerings are in addition to those for the LORD's Sabbaths and[c] in addition to your gifts and whatever you have vowed and all the freewill offerings you give to the LORD.)

[39]" 'So beginning with the fifteenth day of the seventh month, after you have gathered the crops of the land, celebrate the festival to the LORD for seven days; the first day is a day of rest, and the eighth day also is a day of rest. [40]On the first day you are to take choice fruit from the trees, and palm fronds, leafy branches and poplars, and rejoice before the LORD your God for seven days. [41]Celebrate this as a festival to the LORD for seven days each year. This is to be a lasting ordinance for the generations to come; celebrate it in the seventh month. [42]Live in booths for seven days: All native-born Israelites are to live in booths [43]so your descendants will know that I had the Israelites live in booths when I brought them out of Egypt. I am the LORD your God.' "

[44]So Moses announced to the Israelites the appointed feasts of the LORD.

Oil and Bread Set Before the LORD

24 The LORD said to Moses, [2]"Command the Israelites to bring you clear oil of pressed olives for the light so that the lamps may be kept burning continually. [3]Outside the curtain of the Testimony in the Tent of Meeting, Aaron is to tend the lamps before the LORD from evening till morning, continually. This is to be a lasting ordinance for the generations to come. [4]The lamps on the pure gold lampstand before the LORD must be tended continually.

[5]"Take fine flour and bake twelve loaves of bread, using two-tenths of an ephah[d] for each loaf. [6]Set them in two rows, six in each row, on the table of pure gold before the LORD. [7]Along each row put some pure incense as a memorial portion to

---

[a] 19 Traditionally *peace offering*   [b] 27 Or *and fast*; also in verses 29 and 32   [c] 38 Or *These feasts are in addition to the LORD's Sabbaths, and these offerings are*   [d] 5 That is, probably about 4 quarts (about 4.5 liters)

represent the bread and to be an offering made to the LORD by fire. ⁸This bread is to be set out before the LORD regularly, Sabbath after Sabbath, on behalf of the Israelites, as a lasting covenant. ⁹It belongs to Aaron and his sons, who are to eat it in a holy place, because it is a most holy part of their regular share of the offerings made to the LORD by fire."

A Blasphemer Stoned

¹⁰Now the son of an Israelite mother and an Egyptian father went out among the Israelites, and a fight broke out in the camp between him and an Israelite. ¹¹The son of the Israelite woman blasphemed the Name with a curse; so they brought him to Moses. (His mother's name was Shelomith, the daughter of Dibri the Danite.) ¹²They put him in custody until the will of the LORD should be made clear to them.

¹³Then the LORD said to Moses: ¹⁴"Take the blasphemer outside the camp. All those who heard him are to lay their hands on his head, and the entire assembly is to stone him. ¹⁵Say to the Israelites: 'If anyone curses his God, he will be held responsible; ¹⁶anyone who blasphemes the name of the LORD must be put to death. The entire assembly must stone him. Whether an alien or native-born, when he blasphemes the Name, he must be put to death.

¹⁷" 'If anyone takes the life of a human being, he must be put to death. ¹⁸Anyone who takes the life of someone's animal must make restitution—life for life. ¹⁹If anyone injures his neighbor, whatever he has done must be done to him: ²⁰fracture for fracture, eye for eye, tooth for tooth. As he has injured the other, so he is to be injured. ²¹Whoever kills an animal must make restitution, but whoever kills a man must be put to death. ²²You are to have the same law for the alien and the native-born. I am the LORD your God.' "

²³Then Moses spoke to the Israelites, and they took the blasphemer outside the camp and stoned him. The Israelites did as the LORD commanded Moses.

The Sabbath Year

25 The LORD said to Moses on Mount Sinai, ²"Speak to the Israelites and say to them: 'When you enter the land I am going to give you, the land itself must observe a sabbath to the LORD. ³For six years sow your fields, and for six years prune your vineyards and gather their crops. ⁴But in the seventh year the land is to have a sabbath of rest, a sabbath to the LORD. Do not sow your fields or prune your vineyards. ⁵Do not reap what grows of itself or harvest the grapes of your untended vines. The land is to have a year of rest. ⁶Whatever the land yields during the sabbath year will be food for you—for yourself, your manservant and maidservant, and the hired worker and temporary resident who live among you, ⁷as well as for your livestock and the wild animals in your land. Whatever the land produces may be eaten.

Get a Load of This...

A lot of ancient cultures had the death penalty for serious crime, but Israel was the only nation that required stoning, with everyone in the community throwing a stone (see Leviticus 24:14). God wanted to remind the Israelites that they were all responsible to keep the nation holy.

The Year of Jubilee

8" 'Count off seven sabbaths of years—seven times seven years—so that the seven sabbaths of years amount to a period of forty-nine years. ⁹Then have the trumpet sounded everywhere on the tenth day of the seventh month; on the Day of Atonement sound the trumpet throughout your land. ¹⁰Consecrate the fiftieth year and proclaim liberty throughout the land to all its inhabitants. It shall be a jubilee for you; each one of you is to return to his family property and each to his own clan. ¹¹The fiftieth year shall be a jubilee for you; do not sow and do not reap what grows of itself or harvest the untended vines. ¹²For it is a jubilee and is to be holy for you; eat only what is taken directly from the fields.

13" 'In this Year of Jubilee everyone is to return to his own property.

14" 'If you sell land to one of your countrymen or buy any from him, do not take advantage of each other. ¹⁵You are to buy from your countryman on the basis of the number of years since the Jubilee. And he is to sell to you on the basis of the number of years left for harvesting crops. ¹⁶When the years are many, you are to increase the price, and when the years are few, you are to decrease the price, because what he is really selling you is the number of crops. ¹⁷Do not take advantage of each other, but fear your God. I am the LORD your God.

18" 'Follow my decrees and be careful to obey my laws, and you will live safely in the land. ¹⁹Then the land will yield its fruit, and you will eat your fill and live there in safety. ²⁰You may ask, "What will we eat in the seventh year if we do not plant or harvest our crops?" ²¹I will send you such a blessing in the sixth year that the land will yield enough for three years. ²²While you plant during the eighth year, you will eat from the old crop and will continue to eat from it until the harvest of the ninth year comes in.

23" 'The land must not be sold permanently, because the land is mine and you are but aliens and my tenants. ²⁴Throughout the country that you hold as a possession, you must provide for the redemption of the land.

25" 'If one of your countrymen becomes poor and sells some of his property, his nearest relative is to come and redeem what his countryman has sold. ²⁶If, however, a man has no one to redeem it for him but he himself prospers and acquires sufficient means to redeem it, ²⁷he is to determine the value for the years since he sold it and refund the balance to the man to whom he sold it; he can then go back to his own property. ²⁸But if he does not acquire the means to repay him, what he sold will remain in the possession of the buyer until the Year of Jubilee. It will be returned in the Jubilee, and he can then go back to his property.

29" 'If a man sells a house in a walled city, he retains the right of redemption a full year after its sale. During that time he may redeem it. ³⁰If it is not redeemed before a full year has passed, the house in the walled city shall belong permanently to the buyer and his descendants. It is not to be returned in the Jubilee. ³¹But houses in villages without walls around them are to be considered as open country. They can be redeemed, and they are to be returned in the Jubilee.

32" 'The Levites always have the right to redeem their houses in the Levitical towns, which they possess. ³³So the property of the Levites is redeemable—that is, a house sold in any town they hold—and is to be returned in the Jubilee, because the houses in the towns of the Levites are their property among the Israelites. ³⁴But the pastureland belonging to their towns must not be sold; it is their permanent possession.

35" 'If one of your countrymen becomes poor and is unable to support himself among you, help him as you would an alien or a temporary resident, so he can continue to live among you. ³⁶Do not take interest of any kindᵃ from him, but fear your God, so that your countryman may continue to live among you. ³⁷You must not lend him money at interest or sell him food at a profit. ³⁸I am the LORD your God, who brought you out of Egypt to give you the land of Canaan and to be your God.

39" 'If one of your countrymen becomes poor among you and sells himself to you, do not make him work as a slave. ⁴⁰He is to be treated as a hired worker or a temporary resident among you; he is to work for you until the Year of Jubilee.

ᵃ 36 Or take excessive interest; similarly in verse 37

⁴¹Then he and his children are to be released, and he will go back to his own clan and to the property of his forefathers. ⁴²Because the Israelites are my servants, whom I brought out of Egypt, they must not be sold as slaves. ⁴³Do not rule over them ruthlessly, but fear your God.

⁴⁴" 'Your male and female slaves are to come from the nations around you; from them you may buy slaves. ⁴⁵You may also buy some of the temporary residents living among you and members of their clans born in your country, and they will become your property. ⁴⁶You can will them to your children as inherited property and can make them slaves for life, but you must not rule over your fellow Israelites ruthlessly.

⁴⁷" 'If an alien or a temporary resident among you becomes rich and one of your countrymen becomes poor and sells himself to the alien living among you or to a member of the alien's clan, ⁴⁸he retains the right of redemption after he has sold himself. One of his relatives may redeem him: ⁴⁹An uncle or a cousin or any blood relative in his clan may redeem him. Or if he prospers, he may redeem himself. ⁵⁰He and his buyer are to count the time from the year he sold himself up to the Year of Jubilee. The price for his release is to be based on the rate paid to a hired man for that number of years. ⁵¹If many years remain, he must pay for his redemption a larger share of the price paid for him. ⁵²If only a few years remain until the Year of Jubilee, he is to compute that and pay for his redemption accordingly. ⁵³He is to be treated as a man hired from year to year; you must see to it that his owner does not rule over him ruthlessly.

⁵⁴" 'Even if he is not redeemed in any of these ways, he and his children are to be released in the Year of Jubilee, ⁵⁵for the Israelites belong to me as servants. They are my servants, whom I brought out of Egypt. I am the LORD your God.

Reward for Obedience

26 " 'Do not make idols or set up an image or a sacred stone for yourselves, and do not place a carved stone in your land to bow down before it. I am the LORD your God.

²" 'Observe my Sabbaths and have reverence for my sanctuary. I am the LORD.

³" 'If you follow my decrees and are careful to obey my commands, ⁴I will send you rain in its season, and the ground will yield its crops and the trees of the field their fruit. ⁵Your threshing will continue until grape harvest and the grape harvest will continue until planting, and you will eat all the food you want and live in safety in your land.

⁶" 'I will grant peace in the land, and you will lie down and no one will make you afraid. I will remove savage beasts from the land, and the sword will not pass through your country. ⁷You will pursue your enemies, and they will fall by the sword before you. ⁸Five of you will chase a hundred, and a hundred of you will chase ten thousand, and your enemies will fall by the sword before you.

⁹" 'I will look on you with favor and make you fruitful and increase your numbers, and I will keep my covenant with you. ¹⁰You will still be eating last year's harvest when you will have to move it out to make room for the new. ¹¹I will put my dwelling place*ᵃ* among you, and I will not abhor you. ¹²I will walk among you and be your God, and you will be my people. ¹³I am the LORD your God, who brought you out of Egypt so that you would no longer be slaves to the Egyptians; I broke the bars of your yoke and enabled you to walk with heads held high.

Punishment for Disobedience

¹⁴" 'But if you will not listen to me and carry out all these commands, ¹⁵and if you reject my decrees and abhor my laws and fail to carry out all my commands and so violate my covenant, ¹⁶then I will do this to you: I will bring upon you sudden terror, wasting diseases and fever that will destroy your sight and drain away your life. You will plant seed in vain, because your enemies will eat it. ¹⁷I will set my face against you so that you will be defeated by your enemies; those who hate you will rule over you, and you will flee even when no one is pursuing you.

¹⁸" 'If after all this you will not listen to me, I will punish you for your sins seven times over. ¹⁹I will break down your stubborn pride and make the sky above you like iron and the ground beneath you like bronze. ²⁰Your strength will be spent in

ᵃ 11 Or my tabernacle

vain, because your soil will not yield its crops, nor will the trees of the land yield their fruit.

21 " 'If you remain hostile toward me and refuse to listen to me, I will multiply your afflictions seven times over, as your sins deserve. 22 I will send wild animals against you, and they will rob you of your children, destroy your cattle and make you so few in number that your roads will be deserted.

23 " 'If in spite of these things you do not accept my correction but continue to be hostile toward me, 24 I myself will be hostile toward you and will afflict you for your sins seven times over. 25 And I will bring the sword upon you to avenge the breaking of the covenant. When you withdraw into your cities, I will send a plague among you, and you will be given into enemy hands. 26 When I cut off your supply of bread, ten women will be able to bake your bread in one oven, and they will dole out the bread by weight. You will eat, but you will not be satisfied.

27 " 'If in spite of this you still do not listen to me but continue to be hostile toward me, 28 then in my anger I will be hostile toward you, and I myself will punish you for your sins seven times over. 29 You will eat the flesh of your sons and the flesh of your daughters. 30 I will destroy your high places, cut down your incense altars and pile your dead bodies on the lifeless forms of your idols, and I will abhor you. 31 I will turn your cities into ruins and lay waste your sanctuaries, and I will take no delight in the pleasing aroma of your offerings. 32 I will lay waste the land, so that your enemies who live there will be appalled. 33 I will scatter you among the nations and will draw out my sword and pursue you. Your land will be laid waste, and your cities will lie in ruins. 34 Then the land will enjoy its sabbath years all the time that it lies desolate and you are in the country of your enemies; then the land will rest and enjoy its sabbaths. 35 All the time that it lies desolate, the land will have the rest it did not have during the sabbaths you lived in it.

36 " 'As for those of you who are left, I will make their hearts so fearful in the lands of their enemies that the sound of a

Doing Things God's Way

READ LEVITICUS 26:3–13

If you do things God's way, you'll be blessed. It's that simple. Good things will *start* happening to you, and just won't *stop* happening! This doesn't mean you'll never stub your toe or you'll always get "A's" in math or you'll win every school raffle. But God *does* promise that, if you are paying close attention to obeying his commands, he will look on you with favor and help you to walk through life with your head held high (Leviticus 26:3–4, 9, 13). You can't miss with *that*, right? So what does "obeying God's commands" mean? Let's start with one of God's number one commands to kids—"Honor your father and your mother" (Exodus 20:12). This isn't always easy, but if you're interested in having God bless you, start thinking of some practical ways you can honor and obey your parents.

Your next reading is on page 178.

windblown leaf will put them to flight. They will run as though fleeing from the sword, and they will fall, even though no one is pursuing them. ³⁷They will stumble over one another as though fleeing from the sword, even though no one is pursuing them. So you will not be able to stand before your enemies. ³⁸You will perish among the nations; the land of your enemies will devour you. ³⁹Those of you who are left will waste away in the lands of their enemies because of their sins; also because of their fathers' sins they will waste away.

⁴⁰" 'But if they will confess their sins and the sins of their fathers—their treachery against me and their hostility toward me, ⁴¹which made me hostile toward them so that I sent them into the land of their enemies—then when their uncircumcised hearts are humbled and they pay for their sin, ⁴²I will remember my covenant with Jacob and my covenant with Isaac and my covenant with Abraham, and I will remember the land. ⁴³For the land will be deserted by them and will enjoy its sabbaths while it lies desolate without them. They will pay for their sins because they rejected my laws and abhorred my decrees. ⁴⁴Yet in spite of this, when they are in the land of their enemies, I will not reject them or abhor them so as to destroy them completely, breaking my covenant with them. I am the LORD their God. ⁴⁵But for their sake I will remember the covenant with their ancestors whom I brought out of Egypt in the sight of the nations to be their God. I am the LORD.' "

⁴⁶These are the decrees, the laws and the regulations that the LORD established on Mount Sinai between himself and the Israelites through Moses.

Redeeming What Is the LORD's

27 The LORD said to Moses, ²"Speak to the Israelites and say to them: 'If anyone makes a special vow to dedicate persons to the LORD by giving equivalent values, ³set the value of a male between the ages of twenty and sixty at fifty shekels[a] of silver, according to the sanctuary shekel[b]; ⁴and if it is a female, set her value at thirty shekels.[c] ⁵If it is a person between the ages of five and twenty, set the value of a male at twenty shekels[d] and of a female at ten shekels.[e] ⁶If it is a person be-

tween one month and five years, set the value of a male at five shekels[f] of silver and that of a female at three shekels[g] of silver. ⁷If it is a person sixty years old or more, set the value of a male at fifteen shekels[h] and of a female at ten shekels. ⁸If anyone making the vow is too poor to pay the specified amount, he is to present the person to the priest, who will set the value for him according to what the man making the vow can afford.

⁹" 'If what he vowed is an animal that is acceptable as an offering to the LORD, such an animal given to the LORD becomes holy. ¹⁰He must not exchange it or substitute a good one for a bad one, or a bad one for a good one; if he should substitute one animal for another, both it and the substitute become holy. ¹¹If what he vowed is a ceremonially unclean animal—one that is not acceptable as an offering to the LORD—the animal must be presented to the priest, ¹²who will judge its quality as good or bad. Whatever value the priest then sets, that is what it will be. ¹³If the owner wishes to redeem the animal, he must add a fifth to its value.

¹⁴" 'If a man dedicates his house as something holy to the LORD, the priest will judge its quality as good or bad. Whatever value the priest then sets, so it will remain. ¹⁵If the man who dedicates his house redeems it, he must add a fifth to its value, and the house will again become his.

¹⁶" 'If a man dedicates to the LORD part of his family land, its value is to be set according to the amount of seed required for it—fifty shekels of silver to a homer[i] of barley seed. ¹⁷If he dedicates his field during the Year of Jubilee, the value that has been set remains. ¹⁸But if he dedicates his field after the Jubilee, the priest will determine the value according to the number of years that remain until the next Year of Jubilee, and its set value will be reduced. ¹⁹If the man who dedicates the field wishes to redeem it, he must add a fifth to its value, and the field will again become his. ²⁰If, however, he does not redeem the

---

a 3 That is, about 1 1/4 pounds (about 0.6 kilogram); also in verse 16   b 3 That is, about 2/5 ounce (about 11.5 grams); also in verse 25   c 4 That is, about 12 ounces (about 0.3 kilogram)   d 5 That is, about 8 ounces (about 0.2 kilogram)   e 5 That is, about 4 ounces (about 110 grams); also in verse 7   f 6 That is, about 2 ounces (about 55 grams)   g 6 That is, about 1 1/4 ounces (about 35 grams)   h 7 That is, about 6 ounces (about 170 grams)   i 16 That is, probably about 6 bushels (about 220 liters) field, or if he has sold it to someone else, it can never be redeemed. 21When the field is released in the Jubilee, it will become holy, like a field devoted to the LORD; it will become the property of the priests.^a

22" 'If a man dedicates to the LORD a field he has bought, which is not part of his family land, 23the priest will determine its value up to the Year of Jubilee, and the man must pay its value on that day as something holy to the LORD. 24In the Year of Jubilee the field will revert to the person from whom he bought it, the one whose land it was. 25Every value is to be set according to the sanctuary shekel, twenty gerahs to the shekel.

26" 'No one, however, may dedicate the firstborn of an animal, since the firstborn already belongs to the LORD; whether an ox^b or a sheep, it is the LORD's. 27If it is one of the unclean animals, he may buy it back at its set value, adding a fifth of the value to it. If he does not redeem it, it is to be sold at its set value.

28" 'But nothing that a man owns and devotes^c to the LORD—whether man or animal or family land—may be sold or re-deemed; everything so devoted is most holy to the LORD.

29" 'No person devoted to destruction^d may be ransomed; he must be put to death.

30" 'A tithe of everything from the land, whether grain from the soil or fruit from the trees, belongs to the LORD; it is holy to the LORD. 31If a man redeems any of his tithe, he must add a fifth of the value to it. 32The entire tithe of the herd and flock—every tenth animal that passes under the shepherd's rod—will be holy to the LORD. 33He must not pick out the good from the bad or make any substitution. If he does make a substitution, both the animal and its substitute become holy and cannot be redeemed.' "

34These are the commands the LORD gave Moses on Mount Sinai for the Israelites.

---

^a 21 Or priest   ^b 26 The Hebrew word can include both male and female.   ^c 28 The Hebrew term refers to the irrevocable giving over of things or persons to the LORD. ^d 29 The Hebrew term refers to the irrevocable giving over of things or persons to the LORD, often by totally destroying them.

NUMBERS

Who wrote this book?
Moses.

Why was this book written?
Numbers tells how Israel's disobedience kept the Israelites from entering the Promised Land.

What happens in this book?
The Israelites are frightened by the power of the Canaanites. They disobey when God tells them to attack Canaan. The Israelites wander in the desert for 40 years, until all the adults who disobeyed God have died.

What do we learn about God in this book?
God will not bless people who refuse to trust and obey him.

Who is important in this book?
The important people in this book are Moses and Aaron.

When did this happen?
The events in this book happened between 1445 and 1405 B.C.

Where did this happen?
Numbers 1–10 happened at Mount Sinai. Numbers 11–14 happened just outside Canaan. The rest of the book took place in the wilderness and on the way back to Canaan 40 years later.

What are some of the stories in this book?

The Israelites complain	Numbers 11
Aaron and Miriam turn against Moses	Numbers 12
Spies explore Canaan	Numbers 13
The Israelites disobey God	Numbers 14
Korah leads a rebellion	Numbers 16
Aaron's staff buds	Numbers 17
Balaam tries to curse Israel	Numbers 22–24
Israel defeats the Midianites	Numbers 31

The Census

The LORD spoke to Moses in the Tent of Meeting in the Desert of Sinai on the first day of the second month of the second year after the Israelites came out of Egypt. He said: 2"Take a census of the whole Israelite community by their clans and families, listing every man by name, one by one. 3You and Aaron are to number by their divisions all the men in Israel twenty years old or more who are able to serve in the army. 4One man from each tribe, each the head of his family, is to help you. 5These are the names of the men who are to assist you:

from Reuben, Elizur son of Shedeur;
6from Simeon, Shelumiel son of Zurishaddai;
7from Judah, Nahshon son of Amminadab;
8from Issachar, Nethanel son of Zuar;
9from Zebulun, Eliab son of Helon;
10from the sons of Joseph:
   from Ephraim, Elishama son of Ammihud;
   from Manasseh, Gamaliel son of Pedahzur;
11from Benjamin, Abidan son of Gideoni;
12from Dan, Ahiezer son of Ammishaddai;
13from Asher, Pagiel son of Ocran;
14from Gad, Eliasaph son of Deuel;
15from Naphtali, Ahira son of Enan."

16These were the men appointed from the community, the leaders of their ancestral tribes. They were the heads of the clans of Israel. 17Moses and Aaron took these men whose names had been given, 18and they called the whole community together on the first day of the second month. The people indicated their ancestry by their clans and families, and the men twenty years old or more were listed by name, one by one, 19as the LORD commanded Moses. And so he counted them in the Desert of Sinai:

20From the descendants of Reuben the firstborn son of Israel:
   All the men twenty years old or more who were able to serve in the army were listed by name, one by one, according to the records of their clans and families. 21The number from the tribe of Reuben was 46,500.

22From the descendants of Simeon:
   All the men twenty years old or more who were able to serve in the army were counted and listed by name, one by one, according to the records of their clans and families. 23The number from the tribe of Simeon was 59,300.

24From the descendants of Gad:
   All the men twenty years old or more who were able to serve in the army were listed by name, according to the records of their clans and families. 25The number from the tribe of Gad was 45,650.

26From the descendants of Judah:
   All the men twenty years old or more who were able to serve in the army were listed by name, according to the records of their clans and families. 27The number from the tribe of Judah was 74,600.

28From the descendants of Issachar:
   All the men twenty years old or more who were able to serve in the army were listed by name, according to the records of their clans and families. 29The number from the tribe of Issachar was 54,400.

30From the descendants of Zebulun:
   All the men twenty years old or more who were able to serve in the army were listed by name, according to the records of their clans and families. 31The number from the tribe of Zebulun was 57,400.

32From the sons of Joseph:
From the descendants of Ephraim:
   All the men twenty years old or more who were able to serve in the army were listed by name, according to the records of their clans and families. 33The number from the tribe of Ephraim was 40,500.

34From the descendants of Manasseh:
   All the men twenty years old or more who were able to serve in the army were listed by name, according to the records of their clans and families. 35The number from the tribe of Manasseh was 32,200.

³⁶From the descendants of Benjamin: All the men twenty years old or more who were able to serve in the army were listed by name, according to the records of their clans and families. ³⁷The number from the tribe of Benjamin was 35,400.

³⁸From the descendants of Dan: All the men twenty years old or more who were able to serve in the army were listed by name, according to the records of their clans and families. ³⁹The number from the tribe of Dan was 62,700.

⁴⁰From the descendants of Asher: All the men twenty years old or more who were able to serve in the army were listed by name, according to the records of their clans and families. ⁴¹The number from the tribe of Asher was 41,500.

⁴²From the descendants of Naphtali: All the men twenty years old or more who were able to serve in the army were listed by name, according to the records of their clans and families. ⁴³The number from the tribe of Naphtali was 53,400.

⁴⁴These were the men counted by Moses and Aaron and the twelve leaders of Israel, each one representing his family. ⁴⁵All the Israelites twenty years old or more who were able to serve in Israel's army were counted according to their families. ⁴⁶The total number was 603,550.

⁴⁷The families of the tribe of Levi, however, were not counted along with the others. ⁴⁸The LORD had said to Moses: ⁴⁹"You must not count the tribe of Levi or include them in the census of the other Israelites. ⁵⁰Instead, appoint the Levites to be in charge of the tabernacle of the Testimony—over all its furnishings and everything belonging to it. They are to carry the tabernacle and all its furnishings; they are to take care of it and encamp around it. ⁵¹Whenever the tabernacle is to move, the Levites are to take it down, and whenever the tabernacle is to be set up, the Levites shall do it. Anyone else who goes near it shall be put to death. ⁵²The Israelites are to set up their tents by divisions, each man in his own camp under his own standard. ⁵³The Levites, however, are to set up their tents around the tabernacle of the Testimony so that wrath will not fall on the Israelite community. The Levites are to be responsible for the care of the tabernacle of the Testimony."

⁵⁴The Israelites did all this just as the LORD commanded Moses.

The Arrangement of the Tribal Camps

The LORD said to Moses and Aaron: ²"The Israelites are to camp around the Tent of Meeting some distance from it, each man under his standard with the banners of his family."

³On the east, toward the sunrise, the divisions of the camp of Judah are to encamp under their standard. The leader of the people of Judah is Nahshon son of Amminadab. ⁴His division numbers 74,600.

⁵The tribe of Issachar will camp next to them. The leader of the people of Issachar is Nethanel son of Zuar. ⁶His division numbers 54,400.

⁷The tribe of Zebulun will be next. The leader of the people of Zebulun is Eliab son of Helon. ⁸His division numbers 57,400.

⁹All the men assigned to the camp of Judah, according to their divisions, number 186,400. They will set out first.

¹⁰On the south will be the divisions of the camp of Reuben under their standard. The leader of the people of Reuben is Elizur son of Shedeur. ¹¹His division numbers 46,500.

¹²The tribe of Simeon will camp next to them. The leader of the people of Simeon is Shelumiel son of Zurishaddai. ¹³His division numbers 59,300.

¹⁴The tribe of Gad will be next. The leader of the people of Gad is Eliasaph son of Deuel.[a] ¹⁵His division numbers 45,650.

¹⁶All the men assigned to the camp of Reuben, according to their divisions, number 151,450. They will set out second.

¹⁷Then the Tent of Meeting and the camp of the Levites will set out in

---

[a] 14 Many manuscripts of the Masoretic Text, Samaritan Pentateuch and Vulgate (see also Num. 1:14); most manuscripts of the Masoretic Text *Reuel*

the middle of the camps. They will set out in the same order as they encamp, each in his own place under his standard.

18 On the west will be the divisions of the camp of Ephraim under their standard. The leader of the people of Ephraim is Elishama son of Ammihud. 19 His division numbers 40,500.
20 The tribe of Manasseh will be next to them. The leader of the people of Manasseh is Gamaliel son of Pedahzur. 21 His division numbers 32,200.
22 The tribe of Benjamin will be next. The leader of the people of Benjamin is Abidan son of Gideoni. 23 His division numbers 35,400.
24 All the men assigned to the camp of Ephraim, according to their divisions, number 108,100. They will set out third.

25 On the north will be the divisions of the camp of Dan, under their standard. The leader of the people of Dan is Ahiezer son of Ammishaddai. 26 His division numbers 62,700.
27 The tribe of Asher will camp next to them. The leader of the people of Asher is Pagiel son of Ocran. 28 His division numbers 41,500.
29 The tribe of Naphtali will be next. The leader of the people of Naphtali is Ahira son of Enan. 30 His division numbers 53,400.
31 All the men assigned to the camp of Dan number 157,600. They will set out last, under their standards.

32 These are the Israelites, counted according to their families. All those in the camps, by their divisions, number 603,550. 33 The Levites, however, were not counted along with the other Israelites, as the LORD commanded Moses.

34 So the Israelites did everything the LORD commanded Moses; that is the way they encamped under their standards, and that is the way they set out, each with his clan and family.

One Nation Under God

READ NUMBERS 2

Imagine twelve giant football stadiums, side by side, each one packed with 50,000 men. Imagine that all those crowds are ready to go on a road trip together as a team. They're just waiting for the doors to open. Mob riot? No. We are talking about the Israelites and how they were organized. God told them to gather under banners, just like pro sports teams wear jerseys with their logo on them. Their banners identified which of the twelve tribal families they belonged to. In a way, today we stand under banners too, telling the world which crowd we're part of. Are you a skater? A jock? An artist? Whatever banner you fly, make sure God's banner is flying above that. Even with their differences, all of Israel's tribes marched together with God as the leader. They were "one nation under God." And that *is* the main thing: Be sure you're under God's banner.

Your next reading is on page 182.

The Levites

3 This is the account of the family of Aaron and Moses at the time the LORD talked with Moses on Mount Sinai.

²The names of the sons of Aaron were Nadab the firstborn and Abihu, Eleazar and Ithamar. ³Those were the names of Aaron's sons, the anointed priests, who were ordained to serve as priests. ⁴Nadab and Abihu, however, fell dead before the LORD when they made an offering with unauthorized fire before him in the Desert of Sinai. They had no sons; so only Eleazar and Ithamar served as priests during the lifetime of their father Aaron.

⁵The LORD said to Moses, ⁶"Bring the tribe of Levi and present them to Aaron the priest to assist him. ⁷They are to perform duties for him and for the whole community at the Tent of Meeting by doing the work of the tabernacle. ⁸They are to take care of all the furnishings of the Tent of Meeting, fulfilling the obligations of the Israelites by doing the work of the tabernacle. ⁹Give the Levites to Aaron and his sons; they are the Israelites who are to be given wholly to him.[a] ¹⁰Appoint Aaron and his sons to serve as priests; anyone else who approaches the sanctuary must be put to death."

¹¹The LORD also said to Moses, ¹²"I have taken the Levites from among the Israelites in place of the first male offspring of every Israelite woman. The Levites are mine, ¹³for all the firstborn are mine. When I struck down all the firstborn in Egypt, I set apart for myself every firstborn in Israel, whether man or animal. They are to be mine. I am the LORD."

¹⁴The LORD said to Moses in the Desert of Sinai, ¹⁵"Count the Levites by their families and clans. Count every male a month old or more." ¹⁶So Moses counted them, as he was commanded by the word of the LORD.

¹⁷These were the names of the sons of Levi:

Gershon, Kohath and Merari.

¹⁸These were the names of the Gershonite clans:

Libni and Shimei.

¹⁹The Kohathite clans:

Amram, Izhar, Hebron and Uzziel.

²⁰The Merarite clans:

Mahli and Mushi.

These were the Levite clans, according to their families.

²¹To Gershon belonged the clans of the Libnites and Shimeites; these were the Gershonite clans. ²²The number of all the males a month old or more who were counted was 7,500. ²³The Gershonite clans were to camp on the west, behind the tabernacle. ²⁴The leader of the families of the Gershonites was Eliasaph son of Lael. ²⁵At the Tent of Meeting the Gershonites were responsible for the care of the tabernacle and tent, its coverings, the curtain at the entrance to the Tent of Meeting, ²⁶the curtains of the courtyard, the curtain at the entrance to the courtyard surrounding the tabernacle and altar, and the ropes—and everything related to their use.

²⁷To Kohath belonged the clans of the Amramites, Izharites, Hebronites and Uzzielites; these were the Kohathite clans. ²⁸The number of all the males a month old or more was 8,600.[b] The Kohathites were responsible for the care of the sanctuary. ²⁹The Kohathite clans were to camp on the south side of the tabernacle. ³⁰The leader of the families of the Kohathite clans was Elizaphan son of Uzziel. ³¹They were responsible for the care of the ark, the table, the lampstand, the altars, the articles of the sanctuary used in ministering, the curtain, and everything related to their use. ³²The chief leader of the Levites was Eleazar son of Aaron, the priest. He was appointed over those who were responsible for the care of the sanctuary.

³³To Merari belonged the clans of the Mahlites and the Mushites; these were the Merarite clans. ³⁴The number of all the males a month old or more who were counted was 6,200. ³⁵The leader of the families of the Merarite clans was Zuriel son of Abihail; they were to camp on the north side of the tabernacle. ³⁶The Merarites were appointed to take care of the frames of the tabernacle, its crossbars, posts, bases, all its equipment, and everything related to their use, ³⁷as well as the posts of the surrounding courtyard with their bases, tent pegs and ropes.

---

[a] 9 Most manuscripts of the Masoretic Text; some manuscripts of the Masoretic Text, Samaritan Pentateuch and Septuagint (see also Num. 8:16) *to me*   [b] 28 Hebrew; some Septuagint manuscripts *8,300*

38Moses and Aaron and his sons were to camp to the east of the tabernacle, toward the sunrise, in front of the Tent of Meeting. They were responsible for the care of the sanctuary on behalf of the Israelites. Anyone else who approached the sanctuary was to be put to death.

39The total number of Levites counted at the LORD's command by Moses and Aaron according to their clans, including every male a month old or more, was 22,000.

40The LORD said to Moses, "Count all the firstborn Israelite males who are a month old or more and make a list of their names. 41Take the Levites for me in place of all the firstborn of the Israelites, and the livestock of the Levites in place of all the firstborn of the livestock of the Israelites. I am the LORD."

42So Moses counted all the firstborn of the Israelites, as the LORD commanded him. 43The total number of firstborn males a month old or more, listed by name, was 22,273.

44The LORD also said to Moses, 45"Take the Levites in place of all the firstborn of Israel, and the livestock of the Levites in place of their livestock. The Levites are to be mine. I am the LORD. 46To redeem the 273 firstborn Israelites who exceed the number of the Levites, 47collect five shekelsa for each one, according to the sanctuary shekel, which weighs twenty gerahs. 48Give the money for the redemption of the additional Israelites to Aaron and his sons."

49So Moses collected the redemption money from those who exceeded the number redeemed by the Levites. 50From the firstborn of the Israelites he collected silver weighing 1,365 shekels, b according to the sanctuary shekel. 51Moses gave the redemption money to Aaron and his sons, as he was commanded by the word of the LORD.

The Kohathites

4 The LORD said to Moses and Aaron: 2"Take a census of the Kohathite branch of the Levites by their clans and families. 3Count all the men from thirty to fifty years of age who come to serve in the work in the Tent of Meeting.

4"This is the work of the Kohathites in the Tent of Meeting: the care of the most holy things. 5When the camp is to move, Aaron and his sons are to go in and take down the shielding curtain and cover the ark of the Testimony with it. 6Then they are to cover this with hides of sea cows, c spread a cloth of solid blue over that and put the poles in place.

7"Over the table of the Presence they are to spread a blue cloth and put on it the plates, dishes and bowls, and the jars for drink offerings; the bread that is continually there is to remain on it. 8Over these they are to spread a scarlet cloth, cover that with hides of sea cows and put its poles in place.

9"They are to take a blue cloth and cover the lampstand that is for light, together with its lamps, its wick trimmers and trays, and all its jars for the oil used to supply it. 10Then they are to wrap it and all its accessories in a covering of hides of sea cows and put it on a carrying frame.

11"Over the gold altar they are to spread a blue cloth and cover that with hides of sea cows and put its poles in place.

12"They are to take all the articles used for ministering in the sanctuary, wrap them in a blue cloth, cover that with hides of sea cows and put them on a carrying frame.

13"They are to remove the ashes from the bronze altar and spread a purple cloth over it. 14Then they are to place on it all the utensils used for ministering at the altar, including the firepans, meat forks, shovels and sprinkling bowls. Over it they are to spread a covering of hides of sea cows and put its poles in place.

15"After Aaron and his sons have finished covering the holy furnishings and all the holy articles, and when the camp is ready to move, the Kohathites are to come to do the carrying. But they must not touch the holy things or they will die. The Kohathites are to carry those things that are in the Tent of Meeting.

16"Eleazar son of Aaron, the priest, is to have charge of the oil for the light, the fragrant incense, the regular grain offering and the anointing oil. He is to be in

---

a 47 That is, about 2 ounces (about 55 grams)   b 50 That is, about 35 pounds (about 15.5 kilograms)   c 6 That is, dugongs; also in verses 8, 10, 11, 12, 14 and 25 charge of the entire tabernacle and everything in it, including its holy furnishings and articles."

[17] The LORD said to Moses and Aaron, [18] "See that the Kohathite tribal clans are not cut off from the Levites. [19] So that they may live and not die when they come near the most holy things, do this for them: Aaron and his sons are to go into the sanctuary and assign to each man his work and what he is to carry. [20] But the Kohathites must not go in to look at the holy things, even for a moment, or they will die."

The Gershonites

[21] The LORD said to Moses, [22] "Take a census also of the Gershonites by their families and clans. [23] Count all the men from thirty to fifty years of age who come to serve in the work at the Tent of Meeting.

[24] "This is the service of the Gershonite clans as they work and carry burdens: [25] They are to carry the curtains of the tabernacle, the Tent of Meeting, its covering and the outer covering of hides of sea cows, the curtains for the entrance to the Tent of Meeting, [26] the curtains of the courtyard surrounding the tabernacle and altar, the curtain for the entrance, the ropes and all the equipment used in its service. The Gershonites are to do all that needs to be done with these things. [27] All their service, whether carrying or doing other work, is to be done under the direction of Aaron and his sons. You shall assign to them as their responsibility all they are to carry. [28] This is the service of the Gershonite clans at the Tent of Meeting. Their duties are to be under the direction of Ithamar son of Aaron, the priest.

The Merarites

[29] "Count the Merarites by their clans and families. [30] Count all the men from thirty to fifty years of age who come to serve in the work at the Tent of Meeting. [31] This is their duty as they perform service at the Tent of Meeting: to carry the frames of the tabernacle, its crossbars, posts and bases, [32] as well as the posts of the surrounding courtyard with their bases, tent pegs, ropes, all their equipment and everything related to their use. Assign to each man the specific things he is to carry. [33] This is the service of the Merarite clans as they work at the Tent of Meeting under the direction of Ithamar son of Aaron, the priest."

The Numbering of the Levite Clans

[34] Moses, Aaron and the leaders of the community counted the Kohathites by their clans and families. [35] All the men from thirty to fifty years of age who came to serve in the work in the Tent of Meeting, [36] counted by clans, were 2,750. [37] This was the total of all those in the Kohathite clans who served in the Tent of Meeting. Moses and Aaron counted them according to the LORD's command through Moses.

[38] The Gershonites were counted by their clans and families. [39] All the men from thirty to fifty years of age

Get a Load of This...

Check out Numbers 4:11–12. The "hides of sea cows" no doubt came from the East African sea cows ("porpoise" or "dolphin") found in the Red Sea. They were likely expensive because they were hard to get. You had to search the *udder* depths to find a sea cow hide!

who came to serve in the work at the Tent of Meeting, [40]counted by their clans and families, were 2,630. [41]This was the total of those in the Gershonite clans who served at the Tent of Meeting. Moses and Aaron counted them according to the LORD's command.

[42]The Merarites were counted by their clans and families. [43]All the men from thirty to fifty years of age who came to serve in the work at the Tent of Meeting, [44]counted by their clans, were 3,200. [45]This was the total of those in the Merarite clans. Moses and Aaron counted them according to the LORD's command through Moses.

[46]So Moses, Aaron and the leaders of Israel counted all the Levites by their clans and families. [47]All the men from thirty to fifty years of age who came to do the work of serving and carrying the Tent of Meeting [48]numbered 8,580. [49]At the LORD's command through Moses, each was assigned his work and told what to carry.

Thus they were counted, as the LORD commanded Moses.

The Purity of the Camp

5 The LORD said to Moses, [2]"Command the Israelites to send away from the camp anyone who has an infectious skin disease[a] or a discharge of any kind, or who is ceremonially unclean because of a dead body. [3]Send away male and female alike; send them outside the camp so they will not defile their camp, where I dwell among them." [4]The Israelites did this; they sent them outside the camp. They did just as the LORD had instructed Moses.

Restitution for Wrongs

[5]The LORD said to Moses, [6]"Say to the Israelites: 'When a man or woman wrongs another in any way[b] and so is unfaithful to the LORD, that person is guilty [7]and must confess the sin he has committed. He must make full restitution for his wrong, add one fifth to it and give it all to the person he has wronged. [8]But if that

[a] 2 Traditionally *leprosy*; the Hebrew word was used for various diseases affecting the skin—not necessarily leprosy.
[b] 6 Or *woman commits any wrong common to mankind*

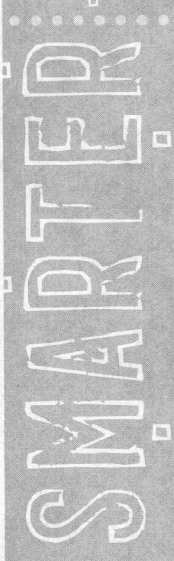

The Blame Game

READ NUMBERS 5:5–10

It's easy to play the *blame game* and try to get others to take the fall for your mistakes. Common "plays" in the blame game include: blaming your friend for daring you to do something wrong; blaming your sister for making you late for school; and blaming the referees at your hockey game for making you lose your temper. Don't play those games. As a man, you need to be responsible for your actions. When you mess up, own up to your mistakes and make things right. God told Moses, "When a man or woman wrongs another ... that person ... must confess the sin he has committed. He must make full restitution for his wrong" (Numbers 5:6–7). When you've hurt someone, you should not only apologize but also do your best to fix the problem. This is called "making restitution." You must do this even when it's tough or embarrassing.

Your next reading is on page 192.

person has no close relative to whom restitution can be made for the wrong, the restitution belongs to the LORD and must be given to the priest, along with the ram with which atonement is made for him. ⁹All the sacred contributions the Israelites bring to a priest will belong to him. ¹⁰Each man's sacred gifts are his own, but what he gives to the priest will belong to the priest.' "

The Test for an Unfaithful Wife

¹¹Then the LORD said to Moses, ¹²"Speak to the Israelites and say to them: 'If a man's wife goes astray and is unfaithful to him ¹³by sleeping with another man, and this is hidden from her husband and her impurity is undetected (since there is no witness against her and she has not been caught in the act), ¹⁴and if feelings of jealousy come over her husband and he suspects his wife and she is impure—or if he is jealous and suspects her even though she is not impure— ¹⁵then he is to take his wife to the priest. He must also take an offering of a tenth of an ephah[a] of barley flour on her behalf. He must not pour oil on it or put incense on it, because it is a grain offering for jealousy, a reminder offering to draw attention to guilt.

¹⁶" 'The priest shall bring her and have her stand before the LORD. ¹⁷Then he shall take some holy water in a clay jar and put some dust from the tabernacle floor into the water. ¹⁸After the priest has had the woman stand before the LORD, he shall loosen her hair and place in her hands the reminder offering, the grain offering for jealousy, while he himself holds the bitter water that brings a curse. ¹⁹Then the priest shall put the woman under oath and say to her, "If no other man has slept with you and you have not gone astray and become impure while married to your husband, may this bitter water that brings a curse not harm you. ²⁰But if you have gone astray while married to your husband and you have defiled yourself by sleeping with a man other than your husband"— ²¹here the priest is to put the woman under this curse of the oath— "may the LORD cause your people to curse and denounce you when he causes your thigh to waste away and your abdomen to swell.[b] ²²May this water that brings a

curse enter your body so that your abdomen swells and your thigh wastes away.[c]"

" 'Then the woman is to say, "Amen. So be it."

²³" 'The priest is to write these curses on a scroll and then wash them off into the bitter water. ²⁴He shall have the woman drink the bitter water that brings a curse, and this water will enter her and cause bitter suffering. ²⁵The priest is to take from her hands the grain offering for jealousy, wave it before the LORD and bring it to the altar. ²⁶The priest is then to take a handful of the grain offering as a memorial offering and burn it on the altar; after that, he is to have the woman drink the water. ²⁷If she has defiled herself and been unfaithful to her husband, then when she is made to drink the water that brings a curse, it will go into her and cause bitter suffering; her abdomen will swell and her thigh waste away,[d] and she will become accursed among her people. ²⁸If, however, the woman has not defiled herself and is free from impurity, she will be cleared of guilt and will be able to have children.

²⁹" 'This, then, is the law of jealousy when a woman goes astray and defiles herself while married to her husband, ³⁰or when feelings of jealousy come over a man because he suspects his wife. The priest is to have her stand before the LORD and is to apply this entire law to her. ³¹The husband will be innocent of any wrongdoing, but the woman will bear the consequences of her sin.' "

The Nazirite

The LORD said to Moses, ²"Speak to the Israelites and say to them: 'If a man or woman wants to make a special vow, a vow of separation to the LORD as a Nazirite, ³he must abstain from wine and other fermented drink and must not drink vinegar made from wine or from other fermented drink. He must not drink grape juice or eat grapes or raisins. ⁴As long as he is a Nazirite, he must not eat anything that comes from the grapevine, not even the seeds or skins.

⁵" 'During the entire period of his vow of separation no razor may be used on his

---

[a] 15 That is, probably about 2 quarts (about 2 liters)
[b] 21 Or causes you to have a miscarrying womb and barrenness   [c] 22 Or body and cause you to be barren and have a miscarrying womb   [d] 27 Or suffering; she will have barrenness and a miscarrying womb

head. He must be holy until the period of his separation to the LORD is over; he must let the hair of his head grow long. 6Throughout the period of his separation to the LORD he must not go near a dead body. 7Even if his own father or mother or brother or sister dies, he must not make himself ceremonially unclean on account of them, because the symbol of his separation to God is on his head. 8Throughout the period of his separation he is consecrated to the LORD.

9" 'If someone dies suddenly in his presence, thus defiling the hair he has dedicated, he must shave his head on the day of his cleansing—the seventh day. 10Then on the eighth day he must bring two doves or two young pigeons to the priest at the entrance to the Tent of Meeting. 11The priest is to offer one as a sin offering and the other as a burnt offering to make atonement for him because he sinned by being in the presence of the dead body. That same day he is to consecrate his head. 12He must dedicate himself to the LORD for the period of his separation and must bring a year-old male lamb as a guilt offering. The previous days do not count, because he became defiled during his separation.

13" 'Now this is the law for the Nazirite when the period of his separation is over. He is to be brought to the entrance to the Tent of Meeting. 14There he is to present his offerings to the LORD: a year-old male lamb without defect for a burnt offering, a year-old ewe lamb without defect for a sin offering, a ram without defect for a fellowship offering,ᵃ 15together with their grain offerings and drink offerings, and a basket of bread made without yeast— cakes made of fine flour mixed with oil, and wafers spread with oil.

16" 'The priest is to present them before the LORD and make the sin offering and the burnt offering. 17He is to present the basket of unleavened bread and is to sacrifice the ram as a fellowship offering to the LORD, together with its grain offering and drink offering.

18" 'Then at the entrance to the Tent of Meeting, the Nazirite must shave off the hair that he dedicated. He is to take the hair and put it in the fire that is under the sacrifice of the fellowship offering.

19" 'After the Nazirite has shaved off the hair of his dedication, the priest is to place in his hands a boiled shoulder of the ram, and a cake and a wafer from the basket, both made without yeast. 20The priest shall then wave them before the LORD as a wave offering; they are holy and belong to the priest, together with the breast that was waved and the thigh that was presented. After that, the Nazirite may drink wine.

21" 'This is the law of the Nazirite who vows his offering to the LORD in accordance with his separation, in addition to whatever else he can afford. He must fulfill the vow he has made, according to the law of the Nazirite.' "

The Priestly Blessing

22The LORD said to Moses, 23"Tell Aaron and his sons, 'This is how you are to bless the Israelites. Say to them:

24" ' "The LORD bless you
and keep you;
25the LORD make his face shine upon you
and be gracious to you;
26the LORD turn his face toward you
and give you peace." '

27"So they will put my name on the Israelites, and I will bless them."

Offerings at the Dedication of the Tabernacle

When Moses finished setting up the tabernacle, he anointed it and consecrated it and all its furnishings. He also anointed and consecrated the altar and all its utensils. 2Then the leaders of Israel, the heads of families who were the tribal leaders in charge of those who were counted, made offerings. 3They brought as their gifts before the LORD six covered carts and twelve oxen—an ox from each leader and a cart from every two. These they presented before the tabernacle.

4The LORD said to Moses, 5"Accept these from them, that they may be used in the work at the Tent of Meeting. Give them to the Levites as each man's work requires."

6So Moses took the carts and oxen and gave them to the Levites. 7He gave two carts and four oxen to the Gershonites, as their work required, 8and he gave four carts and eight oxen to the Merarites, as their work required. They were all under

ᵃ 14 Traditionally *peace offering*; also in verses 17 and 18 the direction of Ithamar son of Aaron, the priest. 9But Moses did not give any to the Kohathites, because they were to carry on their shoulders the holy things, for which they were responsible.

10When the altar was anointed, the leaders brought their offerings for its dedication and presented them before the altar. 11For the LORD had said to Moses, "Each day one leader is to bring his offering for the dedication of the altar."

12The one who brought his offering on the first day was Nahshon son of Amminadab of the tribe of Judah.

13His offering was one silver plate weighing a hundred and thirty shekels,*a* and one silver sprinkling bowl weighing seventy shekels,*b* both according to the sanctuary shekel, each filled with fine flour mixed with oil as a grain offering; 14one gold dish weighing ten shekels,*c* filled with incense; 15one young bull, one ram and one male lamb a year old, for a burnt offering; 16one male goat for a sin offering; 17and two oxen, five rams, five male goats and five male lambs a year old, to be sacrificed as a fellowship offering.*d* This was the offering of Nahshon son of Amminadab.

18On the second day Nethanel son of Zuar, the leader of Issachar, brought his offering.

19The offering he brought was one silver plate weighing a hundred and thirty shekels, and one silver sprinkling bowl weighing seventy shekels, both according to the sanctuary shekel, each filled with fine flour mixed with oil as a grain offering; 20one gold dish weighing ten shek-

a 13 That is, about 3 1/4 pounds (about 1.5 kilograms); also elsewhere in this chapter   *b 13* That is, about 1 3/4 pounds (about 0.8 kilogram); also elsewhere in this chapte
c 14 That is, about 4 ounces (about 110 grams); also elsewhere in this chapter   *d 17* Traditionally *peace offering*; also elsewhere in this chapter

Make It Stick

READ NUMBERS 6:22–27

Rewrite the blessing in verses 24–26. Put the word "me" in place of "you." God wants to bless each and every one of us—past, present and future.

els, filled with incense; 21one young bull, one ram and one male lamb a year old, for a burnt offering; 22one male goat for a sin offering; 23and two oxen, five rams, five male goats and five male lambs a year old, to be sacrificed as a fellowship offering. This was the offering of Nethanel son of Zuar.

24On the third day, Eliab son of Helon, the leader of the people of Zebulun, brought his offering.

25His offering was one silver plate weighing a hundred and thirty shekels, and one silver sprinkling bowl weighing seventy shekels, both according to the sanctuary shekel, each filled with fine flour mixed with oil as a grain offering; 26one gold dish weighing ten shekels, filled with incense; 27one young bull, one ram and one male lamb a year old, for a burnt offering; 28one male goat for a sin offering; 29and two oxen, five rams, five male goats and five male lambs a year old, to be sacrificed as a fellowship offering. This was the offering of Eliab son of Helon.

30On the fourth day Elizur son of Shedeur, the leader of the people of Reuben, brought his offering.

31His offering was one silver plate weighing a hundred and thirty shekels, and one silver sprinkling bowl weighing seventy shekels, both according to the sanctuary shekel, each filled with fine flour mixed with oil as a grain offering; 32one gold dish weighing ten shekels, filled with incense; 33one young bull, one ram and one male lamb a year old, for a burnt offering; 34one male goat for a sin offering; 35and two oxen, five rams, five male goats and five male lambs a year old, to be sacrificed as a fellowship offering. This was the offering of Elizur son of Shedeur.

36On the fifth day Shelumiel son of Zurishaddai, the leader of the people of Simeon, brought his offering.

37His offering was one silver plate weighing a hundred and thirty shekels, and one silver sprinkling bowl weighing seventy shekels, both according to the sanctuary shekel, each filled with fine flour mixed with oil as a grain offering; 38one gold dish weighing ten shekels, filled with incense; 39one young bull, one ram and one male lamb a year old, for a burnt offering; 40one male goat for a sin offering; 41and two oxen, five rams, five male goats and five male lambs a year old, to be sacrificed as a fellowship offering. This was the offering of Shelumiel son of Zurishaddai.

42On the sixth day Eliasaph son of Deuel, the leader of the people of Gad, brought his offering.

43His offering was one silver plate weighing a hundred and thirty shekels, and one silver sprinkling bowl weighing seventy shekels, both according to the sanctuary shekel, each filled with fine flour mixed with oil as a grain offering; 44one gold dish weighing ten shekels, filled with incense; 45one young bull, one ram and one male lamb a year old, for a burnt offering; 46one male goat for a sin offering; 47and two oxen, five rams, five male goats and five male lambs a year old, to be sacrificed as a fellowship offering. This was the offering of Eliasaph son of Deuel.

48On the seventh day Elishama son of Ammihud, the leader of the people of Ephraim, brought his offering.

49His offering was one silver plate weighing a hundred and thirty shekels, and one silver sprinkling bowl weighing seventy shekels, both according to the sanctuary shekel, each filled with fine flour mixed with oil as a grain offering; 50one gold dish weighing ten shekels, filled with incense; 51one young bull, one ram and one male lamb a year old, for a burnt offering; 52one male goat for a sin offering; 53and two oxen, five rams, five male goats and five male lambs a year old, to be sacrificed as a fellowship offering. This was the offering of Elishama son of Ammihud.

54On the eighth day Gamaliel son of Pedahzur, the leader of the people of Manasseh, brought his offering.

55His offering was one silver plate weighing a hundred and thirty shekels, and one silver sprinkling bowl weighing seventy shekels, both according to the sanctuary shekel, each filled with fine flour mixed with oil as a grain offering; ⁵⁶one gold dish weighing ten shekels, filled with incense; ⁵⁷one young bull, one ram and one male lamb a year old, for a burnt offering; ⁵⁸one male goat for a sin offering; ⁵⁹and two oxen, five rams, five male goats and five male lambs a year old, to be sacrificed as a fellowship offering. This was the offering of Gamaliel son of Pedahzur.

⁶⁰On the ninth day Abidan son of Gideoni, the leader of the people of Benjamin, brought his offering. ⁶¹His offering was one silver plate weighing a hundred and thirty shekels, and one silver sprinkling bowl weighing seventy shekels, both according to the sanctuary shekel, each filled with fine flour mixed with oil as a grain offering; ⁶²one gold dish weighing ten shekels, filled with incense; ⁶³one young bull, one ram and one male lamb a year old, for a burnt offering; ⁶⁴one male goat for a sin offering; ⁶⁵and two oxen, five rams, five male goats and five male lambs a year old, to be sacrificed as a fellowship offering. This was the offering of Abidan son of Gideoni.

⁶⁶On the tenth day Ahiezer son of Ammishaddai, the leader of the people of Dan, brought his offering. ⁶⁷His offering was one silver plate weighing a hundred and thirty shekels, and one silver sprinkling bowl weighing seventy shekels, both according to the sanctuary shekel, each filled with fine flour mixed with oil as a grain offering; ⁶⁸one gold dish weighing ten shekels, filled with incense; ⁶⁹one young bull, one ram and one male lamb a year old, for a burnt offering; ⁷⁰one male goat for a sin offering; ⁷¹and two oxen, five rams, five male goats and five male lambs a year old, to be sacrificed as a fellowship offering. This was the offering of Ahiezer son of Ammishaddai.

⁷²On the eleventh day Pagiel son of Ocran, the leader of the people of Asher, brought his offering. ⁷³His offering was one silver plate

weighing a hundred and thirty shekels, and one silver sprinkling bowl weighing seventy shekels, both according to the sanctuary shekel, each filled with fine flour mixed with oil as a grain offering; ⁷⁴one gold dish weighing ten shekels, filled with incense; ⁷⁵one young bull, one ram and one male lamb a year old, for a burnt offering; ⁷⁶one male goat for a sin offering; ⁷⁷and two oxen, five rams, five male goats and five male lambs a year old, to be sacrificed as a fellowship offering. This was the offering of Pagiel son of Ocran.

⁷⁸On the twelfth day Ahira son of Enan, the leader of the people of Naphtali, brought his offering. ⁷⁹His offering was one silver plate weighing a hundred and thirty shekels, and one silver sprinkling bowl weighing seventy shekels, both according to the sanctuary shekel, each filled with fine flour mixed with oil as a grain offering; ⁸⁰one gold dish weighing ten shekels, filled with incense; ⁸¹one young bull, one ram and one male lamb a year old, for a burnt offering; ⁸²one male goat for a sin offering; ⁸³and two oxen, five rams, five male goats and five male lambs a year old, to be sacrificed as a fellowship offering. This was the offering of Ahira son of Enan.

⁸⁴These were the offerings of the Israelite leaders for the dedication of the altar when it was anointed: twelve silver plates, twelve silver sprinkling bowls and twelve gold dishes. ⁸⁵Each silver plate weighed a hundred and thirty shekels, and each sprinkling bowl seventy shekels. Altogether, the silver dishes weighed two thousand four hundred shekels,ᵃ according to the sanctuary shekel. ⁸⁶The twelve gold dishes filled with incense weighed ten shekels each, according to the sanctuary shekel. Altogether, the gold dishes weighed a hundred and twenty shekels.ᵇ ⁸⁷The total number of animals for the burnt offering came to twelve young bulls, twelve rams and twelve male lambs a year old, together with their grain offering. Twelve male goats were used for the

ᵃ 85 That is, about 60 pounds (about 28 kilograms)
ᵇ 86 That is, about 3 pounds (about 1.4 kilograms)

sin offering. 88The total number of animals for the sacrifice of the fellowship offering came to twenty-four oxen, sixty rams, sixty male goats and sixty male lambs a year old. These were the offerings for the dedication of the altar after it was anointed.

89When Moses entered the Tent of Meeting to speak with the LORD, he heard the voice speaking to him from between the two cherubim above the atonement cover on the ark of the Testimony. And he spoke with him.

Setting Up the Lamps

The LORD said to Moses, 2"Speak to Aaron and say to him, 'When you set up the seven lamps, they are to light the area in front of the lampstand.' "

3Aaron did so; he set up the lamps so that they faced forward on the lampstand, just as the LORD commanded Moses. 4This is how the lampstand was made: It was made of hammered gold—from its base to its blossoms. The lampstand was made exactly like the pattern the LORD had shown Moses.

The Setting Apart of the Levites

5The LORD said to Moses: 6"Take the Levites from among the other Israelites and make them ceremonially clean. 7To purify them, do this: Sprinkle the water of cleansing on them; then have them shave their whole bodies and wash their clothes, and so purify themselves. 8Have them take a young bull with its grain offering of fine flour mixed with oil; then you are to take a second young bull for a sin offering. 9Bring the Levites to the front of the Tent of Meeting and assemble the whole Israelite community. 10You are to bring the Levites before the LORD, and the Israelites are to lay their hands on them. 11Aaron is to present the Levites before the LORD as a wave offering from the Israelites, so that they may be ready to do the work of the LORD.

12"After the Levites lay their hands on the heads of the bulls, use the one for a sin offering to the LORD and the other for a burnt offering, to make atonement for the Levites. 13Have the Levites stand in front of Aaron and his sons and then present them as a wave offering to the LORD. 14In this way you are to set the Levites

apart from the other Israelites, and the Levites will be mine.

15"After you have purified the Levites and presented them as a wave offering, they are to come to do their work at the Tent of Meeting. 16They are the Israelites who are to be given wholly to me. I have taken them as my own in place of the firstborn, the first male offspring from every Israelite woman. 17Every firstborn male in Israel, whether man or animal, is mine. When I struck down all the firstborn in Egypt, I set them apart for myself. 18And I have taken the Levites in place of all the firstborn sons in Israel. 19Of all the Israelites, I have given the Levites as gifts to Aaron and his sons to do the work at the Tent of Meeting on behalf of the Israelites and to make atonement for them so that no plague will strike the Israelites when they go near the sanctuary."

20Moses, Aaron and the whole Israelite community did with the Levites just as the LORD commanded Moses. 21The Levites purified themselves and washed their clothes. Then Aaron presented them as a wave offering before the LORD and made atonement for them to purify them. 22After that, the Levites came to do their work at the Tent of Meeting under the supervision of Aaron and his sons. They did with the Levites just as the LORD commanded Moses.

23The LORD said to Moses, 24"This applies to the Levites: Men twenty-five years old or more shall come to take part in the work at the Tent of Meeting, 25but at the age of fifty, they must retire from their regular service and work no longer. 26They may assist their brothers in performing their duties at the Tent of Meeting, but they themselves must not do the work. This, then, is how you are to assign the responsibilities of the Levites."

The Passover

The LORD spoke to Moses in the Desert of Sinai in the first month of the second year after they came out of Egypt. He said, 2"Have the Israelites celebrate the Passover at the appointed time. 3Celebrate it at the appointed time, at twilight on the fourteenth day of this month, in accordance with all its rules and regulations."

4So Moses told the Israelites to celebrate the Passover, 5and they did so in the

Desert of Sinai at twilight on the four-teenth day of the first month. The Israel-ites did everything just as the LORD com-manded Moses.

6But some of them could not celebrate the Passover on that day because they were ceremonially unclean on account of a dead body. So they came to Moses and Aaron that same day 7and said to Moses, "We have become unclean because of a dead body, but why should we be kept from presenting the LORD's offering with the other Israelites at the appointed time?"

8Moses answered them, "Wait until I find out what the LORD commands con-cerning you."

9Then the LORD said to Moses, 10"Tell the Israelites: 'When any of you or your descendants are unclean because of a dead body or are away on a journey, they may still celebrate the LORD's Passover. 11They are to celebrate it on the four-teenth day of the second month at twi-light. They are to eat the lamb, together with unleavened bread and bitter herbs. 12They must not leave any of it till morn-ing or break any of its bones. When they celebrate the Passover, they must follow all the regulations. 13But if a man who is ceremonially clean and not on a journey fails to celebrate the Passover, that person must be cut off from his people because he did not present the LORD's offering at the appointed time. That man will bear the consequences of his sin.

14" 'An alien living among you who wants to celebrate the LORD's Passover must do so in accordance with its rules and reg-ulations. You must have the same regula-tions for the alien and the native-born.' "

The Cloud Above the Tabernacle

15On the day the tabernacle, the Tent of the Testimony, was set up, the cloud cov-ered it. From evening till morning the cloud above the tabernacle looked like fire. 16That is how it continued to be; the cloud covered it, and at night it looked like fire. 17Whenever the cloud lifted from above the Tent, the Israelites set out; wherever the cloud settled, the Israelites encamped. 18At the LORD's command the Israelites set out, and at his command they encamped. As long as the cloud stayed over the tabernacle, they remained in camp. 19When the cloud remained over the tabernacle a long time, the Israelites

obeyed the LORD's order and did not set out. 20Sometimes the cloud was over the tabernacle only a few days; at the LORD's command they would encamp, and then at his command they would set out. 21Sometimes the cloud stayed only from evening till morning, and when it lifted in the morning, they set out. Whether by day or by night, whenever the cloud lift-ed, they set out. 22Whether the cloud stayed over the tabernacle for two days or a month or a year, the Israelites would re-main in camp and not set out; but when it lifted, they would set out. 23At the LORD's command they encamped, and at the LORD's command they set out. They obeyed the LORD's order, in accordance with his command through Moses.

The Silver Trumpets

The LORD said to Moses: 2"Make two trumpets of hammered sil-ver, and use them for calling the community together and for having the camps set out. 3When both are sounded, the whole community is to assemble before you at the entrance to the Tent of Meeting. 4If only one is sound-ed, the leaders—the heads of the clans of Israel—are to assemble before you. 5When a trumpet blast is sounded, the tribes camping on the east are to set out. 6At the sounding of a second blast, the camps on the south are to set out. The blast will be the signal for setting out. 7To gather the assembly, blow the trumpets, but not with the same signal.

8"The sons of Aaron, the priests, are to blow the trumpets. This is to be a lasting ordinance for you and the generations to come. 9When you go into battle in your own land against an enemy who is op-pressing you, sound a blast on the trum-pets. Then you will be remembered by the LORD your God and rescued from your ene-mies. 10Also at your times of rejoicing—your appointed feasts and New Moon fes-tivals—you are to sound the trumpets over your burnt offerings and fellowship offer-ings,a and they will be a memorial for you before your God. I am the LORD your God."

The Israelites Leave Sinai

11On the twentieth day of the second month of the second year, the cloud lifted

---

a 10 Traditionally peace offerings

from above the tabernacle of the Testimony. ¹²Then the Israelites set out from the Desert of Sinai and traveled from place to place until the cloud came to rest in the Desert of Paran. ¹³They set out, this first time, at the LORD's command through Moses.

¹⁴The divisions of the camp of Judah went first, under their standard. Nahshon son of Amminadab was in command. ¹⁵Nethanel son of Zuar was over the division of the tribe of Issachar, ¹⁶and Eliab son of Helon was over the division of the tribe of Zebulun. ¹⁷Then the tabernacle was taken down, and the Gershonites and Merarites, who carried it, set out.

¹⁸The divisions of the camp of Reuben went next, under their standard. Elizur son of Shedeur was in command. ¹⁹Shelumiel son of Zurishaddai was over the division of the tribe of Simeon, ²⁰and Eliasaph son of Deuel was over the division of the tribe of Gad. ²¹Then the Kohathites set out, carrying the holy things. The tabernacle was to be set up before they arrived.

²²The divisions of the camp of Ephraim went next, under their standard. Elishama son of Ammihud was in command. ²³Gamaliel son of Pedahzur was over the division of the tribe of Manasseh, ²⁴and Abidan son of Gideoni was over the division of the tribe of Benjamin.

²⁵Finally, as the rear guard for all the units, the divisions of the camp of Dan set out, under their standard. Ahiezer son of Ammishaddai was in command. ²⁶Pagiel son of Ocran was over the division of the tribe of Asher, ²⁷and Ahira son of Enan was over the division of the tribe of Naphtali. ²⁸This was the order of march for the Israelite divisions as they set out.

²⁹Now Moses said to Hobab son of Reuel the Midianite, Moses' father-in-law, "We are setting out for the place about which the LORD said, 'I will give it to you.' Come with us and we will treat you well, for the LORD has promised good things to Israel."

³⁰He answered, "No, I will not go; I am going back to my own land and my own people."

³¹But Moses said, "Please do not leave us. You know where we should camp in the desert, and you can be our eyes. ³²If you come with us, we will share with you whatever good things the LORD gives us."

³³So they set out from the mountain of the LORD and traveled for three days. The ark of the covenant of the LORD went before them during those three days to find them a place to rest. ³⁴The cloud of the LORD was over them by day when they set out from the camp.

³⁵Whenever the ark set out, Moses said,

"Rise up, O LORD!
   May your enemies be scattered;
   may your foes flee before you."

³⁶Whenever it came to rest, he said,

"Return, O LORD,
   to the countless thousands of Israel."

Fire From the LORD

11 Now the people complained about their hardships in the hearing of the LORD, and when he heard them his anger was aroused. Then fire from the LORD burned among them and consumed some of the outskirts of the camp. ²When the people cried out to Moses, he prayed to the LORD and the fire died down. ³So that place was called Taberah,^a because fire from the LORD had burned among them.

Quail From the LORD

⁴The rabble with them began to crave other food, and again the Israelites started wailing and said, "If only we had meat to eat! ⁵We remember the fish we ate in Egypt at no cost—also the cucumbers, melons, leeks, onions and garlic. ⁶But now we have lost our appetite; we never see anything but this manna!"

⁷The manna was like coriander seed and looked like resin. ⁸The people went around gathering it, and then ground it in a handmill or crushed it in a mortar. They cooked it in a pot or made it into cakes. And it tasted like something made with olive oil. ⁹When the dew settled on the camp at night, the manna also came down.

¹⁰Moses heard the people of every family wailing, each at the entrance to his tent. The LORD became exceedingly angry, and Moses was troubled. ¹¹He asked the LORD, "Why have you brought this trouble on your servant? What have I done to displease you that you put the burden of all these people on me? ¹²Did I conceive all these people? Did I give them birth? Why do you tell me to carry them in my arms,

---

^a 3 Taberah means burning.

as a nurse carries an infant, to the land you promised on oath to their forefathers? ¹³Where can I get meat for all these people? They keep wailing to me, 'Give us meat to eat!' ¹⁴I cannot carry all these people by myself; the burden is too heavy for me. ¹⁵If this is how you are going to treat me, put me to death right now—if I have found favor in your eyes—and do not let me face my own ruin."

¹⁶The LORD said to Moses: "Bring me seventy of Israel's elders who are known to you as leaders and officials among the people. Have them come to the Tent of Meeting, that they may stand there with you. ¹⁷I will come down and speak with you there, and I will take of the Spirit that is on you and put the Spirit on them. They will help you carry the burden of the people so that you will not have to carry it alone.

¹⁸"Tell the people: 'Consecrate yourselves in preparation for tomorrow, when you will eat meat. The LORD heard you when you wailed, "If only we had meat to eat! We were better off in Egypt!" Now the LORD will give you meat, and you will eat it. ¹⁹You will not eat it for just one day, or two days, or five, ten or twenty days, ²⁰but for a whole month—until it comes out of your nostrils and you loathe it—because you have rejected the LORD, who is among you, and have wailed before him, saying, "Why did we ever leave Egypt?" ' "

²¹But Moses said, "Here I am among six hundred thousand men on foot, and you say, 'I will give them meat to eat for a whole month!' ²²Would they have enough if flocks and herds were slaughtered for them? Would they have enough if all the fish in the sea were caught for them?"

²³The LORD answered Moses, "Is the LORD's arm too short? You will now see whether or not what I say will come true for you."

²⁴So Moses went out and told the people what the LORD had said. He brought together seventy of their elders and had them stand around the Tent. ²⁵Then the LORD came down in the cloud and spoke with him, and he took of the Spirit that was on him and put the Spirit on the seventy elders. When the Spirit rested on them, they prophesied, but they did not do so again. ^a

²⁶However, two men, whose names were Eldad and Medad, had remained in the camp. They were listed among the elders, but did not go out to the Tent. Yet the Spirit also rested on them, and they prophesied in the camp. ²⁷A young man ran and told Moses, "Eldad and Medad are prophesying in the camp."

²⁸Joshua son of Nun, who had been Moses' aide since youth, spoke up and said, "Moses, my lord, stop them!"

²⁹But Moses replied, "Are you jealous for my sake? I wish that all the LORD's people were prophets and that the LORD would put his Spirit on them!" ³⁰Then Moses and the elders of Israel returned to the camp.

^a 25 Or *prophesied and continued to do so*

Get a Load of This...

Check out Numbers 11:1–3. You can get hurt if you play with fire. God wasn't playing around here. When the Israelites murmured and God sent fire to burn down some of their tents, he was sending a serious message: Be thankful for what you have.

³¹Now a wind went out from the LORD and drove quail in from the sea. It brought them[a] down all around the camp to about three feet[b] above the ground, as far as a day's walk in any direction. ³²All that day and night and all the next day the people went out and gathered quail. No one gathered less than ten homers.[c] Then they spread them out all around the camp. ³³But while the meat was still between their teeth and before it could be consumed, the anger of the LORD burned against the people, and he struck them with a severe plague. ³⁴Therefore the place was named Kibroth Hattaavah,[d] because there they buried the people who had craved other food.

³⁵From Kibroth Hattaavah the people traveled to Hazeroth and stayed there.

Miriam and Aaron Oppose Moses

12 Miriam and Aaron began to talk against Moses because of his Cushite wife, for he had married a Cushite. ²"Has the LORD spoken only through Moses?" they asked. "Hasn't he also spoken through us?" And the LORD heard this.

³(Now Moses was a very humble man, more humble than anyone else on the face of the earth.)

⁴At once the LORD said to Moses, Aaron and Miriam, "Come out to the Tent of Meeting, all three of you." So the three of them came out. ⁵Then the LORD came down in a pillar of cloud; he stood at the entrance to the Tent and summoned Aaron and Miriam. When both of them stepped forward, ⁶he said, "Listen to my words:

"When a prophet of the LORD is among you,
   I reveal myself to him in visions,
   I speak to him in dreams.
⁷But this is not true of my servant Moses;
   he is faithful in all my house.
⁸With him I speak face to face,
   clearly and not in riddles;

---

a 31 Or *They flew*   *b 31* Hebrew *two cubits* (about 1 meter)
c 32 That is, probably about 60 bushels (about 2.2 kiloliters)
d 34 *Kibroth Hattaavah* means *graves of craving*.

GET SMARTER

Wails, Then Quails

READ NUMBERS 11:4–23, 31–34

God provided the Israelites with miraculous food every day. But for some of them, the manna wasn't good enough. Instead of *asking* God to give them something different, they started to complain. They moaned that they just couldn't go another day without meat, watermelons, onions and garlic. (The meat and melons you can *understand*.) The murmuring spread until *all* the Israelites were wailing. They wanted meat? God *gave* them meat! He dumped so many quails on them that their camp looked like a chicken yard. But a plague from the Lord struck "while the meat was still between their teeth" (verse 33) and killed many of them. Two good lessons here: (1) Be content with what God gives you rather than craving other things; (2) If you really need something, pray for it in the right spirit instead of complaining.

Your next reading is on page 194.

he sees the form of the LORD.
Why then were you not afraid
    to speak against my servant Moses?"

⁹The anger of the LORD burned against them, and he left them.

¹⁰When the cloud lifted from above the Tent, there stood Miriam—leprous,ᵃ like snow. Aaron turned toward her and saw that she had leprosy; ¹¹and he said to Moses, "Please, my lord, do not hold against us the sin we have so foolishly committed. ¹²Do not let her be like a stillborn infant coming from its mother's womb with its flesh half eaten away."

¹³So Moses cried out to the LORD, "O God, please heal her!"

¹⁴The LORD replied to Moses, "If her father had spit in her face, would she not have been in disgrace for seven days? Confine her outside the camp for seven days; after that she can be brought back." ¹⁵So Miriam was confined outside the camp for seven days, and the people did not move on till she was brought back.

¹⁶After that, the people left Hazeroth and encamped in the Desert of Paran.

ᵃ 10 The Hebrew word was used for various diseases affecting the skin—not necessarily leprosy.

Make It Stick

READ NUMBERS 12

If you had to answer to God like Aaron and Miriam did, how would *you* fare? Romans 13 explains that God establishes authorities over us. That's why it's better to encourage (not grumble against) leaders. Write down some ways you can support and honor an authority in your life: parents, principals, teachers, even babysitters.

Exploring Canaan

13 The Lord said to Moses, 2"Send some men to explore the land of Canaan, which I am giving to the Israelites. From each ancestral tribe send one of its leaders."

3So at the Lord's command Moses sent them out from the Desert of Paran. All of them were leaders of the Israelites. 4These are their names:

from the tribe of Reuben, Shammua son of Zaccur;

5from the tribe of Simeon, Shaphat son of Hori;

6from the tribe of Judah, Caleb son of Jephunneh;

7from the tribe of Issachar, Igal son of Joseph;

8from the tribe of Ephraim, Hoshea son of Nun;

9from the tribe of Benjamin, Palti son of Raphu;

10from the tribe of Zebulun, Gaddiel son of Sodi;

11from the tribe of Manasseh (a tribe of Joseph), Gaddi son of Susi;

12from the tribe of Dan, Ammiel son of Gemalli;

13from the tribe of Asher, Sethur son of Michael;

14from the tribe of Naphtali, Nahbi son of Vophsi;

15from the tribe of Gad, Geuel son of Maki.

16These are the names of the men Moses sent to explore the land. (Moses gave Hoshea son of Nun the name Joshua.)

17When Moses sent them to explore Canaan, he said, "Go up through the Negev and on into the hill country. 18See what the land is like and whether the people who live there are strong or weak, few or many. 19What kind of land do they live in? Is it good or bad? What kind of towns do they live in? Are they unwalled or fortified?

Don't Sweat the Other Guy

READ NUMBERS 13:1–3, 26–33

GET STRONGER

Tough but true: There will always be someone who can outdo you. Some kid somewhere is bigger, stronger, faster or smarter. It's easy to get bummed out over that. Case in point: When the Israelites went to investigate the new land, they saw some descendants of a man named Anak who were gigantic dudes. Most of the Israelites were shaken up. Not Caleb. Caleb said, "We should go up and take possession of the land, for we can certainly do it" (Numbers 13:30). Everyone else said, "No way! Those giants will waste us!" They forgot that God was with them and that God could give them the victory no matter how huge their opponents were. Caleb trusted God, and that gave him confidence. It's the same today: If you compare yourself with others, you may be disappointed. Instead, take Caleb's attitude and don't sweat the other guy.

Your next reading is on page 196.

²⁰How is the soil? Is it fertile or poor? Are there trees on it or not? Do your best to bring back some of the fruit of the land." (It was the season for the first ripe grapes.)

²¹So they went up and explored the land from the Desert of Zin as far as Rehob, toward Lebo ᵃ Hamath. ²²They went up through the Negev and came to Hebron, where Ahiman, Sheshai and Talmai, the descendants of Anak, lived. (Hebron had been built seven years before Zoan in Egypt.) ²³When they reached the Valley of Eshcol, ᵇ they cut off a branch bearing a single cluster of grapes. Two of them carried it on a pole between them, along with some pomegranates and figs. ²⁴That place was called the Valley of Eshcol because of the cluster of grapes the Israelites cut off there. ²⁵At the end of forty days they returned from exploring the land.

Report on the Exploration

²⁶They came back to Moses and Aaron and the whole Israelite community at Kadesh in the Desert of Paran. There they reported to them and to the whole assembly and showed them the fruit of the land. ²⁷They gave Moses this account: "We went into the land to which you sent us, and it does flow with milk and honey! Here is its fruit. ²⁸But the people who live there are powerful, and the cities are fortified and very large. We even saw descendants of Anak there. ²⁹The Amalekites live in the Negev; the Hittites, Jebusites and Amorites live in the hill country; and the Canaanites live near the sea and along the Jordan."

³⁰Then Caleb silenced the people before Moses and said, "We should go up and take possession of the land, for we can certainly do it."

³¹But the men who had gone up with him said, "We can't attack those people; they are stronger than we are." ³²And they spread among the Israelites a bad report about the land they had explored. They said, "The land we explored devours those living in it. All the people we saw there are of great size. ³³We saw the Nephilim there (the descendants of Anak come from the Nephilim). We seemed like grasshoppers in our own eyes, and we looked the same to them."

The People Rebel

14 That night all the people of the community raised their voices and wept aloud. ²All the Israelites grumbled against Moses and Aaron, and the whole assembly said to them, "If only we had died in Egypt! Or in this desert! ³Why is the LORD bringing us to this land only to let us fall by the sword? Our wives and children will be taken as plunder. Wouldn't it be better for us to go back to Egypt?" ⁴And they said to each other, "We should choose a leader and go back to Egypt."

⁵Then Moses and Aaron fell facedown in front of the whole Israelite assembly gathered there. ⁶Joshua son of

Get a Load of This...

Check out Numbers 13:28–33. The descendants of Anak, also known as Anakites, were *so* big they would all make the tallest NBA player look shrimpy. Goliath, whom David would kill years later, was likely an Anakite, and he was over nine feet tall. Talk about a shot-blocker!

ᵃ 21 Or *toward the entrance to*   ᵇ 23 *Eshcol* means *cluster*; also in verse 24.

Nun and Caleb son of Jephunneh, who were among those who had explored the land, tore their clothes 7and said to the entire Israelite assembly, "The land we passed through and explored is exceedingly good. 8If the LORD is pleased with us, he will lead us into that land, a land flowing with milk and honey, and will give it to us. 9Only do not rebel against the LORD. And do not be afraid of the people of the land, because we will swallow them up. Their protection is gone, but the LORD is with us. Do not be afraid of them."

10But the whole assembly talked about stoning them. Then the glory of the LORD appeared at the Tent of Meeting to all the Israelites. 11The LORD said to Moses, "How long will these people treat me with contempt? How long will they refuse to believe in me, in spite of all the miraculous signs I have performed among them? 12I will strike them down with a plague and destroy them, but I will make you into a nation greater and stronger than they."

13Moses said to the LORD, "Then the Egyptians will hear about it! By your power you brought these people up from among them. 14And they will tell the inhabitants of this land about it. They have already heard that you, O LORD, are with these people and that you, O LORD, have been seen face to face, that your cloud stays over them, and that you go before them in a pillar of cloud by day and a pillar of fire by night. 15If you put these people to death all at one time, the nations who have heard this report about you will say, 16'The LORD was not able to bring these people into the land he promised them on oath; so he slaughtered them in the desert.'

17"Now may the Lord's strength be displayed, just as you have declared: 18'The LORD is slow to anger, abounding in love and forgiving sin and rebellion. Yet he does not leave the guilty unpunished; he punishes the children for the sin of the fathers to the third and fourth generation.' 19In accordance with your great love, forgive the sin of these people, just as you have pardoned them from the time they left Egypt until now."

20The LORD replied, "I have forgiven them, as you asked. 21Nevertheless, as

Wishing for the Worst

READ NUMBERS 14:1–38

You may have heard the saying, "Be careful what you wish for. You might get it." The idea is that we don't always know what is best for us. The Israelites often wished for the worst possible stuff. For example, they were afraid to enter the Promised Land and moaned, "If only we had died … in this desert!" (verse 2). Caleb and Joshua said, "If the LORD is pleased with us, he will lead us into that land … and will give it to us" (verse 8). Caleb and Joshua trusted God. Everyone else was afraid and rebelled. So guess what? God *gave* the Israelites their wish. He told them they *would* all die in the desert—everyone, that is, except for Joshua and Caleb, who believed that God would give them the victory. When God says he'll do something, believe him and be thankful. Expect him to keep his promises.

Your next reading is on page 204.

surely as I live and as surely as the glory of the LORD fills the whole earth, 22not one of the men who saw my glory and the miraculous signs I performed in Egypt and in the desert but who disobeyed me and tested me ten times— 23not one of them will ever see the land I promised on oath to their forefathers. No one who has treated me with contempt will ever see it. 24But because my servant Caleb has a different spirit and follows me wholeheartedly, I will bring him into the land he went to, and his descendants will inherit it. 25Since the Amalekites and Canaanites are living in the valleys, turn back tomorrow and set out toward the desert along the route to the Red Sea.*a*"

26The LORD said to Moses and Aaron: 27"How long will this wicked community grumble against me? I have heard the complaints of these grumbling Israelites. 28So tell them, 'As surely as I live, declares the LORD, I will do to you the very things I heard you say: 29In this desert your bodies will fall—every one of you twenty years old or more who was counted in the census and who has grumbled against me. 30Not one of you will enter the land I swore with uplifted hand to make your home, except Caleb son of Jephunneh and Joshua son of Nun. 31As for your children that you said would be taken as plunder, I will bring them in to enjoy the land you have rejected. 32But you—your bodies will fall in this desert. 33Your children will be shepherds here for forty years, suffering for your unfaithfulness, until the last of your bodies lies in the desert. 34For forty years—one year for each of the forty days you explored the land—you will suffer for your sins and know what it is like to have me against you.' 35I, the LORD, have spoken, and I will surely do these things to this whole wicked community, which has banded together against me. They will meet their end in this desert; here they will die."

36So the men Moses had sent to explore the land, who returned and made the whole community grumble against him by spreading a bad report about it— 37these men responsible for spreading the bad report about the land were struck down and died of a plague before the LORD. 38Of the men who went to explore the land, only Joshua son of Nun and Caleb son of Jephunneh survived.

39When Moses reported this to all the Israelites, they mourned bitterly. 40Early the next morning they went up toward the high hill country. "We have sinned," they said. "We will go up to the place the LORD promised."

41But Moses said, "Why are you disobeying the LORD's command? This will not succeed! 42Do not go up, because the LORD is not with you. You will be defeated by your enemies, 43for the Amalekites and Canaanites will face you there. Because you have turned away from the LORD, he will not be with you and you will fall by the sword."

44Nevertheless, in their presumption they went up toward the high hill country, though neither Moses nor the ark of the LORD's covenant moved from the camp. 45Then the Amalekites and Canaanites who lived in that hill country came down and attacked them and beat them down all the way to Hormah.

Supplementary Offerings

15 The LORD said to Moses, 2"Speak to the Israelites and say to them: 'After you enter the land I am giving you as a home 3and you present to the LORD offerings made by fire, from the herd or the flock, as an aroma pleasing to the LORD—whether burnt offerings or sacrifices, for special vows or freewill offerings or festival offerings— 4then the one who brings his offering shall present to the LORD a grain offering of a tenth of an ephah*b* of fine flour mixed with a quarter of a hin*c* of oil. 5With each lamb for the burnt offering or the sacrifice, prepare a quarter of a hin of wine as a drink offering.

6" 'With a ram prepare a grain offering of two-tenths of an ephah*d* of fine flour mixed with a third of a hin*e* of oil, 7and a third of a hin of wine as a drink offering. Offer it as an aroma pleasing to the LORD.

8" 'When you prepare a young bull as a burnt offering or sacrifice, for a special vow or a fellowship offering*f* to the LORD, 9bring with the bull a grain offering of three-tenths of an ephah*g* of fine flour

a 25 Hebrew *Yam Suph*; that is, Sea of Reeds   *b 4* That is, probably about 2 quarts (about 2 liters)   *c 4* That is, probably about 1 quart (about 1 liter); also in verse 5   *d 6* That is, probably about 4 quarts (about 4.5 liters)   *e 6* That is, probably about 1 1/4 quarts (about 1.2 liters); also in verse 7   *f 8* Traditionally *peace offering*   *g 9* That is, probably about 6 quarts (about 6.5 liters) mixed with half a hin[a] of oil. ¹⁰Also bring half a hin of wine as a drink offering. It will be an offering made by fire, an aroma pleasing to the Lord. ¹¹Each bull or ram, each lamb or young goat, is to be prepared in this manner. ¹²Do this for each one, for as many as you prepare.

¹³" 'Everyone who is native-born must do these things in this way when he brings an offering made by fire as an aroma pleasing to the Lord. ¹⁴For the generations to come, whenever an alien or anyone else living among you presents an offering made by fire as an aroma pleasing to the Lord, he must do exactly as you do. ¹⁵The community is to have the same rules for you and for the alien living among you; this is a lasting ordinance for the generations to come. You and the alien shall be the same before the Lord: ¹⁶The same laws and regulations will apply both to you and to the alien living among you.' "

¹⁷The Lord said to Moses, ¹⁸"Speak to the Israelites and say to them: 'When you enter the land to which I am taking you ¹⁹and you eat the food of the land, present a portion as an offering to the Lord. ²⁰Present a cake from the first of your ground meal and present it as an offering from the threshing floor. ²¹Throughout the generations to come you are to give this offering to the Lord from the first of your ground meal.

Offerings for Unintentional Sins

²²" 'Now if you unintentionally fail to keep any of these commands the Lord gave Moses— ²³any of the Lord's commands to you through him, from the day the Lord gave them and continuing through the generations to come— ²⁴and if this is done unintentionally without the community being aware of it, then the whole community is to offer a young bull for a burnt offering as an aroma pleasing to the Lord, along with its prescribed grain offering and drink offering, and a male goat for a sin offering. ²⁵The priest is to make atonement for the whole Israelite community, and they will be forgiven, for it was not intentional and they have brought to the Lord for their wrong an offering made by fire and a sin offering. ²⁶The whole Israelite community and the aliens living among them will be forgiven, because all the people were involved in the unintentional wrong.

²⁷" 'But if just one person sins unintentionally, he must bring a year-old female goat for a sin offering. ²⁸The priest is to make atonement before the Lord for the one who erred by sinning unintentionally, and when atonement has been made for him, he will be forgiven. ²⁹One and the same law applies to everyone who sins unintentionally, whether he is a native-born Israelite or an alien.

³⁰" 'But anyone who sins defiantly, whether native-born or alien, blasphemes the Lord, and that person must be cut off from his people. ³¹Because he has despised the Lord's word and broken his commands, that person must surely be cut off; his guilt remains on him.' "

The Sabbath-Breaker Put to Death

³²While the Israelites were in the desert, a man was found gathering wood on the Sabbath day. ³³Those who found him gathering wood brought him to Moses and Aaron and the whole assembly, ³⁴and they kept him in custody, because it was not clear what should be done to him. ³⁵Then the Lord said to Moses, "The man must die. The whole assembly must stone him outside the camp." ³⁶So the assembly took him outside the camp and stoned him to death, as the Lord commanded Moses.

Tassels on Garments

³⁷The Lord said to Moses, ³⁸"Speak to the Israelites and say to them: 'Throughout the generations to come you are to make tassels on the corners of your garments, with a blue cord on each tassel. ³⁹You will have these tassels to look at and so you will remember all the commands of the Lord, that you may obey them and not prostitute yourselves by going after the lusts of your own hearts and eyes. ⁴⁰Then you will remember to obey all my commands and will be consecrated to your God. ⁴¹I am the Lord your God, who brought you out of Egypt to be your God. I am the Lord your God.' "

Korah, Dathan and Abiram

16 Korah son of Izhar, the son of Kohath, the son of Levi, and certain Reubenites—Dathan and Abiram, sons of Eliab, and On

---

[a] 9 That is, probably about 2 quarts (about 2 liters); also in verse 10

son of Peleth—became insolent[a] [2]and rose up against Moses. With them were 250 Israelite men, well-known community leaders who had been appointed members of the council. [3]They came as a group to oppose Moses and Aaron and said to them, "You have gone too far! The whole community is holy, every one of them, and the LORD is with them. Why then do you set yourselves above the LORD's assembly?"

[4]When Moses heard this, he fell facedown. [5]Then he said to Korah and all his followers: "In the morning the LORD will show who belongs to him and who is holy, and he will have that person come near him. The man he chooses he will cause to come near him. [6]You, Korah, and all your followers are to do this: Take censers [7]and tomorrow put fire and incense in them before the LORD. The man the LORD chooses will be the one who is holy. You Levites have gone too far!"

[8]Moses also said to Korah, "Now listen, you Levites! [9]Isn't it enough for you that the God of Israel has separated you from the rest of the Israelite community and brought you near himself to do the work at the LORD's tabernacle and to stand before the community and minister to them? [10]He has brought you and all your fellow Levites near himself, but now you are trying to get the priesthood too. [11]It is against the LORD that you and all your followers have banded together. Who is Aaron that you should grumble against him?"

[12]Then Moses summoned Dathan and Abiram, the sons of Eliab. But they said, "We will not come! [13]Isn't it enough that you have brought us up out of a land flowing with milk and honey to kill us in the desert? And now you also want to lord it over us? [14]Moreover, you haven't brought us into a land flowing with milk and honey or given us an inheritance of fields and vineyards. Will you gouge out the eyes of[b] these men? No, we will not come!"

[15]Then Moses became very angry and said to the LORD, "Do not accept their offering. I have not taken so much as a donkey from them, nor have I wronged any of them."

[16]Moses said to Korah, "You and all your followers are to appear before the LORD tomorrow—you and they and Aaron. [17]Each man is to take his censer and put incense in it—250 censers in all—and present it before the LORD. You and Aaron are to present your censers also." [18]So each man took his censer, put fire and incense in it, and stood with Moses and Aaron at the entrance to the Tent of Meeting. [19]When Korah had gathered all his followers in opposition to them at the entrance to the Tent of Meeting, the glory of the LORD appeared to the entire assembly. [20]The LORD said to Moses and Aaron, [21]"Separate yourselves from this assembly so I can put an end to them at once."

[22]But Moses and Aaron fell facedown and cried out, "O God, God of the spirits of all mankind, will you be

Gross!

Read Numbers 16:1–2, 31–35. God wrote the original recipe to cure rebellion by going extra-crispy on these "Kentucky Fried Rebels." This bunch of people found out that total disobedience to God has a serious price tag.

a 1 Or Peleth—took ¸men¸   b 14 Or you make slaves of; or you deceive angry with the entire assembly when only one man sins?"

23Then the LORD said to Moses, 24"Say to the assembly, 'Move away from the tents of Korah, Dathan and Abiram.' "

25Moses got up and went to Dathan and Abiram, and the elders of Israel followed him. 26He warned the assembly, "Move back from the tents of these wicked men! Do not touch anything belonging to them, or you will be swept away because of all their sins." 27So they moved away from the tents of Korah, Dathan and Abiram. Dathan and Abiram had come out and were standing with their wives, children and little ones at the entrances to their tents.

28Then Moses said, "This is how you will know that the LORD has sent me to do all these things and that it was not my idea: 29If these men die a natural death and experience only what usually happens to men, then the LORD has not sent me. 30But if the LORD brings about something totally new, and the earth opens its mouth and swallows them, with everything that belongs to them, and they go down alive into the grave,a then you will know that these men have treated the LORD with contempt."

31As soon as he finished saying all this, the ground under them split apart 32and the earth opened its mouth and swallowed them, with their households and all Korah's men and all their possessions. 33They went down alive into the grave, with everything they owned; the earth closed over them, and they perished and were gone from the community. 34At their cries, all the Israelites around them fled, shouting, "The earth is going to swallow us too!"

35And fire came out from the LORD and consumed the 250 men who were offering the incense.

36The LORD said to Moses, 37"Tell Eleazar son of Aaron, the priest, to take the censers out of the smoldering remains and scatter the coals some distance away, for the censers are holy— 38the censers of the men who sinned at the cost of their lives. Hammer the censers into sheets to overlay the altar, for they were presented before the LORD and have become holy. Let them be a sign to the Israelites."

39So Eleazar the priest collected the bronze censers brought by those who had been burned up, and he had them ham-

mered out to overlay the altar, 40as the LORD directed him through Moses. This was to remind the Israelites that no one except a descendant of Aaron should come to burn incense before the LORD, or he would become like Korah and his followers.

41The next day the whole Israelite community grumbled against Moses and Aaron. "You have killed the LORD's people," they said.

42But when the assembly gathered in opposition to Moses and Aaron and turned toward the Tent of Meeting, suddenly the cloud covered it and the glory of the LORD appeared. 43Then Moses and Aaron went to the front of the Tent of Meeting, 44and the LORD said to Moses, 45"Get away from this assembly so I can put an end to them at once." And they fell facedown.

46Then Moses said to Aaron, "Take your censer and put incense in it, along with fire from the altar, and hurry to the assembly to make atonement for them. Wrath has come out from the LORD; the plague has started." 47So Aaron did as Moses said, and ran into the midst of the assembly. The plague had already started among the people, but Aaron offered the incense and made atonement for them. 48He stood between the living and the dead, and the plague stopped. 49But 14,700 people died from the plague, in addition to those who had died because of Korah. 50Then Aaron returned to Moses at the entrance to the Tent of Meeting, for the plague had stopped.

The Budding of Aaron's Staff

17 The LORD said to Moses, 2"Speak to the Israelites and get twelve staffs from them, one from the leader of each of their ancestral tribes. Write the name of each man on his staff. 3On the staff of Levi write Aaron's name, for there must be one staff for the head of each ancestral tribe. 4Place them in the Tent of Meeting in front of the Testimony, where I meet with you. 5The staff belonging to the man I choose will sprout, and I will rid myself of this constant grumbling against you by the Israelites."

6So Moses spoke to the Israelites, and their leaders gave him twelve staffs, one for the leader of each of their ancestral

a 30 Hebrew Sheol; also in verse 33

tribes, and Aaron's staff was among them. ⁷Moses placed the staffs before the LORD in the Tent of the Testimony.

⁸The next day Moses entered the Tent of the Testimony and saw that Aaron's staff, which represented the house of Levi, had not only sprouted but had budded, blossomed and produced almonds. ⁹Then Moses brought out all the staffs from the LORD's presence to all the Israelites. They looked at them, and each man took his own staff.

¹⁰The LORD said to Moses, "Put back Aaron's staff in front of the Testimony, to be kept as a sign to the rebellious. This will put an end to their grumbling against me, so that they will not die." ¹¹Moses did just as the LORD commanded him.

¹²The Israelites said to Moses, "We will die! We are lost, we are all lost! ¹³Anyone who even comes near the tabernacle of the LORD will die. Are we all going to die?"

Duties of Priests and Levites

18 The LORD said to Aaron, "You, your sons and your father's family are to bear the responsibility for offenses against the sanctu-

Make It Stick

_____

_____

_____

_____

_____

_____

_____

READ NUMBERS 17

Aaron's blossoming staff was proof that God was working in his life. When you look for a role model or a mentor, check for the blooms and fruit of the Spirit (Galatians 5:22–23) in their life that shows they're obeying and following God. Write down the name of someone you admire and list his or her "fruit."

ary, and you and your sons alone are to bear the responsibility for offenses against the priesthood. [2]Bring your fellow Levites from your ancestral tribe to join you and assist you when you and your sons minister before the Tent of the Testimony. [3]They are to be responsible to you and are to perform all the duties of the Tent, but they must not go near the furnishings of the sanctuary or the altar, or both they and you will die. [4]They are to join you and be responsible for the care of the Tent of Meeting—all the work at the Tent—and no one else may come near where you are.

[5]"You are to be responsible for the care of the sanctuary and the altar, so that wrath will not fall on the Israelites again. [6]I myself have selected your fellow Levites from among the Israelites as a gift to you, dedicated to the LORD to do the work at the Tent of Meeting. [7]But only you and your sons may serve as priests in connection with everything at the altar and inside the curtain. I am giving you the service of the priesthood as a gift. Anyone else who comes near the sanctuary must be put to death."

Offerings for Priests and Levites

[8]Then the LORD said to Aaron, "I myself have put you in charge of the offerings presented to me; all the holy offerings the Israelites give me I give to you and your sons as your portion and regular share. [9]You are to have the part of the most holy offerings that is kept from the fire. From all the gifts they bring me as most holy offerings, whether grain or sin or guilt offerings, that part belongs to you and your sons. [10]Eat it as something most holy; every male shall eat it. You must regard it as holy.

[11]"This also is yours: whatever is set aside from the gifts of all the wave offerings of the Israelites. I give this to you and your sons and daughters as your regular share. Everyone in your household who is ceremonially clean may eat it.

[12]"I give you all the finest olive oil and all the finest new wine and grain they give the LORD as the firstfruits of their harvest. [13]All the land's firstfruits that they bring to the LORD will be yours. Everyone in your household who is ceremonially clean may eat it.

[14]"Everything in Israel that is devoted[a] to the LORD is yours. [15]The first offspring of every womb, both man and animal, that is offered to the LORD is yours. But you must redeem every firstborn son and every firstborn male of unclean animals. [16]When they are a month old, you must redeem them at the redemption price set at five shekels[b] of silver, according to the sanctuary shekel, which weighs twenty gerahs.

[17]"But you must not redeem the firstborn of an ox, a sheep or a goat; they are holy. Sprinkle their blood on the altar and burn their fat as an offering made by fire, an aroma pleasing to the LORD. [18]Their meat is to be yours, just as the breast of the wave offering and the right thigh are yours. [19]Whatever is set aside from the holy offerings the Israelites present to the LORD I give to you and your sons and daughters as your regular share. It is an everlasting covenant of salt before the LORD for both you and your offspring."

[20]The LORD said to Aaron, "You will have no inheritance in their land, nor will you have any share among them; I am your share and your inheritance among the Israelites.

[21]"I give to the Levites all the tithes in Israel as their inheritance in return for the work they do while serving at the Tent of Meeting. [22]From now on the Israelites must not go near the Tent of Meeting, or they will bear the consequences of their sin and will die. [23]It is the Levites who are to do the work at the Tent of Meeting and bear the responsibility for offenses against it. This is a lasting ordinance for the generations to come. They will receive no inheritance among the Israelites. [24]Instead, I give to the Levites as their inheritance the tithes that the Israelites present as an offering to the LORD. That is why I said concerning them: 'They will have no inheritance among the Israelites.' "

[25]The LORD said to Moses, [26]"Speak to the Levites and say to them: 'When you receive from the Israelites the tithe I give you as your inheritance, you must present a tenth of that tithe as the LORD's offering. [27]Your offering will be reckoned to you as grain from the threshing floor or juice from the winepress. [28]In this way you also will present an offering to the LORD from all the tithes you receive from the Israelites. From these tithes you must give the LORD's portion to Aaron the priest. [29]You must

---

[a] 14 The Hebrew term refers to the irrevocable giving over of things or persons to the LORD.   [b] 16 That is, about 2 ounces (about 55 grams)

present as the LORD's portion the best and holiest part of everything given to you.'

30"Say to the Levites: 'When you present the best part, it will be reckoned to you as the product of the threshing floor or the winepress. 31You and your households may eat the rest of it anywhere, for it is your wages for your work at the Tent of Meeting. 32By presenting the best part of it you will not be guilty in this matter; then you will not defile the holy offerings of the Israelites, and you will not die.' "

The Water of Cleansing

19 The LORD said to Moses and Aaron: 2"This is a requirement of the law that the LORD has commanded: Tell the Israelites to bring you a red heifer without defect or blemish and that has never been under a yoke. 3Give it to Eleazar the priest; it is to be taken outside the camp and slaughtered in his presence. 4Then Eleazar the priest is to take some of its blood on his finger and sprin-

kle it seven times toward the front of the Tent of Meeting. 5While he watches, the heifer is to be burned—its hide, flesh, blood and offal. 6The priest is to take some cedar wood, hyssop and scarlet wool and throw them onto the burning heifer. 7After that, the priest must wash his clothes and bathe himself with water. He may then come into the camp, but he will be ceremonially unclean till evening. 8The man who burns it must also wash his clothes and bathe with water, and he too will be unclean till evening.

9"A man who is clean shall gather up the ashes of the heifer and put them in a ceremonially clean place outside the camp. They shall be kept by the Israelite community for use in the water of cleansing; it is for purification from sin. 10The man who gathers up the ashes of the heifer must also wash his clothes, and he too will be unclean till evening. This will be a lasting ordinance both for the Israelites and for the aliens living among them.

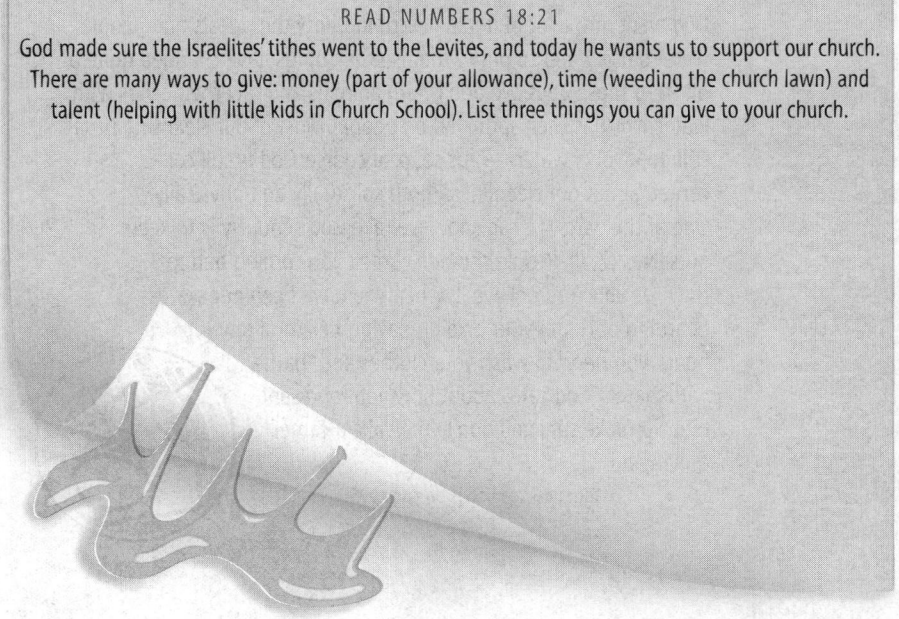

Make It Stick

READ NUMBERS 18:21

God made sure the Israelites' tithes went to the Levites, and today he wants us to support our church. There are many ways to give: money (part of your allowance), time (weeding the church lawn) and talent (helping with little kids in Church School). List three things you can give to your church.

¹¹"Whoever touches the dead body of anyone will be unclean for seven days. ¹²He must purify himself with the water on the third day and on the seventh day; then he will be clean. But if he does not purify himself on the third and seventh days, he will not be clean. ¹³Whoever touches the dead body of anyone and fails to purify himself defiles the LORD's tabernacle. That person must be cut off from Israel. Because the water of cleansing has not been sprinkled on him, he is unclean; his uncleanness remains on him.

¹⁴"This is the law that applies when a person dies in a tent: Anyone who enters the tent and anyone who is in it will be unclean for seven days, ¹⁵and every open container without a lid fastened on it will be unclean.

¹⁶"Anyone out in the open who touches someone who has been killed with a sword or someone who has died a natural death, or anyone who touches a human bone or a grave, will be unclean for seven days.

¹⁷"For the unclean person, put some ashes from the burned purification offering into a jar and pour fresh water over them. ¹⁸Then a man who is ceremonially clean is to take some hyssop, dip it in the water and sprinkle the tent and all the furnishings and the people who were there. He must also sprinkle anyone who has touched a human bone or a grave or someone who has been killed or someone who has died a natural death. ¹⁹The man who is clean is to sprinkle the unclean person on the third and seventh days, and on the seventh day he is to purify him. The person being cleansed must wash his clothes and bathe with water, and that evening he will be clean. ²⁰But if a person who is unclean does not purify himself, he must be cut off from the community, because he has defiled the sanctuary of the LORD. The water of cleansing has not been sprinkled on him, and he is unclean. ²¹This is a lasting ordinance for them.

GET STRONGER.

Clean Up

READ NUMBERS 19

God went into a lot of detail describing how the priests and people were to use water to purify themselves. Things have changed quite a bit from those days: We don't burn animals and mix their ashes with water which is then sprinkled on people. Most of our cleansing rituals still do involve water—plus soap, of course. God is still concerned about our cleanliness, both spiritually and physically. One of the ways we can show we take God seriously is to keep ourselves clean. People shouldn't smell you coming before they see you. And believe it, when you have been out skateboarding or riding your bike or playing ball for a few hours, you *need* to wash your clothes and "bathe with water." God cares about how you represent him. So make sure you don't smell like a camel downwind.

Your next reading is on page 205.

"The man who sprinkles the water of cleansing must also wash his clothes, and anyone who touches the water of cleansing will be unclean till evening. ²²Anything that an unclean person touches becomes unclean, and anyone who touches it becomes unclean till evening."

Water From the Rock

20 In the first month the whole Israelite community arrived at the Desert of Zin, and they stayed at Kadesh. There Miriam died and was buried.

²Now there was no water for the community, and the people gathered in opposition to Moses and Aaron. ³They quarreled with Moses and said, "If only we had died when our brothers fell dead before the LORD! ⁴Why did you bring the LORD's community into this desert, that we and our livestock should die here? ⁵Why did you bring us up out of Egypt to this terrible place? It has no grain or figs, grapevines or pomegranates. And there is no water to drink!"

⁶Moses and Aaron went from the assembly to the entrance to the Tent of Meeting and fell facedown, and the glory of the LORD appeared to them. ⁷The LORD said to Moses, ⁸"Take the staff, and you and your brother Aaron gather the assembly together. Speak to that rock before their eyes and it will pour out its water. You will bring water out of the rock for the community so they and their livestock can drink."

⁹So Moses took the staff from the LORD's presence, just as he commanded him. ¹⁰He and Aaron gathered the assembly together in front of the rock and Moses said to them, "Listen, you rebels, must we bring you water out of this rock?" ¹¹Then Moses raised his arm and struck the rock twice with his staff. Water gushed out, and the community and their livestock drank.

¹²But the LORD said to Moses and Aaron, "Because you did not trust in me enough to honor me as holy in the sight of the Israelites, you will not bring this community into the land I give them."

The Day Moses Lost It

READ NUMBERS 20:1–13

Imagine it's your sister's birthday party but you're mad at her and her friends. Your mom tells you to carry in the birthday cake and set it on the table. You do that—*sort of*. As they're singing "Happy birthday dear ..." you heave the cake on the table, splattering it all over, and shout, "Want cake? Eat!" That's about what Moses did when God told him to speak to the rock. Moses was so mad at the Israelites that instead of speaking to the rock he laid into it with a rod and shouted, "Listen, you rebels, must we bring you water out of this rock?" (verse 10). In spite of the fact that the Israelites were constant complainers, God loved them and gave them water; but it made God look bad when Moses threw a temper tantrum. Moses paid a high price for losing his self-control, as the Lord didn't allow him to enter the Promised Land. So be careful with your actions and words and don't judge others too harshly for their mistakes.

Your next reading is on page 216.

GET COOLER

13These were the waters of Meribah,ᵃ where the Israelites quarreled with the LORD and where he showed himself holy among them.

Edom Denies Israel Passage

14Moses sent messengers from Kadesh to the king of Edom, saying:

"This is what your brother Israel says: You know about all the hardships that have come upon us. 15Our forefathers went down into Egypt, and we lived there many years. The Egyptians mistreated us and our fathers, 16but when we cried out to the LORD, he heard our cry and sent an angel and brought us out of Egypt.

"Now we are here at Kadesh, a town on the edge of your territory. 17Please let us pass through your country. We will not go through any field or vineyard, or drink water from any well. We will travel along the king's highway and not turn to the right or to the left until we have passed through your territory."

ᵃ 13 Meribah means quarreling.

Make It Stick

_____

_____

_____

_____

_____

_____

_____

READ NUMBERS 20:12

Like Moses, everyone makes mistakes. Nobody is perfect, not even our parents, though we sometimes think they should be. Remember, only God is truly perfect, so don't judge others for having some flaws. Make a list of your parents' mistakes, then cross them out.

18 But Edom answered:

"You may not pass through here; if you try, we will march out and attack you with the sword."

19 The Israelites replied:

"We will go along the main road, and if we or our livestock drink any of your water, we will pay for it. We only want to pass through on foot—nothing else."

20 Again they answered:

"You may not pass through."

Then Edom came out against them with a large and powerful army. 21 Since Edom refused to let them go through their territory, Israel turned away from them.

The Death of Aaron

22 The whole Israelite community set out from Kadesh and came to Mount Hor. 23 At Mount Hor, near the border of Edom, the LORD said to Moses and Aaron, 24 "Aaron will be gathered to his people. He will not enter the land I give the Israelites, because both of you rebelled against my command at the waters of Meribah. 25 Get Aaron and his son Eleazar and take them up Mount Hor. 26 Remove Aaron's garments and put them on his son Eleazar, for Aaron will be gathered to his people; he will die there."

27 Moses did as the LORD commanded: They went up Mount Hor in the sight of the whole community. 28 Moses removed Aaron's garments and put them on his son Eleazar. And Aaron died there on top of the mountain. Then Moses and Eleazar came down from the mountain, 29 and when the whole community learned that Aaron had died, the entire house of Israel mourned for him thirty days.

Arad Destroyed

21 When the Canaanite king of Arad, who lived in the Negev, heard that Israel was coming along the road to Atharim, he attacked the Israelites and captured some of them. 2 Then Israel made this vow to the LORD: "If you will deliver these people into our hands, we will totally destroy^a their cities." 3 The LORD listened to Israel's plea and gave the Canaanites over to them. They completely destroyed them and their towns; so the place was named Hormah.^b

The Bronze Snake

4 They traveled from Mount Hor along the route to the Red Sea,^c to go around Edom. But the people grew impatient on the way; 5 they spoke against God and against Moses, and said, "Why have you brought us up out of Egypt to die in the desert? There is no bread!

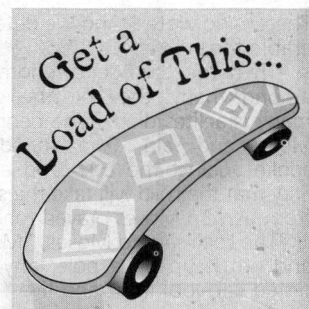

Get a Load of This...

Check out Numbers 21:4–9. Moses lifted up the bronze snake on a pole and those who looked at it were healed. Jesus compared himself to that snake. Oh yes, he did! In John 3:14, he said he had to be "lifted up"—in this case, crucified—just like that desert snake.

---

^a2 The Hebrew term refers to the irrevocable giving over of things or persons to the LORD, often by totally destroying them; also in verse 3.   ^b3 *Hormah* means *destruction*.   ^c4 Hebrew *Yam Suph*; that is, Sea of Reeds

There is no water! And we detest this miserable food!"

⁶Then the LORD sent venomous snakes among them; they bit the people and many Israelites died. ⁷The people came to Moses and said, "We sinned when we spoke against the LORD and against you. Pray that the LORD will take the snakes away from us." So Moses prayed for the people.

⁸The LORD said to Moses, "Make a snake and put it up on a pole; anyone who is bitten can look at it and live." ⁹So Moses made a bronze snake and put it up on a pole. Then when anyone was bitten by a snake and looked at the bronze snake, he lived.

The Journey to Moab

¹⁰The Israelites moved on and camped at Oboth. ¹¹Then they set out from Oboth and camped in Iye Abarim, in the desert that faces Moab toward the sunrise. ¹²From there they moved on and camped in the Zered Valley. ¹³They set out from there and camped alongside the Arnon, which is in the desert extending into Amorite territory. The Arnon is the border of Moab, between Moab and the Amorites. ¹⁴That is why the Book of the Wars of the LORD says:

> ". . . Waheb in Suphah*a* and the
>   ravines,
> the Arnon ¹⁵and*b* the slopes of the
>   ravines
> that lead to the site of Ar
> and lie along the border of Moab."

¹⁶From there they continued on to Beer, the well where the LORD said to Moses, "Gather the people together and I will give them water."

¹⁷Then Israel sang this song:

> "Spring up, O well!
>   Sing about it,
> ¹⁸about the well that the princes dug,
>   that the nobles of the people sank—
>   the nobles with scepters and staffs."

Then they went from the desert to Mattanah, ¹⁹from Mattanah to Nahaliel, from Nahaliel to Bamoth, ²⁰and from Bamoth to the valley in Moab where the top of Pisgah overlooks the wasteland.

Defeat of Sihon and Og

²¹Israel sent messengers to say to Sihon king of the Amorites:

²²"Let us pass through your country. We will not turn aside into any field or vineyard, or drink water from any well. We will travel along the king's highway until we have passed through your territory."

²³But Sihon would not let Israel pass through his territory. He mustered his entire army and marched out into the desert against Israel. When he reached Jahaz, he fought with Israel. ²⁴Israel, however, put him to the sword and took over his land from the Arnon to the Jabbok, but only as far as the Ammonites, because their border was fortified. ²⁵Israel captured all the cities of the Amorites and occupied them, including Heshbon and all its surrounding settlements. ²⁶Heshbon was the city of Sihon king of the Amorites, who had fought against the former king of Moab and had taken from him all his land as far as the Arnon.

²⁷That is why the poets say:

> "Come to Heshbon and let it be rebuilt;
>   let Sihon's city be restored.

²⁸"Fire went out from Heshbon,
>   a blaze from the city of Sihon.
> It consumed Ar of Moab,
>   the citizens of Arnon's heights.
> ²⁹Woe to you, O Moab!
>   You are destroyed, O people of
>   Chemosh!
> He has given up his sons as fugitives
>   and his daughters as captives
> to Sihon king of the Amorites.

³⁰"But we have overthrown them;
>   Heshbon is destroyed all the way to
>   Dibon.
> We have demolished them as far as
>   Nophah,
>   which extends to Medeba."

³¹So Israel settled in the land of the Amorites.

³²After Moses had sent spies to Jazer, the Israelites captured its surrounding settlements and drove out the Amorites who were there. ³³Then they turned and went up along the road toward Bashan, and Og king of Bashan and his whole army marched out to meet them in battle at Edrei.

a 14 The meaning of the Hebrew for this phrase is uncertain.
b 14,15 Or *"I have been given from Suphah and the ravines / of the Arnon ¹⁵to*

³⁴The LORD said to Moses, "Do not be afraid of him, for I have handed him over to you, with his whole army and his land. Do to him what you did to Sihon king of the Amorites, who reigned in Heshbon."

³⁵So they struck him down, together with his sons and his whole army, leaving them no survivors. And they took possession of his land.

Balak Summons Balaam

22 Then the Israelites traveled to the plains of Moab and camped along the Jordan across from Jericho.ᵃ

²Now Balak son of Zippor saw all that Israel had done to the Amorites, ³and Moab was terrified because there were so many people. Indeed, Moab was filled with dread because of the Israelites.

⁴The Moabites said to the elders of Midian, "This horde is going to lick up everything around us, as an ox licks up the grass of the field."

So Balak son of Zippor, who was king of Moab at that time, ⁵sent messengers to summon Balaam son of Beor, who was at Pethor, near the River,ᵇ in his native land. Balak said:

"A people has come out of Egypt; they cover the face of the land and have settled next to me. ⁶Now come and put a curse on these people, because they are too powerful for me. Perhaps then I will be able to defeat them and drive them out of the country. For I know that those you bless are blessed, and those you curse are cursed."

⁷The elders of Moab and Midian left, taking with them the fee for divination. When they came to Balaam, they told him what Balak had said.

⁸"Spend the night here," Balaam said to them, "and I will bring you back the

ᵃ 1 Hebrew *Jordan of Jericho*; possibly an ancient name for the Jordan River   ᵇ 5 That is, the Euphrates

Make It Stick

READ NUMBERS 22:1–7, 21–39

Talk about thick-headed! Even Balaam's donkey had more sense than he did! Have you ever been so stubborn that God had to have one of your pets explain things to you? Draw an animal God might use to speak to you. (Your goldfish?) Write two messages that that animal might give you (feed me, play ball with me, etc.)

answer the LORD gives me." So the Moabite princes stayed with him.

⁹God came to Balaam and asked, "Who are these men with you?"

¹⁰Balaam said to God, "Balak son of Zippor, king of Moab, sent me this message: ¹¹'A people that has come out of Egypt covers the face of the land. Now come and put a curse on them for me. Perhaps then I will be able to fight them and drive them away.' "

¹²But God said to Balaam, "Do not go with them. You must not put a curse on those people, because they are blessed."

¹³The next morning Balaam got up and said to Balak's princes, "Go back to your own country, for the LORD has refused to let me go with you."

¹⁴So the Moabite princes returned to Balak and said, "Balaam refused to come with us."

¹⁵Then Balak sent other princes, more numerous and more distinguished than the first. ¹⁶They came to Balaam and said:

"This is what Balak son of Zippor says: Do not let anything keep you from coming to me, ¹⁷because I will reward you handsomely and do whatever you say. Come and put a curse on these people for me."

¹⁸But Balaam answered them, "Even if Balak gave me his palace filled with silver and gold, I could not do anything great or small to go beyond the command of the LORD my God. ¹⁹Now stay here tonight as the others did, and I will find out what else the LORD will tell me."

²⁰That night God came to Balaam and said, "Since these men have come to summon you, go with them, but do only what I tell you."

Balaam's Donkey

²¹Balaam got up in the morning, saddled his donkey and went with the princes of Moab. ²²But God was very angry when he went, and the angel of the LORD stood in the road to oppose him. Balaam was riding on his donkey, and his two servants were with him. ²³When the donkey saw the angel of the LORD standing in the road with a drawn sword in his hand, she turned off the road into a field. Balaam beat her to get her back on the road.

²⁴Then the angel of the LORD stood in a narrow path between two vineyards, with walls on both sides. ²⁵When the donkey saw the angel of the LORD, she pressed close to the wall, crushing Balaam's foot against it. So he beat her again.

²⁶Then the angel of the LORD moved on ahead and stood in a narrow place where there was no room to turn, either to the right or to the left. ²⁷When the donkey saw the angel of the LORD, she lay down under Balaam, and he was angry and beat her with his staff. ²⁸Then the LORD opened the donkey's mouth, and she said to Balaam, "What have I done to you to make you beat me these three times?"

²⁹Balaam answered the donkey, "You have made a fool of me! If I had a sword in my hand, I would kill you right now."

³⁰The donkey said to Balaam, "Am I not your own donkey, which you have always ridden, to this day? Have I been in the habit of doing this to you?"

"No," he said.

³¹Then the LORD opened Balaam's eyes, and he saw the angel of the LORD standing in the road with his sword drawn. So he bowed low and fell facedown.

³²The angel of the LORD asked him, "Why have you beaten your donkey these three times? I have come here to oppose you because your path is a reckless one before me.ᵃ ³³The donkey saw me and turned away from me these three times. If she had not turned away, I would certainly have killed you by now, but I would have spared her."

³⁴Balaam said to the angel of the LORD, "I have sinned. I did not realize you were standing in the road to oppose me. Now if you are displeased, I will go back."

³⁵The angel of the LORD said to Balaam, "Go with the men, but speak only what I tell you." So Balaam went with the princes of Balak.

³⁶When Balak heard that Balaam was coming, he went out to meet him at the Moabite town on the Arnon border, at the edge of his territory. ³⁷Balak said to Balaam, "Did I not send you an urgent summons? Why didn't you come to me? Am I really not able to reward you?"

³⁸"Well, I have come to you now," Balaam replied. "But can I say just anything? I must speak only what God puts in my mouth."

³⁹Then Balaam went with Balak to Kiri-

ᵃ 32 The meaning of the Hebrew for this clause is uncertain.

ath Huzoth. 40Balak sacrificed cattle and sheep, and gave some to Balaam and the princes who were with him. 41The next morning Balak took Balaam up to Bamoth Baal, and from there he saw part of the people.

Balaam's First Oracle

23 Balaam said, "Build me seven altars here, and prepare seven bulls and seven rams for me." 2Balak did as Balaam said, and the two of them offered a bull and a ram on each altar.

3Then Balaam said to Balak, "Stay here beside your offering while I go aside. Perhaps the LORD will come to meet with me. Whatever he reveals to me I will tell you." Then he went off to a barren height.

4God met with him, and Balaam said, "I have prepared seven altars, and on each altar I have offered a bull and a ram." 5The LORD put a message in Balaam's mouth and said, "Go back to Balak and give him this message."

6So he went back to him and found him standing beside his offering, with all the princes of Moab. 7Then Balaam uttered his oracle:

"Balak brought me from Aram,
    the king of Moab from the eastern mountains.
'Come,' he said, 'curse Jacob for me;
    come, denounce Israel.'
8How can I curse
    those whom God has not cursed?
How can I denounce
    those whom the LORD has not denounced?
9From the rocky peaks I see them,
    from the heights I view them.
I see a people who live apart
    and do not consider themselves one of the nations.
10Who can count the dust of Jacob
    or number the fourth part of Israel?
Let me die the death of the righteous,
    and may my end be like theirs!"

11Balak said to Balaam, "What have you done to me? I brought you to curse my enemies, but you have done nothing but bless them!"

12He answered, "Must I not speak what the LORD puts in my mouth?"

Balaam's Second Oracle

13Then Balak said to him, "Come with me to another place where you can see them; you will see only a part but not all of them. And from there, curse them for me." 14So he took him to the field of Zophim on the top of Pisgah, and there he built seven altars and offered a bull and a ram on each altar.

15Balaam said to Balak, "Stay here beside your offering while I meet with him over there."

16The LORD met with Balaam and put a message in his mouth and said, "Go back to Balak and give him this message."

17So he went to him and found him standing beside his offering, with the princes of Moab. Balak asked him, "What did the LORD say?"

18Then he uttered his oracle:

"Arise, Balak, and listen;
    hear me, son of Zippor.
19God is not a man, that he should lie,
    nor a son of man, that he should change his mind.
Does he speak and then not act?
    Does he promise and not fulfill?
20I have received a command to bless;
    he has blessed, and I cannot change it.

21"No misfortune is seen in Jacob,
    no misery observed in Israel. *a*
The LORD their God is with them;
    the shout of the King is among them.
22God brought them out of Egypt;
    they have the strength of a wild ox.
23There is no sorcery against Jacob,
    no divination against Israel.
It will now be said of Jacob
    and of Israel, 'See what God has done!'
24The people rise like a lioness;
    they rouse themselves like a lion
that does not rest till he devours his prey
    and drinks the blood of his victims."

25Then Balak said to Balaam, "Neither curse them at all nor bless them at all!"

26Balaam answered, "Did I not tell you I must do whatever the LORD says?"

Balaam's Third Oracle

27Then Balak said to Balaam, "Come, let

a 21 Or He has not looked on Jacob's offenses / or on the wrongs found in Israel.

me take you to another place. Perhaps it will please God to let you curse them for me from there." 28And Balak took Balaam to the top of Peor, overlooking the wasteland.

29Balaam said, "Build me seven altars here, and prepare seven bulls and seven rams for me." 30Balak did as Balaam had said, and offered a bull and a ram on each altar.

24 Now when Balaam saw that it pleased the LORD to bless Israel, he did not resort to sorcery as at other times, but turned his face toward the desert. 2When Balaam looked out and saw Israel encamped tribe by tribe, the Spirit of God came upon him 3and he uttered his oracle:

"The oracle of Balaam son of Beor,
    the oracle of one whose eye sees
        clearly,
4 the oracle of one who hears the words
        of God,
    who sees a vision from the Almighty,*a*
    who falls prostrate, and whose eyes
        are opened:

5 "How beautiful are your tents, O Jacob,
    your dwelling places, O Israel!

6 "Like valleys they spread out,
    like gardens beside a river,
like aloes planted by the LORD,
    like cedars beside the waters.
7 Water will flow from their buckets;
    their seed will have abundant water.

"Their king will be greater than Agag;
    their kingdom will be exalted.

8 "God brought them out of Egypt;
    they have the strength of a wild ox.
They devour hostile nations
    and break their bones in pieces;
    with their arrows they pierce them.
9 Like a lion they crouch and lie down,
    like a lioness—who dares to rouse
        them?

"May those who bless you be blessed
    and those who curse you be
        cursed!"

10Then Balak's anger burned against Balaam. He struck his hands together and said to him, "I summoned you to curse my enemies, but you have blessed them these three times. 11Now leave at once and go home! I said I would reward you hand-

somely, but the LORD has kept you from being rewarded."

12Balaam answered Balak, "Did I not tell the messengers you sent me, 13'Even if Balak gave me his palace filled with silver and gold, I could not do anything of my own accord, good or bad, to go beyond the command of the LORD—and I must say only what the LORD says'? 14Now I am going back to my people, but come, let me warn you of what this people will do to your people in days to come."

Balaam's Fourth Oracle

15Then he uttered his oracle:

"The oracle of Balaam son of Beor,
    the oracle of one whose eye sees
        clearly,
16 the oracle of one who hears the words
        of God,
    who has knowledge from the Most
        High,
who sees a vision from the Almighty,
    who falls prostrate, and whose eyes
        are opened:

17 "I see him, but not now;
    I behold him, but not near.
A star will come out of Jacob;
    a scepter will rise out of Israel.
He will crush the foreheads of Moab,
    the skulls*b* of*c* all the sons of Sheth.*d*
18 Edom will be conquered;
    Seir, his enemy, will be conquered,
    but Israel will grow strong.
19 A ruler will come out of Jacob
    and destroy the survivors of the
        city."

Balaam's Final Oracles

20Then Balaam saw Amalek and uttered his oracle:

"Amalek was first among the nations,
    but he will come to ruin at last."

21Then he saw the Kenites and uttered his oracle:

"Your dwelling place is secure,
    your nest is set in a rock;
22 yet you Kenites will be destroyed
    when Asshur takes you captive."

23Then he uttered his oracle:

a 4 Hebrew *Shaddai;* also in verse 16   *b 17* Samaritan Pentateuch (see also Jer. 48:45); the meaning of the word in the Masoretic Text is uncertain.   *c 17* Or possibly *Moab, / batter*   *d 17* Or *all the noisy boasters*

"Ah, who can live when God does this?[a]

24   Ships will come from the shores of Kittim;
they will subdue Asshur and Eber,
    but they too will come to ruin."

25Then Balaam got up and returned home and Balak went his own way.

Moab Seduces Israel

25 While Israel was staying in Shittim, the men began to indulge in sexual immorality with Moabite women, 2who invited them to the sacrifices to their gods. The people ate and bowed down before these gods. 3So Israel joined in worshiping the Baal of Peor. And the LORD's anger burned against them.

4The LORD said to Moses, "Take all the leaders of these people, kill them and expose them in broad daylight before the LORD, so that the LORD's fierce anger may turn away from Israel."

5So Moses said to Israel's judges, "Each of you must put to death those of your men who have joined in worshiping the Baal of Peor."

6Then an Israelite man brought to his family a Midianite woman right before the eyes of Moses and the whole assembly of Israel while they were weeping at the entrance to the Tent of Meeting. 7When Phinehas son of Eleazar, the son of Aaron, the priest, saw this, he left the assembly, took a spear in his hand 8and followed the Israelite into the tent. He drove the spear through both of them—through the Israelite and into the woman's body. Then the plague against the Israelites was stopped; 9but those who died in the plague numbered 24,000.

10The LORD said to Moses, 11"Phinehas son of Eleazar, the son of Aaron, the priest, has turned my anger away from the Israelites; for he was as zealous as I am for my honor among them, so that in my zeal I did not put an end to them. 12Therefore tell him I am making my covenant of peace with him. 13He and his descendants will have a covenant of a lasting priesthood, because he was zealous for the honor of his God and made atonement for the Israelites."

14The name of the Israelite who was killed with the Midianite woman was Zimri son of Salu, the leader of a Simeonite family. 15And the name of the Midianite woman who was put to death was Cozbi daughter of Zur, a tribal chief of a Midianite family.

16The LORD said to Moses, 17"Treat the Midianites as enemies and kill them, 18because they treated you as enemies when they deceived you in the affair of Peor and their sister Cozbi, the daughter of a Midianite leader, the woman who was killed when the plague came as a result of Peor."

The Second Census

26 After the plague the LORD said to Moses and Eleazar son of Aaron, the priest, 2"Take a census of the whole Israelite community by families—all those twenty years old or more who are able to serve in the army of Israel." 3So on the plains of Moab by the Jordan across from Jericho,[b] Moses and Eleazar the priest spoke with them and said, 4"Take a census of the men twenty years old or more, as the LORD commanded Moses."

These were the Israelites who came out of Egypt:

5The descendants of Reuben, the firstborn son of Israel, were:
    through Hanoch, the Hanochite clan;
    through Pallu, the Palluite clan;
    6through Hezron, the Hezronite clan;
    through Carmi, the Carmite clan.
7These were the clans of Reuben; those numbered were 43,730.

8The son of Pallu was Eliab, 9and the sons of Eliab were Nemuel, Dathan and Abiram. The same Dathan and Abiram were the community officials who rebelled against Moses and Aaron and were among Korah's followers when they rebelled against the LORD. 10The earth opened its mouth and swallowed them along with Korah, whose followers died when the fire devoured the 250 men. And they served as a warning sign. 11The line of Korah, however, did not die out.

12The descendants of Simeon by their clans were:

---

[a] 23 Masoretic Text; with a different word division of the Hebrew A people will gather from the north.   [b] 3 Hebrew Jordan of Jericho; possibly an ancient name for the Jordan River; also in verse 63

through Nemuel, the Nemuelite clan;
through Jamin, the Jaminite clan;
through Jakin, the Jakinite clan;
13 through Zerah, the Zerahite clan;
through Shaul, the Shaulite clan.
14 These were the clans of Simeon; there were 22,200 men.

15 The descendants of Gad by their clans were:
through Zephon, the Zephonite clan;
through Haggi, the Haggite clan;
through Shuni, the Shunite clan;
16 through Ozni, the Oznite clan;
through Eri, the Erite clan;
17 through Arodi,ᵃ the Arodite clan;
through Areli, the Arelite clan.
18 These were the clans of Gad; those numbered were 40,500.

19 Er and Onan were sons of Judah, but they died in Canaan.
20 The descendants of Judah by their clans were:
through Shelah, the Shelanite clan;
through Perez, the Perezite clan;
through Zerah, the Zerahite clan.
21 The descendants of Perez were:
through Hezron, the Hezronite clan;
through Hamul, the Hamulite clan.
22 These were the clans of Judah; those numbered were 76,500.

23 The descendants of Issachar by their clans were:
through Tola, the Tolaite clan;
through Puah, the Puiteᵇ clan;
24 through Jashub, the Jashubite clan;
through Shimron, the Shimronite clan.
25 These were the clans of Issachar; those numbered were 64,300.

26 The descendants of Zebulun by their clans were:
through Sered, the Seredite clan;
through Elon, the Elonite clan;
through Jahleel, the Jahleelite clan.
27 These were the clans of Zebulun; those numbered were 60,500.

28 The descendants of Joseph by their clans through Manasseh and Ephraim were:

29 The descendants of Manasseh:
through Makir, the Makirite clan (Makir was the father of Gilead);
through Gilead, the Gileadite clan.
30 These were the descendants of Gilead:
through Iezer, the Iezerite clan;
through Helek, the Helekite clan;

31 through Asriel, the Asrielite clan;
through Shechem, the Shechemite clan;
32 through Shemida, the Shemidaite clan;
through Hepher, the Hepherite clan.
33 (Zelophehad son of Hepher had no sons; he had only daughters, whose names were Mahlah, Noah, Hoglah, Milcah and Tirzah.)
34 These were the clans of Manasseh; those numbered were 52,700.

35 These were the descendants of Ephraim by their clans:
through Shuthelah, the Shuthelahite clan;
through Beker, the Bekerite clan;
through Tahan, the Tahanite clan.
36 These were the descendants of Shuthelah:
through Eran, the Eranite clan.
37 These were the clans of Ephraim; those numbered were 32,500.

These were the descendants of Joseph by their clans.

38 The descendants of Benjamin by their clans were:
through Bela, the Belaite clan;
through Ashbel, the Ashbelite clan;
through Ahiram, the Ahiramite clan;
39 through Shupham,ᶜ the Shuphamite clan;
through Hupham, the Huphamite clan.
40 The descendants of Bela through Ard and Naaman were:
through Ard,ᵈ the Ardite clan;
through Naaman, the Naamite clan.
41 These were the clans of Benjamin; those numbered were 45,600.

42 These were the descendants of Dan by their clans:
through Shuham, the Shuhamite clan.
These were the clans of Dan: 43 All of them were Shuhamite clans; and those numbered were 64,400.

ᵃ 17 Samaritan Pentateuch and Syriac (see also Gen. 46:16);
Masoretic Text Arod   ᵇ 23 Samaritan Pentateuch,
Septuagint, Vulgate and Syriac (see also 1 Chron. 7:1);
Masoretic Text through Puvah, the Punite   ᶜ 39 A few
manuscripts of the Masoretic Text, Samaritan Pentateuch,
Vulgate and Syriac (see also Septuagint); most manuscripts of
the Masoretic Text Shephupham   ᵈ 40 Samaritan
Pentateuch and Vulgate (see also Septuagint); Masoretic Text
does not have through Ard.

44The descendants of Asher by their clans were:

through Imnah, the Imnite clan;
through Ishvi, the Ishvite clan;
through Beriah, the Beriite clan;
45and through the descendants of Beriah:
through Heber, the Heberite clan;
through Malkiel, the Malkielite clan.
46(Asher had a daughter named Serah.)
47These were the clans of Asher; those numbered were 53,400.

48The descendants of Naphtali by their clans were:

through Jahzeel, the Jahzeelite clan;
through Guni, the Gunite clan;
49through Jezer, the Jezerite clan;
through Shillem, the Shillemite clan.
50These were the clans of Naphtali; those numbered were 45,400.

51The total number of the men of Israel was 601,730.

52The LORD said to Moses, 53"The land is to be allotted to them as an inheritance based on the number of names. 54To a larger group give a larger inheritance, and to a smaller group a smaller one; each is to receive its inheritance according to the number of those listed. 55Be sure that the land is distributed by lot. What each group inherits will be according to the names for its ancestral tribe. 56Each inheritance is to be distributed by lot among the larger and smaller groups."

57These were the Levites who were counted by their clans:

through Gershon, the Gershonite clan;
through Kohath, the Kohathite clan;
through Merari, the Merarite clan.
58These also were Levite clans:
the Libnite clan,
the Hebronite clan,
the Mahlite clan,
the Mushite clan,
the Korahite clan.

(Kohath was the forefather of Amram; 59the name of Amram's wife was Jochebed, a descendant of Levi, who was born to the Levites*a* in Egypt. To Amram she bore Aaron, Moses and their sister Miriam. 60Aaron was the father of Nadab and Abihu, Eleazar and Ithamar. 61But Nadab and Abihu died when they made an offering before the LORD with unauthorized fire.)

62All the male Levites a month old or more numbered 23,000. They were not counted along with the other Israelites because they received no inheritance among them.

63These are the ones counted by Moses and Eleazar the priest when they counted the Israelites on the plains of Moab by the Jordan across from Jericho. 64Not one of them was among those counted by Moses and Aaron the priest when they counted the Israelites in the Desert of Sinai. 65For the LORD had told those Israelites they would surely die in the desert, and not one of them was left except Caleb son of Jephunneh and Joshua son of Nun.

Zelophehad's Daughters

27 The daughters of Zelophehad son of Hepher, the son of Gilead, the son of Makir, the son of Manasseh, belonged to the clans of Manasseh son of Joseph. The names of the daughters were Mahlah, Noah, Hoglah, Milcah and Tirzah. They approached 2the entrance to the Tent of Meeting and stood before Moses, Eleazar the priest, the leaders and the whole assembly, and said, 3"Our father died in the desert. He was not among Korah's followers, who banded together against the LORD, but he died for his own sin and left no sons. 4Why should our father's name disappear from his clan because he had no son? Give us property among our father's relatives."

5So Moses brought their case before the LORD 6and the LORD said to him, 7"What Zelophehad's daughters are saying is right. You must certainly give them property as an inheritance among their father's relatives and turn their father's inheritance over to them.

8"Say to the Israelites, 'If a man dies and leaves no son, turn his inheritance over to his daughter. 9If he has no daughter, give his inheritance to his brothers. 10If he has no brothers, give his inheritance to his father's brothers. 11If his father had no brothers, give his inheritance to the nearest relative in his clan, that he may possess it. This is to be a legal re-

a 59 Or Jochebed, a daughter of Levi, who was born to Levi quirement for the Israelites, as the LORD commanded Moses.' "

Joshua to Succeed Moses

¹²Then the LORD said to Moses, "Go up this mountain in the Abarim range and see the land I have given the Israelites. ¹³After you have seen it, you too will be gathered to your people, as your brother Aaron was, ¹⁴for when the community rebelled at the waters in the Desert of Zin, both of you disobeyed my command to honor me as holy before their eyes." (These were the waters of Meribah Kadesh, in the Desert of Zin.)

¹⁵Moses said to the LORD, ¹⁶"May the LORD, the God of the spirits of all mankind, appoint a man over this community ¹⁷to go out and come in before them, one who will lead them out and bring them in, so the LORD's people will not be like sheep without a shepherd."

¹⁸So the LORD said to Moses, "Take Joshua son of Nun, a man in whom is the spirit,ᵃ and lay your hand on him. ¹⁹Have him stand before Eleazar the priest and the entire assembly and commission him in their presence. ²⁰Give him some of your authority so the whole Israelite community will obey him. ²¹He is to stand before Eleazar the priest, who will obtain decisions for him by inquiring of the Urim before the LORD. At his command he and the entire community of the Israelites will go out, and at his command they will come in."

²²Moses did as the LORD commanded him. He took Joshua and had him stand before Eleazar the priest and the whole assembly. ²³Then he laid his hands on him and commissioned him, as the LORD instructed through Moses.

Daily Offerings

28 The LORD said to Moses, ²"Give this command to the Israelites and say to them: 'See that you present to me at the appointed time the food for my offerings made by fire, as an aroma pleasing to me.' ³Say to them: 'This is the offering made by fire that you are to present to the LORD: two lambs a year old without defect, as a regular burnt

ᵃ 18 Or *Spirit*

Zelophehad's Daughters

READ NUMBERS 27:1–11

It's often said, "It's a man's world." That is definitely *not* true of God's kingdom. When God created human beings, he made them both male and female, and he didn't make one more important or valuable than the other. Read Genesis 1:27. God loves all of his people, and women have rights and a place in life, just as much as men. Zelophehad's daughters are proof of this. When their father died without a son, the custom at the time would mean that they would have no land. But God said, "What Zelophehad's daughters are saying is right. You must certainly give them property as an inheritance" (Numbers 27:7). God looks at people's hearts and loves us all as his children. A man who knows God understands this: Women must be honored and treated with respect.

Your next reading is on page 217.

offering each day. ⁴Prepare one lamb in the morning and the other at twilight, ⁵togetherer with a grain offering of a tenth of an ephah ᵃ of fine flour mixed with a quarter of a hin ᵇ of oil from pressed olives. ⁶This is the regular burnt offering instituted at Mount Sinai as a pleasing aroma, an offering made to the LORD by fire. ⁷The accompanying drink offering is to be a quarter of a hin of fermented drink with each lamb. Pour out the drink offering to the LORD at the sanctuary. ⁸Prepare the second lamb at twilight, along with the same kind of grain offering and drink offering that you prepare in the morning. This is an offering made by fire, an aroma pleasing to the LORD.

Sabbath Offerings

⁹" 'On the Sabbath day, make an offering of two lambs a year old without defect, together with its drink offering and a grain offering of two-tenths of an ephah ᶜ of fine flour mixed with oil. ¹⁰This is the burnt offering for every Sabbath, in addition to the regular burnt offering and its drink offering.

Monthly Offerings

¹¹" 'On the first of every month, present to the LORD a burnt offering of two young bulls, one ram and seven male lambs a year old, all without defect. ¹²With each bull there is to be a grain offering of three-tenths of an ephah ᵈ of fine flour mixed with oil; with the ram, a grain offering of two-tenths of an ephah of fine flour mixed with oil; ¹³and with each lamb, a grain offering of a tenth of an ephah of fine flour mixed with oil. This is for a burnt offering, a pleasing aroma, an offering made to the LORD by fire. ¹⁴With each bull there is to be a drink offering of half a hin ᵉ of wine; with the ram, a third of a hin ᶠ; and with each lamb, a quarter of a hin. This is the monthly burnt offering to be made at each new moon during the

ᵃ 5 That is, probably about 2 quarts (about 2 liters); also in verses 13, 21 and 29   ᵇ 5 That is, probably about 1 quart (about 1 liter); also in verses 7 and 14   ᶜ 9 That is, probably about 4 quarts (about 4.5 liters); also in verses 12, 20 and 28   ᵈ 12 That is, probably about 6 quarts (about 6.5 liters); also in verses 20 and 28   ᵉ 14 That is, probably about 2 quarts (about 2 liters)   ᶠ 14 That is, probably about 1 1/4 quarts (about 1.2 liters)

GET SMARTER

Passage Into Manhood

READ NUMBERS 27:12–23

At first, you could only rake leaves. Now, you can run the lawnmower. At first, someone taught you to stand up on a skateboard. Now, you show other skaters how to perform kick-flips and ollies. Joshua started out as an errand boy, Moses' right hand man. The day came when God told Moses that Joshua was ready for a bigger job. God said, "Have him stand before … the entire assembly and commission him in their presence" (Numbers 27:19). God knew it was time for Moses to move on, and for Joshua to replace him as the leader. It's the same for you as you grow up to be a man. Listen to your mentors. They know when you're ready for certain tasks and responsibilities. Do a good job when they give you the chance and, like Joshua, the day will come when they'll tell you it's time for the big leagues.

Your next reading is on page 233.

year. ¹⁵Besides the regular burnt offering with its drink offering, one male goat is to be presented to the LORD as a sin offering.

The Passover

¹⁶" 'On the fourteenth day of the first month the LORD's Passover is to be held. ¹⁷On the fifteenth day of this month there is to be a festival; for seven days eat bread made without yeast. ¹⁸On the first day hold a sacred assembly and do no regular work. ¹⁹Present to the LORD an offering made by fire, a burnt offering of two young bulls, one ram and seven male lambs a year old, all without defect. ²⁰With each bull prepare a grain offering of three-tenths of an ephah of fine flour mixed with oil; with the ram, two-tenths; ²¹and with each of the seven lambs, one-tenth. ²²Include one male goat as a sin offering to make atonement for you. ²³Prepare these in addition to the regular morning burnt offering. ²⁴In this way prepare the food for the offering made by fire every day for seven days as an aroma pleasing to the LORD; it is to be prepared in addition to the regular burnt offering and its drink offering. ²⁵On the seventh day hold a sacred assembly and do no regular work.

Feast of Weeks

²⁶" 'On the day of firstfruits, when you present to the LORD an offering of new grain during the Feast of Weeks, hold a sacred assembly and do no regular work. ²⁷Present a burnt offering of two young bulls, one ram and seven male lambs a year old as an aroma pleasing to the LORD. ²⁸With each bull there is to be a grain offering of three-tenths of an ephah of fine flour mixed with oil; with the ram, two-tenths; ²⁹and with each of the seven lambs, one-tenth. ³⁰Include one male goat to make atonement for you. ³¹Prepare these together with their drink offerings, in addition to the regular burnt offering and its grain offering. Be sure the animals are without defect.

Feast of Trumpets

29 " 'On the first day of the seventh month hold a sacred assembly and do no regular work. It is a day for you to sound the trumpets. ²As an aroma pleasing to the LORD, prepare a burnt offering of one young bull, one ram and seven male lambs a year old, all without defect. ³With the bull prepare a grain offering of three-tenths of an ephah*a* of fine flour mixed with oil; with the ram, two-tenths*b*; ⁴and with each of the seven lambs, one-tenth.*c* ⁵Include one male goat as a sin offering to make atonement for you. ⁶These are in addition to the monthly and daily burnt offerings with their grain offerings and drink offerings as specified. They are offerings made to the LORD by fire—a pleasing aroma.

Day of Atonement

⁷" 'On the tenth day of this seventh month hold a sacred assembly. You must deny yourselves*d* and do no work. ⁸Present as an aroma pleasing to the LORD a burnt offering of one young bull, one ram and seven male lambs a year old, all without defect. ⁹With the bull prepare a grain offering of three-tenths of an ephah of fine flour mixed with oil; with the ram, two-tenths; ¹⁰and with each of the seven lambs, one-tenth. ¹¹Include one male goat as a sin offering, in addition to the sin offering for atonement and the regular burnt offering with its grain offering, and their drink offerings.

Feast of Tabernacles

¹²" 'On the fifteenth day of the seventh month, hold a sacred assembly and do no regular work. Celebrate a festival to the LORD for seven days. ¹³Present an offering made by fire as an aroma pleasing to the LORD, a burnt offering of thirteen young bulls, two rams and fourteen male lambs a year old, all without defect. ¹⁴With each of the thirteen bulls prepare a grain offering of three-tenths of an ephah of fine flour mixed with oil; with each of the two rams, two-tenths; ¹⁵and with each of the fourteen lambs, one-tenth. ¹⁶Include one male goat as a sin offering, in addition to the regular burnt offering with its grain offering and drink offering.

¹⁷" 'On the second day prepare twelve young bulls, two rams and fourteen male lambs a year old, all without defect. ¹⁸With the bulls, rams and lambs, prepare

---

a 3 That is, probably about 6 quarts (about 6.5 liters); also in verses 9 and 14   *b 3* That is, probably about 4 quarts (about 4.5 liters); also in verses 9 and 14   *c 4* That is, probably about 2 quarts (about 2 liters); also in verses 10 and 15   *d 7* Or *must fast* their grain offerings and drink offerings according to the number specified. 19Include one male goat as a sin offering, in addition to the regular burnt offering with its grain offering, and their drink offerings.

20" 'On the third day prepare eleven bulls, two rams and fourteen male lambs a year old, all without defect. 21With the bulls, rams and lambs, prepare their grain offerings and drink offerings according to the number specified. 22Include one male goat as a sin offering, in addition to the regular burnt offering with its grain offering and drink offering.

23" 'On the fourth day prepare ten bulls, two rams and fourteen male lambs a year old, all without defect. 24With the bulls, rams and lambs, prepare their grain offerings and drink offerings according to the number specified. 25Include one male goat as a sin offering, in addition to the regular burnt offering with its grain offering and drink offering.

26" 'On the fifth day prepare nine bulls, two rams and fourteen male lambs a year old, all without defect. 27With the bulls, rams and lambs, prepare their grain offerings and drink offerings according to the number specified. 28Include one male goat as a sin offering, in addition to the regular burnt offering with its grain offering and drink offering.

29" 'On the sixth day prepare eight bulls, two rams and fourteen male lambs a year old, all without defect. 30With the bulls, rams and lambs, prepare their grain offerings and drink offerings according to the number specified. 31Include one male goat as a sin offering, in addition to the regular burnt offering with its grain offering and drink offering.

32" 'On the seventh day prepare seven bulls, two rams and fourteen male lambs a year old, all without defect. 33With the bulls, rams and lambs, prepare their grain offerings and drink offerings according to the number specified. 34Include one male goat as a sin offering, in addition to the regular burnt offering with its grain offering and drink offering.

35" 'On the eighth day hold an assembly and do no regular work. 36Present an offering made by fire as an aroma pleasing to the LORD, a burnt offering of one bull, one ram and seven male lambs a year old, all without defect. 37With the bull, the ram and the lambs, prepare their grain offerings and drink offerings according to the number specified. 38Include one male goat as a sin offering, in addition to the regular burnt offering with its grain offering and drink offering.

39" 'In addition to what you vow and your freewill offerings, prepare these for the LORD at your appointed feasts: your burnt offerings, grain offerings, drink offerings and fellowship offerings.a' "

40Moses told the Israelites all that the LORD commanded him.

Vows

30 Moses said to the heads of the tribes of Israel: "This is what the LORD commands: 2When a man makes a vow to the LORD or takes an oath to obligate himself by a pledge, he must not break his word but must do everything he said.

3"When a young woman still living in her father's house makes a vow to the LORD or obligates herself by a pledge 4and her father hears about her vow or pledge but says nothing to her, then all her vows and every pledge by which she obligated herself will stand. 5But if her father forbids her when he hears about it, none of her vows or the pledges by which she obligated herself will stand; the LORD will release her because her father has forbidden her.

6"If she marries after she makes a vow or after her lips utter a rash promise by which she obligates herself 7and her husband hears about it but says nothing to her, then her vows or the pledges by which she obligated herself will stand. 8But if her husband forbids her when he hears about it, he nullifies the vow that obligates her or the rash promise by which she obligates herself, and the LORD will release her.

9"Any vow or obligation taken by a widow or divorced woman will be binding on her.

10"If a woman living with her husband makes a vow or obligates herself by a pledge under oath 11and her husband hears about it but says nothing to her and does not forbid her, then all her vows or the pledges by which she obligated herself will stand. 12But if her husband nullifies them when he hears about them, then none of the vows or pledges that

a 39 Traditionally peace offerings

came from her lips will stand. Her husband has nullified them, and the LORD will release her. [13]Her husband may confirm or nullify any vow she makes or any sworn pledge to deny herself. [14]But if her husband says nothing to her about it from day to day, then he confirms all her vows or the pledges binding on her. He confirms them by saying nothing to her when he hears about them. [15]If, however, he nullifies them some time after he hears about them, then he is responsible for her guilt."

[16]These are the regulations the LORD gave Moses concerning relationships between a man and his wife, and between a father and his young daughter still living in his house.

Vengeance on the Midianites

31 The LORD said to Moses, [2]"Take vengeance on the Midianites for the Israelites. After that, you will be gathered to your people."

[3]So Moses said to the people, "Arm some of your men to go to war against the Midianites and to carry out the LORD's vengeance on them. [4]Send into battle a thousand men from each of the tribes of Israel." [5]So twelve thousand men armed for battle, a thousand from each tribe, were supplied from the clans of Israel. [6]Moses sent them into battle, a thousand from each tribe, along with Phinehas son of Eleazar, the priest, who took with him articles from the sanctuary and the trumpets for signaling.

[7]They fought against Midian, as the LORD commanded Moses, and killed every man. [8]Among their victims were Evi, Rekem, Zur, Hur and Reba—the five kings of Midian. They also killed Balaam son of Beor with the sword. [9]The Israelites captured the Midianite women and children and took all the Midianite herds, flocks and goods as plunder. [10]They burned all the towns where the Midianites had settled, as well as all their camps. [11]They took all the plunder and spoils, including the people and animals, [12]and brought the captives, spoils and plunder to Moses and Eleazar the priest and the Israelite assembly at their camp on the plains of Moab, by the Jordan across from Jericho. [a]

[13]Moses, Eleazar the priest and all the leaders of the community went to meet them outside the camp. [14]Moses was angry with the officers of the army—the commanders of thousands and commanders of hundreds—who returned from the battle.

[15]"Have you allowed all the women to live?" he asked them. [16]"They were the ones who followed Balaam's advice and were the means of turning the Israelites away from the LORD in what happened at Peor, so that a plague struck the LORD's people. [17]Now kill all the boys. And kill every woman who has slept with a man, [18]but save for yourselves every girl who has never slept with a man.

[19]"All of you who have killed anyone or touched anyone who was killed must stay outside the camp seven days. On the third and seventh days you must purify yourselves and your captives. [20]Purify every garment as well as everything made of leather, goat hair or wood."

[21]Then Eleazar the priest said to the soldiers who had gone into battle, "This is the requirement of the law that the LORD gave Moses: [22]Gold, silver, bronze, iron, tin, lead [23]and anything else that can withstand fire must be put through the fire, and then it will be clean. But it must also be purified with the water of cleansing. And whatever cannot withstand fire must be put through that water. [24]On the seventh day wash your clothes and you will be clean. Then you may come into the camp."

Dividing the Spoils

[25]The LORD said to Moses, [26]"You and Eleazar the priest and the family heads of the community are to count all the people and animals that were captured. [27]Divide the spoils between the soldiers who took part in the battle and the rest of the community. [28]From the soldiers who fought in the battle, set apart as tribute for the LORD one out of every five hundred, whether persons, cattle, donkeys, sheep or goats. [29]Take this tribute from their half share and give it to Eleazar the priest as the LORD's part. [30]From the Israelites' half, select one out of every fifty, whether persons, cattle, donkeys, sheep, goats or other animals. Give them to the Levites, who are responsible for the care of the LORD's tabernacle." [31]So Moses and Eleazar the priest did as the LORD commanded Moses.

[a] 12 Hebrew *Jordan of Jericho*; possibly an ancient name for the Jordan River

32The plunder remaining from the spoils that the soldiers took was 675,000 sheep, 3372,000 cattle, 3461,000 donkeys 35and 32,000 women who had never slept with a man.

36The half share of those who fought in the battle was:

337,500 sheep, 37of which the tribute for the LORD was 675;

3836,000 cattle, of which the tribute for the LORD was 72;

3930,500 donkeys, of which the tribute for the LORD was 61;

4016,000 people, of which the tribute for the LORD was 32.

41Moses gave the tribute to Eleazar the priest as the LORD's part, as the LORD commanded Moses.

42The half belonging to the Israelites, which Moses set apart from that of the fighting men— 43the community's half—was 337,500 sheep, 4436,000 cattle, 4530,500 donkeys 46and 16,000 people. 47From the Israelites' half, Moses selected one out of every fifty persons and animals, as the LORD commanded him, and gave them to the Levites, who were responsible for the care of the LORD's tabernacle.

48Then the officers who were over the units of the army—the commanders of thousands and commanders of hundreds—went to Moses 49and said to him, "Your servants have counted the soldiers under our command, and not one is missing. 50So we have brought as an offering to the LORD the gold articles each of us acquired—armlets, bracelets, signet rings, earrings and necklaces—to make atonement for ourselves before the LORD."

51Moses and Eleazar the priest accepted from them the gold—all the crafted articles. 52All the gold from the commanders of thousands and commanders of hundreds that Moses and Eleazar presented as a gift to the LORD weighed 16,750 shekels.a 53Each soldier had taken plunder for himself. 54Moses and Eleazar the priest accepted the gold from the commanders of thousands and commanders of hundreds and brought it into the Tent of Meeting as a memorial for the Israelites before the LORD.

The Transjordan Tribes

32 The Reubenites and Gadites, who had very large herds and flocks, saw that the lands of Jazer and Gilead were suitable for livestock. 2So they came to Moses and Eleazar the priest and to the leaders of the community, and said, 3"Ataroth, Dibon, Jazer, Nimrah, Heshbon, Elealeh, Sebam, Nebo and Beon— 4the land the LORD subdued before the people of Israel—are suitable for livestock, and your servants have livestock. 5If we have found favor in

In Numbers 31:22–23, all the gold and other precious metals the Israelites captured from their pagan enemies had to be ritually cleansed by being "put through the fire." Great idea! Bet that burned off all the *germs*, too!

a 52 That is, about 420 pounds (about 190 kilograms)

your eyes," they said, "let this land be given to your servants as our possession. Do not make us cross the Jordan."

⁶Moses said to the Gadites and Reubenites, "Shall your countrymen go to war while you sit here? ⁷Why do you discourage the Israelites from going over into the land the LORD has given them? ⁸This is what your fathers did when I sent them from Kadesh Barnea to look over the land. ⁹After they went up to the Valley of Eshcol and viewed the land, they discouraged the Israelites from entering the land the LORD had given them. ¹⁰The LORD's anger was aroused that day and he swore this oath: ¹¹'Because they have not followed me wholeheartedly, not one of the men twenty years old or more who came up out of Egypt will see the land I promised on oath to Abraham, Isaac and Jacob— ¹²not one except Caleb son of Jephunneh the Kenizzite and Joshua son of Nun, for they followed the LORD wholeheartedly.' ¹³The LORD's anger burned against Israel and he made them wander in the desert forty years, until the whole generation of those who had done evil in his sight was gone.

¹⁴"And here you are, a brood of sinners, standing in the place of your fathers and making the LORD even more angry with Israel. ¹⁵If you turn away from following him, he will again leave all this people in the desert, and you will be the cause of their destruction."

¹⁶Then they came up to him and said, "We would like to build pens here for our livestock and cities for our women and children. ¹⁷But we are ready to arm ourselves and go ahead of the Israelites until we have brought them to their place. Meanwhile our women and children will live in fortified cities, for protection from the inhabitants of the land. ¹⁸We will not return to our homes until every Israelite has received his inheritance. ¹⁹We will not receive any inheritance with them on the other side of the Jordan, because our inheritance has come to us on the east side of the Jordan."

²⁰Then Moses said to them, "If you will do this—if you will arm yourselves before the LORD for battle, ²¹and if all of you will go armed over the Jordan before the LORD until he has driven his enemies out before him— ²²then when the land is subdued before the LORD, you may return and be free from your obligation to the LORD and to Israel. And this land will be your possession before the LORD.

²³"But if you fail to do this, you will be sinning against the LORD; and you may be sure that your sin will find you out. ²⁴Build cities for your women and children, and pens for your flocks, but do what you have promised."

²⁵The Gadites and Reubenites said to Moses, "We your servants will do as our lord commands. ²⁶Our children and wives, our flocks and herds will remain here in the cities of Gilead. ²⁷But your servants, every man armed for battle, will cross over to fight before the LORD, just as our lord says."

²⁸Then Moses gave orders about them to Eleazar the priest and Joshua son of Nun and to the family heads of the Israelite tribes. ²⁹He said to them, "If the Gadites and Reubenites, every man armed for battle, cross over the Jordan with you before the LORD, then when the land is subdued before you, give them the land of Gilead as their possession. ³⁰But if they do not cross over with you armed, they must accept their possession with you in Canaan."

³¹The Gadites and Reubenites answered, "Your servants will do what the LORD has said. ³²We will cross over before the LORD into Canaan armed, but the property we inherit will be on this side of the Jordan."

³³Then Moses gave to the Gadites, the Reubenites and the half-tribe of Manasseh son of Joseph the kingdom of Sihon king of the Amorites and the kingdom of Og king of Bashan—the whole land with its cities and the territory around them.

³⁴The Gadites built up Dibon, Ataroth, Aroer, ³⁵Atroth Shophan, Jazer, Jogbehah, ³⁶Beth Nimrah and Beth Haran as fortified cities, and built pens for their flocks. ³⁷And the Reubenites rebuilt Heshbon, Elealeh and Kiriathaim, ³⁸as well as Nebo and Baal Meon (these names were changed) and Sibmah. They gave names to the cities they rebuilt.

³⁹The descendants of Makir son of Manasseh went to Gilead, captured it and drove out the Amorites who were there. ⁴⁰So Moses gave Gilead to the Makirites, the descendants of Manasseh, and they settled there. ⁴¹Jair, a descendant of Manasseh, captured their settlements and

called them Havvoth Jair.[a] 42And Nobah captured Kenath and its surrounding settlements and called it Nobah after himself.

Stages in Israel's Journey

33 Here are the stages in the journey of the Israelites when they came out of Egypt by divisions under the leadership of Moses and Aaron. 2At the LORD's command Moses recorded the stages in their journey. This is their journey by stages:

3The Israelites set out from Rameses on the fifteenth day of the first month, the day after the Passover. They marched out boldly in full view of all the Egyptians, 4who were burying all their firstborn, whom the LORD had struck down among them; for the LORD had brought judgment on their gods.

5The Israelites left Rameses and camped at Succoth.

6They left Succoth and camped at Etham, on the edge of the desert.

7They left Etham, turned back to Pi Hahiroth, to the east of Baal Zephon, and camped near Migdol.

8They left Pi Hahiroth[b] and passed through the sea into the desert, and when they had traveled for three days in the Desert of Etham, they camped at Marah.

9They left Marah and went to Elim, where there were twelve springs and seventy palm trees, and they camped there.

10They left Elim and camped by the Red Sea.[c]

11They left the Red Sea and camped in the Desert of Sin.

12They left the Desert of Sin and camped at Dophkah.

13They left Dophkah and camped at Alush.

14They left Alush and camped at Rephidim, where there was no water for the people to drink.

15They left Rephidim and camped in the Desert of Sinai.

16They left the Desert of Sinai and camped at Kibroth Hattaavah.

17They left Kibroth Hattaavah and camped at Hazeroth.

18They left Hazeroth and camped at Rithmah.

19They left Rithmah and camped at Rimmon Perez.

20They left Rimmon Perez and camped at Libnah.

21They left Libnah and camped at Rissah.

22They left Rissah and camped at Kehelathah.

23They left Kehelathah and camped at Mount Shepher.

24They left Mount Shepher and camped at Haradah.

25They left Haradah and camped at Makheloth.

26They left Makheloth and camped at Tahath.

27They left Tahath and camped at Terah.

28They left Terah and camped at Mithcah.

29They left Mithcah and camped at Hashmonah.

30They left Hashmonah and camped at Moseroth.

31They left Moseroth and camped at Bene Jaakan.

32They left Bene Jaakan and camped at Hor Haggidgad.

33They left Hor Haggidgad and camped at Jotbathah.

34They left Jotbathah and camped at Abronah.

35They left Abronah and camped at Ezion Geber.

36They left Ezion Geber and camped at Kadesh, in the Desert of Zin.

37They left Kadesh and camped at Mount Hor, on the border of Edom. 38At the LORD's command Aaron the priest went up Mount Hor, where he died on the first day of the fifth month of the fortieth year after the Israelites came out of Egypt. 39Aaron was a hundred and twenty-three years old when he died on Mount Hor.

40The Canaanite king of Arad, who lived in the Negev of Canaan, heard that the Israelites were coming.

41They left Mount Hor and camped at Zalmonah.

a 41 Or them the settlements of Jair   b 8 Many manuscripts of the Masoretic Text, Samaritan Pentateuch and Vulgate; most manuscripts of the Masoretic Text left from before Hahiroth   c 10 Hebrew Yam Suph; that is, Sea of Reeds; also in verse 11

42They left Zalmonah and camped at Punon.

43They left Punon and camped at Oboth.

44They left Oboth and camped at Iye Abarim, on the border of Moab.

45They left Iyim[a] and camped at Dibon Gad.

46They left Dibon Gad and camped at Almon Diblathaim.

47They left Almon Diblathaim and camped in the mountains of Abarim, near Nebo.

48They left the mountains of Abarim and camped on the plains of Moab by the Jordan across from Jericho.[b] 49There on the plains of Moab they camped along the Jordan from Beth Jeshimoth to Abel Shittim.

50On the plains of Moab by the Jordan across from Jericho the LORD said to Moses, 51"Speak to the Israelites and say to them: 'When you cross the Jordan into Canaan, 52drive out all the inhabitants of the land before you. Destroy all their carved images and their cast idols, and demolish all their high places. 53Take possession of the land and settle in it, for I have given you the land to possess. 54Distribute the land by lot, according to your clans. To a larger group give a larger inheritance, and to a smaller group a smaller one. Whatever falls to them by lot will be theirs. Distribute it according to your ancestral tribes.

55" 'But if you do not drive out the inhabitants of the land, those you allow to remain will become barbs in your eyes and thorns in your sides. They will give you trouble in the land where you will live. 56And then I will do to you what I plan to do to them.' "

Boundaries of Canaan

34 The LORD said to Moses, 2"Command the Israelites and say to them: 'When you enter Canaan, the land that will be allotted to you as an inheritance will have these boundaries:

3" 'Your southern side will include some of the Desert of Zin along the border of Edom. On the east, your southern boundary will start from the end of the Salt Sea,[c] 4cross south of Scorpion[d] Pass, continue on to Zin and go south of Kadesh Barnea.

Then it will go to Hazar Addar and over to Azmon, 5where it will turn, join the Wadi of Egypt and end at the Sea.[e]

6" 'Your western boundary will be the coast of the Great Sea. This will be your boundary on the west.

7" 'For your northern boundary, run a line from the Great Sea to Mount Hor 8and from Mount Hor to Lebo[f] Hamath. Then the boundary will go to Zedad, 9continue to Ziphron and end at Hazar Enan. This will be your boundary on the north.

10" 'For your eastern boundary, run a line from Hazar Enan to Shepham. 11The boundary will go down from Shepham to Riblah on the east side of Ain and continue along the slopes east of the Sea of Kinnereth.[g] 12Then the boundary will go down along the Jordan and end at the Salt Sea.

" 'This will be your land, with its boundaries on every side.' "

13Moses commanded the Israelites: "Assign this land by lot as an inheritance. The LORD has ordered that it be given to the nine and a half tribes, 14because the families of the tribe of Reuben, the tribe of Gad and the half-tribe of Manasseh have received their inheritance. 15These two and a half tribes have received their inheritance on the east side of the Jordan of Jericho,[h] toward the sunrise."

16The LORD said to Moses, 17"These are the names of the men who are to assign the land for you as an inheritance: Eleazar the priest and Joshua son of Nun. 18And appoint one leader from each tribe to help assign the land. 19These are their names:

Caleb son of Jephunneh,
   from the tribe of Judah;
20Shemuel son of Ammihud,
   from the tribe of Simeon;
21Elidad son of Kislon,
   from the tribe of Benjamin;
22Bukki son of Jogli,
   the leader from the tribe of Dan;
23Hanniel son of Ephod,
   the leader from the tribe of Manasseh son of Joseph;

[a] 45 That is, Iye Abarim   [b] 48 Hebrew Jordan of Jericho; possibly an ancient name for the Jordan River; also in verse 50   [c] 3 That is, the Dead Sea; also in verse 12   [d] 4 Hebrew Akrabbim   [e] 5 That is, the Mediterranean; also in verses 6 and 7   [f] 8 Or to the entrance to   [g] 11 That is, Galilee   [h] 15 Jordan of Jericho was possibly an ancient name for the Jordan River.

24 Kemuel son of Shiphtan,
  the leader from the tribe of Ephraim son of Joseph;
25 Elizaphan son of Parnach,
  the leader from the tribe of Zebulun;
26 Paltiel son of Azzan,
  the leader from the tribe of Issachar;
27 Ahihud son of Shelomi,
  the leader from the tribe of Asher;
28 Pedahel son of Ammihud,
  the leader from the tribe of Naphtali."

29 These are the men the LORD commanded to assign the inheritance to the
Israelites in the land of Canaan.

Towns for the Levites

35 On the plains of Moab by the Jordan across from Jericho,[a] the LORD said to Moses, 2 "Command the Israelites to give the Levites towns to live in from the inheritance the Israelites will possess. And give them pasturelands around the towns. 3 Then they will have towns to live in and pasturelands for their cattle, flocks and all their other livestock.

4 "The pasturelands around the towns that you give the Levites will extend out fifteen hundred feet[b] from the town wall. 5 Outside the town, measure three thousand feet[c] on the east side, three thousand on the south side, three thousand on the west and three thousand on the north, with the town in the center. They will have this area as pastureland for the towns.

Cities of Refuge

6 "Six of the towns you give the Levites will be cities of refuge, to which a person who has killed someone may flee. In addition, give them forty-two other towns. 7 In all you must give the Levites forty-eight towns, together with their pasturelands. 8 The towns you give the Levites from the land the Israelites possess are to be given in proportion to the inheritance of each tribe: Take many towns from a tribe that has many, but few from one that has few."

9 Then the LORD said to Moses: 10 "Speak to the Israelites and say to them: 'When you cross the Jordan into Canaan, 11 select some towns to be your cities of refuge, to which a person who has killed someone

accidentally may flee. 12 They will be places of refuge from the avenger, so that a person accused of murder may not die before he stands trial before the assembly. 13 These six towns you give will be your cities of refuge. 14 Give three on this side of the Jordan and three in Canaan as cities of refuge. 15 These six towns will be a place of refuge for Israelites, aliens and any other people living among them, so that anyone who has killed another accidentally can flee there.

16 " 'If a man strikes someone with an iron object so that he dies, he is a murderer; the murderer shall be put to death. 17 Or if anyone has a stone in his hand that could kill, and he strikes someone so that he dies, he is a murderer; the murderer shall be put to death. 18 Or if anyone has a wooden object in his hand that could kill, and he hits someone so that he dies, he is a murderer; the murderer shall be put to death. 19 The avenger of blood shall put the murderer to death; when he meets him, he shall put him to death. 20 If anyone with malice aforethought shoves another or throws something at him intentionally so that he dies 21 or if in hostility he hits him with his fist so that he dies, that person shall be put to death; he is a murderer. The avenger of blood shall put the murderer to death when he meets him.

22 " 'But if without hostility someone suddenly shoves another or throws something at him unintentionally 23 or, without seeing him, drops a stone on him that could kill him, and he dies, then since he was not his enemy and he did not intend to harm him, 24 the assembly must judge between him and the avenger of blood according to these regulations. 25 The assembly must protect the one accused of murder from the avenger of blood and send him back to the city of refuge to which he fled. He must stay there until the death of the high priest, who was anointed with the holy oil.

26 " 'But if the accused ever goes outside the limits of the city of refuge to which he has fled 27 and the avenger of blood finds him outside the city, the avenger of blood may kill the accused

---

[a] 1 Hebrew *Jordan of Jericho*; possibly an ancient name for the Jordan River   [b] 4 Hebrew *a thousand cubits* (about 450 meters)   [c] 5 Hebrew *two thousand cubits* (about 900 meters)

without being guilty of murder. 28The accused must stay in his city of refuge until the death of the high priest; only after the death of the high priest may he return to his own property.

29" 'These are to be legal requirements for you throughout the generations to come, wherever you live.

30" 'Anyone who kills a person is to be put to death as a murderer only on the testimony of witnesses. But no one is to be put to death on the testimony of only one witness.

31" 'Do not accept a ransom for the life of a murderer, who deserves to die. He must surely be put to death.

32" 'Do not accept a ransom for anyone who has fled to a city of refuge and so allow him to go back and live on his own land before the death of the high priest.

33" 'Do not pollute the land where you are. Bloodshed pollutes the land, and atonement cannot be made for the land on which blood has been shed, except by the blood of the one who shed it. 34Do not defile the land where you live and where I dwell, for I, the LORD, dwell among the Israelites.' "

Make It Stick

READ NUMBERS 35:6
Everyone needs a quiet place, a safe place to go to think. Name three "cities of refuge" you go to when you need a break from your problems. It could be your room or a nearby park or even a person you trust to help you face a tough decision.

Inheritance of Zelophehad's Daughters

36 The family heads of the clan of Gilead son of Makir, the son of Manasseh, who were from the clans of the descendants of Joseph, came and spoke before Moses and the leaders, the heads of the Israelite families. ²They said, "When the LORD commanded my lord to give the land as an inheritance to the Israelites by lot, he ordered you to give the inheritance of our brother Zelophehad to his daughters. ³Now suppose they marry men from other Israelite tribes; then their inheritance will be taken from our ancestral inheritance and added to that of the tribe they marry into. And so part of the inheritance allotted to us will be taken away. ⁴When the Year of Jubilee for the Israelites comes, their inheritance will be added to that of the tribe into which they marry, and their property will be taken from the tribal inheritance of our forefathers."

⁵Then at the LORD's command Moses gave this order to the Israelites: "What the tribe of the descendants of Joseph is saying is right. ⁶This is what the LORD commands for Zelophehad's daughters: They may marry anyone they please as long as they marry within the tribal clan of their father. ⁷No inheritance in Israel is to pass from tribe to tribe, for every Israelite shall keep the tribal land inherited from his forefathers. ⁸Every daughter who inherits land in any Israelite tribe must marry someone in her father's tribal clan, so that every Israelite will possess the inheritance of his fathers. ⁹No inheritance may pass from tribe to tribe, for each Israelite tribe is to keep the land it inherits."

¹⁰So Zelophehad's daughters did as the LORD commanded Moses. ¹¹Zelophehad's daughters—Mahlah, Tirzah, Hoglah, Milcah and Noah—married their cousins on their father's side. ¹²They married within the clans of the descendants of Manasseh son of Joseph, and their inheritance remained in their father's clan and tribe.

¹³These are the commands and regulations the LORD gave through Moses to the Israelites on the plains of Moab by the Jordan across from Jericho.ᵃ

ᵃ 13 Hebrew *Jordan of Jericho*; possibly an ancient name for the Jordan River

DEUTERONOMY

Who wrote this book?
Moses.

Why was this book written?
Deuteronomy tells a new generation of Israelites how to please God, so that God will bless them.

What happens in this book?
Moses speaks to the Israelites. He tells what God has done for them and reviews God's rules for holy living. The Israelites promise to obey God.

What do we learn about God in this book?
God helps people because he loves them. God's rules for living are given in love, and he blesses people who keep his rules.

Who is important in this book?
The important person in this book is Moses.

When did this happen?
These events happened about 1405 B.C.

Where did this happen?
During this time the Israelites were camped across the Jordan River from Canaan, the Promised Land.

What are some of the stories in this book?
Moses tells of Israel's journey	Deuteronomy 1–3
Moses tells of the golden calf	Deuteronomy 9
Moses gives instructions for an altar	Deuteronomy 27
Israel promises to obey God	Deuteronomy 29
Moses dies	Deuteronomy 34

The Command to Leave Horeb

These are the words Moses spoke to all Israel in the desert east of the Jordan—that is, in the Arabah—opposite Suph, between Paran and Tophel, Laban, Hazeroth and Dizahab. ²(It takes eleven days to go from Horeb to Kadesh Barnea by the Mount Seir road.)

³In the fortieth year, on the first day of the eleventh month, Moses proclaimed to the Israelites all that the LORD had commanded him concerning them. ⁴This was after he had defeated Sihon king of the Amorites, who reigned in Heshbon, and at Edrei had defeated Og king of Bashan, who reigned in Ashtaroth.

⁵East of the Jordan in the territory of Moab, Moses began to expound this law, saying:

⁶The LORD our God said to us at Horeb, "You have stayed long enough at this mountain. ⁷Break camp and advance into the hill country of the Amorites; go to all the neighboring peoples in the Arabah, in the mountains, in the western foothills, in the Negev and along the coast, to the land of the Canaanites and to Lebanon, as far as the great river, the Euphrates. ⁸See, I have given you this land. Go in and take possession of the land that the LORD swore he would give to your fathers—to Abraham, Isaac and Jacob—and to their descendants after them."

The Appointment of Leaders

⁹At that time I said to you, "You are too heavy a burden for me to carry alone. ¹⁰The LORD your God has increased your numbers so that today you are as many as the stars in the sky. ¹¹May the LORD, the God of your fathers, increase you a thousand times and bless you as he has promised! ¹²But how can I bear your problems and your burdens and your disputes all by myself? ¹³Choose some wise, understanding and respected men from each of your tribes, and I will set them over you."

¹⁴You answered me, "What you propose to do is good."

¹⁵So I took the leading men of your tribes, wise and respected men, and appointed them to have authority over you—as commanders of thousands, of hundreds, of fifties and of tens and as tribal officials. ¹⁶And I charged your judges at that time: Hear the disputes between your brothers and judge fairly, whether the case is between brother Israelites or between one of them and an alien. ¹⁷Do not show partiality in judging; hear both small and great alike. Do not be afraid of any man, for judgment belongs to God. Bring me any case too hard for you, and I will hear it. ¹⁸And at that time I told you everything you were to do.

Spies Sent Out

¹⁹Then, as the LORD our God commanded us, we set out from Horeb and went toward the hill country of the Amorites through all that vast and dreadful desert that you have seen, and so we reached Kadesh Barnea. ²⁰Then I said to you, "You have reached the hill country of the Amorites, which the LORD our God is giving us. ²¹See, the LORD your God has given you the land. Go up and take possession of it as the LORD, the God of your fathers, told you. Do not be afraid; do not be discouraged."

²²Then all of you came to me and said, "Let us send men ahead to spy out the land for us and bring back a report about the route we are to take and the towns we will come to."

²³The idea seemed good to me; so I selected twelve of you, one man from each tribe. ²⁴They left and went up into the hill country, and came to the Valley of Eshcol and explored it. ²⁵Taking with them some of the fruit of the land, they brought it down to us and reported, "It is a good land that the LORD our God is giving us."

Rebellion Against the LORD

²⁶But you were unwilling to go up; you rebelled against the command of the LORD your God. ²⁷You grumbled in your tents and said, "The LORD hates us; so he brought us out of Egypt to deliver us into the hands of the Amorites to destroy us. ²⁸Where can we go? Our brothers have made us lose heart. They say, 'The people are stronger and taller than we are; the cities are large, with walls up to the sky. We even saw the Anakites there.' "

²⁹Then I said to you, "Do not be terrified; do not be afraid of them. ³⁰The LORD your God, who is going before you, will fight for you, as he did for you in Egypt, before your very eyes, ³¹and in the desert. There you saw how the LORD your God carried you, as a father carries his son, all the way you went until you reached this place."

³²In spite of this, you did not trust in the LORD your God, ³³who went ahead of you on your journey, in fire by night and in a cloud by day, to search out places for you to camp and to show you the way you should go.

³⁴When the LORD heard what you said, he was angry and solemnly swore: ³⁵"Not a man of this evil generation shall see the good land I swore to give your forefathers, ³⁶except Caleb son of Jephunneh. He will see it, and I will give him and his descendants the land he set his feet on, because he followed the LORD wholeheartedly."

³⁷Because of you the LORD became angry with me also and said, "You shall not enter it, either. ³⁸But your assistant, Joshua son of Nun, will enter it. Encourage him, because he will lead Israel to inherit it. ³⁹And the little ones that you said would be taken captive, your children who do not yet know good from bad—they will enter the land. I will give it to them and they will take possession of it. ⁴⁰But as for you, turn around and set out toward the desert along the route to the Red Sea.ᵃ"

⁴¹Then you replied, "We have sinned against the LORD. We will go up and fight, as the LORD our God commanded us." So every one of you put on his weapons, thinking it easy to go up into the hill country.

⁴²But the LORD said to me, "Tell them, 'Do not go up and fight, because I will not be with you. You will be defeated by your enemies.' "

⁴³So I told you, but you would not listen. You rebelled against the LORD's command and in your arrogance you marched up into the hill country. ⁴⁴The Amorites who lived in those hills came out against you; they chased you like a swarm of bees and beat you down from Seir all the way to Hormah. ⁴⁵You came back and wept before the LORD, but he paid no attention to your weeping and turned a deaf ear to you. ⁴⁶And so you stayed in Kadesh many days—all the time you spent there.

Wanderings in the Desert

Then we turned back and set out toward the desert along the route to the Red Sea,ᵃ as the LORD had directed me. For a long time we made our way around the hill country of Seir.

²Then the LORD said to me, ³"You have made your way around this hill country long enough; now turn north. ⁴Give the people these orders: 'You are about to pass through the territory of your brothers the descendants of Esau, who live in Seir. They will be afraid of you, but be very careful. ⁵Do not provoke them to war, for I will not give you any of their land, not even enough to put your foot on. I have given Esau the hill country of Seir as his own. ⁶You are to pay them in silver for the food you eat and the water you drink.' "

⁷The LORD your God has blessed you in all the work of your hands. He has watched over your journey through this vast desert. These forty years the LORD your God has been with you, and you have not lacked anything.

⁸So we went on past our brothers the descendants of Esau, who live in Seir. We turned from the Arabah road, which comes up from Elath and Ezion Geber, and traveled along the desert road of Moab.

⁹Then the LORD said to me, "Do not harass the Moabites or provoke them to war, for I will not give you any part of their land. I have given Ar to the descendants of Lot as a possession."

¹⁰(The Emites used to live there—a people strong and numerous, and as tall as the Anakites. ¹¹Like the Anakites, they too were considered Rephaites, but the Moabites called them Emites. ¹²Horites used to live in Seir, but the descendants of Esau drove them out. They destroyed the Horites from before them and settled in their place, just as Israel did in the land the LORD gave them as their possession.)

¹³And the LORD said, "Now get up and cross the Zered Valley." So we crossed the valley.

¹⁴Thirty-eight years passed from the time we left Kadesh Barnea until we crossed the Zered Valley. By then, that entire generation of fighting men had perished from the camp, as the LORD had sworn to them. ¹⁵The LORD's hand was against them until he had completely eliminated them from the camp.

¹⁶Now when the last of these fighting men among the people had died, ¹⁷the LORD said to me, ¹⁸"Today you are to pass by the region of Moab at Ar. ¹⁹When you come to the Ammonites, do not harass

ᵃ 40,1 Hebrew *Yam Suph*; that is, Sea of Reeds

them or provoke them to war, for I will not give you possession of any land belonging to the Ammonites. I have given it as a possession to the descendants of Lot."

20(That too was considered a land of the Rephaites, who used to live there; but the Ammonites called them Zamzummites. 21They were a people strong and numerous, and as tall as the Anakites. The LORD destroyed them from before the Ammonites, who drove them out and settled in their place. 22The LORD had done the same for the descendants of Esau, who lived in Seir, when he destroyed the Horites from before them. They drove them out and have lived in their place to this day. 23And as for the Avvites who lived in villages as far as Gaza, the Caphtorites coming out from Caphtor[a] destroyed them and settled in their place.)

Defeat of Sihon King of Heshbon

24"Set out now and cross the Arnon Gorge. See, I have given into your hand Sihon the Amorite, king of Heshbon, and his country. Begin to take possession of it and engage him in battle. 25This very day I will begin to put the terror and fear of you on all the nations under heaven. They will hear reports of you and will tremble and be in anguish because of you."

26From the desert of Kedemoth I sent messengers to Sihon king of Heshbon offering peace and saying, 27"Let us pass through your country. We will stay on the main road; we will not turn aside to the right or to the left. 28Sell us food to eat and water to drink for their price in silver. Only let us pass through on foot— 29as the descendants of Esau, who live in Seir, and the Moabites, who live in Ar, did for us—until we cross the Jordan into the land the LORD our God is giving us." 30But Sihon king of Heshbon refused to let us pass through. For the LORD your God had made his spirit stubborn and his heart obstinate in order to give him into your hands, as he has now done.

31The LORD said to me, "See, I have begun to deliver Sihon and his country over to you. Now begin to conquer and possess his land."

32When Sihon and all his army came out to meet us in battle at Jahaz, 33the LORD our God delivered him over to us and we struck him down, together with his

sons and his whole army. 34At that time we took all his towns and completely destroyed[b] them—men, women and children. We left no survivors. 35But the livestock and the plunder from the towns we had captured we carried off for ourselves. 36From Aroer on the rim of the Arnon Gorge, and from the town in the gorge, even as far as Gilead, not one town was too strong for us. The LORD our God gave us all of them. 37But in accordance with the command of the LORD our God, you did not encroach on any of the land of the Ammonites, neither the land along the course of the Jabbok nor that around the towns in the hills.

Defeat of Og King of Bashan

3 Next we turned and went up along the road toward Bashan, and Og king of Bashan with his whole army marched out to meet us in battle at Edrei. 2The LORD said to me, "Do not be afraid of him, for I have handed him over to you with his whole army and his land. Do to him what you did to Sihon king of the Amorites, who reigned in Heshbon."

3So the LORD our God also gave into our hands Og king of Bashan and all his army. We struck them down, leaving no survivors. 4At that time we took all his cities. There was not one of the sixty cities that we did not take from them—the whole region of Argob, Og's kingdom in Bashan. 5All these cities were fortified with high walls and with gates and bars, and there were also a great many unwalled villages. 6We completely destroyed[b] them, as we had done with Sihon king of Heshbon, destroying[b] every city—men, women and children. 7But all the livestock and the plunder from their cities we carried off for ourselves.

8So at that time we took from these two kings of the Amorites the territory east of the Jordan, from the Arnon Gorge as far as Mount Hermon. 9(Hermon is called Sirion by the Sidonians; the Amorites call it Senir.) 10We took all the towns on the plateau, and all Gilead, and all Bashan as far as Salecah and Edrei, towns of Og's kingdom in Bashan. 11(Only Og king of Bashan was left of the remnant of the Rephaites. His bed[c] was made of iron and

---

[a] 23 That is, Crete   [b] 34,6 The Hebrew term refers to the irrevocable giving over of things or persons to the LORD, often by totally destroying them.   [c] 11 Or sarcophagus

Get a Load of This...

Check out Deuteronomy 3:11. If Og's bed was a literal bed, it was truly a king-sized bed—almost as big and as wide as a car! Og would have been one humongous dude! Chances are this "bed" is actually referring to Og's stone coffin, however, his *final* place of rest.

was more than thirteen feet long and six feet wide.[a] It is still in Rabbah of the Ammonites.)

Division of the Land

[12] Of the land that we took over at that time, I gave the Reubenites and the Gadites the territory north of Aroer by the Arnon Gorge, including half the hill country of Gilead, together with its towns. [13] The rest of Gilead and also all of Bashan, the kingdom of Og, I gave to the half-tribe of Manasseh. (The whole region of Argob in Bashan used to be known as a land of the Rephaites. [14] Jair, a descendant of Manasseh, took the whole region of Argob as far as the border of the Geshurites and the Maacathites; it was named after him, so that to this day Bashan is called Havvoth Jair.[b]) [15] And I gave Gilead to Makir. [16] But to the Reubenites and the Gadites I gave the territory extending from Gilead down to the Arnon Gorge (the middle of the gorge being the border) and out to the Jabbok River, which is the border of the Ammonites. [17] Its western border was the Jordan in the Arabah, from Kinnereth to the Sea of the Arabah (the Salt Sea[c]), below the slopes of Pisgah.

[18] I commanded you at that time: "The LORD your God has given you this land to take possession of it. But all your able-bodied men, armed for battle, must cross over ahead of your brother Israelites. [19] However, your wives, your children and your livestock (I know you have much livestock) may stay in the towns I have given you, [20] until the LORD gives rest to your brothers as he has to you, and they too have taken over the land that the LORD your God is giving them, across the Jordan. After that, each of you may go back to the possession I have given you."

Moses Forbidden to Cross the Jordan

[21] At that time I commanded Joshua: "You have seen with your own eyes all that the LORD your God has done to these two kings. The LORD will do the same to all the kingdoms over there where you are going. [22] Do not be afraid of them; the LORD your God himself will fight for you."

[23] At that time I pleaded with the LORD: [24] "O Sovereign LORD, you have begun to show to your servant your greatness and your strong hand. For what god is there in heaven or on earth who can do the deeds and mighty works you do? [25] Let me go over and see the good land beyond the Jordan—that fine hill country and Lebanon."

[26] But because of you the LORD was angry with me and would not listen to me. "That is enough," the LORD said. "Do not speak to me anymore about this matter. [27] Go up to the top of Pisgah and look west and north and south and east. Look at the land with your own eyes, since you are not going to cross this Jordan. [28] But commission Joshua, and encourage and strengthen him, for he will lead this people across and will cause them to in-

---

[a] 11 Hebrew *nine cubits long and four cubits wide* (about 4 meters long and 1.8 meters wide)   [b] 14 Or *called the settlements of Jair*   [c] 17 That is, the Dead Sea

herit the land that you will see." ²⁹So we stayed in the valley near Beth Peor.

Obedience Commanded

4 Hear now, O Israel, the decrees and laws I am about to teach you. Follow them so that you may live and may go in and take possession of the land that the LORD, the God of your fathers, is giving you. ²Do not add to what I command you and do not subtract from it, but keep the commands of the LORD your God that I give you.

³You saw with your own eyes what the LORD did at Baal Peor. The LORD your God destroyed from among you everyone who followed the Baal of Peor, ⁴but all of you who held fast to the LORD your God are still alive today.

⁵See, I have taught you decrees and laws as the LORD my God commanded me, so that you may follow them in the land you are entering to take possession of it. ⁶Observe them carefully, for this will show your wisdom and understanding to the nations, who will hear about all these decrees and say, "Surely this great nation is a wise and understanding people." ⁷What other nation is so great as to have their gods near them the way the LORD our God is near us whenever we pray to him? ⁸And what other nation is so great as to have such righteous decrees and laws as this body of laws I am setting before you today?

⁹Only be careful, and watch yourselves closely so that you do not forget the things your eyes have seen or let them slip from your heart as long as you live. Teach them to your children and to their children after them. ¹⁰Remember the day you stood before the LORD your God at Horeb, when he said to me, "Assemble the people before me to hear my words so that they may learn to revere me as long as they live in the land and may teach them to their children." ¹¹You came near and stood at the foot of the mountain while it blazed with fire to the very heavens, with black clouds and deep darkness. ¹²Then the LORD spoke to you out of the fire. You heard the sound of words but saw no form; there was only a voice. ¹³He declared to you his covenant, the Ten Com-

You Can't Come Over

READ DEUTERONOMY 3:21–28

When we blow it, we know that if we sincerely ask God to forgive us, he will. Unfortunately, there may still be consequences. What if you lied to your dad about studying for a test so you could go play hoop. When you apologize to your dad, he will forgive you. But you may still flunk the test—that's the consequence. Moses blew it, too. He was disobedient to God, so God said that he couldn't enter the Promised Land. Moses begged, but the matter was settled.

God said, "Do not speak to me anymore about this matter" (verse 26). Moses' sin had consequences. It would've been better if Moses had simply obeyed God in the first place. It's the same with you today. It's better to just do what's right to begin with.

Your next reading is on page 236.

mandments, which he commanded you to follow and then wrote them on two stone tablets. [14]And the LORD directed me at that time to teach you the decrees and laws you are to follow in the land that you are crossing the Jordan to possess.

Idolatry Forbidden

[15]You saw no form of any kind the day the LORD spoke to you at Horeb out of the fire. Therefore watch yourselves very carefully, [16]so that you do not become corrupt and make for yourselves an idol, an image of any shape, whether formed like a man or a woman, [17]or like any animal on earth or any bird that flies in the air, [18]or like any creature that moves along the ground or any fish in the waters below. [19]And when you look up to the sky and see the sun, the moon and the stars—all the heavenly array—do not be enticed into bowing down to them and worshiping things the LORD your God has apportioned to all the nations under heaven. [20]But as for you, the LORD took you and brought you out of the iron-smelting furnace, out of Egypt, to be the people of his inheritance, as you now are.

[21]The LORD was angry with me because of you, and he solemnly swore that I would not cross the Jordan and enter the good land the LORD your God is giving you as your inheritance. [22]I will die in this land; I will not cross the Jordan; but you are about to cross over and take possession of that good land. [23]Be careful not to forget the covenant of the LORD your God that he made with you; do not make for yourselves an idol in the form of anything the LORD your God has forbidden. [24]For the LORD your God is a consuming fire, a jealous God.

[25]After you have had children and grandchildren and have lived in the land a long time—if you then become corrupt and make any kind of idol, doing evil in the eyes of the LORD your God and provoking him to anger, [26]I call heaven and earth as witnesses against you this day that you will quickly perish from the land that you are crossing the Jordan to possess. You will not live there long but will certainly be destroyed. [27]The LORD will scatter you among the peoples, and only a few of you will survive among the nations to which the LORD will drive you. [28]There you will worship man-made gods of wood and stone, which cannot see or hear or eat or smell. [29]But if from there you seek the LORD your God, you will find him if you look for him with all your heart and with all your soul. [30]When you are in distress and all these things have happened to you, then in later days you will return to the LORD your God and obey him. [31]For the LORD your God is a merciful God; he will not abandon or destroy you or forget the covenant with your forefathers, which he confirmed to them by oath.

The LORD Is God

[32]Ask now about the former days, long before your time, from the day God created man on the earth; ask from one end of the heavens to the other. Has anything so great as this ever happened, or has anything like it ever been heard of? [33]Has any other people heard the voice of God[a] speaking out of fire, as you have, and lived? [34]Has any god ever tried to take for himself one nation out of another nation, by testings, by miraculous signs and wonders, by war, by a mighty hand and an outstretched arm, or by great and awesome deeds, like all the things the LORD your God did for you in Egypt before your very eyes?

[35]You were shown these things so that you might know that the LORD is God; besides him there is no other. [36]From heaven he made you hear his voice to discipline you. On earth he showed you his great fire, and you heard his words from out of the fire. [37]Because he loved your forefathers and chose their descendants after them, he brought you out of Egypt by his Presence and his great strength, [38]to drive out before you nations greater and stronger than you and to bring you into their land to give it to you for your inheritance, as it is today.

[39]Acknowledge and take to heart this day that the LORD is God in heaven above and on the earth below. There is no other. [40]Keep his decrees and commands, which I am giving you today, so that it may go well with you and your children after you and that you may live long in the land the LORD your God gives you for all time.

Cities of Refuge

[41]Then Moses set aside three cities east of the Jordan, [42]to which anyone who

---

[a] 33 Or of a god

had killed a person could flee if he had unintentionally killed his neighbor without malice aforethought. He could flee into one of these cities and save his life. ⁴³The cities were these: Bezer in the desert plateau, for the Reubenites; Ramoth in Gilead, for the Gadites; and Golan in Bashan, for the Manassites.

Introduction to the Law

⁴⁴This is the law Moses set before the Israelites. ⁴⁵These are the stipulations, decrees and laws Moses gave them when they came out of Egypt ⁴⁶and were in the valley near Beth Peor east of the Jordan, in the land of Sihon king of the Amorites, who reigned in Heshbon and was defeated by Moses and the Israelites as they came out of Egypt. ⁴⁷They took possession of his land and the land of Og king of Bashan, the two Amorite kings east of the Jordan. ⁴⁸This land extended from Aroer on the rim of the Arnon Gorge to Mount Siyon*a* (that is, Hermon), ⁴⁹and included all the Arabah east of the Jordan, as far as the Sea of the Arabah,*b* below the slopes of Pisgah.

The Ten Commandments

5 Moses summoned all Israel and said:

Hear, O Israel, the decrees and laws I declare in your hearing today. Learn them and be sure to follow them. ²The Lord our God made a covenant with us at Horeb. ³It was not with our fathers that the Lord made this covenant, but with us, with all of us who are alive here today. ⁴The Lord spoke to you face to face out of the fire on the mountain. ⁵(At that time I stood between the Lord and you to declare to you the word of the Lord, because you were afraid of the fire and did not go up the mountain.) And he said:

⁶"I am the Lord your God, who brought you out of Egypt, out of the land of slavery.

⁷"You shall have no other gods before*c* me.

⁸"You shall not make for yourself an idol in the form of anything in heaven above or on the earth beneath or in the waters below. ⁹You shall not bow down to them or worship them; for I, the Lord your God, am a jealous God, punishing the children for the sin of the fathers to the third and fourth generation of those who hate me, ¹⁰but showing love to a thousand ⌊generations⌋ of those who love me and keep my commandments.

¹¹"You shall not misuse the name of the Lord your God, for the Lord will not hold anyone guiltless who misuses his name.

¹²"Observe the Sabbath day by keeping it holy, as the Lord your God has commanded you. ¹³Six days you shall labor and do all your work, ¹⁴but the seventh day is a Sabbath to the Lord your God. On it you shall not do any work, neither you, nor your son or daughter, nor your manservant or maidservant, nor your ox, your donkey or any of your animals, nor the alien within your gates, so that your manservant and maidservant may rest, as you do. ¹⁵Remember that you were slaves in Egypt and that the Lord your God brought you out of there with a mighty hand and an outstretched arm. Therefore the Lord your God has commanded you to observe the Sabbath day.

¹⁶"Honor your father and your mother, as the Lord your God has commanded you, so that you may live long and that it may go well with you in the land the Lord your God is giving you.

¹⁷"You shall not murder.

¹⁸"You shall not commit adultery.

¹⁹"You shall not steal.

²⁰"You shall not give false testimony against your neighbor.

²¹"You shall not covet your neighbor's wife. You shall not set your desire on your neighbor's house or land, his manservant or maidservant, his ox or donkey, or anything that belongs to your neighbor."

²²These are the commandments the Lord proclaimed in a loud voice to your whole assembly there on the mountain from out of the fire, the cloud and the

---

a 48 Hebrew; Syriac (see also Deut. 3:9) *Sirion*   *b 49* That is, the Dead Sea   *c 7* Or *besides* deep darkness; and he added nothing more. Then he wrote them on two stone tablets and gave them to me.

²³When you heard the voice out of the darkness, while the mountain was ablaze with fire, all the leading men of your tribes and your elders came to me. ²⁴And you said, "The LORD our God has shown us his glory and his majesty, and we have heard his voice from the fire. Today we have seen that a man can live even if God speaks with him. ²⁵But now, why should we die? This great fire will consume us, and we will die if we hear the voice of the LORD our God any longer. ²⁶For what mortal man has ever heard the voice of the living God speaking out of fire, as we have, and survived? ²⁷Go near and listen to all that the LORD our God says. Then tell us whatever the LORD our God tells you. We will listen and obey."

²⁸The LORD heard you when you spoke to me and the LORD said to me, "I have heard what this people said to you. Everything they said was good. ²⁹Oh, that their hearts would be inclined to fear me and keep all my commands always, so that it might go well with them and their children forever!

³⁰"Go, tell them to return to their tents. ³¹But you stay here with me so that I may give you all the commands, decrees and laws you are to teach them to follow in the land I am giving them to possess."

³²So be careful to do what the LORD your God has commanded you; do not turn aside to the right or to the left. ³³Walk in all the way that the LORD your God has commanded you, so that you may live and prosper and prolong your days in the land that you will possess.

Love the LORD Your God

These are the commands, decrees and laws the LORD your God directed me to teach you to observe in the land that you are crossing the Jordan to possess, ²so that you, your children and their children after them may fear the LORD your God as long as you live by keeping all his decrees and commands that I give you, and so that you may enjoy long life. ³Hear, O Israel, and be careful to obey so that it may go well with you and that

When Parents "Impress" You

READ DEUTERONOMY 6:1–9, 20–25

God gave you guidelines for living, and they're not just a bunch of rules that tell you what you *can't* do. They're encouragement and direction that tell you what's right and how to plug into God's blessings. These guidelines are to be "upon your hearts" (verse 6). You should talk about them when you're sitting, walking, lying down or getting up. In other words, keep them on your mind *all* the time! In fact, your mom and dad are supposed to "impress" them on you (verse 7). So if your parents call you to family devotions, or ask, "Have you read your Bible?" or want you to memorize a verse, remember, they're doing what God told them to do. Respect them for doing their job, and do yours. Be thankful you have parents who love God! Be thankful for your Christian heritage!

Your next reading is on page 239.

you may increase greatly in a land flowing with milk and honey, just as the LORD, the God of your fathers, promised you.

[4]Hear, O Israel: The LORD our God, the LORD is one.[a] [5]Love the LORD your God with all your heart and with all your soul and with all your strength. [6]These commandments that I give you today are to be upon your hearts. [7]Impress them on your children. Talk about them when you sit at home and when you walk along the road, when you lie down and when you get up. [8]Tie them as symbols on your hands and bind them on your foreheads. [9]Write them on the doorframes of your houses and on your gates.

[10]When the LORD your God brings you into the land he swore to your fathers, to Abraham, Isaac and Jacob, to give you—a land with large, flourishing cities you did not build, [11]houses filled with all kinds of good things you did not provide, wells you did not dig, and vineyards and olive groves you did not plant—then when you eat and are satisfied, [12]be careful that you do not forget the LORD, who brought you out of Egypt, out of the land of slavery.

[13]Fear the LORD your God, serve him only and take your oaths in his name. [14]Do not follow other gods, the gods of the peoples around you; [15]for the LORD your God, who is among you, is a jealous God and his anger will burn against you, and he will destroy you from the face of the land. [16]Do not test the LORD your God as you did at Massah. [17]Be sure to keep the commands of the LORD your God and the stipulations and decrees he has given you. [18]Do what is right and good in the LORD's sight, so that it may go well with you and you may go in and take over the good land that the LORD promised on oath to your forefathers, [19]thrusting out all your enemies before you, as the LORD said.

[20]In the future, when your son asks you, "What is the meaning of the stipulations, decrees and laws the LORD our God has commanded you?" [21]tell him: "We were slaves of Pharaoh in Egypt, but the LORD brought us out of Egypt with a mighty hand. [22]Before our eyes the LORD sent miraculous signs and wonders—great and terrible—upon Egypt and Pharaoh and his whole household. [23]But he brought us out from there to bring us in and give us the land that he promised on oath to our forefathers. [24]The LORD com-

manded us to obey all these decrees and to fear the LORD our God, so that we might always prosper and be kept alive, as is the case today. [25]And if we are careful to obey all this law before the LORD our God, as he has commanded us, that will be our righteousness."

Driving Out the Nations

7 When the LORD your God brings you into the land you are entering to possess and drives out before you many nations—the Hittites, Girgashites, Amorites, Canaanites, Perizzites, Hivites and Jebusites, seven nations larger and stronger than you— [2]and when the LORD your God has delivered them over to you and you have defeated them, then you must destroy them totally.[b] Make no treaty with them, and show them no mercy. [3]Do not intermarry with them. Do not give your daughters to their sons or take their daughters for your sons, [4]for they will turn your sons away from following me to serve other gods, and the LORD's anger will burn against you and will quickly destroy you. [5]This is what you are to do to them: Break down their altars, smash their sacred stones, cut down their Asherah poles[c] and burn their idols in the fire. [6]For you are a people holy to the LORD your God. The LORD your God has chosen you out of all the peoples on the face of the earth to be his people, his treasured possession.

[7]The LORD did not set his affection on you and choose you because you were more numerous than other peoples, for you were the fewest of all peoples. [8]But it was because the LORD loved you and kept the oath he swore to your forefathers that he brought you out with a mighty hand and redeemed you from the land of slavery, from the power of Pharaoh king of Egypt. [9]Know therefore that the LORD your God is God; he is the faithful God, keeping his covenant of love to a thousand generations of those who love him and keep his commands. [10]But

those who hate him he will repay to their face by destruction;

[a] 4 Or *The LORD our God is one LORD*; or *The LORD is our God, the LORD is one*; or *The LORD is our God, the LORD alone*
[b] 2 The Hebrew term refers to the irrevocable giving over of things or persons to the LORD, often by totally destroying them; also in verse 26.   [c] 5 That is, symbols of the goddess Asherah; here and elsewhere in Deuteronomy

he will not be slow to repay to their face those who hate him.

[11] Therefore, take care to follow the commands, decrees and laws I give you today.

[12] If you pay attention to these laws and are careful to follow them, then the Lord your God will keep his covenant of love with you, as he swore to your forefathers. [13] He will love you and bless you and increase your numbers. He will bless the fruit of your womb, the crops of your land—your grain, new wine and oil—the calves of your herds and the lambs of your flocks in the land that he swore to your forefathers to give you. [14] You will be blessed more than any other people; none of your men or women will be childless, nor any of your livestock without young. [15] The Lord will keep you free from every disease. He will not inflict on you the horrible diseases you knew in Egypt, but he will inflict them on all who hate you. [16] You must destroy all the peoples the Lord your God gives over to you. Do not look on them with pity and do not serve their gods, for that will be a snare to you.

[17] You may say to yourselves, "These nations are stronger than we are. How can we drive them out?" [18] But do not be afraid of them; remember well what the Lord your God did to Pharaoh and to all Egypt. [19] You saw with your own eyes the great trials, the miraculous signs and wonders, the mighty hand and outstretched arm, with which the Lord your God brought you out. The Lord your God will do the same to all the peoples you now fear. [20] Moreover, the Lord your God will send the hornet among them until even the survivors who hide from you have perished. [21] Do not be terrified by them, for the Lord your God, who is among you, is a great and awesome God. [22] The Lord your God will drive out those nations before you, little by little. You will not be allowed to eliminate them all at once, or the wild animals will multiply around you. [23] But the Lord your God will deliver them over to you, throwing them into great confusion until they are destroyed. [24] He will give their kings into your hand, and you will wipe out their names from under heaven. No one will be able to stand up against you; you will destroy them. [25] The images of their gods you are to burn in the fire. Do not covet the silver and gold on them,

and do not take it for yourselves, or you will be ensnared by it, for it is detestable to the Lord your God. [26] Do not bring a detestable thing into your house or you, like it, will be set apart for destruction. Utterly abhor and detest it, for it is set apart for destruction.

Do Not Forget the Lord

8 Be careful to follow every command I am giving you today, so that you may live and increase and may enter and possess the land that the Lord promised on oath to your forefathers. [2] Remember how the Lord your God led you all the way in the desert these forty years, to humble you and to test you in order to know what was in your heart, whether or not you would keep his commands. [3] He humbled you, causing you to hunger and then feeding you with manna, which neither you nor your fathers had known, to teach you that man does not live on bread alone but on every word that comes from the mouth of the Lord. [4] Your clothes did not wear out and your feet did not swell during these forty years. [5] Know then in your heart that as a man disciplines his son, so the Lord your God disciplines you.

[6] Observe the commands of the Lord your God, walking in his ways and revering him. [7] For the Lord your God is bringing you into a good land—a land with streams and pools of water, with springs flowing in the valleys and hills; [8] a land with wheat and barley, vines and fig trees, pomegranates, olive oil and honey; [9] a land where bread will not be scarce and you will lack nothing; a land where the rocks are iron and you can dig copper out of the hills.

[10] When you have eaten and are satisfied, praise the Lord your God for the good land he has given you. [11] Be careful that you do not forget the Lord your God, failing to observe his commands, his laws and his decrees that I am giving you this day. [12] Otherwise, when you eat and are satisfied, when you build fine houses and settle down, [13] and when your herds and flocks grow large and your silver and gold increase and all you have is multiplied, [14] then your heart will become proud and you will forget the Lord your God, who brought you out of Egypt, out of the land of slavery. [15] He led you through the vast and dreadful desert, that thirsty and wa-

terless land, with its venomous snakes and scorpions. He brought you water out of hard rock. ¹⁶He gave you manna to eat in the desert, something your fathers had never known, to humble and to test you so that in the end it might go well with you. ¹⁷You may say to yourself, "My power and the strength of my hands have produced this wealth for me." ¹⁸But remember the LORD your God, for it is he who gives you the ability to produce wealth, and so confirms his covenant, which he swore to your forefathers, as it is today.

¹⁹If you ever forget the LORD your God and follow other gods and worship and bow down to them, I testify against you today that you will surely be destroyed. ²⁰Like the nations the LORD destroyed before you, so you will be destroyed for not obeying the LORD your God.

Not Because of Israel's Righteousness

9 Hear, O Israel. You are now about to cross the Jordan to go in and dispossess nations greater and stronger than you, with large cities that have walls up to the sky. ²The people are strong and tall—Anakites! You know about them and have heard it said: "Who can stand up against the Anakites?" ³But be assured today that the LORD your God is the one who goes across ahead of you like a devouring fire. He will destroy them; he will subdue them before you. And you will drive them out and annihilate them quickly, as the LORD has promised you.

⁴After the LORD your God has driven them out before you, do not say to yourself, "The LORD has brought me here to take possession of this land because of my righteousness." No, it is on account of the wickedness of these nations that the LORD is going to drive them out before you. ⁵It is not because of your righteousness or your integrity that you are going in to take possession of their land; but on account of the wickedness of these nations, the LORD your God will drive them out before you, to accomplish what he swore to your fathers, to Abraham, Isaac and Jacob. ⁶Understand, then, that it is not because of your righteousness that the LORD your

Loving Learning

READ DEUTERONOMY 8:1–5

All your experiences in life are part of the process of testing, overcoming and learning. And you thought the only tests you had were in school! You have tests at home, too. If your parents tell you to clean up your room and you "forget," you might get grounded. That would teach you to listen better and do what they ask. When God tests you, he's not just picking on you. He wants you to learn, and what he wants you to learn more than anything is that his Word is true. He tested the Israelites for the same reason. Forty years in the desert taught them that they needed to completely depend on God's Word. It taught them that "man does not live on bread alone but on every word that comes from the mouth of the LORD" (Deuteronomy 8:3). Got it? God's Word is the textbook with all the answers to help you get through life's tests.

Your next reading is on page 244.

God is giving you this good land to possess, for you are a stiff-necked people.

The Golden Calf

⁷Remember this and never forget how you provoked the Lord your God to anger in the desert. From the day you left Egypt until you arrived here, you have been rebellious against the Lord. ⁸At Horeb you aroused the Lord's wrath so that he was angry enough to destroy you. ⁹When I went up on the mountain to receive the tablets of stone, the tablets of the covenant that the Lord had made with you, I stayed on the mountain forty days and forty nights; I ate no bread and drank no water. ¹⁰The Lord gave me two stone tablets inscribed by the finger of God. On them were all the commandments the Lord proclaimed to you on the mountain out of the fire, on the day of the assembly.

¹¹At the end of the forty days and forty nights, the Lord gave me the two stone tablets, the tablets of the covenant. ¹²Then the Lord told me, "Go down from here at once, because your people whom you brought out of Egypt have become corrupt. They have turned away quickly from what I commanded them and have made a cast idol for themselves."

¹³And the Lord said to me, "I have seen this people, and they are a stiff-necked people indeed! ¹⁴Let me alone, so that I may destroy them and blot out their name from under heaven. And I will make you into a nation stronger and more numerous than they."

¹⁵So I turned and went down from the mountain while it was ablaze with fire. And the two tablets of the covenant were in my hands.ᵃ ¹⁶When I looked, I saw that you had sinned against the Lord your God; you had made for yourselves an idol cast in the shape of a calf. You had turned aside quickly from the way that the Lord had commanded you. ¹⁷So I took the two tablets and threw them out of my hands, breaking them to pieces before your eyes.

¹⁸Then once again I fell prostrate before the Lord for forty days and forty nights; I ate no bread and drank no water, because of all the sin you had committed, doing what was evil in the Lord's sight and so provoking him to anger. ¹⁹I feared the anger and wrath of the Lord, for he was angry enough with you to destroy you. But again the Lord listened to me. ²⁰And the Lord was angry enough with Aaron to destroy him, but at that time I prayed for Aaron too. ²¹Also I took that sinful thing of yours, the calf you had made, and burned it in the fire. Then I crushed it and ground it to powder as fine as dust and threw the dust into a stream that flowed down the mountain.

²²You also made the Lord angry at Taberah, at Massah and at Kibroth Hattaavah.

²³And when the Lord sent you out from Kadesh Barnea, he said, "Go up and take possession of the land I have given you." But you rebelled against the command of the Lord your God. You did not trust him or obey him. ²⁴You have been rebellious against the Lord ever since I have known you.

²⁵I lay prostrate before the Lord those forty days and forty nights because the Lord had said he would destroy you. ²⁶I prayed to the Lord and said, "O Sovereign Lord, do not destroy your people, your own inheritance that you redeemed by your great power and brought out of Egypt with a mighty hand. ²⁷Remember your servants Abraham, Isaac and Jacob. Overlook the stubbornness of this people, their wickedness and their sin. ²⁸Otherwise, the country from which you brought us will say, 'Because the Lord was not able to take them into the land he had promised them, and because he hated them, he brought them out to put them to death in the desert.' ²⁹But they are your people, your inheritance that you brought out by your great power and your outstretched arm."

Tablets Like the First Ones

10 At that time the Lord said to me, "Chisel out two stone tablets like the first ones and come up to me on the mountain. Also make a wooden chest.ᵇ ²I will write on the tablets the words that were on the first tablets, which you broke. Then you are to put them in the chest."

³So I made the ark out of acacia wood and chiseled out two stone tablets like the first ones, and I went up on the mountain with the two tablets in my hands. ⁴The Lord wrote on these tablets what he had written before, the Ten Commandments

---

ᵃ15 Or And I had the two tablets of the covenant with me, one in each hand   ᵇ1 That is, an ark he had proclaimed to you on the mountain, out of the fire, on the day of the assembly. And the LORD gave them to me. ⁵Then I came back down the mountain and put the tablets in the ark I had made, as the LORD commanded me, and they are there now.

⁶(The Israelites traveled from the wells of the Jaakanites to Moserah. There Aaron died and was buried, and Eleazar his son succeeded him as priest. ⁷From there they traveled to Gudgodah and on to Jotbathah, a land with streams of water. ⁸At that time the LORD set apart the tribe of Levi to carry the ark of the covenant of the LORD, to stand before the LORD to minister and to pronounce blessings in his name, as they still do today. ⁹That is why the Levites have no share or inheritance among their brothers; the LORD is their inheritance, as the LORD your God told them.)

¹⁰Now I had stayed on the mountain forty days and nights, as I did the first time, and the LORD listened to me at this time also. It was not his will to destroy you. ¹¹"Go," the LORD said to me, "and lead the people on their way, so that they may enter and possess the land that I swore to their fathers to give them."

Fear the LORD

¹²And now, O Israel, what does the LORD your God ask of you but to fear the LORD your God, to walk in all his ways, to love him, to serve the LORD your God with all your heart and with all your soul, ¹³and to observe the LORD's commands and decrees that I am giving you today for your own good?

¹⁴To the LORD your God belong the heavens, even the highest heavens, the earth and everything in it. ¹⁵Yet the LORD set his affection on your forefathers and loved them, and he chose you, their descendants, above all the nations, as it is today. ¹⁶Circumcise your hearts, therefore, and do not be stiff-necked any longer. ¹⁷For the LORD your God is God of gods and Lord of lords, the great God, mighty and awesome, who shows no partiality and accepts no bribes. ¹⁸He defends the cause of the fatherless and the widow, and loves the alien, giving him food and clothing. ¹⁹And you are to love those who are aliens, for you yourselves were aliens in Egypt. ²⁰Fear the LORD your God and serve him. Hold fast to him and take your oaths

in his name. ²¹He is your praise; he is your God, who performed for you those great and awesome wonders you saw with your own eyes. ²²Your forefathers who went down into Egypt were seventy in all, and now the LORD your God has made you as numerous as the stars in the sky.

Love and Obey the LORD

11 Love the LORD your God and keep his requirements, his decrees, his laws and his commands always. ²Remember today that your children were not the ones who saw and experienced the discipline of the LORD your God: his majesty, his mighty hand, his outstretched arm; ³the signs he performed and the things he did in the heart of Egypt, both to Pharaoh king of Egypt and to his whole country; ⁴what he did to the Egyptian army, to its horses and chariots, how he overwhelmed them with the waters of the Red Sea[a] as they were pursuing you, and how the LORD brought lasting ruin on them. ⁵It was not your children who saw what he did for you in the desert until you arrived at this place, ⁶and what he did to Dathan and Abiram, sons of Eliab the Reubenite, when the earth opened its mouth right in the middle of all Israel and swallowed them up with their households, their tents and every living thing that belonged to them. ⁷But it was your own eyes that saw all these great things the LORD has done.

⁸Observe therefore all the commands I am giving you today, so that you may have the strength to go in and take over the land that you are crossing the Jordan to possess, ⁹and so that you may live long in the land that the LORD swore to your forefathers to give to them and their descendants, a land flowing with milk and honey. ¹⁰The land you are entering to take over is not like the land of Egypt, from which you have come, where you planted your seed and irrigated it by foot as in a vegetable garden. ¹¹But the land you are crossing the Jordan to take possession of is a land of mountains and valleys that drinks rain from heaven. ¹²It is a land the LORD your God cares for; the eyes of the LORD your God are continually on it from the beginning of the year to its end.

¹³So if you faithfully obey the commands

---

a 4 Hebrew *Yam Suph*; that is, Sea of Reeds

I am giving you today—to love the LORD your God and to serve him with all your heart and with all your soul— 14then I will send rain on your land in its season, both autumn and spring rains, so that you may gather in your grain, new wine and oil. 15I will provide grass in the fields for your cattle, and you will eat and be satisfied.

16Be careful, or you will be enticed to turn away and worship other gods and bow down to them. 17Then the LORD's anger will burn against you, and he will shut the heavens so that it will not rain and the ground will yield no produce, and you will soon perish from the good land the LORD is giving you. 18Fix these words of mine in your hearts and minds; tie them as symbols on your hands and bind them on your foreheads. 19Teach them to your children, talking about them when you sit at home and when you walk along the road, when you lie down and when you get up. 20Write them on the doorframes of your houses and on your gates, 21so that your days and the days of your children may be many in the land that the LORD swore to give your forefathers, as many as the days that the heavens are above the earth.

22If you carefully observe all these commands I am giving you to follow—to love the LORD your God, to walk in all his ways and to hold fast to him— 23then the LORD will drive out all these nations before you, and you will dispossess nations larger and stronger than you. 24Every place where you set your foot will be yours: Your territory will extend from the desert to Lebanon, and from the Euphrates River to the western sea.a 25No man will be able to stand against you. The LORD your God, as he promised you, will put the terror and fear of you on the whole land, wherever you go.

26See, I am setting before you today a blessing and a curse— 27the blessing if you obey the commands of the LORD your God that I am giving you today; 28the curse if you disobey the commands of the LORD your God and turn from the way that I command you today by following other gods, which you have not known. 29When the LORD your God has brought you into the land you are entering to possess, you are to proclaim on Mount Gerizim the blessings, and on Mount Ebal the curses. 30As you know, these mountains are across the Jordan, west of the road,b to-

ward the setting sun, near the great trees of Moreh, in the territory of those Canaanites living in the Arabah in the vicinity of Gilgal. 31You are about to cross the Jordan to enter and take possession of the land the LORD your God is giving you. When you have taken it over and are living there, 32be sure that you obey all the decrees and laws I am setting before you today.

The One Place of Worship

12 These are the decrees and laws you must be careful to follow in the land that the LORD, the God of your fathers, has given you to possess—as long as you live in the land. 2Destroy completely all the places on the high mountains and on the hills and under every spreading tree where the nations you are dispossessing worship their gods. 3Break down their altars, smash their sacred stones and burn their Asherah poles in the fire; cut down the idols of their gods and wipe out their names from those places.

4You must not worship the LORD your God in their way. 5But you are to seek the place the LORD your God will choose from among all your tribes to put his Name there for his dwelling. To that place you must go; 6there bring your burnt offerings and sacrifices, your tithes and special gifts, what you have vowed to give and your freewill offerings, and the firstborn of your herds and flocks. 7There, in the presence of the LORD your God, you and your families shall eat and shall rejoice in everything you have put your hand to, because the LORD your God has blessed you.

8You are not to do as we do here today, everyone as he sees fit, 9since you have not yet reached the resting place and the inheritance the LORD your God is giving you. 10But you will cross the Jordan and settle in the land the LORD your God is giving you as an inheritance, and he will give you rest from all your enemies around you so that you will live in safety. 11Then to the place the LORD your God will choose as a dwelling for his Name—there you are to bring everything I command you: your burnt offerings and sacrifices, your tithes and special gifts, and all the choice possessions you have vowed to the LORD. 12And there rejoice before the LORD your

a 24 That is, the Mediterranean　　b 30 Or Jordan, westward

God, you, your sons and daughters, your menservants and maidservants, and the Levites from your towns, who have no allotment or inheritance of their own. ¹³Be careful not to sacrifice your burnt offerings anywhere you please. ¹⁴Offer them only at the place the Lord will choose in one of your tribes, and there observe everything I command you.

¹⁵Nevertheless, you may slaughter your animals in any of your towns and eat as much of the meat as you want, as if it were gazelle or deer, according to the blessing the Lord your God gives you. Both the ceremonially unclean and the clean may eat it. ¹⁶But you must not eat the blood; pour it out on the ground like water. ¹⁷You must not eat in your own towns the tithe of your grain and new wine and oil, or the firstborn of your herds and flocks, or whatever you have vowed to give, or your freewill offerings or special gifts. ¹⁸Instead, you are to eat them in the presence of the Lord your God at the place the Lord your God will choose—you, your sons and daughters, your menservants and maidservants, and the Levites from your towns—and you are to rejoice before the Lord your God in everything you put your hand to. ¹⁹Be careful not to neglect the Levites as long as you live in your land.

²⁰When the Lord your God has enlarged your territory as he promised you, and you crave meat and say, "I would like some meat," then you may eat as much of it as you want. ²¹If the place where the Lord your God chooses to put his Name is too far away from you, you may slaughter animals from the herds and flocks the Lord has given you, as I have commanded you, and in your own towns you may eat as much of them as you want. ²²Eat them as you would gazelle or deer. Both the ceremonially unclean and the clean may eat. ²³But be sure you do not eat the blood, because the blood is the life, and you must not eat the life with the meat. ²⁴You must not eat the blood; pour it out on the ground like water. ²⁵Do not eat it, so that it may go well with you and your children after you, because you will be doing what is right in the eyes of the Lord.

²⁶But take your consecrated things and whatever you have vowed to give, and go to the place the Lord will choose. ²⁷Present your burnt offerings on the altar of the Lord your God, both the meat and the blood. The blood of your sacrifices must be poured beside the altar of the Lord your God, but you may eat the meat. ²⁸Be careful to obey all these regulations I am giving you, so that it may always go well with you and your children after you, because you will be doing what is good and right in the eyes of the Lord your God.

²⁹The Lord your God will cut off before you the nations you are about to invade and dispossess. But when you have driven them out and settled in their land, ³⁰and after they have been destroyed before you, be careful not to be ensnared by inquiring about their gods, saying, "How do these nations serve their gods? We will do the same." ³¹You must not worship the Lord your God in their way, because in worshiping their gods, they do all kinds of detestable things the Lord hates. They even burn their sons and daughters in the fire as sacrifices to their gods.

³²See that you do all I command you; do not add to it or take away from it.

Worshiping Other Gods

13 If a prophet, or one who foretells by dreams, appears among you and announces to you a miraculous sign or wonder, ²and if the sign or wonder of which he has spoken takes place, and he says, "Let us follow other gods" (gods you have not known) "and let us worship them," ³you must not listen to the words of that prophet or dreamer. The Lord your God is testing you to find out whether you love him with all your heart and with all your soul. ⁴It is the Lord your God you must follow, and him you must revere. Keep his commands and obey him; serve him and hold fast to him. ⁵That prophet or dreamer must be put to death, because he preached rebellion against the Lord your God, who brought you out of Egypt and redeemed you from the land of slavery; he has tried to turn you from the way the Lord your God commanded you to follow. You must purge the evil from among you.

⁶If your very own brother, or your son or daughter, or the wife you love, or your closest friend secretly entices you, saying, "Let us go and worship other gods" (gods that neither you nor your fathers have known, ⁷gods of the peoples around you, whether near or far, from one end of the land to the other), ⁸do not yield to him or

listen to him. Show him no pity. Do not spare him or shield him. ⁹You must certainly put him to death. Your hand must be the first in putting him to death, and then the hands of all the people. ¹⁰Stone him to death, because he tried to turn you away from the LORD your God, who brought you out of Egypt, out of the land of slavery. ¹¹Then all Israel will hear and be afraid, and no one among you will do such an evil thing again.

¹²If you hear it said about one of the towns the LORD your God is giving you to live in ¹³that wicked men have arisen among you and have led the people of their town astray, saying, "Let us go and worship other gods" (gods you have not known), ¹⁴then you must inquire, probe and investigate it thoroughly. And if it is true and it has been proved that this detestable thing has been done among you, ¹⁵you must certainly put to the sword all who live in that town. Destroy it completely,ᵃ both its people and its livestock.

¹⁶Gather all the plunder of the town into the middle of the public square and completely burn the town and all its plunder as a whole burnt offering to the LORD your God. It is to remain a ruin forever, never to be rebuilt. ¹⁷None of those condemned thingsᵃ shall be found in your hands, so that the LORD will turn from his fierce anger; he will show you mercy, have compassion on you, and increase your numbers, as he promised on oath to your forefathers, ¹⁸because you obey the LORD your God, keeping all his commands that I am giving you today and doing what is right in his eyes.

Clean and Unclean Food

14 You are the children of the LORD your God. Do not cut yourselves or shave the front of your heads for the dead, ²for you are a peo-

---

ᵃ 15,17 The Hebrew term refers to the irrevocable giving over of things or persons to the LORD, often by totally destroying them.

GET STRONGER

What's for Supper?

READ DEUTERONOMY 14:3–21

Why was God so concerned about what the Israelites ate that he practically gave them a cookbook? Some people think it was at least partly because he was concerned about the Israelites' health. How would you feel if your mom came in with a big plate of vulture burgers? Eww! OK. God said, "Do not eat any detestable thing" (verse 3). He knew vultures were just loaded with deadly bacteria. Some of the "unclean" critters God outlawed weren't healthy, and some believe they represented sin because they ate the blood of other animals. You might not stick to a strict Jewish "kosher" diet today, but God is still concerned for your health and wants you to take good care of your body. So think: What kind of rules might apply today? How about "Don't just chow down on junk foods and sweets." Today, instead of talking about "clean" and "unclean" food, the emphasis might be more on "junk" and "unjunk" food.

Your next reading is on page 250.

ple holy to the LORD your God. Out of all the peoples on the face of the earth, the LORD has chosen you to be his treasured possession.

³Do not eat any detestable thing. ⁴These are the animals you may eat: the ox, the sheep, the goat, ⁵the deer, the gazelle, the roe deer, the wild goat, the ibex, the antelope and the mountain sheep.ᵃ ⁶You may eat any animal that has a split hoof divided in two and that chews the cud. ⁷However, of those that chew the cud or that have a split hoof completely divided you may not eat the camel, the rabbit or the coney.ᵇ Although they chew the cud, they do not have a split hoof; they are ceremonially unclean for you. ⁸The pig is also unclean; although it has a split hoof, it does not chew the cud. You are not to eat their meat or touch their carcasses.

⁹Of all the creatures living in the water, you may eat any that has fins and scales. ¹⁰But anything that does not have fins and scales you may not eat; for you it is unclean.

¹¹You may eat any clean bird. ¹²But these you may not eat: the eagle, the vulture, the black vulture, ¹³the red kite, the black kite, any kind of falcon, ¹⁴any kind of raven, ¹⁵the horned owl, the screech owl, the gull, any kind of hawk, ¹⁶the little owl, the great owl, the white owl, ¹⁷the desert owl, the osprey, the cormorant, ¹⁸the stork, any kind of heron, the hoopoe and the bat.

¹⁹All flying insects that swarm are unclean to you; do not eat them. ²⁰But any winged creature that is clean you may eat.

²¹Do not eat anything you find already dead. You may give it to an alien living in any of your towns, and he may eat it, or you may sell it to a foreigner. But you are a people holy to the LORD your God.

Do not cook a young goat in its mother's milk.

Tithes

²²Be sure to set aside a tenth of all that your fields produce each year. ²³Eat the tithe of your grain, new wine and oil, and the firstborn of your herds and flocks in the presence of the LORD your God at the place he will choose as a dwelling for his Name, so that you may learn to revere the LORD your God always. ²⁴But if that place is too distant and you have been blessed by the LORD your God and cannot carry your tithe (because the place where the LORD will choose to put his Name is so far away), ²⁵then exchange your tithe for silver, and take the silver with you and go to the place the LORD your God will choose. ²⁶Use the silver to buy whatever you like: cattle, sheep, wine or other fermented drink, or anything you wish. Then you and your household shall eat there in the presence of the LORD your God and rejoice. ²⁷And do not neglect the Levites living in your towns, for they have no allotment or inheritance of their own.

Gross!

Check out Deuteronomy 14:21. Whoa! "Aliens" eating dead animals? Take a closer look next time you see a truck stopped along the side of the road scooping up road kill. It might be ET about to chow down. (Ooonnly joking. "Aliens" means "foreigners.")

ᵃ 5 The precise identification of some of the birds and animals in this chapter is uncertain.   ᵇ 7 That is, the hyrax or rock badger

28At the end of every three years, bring all the tithes of that year's produce and store it in your towns, 29so that the Levites (who have no allotment or inheritance of their own) and the aliens, the fatherless and the widows who live in your towns may come and eat and be satisfied, and so that the LORD your God may bless you in all the work of your hands.

The Year for Canceling Debts

15 At the end of every seven years you must cancel debts. 2This is how it is to be done: Every creditor shall cancel the loan he has made to his fellow Israelite. He shall not require payment from his fellow Israelite or brother, because the LORD's time for canceling debts has been proclaimed. 3You may require payment from a foreigner, but you must cancel any debt your brother owes you. 4However, there should be no poor among you, for in the land the LORD your God is giving you to possess as your inheritance, he will richly bless you, 5if only you fully obey the LORD your God and are careful to follow all these commands I am giving you today. 6For the LORD your God will bless you as he has promised, and you will lend to many nations but will borrow from none. You will rule over many nations but none will rule over you.

7If there is a poor man among your brothers in any of the towns of the land that the LORD your God is giving you, do not be hardhearted or tightfisted toward your poor brother. 8Rather be openhanded and freely lend him whatever he needs. 9Be careful not to harbor this wicked thought: "The seventh year, the year for canceling debts, is near," so that you do not show ill will toward your needy brother and give him nothing. He may then appeal to the LORD against you, and you will be found guilty of sin. 10Give generously to him and do so without a grudging heart; then because of this the LORD your God will bless you in all your work and in everything you put your hand to. 11There will always be poor people in the land. Therefore I command you to be openhanded toward your brothers and toward the poor and needy in your land.

Freeing Servants

12If a fellow Hebrew, a man or a woman, sells himself to you and serves you six years, in the seventh year you must let him go free. 13And when you release him, do not send him away empty-handed. 14Supply him liberally from your flock, your threshing floor and your winepress. Give to him as the LORD your God has blessed you. 15Remember that you were slaves in Egypt and the LORD your God redeemed you. That is why I give you this command today.

16But if your servant says to you, "I do not want to leave you," because he loves you and your family and is well off with you, 17then take an awl and push it through his ear lobe into the door, and he will become your servant for life. Do the same for your maidservant.

18Do not consider it a hardship to set your servant free, because his service to you these six years has been worth twice as much as that of a hired hand. And the LORD your God will bless you in everything you do.

The Firstborn Animals

19Set apart for the LORD your God every firstborn male of your herds and flocks. Do not put the firstborn of your oxen to work, and do not shear the firstborn of your sheep. 20Each year you and your family are to eat them in the presence of the LORD your God at the place he will choose. 21If an animal has a defect, is lame or blind, or has any serious flaw, you must not sacrifice it to the LORD your God. 22You are to eat it in your own towns. Both the ceremonially unclean and the clean may eat it, as if it were gazelle or deer. 23But you must not eat the blood; pour it out on the ground like water.

Passover

16 Observe the month of Abib and celebrate the Passover of the LORD your God, because in the month of Abib he brought you out of Egypt by night. 2Sacrifice as the Passover to the LORD your God an animal from your flock or herd at the place the LORD will choose as a dwelling for his Name. 3Do not eat it with bread made with yeast, but for seven days eat unleavened bread, the bread of affliction, because you left Egypt in haste—so that all the days of your life you may remember the time of your departure from Egypt.

[4]Let no yeast be found in your possession in all your land for seven days. Do not let any of the meat you sacrifice on the evening of the first day remain until morning. [5]You must not sacrifice the Passover in any town the LORD your God gives you [6]except in the place he will choose as a dwelling for his Name. There you must sacrifice the Passover in the evening, when the sun goes down, on the anniversary[a] of your departure from Egypt. [7]Roast it and eat it at the place the LORD your God will choose. Then in the morning return to your tents. [8]For six days eat unleavened bread and on the seventh day hold an assembly to the LORD your God and do no work.

Feast of Weeks

[9]Count off seven weeks from the time you begin to put the sickle to the standing grain. [10]Then celebrate the Feast of Weeks to the LORD your God by giving a freewill offering in proportion to the blessings the LORD your God has given you. [11]And rejoice before the LORD your God at the place he will choose as a dwelling for his Name—you, your sons and daughters, your menservants and maidservants, the Levites in your towns, and the aliens, the fatherless and the widows living among you. [12]Remember that you were slaves in Egypt, and follow carefully these decrees.

Feast of Tabernacles

[13]Celebrate the Feast of Tabernacles for seven days after you have gathered the produce of your threshing floor and your winepress. [14]Be joyful at your Feast—you, your sons and daughters, your menservants and maidservants, and the Levites, the aliens, the fatherless and the widows who live in your towns. [15]For seven days celebrate the Feast to the LORD your God at the place the LORD will choose. For the LORD your God will bless you in all your harvest and in all the work of your hands, and your joy will be complete.

[16]Three times a year all your men must appear before the LORD your God at the place he will choose: at the Feast of Unleavened Bread, the Feast of Weeks and the Feast of Tabernacles. No man should appear before the LORD empty-handed: [17]Each of you must bring a gift in proportion to the way the LORD your God has blessed you.

Judges

[18]Appoint judges and officials for each of your tribes in every town the LORD your God is giving you, and they shall judge the people fairly. [19]Do not pervert justice or show partiality. Do not accept a bribe, for a bribe blinds the eyes of the wise and twists the words of the righteous. [20]Follow justice and justice alone, so that you may live and possess the land the LORD your God is giving you.

Worshiping Other Gods

[21]Do not set up any wooden Asherah pole[b] beside the altar you build to the LORD your God, [22]and do not erect a sacred stone, for these the LORD your God hates.

17 Do not sacrifice to the LORD your God an ox or a sheep that has any defect or flaw in it, for that would be detestable to him.

[2]If a man or woman living among you in one of the towns the LORD gives you is found doing evil in the eyes of the LORD your God in violation of his covenant, [3]and contrary to my command has worshiped other gods, bowing down to them or to the sun or the moon or the stars of the sky, [4]and this has been brought to your attention, then you must investigate it thoroughly. If it is true and it has been proved that this detestable thing has been done in Israel, [5]take the man or woman who has done this evil deed to your city gate and stone that person to death. [6]On the testimony of two or three witnesses a man shall be put to death, but no one shall be put to death on the testimony of only one witness. [7]The hands of the witnesses must be the first in putting him to death, and then the hands of all the people. You must purge the evil from among you.

Law Courts

[8]If cases come before your courts that are too difficult for you to judge—whether bloodshed, lawsuits or assaults—take them to the place the LORD your God will choose. [9]Go to the priests, who are Levites, and to the judge who is in office at that time. Inquire of them and they will give you the verdict. [10]You must act according to the decisions they give you at the place the LORD will choose. Be careful

---

[a] 6 Or down, at the time of day   [b] 21 Or Do not plant any tree dedicated to Asherah

to do everything they direct you to do. [11]Act according to the law they teach you and the decisions they give you. Do not turn aside from what they tell you, to the right or to the left. [12]The man who shows contempt for the judge or for the priest who stands ministering there to the LORD your God must be put to death. You must purge the evil from Israel. [13]All the people will hear and be afraid, and will not be contemptuous again.

The King

[14]When you enter the land the LORD your God is giving you and have taken possession of it and settled in it, and you say, "Let us set a king over us like all the nations around us," [15]be sure to appoint over you the king the LORD your God chooses. He must be from among your own brothers. Do not place a foreigner over you, one who is not a brother Israelite. [16]The king, moreover, must not acquire great numbers of horses for himself or make the people return to Egypt to get more of them, for the LORD has told you, "You are not to go back that way again." [17]He must not take many wives, or his heart will be led astray. He must not accumulate large amounts of silver and gold.

[18]When he takes the throne of his kingdom, he is to write for himself on a scroll a copy of this law, taken from that of the priests, who are Levites. [19]It is to be with him, and he is to read it all the days of his life so that he may learn to revere the LORD his God and follow carefully all the words of this law and these decrees [20]and not consider himself better than his brothers and turn from the law to the right or to the left. Then he and his descendants will reign a long time over his kingdom in Israel.

Offerings for Priests and Levites

18 The priests, who are Levites—indeed the whole tribe of Levi—are to have no allotment or inheritance with Israel. They shall live on the offerings made to the LORD by fire, for that is their inheritance. [2]They shall have no inheritance among their brothers; the LORD is their inheritance, as he promised them.

[3]This is the share due the priests from the people who sacrifice a bull or a sheep: the shoulder, the jowls and the inner parts. [4]You are to give them the firstfruits of your grain, new wine and oil, and the first wool from the shearing of your sheep, [5]for the LORD your God has chosen them and their descendants out of all your tribes to stand and minister in the LORD's name always.

[6]If a Levite moves from one of your towns anywhere in Israel where he is living, and comes in all earnestness to the place the LORD will choose, [7]he may minister in the name of the LORD his God like all his fellow Levites who serve there in the presence of the LORD. [8]He is to share equally in their benefits, even though he has received money from the sale of family possessions.

Detestable Practices

[9]When you enter the land the LORD your God is giving you, do not learn to imitate the detestable ways of the nations there. [10]Let no one be found among you who sacrifices his son or daughter in[a] the fire, who practices divination or sorcery, interprets omens, engages in witchcraft, [11]or casts spells, or who is a medium or spiritist or who consults the dead. [12]Anyone who does these things is detestable to the LORD, and because of these detestable practices the LORD your God will drive out those nations before you. [13]You must be blameless before the LORD your God.

The Prophet

[14]The nations you will dispossess listen to those who practice sorcery or divination. But as for you, the LORD your God has not permitted you to do so. [15]The LORD your God will raise up for you a prophet like me from among your own brothers. You must listen to him. [16]For this is what you asked of the LORD your God at Horeb on the day of the assembly when you said, "Let us not hear the voice of the LORD our God nor see this great fire anymore, or we will die."

[17]The LORD said to me: "What they say is good. [18]I will raise up for them a prophet like you from among their brothers; I will put my words in his mouth, and he will tell them everything I command him. [19]If anyone does not listen to my words that the prophet speaks in my name, I myself will call him to account. [20]But a prophet

[a] 10 Or *who makes his son or daughter pass through*

who presumes to speak in my name anything I have not commanded him to say, or a prophet who speaks in the name of other gods, must be put to death." ²¹You may say to yourselves, "How can we know when a message has not been spoken by the LORD?" ²²If what a prophet proclaims in the name of the LORD does not take place or come true, that is a message the LORD has not spoken. That prophet has spoken presumptuously. Do not be afraid of him.

Cities of Refuge

19 When the LORD your God has destroyed the nations whose land he is giving you, and when you have driven them out and settled in their towns and houses, ²then set aside for yourselves three cities centrally located in the land the LORD your God is giving you to possess. ³Build roads to them and divide into three parts the land the LORD your God is giving you as an inheritance, so that anyone who kills a man may flee there.

⁴This is the rule concerning the man who kills another and flees there to save his life—one who kills his neighbor unintentionally, without malice aforethought. ⁵For instance, a man may go into the forest with his neighbor to cut wood, and as he swings his ax to fell a tree, the head may fly off and hit his neighbor and kill him. That man may flee to one of these cities and save his life. ⁶Otherwise, the avenger of blood might pursue him in a rage, overtake him if the distance is too great, and kill him even though he is not deserving of death, since he did it to his neighbor without malice aforethought. ⁷This is why I command you to set aside for yourselves three cities.

⁸If the LORD your God enlarges your territory, as he promised on oath to your forefathers, and gives you the whole land he promised them, ⁹because you carefully follow all these laws I command you to

Make It Stick

READ DEUTERONOMY 18:9–13

Had to say no to human sacrifices lately? Probably not, but the occult and other perverted things are everywhere today. It can be hard to stay on course when "cool kids" are pressuring you to do something wrong. Think of one thing that God calls detestable—for example, the occult—and write *"No to (that thing)!"* on a sticky note.

day—to love the LORD your God and to walk always in his ways—then you are to set aside three more cities. ¹⁰Do this so that innocent blood will not be shed in your land, which the LORD your God is giving you as your inheritance, and so that you will not be guilty of bloodshed.

¹¹But if a man hates his neighbor and lies in wait for him, assaults and kills him, and then flees to one of these cities, ¹²the elders of his town shall send for him, bring him back from the city, and hand him over to the avenger of blood to die. ¹³Show him no pity. You must purge from Israel the guilt of shedding innocent blood, so that it may go well with you.

¹⁴Do not move your neighbor's boundary stone set up by your predecessors in the inheritance you receive in the land the LORD your God is giving you to possess.

Witnesses

¹⁵One witness is not enough to convict a man accused of any crime or offense he may have committed. A matter must be established by the testimony of two or three witnesses.

¹⁶If a malicious witness takes the stand to accuse a man of a crime, ¹⁷the two men involved in the dispute must stand in the presence of the LORD before the priests and the judges who are in office at the time. ¹⁸The judges must make a thorough investigation, and if the witness proves to be a liar, giving false testimony against his brother, ¹⁹then do to him as he intended to do to his brother. You must purge the evil from among you. ²⁰The rest of the people will hear of this and be afraid, and never again will such an evil thing be done among you. ²¹Show no pity: life for life, eye for eye, tooth for tooth, hand for hand, foot for foot.

Going to War

20 When you go to war against your enemies and see horses and chariots and an army greater than yours, do not be afraid of them, because the LORD your God, who brought you up out of Egypt, will be with you. ²When you are about to go into battle, the priest shall come forward and address the army. ³He shall say:

The Prophet

READ DEUTERONOMY 18:14–19

Even while Moses was speaking to the people of Israel and giving them God's commands, he was telling them about someone even greater who was to come in the future. Think of Moses as a substitute teacher filling in until the real teacher arrived. When the real teacher arrives, everyone sits up straight. No more paper airplanes. Who *was* this Super Prophet mentioned in Deuteronomy 18:18? According to Acts 3:22 and 7:37, it was Jesus! God used Moses to bring the Ten Commandments and many other laws to help the people of Israel govern themselves, but Jesus later narrowed the Law down to just two commandments: "Love God and love your neighbor." Jesus spent his whole adult life teaching people about what it really meant to love God and to love their neighbor. Want to follow Mr. Super Prophet? Live your life according to the teachings of Jesus.

Your next reading is on page 252.

"Hear, O Israel, today you are going into battle against your enemies. Do not be fainthearted or afraid; do not be terrified or give way to panic before them. 4For the LORD your God is the one who goes with you to fight for you against your enemies to give you victory."

5The officers shall say to the army: "Has anyone built a new house and not dedicated it? Let him go home, or he may die in battle and someone else may dedicate it. 6Has anyone planted a vineyard and not begun to enjoy it? Let him go home, or he may die in battle and someone else enjoy it. 7Has anyone become pledged to a woman and not married her? Let him go home, or he may die in battle and someone else marry her." 8Then the officers shall add, "Is any man afraid or fainthearted? Let him go home so that his brothers will not become disheartened too." 9When the officers have finished speaking to the army, they shall appoint commanders over it.

10When you march up to attack a city, make its people an offer of peace. 11If they accept and open their gates, all the people in it shall be subject to forced labor and shall work for you. 12If they refuse to make peace and they engage you in battle, lay siege to that city. 13When the LORD your God delivers it into your hand, put to the sword all the men in it. 14As for the women, the children, the livestock and everything else in the city, you may take these as plunder for yourselves. And you may use the plunder the LORD your God gives you from your enemies. 15This is how you are to treat all the cities that are at a distance from you and do not belong to the nations nearby.

16However, in the cities of the nations the LORD your God is giving you as an inheritance, do not leave alive anything that breathes. 17Completely destroya them— the Hittites, Amorites, Canaanites, Perizzites, Hivites and Jebusites—as the LORD your God has commanded you. 18Otherwise, they will teach you to follow all the detestable things they do in worshiping their gods, and you will sin against the LORD your God.

19When you lay siege to a city for a long time, fighting against it to capture it, do not destroy its trees by putting an ax to them, because you can eat their fruit. Do not cut them down. Are the trees of the field people, that you should besiege them?b 20However, you may cut down trees that you know are not fruit trees and use them to build siege works until the city at war with you falls.

Atonement for an Unsolved Murder

21 If a man is found slain, lying in a field in the land the LORD your God is giving you to possess, and it is not known who killed him, 2your elders and judges shall go out and measure the distance from the body to the neighboring towns. 3Then the elders of the town nearest the body shall take a heifer that has never been worked and has never worn a yoke 4and lead her down to a valley that has not been plowed or planted and where there is a flowing stream. There in the valley they are to break the heifer's neck. 5The priests, the sons of Levi, shall step forward, for the LORD your God has chosen them to minister and to pronounce blessings in the name of the LORD and to decide all cases of dispute and assault. 6Then all the elders of the town nearest the body shall wash their hands over the heifer whose neck was broken in the valley, 7and they shall declare: "Our hands did not shed this blood, nor did our eyes see it done. 8Accept this atonement for your people Israel, whom you have redeemed, O LORD, and do not hold your people guilty of the blood of an innocent man." And the bloodshed will be atoned for. 9So you will purge from yourselves the guilt of shedding innocent blood, since you have done what is right in the eyes of the LORD.

Marrying a Captive Woman

10When you go to war against your enemies and the LORD your God delivers them into your hands and you take captives, 11if you notice among the captives a beautiful woman and are attracted to her, you may take her as your wife. 12Bring her into your home and have her shave her head, trim her nails 13and put aside the clothes she was wearing when captured. After she has lived in your house and mourned her father and mother for a full month, then you may go to her and be her husband and she shall be your wife.

a 17 The Hebrew term refers to the irrevocable giving over of things or persons to the LORD, often by totally destroying them.   b 19 Or down to use in the siege, for the fruit trees are for the benefit of man.

14If you are not pleased with her, let her go wherever she wishes. You must not sell her or treat her as a slave, since you have dishonored her.

The Right of the Firstborn

15If a man has two wives, and he loves one but not the other, and both bear him sons but the firstborn is the son of the wife he does not love, 16when he wills his property to his sons, he must not give the rights of the firstborn to the son of the wife he loves in preference to his actual firstborn, the son of the wife he does not love. 17He must acknowledge the son of his unloved wife as the firstborn by giving him a double share of all he has. That son is the first sign of his father's strength. The right of the firstborn belongs to him.

A Rebellious Son

18If a man has a stubborn and rebellious son who does not obey his father and mother and will not listen to them when they discipline him, 19his father and mother shall take hold of him and bring him to the elders at the gate of his town.

20They shall say to the elders, "This son of ours is stubborn and rebellious. He will not obey us. He is a profligate and a drunkard." 21Then all the men of his town shall stone him to death. You must purge the evil from among you. All Israel will hear of it and be afraid.

Various Laws

22If a man guilty of a capital offense is put to death and his body is hung on a tree, 23you must not leave his body on the tree overnight. Be sure to bury him that same day, because anyone who is hung on a tree is under God's curse. You must not desecrate the land the LORD your God is giving you as an inheritance.

22 If you see your brother's ox or sheep straying, do not ignore it but be sure to take it back to him. 2If the brother does not live near you or if you do not know who he is, take it home with you and keep it until he comes looking for it. Then give it back to him. 3Do the same if you find your brother's donkey or his cloak or anything he loses. Do not ignore it.

Rebellious Kids Rocked Out

READ DEUTERONOMY 21:18–21

Stoning stubborn and rebellious kids might seem like a harsh punishment. *Uh huh.* That's because it *was* harsh. But you've got to understand, these were harsh kids. They didn't merely refuse to clean their rooms or sneak out to a friend's house. We are talking utterly, completely rotten-to-the-very-core, no-hope-left-for-that-kid reprobate wickedness! Today, these kind of juveniles aren't stoned; they end up on the evening news and are slammed into maximum security prisons. But the fact is, *all* rebellion—even the less serious kind kids are tempted with every day—leads to pain, suffering and ultimately self-destruction. All willfulness and stubbornness has consequences. That's why, for your own sake, it's better to obey your parents and God. That puts you in the habit of obeying the laws of the land, and *that* will keep you from causing pain to others and ending up behind bars.

Your next reading is on page 254.

⁴If you see your brother's donkey or his ox fallen on the road, do not ignore it. Help him get it to its feet.

⁵A woman must not wear men's clothing, nor a man wear women's clothing, for the LORD your God detests anyone who does this.

⁶If you come across a bird's nest beside the road, either in a tree or on the ground, and the mother is sitting on the young or on the eggs, do not take the mother with the young. ⁷You may take the young, but be sure to let the mother go, so that it may go well with you and you may have a long life.

⁸When you build a new house, make a parapet around your roof so that you may not bring the guilt of bloodshed on your house if someone falls from the roof.

⁹Do not plant two kinds of seed in your vineyard; if you do, not only the crops you plant but also the fruit of the vineyard will be defiled.ᵃ

¹⁰Do not plow with an ox and a donkey yoked together.

¹¹Do not wear clothes of wool and linen woven together.

¹²Make tassels on the four corners of the cloak you wear.

Marriage Violations

¹³If a man takes a wife and, after lying with her, dislikes her ¹⁴and slanders her and gives her a bad name, saying, "I married this woman, but when I approached her, I did not find proof of her virginity," ¹⁵then the girl's father and mother shall bring proof that she was a virgin to the town elders at the gate. ¹⁶The girl's father will say to the elders, "I gave my daughter in marriage to this man, but he dislikes her. ¹⁷Now he has slandered her and said, 'I did not find your daughter to be a virgin.' But here is the proof of my daughter's virginity." Then her parents shall display the cloth before the elders of the town, ¹⁸and the elders shall take the man and punish him. ¹⁹They shall fine him a hundred shekels of silverᵇ and give them to the girl's father, because this man has given an Israelite virgin a bad name. She shall continue to be his wife; he must not divorce her as long as he lives.

²⁰If, however, the charge is true and no proof of the girl's virginity can be found, ²¹she shall be brought to the door of her father's house and there the men of her town shall stone her to death. She has done a disgraceful thing in Israel by being promiscuous while still in her father's house. You must purge the evil from among you.

²²If a man is found sleeping with another man's wife, both the man who slept with her and the woman must die. You must purge the evil from Israel.

²³If a man happens to meet in a town a virgin pledged to be married and he sleeps with her, ²⁴you shall take both of them to the gate of that town and stone them to death—the girl because she was in a town and did not scream for help, and the man because he violated another man's wife. You must purge the evil from among you.

²⁵But if out in the country a man happens to meet a girl pledged to be married and rapes her, only the man who has done this shall die. ²⁶Do nothing to the girl; she has committed no sin deserving death. This case is like that of someone who attacks and murders his neighbor, ²⁷for the man found the girl out in the country, and though the betrothed girl screamed, there was no one to rescue her.

²⁸If a man happens to meet a virgin who is not pledged to be married and rapes her and they are discovered, ²⁹he shall pay the girl's father fifty shekels of silver.ᶜ He must marry the girl, for he has violated her. He can never divorce her as long as he lives.

³⁰A man is not to marry his father's wife; he must not dishonor his father's bed.

Exclusion From the Assembly

23 No one who has been emasculated by crushing or cutting may enter the assembly of the LORD.

²No one born of a forbidden marriageᵈ nor any of his descendants may enter the assembly of the LORD, even down to the tenth generation.

³No Ammonite or Moabite or any of his descendants may enter the assembly of the LORD, even down to the tenth generation. ⁴For they did not come to meet you with bread and water on your way when you came out of Egypt, and they hired Ba-

ᵃ 9 Or be forfeited to the sanctuary   ᵇ 19 That is, about 2 1/2 pounds (about 1 kilogram)   ᶜ 29 That is, about 1 1/4 pounds (about 0.6 kilogram)   ᵈ 2 Or one of illegitimate birth laam son of Beor from Pethor in Aram Naharaim[a] to pronounce a curse on you. ⁵However, the LORD your God would not listen to Balaam but turned the curse into a blessing for you, because the LORD your God loves you. ⁶Do not seek a treaty of friendship with them as long as you live.

⁷Do not abhor an Edomite, for he is your brother. Do not abhor an Egyptian, because you lived as an alien in his country. ⁸The third generation of children born to them may enter the assembly of the LORD.

Uncleanness in the Camp

⁹When you are encamped against your enemies, keep away from everything impure. ¹⁰If one of your men is unclean because of a nocturnal emission, he is to go outside the camp and stay there. ¹¹But as evening approaches he is to wash himself, and at sunset he may return to the camp. ¹²Designate a place outside the camp where you can go to relieve yourself. ¹³As part of your equipment have something to dig with, and when you relieve yourself, dig a hole and cover up your excrement. ¹⁴For the LORD your God moves about in your camp to protect you and to deliver your enemies to you. Your camp must be holy, so that he will not see among you anything indecent and turn away from you.

Miscellaneous Laws

¹⁵If a slave has taken refuge with you, do not hand him over to his master. ¹⁶Let him live among you wherever he likes and in whatever town he chooses. Do not oppress him.

¹⁷No Israelite man or woman is to become a shrine prostitute. ¹⁸You must not bring the earnings of a female prostitute or of a male prostitute[b] into the house of the LORD your God to pay any vow, because the LORD your God detests them both.

---

[a] 4 That is, Northwest Mesopotamia   [b] 18 Hebrew of a dog

Designated Latrines

READ DEUTERONOMY 23:12–14

Deuteronomy 23:13 says, "When you relieve yourself, dig a hole and cover up your excrement." In other words, don't just relieve yourself any old where. Use designated latrines. God does not like to see human waste laying around. Think hygiene and cleanliness are no big deal? Consider the Black Plague of the 14th century. That disease killed 24,000,000 people—nearly 37% of Europe's entire population! Cleanliness and personal hygiene are still important today. That means don't litter, skip shower time or decorate the lawn with globs of spit. Even when camping, follow the rules, and use the washrooms to prevent disease from spreading. And *pleeaase!* Wash your hands with soap. Then you won't be arrested as a public health hazard (just kidding).

Your next reading is on page 256.

¹⁹Do not charge your brother interest, whether on money or food or anything else that may earn interest. ²⁰You may charge a foreigner interest, but not a brother Israelite, so that the LORD your God may bless you in everything you put your hand to in the land you are entering to possess.

²¹If you make a vow to the LORD your God, do not be slow to pay it, for the LORD your God will certainly demand it of you and you will be guilty of sin. ²²But if you refrain from making a vow, you will not be guilty. ²³Whatever your lips utter you must be sure to do, because you made your vow freely to the LORD your God with your own mouth.

²⁴If you enter your neighbor's vineyard, you may eat all the grapes you want, but do not put any in your basket. ²⁵If you enter your neighbor's grainfield, you may pick kernels with your hands, but you must not put a sickle to his standing grain.

24 If a man marries a woman who becomes displeasing to him because he finds something indecent about her, and he writes her a certificate of divorce, gives it to her and sends her from his house, ²and if after she leaves his house she becomes the wife of another man, ³and her second husband dislikes her and writes her a certificate of divorce, gives it to her and sends her from his house, or if he dies, ⁴then her first husband, who divorced her, is not allowed to marry her again after she has been defiled. That would be detestable in the eyes of the LORD. Do not bring sin upon the land the LORD your God is giving you as an inheritance.

⁵If a man has recently married, he must not be sent to war or have any other duty laid on him. For one year he is to be free to stay at home and bring happiness to the wife he has married.

⁶Do not take a pair of millstones—not even the upper one—as security for a debt, because that would be taking a man's livelihood as security.

⁷If a man is caught kidnapping one of his brother Israelites and treats him as a slave or sells him, the kidnapper must die. You must purge the evil from among you.

⁸In cases of leprous[a] diseases be very careful to do exactly as the priests, who are Levites, instruct you. You must follow carefully what I have commanded them.

⁹Remember what the LORD your God did to Miriam along the way after you came out of Egypt.

¹⁰When you make a loan of any kind to your neighbor, do not go into his house to get what he is offering as a pledge. ¹¹Stay outside and let the man to whom you are making the loan bring the pledge out to you. ¹²If the man is poor, do not go to sleep with his pledge in your possession. ¹³Return his cloak to him by sunset so that he may sleep in it. Then he will thank you, and it will be regarded as a righteous act in the sight of the LORD your God.

¹⁴Do not take advantage of a hired man who is poor and needy, whether he is a brother Israelite or an alien living in one of your towns. ¹⁵Pay him his wages each day before sunset, because he is poor and is counting on it. Otherwise he may cry to the LORD against you, and you will be guilty of sin.

¹⁶Fathers shall not be put to death for their children, nor children put to death for their fathers; each is to die for his own sin.

¹⁷Do not deprive the alien or the fatherless of justice, or take the cloak of the widow as a pledge. ¹⁸Remember that you were slaves in Egypt and the LORD your God redeemed you from there. That is why I command you to do this.

¹⁹When you are harvesting in your field and you overlook a sheaf, do not go back to get it. Leave it for the alien, the fatherless and the widow, so that the LORD your God may bless you in all the work of your hands. ²⁰When you beat the olives from your trees, do not go over the branches a second time. Leave what remains for the alien, the fatherless and the widow. ²¹When you harvest the grapes in your vineyard, do not go over the vines again. Leave what remains for the alien, the fatherless and the widow. ²²Remember that you were slaves in Egypt. That is why I command you to do this.

25 When men have a dispute, they are to take it to court and the judges will decide the case, acquitting the innocent and condemning the guilty. ²If the guilty man deserves to be beaten, the judge shall make him lie down and have him flogged in his presence with the number of lashes

---

a 8 The Hebrew word was used for various diseases affecting the skin—not necessarily leprosy.

his crime deserves, 3but he must not give him more than forty lashes. If he is flogged more than that, your brother will be degraded in your eyes.

4Do not muzzle an ox while it is treading out the grain.

5If brothers are living together and one of them dies without a son, his widow must not marry outside the family. Her husband's brother shall take her and marry her and fulfill the duty of a brother-in-law to her. 6The first son she bears shall carry on the name of the dead brother so that his name will not be blotted out from Israel.

7However, if a man does not want to marry his brother's wife, she shall go to the elders at the town gate and say, "My husband's brother refuses to carry on his brother's name in Israel. He will not fulfill the duty of a brother-in-law to me." 8Then the elders of his town shall summon him and talk to him. If he persists in saying, "I do not want to marry her," 9his brother's widow shall go up to him in the presence of the elders, take off one of his sandals, spit in his face and say, "This is what is done to the man who will not build up his brother's family line." 10That man's line shall be known in Israel as The Family of the Unsandaled.

11If two men are fighting and the wife of one of them comes to rescue her husband from his assailant, and she reaches out and seizes him by his private parts, 12you shall cut off her hand. Show her no pity.

13Do not have two differing weights in your bag—one heavy, one light. 14Do not have two differing measures in your house—one large, one small. 15You must have accurate and honest weights and measures, so that you may live long in the land the LORD your God is giving you. 16For the LORD your God detests anyone who does these things, anyone who deals dishonestly.

17Remember what the Amalekites did to you along the way when you came out of Egypt. 18When you were weary and worn out, they met you on your journey and cut off all who were lagging behind;

GET SMARTER.

Responsible for Your Choices

READ DEUTERONOMY 24:16

Aren't you glad the law doesn't allow a kid to be executed for some crime his dad committed? Whew! And considering the way some kids behave, parents can be happy the law doesn't work the other way either. What it boils down to is this: Each one of us is accountable for what *we* do wrong. Sure, sometimes we can weasel out of punishment when we blow it, but the day is coming when we'll appear before Jesus "that each one may receive what is due him for the things done while in the body, whether good or bad" (2 Corinthians 5:10). Jesus will deal with us in love like a perfect parent, but he will deal with us fairly and firmly. So be wise and be motivated by love when making choices. The consequences of your choices often catch up to you in this life as well. So choose well.

Your next reading is on page 259.

they had no fear of God. [19]When the Lord your God gives you rest from all the enemies around you in the land he is giving you to possess as an inheritance, you shall blot out the memory of Amalek from under heaven. Do not forget!

Firstfruits and Tithes

26 When you have entered the land the Lord your God is giving you as an inheritance and have taken possession of it and settled in it, [2]take some of the firstfruits of all that you produce from the soil of the land the Lord your God is giving you and put them in a basket. Then go to the place the Lord your God will choose as a dwelling for his Name [3]and say to the priest in office at the time, "I declare today to the Lord your God that I have come to the land the Lord swore to our forefathers to give us." [4]The priest shall take the basket from your hands and set it down in front of the altar of the Lord your God. [5]Then you shall declare before the Lord your God: "My father was a wandering Aramean, and he went down into Egypt with a few people and lived there and became a great nation, powerful and numerous. [6]But the Egyptians mistreated us and made us suffer, putting us to hard labor. [7]Then we cried out to the Lord, the God of our fathers, and the Lord heard our voice and saw our misery, toil and oppression. [8]So the Lord brought us out of Egypt with a mighty hand and an outstretched arm, with great terror and with miraculous signs and wonders. [9]He brought us to this place and gave us this land, a land flowing with milk and honey; [10]and now I bring the firstfruits of the soil that you, O Lord, have given me." Place the basket before the Lord your God and bow down before him. [11]And you and the Levites and the aliens among you shall rejoice in all the good things the Lord your God has given to you and your household.

[12]When you have finished setting aside a tenth of all your produce in the third year, the year of the tithe, you shall give it to the Levite, the alien, the fatherless and the widow, so that they may eat in your towns and be satisfied. [13]Then say to the Lord your God: "I have removed from my house the sacred portion and have given it to the Levite, the alien, the fatherless and the widow, according to all you com-

manded. I have not turned aside from your commands nor have I forgotten any of them. [14]I have not eaten any of the sacred portion while I was in mourning, nor have I removed any of it while I was unclean, nor have I offered any of it to the dead. I have obeyed the Lord my God; I have done everything you commanded me. [15]Look down from heaven, your holy dwelling place, and bless your people Israel and the land you have given us as you promised on oath to our forefathers, a land flowing with milk and honey."

Follow the Lord's Commands

[16]The Lord your God commands you this day to follow these decrees and laws; carefully observe them with all your heart and with all your soul. [17]You have declared this day that the Lord is your God and that you will walk in his ways, that you will keep his decrees, commands and laws, and that you will obey him. [18]And the Lord has declared this day that you are his people, his treasured possession as he promised, and that you are to keep all his commands. [19]He has declared that he will set you in praise, fame and honor high above all the nations he has made and that you will be a people holy to the Lord your God, as he promised.

The Altar on Mount Ebal

27 Moses and the elders of Israel commanded the people: "Keep all these commands that I give you today. [2]When you have crossed the Jordan into the land the Lord your God is giving you, set up some large stones and coat them with plaster. [3]Write on them all the words of this law when you have crossed over to enter the land the Lord your God is giving you, a land flowing with milk and honey, just as the Lord, the God of your fathers, promised you. [4]And when you have crossed the Jordan, set up these stones on Mount Ebal, as I command you today, and coat them with plaster. [5]Build there an altar to the Lord your God, an altar of stones. Do not use any iron tool upon them. [6]Build the altar of the Lord your God with fieldstones and offer burnt offerings on it to the Lord your God. [7]Sacrifice fellowship offerings[a] there, eating them and rejoicing in the

---

[a] 7 Traditionally *peace offerings*

presence of the LORD your God. 8And you shall write very clearly all the words of this law on these stones you have set up."

Curses From Mount Ebal

9Then Moses and the priests, who are Levites, said to all Israel, "Be silent, O Israel, and listen! You have now become the people of the LORD your God. 10Obey the LORD your God and follow his commands and decrees that I give you today.

11On the same day Moses commanded the people:

12When you have crossed the Jordan, these tribes shall stand on Mount Gerizim to bless the people: Simeon, Levi, Judah, Issachar, Joseph and Benjamin. 13And these tribes shall stand on Mount Ebal to pronounce curses: Reuben, Gad, Asher, Zebulun, Dan and Naphtali.

14The Levites shall recite to all the people of Israel in a loud voice:

15"Cursed is the man who carves an image or casts an idol—a thing detestable to the LORD, the work of the craftsman's hands—and sets it up in secret."

Then all the people shall say, "Amen!"

16"Cursed is the man who dishonors his father or his mother."

Then all the people shall say, "Amen!"

17"Cursed is the man who moves his neighbor's boundary stone."

Then all the people shall say, "Amen!"

18"Cursed is the man who leads the blind astray on the road."

Then all the people shall say, "Amen!"

19"Cursed is the man who withholds justice from the alien, the fatherless or the widow."

Then all the people shall say, "Amen!"

20"Cursed is the man who sleeps with his father's wife, for he dishonors his father's bed."

Then all the people shall say, "Amen!"

21"Cursed is the man who has sexual relations with any animal."

Then all the people shall say, "Amen!"

22"Cursed is the man who sleeps with his sister, the daughter of his father or the daughter of his mother."

Then all the people shall say, "Amen!"

23"Cursed is the man who sleeps with his mother-in-law."

Then all the people shall say, "Amen!"

24"Cursed is the man who kills his neighbor secretly."

Then all the people shall say, "Amen!"

25"Cursed is the man who accepts a bribe to kill an innocent person."

Then all the people shall say, "Amen!"

26"Cursed is the man who does not uphold the words of this law by carrying them out."

Then all the people shall say, "Amen!"

Blessings for Obedience

28 If you fully obey the LORD your God and carefully follow all his commands I give you today, the LORD your God will set you high above all the nations on earth. 2All these blessings will come upon you and accompany you if you obey the LORD your God:

3You will be blessed in the city and blessed in the country.

4The fruit of your womb will be blessed, and the crops of your land and the young of your livestock—the calves of your herds and the lambs of your flocks.

5Your basket and your kneading trough will be blessed.

6You will be blessed when you come in and blessed when you go out.

7The LORD will grant that the enemies who rise up against you will be defeated before you. They will come at you from one direction but flee from you in seven.

8The LORD will send a blessing on your barns and on everything you put your hand to. The LORD your God will bless you in the land he is giving you.

9The LORD will establish you as his holy people, as he promised you on oath, if you keep the commands of the LORD your God and walk in his ways. 10Then all the peoples on earth will see that you are called by the name of the Lord, and they will fear you. [11]The Lord will grant you abundant prosperity—in the fruit of your womb, the young of your livestock and the crops of your ground—in the land he swore to your forefathers to give you. [12]The Lord will open the heavens, the storehouse of his bounty, to send rain on your land in season and to bless all the work of your hands. You will lend to many nations but will borrow from none. [13]The Lord will make you the head, not the tail. If you pay attention to the commands of the Lord your God that I give you this day and carefully follow them, you will always be at the top, never at the bottom. [14]Do not turn aside from any of the commands I give you today, to the right or to the left, following other gods and serving them.

Curses for Disobedience

[15]However, if you do not obey the Lord your God and do not carefully follow all his commands and decrees I am giving you today, all these curses will come upon you and overtake you:

[16]You will be cursed in the city and cursed in the country.

[17]Your basket and your kneading trough will be cursed.

[18]The fruit of your womb will be cursed, and the crops of your land, and the calves of your herds and the lambs of your flocks.

[19]You will be cursed when you come in and cursed when you go out.

[20]The Lord will send on you curses, confusion and rebuke in everything you put your hand to, until you are destroyed and come to sudden ruin because of the evil you have done in forsaking him.[a] [21]The Lord will plague you with diseases until he has destroyed you from the land you are entering to possess. [22]The Lord will strike you with wasting disease, with fever and inflammation, with scorching heat and

[a] 20 Hebrew me

Blessed Here, Blessed There

READ DEUTERONOMY 28:1–14

It pays to obey God and follow his rules. If a dozen kids were running an obstacle course but you were the only one obeying the rules, in the end everyone else would be disqualified and you would win! It's like that when you obey God: You reap the rewards and you're blessed. Deuteronomy 28:9 promises that "if you keep the commands of the Lord your God and walk in his ways," he would do fabulous things for you. So don't be like a chicken being shooed into the barn, running every possible direction except into the barn. God's way is the best way, so go God's way. Want a better life? Let his principles guide you. That doesn't mean you'll get goodies every time you do the right thing—being a man of integrity is not always Easy Street—but in the long run, God *will* see to it that you're blessed.

Your next reading is on page 268.

Gross!

Read Deuteronomy 28:27–28 to see what God said he'd do if the Israelites didn't obey him …

Question: You accidentally walk toward nuclear testing grounds and you come to a big sign that reads, "Warning! Stop!—or you'll be covered with boils and festering sores, you'll go blind, become a babbling fool and be driven completely insane." What do you do?

drought, with blight and mildew, which will plague you until you perish. ²³The sky over your head will be bronze, the ground beneath you iron. ²⁴The LORD will turn the rain of your country into dust and powder; it will come down from the skies until you are destroyed.

²⁵The LORD will cause you to be defeated before your enemies. You will come at them from one direction but flee from them in seven, and you will become a thing of horror to all the kingdoms on earth. ²⁶Your carcasses will be food for all the birds of the air and the beasts of the earth, and there will be no one to frighten them away. ²⁷The LORD will afflict you with the boils of Egypt and with tumors, festering sores and the itch, from which you cannot be cured. ²⁸The LORD will afflict you with madness, blindness and confusion of mind. ²⁹At midday you will grope about like a blind man in the dark. You will be unsuccessful in everything you do; day after day you will be oppressed and robbed, with no one to rescue you.

³⁰You will be pledged to be married to a woman, but another will take her and ravish her. You will build a house, but you will not live in it. You will plant a vineyard, but you will not even begin to enjoy its fruit. ³¹Your ox will be slaughtered before your eyes, but you will eat none of it. Your donkey will be forcibly taken from you and will not be returned. Your sheep will be given to your enemies, and no one will rescue them. ³²Your sons and daughters will be given to another nation, and you will wear out your eyes watching for them day after day, powerless to lift a hand. ³³A people that you do not know will eat what your land and labor produce, and you will have nothing but cruel oppression all your days. ³⁴The sights you see will drive you mad. ³⁵The LORD will afflict your knees and legs with painful boils that cannot be cured, spreading from the soles of your feet to the top of your head.

³⁶The LORD will drive you and the king you set over you to a nation unknown to you or your fathers. There you will worship other gods, gods of wood and stone. ³⁷You will become a thing of horror and an object of scorn and ridicule to all the nations where the LORD will drive you.

³⁸You will sow much seed in the field but you will harvest little, because locusts will devour it. ³⁹You will plant vineyards and cultivate them but you will not drink the wine or gather the grapes, because worms will eat them. ⁴⁰You will have olive trees throughout your country but you will not use the oil, because the olives will drop off. ⁴¹You will have sons and daughters but you will not keep them, because they will go into captivity. ⁴²Swarms of locusts will take over all your trees and the crops of your land.

⁴³The alien who lives among you will rise above you higher and higher, but you will sink lower and lower. ⁴⁴He will lend to you, but you will not lend to him. He will be the head, but you will be the tail.

⁴⁵All these curses will come upon you. They will pur-

sue you and overtake you until you are destroyed, because you did not obey the LORD your God and observe the commands and decrees he gave you. 46They will be a sign and a wonder to you and your descendants forever. 47Because you did not serve the LORD your God joyfully and gladly in the time of prosperity, 48therefore in hunger and thirst, in nakedness and dire poverty, you will serve the enemies the LORD sends against you. He will put an iron yoke on your neck until he has destroyed you.

49The LORD will bring a nation against you from far away, from the ends of the earth, like an eagle swooping down, a nation whose language you will not understand, 50a fierce-looking nation without respect for the old or pity for the young. 51They will devour the young of your livestock and the crops of your land until you are destroyed. They will leave you no grain, new wine or oil, nor any calves of your herds or lambs of your flocks until you are ruined. 52They will lay siege to all the cities throughout your land until the high fortified walls in which you trust fall down. They will besiege all the cities throughout the land the LORD your God is giving you.

53Because of the suffering that your enemy will inflict on you during the siege, you will eat the fruit of the womb, the flesh of the sons and daughters the LORD your God has given you. 54Even the most gentle and sensitive man among you will have no compassion on his own brother or the wife he loves or his surviving children, 55and he will not give to one of them any of the flesh of his children that he is eating. It will be all he has left because of the suffering your enemy will inflict on you during the siege of all your cities. 56The most gentle and sensitive woman among you—so sensitive and gentle that she would not venture to touch the ground with the sole of her foot—will begrudge the husband she loves and her own son or daughter 57the afterbirth from her womb and the children she bears. For she intends to eat them secretly during the siege and in the distress that your enemy will inflict on you in your cities.

58If you do not carefully follow all the words of this law, which are written in this book, and do not revere this glorious and awesome name—the LORD your God— 59the LORD will send fearful plagues on you and your descendants, harsh and prolonged disasters, and severe and lingering illnesses. 60He will bring upon you all the diseases of Egypt that you dreaded, and they will cling to you. 61The LORD will also bring on you every kind of sickness and disaster not recorded in this Book of the Law, until you are destroyed. 62You who were as numerous as the stars in the sky will be left but few in number, because you did not obey the LORD your God. 63Just as it pleased the LORD to make you prosper and increase in number, so it will please him to ruin and destroy you. You will be uprooted from the land you are entering to possess.

64Then the LORD will scatter you among all nations, from one end of the earth to the other. There you will worship other gods—gods of wood and stone, which neither you nor your fathers have known. 65Among those nations you will find no repose, no resting place for the sole of your foot. There the LORD will give you an anxious mind, eyes weary with longing, and a despairing heart. 66You will live in constant suspense, filled with dread both night and day, never sure of your life. 67In the morning you will say, "If only it were evening!" and in the evening, "If only it were morning!"—because of the terror that will fill your hearts and the sights that your eyes will see. 68The LORD will send you back in ships to Egypt on a journey I said you should never make again. There you will offer yourselves for sale to your enemies as male and female slaves, but no one will buy you.

Renewal of the Covenant

29 These are the terms of the covenant the LORD commanded Moses to make with the Israelites in Moab, in addition to the covenant he had made with them at Horeb.

2Moses summoned all the Israelites and said to them:

Your eyes have seen all that the LORD did in Egypt to Pharaoh, to all his officials and to all his land. 3With your own eyes you saw those great trials, those miraculous signs and great wonders. 4But to this day the LORD has not given you a mind that understands or eyes that see or ears that hear. [5]During the forty years that I led you through the desert, your clothes did not wear out, nor did the sandals on your feet. [6]You ate no bread and drank no wine or other fermented drink. I did this so that you might know that I am the LORD your God.

[7]When you reached this place, Sihon king of Heshbon and Og king of Bashan came out to fight against us, but we defeated them. [8]We took their land and gave it as an inheritance to the Reubenites, the Gadites and the half-tribe of Manasseh.

[9]Carefully follow the terms of this covenant, so that you may prosper in everything you do. [10]All of you are standing today in the presence of the LORD your God—your leaders and chief men, your elders and officials, and all the other men of Israel, [11]together with your children and your wives, and the aliens living in your camps who chop your wood and carry your water. [12]You are standing here in order to enter into a covenant with the LORD your God, a covenant the LORD is making with you this day and sealing with an oath, [13]to confirm you this day as his people, that he may be your God as he promised you and as he swore to your fathers, Abraham, Isaac and Jacob. [14]I am making this covenant, with its oath, not only with you [15]who are standing here with us today in the presence of the LORD our God but also with those who are not here today.

[16]You yourselves know how we lived in Egypt and how we passed through the countries on the way here. [17]You saw among them their detestable images and idols of wood and stone, of silver and gold. [18]Make sure there is no man or woman, clan or tribe among you today whose heart turns away from the LORD our God to go and worship the gods of those nations; make sure there is no root among you that produces such bitter poison.

[19]When such a person hears the words of this oath, he invokes a blessing on himself and therefore thinks, "I will be safe, even though I persist in going my own way." This will bring disaster on the watered land as well as the dry.[a] [20]The LORD will never be willing to forgive him; his wrath and zeal will burn against that man. All the curses written in this book will fall upon him, and the LORD will blot out his name from under heaven. [21]The LORD will single him out from all the tribes of Israel for disaster, according to all the curses of the covenant written in this Book of the Law.

[22]Your children who follow you in later generations and foreigners who come from distant lands will see the calamities that have fallen on the land and the diseases with which the LORD has afflicted it. [23]The whole land will be a burning waste of salt and sulfur—nothing planted, nothing sprouting, no vegetation growing on it. It will be like the destruction of Sodom and Gomorrah, Admah and Zeboiim, which the LORD overthrew in fierce anger. [24]All the nations will ask: "Why has the LORD done this to this land? Why this fierce, burning anger?"

[25]And the answer will be: "It is because this people abandoned the covenant of the LORD, the God of their fathers, the covenant he made with them when he brought them out of Egypt. [26]They went off and worshiped other gods and bowed down to them, gods they did not know, gods he had not given them. [27]Therefore the LORD's anger burned against this land, so that he brought on it all the curses written in this book. [28]In furious anger and in great wrath the LORD uprooted them from their land and thrust them into another land, as it is now."

[29]The secret things belong to the LORD our God, but the things revealed belong to us and to our children forever, that we may follow all the words of this law.

Prosperity After Turning to the LORD

30 When all these blessings and curses I have set before you come upon you and you take them to heart wherever the LORD your God disperses you among the nations, [2]and when you and your children return to the LORD your God and obey him with all your heart and with all your soul according to everything I command you today, [3]then the LORD your God will restore your fortunes[b] and have compassion on you and gather you again from all the nations where he scattered you. [4]Even if you have been banished to the most distant land under the heavens, from there the LORD your God will gather you and bring you back. [5]He will bring you to the

---

[a] 19 Or way, in order to add drunkenness to thirst."
[b] 3 Or will bring you back from captivity

land that belonged to your fathers, and you will take possession of it. He will make you more prosperous and numerous than your fathers. 6The LORD your God will circumcise your hearts and the hearts of your descendants, so that you may love him with all your heart and with all your soul, and live. 7The LORD your God will put all these curses on your enemies who hate and persecute you. 8You will again obey the LORD and follow all his commands I am giving you today. 9Then the LORD your God will make you most prosperous in all the work of your hands and in the fruit of your womb, the young of your livestock and the crops of your land. The LORD will again delight in you and make you prosperous, just as he delighted in your fathers, 10if you obey the LORD your God and keep his commands and decrees that are written in this Book of the Law and turn to the LORD your God with all your heart and with all your soul.

The Offer of Life or Death

11Now what I am commanding you today is not too difficult for you or beyond your reach. 12It is not up in heaven, so that you have to ask, "Who will ascend into heaven to get it and proclaim it to us so we may obey it?" 13Nor is it beyond the sea, so that you have to ask, "Who will cross the sea to get it and proclaim it to us so we may obey it?" 14No, the word is very near you; it is in your mouth and in your heart so you may obey it.

15See, I set before you today life and prosperity, death and destruction. 16For I command you today to love the LORD your God, to walk in his ways, and to keep his commands, decrees and laws; then you will live and increase, and the LORD your God will bless you in the land you are entering to possess.

17But if your heart turns away and you are not obedient, and if you are drawn away to bow down to other gods and worship them, 18I declare to you this day that you will certainly be destroyed. You will not live long in the land you are crossing the Jordan to enter and possess.

19This day I call heaven and earth as witnesses against you that I have set before you life and death, blessings and curses. Now choose life, so that you and your children may live 20and that you may love the LORD your God, listen to his voice,

and hold fast to him. For the LORD is your life, and he will give you many years in the land he swore to give to your fathers, Abraham, Isaac and Jacob.

Joshua to Succeed Moses

31 Then Moses went out and spoke these words to all Israel: 2"I am now a hundred and twenty years old and I am no longer able to lead you. The LORD has said to me, 'You shall not cross the Jordan.' 3The LORD your God himself will cross over ahead of you. He will destroy these nations before you, and you will take possession of their land. Joshua also will cross over ahead of you, as the LORD said. 4And the LORD will do to them what he did to Sihon and Og, the kings of the Amorites, whom he destroyed along with their land. 5The LORD will deliver them to you, and you must do to them all that I have commanded you. 6Be strong and courageous. Do not be afraid or terrified because of them, for the LORD your God goes with you; he will never leave you nor forsake you."

7Then Moses summoned Joshua and said to him in the presence of all Israel, "Be strong and courageous, for you must go with this people into the land that the LORD swore to their forefathers to give them, and you must divide it among them as their inheritance. 8The LORD himself goes before you and will be with you; he will never leave you nor forsake you. Do not be afraid; do not be discouraged."

The Reading of the Law

9So Moses wrote down this law and gave it to the priests, the sons of Levi, who carried the ark of the covenant of the LORD, and to all the elders of Israel. 10Then Moses commanded them: "At the end of every seven years, in the year for canceling debts, during the Feast of Tabernacles, 11when all Israel comes to appear before the LORD your God at the place he will choose, you shall read this law before them in their hearing. 12Assemble the people—men, women and children, and the aliens living in your towns—so they can listen and learn to fear the LORD your God and follow carefully all the words of this law. 13Their children, who do not know this law, must hear it and learn to fear the LORD your God as long as you live in the land you are crossing the Jordan to possess."

Israel's Rebellion Predicted

14The LORD said to Moses, "Now the day of your death is near. Call Joshua and present yourselves at the Tent of Meeting, where I will commission him." So Moses and Joshua came and presented themselves at the Tent of Meeting.

15Then the LORD appeared at the Tent in a pillar of cloud, and the cloud stood over the entrance to the Tent. 16And the LORD said to Moses: "You are going to rest with your fathers, and these people will soon prostitute themselves to the foreign gods of the land they are entering. They will forsake me and break the covenant I made with them. 17On that day I will become angry with them and forsake them; I will hide my face from them, and they will be destroyed. Many disasters and difficulties will come upon them, and on that day they will ask, 'Have not these disasters come upon us because our God is not with us?' 18And I will certainly hide my face on that day because of all their wickedness in turning to other gods.

19"Now write down for yourselves this song and teach it to the Israelites and have them sing it, so that it may be a witness for me against them. 20When I have brought them into the land flowing with milk and honey, the land I promised on oath to their forefathers, and when they eat their fill and thrive, they will turn to other gods and worship them, rejecting me and breaking my covenant. 21And when many disasters and difficulties come upon them, this song will testify against them, because it will not be forgotten by their descendants. I know what they are disposed to do, even before I bring them into the land I promised them on oath." 22So Moses wrote down this song that day and taught it to the Israelites.

23The LORD gave this command to Joshua son of Nun: "Be strong and courageous, for you will bring the Israelites into the land I promised them on oath, and I myself will be with you."

24After Moses finished writing in a book the words of this law from beginning to end, 25he gave this command to the Levites who carried the ark of the covenant of the LORD: 26"Take this Book of the Law and place it beside the ark of the covenant of the LORD your God. There it will remain as a witness against you.

27For I know how rebellious and stiff-necked you are. If you have been rebellious against the LORD while I am still alive and with you, how much more will you rebel after I die! 28Assemble before me all the elders of your tribes and all your officials, so that I can speak these words in their hearing and call heaven and earth to testify against them. 29For I know that after my death you are sure to become utterly corrupt and to turn from the way I have commanded you. In days to come, disaster will fall upon you because you will do evil in the sight of the LORD and provoke him to anger by what your hands have made."

The Song of Moses

30And Moses recited the words of this song from beginning to end in the hearing of the whole assembly of Israel:

32 Listen, O heavens, and I will speak;
  hear, O earth, the words of my mouth.
2 Let my teaching fall like rain
  and my words descend like dew,
 like showers on new grass,
  like abundant rain on tender plants.

3 I will proclaim the name of the LORD.
  Oh, praise the greatness of our God!
4 He is the Rock, his works are perfect,
  and all his ways are just.
 A faithful God who does no wrong,
  upright and just is he.

5 They have acted corruptly toward him;
  to their shame they are no longer his children,
  but a warped and crooked generation. *a*
6 Is this the way you repay the LORD,
  O foolish and unwise people?
 Is he not your Father, your Creator, *b*
  who made you and formed you?

7 Remember the days of old;
  consider the generations long past.
 Ask your father and he will tell you,
  your elders, and they will explain to you.
8 When the Most High gave the nations their inheritance,

a 5 Or Corrupt are they and not his children, / a generation warped and twisted to their shame   *b 6 Or Father, who bought you*

when he divided all mankind,
   he set up boundaries for the peoples
      according to the number of the sons
        of Israel. *a*
9 For the LORD's portion is his people,
   Jacob his allotted inheritance.

10 In a desert land he found him,
   in a barren and howling waste.
He shielded him and cared for him;
   he guarded him as the apple of his
      eye,
11 like an eagle that stirs up its nest
   and hovers over its young,
that spreads its wings to catch them
   and carries them on its pinions.
12 The LORD alone led him;
   no foreign god was with him.

13 He made him ride on the heights of
      the land
   and fed him with the fruit of the
      fields.
He nourished him with honey from the
      rock,
   and with oil from the flinty crag,
14 with curds and milk from herd and flock
   and with fattened lambs and goats,
with choice rams of Bashan
   and the finest kernels of wheat.
You drank the foaming blood of the
      grape.

15 Jeshurun *b* grew fat and kicked;
   filled with food, he became heavy
      and sleek.
He abandoned the God who made him
   and rejected the Rock his Savior.
16 They made him jealous with their
      foreign gods
   and angered him with their
      detestable idols.
17 They sacrificed to demons, which are
      not God—
   gods they had not known,
   gods that recently appeared,
   gods your fathers did not fear.
18 You deserted the Rock, who fathered
      you;
   you forgot the God who gave you
      birth.

19 The LORD saw this and rejected them
   because he was angered by his sons
      and daughters.
20 "I will hide my face from them," he said,
   "and see what their end will be;
for they are a perverse generation,
   children who are unfaithful.

21 They made me jealous by what is no
      god
   and angered me with their worthless
      idols.
I will make them envious by those who
      are not a people;
   I will make them angry by a nation
      that has no understanding.
22 For a fire has been kindled by my wrath,
   one that burns to the realm of
      death *c* below.
It will devour the earth and its harvests
   and set afire the foundations of the
      mountains.

23 "I will heap calamities upon them
   and spend my arrows against them.
24 I will send wasting famine against
      them,
   consuming pestilence and deadly
      plague;
I will send against them the fangs of
      wild beasts,
   the venom of vipers that glide in the
      dust.
25 In the street the sword will make them
      childless;
   in their homes terror will reign.
Young men and young women will
      perish,
   infants and gray-haired men.
26 I said I would scatter them
   and blot out their memory from
      mankind,
27 but I dreaded the taunt of the enemy,
   lest the adversary misunderstand
and say, 'Our hand has triumphed;
   the LORD has not done all this.' "

28 They are a nation without sense,
   there is no discernment in them.
29 If only they were wise and would
      understand this
   and discern what their end will be!
30 How could one man chase a thousand,
   or two put ten thousand to flight,
unless their Rock had sold them,
   unless the LORD had given them up?
31 For their rock is not like our Rock,
   as even our enemies concede.
32 Their vine comes from the vine of
      Sodom
   and from the fields of Gomorrah.
Their grapes are filled with poison,
   and their clusters with bitterness.

a 8 Masoretic Text; Dead Sea Scrolls (see also Septuagint) *sons of God*   *b 15 Jeshurun* means *the upright one,* that is, Israel.   *c 22* Hebrew *to Sheol*

33 Their wine is the venom of serpents,
    the deadly poison of cobras.

34 "Have I not kept this in reserve
    and sealed it in my vaults?
35 It is mine to avenge; I will repay.
    In due time their foot will slip;
  their day of disaster is near
    and their doom rushes upon them."

36 The LORD will judge his people
    and have compassion on his servants
  when he sees their strength is gone
    and no one is left, slave or free.
37 He will say: "Now where are their gods,
    the rock they took refuge in,
38 the gods who ate the fat of their
      sacrifices
    and drank the wine of their drink
      offerings?
  Let them rise up to help you!
  Let them give you shelter!

39 "See now that I myself am He!
    There is no god besides me.
  I put to death and I bring to life,
    I have wounded and I will heal,
    and no one can deliver out of my
      hand.
40 I lift my hand to heaven and declare:
    As surely as I live forever,
41 when I sharpen my flashing sword
    and my hand grasps it in judgment,
  I will take vengeance on my adversaries
    and repay those who hate me.
42 I will make my arrows drunk with blood,
    while my sword devours flesh:
  the blood of the slain and the captives,
    the heads of the enemy leaders."

43 Rejoice, O nations, with his people,[a, b]
    for he will avenge the blood of his
      servants;
  he will take vengeance on his enemies
    and make atonement for his land
      and people.

44 Moses came with Joshua[c] son of Nun
and spoke all the words of this song in the
hearing of the people. 45 When Moses finished reciting all these words to all Israel,
46 he said to them, "Take to heart all the
words I have solemnly declared to you this
day, so that you may command your children to obey carefully all the words of this
law. 47 They are not just idle words for
you—they are your life. By them you will
live long in the land you are crossing the
Jordan to possess."

Moses to Die on Mount Nebo

48 On that same day the LORD told Moses, 49 "Go up into the Abarim Range to
Mount Nebo in Moab, across from Jericho, and view Canaan, the land I am giving the Israelites as their own possession.
50 There on the mountain that you have
climbed you will die and be gathered to
your people, just as your brother Aaron
died on Mount Hor and was gathered to
his people. 51 This is because both of you
broke faith with me in the presence of the
Israelites at the waters of Meribah Kadesh
in the Desert of Zin and because you did
not uphold my holiness among the Israelites. 52 Therefore, you will see the land only
from a distance; you will not enter the
land I am giving to the people of Israel."

Moses Blesses the Tribes

33 This is the blessing that Moses
the man of God pronounced
on the Israelites before his
death. 2 He said:

"The LORD came from Sinai
  and dawned over them from Seir;
  he shone forth from Mount Paran.
He came with[d] myriads of holy ones
  from the south, from his mountain
    slopes.[e]
3 Surely it is you who love the people;
  all the holy ones are in your hand.
At your feet they all bow down,
  and from you receive instruction,
4 the law that Moses gave us,
  the possession of the assembly of
    Jacob.
5 He was king over Jeshurun[f]
  when the leaders of the people
    assembled,
  along with the tribes of Israel.

6 "Let Reuben live and not die,
  nor[g] his men be few."

7 And this he said about Judah:

"Hear, O LORD, the cry of Judah;
  bring him to his people.
With his own hands he defends his
    cause.
  Oh, be his help against his foes!"

---

[a] 43 Or Make his people rejoice, O nations   [b] 43 Masoretic
Text; Dead Sea Scrolls (see also Septuagint) people, / and let
all the angels worship him /   [c] 44 Hebrew Hoshea, a variant
of Joshua   [d] 2 Or from   [e] 2 The meaning of the Hebrew
for this phrase is uncertain.   [f] 5 Jeshurun means the
upright one, that is, Israel; also in verse 26.   [g] 6 Or but let

8 About Levi he said:

"Your Thummim and Urim belong
    to the man you favored.
You tested him at Massah;
    you contended with him at the
        waters of Meribah.
9 He said of his father and mother,
    'I have no regard for them.'
He did not recognize his brothers
    or acknowledge his own children,
but he watched over your word
    and guarded your covenant.
10 He teaches your precepts to Jacob
    and your law to Israel.
He offers incense before you
    and whole burnt offerings on your
        altar.
11 Bless all his skills, O Lord,
    and be pleased with the work of his
        hands.
Smite the loins of those who rise up
    against him;
    strike his foes till they rise no more."

12 About Benjamin he said:

"Let the beloved of the Lord rest secure
    in him,
    for he shields him all day long,
and the one the Lord loves rests
    between his shoulders."

13 About Joseph he said:

"May the Lord bless his land
    with the precious dew from heaven
        above
    and with the deep waters that lie
        below;
14 with the best the sun brings forth
    and the finest the moon can yield;
15 with the choicest gifts of the ancient
        mountains
    and the fruitfulness of the
        everlasting hills;
16 with the best gifts of the earth and its
        fullness
    and the favor of him who dwelt in
        the burning bush.
Let all these rest on the head of Joseph,
    on the brow of the prince among[a]
        his brothers.
17 In majesty he is like a firstborn bull;
    his horns are the horns of a wild ox.
With them he will gore the nations,
    even those at the ends of the earth.
Such are the ten thousands of Ephraim;
    such are the thousands of Manasseh."

18 About Zebulun he said:

"Rejoice, Zebulun, in your going out,
    and you, Issachar, in your tents.
19 They will summon peoples to the
        mountain
    and there offer sacrifices of
        righteousness;
they will feast on the abundance of the
        seas,
    on the treasures hidden in the sand."

20 About Gad he said:

"Blessed is he who enlarges Gad's
        domain!
Gad lives there like a lion,
    tearing at arm or head.
21 He chose the best land for himself;
    the leader's portion was kept for
        him.
When the heads of the people
        assembled,
    he carried out the Lord's righteous
        will,
    and his judgments concerning Israel."

22 About Dan he said:

"Dan is a lion's cub,
    springing out of Bashan."

23 About Naphtali he said:

"Naphtali is abounding with the favor
        of the Lord
    and is full of his blessing;
    he will inherit southward to the lake."

24 About Asher he said:

"Most blessed of sons is Asher;
    let him be favored by his brothers,
    and let him bathe his feet in oil.
25 The bolts of your gates will be iron and
        bronze,
    and your strength will equal your
        days.

26 "There is no one like the God of
        Jeshurun,
    who rides on the heavens to help
        you
    and on the clouds in his majesty.
27 The eternal God is your refuge,
    and underneath are the everlasting
        arms.
He will drive out your enemy before
        you,
    saying, 'Destroy him!'

a 16 Or of the one separated from

GET

Amazing Meek Moses

READ DEUTERONOMY 34

STRONGER.

Moses was an amazing man! He was deep, cool, strong *and* smart. When he was young, however, about all he was was powerful. Oh yeah, and smart. Pharaoh's daughter pulled Moses out of the Nile River and raised him as a royal prince.

SMARTER.

He was "educated in all the wisdom of the Egyptians and was powerful in speech and action" (Acts 7:22). He was smart, he knew how to work the crowds and he had muscle to flex. Moses had it all. Servants attended to his every wish. People bowed down to him. He was like a movie star. That *had* to make him proud. Yet by the time God had finished letting the air out of his ego, "Moses was a very humble man, more humble than anyone else on the face of the earth" (Numbers 12:3). He also went from being tops in Egyptian wisdom to being smart about what really counted—God's Word, which told people how to live godly lives.

COOLER.

Moses' social skills also jumped from a C- average to an A+. Sure, he still blew it a few times, got angry when the Israelites bellyached, but for the most part he had incredible compassion and tender love for his people, like a nurse carrying an infant (Numbers 11:12).

DEEPER.

Where Moses really scored big, however, was in his relationship with God. He gave a whole new meaning to the word "deep." Exodus 33:11 says, "The LORD would speak to Moses face to face, as a man speaks with his friend." After Moses talked to God, he came away looking like a walking lighthouse—he was visibly shining! Yeah. Moses was a pretty amazing man.

Your next reading is on page 271.

28 So Israel will live in safety alone;
      Jacob's spring is secure
  in a land of grain and new wine,
      where the heavens drop dew.
29 Blessed are you, O Israel!
      Who is like you,
      a people saved by the LORD?
  He is your shield and helper
      and your glorious sword.
  Your enemies will cower before you,
      and you will trample down their high places.ᵃ"

The Death of Moses

34 Then Moses climbed Mount Nebo from the plains of Moab to the top of Pisgah, across from Jericho. There the LORD showed him the whole land—from Gilead to Dan, ²all of Naphtali, the territory of Ephraim and Manasseh, all the land of Judah as far as the western sea,ᵇ ³the Negev and the whole region from the Valley of Jericho, the City of Palms, as far as Zoar. ⁴Then the LORD said to him, "This is the land I promised on oath to Abraham, Isaac and Jacob when I said, 'I will give it to your descendants.' I have let you see it with your eyes, but you will not cross over into it."

⁵And Moses the servant of the LORD died there in Moab, as the LORD had said. ⁶He buried himᶜ in Moab, in the valley opposite Beth Peor, but to this day no one knows where his grave is. ⁷Moses was a hundred and twenty years old when he died, yet his eyes were not weak nor his strength gone. ⁸The Israelites grieved for Moses in the plains of Moab thirty days, until the time of weeping and mourning was over.

⁹Now Joshua son of Nun was filled with the spiritᵈ of wisdom because Moses had laid his hands on him. So the Israelites listened to him and did what the LORD had commanded Moses.

¹⁰Since then, no prophet has risen in Israel like Moses, whom the LORD knew face to face, ¹¹who did all those miraculous signs and wonders the LORD sent him to do in Egypt—to Pharaoh and to all his officials and to his whole land. ¹²For no one has ever shown the mighty power or performed the awesome deeds that Moses did in the sight of all Israel.

Get a Load of This...

Check out Deuteronomy 34. Why was Moses' grave hidden from the Israelites? Well, worship of the dead may have been practiced in some Canaanite religions, and God didn't want Israel making a shrine out of Moses' grave and worshiping him. (A golden calf was bad enough!)

ᵃ 29 Or *will tread upon their bodies*   ᵇ 2 That is, the Mediterranean
ᶜ 6 Or *He was buried*   ᵈ 9 Or *Spirit*

JOSHUA

Who wrote this book?
The author of Joshua is not named but probably was someone who witnessed the events described.

Why was this book written?
Joshua tells how God helped the Israelites defeat the Canaanites.

What happens in this book?
Joshua becomes Israel's leader. Joshua leads Israel's armies to victory. Joshua assigns land to Israel's 12 tribes.

What do we learn about God in this book?
God will give victory to his people when they obey him.

Who is important in this book?
The important person in this book is Joshua.

When did this happen?
The Israelite conquest of Canaan probably happened between 1405 and 1390 B.C.

Where did this happen?
The events in this book happened in the land of Canaan. Today we call that land Israel.

What are some of the stories in this book?

The Lord instructs Joshua	Joshua 1
Rahab protects the spies	Joshua 2
Israel crosses the Jordan	Joshua 3–4
Jericho's walls fall down	Joshua 6
Achan's sin brings defeat	Joshua 7
The Gibeonites fool Joshua	Joshua 9
The sun stands still	Joshua 10
Joshua says good-by	Joshua 24

The Lord Commands Joshua

1 After the death of Moses the servant of the Lord, the Lord said to Joshua son of Nun, Moses' aide: ²"Moses my servant is dead. Now then, you and all these people, get ready to cross the Jordan River into the land I am about to give to them—to the Israelites. ³I will give you every place where you set your foot, as I promised Moses. ⁴Your territory will extend from the desert to Lebanon, and from the great river, the Euphrates—all the Hittite country—to the Great Sea^a on the west. ⁵No one will be able to stand up against you all the days of your life. As I was with Moses, so I will be with you; I will never leave you nor forsake you.

⁶"Be strong and courageous, because you will lead these people to inherit the land I swore to their forefathers to give them. ⁷Be strong and very courageous. Be careful to obey all the law my servant Moses gave you; do not turn from it to the right or to the left, that you may be successful wherever you go. ⁸Do not let this Book of the Law depart from your mouth; meditate on it day and night, so that you may be careful to do everything written in it. Then you will be prosperous and successful. ⁹Have I not commanded you? Be strong and courageous. Do not be terrified; do not be discouraged, for the Lord your God will be with you wherever you go."

¹⁰So Joshua ordered the officers of the people: ¹¹"Go through the camp and tell the people, 'Get your supplies ready. Three days from now you will cross the Jordan here to go in and take possession of the land the Lord your God is giving you for your own.' "

¹²But to the Reubenites, the Gadites and the half-tribe of Manasseh, Joshua said, ¹³"Remember the command that Moses the servant of the Lord gave you: 'The Lord your God is giving you rest and has granted you this land.' ¹⁴Your wives, your children and your livestock may stay in the land that Moses gave you east of the Jordan, but all your fighting men, fully armed, must cross over ahead of your brothers.

^a 4 That is, the Mediterranean

GET SMARTER

Headless Chicken Syndrome

READ JOSHUA 1:1–11

As Israel's new leader, Joshua was raring to follow God. He was prepared but he was still nervous about following an act like Moses. God told Joshua, "Be strong and very courageous" (Joshua 1:7). What would *give* him that courage? Moses' next words spelled it out: "Be careful to obey all the law." Obeying God's Word would give Joshua spiritual strength and courage. Think about it. Only NBA players who listen to their coach and play for the good of their team win championships. It's the same with following God. When you fight only for your rights or what you want, you're missing the point. You're like a headless chicken, leaping and jerking around without any direction. When you follow what God says and stand up for righteousness, he will guide and help you. Follow Joshua's example and you can avoid Headless Chicken Syndrome.

Your next reading is on page 272.

You are to help your brothers ¹⁵until the LORD gives them rest, as he has done for you, and until they too have taken possession of the land that the LORD your God is giving them. After that, you may go back and occupy your own land, which Moses the servant of the LORD gave you east of the Jordan toward the sunrise."

¹⁶Then they answered Joshua, "Whatever you have commanded us we will do, and wherever you send us we will go. ¹⁷Just as we fully obeyed Moses, so we will obey you. Only may the LORD your God be with you as he was with Moses. ¹⁸Whoever rebels against your word and does not obey your words, whatever you may command them, will be put to death. Only be strong and courageous!"

Rahab and the Spies

Then Joshua son of Nun secretly sent two spies from Shittim. "Go, look over the land," he said, "especially Jericho." So they went and entered the house of a prostitute^a named Rahab and stayed there.

²The king of Jericho was told, "Look! Some of the Israelites have come here tonight to spy out the land." ³So the king of Jericho sent this message to Rahab: "Bring out the men who came to you and entered your house, because they have come to spy out the whole land."

⁴But the woman had taken the two men and hidden them. She said, "Yes, the men came to me, but I did not know where they had come from. ⁵At dusk, when it was time to close the city gate, the men left. I don't know which way they went. Go after them quickly. You may catch up with them." ⁶(But she had taken them up to the roof and hidden them under the stalks of flax she had laid out on the roof.) ⁷So the men set out in pursuit of the spies on the road that leads to the fords of the Jordan, and as soon as the pursuers had gone out, the gate was shut.

⁸Before the spies lay down for the night, she went up on the roof ⁹and said to them, "I know that the LORD has given this land to you and that a great fear of you has fallen on us, so that all who live in

^a 1 Or possibly *an innkeeper*

Rescuing a Wrecked Rep

READ JOSHUA 2

"The LORD your God is God in heaven above and on the earth below" (Joshua 2:11). Who spoke these words of truth? Moses? Joshua? Nope. The answer is Rahab. She was not only a Canaanite, but a prostitute. It just goes to show, you can't judge someone by his or her reputation. God is in the business of changing people's hearts. It doesn't matter what kind of sin people have been involved with, or how far they've been from God. He can change anyone if they're open to being changed. So even if someone you know is a frog-squashing, dog-collar-wearing, gym-sock-smoking reject, don't count him out, because everyone is valuable to God. Rahab's reputation was once a wreck, but she ended up in God's Hall of Faith (see Hebrews 11:31). On top of that, she had the incredible honor of becoming one of Jesus' ancestors (Matthew 1:5).

Your next reading is on page 276.

this country are melting in fear because of you. ¹⁰We have heard how the LORD dried up the water of the Red Sea[a] for you when you came out of Egypt, and what you did to Sihon and Og, the two kings of the Amorites east of the Jordan, whom you completely destroyed.[b] ¹¹When we heard of it, our hearts melted and everyone's courage failed because of you, for the LORD your God is God in heaven above and on the earth below. ¹²Now then, please swear to me by the LORD that you will show kindness to my family, because I have shown kindness to you. Give me a sure sign ¹³that you will spare the lives of my father and mother, my brothers and sisters, and all who belong to them, and that you will save us from death."

¹⁴"Our lives for your lives!" the men assured her. "If you don't tell what we are doing, we will treat you kindly and faithfully when the LORD gives us the land."

¹⁵So she let them down by a rope through the window, for the house she lived in was part of the city wall. ¹⁶Now she had said to them, "Go to the hills so the pursuers will not find you. Hide yourselves there three days until they return, and then go on your way."

¹⁷The men said to her, "This oath you made us swear will not be binding on us ¹⁸unless, when we enter the land, you have tied this scarlet cord in the window through which you let us down, and unless you have brought your father and mother, your brothers and all your family into your house. ¹⁹If anyone goes outside your house into the street, his blood will be on his own head; we will not be responsible. As for anyone who is in the house with you, his blood will be on our head if a hand is laid on him. ²⁰But if you tell what we are doing, we will be released from the oath you made us swear."

²¹"Agreed," she replied. "Let it be as you say." So she sent them away and they departed. And she tied the scarlet cord in the window.

²²When they left, they went into the hills and stayed there three days, until the pursuers had searched all along the road and returned without finding them. ²³Then the two men started back. They went down out of the hills, forded the river and came to Joshua son of Nun and told him everything that had happened to them. ²⁴They said to Joshua, "The LORD

has surely given the whole land into our hands; all the people are melting in fear because of us."

Crossing the Jordan

3 Early in the morning Joshua and all the Israelites set out from Shittim and went to the Jordan, where they camped before crossing over. ²After three days the officers went throughout the camp, ³giving orders to the people: "When you see the ark of the covenant of the LORD your God, and the priests, who are Levites, carrying it, you are to move out from your positions and follow it. ⁴Then you will know which way to go, since you have never been this way before. But keep a distance of about a thousand yards[c] between you and the ark; do not go near it."

⁵Joshua told the people, "Consecrate yourselves, for tomorrow the LORD will do amazing things among you."

⁶Joshua said to the priests, "Take up the ark of the covenant and pass on ahead of the people." So they took it up and went ahead of them.

⁷And the LORD said to Joshua, "Today I will begin to exalt you in the eyes of all Israel, so they may know that I am with you as I was with Moses. ⁸Tell the priests who carry the ark of the covenant: 'When you reach the edge of the Jordan's waters, go and stand in the river.' "

⁹Joshua said to the Israelites, "Come here and listen to the words of the LORD your God. ¹⁰This is how you will know that the living God is among you and that he will certainly drive out before you the Canaanites, Hittites, Hivites, Perizzites, Girgashites, Amorites and Jebusites. ¹¹See, the ark of the covenant of the Lord of all the earth will go into the Jordan ahead of you. ¹²Now then, choose twelve men from the tribes of Israel, one from each tribe. ¹³And as soon as the priests who carry the ark of the LORD—the Lord of all the earth—set foot in the Jordan, its waters flowing downstream will be cut off and stand up in a heap."

¹⁴So when the people broke camp to cross the Jordan, the priests carrying the

---

a 10 Hebrew *Yam Suph*; that is, Sea of Reeds
b 10 The Hebrew term refers to the irrevocable giving over of things or persons to the LORD, often by totally destroying them.   c 4 Hebrew *about two thousand cubits* (about 900 meters)

ark of the covenant went ahead of them. ¹⁵Now the Jordan is at flood stage all during harvest. Yet as soon as the priests who carried the ark reached the Jordan and their feet touched the water's edge, ¹⁶the water from upstream stopped flowing. It piled up in a heap a great distance away, at a town called Adam in the vicinity of Zarethan, while the water flowing down to the Sea of the Arabah (the Salt Sea ª) was completely cut off. So the people crossed over opposite Jericho. ¹⁷The priests who carried the ark of the covenant of the LORD stood firm on dry ground in the middle of the Jordan, while all Israel passed by until the whole nation had completed the crossing on dry ground.

4 When the whole nation had finished crossing the Jordan, the LORD said to Joshua, ²"Choose twelve men from among the people, one from each tribe, ³and tell them to take up twelve stones from the middle of the Jordan from right where the priests stood and to carry

them over with you and put them down at the place where you stay tonight."

⁴So Joshua called together the twelve men he had appointed from the Israelites, one from each tribe, ⁵and said to them, "Go over before the ark of the LORD your God into the middle of the Jordan. Each of you is to take up a stone on his shoulder, according to the number of the tribes of the Israelites, ⁶to serve as a sign among you. In the future, when your children ask you, 'What do these stones mean?' ⁷tell them that the flow of the Jordan was cut off before the ark of the covenant of the LORD. When it crossed the Jordan, the waters of the Jordan were cut off. These stones are to be a memorial to the people of Israel forever."

⁸So the Israelites did as Joshua commanded them. They took twelve stones from the middle of the Jordan, according to the number of the tribes of the Israel-

ª 16 That is, the Dead Sea

Make It Stick

READ JOSHUA 4:6–7

The Israelites stacked up stones as a memorial so they would always remember what God had done for them at the Jordan River. Think about the three most wonderful and awesome events in your life. Draw three big stones. On each, write something terrific God has done for you, something you want to always remember.

ites, as the Lord had told Joshua; and they carried them over with them to their camp, where they put them down. 9Joshua set up the twelve stones that had been*a* in the middle of the Jordan at the spot where the priests who carried the ark of the covenant had stood. And they are there to this day.

10Now the priests who carried the ark remained standing in the middle of the Jordan until everything the Lord had commanded Joshua was done by the people, just as Moses had directed Joshua. The people hurried over, 11and as soon as all of them had crossed, the ark of the Lord and the priests came to the other side while the people watched. 12The men of Reuben, Gad and the half-tribe of Manasseh crossed over, armed, in front of the Israelites, as Moses had directed them. 13About forty thousand armed for battle crossed over before the Lord to the plains of Jericho for war.

14That day the Lord exalted Joshua in the sight of all Israel; and they revered him all the days of his life, just as they had revered Moses.

15Then the Lord said to Joshua, 16"Command the priests carrying the ark of the Testimony to come up out of the Jordan."

17So Joshua commanded the priests, "Come up out of the Jordan."

18And the priests came up out of the river carrying the ark of the covenant of the Lord. No sooner had they set their feet on the dry ground than the waters of the Jordan returned to their place and ran at flood stage as before.

19On the tenth day of the first month the people went up from the Jordan and camped at Gilgal on the eastern border of Jericho. 20And Joshua set up at Gilgal the twelve stones they had taken out of the Jordan. 21He said to the Israelites, "In the future when your descendants ask their fathers, 'What do these stones mean?' 22tell them, 'Israel crossed the Jordan on dry ground.' 23For the Lord your God dried up the Jordan before you until you had crossed over. The Lord your God did to the Jordan just what he had done to the Red Sea*b* when he dried it up before us until we had crossed over. 24He did this so that all the peoples of the earth might know that the hand of the Lord is powerful and so that you might always fear the Lord your God."

Circumcision at Gilgal

Now when all the Amorite kings west of the Jordan and all the Canaanite kings along the coast heard how the Lord had dried up the Jordan before the Israelites until we had crossed over, their hearts melted and they no longer had the courage to face the Israelites.

2At that time the Lord said to Joshua, "Make flint knives and circumcise the Israelites again." 3So Joshua made flint knives and circumcised the Israelites at Gibeath Haaraloth.*c*

4Now this is why he did so: All those who came out of Egypt—all the men of military age—died in the desert on the way after leaving Egypt. 5All the people that came out had been circumcised, but all the people born in the desert during the journey from Egypt had not. 6The Israelites had moved about in the desert forty years until all the men who were of military age when they left Egypt had died, since they had not obeyed the Lord. For the Lord had sworn to them that they would not see the land that he had solemnly promised their fathers to give us, a land flowing with milk and honey. 7So he raised up their sons in their place, and these were the ones Joshua circumcised. They were still uncircumcised because they had not been circumcised on the way. 8And after the whole nation had been circumcised, they remained where they were in camp until they were healed.

9Then the Lord said to Joshua, "Today I have rolled away the reproach of Egypt from you." So the place has been called Gilgal*d* to this day.

10On the evening of the fourteenth day of the month, while camped at Gilgal on the plains of Jericho, the Israelites celebrated the Passover. 11The day after the Passover, that very day, they ate some of the produce of the land: unleavened bread and roasted grain. 12The manna stopped the day after*e* they ate this food from the land; there was no longer any manna for the Israelites, but that year they ate of the produce of Canaan.

---

a 9 Or Joshua also set up twelve stones   *b 23 Hebrew Yam Suph; that is, Sea of Reeds*   *c 3 Gibeath Haaraloth means hill of foreskins.*   *d 9 Gilgal sounds like the Hebrew for roll.*   *e 12 Or the day*

The Fall of Jericho

13 Now when Joshua was near Jericho, he looked up and saw a man standing in front of him with a drawn sword in his hand. Joshua went up to him and asked, "Are you for us or for our enemies?"

14 "Neither," he replied, "but as commander of the army of the LORD I have now come." Then Joshua fell facedown to the ground in reverence, and asked him, "What message does my Lord[a] have for his servant?"

15 The commander of the LORD's army replied, "Take off your sandals, for the place where you are standing is holy." And Joshua did so.

6 Now Jericho was tightly shut up because of the Israelites. No one went out and no one came in.

2 Then the LORD said to Joshua, "See, I have delivered Jericho into your hands, along with its king and its fighting men. 3 March around the city once with all the armed men. Do this for six days. 4 Have seven priests carry trumpets of rams' horns in front of the ark. On the seventh day, march around the city seven times, with the priests blowing the trumpets. 5 When you hear them sound a long blast on the trumpets, have all the people give a loud shout; then the wall of the city will collapse and the people will go up, every man straight in."

6 So Joshua son of Nun called the priests and said to them, "Take up the ark of the covenant of the LORD and have seven priests carry trumpets in front of it." 7 And he ordered the people, "Advance! March around the city, with the armed guard going ahead of the ark of the LORD."

8 When Joshua had spoken to the people, the seven priests carrying the seven trumpets before the LORD went forward, blowing their trumpets, and the ark of the LORD's covenant followed them. 9 The armed guard marched ahead of the priests who blew the trumpets, and the rear guard followed the ark. All this time the trumpets were sounding. 10 But Joshua had commanded the people, "Do not give a war cry, do not raise your voices, do not

a 14 Or lord

Bringing Down the Walls

READ JOSHUA 6:1–23

"See, I have delivered Jericho into your hands" (Joshua 6:2). God brought down Jericho's towering stone walls without the Israelites lifting a finger. They didn't build siege ramps against the walls. They didn't attack with catapults. They just marched around the city— and their soldiers weren't even at the front of the line! The trumpet-blowing priests were! The Israelites simply did what God had told them to do, then trusted him to bring down the walls. And because they listened to God and obeyed him, he did exactly that. Cool! God is waiting to do cool things for you, too, but he wants you to look to him to help you and tell you what to do. Make a habit of listening to God and you'll never again have to worry about your abilities not being enough, because God will always be there, helping you through.

Your next reading is on page 278.

say a word until the day I tell you to shout. Then shout!" ¹¹So he had the ark of the LORD carried around the city, circling it once. Then the people returned to camp and spent the night there.

¹²Joshua got up early the next morning and the priests took up the ark of the LORD. ¹³The seven priests carrying the seven trumpets went forward, marching before the ark of the LORD and blowing the trumpets. The armed men went ahead of them and the rear guard followed the ark of the LORD, while the trumpets kept sounding. ¹⁴So on the second day they marched around the city once and returned to the camp. They did this for six days.

¹⁵On the seventh day, they got up at daybreak and marched around the city seven times in the same manner, except that on that day they circled the city seven times. ¹⁶The seventh time around, when the priests sounded the trumpet blast, Joshua commanded the people, "Shout! For the LORD has given you the city! ¹⁷The city and all that is in it are to be devoted[a] to the LORD. Only Rahab the prostitute[b] and all who are with her in her house shall be spared, because she hid the spies we sent. ¹⁸But keep away from the devoted things, so that you will not bring about your own destruction by taking any of them. Otherwise you will make the camp of Israel liable to destruction and bring trouble on it. ¹⁹All the silver and gold and the articles of bronze and iron are sacred to the LORD and must go into his treasury."

²⁰When the trumpets sounded, the people shouted, and at the sound of the trumpet, when the people gave a loud shout, the wall collapsed; so every man charged straight in, and they took the city. ²¹They devoted the city to the LORD and destroyed with the sword every living thing in it—men and women, young and old, cattle, sheep and donkeys.

²²Joshua said to the two men who had spied out the land, "Go into the prostitute's house and bring her out and all who belong to her, in accordance with your oath to her." ²³So the young men who had done the spying went in and brought out Rahab, her father and mother and brothers and all who belonged to her. They brought out her entire family and put them in a place outside the camp of Israel.

²⁴Then they burned the whole city and everything in it, but they put the silver and gold and the articles of bronze and iron into the treasury of the LORD's house. ²⁵But Joshua spared Rahab the prostitute, with her family and all who belonged to her, because she hid the men Joshua had sent as spies to Jericho—and she lives among the Israelites to this day.

²⁶At that time Joshua pronounced this solemn oath: "Cursed before the LORD is the man who undertakes to rebuild this city, Jericho:

"At the cost of his firstborn son
   will he lay its foundations;
at the cost of his youngest
   will he set up its gates."

²⁷So the LORD was with Joshua, and his fame spread throughout the land.

Achan's Sin

7 But the Israelites acted unfaithfully in regard to the devoted things[c]; Achan son of Carmi, the son of Zimri,[d] the son of Zerah, of the tribe of Judah, took some of them. So the LORD's anger burned against Israel.

²Now Joshua sent men from Jericho to Ai, which is near Beth Aven to the east of Bethel, and told them, "Go up and spy out the region." So the men went up and spied out Ai.

³When they returned to Joshua, they said, "Not all the people will have to go up against Ai. Send two or three thousand men to take it and do not weary all the people, for only a few men are there." ⁴So about three thousand men went up; but they were routed by the men of Ai, ⁵who killed about thirty-six of them. They chased the Israelites from the city gate as far as the stone quarries[e] and struck them down on the slopes. At this the hearts of the people melted and became like water.

⁶Then Joshua tore his clothes and fell facedown to the ground before the ark of the LORD, remaining there till evening. The elders of Israel did the same, and sprinkled dust on their heads. ⁷And Joshua

---

^a 17 The Hebrew term refers to the irrevocable giving over of things or persons to the LORD, often by totally destroying them; also in verses 18 and 21.   ^b 17 Or possibly *innkeeper*; also in verses 22 and 25   ^c 1 The Hebrew term refers to the irrevocable giving over of things or persons to the LORD, often by totally destroying them; also in verses 11, 12, 13 and 15.   ^d 1 See Septuagint and 1 Chron. 2:6; Hebrew *Zabdi*; also in verses 17 and 18.   ^e 5 Or as far as *Shebarim*

said, "Ah, Sovereign LORD, why did you ever bring this people across the Jordan to deliver us into the hands of the Amorites to destroy us? If only we had been content to stay on the other side of the Jordan! 8O Lord, what can I say, now that Israel has been routed by its enemies? 9The Canaanites and the other people of the country will hear about this and they will surround us and wipe out our name from the earth. What then will you do for your own great name?"

10The LORD said to Joshua, "Stand up! What are you doing down on your face? 11Israel has sinned; they have violated my covenant, which I commanded them to keep. They have taken some of the devoted things; they have stolen, they have lied, they have put them with their own possessions. 12That is why the Israelites cannot stand against their enemies; they turn their backs and run because they have been made liable to destruction. I will not be with you anymore unless you destroy whatever among you is devoted to destruction.

13"Go, consecrate the people. Tell them, 'Consecrate yourselves in preparation for tomorrow; for this is what the LORD, the God of Israel, says: That which is devoted is among you, O Israel. You cannot stand against your enemies until you remove it.

14" 'In the morning, present yourselves tribe by tribe. The tribe that the LORD takes shall come forward clan by clan; the clan that the LORD takes shall come forward family by family; and the family that the LORD takes shall come forward man by man. 15He who is caught with the devoted things shall be destroyed by fire, along with all that belongs to him. He has violated the covenant of the LORD and has done a disgraceful thing in Israel!' "

16Early the next morning Joshua had Israel come forward by tribes, and Judah was taken. 17The clans of Judah came forward, and he took the Zerahites. He had the clan of the Zerahites come forward by families, and Zimri was taken. 18Joshua had his family come forward man by man, and Achan son of Carmi, the son of Zimri,

GET SMARTER.

The Domino Effect

READ JOSHUA 7:1–12, 19–26

Achan disobeyed God and stashed forbidden goods in his tent. "It is true!" he said. "I have sinned against the LORD" (Joshua 7:20). He realized too late that his sin had hurt others, not just himself. Remember, God knows everything. Usually you can't even hide things from your parents. With God, *no way*. So check out your room and get rid of things you know shouldn't be there. Achan thought, "It's OK as long as it doesn't hurt anyone else." But all Israel *was* hurt. When we do wrong things, or don't do right things, we affect our family and those around us. You can't control sin. One sin is like a falling domino—it takes down the next domino and knocks over dominos that you can't even see. So ask God to help you clean up your act. You *will* affect your family and community one way or the other—so make it a positive effect.

Your next reading is on page 282.

the son of Zerah, of the tribe of Judah, was taken.

¹⁹Then Joshua said to Achan, "My son, give glory to the LORD,ᵃ the God of Israel, and give him the praise.ᵇ Tell me what you have done; do not hide it from me."

²⁰Achan replied, "It is true! I have sinned against the LORD, the God of Israel. This is what I have done: ²¹When I saw in the plunder a beautiful robe from Babylonia,ᶜ two hundred shekelsᵈ of silver and a wedge of gold weighing fifty shekels,ᵉ I coveted them and took them. They are hidden in the ground inside my tent, with the silver underneath."

²²So Joshua sent messengers, and they ran to the tent, and there it was, hidden in his tent, with the silver underneath. ²³They took the things from the tent, brought them to Joshua and all the Israelites and spread them out before the LORD. ²⁴Then Joshua, together with all Israel, took Achan son of Zerah, the silver, the robe, the gold wedge, his sons and daughters, his cattle, donkeys and sheep, his tent and all that he had, to the Valley of Achor. ²⁵Joshua said, "Why have you brought this trouble on us? The LORD will bring trouble on you today."

Then all Israel stoned him, and after they had stoned the rest, they burned them. ²⁶Over Achan they heaped up a large pile of rocks, which remains to this day. Then the LORD turned from his fierce anger. Therefore that place has been called the Valley of Achorᶠ ever since.

Ai Destroyed

8 Then the LORD said to Joshua, "Do not be afraid; do not be discouraged. Take the whole army with you, and go up and attack Ai. For I have delivered into your hands the king of Ai, his people, his city and his land. ²You shall do to Ai and its king as you did to Jericho and its king, except that you may carry off their plunder and livestock for yourselves. Set an ambush behind the city."

³So Joshua and the whole army moved out to attack Ai. He chose thirty thousand of his best fighting men and sent them out at night ⁴with these orders: "Listen carefully. You are to set an ambush behind the city. Don't go very far from it. All of you be on the alert. ⁵I and all those with me will advance on the city, and when the men come out against us, as they did be-

fore, we will flee from them. ⁶They will pursue us until we have lured them away from the city, for they will say, 'They are running away from us as they did before.' So when we flee from them, ⁷you are to rise up from ambush and take the city. The LORD your God will give it into your hand. ⁸When you have taken the city, set it on fire. Do what the LORD has commanded. See to it; you have my orders."

⁹Then Joshua sent them off, and they went to the place of ambush and lay in wait between Bethel and Ai, to the west of Ai—but Joshua spent that night with the people.

¹⁰Early the next morning Joshua mustered his men, and he and the leaders of Israel marched before them to Ai. ¹¹The entire force that was with him marched up and approached the city and arrived in front of it. They set up camp north of Ai, with the valley between them and the city. ¹²Joshua had taken about five thousand men and set them in ambush between Bethel and Ai, to the west of the city. ¹³They had the soldiers take up their positions—all those in the camp to the north of the city and the ambush to the west of it. That night Joshua went into the valley.

¹⁴When the king of Ai saw this, he and all the men of the city hurried out early in the morning to meet Israel in battle at a certain place overlooking the Arabah. But he did not know that an ambush had been set against him behind the city. ¹⁵Joshua and all Israel let themselves be driven back before them, and they fled toward the desert. ¹⁶All the men of Ai were called to pursue them, and they pursued Joshua and were lured away from the city. ¹⁷Not a man remained in Ai or Bethel who did not go after Israel. They left the city open and went in pursuit of Israel.

¹⁸Then the LORD said to Joshua, "Hold out toward Ai the javelin that is in your hand, for into your hand I will deliver the city." So Joshua held out his javelin toward Ai. ¹⁹As soon as he did this, the men in the ambush rose quickly from their position and rushed forward. They entered the city and captured it and quickly set it on fire.

²⁰The men of Ai looked back and saw the smoke of the city rising against the

---

ᵃ 19 A solemn charge to tell the truth   ᵇ 19 Or and confess to him   ᶜ 21 Hebrew Shinar   ᵈ 21 That is, about 5 pounds (about 2.3 kilograms)   ᵉ 21 That is, about 1 1/4 pounds (about 0.6 kilogram)   ᶠ 26 Achor means trouble.

sky, but they had no chance to escape in any direction, for the Israelites who had been fleeing toward the desert had turned back against their pursuers. ²¹For when Joshua and all Israel saw that the ambush had taken the city and that smoke was going up from the city, they turned around and attacked the men of Ai. ²²The men of the ambush also came out of the city against them, so that they were caught in the middle, with Israelites on both sides. Israel cut them down, leaving them neither survivors nor fugitives. ²³But they took the king of Ai alive and brought him to Joshua.

²⁴When Israel had finished killing all the men of Ai in the fields and in the desert where they had chased them, and when every one of them had been put to the sword, all the Israelites returned to Ai and killed those who were in it. ²⁵Twelve thousand men and women fell that day—all the people of Ai. ²⁶For Joshua did not draw back the hand that held out his javelin until he had destroyed[a] all who lived in Ai. ²⁷But Israel did carry off for themselves the livestock and plunder of this city, as the LORD had instructed Joshua.

²⁸So Joshua burned Ai and made it a permanent heap of ruins, a desolate place to this day. ²⁹He hung the king of Ai on a tree and left him there until evening. At sunset, Joshua ordered them to take his body from the tree and throw it down at the entrance of the city gate. And they raised a large pile of rocks over it, which remains to this day.

The Covenant Renewed at Mount Ebal

³⁰Then Joshua built on Mount Ebal an altar to the LORD, the God of Israel, ³¹as Moses the servant of the LORD had commanded the Israelites. He built it according to what is written in the Book of the Law of Moses—an altar of uncut stones, on which no iron tool had been used. On it they offered to the LORD burnt offerings and sacrificed fellowship offerings.[b] ³²There, in the presence of the Israelites, Joshua copied on stones the law of Moses, which he had written. ³³All Israel, aliens and citizens alike, with their elders, officials and judges, were standing on both sides of the ark of the covenant of the LORD, facing those who carried it—the priests, who were Levites. Half of the people stood in front of Mount Gerizim and

half of them in front of Mount Ebal, as Moses the servant of the LORD had formerly commanded when he gave instructions to bless the people of Israel.

³⁴Afterward, Joshua read all the words of the law—the blessings and the curses—just as it is written in the Book of the Law. ³⁵There was not a word of all that Moses had commanded that Joshua did not read to the whole assembly of Israel, including the women and children, and the aliens who lived among them.

The Gibeonite Deception

9 Now when all the kings west of the Jordan heard about these things—those in the hill country, in the western foothills, and along the entire coast of the Great Sea[c] as far as Lebanon (the kings of the Hittites, Amorites, Canaanites, Perizzites, Hivites and Jebusites)— ²they came together to make war against Joshua and Israel.

³However, when the people of Gibeon heard what Joshua had done to Jericho and Ai, ⁴they resorted to a ruse: They went as a delegation whose donkeys were loaded[d] with worn-out sacks and old wineskins, cracked and mended. ⁵The men put worn and patched sandals on their feet and wore old clothes. All the bread of their food supply was dry and moldy. ⁶Then they went to Joshua in the camp at Gilgal and said to him and the men of Israel, "We have come from a distant country; make a treaty with us."

⁷The men of Israel said to the Hivites, "But perhaps you live near us. How then can we make a treaty with you?"

⁸"We are your servants," they said to Joshua.

But Joshua asked, "Who are you and where do you come from?"

⁹They answered: "Your servants have come from a very distant country because of the fame of the LORD your God. For we have heard reports of him: all that he did in Egypt, ¹⁰and all that he did to the two kings of the Amorites east of the Jordan—Sihon king of Heshbon, and Og king of Bashan, who reigned in Ashtaroth. ¹¹And our

---

a 26 The Hebrew term refers to the irrevocable giving over of things or persons to the LORD, often by totally destroying them.   *b 31* Traditionally *peace offerings*   *c 1* That is, the Mediterranean   *d 4* Most Hebrew manuscripts; some Hebrew manuscripts, Vulgate and Syriac (see also Septuagint) *They prepared provisions and loaded their donkeys* elders and all those living in our country said to us, 'Take provisions for your journey; go and meet them and say to them, "We are your servants; make a treaty with us." ' ¹²This bread of ours was warm when we packed it at home on the day we left to come to you. But now see how dry and moldy it is. ¹³And these wineskins that we filled were new, but see how cracked they are. And our clothes and sandals are worn out by the very long journey."

¹⁴The men of Israel sampled their provisions but did not inquire of the LORD. ¹⁵Then Joshua made a treaty of peace with them to let them live, and the leaders of the assembly ratified it by oath.

¹⁶Three days after they made the treaty with the Gibeonites, the Israelites heard that they were neighbors, living near them. ¹⁷So the Israelites set out and on the third day came to their cities: Gibeon, Kephirah, Beeroth and Kiriath Jearim. ¹⁸But the Israelites did not attack them, because the leaders of the assembly had sworn an oath to them by the LORD, the God of Israel.

The whole assembly grumbled against the leaders, ¹⁹but all the leaders answered, "We have given them our oath by the LORD, the God of Israel, and we cannot touch them now. ²⁰This is what we will do to them: We will let them live, so that wrath will not fall on us for breaking the oath we swore to them." ²¹They continued, "Let them live, but let them be woodcutters and water carriers for the entire community." So the leaders' promise to them was kept.

²²Then Joshua summoned the Gibeonites and said, "Why did you deceive us by saying, 'We live a long way from you,' while actually you live near us? ²³You are now under a curse: You will never cease to serve as woodcutters and water carriers for the house of my God."

²⁴They answered Joshua, "Your servants were clearly told how the LORD your God had commanded his servant Moses to give you the whole land and to wipe out all its inhabitants from before you. So we feared for our lives because of you, and that is why we did this. ²⁵We are now in your hands. Do to us whatever seems good and right to you."

²⁶So Joshua saved them from the Israelites, and they did not kill them. ²⁷That day he made the Gibeonites woodcutters and water carriers for the community and for the altar of the LORD at the place the LORD would choose. And that is what they are to this day.

The Sun Stands Still

10 Now Adoni-Zedek king of Jerusalem heard that Joshua had taken Ai and totally destroyed[a] it, doing to Ai and its king as he had done to Jericho and its king, and that the people of Gibeon had made a treaty of peace with Israel and were living near them. ²He and his people were very much alarmed at this, because Gibeon was an important city, like one of the royal cities; it was larger than Ai, and all its men were good fighters. ³So Adoni-Zedek king of Jerusalem appealed to Hoham king of Hebron, Piram king of Jarmuth, Japhia king of Lachish and Debir king of Eglon. ⁴"Come up and help me attack Gibeon," he said, "because it has made peace with Joshua and the Israelites."

⁵Then the five kings of the Amorites—the kings of Jerusalem, Hebron, Jarmuth, Lachish and Eglon—joined forces. They moved up with all their troops and took up positions against Gibeon and attacked it.

⁶The Gibeonites then sent word to Joshua in the camp at Gilgal: "Do not abandon your servants. Come up to us quickly and save us! Help us, because all the Amorite kings from the hill country have joined forces against us."

⁷So Joshua marched up from Gilgal with his entire army, including all the best fighting men. ⁸The LORD said to Joshua, "Do not be afraid of them; I have given them into your hand. Not one of them will be able to withstand you."

⁹After an all-night march from Gilgal, Joshua took them by surprise. ¹⁰The LORD threw them into confusion before Israel, who defeated them in a great victory at Gibeon. Israel pursued them along the road going up to Beth Horon and cut them down all the way to Azekah and Makkedah. ¹¹As they fled before Israel on the road down from Beth Horon to Azekah, the LORD hurled large hailstones down on them from the sky, and more of them died from the hailstones than were killed by the swords of the Israelites.

ᵃ 1 The Hebrew term refers to the irrevocable giving over of things or persons to the LORD, often by totally destroying them; also in verses 28, 35, 37, 39 and 40.

¹²On the day the LORD gave the Amorites over to Israel, Joshua said to the LORD in the presence of Israel:

"O sun, stand still over Gibeon,
    O moon, over the Valley of Aijalon."
¹³So the sun stood still,
    and the moon stopped,
    till the nation avenged itself on[a] its
        enemies,

as it is written in the Book of Jashar.

The sun stopped in the middle of the sky and delayed going down about a full day. ¹⁴There has never been a day like it before or since, a day when the LORD listened to a man. Surely the LORD was fighting for Israel!

¹⁵Then Joshua returned with all Israel to the camp at Gilgal.

Five Amorite Kings Killed

¹⁶Now the five kings had fled and hidden in the cave at Makkedah. ¹⁷When Joshua was told that the five kings had been found hiding in the cave at Makkedah, ¹⁸he said, "Roll large rocks up to the mouth of the cave, and post some men there to guard it. ¹⁹But don't stop! Pursue your enemies, attack them from the rear and don't let them reach their cities, for the LORD your God has given them into your hand."

²⁰So Joshua and the Israelites destroyed them completely—almost to a man—but the few who were left reached their fortified cities. ²¹The whole army then returned safely to Joshua in the camp at Makkedah, and no one uttered a word against the Israelites.

²²Joshua said, "Open the mouth of the cave and bring those five kings out to me." ²³So they brought the five kings out of the cave—the kings of Jerusalem, Hebron, Jarmuth, Lachish and Eglon. ²⁴When they had brought these kings to Joshua, he summoned all the men of Israel and said to the army commanders who had

a 13 Or nation triumphed over

Hit the Ground Praying

READ JOSHUA 10:1–14

Joshua needed more time to defeat the Amorites, so God *gave* him time. The Bible says, "the sun stood still, and the moon stopped" (Joshua 10:13)—for almost a full day! We don't know how God did this, but whew, talk about a long day! You've probably been in a pinch like Joshua. Your friends are coming by to pick you up, when your mom reminds you that you need to clean up your room and cut the lawn first. Short deadlines can drive you wild, but hey!—God helped Joshua get around the obstacles and finish *his* job! You may think you don't have the strength or the time to do a job, but God can help you. How did Joshua do it? He plugged into God's power with prayer. So before your feet hit the ground in the morning, talk to God. He's got the power to help you make short work of a long job.

Your next reading is on page 288.

come with him, "Come here and put your feet on the necks of these kings." So they came forward and placed their feet on their necks.

²⁵Joshua said to them, "Do not be afraid; do not be discouraged. Be strong and courageous. This is what the LORD will do to all the enemies you are going to fight." ²⁶Then Joshua struck and killed the kings and hung them on five trees, and they were left hanging on the trees until evening.

²⁷At sunset Joshua gave the order and they took them down from the trees and threw them into the cave where they had been hiding. At the mouth of the cave they placed large rocks, which are there to this day.

²⁸That day Joshua took Makkedah. He put the city and its king to the sword and totally destroyed everyone in it. He left no survivors. And he did to the king of Makkedah as he had done to the king of Jericho.

Southern Cities Conquered

²⁹Then Joshua and all Israel with him moved on from Makkedah to Libnah and attacked it. ³⁰The LORD also gave that city and its king into Israel's hand. The city and everyone in it Joshua put to the sword. He left no survivors there. And he did to its king as he had done to the king of Jericho.

³¹Then Joshua and all Israel with him moved on from Libnah to Lachish; he took up positions against it and attacked it. ³²The LORD handed Lachish over to Israel, and Joshua took it on the second day. The city and everyone in it he put to the sword, just as he had done to Libnah. ³³Meanwhile, Horam king of Gezer had come up to help Lachish, but Joshua defeated him and his army—until no survivors were left.

³⁴Then Joshua and all Israel with him moved on from Lachish to Eglon; they took up positions against it and attacked it. ³⁵They captured it that same day and put it to the sword and totally destroyed everyone in it, just as they had done to Lachish.

³⁶Then Joshua and all Israel with him went up from Eglon to Hebron and attacked it. ³⁷They took the city and put it to the sword, together with its king, its villages and everyone in it. They left no survivors. Just as at Eglon, they totally destroyed it and everyone in it.

³⁸Then Joshua and all Israel with him turned around and attacked Debir. ³⁹They took the city, its king and its villages, and put them to the sword. Everyone in it they totally destroyed. They left no survivors. They did to Debir and its king as they had done to Libnah and its king and to Hebron.

⁴⁰So Joshua subdued the whole region, including the hill country, the Negev, the western foothills and the mountain slopes, together with all their kings. He left no survivors. He totally destroyed all who breathed, just as the LORD, the God of Israel, had commanded. ⁴¹Joshua subdued them from Kadesh Barnea to Gaza and from the whole region of Goshen to Gibeon. ⁴²All these kings and their lands Joshua conquered in one cam-

Gross!

Check out Joshua 10:26. The Amorite kings had powerful armies, but Israel had God. After humongous hailstones pounded the Amorite armies flat, the Amorite kings took off running. Get away? Not a chance. The Israelites tracked them down and hung them from the nearest trees.

paign, because the LORD, the God of Israel, fought for Israel.

⁴³Then Joshua returned with all Israel to the camp at Gilgal.

Northern Kings Defeated

When Jabin king of Hazor heard of this, he sent word to Jobab king of Madon, to the kings of Shimron and Acshaph, ²and to the northern kings who were in the mountains, in the Arabah south of Kinnereth, in the western foothills and in Naphoth Dor ᵃ on the west; ³to the Canaanites in the east and west; to the Amorites, Hittites, Perizzites and Jebusites in the hill country; and to the Hivites below Hermon in the region of Mizpah. ⁴They came out with all their troops and a large number of horses and chariots—a huge army, as numerous as the sand on the seashore. ⁵All these kings joined forces and made camp together at the Waters of Merom, to fight against Israel.

⁶The LORD said to Joshua, "Do not be afraid of them, because by this time tomorrow I will hand all of them over to Israel, slain. You are to hamstring their horses and burn their chariots."

⁷So Joshua and his whole army came against them suddenly at the Waters of Merom and attacked them, ⁸and the LORD gave them into the hand of Israel. They defeated them and pursued them all the way to Greater Sidon, to Misrephoth Maim, and to the Valley of Mizpah on the east, until no survivors were left. ⁹Joshua did to them as the LORD had directed: He hamstrung their horses and burned their chariots.

¹⁰At that time Joshua turned back and captured Hazor and put its king to the sword. (Hazor had been the head of all these kingdoms.) ¹¹Everyone in it they put to the sword. They totally destroyed ᵇ them, not sparing anything that breathed, and he burned up Hazor itself.

ᵃ 2 Or in the heights of Dor   ᵇ 11 The Hebrew term refers to the irrevocable giving over of things or persons to the LORD, often by totally destroying them; also in verses 12, 20 and 21.

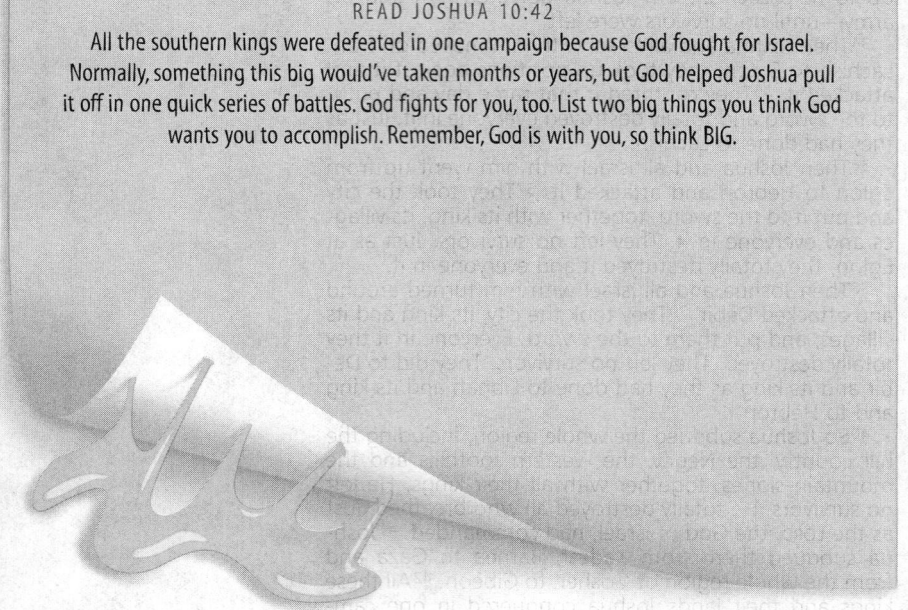

Make It Stick

READ JOSHUA 10:42

All the southern kings were defeated in one campaign because God fought for Israel. Normally, something this big would've taken months or years, but God helped Joshua pull it off in one quick series of battles. God fights for you, too. List two big things you think God wants you to accomplish. Remember, God is with you, so think BIG.

¹²Joshua took all these royal cities and their kings and put them to the sword. He totally destroyed them, as Moses the servant of the Lord had commanded. ¹³Yet Israel did not burn any of the cities built on their mounds—except Hazor, which Joshua burned. ¹⁴The Israelites carried off for themselves all the plunder and livestock of these cities, but all the people they put to the sword until they completely destroyed them, not sparing anyone that breathed. ¹⁵As the Lord commanded his servant Moses, so Moses commanded Joshua, and Joshua did it; he left nothing undone of all that the Lord commanded Moses.

¹⁶So Joshua took this entire land: the hill country, all the Negev, the whole region of Goshen, the western foothills, the Arabah and the mountains of Israel with their foothills, ¹⁷from Mount Halak, which rises toward Seir, to Baal Gad in the Valley of Lebanon below Mount Hermon. He captured all their kings and struck them down, putting them to death. ¹⁸Joshua waged war against all these kings for a long time. ¹⁹Except for the Hivites living in Gibeon, not one city made a treaty of peace with the Israelites, who took them all in battle. ²⁰For it was the Lord himself who hardened their hearts to wage war against Israel, so that he might destroy them totally, exterminating them without mercy, as the Lord had commanded Moses.

²¹At that time Joshua went and destroyed the Anakites from the hill country: from Hebron, Debir and Anab, from all the hill country of Judah, and from all the hill country of Israel. Joshua totally destroyed them and their towns. ²²No Anakites were left in Israelite territory; only in Gaza, Gath and Ashdod did any survive. ²³So Joshua took the entire land, just as the Lord had directed Moses, and he gave it as an inheritance to Israel according to their tribal divisions.

Then the land had rest from war.

List of Defeated Kings

12 These are the kings of the land whom the Israelites had defeated and whose territory they took over east of the Jordan, from the Arnon Gorge to Mount Hermon, including all the eastern side of the Arabah:

²Sihon king of the Amorites,
who reigned in Heshbon. He ruled from Aroer on the rim of the Arnon Gorge—from the middle of the gorge—to the Jabbok River, which is the border of the Ammonites. This included half of Gilead. ³He also ruled over the eastern Arabah from the Sea of Kinnereth*a* to the Sea of the Arabah (the Salt Sea*b*), to Beth Jeshimoth, and then southward below the slopes of Pisgah.

⁴And the territory of Og king of Bashan,
one of the last of the Rephaites, who reigned in Ash-

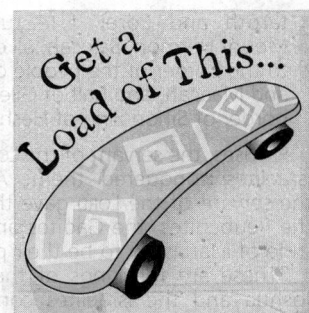

Get a Load of This...

Joshua was a master of military strategy. First he pulled an all-night march to Gibeon in the central part of Canaan (Joshua 10:9). Most leaders would have waited until daylight to march. Not Joshua! Then he took control of the southern region. Next he staged a surprise attack in the north (Joshua 11:7). Joshua's soldiers learned to expect the unexpected—and to win!

a 3 That is, Galilee   *b 3* That is, the Dead Sea

taroth and Edrei. [5]He ruled over Mount Hermon, Salecah, all of Bashan to the border of the people of Geshur and Maacah, and half of Gilead to the border of Sihon king of Heshbon.

[6]Moses, the servant of the LORD, and the Israelites conquered them. And Moses the servant of the LORD gave their land to the Reubenites, the Gadites and the half-tribe of Manasseh to be their possession.

[7]These are the kings of the land that Joshua and the Israelites conquered on the west side of the Jordan, from Baal Gad in the Valley of Lebanon to Mount Halak, which rises toward Seir (their lands Joshua gave as an inheritance to the tribes of Israel according to their tribal divisions— [8]the hill country, the western foothills, the Arabah, the mountain slopes, the desert and the Negev—the lands of the Hittites, Amorites, Canaanites, Perizzites, Hivites and Jebusites):

[9]the king of Jericho	one
the king of Ai (near Bethel)	one
[10]the king of Jerusalem	one
the king of Hebron	one
[11]the king of Jarmuth	one
the king of Lachish	one
[12]the king of Eglon	one
the king of Gezer	one
[13]the king of Debir	one
the king of Geder	one
[14]the king of Hormah	one
the king of Arad	one
[15]the king of Libnah	one
the king of Adullam	one
[16]the king of Makkedah	one
the king of Bethel	one
[17]the king of Tappuah	one
the king of Hepher	one
[18]the king of Aphek	one
the king of Lasharon	one
[19]the king of Madon	one
the king of Hazor	one
[20]the king of Shimron Meron	one
the king of Acshaph	one
[21]the king of Taanach	one
the king of Megiddo	one
[22]the king of Kedesh	one
the king of Jokneam in Carmel	one
[23]the king of Dor (in Naphoth Dor[a])	one
the king of Goyim in Gilgal	one
[24]the king of Tirzah	one

thirty-one kings in all.

Land Still to Be Taken

13 When Joshua was old and well advanced in years, the LORD said to him, "You are very old, and there are still very large areas of land to be taken over.

[2]"This is the land that remains: all the regions of the Philistines and Geshurites: [3]from the Shihor River on the east of Egypt to the territory of Ekron on the north, all of it counted as Canaanite (the territory of the five Philistine rulers in Gaza, Ashdod, Ashkelon, Gath and Ekron—that of the Avvites); [4]from the south, all the land of the Canaanites, from Arah of the Sidonians as far as Aphek, the region of the Amorites, [5]the area of the Gebalites[b]; and all Lebanon to the east, from Baal Gad below Mount Hermon to Lebo[c] Hamath.

[6]"As for all the inhabitants of the mountain regions from Lebanon to Misrephoth Maim, that is, all the Sidonians, I myself will drive them out before the Israelites. Be sure to allocate this land to Israel for an inheritance, as I have instructed you, [7]and divide it as an inheritance among the nine tribes and half of the tribe of Manasseh."

Division of the Land East of the Jordan

[8]The other half of Manasseh,[d] the Reubenites and the Gadites had received the inheritance that Moses had given them east of the Jordan, as he, the servant of the LORD, had assigned it to them.

[9]It extended from Aroer on the rim of the Arnon Gorge, and from the town in the middle of the gorge, and included the whole plateau of Medeba as far as Dibon, [10]and all the towns of Sihon king of the Amorites, who ruled in Heshbon, out to the border of the Ammonites. [11]It also included Gilead, the territory of the people of Geshur and Maacah, all of Mount Hermon and all Bashan as far as Salecah— [12]that is, the whole kingdom of Og in Bashan, who had reigned in Ashtaroth and Edrei and had survived as one of the last of the Rephaites.

[a] 23 Or in the heights of Dor   [b] 5 That is, the area of Byblos   [c] 5 Or to the entrance to   [d] 8 Hebrew With it (that is, with the other half of Manasseh)

Moses had defeated them and taken over their land. 13But the Israelites did not drive out the people of Geshur and Maacah, so they continue to live among the Israelites to this day.

14But to the tribe of Levi he gave no inheritance, since the offerings made by fire to the LORD, the God of Israel, are their inheritance, as he promised them.

15This is what Moses had given to the tribe of Reuben, clan by clan:

16The territory from Aroer on the rim of the Arnon Gorge, and from the town in the middle of the gorge, and the whole plateau past Medeba 17to Heshbon and all its towns on the plateau, including Dibon, Bamoth Baal, Beth Baal Meon, 18Jahaz, Kedemoth, Mephaath, 19Kiriathaim, Sibmah, Zereth Shahar on the hill in the valley, 20Beth Peor, the slopes of Pisgah, and Beth Jeshimoth 21—all the towns on the plateau and the entire realm of Sihon king of the Amorites, who ruled at Heshbon. Moses had defeated him and the Midianite chiefs, Evi, Rekem, Zur, Hur and Reba—princes allied with Sihon—who lived in that country. 22In addition to those slain in battle, the Israelites had put to the sword Balaam son of Beor, who practiced divination. 23The boundary of the Reubenites was the bank of the Jordan. These towns and their villages were the inheritance of the Reubenites, clan by clan.

24This is what Moses had given to the tribe of Gad, clan by clan:

25The territory of Jazer, all the towns of Gilead and half the Ammonite country as far as Aroer, near Rabbah; 26and from Heshbon to Ramath Mizpah and Betonim, and from Mahanaim to the territory of Debir; 27and in the valley, Beth Haram, Beth Nimrah, Succoth and Zaphon with the rest of the realm of Sihon king of Heshbon (the east side of the Jordan, the territory up to the end of the Sea of Kinnereth*a*). 28These towns and their villages were the inheritance of the Gadites, clan by clan.

29This is what Moses had given to the half-tribe of Manasseh, that is, to half the family of the descendants of Manasseh, clan by clan:

30The territory extending from Mahanaim and including all of Bashan, the entire realm of Og king of Bashan— all the settlements of Jair in Bashan, sixty towns, 31half of Gilead, and Ashtaroth and Edrei (the royal cities of Og in Bashan). This was for the descendants of Makir son of Manasseh—for half of the sons of Makir, clan by clan.

32This is the inheritance Moses had given when he was in the plains of Moab across the Jordan east of Jericho. 33But to the tribe of Levi, Moses had given no inheritance; the LORD, the God of Israel, is their inheritance, as he promised them.

Division of the Land West of the Jordan

14 Now these are the areas the Israelites received as an inheritance in the land of Canaan, which Eleazar the priest, Joshua son of Nun and the heads of the tribal clans of Israel allotted to them. 2Their inheritances were assigned by lot to the nine-and-a-half tribes, as the LORD had commanded through Moses. 3Moses had granted the two-and-a-half tribes their inheritance east of the Jordan but had not granted the Levites an inheritance among the rest, 4for the sons of Joseph had become two tribes—Manasseh and Ephraim. The Levites received no share of the land but only towns to live in, with pasturelands for their flocks and herds. 5So the Israelites divided the land, just as the LORD had commanded Moses.

Hebron Given to Caleb

6Now the men of Judah approached Joshua at Gilgal, and Caleb son of Jephunneh the Kenizzite said to him, "You know what the LORD said to Moses the man of God at Kadesh Barnea about you and me. 7I was forty years old when Moses the servant of the LORD sent me from Kadesh Barnea to explore the land. And I brought him back a report according to my convictions, 8but my brothers who went up with me made the hearts of the people melt with fear. I, however, followed the LORD my God wholeheartedly.

a 27 That is, Galilee

⁹So on that day Moses swore to me, 'The land on which your feet have walked will be your inheritance and that of your children forever, because you have followed the LORD my God wholeheartedly.'ᵃ

¹⁰"Now then, just as the LORD promised, he has kept me alive for forty-five years since the time he said this to Moses, while Israel moved about in the desert. So here I am today, eighty-five years old! ¹¹I am still as strong today as the day Moses sent me out; I'm just as vigorous to go out to battle now as I was then. ¹²Now give me this hill country that the LORD promised me that day. You yourself heard then that the Anakites were there and their cities were large and fortified, but, the LORD helping me, I will drive them out just as he said."

¹³Then Joshua blessed Caleb son of Jephunneh and gave him Hebron as his inheritance. ¹⁴So Hebron has belonged to Caleb son of Jephunneh the Kenizzite ever since, because he followed the LORD, the God of Israel, wholeheartedly. ¹⁵(Hebron used to be called Kiriath Arba after Arba, who was the greatest man among the Anakites.)

Then the land had rest from war.

Allotment for Judah

15 The allotment for the tribe of Judah, clan by clan, extended down to the territory of Edom, to the Desert of Zin in the extreme south.

²Their southern boundary started from the bay at the southern end of the Salt Sea,ᵇ ³crossed south of Scorpionᶜ Pass, continued on to Zin and went over to the south of Kadesh Barnea. Then it ran past Hezron up to Addar and curved around to Karka. ⁴It then passed along to Azmon and joined the Wadi of Egypt, ending at the sea. This is theirᵈ southern boundary.

ᵃ9 Deut. 1:36   ᵇ2 That is, the Dead Sea; also in verse 5
ᶜ3 Hebrew *Akrabbim*   ᵈ4 Hebrew *your*

GET STRONGER

Age Doesn't Matter

READ JOSHUA 14:1–15

Forty-five years earlier, Moses had sent spies to look around Canaan and report back. Only two returned with a positive attitude—Joshua and Caleb. On that day through Moses, the Lord promised Caleb some land (see Numbers 14:24). Now Caleb claimed the city of Hebron— and took it by driving out the Anakites. We are talking *armies* of *giants!* At 85 years of age, Caleb flexed his muscles and said, "I am still as strong today as the day Moses sent me out." Imagine your grandfather pounding a *city* full of guys like Goliath! God doesn't care how old you are. He can use you, young *or* old. Some men are called to be kings or prophets when they are kids. Some are called when they are very old. When God is your partner and you're doing what he wants you to do, age doesn't matter. Keep serving God and your whole life will be full of accomplishments.

Your next reading is on page 297.

⁵The eastern boundary is the Salt Sea as far as the mouth of the Jordan.

The northern boundary started from the bay of the sea at the mouth of the Jordan, ⁶went up to Beth Hoglah and continued north of Beth Arabah to the Stone of Bohan son of Reuben. ⁷The boundary then went up to Debir from the Valley of Achor and turned north to Gilgal, which faces the Pass of Adummim south of the gorge. It continued along to the waters of En Shemesh and came out at En Rogel. ⁸Then it ran up the Valley of Ben Hinnom along the southern slope of the Jebusite city (that is, Jerusalem). From there it climbed to the top of the hill west of the Hinnom Valley at the northern end of the Valley of Rephaim. ⁹From the hilltop the boundary headed toward the spring of the waters of Nephtoah, came out at the towns of Mount Ephron and went down toward Baalah (that is, Kiriath Jearim). ¹⁰Then it curved westward from Baalah to Mount Seir, ran along the northern slope of Mount Jearim (that is, Kesalon), continued down to Beth Shemesh and crossed to Timnah. ¹¹It went to the northern slope of Ekron, turned toward Shikkeron, passed along to Mount Baalah and reached Jabneel. The boundary ended at the sea.

¹²The western boundary is the coastline of the Great Sea.ᵃ These are the boundaries around the people of Judah by their clans.

¹³In accordance with the LORD's command to him, Joshua gave to Caleb son of Jephunneh a portion in Judah—Kiriath Arba, that is, Hebron. (Arba was the forefather of Anak.) ¹⁴From Hebron Caleb drove out the three Anakites—Sheshai, Ahiman and Talmai—descendants of Anak. ¹⁵From there he marched against the people living in Debir (formerly called Kiriath Sepher). ¹⁶And Caleb said, "I will give my daughter Acsah in marriage to the man who attacks and captures Kiriath Sepher." ¹⁷Othniel son of Kenaz, Caleb's brother, took it; so Caleb gave his daughter Acsah to him in marriage.

¹⁸One day when she came to Othniel, she urged himᵇ to ask her father for a field. When she got off her donkey, Caleb asked her, "What can I do for you?"

¹⁹She replied, "Do me a special favor. Since you have given me land in the Negev, give me also springs of water." So Caleb gave her the upper and lower springs.

²⁰This is the inheritance of the tribe of Judah, clan by clan:

²¹The southernmost towns of the tribe of Judah in the Negev toward the boundary of Edom were:

Kabzeel, Eder, Jagur, ²²Kinah, Dimonah, Adadah, ²³Kedesh, Hazor, Ithnan, ²⁴Ziph, Telem, Bealoth, ²⁵Hazor Hadattah, Kerioth Hezron (that is, Hazor), ²⁶Amam, Shema, Moladah, ²⁷Hazar Gaddah, Heshmon, Beth Pelet, ²⁸Hazar Shual, Beersheba, Biziothiah, ²⁹Baalah, Iim, Ezem, ³⁰Eltolad, Kesil, Hormah, ³¹Ziklag, Madmannah, Sansannah, ³²Lebaoth, Shilhim, Ain and Rimmon—a total of twenty-nine towns and their villages.

³³In the western foothills:

Eshtaol, Zorah, Ashnah, ³⁴Zanoah, En Gannim, Tappuah, Enam, ³⁵Jarmuth, Adullam, Socoh, Azekah, ³⁶Shaaraim, Adithaim and Gederah (or Gederothaim)ᶜ—fourteen towns and their villages.

³⁷Zenan, Hadashah, Migdal Gad, ³⁸Dilean, Mizpah, Joktheel, ³⁹Lachish, Bozkath, Eglon, ⁴⁰Cabbon, Lahmas, Kitlish, ⁴¹Gederoth, Beth Dagon, Naamah and Makkedah—sixteen towns and their villages.

⁴²Libnah, Ether, Ashan, ⁴³Iphtah, Ashnah, Nezib, ⁴⁴Keilah, Aczib and Mareshah—nine towns and their villages.

⁴⁵Ekron, with its surrounding settlements and villages; ⁴⁶west of Ekron, all that were in the vicinity of Ashdod, together with their villages; ⁴⁷Ashdod, its surrounding settlements and villages; and Gaza, its settlements and villages, as far as the Wadi of Egypt and the coastline of the Great Sea.

⁴⁸In the hill country:

Shamir, Jattir, Socoh, ⁴⁹Dannah, Kir-

ᵃ 12 That is, the Mediterranean; also in verse 47
ᵇ 18 Hebrew and some Septuagint manuscripts; other Septuagint manuscripts (see also note at Judges 1:14) *Othniel, he urged her*   ᶜ 36 Or *Gederah and Gederothaim*

iath Sannah (that is, Debir), ⁵⁰Anab, Eshtemoh, Anim, ⁵¹Goshen, Holon and Giloh—eleven towns and their villages.

⁵²Arab, Dumah, Eshan, ⁵³Janim, Beth Tappuah, Aphekah, ⁵⁴Humtah, Kiriath Arba (that is, Hebron) and Zior—nine towns and their villages.

⁵⁵Maon, Carmel, Ziph, Juttah, ⁵⁶Jezreel, Jokdeam, Zanoah, ⁵⁷Kain, Gibeah and Timnah—ten towns and their villages.

⁵⁸Halhul, Beth Zur, Gedor, ⁵⁹Maarath, Beth Anoth and Eltekon—six towns and their villages.

⁶⁰Kiriath Baal (that is, Kiriath Jearim) and Rabbah—two towns and their villages.

⁶¹In the desert:

Beth Arabah, Middin, Secacah, ⁶²Nibshan, the City of Salt and En Gedi—six towns and their villages.

⁶³Judah could not dislodge the Jebusites, who were living in Jerusalem; to this day the Jebusites live there with the people of Judah.

Allotment for Ephraim and Manasseh

16 The allotment for Joseph began at the Jordan of Jericho,ᵃ east of the waters of Jericho, and went up from there through the desert into the hill country of Bethel. ²It went on from Bethel (that is, Luz),ᵇ crossed over to the territory of the Arkites in Ataroth, ³descended westward to the territory of the Japhletites as far as the region of Lower Beth Horon and on to Gezer, ending at the sea.

⁴So Manasseh and Ephraim, the descendants of Joseph, received their inheritance.

⁵This was the territory of Ephraim, clan by clan:

The boundary of their inheritance went from Ataroth Addar in the east to Upper Beth Horon ⁶and continued to the sea. From Micmethath on the north it curved eastward to Taanath Shiloh, passing by it to Janoah on the east. ⁷Then it went down from Janoah to Ataroth and Naarah, touched Jericho and came out at the Jordan. ⁸From Tappuah the border went west to the Kanah Ravine and ended at the sea. This was the inheritance of the

tribe of the Ephraimites, clan by clan. ⁹It also included all the towns and their villages that were set aside for the Ephraimites within the inheritance of the Manassites.

¹⁰They did not dislodge the Canaanites living in Gezer; to this day the Canaanites live among the people of Ephraim but are required to do forced labor.

17 This was the allotment for the tribe of Manasseh as Joseph's firstborn, that is, for Makir, Manasseh's firstborn. Makir was the ancestor of the Gileadites, who had received Gilead and Bashan because the Makirites were great soldiers. ²So this allotment was for the rest of the people of Manasseh—the clans of Abiezer, Helek, Asriel, Shechem, Hepher and Shemida. These are the other male descendants of Manasseh son of Joseph by their clans.

³Now Zelophehad son of Hepher, the son of Gilead, the son of Makir, the son of Manasseh, had no sons but only daughters, whose names were Mahlah, Noah, Hoglah, Milcah and Tirzah. ⁴They went to Eleazar the priest, Joshua son of Nun, and the leaders and said, "The LORD commanded Moses to give us an inheritance among our brothers." So Joshua gave them an inheritance along with the brothers of their father, according to the LORD's command. ⁵Manasseh's share consisted of ten tracts of land besides Gilead and Bashan east of the Jordan, ⁶because the daughters of the tribe of Manasseh received an inheritance among the sons. The land of Gilead belonged to the rest of the descendants of Manasseh.

⁷The territory of Manasseh extended from Asher to Micmethath east of Shechem. The boundary ran southward from there to include the people living at En Tappuah. ⁸(Manasseh had the land of Tappuah, but Tappuah itself, on the boundary of Manasseh, belonged to the Ephraimites.) ⁹Then the boundary continued south to the Kanah Ravine. There were towns belonging to Ephraim lying among the towns of Manasseh, but the boundary of Manasseh was the northern side of the ravine and ended at the sea. ¹⁰On the south the

---

ᵃ 1 *Jordan of Jericho* was possibly an ancient name for the Jordan River.   ᵇ 2 Septuagint; Hebrew *Bethel to Luz* land belonged to Ephraim, on the north to Manasseh. The territory of Manasseh reached the sea and bordered Asher on the north and Issachar on the east.

11Within Issachar and Asher, Manasseh also had Beth Shan, Ibleam and the people of Dor, Endor, Taanach and Megiddo, together with their surrounding settlements (the third in the list is Naphoth a).

12Yet the Manassites were not able to occupy these towns, for the Canaanites were determined to live in that region. 13However, when the Israelites grew stronger, they subjected the Canaanites to forced labor but did not drive them out completely.

14The people of Joseph said to Joshua, "Why have you given us only one allotment and one portion for an inheritance? We are a numerous people and the LORD has blessed us abundantly."

15"If you are so numerous," Joshua answered, "and if the hill country of Ephraim is too small for you, go up into the forest and clear land for yourselves there in the land of the Perizzites and Rephaites."

16The people of Joseph replied, "The hill country is not enough for us, and all the Canaanites who live in the plain have iron chariots, both those in Beth Shan and its settlements and those in the Valley of Jezreel."

17But Joshua said to the house of Joseph—to Ephraim and Manasseh—"You are numerous and very powerful. You will have not only one allotment 18but the forested hill country as well. Clear it, and its farthest limits will be yours; though the Canaanites have iron chariots and though they are strong, you can drive them out."

Division of the Rest of the Land

18 The whole assembly of the Israelites gathered at Shiloh and set up the Tent of Meeting there. The country was brought under their control, 2but there were still seven Israelite tribes who had not yet received their inheritance.

3So Joshua said to the Israelites: "How long will you wait before you begin to take possession of the land that the LORD, the God of your fathers, has given you? 4Appoint three men from each tribe. I will send them out to make a survey of the land and to write a description of it, according to the inheritance of each. Then they will return to me. 5You are to divide the land into seven parts. Judah is to remain in its territory on the south and the house of Joseph in its territory on the north. 6After you have written descriptions of the seven parts of the land, bring them here to me and I will cast lots for you in the presence of the LORD our God. 7The Levites, however, do not get a portion among you, because the priestly service of the LORD is their inheritance. And Gad, Reuben and the half-tribe of Manasseh have already received their inheritance on the east side of the Jordan. Moses the servant of the LORD gave it to them."

8As the men started on their way to map out the land, Joshua instructed them, "Go and make a survey of the land and write a description of it. Then return to me, and I will cast lots for you here at Shiloh in the presence of the LORD." 9So the men left and went through the land. They wrote its description on a scroll, town by town, in seven parts, and returned to Joshua in the camp at Shiloh. 10Joshua then cast lots for them in Shiloh in the presence of the LORD, and there he distributed the land to the Israelites according to their tribal divisions.

Allotment for Benjamin

11The lot came up for the tribe of Benjamin, clan by clan. Their allotted territory lay between the tribes of Judah and Joseph:

12On the north side their boundary began at the Jordan, passed the northern slope of Jericho and headed west into the hill country, coming out at the desert of Beth Aven. 13From there it crossed to the south slope of Luz (that is, Bethel) and went down to Ataroth Addar on the hill south of Lower Beth Horon.

14From the hill facing Beth Horon on the south the boundary turned south along the western side and came out at Kiriath Baal (that is, Kiriath Jearim), a town of the people of Judah. This was the western side.

15The southern side began at the outskirts of Kiriath Jearim on the west, and the boundary came out at the spring of the waters of Nephtoah. 16The boundary went down to

a 11 That is, Naphoth Dor

the foot of the hill facing the Valley of Ben Hinnom, north of the Valley of Rephaim. It continued down the Hinnom Valley along the southern slope of the Jebusite city and so to En Rogel. 17It then curved north, went to En Shemesh, continued to Geliloth, which faces the Pass of Adummim, and ran down to the Stone of Bohan son of Reuben. 18It continued to the northern slope of Beth Arabaha and on down into the Arabah. 19It then went to the northern slope of Beth Hoglah and came out at the northern bay of the Salt Sea,b at the mouth of the Jordan in the south. This was the southern boundary.

20The Jordan formed the boundary on the eastern side.

These were the boundaries that marked out the inheritance of the clans of Benjamin on all sides.

21The tribe of Benjamin, clan by clan, had the following cities:

Jericho, Beth Hoglah, Emek Keziz, 22Beth Arabah, Zemaraim, Bethel, 23Avvim, Parah, Ophrah, 24Kephar Ammoni, Ophni and Geba—twelve towns and their villages.

25Gibeon, Ramah, Beeroth, 26Mizpah, Kephirah, Mozah, 27Rekem, Irpeel, Taralah, 28Zelah, Haeleph, the Jebusite city (that is, Jerusalem), Gibeah and Kiriath—fourteen towns and their villages.

This was the inheritance of Benjamin for its clans.

Allotment for Simeon

The second lot came out for the tribe of Simeon, clan by clan. Their inheritance lay within the territory of Judah. 2It included:

Beersheba (or Sheba),c Moladah, 3Hazar Shual, Balah, Ezem, 4Eltolad, Bethul, Hormah, 5Ziklag, Beth Marcaboth, Hazar Susah, 6Beth Lebaoth and Sharuhen—thirteen towns and their villages;

7Ain, Rimmon, Ether and Ashan—four towns and their villages— 8and all the villages around these towns as far as Baalath Beer (Ramah in the Negev).

This was the inheritance of the tribe of the Simeonites, clan by clan. 9The inheritance of the Simeonites was taken from the share of Judah, because Judah's portion was more than they needed. So the Simeonites received their inheritance within the territory of Judah.

Allotment for Zebulun

10The third lot came up for Zebulun, clan by clan:

The boundary of their inheritance went as far as Sarid. 11Going west it ran to Maralah, touched Dabbesheth, and extended to the ravine near Jokneam. 12It turned east from Sarid toward the sunrise to the territory of Kisloth Tabor and went on to Daberath and up to Japhia. 13Then it continued eastward to Gath Hepher and Eth Kazin; it came out at Rimmon and turned toward Neah. 14There the boundary went around on the north to Hannathon and ended at the Valley of Iphtah El. 15Included were Kattath, Nahalal, Shimron, Idalah and Bethlehem. There were twelve towns and their villages.

16These towns and their villages were the inheritance of Zebulun, clan by clan.

Allotment for Issachar

17The fourth lot came out for Issachar, clan by clan. 18Their territory included:

Jezreel, Kesulloth, Shunem, 19Hapharaim, Shion, Anaharath, 20Rabbith, Kishion, Ebez, 21Remeth, En Gannim, En Haddah and Beth Pazzez. 22The boundary touched Tabor, Shahazumah and Beth Shemesh, and ended at the Jordan. There were sixteen towns and their villages.

23These towns and their villages were the inheritance of the tribe of Issachar, clan by clan.

Allotment for Asher

24The fifth lot came out for the tribe of Asher, clan by clan. 25Their territory included:

Helkath, Hali, Beten, Acshaph, 26Allammelech, Amad and Mishal. On the west the boundary touched Carmel and Shihor Libnath. 27It then turned east toward Beth Dagon, touched Zebulun and the Valley of Iphtah El,

---

a 18 Septuagint; Hebrew *slope facing the Arabah*
b 19 That is, the Dead Sea   c 2 Or *Beersheba, Sheba;*
1 Chron. 4:28 does not have *Sheba.*

and went north to Beth Emek and Ne-iel, passing Cabul on the left. 28It went to Abdon,*a* Rehob, Hammon and Kanah, as far as Greater Sidon. 29The boundary then turned back toward Ramah and went to the fortified city of Tyre, turned toward Hosah and came out at the sea in the region of Aczib, 30Ummah, Aphek and Rehob. There were twenty-two towns and their villages.

31These towns and their villages were the inheritance of the tribe of Asher, clan by clan.

Allotment for Naphtali

32The sixth lot came out for Naphtali, clan by clan:

33Their boundary went from He-leph and the large tree in Zaanannim, passing Adami Nekeb and Jabneel to Lakkum and ending at the Jordan. 34The boundary ran west through Aznoth Tabor and came out at Huk-kok. It touched Zebulun on the south, Asher on the west and the Jordan*b* on the east. 35The fortified cities were Ziddim, Zer, Hammath, Rak-kath, Kinnereth, 36Adamah, Ramah, Hazor, 37Kedesh, Edrei, En Hazor, 38Iron, Migdal El, Horem, Beth Anath and Beth Shemesh. There were nine-teen towns and their villages.

39These towns and their villages were the inheritance of the tribe of Naphtali, clan by clan.

Allotment for Dan

40The seventh lot came out for the tribe of Dan, clan by clan. 41The territory of their inheritance included:

Zorah, Eshtaol, Ir Shemesh, 42Sha-alabbin, Aijalon, Ithlah, 43Elon, Tim-nah, Ekron, 44Eltekeh, Gibbethon, Baalath, 45Jehud, Bene Berak, Gath Rimmon, 46Me Jarkon and Rakkon, with the area facing Joppa.

47(But the Danites had difficulty taking possession of their territory, so they went up and attacked Leshem, took it, put it to the sword and occupied it. They settled in Leshem and named it Dan after their fore-father.)

48These towns and their villages were the inheritance of the tribe of Dan, clan by clan.

Allotment for Joshua

49When they had finished dividing the land into its allotted portions, the Israel-ites gave Joshua son of Nun an inheri-tance among them, 50as the LORD had commanded. They gave him the town he asked for—Timnath Serah*c* in the hill country of Ephraim. And he built up the town and settled there.

51These are the territories that Eleazar the priest, Joshua son of Nun and the heads of the tribal clans of Israel assigned by lot at Shiloh in the presence of the LORD at the entrance to the Tent of Meeting. And so they finished dividing the land.

Cities of Refuge

20 Then the LORD said to Joshua: 2"Tell the Israelites to designate the cities of refuge, as I in-structed you through Moses, 3so that anyone who kills a person acci-dentally and unintentionally may flee there and find protection from the aveng-er of blood.

4"When he flees to one of these cities, he is to stand in the entrance of the city gate and state his case before the elders of that city. Then they are to admit him into their city and give him a place to live with them. 5If the avenger of blood pur-sues him, they must not surrender the one accused, because he killed his neighbor unintentionally and without malice afore-thought. 6He is to stay in that city until he has stood trial before the assembly and until the death of the high priest who is serving at that time. Then he may go back to his own home in the town from which he fled."

7So they set apart Kedesh in Galilee in the hill country of Naphtali, Shechem in the hill country of Ephraim, and Kiriath Arba (that is, Hebron) in the hill country of Judah. 8On the east side of the Jordan of Jericho*d* they designated Bezer in the des-ert on the plateau in the tribe of Reuben, Ramoth in Gilead in the tribe of Gad, and Golan in Bashan in the tribe of Manasseh. 9Any of the Israelites or any alien living among them who killed someone acci-dentally could flee to these designated cit-

---

a 28 Some Hebrew manuscripts (see also Joshua 21:30); most Hebrew manuscripts *Ebron*   *b 34* Septuagint; Hebrew *west, and Judah, the Jordan,*   *c 50* Also known as *Timnath Heres* (see Judges 2:9)   *d 8* *Jordan of Jericho* was possibly an ancient name for the Jordan River.

ies and not be killed by the avenger of blood prior to standing trial before the assembly.

Towns for the Levites

21 Now the family heads of the Levites approached Eleazar the priest, Joshua son of Nun, and the heads of the other tribal families of Israel ²at Shiloh in Canaan and said to them, "The LORD commanded through Moses that you give us towns to live in, with pasturelands for our livestock." ³So, as the LORD had commanded, the Israelites gave the Levites the following towns and pasturelands out of their own inheritance:

⁴The first lot came out for the Kohathites, clan by clan. The Levites who were descendants of Aaron the priest were allotted thirteen towns from the tribes of Judah, Simeon and Benjamin. ⁵The rest of Kohath's descendants were allotted ten towns from the clans of the tribes of Ephraim, Dan and half of Manasseh.

⁶The descendants of Gershon were allotted thirteen towns from the clans of the tribes of Issachar, Asher, Naphtali and the half-tribe of Manasseh in Bashan.

⁷The descendants of Merari, clan by clan, received twelve towns from the tribes of Reuben, Gad and Zebulun.

⁸So the Israelites allotted to the Levites these towns and their pasturelands, as the LORD had commanded through Moses.

⁹From the tribes of Judah and Simeon they allotted the following towns by name ¹⁰(these towns were assigned to the descendants of Aaron who were from the Kohathite clans of the Levites, because the first lot fell to them):

¹¹They gave them Kiriath Arba (that is, Hebron), with its surrounding pastureland, in the hill country of Judah. (Arba was the forefather of Anak.) ¹²But the fields and villages around the city they had given to Caleb son of Jephunneh as his possession.

¹³So to the descendants of Aaron the priest they gave Hebron (a city of refuge for one accused of murder), Libnah, ¹⁴Jattir, Eshtemoa, ¹⁵Holon, Debir, ¹⁶Ain, Juttah and Beth Shemesh, together with their pasturelands—nine towns from these two tribes.

¹⁷And from the tribe of Benjamin they gave them Gibeon, Geba, ¹⁸Anathoth and Almon, together with their pasturelands—four towns.

¹⁹All the towns for the priests, the descendants of Aaron, were thirteen, together with their pasturelands.

²⁰The rest of the Kohathite clans of the Levites were allotted towns from the tribe of Ephraim:

²¹In the hill country of Ephraim they were given Shechem (a city of refuge for one accused of murder) and Gezer, ²²Kibzaim and Beth Horon, together with their pasturelands—four towns.

²³Also from the tribe of Dan they received Eltekeh, Gibbethon, ²⁴Aijalon and Gath Rimmon, together with their pasturelands—four towns.

²⁵From half the tribe of Manasseh they received Taanach and Gath Rimmon, together with their pasturelands—two towns.

²⁶All these ten towns and their pasturelands were given to the rest of the Kohathite clans.

²⁷The Levite clans of the Gershonites were given:

from the half-tribe of Manasseh,
Golan in Bashan (a city of refuge for one accused of murder) and Be Eshtarah, together with their pasturelands—two towns;

²⁸from the tribe of Issachar,
Kishion, Daberath, ²⁹Jarmuth and En Gannim, together with their pasturelands—four towns;

³⁰from the tribe of Asher,
Mishal, Abdon, ³¹Helkath and Rehob, together with their pasturelands—four towns;

³²from the tribe of Naphtali,
Kedesh in Galilee (a city of refuge for one accused of murder), Hammoth Dor and Kartan, together with their pasturelands—three towns.

³³All the towns of the Gershonite clans were thirteen, together with their pasturelands.

³⁴The Merarite clans (the rest of the Levites) were given:

from the tribe of Zebulun,
Jokneam, Kartah, ³⁵Dimnah and Nahalal, together with their pasturelands—four towns;

36from the tribe of Reuben,
Bezer, Jahaz, 37Kedemoth and Mephaath, together with their pasturelands—four towns;
38from the tribe of Gad,
Ramoth in Gilead (a city of refuge for
one accused of murder), Mahanaim,
39Heshbon and Jazer, together with
their pasturelands—four towns in all.
40All the towns allotted to the Merarite
clans, who were the rest of the Levites,
were twelve.

41The towns of the Levites in the territory held by the Israelites were forty-eight in
all, together with their pasturelands. 42Each
of these towns had pasturelands surrounding it; this was true for all these towns.

43So the LORD gave Israel all the land he
had sworn to give their forefathers, and
they took possession of it and settled
there. 44The LORD gave them rest on every
side, just as he had sworn to their forefathers. Not one of their enemies withstood
them; the LORD handed all their enemies
over to them. 45Not one of all the LORD's
good promises to the house of Israel
failed; every one was fulfilled.

Eastern Tribes Return Home

22 Then Joshua summoned the
Reubenites, the Gadites and
the half-tribe of Manasseh
2and said to them, "You have
done all that Moses the servant of the
LORD commanded, and you have obeyed
me in everything I commanded. 3For a
long time now—to this very day—you
have not deserted your brothers but have
carried out the mission the LORD your God
gave you. 4Now that the LORD your God
has given your brothers rest as he promised, return to your homes in the land that
Moses the servant of the LORD gave you on
the other side of the Jordan. 5But be very
careful to keep the commandment and
the law that Moses the servant of the LORD
gave you: to love the LORD your God, to
walk in all his ways, to obey his commands, to hold fast to him and to serve
him with all your heart and all your soul."

6Then Joshua blessed them and sent
them away, and they went to their homes.
7(To the half-tribe of Manasseh Moses had
given land in Bashan, and to the other
half of the tribe Joshua gave land on the
west side of the Jordan with their broth-

ers.) When Joshua sent them home, he
blessed them, 8saying, "Return to your
homes with your great wealth—with
large herds of livestock, with silver, gold,
bronze and iron, and a great quantity of
clothing—and divide with your brothers
the plunder from your enemies."

9So the Reubenites, the Gadites and the
half-tribe of Manasseh left the Israelites at
Shiloh in Canaan to return to Gilead, their
own land, which they had acquired in accordance with the command of the LORD
through Moses.

10When they came to Geliloth near the
Jordan in the land of Canaan, the Reubenites, the Gadites and the half-tribe of Manasseh built an imposing altar there by
the Jordan. 11And when the Israelites
heard that they had built the altar on the
border of Canaan at Geliloth near the Jordan on the Israelite side, 12the whole assembly of Israel gathered at Shiloh to go
to war against them.

13So the Israelites sent Phinehas son of
Eleazar, the priest, to the land of Gilead—
to Reuben, Gad and the half-tribe of Manasseh. 14With him they sent ten of the
chief men, one for each of the tribes of Israel, each the head of a family division
among the Israelite clans.

15When they went to Gilead—to Reuben, Gad and the half-tribe of Manasseh—they said to them: 16"The whole assembly of the LORD says: 'How could you
break faith with the God of Israel like this?
How could you turn away from the LORD
and build yourselves an altar in rebellion
against him now? 17Was not the sin of
Peor enough for us? Up to this very day
we have not cleansed ourselves from that
sin, even though a plague fell on the community of the LORD! 18And are you now
turning away from the LORD?

" 'If you rebel against the LORD today,
tomorrow he will be angry with the whole
community of Israel. 19If the land you possess is defiled, come over to the LORD's
land, where the LORD's tabernacle stands,
and share the land with us. But do not rebel against the LORD or against us by
building an altar for yourselves, other
than the altar of the LORD our God.
20When Achan son of Zerah acted unfaithfully regarding the devoted things,a

a 20 The Hebrew term refers to the irrevocable giving over of
things or persons to the LORD, often by totally destroying
them.

did not wrath come upon the whole community of Israel? He was not the only one who died for his sin.' "

²¹Then Reuben, Gad and the half-tribe of Manasseh replied to the heads of the clans of Israel: ²²"The Mighty One, God, the LORD! The Mighty One, God, the LORD! He knows! And let Israel know! If this has been in rebellion or disobedience to the LORD, do not spare us this day. ²³If we have built our own altar to turn away from the LORD and to offer burnt offerings and grain offerings, or to sacrifice fellowship offerings*a* on it, may the LORD himself call us to account.

²⁴"No! We did it for fear that some day your descendants might say to ours, 'What do you have to do with the LORD, the God of Israel? ²⁵The LORD has made the Jordan a boundary between us and you—you Reubenites and Gadites! You have no share in the LORD.' So your descendants might cause ours to stop fearing the LORD.

²⁶"That is why we said, 'Let us get ready and build an altar—but not for burnt offerings or sacrifices.' ²⁷On the contrary, it is to be a witness between us and you and the generations that follow, that we will worship the LORD at his sanctuary with our burnt offerings, sacrifices and fellowship offerings. Then in the future your descendants will not be able to say to ours, 'You have no share in the LORD.'

²⁸"And we said, 'If they ever say this to us, or to our descendants, we will answer: Look at the replica of the LORD's altar, which our fathers built, not for burnt offerings and sacrifices, but as a witness between us and you.'

²⁹"Far be it from us to rebel against the LORD and turn away from him today by building an altar for burnt offerings, grain offerings and sacrifices, other than the altar of the LORD our God that stands before his tabernacle."

³⁰When Phinehas the priest and the leaders of the community—the heads of the clans of the Israelites—heard what Reuben, Gad and Manasseh had to say, they were pleased. ³¹And Phinehas son of Eleazar, the priest, said to Reuben, Gad and Manasseh, "Today we know that the LORD is with us, because you have not acted unfaithfully toward the LORD in this matter. Now you have rescued the Israelites from the LORD's hand."

³²Then Phinehas son of Eleazar, the priest, and the leaders returned to Canaan from their meeting with the Reubenites and Gadites in Gilead and reported to the Israelites. ³³They were glad to hear the report and praised God. And they talked no more about going to war against them to devastate the country where the Reubenites and the Gadites lived.

³⁴And the Reubenites and the Gadites gave the altar this name: A Witness Between Us that the LORD is God.

Joshua's Farewell to the Leaders

23 After a long time had passed and the LORD had given Israel rest from all their enemies around them, Joshua, by then old and well advanced in years, ²summoned all Israel—their elders, leaders, judges and officials—and said to them: "I am old and well advanced in years. ³You yourselves have seen everything the LORD your God has done to all these nations for your sake; it was the LORD your God who fought for you. ⁴Remember how I have allotted as an inheritance for your tribes all the land of the nations that remain—the nations I conquered—between the Jordan and the Great Sea*b* in the west. ⁵The LORD your God himself will drive them out of your way. He will push them out before you, and you will take possession of their land, as the LORD your God promised you.

⁶"Be very strong; be careful to obey all that is written in the Book of the Law of Moses, without turning aside to the right or to the left. ⁷Do not associate with these nations that remain among you; do not invoke the names of their gods or swear by them. You must not serve them or bow down to them. ⁸But you are to hold fast to the LORD your God, as you have until now.

⁹"The LORD has driven out before you great and powerful nations; to this day no one has been able to withstand you. ¹⁰One of you routs a thousand, because the LORD your God fights for you, just as he promised. ¹¹So be very careful to love the LORD your God.

¹²"But if you turn away and ally yourselves with the survivors of these nations that remain among you and if you intermarry with them and associate with them,

---

a 23 Traditionally *peace offerings*; also in verse 27   *b 4* That is, the Mediterranean

A Life Well-Lived

READ JOSHUA 24:1, 14–31

"Israel served the LORD throughout the lifetime of Joshua" (Joshua 24:31). This is a tribute to Joshua's leadership—and to the God he served. Joshua started off with the tough task of filling Moses' shoes and leading the people into the Promised Land. He relied on God for *everything*. As a result, he became smart, strong, deep and cool. In his final speech he declared, "As for me and my household, we will serve the LORD" (Joshua 24:15).

SMARTER: All of Joshua's life, God gave him smarts on how to fight battles. Imagine having to conquer an entire land—especially a land full of great cities and giant inhabitants! Strength simply wasn't enough. Smarts were needed, too—and Joshua had 'em. His military tactics, such as his ambush at Ai or marching his army all night to surprise the enemy, were brilliant!

STRONGER: Moses had told Joshua, "Be strong!" (Joshua 1:6), and Joshua was strong. He led his army on long campaigns and sometimes battled all day. When he died at age 110, he had served God energetically his whole life. He was a mighty man in battle, but his true strength came from depending on God to help him.

DEEPER: Moses had told Joshua to meditate on God's Word "day and night" (Joshua 1:8) and obey it, and Joshua did. He obeyed the Lord at every step and always looked to God for help. When ten spies doubted they could take the Promised Land, only he and Caleb believed. Joshua had faith! Result? God answered his prayers in ways he never did for another man (see Joshua 10:14)!

COOLER: When Joshua told the Israelites to ditch anything that came between them and God, they listened up (Joshua 24:14, 16). They respected God *and* Joshua. In the end, Joshua stood up for the truth and reminded the people of their history with the Lord. Joshua's life was extraordinary because he followed God.

Your next reading is on page 302.

¹³then you may be sure that the LORD your God will no longer drive out these nations before you. Instead, they will become snares and traps for you, whips on your backs and thorns in your eyes, until you perish from this good land, which the LORD your God has given you.

¹⁴"Now I am about to go the way of all the earth. You know with all your heart and soul that not one of all the good promises the LORD your God gave you has failed. Every promise has been fulfilled; not one has failed. ¹⁵But just as every good promise of the LORD your God has come true, so the LORD will bring on you all the evil he has threatened, until he has destroyed you from this good land he has given you. ¹⁶If you violate the covenant of the LORD your God, which he commanded you, and go and serve other gods and bow down to them, the LORD's anger will burn against you, and you will quickly perish from the good land he has given you."

The Covenant Renewed at Shechem

24 Then Joshua assembled all the tribes of Israel at Shechem. He summoned the elders, leaders, judges and officials of Israel, and they presented themselves before God.

²Joshua said to all the people, "This is what the LORD, the God of Israel, says: 'Long ago your forefathers, including Terah the father of Abraham and Nahor, lived beyond the River[a] and worshiped other gods. ³But I took your father Abraham from the land beyond the River and led him throughout Canaan and gave him many descendants. I gave him Isaac, ⁴and to Isaac I gave Jacob and Esau. I assigned the hill country of Seir to Esau, but Jacob and his sons went down to Egypt.

⁵" 'Then I sent Moses and Aaron, and I afflicted the Egyptians by what I did there, and I brought you out. ⁶When I brought your fathers out of Egypt, you came to the sea, and the Egyptians pursued them with chariots and horsemen[b] as far as the Red Sea.[c] ⁷But they cried to the LORD for help, and he put darkness between you and the Egyptians; he brought the sea over them and covered them. You saw with your own eyes what I did to the Egyptians. Then you lived in the desert for a long time.

⁸" 'I brought you to the land of the Amorites who lived east of the Jordan. They fought against you, but I gave them into your hands. I destroyed them from before you, and you took possession of their land. ⁹When Balak son of Zippor, the king of Moab, prepared to fight against Israel, he sent for Balaam son of Beor to put a curse on you. ¹⁰But I would not listen to Balaam, so he blessed you again and again, and I delivered you out of his hand.

¹¹" 'Then you crossed the Jordan and came to Jericho. The citizens of Jericho fought against you, as did also the Amorites, Perizzites, Canaanites, Hittites, Girgashites, Hivites and Jebusites, but I gave them into your hands. ¹²I sent the hornet ahead of you, which drove them out before you—also the two Amorite kings. You did not do it with your own sword and bow. ¹³So I gave you a land on which you did not toil and cities you did not build; and you live in them and eat from vineyards and olive groves that you did not plant.'

¹⁴"Now fear the LORD and serve him with all faithfulness. Throw away the gods your forefathers worshiped beyond the River and in Egypt, and serve the LORD. ¹⁵But if serving the LORD seems undesirable to you, then choose for yourselves this day whom you will serve, whether the gods your forefathers served beyond the River, or the gods of the Amorites, in whose land you are living. But as for me and my household, we will serve the LORD."

¹⁶Then the people answered, "Far be it from us to forsake the LORD to serve other gods! ¹⁷It was the LORD our God himself who brought us and our fathers up out of Egypt, from that land of slavery, and performed those great signs before our eyes. He protected us on our entire journey and among all the nations through which we traveled. ¹⁸And the LORD drove out before us all the nations, including the Amorites, who lived in the land. We too will serve the LORD, because he is our God."

¹⁹Joshua said to the people, "You are not able to serve the LORD. He is a holy God; he is a jealous God. He will not forgive your rebellion and your sins. ²⁰If you forsake the LORD and serve foreign gods,

---

[a] 2 That is, the Euphrates; also in verses 3, 14 and 15   [b] 6 Or charioteers   [c] 6 Hebrew Yam Suph; that is, Sea of Reeds

he will turn and bring disaster on you and make an end of you, after he has been good to you."

²¹But the people said to Joshua, "No! We will serve the LORD."

²²Then Joshua said, "You are witnesses against yourselves that you have chosen to serve the LORD."

"Yes, we are witnesses," they replied.

²³"Now then," said Joshua, "throw away the foreign gods that are among you and yield your hearts to the LORD, the God of Israel."

²⁴And the people said to Joshua, "We will serve the LORD our God and obey him."

²⁵On that day Joshua made a covenant for the people, and there at Shechem he drew up for them decrees and laws. ²⁶And Joshua recorded these things in the Book of the Law of God. Then he took a large stone and set it up there under the oak near the holy place of the LORD.

²⁷"See!" he said to all the people. "This stone will be a witness against us. It has heard all the words the LORD has said to us. It will be a witness against you if you are untrue to your God."

Buried in the Promised Land

²⁸Then Joshua sent the people away, each to his own inheritance.

²⁹After these things, Joshua son of Nun, the servant of the LORD, died at the age of a hundred and ten. ³⁰And they buried him in the land of his inheritance, at Timnath Serah*ᵃ* in the hill country of Ephraim, north of Mount Gaash.

³¹Israel served the LORD throughout the lifetime of Joshua and of the elders who outlived him and who had experienced everything the LORD had done for Israel.

³²And Joseph's bones, which the Israelites had brought up from Egypt, were buried at Shechem in the tract of land that Jacob bought for a hundred pieces of silverᵇ from the sons of Hamor, the father of Shechem. This became the inheritance of Joseph's descendants.

³³And Eleazar son of Aaron died and was buried at Gibeah, which had been allotted to his son Phinehas in the hill country of Ephraim.

Get a Load of This...

Check out Joshua 24:32. The mummy returns! More than four hundred years after Joseph told the people to bury his bones in the Promised Land (see Genesis 50:25), his request was finally honored. These weren't just his bones, however—Joseph had been embalmed, Egyptian-style!

ᵃ 30 Also known as *Timnath Heres* (see Judges 2:9)   ᵇ 32 Hebrew *hundred kesitahs*; a kesitah was a unit of money of unknown weight and value.

JUDGES

Who wrote this book?
No one knows for sure. Many people think Samuel is the author.

Why was this book written?
Judges shows what happened when the Israelites abandoned God to worship idols.

What happens in this book?
God's people sin again and again. God lets Israel's enemies win. When the Israelites suffer, they turn to God. Then God sends a "judge" to defeat the enemy and lead Israel.

What do we learn about God in this book?
God is eager to forgive and help people who have sinned if only they will turn to him.

Who is important in this book?
The most important people in this book are Deborah, Gideon, Jephthah and Samson.

When did this happen?
The events in this book happened between 1390 and 1050 B.C.

Where did this happen?
The events of this book happened in different parts of Canaan.

What are some of the stories in this book?
Deborah leads Israel	Judges 4–5
Gideon asks God for a sign	Judges 6
Gideon defeats the Midianites	Judges 7
Jephthah defeats the Ammonites	Judges 11–12
Samson's special birth	Judges 13
Samson's marriage	Judges 14
Samson's revenge	Judges 15
Samson and Delilah	Judges 16

Israel Fights the Remaining Canaanites

After the death of Joshua, the Israelites asked the LORD, "Who will be the first to go up and fight for us against the Canaanites?"

2 The LORD answered, "Judah is to go; I have given the land into their hands."

3 Then the men of Judah said to the Simeonites their brothers, "Come up with us into the territory allotted to us, to fight against the Canaanites. We in turn will go with you into yours." So the Simeonites went with them.

4 When Judah attacked, the LORD gave the Canaanites and Perizzites into their hands and they struck down ten thousand men at Bezek. 5 It was there that they found Adoni-Bezek and fought against him, putting to rout the Canaanites and Perizzites. 6 Adoni-Bezek fled, but they chased him and caught him, and cut off his thumbs and big toes.

7 Then Adoni-Bezek said, "Seventy kings with their thumbs and big toes cut off have picked up scraps under my table. Now God has paid me back for what I did to them." They brought him to Jerusalem, and he died there.

8 The men of Judah attacked Jerusalem also and took it. They put the city to the sword and set it on fire.

9 After that, the men of Judah went down to fight against the Canaanites living in the hill country, the Negev and the western foothills. 10 They advanced against the Canaanites living in Hebron (formerly called Kiriath Arba) and defeated Sheshai, Ahiman and Talmai.

11 From there they advanced against the people living in Debir (formerly called Kiriath Sepher). 12 And Caleb said, "I will give my daughter Acsah in marriage to the man who attacks and captures Kiriath Sepher." 13 Othniel son of Kenaz, Caleb's younger brother, took it; so Caleb gave his daughter Acsah to him in marriage.

14 One day when she came to Othniel, she urged him[a] to ask her father for a field. When she got off her donkey, Caleb asked her, "What can I do for you?"

15 She replied, "Do me a special favor. Since you have given me land in the Negev, give me also springs of water." Then Caleb gave her the upper and lower springs.

16 The descendants of Moses' father-in-law, the Kenite, went up from the City of Palms[b] with the men of Judah to live among the people of the Desert of Judah in the Negev near Arad.

17 Then the men of Judah went with the Simeonites their brothers and attacked the Canaanites living in Zephath, and they totally destroyed[c] the city. Therefore it was called Hormah.[d] 18 The men of Judah also took[e] Gaza, Ashkelon and Ekron—each city with its territory.

19 The LORD was with the men of Judah. They took possession of the hill country, but they were unable to drive the people from the plains, because they had iron chariots. 20 As Moses had promised, Hebron was given to Caleb, who drove from it the three sons of Anak. 21 The Benjamites, however, failed to dislodge the Jebusites, who were living in Jerusalem; to this day the Jebusites live there with the Benjamites.

22 Now the house of Joseph attacked Bethel, and the LORD was with them. 23 When they sent men to spy out Bethel (formerly called Luz), 24 the spies saw a man coming out of the city and they said to him, "Show us how to get into the city and we will see that you are treated well." 25 So he showed them, and they put the city to the sword but spared the man and his whole family. 26 He then went to the land of the Hittites, where he built a city and called it Luz, which is its name to this day.

27 But Manasseh did not drive out the people of Beth Shan or Taanach or Dor or Ibleam or Megiddo and their surrounding settlements, for the Canaanites were determined to live in that land. 28 When Israel became strong, they pressed the Canaanites into forced labor but never drove them out completely. 29 Nor did Ephraim drive out the Canaanites living in Gezer, but the Canaanites continued to live there among them. 30 Neither did Zebulun drive out the Canaanites living in Kitron or Nahalol, who remained among them; but they did subject them to forced labor. 31 Nor did Asher drive out those living in Acco or Sidon or Ahlab or Aczib or Helbah or Aphek or Rehob, 32 and because of this the people of Asher lived among the Canaanite inhabitants of the land. 33 Neither

---

a 14 Hebrew; Septuagint and Vulgate *Othniel, he urged her*   b 16 That is, Jericho   c 17 The Hebrew term refers to the irrevocable giving over of things or persons to the LORD, often by totally destroying them.   d 17 *Hormah* means *destruction*.   e 18 Hebrew; Septuagint *Judah did not take* did Naphtali drive out those living in Beth Shemesh or Beth Anath; but the Naphtalites too lived among the Canaanite inhabitants of the land, and those living in Beth Shemesh and Beth Anath became forced laborers for them. ³⁴The Amorites confined the Danites to the hill country, not allowing them to come down into the plain. ³⁵And the Amorites were determined also to hold out in Mount Heres, Aijalon and Shaalbim, but when the power of the house of Joseph increased, they too were pressed into forced labor. ³⁶The boundary of the Amorites was from Scorpion*a* Pass to Sela and beyond.

The Angel of the LORD at Bokim

The angel of the LORD went up from Gilgal to Bokim and said, "I brought you up out of Egypt and led you into the land that I swore to give to your forefathers. I said, 'I will never break my covenant with you, ²and you shall not make a covenant with the people of this land, but you shall break down their altars.' Yet you have disobeyed me. Why have you done this? ³Now therefore I tell you that I will not drive them out before you; they will be ⌊thorns⌋ in your sides and their gods will be a snare to you."

⁴When the angel of the LORD had spoken these things to all the Israelites, the people wept aloud, ⁵and they called that place Bokim.*b* There they offered sacrifices to the LORD.

Disobedience and Defeat

⁶After Joshua had dismissed the Israelites, they went to take possession of the land, each to his own inheritance. ⁷The people served the LORD throughout the lifetime of Joshua and of the elders who outlived him and who had seen all the great things the LORD had done for Israel.

⁸Joshua son of Nun, the servant of the LORD, died at the age of a hundred and ten. ⁹And they buried him in the land of his inheritance, at Timnath Heres*c* in the hill country of Ephraim, north of Mount Gaash.

¹⁰After that whole generation had been

---

a 36 Hebrew *Akrabbim*   *b 5* *Bokim* means *weepers.*
c 9 Also known as *Timnath Serah* (see Joshua 19:50 and 24:30)

The Vicious Cycle

READ JUDGES 2:1–19

When God led the Israelites into the Promised Land, he simply asked them to worship and obey him. But they constantly ended up worshiping the other gods around them. Every time they did, God judged them by letting their enemies walk all over them. Then the people would come crawling back to God, praying desperately for help. "Whenever the LORD raised up a judge for them, he ... saved them out of the hands of their enemies ... But when the judge died, the people returned to ... following other gods" (verses 18–19). Helllooo! This is God calling Israel! This vicious cycle repeated itself over and over again. Learn from the Israelites' mistake by having a steady relationship with God. Stay close to him all the time. It's a whole lot easier to spend a little time with God each day, than to spend a whole lot of time praying when trouble hits.

Your next reading is on page 305.

gathered to their fathers, another generation grew up, who knew neither the LORD nor what he had done for Israel. ¹¹Then the Israelites did evil in the eyes of the LORD and served the Baals. ¹²They forsook the LORD, the God of their fathers, who had brought them out of Egypt. They followed and worshiped various gods of the peoples around them. They provoked the LORD to anger ¹³because they forsook him and served Baal and the Ashtoreths. ¹⁴In his anger against Israel the LORD handed them over to raiders who plundered them. He sold them to their enemies all around, whom they were no longer able to resist. ¹⁵Whenever Israel went out to fight, the hand of the LORD was against them to defeat them, just as he had sworn to them. They were in great distress.

¹⁶Then the LORD raised up judges,[a] who saved them out of the hands of these raiders. ¹⁷Yet they would not listen to their judges but prostituted themselves to other gods and worshiped them. Unlike their fathers, they quickly turned from the way in which their fathers had walked, the way of obedience to the LORD's commands. ¹⁸Whenever the LORD raised up a judge for them, he was with the judge and saved them out of the hands of their enemies as long as the judge lived; for the LORD had compassion on them as they groaned under those who oppressed and afflicted them. ¹⁹But when the judge died, the people returned to ways even more corrupt than those of their fathers, following other gods and serving and worshiping them. They refused to give up their evil practices and stubborn ways.

²⁰Therefore the LORD was very angry with Israel and said, "Because this nation has violated the covenant that I laid down for their forefathers and has not listened to me, ²¹I will no longer drive out before them any of the nations Joshua left when he died. ²²I will use them to test Israel and see whether they will keep the way of the LORD and walk in it as their forefathers did." ²³The LORD had allowed those nations to remain; he did not drive them out at once by giving them into the hands of Joshua.

3 These are the nations the LORD left to test all those Israelites who had not experienced any of the wars in Canaan ²(he did this only to teach warfare to the descendants of the Israel-

ites who had not had previous battle experience): ³the five rulers of the Philistines, all the Canaanites, the Sidonians, and the Hivites living in the Lebanon mountains from Mount Baal Hermon to Lebo[b] Hamath. ⁴They were left to test the Israelites to see whether they would obey the LORD's commands, which he had given their forefathers through Moses.

⁵The Israelites lived among the Canaanites, Hittites, Amorites, Perizzites, Hivites and Jebusites. ⁶They took their daughters in marriage and gave their own daughters to their sons, and served their gods.

Othniel

⁷The Israelites did evil in the eyes of the LORD; they forgot the LORD their God and served the Baals and the Asherahs. ⁸The anger of the LORD burned against Israel so that he sold them into the hands of Cushan-Rishathaim king of Aram Naharaim,[c] to whom the Israelites were subject for eight years. ⁹But when they cried out to the LORD, he raised up for them a deliverer, Othniel son of Kenaz, Caleb's younger brother, who saved them. ¹⁰The Spirit of the LORD came upon him, so that he became Israel's judge[d] and went to war. The LORD gave Cushan-Rishathaim king of Aram into the hands of Othniel, who overpowered him. ¹¹So the land had peace for forty years, until Othniel son of Kenaz died.

Ehud

¹²Once again the Israelites did evil in the eyes of the LORD, and because they did this evil the LORD gave Eglon king of Moab power over Israel. ¹³Getting the Ammonites and Amalekites to join him, Eglon came and attacked Israel, and they took possession of the City of Palms.[e] ¹⁴The Israelites were subject to Eglon king of Moab for eighteen years.

¹⁵Again the Israelites cried out to the LORD, and he gave them a deliverer—Ehud, a left-handed man, the son of Gera the Benjamite. The Israelites sent him with tribute to Eglon king of Moab. ¹⁶Now Ehud had made a double-edged sword about a foot and a half[f] long, which he strapped to his right thigh under his

---

[a] 16 Or *leaders*; similarly in verses 17–19   [b] 3 Or *to the entrance to*   [c] 8 That is, Northwest Mesopotamia   [d] 10 Or *leader*   [e] 13 That is, Jericho   [f] 16 Hebrew *a cubit* (about 0.5 meter)

clothing. [17]He presented the tribute to Eglon king of Moab, who was a very fat man. [18]After Ehud had presented the tribute, he sent on their way the men who had carried it. [19]At the idols[a] near Gilgal he himself turned back and said, "I have a secret message for you, O king."

The king said, "Quiet!" And all his attendants left him.

[20]Ehud then approached him while he was sitting alone in the upper room of his summer palace[b] and said, "I have a message from God for you." As the king rose from his seat, [21]Ehud reached with his left hand, drew the sword from his right thigh and plunged it into the king's belly. [22]Even the handle sank in after the blade, which came out his back. Ehud did not pull the sword out, and the fat closed in over it. [23]Then Ehud went out to the porch[c]; he shut the doors of the upper room behind him and locked them.

[24]After he had gone, the servants came and found the doors of the upper room locked. They said, "He must be relieving himself in the inner room of the house." [25]They waited to the point of embarrassment, but when he did not open the doors of the room, they took a key and unlocked them. There they saw their lord fallen to the floor, dead.

[26]While they waited, Ehud got away. He passed by the idols and escaped to Seirah. [27]When he arrived there, he blew a trumpet in the hill country of Ephraim, and the Israelites went down with him from the hills, with him leading them.

[28]"Follow me," he ordered, "for the LORD has given Moab, your enemy, into your hands." So they followed him down and, taking possession of the fords of the Jordan that led to Moab, they allowed no one to cross over. [29]At that time they struck down about ten thousand Moabites, all vigorous and strong; not a man escaped. [30]That day Moab was made subject to Israel, and the land had peace for eighty years.

Shamgar

[31]After Ehud came Shamgar son of Anath, who struck down six hundred Philistines with an oxgoad. He too saved Israel.

Deborah

After Ehud died, the Israelites once again did evil in the eyes of the LORD. [2]So the LORD sold them into the hands of Jabin, a king of Canaan, who reigned in Hazor. The commander of his army was Sisera, who lived in Harosheth Haggoyim. [3]Because he had nine hundred iron chariots and had cruelly oppressed the Israelites for twenty years, they cried to the LORD for help.

[4]Deborah, a prophetess, the wife of Lappidoth, was leading[d] Israel at that time. [5]She held court under the

---

Gross!

Check out Judges 3:12–30. Eglon, the evil king of Moab, was so fat that when Ehud stabbed him with an 18-inch sword, it— *Blooop!*—disappeared into Eglon's belly, handle and all! Ehud got away because Eglon's servants thought the king was ... well, *busy*. They were waiting for the air to clear before checking on him.

---

[a] 19 Or *the stone quarries;* also in verse 26   [b] 20 The meaning of the Hebrew for this phrase is uncertain.   [c] 23 The meaning of the Hebrew for this word is uncertain.   [d] 4 Traditionally *judging*

Palm of Deborah between Ramah and Bethel in the hill country of Ephraim, and the Israelites came to her to have their disputes decided. ⁶She sent for Barak son of Abinoam from Kedesh in Naphtali and said to him, "The LORD, the God of Israel, commands you: 'Go, take with you ten thousand men of Naphtali and Zebulun and lead the way to Mount Tabor. ⁷I will lure Sisera, the commander of Jabin's army, with his chariots and his troops to the Kishon River and give him into your hands.' "

⁸Barak said to her, "If you go with me, I will go; but if you don't go with me, I won't go."

⁹"Very well," Deborah said, "I will go with you. But because of the way you are going about this,ᵃ the honor will not be yours, for the LORD will hand Sisera over to a woman." So Deborah went with Barak to Kedesh, ¹⁰where he summoned Zebulun and Naphtali. Ten thousand men followed him, and Deborah also went with him.

¹¹Now Heber the Kenite had left the other Kenites, the descendants of Hobab, Moses' brother-in-law,ᵇ and pitched his tent by the great tree in Zaanannim near Kedesh.

¹²When they told Sisera that Barak son of Abinoam had gone up to Mount Tabor, ¹³Sisera gathered together his nine hundred iron chariots and all the men with him, from Harosheth Haggoyim to the Kishon River.

¹⁴Then Deborah said to Barak, "Go! This is the day the LORD has given Sisera into your hands. Has not the LORD gone ahead of you?" So Barak went down Mount Tabor, followed by ten thousand men. ¹⁵At Barak's advance, the LORD routed Sisera and all his chariots and army by

ᵃ 9 Or But on the expedition you are undertaking
ᵇ 11 Or father-in-law

Warrior Woman and Judge
READ JUDGES 4

The "judges" referred to in the book of Judges did a lot more than what judges today do. They were the leaders of the nation of Israel. Specifically, God used them to bring military deliverance to his people. Deborah was a judge and a warrior in a time when women were looked upon as little more than property. But God showed the Israelites that women are worthy of respect. When Deborah told Barak to go against Sisera's army, "Barak said to her, 'If you go with me, I will go; but if you don't go with me, I won't go' " (verse 8). Deborah didn't bat an eye. She went to battle with him and they won. Deborah was Israel's only female judge, but she wasn't second-rate. She had more guts than Barak, who was supposed to be a mighty warrior. In God's eyes, neither men nor women are better than the other. Neither are closer to God than the other. They're just different (see Acts 2:18 and Galatians 3:28). As men, we need to realize that. Instead of putting down women and girls, we need to work together with them and respect them.

Your next reading is on page 308.

Gross!

Check out Judges 4:21–22. Jael—another tough woman— pounded a tent peg through Sisera's temple, right through his brain, and out the other side into the ground! Some lady! No doubt she chose his temple because it's the weakest part of the skull.

the sword, and Sisera abandoned his chariot and fled on foot. ¹⁶But Barak pursued the chariots and army as far as Harosheth Haggoyim. All the troops of Sisera fell by the sword; not a man was left.

¹⁷Sisera, however, fled on foot to the tent of Jael, the wife of Heber the Kenite, because there were friendly relations between Jabin king of Hazor and the clan of Heber the Kenite.

¹⁸Jael went out to meet Sisera and said to him, "Come, my lord, come right in. Don't be afraid." So he entered her tent, and she put a covering over him.

¹⁹"I'm thirsty," he said. "Please give me some water." She opened a skin of milk, gave him a drink, and covered him up.

²⁰"Stand in the doorway of the tent," he told her. "If someone comes by and asks you, 'Is anyone here?' say 'No.' "

²¹But Jael, Heber's wife, picked up a tent peg and a hammer and went quietly to him while he lay fast asleep, exhausted. She drove the peg through his temple into the ground, and he died.

²²Barak came by in pursuit of Sisera, and Jael went out to meet him. "Come," she said, "I will show you the man you're looking for." So he went in with her, and there lay Sisera with the tent peg through his temple—dead.

²³On that day God subdued Jabin, the Canaanite king, before the Israelites. ²⁴And the hand of the Israelites grew stronger and stronger against Jabin, the Canaanite king, until they destroyed him.

The Song of Deborah

5 On that day Deborah and Barak son of Abinoam sang this song:

²"When the princes in Israel take the lead,
　when the people willingly offer themselves—
　praise the LORD!

³"Hear this, you kings! Listen, you rulers!
　I will sing to*a* the LORD, I will sing;
　I will make music to*b* the LORD, the God of Israel.

⁴"O LORD, when you went out from Seir,
　when you marched from the land of Edom,
the earth shook, the heavens poured,
　the clouds poured down water.
⁵The mountains quaked before the LORD, the One of Sinai,
　before the LORD, the God of Israel.

⁶"In the days of Shamgar son of Anath,
　in the days of Jael, the roads were abandoned;
　travelers took to winding paths.
⁷Village life*c* in Israel ceased,
　ceased until I,*d* Deborah, arose,
　arose a mother in Israel.

a 3 Or of　b 3 Or / with song I will praise　c 7 Or Warriors　d 7 Or you

8 When they chose new gods,
  war came to the city gates,
and not a shield or spear was seen
  among forty thousand in Israel.
9 My heart is with Israel's princes,
  with the willing volunteers among
    the people.
  Praise the LORD!

10 "You who ride on white donkeys,
  sitting on your saddle blankets,
and you who walk along the road,
consider 11 the voice of the singers[a] at
    the watering places.
  They recite the righteous acts of the
    LORD,
  the righteous acts of his warriors[b] in
    Israel.

  "Then the people of the LORD
    went down to the city gates.
12 'Wake up, wake up, Deborah!
    Wake up, wake up, break out in
      song!
  Arise, O Barak!
    Take captive your captives, O son of
      Abinoam.'

13 "Then the men who were left
    came down to the nobles;
  the people of the LORD
    came to me with the mighty.
14 Some came from Ephraim, whose
      roots were in Amalek;
    Benjamin was with the people who
      followed you.
  From Makir captains came down,
    from Zebulun those who bear a
      commander's staff.
15 The princes of Issachar were with
      Deborah;
    yes, Issachar was with Barak,
      rushing after him into the valley.
  In the districts of Reuben
    there was much searching of heart.
16 Why did you stay among the campfires[c]
    to hear the whistling for the flocks?
  In the districts of Reuben
    there was much searching of heart.
17 Gilead stayed beyond the Jordan.
    And Dan, why did he linger by the
      ships?
  Asher remained on the coast
    and stayed in his coves.
18 The people of Zebulun risked their very
      lives;
    so did Naphtali on the heights of the
      field.

19 "Kings came, they fought;
    the kings of Canaan fought
  at Taanach by the waters of Megiddo,
    but they carried off no silver, no
      plunder.
20 From the heavens the stars fought,
    from their courses they fought
      against Sisera.
21 The river Kishon swept them away,
    the age-old river, the river Kishon.
  March on, my soul; be strong!
22 Then thundered the horses' hoofs—
    galloping, galloping go his mighty
      steeds.
23 'Curse Meroz,' said the angel of the
      LORD.
    'Curse its people bitterly,
  because they did not come to help the
      LORD,
    to help the LORD against the mighty.'

24 "Most blessed of women be Jael,
    the wife of Heber the Kenite,
  most blessed of tent-dwelling
      women.
25 He asked for water, and she gave him
      milk;
    in a bowl fit for nobles she brought
      him curdled milk.
26 Her hand reached for the tent peg,
    her right hand for the workman's
      hammer.
  She struck Sisera, she crushed his
      head,
    she shattered and pierced his
      temple.
27 At her feet he sank,
    he fell; there he lay.
  At her feet he sank, he fell;
    where he sank, there he fell—dead.

28 "Through the window peered Sisera's
      mother;
    behind the lattice she cried out,
  'Why is his chariot so long in coming?
    Why is the clatter of his chariots
      delayed?'
29 The wisest of her ladies answer her;
    indeed, she keeps saying to herself,
30 'Are they not finding and dividing the
      spoils:
    a girl or two for each man,
  colorful garments as plunder for
      Sisera,
    colorful garments embroidered,

a 11 Or *archers;* the meaning of the Hebrew for this word is
uncertain.   *b 11* Or *villagers*   *c 16* Or *saddlebags*

highly embroidered garments for my
neck—
all this as plunder?'

31 "So may all your enemies perish,
O Lord!
But may they who love you be like
the sun
when it rises in its strength."

Then the land had peace forty years.

Gideon

6 Again the Israelites did evil in the eyes of the Lord, and for seven years he gave them into the hands of the Midianites. 2Because the power of Midian was so oppressive, the Israelites prepared shelters for themselves in mountain clefts, caves and strongholds. 3Whenever the Israelites planted their crops, the Midianites, Amalekites and other eastern peoples invaded the country. 4They camped on the land and ruined the crops all the way to Gaza and did not spare a living thing for Israel, neither sheep nor cattle nor donkeys. 5They came up with their livestock and their tents like swarms of locusts. It was impossible to count the men and their camels; they invaded the land to ravage it. 6Midian so impoverished the Israelites that they cried out to the Lord for help.

7When the Israelites cried to the Lord because of Midian, 8he sent them a prophet, who said, "This is what the Lord, the God of Israel, says: I brought you up out of Egypt, out of the land of slavery. 9I snatched you from the power of Egypt and from the hand of all your oppressors. I drove them from before you and gave you their land. 10I said to you, 'I am the Lord your God; do not worship the gods of the Amorites, in whose land you live.' But you have not listened to me."

11The angel of the Lord came and sat down under the oak in Ophrah that belonged to Joash the Abiezrite, where his

I'm Just a Pipsqueak

READ JUDGES 6:1–16

Gideon was not what you would call a chest-thumping "he-man." He was just a regular guy who didn't think he amounted to much. But God didn't need a weight lifter for the job he had in mind—to drive off the Midianite oppressors. God knew Gideon would do just fine. Our man wasn't convinced. " 'But Lord,' Gideon asked, 'how can I save Israel? My clan is the weakest in Manasseh, and I am the least in my family' " (verse 15). When Gideon finally stopped looking in his mirror and said "yes" to God, God turned him into such a hero that people were begging him to be king (see Judges 8:22)! So remember, physical strength won't stop you from doing what God calls you to do. Boys and men come in different sizes—some are stronger, some are shrimpier—but God can do great things through you no matter how big or strong you are.

Your next reading is on page 311.

son Gideon was threshing wheat in a winepress to keep it from the Midianites. [12]When the angel of the LORD appeared to Gideon, he said, "The LORD is with you, mighty warrior."

[13]"But sir," Gideon replied, "if the LORD is with us, why has all this happened to us? Where are all his wonders that our fathers told us about when they said, 'Did not the LORD bring us up out of Egypt?' But now the LORD has abandoned us and put us into the hand of Midian."

[14]The LORD turned to him and said, "Go in the strength you have and save Israel out of Midian's hand. Am I not sending you?"

[15]"But Lord,[a] Gideon asked, "how can I save Israel? My clan is the weakest in Manasseh, and I am the least in my family."

[16]The LORD answered, "I will be with you, and you will strike down all the Midianites together."

[17]Gideon replied, "If now I have found favor in your eyes, give me a sign that it is really you talking to me. [18]Please do not go away until I come back and bring my offering and set it before you."

And the LORD said, "I will wait until you return."

[19]Gideon went in, prepared a young goat, and from an ephah[b] of flour he made bread without yeast. Putting the meat in a basket and its broth in a pot, he brought them out and offered them to him under the oak.

[20]The angel of God said to him, "Take the meat and the unleavened bread, place them on this rock, and pour out the broth." And Gideon did so. [21]With the tip of the staff that was in his hand, the angel of the LORD touched the meat and the unleavened bread. Fire flared from the rock, consuming the meat and the bread. And the angel of the LORD disappeared. [22]When Gideon realized that it was the angel of the LORD, he exclaimed, "Ah, Sovereign LORD! I have seen the angel of the LORD face to face!"

[23]But the LORD said to him, "Peace! Do not be afraid. You are not going to die."

[24]So Gideon built an altar to the LORD there and called it The LORD is Peace. To this day it stands in Ophrah of the Abiezrites.

[25]That same night the LORD said to him, "Take the second bull from your father's herd, the one seven years old.[c] Tear down your father's altar to Baal and cut down the Asherah pole[d] beside it. [26]Then build a proper kind of[e] altar to the LORD your God on the top of this height. Using the wood of the Asherah pole that you cut down, offer the second[f] bull as a burnt offering."

[27]So Gideon took ten of his servants and did as the LORD told him. But because he was afraid of his family and the men of the town, he did it at night rather than in the daytime.

[28]In the morning when the men of the town got up, there was Baal's altar, demolished, with the Asherah pole beside it cut down and the second bull sacrificed on the newly built altar!

[29]They asked each other, "Who did this?"

When they carefully investigated, they were told, "Gideon son of Joash did it."

[30]The men of the town demanded of Joash, "Bring out your son. He must die, because he has broken down Baal's altar and cut down the Asherah pole beside it."

[31]But Joash replied to the hostile crowd around him, "Are you going to plead Baal's cause? Are you trying to save him? Whoever fights for him shall be put to death by morning! If Baal really is a god, he can defend himself when someone breaks down his altar." [32]So that day they called Gideon "Jerub-Baal,[g]" saying, "Let Baal contend with him," because he broke down Baal's altar.

[33]Now all the Midianites, Amalekites and other eastern peoples joined forces and crossed over the Jordan and camped in the Valley of Jezreel. [34]Then the Spirit of the LORD came upon Gideon, and he blew a trumpet, summoning the Abiezrites to follow him. [35]He sent messengers throughout Manasseh, calling them to arms, and also into Asher, Zebulun and Naphtali, so that they too went up to meet them.

[36]Gideon said to God, "If you will save Israel by my hand as you have promised— [37]look, I will place a wool fleece on the threshing floor. If there is dew only on the fleece and all the ground is dry, then I will know that you will save Israel by my hand, as you said." [38]And that is what happened. Gideon rose early the next day; he

---

[a] 15 Or sir   [b] 19 That is, probably about 3/5 bushel (about 22 liters)   [c] 25 Or Take a full-grown, mature bull from your father's herd   [d] 25 That is, a symbol of the goddess Asherah; here and elsewhere in Judges   [e] 26 Or build with layers of stone an   [f] 26 Or full-grown; also in verse 28   [g] 32 Jerub-Baal means let Baal contend.

squeezed the fleece and wrung out the dew—a bowlful of water.

³⁹Then Gideon said to God, "Do not be angry with me. Let me make just one more request. Allow me one more test with the fleece. This time make the fleece dry and the ground covered with dew." ⁴⁰That night God did so. Only the fleece was dry; all the ground was covered with dew.

Gideon Defeats the Midianites

Early in the morning, Jerub-Baal (that is, Gideon) and all his men camped at the spring of Harod. The camp of Midian was north of them in the valley near the hill of Moreh. ²The LORD said to Gideon, "You have too many men for me to deliver Midian into their hands. In order that Israel may not boast against me that her own strength has saved her, ³announce now to the people, 'Anyone who trembles with fear may turn back and leave Mount Gilead.' " So twen-

ty-two thousand men left, while ten thousand remained.

⁴But the LORD said to Gideon, "There are still too many men. Take them down to the water, and I will sift them for you there. If I say, 'This one shall go with you,' he shall go; but if I say, 'This one shall not go with you,' he shall not go."

⁵So Gideon took the men down to the water. There the LORD told him, "Separate those who lap the water with their tongues like a dog from those who kneel down to drink." ⁶Three hundred men lapped with their hands to their mouths. All the rest got down on their knees to drink.

⁷The LORD said to Gideon, "With the three hundred men that lapped I will save you and give the Midianites into your hands. Let all the other men go, each to his own place." ⁸So Gideon sent the rest of the Israelites to their tents but kept the three hundred, who took over the provisions and trumpets of the others.

Now the camp of Midian lay below him

Make It Stick

READ JUDGES 6:36–40

Gideon's experiments with the fleece teach two important words: "trust" and "obey." As Gideon learned, God guides in many ways. You just have to trust God to lead you, and leave *how* he does it up to him. And don't forget to obey what he asks! Write "trust and obey" in huge letters on a sticky note.

in the valley. [9]During that night the LORD said to Gideon, "Get up, go down against the camp, because I am going to give it into your hands. [10]If you are afraid to attack, go down to the camp with your servant Purah [11]and listen to what they are saying. Afterward, you will be encouraged to attack the camp." So he and Purah his servant went down to the outposts of the camp. [12]The Midianites, the Amalekites and all the other eastern peoples had settled in the valley, thick as locusts. Their camels could no more be counted than the sand on the seashore.

[13]Gideon arrived just as a man was telling a friend his dream. "I had a dream," he was saying. "A round loaf of barley bread came tumbling into the Midianite camp. It struck the tent with such force that the tent overturned and collapsed."

[14]His friend responded, "This can be nothing other than the sword of Gideon son of Joash, the Israelite. God has given the Midianites and the whole camp into his hands."

[15]When Gideon heard the dream and its interpretation, he worshiped God. He returned to the camp of Israel and called out, "Get up! The LORD has given the Midianite camp into your hands." [16]Dividing the three hundred men into three companies, he placed trumpets and empty jars in the hands of all of them, with torches inside.

[17]"Watch me," he told them. "Follow my lead. When I get to the edge of the camp, do exactly as I do. [18]When I and all who are with me blow our trumpets, then from all around the camp blow yours and shout, 'For the LORD and for Gideon.' "

[19]Gideon and the hundred men with him reached the edge of the camp at the beginning of the middle watch, just after they had changed the guard. They blew their trumpets and broke the jars that were in their hands. [20]The three companies blew the trumpets and smashed the jars. Grasping the torches in their left hands and holding in their right hands the trumpets they were to blow, they shouted, "A sword for the LORD and for Gideon!" [21]While each man held his position

Want Wisdom? It's Yours!

READ JUDGES 7:1–22

If anyone *ever* needed wisdom, Gideon did. God had reduced his army from 32,000 men to 10,000 to a mere 300—and the guys who were left weren't even necessarily the top fighters. The only reason God let them stay was because of the way they drank water. Gideon's enemies, on the other hand, were 135,000 Midianites. Their war-camels "could no more be counted than the sand on the seashore" (verse 12). Gideon didn't even have enough men to fight a battle, but God gave him the wildest battle strategy you ever heard of. And it worked! When Gideon's men blew 300 trumpets at once in the middle of the night, and 300 torches suddenly appeared out of nowhere, the enemy troops were so terrified they started killing each other. Do like Gideon did—ask God for wisdom. He *will* give it to you (see James 1:5).

Your next reading is on page 319.

around the camp, all the Midianites ran, crying out as they fled.

²²When the three hundred trumpets sounded, the LORD caused the men throughout the camp to turn on each other with their swords. The army fled to Beth Shittah toward Zererah as far as the border of Abel Meholah near Tabbath. ²³Israelites from Naphtali, Asher and all Manasseh were called out, and they pursued the Midianites. ²⁴Gideon sent messengers throughout the hill country of Ephraim, saying, "Come down against the Midianites and seize the waters of the Jordan ahead of them as far as Beth Barah."

So all the men of Ephraim were called out and they took the waters of the Jordan as far as Beth Barah. ²⁵They also captured two of the Midianite leaders, Oreb and Zeeb. They killed Oreb at the rock of Oreb, and Zeeb at the winepress of Zeeb. They pursued the Midianites and brought the heads of Oreb and Zeeb to Gideon, who was by the Jordan.

Zebah and Zalmunna

Now the Ephraimites asked Gideon, "Why have you treated us like this? Why didn't you call us when you went to fight Midian?" And they criticized him sharply.

²But he answered them, "What have I accomplished compared to you? Aren't the gleanings of Ephraim's grapes better than the full grape harvest of Abiezer? ³God gave Oreb and Zeeb, the Midianite leaders, into your hands. What was I able to do compared to you?" At this, their resentment against him subsided.

⁴Gideon and his three hundred men, exhausted yet keeping up the pursuit, came to the Jordan and crossed it. ⁵He said to the men of Succoth, "Give my troops some bread; they are worn out, and I am still pursuing Zebah and Zalmunna, the kings of Midian."

⁶But the officials of Succoth said, "Do you already have the hands of Zebah and Zalmunna in your possession? Why should we give bread to your troops?"

⁷Then Gideon replied, "Just for that, when the LORD has given Zebah and Zalmunna into my hand, I will tear your flesh with desert thorns and briers."

⁸From there he went up to Peniel*a* and made the same request of them, but they answered as the men of Succoth had. ⁹So

he said to the men of Peniel, "When I return in triumph, I will tear down this tower."

¹⁰Now Zebah and Zalmunna were in Karkor with a force of about fifteen thousand men, all that were left of the armies of the eastern peoples; a hundred and twenty thousand swordsmen had fallen. ¹¹Gideon went up by the route of the nomads east of Nobah and Jogbehah and fell upon the unsuspecting army. ¹²Zebah and Zalmunna, the two kings of Midian, fled, but he pursued them and captured them, routing their entire army.

¹³Gideon son of Joash then returned from the battle by the Pass of Heres. ¹⁴He caught a young man of Succoth and questioned him, and the young man wrote down for him the names of the seventy-seven officials of Succoth, the elders of the town. ¹⁵Then Gideon came and said to the men of Succoth, "Here are Zebah and Zalmunna, about whom you taunted me by saying, 'Do you already have the hands of Zebah and Zalmunna in your possession? Why should we give bread to your exhausted men?' " ¹⁶He took the elders of the town and taught the men of Succoth a lesson by punishing them with desert thorns and briers. ¹⁷He also pulled down the tower of Peniel and killed the men of the town.

¹⁸Then he asked Zebah and Zalmunna, "What kind of men did you kill at Tabor?"

"Men like you," they answered, "each one with the bearing of a prince."

¹⁹Gideon replied, "Those were my brothers, the sons of my own mother. As surely as the LORD lives, if you had spared their lives, I would not kill you." ²⁰Turning to Jether, his oldest son, he said, "Kill them!" But Jether did not draw his sword, because he was only a boy and was afraid.

²¹Zebah and Zalmunna said, "Come, do it yourself. 'As is the man, so is his strength.' " So Gideon stepped forward and killed them, and took the ornaments off their camels' necks.

Gideon's Ephod

²²The Israelites said to Gideon, "Rule over us—you, your son and your grandson—because you have saved us out of the hand of Midian."

²³But Gideon told them, "I will not rule

---

*a 8 Hebrew Penuel, a variant of Peniel; also in verses 9 and 17 over you, nor will my son rule over you. The LORD will rule over you." 24And he said, "I do have one request, that each of you give me an earring from your share of the plunder." (It was the custom of the Ishmaelites to wear gold earrings.)

25They answered, "We'll be glad to give them." So they spread out a garment, and each man threw a ring from his plunder onto it. 26The weight of the gold rings he asked for came to seventeen hundred shekels, a not counting the ornaments, the pendants and the purple garments worn by the kings of Midian or the chains that were on their camels' necks. 27Gideon made the gold into an ephod, which he placed in Ophrah, his town. All Israel prostituted themselves by worshiping it there, and it became a snare to Gideon and his family.

Gideon's Death

28Thus Midian was subdued before the Israelites and did not raise its head again. During Gideon's lifetime, the land enjoyed peace forty years.

29Jerub-Baal son of Joash went back home to live. 30He had seventy sons of his own, for he had many wives. 31His concubine, who lived in Shechem, also bore him a son, whom he named Abimelech. 32Gideon son of Joash died at a good old age and was buried in the tomb of his father Joash in Ophrah of the Abiezrites.

33No sooner had Gideon died than the Israelites again prostituted themselves to the Baals. They set up Baal-Berith as their god and 34did not remember the LORD their God, who had rescued them from the hands of all their enemies on every side. 35They also failed to show kindness to the family of Jerub-Baal (that is, Gideon) for all the good things he had done for them.

Abimelech

Abimelech son of Jerub-Baal went to his mother's brothers in Shechem and said to them and to all his mother's clan, 2"Ask all the citizens of Shechem, 'Which is better for you: to have all seventy of Jerub-Baal's sons rule over you, or just one man?' Remember, I am your flesh and blood."

3When the brothers repeated all this to the citizens of Shechem, they were inclined to follow Abimelech, for they said, "He is our brother." 4They gave him sev-

enty shekels b of silver from the temple of Baal-Berith, and Abimelech used it to hire reckless adventurers, who became his followers. 5He went to his father's home in Ophrah and on one stone murdered his seventy brothers, the sons of Jerub-Baal. But Jotham, the youngest son of Jerub-Baal, escaped by hiding. 6Then all the citizens of Shechem and Beth Millo gathered beside the great tree at the pillar in Shechem to crown Abimelech king.

7When Jotham was told about this, he climbed up on the top of Mount Gerizim and shouted to them, "Listen to me, citizens of Shechem, so that God may listen to you. 8One day the trees went out to anoint a king for themselves. They said to the olive tree, 'Be our king.'

9"But the olive tree answered, 'Should I give up my oil, by which both gods and men are honored, to hold sway over the trees?'

10"Next, the trees said to the fig tree, 'Come and be our king.'

11"But the fig tree replied, 'Should I give up my fruit, so good and sweet, to hold sway over the trees?'

12"Then the trees said to the vine, 'Come and be our king.'

13"But the vine answered, 'Should I give up my wine, which cheers both gods and men, to hold sway over the trees?'

14"Finally all the trees said to the thornbush, 'Come and be our king.'

15"The thornbush said to the trees, 'If you really want to anoint me king over you, come and take refuge in my shade; but if not, then let fire come out of the thornbush and consume the cedars of Lebanon!'

16"Now if you have acted honorably and in good faith when you made Abimelech king, and if you have been fair to Jerub-Baal and his family, and if you have treated him as he deserves— 17and to think that my father fought for you, risked his life to rescue you from the hand of Midian 18(but today you have revolted against my father's family, murdered his seventy sons on a single stone, and made Abimelech, the son of his slave girl, king over the citizens of Shechem because he is your brother)— 19if then you have acted honorably and in good faith toward Jerub-Baal and his family today, may Abimelech be your joy, and

---

a 26 That is, about 43 pounds (about 19.5 kilograms)
b 4 That is, about 1 3/4 pounds (about 0.8 kilogram)

may you be his, too! ²⁰But if you have not, let fire come out from Abimelech and consume you, citizens of Shechem and Beth Millo, and let fire come out from you, citizens of Shechem and Beth Millo, and consume Abimelech!"

²¹Then Jotham fled, escaping to Beer, and he lived there because he was afraid of his brother Abimelech.

²²After Abimelech had governed Israel three years, ²³God sent an evil spirit between Abimelech and the citizens of Shechem, who acted treacherously against Abimelech. ²⁴God did this in order that the crime against Jerub-Baal's seventy sons, the shedding of their blood, might be avenged on their brother Abimelech and on the citizens of Shechem, who had helped him murder his brothers. ²⁵In opposition to him these citizens of Shechem set men on the hilltops to ambush and rob everyone who passed by, and this was reported to Abimelech.

²⁶Now Gaal son of Ebed moved with his brothers into Shechem, and its citizens put their confidence in him. ²⁷After they had gone out into the fields and gathered the grapes and trodden them, they held a festival in the temple of their god. While they were eating and drinking, they cursed Abimelech. ²⁸Then Gaal son of Ebed said, "Who is Abimelech, and who is Shechem, that we should be subject to him? Isn't he Jerub-Baal's son, and isn't Zebul his deputy? Serve the men of Hamor, Shechem's father! Why should we serve Abimelech? ²⁹If only this people were under my command! Then I would get rid of him. I would say to Abimelech, 'Call out your whole army!'"ᵃ

³⁰When Zebul the governor of the city heard what Gaal son of Ebed said, he was very angry. ³¹Under cover he sent messengers to Abimelech, saying, "Gaal son of Ebed and his brothers have come to Shechem and are stirring up the city against you. ³²Now then, during the night you and your men should come and lie in wait in the fields. ³³In the morning at sunrise, advance against the city. When Gaal and his men come out against you, do whatever your hand finds to do."

³⁴So Abimelech and all his troops set out by night and took up concealed positions near Shechem in four companies. ³⁵Now Gaal son of Ebed had gone out and was standing at the entrance to the

city gate just as Abimelech and his soldiers came out from their hiding place.

³⁶When Gaal saw them, he said to Zebul, "Look, people are coming down from the tops of the mountains!"

Zebul replied, "You mistake the shadows of the mountains for men."

³⁷But Gaal spoke up again: "Look, people are coming down from the center of the land, and a company is coming from the direction of the soothsayers' tree."

³⁸Then Zebul said to him, "Where is your big talk now, you who said, 'Who is Abimelech that we should be subject to him?' Aren't these the men you ridiculed? Go out and fight them!"

³⁹So Gaal led outᵇ the citizens of Shechem and fought Abimelech. ⁴⁰Abimelech chased him, and many fell wounded in the flight—all the way to the entrance to the gate. ⁴¹Abimelech stayed in Arumah, and Zebul drove Gaal and his brothers out of Shechem.

⁴²The next day the people of Shechem went out to the fields, and this was reported to Abimelech. ⁴³So he took his men, divided them into three companies and set an ambush in the fields. When he saw the people coming out of the city, he rose to attack them. ⁴⁴Abimelech and the companies with him rushed forward to a position at the entrance to the city gate. Then two companies rushed upon those in the fields and struck them down. ⁴⁵All that day Abimelech pressed his attack against the city until he had captured it and killed its people. Then he destroyed the city and scattered salt over it.

⁴⁶On hearing this, the citizens in the tower of Shechem went into the stronghold of the temple of El-Berith. ⁴⁷When Abimelech heard that they had assembled there, ⁴⁸he and all his men went up Mount Zalmon. He took an ax and cut off some branches, which he lifted to his shoulders. He ordered the men with him, "Quick! Do what you have seen me do!" ⁴⁹So all the men cut branches and followed Abimelech. They piled them against the stronghold and set it on fire over the people inside. So all the people in the tower of Shechem, about a thousand men and women, also died.

⁵⁰Next Abimelech went to Thebez and

ᵃ 29 Septuagint; Hebrew him." Then he said to Abimelech, "Call out your whole army!"   ᵇ 39 Or Gaal went out in the sight of besieged it and captured it. 51Inside the city, however, was a strong tower, to which all the men and women— all the people of the city—fled. They locked themselves in and climbed up on the tower roof. 52Abimelech went to the tower and stormed it. But as he approached the entrance to the tower to set it on fire, 53a woman dropped an upper millstone on his head and cracked his skull.

54Hurriedly he called to his armor-bearer, "Draw your sword and kill me, so that they can't say, 'A woman killed him.' " So his servant ran him through, and he died. 55When the Israelites saw that Abimelech was dead, they went home.

56Thus God repaid the wickedness that Abimelech had done to his father by murdering his seventy brothers. 57God also made the men of Shechem pay for all their wickedness. The curse of Jotham son of Jerub-Baal came on them.

Tola

After the time of Abimelech a man of Issachar, Tola son of Puah, the son of Dodo, rose to save Israel. He lived in Shamir, in the hill country of Ephraim. 2He led*a* Israel twenty-three years; then he died, and was buried in Shamir.

Jair

3He was followed by Jair of Gilead, who led Israel twenty-two years. 4He had thirty sons, who rode thirty donkeys. They controlled thirty towns in Gilead, which to this day are called Havvoth Jair.*b* 5When Jair died, he was buried in Kamon.

Jephthah

6Again the Israelites did evil in the eyes of the LORD. They served the Baals and the Ashtoreths, and the gods of Aram, the gods of Sidon, the gods of Moab, the gods of the Ammonites and the gods of the Philistines. And because the Israelites forsook the LORD and no longer served him, 7he became angry with them. He sold them into the hands of the Philistines and the Ammonites, 8who that year shattered and crushed them. For eighteen years they oppressed all the Israelites on the east side of the Jordan in Gilead, the land of the Amorites. 9The Ammonites also crossed the Jordan to fight against Judah, Benjamin and the house of Ephraim; and Israel was in great distress. 10Then the Israelites cried out to the LORD, "We have sinned against you, forsaking our God and serving the Baals."

11The LORD replied, "When the Egyptians, the Amorites, the Ammonites, the Philistines, 12the Sidonians, the Amalekites and the Maonites*c* oppressed you and you cried to me for help, did I not save you from their hands? 13But you have forsaken me and served other gods, so I will no longer save you. 14Go and cry out to the gods

Gross!

Check out Judges 9:52–53. Abominable Abimelech had slaughtered nearly all of his brothers, then proclaimed himself king. Three years later, his number was up. He was attacking Thebez—where everyone was holed up in a tower—when a woman saw him below, took aim and dropped a millstone on his head.

---

a 2 Traditionally *judged*; also in verse 3   *b 4* Or *called the settlements of Jair*
c 12 Hebrew; some Septuagint manuscripts *Midianites*

Get a Load of This...

Check out Judges 10:1. Tola was a guy with some strange-sounding names in his family. Can you imagine having a dad named Puah or a grandpa named Dodo? Speaking of strange names, did you know Jesus had a fish in his family tree?—*Salmon* (Matthew 1:4).

you have chosen. Let them save you when you are in trouble!"

15But the Israelites said to the LORD, "We have sinned. Do with us whatever you think best, but please rescue us now." 16Then they got rid of the foreign gods among them and served the LORD. And he could bear Israel's misery no longer.

17When the Ammonites were called to arms and camped in Gilead, the Israelites assembled and camped at Mizpah. 18The leaders of the people of Gilead said to each other, "Whoever will launch the attack against the Ammonites will be the head of all those living in Gilead."

11 Jephthah the Gileadite was a mighty warrior. His father was Gilead; his mother was a prostitute. 2Gilead's wife also bore him sons, and when they were grown up, they drove Jephthah away. "You are not going to get any inheritance in our family," they said, "because you are the son of another woman." 3So Jephthah fled from his brothers and settled in the land of Tob, where a group of adventurers gathered around him and followed him.

4Some time later, when the Ammonites made war on Israel, 5the elders of Gilead went to get Jephthah from the land of Tob. 6"Come," they said, "be our commander, so we can fight the Ammonites."

7Jephthah said to them, "Didn't you hate me and drive me from my father's house? Why do you come to me now, when you're in trouble?"

8The elders of Gilead said to him, "Nevertheless, we are turning to you now; come with us to fight the Ammonites, and you will be our head over all who live in Gilead."

9Jephthah answered, "Suppose you take me back to fight the Ammonites and the LORD gives them to me—will I really be your head?"

10The elders of Gilead replied, "The LORD is our witness; we will certainly do as you say." 11So Jephthah went with the elders of Gilead, and the people made him head and commander over them. And he repeated all his words before the LORD in Mizpah.

12Then Jephthah sent messengers to the Ammonite king with the question: "What do you have against us that you have attacked our country?"

13The king of the Ammonites answered Jephthah's messengers, "When Israel came up out of Egypt, they took away my land from the Arnon to the Jabbok, all the way to the Jordan. Now give it back peaceably."

14Jephthah sent back messengers to the Ammonite king, 15saying:

"This is what Jephthah says: Israel did not take the land of Moab or the land of the Ammonites. 16But when they came up out of Egypt, Israel went through the desert to the Red Sea*a* and on to Kadesh. 17Then Israel sent messengers to the king of Edom, saying, 'Give us permission to go through

a 16 Hebrew Yam Suph; that is, Sea of Reeds

your country,' but the king of Edom would not listen. They sent also to the king of Moab, and he refused. So Israel stayed at Kadesh.

18"Next they traveled through the desert, skirted the lands of Edom and Moab, passed along the eastern side of the country of Moab, and camped on the other side of the Arnon. They did not enter the territory of Moab, for the Arnon was its border.

19"Then Israel sent messengers to Sihon king of the Amorites, who ruled in Heshbon, and said to him, 'Let us pass through your country to our own place.' 20Sihon, however, did not trust Israel[a] to pass through his territory. He mustered all his men and encamped at Jahaz and fought with Israel.

21"Then the LORD, the God of Israel, gave Sihon and all his men into Israel's hands, and they defeated them. Israel took over all the land of the Amorites who lived in that country, 22capturing all of it from the Arnon to the Jabbok and from the desert to the Jordan.

23"Now since the LORD, the God of Israel, has driven the Amorites out before his people Israel, what right have you to take it over? 24Will you not take what your god Chemosh gives you? Likewise, whatever the LORD our God has given us, we will possess. 25Are you better than Balak son of Zippor, king of Moab? Did he ever quarrel with Israel or fight with them? 26For three hundred years Israel occupied Heshbon, Aroer, the surrounding settlements and all the towns along the Arnon. Why didn't you retake them during that time? 27I have not wronged you, but you are doing me wrong by waging war against me. Let the LORD, the Judge,[b] decide the dispute this day between the Israelites and the Ammonites."

28The king of Ammon, however, paid no attention to the message Jephthah sent him.

29Then the Spirit of the LORD came upon Jephthah. He crossed Gilead and Manasseh, passed through Mizpah of Gilead, and from there he advanced against the Ammonites. 30And Jephthah made a vow

to the LORD: "If you give the Ammonites into my hands, 31whatever comes out of the door of my house to meet me when I return in triumph from the Ammonites will be the LORD's, and I will sacrifice it as a burnt offering."

32Then Jephthah went over to fight the Ammonites, and the LORD gave them into his hands. 33He devastated twenty towns from Aroer to the vicinity of Minnith, as far as Abel Keramim. Thus Israel subdued Ammon.

34When Jephthah returned to his home in Mizpah, who should come out to meet him but his daughter, dancing to the sound of tambourines! She was an only child. Except for her he had neither son nor daughter. 35When he saw her, he tore his clothes and cried, "Oh! My daughter! You have made me miserable and wretched, because I have made a vow to the LORD that I cannot break."

36"My father," she replied, "you have given your word to the LORD. Do to me just as you promised, now that the LORD has avenged you of your enemies, the Ammonites. 37But grant me this one request," she said. "Give me two months to roam the hills and weep with my friends, because I will never marry."

38"You may go," he said. And he let her go for two months. She and the girls went into the hills and wept because she would never marry. 39After the two months, she returned to her father and he did to her as he had vowed. And she was a virgin.

From this comes the Israelite custom 40that each year the young women of Israel go out for four days to commemorate the daughter of Jephthah the Gileadite.

Jephthah and Ephraim

The men of Ephraim called out their forces, crossed over to Zaphon and said to Jephthah, "Why did you go to fight the Ammonites without calling us to go with you? We're going to burn down your house over your head."

2Jephthah answered, "I and my people were engaged in a great struggle with the Ammonites, and although I called, you didn't save me out of their hands. 3When

---

a 20 Or however, would not make an agreement for Israel
b 27 Or Ruler

Get a Load of This...

Check out Judges 12:14. Abdon, a judge, had 40 sons and 30 grandsons, and they all rode around on 70 donkeys. Can you imagine how they must have looked? "Make way for 70 donkeys!" Or— "Incoming dust storm! Here comes the royal family!"

I saw that you wouldn't help, I took my life in my hands and crossed over to fight the Ammonites, and the LORD gave me the victory over them. Now why have you come up today to fight me?"

4Jephthah then called together the men of Gilead and fought against Ephraim. The Gileadites struck them down because the Ephraimites had said, "You Gileadites are renegades from Ephraim and Manasseh." 5The Gileadites captured the fords of the Jordan leading to Ephraim, and whenever a survivor of Ephraim said, "Let me cross over," the men of Gilead asked him, "Are you an Ephraimite?" If he replied, "No," 6they said, "All right, say 'Shibboleth.' " If he said, "Sibboleth," because he could not pronounce the word correctly, they seized him and killed him at the fords of the Jordan. Forty-two thousand Ephraimites were killed at that time.

7Jephthah led*a* Israel six years. Then Jephthah the Gileadite died, and was buried in a town in Gilead.

Ibzan, Elon and Abdon

8After him, Ibzan of Bethlehem led Israel. 9He had thirty sons and thirty daughters. He gave his daughters away in marriage to those outside his clan, and for his sons he brought in thirty young women as wives from outside his clan. Ibzan led Israel seven years. 10Then Ibzan died, and was buried in Bethlehem.

11After him, Elon the Zebulunite led Israel ten years. 12Then Elon died, and was buried in Aijalon in the land of Zebulun.

13After him, Abdon son of Hillel, from Pirathon, led Israel. 14He had forty sons and thirty grandsons, who rode on seventy donkeys. He led Israel eight years. 15Then Abdon son of Hillel died, and was buried at Pirathon in Ephraim, in the hill country of the Amalekites.

The Birth of Samson

13 Again the Israelites did evil in the eyes of the LORD, so the LORD delivered them into the hands of the Philistines for forty years.

2A certain man of Zorah, named Manoah, from the clan of the Danites, had a wife who was sterile and remained childless. 3The angel of the LORD appeared to her and said, "You are sterile and childless, but you are going to conceive and have a son. 4Now see to it that you drink no wine or other fermented drink and that you do not eat anything unclean, 5because you will conceive and give birth to a son. No razor may be used on his head, because the boy is to be a Nazirite, set apart to God from birth, and he will begin the deliverance of Israel from the hands of the Philistines."

6Then the woman went to her husband and told him, "A man of God came to me. He looked like an angel of God, very awesome. I didn't ask him where he came from, and he didn't tell me his name. 7But he said to me, 'You will conceive and give birth to a son. Now

a 7 Traditionally judged; also in verses 8–14

then, drink no wine or other fermented drink and do not eat anything unclean, because the boy will be a Nazirite of God from birth until the day of his death.' "

8Then Manoah prayed to the LORD: "O Lord, I beg you, let the man of God you sent to us come again to teach us how to bring up the boy who is to be born."

9God heard Manoah, and the angel of God came again to the woman while she was out in the field; but her husband Manoah was not with her. 10The woman hurried to tell her husband, "He's here! The man who appeared to me the other day!"

11Manoah got up and followed his wife. When he came to the man, he said, "Are you the one who talked to my wife?"

"I am," he said.

12So Manoah asked him, "When your words are fulfilled, what is to be the rule for the boy's life and work?"

13The angel of the LORD answered, "Your wife must do all that I have told her. 14She must not eat anything that comes from the grapevine, nor drink any wine or other fermented drink nor eat anything

unclean. She must do everything I have commanded her."

15Manoah said to the angel of the LORD, "We would like you to stay until we prepare a young goat for you."

16The angel of the LORD replied, "Even though you detain me, I will not eat any of your food. But if you prepare a burnt offering, offer it to the LORD." (Manoah did not realize that it was the angel of the LORD.)

17Then Manoah inquired of the angel of the LORD, "What is your name, so that we may honor you when your word comes true?"

18He replied, "Why do you ask my name? It is beyond understanding. a"

19Then Manoah took a young goat, together with the grain offering, and sacrificed it on a rock to the LORD. And the LORD did an amazing thing while Manoah and his wife watched: 20As the flame blazed up from the altar toward heaven, the angel of the LORD ascended in the flame. Seeing this, Manoah and his wife fell with

a 18 Or is wonderful

Talent: Pounding Philistines

READ JUDGES 13

Before Samson was born, God told his mother her son would be a "Nazirite," a dude with a special calling from God. "No razor may be used on his head, because the boy is to be a Nazirite . . . and he will begin the deliverance of Israel from the hands of the Philistines" (verse 5). God knew the job he had for Samson before Samson was born, just like he knows all of us (see Psalm 139). He gave Samson a special gift—superhuman strength—to match what he was called to do—pound on the Philistines. God also gives us gifts to match what he wants us to do. If you're called to be a doctor, for example, he'll give you gifts and a personality type to match. So pay attention to what you *like* to do and are *good* at. They are clues to what God is calling you to do.

Your next reading is on page 320.

their faces to the ground. ²¹When the angel of the LORD did not show himself again to Manoah and his wife, Manoah realized that it was the angel of the LORD.

²²"We are doomed to die!" he said to his wife. "We have seen God!"

²³But his wife answered, "If the LORD had meant to kill us, he would not have accepted a burnt offering and grain offering from our hands, nor shown us all these things or now told us this."

²⁴The woman gave birth to a boy and named him Samson. He grew and the LORD blessed him, ²⁵and the Spirit of the LORD began to stir him while he was in Mahaneh Dan, between Zorah and Eshtaol.

Samson's Marriage

14 Samson went down to Timnah and saw there a young Philistine woman. ²When he returned, he said to his father and mother, "I have seen a Philistine woman in Timnah; now get her for me as my wife."

³His father and mother replied, "Isn't there an acceptable woman among your relatives or among all our people? Must you go to the uncircumcised Philistines to get a wife?"

But Samson said to his father, "Get her for me. She's the right one for me." ⁴(His parents did not know that this was from the LORD, who was seeking an occasion to confront the Philistines; for at that time they were ruling over Israel.) ⁵Samson went down to Timnah together with his father and mother. As they approached the vineyards of Timnah, suddenly a young lion came roaring toward him. ⁶The Spirit of the LORD came upon him in power so that he tore the lion apart with his bare hands as he might have torn a young goat. But he told neither his father nor his mother what he had done. ⁷Then he went down and talked with the woman, and he liked her.

⁸Some time later, when he went back to marry her, he turned aside to look at

Larger Than Life

READ JUDGES 14

Samson was called by God, sure, but he made some crazy decisions, such as hanging out with the wrong crowd and marrying someone who didn't share his commitment to the Lord. "His father and mother replied, 'Isn't there an acceptable woman among your relatives or among all our people? Must you go to the uncircumcised Philistines to get a wife?'" (verse 3). But Samson wouldn't listen. He was proud and spoiled. He had muscles, he was called by God and he thought, "Man! I am larger than life." He was strong all right, but he made terrible choices when it came to relationships. Time after time, Samson's temper and poor decisions pushed him *out* of favor with others. A man of God should grow *in* favor with people and with God. The key to getting along with others is seeing people as better than yourself (Romans 12:3). Not that you're less important than them, but you need to consider other people's needs before you consider your own.

Your next reading is on page 322.

the lion's carcass. In it was a swarm of bees and some honey, [9]which he scooped out with his hands and ate as he went along. When he rejoined his parents, he gave them some, and they too ate it. But he did not tell them that he had taken the honey from the lion's carcass.

[10]Now his father went down to see the woman. And Samson made a feast there, as was customary for bridegrooms. [11]When he appeared, he was given thirty companions.

[12]"Let me tell you a riddle," Samson said to them. "If you can give me the answer within the seven days of the feast, I will give you thirty linen garments and thirty sets of clothes. [13]If you can't tell me the answer, you must give me thirty linen garments and thirty sets of clothes."

"Tell us your riddle," they said. "Let's hear it."

[14]He replied,

"Out of the eater, something to eat;
    out of the strong, something
        sweet."

For three days they could not give the answer.

[15]On the fourth[a] day, they said to Samson's wife, "Coax your husband into explaining the riddle for us, or we will burn you and your father's household to death. Did you invite us here to rob us?"

[16]Then Samson's wife threw herself on him, sobbing, "You hate me! You don't really love me. You've given my people a riddle, but you haven't told me the answer."

"I haven't even explained it to my father or mother," he replied, "so why should I explain it to you?" [17]She cried the whole seven days of the feast. So on the seventh day he finally told her, because she continued to press him. She in turn explained the riddle to her people.

[18]Before sunset on the seventh day the men of the town said to him,

"What is sweeter than honey?
    What is stronger than a lion?"

Samson said to them,

"If you had not plowed with my heifer,
    you would not have solved my
        riddle."

[19]Then the Spirit of the LORD came upon him in power. He went down to Ashkelon, struck down thirty of their men, stripped them of their belongings and gave their clothes to those who had explained the riddle. Burning with anger, he went up to his father's house. [20]And Samson's wife was given to the friend who had attended him at his wedding.

Samson's Vengeance on the Philistines

15 Later on, at the time of wheat harvest, Samson took a young goat and went to visit his wife. He said, "I'm going to my wife's room." But her father would not let him go in.

[2]"I was so sure you thoroughly hated her," he said, "that I gave her to your friend. Isn't her younger sister more attractive? Take her instead."

[3]Samson said to them, "This time I have a right to get even with the Philistines; I will really harm them." [4]So he went out and caught three hundred foxes and tied them tail to tail in pairs. He then fastened a torch to every pair of tails, [5]lit the torches and let the foxes loose in the standing grain of the Philistines. He burned up the shocks and standing grain, together with the vineyards and olive groves.

[6]When the Philistines asked, "Who did this?" they were told, "Samson, the Timnite's son-in-law, because his wife was given to his friend."

So the Philistines went up and burned her and her father to death. [7]Samson said to them, "Since you've acted like this, I won't stop until I get my revenge on you." [8]He attacked them viciously and slaughtered many of them. Then he went down and stayed in a cave in the rock of Etam.

[9]The Philistines went up and camped in Judah, spreading out near Lehi. [10]The men of Judah asked, "Why have you come to fight us?"

"We have come to take Samson prisoner," they answered, "to do to him as he did to us."

[11]Then three thousand men from Judah went down to the cave in the rock of Etam and said to Samson, "Don't you realize that the Philistines are rulers over us? What have you done to us?"

He answered, "I merely did to them what they did to me."

[a] 15 Some Septuagint manuscripts and Syriac; Hebrew *seventh*

¹²They said to him, "We've come to tie you up and hand you over to the Philistines."

Samson said, "Swear to me that you won't kill me yourselves."

¹³"Agreed," they answered. "We will only tie you up and hand you over to them. We will not kill you." So they bound him with two new ropes and led him up from the rock. ¹⁴As he approached Lehi, the Philistines came toward him shouting. The Spirit of the LORD came upon him in power. The ropes on his arms became like charred flax, and the bindings dropped from his hands. ¹⁵Finding a fresh jawbone of a donkey, he grabbed it and struck down a thousand men.

¹⁶Then Samson said,

"With a donkey's jawbone
    I have made donkeys of them. ᵃ
With a donkey's jawbone
    I have killed a thousand men."

¹⁷When he finished speaking, he threw away the jawbone; and the place was called Ramath Lehi. ᵇ

¹⁸Because he was very thirsty, he cried out to the LORD, "You have given your servant this great victory. Must I now die of thirst and fall into the hands of the uncircumcised?" ¹⁹Then God opened up the hollow place in Lehi, and water came out of it. When Samson drank, his strength returned and he revived. So the spring was called En Hakkore, ᶜ and it is still there in Lehi.

²⁰Samson led ᵈ Israel for twenty years in the days of the Philistines.

Samson and Delilah

16 One day Samson went to Gaza, where he saw a prostitute. He went in to spend the night with her. ²The people of Gaza were

---

ᵃ 16 Or made a heap or two; the Hebrew for donkey sounds like the Hebrew for heap.   ᵇ 17 Ramath Lehi means jawbone hill.   ᶜ 19 En Hakkore means caller's spring.
ᵈ 20 Traditionally judged

GET STRONGER

What's Your "Jawbone"?

READ JUDGES 15:1–16

Samson's conflicts with the Philistines resulted in his own people wanting to hand him over to the enemy. The Philistines came out one thousand strong, armed to the teeth, and went after Samson. Suddenly, before their very eyes, he became like the Incredible Hulk. He reached for a donkey's jawbone and it was "lights out" for the bad guys. "The Spirit of the LORD came upon him in power. The ropes on his arms became like charred flax, and the bindings dropped from his hands. Finding a fresh jawbone of a donkey, he grabbed it and struck down a thousand men" (verses 14–15). Each of us also needs to find the special job God has called us to. Just as Samson reached for the jawbone, we need to reach out for our calling, whether it's a computer mouse or a basketball. As we develop our gifts, we reach the spot where we're doing what God called us to do. Then God's Spirit increases our gifts, making us the best we can possibly be.

Your next reading is on page 324.

told, "Samson is here!" So they surrounded the place and lay in wait for him all night at the city gate. They made no move during the night, saying, "At dawn we'll kill him."

³But Samson lay there only until the middle of the night. Then he got up and took hold of the doors of the city gate, together with the two posts, and tore them loose, bar and all. He lifted them to his shoulders and carried them to the top of the hill that faces Hebron.

⁴Some time later, he fell in love with a woman in the Valley of Sorek whose name was Delilah. ⁵The rulers of the Philistines went to her and said, "See if you can lure him into showing you the secret of his great strength and how we can overpower him so we may tie him up and subdue him. Each one of us will give you eleven hundred shekels\ᵃ of silver."

⁶So Delilah said to Samson, "Tell me the secret of your great strength and how you can be tied up and subdued."

⁷Samson answered her, "If anyone ties me with seven fresh thongs\ᵇ that have not been dried, I'll become as weak as any other man."

⁸Then the rulers of the Philistines brought her seven fresh thongs that had not been dried, and she tied him with them. ⁹With men hidden in the room, she called to him, "Samson, the Philistines are upon you!" But he snapped the thongs as easily as a piece of string snaps when it comes close to a flame. So the secret of his strength was not discovered.

¹⁰Then Delilah said to Samson, "You have made a fool of me; you lied to me. Come now, tell me how you can be tied."

¹¹He said, "If anyone ties me securely with new ropes that have never been used, I'll become as weak as any other man."

¹²So Delilah took new ropes and tied him with them. Then, with men hidden in the room, she called to him, "Samson, the Philistines are upon you!" But he snapped the ropes off his arms as if they were threads.

¹³Delilah then said to Samson, "Until now, you have been making a fool of me and lying to me. Tell me how you can be tied."

He replied, "If you weave the seven braids of my head into the fabric ⌐on the loom⌐ and tighten it with the pin, I'll become as weak as any other man." So while he was sleeping, Delilah took the seven braids of his head, wove them into the fabric ¹⁴andᶜ tightened it with the pin.

Again she called to him, "Samson, the Philistines are upon you!" He awoke from his sleep and pulled up the pin and the loom, with the fabric.

¹⁵Then she said to him, "How can you say, 'I love you,' when you won't confide in me? This is the third time you have made a fool of me and haven't told me the secret of your great strength." ¹⁶With such nagging

Gross!

Check out Judges 15:15. The donkey's jawbone Samson used to kill 1,000 Philistines was "fresh," which means it probably came from a rotting donkey carcass. Yum, Yum. A donkey's jawbone isn't much of a weapon compared to a sword. Then again, it depends on *who's* holding it.

ᵃ 5 That is, about 28 pounds (about 13 kilograms)   ᵇ 7 Or *bowstrings*; also in verses 8 and 9   ᶜ 13,14 Some Septuagint manuscripts; Hebrew "⌐I can⌐ if you weave the seven braids of my head into the fabric ⌐on the loom⌐." ¹⁴So she

she prodded him day after day until he was tired to death.

[17]So he told her everything. "No razor has ever been used on my head," he said, "because I have been a Nazirite set apart to God since birth. If my head were shaved, my strength would leave me, and I would become as weak as any other man."

[18]When Delilah saw that he had told her everything, she sent word to the rulers of the Philistines, "Come back once more; he has told me everything." So the rulers of the Philistines returned with the silver in their hands. [19]Having put him to sleep on her lap, she called a man to shave off the seven braids of his hair, and so began to subdue him. [a] And his strength left him.

[20]Then she called, "Samson, the Philistines are upon you!"

He awoke from his sleep and thought, "I'll go out as before and shake myself free." But he did not know that the LORD had left him.

[21]Then the Philistines seized him, gouged out his eyes and took him down to Gaza. Binding him with bronze shackles, they set him to grinding in the prison. [22]But the hair on his head began to grow again after it had been shaved.

The Death of Samson

[23]Now the rulers of the Philistines assembled to offer a great sacrifice to Dagon their god and to celebrate, saying, "Our god has delivered Samson, our enemy, into our hands."

[24]When the people saw him, they praised their god, saying,

"Our god has delivered our enemy
    into our hands,
the one who laid waste our land
    and multiplied our slain."

[25]While they were in high spirits, they shouted, "Bring out Samson to entertain

[a] 19 Hebrew; some Septuagint manuscripts *and he began to weaken*

Rip and Run

READ JUDGES 16:1–3

The Philistines were trying to kill Samson—again. They thought they would be *verrrry* clever by locking the city gates so he couldn't get out. Not smart. "Samson . . . took hold of the doors of the city gate, together with the two posts, and tore them loose, bar and all. He lifted them to his shoulders and carried them to the top of the hill that faces Hebron" (verse 3). The gate of Gaza was built to withstand a military siege. Not only did Samson bench press that gate—it could've weighed a couple of tons—but he had the sustained strength to carry it up a hill outside the city! Like Samson, sometimes you need sudden bursts of strength. Other times you need long-term endurance. You should develop both types of strength. There's nothing wrong with being strong. You just need to use your strength for good purposes.

Your next reading is on page 325.

us." So they called Samson out of the prison, and he performed for them.

When they stood him among the pillars, 26Samson said to the servant who held his hand, "Put me where I can feel the pillars that support the temple, so that I may lean against them." 27Now the temple was crowded with men and women; all the rulers of the Philistines were there, and on the roof were about three thousand men and women watching Samson perform. 28Then Samson prayed to the LORD, "O Sovereign LORD, remember me. O God, please strengthen me just once more, and let me with one blow get revenge on the Philistines for my two eyes." 29Then Samson reached toward the two central pillars on which the temple stood. Bracing himself against them, his right hand on the one and his left hand on the other, 30Samson said, "Let me die with the Philistines!" Then he pushed with all his might, and down came the temple on the rulers and all the people in it. Thus he killed many more when he died than while he lived.

31Then his brothers and his father's whole family went down to get him. They brought him back and buried him between Zorah and Eshtaol in the tomb of Manoah his father. He had led*a* Israel twenty years.

Micah's Idols

17 Now a man named Micah from the hill country of Ephraim 2said to his mother, "The eleven hundred shekels*b* of silver that were taken from you and about which I heard you utter a curse—I have that silver with me; I took it."

Then his mother said, "The LORD bless you, my son!"

3When he returned the eleven hundred shekels of silver to his mother, she said, "I solemnly consecrate my silver to the LORD for my son to make a carved image and a cast idol. I will give it back to you."

4So he returned the silver to his mother,

a 31 Traditionally *judged*   *b 2* That is, about 28 pounds (about 13 kilograms)

Live Smarter, Not Harder

READ JUDGES 16:4–6, 15–30

Samson suffered terribly for his unwise decisions. After Delilah tricked him, he was captured and tortured by the Philistines. Samson later repented of his mistakes and came back to God. He prayed to God, "Please strengthen me just once more, and let me with one blow get revenge on the Philistines" (verse 28). God gave Samson that final burst of superhuman strength, allowing him to destroy a temple-full of Philistine leaders, plus 3,000 spectators on the roof, in one shot—but it cost Samson his life, too. You can get wisdom one of two ways: Learn it from others—mentors, parents and the Bible—and get it right from the start, and receive the rewards; or you can refuse good advice, make terrible mistakes, then finally repent and get it right. One way is easy; the other hard. Samson learned the hard way, but a man of God can see the wisdom of getting it right the first time.

Your next reading is on page 334.

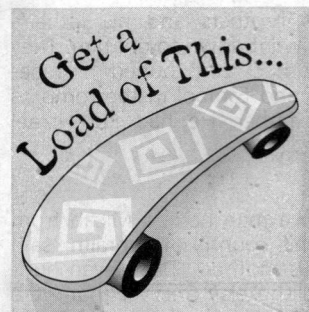

Get a Load of This...

Check out Judges 16:19–20. Samson's long hair was *not* the source of his great strength. *God* was! As a Nazarite, Samson had a vow to God not to cut his hair (Judges 13:5). When he allowed his locks to be snipped, his vow was broken and God left him. When Samson prayed for strength one last time, God made his arms stronger than steel, one last time, and he was able to push the pagan temple's two central wooden pillars from their stone bases. If you could do just one super-natural feat of strength in your lifetime, what would it be?

and she took two hundred shekels[a] of silver and gave them to a silversmith, who made them into the image and the idol. And they were put in Micah's house.

5Now this man Micah had a shrine, and he made an ephod and some idols and installed one of his sons as his priest. 6In those days Israel had no king; everyone did as he saw fit.

7A young Levite from Bethlehem in Judah, who had been living within the clan of Judah, 8left that town in search of some other place to stay. On his way[b] he came to Micah's house in the hill country of Ephraim.

9Micah asked him, "Where are you from?"

"I'm a Levite from Bethlehem in Judah," he said, "and I'm looking for a place to stay."

10Then Micah said to him, "Live with me and be my father and priest, and I'll give you ten shekels[c] of silver a year, your clothes and your food." 11So the Levite agreed to live with him, and the young man was to him like one of his sons. 12Then Micah installed the Levite, and the young man became his priest and lived in his house. 13And Micah said, "Now I know that the LORD will be good to me, since this Levite has become my priest."

Danites Settle in Laish

18 In those days Israel had no king.

And in those days the tribe of the Danites was seeking a place of their own where they might settle, because they had not yet come into an inheritance among the tribes of Israel. 2So the Danites sent five warriors from Zorah and Eshtaol to spy out the land and explore it. These men represented all their clans. They told them, "Go, explore the land."

The men entered the hill country of Ephraim and came to the house of Micah, where they spent the night. 3When they were near Micah's house, they recognized the voice of the young Levite; so they turned in there and asked him, "Who brought you here? What are you doing in this place? Why are you here?"

4He told them what Micah had done for him, and said, "He has hired me and I am his priest."

5Then they said to him, "Please inquire of God to learn whether our journey will be successful."

6The priest answered them, "Go in peace. Your journey has the LORD's approval."

7So the five men left and came to Laish, where they saw that the people were living in safety, like the Sidonians, unsuspecting and secure. And since their land lacked nothing, they were prosperous.[d] Also, they lived a long way from the Sidonians and had no relationship with anyone else.[e]

8When they returned to Zorah and Eshtaol, their brothers asked them, "How did you find things?"

9They answered, "Come on, let's attack them! We

a 4 That is, about 5 pounds (about 2.3 kilograms) b 8 Or To carry on his profession c 10 That is, about 4 ounces (about 110 grams) d 7 The meaning of the Hebrew for this clause is uncertain. e 7 Hebrew; some Septuagint manuscripts with the Arameans have seen that the land is very good. Aren't you going to do something? Don't hesitate to go there and take it over. 10When you get there, you will find an unsuspecting people and a spacious land that God has put into your hands, a land that lacks nothing whatever."

11Then six hundred men from the clan of the Danites, armed for battle, set out from Zorah and Eshtaol. 12On their way they set up camp near Kiriath Jearim in Judah. This is why the place west of Kiriath Jearim is called Mahaneh Dan*a* to this day. 13From there they went on to the hill country of Ephraim and came to Micah's house.

14Then the five men who had spied out the land of Laish said to their brothers, "Do you know that one of these houses has an ephod, other household gods, a carved image and a cast idol? Now you know what to do." 15So they turned in there and went to the house of the young Levite at Micah's place and greeted him. 16The six hundred Danites, armed for battle, stood at the entrance to the gate. 17The five men who had spied out the land went inside and took the carved image, the ephod, the other household gods and the cast idol while the priest and the six hundred armed men stood at the entrance to the gate.

18When these men went into Micah's house and took the carved image, the ephod, the other household gods and the cast idol, the priest said to them, "What are you doing?"

19They answered him, "Be quiet! Don't say a word. Come with us, and be our father and priest. Isn't it better that you serve a tribe and clan in Israel as priest rather than just one man's household?" 20Then the priest was glad. He took the ephod, the other household gods and the carved image and went along with the people. 21Putting their little children, their livestock and their possessions in front of them, they turned away and left.

22When they had gone some distance from Micah's house, the men who lived near Micah were called together and overtook the Danites. 23As they shouted after them, the Danites turned and said to Micah, "What's the matter with you that you called out your men to fight?"

24He replied, "You took the gods I made, and my priest, and went away.

What else do I have? How can you ask, 'What's the matter with you?' "

25The Danites answered, "Don't argue with us, or some hot-tempered men will attack you, and you and your family will lose your lives." 26So the Danites went their way, and Micah, seeing that they were too strong for him, turned around and went back home.

27Then they took what Micah had made, and his priest, and went on to Laish, against a peaceful and unsuspecting people. They attacked them with the sword and burned down their city. 28There was no one to rescue them because they lived a long way from Sidon and had no relationship with anyone else. The city was in a valley near Beth Rehob.

The Danites rebuilt the city and settled there. 29They named it Dan after their forefather Dan, who was born to Israel—though the city used to be called Laish. 30There the Danites set up for themselves the idols, and Jonathan son of Gershom, the son of Moses,*b* and his sons were priests for the tribe of Dan until the time of the captivity of the land. 31They continued to use the idols Micah had made, all the time the house of God was in Shiloh.

A Levite and His Concubine

19 In those days Israel had no king. Now a Levite who lived in a remote area in the hill country of Ephraim took a concubine from Bethlehem in Judah. 2But she was unfaithful to him. She left him and went back to her father's house in Bethlehem, Judah. After she had been there four months, 3her husband went to her to persuade her to return. He had with him his servant and two donkeys. She took him into her father's house, and when her father saw him, he gladly welcomed him. 4His father-in-law, the girl's father, prevailed upon him to stay; so he remained with him three days, eating and drinking, and sleeping there.

5On the fourth day they got up early and he prepared to leave, but the girl's father said to his son-in-law, "Refresh yourself with something to eat; then you can go." 6So the two of them sat down to eat and drink together. Afterward the girl's father

---

a 12 Mahaneh Dan means Dan's camp.   *b 30* An ancient Hebrew scribal tradition, some Septuagint manuscripts and Vulgate; Masoretic Text *Manasseh* said, "Please stay tonight and enjoy yourself." 7And when the man got up to go, his father-in-law persuaded him, so he stayed there that night. 8On the morning of the fifth day, when he rose to go, the girl's father said, "Refresh yourself. Wait till afternoon!" So the two of them ate together.

9Then when the man, with his concubine and his servant, got up to leave, his father-in-law, the girl's father, said, "Now look, it's almost evening. Spend the night here; the day is nearly over. Stay and enjoy yourself. Early tomorrow morning you can get up and be on your way home." 10But, unwilling to stay another night, the man left and went toward Jebus (that is, Jerusalem), with his two saddled donkeys and his concubine.

11When they were near Jebus and the day was almost gone, the servant said to his master, "Come, let's stop at this city of the Jebusites and spend the night."

12His master replied, "No. We won't go into an alien city, whose people are not Israelites. We will go on to Gibeah." 13He added, "Come, let's try to reach Gibeah or Ramah and spend the night in one of those places." 14So they went on, and the sun set as they neared Gibeah in Benjamin. 15There they stopped to spend the night. They went and sat in the city square, but no one took them into his home for the night.

16That evening an old man from the hill country of Ephraim, who was living in Gibeah (the men of the place were Benjamites), came in from his work in the fields. 17When he looked and saw the traveler in the city square, the old man asked, "Where are you going? Where did you come from?"

18He answered, "We are on our way from Bethlehem in Judah to a remote area in the hill country of Ephraim where I live. I have been to Bethlehem in Judah and now I am going to the house of the LORD. No one has taken me into his house. 19We have both straw and fodder for our donkeys and bread and wine for ourselves your servants—me, your maidservant, and the young man with us. We don't need anything."

20"You are welcome at my house," the old man said. "Let me supply whatever you need. Only don't spend the night in the square." 21So he took him into his house and fed his donkeys. After they had

washed their feet, they had something to eat and drink.

22While they were enjoying themselves, some of the wicked men of the city surrounded the house. Pounding on the door, they shouted to the old man who owned the house, "Bring out the man who came to your house so we can have sex with him."

23The owner of the house went outside and said to them, "No, my friends, don't be so vile. Since this man is my guest, don't do this disgraceful thing. 24Look, here is my virgin daughter, and his concubine. I will bring them out to you now, and you can use them and do to them whatever you wish. But to this man, don't do such a disgraceful thing."

25But the men would not listen to him. So the man took his concubine and sent her outside to them, and they raped her and abused her throughout the night, and at dawn they let her go. 26At daybreak the woman went back to the house where her master was staying, fell down at the door and lay there until daylight.

27When her master got up in the morning and opened the door of the house and stepped out to continue on his way, there lay his concubine, fallen in the doorway of the house, with her hands on the threshold. 28He said to her, "Get up; let's go." But there was no answer. Then the man put her on his donkey and set out for home.

29When he reached home, he took a knife and cut up his concubine, limb by limb, into twelve parts and sent them into all the areas of Israel. 30Everyone who saw it said, "Such a thing has never been seen or done, not since the day the Israelites came up out of Egypt. Think about it! Consider it! Tell us what to do!"

Israelites Fight the Benjamites

20 Then all the Israelites from Dan to Beersheba and from the land of Gilead came out as one man and assembled before the LORD in Mizpah. 2The leaders of all the people of the tribes of Israel took their places in the assembly of the people of God, four hundred thousand soldiers armed with swords. 3(The Benjamites heard that the Israelites had gone up to Mizpah.) Then the Israelites said, "Tell us how this awful thing happened."

⁴So the Levite, the husband of the murdered woman, said, "I and my concubine came to Gibeah in Benjamin to spend the night. ⁵During the night the men of Gibeah came after me and surrounded the house, intending to kill me. They raped my concubine, and she died. ⁶I took my concubine, cut her into pieces and sent one piece to each region of Israel's inheritance, because they committed this lewd and disgraceful act in Israel. ⁷Now, all you Israelites, speak up and give your verdict."

⁸All the people rose as one man, saying, "None of us will go home. No, not one of us will return to his house. ⁹But now this is what we'll do to Gibeah: We'll go up against it as the lot directs. ¹⁰We'll take ten men out of every hundred from all the tribes of Israel, and a hundred from a thousand, and a thousand from ten thousand, to get provisions for the army. Then, when the army arrives at Gibeahᵃ in Benjamin, it can give them what they deserve for all this vileness done in Israel." ¹¹So all the men of Israel got together and united as one man against the city.

¹²The tribes of Israel sent men throughout the tribe of Benjamin, saying, "What about this awful crime that was committed among you? ¹³Now surrender those wicked men of Gibeah so that we may put them to death and purge the evil from Israel."

But the Benjamites would not listen to their fellow Israelites. ¹⁴From their towns they came together at Gibeah to fight against the Israelites. ¹⁵At once the Benjamites mobilized twenty-six thousand swordsmen from their towns, in addition to seven hundred chosen men from those living in Gibeah. ¹⁶Among all these soldiers there were seven hundred chosen men who were left-handed, each of whom could sling a stone at a hair and not miss.

¹⁷Israel, apart from Benjamin, mustered four hundred thousand swordsmen, all of them fighting men.

¹⁸The Israelites went up to Bethelᵇ and inquired of God. They said, "Who of us shall go first to fight against the Benjamites?"

The LORD replied, "Judah shall go first."

¹⁹The next morning the Israelites got up and pitched camp near Gibeah. ²⁰The men of Israel went out to fight the Benjamites and took up battle positions against them at Gibeah. ²¹The Benjamites came

out of Gibeah and cut down twenty-two thousand Israelites on the battlefield that day. ²²But the men of Israel encouraged one another and again took up their positions where they had stationed themselves the first day. ²³The Israelites went up and wept before the LORD until evening, and they inquired of the LORD. They said, "Shall we go up again to battle against the Benjamites, our brothers?"

The LORD answered, "Go up against them."

²⁴Then the Israelites drew near to Benjamin the second day. ²⁵This time, when the Benjamites came out from Gibeah to oppose them, they cut down another eighteen thousand Israelites, all of them armed with swords.

²⁶Then the Israelites, all the people, went up to Bethel, and there they sat weeping before the LORD. They fasted that day until evening and presented burnt offerings and fellowship offeringsᶜ to the LORD. ²⁷And the Israelites inquired of the LORD. (In those days the ark of the covenant of God was there, ²⁸with Phinehas son of Eleazar, the son of Aaron, ministering before it.) They asked, "Shall we go up again to battle with Benjamin our brother, or not?"

The LORD responded, "Go, for tomorrow I will give them into your hands."

²⁹Then Israel set an ambush around Gibeah. ³⁰They went up against the Benjamites on the third day and took up positions against Gibeah as they had done before. ³¹The Benjamites came out to meet them and were drawn away from the city. They began to inflict casualties on the Israelites as before, so that about thirty men fell in the open field and on the roads—the one leading to Bethel and the other to Gibeah.

³²While the Benjamites were saying, "We are defeating them as before," the Israelites were saying, "Let's retreat and draw them away from the city to the roads."

³³All the men of Israel moved from their places and took up positions at Baal Tamar, and the Israelite ambush charged out of its place on the westᵈ of Gibeah.ᵉ

ᵃ 10 One Hebrew manuscript; most Hebrew manuscripts *Geba*, a variant of *Gibeah*   ᵇ 18 Or *to the house of God*; also in verse 26   ᶜ 26 Traditionally *peace offerings*   ᵈ 33 Some Septuagint manuscripts and Vulgate; the meaning of the Hebrew for this word is uncertain.   ᵉ 33 Hebrew *Geba*, a variant of *Gibeah*

³⁴Then ten thousand of Israel's finest men made a frontal attack on Gibeah. The fighting was so heavy that the Benjamites did not realize how near disaster was. ³⁵The LORD defeated Benjamin before Israel, and on that day the Israelites struck down 25,100 Benjamites, all armed with swords. ³⁶Then the Benjamites saw that they were beaten.

Now the men of Israel had given way before Benjamin, because they relied on the ambush they had set near Gibeah. ³⁷The men who had been in ambush made a sudden dash into Gibeah, spread out and put the whole city to the sword. ³⁸The men of Israel had arranged with the ambush that they should send up a great cloud of smoke from the city, ³⁹and then the men of Israel would turn in the battle.

The Benjamites had begun to inflict casualties on the men of Israel (about thirty), and they said, "We are defeating them as in the first battle." ⁴⁰But when the column of smoke began to rise from the city, the Benjamites turned and saw the smoke of the whole city going up into the sky. ⁴¹Then the men of Israel turned on them, and the men of Benjamin were terrified, because they realized that disaster had come upon them. ⁴²So they fled before the Israelites in the direction of the desert, but they could not escape the battle. And the men of Israel who came out of the towns cut them down there. ⁴³They surrounded the Benjamites, chased them and easilyᵃ overran them in the vicinity of Gibeah on the east. ⁴⁴Eighteen thousand Benjamites fell, all of them valiant fighters. ⁴⁵As they turned and fled toward the desert to the rock of Rimmon, the Israelites cut down five thousand men along the roads. They kept pressing after the Benjamites as far as Gidom and struck down two thousand more.

⁴⁶On that day twenty-five thousand Benjamite swordsmen fell, all of them valiant fighters. ⁴⁷But six hundred men turned and fled into the desert to the rock of Rimmon, where they stayed four months. ⁴⁸The men of Israel went back to Benjamin and put all the towns to the sword, including the animals and everything else they found. All the towns they came across they set on fire.

Wives for the Benjamites

 The men of Israel had taken an oath at Mizpah: "Not one of us will give his daughter in marriage to a Benjamite."

²The people went to Bethel,ᵇ where they sat before God until evening, raising their voices and weeping bitterly. ³"O LORD, the God of Israel," they cried, "why has this happened to Israel? Why should one tribe be missing from Israel today?"

⁴Early the next day the people built an altar and presented burnt offerings and fellowship offerings.ᶜ

⁵Then the Israelites asked, "Who from all the tribes of Israel has failed to assemble before the LORD?" For they had taken a solemn oath that anyone who failed to assemble before the LORD at Mizpah should certainly be put to death.

⁶Now the Israelites grieved for their brothers, the Benjamites. "Today one tribe is cut off from Israel," they said. ⁷"How can we provide wives for those who are left, since we have taken an oath by the LORD not to give them any of our daughters in marriage?" ⁸Then they asked, "Which one of the tribes of Israel failed to assemble before the LORD at Mizpah?" They discovered that no one from Jabesh Gilead had come to the camp for the assembly. ⁹For when they counted the people, they found that none of the people of Jabesh Gilead were there.

¹⁰So the assembly sent twelve thousand fighting men with instructions to go to Jabesh Gilead and put to the sword those living there, including the women and children. ¹¹"This is what you are to do," they said. "Kill every male and every woman who is not a virgin." ¹²They found among the people living in Jabesh Gilead four hundred young women who had never slept with a man, and they took them to the camp at Shiloh in Canaan.

¹³Then the whole assembly sent an offer of peace to the Benjamites at the rock of Rimmon. ¹⁴So the Benjamites returned at that time and were given the women of Jabesh Gilead who had been spared. But there were not enough for all of them.

¹⁵The people grieved for Benjamin, because the LORD had made a gap in the

ᵃ 43 The meaning of the Hebrew for this word is uncertain.   ᵇ 2 Or to the house of God   ᶜ 4 Traditionally peace offerings tribes of Israel. [16]And the elders of the assembly said, "With the women of Benjamin destroyed, how shall we provide wives for the men who are left? [17]The Benjamite survivors must have heirs," they said, "so that a tribe of Israel will not be wiped out. [18]We can't give them our daughters as wives, since we Israelites have taken this oath: 'Cursed be anyone who gives a wife to a Benjamite.' [19]But look, there is the annual festival of the LORD in Shiloh, to the north of Bethel, and east of the road that goes from Bethel to Shechem, and to the south of Lebonah."

[20]So they instructed the Benjamites, saying, "Go and hide in the vineyards [21]and watch. When the girls of Shiloh come out to join in the dancing, then rush from the vineyards and each of you seize a wife from the girls of Shiloh and go to the land of Benjamin. [22]When their fathers or brothers complain to us, we will say to them, 'Do us a kindness by helping them, because we did not get wives for them during the war, and you are innocent, since you did not give your daughters to them.' "

[23]So that is what the Benjamites did. While the girls were dancing, each man caught one and carried her off to be his wife. Then they returned to their inheritance and rebuilt the towns and settled in them.

[24]At that time the Israelites left that place and went home to their tribes and clans, each to his own inheritance.

[25]In those days Israel had no king; everyone did as he saw fit.

RUTH

Who wrote this book?
The author of Ruth is unknown.

Why was this book written?
Ruth shows that some people trusted God even in the times of the judges.

What happens in this book?
Ruth, a young Moabite widow, travels to Israel with her Jewish mother-in-law and marries a good man there.

What do we learn about God in this book?
God loves people of every nation who put their trust in him.

What people are important in this book?
The important people in this book are Naomi, Ruth and Boaz.

When did this happen?
The story of Ruth took place in the days of the judges, probably about 1100 B.C.

Where did this happen?
Ruth and Naomi lived in Bethlehem, the city where David and Jesus were later born.

What are some of the stories in this book?
Ruth goes with Naomi   Ruth 1
Ruth meets Boaz   Ruth 2
Boaz marries Ruth   Ruth 4

Naomi and Ruth

In the days when the judges ruled,[a] there was a famine in the land, and a man from Bethlehem in Judah, together with his wife and two sons, went to live for a while in the country of Moab. [2]The man's name was Elimelech, his wife's name Naomi, and the names of his two sons were Mahlon and Kilion. They were Ephrathites from Bethlehem, Judah. And they went to Moab and lived there.

[3]Now Elimelech, Naomi's husband, died, and she was left with her two sons. [4]They married Moabite women, one named Orpah and the other Ruth. After they had lived there about ten years, [5]both Mahlon and Kilion also died, and Naomi was left without her two sons and her husband.

[6]When she heard in Moab that the LORD had come to the aid of his people by providing food for them, Naomi and her daughters-in-law prepared to return home from there. [7]With her two daughters-in-law she left the place where she had been living and set out on the road that would take them back to the land of Judah.

[8]Then Naomi said to her two daughters-in-law, "Go back, each of you, to your mother's home. May the LORD show kindness to you, as you have shown to your dead and to me. [9]May the LORD grant that each of you will find rest in the home of another husband."

Then she kissed them and they wept aloud [10]and said to her, "We will go back with you to your people."

[11]But Naomi said, "Return home, my daughters. Why would you come with me? Am I going to have any more sons, who could become your husbands? [12]Return home, my daughters; I am too old to have another husband. Even if I thought there was still hope for me—even if I had a husband tonight and then gave birth to sons— [13]would you wait until they grew up? Would you remain unmarried for them? No, my daughters. It is more bitter for me than for you, because the LORD's hand has gone out against me!"

[14]At this they wept again. Then Orpah kissed her mother-in-law good-by, but Ruth clung to her.

[15]"Look," said Naomi, "your sister-in-law is going back to her people and her gods. Go back with her."

[16]But Ruth replied, "Don't urge me to leave you or to turn back from you. Where you go I will go, and where you stay I will stay. Your people will be my people and your God my God. [17]Where you die I will die, and there I will be buried. May the LORD deal with me, be it ever so severely, if anything but death separates you and me." [18]When Naomi realized that Ruth was determined to go with her, she stopped urging her.

[19]So the two women went on until they came to Bethlehem. When they arrived in Bethlehem, the whole town was stirred because of them, and the women exclaimed, "Can this be Naomi?"

[20]"Don't call me Naomi,[b]" she told them. "Call me Mara,[c] because the Almighty[d] has made my life very bitter. [21]I went away full, but the LORD has brought me back empty. Why call me Naomi? The LORD has afflicted[e] me; the Almighty has brought misfortune upon me."

[22]So Naomi returned from Moab accompanied by Ruth the Moabitess, her daughter-in-law, arriving in Bethlehem as the barley harvest was beginning.

Ruth Meets Boaz

Now Naomi had a relative on her husband's side, from the clan of Elimelech, a man of standing, whose name was Boaz.

[2]And Ruth the Moabitess said to Naomi, "Let me go to the fields and pick up the leftover grain behind anyone in whose eyes I find favor."

Naomi said to her, "Go ahead, my daughter." [3]So she went out and began to glean in the fields behind the harvesters. As it turned out, she found herself working in a field belonging to Boaz, who was from the clan of Elimelech.

[4]Just then Boaz arrived from Bethlehem and greeted the harvesters, "The LORD be with you!"

"The LORD bless you!" they called back.

[5]Boaz asked the foreman of his harvesters, "Whose young woman is that?"

[6]The foreman replied, "She is the Moabitess who came back from Moab with Naomi. [7]She said, 'Please let me glean

---

[a] 1 Traditionally judged   [b] 20 Naomi means pleasant; also in verse 21.   [c] 20 Mara means bitter.   [d] 20 Hebrew Shaddai; also in verse 21   [e] 21 Or has testified against

and gather among the sheaves behind the harvesters.' She went into the field and has worked steadily from morning till now, except for a short rest in the shelter."

⁸So Boaz said to Ruth, "My daughter, listen to me. Don't go and glean in another field and don't go away from here. Stay here with my servant girls. ⁹Watch the field where the men are harvesting, and follow along after the girls. I have told the men not to touch you. And whenever you are thirsty, go and get a drink from the water jars the men have filled."

¹⁰At this, she bowed down with her face to the ground. She exclaimed, "Why have I found such favor in your eyes that you notice me—a foreigner?"

¹¹Boaz replied, "I've been told all about what you have done for your mother-in-law since the death of your husband—how you left your father and mother and your homeland and came to live with a people you did not know before. ¹²May the LORD repay you for what you have done. May you be richly rewarded by the LORD, the God of Israel, under whose wings you have come to take refuge."

¹³"May I continue to find favor in your eyes, my lord," she said. "You have given me comfort and have spoken kindly to your servant—though I do not have the standing of one of your servant girls."

¹⁴At mealtime Boaz said to her, "Come over here. Have some bread and dip it in the wine vinegar."

When she sat down with the harvesters, he offered her some roasted grain. She ate all she wanted and had some left over. ¹⁵As she got up to glean, Boaz gave orders to his men, "Even if she gathers among the sheaves, don't embarrass her. ¹⁶Rather, pull out some stalks for her from the bundles and leave them for her to pick up, and don't rebuke her."

¹⁷So Ruth gleaned in the field until evening. Then she threshed the barley she had gathered, and it amounted to about an ephah.ᵃ ¹⁸She carried it back to town, and her mother-in-law saw how much she had gathered. Ruth also brought out and gave her what she had left over after she had eaten enough.

ᵃ 17 That is, probably about 3/5 bushel (about 22 liters)

One Very Cool Gentleman

READ RUTH 2:1–16

There once was a rich landowner named Boaz. *Boaz* means "in him is strength," and the name fits. Boaz was getting older, but he was still strong. However, his muscles were nothing compared to what an absolutely cool dude he was. He was a good, cheery boss, considerate to his workers, and the kind of gentleman who honored and respected women. He paid attention when his poor relative Naomi came straggling back into town with a young Moabite woman. Sure, Ruth was physically attractive to Boaz, but what impressed him the most was how loyal and hardworking she was, what godly character she had. He knew she had made a great sacrifice to come to a foreign land, without any money, and did everything he could to make life easier for her. His "hello" to Ruth in verses 8–12 is one of the most incredibly beautiful greetings in the Bible.

GET COOLER

Your next reading is on page 340.

[19]Her mother-in-law asked her, "Where did you glean today? Where did you work? Blessed be the man who took notice of you!"

Then Ruth told her mother-in-law about the one at whose place she had been working. "The name of the man I worked with today is Boaz," she said.

[20]"The LORD bless him!" Naomi said to her daughter-in-law. "He has not stopped showing his kindness to the living and the dead." She added, "That man is our close relative; he is one of our kinsman-redeemers."

[21]Then Ruth the Moabitess said, "He even said to me, 'Stay with my workers until they finish harvesting all my grain.' "

[22]Naomi said to Ruth her daughter-in-law, "It will be good for you, my daughter, to go with his girls, because in someone else's field you might be harmed."

[23]So Ruth stayed close to the servant girls of Boaz to glean until the barley and wheat harvests were finished. And she lived with her mother-in-law.

Ruth and Boaz at the Threshing Floor

3 One day Naomi her mother-in-law said to her, "My daughter, should I not try to find a home[a] for you, where you will be well provided for? [2]Is not Boaz, with whose servant girls you have been, a kinsman of ours? Tonight he will be winnowing barley on the threshing floor. [3]Wash and perfume yourself, and put on your best clothes. Then go down to the threshing floor, but don't let him know you are there until he has finished eating and drinking. [4]When he lies down, note the place where he is lying. Then go and uncover his feet and lie down. He will tell you what to do."

[5]"I will do whatever you say," Ruth answered. [6]So she went down to the threshing floor and did everything her mother-in-law told her to do.

[7]When Boaz had finished eating and drinking and was in good spirits, he went over to lie down at the far end of the grain pile. Ruth approached quietly, uncovered his feet and lay down. [8]In the middle of the night something startled the man, and he turned and discovered a woman lying at his feet.

[9]"Who are you?" he asked.

"I am your servant Ruth," she said.

"Spread the corner of your garment over me, since you are a kinsman-redeemer."

[10]"The LORD bless you, my daughter," he replied. "This kindness is greater than that which you showed earlier: You have not run after the younger men, whether rich or poor. [11]And now, my daughter, don't be afraid. I will do for you all you ask. All my fellow townsmen know that you are a woman of noble character. [12]Although it is true that I am near of kin, there is a kinsman-redeemer nearer than I. [13]Stay here for the night, and in the morning if he wants to redeem, good; let him redeem. But if he is not willing, as surely as the LORD lives I will do it. Lie here until morning."

[14]So she lay at his feet until morning, but got up before anyone could be recognized; and he said, "Don't let it be known that a woman came to the threshing floor."

[15]He also said, "Bring me the shawl you are wearing and hold it out." When she did so, he poured into it six measures of barley and put it on her. Then he[b] went back to town.

[16]When Ruth came to her mother-in-law, Naomi asked, "How did it go, my daughter?"

Then she told her everything Boaz had done for her [17]and added, "He gave me these six measures of barley, saying, 'Don't go back to your mother-in-law empty-handed.' "

[18]Then Naomi said, "Wait, my daughter, until you find out what happens. For the man will not rest until the matter is settled today."

Boaz Marries Ruth

4 Meanwhile Boaz went up to the town gate and sat there. When the kinsman-redeemer he had mentioned came along, Boaz said, "Come over here, my friend, and sit down." So he went over and sat down.

[2]Boaz took ten of the elders of the town and said, "Sit here," and they did so. [3]Then he said to the kinsman-redeemer, "Naomi, who has come back from Moab, is selling the piece of land that belonged to our brother Elimelech. [4]I thought I should bring the matter to your

---

[a] 1 Hebrew *find rest* (see Ruth 1:9)   [b] 15 Most Hebrew manuscripts; many Hebrew manuscripts, Vulgate and Syriac *she*

Get a Load of This...

Check out Ruth 4:6–7. In Boaz's day, when an Israelite transferred property rights, he would finalize the deal by taking off one sandal and giving it to the other person. Other, well, *interesting* Israelite customs included a woman publicly spitting in a man's face *and* taking one of his sandals! (see Deuteronomy 25:7–10).

attention and suggest that you buy it in the presence of these seated here and in the presence of the elders of my people. If you will redeem it, do so. But if you[a] will not, tell me, so I will know. For no one has the right to do it except you, and I am next in line."

"I will redeem it," he said.

⁵Then Boaz said, "On the day you buy the land from Naomi and from Ruth the Moabitess, you acquire[b] the dead man's widow, in order to maintain the name of the dead with his property."

⁶At this, the kinsman-redeemer said, "Then I cannot redeem it because I might endanger my own estate. You redeem it yourself. I cannot do it."

⁷(Now in earlier times in Israel, for the redemption and transfer of property to become final, one party took off his sandal and gave it to the other. This was the method of legalizing transactions in Israel.)

⁸So the kinsman-redeemer said to Boaz, "Buy it yourself." And he removed his sandal.

⁹Then Boaz announced to the elders and all the people, "Today you are witnesses that I have bought from Naomi all the property of Elimelech, Kilion and Mahlon. ¹⁰I have also acquired Ruth the Moabitess, Mahlon's widow, as my wife, in order to maintain the name of the dead with his property, so that his name will not disappear from among his family or from the town records. Today you are witnesses!"

¹¹Then the elders and all those at the gate said, "We are witnesses. May the LORD make the woman who is coming into your home like Rachel and Leah, who together built up the house of Israel. May you have standing in Ephrathah and be famous in Bethlehem. ¹²Through the offspring the LORD gives you by this young woman, may your family be like that of Perez, whom Tamar bore to Judah."

The Genealogy of David

¹³So Boaz took Ruth and she became his wife. Then he went to her, and the LORD enabled her to conceive, and she gave birth to a son. ¹⁴The women said to Naomi: "Praise be to the LORD, who this day has not left you without a kinsman-redeemer. May he become famous throughout Israel! ¹⁵He will renew your life and sustain you in your old age. For your daughter-in-law, who loves you and who is better to you than seven sons, has given him birth."

¹⁶Then Naomi took the child, laid him in her lap and cared for him. ¹⁷The women living there said, "Naomi has a son." And they named him Obed. He was the father of Jesse, the father of David.

¹⁸This, then, is the family line of Perez:

Perez was the father of Hezron,
¹⁹Hezron the father of Ram,

---

a 4 Many Hebrew manuscripts, Septuagint, Vulgate and Syriac; most Hebrew manuscripts *he*   b 5 Hebrew; Vulgate and Syriac *Naomi, you acquire Ruth the Moabitess,*

Ram the father of Amminadab,
20 Amminadab the father of Nahshon,
Nahshon the father of Salmon,[a]
21 Salmon the father of Boaz,
Boaz the father of Obed,
22 Obed the father of Jesse,
and Jesse the father of David.

Get a Load of This...

Boaz was what was called a "kinsman-redeemer," which was someone who looked out for his family. Hebrew customs said that when an Israelite man died, his brother or near relative should marry the widow and buy her land. Boaz was tickled pink to do that good deed.

[a] 20 A few Hebrew manuscripts, some Septuagint manuscripts and Vulgate (see also verse 21 and Septuagint of 1 Chron. 2:11); most Hebrew manuscripts *Salma*

1 SAMUEL

Who wrote this book?
The author of this book is unknown.

Why was this book written?
The book of 1 Samuel shows how the Israelites became a kingdom.

What happens in this book?
Samuel serves as Israel's last judge. Saul becomes Israel's first king. David kills Goliath and joins Saul's army. Saul disobeys God and is killed.

What do we learn about God in this book?
God wants leaders who will obey him.

Who is important in this book?
The important people in this book are Samuel, Saul and David.

When did this happen?
The events of this book happened between 1105 and 1010 B.C.

Where did this happen?
The stories in this book happened in the land of Israel.

What are some of the stories in this book?

God calls the boy Samuel	1 Samuel 3
The ark is captured	1 Samuel 4
The ark is returned	1 Samuel 5–6
Samuel anoints Saul king	1 Samuel 9
Saul disobeys	1 Samuel 13; 15
Samuel anoints David king	1 Samuel 16
David kills Goliath	1 Samuel 17
Saul is jealous of David	1 Samuel 18
David and Jonathan	1 Samuel 20
David spares Saul's life	1 Samuel 24
Abigail faces David	1 Samuel 25
David spares Saul again	1 Samuel 26
Saul dies in battle	1 Samuel 31

The Birth of Samuel

There was a certain man from Ramathaim, a Zuphite[a] from the hill country
of Ephraim, whose name was Elkanah
son of Jeroham, the son of Elihu, the
son of Tohu, the son of Zuph, an Ephraimite. ²He had two wives; one was called
Hannah and the other Peninnah. Peninnah
had children, but Hannah had none.

³Year after year this man went up from
his town to worship and sacrifice to the
LORD Almighty at Shiloh, where Hophni
and Phinehas, the two sons of Eli, were
priests of the LORD. ⁴Whenever the day
came for Elkanah to sacrifice, he would
give portions of the meat to his wife Peninnah and to all her sons and daughters.
⁵But to Hannah he gave a double portion
because he loved her, and the LORD had
closed her womb. ⁶And because the LORD
had closed her womb, her rival kept provoking her in order to irritate her. ⁷This
went on year after year. Whenever Hannah went up to the house of the LORD, her
rival provoked her till she wept and would
not eat. ⁸Elkanah her husband would say
to her, "Hannah, why are you weeping?
Why don't you eat? Why are you down-
hearted? Don't I mean more to you than
ten sons?"

⁹Once when they had finished eating
and drinking in Shiloh, Hannah stood up.
Now Eli the priest was sitting on a chair by
the doorpost of the LORD's temple.[b] ¹⁰In
bitterness of soul Hannah wept much and
prayed to the LORD. ¹¹And she made a
vow, saying, "O LORD Almighty, if you will
only look upon your servant's misery and
remember me, and not forget your servant but give her a son, then I will give
him to the LORD for all the days of his life,
and no razor will ever be used on his
head."

¹²As she kept on praying to the LORD, Eli
observed her mouth. ¹³Hannah was pray-

---

a 1 Or from Ramathaim Zuphim   b 9 That is, tabernacle

Make It Stick

READ 1 SAMUEL 1:16

Hannah was seeking God so passionately and whole-heartedly that the priest thought she
was drunk—but her prayer was powerful and effective (see Jeremiah 29:12–13; James 5:16).
What is something that *you* really want God to do? Write it on a sticky note. Make a copy of the
sticky note, put it near your bed and pray about it.

GET

Samuel—The 252 Man

READ 1 SAMUEL 1:1–5, 10–11, 20–28

Samuel was a great example of how to grow up into a godly man. First Samuel 2:26 says, "And the boy Samuel continued to grow in stature and in favor with the Lord and with men." Guess what? Luke was thinking of this verse when he wrote Luke 2:52 about Jesus.

GOD'S CARE

(read 1 Samuel 2:12–21). "The boy Samuel grew up in the presence of the Lord" (verse 21). During the ages of 7–9, boys go through big changes. They become more independent, and that's a good thing. This is when you learn to trust God yourself. Like Samuel did. He trusted God to care for him and ate the food the people gave to the priests.

PERSONAL GROWTH

(read 1 Samuel 2:22–26). Eli heard about the bad stuff his sons were into and confronted them, but did they listen? Nope! The people were mad at Eli's wicked sons, but they thought Samuel was cool. "Samuel continued to grow in stature and in favor with the Lord and with men" (verse 26). When boys are ages 10–11, it's a mega-important time to learn from the Bible what God expects of you—how you should act and behave. Samuel not only learned God's Word, but he had the humility to listen to those older and wiser than himself.

DIRECTION AND OBEDIENCE

(read 1 Samuel 2:27—3:19). Eli's sons Hophni and Phinehas put zero value on being in God's presence and obeying him. But Samuel, who was now 12 or a little older, loved God and listened to him. When God called to him in the night, Samuel said, "Speak, for your servant is listening" (verse 10). He didn't just listen, he hung on to God's Word. "The Lord was with Samuel as he grew up, and he let none of his words fall to the ground" (verse 19).

DEEPER

(read 1 Samuel 3:20—4:1). Samuel was now no longer just in the house of the Lord learning; he was out living life. When he was an adult, "Samuel's word came to all Israel" (chapter 4:1). When you become a man like Samuel, you can walk in God's will and have a life that counts. But that doesn't happen by accident. It wasn't by chance that Samuel became a leader and judge in Israel; God made sure Samuel's message came to all Israel because Samuel had spent years valuing and obeying God's Word.

Your next reading is on page 347.

ing in her heart, and her lips were moving but her voice was not heard. Eli thought she was drunk [14]and said to her, "How long will you keep on getting drunk? Get rid of your wine."

[15]"Not so, my lord," Hannah replied, "I am a woman who is deeply troubled. I have not been drinking wine or beer; I was pouring out my soul to the LORD. [16]Do not take your servant for a wicked woman; I have been praying here out of my great anguish and grief."

[17]Eli answered, "Go in peace, and may the God of Israel grant you what you have asked of him."

[18]She said, "May your servant find favor in your eyes." Then she went her way and ate something, and her face was no longer downcast.

[19]Early the next morning they arose and worshiped before the LORD and then went back to their home at Ramah. Elkanah lay with Hannah his wife, and the LORD remembered her. [20]So in the course of time Hannah conceived and gave birth to a son. She named him Samuel,[a] saying, "Because I asked the LORD for him."

Hannah Dedicates Samuel

[21]When the man Elkanah went up with all his family to offer the annual sacrifice to the LORD and to fulfill his vow, [22]Hannah did not go. She said to her husband, "After the boy is weaned, I will take him and present him before the LORD, and he will live there always."

[23]"Do what seems best to you," Elkanah her husband told her. "Stay here until you have weaned him; only may the LORD make good his[b] word." So the woman stayed at home and nursed her son until she had weaned him.

[24]After he was weaned, she took the boy with her, young as he was, along with a three-year-old bull,[c] an ephah[d] of flour and a skin of wine, and brought him to the house of the LORD at Shiloh. [25]When they had slaughtered the bull, they brought the boy to Eli, [26]and she said to him, "As surely as you live, my lord, I am the woman who stood here beside you praying to the LORD. [27]I prayed for this child, and the LORD has granted me what I asked of him. [28]So now I give him to the LORD. For his whole life he will be given over to the LORD." And he worshiped the LORD there.

Hannah's Prayer

Then Hannah prayed and said:

"My heart rejoices in the LORD;
  in the LORD my horn[e] is lifted high.
My mouth boasts over my enemies,
  for I delight in your deliverance.

[2]"There is no one holy[f] like the LORD;
  there is no one besides you;
  there is no Rock like our God.

[3]"Do not keep talking so proudly
  or let your mouth speak such arrogance,
for the LORD is a God who knows,
  and by him deeds are weighed.

[4]"The bows of the warriors are broken,
  but those who stumbled are armed with strength.
[5]Those who were full hire themselves out for food,
  but those who were hungry hunger no more.
She who was barren has borne seven children,
  but she who has had many sons pines away.

[6]"The LORD brings death and makes alive;
  he brings down to the grave[g] and raises up.
[7]The LORD sends poverty and wealth;
  he humbles and he exalts.
[8]He raises the poor from the dust
  and lifts the needy from the ash heap;
he seats them with princes
  and has them inherit a throne of honor.

"For the foundations of the earth are the LORD's;
  upon them he has set the world.
[9]He will guard the feet of his saints,
  but the wicked will be silenced in darkness.

"It is not by strength that one prevails;
10 those who oppose the LORD will be shattered.

---

[a] 20 *Samuel* sounds like the Hebrew for *heard of God.*
[b] 23 Masoretic Text; Dead Sea Scrolls, Septuagint and Syriac *your*   [c] 24 Dead Sea Scrolls and Syriac; Masoretic Text *with three bulls*   [d] 24 That is, probably about 3/5 bushel (about 22 liters)   [e] 1 *Horn* here symbolizes strength; also in verse 10.   [f] 2 Or *no Holy One*   [g] 6 Hebrew *Sheol*

He will thunder against them from
heaven;
  the LORD will judge the ends of the
earth.

"He will give strength to his king
  and exalt the horn of his anointed."

¹¹Then Elkanah went home to Ramah,
but the boy ministered before the LORD
under Eli the priest.

Eli's Wicked Sons

¹²Eli's sons were wicked men; they had
no regard for the LORD. ¹³Now it was the
practice of the priests with the people
that whenever anyone offered a sacrifice
and while the meat was being boiled, the
servant of the priest would come with a
three-pronged fork in his hand. ¹⁴He
would plunge it into the pan or kettle or
caldron or pot, and the priest would take
for himself whatever the fork brought up.
This is how they treated all the Israelites
who came to Shiloh. ¹⁵But even before
the fat was burned, the servant of the
priest would come and say to the man
who was sacrificing, "Give the priest some
meat to roast; he won't accept boiled
meat from you, but only raw."

¹⁶If the man said to him, "Let the fat be
burned up first, and then take whatever
you want," the servant would then answer, "No, hand it over now; if you don't,
I'll take it by force."

¹⁷This sin of the young men was very
great in the LORD's sight, for they^a were
treating the LORD's offering with contempt.

¹⁸But Samuel was ministering before
the LORD—a boy wearing a linen ephod.
¹⁹Each year his mother made him a little
robe and took it to him when she went up
with her husband to offer the annual sacrifice. ²⁰Eli would bless Elkanah and his
wife, saying, "May the LORD give you children by this woman to take the place of
the one she prayed for and gave to the
LORD." Then they would go home. ²¹And
the LORD was gracious to Hannah; she conceived and gave birth to three sons and
two daughters. Meanwhile, the boy Samuel grew up in the presence of the LORD.

²²Now Eli, who was very old, heard
about everything his sons were doing to all
Israel and how they slept with the women
who served at the entrance to the Tent of
Meeting. ²³So he said to them, "Why do
you do such things? I hear from all the

people about these wicked deeds of yours.
²⁴No, my sons; it is not a good report that
I hear spreading among the LORD's people.
²⁵If a man sins against another man, God^b
may mediate for him; but if a man sins
against the LORD, who will intercede for
him?" His sons, however, did not listen to
their father's rebuke, for it was the LORD's
will to put them to death.

²⁶And the boy Samuel continued to
grow in stature and in favor with the LORD
and with men.

Prophecy Against the House of Eli

²⁷Now a man of God came to Eli and
said to him, "This is what the LORD says:
'Did I not clearly reveal myself to your father's house when they were in Egypt under Pharaoh? ²⁸I chose your father out of
all the tribes of Israel to be my priest, to
go up to my altar, to burn incense, and to
wear an ephod in my presence. I also gave
your father's house all the offerings made
with fire by the Israelites. ²⁹Why do you^c
scorn my sacrifice and offering that I pre-
scribed for my dwelling? Why do you
honor your sons more than me by fatten-
ing yourselves on the choice parts of every
offering made by my people Israel?'

³⁰"Therefore the LORD, the God of Israel,
declares: 'I promised that your house and
your father's house would minister before
me forever.' But now the LORD declares:
'Far be it from me! Those who honor me I
will honor, but those who despise me will
be disdained. ³¹The time is coming when
I will cut short your strength and the
strength of your father's house, so that
there will not be an old man in your family line ³²and you will see distress in my
dwelling. Although good will be done to
Israel, in your family line there will never
be an old man. ³³Every one of you that I
do not cut off from my altar will be spared
only to blind your eyes with tears and to
grieve your heart, and all your descendants will die in the prime of life.

³⁴"'And what happens to your two
sons, Hophni and Phinehas, will be a sign
to you—they will both die on the same
day. ³⁵I will raise up for myself a faithful
priest, who will do according to what is in
my heart and mind. I will firmly establish
his house, and he will minister before my

---

^a17 Or men ^b25 Or the judges ^c29 The Hebrew is
plural.

anointed one always. 36Then everyone left in your family line will come and bow down before him for a piece of silver and a crust of bread and plead, "Appoint me to some priestly office so I can have food to eat." ' "

The LORD Calls Samuel

The boy Samuel ministered before the LORD under Eli. In those days the word of the LORD was rare; there were not many visions.

2One night Eli, whose eyes were becoming so weak that he could barely see, was lying down in his usual place. 3The lamp of God had not yet gone out, and Samuel was lying down in the temple*a* of the LORD, where the ark of God was. 4Then the LORD called Samuel.

Samuel answered, "Here I am." 5And he ran to Eli and said, "Here I am; you called me."

But Eli said, "I did not call; go back and lie down." So he went and lay down.

6Again the LORD called, "Samuel!" And Samuel got up and went to Eli and said, "Here I am; you called me."

"My son," Eli said, "I did not call; go back and lie down."

7Now Samuel did not yet know the LORD: The word of the LORD had not yet been revealed to him.

8The LORD called Samuel a third time, and Samuel got up and went to Eli and said, "Here I am; you called me."

Then Eli realized that the LORD was calling the boy. 9So Eli told Samuel, "Go and lie down, and if he calls you, say, 'Speak, LORD, for your servant is listening.' " So Samuel went and lay down in his place.

10The LORD came and stood there, calling as at the other times, "Samuel! Samuel!"

Then Samuel said, "Speak, for your servant is listening."

11And the LORD said to Samuel: "See, I am about to do something in Israel that will make the ears of everyone who hears of it tingle. 12At that time I will carry out against Eli everything I spoke against his family—from beginning to end. 13For I told him that I would judge his family forever because of the sin he knew about; his sons made themselves contemptible,*b* and he failed to restrain them. 14Therefore, I swore to the house of Eli, 'The guilt of Eli's house will never be atoned for by sacrifice or offering.' "

15Samuel lay down until morning and then opened the doors of the house of the LORD. He was afraid to tell Eli the vision, 16but Eli called him and said, "Samuel, my son."

Samuel answered, "Here I am."

17"What was it he said to you?" Eli asked. "Do not hide it from me. May God deal with you, be it ever so severely, if you hide from me anything he told you." 18So Samuel told him everything, hiding nothing from him. Then Eli said, "He is the LORD; let him do what is good in his eyes."

19The LORD was with Samuel as he grew up, and he let none of his words fall to the ground. 20And all Israel from Dan to Beersheba recognized that Samuel was attested as a prophet of the LORD. 21The LORD continued to appear at Shiloh, and there he revealed himself to Samuel through his word.

And Samuel's word came to all Israel.

The Philistines Capture the Ark

Now the Israelites went out to fight against the Philistines. The Israelites camped at Ebenezer, and the Philistines at Aphek. 2The Philistines deployed their forces to meet Israel, and as the battle spread, Israel was defeated by the Philistines, who killed about four thousand of them on the battlefield. 3When the soldiers returned to camp, the elders of Israel asked, "Why did the LORD bring defeat upon us today before the Philistines? Let us bring the ark of the LORD's covenant from Shiloh, so that it*c* may go with us and save us from the hand of our enemies."

4So the people sent men to Shiloh, and they brought back the ark of the covenant of the LORD Almighty, who is enthroned between the cherubim. And Eli's two sons, Hophni and Phinehas, were there with the ark of the covenant of God.

5When the ark of the LORD's covenant came into the camp, all Israel raised such a great shout that the ground shook. 6Hearing the uproar, the Philistines asked, "What's all this shouting in the Hebrew camp?"

When they learned that the ark of the LORD had come into the camp, 7the Philistines were afraid. "A god has come into

---

a 3 That is, tabernacle　　*b 13* Masoretic Text; an ancient Hebrew scribal tradition and Septuagint *sons blasphemed God*　　*c 3* Or *he* the camp," they said. "We're in trouble! Nothing like this has happened before. [8]Woe to us! Who will deliver us from the hand of these mighty gods? They are the gods who struck the Egyptians with all kinds of plagues in the desert. [9]Be strong, Philistines! Be men, or you will be subject to the Hebrews, as they have been to you. Be men, and fight!"

[10]So the Philistines fought, and the Israelites were defeated and every man fled to his tent. The slaughter was very great; Israel lost thirty thousand foot soldiers. [11]The ark of God was captured, and Eli's two sons, Hophni and Phinehas, died.

Death of Eli

[12]That same day a Benjamite ran from the battle line and went to Shiloh, his clothes torn and dust on his head. [13]When he arrived, there was Eli sitting on his chair by the side of the road, watching, because his heart feared for the ark of God. When the man entered the town and told what had happened, the whole town sent up a cry.

[14]Eli heard the outcry and asked, "What is the meaning of this uproar?"

The man hurried over to Eli, [15]who was ninety-eight years old and whose eyes were set so that he could not see. [16]He told Eli, "I have just come from the battle line; I fled from it this very day."

Eli asked, "What happened, my son?"

[17]The man who brought the news replied, "Israel fled before the Philistines, and the army has suffered heavy losses. Also your two sons, Hophni and Phinehas, are dead, and the ark of God has been captured."

[18]When he mentioned the ark of God, Eli fell backward off his chair by the side of the gate. His neck was broken and he died, for he was an old man and heavy. He had led[a] Israel forty years.

[19]His daughter-in-law, the wife of Phinehas, was pregnant and near the time of delivery. When she heard the news that the ark of God had been captured and that her father-in-law and her husband were dead, she went into labor and gave birth, but was overcome by her labor pains. [20]As she was dying, the women attending her said, "Don't despair; you have given birth to a son." But she did not respond or pay any attention.

[21]She named the boy Ichabod,[b] saying,

"The glory has departed from Israel"—because of the capture of the ark of God and the deaths of her father-in-law and her husband. [22]She said, "The glory has departed from Israel, for the ark of God has been captured."

The Ark in Ashdod and Ekron

5 After the Philistines had captured the ark of God, they took it from Ebenezer to Ashdod. [2]Then they carried the ark into Dagon's temple and set it beside Dagon. [3]When the people of Ashdod rose early the next day, there was Dagon, fallen on his face on the ground before the ark of the Lord! They took Dagon and put him back in his place. [4]But the following morning when they rose, there was Dagon, fallen on his face on the ground before the ark of the Lord! His head and hands had been broken off and were lying on the threshold; only his body remained. [5]That is why to this day neither the priests of Dagon nor any others who enter Dagon's temple at Ashdod step on the threshold.

[6]The Lord's hand was heavy upon the people of Ashdod and its vicinity; he brought devastation upon them and afflicted them with tumors.[c] [7]When the men of Ashdod saw what was happening, they said, "The ark of the god of Israel must not stay here with us, because his hand is heavy upon us and upon Dagon our god." [8]So they called together all the rulers of the Philistines and asked them, "What shall we do with the ark of the god of Israel?"

They answered, "Have the ark of the god of Israel moved to Gath." So they moved the ark of the God of Israel.

[9]But after they had moved it, the Lord's hand was against that city, throwing it into a great panic. He afflicted the people of the city, both young and old, with an outbreak of tumors.[d] [10]So they sent the ark of God to Ekron.

As the ark of God was entering Ekron, the people of Ekron cried out, "They have brought the ark of the god of Israel around to us to kill us and our people." [11]So they called together all the rulers of

---

[a] 18 Traditionally *judged*   [b] 21 *Ichabod* means *no glory.*
[c] 6 Hebrew; Septuagint and Vulgate *tumors. And rats appeared in their land, and death and destruction were throughout the city*   [d] 9 Or *with tumors in the groin* (see Septuagint)

the Philistines and said, "Send the ark of the god of Israel away; let it go back to its own place, or it[a] will kill us and our people." For death had filled the city with panic; God's hand was very heavy upon it. 12 Those who did not die were afflicted with tumors, and the outcry of the city went up to heaven.

The Ark Returned to Israel

6 When the ark of the Lord had been in Philistine territory seven months, 2 the Philistines called for the priests and the diviners and said, "What shall we do with the ark of the Lord? Tell us how we should send it back to its place."

3 They answered, "If you return the ark of the god of Israel, do not send it away empty, but by all means send a guilt offering to him. Then you will be healed, and you will know why his hand has not been lifted from you."

4 The Philistines asked, "What guilt offering should we send to him?"

They replied, "Five gold tumors and five gold rats, according to the number of the Philistine rulers, because the same plague has struck both you and your rulers. 5 Make models of the tumors and of the rats that are destroying the country, and pay honor to Israel's god. Perhaps he will lift his hand from you and your gods and your land. 6 Why do you harden your hearts as the Egyptians and Pharaoh did? When he[b] treated them harshly, did they not send the Israelites out so they could go on their way?

7 "Now then, get a new cart ready, with two cows that have calved and have never been yoked. Hitch the cows to the cart, but take their calves away and pen them up. 8 Take the ark of the Lord and put it on the cart, and in a chest beside it put the gold objects you are sending back to him as a guilt offering. Send it on its way, 9 but keep watching it. If it goes up to its own territory, toward Beth Shemesh, then the Lord has brought this great disaster on us. But if it does not, then we will know that it was not his hand that struck us and that it happened to us by chance."

10 So they did this. They took two such cows and hitched them to the cart and penned up their calves. 11 They placed the ark of the Lord on the cart and along with it the chest containing the gold rats and the models of the tumors. 12 Then the cows went straight up toward Beth Shemesh, keeping on the road and lowing all the way; they did not turn to the right or to the left. The rulers of the Philistines followed them as far as the border of Beth Shemesh.

13 Now the people of Beth Shemesh were harvesting their wheat in the valley, and when they looked up and saw the ark, they rejoiced at the sight. 14 The cart came to the field of Joshua of Beth Shemesh, and there it stopped beside a large rock. The people chopped up the wood of the cart and sacrificed the cows as a burnt offering to the

Gross!

From a classified ad in the *Philistine Times*: "Free! One acacia wood ark. Gold overlay lid. Formerly belonged to Israelites. Warning: may cause tumors and terrible plagues. Bonus! Comes with peace offering—gold rats and gold tumors. Yours if you'll simply take it away. Call priests of Dagon ASAP."
For the real story, check out 1 Samuel 6:11.

a 11 Or *he*   b 6 That is, God

Get a Load of This...

In Uganda, it thundered a record 251 days in 1967. Imagine all of that packed into one single day and you might have a clue as to what the Philistines experienced. The thunder they heard was God rolling up his sleeves, and man, were they freaked! Check out 1 Samuel 7:10.

LORD. [15]The Levites took down the ark of the LORD, together with the chest containing the gold objects, and placed them on the large rock. On that day the people of Beth Shemesh offered burnt offerings and made sacrifices to the LORD. [16]The five rulers of the Philistines saw all this and then returned that same day to Ekron.

[17]These are the gold tumors the Philistines sent as a guilt offering to the LORD—one each for Ashdod, Gaza, Ashkelon, Gath and Ekron. [18]And the number of the gold rats was according to the number of Philistine towns belonging to the five rulers—the fortified towns with their country villages. The large rock, on which[a] they set the ark of the LORD, is a witness to this day in the field of Joshua of Beth Shemesh.

[19]But God struck down some of the men of Beth Shemesh, putting seventy[b] of them to death because they had looked into the ark of the LORD. The people mourned because of the heavy blow the LORD had dealt them, [20]and the men of Beth Shemesh asked, "Who can stand in the presence of the LORD, this holy God? To whom will the ark go up from here?"

[21]Then they sent messengers to the people of Kiriath Jearim, saying, "The Philistines have returned the ark of the LORD. Come down and take it up to your place." [1]So the men of Kiriath Jearim came and took up the ark of the LORD. They took it to Abinadab's house on the hill and consecrated Eleazar his son to guard the ark of the LORD.

Samuel Subdues the Philistines at Mizpah

[2]It was a long time, twenty years in all, that the ark remained at Kiriath Jearim, and all the people of Israel mourned and sought after the LORD. [3]And Samuel said to the whole house of Israel, "If you are returning to the LORD with all your hearts, then rid yourselves of the foreign gods and the Ashtoreths and commit yourselves to the LORD and serve him only, and he will deliver you out of the hand of the Philistines." [4]So the Israelites put away their Baals and Ashtoreths, and served the LORD only.

[5]Then Samuel said, "Assemble all Israel at Mizpah and I will intercede with the LORD for you." [6]When they had assembled at Mizpah, they drew water and poured it out before the LORD. On that day they fasted and there they confessed, "We have sinned against the LORD." And Samuel was leader[c] of Israel at Mizpah.

[7]When the Philistines heard that Israel had assembled at Mizpah, the rulers of the Philistines came up to attack them. And when the Israelites heard of it, they were afraid because of the Philistines. [8]They said to Samuel, "Do not stop crying out to the LORD our God for us, that he may rescue us from the hand of the Philistines." [9]Then Samuel took a suckling lamb and offered it up as a whole burnt offering to the LORD. He cried out to the

---

[a] 18 A few Hebrew manuscripts (see also Septuagint); most Hebrew manuscripts *villages as far as Greater Abel, where*   [b] 19 A few Hebrew manuscripts; most Hebrew manuscripts and Septuagint *50,070*   [c] 6 Traditionally *judge*

LORD on Israel's behalf, and the LORD answered him.

[10]While Samuel was sacrificing the burnt offering, the Philistines drew near to engage Israel in battle. But that day the LORD thundered with loud thunder against the Philistines and threw them into such a panic that they were routed before the Israelites. [11]The men of Israel rushed out of Mizpah and pursued the Philistines, slaughtering them along the way to a point below Beth Car.

[12]Then Samuel took a stone and set it up between Mizpah and Shen. He named it Ebenezer,[a] saying, "Thus far has the LORD helped us." [13]So the Philistines were subdued and did not invade Israelite territory again.

Throughout Samuel's lifetime, the hand of the LORD was against the Philistines. [14]The towns from Ekron to Gath that the Philistines had captured from Israel were restored to her, and Israel delivered the neighboring territory from the power of the Philistines. And there was peace between Israel and the Amorites.

[15]Samuel continued as judge over Israel all the days of his life. [16]From year to year he went on a circuit from Bethel to Gilgal to Mizpah, judging Israel in all those places. [17]But he always went back to Ramah, where his home was, and there he also judged Israel. And he built an altar there to the LORD.

Israel Asks for a King

When Samuel grew old, he appointed his sons as judges for Israel. [2]The name of his firstborn was Joel and the name of his second was Abijah, and they served at Beersheba. [3]But his sons did not walk in his ways. They turned aside after dishonest gain and accepted bribes and perverted justice.

[4]So all the elders of Israel gathered together and came to Samuel at Ramah. [5]They said to him, "You are old, and your sons do not walk in your ways; now appoint a king to lead[b] us, such as all the other nations have."

[6]But when they said, "Give us a king to

---

[a] 12 Ebenezer means stone of help.   [b] 5 Traditionally judge; also in verses 6 and 20

The Ball's in Your Court

READ 1 SAMUEL 8:1–22

The Israelites kept choosing worldly ways instead of God's way. "The other nations have kings," they said. "We want a king, too!" Samuel warned them that having a king would cost them big time. But they insisted, "We want a man to lead us." God told Samuel, "They have rejected me as their king" (1 Samuel 8:7). The same principle applies if you always want others to lead you, or *just* rely on your parents to tell you what to do. You need to have your *own* relationship with God. Yes, ask advice of godly adults, but first go to God and his Word. Get things from God yourself, then run it by adults. You needed your dad's help to learn to shoot a basketball, right? But now, would you want him to pick you up and carry you to the rim like he did when you were four? That's not cool. So develop your relationship with God.

Your next reading is on page 351.

lead us," this displeased Samuel; so he prayed to the LORD. 7And the LORD told him: "Listen to all that the people are saying to you; it is not you they have rejected, but they have rejected me as their king. 8As they have done from the day I brought them up out of Egypt until this day, forsaking me and serving other gods, so they are doing to you. 9Now listen to them; but warn them solemnly and let them know what the king who will reign over them will do."

10Samuel told all the words of the LORD to the people who were asking him for a king. 11He said, "This is what the king who will reign over you will do: He will take your sons and make them serve with his chariots and horses, and they will run in front of his chariots. 12Some he will assign to be commanders of thousands and commanders of fifties, and others to plow his ground and reap his harvest, and still others to make weapons of war and equipment for his chariots. 13He will take your daughters to be perfumers and cooks and bakers. 14He will take the best of your fields and vineyards and olive groves and give them to his attendants. 15He will take a tenth of your grain and of your vintage and give it to his officials and attendants. 16Your menservants and maidservants and the best of your cattle*a* and donkeys he will take for his own use. 17He will take a tenth of your flocks, and you yourselves will become his slaves. 18When that day comes, you will cry out for relief from the king you have chosen, and the LORD will not answer you in that day."

19But the people refused to listen to Samuel. "No!" they said. "We want a king over us. 20Then we will be like all the other nations, with a king to lead us and to go out before us and fight our battles."

21When Samuel heard all that the people said, he repeated it before the LORD. 22The LORD answered, "Listen to them and give them a king."

Then Samuel said to the men of Israel, "Everyone go back to his town."

Samuel Anoints Saul

There was a Benjamite, a man of standing, whose name was Kish son of Abiel, the son of Zeror, the son of Becorath, the son of Aphiah of Benjamin. 2He had a son named Saul, an impressive young man without equal among the Israelites—a head taller than any of the others.

3Now the donkeys belonging to Saul's father Kish were lost, and Kish said to his son Saul, "Take one of the servants with you and go and look for the donkeys." 4So he passed through the hill country of Ephraim and through the area around Shalisha, but they did not find them. They went on into the district of Shaalim, but the donkeys were not there. Then he passed through the territory of Benjamin, but they did not find them.

5When they reached the district of Zuph, Saul said to the servant who was with him, "Come, let's go back, or my father will stop thinking about the donkeys and start worrying about us."

6But the servant replied, "Look, in this town there is a man of God; he is highly respected, and everything he says comes true. Let's go there now. Perhaps he will tell us what way to take."

7Saul said to his servant, "If we go, what can we give the man? The food in our sacks is gone. We have no gift to take to the man of God. What do we have?"

8The servant answered him again. "Look," he said, "I have a quarter of a shekel*b* of silver. I will give it to the man of God so that he will tell us what way to take." 9(Formerly in Israel, if a man went to inquire of God, he would say, "Come, let us go to the seer," because the prophet of today used to be called a seer.)

10"Good," Saul said to his servant. "Come, let's go." So they set out for the town where the man of God was.

11As they were going up the hill to the town, they met some girls coming out to draw water, and they asked them, "Is the seer here?"

12"He is," they answered. "He's ahead of you. Hurry now; he has just come to our town today, for the people have a sacrifice at the high place. 13As soon as you enter the town, you will find him before he goes up to the high place to eat. The people will not begin eating until he comes, because he must bless the sacrifice; afterward, those who are invited will eat. Go up now; you should find him about this time."

14They went up to the town, and as

---

a 16 Septuagint; Hebrew *young men*   *b 8* That is, about 1/10 ounce (about 3 grams) they were entering it, there was Samuel, coming toward them on his way up to the high place.

¹⁵Now the day before Saul came, the LORD had revealed this to Samuel: ¹⁶"About this time tomorrow I will send you a man from the land of Benjamin. Anoint him leader over my people Israel; he will deliver my people from the hand of the Philistines. I have looked upon my people, for their cry has reached me."

¹⁷When Samuel caught sight of Saul, the LORD said to him, "This is the man I spoke to you about; he will govern my people."

¹⁸Saul approached Samuel in the gateway and asked, "Would you please tell me where the seer's house is?"

¹⁹"I am the seer," Samuel replied. "Go up ahead of me to the high place, for today you are to eat with me, and in the morning I will let you go and will tell you all that is in your heart. ²⁰As for the donkeys you lost three days ago, do not worry about them; they have been found. And to whom is all the desire of Israel turned, if not to you and all your father's family?"

²¹Saul answered, "But am I not a Benjamite, from the smallest tribe of Israel, and is not my clan the least of all the clans of the tribe of Benjamin? Why do you say such a thing to me?"

²²Then Samuel brought Saul and his servant into the hall and seated them at the head of those who were invited—about thirty in number. ²³Samuel said to the cook, "Bring the piece of meat I gave you, the one I told you to lay aside."

²⁴So the cook took up the leg with what was on it and set it in front of Saul. Samuel said, "Here is what has been kept for you. Eat, because it was set aside for you for this occasion, from the time I said, 'I have invited guests.' " And Saul dined with Samuel that day.

²⁵After they came down from the high place to the town, Samuel talked with Saul on the roof of his house. ²⁶They rose about daybreak and Samuel called to Saul on the roof, "Get ready, and I will send you on your way." When Saul got ready, he and Samuel went outside together. ²⁷As they were going down to the edge of the town, Samuel said to Saul, "Tell the servant to go on ahead of us"—and the servant did so—"but you stay here awhile, so that I may give you a message from God."

10 Then Samuel took a flask of oil and poured it on Saul's head and kissed him, saying, "Has not the LORD anointed you leader over his inheritance?ᵃ ²When you leave me today, you will meet two men near Rachel's tomb, at Zelzah on the border of Benjamin. They will say to you, 'The donkeys you set out to look for have been found. And now your father has stopped thinking about them and is worried about you. He is asking, "What shall I do about my son?" '

³"Then you will go on from there until you reach the great tree of Tabor. Three men going up to God at Bethel will meet you there. One will be carrying three young goats, another three loaves of bread, and another a skin of wine. ⁴They will greet you and offer you two loaves of bread, which you will accept from them.

⁵"After that you will go to Gibeah of God, where there is a Philistine outpost. As you approach the town, you will meet a procession of prophets coming down from the high place with lyres, tambourines, flutes and harps being played before them, and they will be prophesying. ⁶The Spirit of the LORD will come upon you in power, and you will prophesy with them; and you will be changed into a different person. ⁷Once these signs are fulfilled, do whatever your hand finds to do, for God is with you.

⁸"Go down ahead of me to Gilgal. I will surely come down to you to sacrifice burnt offerings and fellowship offerings,ᵇ but you must wait seven days until I come to you and tell you what you are to do."

Saul Made King

⁹As Saul turned to leave Samuel, God changed Saul's heart, and all these signs were fulfilled that day. ¹⁰When they arrived at Gibeah, a procession of prophets met him; the Spirit of God came upon him in power, and he joined in their prophesying. ¹¹When all those who had formerly known him saw him prophesying with the prophets, they asked each other,

---

ᵃ 1 Hebrew; Septuagint and Vulgate *over his people Israel? You will reign over the LORD's people and save them from the power of their enemies round about. And this will be a sign to you that the LORD has anointed you leader over his inheritance:* ᵇ 8 Traditionally *peace offerings*

"What is this that has happened to the son of Kish? Is Saul also among the prophets?"

12A man who lived there answered, "And who is their father?" So it became a saying: "Is Saul also among the prophets?" 13After Saul stopped prophesying, he went to the high place.

14Now Saul's uncle asked him and his servant, "Where have you been?"

"Looking for the donkeys," he said. "But when we saw they were not to be found, we went to Samuel."

15Saul's uncle said, "Tell me what Samuel said to you."

16Saul replied, "He assured us that the donkeys had been found." But he did not tell his uncle what Samuel had said about the kingship.

17Samuel summoned the people of Israel to the LORD at Mizpah 18and said to them, "This is what the LORD, the God of Israel, says: 'I brought Israel up out of Egypt, and I delivered you from the pow-er of Egypt and all the kingdoms that oppressed you.' 19But you have now rejected your God, who saves you out of all your calamities and distresses. And you have said, 'No, set a king over us.' So now present yourselves before the LORD by your tribes and clans."

20When Samuel brought all the tribes of Israel near, the tribe of Benjamin was chosen. 21Then he brought forward the tribe of Benjamin, clan by clan, and Ma-tri's clan was chosen. Finally Saul son of Kish was chosen. But when they looked for him, he was not to be found. 22So they inquired further of the LORD, "Has the man come here yet?"

And the LORD said, "Yes, he has hidden himself among the baggage."

23They ran and brought him out, and as he stood among the people he was a head taller than any of the others. 24Samuel said to all the people, "Do you see the man the LORD has chosen? There is no one like him among all the people."

Make It Stick

READ 1 SAMUEL 10:1

When Israelite kings were anointed with oil, God's Spirit gave them the power and ability to lead the people. Write "My Life" on your sticky note. Smear one drop of cooking oil over the words. Let it dry, then stick it in the Bible. Remember, the oil represents the Holy Spirit helping and guiding you.

Then the people shouted, "Long live the king!"

²⁵Samuel explained to the people the regulations of the kingship. He wrote them down on a scroll and deposited it before the LORD. Then Samuel dismissed the people, each to his own home.

²⁶Saul also went to his home in Gibeah, accompanied by valiant men whose hearts God had touched. ²⁷But some troublemakers said, "How can this fellow save us?" They despised him and brought him no gifts. But Saul kept silent.

Saul Rescues the City of Jabesh

11 Nahash the Ammonite went up and besieged Jabesh Gilead. And all the men of Jabesh said to him, "Make a treaty with us, and we will be subject to you."

²But Nahash the Ammonite replied, "I will make a treaty with you only on the condition that I gouge out the right eye of every one of you and so bring disgrace on all Israel."

³The elders of Jabesh said to him, "Give us seven days so we can send messengers throughout Israel; if no one comes to rescue us, we will surrender to you."

⁴When the messengers came to Gibeah of Saul and reported these terms to the people, they all wept aloud. ⁵Just then Saul was returning from the fields, behind his oxen, and he asked, "What is wrong with the people? Why are they weeping?" Then they repeated to him what the men of Jabesh had said.

⁶When Saul heard their words, the Spirit of God came upon him in power, and he burned with anger. ⁷He took a pair of oxen, cut them into pieces, and sent the pieces by messengers throughout Israel, proclaiming, "This is what will be done to the oxen of anyone who does not follow Saul and Samuel." Then the terror of the LORD fell on the people, and they turned out as one man. ⁸When Saul mustered

---

GET STRONGER

Heart Check

READ 1 SAMUEL 10:23–24

Saul seemed to have it all—looks, height and popularity. Women swooned, men cheered. The prophet Samuel declared, "There is no one like him among all the people" (verse 24). Yes, Saul was a head taller than anyone else (see also 1 Samuel 9:2), and the scouting report would've listed him as a first-round pick if they'd had pro basketball back then. But because of Saul's disobedient heart, it wasn't long before the Lord was grieved that he had made Saul king. So God sought out a new king—a "man after his own heart" (1 Samuel 13:14). Remember, there's nothing wrong with being strong physically. God has given us strength, and as men, we should take care of our appearance. But what really makes a man is not what's outside but what's inside. We may score points for looking like Hercules—young, buff and tough—but what matters most is that we are like God in character and love. What does your scouting report say? If you've got God's heart, the rest matters less.

Your next reading is on page 353.

them at Bezek, the men of Israel numbered three hundred thousand and the men of Judah thirty thousand.

9They told the messengers who had come, "Say to the men of Jabesh Gilead, 'By the time the sun is hot tomorrow, you will be delivered.' " When the messengers went and reported this to the men of Jabesh, they were elated. 10They said to the Ammonites, "Tomorrow we will surrender to you, and you can do to us whatever seems good to you."

11The next day Saul separated his men into three divisions; during the last watch of the night they broke into the camp of the Ammonites and slaughtered them until the heat of the day. Those who survived were scattered, so that no two of them were left together.

Saul Confirmed as King

12The people then said to Samuel, "Who was it that asked, 'Shall Saul reign over us?' Bring these men to us and we will put them to death."

13But Saul said, "No one shall be put to death today, for this day the LORD has rescued Israel."

14Then Samuel said to the people, "Come, let us go to Gilgal and there reaffirm the kingship." 15So all the people went to Gilgal and confirmed Saul as king in the presence of the LORD. There they sacrificed fellowship offeringsa before the LORD, and Saul and all the Israelites held a great celebration.

Samuel's Farewell Speech

12 Samuel said to all Israel, "I have listened to everything you said to me and have set a king over you. 2Now you have a king as your leader. As for me, I am old and gray, and my sons are here with me. I have been your leader from my youth until this day. 3Here I stand. Testify against me in the presence of the LORD and his anointed. Whose ox have I taken? Whose donkey have I taken? Whom have I cheated? Whom have I oppressed? From whose hand have I accepted a bribe to make me shut my eyes? If I have done any of these, I will make it right."

4"You have not cheated or oppressed us," they replied. "You have not taken anything from anyone's hand."

5Samuel said to them, "The LORD is wit-

ness against you, and also his anointed is witness this day, that you have not found anything in my hand."

"He is witness," they said.

6Then Samuel said to the people, "It is the LORD who appointed Moses and Aaron and brought your forefathers up out of Egypt. 7Now then, stand here, because I am going to confront you with evidence before the LORD as to all the righteous acts performed by the LORD for you and your fathers.

8"After Jacob entered Egypt, they cried to the LORD for help, and the LORD sent Moses and Aaron, who brought your forefathers out of Egypt and settled them in this place.

9"But they forgot the LORD their God; so he sold them into the hand of Sisera, the commander of the army of Hazor, and into the hands of the Philistines and the king of Moab, who fought against them. 10They cried out to the LORD and said, 'We have sinned; we have forsaken the LORD and served the Baals and the Ashtoreths. But now deliver us from the hands of our enemies, and we will serve you.' 11Then the LORD sent Jerub-Baal,b Barak,c Jephthah and Samuel,d and he delivered you from the hands of your enemies on every side, so that you lived securely.

12"But when you saw that Nahash king of the Ammonites was moving against you, you said to me, 'No, we want a king to rule over us'—even though the LORD your God was your king. 13Now here is the king you have chosen, the one you asked for; see, the LORD has set a king over you. 14If you fear the LORD and serve and obey him and do not rebel against his commands, and if both you and the king who reigns over you follow the LORD your God—good! 15But if you do not obey the LORD, and if you rebel against his commands, his hand will be against you, as it was against your fathers.

16"Now then, stand still and see this great thing the LORD is about to do before your eyes! 17Is it not wheat harvest now? I will call upon the LORD to send thunder and rain. And you will realize what an evil thing you did in the eyes of the LORD when you asked for a king."

---

a 15 Traditionally peace offerings   b 11 Also called Gideon
c 11 Some Septuagint manuscripts and Syriac; Hebrew Bedan
d 11 Hebrew; some Septuagint manuscripts and Syriac Samson

18Then Samuel called upon the LORD, and that same day the LORD sent thunder and rain. So all the people stood in awe of the LORD and of Samuel.

19The people all said to Samuel, "Pray to the LORD your God for your servants so that we will not die, for we have added to all our other sins the evil of asking for a king."

20"Do not be afraid," Samuel replied. "You have done all this evil; yet do not turn away from the LORD, but serve the LORD with all your heart. 21Do not turn away after useless idols. They can do you no good, nor can they rescue you, because they are useless. 22For the sake of his great name the LORD will not reject his people, because the LORD was pleased to make you his own. 23As for me, far be it from me that I should sin against the LORD by failing to pray for you. And I will teach you the way that is good and right. 24But be sure to fear the LORD and serve him faithfully with all your heart; consider what great things he has done for you. 25Yet if you persist in doing evil, both you and your king will be swept away."

Samuel Rebukes Saul

13 Saul was ˻thirty˼a years old when he became king, and he reigned over Israel ˻forty-˼b two years. 2Saulc chose three thousand men from Israel; two thousand were with him at Micmash and in the hill country of Bethel, and a thousand were with Jonathan at Gibeah in Benjamin. The rest of the men he sent back to their homes.

3Jonathan attacked the Philistine outpost at Geba, and the Philistines heard about it. Then Saul had the trumpet blown throughout the land and said, "Let the Hebrews hear!" 4So all Israel heard the news: "Saul has attacked the Philistine outpost, and now Israel has become a stench to the Philistines." And the people were summoned to join Saul at Gilgal.

5The Philistines assembled to fight Israel, with three thousandd chariots, six thousand charioteers, and soldiers as nu-

---

a 1 A few late manuscripts of the Septuagint; Hebrew does not have thirty.   b 1 See the round number in Acts 13:21; Hebrew does not have forty-.   c 1,2 Or and when he had reigned over Israel two years, 2he   d 5 Some Septuagint manuscripts and Syriac; Hebrew thirty thousand

---

GET SMARTER

Patience, Patience

READ 1 SAMUEL 13:1–14

One of Saul's major character flaws was impatience. "Saul's men began to scatter. So … Saul offered up the burnt offering" (verses 8–9). He thought he just couldn't wait any longer, and his impatience cost him the kingdom. Patience with God, with yourself and with others is SO important. When you jump the gun, you can miss God's best and sometimes you just plain lose. "Love is patient, love is kind" (1 Corinthians 13:4). Often, being patient means being kind. If you were teaching someone to juggle a soccer ball, you'd be cool about it, right? You'd cut him some slack, because you know he can only learn so much at a time. Losing your cool would only ruin your relationship. God knows what you can handle and when you're ready. So be patient with God too and wait, even if you really, really prayed hard for something.

Your next reading is on page 355.

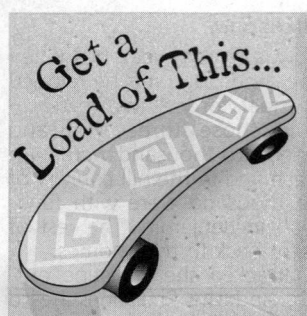

Get a Load of This...

Check out 1 Samuel 13:19–22. The Philistines had a technological advantage. They didn't let the Israelites have any iron weapons. The Israelites had bows and arrows and slings . . . oh yeah, and farming tools. But hoes and bows were no match against iron chariots, iron swords, iron spears and well-trained armies in armor.

merous as the sand on the seashore. They went up and camped at Micmash, east of Beth Aven. ⁶When the men of Israel saw that their situation was critical and that their army was hard pressed, they hid in caves and thickets, among the rocks, and in pits and cisterns. ⁷Some Hebrews even crossed the Jordan to the land of Gad and Gilead.

Saul remained at Gilgal, and all the troops with him were quaking with fear. ⁸He waited seven days, the time set by Samuel; but Samuel did not come to Gilgal, and Saul's men began to scatter. ⁹So he said, "Bring me the burnt offering and the fellowship offerings.ᵃ" And Saul offered up the burnt offering. ¹⁰Just as he finished making the offering, Samuel arrived, and Saul went out to greet him.

¹¹"What have you done?" asked Samuel.

Saul replied, "When I saw that the men were scattering, and that you did not come at the set time, and that the Philistines were assembling at Micmash, ¹²I thought, 'Now the Philistines will come down against me at Gilgal, and I have not sought the LORD's favor.' So I felt compelled to offer the burnt offering."

¹³"You acted foolishly," Samuel said. "You have not kept the command the LORD your God gave you; if you had, he would have established your kingdom over Israel for all time. ¹⁴But now your kingdom will not endure; the LORD has sought out a man after his own heart and appointed him leader of his people, because you have not kept the LORD's command."

¹⁵Then Samuel left Gilgalᵇ and went up to Gibeah in Benjamin, and Saul counted the men who were with him. They numbered about six hundred.

Israel Without Weapons

¹⁶Saul and his son Jonathan and the men with them were staying in Gibeahᶜ in Benjamin, while the Philistines camped at Micmash. ¹⁷Raiding parties went out from the Philistine camp in three detachments. One turned toward Ophrah in the vicinity of Shual, ¹⁸another toward Beth Horon, and the third toward the borderland overlooking the Valley of Zeboim facing the desert.

¹⁹Not a blacksmith could be found in the whole land of Israel, because the Philistines had said, "Otherwise the Hebrews will make swords or spears!" ²⁰So all Israel went down to the Philistines to have their plowshares, mattocks, axes and sicklesᵈ sharpened. ²¹The price was two thirds of a shekelᵉ for sharpening plowshares and mattocks, and a third of a shekelᶠ for sharpening forks and axes and for repointing goads.

²²So on the day of the battle not a soldier with Saul

ᵃ9 Traditionally *peace offerings* ᵇ15 Hebrew; Septuagint *Gilgal and went his way; the rest of the people went after Saul to meet the army, and they went out of Gilgal* ᶜ16 Two Hebrew manuscripts; most Hebrew manuscripts *Geba*, a variant of *Gibeah* ᵈ20 Septuagint; Hebrew *plowshares* ᵉ21 Hebrew *pim*; that is, about 1/4 ounce (about 8 grams) ᶠ21 That is, about 1/8 ounce (about 4 grams) and Jonathan had a sword or spear in his hand; only Saul and his son Jonathan had them.

Jonathan Attacks the Philistines

23Now a detachment of Philistines had gone out to the pass at Micmash. 1One day Jonathan son of Saul said to the young man bearing his armor, "Come, let's go over to the Philistine outpost on the other side." But he did not tell his father.

2Saul was staying on the outskirts of Gibeah under a pomegranate tree in Migron. With him were about six hundred men, 3among whom was Ahijah, who was wearing an ephod. He was a son of Ichabod's brother Ahitub son of Phinehas, the son of Eli, the LORD's priest in Shiloh. No one was aware that Jonathan had left.

4On each side of the pass that Jonathan intended to cross to reach the Philistine outpost was a cliff; one was called Bozez, and the other Seneh. 5One cliff stood to the north toward Micmash, the other to the south toward Geba.

6Jonathan said to his young armor-bearer, "Come, let's go over to the outpost of those uncircumcised fellows. Perhaps the LORD will act in our behalf. Nothing can hinder the LORD from saving, whether by many or by few."

7"Do all that you have in mind," his armor-bearer said. "Go ahead; I am with you heart and soul."

8Jonathan said, "Come, then; we will cross over toward the men and let them see us. 9If they say to us, 'Wait there until we come to you,' we will stay where we are and not go up to them. 10But if they say, 'Come up to us,' we will climb up, because that will be our sign that the LORD has given them into our hands."

11So both of them showed themselves to the Philistine outpost. "Look!" said the Philistines. "The Hebrews are crawling out of the holes they were hiding in." 12The men of the outpost shouted to Jonathan

Soldier Under Command

READ 1 SAMUEL 14:1–23

Jonathan had it going—the ultimate combination of warrior strength and godly character. When he and his armor-bearer went rock-climbing up the cliff, looking for some Philistine enemies, he trusted that God was with him. "Perhaps the LORD will act in our behalf. Nothing can hinder the LORD from saving, whether by many or by few" (verse 6). Jonathan was confident in his strength and ability as a soldier, but more than anything else, his confidence was in God. He was well prepared, both physically and spiritually. Jonathan loved excellence and strong character. He trained hard as a warrior, and was skilled and fit. By himself, he knew he could take on half a dozen Philistines. With God's help, he could take on a whole army. A real man believes that, with God, all things are possible. The size of the problem doesn't matter.

Your next reading is on page 358.

and his armor-bearer, "Come up to us and we'll teach you a lesson."

So Jonathan said to his armor-bearer, "Climb up after me; the LORD has given them into the hand of Israel."

¹³Jonathan climbed up, using his hands and feet, with his armor-bearer right behind him. The Philistines fell before Jonathan, and his armor-bearer followed and killed behind him. ¹⁴In that first attack Jonathan and his armor-bearer killed some twenty men in an area of about half an acre.ᵃ

Israel Routs the Philistines

¹⁵Then panic struck the whole army—those in the camp and field, and those in the outposts and raiding parties—and the ground shook. It was a panic sent by God.ᵇ

¹⁶Saul's lookouts at Gibeah in Benjamin saw the army melting away in all directions. ¹⁷Then Saul said to the men who were with him, "Muster the forces and see who has left us." When they did, it was Jonathan and his armor-bearer who were not there.

¹⁸Saul said to Ahijah, "Bring the ark of God." (At that time it was with the Israelites.)ᶜ ¹⁹While Saul was talking to the priest, the tumult in the Philistine camp increased more and more. So Saul said to the priest, "Withdraw your hand."

²⁰Then Saul and all his men assembled and went to the battle. They found the Philistines in total confusion, striking each other with their swords. ²¹Those Hebrews who had previously been with the Philistines and had gone up with them to their camp went over to the Israelites who were with Saul and Jonathan. ²²When all the Israelites who had hidden in the hill country of Ephraim heard that the Philistines were on the run, they joined the battle in hot pursuit. ²³So the LORD rescued Israel that day, and the battle moved on beyond Beth Aven.

Jonathan Eats Honey

²⁴Now the men of Israel were in distress that day, because Saul had bound the people under an oath, saying, "Cursed be any man who eats food before evening comes, before I have avenged myself on my enemies!" So none of the troops tasted food.

²⁵The entire armyᵈ entered the woods, and there was honey on the ground. ²⁶When they went into the woods, they saw the honey oozing out, yet no one put his hand to his mouth, because they feared the oath. ²⁷But Jonathan had not heard that his father had bound the people with the oath, so he reached out the end of the staff that was in his hand and dipped it into the honeycomb. He raised his hand to his mouth, and his eyes brightened.ᵉ ²⁸Then one of the soldiers told him, "Your father bound the army under a strict oath, saying, 'Cursed be any man who eats food today!' That is why the men are faint."

²⁹Jonathan said, "My father has made trouble for the country. See how my eyes brightenedᶠ when I tasted a little of this honey. ³⁰How much better it would have been if the men had eaten today some of the plunder they took from their enemies. Would not the slaughter of the Philistines have been even greater?"

³¹That day, after the Israelites had struck down the Philistines from Micmash to Aijalon, they were exhausted. ³²They pounced on the plunder and, taking sheep, cattle and calves, they butchered them on the ground and ate them, together with the blood. ³³Then someone said to Saul, "Look, the men are sinning against the LORD by eating meat that has blood in it."

"You have broken faith," he said. "Roll a large stone over here at once." ³⁴Then he said, "Go out among the men and tell them, 'Each of you bring me your cattle and sheep, and slaughter them here and eat them. Do not sin against the LORD by eating meat with blood still in it.' "

So everyone brought his ox that night and slaughtered it there. ³⁵Then Saul built an altar to the LORD; it was the first time he had done this.

³⁶Saul said, "Let us go down after the Philistines by night and plunder them till dawn, and let us not leave one of them alive."

"Do whatever seems best to you," they replied.

But the priest said, "Let us inquire of God here."

ᵃ 14 Hebrew *half a yoke*; a "yoke" was the land plowed by a yoke of oxen in one day.   ᵇ 15 Or *a terrible panic*   ᶜ 18 Hebrew; Septuagint *"Bring the ephod."* (At that time he wore the ephod before the Israelites.)   ᵈ 25 Or *Now all the people of the land*   ᵉ 27 Or *his strength was renewed*   ᶠ 29 Or *my strength was renewed*

37So Saul asked God, "Shall I go down after the Philistines? Will you give them into Israel's hand?" But God did not answer him that day. 38Saul therefore said, "Come here, all you who are leaders of the army, and let us find out what sin has been committed today. 39As surely as the LORD who rescues Israel lives, even if it lies with my son Jonathan, he must die." But not one of the men said a word.

40Saul then said to all the Israelites, "You stand over there; I and Jonathan my son will stand over here."

"Do what seems best to you," the men replied.

41Then Saul prayed to the LORD, the God of Israel, "Give me the right answer."a And Jonathan and Saul were taken by lot, and the men were cleared. 42Saul said, "Cast the lot between me and Jonathan my son." And Jonathan was taken.

43Then Saul said to Jonathan, "Tell me what you have done."

So Jonathan told him, "I merely tasted a little honey with the end of my staff. And now must I die?"

44Saul said, "May God deal with me, be it ever so severely, if you do not die, Jonathan."

45But the men said to Saul, "Should Jonathan die—he who has brought about this great deliverance in Israel? Never! As surely as the LORD lives, not a hair of his head will fall to the ground, for he did this today with God's help." So the men rescued Jonathan, and he was not put to death.

46Then Saul stopped pursuing the Philistines, and they withdrew to their own land.

47After Saul had assumed rule over Israel, he fought against their enemies on every side: Moab, the Ammonites, Edom, the kingsb of Zobah, and the Philistines. Wherever he turned, he inflicted punishment on them.c 48He fought valiantly and defeated the Amalekites, delivering Israel from the hands of those who had plundered them.

Saul's Family

49Saul's sons were Jonathan, Ishvi and Malki-Shua. The name of his older daughter was Merab, and that of the younger was Michal. 50His wife's name was Ahinoam daughter of Ahimaaz. The name of the commander of Saul's army was Abner son of Ner, and Ner was Saul's uncle. 51Saul's father Kish and Abner's father Ner were sons of Abiel.

52All the days of Saul there was bitter war with the Philistines, and whenever Saul saw a mighty or brave man, he took him into his service.

The LORD Rejects Saul as King

15 Samuel said to Saul, "I am the one the LORD sent to anoint you king over his people Israel; so listen now to the message from the LORD. 2This is what the LORD Almighty says: 'I will punish the Amalekites for what they did to Israel when they waylaid them as they came up from Egypt. 3Now go, attack the Amalekites and totally destroyd everything that belongs to them. Do not spare them; put to death men and women, children and infants, cattle and sheep, camels and donkeys.' "

4So Saul summoned the men and mustered them at Telaim—two hundred thousand foot soldiers and ten thousand men from Judah. 5Saul went to the city of Amalek and set an ambush in the ravine. 6Then he said to the Kenites, "Go away, leave the Amalekites so that I do not destroy you along with them; for you showed kindness to all the Israelites when they came up out of Egypt." So the Kenites moved away from the Amalekites.

7Then Saul attacked the Amalekites all the way from Havilah to Shur, to the east of Egypt. 8He took Agag king of the Amalekites alive, and all his people he totally destroyed with the sword. 9But Saul and the army spared Agag and the best of the sheep and cattle, the fat calvese and lambs—everything that was good. These they were unwilling to destroy completely, but everything that was despised and weak they totally destroyed.

10Then the word of the LORD came to Samuel: 11"I am grieved that I have made Saul king, because he has turned away from me and has not carried out my in-

---

a 41 Hebrew; Septuagint "Why have you not answered your servant today? If the fault is in me or my son Jonathan, respond with Urim, but if the men of Israel are at fault, respond with Thummim."   b 47 Masoretic Text; Dead Sea Scrolls and Septuagint king   c 47 Hebrew; Septuagint he was victorious   d 3 The Hebrew term refers to the irrevocable giving over of things or persons to the LORD, often by totally destroying them; also in verses 8, 9, 15, 18, 20 and 21.   e 9 Or the grown bulls; the meaning of the Hebrew for this phrase is uncertain.

structions." Samuel was troubled, and he cried out to the LORD all that night.

¹²Early in the morning Samuel got up and went to meet Saul, but he was told, "Saul has gone to Carmel. There he has set up a monument in his own honor and has turned and gone on down to Gilgal."

¹³When Samuel reached him, Saul said, "The LORD bless you! I have carried out the LORD's instructions."

¹⁴But Samuel said, "What then is this bleating of sheep in my ears? What is this lowing of cattle that I hear?"

¹⁵Saul answered, "The soldiers brought them from the Amalekites; they spared the best of the sheep and cattle to sacrifice to the LORD your God, but we totally destroyed the rest."

¹⁶"Stop!" Samuel said to Saul. "Let me tell you what the LORD said to me last night."

"Tell me," Saul replied.

¹⁷Samuel said, "Although you were once small in your own eyes, did you not become the head of the tribes of Israel? The LORD anointed you king over Israel.

¹⁸And he sent you on a mission, saying, 'Go and completely destroy those wicked people, the Amalekites; make war on them until you have wiped them out.' ¹⁹Why did you not obey the LORD? Why did you pounce on the plunder and do evil in the eyes of the LORD?"

²⁰"But I did obey the LORD," Saul said. "I went on the mission the LORD assigned me. I completely destroyed the Amalekites and brought back Agag their king. ²¹The soldiers took sheep and cattle from the plunder, the best of what was devoted to God, in order to sacrifice them to the LORD your God at Gilgal."

²²But Samuel replied:

"Does the LORD delight in burnt
    offerings and sacrifices
  as much as in obeying the voice of
    the LORD?
To obey is better than sacrifice,
  and to heed is better than the fat of
    rams.
²³For rebellion is like the sin of divination,
  and arrogance like the evil of
    idolatry.

GET SMARTER

God Makes Sense

READ 1 SAMUEL 15:1–26

Saul just didn't *get* it. He thought he knew better than God. He didn't obey God because he couldn't see the sense in God's commands. Men struggle with this today, too. God says not to lie (it's the ninth commandment; see Exodus 20:16). But people say it's OK anyway. Lies don't hurt anyone, right? Wrong. You need to trust God and say, "No." What his Word says is the truth and for your good. You need to obey even if you don't understand. God told Saul, "Because you have rejected the word of the LORD, he has rejected you as king" (verse 23). If you watch the news, go to the mall, hang out at the local skate park, you'll see guys who want to "do their own thing" but are totally clueless about the consequences of their actions. Don't play that game. Ask Saul—there are no winners.

Your next reading is on page 360.

Because you have rejected the word of
        the Lord,
    he has rejected you as king."

²⁴Then Saul said to Samuel, "I have
sinned. I violated the Lord's command
and your instructions. I was afraid of the
people and so I gave in to them. ²⁵Now I
beg you, forgive my sin and come back
with me, so that I may worship the Lord."
²⁶But Samuel said to him, "I will not go
back with you. You have rejected the
word of the Lord, and the Lord has rejected you as king over Israel!"

²⁷As Samuel turned to leave, Saul
caught hold of the hem of his robe, and it
tore. ²⁸Samuel said to him, "The Lord has
torn the kingdom of Israel from you today
and has given it to one of your neighbors—to one better than you. ²⁹He who is
the Glory of Israel does not lie or change
his mind; for he is not a man, that he
should change his mind."

³⁰Saul replied, "I have sinned. But
please honor me before the elders of my
people and before Israel; come back with
me, so that I may worship the Lord your
God." ³¹So Samuel went back with Saul,
and Saul worshiped the Lord.

³²Then Samuel said, "Bring me Agag
king of the Amalekites."

Agag came to him confidently,^a thinking, "Surely the bitterness of death is
past."

³³But Samuel said,

"As your sword has made women
        childless,
    so will your mother be childless
        among women."

And Samuel put Agag to death before the
Lord at Gilgal.

³⁴Then Samuel left for Ramah, but Saul
went up to his home in Gibeah of Saul.
³⁵Until the day Samuel died, he did not go
to see Saul again, though Samuel mourned
for him. And the Lord was grieved that he
had made Saul king over Israel.

Samuel Anoints David

16 The Lord said to Samuel, "How
long will you mourn for Saul,
since I have rejected him as king
over Israel? Fill your horn with oil
and be on your way; I am sending you to
Jesse of Bethlehem. I have chosen one of
his sons to be king."

²But Samuel said, "How can I go? Saul
will hear about it and kill me."

The Lord said, "Take a heifer with you
and say, 'I have come to sacrifice to the
Lord.' ³Invite Jesse to the sacrifice, and I
will show you what to do. You are to
anoint for me the one I indicate."

⁴Samuel did what the Lord said. When
he arrived at Bethlehem, the elders of the
town trembled when they met him. They
asked, "Do you come in peace?"

⁵Samuel replied, "Yes, in peace; I have
come to sacrifice to the Lord. Consecrate
yourselves and come to the sacrifice with
me." Then he consecrated Jesse and his
sons and invited them to the sacrifice.

⁶When they arrived, Samuel saw Eliab
and thought, "Surely the Lord's anointed
stands here before the Lord."

⁷But the Lord said to Samuel, "Do not
consider his appearance or his height, for
I have rejected him. The Lord does not
look at the things man looks at. Man
looks at the outward appearance, but the
Lord looks at the heart."

⁸Then Jesse called Abinadab and had
him pass in front of Samuel. But Samuel
said, "The Lord has not chosen this one either." ⁹Jesse then had Shammah pass by,
but Samuel said, "Nor has the Lord chosen this one." ¹⁰Jesse had seven of his
sons pass before Samuel, but Samuel said
to him, "The Lord has not chosen these."
¹¹So he asked Jesse, "Are these all the
sons you have?"

"There is still the youngest," Jesse answered, "but he is tending the sheep."

Samuel said, "Send for him; we will not
sit down^b until he arrives."

¹²So he sent and had him brought in.
He was ruddy, with a fine appearance and
handsome features.

Then the Lord said, "Rise and anoint
him; he is the one."

¹³So Samuel took the horn of oil and
anointed him in the presence of his brothers, and from that day on the Spirit of the
Lord came upon David in power. Samuel
then went to Ramah.

David in Saul's Service

¹⁴Now the Spirit of the Lord had de-
parted from Saul, and an evil^c spirit from
the Lord tormented him.

---

^a 32 Or him trembling, yet   ^b 11 Some Septuagint
manuscripts; Hebrew not gather around   ^c 14 Or injurious;
also in verses 15, 16 and 23

¹⁵Saul's attendants said to him, "See, an evil spirit from God is tormenting you. ¹⁶Let our lord command his servants here to search for someone who can play the harp. He will play when the evil spirit from God comes upon you, and you will feel better."

¹⁷So Saul said to his attendants, "Find someone who plays well and bring him to me."

¹⁸One of the servants answered, "I have seen a son of Jesse of Bethlehem who knows how to play the harp. He is a brave man and a warrior. He speaks well and is a fine-looking man. And the LORD is with him."

¹⁹Then Saul sent messengers to Jesse and said, "Send me your son David, who is with the sheep." ²⁰So Jesse took a donkey loaded with bread, a skin of wine and a young goat and sent them with his son David to Saul.

²¹David came to Saul and entered his service. Saul liked him very much, and David became one of his armor-bearers. ²²Then Saul sent word to Jesse, saying, "Allow David to remain in my service, for I am pleased with him."

²³Whenever the spirit from God came upon Saul, David would take his harp and play. Then relief would come to Saul; he would feel better, and the evil spirit would leave him.

David and Goliath

17 Now the Philistines gathered their forces for war and assembled at Socoh in Judah. They pitched camp at Ephes Dammim, between Socoh and Azekah. ²Saul and the Israelites assembled and camped in the Valley of Elah and drew up their battle line to meet the Philistines. ³The Philistines occupied one hill and the Israelites another, with the valley between them.

⁴A champion named Goliath, who was from Gath, came out of the Philistine camp. He was over nine feet*a* tall. ⁵He had a bronze helmet on his head and wore a coat of scale armor of bronze weighing five thousand shekels*b*; ⁶on his legs he wore bronze greaves, and a

a 4 Hebrew *was six cubits and a span* (about 3 meters)
b 5 That is, about 125 pounds (about 57 kilograms)

Building From the Inside Out

READ 1 SAMUEL 16

Like Saul, David was a handsome warrior. He was also brave, and a musician. As Israel's new king, he had it all. And what David had that Saul *didn't* have was a heart that loved God. David was cool, but best of all, the Lord was with him (verse 18). That was his foundation. His coolness was built on God. You wouldn't build a house without a foundation or a framework, would you? The first strong wind comes along, and you're one of the three little pigs, looking for a place to live. It's the same with building yourself as a man. Your foundation is your relationship with Jesus Christ, and your framework is made of the talents and abilities God has given you. Build yourself from the inside out. Take care of yourself, look your best, get an education and training for a career, *but* base all of this on your relationship with Jesus.

Your next reading is on page 362.

bronze javelin was slung on his back. [7]His spear shaft was like a weaver's rod, and its iron point weighed six hundred shekels.[a] His shield bearer went ahead of him.

[8]Goliath stood and shouted to the ranks of Israel, "Why do you come out and line up for battle? Am I not a Philistine, and are you not the servants of Saul? Choose a man and have him come down to me. [9]If he is able to fight and kill me, we will become your subjects; but if I overcome him and kill him, you will become our subjects and serve us." [10]Then the Philistine said, "This day I defy the ranks of Israel! Give me a man and let us fight each other." [11]On hearing the Philistine's words, Saul and all the Israelites were dismayed and terrified.

[12]Now David was the son of an Ephrathite named Jesse, who was from Bethlehem in Judah. Jesse had eight sons, and in Saul's time he was old and well advanced in years. [13]Jesse's three oldest sons had followed Saul to the war: The firstborn was Eliab; the second, Abinadab; and the third, Shammah. [14]David was the youngest. The three oldest followed Saul, [15]but David went back and forth from Saul to tend his father's sheep at Bethlehem.

[16]For forty days the Philistine came forward every morning and evening and took his stand.

[17]Now Jesse said to his son David, "Take this ephah[b] of roasted grain and these ten loaves of bread for your brothers and hurry to their camp. [18]Take along these ten cheeses to the commander of their unit.[c] See how your brothers are and bring back some assurance[d] from them. [19]They are with Saul and all the men of Israel in the Valley of Elah, fighting against the Philistines."

[20]Early in the morning David left the flock with a shepherd, loaded up and set

[a] 7 That is, about 15 pounds (about 7 kilograms)
[b] 17 That is, probably about 3/5 bushel (about 22 liters)
[c] 18 Hebrew *thousand*   [d] 18 Or *some token; or some pledge of spoils*

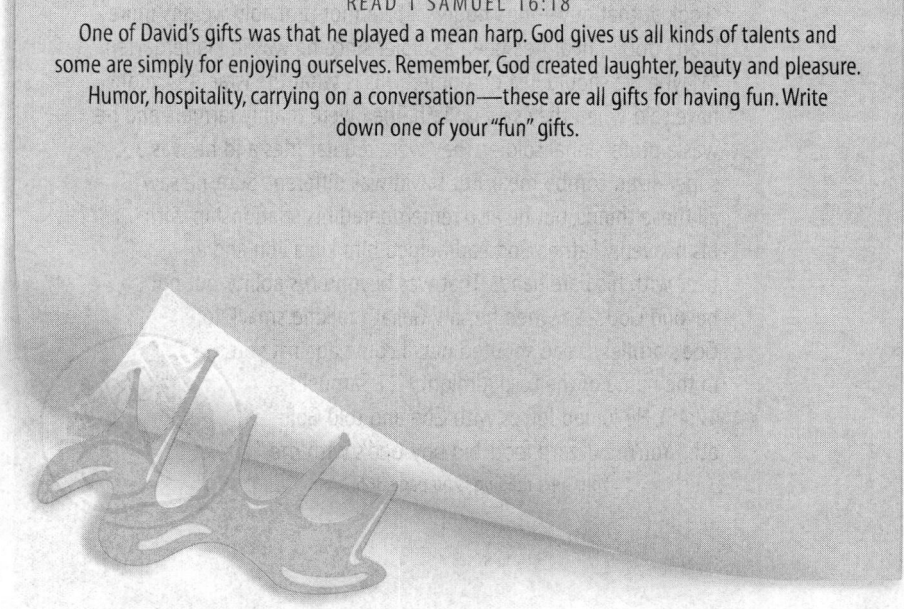

Make It Stick

READ 1 SAMUEL 16:18

One of David's gifts was that he played a mean harp. God gives us all kinds of talents and some are simply for enjoying ourselves. Remember, God created laughter, beauty and pleasure. Humor, hospitality, carrying on a conversation—these are all gifts for having fun. Write down one of your "fun" gifts.

out, as Jesse had directed. He reached the camp as the army was going out to its battle positions, shouting the war cry. ²¹Israel and the Philistines were drawing up their lines facing each other. ²²David left his things with the keeper of supplies, ran to the battle lines and greeted his brothers. ²³As he was talking with them, Goliath, the Philistine champion from Gath, stepped out from his lines and shouted his usual defiance, and David heard it. ²⁴When the Israelites saw the man, they all ran from him in great fear.

²⁵Now the Israelites had been saying, "Do you see how this man keeps coming out? He comes out to defy Israel. The king will give great wealth to the man who kills him. He will also give him his daughter in marriage and will exempt his father's family from taxes in Israel."

²⁶David asked the men standing near him, "What will be done for the man who kills this Philistine and removes this disgrace from Israel? Who is this uncircumcised Philistine that he should defy the armies of the living God?"

²⁷They repeated to him what they had been saying and told him, "This is what will be done for the man who kills him."

²⁸When Eliab, David's oldest brother, heard him speaking with the men, he burned with anger at him and asked, "Why have you come down here? And with whom did you leave those few sheep in the desert? I know how conceited you are and how wicked your heart is; you came down only to watch the battle."

²⁹"Now what have I done?" said David. "Can't I even speak?" ³⁰He then turned away to someone else and brought up the same matter, and the men answered him as before. ³¹What David said was overheard and reported to Saul, and Saul sent for him.

³²David said to Saul, "Let no one lose heart on account of this Philistine; your servant will go and fight him."

³³Saul replied, "You are not able to go

GET STRONGER

My Daddy Can Whip Yours!

READ 1 SAMUEL 17:1–11, 32–51

"Look at that guy—he's huge!" "His armor probably weighs more than I do!" "I hear he's been a soldier since he was in kindergarten." "Maybe we should just go home." This is what the Israelites might have said when they saw Goliath. They were mainly farmers and he was a professional soldier. They were regular fries and he was a super-sized combo meal. But David was different. Sure, he saw all those things, but he also remembered his relationship with his heavenly Father. God had helped him kill a lion and a bear with his bare hands. That was beyond *his* ability, but not beyond God's. So when he saw Goliath talking smack to God's armies, David shouted out, "I come against you in the name of the Lord Almighty" (1 Samuel 17:45). He joined forces with God and told Goliath, "You're buzzard food, big boy. God's with *me*."

Your next reading is on page 366.

out against this Philistine and fight him; you are only a boy, and he has been a fighting man from his youth."

³⁴But David said to Saul, "Your servant has been keeping his father's sheep. When a lion or a bear came and carried off a sheep from the flock, ³⁵I went after it, struck it and rescued the sheep from its mouth. When it turned on me, I seized it by its hair, struck it and killed it. ³⁶Your servant has killed both the lion and the bear; this uncircumcised Philistine will be like one of them, because he has defied the armies of the living God. ³⁷The LORD who delivered me from the paw of the lion and the paw of the bear will deliver me from the hand of this Philistine."

Saul said to David, "Go, and the LORD be with you."

³⁸Then Saul dressed David in his own tunic. He put a coat of armor on him and a bronze helmet on his head. ³⁹David fastened on his sword over the tunic and tried walking around, because he was not used to them.

"I cannot go in these," he said to Saul, "because I am not used to them." So he took them off. ⁴⁰Then he took his staff in his hand, chose five smooth stones from the stream, put them in the pouch of his shepherd's bag and, with his sling in his hand, approached the Philistine.

⁴¹Meanwhile, the Philistine, with his shield bearer in front of him, kept coming closer to David. ⁴²He looked David over and saw that he was only a boy, ruddy and handsome, and he despised him. ⁴³He said to David, "Am I a dog, that you come at me with sticks?" And the Philistine cursed David by his gods. ⁴⁴"Come here," he said, "and I'll give your flesh to the birds of the air and the beasts of the field!"

⁴⁵David said to the Philistine, "You come against me with sword and spear and javelin, but I come against you in the name of the LORD Almighty, the God of the armies of Israel, whom you have defied. ⁴⁶This day the LORD will hand you over to me, and I'll strike you down and cut off your head. Today I will give the carcasses of the Philistine army to the birds of the air and the beasts of the earth, and the whole world will know that there is a God in Israel. ⁴⁷All those gathered here will know that it is not by sword or spear that the LORD saves; for the battle is the LORD's, and he will give all of you into our hands."

⁴⁸As the Philistine moved closer to attack him, David ran quickly toward the battle line to meet him. ⁴⁹Reaching into his bag and taking out a stone, he slung it and struck the Philistine on the forehead. The stone sank into his forehead, and he fell facedown on the ground.

⁵⁰So David triumphed over the Philistine with a sling and a stone; without a sword in his hand he struck down the Philistine and killed him.

⁵¹David ran and stood over him. He took hold of the Philistine's sword and drew it from the scabbard. After he killed him, he cut off his head with the sword.

When the Philistines saw that their hero was dead,

Gross!

Check out 1 Samuel 17:51. Nobody said giant-killing was clean business. When David hoisted the monster doorstop that used to be Goliath's head, he probably got blood everywhere. There are some big blood vessels in the neck region, and a giant's are probably like hoses. Messy, messy!

they turned and ran. ⁵²Then the men of Israel and Judah surged forward with a shout and pursued the Philistines to the entrance of Gath*a* and to the gates of Ekron. Their dead were strewn along the Shaaraim road to Gath and Ekron. ⁵³When the Israelites returned from chasing the Philistines, they plundered their camp. ⁵⁴David took the Philistine's head and brought it to Jerusalem, and he put the Philistine's weapons in his own tent.

⁵⁵As Saul watched David going out to meet the Philistine, he said to Abner, commander of the army, "Abner, whose son is that young man?"

Abner replied, "As surely as you live, O king, I don't know."

⁵⁶The king said, "Find out whose son this young man is."

⁵⁷As soon as David returned from killing the Philistine, Abner took him and brought him before Saul, with David still holding the Philistine's head.

⁵⁸"Whose son are you, young man?" Saul asked him.

David said, "I am the son of your servant Jesse of Bethlehem."

Saul's Jealousy of David

18 After David had finished talking with Saul, Jonathan became one in spirit with David, and he loved him as himself. ²From that day Saul kept David with him and did not let him return to his father's house. ³And Jonathan made a covenant with David because he loved him as himself. ⁴Jonathan took off the robe he was wearing and gave it to David, along with his tunic, and even his sword, his bow and his belt.

⁵Whatever Saul sent him to do, David did it so successfully*b* that Saul gave him a high rank in the army. This pleased all the people, and Saul's officers as well.

⁶When the men were returning home after David had killed the Philistine, the women came out from all the towns of Israel to meet King Saul with singing and dancing, with joyful songs and with tambourines and lutes. ⁷As they danced, they sang:

"Saul has slain his thousands,
    and David his tens of thousands."

⁸Saul was very angry; this refrain galled him. "They have credited David with tens of thousands," he thought, "but me with

only thousands. What more can he get but the kingdom?" ⁹And from that time on Saul kept a jealous eye on David.

¹⁰The next day an evil*c* spirit from God came forcefully upon Saul. He was prophesying in his house, while David was playing the harp, as he usually did. Saul had a spear in his hand ¹¹and he hurled it, saying to himself, "I'll pin David to the wall." But David eluded him twice.

¹²Saul was afraid of David, because the LORD was with David but had left Saul. ¹³So he sent David away from him and gave him command over a thousand men, and David led the troops in their campaigns. ¹⁴In everything he did he had great success,*d* because the LORD was with him. ¹⁵When Saul saw how successful*e* he was, he was afraid of him. ¹⁶But all Israel and Judah loved David, because he led them in their campaigns.

¹⁷Saul said to David, "Here is my older daughter Merab. I will give her to you in marriage; only serve me bravely and fight the battles of the LORD." For Saul said to himself, "I will not raise a hand against him. Let the Philistines do that!"

¹⁸But David said to Saul, "Who am I, and what is my family or my father's clan in Israel, that I should become the king's son-in-law?" ¹⁹So*f* when the time came for Merab, Saul's daughter, to be given to David, she was given in marriage to Adriel of Meholah.

²⁰Now Saul's daughter Michal was in love with David, and when they told Saul about it, he was pleased. ²¹"I will give her to him," he thought, "so that she may be a snare to him and so that the hand of the Philistines may be against him." So Saul said to David, "Now you have a second opportunity to become my son-in-law."

²²Then Saul ordered his attendants: "Speak to David privately and say, 'Look, the king is pleased with you, and his attendants all like you; now become his son-in-law.'"

²³They repeated these words to David. But David said, "Do you think it is a small matter to become the king's son-in-law? I'm only a poor man and little known."

²⁴When Saul's servants told him what David had said, ²⁵Saul replied, "Say to Da-

---

a 52 Some Septuagint manuscripts; Hebrew *a valley*
b 5 Or *wisely*   *c 10* Or *injurious*   *d 14* Or *he was very wise*   *e 15* Or *wise*   *f 19* Or *However,*

vid, 'The king wants no other price for the bride than a hundred Philistine foreskins, to take revenge on his enemies.' " Saul's plan was to have David fall by the hands of the Philistines.

26When the attendants told David these things, he was pleased to become the king's son-in-law. So before the allotted time elapsed, 27David and his men went out and killed two hundred Philistines. He brought their foreskins and presented the full number to the king so that he might become the king's son-in-law. Then Saul gave him his daughter Michal in marriage.

28When Saul realized that the LORD was with David and that his daughter Michal loved David, 29Saul became still more afraid of him, and he remained his enemy the rest of his days.

30The Philistine commanders continued to go out to battle, and as often as they did, David met with more successª than the rest of Saul's officers, and his name became well known.

Saul Tries to Kill David

19 Saul told his son Jonathan and all the attendants to kill David. But Jonathan was very fond of David 2and warned him, "My father Saul is looking for a chance to kill you. Be on your guard tomorrow morning; go into hiding and stay there. 3I will go out and stand with my father in the field where you are. I'll speak to him about you and will tell you what I find out."

4Jonathan spoke well of David to Saul his father and said to him, "Let not the king do wrong to his servant David; he has not wronged you, and what he has done has benefited you greatly. 5He took his life in his hands when he killed the Philistine. The LORD won a great victory for all Israel, and you saw it and were glad. Why then would you do wrong to an innocent man like David by killing him for no reason?"

ª 30 Or David acted more wisely

Make It Stick

READ 1 SAMUEL 18:9

Saul felt threatened by David. His jealousy led to fear, and fear led to spear-throwing. That's the wrong reaction. When you see someone who's good at something, be encouraged. They've worked hard to succeed and are proof that you can, too. Write the name of someone you know and his or her gift. Thank him or her for inspiring you.

⁶Saul listened to Jonathan and took this oath: "As surely as the LORD lives, David will not be put to death."

⁷So Jonathan called David and told him the whole conversation. He brought him to Saul, and David was with Saul as before.

⁸Once more war broke out, and David went out and fought the Philistines. He struck them with such force that they fled before him.

⁹But an evil*ᵃ* spirit from the LORD came upon Saul as he was sitting in his house with his spear in his hand. While David was playing the harp, ¹⁰Saul tried to pin him to the wall with his spear, but David eluded him as Saul drove the spear into the wall. That night David made good his escape.

¹¹Saul sent men to David's house to watch it and to kill him in the morning. But Michal, David's wife, warned him, "If you don't run for your life tonight, tomorrow you'll be killed." ¹²So Michal let David down through a window, and he fled and escaped. ¹³Then Michal took an idol*ᵇ* and laid it on the bed, covering it with a garment and putting some goats' hair at the head.

¹⁴When Saul sent the men to capture David, Michal said, "He is ill."

¹⁵Then Saul sent the men back to see David and told them, "Bring him up to me in his bed so that I may kill him." ¹⁶But when the men entered, there was the idol in the bed, and at the head was some goats' hair.

¹⁷Saul said to Michal, "Why did you deceive me like this and send my enemy away so that he escaped?"

Michal told him, "He said to me, 'Let me get away. Why should I kill you?' "

¹⁸When David had fled and made his escape, he went to Samuel at Ramah and told him all that Saul had done to him. Then he and Samuel went to Naioth and stayed there. ¹⁹Word came to Saul: "Da-

---

ᵃ 9 Or *injurious*　　ᵇ 13 Hebrew *teraphim*; also in verse 16

Spearmania 1025 B.C.

READ 1 SAMUEL 19:1–10

David honored Saul as God's chosen king. David was always there to play Saul a soothing melody when he was depressed. And how did Saul respond? "Saul tried to pin him to the wall with his spear" (verse 10). Saul had serious problems, but David had the right attitude. When you're tag-teaming with God and he's in your corner, that does NOT mean that everything is always going to go well. But it does mean that when you've been elbow-dropped by life or hit over the head by one of life's folding chairs, you can go to God. Stuff happens, right? When it does, don't ask, "Where was God? Why did that happen?" Instead, talk to God and trust him—as David did—to work on your behalf. Even if you're getting creamed today, God is still in control of the whole show. In the end, that means you'll come out ahead.

Your next reading is on page 368.

vid is in Naioth at Ramah"; 20so he sent men to capture him. But when they saw a group of prophets prophesying, with Samuel standing there as their leader, the Spirit of God came upon Saul's men and they also prophesied. 21Saul was told about it, and he sent more men, and they prophesied too. Saul sent men a third time, and they also prophesied. 22Finally, he himself left for Ramah and went to the great cistern at Secu. And he asked, "Where are Samuel and David?"

"Over in Naioth at Ramah," they said.

23So Saul went to Naioth at Ramah. But the Spirit of God came even upon him, and he walked along prophesying until he came to Naioth. 24He stripped off his robes and also prophesied in Samuel's presence. He lay that way all that day and night. This is why people say, "Is Saul also among the prophets?"

David and Jonathan

20 Then David fled from Naioth at Ramah and went to Jonathan and asked, "What have I done? What is my crime? How have I wronged your father, that he is trying to take my life?"

2"Never!" Jonathan replied. "You are not going to die! Look, my father doesn't do anything, great or small, without confiding in me. Why would he hide this from me? It's not so!"

3But David took an oath and said, "Your father knows very well that I have found favor in your eyes, and he has said to himself, 'Jonathan must not know this or he will be grieved.' Yet as surely as the LORD lives and as you live, there is only a step between me and death."

4Jonathan said to David, "Whatever you want me to do, I'll do for you."

5So David said, "Look, tomorrow is the New Moon festival, and I am supposed to dine with the king; but let me go and hide in the field until the evening of the day after tomorrow. 6If your father misses me at all, tell him, 'David earnestly asked my permission to hurry to Bethlehem, his hometown, because an annual sacrifice is being made there for his whole clan.' 7If he says, 'Very well,' then your servant is safe. But if he loses his temper, you can be sure that he is determined to harm me. 8As for you, show kindness to your servant, for you have brought him into a cov-

enant with you before the LORD. If I am guilty, then kill me yourself! Why hand me over to your father?"

9"Never!" Jonathan said. "If I had the least inkling that my father was determined to harm you, wouldn't I tell you?"

10David asked, "Who will tell me if your father answers you harshly?"

11"Come," Jonathan said, "let's go out into the field." So they went there together.

12Then Jonathan said to David: "By the LORD, the God of Israel, I will surely sound out my father by this time the day after tomorrow! If he is favorably disposed toward you, will I not send you word and let you know? 13But if my father is inclined to harm you, may the LORD deal with me, be it ever so severely, if I do not let you know and send you away safely. May the LORD be with you as he has been with my father. 14But show me unfailing kindness like that of the LORD as long as I live, so that I may not be killed, 15and do not ever cut off your kindness from my family—not even when the LORD has cut off every one of David's enemies from the face of the earth."

16So Jonathan made a covenant with the house of David, saying, "May the LORD call David's enemies to account." 17And Jonathan had David reaffirm his oath out of love for him, because he loved him as he loved himself.

18Then Jonathan said to David: "Tomorrow is the New Moon festival. You will be missed, because your seat will be empty. 19The day after tomorrow, toward evening, go to the place where you hid when this trouble began, and wait by the stone Ezel. 20I will shoot three arrows to the side of it, as though I were shooting at a target. 21Then I will send a boy and say, 'Go, find the arrows.' If I say to him, 'Look, the arrows are on this side of you; bring them here,' then come, because, as surely as the LORD lives, you are safe; there is no danger. 22But if I say to the boy, 'Look, the arrows are beyond you,' then you must go, because the LORD has sent you away. 23And about the matter you and I discussed—remember, the LORD is witness between you and me forever."

24So David hid in the field, and when the New Moon festival came, the king sat down to eat. 25He sat in his customary place by the wall, opposite Jonathan,*a*

---

a 25 Septuagint; Hebrew *wall. Jonathan arose*

and Abner sat next to Saul, but David's place was empty. 26Saul said nothing that day, for he thought, "Something must have happened to David to make him ceremonially unclean—surely he is unclean." 27But the next day, the second day of the month, David's place was empty again. Then Saul said to his son Jonathan, "Why hasn't the son of Jesse come to the meal, either yesterday or today?"

28Jonathan answered, "David earnestly asked me for permission to go to Bethlehem. 29He said, 'Let me go, because our family is observing a sacrifice in the town and my brother has ordered me to be there. If I have found favor in your eyes, let me get away to see my brothers.' That is why he has not come to the king's table."

30Saul's anger flared up at Jonathan and he said to him, "You son of a perverse and rebellious woman! Don't I know that you have sided with the son of Jesse to your own shame and to the shame of the mother who bore you? 31As long as the son of Jesse lives on this earth, neither you nor your kingdom will be established.

Now send and bring him to me, for he must die!"

32"Why should he be put to death? What has he done?" Jonathan asked his father. 33But Saul hurled his spear at him to kill him. Then Jonathan knew that his father intended to kill David.

34Jonathan got up from the table in fierce anger; on that second day of the month he did not eat, because he was grieved at his father's shameful treatment of David.

35In the morning Jonathan went out to the field for his meeting with David. He had a small boy with him, 36and he said to the boy, "Run and find the arrows I shoot." As the boy ran, he shot an arrow beyond him. 37When the boy came to the place where Jonathan's arrow had fallen, Jonathan called out after him, "Isn't the arrow beyond you?" 38Then he shouted, "Hurry! Go quickly! Don't stop!" The boy picked up the arrow and returned to his master. 39(The boy knew nothing of all this; only Jonathan and David knew.) 40Then Jonathan gave his weapons to the boy and said, "Go, carry them back to town."

Warrior Prince and Perfect Friend

READ 1 SAMUEL 20:1–9, 41–42; 23:15–18

One of the absolutely coolest guys in the Bible was the warrior-prince Jonathan. When a young shepherd named David came to the palace, he and Jonathan became best friends (see 1 Samuel 18:1–4). Later, when King Saul got mad at David and tried to kill him, Jonathan met David secretly and said, "You will be king over Israel, and I will be second to you" (1 Samuel 23:17). Talk about a friend! In those days, men often killed one another so *they* could be king. Jonathan was the king's son and therefore Mr. King-to-be, yet he knew that it was God's will for David to be king, not him. He wanted to see God's will done in David's life and he risked his life to protect him. Want to be a true friend to someone? Always encourage your friend to do things God's way, and pray that they find God's will for their life.

Your next reading is on page 372.

⁴¹After the boy had gone, David got up from the south side ⌊of the stone⌋ and bowed down before Jonathan three times, with his face to the ground. Then they kissed each other and wept together—but David wept the most.

⁴²Jonathan said to David, "Go in peace, for we have sworn friendship with each other in the name of the LORD, saying, 'The LORD is witness between you and me, and between your descendants and my descendants forever.' " Then David left, and Jonathan went back to the town.

David at Nob

²¹ David went to Nob, to Ahimelech the priest. Ahimelech trembled when he met him, and asked, "Why are you alone? Why is no one with you?"

²David answered Ahimelech the priest, "The king charged me with a certain matter and said to me, 'No one is to know anything about your mission and your instructions.' As for my men, I have told them to meet me at a certain place. ³Now then, what do you have on hand? Give me five loaves of bread, or whatever you can find."

⁴But the priest answered David, "I don't have any ordinary bread on hand; however, there is some consecrated bread here—provided the men have kept themselves from women."

⁵David replied, "Indeed women have been kept from us, as usual whenever*a* I set out. The men's things*b* are holy even on missions that are not holy. How much more so today!" ⁶So the priest gave him the consecrated bread, since there was no bread there except the bread of the Presence that had been removed from before the LORD and replaced by hot bread on the day it was taken away.

⁷Now one of Saul's servants was there that day, detained before the LORD; he was Doeg the Edomite, Saul's head shepherd.

⁸David asked Ahimelech, "Don't you have a spear or a sword here? I haven't brought my sword or any other weapon, because the king's business was urgent."

⁹The priest replied, "The sword of Goliath the Philistine, whom you killed in the Valley of Elah, is here; it is wrapped in a cloth behind the ephod. If you want it, take it; there is no sword here but that one."

David said, "There is none like it; give it to me."

David at Gath

¹⁰That day David fled from Saul and went to Achish king of Gath. ¹¹But the servants of Achish said to him, "Isn't this David, the king of the land? Isn't he the one they sing about in their dances:

" 'Saul has slain his thousands,
    and David his tens of thousands'?"

a 5 Or from us in the past few days since   *b 5 Or bodies*

Gross!

Check out 1 Samuel 21:10–15. When David arrived in Gath, Achish's servants dragged him before the king and said, "Look! It's David!" Achish looked at the madman rolling his eyes, slobbering all over his beard and clawing the gates like a dog. "Yeah, *right!*" he thought. He threw David out in disgust.

¹²David took these words to heart and was very much afraid of Achish king of Gath. ¹³So he pretended to be insane in their presence; and while he was in their hands he acted like a madman, making marks on the doors of the gate and letting saliva run down his beard.

¹⁴Achish said to his servants, "Look at the man! He is insane! Why bring him to me? ¹⁵Am I so short of madmen that you have to bring this fellow here to carry on like this in front of me? Must this man come into my house?"

David at Adullam and Mizpah

22 David left Gath and escaped to the cave of Adullam. When his brothers and his father's household heard about it, they went down to him there. ²All those who were in distress or in debt or discontented gathered around him, and he became their leader. About four hundred men were with him.

³From there David went to Mizpah in Moab and said to the king of Moab, "Would you let my father and mother come and stay with you until I learn what God will do for me?" ⁴So he left them with the king of Moab, and they stayed with him as long as David was in the stronghold.

⁵But the prophet Gad said to David, "Do not stay in the stronghold. Go into the land of Judah." So David left and went to the forest of Hereth.

Saul Kills the Priests of Nob

⁶Now Saul heard that David and his men had been discovered. And Saul, spear in hand, was seated under the tamarisk tree on the hill at Gibeah, with all his officials standing around him. ⁷Saul said to them, "Listen, men of Benjamin! Will the son of Jesse give all of you fields and vineyards? Will he make all of you commanders of thousands and commanders of hundreds? ⁸Is that why you have all conspired against me? No one tells me when my son makes a covenant with the son of Jesse. None of you is concerned about me or tells me that my son has incited my servant to lie in wait for me, as he does today."

⁹But Doeg the Edomite, who was standing with Saul's officials, said, "I saw the son of Jesse come to Ahimelech son of Ahitub at Nob. ¹⁰Ahimelech inquired of the LORD for him; he also gave him provisions and the sword of Goliath the Philistine."

¹¹Then the king sent for the priest Ahimelech son of Ahitub and his father's whole family, who were the priests at Nob, and they all came to the king. ¹²Saul said, "Listen now, son of Ahitub."

"Yes, my lord," he answered.

¹³Saul said to him, "Why have you conspired against me, you and the son of Jesse, giving him bread and a sword and inquiring of God for him, so that he has rebelled against me and lies in wait for me, as he does today?"

¹⁴Ahimelech answered the king, "Who of all your servants is as loyal as David, the king's son-in-law, captain of your bodyguard and highly respected in your household? ¹⁵Was that day the first time I inquired of God for him? Of course not! Let not the king accuse your servant or any of his father's family, for your servant knows nothing at all about this whole affair."

¹⁶But the king said, "You will surely die, Ahimelech, you and your father's whole family."

¹⁷Then the king ordered the guards at his side: "Turn and kill the priests of the LORD, because they too have sided with David. They knew he was fleeing, yet they did not tell me."

But the king's officials were not willing to raise a hand to strike the priests of the LORD.

¹⁸The king then ordered Doeg, "You turn and strike down the priests." So Doeg the Edomite turned and struck them down. That day he killed eighty-five men who wore the linen ephod. ¹⁹He also put to the sword Nob, the town of the priests, with its men and women, its children and infants, and its cattle, donkeys and sheep.

²⁰But Abiathar, a son of Ahimelech son of Ahitub, escaped and fled to join David. ²¹He told David that Saul had killed the priests of the LORD. ²²Then David said to Abiathar: "That day, when Doeg the Edomite was there, I knew he would be sure to tell Saul. I am responsible for the death of your father's whole family. ²³Stay with me; don't be afraid; the man who is seeking your life is seeking mine also. You will be safe with me."

David Saves Keilah

23 When David was told, "Look, the Philistines are fighting against Keilah and are looting the threshing floors," ²he inquired of the LORD, saying, "Shall I go and attack these Philistines?"

The LORD answered him, "Go, attack the Philistines and save Keilah."

³But David's men said to him, "Here in Judah we are afraid. How much more, then, if we go to Keilah against the Philistine forces!"

⁴Once again David inquired of the LORD, and the LORD answered him, "Go down to Keilah, for I am going to give the Philistines into your hand." ⁵So David and his men went to Keilah, fought the Philistines and carried off their livestock. He inflicted heavy losses on the Philistines and saved the people of Keilah. ⁶(Now Abiathar son of Ahimelech had brought the ephod down with him when he fled to David at Keilah.)

Saul Pursues David

⁷Saul was told that David had gone to Keilah, and he said, "God has handed him over to me, for David has imprisoned himself by entering a town with gates and bars." ⁸And Saul called up all his forces for battle, to go down to Keilah to besiege David and his men.

⁹When David learned that Saul was plotting against him, he said to Abiathar the priest, "Bring the ephod." ¹⁰David said, "O LORD, God of Israel, your servant has heard definitely that Saul plans to come to Keilah and destroy the town on account of me. ¹¹Will the citizens of Keilah surrender me to him? Will Saul come down, as your servant has heard? O LORD, God of Israel, tell your servant."

And the LORD said, "He will."

¹²Again David asked, "Will the citizens of Keilah surrender me and my men to Saul?"

And the LORD said, "They will."

¹³So David and his men, about six hundred in number, left Keilah and kept moving from place to place. When Saul was told that David had escaped from Keilah, he did not go there.

¹⁴David stayed in the desert strongholds and in the hills of the Desert of Ziph.

Day after day Saul searched for him, but God did not give David into his hands.

¹⁵While David was at Horesh in the Desert of Ziph, he learned that Saul had come out to take his life. ¹⁶And Saul's son Jonathan went to David at Horesh and helped him find strength in God. ¹⁷"Don't be afraid," he said. "My father Saul will not lay a hand on you. You will be king over Israel, and I will be second to you. Even my father Saul knows this." ¹⁸The two of them made a covenant before the LORD. Then Jonathan went home, but David remained at Horesh.

¹⁹The Ziphites went up to Saul at Gibeah and said, "Is not David hiding among us in the strongholds at Horesh, on the hill of Hakilah, south of Jeshimon? ²⁰Now, O king, come down whenever it pleases you to do so, and we will be responsible for handing him over to the king."

²¹Saul replied, "The LORD bless you for your concern for me. ²²Go and make further preparation. Find out where David usually goes and who has seen him there. They tell me he is very crafty. ²³Find out about all the hiding places he uses and come back to me with definite information.ᵃ Then I will go with you; if he is in the area, I will track him down among all the clans of Judah."

²⁴So they set out and went to Ziph ahead of Saul. Now David and his men were in the Desert of Maon, in the Arabah south of Jeshimon. ²⁵Saul and his men began the search, and when David was told about it, he went down to the rock and stayed in the Desert of Maon. When Saul heard this, he went into the Desert of Maon in pursuit of David.

²⁶Saul was going along one side of the mountain, and David and his men were on the other side, hurrying to get away from Saul. As Saul and his forces were closing in on David and his men to capture them, ²⁷a messenger came to Saul, saying, "Come quickly! The Philistines are raiding the land." ²⁸Then Saul broke off his pursuit of David and went to meet the Philistines. That is why they call this place Sela Hammahlekoth.ᵇ ²⁹And David went up from there and lived in the strongholds of En Gedi.

ᵃ 23 Or me at Nacon   ᵇ 28 Sela Hammahlekoth means rock of parting.

David Spares Saul's Life

24 After Saul returned from pursuing the Philistines, he was told, "David is in the Desert of En Gedi." ²So Saul took three thousand chosen men from all Israel and set out to look for David and his men near the Crags of the Wild Goats.

³He came to the sheep pens along the way; a cave was there, and Saul went in to relieve himself. David and his men were far back in the cave. ⁴The men said, "This is the day the LORD spoke of when he said *a* to you, 'I will give your enemy into your hands for you to deal with as you wish.' " Then David crept up unnoticed and cut off a corner of Saul's robe.

⁵Afterward, David was conscience-stricken for having cut off a corner of his robe. ⁶He said to his men, "The LORD forbid that I should do such a thing to my master, the LORD's anointed, or lift my hand against him; for he is the anointed of the LORD." ⁷With these words David rebuked his men and did not allow them to attack Saul. And Saul left the cave and went his way.

⁸Then David went out of the cave and called out to Saul, "My lord the king!" When Saul looked behind him, David bowed down and prostrated himself with his face to the ground. ⁹He said to Saul, "Why do you listen when men say, 'David is bent on harming you'? ¹⁰This day you have seen with your own eyes how the LORD delivered you into my hands in the cave. Some urged me to kill you, but I spared you; I said, 'I will not lift my hand against my master, because he is the LORD's anointed.' ¹¹See, my father, look at this piece of your robe in my hand! I cut off the corner of your robe but did not kill you. Now understand and recognize that I am not guilty of wrongdoing or rebellion. I have not wronged you, but you are hunting me down to take my life. ¹²May the LORD judge between you and me. And may the LORD avenge the wrongs you have done to me, but my hand will not touch you. ¹³As the old saying goes, 'From evildoers come evil deeds,' so my hand will not touch you.

a 4 Or *"Today the LORD is saying*

Fighting Fire With Mercy

READ 1 SAMUEL 24:1–12; 26:1–11

David had two chances to take revenge on Saul—but he refused to. David knew that Saul was wrong in everything he was doing, but when he had the chance to try the spear trick on Saul, he didn't. Instead of returning evil for evil, David returned kindness and mercy. He said, "The LORD himself will strike him … But the LORD forbid that I should lay a hand on the LORD's anointed" (1 Samuel 26:10–11). If someone calls you names, you might want to call names back. If someone fouls you hard, you might want to foul him hard. But you shouldn't. Revenge sounds like fun, but Jesus taught us to turn the other cheek. Godly men lead by example. When you refuse to fight fire with fire, you'll show others that what they're doing is wrong. *You* are responsible to God, and God will take care of you.

Your next reading is on page 374.

14"Against whom has the king of Israel come out? Whom are you pursuing? A dead dog? A flea? 15May the LORD be our judge and decide between us. May he consider my cause and uphold it; may he vindicate me by delivering me from your hand."

16When David finished saying this, Saul asked, "Is that your voice, David my son?" And he wept aloud. 17"You are more righteous than I," he said. "You have treated me well, but I have treated you badly. 18You have just now told me of the good you did to me; the LORD delivered me into your hands, but you did not kill me. 19When a man finds his enemy, does he let him get away unharmed? May the LORD reward you well for the way you treated me today. 20I know that you will surely be king and that the kingdom of Israel will be established in your hands. 21Now swear to me by the LORD that you will not cut off my descendants or wipe out my name from my father's family."

22So David gave his oath to Saul. Then Saul returned home, but David and his men went up to the stronghold.

David, Nabal and Abigail

25 Now Samuel died, and all Israel assembled and mourned for him; and they buried him at his home in Ramah.

Then David moved down into the Desert of Maon.a 2A certain man in Maon, who had property there at Carmel, was very wealthy. He had a thousand goats and three thousand sheep, which he was shearing in Carmel. 3His name was Nabal and his wife's name was Abigail. She was an intelligent and beautiful woman, but her husband, a Calebite, was surly and mean in his dealings.

4While David was in the desert, he heard that Nabal was shearing sheep. 5So he sent ten young men and said to them, "Go up to Nabal at Carmel and greet him in my name. 6Say to him: 'Long life to you! Good health to you and your household! And good health to all that is yours!

7" 'Now I hear that it is sheep-shearing time. When your shepherds were with us, we did not mistreat them, and the whole time they were at Carmel nothing of theirs was missing. 8Ask your own servants and they will tell you. Therefore be favorable toward my young men, since we come at a festive time. Please give your servants and your son David whatever you can find for them.' "

9When David's men arrived, they gave Nabal this message in David's name. Then they waited.

10Nabal answered David's servants, "Who is this David? Who is this son of Jesse? Many servants are breaking away from their masters these days. 11Why should I take my bread and water, and the meat I have slaughtered for my shearers, and give it to men coming from who knows where?"

12David's men turned around and went back. When they arrived, they reported every word. 13David said to his men, "Put on your swords!" So they put on their swords, and David put on his. About four hundred men went up with David, while two hundred stayed with the supplies.

14One of the servants told Nabal's wife Abigail: "David sent messengers from the desert to give our master his greetings, but he hurled insults at them. 15Yet these men were very good to us. They did not mistreat us, and the whole time we were out in the fields near them nothing was missing. 16Night and day they were a wall around us all the time we were herding our sheep near them. 17Now think it over and see what you can do, because disaster is hanging over our master and his whole household. He is such a wicked man that no one can talk to him."

18Abigail lost no time. She took two hundred loaves of bread, two skins of wine, five dressed sheep, five seahsb of roasted grain, a hundred cakes of raisins and two hundred cakes of pressed figs, and loaded them on donkeys. 19Then she told her servants, "Go on ahead; I'll follow you." But she did not tell her husband Nabal.

20As she came riding her donkey into a mountain ravine, there were David and his men descending toward her, and she met them. 21David had just said, "It's been useless—all my watching over this fellow's property in the desert so that nothing of his was missing. He has paid me back evil for good. 22May God deal with David,c be it ever so severely, if by morn-

a 1 Some Septuagint manuscripts; Hebrew Paran
b 18 That is, probably about a bushel (about 37 liters)
c 22 Some Septuagint manuscripts; Hebrew with David's enemies

ing I leave alive one male of all who belong to him!"

23When Abigail saw David, she quickly got off her donkey and bowed down before David with her face to the ground. 24She fell at his feet and said: "My lord, let the blame be on me alone. Please let your servant speak to you; hear what your servant has to say. 25May my lord pay no attention to that wicked man Nabal. He is just like his name—his name is Fool, and folly goes with him. But as for me, your servant, I did not see the men my master sent.

26"Now since the LORD has kept you, my master, from bloodshed and from avenging yourself with your own hands, as surely as the LORD lives and as you live, may your enemies and all who intend to harm my master be like Nabal. 27And let this gift, which your servant has brought to my master, be given to the men who follow you. 28Please forgive your servant's offense, for the LORD will certainly make a lasting dynasty for my master, because he fights the LORD's battles. Let no wrongdoing be found in you as long as you live.

29Even though someone is pursuing you to take your life, the life of my master will be bound securely in the bundle of the living by the LORD your God. But the lives of your enemies he will hurl away as from the pocket of a sling. 30When the LORD has done for my master every good thing he promised concerning him and has appointed him leader over Israel, 31my master will not have on his conscience the staggering burden of needless bloodshed or of having avenged himself. And when the LORD has brought my master success, remember your servant."

32David said to Abigail, "Praise be to the LORD, the God of Israel, who has sent you today to meet me. 33May you be blessed for your good judgment and for keeping me from bloodshed this day and from avenging myself with my own hands. 34Otherwise, as surely as the LORD, the God of Israel, lives, who has kept me from harming you, if you had not come quickly to meet me, not one male belonging to Nabal would have been left alive by daybreak."

Hey! I Was Nice to You!

READ 1 SAMUEL 25:1–35

David looked out for Nabal's flocks and Nabal should have rewarded David. On the other hand, David should have handled Nabal's disrespect more gracefully. Nabal lived up to his name—Nabal meant "Fool"—but David's attitude was wrong, too. Only Abigail did the right thing. After she saved the day, David told her, "May you be blessed for your good judgment and for keeping me … from avenging myself with my own hands" (verse 33). Your life isn't WrestleBonanza 22, where revenge and reward are all that matters. You just do the right thing. When you do something nice for someone, don't get upset if they don't pay you back. Maybe they can't. Maybe they don't care. In either case, God wants you to do the right thing *because it's right*. Sooner or later, God will reward you. If someone returns your kindness, that's a bonus, but a real man of God is kind and good to everyone regardless of how they act toward him.

Your next reading is on page 380.

³⁵Then David accepted from her hand what she had brought him and said, "Go home in peace. I have heard your words and granted your request."

³⁶When Abigail went to Nabal, he was in the house holding a banquet like that of a king. He was in high spirits and very drunk. So she told him nothing until daybreak. ³⁷Then in the morning, when Nabal was sober, his wife told him all these things, and his heart failed him and he became like a stone. ³⁸About ten days later, the LORD struck Nabal and he died.

³⁹When David heard that Nabal was dead, he said, "Praise be to the LORD, who has upheld my cause against Nabal for treating me with contempt. He has kept his servant from doing wrong and has brought Nabal's wrongdoing down on his own head."

Then David sent word to Abigail, asking her to become his wife. ⁴⁰His servants went to Carmel and said to Abigail, "David has sent us to you to take you to become his wife."

⁴¹She bowed down with her face to the ground and said, "Here is your maidservant, ready to serve you and wash the feet of my master's servants." ⁴²Abigail quickly got on a donkey and, attended by her five maids, went with David's messengers and became his wife. ⁴³David had also married Ahinoam of Jezreel, and they both were his wives. ⁴⁴But Saul had given his daughter Michal, David's wife, to Paltiel*a* son of Laish, who was from Gallim.

David Again Spares Saul's Life

26 The Ziphites went to Saul at Gibeah and said, "Is not David hiding on the hill of Hakilah, which faces Jeshimon?"

²So Saul went down to the Desert of Ziph, with his three thousand chosen men of Israel, to search there for David. ³Saul made his camp beside the road on the hill of Hakilah facing Jeshimon, but David stayed in the desert. When he saw that Saul had followed him there, ⁴he sent out scouts and learned that Saul had definitely arrived.*b*

⁵Then David set out and went to the place where Saul had camped. He saw where Saul and Abner son of Ner, the commander of the army, had lain down. Saul was lying inside the camp, with the army encamped around him.

⁶David then asked Ahimelech the Hittite and Abishai son of Zeruiah, Joab's brother, "Who will go down into the camp with me to Saul?"

"I'll go with you," said Abishai.

⁷So David and Abishai went to the army by night, and there was Saul, lying asleep inside the camp with his spear stuck in the ground near his head. Abner and the soldiers were lying around him.

⁸Abishai said to David, "Today God has delivered your enemy into your hands. Now let me pin him to the

Gross!

Check out 1 Samuel 25:37–38. While Nabal was as drunk as a skunk, Abigail didn't tell him that he had come *oh-so-close* to being killed. He would have laughed it off. She told him the next morning when he was sober, with a hangover. Nabal was so shocked he had a heart attack or a stroke, and about ten days later he died.

---

a 44 Hebrew Palti, a variant of Paltiel · b 4 Or had come to Nacon ground with one thrust of my spear; I won't strike him twice."

⁹But David said to Abishai, "Don't destroy him! Who can lay a hand on the Lᴏʀᴅ's anointed and be guiltless? ¹⁰As surely as the Lᴏʀᴅ lives," he said, "the Lᴏʀᴅ himself will strike him; either his time will come and he will die, or he will go into battle and perish. ¹¹But the Lᴏʀᴅ forbid that I should lay a hand on the Lᴏʀᴅ's anointed. Now get the spear and water jug that are near his head, and let's go."

¹²So David took the spear and water jug near Saul's head, and they left. No one saw or knew about it, nor did anyone wake up. They were all sleeping, because the Lᴏʀᴅ had put them into a deep sleep.

¹³Then David crossed over to the other side and stood on top of the hill some distance away; there was a wide space between them. ¹⁴He called out to the army and to Abner son of Ner, "Aren't you going to answer me, Abner?"

Abner replied, "Who are you who calls to the king?"

¹⁵David said, "You're a man, aren't you? And who is like you in Israel? Why didn't you guard your lord the king? Someone came to destroy your lord the king. ¹⁶What you have done is not good. As surely as the Lᴏʀᴅ lives, you and your men deserve to die, because you did not guard your master, the Lᴏʀᴅ's anointed. Look around you. Where are the king's spear and water jug that were near his head?"

¹⁷Saul recognized David's voice and said, "Is that your voice, David my son?"

David replied, "Yes it is, my lord the king." ¹⁸And he added, "Why is my lord pursuing his servant? What have I done, and what wrong am I guilty of? ¹⁹Now let my lord the king listen to his servant's words. If the Lᴏʀᴅ has incited you against me, then may he accept an offering. If, however, men have done it, may they be cursed before the Lᴏʀᴅ! They have now driven me from my share in the Lᴏʀᴅ's inheritance and have said, 'Go, serve other gods.' ²⁰Now do not let my blood fall to the ground far from the presence of the Lᴏʀᴅ. The king of Israel has come out to look for a flea—as one hunts a partridge in the mountains."

²¹Then Saul said, "I have sinned. Come back, David my son. Because you considered my life precious today, I will not try to

harm you again. Surely I have acted like a fool and have erred greatly."

²²"Here is the king's spear," David answered. "Let one of your young men come over and get it. ²³The Lᴏʀᴅ rewards every man for his righteousness and faithfulness. The Lᴏʀᴅ delivered you into my hands today, but I would not lay a hand on the Lᴏʀᴅ's anointed. ²⁴As surely as I valued your life today, so may the Lᴏʀᴅ value my life and deliver me from all trouble."

²⁵Then Saul said to David, "May you be blessed, my son David; you will do great things and surely triumph."

So David went on his way, and Saul returned home.

David Among the Philistines

27 But David thought to himself, "One of these days I will be destroyed by the hand of Saul. The best thing I can do is to escape to the land of the Philistines. Then Saul will give up searching for me anywhere in Israel, and I will slip out of his hand."

²So David and the six hundred men with him left and went over to Achish son of Maoch king of Gath. ³David and his men settled in Gath with Achish. Each man had his family with him, and David had his two wives: Ahinoam of Jezreel and Abigail of Carmel, the widow of Nabal. ⁴When Saul was told that David had fled to Gath, he no longer searched for him.

⁵Then David said to Achish, "If I have found favor in your eyes, let a place be assigned to me in one of the country towns, that I may live there. Why should your servant live in the royal city with you?"

⁶So on that day Achish gave him Ziklag, and it has belonged to the kings of Judah ever since. ⁷David lived in Philistine territory a year and four months.

⁸Now David and his men went up and raided the Geshurites, the Girzites and the Amalekites. (From ancient times these peoples had lived in the land extending to Shur and Egypt.) ⁹Whenever David attacked an area, he did not leave a man or woman alive, but took sheep and cattle, donkeys and camels, and clothes. Then he returned to Achish.

¹⁰When Achish asked, "Where did you go raiding today?" David would say, "Against the Negev of Judah" or "Against

the Negev of Jerahmeel" or "Against the Negev of the Kenites." [11]He did not leave a man or woman alive to be brought to Gath, for he thought, "They might inform on us and say, 'This is what David did.' " And such was his practice as long as he lived in Philistine territory. [12]Achish trusted David and said to himself, "He has become so odious to his people, the Israelites, that he will be my servant forever."

Saul and the Witch of Endor

28 In those days the Philistines gathered their forces to fight against Israel. Achish said to David, "You must understand that you and your men will accompany me in the army."

[2]David said, "Then you will see for yourself what your servant can do."

Achish replied, "Very well, I will make you my bodyguard for life."

[3]Now Samuel was dead, and all Israel had mourned for him and buried him in his own town of Ramah. Saul had expelled the mediums and spiritists from the land.

[4]The Philistines assembled and came and set up camp at Shunem, while Saul gathered all the Israelites and set up camp at Gilboa. [5]When Saul saw the Philistine army, he was afraid; terror filled his heart. [6]He inquired of the LORD, but the LORD did not answer him by dreams or Urim or prophets. [7]Saul then said to his attendants, "Find me a woman who is a medium, so I may go and inquire of her."

"There is one in Endor," they said.

[8]So Saul disguised himself, putting on other clothes, and at night he and two men went to the woman. "Consult a spirit for me," he said, "and bring up for me the one I name."

[9]But the woman said to him, "Surely you know what Saul has done. He has cut off the mediums and spiritists from the land. Why have you set a trap for my life to bring about my death?"

[10]Saul swore to her by the LORD, "As surely as the LORD lives, you will not be punished for this."

[11]Then the woman asked, "Whom shall I bring up for you?"

"Bring up Samuel," he said.

[12]When the woman saw Samuel, she cried out at the top of her voice and said to Saul, "Why have you deceived me? You are Saul!"

[13]The king said to her, "Don't be afraid. What do you see?"

The woman said, "I see a spirit[a] coming up out of the ground."

[14]"What does he look like?" he asked.

"An old man wearing a robe is coming up," she said.

Then Saul knew it was Samuel, and he bowed down and prostrated himself with his face to the ground.

[15]Samuel said to Saul, "Why have you disturbed me by bringing me up?"

"I am in great distress," Saul said. "The Philistines are fighting against me, and God has turned away from me. He no longer answers me, either by prophets or by dreams. So I have called on you to tell me what to do."

[16]Samuel said, "Why do you consult me, now that the LORD has turned away from you and become your enemy? [17]The LORD has done what he predicted through me. The LORD has torn the kingdom out of your hands and given it to one of your neighbors—to David. [18]Because you did not obey the LORD or carry out his fierce wrath against the Amalekites, the LORD has done this to you today. [19]The LORD will hand over both Israel and you to the Philistines, and tomorrow you and your sons will be with me. The LORD will also hand over the army of Israel to the Philistines."

[20]Immediately Saul fell full length on the ground, filled with fear because of Samuel's words. His strength was gone, for he had eaten nothing all that day and night.

[21]When the woman came to Saul and saw that he was greatly shaken, she said, "Look, your maidservant has obeyed you. I took my life in my hands and did what you told me to do. [22]Now please listen to your servant and let me give you some food so you may eat and have the strength to go on your way."

[23]He refused and said, "I will not eat."

But his men joined the woman in urging him, and he listened to them. He got up from the ground and sat on the couch.

[24]The woman had a fattened calf at the house, which she butchered at once. She took some flour, kneaded it and baked bread without yeast. [25]Then she set it before Saul and his men, and they ate. That same night they got up and left.

---

[a] 13 Or see spirits; or see gods

Achish Sends David Back to Ziklag

29 The Philistines gathered all their forces at Aphek, and Israel camped by the spring in Jezreel. ²As the Philistine rulers marched with their units of hundreds and thousands, David and his men were marching at the rear with Achish. ³The commanders of the Philistines asked, "What about these Hebrews?"

Achish replied, "Is this not David, who was an officer of Saul king of Israel? He has already been with me for over a year, and from the day he left Saul until now, I have found no fault in him."

⁴But the Philistine commanders were angry with him and said, "Send the man back, that he may return to the place you assigned him. He must not go with us into battle, or he will turn against us during the fighting. How better could he regain his master's favor than by taking the heads of our own men? ⁵Isn't this the David they sang about in their dances:

" 'Saul has slain his thousands,
    and David his tens of thousands'?"

Make It Stick

_____

_____

_____

_____

_____

_____

_____

READ 1 SAMUEL 28:7
When Saul didn't listen to or obey God, God stopped speaking to him. Saul's solution? Visit a "psychic friend." Today, people try to learn their future through astrology, tarot cards, psychics, etc. Wrong? Yes. One, they're worthless. Two, they're dangerous. God's system works—trust *him* for your future. List a few occult things you should avoid (like psychic hotlines and astrology charts).

6So Achish called David and said to him, "As surely as the LORD lives, you have been reliable, and I would be pleased to have you serve with me in the army. From the day you came to me until now, I have found no fault in you, but the rulers don't approve of you. 7Turn back and go in peace; do nothing to displease the Philistine rulers."

8"But what have I done?" asked David. "What have you found against your servant from the day I came to you until now? Why can't I go and fight against the enemies of my lord the king?"

9Achish answered, "I know that you have been as pleasing in my eyes as an angel of God; nevertheless, the Philistine commanders have said, 'He must not go up with us into battle.' 10Now get up early, along with your master's servants who have come with you, and leave in the morning as soon as it is light."

11So David and his men got up early in the morning to go back to the land of the Philistines, and the Philistines went up to Jezreel.

David Destroys the Amalekites

30 David and his men reached Ziklag on the third day. Now the Amalekites had raided the Negev and Ziklag. They had attacked Ziklag and burned it, 2and had taken captive the women and all who were in it, both young and old. They killed none of them, but carried them off as they went on their way.

3When David and his men came to Ziklag, they found it destroyed by fire and their wives and sons and daughters taken captive. 4So David and his men wept aloud until they had no strength left to weep. 5David's two wives had been captured—Ahinoam of Jezreel and Abigail, the widow of Nabal of Carmel. 6David was greatly distressed because the men were talking of stoning him; each one was bitter in spirit because of his sons and daughters. But David found strength in the LORD his God.

7Then David said to Abiathar the priest, the son of Ahimelech, "Bring me the ephod." Abiathar brought it to him, 8and David inquired of the LORD, "Shall I pursue this raiding party? Will I overtake them?"

"Pursue them," he answered. "You will certainly overtake them and succeed in the rescue."

9David and the six hundred men with him came to the Besor Ravine, where some stayed behind, 10for two hundred men were too exhausted to cross the ravine. But David and four hundred men continued the pursuit.

11They found an Egyptian in a field and brought him to David. They gave him water to drink and food to eat— 12part of a cake of pressed figs and two cakes of raisins. He ate and was revived, for he had not eaten any food or drunk any water for three days and three nights.

13David asked him, "To whom do you belong, and where do you come from?"

He said, "I am an Egyptian, the slave of an Amalekite. My master abandoned me when I became ill three days ago. 14We raided the Negev of the Kerethites and the territory belonging to Judah and the Negev of Caleb. And we burned Ziklag."

15David asked him, "Can you lead me down to this raiding party?"

He answered, "Swear to me before God that you will not kill me or hand me over to my master, and I will take you down to them."

16He led David down, and there they were, scattered over the countryside, eating, drinking and reveling because of the great amount of plunder they had taken from the land of the Philistines and from Judah. 17David fought them from dusk until the evening of the next day, and none of them got away, except four hundred young men who rode off on camels and fled. 18David recovered everything the Amalekites had taken, including his two wives. 19Nothing was missing: young or old, boy or girl, plunder or anything else they had taken. David brought everything back. 20He took all the flocks and herds, and his men drove them ahead of the other livestock, saying, "This is David's plunder."

21Then David came to the two hundred men who had been too exhausted to follow him and who were left behind at the Besor Ravine. They came out to meet David and the people with him. As David and his men approached, he greeted them. 22But all the evil men and troublemakers among David's followers said, "Because they did not go out with us, we will not share with them the plunder we recovered. However, each man may take his wife and children and go."

²³David replied, "No, my brothers, you must not do that with what the LORD has given us. He has protected us and handed over to us the forces that came against us. ²⁴Who will listen to what you say? The share of the man who stayed with the supplies is to be the same as that of him who went down to the battle. All will share alike." ²⁵David made this a statute and ordinance for Israel from that day to this.

²⁶When David arrived in Ziklag, he sent some of the plunder to the elders of Judah, who were his friends, saying, "Here is a present for you from the plunder of the LORD's enemies."

²⁷He sent it to those who were in Bethel, Ramoth Negev and Jattir; ²⁸to those in Aroer, Siphmoth, Eshtemoa ²⁹and Racal; to those in the towns of the Jerahmeelites and the Kenites; ³⁰to those in Hormah, Bor Ashan, Athach ³¹and Hebron; and to those in all the other places where David and his men had roamed.

Saul Takes His Life

31 Now the Philistines fought against Israel; the Israelites fled before them, and many fell slain on Mount Gilboa. ²The Philistines pressed hard after Saul and his sons, and they killed his sons Jonathan, Abinadab and Malki-Shua. ³The fighting grew fierce around Saul, and when the archers overtook him, they wounded him critically.

⁴Saul said to his armor-bearer, "Draw your sword and run me through, or these uncircumcised fellows will come and run me through and abuse me."

But his armor-bearer was terrified and would not do it; so Saul took his own sword and fell on it. ⁵When the armor-bearer saw that Saul was dead, he too fell on his sword and died with him. ⁶So Saul and his three sons and his armor-bearer

Don't Fall on Your Sword

READ 1 SAMUEL 31

"Saul took his own sword and fell on it" (verse 4). When Saul committed suicide, that was the ultimate failure. Never forget that you are God's "temple" (1 Corinthians 3:16–17). God gave you life and God decides when it's checkout time. No joke—it's murder to kill yourself. If any of your friends are thinking about suicide, tell them not to do it. Also, talk to an adult, even if your friend says, "Don't tell anybody." The Kids' Code of Silence does *not* apply when someone is in danger. And don't buy the line, "That's their decision." *It's not.* Get a grown-up involved and get that person help. Remember, some people have become depressed and thought they wanted to end their life. But they made it through, and looked back later and were very thankful they didn't end it all. Be God's light when friends are down.

Your next reading is on page 383.

and all his men died together that same day.

7When the Israelites along the valley and those across the Jordan saw that the Israelite army had fled and that Saul and his sons had died, they abandoned their towns and fled. And the Philistines came and occupied them.

8The next day, when the Philistines came to strip the dead, they found Saul and his three sons fallen on Mount Gilboa. 9They cut off his head and stripped off his armor, and they sent messengers throughout the land of the Philistines to proclaim the news in the temple of their idols and among their people. 10They put his armor in the temple of the Ashtoreths and fastened his body to the wall of Beth Shan.

11When the people of Jabesh Gilead heard of what the Philistines had done to Saul, 12all their valiant men journeyed through the night to Beth Shan. They took down the bodies of Saul and his sons from the wall of Beth Shan and went to Jabesh, where they burned them. 13Then they took their bones and buried them under a tamarisk tree at Jabesh, and they fasted seven days.

2 SAMUEL

Who wrote this book?
The writer is unknown.

Why was this book written?
The book of 2 Samuel tells the story of David's 40-year reign as Israel's king.

What happens in this book?
David becomes king of Israel. During his reign foreign enemies are defeated and Israel becomes a great nation.

What do we learn about God in this book?
God uses people who love and want to please him, as King David did.

Who is important in this book?
The important person in this book is King David.

When did this happen?
Events of this book happened between 1010 and 970 B.C.

Where did this happen?
These events took place in Israel.

What are some of the stories in this book?

David conquers Jerusalem	2 Samuel 5
David brings the ark to Jerusalem	2 Samuel 6
David helps Mephibosheth	2 Samuel 9
David sins with Bathsheba	2 Samuel 11
David confesses his sin	2 Samuel 12
Absalom leads a rebellion	2 Samuel 15–18
David builds an altar	2 Samuel 24

David Hears of Saul's Death

After the death of Saul, David returned from defeating the Amalekites and stayed in Ziklag two days. 2On the third day a man arrived from Saul's camp, with his clothes torn and with dust on his head. When he came to David, he fell to the ground to pay him honor.

3"Where have you come from?" David asked him.

He answered, "I have escaped from the Israelite camp."

4"What happened?" David asked. "Tell me."

He said, "The men fled from the battle. Many of them fell and died. And Saul and his son Jonathan are dead."

5Then David said to the young man who brought him the report, "How do you know that Saul and his son Jonathan are dead?"

6"I happened to be on Mount Gilboa," the young man said, "and there was Saul, leaning on his spear, with the chariots and riders almost upon him. 7When he turned around and saw me, he called out to me, and I said, 'What can I do?'

8"He asked me, 'Who are you?'

" 'An Amalekite,' I answered.

9"Then he said to me, 'Stand over me and kill me! I am in the throes of death, but I'm still alive.'

10"So I stood over him and killed him, because I knew that after he had fallen he could not survive. And I took the crown that was on his head and the band on his arm and have brought them here to my lord."

11Then David and all the men with him took hold of their clothes and tore them. 12They mourned and wept and fasted till evening for Saul and his son Jonathan, and for the army of the LORD and the house of Israel, because they had fallen by the sword.

13David said to the young man who brought him the report, "Where are you from?"

"I am the son of an alien, an Amalekite," he answered.

14David asked him, "Why were you not

GET SMARTER

Saul Dies; David Cries

READ 2 SAMUEL 1:1–16, 23–25

Would you cry if your worst enemy broke his leg? No? Well, Saul had been trying to kill David, yet David mourned when Saul died. Obviously David didn't love it when Saul was trying to put a spear through him, but he did love Saul. How *could* he?—because God loves everyone, so everyone is worthy of our love as well. So don't rejoice in your enemy's defeat; feel sorry for that person instead. When others act like jerks or try to trash you, try to see the difference between them as a person whom God loves, and the bad they're up to. Remember: God created everyone to be like him in his or her own unique way. Pray that your enemies will change and live up to their God-given potential.

Your next reading is on page 389.

afraid to lift your hand to destroy the LORD's anointed?"

15Then David called one of his men and said, "Go, strike him down!" So he struck him down, and he died. 16For David had said to him, "Your blood be on your own head. Your own mouth testified against you when you said, 'I killed the LORD's anointed.' "

David's Lament for Saul and Jonathan

17David took up this lament concerning Saul and his son Jonathan, 18and ordered that the men of Judah be taught this lament of the bow (it is written in the Book of Jashar):

19 "Your glory, O Israel, lies slain on your
    heights.
  How the mighty have fallen!

20 "Tell it not in Gath,
    proclaim it not in the streets of
      Ashkelon,
lest the daughters of the Philistines be
    glad,
  lest the daughters of the
    uncircumcised rejoice.

Make It Stick

_____

_____

_____

_____

_____

_____

READ 2 SAMUEL
1:17–27

David was heartbroken when his best friend, Jonathan, died. Have you ever lost a friend? Has one of your friends moved away? If so, write a brief note about a fun experience you shared. Focus on what you *had* rather than what you've lost, and look forward to when you'll see your friend again.

21 "O mountains of Gilboa,
      may you have neither dew nor rain,
      nor fields that yield offerings ⌊of grain⌋.
   For there the shield of the mighty was defiled,
      the shield of Saul—no longer rubbed with oil.
22 From the blood of the slain,
      from the flesh of the mighty,
   the bow of Jonathan did not turn back,
      the sword of Saul did not return unsatisfied.

23 "Saul and Jonathan—
      in life they were loved and gracious,
      and in death they were not parted.
   They were swifter than eagles,
      they were stronger than lions.

24 "O daughters of Israel,
      weep for Saul,
   who clothed you in scarlet and finery,
      who adorned your garments with ornaments of
         gold.

25 "How the mighty have fallen in battle!
      Jonathan lies slain on your heights.
26 I grieve for you, Jonathan my brother;
      you were very dear to me.
   Your love for me was wonderful,
      more wonderful than that of women.

27 "How the mighty have fallen!
      The weapons of war have perished!"

David Anointed King Over Judah

2 In the course of time, David inquired of the LORD.
   "Shall I go up to one of the towns of Judah?" he
   asked.
   The LORD said, "Go up."
   David asked, "Where shall I go?"
   "To Hebron," the LORD answered.
   2 So David went up there with his two wives, Ahinoam of Jezreel and Abigail, the widow of Nabal of Carmel. 3 David also took the men who were with him, each
with his family, and they settled in Hebron and its
towns. 4 Then the men of Judah came to Hebron and
there they anointed David king over the house of Judah.
   When David was told that it was the men of Jabesh
Gilead who had buried Saul, 5 he sent messengers to the
men of Jabesh Gilead to say to them, "The LORD bless
you for showing this kindness to Saul your master by
burying him. 6 May the LORD now show you kindness
and faithfulness, and I too will show you the same favor
because you have done this. 7 Now then, be strong and
brave, for Saul your master is dead, and the house of Judah has anointed me king over them."

War Between the Houses of David and Saul

8 Meanwhile, Abner son of Ner, the commander of
Saul's army, had taken Ish-Bosheth son of Saul and
brought him over to Mahanaim. 9 He made him king

Get a Load of This...

Check out 2 Samuel
2:1–7. Time for an oil
change! David was
anointed with oil as
king of Judah. When he
had been a boy, he had
already gone through
this with Samuel.
"Thanks for making me
king," David probably
thought, "but do you
know how hard it is to
wash this stuff out?"

over Gilead, Ashuri*a* and Jezreel, and also over Ephraim, Benjamin and all Israel.

¹⁰Ish-Bosheth son of Saul was forty years old when he became king over Israel, and he reigned two years. The house of Judah, however, followed David. ¹¹The length of time David was king in Hebron over the house of Judah was seven years and six months.

¹²Abner son of Ner, together with the men of Ish-Bosheth son of Saul, left Mahanaim and went to Gibeon. ¹³Joab son of Zeruiah and David's men went out and met them at the pool of Gibeon. One group sat down on one side of the pool and one group on the other side.

¹⁴Then Abner said to Joab, "Let's have some of the young men get up and fight hand to hand in front of us."

"All right, let them do it," Joab said.

¹⁵So they stood up and were counted off—twelve men for Benjamin and Ish-Bosheth son of Saul, and twelve for David. ¹⁶Then each man grabbed his opponent by the head and thrust his dagger into his opponent's side, and they fell down together. So that place in Gibeon was called Helkath Hazzurim.*b*

¹⁷The battle that day was very fierce, and Abner and the men of Israel were defeated by David's men.

¹⁸The three sons of Zeruiah were there: Joab, Abishai and Asahel. Now Asahel was as fleet-footed as a wild gazelle. ¹⁹He chased Abner, turning neither to the right nor to the left as he pursued him. ²⁰Abner looked behind him and asked, "Is that you, Asahel?"

"It is," he answered.

²¹Then Abner said to him, "Turn aside to the right or to the left; take on one of the young men and strip him of his weapons." But Asahel would not stop chasing him.

²²Again Abner warned Asahel, "Stop chasing me! Why should I strike you down? How could I look your brother Joab in the face?"

²³But Asahel refused to give up the pursuit; so Abner thrust the butt of his spear into Asahel's stomach, and the spear came out through his back. He fell there and died on the spot. And every man stopped when he came to the place where Asahel had fallen and died.

²⁴But Joab and Abishai pursued Abner, and as the sun was setting, they came to the hill of Ammah, near Giah on the way to the wasteland of Gibeon. ²⁵Then the men of Benjamin rallied behind Abner. They formed themselves into a group and took their stand on top of a hill.

²⁶Abner called out to Joab, "Must the sword devour forever? Don't you realize that this will end in bitterness? How long before you order your men to stop pursuing their brothers?"

²⁷Joab answered, "As surely as God lives, if you had not spoken, the men would have continued the pursuit of their brothers until morning.*c*"

²⁸So Joab blew the trumpet, and all the men came to a halt; they no longer pursued Israel, nor did they fight anymore.

²⁹All that night Abner and his men marched through the Arabah. They crossed the Jordan, continued through the whole Bithron*d* and came to Mahanaim.

³⁰Then Joab returned from pursuing Abner and assembled all his men. Besides Asahel, nineteen of David's men were found missing. ³¹But David's men had killed three hundred and sixty Benjamites who were with Abner. ³²They took Asahel and buried him in his father's tomb at Bethlehem. Then Joab and his men marched all night and arrived at Hebron by daybreak.

3 The war between the house of Saul and the house of David lasted a long time. David grew stronger and stronger, while the house of Saul grew weaker and weaker.

²Sons were born to David in Hebron:

His firstborn was Amnon the son of Ahinoam of Jezreel;

³his second, Kileab the son of Abigail the widow of Nabal of Carmel;

the third, Absalom the son of Maacah daughter of Talmai king of Geshur;

⁴the fourth, Adonijah the son of Haggith;

the fifth, Shephatiah the son of Abital;

⁵and the sixth, Ithream the son of David's wife Eglah.

a 9 Or *Asher*   *b 16 Helkath Hazzurim* means *field of daggers* or *field of hostilities.*   *c 27* Or *spoken this morning, the men would not have taken up the pursuit of their brothers; or spoken, the men would have given up the pursuit of their brothers by morning*   *d 29* Or *morning;* or *ravine;* the meaning of the Hebrew for this word is uncertain.

These were born to David in Hebron.

Abner Goes Over to David

6During the war between the house of Saul and the house of David, Abner had been strengthening his own position in the house of Saul. 7Now Saul had had a concubine named Rizpah daughter of Aiah. And Ish-Bosheth said to Abner, "Why did you sleep with my father's concubine?"

8Abner was very angry because of what Ish-Bosheth said and he answered, "Am I a dog's head—on Judah's side? This very day I am loyal to the house of your father Saul and to his family and friends. I haven't handed you over to David. Yet now you accuse me of an offense involving this woman! 9May God deal with Abner, be it ever so severely, if I do not do for David what the LORD promised him on oath 10and transfer the kingdom from the house of Saul and establish David's throne over Israel and Judah from Dan to Beersheba." 11Ish-Bosheth did not dare to say another word to Abner, because he was afraid of him.

12Then Abner sent messengers on his behalf to say to David, "Whose land is it? Make an agreement with me, and I will help you bring all Israel over to you."

13"Good," said David. "I will make an agreement with you. But I demand one thing of you: Do not come into my presence unless you bring Michal daughter of Saul when you come to see me." 14Then David sent messengers to Ish-Bosheth son of Saul, demanding, "Give me my wife Michal, whom I betrothed to myself for the price of a hundred Philistine foreskins."

15So Ish-Bosheth gave orders and had her taken away from her husband Paltiel son of Laish. 16Her husband, however, went with her, weeping behind her all the way to Bahurim. Then Abner said to him, "Go back home!" So he went back.

Make It Stick

READ 2 SAMUEL 3

Revenge is like knocking over a row of dominoes: When one domino goes down, it keeps on knocking down others. The story of Joab and Abner shows this effect. Write down two "dominoes" in your life—things you might want revenge for. Wanting to get even is natural. But Jesus says to forgive those who wrong us. Don't let the next domino go down!

¹⁷Abner conferred with the elders of Israel and said, "For some time you have wanted to make David your king. ¹⁸Now do it! For the LORD promised David, 'By my servant David I will rescue my people Israel from the hand of the Philistines and from the hand of all their enemies.' "

¹⁹Abner also spoke to the Benjamites in person. Then he went to Hebron to tell David everything that Israel and the whole house of Benjamin wanted to do. ²⁰When Abner, who had twenty men with him, came to David at Hebron, David prepared a feast for him and his men. ²¹Then Abner said to David, "Let me go at once and assemble all Israel for my lord the king, so that they may make a compact with you, and that you may rule over all that your heart desires." So David sent Abner away, and he went in peace.

Joab Murders Abner

²²Just then David's men and Joab returned from a raid and brought with them a great deal of plunder. But Abner was no longer with David in Hebron, because David had sent him away, and he had gone in peace. ²³When Joab and all the soldiers with him arrived, he was told that Abner son of Ner had come to the king and that the king had sent him away and that he had gone in peace.

²⁴So Joab went to the king and said, "What have you done? Look, Abner came to you. Why did you let him go? Now he is gone! ²⁵You know Abner son of Ner; he came to deceive you and observe your movements and find out everything you are doing."

²⁶Joab then left David and sent messengers after Abner, and they brought him back from the well of Sirah. But David did not know it. ²⁷Now when Abner returned to Hebron, Joab took him aside into the gateway, as though to speak with him privately. And there, to avenge the blood of his brother Asahel, Joab stabbed him in the stomach, and he died.

²⁸Later, when David heard about this, he said, "I and my kingdom are forever innocent before the LORD concerning the blood of Abner son of Ner. ²⁹May his blood fall upon the head of Joab and upon all his father's house! May Joab's house never be without someone who has a running sore or leprosyᵃ or who

leans on a crutch or who falls by the sword or who lacks food."

³⁰(Joab and his brother Abishai murdered Abner because he had killed their brother Asahel in the battle at Gibeon.)

³¹Then David said to Joab and all the people with him, "Tear your clothes and put on sackcloth and walk in mourning in front of Abner." King David himself walked behind the bier. ³²They buried Abner in Hebron, and the king wept aloud at Abner's tomb. All the people wept also.

³³The king sang this lament for Abner:

"Should Abner have died as the
        lawless die?
³⁴   Your hands were not bound,
        your feet were not fettered.
You fell as one falls before wicked men."

And all the people wept over him again. ³⁵Then they all came and urged David to eat something while it was still day; but David took an oath, saying, "May God deal with me, be it ever so severely, if I taste bread or anything else before the sun sets!"

³⁶All the people took note and were pleased; indeed, everything the king did pleased them. ³⁷So on that day all the people and all Israel knew that the king had no part in the murder of Abner son of Ner.

³⁸Then the king said to his men, "Do you not realize that a prince and a great man has fallen in Israel this day? ³⁹And today, though I am the anointed king, I am weak, and these sons of Zeruiah are too strong for me. May the LORD repay the evildoer according to his evil deeds!"

Ish-Bosheth Murdered

4 When Ish-Bosheth son of Saul heard that Abner had died in Hebron, he lost courage, and all Israel became alarmed. ²Now Saul's son had two men who were leaders of raiding bands. One was named Baanah and the other Recab; they were sons of Rimmon the Beerothite from the tribe of Benjamin—Beeroth is considered part of Benjamin, ³because the people of Beeroth fled to Gittaim and have lived there as aliens to this day.

⁴(Jonathan son of Saul had a son who was lame in both feet. He was five years

---

ᵃ 29 The Hebrew word was used for various diseases affecting the skin—not necessarily leprosy.

old when the news about Saul and Jonathan came from Jezreel. His nurse picked him up and fled, but as she hurried to leave, he fell and became crippled. His name was Mephibosheth.)

⁵Now Recab and Baanah, the sons of Rimmon the Beerothite, set out for the house of Ish-Bosheth, and they arrived there in the heat of the day while he was taking his noonday rest. ⁶They went into the inner part of the house as if to get some wheat, and they stabbed him in the stomach. Then Recab and his brother Baanah slipped away.

⁷They had gone into the house while he was lying on the bed in his bedroom. After they stabbed and killed him, they cut off his head. Taking it with them, they traveled all night by way of the Arabah. ⁸They brought the head of Ish-Bosheth to David at Hebron and said to the king, "Here is the head of Ish-Bosheth son of Saul, your enemy, who tried to take your life. This day the LORD has avenged my lord the king against Saul and his offspring."

⁹David answered Recab and his brother Baanah, the sons of Rimmon the Beerothite, "As surely as the LORD lives, who has delivered me out of all trouble, ¹⁰when a man told me, 'Saul is dead,' and thought he was bringing good news, I seized him and put him to death in Ziklag. That was the reward I gave him for his news! ¹¹How much more—when wicked men have killed an innocent man in his own house and on his own bed—should I not now demand his blood from your hand and rid the earth of you!"

¹²So David gave an order to his men, and they killed them. They cut off their hands and feet and hung the bodies by the pool in Hebron. But they took the head of Ish-Bosheth and buried it in Abner's tomb at Hebron.

David Becomes King Over Israel

All the tribes of Israel came to David at Hebron and said, "We are your own flesh and blood. ²In the past, while Saul was king over us, you were the one who led Israel on their military campaigns. And the LORD said to you, 'You will shepherd my people Israel, and you will become their ruler.'"

Remember the Three "P's"

READ 2 SAMUEL 5:1–5

David's life can be summed up in three words: "patience," "perseverance" and "preparation." When he was first anointed as king by Samuel, he didn't run out and try to get himself crowned. Instead, he was patient and relied on God to show him when the timing was right. David also persevered through a lot of tough stuff, and he prepared himself to lead the country by leading smaller groups of men. It all paid off big time. "When all the elders of Israel had come to King David at Hebron . . . they anointed David king over Israel" (verse 3). Patience, perseverance and preparation will help you do well at everything you try, too, from playing sports to studying in school. Just don't go around telling everyone how great you are; let God do that. Others will recognize you if you just live by these three words.

Your next reading is on page 392.

³When all the elders of Israel had come to King David at Hebron, the king made a compact with them at Hebron before the LORD, and they anointed David king over Israel.

⁴David was thirty years old when he became king, and he reigned forty years. ⁵In Hebron he reigned over Judah seven years and six months, and in Jerusalem he reigned over all Israel and Judah thirty-three years.

David Conquers Jerusalem

⁶The king and his men marched to Jerusalem to attack the Jebusites, who lived there. The Jebusites said to David, "You will not get in here; even the blind and the lame can ward you off." They thought, "David cannot get in here." ⁷Nevertheless, David captured the fortress of Zion, the City of David.

⁸On that day, David said, "Anyone who conquers the Jebusites will have to use the water shaft[a] to reach those 'lame and blind' who are David's enemies.[b]" That is why they say, "The 'blind and lame' will not enter the palace."

⁹David then took up residence in the fortress and called it the City of David. He built up the area around it, from the supporting terraces[c] inward. ¹⁰And he became more and more powerful, because the LORD God Almighty was with him.

¹¹Now Hiram king of Tyre sent messengers to David, along with cedar logs and carpenters and stonemasons, and they built a palace for David. ¹²And David knew that the LORD had established him as king over Israel and had exalted his kingdom for the sake of his people Israel.

¹³After he left Hebron, David took more concubines and wives in Jerusalem, and more sons and daughters were born to him. ¹⁴These are the names of the children born to him there: Shammua, Shobab, Nathan, Solomon, ¹⁵Ibhar, Elishua, Nepheg, Japhia, ¹⁶Elishama, Eliada and Eliphelet.

David Defeats the Philistines

¹⁷When the Philistines heard that David had been anointed king over Israel, they went up in full force to search for him, but David heard about it and went down to the stronghold. ¹⁸Now the Philistines had come and spread out in the Valley of Rephaim; ¹⁹so David inquired of the LORD,

"Shall I go and attack the Philistines? Will you hand them over to me?"

The LORD answered him, "Go, for I will surely hand the Philistines over to you."

²⁰So David went to Baal Perazim, and there he defeated them. He said, "As waters break out, the LORD has broken out against my enemies before me." So that place was called Baal Perazim.[d] ²¹The Philistines abandoned their idols there, and David and his men carried them off.

²²Once more the Philistines came up and spread out in the Valley of Rephaim; ²³so David inquired of the LORD, and he answered, "Do not go straight up, but circle around behind them and attack them in front of the balsam trees. ²⁴As soon as you hear the sound of marching in the tops of the balsam trees, move quickly, because that will mean the LORD has gone out in front of you to strike the Philistine army." ²⁵So David did as the LORD commanded him, and he struck down the Philistines all the way from Gibeon[e] to Gezer.

The Ark Brought to Jerusalem

6 David again brought together out of Israel chosen men, thirty thousand in all. ²He and all his men set out from Baalah of Judah[f] to bring up from there the ark of God, which is called by the Name,[g] the name of the LORD Almighty, who is enthroned between the cherubim that are on the ark. ³They set the ark of God on a new cart and brought it from the house of Abinadab, which was on the hill. Uzzah and Ahio, sons of Abinadab, were guiding the new cart ⁴with the ark of God on it,[h] and Ahio was walking in front of it. ⁵David and the whole house of Israel were celebrating with all their might before the LORD, with songs[i] and with harps, lyres, tambourines, sistrums and cymbals.

⁶When they came to the threshing floor of Nacon, Uzzah reached out and took

---

a 8 Or use scaling hooks   b 8 Or are hated by David
c 9 Or the Millo   d 20 Baal Perazim means the lord who breaks out.   e 25 Septuagint (see also 1 Chron. 14:16); Hebrew Geba   f 2 That is, Kiriath Jearim; Hebrew Baale Judah, a variant of Baalah of Judah   g 2 Hebrew; Septuagint and Vulgate do not have the Name.   h 3,4 Dead Sea Scrolls and some Septuagint manuscripts; Masoretic Text cart ⁴and they brought it with the ark of God from the house of Abinadab, which was on the hill   i 5 See Dead Sea Scrolls, Septuagint and 1 Chronicles 13:8; Masoretic Text celebrating before the LORD with all kinds of instruments made of pine.

hold of the ark of God, because the oxen stumbled. 7The Lord's anger burned against Uzzah because of his irreverent act; therefore God struck him down and he died there beside the ark of God.

8Then David was angry because the Lord's wrath had broken out against Uzzah, and to this day that place is called Perez Uzzah.a

9David was afraid of the Lord that day and said, "How can the ark of the Lord ever come to me?" 10He was not willing to take the ark of the Lord to be with him in the City of David. Instead, he took it aside to the house of Obed-Edom the Gittite. 11The ark of the Lord remained in the house of Obed-Edom the Gittite for three months, and the Lord blessed him and his entire household.

12Now King David was told, "The Lord has blessed the household of Obed-Edom and everything he has, because of the ark of God." So David went down and brought up the ark of God from the house of Obed-Edom to the City of David with rejoicing. 13When those who were carrying the ark of the Lord had taken six steps, he sacrificed a bull and a fattened calf. 14David, wearing a linen ephod, danced before the Lord with all his might, 15while he and the entire house of Israel brought up the ark of the Lord with shouts and the sound of trumpets.

16As the ark of the Lord was entering the City of David, Michal daughter of Saul watched from a window. And when she saw King David leaping and dancing before the Lord, she despised him in her heart.

17They brought the ark of the Lord and set it in its place inside the tent that David had pitched for it, and David sacrificed burnt offerings and fellowship offeringsb before the Lord. 18After he had finished sacrificing the burnt offerings and fellowship offerings, he blessed the people in the name of the Lord Almighty. 19Then he gave a loaf of bread, a cake of dates and a cake of raisins to each person in the whole crowd of Israelites, both men and women. And all the people went to their homes.

20When David returned home to bless his household, Michal daughter of Saul came out to meet him and said, "How the king of Israel has distinguished himself today, disrobing in the sight of the slave girls of his servants as any vulgar fellow would!"

21David said to Michal, "It was before the Lord, who chose me rather than your father or anyone from his house when he appointed me ruler over the Lord's people Israel—I will celebrate before the Lord. 22I will become even more undignified than this, and I will be humiliated in my own eyes. But by these slave girls you spoke of, I will be held in honor."

23And Michal daughter of Saul had no children to the day of her death.

Get a Load of This...

Check out 2 Samuel 6:1–10. When God says something, he *means* it. In this case, he said, "Don't touch the ark. It's sacred." Uzzah didn't listen and got ker-zapped! Oops. Remember: Doing things God's way is important. God won't strike you dead if you don't, but your life will go better if you do.

---

a 8 Perez Uzzah means outbreak against Uzzah.   b 17 Traditionally peace offerings; also in verse 18

God's Promise to David

7 After the king was settled in his palace and the LORD had given him rest from all his enemies around him, [2] he said to Nathan the prophet, "Here I am, living in a palace of cedar, while the ark of God remains in a tent."

[3] Nathan replied to the king, "Whatever you have in mind, go ahead and do it, for the LORD is with you."

[4] That night the word of the LORD came to Nathan, saying:

[5] "Go and tell my servant David, 'This is what the LORD says: Are you the one to build me a house to dwell in? [6] I have not dwelt in a house from the day I brought the Israelites up out of Egypt to this day. I have been moving from place to place with a tent as my dwelling. [7] Wherever I have moved with all the Israelites, did I ever say to any of their rulers whom I commanded to shepherd my people Israel, "Why have you not built me a house of cedar?" '

[8] "Now then, tell my servant David, 'This is what the LORD Almighty says: I took you from the pasture and from following the flock to be ruler over my people Israel. [9] I have been with you wherever you have gone, and I have cut off all your enemies from before you. Now I will make your name great, like the names of the greatest men of the earth. [10] And I will provide a place for my people Israel and will plant them so that they can have a home of their own and no longer be disturbed. Wicked people will not oppress them anymore, as they did at the beginning [11] and have done ever since the time I appointed leaders[a] over my people Israel. I will also give you rest from all your enemies.

" 'The LORD declares to you that the LORD himself will establish a house for you: [12] When your days are over and you rest with your fathers, I will raise up your offspring to succeed you, who will come from your own body, and I will establish his kingdom. [13] He

---

[a] 11 Traditionally *judges*

David's Praise & Worship Concert

READ 2 SAMUEL 6:11–21

If you feel like worshiping God, just do it! Kneel. Sing. Shout! Raise your hands! David went even further: He was dancing with all his might. His wife, Saul's daughter Michal, didn't approve. But David didn't care. He wasn't worshiping God to please her, but to please God. Michal made exaggerated accusations, saying David was "disrobing" or naked (verse 20). It sounds like David *had* ditched his ankle-length rich royal robes (you can't "leap and dance" in *those*!), but give the guy a break: He *was* still wearing a priestly garment made of linen. The lesson? Don't be embarrassed to love God. Respect other people's views, of course, especially when you're among unbelievers. You shouldn't hide your faith when you're around them, but don't go to the opposite extreme either. Find a balance between being true to God and being sensitive to others.

Your next reading is on page 394.

is the one who will build a house for my Name, and I will establish the throne of his kingdom forever. [14]I will be his father, and he will be my son. When he does wrong, I will punish him with the rod of men, with floggings inflicted by men. [15]But my love will never be taken away from him, as I took it away from Saul, whom I removed from before you. [16]Your house and your kingdom will endure forever before me[a]; your throne will be established forever.' "

[17]Nathan reported to David all the words of this entire revelation.

David's Prayer

[18]Then King David went in and sat before the LORD, and he said:

"Who am I, O Sovereign LORD, and what is my family, that you have brought me this far? [19]And as if this were not enough in your sight,

O Sovereign LORD, you have also spoken about the future of the house of your servant. Is this your usual way of dealing with man, O Sovereign LORD? [20]"What more can David say to you? For you know your servant, O Sovereign LORD. [21]For the sake of your word and according to your will, you have done this great thing and made it known to your servant.

[22]"How great you are, O Sovereign LORD! There is no one like you, and there is no God but you, as we have heard with our own ears. [23]And who is like your people Israel—the one nation on earth that God went out to redeem as a people for himself, and to make a name for himself, and to perform great and awesome wonders by driving out nations and their gods from before your people, whom

[a] 16 Some Hebrew manuscripts and Septuagint; most Hebrew manuscripts you

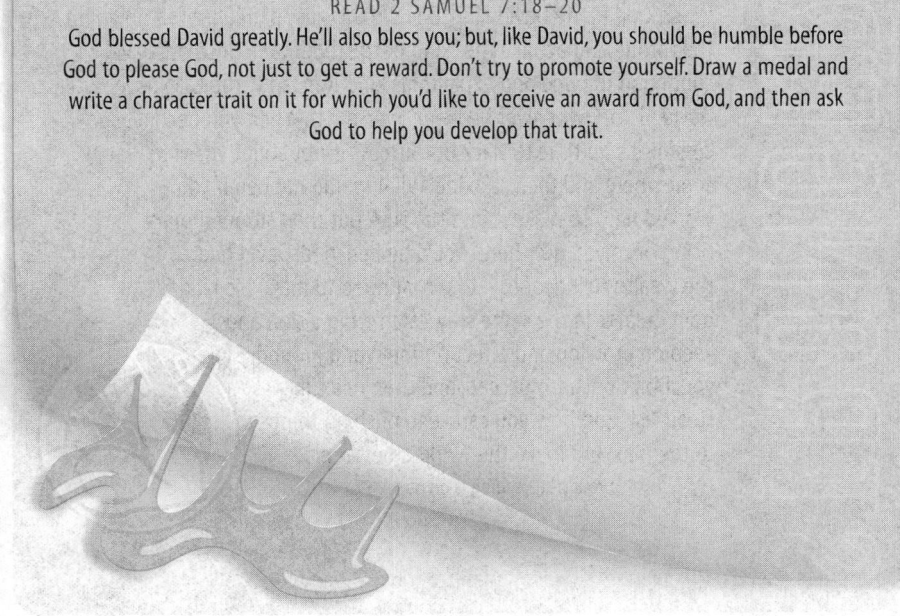

Make It Stick

READ 2 SAMUEL 7:18–20

God blessed David greatly. He'll also bless you; but, like David, you should be humble before God to please God, not just to get a reward. Don't try to promote yourself. Draw a medal and write a character trait on it for which you'd like to receive an award from God, and then ask God to help you develop that trait.

you redeemed from Egypt?[a] 24You have established your people Israel as your very own forever, and you, O LORD, have become their God.

25"And now, LORD God, keep forever the promise you have made concerning your servant and his house. Do as you promised, 26so that your name will be great forever. Then men will say, 'The LORD Almighty is God over Israel!' And the house of your servant David will be established before you.

27"O LORD Almighty, God of Israel, you have revealed this to your servant, saying, 'I will build a house for you.' So your servant has found courage to offer you this prayer. 28O Sovereign LORD, you are God! Your words are trustworthy, and you have promised these good things to your servant. 29Now be pleased to bless the house of your servant, that it may continue forever in your sight; for

you, O Sovereign LORD, have spoken, and with your blessing the house of your servant will be blessed forever."

David's Victories

8 In the course of time, David defeated the Philistines and subdued them, and he took Metheg Ammah from the control of the Philistines.

2David also defeated the Moabites. He made them lie down on the ground and measured them off with a length of cord. Every two lengths of them were put to death, and the third length was allowed to live. So the Moabites became subject to David and brought tribute.

3Moreover, David fought Hadadezer son of Rehob, king of Zobah, when he went to restore his control along the Euphrates River. 4David captured a thousand of his chariots, seven thousand chariot-

---

[a] 23 See Septuagint and 1 Chron. 17:21; Hebrew *wonders for your land and before your people, whom you redeemed from Egypt, from the nations and their gods.*

GET STRONGER

Don't Stop at the Top!

READ 2 SAMUEL 8:1–14

When God made David king, David didn't just plunk himself down on the throne and act like the "king of the mountain." Instead, David continued to build and expand his kingdom, and "The LORD gave David victory wherever he went" (verse 14). When you become successful, it's no time to slack off. Success is not about "arriving" somewhere and then relaxing. What would happen if you worked hard to make it into the NBA but then stopped practicing once you got there? You'd be benched. David had all the wealth he needed, yet he continued to make his kingdom greater. In the same way, catch a big vision and keep on growing and affecting the world around you. Don't push to succeed, and then relax. Instead, ask God how you can keep pushing things to the max and make the world a better place.

Your next reading is on page 397.

eers[a] and twenty thousand foot soldiers. He hamstrung all but a hundred of the chariot horses.

5When the Arameans of Damascus came to help Hadadezer king of Zobah, David struck down twenty-two thousand of them. 6He put garrisons in the Aramean kingdom of Damascus, and the Arameans became subject to him and brought tribute. The LORD gave David victory wherever he went.

7David took the gold shields that belonged to the officers of Hadadezer and brought them to Jerusalem. 8From Tebah[b] and Berothai, towns that belonged to Hadadezer, King David took a great quantity of bronze.

9When Tou[c] king of Hamath heard that David had defeated the entire army of Hadadezer, 10he sent his son Joram[d] to King David to greet him and congratulate him on his victory in battle over Hadadezer, who had been at war with Tou. Joram brought with him articles of silver and gold and bronze.

11King David dedicated these articles to the LORD, as he had done with the silver and gold from all the nations he had subdued: 12Edom[e] and Moab, the Ammonites and the Philistines, and Amalek. He also dedicated the plunder taken from Hadadezer son of Rehob, king of Zobah.

13And David became famous after he returned from striking down eighteen thousand Edomites[f] in the Valley of Salt.

14He put garrisons throughout Edom, and all the Edomites became subject to David. The LORD gave David victory wherever he went.

David's Officials

15David reigned over all Israel, doing what was just and right for all his people. 16Joab son of Zeruiah was over the army; Jehoshaphat son of Ahilud was recorder; 17Zadok son of Ahitub and Ahimelech son of Abiathar were priests; Seraiah was secretary; 18Benaiah son of Jehoiada was over the Kerethites and Pelethites; and David's sons were royal advisers.[g]

David and Mephibosheth

9David asked, "Is there anyone still left of the house of Saul to whom I can show kindness for Jonathan's sake?"

2Now there was a servant of Saul's household named Ziba. They called him to appear before David, and the king said to him, "Are you Ziba?"

"Your servant," he replied.

3The king asked, "Is there no one still left of the house of Saul to whom I can show God's kindness?"

Ziba answered the king, "There is still a son of Jonathan; he is crippled in both feet."

4"Where is he?" the king asked.

Ziba answered, "He is at the house of Makir son of Ammiel in Lo Debar."

5So King David had him brought from Lo Debar, from the house of Makir son of Ammiel.

6When Mephibosheth son of Jonathan, the son of Saul, came to David, he bowed down to pay him honor.

David said, "Mephibosheth!"

"Your servant," he replied.

7"Don't be afraid," David said to him, "for I will surely show you kindness for the sake of your father Jonathan. I will restore to you all the land that belonged to your grandfather Saul, and you will always eat at my table."

8Mephibosheth bowed down and said, "What is your servant, that you should notice a dead dog like me?"

9Then the king summoned Ziba, Saul's servant, and said to him, "I have given your master's grandson everything that belonged to Saul and his family. 10You and your sons and your servants are to farm the land for him and bring in the crops, so that your master's grandson may be provided for. And Mephibosheth, grandson of your master, will always eat at my table." (Now Ziba had fifteen sons and twenty servants.)

11Then Ziba said to the king, "Your servant will do whatever my lord the king commands his servant to do." So Mephibosheth ate at David's[h] table like one of the king's sons.

12Mephibosheth had a young son named Mica, and all the members of Zi-

a 4 Septuagint (see also Dead Sea Scrolls and 1 Chron. 18:4); Masoretic Text captured seventeen hundred of his charioteers   b 8 See some Septuagint manuscripts (see also 1 Chron. 18:8); Hebrew Betah.   c 9 Hebrew Toi, a variant of Tou; also in verse 10   d 10 A variant of Hadoram   e 12 Some Hebrew manuscripts, Septuagint and Syriac (see also 1 Chron. 18:11); most Hebrew manuscripts Aram   f 13 A few Hebrew manuscripts, Septuagint and Syriac (see also 1 Chron. 18:12); most Hebrew manuscripts Aram (that is, Arameans)   g 18 Or were priests   h 11 Septuagint; Hebrew my ba's household were servants of Mephibosheth. [13]And Mephibosheth lived in Jerusalem, because he always ate at the king's table, and he was crippled in both feet.

David Defeats the Ammonites

10 In the course of time, the king of the Ammonites died, and his son Hanun succeeded him as king. [2]David thought, "I will show kindness to Hanun son of Nahash, just as his father showed kindness to me." So David sent a delegation to express his sympathy to Hanun concerning his father.

When David's men came to the land of the Ammonites, [3]the Ammonite nobles said to Hanun their lord, "Do you think David is honoring your father by sending men to you to express sympathy? Hasn't David sent them to you to explore the city and spy it out and overthrow it?" [4]So Hanun seized David's men, shaved off half of each man's beard, cut off their garments in the middle at the buttocks, and sent them away.

[5]When David was told about this, he sent messengers to meet the men, for they were greatly humiliated. The king said, "Stay at Jericho till your beards have grown, and then come back."

[6]When the Ammonites realized that they had become a stench in David's nostrils, they hired twenty thousand Aramean foot soldiers from Beth Rehob and Zobah, as well as the king of Maacah with a thousand men, and also twelve thousand men from Tob.

[7]On hearing this, David sent Joab out with the entire army of fighting men. [8]The Ammonites came out and drew up in battle formation at the entrance to their city gate, while the Arameans of Zobah and Rehob and the men of Tob and Maacah were by themselves in the open country.

[9]Joab saw that there were battle lines in front of him and behind him; so he selected some of the best troops in Israel and deployed them against the Arameans. [10]He put the rest of the men under the

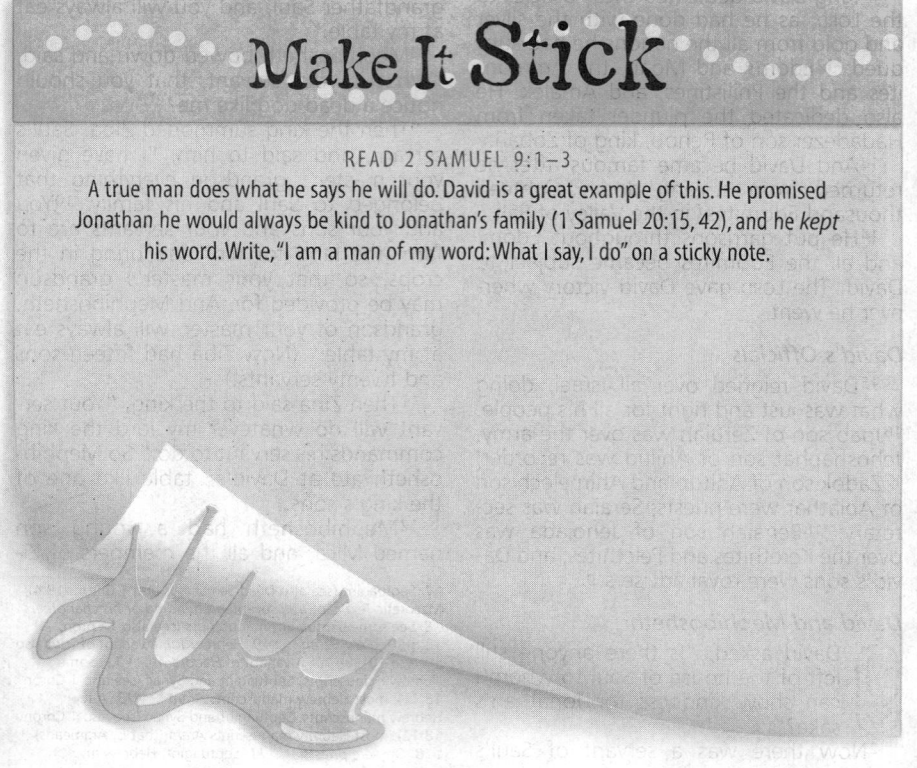

Make It Stick

READ 2 SAMUEL 9:1–3

A true man does what he says he will do. David is a great example of this. He promised Jonathan he would always be kind to Jonathan's family (1 Samuel 20:15, 42), and he *kept* his word. Write, "I am a man of my word: What I say, I do" on a sticky note.

command of Abishai his brother and deployed them against the Ammonites. [11]Joab said, "If the Arameans are too strong for me, then you are to come to my rescue; but if the Ammonites are too strong for you, then I will come to rescue you. [12]Be strong and let us fight bravely for our people and the cities of our God. The LORD will do what is good in his sight."

[13]Then Joab and the troops with him advanced to fight the Arameans, and they fled before him. [14]When the Ammonites saw that the Arameans were fleeing, they fled before Abishai and went inside the city. So Joab returned from fighting the Ammonites and came to Jerusalem.

[15]After the Arameans saw that they had been routed by Israel, they regrouped. [16]Hadadezer had Arameans brought from beyond the River[a]; they went to Helam, with Shobach the commander of Hadadezer's army leading them.

[17]When David was told of this, he gathered all Israel, crossed the Jordan and went to Helam. The Arameans formed their battle lines to meet David and fought against him. [18]But they fled before Israel, and David killed seven hundred of their charioteers and forty thousand of their foot soldiers.[b] He also struck down Shobach the commander of their army, and he died there. [19]When all the kings who were vassals of Hadadezer saw that they had been defeated by Israel, they made peace with the Israelites and became subject to them.

So the Arameans were afraid to help the Ammonites anymore.

David and Bathsheba

In the spring, at the time when kings go off to war, David sent Joab out with the king's men and the whole Israelite army. They destroyed the Ammonites and besieged Rabbah. But David remained in Jerusalem.

[2]One evening David got up from his bed and walked around on the roof of the palace. From the roof he saw a woman bathing. The woman was very beautiful, [3]and David sent someone to find out

a 16 That is, the Euphrates   *b 18* Some Septuagint manuscripts (see also 1 Chron. 19:18); Hebrew *horsemen*

Just Like Everyone Else

READ 2 SAMUEL 9:1–13

David did more than just befriend Mephibosheth. He gave him all the lands his grandfather Saul owned, and even let him eat at his own table. "And Mephibosheth lived in Jerusalem, because he always ate at the king's table, and he was crippled in both feet" (verse 13). David did this because Mephibosheth was the son of his best friend, not because he was physically challenged. This is how you should treat those who are physically or mentally disabled today. All they want is to be treated like regular people, no better, no worse. Is there someone like that in your life? Do you have a difficult time knowing how to act around them? It's no big deal: just treat them like everyone else, and you'll do fine. Remember, in God's eyes they *are* just like everyone else.

Your next reading is on page 399.

Gross!

Check out 2 Samuel 10:4. Through a gross misunderstanding, David's men were seized and had their beards shaved and buttocks exposed. Both actions were considered great insults in David's time. To keep the men from being dishonored and embarrassed, David told them to keep their "buttocks in the barracks" until their beards grew back.

about her. The man said, "Isn't this Bathsheba, the daughter of Eliam and the wife of Uriah the Hittite?" ⁴Then David sent messengers to get her. She came to him, and he slept with her. (She had purified herself from her uncleanness.) Then*a* she went back home. ⁵The woman conceived and sent word to David, saying, "I am pregnant."

⁶So David sent this word to Joab: "Send me Uriah the Hittite." And Joab sent him to David. ⁷When Uriah came to him, David asked him how Joab was, how the soldiers were and how the war was going. ⁸Then David said to Uriah, "Go down to your house and wash your feet." So Uriah left the palace, and a gift from the king was sent after him. ⁹But Uriah slept at the entrance to the palace with all his master's servants and did not go down to his house.

¹⁰When David was told, "Uriah did not go home," he asked him, "Haven't you just come from a distance? Why didn't you go home?"

¹¹Uriah said to David, "The ark and Israel and Judah are staying in tents, and my master Joab and my lord's men are camped in the open fields. How could I go to my house to eat and drink and lie with my wife? As surely as you live, I will not do such a thing!"

¹²Then David said to him, "Stay here one more day, and tomorrow I will send you back." So Uriah remained in Jerusalem that day and the next. ¹³At David's invitation, he ate and drank with him, and David made him drunk. But in the evening Uriah went out to sleep on his mat among his master's servants; he did not go home.

¹⁴In the morning David wrote a letter to Joab and sent it with Uriah. ¹⁵In it he wrote, "Put Uriah in the front line where the fighting is fiercest. Then withdraw from him so he will be struck down and die."

¹⁶So while Joab had the city under siege, he put Uriah at a place where he knew the strongest defenders were. ¹⁷When the men of the city came out and fought against Joab, some of the men in David's army fell; moreover, Uriah the Hittite died.

¹⁸Joab sent David a full account of the battle. ¹⁹He instructed the messenger: "When you have finished giving the king this account of the battle, ²⁰the king's anger may flare up, and he may ask you, 'Why did you get so close to the city to fight? Didn't you know they would shoot arrows from the wall? ²¹Who killed Abimelech son of Jerub-Besheth*b*? Didn't a woman throw an upper millstone on him from the wall, so that he died in Thebez? Why did you get so close to the wall?' If he asks you this, then say to him, 'Also, your servant Uriah the Hittite is dead.' "

²²The messenger set out, and when he arrived he told David everything Joab had sent him to say. ²³The messenger said to David, "The men overpowered us and came out against us in the open, but we drove them

a 4 Or *with her. When she purified herself from her uncleanness,*   *b 21* Also known as *Jerub-Baal* (that is, Gideon) back to the entrance to the city gate. [24]Then the archers shot arrows at your servants from the wall, and some of the king's men died. Moreover, your servant Uriah the Hittite is dead."

[25]David told the messenger, "Say this to Joab: 'Don't let this upset you; the sword devours one as well as another. Press the attack against the city and destroy it.' Say this to encourage Joab."

[26]When Uriah's wife heard that her husband was dead, she mourned for him. [27]After the time of mourning was over, David had her brought to his house, and she became his wife and bore him a son. But the thing David had done displeased the LORD.

Nathan Rebukes David

12 The LORD sent Nathan to David. When he came to him, he said, "There were two men in a certain town, one rich and the other poor. [2]The rich man had a very large number of sheep and cattle, [3]but the poor man had nothing except one little ewe lamb he had bought. He raised it, and it grew up with him and his children. It shared his food, drank from his cup and even slept in his arms. It was like a daughter to him.

[4]"Now a traveler came to the rich man, but the rich man refrained from taking one of his own sheep or cattle to prepare a meal for the traveler who had come to him. Instead, he took the ewe lamb that belonged to the poor man and prepared it for the one who had come to him."

[5]David burned with anger against the man and said to Nathan, "As surely as the LORD lives, the man who did this deserves to die! [6]He must pay for that lamb four times over, because he did such a thing and had no pity."

[7]Then Nathan said to David, "You are the man! This is what the LORD, the God of Israel, says: 'I anointed you king over Israel, and I delivered you from the hand of

Peeking From the Palace
READ 2 SAMUEL 11:1–17, 26–27; 12:13–14

GET

STRONGER

It's dangerous to let your eyes wander. David got in heaps of trouble before he learned this lesson. "One evening David got up from his bed and walked around on the roof of the palace. From the roof he saw a woman bathing. The woman was very beautiful" (2 Samuel 11:2). That first look eventually led to David taking away another man's wife, then murdering her husband. God made women beautiful, but part of that beauty is to be revealed only in marriage. We need to honor the purpose of that beauty and turn away from sinful opinions and actions about sex that don't match up with what God says. Women and girls are created in the image of God, just as men are, and they should be honored and respected.

Your next reading is on page 403.

Saul. 8I gave your master's house to you, and your master's wives into your arms. I gave you the house of Israel and Judah. And if all this had been too little, I would have given you even more. 9Why did you despise the word of the LORD by doing what is evil in his eyes? You struck down Uriah the Hittite with the sword and took his wife to be your own. You killed him with the sword of the Ammonites. 10Now, therefore, the sword will never depart from your house, because you despised me and took the wife of Uriah the Hittite to be your own.'

11"This is what the LORD says: 'Out of your own household I am going to bring calamity upon you. Before your very eyes I will take your wives and give them to one who is close to you, and he will lie with your wives in broad daylight. 12You did it in secret, but I will do this thing in broad daylight before all Israel.' "

13Then David said to Nathan, "I have sinned against the LORD."

Nathan replied, "The LORD has taken away your sin. You are not going to die. 14But because by doing this you have made the enemies of the LORD show utter contempt,a the son born to you will die."

15After Nathan had gone home, the LORD struck the child that Uriah's wife had borne to David, and he became ill. 16David pleaded with God for the child. He fasted and went into his house and spent the nights lying on the ground. 17The elders of his household stood beside him to get him up from the ground, but he refused, and he would not eat any food with them.

18On the seventh day the child died. David's servants were afraid to tell him that the child was dead, for they thought, "While the child was still living, we spoke to David but he would not listen to us. How can we tell him the child is dead? He may do something desperate."

a 14 Masoretic Text; an ancient Hebrew scribal tradition *this you have shown utter contempt for the LORD*

Make It Stick

READ 2 SAMUEL 12:7–10

Nathan stood up for what was right and did some very straight talking with King David. You need the guts to do that, too, if a friend has done something seriously wrong or is about to do so. On a sticky note, write one extreme circumstance where you'd speak up to a friend.

¹⁹David noticed that his servants were whispering among themselves and he realized the child was dead. "Is the child dead?" he asked.

"Yes," they replied, "he is dead."

²⁰Then David got up from the ground. After he had washed, put on lotions and changed his clothes, he went into the house of the LORD and worshiped. Then he went to his own house, and at his request they served him food, and he ate.

²¹His servants asked him, "Why are you acting this way? While the child was alive, you fasted and wept, but now that the child is dead, you get up and eat!"

²²He answered, "While the child was still alive, I fasted and wept. I thought, 'Who knows? The LORD may be gracious to me and let the child live.' ²³But now that he is dead, why should I fast? Can I bring him back again? I will go to him, but he will not return to me."

²⁴Then David comforted his wife Bathsheba, and he went to her and lay with her. She gave birth to a son, and they named him Solomon. The LORD loved him; ²⁵and because the LORD loved him, he sent word through Nathan the prophet to name him Jedidiah.ᵃ

²⁶Meanwhile Joab fought against Rabbah of the Ammonites and captured the royal citadel. ²⁷Joab then sent messengers to David, saying, "I have fought against Rabbah and taken its water supply. ²⁸Now muster the rest of the troops and besiege the city and capture it. Otherwise I will take the city, and it will be named after me."

²⁹So David mustered the entire army and went to Rabbah, and attacked and captured it. ³⁰He took the crown from the head of their kingᵇ—its weight was a talentᶜ of gold, and it was set with precious stones—and it was placed on David's head. He took a great quantity of plunder from the city ³¹and brought out the people who were there, consigning them to labor with saws and with iron picks and axes, and he made them work at brickmaking.ᵈ He did this to all the Ammonite towns. Then David and his entire army returned to Jerusalem.

Amnon and Tamar

13 In the course of time, Amnon son of David fell in love with Tamar, the beautiful sister of Absalom son of David.

²Amnon became frustrated to the point of illness on account of his sister Tamar, for she was a virgin, and it seemed impossible for him to do anything to her.

³Now Amnon had a friend named Jonadab son of Shimeah, David's brother. Jonadab was a very shrewd man. ⁴He asked Amnon, "Why do you, the king's son, look so haggard morning after morning? Won't you tell me?"

Amnon said to him, "I'm in love with Tamar, my brother Absalom's sister."

⁵"Go to bed and pretend to be ill," Jonadab said. "When your father comes to see you, say to him, 'I would like my sister Tamar to come and give me something to eat. Let her prepare the food in my sight so I may watch her and then eat it from her hand.' "

⁶So Amnon lay down and pretended to be ill. When the king came to see him, Amnon said to him, "I would like my sister Tamar to come and make some special bread in my sight, so I may eat from her hand."

⁷David sent word to Tamar at the palace: "Go to the house of your brother Amnon and prepare some food for him." ⁸So Tamar went to the house of her brother Amnon, who was lying down. She took some dough, kneaded it, made the bread in his sight and baked it. ⁹Then she took the pan and served him the bread, but he refused to eat.

"Send everyone out of here," Amnon said. So everyone left him. ¹⁰Then Amnon said to Tamar, "Bring the food here into my bedroom so I may eat from your hand." And Tamar took the bread she had prepared and brought it to her brother Amnon in his bedroom. ¹¹But when she took it to him to eat, he grabbed her and said, "Come to bed with me, my sister."

¹²"Don't, my brother!" she said to him. "Don't force me. Such a thing should not be done in Israel! Don't do this wicked thing. ¹³What about me? Where could I get rid of my disgrace? And what about you? You would be like one of the wicked fools in Israel. Please speak to the king; he will not keep me from being married to you." ¹⁴But he refused to listen to her, and since he was stronger than she, he raped her.

ᵃ 25 *Jedidiah* means *loved by the LORD.*   ᵇ 30 Or *of Milcom* (that is, Molech)   ᶜ 30 That is, about 75 pounds (about 34 kilograms)   ᵈ 31 The meaning of the Hebrew for this clause is uncertain.

¹⁵Then Amnon hated her with intense hatred. In fact, he hated her more than he had loved her. Amnon said to her, "Get up and get out!"

¹⁶"No!" she said to him. "Sending me away would be a greater wrong than what you have already done to me."

But he refused to listen to her. ¹⁷He called his personal servant and said, "Get this woman out of here and bolt the door after her." ¹⁸So his servant put her out and bolted the door after her. She was wearing a richly ornamented*ᵃ* robe, for this was the kind of garment the virgin daughters of the king wore. ¹⁹Tamar put ashes on her head and tore the ornamented*ᵇ* robe she was wearing. She put her hand on her head and went away, weeping aloud as she went.

²⁰Her brother Absalom said to her, "Has that Amnon, your brother, been with you? Be quiet now, my sister; he is your brother. Don't take this thing to heart." And Tamar lived in her brother Absalom's house, a desolate woman.

²¹When King David heard all this, he was furious. ²²Absalom never said a word to Amnon, either good or bad; he hated Amnon because he had disgraced his sister Tamar.

Absalom Kills Amnon

²³Two years later, when Absalom's sheepshearers were at Baal Hazor near the border of Ephraim, he invited all the king's sons to come there. ²⁴Absalom went to the king and said, "Your servant has had shearers come. Will the king and his officials please join me?"

²⁵"No, my son," the king replied. "All of us should not go; we would only be a burden to you." Although Absalom urged him, he still refused to go, but gave him his blessing.

²⁶Then Absalom said, "If not, please let my brother Amnon come with us."

The king asked him, "Why should he go with you?" ²⁷But Absalom urged him, so he sent with him Amnon and the rest of the king's sons.

²⁸Absalom ordered his men, "Listen! When Amnon is in high spirits from drinking wine and I say to you, 'Strike Amnon down,' then kill him. Don't be afraid. Have not I given you this order? Be strong and brave." ²⁹So Absalom's men did to Amnon what Absalom had ordered. Then all the king's sons got up, mounted their mules and fled.

³⁰While they were on their way, the report came to David: "Absalom has struck down all the king's sons; not one of them is left." ³¹The king stood up, tore his clothes and lay down on the ground; and all his servants stood by with their clothes torn.

³²But Jonadab son of Shimeah, David's brother, said, "My lord should not think that they killed all the princes; only Amnon is dead. This has been Absalom's expressed intention ever since the day Amnon raped his sister Tamar. ³³My lord the king should not be concerned about the report that all the king's sons are dead. Only Amnon is dead."

³⁴Meanwhile, Absalom had fled.

Now the man standing watch looked up and saw many people on the road west of him, coming down the side of the hill. The watchman went and told the king, "I see men in the direction of Horonaim, on the side of the hill."*ᶜ*

³⁵Jonadab said to the king, "See, the king's sons are here; it has happened just as your servant said."

³⁶As he finished speaking, the king's sons came in, wailing loudly. The king, too, and all his servants wept very bitterly.

³⁷Absalom fled and went to Talmai son of Ammihud, the king of Geshur. But King David mourned for his son every day.

³⁸After Absalom fled and went to Geshur, he stayed there three years. ³⁹And the spirit of the king*ᵈ* longed to go to Absalom, for he was consoled concerning Amnon's death.

Absalom Returns to Jerusalem

14 Joab son of Zeruiah knew that the king's heart longed for Absalom. ²So Joab sent someone to Tekoa and had a wise woman brought from there. He said to her, "Pretend you are in mourning. Dress in mourning clothes, and don't use any cosmetic lotions. Act like a woman who has spent many days grieving for the dead. ³Then go to the king and speak these words to him." And Joab put the words in her mouth.

ᵃ18 The meaning of the Hebrew for this phrase is uncertain.
ᵇ19 The meaning of the Hebrew for this word is uncertain.
ᶜ34 Septuagint; Hebrew does not have this sentence.
ᵈ39 Dead Sea Scrolls and some Septuagint manuscripts; Masoretic Text *But the spirit of David the king*

⁴When the woman from Tekoa went*a* to the king, she fell with her face to the ground to pay him honor, and she said, "Help me, O king!"

⁵The king asked her, "What is troubling you?"

She said, "I am indeed a widow; my husband is dead. ⁶I your servant had two sons. They got into a fight with each other in the field, and no one was there to separate them. One struck the other and killed him. ⁷Now the whole clan has risen up against your servant; they say, 'Hand over the one who struck his brother down, so that we may put him to death for the life of his brother whom he killed; then we will get rid of the heir as well.' They would put out the only burning coal I have left, leaving my husband neither name nor descendant on the face of the earth."

⁸The king said to the woman, "Go home, and I will issue an order in your behalf."

⁹But the woman from Tekoa said to him, "My lord the king, let the blame rest on me and on my father's family, and let the king and his throne be without guilt."

¹⁰The king replied, "If anyone says anything to you, bring him to me, and he will not bother you again."

¹¹She said, "Then let the king invoke the LORD his God to prevent the avenger of blood from adding to the destruction, so that my son will not be destroyed."

"As surely as the LORD lives," he said, "not one hair of your son's head will fall to the ground."

¹²Then the woman said, "Let your servant speak a word to my lord the king."

"Speak," he replied.

¹³The woman said, "Why then have you devised a thing like this against the people of God? When the king says this, does he not convict himself, for the king has not brought back his banished son? ¹⁴Like water spilled on the ground, which cannot be recovered, so we must die. But God does not take away life; instead, he devises ways so that a banished person may not remain estranged from him.

¹⁵"And now I have come to say this to

a 4 Many Hebrew manuscripts, Septuagint, Vulgate and Syriac; most Hebrew manuscripts *spoke*

Kissing Up
READ 2 SAMUEL 14:1–12

Imagine this new kid comes to your school: He's tall, athletic, handsome and . . . get a load of that *hair!*—Long curly locks halfway down his back! He's so arrogant about being Mr. Cool that he treats everyone else like scum. Then he decides to run for school president. Suddenly—*ho!*—he's everybody's best pal. He pulls you over in the hallway, tells you he's your buddy-bud and says you deserve an "A" in math. *Like, what is* wrong *with this picture?* Absalom was kissing up (verse 5). It's great to be genuinely kind to others and say good things about them to encourage them, but it's dishonest to lay it on thick, flattering others just so they'll like you and give you what you want. That's manipulation. Got a genuine compliment? *Give* it! Have an encouraging word? *Say* it! But just skip the Absalom stuff.

Your next reading is on page 405.

my lord the king because the people have made me afraid. Your servant thought, 'I will speak to the king; perhaps he will do what his servant asks. ¹⁶Perhaps the king will agree to deliver his servant from the hand of the man who is trying to cut off both me and my son from the inheritance God gave us.'

¹⁷"And now your servant says, 'May the word of my lord the king bring me rest, for my lord the king is like an angel of God in discerning good and evil. May the LORD your God be with you.' "

¹⁸Then the king said to the woman, "Do not keep from me the answer to what I am going to ask you."

"Let my lord the king speak," the woman said.

¹⁹The king asked, "Isn't the hand of Joab with you in all this?"

The woman answered, "As surely as you live, my lord the king, no one can turn to the right or to the left from anything my lord the king says. Yes, it was your servant Joab who instructed me to do this and who put all these words into the mouth of your servant. ²⁰Your servant Joab did this to change the present situation. My lord has wisdom like that of an angel of God—he knows everything that happens in the land."

²¹The king said to Joab, "Very well, I will do it. Go, bring back the young man Absalom."

²²Joab fell with his face to the ground to pay him honor, and he blessed the king. Joab said, "Today your servant knows that he has found favor in your eyes, my lord the king, because the king has granted his servant's request."

²³Then Joab went to Geshur and brought Absalom back to Jerusalem. ²⁴But the king said, "He must go to his own house; he must not see my face." So Absalom went to his own house and did not see the face of the king.

²⁵In all Israel there was not a man so highly praised for his handsome appearance as Absalom. From the top of his head to the sole of his foot there was no blemish in him. ²⁶Whenever he cut the hair of his head—he used to cut his hair from time to time when it became too heavy for him—he would weigh it, and its weight was two hundred shekels[a] by the royal standard.

²⁷Three sons and a daughter were born to Absalom. The daughter's name was Tamar, and she became a beautiful woman.

²⁸Absalom lived two years in Jerusalem without seeing the king's face. ²⁹Then Absalom sent for Joab in order to send him to the king, but Joab refused to come to him. So he sent a second time, but he refused to come. ³⁰Then he said to his servants, "Look, Joab's field is next to mine, and he has barley there. Go and set it on fire." So Absalom's servants set the field on fire.

³¹Then Joab did go to Absalom's house and he said to him, "Why have your servants set my field on fire?"

³²Absalom said to Joab, "Look, I sent word to you and said, 'Come here so I can send you to the king to ask, "Why have I come from Geshur? It would be better for me if I were still there!" ' Now then, I want to see the king's face, and if I am guilty of anything, let him put me to death."

³³So Joab went to the king and told him this. Then the king summoned Absalom, and he came in and bowed down with his face to the ground before the king. And the king kissed Absalom.

Absalom's Conspiracy

15 In the course of time, Absalom provided himself with a chariot and horses and with fifty men to run ahead of him. ²He would get up early and stand by the side of the road leading to the city gate. Whenever anyone came with a complaint to be placed before the king for a decision, Absalom would call out to him, "What town are you from?" He would answer, "Your servant is from one of the tribes of Israel." ³Then Absalom would say to him, "Look, your claims are valid and proper, but there is no representative of the king to hear you." ⁴And Absalom would add, "If only I were appointed judge in the land! Then everyone who has a complaint or case could come to me and I would see that he gets justice."

⁵Also, whenever anyone approached him to bow down before him, Absalom would reach out his hand, take hold of him and kiss him. ⁶Absalom behaved in this way toward all the Israelites who came to the king asking for justice, and so he stole the hearts of the men of Israel.

ᵃ 26 That is, about 5 pounds (about 2.3 kilograms)

[7]At the end of four[a] years, Absalom said to the king, "Let me go to Hebron and fulfill a vow I made to the LORD. [8]While your servant was living at Geshur in Aram, I made this vow: 'If the LORD takes me back to Jerusalem, I will worship the LORD in Hebron.[b]' "

[9]The king said to him, "Go in peace." So he went to Hebron.

[10]Then Absalom sent secret messengers throughout the tribes of Israel to say, "As soon as you hear the sound of the trumpets, then say, 'Absalom is king in Hebron.' " [11]Two hundred men from Jerusalem had accompanied Absalom. They had been invited as guests and went quite innocently, knowing nothing about the matter. [12]While Absalom was offering sacrifices, he also sent for Ahithophel the Gilonite, David's counselor, to come from Giloh, his hometown. And so the conspiracy gained strength, and Absalom's following kept on increasing.

David Flees

[13]A messenger came and told David, "The hearts of the men of Israel are with Absalom."

[14]Then David said to all his officials who were with him in Jerusalem, "Come! We must flee, or none of us will escape from Absalom. We must leave immediately, or he will move quickly to overtake us and bring ruin upon us and put the city to the sword."

[15]The king's officials answered him, "Your servants are ready to do whatever our lord the king chooses."

[16]The king set out, with his entire household following him; but he left ten concubines to take care of the palace. [17]So the king set out, with all the people following him, and they halted at a place some distance away. [18]All his men marched past him, along with all the Ker-

---

a 7 Some Septuagint manuscripts, Syriac and Josephus; Hebrew *forty*   *b 8* Some Septuagint manuscripts; Hebrew does not have *in Hebron.*

In Love With Your Reflection

READ 2 SAMUEL 14:25–26; 15:10–12; 18:9–17

Everyone wants to look their best, but some people take things too far—like Absalom. "In all Israel there was not a man so highly praised for his handsome appearance as Absalom. From the top of his head to the sole of his foot there was no blemish in him" (2 Samuel 14:25). Absalom was one good-looking dude, but his handsome head and his long, long hair—his greatest pride—became his downfall. After leading a rebellion against his own father, during a battle his mule went under a tree with thick branches and Absalom's head got caught in the tree, resulting in his death. Character is far more important than physical appearance. It's good to groom yourself and look your best. But remember that looks are only a small part of what life is about. It's what's *inside* that really counts.

Your next reading is on page 419.

ethites and Pelethites; and all the six hundred Gittites who had accompanied him from Gath marched before the king.

¹⁹The king said to Ittai the Gittite, "Why should you come along with us? Go back and stay with King Absalom. You are a foreigner, an exile from your homeland. ²⁰You came only yesterday. And today shall I make you wander about with us, when I do not know where I am going? Go back, and take your countrymen. May kindness and faithfulness be with you."

²¹But Ittai replied to the king, "As surely as the Lord lives, and as my lord the king lives, wherever my lord the king may be, whether it means life or death, there will your servant be."

²²David said to Ittai, "Go ahead, march on." So Ittai the Gittite marched on with all his men and the families that were with him.

²³The whole countryside wept aloud as all the people passed by. The king also crossed the Kidron Valley, and all the people moved on toward the desert.

²⁴Zadok was there, too, and all the Levites who were with him were carrying the ark of the covenant of God. They set down the ark of God, and Abiathar offered sacrifices[a] until all the people had finished leaving the city.

²⁵Then the king said to Zadok, "Take the ark of God back into the city. If I find favor in the Lord's eyes, he will bring me back and let me see it and his dwelling place again. ²⁶But if he says, 'I am not pleased with you,' then I am ready; let him do to me whatever seems good to him."

²⁷The king also said to Zadok the priest, "Aren't you a seer? Go back to the city in peace, with your son Ahimaaz and Jonathan son of Abiathar. You and Abiathar take your two sons with you. ²⁸I will wait at the fords in the desert until word comes from you to inform me." ²⁹So Zadok and Abiathar took the ark of God back to Jerusalem and stayed there.

³⁰But David continued up the Mount of Olives, weeping as he went; his head was covered and he was barefoot. All the people with him covered their heads too and were weeping as they went up. ³¹Now David had been told, "Ahithophel is among the conspirators with Absalom." So David prayed, "O Lord, turn Ahithophel's counsel into foolishness."

³²When David arrived at the summit, where people used to worship God, Hushai the Arkite was there to meet him, his robe torn and dust on his head. ³³David said to him, "If you go with me, you will be a burden to me. ³⁴But if you return to the city and say to Absalom, 'I will be your servant, O king; I was your father's servant in the past, but now I will be your servant,' then you can help me by frustrating Ahithophel's advice. ³⁵Won't the priests Zadok and Abiathar be there with you? Tell them anything you hear in the king's palace. ³⁶Their two sons, Ahimaaz son of Zadok and Jonathan son of Abiathar, are there with them. Send them to me with anything you hear."

³⁷So David's friend Hushai arrived at Jerusalem as Absalom was entering the city.

David and Ziba

16 When David had gone a short distance beyond the summit, there was Ziba, the steward of Mephibosheth, waiting to meet him. He had a string of donkeys saddled and loaded with two hundred loaves of bread, a hundred cakes of raisins, a hundred cakes of figs and a skin of wine.

²The king asked Ziba, "Why have you brought these?"

Ziba answered, "The donkeys are for the king's household to ride on, the bread and fruit are for the men to eat, and the wine is to refresh those who become exhausted in the desert."

³The king then asked, "Where is your master's grandson?"

Ziba said to him, "He is staying in Jerusalem, because he thinks, 'Today the house of Israel will give me back my grandfather's kingdom.' "

⁴Then the king said to Ziba, "All that belonged to Mephibosheth is now yours."

"I humbly bow," Ziba said. "May I find favor in your eyes, my lord the king."

Shimei Curses David

⁵As King David approached Bahurim, a man from the same clan as Saul's family came out from there. His name was Shimei son of Gera, and he cursed as he came out. ⁶He pelted David and all the king's officials with stones, though all the troops and the special guard were on David's right and left. ⁷As he cursed, Shimei said,

---

ª 24 Or *Abiathar went up*

"Get out, get out, you man of blood, you scoundrel! 8The LORD has repaid you for all the blood you shed in the household of Saul, in whose place you have reigned. The LORD has handed the kingdom over to your son Absalom. You have come to ruin because you are a man of blood!"

9Then Abishai son of Zeruiah said to the king, "Why should this dead dog curse my lord the king? Let me go over and cut off his head."

10But the king said, "What do you and I have in common, you sons of Zeruiah? If he is cursing because the LORD said to him, 'Curse David,' who can ask, 'Why do you do this?' "

11David then said to Abishai and all his officials, "My son, who is of my own flesh, is trying to take my life. How much more, then, this Benjamite! Leave him alone; let him curse, for the LORD has told him to. 12It may be that the LORD will see my distress and repay me with good for the cursing I am receiving today."

13So David and his men continued along the road while Shimei was going along the hillside opposite him, cursing as he went and throwing stones at him and showering him with dirt. 14The king and all the people with him arrived at their destination exhausted. And there he refreshed himself.

The Advice of Ahithophel and Hushai

15Meanwhile, Absalom and all the men of Israel came to Jerusalem, and Ahithophel was with him. 16Then Hushai the Arkite, David's friend, went to Absalom and said to him, "Long live the king! Long live the king!"

17Absalom asked Hushai, "Is this the love you show your friend? Why didn't you go with your friend?"

18Hushai said to Absalom, "No, the one chosen by the LORD, by these people, and by all the men of Israel—his I will be, and I will remain with him. 19Furthermore, whom should I serve? Should I not serve the son? Just as I served your father, so I will serve you."

20Absalom said to Ahithophel, "Give us your advice. What should we do?"

21Ahithophel answered, "Lie with your father's concubines whom he left to take care of the palace. Then all Israel will hear that you have made yourself a stench in your father's nostrils, and the hands of everyone with you will be strengthened." 22So they pitched a tent for Absalom on the roof, and he lay with his father's concubines in the sight of all Israel.

23Now in those days the advice Ahithophel gave was like that of one who inquires of God. That was how both David and Absalom regarded all of Ahithophel's advice.

17 Ahithophel said to Absalom, "I would*a* choose twelve thousand men and set out tonight in pursuit of David. 2I would*b* attack him while he is weary and weak. I would*b* strike him with terror, and then all the people with him will flee. I

Get a Load of This...

Wow! Shimei was *pushing* it by cursing the king, "throwing stones at him and showering him with dirt" (2 Samuel 16:13). David left the situation to God, but he didn't always respond like this to his enemies. Good thing Shimei caught David in a godly mood.

a 1 Or Let me   b 2 Or will

would[a] strike down only the king ³and bring all the people back to you. The death of the man you seek will mean the return of all; all the people will be unharmed." ⁴This plan seemed good to Absalom and to all the elders of Israel.

⁵But Absalom said, "Summon also Hushai the Arkite, so we can hear what he has to say." ⁶When Hushai came to him, Absalom said, "Ahithophel has given this advice. Should we do what he says? If not, give us your opinion."

⁷Hushai replied to Absalom, "The advice Ahithophel has given is not good this time. ⁸You know your father and his men; they are fighters, and as fierce as a wild bear robbed of her cubs. Besides, your father is an experienced fighter; he will not spend the night with the troops. ⁹Even now, he is hidden in a cave or some other place. If he should attack your troops first,[b] whoever hears about it will say, 'There has been a slaughter among the troops who follow Absalom.' ¹⁰Then even the bravest soldier, whose heart is like the heart of a lion, will melt with fear, for all Israel knows that your father is a fighter and that those with him are brave.

¹¹"So I advise you: Let all Israel, from Dan to Beersheba—as numerous as the sand on the seashore—be gathered to you, with you yourself leading them into battle. ¹²Then we will attack him wherever he may be found, and we will fall on him as dew settles on the ground. Neither he nor any of his men will be left alive. ¹³If he withdraws into a city, then all Israel will bring ropes to that city, and we will drag it down to the valley until not even a piece of it can be found."

¹⁴Absalom and all the men of Israel said, "The advice of Hushai the Arkite is better than that of Ahithophel." For the LORD had determined to frustrate the good advice of Ahithophel in order to bring disaster on Absalom.

¹⁵Hushai told Zadok and Abiathar, the priests, "Ahithophel has advised Absalom and the elders of Israel to do such and such, but I have advised them to do so and so. ¹⁶Now send a message immediately and tell David, 'Do not spend the night at the fords in the desert; cross over without fail, or the king and all the people with him will be swallowed up.' "

¹⁷Jonathan and Ahimaaz were staying at En Rogel. A servant girl was to go and inform them, and they were to go and tell King David, for they could not risk being seen entering the city. ¹⁸But a young man saw them and told Absalom. So the two of them left quickly and went to the house of a man in Bahurim. He had a well in his courtyard, and they climbed down into it. ¹⁹His wife took a covering and spread it out over the opening of the well and scattered grain over it. No one knew anything about it.

²⁰When Absalom's men came to the woman at the house, they asked, "Where are Ahimaaz and Jonathan?"

The woman answered them, "They crossed over the brook."[c] The men searched but found no one, so they returned to Jerusalem.

²¹After the men had gone, the two climbed out of the well and went to inform King David. They said to him, "Set out and cross the river at once; Ahithophel has advised such and such against you." ²²So David and all the people with him set out and crossed the Jordan. By daybreak, no one was left who had not crossed the Jordan.

²³When Ahithophel saw that his advice had not been followed, he saddled his donkey and set out for his house in his hometown. He put his house in order and then hanged himself. So he died and was buried in his father's tomb.

²⁴David went to Mahanaim, and Absalom crossed the Jordan with all the men of Israel. ²⁵Absalom had appointed Amasa over the army in place of Joab. Amasa was the son of a man named Jether,[d] an Israelite[e] who had married Abigail,[f] the daughter of Nahash and sister of Zeruiah the mother of Joab. ²⁶The Israelites and Absalom camped in the land of Gilead.

²⁷When David came to Mahanaim, Shobi son of Nahash from Rabbah of the Ammonites, and Makir son of Ammiel from Lo Debar, and Barzillai the Gileadite from Rogelim ²⁸brought bedding and bowls and articles of pottery. They also brought wheat and barley, flour and roasted grain, beans and lentils,[g] ²⁹honey

ᵃ 2 Or will   ᵇ 9 Or When some of the men fall at the first attack   ᶜ 20 Or "They passed by the sheep pen toward the water."   ᵈ 25 Hebrew Ithra, a variant of Jether
ᵉ 25 Hebrew and some Septuagint manuscripts; other Septuagint manuscripts (see also 1 Chron. 2:17) Ishmaelite or Jezreelite   ᶠ 25 Hebrew Abigal, a variant of Abigail
ᵍ 28 Most Septuagint manuscripts and Syriac; Hebrew lentils, and roasted grain

and curds, sheep, and cheese from cows' milk for David and his people to eat. For they said, "The people have become hungry and tired and thirsty in the desert."

Absalom's Death

18 David mustered the men who were with him and appointed over them commanders of thousands and commanders of hundreds. ²David sent the troops out—a third under the command of Joab, a third under Joab's brother Abishai son of Zeruiah, and a third under Ittai the Gittite. The king told the troops, "I myself will surely march out with you."

³But the men said, "You must not go out; if we are forced to flee, they won't care about us. Even if half of us die, they won't care; but you are worth ten thousand of us.ᵃ It would be better now for you to give us support from the city."

⁴The king answered, "I will do whatever seems best to you."

So the king stood beside the gate while all the men marched out in units of hundreds and of thousands. ⁵The king commanded Joab, Abishai and Ittai, "Be gentle with the young man Absalom for my sake." And all the troops heard the king giving orders concerning Absalom to each of the commanders.

⁶The army marched into the field to fight Israel, and the battle took place in the forest of Ephraim. ⁷There the army of Israel was defeated by David's men, and the casualties that day were great—twenty thousand men. ⁸The battle spread out over the whole countryside, and the forest claimed more lives that day than the sword.

⁹Now Absalom happened to meet David's men. He was riding his mule, and as the mule went under the thick branches of a large oak, Absalom's head got caught in the tree. He was left hanging in midair, while the mule he was riding kept on going.

¹⁰When one of the men saw this, he told Joab, "I just saw Absalom hanging in an oak tree."

¹¹Joab said to the man who had told him this, "What! You saw him? Why didn't you strike him to the ground right there? Then I would have had to give you ten shekelsᵇ of silver and a warrior's belt."

¹²But the man replied, "Even if a thousand shekelsᶜ were weighed out into my hands, I would not lift my hand against the king's son. In our hearing the king commanded you and Abishai and Ittai, 'Protect the young man Absalom for my sake.ᵈ ¹³And if I had put my life in jeopardyᵉ—and nothing is hidden from the king—you would have kept your distance from me."

¹⁴Joab said, "I'm not going to wait like this for you."

ᵃ 3 Two Hebrew manuscripts, some Septuagint manuscripts and Vulgate; most Hebrew manuscripts *care; for now there are ten thousand like us*   ᵇ 11 That is, about 4 ounces (about 115 grams)   ᶜ 12 That is, about 25 pounds (about 11 kilograms)   ᵈ 12 A few Hebrew manuscripts, Septuagint, Vulgate and Syriac; most Hebrew manuscripts may be translated *Absalom, whoever you may be.*
ᵉ 13 Or *Otherwise, if I had acted treacherously toward him*

Gross!

Check out 2 Samuel 18:14. Joab jabbed three javelins through Absalom's heart while he was hanging in the tree by his head. Javelins were like spears, only lighter and shorter. One javelin would probably have done the job, but Joab obviously wanted to make sure Absalom was dead.

So he took three javelins in his hand and plunged them into Absalom's heart while Absalom was still alive in the oak tree. 15And ten of Joab's armor-bearers surrounded Absalom, struck him and killed him.

16Then Joab sounded the trumpet, and the troops stopped pursuing Israel, for Joab halted them. 17They took Absalom, threw him into a big pit in the forest and piled up a large heap of rocks over him. Meanwhile, all the Israelites fled to their homes.

18During his lifetime Absalom had taken a pillar and erected it in the King's Valley as a monument to himself, for he thought, "I have no son to carry on the memory of my name." He named the pillar after himself, and it is called Absalom's Monument to this day.

David Mourns

19Now Ahimaaz son of Zadok said, "Let me run and take the news to the king that the LORD has delivered him from the hand of his enemies."

20"You are not the one to take the news today," Joab told him. "You may take the news another time, but you must not do so today, because the king's son is dead."

21Then Joab said to a Cushite, "Go, tell the king what you have seen." The Cushite bowed down before Joab and ran off.

22Ahimaaz son of Zadok again said to Joab, "Come what may, please let me run behind the Cushite."

But Joab replied, "My son, why do you want to go? You don't have any news that will bring you a reward."

23He said, "Come what may, I want to run."

So Joab said, "Run!" Then Ahimaaz ran by way of the plain a and outran the Cushite.

24While David was sitting between the inner and outer gates, the watchman went up to the roof of the gateway by the wall. As he looked out, he saw a man running alone. 25The watchman called out to the king and reported it.

The king said, "If he is alone, he must have good news." And the man came closer and closer.

26Then the watchman saw another man running, and he called down to the gatekeeper, "Look, another man running alone!"

The king said, "He must be bringing good news, too."

27The watchman said, "It seems to me that the first one runs like Ahimaaz son of Zadok."

"He's a good man," the king said. "He comes with good news."

28Then Ahimaaz called out to the king, "All is well!" He bowed down before the king with his face to the ground and said, "Praise be to the LORD your God! He has delivered up the men who lifted their hands against my lord the king."

29The king asked, "Is the young man Absalom safe?"

Ahimaaz answered, "I saw great confusion just as Joab was about to send the king's servant and me, your servant, but I don't know what it was."

30The king said, "Stand aside and wait here." So he stepped aside and stood there.

31Then the Cushite arrived and said, "My lord the king, hear the good news! The LORD has delivered you today from all who rose up against you."

32The king asked the Cushite, "Is the young man Absalom safe?"

The Cushite replied, "May the enemies of my lord the king and all who rise up to harm you be like that young man."

33The king was shaken. He went up to the room over the gateway and wept. As he went, he said: "O my son Absalom! My son, my son Absalom! If only I had died instead of you—O Absalom, my son, my son!"

19 Joab was told, "The king is weeping and mourning for Absalom." 2And for the whole army the victory that day was turned into mourning, because on that day the troops heard it said, "The king is grieving for his son." 3The men stole into the city that day as men steal in who are ashamed when they flee from battle. 4The king covered his face and cried aloud, "O my son Absalom! O Absalom, my son, my son!"

5Then Joab went into the house to the king and said, "Today you have humiliated all your men, who have just saved your life and the lives of your sons and daughters and the lives of your wives and concubines. 6You love those who hate you and hate those who love you. You have made

a 23 That is, the plain of the Jordan

it clear today that the commanders and their men mean nothing to you. I see that you would be pleased if Absalom were alive today and all of us were dead. 7Now go out and encourage your men. I swear by the LORD that if you don't go out, not a man will be left with you by nightfall. This will be worse for you than all the calamities that have come upon you from your youth till now."

8So the king got up and took his seat in the gateway. When the men were told, "The king is sitting in the gateway," they all came before him.

David Returns to Jerusalem

Meanwhile, the Israelites had fled to their homes. 9Throughout the tribes of Israel, the people were all arguing with each other, saying, "The king delivered us from the hand of our enemies; he is the one who rescued us from the hand of the Philistines. But now he has fled the country because of Absalom; 10and Absalom, whom we anointed to rule over us, has died in battle. So why do you say nothing about bringing the king back?"

11King David sent this message to Zadok and Abiathar, the priests: "Ask the elders of Judah, 'Why should you be the last to bring the king back to his palace, since what is being said throughout Israel has reached the king at his quarters? 12You are my brothers, my own flesh and blood. So why should you be the last to bring back the king?' 13And say to Amasa, 'Are you not my own flesh and blood? May God deal with me, be it ever so severely, if from now on you are not the commander of my army in place of Joab.' "

14He won over the hearts of all the men of Judah as though they were one man. They sent word to the king, "Return, you and all your men." 15Then the king returned and went as far as the Jordan.

Now the men of Judah had come to Gilgal to go out and meet the king and bring him across the Jordan. 16Shimei son of Gera, the Benjamite from Bahurim, hurried down with the men of Judah to meet King David. 17With him were a thousand Benjamites, along with Ziba, the steward of Saul's household, and his fifteen sons and twenty servants. They rushed to the Jordan, where the king was. 18They crossed at the ford to take the king's household over and to do whatever he wished.

When Shimei son of Gera crossed the Jordan, he fell prostrate before the king 19and said to him, "May my lord not hold me guilty. Do not remember how your servant did wrong on the day my lord the king left Jerusalem. May the king put it out of his mind. 20For I your servant know that I have sinned, but today I have come here as the first of the whole house of Joseph to come down and meet my lord the king."

21Then Abishai son of Zeruiah said, "Shouldn't Shimei be put to death for this? He cursed the LORD's anointed."

22David replied, "What do you and I have in common, you sons of Zeruiah? This day you have become my adversaries! Should anyone be put to death in Israel today? Do I not know that today I am king over Israel?" 23So the king said to Shimei, "You shall not die." And the king promised him on oath.

24Mephibosheth, Saul's grandson, also went down to meet the king. He had not taken care of his feet or trimmed his mustache or washed his clothes from the day the king left until the day he returned safely. 25When he came from Jerusalem to meet the king, the king asked him, "Why didn't you go with me, Mephibosheth?"

26He said, "My lord the king, since I your servant am lame, I said, 'I will have my donkey saddled and will ride on it, so I can go with the king.' But Ziba my servant betrayed me. 27And he has slandered your servant to my lord the king. My lord the king is like an angel of God; so do whatever pleases you. 28All my grandfather's descendants deserved nothing but death from my lord the king, but you gave your servant a place among those who eat at your table. So what right do I have to make any more appeals to the king?"

29The king said to him, "Why say more? I order you and Ziba to divide the fields."

30Mephibosheth said to the king, "Let him take everything, now that my lord the king has arrived home safely."

31Barzillai the Gileadite also came down from Rogelim to cross the Jordan with the king and to send him on his way from there. 32Now Barzillai was a very old man, eighty years of age. He had provided for the king during his stay in Mahanaim, for he was a very wealthy man. 33The king said to Barzillai, "Cross over with me and stay with me in Jerusalem, and I will provide for you."

³⁴But Barzillai answered the king, "How many more years will I live, that I should go up to Jerusalem with the king? ³⁵I am now eighty years old. Can I tell the difference between what is good and what is not? Can your servant taste what he eats and drinks? Can I still hear the voices of men and women singers? Why should your servant be an added burden to my lord the king? ³⁶Your servant will cross over the Jordan with the king for a short distance, but why should the king reward me in this way? ³⁷Let your servant return, that I may die in my own town near the tomb of my father and mother. But here is your servant Kimham. Let him cross over with my lord the king. Do for him whatever pleases you."

³⁸The king said, "Kimham shall cross over with me, and I will do for him whatever pleases you. And anything you desire from me I will do for you."

³⁹So all the people crossed the Jordan, and then the king crossed over. The king kissed Barzillai and gave him his blessing, and Barzillai returned to his home.

⁴⁰When the king crossed over to Gilgal, Kimham crossed with him. All the troops of Judah and half the troops of Israel had taken the king over.

⁴¹Soon all the men of Israel were coming to the king and saying to him, "Why did our brothers, the men of Judah, steal the king away and bring him and his household across the Jordan, together with all his men?"

⁴²All the men of Judah answered the men of Israel, "We did this because the king is closely related to us. Why are you angry about it? Have we eaten any of the king's provisions? Have we taken anything for ourselves?"

⁴³Then the men of Israel answered the men of Judah, "We have ten shares in the king; and besides, we have a greater claim on David than you have. So why do you treat us with contempt? Were we not the first to speak of bringing back our king?"

But the men of Judah responded even more harshly than the men of Israel.

Sheba Rebels Against David

 Now a troubleman named Sheba son of Bicri, a Benjamite, happened to be there. He sounded the trumpet and shouted,

"We have no share in David,
    no part in Jesse's son!
Every man to his tent, O Israel!"

²So all the men of Israel deserted David to follow Sheba son of Bicri. But the men of Judah stayed by their king all the way from the Jordan to Jerusalem.

³When David returned to his palace in Jerusalem, he took the ten concubines he had left to take care of the palace and put them in a house under guard. He provided for them, but did not lie with them. They were kept in confinement till the day of their death, living as widows.

⁴Then the king said to Amasa, "Summon the men of Judah to come to me within three days, and be here yourself." ⁵But when Amasa went to summon Judah, he took longer than the time the king had set for him.

⁶David said to Abishai, "Now Sheba son of Bicri will do us more harm than Absalom did. Take your master's men and pursue him, or he will find fortified cities and escape from us." ⁷So Joab's men and the Kerethites and Pelethites and all the mighty warriors went out under the command of Abishai. They marched out from Jerusalem to pursue Sheba son of Bicri.

⁸While they were at the great rock in Gibeon, Amasa came to meet them. Joab was wearing his military tunic, and strapped over it at his waist was a belt with a dagger in its sheath. As he stepped forward, it dropped out of its sheath.

⁹Joab said to Amasa, "How are you, my brother?" Then Joab took Amasa by the beard with his right hand to kiss him. ¹⁰Amasa was not on his guard against the dagger in Joab's hand, and Joab plunged it into his belly, and his intestines spilled out on the ground. Without being stabbed again, Amasa died. Then Joab and his brother Abishai pursued Sheba son of Bicri.

¹¹One of Joab's men stood beside Amasa and said, "Whoever favors Joab, and whoever is for David, let him follow Joab!" ¹²Amasa lay wallowing in his

blood in the middle of the road, and the man saw that all the troops came to a halt there. When he realized that everyone who came up to Amasa stopped, he dragged him from the road into a field and threw a garment over him. ¹³After Amasa had been removed from the road, all the men went on with Joab to pursue Sheba son of Bicri.

¹⁴Sheba passed through all the tribes of Israel to Abel Beth Maacah ᵃ and through the entire region of the Berites, who gathered together and followed him. ¹⁵All the troops with Joab came and besieged Sheba in Abel Beth Maacah. They built a siege ramp up to the city, and it stood against the outer fortifications. While they were battering the wall to bring it down, ¹⁶a wise woman called from the city, "Listen! Listen! Tell Joab to come here so I can speak to him." ¹⁷He went toward her, and she asked, "Are you Joab?"

"I am," he answered.

She said, "Listen to what your servant has to say."

"I'm listening," he said.

¹⁸She continued, "Long ago they used to say, 'Get your answer at Abel,' and that settled it. ¹⁹We are the peaceful and faithful in Israel. You are trying to destroy a city that is a mother in Israel. Why do you want to swallow up the LORD's inheritance?"

²⁰"Far be it from me!" Joab replied, "Far be it from me to swallow up or destroy! ²¹That is not the case. A man named Sheba son of Bicri, from the hill country of Ephraim, has lifted up his hand against the king, against David. Hand over this one man, and I'll withdraw from the city."

The woman said to Joab, "His head will be thrown to you from the wall."

²²Then the woman went to all the people with her wise advice, and they cut off the head of Sheba son of Bicri and threw it to Joab. So he sounded the trumpet, and his men dispersed from the city, each returning to his home. And Joab went back to the king in Jerusalem.

²³Joab was over Israel's entire army; Benaiah son of Jehoiada was over the Kerethites and Pelethites; ²⁴Adoniram ᵇ was in charge of forced labor; Jehoshaphat son of Ahilud was recorder; ²⁵Sheva was secretary; Zadok and Abiathar were priests; ²⁶and Ira the Jairite was David's priest.

The Gibeonites Avenged

During the reign of David, there was a famine for three successive years; so David sought the face of the LORD. The LORD said, "It is on account of Saul and his blood-stained house; it is because he put the Gibeonites to death."

²The king summoned the Gibeonites and spoke to them. (Now the Gibeonites were not a part of Israel but were survivors of the Amorites; the Israelites had sworn to ⌊spare⌋ them, but Saul in his zeal for Israel and Judah

Gross!

Check out 2 Samuel 20:10. When Amasa met Joab, he thought they would be "buddy-buddy." So when Joab took Amasa by the beard, Amasa thought, "Oh, he just wants to kiss me." (That's how men greeted each other back then.) Surprise! Joab stabbed him instead and spilled his intestines onto the road.

ᵃ 14 Or *Abel, even Beth Maacah;* also in verse 15   ᵇ 24 Some Septuagint manuscripts (see also 1 Kings 4:6 and 5:14); Hebrew *Adoram*

Gross!

Check out 2 Samuel 20:22. There were some tough women in Abel Beth Maacah. Wise ones, too. When Joab's army besieged the city, a wise woman found out what he was after and then took action—by getting the people to cut off Sheba's head and—"Here, Joab, catch!"— toss it over the wall.

had tried to annihilate them.) ³David asked the Gibeonites, "What shall I do for you? How shall I make amends so that you will bless the LORD's inheritance?"

⁴The Gibeonites answered him, "We have no right to demand silver or gold from Saul or his family, nor do we have the right to put anyone in Israel to death."

"What do you want me to do for you?" David asked.

⁵They answered the king, "As for the man who destroyed us and plotted against us so that we have been decimated and have no place anywhere in Israel, ⁶let seven of his male descendants be given to us to be killed and exposed before the LORD at Gibeah of Saul—the LORD's chosen one."

So the king said, "I will give them to you."

⁷The king spared Mephibosheth son of Jonathan, the son of Saul, because of the oath before the LORD between David and Jonathan son of Saul. ⁸But the king took Armoni and Mephibosheth, the two sons of Aiah's daughter Rizpah, whom she had borne to Saul, together with the five sons of Saul's daughter Merab,ᵃ whom she had borne to Adriel son of Barzillai the Meholathite. ⁹He handed them over to the Gibeonites, who killed and exposed them on a hill before the LORD. All seven of them fell together; they were put to death during the first days of the harvest, just as the barley harvest was beginning.

¹⁰Rizpah daughter of Aiah took sackcloth and spread it out for herself on a rock. From the beginning of the harvest till the rain poured down from the heavens on the bodies, she did not let the birds of the air touch them by day or the wild animals by night. ¹¹When David was told what Aiah's daughter Rizpah, Saul's concubine, had done, ¹²he went and took the bones of Saul and his son Jonathan from the citizens of Jabesh Gilead. (They had taken them secretly from the public square at Beth Shan, where the Philistines had hung them after they struck Saul down on Gilboa.) ¹³David brought the bones of Saul and his son Jonathan from there, and the bones of those who had been killed and exposed were gathered up.

¹⁴They buried the bones of Saul and his son Jonathan in the tomb of Saul's father Kish, at Zela in Benjamin, and did everything the king commanded. After that, God answered prayer in behalf of the land.

Wars Against the Philistines

¹⁵Once again there was a battle between the Philistines and Israel. David went down with his men to fight against the Philistines, and he became exhausted. ¹⁶And Ishbi-Benob, one of the descendants of Rapha, whose bronze spearhead weighed three hundred shekelsᵇ and who was armed with a new ⌊sword⌋, said he would kill David. ¹⁷But Abishai son of Zeruiah came to David's rescue; he struck the Philistine down and killed him. Then

ᵃ 8 Two Hebrew manuscripts, some Septuagint manuscripts and Syriac (see also 1 Samuel 18:19); most Hebrew and Septuagint manuscripts *Michal* ᵇ 16 That is, about 7 1/2 pounds (about 3.5 kilograms)

David's men swore to him, saying, "Never again will you go out with us to battle, so that the lamp of Israel will not be extinguished."

¹⁸In the course of time, there was another battle with the Philistines, at Gob. At that time Sibbecai the Hushathite killed Saph, one of the descendants of Rapha.

¹⁹In another battle with the Philistines at Gob, Elhanan son of Jaare-Oregimᵃ the Bethlehemite killed Goliathᵇ the Gittite, who had a spear with a shaft like a weaver's rod.

²⁰In still another battle, which took place at Gath, there was a huge man with six fingers on each hand and six toes on each foot—twenty-four in all. He also was descended from Rapha. ²¹When he taunted Israel, Jonathan son of Shimeah, David's brother, killed him.

²²These four were descendants of Rapha in Gath, and they fell at the hands of David and his men. .

David's Song of Praise

22 David sang to the Lᴏʀᴅ the words of this song when the Lᴏʀᴅ delivered him from the hand of all his enemies and from the hand of Saul. ²He said:

"The Lᴏʀᴅ is my rock, my fortress and
     my deliverer;
3   my God is my rock, in whom I take
         refuge,
     my shield and the hornᶜ of my
         salvation.
He is my stronghold, my refuge and
     my savior—
     from violent men you save me.
⁴I call to the Lᴏʀᴅ, who is worthy of
     praise,
     and I am saved from my enemies.

⁵"The waves of death swirled about
     me;

ᵃ 19 Or son of Jair the weaver   ᵇ 19 Hebrew and Septuagint; 1 Chron. 20:5 son of Jair killed Lahmi the brother of Goliath   ᶜ 3 Horn here symbolizes strength.

Make It Stick

READ 2 SAMUEL 21:1–2

In 2 Samuel 21:1–2, Saul nearly wiped out the Gibeonites. After all, God told Israel to get rid of them, right? Problem was, Saul deliberately "forgot" that Israel had a *covenant* to spare the Gibeonites (see Joshua 9). Don't go back on your promises. On a sticky note, write something you've promised recently.

the torrents of destruction
  overwhelmed me.
⁶The cords of the grave*a* coiled around
    me;
  the snares of death confronted me.
⁷In my distress I called to the Lord;
  I called out to my God.
From his temple he heard my voice;
  my cry came to his ears.
⁸"The earth trembled and quaked,
  the foundations of the heavens*b*
    shook;
  they trembled because he was angry.
⁹Smoke rose from his nostrils;
  consuming fire came from his mouth,
  burning coals blazed out of it.
¹⁰He parted the heavens and came down;
  dark clouds were under his feet.
¹¹He mounted the cherubim and flew;
  he soared*c* on the wings of the wind.
¹²He made darkness his canopy around
    him—
  the dark*d* rain clouds of the sky.

¹³Out of the brightness of his presence
  bolts of lightning blazed forth.
¹⁴The Lord thundered from heaven;
  the voice of the Most High
    resounded.
¹⁵He shot arrows and scattered ⌊the
    enemies⌋,
  bolts of lightning and routed them.
¹⁶The valleys of the sea were exposed
  and the foundations of the earth
    laid bare
at the rebuke of the Lord,
  at the blast of breath from his
    nostrils.

¹⁷"He reached down from on high and
    took hold of me;
  he drew me out of deep waters.
¹⁸He rescued me from my powerful
    enemy,

a 6 Hebrew *Sheol*   *b 8* Hebrew; Vulgate and Syriac (see also
Psalm 18:7) *mountains*   *c 11* Many Hebrew manuscripts
(see also Psalm 18:10); most Hebrew manuscripts *appeared*
d 12 Septuagint and Vulgate (see also Psalm 18:11); Hebrew
massed

Make It Stick

READ 2 SAMUEL 21:15–22

Remember how Israel was afraid to enter the Promised Land because of the giants (Numbers
13:31–33)? These verses show who won in the end. What are two "giants" in your life that you're
afraid of? Write them on a sticky note, and then cross them out as a reminder that, with God,
you can defeat anything.

from my foes, who were too strong for me.

19 They confronted me in the day of my
disaster,
but the LORD was my support.

20 He brought me out into a spacious
place;
he rescued me because he delighted
in me.

21 "The LORD has dealt with me according
to my righteousness;
according to the cleanness of my
hands he has rewarded me.

22 For I have kept the ways of the LORD;
I have not done evil by turning from
my God.

23 All his laws are before me;
I have not turned away from his
decrees.

24 I have been blameless before him
and have kept myself from sin.

25 The LORD has rewarded me according
to my righteousness,
according to my cleanness*a* in his
sight.

26 "To the faithful you show yourself
faithful,
to the blameless you show yourself
blameless,

27 to the pure you show yourself pure,
but to the crooked you show
yourself shrewd.

28 You save the humble,
but your eyes are on the haughty to
bring them low.

29 You are my lamp, O LORD;
the LORD turns my darkness into light.

30 With your help I can advance against a
troop*b*;
with my God I can scale a wall.

31 "As for God, his way is perfect;
the word of the LORD is flawless.
He is a shield
for all who take refuge in him.

32 For who is God besides the LORD?
And who is the Rock except our God?

33 It is God who arms me with strength*c*
and makes my way perfect.

34 He makes my feet like the feet of a
deer;
he enables me to stand on the
heights.

35 He trains my hands for battle;
my arms can bend a bow of bronze.

36 You give me your shield of victory;

you stoop down to make me great.

37 You broaden the path beneath me,
so that my ankles do not turn.

38 "I pursued my enemies and crushed
them;
I did not turn back till they were
destroyed.

39 I crushed them completely, and they
could not rise;
they fell beneath my feet.

40 You armed me with strength for battle;
you made my adversaries bow at my
feet.

41 You made my enemies turn their backs
in flight,
and I destroyed my foes.

42 They cried for help, but there was no
one to save them—
to the LORD, but he did not answer.

43 I beat them as fine as the dust of the
earth;
I pounded and trampled them like
mud in the streets.

44 "You have delivered me from the
attacks of my people;
you have preserved me as the head
of nations.
People I did not know are subject to
me,

45 and foreigners come cringing to me;
as soon as they hear me, they obey
me.

46 They all lose heart;
they come trembling*d* from their
strongholds.

47 "The LORD lives! Praise be to my Rock!
Exalted be God, the Rock, my Savior!

48 He is the God who avenges me,
who puts the nations under me,

49 who sets me free from my enemies.
You exalted me above my foes;
from violent men you rescued me.

50 Therefore I will praise you, O LORD,
among the nations;
I will sing praises to your name.

51 He gives his king great victories;
he shows unfailing kindness to his
anointed,
to David and his descendants forever."

a 25 Hebrew; Septuagint and Vulgate (see also Psalm 18:24)
to the cleanness of my hands   *b 30* Or *can run through a
barricade*   *c 33* Dead Sea Scrolls, some Septuagint
manuscripts, Vulgate and Syriac (see also Psalm 18:32);
Masoretic Text *who is my strong refuge*   *d 46* Some
Septuagint manuscripts and Vulgate (see also Psalm 18:45);
Masoretic Text *they arm themselves.*

The Last Words of David

23 These are the last words of David:

"The oracle of David son of Jesse,
the oracle of the man exalted by the Most High,
the man anointed by the God of Jacob,
Israel's singer of songs[a]:

2 "The Spirit of the LORD spoke through me;
his word was on my tongue.
3 The God of Israel spoke,
the Rock of Israel said to me:
'When one rules over men in righteousness,
when he rules in the fear of God,
4 he is like the light of morning at sunrise
on a cloudless morning,
like the brightness after rain
that brings the grass from the earth.'

5 "Is not my house right with God?
Has he not made with me an everlasting covenant,
arranged and secured in every part?
Will he not bring to fruition my salvation
and grant me my every desire?
6 But evil men are all to be cast aside like thorns,
which are not gathered with the hand.
7 Whoever touches thorns
uses a tool of iron or the shaft of a spear;
they are burned up where they lie."

David's Mighty Men

8 These are the names of David's mighty men:

Josheb-Basshebeth,[b] a Tahkemonite,[c] was chief of the Three; he raised his spear against eight hundred men, whom he killed[d] in one encounter. 9 Next to him was Eleazar son of Dodai the Ahohite. As one of the three mighty men, he was with David when they taunted the Philistines gathered ⌊at Pas Dammim⌋[e] for battle. Then the men of Israel retreated, 10 but he stood his ground and struck down the Philistines till his hand grew tired and froze to the sword. The LORD brought about a great victory that day. The troops returned to Eleazar, but only to strip the dead.

11 Next to him was Shammah son of Agee the Hararite. When the Philistines banded together at a place where there was a field full of lentils, Israel's troops fled from them. 12 But Shammah took his stand in the middle of the field. He defended it and struck the Philistines down, and the LORD brought about a great victory.

13 During harvest time, three of the thirty chief men came down to David at the cave of Adullam, while a band of Philistines was encamped in the Valley of Rephaim. 14 At that time David was in the stronghold, and the Philistine garrison was at Bethlehem. 15 David longed for water and said, "Oh, that someone would get me a drink of water from the well near the gate of Bethlehem!" 16 So the three mighty men broke through the Philistine lines, drew water from the well near the gate of Bethlehem and carried it back to David. But he refused to drink it; instead, he poured it out before the LORD. 17 "Far be it from me, O LORD, to do this!" he said. "Is it not the blood of men who went at the risk of their lives?" And David would not drink it.

Such were the exploits of the three mighty men.

18 Abishai the brother of Joab son of Zeruiah was chief of the Three.[f] He raised his spear against three hundred men, whom he killed, and so he became as famous as the Three. 19 Was he not held in greater honor than the Three? He became their commander, even though he was not included among them.

20 Benaiah son of Jehoiada was a valiant fighter from Kabzeel, who performed great exploits. He struck down two of Moab's best men. He also went down into a pit on a snowy day and killed a lion. 21 And he struck down a huge Egyptian. Although the Egyptian had a spear in his hand, Benaiah went against him with a club. He snatched the spear from the Egyptian's hand and killed him with his own spear.

---

a 1 Or *Israel's beloved singer* *b 8* Hebrew; some Septuagint manuscripts suggest *Ish-Bosheth,* that is, *Esh-Baal* (see also 1 Chron. 11:11 *Jashobeam*). *c 8* Probably a variant of *Hacmonite* (see 1 Chron. 11:11) *d 8* Some Septuagint manuscripts (see also 1 Chron. 11:11); Hebrew and other Septuagint manuscripts *Three; it was Adino the Eznite who killed eight hundred men* *e 9* See 1 Chron. 11:13; Hebrew *gathered there.* *f 18* Most Hebrew manuscripts (see also 1 Chron. 11:20); two Hebrew manuscripts and Syriac *Thirty*

22 Such were the exploits of Benaiah son of Jehoiada; he too was as famous as the three mighty men. 23 He was held in greater honor than any of the Thirty, but he was not included among the Three. And David put him in charge of his bodyguard.

24 Among the Thirty were:

Asahel the brother of Joab,
Elhanan son of Dodo from Bethlehem,
25 Shammah the Harodite,
Elika the Harodite,
26 Helez the Paltite,
Ira son of Ikkesh from Tekoa,
27 Abiezer from Anathoth,
Mebunnai*a* the Hushathite,
28 Zalmon the Ahohite,
Maharai the Netophathite,
29 Heled*b* son of Baanah the Netophathite,
Ithai son of Ribai from Gibeah in Benjamin,
30 Benaiah the Pirathonite,
Hiddai*c* from the ravines of Gaash,
31 Abi-Albon the Arbathite,
Azmaveth the Barhumite,
32 Eliahba the Shaalbonite,
the sons of Jashen,

a 27 Hebrew; some Septuagint manuscripts (see also 1 Chron. 11:29) *Sibbecai* *b 29* Some Hebrew manuscripts and Vulgate (see also 1 Chron. 11:30); most Hebrew manuscripts *Heleb* *c 30* Hebrew; some Septuagint manuscripts (see also 1 Chron. 11:32) *Hurai*

David's Super Heroes!

READ 2 SAMUEL 23:8–23

When David was hiding from Saul in the cave of Adullam, four hundred men came to join him (1 Samuel 22:1–2; see also 2 Samuel 23:13). Chapter 23 of 2 Samuel lists 37 of these men who became great warriors. These men were war heroes, tough guys, GI Joe material. They were also men of great faith who strove for excellence in all things. As a result, they did all sorts of fantastic stuff (see below). In the same way, you need to strive for excellence at whatever God has called you to do. The difference between a super hero and "just another person" is the commitment to grow, learn and improve yourself. So go out there and do your stuff!

David's Super Heroes

Josheb-Basshebeth—killed 800 men with his spear in one encounter

Eleazar—struck down the Philistines until his hand grew tired and froze to the sword

Shammah—defended a lentil field from the Philistines and killed them all

Abishai—killed 300 men with his spear

Benaiah—struck down two of Moab's best men, killed a lion in a pit on a snowy day, killed a huge Egyptian warrior, and was put in charge of David's bodyguard

Your next reading is on page 423.

Jonathan [33]son of[a] Shammah the
  Hararite,
Ahiam son of Sharar[b] the Hararite,
[34]Eliphelet son of Ahasbai the Maacathite,
Eliam son of Ahithophel the Gilonite,
[35]Hezro the Carmelite,
Paarai the Arbite,
[36]Igal son of Nathan from Zobah,
  the son of Hagri,[c]
[37]Zelek the Ammonite,
Naharai the Beerothite, the armor-
  bearer of Joab son of Zeruiah,
[38]Ira the Ithrite,
Gareb the Ithrite
[39]and Uriah the Hittite.
There were thirty-seven in all.

David Counts the Fighting Men

24 Again the anger of the Lord
burned against Israel, and he
incited David against them,
saying, "Go and take a census
of Israel and Judah."

[2]So the king said to Joab and the army
commanders[d] with him, "Go throughout
the tribes of Israel from Dan to Beersheba
and enroll the fighting men, so that I may
know how many there are."

[3]But Joab replied to the king, "May the
Lord your God multiply the troops a hundred times over, and may the eyes of my
lord the king see it. But why does my lord
the king want to do such a thing?"

[4]The king's word, however, overruled
Joab and the army commanders; so they
left the presence of the king to enroll the
fighting men of Israel.

[5]After crossing the Jordan, they
camped near Aroer, south of the town in
the gorge, and then went through Gad
and on to Jazer. [6]They went to Gilead and
the region of Tahtim Hodshi, and on to
Dan Jaan and around toward Sidon.
[7]Then they went toward the fortress of
Tyre and all the towns of the Hivites and
Canaanites. Finally, they went on to Beersheba in the Negev of Judah.

[8]After they had gone through the entire
land, they came back to Jerusalem at the
end of nine months and twenty days.

[9]Joab reported the number of the fighting men to the king: In Israel there were
eight hundred thousand able-bodied men
who could handle a sword, and in Judah
five hundred thousand.

[10]David was conscience-stricken after
he had counted the fighting men, and he
said to the Lord, "I have sinned greatly in
what I have done. Now, O Lord, I beg you,
take away the guilt of your servant. I have
done a very foolish thing."

[11]Before David got up the next morning, the word of the Lord had come to
Gad the prophet, David's seer: [12]"Go and
tell David, 'This is what the Lord says: I am
giving you three options. Choose one of
them for me to carry out against you.' "

[13]So Gad went to David and said to him,
"Shall there come upon you three[e] years of
famine in your land? Or three months of
fleeing from your enemies while they pursue
you? Or three days of plague in your land?
Now then, think it over and decide how I
should answer the one who sent me."

[14]David said to Gad, "I am in deep distress. Let us fall into the hands of the Lord,
for his mercy is great; but do not let me
fall into the hands of men."

[15]So the Lord sent a plague on Israel
from that morning until the end of the
time designated, and seventy thousand of
the people from Dan to Beersheba died.
[16]When the angel stretched out his hand
to destroy Jerusalem, the Lord was grieved
because of the calamity and said to the
angel who was afflicting the people,
"Enough! Withdraw your hand." The angel of the Lord was then at the threshing
floor of Araunah the Jebusite.

[17]When David saw the angel who was
striking down the people, he said to the
Lord, "I am the one who has sinned and
done wrong. These are but sheep. What
have they done? Let your hand fall upon
me and my family."

David Builds an Altar

[18]On that day Gad went to David and
said to him, "Go up and build an altar to
the Lord on the threshing floor of Araunah the Jebusite." [19]So David went up, as
the Lord had commanded through Gad.
[20]When Araunah looked and saw the king
and his men coming toward him, he went
out and bowed down before the king
with his face to the ground.

[a] 33 Some Septuagint manuscripts (see also 1 Chron. 11:34);
Hebrew does not have son of.   [b] 33 Hebrew; some
Septuagint manuscripts (see also 1 Chron. 11:35) Sacar
[c] 36 Some Septuagint manuscripts (see also 1 Chron. 11:38);
Hebrew Haggadi   [d] 2 Septuagint (see also verse 4 and
1 Chron. 21:2); Hebrew Joab the army commander
[e] 13 Septuagint (see also 1 Chron. 21:12); Hebrew seven

²¹Araunah said, "Why has my lord the king come to his servant?"

"To buy your threshing floor," David answered, "so I can build an altar to the Lord, that the plague on the people may be stopped."

²²Araunah said to David, "Let my lord the king take whatever pleases him and offer it up. Here are oxen for the burnt offering, and here are threshing sledges and ox yokes for the wood. ²³O king, Araunah gives all this to the king." Araunah also said to him, "May the Lord your God accept you."

²⁴But the king replied to Araunah, "No, I insist on paying you for it. I will not sacrifice to the Lord my God burnt offerings that cost me nothing."

So David bought the threshing floor and the oxen and paid fifty shekels[a] of silver for them. ²⁵David built an altar to the Lord there and sacrificed burnt offerings and fellowship offerings.[b] Then the Lord answered prayer in behalf of the land, and the plague on Israel was stopped.

[a] 24 That is, about 1 1/4 pounds (about 0.6 kilogram)
[b] 25 Traditionally *peace offerings*

Make It Stick

_____

_____

_____

_____

_____

_____

_____

READ 2 SAMUEL 24:2

God gave David many great victories, but toward the end, David wanted to count his fighting men to see just exactly how strong he was. Knowing your strengths can be helpful, but *not* if you're doing it to show off. Write some of your strengths on a sticky note. Thank God for them, and ask him to help you be humble about them.

1 KINGS

Who wrote this book?
The author of this book is unknown.

Why was this book written?
The book of 1 Kings shows how the kings of Israel and Judah obeyed or disobeyed God.

What happens in this book?
Solomon rules for 40 years. When he dies his kingdom is divided. The northern ten tribes are called Israel. The southern two tribes are called Judah.

What do we learn about God in this book?
God sends prophets to turn disobedient people back to him.

What people are important in this book?
The important people in this book are Solomon, Elijah, and evil King Ahab of Israel.

When did this happen?
The stories in this book took place between 970 and 853 B.C.

What are some of the stories in this book?
Solomon asks for wisdom	1 Kings 3
Solomon builds the temple	1 Kings 6
Solomon dedicates the temple	1 Kings 8
A queen visits Solomon	1 Kings 10
A prophet warns Jeroboam	1 Kings 13
Elijah is fed by ravens	1 Kings 17
Elijah on Mount Carmel	1 Kings 18
Elijah runs away	1 Kings 19
Ahab steals a vineyard	1 Kings 21
Ahab dies in battle	1 Kings 22

Adonijah Sets Himself Up as King

1 When King David was old and well advanced in years, he could not keep warm even when they put covers over him. [2]So his servants said to him, "Let us look for a young virgin to attend the king and take care of him. She can lie beside him so that our lord the king may keep warm."

[3]Then they searched throughout Israel for a beautiful girl and found Abishag, a Shunammite, and brought her to the king. [4]The girl was very beautiful; she took care of the king and waited on him, but the king had no intimate relations with her.

[5]Now Adonijah, whose mother was Haggith, put himself forward and said, "I will be king." So he got chariots and horses[a] ready, with fifty men to run ahead of him. [6](His father had never interfered with him by asking, "Why do you behave as you do?" He was also very handsome and was born next after Absalom.)

[7]Adonijah conferred with Joab son of Zeruiah and with Abiathar the priest, and they gave him their support. [8]But Zadok the priest, Benaiah son of Jehoiada, Nathan the prophet, Shimei and Rei[b] and David's special guard did not join Adonijah.

[9]Adonijah then sacrificed sheep, cattle and fattened calves at the Stone of Zoheleth near En Rogel. He invited all his brothers, the king's sons, and all the men of Judah who were royal officials, [10]but he did not invite Nathan the prophet or Benaiah or the special guard or his brother Solomon.

[11]Then Nathan asked Bathsheba, Solomon's mother, "Have you not heard that Adonijah, the son of Haggith, has become king without our lord David's knowing it? [12]Now then, let me advise you how you can save your own life and the life of your son Solomon. [13]Go in to King David and say to him, 'My lord the king, did you not swear to me your servant: "Surely Solomon your son shall be king after me, and he will sit on my throne"? Why then has Adonijah become king?' [14]While you are still there talking to the king, I will come in and confirm what you have said."

[a] 5 Or charioteers   [b] 8 Or and his friends

The Spoiled Brat

READ 1 KINGS 1:5–6

You might think sometimes it would be great if your dad and mom *never* disciplined you. You could skip school, watch any video you wanted and stay up late. (Sounds like Pinnochio just before he started growing donkey ears!) King David never corrected or disciplined his son, Adonijah. Verse 6 says, "His father had never interfered with him by asking, 'Why do you behave as you do?' " Result? Adonijah became strong willed, selfish and rebellious. The Bible tells us that when parents *don't* discipline their children, the kids don't learn or grow. They can end up spoiled brats and fail in life. But if parents *care* about their kids, they take the time to teach and discipline them. So be thankful your parents love you enough to discipline you; it's because they want your life to turn out well.

Your next reading is on page 424.

¹⁵So Bathsheba went to see the aged king in his room, where Abishag the Shunammite was attending him. ¹⁶Bathsheba bowed low and knelt before the king.

"What is it you want?" the king asked.

¹⁷She said to him, "My lord, you yourself swore to me your servant by the LORD your God: 'Solomon your son shall be king after me, and he will sit on my throne.' ¹⁸But now Adonijah has become king, and you, my lord the king, do not know about it. ¹⁹He has sacrificed great numbers of cattle, fattened calves, and sheep, and has invited all the king's sons, Abiathar the priest and Joab the commander of the army, but he has not invited Solomon your servant. ²⁰My lord the king, the eyes of all Israel are on you, to learn from you who will sit on the throne of my lord the king after him. ²¹Otherwise, as soon as my lord the king is laid to rest with his fathers, I and my son Solomon will be treated as criminals."

²²While she was still speaking with the king, Nathan the prophet arrived. ²³And they told the king, "Nathan the prophet is here." So he went before the king and bowed with his face to the ground.

²⁴Nathan said, "Have you, my lord the king, declared that Adonijah shall be king after you, and that he will sit on your throne? ²⁵Today he has gone down and sacrificed great numbers of cattle, fattened calves, and sheep. He has invited all the king's sons, the commanders of the army and Abiathar the priest. Right now they are eating and drinking with him and saying, 'Long live King Adonijah!' ²⁶But me your servant, and Zadok the priest, and Benaiah son of Jehoiada, and your servant Solomon he did not invite. ²⁷Is this something my lord the king has done without letting his servants know who should sit on the throne of my lord the king after him?"

David Makes Solomon King

²⁸Then King David said, "Call in Bathsheba." So she came into the king's presence and stood before him.

²⁹The king then took an oath: "As surely as the LORD lives, who has delivered me out of every trouble, ³⁰I will surely carry

The Out-of-bounds King

READ 1 KINGS 1

While his old, sick dad was shivering in bed, David's son Adonijah decided it was time to make his move and steal the throne from Solomon. Adonijah held a big barbecue, invited all his friends and set himself up as the new king. But the prophet Nathan had Solomon's mom blow the whistle on Adonijah: "Did you not swear to me your servant: 'Surely Solomon your son shall be king after me …'? Why then has Adonijah become king?" (verse 13).

David quickly crashed Adonijah's party and put Solomon on the throne. Remember: Competition is good and healthy as long as everyone plays by the rules and stays in bounds. But if you get in the habit of lying, cheating, taking out-of-bound shortcuts, or hurting others to get ahead, you'll wind up the loser.

Your next reading is on page 426.

out today what I swore to you by the LORD, the God of Israel: Solomon your son shall be king after me, and he will sit on my throne in my place."

31 Then Bathsheba bowed low with her face to the ground and, kneeling before the king, said, "May my lord King David live forever!"

32 King David said, "Call in Zadok the priest, Nathan the prophet and Benaiah son of Jehoiada." When they came before the king, 33 he said to them: "Take your lord's servants with you and set Solomon my son on my own mule and take him down to Gihon. 34 There have Zadok the priest and Nathan the prophet anoint him king over Israel. Blow the trumpet and shout, 'Long live King Solomon!' 35 Then you are to go up with him, and he is to come and sit on my throne and reign in my place. I have appointed him ruler over Israel and Judah."

36 Benaiah son of Jehoiada answered the king, "Amen! May the LORD, the God of my lord the king, so declare it. 37 As the LORD was with my lord the king, so may he be with Solomon to make his throne even greater than the throne of my lord King David!"

38 So Zadok the priest, Nathan the prophet, Benaiah son of Jehoiada, the Kerethites and the Pelethites went down and put Solomon on King David's mule and escorted him to Gihon. 39 Zadok the priest took the horn of oil from the sacred tent and anointed Solomon. Then they sounded the trumpet and all the people shouted, "Long live King Solomon!" 40 And all the people went up after him, playing flutes and rejoicing greatly, so that the ground shook with the sound.

41 Adonijah and all the guests who were with him heard it as they were finishing their feast. On hearing the sound of the trumpet, Joab asked, "What's the meaning of all the noise in the city?"

42 Even as he was speaking, Jonathan son of Abiathar the priest arrived. Adonijah said, "Come in. A worthy man like you must be bringing good news."

43 "Not at all!" Jonathan answered. "Our lord King David has made Solomon king. 44 The king has sent with him Zadok the priest, Nathan the prophet, Benaiah son of Jehoiada, the Kerethites and the Pelethites, and they have put him on the king's mule, 45 and Zadok the priest and Nathan the prophet have anointed him king at Gihon. From there they have gone up cheering, and the city resounds with it. That's the noise you hear. 46 Moreover, Solomon has taken his seat on the royal throne. 47 Also, the royal officials have come to congratulate our lord King David, saying, 'May your God make Solomon's name more famous than yours and his throne greater than yours!' And the king bowed in worship on his bed 48 and said, 'Praise be to the LORD, the God of Israel, who has allowed my eyes to see a successor on my throne today.' "

49 At this, all Adonijah's guests rose in alarm and dispersed. 50 But Adonijah, in fear of Solomon, went and took hold of the horns of the altar. 51 Then Solomon was told, "Adonijah is afraid of King Solomon and is clinging to the horns of the altar. He says, 'Let King Solomon swear to me today that he will not put his servant to death with the sword.' "

52 Solomon replied, "If he shows himself to be a worthy man, not a hair of his head will fall to the ground; but if evil is found in him, he will die." 53 Then King Solomon sent men, and they brought him down from the altar. And Adonijah came and bowed down to King Solomon, and Solomon said, "Go to your home."

David's Charge to Solomon

2 When the time drew near for David to die, he gave a charge to Solomon his son.

2 "I am about to go the way of all the earth," he said. "So be strong, show yourself a man, 3 and observe what the LORD your God requires: Walk in his ways, and keep his decrees and commands, his laws and requirements, as written in the Law of Moses, so that you may prosper in all you do and wherever you go, 4 and that the LORD may keep his promise to me: 'If your descendants watch how they live, and if they walk faithfully before me with all their heart and soul, you will never fail to have a man on the throne of Israel.'

5 "Now you yourself know what Joab son of Zeruiah did to me—what he did to the two commanders of Israel's armies, Abner son of Ner and Amasa son of Jether. He killed them, shedding their blood in peacetime as if in battle, and with that blood stained the belt around his waist and the sandals on his feet. 6 Deal with

An Amazing King

READ 1 KINGS 2:1–10

What made David so amazing? Read on.

DEEPER David was "a man after [God's] own heart" (1 Samuel 13:14). This means he sought to know God to the max. When he sinned, he sinned big, but when he repented and asked God for forgiveness, he meant it with all his heart. And he really worshiped God. Right from the start when he first chose David as king, God told Samuel that he looked on men's hearts (see 1 Samuel 16:7), and he obviously saw things in David's heart he liked. What a compliment! This character trait eventually became David's number one calling card as king: He truly and deeply loved God.

COOLER David was good at working with people and running the country. He was also way out front, leading his people to worship God. David was also a great friend to Jonathan and was kind to Saul, even though Saul tried to kill him! David wasn't perfect: He sinned with Bathsheba, lost his temper with Nabal and failed to discipline his children when they did wrong things. But from the time he appeared on the national scene, "all Israel and Judah loved David" (1 Samuel 18:16).

STRONGER When he was young, David spent hours and hours perfecting his use of the slingshot. So when Goliath asked for it, David gave it to him—right in the head. As David grew up, he worked just as hard to learn how to use other weapons. However, David didn't win battles just because he was a lean, mean fighting machine. He won them because he trusted God to help him. This dynamic combination of a strong body, a strong mind, and a strong spirit helped David to win wars, expand his kingdom as far as Egypt and the Euphrates River, and strike living terror into his enemies.

SMARTER David was a very smart guy and had great talents and abilities. He was a skilled musician who wrote scores of songs called psalms. David was also a talented actor (see 1 Samuel 21:10–15) and a brilliant engineer. He drew up the architectural plans for God's awesome temple. He was also a good politician. After Saul died and the kingdom was falling apart and the people were disorganized, David was able to really get things back on track.

David was an incredible man. He made mistakes in each area of his life, but because his heart was focused on God, he always repented, moved past his mistakes and punishments, and continued to grow. That is what a man of God should do.

Your next reading is on page 429.

him according to your wisdom, but do not let his gray head go down to the grave[a] in peace.

7"But show kindness to the sons of Barzillai of Gilead and let them be among those who eat at your table. They stood by me when I fled from your brother Absalom.

8"And remember, you have with you Shimei son of Gera, the Benjamite from Bahurim, who called down bitter curses on me the day I went to Mahanaim. When he came down to meet me at the Jordan, I swore to him by the Lord: 'I will not put you to death by the sword.' 9But now, do not consider him innocent. You are a man of wisdom; you will know what to do to him. Bring his gray head down to the grave in blood."

10Then David rested with his fathers and was buried in the City of David. 11He had reigned forty years over Israel—seven years in Hebron and thirty-three in Jerusalem. 12So Solomon sat on the throne of his father David, and his rule was firmly established.

Solomon's Throne Established

13Now Adonijah, the son of Haggith, went to Bathsheba, Solomon's mother. Bathsheba asked him, "Do you come peacefully?"

He answered, "Yes, peacefully." 14Then he added, "I have something to say to you."

"You may say it," she replied.

15"As you know," he said, "the kingdom was mine. All Israel looked to me as their king. But things changed, and the kingdom has gone to my brother; for it has come to him from the Lord. 16Now I have one request to make of you. Do not refuse me."

"You may make it," she said.

17So he continued, "Please ask King Solomon—he will not refuse you—to give me Abishag the Shunammite as my wife."

18"Very well," Bathsheba replied, "I will speak to the king for you."

19When Bathsheba went to King Solomon to speak to him for Adonijah, the king stood up to meet her, bowed down to her and sat down on his throne. He had a throne brought for the king's mother, and she sat down at his right hand.

20"I have one small request to make of you," she said. "Do not refuse me."

The king replied, "Make it, my mother; I will not refuse you."

21So she said, "Let Abishag the Shunammite be given in marriage to your brother Adonijah."

22King Solomon answered his mother, "Why do you request Abishag the Shunammite for Adonijah? You might as well request the kingdom for him—after all, he is my older brother—yes, for him and for Abiathar the priest and Joab son of Zeruiah!"

23Then King Solomon swore by the Lord: "May God

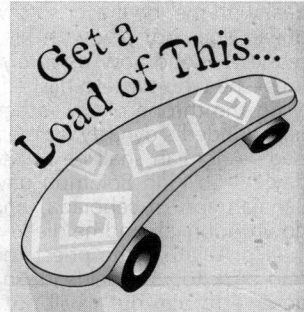

Get a Load of This...

In 2 Samuel 7:16, God promised that David's kingdom would "endure forever." That's why the Jewish people believed the Messiah would be a descendant of David and would establish David's eternal kingdom. Now do you get why the people shouted that Jesus was the "Son of David"? (Matthew 21:9).

[a] 6 Hebrew *Sheol*; also in verse 9

deal with me, be it ever so severely, if Adonijah does not pay with his life for this request! ²⁴And now, as surely as the Lord lives—he who has established me securely on the throne of my father David and has founded a dynasty for me as he promised—Adonijah shall be put to death today!" ²⁵So King Solomon gave orders to Benaiah son of Jehoiada, and he struck down Adonijah and he died.

²⁶To Abiathar the priest the king said, "Go back to your fields in Anathoth. You deserve to die, but I will not put you to death now, because you carried the ark of the Sovereign Lord before my father David and shared all my father's hardships." ²⁷So Solomon removed Abiathar from the priesthood of the Lord, fulfilling the word the Lord had spoken at Shiloh about the house of Eli.

²⁸When the news reached Joab, who had conspired with Adonijah though not with Absalom, he fled to the tent of the Lord and took hold of the horns of the altar. ²⁹King Solomon was told that Joab had fled to the tent of the Lord and was beside the altar. Then Solomon ordered Benaiah son of Jehoiada, "Go, strike him down!"

³⁰So Benaiah entered the tent of the Lord and said to Joab, "The king says, 'Come out!'"

But he answered, "No, I will die here."

Benaiah reported to the king, "This is how Joab answered me."

³¹Then the king commanded Benaiah, "Do as he says. Strike him down and bury him, and so clear me and my father's house of the guilt of the innocent blood that Joab shed. ³²The Lord will repay him for the blood he shed, because without the knowledge of my father David he attacked two men and killed them with the sword. Both of them—Abner son of Ner, commander of Israel's army, and Amasa son of Jether, commander of Judah's army—were better men and more upright than he. ³³May the guilt of their blood rest on the head of Joab and his descendants forever. But on David and his descendants, his house and his throne, may there be the Lord's peace forever."

³⁴So Benaiah son of Jehoiada went up and struck down Joab and killed him, and he was buried on his own land*a* in the desert. ³⁵The king put Benaiah son of Jehoiada over the army in Joab's position and replaced Abiathar with Zadok the priest.

³⁶Then the king sent for Shimei and said to him, "Build yourself a house in Jerusalem and live there, but do not go anywhere else. ³⁷The day you leave and cross the Kidron Valley, you can be sure you will die; your blood will be on your own head."

³⁸Shimei answered the king, "What you say is good. Your servant will do as my lord the king has said." And Shimei stayed in Jerusalem for a long time.

³⁹But three years later, two of Shimei's slaves ran off to Achish son of Maacah, king of Gath, and Shimei was told, "Your slaves are in Gath." ⁴⁰At this, he saddled his donkey and went to Achish at Gath in search of his slaves. So Shimei went away and brought the slaves back from Gath.

⁴¹When Solomon was told that Shimei had gone from Jerusalem to Gath and had returned, ⁴²the king summoned Shimei and said to him, "Did I not make you swear by the Lord and warn you, 'On the day you leave to go anywhere else, you can be sure you will die'? At that time you said to me, 'What you say is good. I will obey.' ⁴³Why then did you not keep your oath to the Lord and obey the command I gave you?"

⁴⁴The king also said to Shimei, "You know in your heart all the wrong you did to my father David. Now the Lord will repay you for your wrongdoing. ⁴⁵But King Solomon will be blessed, and David's throne will remain secure before the Lord forever."

⁴⁶Then the king gave the order to Benaiah son of Jehoiada, and he went out and struck Shimei down and killed him.

The kingdom was now firmly established in Solomon's hands.

Solomon Asks for Wisdom

3 Solomon made an alliance with Pharaoh king of Egypt and married his daughter. He brought her to the City of David until he finished building his palace and the temple of the Lord, and the wall around Jerusalem. ²The people, however, were still sacrificing at the high places, because a temple had not yet been built for the Name of the Lord. ³Solomon showed his love for the Lord by walking according to the statutes of his father David, except that he offered sacrifices and burned incense on the high places.

a 34 Or *buried in his tomb*

4The king went to Gibeon to offer sacrifices, for that was the most important high place, and Solomon offered a thousand burnt offerings on that altar. 5At Gibeon the LORD appeared to Solomon during the night in a dream, and God said, "Ask for whatever you want me to give you."

6Solomon answered, "You have shown great kindness to your servant, my father David, because he was faithful to you and righteous and upright in heart. You have continued this great kindness to him and have given him a son to sit on his throne this very day.

7"Now, O LORD my God, you have made your servant king in place of my father David. But I am only a little child and do not know how to carry out my duties. 8Your servant is here among the people you have chosen, a great people, too numerous to count or number. 9So give your servant a discerning heart to govern your people and to distinguish between right and wrong. For who is able to govern this great people of yours?"

10The Lord was pleased that Solomon had asked for this. 11So God said to him, "Since you have asked for this and not for long life or wealth for yourself, nor have asked for the death of your enemies but for discernment in administering justice, 12I will do what you have asked. I will give you a wise and discerning heart, so that there will never have been anyone like you, nor will there ever be. 13Moreover, I will give you what you have not asked for—both riches and honor—so that in your lifetime you will have no equal among kings. 14And if you walk in my ways and obey my statutes and commands as David your father did, I will give you a long life." 15Then Solomon awoke—and he realized it had been a dream.

He returned to Jerusalem, stood before the ark of the Lord's covenant and sacrificed burnt offerings and fellowship offerings.*a* Then he gave a feast for all his court.

A Wise Ruling

16Now two prostitutes came to the king and stood before him. 17One of them

a 15 Traditionally peace offerings

Go Ahead, Be a Wise Guy

GET SMARTER

READ 1 KINGS 3

When Solomon became king, he was just a young man. He hardly had a clue what to do. But instead of guessing, he asked God for help. "Give your servant a discerning heart to govern your people and to distinguish between right and wrong" (1 Kings 3:9). Solomon asked God for wisdom, and not just *any* old wisdom—he asked for the smarts to do the specific job that God had called him to do. A prayer like that took humility. Many people are too proud to admit their ignorance, but James 1:5 says that if anyone lacks wisdom, just *ask* God for it. Another thing: you usually don't get zapped by a bolt of wisdom. Even Solomon got wiser by learning God's Word and listening to counselors who were older and more experienced than himself, so you should be willing to do the same thing.

Your next reading is on page 434.

Gross!

When two women both claimed a baby was theirs, bright-minded Solomon said to settle it by suggesting that the kid be cut in half (1 Kings 3:25). Uh ... was that lengthwise or crosswise? This so shocked the women that they blurted out the first thing on their mind. It suddenly became very clear which woman was the mother.

said, "My lord, this woman and I live in the same house. I had a baby while she was there with me. 18The third day after my child was born, this woman also had a baby. We were alone; there was no one in the house but the two of us.

19"During the night this woman's son died because she lay on him. 20So she got up in the middle of the night and took my son from my side while I your servant was asleep. She put him by her breast and put her dead son by my breast. 21The next morning, I got up to nurse my son—and he was dead! But when I looked at him closely in the morning light, I saw that it wasn't the son I had borne."

22The other woman said, "No! The living one is my son; the dead one is yours."

But the first one insisted, "No! The dead one is yours; the living one is mine." And so they argued before the king.

23The king said, "This one says, 'My son is alive and your son is dead,' while that one says, 'No! Your son is dead and mine is alive.' "

24Then the king said, "Bring me a sword." So they brought a sword for the king. 25He then gave an order: "Cut the living child in two and give half to one and half to the other."

26The woman whose son was alive was filled with compassion for her son and said to the king, "Please, my lord, give her the living baby! Don't kill him!"

But the other said, "Neither I nor you shall have him. Cut him in two!"

27Then the king gave his ruling: "Give the living baby to the first woman. Do not kill him; she is his mother."

28When all Israel heard the verdict the king had given, they held the king in awe, because they saw that he had wisdom from God to administer justice.

Solomon's Officials and Governors

So King Solomon ruled over all Israel. 2And these were his chief officials:

Azariah son of Zadok—the priest;
3 Elihoreph and Ahijah, sons of Shisha—secretaries;
Jehoshaphat son of Ahilud—recorder;
4 Benaiah son of Jehoiada—commander in chief;
Zadok and Abiathar—priests;
5 Azariah son of Nathan—in charge of the district officers;
Zabud son of Nathan—a priest and personal adviser to the king;
6 Ahishar—in charge of the palace;
Adoniram son of Abda—in charge of forced labor.

7Solomon also had twelve district governors over all Israel, who supplied provisions for the king and the royal household. Each one had to provide supplies for one month in the year. 8These are their names:

Ben-Hur—in the hill country of Ephraim;

9 Ben-Deker—in Makaz, Shaalbim, Beth Shemesh and Elon Bethhanan;

10 Ben-Hesed—in Arubboth (Socoh and all the land of Hepher were his);

11 Ben-Abinadab—in Naphoth Dor^a (he was married to Taphath daughter of Solomon);

12 Baana son of Ahilud—in Taanach and Megiddo, and in all of Beth Shan next to Zarethan below Jezreel, from Beth Shan to Abel Meholah across to Jokmeam;

13 Ben-Geber—in Ramoth Gilead (the settlements of Jair son of Manasseh in Gilead were his, as well as the district of Argob in Bashan and its sixty large walled cities with bronze gate bars);

14 Ahinadab son of Iddo—in Mahanaim;

15 Ahimaaz—in Naphtali (he had married Basemath daughter of Solomon);

16 Baana son of Hushai—in Asher and in Aloth;

17 Jehoshaphat son of Paruah—in Issachar;

18 Shimei son of Ela—in Benjamin;

19 Geber son of Uri—in Gilead (the country of Sihon king of the Amorites and the country of Og king of Bashan). He was the only governor over the district.

Solomon's Daily Provisions

20 The people of Judah and Israel were as numerous as the sand on the seashore; they ate, they drank and they were happy. 21 And Solomon ruled over all the kingdoms from the River^b to the land of the Philistines, as far as the border of Egypt. These countries brought tribute and were Solomon's subjects all his life.

22 Solomon's daily provisions were thirty cors^c of fine flour and sixty cors^d of meal, 23 ten head of stall-fed cattle, twenty of pasture-fed cattle and a hundred sheep and goats, as well as deer, gazelles, roebucks and choice fowl. 24 For he ruled over all the kingdoms west of the River, from Tiphsah to Gaza, and had peace on all sides. 25 During Solomon's lifetime Judah and Israel, from Dan to Beersheba, lived in safety, each man under his own vine and fig tree.

26 Solomon had four^e thousand stalls for chariot horses, and twelve thousand horses.^f

27 The district officers, each in his month, supplied provisions for King Solomon and all who came to the king's table. They saw to it that nothing was lacking. 28 They also brought to the proper place their quotas of barley and straw for the chariot horses and the other horses.

Solomon's Wisdom

29 God gave Solomon wisdom and very great insight, and a breadth of understanding as measureless as the sand on the seashore. 30 Solomon's wisdom was greater than the wisdom of all the men of the East, and greater than all the wisdom of Egypt. 31 He was wiser than any other man, including Ethan the Ezrahite—wiser than Heman, Calcol and Darda, the sons of Mahol. And his fame spread to all the surrounding nations. 32 He spoke three thousand proverbs and his songs numbered a thousand and five. 33 He described plant life, from the cedar of Lebanon to the hyssop that grows out of walls. He also taught about animals and birds, reptiles and fish. 34 Men of all nations came to listen to Solomon's wisdom, sent by all the kings of the world, who had heard of his wisdom.

Preparations for Building the Temple

5 When Hiram king of Tyre heard that Solomon had been anointed king to succeed his father David, he sent his envoys to Solomon, because he had always been on friendly terms with David. 2 Solomon sent back this message to Hiram:

3 "You know that because of the wars waged against my father David from all sides, he could not build a temple for the Name of the LORD his God until the LORD put his enemies under his feet. 4 But now the LORD my God has given me rest on every side, and there is no adversary or disaster. 5 I intend, therefore, to build a temple for the Name of the LORD my God, as the LORD told my father David, when he said, 'Your son whom I will put on the throne in your place will build the temple for my Name.'

---

a 11 Or in the heights of Dor   b 21 That is, the Euphrates; also in verse 24   c 22 That is, probably about 185 bushels (about 6.6 kiloliters)   d 22 That is, probably about 375 bushels (about 13.2 kiloliters)   e 26 Some Septuagint manuscripts (see also 2 Chron. 9:25); Hebrew forty   f 26 Or charioteers

6 "So give orders that cedars of Lebanon be cut for me. My men will work with yours, and I will pay you for your men whatever wages you set. You know that we have no one so skilled in felling timber as the Sidonians."

7 When Hiram heard Solomon's message, he was greatly pleased and said, "Praise be to the LORD today, for he has given David a wise son to rule over this great nation."

8 So Hiram sent word to Solomon:

"I have received the message you sent me and will do all you want in providing the cedar and pine logs. 9 My men will haul them down from Lebanon to the sea, and I will float them in rafts by sea to the place you specify. There I will separate them and you can take them away. And you are to grant my wish by providing food for my royal household."

10 In this way Hiram kept Solomon supplied with all the cedar and pine logs he wanted, 11 and Solomon gave Hiram twenty thousand cors *a* of wheat as food

a 11 That is, probably about 125,000 bushels (about 4,400 kiloliters)

Make It Stick

_____

_____

_____

_____

_____

_____

READ 1 KINGS 4:29–34
When Solomon asked God for wisdom, God gave it to him big-time. Solomon became like a walking, talking encyclopedia. He became an expert in science and nature. What natural or scientific things interest *you*? Make a list, put it on your wall, and try to learn more about those things.

for his household, in addition to twenty thousand baths[a,b] of pressed olive oil. Solomon continued to do this for Hiram year after year. [12]The LORD gave Solomon wisdom, just as he had promised him. There were peaceful relations between Hiram and Solomon, and the two of them made a treaty.

[13]King Solomon conscripted laborers from all Israel—thirty thousand men. [14]He sent them off to Lebanon in shifts of ten thousand a month, so that they spent one month in Lebanon and two months at home. Adoniram was in charge of the forced labor. [15]Solomon had seventy thousand carriers and eighty thousand stonecutters in the hills, [16]as well as thirty-three hundred[c] foremen who supervised the project and directed the workmen. [17]At the king's command they removed from the quarry large blocks of quality stone to provide a foundation of dressed stone for the temple. [18]The craftsmen of Solomon and Hiram and the men of Gebal[d] cut and prepared the timber and stone for the building of the temple.

Solomon Builds the Temple

In the four hundred and eightieth[e] year after the Israelites had come out of Egypt, in the fourth year of Solomon's reign over Israel, in the month of Ziv, the second month, he began to build temple of the LORD.

[2]The temple that King Solomon built for the LORD was sixty cubits long, twenty wide and thirty high.[f] [3]The portico at the front of the main hall of the temple extended the width of the temple, that is twenty cubits,[g] and projected ten cubits[h] from the front of the temple. [4]He made narrow clerestory windows in the temple. [5]Against the walls of the main hall and inner sanctuary he built a structure around the building, in which there were side rooms. [6]The lowest floor was five cubits[i] wide, the middle floor six cubits[j] and the third floor seven.[k] He made offset ledges around the outside of the temple so that nothing would be inserted into the temple walls.

[7]In building the temple, only blocks dressed at the quarry were used, and no hammer, chisel or any other iron tool was heard at the temple site while it was being built.

[8]The entrance to the lowest[l] floor was on the south side of the temple; a stairway led up to the middle level and from there to the third. [9]So he built the temple and completed it, roofing it with beams and cedar planks.

Get a Load of This...

Check out 1 Kings 5:13–16. To get an idea of how much work was involved in gathering materials for the temple, take a look at these numbers: 30,000 men just to get the logs, 70,000 men to carry other materials, 80,000 men to quarry stones and 3,300 men to supervise the work. Talk about a *lot* of aching backs!

---

[a] 11 Septuagint (see also 2 Chron. 2:10); Hebrew *twenty cors*   [b] 11 That is, about 115,000 gallons (about 440 kiloliters)   [c] 16 Hebrew; some Septuagint manuscripts (see also 2 Chron. 2:2, 18) *thirty-six hundred*   [d] 18 That is, Byblos   [e] 1 Hebrew; Septuagint *four hundred and fortieth*   [f] 2 That is, about 90 feet (about 27 meters) long and 30 feet (about 9 meters) wide and 45 feet (about 13.5 meters) high   [g] 3 That is, about 30 feet (about 9 meters)   [h] 3 That is, about 15 feet (about 4.5 meters)   [i] 6 That is, about 7 1/2 feet (about 2.3 meters); also in verses 10 and 24   [j] 6 That is, about 9 feet (about 2.7 meters)   [k] 6 That is, about 10 1/2 feet (about 3.1 meters)   [l] 8 Septuagint; Hebrew *middle*

10And he built the side rooms all along the temple. The height of each was five cubits, and they were attached to the temple by beams of cedar.

11The word of the LORD came to Solomon: 12"As for this temple you are building, if you follow my decrees, carry out my regulations and keep all my commands and obey them, I will fulfill through you the promise I gave to David your father. 13And I will live among the Israelites and will not abandon my people Israel."

14So Solomon built the temple and completed it. 15He lined its interior walls with cedar boards, paneling them from the floor of the temple to the ceiling, and covered the floor of the temple with planks of pine. 16He partitioned off twenty cubits*a* at the rear of the temple with cedar boards from floor to ceiling to form within the temple an inner sanctuary, the Most Holy Place. 17The main hall in front of this room was forty cubits*b* long. 18The inside of the temple was cedar, carved with gourds and open flowers. Everything was cedar; no stone was to be seen.

19He prepared the inner sanctuary with-in the temple to set the ark of the covenant of the LORD there. 20The inner sanctuary was twenty cubits long, twenty wide and twenty high.*c* He overlaid the inside with pure gold, and he also overlaid the altar of cedar. 21Solomon covered the inside of the temple with pure gold, and he extended gold chains across the front of the inner sanctuary, which was overlaid with gold. 22So he overlaid the whole interior with gold. He also overlaid with gold the altar that belonged to the inner sanctuary.

23In the inner sanctuary he made a pair of cherubim of olive wood, each ten cubits*d* high. 24One wing of the first cherub was five cubits long, and the other wing five cubits—ten cubits from wing tip to wing tip. 25The second cherub also measured ten cubits, for the two cherubim were identical in size and shape. 26The height of each cherub was ten cubits. 27He placed the cherubim inside the in-

a 16 That is, about 30 feet (about 9 meters)   *b 17* That is, about 60 feet (about 18 meters)   *c 20* That is, about 30 feet (about 9 meters) long, wide and high   *d 23* That is, about 15 feet (about 4.5 meters)

Negotiation Know-how

READ 1 KINGS 5:1–12

"Hey, it's my turn to watch my show!" "No it's not! You had your turn! Now it's mine!" Sound familiar? How do *you* solve these kind of problems? Solomon was a peacemaker. In fact his name means "peace." Solomon's negotiating skills with Hiram, king of Tyre, are a good example. Solomon needed the wood from cedars growing in Lebanon, and Hiram needed food from Israel. Solomon showed that the key to negotiation is this: 1) Be willing to give and not just take, (2) compliment the other party and (3) work out an agreement that benefits both sides. Want a challenge? Practice being a peacemaker with your brother or sister. Instead of making them lose out, use negotiation skills to create a win-win situation for both of you. Next time you want to watch different shows at the same time apply these three points. They might help.

Your next reading is on page 435.

nermost room of the temple, with their wings spread out. The wing of one cherub touched one wall, while the wing of the other touched the other wall, and their wings touched each other in the middle of the room. 28He overlaid the cherubim with gold.

29On the walls all around the temple, in both the inner and outer rooms, he carved cherubim, palm trees and open flowers. 30He also covered the floors of both the inner and outer rooms of the temple with gold.

31For the entrance of the inner sanctuary he made doors of olive wood with five-sided jambs. 32And on the two olive wood doors he carved cherubim, palm trees and open flowers, and overlaid the cherubim and palm trees with beaten gold. 33In the same way he made four-sided jambs of olive wood for the entrance to the main hall. 34He also made two pine doors, each having two leaves that turned in sockets. 35He carved cherubim, palm trees and open

flowers on them and overlaid them with gold hammered evenly over the carvings.

36And he built the inner courtyard of three courses of dressed stone and one course of trimmed cedar beams.

37The foundation of the temple of the LORD was laid in the fourth year, in the month of Ziv. 38In the eleventh year in the month of Bul, the eighth month, the temple was finished in all its details according to its specifications. He had spent seven years building it.

Solomon Builds His Palace

7 It took Solomon thirteen years, however, to complete the construction of his palace. 2He built the Palace of the Forest of Lebanon a hundred cubits long, fifty wide and thirty high,*a* with four rows of cedar columns supporting trimmed cedar beams. 3It was roofed with cedar above the beams that rested on the

a 2 That is, about 150 feet (about 46 meters) long, 75 feet (about 23 meters) wide and 45 feet (about 13.5 meters) high

Putting on the Work Gloves

READ 1 KINGS 6:1–7, 14–18, 37–38

Ready, set, set, set, set, set ... Imagine if you *never* went *go*! All you did was get ready all day long. When men want to accomplish things in life they have to remember the phrase, "Ready, set, go!" David and Solomon did this when they built the temple. When King David did the planning and prepared material for the temple it was "ready, set." Then Solomon came along and went "go." First Kings 6:14 sums it up: "Solomon built the temple and completed it." The key to tackling any project is the same—whether it's a humongous homework assignment or building a new skateboard ramp. You plan and prepare, then there comes the time when you put on the work gloves, get dirty and do the job. The more you plan and prepare, the better you'll do things. But you *do* have to do them.

Your next reading is on page 443.

Get a Load of This...

Check out 1 Kings 6:2. The temple was about 90 feet long by 30 feet wide and 45 feet tall—about the same size as many churches today (except mega-churches). The 8 million pounds of gold used in building the temple would cost (are you ready for this?) over $30 *billion* dollars today!

columns—forty-five beams, fifteen to a row. [4]Its windows were placed high in sets of three, facing each other. [5]All the doorways had rectangular frames; they were in the front part in sets of three, facing each other.[a]

[6]He made a colonnade fifty cubits long and thirty wide.[b] In front of it was a portico, and in front of that were pillars and an overhanging roof.

[7]He built the throne hall, the Hall of Justice, where he was to judge, and he covered it with cedar from floor to ceiling.[c] [8]And the palace in which he was to live, set farther back, was similar in design. Solomon also made a palace like this hall for Pharaoh's daughter, whom he had married.

[9]All these structures, from the outside to the great courtyard and from foundation to eaves, were made of blocks of high-grade stone cut to size and trimmed with a saw on their inner and outer faces. [10]The foundations were laid with large stones of good quality, some measuring ten cubits[d] and some eight.[e] [11]Above were high-grade stones, cut to size, and cedar beams. [12]The great courtyard was surrounded by a wall of three courses of dressed stone and one course of trimmed cedar beams, as was the inner courtyard of the temple of the LORD with its portico.

The Temple's Furnishings

[13]King Solomon sent to Tyre and brought Huram,[f] [14]whose mother was a widow from the tribe of Naphtali and whose father was a man of Tyre and a craftsman in bronze. Huram was highly skilled and experienced in all kinds of bronze work. He came to King Solomon and did all the work assigned to him.

[15]He cast two bronze pillars, each eighteen cubits high and twelve cubits around,[g] by line. [16]He also made two capitals of cast bronze to set on the tops of the pillars; each capital was five cubits[h] high. [17]A network of interwoven chains festooned the capitals on top of the pillars, seven for each capital. [18]He made pomegranates in two rows[i] encircling each network to decorate the capitals on top of the pillars.[j] He did the same for each capital. [19]The capitals on top of the pillars in the portico were in the shape of lilies, four cubits[k] high. [20]On the capitals of both pillars, above the bowl-shaped part next to the network, were the two hundred pomegranates in rows all around. [21]He erected the pillars at the portico of the temple. The pillar to the south he named Jakin[l] and the one to the north Boaz.[m] [22]The capitals on

a 5 The meaning of the Hebrew for this verse is uncertain.   *b 6* That is, about 75 feet (about 23 meters) long and 45 feet (about 13.5 meters) wide   *c 7* Vulgate and Syriac; Hebrew *floor*   *d 10* That is, about 15 feet (about 4.5 meters)   *e 10* That is, about 12 feet (about 3.6 meters)   *f 13* Hebrew *Hiram,* a variant of *Huram;* also in verses 40 and 45   *g 15* That is, about 27 feet (about 8.1 meters) high and 18 feet (about 5.4 meters) around   *h 16* That is, about 7 1/2 feet (about 2.3 meters); also in verse 23   *i 18* Two Hebrew manuscripts and Septuagint; most Hebrew manuscripts *made the pillars, and there were two rows*   *j 18* Many Hebrew manuscripts and Syriac; most Hebrew manuscripts *pomegranates*   *k 19* That is, about 6 feet (about 1.8 meters); also in verse 38   *l 21* Jakin probably means *he establishes.*   *m 21* Boaz probably means *in him is strength.*

top were in the shape of lilies. And so the work on the pillars was completed.

23He made the Sea of cast metal, circular in shape, measuring ten cubits*a* from rim to rim and five cubits high. It took a line of thirty cubits*b* to measure around it. 24Below the rim, gourds encircled it—ten to a cubit. The gourds were cast in two rows in one piece with the Sea.

25The Sea stood on twelve bulls, three facing north, three facing west, three facing south and three facing east. The Sea rested on top of them, and their hindquarters were toward the center. 26It was a handbreadth*c* in thickness, and its rim was like the rim of a cup, like a lily blossom. It held two thousand baths.*d*

27He also made ten movable stands of bronze; each was four cubits long, four wide and three high.*e* 28This is how the stands were made: They had side panels attached to uprights. 29On the panels between the uprights were lions, bulls and cherubim—and on the uprights as well. Above and below the lions and bulls were wreaths of hammered work. 30Each stand had four bronze wheels with bronze axles, and each had a basin resting on four supports, cast with wreaths on each side. 31On the inside of the stand there was an opening that had a circular frame one cubit*f* deep. This opening was round, and with its basework it measured a cubit and a half.*g* Around its opening there was engraving. The panels of the stands were square, not round. 32The four wheels were under the panels, and the axles of the wheels were attached to the stand. The diameter of each wheel was a cubit and a half. 33The wheels were made like chariot wheels; the axles, rims, spokes and hubs were all of cast metal.

34Each stand had four handles, one on each corner, projecting from the stand. 35At the top of the stand there was a circular band half a cubit*h* deep. The supports and panels were attached to the top of the stand. 36He engraved cherubim, lions and palm trees on the surfaces of the supports and on the panels, in every available space, with wreaths all around. 37This is the way he made the ten stands. They were all cast in the same molds and were identical in size and shape.

38He then made ten bronze basins, each holding forty baths*i* and measuring four cubits across, one basin to go on each of the ten stands. 39He placed five of the stands on the south side of the temple and five on the north. He placed the Sea on the south side, at the southeast corner of the temple. 40He also made the basins and shovels and sprinkling bowls.

So Huram finished all the work he had undertaken for King Solomon in the temple of the LORD:

Get a Load of This...

Check out 1 Kings 7. Solomon spent only seven years building the temple of God, so why did it take him thirteen years to build his *own* palace? One, his palace was bigger. Two, David had drawn up blueprints and gotten materials for the temple, but Solomon had to prepare for his palace himself. There were a whole lot of gold and silver utensils used in the temple. Look at this list from Ezra 1:9–10 of the items the Babylonians seized when they later destroyed the temple: 30 gold dishes; 1,000 silver dishes; 29 silver pans; 30 gold bowls; 410 silver bowls; 1,000 other articles.

---

a 23 That is, about 15 feet (about 4.5 meters)   *b 23* That is, about 45 feet (about 13.5 meters)   *c 26* That is, about 3 inches (about 8 centimeters)
d 26 That is, probably about 11,500 gallons (about 44 kiloliters); the Septuagint does not have this sentence.   *e 27* That is, about 6 feet (about 1.8 meters) long and wide and about 4 1/2 feet (about 1.3 meters) high   *f 31* That is, about 1 1/2 feet (about 0.5 meter)   *g 31* That is, about 2 1/4 feet (about 0.7 meter); also in verse 32   *h 35* That is, about 3/4 foot (about 0.2 meter)   *i 38* That is, about 230 gallons (about 880 liters)

⁴¹the two pillars;

the two bowl-shaped capitals on top
of the pillars;

the two sets of network decorating
the two bowl-shaped capitals on
top of the pillars;

⁴²the four hundred pomegranates for
the two sets of network (two rows
of pomegranates for each network, decorating the bowl-shaped
capitals on top of the pillars);

⁴³the ten stands with their ten basins;

⁴⁴the Sea and the twelve bulls under it;

⁴⁵the pots, shovels and sprinkling bowls.

All these objects that Huram made for
King Solomon for the temple of the LORD
were of burnished bronze. ⁴⁶The king had
them cast in clay molds in the plain of the
Jordan between Succoth and Zarethan.
⁴⁷Solomon left all these things un-
weighed, because there were so many;
the weight of the bronze was not determined.

⁴⁸Solomon also made all the furnishings that were in the LORD's temple:

the golden altar;

the golden table on which was the
bread of the Presence;

⁴⁹the lampstands of pure gold (five on
the right and five on the left, in
front of the inner sanctuary);

the gold floral work and lamps and
tongs;

⁵⁰the pure gold basins, wick trimmers,
sprinkling bowls, dishes and censers;

and the gold sockets for the doors of
the innermost room, the Most
Holy Place, and also for the doors
of the main hall of the temple.

⁵¹When all the work King Solomon had
done for the temple of the LORD was finished, he brought in the things his father
David had dedicated—the silver and gold
and the furnishings—and he placed them
in the treasuries of the LORD's temple.

The Ark Brought to the Temple

Then King Solomon summoned into
his presence at Jerusalem the elders
of Israel, all the heads of the tribes
and the chiefs of the Israelite families, to bring up the ark of the LORD's covenant from Zion, the City of David. ²All
the men of Israel came together to King
Solomon at the time of the festival in the
month of Ethanim, the seventh month.

³When all the elders of Israel had arrived, the priests took up the ark, ⁴and
they brought up the ark of the LORD and
the Tent of Meeting and all the sacred furnishings in it. The priests and Levites carried them up, ⁵and King Solomon and the
entire assembly of Israel that had gathered about him were before the ark, sacrificing so many sheep and cattle that they
could not be recorded or counted.

⁶The priests then brought the ark of the
LORD's covenant to its place in the inner
sanctuary of the temple, the Most Holy
Place, and put it beneath the wings of the
cherubim. ⁷The cherubim spread their
wings over the place of the ark and over-
shadowed the ark and its carrying poles.
⁸These poles were so long that their ends
could be seen from the Holy Place in front
of the inner sanctuary, but not from outside the Holy Place; and they are still there
today. ⁹There was nothing in the ark except the two stone tablets that Moses had
placed in it at Horeb, where the LORD
made a covenant with the Israelites after
they came out of Egypt.

¹⁰When the priests withdrew from the
Holy Place, the cloud filled the temple of
the LORD. ¹¹And the priests could not perform their service because of the cloud,
for the glory of the LORD filled his temple.

¹²Then Solomon said, "The LORD has
said that he would dwell in a dark cloud;
¹³I have indeed built a magnificent temple
for you, a place for you to dwell forever."

¹⁴While the whole assembly of Israel
was standing there, the king turned
around and blessed them. ¹⁵Then he said:

"Praise be to the LORD, the God of
Israel, who with his own hand has
fulfilled what he promised with his
own mouth to my father David. For
he said, ¹⁶'Since the day I brought
my people Israel out of Egypt, I have
not chosen a city in any tribe of Israel
to have a temple built for my Name
to be there, but I have chosen David
to rule my people Israel.'

¹⁷"My father David had it in his
heart to build a temple for the Name
of the LORD, the God of Israel. ¹⁸But
the LORD said to my father David, 'Because it was in your heart to build a
temple for my Name, you did well to

have this in your heart. ¹⁹Nevertheless, you are not the one to build the temple, but your son, who is your own flesh and blood—he is the one who will build the temple for my Name.'

²⁰"The LORD has kept the promise he made: I have succeeded David my father and now I sit on the throne of Israel, just as the LORD promised, and I have built the temple for the Name of the LORD, the God of Israel. ²¹I have provided a place there for the ark, in which is the covenant of the LORD that he made with our fathers when he brought them out of Egypt."

Solomon's Prayer of Dedication

²²Then Solomon stood before the altar of the LORD in front of the whole assembly of Israel, spread out his hands toward heaven ²³and said:

"O LORD, God of Israel, there is no God like you in heaven above or on earth below—you who keep your covenant of love with your servants who continue wholeheartedly in your way. ²⁴You have kept your promise to your servant David my father; with your mouth you have promised and with your hand you have fulfilled it—as it is today.

²⁵"Now LORD, God of Israel, keep for your servant David my father the promises you made to him when you said, 'You shall never fail to have a man to sit before me on the throne of Israel, if only your sons are careful in all they do to walk before me as you have done.' ²⁶And now, O God of Israel, let your word that you promised your servant David my father come true.

²⁷"But will God really dwell on earth? The heavens, even the highest heaven, cannot contain you. How much less this temple I have built! ²⁸Yet give attention to your servant's prayer and his plea for mercy, O LORD my God. Hear the cry and the prayer that your servant is praying in your presence this day. ²⁹May your eyes be open toward this temple night and day, this place of which you said, 'My Name shall be there,' so that you will hear the prayer your servant prays toward this place. ³⁰Hear the supplication of your servant and of your people Israel when they pray toward this place. Hear from heaven, your dwelling place, and when you hear, forgive.

³¹"When a man wrongs his neighbor and is required to take an oath and he comes and swears the oath before your altar in this temple, ³²then hear from heaven and act. Judge between your servants, condemning the guilty and bringing down on his own head what he has done. Declare the innocent not guilty, and so establish his innocence.

³³"When your people Israel have been defeated by an enemy because they have sinned against you, and when they turn back to you and confess your name, praying and making supplication to you in this temple, ³⁴then hear from heaven and forgive the sin of your people Israel and bring them back to the land you gave to their fathers.

³⁵"When the heavens are shut up and there is no rain because your people have sinned against you, and when they pray toward this place and confess your name and turn from their sin because you have afflicted them, ³⁶then hear from heaven and forgive the sin of your servants, your people Israel. Teach them the right way to live, and send rain on the land you gave your people for an inheritance.

³⁷"When famine or plague comes to the land, or blight or mildew, locusts or grasshoppers, or when an enemy besieges them in any of their cities, whatever disaster or disease may come, ³⁸and when a prayer or plea is made by any of your people Israel—each one aware of the afflictions of his own heart, and spreading out his hands toward this temple—³⁹then hear from heaven, your dwelling place. Forgive and act; deal with each man according to all he does, since you know his heart (for you alone know the hearts of all men), ⁴⁰so that they will fear you all the time they live in the land you gave our fathers.

⁴¹"As for the foreigner who does not belong to your people Israel but

has come from a distant land because of your name— ⁴²for men will hear of your great name and your mighty hand and your outstretched arm—when he comes and prays toward this temple, ⁴³then hear from heaven, your dwelling place, and do whatever the foreigner asks of you, so that all the peoples of the earth may know your name and fear you, as do your own people Israel, and may know that this house I have built bears your Name.

⁴⁴"When your people go to war against their enemies, wherever you send them, and when they pray to the LORD toward the city you have chosen and the temple I have built for your Name, ⁴⁵then hear from heaven their prayer and their plea, and uphold their cause.

⁴⁶"When they sin against you—for there is no one who does not sin—and you become angry with them and give them over to the enemy, who takes them captive to his own land, far away or near; ⁴⁷and if they have a change of heart in the land where they are held captive, and repent and plead with you in the land of their conquerors and say, 'We have sinned, we have done wrong, we have acted wickedly'; ⁴⁸and if they turn back to you with all their heart and soul in the land of their enemies who took them captive, and pray to you toward the land you gave their fathers, toward the city you have chosen and the temple I have built for your Name; ⁴⁹then from heaven, your dwelling place, hear their prayer and their plea, and uphold their cause. ⁵⁰And forgive your people, who have sinned against you; forgive all the offenses they have committed against you, and cause their conquerors to show them mercy; ⁵¹for they are your people and your inheritance, whom you brought out of Egypt, out of that iron-smelting furnace.

⁵²"May your eyes be open to your servant's plea and to the plea of your people Israel, and may you listen to them whenever they cry out to you. ⁵³For you singled them out from all the nations of the world to be your own inheritance, just as you declared through your servant Moses when you, O Sovereign LORD, brought our fathers out of Egypt."

⁵⁴When Solomon had finished all these prayers and supplications to the LORD, he rose from before the altar of the LORD, where he had been kneeling with his hands spread out toward heaven. ⁵⁵He stood and blessed the whole assembly of Israel in a loud voice, saying:

⁵⁶"Praise be to the LORD, who has given rest to his people Israel just as he promised. Not one word has failed of all the good promises he gave through his servant Moses. ⁵⁷May the LORD our God be with us as he was with our fathers; may he never leave us nor forsake us. ⁵⁸May he turn our hearts to him, to walk in all his ways and to keep the commands, decrees and regulations he gave our fathers. ⁵⁹And may these words of mine, which I have prayed before the LORD, be near to the LORD our God day and night, that he may uphold the cause of his servant and the cause of his people Israel according to each day's need, ⁶⁰so that all the peoples of the earth may know that the LORD is God and that there is no other. ⁶¹But your hearts must be fully committed to the LORD our God, to live by his decrees and obey his commands, as at this time."

The Dedication of the Temple

⁶²Then the king and all Israel with him offered sacrifices before the LORD. ⁶³Solomon offered a sacrifice of fellowship offerings[a] to the LORD: twenty-two thousand cattle and a hundred and twenty thousand sheep and goats. So the king and all the Israelites dedicated the temple of the LORD.

⁶⁴On that same day the king consecrated the middle part of the courtyard in front of the temple of the LORD, and there he offered burnt offerings, grain offerings and the fat of the fellowship offerings, because the bronze altar before the LORD was too small to hold the burnt offerings, the grain offerings and the fat of the fellowship offerings.

⁶⁵So Solomon observed the festival at

ᵃ 63 Traditionally peace offerings; also in verse 64

that time, and all Israel with him—a vast assembly, people from Lebo[a] Hamath to the Wadi of Egypt. They celebrated it before the LORD our God for seven days and seven days more, fourteen days in all. [66]On the following day he sent the people away. They blessed the king and then went home, joyful and glad in heart for all the good things the LORD had done for his servant David and his people Israel.

The LORD Appears to Solomon

When Solomon had finished building the temple of the LORD and the royal palace, and had achieved all he had desired to do, [2]the LORD appeared to him a second time, as he had appeared to him at Gibeon. [3]The LORD said to him:

"I have heard the prayer and plea you have made before me; I have consecrated this temple, which you have built, by putting my Name there forever. My eyes and my heart will always be there.

[4]"As for you, if you walk before me in integrity of heart and uprightness, as David your father did, and do all I command and observe my decrees and laws, [5]I will establish your royal throne over Israel forever, as I promised David your father when I said, 'You shall never fail to have a man on the throne of Israel.'

[6]"But if you[b] or your sons turn away from me and do not observe the commands and decrees I have given you[b] and go off to serve other gods and worship them, [7]then I will cut off Israel from the land I have given them and will reject this temple I have consecrated for my Name. Israel will then become a byword and an object of ridicule among all peoples. [8]And though this temple is now imposing, all who pass by will be appalled and will scoff and say, 'Why has the LORD done such a thing to this land and to this temple?' [9]People will answer, 'Because they have forsaken the LORD their God, who brought their fathers out of Egypt, and have embraced other gods, worshiping and serving them—that is why the LORD brought all this disaster on them.' "

Solomon's Other Activities

[10]At the end of twenty years, during which Solomon built these two buildings—the temple of the LORD and the royal palace— [11]King Solomon gave twenty towns in Galilee to Hiram king of Tyre, because Hiram had supplied him with all the cedar and pine and gold he wanted. [12]But when Hiram went from Tyre to see the towns that Solomon had given him, he was not pleased with them. [13]"What kind of towns are these you have given me, my brother?" he asked. And he called them the Land of Cabul,[c] a name they have to this day. [14]Now Hiram had sent to the king 120 talents[d] of gold.

[15]Here is the account of the forced labor King Solomon conscripted to build the LORD's temple, his own palace, the supporting terraces,[e] the wall of Jerusalem, and Hazor, Megiddo and Gezer. [16](Pharaoh king of Egypt had attacked and captured Gezer. He had set it on fire. He killed its Canaanite inhabitants and then gave it as a wedding gift to his daughter, Solomon's wife. [17]And Solomon rebuilt Gezer.) He built up Lower Beth Horon, [18]Baalath, and Tadmor[f] in the desert, within his land, [19]as well as all his store cities and the towns for his chariots and for his horses[g]—whatever he desired to build in Jerusalem, in Lebanon and throughout all the territory he ruled.

[20]All the people left from the Amorites, Hittites, Perizzites, Hivites and Jebusites (these peoples were not Israelites), [21]that is, their descendants remaining in the land, whom the Israelites could not exterminate[h]—these Solomon conscripted for his slave labor force, as it is to this day. [22]But Solomon did not make slaves of any of the Israelites; they were his fighting men, his government officials, his officers, his captains, and the commanders of his chariots and charioteers. [23]They were also the chief officials in charge of Solomon's projects—550 officials supervising the men who did the work.

[24]After Pharaoh's daughter had come up from the City of David to the palace

---

[a] 65 Or *from the entrance to*   [b] 6 The Hebrew is plural.
[c] 13 *Cabul* sounds like the Hebrew for *good-for-nothing.*
[d] 14 That is, about 4 1/2 tons (about 4 metric tons)
[e] 15 Or *the Millo*; also in verse 24   [f] 18 The Hebrew may also be read *Tamar.*   [g] 19 Or *charioteers*
[h] 21 The Hebrew term refers to the irrevocable giving over of things or persons to the LORD, often by totally destroying them.

Gross!

Check out 1 Kings 9:19. First Kings 4:26 says that Solomon had 4,000 horse stalls and 12,000 horses. Solomon's numerous building projects included several towns where he kept his horses and chariots. Just think, all those horses created a lot of horse manure—yet everyone back then walked around town in sandals! Yuck!

Solomon had built for her, he constructed the supporting terraces.

²⁵Three times a year Solomon sacrificed burnt offerings and fellowship offerings[a] on the altar he had built for the LORD, burning incense before the LORD along with them, and so fulfilled the temple obligations.

²⁶King Solomon also built ships at Ezion Geber, which is near Elath in Edom, on the shore of the Red Sea.[b] ²⁷And Hiram sent his men—sailors who knew the sea—to serve in the fleet with Solomon's men. ²⁸They sailed to Ophir and brought back 420 talents[c] of gold, which they delivered to King Solomon.

The Queen of Sheba Visits Solomon

10 When the queen of Sheba heard about the fame of Solomon and his relation to the name of the LORD, she came to test him with hard questions. ²Arriving at Jerusalem with a very great caravan—with camels carrying spices, large quantities of gold, and precious stones—she came to Solomon and talked with him about all that she had on her mind. ³Solomon answered all her questions; nothing was too hard for the king to explain to her. ⁴When the queen of Sheba saw all the wisdom of Solomon and the palace he had built, ⁵the food on his table, the seating of his officials, the attending servants in their robes, his cupbearers, and the burnt offerings he made at[d] the temple of the LORD, she was overwhelmed.

⁶She said to the king, "The report I heard in my own country about your achievements and your wisdom is true. ⁷But I did not believe these things until I came and saw with my own eyes. Indeed, not even half was told me; in wisdom and wealth you have far exceeded the report I heard. ⁸How happy your men must be! How happy your officials, who continually stand before you and hear your wisdom! ⁹Praise be to the LORD your God, who has delighted in you and placed you on the throne of Israel. Because of the LORD's eternal love for Israel, he has made you king, to maintain justice and righteousness."

¹⁰And she gave the king 120 talents[e] of gold, large quantities of spices, and precious stones. Never again were so many spices brought in as those the queen of Sheba gave to King Solomon.

¹¹(Hiram's ships brought gold from Ophir; and from there they brought great cargoes of almugwood[f] and precious stones. ¹²The king used the almugwood to make supports for the temple of the LORD and for the royal palace, and to make harps and lyres for the musicians. So much almugwood has never been imported or seen since that day.)

¹³King Solomon gave the queen of Sheba all she desired and asked for, besides what he had given her out of

ᵃ 25 Traditionally peace offerings   ᵇ 26 Hebrew Yam Suph; that is, Sea of Reeds   ᶜ 28 That is, about 16 tons (about 14.5 metric tons)   ᵈ 5 Or the ascent by which he went up to   ᵉ 10 That is, about 4 1/2 tons (about 4 metric tons)   ᶠ 11 Probably a variant of algumwood; also in verse 12 his royal bounty. Then she left and returned with her retinue to her own country.

Solomon's Splendor

¹⁴The weight of the gold that Solomon received yearly was 666 talents,ᵃ ¹⁵not including the revenues from merchants and traders and from all the Arabian kings and the governors of the land.

¹⁶King Solomon made two hundred large shields of hammered gold; six hundred bekasᵇ of gold went into each shield. ¹⁷He also made three hundred small shields of hammered gold, with three minasᶜ of gold in each shield. The king put them in the Palace of the Forest of Lebanon.

¹⁸Then the king made a great throne inlaid with ivory and overlaid with fine gold. ¹⁹The throne had six steps, and its back had a rounded top. On both sides of the seat were armrests, with a lion standing beside each of them. ²⁰Twelve lions stood on the six steps, one at either end of each step. Nothing like it had ever been made for any other kingdom. ²¹All King Solo-

mon's goblets were gold, and all the household articles in the Palace of the Forest of Lebanon were pure gold. Nothing was made of silver, because silver was considered of little value in Solomon's days. ²²The king had a fleet of trading shipsᵈ at sea along with the ships of Hiram. Once every three years it returned, carrying gold, silver and ivory, and apes and baboons.

²³King Solomon was greater in riches and wisdom than all the other kings of the earth. ²⁴The whole world sought audience with Solomon to hear the wisdom God had put in his heart. ²⁵Year after year, everyone who came brought a gift—articles of silver and gold, robes, weapons and spices, and horses and mules.

²⁶Solomon accumulated chariots and horses; he had fourteen hundred chariots and twelve thousand horses,ᵉ which he kept in the chariot cities and also with him in Jerusalem. ²⁷The king made silver as common in Jerusalem as stones, and ce-

ᵃ 14 That is, about 25 tons (about 23 metric tons)
ᵇ 16 That is, about 7 1/2 pounds (about 3.5 kilograms)
ᶜ 17 That is, about 3 3/4 pounds (about 1.7 kilograms)
ᵈ 22 Hebrew of ships of Tarshish   ᵉ 26 Or charioteers

Be a People Person

READ 1 KINGS 10:14–29

GET SMARTER

Solomon was "greater in riches and wisdom than all the other kings of the earth" (verse 23). His splendor and wealth didn't happen by accident either. Remember, it was God who gave Solomon wisdom and told him he was going to get mega-wealth, too (see 1 Kings 3:10–13). God gave Solomon the wisdom to do business, to get along with people, and make smart trade treaties. He was a real "people person" and his diplomatic dealings with others resulted in incredible international trade and shipping. All that brought lots of money into the country. This benefited Solomon, and, in the beginning, *all* Israelites. The size of Solomon's bank account was a direct result of him using his wisdom to relate to others and do productive business. God blesses hard work—especially *smart* hard work that benefits others. Do you use your wisdom to do things that please God and help others?

Your next reading is on page 445.

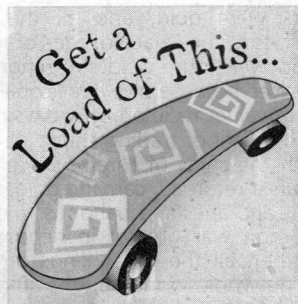

Get a Load of This...

Check out 1 Kings 11:4–6 and 12:4. God gave Solomon great wealth, but in his later years Solomon decided he couldn't get enough of a good thing. He became greedy and over-taxed and oppressed his people. He also wor-shiped the false gods his foreign wives wor-shiped. Solomon was straying away from God, and *Whoa!* That was *not* good.

dar as plentiful as sycamore-fig trees in the foothills. ²⁸Solomon's horses were imported from Egypt[a] and from Kue[b]—the royal merchants purchased them from Kue. ²⁹They imported a chariot from Egypt for six hundred shekels[c] of silver, and a horse for a hundred and fifty.[d] They also exported them to all the kings of the Hittites and of the Arameans.

Solomon's Wives

11 King Solomon, however, loved many foreign women besides Pharaoh's daughter—Moabites, Ammonites, Edomites, Sidonians and Hittites. ²They were from nations about which the LORD had told the Israelites, "You must not intermarry with them, because they will surely turn your hearts after their gods." Nevertheless, Solomon held fast to them in love. ³He had seven hundred wives of royal birth and three hundred concubines, and his wives led him astray. ⁴As Solomon grew old, his wives turned his heart after other gods, and his heart was not fully devoted to the LORD his God, as the heart of David his father had been. ⁵He followed Ashtoreth the goddess of the Sidonians, and Molech[e] the detestable god of the Ammonites. ⁶So Solomon did evil in the eyes of the LORD; he did not follow the LORD completely, as David his father had done.

⁷On a hill east of Jerusalem, Solomon built a high place for Chemosh the detestable god of Moab, and for Molech the detestable god of the Ammonites. ⁸He did the same for all his foreign wives, who burned incense and offered sacrifices to their gods.

⁹The LORD became angry with Solomon because his heart had turned away from the LORD, the God of Israel, who had appeared to him twice. ¹⁰Although he had forbidden Solomon to follow other gods, Solomon did not keep the LORD's command. ¹¹So the LORD said to Solomon, "Since this is your attitude and you have not kept my covenant and my decrees, which I commanded you, I will most certainly tear the kingdom away from you and give it to one of your subordinates. ¹²Nevertheless, for the sake of David your father, I will not do it during your lifetime. I will tear it out of the hand of your son. ¹³Yet I will not tear the whole kingdom from him, but will give him one tribe for the sake of David my servant and for the sake of Jerusalem, which I have chosen."

Solomon's Adversaries

¹⁴Then the LORD raised up against Solomon an adversary, Hadad the Edomite, from the royal line of Edom. ¹⁵Earlier when David was fighting with Edom, Joab the commander of the army, who had gone up to bury the dead, had struck down all the men in Edom. ¹⁶Joab and all the Israelites stayed there for six months, until they had destroyed all the men in Edom. ¹⁷But Hadad, still only a boy, fled to Egypt with some Edomite officials

---

^a *28* Or possibly *Muzur*, a region in Cilicia; also in verse 29   ^b *28* Probably *Cilicia*   ^c *29* That is, about 15 pounds (about 7 kilograms)   ^d *29* That is, about 3 3/4 pounds (about 1.7 kilograms)   ^e *5* Hebrew *Milcom*; also in verse 33

who had served his father. ¹⁸They set out from Midian and went to Paran. Then taking men from Paran with them, they went to Egypt, to Pharaoh king of Egypt, who gave Hadad a house and land and provided him with food.

¹⁹Pharaoh was so pleased with Hadad that he gave him a sister of his own wife, Queen Tahpenes, in marriage. ²⁰The sister of Tahpenes bore him a son named Genubath, whom Tahpenes brought up in the royal palace. There Genubath lived with Pharaoh's own children.

²¹While he was in Egypt, Hadad heard that David rested with his fathers and that Joab the commander of the army was also dead. Then Hadad said to Pharaoh, "Let me go, that I may return to my own country."

²²"What have you lacked here that you want to go back to your own country?" Pharaoh asked.

"Nothing," Hadad replied, "but do let me go!"

²³And God raised up against Solomon another adversary, Rezon son of Eliada, who had fled from his master, Hadadezer king of Zobah. ²⁴He gathered men around him and became the leader of a band of rebels when David destroyed the forces ᵃ ⌐of Zobah⌐; the rebels went to Damascus, where they settled and took control. ²⁵Rezon was Israel's adversary as long as Solomon lived, adding to the trouble caused by Hadad. So Rezon ruled in Aram and was hostile toward Israel.

Jeroboam Rebels Against Solomon

²⁶Also, Jeroboam son of Nebat rebelled against the king. He was one of Solomon's officials, an Ephraimite from Zeredah, and his mother was a widow named Zeruah.

²⁷Here is the account of how he rebelled against the king: Solomon had built the supporting terraces ᵇ and had filled in the gap in the wall of the city of David his father. ²⁸Now Jeroboam was a

ᵃ 24 Hebrew *destroyed them*   ᵇ 27 Or *the Millo*

Nightmare in the Palace

READ 1 KINGS 11:1–4

"As Solomon grew old, his wives turned his heart after other gods" (1 Kings 11:4). Solomon had 700 wives and 300 concubines (women who were legally married to Solomon but had less rights than the other wives), which is a *crowd* whichever way you look at it. Obviously it was the *wrong* crowd. Solomon was not even supposed to *have* foreign wives, but marrying pagan princesses had helped bring him peace treaties and trade agreements with other nations. He shouldn't have done it, but Solomon probably thought he was strong enough to get away with it. But soon what God said *would* happen, *did* happen: Solomon began to compromise his faith and forgot the number one rule of wisdom—"Fear God." He finally ended up worshiping his wives' gods. The moral? Don't hang out with the wrong crowd or choose unbelievers as your closest friends. Don't think, "I'm strong enough. It will be OK." God wants your closest relationships to be with other believers.

Your next reading is on page 447.

man of standing, and when Solomon saw how well the young man did his work, he put him in charge of the whole labor force of the house of Joseph.

²⁹About that time Jeroboam was going out of Jerusalem, and Ahijah the prophet of Shiloh met him on the way, wearing a new cloak. The two of them were alone out in the country, ³⁰and Ahijah took hold of the new cloak he was wearing and tore it into twelve pieces. ³¹Then he said to Jeroboam, "Take ten pieces for yourself, for this is what the LORD, the God of Israel, says: 'See, I am going to tear the kingdom out of Solomon's hand and give you ten tribes. ³²But for the sake of my servant David and the city of Jerusalem, which I have chosen out of all the tribes of Israel, he will have one tribe. ³³I will do this because they have^a forsaken me and worshiped Ashtoreth the goddess of the Sidonians, Chemosh the god of the Moabites, and Molech the god of the Ammonites, and have not walked in my ways, nor done what is right in my eyes, nor kept my statutes and laws as David, Solomon's father, did.

³⁴" 'But I will not take the whole kingdom out of Solomon's hand; I have made him ruler all the days of his life for the sake of David my servant, whom I chose and who observed my commands and statutes. ³⁵I will take the kingdom from his son's hands and give you ten tribes. ³⁶I will give one tribe to his son so that David my servant may always have a lamp before me in Jerusalem, the city where I chose to put my Name. ³⁷However, as for you, I will take you, and you will rule over all that your heart desires; you will be king over Israel. ³⁸If you do whatever I command you and walk in my ways and do what is right in my eyes by keeping my statutes and commands, as David my servant did, I will be with you. I will build you a dynasty as enduring as the one I built for David and will give Israel to you. ³⁹I will humble David's descendants because of this, but not forever.' "

⁴⁰Solomon tried to kill Jeroboam, but Jeroboam fled to Egypt, to Shishak the king, and stayed there until Solomon's death.

Solomon's Death

⁴¹As for the other events of Solomon's reign—all he did and the wisdom he displayed—are they not written in the book of the annals of Solomon? ⁴²Solomon reigned in Jerusalem over all Israel forty years. ⁴³Then he rested with his fathers and was buried in the city of David his father. And Rehoboam his son succeeded him as king.

Israel Rebels Against Rehoboam

12 Rehoboam went to Shechem, for all the Israelites had gone there to make him king. ²When Jeroboam son of Nebat heard this (he was still in Egypt, where he had fled from King Solomon), he returned from^b Egypt. ³So they sent for Jeroboam, and he and the whole assembly of Israel went to Rehoboam and said to him: ⁴"Your father put a heavy yoke on us, but now lighten the harsh labor and the heavy yoke he put on us, and we will serve you."

⁵Rehoboam answered, "Go away for three days and then come back to me." So the people went away.

⁶Then King Rehoboam consulted the elders who had served his father Solomon during his lifetime. "How would you advise me to answer these people?" he asked.

⁷They replied, "If today you will be a servant to these people and serve them and give them a favorable answer, they will always be your servants."

⁸But Rehoboam rejected the advice the elders gave him and consulted the young men who had grown up with him and were serving him. ⁹He asked them, "What is your advice? How should we answer these people who say to me, 'Lighten the yoke your father put on us'?"

¹⁰The young men who had grown up with him replied, "Tell these people who have said to you, 'Your father put a heavy yoke on us, but make our yoke lighter'— tell them, 'My little finger is thicker than my father's waist. ¹¹My father laid on you a heavy yoke; I will make it even heavier. My father scourged you with whips; I will scourge you with scorpions.' "

¹²Three days later Jeroboam and all the people returned to Rehoboam, as the king had said, "Come back to me in three days." ¹³The king answered the people harshly. Rejecting the advice given him by the elders, ¹⁴he followed the advice of the young men and said, "My father made

^a 33 Hebrew; Septuagint, Vulgate and Syriac *because he has*
^b 2 Or *he remained in*

your yoke heavy; I will make it even heavier. My father scourged you with whips; I will scourge you with scorpions." ¹⁵So the king did not listen to the people, for this turn of events was from the LORD, to fulfill the word the LORD had spoken to Jeroboam son of Nebat through Ahijah the Shilonite.

¹⁶When all Israel saw that the king refused to listen to them, they answered the king:

"What share do we have in David,
    what part in Jesse's son?
To your tents, O Israel!
    Look after your own house, O David!"

So the Israelites went home. ¹⁷But as for the Israelites who were living in the towns of Judah, Rehoboam still ruled over them.

¹⁸King Rehoboam sent out Adoniram,ᵃ who was in charge of forced labor, but all Israel stoned him to death. King Rehoboam, however, managed to get into his chariot and escape to Jerusalem. ¹⁹So Israel has been in rebellion against the house of David to this day.

²⁰When all the Israelites heard that Jeroboam had returned, they sent and called him to the assembly and made him king over all Israel. Only the tribe of Judah remained loyal to the house of David.

²¹When Rehoboam arrived in Jerusalem, he mustered the whole house of Judah and the tribe of Benjamin—a hundred and eighty thousand fighting men—to make war against the house of Israel and to regain the kingdom for Rehoboam son of Solomon.

²²But this word of God came to Shemaiah the man of God: ²³"Say to Rehoboam son of Solomon king of Judah, to the whole house of Judah and Benjamin, and to the rest of the people, ²⁴'This is what the LORD says: Do not go up to fight against your brothers, the Israelites. Go home, every one of you, for this is my doing.' " So they obeyed the word of the LORD and went home again, as the LORD had ordered.

Golden Calves at Bethel and Dan

²⁵Then Jeroboam fortified Shechem in

ᵃ *18* Some Septuagint manuscripts and Syriac (see also 1 Kings 4:6 and 5:14); Hebrew *Adoram*

Listening to Fools

READ 1 KINGS 12:1–24

When Rehoboam needed answers, he listened to unwise advice from a bunch of young guys. They helped him all right. They helped him lose everything that his family had spent two generations working for! Older, wiser men had told him to get along with the people and treat them with respect. But Rehoboam's buddies pushed him to bully the people. If you wanted to improve your slapshot, would you ask your kid sister? You'd be wiser to talk to your hockey coach. Or even email an NHL player. If you wanted to know how to become a successful businessman, it would be smart to ask someone who has spent time learning what to do and what *not* to do. The fast track to wisdom starts with God and his Word. Then, when you need advice, ask godly people who have succeeded through listening to God and by working hard.

Your next reading is on page 450.

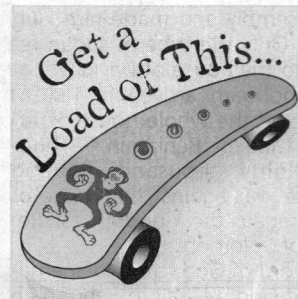

Get a Load of This...

Check out 1 Kings 13:4–5. When Jeroboam raised his hand against God's prophet, it immediately shriveled up like a grape turning into a raisin. The altar then split right down the middle as if it had just taken a major karate chop. Then it spilled its guts—ashes—over the whole scene.

the hill country of Ephraim and lived there. From there he went out and built up Peniel.ª

26Jeroboam thought to himself, "The kingdom will now likely revert to the house of David. 27If these people go up to offer sacrifices at the temple of the LORD in Jerusalem, they will again give their allegiance to their lord, Rehoboam king of Judah. They will kill me and return to King Rehoboam."

28After seeking advice, the king made two golden calves. He said to the people, "It is too much for you to go up to Jerusalem. Here are your gods, O Israel, who brought you up out of Egypt." 29One he set up in Bethel, and the other in Dan. 30And this thing became a sin; the people went even as far as Dan to worship the one there.

31Jeroboam built shrines on high places and appointed priests from all sorts of people, even though they were not Levites. 32He instituted a festival on the fifteenth day of the eighth month, like the festival held in Judah, and offered sacrifices on the altar. This he did in Bethel, sacrificing to the calves he had made. And at Bethel he also installed priests at the high places he had made. 33On the fifteenth day of the eighth month, a month of his own choosing, he offered sacrifices on the altar he had built at Bethel. So he instituted the festival for the Israelites and went up to the altar to make offerings.

The Man of God From Judah

13 By the word of the LORD a man of God came from Judah to Bethel, as Jeroboam was standing by the altar to make an offering. 2He cried out against the altar by the word of the LORD: "O altar, altar! This is what the LORD says: 'A son named Josiah will be born to the house of David. On you he will sacrifice the priests of the high places who now make offerings here, and human bones will be burned on you.' " 3That same day the man of God gave a sign: "This is the sign the LORD has declared: The altar will be split apart and the ashes on it will be poured out."

4When King Jeroboam heard what the man of God cried out against the altar at Bethel, he stretched out his hand from the altar and said, "Seize him!" But the hand he stretched out toward the man shriveled up, so that he could not pull it back. 5Also, the altar was split apart and its ashes poured out according to the sign given by the man of God by the word of the LORD.

6Then the king said to the man of God, "Intercede with the LORD your God and pray for me that my hand may be restored." So the man of God interceded with the LORD, and the king's hand was restored and became as it was before.

7The king said to the man of God, "Come home with me and have something to eat, and I will give you a gift."

ª 25 Hebrew Penuel, a variant of Peniel

8But the man of God answered the king, "Even if you were to give me half your possessions, I would not go with you, nor would I eat bread or drink water here. 9For I was commanded by the word of the LORD: 'You must not eat bread or drink water or return by the way you came.' " 10So he took another road and did not return by the way he had come to Bethel.

11Now there was a certain old prophet living in Bethel, whose sons came and told him all that the man of God had done there that day. They also told their father what he had said to the king. 12Their father asked them, "Which way did he go?" And his sons showed him which road the man of God from Judah had taken. 13So he said to his sons, "Saddle the donkey for me." And when they had saddled the donkey for him, he mounted it 14and rode after the man of God. He found him sitting under an oak tree and asked, "Are you the man of God who came from Judah?"

"I am," he replied.

15So the prophet said to him, "Come home with me and eat."

16The man of God said, "I cannot turn back and go with you, nor can I eat bread or drink water with you in this place. 17I have been told by the word of the LORD: 'You must not eat bread or drink water there or return by the way you came.' "

18The old prophet answered, "I too am a prophet, as you are. And an angel said to me by the word of the LORD: 'Bring him back with you to your house so that he may eat bread and drink water.' " (But he was lying to him.) 19So the man of God returned with him and ate and drank in his house.

20While they were sitting at the table, the word of the LORD came to the old prophet who had brought him back. 21He cried out to the man of God who had come from Judah, "This is what the LORD says: 'You have defied the word of the LORD and have not kept the command the LORD your God gave you. 22You came back and ate bread and drank water in the place where he told you not to eat or drink. Therefore your body will not be buried in the tomb of your fathers.' "

23When the man of God had finished eating and drinking, the prophet who had brought him back saddled his donkey for him. 24As he went on his way, a lion met him on the road and killed him, and his body was thrown down on the road, with both the donkey and the lion standing beside it. 25Some people who passed by saw the body thrown down there, with the lion standing beside the body, and they went and reported it in the city where the old prophet lived.

26When the prophet who had brought him back from his journey heard of it, he said, "It is the man of God who defied the word of the LORD. The LORD has given him over to the lion, which has mauled him and killed him, as the word of the LORD had warned him."

27The prophet said to his sons, "Saddle the donkey for me," and they did so. 28Then he went out and found the body thrown down on the road, with the donkey and the lion standing beside it. The lion had neither eaten the body nor mauled the donkey. 29So the prophet picked up the body of the man of God, laid it on the donkey, and brought it back to his own city to mourn for him and bury him. 30Then he laid the body in his own tomb, and they mourned over him and said, "Oh, my brother!"

31After burying him, he said to his sons, "When I die, bury me in the grave where the man of God is buried; lay my bones beside his bones. 32For the message he declared by the word of the LORD against the altar in Bethel and against all the shrines on the high places in the towns of Samaria will certainly come true."

33Even after this, Jeroboam did not change his evil ways, but once more appointed priests for the high places from all sorts of people. Anyone who wanted to become a priest he consecrated for the high places. 34This was the sin of the house of Jeroboam that led to its downfall and to its destruction from the face of the earth.

Ahijah's Prophecy Against Jeroboam

14 At that time Abijah son of Jeroboam became ill, 2and Jeroboam said to his wife, "Go, disguise yourself, so you won't be recognized as the wife of Jeroboam. Then go to Shiloh. Ahijah the prophet is there—the one who told me I would be king over this people. 3Take ten loaves of bread with you, some cakes and a jar of honey, and go to him. He will tell you what will happen to the boy." 4So Jeroboam's wife did what he said and went to Ahijah's house in Shiloh.

Now Ahijah could not see; his sight was gone because of his age. ⁵But the LORD had told Ahijah, "Jeroboam's wife is coming to ask you about her son, for he is ill, and you are to give her such and such an answer. When she arrives, she will pretend to be someone else."

⁶So when Ahijah heard the sound of her footsteps at the door, he said, "Come in, wife of Jeroboam. Why this pretense? I have been sent to you with bad news. ⁷Go, tell Jeroboam that this is what the LORD, the God of Israel, says: 'I raised you up from among the people and made you a leader over my people Israel. ⁸I tore the kingdom away from the house of David and gave it to you, but you have not been like my servant David, who kept my commands and followed me with all his heart, doing only what was right in my eyes. ⁹You have done more evil than all who lived before you. You have made for yourself other gods, idols made of metal; you have provoked me to anger and thrust me behind your back.

¹⁰" 'Because of this, I am going to bring disaster on the house of Jeroboam. I will cut off from Jeroboam every last male in Israel—slave or free. I will burn up the house of Jeroboam as one burns dung, until it is all gone. ¹¹Dogs will eat those belonging to Jeroboam who die in the city, and the birds of the air will feed on those who die in the country. The LORD has spoken!'

¹²"As for you, go back home. When you set foot in your city, the boy will die. ¹³All Israel will mourn for him and bury him. He is the only one belonging to Jeroboam who will be buried, because he is the only one in the house of Jeroboam in whom the LORD, the God of Israel, has found anything good.

¹⁴"The LORD will raise up for himself a king over Israel who will cut off the family of Jeroboam. This is the day! What? Yes, even now. ᵃ ¹⁵And the LORD will strike Israel, so that it will be like a reed swaying in the water. He will uproot Israel from this good land that he gave to their forefa-

ᵃ 14 The meaning of the Hebrew for this sentence is uncertain.

Choosing a Deadly Path

READ 1 KINGS 14:1–20

Imagine you're tramping through the bush on the way to your best fishing spot. You see another path which looks like a shortcut. Even though a "No Trespassing" sign sits at the trail's head, you go anyway—and end up totally lost in a swamp! Jeroboam disobeyed and started the Israelites worshiping golden calves, and eventually they became a nation of idol-worshipers. Ahijah prophesied that, as a result, God would send judgment on Israel. That didn't happen for many years but, step by step, that was exactly where Israel was headed. Just like you can make good choices, step by step, and end up helping the world, you can follow the road to ruin by taking the first steps in the wrong direction. Both paths look good at the beginning—hey, who wouldn't want to get a few extra casts in at the fishing hole?—but a journey to danger starts with that first step into disobedience.

Your next reading is on page 453.

thers and scatter them beyond the River,[a] because they provoked the LORD to anger by making Asherah poles.[b] [16]And he will give Israel up because of the sins Jeroboam has committed and has caused Israel to commit."

[17]Then Jeroboam's wife got up and left and went to Tirzah. As soon as she stepped over the threshold of the house, the boy died. [18]They buried him, and all Israel mourned for him, as the LORD had said through his servant the prophet Ahijah.

[19]The other events of Jeroboam's reign, his wars and how he ruled, are written in the book of the annals of the kings of Israel. [20]He reigned for twenty-two years and then rested with his fathers. And Nadab his son succeeded him as king.

Rehoboam King of Judah

[21]Rehoboam son of Solomon was king in Judah. He was forty-one years old when he became king, and he reigned seventeen years in Jerusalem, the city the LORD had chosen out of all the tribes of Israel in which to put his Name. His mother's name was Naamah; she was an Ammonite.

[22]Judah did evil in the eyes of the LORD. By the sins they committed they stirred up his jealous anger more than their fathers had done. [23]They also set up for themselves high places, sacred stones and Asherah poles on every high hill and under every spreading tree. [24]There were even male shrine prostitutes in the land; the people engaged in all the detestable practices of the nations the LORD had driven out before the Israelites.

[25]In the fifth year of King Rehoboam, Shishak king of Egypt attacked Jerusalem. [26]He carried off the treasures of the temple of the LORD and the treasures of the royal palace. He took everything, including all the gold shields Solomon had made. [27]So King Rehoboam made bronze shields to replace them and assigned these to the commanders of the guard on duty at the entrance to the royal palace. [28]Whenever the king went to the LORD's temple, the guards bore the shields, and afterward they returned them to the guardroom.

[29]As for the other events of Rehoboam's reign, and all he did, are they not written in the book of the annals of the kings of Judah? [30]There was continual warfare between Rehoboam and Jerobo-

am. [31]And Rehoboam rested with his fathers and was buried with them in the City of David. His mother's name was Naamah; she was an Ammonite. And Abijah[c] his son succeeded him as king.

Abijah King of Judah

15 In the eighteenth year of the reign of Jeroboam son of Nebat, Abijah[d] became king of Judah, [2]and he reigned in Jerusalem three years. His mother's name was Maacah daughter of Abishalom.[e]

[3]He committed all the sins his father had done before him; his heart was not fully devoted to the LORD his God, as the heart of David his forefather had been. [4]Nevertheless, for David's sake the LORD his God gave him a lamp in Jerusalem by raising up a son to succeed him and by making Jerusalem strong. [5]For David had done what was right in the eyes of the LORD and had not failed to keep any of the LORD's commands all the days of his life—except in the case of Uriah the Hittite.

[6]There was war between Rehoboam[f] and Jeroboam throughout Abijah's lifetime. [7]As for the other events of Abijah's reign, and all he did, are they not written in the book of the annals of the kings of Judah? There was war between Abijah and Jeroboam. [8]And Abijah rested with his fathers and was buried in the City of David. And Asa his son succeeded him as king.

Asa King of Judah

[9]In the twentieth year of Jeroboam king of Israel, Asa became king of Judah, [10]and he reigned in Jerusalem forty-one years. His grandmother's name was Maacah daughter of Abishalom.

[11]Asa did what was right in the eyes of the LORD, as his father David had done. [12]He expelled the male shrine prostitutes from the land and got rid of all the idols his fathers had made. [13]He even deposed his grandmother Maacah from her position as queen mother, because she had made a repulsive Asherah pole. Asa cut

---

[a] 15 That is, the Euphrates   [b] 15 That is, symbols of the goddess Asherah; here and elsewhere in 1 Kings   [c] 31 Some Hebrew manuscripts and Septuagint (see also 2 Chron. 12:16); most Hebrew manuscripts *Abijam*   [d] 1 Some Hebrew manuscripts and Septuagint (see also 2 Chron. 12:16); most Hebrew manuscripts *Abijam*; also in verses 7 and 8   [e] 2 A variant of *Absalom*; also in verse 10   [f] 6 Most Hebrew manuscripts; some Hebrew manuscripts and Syriac *Abijam* (that is, Abijah)

the pole down and burned it in the Kidron Valley. ¹⁴Although he did not remove the high places, Asa's heart was fully committed to the LORD all his life. ¹⁵He brought into the temple of the LORD the silver and gold and the articles that he and his father had dedicated.

¹⁶There was war between Asa and Baasha king of Israel throughout their reigns. ¹⁷Baasha king of Israel went up against Judah and fortified Ramah to prevent anyone from leaving or entering the territory of Asa king of Judah.

¹⁸Asa then took all the silver and gold that was left in the treasuries of the LORD's temple and of his own palace. He entrusted it to his officials and sent them to Ben-Hadad son of Tabrimmon, the son of Hezion, the king of Aram, who was ruling in Damascus. ¹⁹"Let there be a treaty between me and you," he said, "as there was between my father and your father. See, I am sending you a gift of silver and gold. Now break your treaty with Baasha king of Israel so he will withdraw from me."

²⁰Ben-Hadad agreed with King Asa and sent the commanders of his forces against the towns of Israel. He conquered Ijon, Dan, Abel Beth Maacah and all Kinnereth in addition to Naphtali. ²¹When Baasha heard this, he stopped building Ramah and withdrew to Tirzah. ²²Then King Asa issued an order to all Judah—no one was exempt—and they carried away from Ramah the stones and timber Baasha had been using there. With them King Asa built up Geba in Benjamin, and also Mizpah.

²³As for all the other events of Asa's reign, all his achievements, all he did and the cities he built, are they not written in the book of the annals of the kings of Judah? In his old age, however, his feet became diseased. ²⁴Then Asa rested with his fathers and was buried with them in the city of his father David. And Jehoshaphat his son succeeded him as king.

Nadab King of Israel

²⁵Nadab son of Jeroboam became king of Israel in the second year of Asa king of Judah, and he reigned over Israel two years. ²⁶He did evil in the eyes of the LORD, walking in the ways of his father and in his sin, which he had caused Israel to commit.

²⁷Baasha son of Ahijah of the house of Issachar plotted against him, and he struck him down at Gibbethon, a Philistine town, while Nadab and all Israel were besieging it. ²⁸Baasha killed Nadab in the third year of Asa king of Judah and succeeded him as king.

²⁹As soon as he began to reign, he killed Jeroboam's whole family. He did not leave Jeroboam anyone that breathed, but destroyed them all, according to the word of the LORD given through his servant Ahijah the Shilonite— ³⁰because of the sins Jeroboam had committed and had caused Israel to commit, and because he provoked the LORD, the God of Israel, to anger.

³¹As for the other events of Nadab's reign, and all he did, are they not written in the book of the annals of the kings of Israel? ³²There was war between Asa and Baasha king of Israel throughout their reigns.

Baasha King of Israel

³³In the third year of Asa king of Judah, Baasha son of Ahijah became king of all Israel in Tirzah, and he reigned twenty-four years. ³⁴He did evil in the eyes of the LORD, walking in the ways of Jeroboam and in his sin, which he had caused Israel to commit.

16 Then the word of the LORD came to Jehu son of Hanani against Baasha: ²"I lifted you up from the dust and made you leader of my people Israel, but you walked in the ways of Jeroboam and caused my people Israel to sin and to provoke me to anger by their sins. ³So I am about to consume Baasha and his house, and I will make your house like that of Jeroboam son of Nebat. ⁴Dogs will eat those belonging to Baasha who die in the city, and the birds of the air will feed on those who die in the country."

⁵As for the other events of Baasha's reign, what he did and his achievements, are they not written in the book of the annals of the kings of Israel? ⁶Baasha rested with his fathers and was buried in Tirzah. And Elah his son succeeded him as king.

⁷Moreover, the word of the LORD came through the prophet Jehu son of Hanani to Baasha and his house, because of all the evil he had done in the eyes of the LORD, provoking him to anger by the things he did, and becoming like the house of Jeroboam—and also because he destroyed it.

Elah King of Israel

8In the twenty-sixth year of Asa king of Judah, Elah son of Baasha became king of Israel, and he reigned in Tirzah two years.

9Zimri, one of his officials, who had command of half his chariots, plotted against him. Elah was in Tirzah at the time, getting drunk in the home of Arza, the man in charge of the palace at Tirzah. 10Zimri came in, struck him down and killed him in the twenty-seventh year of Asa king of Judah. Then he succeeded him as king.

11As soon as he began to reign and was seated on the throne, he killed off Baasha's whole family. He did not spare a single male, whether relative or friend. 12So Zimri destroyed the whole family of Baasha, in accordance with the word of the LORD spoken against Baasha through the prophet Jehu— 13because of all the sins Baasha and his son Elah had committed and had caused Israel to commit, so that they provoked the LORD, the God of Israel, to anger by their worthless idols.

14As for the other events of Elah's reign, and all he did, are they not written in the book of the annals of the kings of Israel?

Zimri King of Israel

15In the twenty-seventh year of Asa king of Judah, Zimri reigned in Tirzah seven days. The army was encamped near Gibbethon, a Philistine town. 16When the Israelites in the camp heard that Zimri had plotted against the king and murdered him, they proclaimed Omri, the commander of the army, king over Israel that very day there in the camp. 17Then Omri and all the Israelites with him withdrew from Gibbethon and laid siege to Tirzah. 18When Zimri saw that the city was taken, he went into the citadel of the royal palace and set the palace on fire around him. So he died, 19because of the sins he had committed, doing evil in the eyes of the

GET STRONGER

Power Play

READ 1 KINGS 15:25—16:28

When one of your teammates becomes captain of the squad, should you try to get him cut from the team so you can take his place? No way. But at one time, Israel's kings were constantly fighting for power. If you wanted to be king in those days, qualities listed on your résumé could include being a self-centered traitor. When Israel's rulers (and wanna-bes) were busy playing king-of-the-hill, they were making the world a rotten place to live.

God gives a man physical and mental strength so that he can use it to lift others up, not knock them down—except in boxing, but that's another story. Success in your career, in music, athletics and anything else, comes by using your talents to work with other people. Being top dog will leave you feeling empty inside if you get there by stepping on others.

Your next reading is on page 455.

LORD and walking in the ways of Jeroboam and in the sin he had committed and had caused Israel to commit.

²⁰As for the other events of Zimri's reign, and the rebellion he carried out, are they not written in the book of the annals of the kings of Israel?

Omri King of Israel

²¹Then the people of Israel were split into two factions; half supported Tibni son of Ginath for king, and the other half supported Omri. ²²But Omri's followers proved stronger than those of Tibni son of Ginath. So Tibni died and Omri became king.

²³In the thirty-first year of Asa king of Judah, Omri became king of Israel, and he reigned twelve years, six of them in Tirzah. ²⁴He bought the hill of Samaria from Shemer for two talents*a* of silver and built a city on the hill, calling it Samaria, after Shemer, the name of the former owner of the hill.

²⁵But Omri did evil in the eyes of the LORD and sinned more than all those before him. ²⁶He walked in all the ways of Jeroboam son of Nebat and in his sin, which he had caused Israel to commit, so that they provoked the LORD, the God of Israel, to anger by their worthless idols.

²⁷As for the other events of Omri's reign, what he did and the things he achieved, are they not written in the book of the annals of the kings of Israel? ²⁸Omri rested with his fathers and was buried in Samaria. And Ahab his son succeeded him as king.

Ahab Becomes King of Israel

²⁹In the thirty-eighth year of Asa king of Judah, Ahab son of Omri became king of Israel, and he reigned in Samaria over Israel twenty-two years. ³⁰Ahab son of Omri did more evil in the eyes of the LORD than any of those before him. ³¹He not only considered it trivial to commit the sins of Jeroboam son of Nebat, but he also married Jezebel daughter of Ethbaal king of the Sidonians, and began to serve Baal and worship him. ³²He set up an altar for Baal in the temple of Baal that he built in Samaria. ³³Ahab also made an Asherah pole and did more to provoke the LORD, the God of Israel, to anger than did all the kings of Israel before him.

³⁴In Ahab's time, Hiel of Bethel rebuilt Jericho. He laid its foundations at the cost of his firstborn son Abiram, and he set up its gates at the cost of his youngest son Segub, in accordance with the word of the LORD spoken by Joshua son of Nun.

Elijah Fed by Ravens

17 Now Elijah the Tishbite, from Tishbe*b* in Gilead, said to Ahab, "As the LORD, the God of Israel, lives, whom I serve, there will be neither dew nor rain in the next few years except at my word."

²Then the word of the LORD came to Elijah: ³"Leave here, turn eastward and hide in the Kerith Ravine, east of the Jordan. ⁴You will drink from the brook, and I have ordered the ravens to feed you there."

⁵So he did what the LORD had told him. He went to the Kerith Ravine, east of the Jordan, and stayed there. ⁶The ravens brought him bread and meat in the morning and bread and meat in the evening, and he drank from the brook.

The Widow at Zarephath

⁷Some time later the brook dried up because there had been no rain in the land. ⁸Then the word of the LORD came to him: ⁹"Go at once to Zarephath of Sidon and stay there. I have commanded a widow in that place to supply you with food." ¹⁰So he went to Zarephath. When he came to the town gate, a widow was there gathering sticks. He called to her and asked, "Would you bring me a little water in a jar so I may have a drink?" ¹¹As she was going to get it, he called, "And bring me, please, a piece of bread."

¹²"As surely as the LORD your God lives," she replied, "I don't have any bread—only a handful of flour in a jar and a little oil in a jug. I am gathering a few sticks to take home and make a meal for myself and my son, that we may eat it—and die."

¹³Elijah said to her, "Don't be afraid. Go home and do as you have said. But first make a small cake of bread for me from what you have and bring it to me, and then make something for yourself and your son. ¹⁴For this is what the LORD, the God of Israel, says: 'The jar of flour will not be used up and the jug of oil will not run dry until the day the LORD gives rain on the land.' "

¹⁵She went away and did as Elijah had

---

a 24 That is, about 150 pounds (about 70 kilograms)
b 1 Or *Tishbite, of the settlers*

told her. So there was food every day for Elijah and for the woman and her family. ¹⁶For the jar of flour was not used up and the jug of oil did not run dry, in keeping with the word of the LORD spoken by Elijah.

¹⁷Some time later the son of the woman who owned the house became ill. He grew worse and worse, and finally stopped breathing. ¹⁸She said to Elijah, "What do you have against me, man of God? Did you come to remind me of my sin and kill my son?"

¹⁹"Give me your son," Elijah replied. He took him from her arms, carried him to the upper room where he was staying, and laid him on his bed. ²⁰Then he cried out to the LORD, "O LORD my God, have you brought tragedy also upon this widow I am staying with, by causing her son to die?" ²¹Then he stretched himself out on the boy three times and cried to the LORD, "O LORD my God, let this boy's life return to him!"

²²The LORD heard Elijah's cry, and the boy's life returned to him, and he lived. ²³Elijah picked up the child and carried him down from the room into the house. He gave him to his mother and said, "Look, your son is alive!"

²⁴Then the woman said to Elijah, "Now I know that you are a man of God and that the word of the LORD from your mouth is the truth."

Elijah and Obadiah

After a long time, in the third year, the word of the LORD came to Elijah: "Go and present yourself to Ahab, and I will send rain on the land." ²So Elijah went to present himself to Ahab.

Now the famine was severe in Samaria, ³and Ahab had summoned Obadiah, who was in charge of his palace. (Obadiah was a devout believer in the LORD. ⁴While Jezebel was killing off the LORD's prophets, Obadiah had taken a hundred prophets

Day by Day

READ 1 KINGS 16:29—17:24

In one of the first recorded cases of take-out food, God told ravens to drop off meat and bread to Elijah twice a day. When the famine got worse, God provided his prophet and a poor widow and her son with a non-stop bread buffet. Elijah wanted to serve God above everything else, so God took good care of him by giving him the things he needed. God isn't against you enjoying cool stuff—after all, he made all those rugged forests perfect for mountain biking and crashing waves the ultimate place to surf. He just wants you to have your priorities straight. God is not against these things; they're just not supposed to be your main reason for being alive. So put serving God at the top of the list and he'll meet all your needs, with plenty to spare! (see Matthew 6:32–33).

Your next reading is on page 456.

and hidden them in two caves, fifty in each, and had supplied them with food and water.) ⁵Ahab had said to Obadiah, "Go through the land to all the springs and valleys. Maybe we can find some grass to keep the horses and mules alive so we will not have to kill any of our animals." ⁶So they divided the land they were to cover, Ahab going in one direction and Obadiah in another.

⁷As Obadiah was walking along, Elijah met him. Obadiah recognized him, bowed down to the ground, and said, "Is it really you, my lord Elijah?"

⁸"Yes," he replied. "Go tell your master, 'Elijah is here.' "

⁹"What have I done wrong," asked Obadiah, "that you are handing your servant over to Ahab to be put to death? ¹⁰As surely as the LORD your God lives, there is not a nation or kingdom where my master has not sent someone to look for you. And whenever a nation or kingdom claimed you were not there, he made them swear they could not find you. ¹¹But now you tell me to go to my master and say, 'Elijah is here.' ¹²I don't

know where the Spirit of the LORD may carry you when I leave you. If I go and tell Ahab and he doesn't find you, he will kill me. Yet I your servant have worshiped the LORD since my youth. ¹³Haven't you heard, my lord, what I did while Jezebel was killing the prophets of the LORD? I hid a hundred of the LORD's prophets in two caves, fifty in each, and supplied them with food and water. ¹⁴And now you tell me to go to my master and say, 'Elijah is here.' He will kill me!"

¹⁵Elijah said, "As the LORD Almighty lives, whom I serve, I will surely present myself to Ahab today."

Elijah on Mount Carmel

¹⁶So Obadiah went to meet Ahab and told him, and Ahab went to meet Elijah. ¹⁷When he saw Elijah, he said to him, "Is that you, you troubler of Israel?"

¹⁸"I have not made trouble for Israel," Elijah replied. "But you and your father's family have. You have abandoned the LORD's commands and have followed the Baals. ¹⁹Now summon the people from all over Israel to meet me on Mount Carmel.

Falling off the Fence

READ 1 KINGS 18:16–46

The Israelites tried to worship both God *and* Baal because they wanted to have all of their bases covered. That didn't work. By worshiping Baal, too, they were insulting God. It's the same today. Don't be a fence sitter. Making fun of your classmates or listening to raunchy tunes with friends during the week so they'll think you're "cool" doesn't mix with going to church or living like a Christian. It's like trying to "half-sub" into a basketball game, with half your body on the court and the other half in the stands. If you do "God stuff" just to please your parents, you'll end up on the losing side. Choose to be serious about your faith right now—don't put it off until you're older—and you'll start on a winning streak.

Your next reading is on page 459.

And bring the four hundred and fifty prophets of Baal and the four hundred prophets of Asherah, who eat at Jezebel's table."

20So Ahab sent word throughout all Israel and assembled the prophets on Mount Carmel. 21Elijah went before the people and said, "How long will you waver between two opinions? If the LORD is God, follow him; but if Baal is God, follow him."

But the people said nothing.

22Then Elijah said to them, "I am the only one of the LORD's prophets left, but Baal has four hundred and fifty prophets. 23Get two bulls for us. Let them choose one for themselves, and let them cut it into pieces and put it on the wood but not set fire to it. I will prepare the other bull and put it on the wood but not set fire to it. 24Then you call on the name of your god, and I will call on the name of the LORD. The god who answers by fire—he is God."

Then all the people said, "What you say is good."

25Elijah said to the prophets of Baal, "Choose one of the bulls and prepare it first, since there are so many of you. Call on the name of your god, but do not light the fire." 26So they took the bull given them and prepared it.

Then they called on the name of Baal from morning till noon. "O Baal, answer us!" they shouted. But there was no response; no one answered. And they danced around the altar they had made.

27At noon Elijah began to taunt them. "Shout louder!" he said. "Surely he is a god! Perhaps he is deep in thought, or busy, or traveling. Maybe he is sleeping and must be awakened." 28So they shouted louder and slashed themselves with swords and spears, as was their custom, until their blood flowed. 29Midday passed, and they continued their frantic prophesying until the time for the evening sacrifice. But there was no response, no one answered, no one paid attention.

30Then Elijah said to all the people, "Come here to me." They came to him, and he repaired the altar of the LORD, which was in ruins. 31Elijah took twelve stones, one for each of the tribes descended from Jacob, to whom the word of the LORD had come, saying, "Your name shall be Israel." 32With the stones he built an altar in the name of the LORD, and he dug a trench around it large enough to hold two seahsa of seed. 33He arranged the wood, cut the bull into pieces and laid it on the wood. Then he said to them, "Fill four large jars with water and pour it on the offering and on the wood."

34"Do it again," he said, and they did it again.

"Do it a third time," he ordered, and they did it the third time. 35The water ran down around the altar and even filled the trench.

36At the time of sacrifice, the prophet Elijah stepped forward and prayed: "O LORD, God of Abraham, Isaac and Israel, let it be known today that you are God in Israel and that I am your servant and have done all these

Get a Load of This...

Check out 1 Kings 18:27–29. Statues and drawings of Baal often showed him carrying a thunderbolt, but this no-show "weather god" proved to be a fake. The forecast that day: periods of stunned silence and inactivity followed by acts of God—super-hot, stone-burning, water-scorching fire from the sky!

a 32 That is, probably about 13 quarts (about 15 liters)

things at your command. 37Answer me, O LORD, answer me, so these people will know that you, O LORD, are God, and that you are turning their hearts back again."

38Then the fire of the LORD fell and burned up the sacrifice, the wood, the stones and the soil, and also licked up the water in the trench.

39When all the people saw this, they fell prostrate and cried, "The LORD—he is God! The LORD—he is God!"

40Then Elijah commanded them, "Seize the prophets of Baal. Don't let anyone get away!" They seized them, and Elijah had them brought down to the Kishon Valley and slaughtered there.

41And Elijah said to Ahab, "Go, eat and drink, for there is the sound of a heavy rain." 42So Ahab went off to eat and drink, but Elijah climbed to the top of Carmel, bent down to the ground and put his face between his knees.

43"Go and look toward the sea," he told his servant. And he went up and looked.

"There is nothing there," he said.

Seven times Elijah said, "Go back."

44The seventh time the servant reported, "A cloud as small as a man's hand is rising from the sea."

So Elijah said, "Go and tell Ahab, 'Hitch up your chariot and go down before the rain stops you.' "

45Meanwhile, the sky grew black with clouds, the wind rose, a heavy rain came on and Ahab rode off to Jezreel. 46The power of the LORD came upon Elijah and, tucking his cloak into his belt, he ran ahead of Ahab all the way to Jezreel.

Elijah Flees to Horeb

19 Now Ahab told Jezebel everything Elijah had done and how he had killed all the prophets with the sword. 2So Jezebel sent a messenger to Elijah to say, "May the gods deal with me, be it ever so severely, if by this time tomorrow I do not make your life like that of one of them."

Make It Stick

READ 1 KINGS 18:41–46

It took seven tries, but Elijah kept praying for rain. Finally God sent a real gully-washer of a cloudburst. James 5:16 says, "The prayer of a righteous man is powerful and effective." What are two things can you pray about and *keep* praying about? Pray over them every day for this week. Then write two more to pray about next week. Try to keep the habit going.

³Elijah was afraid[a] and ran for his life. When he came to Beersheba in Judah, he left his servant there, ⁴while he himself went a day's journey into the desert. He came to a broom tree, sat down under it and prayed that he might die. "I have had enough, LORD," he said. "Take my life; I am no better than my ancestors." ⁵Then he lay down under the tree and fell asleep.

All at once an angel touched him and said, "Get up and eat." ⁶He looked around, and there by his head was a cake of bread baked over hot coals, and a jar of water. He ate and drank and then lay down again.

⁷The angel of the LORD came back a second time and touched him and said, "Get up and eat, for the journey is too much for you." ⁸So he got up and ate and drank. Strengthened by that food, he traveled forty days and forty nights until he reached Horeb, the mountain of God. ⁹There he went into a cave and spent the night.

The LORD Appears to Elijah

And the word of the LORD came to him: "What are you doing here, Elijah?"

¹⁰He replied, "I have been very zealous for the LORD God Almighty. The Israelites have rejected your covenant, broken down your altars, and put your prophets to death with the sword. I am the only one left, and now they are trying to kill me too."

¹¹The LORD said, "Go out and stand on the mountain in the presence of the LORD, for the LORD is about to pass by."

Then a great and powerful wind tore the mountains apart and shattered the rocks before the LORD, but the LORD was not in the wind. After the wind there was an earthquake, but the LORD was not in the earthquake. ¹²After the earthquake came a fire, but the LORD was not in the fire. And after the fire came a gentle whisper. ¹³When Elijah heard it, he pulled his cloak over his face and went out and stood at the mouth of the cave.

Then a voice said to him, "What are you doing here, Elijah?"

¹⁴He replied, "I have been very zealous for the LORD God Almighty. The Israelites

a 3 Or Elijah saw

Not All Special Effects

READ 1 KINGS 19:1–18

When a man's looking for God, he often hopes for a *Jurassic Park* style entrance—chaos, shaking earth and some real noise. When Elijah was worried about being taken out by Jezebel and her prophet-killers, God passed by for a little chat to comfort him. Earthquakes shook the mountain. Fire and wind blasted the rocks. Then God followed all the mayhem by breezing by in a gentle whisper. God has a lot of different styles. He can do the big stuff, but he also makes miracles happen in small ways: You get a job and earn some needed money; God helps you to study extra hard, so you ace the final math test; you pray, and suddenly you understand something. So be quiet and still. It gives God a chance to speak to you. He can shake mountains, but he also whispers quietly.

Your next reading is on page 468.

have rejected your covenant, broken down your altars, and put your prophets to death with the sword. I am the only one left, and now they are trying to kill me too."

15The LORD said to him, "Go back the way you came, and go to the Desert of Damascus. When you get there, anoint Hazael king over Aram. 16Also, anoint Jehu son of Nimshi king over Israel, and anoint Elisha son of Shaphat from Abel Meholah to succeed you as prophet. 17Jehu will put to death any who escape the sword of Hazael, and Elisha will put to death any who escape the sword of Jehu. 18Yet I reserve seven thousand in Israel— all whose knees have not bowed down to Baal and all whose mouths have not kissed him."

The Call of Elisha

19So Elijah went from there and found Elisha son of Shaphat. He was plowing with twelve yoke of oxen, and he himself was driving the twelfth pair. Elijah went up to him and threw his cloak around him. 20Elisha then left his oxen and ran after Elijah. "Let me kiss my father and mother good-by," he said, "and then I will come with you."

"Go back," Elijah replied. "What have I done to you?"

21So Elisha left him and went back. He took his yoke of oxen and slaughtered them. He burned the plowing equipment to cook the meat and gave it to the people, and they ate. Then he set out to follow Elijah and became his attendant.

Ben-Hadad Attacks Samaria

20 Now Ben-Hadad king of Aram mustered his entire army. Accompanied by thirty-two kings with their horses and chariots, he went up and besieged Samaria and attacked it. 2He sent messengers into the city to Ahab king of Israel, saying, "This is what Ben-Hadad says: 3'Your silver and gold are mine, and the best of your wives and children are mine.' "

4The king of Israel answered, "Just as you say, my lord the king. I and all I have are yours."

5The messengers came again and said, "This is what Ben-Hadad says: 'I sent to demand your silver and gold, your wives and your children. 6But about this time tomorrow I am going to send my officials

to search your palace and the houses of your officials. They will seize everything you value and carry it away.' "

7The king of Israel summoned all the elders of the land and said to them, "See how this man is looking for trouble! When he sent for my wives and my children, my silver and my gold, I did not refuse him."

8The elders and the people all answered, "Don't listen to him or agree to his demands."

9So he replied to Ben-Hadad's messengers, "Tell my lord the king, 'Your servant will do all you demanded the first time, but this demand I cannot meet.' " They left and took the answer back to Ben-Hadad.

10Then Ben-Hadad sent another message to Ahab: "May the gods deal with me, be it ever so severely, if enough dust remains in Samaria to give each of my men a handful."

11The king of Israel answered, "Tell him: 'One who puts on his armor should not boast like one who takes it off.' "

12Ben-Hadad heard this message while he and the kings were drinking in their tents,a and he ordered his men: "Prepare to attack." So they prepared to attack the city.

Ahab Defeats Ben-Hadad

13Meanwhile a prophet came to Ahab king of Israel and announced, "This is what the LORD says: 'Do you see this vast army? I will give it into your hand today, and then you will know that I am the LORD.' "

14"But who will do this?" asked Ahab.

The prophet replied, "This is what the LORD says: 'The young officers of the provincial commanders will do it.' "

"And who will start the battle?" he asked.

The prophet answered, "You will."

15So Ahab summoned the young officers of the provincial commanders, 232 men. Then he assembled the rest of the Israelites, 7,000 in all. 16They set out at noon while Ben-Hadad and the 32 kings allied with him were in their tents getting drunk. 17The young officers of the provincial commanders went out first.

Now Ben-Hadad had dispatched scouts, who reported, "Men are advancing from Samaria."

18He said, "If they have come out for

a 12 Or in Succoth; also in verse 16

peace, take them alive; if they have come out for war, take them alive."

¹⁹The young officers of the provincial commanders marched out of the city with the army behind them ²⁰and each one struck down his opponent. At that, the Arameans fled, with the Israelites in pursuit. But Ben-Hadad king of Aram escaped on horseback with some of his horsemen. ²¹The king of Israel advanced and overpowered the horses and chariots and inflicted heavy losses on the Arameans.

²²Afterward, the prophet came to the king of Israel and said, "Strengthen your position and see what must be done, because next spring the king of Aram will attack you again."

²³Meanwhile, the officials of the king of Aram advised him, "Their gods are gods of the hills. That is why they were too strong for us. But if we fight them on the plains, surely we will be stronger than they. ²⁴Do this: Remove all the kings from their commands and replace them with other officers. ²⁵You must also raise an army like the one you lost—horse for horse and chariot for chariot—so we can fight Israel on the plains. Then surely we will be stronger than they." He agreed with them and acted accordingly.

²⁶The next spring Ben-Hadad mustered the Arameans and went up to Aphek to fight against Israel. ²⁷When the Israelites were also mustered and given provisions, they marched out to meet them. The Israelites camped opposite them like two small flocks of goats, while the Arameans covered the countryside.

²⁸The man of God came up and told the king of Israel, "This is what the LORD says: 'Because the Arameans think the LORD is a god of the hills and not a god of the valleys, I will deliver this vast army into your hands, and you will know that I am the LORD.' "

²⁹For seven days they camped opposite each other, and on the seventh day the battle was joined. The Israelites inflicted a hundred thousand casualties on the Aramean foot soldiers in one day. ³⁰The rest of them escaped to the city of Aphek, where the wall collapsed on twenty-seven thousand of them. And Ben-Hadad fled to the city and hid in an inner room.

³¹His officials said to him, "Look, we have heard that the kings of the house of Israel are merciful. Let us go to the king of Israel with sackcloth around our waists and ropes around our heads. Perhaps he will spare your life."

³²Wearing sackcloth around their waists and ropes around their heads, they went to the king of Israel and said, "Your servant Ben-Hadad says: 'Please let me live.' "

The king answered, "Is he still alive? He is my brother."

³³The men took this as a good sign and were quick to pick up his word. "Yes, your brother Ben-Hadad!" they said.

"Go and get him," the king said. When Ben-Hadad came out, Ahab had him come up into his chariot.

³⁴"I will return the cities my father took from your father," Ben-Hadad offered. "You may set up your own market areas in Damascus, as my father did in Samaria."

⌊Ahab said,⌋ "On the basis of a treaty I will set you free." So he made a treaty with him, and let him go.

A Prophet Condemns Ahab

³⁵By the word of the LORD one of the sons of the prophets said to his companion, "Strike me with your weapon," but the man refused.

³⁶So the prophet said, "Because you have not obeyed the LORD, as soon as you leave me a lion will kill you." And after the man went away, a lion found him and killed him.

³⁷The prophet found another man and said, "Strike me, please." So the man struck him and wounded him. ³⁸Then the prophet went and stood by the road waiting for the king. He disguised himself with his headband down over his eyes. ³⁹As the king passed by, the prophet called out to him, "Your servant went into the thick of the battle, and someone came to me with a captive and said, 'Guard this man. If he is missing, it will be your life for his life, or you must pay a talent*a* of silver.' ⁴⁰While your servant was busy here and there, the man disappeared."

"That is your sentence," the king of Israel said. "You have pronounced it yourself."

⁴¹Then the prophet quickly removed the headband from his eyes, and the king of Israel recognized him as one of the prophets. ⁴²He said to the king, "This is what the LORD says: 'You have set free a man I had

---

a 39 That is, about 75 pounds (about 34 kilograms)

determined should die.ᵃ Therefore it is your life for his life, your people for his people.' " ⁴³Sullen and angry, the king of Israel went to his palace in Samaria.

Naboth's Vineyard

21 Some time later there was an incident involving a vineyard belonging to Naboth the Jezreelite. The vineyard was in Jezreel, close to the palace of Ahab king of Samaria. ²Ahab said to Naboth, "Let me have your vineyard to use for a vegetable garden, since it is close to my palace. In exchange I will give you a better vineyard or, if you prefer, I will pay you whatever it is worth."

³But Naboth replied, "The LORD forbid that I should give you the inheritance of my fathers."

⁴So Ahab went home, sullen and angry because Naboth the Jezreelite had said, "I will not give you the inheritance of my fathers." He lay on his bed sulking and refused to eat.

⁵His wife Jezebel came in and asked him, "Why are you so sullen? Why won't you eat?"

⁶He answered her, "Because I said to Naboth the Jezreelite, 'Sell me your vineyard; or if you prefer, I will give you another vineyard in its place.' But he said, 'I will not give you my vineyard.' "

⁷Jezebel his wife said, "Is this how you act as king over Israel? Get up and eat! Cheer up. I'll get you the vineyard of Naboth the Jezreelite."

⁸So she wrote letters in Ahab's name, placed his seal on them, and sent them to the elders and nobles who lived in Naboth's city with him. ⁹In those letters she wrote:

"Proclaim a day of fasting and seat Naboth in a prominent place among the people. ¹⁰But seat two scoundrels opposite him and have them testify that he has cursed both God and the king. Then take him out and stone him to death."

¹¹So the elders and nobles who lived in Naboth's city did as Jezebel directed in the letters she had written to them. ¹²They proclaimed a fast and seated Naboth in a prominent place among the people. ¹³Then two scoundrels came and sat opposite him and brought charges against Naboth before the people, saying, "Naboth has cursed both God and the king."

So they took him outside the city and stoned him to death. ¹⁴Then they sent word to Jezebel: "Naboth has been stoned and is dead."

¹⁵As soon as Jezebel heard that Naboth had been stoned to death, she said to Ahab, "Get up and take possession of the vineyard of Naboth the Jezreelite that he refused to sell you. He is no longer alive, but dead." ¹⁶When Ahab heard that Naboth was dead, he got up and went down to take possession of Naboth's vineyard.

¹⁷Then the word of the LORD came to Elijah the Tishbite: ¹⁸"Go down to meet Ahab king of Israel, who rules in Samaria. He is now in Naboth's vineyard, where he has gone to take possession of it. ¹⁹Say to him, 'This is what the LORD says: Have you not murdered a man and seized his property?' Then say to him, 'This is what the LORD says: In the place where dogs licked up Naboth's blood, dogs will lick up your blood—yes, yours!' "

²⁰Ahab said to Elijah, "So you have found me, my enemy!"

"I have found you," he answered, "because you have sold yourself to do evil in the eyes of the LORD. ²¹I am going to bring disaster on you. I will consume your descendants and cut off from Ahab every last male in Israel—slave or free. ²²I will make your house like that of Jeroboam son of Nebat and that of Baasha son of Ahijah, because you have provoked me to anger and have caused Israel to sin.'

²³"And also concerning Jezebel the LORD says: 'Dogs will devour Jezebel by the wall ofᵇ Jezreel.'

²⁴"Dogs will eat those belonging to Ahab who die in the city, and the birds of the air will feed on those who die in the country."

²⁵(There was never a man like Ahab, who sold himself to do evil in the eyes of the LORD, urged on by Jezebel his wife. ²⁶He behaved in the vilest manner by going after idols, like the Amorites the LORD drove out before Israel.)

²⁷When Ahab heard these words, he tore his clothes, put on sackcloth and fasted. He lay in sackcloth and went around meekly.

ᵃ 42 The Hebrew term refers to the irrevocable giving over of things or persons to the LORD, often by totally destroying them.   ᵇ 23 Most Hebrew manuscripts; a few Hebrew manuscripts, Vulgate and Syriac (see also 2 Kings 9:26) the plot of ground at

28Then the word of the LORD came to Elijah the Tishbite: 29"Have you noticed how Ahab has humbled himself before me? Because he has humbled himself, I will not bring this disaster in his day, but I will bring it on his house in the days of his son."

Micaiah Prophesies Against Ahab

22 For three years there was no war between Aram and Israel. 2But in the third year Jehoshaphat king of Judah went down to see the king of Israel. 3The king of Israel had said to his officials, "Don't you know that Ramoth Gilead belongs to us and yet we are doing nothing to retake it from the king of Aram?"

4So he asked Jehoshaphat, "Will you go with me to fight against Ramoth Gilead?"

Jehoshaphat replied to the king of Israel, "I am as you are, my people as your people, my horses as your horses." 5But Jehoshaphat also said to the king of Israel, "First seek the counsel of the LORD."

6So the king of Israel brought together the prophets—about four hundred men—and asked them, "Shall I go to war against Ramoth Gilead, or shall I refrain?"

"Go," they answered, "for the Lord will give it into the king's hand."

7But Jehoshaphat asked, "Is there not a prophet of the LORD here whom we can inquire of?"

8The king of Israel answered Jehoshaphat, "There is still one man through whom we can inquire of the LORD, but I hate him because he never prophesies anything good about me, but always bad. He is Micaiah son of Imlah."

"The king should not say that," Jehoshaphat replied.

9So the king of Israel called one of his officials and said, "Bring Micaiah son of Imlah at once."

10Dressed in their royal robes, the king of Israel and Jehoshaphat king of Judah were sitting on their thrones at the threshing floor by the entrance of the gate of Samaria, with all the prophets prophesying before them. 11Now Zedekiah son of Kenaanah had made iron horns and he declared, "This is what the LORD says: 'With these you will gore the Arameans until they are destroyed.' "

12All the other prophets were prophesying the same thing. "Attack Ramoth Gil-

ead and be victorious," they said, "for the LORD will give it into the king's hand."

13The messenger who had gone to summon Micaiah said to him, "Look, as one man the other prophets are predicting success for the king. Let your word agree with theirs, and speak favorably."

14But Micaiah said, "As surely as the LORD lives, I can tell him only what the LORD tells me."

15When he arrived, the king asked him, "Micaiah, shall we go to war against Ramoth Gilead, or shall I refrain?"

"Attack and be victorious," he answered, "for the LORD will give it into the king's hand."

16The king said to him, "How many times must I make you swear to tell me nothing but the truth in the name of the LORD?"

17Then Micaiah answered, "I saw all Israel scattered on the hills like sheep without a shepherd, and the LORD said, 'These people have no master. Let each one go home in peace.' "

18The king of Israel said to Jehoshaphat, "Didn't I tell you that he never prophesies anything good about me, but only bad?"

19Micaiah continued, "Therefore hear the word of the LORD: I saw the LORD sitting on his throne with all the host of heaven standing around him on his right and on his left. 20And the LORD said, 'Who will entice Ahab into attacking Ramoth Gilead and going to his death there?'

"One suggested this, and another that. 21Finally, a spirit came forward, stood before the LORD and said, 'I will entice him.'

22" 'By what means?' the LORD asked.

" 'I will go out and be a lying spirit in the mouths of all his prophets,' he said.

" 'You will succeed in enticing him,' said the LORD. 'Go and do it.'

23"So now the LORD has put a lying spirit in the mouths of all these prophets of yours. The LORD has decreed disaster for you."

24Then Zedekiah son of Kenaanah went up and slapped Micaiah in the face. "Which way did the spirit from*a* the LORD go when he went from me to speak to you?" he asked.

25Micaiah replied, "You will find out on the day you go to hide in an inner room."

a 24 Or Spirit of

Gross!

Check out 1 Kings 22:38. The next time you take Rover for a walk and he stops to lap at a puddle, think about Ahab. Ahab had killed Naboth (and stole his property), so Elijah predicted that "dogs would lick up his blood." Yup. Dogs are not real particular about what they drink.

26The king of Israel then ordered, "Take Micaiah and send him back to Amon the ruler of the city and to Joash the king's son 27and say, 'This is what the king says: Put this fellow in prison and give him nothing but bread and water until I return safely.' "

28Micaiah declared, "If you ever return safely, the LORD has not spoken through me." Then he added, "Mark my words, all you people!"

Ahab Killed at Ramoth Gilead

29So the king of Israel and Jehoshaphat king of Judah went up to Ramoth Gilead. 30The king of Israel said to Jehoshaphat, "I will enter the battle in disguise, but you wear your royal robes." So the king of Israel disguised himself and went into battle.

31Now the king of Aram had ordered his thirty-two chariot commanders, "Do not fight with anyone, small or great, except the king of Israel." 32When the chariot commanders saw Jehoshaphat, they thought, "Surely this is the king of Israel." So they turned to attack him, but when Jehoshaphat cried out, 33the chariot commanders saw that he was not the king of Israel and stopped pursuing him.

34But someone drew his bow at random and hit the king of Israel between the sections of his armor. The king told his chariot driver, "Wheel around and get me out of the fighting. I've been wounded." 35All day long the battle raged, and the king was propped up in his chariot facing the Arameans. The blood from his wound ran onto the floor of the chariot, and that evening he died. 36As the sun was setting, a cry spread through the army: "Every man to his town; everyone to his land!"

37So the king died and was brought to Samaria, and they buried him there. 38They washed the chariot at a pool in Samaria (where the prostitutes bathed),[a] and the dogs licked up his blood, as the word of the LORD had declared.

39As for the other events of Ahab's reign, including all he did, the palace he built and inlaid with ivory, and the cities he fortified, are they not written in the book of the annals of the kings of Israel? 40Ahab rested with his fathers. And Ahaziah his son succeeded him as king.

Jehoshaphat King of Judah

41Jehoshaphat son of Asa became king of Judah in the fourth year of Ahab king of Israel. 42Jehoshaphat was thirty-five years old when he became king, and he reigned in Jerusalem twenty-five years. His mother's name was Azubah daughter of Shilhi. 43In everything he walked in the ways of his father Asa and did not stray from them; he did what was right in the eyes of the LORD. The high places, however, were not removed, and the people continued to offer sacrifices and burn incense there. 44Jehoshaphat was also at peace with the king of Israel.

a 38 Or Samaria and cleaned the weapons

45As for the other events of Jehosha-phat's reign, the things he achieved and his military exploits, are they not written in the book of the annals of the kings of Judah? 46He rid the land of the rest of the male shrine prostitutes who remained there even after the reign of his father Asa. 47There was then no king in Edom; a deputy ruled.

48Now Jehoshaphat built a fleet of trading ships[a] to go to Ophir for gold, but they never set sail—they were wrecked at Ezion Geber. 49At that time Ahaziah son of Ahab said to Jehoshaphat, "Let my men sail with your men," but Jehoshaphat refused.

50Then Jehoshaphat rested with his fathers and was buried with them in the city of David his father. And Jehoram his son succeeded him.

Ahaziah King of Israel

51Ahaziah son of Ahab became king of Israel in Samaria in the seventeenth year of Jehoshaphat king of Judah, and he reigned over Israel two years. 52He did evil in the eyes of the LORD, because he walked in the ways of his father and mother and in the ways of Jeroboam son of Nebat, who caused Israel to sin. 53He served and worshiped Baal and provoked the LORD, the God of Israel, to anger, just as his father had done.

---

a 48 Hebrew *of ships of Tarshish*

2 KINGS

Who wrote this book?
The author of this book is unknown.

Why was this book written?
The book of 2 Kings shows why God finally exiled Israel and Judah from the Promised Land.

What happens in this book?
The stories of many kings of Judah and Israel are told in this book.

What do we learn about God in this book?
God is very patient. But God will punish his people if they keep on disobeying him.

What people are important in this book?
The most important people in this book are Elisha, Joash, Hezekiah and Josiah.

When did this happen?
The events in this book happened between 853 and 586 B.C.

Where did this happen?
These stories happened in Israel and Judah.

What are some of the stories in this book?

The LORD's Judgment on Ahaziah

1 After Ahab's death, Moab rebelled against Israel. ²Now Ahaziah had fallen through the lattice of his upper room in Samaria and injured himself. So he sent messengers, saying to them, "Go and consult Baal-Zebub, the god of Ekron, to see if I will recover from this injury."

³But the angel of the LORD said to Elijah the Tishbite, "Go up and meet the messengers of the king of Samaria and ask them, 'Is it because there is no God in Israel that you are going off to consult Baal-Zebub, the god of Ekron?' ⁴Therefore this is what the LORD says: 'You will not leave the bed you are lying on. You will certainly die!' " So Elijah went.

⁵When the messengers returned to the king, he asked them, "Why have you come back?"

⁶"A man came to meet us," they replied. "And he said to us, 'Go back to the king who sent you and tell him, "This is what the LORD says: Is it because there is no God in Israel that you are sending men to consult Baal-Zebub, the god of Ekron? Therefore you will not leave the bed you are lying on. You will certainly die!" ' "

⁷The king asked them, "What kind of man was it who came to meet you and told you this?"

⁸They replied, "He was a man with a garment of hair and with a leather belt around his waist."

The king said, "That was Elijah the Tishbite."

⁹Then he sent to Elijah a captain with his company of fifty men. The captain went up to Elijah, who was sitting on the top of a hill, and said to him, "Man of God, the king says, 'Come down!' "

¹⁰Elijah answered the captain, "If I am a man of God, may fire come down from heaven and consume you and your fifty men!" Then fire fell from heaven and consumed the captain and his men.

¹¹At this the king sent to Elijah another captain with his fifty men. The captain said to him, "Man of God, this is what the king says, 'Come down at once!' "

¹²"If I am a man of God," Elijah replied, "may fire come down from heaven and consume you and your fifty men!" Then the fire of God fell from heaven and consumed him and his fifty men.

¹³So the king sent a third captain with his fifty men. This third captain went up and fell on his knees before Elijah. "Man of God," he begged, "please have respect for my life and the lives of these fifty men, your servants! ¹⁴See, fire has fallen from heaven and consumed the first two captains and all their men. But now have respect for my life!"

¹⁵The angel of the LORD said to Elijah, "Go down with him; do not be afraid of him." So Elijah got up and went down with him to the king.

¹⁶He told the king, "This is what the LORD says: Is it because there is no God in Israel for you to consult that you have sent messengers to consult Baal-Zebub, the god of Ekron? Because you have done this, you will never leave

Gross!

Check out 2 Kings 1:9–15. When Ahaziah sent soldiers to capture Elijah, God burned them to a crisp. Imagine the second and third group of fifty men coming along and seeing the charred earth and remains of the other soldiers' armor! No wonder the third captain figured he had better beg for mercy.

the bed you are lying on. You will certainly die!" ¹⁷So he died, according to the word of the LORD that Elijah had spoken.

Because Ahaziah had no son, Joram*ᵃ* succeeded him as king in the second year of Jehoram son of Jehoshaphat king of Judah. ¹⁸As for all the other events of Ahaziah's reign, and what he did, are they not written in the book of the annals of the kings of Israel?

Elijah Taken Up to Heaven

When the LORD was about to take Elijah up to heaven in a whirlwind, Elijah and Elisha were on their way from Gilgal. ²Elijah said to Elisha, "Stay here; the LORD has sent me to Bethel."

But Elisha said, "As surely as the LORD lives and as you live, I will not leave you." So they went down to Bethel.

³The company of the prophets at Bethel came out to Elisha and asked, "Do you know that the LORD is going to take your master from you today?"

"Yes, I know," Elisha replied, "but do not speak of it."

⁴Then Elijah said to him, "Stay here, Elisha; the LORD has sent me to Jericho."

And he replied, "As surely as the LORD lives and as you live, I will not leave you." So they went to Jericho.

⁵The company of the prophets at Jericho went up to Elisha and asked him, "Do you know that the LORD is going to take your master from you today?"

"Yes, I know," he replied, "but do not speak of it."

⁶Then Elijah said to him, "Stay here; the LORD has sent me to the Jordan."

And he replied, "As surely as the LORD lives and as you live, I will not leave you." So the two of them walked on.

⁷Fifty men of the company of the prophets went and stood at a distance, facing the place where Elijah and Elisha had stopped at the Jordan. ⁸Elijah took his cloak, rolled it up and struck the water with it. The water divided to the right and to the left, and the two of them crossed over on dry ground.

⁹When they had crossed, Elijah said to

ᵃ 17 Hebrew *Jehoram,* a variant of *Joram*

Jump Into the Game

READ 2 KINGS 2:1–18

Elisha wasn't the kind of guy to go for seconds; he got everything he wanted the first time around. Just before Elijah got transported into heaven in a whirlwind, he asked Elisha if there was anything he could do for him. Did he really mean it? Yep. In that case, Elisha's thinking, "Pour it on! I want my life to really count for God! I want double the spirit you received" (verse 9). It was a bold request, but God honored it. Elisha was serious about following God and doing what God wanted him to do. What about you? Are you sitting on the sidelines? Why not jump into the game? God has an important position for you to play. Just tell him, "God, I want to play on your team. Please show me what you want me to do and help me to be wholehearted about doing it."

Your next reading is on page 473.

Elisha, "Tell me, what can I do for you before I am taken from you?"

"Let me inherit a double portion of your spirit," Elisha replied.

10 "You have asked a difficult thing," Elijah said, "yet if you see me when I am taken from you, it will be yours—otherwise not."

11 As they were walking along and talking together, suddenly a chariot of fire and horses of fire appeared and separated the two of them, and Elijah went up to heaven in a whirlwind. 12 Elisha saw this and cried out, "My father! My father! The chariots and horsemen of Israel!" And Elisha saw him no more. Then he took hold of his own clothes and tore them apart.

13 He picked up the cloak that had fallen from Elijah and went back and stood on the bank of the Jordan. 14 Then he took the cloak that had fallen from him and struck the water with it. "Where now is the LORD, the God of Elijah?" he asked. When he struck the water, it divided to the right and to the left, and he crossed over.

15 The company of the prophets from Jericho, who were watching, said, "The spirit of Elijah is resting on Elisha." And they went to meet him and bowed to the ground before him. 16 "Look," they said, "we your servants have fifty able men. Let them go and look for your master. Perhaps the Spirit of the LORD has picked him up and set him down on some mountain or in some valley."

"No," Elisha replied, "do not send them."

17 But they persisted until he was too ashamed to refuse. So he said, "Send them." And they sent fifty men, who searched for three days but did not find him. 18 When they returned to Elisha, who was staying in Jericho, he said to them, "Didn't I tell you not to go?"

Healing of the Water

19 The men of the city said to Elisha, "Look, our lord, this town is well situated, as you can see, but the water is bad and the land is unproductive."

20 "Bring me a new bowl," he said, "and put salt in it." So they brought it to him.

21 Then he went out to the spring and threw the salt into it, saying, "This is what the LORD says: 'I have healed this water. Never again will it cause death or make the land unproductive.' " 22 And the water

has remained wholesome to this day, according to the word Elisha had spoken.

Elisha Is Jeered

23 From there Elisha went up to Bethel. As he was walking along the road, some youths came out of the town and jeered at him. "Go on up, you baldhead!" they said. "Go on up, you baldhead!" 24 He turned around, looked at them and called down a curse on them in the name of the LORD. Then two bears came out of the woods and mauled forty-two of the youths. 25 And he went on to Mount Carmel and from there returned to Samaria.

Moab Revolts

3 Joram[a] son of Ahab became king of Israel in Samaria in the eighteenth year of Jehoshaphat king of Judah, and he reigned twelve years. 2 He did evil in the eyes of the LORD, but not as his father and mother had done. He got rid of the sacred stone of Baal that his father had made. 3 Nevertheless he clung to the sins of Jeroboam son of Nebat, which he had caused Israel to commit; he did not turn away from them.

4 Now Mesha king of Moab raised sheep, and he had to supply the king of Israel with a hundred thousand lambs and with the wool of a hundred thousand rams. 5 But after Ahab died, the king of Moab rebelled against the king of Israel. 6 So at that time King Joram set out from Samaria and mobilized all Israel. 7 He also sent this message to Jehoshaphat king of Judah: "The king of Moab has rebelled against me. Will you go with me to fight against Moab?"

"I will go with you," he replied. "I am as you are, my people as your people, my horses as your horses."

8 "By what route shall we attack?" he asked.

"Through the Desert of Edom," he answered.

9 So the king of Israel set out with the king of Judah and the king of Edom. After a roundabout march of seven days, the army had no more water for themselves or for the animals with them.

10 "What!" exclaimed the king of Israel. "Has the LORD called us three kings together only to hand us over to Moab?"

a 1 Hebrew *Jehoram*, a variant of *Joram*; also in verse 6

¹¹But Jehoshaphat asked, "Is there no prophet of the LORD here, that we may inquire of the LORD through him?"

An officer of the king of Israel answered, "Elisha son of Shaphat is here. He used to pour water on the hands of Elijah.ᵃ"

¹²Jehoshaphat said, "The word of the LORD is with him." So the king of Israel and Jehoshaphat and the king of Edom went down to him.

¹³Elisha said to the king of Israel, "What do we have to do with each other? Go to the prophets of your father and the prophets of your mother."

"No," the king of Israel answered, "because it was the LORD who called us three kings together to hand us over to Moab."

¹⁴Elisha said, "As surely as the LORD Almighty lives, whom I serve, if I did not have respect for the presence of Jehoshaphat king of Judah, I would not look at you or even notice you. ¹⁵But now bring me a harpist."

While the harpist was playing, the hand of the LORD came upon Elisha ¹⁶and he said, "This is what the LORD says: Make this valley full of ditches. ¹⁷For this is what the LORD says: You will see neither wind nor rain, yet this valley will be filled with water, and you, your cattle and your other animals will drink. ¹⁸This is an easy thing in the eyes of the LORD; he will also hand Moab over to you. ¹⁹You will overthrow every fortified city and every major town. You will cut down every good tree, stop up all the springs, and ruin every good field with stones."

²⁰The next morning, about the time for offering the sacrifice, there it was—water flowing from the direction of Edom! And the land was filled with water.

²¹Now all the Moabites had heard that the kings had come to fight against them; so every man, young and old, who could bear arms was called up and stationed on the border. ²²When they got up early in the morning, the sun was shining on the water. To the Moabites across the way, the water looked red—like blood. ²³"That's blood!" they said. "Those kings must have fought and slaughtered each other. Now to the plunder, Moab!"

²⁴But when the Moabites came to the camp of Israel, the Israelites rose up and fought them until they fled. And the Israelites invaded the land and slaughtered the Moabites. ²⁵They destroyed the towns, and each man threw a stone on every good field until it was covered. They stopped up all the springs and cut down every good tree. Only Kir Hareseth was left with its stones in place, but men armed with slings surrounded it and attacked it as well.

²⁶When the king of Moab saw that the battle had gone against him, he took with him seven hundred swordsmen to break through to the king of Edom, but they failed. ²⁷Then he took his firstborn son, who was to succeed him as king, and offered him as a sacrifice on the city wall. The fury against Israel was great; they withdrew and returned to their own land.

The Widow's Oil

4 The wife of a man from the company of the prophets cried out to Elisha, "Your servant my husband is dead, and you know that he revered the LORD. But now his creditor is coming to take my two boys as his slaves."

²Elisha replied to her, "How can I help you? Tell me, what do you have in your house?"

"Your servant has nothing there at all," she said, "except a little oil."

³Elisha said, "Go around and ask all your neighbors for empty jars. Don't ask for just a few. ⁴Then go inside and shut the door behind you and your sons. Pour oil into all the jars, and as each is filled, put it to one side."

⁵She left him and afterward shut the door behind her and her sons. They brought the jars to her and she kept pouring. ⁶When all the jars were full, she said to her son, "Bring me another one."

But he replied, "There is not a jar left." Then the oil stopped flowing.

⁷She went and told the man of God, and he said, "Go, sell the oil and pay your debts. You and your sons can live on what is left."

The Shunammite's Son Restored to Life

⁸One day Elisha went to Shunem. And a well-to-do woman was there, who urged him to stay for a meal. So whenever he came by, he stopped there to eat. ⁹She said to her husband, "I know that this man who often comes our way is a holy man of God. ¹⁰Let's make a small room on the

---

ᵃ 11 That is, he was Elijah's personal servant.

roof and put in it a bed and a table, a chair and a lamp for him. Then he can stay there whenever he comes to us."

¹¹One day when Elisha came, he went up to his room and lay down there. ¹²He said to his servant Gehazi, "Call the Shunammite." So he called her, and she stood before him. ¹³Elisha said to him, "Tell her, 'You have gone to all this trouble for us. Now what can be done for you? Can we speak on your behalf to the king or the commander of the army?' "

She replied, "I have a home among my own people."

¹⁴"What can be done for her?" Elisha asked.

Gehazi said, "Well, she has no son and her husband is old."

¹⁵Then Elisha said, "Call her." So he called her, and she stood in the doorway. ¹⁶"About this time next year," Elisha said, "you will hold a son in your arms."

"No, my lord," she objected. "Don't mislead your servant, O man of God!"

¹⁷But the woman became pregnant, and the next year about that same time she gave birth to a son, just as Elisha had told her.

Make It Stick

READ 2 KINGS 4:1–7

Ever heard the saying, "Don't make a mountain out of a mole hill"? Well, God specializes in doing that sort of thing, in a good way—like he did with the widow's oil. Write down some small good things you have (allowance money, talents, volunteer time) and then ask God to turn your "mole hills" into "mountains."

18The child grew, and one day he went out to his father, who was with the reapers. 19"My head! My head!" he said to his father.

His father told a servant, "Carry him to his mother." 20After the servant had lifted him up and carried him to his mother, the boy sat on her lap until noon, and then he died. 21She went up and laid him on the bed of the man of God, then shut the door and went out.

22She called her husband and said, "Please send me one of the servants and a donkey so I can go to the man of God quickly and return."

23"Why go to him today?" he asked. "It's not the New Moon or the Sabbath."

"It's all right," she said.

24She saddled the donkey and said to her servant, "Lead on; don't slow down for me unless I tell you." 25So she set out and came to the man of God at Mount Carmel.

When he saw her in the distance, the man of God said to his servant Gehazi, "Look! There's the Shunammite! 26Run to meet her and ask her, 'Are you all right? Is your husband all right? Is your child all right?' "

"Everything is all right," she said.

27When she reached the man of God at the mountain, she took hold of his feet. Gehazi came over to push her away, but the man of God said, "Leave her alone! She is in bitter distress, but the LORD has hidden it from me and has not told me why."

28"Did I ask you for a son, my lord?" she said. "Didn't I tell you, 'Don't raise my hopes'?"

29Elisha said to Gehazi, "Tuck your cloak into your belt, take my staff in your hand and run. If you meet anyone, do not greet him, and if anyone greets you, do not answer. Lay my staff on the boy's face."

30But the child's mother said, "As surely as the LORD lives and as you live, I will not leave you." So he got up and followed her.

31Gehazi went on ahead and laid the staff on the boy's face, but there was no sound or response. So Gehazi went back to meet Elisha and told him, "The boy has not awakened."

32When Elisha reached the house, there was the boy lying dead on his couch. 33He went in, shut the door on the two of them and prayed to the LORD. 34Then he got on the bed and lay upon the boy, mouth to mouth, eyes to eyes, hands to hands. As he stretched himself out upon him, the boy's body grew warm. 35Elisha turned away and walked back and forth in the room and then got on the bed and stretched out upon him once more. The boy sneezed seven times and opened his eyes.

36Elisha summoned Gehazi and said, "Call the Shunammite." And he did. When she came, he said, "Take your son." 37She came in, fell at his feet and bowed to the ground. Then she took her son and went out.

Death in the Pot

38Elisha returned to Gilgal and there was a famine in that region. While the company of the prophets was meeting with him, he said to his servant, "Put on the large pot and cook some stew for these men."

39One of them went out into the fields to gather herbs and found a wild vine. He gathered some of its gourds and filled the fold of his cloak. When he returned, he cut them up into the pot of stew, though no one knew what they were. 40The stew was poured out for the men, but as they began to eat it, they cried out, "O man of God, there is death in the pot!" And they could not eat it.

41Elisha said, "Get some flour." He put it into the pot and said, "Serve it to the people to eat." And there was nothing harmful in the pot.

Feeding of a Hundred

42A man came from Baal Shalishah, bringing the man of God twenty loaves of barley bread baked from the first ripe grain, along with some heads of new grain. "Give it to the people to eat," Elisha said.

43"How can I set this before a hundred men?" his servant asked.

But Elisha answered, "Give it to the people to eat. For this is what the LORD says: 'They will eat and have some left over.' " 44Then he set it before them, and they ate and had some left over, according to the word of the LORD.

Naaman Healed of Leprosy

5 Now Naaman was commander of the army of the king of Aram. He was a great man in the sight of his master and highly regarded, because through him the LORD had given vic-

tory to Aram. He was a valiant soldier, but he had leprosy. [a]

2Now bands from Aram had gone out and had taken captive a young girl from Israel, and she served Naaman's wife. 3She said to her mistress, "If only my master would see the prophet who is in Samaria! He would cure him of his leprosy."

4Naaman went to his master and told him what the girl from Israel had said. 5"By all means, go," the king of Aram replied. "I will send a letter to the king of Israel." So Naaman left, taking with him ten talents [b] of silver, six thousand shekels [c] of gold and ten sets of clothing. 6The letter that he took to the king of Israel read: "With this letter I am sending my servant Naaman to you so that you may cure him of his leprosy."

7As soon as the king of Israel read the letter, he tore his robes and said, "Am I God? Can I kill and bring back to life? Why does this fellow send someone to me to be cured of his leprosy? See how he is trying to pick a quarrel with me!"

8When Elisha the man of God heard that the king of Israel had torn his robes, he sent him this message: "Why have you torn your robes? Have the man come to me and he will know that there is a prophet in Israel." 9So Naaman went with his horses and chariots and stopped at the door of Elisha's house. 10Elisha sent a messenger to say to him, "Go, wash yourself seven times in the Jordan, and your flesh will be restored and you will be cleansed."

11But Naaman went away angry and said, "I thought that he would surely come out to me and stand and call on the name of the LORD his God, wave his hand over the spot and cure me of my leprosy. 12Are not Abana and Pharpar, the rivers of Damascus, better than any of the waters of Israel? Couldn't I wash in them and be cleansed?" So he turned and went off in a rage.

13Naaman's servants went to him and said, "My father, if the prophet had told

[a] 1 The Hebrew word was used for various diseases affecting the skin—not necessarily leprosy; also in verses 3, 6, 7, 11 and 27.   [b] 5 That is, about 750 pounds (about 340 kilograms)   [c] 5 That is, about 150 pounds (about 70 kilograms)

GET SMARTER

You Want Me to Do What?

READ 2 KINGS 5

When Naaman asked Elisha to cure his leprosy, he was expecting some spectacular show. *Not*. Elisha didn't even come out and look at him. Elisha's messenger told Naaman to dip in the Jordan River seven times. Naaman was too proud to do such a ridiculous thing. "So he turned and went off in a rage" (verse 12). Like Naaman, you might sometimes feel that certain humble tasks are beneath you. "Why does God have me cleaning toilets?" you may ask. "I asked him to make me class president!" But God needs to know if you're willing to do *anything* for him, not just jobs that will earn you praise. If you're faithful in the little things, God will trust you with big things (see Matthew 25:14–29). So have a humble attitude. If you can't scrub a toilet that needs cleaning, how can you inspire others to do what needs to be done?

Your next reading is on page 476.

you to do some great thing, would you not have done it? How much more, then, when he tells you, 'Wash and be cleansed'!" [14]So he went down and dipped himself in the Jordan seven times, as the man of God had told him, and his flesh was restored and became clean like that of a young boy.

[15]Then Naaman and all his attendants went back to the man of God. He stood before him and said, "Now I know that there is no God in all the world except in Israel. Please accept now a gift from your servant."

[16]The prophet answered, "As surely as the LORD lives, whom I serve, I will not accept a thing." And even though Naaman urged him, he refused.

[17]"If you will not," said Naaman, "please let me, your servant, be given as much earth as a pair of mules can carry, for your servant will never again make burnt offerings and sacrifices to any other god but the LORD. [18]But may the LORD forgive your servant for this one thing: When my master enters the temple of Rimmon to bow down and he is leaning on my arm and I bow there also—when I bow down in the temple of Rimmon, may the LORD forgive your servant for this."

[19]"Go in peace," Elisha said.

After Naaman had traveled some distance, [20]Gehazi, the servant of Elisha the man of God, said to himself, "My master was too easy on Naaman, this Aramean, by not accepting from him what he brought. As surely as the LORD lives, I will run after him and get something from him."

[21]So Gehazi hurried after Naaman. When Naaman saw him running toward him, he got down from the chariot to meet him. "Is everything all right?" he asked.

[22]"Everything is all right," Gehazi answered. "My master sent me to say, 'Two young men from the company of the prophets have just come to me from the hill country of Ephraim. Please give them a talent[a] of silver and two sets of clothing.' "

[23]"By all means, take two talents," said Naaman. He urged Gehazi to accept them, and then tied up the two talents of silver in two bags, with two sets of clothing. He gave them to two of his servants, and they carried them ahead of Gehazi. [24]When Gehazi came to the hill, he took the things from the servants and put them away in the house. He sent the men away and they left. [25]Then he went in and stood before his master Elisha.

"Where have you been, Gehazi?" Elisha asked.

"Your servant didn't go anywhere," Gehazi answered.

[26]But Elisha said to him, "Was not my spirit with you when the man got down from his chariot to meet you? Is this the time to take money, or to accept clothes, olive groves, vineyards, flocks, herds, or menservants and maidservants? [27]Naaman's leprosy will cling to you and to your descendants forever." Then Gehazi went from Elisha's presence and he was leprous, as white as snow.

An Axhead Floats

6 The company of the prophets said to Elisha, "Look, the place where we meet with you is too small for us. [2]Let us go to the Jordan, where each of us can get a pole; and let us build a place there for us to live."

And he said, "Go."

[3]Then one of them said, "Won't you please come with your servants?"

"I will," Elisha replied. [4]And he went with them.

They went to the Jordan and began to cut down trees. [5]As one of them was cutting down a tree, the iron axhead fell into the water. "Oh, my lord," he cried out, "it was borrowed!"

[6]The man of God asked, "Where did it fall?" When he showed him the place, Elisha cut a stick and threw it there, and made the iron float. [7]"Lift it out," he said. Then the man reached out his hand and took it.

Elisha Traps Blinded Arameans

[8]Now the king of Aram was at war with Israel. After conferring with his officers, he said, "I will set up my camp in such and such a place."

[9]The man of God sent word to the king of Israel: "Beware of passing that place, because the Arameans are going down there." [10]So the king of Israel checked on the place indicated by the man of God. Time and again Elisha warned the king, so that he was on his guard in such places.

[11]This enraged the king of Aram. He

a 22 That is, about 75 pounds (about 34 kilograms)

summoned his officers and demanded of them, "Will you not tell me which of us is on the side of the king of Israel?"

12"None of us, my lord the king," said one of his officers, "but Elisha, the prophet who is in Israel, tells the king of Israel the very words you speak in your bedroom."

13"Go, find out where he is," the king ordered, "so I can send men and capture him." The report came back: "He is in Dothan." 14Then he sent horses and chariots and a strong force there. They went by night and surrounded the city.

15When the servant of the man of God got up and went out early the next morning, an army with horses and chariots had surrounded the city. "Oh, my lord, what shall we do?" the servant asked.

16"Don't be afraid," the prophet answered. "Those who are with us are more than those who are with them."

17And Elisha prayed, "O LORD, open his eyes so he may see." Then the LORD opened the servant's eyes, and he looked and saw the hills full of horses and chariots of fire all around Elisha.

18As the enemy came down toward him, Elisha prayed to the LORD, "Strike these people with blindness." So he struck them with blindness, as Elisha had asked.

19Elisha told them, "This is not the road and this is not the city. Follow me, and I will lead you to the man you are looking for." And he led them to Samaria.

20After they entered the city, Elisha said, "LORD, open the eyes of these men so they can see." Then the LORD opened their eyes and they looked, and there they were, inside Samaria.

21When the king of Israel saw them, he asked Elisha, "Shall I kill them, my father? Shall I kill them?"

22"Do not kill them," he answered. "Would you kill men you have captured with your own sword or bow? Set food and water before them so that they may eat and drink and then go back to their master." 23So he prepared a great feast for them, and after they had finished eating and drinking, he sent them away, and they returned to their master. So the bands from Aram stopped raiding Israel's territory.

Famine in Besieged Samaria

24Some time later, Ben-Hadad king of Aram mobilized his entire army and marched up and laid siege to Samaria. 25There was a great famine in the city; the siege lasted so long that a donkey's head sold for eighty shekels[a] of silver, and a quarter of a cab[b] of seed pods[c] for five shekels.[d]

26As the king of Israel was passing by on the wall, a woman cried to him, "Help me, my lord the king!"

27The king replied, "If the LORD does not help you,

Get a Load of This...

Check out 2 Kings 6:1–7. "I knew I should have tightened that thing." That's what Elisha's buddy must have thought when his ax head flew off and fell into the river. He was just about to swim for it when Elisha bailed him out with the "floating ax head" miracle.

---

[a] 25 That is, about 2 pounds (about 1 kilogram)   [b] 25 That is, probably about 1/2 pint (about 0.3 liter)   [c] 25 Or of doves' dung   [d] 25 That is, about 2 ounces (about 55 grams)

where can I get help for you? From the threshing floor? From the winepress?" 28Then he asked her, "What's the matter?"

She answered, "This woman said to me, 'Give up your son so we may eat him today, and tomorrow we'll eat my son.' 29So we cooked my son and ate him. The next day I said to her, 'Give up your son so we may eat him,' but she had hidden him."

30When the king heard the woman's words, he tore his robes. As he went along the wall, the people looked, and there, underneath, he had sackcloth on his body. 31He said, "May God deal with me, be it ever so severely, if the head of Elisha son of Shaphat remains on his shoulders today!"

32Now Elisha was sitting in his house, and the elders were sitting with him. The king sent a messenger ahead, but before he arrived, Elisha said to the elders, "Don't you see how this murderer is sending someone to cut off my head? Look, when the messenger comes, shut the door and hold it shut against him. Is not the sound of his master's footsteps behind him?"

33While he was still talking to them, the messenger came down to him. And the king said, "This disaster is from the LORD. Why should I wait for the LORD any longer?"

7 Elisha said, "Hear the word of the LORD. This is what the LORD says: About this time tomorrow, a seah*a* of flour will sell for a shekel*b* and two seahs*c* of barley for a shekel at the gate of Samaria."

2The officer on whose arm the king was leaning said to the man of God, "Look, even if the LORD should open the floodgates of the heavens, could this happen?"

"You will see it with your own eyes," answered Elisha, "but you will not eat any of it!"

---

a 1 That is, probably about 7 quarts (about 7.3 liters); also in verses 16 and 18   *b 1* That is, about 2/5 ounce (about 11 grams); also in verses 16 and 18   *c 1* That is, probably about 13 quarts (about 15 liters); also in verses 16 and 18

In God We Trust

READ 2 KINGS 6:24–25; 7:1–20

After being surrounded by the Aramean army for what seemed like eternity, the people of Samaria were starving. They were eating "seed pods" (2 Kings 6:25), which some translators say is actually *dove's dung*! At about that point, God told Elisha that things would get better the next day. One of the king's officers didn't believe it, but God came through with the volume turned up high. Sometimes things may look hopeless to you, but don't doubt God like that man did. Remember, you're not just limited to *your* resources. God can make huge changes happen instantly! He can make today's big problems literally disappear tomorrow. God doesn't always work fast—he may just move you one step down the road—but you can still trust him to take you the rest of the way. Don't worry when you're in a pinch. Trust God and things will work out.

Your next reading is on page 489.

The Siege Lifted

3 Now there were four men with leprosy[a] at the entrance of the city gate. They said to each other, "Why stay here until we die? 4 If we say, 'We'll go into the city'—the famine is there, and we will die. And if we stay here, we will die. So let's go over to the camp of the Arameans and surrender. If they spare us, we live; if they kill us, then we die."

5 At dusk they got up and went to the camp of the Arameans. When they reached the edge of the camp, not a man was there, 6 for the Lord had caused the Arameans to hear the sound of chariots and horses and a great army, so that they said to one another, "Look, the king of Israel has hired the Hittite and Egyptian kings to attack us!" 7 So they got up and fled in the dusk and abandoned their tents and their horses and donkeys. They left the camp as it was and ran for their lives.

8 The men who had leprosy reached the edge of the camp and entered one of the tents. They ate and drank, and carried away silver, gold and clothes, and went off and hid them. They returned and entered another tent and took some things from it and hid them also.

9 Then they said to each other, "We're not doing right. This is a day of good news and we are keeping it to ourselves. If we wait until daylight, punishment will overtake us. Let's go at once and report this to the royal palace."

10 So they went and called out to the city gatekeepers and told them, "We went into the Aramean camp and not a man was there—not a sound of anyone—only tethered horses and donkeys, and the tents left just as they were." 11 The gatekeepers shouted the news, and it was reported within the palace.

12 The king got up in the night and said to his officers, "I will tell you what the Arameans have done to us. They know we are starving; so they have left the camp to hide in the countryside, thinking, 'They will surely come out, and then we will take them alive and get into the city.'"

13 One of his officers answered, "Have some men take five of the horses that are left in the city. Their plight will be like that of all the Israelites left here—yes, they will only be like all these Israelites who are doomed. So let us send them to find out what happened."

14 So they selected two chariots with their horses, and the king sent them after the Aramean army. He commanded the drivers, "Go and find out what has happened." 15 They followed them as far as the Jordan, and they found the whole road strewn with the clothing and equipment the Arameans had thrown away in their headlong flight. So the messengers returned and reported to the king. 16 Then the people went out and plundered the camp of the Arameans. So a seah of flour sold for a shekel, and two seahs of barley sold for a shekel, as the Lord had said.

17 Now the king had put the officer on whose arm he leaned in charge of the gate, and the people trampled him in the gateway, and he died, just as the man of God had foretold when the king came down to his house. 18 It happened as the man of God had said to the king: "About this time tomorrow, a seah of flour will sell for a shekel and two seahs of barley for a shekel at the gate of Samaria."

19 The officer had said to the man of God, "Look, even if the Lord should open the floodgates of the heavens, could this happen?" The man of God had replied, "You will see it with your own eyes, but you will not eat any of it!" 20 And that is exactly what happened to him, for the people trampled him in the gateway, and he died.

The Shunammite's Land Restored

8 Now Elisha had said to the woman whose son he had restored to life, "Go away with your family and stay for a while wherever you can, because the Lord has decreed a famine in the land that will last seven years." 2 The woman proceeded to do as the man of God said. She and her family went away and stayed in the land of the Philistines seven years.

3 At the end of the seven years she came back from the land of the Philistines and went to the king to beg for her house and land. 4 The king was talking to Gehazi, the servant of the man of God, and had said, "Tell me about all the great things Elisha has done." 5 Just as Gehazi was telling the king how Elisha had restored the dead to

---

a 3 The Hebrew word is used for various diseases affecting the skin—not necessarily leprosy; also in verse 8.

life, the woman whose son Elisha had brought back to life came to beg the king for her house and land.

Gehazi said, "This is the woman, my lord the king, and this is her son whom Elisha restored to life." 6The king asked the woman about it, and she told him.

Then he assigned an official to her case and said to him, "Give back everything that belonged to her, including all the income from her land from the day she left the country until now."

Hazael Murders Ben-Hadad

7Elisha went to Damascus, and Ben-Hadad king of Aram was ill. When the king was told, "The man of God has come all the way up here," 8he said to Hazael, "Take a gift with you and go to meet the man of God. Consult the LORD through him; ask him, 'Will I recover from this illness?' "

9Hazael went to meet Elisha, taking with him as a gift forty camel-loads of all the finest wares of Damascus. He went in and stood before him, and said, "Your son Ben-Hadad king of Aram has sent me to ask, 'Will I recover from this illness?' "

10Elisha answered, "Go and say to him, 'You will certainly recover'; buta the LORD has revealed to me that he will in fact die." 11He stared at him with a fixed gaze until Hazael felt ashamed. Then the man of God began to weep.

12"Why is my lord weeping?" asked Hazael.

"Because I know the harm you will do to the Israelites," he answered. "You will set fire to their fortified places, kill their young men with the sword, dash their little children to the ground, and rip open their pregnant women."

13Hazael said, "How could your servant, a mere dog, accomplish such a feat?"

"The LORD has shown me that you will become king of Aram," answered Elisha.

14Then Hazael left Elisha and returned to his master. When Ben-Hadad asked, "What did Elisha say to you?" Hazael replied, "He told me that you would certainly recover." 15But the next day he took a thick cloth, soaked it in water and spread it over the king's face, so that he died. Then Hazael succeeded him as king.

Jehoram King of Judah

16In the fifth year of Joram son of Ahab king of Israel, when Jehoshaphat was king of Judah, Jehoram son of Jehoshaphat began his reign as king of Judah. 17He was thirty-two years old when he became king, and he reigned in Jerusalem eight years. 18He walked in the ways of the kings of Israel, as the house of Ahab had done, for he married a daughter of Ahab. He did evil in the eyes of the LORD. 19Nevertheless, for the sake of his servant David, the LORD was not willing to destroy Judah. He had promised to maintain a lamp for David and his descendants forever.

20In the time of Jehoram, Edom rebelled against Judah and set up its own king. 21So Jehoramb went to Zair with all his chariots. The Edomites surrounded him and his chariot commanders, but he rose up and broke through by night; his army, however, fled back home. 22To this day Edom has been in rebellion against Judah. Libnah revolted at the same time.

23As for the other events of Jehoram's reign, and all he did, are they not written in the book of the annals of the kings of Judah? 24Jehoram rested with his fathers and was buried with them in the City of David. And Ahaziah his son succeeded him as king.

Ahaziah King of Judah

25In the twelfth year of Joram son of Ahab king of Israel, Ahaziah son of Jehoram king of Judah began to reign. 26Ahaziah was twenty-two years old when he became king, and he reigned in Jerusalem one year. His mother's name was Athaliah, a granddaughter of Omri king of Israel. 27He walked in the ways of the house of Ahab and did evil in the eyes of the LORD, as the house of Ahab had done, for he was related by marriage to Ahab's family.

28Ahaziah went with Joram son of Ahab to war against Hazael king of Aram at Ramoth Gilead. The Arameans wounded Joram; 29so King Joram returned to Jezreel to recover from the wounds the Arameans had inflicted on him at Ramothc in his battle with Hazael king of Aram.

Then Ahaziah son of Jehoram king of Judah went down to Jezreel to see Joram son of Ahab, because he had been wounded.

---

a 10 The Hebrew may also be read Go and say, 'You will certainly not recover,' for. b 21 Hebrew Joram, a variant of Jehoram; also in verses 23 and 24 c 29 Hebrew Ramah, a variant of Ramoth

Jehu Anointed King of Israel

9 The prophet Elisha summoned a man from the company of the prophets and said to him, "Tuck your cloak into your belt, take this flask of oil with you and go to Ramoth Gilead. ²When you get there, look for Jehu son of Jehoshaphat, the son of Nimshi. Go to him, get him away from his companions and take him into an inner room. ³Then take the flask and pour the oil on his head and declare, 'This is what the LORD says: I anoint you king over Israel.' Then open the door and run; don't delay!"

⁴So the young man, the prophet, went to Ramoth Gilead. ⁵When he arrived, he found the army officers sitting together. "I have a message for you, commander," he said.

"For which of us?" asked Jehu.

"For you, commander," he replied.

⁶Jehu got up and went into the house. Then the prophet poured the oil on Jehu's head and declared, "This is what the LORD, the God of Israel, says: 'I anoint you king over the LORD's people Israel. ⁷You are to destroy the house of Ahab your master, and I will avenge the blood of my servants the prophets and the blood of all the LORD's servants shed by Jezebel. ⁸The whole house of Ahab will perish. I will cut off from Ahab every last male in Israel—slave or free. ⁹I will make the house of Ahab like the house of Jeroboam son of Nebat and like the house of Baasha son of Ahijah. ¹⁰As for Jezebel, dogs will devour her on the plot of ground at Jezreel, and no one will bury her.' " Then he opened the door and ran.

¹¹When Jehu went out to his fellow officers, one of them asked him, "Is everything all right? Why did this madman come to you?"

"You know the man and the sort of things he says," Jehu replied.

¹²"That's not true!" they said. "Tell us."

Jehu said, "Here is what he told me: 'This is what the LORD says: I anoint you king over Israel.' "

¹³They hurried and took their cloaks and spread them under him on the bare steps. Then they blew the trumpet and shouted, "Jehu is king!"

Jehu Kills Joram and Ahaziah

¹⁴So Jehu son of Jehoshaphat, the son of Nimshi, conspired against Joram. (Now Joram and all Israel had been defending Ramoth Gilead against Hazael king of Aram, ¹⁵but King Joramª had returned to Jezreel to recover from the wounds the Arameans had inflicted on him in the battle with Hazael king of Aram.) Jehu said, "If this is the way you feel, don't let anyone slip out of the city to go and tell the news in Jezreel." ¹⁶Then he got into his chariot and rode to Jezreel, because Joram was resting there and Ahaziah king of Judah had gone down to see him.

ª 15 Hebrew *Jehoram*, a variant of *Joram*; also in verses 17 and 21–24

Get a Load of This...

Check out 2 Kings 9:10. You've heard of drive-thru restaurants, but what about drive-thru prophecy? OK, Elisha's prophet didn't exactly drive into Jehu's house to anoint him as king, but he didn't waste any time there either. He just dumped the oil and ran. It's a wonder he didn't slip on his way out!

Gross!

Check out 2 Kings 9:30–36. Jezebel shouldn't have bothered putting on makeup. It was only going to get smeared in a moment anyway. When Jehu's men went to bury her body, her face was nowhere to be found!

17When the lookout standing on the tower in Jezreel saw Jehu's troops approaching, he called out, "I see some troops coming."

"Get a horseman," Joram ordered. "Send him to meet them and ask, 'Do you come in peace?' "

18The horseman rode off to meet Jehu and said, "This is what the king says: 'Do you come in peace?' "

"What do you have to do with peace?" Jehu replied. "Fall in behind me."

The lookout reported, "The messenger has reached them, but he isn't coming back."

19So the king sent out a second horseman. When he came to them he said, "This is what the king says: 'Do you come in peace?' "

Jehu replied, "What do you have to do with peace? Fall in behind me."

20The lookout reported, "He has reached them, but he isn't coming back either. The driving is like that of Jehu son of Nimshi—he drives like a madman."

21"Hitch up my chariot," Joram ordered. And when it was hitched up, Joram king of Israel and Ahaziah king of Judah rode out, each in his own chariot, to meet Jehu. They met him at the plot of ground that had belonged to Naboth the Jezreelite. 22When Joram saw Jehu he asked, "Have you come in peace, Jehu?"

"How can there be peace," Jehu replied, "as long as all the idolatry and witchcraft of your mother Jezebel abound?"

23Joram turned about and fled, calling out to Ahaziah, "Treachery, Ahaziah!"

24Then Jehu drew his bow and shot Joram between the shoulders. The arrow pierced his heart and he slumped down in his chariot. 25Jehu said to Bidkar, his chariot officer, "Pick him up and throw him on the field that belonged to Naboth the Jezreelite. Remember how you and I were riding together in chariots behind Ahab his father when the LORD made this prophecy about him: 26'Yesterday I saw the blood of Naboth and the blood of his sons, declares the LORD, and I will surely make you pay for it on this plot of ground, declares the LORD.'ᵃ Now then, pick him up and throw him on that plot, in accordance with the word of the LORD."

27When Ahaziah king of Judah saw what had happened, he fled up the road to Beth Haggan.ᵇ Jehu chased him, shouting, "Kill him too!" They wounded him in his chariot on the way up to Gur near Ibleam, but he escaped to Megiddo and died there. 28His servants took him by chariot to Jerusalem and buried him with his fathers in his tomb in the City of David. 29(In the eleventh year of Joram son of Ahab, Ahaziah had become king of Judah.)

Jezebel Killed

30Then Jehu went to Jezreel. When Jezebel heard about it, she painted her eyes, arranged her hair and

ᵃ 26 See 1 Kings 21:19.　　ᵇ 27 Or fled by way of the garden house looked out of a window. ³¹As Jehu entered the gate, she asked, "Have you come in peace, Zimri, you murderer of your master?"ᵃ

³²He looked up at the window and called out, "Who is on my side? Who?" Two or three eunuchs looked down at him. ³³"Throw her down!" Jehu said. So they threw her down, and some of her blood spattered the wall and the horses as they trampled her underfoot.

³⁴Jehu went in and ate and drank. "Take care of that cursed woman," he said, "and bury her, for she was a king's daughter." ³⁵But when they went out to bury her, they found nothing except her skull, her feet and her hands. ³⁶They went back and told Jehu, who said, "This is the word of the LORD that he spoke through his servant Elijah the Tishbite: On the plot of ground at Jezreel dogs will devour Jezebel's flesh.ᵇ ³⁷Jezebel's body will be like refuse on the ground in the plot at Jezreel, so that no one will be able to say, 'This is Jezebel.' "

Ahab's Family Killed

10 Now there were in Samaria seventy sons of the house of Ahab. So Jehu wrote letters and sent them to Samaria: to the officials of Jezreel,ᶜ to the elders and to the guardians of Ahab's children. He said, ²"As soon as this letter reaches you, since your master's sons are with you and you have chariots and horses, a fortified city and weapons, ³choose the best and most worthy of your master's sons and set him on his father's throne. Then fight for your master's house."

⁴But they were terrified and said, "If two kings could not resist him, how can we?"

⁵So the palace administrator, the city governor, the elders and the guardians sent this message to Jehu: "We are your servants and we will do anything you say. We will not appoint anyone as king; you do whatever you think best."

⁶Then Jehu wrote them a second letter, saying, "If you are on my side and will obey me, take the heads of your master's sons and come to me in Jezreel by this time tomorrow."

Now the royal princes, seventy of them, were with the leading men of the city, who were rearing them. ⁷When the letter arrived, these men took the princes and slaughtered all seventy of them. They put their heads in baskets and sent them to Jehu in Jezreel. ⁸When the messenger arrived, he told Jehu, "They have brought the heads of the princes."

Then Jehu ordered, "Put them in two piles at the entrance of the city gate until morning."

⁹The next morning Jehu went out. He stood before all the people and said, "You are innocent. It was I who conspired against my master and killed him, but who killed all these? ¹⁰Know then, that not a word the LORD has spoken against the house of Ahab will fail. The LORD has done what he promised through his servant Elijah." ¹¹So Jehu killed everyone in Jezreel who remained of the house of Ahab, as well as all his chief men, his close friends and his priests, leaving him no survivor.

¹²Jehu then set out and went toward Samaria. At Beth Eked of the Shepherds, ¹³he met some relatives of Ahaziah king of Judah and asked, "Who are you?"

They said, "We are relatives of Ahaziah, and we have come down to greet the families of the king and of the queen mother."

¹⁴"Take them alive!" he ordered. So they took them alive and slaughtered them by the well of Beth Eked—forty-two men. He left no survivor.

¹⁵After he left there, he came upon Jehonadab son of Recab, who was on his way to meet him. Jehu greeted him and said, "Are you in accord with me, as I am with you?"

"I am," Jehonadab answered.

"If so," said Jehu, "give me your hand." So he did, and Jehu helped him up into the chariot. ¹⁶Jehu said, "Come with me and see my zeal for the LORD." Then he had him ride along in his chariot.

¹⁷When Jehu came to Samaria, he killed all who were left there of Ahab's family; he destroyed them, according to the word of the LORD spoken to Elijah.

Ministers of Baal Killed

¹⁸Then Jehu brought all the people together and said to them, "Ahab served Baal a little; Jehu will serve him much.

ᵃ 31 Or "Did Zimri have peace, who murdered his master?"   ᵇ 36 See 1 Kings 21:23.   ᶜ 1 Hebrew; some Septuagint manuscripts and Vulgate of the city

"Stay off the sidewalks!" That's about what people used to say when they saw Jehu come driving in his chariot. He was a wild man in lots of other ways, too, including how he whopped on God's enemies, the prophets of Baal (2 Kings 10:25).

19Now summon all the prophets of Baal, all his ministers and all his priests. See that no one is missing, because I am going to hold a great sacrifice for Baal. Anyone who fails to come will no longer live." But Jehu was acting deceptively in order to destroy the ministers of Baal.

20Jehu said, "Call an assembly in honor of Baal." So they proclaimed it. 21Then he sent word throughout Israel, and all the ministers of Baal came; not one stayed away. They crowded into the temple of Baal until it was full from one end to the other. 22And Jehu said to the keeper of the wardrobe, "Bring robes for all the ministers of Baal." So he brought out robes for them.

23Then Jehu and Jehonadab son of Recab went into the temple of Baal. Jehu said to the ministers of Baal, "Look around and see that no servants of the LORD are here with you—only ministers of Baal." 24So they went in to make sacrifices and burnt offerings. Now Jehu had posted eighty men outside with this warning: "If one of you lets any of the men I am placing in your hands escape, it will be your life for his life."

25As soon as Jehu had finished making the burnt offering, he ordered the guards and officers: "Go in and kill them; let no one escape." So they cut them down with the sword. The guards and officers threw the bodies out and then entered the inner shrine of the temple of Baal. 26They brought the sacred stone out of the temple of Baal and burned it. 27They demolished the sacred stone of Baal and tore down the temple of Baal, and people have used it for a latrine to this day.

28So Jehu destroyed Baal worship in Israel. 29However, he did not turn away from the sins of Jeroboam son of Nebat, which he had caused Israel to commit—the worship of the golden calves at Bethel and Dan.

30The LORD said to Jehu, "Because you have done well in accomplishing what is right in my eyes and have done to the house of Ahab all I had in mind to do, your descendants will sit on the throne of Israel to the fourth generation." 31Yet Jehu was not careful to keep the law of the LORD, the God of Israel, with all his heart. He did not turn away from the sins of Jeroboam, which he had caused Israel to commit.

32In those days the LORD began to reduce the size of Israel. Hazael overpowered the Israelites throughout their territory 33east of the Jordan in all the land of Gilead (the region of Gad, Reuben and Manasseh), from Aroer by the Arnon Gorge through Gilead to Bashan.

34As for the other events of Jehu's reign, all he did, and all his achievements, are they not written in the book of the annals of the kings of Israel?

35Jehu rested with his fathers and was buried in Samaria. And Jehoahaz his son succeeded him as king. 36The time that Jehu reigned over Israel in Samaria was twenty-eight years.

Athaliah and Joash

11 When Athaliah the mother of Ahaziah saw that her son was dead, she proceeded to destroy the whole royal family. ²But Jehosheba, the daughter of King Jehoram[a] and sister of Ahaziah, took Joash son of Ahaziah and stole him away from among the royal princes, who were about to be murdered. She put him and his nurse in a bedroom to hide him from Athaliah; so he was not killed. ³He remained hidden with his nurse at the temple of the LORD for six years while Athaliah ruled the land.

⁴In the seventh year Jehoiada sent for the commanders of units of a hundred, the Carites and the guards and had them brought to him at the temple of the LORD. He made a covenant with them and put them under oath at the temple of the LORD. Then he showed them the king's son. ⁵He commanded them, saying, "This is what you are to do: You who are in the three companies that are going on duty on the Sabbath—a third of you guarding the royal palace, ⁶a third at the Sur Gate, and a third at the gate behind the guard, who take turns guarding the temple—⁷and you who are in the other two companies that normally go off Sabbath duty are all to guard the temple for the king. ⁸Station yourselves around the king, each man with his weapon in his hand. Anyone who approaches your ranks[b] must be put to death. Stay close to the king wherever he goes."

⁹The commanders of units of a hundred did just as Jehoiada the priest ordered. Each one took his men—those who were going on duty on the Sabbath and those who were going off duty—and came to Jehoiada the priest. ¹⁰Then he gave the commanders the spears and shields that had belonged to King David and that were in the temple of the LORD. ¹¹The guards, each with his weapon in his hand, stationed themselves around the king—near the altar and the temple, from the south side to the north side of the temple.

¹²Jehoiada brought out the king's son and put the crown on him; he presented him with a copy of the covenant and proclaimed him king. They anointed him, and the people clapped their hands and shouted, "Long live the king!"

¹³When Athaliah heard the noise made by the guards and the people, she went to the people at the temple of the LORD. ¹⁴She looked and there was the king, standing by the pillar, as the custom was. The officers and the trumpeters were beside the king, and all the people of the land were rejoicing and blowing trumpets. Then Athaliah tore her robes and called out, "Treason! Treason!"

¹⁵Jehoiada the priest ordered the commanders of units of a hundred, who were in charge of the troops: "Bring her out between the ranks[c] and put to the sword anyone who follows her." For the priest had said, "She must not be put to death in the temple of the LORD." ¹⁶So they seized her as she reached the place where the horses enter the palace grounds, and there she was put to death.

¹⁷Jehoiada then made a covenant between the LORD and the king and people that they would be the LORD's people. He also made a covenant between the king and the people. ¹⁸All the people of the land went to the temple of Baal and tore it down. They smashed the altars and idols to pieces and killed Mattan the priest of Baal in front of the altars.

Then Jehoiada the priest posted guards at the temple of the LORD. ¹⁹He took with him the commanders of hundreds, the Carites, the guards and all the people of the land, and together they brought the king down from the temple of the LORD and went into the palace, entering by way of the gate of the guards. The king then took his place on the royal throne, ²⁰and all the people of the land rejoiced. And the city was quiet, because Athaliah had been slain with the sword at the palace.

²¹Joash[d] was seven years old when he began to reign.

Joash Repairs the Temple

12 In the seventh year of Jehu, Joash[e] became king, and he reigned in Jerusalem forty years. His mother's name was Zibiah; she was from Beersheba. ²Joash did what was right in the eyes of the LORD all the years Jehoiada the priest instructed him. ³The high places, however, were not removed;

---

a 2 Hebrew *Joram,* a variant of *Jehoram*   *b 8* Or *approaches the precincts*   *c 15* Or *out from the precincts*
d 21 Hebrew *Jehoash,* a variant of *Joash*   *e 1* Hebrew *Jehoash,* a variant of *Joash*; also in verses 2, 4, 6, 7 and 18

the people continued to offer sacrifices and burn incense there.

⁴Joash said to the priests, "Collect all the money that is brought as sacred offerings to the temple of the LORD—the money collected in the census, the money received from personal vows and the money brought voluntarily to the temple. ⁵Let every priest receive the money from one of the treasurers, and let it be used to repair whatever damage is found in the temple."

⁶But by the twenty-third year of King Joash the priests still had not repaired the temple. ⁷Therefore King Joash summoned Jehoiada the priest and the other priests and asked them, "Why aren't you repairing the damage done to the temple? Take no more money from your treasurers, but hand it over for repairing the temple." ⁸The priests agreed that they would not collect any more money from the people and that they would not repair the temple themselves.

⁹Jehoiada the priest took a chest and bored a hole in its lid. He placed it beside the altar, on the right side as one enters the temple of the LORD. The priests who guarded the entrance put into the chest all the money that was brought to the temple of the LORD. ¹⁰Whenever they saw that there was a large amount of money in the chest, the royal secretary and the high priest came, counted the money that had been brought into the temple of the LORD and put it into bags. ¹¹When the amount had been determined, they gave the money to the men appointed to supervise the work on the temple. With it they paid those who worked on the temple of the LORD—the carpenters and builders, ¹²the masons and stonecutters. They purchased timber and dressed stone for the repair of the temple of the LORD, and met all the other expenses of restoring the temple.

¹³The money brought into the temple was not spent for making silver basins, wick trimmers, sprinkling bowls, trumpets or any other articles of gold or silver for the temple of the LORD; ¹⁴it was paid to the workmen, who used it to repair the temple. ¹⁵They did not require an accounting from those to whom they gave the money to pay the workers, because they acted with complete honesty. ¹⁶The money from the guilt offerings and sin offerings was not brought into the temple of the LORD; it belonged to the priests.

¹⁷About this time Hazael king of Aram went up and attacked Gath and captured it. Then he turned to attack Jerusalem. ¹⁸But Joash king of Judah took all the sacred objects dedicated by his fathers—Jehoshaphat, Jehoram and Ahaziah, the kings of Judah—and the gifts he himself had dedicated and all the gold found in the treasuries of the temple of the LORD and of the royal palace, and he sent them to Hazael king of Aram, who then withdrew from Jerusalem.

¹⁹As for the other events of the reign of Joash, and all he did, are they not written in the book of the annals of the kings of Judah? ²⁰His officials conspired against him and assassinated him at Beth Millo, on the road down to Silla. ²¹The officials who murdered him were Jozabad son of Shimeath and Jehozabad son of Shomer. He died and was buried with his fathers in the City of David. And Amaziah his son succeeded him as king.

Jehoahaz King of Israel

13 In the twenty-third year of Joash son of Ahaziah king of Judah, Jehoahaz son of Jehu became king of Israel in Samaria, and he reigned seventeen years. ²He did evil in the eyes of the LORD by following the sins of Jeroboam son of Nebat, which he had caused Israel to commit, and he did not turn away from them. ³So the LORD's anger burned against Israel, and for a long time he kept them under the power of Hazael king of Aram and Ben-Hadad his son.

⁴Then Jehoahaz sought the LORD's favor, and the LORD listened to him, for he saw how severely the king of Aram was oppressing Israel. ⁵The LORD provided a deliverer for Israel, and they escaped from the power of Aram. So the Israelites lived in their own homes as they had before. ⁶But they did not turn away from the sins of the house of Jeroboam, which he had caused Israel to commit; they continued in them. Also, the Asherah pole[a] remained standing in Samaria.

⁷Nothing had been left of the army of Jehoahaz except fifty horsemen, ten chariots and ten thousand foot soldiers, for

---

[a] 6 That is, a symbol of the goddess Asherah; here and elsewhere in 2 Kings

the king of Aram had destroyed the rest and made them like the dust at threshing time.

⁸As for the other events of the reign of Jehoahaz, all he did and his achievements, are they not written in the book of the annals of the kings of Israel? ⁹Jehoahaz rested with his fathers and was buried in Samaria. And Jehoash*a* his son succeeded him as king.

Jehoash King of Israel

¹⁰In the thirty-seventh year of Joash king of Judah, Jehoash son of Jehoahaz became king of Israel in Samaria, and he reigned sixteen years. ¹¹He did evil in the eyes of the LORD and did not turn away from any of the sins of Jeroboam son of Nebat, which he had caused Israel to commit; he continued in them.

¹²As for the other events of the reign of Jehoash, all he did and his achievements, including his war against Amaziah king of Judah, are they not written in the book of the annals of the kings of Israel? ¹³Jehoash rested with his fathers, and Jeroboam succeeded him on the throne. Jehoash was buried in Samaria with the kings of Israel.

¹⁴Now Elisha was suffering from the illness from which he died. Jehoash king of Israel went down to see him and wept over him. "My father! My father!" he cried. "The chariots and horsemen of Israel!"

¹⁵Elisha said, "Get a bow and some arrows," and he did so. ¹⁶"Take the bow in your hands," he said to the king of Israel. When he had taken it, Elisha put his hands on the king's hands.

¹⁷"Open the east window," he said, and he opened it. "Shoot!" Elisha said, and he shot. "The LORD's arrow of victory, the arrow of victory over Aram!" Elisha declared. "You will completely destroy the Arameans at Aphek."

¹⁸Then he said, "Take the arrows," and the king took them. Elisha told him, "Strike the ground." He struck it three times and stopped. ¹⁹The man of God was angry with him and said, "You should have struck the ground five or six times; then you would have defeated Aram and completely destroyed it. But now you will defeat it only three times."

²⁰Elisha died and was buried.

Now Moabite raiders used to enter the country every spring. ²¹Once while some Israelites were burying a man, suddenly they saw a band of raiders; so they threw the man's body into Elisha's tomb. When the body touched Elisha's bones, the man came to life and stood up on his feet.

²²Hazael king of Aram oppressed Israel throughout the reign of Jehoahaz. ²³But the LORD was gracious to them and had compassion and showed concern for them because of his covenant with Abraham, Isaac and Jacob. To this day he has been unwilling to destroy them or banish them from his presence.

²⁴Hazael king of Aram died, and Ben-Hadad his son succeeded him as king. ²⁵Then Jehoash son of Jehoahaz

Get a Load of This...

Elisha "supersized" his order of anointing so that he had twice the power of Elijah (2 Kings 2:9). Sure enough, he did exactly twice as many miracles as Elijah, when you include the final one when his bones pulled off after he was dead (2 Kings 13:21). Imagine how surprised his friends were when he scrambled back out of the tomb—alive!

---

a 9 Hebrew Joash, a variant of *Jehoash;* also in verses 12–14 and 25 recaptured from Ben-Hadad son of Hazael the towns he had taken in battle from his father Jehoahaz. Three times Jehoash defeated him, and so he recovered the Israelite towns.

Amaziah King of Judah

In the second year of Jehoash[a] son of Jehoahaz king of Israel, Amaziah son of Joash king of Judah began to reign. 2He was twenty-five years old when he became king, and he reigned in Jerusalem twenty-nine years. His mother's name was Jehoaddin; she was from Jerusalem. 3He did what was right in the eyes of the LORD, but not as his father David had done. In everything he followed the example of his father Joash. 4The high places, however, were not removed; the people continued to offer sacrifices and burn incense there.

5After the kingdom was firmly in his grasp, he executed the officials who had murdered his father the king. 6Yet he did not put the sons of the assassins to death, in accordance with what is written in the Book of the Law of Moses where the LORD commanded: "Fathers shall not be put to death for their children, nor children put to death for their fathers; each is to die for his own sins."[b]

7He was the one who defeated ten thousand Edomites in the Valley of Salt and captured Sela in battle, calling it Joktheel, the name it has to this day.

8Then Amaziah sent messengers to Jehoash son of Jehoahaz, the son of Jehu, king of Israel, with the challenge: "Come, meet me face to face."

9But Jehoash king of Israel replied to Amaziah king of Judah: "A thistle in Lebanon sent a message to a cedar in Lebanon, 'Give your daughter to my son in marriage.' Then a wild beast in Lebanon came along and trampled the thistle underfoot. 10You have indeed defeated Edom and now you are arrogant. Glory in your victory, but stay at home! Why ask for trouble and cause your own downfall and that of Judah also?"

11Amaziah, however, would not listen, so Jehoash king of Israel attacked. He and Amaziah king of Judah faced each other at Beth Shemesh in Judah. 12Judah was routed by Israel, and every man fled to his home. 13Jehoash king of Israel captured Amaziah king of Judah, the son of Joash, the son of Ahaziah, at Beth Shemesh. Then Jehoash went to Jerusalem and broke down the wall of Jerusalem from the Ephraim Gate to the Corner Gate—a section about six hundred feet long.[c] 14He took all the gold and silver and all the articles found in the temple of the LORD and in the treasuries of the royal palace. He also took hostages and returned to Samaria.

15As for the other events of the reign of Jehoash, what he did and his achievements, including his war against Amaziah king of Judah, are they not written in the book of the annals of the kings of Israel? 16Jehoash rested with his fathers and was buried in Samaria with the kings of Israel. And Jeroboam his son succeeded him as king.

17Amaziah son of Joash king of Judah lived for fifteen years after the death of Jehoash son of Jehoahaz king of Israel. 18As for the other events of Amaziah's reign, are they not written in the book of the annals of the kings of Judah?

19They conspired against him in Jerusalem, and he fled to Lachish, but they sent men after him to Lachish and killed him there. 20He was brought back by horse and was buried in Jerusalem with his fathers, in the City of David.

21Then all the people of Judah took Azariah,[d] who was sixteen years old, and made him king in place of his father Amaziah. 22He was the one who rebuilt Elath and restored it to Judah after Amaziah rested with his fathers.

Jeroboam II King of Israel

23In the fifteenth year of Amaziah son of Joash king of Judah, Jeroboam son of Jehoash king of Israel became king in Samaria, and he reigned forty-one years. 24He did evil in the eyes of the LORD and did not turn away from any of the sins of Jeroboam son of Nebat, which he had caused Israel to commit. 25He was the one who restored the boundaries of Israel from Lebo[e] Hamath to the Sea of the Arabah,[f] in accordance with the word of the LORD, the God of Israel, spoken through his servant Jonah son of Amittai, the prophet from Gath Hepher. 26The LORD had seen how bitterly every-

---

a 1 Hebrew Joash, a variant of Jehoash; also in verses 13, 23 and 27　b 6 Deut. 24:16　c 13 Hebrew four hundred cubits (about 180 meters)　d 21 Also called Uzziah
e 25 Or from the entrance to　f 25 That is, the Dead Sea

one in Israel, whether slave or free, was suffering; there was no one to help them. [27]And since the LORD had not said he would blot out the name of Israel from under heaven, he saved them by the hand of Jeroboam son of Jehoash.

[28]As for the other events of Jeroboam's reign, all he did, and his military achievements, including how he recovered for Israel both Damascus and Hamath, which had belonged to Yaudi,[a] are they not written in the book of the annals of the kings of Israel? [29]Jeroboam rested with his fathers, the kings of Israel. And Zechariah his son succeeded him as king.

Azariah King of Judah

In the twenty-seventh year of Jeroboam king of Israel, Azariah son of Amaziah king of Judah began to reign. [2]He was sixteen years old when he became king, and he reigned in Jerusalem fifty-two years. His mother's name was Jecoliah; she was from Jerusalem. [3]He did what was right in the eyes of the LORD, just as his father Amaziah had done. [4]The high places, however, were not removed; the people continued to offer sacrifices and burn incense there.

[5]The LORD afflicted the king with leprosy[b] until the day he died, and he lived in a separate house.[c] Jotham the king's son had charge of the palace and governed the people of the land.

[6]As for the other events of Azariah's reign, and all he did, are they not written in the book of the annals of the kings of Judah? [7]Azariah rested with his fathers and was buried near them in the City of David. And Jotham his son succeeded him as king.

Zechariah King of Israel

[8]In the thirty-eighth year of Azariah king of Judah, Zechariah son of Jeroboam became king of Israel in Samaria, and he reigned six months. [9]He did evil in the eyes of the LORD, as his fathers had done. He did not turn away from the sins of Jeroboam son of Nebat, which he had caused Israel to commit.

[10]Shallum son of Jabesh conspired against Zechariah. He attacked him in front of the people,[d] assassinated him and succeeded him as king. [11]The other events of Zechariah's reign are written in the book of the annals of the kings of Israel. [12]So the word of the LORD spoken to Jehu was fulfilled: "Your descendants will sit on the throne of Israel to the fourth generation."[e]

Shallum King of Israel

[13]Shallum son of Jabesh became king in the thirty-ninth year of Uzziah king of Judah, and he reigned in Samaria one month. [14]Then Menahem son of Gadi went from Tirzah up to Samaria. He attacked Shallum son of Jabesh in Samaria, assassinated him and succeeded him as king.

[15]The other events of Shallum's reign, and the conspiracy he led, are written in the book of the annals of the kings of Israel.

[16]At that time Menahem, starting out from Tirzah, attacked Tiphsah and everyone in the city and its vicinity, because they refused to open their gates. He sacked Tiphsah and ripped open all the pregnant women.

Menahem King of Israel

[17]In the thirty-ninth year of Azariah king of Judah, Menahem son of Gadi became king of Israel, and he reigned in Samaria ten years. [18]He did evil in the eyes of the LORD. During his entire reign he did not turn away from the sins of Jeroboam son of Nebat, which he had caused Israel to commit.

[19]Then Pul[f] king of Assyria invaded the land, and Menahem gave him a thousand talents[g] of silver to gain his support and strengthen his own hold on the kingdom. [20]Menahem exacted this money from Israel. Every wealthy man had to contribute fifty shekels[h] of silver to be given to the king of Assyria. So the king of Assyria withdrew and stayed in the land no longer.

[21]As for the other events of Menahem's reign, and all he did, are they not written in the book of the annals of the kings of Israel? [22]Menahem rested with his fathers. And Pekahiah his son succeeded him as king.

---

[a] 28 Or Judah   [b] 5 The Hebrew word was used for various diseases affecting the skin—not necessarily leprosy.
[c] 5 Or in a house where he was relieved of responsibility
[d] 10 Hebrew; some Septuagint manuscripts in Ibleam
[e] 12 2 Kings 10:30   [f] 19 Also called Tiglath-Pileser
[g] 19 That is, about 37 tons (about 34 metric tons)
[h] 20 That is, about 1 1/4 pounds (about 0.6 kilogram)

Pekahiah King of Israel

23 In the fiftieth year of Azariah king of Judah, Pekahiah son of Menahem became king of Israel in Samaria, and he reigned two years. 24 Pekahiah did evil in the eyes of the LORD. He did not turn away from the sins of Jeroboam son of Nebat, which he had caused Israel to commit. 25 One of his chief officers, Pekah son of Remaliah, conspired against him. Taking fifty men of Gilead with him, he assassinated Pekahiah, along with Argob and Arieh, in the citadel of the royal palace at Samaria. So Pekah killed Pekahiah and succeeded him as king.

26 The other events of Pekahiah's reign, and all he did, are written in the book of the annals of the kings of Israel.

Pekah King of Israel

27 In the fifty-second year of Azariah king of Judah, Pekah son of Remaliah became king of Israel in Samaria, and he reigned twenty years. 28 He did evil in the eyes of the LORD. He did not turn away from the sins of Jeroboam son of Nebat, which he had caused Israel to commit.

29 In the time of Pekah king of Israel, Tiglath-Pileser king of Assyria came and took Ijon, Abel Beth Maacah, Janoah, Kedesh and Hazor. He took Gilead and Galilee, including all the land of Naphtali, and deported the people to Assyria. 30 Then Hoshea son of Elah conspired against Pekah son of Remaliah. He attacked and assassinated him, and then succeeded him as king in the twentieth year of Jotham son of Uzziah.

31 As for the other events of Pekah's reign, and all he did, are they not written in the book of the annals of the kings of Israel?

Jotham King of Judah

32 In the second year of Pekah son of Remaliah king of Israel, Jotham son of Uzziah king of Judah began to reign. 33 He was twenty-five years old when he became king, and he reigned in Jerusalem sixteen years. His mother's name was Jerusha daughter of Zadok. 34 He did what was right in the eyes of the LORD, just as his father Uzziah had done. 35 The high places, however, were not removed; the people continued to offer sacrifices and burn incense there. Jotham rebuilt the Upper Gate of the temple of the LORD.

36 As for the other events of Jotham's reign, and what he did, are they not written in the book of the annals of the kings of Judah? 37 (In those days the LORD began to send Rezin king of Aram and Pekah son of Remaliah against Judah.) 38 Jotham rested with his fathers and was buried with them in the City of David, the city of his father. And Ahaz his son succeeded him as king.

Ahaz King of Judah

16 In the seventeenth year of Pekah son of Remaliah, Ahaz son of Jotham king of Judah began to reign. 2 Ahaz was twenty years old when he became king, and he reigned in Jerusalem sixteen years. Unlike David his father, he did not do what was right in the eyes of the LORD his God. 3 He walked in the ways of the kings of Israel and even sacrificed his son in*a* the fire, following the detestable ways of the nations the LORD had driven out before the Israelites. 4 He offered sacrifices and burned incense at the high places, on the hilltops and under every spreading tree.

5 Then Rezin king of Aram and Pekah son of Remaliah king of Israel marched up to fight against Jerusalem and besieged Ahaz, but they could not overpower him. 6 At that time, Rezin king of Aram recovered Elath for Aram by driving out the men of Judah. Edomites then moved into Elath and have lived there to this day.

7 Ahaz sent messengers to say to Tiglath-Pileser king of Assyria, "I am your servant and vassal. Come up and save me out of the hand of the king of Aram and of the king of Israel, who are attacking me." 8 And Ahaz took the silver and gold found in the temple of the LORD and in the treasuries of the royal palace and sent it as a gift to the king of Assyria. 9 The king of Assyria complied by attacking Damascus and capturing it. He deported its inhabitants to Kir and put Rezin to death.

10 Then King Ahaz went to Damascus to meet Tiglath-Pileser king of Assyria. He saw an altar in Damascus and sent to Uriah the priest a sketch of the altar, with detailed plans for its construction. 11 So Uriah the priest built an altar in accordance with all the plans that King Ahaz had sent from Damascus and finished it before

a 3 Or even made his son pass through

King Ahaz returned. 12When the king came back from Damascus and saw the altar, he approached it and presented offerings[a] on it. 13He offered up his burnt offering and grain offering, poured out his drink offering, and sprinkled the blood of his fellowship offerings[b] on the altar. 14The bronze altar that stood before the LORD he brought from the front of the temple—from between the new altar and the temple of the LORD—and put it on the north side of the new altar.

15King Ahaz then gave these orders to Uriah the priest: "On the large new altar, offer the morning burnt offering and the evening grain offering, the king's burnt offering and his grain offering, and the burnt offering of all the people of the land, and their grain offering and their drink offering. Sprinkle on the altar all the blood of the burnt offerings and sacrifices. But I will use the bronze altar for seeking guidance." 16And Uriah the priest did just as King Ahaz had ordered.

17King Ahaz took away the side panels and removed the basins from the movable stands. He removed the Sea from the bronze bulls that supported it and set it on a stone base. 18He took away the Sabbath canopy[c] that had been built at the temple and removed the royal entryway outside the temple of the LORD, in deference to the king of Assyria.

19As for the other events of the reign of Ahaz, and what he did, are they not written in the book of the annals of the kings of Judah? 20Ahaz rested with his fathers and was buried with them in the City of David. And Hezekiah his son succeeded him as king.

Hoshea Last King of Israel

17 In the twelfth year of Ahaz king of Judah, Hoshea son of Elah became king of Israel in Samaria, and he reigned nine years. 2He

a 12 Or and went up   b 13 Traditionally peace offerings
c 18 Or the dais of his throne (see Septuagint)

Compromise Quicksand

READ 2 KINGS 17

Murderers, idol worshipers, baby-sacrificers. These were the rulers of Israel. The Israelites were destroyed by the Assyrians because they and their kings "persisted in all the sins of Jeroboam" (verse 22). Remember Jeroboam? When the kingdom was split into two nations after King Solomon, Jeroboam became the first king of the northern kingdom of Israel. He started the nation worshiping the golden calves (1 Kings 12:26–32). Then, slowly but surely, they made more compromises and became worse and worse until they were so far gone they didn't know right from wrong anymore. Compromise starts small, but it soon grows out of control until one day people find themselves in a situation they never dreamed they'd be in. It's like a kid who only tells "little" lies and cheats on his tests. No big deal? Well, when he's an adult, Little Cheater might end up in jail for fraud. Don't get caught in compromise quicksand. Be radical for God, and stop compromise before it starts.

Your next reading is on page 504.

did evil in the eyes of the LORD, but not like the kings of Israel who preceded him.

³Shalmaneser king of Assyria came up to attack Hoshea, who had been Shalmaneser's vassal and had paid him tribute. ⁴But the king of Assyria discovered that Hoshea was a traitor, for he had sent envoys to So[a] king of Egypt, and he no longer paid tribute to the king of Assyria, as he had done year by year. Therefore Shalmaneser seized him and put him in prison. ⁵The king of Assyria invaded the entire land, marched against Samaria and laid siege to it for three years. ⁶In the ninth year of Hoshea, the king of Assyria captured Samaria and deported the Israelites to Assyria. He settled them in Halah, in Gozan on the Habor River and in the towns of the Medes.

Israel Exiled Because of Sin

⁷All this took place because the Israelites had sinned against the LORD their God, who had brought them up out of Egypt from under the power of Pharaoh king of Egypt. They worshiped other gods ⁸and followed the practices of the nations the LORD had driven out before them, as well as the practices that the kings of Israel had introduced. ⁹The Israelites secretly did things against the LORD their God that were not right. From watchtower to fortified city they built themselves high places in all their towns. ¹⁰They set up sacred stones and Asherah poles on every high hill and under every spreading tree. ¹¹At every high place they burned incense, as the nations whom the LORD had driven out before them had done. They did wicked things that provoked the LORD to anger. ¹²They worshiped idols, though the LORD had said, "You shall not do this."[b] ¹³The LORD warned Israel and Judah through all his prophets and seers: "Turn from your evil ways. Observe my commands and de-

[a] 4 Or to Sais, to the; So is possibly an abbreviation for Osorkon.   [b] 12 Exodus 20:4,5

Make It Stick

READ 2 KINGS 17:1–6

The northern kingdom was gone! Why? As verses 7–23 say, they absolutely refused to listen to God's warnings, so God allowed Assyria to carry them away. We need to be careful not to close our ears to God's Word. On a sticky note, write down one thing you need to listen to God about today.

crees, in accordance with the entire Law that I commanded your fathers to obey and that I delivered to you through my servants the prophets."

14But they would not listen and were as stiff-necked as their fathers, who did not trust in the LORD their God. 15They rejected his decrees and the covenant he had made with their fathers and the warnings he had given them. They followed worthless idols and themselves became worthless. They imitated the nations around them although the LORD had ordered them, "Do not do as they do," and they did the things the LORD had forbidden them to do.

16They forsook all the commands of the LORD their God and made for themselves two idols cast in the shape of calves, and an Asherah pole. They bowed down to all the starry hosts, and they worshiped Baal. 17They sacrificed their sons and daughters in[a] the fire. They practiced divination and sorcery and sold themselves to do evil in the eyes of the LORD, provoking him to anger.

18So the LORD was very angry with Israel and removed them from his presence. Only the tribe of Judah was left, 19and even Judah did not keep the commands of the LORD their God. They followed the practices Israel had introduced. 20Therefore the LORD rejected all the people of Israel; he afflicted them and gave them into the hands of plunderers, until he thrust them from his presence.

21When he tore Israel away from the house of David, they made Jeroboam son of Nebat their king. Jeroboam enticed Israel away from following the LORD and caused them to commit a great sin. 22The Israelites persisted in all the sins of Jeroboam and did not turn away from them 23until the LORD removed them from his presence, as he had warned through all his servants the prophets. So the people of Israel were taken from their homeland into exile in Assyria, and they are still there.

Samaria Resettled

24The king of Assyria brought people from Babylon, Cuthah, Avva, Hamath and Sepharvaim and settled them in the towns of Samaria to replace the Israelites. They took over Samaria and lived in its towns. 25When they first lived there, they did not worship the LORD; so he sent lions among them and they killed some of the people.

26It was reported to the king of Assyria: "The people you deported and resettled in the towns of Samaria do not know what the god of that country requires. He has sent lions among them, which are killing them off, because the people do not know what he requires."

27Then the king of Assyria gave this order: "Have one of the priests you took captive from Samaria go back to live there and teach the people what the god of the land requires." 28So one of the priests who had been exiled from Samaria came to live in Bethel and taught them how to worship the LORD.

29Nevertheless, each national group made its own gods in the several towns where they settled, and set them up in the shrines the people of Samaria had made at the high places. 30The men from Babylon made Succoth Benoth, the men from Cuthah made Nergal, and the men from Hamath made Ashima; 31the Avvites made Nibhaz and Tartak, and the Sepharvites burned their children in the fire as sacrifices to Adrammelech and Anammelech, the gods of Sepharvaim. 32They worshiped the LORD, but they also appointed all sorts of their own people to officiate for them as priests in the shrines at the high places. 33They worshiped the LORD, but they also served their own gods in accordance with the customs of the nations from which they had been brought.

34To this day they persist in their former practices. They neither worship the LORD nor adhere to the decrees and ordinances, the laws and commands that the LORD gave the descendants of Jacob, whom he named Israel. 35When the LORD made a covenant with the Israelites, he commanded them: "Do not worship any other gods or bow down to them, serve them or sacrifice to them. 36But the LORD, who brought you up out of Egypt with mighty power and outstretched arm, is the one you must worship. To him you shall bow down and to him offer sacrifices. 37You must always be careful to keep the decrees and ordinances, the laws and commands he wrote for you. Do not worship other gods. 38Do not forget the covenant I have made with you, and do not worship other gods. 39Rather, worship the LORD

a 17 Or They made their sons and daughters pass through

your God; it is he who will deliver you from the hand of all your enemies."

⁴⁰They would not listen, however, but persisted in their former practices. ⁴¹Even while these people were worshiping the LORD, they were serving their idols. To this day their children and grandchildren continue to do as their fathers did.

Hezekiah King of Judah

18 In the third year of Hoshea son of Elah king of Israel, Hezekiah son of Ahaz king of Judah began to reign. ²He was twenty-five years old when he became king, and he reigned in Jerusalem twenty-nine years. His mother's name was Abijahᵃ daughter of Zechariah. ³He did what was right in the eyes of the LORD, just as his father David had done. ⁴He removed the high places, smashed the sacred stones and cut down the Asherah poles. He broke into pieces the bronze snake Moses had made, for up to that time the Israelites had been burning incense to it. (It was calledᵇ Nehushtan.ᶜ)

⁵Hezekiah trusted in the LORD, the God of Israel. There was no one like him among all the kings of Judah, either before him or after him. ⁶He held fast to the LORD and did not cease to follow him; he kept the commands the LORD had given Moses. ⁷And the LORD was with him; he was successful in whatever he undertook. He rebelled against the king of Assyria and did not serve him. ⁸From watchtower to fortified city, he defeated the Philistines, as far as Gaza and its territory.

⁹In King Hezekiah's fourth year, which was the seventh year of Hoshea son of Elah king of Israel, Shalmaneser king of Assyria marched against Samaria and laid siege to it. ¹⁰At the end of three years the Assyrians took it. So Samaria was captured in Hezekiah's sixth year, which was the ninth year of Hoshea king of Israel. ¹¹The king of Assyria deported Israel to Assyria and settled them in Halah, in Gozan on the Habor River and in towns of the Medes. ¹²This happened because they had not obeyed the LORD their God, but had violated his covenant—all that Moses the servant of the LORD commanded. They neither listened to the commands nor carried them out.

¹³In the fourteenth year of King Hezekiah's reign, Sennacherib king of Assyria attacked all the fortified cities of Judah and captured them. ¹⁴So Hezekiah king of Judah sent this message to the king of Assyria at Lachish: "I have done wrong. Withdraw from me, and I will pay whatever you demand of me." The king of Assyria exacted from Hezekiah king of Judah three hundred talentsᵈ of silver and thirty talentsᵉ of gold. ¹⁵So Hezekiah gave him all the silver that was found in the temple of the LORD and in the treasuries of the royal palace.

¹⁶At this time Hezekiah king of Judah stripped off the gold with which he had covered the doors and doorposts of the temple of the LORD, and gave it to the king of Assyria.

Sennacherib Threatens Jerusalem

¹⁷The king of Assyria sent his supreme commander, his chief officer and his field commander with a large army, from Lachish to King Hezekiah at Jerusalem. They came up to Jerusalem and stopped at the aqueduct of the Upper Pool, on the road to the Washerman's Field. ¹⁸They called for the king; and Eliakim son of Hilkiah the palace administrator, Shebna the secretary, and Joah son of Asaph the recorder went out to them.

¹⁹The field commander said to them, "Tell Hezekiah:

" 'This is what the great king, the king of Assyria, says: On what are you basing this confidence of yours? ²⁰You say you have strategy and military strength—but you speak only empty words. On whom are you depending, that you rebel against me? ²¹Look now, you are depending on Egypt, that splintered reed of a staff, which pierces a man's hand and wounds him if he leans on it! Such is Pharaoh king of Egypt to all who depend on him. ²²And if you say to me, "We are depending on the LORD our God"—isn't he the one whose high places and altars Hezekiah removed, saying to Judah and Jerusalem, "You must worship before this altar in Jerusalem"?

²³" 'Come now, make a bargain

ᵃ 2 Hebrew Abi, a variant of Abijah　ᵇ 4 Or He called it
ᶜ 4 Nehushtan sounds like the Hebrew for bronze and snake and unclean thing.　ᵈ 14 That is, about 11 tons (about 10 metric tons)　ᵉ 14 That is, about 1 ton (about 1 metric ton)

with my master, the king of Assyria: I will give you two thousand horses— if you can put riders on them! 24How can you repulse one officer of the least of my master's officials, even though you are depending on Egypt for chariots and horsemen*a*? 25Furthermore, have I come to attack and destroy this place without word from the LORD? The LORD himself told me to march against this country and destroy it.' "

26Then Eliakim son of Hilkiah, and Shebna and Joah said to the field commander, "Please speak to your servants in Aramaic, since we understand it. Don't speak to us in Hebrew in the hearing of the people on the wall."

27But the commander replied, "Was it only to your master and you that my master sent me to say these things, and not to the men sitting on the wall—who, like you, will have to eat their own filth and drink their own urine?"

28Then the commander stood and called out in Hebrew: "Hear the word of the great king, the king of Assyria! 29This is what the king says: Do not let Hezekiah deceive you. He cannot deliver you from my hand. 30Do not let Hezekiah persuade you to trust in the LORD when he says, 'The LORD will surely deliver us; this city will not be given into the hand of the king of Assyria.'

31"Do not listen to Hezekiah. This is what the king of Assyria says: Make peace with me and come out to me. Then every one of you will eat from his own vine and fig tree and drink water from his own cistern, 32until I come and take you to a land like your own, a land of grain and new wine, a land of bread and vineyards, a land of olive trees and honey. Choose life and not death!

"Do not listen to Hezekiah, for he is misleading you when he says, 'The LORD will deliver us.' 33Has the god of any nation ever delivered his land from the hand of the king of Assyria? 34Where are the gods of Hamath and Arpad? Where are the gods of Sepharvaim, Hena and Ivvah? Have they rescued Samaria from my hand? 35Who of all the gods of these countries has been able to save his land from me? How then can the LORD deliver Jerusalem from my hand?"

36But the people remained silent and said nothing in reply, because the king had commanded, "Do not answer him."

37Then Eliakim son of Hilkiah the palace administrator, Shebna the secretary and Joah son of Asaph the recorder went to Hezekiah, with their clothes torn, and told him what the field commander had said.

Jerusalem's Deliverance Foretold

19 When King Hezekiah heard this, he tore his clothes and put on sackcloth and went into the temple of the LORD. 2He sent Eliakim the palace administrator, Shebna the secretary and the leading priests, all wearing sackcloth, to the prophet Isaiah son of Amoz. 3They told him, "This is what Hezekiah says: This day is a day of distress and rebuke and disgrace, as when children come to the point of birth and there is no strength to deliver them. 4It may be that the LORD your God will hear all the words of the field commander, whom his master, the king of Assyria, has sent to ridicule the living God, and that he will rebuke him for the words the LORD your God has heard. Therefore pray for the remnant that still survives."

5When King Hezekiah's officials came to Isaiah, 6Isaiah said to them, "Tell your master, 'This is what the LORD says: Do not be afraid of what you have heard—those words with which the underlings of the king of Assyria have blasphemed me. 7Listen! I am going to put such a spirit in him that when he hears a certain report, he will return to his own country, and there I will have him cut down with the sword.' "

8When the field commander heard that the king of Assyria had left Lachish, he withdrew and found the king fighting against Libnah.

9Now Sennacherib received a report that Tirhakah, the Cushite*b* king ˌof Egyptˌ, was marching out to fight against him. So he again sent messengers to Hezekiah with this word: 10"Say to Hezekiah king of Judah: Do not let the god you depend on deceive you when he says, 'Jerusalem will not be handed over to the king of Assyria.' 11Surely you have heard what the kings of Assyria have done to all the countries, destroying them completely. And will you be delivered? 12Did the gods of the nations

---

a 24 Or *charioteers*   *b 9* That is, from the upper Nile region that were destroyed by my forefathers deliver them: the gods of Gozan, Haran, Rezeph and the people of Eden who were in Tel Assar? ¹³Where is the king of Hamath, the king of Arpad, the king of the city of Sepharvaim, or of Hena or Ivvah?"

Hezekiah's Prayer

¹⁴Hezekiah received the letter from the messengers and read it. Then he went up to the temple of the LORD and spread it out before the LORD. ¹⁵And Hezekiah prayed to the LORD: "O LORD, God of Israel, enthroned between the cherubim, you alone are God over all the kingdoms of the earth. You have made heaven and earth. ¹⁶Give ear, O LORD, and hear; open your eyes, O LORD, and see; listen to the words Sennacherib has sent to insult the living God.

¹⁷"It is true, O LORD, that the Assyrian kings have laid waste these nations and their lands. ¹⁸They have thrown their gods into the fire and destroyed them, for they were not gods but only wood and stone, fashioned by men's hands. ¹⁹Now, O LORD our God, deliver us from his hand, so that all kingdoms on earth may know that you alone, O LORD, are God."

Isaiah Prophesies Sennacherib's Fall

²⁰Then Isaiah son of Amoz sent a message to Hezekiah: "This is what the LORD, the God of Israel, says: I have heard your prayer concerning Sennacherib king of Assyria. ²¹This is the word that the LORD has spoken against him:

" 'The Virgin Daughter of Zion
　　despises you and mocks you.
The Daughter of Jerusalem
　　tosses her head as you flee.
²²Who is it you have insulted and
　　　blasphemed?
　　Against whom have you raised your
　　　voice
and lifted your eyes in pride?
　　Against the Holy One of Israel!
²³By your messengers
　　you have heaped insults on the Lord.
And you have said,
　　"With my many chariots
I have ascended the heights of the
　　　mountains,
　　the utmost heights of Lebanon.
I have cut down its tallest cedars,
　　the choicest of its pines.
I have reached its remotest parts,

the finest of its forests.
²⁴I have dug wells in foreign lands
　　and drunk the water there.
With the soles of my feet
　　I have dried up all the streams of
　　　Egypt."

²⁵" 'Have you not heard?
　　Long ago I ordained it.
In days of old I planned it;
　　now I have brought it to pass,
that you have turned fortified cities
　　into piles of stone.
²⁶Their people, drained of power,
　　are dismayed and put to shame.
They are like plants in the field,
　　like tender green shoots,
like grass sprouting on the roof,
　　scorched before it grows up.

²⁷" 'But I know where you stay
　　and when you come and go
　　and how you rage against me.
²⁸Because you rage against me
　　and your insolence has reached my
　　　ears,
I will put my hook in your nose
　　and my bit in your mouth,
and I will make you return
　　by the way you came.'

²⁹"This will be the sign for you, O Hezekiah:

"This year you will eat what grows by
　　　itself,
　　and the second year what springs
　　　from that.
But in the third year sow and reap,
　　plant vineyards and eat their fruit.
³⁰Once more a remnant of the house of
　　　Judah
　　will take root below and bear fruit
　　　above.
³¹For out of Jerusalem will come a
　　　remnant,
　　and out of Mount Zion a band of
　　　survivors.

The zeal of the LORD Almighty will accomplish this.

³²"Therefore this is what the LORD says concerning the king of Assyria:

"He will not enter this city
　　or shoot an arrow here.
He will not come before it with shield
　　or build a siege ramp against it.
³³By the way that he came he will return;

he will not enter this city,
            declares the LORD.
34I will defend this city and save it,
    for my sake and for the sake of
        David my servant."

35That night the angel of the LORD went out and put to death a hundred and eighty-five thousand men in the Assyrian camp. When the people got up the next morning—there were all the dead bodies! 36So Sennacherib king of Assyria broke camp and withdrew. He returned to Nineveh and stayed there.

37One day, while he was worshiping in the temple of his god Nisroch, his sons Adrammelech and Sharezer cut him down with the sword, and they escaped to the land of Ararat. And Esarhaddon his son succeeded him as king.

Hezekiah's Illness

In those days Hezekiah became ill and was at the point of death. The prophet Isaiah son of Amoz went to him and said, "This is what the LORD says: Put your house in order, because you are going to die; you will not recover."

2Hezekiah turned his face to the wall and prayed to the LORD, 3"Remember, O LORD, how I have walked before you faithfully and with wholehearted devotion and have done what is good in your eyes." And Hezekiah wept bitterly.

4Before Isaiah had left the middle court, the word of the LORD came to him: 5"Go back and tell Hezekiah, the leader of my people, 'This is what the LORD, the God of your father David, says: I have heard your prayer and seen your tears; I will heal you. On the third day from now you will go up to the temple of the LORD. 6I will add fifteen years to your life. And I will deliver you and this city from the hand of the king of Assyria. I will defend this city for my sake and for the sake of my servant David.' "

7Then Isaiah said, "Prepare a poultice of figs." They did so and applied it to the boil, and he recovered.

8Hezekiah had asked Isaiah, "What will be the sign that the LORD will heal me and that I will go up to the temple of the LORD on the third day from now?"

9Isaiah answered, "This is the LORD's sign to you that the LORD will do what he has promised: Shall the shadow go forward ten steps, or shall it go back ten steps?"

10"It is a simple matter for the shadow to go forward ten steps," said Hezekiah. "Rather, have it go back ten steps."

11Then the prophet Isaiah called upon the LORD, and the LORD made the shadow go back the ten steps it had gone down on the stairway of Ahaz.

Envoys From Babylon

12At that time Merodach-Baladan son of Baladan king of Babylon sent Hezekiah letters and a gift, because he had heard of Hezekiah's illness. 13Hezekiah received the messengers and showed them all that was in his storehouses—the silver, the gold, the spices and the fine oil—his armory and everything found among his treasures. There was nothing in his palace or in all his kingdom that Hezekiah did not show them.

14Then Isaiah the prophet went to King Hezekiah and asked, "What did those men say, and where did they come from?"

"From a distant land," Hezekiah replied. "They came from Babylon."

15The prophet asked, "What did they see in your palace?"

"They saw everything in my palace," Hezekiah said. "There is nothing among my treasures that I did not show them."

16Then Isaiah said to Hezekiah, "Hear the word of the LORD: 17The time will surely come when everything in your palace, and all that your fathers have stored up until this day, will be carried off to Babylon. Nothing will be left, says the LORD. 18And some of your descendants, your own flesh and blood, that will be born to you, will be taken away, and they will become eunuchs in the palace of the king of Babylon."

19"The word of the LORD you have spoken is good," Hezekiah replied. For he thought, "Will there not be peace and security in my lifetime?"

20As for the other events of Hezekiah's reign, all his achievements and how he made the pool and the tunnel by which he brought water into the city, are they not written in the book of the annals of the kings of Judah? 21Hezekiah rested with his fathers. And Manasseh his son succeeded him as king.

Manasseh King of Judah

21 Manasseh was twelve years old when he became king, and he reigned in Jerusalem fifty-five years. His mother's name was Hephzibah. ²He did evil in the eyes of the LORD, following the detestable practices of the nations the LORD had driven out before the Israelites. ³He rebuilt the high places his father Hezekiah had destroyed; he also erected altars to Baal and made an Asherah pole, as Ahab king of Israel had done. He bowed down to all the starry hosts and worshiped them. ⁴He built altars in the temple of the LORD, of which the LORD had said, "In Jerusalem I will put my Name." ⁵In both courts of the temple of the LORD, he built altars to all the starry hosts. ⁶He sacrificed his own son in a the fire, practiced sorcery and divination, and consulted mediums and spiritists. He did much evil in the eyes of the LORD, provoking him to anger.

⁷He took the carved Asherah pole he had made and put it in the temple, of which the LORD had said to David and to his son Solomon, "In this temple and in Jerusalem, which I have chosen out of all the tribes of Israel, I will put my Name forever. ⁸I will not again make the feet of the Israelites wander from the land I gave their forefathers, if only they will be careful to do everything I commanded them and will keep the whole Law that my servant Moses gave them." ⁹But the people did not listen. Manasseh led them astray, so that they did more evil than the nations the LORD had destroyed before the Israelites.

¹⁰The LORD said through his servants the prophets: ¹¹"Manasseh king of Judah has committed these detestable sins. He has done more evil than the Amorites who preceded him and has led Judah into sin with his idols. ¹²Therefore this is what the LORD, the God of Israel, says: I am going to bring such disaster on Jerusalem and Judah that the ears of everyone who hears of it will tingle. ¹³I will stretch out over Jerusalem the measuring line used against Samaria and the plumb line used against the house of Ahab. I will wipe out Jerusalem as one wipes a dish, wiping it and turning it upside down. ¹⁴I will forsake the remnant of my inheritance and hand them over to their enemies. They will be looted and plundered by all their foes,

¹⁵because they have done evil in my eyes and have provoked me to anger from the day their forefathers came out of Egypt until this day."

¹⁶Moreover, Manasseh also shed so much innocent blood that he filled Jerusalem from end to end—besides the sin that he had caused Judah to commit, so that they did evil in the eyes of the LORD.

¹⁷As for the other events of Manasseh's reign, and all he did, including the sin he committed, are they not written in the book of the annals of the kings of Judah? ¹⁸Manasseh rested with his fathers and was buried in his palace garden, the garden of Uzza. And Amon his son succeeded him as king.

Amon King of Judah

¹⁹Amon was twenty-two years old when he became king, and he reigned in Jerusalem two years. His mother's name was Meshullemeth daughter of Haruz; she was from Jotbah. ²⁰He did evil in the eyes of the LORD, as his father Manasseh had done. ²¹He walked in all the ways of his father; he worshiped the idols his father had worshiped, and bowed down to them. ²²He forsook the LORD, the God of his fathers, and did not walk in the way of the LORD.

²³Amon's officials conspired against him and assassinated the king in his palace. ²⁴Then the people of the land killed all who had plotted against King Amon, and they made Josiah his son king in his place.

²⁵As for the other events of Amon's reign, and what he did, are they not written in the book of the annals of the kings of Judah? ²⁶He was buried in his grave in the garden of Uzza. And Josiah his son succeeded him as king.

The Book of the Law Found

22 Josiah was eight years old when he became king, and he reigned in Jerusalem thirty-one years. His mother's name was Jedidah daughter of Adaiah; she was from Bozkath. ²He did what was right in the eyes of the LORD and walked in all the ways of his father David, not turning aside to the right or to the left.

³In the eighteenth year of his reign, King Josiah sent the secretary, Shaphan

---

a 6 Or He made his own son pass through

son of Azaliah, the son of Meshullam, to the temple of the LORD. He said: 4"Go up to Hilkiah the high priest and have him get ready the money that has been brought into the temple of the LORD, which the doorkeepers have collected from the people. 5Have them entrust it to the men appointed to supervise the work on the temple. And have these men pay the workers who repair the temple of the LORD— 6the carpenters, the builders and the masons. Also have them purchase timber and dressed stone to repair the temple. 7But they need not account for the money entrusted to them, because they are acting faithfully."

8Hilkiah the high priest said to Shaphan the secretary, "I have found the Book of the Law in the temple of the LORD." He gave it to Shaphan, who read it. 9Then Shaphan the secretary went to the king and reported to him: "Your officials have paid out the money that was in the temple of the LORD and have entrusted it to the workers and supervisors at the temple." 10Then Shaphan the secretary informed the king, "Hilkiah the priest has given me a book." And Shaphan read from it in the presence of the king.

11When the king heard the words of the Book of the Law, he tore his robes. 12He gave these orders to Hilkiah the priest, Ahikam son of Shaphan, Acbor son of Micaiah, Shaphan the secretary and Asaiah the king's attendant: 13"Go and inquire of the LORD for me and for the people and for all Judah about what is written in this book that has been found. Great is the LORD's anger that burns against us because our fathers have not obeyed the words of this book; they have not acted in accordance with all that is written there concerning us."

14Hilkiah the priest, Ahikam, Acbor, Shaphan and Asaiah went to speak to the prophetess Huldah, who was the wife of Shallum son of Tikvah, the son of Harhas, keeper of the wardrobe. She lived in Jerusalem, in the Second District.

15She said to them, "This is what the LORD, the God of Israel, says: Tell the man who sent you to me, 16'This is what the LORD says: I am going to bring disaster on this place and its people, according to everything written in the book the king of Judah has read. 17Because they have forsaken me and burned incense to other gods and provoked me to anger by all the idols their hands have made,ᵃ my anger will burn against this place and will not be quenched.' 18Tell the king of Judah, who sent you to inquire of the LORD, 'This is what the LORD, the God of Israel, says concerning the words you heard: 19Because your heart was responsive and you humbled yourself before the LORD when you heard what I have spoken against this place and its people, that they would become accursed and laid waste, and because you tore your robes and wept in my presence, I have heard you, declares the LORD. 20Therefore I will gather you to your fathers, and you will be buried in peace.

ᵃ 17 Or by everything they have done

Get a Load of This...

Manasseh did evil-- more evil than even the heathen (see 2 Kings 21:1–18). And he suffered for it. Big time! God is merciful and full of grace but he's no softie pushover. When he draws the line and says, "No more!" and people cross the line, they're in for it.

Your eyes will not see all the disaster I am going to bring on this place.' "

So they took her answer back to the king.

Josiah Renews the Covenant

23 Then the king called together all the elders of Judah and Jerusalem. ²He went up to the temple of the LORD with the men of Judah, the people of Jerusalem, the priests and the prophets—all the people from the least to the greatest. He read in their hearing all the words of the Book of the Covenant, which had been found in the temple of the LORD. ³The king stood by the pillar and renewed the covenant in the presence of the LORD—to follow the LORD and keep his commands, regulations and decrees with all his heart and all his soul, thus confirming the words of the covenant written in this book. Then all the people pledged themselves to the covenant.

⁴The king ordered Hilkiah the high priest, the priests next in rank and the doorkeepers to remove from the temple of the LORD all the articles made for Baal and Asherah and all the starry hosts. He burned them outside Jerusalem in the fields of the Kidron Valley and took the ashes to Bethel. ⁵He did away with the pagan priests appointed by the kings of Judah to burn incense on the high places of the towns of Judah and on those around Jerusalem—those who burned incense to Baal, to the sun and moon, to the constellations and to all the starry hosts. ⁶He took the Asherah pole from the temple of the LORD to the Kidron Valley outside Jerusalem and burned it there. He ground it to powder and scattered the dust over the graves of the common people. ⁷He also tore down the quarters of the male shrine prostitutes, which were in the temple of the LORD and where women did weaving for Asherah.

⁸Josiah brought all the priests from the towns of Judah and desecrated the high places, from Geba to Beersheba, where the priests had burned incense. He broke down the shrines*a* at the gates—at the entrance to the Gate of Joshua, the city governor, which is on the left of the city gate. ⁹Although the priests of the high places did not serve at the altar of the LORD in Jerusalem, they ate unleavened bread with their fellow priests.

¹⁰He desecrated Topheth, which was in the Valley of Ben Hinnom, so no one could use it to sacrifice his son or daughter in*b* the fire to Molech. ¹¹He removed from the entrance to the temple of the LORD the horses that the kings of Judah had dedicated to the sun. They were in the court near the room of an official named Nathan-Melech. Josiah then burned the chariots dedicated to the sun.

¹²He pulled down the altars the kings of Judah had erected on the roof near the upper room of Ahaz, and the altars Manasseh had built in the two courts of the temple of the LORD. He removed them from there, smashed them to pieces and threw the rubble into the Kidron Valley. ¹³The king also desecrated the high places that were east of Jerusalem on the south of the Hill of Corruption—the ones Solomon king of Israel had built for Ashtoreth the vile goddess of the Sidonians, for Chemosh the vile god of Moab, and for Molech*c* the detestable god of the people of Ammon. ¹⁴Josiah smashed the sacred stones and cut down the Asherah poles and covered the sites with human bones.

¹⁵Even the altar at Bethel, the high place made by Jeroboam son of Nebat, who had caused Israel to sin—even that altar and high place he demolished. He burned the high place and ground it to powder, and burned the Asherah pole also. ¹⁶Then Josiah looked around, and when he saw the tombs that were there on the hillside, he had the bones removed from them and burned on the altar to defile it, in accordance with the word of the LORD proclaimed by the man of God who foretold these things.

¹⁷The king asked, "What is that tombstone I see?"

The men of the city said, "It marks the tomb of the man of God who came from Judah and pronounced against the altar of Bethel the very things you have done to it."

¹⁸"Leave it alone," he said. "Don't let anyone disturb his bones." So they spared his bones and those of the prophet who had come from Samaria.

¹⁹Just as he had done at Bethel, Josiah removed and defiled all the shrines at the high places that the kings of Israel had

---

a 8 Or *high places*   *b 10* Or *to make his son or daughter pass through*   *c 13* Hebrew *Milcom* built in the towns of Samaria that had provoked the LORD to anger. 20Josiah slaughtered all the priests of those high places on the altars and burned human bones on them. Then he went back to Jerusalem.

21The king gave this order to all the people: "Celebrate the Passover to the LORD your God, as it is written in this Book of the Covenant." 22Not since the days of the judges who led Israel, nor throughout the days of the kings of Israel and the kings of Judah, had any such Passover been observed. 23But in the eighteenth year of King Josiah, this Passover was celebrated to the LORD in Jerusalem.

24Furthermore, Josiah got rid of the mediums and spiritists, the household gods, the idols and all the other detestable things seen in Judah and Jerusalem. This he did to fulfill the requirements of the law written in the book that Hilkiah the priest had discovered in the temple of the LORD. 25Neither before nor after Josiah was there a king like him who turned to the LORD as he did—with all his heart and with all his soul and with all his strength, in accordance with all the Law of Moses.

26Nevertheless, the LORD did not turn away from the heat of his fierce anger, which burned against Judah because of all that Manasseh had done to provoke him to anger. 27So the LORD said, "I will remove Judah also from my presence as I removed Israel, and I will reject Jerusalem, the city I chose, and this temple, about which I said, 'There shall my Name be.'a"

28As for the other events of Josiah's reign, and all he did, are they not written in the book of the annals of the kings of Judah?

29While Josiah was king, Pharaoh Neco king of Egypt went up to the Euphrates River to help the king of Assyria. King Josiah marched out to meet him in battle, but Neco faced him and killed him at Megiddo. 30Josiah's servants brought his body in a chariot from Megiddo to Jerusalem and buried him in his own tomb. And the people of the land took Jehoahaz son of Josiah and anointed him and made him king in place of his father.

Jehoahaz King of Judah

31Jehoahaz was twenty-three years old when he became king, and he reigned in Jerusalem three months. His mother's name was Hamutal daughter of Jeremiah; she was from Libnah. 32He did evil in the eyes of the LORD, just as his fathers had done. 33Pharaoh Neco put him in chains at Riblah in the land of Hamathb so that he might not reign in Jerusalem, and he imposed on Judah a levy of a hundred talentsc of silver and a talentd of gold. 34Pharaoh Neco made Eliakim son of Josiah king in place of his father Josiah and changed Eliakim's name to Jehoiakim. But he took Jehoahaz and carried him off to Egypt, and there he died. 35Jehoiakim paid Pharaoh Neco the silver and gold he demanded. In order to do so, he taxed the land and exacted the silver and gold from the people of the land according to their assessments.

Jehoiakim King of Judah

36Jehoiakim was twenty-five years old when he became king, and he reigned in Jerusalem eleven years. His mother's name was Zebidah daughter of Pedaiah; she was from Rumah. 37And he did evil in the eyes of the LORD, just as his fathers had done.

During Jehoiakim's reign, Nebuchadnezzar king of Babylon invaded the land, and Jehoiakim became his vassal for three years. But then he changed his mind and rebelled against Nebuchadnezzar. 2The LORD sent Babylonian,e Aramean, Moabite and Ammonite raiders against him. He sent them to destroy Judah, in accordance with the word of the LORD proclaimed by his servants the prophets. 3Surely these things happened to Judah according to the LORD's command, in order to remove them from his presence because of the sins of Manasseh and all he had done, 4including the shedding of innocent blood. For he had filled Jerusalem with innocent blood, and the LORD was not willing to forgive.

5As for the other events of Jehoiakim's reign, and all he did, are they not written in the book of the annals of the kings of Judah? 6Jehoiakim rested with his fathers. And Jehoiachin his son succeeded him as king.

a 27 1 Kings 8:29   b 33 Hebrew; Septuagint (see also 2 Chron. 36:3) *Neco at Riblah in Hamath removed him*   c 33 That is, about 3 3/4 tons (about 3.4 metric tons)   d 33 That is, about 75 pounds (about 34 kilograms)   e 2 Or *Chaldean*

[7]The king of Egypt did not march out from his own country again, because the king of Babylon had taken all his territory, from the Wadi of Egypt to the Euphrates River.

Jehoiachin King of Judah

[8]Jehoiachin was eighteen years old when he became king, and he reigned in Jerusalem three months. His mother's name was Nehushta daughter of Elnathan; she was from Jerusalem. [9]He did evil in the eyes of the LORD, just as his father had done.

[10]At that time the officers of Nebuchadnezzar king of Babylon advanced on Jerusalem and laid siege to it, [11]and Nebuchadnezzar himself came up to the city while his officers were besieging it. [12]Jehoiachin king of Judah, his mother, his attendants, his nobles and his officials all surrendered to him.

In the eighth year of the reign of the king of Babylon, he took Jehoiachin prisoner. [13]As the LORD had declared, Nebuchadnezzar removed all the treasures from the temple of the LORD and from the royal palace, and took away all the gold articles that Solomon king of Israel had made for the temple of the LORD. [14]He carried into exile all Jerusalem: all the officers and fighting men, and all the craftsmen and artisans—a total of ten thousand. Only the poorest people of the land were left.

[15]Nebuchadnezzar took Jehoiachin captive to Babylon. He also took from Jerusalem to Babylon the king's mother, his wives, his officials and the leading men of the land. [16]The king of Babylon also deported to Babylon the entire force of seven thousand fighting men, strong and fit for war, and a thousand craftsmen and artisans. [17]He made Mattaniah, Jehoiachin's uncle, king in his place and changed his name to Zedekiah.

Zedekiah King of Judah

[18]Zedekiah was twenty-one years old when he became king, and he reigned in Jerusalem eleven years. His mother's name was Hamutal daughter of Jeremiah; she was from Libnah. [19]He did evil in the eyes of the LORD, just as Jehoiakim had done. [20]It was because of the LORD's anger that all this happened to Jerusalem and Judah, and in the end he thrust them from his presence.

The Fall of Jerusalem

Now Zedekiah rebelled against the king of Babylon.

25 So in the ninth year of Zedekiah's reign, on the tenth day of the tenth month, Nebuchadnezzar king of Babylon marched against Jerusalem with his whole army. He encamped outside the city and built siege works all around it. [2]The city was kept under siege until the eleventh year of King Zedekiah. [3]By the ninth day of the ⌊fourth⌋[a] month the famine in the city had become so severe that there was no food for the people to eat. [4]Then the city wall was broken through, and the whole army fled at night through the gate between the two walls near the king's garden, though the Babylonians[b] were surrounding the city. They fled toward the Arabah,[c] [5]but the Babylonian[d] army pursued the king and overtook him in the plains of Jericho. All his soldiers were separated from him and scattered, [6]and he was captured. He was taken to the king of Babylon at Riblah, where sentence was pronounced on him. [7]They killed the sons of Zedekiah before his eyes. Then they put out his eyes, bound him with bronze shackles and took him to Babylon.

[8]On the seventh day of the fifth month, in the nineteenth year of Nebuchadnezzar king of Babylon, Nebuzaradan commander of the imperial guard, an official of the king of Babylon, came to Jerusalem. [9]He set fire to the temple of the LORD, the royal palace and all the houses of Jerusalem. Every important building he burned down. [10]The whole Babylonian army, under the commander of the imperial guard, broke down the walls around Jerusalem. [11]Nebuzaradan the commander of the guard carried into exile the people who remained in the city, along with the rest of the populace and those who had gone over to the king of Babylon. [12]But the commander left behind some of the poorest people of the land to work the vineyards and fields.

[13]The Babylonians broke up the bronze pillars, the movable stands and the bronze Sea that were at the temple of the LORD and they carried the bronze to Bab-

---

[a] 3 See Jer. 52:6.   [b] 4 Or Chaldeans; also in verses 13, 25 and 26   [c] 4 Or the Jordan Valley   [d] 5 Or Chaldean; also in verses 10 and 24

ylon. ¹⁴They also took away the pots, shovels, wick trimmers, dishes and all the bronze articles used in the temple service. ¹⁵The commander of the imperial guard took away the censers and sprinkling bowls—all that were made of pure gold or silver.

¹⁶The bronze from the two pillars, the Sea and the movable stands, which Solomon had made for the temple of the LORD, was more than could be weighed. ¹⁷Each pillar was twenty-seven feet[a] high. The bronze capital on top of one pillar was four and a half feet[b] high and was decorated with a network and pomegranates of bronze all around. The other pillar, with its network, was similar.

¹⁸The commander of the guard took as prisoners Seraiah the chief priest, Zephaniah the priest next in rank and the three doorkeepers. ¹⁹Of those still in the city, he took the officer in charge of the fighting men and five royal advisers. He also took the secretary who was chief officer in charge of conscripting the people of the land and sixty of his men who were found in the city. ²⁰Nebuzaradan the commander took them all and brought them to the king of Babylon at Riblah. ²¹There at Riblah, in the land of Hamath, the king had them executed.

So Judah went into captivity, away from her land.

²²Nebuchadnezzar king of Babylon appointed Gedaliah son of Ahikam, the son of Shaphan, to be over the people he had left behind in Judah. ²³When all the army officers and their men heard that the king of Babylon had appointed Gedaliah as governor, they came to Gedaliah at Mizpah—Ishmael son of Nethaniah, Johanan son of Kareah, Seraiah son of Tanhumeth the Netophathite, Jaazaniah the son of the Maacathite, and their men. ²⁴Gedaliah took an oath to reassure them and their men. "Do not be afraid of the Babylonian officials," he said. "Settle down in the land and serve the king of Babylon, and it will go well with you."

²⁵In the seventh month, however, Ishmael son of Nethaniah, the son of Elishama, who was of royal blood, came with ten men and assassinated Gedaliah and also the men of Judah and the Babylonians who were with him at Mizpah. ²⁶At this, all the people from the least to the greatest, together with the army officers, fled to Egypt for fear of the Babylonians.

Jehoiachin Released

²⁷In the thirty-seventh year of the exile of Jehoiachin king of Judah, in the year Evil-Merodach[c] became king of Babylon, he released Jehoiachin from prison on the twenty-seventh day of the twelfth month. ²⁸He spoke kindly to him and gave him a seat of honor higher than those of the other kings who were with him in Babylon. ²⁹So Jehoiachin put aside his prison clothes and for the rest of his life ate regularly at the king's table. ³⁰Day by day the king gave Jehoiachin a regular allowance as long as he lived.

---

[a] 17 Hebrew *eighteen cubits* (about 8.1 meters)
[b] 17 Hebrew *three cubits* (about 1.3 meters)   [c] 27 Also called *Amel-Marduk*

1 CHRONICLES

Who wrote this book?

The author is unknown. Many think the book was written by Ezra.

Why was this book written?

The book of 1 Chronicles gives God's evaluation of David's rule.

What happens in this book?

David becomes king of Israel. He defeats Israel's enemies and works to make Israel a mighty nation.

What do we learn about God in this book?

God gives people who serve him many different abilities.

Who is important in this book?

The important person in this book is David.

When did this happen?

The events in this book happened between 1010 and 970 B.C.

Where did this happen?

These events took place in the land of Israel, united by David into a powerful nation.

What are some of the stories in this book?

The ark comes to Jerusalem	1 Chronicles 15
God's promise to David	1 Chronicles 17
David counts his army	1 Chronicles 21
David's plans for the temple	1 Chronicles 28

Historical Records From Adam to Abraham

To Noah's Sons

1 Adam, Seth, Enosh, [2]Kenan, Mahalalel, Jared, [3]Enoch, Methuselah, Lamech, Noah.

[4]The sons of Noah:[a]
Shem, Ham and Japheth.

The Japhethites

[5]The sons[b] of Japheth:
Gomer, Magog, Madai, Javan, Tubal, Meshech and Tiras.
[6]The sons of Gomer:
Ashkenaz, Riphath[c] and Togarmah.
[7]The sons of Javan:
Elishah, Tarshish, the Kittim and the Rodanim.

The Hamites

[8]The sons of Ham:
Cush, Mizraim,[d] Put and Canaan.
[9]The sons of Cush:
Seba, Havilah, Sabta, Raamah and Sabteca.
The sons of Raamah:
Sheba and Dedan.
[10]Cush was the father[e] of
Nimrod, who grew to be a mighty warrior on earth.
[11]Mizraim was the father of
the Ludites, Anamites, Lehabites, Naphtuhites, [12]Pathrusites, Casluhites (from whom the Philistines came) and Caphtorites.
[13]Canaan was the father of
Sidon his firstborn,[f] and of the Hittites, [14]Jebusites, Amorites, Girgashites, [15]Hivites, Arkites, Sinites, [16]Arvadites, Zemarites and Hamathites.

The Semites

[17]The sons of Shem:
Elam, Asshur, Arphaxad, Lud and Aram.
The sons of Aram:[g]
Uz, Hul, Gether and Meshech.
[18]Arphaxad was the father of Shelah, and Shelah the father of Eber.
[19]Two sons were born to Eber:
One was named Peleg,[h] because in his time the earth was divided; his brother was named Joktan.

[20]Joktan was the father of
Almodad, Sheleph, Hazarmaveth, Jerah, [21]Hadoram, Uzal, Diklah, [22]Obal,[i] Abimael, Sheba, [23]Ophir, Havilah and Jobab. All these were sons of Joktan.

[24]Shem, Arphaxad,[j] Shelah,
[25]Eber, Peleg, Reu,
[26]Serug, Nahor, Terah
[27]and Abram (that is, Abraham).

The Family of Abraham

[28]The sons of Abraham:
Isaac and Ishmael.

Descendants of Hagar

[29]These were their descendants:
Nebaioth the firstborn of Ishmael, Kedar, Adbeel, Mibsam, [30]Mishma, Dumah, Massa, Hadad, Tema, [31]Jetur, Naphish and Kedemah. These were the sons of Ishmael.

Descendants of Keturah

[32]The sons born to Keturah, Abraham's concubine:
Zimran, Jokshan, Medan, Midian, Ishbak and Shuah.
The sons of Jokshan:
Sheba and Dedan.
[33]The sons of Midian:
Ephah, Epher, Hanoch, Abida and Eldaah.
All these were descendants of Keturah.

Descendants of Sarah

[34]Abraham was the father of Isaac.
The sons of Isaac:
Esau and Israel.

Esau's Sons

[35]The sons of Esau:
Eliphaz, Reuel, Jeush, Jalam and Korah.

---

[a] 4 Septuagint; Hebrew does not have this line   [b] 5 *Sons* may mean *descendants* or *successors* or *nations*; also in verses 6–10, 17 and 20.   [c] 6 Many Hebrew manuscripts and Vulgate (see also Septuagint and Gen. 10:3); most Hebrew manuscripts *Diphath*   [d] 8 That is, Egypt; also in verse 11   [e] 10 *Father* may mean *ancestor* or *predecessor* or *founder*; also in verses 11, 13, 18 and 20.   [f] 13 Or *of the Sidonians, the foremost*   [g] 17 One Hebrew manuscript and some Septuagint manuscripts (see also Gen. 10:23); most Hebrew manuscripts do not have this line.   [h] 19 *Peleg* means *division*.   [i] 22 Some Hebrew manuscripts and Syriac (see also Gen. 10:28); most Hebrew manuscripts *Ebal*   [j] 24 Hebrew; some Septuagint manuscripts *Arphaxad, Cainan* (see also note at Gen. 11:10)

36 The sons of Eliphaz:
      Teman, Omar, Zepho,*a* Gatam and
      Kenaz;
      by Timna: Amalek.*b*
37 The sons of Reuel:
      Nahath, Zerah, Shammah and
      Mizzah.

The People of Seir in Edom

38 The sons of Seir:
      Lotan, Shobal, Zibeon, Anah, Di-
      shon, Ezer and Dishan.
39 The sons of Lotan:
      Hori and Homam. Timna was Lo-
      tan's sister.
40 The sons of Shobal:
      Alvan,*c* Manahath, Ebal, Shepho
      and Onam.
   The sons of Zibeon:
      Aiah and Anah.
41 The son of Anah:
      Dishon.
   The sons of Dishon:
      Hemdan,*d* Eshban, Ithran and Ke-
      ran.

42 The sons of Ezer:
      Bilhan, Zaavan and Akan.*e*
   The sons of Dishan*f*:
      Uz and Aran.

The Rulers of Edom

43 These were the kings who reigned in
      Edom before any Israelite king
      reigned*g*:
      Bela son of Beor, whose city was
      named Dinhabah.
44 When Bela died, Jobab son of Zerah
      from Bozrah succeeded him as king.
45 When Jobab died, Husham from the
      land of the Temanites succeeded
      him as king.

a 36 Many Hebrew manuscripts, some Septuagint
manuscripts and Syriac (see also Gen. 36:11); most Hebrew
manuscripts *Zephi*   *b 36* Some Septuagint manuscripts (see
also Gen. 36:12); Hebrew *Gatam, Kenaz, Timna and Amalek*
c 40 Many Hebrew manuscripts and some Septuagint
manuscripts (see also Gen. 36:23); most Hebrew manuscripts
Alian   *d 41* Many Hebrew manuscripts and some
Septuagint manuscripts (see also Gen. 36:26); most Hebrew
manuscripts *Hamran*   *e 42* Many Hebrew and Septuagint
manuscripts (see also Gen. 36:27); most Hebrew manuscripts
Zaavan, Jaakan   *f 42* Hebrew *Dishon,* a variant of *Dishan*
g 43 Or *before an Israelite king reigned over them*

Jolly Genealogy

READ 1 CHRONICLES 1:1–4, 17–28, 34; 2:1–15

"Adam, Seth, Enosh, Kenan, Mahalalel, Jared . . ." Enough already! Why
are there so many long lists of names in the Bible? Who cares who
David's great-great-great-great-great grandfather was? Believe it or
not, *God* does, and we should, too. These lists of names are called "genealogies." The verses you were asked to read list everyone
from Adam to David. That's a lot of names! The Jews realized
that genealogies were important, because part of knowing
who you are is knowing where you come from. This includes
what country your ancestors were from, what culture they
were raised in, and so on. So learn about your roots. Ask your
parents to fill you in on your family history. Your ancestors may come from many different cultures, so
your parents will have some interesting stories to
tell. You'll understand yourself better by learning
where you come from, and all the ingredients
that God used to make you with.

Your next reading is on page 527.

46 When Husham died, Hadad son of Bedad, who defeated Midian in the country of Moab, succeeded him as king. His city was named Avith. 47 When Hadad died, Samlah from Masrekah succeeded him as king. 48 When Samlah died, Shaul from Rehoboth on the river[a] succeeded him as king. 49 When Shaul died, Baal-Hanan son of Acbor succeeded him as king. 50 When Baal-Hanan died, Hadad succeeded him as king. His city was named Pau,[b] and his wife's name was Mehetabel daughter of Matred, the daughter of Me-Zahab. 51 Hadad also died.

The chiefs of Edom were:

Timna, Alvah, Jetheth, 52 Oholibamah, Elah, Pinon, 53 Kenaz, Teman, Mibzar, 54 Magdiel and Iram. These were the chiefs of Edom.

Israel's Sons

2 These were the sons of Israel: Reuben, Simeon, Levi, Judah, Issachar, Zebulun, 2 Dan, Joseph, Benjamin, Naphtali, Gad and Asher.

Judah

To Hezron's Sons

3 The sons of Judah:

Er, Onan and Shelah. These three were born to him by a Canaanite woman, the daughter of Shua. Er, Judah's firstborn, was wicked in the LORD's sight; so the LORD put him to death. 4 Tamar, Judah's daughter-in-law, bore him Perez and Zerah. Judah had five sons in all.

5 The sons of Perez:

Hezron and Hamul.

6 The sons of Zerah:

Zimri, Ethan, Heman, Calcol and Darda[c]—five in all.

7 The son of Carmi:

Achar,[d] who brought trouble on Israel by violating the ban on taking devoted things.[e]

8 The son of Ethan:

Azariah.

9 The sons born to Hezron were:

Jerahmeel, Ram and Caleb.[f]

From Ram Son of Hezron

10 Ram was the father of

Amminadab, and Amminadab the father of Nahshon, the leader of the people of Judah. 11 Nahshon was the father of Salmon,[g] Salmon the father of Boaz, 12 Boaz the father of Obed and Obed the father of Jesse.

13 Jesse was the father of

Eliab his firstborn; the second son was Abinadab, the third Shimea, 14 the fourth Nethanel, the fifth Raddai, 15 the sixth Ozem and the seventh David. 16 Their sisters were Zeruiah and Abigail. Zeruiah's three sons were Abishai, Joab and Asahel. 17 Abigail was the mother of Amasa, whose father was Jether the Ishmaelite.

Caleb Son of Hezron

18 Caleb son of Hezron had children by his wife Azubah (and by Jerioth). These were her sons: Jesher, Shobab and Ardon. 19 When Azubah died, Caleb married Ephrath, who bore him Hur. 20 Hur was the father of Uri, and Uri the father of Bezalel.

21 Later, Hezron lay with the daughter of Makir the father of Gilead (he had married her when he was sixty years old), and she bore him Segub. 22 Segub was the father of Jair, who controlled twenty-three towns in Gilead. 23 (But Geshur and Aram captured Havvoth Jair,[h] as well as Kenath with its surrounding settlements—sixty towns.) All these were descendants of Makir the father of Gilead.

24 After Hezron died in Caleb Ephrathah, Abijah the wife of Hezron bore him Ashhur the father[i] of Tekoa.

---

a 48 Possibly the Euphrates   b 50 Many Hebrew manuscripts, some Septuagint manuscripts, Vulgate and Syriac (see also Gen. 36:39); most Hebrew manuscripts *Pai*   c 6 Many Hebrew manuscripts, some Septuagint manuscripts and Syriac (see also 1 Kings 4:31); most Hebrew manuscripts *Dara*   d 7 *Achar* means *trouble*; *Achar* is called *Achan* in Joshua.   e 7 The Hebrew term refers to the irrevocable giving over of things or persons to the LORD, often by totally destroying them.   f 9 Hebrew *Kelubai*, a variant of *Caleb*   g 11 Septuagint (see also Ruth 4:21); Hebrew *Salma*   h 23 Or *captured the settlements of Jair*   i 24 *Father* may mean *civic leader* or *military leader*; also in verses 42, 45, 49–52 and possibly elsewhere.

Jerahmeel Son of Hezron

25 The sons of Jerahmeel the firstborn of Hezron:
   Ram his firstborn, Bunah, Oren, Ozem and[a] Ahijah. 26 Jerahmeel had another wife, whose name was Atarah; she was the mother of Onam.

27 The sons of Ram the firstborn of Jerahmeel:
   Maaz, Jamin and Eker.

28 The sons of Onam:
   Shammai and Jada.
   The sons of Shammai:
   Nadab and Abishur.

29 Abishur's wife was named Abihail, who bore him Ahban and Molid.

30 The sons of Nadab:
   Seled and Appaim. Seled died without children.

31 The son of Appaim:
   Ishi, who was the father of Sheshan.
   Sheshan was the father of Ahlai.

32 The sons of Jada, Shammai's brother:
   Jether and Jonathan. Jether died without children.

33 The sons of Jonathan:
   Peleth and Zaza.
   These were the descendants of Jerahmeel.

34 Sheshan had no sons—only daughters.
   He had an Egyptian servant named Jarha. 35 Sheshan gave his daughter in marriage to his servant Jarha, and she bore him Attai.

36 Attai was the father of Nathan, Nathan the father of Zabad,

37 Zabad the father of Ephlal, Ephlal the father of Obed,

38 Obed the father of Jehu, Jehu the father of Azariah,

39 Azariah the father of Helez, Helez the father of Eleasah,

40 Eleasah the father of Sismai, Sismai the father of Shallum,

41 Shallum the father of Jekamiah, and Jekamiah the father of Elishama.

The Clans of Caleb

42 The sons of Caleb the brother of Jerahmeel:
   Mesha his firstborn, who was the father of Ziph, and his son Mareshah,[b] who was the father of Hebron.

43 The sons of Hebron:
   Korah, Tappuah, Rekem and Shema. 44 Shema was the father of Raham, and Raham the father of Jorkeam. Rekem was the father of Shammai. 45 The son of Shammai was Maon, and Maon was the father of Beth Zur.

46 Caleb's concubine Ephah was the mother of Haran, Moza and Gazez. Haran was the father of Gazez.

47 The sons of Jahdai:
   Regem, Jotham, Geshan, Pelet, Ephah and Shaaph.

48 Caleb's concubine Maacah was the mother of Sheber and Tirhanah. 49 She also gave birth to Shaaph the father of Madmannah and to Sheva the father of Macbenah and Gibea. Caleb's daughter was Acsah. 50 These were the descendants of Caleb.

The sons of Hur the firstborn of Ephrathah:
   Shobal the father of Kiriath Jearim, 51 Salma the father of Bethlehem, and Hareph the father of Beth Gader.

52 The descendants of Shobal the father of Kiriath Jearim were:
   Haroeh, half the Manahathites, 53 and the clans of Kiriath Jearim: the Ithrites, Puthites, Shumathites and Mishraites. From these descended the Zorathites and Eshtaolites.

54 The descendants of Salma:
   Bethlehem, the Netophathites, Atroth Beth Joab, half the Manahathites, the Zorites, 55 and the clans of scribes[c] who lived at Jabez: the Tirathites, Shimeathites and Sucathites. These are the Kenites who came from Hammath, the father of the house of Recab.[d]

The Sons of David

3 These were the sons of David born to him in Hebron:
   The firstborn was Amnon the son of Ahinoam of Jezreel;
   the second, Daniel the son of Abigail of Carmel;

---

a 25 Or *Oren and Ozem, by* b 42 The meaning of the Hebrew for this phrase is uncertain. c 55 Or *of the Sopherites* d 55 Or *father of Beth Recab*

² the third, Absalom the son of Maacah daughter of Talmai king of Geshur;
the fourth, Adonijah the son of Haggith;
³ the fifth, Shephatiah the son of Abital;
and the sixth, Ithream, by his wife Eglah.
⁴ These six were born to David in Hebron, where he reigned seven years and six months.

David reigned in Jerusalem thirty-three years, ⁵ and these were the children born to him there:
Shammua,ᵃ Shobab, Nathan and Solomon. These four were by Bathshebaᵇ daughter of Ammiel.
⁶ There were also Ibhar, Elishua,ᶜ Eliphelet, ⁷ Nogah, Nepheg, Japhia, ⁸ Elishama, Eliada and Eliphelet—nine in all. ⁹ All these were the sons of David, besides his sons by his concubines. And Tamar was their sister.

The Kings of Judah

¹⁰ Solomon's son was Rehoboam,
Abijah his son,
Asa his son,
Jehoshaphat his son,
¹¹ Jehoramᵈ his son,
Ahaziah his son,
Joash his son,
¹² Amaziah his son,
Azariah his son,
Jotham his son,
¹³ Ahaz his son,
Hezekiah his son,
Manasseh his son,
¹⁴ Amon his son,
Josiah his son.
¹⁵ The sons of Josiah:
Johanan the firstborn,
Jehoiakim the second son,
Zedekiah the third,
Shallum the fourth.
¹⁶ The successors of Jehoiakim:
Jehoiachinᵉ his son,
and Zedekiah.

The Royal Line After the Exile

¹⁷ The descendants of Jehoiachin the captive:
Shealtiel his son, ¹⁸ Malkiram, Pedaiah, Shenazzar, Jekamiah, Hoshama and Nedabiah.

¹⁹ The sons of Pedaiah:
Zerubbabel and Shimei.
The sons of Zerubbabel:
Meshullam and Hananiah.
Shelomith was their sister.
²⁰ There were also five others:
Hashubah, Ohel, Berekiah, Hasadiah and Jushab-Hesed.
²¹ The descendants of Hananiah:
Pelatiah and Jeshaiah, and the sons of Rephaiah, of Arnan, of Obadiah and of Shecaniah.
²² The descendants of Shecaniah:
Shemaiah and his sons:
Hattush, Igal, Bariah, Neariah and Shaphat—six in all.
²³ The sons of Neariah:
Elioenai, Hizkiah and Azrikam—three in all.
²⁴ The sons of Elioenai:
Hodaviah, Eliashib, Pelaiah, Akkub, Johanan, Delaiah and Anani—seven in all.

Other Clans of Judah

The descendants of Judah:
Perez, Hezron, Carmi, Hur and Shobal.
² Reaiah son of Shobal was the father of Jahath, and Jahath the father of Ahumai and Lahad. These were the clans of the Zorathites.
³ These were the sonsᶠ of Etam:
Jezreel, Ishma and Idbash. Their sister was named Hazzelelponi.
⁴ Penuel was the father of Gedor, and Ezer the father of Hushah.
These were the descendants of Hur, the firstborn of Ephrathah and fatherᵍ of Bethlehem.
⁵ Ashhur the father of Tekoa had two wives, Helah and Naarah.
⁶ Naarah bore him Ahuzzam, Hepher, Temeni and Haahashtari. These were the descendants of Naarah.
⁷ The sons of Helah:
Zereth, Zohar, Ethnan, ⁸ and Koz, who was the father of Anub and

---

ᵃ 5 Hebrew *Shimea*, a variant of *Shammua*
ᵇ 5 One Hebrew manuscript and Vulgate (see also Septuagint and 2 Samuel 11:3); most Hebrew manuscripts *Bathshua*
ᶜ 6 Two Hebrew manuscripts (see also 2 Samuel 5:15 and 1 Chron. 14:5); most Hebrew manuscripts *Elishama*
ᵈ 11 Hebrew *Joram*, a variant of *Jehoram*   ᵉ 16 Hebrew *Jeconiah*, a variant of *Jehoiachin*; also in verse 17   ᶠ 3 Some Septuagint manuscripts (see also Vulgate); Hebrew *father*
ᵍ 4 *Father* may mean *civic leader* or *military leader*; also in verses 12, 14, 17, 18 and possibly elsewhere.

Hazzobebah and of the clans of Aharhel son of Harum.

⁹Jabez was more honorable than his brothers. His mother had named him Jabez,ᵃ saying, "I gave birth to him in pain." ¹⁰Jabez cried out to the God of Israel, "Oh, that you would bless me and enlarge my territory! Let your hand be with me, and keep me from harm so that I will be free from pain." And God granted his request.

¹¹Kelub, Shuhah's brother, was the father of Mehir, who was the father of Eshton. ¹²Eshton was the father of Beth Rapha, Paseah and Tehinnah the father of Ir Nahash.ᵇ These were the men of Recah.

¹³The sons of Kenaz:
Othniel and Seraiah.
The sons of Othniel:
Hathath and Meonothai.ᶜ ¹⁴Meonothai was the father of Ophrah.
Seraiah was the father of Joab,
the father of Ge Harashim.ᵈ It was called this because its people were craftsmen.

¹⁵The sons of Caleb son of Jephunneh:
Iru, Elah and Naam.
The son of Elah:
Kenaz.

¹⁶The sons of Jehallelel:
Ziph, Ziphah, Tiria and Asarel.

¹⁷The sons of Ezrah:
Jether, Mered, Epher and Jalon. One of Mered's wives gave birth to Miriam, Shammai and Ishbah the father of Eshtemoa. ¹⁸(His Judean wife gave birth to Jered the father of Gedor, Heber the father of Soco, and Jekuthiel the father of Zanoah.) These were the children of Pharaoh's daughter Bithiah, whom Mered had married.

¹⁹The sons of Hodiah's wife, the sister of Naham:
the father of Keilah the Garmite, and Eshtemoa the Maacathite.

²⁰The sons of Shimon:
Amnon, Rinnah, Ben-Hanan and Tilon.
The descendants of Ishi:
Zoheth and Ben-Zoheth.

²¹The sons of Shelah son of Judah:
Er the father of Lecah, Laadah the father of Mareshah and the clans of the linen workers at Beth Ashbea,

²²Jokim, the men of Cozeba, and Joash and Saraph, who ruled in Moab and Jashubi Lehem. (These records are from ancient times.) ²³They were the potters who lived at Netaim and Gederah; they stayed there and worked for the king.

Simeon

²⁴The descendants of Simeon:
Nemuel, Jamin, Jarib, Zerah and Shaul;
²⁵Shallum was Shaul's son, Mibsam his son and Mishma his son.
²⁶The descendants of Mishma:
Hammuel his son, Zaccur his son and Shimei his son.
²⁷Shimei had sixteen sons and six daughters, but his brothers did not have many children; so their entire clan did not become as numerous as the people of Judah. ²⁸They lived in Beersheba, Moladah, Hazar Shual, ²⁹Bilhah, Ezem, Tolad, ³⁰Bethuel, Hormah, Ziklag, ³¹Beth Marcaboth, Hazar Susim, Beth Biri and Shaaraim. These were their towns until the reign of David. ³²Their surrounding villages were Etam, Ain, Rimmon, Token and Ashan— five towns— ³³and all the villages around these towns as far as Baalath.ᵉ These were their settlements. And they kept a genealogical record.

³⁴Meshobab, Jamlech, Joshah son of Amaziah, ³⁵Joel, Jehu son of Joshibiah, the son of Seraiah, the son of Asiel, ³⁶also Elioenai, Jaakobah, Jeshohaiah, Asaiah, Adiel, Jesimiel, Benaiah, ³⁷and Ziza son of Shiphi, the son of Allon, the son of Jedaiah, the son of Shimri, the son of Shemaiah.

³⁸The men listed above by name were leaders of their clans. Their families increased greatly, ³⁹and they went to the outskirts of Gedor to the east of the valley in search of pasture for their flocks. ⁴⁰They found rich, good pasture, and the land was spacious, peaceful and quiet. Some Hamites had lived there formerly.

⁴¹The men whose names were listed came in the days of Hezekiah king of Judah. They attacked the Hamites in their

---

dwellings and also the Meunites who were there and completely destroyed[a] them, as is evident to this day. Then they settled in their place, because there was pasture for their flocks. 42And five hundred of these Simeonites, led by Pelatiah, Neariah, Rephaiah and Uzziel, the sons of Ishi, invaded the hill country of Seir. 43They killed the remaining Amalekites who had escaped, and they have lived there to this day.

Reuben

5 The sons of Reuben the firstborn of Israel (he was the firstborn, but when he defiled his father's marriage bed, his rights as firstborn were given to the sons of Joseph son of Israel; so he could not be listed in the genealogical record in accordance with his birthright, 2and though Judah was the strongest of his brothers and a ruler came from him, the rights of the firstborn belonged to Joseph)— 3the sons of Reuben the firstborn of Israel:

Hanoch, Pallu, Hezron and Carmi.
4The descendants of Joel:
Shemaiah his son, Gog his son, Shimei his son, 5Micah his son, Reaiah his son, Baal his son,
6and Beerah his son, whom Tiglath-Pileser[b] king of Assyria took into exile. Beerah was a leader of the Reubenites.
7Their relatives by clans, listed according to their genealogical records:
Jeiel the chief, Zechariah, 8and Bela son of Azaz, the son of Shema, the son of Joel. They settled in the area from Aroer to Nebo and Baal Meon. 9To the east they occupied the land up to the edge of the desert that extends to the Euphrates River, because their livestock had increased in Gilead.
10During Saul's reign they waged war against the Hagrites, who were defeated at their hands; they occupied the dwellings of the Hagrites throughout the entire region east of Gilead.

Gad

11The Gadites lived next to them in Bashan, as far as Salecah:
12Joel was the chief, Shapham the second, then Janai and Shaphat, in Bashan.

13Their relatives, by families, were:
Michael, Meshullam, Sheba, Jorai, Jacan, Zia and Eber—seven in all.
14These were the sons of Abihail son of Huri, the son of Jaroah, the son of Gilead, the son of Michael, the son of Jeshishai, the son of Jahdo, the son of Buz.
15Ahi son of Abdiel, the son of Guni, was head of their family.
16The Gadites lived in Gilead, in Bashan and its outlying villages, and on all the pasturelands of Sharon as far as they extended.
17All these were entered in the genealogical records during the reigns of Jotham king of Judah and Jeroboam king of Israel.

18The Reubenites, the Gadites and the half-tribe of Manasseh had 44,760 men ready for military service—able-bodied men who could handle shield and sword, who could use a bow, and who were trained for battle. 19They waged war against the Hagrites, Jetur, Naphish and Nodab. 20They were helped in fighting them, and God handed the Hagrites and all their allies over to them, because they cried out to him during the battle. He answered their prayers, because they trusted in him. 21They seized the livestock of the Hagrites—fifty thousand camels, two hundred fifty thousand sheep and two thousand donkeys. They also took one hundred thousand people captive, 22and many others fell slain, because the battle was God's. And they occupied the land until the exile.

The Half-Tribe of Manasseh

23The people of the half-tribe of Manasseh were numerous; they settled in the land from Bashan to Baal Hermon, that is, to Senir (Mount Hermon).
24These were the heads of their families: Epher, Ishi, Eliel, Azriel, Jeremiah, Hodaviah and Jahdiel. They were brave warriors, famous men, and heads of their families. 25But they were unfaithful to the God of their fathers and prostituted themselves to the gods of the peoples of the land, whom God had destroyed be-

---

a 41 The Hebrew term refers to the irrevocable giving over of things or persons to the Lord, often by totally destroying them. b 6 Hebrew *Tilgath-Pilneser*, a variant of *Tiglath-Pileser*; also in verse 26 fore them. ²⁶So the God of Israel stirred up the spirit of Pul king of Assyria (that is, Tiglath-Pileser king of Assyria), who took the Reubenites, the Gadites and the half-tribe of Manasseh into exile. He took them to Halah, Habor, Hara and the river of Gozan, where they are to this day.

Levi

6 The sons of Levi:
Gershon, Kohath and Merari.
²The sons of Kohath:
Amram, Izhar, Hebron and Uzziel.
³The children of Amram:
Aaron, Moses and Miriam.
The sons of Aaron:
Nadab, Abihu, Eleazar and Ithamar.
⁴Eleazar was the father of Phinehas,
Phinehas the father of Abishua,
⁵Abishua the father of Bukki,
Bukki the father of Uzzi,
⁶Uzzi the father of Zerahiah,
Zerahiah the father of Meraioth,
⁷Meraioth the father of Amariah,

Amariah the father of Ahitub,
⁸Ahitub the father of Zadok,
Zadok the father of Ahimaaz,
⁹Ahimaaz the father of Azariah,
Azariah the father of Johanan,
¹⁰Johanan the father of Azariah (it was he who served as priest in the temple Solomon built in Jerusalem),
¹¹Azariah the father of Amariah,
Amariah the father of Ahitub,
¹²Ahitub the father of Zadok,
Zadok the father of Shallum,
¹³Shallum the father of Hilkiah,
Hilkiah the father of Azariah,
¹⁴Azariah the father of Seraiah,
and Seraiah the father of Jehozadak.
¹⁵Jehozadak was deported when the LORD sent Judah and Jerusalem into exile by the hand of Nebuchadnezzar.

¹⁶The sons of Levi:
Gershon,ᵃ Kohath and Merari.

ᵃ 16 Hebrew *Gershom,* a variant of *Gershon*; also in verses 17, 20, 43, 62 and 71

Make It Stick

READ 1 CHRONICLES 6

Have you ever looked up your own family tree? Anyone who ever did something totally incredible or mind-boggling? Hey, you never know! Write three names of very interesting characters from the family tree, whether from your mom's or your dad's side.

17 These are the names of the sons of Gershon:
Libni and Shimei.
18 The sons of Kohath:
Amram, Izhar, Hebron and Uzziel.
19 The sons of Merari:
Mahli and Mushi.
These are the clans of the Levites listed according to their fathers:
20 Of Gershon:
Libni his son, Jehath his son,
Zimmah his son, 21 Joah his son,
Iddo his son, Zerah his son
and Jeatherai his son.
22 The descendants of Kohath:
Amminadab his son, Korah his son,
Assir his son, 23 Elkanah his son,
Ebiasaph his son, Assir his son,
24 Tahath his son, Uriel his son,
Uzziah his son and Shaul his son.
25 The descendants of Elkanah:
Amasai, Ahimoth,
26 Elkanah his son,[a] Zophai his son,
Nahath his son, 27 Eliab his son,
Jeroham his son, Elkanah his son
and Samuel his son.[b]
28 The sons of Samuel:
Joel[c] the firstborn
and Abijah the second son.
29 The descendants of Merari:
Mahli, Libni his son,
Shimei his son, Uzzah his son,
30 Shimea his son, Haggiah his son
and Asaiah his son.

The Temple Musicians

31 These are the men David put in charge of the music in the house of the LORD after the ark came to rest there. 32 They ministered with music before the tabernacle, the Tent of Meeting, until Solomon built the temple of the LORD in Jerusalem. They performed their duties according to the regulations laid down for them.
33 Here are the men who served, together with their sons:
From the Kohathites:
Heman, the musician,
the son of Joel, the son of Samuel,
34 the son of Elkanah, the son of Jeroham,
the son of Eliel, the son of Toah,
35 the son of Zuph, the son of Elkanah,
the son of Mahath, the son of Amasai,
36 the son of Elkanah, the son of Joel,

the son of Azariah, the son of Zephaniah,
37 the son of Tahath, the son of Assir,
the son of Ebiasaph, the son of Korah,
38 the son of Izhar, the son of Kohath,
the son of Levi, the son of Israel;
39 and Heman's associate Asaph, who served at his right hand:
Asaph son of Berekiah, the son of Shimea,
40 the son of Michael, the son of Baaseiah,[d]
the son of Malkijah, 41 the son of Ethni,
the son of Zerah, the son of Adaiah,
42 the son of Ethan, the son of Zimmah,
the son of Shimei, 43 the son of Jahath,
the son of Gershon, the son of Levi;
44 and from their associates, the Merarites, at his left hand:
Ethan son of Kishi, the son of Abdi,
the son of Malluch, 45 the son of Hashabiah,
the son of Amaziah, the son of Hilkiah,
46 the son of Amzi, the son of Bani,
the son of Shemer, 47 the son of Mahli,
the son of Mushi, the son of Merari, the son of Levi.

48 Their fellow Levites were assigned to all the other duties of the tabernacle, the house of God. 49 But Aaron and his descendants were the ones who presented offerings on the altar of burnt offering and on the altar of incense in connection with all that was done in the Most Holy Place, making atonement for Israel, in accordance with all that Moses the servant of God had commanded.

50 These were the descendants of Aaron:
Eleazar his son, Phinehas his son,
Abishua his son, 51 Bukki his son,
Uzzi his son, Zerahiah his son,

a 26 Some Hebrew manuscripts, Septuagint and Syriac; most Hebrew manuscripts Ahimoth 26 and Elkanah. The sons of Elkanah: b 27 Some Septuagint manuscripts (see also 1 Samuel 1:19,20 and 1 Chron. 6:33,34); Hebrew does not have and Samuel his son.   c 28 Some Septuagint manuscripts and Syriac (see also 1 Samuel 8:2 and 1 Chron. 6:33); Hebrew does not have Joel.   d 40 Most Hebrew manuscripts; some Hebrew manuscripts, one Septuagint manuscript and Syriac Maaseiah

52 Meraioth his son, Amariah his son, Ahitub his son, 53 Zadok his son and Ahimaaz his son.

54 These were the locations of their settlements allotted as their territory (they were assigned to the descendants of Aaron who were from the Kohathite clan, because the first lot was for them): 55 They were given Hebron in Judah with its surrounding pasturelands. 56 But the fields and villages around the city were given to Caleb son of Jephunneh. 57 So the descendants of Aaron were given Hebron (a city of refuge), and Libnah,*a* Jattir, Eshtemoa, 58 Hilen, Debir, 59 Ashan, Juttah*b* and Beth Shemesh, together with their pasturelands. 60 And from the tribe of Benjamin they were given Gibeon,*c* Geba, Alemeth and Anathoth, together with their pasturelands.

These towns, which were distributed among the Kohathite clans, were thirteen in all.

61 The rest of Kohath's descendants were allotted ten towns from the clans of half the tribe of Manasseh.

62 The descendants of Gershon, clan by clan, were allotted thirteen towns from the tribes of Issachar, Asher and Naphtali, and from the part of the tribe of Manasseh that is in Bashan.

63 The descendants of Merari, clan by clan, were allotted twelve towns from the tribes of Reuben, Gad and Zebulun.

64 So the Israelites gave the Levites these towns and their pasturelands. 65 From the tribes of Judah, Simeon and Benjamin they allotted the previously named towns. 66 Some of the Kohathite clans were given as their territory towns from the tribe of Ephraim.

67 In the hill country of Ephraim they were given Shechem (a city of refuge), and Gezer,*d* 68 Jokmeam, Beth Horon, 69 Aijalon and Gath Rimmon, together with their pasturelands.

70 And from half the tribe of Manasseh the Israelites gave Aner and Bileam, together with their pasturelands, to the rest of the Kohathite clans.

71 The Gershonites received the following:

From the clan of the half-tribe of Manasseh they received Golan in Bashan and also Ashtaroth, together with their pasturelands;

72 from the tribe of Issachar they received Kedesh, Daberath, 73 Ramoth and Anem, together with their pasturelands;

74 from the tribe of Asher they received Mashal, Abdon, 75 Hukok and Rehob, together with their pasturelands;

76 and from the tribe of Naphtali they received Kedesh in Galilee, Hammon and Kiriathaim, together with their pasturelands.

77 The Merarites (the rest of the Levites) received the following:

From the tribe of Zebulun they received Jokneam, Kartah,*e* Rimmono and Tabor, together with their pasturelands;

78 from the tribe of Reuben across the Jordan east of Jericho they received Bezer in the desert, Jahzah, 79 Kedemoth and Mephaath, together with their pasturelands;

80 and from the tribe of Gad they received Ramoth in Gilead, Mahanaim, 81 Heshbon and Jazer, together with their pasturelands.

Issachar

7 The sons of Issachar:

Tola, Puah, Jashub and Shimron—four in all.

2 The sons of Tola:

Uzzi, Rephaiah, Jeriel, Jahmai, Ibsam and Samuel—heads of their families. During the reign of David, the descendants of Tola listed as fighting men in their genealogy numbered 22,600.

3 The son of Uzzi:

Izrahiah.

The sons of Izrahiah:

Michael, Obadiah, Joel and Isshiah. All five of them were chiefs. 4 According to their family genealogy, they had 36,000 men ready for

---

a 57 See Joshua 21:13; Hebrew *given the cities of refuge: Hebron, Libnah.*   *b 59* Syriac (see also Septuagint and Joshua 21:16); Hebrew does not have *Juttah.*
c 60 See Joshua 21:17; Hebrew does not have *Gibeon.*
d 67 See Joshua 21:21; Hebrew *given the cities of refuge: Shechem, Gezer.*   *e 77* See Septuagint and Joshua 21:34; Hebrew does not have *Jokneam, Kartah.*

battle, for they had many wives and children.

5 The relatives who were fighting men belonging to all the clans of Issachar, as listed in their genealogy, were 87,000 in all.

Benjamin

6 Three sons of Benjamin:
Bela, Beker and Jediael.

7 The sons of Bela:
Ezbon, Uzzi, Uzziel, Jerimoth and Iri, heads of families—five in all. Their genealogical record listed 22,034 fighting men.

8 The sons of Beker:
Zemirah, Joash, Eliezer, Elioenai, Omri, Jeremoth, Abijah, Anathoth and Alemeth. All these were the sons of Beker. 9 Their genealogical record listed the heads of families and 20,200 fighting men.

10 The son of Jediael:
Bilhan.
The sons of Bilhan:
Jeush, Benjamin, Ehud, Kenaanah, Zethan, Tarshish and Ahishahar. 11 All these sons of Jediael were heads of families. There were 17,200 fighting men ready to go out to war.

12 The Shuppites and Huppites were the descendants of Ir, and the Hushites the descendants of Aher.

Naphtali

13 The sons of Naphtali:
Jahziel, Guni, Jezer and Shillem[a]— the descendants of Bilhah.

Manasseh

14 The descendants of Manasseh:
Asriel was his descendant through his Aramean concubine. She gave birth to Makir the father of Gilead. 15 Makir took a wife from among the Huppites and Shuppites. His sister's name was Maacah.

Another descendant was named Zelophehad, who had only daughters.

16 Makir's wife Maacah gave birth to a son and named him Peresh. His brother was named Sheresh, and his sons were Ulam and Rakem.

17 The son of Ulam:
Bedan.
These were the sons of Gilead son of Makir, the son of Manasseh. 18 His sister Hammoleketh gave birth to Ishhod, Abiezer and Mahlah.

19 The sons of Shemida were:
Ahian, Shechem, Likhi and Aniam.

Ephraim

20 The descendants of Ephraim:
Shuthelah, Bered his son,
Tahath his son, Eleadah his son,
Tahath his son, 21 Zabad his son
and Shuthelah his son.

Ezer and Elead were killed by the native-born men of Gath, when they went down to seize their livestock. 22 Their father Ephraim mourned for them many days, and his relatives came to comfort him. 23 Then he lay with his wife again, and she became pregnant and gave birth to a son. He named him Beriah,[b] because there had been misfortune in his family. 24 His daughter was Sheerah, who built Lower and Upper Beth Horon as well as Uzzen Sheerah.

25 Rephah was his son, Resheph his son,[c]
Telah his son, Tahan his son,
26 Ladan his son, Ammihud his son,
Elishama his son, 27 Nun his son
and Joshua his son.

28 Their lands and settlements included Bethel and its surrounding villages, Naaran to the east, Gezer and its villages to the west, and Shechem and its villages all the way to Ayyah and its villages. 29 Along the borders of Manasseh were Beth Shan, Taanach, Megiddo and Dor, together with their villages. The descendants of Joseph son of Israel lived in these towns.

Asher

30 The sons of Asher:
Imnah, Ishvah, Ishvi and Beriah. Their sister was Serah.

31 The sons of Beriah:
Heber and Malkiel, who was the father of Birzaith.

32 Heber was the father of Japhlet, Shomer and Hotham and of their sister Shua.

33 The sons of Japhlet:
Pasach, Bimhal and Ashvath.

---

[a] 13 Some Hebrew and Septuagint manuscripts (see also Gen. 46:24 and Num. 26:49); most Hebrew manuscripts *Shallum*
[b] 23 *Beriah* sounds like the Hebrew for *misfortune*.
[c] 25 Some Septuagint manuscripts; Hebrew does not have *his son*.

These were Japhlet's sons.

34 The sons of Shomer:

Ahi, Rohgah,[a] Hubbah and Aram.

35 The sons of his brother Helem:

Zophah, Imna, Shelesh and Amal.

36 The sons of Zophah:

Suah, Harnepher, Shual, Beri, Imrah, 37 Bezer, Hod, Shamma, Shilshah, Ithran[b] and Beera.

38 The sons of Jether:

Jephunneh, Pispah and Ara.

39 The sons of Ulla:

Arah, Hanniel and Rizia.

40 All these were descendants of Asher—heads of families, choice men, brave warriors and outstanding leaders. The number of men ready for battle, as listed in their genealogy, was 26,000.

The Genealogy of Saul the Benjamite

8 Benjamin was the father of Bela his firstborn, Ashbel the second son, Aharah the third, 2 Nohah the fourth and Rapha the fifth.

3 The sons of Bela were:

Addar, Gera, Abihud,[c] 4 Abishua, Naaman, Ahoah, 5 Gera, Shephuphan and Huram.

6 These were the descendants of Ehud, who were heads of families of those living in Geba and were deported to Manahath:

7 Naaman, Ahijah, and Gera, who deported them and who was the father of Uzza and Ahihud.

8 Sons were born to Shaharaim in Moab after he had divorced his wives Hushim and Baara. 9 By his wife Hodesh he had Jobab, Zibia, Mesha, Malcam, 10 Jeuz, Sakia and Mirmah. These were his sons, heads of families. 11 By Hushim he had Abitub and Elpaal.

12 The sons of Elpaal:

Eber, Misham, Shemed (who built Ono and Lod with its surrounding villages), 13 and Beriah and Shema, who were heads of families of those living in Aijalon and who drove out the inhabitants of Gath.

14 Ahio, Shashak, Jeremoth, 15 Zebadiah, Arad, Eder, 16 Michael, Ishpah and Joha were the sons of Beriah.

17 Zebadiah, Meshullam, Hizki, Heber, 18 Ishmerai, Izliah and Jobab were the sons of Elpaal.

19 Jakim, Zicri, Zabdi, 20 Elienai, Zillethai, Eliel, 21 Adaiah, Beraiah and Shimrath were the sons of Shimei.

22 Ishpan, Eber, Eliel, 23 Abdon, Zicri, Hanan, 24 Hananiah, Elam, Anthothijah, 25 Iphdeiah and Penuel were the sons of Shashak.

26 Shamsherai, Shehariah, Athaliah, 27 Jaareshiah, Elijah and Zicri were the sons of Jeroham.

28 All these were heads of families, chiefs as listed in their genealogy, and they lived in Jerusalem.

29 Jeiel[d] the father[e] of Gibeon lived in Gibeon.

His wife's name was Maacah, 30 and his firstborn son was Abdon, followed by Zur, Kish, Baal, Ner,[f] Nadab, 31 Gedor, Ahio, Zeker 32 and Mikloth, who was the father of Shimeah. They too lived near their relatives in Jerusalem.

33 Ner was the father of Kish, Kish the father of Saul, and Saul the father of Jonathan, Malki-Shua, Abinadab and Esh-Baal.[g]

34 The son of Jonathan:

Merib-Baal,[h] who was the father of Micah.

35 The sons of Micah:

Pithon, Melech, Tarea and Ahaz.

36 Ahaz was the father of Jehoaddah, Jehoaddah was the father of Alemeth, Azmaveth and Zimri, and Zimri was the father of Moza. 37 Moza was the father of Binea; Raphah was his son, Eleasah his son and Azel his son.

38 Azel had six sons, and these were their names:

Azrikam, Bokeru, Ishmael, Sheariah, Obadiah and Hanan. All these were the sons of Azel.

39 The sons of his brother Eshek:

Ulam his firstborn, Jeush the second son and Eliphelet the third. 40 The sons of Ulam were brave

a 34 Or of his brother Shomer: Rohgah   b 37 Possibly a variant of Jether   c 3 Or Gera the father of Ehud   d 29 Some Septuagint manuscripts (see also 1 Chron. 9:35); Hebrew does not have Jeiel.   e 29 Father may mean civic leader or military leader.   f 30 Some Septuagint manuscripts (see also 1 Chron. 9:36); Hebrew does not have Ner.   g 33 Also known as Ish-Bosheth   h 34 Also known as Mephibosheth warriors who could handle the bow. They had many sons and grandsons—150 in all.

All these were the descendants of Benjamin.

9 All Israel was listed in the genealogies recorded in the book of the kings of Israel.

The People in Jerusalem

The people of Judah were taken captive to Babylon because of their unfaithfulness. ²Now the first to resettle on their own property in their own towns were some Israelites, priests, Levites and temple servants.

³Those from Judah, from Benjamin, and from Ephraim and Manasseh who lived in Jerusalem were:

⁴Uthai son of Ammihud, the son of Omri, the son of Imri, the son of Bani, a descendant of Perez son of Judah.

⁵Of the Shilonites:

Asaiah the firstborn and his sons.

⁶Of the Zerahites:

Jeuel.

The people from Judah numbered 690.

⁷Of the Benjamites:

Sallu son of Meshullam, the son of Hodaviah, the son of Hassenuah;

⁸Ibneiah son of Jeroham; Elah son of Uzzi, the son of Micri; and Meshullam son of Shephatiah, the son of Reuel, the son of Ibnijah.

⁹The people from Benjamin, as listed in their genealogy, numbered 956. All these men were heads of their families.

¹⁰Of the priests:

Jedaiah; Jehoiarib; Jakin;

¹¹Azariah son of Hilkiah, the son of Meshullam, the son of Zadok, the son of Meraioth, the son of Ahitub, the official in charge of the house of God;

¹²Adaiah son of Jeroham, the son of Pashhur, the son of Malkijah; and Maasai son of Adiel, the son of Jahzerah, the son of Meshullam, the son of Meshillemith, the son of Immer.

¹³The priests, who were heads of families, numbered 1,760. They were able men, responsible for ministering in the house of God.

¹⁴Of the Levites:

Shemaiah son of Hasshub, the son of Azrikam, the son of Hashabiah, a Merarite; ¹⁵Bakbakkar, Heresh, Galal and Mattaniah son of Mica, the son of Zicri, the son of Asaph; ¹⁶Obadiah son of Shemaiah, the son of Galal, the son of Jeduthun; and Berekiah son of Asa, the son of Elkanah, who lived in the villages of the Netophathites.

¹⁷The gatekeepers:

Shallum, Akkub, Talmon, Ahiman and their brothers, Shallum their chief ¹⁸being stationed at the King's Gate on the east, up to the present time. These were the gatekeepers belonging to the camp of the Levites. ¹⁹Shallum son of Kore, the son of Ebiasaph, the son of Korah, and his fellow gatekeepers from his family (the Korahites) were responsible for guarding the thresholds of the Tent[a] just as their fathers had been responsible for guarding the entrance to the dwelling of the LORD. ²⁰In earlier times Phinehas son of Eleazar was in charge of the gatekeepers, and the LORD was with him. ²¹Zechariah son of Meshelemiah was the gatekeeper at the entrance to the Tent of Meeting.

²²Altogether, those chosen to be gatekeepers at the thresholds numbered 212. They were registered by genealogy in their villages. The gatekeepers had been assigned to their positions of trust by David and Samuel the seer. ²³They and their descendants were in charge of guarding the gates of the house of the LORD—the house called the Tent. ²⁴The gatekeepers were on the four sides: east, west, north and south. ²⁵Their brothers in their villages had to come from time to time and share their duties for seven-day periods. ²⁶But the four principal gatekeepers, who were Levites, were entrusted with the responsibility for the rooms and treasuries in the house of God. ²⁷They would spend the night stationed around the house of God, because they had to guard it; and they had charge of the key for opening it each morning.

²⁸Some of them were in charge of the

---

a 19 That is, the temple; also in verses 21 and 23

articles used in the temple service; they counted them when they were brought in and when they were taken out. ²⁹Others were assigned to take care of the furnishings and all the other articles of the sanctuary, as well as the flour and wine, and the oil, incense and spices. ³⁰But some of the priests took care of mixing the spices. ³¹A Levite named Mattithiah, the firstborn son of Shallum the Korahite, was entrusted with the responsibility for baking the offering bread. ³²Some of their Kohathite brothers were in charge of preparing for every Sabbath the bread set out on the table.

³³Those who were musicians, heads of Levite families, stayed in the rooms of the temple and were exempt from other duties because they were responsible for the work day and night.

³⁴All these were heads of Levite families, chiefs as listed in their genealogy, and they lived in Jerusalem.

The Genealogy of Saul

³⁵Jeiel the father*ᵃ* of Gibeon lived in Gibeon.

His wife's name was Maacah, ³⁶and his firstborn son was Abdon, followed by Zur, Kish, Baal, Ner, Nadab, ³⁷Gedor, Ahio, Zechariah and Mikloth. ³⁸Mikloth was the father of Shimeam. They too lived near their relatives in Jerusalem.

³⁹Ner was the father of Kish, Kish the father of Saul, and Saul the father of Jonathan, Malki-Shua, Abinadab and Esh-Baal.*ᵇ*

⁴⁰The son of Jonathan:

Merib-Baal,*ᶜ* who was the father of Micah.

⁴¹The sons of Micah:

Pithon, Melech, Tahrea and Ahaz.*ᵈ*

⁴²Ahaz was the father of Jadah, Jadah*ᵉ* was the father of Alemeth, Azmaveth and Zimri, and Zimri was the father of Moza. ⁴³Moza was the father of Binea; Rephaiah was his son, Eleasah his son and Azel his son.

⁴⁴Azel had six sons, and these were their names:

Azrikam, Bokeru, Ishmael, Sheariah, Obadiah and Hanan. These were the sons of Azel.

Saul Takes His Life

10 Now the Philistines fought against Israel; the Israelites fled before them, and many fell slain on Mount Gilboa. ²The Philistines pressed hard after Saul and his sons, and they killed his sons Jonathan, Abinadab and Malki-Shua. ³The fighting grew fierce around Saul, and when the archers overtook him, they wounded him.

⁴Saul said to his armor-bearer, "Draw your sword and run me through, or these uncircumcised fellows will come and abuse me."

But his armor-bearer was terrified and would not do it; so Saul took his own sword and fell on it. ⁵When the armor-bearer saw that Saul was dead, he too fell on his sword and died. ⁶So Saul and his three sons died, and all his house died together.

⁷When all the Israelites in the valley saw that the army had fled and that Saul and his sons had died, they abandoned their towns and fled. And the Philistines came and occupied them.

⁸The next day, when the Philistines came to strip the dead, they found Saul and his sons fallen on Mount Gilboa. ⁹They stripped him and took his head and his armor, and sent messengers throughout the land of the Philistines to proclaim the news among their idols and their people. ¹⁰They put his armor in the temple of their gods and hung up his head in the temple of Dagon.

¹¹When all the inhabitants of Jabesh Gilead heard of everything the Philistines had done to Saul, ¹²all their valiant men went and took the bodies of Saul and his sons and brought them to Jabesh. Then they buried their bones under the great tree in Jabesh, and they fasted seven days.

¹³Saul died because he was unfaithful to the LORD; he did not keep the word of the LORD and even consulted a medium for guidance, ¹⁴and did not inquire of the LORD. So the LORD put him to death and turned the kingdom over to David son of Jesse.

ᵃ 35 *Father* may mean *civic leader* or *military leader.*
ᵇ 39 Also known as *Ish-Bosheth*   *ᶜ 40* Also known as *Mephibosheth*   *ᵈ 41* Vulgate and Syriac (see also Septuagint and 1 Chron. 8:35); Hebrew does not have *and Ahaz.*   *ᵉ 42* Some Hebrew manuscripts and Septuagint (see also 1 Chron. 8:36); most Hebrew manuscripts *Jarah, Jarah*

David Becomes King Over Israel

11 All Israel came together to David at Hebron and said, "We are your own flesh and blood. ²In the past, even while Saul was king, you were the one who led Israel on their military campaigns. And the LORD your God said to you, 'You will shepherd my people Israel, and you will become their ruler.' "

³When all the elders of Israel had come to King David at Hebron, he made a compact with them at Hebron before the LORD, and they anointed David king over Israel, as the LORD had promised through Samuel.

David Conquers Jerusalem

⁴David and all the Israelites marched to Jerusalem (that is, Jebus). The Jebusites who lived there ⁵said to David, "You will not get in here." Nevertheless, David captured the fortress of Zion, the City of David.

⁶David had said, "Whoever leads the attack on the Jebusites will become commander-in-chief." Joab son of Zeruiah went up first, and so he received the command.

⁷David then took up residence in the fortress, and so it was called the City of David. ⁸He built up the city around it, from the supporting terraces*a* to the surrounding wall, while Joab restored the rest of the city. ⁹And David became more and more powerful, because the LORD Almighty was with him.

David's Mighty Men

¹⁰These were the chiefs of David's mighty men—they, together with all Israel, gave his kingship strong support to extend it over the whole land, as the LORD had promised— ¹¹this is the list of David's mighty men:

Jashobeam,*b* a Hacmonite, was chief of the officers*c*; he raised his spear against three hundred men, whom he killed in one encounter.

¹²Next to him was Eleazar son of Dodai the Ahohite, one of the three mighty men. ¹³He was with David at Pas Dammim when the Philistines gathered there for battle. At a place where there was a field full of barley, the troops fled from the Philistines. ¹⁴But they took their stand in the middle of the field. They defended it and struck the Philistines down, and the LORD brought about a great victory.

¹⁵Three of the thirty chiefs came down to David to the rock at the cave of Adullam, while a band of Philistines was encamped in the Valley of Rephaim. ¹⁶At that time David was in the stronghold, and the Philistine garrison was at Bethlehem. ¹⁷David longed for water and said, "Oh, that someone would get me a drink of water from the well near the gate of Bethlehem!" ¹⁸So the Three broke through the Philistine lines, drew water from the well near the gate of Bethlehem and carried it back to David. But he refused to drink it; instead, he poured it out before the LORD. ¹⁹"God forbid that I

Get a Load of This...

Check out 1 Chronicles 11:4–9. The only way David's men could get inside Jerusalem was through a water shaft (see 2 Samuel 5:6–8). It was a slippery, dangerous, claustrophobic tunnel, and David said the guy with guts enough to go first would become his second-in-command. Joab successfully completed the mission and got the job.

---

a 8 Or the Millo   b 11 Possibly a variant of Jashob-Baal   c 11 Or Thirty; some Septuagint manuscripts Three (see also 2 Samuel 23:8) should do this!" he said. "Should I drink the blood of these men who went at the risk of their lives?" Because they risked their lives to bring it back, David would not drink it.

Such were the exploits of the three mighty men.

²⁰Abishai the brother of Joab was chief of the Three. He raised his spear against three hundred men, whom he killed, and so he became as famous as the Three. ²¹He was doubly honored above the Three and became their commander, even though he was not included among them.

²²Benaiah son of Jehoiada was a valiant fighter from Kabzeel, who performed great exploits. He struck down two of Moab's best men. He also went down into a pit on a snowy day and killed a lion. ²³And he struck down an Egyptian who was seven and a half feet*a* tall. Although the Egyptian had a spear like a weaver's rod in his hand, Benaiah went against him with a club. He snatched the spear from the Egyptian's hand and killed him with his own spear. ²⁴Such were the exploits of Benaiah son of Jehoiada; he too was as famous as the three mighty men. ²⁵He was held in greater honor than any of the Thirty, but he was not included among the Three. And David put him in charge of his bodyguard.

²⁶The mighty men were:

Asahel the brother of Joab,
Elhanan son of Dodo from Bethlehem,
²⁷Shammoth the Harorite,
Helez the Pelonite,
²⁸Ira son of Ikkesh from Tekoa,
Abiezer from Anathoth,
²⁹Sibbecai the Hushathite,
Ilai the Ahohite,
³⁰Maharai the Netophathite,
Heled son of Baanah the Netophathite,
³¹Ithai son of Ribai from Gibeah in Benjamin,
Benaiah the Pirathonite,
³²Hurai from the ravines of Gaash,
Abiel the Arbathite,
³³Azmaveth the Baharumite,
Eliahba the Shaalbonite,
³⁴the sons of Hashem the Gizonite,
Jonathan son of Shagee the Hararite,
³⁵Ahiam son of Sacar the Hararite,

Eliphal son of Ur,
³⁶Hepher the Mekerathite,
Ahijah the Pelonite,
³⁷Hezro the Carmelite,
Naarai son of Ezbai,
³⁸Joel the brother of Nathan,
Mibhar son of Hagri,
³⁹Zelek the Ammonite,
Naharai the Berothite, the armor-bearer of Joab son of Zeruiah,
⁴⁰Ira the Ithrite,
Gareb the Ithrite,
⁴¹Uriah the Hittite,
Zabad son of Ahlai,
⁴²Adina son of Shiza the Reubenite, who was chief of the Reubenites, and the thirty with him,
⁴³Hanan son of Maacah,
Joshaphat the Mithnite,
⁴⁴Uzzia the Ashterathite,
Shama and Jeiel the sons of Hotham the Aroerite,
⁴⁵Jediael son of Shimri,
his brother Joha the Tizite,
⁴⁶Eliel the Mahavite,
Jeribai and Joshaviah the sons of Elnaam,
Ithmah the Moabite,
⁴⁷Eliel, Obed and Jaasiel the Mezobaite.

Warriors Join David

These were the men who came to David at Ziklag, while he was banished from the presence of Saul son of Kish (they were among the warriors who helped him in battle; ²they were armed with bows and were able to shoot arrows or to sling stones right-handed or left-handed; they were kinsmen of Saul from the tribe of Benjamin):

³Ahiezer their chief and Joash the sons of Shemaah the Gibeathite; Jeziel and Pelet the sons of Azmaveth; Beracah, Jehu the Anathothite, ⁴and Ishmaiah the Gibeonite, a mighty man among the Thirty, who was a leader of the Thirty; Jeremiah, Jahaziel, Johanan, Jozabad the Gederathite, ⁵Eluzai, Jerimoth, Bealiah, Shemariah and Shephatiah the Haruphite; ⁶Elkanah, Isshiah, Azarel, Joezer and Jashobeam the Korahites;

a 23 Hebrew *five cubits* (about 2.3 meters)

7and Joelah and Zebadiah the sons of Jeroham from Gedor.

8Some Gadites defected to David at his stronghold in the desert. They were brave warriors, ready for battle and able to handle the shield and spear. Their faces were the faces of lions, and they were as swift as gazelles in the mountains.
9Ezer was the chief,
Obadiah the second in command, Eliab the third,
10Mishmannah the fourth, Jeremiah the fifth,
11Attai the sixth, Eliel the seventh,
12Johanan the eighth, Elzabad the ninth,
13Jeremiah the tenth and Macbannai the eleventh.

14These Gadites were army commanders; the least was a match for a hundred, and the greatest for a thousand. 15It was they who crossed the Jordan in the first month when it was overflowing all its banks, and they put to flight everyone living in the valleys, to the east and to the west.

16Other Benjamites and some men from Judah also came to David in his stronghold. 17David went out to meet them and said to them, "If you have come to me in peace, to help me, I am ready to have you unite with me. But if you have come to betray me to my enemies when my hands are free from violence, may the God of our fathers see it and judge you."

18Then the Spirit came upon Amasai, chief of the Thirty, and he said:

"We are yours, O David!
We are with you, O son of Jesse!
Success, success to you,
and success to those who help you,
for your God will help you."

So David received them and made them leaders of his raiding bands.

19Some of the men of Manasseh defected to David when he went with the Philistines to fight against Saul. (He and his men did not help the Philistines because, after consultation, their rulers sent him away. They said, "It will cost us our heads if he deserts to his master Saul.") 20When David went to Ziklag, these were the men of Manasseh who defected to him: Adnah, Jozabad, Jediael, Michael, Jozabad, Elihu and Zillethai, leaders of units of a thousand in Manasseh. 21They helped David against raiding bands, for all of them were brave warriors, and they were commanders in his army. 22Day after day men came to help David, until he had a great army, like the army of God.ᵃ

Others Join David at Hebron

23These are the numbers of the men armed for battle who came to David at Hebron to turn Saul's kingdom over to him, as the LORD had said:
24men of Judah, carrying shield and spear—6,800 armed for battle;
25men of Simeon, warriors ready for battle—7,100;
26men of Levi—4,600, 27including Jehoiada, leader of the family of Aaron, with 3,700 men, 28and Zadok, a brave young warrior, with 22 officers from his family;
29men of Benjamin, Saul's kinsmen—3,000, most of whom had remained loyal to Saul's house until then;
30men of Ephraim, brave warriors, famous in their own clans—20,800;
31men of half the tribe of Manasseh, designated by name to come and make David king—18,000;
32men of Issachar, who understood the times and knew what Israel should do—200 chiefs, with all their relatives under their command;
33men of Zebulun, experienced soldiers prepared for battle with every type of weapon, to help David with undivided loyalty—50,000;
34men of Naphtali—1,000 officers, together with 37,000 men carrying shields and spears;
35men of Dan, ready for battle—28,600;
36men of Asher, experienced soldiers prepared for battle—40,000;
37and from east of the Jordan, men of Reuben, Gad and the half-tribe of Manasseh, armed with every type of weapon—120,000.

38All these were fighting men who volunteered to serve in the ranks. They came to Hebron fully determined to make David king over all Israel. All the rest of the Israelites were also of one mind to make David king. 39The men spent three days there with David, eating and drinking, for their families had supplied provisions for them.

ᵃ 22 Or a great and mighty army

⁴⁰Also, their neighbors from as far away as Issachar, Zebulun and Naphtali came bringing food on donkeys, camels, mules and oxen. There were plentiful supplies of flour, fig cakes, raisin cakes, wine, oil, cattle and sheep, for there was joy in Israel.

Bringing Back the Ark

13 David conferred with each of his officers, the commanders of thousands and commanders of hundreds. ²He then said to the whole assembly of Israel, "If it seems good to you and if it is the will of the LORD our God, let us send word far and wide to the rest of our brothers throughout the territories of Israel, and also to the priests and Levites who are with them in their towns and pasturelands, to come and join us. ³Let us bring the ark of our God back to us, for we did not inquire of ͣ it ᵇ during the reign of Saul." ⁴The whole assembly agreed to do this, because it seemed right to all the people.

⁵So David assembled all the Israelites, from the Shihor River in Egypt to Lebo ͨ Hamath, to bring the ark of God from Kiriath Jearim. ⁶David and all the Israelites with him went to Baalah of Judah (Kiriath Jearim) to bring up from there the ark of God the LORD, who is enthroned between the cherubim—the ark that is called by the Name.

⁷They moved the ark of God from Abinadab's house on a new cart, with Uzzah and Ahio guiding it. ⁸David and all the Israelites were celebrating with all their might before God, with songs and with harps, lyres, tambourines, cymbals and trumpets.

⁹When they came to the threshing floor of Kidon, Uzzah reached out his hand to steady the ark, because the oxen stumbled. ¹⁰The LORD's anger burned against Uzzah, and he struck him down because he had put his hand on the ark. So he died there before God.

¹¹Then David was angry because the LORD's wrath had broken out against Uzzah, and to this day that place is called Perez Uzzah. ͩ

¹²David was afraid of God that day and asked, "How can I ever bring the ark of God to me?" ¹³He did not take the ark to be with him in the City of David. Instead, he took it aside to the house of Obed-Edom the Gittite. ¹⁴The ark of God remained with the family of Obed-Edom in his house for three months, and the LORD blessed his household and everything he had.

David's House and Family

14 Now Hiram king of Tyre sent messengers to David, along with cedar logs, stonemasons and carpenters to build a palace for him. ²And David knew that the LORD had established him as king over Israel and that his kingdom had been highly exalted for the sake of his people Israel.

³In Jerusalem David took more wives and became the father of more sons and daughters. ⁴These are the names of the children born to him there: Shammua, Shobab, Nathan, Solomon, ⁵Ibhar, Elishua, Elpelet, ⁶Nogah, Nepheg, Japhia, ⁷Elishama, Beeliada ͤ and Eliphelet.

David Defeats the Philistines

⁸When the Philistines heard that David had been anointed king over all Israel, they went up in full force to search for him, but David heard about it and went out to meet them. ⁹Now the Philistines had come and raided the Valley of Rephaim; ¹⁰so David inquired of God: "Shall I go and attack the Philistines? Will you hand them over to me?"

The LORD answered him, "Go, I will hand them over to you."

¹¹So David and his men went up to Baal Perazim, and there he defeated them. He said, "As waters break out, God has broken out against my enemies by my hand." So that place was called Baal Perazim. ͬ ¹²The Philistines had abandoned their gods there, and David gave orders to burn them in the fire.

¹³Once more the Philistines raided the valley; ¹⁴so David inquired of God again, and God answered him, "Do not go straight up, but circle around them and attack them in front of the balsam trees. ¹⁵As soon as you hear the sound of marching in the tops of the balsam trees, move out to battle, because that will mean God has gone out in front of you to strike the Philistine army." ¹⁶So David did as God commanded him, and they struck

---

ͣ 3 Or we neglected   ᵇ 3 Or him   ͨ 5 Or to the entrance to   ͩ 11 Perez Uzzah means outbreak against Uzzah.
ͤ 7 A variant of Eliada   ͬ 11 Baal Perazim means the lord who breaks out.

down the Philistine army, all the way from Gibeon to Gezer.

[17]So David's fame spread throughout every land, and the LORD made all the nations fear him.

The Ark Brought to Jerusalem

15 After David had constructed buildings for himself in the City of David, he prepared a place for the ark of God and pitched a tent for it. [2]Then David said, "No one but the Levites may carry the ark of God, because the LORD chose them to carry the ark of the LORD and to minister before him forever."

[3]David assembled all Israel in Jerusalem to bring up the ark of the LORD to the place he had prepared for it. [4]He called together the descendants of Aaron and the Levites:

[5]From the descendants of Kohath,
   Uriel the leader and 120 relatives;
[6]from the descendants of Merari,
   Asaiah the leader and 220 relatives;
[7]from the descendants of Gershon,[a]
   Joel the leader and 130 relatives;
[8]from the descendants of Elizaphan,
   Shemaiah the leader and 200 relatives;
[9]from the descendants of Hebron,
   Eliel the leader and 80 relatives;
[10]from the descendants of Uzziel,
   Amminadab the leader and 112 relatives.

[11]Then David summoned Zadok and Abiathar the priests, and Uriel, Asaiah, Joel, Shemaiah, Eliel and Amminadab the Levites. [12]He said to them, "You are the heads of the Levitical families; you and your fellow Levites are to consecrate yourselves and bring up the ark of the LORD, the God of Israel, to the place I have prepared for it. [13]It was because you, the Levites, did not bring it up the first time that the LORD our God broke out in anger against us. We did not inquire of him about how to do it in the prescribed way." [14]So the priests and Levites consecrated themselves in order to bring up the ark of the LORD, the God of Israel. [15]And the Levites carried the ark of God with the poles on their shoulders, as Moses had commanded in accordance with the word of the LORD.

[16]David told the leaders of the Levites to appoint their brothers as singers to sing joyful songs, accompanied by musical instruments: lyres, harps and cymbals.

[17]So the Levites appointed Heman son of Joel; from his brothers, Asaph son of Berekiah; and from their brothers the Merarites, Ethan son of Kushaiah; [18]and with them their brothers next in rank: Zechariah,[b] Jaaziel, Shemiramoth, Jehiel, Unni, Eliab, Benaiah, Maaseiah, Mattithiah, Eliphelehu, Mikneiah, Obed-Edom and Jeiel,[c] the gatekeepers.

[19]The musicians Heman, Asaph and Ethan were to sound the bronze cymbals; [20]Zechariah, Aziel, Shemiramoth, Jehiel, Unni, Eliab, Maaseiah and Benaiah were to play the lyres according to *alamoth,*[d] [21]and Mattithiah, Eliphelehu, Mikneiah, Obed-Edom, Jeiel and Azaziah were to play the harps, directing according to *sheminith.*[d] [22]Kenaniah the head Levite was in charge of the singing; that was his responsibility because he was skillful at it.

[23]Berekiah and Elkanah were to be doorkeepers for the ark. [24]Shebaniah, Joshaphat, Nethanel, Amasai, Zechariah, Benaiah and Eliezer the priests were to blow trumpets before the ark of God. Obed-Edom and Jehiah were also to be doorkeepers for the ark.

[25]So David and the elders of Israel and the commanders of units of a thousand went to bring up the ark of the covenant of the LORD from the house of Obed-Edom, with rejoicing. [26]Because God had helped the Levites who were carrying the ark of the covenant of the LORD, seven bulls and seven rams were sacrificed. [27]Now David was clothed in a robe of fine linen, as were all the Levites who were carrying the ark, and as were the singers, and Kenaniah, who was in charge of the singing of the choirs. David also wore a linen ephod. [28]So all Israel brought up the ark of the covenant of the LORD with shouts, with the sounding of rams' horns and trumpets, and of cymbals, and the playing of lyres and harps.

[29]As the ark of the covenant of the LORD was entering the City of David, Michal daughter of Saul watched from a window. And when she saw King David dancing and celebrating, she despised him in her heart.

---

[a] 7 Hebrew *Gershom*, a variant of *Gershon*   [b] 18 Three Hebrew manuscripts and most Septuagint manuscripts (see also verse 20 and 1 Chron. 16:5); most Hebrew manuscripts *Zechariah son and* or *Zechariah, Ben and*   [c] 18 Hebrew; Septuagint (see also verse 21) *Jeiel and Azaziah*   [d] 20,21 Probably a musical term

16 They brought the ark of God and set it inside the tent that David had pitched for it, and they presented burnt offerings and fellowship offerings[a] before God. [2] After David had finished sacrificing the burnt offerings and fellowship offerings, he blessed the people in the name of the LORD. [3] Then he gave a loaf of bread, a cake of dates and a cake of raisins to each Israelite man and woman.

[4] He appointed some of the Levites to minister before the ark of the LORD, to make petition, to give thanks, and to praise the LORD, the God of Israel: [5] Asaph was the chief, Zechariah second, then Jeiel, Shemiramoth, Jehiel, Mattithiah, Eliab, Benaiah, Obed-Edom and Jeiel. They were to play the lyres and harps, Asaph was to sound the cymbals, [6] and Benaiah and Jahaziel the priests were to blow the trumpets regularly before the ark of the covenant of God.

David's Psalm of Thanks

[7] That day David first committed to Asaph and his associates this psalm of thanks to the LORD:

[8] Give thanks to the LORD, call on his
         name;
     make known among the nations
         what he has done.
[9] Sing to him, sing praise to him;
     tell of all his wonderful acts.
[10] Glory in his holy name;
     let the hearts of those who seek the
         LORD rejoice.
[11] Look to the LORD and his strength;
     seek his face always.
[12] Remember the wonders he has done,
     his miracles, and the judgments he
         pronounced,
[13] O descendants of Israel his servant,
     O sons of Jacob, his chosen ones.

[14] He is the LORD our God;
     his judgments are in all the earth.
[15] He remembers[b] his covenant forever,
     the word he commanded, for a
         thousand generations,
[16] the covenant he made with Abraham,
     the oath he swore to Isaac.
[17] He confirmed it to Jacob as a decree,
     to Israel as an everlasting covenant:
[18] "To you I will give the land of Canaan
     as the portion you will inherit."

[19] When they were but few in number,
     few indeed, and strangers in it,
[20] they[c] wandered from nation to nation,
     from one kingdom to another.
[21] He allowed no man to oppress them;
     for their sake he rebuked kings:
[22] "Do not touch my anointed ones;
     do my prophets no harm."

[23] Sing to the LORD, all the earth;
     proclaim his salvation day after day.
[24] Declare his glory among the nations,
     his marvelous deeds among all
         peoples.
[25] For great is the LORD and most worthy
         of praise;
     he is to be feared above all gods.
[26] For all the gods of the nations are
         idols,
     but the LORD made the heavens.
[27] Splendor and majesty are before him;
     strength and joy in his dwelling place.
[28] Ascribe to the LORD, O families of
         nations,
     ascribe to the LORD glory and strength,
[29] ascribe to the LORD the glory due his
         name.
     Bring an offering and come before him;
     worship the LORD in the splendor of
         his[d] holiness.
[30] Tremble before him, all the earth!
     The world is firmly established; it
         cannot be moved.
[31] Let the heavens rejoice, let the earth be
         glad;
     let them say among the nations,
         "The LORD reigns!"
[32] Let the sea resound, and all that is in it;
     let the fields be jubilant, and
         everything in them!
[33] Then the trees of the forest will sing,
     they will sing for joy before the LORD,
     for he comes to judge the earth.

[34] Give thanks to the LORD, for he is good;
     his love endures forever.
[35] Cry out, "Save us, O God our Savior;
     gather us and deliver us from the
         nations,
     that we may give thanks to your holy
         name,
     that we may glory in your praise."

36 Praise be to the LORD, the God of Israel,
from everlasting to everlasting.

Then all the people said "Amen" and "Praise the LORD."

37 David left Asaph and his associates before the ark of the covenant of the LORD to minister there regularly, according to each day's requirements. 38 He also left Obed-Edom and his sixty-eight associates to minister with them. Obed-Edom son of Jeduthun, and also Hosah, were gatekeepers.

39 David left Zadok the priest and his fellow priests before the tabernacle of the LORD at the high place in Gibeon 40 to present burnt offerings to the LORD on the altar of burnt offering regularly, morning and evening, in accordance with everything written in the Law of the LORD, which he had given Israel. 41 With them were Heman and Jeduthun and the rest of those chosen and designated by name to give thanks to the LORD, "for his love endures forever." 42 Heman and Jeduthun were responsible for the sounding of the trumpets and cymbals and for the playing of the other instruments for sacred song. The sons of Jeduthun were stationed at the gate.

43 Then all the people left, each for his own home, and David returned home to bless his family.

God's Promise to David

17 After David was settled in his palace, he said to Nathan the prophet, "Here I am, living in a palace of cedar, while the ark of the covenant of the LORD is under a tent."

2 Nathan replied to David, "Whatever you have in mind, do it, for God is with you."

3 That night the word of God came to Nathan, saying:

4 "Go and tell my servant David, 'This is what the LORD says: You are not the one to build me a house to dwell in. 5 I have not dwelt in a house from the day I brought Israel up out of Egypt to this day. I have moved from one tent site to another, from one dwelling place to another. 6 Wherever I have moved with all the Israelites, did I ever say to any of their leaders[a] whom I commanded to shepherd my people, "Why have you not built me a house of cedar?" '

7 "Now then, tell my servant David,

'This is what the LORD Almighty says: I took you from the pasture and from following the flock, to be ruler over my people Israel. 8 I have been with you wherever you have gone, and I have cut off all your enemies from before you. Now I will make your name like the names of the greatest men of the earth. 9 And I will provide a place for my people Israel and will plant them so that they can have a home of their own and no longer be disturbed. Wicked people will not oppress them anymore, as they did at the beginning 10 and have done ever since the time I appointed leaders over my people Israel. I will also subdue all your enemies.

" 'I declare to you that the LORD will build a house for you: 11 When your days are over and you go to be with your fathers, I will raise up your offspring to succeed you, one of your own sons, and I will establish his kingdom. 12 He is the one who will build a house for me, and I will establish his throne forever. 13 I will be his father, and he will be my son. I will never take my love away from him, as I took it away from your predecessor. 14 I will set him over my house and my kingdom forever; his throne will be established forever.' "

15 Nathan reported to David all the words of this entire revelation.

David's Prayer

16 Then King David went in and sat before the LORD, and he said:

"Who am I, O LORD God, and what is my family, that you have brought me this far? 17 And as if this were not enough in your sight, O God, you have spoken about the future of the house of your servant. You have looked on me as though I were the most exalted of men, O LORD God.

18 "What more can David say to you for honoring your servant? For you know your servant, 19 O LORD. For the sake of your servant and according to your will, you have done this great thing and made known all these great promises.

---

a 6 Traditionally judges; also in verse 10

20"There is no one like you, O LORD, and there is no God but you, as we have heard with our own ears. 21And who is like your people Israel—the one nation on earth whose God went out to redeem a people for himself, and to make a name for yourself, and to perform great and awesome wonders by driving out nations from before your people, whom you redeemed from Egypt? 22You made your people Israel your very own forever, and you, O LORD, have become their God.

23"And now, LORD, let the promise you have made concerning your servant and his house be established forever. Do as you promised, 24so that it will be established and that your name will be great forever. Then men will say, 'The LORD Almighty, the God over Israel, is Israel's God!' And the house of your servant David will be established before you.

25"You, my God, have revealed to your servant that you will build a house for him. So your servant has found courage to pray to you. 26O LORD, you are God! You have promised these good things to your servant. 27Now you have been pleased to bless the house of your servant, that it may continue forever in your sight; for you, O LORD, have blessed it, and it will be blessed forever."

David's Victories

18 In the course of time, David defeated the Philistines and subdued them, and he took Gath and its surrounding villages from the control of the Philistines.

2David also defeated the Moabites, and they became subject to him and brought tribute.

3Moreover, David fought Hadadezer king of Zobah, as far as Hamath, when he went to establish his control along the Euphrates River. 4David captured a thousand of his chariots, seven thousand charioteers and twenty thousand foot soldiers. He hamstrung all but a hundred of the chariot horses.

5When the Arameans of Damascus came to help Hadadezer king of Zobah, David struck down twenty-two thousand of them. 6He put garrisons in the Arame-

an kingdom of Damascus, and the Arameans became subject to him and brought tribute. The LORD gave David victory everywhere he went.

7David took the gold shields carried by the officers of Hadadezer and brought them to Jerusalem. 8From Tebah[a] and Cun, towns that belonged to Hadadezer, David took a great quantity of bronze, which Solomon used to make the bronze Sea, the pillars and various bronze articles.

9When Tou king of Hamath heard that David had defeated the entire army of Hadadezer king of Zobah, 10he sent his son Hadoram to King David to greet him and congratulate him on his victory in battle over Hadadezer, who had been at war with Tou. Hadoram brought all kinds of articles of gold and silver and bronze.

11King David dedicated these articles to the LORD, as he had done with the silver and gold he had taken from all these nations: Edom and Moab, the Ammonites and the Philistines, and Amalek.

12Abishai son of Zeruiah struck down eighteen thousand Edomites in the Valley of Salt. 13He put garrisons in Edom, and all the Edomites became subject to David. The LORD gave David victory everywhere he went.

David's Officials

14David reigned over all Israel, doing what was just and right for all his people. 15Joab son of Zeruiah was over the army; Jehoshaphat son of Ahilud was recorder; 16Zadok son of Ahitub and Ahimelech[b] son of Abiathar were priests; Shavsha was secretary; 17Benaiah son of Jehoiada was over the Kerethites and Pelethites; and David's sons were chief officials at the king's side.

The Battle Against the Ammonites

19 In the course of time, Nahash king of the Ammonites died, and his son succeeded him as king. 2David thought, "I will show kindness to Hanun son of Nahash, because his father showed kindness to me." So David sent a delegation to express his sympathy to Hanun concerning his father.

When David's men came to Hanun in the land of the Ammonites to express

---

a 8 Hebrew *Tibhath*, a variant of *Tebah*   b 16 Some Hebrew manuscripts, Vulgate and Syriac (see also 2 Samuel 8:17); most Hebrew manuscripts *Abimelech* sympathy to him, ³the Ammonite nobles said to Hanun, "Do you think David is honoring your father by sending men to you to express sympathy? Haven't his men come to you to explore and spy out the country and overthrow it?" ⁴So Hanun seized David's men, shaved them, cut off their garments in the middle at the buttocks, and sent them away.

⁵When someone came and told David about the men, he sent messengers to meet them, for they were greatly humiliated. The king said, "Stay at Jericho till your beards have grown, and then come back."

⁶When the Ammonites realized that they had become a stench in David's nostrils, Hanun and the Ammonites sent a thousand talents^a of silver to hire chariots and charioteers from Aram Naharaim,^{b} Aram Maacah and Zobah. ⁷They hired thirty-two thousand chariots and charioteers, as well as the king of Maacah with his troops, who came and camped near Medeba, while the Ammonites were mustered from their towns and moved out for battle.

⁸On hearing this, David sent Joab out with the entire army of fighting men. ⁹The Ammonites came out and drew up in battle formation at the entrance to their city, while the kings who had come were by themselves in the open country.

¹⁰Joab saw that there were battle lines in front of him and behind him; so he selected some of the best troops in Israel and deployed them against the Arameans. ¹¹He put the rest of the men under the command of Abishai his brother, and they were deployed against the Ammonites. ¹²Joab said, "If the Arameans are too strong for me, then you are to rescue me; but if the Ammonites are too strong for you, then I will rescue you. ¹³Be strong and let us fight bravely for our people and the cities of our God. The LORD will do what is good in his sight."

¹⁴Then Joab and the troops with him advanced to fight the Arameans, and they fled before him. ¹⁵When the Ammonites saw that the Arameans were fleeing, they too fled before his brother Abishai and went inside the city. So Joab went back to Jerusalem.

¹⁶After the Arameans saw that they had been routed by Israel, they sent messengers and had Arameans brought from beyond the River,^{c} with Shophach the commander of Hadadezer's army leading them.

¹⁷When David was told of this, he gathered all Israel and crossed the Jordan; he advanced against them and formed his battle lines opposite them. David formed his lines to meet the Arameans in battle, and they fought against him. ¹⁸But they fled before Israel, and David killed seven thousand of their charioteers and forty thousand of their foot soldiers. He also killed Shophach the commander of their army.

¹⁹When the vassals of Hadadezer saw that they had been defeated by Israel, they made peace with David and became subject to him.

So the Arameans were not willing to help the Ammonites anymore.

The Capture of Rabbah

20 In the spring, at the time when kings go off to war, Joab led out the armed forces. He laid waste the land of the Ammonites and went to Rabbah and besieged it, but David remained in Jerusalem. Joab attacked Rabbah and left it in ruins. ²David took the crown from the head of their king^d—its weight was found to be a talent^e of gold, and it was set with precious stones—and it was placed on David's head. He took a great quantity of plunder from the city ³and brought out the people who were there, consigning them to labor with saws and with iron picks and axes. David did this to all the Ammonite towns. Then David and his entire army returned to Jerusalem.

War With the Philistines

⁴In the course of time, war broke out with the Philistines, at Gezer. At that time Sibbecai the Hushathite killed Sippai, one of the descendants of the Rephaites, and the Philistines were subjugated.

⁵In another battle with the Philistines, Elhanan son of Jair killed Lahmi the brother of Goliath the Gittite, who had a spear with a shaft like a weaver's rod.

⁶In still another battle, which took place at Gath, there was a huge man with six fingers on each hand and six toes on each foot—twenty-four in all. He also was descended from Rapha. ⁷When he taunted

---

^{a} 6 That is, about 37 tons (about 34 metric tons) ^{b} 6 That is, Northwest Mesopotamia ^{c} 16 That is, the Euphrates ^{d} 2 Or of Milcom, that is, Molech ^{e} 2 That is, about 75 pounds (about 34 kilograms)

Israel, Jonathan son of Shimea, David's brother, killed him.

⁸These were descendants of Rapha in Gath, and they fell at the hands of David and his men.

David Numbers the Fighting Men

21 Satan rose up against Israel and incited David to take a census of Israel. ²So David said to Joab and the commanders of the troops, "Go and count the Israelites from Beersheba to Dan. Then report back to me so that I may know how many there are."

³But Joab replied, "May the LORD multiply his troops a hundred times over. My lord the king, are they not all my lord's subjects? Why does my lord want to do this? Why should he bring guilt on Israel?"

⁴The king's word, however, overruled Joab; so Joab left and went throughout Israel and then came back to Jerusalem. ⁵Joab reported the number of the fighting men to David: In all Israel there were one million one hundred thousand men who could handle a sword, including four hundred and seventy thousand in Judah.

⁶But Joab did not include Levi and Benjamin in the numbering, because the king's command was repulsive to him. ⁷This command was also evil in the sight of God; so he punished Israel.

⁸Then David said to God, "I have sinned greatly by doing this. Now, I beg you, take away the guilt of your servant. I have done a very foolish thing."

⁹The LORD said to Gad, David's seer, ¹⁰"Go and tell David, 'This is what the LORD says: I am giving you three options. Choose one of them for me to carry out against you.' "

¹¹So Gad went to David and said to him, "This is what the LORD says: 'Take your choice: ¹²three years of famine, three months of being swept away[a] before your enemies, with their swords overtaking you, or three days of the sword of the LORD—days of plague in the land, with the angel of the LORD ravaging every part of Israel.' Now then, decide how I should answer the one who sent me."

¹³David said to Gad, "I am in deep distress. Let me fall into the hands of the LORD, for his mercy is very great; but do not let me fall into the hands of men."

¹⁴So the LORD sent a plague on Israel, and seventy thousand men of Israel fell dead. ¹⁵And God sent an angel to destroy Jerusalem. But as the angel was doing so, the LORD saw it and was grieved because of the calamity and said to the angel who was destroying the people, "Enough! Withdraw your hand." The angel of the LORD was then standing at the threshing floor of Araunah[b] the Jebusite.

¹⁶David looked up and saw the angel of the LORD standing between heaven and earth, with a drawn sword in his hand extended over Jerusalem. Then David and the elders, clothed in sackcloth, fell facedown.

¹⁷David said to God, "Was it not I who ordered the fighting men to be counted? I am the one who has sinned and done wrong. These are but sheep. What have they done? O LORD my God, let your hand fall upon me and my family, but do not let this plague remain on your people."

¹⁸Then the angel of the LORD ordered Gad to tell David to go up and build an altar to the LORD on the threshing floor of Araunah the Jebusite. ¹⁹So David went up in obedience to the word that Gad had spoken in the name of the LORD.

²⁰While Araunah was threshing wheat, he turned and saw the angel; his four sons who were with him hid themselves. ²¹Then David approached, and when Araunah looked and saw him, he left the threshing floor and bowed down before David with his face to the ground.

²²David said to him, "Let me have the site of your threshing floor so I can build an altar to the LORD, that the plague on the people may be stopped. Sell it to me at the full price."

²³Araunah said to David, "Take it! Let my lord the king do whatever pleases him. Look, I will give the oxen for the burnt offerings, the threshing sledges for the wood, and the wheat for the grain offering. I will give all this."

²⁴But King David replied to Araunah, "No, I insist on paying the full price. I will not take for the LORD what is yours, or sacrifice a burnt offering that costs me nothing."

²⁵So David paid Araunah six hundred shekels[c] of gold for the site. ²⁶David built an altar to the LORD there and sacrificed

---

[a] 12 Hebrew; Septuagint and Vulgate (see also 2 Samuel 24:13) of fleeing   [b] 15 Hebrew Ornan, a variant of Araunah; also in verses 18–28   [c] 25 That is, about 15 pounds (about 7 kilograms)

burnt offerings and fellowship offerings.[a] He called on the LORD, and the LORD answered him with fire from heaven on the altar of burnt offering.

27Then the LORD spoke to the angel, and he put his sword back into its sheath. 28At that time, when David saw that the LORD had answered him on the threshing floor of Araunah the Jebusite, he offered sacrifices there. 29The tabernacle of the LORD, which Moses had made in the desert, and the altar of burnt offering were at that time on the high place at Gibeon. 30But David could not go before it to inquire of God, because he was afraid of the sword of the angel of the LORD.

22 Then David said, "The house of the LORD God is to be here, and also the altar of burnt offering for Israel."

Preparations for the Temple

2So David gave orders to assemble the aliens living in Israel, and from among them he appointed stonecutters to prepare dressed stone for building the house of God. 3He provided a large amount of iron to make nails for the doors of the gateways and for the fittings, and more bronze than could be weighed. 4He also provided more cedar logs than could be counted, for the Sidonians and Tyrians had brought large numbers of them to David.

5David said, "My son Solomon is young and inexperienced, and the house to be built for the LORD should be of great magnificence and fame and splendor in the sight of all the nations. Therefore I will make preparations for it." So David made extensive preparations before his death.

6Then he called for his son Solomon and charged him to build a house for the LORD, the God of Israel. 7David said to Solomon: "My son, I had it in my heart to build a house for the Name of the LORD my God. 8But this word of the LORD came to me: 'You have shed much blood and have fought many wars. You are not to build a house for my Name, because you have shed much blood on the earth in my sight. 9But you will have a son who will be a man of peace and rest, and I will give him rest

a 26 Traditionally peace offerings

Do What You Can

READ 1 CHRONICLES 22

Ever really wanted to do something, made all the preparations beforehand, only to have everything called off? That's what happened to David. He wanted to build a magnificent temple for God, but God said no. David had killed far too many people to qualify for the job. Solomon would build it instead. David didn't take his football and huff off toward home, pouting. Instead, he said, "I will make preparations for it" (1 Chronicles 22:5). David drew up detailed blueprints for the temple and gathered all the building materials Solomon would need. Sure, David was told to stop the construction, but he still helped all he could. As Christians, we are all a team. We all have a part to play. You may not be the one to run the football across the goal line, but you *can* throw it to the guy who does.

Your next reading is on page 543.

from all his enemies on every side. His name will be Solomon,[a] and I will grant Israel peace and quiet during his reign. ¹⁰He is the one who will build a house for my Name. He will be my son, and I will be his father. And I will establish the throne of his kingdom over Israel forever.'

¹¹"Now, my son, the LORD be with you, and may you have success and build the house of the LORD your God, as he said you would. ¹²May the LORD give you discretion and understanding when he puts you in command over Israel, so that you may keep the law of the LORD your God. ¹³Then you will have success if you are careful to observe the decrees and laws that the LORD gave Moses for Israel. Be strong and courageous. Do not be afraid or discouraged.

¹⁴"I have taken great pains to provide for the temple of the LORD a hundred thousand talents[b] of gold, a million talents[c] of silver, quantities of bronze and iron too great to be weighed, and wood and stone. And you may add to them. ¹⁵You have many workmen: stonecutters, masons and carpenters, as well as men skilled in every kind of work ¹⁶in gold and silver, bronze and iron—craftsmen beyond number. Now begin the work, and the LORD be with you."

¹⁷Then David ordered all the leaders of Israel to help his son Solomon. ¹⁸He said to them, "Is not the LORD your God with you? And has he not granted you rest on every side? For he has handed the inhabitants of the land over to me, and the land is subject to the LORD and to his people. ¹⁹Now devote your heart and soul to seeking the LORD your God. Begin to build the sanctuary of the LORD God, so that you may bring the ark of the covenant of the LORD and the sacred articles belonging to God into the temple that will be built for the Name of the LORD."

The Levites

23 When David was old and full of years, he made his son Solomon king over Israel.

²He also gathered together all the leaders of Israel, as well as the priests and Levites. ³The Levites thirty years old or more were counted, and the total number of men was thirty-eight thousand. ⁴David said, "Of these, twenty-four thousand are to supervise the work of the temple of the LORD and six thousand are to be officials and judges. ⁵Four thousand are to be gatekeepers and four thousand are to praise the LORD with the musical instruments I have provided for that purpose."

⁶David divided the Levites into groups corresponding to the sons of Levi: Gershon, Kohath and Merari.

Gershonites

⁷Belonging to the Gershonites:
Ladan and Shimei.

⁸The sons of Ladan:
Jehiel the first, Zetham and Joel—three in all.

⁹The sons of Shimei:
Shelomoth, Haziel and Haran—three in all.
These were the heads of the families of Ladan.

¹⁰And the sons of Shimei:
Jahath, Ziza,[d] Jeush and Beriah.
These were the sons of Shimei—four in all.

¹¹Jahath was the first and Ziza the second, but Jeush and Beriah did not have many sons; so they were counted as one family with one assignment.

Kohathites

¹²The sons of Kohath:
Amram, Izhar, Hebron and Uzziel—four in all.

¹³The sons of Amram:
Aaron and Moses.
Aaron was set apart, he and his descendants forever, to consecrate the most holy things, to offer sacrifices before the LORD, to minister before him and to pronounce blessings in his name forever. ¹⁴The sons of Moses the man of God were counted as part of the tribe of Levi.

¹⁵The sons of Moses:
Gershom and Eliezer.

¹⁶The descendants of Gershom:
Shubael was the first.

¹⁷The descendants of Eliezer:
Rehabiah was the first.

---

[a] 9 *Solomon* sounds like and may be derived from the Hebrew for *peace*.   [b] 14 That is, about 3,750 tons (about 3,450 metric tons)   [c] 14 That is, about 37,500 tons (about 34,500 metric tons)   [d] 10 One Hebrew manuscript, Septuagint and Vulgate (see also verse 11); most Hebrew manuscripts *Zina*

Eliezer had no other sons, but the sons of Rehabiah were very numerous.

18 The sons of Izhar:

Shelomith was the first.

19 The sons of Hebron:

Jeriah the first, Amariah the second, Jahaziel the third and Jekameam the fourth.

20 The sons of Uzziel:

Micah the first and Isshiah the second.

Merarites

21 The sons of Merari:

Mahli and Mushi.

The sons of Mahli:

Eleazar and Kish.

22 Eleazar died without having sons: he had only daughters. Their cousins, the sons of Kish, married them.

23 The sons of Mushi:

Mahli, Eder and Jerimoth—three in all.

24 These were the descendants of Levi by their families—the heads of families as they were registered under their names and counted individually, that is, the workers twenty years old or more who served in the temple of the LORD. 25 For David had said, "Since the LORD, the God of Israel, has granted rest to his people and has come to dwell in Jerusalem forever, 26 the Levites no longer need to carry the tabernacle or any of the articles used in its service." 27 According to the last instructions of David, the Levites were counted from those twenty years old or more.

28 The duty of the Levites was to help Aaron's descendants in the service of the temple of the LORD: to be in charge of the courtyards, the side rooms, the purification of all sacred things and the performance of other duties at the house of God. 29 They were in charge of the bread set out on the table, the flour for the grain offerings, the unleavened wafers, the baking and the mixing, and all measurements of quantity and size. 30 They were also to stand every morning to thank and praise the LORD. They were to do the same in the evening 31 and whenever burnt offerings were presented to the LORD on Sabbaths and at New Moon festivals and at appointed feasts. They were to serve before

the LORD regularly in the proper number and in the way prescribed for them.

32 And so the Levites carried out their responsibilities for the Tent of Meeting, for the Holy Place and, under their brothers the descendants of Aaron, for the service of the temple of the LORD.

The Divisions of Priests

24 These were the divisions of the sons of Aaron:

The sons of Aaron were Nadab, Abihu, Eleazar and Ithamar. 2 But Nadab and Abihu died before their father did, and they had no sons; so Eleazar and Ithamar served as the priests. 3 With the help of Zadok a descendant of Eleazar and Ahimelech a descendant of Ithamar, David separated them into divisions for their appointed order of ministering. 4 A larger number of leaders were found among Eleazar's descendants than among Ithamar's, and they were divided accordingly: sixteen heads of families from Eleazar's descendants and eight heads of families from Ithamar's descendants. 5 They divided them impartially by drawing lots, for there were officials of the sanctuary and officials of God among the descendants of both Eleazar and Ithamar.

6 The scribe Shemaiah son of Nethanel, a Levite, recorded their names in the presence of the king and of the officials: Zadok the priest, Ahimelech son of Abiathar and the heads of families of the priests and of the Levites—one family being taken from Eleazar and then one from Ithamar.

7 The first lot fell to Jehoiarib,
the second to Jedaiah,
8 the third to Harim,
the fourth to Seorim,
9 the fifth to Malkijah,
the sixth to Mijamin,
10 the seventh to Hakkoz,
the eighth to Abijah,
11 the ninth to Jeshua,
the tenth to Shecaniah,
12 the eleventh to Eliashib,
the twelfth to Jakim,
13 the thirteenth to Huppah,
the fourteenth to Jeshebeab,
14 the fifteenth to Bilgah,
the sixteenth to Immer,
15 the seventeenth to Hezir,
the eighteenth to Happizzez,
16 the nineteenth to Pethahiah,

the twentieth to Jehezkel,
17 the twenty-first to Jakin,
the twenty-second to Gamul,
18 the twenty-third to Delaiah
and the twenty-fourth to Maaziah.

19 This was their appointed order of ministering when they entered the temple of the Lord, according to the regulations prescribed for them by their forefather Aaron, as the Lord, the God of Israel, had commanded him.

The Rest of the Levites

20 As for the rest of the descendants of Levi:
　　from the sons of Amram: Shubael;
　　from the sons of Shubael: Jehde-
　　　iah.
　　21 As for Rehabiah, from his sons:
　　　Isshiah was the first.
22 From the Izharites: Shelomoth;
　　from the sons of Shelomoth: Ja-
　　hath.
23 The sons of Hebron: Jeriah the first,a
　　Amariah the second, Jahaziel the
　　third and Jekameam the fourth.
24 The son of Uzziel: Micah;
　　from the sons of Micah: Shamir.
　　25 The brother of Micah: Isshiah;
　　from the sons of Isshiah: Zechariah.
26 The sons of Merari: Mahli and Mushi.
　　The son of Jaaziah: Beno.
27 The sons of Merari:
　　from Jaaziah: Beno, Shoham, Zac-
　　cur and Ibri.
28 From Mahli: Eleazar, who had no
　　sons.
29 From Kish: the son of Kish:
　　Jerahmeel.
30 And the sons of Mushi: Mahli, Eder
　　and Jerimoth.

These were the Levites, according to their families. 31 They also cast lots, just as their brothers the descendants of Aaron did, in the presence of King David and of Zadok, Ahimelech, and the heads of families of the priests and of the Levites. The families of the oldest brother were treated the same as those of the youngest.

The Singers

25 David, together with the commanders of the army, set apart some of the sons of Asaph, Heman and Jeduthun for the ministry of prophesying, accompanied by harps, lyres and cymbals. Here is the list of the men who performed this service:

2 From the sons of Asaph:
　　Zaccur, Joseph, Nethaniah and Asare-
　　lah. The sons of Asaph were under
　　the supervision of Asaph, who proph-
　　esied under the king's supervision.
3 As for Jeduthun, from his sons:
　　Gedaliah, Zeri, Jeshaiah, Shimei,b
　　Hashabiah and Mattithiah, six in all,
　　under the supervision of their father
　　Jeduthun, who prophesied, using the
　　harp in thanking and praising the
　　Lord.
4 As for Heman, from his sons:
　　Bukkiah, Mattaniah, Uzziel, Shubael
　　and Jerimoth; Hananiah, Hanani, Eli-
　　athah, Giddalti and Romamti-Ezer;
　　Joshbekashah, Mallothi, Hothir and
　　Mahazioth. 5 All these were sons of
　　Heman the king's seer. They were giv-
　　en him through the promises of God
　　to exalt him.c God gave Heman four-
　　teen sons and three daughters.

6 All these men were under the supervision of their fathers for the music of the temple of the Lord, with cymbals, lyres and harps, for the ministry at the house of God. Asaph, Jeduthun and Heman were under the supervision of the king. 7 Along with their relatives—all of them trained and skilled in music for the Lord—they numbered 288. 8 Young and old alike, teacher as well as student, cast lots for their duties.

9 The first lot, which was for Asaph,
　　fell to Joseph,
　　his sons and relatives,d 12e
　　the second to Gedaliah,
　　he and his relatives and sons, 12
10 the third to Zaccur,
　　his sons and relatives, 12
11 the fourth to Izri,f
　　his sons and relatives, 12
12 the fifth to Nethaniah,
　　his sons and relatives, 12
13 the sixth to Bukkiah,
　　his sons and relatives, 12

---

a 23 Two Hebrew manuscripts and some Septuagint manuscripts (see also 1 Chron. 23:19); most Hebrew manuscripts The sons of Jeriah.　b 3 One Hebrew manuscript and some Septuagint manuscripts (see also verse 17); most Hebrew manuscripts do not have Shimei.　c 5 Hebrew exalt the horn　d 9 See Septuagint; Hebrew does not have his sons and relatives.　e 9 See the total in verse 7; Hebrew does not have twelve.　f 11 A variant of Zeri

¹⁴the seventh to Jesarelah,ᵃ
  his sons and relatives,   12
¹⁵the eighth to Jeshaiah,
  his sons and relatives,   12
¹⁶the ninth to Mattaniah,
  his sons and relatives,   12
¹⁷the tenth to Shimei,
  his sons and relatives,   12
¹⁸the eleventh to Azarel,ᵇ
  his sons and relatives,   12
¹⁹the twelfth to Hashabiah,
  his sons and relatives,   12
²⁰the thirteenth to Shubael,
  his sons and relatives,   12
²¹the fourteenth to Mattithiah,
  his sons and relatives,   12
²²the fifteenth to Jerimoth,
  his sons and relatives,   12
²³the sixteenth to Hananiah,
  his sons and relatives,   12
²⁴the seventeenth to
  Joshbekashah,
  his sons and relatives,   12
²⁵the eighteenth to Hanani,
  his sons and relatives,   12
²⁶the nineteenth to Mallothi,
  his sons and relatives,   12
²⁷the twentieth to Eliathah,
  his sons and relatives,   12
²⁸the twenty-first to Hothir,
  his sons and relatives,   12
²⁹the twenty-second to Giddalti,
  his sons and relatives,   12
³⁰the twenty-third to Mahazioth,
  his sons and relatives,   12
³¹the twenty-fourth to
  Romamti-Ezer,
  his sons and relatives,   12

The Gatekeepers

26 The divisions of the gate-keepers:

From the Korahites: Meshelemiah son of Kore, one of the sons of Asaph.

²Meshelemiah had sons:
  Zechariah the firstborn,
  Jediael the second,
  Zebadiah the third,
  Jathniel the fourth,
  ³Elam the fifth,
  Jehohanan the sixth
  and Eliehoenai the seventh.
⁴Obed-Edom also had sons:
  Shemaiah the firstborn,
  Jehozabad the second,

  Joah the third,
  Sacar the fourth,
  Nethanel the fifth,
  ⁵Ammiel the sixth,
  Issachar the seventh
  and Peullethai the eighth.
  (For God had blessed Obed-Edom.)

⁶His son Shemaiah also had sons, who were leaders in their father's family because they were very capable men. ⁷The sons of Shemaiah: Othni, Rephael, Obed and Elzabad; his relatives Elihu and Semakiah were also able men. ⁸All these were descendants of Obed-Edom; they and their sons and their relatives were capable men with the strength to do the work—descendants of Obed-Edom, 62 in all.

⁹Meshelemiah had sons and relatives, who were able men—18 in all.

¹⁰Hosah the Merarite had sons: Shimri the first (although he was not the firstborn, his father had appointed him the first), ¹¹Hilkiah the second, Tabaliah the third and Zechariah the fourth. The sons and relatives of Hosah were 13 in all.

¹²These divisions of the gatekeepers, through their chief men, had duties for ministering in the temple of the Lord, just as their relatives had. ¹³Lots were cast for each gate, according to their families, young and old alike.

¹⁴The lot for the East Gate fell to Shelemiah.ᶜ Then lots were cast for his son Zechariah, a wise counselor, and the lot for the North Gate fell to him. ¹⁵The lot for the South Gate fell to Obed-Edom, and the lot for the storehouse fell to his sons. ¹⁶The lots for the West Gate and the Shalleketh Gate on the upper road fell to Shuppim and Hosah.

Guard was alongside of guard: ¹⁷There were six Levites a day on the east, four a day on the north, four a day on the south and two at a time at the storehouse. ¹⁸As for the court to the west, there were four at the road and two at the court itself.

¹⁹These were the divisions of the gatekeepers who were descendants of Korah and Merari.

ᵃ 14 A variant of *Asarelah*   ᵇ 18 A variant of *Uzziel*
ᶜ 14 A variant of *Meshelemiah*

The Treasurers and Other Officials

20Their fellow Levites were*a* in charge of the treasuries of the house of God and the treasuries for the dedicated things.

21The descendants of Ladan, who were Gershonites through Ladan and who were heads of families belonging to Ladan the Gershonite, were Jehieli, 22the sons of Jehieli, Zetham and his brother Joel. They were in charge of the treasuries of the temple of the LORD.

23From the Amramites, the Izharites, the Hebronites and the Uzzielites:

24Shubael, a descendant of Gershom son of Moses, was the officer in charge of the treasuries. 25His relatives through Eliezer: Rehabiah his son, Jeshaiah his son, Joram his son, Zicri his son and Shelomith his son. 26Shelomith and his relatives were in charge of all the treasuries for the things dedicated by King David, by the heads of families who were the commanders of thousands and commanders of hundreds, and by the other army commanders. 27Some of the plunder taken in battle they dedicated for the repair of the temple of the LORD. 28And everything dedicated by Samuel the seer and by Saul son of Kish, Abner son of Ner and Joab son of Zeruiah, and all the other dedicated things were in the care of Shelomith and his relatives.

29From the Izharites: Kenaniah and his sons were assigned duties away from the temple, as officials and judges over Israel.

30From the Hebronites: Hashabiah and his relatives—seventeen hundred able men—were responsible in Israel west of the Jordan for all the work of the LORD and for the king's service. 31As for the Hebronites, Jeriah was their chief according to the genealogical records of their families. In the fortieth year of David's reign a search was made in the records, and capable men among the Hebronites were found at Jazer in Gilead. 32Jeriah had twenty-seven hundred relatives, who were able men and heads of families, and King David put them in charge of the Reubenites, the Gadites and the half-tribe of Manasseh for every matter pertaining to God and for the affairs of the king.

Army Divisions

27 This is the list of the Israelites—heads of families, commanders of thousands and commanders of hundreds, and their officers, who served the king in all that concerned the army divisions that were on duty month by month throughout the year. Each division consisted of 24,000 men.

2In charge of the first division, for the first month, was Jashobeam son of Zabdiel. There were 24,000 men in his division. 3He was a descendant of Perez and chief of all the army officers for the first month.

4In charge of the division for the second month was Dodai the Ahohite; Mikloth was the leader of his division. There were 24,000 men in his division.

5The third army commander, for the third month, was Benaiah son of Jehoiada the priest. He was chief and there were 24,000 men in his division. 6This was the Benaiah who was a mighty man among the Thirty and was over the Thirty. His son Ammizabad was in charge of his division.

7The fourth, for the fourth month, was Asahel the brother of Joab; his son Zebadiah was his successor. There were 24,000 men in his division.

8The fifth, for the fifth month, was the commander Shamhuth the Izrahite. There were 24,000 men in his division.

9The sixth, for the sixth month, was Ira the son of Ikkesh the Tekoite. There were 24,000 men in his division.

10The seventh, for the seventh month, was Helez the Pelonite, an Ephraimite. There were 24,000 men in his division.

11The eighth, for the eighth month, was Sibbecai the Hushathite, a Zerahite. There were 24,000 men in his division.

12The ninth, for the ninth month, was Abiezer the Anathothite, a Benjamite. There were 24,000 men in his division.

13The tenth, for the tenth month, was Maharai the Netophathite, a Zerahite. There were 24,000 men in his division.

a 20 Septuagint; Hebrew *As for the Levites, Ahijah was*

14 The eleventh, for the eleventh month, was Benaiah the Pirathonite, an Ephraimite. There were 24,000 men in his division.
15 The twelfth, for the twelfth month, was Heldai the Netophathite, from the family of Othniel. There were 24,000 men in his division.

Officers of the Tribes

16 The officers over the tribes of Israel:

over the Reubenites: Eliezer son of Zicri;

over the Simeonites: Shephatiah son of Maacah;

17 over Levi: Hashabiah son of Kemuel; over Aaron: Zadok;

18 over Judah: Elihu, a brother of David; over Issachar: Omri son of Michael;

19 over Zebulun: Ishmaiah son of Obadiah;

over Naphtali: Jerimoth son of Azriel;

20 over the Ephraimites: Hoshea son of Azaziah;

over half the tribe of Manasseh: Joel son of Pedaiah;

21 over the half-tribe of Manasseh in Gilead: Iddo son of Zechariah;

over Benjamin: Jaasiel son of Abner;

22 over Dan: Azarel son of Jeroham.

These were the officers over the tribes of Israel.

23 David did not take the number of the men twenty years old or less, because the LORD had promised to make Israel as numerous as the stars in the sky. 24 Joab son of Zeruiah began to count the men but did not finish. Wrath came on Israel on account of this numbering, and the number was not entered in the book[a] of the annals of King David.

The King's Overseers

25 Azmaveth son of Adiel was in charge of the royal storehouses.

Jonathan son of Uzziah was in charge of the storehouses in the outlying districts, in the towns, the villages and the watchtowers.

26 Ezri son of Kelub was in charge of the field workers who farmed the land.

27 Shimei the Ramathite was in charge of the vineyards.

Zabdi the Shiphmite was in charge of the produce of the vineyards for the wine vats.

28 Baal-Hanan the Gederite was in charge of the olive and sycamore-fig trees in the western foothills.

Joash was in charge of the supplies of olive oil.

29 Shitrai the Sharonite was in charge of the herds grazing in Sharon.

Shaphat son of Adlai was in charge of the herds in the valleys.

30 Obil the Ishmaelite was in charge of the camels.

Jehdeiah the Meronothite was in charge of the donkeys.

31 Jaziz the Hagrite was in charge of the flocks.

All these were the officials in charge of King David's property.

32 Jonathan, David's uncle, was a counselor, a man of insight and a scribe. Jehiel son of Hacmoni took care of the king's sons.

33 Ahithophel was the king's counselor. Hushai the Arkite was the king's friend.

34 Ahithophel was succeeded by Jehoiada son of Benaiah and by Abiathar.

Joab was the commander of the royal army.

David's Plans for the Temple

28 David summoned all the officials of Israel to assemble at Jerusalem: the officers over the tribes, the commanders of the divisions in the service of the king, the commanders of thousands and commanders of hundreds, and the officials in charge of all the property and livestock belonging to the king and his sons, together with the palace officials, the mighty men and all the brave warriors.

2 King David rose to his feet and said: "Listen to me, my brothers and my people. I had it in my heart to build a house as a place of rest for the ark of the covenant of the LORD, for the footstool of our God, and I made plans to build it. 3 But God said to me, 'You are not to build a house for my Name, because you are a warrior and have shed blood.'

4 "Yet the LORD, the God of Israel, chose me from my whole family to be king over Israel forever. He chose Judah as leader, and from the house of Judah he chose my family, and from my father's sons he was pleased to make me king over all Israel.

---

a 24 Septuagint; Hebrew *number*

⁵Of all my sons—and the Lᴏʀᴅ has given me many—he has chosen my son Solomon to sit on the throne of the kingdom of the Lᴏʀᴅ over Israel. ⁶He said to me: 'Solomon your son is the one who will build my house and my courts, for I have chosen him to be my son, and I will be his father. ⁷I will establish his kingdom forever if he is unswerving in carrying out my commands and laws, as is being done at this time.'

⁸"So now I charge you in the sight of all Israel and of the assembly of the Lᴏʀᴅ, and in the hearing of our God: Be careful to follow all the commands of the Lᴏʀᴅ your God, that you may possess this good land and pass it on as an inheritance to your descendants forever.

⁹"And you, my son Solomon, acknowledge the God of your father, and serve him with wholehearted devotion and with a willing mind, for the Lᴏʀᴅ searches every heart and understands every motive behind the thoughts. If you seek him, he will be found by you; but if you forsake him, he will reject you forever. ¹⁰Consider now, for the Lᴏʀᴅ has chosen you to build a temple as a sanctuary. Be strong and do the work."

¹¹Then David gave his son Solomon the plans for the portico of the temple, its buildings, its storerooms, its upper parts, its inner rooms and the place of atonement. ¹²He gave him the plans of all that the Spirit had put in his mind for the courts of the temple of the Lᴏʀᴅ and all the surrounding rooms, for the treasuries of the temple of God and for the treasuries for the dedicated things. ¹³He gave him instructions for the divisions of the priests and Levites, and for all the work of serving in the temple of the Lᴏʀᴅ, as well as for all the articles to be used in its service. ¹⁴He designated the weight of gold for all the gold articles to be used in various kinds of service, and the weight of silver for all the silver articles to be used in various kinds of service: ¹⁵the weight of gold for the gold lampstands and their lamps, with the weight for each lampstand and its lamps; and the weight of silver for each silver lampstand and its lamps, according to the use of each lampstand; ¹⁶the weight of gold for each table for consecrated bread; the weight of silver for the silver tables; ¹⁷the weight of pure gold for the forks, sprinkling bowls and pitchers; the weight of gold for each gold dish; the weight of silver for each silver dish; ¹⁸and the weight of the refined gold for the altar of incense. He also gave him the plan for the chariot, that is, the cherubim of gold that spread their wings and shelter the ark of the covenant of the Lᴏʀᴅ.

¹⁹"All this," David said, "I have in writing from the hand of the Lᴏʀᴅ upon me, and he gave me understanding in all the details of the plan."

²⁰David also said to Solomon his son, "Be strong and courageous, and do the work. Do not be afraid or discouraged, for the Lᴏʀᴅ God, my God, is with you. He will not fail you or forsake you until all the work for the service of the temple of the Lᴏʀᴅ is finished. ²¹The divisions of the priests and Levites are ready for all the work on the temple of God, and every willing man skilled in any craft will help you in all the work. The officials and all the people will obey your every command."

Gifts for Building the Temple

29 Then King David said to the whole assembly: "My son Solomon, the one whom God has chosen, is young and inexperienced. The task is great, because this palatial structure is not for man but for the Lᴏʀᴅ God. ²With all my resources I have provided for the temple of my God—gold for the gold work, silver for the silver, bronze for the bronze, iron for the iron and wood for the wood, as well as onyx for the settings, turquoise,ᵃ stones of various colors, and all kinds of fine stone and marble—all of these in large quantities. ³Besides, in my devotion to the temple of my God I now give my personal treasures of gold and silver for the temple of my God, over and above everything I have provided for this holy temple: ⁴three thousand talentsᵇ of gold (gold of Ophir) and seven thousand talentsᶜ of refined silver, for the overlaying of the walls of the buildings, ⁵for the gold work and the silver work, and for all the work to be done by the craftsmen. Now, who is willing to consecrate himself today to the Lᴏʀᴅ?"

⁶Then the leaders of families, the officers of the tribes of Israel, the command-

---

ᵃ 2 The meaning of the Hebrew for this word is uncertain.
ᵇ 4 That is, about 110 tons (about 100 metric tons)
ᶜ 4 That is, about 260 tons (about 240 metric tons)

ers of thousands and commanders of hundreds, and the officials in charge of the king's work gave willingly. [7]They gave toward the work on the temple of God five thousand talents[a] and ten thousand darics[b] of gold, ten thousand talents[c] of silver, eighteen thousand talents[d] of bronze and a hundred thousand talents[e] of iron. [8]Any who had precious stones gave them to the treasury of the temple of the LORD in the custody of Jehiel the Gershonite. [9]The people rejoiced at the willing response of their leaders, for they had given freely and wholeheartedly to the LORD. David the king also rejoiced greatly.

David's Prayer

[10]David praised the LORD in the presence of the whole assembly, saying,

"Praise be to you, O LORD,
    God of our father Israel,
    from everlasting to everlasting.
[11]Yours, O LORD, is the greatness and the power
    and the glory and the majesty and the splendor,
    for everything in heaven and earth is yours.
Yours, O LORD, is the kingdom;
    you are exalted as head over all.
[12]Wealth and honor come from you;
    you are the ruler of all things.
In your hands are strength and power
    to exalt and give strength to all.
[13]Now, our God, we give you thanks,
    and praise your glorious name.

[14]"But who am I, and who are my people, that we should be able to give as generously as this? Everything comes from you, and we have given you only what comes from your hand. [15]We are aliens and strangers in your sight, as were all our forefathers. Our days on earth are like a shadow, without hope. [16]O LORD our God, as for all this abundance that we have provided for building you a temple for your Holy Name, it comes from your hand, and all of it belongs to you. [17]I know, my God, that you test the heart and are pleased with integrity. All these things have I given willingly and with honest intent. And now I have seen with joy how willingly your people who are here have given to you. [18]O LORD, God of our fathers Abraham, Isaac and Israel, keep this desire in the hearts of your people

forever, and keep their hearts loyal to you. [19]And give my son Solomon the wholehearted devotion to keep your commands, requirements and decrees and to do everything to build the palatial structure for which I have provided."

[20]Then David said to the whole assembly, "Praise the LORD your God." So they all praised the LORD, the God of their fathers; they bowed low and fell prostrate before the LORD and the king.

Solomon Acknowledged as King

[21]The next day they made sacrifices to the LORD and presented burnt offerings to him: a thousand bulls, a thousand rams and a thousand male lambs, together with their drink offerings, and other sacrifices in abundance for all Israel. [22]They ate and drank with great joy in the presence of the LORD that day.

Then they acknowledged Solomon son of David as king a second time, anointing him before the LORD to be ruler and Zadok to be priest. [23]So Solomon sat on the throne of the LORD as king in place of his father David. He prospered and all Israel obeyed him. [24]All the officers and mighty men, as well as all of King David's sons, pledged their submission to King Solomon.

[25]The LORD highly exalted Solomon in the sight of all Israel and bestowed on him royal splendor such as no king over Israel ever had before.

The Death of David

[26]David son of Jesse was king over all Israel. [27]He ruled over Israel forty years—seven in Hebron and thirty-three in Jerusalem. [28]He died at a good old age, having enjoyed long life, wealth and honor. His son Solomon succeeded him as king.

[29]As for the events of King David's reign, from beginning to end, they are written in the records of Samuel the seer, the records of Nathan the prophet and the records of Gad the seer, [30]together with the details of his reign and power, and the circumstances that surrounded him and Israel and the kingdoms of all the other lands.

---

a 7 That is, about 190 tons (about 170 metric tons)
b 7 That is, about 185 pounds (about 84 kilograms)
c 7 That is, about 375 tons (about 345 metric tons)
d 7 That is, about 675 tons (about 610 metric tons)
e 7 That is, about 3,750 tons (about 3,450 metric tons)

2 CHRONICLES

Who wrote this book?
The author of this book is unknown. Some think he was Ezra.

Why was this book written?
The book of 2 Chronicles tells what God thought of the kings of Israel and Judah.

What happens in this book?
Solomon is king for 40 years. When he dies, his kingdom is divided into two nations. The people of both Hebrew nations sin, and God punishes them by sending them into exile.

What do we learn about God in this book?
God rescues godly leaders who depend on him for help.

What people are important in this book?
The important people in this book are Solomon, Ahab, Jehoshaphat, Joash, Hezekiah and Josiah.

When did this happen?
The events in this book happened between 970 and 586 B.C.

Where did this happen?
These things happened in the two kingdoms of Israel and Judah.

What are some of the stories in this book?
Solomon builds the temple	2 Chronicles 3
Solomon dedicates the temple	2 Chronicles 7
Egypt attacks Judah	2 Chronicles 12
Asa worships God	2 Chronicles 15
Ahab is killed	2 Chronicles 18
Jehoshaphat wins a war	2 Chronicles 20
Joash repairs the temple	2 Chronicles 24
Hezekiah trusts God	2 Chronicles 29–32
Josiah reforms Judah	2 Chronicles 34–35

Solomon Asks for Wisdom

Solomon son of David established himself firmly over his kingdom, for the LORD his God was with him and made him exceedingly great.

2Then Solomon spoke to all Israel—to the commanders of thousands and commanders of hundreds, to the judges and to all the leaders in Israel, the heads of families— 3and Solomon and the whole assembly went to the high place at Gibeon, for God's Tent of Meeting was there, which Moses the LORD's servant had made in the desert. 4Now David had brought up the ark of God from Kiriath Jearim to the place he had prepared for it, because he had pitched a tent for it in Jerusalem. 5But the bronze altar that Bezalel son of Uri, the son of Hur, had made was in Gibeon in front of the tabernacle of the LORD; so Solomon and the assembly inquired of him there. 6Solomon went up to the bronze altar before the LORD in the Tent of Meeting and offered a thousand burnt offerings on it.

7That night God appeared to Solomon and said to him, "Ask for whatever you want me to give you."

8Solomon answered God, "You have shown great kindness to David my father and have made me king in his place. 9Now, LORD God, let your promise to my father David be confirmed, for you have made me king over a people who are as numerous as the dust of the earth. 10Give me wisdom and knowledge, that I may lead this people, for who is able to govern this great people of yours?"

11God said to Solomon, "Since this is your heart's desire and you have not asked for wealth, riches or honor, nor for the death of your enemies, and since you have not asked for a long life but for wisdom and knowledge to govern my people over whom I have made you king, 12therefore wisdom and knowledge will be given you. And I will also give you wealth, riches and honor, such as no king who was before you ever had and none after you will have."

13Then Solomon went to Jerusalem from the high place at Gibeon, from before the Tent of Meeting. And he reigned over Israel.

14Solomon accumulated chariots and horses; he had fourteen hundred chariots and twelve thousand horses,a which he kept in the chariot cities and also with him in Jerusalem. 15The king made silver and gold as common in Jerusalem as stones, and cedar as plentiful as sycamore-fig trees in the foothills. 16Solomon's horses were imported from Egyptb and from Kuec—the royal merchants purchased them from Kue. 17They imported a chariot from Egypt for six hundred shekelsd of silver, and a horse for a hundred and fifty.e They also exported them to all the kings of the Hittites and of the Arameans.

Preparations for Building the Temple

Solomon gave orders to build a temple for the Name of the LORD and a royal palace for himself. 2He conscripted seventy thousand men as carriers and eighty thousand as stonecutters in the hills and thirty-six hundred as foremen over them.

3Solomon sent this message to Hiramf king of Tyre:

"Send me cedar logs as you did for my father David when you sent him cedar to build a palace to live in. 4Now I am about to build a temple for the Name of the LORD my God and to dedicate it to him for burning fragrant incense before him, for setting out the consecrated bread regularly, and for making burnt offerings every morning and evening and on Sabbaths and New Moons and at the appointed feasts of the LORD our God. This is a lasting ordinance for Israel.

5"The temple I am going to build will be great, because our God is greater than all other gods. 6But who is able to build a temple for him, since the heavens, even the highest heavens, cannot contain him? Who then am I to build a temple for him, except as a place to burn sacrifices before him?

7"Send me, therefore, a man skilled to work in gold and silver, bronze and iron, and in purple, crimson and blue yarn, and experienced in the art of engraving, to work in Judah and Jerusalem with my skilled craftsmen, whom my father David provided.

---

a 14 Or charioteers   b 16 Or possibly Muzur, a region in Cilicia; also in verse 17   c 16 Probably Cilicia   d 17 That is, about 15 pounds (about 7 kilograms)   e 17 That is, about 3 3/4 pounds (about 1.7 kilograms)   f 3 Hebrew Huram, a variant of Hiram; also in verses 11 and 12

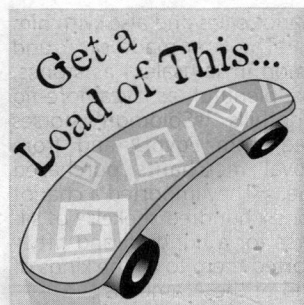

Get a Load of This...

Lebanon was famous for its cedars, just like McDonald's is famous for its hamburgers. The giant cedars for Solomon's temple were transported in part by water (2 Chronicles 2:16). They were lashed together and floated down the Mediterranean Sea to Joppa, then dragged 35 miles inland to Jerusalem.

8"Send me also cedar, pine and algum[a] logs from Lebanon, for I know that your men are skilled in cutting timber there. My men will work with yours 9to provide me with plenty of lumber, because the temple I build must be large and magnificent. 10I will give your servants, the woodsmen who cut the timber, twenty thousand cors[b] of ground wheat, twenty thousand cors of barley, twenty thousand baths[c] of wine and twenty thousand baths of olive oil."

11Hiram king of Tyre replied by letter to Solomon:

"Because the LORD loves his people, he has made you their king."

12And Hiram added:

"Praise be to the LORD, the God of Israel, who made heaven and earth! He has given King David a wise son, endowed with intelligence and discernment, who will build a temple for the LORD and a palace for himself.

13"I am sending you Huram-Abi, a man of great skill, 14whose mother was from Dan and whose father was from Tyre. He is trained to work in gold and silver, bronze and iron, stone and wood, and with purple and blue and crimson yarn and fine linen. He is experienced in all kinds of engraving and can execute any design given to him. He will work with your craftsmen and with those of my lord, David your father.

15"Now let my lord send his servants the wheat and barley and the olive oil and wine he promised, 16and we will cut all the logs from Lebanon that you need and will float them in rafts by sea down to Joppa. You can then take them up to Jerusalem."

17Solomon took a census of all the aliens who were in Israel, after the census his father David had taken; and they were found to be 153,600. 18He assigned 70,000 of them to be carriers and 80,000 to be stonecutters in the hills, with 3,600 foremen over them to keep the people working.

Solomon Builds the Temple

3 Then Solomon began to build the temple of the LORD in Jerusalem on Mount Moriah, where the LORD had appeared to his father David. It was on the threshing floor of Araunah[d] the Jebusite, the place provided by David. 2He began building on the second day of the second month in the fourth year of his reign.

3The foundation Solomon laid for building the temple of God was sixty cubits long and twenty cubits wide[e]

---

a 8 Probably a variant of almug; possibly juniper   b 10 That is, probably about 125,000 bushels (about 4,400 kiloliters)   c 10 That is, probably about 115,000 gallons (about 440 kiloliters)   d 1 Hebrew Ornan, a variant of Araunah   e 3 That is, about 90 feet (about 27 meters) long and 30 feet (about 9 meters) wide (using the cubit of the old standard). ⁴The portico at the front of the temple was twenty cubits*a* long across the width of the building and twenty cubits*b* high.

He overlaid the inside with pure gold. ⁵He paneled the main hall with pine and covered it with fine gold and decorated it with palm tree and chain designs. ⁶He adorned the temple with precious stones. And the gold he used was gold of Parvaim. ⁷He overlaid the ceiling beams, doorframes, walls and doors of the temple with gold, and he carved cherubim on the walls.

⁸He built the Most Holy Place, its length corresponding to the width of the temple—twenty cubits long and twenty cubits wide. He overlaid the inside with six hundred talents*c* of fine gold. ⁹The gold nails weighed fifty shekels.*d* He also overlaid the upper parts with gold.

¹⁰In the Most Holy Place he made a pair of sculptured cherubim and overlaid them with gold. ¹¹The total wingspan of the cherubim was twenty cubits. One wing of the first cherub was five cubits*e* long and touched the temple wall, while its other wing, also five cubits long, touched the wing of the other cherub. ¹²Similarly one wing of the second cherub was five cubits long and touched the other temple wall, and its other wing, also five cubits long, touched the wing of the first cherub. ¹³The wings of these cherubim extended twenty cubits. They stood on their feet, facing the main hall.*f*

¹⁴He made the curtain of blue, purple and crimson yarn and fine linen, with cherubim worked into it.

¹⁵In the front of the temple he made two pillars, which ⌐together⌐ were thirty-five cubits*g* long, each with a capital on top measuring five cubits. ¹⁶He made interwoven chains*h* and put them on top of the pillars. He also made a hundred pomegranates and attached them to the chains. ¹⁷He erected the pillars in the front of the temple, one to the south and one to the north. The one to the south he named Jakin*i* and the one to the north Boaz.*j*

The Temple's Furnishings

He made a bronze altar twenty cubits long, twenty cubits wide and ten cubits high.*k* ²He made the Sea of cast metal, circular in shape, measuring ten cubits from rim to rim and five cubits*l* high. It took a line of thirty cubits*m* to measure around it. ³Below the rim, figures of bulls encircled it—ten to a cubit.*n* The bulls were cast in two rows in one piece with the Sea.

⁴The Sea stood on twelve bulls, three facing north, three facing west, three facing south and three facing

Get a Load of This...

Check out 2 Chronicles 4:2. The first jacuzzi!— three thousand baths on top of twelve bulls! The "Sea of cast metal," which was used by the priests for ritual washing, was a round pool fifteen feet across and seven and a half feet deep. It held "3,000 baths"—about 17,500 gallons of water.

---

a 4 That is, about 30 feet (about 9 meters); also in verses 8, 11 and 13   *b 4* Some Septuagint and Syriac manuscripts; Hebrew *and a hundred and twenty*   *c 8* That is, about 23 tons (about 21 metric tons)   *d 9* That is, about 1 1/4 pounds (about 0.6 kilogram)   *e 11* That is, about 7 1/2 feet (about 2.3 meters); also in verse 15   *f 13* Or *facing inward*   *g 15* That is, about 52 feet (about 16 meters)   *h 16* Or possibly *made chains in the inner sanctuary*; the meaning of the Hebrew for this phrase is uncertain.   *i 17* Jakin probably means *he establishes.*   *j 17* Boaz probably means *in him is strength.*   *k 1* That is, about 30 feet (about 9 meters) long and wide, and about 15 feet (about 4.5 meters) high   *l 2* That is, about 7 1/2 feet (about 2.3 meters)   *m 2* That is, about 45 feet (about 13.5 meters)   *n 3* That is, about 1 1/2 feet (about 0.5 meter) east. The Sea rested on top of them, and their hindquarters were toward the center. [5]It was a handbreadth[a] in thickness, and its rim was like the rim of a cup, like a lily blossom. It held three thousand baths.[b]

[6]He then made ten basins for washing and placed five on the south side and five on the north. In them the things to be used for the burnt offerings were rinsed, but the Sea was to be used by the priests for washing.

[7]He made ten gold lampstands according to the specifications for them and placed them in the temple, five on the south side and five on the north.

[8]He made ten tables and placed them in the temple, five on the south side and five on the north. He also made a hundred gold sprinkling bowls.

[9]He made the courtyard of the priests, and the large court and the doors for the court, and overlaid the doors with bronze. [10]He placed the Sea on the south side, at the southeast corner.

[11]He also made the pots and shovels and sprinkling bowls.

So Huram finished the work he had undertaken for King Solomon in the temple of God:

[12]the two pillars;

the two bowl-shaped capitals on top of the pillars;

the two sets of network decorating the two bowl-shaped capitals on top of the pillars;

[13]the four hundred pomegranates for the two sets of network (two rows of pomegranates for each network, decorating the bowl-shaped capitals on top of the pillars);

[14]the stands with their basins;

[15]the Sea and the twelve bulls under it;

[16]the pots, shovels, meat forks and all related articles.

All the objects that Huram-Abi made for King Solomon for the temple of the LORD were of polished bronze. [17]The king had them cast in clay molds in the plain of the Jordan between Succoth and Zarethan.[c] [18]All these things that Solomon made amounted to so much that the weight of the bronze was not determined.

[19]Solomon also made all the furnishings that were in God's temple:

the golden altar;

the tables on which was the bread of the Presence;

[20]the lampstands of pure gold with their lamps, to burn in front of the inner sanctuary as prescribed;

[21]the gold floral work and lamps and tongs (they were solid gold);

[22]the pure gold wick trimmers, sprinkling bowls, dishes and censers; and the gold doors of the temple: the inner doors to the Most Holy Place and the doors of the main hall.

5 When all the work Solomon had done for the temple of the LORD was finished, he brought in the things his father David had dedicated—the silver and gold and all the furnishings—and he placed them in the treasuries of God's temple.

The Ark Brought to the Temple

[2]Then Solomon summoned to Jerusalem the elders of Israel, all the heads of the tribes and the chiefs of the Israelite families, to bring up the ark of the LORD's covenant from Zion, the City of David. [3]And all the men of Israel came together to the king at the time of the festival in the seventh month.

[4]When all the elders of Israel had arrived, the Levites took up the ark, [5]and they brought up the ark and the Tent of Meeting and all the sacred furnishings in it. The priests, who were Levites, carried them up; [6]and King Solomon and the entire assembly of Israel that had gathered about him were before the ark, sacrificing so many sheep and cattle that they could not be recorded or counted.

[7]The priests then brought the ark of the LORD's covenant to its place in the inner sanctuary of the temple, the Most Holy Place, and put it beneath the wings of the cherubim. [8]The cherubim spread their wings over the place of the ark and covered the ark and its carrying poles. [9]These poles were so long that their ends, extending from the ark, could be seen from in front of the inner sanctuary, but not from outside the Holy Place; and they are still there today. [10]There was nothing in the ark except the two tablets that Moses

---

[a]5 That is, about 3 inches (about 8 centimeters)　　[b]5 That is, about 17,500 gallons (about 66 kiloliters)　　[c]17 Hebrew *Zeredatha*, a variant of *Zarethan*

had placed in it at Horeb, where the Lord made a covenant with the Israelites after they came out of Egypt.

¹¹The priests then withdrew from the Holy Place. All the priests who were there had consecrated themselves, regardless of their divisions. ¹²All the Levites who were musicians—Asaph, Heman, Jeduthun and their sons and relatives—stood on the east side of the altar, dressed in fine linen and playing cymbals, harps and lyres. They were accompanied by 120 priests sounding trumpets. ¹³The trumpeters and singers joined in unison, as with one voice, to give praise and thanks to the Lord. Accompanied by trumpets, cymbals and other instruments, they raised their voices in praise to the Lord and sang:

"He is good;
　his love endures forever."

Then the temple of the Lord was filled with a cloud, ¹⁴and the priests could not perform their service because of the cloud, for the glory of the Lord filled the temple of God.

6 Then Solomon said, "The Lord has said that he would dwell in a dark cloud; ²I have built a magnificent temple for you, a place for you to dwell forever."

³While the whole assembly of Israel was standing there, the king turned around and blessed them. ⁴Then he said:

"Praise be to the Lord, the God of Israel, who with his hands has fulfilled what he promised with his mouth to my father David. For he said, ⁵'Since the day I brought my people out of Egypt, I have not chosen a city in any tribe of Israel to have a temple built for my Name to be there, nor have I chosen anyone to be the leader over my people Israel. ⁶But now I have chosen Jerusalem for my Name to be there, and I have chosen David to rule my people Israel.'

⁷"My father David had it in his heart to build a temple for the Name of the Lord, the God of Israel. ⁸But the Lord said to my father David, 'Because it was in your heart to build a temple for my Name, you did well to have this in your heart. ⁹Nevertheless, you are not the one to build the temple, but your son, who is your own

flesh and blood—he is the one who will build the temple for my Name.'

¹⁰"The Lord has kept the promise he made. I have succeeded David my father and now I sit on the throne of Israel, just as the Lord promised, and I have built the temple for the Name of the Lord, the God of Israel. ¹¹There I have placed the ark, in which is the covenant of the Lord that he made with the people of Israel."

Solomon's Prayer of Dedication

¹²Then Solomon stood before the altar of the Lord in front of the whole assembly of Israel and spread out his hands. ¹³Now he had made a bronze platform, five cubits[a] long, five cubits wide and three cubits[b] high, and had placed it in the center of the outer court. He stood on the platform and then knelt down before the whole assembly of Israel and spread out his hands toward heaven. ¹⁴He said:

"O Lord, God of Israel, there is no God like you in heaven or on earth— you who keep your covenant of love with your servants who continue wholeheartedly in your way. ¹⁵You have kept your promise to your servant David my father; with your mouth you have promised and with your hand you have fulfilled it—as it is today.

¹⁶"Now Lord, God of Israel, keep for your servant David my father the promises you made to him when you said, 'You shall never fail to have a man to sit before me on the throne of Israel, if only your sons are careful in all they do to walk before me according to my law, as you have done.' ¹⁷And now, O Lord, God of Israel, let your word that you promised your servant David come true.

¹⁸"But will God really dwell on earth with men? The heavens, even the highest heavens, cannot contain you. How much less this temple I have built! ¹⁹Yet give attention to your servant's prayer and his plea for mercy, O Lord my God. Hear the cry and the prayer that your servant is praying in your presence. ²⁰May your eyes be open toward this temple day and

---

a 13 That is, about 7 1/2 feet (about 2.3 meters)　　*b 13* That is, about 4 1/2 feet (about 1.3 meters) night, this place of which you said you would put your Name there. May you hear the prayer your servant prays toward this place. ²¹Hear the supplications of your servant and of your people Israel when they pray toward this place. Hear from heaven, your dwelling place; and when you hear, forgive.

²²"When a man wrongs his neighbor and is required to take an oath and he comes and swears the oath before your altar in this temple, ²³then hear from heaven and act. Judge between your servants, repaying the guilty by bringing down on his own head what he has done. Declare the innocent not guilty and so establish his innocence.

²⁴"When your people Israel have been defeated by an enemy because they have sinned against you and when they turn back and confess your name, praying and making supplication before you in this temple, ²⁵then hear from heaven and forgive the sin of your people Israel and bring them back to the land you gave to them and their fathers.

²⁶"When the heavens are shut up and there is no rain because your people have sinned against you, and when they pray toward this place and confess your name and turn from their sin because you have afflicted them, ²⁷then hear from heaven and forgive the sin of your servants, your people Israel. Teach them the right way to live, and send rain on the land you gave your people for an inheritance.

²⁸"When famine or plague comes to the land, or blight or mildew, locusts or grasshoppers, or when enemies besiege them in any of their cities, whatever disaster or disease may come, ²⁹and when a prayer or plea is made by any of your people Israel— each one aware of his afflictions and pains, and spreading out his hands toward this temple— ³⁰then hear from heaven, your dwelling place. Forgive, and deal with each man according to all he does, since you know his heart (for you alone know the hearts of men), ³¹so that they will fear you and walk in your ways all the time they live in the land you gave our fathers.

³²"As for the foreigner who does not belong to your people Israel but has come from a distant land because of your great name and your mighty hand and your outstretched arm—when he comes and prays toward this temple, ³³then hear from heaven, your dwelling place, and do whatever the foreigner asks of you, so that all the peoples of the earth may know your name and fear you, as do your own people Israel, and may know that this house I have built bears your Name.

³⁴"When your people go to war against their enemies, wherever you send them, and when they pray to you toward this city you have chosen and the temple I have built for your Name, ³⁵then hear from heaven their prayer and their plea, and uphold their cause.

³⁶"When they sin against you—for there is no one who does not sin— and you become angry with them and give them over to the enemy, who takes them captive to a land far away or near; ³⁷and if they have a change of heart in the land where they are held captive, and repent and plead with you in the land of their captivity and say, 'We have sinned, we have done wrong and acted wickedly'; ³⁸and if they turn back to you with all their heart and soul in the land of their captivity where they were taken, and pray toward the land you gave their fathers, toward the city you have chosen and toward the temple I have built for your Name; ³⁹then from heaven, your dwelling place, hear their prayer and their pleas, and uphold their cause. And forgive your people, who have sinned against you.

⁴⁰"Now, my God, may your eyes be open and your ears attentive to the prayers offered in this place.

⁴¹"Now arise, O Lᴏʀᴅ God, and
　　come to your resting place,
　　you and the ark of your might.
May your priests, O Lᴏʀᴅ God, be
　　clothed with salvation,
　　may your saints rejoice in your
　　goodness.

⁴²O Lᴏʀᴅ God, do not reject your
     anointed one.
   Remember the great love
     promised to David your
     servant."

The Dedication of the Temple

When Solomon finished praying, fire came down from heaven and consumed the burnt offering and the sacrifices, and the glory of the Lᴏʀᴅ filled the temple. ²The priests could not enter the temple of the Lᴏʀᴅ because the glory of the Lᴏʀᴅ filled it. ³When all the Israelites saw the fire coming down and the glory of the Lᴏʀᴅ above the temple, they knelt on the pavement with their faces to the ground, and they worshiped and gave thanks to the Lᴏʀᴅ, saying,

"He is good;
   his love endures forever."

⁴Then the king and all the people offered sacrifices before the Lᴏʀᴅ. ⁵And King Solomon offered a sacrifice of twenty-two thousand head of cattle and a hundred and twenty thousand sheep and goats. So

the king and all the people dedicated the temple of God. ⁶The priests took their positions, as did the Levites with the Lᴏʀᴅ's musical instruments, which King David had made for praising the Lᴏʀᴅ and which were used when he gave thanks, saying, "His love endures forever." Opposite the Levites, the priests blew their trumpets, and all the Israelites were standing.

⁷Solomon consecrated the middle part of the courtyard in front of the temple of the Lᴏʀᴅ, and there he offered burnt offerings and the fat of the fellowship offerings,ᵃ because the bronze altar he had made could not hold the burnt offerings, the grain offerings and the fat portions.

⁸So Solomon observed the festival at that time for seven days, and all Israel with him—a vast assembly, people from Lebᵇ Hamath to the Wadi of Egypt. ⁹On the eighth day they held an assembly, for they had celebrated the dedication of the altar for seven days and the festival for seven days more. ¹⁰On the twenty-third day of the seventh month he sent the people to

ᵃ 7 Traditionally peace offerings   ᵇ 8 Or from the entrance to

All on Your Knees

READ 2 CHRONICLES 7:1–3

Have you ever met a big movie star or professional athletes? Maybe you got their autograph or shook their hand. Were you nervous or scared? When the people of Israel attended the grand opening of the new temple, they had an encounter with someone way bigger than a movie star. They met God! When you get really close to God, your automatic reaction is to drop to your knees and worship him. Worship is not about being scared or nervous around God. It's being in total, blown-away awe of him. It's surrendering your will to his care and letting him be in charge of your life. When you do that, God comes deeper into your life. The more you get to know God, the more you want to say, "wow!" and worship him. That moves you in a cycle, closer and closer to God.

Your next reading is on page 545.

their homes, joyful and glad in heart for the good things the Lord had done for David and Solomon and for his people Israel.

The Lord Appears to Solomon

[11]When Solomon had finished the temple of the Lord and the royal palace, and had succeeded in carrying out all he had in mind to do in the temple of the Lord and in his own palace, [12]the Lord appeared to him at night and said:

"I have heard your prayer and have chosen this place for myself as a temple for sacrifices.

[13]"When I shut up the heavens so that there is no rain, or command locusts to devour the land or send a plague among my people, [14]if my people, who are called by my name, will humble themselves and pray and seek my face and turn from their wicked ways, then will I hear from heaven and will forgive their sin and will heal their land. [15]Now my eyes will be open and my ears attentive to the prayers offered in this place. [16]I have chosen and consecrated this temple so that my Name may be there forever. My eyes and my heart will always be there.

[17]"As for you, if you walk before me as David your father did, and do all I command, and observe my decrees and laws, [18]I will establish your royal throne, as I covenanted with David your father when I said, 'You shall never fail to have a man to rule over Israel.'

[19]"But if you[a] turn away and forsake the decrees and commands I have given you[a] and go off to serve other gods and worship them, [20]then I will uproot Israel from my land, which I have given them, and will reject this temple I have consecrated for my Name. I will make it a byword and an object of ridicule among all peoples. [21]And though this temple is now so imposing, all who pass by will be appalled and say, 'Why has the Lord done such a thing to this land and to this temple?' [22]People will answer, 'Because they have forsaken the Lord, the God of their fathers, who brought them out of Egypt, and have embraced other gods, worshiping and serving them—that is why he brought all this disaster on them.' "

Solomon's Other Activities

At the end of twenty years, during which Solomon built the temple of the Lord and his own palace, [2]Solomon rebuilt the villages that Hiram[b] had given him, and settled Israelites in them. [3]Solomon then went to Hamath Zobah and captured it. [4]He also built up Tadmor in the desert and all the store cities he had built in Hamath. [5]He rebuilt Upper Beth Horon and Lower Beth Horon as fortified cities, with walls and with gates and bars, [6]as well as Baalath and all his store cities, and all the cities for his chariots and for his horses[c]—whatever he desired to build in Jerusalem, in Lebanon and throughout all the territory he ruled.

[7]All the people left from the Hittites, Amorites, Perizzites, Hivites and Jebusites (these peoples were not Israelites), [8]that is, their descendants remaining in the land, whom the Israelites had not destroyed—these Solomon conscripted for his slave labor force, as it is to this day. [9]But Solomon did not make slaves of the Israelites for his work; they were his fighting men, commanders of his captains, and commanders of his chariots and charioteers. [10]They were also King Solomon's chief officials—two hundred and fifty officials supervising the men.

[11]Solomon brought Pharaoh's daughter up from the City of David to the palace he had built for her, for he said, "My wife must not live in the palace of David king of Israel, because the places the ark of the Lord has entered are holy."

[12]On the altar of the Lord that he had built in front of the portico, Solomon sacrificed burnt offerings to the Lord, [13]according to the daily requirement for offerings commanded by Moses for Sabbaths, New Moons and the three annual feasts—the Feast of Unleavened Bread, the Feast of Weeks and the Feast of Tabernacles. [14]In keeping with the ordinance of his father David, he appointed the divisions of the priests for their duties, and the Levites to lead the praise and to assist the priests according to each day's requirement. He

---

[a] 19 The Hebrew is plural.   [b] 2 Hebrew Huram, a variant of Hiram; also in verse 18   [c] 6 Or charioteers

also appointed the gatekeepers by divisions for the various gates, because this was what David the man of God had ordered. ¹⁵They did not deviate from the king's commands to the priests or to the Levites in any matter, including that of the treasuries.

¹⁶All Solomon's work was carried out, from the day the foundation of the temple of the LORD was laid until its completion. So the temple of the LORD was finished.

¹⁷Then Solomon went to Ezion Geber and Elath on the coast of Edom. ¹⁸And Hiram sent him ships commanded by his own officers, men who knew the sea. These, with Solomon's men, sailed to Ophir and brought back four hundred and fifty talents*a* of gold, which they delivered to King Solomon.

The Queen of Sheba Visits Solomon

When the queen of Sheba heard of Solomon's fame, she came to Jerusalem to test him with hard questions. Arriving with a very great caravan—with camels carrying spices, large quantities of gold, and precious stones— she came to Solomon and talked with him about all she had on her mind. ²Solomon answered all her questions; nothing was too hard for him to explain to her. ³When the queen of Sheba saw the wisdom of Solomon, as well as the palace he had built, ⁴the food on his table, the seating of his officials, the attending servants in their robes, the cupbearers in their robes and the burnt offerings he made at*b* the temple of the LORD, she was overwhelmed.

⁵She said to the king, "The report I heard in my own country about your achievements and your wisdom is true. ⁶But I did not believe what they said until I came and saw with my own eyes. Indeed, not even half the greatness of your wisdom was told me; you have far exceeded the report I heard. ⁷How happy your men must be! How happy your officials, who continually stand before you and hear your wisdom! ⁸Praise be to the LORD your God, who has delighted in you

a 18 That is, about 17 tons (about 16 metric tons)
b 4 Or the ascent by which he went up to

Smarter Than Smart

READ 1 CHRONICLES 9:1–12

Just imagine the fun Solomon would have answering questions on "Jeopardy." The queen of Sheba asked him some tough questions and was amazed by the answers she received. She was so impressed that she told Solomon, "Indeed, not even half the greatness of your wisdom was told me; you have far exceeded the report I heard" (verse 6). She was also impressed with Solomon's leadership. He was genuinely concerned for the people, and he was kind, understanding, considerate and righteous. This is what God is looking for in real men. Solomon could have used his power and wisdom to serve himself, but—at least early in his reign—he didn't. That's why the queen praised God: she saw him as the source of Solomon's good leadership and wisdom. When you use your smarts and talents to serve others, people will know you're plugged in to God.

Your next reading is on page 548.

Get a Load of This...

Check out 2 Chronicles 9:21. What's more fun than a barrel of monkeys? A boatload of apes! Solomon might have been starting a zoo in Jerusalem, since he shipped in exotic animals such as baboons and apes on his ships.

and placed you on his throne as king to rule for the Lord your God. Because of the love of your God for Israel and his desire to uphold them forever, he has made you king over them, to maintain justice and righteousness."

⁹Then she gave the king 120 talents[a] of gold, large quantities of spices, and precious stones. There had never been such spices as those the queen of Sheba gave to King Solomon.

¹⁰(The men of Hiram and the men of Solomon brought gold from Ophir; they also brought algumwood[b] and precious stones. ¹¹The king used the algumwood to make steps for the temple of the Lord and for the royal palace, and to make harps and lyres for the musicians. Nothing like them had ever been seen in Judah.)

¹²King Solomon gave the queen of Sheba all she desired and asked for; he gave her more than she had brought to him. Then she left and returned with her retinue to her own country.

Solomon's Splendor

¹³The weight of the gold that Solomon received yearly was 666 talents,[c] ¹⁴not including the revenues brought in by merchants and traders. Also all the kings of Arabia and the governors of the land brought gold and silver to Solomon.

¹⁵King Solomon made two hundred large shields of hammered gold; six hundred bekas[d] of hammered gold went into each shield. ¹⁶He also made three hundred small shields of hammered gold, with three hundred bekas[e] of gold in each shield. The king put them in the Palace of the Forest of Lebanon.

¹⁷Then the king made a great throne inlaid with ivory and overlaid with pure gold. ¹⁸The throne had six steps, and a footstool of gold was attached to it. On both sides of the seat were armrests, with a lion standing beside each of them. ¹⁹Twelve lions stood on the six steps, one at either end of each step. Nothing like it had ever been made for any other kingdom. ²⁰All King Solomon's goblets were gold, and all the household articles in the Palace of the Forest of Lebanon were pure gold. Nothing was made of silver, because silver was considered of little value in Solomon's day. ²¹The king had a fleet of trading ships[f] manned by Hiram's[g] men. Once every three years it returned, carrying gold, silver and ivory, and apes and baboons.

²²King Solomon was greater in riches and wisdom than all the other kings of the earth. ²³All the kings of the earth sought audience with Solomon to hear the wisdom God had put in his heart. ²⁴Year after year, everyone who came brought a gift—articles of silver and gold, and robes, weapons and spices, and horses and mules.

9 That is, about 4 1/2 tons (about 4 metric tons)   b 10 Probably a variant of *almugwood*   c 13 That is, about 25 tons (about 23 metric tons)   d 15 That is, about 7 1/2 pounds (about 3.5 kilograms)   e 16 That is, about 3 3/4 pounds (about 1.7 kilograms)   f 21 Hebrew of *ships that could go to Tarshish*   g 21 Hebrew *Huram*, a variant of *Hiram*

²⁵Solomon had four thousand stalls for horses and chariots, and twelve thousand horses,^a which he kept in the chariot cities and also with him in Jerusalem. ²⁶He ruled over all the kings from the River^b to the land of the Philistines, as far as the border of Egypt. ²⁷The king made silver as common in Jerusalem as stones, and cedar as plentiful as sycamore-fig trees in the foothills. ²⁸Solomon's horses were imported from Egypt^c and from all other countries.

Solomon's Death

²⁹As for the other events of Solomon's reign, from beginning to end, are they not written in the records of Nathan the prophet, in the prophecy of Ahijah the Shilonite and in the visions of Iddo the seer concerning Jeroboam son of Nebat? ³⁰Solomon reigned in Jerusalem over all Israel forty years. ³¹Then he rested with his fathers and was buried in the city of David his father. And Rehoboam his son succeeded him as king.

Israel Rebels Against Rehoboam

10 Rehoboam went to Shechem, for all the Israelites had gone there to make him king. ²When Jeroboam son of Nebat heard this (he was in Egypt, where he had fled from King Solomon), he returned from Egypt. ³So they sent for Jeroboam, and he and all Israel went to Rehoboam and said to him: ⁴"Your father put a heavy yoke on us, but now lighten the harsh labor and the heavy yoke he put on us, and we will serve you."

⁵Rehoboam answered, "Come back to me in three days." So the people went away.

⁶Then King Rehoboam consulted the elders who had served his father Solomon during his lifetime. "How would you advise me to answer these people?" he asked.

⁷They replied, "If you will be kind to these people and please them and give them a favorable answer, they will always be your servants."

⁸But Rehoboam rejected the advice the elders gave him and consulted the young men who had grown up with him and were serving him. ⁹He asked them, "What is your advice? How should we answer these people who say to me, 'Lighten the yoke your father put on us'?"

¹⁰The young men who had grown up with him replied, "Tell the people who have said to you, 'Your father put a heavy yoke on us, but make our yoke lighter'—tell them, 'My little finger is thicker than my father's waist. ¹¹My father laid on you a heavy yoke; I will make it even heavier. My father scourged you with whips; I will scourge you with scorpions.' "

¹²Three days later Jeroboam and all the people returned to Rehoboam, as the king had said, "Come back to me in three days." ¹³The king answered them harshly. Rejecting the advice of the elders, ¹⁴he followed the

Get a Load of This...

Check out 2 Chronicles 9:25. God had said that no Israelite king should gather "great numbers of horses" (Deuteronomy 17:16), yet Solomon had *twelve thousand*! Either (a) Solomon couldn't count or (b) he didn't think 12,000 was "great numbers" or (c) he was just plain disobedient.

^a 25 Or charioteers   ^b 26 That is, the Euphrates   ^c 28 Or possibly Muzur, a region in Cilicia

GET
Solomon's Statistics

READ 2 CHRONICLES 9:29–31

By the time Solomon "rested with his fathers" (verse 31), he had been all over the scoreboard, from good to bad, in a major way. Let's see what his report card looks like.

DEEPER: Solomon started off deep with God, but ended up shallow. At first he followed his father David's example and did a great job of worshiping and obeying God. When he prayed, fire fell from heaven and the glory of God filled the temple (see 2 Chronicles 7:1). So why did Solomon hit the mat in the eleventh round? He knew lots about God, sure, but he didn't have the character that David had. He didn't have that same deep, long-term relationship called *commitment*.

SMARTER: Smart? Hey! Solomon was *the* smartest of all (see 1 Kings 4:31)! After God gave Solomon a serious download of wisdom, he became a walking encyclopedia. He studied plants, animals and—get this—even became an expert on *reptiles* (see 1 Kings 4:33–34). Cool. Solomon wrote over a thousand songs and most of the book of Proverbs. He probably also wrote Ecclesiastes and Song of Songs. But suddenly his brains seemed to bail out on him, and he did *d-u-m-b* things like disobey God. He had lots of wisdom about the things of this life, but not enough personal knowledge of God.

COOLER: Solomon was superb at international diplomacy and the queen of Sheba was amazed by how he handled his servants and staff (see 1 Kings 10:4–5, 8). Solomon also built the temple that brought about great group worship. The downside was that he was too much of a crowd-pleaser. He compromised in order to have people say, "Look, man, here comes our very cool king." God had made it clear that it is *not* acceptable to marry foreigners who didn't follow the Lord. But Solomon did it anyway—hundreds of times!

STRONGER: Solomon was a strong leader. He was also very strong in the massive building projects he completed: building the temple, constructing his own palace and fortifying Jerusalem, and other cities—not to mention holding together a great empire. Solomon accomplished amazing things. This guy was no couch potato. In the end, however, he used his strength and building power to build pagan altars (see 1 Kings 11:7–8). Hmmmm . . . he would have been better off working out in the gym.

Your next reading is on page 551.

advice of the young men and said, "My father made your yoke heavy; I will make it even heavier. My father scourged you with whips; I will scourge you with scorpions." ¹⁵So the king did not listen to the people, for this turn of events was from God, to fulfill the word the LORD had spoken to Jeroboam son of Nebat through Ahijah the Shilonite.

¹⁶When all Israel saw that the king refused to listen to them, they answered the king:

"What share do we have in David,
    what part in Jesse's son?
To your tents, O Israel!
    Look after your own house, O David!"

So all the Israelites went home. ¹⁷But as for the Israelites who were living in the towns of Judah, Rehoboam still ruled over them.

¹⁸King Rehoboam sent out Adoniram,ᵃ who was in charge of forced labor, but the Israelites stoned him to death. King Rehoboam, however, managed to get into his chariot and escape to Jerusalem. ¹⁹So Israel has been in rebellion against the house of David to this day.

11 When Rehoboam arrived in Jerusalem, he mustered the house of Judah and Benjamin—a hundred and eighty thousand fighting men—to make war against Israel and to regain the kingdom for Rehoboam. ²But this word of the LORD came to Shemaiah the man of God: ³"Say to Rehoboam son of Solomon king of Judah and to all the Israelites in Judah and Benjamin, ⁴'This is what the LORD says: Do not go up to fight against your brothers. Go home, every one of you, for this is my doing.' " So they obeyed the words of the LORD and turned back from marching against Jeroboam.

Rehoboam Fortifies Judah

⁵Rehoboam lived in Jerusalem and built up towns for defense in Judah: ⁶Bethlehem, Etam, Tekoa, ⁷Beth Zur, Soco, Adullam, ⁸Gath, Mareshah, Ziph, ⁹Adoraim, Lachish, Azekah, ¹⁰Zorah, Aijalon and Hebron. These were fortified cities in Judah and Benjamin. ¹¹He strengthened their defenses and put commanders in them, with supplies of food, olive oil and wine. ¹²He put shields and spears in all the cities, and made them very strong. So Judah and Benjamin were his.

¹³The priests and Levites from all their districts throughout Israel sided with him. ¹⁴The Levites even abandoned their pasturelands and property, and came to Judah and Jerusalem because Jeroboam and his sons had rejected them as priests of the LORD. ¹⁵And he appointed his own priests for the high places and for the goat and calf idols he had made. ¹⁶Those from every tribe of Israel who set their hearts on seeking the LORD, the God of Israel, followed the Levites to Jerusalem to offer sacrifices to the LORD, the God of their fathers. ¹⁷They strengthened the kingdom of Judah and supported Rehoboam son of Solomon three years, walking in the ways of David and Solomon during this time.

Rehoboam's Family

¹⁸Rehoboam married Mahalath, who was the daughter of David's son Jerimoth and of Abihail, the daughter of Jesse's son Eliab. ¹⁹She bore him sons: Jeush, Shemariah and Zaham. ²⁰Then he married Maacah daughter of Absalom, who bore him Abijah, Attai, Ziza and Shelomith. ²¹Rehoboam loved Maacah daughter of Absalom more than any of his other wives and concubines. In all, he had eighteen wives and sixty concubines, twenty-eight sons and sixty daughters.

²²Rehoboam appointed Abijah son of Maacah to be the chief prince among his brothers, in order to make him king. ²³He acted wisely, dispersing some of his sons throughout the districts of Judah and Benjamin, and to all the fortified cities. He gave them abundant provisions and took many wives for them.

Shishak Attacks Jerusalem

12 After Rehoboam's position as king was established and he had become strong, he and all Israelᵇ with him abandoned the law of the LORD. ²Because they had been unfaithful to the LORD, Shishak king of Egypt attacked Jerusalem in the fifth year of King Rehoboam. ³With twelve hundred chariots and sixty thousand horsemen and the innumerable troops of Libyans, Sukkites and Cushitesᶜ that came with him from

---

ᵃ 18 Hebrew Hadoram, a variant of Adoniram   ᵇ 1 That is, Judah, as frequently in 2 Chronicles   ᶜ 3 That is, people from the upper Nile region

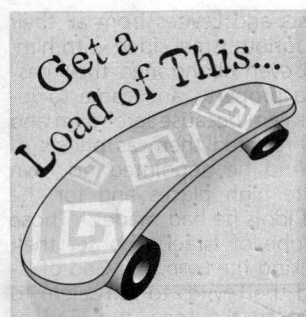

Get a Load of This...

Check out 2 Chronicles 12:9. Several hundred years after God gave the Israelites tons of Egyptian gold and treasures (Exodus 12:35–36), Pharaoh Shishak came along and snagged tons of gold from *them*. Why didn't God help Judah keep all that treasure? Because the people of Judah had cut out on God. He wasn't number one in their life anymore.

Egypt, ⁴he captured the fortified cities of Judah and came as far as Jerusalem.

⁵Then the prophet Shemaiah came to Rehoboam and to the leaders of Judah who had assembled in Jerusalem for fear of Shishak, and he said to them, "This is what the LORD says, 'You have abandoned me; therefore, I now abandon you to Shishak.' "

⁶The leaders of Israel and the king humbled themselves and said, "The LORD is just."

⁷When the LORD saw that they humbled themselves, this word of the LORD came to Shemaiah: "Since they have humbled themselves, I will not destroy them but will soon give them deliverance. My wrath will not be poured out on Jerusalem through Shishak. ⁸They will, however, become subject to him, so that they may learn the difference between serving me and serving the kings of other lands."

⁹When Shishak king of Egypt attacked Jerusalem, he carried off the treasures of the temple of the LORD and the treasures of the royal palace. He took everything, including the gold shields Solomon had made. ¹⁰So King Rehoboam made bronze shields to replace them and assigned these to the commanders of the guard on duty at the entrance to the royal palace. ¹¹Whenever the king went to the LORD's temple, the guards went with him, bearing the shields, and afterward they returned them to the guardroom.

¹²Because Rehoboam humbled himself, the LORD's anger turned from him, and he was not totally destroyed. Indeed, there was some good in Judah.

¹³King Rehoboam established himself firmly in Jerusalem and continued as king. He was forty-one years old when he became king, and he reigned seventeen years in Jerusalem, the city the LORD had chosen out of all the tribes of Israel in which to put his Name. His mother's name was Naamah; she was an Ammonite. ¹⁴He did evil because he had not set his heart on seeking the LORD.

¹⁵As for the events of Rehoboam's reign, from beginning to end, are they not written in the records of Shemaiah the prophet and of Iddo the seer that deal with genealogies? There was continual warfare between Rehoboam and Jeroboam. ¹⁶Rehoboam rested with his fathers and was buried in the City of David. And Abijah his son succeeded him as king.

Abijah King of Judah

13 In the eighteenth year of the reign of Jeroboam, Abijah became king of Judah, ²and he reigned in Jerusalem three years. His mother's name was Maacah,ᵃ a daughterᵇ of Uriel of Gibeah.

There was war between Abijah and Jeroboam. ³Abijah went into battle with a force of four hundred thousand able fighting men, and Jeroboam drew up a battle

---

ᵃ 2 Most Septuagint manuscripts and Syriac (see also 2 Chron. 11:20 and 1 Kings 15:2); Hebrew *Micaiah*   ᵇ 2 Or *granddaughter* line against him with eight hundred thousand able troops.

⁴Abijah stood on Mount Zemaraim, in the hill country of Ephraim, and said, "Jeroboam and all Israel, listen to me! ⁵Don't you know that the Lᴏʀᴅ, the God of Israel, has given the kingship of Israel to David and his descendants forever by a covenant of salt? ⁶Yet Jeroboam son of Nebat, an official of Solomon son of David, rebelled against his master. ⁷Some worthless scoundrels gathered around him and opposed Rehoboam son of Solomon when he was young and indecisive and not strong enough to resist them.

⁸"And now you plan to resist the kingdom of the Lᴏʀᴅ, which is in the hands of David's descendants. You are indeed a vast army and have with you the golden calves that Jeroboam made to be your gods. ⁹But didn't you drive out the priests of the Lᴏʀᴅ, the sons of Aaron, and the Levites, and make priests of your own as the peoples of other lands do? Whoever comes to consecrate himself with a young bull and seven rams may become a priest of what are not gods.

¹⁰"As for us, the Lᴏʀᴅ is our God, and we have not forsaken him. The priests who serve the Lᴏʀᴅ are sons of Aaron, and the Levites assist them. ¹¹Every morning and evening they present burnt offerings and fragrant incense to the Lᴏʀᴅ. They set out the bread on the ceremonially clean table and light the lamps on the gold lampstand every evening. We are observing the requirements of the Lᴏʀᴅ our God. But you have forsaken him. ¹²God is with us; he is our leader. His priests with their trumpets will sound the battle cry against you. Men of Israel, do not fight against the Lᴏʀᴅ, the God of your fathers, for you will not succeed."

¹³Now Jeroboam had sent troops around to the rear, so that while he was in front of Judah the ambush was behind them. ¹⁴Judah turned and saw that they were being attacked at both front and rear. Then they cried out to the Lᴏʀᴅ. The priests blew their trumpets ¹⁵and the men of Judah raised the battle cry. At the sound of their battle cry, God routed Jeroboam and all Israel before Abijah and Judah. ¹⁶The Israelites fled before Judah,

God-time Can't Slide

READ 2 CHRONICLES 13:1–20

Wow, what a battle! Jeroboam, the bad guy, had 800,000 men compared to Abijah's 400,000 men. In the end, "the men of Judah were victorious because they relied on the Lᴏʀᴅ " (verse 18). Jeroboam's men had forgotten God and relied on their superior numbers and sneak attacks, but the army of Judah put their trust in God. Sometimes Christians are tempted to let their relationship with God slide and only yell for his help when an emergency hits. That's like not doing your math homework for two weeks, then trying to cram for the test the night before. Not good. When you rely on God, his blessing will automatically be in your life—and be there when you need it. Don't let your God-time slide. Day by day, build your relationship with him, and his blessings will come as part of the package.

Your next reading is on page 553.

and God delivered them into their hands. [17]Abijah and his men inflicted heavy losses on them, so that there were five hundred thousand casualties among Israel's able men. [18]The men of Israel were subdued on that occasion, and the men of Judah were victorious because they relied on the LORD, the God of their fathers.

[19]Abijah pursued Jeroboam and took from him the towns of Bethel, Jeshanah and Ephron, with their surrounding villages. [20]Jeroboam did not regain power during the time of Abijah. And the LORD struck him down and he died.

[21]But Abijah grew in strength. He married fourteen wives and had twenty-two sons and sixteen daughters.

[22]The other events of Abijah's reign, what he did and what he said, are written in the annotations of the prophet Iddo.

14 And Abijah rested with his fathers and was buried in the City of David. Asa his son succeeded him as king, and in his days the country was at peace for ten years.

Asa King of Judah

[2]Asa did what was good and right in the eyes of the LORD his God. [3]He removed the foreign altars and the high places, smashed the sacred stones and cut down the Asherah poles.[a] [4]He commanded Judah to seek the LORD, the God of their fathers, and to obey his laws and commands. [5]He removed the high places and incense altars in every town in Judah, and the kingdom was at peace under him. [6]He built up the fortified cities of Judah, since the land was at peace. No one was at war with him during those years, for the LORD gave him rest.

[7]"Let us build up these towns," he said to Judah, "and put walls around them, with towers, gates and bars. The land is still ours, because we have sought the LORD our God; we sought him and he has given us rest on every side." So they built and prospered.

[8]Asa had an army of three hundred thousand men from Judah, equipped with large shields and with spears, and two hundred and eighty thousand from Benjamin, armed with small shields and with bows. All these were brave fighting men.

[9]Zerah the Cushite marched out against them with a vast army[b] and three hundred chariots, and came as far as Mare-

shah. [10]Asa went out to meet him, and they took up battle positions in the Valley of Zephathah near Mareshah.

[11]Then Asa called to the LORD his God and said, "LORD, there is no one like you to help the powerless against the mighty. Help us, O LORD our God, for we rely on you, and in your name we have come against this vast army. O LORD, you are our God; do not let man prevail against you."

[12]The LORD struck down the Cushites before Asa and Judah. The Cushites fled, [13]and Asa and his army pursued them as far as Gerar. Such a great number of Cushites fell that they could not recover; they were crushed before the LORD and his forces. The men of Judah carried off a large amount of plunder. [14]They destroyed all the villages around Gerar, for the terror of the LORD had fallen upon them. They plundered all these villages, since there was much booty there. [15]They also attacked the camps of the herdsmen and carried off droves of sheep and goats and camels. Then they returned to Jerusalem.

Asa's Reform

15 The Spirit of God came upon Azariah son of Oded. [2]He went out to meet Asa and said to him, "Listen to me, Asa and all Judah and Benjamin. The LORD is with you when you are with him. If you seek him, he will be found by you, but if you forsake him, he will forsake you. [3]For a long time Israel was without the true God, without a priest to teach and without the law. [4]But in their distress they turned to the LORD, the God of Israel, and sought him, and he was found by them. [5]In those days it was not safe to travel about, for all the inhabitants of the lands were in great turmoil. [6]One nation was being crushed by another and one city by another, because God was troubling them with every kind of distress. [7]But as for you, be strong and do not give up, for your work will be rewarded."

[8]When Asa heard these words and the prophecy of Azariah son of[c] Oded the prophet, he took courage. He removed the detestable idols from the whole land of Judah and Benjamin and from the towns he

---

[a] 3 That is, symbols of the goddess Asherah; here and elsewhere in 2 Chronicles   [b] 9 Hebrew *with an army of a thousand thousands* or *with an army of thousands upon thousands*   [c] 8 Vulgate and Syriac (see also Septuagint and verse 1); Hebrew does not have *Azariah son of*.

had captured in the hills of Ephraim. He repaired the altar of the LORD that was in front of the portico of the LORD's temple.

⁹Then he assembled all Judah and Benjamin and the people from Ephraim, Manasseh and Simeon who had settled among them, for large numbers had come over to him from Israel when they saw that the LORD his God was with him.

¹⁰They assembled at Jerusalem in the third month of the fifteenth year of Asa's reign. ¹¹At that time they sacrificed to the LORD seven hundred head of cattle and seven thousand sheep and goats from the plunder they had brought back. ¹²They entered into a covenant to seek the LORD, the God of their fathers, with all their heart and soul. ¹³All who would not seek the LORD, the God of Israel, were to be put to death, whether small or great, man or woman. ¹⁴They took an oath to the LORD with loud acclamation, with shouting and with trumpets and horns. ¹⁵All Judah rejoiced about the oath because they had sworn it wholeheartedly. They sought God eagerly, and he was found by them. So the LORD gave them rest on every side.

¹⁶King Asa also deposed his grandmother Maacah from her position as queen mother, because she had made a repulsive Asherah pole. Asa cut the pole down, broke it up and burned it in the Kidron Valley. ¹⁷Although he did not remove the high places from Israel, Asa's heart was fully committed ⌊to the LORD⌋ all his life. ¹⁸He brought into the temple of God the silver and gold and the articles that he and his father had dedicated.

¹⁹There was no more war until the thirty-fifth year of Asa's reign.

Asa's Last Years

In the thirty-sixth year of Asa's reign Baasha king of Israel went up against Judah and fortified Ramah to prevent anyone from leaving or entering the territory of Asa king of Judah.

²Asa then took the silver and gold out of the treasuries of the LORD's temple and of his own palace and sent it to Ben-Hadad king of Aram, who was ruling in Damascus. ³"Let there be a treaty between me and you," he said, "as there was be-

Idol-smashing Spree

READ 2 CHRONICLES 15

Asa, King of Judah, picked up a sledge hammer and went on an idol-smashing spree. He probably enjoyed taking the heads off statues of Baal. God hated idols because people put their trust in a piece of wood or rock that could never help them live their lives right. God is the only one who can bless people and make their lives work. You probably don't worship wooden or stone idols, but modern "idols" can be made out of circuit boards and memory chips. Modern-day idols can be *anything* that gets in the way of your relationship with God and others—even a game you play that takes up most of your time. Or a toy you absolutely refuse to let anyone touch. If you went on an idol-smashing spree in your life, what would the garbage man find at the curb?

Your next reading is on page 557.

tween my father and your father. See, I am sending you silver and gold. Now break your treaty with Baasha king of Israel so he will withdraw from me."

4Ben-Hadad agreed with King Asa and sent the commanders of his forces against the towns of Israel. They conquered Ijon, Dan, Abel Maim*a* and all the store cities of Naphtali. 5When Baasha heard this, he stopped building Ramah and abandoned his work. 6Then King Asa brought all the men of Judah, and they carried away from Ramah the stones and timber Baasha had been using. With them he built up Geba and Mizpah.

7At that time Hanani the seer came to Asa king of Judah and said to him: "Because you relied on the king of Aram and not on the LORD your God, the army of the king of Aram has escaped from your hand. 8Were not the Cushites*b* and Libyans a mighty army with great numbers of chariots and horsemen*c*? Yet when you relied on the LORD, he delivered them into your hand. 9For the eyes of the LORD range throughout the earth to strengthen those whose hearts are fully committed to him. You have done a foolish thing, and from now on you will be at war."

10Asa was angry with the seer because of this; he was so enraged that he put him in prison. At the same time Asa brutally oppressed some of the people.

11The events of Asa's reign, from beginning to end, are written in the book of the kings of Judah and Israel. 12In the thirty-ninth year of his reign Asa was afflicted with a disease in his feet. Though his disease was severe, even in his illness he did not seek help from the LORD, but only from the physicians. 13Then in the forty-first year of his reign Asa died and rested with his fathers. 14They buried him in the tomb that he had cut out for himself in the City of David. They laid him on a bier covered with spices and various blended perfumes, and they made a huge fire in his honor.

Jehoshaphat King of Judah

17 Jehoshaphat his son succeeded him as king and strengthened himself against Israel. 2He stationed troops in all the fortified cities of Judah and put garrisons in Judah and in the towns of Ephraim that his father Asa had captured.

3The LORD was with Jehoshaphat because in his early years he walked in the ways his father David had followed. He did not consult the Baals 4but sought the God of his father and followed his commands rather than the practices of Israel. 5The LORD established the kingdom under his control; and all Judah brought gifts to Jehoshaphat, so that he had great wealth and honor. 6His heart was devoted to the ways of the LORD; furthermore, he removed the high places and the Asherah poles from Judah.

7In the third year of his reign he sent his officials Ben-Hail, Obadiah, Zechariah, Nethanel and Micaiah to teach in the towns of Judah. 8With them were certain Levites—Shemaiah, Nethaniah, Zebadiah, Asahel, Shemiramoth, Jehonathan, Adonijah, Tobijah and Tob-Adonijah—and the priests Elishama and Jehoram. 9They taught throughout Judah, taking with them the Book of the Law of the LORD; they went around to all the towns of Judah and taught the people.

10The fear of the LORD fell on all the kingdoms of the lands surrounding Judah, so that they did not make war with Jehoshaphat. 11Some Philistines brought Jehoshaphat gifts and silver as tribute, and the Arabs brought him flocks: seven thousand seven hundred rams and seven thousand seven hundred goats.

12Jehoshaphat became more and more powerful; he built forts and store cities in Judah 13and had large supplies in the towns of Judah. He also kept experienced fighting men in Jerusalem. 14Their enrollment by families was as follows:

From Judah, commanders of units of 1,000:
  Adnah the commander, with 300,000 fighting men;
15next, Jehohanan the commander, with 280,000;
16next, Amasiah son of Zicri, who volunteered himself for the service of the LORD, with 200,000.
17From Benjamin:
  Eliada, a valiant soldier, with 200,000 men armed with bows and shields;
18next, Jehozabad, with 180,000 men armed for battle.

a 4 Also known as *Abel Beth Maacah*   *b 8* That is, people from the upper Nile region   *c 8* Or *charioteers*

19These were the men who served the king, besides those he stationed in the fortified cities throughout Judah.

Micaiah Prophesies Against Ahab

18 Now Jehoshaphat had great wealth and honor, and he allied himself with Ahab by marriage. 2Some years later he went down to visit Ahab in Samaria. Ahab slaughtered many sheep and cattle for him and the people with him and urged him to attack Ramoth Gilead. 3Ahab king of Israel asked Jehoshaphat king of Judah, "Will you go with me against Ramoth Gilead?"

Jehoshaphat replied, "I am as you are, and my people as your people; we will join you in the war." 4But Jehoshaphat also said to the king of Israel, "First seek the counsel of the LORD."

5So the king of Israel brought together the prophets—four hundred men—and asked them, "Shall we go to war against Ramoth Gilead, or shall I refrain?"

"Go," they answered, "for God will give it into the king's hand."

6But Jehoshaphat asked, "Is there not a prophet of the LORD here whom we can inquire of?"

7The king of Israel answered Jehoshaphat, "There is still one man through whom we can inquire of the LORD, but I hate him because he never prophesies anything good about me, but always bad. He is Micaiah son of Imlah."

"The king should not say that," Jehoshaphat replied.

8So the king of Israel called one of his officials and said, "Bring Micaiah son of Imlah at once."

9Dressed in their royal robes, the king of Israel and Jehoshaphat king of Judah were sitting on their thrones at the threshing floor by the entrance to the gate of Samaria, with all the prophets prophesying before them. 10Now Zedekiah son of Kenaanah had made iron horns, and he declared, "This is what the LORD says: 'With these you will gore the Arameans until they are destroyed.' "

11All the other prophets were prophesying the same thing. "Attack Ramoth Gilead and be victorious," they said, "for the LORD will give it into the king's hand."

12The messenger who had gone to summon Micaiah said to him, "Look, as one man the other prophets are predict-

ing success for the king. Let your word agree with theirs, and speak favorably."

13But Micaiah said, "As surely as the LORD lives, I can tell him only what my God says."

14When he arrived, the king asked him, "Micaiah, shall we go to war against Ramoth Gilead, or shall I refrain?"

"Attack and be victorious," he answered, "for they will be given into your hand."

15The king said to him, "How many times must I make you swear to tell me nothing but the truth in the name of the LORD?"

16Then Micaiah answered, "I saw all Israel scattered on the hills like sheep without a shepherd, and the LORD said, 'These people have no master. Let each one go home in peace.' "

17The king of Israel said to Jehoshaphat, "Didn't I tell you that he never prophesies anything good about me, but only bad?"

18Micaiah continued, "Therefore hear the word of the LORD: I saw the LORD sitting on his throne with all the host of heaven standing on his right and on his left. 19And the LORD said, 'Who will entice Ahab king of Israel into attacking Ramoth Gilead and going to his death there?'

"One suggested this, and another that. 20Finally, a spirit came forward, stood before the LORD and said, 'I will entice him.'

" 'By what means?' the LORD asked.

21" 'I will go and be a lying spirit in the mouths of all his prophets,' he said.

" 'You will succeed in enticing him,' said the LORD. 'Go and do it.'

22"So now the LORD has put a lying spirit in the mouths of these prophets of yours. The LORD has decreed disaster for you."

23Then Zedekiah son of Kenaanah went up and slapped Micaiah in the face. "Which way did the spirit from[a] the LORD go when he went from me to speak to you?" he asked.

24Micaiah replied, "You will find out on the day you go to hide in an inner room."

25The king of Israel then ordered, "Take Micaiah and send him back to Amon the ruler of the city and to Joash the king's son, 26and say, 'This is what the king says: Put this fellow in prison and give him nothing but bread and water until I return safely.' "

27Micaiah declared, "If you ever return

a 23 Or Spirit of

safely, the LORD has not spoken through me." Then he added, "Mark my words, all you people!"

Ahab Killed at Ramoth Gilead

28So the king of Israel and Jehoshaphat king of Judah went up to Ramoth Gilead. 29The king of Israel said to Jehoshaphat, "I will enter the battle in disguise, but you wear your royal robes." So the king of Israel disguised himself and went into battle.

30Now the king of Aram had ordered his chariot commanders, "Do not fight with anyone, small or great, except the king of Israel." 31When the chariot commanders saw Jehoshaphat, they thought, "This is the king of Israel." So they turned to attack him, but Jehoshaphat cried out, and the LORD helped him. God drew them away from him, 32for when the chariot commanders saw that he was not the king of Israel, they stopped pursuing him.

33But someone drew his bow at random and hit the king of Israel between the sections of his armor. The king told the chariot driver, "Wheel around and get me out of the fighting. I've been wounded." 34All day long the battle raged, and the king of Israel propped himself up in his chariot facing the Arameans until evening. Then at sunset he died.

19 When Jehoshaphat king of Judah returned safely to his palace in Jerusalem, 2Jehu the seer, the son of Hanani, went out to meet him and said to the king, "Should you help the wicked and lovea those who hate the LORD? Because of this, the wrath of the LORD is upon you. 3There is, however, some good in you, for you have rid the land of the Asherah poles and have set your heart on seeking God."

Jehoshaphat Appoints Judges

4Jehoshaphat lived in Jerusalem, and he went out again among the people from

a 2 Or and make alliances with

Make It Stick

READ 2 CHRONICLES 18:34

Nothing gets past God. A prophet of the Lord had predicted that evil King Ahab would die in this battle. So the random arrow that struck Ahab between the sections of his armor wasn't a "lucky shot" at all, but was indeed God's doing. Think of something you're doing that *pleases* God, and draw an arrow bouncing off a shield.

Beersheba to the hill country of Ephraim and turned them back to the LORD, the God of their fathers. ⁵He appointed judges in the land, in each of the fortified cities of Judah. ⁶He told them, "Consider carefully what you do, because you are not judging for man but for the LORD, who is with you whenever you give a verdict. ⁷Now let the fear of the LORD be upon you. Judge carefully, for with the LORD our God there is no injustice or partiality or bribery."

⁸In Jerusalem also, Jehoshaphat appointed some of the Levites, priests and heads of Israelite families to administer the law of the LORD and to settle disputes. And they lived in Jerusalem. ⁹He gave them these orders: "You must serve faithfully and wholeheartedly in the fear of the LORD. ¹⁰In every case that comes before you from your fellow countrymen who live in the cities—whether bloodshed or other concerns of the law, commands, decrees or ordinances—you are to warn them not to sin against the LORD; otherwise his wrath will come on you and your brothers. Do this, and you will not sin.

¹¹"Amariah the chief priest will be over you in any matter concerning the LORD, and Zebadiah son of Ishmael, the leader of the tribe of Judah, will be over you in any matter concerning the king, and the Levites will serve as officials before you. Act with courage, and may the LORD be with those who do well."

Jehoshaphat Defeats Moab and Ammon

20 After this, the Moabites and Ammonites with some of the Meunites*ᵃ* came to make war on Jehoshaphat.

²Some men came and told Jehoshaphat, "A vast army is coming against you from Edom,*ᵇ* from the other side of the Sea.*ᶜ* It is already in Hazazon Tamar" (that is, En Gedi). ³Alarmed, Jehoshaphat resolved to inquire of the LORD, and he proclaimed a fast for all Judah. ⁴The people of Judah came together to seek help from the LORD; indeed, they came from every town in Judah to seek him.

ᵃ 1 Some Septuagint manuscripts; Hebrew *Ammonites*
ᵇ 2 One Hebrew manuscript; most Hebrew manuscripts, Septuagint and Vulgate *Aram*   *ᶜ 2* That is, the Dead Sea

---

Jehoshaphat's Eyeballs

READ 2 CHRONICLES 20:1–25

"We do not know what to do" (verse 12). Not quite what you want to hear from your leader just before plunging into battle! But Jehoshaphat said the right thing. He admitted that he was in way over his head. He reminded God, "You *told* us to pray to you when we had a desperate need. Well, here's our need: We're being invaded and we're as good as dead meat." Jehoshaphat knew he needed help big time. That's why he told God, "Our eyes are upon you" (verse 12). Result? The men of Judah didn't even have to fight. God went like a bowling ball across the battlefield and *Strike!*—all the pins went down! You don't always have to know what to do, but if you keep your eyes on God in prayer, he will always see you through.

Your next reading is on page 561.

⁵Then Jehoshaphat stood up in the assembly of Judah and Jerusalem at the temple of the LORD in the front of the new courtyard ⁶and said:

"O LORD, God of our fathers, are you not the God who is in heaven? You rule over all the kingdoms of the nations. Power and might are in your hand, and no one can withstand you. ⁷O our God, did you not drive out the inhabitants of this land before your people Israel and give it forever to the descendants of Abraham your friend? ⁸They have lived in it and have built in it a sanctuary for your Name, saying, ⁹'If calamity comes upon us, whether the sword of judgment, or plague or famine, we will stand in your presence before this temple that bears your Name and will cry out to you in our distress, and you will hear us and save us.'

¹⁰"But now here are men from Ammon, Moab and Mount Seir, whose territory you would not allow Israel to invade when they came from Egypt; so they turned away from them and did not destroy them. ¹¹See how they are repaying us by coming to drive us out of the possession you gave us as an inheritance. ¹²O our God, will you not judge them? For we have no power to face this vast army that is attacking us. We do not know what to do, but our eyes are upon you."

¹³All the men of Judah, with their wives and children and little ones, stood there before the LORD.

¹⁴Then the Spirit of the LORD came upon Jahaziel son of Zechariah, the son of Benaiah, the son of Jeiel, the son of Mattaniah, a Levite and descendant of Asaph, as he stood in the assembly.

¹⁵He said: "Listen, King Jehoshaphat and all who live in Judah and Jerusalem! This is what the LORD says to you: 'Do not be afraid or discouraged because of this vast army. For the battle is not yours, but God's. ¹⁶Tomorrow march down against them. They will be climbing up by the Pass of Ziz, and you will find them at the end of the gorge in the Desert of Jeruel. ¹⁷You will not have to fight this battle. Take up your positions; stand firm and see the deliverance the LORD will give you, O Judah and Jerusalem. Do not be afraid; do not

be discouraged. Go out to face them tomorrow, and the LORD will be with you.' "

¹⁸Jehoshaphat bowed with his face to the ground, and all the people of Judah and Jerusalem fell down in worship before the LORD. ¹⁹Then some Levites from the Kohathites and Korahites stood up and praised the LORD, the God of Israel, with a very loud voice.

²⁰Early in the morning they left for the Desert of Tekoa. As they set out, Jehoshaphat stood and said, "Listen to me, Judah and people of Jerusalem! Have faith in the LORD your God and you will be upheld; have faith in his prophets and you will be successful." ²¹After consulting the people, Jehoshaphat appointed men to sing to the LORD and to praise him for the splendor of his*a* holiness as they went out at the head of the army, saying:

"Give thanks to the LORD,
   for his love endures forever."

²²As they began to sing and praise, the LORD set ambushes against the men of Ammon and Moab and Mount Seir who were invading Judah, and they were defeated. ²³The men of Ammon and Moab rose up against the men from Mount Seir to destroy and annihilate them. After they finished slaughtering the men from Seir, they helped to destroy one another.

²⁴When the men of Judah came to the place that overlooks the desert and looked toward the vast army, they saw only dead bodies lying on the ground; no one had escaped. ²⁵So Jehoshaphat and his men went to carry off their plunder, and they found among them a great amount of equipment and clothing*b* and also articles of value—more than they could take away. There was so much plunder that it took three days to collect it. ²⁶On the fourth day they assembled in the Valley of Beracah, where they praised the LORD. This is why it is called the Valley of Beracah*c* to this day.

²⁷Then, led by Jehoshaphat, all the men of Judah and Jerusalem returned joyfully to Jerusalem, for the LORD had given them cause to rejoice over their enemies. ²⁸They entered Jerusalem and went to the temple of the LORD with harps and lutes and trumpets.

²⁹The fear of God came upon all the

---

a 21 Or *him with the splendor of*   *b 25* Some Hebrew manuscripts and Vulgate; most Hebrew manuscripts *corpses*   *c 26 Beracah* means *praise.*

kingdoms of the countries when they heard how the LORD had fought against the enemies of Israel. ³⁰And the kingdom of Jehoshaphat was at peace, for his God had given him rest on every side.

The End of Jehoshaphat's Reign

³¹So Jehoshaphat reigned over Judah. He was thirty-five years old when he became king of Judah, and he reigned in Jerusalem twenty-five years. His mother's name was Azubah daughter of Shilhi. ³²He walked in the ways of his father Asa and did not stray from them; he did what

was right in the eyes of the LORD. ³³The high places, however, were not removed, and the people still had not set their hearts on the God of their fathers.

³⁴The other events of Jehoshaphat's reign, from beginning to end, are written in the annals of Jehu son of Hanani, which are recorded in the book of the kings of Israel.

³⁵Later, Jehoshaphat king of Judah made an alliance with Ahaziah king of Israel, who was guilty of wickedness. ³⁶He agreed with him to construct a fleet of trading ships.ᵃ After these were built at Ezion Geber, ³⁷Eli-

---

ᵃ 36 Hebrew of ships that could go to Tarshish

Make It Stick

READ 2 CHRONICLES 20:21

Jehoshaphat knew that God would make them victorious, so he sent the musicians out in front of the army to sing songs of praise. Write down a couple of problems that you're thankful God is taking care of. Then put the pen down and tell him how thankful you are. That's called praise.

_____

_____

_____

_____

_____

_____

_____

ezer son of Dodavahu of Mareshah prophesied against Jehoshaphat, saying, "Because you have made an alliance with Ahaziah, the LORD will destroy what you have made." The ships were wrecked and were not able to set sail to trade.[a]

21 Then Jehoshaphat rested with his fathers and was buried with them in the City of David. And Jehoram his son succeeded him as king. ²Jehoram's brothers, the sons of Jehoshaphat, were Azariah, Jehiel, Zechariah, Azariahu, Michael and Shephatiah. All these were sons of Jehoshaphat king of Israel.[b] ³Their father had given them many gifts of silver and gold and articles of value, as well as fortified cities in Judah, but he had given the kingdom to Jehoram because he was his firstborn son.

Jehoram King of Judah

⁴When Jehoram established himself firmly over his father's kingdom, he put all his brothers to the sword along with some of the princes of Israel. ⁵Jehoram was thirty-two years old when he became king, and he reigned in Jerusalem eight years. ⁶He walked in the ways of the kings of Israel, as the house of Ahab had done, for he married a daughter of Ahab. He did evil in the eyes of the LORD. ⁷Nevertheless, because of the covenant the LORD had made with David, the LORD was not willing to destroy the house of David. He had promised to maintain a lamp for him and his descendants forever.

⁸In the time of Jehoram, Edom rebelled against Judah and set up its own king. ⁹So Jehoram went there with his officers and all his chariots. The Edomites surrounded him and his chariot commanders, but he rose up and broke through by night. ¹⁰To this day Edom has been in rebellion against Judah.

Libnah revolted at the same time, because Jehoram had forsaken the LORD, the God of his fathers. ¹¹He had also built high places on the hills of Judah and had caused the people of Jerusalem to prostitute themselves and had led Judah astray.

¹²Jehoram received a letter from Elijah the prophet, which said:

"This is what the LORD, the God of your father David, says: 'You have not walked in the ways of your father Jehoshaphat or of Asa king of Judah.

¹³But you have walked in the ways of the kings of Israel, and you have led Judah and the people of Jerusalem to prostitute themselves, just as the house of Ahab did. You have also murdered your own brothers, members of your father's house, men who were better than you. ¹⁴So now the LORD is about to strike your people, your sons, your wives and everything that is yours, with a heavy blow. ¹⁵You yourself will be very ill with a lingering disease of the bowels, until the disease causes your bowels to come out.' "

¹⁶The LORD aroused against Jehoram the hostility of the Philistines and of the Arabs who lived near the Cushites. ¹⁷They attacked Judah, invaded it and carried off all the goods found in the king's palace, together with his sons and wives. Not a son was left to him except Ahaziah,[c] the youngest.

¹⁸After all this, the LORD afflicted Jehoram with an incurable disease of the bowels. ¹⁹In the course of time, at the end of the second year, his bowels came out because of the disease, and he died in great pain. His people made no fire in his honor, as they had for his fathers.

²⁰Jehoram was thirty-two years old when he became king, and he reigned in Jerusalem eight years. He passed away, to no one's regret, and was buried in the City of David, but not in the tombs of the kings.

Ahaziah King of Judah

22 The people of Jerusalem made Ahaziah, Jehoram's youngest son, king in his place, since the raiders, who came with the Arabs into the camp, had killed all the older sons. So Ahaziah son of Jehoram king of Judah began to reign.

²Ahaziah was twenty-two[d] years old when he became king, and he reigned in Jerusalem one year. His mother's name was Athaliah, a granddaughter of Omri.

³He too walked in the ways of the house of Ahab, for his mother encouraged him in doing wrong. ⁴He did evil in the eyes of the LORD, as the house of Ahab

---

[a] 37 Hebrew *sail for Tarshish*   [b] 2 That is, Judah, as frequently in 2 Chronicles   [c] 17 Hebrew *Jehoahaz,* a variant of *Ahaziah*   [d] 2 Some Septuagint manuscripts and Syriac (see also 2 Kings 8:26); Hebrew *forty-two*

had done, for after his father's death they became his advisers, to his undoing. ⁵He also followed their counsel when he went with Joram*ᵃ* son of Ahab king of Israel to war against Hazael king of Aram at Ramoth Gilead. The Arameans wounded Joram; ⁶so he returned to Jezreel to recover from the wounds they had inflicted on him at Ramoth*ᵇ* in his battle with Hazael king of Aram.

Then Ahaziah*ᶜ* son of Jehoram king of Judah went down to Jezreel to see Joram son of Ahab because he had been wounded.

⁷Through Ahaziah's visit to Joram, God brought about Ahaziah's downfall. When Ahaziah arrived, he went out with Joram to meet Jehu son of Nimshi, whom the LORD had anointed to destroy the house of Ahab. ⁸While Jehu was executing judgment on the house of Ahab, he found the princes of Judah and the sons of Ahaziah's relatives, who had been attending Ahaziah, and he killed them. ⁹He then went in search of Ahaziah, and his men captured him while he was hiding in Samaria. He was brought to Jehu and put to death. They buried him, for they said, "He was a son of Jehoshaphat, who sought the LORD with all his heart." So there was no one in the house of Ahaziah powerful enough to retain the kingdom.

Athaliah and Joash

¹⁰When Athaliah the mother of Ahaziah saw that her son was dead, she proceeded to destroy the whole royal family of the house of Judah. ¹¹But Jehosheba,*ᵈ* the daughter of King Jehoram, took Joash son of Ahaziah and stole him away from among the royal princes who were about to be murdered and put him and his nurse in a bedroom. Because Jehosheba,*ᵈ* the daughter of King Jehoram and wife of the priest Jehoiada, was Ahaziah's sister, she hid the child from Athaliah so she could not kill him. ¹²He remained hidden with them at the temple of God for six years while Athaliah ruled the land.

ᵃ 5 Hebrew *Jehoram,* a variant of *Joram;* also in verses 6 and 7   *ᵇ 6* Hebrew *Ramah,* a variant of *Ramoth*
ᶜ 6 Some Hebrew manuscripts, Septuagint, Vulgate and Syriac (see also 2 Kings 8:29); most Hebrew manuscripts *Azariah*
ᵈ 11 Hebrew *Jehoshabeath,* a variant of *Jehosheba*

Joash's Mentor

READ 2 CHRONICLES 22:10—23:16; 24:1-2

A *mentor* is a person you look up to, a role model or a "big brother" who teaches you about being a man. Don't confuse this with a *tormentor* who teases and bugs you and drives you crazy! A godly mentor can help prepare you to be a godly man. It could be your dad, a coach or a church school teacher. That is what Joash had in the high priest Jehoiada. The high priest was wise, obeyed God and was *very* gutsy. (He planned and pulled off a military coup!) He taught Joash so well that Joash become a powerful ruler. You also must listen to the advice of mentors while you're growing up. Childhood is a time for fun and games, true, but it is *also* a time to grow and learn. That way, when you become a man, you'll know what's expected of you and you'll be ready.

Your next reading is on page 569.

Get a Load of This...

Evil Athalia became queen after killing all of her grandchildren. Talk about a wicked witch! The only child to escape was baby Joash. His aunt Jehosheba scooped him from his cradle, ran to God's temple and hid him there (2 Chronicles 22:10–12).

23 In the seventh year Jehoiada showed his strength. He made a covenant with the commanders of units of a hundred: Azariah son of Jeroham, Ishmael son of Jehohanan, Azariah son of Obed, Maaseiah son of Adaiah, and Elishaphat son of Zicri. ²They went throughout Judah and gathered the Levites and the heads of Israelite families from all the towns. When they came to Jerusalem, ³the whole assembly made a covenant with the king at the temple of God.

Jehoiada said to them, "The king's son shall reign, as the LORD promised concerning the descendants of David. ⁴Now this is what you are to do: A third of you priests and Levites who are going on duty on the Sabbath are to keep watch at the doors, ⁵a third of you at the royal palace and a third at the Foundation Gate, and all the other men are to be in the courtyards of the temple of the LORD. ⁶No one is to enter the temple of the LORD except the priests and Levites on duty; they may enter because they are consecrated, but all the other men are to guard what the LORD has assigned to them.ᵃ ⁷The Levites are to station themselves around the king, each man with his weapons in his hand. Anyone who enters the temple must be put to death. Stay close to the king wherever he goes."

⁸The Levites and all the men of Judah did just as Jehoiada the priest ordered. Each one took his men—those who were going on duty on the Sabbath and those who were going off duty—for Jehoiada the priest had not released any of the divisions. ⁹Then he gave the commanders of units of a hundred the spears and the large and small shields that had belonged to King David and that were in the temple of God. ¹⁰He stationed all the men, each with his weapon in his hand, around the king—near the altar and the temple, from the south side to the north side of the temple.

¹¹Jehoiada and his sons brought out the king's son and put the crown on him; they presented him with a copy of the covenant and proclaimed him king. They anointed him and shouted, "Long live the king!"

¹²When Athaliah heard the noise of the people running and cheering the king, she went to them at the temple of the LORD. ¹³She looked, and there was the king, standing by his pillar at the entrance. The officers and the trumpeters were beside the king, and all the people of the land were rejoicing and blowing trumpets, and singers with musical instruments were leading the praises. Then Athaliah tore her robes and shouted, "Treason! Treason!"

¹⁴Jehoiada the priest sent out the commanders of units of a hundred, who were in charge of the troops, and said to them: "Bring her out between the ranksᵇ and put to the sword anyone who follows her." For the priest had said, "Do not put her to death at the temple

ᵃ 6 Or to observe the LORD's command not to enter,   ᵇ 14 Or out from the precincts of the LORD." ¹⁵So they seized her as she reached the entrance of the Horse Gate on the palace grounds, and there they put her to death.

¹⁶Jehoiada then made a covenant that he and the people and the king[a] would be the LORD's people. ¹⁷All the people went to the temple of Baal and tore it down. They smashed the altars and idols and killed Mattan the priest of Baal in front of the altars.

¹⁸Then Jehoiada placed the oversight of the temple of the LORD in the hands of the priests, who were Levites, to whom David had made assignments in the temple, to present the burnt offerings of the LORD as written in the Law of Moses, with rejoicing and singing, as David had ordered. ¹⁹He also stationed doorkeepers at the gates of the LORD's temple so that no one who was in any way unclean might enter.

²⁰He took with him the commanders of hundreds, the nobles, the rulers of the people and all the people of the land and brought the king down from the temple of the LORD. They went into the palace through the Upper Gate and seated the king on the royal throne, ²¹and all the people of the land rejoiced. And the city was quiet, because Athaliah had been slain with the sword.

Joash Repairs the Temple

24 Joash was seven years old when he became king, and he reigned in Jerusalem forty years. His mother's name was Zibiah; she was from Beersheba. ²Joash did what was right in the eyes of the LORD all the years of Jehoiada the priest. ³Jehoiada chose two wives for him, and he had sons and daughters.

⁴Some time later Joash decided to restore the temple of the LORD. ⁵He called together the priests and Levites and said to them, "Go to the towns of Judah and collect the money due annually from all Israel, to repair the temple of your God. Do it now." But the Levites did not act at once.

⁶Therefore the king summoned Jehoiada the chief priest and said to him, "Why haven't you required the Levites to bring in from Judah and Jerusalem the tax imposed by Moses the servant of the LORD and by the assembly of Israel for the Tent of the Testimony?"

⁷Now the sons of that wicked woman Athaliah had broken into the temple of God and had used even its sacred objects for the Baals.

⁸At the king's command, a chest was made and placed outside, at the gate of the temple of the LORD. ⁹A proclamation was then issued in Judah and Jerusalem that they should bring to the LORD the tax that Moses the servant of God had required of Israel in the desert. ¹⁰All the officials and all the people brought their contributions gladly, dropping them into the chest until it was full. ¹¹Whenever the chest was brought in by the Levites to the king's officials and they saw that there was a large amount of money, the royal secretary and the officer of the chief priest would come and empty the chest and carry it back to its place. They did this regularly and collected a great amount of money. ¹²The king and Jehoiada gave it to the men who carried out the work required for the temple of the LORD. They hired masons and carpenters to restore the LORD's temple, and also workers in iron and bronze to repair the temple.

¹³The men in charge of the work were diligent, and the repairs progressed under them. They rebuilt the temple of God according to its original design and reinforced it. ¹⁴When they had finished, they brought the rest of the money to the king and Jehoiada, and with it were made articles for the LORD's temple: articles for the service and for the burnt offerings, and also dishes and other objects of gold and silver. As long as Jehoiada lived, burnt offerings were presented continually in the temple of the LORD.

¹⁵Now Jehoiada was old and full of years, and he died at the age of a hundred and thirty. ¹⁶He was buried with the kings in the City of David, because of the good he had done in Israel for God and his temple.

The Wickedness of Joash

¹⁷After the death of Jehoiada, the officials of Judah came and paid homage to the king, and he listened to them. ¹⁸They abandoned the temple of the LORD, the God of their fathers, and worshiped Asherah poles and idols. Because of their guilt, God's anger came upon Judah and Jeru-

---

a 16 Or covenant between ‚the LORD‚ and the people and the king that they (see 2 Kings 11:17) salem. ¹⁹Although the LORD sent prophets to the people to bring them back to him, and though they testified against them, they would not listen.

²⁰Then the Spirit of God came upon Zechariah son of Jehoiada the priest. He stood before the people and said, "This is what God says: 'Why do you disobey the LORD's commands? You will not prosper. Because you have forsaken the LORD, he has forsaken you.' "

²¹But they plotted against him, and by order of the king they stoned him to death in the courtyard of the LORD's temple. ²²King Joash did not remember the kindness Zechariah's father Jehoiada had shown him but killed his son, who said as he lay dying, "May the LORD see this and call you to account."

²³At the turn of the year,ᵃ the army of Aram marched against Joash; it invaded Judah and Jerusalem and killed all the leaders of the people. They sent all the plunder to their king in Damascus. ²⁴Al-though the Aramean army had come with only a few men, the LORD delivered into their hands a much larger army. Because Judah had forsaken the LORD, the God of their fathers, judgment was executed on Joash. ²⁵When the Arameans withdrew, they left Joash severely wounded. His officials conspired against him for murdering the son of Jehoiada the priest, and they killed him in his bed. So he died and was buried in the City of David, but not in the tombs of the kings.

²⁶Those who conspired against him were Zabad,ᵇ son of Shimeath an Ammonite woman, and Jehozabad, son of Shimrithᶜ a Moabite woman. ²⁷The account of his sons, the many prophecies about him, and the record of the restoration of the temple of God are written in the annotations on the book of the kings. And Amaziah his son succeeded him as king.

ᵃ 23 Probably in the spring   ᵇ 26 A variant of *Jozabad*
ᶜ 26 A variant of *Shomer*

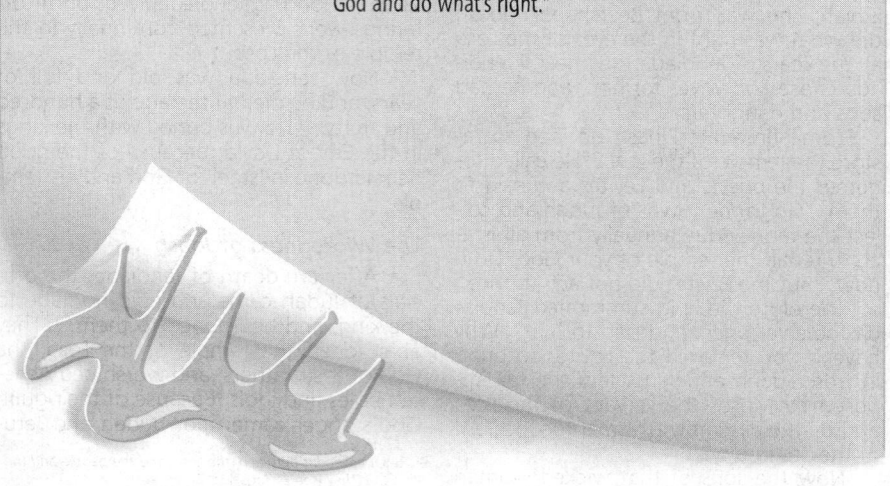

Make It Stick

READ 2 CHRONICLES 24:17–18

After godly Jehoiada died, Joash stopped doing the right thing (2 Chronicles 24:17–18). Instead of doing good things just to please others, our aim should be to please God. Then when we're tempted to do wrong, we won't give in. Write on a sticky note, "I want to please God and do what's right."

Amaziah King of Judah

25 Amaziah was twenty-five years old when he became king, and he reigned in Jerusalem twenty-nine years. His mother's name was Jehoaddin[a]; she was from Jerusalem. [2]He did what was right in the eyes of the LORD, but not wholeheartedly. [3]After the kingdom was firmly in his control, he executed the officials who had murdered his father the king. [4]Yet he did not put their sons to death, but acted in accordance with what is written in the Law, in the Book of Moses, where the LORD commanded: "Fathers shall not be put to death for their children, nor children put to death for their fathers; each is to die for his own sins."[b]

[5]Amaziah called the people of Judah together and assigned them according to their families to commanders of thousands and commanders of hundreds for all Judah and Benjamin. He then mustered those twenty years old or more and found that there were three hundred thousand men ready for military service, able to handle the spear and shield. [6]He also hired a hundred thousand fighting men from Israel for a hundred talents[c] of silver.

[7]But a man of God came to him and said, "O king, these troops from Israel must not march with you, for the LORD is not with Israel—not with any of the people of Ephraim. [8]Even if you go and fight courageously in battle, God will overthrow you before the enemy, for God has the power to help or to overthrow."

[9]Amaziah asked the man of God, "But what about the hundred talents I paid for these Israelite troops?"

The man of God replied, "The LORD can give you much more than that."

[10]So Amaziah dismissed the troops who had come to him from Ephraim and sent them home. They were furious with Judah and left for home in a great rage.

[11]Amaziah then marshaled his strength and led his army to the Valley of Salt, where he killed ten thousand men of Seir. [12]The army of Judah also captured ten thousand men alive, took them to the top of a cliff and threw them down so that all were dashed to pieces.

[13]Meanwhile the troops that Amaziah had sent back and had not allowed to take part in the war raided Judean towns from Samaria to Beth Horon. They killed three thousand people and carried off great quantities of plunder.

[14]When Amaziah returned from slaughtering the Edomites, he brought back the gods of the people of Seir. He set them up as his own gods, bowed down to them and burned sacrifices to them. [15]The anger of the LORD burned against Amaziah, and he sent a prophet to him, who said, "Why do you consult this people's gods, which could not save their own people from your hand?"

Get a Load of This...

Amaziah "did was right in the eyes of the LORD, but not wholeheartedly" (2 Chronicles 25:2). Is there a problem here? You betcha! It wasn't long before Amaziah did a belly flop in the dust before the idols of Edom and worshiped them (verses 14–15). Big mistake!

---

[a] 1 Hebrew *Jehoaddan*, a variant of *Jehoaddin*   [b] 4 Deut. 24:16   [c] 6 That is, about 3 3/4 tons (about 3.4 metric tons); also in verse 9

¹⁶While he was still speaking, the king said to him, "Have we appointed you an adviser to the king? Stop! Why be struck down?"

So the prophet stopped but said, "I know that God has determined to destroy you, because you have done this and have not listened to my counsel."

¹⁷After Amaziah king of Judah consulted his advisers, he sent this challenge to Jehoash^a son of Jehoahaz, the son of Jehu, king of Israel: "Come, meet me face to face."

¹⁸But Jehoash king of Israel replied to Amaziah king of Judah: "A thistle in Lebanon sent a message to a cedar in Lebanon, 'Give your daughter to my son in marriage.' Then a wild beast in Lebanon came along and trampled the thistle underfoot. ¹⁹You say to yourself that you have defeated Edom, and now you are arrogant and proud. But stay at home! Why ask for trouble and cause your own downfall and that of Judah also?"

²⁰Amaziah, however, would not listen, for God so worked that he might hand them over to Jehoash, because they sought the gods of Edom. ²¹So Jehoash king of Israel attacked. He and Amaziah king of Judah faced each other at Beth Shemesh in Judah. ²²Judah was routed by Israel, and every man fled to his home. ²³Jehoash king of Israel captured Amaziah king of Judah, the son of Joash, the son of Ahaziah,^b at Beth Shemesh. Then Jehoash brought him to Jerusalem and broke down the wall of Jerusalem from the Ephraim Gate to the Corner Gate—a section about six hundred feet^c long. ²⁴He took all the gold and silver and all the articles found in the temple of God that had been in the care of Obed-Edom, together with the palace treasures and the hostages, and returned to Samaria.

²⁵Amaziah son of Joash king of Judah lived for fifteen years after the death of Jehoash son of Jehoahaz king of Israel. ²⁶As for the other events of Amaziah's reign, from beginning to end, are they not written in the book of the kings of Judah and Israel? ²⁷From the time that Amaziah turned away from following the LORD, they conspired against him in Jerusalem and he fled to Lachish, but they sent men after him to Lachish and killed him there. ²⁸He was brought back by horse and was buried with his fathers in the City of Judah.

Uzziah King of Judah

26 Then all the people of Judah took Uzziah,^d who was sixteen years old, and made him king in place of his father Amaziah. ²He was the one who rebuilt Elath and restored it to Judah after Amaziah rested with his fathers.

³Uzziah was sixteen years old when he became king, and he reigned in Jerusalem fifty-two years. His mother's name was Jecoliah; she was from Jerusalem. ⁴He did what was right in the eyes of the LORD, just as his father Amaziah had done. ⁵He sought God during the days of Zechariah, who instructed him in the fear^e of God. As long as he sought the LORD, God gave him success.

⁶He went to war against the Philistines and broke down the walls of Gath, Jabneh and Ashdod. He then rebuilt towns near Ashdod and elsewhere among the Philistines. ⁷God helped him against the Philistines and against the Arabs who lived in Gur Baal and against the Meunites. ⁸The Ammonites brought tribute to Uzziah, and his fame spread as far as the border of Egypt, because he had become very powerful.

⁹Uzziah built towers in Jerusalem at the Corner Gate, at the Valley Gate and at the angle of the wall, and he fortified them. ¹⁰He also built towers in the desert and dug many cisterns, because he had much livestock in the foothills and in the plain. He had people working his fields and vineyards in the hills and in the fertile lands, for he loved the soil.

¹¹Uzziah had a well-trained army, ready to go out by divisions according to their numbers as mustered by Jeiel the secretary and Maaseiah the officer under the direction of Hananiah, one of the royal officials. ¹²The total number of family leaders over the fighting men was 2,600. ¹³Under their command was an army of 307,500 men trained for war, a powerful force to support the king against his enemies. ¹⁴Uzziah provided shields, spears, helmets, coats of armor, bows and slingstones for the entire army. ¹⁵In Jerusalem

^a 17 Hebrew *Joash*, a variant of *Jehoash*; also in verses 18, 21, 23 and 25   ^b 23 Hebrew *Jehoahaz*, a variant of *Ahaziah*   ^c 23 Hebrew *four hundred cubits* (about 180 meters)   ^d 1 Also called *Azariah*   ^e 5 Many Hebrew manuscripts, Septuagint and Syriac; other Hebrew manuscripts *vision*

he made machines designed by skillful men for use on the towers and on the corner defenses to shoot arrows and hurl large stones. His fame spread far and wide, for he was greatly helped until he became powerful.

¹⁶But after Uzziah became powerful, his pride led to his downfall. He was unfaithful to the LORD his God, and entered the temple of the LORD to burn incense on the altar of incense. ¹⁷Azariah the priest with eighty other courageous priests of the LORD followed him in. ¹⁸They confronted him and said, "It is not right for you, Uzziah, to burn incense to the LORD. That is for the priests, the descendants of Aaron, who have been consecrated to burn incense. Leave the sanctuary, for you have been unfaithful; and you will not be honored by the LORD God."

¹⁹Uzziah, who had a censer in his hand ready to burn incense, became angry. While he was raging at the priests in their presence before the incense altar in the LORD's temple, leprosy^a broke out on his forehead. ²⁰When Azariah the chief priest and all the other priests looked at him, they saw that he had leprosy on his forehead, so they hurried him out. Indeed, he himself was eager to leave, because the LORD had afflicted him.

²¹King Uzziah had leprosy until the day he died. He lived in a separate house^b—leprous, and excluded from the temple of the LORD. Jotham his son had charge of the palace and governed the people of the land.

²²The other events of Uzziah's reign, from beginning to end, are recorded by the prophet Isaiah son of Amoz. ²³Uzziah rested with his fathers and was buried near them in a field for burial that belonged to the kings, for people said, "He had leprosy." And Jotham his son succeeded him as king.

Jotham King of Judah

27 Jotham was twenty-five years old when he became king, and he reigned in Jerusalem sixteen years. His mother's name was Jerusha daughter of Zadok. ²He did what was right in the eyes of the LORD, just as his father Uzziah had done, but unlike him he did not enter the temple of the LORD. The people, however, continued their corrupt practices. ³Jotham rebuilt the Upper Gate of the temple of the LORD and did extensive work on the wall at the hill of Ophel. ⁴He built towns in the Judean hills and forts and towers in the wooded areas.

⁵Jotham made war on the king of the Ammonites and conquered them. That year the Ammonites paid him a hundred talents^c of silver, ten thousand cors^d of wheat and ten thousand cors of barley. The Ammonites brought him the same amount also in the second and third years.

⁶Jotham grew powerful because he walked steadfastly before the LORD his God.

Get a Load of This...

Uzziah was unbeatable in battle and "as long as he sought the LORD, God gave him success" (2 Chronicles 26:5). Then came trouble: "After Uzziah became powerful, his pride led to his downfall" (verse 16). The king entered the temple to do what only the priests were allowed to do. *WHAM!*— God turned him into a leper to humble him.

---

^{a} *19* The Hebrew word was used for various diseases affecting the skin—not necessarily leprosy; also in verses 20, 21 and 23. ^{b} *21* Or *in a house where he was relieved of responsibilities* ^{c} *5* That is, about 3 3/4 tons (about 3.4 metric tons) ^{d} *5* That is, probably about 62,000 bushels (about 2,200 kiloliters)

7The other events in Jotham's reign, including all his wars and the other things he did, are written in the book of the kings of Israel and Judah. 8He was twenty-five years old when he became king, and he reigned in Jerusalem sixteen years. 9Jotham rested with his fathers and was buried in the City of David. And Ahaz his son succeeded him as king.

Ahaz King of Judah

28 Ahaz was twenty years old when he became king, and he reigned in Jerusalem sixteen years. Unlike David his father, he did not do what was right in the eyes of the LORD. 2He walked in the ways of the kings of Israel and also made cast idols for worshiping the Baals. 3He burned sacrifices in the Valley of Ben Hinnom and sacrificed his sons in the fire, following the detestable ways of the nations the LORD had driven out before the Israelites. 4He offered sacrifices and burned incense at the high places, on the hilltops and under every spreading tree.

5Therefore the LORD his God handed him over to the king of Aram. The Arameans defeated him and took many of his people as prisoners and brought them to Damascus.

He was also given into the hands of the king of Israel, who inflicted heavy casualties on him. 6In one day Pekah son of Remaliah killed a hundred and twenty thousand soldiers in Judah—because Judah had forsaken the LORD, the God of their fathers. 7Zicri, an Ephraimite warrior, killed Maaseiah the king's son, Azrikam the officer in charge of the palace, and Elkanah, second to the king. 8The Israelites took captive from their kinsmen two hundred thousand wives, sons and daughters. They also took a great deal of plunder, which they carried back to Samaria.

9But a prophet of the LORD named Oded was there, and he went out to meet the army when it returned to Samaria. He said to them, "Because the LORD, the God of your fathers, was angry with Judah, he gave them into your hand. But you have slaughtered them in a rage that reaches to heaven. 10And now you intend to make the men and women of Judah and Jerusalem your slaves. But aren't you also guilty of sins against the LORD your God? 11Now listen to me! Send back your fellow countrymen you have taken as prisoners, for the LORD's fierce anger rests on you."

12Then some of the leaders in Ephraim—Azariah son of Jehohanan, Berekiah son of Meshillemoth, Jehizkiah son of Shallum, and Amasa son of Hadlai—confronted those who were arriving from the war. 13"You must not bring those prisoners here," they said, "or we will be guilty before the LORD. Do you intend to add to our sin and guilt? For our guilt is already great, and his fierce anger rests on Israel."

14So the soldiers gave up the prisoners and plunder in the presence of the officials and all the assembly. 15The men designated by name took the prisoners, and from the plunder they clothed all who were naked. They provided them with clothes and sandals, food and drink, and healing balm. All those who were weak they put on donkeys. So they took them back to their fellow countrymen at Jericho, the City of Palms, and returned to Samaria.

16At that time King Ahaz sent to the king*a* of Assyria for help. 17The Edomites had again come and attacked Judah and carried away prisoners, 18while the Philistines had raided towns in the foothills and in the Negev of Judah. They captured and occupied Beth Shemesh, Aijalon and Gederoth, as well as Soco, Timnah and Gimzo, with their surrounding villages. 19The LORD had humbled Judah because of Ahaz king of Israel,*b* for he had promoted wickedness in Judah and had been most unfaithful to the LORD. 20Tiglath-Pileser*c* king of Assyria came to him, but he gave him trouble instead of help. 21Ahaz took some of the things from the temple of the LORD and from the royal palace and from the princes and presented them to the king of Assyria, but that did not help him.

22In his time of trouble King Ahaz became even more unfaithful to the LORD. 23He offered sacrifices to the gods of Damascus, who had defeated him; for he thought, "Since the gods of the kings of Aram have helped them, I will sacrifice to them so they will help me." But they were his downfall and the downfall of all Israel.

24Ahaz gathered together the furnishings from the temple of God and took

---

a 16 One Hebrew manuscript, Septuagint and Vulgate (see also 2 Kings 16:7); most Hebrew manuscripts *kings*
b 19 That is, Judah, as frequently in 2 Chronicles
c 20 Hebrew *Tilgath-Pilneser,* a variant of *Tiglath-Pileser*

them away.^a He shut the doors of the LORD's temple and set up altars at every street corner in Jerusalem. ²⁵In every town in Judah he built high places to burn sacrifices to other gods and provoked the LORD, the God of his fathers, to anger.

²⁶The other events of his reign and all his ways, from beginning to end, are written in the book of the kings of Judah and Israel. ²⁷Ahaz rested with his fathers and was buried in the city of Jerusalem, but he was not placed in the tombs of the kings of Israel. And Hezekiah his son succeeded him as king.

Hezekiah Purifies the Temple

29 Hezekiah was twenty-five years old when he became king, and he reigned in Jerusalem twenty-nine years. His mother's name was Abijah daughter of Zechariah. ²He did what was right in the eyes of the LORD, just as his father David had done.

³In the first month of the first year of his reign, he opened the doors of the temple of the LORD and repaired them. ⁴He brought in the priests and the Levites, as-

sembled them in the square on the east side ⁵and said: "Listen to me, Levites! Consecrate yourselves now and consecrate the temple of the LORD, the God of your fathers. Remove all defilement from the sanctuary. ⁶Our fathers were unfaithful; they did evil in the eyes of the LORD our God and forsook him. They turned their faces away from the LORD's dwelling place and turned their backs on him. ⁷They also shut the doors of the portico and put out the lamps. They did not burn incense or present any burnt offerings at the sanctuary to the God of Israel. ⁸Therefore, the anger of the LORD has fallen on Judah and Jerusalem; he has made them an object of dread and horror and scorn, as you can see with your own eyes. ⁹This is why our fathers have fallen by the sword and why our sons and daughters and our wives are in captivity. ¹⁰Now I intend to make a covenant with the LORD, the God of Israel, so that his fierce anger will turn away from us. ¹¹My sons, do not be negligent now, for the LORD has chosen you to stand be-

^a 24 Or and cut them up

Back on Track

READ 2 CHRONICLES 29:1–10; 30:1–5, 10–14, 25–27

Smash! Hezekiah and his men must have had a blast hurling the altars and idols into the Kidron Valley. Hezekiah wanted to get his nation back on track, and that meant doing some serious housecleaning, as well as getting all the Israelites together for a huge Passover feast. He even invited folks from the recently conquered northern kingdom. Sure, lots of people probably made jokes about him—"How many Hezekiahs does it take to screw in a light bulb?" Stuff like that—but he stood for what was right. Doing the right thing, even when it could be labeled "uncool" by your classmates, is important to God. It might seem useless at the time, but Hezekiah proved you can have a great effect for God. He even turned many in the former northern kingdom back to God. Be like Hezekiah: Stand up for what is right and make a difference.

Your next reading is on page 573.

fore him and serve him, to minister before him and to burn incense."

¹²Then these Levites set to work:

from the Kohathites,
Mahath son of Amasai and Joel son of Azariah;

from the Merarites,
Kish son of Abdi and Azariah son of Jehallelel;

from the Gershonites,
Joah son of Zimmah and Eden son of Joah;

¹³from the descendants of Elizaphan,
Shimri and Jeiel;

from the descendants of Asaph,
Zechariah and Mattaniah;

¹⁴from the descendants of Heman,
Jehiel and Shimei;

from the descendants of Jeduthun,
Shemaiah and Uzziel.

¹⁵When they had assembled their brothers and consecrated themselves, they went in to purify the temple of the LORD, as the king had ordered, following the word of the LORD. ¹⁶The priests went into the sanctuary of the LORD to purify it. They brought out to the courtyard of the LORD's temple everything unclean that they found in the temple of the LORD. The Levites took it and carried it out to the Kidron Valley. ¹⁷They began the consecration on the first day of the first month, and by the eighth day of the month they reached the portico of the LORD. For eight more days they consecrated the temple of the LORD itself, finishing on the sixteenth day of the first month.

¹⁸Then they went in to King Hezekiah and reported: "We have purified the entire temple of the LORD, the altar of burnt offering with all its utensils, and the table for setting out the consecrated bread, with all its articles. ¹⁹We have prepared and consecrated all the articles that King Ahaz removed in his unfaithfulness while he was king. They are now in front of the LORD's altar."

²⁰Early the next morning King Hezekiah gathered the city officials together and went up to the temple of the LORD. ²¹They brought seven bulls, seven rams, seven male lambs and seven male goats as a sin offering for the kingdom, for the sanctuary and for Judah. The king commanded the priests, the descendants of Aaron, to offer these on the altar of the LORD. ²²So they slaughtered the bulls, and the priests took the blood and sprinkled it on the altar; next they slaughtered the rams and sprinkled their blood on the altar; then they slaughtered the lambs and sprinkled their blood on the altar. ²³The goats for the sin offering were brought before the king and the assembly, and they laid their hands on them. ²⁴The priests then slaughtered the goats and presented their blood on the altar for a sin offering to atone for all Israel, because the king had ordered the burnt offering and the sin offering for all Israel.

²⁵He stationed the Levites in the temple of the LORD with cymbals, harps and lyres in the way prescribed by David and Gad the king's seer and Nathan the prophet; this was commanded by the LORD through his prophets. ²⁶So the Levites stood ready with David's instruments, and the priests with their trumpets.

²⁷Hezekiah gave the order to sacrifice the burnt offering on the altar. As the offering began, singing to the LORD began also, accompanied by trumpets and the instruments of David king of Israel. ²⁸The whole assembly bowed in worship, while the singers sang and the trumpeters played. All this continued until the sacrifice of the burnt offering was completed.

²⁹When the offerings were finished, the king and everyone present with him knelt down and worshiped. ³⁰King Hezekiah and his officials ordered the Levites to praise the LORD with the words of David and of Asaph the seer. So they sang praises with gladness and bowed their heads and worshiped.

³¹Then Hezekiah said, "You have now dedicated yourselves to the LORD. Come and bring sacrifices and thank offerings to the temple of the LORD." So the assembly brought sacrifices and thank offerings, and all whose hearts were willing brought burnt offerings.

³²The number of burnt offerings the assembly brought was seventy bulls, a hundred rams and two hundred male lambs—all of them for burnt offerings to the LORD. ³³The animals consecrated as sacrifices amounted to six hundred bulls and three thousand sheep and goats. ³⁴The priests, however, were too few to skin all the burnt offerings; so their kinsmen the Levites helped them until the task was finished and until other priests had been consecrated, for the Levites had

been more conscientious in consecrating themselves than the priests had been. ³⁵There were burnt offerings in abundance, together with the fat of the fellowship offerings^a and the drink offerings that accompanied the burnt offerings.

So the service of the temple of the LORD was reestablished. ³⁶Hezekiah and all the people rejoiced at what God had brought about for his people, because it was done so quickly.

Hezekiah Celebrates the Passover

30 Hezekiah sent word to all Israel and Judah and also wrote letters to Ephraim and Manasseh, inviting them to come to the temple of the LORD in Jerusalem and celebrate the Passover to the LORD, the God of Israel. ²The king and his officials and the whole assembly in Jerusalem decided to celebrate the Passover in the second month. ³They had not been able to celebrate it at the regular time because not enough priests had consecrated themselves and the people had not assembled in Jerusalem. ⁴The plan seemed right both to the king and to the whole assembly. ⁵They decided to send a proclamation throughout Israel, from Beersheba to Dan, calling the people to come to Jerusalem and celebrate the Passover to the LORD, the God of Israel. It had not been celebrated in large numbers according to what was written.

⁶At the king's command, couriers went throughout Israel and Judah with letters from the king and from his officials, which read:

"People of Israel, return to the LORD, the God of Abraham, Isaac and Israel, that he may return to you who are left, who have escaped from the hand of the kings of Assyria. ⁷Do not be like your fathers and brothers, who were unfaithful to the LORD, the God of their fathers, so that he made them an object of horror, as you see. ⁸Do not be stiff-necked, as your fathers were; submit to the LORD. Come to the sanctuary, which he has consecrated forever. Serve the LORD your God, so that his fierce anger will turn away from you. ⁹If you return to the LORD, then your brothers and your children will be shown compassion by their captors and will come back to this land, for the LORD your God is gracious and compassionate. He will not turn his face from you if you return to him."

¹⁰The couriers went from town to town in Ephraim and Manasseh, as far as Zebulun, but the people scorned and ridiculed them. ¹¹Nevertheless, some men of Asher, Manasseh and Zebulun humbled themselves and went to Jerusalem. ¹²Also in Judah the hand of God was on the people to give them unity of mind to carry out what the king and his officials had ordered, following the word of the LORD.

¹³A very large crowd of people assembled in Jerusalem to celebrate the Feast of Unleavened Bread in the second month. ¹⁴They removed the altars in Jerusalem and cleared away the incense altars and threw them into the Kidron Valley.

¹⁵They slaughtered the Passover lamb on the fourteenth day of the second month. The priests and the Levites were ashamed and consecrated themselves and brought burnt offerings to the temple of the LORD. ¹⁶Then they took up their regular positions as prescribed in the Law of Moses the man of God. The priests sprinkled the blood handed to them by the Levites. ¹⁷Since many in the crowd had not consecrated themselves, the Levites had to kill the Passover lambs for all those who were not ceremonially clean and could not consecrate ⌊their lambs⌋ to the LORD. ¹⁸Although most of the many people who came from Ephraim, Manasseh, Issachar and Zebulun had not purified themselves, yet they ate the Passover, contrary to what was written. But Hezekiah prayed for them, saying, "May the LORD, who is good, pardon everyone ¹⁹who sets his heart on seeking God—the LORD, the God of his fathers—even if he is not clean according to the rules of the sanctuary." ²⁰And the LORD heard Hezekiah and healed the people.

²¹The Israelites who were present in Jerusalem celebrated the Feast of Unleavened Bread for seven days with great rejoicing, while the Levites and priests sang to the LORD every day, accompanied by the LORD's instruments of praise.^b

---

^a 35 Traditionally *peace offerings*   ^b 21 Or *priests praised the LORD every day with resounding instruments belonging to the LORD*

²²Hezekiah spoke encouragingly to all the Levites, who showed good understanding of the service of the LORD. For the seven days they ate their assigned portion and offered fellowship offerings[a] and praised the LORD, the God of their fathers. ²³The whole assembly then agreed to celebrate the festival seven more days; so for another seven days they celebrated joyfully. ²⁴Hezekiah king of Judah provided a thousand bulls and seven thousand sheep and goats for the assembly, and the officials provided them with a thousand bulls and ten thousand sheep and goats. A great number of priests consecrated themselves. ²⁵The entire assembly of Judah rejoiced, along with the priests and Levites and all who had assembled from Israel, including the aliens who had come from Israel and those who lived in Judah. ²⁶There was great joy in Jerusalem, for since the days of Solomon son of David king of Israel there had been nothing like this in Jerusalem. ²⁷The priests and the Levites stood to bless the people, and God heard them, for their prayer reached heaven, his holy dwelling place.

31 When all this had ended, the Israelites who were there went out to the towns of Judah, smashed the sacred stones and cut down the Asherah poles. They destroyed the high places and the altars throughout Judah and Benjamin and in Ephraim and Manasseh. After they had destroyed all of them, the Israelites returned to their own towns and to their own property.

Contributions for Worship

²Hezekiah assigned the priests and Levites to divisions—each of them according to their duties as priests or Levites—to offer burnt offerings and fellowship offerings,[a] to minister, to give thanks and to sing praises at the gates of the LORD's dwelling. ³The king contributed from his own possessions for the morning and evening burnt offerings and for the burnt offerings on the Sabbaths, New Moons and appointed feasts as written in the Law of the LORD. ⁴He ordered the people living in Jerusalem to give the portion due the priests and Levites so they could devote themselves to the Law of the LORD. ⁵As soon as the order went out, the Israelites generously gave the firstfruits of their grain, new wine, oil and honey and all that the fields produced. They brought a great amount, a tithe of everything. ⁶The men of Israel and Judah who lived in the towns of Judah also brought a tithe of their herds and flocks and a tithe of the holy things dedicated to the LORD their God, and they piled them in heaps. ⁷They began doing this in the third month and finished in the seventh month. ⁸When Hezekiah and his officials came and saw the heaps, they praised the LORD and blessed his people Israel.

⁹Hezekiah asked the priests and Levites about the heaps; ¹⁰and Azariah the chief priest, from the family of Zadok, answered, "Since the people began to bring their contributions to the temple of the LORD, we have had enough to eat and plenty to spare, because the LORD has blessed his people, and this great amount is left over."

¹¹Hezekiah gave orders to prepare storerooms in the temple of the LORD, and this was done. ¹²Then they faithfully brought in the contributions, tithes and dedicated gifts. Conaniah, a Levite, was in charge of these things, and his brother Shimei was next in rank. ¹³Jehiel, Azaziah, Nahath, Asahel, Jerimoth, Jozabad, Eliel, Ismakiah, Mahath and Benaiah were supervisors under Conaniah and Shimei his brother, by appointment of King Hezekiah and Azariah the official in charge of the temple of God.

¹⁴Kore son of Imnah the Levite, keeper of the East Gate, was in charge of the freewill offerings given to God, distributing the contributions made to the LORD and also the consecrated gifts. ¹⁵Eden, Miniamin, Jeshua, Shemaiah, Amariah and Shecaniah assisted him faithfully in the towns of the priests, distributing to their fellow priests according to their divisions, old and young alike.

¹⁶In addition, they distributed to the males three years old or more whose names were in the genealogical records— all who would enter the temple of the LORD to perform the daily duties of their various tasks, according to their responsibilities and their divisions. ¹⁷And they distributed to the priests enrolled by their families in the genealogical records and likewise to the Levites twenty years old or more, according to their responsibilities and their divisions. ¹⁸They included all the little ones, the wives, and the sons and

---

a 22,2 Traditionally *peace offerings*

daughters of the whole community listed in these genealogical records. For they were faithful in consecrating themselves.

¹⁹As for the priests, the descendants of Aaron, who lived on the farm lands around their towns or in any other towns, men were designated by name to distribute portions to every male among them and to all who were recorded in the genealogies of the Levites.

²⁰This is what Hezekiah did throughout Judah, doing what was good and right and faithful before the LORD his God. ²¹In everything that he undertook in the service of God's temple and in obedience to the law and the commands, he sought his God and worked wholeheartedly. And so he prospered.

Sennacherib Threatens Jerusalem

32 After all that Hezekiah had so faithfully done, Sennacherib king of Assyria came and invaded Judah. He laid siege to the fortified cities, thinking to conquer them for himself. ²When Hezekiah saw that Sennacherib had come and that he intended to make war on Jerusalem, ³he consulted with his officials and military staff about blocking off the water from the springs outside the city, and they helped him. ⁴A large force of men assembled, and they blocked all the springs and the stream that flowed through the land. "Why should the kingsª of Assyria come and find plenty of water?" they said. ⁵Then he worked hard repairing all the broken sections of the wall and building towers on it. He built another wall outside that one and reinforced the supporting terracesᵇ of the City of David. He also made large numbers of weapons and shields.

⁶He appointed military officers over the people and assembled them before him in the square at the city gate and encouraged them with these words: ⁷"Be strong and courageous. Do not be afraid or dis-

ª 4 Hebrew; Septuagint and Syriac *king*   ᵇ 5 Or *the Millo*

GET STRONGER

When God Flexes His Muscles

READ 2 CHRONICLES 32:1–23

It looked like a done deal. The battle hadn't even started, but Sennacherib was already making plans for his new city. He'd blown away everyone else he fought against. Why would Jerusalem be any different? After Sennacherib finished insulting God and bragging, God flexed his muscles in a way that the Assyrians couldn't ignore; he sent one—that's right, *one*—angel who annihilated every fighter and leader in their camp. The gladiators had nothing on this angel. The people of Jerusalem were ready to fight the Assyrians, but they relied on God's strength first. No matter how strong you are, God can push the limits way beyond your personal best. The trick is to yield your strength to him. Sometimes he'll ask you to sit back and watch the dust fly. Other times, you'll combine forces. However God chooses to act, he's going to come out on top.

Your next reading is on page 577.

couraged because of the king of Assyria and the vast army with him, for there is a greater power with us than with him. [8]With him is only the arm of flesh, but with us is the LORD our God to help us and to fight our battles." And the people gained confidence from what Hezekiah the king of Judah said.

[9]Later, when Sennacherib king of Assyria and all his forces were laying siege to Lachish, he sent his officers to Jerusalem with this message for Hezekiah king of Judah and for all the people of Judah who were there:

[10]"This is what Sennacherib king of Assyria says: On what are you basing your confidence, that you remain in Jerusalem under siege? [11]When Hezekiah says, 'The LORD our God will save us from the hand of the king of Assyria,' he is misleading you, to let you die of hunger and thirst. [12]Did not Hezekiah himself remove this god's high places and altars, saying to Judah and Jerusalem, 'You must worship before one altar and burn sacrifices on it'?

[13]"Do you not know what I and my fathers have done to all the peoples of the other lands? Were the gods of those nations ever able to deliver their land from my hand? [14]Who of all the gods of these nations that my fathers destroyed has been able to save his people from me? How then can your god deliver you from my hand? [15]Now do not let Hezekiah deceive you and mislead you like this. Do not believe him, for no god of any nation or kingdom has been able to deliver his people from my hand or the hand of my fathers. How much less will your god deliver you from my hand!"

[16]Sennacherib's officers spoke further against the LORD God and against his servant Hezekiah. [17]The king also wrote letters insulting the LORD, the God of Israel, and saying this against him: "Just as the gods of the peoples of the other lands did not rescue their people from my hand, so the god of Hezekiah will not rescue his people from my hand." [18]Then they called out in Hebrew to the people of Jerusalem who were on the wall, to terrify them and make them afraid in order to capture the city. [19]They spoke about the God of Jerusalem as they did about the gods of the other peoples of the world—the work of men's hands.

[20]King Hezekiah and the prophet Isaiah son of Amoz cried out in prayer to heaven about this. [21]And the LORD sent an angel, who annihilated all the fighting men and the leaders and officers in the camp of the Assyrian king. So he withdrew to his own land in disgrace. And when he went into the temple of his god, some of his sons cut him down with the sword.

[22]So the LORD saved Hezekiah and the people of Jerusalem from the hand of Sennacherib king of Assyria and from the hand of all others. He took care of them[a] on every side. [23]Many brought offerings to Jerusalem for the LORD and valuable gifts for Hezekiah king of Judah. From then on he was highly regarded by all the nations.

Hezekiah's Pride, Success and Death

[24]In those days Hezekiah became ill and was at the point of death. He prayed to the LORD, who answered him and gave him a miraculous sign. [25]But Hezekiah's heart was proud and he did not respond to the kindness shown him; therefore the LORD's wrath was on him and on Judah and Jerusalem. [26]Then Hezekiah repented of the pride of his heart, as did the people of Jerusalem; therefore the LORD's wrath did not come upon them during the days of Hezekiah.

[27]Hezekiah had very great riches and honor, and he made treasuries for his silver and gold and for his precious stones, spices, shields and all kinds of valuables. [28]He also made buildings to store the harvest of grain, new wine and oil; and he made stalls for various kinds of cattle, and pens for the flocks. [29]He built villages and acquired great numbers of flocks and herds, for God had given him very great riches.

[30]It was Hezekiah who blocked the upper outlet of the Gihon spring and channeled the water down to the west side of the City of David. He succeeded in everything he undertook. [31]But when envoys were sent by the rulers of Babylon to ask him about the miraculous sign that had occurred in the land, God left him to test him and to know everything that was in his heart.

[32]The other events of Hezekiah's reign and his acts of devotion are written in the

---

[a] 22 Hebrew; Septuagint and Vulgate *He gave them rest*

vision of the prophet Isaiah son of Amoz in the book of the kings of Judah and Israel. ³³Hezekiah rested with his fathers and was buried on the hill where the tombs of David's descendants are. All Judah and the people of Jerusalem honored him when he died. And Manasseh his son succeeded him as king.

Manasseh King of Judah

33 Manasseh was twelve years old when he became king, and he reigned in Jerusalem fifty-five years. ²He did evil in the eyes of the LORD, following the detestable practices of the nations the LORD had driven out before the Israelites. ³He rebuilt the high places his father Hezekiah had demolished; he also erected altars to the Baals and made Asherah poles. He bowed down to all the starry hosts and worshiped them. ⁴He built altars in the temple of the LORD, of which the LORD had said, "My Name will remain in Jerusalem forever." ⁵In both courts of the temple of the LORD, he built altars to all the starry hosts. ⁶He sacrificed his sons in ᵃ the fire in the Valley of Ben Hinnom, practiced sorcery, divination and witchcraft, and consulted mediums and spiritists. He did much evil in the eyes of the LORD, provoking him to anger.

⁷He took the carved image he had made and put it in God's temple, of which God had said to David and to his son Solomon, "In this temple and in Jerusalem, which I have chosen out of all the tribes of Israel, I will put my Name forever. ⁸I will not again make the feet of the Israelites leave the land I assigned to your forefathers, if only they will be careful to do everything I commanded them concerning all the laws, decrees and ordinances given through Moses." ⁹But Manasseh led Judah and the people of Jerusalem astray, so that they did more evil than the nations the LORD had destroyed before the Israelites.

¹⁰The LORD spoke to Manasseh and his people, but they paid no attention. ¹¹So the LORD brought against them the army commanders of the king of Assyria, who took Manasseh prisoner, put a hook in his nose, bound him with bronze shackles and took him to Babylon. ¹²In his distress he sought the favor of the LORD his God and humbled himself greatly before the God of his fathers. ¹³And when he prayed to him, the LORD was moved by his entreaty and listened to his plea; so he brought him back to Jerusalem and to his kingdom. Then Manasseh knew that the LORD is God.

¹⁴Afterward he rebuilt the outer wall of the City of David, west of the Gihon spring in the valley, as far as the entrance of the Fish Gate and encircling the hill of Ophel; he also made it much higher. He stationed military commanders in all the fortified cities in Judah.

¹⁵He got rid of the foreign gods and removed the image from the temple of the LORD, as well as all the altars he had built on the temple hill and in Jerusalem; and he

ᵃ 6 Or *He made his sons pass through*

Get a Load of This...

Manasseh "did more evil" than even the heathen (2 Chronicles 33:9). And he *suffered* for it. Big time! God is merciful and full of grace but he's no softie pushover. When he draws the line and says, "No more!" and people *cross* the line, they're in for it.

Get a Load of This...

"Josiah was eight years old when he became king" (2 Chronicles 34:1). Now *that* is cool! But even better, "while he was still *young*, he began to seek . . . God" (verse 3). That's when he jumped off his throne, grabbed a sledgehammer and began smashing idols!

threw them out of the city. ¹⁶Then he restored the altar of the Lord and sacrificed fellowship offerings*a* and thank offerings on it, and told Judah to serve the Lord, the God of Israel. ¹⁷The people, however, continued to sacrifice at the high places, but only to the Lord their God.

¹⁸The other events of Manasseh's reign, including his prayer to his God and the words the seers spoke to him in the name of the Lord, the God of Israel, are written in the annals of the kings of Israel.*b* ¹⁹His prayer and how God was moved by his entreaty, as well as all his sins and unfaithfulness, and the sites where he built high places and set up Asherah poles and idols before he humbled himself—all are written in the records of the seers.*c* ²⁰Manasseh rested with his fathers and was buried in his palace. And Amon his son succeeded him as king.

Amon King of Judah

²¹Amon was twenty-two years old when he became king, and he reigned in Jerusalem two years. ²²He did evil in the eyes of the Lord, as his father Manasseh had done. Amon worshiped and offered sacrifices to all the idols Manasseh had made. ²³But unlike his father Manasseh, he did not humble himself before the Lord; Amon increased his guilt.

²⁴Amon's officials conspired against him and assassinated him in his palace. ²⁵Then the people of the land killed all who had plotted against King Amon, and they made Josiah his son king in his place.

Josiah's Reforms

34 Josiah was eight years old when he became king, and he reigned in Jerusalem thirty-one years. ²He did what was right in the eyes of the Lord and walked in the ways of his father David, not turning aside to the right or to the left.

³In the eighth year of his reign, while he was still young, he began to seek the God of his father David. In his twelfth year he began to purge Judah and Jerusalem of high places, Asherah poles, carved idols and cast images. ⁴Under his direction the altars of the Baals were torn down; he cut to pieces the incense altars that were above them, and smashed the Asherah poles, the idols and the images. These he broke to pieces and scattered over the graves of those who had sacrificed to them. ⁵He burned the bones of the priests on their altars, and so he purged Judah and Jerusalem. ⁶In the towns of Manasseh, Ephraim and Simeon, as far as Naphtali, and in the ruins around them, ⁷he tore down the altars and the Asherah poles and crushed the idols to powder and cut to pieces all the incense altars throughout Israel. Then he went back to Jerusalem.

⁸In the eighteenth year of Josiah's reign, to purify the land and the temple, he sent Shaphan son of Azaliah

a 16 Traditionally *peace offerings*   *b 18* That is, Judah, as frequently in 2 Chronicles   *c 19* One Hebrew manuscript and Septuagint; most Hebrew manuscripts of *Hozai* and Maaseiah the ruler of the city, with Joah son of Joahaz, the recorder, to repair the temple of the LORD his God.

⁹They went to Hilkiah the high priest and gave him the money that had been brought into the temple of God, which the Levites who were the doorkeepers had collected from the people of Manasseh, Ephraim and the entire remnant of Israel and from all the people of Judah and Benjamin and the inhabitants of Jerusalem. ¹⁰Then they entrusted it to the men appointed to supervise the work on the LORD's temple. These men paid the workers who repaired and restored the temple. ¹¹They also gave money to the carpenters and builders to purchase dressed stone, and timber for joists and beams for the buildings that the kings of Judah had allowed to fall into ruin.

¹²The men did the work faithfully. Over them to direct them were Jahath and Obadiah, Levites descended from Merari, and Zechariah and Meshullam, descended

from Kohath. The Levites—all who were skilled in playing musical instruments—¹³had charge of the laborers and supervised all the workers from job to job. Some of the Levites were secretaries, scribes and doorkeepers.

The Book of the Law Found

¹⁴While they were bringing out the money that had been taken into the temple of the LORD, Hilkiah the priest found the Book of the Law of the LORD that had been given through Moses. ¹⁵Hilkiah said to Shaphan the secretary, "I have found the Book of the Law in the temple of the LORD." He gave it to Shaphan.

¹⁶Then Shaphan took the book to the king and reported to him: "Your officials are doing everything that has been committed to them. ¹⁷They have paid out the money that was in the temple of the LORD and have entrusted it to the supervisors and workers." ¹⁸Then Shaphan the secretary informed the king, "Hilkiah the priest

Wisdom From the Rubble

READ 2 CHRONICLES 34:1–8, 14–19, 29–33

When Josiah started looking for God, he started with the basics, smashing and burning idols and other things that were wrong. Next on the list was cleaning up the rubble of the neglected temple and making needed repairs. That's when they found the Book of the Law. Josiah had already been doing the right thing, even though the Book of the Law had been lost and there was no Bible to say what was right or wrong. Suddenly he had a whole lot more truth! (Ever wonder what surprises you'd find under the rubble on your bedroom floor?) Because Josiah looked for truth, God led him back to the Law and into a friendship with him. Finding God's truth is a step-by-step hike. You just start where you are. Act on the truth you already have. Then God will give you more truth and wisdom as you move ahead.

Your next reading is on page 580.

has given me a book." And Shaphan read from it in the presence of the king.

¹⁹When the king heard the words of the Law, he tore his robes. ²⁰He gave these orders to Hilkiah, Ahikam son of Shaphan, Abdon son of Micah,ᵃ Shaphan the secretary and Asaiah the king's attendant: ²¹"Go and inquire of the Lᴏʀᴅ for me and for the remnant in Israel and Judah about what is written in this book that has been found. Great is the Lᴏʀᴅ's anger that is poured out on us because our fathers have not kept the word of the Lᴏʀᴅ; they have not acted in accordance with all that is written in this book."

²²Hilkiah and those the king had sent with himᵇ went to speak to the prophetess Huldah, who was the wife of Shallum son of Tokhath,ᶜ the son of Hasrah,ᵈ keeper of the wardrobe. She lived in Jerusalem, in the Second District.

²³She said to them, "This is what the Lᴏʀᴅ, the God of Israel, says: Tell the man who sent you to me, ²⁴'This is what the Lᴏʀᴅ says: I am going to bring disaster on this place and its people—all the curses written in the book that has been read in the presence of the king of Judah. ²⁵Because they have forsaken me and burned incense to other gods and provoked me to anger by all that their hands have made,ᵉ my anger will be poured out on this place and will not be quenched.' ²⁶Tell the king of Judah, who sent you to inquire of the Lᴏʀᴅ, 'This is what the Lᴏʀᴅ, the God of Israel, says concerning the words you heard: ²⁷Because your heart was responsive and you humbled yourself before God when you heard what he spoke against this place and its people, and because you humbled yourself before me and tore your robes and wept in my presence, I have heard you, declares the Lᴏʀᴅ. ²⁸Now I will gather you to your fathers, and you will be buried in peace. Your eyes will not see all the disaster I am going to bring on this place and on those who live here.' "

So they took her answer back to the king.

²⁹Then the king called together all the elders of Judah and Jerusalem. ³⁰He went up to the temple of the Lᴏʀᴅ with the men of Judah, the people of Jerusalem, the priests and the Levites—all the people from the least to the greatest. He read in their hearing all the words of the Book of the Covenant, which had been found in the temple of the Lᴏʀᴅ. ³¹The king stood by his pillar and renewed the covenant in the presence of the Lᴏʀᴅ—to follow the Lᴏʀᴅ and keep his commands, regulations and decrees with all his heart and all his soul, and to obey the words of the covenant written in this book.

³²Then he had everyone in Jerusalem and Benjamin pledge themselves to it; the people of Jerusalem did this in accordance with the covenant of God, the God of their fathers.

³³Josiah removed all the detestable idols from all the territory belonging to the Israelites, and he had all who were present in Israel serve the Lᴏʀᴅ their God. As long as he lived, they did not fail to follow the Lᴏʀᴅ, the God of their fathers.

Josiah Celebrates the Passover

35 Josiah celebrated the Passover to the Lᴏʀᴅ in Jerusalem, and the Passover lamb was slaughtered on the fourteenth day of the first month. ²He appointed the priests to their duties and encouraged them in the service of the Lᴏʀᴅ's temple. ³He said to the Levites, who instructed all Israel and who had been consecrated to the Lᴏʀᴅ: "Put the sacred ark in the temple that Solomon son of David king of Israel built. It is not to be carried about on your shoulders. Now serve the Lᴏʀᴅ your God and his people Israel. ⁴Prepare yourselves by families in your divisions, according to the directions written by David king of Israel and by his son Solomon.

⁵"Stand in the holy place with a group of Levites for each subdivision of the families of your fellow countrymen, the lay people. ⁶Slaughter the Passover lambs, consecrate yourselves and prepare ⌊the lambs⌋ for your fellow countrymen, doing what the Lᴏʀᴅ commanded through Moses."

⁷Josiah provided for all the lay people who were there a total of thirty thousand sheep and goats for the Passover offerings, and also three thousand cattle—all from the king's own possessions.

⁸His officials also contributed voluntari-

ᵃ 20 Also called Acbor son of Micaiah   ᵇ 22 One Hebrew manuscript, Vulgate and Syriac; most Hebrew manuscripts do not have had sent with him.   ᶜ 22 Also called Tikvah   ᵈ 22 Also called Harhas   ᵉ 25 Or by everything they have done ly to the people and the priests and Levites. Hilkiah, Zechariah and Jehiel, the administrators of God's temple, gave the priests twenty-six hundred Passover offerings and three hundred cattle. 9Also Conaniah along with Shemaiah and Nethanel, his brothers, and Hashabiah, Jeiel and Jozabad, the leaders of the Levites, provided five thousand Passover offerings and five hundred head of cattle for the Levites.

10The service was arranged and the priests stood in their places with the Levites in their divisions as the king had ordered. 11The Passover lambs were slaughtered, and the priests sprinkled the blood handed to them, while the Levites skinned the animals. 12They set aside the burnt offerings to give them to the subdivisions of the families of the people to offer to the LORD, as is written in the Book of Moses. They did the same with the cattle. 13They roasted the Passover animals over the fire as prescribed, and boiled the holy offerings in pots, caldrons and pans and served them quickly to all the people. 14After this, they made preparations for themselves and for the priests, because the priests, the descendants of Aaron, were sacrificing the burnt offerings and the fat portions until nightfall. So the Levites made preparations for themselves and for the Aaronic priests.

15The musicians, the descendants of Asaph, were in the places prescribed by David, Asaph, Heman and Jeduthun the king's seer. The gatekeepers at each gate did not need to leave their posts, because their fellow Levites made the preparations for them.

16So at that time the entire service of the LORD was carried out for the celebration of the Passover and the offering of burnt offerings on the altar of the LORD, as King Josiah had ordered. 17The Israelites who were present celebrated the Passover at that time and observed the Feast of Unleavened Bread for seven days. 18The Passover had not been observed like this in Israel since the days of the prophet Samuel; and none of the kings of Israel had ever celebrated such a Passover as did Josiah, with the priests, the Levites and all Judah and Israel who were there with the people of Jerusalem. 19This Passover was celebrated in the eighteenth year of Josiah's reign.

The Death of Josiah

20After all this, when Josiah had set the temple in order, Neco king of Egypt went up to fight at Carchemish on the Euphrates, and Josiah marched out to meet him in battle. 21But Neco sent messengers to him, saying, "What quarrel is there between you and me, O king of Judah? It is not you I am attacking at this time, but the house with which I am at war. God has told me to hurry; so stop opposing God, who is with me, or he will destroy you."

22Josiah, however, would not turn away from him, but disguised himself to engage him in battle. He would not listen to what Neco had said at God's command but went to fight him on the plain of Megiddo.

23Archers shot King Josiah, and he told his officers, "Take me away; I am badly wounded." 24So they took him out of his chariot, put him in the other chariot he had and brought him to Jerusalem, where he died. He was buried in the tombs of his fathers, and all Judah and Jerusalem mourned for him.

25Jeremiah composed laments for Josiah, and to this day all the men and women singers commemorate Josiah in the laments. These became a tradition in Israel and are written in the Laments.

26The other events of Josiah's reign and his acts of devotion, according to what is written in the Law of the LORD— 27all the events, from beginning to end, are written in the book of the kings of Israel and Judah. 1And the people of the land took Jehoahaz son of Josiah and made him king in Jerusalem in place of his father.

Jehoahaz King of Judah

2Jehoahaza was twenty-three years old when he became king, and he reigned in Jerusalem three months. 3The king of Egypt dethroned him in Jerusalem and imposed on Judah a levy of a hundred talentsb of silver and a talentc of gold. 4The king of Egypt made Eliakim, a brother of Jehoahaz, king over Judah and Jerusalem and changed Eliakim's name to Jehoiakim. But Neco took Eliakim's brother Jehoahaz and carried him off to Egypt.

a 2 Hebrew Joahaz, a variant of Jehoahaz; also in verse 4
b 3 That is, about 3 3/4 tons (about 3.4 metric tons)
c 3 That is, about 75 pounds (about 34 kilograms)

Jehoiakim King of Judah

⁵Jehoiakim was twenty-five years old when he became king, and he reigned in Jerusalem eleven years. He did evil in the eyes of the LORD his God. ⁶Nebuchadnezzar king of Babylon attacked him and bound him with bronze shackles to take him to Babylon. ⁷Nebuchadnezzar also took to Babylon articles from the temple of the LORD and put them in his temple*a* there.

⁸The other events of Jehoiakim's reign, the detestable things he did and all that was found against him, are written in the book of the kings of Israel and Judah. And Jehoiachin his son succeeded him as king.

Jehoiachin King of Judah

⁹Jehoiachin was eighteen*b* years old when he became king, and he reigned in Jerusalem three months and ten days. He did evil in the eyes of the LORD. ¹⁰In the spring, King Nebuchadnezzar sent for him and brought him to Babylon, together with articles of value from the temple of the LORD, and he made Jehoiachin's uncle,*c* Zedekiah, king over Judah and Jerusalem.

Zedekiah King of Judah

¹¹Zedekiah was twenty-one years old when he became king, and he reigned in Jerusalem eleven years. ¹²He did evil in the eyes of the LORD his God and did not humble himself before Jeremiah the prophet, who spoke the word of the LORD. ¹³He also rebelled against King Nebuchadnezzar, who had made him take an oath in God's name. He became stiff-necked and hardened his heart and would not turn to the LORD, the God of Israel. ¹⁴Furthermore, all the leaders of the priests and the people became more and more unfaithful, following all the detestable practices of the nations and defiling the temple of the LORD, which he had consecrated in Jerusalem.

The Fall of Jerusalem

¹⁵The LORD, the God of their fathers, sent word to them through his messengers again and again, because he had pity

a 7 Or *palace*   *b 9* One Hebrew manuscript, some Septuagint manuscripts and Syriac (see also 2 Kings 24:8); most Hebrew manuscripts *eight*   *c 10* Hebrew *brother,* that is, relative (see 2 Kings 24:17)

No Time Like the Present

READ 2 CHRONICLES 36:11–20

Ever get in big trouble because you didn't do something your parents asked you to do? That's kind of what happened to Judah. It all really started with King Manasseh (see 2 Kings 21:10–15; Jeremiah 15:1–4). He led the Israelites into incredibly evil things, like sacrificing children and worshiping idols. God sent prophets to try to get the people to repent. But did they? No way (verses 15–16). They just kept doing their own thing. After a while, they couldn't have repented if they had wanted to. They didn't know right from wrong anymore, and they just didn't care. *Repent? Of what?* That's when God brought the hammer down, and there was no way Judah's final kings were going to permanently turn the nation around. It was too little, too late. Do yourself a favor: learn from Judah's mistake. When it comes to repentance, never put off until tomorrow what you can do today.

Your next reading is on page 583.

on his people and on his dwelling place.
¹⁶But they mocked God's messengers, despised his words and scoffed at his prophets until the wrath of the LORD was aroused against his people and there was no remedy. ¹⁷He brought up against them the king of the Babylonians,ᵃ who killed their young men with the sword in the sanctuary, and spared neither young man nor young woman, old man or aged. God handed all of them over to Nebuchadnezzar. ¹⁸He carried to Babylon all the articles from the temple of God, both large and small, and the treasures of the LORD's temple and the treasures of the king and his officials. ¹⁹They set fire to God's temple and broke down the wall of Jerusalem; they burned all the palaces and destroyed everything of value there.

²⁰He carried into exile to Babylon the remnant, who escaped from the sword, and they became servants to him and his sons until the kingdom of Persia came to power. ²¹The land enjoyed its sabbath rests; all the time of its desolation it rested, until the seventy years were completed in fulfillment of the word of the LORD spoken by Jeremiah.

²²In the first year of Cyrus king of Persia, in order to fulfill the word of the LORD spoken by Jeremiah, the LORD moved the heart of Cyrus king of Persia to make a proclamation throughout his realm and to put it in writing:

²³"This is what Cyrus king of Persia says:

" 'The LORD, the God of heaven, has given me all the kingdoms of the earth and he has appointed me to build a temple for him at Jerusalem in Judah. Anyone of his people among you—may the LORD his God be with him, and let him go up.' "

ᵃ 17 Or Chaldeans

EZRA

Who wrote this book?
The author is unknown. Many people think Ezra wrote much of this book.

Why was this book written?
Ezra shows how God kept his promise and brought the Jews back to their homeland.

What happens in this book?
The Persian ruler Cyrus lets captive people return home. Some of the Jews in Babylon go back to Judah. They rebuild God's temple. Later Ezra comes from Babylon to teach God's law.

What do we learn about God in this book?
God is faithful and keeps his promises.

What people are important in this book?
The important people in this book are King Cyrus and Ezra.

When did this happen?
The first Jews returned to Judah in 538 B.C. Ezra returned in 458 B.C.

Where did this happen?
The events of this book happened in the land of Judah and the city of Jerusalem.

What are some of the stories in this book?

Exiled Jews return home	Ezra 1–2
Rebuilding the temple	Ezra 3–6
Ezra returns to Jerusalem	Ezra 7–8
Ezra confesses Judah's sins	Ezra 9
The people of Judah confess	Ezra 10

Cyrus Helps the Exiles to Return

In the first year of Cyrus king of Persia, in order to fulfill the word of the LORD spoken by Jeremiah, the LORD moved the heart of Cyrus king of Persia to make a proclamation throughout his realm and to put it in writing:

2 "This is what Cyrus king of Persia says:

" 'The LORD, the God of heaven, has given me all the kingdoms of the earth and he has appointed me to build a temple for him at Jerusalem in Judah. 3 Anyone of his people among you—may his God be with him, and let him go up to Jerusalem in Judah and build the temple of the LORD, the God of Israel, the God who is in Jerusalem. 4 And the people of any place where survivors may now be living are to provide him with silver and gold, with goods and livestock, and with freewill offerings for the temple of God in Jerusalem.' "

5 Then the family heads of Judah and Benjamin, and the priests and Levites—everyone whose heart God had moved—prepared to go up and build the house of the LORD in Jerusalem. 6 All their neighbors assisted them with articles of silver and gold, with goods and livestock, and with valuable gifts, in addition to all the freewill offerings. 7 Moreover, King Cyrus brought out the articles belonging to the temple of the LORD, which Nebuchadnezzar had carried away from Jerusalem and had placed in the temple of his god.ª 8 Cyrus king of Persia had them brought by Mithredath the treasurer, who counted them out to Sheshbazzar the prince of Judah.

9 This was the inventory:

gold dishes	30
silver dishes	1,000
silver pans[b]	29
10 gold bowls	30
matching silver bowls	410
other articles	1,000

11 In all, there were 5,400 articles of gold and of silver. Sheshbazzar brought

---

ª 7 Or *gods*   b 9 The meaning of the Hebrew for this word is uncertain.

God Calls the Shots

READ EZRA 1

When the Persians conquered Babylon, King Cyrus had the muscle to force the Jews to stay and serve him. But instead, "the LORD moved the heart of Cyrus" (verse 1), and he freed the Jews, let them return to their homeland and told them to rebuild God's temple. Cool? Hey, Cyrus was just doing what God had created him for. God spelled out his plans for Cyrus over a hundred years before Cyrus was born, and—get this—even mentioned him *by name* (see Isaiah 41:2, 25; 44:28; 45:1–6, 13; 46:11). Wow! Talk about being in control! Cyrus was top dog, but God was the dog's owner and when he said, "Fetch!" Cyrus fetched. God can make huge changes in the world. When you stay close to him and pray, God can do phenomenal miracles to fulfill his promises. You do your part by praying and believing, and God does the rest.

Your next reading is on page 584.

all these along when the exiles came up from Babylon to Jerusalem.

The List of the Exiles Who Returned

2 Now these are the people of the province who came up from the captivity of the exiles, whom Nebuchadnezzar king of Babylon had taken captive to Babylon (they returned to Jerusalem and Judah, each to his own town, ²in company with Zerubbabel, Jeshua, Nehemiah, Seraiah, Reelaiah, Mordecai, Bilshan, Mispar, Bigvai, Rehum and Baanah):

The list of the men of the people of Israel:

³ the descendants of Parosh	2,172
⁴ of Shephatiah	372
⁵ of Arah	775
⁶ of Pahath-Moab (through the line of Jeshua and Joab)	2,812
⁷ of Elam	1,254
⁸ of Zattu	945
⁹ of Zaccai	760
¹⁰ of Bani	642
¹¹ of Bebai	623
¹² of Azgad	1,222
¹³ of Adonikam	666
¹⁴ of Bigvai	2,056
¹⁵ of Adin	454
¹⁶ of Ater (through Hezekiah)	98
¹⁷ of Bezai	323
¹⁸ of Jorah	112
¹⁹ of Hashum	223
²⁰ of Gibbar	95
²¹ the men of Bethlehem	123
²² of Netophah	56
²³ of Anathoth	128
²⁴ of Azmaveth	42
²⁵ of Kiriath Jearim,ᵃ Kephirah and Beeroth	743
²⁶ of Ramah and Geba	621
²⁷ of Micmash	122
²⁸ of Bethel and Ai	223
²⁹ of Nebo	52
³⁰ of Magbish	156
³¹ of the other Elam	1,254
³² of Harim	320
³³ of Lod, Hadid and Ono	725

ᵃ 25 See Septuagint (see also Neh. 7:29); Hebrew *Kiriath Arim.*

No Apologies

READ EZRA 2:1–2; 3:1–6

What if your church's youth group reserved a baseball diamond for a weekend game, but when you got there, you found some tough kids sitting on the bleachers, waiting to make fun of you? That's about what happened to the Jews. They returned to Judah—which had once been *their* home—to find it filled with enemies. The Jews were afraid, but they knew they were in the right. "Despite their fear of the peoples around them, they built the altar . . . and sacrificed burnt offerings on it to the LORD" (Ezra 3:3). As a man, you should stand up for what you believe. You should be respectful of other people's beliefs, but you should never hide who you are as a Christian. This doesn't mean being pushy or weird, just being a Christian, no apologies. Some people won't like you? No sweat. Just be who you are.

Your next reading is on page 586.

³⁴of Jericho   345
³⁵of Senaah   3,630

³⁶The priests:

the descendants of Jedaiah
(through the family of
Jeshua)   973
³⁷of Immer   1,052
³⁸of Pashhur   1,247
³⁹of Harim   1,017

⁴⁰The Levites:

the descendants of Jeshua
and Kadmiel (through the
line of Hodaviah)   74

⁴¹The singers:

the descendants of Asaph   128

⁴²The gatekeepers of the temple:

the descendants of
Shallum, Ater, Talmon,
Akkub, Hatita and Shobai   139

⁴³The temple servants:

the descendants of
Ziha, Hasupha, Tabbaoth,
⁴⁴Keros, Siaha, Padon,
⁴⁵Lebanah, Hagabah, Akkub,
⁴⁶Hagab, Shalmai, Hanan,
⁴⁷Giddel, Gahar, Reaiah,
⁴⁸Rezin, Nekoda, Gazzam,
⁴⁹Uzza, Paseah, Besai,
⁵⁰Asnah, Meunim, Nephusim,
⁵¹Bakbuk, Hakupha, Harhur,
⁵²Bazluth, Mehida, Harsha,
⁵³Barkos, Sisera, Temah,
⁵⁴Neziah and Hatipha

⁵⁵The descendants of the servants of
Solomon:

the descendants of
Sotai, Hassophereth, Peruda,
⁵⁶Jaala, Darkon, Giddel,
⁵⁷Shephatiah, Hattil,
Pokereth-Hazzebaim and Ami

⁵⁸The temple servants and the
descendants of the servants
of Solomon   392

⁵⁹The following came up from the
towns of Tel Melah, Tel Harsha, Ke-
rub, Addon and Immer, but they
could not show that their families
were descended from Israel:

⁶⁰The descendants of
Delaiah, Tobiah and
Nekoda   652

⁶¹And from among the priests:

The descendants of
Hobaiah, Hakkoz and Barzillai
(a man who had married a
daughter of Barzillai the Gileadite
and was called by that name).
⁶²These searched for their family
records, but they could not find them
and so were excluded from the
priesthood as unclean. ⁶³The governor ordered them not to eat any of
the most sacred food until there was
a priest ministering with the Urim
and Thummim.

⁶⁴The whole company numbered
42,360, ⁶⁵besides their 7,337 menservants and maidservants; and they also
had 200 men and women singers.
⁶⁶They had 736 horses, 245 mules,
⁶⁷435 camels and 6,720 donkeys.

⁶⁸When they arrived at the house of the
Lord in Jerusalem, some of the heads of
the families gave freewill offerings toward
the rebuilding of the house of God on its
site. ⁶⁹According to their ability they gave
to the treasury for this work 61,000
drachmas^a of gold, 5,000 minas^b of silver
and 100 priestly garments.
⁷⁰The priests, the Levites, the singers,
the gatekeepers and the temple servants
settled in their own towns, along with
some of the other people, and the rest of
the Israelites settled in their towns.

Rebuilding the Altar

When the seventh month came and
the Israelites had settled in their
towns, the people assembled as
one man in Jerusalem. ²Then Jeshua
son of Jozadak and his fellow priests and
Zerubbabel son of Shealtiel and his associates began to build the altar of the God of
Israel to sacrifice burnt offerings on it, in
accordance with what is written in the
Law of Moses the man of God. ³Despite
their fear of the peoples around them,
they built the altar on its foundation and
sacrificed burnt offerings on it to the Lord,
both the morning and evening sacrifices.

^a 69 That is, about 1,100 pounds (about 500 kilograms)
^b 69 That is, about 3 tons (about 2.9 metric tons)

4Then in accordance with what is written, they celebrated the Feast of Tabernacles with the required number of burnt offerings prescribed for each day. 5After that, they presented the regular burnt offerings, the New Moon sacrifices and the sacrifices for all the appointed sacred feasts of the LORD, as well as those brought as freewill offerings to the LORD. 6On the first day of the seventh month they began to offer burnt offerings to the LORD, though the foundation of the LORD's temple had not yet been laid.

Rebuilding the Temple

7Then they gave money to the masons and carpenters, and gave food and drink and oil to the people of Sidon and Tyre, so that they would bring cedar logs by sea from Lebanon to Joppa, as authorized by Cyrus king of Persia.

8In the second month of the second year after their arrival at the house of God in Jerusalem, Zerubbabel son of Shealtiel, Jeshua son of Jozadak and the rest of their brothers (the priests and the Levites and all who had returned from the captivity to Jerusalem) began the work, appointing Levites twenty years of age and older to supervise the building of the house of the LORD. 9Jeshua and his sons and brothers and Kadmiel and his sons (descendants of Hodaviah[a]) and the sons of Henadad and their sons and brothers—all Levites—joined together in supervising those working on the house of God.

10When the builders laid the foundation of the temple of the LORD, the priests in their vestments and with trumpets, and the Levites (the sons of Asaph) with cymbals, took their places to praise the LORD, as prescribed by David king of Israel. 11With praise and thanksgiving they sang to the LORD:

a 9 Hebrew *Yehudah*, probably a variant of *Hodaviah*

Not Much to Look at?

READ EZRA 3:7–13

If your sister smashed your giant model plane, how would you feel if you finally rebuilt it, but pieces were missing and it looked cheap and glommed together with glue? Well, when the Jews started rebuilding their *economy-version* temple, the older folks who had seen Solomon's glorious temple were so bummed out they wept. They knew that the new temple was going to be *peanuts* compared to the old one! But the younger people whooped for joy! They had never had *any* temple and now they were finally going to have one (verses 11–12). Sure, you should have a big vision and want God to help you build top-of-the-line stuff, but you should also accept the times when you need to focus on less-than-grand huge plans that other people might not notice but are still important. Like the Jews, you may not have much to work with. Does that mean you can't accomplish anything worthwhile? Think again. Push for excellence, but when you've done your best, both you and God can be happy with the results.

Your next reading is on page 588.

"He is good;
    his love to Israel endures forever."

And all the people gave a great shout of praise to the LORD, because the foundation of the house of the LORD was laid. ¹²But many of the older priests and Levites and family heads, who had seen the former temple, wept aloud when they saw the foundation of this temple being laid, while many others shouted for joy. ¹³No one could distinguish the sound of the shouts of joy from the sound of weeping, because the people made so much noise. And the sound was heard far away.

Opposition to the Rebuilding

When the enemies of Judah and Benjamin heard that the exiles were building a temple for the LORD, the God of Israel, ²they came to Zerubbabel and to the heads of the families and said, "Let us help you build because, like you, we seek your God and have been sacrificing to him since the time of Esarhaddon king of Assyria, who brought us here." ³But Zerubbabel, Jeshua and the rest of the heads of the families of Israel answered, "You have no part with us in building a temple to our God. We alone will build it for the LORD, the God of Israel, as King Cyrus, the king of Persia, commanded us."

⁴Then the peoples around them set out to discourage the people of Judah and make them afraid to go on building.ᵃ ⁵They hired counselors to work against them and frustrate their plans during the entire reign of Cyrus king of Persia and down to the reign of Darius king of Persia.

Later Opposition Under Xerxes and Artaxerxes

⁶At the beginning of the reign of Xerxes,ᵇ they lodged an accusation against the people of Judah and Jerusalem.

⁷And in the days of Artaxerxes king of Persia, Bishlam, Mithredath, Tabeel and the rest of his associates wrote a letter to Artaxerxes. The letter was written in Aramaic script and in the Aramaic language.ᶜᵈ

⁸Rehum the commanding officer and Shimshai the secretary wrote a letter against Jerusalem to Artaxerxes the king as follows:

⁹Rehum the commanding officer and Shimshai the secretary, together with the rest of their associates—the judges and officials over the men from Tripolis, Persia,ᵉ Erech and Babylon, the Elamites of Susa, ¹⁰and the other people whom the great and honorable Ashurbanipalᶠ deported and settled in the city of Samaria and elsewhere in Trans-Euphrates.

¹¹(This is a copy of the letter they sent him.)

To King Artaxerxes,

From your servants, the men of Trans-Euphrates:

¹²The king should know that the Jews who came up to us from you have gone to Jerusalem and are rebuilding that rebellious and wicked city. They are restoring the walls and repairing the foundations.

¹³Furthermore, the king should know that if this city is built and its walls are restored, no more taxes, tribute or duty will be paid, and the royal revenues will suffer. ¹⁴Now since we are under obligation to the palace and it is not proper for us to see the king dishonored, we are sending this message to inform the king, ¹⁵so that a search may be made in the archives of your predecessors. In these records you will find that this city is a rebellious city, troublesome to kings and provinces, a place of rebellion from ancient times. That is why this city was destroyed. ¹⁶We inform the king that if this city is built and its walls are restored, you will be left with nothing in Trans-Euphrates.

¹⁷The king sent this reply:

To Rehum the commanding officer, Shimshai the secretary and the rest of their associates living in Samaria and elsewhere in Trans-Euphrates:

Greetings.

¹⁸The letter you sent us has been read and translated in my presence. ¹⁹I issued an order and a search was

---

ᵃ4 Or and troubled them as they built   ᵇ6 Hebrew
Ahasuerus, a variant of Xerxes' Persian name   ᶜ7 Or written
in Aramaic and translated   ᵈ7 The text of Ezra 4:8—6:18 is
in Aramaic.   ᵉ9 Or officials, magistrates and governors over
the men from   ᶠ10 Aramaic Osnappar, a variant of
Ashurbanipal

made, and it was found that this city has a long history of revolt against kings and has been a place of rebellion and sedition. [20]Jerusalem has had powerful kings ruling over the whole of Trans-Euphrates, and taxes, tribute and duty were paid to them. [21]Now issue an order to these men to stop work, so that this city will not be rebuilt until I so order. [22]Be careful not to neglect this matter. Why let this threat grow, to the detriment of the royal interests?

[23]As soon as the copy of the letter of King Artaxerxes was read to Rehum and Shimshai the secretary and their associates, they went immediately to the Jews in Jerusalem and compelled them by force to stop.

[24]Thus the work on the house of God in Jerusalem came to a standstill until the second year of the reign of Darius king of Persia.

Tattenai's Letter to Darius

Now Haggai the prophet and Zechariah the prophet, a descendant of Iddo, prophesied to the Jews in Judah and Jerusalem in the name of the God of Israel, who was over them. [2]Then Zerubbabel son of Shealtiel and Jeshua son of Jozadak set to work to rebuild the house of God in Jerusalem. And the prophets of God were with them, helping them.

[3]At that time Tattenai, governor of Trans-Euphrates, and Shethar-Bozenai and their associates went to them and asked, "Who authorized you to rebuild this temple and restore this structure?" [4]They also asked, "What are the names of the men constructing this building?"[a] [5]But the eye of their God was watching over the elders of the Jews, and they were not stopped until a report could go to Darius and his written reply be received.

[a] 4 See Septuagint; Aramaic [4]*We told them the names of the men constructing this building.*

Standing up to Bullies

READ EZRA 4:1–6, 17–24; 5:1–5

The Jews' enemies did everything possible to stop them from building God's temple. "Then the peoples around them set out to discourage the people of Judah and make them afraid to go on building" (Ezra 4:4). But the Jews just refused to be bullied. They didn't lie down and go into doormat mode. Neither should you. As a man, it's important to stand up for what's right. You should stand up not just for yourself but also for your family, city and country. Don't be intimidated just because people bully you. If you're doing what God wants you to, keep at it. Another thing: Bullying is wrong. So if someone is being bullied at school, speak out against it. Don't let it slide just because speaking out might make you unpopular.

Your next reading is on page 591.

6This is a copy of the letter that Tattenai, governor of Trans-Euphrates, and Shethar-Bozenai and their associates, the officials of Trans-Euphrates, sent to King Darius. 7The report they sent him read as follows:

To King Darius:

Cordial greetings.

8The king should know that we went to the district of Judah, to the temple of the great God. The people are building it with large stones and placing the timbers in the walls. The work is being carried on with diligence and is making rapid progress under their direction.

9We questioned the elders and asked them, "Who authorized you to rebuild this temple and restore this structure?" 10We also asked them their names, so that we could write down the names of their leaders for your information.

11This is the answer they gave us:

"We are the servants of the God of heaven and earth, and we are rebuilding the temple that was built many years ago, one that a great king of Israel built and finished. 12But because our fathers angered the God of heaven, he handed them over to Nebuchadnezzar the Chaldean, king of Babylon, who destroyed this temple and deported the people to Babylon.

13"However, in the first year of Cyrus king of Babylon, King Cyrus issued a decree to rebuild this house of God. 14He even removed from the templeᵃ of Babylon the gold and silver articles of the house of God, which Nebuchadnezzar had taken from the temple in Jerusalem and brought to the templeᵃ in Babylon.

"Then King Cyrus gave them to a man named Sheshbazzar, whom he had appointed governor, 15and he told him, 'Take these articles and go and deposit them in the temple in Jerusalem. And rebuild the house of God on its site.' 16So this Sheshbazzar came and laid the foundations of the house of God in Jerusalem. From that day to the present it has been under construction but is not yet finished."

17Now if it pleases the king, let a search be made in the royal archives of Babylon to see if King Cyrus did in fact issue a decree to rebuild this house of God in Jerusalem. Then let the king send us his decision in this matter.

The Decree of Darius

6 King Darius then issued an order, and they searched in the archives stored in the treasury at Babylon. 2A scroll was found in the citadel of Ecbatana in the province of Media, and this was written on it:

Memorandum:

3In the first year of King Cyrus, the king issued a decree concerning the temple of God in Jerusalem:

Let the temple be rebuilt as a place to present sacrifices, and let its foundations be laid. It is to be ninety feetᵇ high and ninety feet wide, 4with three courses of large stones and one of timbers. The costs are to be paid by the royal treasury. 5Also, the gold and silver articles of the house of God, which Nebuchadnezzar took from the temple in Jerusalem and brought to Babylon, are to be returned to their places in the temple in Jerusalem; they are to be deposited in the house of God.

6Now then, Tattenai, governor of Trans-Euphrates, and Shethar-Bozenai and you, their fellow officials of that province, stay away from there. 7Do not interfere with the work on this temple of God. Let the governor of the Jews and the Jewish elders rebuild this house of God on its site.

8Moreover, I hereby decree what you are to do for these elders of the Jews in the construction of this house of God:

The expenses of these men are to be fully paid out of the royal treasury, from the revenues of Trans-Euphrates, so that the work will not stop. 9Whatever is needed—young bulls, rams, male lambs for burnt offerings to the God of heaven, and wheat, salt, wine and oil, as requested by the

---

ᵃ 14 Or palace   ᵇ 3 Aramaic sixty cubits (about 27 meters) priests in Jerusalem—must be given them daily without fail, ¹⁰so that they may offer sacrifices pleasing to the God of heaven and pray for the well-being of the king and his sons.

¹¹Furthermore, I decree that if anyone changes this edict, a beam is to be pulled from his house and he is to be lifted up and impaled on it. And for this crime his house is to be made a pile of rubble. ¹²May God, who has caused his Name to dwell there, overthrow any king or people who lifts a hand to change this decree or to destroy this temple in Jerusalem.

I Darius have decreed it. Let it be carried out with diligence.

Completion and Dedication of the Temple

¹³Then, because of the decree King Darius had sent, Tattenai, governor of Trans-Euphrates, and Shethar-Bozenai and their associates carried it out with diligence.

¹⁴So the elders of the Jews continued to build and prosper under the preaching of Haggai the prophet and Zechariah, a descendant of Iddo. They finished building the temple according to the command of the God of Israel and the decrees of Cyrus, Darius and Artaxerxes, kings of Persia. ¹⁵The temple was completed on the third day of the month Adar, in the sixth year of the reign of King Darius.

¹⁶Then the people of Israel—the priests, the Levites and the rest of the exiles—celebrated the dedication of the house of God with joy. ¹⁷For the dedication of this house of God they offered a hundred bulls, two hundred rams, four hundred male lambs and, as a sin offering for all Israel, twelve male goats, one for each of the tribes of Israel. ¹⁸And they installed the priests in their divisions and the Levites in their groups for the service of God at Jerusalem, according to what is written in the Book of Moses.

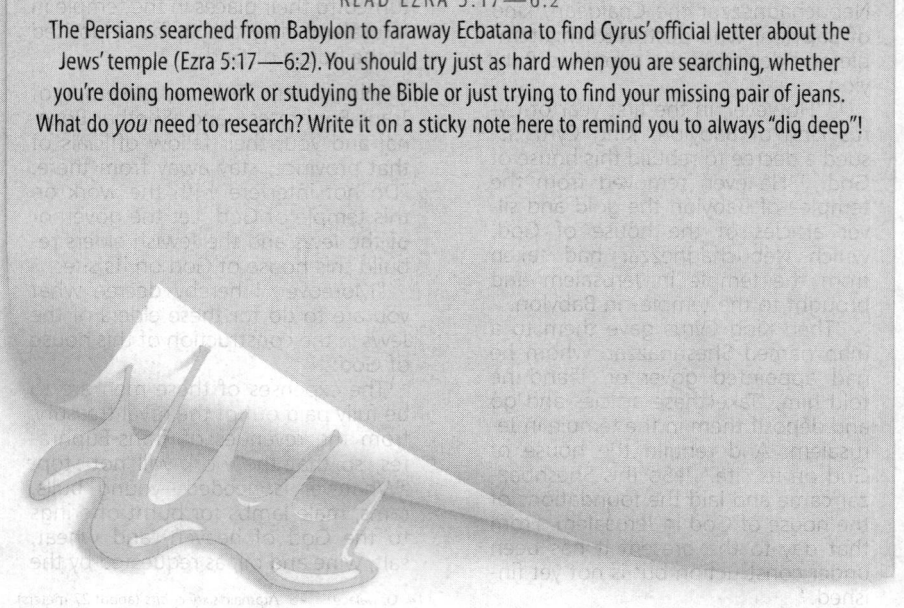

Make It Stick

READ EZRA 5:17—6:2

The Persians searched from Babylon to faraway Ecbatana to find Cyrus' official letter about the Jews' temple (Ezra 5:17—6:2). You should try just as hard when you are searching, whether you're doing homework or studying the Bible or just trying to find your missing pair of jeans. What do *you* need to research? Write it on a sticky note here to remind you to always "dig deep"!

The Passover

¹⁹On the fourteenth day of the first month, the exiles celebrated the Passover. ²⁰The priests and Levites had purified themselves and were all ceremonially clean. The Levites slaughtered the Passover lamb for all the exiles, for their brothers the priests and for themselves. ²¹So the Israelites who had returned from the exile ate it, together with all who had separated themselves from the unclean practices of their Gentile neighbors in order to seek the LORD, the God of Israel. ²²For seven days they celebrated with joy the Feast of Unleavened Bread, because the LORD had filled them with joy by changing the attitude of the king of Assyria, so that he assisted them in the work on the house of God, the God of Israel.

Ezra Comes to Jerusalem

7 After these things, during the reign of Artaxerxes king of Persia, Ezra son of Seraiah, the son of Azariah, the son of Hilkiah, ²the son of Shallum, the son of Zadok, the son of Ahitub, ³the son of Amariah, the son of Azariah, the son of Meraioth, ⁴the son of Zerahiah, the son of Uzzi, the son of Bukki, ⁵the son of Abishua, the son of Phinehas, the son of Eleazar, the son of Aaron the chief priest— ⁶this Ezra came up from Babylon. He was a teacher well versed in the Law of Moses, which the LORD, the God of Israel, had given. The king had granted him everything he asked, for the hand of the LORD his God was on him. ⁷Some of the Israelites, including priests, Levites, singers, gatekeepers and temple servants, also came up to Jerusalem in the seventh year of King Artaxerxes.

⁸Ezra arrived in Jerusalem in the fifth month of the seventh year of the king. ⁹He had begun his journey from Babylon on the first day of the first month, and he arrived in Jerusalem on the first day of the fifth month, for the gracious hand of his God was on him. ¹⁰For Ezra had devoted himself to the study and observance of the Law of the LORD, and to teaching its decrees and laws in Israel.

Obeying the Law
READ EZRA 7:1–12, 25–26

Artaxerxes, king of Persia, told Ezra, "Whoever does not obey the law of your God and the law of the king must surely be punished by death . . . or imprisonment" (verse 26). Yikes, they didn't mess around! Like Ezra, one day you may be in a position of authority as a policeman, judge or politician. If so, your full-time job will be enforcing what's right and punishing what's wrong. But Romans 13 tells us that keeping order in society is not just a job for authorities. It's everyone's responsibility. You may think it's OK to break one little law, but don't do it (unless, of course, the government tells you to do something contrary to God's Word). The whole setup of laws and punishments comes from God. Why? Because obeying the law makes society work better. So take responsibility for your actions and obey the rules. This starts at home by obeying your parents.

Your next reading is on page 594.

King Artaxerxes' Letter to Ezra

¹¹This is a copy of the letter King Artaxerxes had given to Ezra the priest and teacher, a man learned in matters concerning the commands and decrees of the LORD for Israel:

¹²ᵃ Artaxerxes, king of kings,

To Ezra the priest, a teacher of the Law of the God of heaven:

Greetings.

¹³Now I decree that any of the Israelites in my kingdom, including priests and Levites, who wish to go to Jerusalem with you, may go. ¹⁴You are sent by the king and his seven advisers to inquire about Judah and Jerusalem with regard to the Law of your God, which is in your hand. ¹⁵Moreover, you are to take with you the silver and gold that the king and his advisers have freely given to the God of Israel, whose dwelling is in Jerusalem, ¹⁶together with all the silver and gold you may obtain from the province of Babylon, as well as the freewill offerings of the people and priests for the temple of their God in Jerusalem. ¹⁷With this money be sure to buy bulls, rams and male lambs, together with their grain offerings and drink offerings, and sacrifice them on the altar of the temple of your God in Jerusalem.

¹⁸You and your brother Jews may then do whatever seems best with the rest of the silver and gold, in accordance with the will of your God. ¹⁹Deliver to the God of Jerusalem all the articles entrusted to you for worship in the temple of your God. ²⁰And anything else needed for the temple of your God that you may have occasion to supply, you may provide from the royal treasury.

²¹Now I, King Artaxerxes, order all the treasurers of Trans-Euphrates to provide with diligence whatever Ezra the priest, a teacher of the Law of the God of heaven, may ask of you— ²²up to a hundred talentsᵇ of silver, a hundred corsᶜ of wheat, a hundred bathsᵈ of wine, a hundred bathsᵈ of olive oil, and salt without limit. ²³Whatever the God of heaven has prescribed, let it be done with diligence for the temple of the God of heaven. Why should there be wrath against the realm of the king and of his sons? ²⁴You are also to know that you have no authority to impose taxes, tribute or duty on any of the priests, Levites, singers, gatekeepers, temple servants or other workers at this house of God.

²⁵And you, Ezra, in accordance with the wisdom of your God, which you possess, appoint magistrates and judges to administer justice to all the people of Trans-Euphrates—all who know the laws of your God. And you are to teach any who do not know them. ²⁶Whoever does not obey the law of your God and the law of the king must surely be punished by death, banishment, confiscation of property, or imprisonment.

²⁷Praise be to the LORD, the God of our fathers, who has put it into the king's heart to bring honor to the house of the LORD in Jerusalem in this way ²⁸and who has extended his good favor to me before the king and his advisers and all the king's powerful officials. Because the hand of the LORD my God was on me, I took courage and gathered leading men from Israel to go up with me.

List of the Family Heads Returning With Ezra

8 These are the family heads and those registered with them who came up with me from Babylon during the reign of King Artaxerxes: ²of the descendants of Phinehas, Gershom;

of the descendants of Ithamar, Daniel;

of the descendants of David, Hattush ³of the descendants of Shecaniah;

of the descendants of Parosh, Zechariah, and with him were registered 150 men;

⁴of the descendants of Pahath-Moab, Eliehoenai son of Zerahiah, and with him 200 men;

ᵃ 12 The text of Ezra 7:12–26 is in Aramaic.   ᵇ 22 That is, about 3 3/4 tons (about 3.4 metric tons)   ᶜ 22 That is, probably about 600 bushels (about 22 kiloliters)   ᵈ 22 That is, probably about 600 gallons (about 2.2 kiloliters)

5 of the descendants of Zattu,[a] Shecaniah son of Jahaziel, and with him 300 men;

6 of the descendants of Adin, Ebed son of Jonathan, and with him 50 men;

7 of the descendants of Elam, Jeshaiah son of Athaliah, and with him 70 men;

8 of the descendants of Shephatiah, Zebadiah son of Michael, and with him 80 men;

9 of the descendants of Joab, Obadiah son of Jehiel, and with him 218 men;

10 of the descendants of Bani,[b] Shelomith son of Josiphiah, and with him 160 men;

11 of the descendants of Bebai, Zechariah son of Bebai, and with him 28 men;

12 of the descendants of Azgad, Johanan son of Hakkatan, and with him 110 men;

13 of the descendants of Adonikam, the last ones, whose names were Eliphelet, Jeuel and Shemaiah, and with them 60 men;

14 of the descendants of Bigvai, Uthai and Zaccur, and with them 70 men.

The Return to Jerusalem

15 I assembled them at the canal that flows toward Ahava, and we camped there three days. When I checked among the people and the priests, I found no Levites there. 16 So I summoned Eliezer, Ariel, Shemaiah, Elnathan, Jarib, Elnathan, Nathan, Zechariah and Meshullam, who were leaders, and Joiarib and Elnathan, who were men of learning, 17 and I sent them to Iddo, the leader in Casiphia. I told them what to say to Iddo and his kinsmen, the temple servants in Casiphia, so that they might bring attendants to us for the house of our God. 18 Because the gracious hand of our God was on us, they brought us Sherebiah, a capable man, from the descendants of Mahli son of Levi, the son of Israel, and Sherebiah's sons and brothers, 18 men; 19 and Hashabiah, together with Jeshaiah from the descendants of Merari, and his brothers and nephews, 20 men. 20 They also brought 220 of the temple servants—a body that David and the officials had established to assist the Levites. All were registered by name.

21 There, by the Ahava Canal, I proclaimed a fast, so that we might humble ourselves before our God and ask him for a safe journey for us and our children, with all our possessions. 22 I was ashamed to ask the king for soldiers and horsemen to protect us from enemies on the road, because we had told the king, "The gracious hand of our God is on everyone who looks to him, but his great anger is against all who forsake him." 23 So we fasted and petitioned our God about this, and he answered our prayer.

24 Then I set apart twelve of the leading priests, together with Sherebiah, Hashabiah and ten of their

Get a Load of This...

These names may have been common names back then, but some of them, like Hattush (Ezra 8:3), sound funny today. (Knock knock. Who's there? Hattush. Hattush-who? Hey! Don't sneeze on me!)

---

a 5 Some Septuagint manuscripts (also 1 Esdras 8:32); Hebrew does not have *Zattu.*   b 10 Some Septuagint manuscripts (also 1 Esdras 8:36); Hebrew does not have *Bani.*

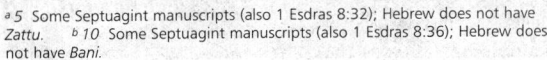

brothers, 25and I weighed out to them the offering of silver and gold and the articles that the king, his advisers, his officials and all Israel present there had donated for the house of our God. 26I weighed out to them 650 talents*a* of silver, silver articles weighing 100 talents,*b* 100 talents*b* of gold, 2720 bowls of gold valued at 1,000 darics,*c* and two fine articles of polished bronze, as precious as gold.

28I said to them, "You as well as these articles are consecrated to the Lord. The silver and gold are a freewill offering to the Lord, the God of your fathers. 29Guard them carefully until you weigh them out in the chambers of the house of the Lord in Jerusalem before the leading priests and the Levites and the family heads of Israel." 30Then the priests and Levites received the silver and gold and sacred articles that had been weighed out to be taken to the house of our God in Jerusalem.

31On the twelfth day of the first month we set out from the Ahava Canal to go to Jerusalem. The hand of our God was on us, and he protected us from enemies and bandits along the way. 32So we arrived in Jerusalem, where we rested three days.

33On the fourth day, in the house of our God, we weighed out the silver and gold and the sacred articles into the hands of Meremoth son of Uriah, the priest. Eleazar son of Phinehas was with him, and so were the Levites Jozabad son of Jeshua and Noadiah son of Binnui. 34Everything was accounted for by number and weight, and the entire weight was recorded at that time.

35Then the exiles who had returned from captivity sacrificed burnt offerings to the God of Israel: twelve bulls for all Israel, ninety-six rams, seventy-seven male lambs and, as a sin offering, twelve male goats. All this was a burnt offering to the Lord. 36They also delivered the king's orders to the royal satraps and to the governors of Trans-Euphrates, who then gave assistance to the people and to the house of God.

a 26 That is, about 25 tons (about 22 metric tons)
b 26 That is, about 3 3/4 tons (about 3.4 metric tons)
c 27 That is, about 19 pounds (about 8.5 kilograms)

A Major Long Journey
READ EZRA 1

Can you imagine you and your whole school (or a couple of schools) walking across two whole states (like from Ohio to Wisconsin)? Hey, it's one thing to watch those survival shows on TV, it's quite another to tie your boots up and do it! Take Ezra. He led a couple thousand people on a trip from Babylon to Jerusalem (their Jewish homeland). They traveled about 900 miles, and in those days everybody had to walk! Before they left, they prayed to God for his protection (see verses 21–22). And God gave it (see verse 31). How cool is that? Who knows if you'll ever take a 900-mile hike. But don't wait to ask God for protection just during those "extreme" times in your life. Try asking him in the middle of a normal day, like before you study, before a big game or when you go out with your friends. God is only a prayer away. He'd love to hear from you!

Your next reading is on page 596.

Ezra's Prayer About Intermarriage

After these things had been done, the leaders came to me and said, "The people of Israel, including the priests and the Levites, have not kept themselves separate from the neighboring peoples with their detestable practices, like those of the Canaanites, Hittites, Perizzites, Jebusites, Ammonites, Moabites, Egyptians and Amorites. ²They have taken some of their daughters as wives for themselves and their sons, and have mingled the holy race with the peoples around them. And the leaders and officials have led the way in this unfaithfulness."

³When I heard this, I tore my tunic and cloak, pulled hair from my head and beard and sat down appalled. ⁴Then everyone who trembled at the words of the God of Israel gathered around me because of this unfaithfulness of the exiles. And I sat there appalled until the evening sacrifice.

⁵Then, at the evening sacrifice, I rose from my self-abasement, with my tunic and cloak torn, and fell on my knees with my hands spread out to the LORD my God ⁶and prayed:

"O my God, I am too ashamed and disgraced to lift up my face to you, my God, because our sins are higher than our heads and our guilt has reached to the heavens. ⁷From the days of our forefathers until now, our guilt has been great. Because of our sins, we and our kings and our priests have been subjected to the sword and captivity, to pillage and humiliation at the hand of foreign kings, as it is today.

⁸"But now, for a brief moment, the LORD our God has been gracious in leaving us a remnant and giving us a firm place in his sanctuary, and so our God gives light to our eyes and a little relief in our bondage. ⁹Though we are slaves, our God has not deserted

Make It Stick

READ EZRA 9:9–10

Like the Jewish exiles, sometimes after we've been forgiven for a mistake, we forget how rough our punishment was. Write down one dumb thing you've done as a reminder not to do it again.

us in our bondage. He has shown us kindness in the sight of the kings of Persia: He has granted us new life to rebuild the house of our God and repair its ruins, and he has given us a wall of protection in Judah and Jerusalem.

¹⁰"But now, O our God, what can we say after this? For we have disregarded the commands ¹¹you gave through your servants the prophets when you said: 'The land you are entering to possess is a land polluted by the corruption of its peoples. By their detestable practices they have filled it with their impurity from one end to the other. ¹²Therefore, do not give your daughters in marriage to their sons or take their daughters for your sons. Do not seek a treaty of friendship with them at any time, that you may be strong and eat the good things of the land and leave it to your children as an everlasting inheritance.'

¹³"What has happened to us is a result of our evil deeds and our great guilt, and yet, our God, you have punished us less than our sins have deserved and have given us a remnant like this. ¹⁴Shall we again break your commands and intermarry with the peoples who commit such detestable practices? Would you not be angry enough with us to destroy us, leaving us no remnant or survivor? ¹⁵O LORD, God of Israel, you are righteous! We are left this day as a remnant. Here we are before you in our guilt, though because of it not one of us can stand in your presence."

The People's Confession of Sin

10 While Ezra was praying and confessing, weeping and throwing himself down before the house of God, a large crowd of Israelites—men, women and children—gathered around him. They too wept bitterly. ²Then Shecaniah son of Jehiel, one of the descendants of Elam, said to Ezra, "We

---

Part of the Solution

READ EZRA 10:1–17

Sometimes you might think it's OK to do something wrong as long as it's "not hurting anyone else." But you're part of a community and your attitude affects others, so it's impossible not to hurt someone else when you sin. For example, if enough people in society do something wrong—such as buying magazines or hitting websites that promote immorality—often society's laws change and make that sin "legal." So don't be part of the problem. Another thing: If you get in the habit of doing wrong, like pocketing things that aren't yours, it takes a bit of doing to make things right. The Israelites had disobeyed God big time, and confessed, "This matter cannot be taken care of in a day or two, because we have sinned greatly in this thing" (verse 13). Don't go against God's law or you'll hurt yourself and others who follow your example. Obey God and be part of the solution.

Your next reading is on page 601.

have been unfaithful to our God by marrying foreign women from the peoples
around us. But in spite of this, there is still
hope for Israel. ³Now let us make a covenant before our God to send away all
these women and their children, in accordance with the counsel of my lord and of
those who fear the commands of our
God. Let it be done according to the Law.
⁴Rise up; this matter is in your hands. We
will support you, so take courage and
do it."

⁵So Ezra rose up and put the leading
priests and Levites and all Israel under
oath to do what had been suggested.
And they took the oath. ⁶Then Ezra withdrew from before the house of God and
went to the room of Jehohanan son of Eliashib. While he was there, he ate no food
and drank no water, because he continued to mourn over the unfaithfulness of
the exiles.

⁷A proclamation was then issued
throughout Judah and Jerusalem for all the
exiles to assemble in Jerusalem. ⁸Anyone
who failed to appear within three days
would forfeit all his property, in accordance
with the decision of the officials and elders,
and would himself be expelled from the assembly of the exiles.

⁹Within the three days, all the men of
Judah and Benjamin had gathered in Jerusalem. And on the twentieth day of the
ninth month, all the people were sitting in
the square before the house of God, greatly distressed by the occasion and because
of the rain. ¹⁰Then Ezra the priest stood up
and said to them, "You have been unfaithful; you have married foreign women,
adding to Israel's guilt. ¹¹Now make confession to the Lᴏʀᴅ, the God of your fathers, and do his will. Separate yourselves
from the peoples around you and from
your foreign wives."

¹²The whole assembly responded with
a loud voice: "You are right! We must do
as you say. ¹³But there are many people
here and it is the rainy season; so we cannot stand outside. Besides, this matter
cannot be taken care of in a day or two,
because we have sinned greatly in this
thing. ¹⁴Let our officials act for the whole
assembly. Then let everyone in our towns
who has married a foreign woman come
at a set time, along with the elders and
judges of each town, until the fierce anger

of our God in this matter is turned away
from us." ¹⁵Only Jonathan son of Asahel
and Jahzeiah son of Tikvah, supported by
Meshullam and Shabbethai the Levite, opposed this.

¹⁶So the exiles did as was proposed.
Ezra the priest selected men who were
family heads, one from each family division, and all of them designated by name.
On the first day of the tenth month they
sat down to investigate the cases, ¹⁷and
by the first day of the first month they finished dealing with all the men who had
married foreign women.

Those Guilty of Intermarriage

¹⁸Among the descendants of the
priests, the following had married
foreign women:

From the descendants of Jeshua son
of Jozadak, and his brothers: Maaseiah, Eliezer, Jarib and Gedaliah.
¹⁹(They all gave their hands in
pledge to put away their wives,
and for their guilt they each presented a ram from the flock as a
guilt offering.)
²⁰From the descendants of Immer:
Hanani and Zebadiah.
²¹From the descendants of Harim:
Maaseiah, Elijah, Shemaiah, Jehiel
and Uzziah.
²²From the descendants of Pashhur:
Elioenai, Maaseiah, Ishmael, Nethanel, Jozabad and Elasah.

²³Among the Levites:

Jozabad, Shimei, Kelaiah (that is,
Kelita), Pethahiah, Judah and Elie-
zer.
²⁴From the singers:
Eliashib.
From the gatekeepers:
Shallum, Telem and Uri.

²⁵And among the other Israelites:

From the descendants of Parosh:
Ramiah, Izziah, Malkijah, Mijamin,
Eleazar, Malkijah and Benaiah.
²⁶From the descendants of Elam:
Mattaniah, Zechariah, Jehiel, Abdi,
Jeremoth and Elijah.
²⁷From the descendants of Zattu:
Elioenai, Eliashib, Mattaniah, Jere-
moth, Zabad and Aziza.
²⁸From the descendants of Bebai:

Get a Load of This...

Check out Ezra 10:3. It was rough to send away their foreign, pagan wives, but God had absolutely, flat-out forbidden the Israelites to marry them in the first place. Pagan wives almost always led Israelite men into idol-worship. God wants our closest relationships in life to be with fellow believers.

Jehohanan, Hananiah, Zabbai and Athlai.
²⁹ From the descendants of Bani:
Meshullam, Malluch, Adaiah, Jashub, Sheal and Jeremoth.
³⁰ From the descendants of Pahath-Moab:
Adna, Kelal, Benaiah, Maaseiah, Mattaniah, Bezalel, Binnui and Manasseh.
³¹ From the descendants of Harim:
Eliezer, Ishijah, Malkijah, Shemaiah, Shimeon, ³² Benjamin, Malluch and Shemariah.
³³ From the descendants of Hashum:
Mattenai, Mattattah, Zabad, Eliphelet, Jeremai, Manasseh and Shimei.
³⁴ From the descendants of Bani:
Maadai, Amram, Uel, ³⁵ Benaiah, Bedeiah, Keluhi, ³⁶ Vaniah, Meremoth, Eliashib, ³⁷ Mattaniah, Mattenai and Jaasu.
³⁸ From the descendants of Binnui:^a
Shimei, ³⁹ Shelemiah, Nathan, Adaiah, ⁴⁰ Macnadebai, Shashai, Sharai, ⁴¹ Azarel, Shelemiah, Shemariah, ⁴² Shallum, Amariah and Joseph.
⁴³ From the descendants of Nebo:
Jeiel, Mattithiah, Zabad, Zebina, Jaddai, Joel and Benaiah.

⁴⁴ All these had married foreign women, and some of them had children by these wives.^b

---

^a 37,38 See Septuagint (also 1 Esdras 9:34); Hebrew *Jaasu* ³⁸*and Bani and Binnui,*
^b 44 Or *and they sent them away with their children*

NEHEMIAH

Who wrote this book?

The author of Nehemiah is unknown. Many people think the book was written by Ezra.

Why was this book written?

The book of Nehemiah tells how God used Nehemiah to rebuild the walls of Jerusalem.

What happens in this book?

Nehemiah is made governor of Judah. He has the Jews rebuild the city walls. Nehemiah also makes the people of Judah stop sinning.

What do we learn about God in this book?

God wants his people to be courageous and keep on doing his work.

Who is important in this book?

The important person in this book is Nehemiah.

When did this happen?

The events of this book happened between 444 and 430 B.C.

What are some of the stories in this book?

The walls are rebuilt   Nehemiah 3
Nehemiah helps the poor   Nehemiah 5
Opposition to the rebuilding   Nehemiah 6
Ezra reads God's law   Nehemiah 8
The Israelites confess their sins   Nehemiah 9
Nehemiah asks to be remembered   Nehemiah 13

Get a Load of This...

Nehemiah's job as "cupbearer" (Nehemiah 1:11) was to taste the king's wine before passing the cup to the king, to make sure it hadn't been poisoned by an enemy. It's a good thing the wine was never poisoned; otherwise we wouldn't have the book of Nehemiah.

Nehemiah's Prayer

1 The words of Nehemiah son of Hacaliah:

In the month of Kislev in the twentieth year, while I was in the citadel of Susa, ²Hanani, one of my brothers, came from Judah with some other men, and I questioned them about the Jewish remnant that survived the exile, and also about Jerusalem.

³They said to me, "Those who survived the exile and are back in the province are in great trouble and disgrace. The wall of Jerusalem is broken down, and its gates have been burned with fire."

⁴When I heard these things, I sat down and wept. For some days I mourned and fasted and prayed before the God of heaven. ⁵Then I said:

"O LORD, God of heaven, the great and awesome God, who keeps his covenant of love with those who love him and obey his commands, ⁶let your ear be attentive and your eyes open to hear the prayer your servant is praying before you day and night for your servants, the people of Israel. I confess the sins we Israelites, including myself and my father's house, have committed against you. ⁷We have acted very wickedly toward you. We have not obeyed the commands, decrees and laws you gave your servant Moses.

⁸"Remember the instruction you gave your servant Moses, saying, 'If you are unfaithful, I will scatter you among the nations, ⁹but if you return to me and obey my commands, then even if your exiled people are at the farthest horizon, I will gather them from there and bring them to the place I have chosen as a dwelling for my Name.'

¹⁰"They are your servants and your people, whom you redeemed by your great strength and your mighty hand. ¹¹O Lord, let your ear be attentive to the prayer of this your servant and to the prayer of your servants who delight in revering your name. Give your servant success today by granting him favor in the presence of this man."

I was cupbearer to the king.

Artaxerxes Sends Nehemiah to Jerusalem

2 In the month of Nisan in the twentieth year of King Artaxerxes, when wine was brought for him, I took the wine and gave it to the king. I had not been sad in his presence before; ²so the king asked me, "Why does your face look so sad when you are not ill? This can be nothing but sadness of heart."

I was very much afraid, ³but I said to the king, "May the king live forever! Why should my face not look sad when the city where my fathers are buried lies in ruins, and its gates have been destroyed by fire?"

⁴The king said to me, "What is it you want?"

Then I prayed to the God of heaven, ⁵and I answered

the king, "If it pleases the king and if your servant has found favor in his sight, let him send me to the city in Judah where my fathers are buried so that I can rebuild it."

6Then the king, with the queen sitting beside him, asked me, "How long will your journey take, and when will you get back?" It pleased the king to send me; so I set a time.

7I also said to him, "If it pleases the king, may I have letters to the governors of Trans-Euphrates, so that they will provide me safe-conduct until I arrive in Judah? 8And may I have a letter to Asaph, keeper of the king's forest, so he will give me timber to make beams for the gates of the citadel by the temple and for the city wall and for the residence I will occupy?" And because the gracious hand of my God was upon me, the king granted my requests. 9So I went to the governors of Trans-Euphrates and gave them the king's letters. The king had also sent army officers and cavalry with me.

10When Sanballat the Horonite and Tobiah the Ammonite official heard about this, they were very much disturbed that someone had come to promote the welfare of the Israelites.

Nehemiah Inspects Jerusalem's Walls

11I went to Jerusalem, and after staying there three days 12I set out during the night with a few men. I had not told anyone what my God had put in my heart to do for Jerusalem. There were no mounts with me except the one I was riding on.

13By night I went out through the Valley Gate toward the Jackal[a] Well and the Dung Gate, examining the walls of Jerusalem, which had been broken down, and its gates, which had been destroyed by fire. 14Then I moved on toward the Fountain Gate and the King's Pool, but there was not enough room for my mount to get through; 15so I went up the valley by night, examining the wall. Finally, I turned back and reentered through the Valley Gate. 16The officials did not know where I had gone or what I was doing, because as yet I had said nothing to the Jews or the

[a] 13 Or *Serpent* or *Fig*

Everyone Pitching In

READ NEHEMIAH 2:11–18; 3:1–2, 28–32

Big jobs can get done in no time when everyone pitches in. Rebuilding Jerusalem's walls was all about teamwork. It would've taken forever if most of the guys had just snoozed in the shade. We *all* need to do our part in God's work. Even *important* people like lawyers, doctors and professional athletes shouldn't be excused from setting up chairs in church or feeding street people in a soup kitchen. So why should *we*? Sure, you might work hard at school and at an after-school job, but you still need to help out in your church and community—*and* at home! It's pathetic to say: "I went to school and did my paper route, so I shouldn't have to do the dishes, take out the trash, mow the lawn or even pick up my clothes." A man of God doesn't expect others to wait on him. He's a team player. He does his part.

Your next reading is on page 604.

priests or nobles or officials or any others who would be doing the work.

¹⁷Then I said to them, "You see the trouble we are in: Jerusalem lies in ruins, and its gates have been burned with fire. Come, let us rebuild the wall of Jerusalem, and we will no longer be in disgrace." ¹⁸I also told them about the gracious hand of my God upon me and what the king had said to me.

They replied, "Let us start rebuilding." So they began this good work.

¹⁹But when Sanballat the Horonite, Tobiah the Ammonite official and Geshem the Arab heard about it, they mocked and ridiculed us. "What is this you are doing?" they asked. "Are you rebelling against the king?"

²⁰I answered them by saying, "The God of heaven will give us success. We his servants will start rebuilding, but as for you, you have no share in Jerusalem or any claim or historic right to it."

Builders of the Wall

3 Eliashib the high priest and his fellow priests went to work and rebuilt the Sheep Gate. They dedicated it and set its doors in place, building as far as the Tower of the Hundred, which they dedicated, and as far as the Tower of Hananel. ²The men of Jericho built the adjoining section, and Zaccur son of Imri built next to them.

³The Fish Gate was rebuilt by the sons of Hassenaah. They laid its beams and put its doors and bolts and bars in place. ⁴Meremoth son of Uriah, the son of Hakkoz, repaired the next section. Next to him Meshullam son of Berekiah, the son of Meshezabel, made repairs, and next to him Zadok son of Baana also made repairs. ⁵The next section was repaired by the men of Tekoa, but their nobles would not put their shoulders to the work under their supervisors.^a

⁶The Jeshanah^b Gate was repaired by Joiada son of Paseah and Meshullam son of Besodeiah. They laid its beams and put its doors and bolts and bars in place. ⁷Next to them, repairs were made by men from Gibeon and Mizpah—Melatiah of Gibeon and Jadon of Meronoth—places under the authority of the governor of Trans-Euphrates. ⁸Uzziel son of Harhaiah, one of the goldsmiths, repaired the next

section; and Hananiah, one of the perfume-makers, made repairs next to that. They restored^c Jerusalem as far as the Broad Wall. ⁹Rephaiah son of Hur, ruler of a half-district of Jerusalem, repaired the next section. ¹⁰Adjoining this, Jedaiah son of Harumaph made repairs opposite his house, and Hattush son of Hashabneiah made repairs next to him. ¹¹Malkijah son of Harim and Hasshub son of Pahath-Moab repaired another section and the Tower of the Ovens. ¹²Shallum son of Hallohesh, ruler of a half-district of Jerusalem, repaired the next section with the help of his daughters.

¹³The Valley Gate was repaired by Hanun and the residents of Zanoah. They rebuilt it and put its doors and bolts and bars in place. They also repaired five hundred yards^d of the wall as far as the Dung Gate.

¹⁴The Dung Gate was repaired by Malkijah son of Recab, ruler of the district of Beth Hakkerem. He rebuilt it and put its doors and bolts and bars in place.

¹⁵The Fountain Gate was repaired by Shallun son of Col-Hozeh, ruler of the district of Mizpah. He rebuilt it, roofing it over and putting its doors and bolts and bars in place. He also repaired the wall of the Pool of Siloam,^e by the King's Garden, as far as the steps going down from the City of David. ¹⁶Beyond him, Nehemiah son of Azbuk, ruler of a half-district of Beth Zur, made repairs up to a point opposite the tombs^f of David, as far as the artificial pool and the House of the Heroes.

¹⁷Next to him, the repairs were made by the Levites under Rehum son of Bani. Beside him, Hashabiah, ruler of half the district of Keilah, carried out repairs for his district. ¹⁸Next to him, the repairs were made by their countrymen under Binnui^g son of Henadad, ruler of the other half-district of Keilah. ¹⁹Next to him, Ezer son of Jeshua, ruler of Mizpah, repaired another section, from a point facing the ascent to the armory as far as the angle. ²⁰Next to him, Baruch son of Zabbai zeal-

---

^a 5 Or their Lord or the governor   ^b 6 Or Old
^c 8 Or They left out part of   ^d 13 Hebrew a thousand cubits
(about 450 meters)   ^e 15 Hebrew Shelah, a variant of
Shiloah, that is, Siloam   ^f 16 Hebrew; Septuagint, some
Vulgate manuscripts and Syriac tomb   ^g 18 Two Hebrew
manuscripts and Syriac (see also Septuagint and verse 24);
most Hebrew manuscripts Bavvai

ously repaired another section, from the angle to the entrance of the house of Eliashib the high priest. [21]Next to him, Meremoth son of Uriah, the son of Hakkoz, repaired another section, from the entrance of Eliashib's house to the end of it. [22]The repairs next to him were made by the priests from the surrounding region. [23]Beyond them, Benjamin and Hasshub made repairs in front of their house; and next to them, Azariah son of Maaseiah, the son of Ananiah, made repairs beside his house. [24]Next to him, Binnui son of Henadad repaired another section, from Azariah's house to the angle and the corner, [25]and Palal son of Uzai worked opposite the angle and the tower projecting from the upper palace near the court of the guard. Next to him, Pedaiah son of Parosh [26]and the temple servants living on the hill of Ophel made repairs up to a point opposite the Water Gate toward the east and the projecting tower. [27]Next to them, the men of Tekoa repaired another section, from the great projecting tower to the wall of Ophel.

[28]Above the Horse Gate, the priests made repairs, each in front of his own house. [29]Next to them, Zadok son of Immer made repairs opposite his house. Next to him, Shemaiah son of Shecaniah, the guard at the East Gate, made repairs. [30]Next to him, Hananiah son of Shelemiah, and Hanun, the sixth son of Zalaph, repaired another section. Next to them, Meshullam son of Berekiah made repairs opposite his living quarters. [31]Next to him, Malkijah, one of the goldsmiths, made repairs as far as the house of the temple servants and the merchants, opposite the Inspection Gate, and as far as the room above the corner; [32]and between the room above the corner and the Sheep Gate the goldsmiths and merchants made repairs.

Opposition to the Rebuilding

When Sanballat heard that we were rebuilding the wall, he became angry and was greatly incensed. He ridiculed the Jews, [2]and in the presence of his associates and the army of Samaria, he said, "What are those feeble Jews doing? Will they restore their wall? Will they offer sacrifices? Will they finish in a day? Can they bring the stones back to life from those heaps of rubble—burned as they are?"

[3]Tobiah the Ammonite, who was at his side, said, "What they are building—if even a fox climbed up on it, he would break down their wall of stones!"

[4]Hear us, O our God, for we are despised. Turn their insults back on their own heads. Give them over as plunder in a land of captivity. [5]Do not cover up their guilt or blot out their sins from your sight, for they have thrown insults in the face of[a] the builders.

[6]So we rebuilt the wall till all of it reached half its height, for the people worked with all their heart.

[7]But when Sanballat, Tobiah, the Arabs, the Ammonites and the men of Ashdod heard that the repairs to Jerusalem's walls had gone ahead and that the gaps were being closed, they were very angry. [8]They all plotted together to come and fight against Jerusalem and stir up trouble against it. [9]But we prayed to our God and posted a guard day and night to meet this threat.

[10]Meanwhile, the people in Judah said, "The strength of the laborers is giving out, and there is so much rubble that we cannot rebuild the wall."

[11]Also our enemies said, "Before they know it or see us, we will be right there among them and will kill them and put an end to the work."

[12]Then the Jews who lived near them came and told us ten times over, "Wherever you turn, they will attack us."

[13]Therefore I stationed some of the people behind the lowest points of the wall at the exposed places, posting them by families, with their swords, spears and bows. [14]After I looked things over, I stood up and said to the nobles, the officials and the rest of the people, "Don't be afraid of them. Remember the Lord, who is great and awesome, and fight for your brothers, your sons and your daughters, your wives and your homes."

[15]When our enemies heard that we were aware of their plot and that God had frustrated it, we all returned to the wall, each to his own work.

[16]From that day on, half of my men did the work, while the other half were

---

a 5 Or *have provoked you to anger before*

equipped with spears, shields, bows and armor. The officers posted themselves behind all the people of Judah [17]who were building the wall. Those who carried materials did their work with one hand and held a weapon in the other, [18]and each of the builders wore his sword at his side as he worked. But the man who sounded the trumpet stayed with me.

[19]Then I said to the nobles, the officials and the rest of the people, "The work is extensive and spread out, and we are widely separated from each other along the wall. [20]Wherever you hear the sound of the trumpet, join us there. Our God will fight for us!"

[21]So we continued the work with half the men holding spears, from the first light of dawn till the stars came out. [22]At that time I also said to the people, "Have every man and his helper stay inside Jerusalem at night, so they can serve us as guards by night and workmen by day." [23]Neither I nor my brothers nor my men nor the guards with me took off our clothes; each had his weapon, even when he went for water.[a]

Nehemiah Helps the Poor

5 Now the men and their wives raised a great outcry against their Jewish brothers. [2]Some were saying, "We and our sons and daughters are numerous; in order for us to eat and stay alive, we must get grain."

[3]Others were saying, "We are mortgaging our fields, our vineyards and our homes to get grain during the famine."

[4]Still others were saying, "We have had to borrow money to pay the king's tax on our fields and vineyards. [5]Although we are of the same flesh and blood as our countrymen and though our sons are as good as theirs, yet we have to subject our sons and daughters to slavery. Some of our daughters have already been enslaved, but we are powerless, because our fields and our vineyards belong to others."

[a] 23 The meaning of the Hebrew for this clause is uncertain.

GET STRONGER.

Sanballat Sandblaster

READ NEHEMIAH 4

It's hard to do a good job while someone is laying on the peer pressure and threatening you. Just when the Jews started to get their hands dirty rebuilding the wall, Sanballat (the "Sandblaster") and his buddies tried to intimidate them to make them quit. When someone intimidates you, they get really loud, push you around (especially if you're smaller than they are) or glare at you. They try to get you to obey them by making you afraid to stand up to them. But threatening people is for losers. As a man of God, you can have an inner strength so you won't need to intimidate others or push your opinions on them. Even when you disagree with people, you can still treat them with respect. Proverbs 17:27 says, "A man of knowledge uses words with restraint." So take a tip: don't be a sandblaster.

Your next reading is on page 606.

6When I heard their outcry and these charges, I was very angry. 7I pondered them in my mind and then accused the nobles and officials. I told them, "You are exacting usury from your own countrymen!" So I called together a large meeting to deal with them 8and said: "As far as possible, we have bought back our Jewish brothers who were sold to the Gentiles. Now you are selling your brothers, only for them to be sold back to us!" They kept quiet, because they could find nothing to say.

9So I continued, "What you are doing is not right. Shouldn't you walk in the fear of our God to avoid the reproach of our Gentile enemies? 10I and my brothers and my men are also lending the people money and grain. But let the exacting of usury stop! 11Give back to them immediately their fields, vineyards, olive groves and houses, and also the usury you are charging them—the hundredth part of the money, grain, new wine and oil."

12"We will give it back," they said. "And we will not demand anything more from them. We will do as you say."

Then I summoned the priests and made the nobles and officials take an oath to do what they had promised. 13I also shook out the folds of my robe and said, "In this way may God shake out of his house and possessions every man who does not keep this promise. So may such a man be shaken out and emptied!"

At this the whole assembly said, "Amen," and praised the LORD. And the people did as they had promised.

14Moreover, from the twentieth year of King Artaxerxes, when I was appointed to be their governor in the land of Judah, until his thirty-second year—twelve years—neither I nor my brothers ate the food allotted to the governor. 15But the earlier governors—those preceding me—placed a heavy burden on the people and took forty shekels*a* of silver from them in addition to food and wine. Their assistants also lorded it over the people. But out of reverence for God I did not act like that. 16Instead, I devoted myself to the work on this wall. All my men were assembled there for the work; we*b* did not acquire any land.

17Furthermore, a hundred and fifty Jews and officials ate at my table, as well as those who came to us from the sur-

rounding nations. 18Each day one ox, six choice sheep and some poultry were prepared for me, and every ten days an abundant supply of wine of all kinds. In spite of all this, I never demanded the food allotted to the governor, because the demands were heavy on these people.

19Remember me with favor, O my God, for all I have done for these people.

Further Opposition to the Rebuilding

6 When word came to Sanballat, Tobiah, Geshem the Arab and the rest of our enemies that I had rebuilt the wall and not a gap was left in it—though up to that time I had not set the doors in the gates— 2Sanballat and Geshem sent me this message: "Come, let us meet together in one of the villages*c* on the plain of Ono."

But they were scheming to harm me; 3so I sent messengers to them with this reply: "I am carrying on a great project and cannot go down. Why should the work stop while I leave it and go down to you?" 4Four times they sent me the same message, and each time I gave them the same answer.

5Then, the fifth time, Sanballat sent his aide to me with the same message, and in his hand was an unsealed letter 6in which was written:

"It is reported among the nations—and Geshem*d* says it is true—that you and the Jews are plotting to revolt, and therefore you are building the wall. Moreover, according to these reports you are about to become their king 7and have even appointed prophets to make this proclamation about you in Jerusalem: 'There is a king in Judah!' Now this report will get back to the king; so come, let us confer together."

8I sent him this reply: "Nothing like what you are saying is happening; you are just making it up out of your head."

9They were all trying to frighten us, thinking, "Their hands will get too weak for the work, and it will not be completed."

ˌBut I prayed,ˌ "Now strengthen my hands."

a 15 That is, about 1 pound (about 0.5 kilogram)
b 16 Most Hebrew manuscripts; some Hebrew manuscripts, Septuagint, Vulgate and Syriac *I*   *c 2* Or *in Kephirim*
d 6 Hebrew *Gashmu*, a variant of *Geshem*

¹⁰One day I went to the house of Shemaiah son of Delaiah, the son of Mehetabel, who was shut in at his home. He said, "Let us meet in the house of God, inside the temple, and let us close the temple doors, because men are coming to kill you—by night they are coming to kill you."

¹¹But I said, "Should a man like me run away? Or should one like me go into the temple to save his life? I will not go!" ¹²I realized that God had not sent him, but that he had prophesied against me because Tobiah and Sanballat had hired him. ¹³He had been hired to intimidate me so that I would commit a sin by doing this, and then they would give me a bad name to discredit me.

¹⁴Remember Tobiah and Sanballat, O my God, because of what they have done; remember also the prophetess Noadiah and the rest of the prophets who have been trying to intimidate me.

The Completion of the Wall

¹⁵So the wall was completed on the twenty-fifth of Elul, in fifty-two days.

¹⁶When all our enemies heard about this, all the surrounding nations were afraid and lost their self-confidence, because they realized that this work had been done with the help of our God.

¹⁷Also, in those days the nobles of Judah were sending many letters to Tobiah, and replies from Tobiah kept coming to them. ¹⁸For many in Judah were under oath to him, since he was son-in-law to Shecaniah son of Arah, and his son Jehohanan had married the daughter of Meshullam son of Berekiah. ¹⁹Moreover, they kept reporting to me his good deeds and then telling him what I said. And Tobiah sent letters to intimidate me.

After the wall had been rebuilt and I had set the doors in place, the gatekeepers and the singers and the Levites were appointed. 2I put in charge of Jerusalem my brother Hanani, along with[a] Hananiah the commander of the citadel, because he was a man of integrity and feared God more than most men do. 3I said to them, "The gates of Je-

ᵃ 2 Or Hanani, that is,

Me? Chicken?

READ NEHEMIAH 6:1–16

Sanballat and his buddies just wouldn't quit. They were still trying to push Nehemiah around, even when he was putting the finishing touches on the wall. They figured if they could get him to stop working and travel to a meeting with them, they could put him out of commission. Nehemiah saw right through their scheme. He didn't give in to their threats because he knew he was doing the right thing. Sometimes other kids will use the same ancient tactics that Sanballat did. They'll call you a chicken or say, "You're not cool if you don't do things our way" or "Do it, buddy, or else!" Sometimes you have to give fools a straight answer and tell them, "No." But most of the time you can ignore them. Be like Nehemiah: He walked away from trouble and refused to cave in to pressure.

Your next reading is on page 613.

rusalem are not to be opened until the sun is hot. While the gatekeepers are still on duty, have them shut the doors and bar them. Also appoint residents of Jerusalem as guards, some at their posts and some near their own houses."

The List of the Exiles Who Returned

4Now the city was large and spacious, but there were few people in it, and the houses had not yet been rebuilt. 5So my God put it into my heart to assemble the nobles, the officials and the common people for registration by families. I found the genealogical record of those who had been the first to return. This is what I found written there:

6These are the people of the province who came up from the captivity of the exiles whom Nebuchadnezzar king of Babylon had taken captive (they returned to Jerusalem and Judah, each to his own town, 7in company with Zerubbabel, Jeshua, Nehemiah, Azariah, Raamiah, Nahamani, Mordecai, Bilshan, Mispereth, Bigvai, Nehum and Baanah):

The list of the men of Israel:

8the descendants of Parosh	2,172
9of Shephatiah	372
10of Arah	652
11of Pahath-Moab (through the line of Jeshua and Joab)	2,818
12of Elam	1,254
13of Zattu	845
14of Zaccai	760
15of Binnui	648
16of Bebai	628
17of Azgad	2,322
18of Adonikam	667
19of Bigvai	2,067
20of Adin	655
21of Ater (through Hezekiah)	98
22of Hashum	328
23of Bezai	324
24of Hariph	112
25of Gibeon	95
26the men of Bethlehem and Netophah	188
27of Anathoth	128
28of Beth Azmaveth	42
29of Kiriath Jearim, Kephirah and Beeroth	743
30of Ramah and Geba	621
31of Micmash	122
32of Bethel and Ai	123
33of the other Nebo	52
34of the other Elam	1,254
35of Harim	320
36of Jericho	345
37of Lod, Hadid and Ono	721
38of Senaah	3,930

39The priests:

the descendants of Jedaiah (through the family of Jeshua)	973
40of Immer	1,052
41of Pashhur	1,247
42of Harim	1,017

43The Levites:

the descendants of Jeshua (through Kadmiel through the line of Hodaviah)	74

44The singers:

the descendants of Asaph	148

45The gatekeepers:

the descendants of Shallum, Ater, Talmon, Akkub, Hatita and Shobai	138

46The temple servants:

the descendants of Ziha, Hasupha, Tabbaoth, 47Keros, Sia, Padon, 48Lebana, Hagaba, Shalmai, 49Hanan, Giddel, Gahar, 50Reaiah, Rezin, Nekoda, 51Gazzam, Uzza, Paseah, 52Besai, Meunim, Nephusim, 53Bakbuk, Hakupha, Harhur, 54Bazluth, Mehida, Harsha, 55Barkos, Sisera, Temah, 56Neziah and Hatipha

57The descendants of the servants of Solomon:

the descendants of Sotai, Sophereth, Perida, 58Jaala, Darkon, Giddel, 59Shephatiah, Hattil, Pokereth-Hazzebaim and Amon

60The temple servants and the descendants of the servants of Solomon	392

61The following came up from the towns of Tel Melah, Tel Harsha, Ke-

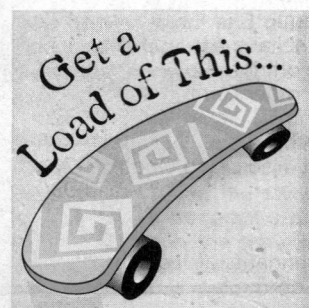

Get a Load of This...

You have to wonder about some of the names these people came up with! Take Nehemiah 7:53 for example. *Bakbuk* sounds like a name someone would give a chicken, but it means "jar." Then there's *Hakupha*; his name means "crooked." His parents must not have had high hopes for how he'd turn out!

rub, Addon and Immer, but they could not show that their families were descended from Israel:

62 the descendants of
   Delaiah, Tobiah and Nekoda   642

63 And from among the priests:

   the descendants of
      Hobaiah, Hakkoz and Barzillai (a man who had married a daughter of Barzillai the Gileadite and was called by that name).

64 These searched for their family records, but they could not find them and so were excluded from the priesthood as unclean. 65 The governor, therefore, ordered them not to eat any of the most sacred food until there should be a priest ministering with the Urim and Thummim.

66 The whole company numbered 42,360, 67 besides their 7,337 menservants and maidservants; and they also had 245 men and women singers. 68 There were 736 horses, 245 mules,[a] 69 435 camels and 6,720 donkeys.

70 Some of the heads of the families contributed to the work. The governor gave to the treasury 1,000 drachmas[b] of gold, 50 bowls and 530 garments for priests. 71 Some of the heads of the families gave to the treasury for the work 20,000 drachmas[c] of gold and 2,200 minas[d] of silver. 72 The total given by the rest of the people was 20,000 drachmas of gold, 2,000 minas[e] of silver and 67 garments for priests. 73 The priests, the Levites, the gatekeepers, the singers and the temple servants, along with certain of the people and the rest of the Israelites, settled in their own towns.

Ezra Reads the Law

When the seventh month came and the Israelites had settled in their towns, 1 all the people assembled as one man in the square before the Water Gate. They told Ezra the scribe to bring out the Book of the Law of Moses, which the LORD had commanded for Israel.

2 So on the first day of the seventh month Ezra the priest brought the Law before the assembly, which was made up of men and women and all who were able to understand. 3 He read it aloud from daybreak till noon as he faced the square before the Water Gate in the presence of the men, women and others who could understand. And all the people listened attentively to the Book of the Law.

4 Ezra the scribe stood on a high wooden platform built

---

a 68 Some Hebrew manuscripts (see also Ezra 2:66); most Hebrew manuscripts do not have this verse.   *b 70* That is, about 19 pounds (about 8.5 kilograms)
c 71 That is, about 375 pounds (about 170 kilograms); also in verse 72
d 71 That is, about 1 1/3 tons (about 1.2 metric tons)   *e 72* That is, about 1 1/4 tons (about 1.1 metric tons)

for the occasion. Beside him on his right stood Mattithiah, Shema, Anaiah, Uriah, Hilkiah and Maaseiah; and on his left were Pedaiah, Mishael, Malkijah, Hashum, Hashbaddanah, Zechariah and Meshullam.

⁵Ezra opened the book. All the people could see him because he was standing above them; and as he opened it, the people all stood up. ⁶Ezra praised the Lord, the great God; and all the people lifted their hands and responded, "Amen! Amen!" Then they bowed down and worshiped the Lord with their faces to the ground.

⁷The Levites—Jeshua, Bani, Sherebiah, Jamin, Akkub, Shabbethai, Hodiah, Maaseiah, Kelita, Azariah, Jozabad, Hanan and Pelaiah—instructed the people in the Law while the people were standing there. ⁸They read from the Book of the Law of God, making it clear[a] and giving the meaning so that the people could understand what was being read.

⁹Then Nehemiah the governor, Ezra the priest and scribe, and the Levites who were instructing the people said to them

[a] 8 Or God, translating it

Make It Stick

B _____

I _____

B _____

L _____

E _____

_____

_____

READ NEHEMIAH 8:8

The assistants to the priests read the Book of the Law, "making it clear and giving the meaning" (Nehemiah 8:8). Ask God to help you understand the Bible. Read explanatory notes in a Bible like this one, or ask an adult to explain. Use the word "BIBLE" as an acronym and write a word under each letter. Example: Believing In Big Lessons Everywhere.

Do you start to get antsy if the pastor goes on preaching for an extra fifteen minutes? Ho! Try sitting in church *all day!* In Nehemiah 8:3, God's people had three hours of Scripture reading followed by three hours of confession and worship.

all, "This day is sacred to the LORD your God. Do not mourn or weep." For all the people had been weeping as they listened to the words of the Law.

¹⁰Nehemiah said, "Go and enjoy choice food and sweet drinks, and send some to those who have nothing prepared. This day is sacred to our Lord. Do not grieve, for the joy of the LORD is your strength."

¹¹The Levites calmed all the people, saying, "Be still, for this is a sacred day. Do not grieve."

¹²Then all the people went away to eat and drink, to send portions of food and to celebrate with great joy, because they now understood the words that had been made known to them.

¹³On the second day of the month, the heads of all the families, along with the priests and the Levites, gathered around Ezra the scribe to give attention to the words of the Law. ¹⁴They found written in the Law, which the LORD had commanded through Moses, that the Israelites were to live in booths during the feast of the seventh month ¹⁵and that they should proclaim this word and spread it throughout their towns and in Jerusalem: "Go out into the hill country and bring back branches from olive and wild olive trees, and from myrtles, palms and shade trees, to make booths"—as it is written.ᵃ

¹⁶So the people went out and brought back branches and built themselves booths on their own roofs, in their courtyards, in the courts of the house of God and in the square by the Water Gate and the one by the Gate of Ephraim. ¹⁷The whole company that had returned from exile built booths and lived in them. From the days of Joshua son of Nun until that day, the Israelites had not celebrated it like this. And their joy was very great.

¹⁸Day after day, from the first day to the last, Ezra read from the Book of the Law of God. They celebrated the feast for seven days, and on the eighth day, in accordance with the regulation, there was an assembly.

The Israelites Confess Their Sins

On the twenty-fourth day of the same month, the Israelites gathered together, fasting and wearing sackcloth and having dust on their heads. ²Those of Israelite descent had separated themselves from all foreigners. They stood in their places and confessed their sins and the wickedness of their fathers. ³They stood where they were and read from the Book of the Law of the LORD their God for a quarter of the day, and spent another quarter in confession and in worshiping the LORD their God. ⁴Standing on the stairs were the Levites—Jeshua, Bani, Kadmiel, Shebaniah, Bunni, Sherebiah, Bani and Kenani—who called with loud voices to the LORD their God. ⁵And the Levites—Jeshua, Kadmiel, Bani, Hashabneiah, Sherebiah, Hodiah, Shebaniah and Pethahiah—said: "Stand up and praise the LORD your God, who is from everlasting to everlasting.ᵇ"

"Blessed be your glorious name, and may it be

ᵃ 15 See Lev. 23:37–40. ᵇ 5 Or God for ever and ever

exalted above all blessing and praise. ⁶You alone are the Lord. You made the heavens, even the highest heavens, and all their starry host, the earth and all that is on it, the seas and all that is in them. You give life to everything, and the multitudes of heaven worship you.

⁷"You are the Lord God, who chose Abram and brought him out of Ur of the Chaldeans and named him Abraham. ⁸You found his heart faithful to you, and you made a covenant with him to give to his descendants the land of the Canaanites, Hittites, Amorites, Perizzites, Jebusites and Girgashites. You have kept your promise because you are righteous.

⁹"You saw the suffering of our forefathers in Egypt; you heard their cry at the Red Sea.ᵃ ¹⁰You sent miraculous signs and wonders against Pharaoh, against all his officials and all the people of his land, for you knew how arrogantly the Egyptians treated them. You made a name for yourself, which remains to this day. ¹¹You divided the sea before them, so that they passed through it on dry ground, but you hurled their pursuers into the depths, like a stone into mighty waters. ¹²By day you led them with a pillar of cloud, and by night with a pillar of fire to give them light on the way they were to take.

¹³"You came down on Mount Sinai; you spoke to them from heaven. You gave them regulations and laws that are just and right, and decrees and commands that are good. ¹⁴You made known to them your holy Sabbath and gave them commands, decrees and laws through your servant Moses. ¹⁵In their hunger you gave them bread from heaven and in their thirst you brought them water from the rock; you told them to go in and take possession of the land you had sworn with uplifted hand to give them.

¹⁶"But they, our forefathers, became arrogant and stiff-necked, and did not obey your commands. ¹⁷They refused to listen and failed to remember the miracles you performed among them. They became stiff-necked and in their rebellion appointed a leader in order to return to their slavery. But you are a forgiving God, gracious and compassionate, slow to anger and abounding in love. Therefore you did not desert them, ¹⁸even when they cast for themselves an image of a calf and said, 'This is your god, who brought you up out of Egypt,' or when they committed awful blasphemies.

¹⁹"Because of your great compassion you did not abandon them in the desert. By day the pillar of cloud did not cease to guide them on their path, nor the pillar of fire by night to shine on the way they were to take. ²⁰You gave your good Spirit to instruct them. You did not withhold your manna from their mouths, and you gave them water for their thirst. ²¹For forty years you sustained them in the desert; they lacked nothing, their clothes did not wear out nor did their feet become swollen.

²²"You gave them kingdoms and nations, allotting to them even the remotest frontiers. They took over the country of Sihonᵇ king of Heshbon and the country of Og king of Bashan. ²³You made their sons as numerous as the stars in the sky, and you brought them into the land that you told their fathers to enter and possess. ²⁴Their sons went in and took possession of the land. You subdued before them the Canaanites, who lived in the land; you handed the Canaanites over to them, along with their kings and the peoples of the land, to deal with them as they pleased. ²⁵They captured fortified cities and fertile land; they took possession of houses filled with all kinds of good things, wells already dug, vineyards, olive groves and fruit trees in abundance. They ate to the full and were well-nourished; they reveled in your great goodness.

²⁶"But they were disobedient and rebelled against you; they put your law behind their backs. They killed your prophets, who had admonished them in order to turn them back to you; they committed awful blasphe-

ᵃ 9 Hebrew *Yam Suph*; that is, Sea of Reeds
ᵇ 22 One Hebrew manuscript and Septuagint; most Hebrew manuscripts *Sihon, that is, the country of the*

mies. ²⁷So you handed them over to their enemies, who oppressed them. But when they were oppressed they cried out to you. From heaven you heard them, and in your great compassion you gave them deliverers, who rescued them from the hand of their enemies.

²⁸"But as soon as they were at rest, they again did what was evil in your sight. Then you abandoned them to the hand of their enemies so that they ruled over them. And when they cried out to you again, you heard from heaven, and in your compassion you delivered them time after time.

²⁹"You warned them to return to your law, but they became arrogant and disobeyed your commands. They sinned against your ordinances, by which a man will live if he obeys them. Stubbornly they turned their backs on you, became stiff-necked and refused to listen. ³⁰For many years you were patient with them. By your Spirit you admonished them through your prophets. Yet they paid no attention, so you handed them over to the neighboring peoples. ³¹But in your great mercy you did not put an end to them or abandon them, for you are a gracious and merciful God.

³²"Now therefore, O our God, the great, mighty and awesome God, who keeps his covenant of love, do not let all this hardship seem trifling in your eyes—the hardship that has come upon us, upon our kings and leaders, upon our priests and prophets, upon our fathers and all your people, from the days of the kings of Assyria until today. ³³In all that has happened to us, you have been just; you have acted faithfully, while we did wrong. ³⁴Our kings, our leaders, our priests and our fathers did not follow your law; they did not pay attention to your commands or the warnings you gave them. ³⁵Even while they were in their kingdom, enjoying your great goodness to them in the spacious and fertile land you gave them, they did not serve you or turn from their evil ways.

³⁶"But see, we are slaves today, slaves in the land you gave our fore-fathers so they could eat its fruit and the other good things it produces. ³⁷Because of our sins, its abundant harvest goes to the kings you have placed over us. They rule over our bodies and our cattle as they please. We are in great distress.

The Agreement of the People

³⁸"In view of all this, we are making a binding agreement, putting it in writing, and our leaders, our Levites and our priests are affixing their seals to it."

 Those who sealed it were:

Nehemiah the governor, the son of Hacaliah.

Zedekiah, ²Seraiah, Azariah, Jeremiah, ³Pashhur, Amariah, Malkijah, ⁴Hattush, Shebaniah, Malluch, ⁵Harim, Meremoth, Obadiah, ⁶Daniel, Ginnethon, Baruch, ⁷Meshullam, Abijah, Mijamin, ⁸Maaziah, Bilgai and Shemaiah. These were the priests.

⁹The Levites:

Jeshua son of Azaniah, Binnui of the sons of Henadad, Kadmiel, ¹⁰and their associates: Shebaniah, Hodiah, Kelita, Pelaiah, Hanan, ¹¹Mica, Rehob, Hashabiah, ¹²Zaccur, Sherebiah, Shebaniah, ¹³Hodiah, Bani and Beninu.

¹⁴The leaders of the people:

Parosh, Pahath-Moab, Elam, Zattu, Bani, ¹⁵Bunni, Azgad, Bebai, ¹⁶Adonijah, Bigvai, Adin, ¹⁷Ater, Hezekiah, Azzur, ¹⁸Hodiah, Hashum, Bezai, ¹⁹Hariph, Anathoth, Nebai, ²⁰Magpiash, Meshullam, Hezir, ²¹Meshezabel, Zadok, Jaddua, ²²Pelatiah, Hanan, Anaiah, ²³Hoshea, Hananiah, Hasshub, ²⁴Hallohesh, Pilha, Shobek, ²⁵Rehum, Hashabnah, Maaseiah, ²⁶Ahiah, Hanan, Anan, ²⁷Malluch, Harim and Baanah.

²⁸"The rest of the people—priests, Levites, gatekeepers, singers, temple servants and all who separated themselves from the neighboring peoples

for the sake of the Law of God, together with their wives and all their sons and daughters who are able to understand— ²⁹all these now join their brothers the nobles, and bind themselves with a curse and an oath to follow the Law of God given through Moses the servant of God and to obey carefully all the commands, regulations and decrees of the LORD our Lord.

³⁰"We promise not to give our daughters in marriage to the peoples around us or take their daughters for our sons.

³¹"When the neighboring peoples bring merchandise or grain to sell on the Sabbath, we will not buy from them on the Sabbath or on any holy day. Every seventh year we will forgo working the land and will cancel all debts.

³²"We assume the responsibility for carrying out the commands to give a third of a shekel*a* each year for the service of the house of our God:
³³for the bread set out on the table;

for the regular grain offerings and burnt offerings; for the offerings on the Sabbaths, New Moon festivals and appointed feasts; for the holy offerings; for sin offerings to make atonement for Israel; and for all the duties of the house of our God.

³⁴"We—the priests, the Levites and the people—have cast lots to determine when each of our families is to bring to the house of our God at set times each year a contribution of wood to burn on the altar of the LORD our God, as it is written in the Law.

³⁵"We also assume responsibility for bringing to the house of the LORD each year the firstfruits of our crops and of every fruit tree.

³⁶"As it is also written in the Law, we will bring the firstborn of our sons and of our cattle, of our herds and of our flocks to the house of our God, to the priests ministering there.

³⁷"Moreover, we will bring to the storerooms of the house of our God,

a 32 That is, about 1/8 ounce (about 4 grams)

Assuming Responsibility

READ NEHEMIAH 10:28–39

Putting up with dogs chasing you on your paper route or the hot sun beating down on you when you cut the grass is all worth it when you get that cold, hard cash in your hand. Have fun with your earnings! Just remember, God also wants you to use part of it to support the church. God helped you get that job and earn that money, so giving some of it back to God is a good way of showing your thankfulness to him. The money that you place in the offering should be put there (willingly) on a regular basis. In Nehemiah's day, godly men and women "assumed responsibility" (verses 32 and 35) to give money to the temple. They promised, "We will not neglect the house of our God" (verse 38). Starting right now, make a commitment to support *your* church.

Your next reading is on page 617.

to the priests, the first of our ground meal, of our grain offerings, of the fruit of all our trees and of our new wine and oil. And we will bring a tithe of our crops to the Levites, for it is the Levites who collect the tithes in all the towns where we work. [38]A priest descended from Aaron is to accompany the Levites when they receive the tithes, and the Levites are to bring a tenth of the tithes up to the house of our God, to the storerooms of the treasury. [39]The people of Israel, including the Levites, are to bring their contributions of grain, new wine and oil to the storerooms where the articles for the sanctuary are kept and where the ministering priests, the gatekeepers and the singers stay.

"We will not neglect the house of our God."

The New Residents of Jerusalem

Now the leaders of the people settled in Jerusalem, and the rest of the people cast lots to bring one out of every ten to live in Jerusalem, the holy city, while the remaining nine were to stay in their own towns. [2]The people commended all the men who volunteered to live in Jerusalem.

[3]These are the provincial leaders who settled in Jerusalem (now some Israelites, priests, Levites, temple servants and descendants of Solomon's servants lived in the towns of Judah, each on his own property in the various towns, [4]while other people from both Judah and Benjamin lived in Jerusalem):

From the descendants of Judah:

Athaiah son of Uzziah, the son of Zechariah, the son of Amariah, the son of Shephatiah, the son of Mahalalel, a descendant of Perez; [5]and Maaseiah son of Baruch, the son of Col-Hozeh, the son of Hazaiah, the son of Adaiah, the son of Joiarib, the son of Zechariah, a descendant of Shelah. [6]The descendants of Perez who lived in Jerusalem totaled 468 able men.

[7]From the descendants of Benjamin:

Sallu son of Meshullam, the son of Joed, the son of Pedaiah, the son of Kolaiah, the son of Maaseiah, the son of Ithiel, the son of Jeshaiah, [8]and his followers, Gabbai and Sallai—928 men. [9]Joel son of Zicri was their chief officer, and Judah son of Hassenuah was over the Second District of the city.

[10]From the priests:

Jedaiah; the son of Joiarib; Jakin; [11]Seraiah son of Hilkiah, the son of Meshullam, the son of Zadok, the son of Meraioth, the son of Ahitub, supervisor in the house of God, [12]and their associates, who carried on work for the temple—822 men; Adaiah son of Jeroham, the son of Pelaliah, the son of Amzi, the son of Zechariah, the son of Pashhur, the son of Malkijah, [13]and his associates, who were heads of families—242 men; Amashsai son of Azarel, the son of Ahzai, the son of Meshillemoth, the son of Immer, [14]and his[a] associates, who were able men—128. Their chief officer was Zabdiel son of Haggedolim.

[15]From the Levites:

Shemaiah son of Hasshub, the son of Azrikam, the son of Hashabiah, the son of Bunni; [16]Shabbethai and Jozabad, two of the heads of the Levites, who had charge of the outside work of the house of God; [17]Mattaniah son of Mica, the son of Zabdi, the son of Asaph, the director who led in thanksgiving and prayer; Bakbukiah, second among his associates; and Abda son of Shammua, the son of Galal, the son of Jeduthun. [18]The Levites in the holy city totaled 284.

[19]The gatekeepers:

Akkub, Talmon and their associates, who kept watch at the gates—172 men.

[20]The rest of the Israelites, with the priests and Levites, were in all the towns of Judah, each on his ancestral property.

[21]The temple servants lived on the hill of Ophel, and Ziha and Gishpa were in charge of them.

[22]The chief officer of the Levites in Jerusalem was Uzzi son of Bani, the son of Hashabiah, the son of Mattaniah, the son of Mica. Uzzi was one of Asaph's descendants, who were the singers responsible

[a] 14 Most Septuagint manuscripts; Hebrew *their*

for the service of the house of God. 23The singers were under the king's orders, which regulated their daily activity.

24Pethahiah son of Meshezabel, one of the descendants of Zerah son of Judah, was the king's agent in all affairs relating to the people.

25As for the villages with their fields, some of the people of Judah lived in Kiriath Arba and its surrounding settlements, in Dibon and its settlements, in Jekabzeel and its villages, 26in Jeshua, in Moladah, in Beth Pelet, 27in Hazar Shual, in Beersheba and its settlements, 28in Ziklag, in Meconah and its settlements, 29in En Rimmon, in Zorah, in Jarmuth, 30Zanoah, Adullam and their villages, in Lachish and its fields, and in Azekah and its settlements. So they were living all the way from Beersheba to the Valley of Hinnom.

31The descendants of the Benjamites from Geba lived in Micmash, Aija, Bethel and its settlements, 32in Anathoth, Nob and Ananiah, 33in Hazor, Ramah and Gittaim, 34in Hadid, Zeboim and Neballat, 35in Lod and Ono, and in the Valley of the Craftsmen.

36Some of the divisions of the Levites of Judah settled in Benjamin.

Priests and Levites

These were the priests and Levites who returned with Zerubbabel son of Shealtiel and with Jeshua:

Seraiah, Jeremiah, Ezra,
2Amariah, Malluch, Hattush,
3Shecaniah, Rehum, Meremoth,
4Iddo, Ginnethon,a Abijah,
5Mijamin,b Moadiah, Bilgah,
6Shemaiah, Joiarib, Jedaiah,
7Sallu, Amok, Hilkiah and Jedaiah.
These were the leaders of the priests and their associates in the days of Jeshua.

8The Levites were Jeshua, Binnui, Kadmiel, Sherebiah, Judah, and also Mattaniah, who, together with his associates, was in charge of the songs of thanksgiving. 9Bakbukiah and Unni, their associates, stood opposite them in the services.

10Jeshua was the father of Joiakim, Joiakim the father of Eliashib, Eliashib the father of Joiada, 11Joiada the father of Jonathan, and Jonathan the father of Jaddua.

12In the days of Joiakim, these were the heads of the priestly families:
of Seraiah's family, Meraiah;

of Jeremiah's, Hananiah;
13of Ezra's, Meshullam;
of Amariah's, Jehohanan;
14of Malluch's, Jonathan;
of Shecaniah's,c Joseph;
15of Harim's, Adna;
of Meremoth's,d Helkai;
16of Iddo's, Zechariah;
of Ginnethon's, Meshullam;
17of Abijah's, Zicri;
of Miniamin's and of Moadiah's, Piltai;
18of Bilgah's, Shammua;
of Shemaiah's, Jehonathan;
19of Joiarib's, Mattenai;
of Jedaiah's, Uzzi;
20of Sallu's, Kallai;
of Amok's, Eber;
21of Hilkiah's, Hashabiah;
of Jedaiah's, Nethanel.

22The family heads of the Levites in the days of Eliashib, Joiada, Johanan and Jaddua, as well as those of the priests, were recorded in the reign of Darius the Persian. 23The family heads among the descendants of Levi up to the time of Johanan son of Eliashib were recorded in the book of the annals. 24And the leaders of the Levites were Hashabiah, Sherebiah, Jeshua son of Kadmiel, and their associates, who stood opposite them to give praise and thanksgiving, one section responding to the other, as prescribed by David the man of God.

25Mattaniah, Bakbukiah, Obadiah, Meshullam, Talmon and Akkub were gatekeepers who guarded the storerooms at the gates. 26They served in the days of Joiakim son of Jeshua, the son of Jozadak, and in the days of Nehemiah the governor and of Ezra the priest and scribe.

Dedication of the Wall of Jerusalem

27At the dedication of the wall of Jerusalem, the Levites were sought out from where they lived and were brought to Jerusalem to celebrate joyfully the dedication with songs of thanksgiving and with the music of cymbals, harps and lyres. 28The singers also were brought together from the region around Jerusalem—from the villages of the Netophathites, 29from

---

a4 Many Hebrew manuscripts and Vulgate (see also Neh. 12:16); most Hebrew manuscripts *Ginnethoi*   b5 A variant of *Miniamin*   c14 Very many Hebrew manuscripts, some Septuagint manuscripts and Syriac (see also Neh. 12:3); most Hebrew manuscripts *Shebaniah's*   d15 Some Septuagint manuscripts (see also Neh. 12:3); Hebrew *Meraioth's*

Beth Gilgal, and from the area of Geba and Azmaveth, for the singers had built villages for themselves around Jerusalem. ³⁰When the priests and Levites had purified themselves ceremonially, they purified the people, the gates and the wall.

³¹I had the leaders of Judah go up on top*ᵃ* of the wall. I also assigned two large choirs to give thanks. One was to proceed on top*ᵇ* of the wall to the right, toward the Dung Gate. ³²Hoshaiah and half the leaders of Judah followed them, ³³along with Azariah, Ezra, Meshullam, ³⁴Judah, Benjamin, Shemaiah, Jeremiah, ³⁵as well as some priests with trumpets, and also Zechariah son of Jonathan, the son of Shemaiah, the son of Mattaniah, the son of Micaiah, the son of Zaccur, the son of Asaph, ³⁶and his associates—Shemaiah, Azarel, Milalai, Gilalai, Maai, Nethanel, Judah and Hanani—with musical instruments prescribed by David the man of God. Ezra the scribe led the procession. ³⁷At the Fountain Gate they continued directly up the steps of the City of David on the ascent to the wall and passed above the house of David to the Water Gate on the east.

³⁸The second choir proceeded in the opposite direction. I followed them on top*ᶜ* of the wall, together with half the people—past the Tower of the Ovens to the Broad Wall, ³⁹over the Gate of Ephraim, the Jeshanah*ᵈ* Gate, the Fish Gate, the Tower of Hananel and the Tower of the Hundred, as far as the Sheep Gate. At the Gate of the Guard they stopped.

⁴⁰The two choirs that gave thanks then took their places in the house of God; so did I, together with half the officials, ⁴¹as well as the priests—Eliakim, Maaseiah, Miniamin, Micaiah, Elioenai, Zechariah and Hananiah with their trumpets— ⁴²and also Maaseiah, Shemaiah, Eleazar, Uzzi, Jehohanan, Malkijah, Elam and Ezer. The choirs sang under the direction of Jezrahiah. ⁴³And on that day they offered great sacrifices, rejoicing because God had given them great joy. The women and children also rejoiced. The sound of rejoicing in Jerusalem could be heard far away.

⁴⁴At that time men were appointed to be in charge of the storerooms for the contributions, firstfruits and tithes. From the fields around the towns they were to bring into the storerooms the portions required by the Law for the priests and the Levites, for Judah was pleased with the ministering priests and Levites. ⁴⁵They performed the service of their God and the service of purification, as did also the singers and gatekeepers, according to the commands of David and his son Solomon. ⁴⁶For long ago, in the days of David and Asaph, there had been directors for the singers and for the songs of praise and thanksgiving to God. ⁴⁷So in the days of Zerubbabel and of Nehemiah, all Israel contributed the daily portions for the singers and gatekeepers. They also set aside the portion for the other Levites, and the Levites set aside the portion for the descendants of Aaron.

Nehemiah's Final Reforms

13 On that day the Book of Moses was read aloud in the hearing of the people and there it was found written that no Ammonite or Moabite should ever be admitted into the assembly of God, ²because they had not met the Israelites with food and water but had hired Balaam to call a curse down on them. (Our God, however, turned the curse into a blessing.) ³When the people heard this law, they excluded from Israel all who were of foreign descent.

⁴Before this, Eliashib the priest had been put in charge of the storerooms of the house of our God. He was closely associated with Tobiah, ⁵and he had provided him with a large room formerly used to store the grain offerings and incense and temple articles, and also the tithes of grain, new wine and oil prescribed for the Levites, singers and gatekeepers, as well as the contributions for the priests.

⁶But while all this was going on, I was not in Jerusalem, for in the thirty-second year of Artaxerxes king of Babylon I had returned to the king. Some time later I asked his permission ⁷and came back to Jerusalem. Here I learned about the evil thing Eliashib had done in providing Tobiah a room in the courts of the house of God. ⁸I was greatly displeased and threw all Tobiah's household goods out of the room. ⁹I gave orders to purify the rooms, and then I put back into them the equipment of the house of God, with the grain offerings and the incense.

ᵃ 31 Or *go alongside*　*ᵇ 31* Or *proceed alongside*
ᶜ 38 Or *them alongside*　*ᵈ 39* Or *Old*

10I also learned that the portions assigned to the Levites had not been given to them, and that all the Levites and singers responsible for the service had gone back to their own fields. 11So I rebuked the officials and asked them, "Why is the house of God neglected?" Then I called them together and stationed them at their posts.

12All Judah brought the tithes of grain, new wine and oil into the storerooms. 13I put Shelemiah the priest, Zadok the scribe, and a Levite named Pedaiah in charge of the storerooms and made Hanan son of Zaccur, the son of Mattaniah, their assistant, because these men were considered trustworthy. They were made responsible for distributing the supplies to their brothers.

14Remember me for this, O my God, and do not blot out what I have so faithfully done for the house of my God and its services.

15In those days I saw men in Judah treading winepresses on the Sabbath and bringing in grain and loading it on don-

keys, together with wine, grapes, figs and all other kinds of loads. And they were bringing all this into Jerusalem on the Sabbath. Therefore I warned them against selling food on that day. 16Men from Tyre who lived in Jerusalem were bringing in fish and all kinds of merchandise and selling them in Jerusalem on the Sabbath to the people of Judah. 17I rebuked the nobles of Judah and said to them, "What is this wicked thing you are doing—desecrating the Sabbath day? 18Didn't your forefathers do the same things, so that our God brought all this calamity upon us and upon this city? Now you are stirring up more wrath against Israel by desecrating the Sabbath."

19When evening shadows fell on the gates of Jerusalem before the Sabbath, I ordered the doors to be shut and not opened until the Sabbath was over. I stationed some of my own men at the gates so that no load could be brought in on the Sabbath day. 20Once or twice the merchants and sellers of all kinds of goods spent the night outside Jerusalem. 21But I warned them and said, "Why do you

Bad Company

READ NEHEMIAH 13:1–13

Eliashib, the high priest, made the serious blunder of getting buddy-buddy with an ungodly guy named Tobiah. You really have to wonder what on earth Eliashib was *thinking*! Everyone knew that Tobiah was an enemy of God's people (see Nehemiah 2:19; 4:3–8). So why did Eliashib do it? Well, Tobiah was a very powerful man, probably even the Governor of the whole region. It paid to be tight with Tobiah. Next thing you know, Eliashib actually gave Tobiah a large room in God's temple to store his household stuff! *Huh*? That cost Eliashib big-time! Don't hang out with a Tobiah or have him over at your house every day after school, camped out in your bedroom. Sure, it's OK to play pick-up basketball with non-Christian friends. But your best buddies should be godly dudes who share your faith. When you go to choose your closest friends, choose carefully.

Your next reading is on page 621.

spend the night by the wall? If you do this again, I will lay hands on you." From that time on they no longer came on the Sabbath. ²²Then I commanded the Levites to purify themselves and go and guard the gates in order to keep the Sabbath day holy.

Remember me for this also, O my God, and show mercy to me according to your great love.

²³Moreover, in those days I saw men of Judah who had married women from Ashdod, Ammon and Moab. ²⁴Half of their children spoke the language of Ashdod or the language of one of the other peoples, and did not know how to speak the language of Judah. ²⁵I rebuked them and called curses down on them. I beat some of the men and pulled out their hair. I made them take an oath in God's name and said: "You are not to give your daughters in marriage to their sons, nor are you to take their daughters in marriage for your sons or for yourselves.

²⁶Was it not because of marriages like these that Solomon king of Israel sinned? Among the many nations there was no king like him. He was loved by his God, and God made him king over all Israel, but even he was led into sin by foreign women. ²⁷Must we hear now that you too are doing all this terrible wickedness and are being unfaithful to our God by marrying foreign women?"

²⁸One of the sons of Joiada son of Eliashib the high priest was son-in-law to Sanballat the Horonite. And I drove him away from me.

²⁹Remember them, O my God, because they defiled the priestly office and the covenant of the priesthood and of the Levites.

³⁰So I purified the priests and the Levites of everything foreign, and assigned them duties, each to his own task. ³¹I also made provision for contributions of wood at designated times, and for the firstfruits.

Remember me with favor, O my God.

ESTHER

Who wrote this book?

The author of this book is unknown.

Why was this book written?

Esther reveals how God takes care of his people.

What happens in this book?

A Jewish girl, Esther, becomes queen of Persia. An evil man named Haman plots to kill all Jews everywhere. Esther saves her people.

What do we learn about God in this book?

God does not need to do miracles to rescue his people. He is able to work through ordinary events and ordinary people.

What people are important in this book?

The important people in this book are King Xerxes, Haman, Esther and Mordecai.

When did this happen?

The events in this book happened between 483 and 471 B.C.

Where did this happen?

These events happened in Persia's capital, Susa, a royal city built by the king.

What are some of the stories in this book?

Xerxes divorces Vashti	Esther 1
Esther becomes queen	Esther 2
Haman's plot	Esther 3
Esther's courage	Esther 4–5
Xerxes honors Mordecai	Esther 6
Haman is hanged	Esther 7
The Jews are saved	Esther 8–9

Queen Vashti Deposed

1 This is what happened during the time of Xerxes,[a] the Xerxes who ruled over 127 provinces stretching from India to Cush[b]: 2At that time King Xerxes reigned from his royal throne in the citadel of Susa, 3and in the third year of his reign he gave a banquet for all his nobles and officials. The military leaders of Persia and Media, the princes, and the nobles of the provinces were present.

4For a full 180 days he displayed the vast wealth of his kingdom and the splendor and glory of his majesty. 5When these days were over, the king gave a banquet, lasting seven days, in the enclosed garden of the king's palace, for all the people from the least to the greatest, who were in the citadel of Susa. 6The garden had hangings of white and blue linen, fastened with cords of white linen and purple material to silver rings on marble pillars. There were couches of gold and silver on a mosaic pavement of porphyry, marble, mother-of-pearl and other costly stones. 7Wine was served in goblets of gold, each one different from the other, and the royal wine was abundant, in keeping with the king's liberality. 8By the king's command each guest was allowed to drink in his own way, for the king instructed all the wine stewards to serve each man what he wished.

9Queen Vashti also gave a banquet for the women in the royal palace of King Xerxes.

10On the seventh day, when King Xerxes was in high spirits from wine, he commanded the seven eunuchs who served him—Mehuman, Biztha, Harbona, Bigtha, Abagtha, Zethar and Carcas— 11to bring before him Queen Vashti, wearing her royal crown, in order to display her beauty to the people and nobles, for she was lovely to look at. 12But when the attendants delivered the king's command, Queen Vashti refused to come. Then the king became furious and burned with anger.

13Since it was customary for the king to consult experts in matters of law and justice, he spoke with the wise men who understood the times 14and were closest to the king—Carshena, Shethar, Admatha, Tarshish, Meres, Marsena and Memucan, the seven nobles of Persia and Media who had special access to the king and were highest in the kingdom.

15"According to law, what must be done to Queen Vashti?" he asked. "She has not obeyed the command of King Xerxes that the eunuchs have taken to her."

16Then Memucan replied in the presence of the king and the nobles, "Queen Vashti has done wrong, not only against the king but also against all the nobles and the peoples of all the provinces of King Xerxes. 17For the queen's conduct will become known to all the women, and so they will despise their husbands and say, 'King Xerxes commanded Queen Vashti to be brought before him, but she would not come.' 18This very day the Persian and Median women of the nobility who have heard about the queen's conduct will respond to all the king's nobles in the same way. There will be no end of disrespect and discord.

19"Therefore, if it pleases the king, let him issue a royal decree and let it be written in the laws of Persia and Media, which cannot be repealed, that Vashti is never again to enter the presence of King Xerxes. Also let the king give her royal position to someone else who is better than she. 20Then when the king's edict is proclaimed throughout all his vast realm, all the women will respect their husbands, from the least to the greatest."

21The king and his nobles were pleased with this advice, so the king did as Memucan proposed. 22He sent dispatches to all parts of the kingdom, to each province in its own script and to each people in its own language, proclaiming in each people's tongue that every man should be ruler over his own household.

Esther Made Queen

2 Later when the anger of King Xerxes had subsided, he remembered Vashti and what she had done and what he had decreed about her. 2Then the king's personal attendants proposed, "Let a search be made for beautiful young virgins for the king. 3Let the king appoint commissioners in every province of his realm to bring all these beautiful girls into the harem at the citadel of Susa. Let them be placed under the care

a 1 Hebrew Ahasuerus, a variant of Xerxes' Persian name; here and throughout Esther   b 1 That is, the upper Nile region of Hegai, the king's eunuch, who is in charge of the women; and let beauty treatments be given to them. ⁴Then let the girl who pleases the king be queen instead of Vashti." This advice appealed to the king, and he followed it.

⁵Now there was in the citadel of Susa a Jew of the tribe of Benjamin, named Mordecai son of Jair, the son of Shimei, the son of Kish, ⁶who had been carried into exile from Jerusalem by Nebuchadnezzar king of Babylon, among those taken captive with Jehoiachinᵃ king of Judah. ⁷Mordecai had a cousin named Hadassah, whom he had brought up because she had neither father nor mother. This girl, who was also known as Esther, was lovely in form and features, and Mordecai had taken her as his own daughter when her father and mother died.

⁸When the king's order and edict had been proclaimed, many girls were brought to the citadel of Susa and put under the care of Hegai. Esther also was taken to the king's palace and entrusted to Hegai, who had charge of the harem. ⁹The girl pleased him and won his favor. Immediately he provided her with her beauty treatments and special food. He assigned to her seven maids selected from the king's palace and moved her and her maids into the best place in the harem.

¹⁰Esther had not revealed her nationality and family background, because Mordecai had forbidden her to do so. ¹¹Every day he walked back and forth near the courtyard of the harem to find out how Esther was and what was happening to her.

¹²Before a girl's turn came to go in to King Xerxes, she had to complete twelve months of beauty treatments prescribed for the women, six months with oil of myrrh and six with perfumes and cosmetics. ¹³And this is how she would go to the king: Anything she wanted was given her

---

ᵃ 6 Hebrew *Jeconiah*, a variant of *Jehoiachin*

GET STRONGER

Be a Guardian

READ ESTHER 2:1–11, 20

Ever have someone give you something for safekeeping, and say, "Guard this with your life"? When Esther's mother and father died, her cousin Mordecai took over the responsibility of protecting and looking after her. He was her "guardian." God gives men physical strength and an instinct to guard their families. Guards have power and strength because of their weapons. That power can be used to protect others or it can be used to push people around and get your own way. Do you treat your mom with respect and help her? Do you look out for your brothers and sisters? Never use your size to bully them, no matter how tempting it might be. Watch out for them and protect them like an armed guard.

Your next reading is on page 622.

to take with her from the harem to the king's palace. ¹⁴In the evening she would go there and in the morning return to another part of the harem to the care of Shaashgaz, the king's eunuch who was in charge of the concubines. She would not return to the king unless he was pleased with her and summoned her by name.

¹⁵When the turn came for Esther (the girl Mordecai had adopted, the daughter of his uncle Abihail) to go to the king, she asked for nothing other than what Hegai, the king's eunuch who was in charge of the harem, suggested. And Esther won the favor of everyone who saw her. ¹⁶She was taken to King Xerxes in the royal residence in the tenth month, the month of Tebeth, in the seventh year of his reign.

¹⁷Now the king was attracted to Esther more than to any of the other women, and she won his favor and approval more than any of the other virgins. So he set a royal crown on her head and made her queen instead of Vashti. ¹⁸And the king gave a great banquet, Esther's banquet, for all his nobles and officials. He proclaimed a holiday throughout the provinces and distributed gifts with royal liberality.

Mordecai Uncovers a Conspiracy

¹⁹When the virgins were assembled a second time, Mordecai was sitting at the king's gate. ²⁰But Esther had kept secret her family background and nationality just as Mordecai had told her to do, for she continued to follow Mordecai's instructions as she had done when he was bringing her up.

²¹During the time Mordecai was sitting at the king's gate, Bigthana*a* and Teresh, two of the king's officers who guarded the doorway, became angry and conspired to assassinate King Xerxes. ²²But Mordecai found out about the plot and told Queen Esther, who in turn reported it to the king, giving credit to Mordecai. ²³And when the report was investigated and found to be true, the two officials were hanged on a gallows.*b* All this was recorded in the book of the annals in the presence of the king.

a 21 Hebrew *Bigthan*, a variant of *Bigthana*　　*b 23* Or *were hung* (or *impaled*) *on poles*; similarly elsewhere in Esther

Blowing the Whistle

READ ESTHER 2:21–23

Mordecai overheard a plot to kill the king. What should he have done? Have you ever found out that somebody was planning something bad? Did you hesitate to tell an adult because you didn't want kids to say you had told on them? Nobody wants to be called a squealer or tattletale, but what's so "cool" about a boy who's too afraid to speak up for what's right? What's so great about a referee who sees a major bone-smashing foul, but is too chicken to blow the whistle? There are times when we *have* to speak up. If a friend is planning to leap off his roof with a cape around his neck or seriously pound on someone, blowing the whistle is the *right* thing to do. Forget what other kids think. Just do what you know is right.

Your next reading is on page 623.

Haman's Plot to Destroy the Jews

After these events, King Xerxes honored Haman son of Hammedatha, the Agagite, elevating him and giving him a seat of honor higher than that of all the other nobles. 2All the royal officials at the king's gate knelt down and paid honor to Haman, for the king had commanded this concerning him. But Mordecai would not kneel down or pay him honor.

3Then the royal officials at the king's gate asked Mordecai, "Why do you disobey the king's command?" 4Day after day they spoke to him but he refused to comply. Therefore they told Haman about it to see whether Mordecai's behavior would be tolerated, for he had told them he was a Jew.

5When Haman saw that Mordecai would not kneel down or pay him honor, he was enraged. 6Yet having learned who Mordecai's people were, he scorned the idea of killing only Mordecai. Instead Haman looked for a way to destroy all Mordecai's people, the Jews, throughout the whole kingdom of Xerxes.

7In the twelfth year of King Xerxes, in the first month, the month of Nisan, they cast the *pur* (that is, the lot) in the presence of Haman to select a day and month. And the lot fell on[a] the twelfth month, the month of Adar.

8Then Haman said to King Xerxes, "There is a certain people dispersed and scattered among the peoples in all the provinces of your kingdom whose customs are different from those of all other people and who do not obey the king's laws; it is not in the king's best interest to tolerate them. 9If it pleases the king, let a decree be issued to destroy them, and I will put ten thousand talents[b] of silver into the royal treasury for the men who carry out this business."

10So the king took his signet ring from his finger and gave it to Haman son of Hammedatha, the Agagite, the enemy of the Jews. 11"Keep the money," the king said to Haman, "and do with the people as you please."

---

[a] 7 Septuagint; Hebrew does not have *And the lot fell on.*
[b] 9 That is, about 375 tons (about 345 metric tons)

GET SMARTER

What Can I Do?

READ ESTHER 3:8–11; 4:1–16

When you hear news on the TV about an emergency in your country or community, what's your reaction? Do you pray about it and ask yourself, "What can I do to help?" or do you yawn, hit the clicker and move to the cartoon channel? If you've ever dreamed of being the one who stands up and saves the day, you need to be ready. Mordecai was ready when his chance came. He was a man of action, not a channel surfer. When his people were in trouble, he immediately prayed, "What is my part? What can I do?" He encouraged Esther to risk her life as well, saying, "Who knows but that you have come to royal position for such a time as this?" (Esther 4:14). Our attitude needs to be like Mordecai's—ready to do whatever we can. A real man stands up and helps.

Your next reading is on page 626.

12Then on the thirteenth day of the first month the royal secretaries were summoned. They wrote out in the script of each province and in the language of each people all Haman's orders to the king's satraps, the governors of the various provinces and the nobles of the various peoples. These were written in the name of King Xerxes himself and sealed with his own ring. 13Dispatches were sent by couriers to all the king's provinces with the order to destroy, kill and annihilate all the Jews—young and old, women and little children—on a single day, the thirteenth day of the twelfth month, the month of Adar, and to plunder their goods. 14A copy of the text of the edict was to be issued as law in every province and made known to the people of every nationality so they would be ready for that day.

15Spurred on by the king's command, the couriers went out, and the edict was issued in the citadel of Susa. The king and Haman sat down to drink, but the city of Susa was bewildered.

Mordecai Persuades Esther to Help

When Mordecai learned of all that had been done, he tore his clothes, put on sackcloth and ashes, and went out into the city, wailing loudly and bitterly. 2But he went only as far as the king's gate, because no one clothed in sackcloth was allowed to enter it. 3In every province to which the edict and order of the king came, there was great mourning among the Jews, with fasting, weeping and wailing. Many lay in sackcloth and ashes.

4When Esther's maids and eunuchs came and told her about Mordecai, she was in great distress. She sent clothes for him to put on instead of his sackcloth, but he would not accept them. 5Then Esther summoned Hathach, one of the king's eunuchs assigned to attend her, and ordered him to find out what was troubling Mordecai and why.

6So Hathach went out to Mordecai in the open square of the city in front of the king's gate. 7Mordecai told him everything that had happened to him, including the exact amount of money Haman had promised to pay into the royal treasury for the destruction of the Jews. 8He also gave him a copy of the text of the edict for their annihilation, which had been published in Susa, to show to Esther and explain it to her, and he told him to urge her to go into the king's presence to beg for mercy and plead with him for her people.

9Hathach went back and reported to Esther what Mordecai had said. 10Then she instructed him to say to Mordecai, 11"All the king's officials and the people of the royal provinces know that for any man or woman who approaches the king in the inner court without being summoned the king has but one law: that he be put to death. The only exception to this is for the king to extend the gold scepter to him and spare his life. But thirty days have passed since I was called to go to the king."

12When Esther's words were reported to Mordecai, 13he sent back this answer: "Do not think that because you are in the king's house you alone of all the Jews will escape. 14For if you remain silent at this time, relief and deliverance for the Jews will arise from another place, but you and your father's family will perish. And who knows but that you have come to royal position for such a time as this?"

15Then Esther sent this reply to Mordecai: 16"Go, gather together all the Jews who are in Susa, and fast for me. Do not eat or drink for three days, night or day. I and my maids will fast as you do. When this is done, I will go to the king, even though it is against the law. And if I perish, I perish."

17So Mordecai went away and carried out all of Esther's instructions.

Esther's Request to the King

On the third day Esther put on her royal robes and stood in the inner court of the palace, in front of the king's hall. The king was sitting on his royal throne in the hall, facing the entrance. 2When he saw Queen Esther standing in the court, he was pleased with her and held out to her the gold scepter that was in his hand. So Esther approached and touched the tip of the scepter.

3Then the king asked, "What is it, Queen Esther? What is your request? Even up to half the kingdom, it will be given you."

4"If it pleases the king," replied Esther, "let the king, together with Haman, come today to a banquet I have prepared for him."

5"Bring Haman at once," the king said, "so that we may do what Esther asks."

So the king and Haman went to the banquet Esther had prepared. 6As they were drinking wine, the king again asked Esther, "Now what is your petition? It will be given you. And what is your request? Even up to half the kingdom, it will be granted."

7Esther replied, "My petition and my request is this: 8If the king regards me with favor and if it pleases the king to grant my petition and fulfill my request, let the king and Haman come tomorrow to the banquet I will prepare for them. Then I will answer the king's question."

Haman's Rage Against Mordecai

9Haman went out that day happy and in high spirits. But when he saw Mordecai at the king's gate and observed that he neither rose nor showed fear in his presence, he was filled with rage against Mordecai. 10Nevertheless, Haman restrained himself and went home.

Calling together his friends and Zeresh, his wife, 11Haman boasted to them about his vast wealth, his many sons, and all the ways the king had honored him and how he had elevated him above the other nobles and officials. 12"And that's not all," Haman added. "I'm the only person Queen Esther invited to accompany the king to the banquet she gave. And she has invited me along with the king tomorrow. 13But all this gives me no satisfaction as long as I see that Jew Mordecai sitting at the king's gate."

14His wife Zeresh and all his friends said to him, "Have a gallows built, seventy-five feet[a] high, and ask the king in the morning to have Mordecai hanged on it. Then go with the king to the dinner and be happy." This suggestion delighted Haman, and he had the gallows built.

Mordecai Honored

6 That night the king could not sleep; so he ordered the book of the chronicles, the record of his reign, to be brought in and read to him. 2It was found recorded there that Mordecai had exposed Bigthana and Teresh, two of the king's officers who guarded the doorway, who had conspired to assassinate King Xerxes.

3"What honor and recognition has Mordecai received for this?" the king asked.

"Nothing has been done for him," his attendants answered.

4The king said, "Who is in the court?" Now Haman had just entered the outer court of the palace to speak to the king about hanging Mordecai on the gallows he had erected for him.

5His attendants answered, "Haman is standing in the court."

"Bring him in," the king ordered.

6When Haman entered, the king asked him, "What should be done for the man the king delights to honor?"

Now Haman thought to himself, "Who is there that the king would rather honor than me?" 7So he answered the king, "For the man the king delights to honor, 8have them bring a royal robe the king has worn and a horse the king has ridden, one with a royal crest placed on its head. 9Then let the robe and horse be entrusted to one of the king's most noble princes. Let them robe the man the king delights to honor, and lead him on the horse through the city streets, proclaiming before him, 'This is what is done for the man the king delights to honor!' "

10"Go at once," the king commanded Haman. "Get the robe and the horse and do just as you have suggested for Mordecai the Jew, who sits at the king's gate. Do not neglect anything you have recommended."

11So Haman got the robe and the horse. He robed Mordecai, and led him on horseback through the city streets, proclaiming before him, "This is what is done for the man the king delights to honor!"

12Afterward Mordecai returned to the king's gate. But Haman rushed home, with his head covered in grief, 13and told Zeresh his wife and all his friends everything that had happened to him.

His advisers and his wife Zeresh said to him, "Since Mordecai, before whom your downfall has started, is of Jewish origin, you cannot stand against him—you will surely come to ruin!" 14While they were still talking with him, the king's eunuchs arrived and hurried Haman away to the banquet Esther had prepared.

Haman Hanged

7 So the king and Haman went to dine with Queen Esther, 2and as they were drinking wine on that second day, the king again asked,

a 14 Hebrew fifty cubits (about 23 meters)

"Queen Esther, what is your petition? It will be given you. What is your request? Even up to half the kingdom, it will be granted."

³Then Queen Esther answered, "If I have found favor with you, O king, and if it pleases your majesty, grant me my life— this is my petition. And spare my people— this is my request. ⁴For I and my people have been sold for destruction and slaughter and annihilation. If we had merely been sold as male and female slaves, I would have kept quiet, because no such distress would justify disturbing the king. *ᵃ*

⁵King Xerxes asked Queen Esther, "Who is he? Where is the man who has dared to do such a thing?"

⁶Esther said, "The adversary and enemy is this vile Haman."

Then Haman was terrified before the king and queen. ⁷The king got up in a rage, left his wine and went out into the palace garden. But Haman, realizing that the king had already decided his fate, stayed behind to beg Queen Esther for his life.

⁸Just as the king returned from the palace garden to the banquet hall, Haman was falling on the couch where Esther was reclining.

The king exclaimed, "Will he even molest the queen while she is with me in the house?"

As soon as the word left the king's mouth, they covered Haman's face. ⁹Then Harbona, one of the eunuchs attending the king, said, "A gallows seventy-five feet *ᵇ* high stands by Haman's house. He had it made for Mordecai, who spoke up to help the king."

The king said, "Hang him on it!" ¹⁰So they hanged Haman on the gallows he had prepared for Mordecai. Then the king's fury subsided.

The King's Edict in Behalf of the Jews

That same day King Xerxes gave Queen Esther the estate of Haman, the enemy of the Jews. And Mordecai came into the presence of the

---

ᵃ 4 Or *quiet, but the compensation our adversary offers cannot be compared with the loss the king would suffer*
ᵇ 9 Hebrew *fifty cubits* (about 23 meters)

Who's First?
READ ESTHER 6:1—8:2

What a difference between Haman and Mordecai! Haman spent his whole life thinking about himself and how he could get people to bow down to him. Mordecai spent his life thinking about how he could help others. A whole nationality of people were about to be killed and all Haman could do was smirk and strut around. But let Haman himself be in danger and immediately he's on his knees, blubbering like a baby, begging for his life. Man! All this crybaby ever thought about was being first in line. Jesus said, "Whoever exalts himself will be humbled" (Matthew 23:12). In other words, if you do everything to be number one and try to impress people, you may end up as number zero. Live for others and you'll end up being remembered and loved.

Your next reading is on page 631.

king, for Esther had told how he was related to her. ²The king took off his signet ring, which he had reclaimed from Haman, and presented it to Mordecai. And Esther appointed him over Haman's estate.

³Esther again pleaded with the king, falling at his feet and weeping. She begged him to put an end to the evil plan of Haman the Agagite, which he had devised against the Jews. ⁴Then the king extended the gold scepter to Esther and she arose and stood before him.

⁵"If it pleases the king," she said, "and if he regards me with favor and thinks it the right thing to do, and if he is pleased with me, let an order be written overruling the dispatches that Haman son of Hammedatha, the Agagite, devised and wrote to destroy the Jews in all the king's provinces. ⁶For how can I bear to see disaster fall on my people? How can I bear to see the destruction of my family?"

⁷King Xerxes replied to Queen Esther and to Mordecai the Jew, "Because Haman attacked the Jews, I have given his estate to Esther, and they have hanged him on the gallows. ⁸Now write another decree in the king's name in behalf of the Jews as seems best to you, and seal it with the king's signet ring—for no document written in the king's name and sealed with his ring can be revoked."

⁹At once the royal secretaries were summoned—on the twenty-third day of the third month, the month of Sivan. They wrote out all Mordecai's orders to the Jews, and to the satraps, governors and nobles of the 127 provinces stretching from India to Cush.ᵃ These orders were written in the script of each province and the language of each people and also to the Jews in their own script and language. ¹⁰Mordecai wrote in the name of King Xerxes, sealed the dispatches with the king's signet ring, and sent them by mounted couriers, who rode fast horses especially bred for the king.

¹¹The king's edict granted the Jews in every city the right to assemble and protect themselves; to destroy, kill and annihilate any armed force of any nationality or province that might attack them and their women and children; and to plunder the property of their enemies. ¹²The day appointed for the Jews to do this in all the provinces of King Xerxes was the thirteenth day of the twelfth month, the month of Adar. ¹³A copy of the text of the edict was to be issued as law in every province and made known to the people of every nationality so that the Jews would be ready on that day to avenge themselves on their enemies.

¹⁴The couriers, riding the royal horses, raced out, spurred on by the king's command. And the edict was also issued in the citadel of Susa.

¹⁵Mordecai left the king's presence wearing royal garments of blue and white, a large crown of gold and a purple robe of fine linen. And the city of Susa held a joyous celebration. ¹⁶For the Jews it was a time of happi-

Gross!

Check out Esther 7:9. Question: How did Haman finally get all the people of Persia to look up to him? Answer: He climbed to the top of the 75-foot high gallows and was hung.

ᵃ 9 That is, the upper Nile region

ness and joy, gladness and honor. ¹⁷In every province and in every city, wherever the edict of the king went, there was joy and gladness among the Jews, with feasting and celebrating. And many people of other nationalities became Jews because fear of the Jews had seized them.

Triumph of the Jews

On the thirteenth day of the twelfth month, the month of Adar, the edict commanded by the king was to be carried out. On this day the enemies of the Jews had hoped to overpower them, but now the tables were turned and the Jews got the upper hand over those who hated them. ²The Jews assembled in their cities in all the provinces of King Xerxes to attack those seeking their destruction. No one could stand against them, because the people of all the other nationalities were afraid of them. ³And all the nobles of the provinces, the satraps, the governors and the king's administrators helped the Jews, because fear of Mordecai had seized them. ⁴Mordecai was prominent in the palace; his reputation spread throughout the provinces, and he became more and more powerful.

⁵The Jews struck down all their enemies with the sword, killing and destroying them, and they did what they pleased to those who hated them. ⁶In the citadel of Susa, the Jews killed and destroyed five hundred men. ⁷They also killed Parshandatha, Dalphon, Aspatha, ⁸Poratha, Adalia, Aridatha, ⁹Parmashta, Arisai, Aridai and Vaizatha, ¹⁰the ten sons of Haman son of Hammedatha, the enemy of the Jews. But they did not lay their hands on the plunder.

¹¹The number of those slain in the citadel of Susa was reported to the king that same day. ¹²The king said to Queen Esther, "The Jews have killed and destroyed five hundred men and the ten sons of Haman in the citadel of Susa. What have they done in the rest of the king's provinces? Now what is your petition? It will be given you. What is your request? It will also be granted."

¹³"If it pleases the king," Esther answered, "give the Jews in Susa permission to carry out this day's edict tomorrow also, and let Haman's ten sons be hanged on gallows."

¹⁴So the king commanded that this be done. An edict was issued in Susa, and they hanged the ten sons of Haman. ¹⁵The Jews in Susa came together on the fourteenth day of the month of Adar, and they put to death in Susa three hundred men, but they did not lay their hands on the plunder.

¹⁶Meanwhile, the remainder of the Jews who were in the king's provinces also assembled to protect themselves and get relief from their enemies. They killed seventy-five thousand of them but did not lay their hands on the plunder. ¹⁷This happened on the thirteenth day of the month of Adar, and on the fourteenth they rested and made it a day of feasting and joy.

Purim Celebrated

¹⁸The Jews in Susa, however, had assembled on the thirteenth and fourteenth, and then on the fifteenth they rested and made it a day of feasting and joy.

¹⁹That is why rural Jews—those living in villages—observe the fourteenth of the month of Adar as a day of joy and feasting, a day for giving presents to each other.

²⁰Mordecai recorded these events, and he sent letters to all the Jews throughout the provinces of King Xerxes, near and far, ²¹to have them celebrate annually the fourteenth and fifteenth days of the month of Adar ²²as the time when the Jews got relief from their enemies, and as the month when their sorrow was turned into joy and their mourning into a day of celebration. He wrote them to observe the days as days of feasting and joy and giving presents of food to one another and gifts to the poor.

²³So the Jews agreed to continue the celebration they had begun, doing what Mordecai had written to them. ²⁴For Haman son of Hammedatha, the Agagite, the enemy of all the Jews, had plotted against the Jews to destroy them and had cast the *pur* (that is, the lot) for their ruin and destruction. ²⁵But when the plot came to the king's attention,[a] he issued written orders that the evil scheme Haman had devised against the Jews should come back onto his own head, and that he and his sons should be hanged on the gallows. ²⁶(Therefore these days were called Purim, from the word *pur*.) Because

---

a 25 Or *when Esther came before the king*

of everything written in this letter and because of what they had seen and what had happened to them, 27the Jews took it upon themselves to establish the custom that they and their descendants and all who join them should without fail observe these two days every year, in the way prescribed and at the time appointed. 28These days should be remembered and observed in every generation by every family, and in every province and in every city. And these days of Purim should never cease to be celebrated by the Jews, nor should the memory of them die out among their descendants.

29So Queen Esther, daughter of Abihail, along with Mordecai the Jew, wrote with full authority to confirm this second letter concerning Purim. 30And Mordecai sent letters to all the Jews in the 127 provinces of the kingdom of Xerxes—words of goodwill and assurance— 31to establish these days of Purim at their designated times, as Mordecai the Jew and Queen Esther had decreed for them, and as they had established for themselves and their descendants in regard to their times of fasting and lamentation. 32Esther's decree confirmed these regulations about Purim, and it was written down in the records.

The Greatness of Mordecai

King Xerxes imposed tribute throughout the empire, to its distant shores. 2And all his acts of power and might, together with a full account of the greatness of Mordecai to which the king had raised him, are they not written in the book of the annals of the kings of Media and Persia? 3Mordecai the Jew was second in rank to King Xerxes, preeminent among the Jews, and held in high esteem by his many fellow Jews, because he worked for the good of his people and spoke up for the welfare of all the Jews.

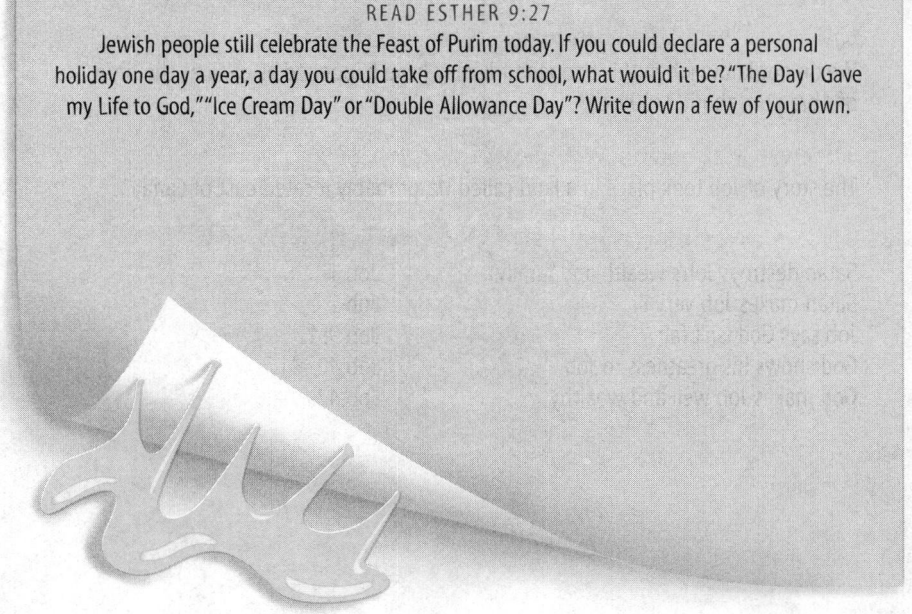

Make It Stick

READ ESTHER 9:27

Jewish people still celebrate the Feast of Purim today. If you could declare a personal holiday one day a year, a day you could take off from school, what would it be? "The Day I Gave my Life to God," "Ice Cream Day" or "Double Allowance Day"? Write down a few of your own.

JOB

Who wrote this book?
The writer of Job is unknown.

Why was this book written?
Job was written to help people learn that suffering is not always punishment from God.

What happens in this book?
Terrible things happen to Job. Job and his three friends discuss why God has let these things happen. God tells Job and his friends to just trust him. God then heals Job and makes him wealthy again.

What do we learn about God in this book?
God does let bad things happen to good people. When bad things happen, it does not mean that God is punishing them for some sin.

Who is important in this book?
Job is the most important person in this book.

When did this happen?
We do not know when this happened. It may have happened as early as the time of Abraham, about 2100 B.C.

Where did this happen?
The story of Job took place in a land called Uz, probably located east of Canaan.

What are some of the stories in this book?
Satan destroys Job's wealth and family	Job 1
Satan makes Job very ill	Job 2
Job says God isn't fair	Job 9; 12
God shows his greatness to Job	Job 40–41
God makes Job well and wealthy	Job 42

Prologue

1 In the land of Uz there lived a man whose name was Job. This man was blameless and upright; he feared God and shunned evil. ²He had seven sons and three daughters, ³and he owned seven thousand sheep, three thousand camels, five hundred yoke of oxen and five hundred donkeys, and had a large number of servants. He was the greatest man among all the people of the East.

⁴His sons used to take turns holding feasts in their homes, and they would invite their three sisters to eat and drink with them. ⁵When a period of feasting had run its course, Job would send and have them purified. Early in the morning he would sacrifice a burnt offering for each of them, thinking, "Perhaps my children have sinned and cursed God in their hearts." This was Job's regular custom.

Job's First Test

⁶One day the angels[a] came to present themselves before the LORD, and Satan[b] also came with them. ⁷The LORD said to Satan, "Where have you come from?"

Satan answered the LORD, "From roaming through the earth and going back and forth in it."

⁸Then the LORD said to Satan, "Have you considered my servant Job? There is no one on earth like him; he is blameless and upright, a man who fears God and shuns evil."

⁹"Does Job fear God for nothing?" Satan replied. ¹⁰"Have you not put a hedge around him and his household and everything he has? You have blessed the work of his hands, so that his flocks and herds are spread throughout the land. ¹¹But stretch out your hand and strike everything he has, and he will surely curse you to your face."

¹²The LORD said to Satan, "Very well, then, everything he has is in your hands, but on the man himself do not lay a finger."

Then Satan went out from the presence of the LORD.

---

[a] 6 Hebrew the sons of God   [b] 6 Satan means accuser.

Job's Big Ranch

READ JOB 1:1–5, 10–11

If someone made a movie about a godly man who had it all, Job would be the star. "This man was blameless and upright; he feared God and shunned evil" (verse 1). Picture the opening scene: a vast landscape of crops and pastures, thousands of sheep and camels covering the hillsides, five hundred oxen pulling plows, servants busy at work, Job's sons and daughters partying in their mansions and living large. Then Job, a handsome, middle-aged man, dressed in fine robes, comes riding over the crest of a hill and looks out at everything. Like Jesus, Job was smart, strong, deep and cool (Luke 2:52). God honored Job because Job held to what was true and right. Aim to be that kind of man. Don't do what's right in the hopes that God will bless you. Do it because it's *right*. Then God will notice you and honor you.

Your next reading is on page 635.

GET DEEPER

Get a Load of This...

Don't get mixed up— Job was the wise man of Uz (Job 1:1), not the wizard of Oz. Uz was an ancient, far-off kingdom. Still, if a tornado picked up your house and dropped it in Uz, you could say, "I guess we're not in Kansas any more."

¹³One day when Job's sons and daughters were feasting and drinking wine at the oldest brother's house, ¹⁴a messenger came to Job and said, "The oxen were plowing and the donkeys were grazing nearby, ¹⁵and the Sabeans attacked and carried them off. They put the servants to the sword, and I am the only one who has escaped to tell you!"

¹⁶While he was still speaking, another messenger came and said, "The fire of God fell from the sky and burned up the sheep and the servants, and I am the only one who has escaped to tell you!"

¹⁷While he was still speaking, another messenger came and said, "The Chaldeans formed three raiding parties and swept down on your camels and carried them off. They put the servants to the sword, and I am the only one who has escaped to tell you!"

¹⁸While he was still speaking, yet another messenger came and said, "Your sons and daughters were feasting and drinking wine at the oldest brother's house, ¹⁹when suddenly a mighty wind swept in from the desert and struck the four corners of the house. It collapsed on them and they are dead, and I am the only one who has escaped to tell you!"

²⁰At this, Job got up and tore his robe and shaved his head. Then he fell to the ground in worship ²¹and said:

"Naked I came from my mother's womb,
  and naked I will depart.ᵃ
The Lord gave and the Lord has taken away;
  may the name of the Lord be praised."

²²In all this, Job did not sin by charging God with wrongdoing.

Job's Second Test

On another day the angelsᵇ came to present themselves before the Lord, and Satan also came with them to present himself before him. ²And the Lord said to Satan, "Where have you come from?"

Satan answered the Lord, "From roaming through the earth and going back and forth in it."

³Then the Lord said to Satan, "Have you considered my servant Job? There is no one on earth like him; he is blameless and upright, a man who fears God and shuns evil. And he still maintains his integrity, though you incited me against him to ruin him without any reason."

⁴"Skin for skin!" Satan replied. "A man will give all he has for his own life. ⁵But stretch out your hand and strike his flesh and bones, and he will surely curse you to your face."

⁶The Lord said to Satan, "Very well, then, he is in your hands; but you must spare his life."

⁷So Satan went out from the presence of the Lord and afflicted Job with painful sores from the soles of his feet to the top of his head. ⁸Then Job took a piece of

---

ᵃ 21 Or will return there   ᵇ 1 Hebrew the sons of God

broken pottery and scraped himself with it as he sat among the ashes.

⁹His wife said to him, "Are you still holding on to your integrity? Curse God and die!"

¹⁰He replied, "You are talking like a foolish ᵃ woman. Shall we accept good from God, and not trouble?"

In all this, Job did not sin in what he said.

Job's Three Friends

¹¹When Job's three friends, Eliphaz the Temanite, Bildad the Shuhite and Zophar the Naamathite, heard about all the troubles that had come upon him, they set out from their homes and met together by agreement to go and sympathize with him and comfort him. ¹²When they saw him from a distance, they could hardly recognize him; they began to weep aloud, and they tore their robes and sprinkled dust on their heads. ¹³Then they sat on the ground with him for seven days and seven nights.

No one said a word to him, because they saw how great his suffering was.

Job Speaks

3 After this, Job opened his mouth and cursed the day of his birth. ²He said:

³ "May the day of my birth perish,
   and the night it was said, 'A boy is
      born!'
⁴That day—may it turn to darkness;
   may God above not care about it;
   may no light shine upon it.
⁵May darkness and deep shadow ᵇ claim
      it once more;
   may a cloud settle over it;
   may blackness overwhelm its light.
⁶That night—may thick darkness seize it;
   may it not be included among the
      days of the year

ᵃ 10 The Hebrew word rendered *foolish* denotes moral deficiency.   ᵇ 5 Or *and the shadow of death*

Make It Stick

READ JOB 1:6–12

Hollywood says Satan is a "loose cannon," doing what he wants. But Satan is powerless to do a thing unless God signs his permission slip. God is in total control (see verses 6–12). Write about an area of your life you don't want to face, then pray about it, and ask God to protect you.

nor be entered in any of the months.
⁷May that night be barren;
    may no shout of joy be heard in it.
⁸May those who curse days^a curse that day,
    those who are ready to rouse Leviathan.
⁹May its morning stars become dark;
    may it wait for daylight in vain
    and not see the first rays of dawn,
¹⁰for it did not shut the doors of the womb on me
    to hide trouble from my eyes.

¹¹"Why did I not perish at birth,
    and die as I came from the womb?
¹²Why were there knees to receive me
    and breasts that I might be nursed?
¹³For now I would be lying down in peace;
    I would be asleep and at rest
¹⁴with kings and counselors of the earth,
    who built for themselves places now lying in ruins,
¹⁵with rulers who had gold,
    who filled their houses with silver.
¹⁶Or why was I not hidden in the ground like a
        stillborn child,
    like an infant who never saw the light of day?
¹⁷There the wicked cease from turmoil,
    and there the weary are at rest.
¹⁸Captives also enjoy their ease;
    they no longer hear the slave driver's shout.
¹⁹The small and the great are there,
    and the slave is freed from his master.

²⁰"Why is light given to those in misery,
    and life to the bitter of soul,
²¹to those who long for death that does not come,
    who search for it more than for hidden treasure,
²²who are filled with gladness
    and rejoice when they reach the grave?
²³Why is life given to a man
    whose way is hidden,
    whom God has hedged in?
²⁴For sighing comes to me instead of food;
    my groans pour out like water.
²⁵What I feared has come upon me;
    what I dreaded has happened to me.
²⁶I have no peace, no quietness;
    I have no rest, but only turmoil."

Eliphaz

Then Eliphaz the Temanite replied:

²"If someone ventures a word with you, will you
        be impatient?
    But who can keep from speaking?
³Think how you have instructed many,
    how you have strengthened feeble hands.
⁴Your words have supported those who stumbled;

Gross!

Job had horrible, painful, festering sores—probably boils—covering every part of his body (Job 2:7). He sat in a heap of oven ashes that had been dumped behind his house, scraping the pus out of all his boils with broken pieces of pottery.

^a 8 Or the sea

you have strengthened faltering
knees.
5 But now trouble comes to you, and
you are discouraged;
it strikes you, and you are dismayed.
6 Should not your piety be your
confidence
and your blameless ways your hope?

7 "Consider now: Who, being innocent,
has ever perished?
Where were the upright ever
destroyed?
8 As I have observed, those who plow
evil
and those who sow trouble reap it.
9 At the breath of God they are
destroyed;
at the blast of his anger they perish.
10 The lions may roar and growl,
yet the teeth of the great lions are
broken.
11 The lion perishes for lack of prey,
and the cubs of the lioness are
scattered.

12 "A word was secretly brought to me,
my ears caught a whisper of it.

13 Amid disquieting dreams in the
night,
when deep sleep falls on men,
14 fear and trembling seized me
and made all my bones shake.
15 A spirit glided past my face,
and the hair on my body stood on
end.
16 It stopped,
but I could not tell what it was.
A form stood before my eyes,
and I heard a hushed voice:
17 'Can a mortal be more righteous than
God?
Can a man be more pure than his
Maker?
18 If God places no trust in his servants,
if he charges his angels with error,
19 how much more those who live in
houses of clay,
whose foundations are in the dust,
who are crushed more readily than
a moth!
20 Between dawn and dusk they are
broken to pieces;
unnoticed, they perish forever.

Being There

READ JOB 2:11-13

Ignore for a moment that Job's friends ended up giving some pretty
lame advice. Focus on what they did when they heard their friend
was suffering. "They set out from their homes and met together by
agreement to go and ... comfort him" (verse 11). They didn't just say,
"Wow, hope he's okay." And they didn't just hang out for a few
minutes. They felt so much pain for Job that they sat on the
ground with him for a week—saying *nothing*! And they
probably stayed for weeks and weeks after that, talking to
him. The best way to support your friends is to "be there."
When there's nothing you can say or do, just being there
means a lot. Saying nothing is better than saying
something fakey and worn-out, right? Being a
good friend is part of being a man. It's being part
of a community that needs you.

Your next reading is on page 639.

²¹ Are not the cords of their tent pulled
up,
   so that they die without wisdom?'ᵃ

5 "Call if you will, but who will
answer you?
   To which of the holy ones will you
turn?
² Resentment kills a fool,
   and envy slays the simple.
³ I myself have seen a fool taking root,
   but suddenly his house was cursed.
⁴ His children are far from safety,
   crushed in court without a defender.
⁵ The hungry consume his harvest,
   taking it even from among thorns,
   and the thirsty pant after his wealth.
⁶ For hardship does not spring from the
soil,
   nor does trouble sprout from the
ground.
⁷ Yet man is born to trouble
   as surely as sparks fly upward.

⁸ "But if it were I, I would appeal to
God;
   I would lay my cause before him.
⁹ He performs wonders that cannot be
fathomed,
   miracles that cannot be counted.
¹⁰ He bestows rain on the earth;
   he sends water upon the
countryside.
¹¹ The lowly he sets on high,
   and those who mourn are lifted to
safety.
¹² He thwarts the plans of the crafty,
   so that their hands achieve no
success.
¹³ He catches the wise in their craftiness,
   and the schemes of the wily are
swept away.
¹⁴ Darkness comes upon them in the
daytime;
   at noon they grope as in the night.
¹⁵ He saves the needy from the sword in
their mouth;
   he saves them from the clutches of
the powerful.
¹⁶ So the poor have hope,
   and injustice shuts its mouth.

¹⁷ "Blessed is the man whom God
corrects;
   so do not despise the discipline of
the Almighty.ᵇ
¹⁸ For he wounds, but he also binds up;
   he injures, but his hands also heal.

¹⁹ From six calamities he will rescue you;
   in seven no harm will befall you.
²⁰ In famine he will ransom you from
death,
   and in battle from the stroke of the
sword.
²¹ You will be protected from the lash of
the tongue,
   and need not fear when destruction
comes.
²² You will laugh at destruction and
famine,
   and need not fear the beasts of the
earth.
²³ For you will have a covenant with the
stones of the field,
   and the wild animals will be at
peace with you.
²⁴ You will know that your tent is secure;
   you will take stock of your property
and find nothing missing.
²⁵ You will know that your children will
be many,
   and your descendants like the grass
of the earth.
²⁶ You will come to the grave in full vigor,
   like sheaves gathered in season.

²⁷ "We have examined this, and it is true.
   So hear it and apply it to yourself."

Job

6 Then Job replied:

² "If only my anguish could be
weighed
   and all my misery be placed on the
scales!
³ It would surely outweigh the sand of
the seas—
   no wonder my words have been
impetuous.
⁴ The arrows of the Almighty are in me,
   my spirit drinks in their poison;
   God's terrors are marshaled against
me.
⁵ Does a wild donkey bray when it has
grass,
   or an ox bellow when it has fodder?
⁶ Is tasteless food eaten without salt,
   or is there flavor in the white of an
eggᶜ?
⁷ I refuse to touch it;
   such food makes me ill.

ᵃ 21 Some interpreters end the quotation after verse 17.
ᵇ 17 Hebrew *Shaddai*; here and throughout Job
ᶜ 6 The meaning of the Hebrew for this phrase is uncertain.

8 "Oh, that I might have my request,
    that God would grant what I hope
    for,
9 that God would be willing to crush me,
    to let loose his hand and cut me off!
10 Then I would still have this
    consolation—
    my joy in unrelenting pain—
    that I had not denied the words of
    the Holy One.

11 "What strength do I have, that I
    should still hope?
    What prospects, that I should be
    patient?
12 Do I have the strength of stone?
    Is my flesh bronze?
13 Do I have any power to help myself,
    now that success has been driven
    from me?

14 "A despairing man should have the
    devotion of his friends,
    even though he forsakes the fear of
    the Almighty.

15 But my brothers are as undependable
    as intermittent streams,
    as the streams that overflow
16 when darkened by thawing ice
    and swollen with melting snow,
17 but that cease to flow in the dry
    season,
    and in the heat vanish from their
    channels.
18 Caravans turn aside from their routes;
    they go up into the wasteland and
    perish.
19 The caravans of Tema look for water,
    the traveling merchants of Sheba
    look in hope.
20 They are distressed, because they had
    been confident;
    they arrive there, only to be
    disappointed.
21 Now you too have proved to be of no
    help;
    you see something dreadful and are
    afraid.

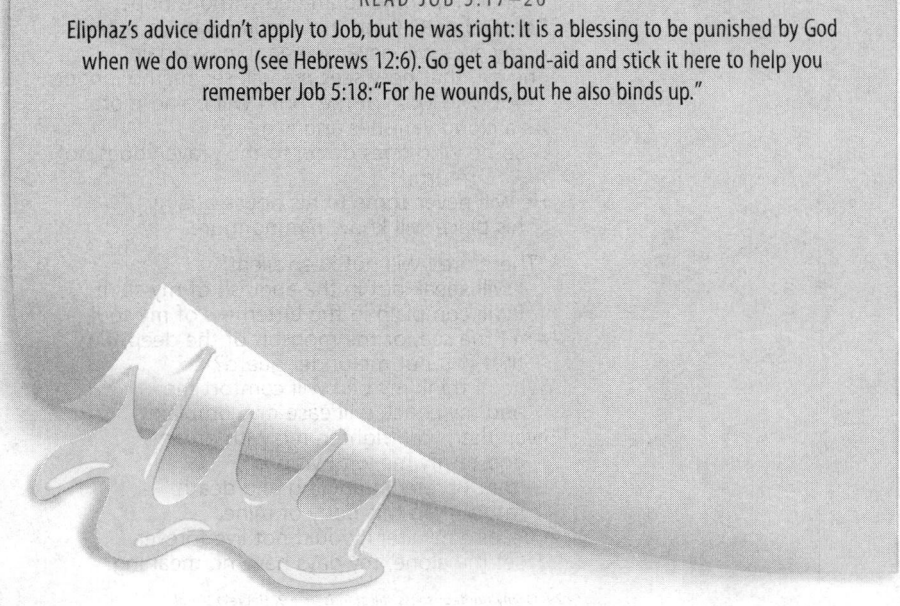

Make It Stick

READ JOB 5:17–26

Eliphaz's advice didn't apply to Job, but he was right: It is a blessing to be punished by God
when we do wrong (see Hebrews 12:6). Go get a band-aid and stick it here to help you
remember Job 5:18: "For he wounds, but he also binds up."

Gross!

We've talked about Job's boils (see Job 2:7). Want to really get grossed out now? Apparently, worms were hatching inside Job's festering sores!— Possibly fly maggots! Job was literally "clothed" with scabs and worms (Job 7:5). No wonder he was scraping his boils to get them out.

22 Have I ever said, 'Give something on my behalf,
    pay a ransom for me from your wealth,
23 deliver me from the hand of the enemy,
    ransom me from the clutches of the ruthless'?

24 "Teach me, and I will be quiet;
    show me where I have been wrong.
25 How painful are honest words!
    But what do your arguments prove?
26 Do you mean to correct what I say,
    and treat the words of a despairing man as wind?
27 You would even cast lots for the fatherless
    and barter away your friend.

28 "But now be so kind as to look at me.
    Would I lie to your face?
29 Relent, do not be unjust;
    reconsider, for my integrity is at stake. *a*
30 Is there any wickedness on my lips?
    Can my mouth not discern malice?

7 "Does not man have hard service on earth?
    Are not his days like those of a hired man?
2 Like a slave longing for the evening shadows,
    or a hired man waiting eagerly for his wages,
3 so I have been allotted months of futility,
    and nights of misery have been assigned to me.
4 When I lie down I think, 'How long before I get up?'
    The night drags on, and I toss till dawn.
5 My body is clothed with worms and scabs,
    my skin is broken and festering.

6 "My days are swifter than a weaver's shuttle,
    and they come to an end without hope.
7 Remember, O God, that my life is but a breath;
    my eyes will never see happiness again.
8 The eye that now sees me will see me no longer;
    you will look for me, but I will be no more.
9 As a cloud vanishes and is gone,
    so he who goes down to the grave *b* does not
      return.
10 He will never come to his house again;
    his place will know him no more.

11 "Therefore I will not keep silent;
    I will speak out in the anguish of my spirit,
    I will complain in the bitterness of my soul.
12 Am I the sea, or the monster of the deep,
    that you put me under guard?
13 When I think my bed will comfort me
    and my couch will ease my complaint,
14 even then you frighten me with dreams
    and terrify me with visions,
15 so that I prefer strangling and death,
    rather than this body of mine.
16 I despise my life; I would not live forever.
    Let me alone; my days have no meaning.

a 29 Or my righteousness still stands   *b 9 Hebrew Sheol*

17 "What is man that you make so much
   of him,
   that you give him so much attention,
18 that you examine him every morning
   and test him every moment?
19 Will you never look away from me,
   or let me alone even for an instant?
20 If I have sinned, what have I done to
   you,
   O watcher of men?
   Why have you made me your target?
   Have I become a burden to you?[a]
21 Why do you not pardon my offenses
   and forgive my sins?
   For I will soon lie down in the dust;
   you will search for me, but I will be
   no more."

Bildad

Then Bildad the Shuhite replied:

2 "How long will you say such
   things?
   Your words are a blustering wind.
3 Does God pervert justice?
   Does the Almighty pervert what is
   right?

4 When your children sinned against
   him,
   he gave them over to the penalty of
   their sin.
5 But if you will look to God
   and plead with the Almighty,
6 if you are pure and upright,
   even now he will rouse himself on
   your behalf
   and restore you to your rightful
   place.
7 Your beginnings will seem humble,
   so prosperous will your future be.

8 "Ask the former generations
   and find out what their fathers
   learned,
9 for we were born only yesterday and
   know nothing,
   and our days on earth are but a
   shadow.
10 Will they not instruct you and tell you?
   Will they not bring forth words from
   their understanding?

[a] 20 A few manuscripts of the Masoretic Text, an ancient
Hebrew scribal tradition and Septuagint; most manuscripts of
the Masoretic Text *I have become a burden to myself.*

Babble-bombs

READ JOB 4:1–2; 8:1–6

Job's friends couldn't keep quiet and now they're dropping babble-
bombs all over. Bildad told Job, "Your words are a blustering wind" (Job
8:2). Right back at you, Bil! Job's situation was like those monster
movies where the giant lizard crushes the city, but then saves everyone
from the giant cockroach. Which is worse—being crushed by a
lizard or a cockroach? Job got smashed on all three sides. With
friends like these, who needs monsters? When God is letting
tough stuff happen to your friends, be humble when you go
to talk to them, and comfort them. It's easy to say, "Here's
where you're missing it, man. This is your problem." Job's
friends weren't really giving Job helpful advice. None
of them (including Job) knew the reason for what
had happened. You don't always know what's
really troubling your friend, right? So concentrate
on being a good friend, and skip the sermons.

Your next reading is on page 641.

¹¹Can papyrus grow tall where there is
   no marsh?
   Can reeds thrive without water?
¹²While still growing and uncut,
   they wither more quickly than grass.
¹³Such is the destiny of all who forget
   God;
   so perishes the hope of the godless.
¹⁴What he trusts in is fragile*a*;
   what he relies on is a spider's web.
¹⁵He leans on his web, but it gives way;
   he clings to it, but it does not hold.
¹⁶He is like a well-watered plant in the
   sunshine,
   spreading its shoots over the garden;
¹⁷it entwines its roots around a pile of
   rocks
   and looks for a place among the
   stones.
¹⁸But when it is torn from its spot,
   that place disowns it and says, 'I
   never saw you.'
¹⁹Surely its life withers away,
   and*b* from the soil other plants grow.

²⁰"Surely God does not reject a
   blameless man
   or strengthen the hands of evildoers.
²¹He will yet fill your mouth with
   laughter
   and your lips with shouts of joy.
²²Your enemies will be clothed in shame,
   and the tents of the wicked will be
   no more."

Job

Then Job replied:

²"Indeed, I know that this is true.
   But how can a mortal be righteous
   before God?
³Though one wished to dispute with
   him,
   he could not answer him one time
   out of a thousand.
⁴His wisdom is profound, his power is
   vast.
   Who has resisted him and come out
   unscathed?
⁵He moves mountains without their
   knowing it
   and overturns them in his anger.
⁶He shakes the earth from its place
   and makes its pillars tremble.
⁷He speaks to the sun and it does not
   shine;
   he seals off the light of the stars.

⁸He alone stretches out the heavens
   and treads on the waves of the sea.
⁹He is the Maker of the Bear and Orion,
   the Pleiades and the constellations
   of the south.
¹⁰He performs wonders that cannot be
   fathomed,
   miracles that cannot be counted.
¹¹When he passes me, I cannot see him;
   when he goes by, I cannot perceive
   him.
¹²If he snatches away, who can stop him?
   Who can say to him, 'What are you
   doing?'
¹³God does not restrain his anger;
   even the cohorts of Rahab cowered
   at his feet.

¹⁴"How then can I dispute with him?
   How can I find words to argue with
   him?
¹⁵Though I were innocent, I could not
   answer him;
   I could only plead with my Judge for
   mercy.
¹⁶Even if I summoned him and he
   responded,
   I do not believe he would give me a
   hearing.
¹⁷He would crush me with a storm
   and multiply my wounds for no
   reason.
¹⁸He would not let me regain my breath
   but would overwhelm me with
   misery.
¹⁹If it is a matter of strength, he is
   mighty!
   And if it is a matter of justice, who
   will summon him*c*?
²⁰Even if I were innocent, my mouth
   would condemn me;
   if I were blameless, it would
   pronounce me guilty.

²¹"Although I am blameless,
   I have no concern for myself;
   I despise my own life.
²²It is all the same; that is why I say,
   'He destroys both the blameless and
   the wicked.'
²³When a scourge brings sudden death,
   he mocks the despair of the
   innocent.
²⁴When a land falls into the hands of the
   wicked,

---

a 14 The meaning of the Hebrew for this word is uncertain.
b 19 Or *Surely all the joy it has / is that*
c 19 See Septuagint; Hebrew *me*.

he blindfolds its judges.
If it is not he, then who is it?

25 "My days are swifter than a runner;
they fly away without a glimpse of
joy.
26 They skim past like boats of papyrus,
like eagles swooping down on their
prey.
27 If I say, 'I will forget my complaint,
I will change my expression, and
smile,'
28 I still dread all my sufferings,
for I know you will not hold me
innocent.
29 Since I am already found guilty,
why should I struggle in vain?
30 Even if I washed myself with soap*a*
and my hands with washing soda,
31 you would plunge me into a slime pit
so that even my clothes would
detest me.

32 "He is not a man like me that I might
answer him,
that we might confront each other
in court.

33 If only there were someone to arbitrate
between us,
to lay his hand upon us both,
34 someone to remove God's rod from
me,
so that his terror would frighten me
no more.
35 Then I would speak up without fear of
him,
but as it now stands with me,
I cannot.

10 I loathe my very life;
therefore I will give free rein to
my complaint
and speak out in the bitterness
of my soul.
2 I will say to God: Do not condemn me,
but tell me what charges you have
against me.
3 Does it please you to oppress me,
to spurn the work of your hands,
while you smile on the schemes of
the wicked?
4 Do you have eyes of flesh?
Do you see as a mortal sees?

a 30 Or snow

Arbitrator and Mediator

READ JOB 9:1–15, 32–35

When Job was being tested to the limit, he longed for someone to speak for him—to plead his case to God—to mediate between him and God (verse 33). Eventually, Jesus Christ became that mediator for us. When God made Jesus our mediator, he gave us someone who could see both sides of the story—God's side (since Jesus is God) and our side (since Jesus was a man on earth). Jesus understands us. He speaks up for us to God, he prays for us, he intercedes for us (see Romans 8:34). Jesus also strengthens us when hard times hit. He told Simon Peter that Satan wanted to crush him, but then told him, "I have prayed for you, Simon, that your faith may not fail" (Luke 22:32). Despite everything Job went through, he stood firm in his faith and never gave up. With Jesus helping us, we can stand firm, too.

Your next reading is on page 643.

⁵Are your days like those of a mortal
    or your years like those of a man,
⁶that you must search out my faults
    and probe after my sin—
⁷though you know that I am not guilty
    and that no one can rescue me from
        your hand?

⁸"Your hands shaped me and made me.
    Will you now turn and destroy me?
⁹Remember that you molded me like
        clay.
    Will you now turn me to dust again?
¹⁰Did you not pour me out like milk
    and curdle me like cheese,
¹¹clothe me with skin and flesh
    and knit me together with bones
        and sinews?
¹²You gave me life and showed me
        kindness,
    and in your providence watched
        over my spirit.

¹³"But this is what you concealed in your
        heart,
    and I know that this was in your
        mind:
¹⁴If I sinned, you would be watching me
    and would not let my offense go
        unpunished.
¹⁵If I am guilty—woe to me!
    Even if I am innocent, I cannot lift
        my head,
  for I am full of shame
    and drowned inª my affliction.
¹⁶If I hold my head high, you stalk me
        like a lion
    and again display your awesome
        power against me.
¹⁷You bring new witnesses against me
    and increase your anger toward me;
    your forces come against me wave
        upon wave.

¹⁸"Why then did you bring me out of
        the womb?
    I wish I had died before any eye saw
        me.
¹⁹If only I had never come into being,
    or had been carried straight from
        the womb to the grave!
²⁰Are not my few days almost over?
    Turn away from me so I can have a
        moment's joy
²¹before I go to the place of no return,
    to the land of gloom and deep
        shadow,ᵇ
²²to the land of deepest night,

of deep shadow and disorder,
    where even the light is like darkness."

Zophar

11 Then Zophar the Naamathite re-
        plied:

²"Are all these words to go
        unanswered?
    Is this talker to be vindicated?
³Will your idle talk reduce men to
        silence?
    Will no one rebuke you when you
        mock?
⁴You say to God, 'My beliefs are
        flawless
    and I am pure in your sight.'
⁵Oh, how I wish that God would speak,
    that he would open his lips against
        you
⁶and disclose to you the secrets of
        wisdom,
    for true wisdom has two sides.
    Know this: God has even forgotten
        some of your sin.

⁷"Can you fathom the mysteries of God?
    Can you probe the limits of the
        Almighty?
⁸They are higher than the heavens—
        what can you do?
    They are deeper than the depths of
        the graveᶜ—what can you
        know?
⁹Their measure is longer than the earth
    and wider than the sea.

¹⁰"If he comes along and confines you in
        prison
    and convenes a court, who can
        oppose him?
¹¹Surely he recognizes deceitful men;
    and when he sees evil, does he not
        take note?
¹²But a witless man can no more
        become wise
    than a wild donkey's colt can be
        born a man.ᵈ

¹³"Yet if you devote your heart to him
    and stretch out your hands to him,
¹⁴if you put away the sin that is in your
        hand
    and allow no evil to dwell in your
        tent,

ª 15 Or and aware of   ᵇ 21 Or and the shadow of death;
also in verse 22   ᶜ 8 Hebrew than Sheol   ᵈ 12 Or wild
donkey can be born tame

15 then you will lift up your face without
    shame;
  you will stand firm and without fear.
16 You will surely forget your trouble,
  recalling it only as waters gone by.
17 Life will be brighter than noonday,
  and darkness will become like
    morning.
18 You will be secure, because there is
    hope;
  you will look about you and take
    your rest in safety.
19 You will lie down, with no one to
    make you afraid,
  and many will court your favor.
20 But the eyes of the wicked will fail,
  and escape will elude them;
  their hope will become a dying
    gasp."

Job

12 Then Job replied:

2 "Doubtless you are the people,
  and wisdom will die with you!
3 But I have a mind as well as you;

  I am not inferior to you.
  Who does not know all these things?

4 "I have become a laughingstock to my
    friends,
  though I called upon God and he
    answered—
  a mere laughingstock, though
    righteous and blameless!
5 Men at ease have contempt for
    misfortune
  as the fate of those whose feet are
    slipping.
6 The tents of marauders are undisturbed,
  and those who provoke God are
    secure—
  those who carry their god in their
    hands. [a]

7 "But ask the animals, and they will
    teach you,
  or the birds of the air, and they will
    tell you;
8 or speak to the earth, and it will teach
    you,
  or let the fish of the sea inform you.

[a] 6 Or secure / in what God's hand brings them

GET SMARTER

Don't Be a Cabbage-head

READ JOB 12:1–3; 13:1–5

Job finally got fed up with his friends' so-called advice: "I have a mind as well as you ... Who does not know all these things?" (Job 12:3). Basically he said, "You guys are real know-it-alls, and you think I'm a cabbage-head." Nobody likes being treated like they're stupid, right? It's one thing explaining when someone says, "I don't get it." It's another thing when you lecture them on really basic stuff. Job's friends were preaching to him about God, but it was like first grade writing practice for Job. *Not* helpful. Give people credit. If it's their problem, chances are good they know the ABCs of the situation. As a man, approach them with re-spect. Treat people as if they are intelligent and can think. Check out both sides of the story and be a good listener. Know-it-alls are the *real* cabbage-heads.

Your next reading is on page 647.

⁹Which of all these does not know
    that the hand of the LORD has done
        this?
¹⁰In his hand is the life of every creature
    and the breath of all mankind.
¹¹Does not the ear test words
    as the tongue tastes food?
¹²Is not wisdom found among the aged?
    Does not long life bring
        understanding?

¹³"To God belong wisdom and power;
    counsel and understanding are his.
¹⁴What he tears down cannot be rebuilt;
    the man he imprisons cannot be
        released.
¹⁵If he holds back the waters, there is
        drought;
    if he lets them loose, they devastate
        the land.
¹⁶To him belong strength and victory;
    both deceived and deceiver are his.
¹⁷He leads counselors away stripped
    and makes fools of judges.
¹⁸He takes off the shackles put on by
        kings
    and ties a loincloth[a] around their
        waist.
¹⁹He leads priests away stripped
    and overthrows men long
        established.
²⁰He silences the lips of trusted advisers
    and takes away the discernment of
        elders.
²¹He pours contempt on nobles
    and disarms the mighty.
²²He reveals the deep things of darkness
    and brings deep shadows into the
        light.
²³He makes nations great, and destroys
        them;
    he enlarges nations, and disperses
        them.
²⁴He deprives the leaders of the earth of
        their reason;
    he sends them wandering through a
        trackless waste.
²⁵They grope in darkness with no light;
    he makes them stagger like
        drunkards.

13 "My eyes have seen all this,
    my ears have heard and
        understood it.
²What you know, I also know;
    I am not inferior to you.
³But I desire to speak to the Almighty
    and to argue my case with God.

⁴You, however, smear me with lies;
    you are worthless physicians, all of
        you!
⁵If only you would be altogether silent!
    For you, that would be wisdom.
⁶Hear now my argument;
    listen to the plea of my lips.
⁷Will you speak wickedly on God's
        behalf?
    Will you speak deceitfully for him?
⁸Will you show him partiality?
    Will you argue the case for God?
⁹Would it turn out well if he examined
        you?
    Could you deceive him as you might
        deceive men?
¹⁰He would surely rebuke you
    if you secretly showed partiality.
¹¹Would not his splendor terrify you?
    Would not the dread of him fall on
        you?
¹²Your maxims are proverbs of ashes;
    your defenses are defenses of clay.

¹³"Keep silent and let me speak;
    then let come to me what may.
¹⁴Why do I put myself in jeopardy
    and take my life in my hands?
¹⁵Though he slay me, yet will I hope in
        him;
    I will surely[b] defend my ways to his
        face.
¹⁶Indeed, this will turn out for my
        deliverance,
    for no godless man would dare
        come before him!
¹⁷Listen carefully to my words;
    let your ears take in what I say.
¹⁸Now that I have prepared my case,
    I know I will be vindicated.
¹⁹Can anyone bring charges against me?
    If so, I will be silent and die.

²⁰"Only grant me these two things,
        O God,
    and then I will not hide from you:
²¹Withdraw your hand far from me,
    and stop frightening me with your
        terrors.
²²Then summon me and I will answer,
    or let me speak, and you reply.
²³How many wrongs and sins have I
        committed?
    Show me my offense and my sin.
²⁴Why do you hide your face

---

[a] 18 Or shackles of kings / and ties a belt   [b] 15 Or He will
surely slay me; I have no hope — / yet I will

and consider me your enemy?
25 Will you torment a windblown leaf?
    Will you chase after dry chaff?
26 For you write down bitter things
        against me
    and make me inherit the sins of my
        youth.
27 You fasten my feet in shackles;
    you keep close watch on all my paths
    by putting marks on the soles of my
        feet.

28 "So man wastes away like something
        rotten,
    like a garment eaten by moths.

14 "Man born of woman
    is of few days and full of trouble.
2 He springs up like a flower and
    withers away;
    like a fleeting shadow, he does not
        endure.
3 Do you fix your eye on such a one?
    Will you bring him*a* before you for
        judgment?
4 Who can bring what is pure from the
        impure?
    No one!
5 Man's days are determined;
    you have decreed the number of his
        months
    and have set limits he cannot exceed.
6 So look away from him and let him
        alone,
    till he has put in his time like a hired
        man.

7 "At least there is hope for a tree:
    If it is cut down, it will sprout again,
    and its new shoots will not fail.
8 Its roots may grow old in the ground
    and its stump die in the soil,
9 yet at the scent of water it will bud
    and put forth shoots like a plant.
10 But man dies and is laid low;
    he breathes his last and is no more.
11 As water disappears from the sea
    or a riverbed becomes parched and
        dry,
12 so man lies down and does not rise;
    till the heavens are no more, men
        will not awake
    or be roused from their sleep.

13 "If only you would hide me in the
        grave*b*
    and conceal me till your anger has
        passed!
    If only you would set me a time

and then remember me!
14 If a man dies, will he live again?
    All the days of my hard service
    I will wait for my renewal*c* to come.
15 You will call and I will answer you;
    you will long for the creature your
        hands have made.
16 Surely then you will count my steps
    but not keep track of my sin.
17 My offenses will be sealed up in a bag;
    you will cover over my sin.

18 "But as a mountain erodes and
        crumbles
    and as a rock is moved from its
        place,
19 as water wears away stones
    and torrents wash away the soil,
    so you destroy man's hope.
20 You overpower him once for all, and
        he is gone;
    you change his countenance and
        send him away.
21 If his sons are honored, he does not
        know it;
    if they are brought low, he does not
        see it.
22 He feels but the pain of his own body
    and mourns only for himself."

Eliphaz

15 Then Eliphaz the Temanite re-
    plied:

2 "Would a wise man answer
        with empty notions
    or fill his belly with the hot east
        wind?
3 Would he argue with useless words,
    with speeches that have no value?
4 But you even undermine piety
    and hinder devotion to God.
5 Your sin prompts your mouth;
    you adopt the tongue of the crafty.
6 Your own mouth condemns you, not
        mine;
    your own lips testify against you.

7 "Are you the first man ever born?
    Were you brought forth before the
        hills?
8 Do you listen in on God's council?
    Do you limit wisdom to yourself?
9 What do you know that we do not
        know?

a 3 Septuagint, Vulgate and Syriac; Hebrew *me*
b 13 Hebrew *Sheol*   *c 14* Or *release*

What insights do you have that we
　　do not have?
10 The gray-haired and the aged are on
　　our side,
　　men even older than your father.
11 Are God's consolations not enough for
　　you,
　　words spoken gently to you?
12 Why has your heart carried you away,
　　and why do your eyes flash,
13 so that you vent your rage against God
　　and pour out such words from your
　　mouth?

14 "What is man, that he could be pure,
　　or one born of woman, that he
　　could be righteous?
15 If God places no trust in his holy
　　ones,
　　if even the heavens are not pure in
　　his eyes,
16 how much less man, who is vile and
　　corrupt,
　　who drinks up evil like water!

17 "Listen to me and I will explain to you;
　　let me tell you what I have seen,
18 what wise men have declared,
　　hiding nothing received from their
　　fathers
19 (to whom alone the land was given
　　when no alien passed among them):
20 All his days the wicked man suffers
　　torment,
　　the ruthless through all the years
　　stored up for him.
21 Terrifying sounds fill his ears;
　　when all seems well, marauders
　　attack him.
22 He despairs of escaping the darkness;
　　he is marked for the sword.
23 He wanders about—food for vultures[a];
　　he knows the day of darkness is at
　　hand.
24 Distress and anguish fill him with terror;
　　they overwhelm him, like a king
　　poised to attack,

a 23 Or about, looking for food

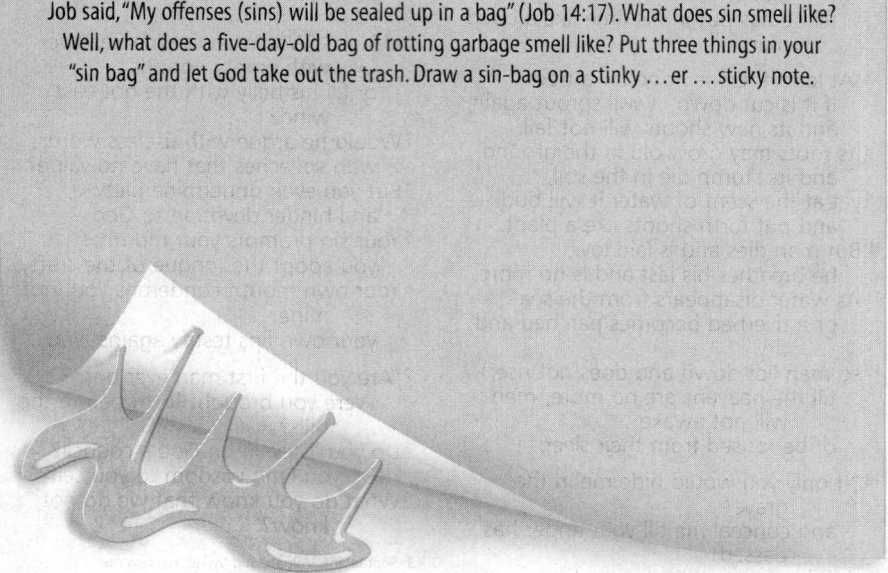

Make It Stick

READ JOB 14:17

Job said, "My offenses (sins) will be sealed up in a bag" (Job 14:17). What does sin smell like?
Well, what does a five-day-old bag of rotting garbage smell like? Put three things in your
"sin bag" and let God take out the trash. Draw a sin-bag on a stinky ... er ... sticky note.

25 because he shakes his fist at God
  and vaunts himself against the
    Almighty,
26 defiantly charging against him
  with a thick, strong shield.

27 "Though his face is covered with fat
  and his waist bulges with flesh,
28 he will inhabit ruined towns
  and houses where no one lives,
  houses crumbling to rubble.
29 He will no longer be rich and his
    wealth will not endure,
  nor will his possessions spread over
    the land.
30 He will not escape the darkness;
  a flame will wither his shoots,
  and the breath of God's mouth will
    carry him away.
31 Let him not deceive himself by trusting
    what is worthless,
  for he will get nothing in return.
32 Before his time he will be paid in full,
  and his branches will not flourish.

33 He will be like a vine stripped of its
    unripe grapes,
  like an olive tree shedding its
    blossoms.
34 For the company of the godless will be
    barren,
  and fire will consume the tents of
    those who love bribes.
35 They conceive trouble and give birth to
    evil;
  their womb fashions deceit."

Job

16 Then Job replied:

2 "I have heard many things like
    these;
  miserable comforters are you all!
3 Will your long-winded speeches never
    end?
  What ails you that you keep on
    arguing?
4 I also could speak like you,
  if you were in my place;

Dive-bombing Criticism

READ JOB 16:2–5

Imagine that you're having a rough time today—nasty school lunch, flattened by a tough pop quiz. But wait! Here comes your best bud—he always makes you laugh. You could use some encouragement about now. But no! He dive-bombs you—saying how you should act more like a Christian and stop being so bummed out. He doesn't care what's wrong. He doesn't ask if he can do anything to help. Maaaan, now you're *really* bummed! Now you get what Job meant when he exclaimed what he would do if he were in his friends' place, "But my mouth would encourage you; comfort from my lips would bring you relief" (Job 16:5). But calm down before you get too angry with your friend for not being there for you. "The Lord's servant must not quarrel; instead, he must be kind to everyone ... not resentful" (2 Timothy 2:24). The next time one of your friends is down, encourage him. Don't dive-bomb him with criticism.

Your next reading is on page 650.

I could make fine speeches against you
  and shake my head at you.
5 But my mouth would encourage you;
  comfort from my lips would bring
    you relief.

6 "Yet if I speak, my pain is not relieved;
  and if I refrain, it does not go away.
7 Surely, O God, you have worn me out;
  you have devastated my entire
    household.
8 You have bound me—and it has
    become a witness;
  my gauntness rises up and testifies
    against me.
9 God assails me and tears me in his
    anger
  and gnashes his teeth at me;
  my opponent fastens on me his
    piercing eyes.
10 Men open their mouths to jeer at me;
  they strike my cheek in scorn
  and unite together against me.
11 God has turned me over to evil men
  and thrown me into the clutches of
    the wicked.
12 All was well with me, but he shattered
    me;
  he seized me by the neck and
    crushed me.
  He has made me his target;
13   his archers surround me.
  Without pity, he pierces my kidneys
  and spills my gall on the ground.
14 Again and again he bursts upon me;
  he rushes at me like a warrior.

15 "I have sewed sackcloth over my skin
  and buried my brow in the dust.
16 My face is red with weeping,
  deep shadows ring my eyes;
17 yet my hands have been free of
    violence
  and my prayer is pure.

18 "O earth, do not cover my blood;
  may my cry never be laid to rest!
19 Even now my witness is in heaven;
  my advocate is on high.
20 My intercessor is my friend[a]
  as my eyes pour out tears to God;
21 on behalf of a man he pleads with
    God
  as a man pleads for his friend.

22 "Only a few years will pass
  before I go on the journey of no
    return.

17 ¹ My spirit is broken,
  my days are cut short,
  the grave awaits me.
² Surely mockers surround me;
  my eyes must dwell on their hostility.

3 "Give me, O God, the pledge you
    demand.
  Who else will put up security for me?
4 You have closed their minds to
    understanding;
  therefore you will not let them
    triumph.
5 If a man denounces his friends for
    reward,
  the eyes of his children will fail.

6 "God has made me a byword to
    everyone,
  a man in whose face people spit.
7 My eyes have grown dim with grief;
  my whole frame is but a shadow.
8 Upright men are appalled at this;
  the innocent are aroused against the
    ungodly.
9 Nevertheless, the righteous will hold to
    their ways,
  and those with clean hands will
    grow stronger.

10 "But come on, all of you, try again!
  I will not find a wise man among you.
11 My days have passed, my plans are
    shattered,
  and so are the desires of my heart.
12 These men turn night into day;
  in the face of darkness they say,
    'Light is near.'
13 If the only home I hope for is the
    grave,[b]
  if I spread out my bed in darkness,
14 if I say to corruption, 'You are my
    father,'
  and to the worm, 'My mother' or
    'My sister,'
15 where then is my hope?
  Who can see any hope for me?
16 Will it go down to the gates of death[b]?
  Will we descend together into the
    dust?"

Bildad

18 Then Bildad the Shuhite replied:

² "When will you end these
    speeches?

a 20 Or My friends treat me with scorn   b 13,16 Hebrew
Sheol

Be sensible, and then we can talk.
³ Why are we regarded as cattle
     and considered stupid in your sight?
⁴ You who tear yourself to pieces in your anger,
     is the earth to be abandoned for your sake?
     Or must the rocks be moved from their place?

⁵ "The lamp of the wicked is snuffed out;
     the flame of his fire stops burning.
⁶ The light in his tent becomes dark;
     the lamp beside him goes out.
⁷ The vigor of his step is weakened;
     his own schemes throw him down.
⁸ His feet thrust him into a net
     and he wanders into its mesh.
⁹ A trap seizes him by the heel;
     a snare holds him fast.
¹⁰ A noose is hidden for him on the ground;
     a trap lies in his path.
¹¹ Terrors startle him on every side
     and dog his every step.
¹² Calamity is hungry for him;
     disaster is ready for him when he falls.
¹³ It eats away parts of his skin;
     death's firstborn devours his limbs.
¹⁴ He is torn from the security of his tent
     and marched off to the king of terrors.
¹⁵ Fire resides[a] in his tent;
     burning sulfur is scattered over his dwelling.
¹⁶ His roots dry up below
     and his branches wither above.
¹⁷ The memory of him perishes from the earth;
     he has no name in the land.
¹⁸ He is driven from light into darkness
     and is banished from the world.
¹⁹ He has no offspring or descendants among his
         people,
     no survivor where once he lived.
²⁰ Men of the west are appalled at his fate;
     men of the east are seized with horror.
²¹ Surely such is the dwelling of an evil man;
     such is the place of one who knows not God."

Job

19 Then Job replied:

² "How long will you torment me
     and crush me with words?
³ Ten times now you have reproached me;
     shamelessly you attack me.
⁴ If it is true that I have gone astray,
     my error remains my concern alone.
⁵ If indeed you would exalt yourselves above me
     and use my humiliation against me,
⁶ then know that God has wronged me
     and drawn his net around me.

---

a 15 Or *Nothing he had remains*

Get a Load of This...

"He is ... banished from the world" (Job 18:18). What is this?—Exile to Pluto? Being shipped off to a prison colony on the fourth moon of Neptune? Actually, as you probably guessed, it's talking about someone leaving this world by dying.

7 "Though I cry, 'I've been wronged!' I
    get no response;
  though I call for help, there is no
    justice.
8 He has blocked my way so I cannot
    pass;
  he has shrouded my paths in darkness.
9 He has stripped me of my honor
  and removed the crown from my
    head.
10 He tears me down on every side till I
    am gone;
  he uproots my hope like a tree.
11 His anger burns against me;
  he counts me among his enemies.
12 His troops advance in force;
  they build a siege ramp against me
  and encamp around my tent.

13 "He has alienated my brothers from me;
  my acquaintances are completely
    estranged from me.
14 My kinsmen have gone away;
  my friends have forgotten me.
15 My guests and my maidservants count
    me a stranger;
  they look upon me as an alien.

16 I summon my servant, but he does not
    answer,
  though I beg him with my own
    mouth.
17 My breath is offensive to my wife;
  I am loathsome to my own brothers.
18 Even the little boys scorn me;
  when I appear, they ridicule me.
19 All my intimate friends detest me;
  those I love have turned against me.
20 I am nothing but skin and bones;
  I have escaped with only the skin of
    my teeth. [a]

21 "Have pity on me, my friends, have pity,
  for the hand of God has struck me.
22 Why do you pursue me as God does?
  Will you never get enough of my
    flesh?
23 "Oh, that my words were recorded,
  that they were written on a scroll,
24 that they were inscribed with an iron
    tool on [b] lead,
  or engraved in rock forever!
25 I know that my Redeemer [c] lives,

[a] 20 Or only my gums   [b] 24 Or and   [c] 25 Or defender

On the Run . . . Alone

READ JOB 19:13–20

Ever seen a movie where some guy uncovers this incredible plot—
some conspiracy to take over the government—and he tries to warn
people, but no one believes him, and he's on the run for his life? He
goes to his friends, but even they don't believe him and *man!*—Now
he *really* feels alone! The fate of the country may not rest in
our hands, but all of us feel lonely and misunderstood at
times. We get down on ourselves and think no one cares. People *do* care. God cares. Don't hide from God or your
friends—let them help. Job said, "My friends have forgotten
me" (verse 14). In Job's case, it was true, but 99% of the
time, we really can turn to our friends. And like the
guy in the movie, you'll always find at least *one*
friend who believes in you and cares.

Your next reading is on page 653.

GET COOLER

and that in the end he will stand
  upon the earth.[a]

26 And after my skin has been destroyed,
  yet[b] in[c] my flesh I will see God;

27 I myself will see him
  with my own eyes—I, and not
    another.
  How my heart yearns within me!

28 "If you say, 'How we will hound him,
  since the root of the trouble lies in
    him,[d]'

29 you should fear the sword yourselves;
  for wrath will bring punishment by
    the sword,
  and then you will know that there is
    judgment.[e]"

Zophar

20 Then Zophar the Naamathite
replied:

2 "My troubled thoughts
prompt me to answer

because I am greatly disturbed.

3 I hear a rebuke that dishonors me,
  and my understanding inspires me
    to reply.

4 "Surely you know how it has been
    from of old,
  ever since man[f] was placed on the
    earth,

5 that the mirth of the wicked is brief,
  the joy of the godless lasts but a
    moment.

6 Though his pride reaches to the heavens
  and his head touches the clouds,

7 he will perish forever, like his own dung;
  those who have seen him will say,
    'Where is he?'

8 Like a dream he flies away, no more to
    be found,
  banished like a vision of the night.

---

[a] 25 Or upon my grave   [b] 26 Or And after I awake, /
though this ⌊body⌋ has been destroyed, / then   [c] 26 Or /
apart from   [d] 28 Many Hebrew manuscripts, Septuagint
and Vulgate; most Hebrew manuscripts me   [e] 29 Or / that
you may come to know the Almighty   [f] 4 Or Adam

Make It Stick

READ JOB 19:17

Is your breath "offensive" like Job's was (Job 19:17)? Take the Raunchy Breath Test: lick your arm,
then breathe on the spot. Rate your mouth odor from 1 to 10 (1 being "smells like a rose,"
10 being "gag a maggot"). If you want people to be able to listen to you without gagging, brush
and floss—even brush your tongue. Bad breath comes from bacteria on the back of your tongue.

Get a Load of This...

Check out Job 19:25–27. Job lived thousands of years ago and yet look at this! Way back then God had already given him a revelation about Jesus—the Redeemer—coming back to earth, and the resurrection from the dead! Cool!

9 The eye that saw him will not see him again;
   his place will look on him no more.
10 His children must make amends to the poor;
   his own hands must give back his wealth.
11 The youthful vigor that fills his bones
   will lie with him in the dust.

12 "Though evil is sweet in his mouth
   and he hides it under his tongue,
13 though he cannot bear to let it go
   and keeps it in his mouth,
14 yet his food will turn sour in his stomach;
   it will become the venom of serpents within him.
15 He will spit out the riches he swallowed;
   God will make his stomach vomit them up.
16 He will suck the poison of serpents;
   the fangs of an adder will kill him.
17 He will not enjoy the streams,
   the rivers flowing with honey and cream.
18 What he toiled for he must give back uneaten;
   he will not enjoy the profit from his trading.
19 For he has oppressed the poor and left them destitute;
   he has seized houses he did not build.

20 "Surely he will have no respite from his craving;
   he cannot save himself by his treasure.
21 Nothing is left for him to devour;
   his prosperity will not endure.
22 In the midst of his plenty, distress will overtake him;
   the full force of misery will come upon him.
23 When he has filled his belly,
   God will vent his burning anger against him
   and rain down his blows upon him.
24 Though he flees from an iron weapon,
   a bronze-tipped arrow pierces him.
25 He pulls it out of his back,
   the gleaming point out of his liver.
   Terrors will come over him;
26   total darkness lies in wait for his treasures.
   A fire unfanned will consume him
   and devour what is left in his tent.
27 The heavens will expose his guilt;
   the earth will rise up against him.
28 A flood will carry off his house,
   rushing waters[a] on the day of God's wrath.
29 Such is the fate God allots the wicked,
   the heritage appointed for them by God."

Job

21

Then Job replied:

2 "Listen carefully to my words;
   let this be the consolation you give me.
3 Bear with me while I speak,
   and after I have spoken, mock on.

---

[a] 28 Or The possessions in his house will be carried off, / washed away

4 "Is my complaint directed to man?
  Why should I not be impatient?
5 Look at me and be astonished;
  clap your hand over your mouth.
6 When I think about this, I am terrified;
  trembling seizes my body.
7 Why do the wicked live on,
  growing old and increasing in
  power?
8 They see their children established
  around them,
  their offspring before their eyes.
9 Their homes are safe and free from
  fear;
  the rod of God is not upon them.
10 Their bulls never fail to breed;
  their cows calve and do not miscarry.
11 They send forth their children as a
  flock;
  their little ones dance about.
12 They sing to the music of tambourine
  and harp;
  they make merry to the sound of the
  flute.

13 They spend their years in prosperity
  and go down to the grave[a] in
  peace.[b]
14 Yet they say to God, 'Leave us alone!
  We have no desire to know your
  ways.
15 Who is the Almighty, that we should
  serve him?
  What would we gain by praying to
  him?'
16 But their prosperity is not in their own
  hands,
  so I stand aloof from the counsel of
  the wicked.

17 "Yet how often is the lamp of the
  wicked snuffed out?
  How often does calamity come upon
  them,
  the fate God allots in his anger?
18 How often are they like straw before
  the wind,
  like chaff swept away by a gale?

a 13 Hebrew *Sheol*   b 13 Or *in an instant*

The Big Picture

READ JOB 21:7–20

You see it everywhere—worldly people, having fun doing whatever they want. Job saw it, too. He wondered what was the point of being good if wicked people were allowed to run around thumbing their noses at God. But Job already knew the answer: He knew that God would judge the wicked. Job was a godly man and he acted responsibly. Sure, he enjoyed fun and humor and owning cool things, but he also knew how to find a balance in life. You can, too. Getting caught up in always living for the moment is dangerous. A righteous man takes the big picture into account. There are times to enjoy the moment and have fun, but there's more … like loving God, genuinely loving others and do what's right. When God is ready, he'll pull out his set of scales and judge the wicked. Maybe not until eternity. That's the *big* picture.

Your next reading is on page 656.

GET SMARTER.

¹⁹ₗIt is said,₁ 'God stores up a man's
    punishment for his sons.'
  Let him repay the man himself, so
    that he will know it!
²⁰ Let his own eyes see his destruction;
    let him drink of the wrath of the
    Almighty.ᵃ
²¹ For what does he care about the family
    he leaves behind
  when his allotted months come to
    an end?

²² "Can anyone teach knowledge to God,
    since he judges even the highest?
²³ One man dies in full vigor,
    completely secure and at ease,
²⁴ his bodyᵇ well nourished,
    his bones rich with marrow.
²⁵ Another man dies in bitterness of soul,
    never having enjoyed anything good.
²⁶ Side by side they lie in the dust,
    and worms cover them both.

²⁷ "I know full well what you are thinking,
    the schemes by which you would
    wrong me.
²⁸ You say, 'Where now is the great
    man's house,
    the tents where wicked men lived?'
²⁹ Have you never questioned those who
    travel?
  Have you paid no regard to their
    accounts—
³⁰ that the evil man is spared from the
    day of calamity,
  that he is delivered fromᶜ the day of
    wrath?
³¹ Who denounces his conduct to his face?
    Who repays him for what he has
    done?
³² He is carried to the grave,
    and watch is kept over his tomb.
³³ The soil in the valley is sweet to him;
    all men follow after him,
  and a countless throng goesᵈ before
    him.

³⁴ "So how can you console me with your
    nonsense?
  Nothing is left of your answers but
    falsehood!"

Eliphaz

22 Then Eliphaz the Temanite re-
    plied:

² "Can a man be of benefit to
    God?

Can even a wise man benefit him?
³ What pleasure would it give the
    Almighty if you were righteous?
  What would he gain if your ways
    were blameless?
⁴ "Is it for your piety that he rebukes you
    and brings charges against you?
⁵ Is not your wickedness great?
    Are not your sins endless?
⁶ You demanded security from your
    brothers for no reason;
  you stripped men of their clothing,
    leaving them naked.
⁷ You gave no water to the weary
    and you withheld food from the
    hungry,
⁸ though you were a powerful man,
    owning land—
  an honored man, living on it.
⁹ And you sent widows away
    empty-handed
  and broke the strength of the
    fatherless.
¹⁰ That is why snares are all around you,
    why sudden peril terrifies you,
¹¹ why it is so dark you cannot see,
    and why a flood of water covers you.

¹² "Is not God in the heights of heaven?
    And see how lofty are the highest
    stars!
¹³ Yet you say, 'What does God know?
    Does he judge through such
    darkness?
¹⁴ Thick clouds veil him, so he does not
    see us
  as he goes about in the vaulted
    heavens.'
¹⁵ Will you keep to the old path
    that evil men have trod?
¹⁶ They were carried off before their time,
    their foundations washed away by a
    flood.
¹⁷ They said to God, 'Leave us alone!
    What can the Almighty do to us?'
¹⁸ Yet it was he who filled their houses
    with good things,
  so I stand aloof from the counsel of
    the wicked.

¹⁹ "The righteous see their ruin and
    rejoice;
  the innocent mock them, saying,

ᵃ 17–20 Verses 17 and 18 may be taken as exclamations and
19 and 20 as declarations.   ᵇ 24 The meaning of the
Hebrew for this word is uncertain.   ᶜ 30 Or man is reserved
for the day of calamity, / that he is brought forth to
ᵈ 33 Or / as a countless throng went

20 'Surely our foes are destroyed,
and fire devours their wealth.'

21 "Submit to God and be at peace with
him;
in this way prosperity will come to
you.
22 Accept instruction from his mouth
and lay up his words in your heart.
23 If you return to the Almighty, you will
be restored:
If you remove wickedness far from
your tent
24 and assign your nuggets to the dust,
your gold of Ophir to the rocks in
the ravines,
25 then the Almighty will be your gold,
the choicest silver for you.
26 Surely then you will find delight in the
Almighty
and will lift up your face to God.
27 You will pray to him, and he will hear
you,
and you will fulfill your vows.
28 What you decide on will be done,
and light will shine on your ways.
29 When men are brought low and you
say, 'Lift them up!'
then he will save the downcast.
30 He will deliver even one who is not
innocent,
who will be delivered through the
cleanness of your hands."

Job

23 Then Job replied:

2 "Even today my complaint is
bitter;
his hand[a] is heavy in spite of[b] my
groaning.
3 If only I knew where to find him;
if only I could go to his dwelling!
4 I would state my case before him
and fill my mouth with arguments.
5 I would find out what he would
answer me,
and consider what he would say.
6 Would he oppose me with great power?
No, he would not press charges
against me.
7 There an upright man could present
his case before him,
and I would be delivered forever
from my judge.

8 "But if I go to the east, he is not there;
if I go to the west, I do not find him.

9 When he is at work in the north, I do
not see him;
when he turns to the south, I catch
no glimpse of him.
10 But he knows the way that I take;
when he has tested me, I will come
forth as gold.
11 My feet have closely followed his steps;
I have kept to his way without
turning aside.
12 I have not departed from the
commands of his lips;
I have treasured the words of his
mouth more than my daily
bread.

13 "But he stands alone, and who can
oppose him?
He does whatever he pleases.
14 He carries out his decree against me,
and many such plans he still has in
store.
15 That is why I am terrified before him;
when I think of all this, I fear him.
16 God has made my heart faint;
the Almighty has terrified me.
17 Yet I am not silenced by the darkness,
by the thick darkness that covers my
face.

24 "Why does the Almighty not
set times for judgment?
Why must those who know
him look in vain for such days?
2 Men move boundary stones;
they pasture flocks they have stolen.
3 They drive away the orphan's donkey
and take the widow's ox in pledge.
4 They thrust the needy from the path
and force all the poor of the land
into hiding.
5 Like wild donkeys in the desert,
the poor go about their labor of
foraging food;
the wasteland provides food for
their children.
6 They gather fodder in the fields
and glean in the vineyards of the
wicked.
7 Lacking clothes, they spend the night
naked;
they have nothing to cover
themselves in the cold.
8 They are drenched by mountain rains
and hug the rocks for lack of shelter.

a 2 Septuagint and Syriac; Hebrew / the hand on me
b 2 Or heavy on me in

⁹The fatherless child is snatched from
    the breast;
  the infant of the poor is seized for a
    debt.
¹⁰Lacking clothes, they go about naked;
  they carry the sheaves, but still go
    hungry.
¹¹They crush olives among the terraces ᵃ;
  they tread the winepresses, yet
    suffer thirst.
¹²The groans of the dying rise from the
    city,
  and the souls of the wounded cry
    out for help.
  But God charges no one with
    wrongdoing.

¹³"There are those who rebel against the
    light,
  who do not know its ways
    or stay in its paths.
¹⁴When daylight is gone, the murderer
    rises up
  and kills the poor and needy;
    in the night he steals forth like a thief.
¹⁵The eye of the adulterer watches for
    dusk;

he thinks, 'No eye will see me,'
  and he keeps his face concealed.
¹⁶In the dark, men break into houses,
  but by day they shut themselves in;
    they want nothing to do with the
    light.
¹⁷For all of them, deep darkness is their
    morning ᵇ;
  they make friends with the terrors of
    darkness. ᶜ

¹⁸"Yet they are foam on the surface of
    the water;
  their portion of the land is cursed,
    so that no one goes to the vineyards.
¹⁹As heat and drought snatch away the
    melted snow,
  so the grave ᵈ snatches away those
    who have sinned.
²⁰The womb forgets them,
  the worm feasts on them;
  evil men are no longer remembered
    but are broken like a tree.

ᵃ 11 Or *olives between the millstones;* the meaning of the
Hebrew for this word is uncertain.   ᵇ 17 Or *them, their
morning is like the shadow of death*   ᶜ 17 Or *of the
shadow of death*   ᵈ 19 Hebrew *Sheol*

Buried in a Happy Life

READ JOB 24:2–11, 21–24

Check this out. Did you eat today? Wearing clothes today? Roll out of bed in a room with four walls and a roof? If you answered yes to these, you're better off than most people in the world. So don't be so buried in your own happy life that you can't see the needs in the world around you. God says that "pure religion" is to help others in their time of need (James 1:27). One huge reason God has blessed you is so you can bless others, like Job did (Job 29:11–17). How can you help? Sponsor a child with your family or church school class. Have a car wash to raise money for a family who lost their home. You can *find* ways.

Here's what's important: When you hear about someone in need, ask, "What can I do to help?" You can't save the world, but you *can* do your part.

Your next reading is on page 662.

21 They prey on the barren and childless
      woman,
   and to the widow show no kindness.
22 But God drags away the mighty by his
      power;
   though they become established,
      they have no assurance of life.
23 He may let them rest in a feeling of
      security,
   but his eyes are on their ways.
24 For a little while they are exalted, and
      then they are gone;
   they are brought low and gathered
      up like all others;
   they are cut off like heads of grain.
25 "If this is not so, who can prove me
      false
   and reduce my words to nothing?"

Bildad

25 Then Bildad the Shuhite re-
      plied:

2 "Dominion and awe belong
      to God;
   he establishes order in the heights of
      heaven.
3 Can his forces be numbered?
   Upon whom does his light not rise?
4 How then can a man be righteous
      before God?
   How can one born of woman be
      pure?
5 If even the moon is not bright
   and the stars are not pure in his eyes,
6 how much less man, who is but a
      maggot—
   a son of man, who is only a worm!"

Job

26 Then Job replied:

2 "How you have helped the
      powerless!
   How you have saved the arm that is
      feeble!
3 What advice you have offered to one
      without wisdom!
   And what great insight you have
      displayed!
4 Who has helped you utter these words?
   And whose spirit spoke from your
      mouth?
5 "The dead are in deep anguish,
   those beneath the waters and all
      that live in them.

6 Death*a* is naked before God;
   Destruction*b* lies uncovered.
7 He spreads out the northern ⌊skies⌋
      over empty space;
   he suspends the earth over nothing.
8 He wraps up the waters in his clouds,
   yet the clouds do not burst under
      their weight.
9 He covers the face of the full moon,
   spreading his clouds over it.
10 He marks out the horizon on the face
      of the waters
   for a boundary between light and
      darkness.
11 The pillars of the heavens quake,
   aghast at his rebuke.
12 By his power he churned up the sea;
   by his wisdom he cut Rahab to
      pieces.
13 By his breath the skies became fair;
   his hand pierced the gliding serpent.
14 And these are but the outer fringe of
      his works;
   how faint the whisper we hear of
      him!
   Who then can understand the
      thunder of his power?"

27 And Job continued his dis-
      course:

2 "As surely as God lives, who
      has denied me justice,
   the Almighty, who has made me
      taste bitterness of soul,
3 as long as I have life within me,
   the breath of God in my nostrils,
4 my lips will not speak wickedness,
   and my tongue will utter no deceit.
5 I will never admit you are in the right;
   till I die, I will not deny my integrity.
6 I will maintain my righteousness and
      never let go of it;
   my conscience will not reproach me
      as long as I live.

7 "May my enemies be like the wicked,
   my adversaries like the unjust!
8 For what hope has the godless when
      he is cut off,
   when God takes away his life?
9 Does God listen to his cry
   when distress comes upon him?
10 Will he find delight in the Almighty?
   Will he call upon God at all times?

a 6 Hebrew *Sheol*   *b* 6 Hebrew *Abaddon*

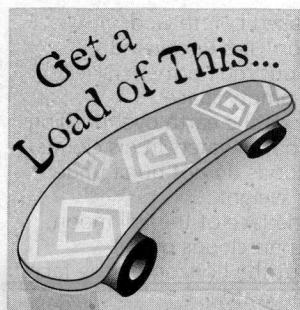

Get a Load of This...

Check out Job 28:9–10. Cool! There were miners even way back in Job's day. Picture muscle-man miners sweating like crazy underground, looking for gold and diamonds. It can be like that when looking for nuggets and gems of wisdom in the Bible. Have you ever worked that hard to "mine" gold from God's Word?

11 "I will teach you about the power of God;
    the ways of the Almighty I will not conceal.
12 You have all seen this yourselves.
    Why then this meaningless talk?

13 "Here is the fate God allots to the wicked,
    the heritage a ruthless man receives from the Almighty:
14 However many his children, their fate is the sword;
    his offspring will never have enough to eat.
15 The plague will bury those who survive him,
    and their widows will not weep for them.
16 Though he heaps up silver like dust
    and clothes like piles of clay,
17 what he lays up the righteous will wear,
    and the innocent will divide his silver.
18 The house he builds is like a moth's cocoon,
    like a hut made by a watchman.
19 He lies down wealthy, but will do so no more;
    when he opens his eyes, all is gone.
20 Terrors overtake him like a flood;
    a tempest snatches him away in the night.
21 The east wind carries him off, and he is gone;
    it sweeps him out of his place.
22 It hurls itself against him without mercy
    as he flees headlong from its power.
23 It claps its hands in derision
    and hisses him out of his place.

28 "There is a mine for silver
    and a place where gold is refined.
2 Iron is taken from the earth,
    and copper is smelted from ore.
3 Man puts an end to the darkness;
    he searches the farthest recesses
    for ore in the blackest darkness.
4 Far from where people dwell he cuts a shaft,
    in places forgotten by the foot of man;
    far from men he dangles and sways.
5 The earth, from which food comes,
    is transformed below as by fire;
6 sapphires[a] come from its rocks,
    and its dust contains nuggets of gold.
7 No bird of prey knows that hidden path,
    no falcon's eye has seen it.
8 Proud beasts do not set foot on it,
    and no lion prowls there.
9 Man's hand assaults the flinty rock
    and lays bare the roots of the mountains.
10 He tunnels through the rock;
    his eyes see all its treasures.
11 He searches[b] the sources of the rivers
    and brings hidden things to light.

12 "But where can wisdom be found?
    Where does understanding dwell?

---

[a] 6 Or *lapis lazuli*; also in verse 16   [b] 11 Septuagint, Aquila and Vulgate; Hebrew *He dams up*

¹³ Man does not comprehend its worth;
　　it cannot be found in the land of the
　　living.
¹⁴ The deep says, 'It is not in me';
　　the sea says, 'It is not with me.'
¹⁵ It cannot be bought with the finest
　　gold,
　　nor can its price be weighed in silver.
¹⁶ It cannot be bought with the gold of
　　Ophir,
　　with precious onyx or sapphires.
¹⁷ Neither gold nor crystal can compare
　　with it,
　　nor can it be had for jewels of gold.
¹⁸ Coral and jasper are not worthy of
　　mention;
　　the price of wisdom is beyond rubies.
¹⁹ The topaz of Cush cannot compare
　　with it;
　　it cannot be bought with pure gold.

²⁰ "Where then does wisdom come from?
　　Where does understanding dwell?
²¹ It is hidden from the eyes of every
　　living thing,
　　concealed even from the birds of the
　　air.
²² Destruction[a] and Death say,
　　'Only a rumor of it has reached our
　　ears.'
²³ God understands the way to it
　　and he alone knows where it dwells,
²⁴ for he views the ends of the earth
　　and sees everything under the
　　heavens.
²⁵ When he established the force of the
　　wind
　　and measured out the waters,
²⁶ when he made a decree for the rain
　　and a path for the thunderstorm,
²⁷ then he looked at wisdom and
　　appraised it;
　　he confirmed it and tested it.
²⁸ And he said to man,
　　'The fear of the Lord—that is wisdom,
　　and to shun evil is understanding.' "

29 Job continued his discourse:

² "How I long for the months
　　gone by,
　for the days when God watched
　　over me,
³ when his lamp shone upon my head
　and by his light I walked through
　　darkness!
⁴ Oh, for the days when I was in my
　　prime,

when God's intimate friendship
　　blessed my house,
⁵ when the Almighty was still with me
　　and my children were around me,
⁶ when my path was drenched with
　　cream
　　and the rock poured out for me
　　streams of olive oil.

⁷ "When I went to the gate of the city
　　and took my seat in the public
　　square,
⁸ the young men saw me and stepped
　　aside
　　and the old men rose to their feet;
⁹ the chief men refrained from speaking
　　and covered their mouths with their
　　hands;
¹⁰ the voices of the nobles were hushed,
　　and their tongues stuck to the roof
　　of their mouths.
¹¹ Whoever heard me spoke well of me,
　　and those who saw me commended
　　me,
¹² because I rescued the poor who cried
　　for help,
　　and the fatherless who had none to
　　assist him.
¹³ The man who was dying blessed me;
　　I made the widow's heart sing.
¹⁴ I put on righteousness as my clothing;
　　justice was my robe and my turban.
¹⁵ I was eyes to the blind
　　and feet to the lame.
¹⁶ I was a father to the needy;
　　I took up the case of the stranger.
¹⁷ I broke the fangs of the wicked
　　and snatched the victims from their
　　teeth.

¹⁸ "I thought, 'I will die in my own house,
　　my days as numerous as the grains
　　of sand.
¹⁹ My roots will reach to the water,
　　and the dew will lie all night on my
　　branches.
²⁰ My glory will remain fresh in me,
　　the bow ever new in my hand.'

²¹ "Men listened to me expectantly,
　　waiting in silence for my counsel.
²² After I had spoken, they spoke no
　　more;
　　my words fell gently on their ears.
²³ They waited for me as for showers
　　and drank in my words as the spring
　　rain.

---

a 22 Hebrew *Abaddon*

²⁴When I smiled at them, they scarcely
    believed it;
  the light of my face was precious to
    them. ᵃ
²⁵I chose the way for them and sat as
    their chief;
  I dwelt as a king among his troops;
  I was like one who comforts
    mourners.

30 "But now they mock me,
    men younger than I,
  whose fathers I would have
    disdained
to put with my sheep dogs.

²Of what use was the strength of their
    hands to me,
  since their vigor had gone from
    them?
³Haggard from want and hunger,
  they roamedᵇ the parched land
  in desolate wastelands at night.
⁴In the brush they gathered salt herbs,
  and their foodᶜ was the root of the
    broom tree.
⁵They were banished from their fellow
    men,

ᵃ 24 The meaning of the Hebrew for this clause is uncertain.
ᵇ 3 Or gnawed   ᶜ 4 Or fuel

Make It Stick

_____

_____

_____

_____

_____

_____

_____

READ JOB 29:11–17
Narrow this passage down
to a couple of sentences in
your own words and write it
on a sticky note. This is what
you should be able to say
about yourself. Follow Job's
words but put in the details
from your life—your rela-
tionships and the things
you've done for people.

shouted at as if they were thieves.
6 They were forced to live in the dry stream beds,
    among the rocks and in holes in the ground.
7 They brayed among the bushes
    and huddled in the undergrowth.
8 A base and nameless brood,
    they were driven out of the land.

9 "And now their sons mock me in song;
    I have become a byword among them.
10 They detest me and keep their distance;
    they do not hesitate to spit in my face.
11 Now that God has unstrung my bow and afflicted
        me,
    they throw off restraint in my presence.
12 On my right the tribe*a* attacks;
    they lay snares for my feet,
    they build their siege ramps against me.
13 They break up my road;
    they succeed in destroying me—
    without anyone's helping them. *b*
14 They advance as through a gaping breach;
    amid the ruins they come rolling in.
15 Terrors overwhelm me;
    my dignity is driven away as by the wind,
    my safety vanishes like a cloud.

16 "And now my life ebbs away;
    days of suffering grip me.
17 Night pierces my bones;
    my gnawing pains never rest.
18 In his great power ⌊God⌋ becomes like clothing to
        me*c*;
    he binds me like the neck of my garment.
19 He throws me into the mud,
    and I am reduced to dust and ashes.

20 "I cry out to you, O God, but you do not answer;
    I stand up, but you merely look at me.
21 You turn on me ruthlessly;
    with the might of your hand you attack me.
22 You snatch me up and drive me before the wind;
    you toss me about in the storm.
23 I know you will bring me down to death,
    to the place appointed for all the living.

24 "Surely no one lays a hand on a broken man
    when he cries for help in his distress.
25 Have I not wept for those in trouble?
    Has not my soul grieved for the poor?
26 Yet when I hoped for good, evil came;
    when I looked for light, then came darkness.
27 The churning inside me never stops;
    days of suffering confront me.
28 I go about blackened, but not by the sun;
    I stand up in the assembly and cry for help.

Gross!

Check out Job 30:19. Job said, "He throws me into the mud." This just goes to show you that Job was smart, sure, but he was no pro at mud wrestling. And for *sure* he was too skinny for Sumo mud wrestling.

---

a 12 The meaning of the Hebrew for this word is uncertain.   *b* 13 Or me. / 'No one can help him,' ⌊they say⌋.   *c* 18 Hebrew; Septuagint ⌊God⌋ grasps my clothing

29 I have become a brother of jackals,
    a companion of owls.
30 My skin grows black and peels;
    my body burns with fever.
31 My harp is tuned to mourning,
    and my flute to the sound of wailing.

31 "I made a covenant with my
    eyes
    not to look lustfully at a girl.
2 For what is man's lot from
    God above,
    his heritage from the Almighty on
    high?
3 Is it not ruin for the wicked,
    disaster for those who do wrong?
4 Does he not see my ways
    and count my every step?

5 "If I have walked in falsehood
    or my foot has hurried after deceit—
6 let God weigh me in honest scales
    and he will know that I am
    blameless—
7 if my steps have turned from the path,

if my heart has been led by my eyes,
    or if my hands have been defiled,
8 then may others eat what I have sown,
    and may my crops be uprooted.

9 "If my heart has been enticed by a
    woman,
    or if I have lurked at my neighbor's
    door,
10 then may my wife grind another man's
    grain,
    and may other men sleep with her.
11 For that would have been shameful,
    a sin to be judged.
12 It is a fire that burns to Destruction[a];
    it would have uprooted my harvest.

13 "If I have denied justice to my
    menservants and maidservants
    when they had a grievance against
    me,
14 what will I do when God confronts
    me?

---

a 12 Hebrew *Abaddon*

What will I answer when called to account?
15 Did not he who made me in the womb make them?
   Did not the same one form us both within our
      mothers?

16 "If I have denied the desires of the poor
   or let the eyes of the widow grow weary,
17 if I have kept my bread to myself,
   not sharing it with the fatherless—
18 but from my youth I reared him as would a father,
   and from my birth I guided the widow—
19 if I have seen anyone perishing for lack of clothing,
   or a needy man without a garment,
20 and his heart did not bless me
   for warming him with the fleece from my sheep,
21 if I have raised my hand against the fatherless,
   knowing that I had influence in court,
22 then let my arm fall from the shoulder,
   let it be broken off at the joint.
23 For I dreaded destruction from God,
   and for fear of his splendor I could not do such
      things.

24 "If I have put my trust in gold
   or said to pure gold, 'You are my security,'
25 if I have rejoiced over my great wealth,
   the fortune my hands had gained,
26 if I have regarded the sun in its radiance
   or the moon moving in splendor,
27 so that my heart was secretly enticed
   and my hand offered them a kiss of homage,
28 then these also would be sins to be judged,
   for I would have been unfaithful to God on high.

29 "If I have rejoiced at my enemy's misfortune
   or gloated over the trouble that came to him—
30 I have not allowed my mouth to sin
   by invoking a curse against his life—
31 if the men of my household have never said,
   'Who has not had his fill of Job's meat?'—
32 but no stranger had to spend the night in the street,
   for my door was always open to the traveler—
33 if I have concealed my sin as men do,ᵃ
   by hiding my guilt in my heart
34 because I so feared the crowd
   and so dreaded the contempt of the clans
   that I kept silent and would not go outside—

35 ("Oh, that I had someone to hear me!
   I sign now my defense—let the Almighty answer
      me;
   let my accuser put his indictment in writing.
36 Surely I would wear it on my shoulder,
   I would put it on like a crown.
37 I would give him an account of my every step;
   like a prince I would approach him.)—

ᵃ 33 Or as Adam did

Gross!

Job said, "If I have raised my hand against the fatherless ... let my arm ... be broken off at the joint" (Job 31:22–23). We are talking major pain! What about you? Do you tease loners? Bully small kids? Would you behave differently if *this* were the punishment?

38 "if my land cries out against me
   and all its furrows are wet with tears,
39 if I have devoured its yield without
      payment
   or broken the spirit of its tenants,
40 then let briers come up instead of
      wheat
   and weeds instead of barley."

The words of Job are ended.

Elihu

32 So these three men stopped answering Job, because he was righteous in his own eyes. 2 But Elihu son of Barakel the Buzite, of the family of Ram, became very angry with Job for justifying himself rather than God. 3 He was also angry with the three friends, because they had found no way to refute Job, and yet had condemned him.[a] 4 Now Elihu had waited before speaking to Job because they were older than he. 5 But when he saw that the three men had nothing more to say, his anger was aroused.

6 So Elihu son of Barakel the Buzite said:

"I am young in years,
   and you are old;
that is why I was fearful,
   not daring to tell you what I know.
7 I thought, 'Age should speak;
   advanced years should teach
      wisdom.'
8 But it is the spirit[b] in a man,
   the breath of the Almighty, that
      gives him understanding.
9 It is not only the old[c] who are wise,
   not only the aged who understand
      what is right.

10 "Therefore I say: Listen to me;
   I too will tell you what I know.
11 I waited while you spoke,
   I listened to your reasoning;
   while you were searching for words,
12   I gave you my full attention.
   But not one of you has proved Job
      wrong;
   none of you has answered his
      arguments.

---

[a] 3 Masoretic Text; an ancient Hebrew scribal tradition *Job, and so had condemned God*   [b] 8 Or *Spirit*; also in verse 18
[c] 9 Or *many*; or *great*

GET SMARTER

Youth and Wisdom

READ JOB 32:1–14

The best young pro athletes are the ones who listen to the veteran players and coaches. They combine energy and fresh skills with the smarts of men who have learned how to play the game. That's a winning combo—youth and wisdom. Elihu was patient and respectful toward these guys because they were older and supposedly had more wisdom. But age doesn't necessarily make you wise. Real wisdom begins with listening, and you can't listen if you're talking. Elihu didn't shoot his mouth off. He first took the time to listen patiently and to think about what everyone was saying. Then when he finally did speak, he had something worth saying. Even if you're young, God can give you wisdom. Elihu had it, and so can you.

Your next reading is on page 667.

¹³ Do not say, 'We have found wisdom;
   let God refute him, not man.'
¹⁴ But Job has not marshaled his words
         against me,
   and I will not answer him with your
         arguments.

¹⁵ "They are dismayed and have no more
         to say;
   words have failed them.
¹⁶ Must I wait, now that they are silent,
   now that they stand there with no
         reply?
¹⁷ I too will have my say;
   I too will tell what I know.
¹⁸ For I am full of words,
   and the spirit within me compels me;
¹⁹ inside I am like bottled-up wine,
   like new wineskins ready to burst.
²⁰ I must speak and find relief;
   I must open my lips and reply.
²¹ I will show partiality to no one,
   nor will I flatter any man;
²² for if I were skilled in flattery,
   my Maker would soon take me away.

33 "But now, Job, listen to my
      words;
   pay attention to everything I
      say.
² I am about to open my mouth;
   my words are on the tip of my
      tongue.
³ My words come from an upright heart;
   my lips sincerely speak what I know.
⁴ The Spirit of God has made me;
   the breath of the Almighty gives me
      life.
⁵ Answer me then, if you can;
   prepare yourself and confront me.
⁶ I am just like you before God;
   I too have been taken from clay.
⁷ No fear of me should alarm you,
   nor should my hand be heavy upon
      you.

⁸ "But you have said in my hearing—
   I heard the very words—
⁹ 'I am pure and without sin;
   I am clean and free from guilt.
¹⁰ Yet God has found fault with me;
   he considers me his enemy.
¹¹ He fastens my feet in shackles;
   he keeps close watch on all my
      paths.'

¹² "But I tell you, in this you are not right,
   for God is greater than man.
¹³ Why do you complain to him

that he answers none of man's
   words[a]?
¹⁴ For God does speak—now one way,
         now another—
   though man may not perceive it.
¹⁵ In a dream, in a vision of the night,
   when deep sleep falls on men
      as they slumber in their beds,
¹⁶ he may speak in their ears
   and terrify them with warnings,
¹⁷ to turn man from wrongdoing
   and keep him from pride,
¹⁸ to preserve his soul from the pit,[b]
   his life from perishing by the sword.[c]
¹⁹ Or a man may be chastened on a bed
         of pain
   with constant distress in his bones,
²⁰ so that his very being finds food
         repulsive
   and his soul loathes the choicest
         meal.
²¹ His flesh wastes away to nothing,
   and his bones, once hidden, now
      stick out.
²² His soul draws near to the pit,[d]
   and his life to the messengers of
      death.[e]

²³ "Yet if there is an angel on his side
   as a mediator, one out of a thousand,
   to tell a man what is right for him,
²⁴ to be gracious to him and say,
   'Spare him from going down to the
      pit[f];
   I have found a ransom for him'—
²⁵ then his flesh is renewed like a child's;
   it is restored as in the days of his
      youth.
²⁶ He prays to God and finds favor with
      him,
   he sees God's face and shouts for joy;
   he is restored by God to his
      righteous state.
²⁷ Then he comes to men and says,
   'I sinned, and perverted what was
      right,
   but I did not get what I deserved.
²⁸ He redeemed my soul from going
         down to the pit,[g]
   and I will live to enjoy the light.'

²⁹ "God does all these things to a man—
   twice, even three times—

---

[a] 13 Or that he does not answer for any of his actions
[b] 18 Or preserve him from the grave   [c] 18 Or from crossing
the River   [d] 22 Or He draws near to the grave
[e] 22 Or to the dead   [f] 24 Or grave   [g] 28 Or redeemed
me from going down to the grave

30 to turn back his soul from the pit,[a]
     that the light of life may shine on
       him.
31 "Pay attention, Job, and listen to me;
     be silent, and I will speak.
32 If you have anything to say, answer me;
     speak up, for I want you to be
       cleared.
33 But if not, then listen to me;
     be silent, and I will teach you
       wisdom."

34

Then Elihu said:

2 "Hear my words, you wise
     men;
listen to me, you men of learning.
3 For the ear tests words
     as the tongue tastes food.
4 Let us discern for ourselves what is
       right;
     let us learn together what is good.

5 "Job says, 'I am innocent,
     but God denies me justice.
6 Although I am right,
     I am considered a liar;
although I am guiltless,
     his arrow inflicts an incurable wound.'
7 What man is like Job,
     who drinks scorn like water?
8 He keeps company with evildoers;
     he associates with wicked men.
9 For he says, 'It profits a man nothing
     when he tries to please God.'

10 "So listen to me, you men of
       understanding.
     Far be it from God to do evil,
     from the Almighty to do wrong.
11 He repays a man for what he has done;
     he brings upon him what his
       conduct deserves.
12 It is unthinkable that God would do
       wrong,
     that the Almighty would pervert
       justice.
13 Who appointed him over the earth?
     Who put him in charge of the whole
       world?
14 If it were his intention
     and he withdrew his spirit[b] and
       breath,
15 all mankind would perish together
     and man would return to the dust.

16 "If you have understanding, hear this;
     listen to what I say.

17 Can he who hates justice govern?
     Will you condemn the just and
       mighty One?
18 Is he not the One who says to kings,
     'You are worthless,'
     and to nobles, 'You are wicked,'
19 who shows no partiality to princes
     and does not favor the rich over the
       poor,
     for they are all the work of his
       hands?
20 They die in an instant, in the middle of
       the night;
     the people are shaken and they pass
       away;
     the mighty are removed without
       human hand.

21 "His eyes are on the ways of men;
     he sees their every step.
22 There is no dark place, no deep
       shadow,
     where evildoers can hide.
23 God has no need to examine men
       further,
     that they should come before him
       for judgment.
24 Without inquiry he shatters the mighty
     and sets up others in their place.
25 Because he takes note of their deeds,
     he overthrows them in the night and
       they are crushed.
26 He punishes them for their wickedness
     where everyone can see them,
27 because they turned from following him
     and had no regard for any of his
       ways.
28 They caused the cry of the poor to
       come before him,
     so that he heard the cry of the needy.
29 But if he remains silent, who can
       condemn him?
     If he hides his face, who can see
       him?
     Yet he is over man and nation alike,
30   to keep a godless man from ruling,
     from laying snares for the people.

31 "Suppose a man says to God,
     'I am guilty but will offend no more.
32 Teach me what I cannot see;
     if I have done wrong, I will not do
       so again.'
33 Should God then reward you on your
       terms,
     when you refuse to repent?

---

a 30 Or turn him back from the grave   b 14 Or Spirit

You must decide, not I;
  so tell me what you know.

34 "Men of understanding declare,
  wise men who hear me say to me,
35 'Job speaks without knowledge;
  his words lack insight.'
36 Oh, that Job might be tested to the utmost
  for answering like a wicked man!
37 To his sin he adds rebellion;
  scornfully he claps his hands among us
  and multiplies his words against God."

35 Then Elihu said:

2 "Do you think this is just?
  You say, 'I will be cleared by God.'*a*
3 Yet you ask him, 'What profit is it to me,*b*
  and what do I gain by not sinning?'

4 "I would like to reply to you
  and to your friends with you.
5 Look up at the heavens and see;
  gaze at the clouds so high above you.
6 If you sin, how does that affect him?
  If your sins are many, what does that do to him?
7 If you are righteous, what do you give to him,
  or what does he receive from your hand?
8 Your wickedness affects only a man like yourself,
  and your righteousness only the sons of men.

9 "Men cry out under a load of oppression;
  they plead for relief from the arm of the powerful.
10 But no one says, 'Where is God my Maker,
  who gives songs in the night,
11 who teaches more to us than to*c* the beasts of the earth
  and makes us wiser than*d* the birds of the air?'
12 He does not answer when men cry out

a 2 Or My righteousness is more than God's *b 3 Or you* *c 11 Or teaches us by* *d 11 Or us wise by*

Flash Flood Warning

READ JOB 34:31–33

If you were skateboarding in a half-pipe, then realized that it was a storm sewer—just before a flash flood hit, you'd want to get out of there in a hurry, right? That's what true repenting is like: When you find out you're doing something wrong, you turn back. You stop what you're doing and avoid it in the future. "Teach me what I cannot see; if I have done wrong, I will not do so again" (Job 34:32). God promised in 1 John 1:9 that he forgives those who confess their sins. Sometimes you might sin in ways you're not aware of and "cannot see," so ask God to show you. He will. Remember, sin can turn skate parks into storm sewers in a flash, so don't hesitate to turn back when you realize you're in the wrong place.

Your next reading is on page 670.

because of the arrogance of the
  wicked.
13 Indeed, God does not listen to their
    empty plea;
  the Almighty pays no attention to it.
14 How much less, then, will he listen
    when you say that you do not see
    him,
  that your case is before him
  and you must wait for him,
15 and further, that his anger never
    punishes
  and he does not take the least
    notice of wickedness. *a*
16 So Job opens his mouth with empty
    talk;
  without knowledge he multiplies
    words."

36 Elihu continued:

2 "Bear with me a little longer
  and I will show you
  that there is more to be said in
    God's behalf.
3 I get my knowledge from afar;
  I will ascribe justice to my Maker.
4 Be assured that my words are not false;
  one perfect in knowledge is with you.

5 "God is mighty, but does not despise
    men;
  he is mighty, and firm in his purpose.
6 He does not keep the wicked alive
  but gives the afflicted their rights.
7 He does not take his eyes off the
    righteous;
  he enthrones them with kings
  and exalts them forever.
8 But if men are bound in chains,
  held fast by cords of affliction,
9 he tells them what they have done—
  that they have sinned arrogantly.
10 He makes them listen to correction
  and commands them to repent of
    their evil.
11 If they obey and serve him,
  they will spend the rest of their days
    in prosperity
  and their years in contentment.
12 But if they do not listen,
  they will perish by the sword *b*
  and die without knowledge.

13 "The godless in heart harbor
    resentment;
  even when he fetters them, they do
    not cry for help.

14 They die in their youth,
  among male prostitutes of the
    shrines.
15 But those who suffer he delivers in
    their suffering;
  he speaks to them in their affliction.

16 "He is wooing you from the jaws of
    distress
  to a spacious place free from
    restriction,
  to the comfort of your table laden
    with choice food.
17 But now you are laden with the
    judgment due the wicked;
  judgment and justice have taken
    hold of you.
18 Be careful that no one entices you by
    riches;
  do not let a large bribe turn you
    aside.
19 Would your wealth
  or even all your mighty efforts
  sustain you so you would not be in
    distress?
20 Do not long for the night,
  to drag people away from their
    homes. *c*
21 Beware of turning to evil,
  which you seem to prefer to
    affliction.

22 "God is exalted in his power.
  Who is a teacher like him?
23 Who has prescribed his ways for him,
  or said to him, 'You have done
    wrong'?
24 Remember to extol his work,
  which men have praised in song.
25 All mankind has seen it;
  men gaze on it from afar.
26 How great is God—beyond our
    understanding!
  The number of his years is past
    finding out.

27 "He draws up the drops of water,
  which distill as rain to the streams *d*;
28 the clouds pour down their moisture
  and abundant showers fall on
    mankind.
29 Who can understand how he spreads
    out the clouds,
  how he thunders from his pavilion?

---

a 15 Symmachus, Theodotion and Vulgate; the meaning of
the Hebrew for this word is uncertain.   *b 12* Or *will cross
the River*   *c 20* The meaning of the Hebrew for verses
18–20 is uncertain.   *d 27* Or *distill from the mist as rain*

30 See how he scatters his lightning about him,
   bathing the depths of the sea.
31 This is the way he governs[a] the nations
   and provides food in abundance.
32 He fills his hands with lightning
   and commands it to strike its mark.
33 His thunder announces the coming storm;
   even the cattle make known its approach.[b]

37 "At this my heart pounds
   and leaps from its place.
2 Listen! Listen to the roar of his voice,
   to the rumbling that comes from his mouth.
3 He unleashes his lightning beneath the whole heaven
   and sends it to the ends of the earth.
4 After that comes the sound of his roar;
   he thunders with his majestic voice.
   When his voice resounds,
   he holds nothing back.
5 God's voice thunders in marvelous ways;
   he does great things beyond our understanding.
6 He says to the snow, 'Fall on the earth,'
   and to the rain shower, 'Be a mighty downpour.'
7 So that all men he has made may know his work,
   he stops every man from his labor.[c]
8 The animals take cover;
   they remain in their dens.
9 The tempest comes out from its chamber,
   the cold from the driving winds.
10 The breath of God produces ice,
   and the broad waters become frozen.
11 He loads the clouds with moisture;
   he scatters his lightning through them.
12 At his direction they swirl around
   over the face of the whole earth
   to do whatever he commands them.
13 He brings the clouds to punish men,
   or to water his earth[d] and show his love.

14 "Listen to this, Job;
   stop and consider God's wonders.
15 Do you know how God controls the clouds
   and makes his lightning flash?
16 Do you know how the clouds hang poised,
   those wonders of him who is perfect in
   knowledge?
17 You who swelter in your clothes
   when the land lies hushed under the south wind,
18 can you join him in spreading out the skies,
   hard as a mirror of cast bronze?

19 "Tell us what we should say to him;
   we cannot draw up our case because of our
   darkness.
20 Should he be told that I want to speak?
   Would any man ask to be swallowed up?

Get a Load of This...

Check out Job 37:5, 11. The temperature of one bolt of lightning is about seven times hotter than the sun's surface. It has an electrical potential of over a billion volts. And it's all under God's command—a *sliver* of his power. Now that's some serious heat!

---

[a] 31 Or *nourishes* [b] 33 Or *announces his coming— / the One zealous against evil* [c] 7 Or / *he fills all men with fear by his power* [d] 13 Or *to favor them*

21 Now no one can look at the sun,
   bright as it is in the skies
   after the wind has swept them clean.
22 Out of the north he comes in golden
    splendor;
   God comes in awesome majesty.
23 The Almighty is beyond our reach and
    exalted in power;
   in his justice and great righteousness,
   he does not oppress.
24 Therefore, men revere him,
   for does he not have regard for all
    the wise in heart? [a]"

The Lord Speaks

38 Then the Lord answered Job out of the storm. He said:

2 "Who is this that darkens my counsel
with words without knowledge?
3 Brace yourself like a man;
   I will question you,
   and you shall answer me.

4 "Where were you when I laid the
   earth's foundation?

Tell me, if you understand.
5 Who marked off its dimensions? Surely
   you know!
   Who stretched a measuring line
    across it?
6 On what were its footings set,
   or who laid its cornerstone—
7 while the morning stars sang together
   and all the angels [b] shouted for joy?

8 "Who shut up the sea behind doors
   when it burst forth from the womb,
9 when I made the clouds its garment
   and wrapped it in thick darkness,
10 when I fixed limits for it
   and set its doors and bars in place,
11 when I said, 'This far you may come
    and no farther;
   here is where your proud waves halt'?

12 "Have you ever given orders to the
    morning,
   or shown the dawn its place,
13 that it might take the earth by the edges
   and shake the wicked out of it?

---

[a] 24 Or for he does not have regard for any who think they are wise.   [b] 7 Hebrew the sons of God

Brace Yourself Like a Man

READ JOB 38:1–18

And now for the conclusion: After all of the "wise" arguments between Job and his friends, it was God's turn. Imagine the gale force wind when God spoke out of the storm: "Brace yourself like a man ... answer me. Where were you when I laid the earth's foundation? Tell me, if you understand" (verses 3–4). Of course, Job didn't have a clue. The bottom line was that Job and all his friends didn't know *beans*. God is so much bigger than mere humans. Boil that thought down and it means two things: First, no way can you understand everything God thinks and does. Second, God is big enough to take care of you. This is the biggest lesson you can learn. Ask God to help you understand things, and if you *can't* understand, ask him to help you trust. That's faith, and that's what life is all about.

Your next reading is on page 675.

14 The earth takes shape like clay under a seal;
   its features stand out like those of a garment.
15 The wicked are denied their light,
   and their upraised arm is broken.

16 "Have you journeyed to the springs of the sea
   or walked in the recesses of the deep?
17 Have the gates of death been shown to you?
   Have you seen the gates of the shadow of death[a]?
18 Have you comprehended the vast expanses of the
   earth?
   Tell me, if you know all this.

19 "What is the way to the abode of light?
   And where does darkness reside?
20 Can you take them to their places?
   Do you know the paths to their dwellings?
21 Surely you know, for you were already born!
   You have lived so many years!

22 "Have you entered the storehouses of the snow
   or seen the storehouses of the hail,
23 which I reserve for times of trouble,
   for days of war and battle?
24 What is the way to the place where the lightning is
   dispersed,
   or the place where the east winds are scattered
   over the earth?
25 Who cuts a channel for the torrents of rain,
   and a path for the thunderstorm,
26 to water a land where no man lives,
   a desert with no one in it,
27 to satisfy a desolate wasteland
   and make it sprout with grass?
28 Does the rain have a father?
   Who fathers the drops of dew?
29 From whose womb comes the ice?
   Who gives birth to the frost from the heavens
30 when the waters become hard as stone,
   when the surface of the deep is frozen?

31 "Can you bind the beautiful[b] Pleiades?
   Can you loose the cords of Orion?
32 Can you bring forth the constellations in their
   seasons[c]
   or lead out the Bear[d] with its cubs?
33 Do you know the laws of the heavens?
   Can you set up ⌊God's[e]⌋ dominion over the earth?

34 "Can you raise your voice to the clouds
   and cover yourself with a flood of water?
35 Do you send the lightning bolts on their way?
   Do they report to you, 'Here we are'?
36 Who endowed the heart[f] with wisdom
   or gave understanding to the mind[f]?
37 Who has the wisdom to count the clouds?

Get a Load of This...

"Have you entered the storehouses of the snow" (Job 38:22)? God was not asking Job if he'd ever been on an Arctic expedition. The Hebrew word for "storehouse" can also mean "armory," a place where *weapons* are stored. God sometimes uses ice, hail and snow as sweapons. Cool!

---

a 17 Or *gates of deep shadows*   b 31 Or *the twinkling*; or *the chains of the*
c 32 Or *the morning star in its season*   d 32 Or *out Leo*   e 33 Or *his*; or *their*
f 36 The meaning of the Hebrew for this word is uncertain.

Who can tip over the water jars of
the heavens
38 when the dust becomes hard
and the clods of earth stick together?

39 "Do you hunt the prey for the lioness
and satisfy the hunger of the lions
40 when they crouch in their dens
or lie in wait in a thicket?
41 Who provides food for the raven
when its young cry out to God
and wander about for lack of food?

39

"Do you know when the
mountain goats give birth?
Do you watch when the doe
bears her fawn?
2 Do you count the months till they
bear?
Do you know the time they give
birth?
3 They crouch down and bring forth
their young;
their labor pains are ended.
4 Their young thrive and grow strong in
the wilds;
they leave and do not return.

5 "Who let the wild donkey go free?
Who untied his ropes?
6 I gave him the wasteland as his home,
the salt flats as his habitat.
7 He laughs at the commotion in the
town;
he does not hear a driver's shout.
8 He ranges the hills for his pasture
and searches for any green thing.

9 "Will the wild ox consent to serve you?
Will he stay by your manger at night?
10 Can you hold him to the furrow with a
harness?
Will he till the valleys behind you?
11 Will you rely on him for his great
strength?
Will you leave your heavy work to
him?
12 Can you trust him to bring in your grain
and gather it to your threshing floor?

13 "The wings of the ostrich flap joyfully,
but they cannot compare with the
pinions and feathers of the
stork.
14 She lays her eggs on the ground
and lets them warm in the sand,
15 unmindful that a foot may crush them,
that some wild animal may trample
them.

16 She treats her young harshly, as if they
were not hers;
she cares not that her labor was in
vain,
17 for God did not endow her with
wisdom
or give her a share of good sense.
18 Yet when she spreads her feathers to
run,
she laughs at horse and rider.

19 "Do you give the horse his strength
or clothe his neck with a flowing
mane?
20 Do you make him leap like a locust,
striking terror with his proud
snorting?
21 He paws fiercely, rejoicing in his
strength,
and charges into the fray.
22 He laughs at fear, afraid of nothing;
he does not shy away from the
sword.
23 The quiver rattles against his side,
along with the flashing spear and
lance.
24 In frenzied excitement he eats up the
ground;
he cannot stand still when the
trumpet sounds.
25 At the blast of the trumpet he snorts,
'Aha!'
He catches the scent of battle from
afar,
the shout of commanders and the
battle cry.

26 "Does the hawk take flight by your
wisdom
and spread his wings toward the
south?
27 Does the eagle soar at your command
and build his nest on high?
28 He dwells on a cliff and stays there at
night;
a rocky crag is his stronghold.
29 From there he seeks out his food;
his eyes detect it from afar.
30 His young ones feast on blood,
and where the slain are, there is he."

40

The LORD said to Job:

2 "Will the one who contends
with the Almighty correct
him?
Let him who accuses God answer
him!"

³Then Job answered the LORD:

⁴"I am unworthy—how can I reply to you?
　　I put my hand over my mouth.
⁵I spoke once, but I have no answer—
　　twice, but I will say no more."

⁶Then the LORD spoke to Job out of the storm:

⁷"Brace yourself like a man;
　　I will question you,
　　and you shall answer me.

⁸"Would you discredit my justice?
　　Would you condemn me to justify yourself?
⁹Do you have an arm like God's,
　　and can your voice thunder like his?
¹⁰Then adorn yourself with glory and splendor,
　　and clothe yourself in honor and majesty.
¹¹Unleash the fury of your wrath,
　　look at every proud man and bring him low,
¹²look at every proud man and humble him,
　　crush the wicked where they stand.
¹³Bury them all in the dust together;
　　shroud their faces in the grave.
¹⁴Then I myself will admit to you
　　that your own right hand can save you.

¹⁵"Look at the behemoth,ᵃ
　　which I made along with you
　　and which feeds on grass like an ox.
¹⁶What strength he has in his loins,
　　what power in the muscles of his belly!
¹⁷His tailᵇ sways like a cedar;
　　the sinews of his thighs are close-knit.
¹⁸His bones are tubes of bronze,
　　his limbs like rods of iron.
¹⁹He ranks first among the works of God,
　　yet his Maker can approach him with his sword.
²⁰The hills bring him their produce,
　　and all the wild animals play nearby.
²¹Under the lotus plants he lies,
　　hidden among the reeds in the marsh.
²²The lotuses conceal him in their shadow;
　　the poplars by the stream surround him.
²³When the river rages, he is not alarmed;
　　he is secure, though the Jordan should surge
　　　against his mouth.
²⁴Can anyone capture him by the eyes,ᶜ
　　or trap him and pierce his nose?

41 "Can you pull in the leviathanᵈ with a fishhook
　　or tie down his tongue with a rope?
²Can you put a cord through his nose
　　or pierce his jaw with a hook?
³Will he keep begging you for mercy?

ᵃ 15 Possibly the hippopotamus or the elephant　　ᵇ 17 Possibly trunk
ᶜ 24 Or by a water hole　　ᵈ 1 Possibly the crocodile

Get a Load of This...

Check out Job 41. What have we got here? *Leviathan?* What *is* this monster? One theory is that it's a giant crocodile. Other Bible scholars think it was a giant prehistoric sea monster of some kind. And the fiery dragon breath? Wow! Now *that's* wild!

Will he speak to you with gentle
words?
⁴Will he make an agreement with you
for you to take him as your slave for
life?
⁵Can you make a pet of him like a bird
or put him on a leash for your girls?
⁶Will traders barter for him?
Will they divide him up among the
merchants?
⁷Can you fill his hide with harpoons
or his head with fishing spears?
⁸If you lay a hand on him,
you will remember the struggle and
never do it again!
⁹Any hope of subduing him is false;
the mere sight of him is
overpowering.
¹⁰No one is fierce enough to rouse him.
Who then is able to stand against
me?
¹¹Who has a claim against me that I
must pay?

Everything under heaven belongs to
me.
¹²"I will not fail to speak of his limbs,
his strength and his graceful form.
¹³Who can strip off his outer coat?
Who would approach him with a
bridle?
¹⁴Who dares open the doors of his
mouth,
ringed about with his fearsome
teeth?
¹⁵His back has ᵃ rows of shields
tightly sealed together;
¹⁶each is so close to the next
that no air can pass between.
¹⁷They are joined fast to one another;
they cling together and cannot be
parted.
¹⁸His snorting throws out flashes of
light;
his eyes are like the rays of dawn.
¹⁹Firebrands stream from his mouth;

ᵃ 15 Or *His pride is his*

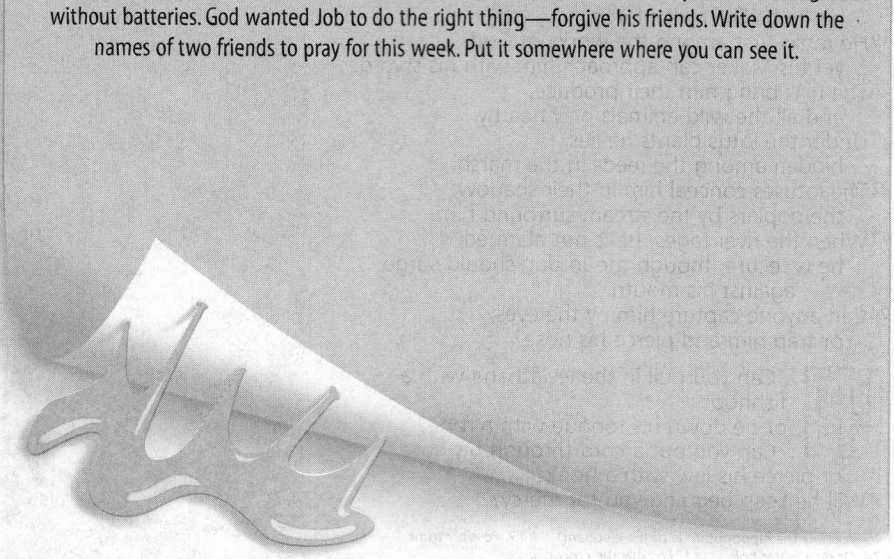

Make It Stick

READ JOB 42:8

God had Job pray for his friends, even though they had been about as helpful as a flashlight
without batteries. God wanted Job to do the right thing—forgive his friends. Write down the
names of two friends to pray for this week. Put it somewhere where you can see it.

sparks of fire shoot out.

20 Smoke pours from his nostrils
   as from a boiling pot over a fire of
      reeds.
21 His breath sets coals ablaze,
   and flames dart from his mouth.
22 Strength resides in his neck;
   dismay goes before him.
23 The folds of his flesh are tightly joined;
   they are firm and immovable.
24 His chest is hard as rock,
   hard as a lower millstone.
25 When he rises up, the mighty are
      terrified;
   they retreat before his thrashing.
26 The sword that reaches him has no
      effect,
   nor does the spear or the dart or the
      javelin.
27 Iron he treats like straw
   and bronze like rotten wood.
28 Arrows do not make him flee;
   slingstones are like chaff to him.

29 A club seems to him but a piece of
      straw;
   he laughs at the rattling of the lance.
30 His undersides are jagged potsherds,
   leaving a trail in the mud like a
      threshing sledge.
31 He makes the depths churn like a
      boiling caldron
   and stirs up the sea like a pot of
      ointment.
32 Behind him he leaves a glistening wake;
   one would think the deep had white
      hair.
33 Nothing on earth is his equal—
   a creature without fear.
34 He looks down on all that are haughty;
   he is king over all that are proud."

Job

42 Then Job replied to the LORD:

2 "I know that you can do all
      things;
   no plan of yours can be thwarted.

Worth the Grief

READ JOB 42:10–17

Job's whole ordeal probably lasted months and months. And you thought *school* was tough! In the end, Satan was proved wrong. Remember how this all started? Satan said Job would curse God if God afflicted Job. *Not.* Job remained faithful. He lost everything, he was infested with worms, but he hung in there. It's hard to keep trusting when you're sick and your emotions are raw. You feel like you've been body-slammed off the third floor. But Job proved you can get through it. If you just keep going and hang in there, God will bless you, too (see James 5:11). When it was clear that taking everything away from Job didn't make him turn away from God, God gave Job twice as much riches as he'd had before!

Your next reading is on page 678.

Get a Load of This...

Job finally repented! (Job 42:6) But he wasn't repenting (like his friends advised) for some supposed "sin" that had caused his suffering. Nope. He was innocent on *that* score. Job was repenting of his attitude and harsh words *after* he began suffering.

³ₗYou asked,ₗ 'Who is this that obscures my counsel
    without knowledge?'
Surely I spoke of things I did not understand,
    things too wonderful for me to know.

⁴ₗ"You said,ₗ 'Listen now, and I will speak;
   I will question you,
   and you shall answer me.'
⁵ My ears had heard of you
   but now my eyes have seen you.
⁶ Therefore I despise myself
   and repent in dust and ashes."

Epilogue

⁷ After the Lord had said these things to Job, he said to Eliphaz the Temanite, "I am angry with you and your two friends, because you have not spoken of me what is right, as my servant Job has. ⁸ So now take seven bulls and seven rams and go to my servant Job and sacrifice a burnt offering for yourselves. My servant Job will pray for you, and I will accept his prayer and not deal with you according to your folly. You have not spoken of me what is right, as my servant Job has." ⁹ So Eliphaz the Temanite, Bildad the Shuhite and Zophar the Naamathite did what the Lord told them; and the Lord accepted Job's prayer.

¹⁰ After Job had prayed for his friends, the Lord made him prosperous again and gave him twice as much as he had before. ¹¹ All his brothers and sisters and everyone who had known him before came and ate with him in his house. They comforted and consoled him over all the trouble the Lord had brought upon him, and each one gave him a piece of silver*ᵃ* and a gold ring.

¹² The Lord blessed the latter part of Job's life more than the first. He had fourteen thousand sheep, six thousand camels, a thousand yoke of oxen and a thousand donkeys. ¹³ And he also had seven sons and three daughters. ¹⁴ The first daughter he named Jemimah, the second Keziah and the third Keren-Happuch. ¹⁵ Nowhere in all the land were there found women as beautiful as Job's daughters, and their father granted them an inheritance along with their brothers.

¹⁶ After this, Job lived a hundred and forty years; he saw his children and their children to the fourth generation. ¹⁷ And so he died, old and full of years.

ᵃ 11 Hebrew *him a kesitah*; a kesitah was a unit of money of unknown weight and value.

PSALMS

Who wrote this book?
David wrote 73 of the 150 psalms. Several different people wrote the others.

Why was this book written?
The Psalms show God's people how to talk to him and to worship him.

What kinds of psalms are there?

There are seven kinds of psalms:
1. Praise psalms like Psalms 33 and 103 show us how to thank God for who he is.
2. History psalms like Psalms 68 and 106 tell what God has done for his people.
3. Friendship psalms like Psalms 8 and 23 remind us that God loves us and tell us how we can show our love to him.
4. Anger psalms like Psalms 35 and 137 ask God to punish evil people.
5. Confession psalms like Psalms 32 and 51 show how to talk to God about our sins.
6. Messiah psalms like Psalms 22 and 89 tell us about Jesus.
7. Worship psalms like Psalms 30 and 122 were used on special religious holidays to worship God with other people.

What kind of poetry is used in this book?
The Psalms do not rhyme. Hebrew poetry repeats ideas instead of repeating sounds.

When were the Psalms written?
The Psalms were probably written between about 1400 and 500 B.C.

What are some favorite psalms?

God's creation and Word	Psalm 19
God is our shepherd	Psalm 23
Confessing sin to God	Psalm 32
Trusting God	Psalm 37
Don't be jealous	Psalm 73
God's great love	Psalm 89
How great God is	Psalm 104
Loving God's Word	Psalm 119

BOOK I

Psalms 1–41

PSALM 1

¹ Blessed is the man
who does not walk in the counsel of
the wicked
or stand in the way of sinners
or sit in the seat of mockers.
² But his delight is in the law of the
LORD,
and on his law he meditates day and
night.
³ He is like a tree planted by streams of
water,
which yields its fruit in season
and whose leaf does not wither.
Whatever he does prospers.

⁴ Not so the wicked!
They are like chaff
that the wind blows away.
⁵ Therefore the wicked will not stand in
the judgment,
nor sinners in the assembly of the
righteous.

⁶ For the LORD watches over the way of
the righteous,
but the way of the wicked will perish.

PSALM 2

¹ Why do the nations conspire[a]
and the peoples plot in vain?
² The kings of the earth take their stand
and the rulers gather together
against the LORD
and against his Anointed One.[b]
³ "Let us break their chains," they say,
"and throw off their fetters."

⁴ The One enthroned in heaven laughs;
the Lord scoffs at them.
⁵ Then he rebukes them in his anger
and terrifies them in his wrath, saying,
⁶ "I have installed my King[c]
on Zion, my holy hill."

⁷ I will proclaim the decree of the LORD:

He said to me, "You are my Son[d];
today I have become your Father.[e]

*a 1 Hebrew; Septuagint rage   b 2 Or anointed one
c 6 Or king   d 7 Or son; also in verse 12   e 7 Or have
begotten you*

The Worldly and the Righteous

READ PSALM 1

This opening psalm gives a good look at the difference between
worldly men and righteous men. The righteous man doesn't "walk in
the counsel of the wicked." You have to live your life according to the
beat of God's drum, not according to the world around you. The righteous man doesn't "stand in the way of sinners." Don't go
along with kids who are doing wrong. Don't say, "Ahhhh, it
doesn't matter. God understands we're weak." The righteous
man doesn't "sit in the seat of mockers." Mockers say things
like, "Good guys finish last." (Wrong. In the end, good guys
finish first.) Or, "You don't believe in that God stuff, do
you?" (Oh yeah! We do. But God isn't a crutch.) As
Christians, the temptation sometimes is to not
stand up for God, to just go along with the world
to be cool and accepted. Don't do it. Delight yourself in *God's* way (see verse 2). His way is the best.

Your next reading is on page 680.

8 Ask of me,
>   and I will make the nations your inheritance,
>   the ends of the earth your possession.
9 You will rule them with an iron scepter[a];
>   you will dash them to pieces like pottery."

10 Therefore, you kings, be wise;
>   be warned, you rulers of the earth.
11 Serve the LORD with fear
>   and rejoice with trembling.
12 Kiss the Son, lest he be angry
>   and you be destroyed in your way,
> for his wrath can flare up in a moment.
>   Blessed are all who take refuge in him.

PSALM 3

A psalm of David. When he fled from his son Absalom.

1 O LORD, how many are my foes!
>   How many rise up against me!
2 Many are saying of me,
>   "God will not deliver him."   *Selah*[b]

3 But you are a shield around me, O LORD;
>   you bestow glory on me and lift[c] up my head.
4 To the LORD I cry aloud,
>   and he answers me from his holy hill.   *Selah*

5 I lie down and sleep;
>   I wake again, because the LORD sustains me.
6 I will not fear the tens of thousands
>   drawn up against me on every side.

7 Arise, O LORD!
>   Deliver me, O my God!
> Strike all my enemies on the jaw;
>   break the teeth of the wicked.

8 From the LORD comes deliverance.
>   May your blessing be on your people.   *Selah*

PSALM 4

For the director of music. With stringed instruments.
A psalm of David.

1 Answer me when I call to you,
>   O my righteous God.
> Give me relief from my distress;
>   be merciful to me and hear my prayer.

2 How long, O men, will you turn my glory into
>   shame[d]?
> How long will you love delusions and seek false
>   gods[e]?   *Selah*
3 Know that the LORD has set apart the godly for
>   himself;
>   the LORD will hear when I call to him.

Get a Load of This...

What a picture!—God sitting on his throne, throwing his head back and laughing at the foolish men who oppose him, who think they can get away with anything (Psalm 2:4). Can't you just picture God saying, "Go ahead—Make my day"?

In Other Words...

---

[a] 9 Or *will break them with a rod of iron*   [b] 2 A word of uncertain meaning, occurring frequently in the Psalms; possibly a musical term   [c] 3 Or *LORD, / my Glorious One, who lifts*   [d] 2 Or *you dishonor my Glorious One*   [e] 2 Or *seek lies*

⁴ In your anger do not sin;
     when you are on your beds,
     search your hearts and be silent.
                    Selah

⁵ Offer right sacrifices
     and trust in the LORD.

⁶ Many are asking, "Who can show us
         any good?"
     Let the light of your face shine upon
         us, O LORD.
⁷ You have filled my heart with greater
         joy
     than when their grain and new wine
         abound.
⁸ I will lie down and sleep in peace,
     for you alone, O LORD,
     make me dwell in safety.

PSALM 5

For the director of music. For flutes.
A psalm of David.

¹ Give ear to my words, O LORD,
     consider my sighing.
² Listen to my cry for help,
     my King and my God,
     for to you I pray.

³ In the morning, O LORD, you hear my
         voice;
     in the morning I lay my requests
         before you
     and wait in expectation.

⁴ You are not a God who takes pleasure
         in evil;
     with you the wicked cannot dwell.
⁵ The arrogant cannot stand in your
         presence;
     you hate all who do wrong.
⁶ You destroy those who tell lies;
     bloodthirsty and deceitful men
     the LORD abhors.

⁷ But I, by your great mercy,
     will come into your house;
    in reverence will I bow down
     toward your holy temple.
⁸ Lead me, O LORD, in your righteousness
     because of my enemies—
     make straight your way before me.

⁹ Not a word from their mouth can be
         trusted;
     their heart is filled with destruction.
     Their throat is an open grave;

Unwinding With God

READ PSALM 4

When you've had a busy day and finally crawl into bed, don't just pull up the sheets and count sheep. Take time to unwind and give God your thoughts. Seek God and let him know you really want to hear from him. That's what David did, and he said, "The LORD will hear when I call to him" (verse 3). So tell God what's on your mind, then be quiet, listen and expect him to answer. God can speak to you in your thoughts. His peace and presence can fill your heart with joy so you can "lie down and sleep in peace" (verses 7–8). Morning is a cool time to pray, too, and give a whole new day to God (see Psalm 5:3). Whether you're a morning or a night person—talk to God.

Your next reading is on page 683.

with their tongue they speak deceit.
10 Declare them guilty, O God!
   Let their intrigues be their downfall.
Banish them for their many sins,
   for they have rebelled against you.

11 But let all who take refuge in you be glad;
   let them ever sing for joy.
Spread your protection over them,
   that those who love your name may rejoice in you.
12 For surely, O LORD, you bless the righteous;
   you surround them with your favor as with a shield.

PSALM 6

For the director of music. With stringed instruments.
According to *sheminith*. *a* A psalm of David.

1 O LORD, do not rebuke me in your anger
   or discipline me in your wrath.
2 Be merciful to me, LORD, for I am faint;
   O LORD, heal me, for my bones are in agony.
3 My soul is in anguish.
   How long, O LORD, how long?

4 Turn, O LORD, and deliver me;
   save me because of your unfailing love.
5 No one remembers you when he is dead.
   Who praises you from the grave *b*?

6 I am worn out from groaning;
   all night long I flood my bed with weeping
   and drench my couch with tears.
7 My eyes grow weak with sorrow;
   they fail because of all my foes.

8 Away from me, all you who do evil,
   for the LORD has heard my weeping.
9 The LORD has heard my cry for mercy;
   the LORD accepts my prayer.
10 All my enemies will be ashamed and dismayed;
   they will turn back in sudden disgrace.

PSALM 7

A *shiggaion* *c* of David, which he sang to the LORD concerning
Cush, a Benjamite.

1 O LORD my God, I take refuge in you;
   save and deliver me from all who pursue me,
2 or they will tear me like a lion
   and rip me to pieces with no one to rescue me.

3 O LORD my God, if I have done this
   and there is guilt on my hands—
4 if I have done evil to him who is at peace with me
   or without cause have robbed my foe—
5 then let my enemy pursue and overtake me;
   let him trample my life to the ground
   and make me sleep in the dust.   *Selah*

a Title: Probably a musical term   b 5 Hebrew *Sheol*   c Title: Probably a literary
or musical term

Get a Load of This...

Check out Psalm 6:6. With some kids, "flooding their bed" happens when they drink too much water before turning in for the night— not from crying out to God with tears all night. If your bed turns into Niagara Falls for reason number one, 'fess up and tell your mom. If it happens for reason number two, talk about what's bothering you with a friend or parent. They care.

Get a Load of This...

Check out Psalm 7:10. "My shield is God." The Israelites carried two different kinds of shields into battle: the *maghen* (a small, round, light shield used for fast sword fighting) and the *tsinnah* (a larger, heavy-duty body shield). In today's terms, you might compare God to a bicycle helmet or a bulletproof window.

⁶ Arise, O Lᴏʀᴅ, in your anger;
      rise up against the rage of my enemies.
      Awake, my God; decree justice.
⁷ Let the assembled peoples gather around you.
      Rule over them from on high;
⁸   let the Lᴏʀᴅ judge the peoples.
   Judge me, O Lᴏʀᴅ, according to my righteousness,
      according to my integrity, O Most High.
⁹ O righteous God,
      who searches minds and hearts,
   bring to an end the violence of the wicked
      and make the righteous secure.

¹⁰ My shieldᵃ is God Most High,
      who saves the upright in heart.
¹¹ God is a righteous judge,
      a God who expresses his wrath every day.
¹² If he does not relent,
      heᵇ will sharpen his sword;
      he will bend and string his bow.
¹³ He has prepared his deadly weapons;
      he makes ready his flaming arrows.

¹⁴ He who is pregnant with evil
      and conceives trouble gives birth to disillusionment.
¹⁵ He who digs a hole and scoops it out
      falls into the pit he has made.
¹⁶ The trouble he causes recoils on himself;
      his violence comes down on his own head.

¹⁷ I will give thanks to the Lᴏʀᴅ because of his
      righteousness
   and will sing praise to the name of the Lᴏʀᴅ Most
      High.

PSALM 8

For the director of music. According to gittith.ᶜ
A psalm of David.

¹ O Lᴏʀᴅ, our Lord,
      how majestic is your name in all the earth!

   You have set your glory
      above the heavens.
² From the lips of children and infants
      you have ordained praiseᵈ
   because of your enemies,
      to silence the foe and the avenger.

³ When I consider your heavens,
      the work of your fingers,
   the moon and the stars,
      which you have set in place,
⁴ what is man that you are mindful of him,
      the son of man that you care for him?
⁵ You made him a little lower than the heavenly
      beingsᵉ
   and crowned him with glory and honor.

ᵃ 10 Or sovereign   ᵇ 12 Or If a man does not repent, / God   ᶜ Title: Probably a
musical term   ᵈ 2 Or strength   ᵉ 5 Or than God

⁶You made him ruler over the works of
  your hands;
  you put everything under his feet:
⁷all flocks and herds,
  and the beasts of the field,
⁸the birds of the air,
  and the fish of the sea,
  all that swim the paths of the seas.

⁹O LORD, our Lord,
  how majestic is your name in all the
  earth!

PSALM 9 ᵃ

For the director of music. To the tune of,
"The Death of the Son." A psalm of David.

¹I will praise you, O LORD, with all my
  heart;
  I will tell of all your wonders.
²I will be glad and rejoice in you;
  I will sing praise to your name,
  O Most High.

³My enemies turn back;
  they stumble and perish before you.
⁴For you have upheld my right and my
  cause;

you have sat on your throne,
  judging righteously.
⁵You have rebuked the nations and
  destroyed the wicked;
  you have blotted out their name for
  ever and ever.
⁶Endless ruin has overtaken the enemy,
  you have uprooted their cities;
  even the memory of them has
  perished.

⁷The LORD reigns forever;
  he has established his throne for
  judgment.
⁸He will judge the world in righteousness;
  he will govern the peoples with
  justice.
⁹The LORD is a refuge for the oppressed,
  a stronghold in times of trouble.
¹⁰Those who know your name will trust
  in you,
  for you, LORD, have never forsaken
  those who seek you.

ᵃ Psalms 9 and 10 may have been originally a single acrostic
poem, the stanzas of which begin with the successive letters
of the Hebrew alphabet. In the Septuagint they constitute one
psalm.

Trusting Trusty God

READ PSALM 9

The psalms are not all sweetness and praise. Parts of it sound like a big screen war movie—God breaking the teeth of the ungodly (3:7), snapping their arms (10:15) and shedding their blood (58:10). In this psalm, David talks about his enemies being wiped out and their cities being destroyed, but he starts off by saying, "I will praise you, O LORD, with all my heart; I will tell of all your wonders" (verse 1). You may have lots of troubles, but like David, remember that God is the one who constantly delivers you from them. Take the time to count the good stuff God has done for you. You can trust God! Why? Because he has never forsaken those who trust him (verse 10). God is trust-worthy—which means he's worth trusting! What a great reason to pray!

Your next reading is on page 689.

¹¹ Sing praises to the LORD, enthroned in
    Zion;
  proclaim among the nations what
    he has done.
¹² For he who avenges blood remembers;
  he does not ignore the cry of the
    afflicted.

¹³ O LORD, see how my enemies persecute
    me!
  Have mercy and lift me up from the
    gates of death,
¹⁴ that I may declare your praises
  in the gates of the Daughter of Zion
  and there rejoice in your salvation.

¹⁵ The nations have fallen into the pit
    they have dug;
  their feet are caught in the net they
    have hidden.
¹⁶ The LORD is known by his justice;
  the wicked are ensnared by the work
    of their hands.   *Higgaion.* [a] *Selah*

¹⁷ The wicked return to the grave, [b]
  all the nations that forget God.
¹⁸ But the needy will not always be
    forgotten,
  nor the hope of the afflicted ever
    perish.

¹⁹ Arise, O LORD, let not man triumph;
  let the nations be judged in your
    presence.
²⁰ Strike them with terror, O LORD;
  let the nations know they are but
    men.   *Selah*

PSALM 10 [c]

¹ Why, O LORD, do you stand far off?
  Why do you hide yourself in times of
    trouble?

² In his arrogance the wicked man hunts
    down the weak,
  who are caught in the schemes he
    devises.
³ He boasts of the cravings of his heart;
  he blesses the greedy and reviles the
    LORD.
⁴ In his pride the wicked does not seek
    him;
  in all his thoughts there is no room
    for God.
⁵ His ways are always prosperous;
  he is haughty and your laws are far
    from him;
  he sneers at all his enemies.
⁶ He says to himself, "Nothing will shake
    me;

  I'll always be happy and never have
    trouble."
⁷ His mouth is full of curses and lies and
    threats;
  trouble and evil are under his
    tongue.
⁸ He lies in wait near the villages;
  from ambush he murders the
    innocent,
  watching in secret for his victims.
⁹ He lies in wait like a lion in cover;
  he lies in wait to catch the helpless;
  he catches the helpless and drags
    them off in his net.
¹⁰ His victims are crushed, they collapse;
  they fall under his strength.
¹¹ He says to himself, "God has
    forgotten;
  he covers his face and never sees."

¹² Arise, LORD! Lift up your hand, O God.
  Do not forget the helpless.
¹³ Why does the wicked man revile God?
  Why does he say to himself,
  "He won't call me to account"?
¹⁴ But you, O God, do see trouble and
    grief;
  you consider it to take it in hand.
  The victim commits himself to you;
  you are the helper of the fatherless.
¹⁵ Break the arm of the wicked and evil
    man;
  call him to account for his
    wickedness
  that would not be found out.

¹⁶ The LORD is King for ever and ever;
  the nations will perish from his
    land.
¹⁷ You hear, O LORD, the desire of the
    afflicted;
  you encourage them, and you listen
    to their cry,
¹⁸ defending the fatherless and the
    oppressed,
  in order that man, who is of the
    earth, may terrify no more.

PSALM 11

For the director of music. Of David.

¹ In the LORD I take refuge.
  How then can you say to me:
  "Flee like a bird to your mountain.

---

[a] 16 Or *Meditation*; possibly a musical notation
[b] 17 Hebrew *Sheol*   [c] Psalms 9 and 10 may have been
originally a single acrostic poem, the stanzas of which begin
with the successive letters of the Hebrew alphabet. In the
Septuagint they constitute one psalm.

2 For look, the wicked bend their bows;
  they set their arrows against the
    strings
to shoot from the shadows
  at the upright in heart.
3 When the foundations are being
    destroyed,
  what can the righteous do*a*?"

4 The LORD is in his holy temple;
  the LORD is on his heavenly throne.
He observes the sons of men;
  his eyes examine them.
5 The LORD examines the righteous,
  but the wicked*b* and those who love
    violence
  his soul hates.
6 On the wicked he will rain
  fiery coals and burning sulfur;
  a scorching wind will be their lot.

7 For the LORD is righteous,
  he loves justice;
  upright men will see his face.

PSALM 12

For the director of music. According to
  sheminith. c A psalm of David.

1 Help, LORD, for the godly are no more;
  the faithful have vanished from
    among men.
2 Everyone lies to his neighbor;
  their flattering lips speak with
    deception.

3 May the LORD cut off all flattering lips
  and every boastful tongue
4 that says, "We will triumph with our
    tongues;
  we own our lips*d*—who is our
    master?"

5 "Because of the oppression of the
    weak
  and the groaning of the needy,
  I will now arise," says the LORD.

a 3 Or *what is the Righteous One doing*   *b 5* Or *The LORD,
the Righteous One, examines the wicked, /*   *c* Title: Probably
a musical term   *d 4* Or */ our lips are our plowshares*

Make It Stick

READ PSALM 12:2

We all want to be encouraged and to be told we're great at something. But some kids use flattery to manipulate others into doing things (see Psalm 12:2). If someone says, "You look *sooo* cool! Hey, you'd look even cooler with a ring in your tongue!"—Are they really praising you? No way. Write on a sticky note, "Without sincerity, flattery falls flat."

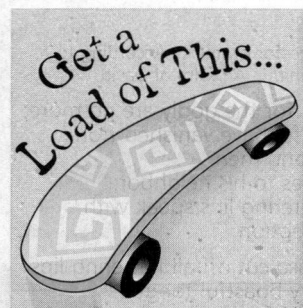

Get a Load of This...

Think there are mistakes in God's Word? Think again! God's Word is like silver that has been melted down so the impurities can be skimmed off the top and dumped—not once, but *seven* times! (see Psalm 12:6.) Talk about being pure!

"I will protect them from those who malign them."

6 And the words of the LORD are flawless,
  like silver refined in a furnace of clay,
  purified seven times.

7 O LORD, you will keep us safe
  and protect us from such people forever.
8 The wicked freely strut about
  when what is vile is honored among men.

PSALM 13

For the director of music. A psalm of David.

1 How long, O LORD? Will you forget me forever?
  How long will you hide your face from me?
2 How long must I wrestle with my thoughts
  and every day have sorrow in my heart?
  How long will my enemy triumph over me?

3 Look on me and answer, O LORD my God.
  Give light to my eyes, or I will sleep in death;
4 my enemy will say, "I have overcome him,"
  and my foes will rejoice when I fall.

5 But I trust in your unfailing love;
  my heart rejoices in your salvation.
6 I will sing to the LORD,
  for he has been good to me.

PSALM 14

For the director of music. Of David.

1 The fool[a] says in his heart,
  "There is no God."
They are corrupt, their deeds are vile;
  there is no one who does good.

2 The LORD looks down from heaven
  on the sons of men
to see if there are any who understand,
  any who seek God.
3 All have turned aside,
  they have together become corrupt;
there is no one who does good,
  not even one.

4 Will evildoers never learn—
  those who devour my people as men eat bread
  and who do not call on the LORD?
5 There they are, overwhelmed with dread,
  for God is present in the company of the
    righteous.
6 You evildoers frustrate the plans of the poor,
  but the LORD is their refuge.

7 Oh, that salvation for Israel would come out of Zion!
  When the LORD restores the fortunes of his people,
  let Jacob rejoice and Israel be glad!

a 1 The Hebrew words rendered *fool* in Psalms denote one who is morally deficient.

PSALM 15

A psalm of David.

1 LORD, who may dwell in your sanctuary?
   Who may live on your holy hill?

2 He whose walk is blameless
   and who does what is righteous,
who speaks the truth from his heart
3   and has no slander on his tongue,
   who does his neighbor no wrong
   and casts no slur on his fellowman,
4 who despises a vile man
   but honors those who fear the LORD,
who keeps his oath
   even when it hurts,
5 who lends his money without usury
   and does not accept a bribe against
      the innocent.

He who does these things
   will never be shaken.

PSALM 16

A *miktam*[a] of David.

1 Keep me safe, O God,
   for in you I take refuge.

2 I said to the LORD, "You are my Lord;
   apart from you I have no good thing."
3 As for the saints who are in the land,
   they are the glorious ones in whom
      is all my delight.[b]
4 The sorrows of those will increase
   who run after other gods.
I will not pour out their libations of
      blood
   or take up their names on my lips.

5 LORD, you have assigned me my portion
      and my cup;
   you have made my lot secure.
6 The boundary lines have fallen for me
      in pleasant places;
   surely I have a delightful inheritance.

7 I will praise the LORD, who counsels me;
   even at night my heart instructs me.
8 I have set the LORD always before me.
   Because he is at my right hand,
   I will not be shaken.

9 Therefore my heart is glad and my
      tongue rejoices;
   my body also will rest secure,
10 because you will not abandon me to
      the grave,[c]
   nor will you let your Holy One[d] see
      decay.

11 You have made[e] known to me the
      path of life;
   you will fill me with joy in your
      presence,
   with eternal pleasures at your right
      hand.

PSALM 17

A prayer of David.

1 Hear, O LORD, my righteous plea;
   listen to my cry.
Give ear to my prayer—
   it does not rise from deceitful lips.
2 May my vindication come from you;
   may your eyes see what is right.

3 Though you probe my heart and
      examine me at night,
   though you test me, you will find
      nothing;
   I have resolved that my mouth will
      not sin.
4 As for the deeds of men—
   by the word of your lips
   I have kept myself
   from the ways of the violent.
5 My steps have held to your paths;
   my feet have not slipped.

6 I call on you, O God, for you will
      answer me;
   give ear to me and hear my prayer.
7 Show the wonder of your great love,
   you who save by your right hand
   those who take refuge in you from
      their foes.
8 Keep me as the apple of your eye;
   hide me in the shadow of your wings
9 from the wicked who assail me,
   from my mortal enemies who
      surround me.

10 They close up their callous hearts,
   and their mouths speak with
      arrogance.
11 They have tracked me down, they now
      surround me,
   with eyes alert, to throw me to the
      ground.
12 They are like a lion hungry for prey,
   like a great lion crouching in cover.

13 Rise up, O LORD, confront them, bring
      them down;

a Title: Probably a literary or musical term   b 3 Or As for the
pagan priests who are in the land / and the nobles in whom
all delight, I said: c 10 Hebrew Sheol   d 10 Or your
faithful one   e 11 Or You will make

rescue me from the wicked by your
sword.
¹⁴ O Lord, by your hand save me from
such men,
from men of this world whose
reward is in this life.

You still the hunger of those you cherish;
their sons have plenty,
and they store up wealth for their
children.
¹⁵ And I—in righteousness I will see your
face;
when I awake, I will be satisfied with
seeing your likeness.

PSALM 18

For the director of music. Of David the servant
of the Lord. He sang to the Lord the words of
this song when the Lord delivered him from
the hand of all his enemies and from the
hand of Saul. He said:

¹ I love you, O Lord, my strength.

² The Lord is my rock, my fortress and
my deliverer;
my God is my rock, in whom I take
refuge.
He is my shield and the horn^a of my
salvation, my stronghold.
³ I call to the Lord, who is worthy of
praise,
and I am saved from my enemies.

⁴ The cords of death entangled me;
the torrents of destruction
overwhelmed me.
⁵ The cords of the grave^b coiled around
me;
the snares of death confronted me.
⁶ In my distress I called to the Lord;
I cried to my God for help.
From his temple he heard my voice;
my cry came before him, into his ears.

⁷ The earth trembled and quaked,
and the foundations of the
mountains shook;
they trembled because he was angry.
⁸ Smoke rose from his nostrils;

---

^a 2 *Horn* here symbolizes strength.   ^b 5 Hebrew *Sheol*

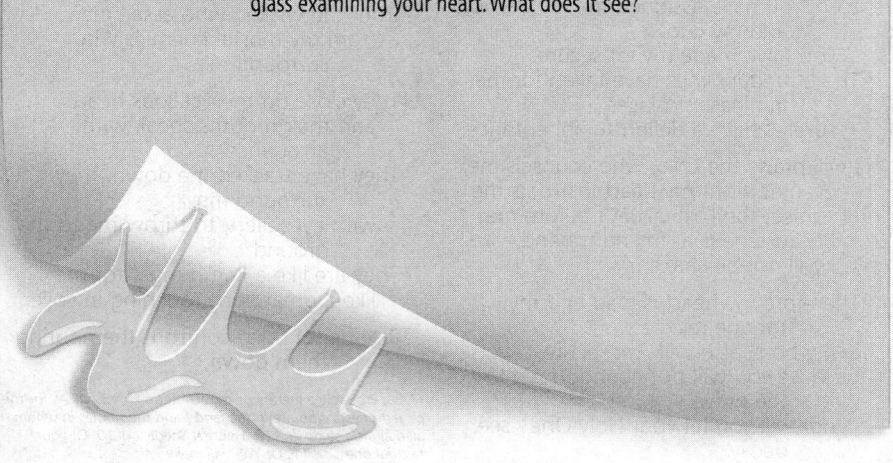

Make It Stick

READ PSALM 17:3–5

Here's a guy committed to having godly character! David had so totally made up his mind
to do the right thing—to only speak good things—that he could tell God, "Probe me. Test me.
You won't find a thing. I'm keeping myself from wrong things." (Psalm 17:3.) Draw a magnifying
glass examining your heart. What does it see?

consuming fire came from his mouth,
burning coals blazed out of it.
⁹ He parted the heavens and came down;
dark clouds were under his feet.
¹⁰ He mounted the cherubim and flew;
he soared on the wings of the wind.
¹¹ He made darkness his covering, his
canopy around him—
the dark rain clouds of the sky.
¹² Out of the brightness of his presence
clouds advanced,
with hailstones and bolts of lightning.
¹³ The LORD thundered from heaven;
the voice of the Most High
resounded. ª
¹⁴ He shot his arrows and scattered ⌞the
enemies⌟,
great bolts of lightning and routed
them.
¹⁵ The valleys of the sea were exposed
and the foundations of the earth
laid bare
at your rebuke, O LORD,
at the blast of breath from your
nostrils.

¹⁶ He reached down from on high and
took hold of me;
he drew me out of deep waters.
¹⁷ He rescued me from my powerful
enemy,
from my foes, who were too strong
for me.
¹⁸ They confronted me in the day of my
disaster,
but the LORD was my support.
¹⁹ He brought me out into a spacious
place;
he rescued me because he delighted
in me.

²⁰ The LORD has dealt with me according
to my righteousness;
according to the cleanness of my
hands he has rewarded me.
²¹ For I have kept the ways of the LORD;
I have not done evil by turning from
my God.
²² All his laws are before me;

ª 13 Some Hebrew manuscripts and Septuagint (see also
2 Samuel 22:14); most Hebrew manuscripts *resounded, /
amid hailstones and bolts of lightning*

The Mighty Fortress

PSALM 18:1–6, 16–36

Picture a mighty fortress built from heavy blocks of stone, towering on top of a mountain, completely secure, in zero danger from enemy armies. David said, "The LORD is my rock, my fortress" (verse 2). David wasn't thinking of a snow fort, not even a city with high walls—he was thinking *fortress*. Listen, David *knew* what it took to capture a fortified city. Half his life had been spent shouting orders as he and his men swarmed up siege ramps and over city walls—or took a battering ram through a city gate. David had enemies, too, and when they attacked, he didn't want to be caught in a sand castle. He wanted to be protected inside a *super* fortress higher and safer than any other. His fortress was God. David knew that if he was faithful, if he followed closely, God would protect him. What about you? Is God *your* fortress?

Your next reading is on page 694.

Get a Load of This...

"With my God I can scale a wall" (Psalm 18:29). And you didn't think God liked extreme sports? It sounds like every time David scaled a wall or went rock-climbing, God had his fingers in the cracks right beside him. (Don't try this without your mom's permission though!)

I have not turned away from his decrees.
²³ I have been blameless before him
    and have kept myself from sin.
²⁴ The LORD has rewarded me according to my
    righteousness,
    according to the cleanness of my hands in his sight.

²⁵ To the faithful you show yourself faithful,
    to the blameless you show yourself blameless,
²⁶ to the pure you show yourself pure,
    but to the crooked you show yourself shrewd.
²⁷ You save the humble
    but bring low those whose eyes are haughty.
²⁸ You, O LORD, keep my lamp burning;
    my God turns my darkness into light.
²⁹ With your help I can advance against a troop ᵃ;
    with my God I can scale a wall.

³⁰ As for God, his way is perfect;
    the word of the LORD is flawless.
  He is a shield
    for all who take refuge in him.
³¹ For who is God besides the LORD?
    And who is the Rock except our God?
³² It is God who arms me with strength
    and makes my way perfect.
³³ He makes my feet like the feet of a deer;
    he enables me to stand on the heights.
³⁴ He trains my hands for battle;
    my arms can bend a bow of bronze.
³⁵ You give me your shield of victory,
    and your right hand sustains me;
    you stoop down to make me great.
³⁶ You broaden the path beneath me,
    so that my ankles do not turn.

³⁷ I pursued my enemies and overtook them;
    I did not turn back till they were destroyed.
³⁸ I crushed them so that they could not rise;
    they fell beneath my feet.
³⁹ You armed me with strength for battle;
    you made my adversaries bow at my feet.
⁴⁰ You made my enemies turn their backs in flight,
    and I destroyed my foes.
⁴¹ They cried for help, but there was no one to save
    them—
    to the LORD, but he did not answer.
⁴² I beat them as fine as dust borne on the wind;
    I poured them out like mud in the streets.

⁴³ You have delivered me from the attacks of the people;
    you have made me the head of nations;
    people I did not know are subject to me.
⁴⁴ As soon as they hear me, they obey me;
    foreigners cringe before me.
⁴⁵ They all lose heart;
    they come trembling from their strongholds.

ᵃ 29 Or can run through a barricade

46 The Lord lives! Praise be to my Rock!
　Exalted be God my Savior!
47 He is the God who avenges me,
　who subdues nations under me,
48 　who saves me from my enemies.
　You exalted me above my foes;
　from violent men you rescued me.
49 Therefore I will praise you among the
　nations, O Lord;
　I will sing praises to your name.
50 He gives his king great victories;
　he shows unfailing kindness to his
　anointed,
　to David and his descendants forever.

PSALM 19

For the director of music. A psalm of David.

1 The heavens declare the glory of God;
　the skies proclaim the work of his
　hands.
2 Day after day they pour forth speech;
　night after night they display
　knowledge.

3 There is no speech or language
　where their voice is not heard.[a]
4 Their voice[b] goes out into all the earth,
　their words to the ends of the world.

In the heavens he has pitched a tent
　for the sun,
5 　which is like a bridegroom coming
　forth from his pavilion,
　like a champion rejoicing to run his
　course.
6 It rises at one end of the heavens
　and makes its circuit to the other;
　nothing is hidden from its heat.

7 The law of the Lord is perfect,
　reviving the soul.
The statutes of the Lord are
　trustworthy,
　making wise the simple.
8 The precepts of the Lord are right,
　giving joy to the heart.

[a] 3 Or They have no speech, there are no words; / no sound
is heard from them   [b] 4 Septuagint, Jerome and Syriac;
Hebrew line

Make It Stick

READ PSALM 19:1–3

Watch a sunset or a thunderstorm and you'll see "the heavens declare the glory of God" (Psalm 19:1).
You can learn about God's invisible qualities by looking at the world he created (Romans 1:20). What
are a few things in nature that show you how awesome God is, or what a great artist he is?

The commands of the LORD are radiant,
giving light to the eyes.
⁹ The fear of the LORD is pure,
enduring forever.
The ordinances of the LORD are sure
and altogether righteous.
¹⁰ They are more precious than gold,
than much pure gold;
they are sweeter than honey,
than honey from the comb.
¹¹ By them is your servant warned;
in keeping them there is great
reward.

¹² Who can discern his errors?
Forgive my hidden faults.
¹³ Keep your servant also from willful sins;
may they not rule over me.
Then will I be blameless,
innocent of great transgression.

¹⁴ May the words of my mouth and the
meditation of my heart
be pleasing in your sight,
O LORD, my Rock and my Redeemer.

PSALM 20

For the director of music. A psalm of David.

¹ May the LORD answer you when you
are in distress;
may the name of the God of Jacob
protect you.
² May he send you help from the
sanctuary
and grant you support from Zion.
³ May he remember all your sacrifices
and accept your burnt offerings.

Selah

⁴ May he give you the desire of your
heart
and make all your plans succeed.
⁵ We will shout for joy when you are
victorious
and will lift up our banners in the
name of our God.
May the LORD grant all your requests.

⁶ Now I know that the LORD saves his
anointed;

Make It Stick

READ PSALM 19:13–14

How can you be sure that what you say and think is pleasing to God? Easy. Tank your heart up with God's truth and make a decision to watch your thoughts (see Psalm 19:13–14). It's your choice what you fill your mind with. Write on a sticky note, "God rules! Willful sins and thoughts do not!"

he answers him from his holy heaven
    with the saving power of his right
    hand.
7 Some trust in chariots and some in
    horses,
    but we trust in the name of the LORD
    our God.
8 They are brought to their knees and fall,
    but we rise up and stand firm.

9 O LORD, save the king!
    Answer*a* us when we call!

PSALM 21

For the director of music. A psalm of David.

1 O LORD, the king rejoices in your
    strength.
    How great is his joy in the victories
    you give!
2 You have granted him the desire of his
    heart
    and have not withheld the request
    of his lips.   *Selah*
3 You welcomed him with rich blessings
    and placed a crown of pure gold on
    his head.
4 He asked you for life, and you gave it
    to him—
    length of days, for ever and ever.
5 Through the victories you gave, his
    glory is great;
    you have bestowed on him splendor
    and majesty.
6 Surely you have granted him eternal
    blessings
    and made him glad with the joy of
    your presence.
7 For the king trusts in the LORD;
    through the unfailing love of the
    Most High
    he will not be shaken.

8 Your hand will lay hold on all your
    enemies;
    your right hand will seize your foes.
9 At the time of your appearing
    you will make them like a fiery
    furnace.
    In his wrath the LORD will swallow
    them up,
    and his fire will consume them.
10 You will destroy their descendants
    from the earth,
    their posterity from mankind.
11 Though they plot evil against you
    and devise wicked schemes, they
    cannot succeed;

12 for you will make them turn their
    backs
    when you aim at them with drawn
    bow.
13 Be exalted, O LORD, in your strength;
    we will sing and praise your might.

PSALM 22

For the director of music. To ⌊the tune of⌋
"The Doe of the Morning." A psalm of David.

1 My God, my God, why have you
    forsaken me?
    Why are you so far from saving me,
    so far from the words of my
    groaning?
2 O my God, I cry out by day, but you do
    not answer,
    by night, and am not silent.

3 Yet you are enthroned as the Holy One;
    you are the praise of Israel.*b*
4 In you our fathers put their trust;
    they trusted and you delivered them.
5 They cried to you and were saved;
    in you they trusted and were not
    disappointed.

6 But I am a worm and not a man,
    scorned by men and despised by the
    people.
7 All who see me mock me;
    they hurl insults, shaking their heads:
8 "He trusts in the LORD;
    let the LORD rescue him.
    Let him deliver him,
    since he delights in him."

9 Yet you brought me out of the womb;
    you made me trust in you
    even at my mother's breast.
10 From birth I was cast upon you;
    from my mother's womb you have
    been my God.
11 Do not be far from me,
    for trouble is near
    and there is no one to help.

12 Many bulls surround me;
    strong bulls of Bashan encircle me.
13 Roaring lions tearing their prey
    open their mouths wide against me.
14 I am poured out like water,
    and all my bones are out of joint.
    My heart has turned to wax;
    it has melted away within me.
15 My strength is dried up like a potsherd,

*a 9 Or save! / O King, answer   b 3 Or Yet you are holy, /
enthroned on the praises of Israel*

and my tongue sticks to the roof of
    my mouth;
you lay me[a] in the dust of death.
16 Dogs have surrounded me;
    a band of evil men has encircled me,
    they have pierced[b] my hands and
        my feet.
17 I can count all my bones;
    people stare and gloat over me.
18 They divide my garments among them
    and cast lots for my clothing.

19 But you, O LORD, be not far off;
    O my Strength, come quickly to help
        me.
20 Deliver my life from the sword,
    my precious life from the power of
        the dogs.
21 Rescue me from the mouth of the lions;
    save[c] me from the horns of the wild
        oxen.

22 I will declare your name to my brothers;
    in the congregation I will praise you.
23 You who fear the LORD, praise him!
    All you descendants of Jacob, honor
        him!

Revere him, all you descendants of
    Israel!
24 For he has not despised or disdained
    the suffering of the afflicted one;
he has not hidden his face from him
    but has listened to his cry for help.

25 From you comes the theme of my
    praise in the great assembly;
before those who fear you[d] will I
    fulfill my vows.
26 The poor will eat and be satisfied;
    they who seek the LORD will praise
        him—
    may your hearts live forever!
27 All the ends of the earth
    will remember and turn to the LORD,
and all the families of the nations
    will bow down before him,
28 for dominion belongs to the LORD
    and he rules over the nations.

29 All the rich of the earth will feast and
    worship;

[a] 15 Or / I am laid   [b] 16 Some Hebrew manuscripts,
Septuagint and Syriac; most Hebrew manuscripts / like the
lion,   [c] 21 Or / you have heard   [d] 25 Hebrew him

The Master's Master Plan

READ PSALM 22

GET SMARTER.

David wrote his psalms one thousand years before Jesus the Messiah
was born, yet by God's Spirit David prophesied exactly what Jesus
would suffer. Verse 1, "My God, my God, why have you forsaken me?"
was quoted by Jesus as he died on the cross (Matthew 27:46). Even
the mockery of Jesus' enemies (Matthew 27:43) was prophesied in verse 8—"He trusts in the LORD; let the LORD rescue
him." Verse 16, "They have pierced my hands and my feet,"
was fulfilled when the Romans nailed Jesus to the cross
(Matthew 27:35). Verse 14, "All my bones are out of joint," describes what happens when someone hangs on a cross.
God knows what's going to happen before we do.
He has the master plan, and it's perfect. He knows
the beginning from the end and every little thing
in between. If God knows *this* much, you can
sure trust him with *your* life.

Your next reading is on page 696.

all who go down to the dust will
    kneel before him—
those who cannot keep themselves
    alive.
30 Posterity will serve him;
    future generations will be told about
      the Lord.
31 They will proclaim his righteousness
    to a people yet unborn—
    for he has done it.

PSALM 23

A psalm of David.

1 The Lord is my shepherd, I shall not be
    in want.
2   He makes me lie down in green
      pastures,
he leads me beside quiet waters,
3   he restores my soul.
He guides me in paths of
    righteousness
    for his name's sake.
4 Even though I walk

through the valley of the shadow of
    death, [a]
I will fear no evil,
    for you are with me;
your rod and your staff,
    they comfort me.

5 You prepare a table before me
    in the presence of my enemies.
You anoint my head with oil;
    my cup overflows.
6 Surely goodness and love will follow me
    all the days of my life,
and I will dwell in the house of the Lord
    forever.

PSALM 24

Of David. A psalm.

1 The earth is the Lord's, and everything
    in it,
    the world, and all who live in it;
2 for he founded it upon the seas

[a] 4 Or through the darkest valley

Make It Stick

READ PSALM 23

In Psalm 23, David said that God loves us like a shepherd cares for his sheep. Think of some other examples. "The Lord is like Superman watching over the city of Metropolis," or "The Lord takes care of me the way the water takes care of my fish." Your turn. Choose a few examples that work for you, even if they seem goofy.

and established it upon the waters.

³Who may ascend the hill of the LORD?
  Who may stand in his holy place?
⁴He who has clean hands and a pure
    heart,
  who does not lift up his soul to an
    idol
  or swear by what is false. ͣ
⁵He will receive blessing from the LORD
  and vindication from God his Savior.
⁶Such is the generation of those who
    seek him,
  who seek your face, O God of
    Jacob. ᵇ   Selah

⁷Lift up your heads, O you gates;
  be lifted up, you ancient doors,
  that the King of glory may come in.
⁸Who is this King of glory?
  The LORD strong and mighty,
  the LORD mighty in battle.
⁹Lift up your heads, O you gates;
  lift them up, you ancient doors,
  that the King of glory may come in.
¹⁰Who is he, this King of glory?
  The LORD Almighty—
  he is the King of glory.   Selah

PSALM 25 ᶜ

Of David.

¹To you, O LORD, I lift up my soul;
² in you I trust, O my God.
  Do not let me be put to shame,
  nor let my enemies triumph over me.
³No one whose hope is in you
  will ever be put to shame,
  but they will be put to shame
  who are treacherous without excuse.

⁴Show me your ways, O LORD,
  teach me your paths;
⁵guide me in your truth and teach me,
  for you are God my Savior,
  and my hope is in you all day long.
⁶Remember, O LORD, your great mercy
    and love,
  for they are from of old.
⁷Remember not the sins of my youth
  and my rebellious ways;
  according to your love remember me,
  for you are good, O LORD.

ͣ 4 Or *swear falsely*   ᵇ 6 Two Hebrew manuscripts and
Syriac (see also Septuagint); most Hebrew manuscripts *face,
Jacob*   ᶜ This psalm is an acrostic poem, the verses of which
begin with the successive letters of the Hebrew alphabet.

The Blame/Shame Game

READ PSALM 25:1–2, 20–21

David did not like people giving him the hairy eyeball as he stood there with hot red cheeks, feeling two inches high, and wishing he could crawl under the nearest rug. He prayed to God, "Do not let me be put to shame" (verse 2). As a man, it's right to want to be respected and looked up to. Having a good reputation is a cool thing. You *sure* don't want a bad reputation! The good news is that it's up to *you!* You can choose if you have a good rep or bring shame to yourself and others. How? By the way you live. And get this—there's a *huge* difference between genuine shame (when you're sorry for stuff you've done wrong) and false shame (when people dump guilt on you and blame you for things that aren't even wrong or aren't your fault.) Know the difference.

Your next reading is on page 698.

8 Good and upright is the LORD;
  therefore he instructs sinners in his
    ways.
9 He guides the humble in what is right
  and teaches them his way.
10 All the ways of the LORD are loving and
     faithful
  for those who keep the demands of
    his covenant.
11 For the sake of your name, O LORD,
  forgive my iniquity, though it is great.
12 Who, then, is the man that fears the
     LORD?
  He will instruct him in the way
    chosen for him.
13 He will spend his days in prosperity,
  and his descendants will inherit the
    land.
14 The LORD confides in those who fear
     him;
  he makes his covenant known to
    them.
15 My eyes are ever on the LORD,
  for only he will release my feet from
    the snare.

16 Turn to me and be gracious to me,
  for I am lonely and afflicted.
17 The troubles of my heart have
     multiplied;
  free me from my anguish.
18 Look upon my affliction and my distress
  and take away all my sins.
19 See how my enemies have increased
  and how fiercely they hate me!
20 Guard my life and rescue me;
  let me not be put to shame,
  for I take refuge in you.
21 May integrity and uprightness protect
     me,
  because my hope is in you.

22 Redeem Israel, O God,
  from all their troubles!

PSALM 26

Of David.

1 Vindicate me, O LORD,
  for I have led a blameless life;
  I have trusted in the LORD
    without wavering.
2 Test me, O LORD, and try me,
  examine my heart and my mind;
3 for your love is ever before me,
  and I walk continually in your truth.
4 I do not sit with deceitful men,
  nor do I consort with hypocrites;

5 I abhor the assembly of evildoers
  and refuse to sit with the wicked.
6 I wash my hands in innocence,
  and go about your altar, O LORD,
7 proclaiming aloud your praise
  and telling of all your wonderful
    deeds.
8 I love the house where you live, O LORD,
  the place where your glory dwells.

9 Do not take away my soul along with
     sinners,
  my life with bloodthirsty men,
10 in whose hands are wicked schemes,
  whose right hands are full of bribes.
11 But I lead a blameless life;
  redeem me and be merciful to me.

12 My feet stand on level ground;
  in the great assembly I will praise the
    LORD.

PSALM 27

Of David.

1 The LORD is my light and my salvation—
    whom shall I fear?
  The LORD is the stronghold of my life—
    of whom shall I be afraid?
2 When evil men advance against me
    to devour my flesh,[a]
  when my enemies and my foes attack
     me,
    they will stumble and fall.
3 Though an army besiege me,
    my heart will not fear;
  though war break out against me,
    even then will I be confident.

4 One thing I ask of the LORD,
    this is what I seek:
  that I may dwell in the house of the
     LORD
    all the days of my life,
  to gaze upon the beauty of the LORD
    and to seek him in his temple.
5 For in the day of trouble
    he will keep me safe in his dwelling;
  he will hide me in the shelter of his
     tabernacle
    and set me high upon a rock.
6 Then my head will be exalted
    above the enemies who surround me;
  at his tabernacle will I sacrifice with
     shouts of joy;
  I will sing and make music to the
     LORD.

a 2 Or to slander me

7 Hear my voice when I call, O LORD;
    be merciful to me and answer me.
8 My heart says of you, "Seek his[a] face!"
    Your face, LORD, I will seek.
9 Do not hide your face from me,
    do not turn your servant away in
        anger;
    you have been my helper.
  Do not reject me or forsake me,
    O God my Savior.
10 Though my father and mother forsake
        me,
    the LORD will receive me.
11 Teach me your way, O LORD;
    lead me in a straight path
    because of my oppressors.
12 Do not turn me over to the desire of
        my foes,
    for false witnesses rise up against me,
    breathing out violence.

13 I am still confident of this:
    I will see the goodness of the LORD
    in the land of the living.
14 Wait for the LORD;
    be strong and take heart
    and wait for the LORD.

PSALM 28

Of David.

1 To you I call, O LORD my Rock;
    do not turn a deaf ear to me.
  For if you remain silent,
    I will be like those who have gone
        down to the pit.
2 Hear my cry for mercy
    as I call to you for help,
  as I lift up my hands
    toward your Most Holy Place.

3 Do not drag me away with the wicked,
    with those who do evil,
  who speak cordially with their neighbors
    but harbor malice in their hearts.
4 Repay them for their deeds
    and for their evil work;
  repay them for what their hands have
        done
    and bring back upon them what
        they deserve.
5 Since they show no regard for the
    works of the LORD

a 8 Or To you, O my heart, he has said, "Seek my

They Will Trip Up!

READ PSALM 27

David was waiting for the evening news, but not to catch the latest baseball scores. He was expecting all-out war any minute. Did he worry? Nope! Come what may, he believed that God would protect him. "Though war break out against me, even then will I be confident" (verse 3). How so?—Because David trusted that God would make his enemies trip up (verse 2). We all have troubles, but if you have faith in God, he'll help you. Trusting God is the big picture—it's the lifelong attitude. Faith?—That's when the pressure is on and you trust that God's in control right *now*! Prayer is more than just sending words into the air. You need to believe that God *hears* you and is *doing* something. You can't put him in a box or tell him how he should answer, but you can tell him your needs.

Your next reading is on page 700.

and what his hands have done,
he will tear them down
and never build them up again.

6 Praise be to the LORD,
for he has heard my cry for mercy.
7 The LORD is my strength and my shield;
my heart trusts in him, and I am
helped.
My heart leaps for joy
and I will give thanks to him in song.

8 The LORD is the strength of his people,
a fortress of salvation for his
anointed one.
9 Save your people and bless your
inheritance;
be their shepherd and carry them
forever.

PSALM 29

A psalm of David.

1 Ascribe to the LORD, O mighty ones,
ascribe to the LORD glory and
strength.
2 Ascribe to the LORD the glory due his
name;
worship the LORD in the splendor of
his *a* holiness.

3 The voice of the LORD is over the waters;
the God of glory thunders,
the LORD thunders over the mighty
waters.
4 The voice of the LORD is powerful;
the voice of the LORD is majestic.
5 The voice of the LORD breaks the
cedars;
the LORD breaks in pieces the cedars
of Lebanon.
6 He makes Lebanon skip like a calf,
Sirion *b* like a young wild ox.
7 The voice of the LORD strikes
with flashes of lightning.
8 The voice of the LORD shakes the
desert;
the LORD shakes the Desert of
Kadesh.
9 The voice of the LORD twists the oaks *c*
and strips the forests bare.
And in his temple all cry, "Glory!"

10 The LORD sits *d* enthroned over the
flood;
the LORD is enthroned as King forever.
11 The LORD gives strength to his people;
the LORD blesses his people with
peace.

PSALM 30

A psalm. A song. For the dedication of the
temple. *e* Of David.

1 I will exalt you, O LORD,
for you lifted me out of the depths
and did not let my enemies gloat
over me.
2 O LORD my God, I called to you for help
and you healed me.
3 O LORD, you brought me up from the
grave *f*;
you spared me from going down
into the pit.

4 Sing to the LORD, you saints of his;
praise his holy name.
5 For his anger lasts only a moment,
but his favor lasts a lifetime;
weeping may remain for a night,
but rejoicing comes in the morning.

6 When I felt secure, I said,
"I will never be shaken."
7 O LORD, when you favored me,
you made my mountain *g* stand firm;
but when you hid your face,
I was dismayed.

8 To you, O LORD, I called;
to the Lord I cried for mercy:
9 "What gain is there in my destruction, *h*
in my going down into the pit?
Will the dust praise you?
Will it proclaim your faithfulness?
10 Hear, O LORD, and be merciful to me;
O LORD, be my help."

11 You turned my wailing into dancing;
you removed my sackcloth and
clothed me with joy,
12 that my heart may sing to you and not
be silent.
O LORD my God, I will give you
thanks forever.

PSALM 31

For the director of music. A psalm of David.

1 In you, O LORD, I have taken refuge;
let me never be put to shame;
deliver me in your righteousness.
2 Turn your ear to me,
come quickly to my rescue;
be my rock of refuge,
a strong fortress to save me.

---

a 2 Or LORD *with the splendor of*   *b 6* That is, Mount
Hermon   *c 9* Or LORD *makes the deer give birth*
d 10 Or *sat*   *e Title:* Or *palace*   *f 3* Hebrew *Sheol*
g 7 Or *hill country*   *h 9* Or *there if I am silenced*

3 Since you are my rock and my fortress,
　for the sake of your name lead and
　　guide me.
4 Free me from the trap that is set for me,
　for you are my refuge.
5 Into your hands I commit my spirit;
　redeem me, O LORD, the God of truth.

6 I hate those who cling to worthless
　　idols;
　I trust in the LORD.
7 I will be glad and rejoice in your love,
　for you saw my affliction
　and knew the anguish of my soul.
8 You have not handed me over to the
　　enemy
　but have set my feet in a spacious
　　place.

9 Be merciful to me, O LORD, for I am in
　　distress;
　my eyes grow weak with sorrow,
　my soul and my body with grief.
10 My life is consumed by anguish
　and my years by groaning;
　my strength fails because of my
　　affliction, a
　and my bones grow weak.

11 Because of all my enemies,
　I am the utter contempt of my
　　neighbors;
　I am a dread to my friends—
　　those who see me on the street flee
　　from me.
12 I am forgotten by them as though I
　　were dead;
　I have become like broken pottery.
13 For I hear the slander of many;
　there is terror on every side;
　they conspire against me
　and plot to take my life.

14 But I trust in you, O LORD;
　I say, "You are my God."
15 My times are in your hands;
　deliver me from my enemies
　and from those who pursue me.
16 Let your face shine on your servant;
　save me in your unfailing love.
17 Let me not be put to shame, O LORD,
　for I have cried out to you;
　but let the wicked be put to shame
　and lie silent in the grave. b
18 Let their lying lips be silenced,

a 10 Or *guilt*　　b 17 Hebrew *Sheol*

Dumped and Rejected

READ PSALM 31

Hardly anything is tougher than having a close friend dump you.
When David felt rejected, he went to God and talked about how his
friends were treating him: "I am a dread to my friends—those who
see me on the street flee from me" (verse 11). Wow! Ever had *that*
happen? David knew God would listen to his cries and help
him, and God did. David then even encouraged others,
"Be strong and take heart, all you who hope in the LORD"
(verse 24). Jesus went through abandonment and rejection,
too. Big time. He suffered the ultimate rejection on the cross.
His friends deserted him. The religious leaders of his
people called for his death. That's why you can go
to Jesus when you're feeling rejected. He knows
what you're going through. He's been there.
When friends you thought you'd be tight with
forever leave you, take your feelings to God.

Your next reading is on page 704.

for with pride and contempt
they speak arrogantly against the
righteous.

19 How great is your goodness,
which you have stored up for those
who fear you,
which you bestow in the sight of men
on those who take refuge in you.
20 In the shelter of your presence you
hide them
from the intrigues of men;
in your dwelling you keep them safe
from accusing tongues.

21 Praise be to the LORD,
for he showed his wonderful love to
me
when I was in a besieged city.
22 In my alarm I said,
"I am cut off from your sight!"
Yet you heard my cry for mercy
when I called to you for help.

23 Love the LORD, all his saints!
The LORD preserves the faithful,
but the proud he pays back in full.
24 Be strong and take heart,
all you who hope in the LORD.

PSALM 32

Of David. A *maskil*. ᵃ

1 Blessed is he
whose transgressions are forgiven,
whose sins are covered.
2 Blessed is the man
whose sin the LORD does not count
against him
and in whose spirit is no deceit.

3 When I kept silent,
my bones wasted away
through my groaning all day long.
4 For day and night
your hand was heavy upon me;
my strength was sapped
as in the heat of summer.   *Selah*
5 Then I acknowledged my sin to you
and did not cover up my iniquity.
I said, "I will confess
my transgressions to the LORD"—
and you forgave
the guilt of my sin.   *Selah*

6 Therefore let everyone who is godly
pray to you
while you may be found;
surely when the mighty waters rise,
they will not reach him.

7 You are my hiding place;
you will protect me from trouble
and surround me with songs of
deliverance.   *Selah*
8 I will instruct you and teach you in the
way you should go;
I will counsel you and watch over
you.
9 Do not be like the horse or the mule,
which have no understanding
but must be controlled by bit and
bridle
or they will not come to you.
10 Many are the woes of the wicked,
but the LORD's unfailing love
surrounds the man who trusts in
him.

11 Rejoice in the LORD and be glad, you
righteous;
sing, all you who are upright in
heart!

PSALM 33

1 Sing joyfully to the LORD, you righteous;
it is fitting for the upright to praise
him.
2 Praise the LORD with the harp;
make music to him on the ten-
stringed lyre.
3 Sing to him a new song;
play skillfully, and shout for joy.

4 For the word of the LORD is right and
true;
he is faithful in all he does.
5 The LORD loves righteousness and
justice;
the earth is full of his unfailing love.

6 By the word of the LORD were the
heavens made,
their starry host by the breath of his
mouth.
7 He gathers the waters of the sea into
jars ᵇ;
he puts the deep into storehouses.
8 Let all the earth fear the LORD;
let all the people of the world revere
him.
9 For he spoke, and it came to be;
he commanded, and it stood firm.
10 The LORD foils the plans of the nations;
he thwarts the purposes of the
peoples.

ᵃ Title: Probably a literary or musical term   ᵇ 7 Or *sea as into
a heap*

¹¹ But the plans of the Lord stand firm
forever,
    the purposes of his heart through all
generations.

¹² Blessed is the nation whose God is the
Lord,
    the people he chose for his
inheritance.
¹³ From heaven the Lord looks down
    and sees all mankind;
¹⁴ from his dwelling place he watches
    all who live on earth—
¹⁵ he who forms the hearts of all,

    who considers everything they do.
¹⁶ No king is saved by the size of his
army;
    no warrior escapes by his great
strength.
¹⁷ A horse is a vain hope for deliverance;
    despite all its great strength it
cannot save.
¹⁸ But the eyes of the Lord are on those
who fear him,
    on those whose hope is in his
unfailing love,
¹⁹ to deliver them from death
    and keep them alive in famine.

Make It Stick

_____

_____

_____

_____

_____

_____

READ PSALM 32:2
There are out-and-out lies and then there are distortions of the truth. When a man's spirit has "no deceit" (verse 2) he avoids both and speaks only the truth. Write down three times you've told a half-truth and why you did it. If you haven't confessed those sins to God, consider doing so now.

20 We wait in hope for the LORD;
   he is our help and our shield.
21 In him our hearts rejoice,
   for we trust in his holy name.
22 May your unfailing love rest upon us, O LORD,
   even as we put our hope in you.

PSALM 34 *a*

Of David. When he pretended to be insane before Abimelech,
who drove him away, and he left.

1 I will extol the LORD at all times;
   his praise will always be on my lips.
2 My soul will boast in the LORD;
   let the afflicted hear and rejoice.
3 Glorify the LORD with me;
   let us exalt his name together.

4 I sought the LORD, and he answered me;
   he delivered me from all my fears.
5 Those who look to him are radiant;
   their faces are never covered with shame.
6 This poor man called, and the LORD heard him;
   he saved him out of all his troubles.
7 The angel of the LORD encamps around those who
      fear him,
   and he delivers them.

8 Taste and see that the LORD is good;
   blessed is the man who takes refuge in him.
9 Fear the LORD, you his saints,
   for those who fear him lack nothing.
10 The lions may grow weak and hungry,
   but those who seek the LORD lack no good thing.

11 Come, my children, listen to me;
   I will teach you the fear of the LORD.
12 Whoever of you loves life
   and desires to see many good days,
13 keep your tongue from evil
   and your lips from speaking lies.
14 Turn from evil and do good;
   seek peace and pursue it.

15 The eyes of the LORD are on the righteous
   and his ears are attentive to their cry;
16 the face of the LORD is against those who do evil,
   to cut off the memory of them from the earth.

17 The righteous cry out, and the LORD hears them;
   he delivers them from all their troubles.
18 The LORD is close to the brokenhearted
   and saves those who are crushed in spirit.

19 A righteous man may have many troubles,
   but the LORD delivers him from them all;
20 he protects all his bones,
   not one of them will be broken.

a This psalm is an acrostic poem, the verses of which begin with the successive
letters of the Hebrew alphabet.

Get a Load of This...

Ever heard someone say, "God's gotta smack me on the head to get through to me"? Read Psalm 32:8–9. God doesn't want us to be like that. Being mule-headed (stubborn) is not a "manly" attitude. A man of God should have a soft heart toward God.

21 Evil will slay the wicked;
    the foes of the righteous will be
    condemned.
22 The LORD redeems his servants;
    no one will be condemned who
    takes refuge in him.

PSALM 35

Of David.

1 Contend, O LORD, with those who
    contend with me;
    fight against those who fight against
    me.
2 Take up shield and buckler;
    arise and come to my aid.
3 Brandish spear and javelina
    against those who pursue me.
  Say to my soul,
    "I am your salvation."

4 May those who seek my life
    be disgraced and put to shame;
  may those who plot my ruin
    be turned back in dismay.

5 May they be like chaff before the wind,
    with the angel of the LORD driving
    them away;
6 may their path be dark and slippery,
    with the angel of the LORD pursuing
    them.
7 Since they hid their net for me without
    cause
  and without cause dug a pit for me,
8 may ruin overtake them by surprise—
    may the net they hid entangle them,
    may they fall into the pit, to their
    ruin.
9 Then my soul will rejoice in the LORD
    and delight in his salvation.
10 My whole being will exclaim,
    "Who is like you, O LORD?
  You rescue the poor from those too
    strong for them,
    the poor and needy from those who
    rob them."

11 Ruthless witnesses come forward;

a 3 Or and block the way

Stronger than Cyborgs

READ PSALM 33:13–22

In Bible times, if you were a king with a big army, you were pretty hard to stop. The more guys you had, the better your chances were to be left standing at the end of the battle. But God isn't impressed with numbers. "No king is saved by the size of his army; no warrior escapes by his great strength" (verse 16). God gave you strength, abilities and a brain, and wants you to be strong and successful, but he knows that a lot of times your strength just won't be enough. Not a problem. When God is your partner, even an army of a million killer cyborgs can't destroy you. Guys like Gideon and Joshua knew that, once God hooked them up to his power (see Joshua 6 and Judges 7). God is totally there for you, so let him do the really big "strong stuff" for you.

Your next reading is on page 708.

they question me on things I know
nothing about.
¹²They repay me evil for good
and leave my soul forlorn.
¹³Yet when they were ill, I put on
sackcloth
and humbled myself with fasting.
When my prayers returned to me
unanswered,
¹⁴ I went about mourning
as though for my friend or brother.
I bowed my head in grief
as though weeping for my mother.
¹⁵But when I stumbled, they gathered in
glee;
attackers gathered against me when
I was unaware.
They slandered me without ceasing.
¹⁶Like the ungodly they maliciously
mocked[a];
they gnashed their teeth at me.
¹⁷O Lord, how long will you look on?
Rescue my life from their ravages,
my precious life from these lions.

¹⁸I will give you thanks in the great
assembly;
among throngs of people I will
praise you.

¹⁹Let not those gloat over me
who are my enemies without cause;
let not those who hate me without
reason
maliciously wink the eye.
²⁰They do not speak peaceably,
but devise false accusations
against those who live quietly in the
land.
²¹They gape at me and say, "Aha! Aha!
With our own eyes we have seen it."

²²O Lord, you have seen this; be not
silent.
Do not be far from me, O Lord.
²³Awake, and rise to my defense!
Contend for me, my God and Lord.

[a] 16 Septuagint; Hebrew may mean *ungodly circle of mockers.*

Make It Stick

READ PSALM 34:8

"Taste and see" (Psalm 34:8). Write on a sticky note three of the best things you've ever tasted.
God is the same. As you get to know him, your relationship with him gets better, better than
the best Supreme Pizza you've ever had. Now go to the kitchen and have a tasty snack.

24 Vindicate me in your righteousness,
      O Lord my God;
   do not let them gloat over me.
25 Do not let them think, "Aha, just what
      we wanted!"
   or say, "We have swallowed him up."

26 May all who gloat over my distress
      be put to shame and confusion;
   may all who exalt themselves over me
      be clothed with shame and disgrace.
27 May those who delight in my
      vindication
   shout for joy and gladness;
   may they always say, "The Lord be
      exalted,
   who delights in the well-being of his
      servant."
28 My tongue will speak of your
      righteousness
   and of your praises all day long.

PSALM 36

For the director of music. Of David the
servant of the Lord.

1 An oracle is within my heart
   concerning the sinfulness of the
      wicked:[a]
   There is no fear of God
      before his eyes.
2 For in his own eyes he flatters himself
   too much to detect or hate his sin.
3 The words of his mouth are wicked
      and deceitful;
   he has ceased to be wise and to do
      good.
4 Even on his bed he plots evil;
   he commits himself to a sinful
      course
   and does not reject what is wrong.

5 Your love, O Lord, reaches to the
      heavens,
   your faithfulness to the skies.
6 Your righteousness is like the mighty
      mountains,
   your justice like the great deep.
   O Lord, you preserve both man and
      beast.
7   How priceless is your unfailing love!
   Both high and low among men
      find[b] refuge in the shadow of your
         wings.
8 They feast on the abundance of your
      house;
   you give them drink from your river
      of delights.

9 For with you is the fountain of life;
   in your light we see light.

10 Continue your love to those who know
      you,
   your righteousness to the upright in
      heart.
11 May the foot of the proud not come
      against me,
   nor the hand of the wicked drive me
      away.
12 See how the evildoers lie fallen—
   thrown down, not able to rise!

PSALM 37[c]

Of David.

1 Do not fret because of evil men
   or be envious of those who do
      wrong;
2 for like the grass they will soon wither,
   like green plants they will soon die
      away.

3 Trust in the Lord and do good;
   dwell in the land and enjoy safe
      pasture.
4 Delight yourself in the Lord
   and he will give you the desires of
      your heart.

5 Commit your way to the Lord;
   trust in him and he will do this:
6 He will make your righteousness shine
      like the dawn,
   the justice of your cause like the
      noonday sun.

7 Be still before the Lord and wait
      patiently for him;
   do not fret when men succeed in
      their ways,
   when they carry out their wicked
      schemes.

8 Refrain from anger and turn from
      wrath;
   do not fret—it leads only to evil.
9 For evil men will be cut off,
   but those who hope in the Lord will
      inherit the land.

10 A little while, and the wicked will be
      no more;
   though you look for them, they will
      not be found.

a 1 Or heart: / Sin proceeds from the wicked.   b 7 Or love,
O God! / Men find; or love! / Both heavenly beings and men /
find   c This psalm is an acrostic poem, the stanzas of which
begin with the successive letters of the Hebrew alphabet.

11 But the meek will inherit the land
　and enjoy great peace.

12 The wicked plot against the righteous
　and gnash their teeth at them;
13 but the Lord laughs at the wicked,
　for he knows their day is coming.

14 The wicked draw the sword
　and bend the bow
　to bring down the poor and needy,
　to slay those whose ways are upright.
15 But their swords will pierce their own
　hearts,
　and their bows will be broken.

16 Better the little that the righteous have
　than the wealth of many wicked;
17 for the power of the wicked will be
　broken,
　but the Lord upholds the righteous.

18 The days of the blameless are known
　to the Lord,
　and their inheritance will endure
　forever.

19 In times of disaster they will not
　wither;
　in days of famine they will enjoy
　plenty.

20 But the wicked will perish:
　The Lord's enemies will be like the
　beauty of the fields,
　they will vanish—vanish like smoke.

21 The wicked borrow and do not repay,
　but the righteous give generously;
22 those the Lord blesses will inherit the
　land,
　but those he curses will be cut off.

23 If the Lord delights in a man's way,
　he makes his steps firm;
24 though he stumble, he will not fall,
　for the Lord upholds him with his
　hand.

25 I was young and now I am old,
　yet I have never seen the righteous
　forsaken
　or their children begging bread.

Make It Stick

READ PSALM 37:4

The "desires of your heart" (Psalm 37:4) isn't referring to a video game or toy you want for Christmas. It's a longing that God places deep inside your heart, something that would cause your life to be fulfilled. On a sticky note, write down a "desire of your heart."

26 They are always generous and lend
     freely;
       their children will be blessed.

27 Turn from evil and do good;
       then you will dwell in the land
         forever.
28 For the LORD loves the just
       and will not forsake his faithful ones.

They will be protected forever,
       but the offspring of the wicked will
         be cut off;
29 the righteous will inherit the land
       and dwell in it forever.

30 The mouth of the righteous man utters
       wisdom,
       and his tongue speaks what is just.
31 The law of his God is in his heart;
       his feet do not slip.

32 The wicked lie in wait for the righteous,
       seeking their very lives;
33 but the LORD will not leave them in
       their power
       or let them be condemned when
         brought to trial.

34 Wait for the LORD
       and keep his way.
He will exalt you to inherit the land;
       when the wicked are cut off, you
         will see it.

35 I have seen a wicked and ruthless man
       flourishing like a green tree in its
         native soil,
36 but he soon passed away and was no
       more;
       though I looked for him, he could
         not be found.

37 Consider the blameless, observe the
       upright;
       there is a future[a] for the man of
         peace.
38 But all sinners will be destroyed;
       the future[b] of the wicked will be cut
         off.

39 The salvation of the righteous comes
       from the LORD;
       he is their stronghold in time of
         trouble.

[a] 37 Or there will be posterity   [b] 38 Or posterity

GET SMARTER

Packers, Punchers and Peacemakers

READ PSALM 37:1–17, 32–38

Many Christian men think that when they blow up it's "righteous anger." *Yeah, right.* You don't have to blow a fuse when someone irritates you. You can control yourself. It's not a sin to *feel* anger. Everyone gets angry at times—sometimes rightly so—but it's how you handle it. There are Packers, Punchers and Peacemakers. Packers hold all their frustration in until they become bitter. Punchers make fists and start swinging (or make harsh words and start spouting off). Peacemakers follow God's advice: " 'In your anger do not sin': Do not let the sun go down while you are still angry" (Ephesians 4:26). When you get mad, take some time to cool down, listen carefully to others, and talk about what's making you angry. You don't have to be a Packer or a Puncher. With God's help, you can be a Peacemaker.

Your next reading is on page 714.

40 The Lord helps them and delivers them;
　　he delivers them from the wicked
　　　and saves them,
　　because they take refuge in him.

PSALM 38

A psalm of David. A petition.

1 O Lord, do not rebuke me in your anger
　　or discipline me in your wrath.
2 For your arrows have pierced me,
　　and your hand has come down
　　　upon me.
3 Because of your wrath there is no
　　　health in my body;
　　my bones have no soundness
　　　because of my sin.
4 My guilt has overwhelmed me
　　like a burden too heavy to bear.

5 My wounds fester and are loathsome
　　because of my sinful folly.
6 I am bowed down and brought very
　　　low;
　　all day long I go about mourning.
7 My back is filled with searing pain;
　　there is no health in my body.
8 I am feeble and utterly crushed;
　　I groan in anguish of heart.

9 All my longings lie open before you,
　　　O Lord;
　　my sighing is not hidden from you.
10 My heart pounds, my strength fails me;
　　even the light has gone from my eyes.
11 My friends and companions avoid me
　　　because of my wounds;
　　my neighbors stay far away.
12 Those who seek my life set their traps,
　　those who would harm me talk of
　　　my ruin;
　　all day long they plot deception.

13 I am like a deaf man, who cannot hear,
　　like a mute, who cannot open his
　　　mouth;
14 I have become like a man who does
　　　not hear,
　　whose mouth can offer no reply.
15 I wait for you, O Lord;
　　you will answer, O Lord my God.
16 For I said, "Do not let them gloat
　　or exalt themselves over me when
　　　my foot slips."

17 For I am about to fall,
　　and my pain is ever with me.
18 I confess my iniquity;
　　I am troubled by my sin.

19 Many are those who are my vigorous
　　　enemies;
　　those who hate me without reason
　　　are numerous.
20 Those who repay my good with evil
　　slander me when I pursue what is
　　　good.

21 O Lord, do not forsake me;
　　be not far from me, O my God.
22 Come quickly to help me,
　　O Lord my Savior.

PSALM 39

For the director of music. For Jeduthun.
A psalm of David.

1 I said, "I will watch my ways
　　and keep my tongue from sin;
　　I will put a muzzle on my mouth
　　as long as the wicked are in my
　　　presence."
2 But when I was silent and still,
　　not even saying anything good,
　　my anguish increased.
3 My heart grew hot within me,
　　and as I meditated, the fire burned;
　　then I spoke with my tongue:

4 "Show me, O Lord, my life's end
　　and the number of my days;
　　let me know how fleeting is my life.
5 You have made my days a mere
　　　handbreadth;
　　the span of my years is as nothing
　　　before you.
　　Each man's life is but a breath. *Selah*
6 Man is a mere phantom as he goes to
　　　and fro:
　　He bustles about, but only in vain;
　　he heaps up wealth, not knowing
　　　who will get it.

7 "But now, Lord, what do I look for?
　　My hope is in you.
8 Save me from all my transgressions;
　　do not make me the scorn of fools.
9 I was silent; I would not open my
　　　mouth,
　　for you are the one who has done
　　　this.
10 Remove your scourge from me;
　　I am overcome by the blow of your
　　　hand.
11 You rebuke and discipline men for their
　　　sin;
　　you consume their wealth like a
　　　moth—
　　each man is but a breath.　　　*Selah*

Get a Load of This...

David said, "I will put a muzzle on my mouth" (Psalm 39:1). Cool! Can't you see the king of Israel sitting on his throne, wearing a dog muzzle? Seriously though, David was making a good point here: It's better to be a muzzle-mouth than a motor-mouth.

¹² "Hear my prayer, O LORD,
    listen to my cry for help;
    be not deaf to my weeping.
For I dwell with you as an alien,
    a stranger, as all my fathers were.
¹³ Look away from me, that I may rejoice again
    before I depart and am no more."

PSALM 40

For the director of music. Of David. A psalm.

¹ I waited patiently for the LORD;
    he turned to me and heard my cry.
² He lifted me out of the slimy pit,
    out of the mud and mire;
he set my feet on a rock
    and gave me a firm place to stand.
³ He put a new song in my mouth,
    a hymn of praise to our God.
Many will see and fear
    and put their trust in the LORD.

⁴ Blessed is the man
    who makes the LORD his trust,
who does not look to the proud,
    to those who turn aside to false gods.^a
⁵ Many, O LORD my God,
    are the wonders you have done.
The things you planned for us
    no one can recount to you;
were I to speak and tell of them,
    they would be too many to declare.

⁶ Sacrifice and offering you did not desire,
    but my ears you have pierced^{b, c};
burnt offerings and sin offerings
    you did not require.
⁷ Then I said, "Here I am, I have come—
    it is written about me in the scroll.^d
⁸ I desire to do your will, O my God;
    your law is within my heart."

⁹ I proclaim righteousness in the great assembly;
    I do not seal my lips,
    as you know, O LORD.
¹⁰ I do not hide your righteousness in my heart;
    I speak of your faithfulness and salvation.
I do not conceal your love and your truth
    from the great assembly.

¹¹ Do not withhold your mercy from me, O LORD;
    may your love and your truth always protect me.
¹² For troubles without number surround me;
    my sins have overtaken me, and I cannot see.
They are more than the hairs of my head,
    and my heart fails within me.

---

^a 4 Or *to falsehood*   ^b 6 Hebrew; Septuagint *but a body you have prepared for me* (see also Symmachus and Theodotion)   ^c 6 Or *opened*   ^d 7 Or *come / with the scroll written for me*

13 Be pleased, O LORD, to save me;
     O LORD, come quickly to help me.
14 May all who seek to take my life
     be put to shame and confusion;
  may all who desire my ruin
     be turned back in disgrace.
15 May those who say to me, "Aha! Aha!"
     be appalled at their own shame.
16 But may all who seek you
     rejoice and be glad in you;
  may those who love your salvation
         always say,
     "The LORD be exalted!"

17 Yet I am poor and needy;
     may the Lord think of me.
  You are my help and my deliverer;
     O my God, do not delay.

PSALM 41

For the director of music. A psalm of David.

1 Blessed is he who has regard for the
         weak;
     the LORD delivers him in times of
         trouble.
2 The LORD will protect him and preserve
         his life;
     he will bless him in the land
  and not surrender him to the desire
         of his foes.
3 The LORD will sustain him on his sickbed
     and restore him from his bed of
         illness.

4 I said, "O LORD, have mercy on me;
     heal me, for I have sinned against
         you."
5 My enemies say of me in malice,
     "When will he die and his name
         perish?"
6 Whenever one comes to see me,
     he speaks falsely, while his heart
         gathers slander;
  then he goes out and spreads it
         abroad.

7 All my enemies whisper together
         against me;
     they imagine the worst for me, saying,
8 "A vile disease has beset him;
     he will never get up from the place
         where he lies."
9 Even my close friend, whom I trusted,
     he who shared my bread,
  has lifted up his heel against me.

10 But you, O LORD, have mercy on me;
     raise me up, that I may repay them.

11 I know that you are pleased with me,
     for my enemy does not triumph over
         me.
12 In my integrity you uphold me
     and set me in your presence forever.

13 Praise be to the LORD, the God of Israel,
     from everlasting to everlasting.
         Amen and Amen.

BOOK II

Psalms 42–72

PSALM 42 [a]

*For the director of music. A maskil [b] of
the Sons of Korah.*

1 As the deer pants for streams of water,
     so my soul pants for you, O God.
2 My soul thirsts for God, for the living
         God.
     When can I go and meet with God?
3 My tears have been my food
         day and night,
  while men say to me all day long,
     "Where is your God?"
4 These things I remember
     as I pour out my soul:
  how I used to go with the multitude,
     leading the procession to the house
         of God,
  with shouts of joy and thanksgiving
     among the festive throng.

5 Why are you downcast, O my soul?
     Why so disturbed within me?
  Put your hope in God,
     for I will yet praise him,
     my Savior and 6 my God.

My [c] soul is downcast within me;
     therefore I will remember you
  from the land of the Jordan,
     the heights of Hermon—from
         Mount Mizar.
7 Deep calls to deep
     in the roar of your waterfalls;
  all your waves and breakers
     have swept over me.

8 By day the LORD directs his love,
     at night his song is with me—
     a prayer to the God of my life.

---

[a] In many Hebrew manuscripts Psalms 42 and 43 constitute
one psalm.   [b] Title: Probably a literary or musical term
[c] 5,6 A few Hebrew manuscripts, Septuagint and Syriac; most
Hebrew manuscripts *praise him for his saving help. / 6O my
God, my*

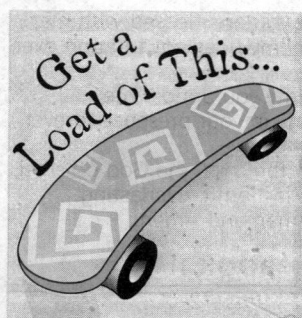

Get a Load of This...

"Deer pants" (Psalm 42:1)? What are *those*? Are they like buckskin cowboy chaps? And what about "soul pants"? Is that what you wear when you eat soul food? *Just joking!* This is actually a terrific psalm about being thirsty for God.

⁹ I say to God my Rock,
    "Why have you forgotten me?
Why must I go about mourning,
    oppressed by the enemy?"
¹⁰ My bones suffer mortal agony
    as my foes taunt me,
saying to me all day long,
    "Where is your God?"

¹¹ Why are you downcast, O my soul?
    Why so disturbed within me?
Put your hope in God,
    for I will yet praise him,
    my Savior and my God.

PSALM 43 ᵃ

¹ Vindicate me, O God,
    and plead my cause against an ungodly nation;
    rescue me from deceitful and wicked men.
² You are God my stronghold.
    Why have you rejected me?
Why must I go about mourning,
    oppressed by the enemy?
³ Send forth your light and your truth,
    let them guide me;
let them bring me to your holy mountain,
    to the place where you dwell.
⁴ Then will I go to the altar of God,
    to God, my joy and my delight.
I will praise you with the harp,
    O God, my God.

⁵ Why are you downcast, O my soul?
    Why so disturbed within me?
Put your hope in God,
    for I will yet praise him,
    my Savior and my God.

PSALM 44

For the director of music. Of the Sons of Korah. A *maskil.* ᵇ

¹ We have heard with our ears, O God;
    our fathers have told us
what you did in their days,
    in days long ago.
² With your hand you drove out the nations
    and planted our fathers;
you crushed the peoples
    and made our fathers flourish.
³ It was not by their sword that they won the land,
    nor did their arm bring them victory;
it was your right hand, your arm,
    and the light of your face, for you loved them.

⁴ You are my King and my God,
    who decrees ᶜ victories for Jacob.

ᵃ In many Hebrew manuscripts Psalms 42 and 43 constitute one psalm.   ᵇ Title: Probably a literary or musical term   ᶜ 4 Septuagint, Aquila and Syriac; Hebrew *King, O God; / command*

5 Through you we push back our enemies;
  through your name we trample our
    foes.
6 I do not trust in my bow,
  my sword does not bring me victory;
7 but you give us victory over our
    enemies,
  you put our adversaries to shame.
8 In God we make our boast all day
    long,
  and we will praise your name
    forever.   *Selah*

9 But now you have rejected and
    humbled us;
  you no longer go out with our
    armies.
10 You made us retreat before the enemy,
   and our adversaries have plundered
     us.
11 You gave us up to be devoured like
     sheep
   and have scattered us among the
     nations.
12 You sold your people for a pittance,
   gaining nothing from their sale.

13 You have made us a reproach to our
     neighbors,
   the scorn and derision of those
     around us.
14 You have made us a byword among
     the nations;
   the peoples shake their heads at us.
15 My disgrace is before me all day long,
   and my face is covered with shame
16 at the taunts of those who reproach
     and revile me,
   because of the enemy, who is bent
     on revenge.

17 All this happened to us,
   though we had not forgotten you
   or been false to your covenant.
18 Our hearts had not turned back;
   our feet had not strayed from your
     path.
19 But you crushed us and made us a
     haunt for jackals
   and covered us over with deep
     darkness.
20 If we had forgotten the name of our
     God
   or spread out our hands to a foreign
     god,
21 would not God have discovered it,
   since he knows the secrets of the
     heart?

22 Yet for your sake we face death all day
     long;
   we are considered as sheep to be
     slaughtered.
23 Awake, O Lord! Why do you sleep?
   Rouse yourself! Do not reject us
     forever.
24 Why do you hide your face
   and forget our misery and
     oppression?
25 We are brought down to the dust;
   our bodies cling to the ground.
26 Rise up and help us;
   redeem us because of your unfailing
     love.

PSALM 45

For the director of music. To ⌊the tune of⌋
"Lilies." Of the Sons of Korah. A *maskil*. [a]
A wedding song.

1 My heart is stirred by a noble theme
  as I recite my verses for the king;
  my tongue is the pen of a skillful
    writer.

2 You are the most excellent of men
  and your lips have been anointed
    with grace,
  since God has blessed you forever.
3 Gird your sword upon your side,
    O mighty one;
  clothe yourself with splendor and
    majesty.
4 In your majesty ride forth victoriously
  in behalf of truth, humility and
    righteousness;
  let your right hand display awesome
    deeds.
5 Let your sharp arrows pierce the hearts
    of the king's enemies;
  let the nations fall beneath your
    feet.
6 Your throne, O God, will last for ever
    and ever;
  a scepter of justice will be the
    scepter of your kingdom.
7 You love righteousness and hate
    wickedness;
  therefore God, your God, has set
    you above your companions
  by anointing you with the oil of joy.
8 All your robes are fragrant with myrrh
    and aloes and cassia;
  from palaces adorned with ivory

a Title: Probably a literary or musical term

the music of the strings makes you
glad.
9 Daughters of kings are among your
honored women;
at your right hand is the royal bride
in gold of Ophir.

10 Listen, O daughter, consider and give ear:
Forget your people and your father's
house.
11 The king is enthralled by your beauty;
honor him, for he is your lord.
12 The Daughter of Tyre will come with a
gift,ᵃ
men of wealth will seek your favor.
13 All glorious is the princess within her
chamber.;
her gown is interwoven with gold.
14 In embroidered garments she is led to
the king;
her virgin companions follow her
and are brought to you.
15 They are led in with joy and gladness;
they enter the palace of the king.
16 Your sons will take the place of your
fathers;

you will make them princes
throughout the land.
17 I will perpetuate your memory through
all generations;
therefore the nations will praise you
for ever and ever.

PSALM 46

For the director of music. Of the Sons of
Korah. According to *alamoth*.ᵇ A song.

1 God is our refuge and strength,
an ever-present help in trouble.
2 Therefore we will not fear, though the
earth give way
and the mountains fall into the heart
of the sea,
3 though its waters roar and foam
and the mountains quake with their
surging.   *Selah*

4 There is a river whose streams make
glad the city of God,
the holy place where the Most High
dwells.

ᵃ 12 Or *A Tyrian robe is among the gifts*   ᵇ Title: Probably a
musical term

The Skillful Tongue

READ PSALM 45:1–2

"My heart is stirred by a noble theme ... my tongue is the pen of a skillful writer" (verse 1). Jesus is the most "noble theme" you can have—the best possible thing you can talk about. When you represent Jesus, shouldn't everything you say and do show others that he is real? You bet! God wants you to speak up for him, so that makes you his representative. So first of all, do your best to live a godly life. Second, don't just open your mouth and start babbling. Speaking is an important skill, so seriously study how to talk and present things. You can't just talk about the right things; you also need to talk about them in the right way. Learn to speak in love so people will tune in to you, and ask God for your lips to be "anointed with grace" (verse 2). That's *grace*, not grease.

Your next reading is on page 719.

⁵ God is within her, she will not fall;
    God will help her at break of day.
⁶ Nations are in uproar, kingdoms fall;
    he lifts his voice, the earth melts.

⁷ The LORD Almighty is with us;
    the God of Jacob is our fortress.
                      Selah

⁸ Come and see the works of the LORD,
    the desolations he has brought on
    the earth.
⁹ He makes wars cease to the ends of
    the earth;
    he breaks the bow and shatters the
    spear,
    he burns the shields*ᵃ* with fire.
¹⁰ "Be still, and know that I am God;
    I will be exalted among the
    nations,
    I will be exalted in the earth."

¹¹ The LORD Almighty is with us;
    the God of Jacob is our fortress.
                      Selah

PSALM 47

For the director of music. Of the
Sons of Korah. A psalm.

¹ Clap your hands, all you nations;
    shout to God with cries of joy.
² How awesome is the LORD Most High,
    the great King over all the earth!
³ He subdued nations under us,
    peoples under our feet.
⁴ He chose our inheritance for us,
    the pride of Jacob, whom he loved.
                      Selah

⁵ God has ascended amid shouts of joy,
    the LORD amid the sounding of
    trumpets.
⁶ Sing praises to God, sing praises;
    sing praises to our King, sing praises.

⁷ For God is the King of all the earth;
    sing to him a psalm*ᵇ* of praise.
⁸ God reigns over the nations;

ᵃ 9 Or chariots   *ᵇ 7 Or a maskil (probably a literary or
musical term)*

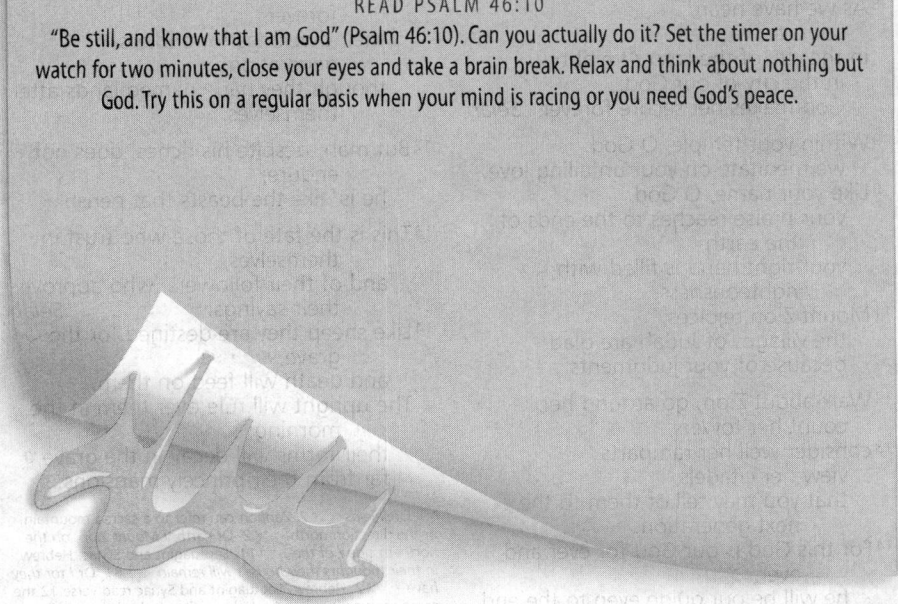

Make It Stick

READ PSALM 46:10

"Be still, and know that I am God" (Psalm 46:10). Can you actually do it? Set the timer on your watch for two minutes, close your eyes and take a brain break. Relax and think about nothing but God. Try this on a regular basis when your mind is racing or you need God's peace.

God is seated on his holy throne.
⁹ The nobles of the nations assemble
  as the people of the God of
  Abraham,
for the kingsᵃ of the earth belong to
  God;
he is greatly exalted.

PSALM 48

A song. A psalm of the Sons of Korah.

¹ Great is the Lᴏʀᴅ, and most worthy of
  praise,
  in the city of our God, his holy
  mountain.
² It is beautiful in its loftiness,
  the joy of the whole earth.
Like the utmost heights of Zaphonᵇ is
  Mount Zion,
  theᶜ city of the Great King.
³ God is in her citadels;
  he has shown himself to be her
  fortress.

⁴ When the kings joined forces,
  when they advanced together,
⁵ they saw ⌊her⌋ and were astounded;
  they fled in terror.
⁶ Trembling seized them there,
  pain like that of a woman in labor.
⁷ You destroyed them like ships of Tarshish
  shattered by an east wind.

⁸ As we have heard,
  so have we seen
in the city of the Lᴏʀᴅ Almighty,
  in the city of our God:
  God makes her secure forever. *Selah*

⁹ Within your temple, O God,
  we meditate on your unfailing love.
¹⁰ Like your name, O God,
  your praise reaches to the ends of
  the earth;
  your right hand is filled with
  righteousness.
¹¹ Mount Zion rejoices,
  the villages of Judah are glad
  because of your judgments.

¹² Walk about Zion, go around her,
  count her towers,
¹³ consider well her ramparts,
  view her citadels,
  that you may tell of them to the
  next generation.
¹⁴ For this God is our God for ever and
  ever;
  he will be our guide even to the end.

PSALM 49

*For the director of music. Of the Sons of
Korah. A psalm.*

¹ Hear this, all you peoples;
  listen, all who live in this world,
² both low and high,
  rich and poor alike:
³ My mouth will speak words of
  wisdom;
  the utterance from my heart will
  give understanding.
⁴ I will turn my ear to a proverb;
  with the harp I will expound my
  riddle:

⁵ Why should I fear when evil days come,
  when wicked deceivers surround
  me—
⁶ those who trust in their wealth
  and boast of their great riches?
⁷ No man can redeem the life of another
  or give to God a ransom for him—
⁸ the ransom for a life is costly,
  no payment is ever enough—
⁹ that he should live on forever
  and not see decay.

¹⁰ For all can see that wise men die;
  the foolish and the senseless alike
  perish
  and leave their wealth to others.
¹¹ Their tombs will remain their housesᵈ
  forever,
  their dwellings for endless
  generations,
  though they hadᵉ named lands after
  themselves.

¹² But man, despite his riches, does not
  endure;
  he isᶠ like the beasts that perish.

¹³ This is the fate of those who trust in
  themselves,
  and of their followers, who approve
  their sayings.   *Selah*
¹⁴ Like sheep they are destined for the
  grave,ᵍ
  and death will feed on them.
The upright will rule over them in the
  morning;
  their forms will decay in the grave,ᵍ
  far from their princely mansions.

ᵃ 9 Or *shields*   ᵇ 2 *Zaphon* can refer to a sacred mountain
or the direction north.   ᶜ 2 Or *earth, / Mount Zion, on the
northern side / of the*   ᵈ 11 Septuagint and Syriac; Hebrew
In their thoughts their houses will remain   ᵉ 11 Or / *for they
have*   ᶠ 12 Hebrew; Septuagint and Syriac read verse 12 the
same as verse 20.   ᵍ 14 Hebrew *Sheol*; also in verse 15

15 But God will redeem my life[a] from the grave; *Selah*
  he will surely take me to himself.

16 Do not be overawed when a man grows rich,
  when the splendor of his house increases;
17 for he will take nothing with him when he dies,
  his splendor will not descend with him.
18 Though while he lived he counted himself blessed—
  and men praise you when you prosper—
19 he will join the generation of his fathers,
  who will never see the light ⌐of life⌐.

20 A man who has riches without understanding
  is like the beasts that perish.

PSALM 50

A psalm of Asaph.

1 The Mighty One, God, the Lᴏʀᴅ,
  speaks and summons the earth
  from the rising of the sun to the place where it
    sets.
2 From Zion, perfect in beauty,
  God shines forth.
3 Our God comes and will not be silent;
  a fire devours before him,
  and around him a tempest rages.
4 He summons the heavens above,
  and the earth, that he may judge his people:
5 "Gather to me my consecrated ones,
  who made a covenant with me by sacrifice."
6 And the heavens proclaim his righteousness,
  for God himself is judge. *Selah*

7 "Hear, O my people, and I will speak,
  O Israel, and I will testify against you:
  I am God, your God.
8 I do not rebuke you for your sacrifices
  or your burnt offerings, which are ever before me.
9 I have no need of a bull from your stall
  or of goats from your pens,
10 for every animal of the forest is mine,
  and the cattle on a thousand hills.
11 I know every bird in the mountains,
  and the creatures of the field are mine.
12 If I were hungry I would not tell you,
  for the world is mine, and all that is in it.
13 Do I eat the flesh of bulls
  or drink the blood of goats?
14 Sacrifice thank offerings to God,
  fulfill your vows to the Most High,
15 and call upon me in the day of trouble;
  I will deliver you, and you will honor me."

16 But to the wicked, God says:

  "What right have you to recite my laws
  or take my covenant on your lips?

a 15 Or *soul*

Get a Load of This...

Read Psalm 49:16–20. Zero in on verse 20, which says, "A man who has riches without understanding is like the beasts that perish." This is another way of saying that a rich guy with no appreciation for God lives and dies like a mere animal.

In other words...

17 You hate my instruction
    and cast my words behind you.
18 When you see a thief, you join with
        him;
    you throw in your lot with adulterers.
19 You use your mouth for evil
    and harness your tongue to deceit.
20 You speak continually against your
        brother
    and slander your own mother's son.
21 These things you have done and I kept
        silent;
    you thought I was altogether[a] like
        you.
  But I will rebuke you
    and accuse you to your face.

22 "Consider this, you who forget God,
    or I will tear you to pieces, with
        none to rescue:
23 He who sacrifices thank offerings
        honors me,
    and he prepares the way
    so that I may show him[b] the
        salvation of God."

PSALM 51

*For the director of music. A psalm of David.
When the prophet Nathan came to him
after David had committed adultery
with Bathsheba.*

1 Have mercy on me, O God,
    according to your unfailing love;
  according to your great compassion
    blot out my transgressions.
2 Wash away all my iniquity
    and cleanse me from my sin.

3 For I know my transgressions,
    and my sin is always before me.
4 Against you, you only, have I sinned
    and done what is evil in your sight,
  so that you are proved right when you
        speak
    and justified when you judge.
5 Surely I was sinful at birth,
    sinful from the time my mother
        conceived me.
6 Surely you desire truth in the inner
        parts[c];
    you teach[d] me wisdom in the
        inmost place.

7 Cleanse me with hyssop, and I will be
        clean;
    wash me, and I will be whiter than
        snow.
8 Let me hear joy and gladness;

    let the bones you have crushed
        rejoice.
9 Hide your face from my sins
    and blot out all my iniquity.

10 Create in me a pure heart, O God,
    and renew a steadfast spirit within
        me.
11 Do not cast me from your presence
    or take your Holy Spirit from me.
12 Restore to me the joy of your salvation
    and grant me a willing spirit, to
        sustain me.

13 Then I will teach transgressors your
        ways,
    and sinners will turn back to you.
14 Save me from bloodguilt, O God,
    the God who saves me,
    and my tongue will sing of your
        righteousness.
15 O Lord, open my lips,
    and my mouth will declare your
        praise.
16 You do not delight in sacrifice, or I
        would bring it;
    you do not take pleasure in burnt
        offerings.
17 The sacrifices of God are[e] a broken
        spirit;
    a broken and contrite heart,
    O God, you will not despise.

18 In your good pleasure make Zion
        prosper;
    build up the walls of Jerusalem.
19 Then there will be righteous sacrifices,
    whole burnt offerings to delight
        you;
    then bulls will be offered on your
        altar.

PSALM 52

*For the director of music. A maskil[f] of David.
When Doeg the Edomite had gone to Saul
and told him: "David has gone to the
house of Ahimelech."*

1 Why do you boast of evil, you mighty
        man?
  Why do you boast all day long,
    you who are a disgrace in the eyes
        of God?
2 Your tongue plots destruction;

---

[a] 21 Or thought the 'I AM' was   [b] 23 Or and to him who
considers his way / I will show   [c] 6 The meaning of the
Hebrew for this phrase is uncertain.   [d] 6 Or you
desired . . .; / you taught   [e] 17 Or My sacrifice, O God, is
[f] Title: Probably a literary or musical term

it is like a sharpened razor,
you who practice deceit.
³You love evil rather than good,
falsehood rather than speaking the
truth.   *Selah*
⁴You love every harmful word,
O you deceitful tongue!

⁵Surely God will bring you down to
everlasting ruin:
He will snatch you up and tear you
from your tent;
he will uproot you from the land of
the living.   *Selah*
⁶The righteous will see and fear;
they will laugh at him, saying,
⁷"Here now is the man
who did not make God his stronghold
but trusted in his great wealth
and grew strong by destroying
others!"

⁸But I am like an olive tree
flourishing in the house of God;
I trust in God's unfailing love
for ever and ever.
⁹I will praise you forever for what you
have done;

in your name I will hope, for your
name is good.
I will praise you in the presence of
your saints.

PSALM 53

For the director of music. According to
mahalath.[a] A *maskil*[b] of David.

¹The fool says in his heart,
"There is no God."
They are corrupt, and their ways are
vile;
there is no one who does good.

²God looks down from heaven
on the sons of men
to see if there are any who
understand,
any who seek God.
³Everyone has turned away,
they have together become
corrupt;
there is no one who does good,
not even one.

[a] Title: Probably a musical term   [b] Title: Probably a literary or
musical term

Power Wash

READ PSALM 51

When a man of God wrongs God or others, he's quick to go and confess. But a lot of machos have the attitude that "a real man never says he's sorry." Yeah? Ever wonder why those men don't have many close friends? It's their attitude. Now look at David. He made a big-time mistake and God called him on it (see 2 Samuel 11–12). David's response was Psalm 51: "Create in me a pure heart, O God" (verse 10). Hiding his sins had only made things worse, so David owned up to his sins, admitted what he had done wrong, then gave his sin to God like a hot potato. "He who conceals his sins does not prosper, but whoever confesses and renounces them finds mercy" (Proverbs 28:13). Learn from David. He was the real article.

Your next reading is on page 725.

Get a Load of This...

Look at the glorious creation of God! Isn't it foolish for people to say there is no God (Psalm 53:1)? Did you know that only 3% of the U.S. population says they don't believe in God?

4 Will the evildoers never learn—
　　those who devour my people as men eat bread
　　and who do not call on God?
5 There they were, overwhelmed with dread,
　　where there was nothing to dread.
　God scattered the bones of those who attacked you;
　　you put them to shame, for God despised them.

6 Oh, that salvation for Israel would come out of Zion!
　　When God restores the fortunes of his people,
　　let Jacob rejoice and Israel be glad!

PSALM 54

*For the director of music. With stringed instruments.
A maskil[a] of David. When the Ziphites had gone to Saul
and said, "Is not David hiding among us?"*

1 Save me, O God, by your name;
　　vindicate me by your might.
2 Hear my prayer, O God;
　　listen to the words of my mouth.

3 Strangers are attacking me;
　　ruthless men seek my life—
　　men without regard for God.　　　　　　*Selah*

4 Surely God is my help;
　　the Lord is the one who sustains me.

5 Let evil recoil on those who slander me;
　　in your faithfulness destroy them.

6 I will sacrifice a freewill offering to you;
　　I will praise your name, O LORD,
　　for it is good.
7 For he has delivered me from all my troubles,
　　and my eyes have looked in triumph on my foes.

PSALM 55

*For the director of music. With stringed instruments.
A maskil[a] of David.*

1 Listen to my prayer, O God,
　　do not ignore my plea;
2 　hear me and answer me.
　My thoughts trouble me and I am distraught
3 　at the voice of the enemy,
　　at the stares of the wicked;
　for they bring down suffering upon me
　　and revile me in their anger.

4 My heart is in anguish within me;
　　the terrors of death assail me.
5 Fear and trembling have beset me;
　　horror has overwhelmed me.
6 I said, "Oh, that I had the wings of a dove!
　　I would fly away and be at rest—
7 I would flee far away
　　and stay in the desert;　　　　　　*Selah*
8 I would hurry to my place of shelter,
　　far from the tempest and storm."

a Title: Probably a literary or musical term

9 Confuse the wicked, O Lord, confound
　　their speech,
　　for I see violence and strife in the
　　　city.
10 Day and night they prowl about on its
　　walls;
　　malice and abuse are within it.
11 Destructive forces are at work in the
　　city;
　　threats and lies never leave its
　　　streets.

12 If an enemy were insulting me,
　　I could endure it;
　if a foe were raising himself against
　　　me,
　　I could hide from him.
13 But it is you, a man like myself,
　　my companion, my close friend,
14 with whom I once enjoyed sweet
　　fellowship
　　as we walked with the throng at the
　　　house of God.

15 Let death take my enemies by surprise;
　　let them go down alive to the
　　　grave,[a]
　　for evil finds lodging among them.

16 But I call to God,
　　and the LORD saves me.
17 Evening, morning and noon
　　I cry out in distress,
　　and he hears my voice.
18 He ransoms me unharmed
　　from the battle waged against me,
　　even though many oppose me.
19 God, who is enthroned forever,
　　will hear them and afflict them—
　　　　　　　　　　　　　　　Selah

　men who never change their ways
　　and have no fear of God.

20 My companion attacks his friends;
　　he violates his covenant.
21 His speech is smooth as butter,
　　yet war is in his heart;
　his words are more soothing than oil,
　　yet they are drawn swords.

22 Cast your cares on the LORD
　　and he will sustain you;
　　he will never let the righteous fall.
23 But you, O God, will bring down the
　　wicked
　　into the pit of corruption;
　bloodthirsty and deceitful men
　　will not live out half their days.

But as for me, I trust in you.

PSALM 56

For the director of music. To ⌊the tune of⌋ "A
Dove on Distant Oaks." Of David. A *miktam*.[b]
When the Philistines had seized him in Gath.

1 Be merciful to me, O God, for men
　　hotly pursue me;
　　all day long they press their attack.
2 My slanderers pursue me all day long;
　　many are attacking me in their pride.

3 When I am afraid,
　　I will trust in you.
4 In God, whose word I praise,
　　in God I trust; I will not be afraid.
　　What can mortal man do to me?

5 All day long they twist my words;
　　they are always plotting to harm me.
6 They conspire, they lurk,
　　they watch my steps,
　　eager to take my life.

7 On no account let them escape;
　　in your anger, O God, bring down
　　　the nations.
8 Record my lament;
　　list my tears on your scroll[c]—
　　are they not in your record?

9 Then my enemies will turn back
　　when I call for help.
　By this I will know that God is for me.
10 In God, whose word I praise,
　　in the LORD, whose word I praise—
11 in God I trust; I will not be afraid.
　　What can man do to me?

12 I am under vows to you, O God;
　　I will present my thank offerings to
　　　you.
13 For you have delivered me[d] from death
　　and my feet from stumbling,
　　that I may walk before God
　　in the light of life.[e]

PSALM 57

For the director of music. ⌊To the tune of⌋ "Do
Not Destroy." Of David. A *miktam*.[b] When he
had fled from Saul into the cave.

1 Have mercy on me, O God, have mercy
　　on me,
　　for in you my soul takes refuge.
　I will take refuge in the shadow of
　　your wings
　　until the disaster has passed.

---

a 15 Hebrew *Sheol*　　*b Title:* Probably a literary or musical
term　　*c 8* Or / *put my tears in your wineskin*　　*d 13* Or *my
soul*　　*e 13* Or *the land of the living*

Gross!

What does lying "among ravenous beasts" whose teeth are "spears and arrows" (Psalm 57:4) sound like to *you*?— a slumber party in the zoo where *you* are the midnight snack?

²I cry out to God Most High,
   to God, who fulfills ⌊his purpose⌋ for me.
³He sends from heaven and saves me,
   rebuking those who hotly pursue me;   *Selah*
   God sends his love and his faithfulness.

⁴I am in the midst of lions;
   I lie among ravenous beasts—
men whose teeth are spears and arrows,
   whose tongues are sharp swords.

⁵Be exalted, O God, above the heavens;
   let your glory be over all the earth.

⁶They spread a net for my feet—
   I was bowed down in distress.
They dug a pit in my path—
   but they have fallen into it themselves.   *Selah*

⁷My heart is steadfast, O God,
   my heart is steadfast;
I will sing and make music.
⁸Awake, my soul!
   Awake, harp and lyre!
   I will awaken the dawn.

⁹I will praise you, O Lord, among the nations;
   I will sing of you among the peoples.
¹⁰For great is your love, reaching to the heavens;
   your faithfulness reaches to the skies.

¹¹Be exalted, O God, above the heavens;
   let your glory be over all the earth.

PSALM 58

For the director of music. ⌊To the tune of⌋ "Do Not Destroy."
Of David. A *miktam*. ^a

¹Do you rulers indeed speak justly?
   Do you judge uprightly among men?
²No, in your heart you devise injustice,
   and your hands mete out violence on the earth.
³Even from birth the wicked go astray;
   from the womb they are wayward and speak
     lies.
⁴Their venom is like the venom of a snake,
   like that of a cobra that has stopped its ears,
⁵that will not heed the tune of the charmer,
   however skillful the enchanter may be.

⁶Break the teeth in their mouths, O God;
   tear out, O LORD, the fangs of the lions!
⁷Let them vanish like water that flows away;
   when they draw the bow, let their arrows be
     blunted.
⁸Like a slug melting away as it moves along,
   like a stillborn child, may they not see the sun.

⁹Before your pots can feel ⌊the heat of⌋ the thorns—

^a Title: Probably a literary or musical term

whether they be green or dry—the
wicked will be swept away. [a]
10 The righteous will be glad when they
are avenged,
when they bathe their feet in the
blood of the wicked.
11 Then men will say,
"Surely the righteous still are
rewarded;
surely there is a God who judges the
earth."

PSALM 59

For the director of music. ˌTo the tune ofˌ "Do
Not Destroy." Of David. A *miktam.* [b] When
Saul had sent men to watch David's house in
order to kill him.

1 Deliver me from my enemies, O God;
protect me from those who rise up
against me.
2 Deliver me from evildoers
and save me from bloodthirsty men.

3 See how they lie in wait for me!
Fierce men conspire against me
for no offense or sin of mine, O LORD.
4 I have done no wrong, yet they are
ready to attack me.
Arise to help me; look on my plight!
5 O LORD God Almighty, the God of Israel,
rouse yourself to punish all the
nations;
show no mercy to wicked traitors.
Selah

6 They return at evening,
snarling like dogs,
and prowl about the city.
7 See what they spew from their
mouths—
they spew out swords from their lips,
and they say, "Who can hear us?"
8 But you, O LORD, laugh at them;
you scoff at all those nations.

9 O my Strength, I watch for you;
you, O God, are my fortress, 10 my
loving God.

God will go before me
and will let me gloat over those who
slander me.
11 But do not kill them, O Lord our
shield, [c]
or my people will forget.
In your might make them wander
about,
and bring them down.

12 For the sins of their mouths,
for the words of their lips,
let them be caught in their pride.
For the curses and lies they utter,
13 consume them in wrath,
consume them till they are no more.
Then it will be known to the ends of
the earth
that God rules over Jacob. *Selah*

14 They return at evening,
snarling like dogs,
and prowl about the city.
15 They wander about for food
and howl if not satisfied.
16 But I will sing of your strength,
in the morning I will sing of your love;
for you are my fortress,
my refuge in times of trouble.

17 O my Strength, I sing praise to you;
you, O God, are my fortress, my
loving God.

PSALM 60

For the director of music. To ˌthe tune ofˌ
"The Lily of the Covenant." A *miktam* [b] of
David. For teaching. When he fought Aram
Naharaim [d] and Aram Zobah, [e] and when Joab
returned and struck down twelve thousand
Edomites in the Valley of Salt.

1 You have rejected us, O God, and burst
forth upon us;
you have been angry—now restore
us!
2 You have shaken the land and torn it
open;
mend its fractures, for it is quaking.
3 You have shown your people desperate
times;
you have given us wine that makes
us stagger.
4 But for those who fear you, you have
raised a banner
to be unfurled against the bow.
Selah

5 Save us and help us with your right
hand,
that those you love may be delivered.
6 God has spoken from his sanctuary:
"In triumph I will parcel out Shechem
and measure off the Valley of
Succoth.

[a] 9 The meaning of the Hebrew for this verse is uncertain.
[b] Title: Probably a literary or musical term
[c] 11 Or *sovereign*   [d] Title: That is, Arameans of Northwest
Mesopotamia   [e] Title: That is, Arameans of central Syria

7 Gilead is mine, and Manasseh is mine;
    Ephraim is my helmet,
    Judah my scepter.
8 Moab is my washbasin,
    upon Edom I toss my sandal;
    over Philistia I shout in triumph."

9 Who will bring me to the fortified city?
    Who will lead me to Edom?
10 Is it not you, O God, you who have
        rejected us
    and no longer go out with our
        armies?
11 Give us aid against the enemy,
    for the help of man is worthless.
12 With God we will gain the victory,
    and he will trample down our
        enemies.

PSALM 61

*For the director of music. With stringed
instruments. Of David.*

1 Hear my cry, O God;
    listen to my prayer.

2 From the ends of the earth I call to
        you,
    I call as my heart grows faint;
    lead me to the rock that is higher
        than I.
3 For you have been my refuge,
    a strong tower against the foe.

4 I long to dwell in your tent forever
    and take refuge in the shelter of
        your wings.   *Selah*
5 For you have heard my vows, O God;
    you have given me the heritage of
        those who fear your name.

6 Increase the days of the king's life,
    his years for many generations.
7 May he be enthroned in God's
        presence forever;
    appoint your love and faithfulness to
        protect him.

8 Then will I ever sing praise to your name
    and fulfill my vows day after day.

PSALM 62

*For the director of music. For Jeduthun.
A psalm of David.*

1 My soul finds rest in God alone;
    my salvation comes from him.
2 He alone is my rock and my salvation;
    he is my fortress, I will never be
        shaken.

3 How long will you assault a man?
    Would all of you throw him down—
    this leaning wall, this tottering fence?
4 They fully intend to topple him
    from his lofty place;
    they take delight in lies.
With their mouths they bless,
    but in their hearts they curse.   *Selah*

5 Find rest, O my soul, in God alone;
    my hope comes from him.
6 He alone is my rock and my salvation;
    he is my fortress, I will not be shaken.
7 My salvation and my honor depend on
        God *a*;
    he is my mighty rock, my refuge.
8 Trust in him at all times, O people;
    pour out your hearts to him,
    for God is our refuge.   *Selah*

9 Lowborn men are but a breath,
    the highborn are but a lie;
    if weighed on a balance, they are
        nothing;
    together they are only a breath.
10 Do not trust in extortion
    or take pride in stolen goods;
    though your riches increase,
    do not set your heart on them.

11 One thing God has spoken,
    two things have I heard:
that you, O God, are strong,
12   and that you, O Lord, are loving.
Surely you will reward each person
    according to what he has done.

PSALM 63

*A psalm of David. When he was in
the Desert of Judah.*

1 O God, you are my God,
    earnestly I seek you;
my soul thirsts for you,
    my body longs for you,
in a dry and weary land
    where there is no water.

2 I have seen you in the sanctuary
    and beheld your power and your
        glory.
3 Because your love is better than life,
    my lips will glorify you.
4 I will praise you as long as I live,
    and in your name I will lift up my
        hands.
5 My soul will be satisfied as with the
        richest of foods;

a 7 Or / God Most High is my salvation and my honor

with singing lips my mouth will
    praise you.

6 On my bed I remember you;
    I think of you through the watches
      of the night.
7 Because you are my help,
    I sing in the shadow of your wings.
8 My soul clings to you;
    your right hand upholds me.

9 They who seek my life will be
      destroyed;
    they will go down to the depths of
      the earth.
10 They will be given over to the sword
    and become food for jackals.

11 But the king will rejoice in God;
    all who swear by God's name will
      praise him,
    while the mouths of liars will be
      silenced.

PSALM 64

For the director of music. A psalm of David.

1 Hear me, O God, as I voice my
      complaint;

protect my life from the threat of
    the enemy.
2 Hide me from the conspiracy of the
      wicked,
    from that noisy crowd of evildoers.

3 They sharpen their tongues like swords
    and aim their words like deadly
      arrows.
4 They shoot from ambush at the
      innocent man;
    they shoot at him suddenly, without
      fear.

5 They encourage each other in evil
      plans,
    they talk about hiding their snares;
    they say, "Who will see them *a* ?"
6 They plot injustice and say,
    "We have devised a perfect plan!"
    Surely the mind and heart of man
      are cunning.

7 But God will shoot them with arrows;
    suddenly they will be struck down.
8 He will turn their own tongues against
    them

a 5 Or us

Tanking Up With God

READ PSALM 63

Have you ever gone on a marathon hike and someone forgot the
sports drink? Aaack! Now *that's* thirst! Life's like a long hike, too. We
get thirsty every day. We need something to quench that dryness,
that burning inside. Only, instead of a sports drink, we need God. It's
one thing to *believe* in God, but genuine Christians also want
to *seek* God. What really makes life worthwhile is having a
close relationship with him and praying to him every day—
not just when you're in trouble. Do you have a strong desire
to know God better? Do you pray to him daily, wanting to
know him better? Do it today. Walk up to your Bible as if
it were a big old water trough and you were a
thirsty camel.

Your next reading is on page 729.

and bring them to ruin;
all who see them will shake their
heads in scorn.
⁹All mankind will fear;
they will proclaim the works of God
and ponder what he has done.
¹⁰Let the righteous rejoice in the LORD
and take refuge in him;
let all the upright in heart praise him!

PSALM 65

*For the director of music. A psalm of David.
A song.*

¹Praise awaits*ᵃ* you, O God, in Zion;
to you our vows will be fulfilled.
²O you who hear prayer,
to you all men will come.
³When we were overwhelmed by sins,
you forgave*ᵇ* our transgressions.
⁴Blessed are those you choose
and bring near to live in your courts!
We are filled with the good things of
your house,
of your holy temple.

⁵You answer us with awesome deeds of
righteousness,
O God our Savior,
the hope of all the ends of the earth
and of the farthest seas,
⁶who formed the mountains by your
power,
having armed yourself with strength,
⁷who stilled the roaring of the seas,
the roaring of their waves,
and the turmoil of the nations.
⁸Those living far away fear your
wonders;
where morning dawns and evening
fades
you call forth songs of joy.

⁹You care for the land and water it;
you enrich it abundantly.
The streams of God are filled with
water
to provide the people with grain,
for so you have ordained it.*ᶜ*
¹⁰You drench its furrows
and level its ridges;
you soften it with showers
and bless its crops.
¹¹You crown the year with your bounty,
and your carts overflow with
abundance.
¹²The grasslands of the desert overflow;
the hills are clothed with gladness.

¹³The meadows are covered with flocks
and the valleys are mantled with
grain;
they shout for joy and sing.

PSALM 66

For the director of music. A song. A psalm.

¹Shout with joy to God, all the earth!
² Sing the glory of his name;
make his praise glorious!
³Say to God, "How awesome are your
deeds!
So great is your power
that your enemies cringe before you.
⁴All the earth bows down to you;
they sing praise to you,
they sing praise to your name." *Selah*

⁵Come and see what God has done,
how awesome his works in man's
behalf!
⁶He turned the sea into dry land,
they passed through the waters on
foot—
come, let us rejoice in him.
⁷He rules forever by his power,
his eyes watch the nations—
let not the rebellious rise up against
him. *Selah*

⁸Praise our God, O peoples,
let the sound of his praise be
heard;
⁹he has preserved our lives
and kept our feet from slipping.
¹⁰For you, O God, tested us;
you refined us like silver.
¹¹You brought us into prison
and laid burdens on our backs.
¹²You let men ride over our heads;
we went through fire and water,
but you brought us to a place of
abundance.

¹³I will come to your temple with burnt
offerings
and fulfill my vows to you—
¹⁴vows my lips promised and my mouth
spoke
when I was in trouble.
¹⁵I will sacrifice fat animals to you
and an offering of rams;
I will offer bulls and goats. *Selah*

ᵃ 1 Or *befits;* the meaning of the Hebrew for this word is
uncertain.   *ᵇ 3* Or *made atonement for*   *ᶜ 9* Or *for that is
how you prepare the land*

16 Come and listen, all you who fear God;
　let me tell you what he has done for
　me.
17 I cried out to him with my mouth;
　his praise was on my tongue.
18 If I had cherished sin in my heart,
　the Lord would not have listened;
19 but God has surely listened
　and heard my voice in prayer.
20 Praise be to God,
　who has not rejected my prayer
　or withheld his love from me!

PSALM 67

For the director of music. With stringed
instruments. A psalm. A song.

1 May God be gracious to us and bless us
　and make his face shine upon us,
　　　　　　　　　　　　　　Selah
2 that your ways may be known on earth,
　your salvation among all nations.

3 May the peoples praise you, O God;
　may all the peoples praise you.
4 May the nations be glad and sing for joy,
　for you rule the peoples justly
　and guide the nations of the earth.
　　　　　　　　　　　　　　Selah
5 May the peoples praise you, O God;
　may all the peoples praise you.

6 Then the land will yield its harvest,
　and God, our God, will bless us.
7 God will bless us,
　and all the ends of the earth will
　fear him.

PSALM 68

For the director of music. Of David. A psalm.
A song.

1 May God arise, may his enemies be
　scattered;
　may his foes flee before him.
2 As smoke is blown away by the wind,
　may you blow them away;
　as wax melts before the fire,
　may the wicked perish before God.
3 But may the righteous be glad
　and rejoice before God;
　may they be happy and joyful.

4 Sing to God, sing praise to his name,
　extol him who rides on the clouds[a]—
　his name is the LORD—
　and rejoice before him.
5 A father to the fatherless, a defender
　of widows,

is God in his holy dwelling.
6 God sets the lonely in families,[b]
　he leads forth the prisoners with
　singing;
　but the rebellious live in a
　sun-scorched land.

7 When you went out before your
　people, O God,
　when you marched through the
　wasteland,　　　　　　　*Selah*
8 the earth shook,
　the heavens poured down rain,
　before God, the One of Sinai,
　before God, the God of Israel.
9 You gave abundant showers, O God;
　you refreshed your weary inheritance.
10 Your people settled in it,
　and from your bounty, O God, you
　provided for the poor.

11 The Lord announced the word,
　and great was the company of those
　who proclaimed it:
12 "Kings and armies flee in haste;
　in the camps men divide the plunder.
13 Even while you sleep among the
　campfires,[c]
　the wings of ⌊my⌋ dove are sheathed
　with silver,
　its feathers with shining gold."
14 When the Almighty[d] scattered the
　kings in the land,
　it was like snow fallen on Zalmon.

15 The mountains of Bashan are majestic
　mountains;
　rugged are the mountains of Bashan.
16 Why gaze in envy, O rugged mountains,
　at the mountain where God chooses
　to reign,
　where the LORD himself will dwell
　forever?
17 The chariots of God are tens of
　thousands
　and thousands of thousands;
　the Lord ⌊has come⌋ from Sinai into
　his sanctuary.
18 When you ascended on high,
　you led captives in your train;
　you received gifts from men,
　even from[e] the rebellious—
　that you,[f] O LORD God, might dwell
　there.

a 4 Or / *prepare the way for him who rides through the*
deserts　　*b 6* Or *the desolate in a homeland*
c 13 Or *saddlebags*　　*d 14* Hebrew *Shaddai*　　*e 18* Or *gifts*
for men, / even　　*f 18* Or *they*

Gross!

"You may plunge your feet in the blood of your foes, while the tongues of your dogs have their share" (Psalm 68:23). Ah, y'know, guys, I think I'll give this wading pool a miss. I have to go and …do some homework. Yeah, homework. Come on, Rover, let's go.

¹⁹ Praise be to the Lord, to God our Savior,
     who daily bears our burdens.   *Selah*
²⁰ Our God is a God who saves;
     from the Sovereign LORD comes escape from death.

²¹ Surely God will crush the heads of his enemies,
     the hairy crowns of those who go on in their sins.
²² The Lord says, "I will bring them from Bashan;
     I will bring them from the depths of the sea,
²³ that you may plunge your feet in the blood of your foes,
     while the tongues of your dogs have their share."

²⁴ Your procession has come into view, O God,
     the procession of my God and King into the sanctuary.
²⁵ In front are the singers, after them the musicians;
     with them are the maidens playing tambourines.
²⁶ Praise God in the great congregation;
     praise the LORD in the assembly of Israel.
²⁷ There is the little tribe of Benjamin, leading them,
     there the great throng of Judah's princes,
     and there the princes of Zebulun and of Naphtali.

²⁸ Summon your power, O God[a];
     show us your strength, O God, as you have done before.
²⁹ Because of your temple at Jerusalem
     kings will bring you gifts.
³⁰ Rebuke the beast among the reeds,
     the herd of bulls among the calves of the nations.
   Humbled, may it bring bars of silver.
     Scatter the nations who delight in war.
³¹ Envoys will come from Egypt;
     Cush[b] will submit herself to God.

³² Sing to God, O kingdoms of the earth,
     sing praise to the Lord,   *Selah*
³³ to him who rides the ancient skies above,
     who thunders with mighty voice.
³⁴ Proclaim the power of God,
     whose majesty is over Israel,
     whose power is in the skies.
³⁵ You are awesome, O God, in your sanctuary;
     the God of Israel gives power and strength to his people.

     Praise be to God!

PSALM 69

For the director of music. To the tune of, "Lilies." Of David.

¹ Save me, O God,
     for the waters have come up to my neck.
² I sink in the miry depths,
     where there is no foothold.
   I have come into the deep waters;

---

[a] *28* Many Hebrew manuscripts, Septuagint and Syriac; most Hebrew manuscripts *Your God has summoned power for you*   [b] *31* That is, the upper Nile region

the floods engulf me.
3 I am worn out calling for help;
    my throat is parched.
My eyes fail,
    looking for my God.
4 Those who hate me without reason
    outnumber the hairs of my head;
many are my enemies without cause,
    those who seek to destroy me.
I am forced to restore
    what I did not steal.

5 You know my folly, O God;
    my guilt is not hidden from you.

6 May those who hope in you
    not be disgraced because of me,
    O Lord, the LORD Almighty;
may those who seek you
    not be put to shame because of
    me,
    O God of Israel.
7 For I endure scorn for your sake,
    and shame covers my face.
8 I am a stranger to my brothers,
    an alien to my own mother's sons;
9 for zeal for your house consumes me,

and the insults of those who insult
    you fall on me.
10 When I weep and fast,
    I must endure scorn;
11 when I put on sackcloth,
    people make sport of me.
12 Those who sit at the gate mock me,
    and I am the song of the drunkards.

13 But I pray to you, O LORD,
    in the time of your favor;
in your great love, O God,
    answer me with your sure salvation.
14 Rescue me from the mire,
    do not let me sink;
deliver me from those who hate me,
    from the deep waters.
15 Do not let the floodwaters engulf me
    or the depths swallow me up
    or the pit close its mouth over me.
16 Answer me, O LORD, out of the
    goodness of your love;
in your great mercy turn to me.
17 Do not hide your face from your
    servant;
answer me quickly, for I am in
    trouble.

GET SMARTER

No Water Too Deep

READ PSALM 69:1–20

Many people say men should be "strong and silent." But it's *OK* to feel bad when you're discouraged. How do *you* handle being down? You don't want to be a whiner, but playing the Rock doesn't help either. So take your problems to God like David did. Look at what a prayer warrior he was! He *had* to be. David was mocked, insulted, humiliated and viciously attacked. Small wonder he poured his heart out to God: "Rescue me . . . do not let me sink; deliver me from those who hate me, from the deep waters" (verse 14). He trusted God to rescue him and help him see things put right. We all go through that feeling—that the water is up to our necks and rising fast (verse 1). When you're there, tell God how you feel. There's no water too deep for God.

Your next reading is on page 733.

¹⁸Come near and rescue me;
  redeem me because of my foes.

¹⁹You know how I am scorned,
    disgraced and shamed;
  all my enemies are before you.
²⁰Scorn has broken my heart
    and has left me helpless;
  I looked for sympathy, but there was
    none,
  for comforters, but I found none.
²¹They put gall in my food
    and gave me vinegar for my thirst.

²²May the table set before them become
    a snare;
    may it become retribution and[a] a
    trap.
²³May their eyes be darkened so they
    cannot see,
  and their backs be bent forever.
²⁴Pour out your wrath on them;
    let your fierce anger overtake them.
²⁵May their place be deserted;
    let there be no one to dwell in their
    tents.
²⁶For they persecute those you wound
    and talk about the pain of those you
    hurt.
²⁷Charge them with crime upon crime;
    do not let them share in your
    salvation.
²⁸May they be blotted out of the book of
    life
  and not be listed with the righteous.

²⁹I am in pain and distress;
    may your salvation, O God, protect
    me.

³⁰I will praise God's name in song
    and glorify him with thanksgiving.
³¹This will please the Lord more than an
    ox,
    more than a bull with its horns and
    hoofs.
³²The poor will see and be glad—
    you who seek God, may your hearts
    live!
³³The Lord hears the needy
    and does not despise his captive
    people.

³⁴Let heaven and earth praise him,
    the seas and all that move in them,
³⁵for God will save Zion
    and rebuild the cities of Judah.
  Then people will settle there and
    possess it;

³⁶the children of his servants will
    inherit it,
  and those who love his name will
    dwell there.

PSALM 70

*For the director of music. Of David.
A petition.*

¹Hasten, O God, to save me;
  O Lord, come quickly to help me.
²May those who seek my life
    be put to shame and confusion;
  may all who desire my ruin
    be turned back in disgrace.
³May those who say to me, "Aha! Aha!"
    turn back because of their shame.
⁴But may all who seek you
    rejoice and be glad in you;
  may those who love your salvation
    always say,
  "Let God be exalted!"

⁵Yet I am poor and needy;
    come quickly to me, O God.
  You are my help and my deliverer;
    O Lord, do not delay.

PSALM 71

¹In you, O Lord, I have taken refuge;
    let me never be put to shame.
²Rescue me and deliver me in your
    righteousness;
    turn your ear to me and save me.
³Be my rock of refuge,
    to which I can always go;
  give the command to save me,
    for you are my rock and my fortress.
⁴Deliver me, O my God, from the hand
    of the wicked,
    from the grasp of evil and cruel men.

⁵For you have been my hope,
    O Sovereign Lord,
  my confidence since my youth.
⁶From birth I have relied on you;
    you brought me forth from my
    mother's womb.
  I will ever praise you.
⁷I have become like a portent to many,
    but you are my strong refuge.
⁸My mouth is filled with your praise,
    declaring your splendor all day long.

⁹Do not cast me away when I am old;
    do not forsake me when my
    strength is gone.

[a] 22 Or *snare / and their fellowship become*

¹⁰ For my enemies speak against me;
  those who wait to kill me conspire
  together.
¹¹ They say, "God has forsaken him;
  pursue him and seize him,
  for no one will rescue him."
¹² Be not far from me, O God;
  come quickly, O my God, to help
  me.
¹³ May my accusers perish in shame;
  may those who want to harm me
  be covered with scorn and disgrace.

¹⁴ But as for me, I will always have hope;
  I will praise you more and more.

¹⁵ My mouth will tell of your
  righteousness,
  of your salvation all day long,
  though I know not its measure.
¹⁶ I will come and proclaim your mighty
  acts, O Sovereign LORD;
  I will proclaim your righteousness,
  yours alone.
¹⁷ Since my youth, O God, you have
  taught me,
  and to this day I declare your
  marvelous deeds.
¹⁸ Even when I am old and gray,
  do not forsake me, O God,

Make It Stick

READ PSALM 71:20–24
The author of Psalm 71 was not being respected, and God promised to restore his honor and comfort him (see Psalm 71:21). Think over the last week. Did you fight with a friend? Were you picked on? Ask God to comfort you. Write a note to God, telling him what's on your mind, and believe that he's there for you.

till I declare your power to the next
generation,
    your might to all who are to come.

19 Your righteousness reaches to the
skies, O God,
    you who have done great things.
    Who, O God, is like you?
20 Though you have made me see
troubles, many and bitter,
    you will restore my life again;
from the depths of the earth
    you will again bring me up.
21 You will increase my honor
    and comfort me once again.

22 I will praise you with the harp
    for your faithfulness, O my God;
I will sing praise to you with the lyre,
    O Holy One of Israel.
23 My lips will shout for joy
    when I sing praise to you—
    I, whom you have redeemed.
24 My tongue will tell of your righteous
acts
    all day long,
for those who wanted to harm me
    have been put to shame and
confusion.

PSALM 72

Of Solomon.

1 Endow the king with your justice,
    O God,
    the royal son with your
righteousness.
2 He will[a] judge your people in
righteousness,
    your afflicted ones with justice.
3 The mountains will bring prosperity to
the people,
    the hills the fruit of righteousness.
4 He will defend the afflicted among the
people
    and save the children of the needy;
    he will crush the oppressor.

5 He will endure[b] as long as the sun,
    as long as the moon, through all
generations.
6 He will be like rain falling on a mown
field,
    like showers watering the earth.
7 In his days the righteous will flourish;
    prosperity will abound till the moon
is no more.

8 He will rule from sea to sea
    and from the River[c] to the ends of
the earth.[d]
9 The desert tribes will bow before him
    and his enemies will lick the dust.
10 The kings of Tarshish and of distant
shores
    will bring tribute to him;
the kings of Sheba and Seba
    will present him gifts.
11 All kings will bow down to him
    and all nations will serve him.

12 For he will deliver the needy who cry out,
    the afflicted who have no one to help.
13 He will take pity on the weak and the
needy
    and save the needy from death.
14 He will rescue them from oppression
and violence,
    for precious is their blood in his sight.

15 Long may he live!
    May gold from Sheba be given him.
May people ever pray for him
    and bless him all day long.
16 Let grain abound throughout the land;
    on the tops of the hills may it sway.
Let its fruit flourish like Lebanon;
    let it thrive like the grass of the field.
17 May his name endure forever;
    may it continue as long as the sun.

All nations will be blessed through him,
    and they will call him blessed.

18 Praise be to the LORD God, the God of
Israel,
    who alone does marvelous deeds.
19 Praise be to his glorious name forever;
    may the whole earth be filled with
his glory.
    Amen and Amen.

20 This concludes the prayers of David son
of Jesse.

BOOK III

Psalms 73–89

PSALM 73

A psalm of Asaph.

1 Surely God is good to Israel,
    to those who are pure in heart.

---

a 2 Or May he; similarly in verses 3–11 and 17
b 5 Septuagint; Hebrew You will be feared   c 8 That is, the
Euphrates   d 8 Or the end of the land

2 But as for me, my feet had almost
  slipped;
  I had nearly lost my foothold.
3 For I envied the arrogant
  when I saw the prosperity of the
  wicked.
4 They have no struggles;
  their bodies are healthy and strong. *a*
5 They are free from the burdens
  common to man;
  they are not plagued by human ills.
6 Therefore pride is their necklace;
  they clothe themselves with violence.
7 From their callous hearts comes
  iniquity *b*;
  the evil conceits of their minds know
  no limits.
8 They scoff, and speak with malice;
  in their arrogance they threaten
  oppression.
9 Their mouths lay claim to heaven,
  and their tongues take possession of
  the earth.
10 Therefore their people turn to them
  and drink up waters in abundance. *c*
11 They say, "How can God know?

Does the Most High have
  knowledge?"
12 This is what the wicked are like—
  always carefree, they increase in
  wealth.
13 Surely in vain have I kept my heart
  pure;
  in vain have I washed my hands in
  innocence.
14 All day long I have been plagued;
  I have been punished every morning.
15 If I had said, "I will speak thus,"
  I would have betrayed your children.
16 When I tried to understand all this,
  it was oppressive to me
17 till I entered the sanctuary of God;
  then I understood their final destiny.

18 Surely you place them on slippery
  ground;
  you cast them down to ruin.

a 4 With a different word division of the Hebrew; Masoretic
Text *struggles at their death; / their bodies are healthy*
b 7 Syriac (see also Septuagint); Hebrew *Their eyes bulge with
fat   c 10* The meaning of the Hebrew for this verse is
uncertain.

Wow! Nice Car!

READ PSALM 73

Ever seen a non-Christian celebrity who looks like he has it all—
money, women, fame, cars? That's how the guy who wrote this psalm
was feeling. It bugged him that people ignored God, yet were rolling
in the dough. But the psalm writer decided that knowing God was
better than having everything the world had to offer (verses
25–26). They were having fun with their toys, sure, but it was
only for the moment. In the big picture—the eternal one—
those guys pay an incredible price. Jesus asked what good is
it to "have it all" if it costs you your *soul* (Matthew 16:26). "Do
not ... be envious of the wicked, for the evil man has no
future hope" (Proverbs 24:19–20). You might not
think you have much; but if you have Christ in
your life, your future is fabulous.

Your next reading is on page 742.

19 How suddenly are they destroyed,
　　completely swept away by terrors!
20 As a dream when one awakes,
　　so when you arise, O Lord,
　　you will despise them as fantasies.

21 When my heart was grieved
　　and my spirit embittered,
22 I was senseless and ignorant;
　　I was a brute beast before you.

23 Yet I am always with you;
　　you hold me by my right hand.
24 You guide me with your counsel,
　　and afterward you will take me into
　　　glory.
25 Whom have I in heaven but you?
　　And earth has nothing I desire
　　　besides you.
26 My flesh and my heart may fail,
　　but God is the strength of my heart
　　and my portion forever.

27 Those who are far from you will perish;
　　you destroy all who are unfaithful to
　　　you.
28 But as for me, it is good to be near
　　　God.
　　I have made the Sovereign LORD my
　　　refuge;
　　I will tell of all your deeds.

PSALM 74

A maskil[a] of Asaph.

1 Why have you rejected us forever,
　　O God?
　　Why does your anger smolder
　　　against the sheep of your
　　　pasture?
2 Remember the people you purchased
　　of old,
　　the tribe of your inheritance, whom
　　　you redeemed—
　　Mount Zion, where you dwelt.
3 Turn your steps toward these
　　　everlasting ruins,
　　all this destruction the enemy has
　　　brought on the sanctuary.

4 Your foes roared in the place where
　　　you met with us;
　　they set up their standards as signs.
5 They behaved like men wielding axes
　　to cut through a thicket of trees.
6 They smashed all the carved paneling
　　with their axes and hatchets.
7 They burned your sanctuary to the
　　　ground;

they defiled the dwelling place of
　　your Name.
8 They said in their hearts, "We will
　　crush them completely!"
　　They burned every place where God
　　was worshiped in the land.
9 We are given no miraculous signs;
　　no prophets are left,
　　and none of us knows how long this
　　will be.

10 How long will the enemy mock you,
　　O God?
　　Will the foe revile your name
　　forever?
11 Why do you hold back your hand, your
　　right hand?
　　Take it from the folds of your
　　garment and destroy them!

12 But you, O God, are my king from of
　　old;
　　you bring salvation upon the earth.
13 It was you who split open the sea by
　　your power;
　　you broke the heads of the monster
　　in the waters.
14 It was you who crushed the heads of
　　Leviathan
　　and gave him as food to the
　　creatures of the desert.
15 It was you who opened up springs and
　　streams;
　　you dried up the ever flowing rivers.
16 The day is yours, and yours also the
　　night;
　　you established the sun and moon.
17 It was you who set all the boundaries
　　of the earth;
　　you made both summer and winter.

18 Remember how the enemy has
　　mocked you, O LORD,
　　how foolish people have reviled your
　　name.
19 Do not hand over the life of your dove
　　to wild beasts;
　　do not forget the lives of your
　　afflicted people forever.
20 Have regard for your covenant,
　　because haunts of violence fill the
　　dark places of the land.
21 Do not let the oppressed retreat in
　　disgrace;
　　may the poor and needy praise your
　　name.

---

a Title: Probably a literary or musical term

22 Rise up, O God, and defend your
      cause;
    remember how fools mock you all
      day long.
23 Do not ignore the clamor of your
      adversaries,
    the uproar of your enemies, which
      rises continually.

PSALM 75

*For the director of music. To the tune of "Do
Not Destroy." A psalm of Asaph. A song.*

1 We give thanks to you, O God,
    we give thanks, for your Name is
      near;
    men tell of your wonderful deeds.

2 You say, "I choose the appointed
      time;
    it is I who judge uprightly.
3 When the earth and all its people
      quake,
    it is I who hold its pillars firm.   *Selah*
4 To the arrogant I say, 'Boast no more,'

and to the wicked, 'Do not lift up
    your horns.
5 Do not lift your horns against heaven;
    do not speak with outstretched
      neck.' "

6 No one from the east or the west
    or from the desert can exalt a man.
7 But it is God who judges:
    He brings one down, he exalts
      another.
8 In the hand of the LORD is a cup
    full of foaming wine mixed with
      spices;
    he pours it out, and all the wicked of
      the earth
    drink it down to its very dregs.

9 As for me, I will declare this forever;
    I will sing praise to the God of
      Jacob.
10 I will cut off the horns of all the
      wicked,
    but the horns of the righteous will
      be lifted up.

Make It Stick

READ PSALM 75:6–7

In society, people seek promotions and fame, but following God's ways is the only path to *true*
promotion. Pretend God just told you, "Hey, good job on dishwashing! Now I want you to run the
whole restaurant and have all-you-can-eat privileges." What kind of restaurant it would be?
Then write in big letters, "God's my ultimate boss!"

PSALM 76

For the director of music. With stringed instruments. A psalm of Asaph. A song.

1 In Judah God is known;
  his name is great in Israel.
2 His tent is in Salem,
  his dwelling place in Zion.
3 There he broke the flashing arrows,
  the shields and the swords, the
    weapons of war.   *Selah*

4 You are resplendent with light,
  more majestic than mountains rich
    with game.
5 Valiant men lie plundered,
  they sleep their last sleep;
 not one of the warriors
  can lift his hands.
6 At your rebuke, O God of Jacob,
  both horse and chariot lie still.
7 You alone are to be feared.
  Who can stand before you when
    you are angry?
8 From heaven you pronounced
    judgment,
  and the land feared and was quiet—
9 when you, O God, rose up to judge,
  to save all the afflicted of the land.
            Selah
10 Surely your wrath against men brings
    you praise,
  and the survivors of your wrath are
    restrained. *a*

11 Make vows to the LORD your God and
    fulfill them;
  let all the neighboring lands
    bring gifts to the One to be feared.
12 He breaks the spirit of rulers;
  he is feared by the kings of the earth.

PSALM 77

For the director of music. For Jeduthun.
Of Asaph. A psalm.

1 I cried out to God for help;
  I cried out to God to hear me.
2 When I was in distress, I sought the
    Lord;
  at night I stretched out untiring hands
  and my soul refused to be comforted.

3 I remembered you, O God, and I
    groaned;
  I mused, and my spirit grew faint.
            Selah
4 You kept my eyes from closing;
  I was too troubled to speak.

5 I thought about the former days,
  the years of long ago;
6 I remembered my songs in the night.
  My heart mused and my spirit
    inquired:

7 "Will the Lord reject forever?
  Will he never show his favor again?
8 Has his unfailing love vanished forever?
  Has his promise failed for all time?
9 Has God forgotten to be merciful?
  Has he in anger withheld his
    compassion?"   *Selah*

10 Then I thought, "To this I will appeal:
  the years of the right hand of the
    Most High."
11 I will remember the deeds of the LORD;
  yes, I will remember your miracles of
    long ago.
12 I will meditate on all your works
  and consider all your mighty deeds.

13 Your ways, O God, are holy.
  What god is so great as our God?
14 You are the God who performs miracles;
  you display your power among the
    peoples.
15 With your mighty arm you redeemed
    your people,
  the descendants of Jacob and
    Joseph.   *Selah*

16 The waters saw you, O God,
  the waters saw you and writhed;
  the very depths were convulsed.
17 The clouds poured down water,
  the skies resounded with thunder;
  your arrows flashed back and forth.
18 Your thunder was heard in the
    whirlwind,
  your lightning lit up the world;
  the earth trembled and quaked.
19 Your path led through the sea,
  your way through the mighty
    waters,
  though your footprints were not
    seen.

20 You led your people like a flock
  by the hand of Moses and Aaron.

PSALM 78

A *maskil* *b* of Asaph.

1 O my people, hear my teaching;
  listen to the words of my mouth.

*a 10 Or Surely the wrath of men brings you praise, / and with
the remainder of wrath you arm yourself   b Title: Probably a
literary or musical term*

2 I will open my mouth in parables,
  I will utter hidden things, things
    from of old—
3 what we have heard and known,
  what our fathers have told us.
4 We will not hide them from their
    children;
  we will tell the next generation
the praiseworthy deeds of the LORD,
  his power, and the wonders he has
    done.
5 He decreed statutes for Jacob
  and established the law in Israel,
which he commanded our forefathers
  to teach their children,
6 so the next generation would know
    them,
  even the children yet to be born,
  and they in turn would tell their
    children.
7 Then they would put their trust in God
  and would not forget his deeds
  but would keep his commands.
8 They would not be like their
    forefathers—
  a stubborn and rebellious generation,
whose hearts were not loyal to God,
  whose spirits were not faithful to
    him.

9 The men of Ephraim, though armed
    with bows,
  turned back on the day of battle;
10 they did not keep God's covenant
  and refused to live by his law.
11 They forgot what he had done,
  the wonders he had shown them.
12 He did miracles in the sight of their
    fathers
  in the land of Egypt, in the region of
    Zoan.
13 He divided the sea and led them
    through;
  he made the water stand firm like a
    wall.
14 He guided them with the cloud by day
  and with light from the fire all night.
15 He split the rocks in the desert
  and gave them water as abundant
    as the seas;
16 he brought streams out of a rocky crag
  and made water flow down like
    rivers.
17 But they continued to sin against him,
  rebelling in the desert against the
    Most High.
18 They willfully put God to the test

by demanding the food they craved.
19 They spoke against God, saying,
  "Can God spread a table in the
    desert?
20 When he struck the rock, water
    gushed out,
  and streams flowed abundantly.
But can he also give us food?
  Can he supply meat for his people?"
21 When the LORD heard them, he was
    very angry;
  his fire broke out against Jacob,
  and his wrath rose against Israel,
22 for they did not believe in God
  or trust in his deliverance.
23 Yet he gave a command to the skies
    above
  and opened the doors of the
    heavens;
24 he rained down manna for the people
    to eat,
  he gave them the grain of heaven.
25 Men ate the bread of angels;
  he sent them all the food they could
    eat.
26 He let loose the east wind from the
    heavens
  and led forth the south wind by his
    power.
27 He rained meat down on them like
    dust,
  flying birds like sand on the seashore.
28 He made them come down inside their
    camp,
  all around their tents.
29 They ate till they had more than
    enough,
  for he had given them what they
    craved.
30 But before they turned from the food
    they craved,
  even while it was still in their mouths,
31 God's anger rose against them;
  he put to death the sturdiest among
    them,
  cutting down the young men of
    Israel.

32 In spite of all this, they kept on
    sinning;
  in spite of his wonders, they did not
    believe.
33 So he ended their days in futility
  and their years in terror.
34 Whenever God slew them, they would
    seek him;
  they eagerly turned to him again.

35 They remembered that God was their
    Rock,
      that God Most High was their
        Redeemer.
36 But then they would flatter him with
    their mouths,
      lying to him with their tongues;
37 their hearts were not loyal to him,
      they were not faithful to his
        covenant.
38 Yet he was merciful;
      he forgave their iniquities
      and did not destroy them.
    Time after time he restrained his anger
      and did not stir up his full wrath.
39 He remembered that they were but
    flesh,
      a passing breeze that does not
        return.

40 How often they rebelled against him in
    the desert
      and grieved him in the wasteland!
41 Again and again they put God to the
    test;
      they vexed the Holy One of Israel.
42 They did not remember his power—
      the day he redeemed them from the
        oppressor,
43 the day he displayed his miraculous
      signs in Egypt,
      his wonders in the region of Zoan.
44 He turned their rivers to blood;
      they could not drink from their
        streams.
45 He sent swarms of flies that devoured
    them,
      and frogs that devastated them.
46 He gave their crops to the grasshopper,
      their produce to the locust.
47 He destroyed their vines with hail
      and their sycamore-figs with sleet.
48 He gave over their cattle to the hail,
      their livestock to bolts of lightning.
49 He unleashed against them his hot
    anger,
      his wrath, indignation and hostility—
      a band of destroying angels.
50 He prepared a path for his anger;
      he did not spare them from death
      but gave them over to the plague.
51 He struck down all the firstborn of
    Egypt,
      the firstfruits of manhood in the
        tents of Ham.
52 But he brought his people out like a
    flock;

he led them like sheep through the
    desert.
53 He guided them safely, so they were
    unafraid;
      but the sea engulfed their enemies.
54 Thus he brought them to the border of
    his holy land,
      to the hill country his right hand had
        taken.
55 He drove out nations before them
      and allotted their lands to them as
        an inheritance;
      he settled the tribes of Israel in their
        homes.

56 But they put God to the test
      and rebelled against the Most High;
      they did not keep his statutes.
57 Like their fathers they were disloyal
    and faithless,
      as unreliable as a faulty bow.
58 They angered him with their high
    places;
      they aroused his jealousy with their
        idols.
59 When God heard them, he was very
    angry;
      he rejected Israel completely.
60 He abandoned the tabernacle of
    Shiloh,
      the tent he had set up among men.
61 He sent ⌊the ark of⌋ his might into
    captivity,
      his splendor into the hands of the
        enemy.
62 He gave his people over to the sword;
      he was very angry with his
        inheritance.
63 Fire consumed their young men,
      and their maidens had no wedding
        songs;
64 their priests were put to the sword,
      and their widows could not weep.

65 Then the Lord awoke as from sleep,
      as a man wakes from the stupor of
        wine.
66 He beat back his enemies;
      he put them to everlasting shame.
67 Then he rejected the tents of Joseph,
      he did not choose the tribe of
        Ephraim;
68 but he chose the tribe of Judah,
      Mount Zion, which he loved.
69 He built his sanctuary like the heights,
      like the earth that he established
        forever.
70 He chose David his servant

and took him from the sheep pens;
71 from tending the sheep he brought him
    to be the shepherd of his people Jacob,
    of Israel his inheritance.
72 And David shepherded them with integrity of heart;
    with skillful hands he led them.

PSALM 79

A psalm of Asaph.

1 O God, the nations have invaded your inheritance;
    they have defiled your holy temple,
    they have reduced Jerusalem to rubble.
2 They have given the dead bodies of your servants
    as food to the birds of the air,
    the flesh of your saints to the beasts of the earth.
3 They have poured out blood like water
    all around Jerusalem,
    and there is no one to bury the dead.
4 We are objects of reproach to our neighbors,
    of scorn and derision to those around us.

5 How long, O Lord? Will you be angry forever?
    How long will your jealousy burn like fire?
6 Pour out your wrath on the nations
    that do not acknowledge you,
  on the kingdoms
    that do not call on your name;
7 for they have devoured Jacob
    and destroyed his homeland.
8 Do not hold against us the sins of the fathers;
    may your mercy come quickly to meet us,
    for we are in desperate need.

9 Help us, O God our Savior,
    for the glory of your name;
  deliver us and forgive our sins
    for your name's sake.
10 Why should the nations say,
    "Where is their God?"
  Before our eyes, make known among the nations
    that you avenge the outpoured blood of your
        servants.
11 May the groans of the prisoners come before you;
    by the strength of your arm
    preserve those condemned to die.

12 Pay back into the laps of our neighbors seven times
    the reproach they have hurled at you, O Lord.
13 Then we your people, the sheep of your pasture,
    will praise you forever;
  from generation to generation
    we will recount your praise.

PSALM 80

*For the director of music. To the tune of, "The Lilies of the
Covenant." Of Asaph. A psalm.*

1 Hear us, O Shepherd of Israel,
    you who lead Joseph like a flock;

Get a Load of This...

A man of God has integrity of heart and skillful hands (see Psalm 78:72). Whether sling-twirling, sheep-guarding, harp-playing or psalm-writing, David rocked. You too can have an awesome pure heart and be skillful in what God calls you to do.

In Other Words...

you who sit enthroned between the
cherubim, shine forth
2   before Ephraim, Benjamin and
Manasseh.
Awaken your might;
come and save us.

3 Restore us, O God;
make your face shine upon us,
that we may be saved.

4 O Lord God Almighty,
how long will your anger smolder
against the prayers of your people?
5 You have fed them with the bread of
tears;
you have made them drink tears by
the bowlful.
6 You have made us a source of
contention to our neighbors,
and our enemies mock us.

7 Restore us, O God Almighty;
make your face shine upon us,
that we may be saved.

8 You brought a vine out of Egypt;
you drove out the nations and
planted it.
9 You cleared the ground for it,
and it took root and filled the land.
10 The mountains were covered with its
shade,
the mighty cedars with its branches.
11 It sent out its boughs to the Sea,^{a}
its shoots as far as the River.^{b}

12 Why have you broken down its walls
so that all who pass by pick its
grapes?
13 Boars from the forest ravage it
and the creatures of the field feed
on it.
14 Return to us, O God Almighty!
Look down from heaven and see!
Watch over this vine,
15   the root your right hand has planted,
the son^c you have raised up for
yourself.

16 Your vine is cut down, it is burned with
fire;
at your rebuke your people perish.
17 Let your hand rest on the man at your
right hand,
the son of man you have raised up
for yourself.
18 Then we will not turn away from you;
revive us, and we will call on your
name.

19 Restore us, O Lord God Almighty;
make your face shine upon us,
that we may be saved.

PSALM 81

For the director of music. According to
gittith. ^{d} Of Asaph.

1 Sing for joy to God our strength;
shout aloud to the God of Jacob!
2 Begin the music, strike the tambourine,
play the melodious harp and lyre.
3 Sound the ram's horn at the New
Moon,
and when the moon is full, on the
day of our Feast;
4 this is a decree for Israel,
an ordinance of the God of Jacob.
5 He established it as a statute for Joseph
when he went out against Egypt,
where we heard a language we did
not understand.^{e}

6 He says, "I removed the burden from
their shoulders;
their hands were set free from the
basket.
7 In your distress you called and I
rescued you,
I answered you out of a
thundercloud;
I tested you at the waters of
Meribah.   *Selah*

8 "Hear, O my people, and I will warn
you—
if you would but listen to me,
O Israel!
9 You shall have no foreign god among
you;
you shall not bow down to an alien
god.
10 I am the Lord your God,
who brought you up out of Egypt.
Open wide your mouth and I will fill
it.

11 "But my people would not listen to
me;
Israel would not submit to me.
12 So I gave them over to their stubborn
hearts
to follow their own devices.

13 "If my people would but listen to me,
if Israel would follow my ways,

---

^{a} 11 Probably the Mediterranean ^{b} 11 That is, the
Euphrates ^{c} 15 Or *branch* ^{d} Title: Probably a musical
term ^{e} 5 Or / *and we heard a voice we had not known*

14 how quickly would I subdue their
        enemies
    and turn my hand against their foes!
15 Those who hate the LORD would cringe
        before him,
    and their punishment would last
        forever.
16 But you would be fed with the finest
        of wheat;
    with honey from the rock I would
        satisfy you."

PSALM 82

A psalm of Asaph.

1 God presides in the great assembly;
    he gives judgment among the
        "gods":

2 "How long will you[a] defend the unjust
    and show partiality to the wicked?
                                Selah
3 Defend the cause of the weak and
        fatherless;
    maintain the rights of the poor and
        oppressed.
4 Rescue the weak and needy;
    deliver them from the hand of the
        wicked.

5 "They know nothing, they understand
        nothing.
    They walk about in darkness;
    all the foundations of the earth are
        shaken.

6 "I said, 'You are "gods";
    you are all sons of the Most High.'
7 But you will die like mere men;
    you will fall like every other ruler."

8 Rise up, O God, judge the earth,
    for all the nations are your
        inheritance.

PSALM 83

A song. A psalm of Asaph.

1 O God, do not keep silent;
    be not quiet, O God, be not still.
2 See how your enemies are astir,
    how your foes rear their heads.
3 With cunning they conspire against
        your people;
    they plot against those you cherish.
4 "Come," they say, "let us destroy them
        as a nation,
    that the name of Israel be
        remembered no more."

5 With one mind they plot together;
    they form an alliance against you—
6 the tents of Edom and the Ishmaelites,
    of Moab and the Hagrites,
7 Gebal,[b] Ammon and Amalek,
    Philistia, with the people of Tyre.
8 Even Assyria has joined them
    to lend strength to the descendants
        of Lot.   *Selah*

9 Do to them as you did to Midian,
    as you did to Sisera and Jabin at the
        river Kishon,
10 who perished at Endor
    and became like refuse on the
        ground.
11 Make their nobles like Oreb and Zeeb,
    all their princes like Zebah and
        Zalmunna,
12 who said, "Let us take possession
    of the pasturelands of God."

13 Make them like tumbleweed, O my
        God,
    like chaff before the wind.
14 As fire consumes the forest
    or a flame sets the mountains
        ablaze,
15 so pursue them with your tempest
    and terrify them with your storm.
16 Cover their faces with shame
    so that men will seek your name,
        O LORD.

17 May they ever be ashamed and
        dismayed;
    may they perish in disgrace.
18 Let them know that you, whose name
        is the LORD—
    that you alone are the Most High
        over all the earth.

PSALM 84

*For the director of music. According to
gittith.[c] Of the Sons of Korah. A psalm.*

1 How lovely is your dwelling place,
    O LORD Almighty!
2 My soul yearns, even faints,
    for the courts of the LORD;
    my heart and my flesh cry out
        for the living God.

3 Even the sparrow has found a home,
    and the swallow a nest for herself,
    where she may have her young—
    a place near your altar,

a 2 The Hebrew is plural.   *b 7* That is, Byblos   *c Title:*
Probably a musical term

O Lᴏʀᴅ Almighty, my King and my
God.
4 Blessed are those who dwell in your
house;
they are ever praising you.   *Selah*

5 Blessed are those whose strength is in
you,
who have set their hearts on
pilgrimage.
6 As they pass through the Valley of Baca,
they make it a place of springs;
the autumn rains also cover it with
pools.ᵃ
7 They go from strength to strength,
till each appears before God in Zion.

8 Hear my prayer, O Lᴏʀᴅ God Almighty;
listen to me, O God of Jacob.   *Selah*
9 Look upon our shield,ᵇ O God;
look with favor on your anointed
one.

10 Better is one day in your courts
than a thousand elsewhere;
I would rather be a doorkeeper in the
house of my God
than dwell in the tents of the wicked.

11 For the Lᴏʀᴅ God is a sun and shield;
the Lᴏʀᴅ bestows favor and honor;
no good thing does he withhold
from those whose walk is blameless.

12 O Lᴏʀᴅ Almighty,
blessed is the man who trusts in you.

PSALM 85

For the director of music. Of the Sons of
Korah. A psalm.

1 You showed favor to your land, O Lᴏʀᴅ;
you restored the fortunes of Jacob.
2 You forgave the iniquity of your people
and covered all their sins.   *Selah*
3 You set aside all your wrath
and turned from your fierce anger.

4 Restore us again, O God our Savior,
and put away your displeasure
toward us.
5 Will you be angry with us forever?
Will you prolong your anger through
all generations?
6 Will you not revive us again,
that your people may rejoice in you?

ᵃ 6 Or *blessings*   ᵇ 9 Or *sovereign*

Super Power Hideout

READ PSALM 84

Superheroes have secret hideouts—places to recover from fighting evil and to make plans for the future. As Christians, we don't have high-tech caves or frozen fortresses we can sneak away to when things get to be too much. But we can go straight into the presence of the God of the Universe! The poor guy who wrote this psalm felt that he just had to be in the temple in Jerusalem to be with God. He lamented, "Better is one day in your courts than a thousand elsewhere" (verse 10). As Christians, all we have to do is close our eyes and we can—*Whoosh!*—immediately come before God! We can go to him daily in prayer and worship. God is the only true superpower—he can charge our batteries so full that we'll walk away sparking. Feeling low or discouraged? Go to your "secret hideout," the presence of God, and get recharged.

Your next reading is on page 747.

7 Show us your unfailing love, O LORD,
   and grant us your salvation.

8 I will listen to what God the LORD will
      say;
   he promises peace to his people, his
      saints—
   but let them not return to folly.
9 Surely his salvation is near those who
      fear him,
   that his glory may dwell in our land.

10 Love and faithfulness meet together;
   righteousness and peace kiss each
      other.
11 Faithfulness springs forth from the
      earth,
   and righteousness looks down from
      heaven.
12 The LORD will indeed give what is good,
   and our land will yield its harvest.
13 Righteousness goes before him
   and prepares the way for his steps.

PSALM 86

A prayer of David.

1 Hear, O LORD, and answer me,
   for I am poor and needy.
2 Guard my life, for I am devoted to you.
   You are my God; save your servant
      who trusts in you.
3 Have mercy on me, O Lord,
   for I call to you all day long.
4 Bring joy to your servant,
   for to you, O Lord,
   I lift up my soul.

5 You are forgiving and good, O Lord,
   abounding in love to all who call to
      you.
6 Hear my prayer, O LORD;
   listen to my cry for mercy.
7 In the day of my trouble I will call to
      you,
   for you will answer me.

8 Among the gods there is none like
      you, O Lord;
   no deeds can compare with yours.
9 All the nations you have made
   will come and worship before you,
      O Lord;
   they will bring glory to your name.
10 For you are great and do marvelous
      deeds;
   you alone are God.

11 Teach me your way, O LORD,
   and I will walk in your truth;

give me an undivided heart,
   that I may fear your name.
12 I will praise you, O Lord my God, with
      all my heart;
   I will glorify your name forever.
13 For great is your love toward me;
   you have delivered me from the
      depths of the grave. a

14 The arrogant are attacking me, O God;
   a band of ruthless men seeks my
      life—
   men without regard for you.
15 But you, O Lord, are a compassionate
      and gracious God,
   slow to anger, abounding in love
      and faithfulness.
16 Turn to me and have mercy on me;
   grant your strength to your servant
   and save the son of your
      maidservant. b
17 Give me a sign of your goodness,
   that my enemies may see it and be
      put to shame,
   for you, O LORD, have helped me and
      comforted me.

PSALM 87

Of the Sons of Korah. A psalm. A song.

1 He has set his foundation on the holy
      mountain;
2   the LORD loves the gates of Zion
   more than all the dwellings of Jacob.
3 Glorious things are said of you,
   O city of God: Selah
4 "I will record Rahab c and Babylon
   among those who acknowledge
      me—
   Philistia too, and Tyre, along with
      Cush d—
   and will say, 'This e one was born in
      Zion.' "

5 Indeed, of Zion it will be said,
   "This one and that one were born in
      her,
   and the Most High himself will
      establish her."
6 The LORD will write in the register of
      the peoples:
   "This one was born in Zion."   Selah
7 As they make music they will sing,
   "All my fountains are in you."

a 13 Hebrew Sheol   b 16 Or save your faithful son
c 4 A poetic name for Egypt   d 4 That is, the upper Nile
region   e 4 Or "O Rahab and Babylon, / Philistia, Tyre and
Cush, / I will record concerning those who acknowledge me: /
'This

PSALM 88

A song. A psalm of the Sons of Korah. For the director of music. According to *mahalath leannoth*. *a* A *maskil* *b* of Heman the Ezrahite.

¹ O LORD, the God who saves me,
   day and night I cry out before you.
² May my prayer come before you;
   turn your ear to my cry.

³ For my soul is full of trouble
   and my life draws near the grave. *c*
⁴ I am counted among those who go
      down to the pit;
   I am like a man without strength.
⁵ I am set apart with the dead,
   like the slain who lie in the grave,
   whom you remember no more,
   who are cut off from your care.

⁶ You have put me in the lowest pit,
   in the darkest depths.
⁷ Your wrath lies heavily upon me;
   you have overwhelmed me with all
      your waves.   *Selah*

⁸ You have taken from me my closest
      friends
   and have made me repulsive to them.
   I am confined and cannot escape;
⁹   my eyes are dim with grief.

   I call to you, O LORD, every day;
   I spread out my hands to you.
¹⁰ Do you show your wonders to the
      dead?
   Do those who are dead rise up and
      praise you?   *Selah*
¹¹ Is your love declared in the grave,
   your faithfulness in Destruction *d*?
¹² Are your wonders known in the place
      of darkness,
   or your righteous deeds in the land
      of oblivion?

¹³ But I cry to you for help, O LORD;
   in the morning my prayer comes
      before you.

a Title: Possibly a tune, "The Suffering of Affliction"   *b* Title: Probably a literary or musical term   *c 3* Hebrew *Sheol*   *d 11* Hebrew *Abaddon*

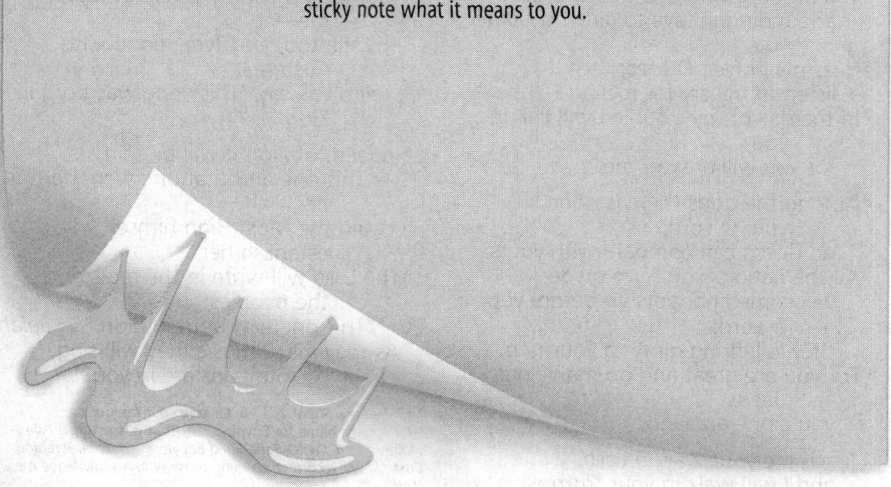

Make It Stick

READ PSALM 86:11

What *is* an "undivided heart" (Psalm 86:11)? One thing it means is to be fully committed to God, no longer wrestling between the world and God, but being totally in God's corner. If *you* were asking God for an "undivided heart," what would you be asking for? Write on a sticky note what it means to you.

14 Why, O LORD, do you reject me
   and hide your face from me?

15 From my youth I have been afflicted
   and close to death;
   I have suffered your terrors and am
   in despair.
16 Your wrath has swept over me;
   your terrors have destroyed me.
17 All day long they surround me like a
   flood;
   they have completely engulfed me.
18 You have taken my companions and
   loved ones from me;
   the darkness is my closest friend.

PSALM 89

A *maskil*[a] of Ethan the Ezrahite.

1 I will sing of the LORD's great love
   forever;
   with my mouth I will make your
   faithfulness known through all
   generations.
2 I will declare that your love stands firm
   forever,
   that you established your
   faithfulness in heaven itself.

3 You said, "I have made a covenant
   with my chosen one,
   I have sworn to David my servant,
4 'I will establish your line forever
   and make your throne firm through
   all generations.' "   *Selah*

5 The heavens praise your wonders,
   O LORD,
   your faithfulness too, in the
   assembly of the holy ones.
6 For who in the skies above can
   compare with the LORD?
   Who is like the LORD among the
   heavenly beings?
7 In the council of the holy ones God is
   greatly feared;
   he is more awesome than all who
   surround him.
8 O LORD God Almighty, who is like you?
   You are mighty, O LORD, and your
   faithfulness surrounds you.

9 You rule over the surging sea;
   when its waves mount up, you still
   them.
10 You crushed Rahab like one of the
   slain;
   with your strong arm you scattered
   your enemies.

11 The heavens are yours, and yours also
   the earth;
   you founded the world and all that
   is in it.
12 You created the north and the south;
   Tabor and Hermon sing for joy at
   your name.
13 Your arm is endued with power;
   your hand is strong, your right hand
   exalted.

14 Righteousness and justice are the
   foundation of your throne;
   love and faithfulness go before you.
15 Blessed are those who have learned to
   acclaim you,
   who walk in the light of your
   presence, O LORD.
16 They rejoice in your name all day long;
   they exult in your righteousness.
17 For you are their glory and strength,
   and by your favor you exalt our
   horn.[b]
18 Indeed, our shield[c] belongs to the LORD,
   our king to the Holy One of Israel.

19 Once you spoke in a vision,
   to your faithful people you said:
   "I have bestowed strength on a
   warrior;
   I have exalted a young man from
   among the people.
20 I have found David my servant;
   with my sacred oil I have anointed
   him.
21 My hand will sustain him;
   surely my arm will strengthen him.
22 No enemy will subject him to tribute;
   no wicked man will oppress him.
23 I will crush his foes before him
   and strike down his adversaries.
24 My faithful love will be with him,
   and through my name his horn[d] will
   be exalted.
25 I will set his hand over the sea,
   his right hand over the rivers.
26 He will call out to me, 'You are my
   Father,
   my God, the Rock my Savior.'
27 I will also appoint him my firstborn,
   the most exalted of the kings of the
   earth.
28 I will maintain my love to him forever,
   and my covenant with him will never
   fail.

---

a Title: Probably a literary or musical term   *b 17* *Horn* here
symbolizes strong one.   *c 18* Or *sovereign*   *d 24* *Horn*
here symbolizes strength.

²⁹ I will establish his line forever,
    his throne as long as the heavens
        endure.

³⁰ "If his sons forsake my law
    and do not follow my statutes,
³¹ if they violate my decrees
    and fail to keep my commands,
³² I will punish their sin with the rod,
    their iniquity with flogging;
³³ but I will not take my love from him,
    nor will I ever betray my faithfulness.
³⁴ I will not violate my covenant
    or alter what my lips have uttered.
³⁵ Once for all, I have sworn by my
        holiness—
    and I will not lie to David—
³⁶ that his line will continue forever
    and his throne endure before me
        like the sun;
³⁷ it will be established forever like the
        moon,
    the faithful witness in the sky." *Selah*

³⁸ But you have rejected, you have
        spurned,
    you have been very angry with your
        anointed one.
³⁹ You have renounced the covenant with
        your servant
    and have defiled his crown in the
        dust.
⁴⁰ You have broken through all his walls
    and reduced his strongholds to
        ruins.
⁴¹ All who pass by have plundered him;
    he has become the scorn of his
        neighbors.
⁴² You have exalted the right hand of his
        foes;
    you have made all his enemies
        rejoice.
⁴³ You have turned back the edge of his
        sword
    and have not supported him in
        battle.
⁴⁴ You have put an end to his splendor
    and cast his throne to the ground.
⁴⁵ You have cut short the days of his
        youth;
    you have covered him with a mantle
        of shame.   *Selah*

⁴⁶ How long, O Lᴏʀᴅ? Will you hide
        yourself forever?
    How long will your wrath burn like
        fire?
⁴⁷ Remember how fleeting is my life.

For what futility you have created all
        men!
⁴⁸ What man can live and not see death,
    or save himself from the power of
        the grave*ᵃ*?   *Selah*
⁴⁹ O Lord, where is your former great love,
    which in your faithfulness you swore
        to David?
⁵⁰ Remember, Lord, how your servant
        has*ᵇ* been mocked,
    how I bear in my heart the taunts of
        all the nations,
⁵¹ the taunts with which your enemies
    have mocked, O Lᴏʀᴅ,
    with which they have mocked every
        step of your anointed one.

⁵² Praise be to the Lᴏʀᴅ forever!
    Amen and Amen.

BOOK IV

Psalms 90–106

PSALM 90

A prayer of Moses the man of God.

¹ Lord, you have been our dwelling place
    throughout all generations.
² Before the mountains were born
    or you brought forth the earth and
        the world,
    from everlasting to everlasting you
        are God.

³ You turn men back to dust,
    saying, "Return to dust, O sons of
        men."
⁴ For a thousand years in your sight
    are like a day that has just gone by,
    or like a watch in the night.
⁵ You sweep men away in the sleep of
        death;
    they are like the new grass of the
        morning—
⁶ though in the morning it springs up
        new,
    by evening it is dry and withered.

⁷ We are consumed by your anger
    and terrified by your indignation.
⁸ You have set our iniquities before you,
    our secret sins in the light of your
        presence.
⁹ All our days pass away under your
        wrath;
    we finish our years with a moan.

ᵃ 48 Hebrew *Sheol*   *ᵇ 50* Or *your servants have*

¹⁰The length of our days is seventy
  years—
 or eighty, if we have the strength;
 yet their span*ᵃ* is but trouble and
  sorrow,
  for they quickly pass, and we fly
   away.
¹¹Who knows the power of your anger?
  For your wrath is as great as the fear
   that is due you.
¹²Teach us to number our days aright,
  that we may gain a heart of
   wisdom.
¹³Relent, O Lᴏʀᴅ! How long will it be?
  Have compassion on your servants.
¹⁴Satisfy us in the morning with your
  unfailing love,
  that we may sing for joy and be glad
   all our days.
¹⁵Make us glad for as many days as you
  have afflicted us,
  for as many years as we have seen
   trouble.
¹⁶May your deeds be shown to your
  servants,
 your splendor to their children.

¹⁷May the favor*ᵇ* of the Lord our God
  rest upon us;
 establish the work of our hands for
  us—
 yes, establish the work of our hands.

PSALM 91

¹He who dwells in the shelter of the
  Most High
 will rest in the shadow of the
  Almighty.*ᶜ*
²I will say*ᵈ* of the Lᴏʀᴅ, "He is my refuge
  and my fortress,
 my God, in whom I trust."

³Surely he will save you from the
  fowler's snare
 and from the deadly pestilence.
⁴He will cover you with his feathers,
 and under his wings you will find
  refuge;
 his faithfulness will be your shield
  and rampart.
⁵You will not fear the terror of night,
 nor the arrow that flies by day,

ᵃ 10 Or *yet the best of them*   *ᵇ 17* Or *beauty*
ᶜ 1 Hebrew *Shaddai*   *ᵈ 2* Or *He says*

Living in the Shelter

READ PSALM 91

God blesses and protects those who love him." 'Because he loves me,'
says the Lᴏʀᴅ, 'I will rescue him; I will protect him, for he acknowledges my name' " (verse 14). You shouldn't just love God and acknowledge him when bullets are flying past your head. Hanging out
with God once in a while won't cut it. God is looking for the
man who "dwells in the shelter of the Most High" (verse 1).
That means you're not only looking to God in hard times but
also during the good times. Do that and God will respond by
giving you all the blessings that he promises in this psalm. As
you get closer to God, your faith increases, and then his
blessings just come flowing into your life. When you
stick to God like a shadow, you're choosing for
God to protect you and honor you.

Your next reading is on page 753.

6 nor the pestilence that stalks in the
   darkness,
   nor the plague that destroys at
   midday.
7 A thousand may fall at your side,
   ten thousand at your right hand,
   but it will not come near you.
8 You will only observe with your eyes
   and see the punishment of the
   wicked.

9 If you make the Most High your
   dwelling—
   even the LORD, who is my refuge—
10 then no harm will befall you,
   no disaster will come near your tent.
11 For he will command his angels
   concerning you
   to guard you in all your ways;
12 they will lift you up in their hands,
   so that you will not strike your foot
   against a stone.
13 You will tread upon the lion and the
   cobra;
   you will trample the great lion and
   the serpent.

14 "Because he loves me," says the LORD,
   "I will rescue him;
   I will protect him, for he
   acknowledges my name.
15 He will call upon me, and I will answer
   him;
   I will be with him in trouble,
   I will deliver him and honor him.
16 With long life will I satisfy him
   and show him my salvation."

PSALM 92

A psalm. A song. For the Sabbath day.

1 It is good to praise the LORD
   and make music to your name,
   O Most High,
2 to proclaim your love in the morning
   and your faithfulness at night,
3 to the music of the ten-stringed lyre
   and the melody of the harp.

4 For you make me glad by your deeds,
   O LORD;
   I sing for joy at the works of your
   hands.
5 How great are your works, O LORD,
   how profound your thoughts!
6 The senseless man does not know,
   fools do not understand,
7 that though the wicked spring up like
   grass

and all evildoers flourish,
   they will be forever destroyed.

8 But you, O LORD, are exalted forever.

9 For surely your enemies, O LORD,
   surely your enemies will perish;
   all evildoers will be scattered.
10 You have exalted my horn[a] like that of
   a wild ox;
   fine oils have been poured upon me.
11 My eyes have seen the defeat of my
   adversaries;
   my ears have heard the rout of my
   wicked foes.

12 The righteous will flourish like a palm
   tree,
   they will grow like a cedar of
   Lebanon;
13 planted in the house of the LORD,
   they will flourish in the courts of our
   God.
14 They will still bear fruit in old age,
   they will stay fresh and green,
15 proclaiming, "The LORD is upright;
   he is my Rock, and there is no
   wickedness in him."

PSALM 93

1 The LORD reigns, he is robed in majesty;
   the LORD is robed in majesty
   and is armed with strength.
   The world is firmly established;
   it cannot be moved.
2 Your throne was established long ago;
   you are from all eternity.

3 The seas have lifted up, O LORD,
   the seas have lifted up their voice;
   the seas have lifted up their
   pounding waves.
4 Mightier than the thunder of the great
   waters,
   mightier than the breakers of the
   sea—
   the LORD on high is mighty.

5 Your statutes stand firm;
   holiness adorns your house
   for endless days, O LORD.

PSALM 94

1 O LORD, the God who avenges,
   O God who avenges, shine forth.
2 Rise up, O Judge of the earth;
   pay back to the proud what they
   deserve.

a 10 Horn here symbolizes strength.

3 How long will the wicked, O Lord,
  how long will the wicked be jubilant?

4 They pour out arrogant words;
  all the evildoers are full of boasting.
5 They crush your people, O Lord;
  they oppress your inheritance.
6 They slay the widow and the alien;
  they murder the fatherless.
7 They say, "The Lord does not see;
  the God of Jacob pays no heed."

8 Take heed, you senseless ones among
    the people;
  you fools, when will you become
    wise?
9 Does he who implanted the ear not
    hear?
  Does he who formed the eye not
    see?
10 Does he who disciplines nations not
    punish?
  Does he who teaches man lack
    knowledge?
11 The Lord knows the thoughts of man;
  he knows that they are futile.

12 Blessed is the man you discipline,
    O Lord,
  the man you teach from your law;
13 you grant him relief from days of
    trouble,
  till a pit is dug for the wicked.
14 For the Lord will not reject his people;
  he will never forsake his inheritance.
15 Judgment will again be founded on
    righteousness,
  and all the upright in heart will
    follow it.

16 Who will rise up for me against the
    wicked?
  Who will take a stand for me against
    evildoers?
17 Unless the Lord had given me help,
  I would soon have dwelt in the
    silence of death.
18 When I said, "My foot is slipping,"
  your love, O Lord, supported me.
19 When anxiety was great within me,
  your consolation brought joy to my
    soul.

20 Can a corrupt throne be allied with
    you—
  one that brings on misery by its
    decrees?
21 They band together against the
    righteous

and condemn the innocent to death.
22 But the Lord has become my fortress,
  and my God the rock in whom I take
    refuge.
23 He will repay them for their sins
  and destroy them for their
    wickedness;
  the Lord our God will destroy them.

PSALM 95

1 Come, let us sing for joy to the Lord;
  let us shout aloud to the Rock of our
    salvation.
2 Let us come before him with
    thanksgiving
  and extol him with music and song.

3 For the Lord is the great God,
  the great King above all gods.
4 In his hand are the depths of the earth,
  and the mountain peaks belong to
    him.
5 The sea is his, for he made it,
  and his hands formed the dry land.

6 Come, let us bow down in worship,
  let us kneel before the Lord our
    Maker;
7 for he is our God
  and we are the people of his
    pasture,
  the flock under his care.

Today, if you hear his voice,
8 do not harden your hearts as you
      did at Meribah,[a]
    as you did that day at Massah[b] in
      the desert,
9 where your fathers tested and tried me,
  though they had seen what I did.
10 For forty years I was angry with that
    generation;
  I said, "They are a people whose
    hearts go astray,
  and they have not known my ways."
11 So I declared on oath in my anger,
  "They shall never enter my rest."

PSALM 96

1 Sing to the Lord a new song;
  sing to the Lord, all the earth.
2 Sing to the Lord, praise his name;
  proclaim his salvation day after day.
3 Declare his glory among the nations,
  his marvelous deeds among all
    peoples.

a 8 Meribah means *quarreling.*   *b 8 Massah* means *testing.*

⁴For great is the Lord and most worthy
    of praise;
  he is to be feared above all gods.
⁵For all the gods of the nations are
    idols,
  but the Lord made the heavens.
⁶Splendor and majesty are before him;
  strength and glory are in his
    sanctuary.

⁷Ascribe to the Lord, O families of
    nations,
  ascribe to the Lord glory and
    strength.
⁸Ascribe to the Lord the glory due his
    name;
  bring an offering and come into his
    courts.
⁹Worship the Lord in the splendor of
    his[a] holiness;
  tremble before him, all the earth.

¹⁰Say among the nations, "The Lord
    reigns."
  The world is firmly established, it
    cannot be moved;
  he will judge the peoples with equity.
¹¹Let the heavens rejoice, let the earth be
    glad;
  let the sea resound, and all that is in
    it;
¹²   let the fields be jubilant, and
    everything in them.
  Then all the trees of the forest will sing
    for joy;
¹³   they will sing before the Lord, for he
    comes,
  he comes to judge the earth.
  He will judge the world in righteousness
    and the peoples in his truth.

PSALM 97

¹The Lord reigns, let the earth be glad;
  let the distant shores rejoice.

²Clouds and thick darkness surround
    him;
  righteousness and justice are the
    foundation of his throne.
³Fire goes before him
  and consumes his foes on every side.
⁴His lightning lights up the world;
  the earth sees and trembles.
⁵The mountains melt like wax before
    the Lord,
  before the Lord of all the earth.
⁶The heavens proclaim his righteousness,
  and all the peoples see his glory.

⁷All who worship images are put to
    shame,
  those who boast in idols—
  worship him, all you gods!

⁸Zion hears and rejoices
  and the villages of Judah are glad
  because of your judgments, O Lord.
⁹For you, O Lord, are the Most High
    over all the earth;
  you are exalted far above all gods.

¹⁰Let those who love the Lord hate evil,
  for he guards the lives of his faithful
    ones
  and delivers them from the hand of
    the wicked.
¹¹Light is shed upon the righteous
  and joy on the upright in heart.
¹²Rejoice in the Lord, you who are
    righteous,
  and praise his holy name.

PSALM 98

A psalm.

¹Sing to the Lord a new song,
  for he has done marvelous things;
  his right hand and his holy arm
  have worked salvation for him.
²The Lord has made his salvation known
  and revealed his righteousness to
    the nations.
³He has remembered his love
  and his faithfulness to the house of
    Israel;
  all the ends of the earth have seen
  the salvation of our God.

⁴Shout for joy to the Lord, all the earth,
  burst into jubilant song with music;
⁵make music to the Lord with the harp,
  with the harp and the sound of
    singing,
⁶with trumpets and the blast of the
    ram's horn—
  shout for joy before the Lord, the
    King.

⁷Let the sea resound, and everything in it,
  the world, and all who live in it.
⁸Let the rivers clap their hands,
  let the mountains sing together for
    joy;
⁹let them sing before the Lord,
  for he comes to judge the earth.
  He will judge the world in righteousness
    and the peoples with equity.

ᵃ 9 Or Lord with the splendor of

PSALM 99

[1] The LORD reigns,
　　let the nations tremble;
he sits enthroned between the
　　cherubim,
　　let the earth shake.
[2] Great is the LORD in Zion;
　　he is exalted over all the nations.
[3] Let them praise your great and
　　awesome name—
　　he is holy.

[4] The King is mighty, he loves justice—
　　you have established equity;
in Jacob you have done
　　what is just and right.
[5] Exalt the LORD our God
　　and worship at his footstool;
　　he is holy.

[6] Moses and Aaron were among his
　　priests,
　　Samuel was among those who
　　called on his name;
they called on the LORD
　　and he answered them.
[7] He spoke to them from the pillar of
　　cloud;
　　they kept his statutes and the
　　decrees he gave them.

[8] O LORD our God,
　　you answered them;
you were to Israel[a] a forgiving God,
　　though you punished their misdeeds.[b]
[9] Exalt the LORD our God
　　and worship at his holy mountain,
　　for the LORD our God is holy.

PSALM 100

A psalm. For giving thanks.

[1] Shout for joy to the LORD, all the earth.
[2] 　Worship the LORD with gladness;
　　come before him with joyful songs.
[3] Know that the LORD is God.
　　It is he who made us, and we are
　　his[c];
we are his people, the sheep of his
　　pasture.

[4] Enter his gates with thanksgiving
　　and his courts with praise;
give thanks to him and praise his
　　name.
[5] For the LORD is good and his love
　　endures forever;
　　his faithfulness continues through all
　　generations.

PSALM 101

Of David. A psalm.

[1] I will sing of your love and justice;
　　to you, O LORD, I will sing praise.
[2] I will be careful to lead a blameless
　　life—
　　when will you come to me?

I will walk in my house
　　with blameless heart.
[3] I will set before my eyes
　　no vile thing.

The deeds of faithless men I hate;
　　they will not cling to me.
[4] Men of perverse heart shall be far from
　　me;
　　I will have nothing to do with evil.

[5] Whoever slanders his neighbor in secret,
　　him will I put to silence;
whoever has haughty eyes and a proud
　　heart,
　　him will I not endure.

[6] My eyes will be on the faithful in the
　　land,
　　that they may dwell with me;
he whose walk is blameless
　　will minister to me.

[7] No one who practices deceit
　　will dwell in my house;
no one who speaks falsely
　　will stand in my presence.

[8] Every morning I will put to silence
　　all the wicked in the land;
I will cut off every evildoer
　　from the city of the LORD.

PSALM 102

*A prayer of an afflicted man. When he is faint
and pours out his lament before the LORD.*

[1] Hear my prayer, O LORD;
　　let my cry for help come to you.
[2] Do not hide your face from me
　　when I am in distress.
Turn your ear to me;
　　when I call, answer me quickly.

[3] For my days vanish like smoke;
　　my bones burn like glowing embers.
[4] My heart is blighted and withered like
　　grass;
　　I forget to eat my food.
[5] Because of my loud groaning

---

[a] 8 Hebrew *them*　　[b] 8 Or / *an avenger of the wrongs done
to them*　　[c] 3 Or *and not we ourselves*

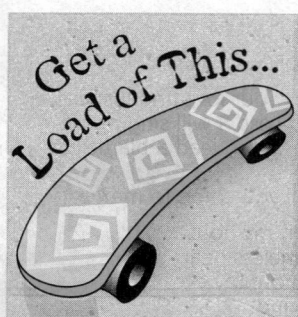

Get a Load of This...

How bad do you have to feel to describe yourself as a "desert owl" hanging out in the busted-up walls of an old, abandoned building (Psalm 102:6)? The guy who wrote this psalm didn't just feel like a *lonely* owl. He felt like an I-got-the-blues, living-in-the-duststorm, completely lonesome old bird.

I am reduced to skin and bones.
6 I am like a desert owl,
    like an owl among the ruins.
7 I lie awake; I have become
    like a bird alone on a roof.
8 All day long my enemies taunt me;
    those who rail against me use my name as a
        curse.
9 For I eat ashes as my food
    and mingle my drink with tears
10 because of your great wrath,
    for you have taken me up and thrown me aside.
11 My days are like the evening shadow;
    I wither away like grass.

12 But you, O LORD, sit enthroned forever;
    your renown endures through all generations.
13 You will arise and have compassion on Zion,
    for it is time to show favor to her;
    the appointed time has come.
14 For her stones are dear to your servants;
    her very dust moves them to pity.
15 The nations will fear the name of the LORD,
    all the kings of the earth will revere your glory.
16 For the LORD will rebuild Zion
    and appear in his glory.
17 He will respond to the prayer of the destitute;
    he will not despise their plea.

18 Let this be written for a future generation,
    that a people not yet created may praise the LORD:
19 "The LORD looked down from his sanctuary on high,
    from heaven he viewed the earth,
20 to hear the groans of the prisoners
    and release those condemned to death."
21 So the name of the LORD will be declared in Zion
    and his praise in Jerusalem
22 when the peoples and the kingdoms
    assemble to worship the LORD.

23 In the course of my life*a* he broke my strength;
    he cut short my days.
24 So I said:
    "Do not take me away, O my God, in the midst of
        my days;
    your years go on through all generations.
25 In the beginning you laid the foundations of the
        earth,
    and the heavens are the work of your hands.
26 They will perish, but you remain;
    they will all wear out like a garment.
  Like clothing you will change them
    and they will be discarded.
27 But you remain the same,
    and your years will never end.
28 The children of your servants will live in your presence;
    their descendants will be established before you."

---

a 23 Or By his power

PSALM 103

Of David.

1 Praise the LORD, O my soul;
    all my inmost being, praise his holy
        name.
2 Praise the LORD, O my soul,
    and forget not all his benefits—
3 who forgives all your sins
    and heals all your diseases,
4 who redeems your life from the pit
    and crowns you with love and
        compassion,
5 who satisfies your desires with good
        things
    so that your youth is renewed like
        the eagle's.

6 The LORD works righteousness
    and justice for all the oppressed.

7 He made known his ways to Moses,
    his deeds to the people of Israel:
8 The LORD is compassionate and
        gracious,
    slow to anger, abounding in love.
9 He will not always accuse,
    nor will he harbor his anger forever;

10 he does not treat us as our sins deserve
    or repay us according to our
        iniquities.
11 For as high as the heavens are above
        the earth,
    so great is his love for those who
        fear him;
12 as far as the east is from the west,
    so far has he removed our
        transgressions from us.
13 As a father has compassion on his
        children,
    so the LORD has compassion on
        those who fear him;
14 for he knows how we are formed,
    he remembers that we are dust.
15 As for man, his days are like grass,
    he flourishes like a flower of the field;
16 the wind blows over it and it is gone,
    and its place remembers it no more.
17 But from everlasting to everlasting
    the LORD's love is with those who
        fear him,
    and his righteousness with their
        children's children—
18 with those who keep his covenant
    and remember to obey his precepts.

Expect a Blessing

READ PSALM 103

Many people go through life not expecting a thing from God. They may not think God is against them, but they don't expect God to bless them either. You know what? These people are missing out. Big time. God *wants* you to expect a blessing, because he has promised to do you good. Psalm 103 says, God "satisfies your desires with good things" (verse 5). It also tells us not to forget all of God's benefits (verse 2). Here's an important formula to remember: 1) expect a blessing, 2) be thankful when it comes, and 3) don't forget it. God is a compassionate, loving Father. He wants to give you wonderful gifts, including peace of mind in this world and eternal life in the next. So be expectant, be thankful, and remember how good God has been to you.

Your next reading is on page 765.

¹⁹The LORD has established his throne in
  heaven,
  and his kingdom rules over all.

²⁰Praise the LORD, you his angels,
  you mighty ones who do his bidding,
  who obey his word.
²¹Praise the LORD, all his heavenly hosts,
  you his servants who do his will.
²²Praise the LORD, all his works
  everywhere in his dominion.

Praise the LORD, O my soul.

PSALM 104

¹Praise the LORD, O my soul.

O LORD my God, you are very great;
  you are clothed with splendor and
  majesty.
²He wraps himself in light as with a
  garment;
  he stretches out the heavens like a
  tent
³ and lays the beams of his upper
  chambers on their waters.
He makes the clouds his chariot
  and rides on the wings of the wind.
⁴He makes winds his messengers,ᵃ
  flames of fire his servants.

⁵He set the earth on its foundations;
  it can never be moved.
⁶You covered it with the deep as with a
  garment;
  the waters stood above the
  mountains.
⁷But at your rebuke the waters fled,
  at the sound of your thunder they
  took to flight;
⁸they flowed over the mountains,
  they went down into the valleys,
  to the place you assigned for them.
⁹You set a boundary they cannot cross;
  never again will they cover the earth.

¹⁰He makes springs pour water into the
  ravines;
  it flows between the mountains.
¹¹They give water to all the beasts of the
  field;
  the wild donkeys quench their thirst.
¹²The birds of the air nest by the waters;
  they sing among the branches.
¹³He waters the mountains from his
  upper chambers;
  the earth is satisfied by the fruit of
  his work.
¹⁴He makes grass grow for the cattle,

and plants for man to cultivate—
  bringing forth food from the earth:
¹⁵wine that gladdens the heart of man,
  oil to make his face shine,
  and bread that sustains his heart.
¹⁶The trees of the LORD are well watered,
  the cedars of Lebanon that he
  planted.
¹⁷There the birds make their nests;
  the stork has its home in the pine
  trees.
¹⁸The high mountains belong to the wild
  goats;
  the crags are a refuge for the coneys. ᵇ

¹⁹The moon marks off the seasons,
  and the sun knows when to go
  down.
²⁰You bring darkness, it becomes night,
  and all the beasts of the forest prowl.
²¹The lions roar for their prey
  and seek their food from God.
²²The sun rises, and they steal away;
  they return and lie down in their
  dens.
²³Then man goes out to his work,
  to his labor until evening.

²⁴How many are your works, O LORD!
  In wisdom you made them all;
  the earth is full of your creatures.
²⁵There is the sea, vast and spacious,
  teeming with creatures beyond
  number—
  living things both large and small.
²⁶There the ships go to and fro,
  and the leviathan, which you formed
  to frolic there.

²⁷These all look to you
  to give them their food at the
  proper time.
²⁸When you give it to them,
  they gather it up;
when you open your hand,
  they are satisfied with good things.
²⁹When you hide your face,
  they are terrified;
when you take away their breath,
  they die and return to the dust.
³⁰When you send your Spirit,
  they are created,
  and you renew the face of the earth.

³¹May the glory of the LORD endure
  forever;
  may the LORD rejoice in his works—

ᵃ4 Or angels   ᵇ18 That is, the hyrax or rock badger

32 he who looks at the earth, and it
	trembles,
	who touches the mountains, and
	they smoke.
33 I will sing to the Lord all my life;
	I will sing praise to my God as long
	as I live.
34 May my meditation be pleasing to him,
	as I rejoice in the Lord.
35 But may sinners vanish from the earth
	and the wicked be no more.

Praise the Lord, O my soul.

Praise the Lord. [a]

PSALM 105

1 Give thanks to the Lord, call on his
	name;
	make known among the nations
	what he has done.
2 Sing to him, sing praise to him;
	tell of all his wonderful acts.
3 Glory in his holy name;
	let the hearts of those who seek the
	Lord rejoice.
4 Look to the Lord and his strength;
	seek his face always.

5 Remember the wonders he has done,
	his miracles, and the judgments he
	pronounced,
6 O descendants of Abraham his servant,
	O sons of Jacob, his chosen ones.
7 He is the Lord our God;
	his judgments are in all the earth.

8 He remembers his covenant forever,
	the word he commanded, for a
	thousand generations,
9 the covenant he made with Abraham,
	the oath he swore to Isaac.
10 He confirmed it to Jacob as a decree,
	to Israel as an everlasting covenant:
11 "To you I will give the land of Canaan
	as the portion you will inherit."

12 When they were but few in number,
	few indeed, and strangers in it,
13 they wandered from nation to nation,
	from one kingdom to another.
14 He allowed no one to oppress them;
	for their sake he rebuked kings:
15 "Do not touch my anointed ones;
	do my prophets no harm."

16 He called down famine on the land
	and destroyed all their supplies of
	food;

17 and he sent a man before them—
	Joseph, sold as a slave.
18 They bruised his feet with shackles,
	his neck was put in irons,
19 till what he foretold came to pass,
	till the word of the Lord proved him
	true.
20 The king sent and released him,
	the ruler of peoples set him free.
21 He made him master of his household,
	ruler over all he possessed,
22 to instruct his princes as he pleased
	and teach his elders wisdom.

23 Then Israel entered Egypt;
	Jacob lived as an alien in the land of
	Ham.
24 The Lord made his people very fruitful;
	he made them too numerous for
	their foes,
25 whose hearts he turned to hate his
	people,
	to conspire against his servants.
26 He sent Moses his servant,
	and Aaron, whom he had chosen.
27 They performed his miraculous signs
	among them,
	his wonders in the land of Ham.
28 He sent darkness and made the land
	dark—
	for had they not rebelled against his
	words?
29 He turned their waters into blood,
	causing their fish to die.
30 Their land teemed with frogs,
	which went up into the bedrooms of
	their rulers.
31 He spoke, and there came swarms of
	flies,
	and gnats throughout their country.
32 He turned their rain into hail,
	with lightning throughout their
	land;
33 he struck down their vines and fig
	trees
	and shattered the trees of their
	country.
34 He spoke, and the locusts came,
	grasshoppers without number;
35 they ate up every green thing in their
	land,
	ate up the produce of their soil.
36 Then he struck down all the firstborn
	in their land,
	the firstfruits of all their manhood.

a 35 Hebrew Hallelu Yah; in the Septuagint this line stands at
the beginning of Psalm 105.

37 He brought out Israel, laden with silver
 and gold,
  and from among their tribes no one
   faltered.
38 Egypt was glad when they left,
  because dread of Israel had fallen on
   them.
39 He spread out a cloud as a covering,
  and a fire to give light at night.
40 They asked, and he brought them quail
  and satisfied them with the bread of
   heaven.
41 He opened the rock, and water gushed
   out;
  like a river it flowed in the desert.

42 For he remembered his holy promise
  given to his servant Abraham.
43 He brought out his people with
   rejoicing,
  his chosen ones with shouts of joy;
44 he gave them the lands of the nations,
  and they fell heir to what others had
   toiled for—
45 that they might keep his precepts
  and observe his laws.

Praise the LORD. *a*

PSALM 106

1 Praise the LORD. *b*

Give thanks to the LORD, for he is good;
 his love endures forever.
2 Who can proclaim the mighty acts of
  the LORD
 or fully declare his praise?
3 Blessed are they who maintain justice,
 who constantly do what is right.
4 Remember me, O LORD, when you
  show favor to your people,
 come to my aid when you save
  them,
5 that I may enjoy the prosperity of your
  chosen ones,
 that I may share in the joy of your
  nation
 and join your inheritance in giving
  praise.

6 We have sinned, even as our fathers
  did;
 we have done wrong and acted
  wickedly.
7 When our fathers were in Egypt,
 they gave no thought to your
  miracles;
 they did not remember your many
  kindnesses,

and they rebelled by the sea, the
 Red Sea. *c*
8 Yet he saved them for his name's sake,
 to make his mighty power known.
9 He rebuked the Red Sea, and it dried up;
 he led them through the depths as
  through a desert.
10 He saved them from the hand of the
  foe;
 from the hand of the enemy he
  redeemed them.
11 The waters covered their adversaries;
 not one of them survived.
12 Then they believed his promises
 and sang his praise.

13 But they soon forgot what he had done
 and did not wait for his counsel.
14 In the desert they gave in to their
  craving;
 in the wasteland they put God to
  the test.
15 So he gave them what they asked for,
 but sent a wasting disease upon
  them.

16 In the camp they grew envious of
  Moses
 and of Aaron, who was consecrated
  to the LORD.
17 The earth opened up and swallowed
  Dathan;
 it buried the company of Abiram.
18 Fire blazed among their followers;
 a flame consumed the wicked.

19 At Horeb they made a calf
 and worshiped an idol cast from
  metal.
20 They exchanged their Glory
 for an image of a bull, which eats
  grass.
21 They forgot the God who saved them,
 who had done great things in Egypt,
22 miracles in the land of Ham
 and awesome deeds by the Red Sea.
23 So he said he would destroy them—
 had not Moses, his chosen one,
 stood in the breach before him
  to keep his wrath from destroying
   them.

24 Then they despised the pleasant land;
 they did not believe his promise.
25 They grumbled in their tents
 and did not obey the LORD.

a 45 Hebrew *Hallelu Yah*   *b 1* Hebrew *Hallelu Yah*; also in
verse 48   *c 7* Hebrew *Yam Suph*; that is, Sea of Reeds; also
in verses 9 and 22

26 So he swore to them with uplifted hand
    that he would make them fall in the
        desert,
27 make their descendants fall among the
        nations
    and scatter them throughout the
        lands.

28 They yoked themselves to the Baal of
        Peor
    and ate sacrifices offered to lifeless
        gods;
29 they provoked the LORD to anger by
        their wicked deeds,
    and a plague broke out among them.
30 But Phinehas stood up and intervened,
    and the plague was checked.
31 This was credited to him as
        righteousness
    for endless generations to come.

32 By the waters of Meribah they angered
        the LORD,
    and trouble came to Moses because
        of them;

33 for they rebelled against the Spirit of
        God,
    and rash words came from Moses'
        lips. a

34 They did not destroy the peoples
    as the LORD had commanded them,
35 but they mingled with the nations
    and adopted their customs.
36 They worshiped their idols,
    which became a snare to them.
37 They sacrificed their sons
    and their daughters to demons.
38 They shed innocent blood,
    the blood of their sons and daughters,
    whom they sacrificed to the idols of
        Canaan,
    and the land was desecrated by their
        blood.
39 They defiled themselves by what they
        did;
    by their deeds they prostituted
        themselves.

a 33 Or *against his spirit, / and rash words came from his lips*

Make It Stick

READ PSALM 106:32–33

Psalm 106:32–33 recalls a story when Moses messed up and spoke "rash words" (see also
Numbers 20:7–13). Men of God control their anger in different ways. Some count to ten.
Others follow this rule: Stop, think, and *then* act. Write these words (or words similar to them)
on a sticky note as a reminder to keep your cool.

40 Therefore the LORD was angry with his
     people
     and abhorred his inheritance.
41 He handed them over to the nations,
     and their foes ruled over them.
42 Their enemies oppressed them
     and subjected them to their power.
43 Many times he delivered them,
     but they were bent on rebellion
     and they wasted away in their sin.

44 But he took note of their distress
     when he heard their cry;
45 for their sake he remembered his
     covenant
     and out of his great love he
     relented.
46 He caused them to be pitied
     by all who held them captive.

47 Save us, O LORD our God,
     and gather us from the nations,
     that we may give thanks to your holy
     name
     and glory in your praise.

48 Praise be to the LORD, the God of Israel,
     from everlasting to everlasting.
     Let all the people say, "Amen!"

     Praise the LORD.

BOOK V

Psalms 107–150

PSALM 107

1 Give thanks to the LORD, for he is good;
     his love endures forever.
2 Let the redeemed of the LORD say this—
     those he redeemed from the hand
     of the foe,
3 those he gathered from the lands,
     from east and west, from north and
     south. *a*

4 Some wandered in desert wastelands,
     finding no way to a city where they
     could settle.
5 They were hungry and thirsty,
     and their lives ebbed away.
6 Then they cried out to the LORD in their
     trouble,
     and he delivered them from their
     distress.
7 He led them by a straight way
     to a city where they could settle.
8 Let them give thanks to the LORD for
     his unfailing love
     and his wonderful deeds for men,

9 for he satisfies the thirsty
     and fills the hungry with good things.

10 Some sat in darkness and the deepest
     gloom,
     prisoners suffering in iron chains,
11 for they had rebelled against the words
     of God
     and despised the counsel of the
     Most High.
12 So he subjected them to bitter labor;
     they stumbled, and there was no
     one to help.
13 Then they cried to the LORD in their
     trouble,
     and he saved them from their
     distress.
14 He brought them out of darkness and
     the deepest gloom
     and broke away their chains.
15 Let them give thanks to the LORD for
     his unfailing love
     and his wonderful deeds for men,
16 for he breaks down gates of bronze
     and cuts through bars of iron.

17 Some became fools through their
     rebellious ways
     and suffered affliction because of
     their iniquities.
18 They loathed all food
     and drew near the gates of death.
19 Then they cried to the LORD in their
     trouble,
     and he saved them from their
     distress.
20 He sent forth his word and healed
     them;
     he rescued them from the grave.
21 Let them give thanks to the LORD for
     his unfailing love
     and his wonderful deeds for men.
22 Let them sacrifice thank offerings
     and tell of his works with songs of
     joy.

23 Others went out on the sea in ships;
     they were merchants on the mighty
     waters.
24 They saw the works of the LORD,
     his wonderful deeds in the deep.
25 For he spoke and stirred up a tempest
     that lifted high the waves.
26 They mounted up to the heavens and
     went down to the depths;
     in their peril their courage melted
     away.

a 3 Hebrew *north and the sea*

27 They reeled and staggered like drunken
    men;
    they were at their wits' end.
28 Then they cried out to the LORD in their
    trouble,
    and he brought them out of their
    distress.
29 He stilled the storm to a whisper;
    the waves of the sea were hushed.
30 They were glad when it grew calm,
    and he guided them to their desired
    haven.
31 Let them give thanks to the LORD for
    his unfailing love
    and his wonderful deeds for men.
32 Let them exalt him in the assembly of
    the people
    and praise him in the council of the
    elders.

33 He turned rivers into a desert,
    flowing springs into thirsty ground,
34 and fruitful land into a salt waste,
    because of the wickedness of those
    who lived there.
35 He turned the desert into pools of
    water
    and the parched ground into
    flowing springs;
36 there he brought the hungry to live,
    and they founded a city where they
    could settle.
37 They sowed fields and planted
    vineyards
    that yielded a fruitful harvest;
38 he blessed them, and their numbers
    greatly increased,
    and he did not let their herds
    diminish.

39 Then their numbers decreased, and
    they were humbled
    by oppression, calamity and
    sorrow;
40 he who pours contempt on nobles
    made them wander in a trackless
    waste.
41 But he lifted the needy out of their
    affliction
    and increased their families like
    flocks.
42 The upright see and rejoice,
    but all the wicked shut their mouths.

43 Whoever is wise, let him heed these
    things
    and consider the great love of the
    LORD.

PSALM 108

A song. A psalm of David.

1 My heart is steadfast, O God;
    I will sing and make music with all
    my soul.
2 Awake, harp and lyre!
    I will awaken the dawn.
3 I will praise you, O LORD, among the
    nations;
    I will sing of you among the peoples.
4 For great is your love, higher than the
    heavens;
    your faithfulness reaches to the skies.
5 Be exalted, O God, above the heavens,
    and let your glory be over all the
    earth.

6 Save us and help us with your right
    hand,
    that those you love may be delivered.
7 God has spoken from his sanctuary:
    "In triumph I will parcel out Shechem
    and measure off the Valley of
    Succoth.
8 Gilead is mine, Manasseh is mine;
    Ephraim is my helmet,
    Judah my scepter.
9 Moab is my washbasin,
    upon Edom I toss my sandal;
    over Philistia I shout in triumph."
10 Who will bring me to the fortified city?
    Who will lead me to Edom?
11 Is it not you, O God, you who have
    rejected us
    and no longer go out with our
    armies?
12 Give us aid against the enemy,
    for the help of man is worthless.
13 With God we will gain the victory,
    and he will trample down our
    enemies.

PSALM 109

For the director of music. Of David. A psalm.

1 O God, whom I praise,
    do not remain silent,
2 for wicked and deceitful men
    have opened their mouths against
    me;
    they have spoken against me with
    lying tongues.
3 With words of hatred they surround me;
    they attack me without cause.
4 In return for my friendship they accuse
    me,

but I am a man of prayer.
⁵They repay me evil for good,
    and hatred for my friendship.

⁶Appoint*a* an evil man*b* to oppose him;
    let an accuser*c* stand at his right
        hand.
⁷When he is tried, let him be found
        guilty,
    and may his prayers condemn him.
⁸May his days be few;
    may another take his place of
        leadership.
⁹May his children be fatherless
    and his wife a widow.
¹⁰May his children be wandering beggars;
    may they be driven*d* from their
        ruined homes.
¹¹May a creditor seize all he has;
    may strangers plunder the fruits of
        his labor.
¹²May no one extend kindness to him
    or take pity on his fatherless
        children.
¹³May his descendants be cut off,
    their names blotted out from the
        next generation.
¹⁴May the iniquity of his fathers be
        remembered before the LORD;
    may the sin of his mother never be
        blotted out.
¹⁵May their sins always remain before
        the LORD,
    that he may cut off the memory of
        them from the earth.

¹⁶For he never thought of doing a
        kindness,
    but hounded to death the poor
    and the needy and the
        brokenhearted.
¹⁷He loved to pronounce a curse—
    may it*e* come on him;
    he found no pleasure in blessing—
    may it be*f* far from him.
¹⁸He wore cursing as his garment;
    it entered into his body like water,
        into his bones like oil.
¹⁹May it be like a cloak wrapped about
        him,
    like a belt tied forever around him.
²⁰May this be the LORD's payment to my
        accusers,
    to those who speak evil of me.

²¹But you, O Sovereign LORD,
    deal well with me for your name's
        sake;

out of the goodness of your love,
    deliver me.
²²For I am poor and needy,
    and my heart is wounded within me.
²³I fade away like an evening shadow;
    I am shaken off like a locust.
²⁴My knees give way from fasting;
    my body is thin and gaunt.
²⁵I am an object of scorn to my accusers;
    when they see me, they shake their
        heads.

²⁶Help me, O LORD my God;
    save me in accordance with your love.
²⁷Let them know that it is your hand,
    that you, O LORD, have done it.
²⁸They may curse, but you will bless;
    when they attack they will be put to
        shame,
    but your servant will rejoice.
²⁹My accusers will be clothed with
        disgrace
    and wrapped in shame as in a cloak.

³⁰With my mouth I will greatly extol the
        LORD;
    in the great throng I will praise him.
³¹For he stands at the right hand of the
        needy one,
    to save his life from those who
        condemn him.

PSALM 110

Of David. A psalm.

¹The LORD says to my Lord:
    "Sit at my right hand
until I make your enemies
    a footstool for your feet."

²The LORD will extend your mighty
        scepter from Zion;
    you will rule in the midst of your
        enemies.
³Your troops will be willing
    on your day of battle.
Arrayed in holy majesty,
    from the womb of the dawn
    you will receive the dew of your
        youth.*g*

⁴The LORD has sworn
    and will not change his mind:
"You are a priest forever,
    in the order of Melchizedek."

a 6 Or *They say:* "*Appoint* (with quotation marks at the end
of verse 19)   *b 6* Or *the Evil One*   *c 6* Or *let Satan*
d 10 Septuagint; Hebrew *sought*   *e 17* Or *curse, / and it
has*   *f 17* Or *blessing, / and it is*   *g 3* Or / *your young
men will come to you like the dew*

5 The Lord is at your right hand;
    he will crush kings on the day of his
        wrath.
6 He will judge the nations, heaping up
        the dead
    and crushing the rulers of the whole
        earth.
7 He will drink from a brook beside the
        way *a*;
    therefore he will lift up his head.

PSALM 111 *b*

1 Praise the LORD. *c*

I will extol the LORD with all my heart
    in the council of the upright and in
        the assembly.

2 Great are the works of the LORD;
    they are pondered by all who delight
        in them.
3 Glorious and majestic are his deeds,
    and his righteousness endures forever.
4 He has caused his wonders to be
        remembered;
    the LORD is gracious and
        compassionate.
5 He provides food for those who fear
        him;
    he remembers his covenant forever.
6 He has shown his people the power of
        his works,
    giving them the lands of other
        nations.
7 The works of his hands are faithful and
        just;
    all his precepts are trustworthy.
8 They are steadfast for ever and ever,
    done in faithfulness and uprightness.
9 He provided redemption for his people;
    he ordained his covenant forever—
    holy and awesome is his name.

10 The fear of the LORD is the beginning of
        wisdom;
    all who follow his precepts have
        good understanding.
    To him belongs eternal praise.

PSALM 112 *b*

1 Praise the LORD. *c*

Blessed is the man who fears the LORD,
    who finds great delight in his
        commands.

2 His children will be mighty in the land;
    the generation of the upright will be
        blessed.

3 Wealth and riches are in his house,
    and his righteousness endures
        forever.
4 Even in darkness light dawns for the
        upright,
    for the gracious and compassionate
        and righteous man. *d*
5 Good will come to him who is
        generous and lends freely,
    who conducts his affairs with justice.
6 Surely he will never be shaken;
    a righteous man will be remembered
        forever.
7 He will have no fear of bad news;
    his heart is steadfast, trusting in the
        LORD.
8 His heart is secure, he will have no
        fear;
    in the end he will look in triumph on
        his foes.
9 He has scattered abroad his gifts to the
        poor,
    his righteousness endures forever;
    his horn *e* will be lifted high in honor.

10 The wicked man will see and be vexed,
    he will gnash his teeth and waste
        away;
    the longings of the wicked will come
        to nothing.

PSALM 113

1 Praise the LORD. *f*

Praise, O servants of the LORD,
    praise the name of the LORD.
2 Let the name of the LORD be praised,
    both now and forevermore.
3 From the rising of the sun to the place
        where it sets,
    the name of the LORD is to be
        praised.

4 The LORD is exalted over all the nations,
    his glory above the heavens.
5 Who is like the LORD our God,
    the One who sits enthroned on
        high,
6 who stoops down to look
    on the heavens and the earth?

7 He raises the poor from the dust
    and lifts the needy from the ash heap;

a 7 Or / The One who grants succession will set him in authority   b This psalm is an acrostic poem, the lines of which begin with the successive letters of the Hebrew alphabet.   c 1 Hebrew Hallelu Yah   d 4 Or / for the LORD, is gracious and compassionate and righteous   e 9 Horn here symbolizes dignity.   f 1 Hebrew Hallelu Yah; also in verse 9

8he seats them with princes,
with the princes of their people.
9He settles the barren woman in her
home
as a happy mother of children.

Praise the LORD.

PSALM 114

1When Israel came out of Egypt,
the house of Jacob from a people of
foreign tongue,
2Judah became God's sanctuary,
Israel his dominion.

3The sea looked and fled,
the Jordan turned back;
4the mountains skipped like rams,
the hills like lambs.

5Why was it, O sea, that you fled,
O Jordan, that you turned back,
6you mountains, that you skipped like
rams,
you hills, like lambs?

7Tremble, O earth, at the presence of
the Lord,
at the presence of the God of Jacob,
8who turned the rock into a pool,
the hard rock into springs of water.

PSALM 115

1Not to us, O LORD, not to us
but to your name be the glory,
because of your love and faithfulness.

2Why do the nations say,
"Where is their God?"
3Our God is in heaven;
he does whatever pleases him.
4But their idols are silver and gold,
made by the hands of men.
5They have mouths, but cannot speak,
eyes, but they cannot see;
6they have ears, but cannot hear,
noses, but they cannot smell;
7they have hands, but cannot feel,
feet, but they cannot walk;
nor can they utter a sound with their
throats.
8Those who make them will be like them,
and so will all who trust in them.

9O house of Israel, trust in the LORD—
he is their help and shield.
10O house of Aaron, trust in the LORD—
he is their help and shield.
11You who fear him, trust in the LORD—
he is their help and shield.

12The LORD remembers us and will bless us:
He will bless the house of Israel,
he will bless the house of Aaron,
13he will bless those who fear the LORD—
small and great alike.

14May the LORD make you increase,
both you and your children.
15May you be blessed by the LORD,
the Maker of heaven and earth.

16The highest heavens belong to the LORD,
but the earth he has given to man.
17It is not the dead who praise the LORD,
those who go down to silence;
18it is we who extol the LORD,
both now and forevermore.

Praise the LORD. *a*

PSALM 116

1I love the LORD, for he heard my voice;
he heard my cry for mercy.
2Because he turned his ear to me,
I will call on him as long as I live.

3The cords of death entangled me,
the anguish of the grave*b* came
upon me;
I was overcome by trouble and
sorrow.
4Then I called on the name of the LORD:
"O LORD, save me!"

5The LORD is gracious and righteous;
our God is full of compassion.
6The LORD protects the simplehearted;
when I was in great need, he saved
me.

7Be at rest once more, O my soul,
for the LORD has been good to you.

8For you, O LORD, have delivered my soul
from death,
my eyes from tears,
my feet from stumbling,
9that I may walk before the LORD
in the land of the living.
10I believed; therefore*c* I said,
"I am greatly afflicted."
11And in my dismay I said,
"All men are liars."

12How can I repay the LORD
for all his goodness to me?
13I will lift up the cup of salvation
and call on the name of the LORD.

a 18 Hebrew *Hallelu Yah*   *b 3* Hebrew *Sheol*
c 10 Or *believed even when*

14 I will fulfill my vows to the LORD
    in the presence of all his people.

15 Precious in the sight of the LORD
    is the death of his saints.
16 O LORD, truly I am your servant;
    I am your servant, the son of your
        maidservant[a];
    you have freed me from my chains.

17 I will sacrifice a thank offering to you
    and call on the name of the LORD.
18 I will fulfill my vows to the LORD
    in the presence of all his people,
19 in the courts of the house of the LORD—
    in your midst, O Jerusalem.

    Praise the LORD.[b]

PSALM 117

1 Praise the LORD, all you nations;
    extol him, all you peoples.
2 For great is his love toward us,
    and the faithfulness of the LORD
        endures forever.

    Praise the LORD.[b]

PSALM 118

1 Give thanks to the LORD, for he is good;
    his love endures forever.

2 Let Israel say:
    "His love endures forever."
3 Let the house of Aaron say:
    "His love endures forever."
4 Let those who fear the LORD say:
    "His love endures forever."

5 In my anguish I cried to the LORD,
    and he answered by setting me free.
6 The LORD is with me; I will not be afraid.
    What can man do to me?
7 The LORD is with me; he is my helper.
    I will look in triumph on my
        enemies.

8 It is better to take refuge in the LORD
    than to trust in man.
9 It is better to take refuge in the LORD
    than to trust in princes.

10 All the nations surrounded me,
    but in the name of the LORD I cut
        them off.
11 They surrounded me on every side,
    but in the name of the LORD I cut
        them off.
12 They swarmed around me like bees,
    but they died out as quickly as
        burning thorns;

in the name of the LORD I cut them
    off.
13 I was pushed back and about to fall,
    but the LORD helped me.
14 The LORD is my strength and my song;
    he has become my salvation.

15 Shouts of joy and victory
    resound in the tents of the righteous:
    "The LORD's right hand has done
        mighty things!
16   The LORD's right hand is lifted high;
    the LORD's right hand has done
        mighty things!"

17 I will not die but live,
    and will proclaim what the LORD has
        done.
18 The LORD has chastened me severely,
    but he has not given me over to
        death.

19 Open for me the gates of
        righteousness;
    I will enter and give thanks to the
        LORD.
20 This is the gate of the LORD
    through which the righteous may
        enter.
21 I will give you thanks, for you
        answered me;
    you have become my salvation.

22 The stone the builders rejected
    has become the capstone;
23 the LORD has done this,
    and it is marvelous in our eyes.
24 This is the day the LORD has made;
    let us rejoice and be glad in it.

25 O LORD, save us;
    O LORD, grant us success.
26 Blessed is he who comes in the name
        of the LORD.
    From the house of the LORD we bless
        you.[c]
27 The LORD is God,
    and he has made his light shine
        upon us.
    With boughs in hand, join in the festal
        procession
    up[d] to the horns of the altar.

28 You are my God, and I will give you
        thanks;
    you are my God, and I will exalt you.

---

a 16 Or *servant, your faithful son*   *b 19,2* Hebrew *Hallelu
Yah*   *c 26* The Hebrew is plural.   *d 27* Or *Bind the festal
sacrifice with ropes / and take it*

29 Give thanks to the LORD, for he is good;
　his love endures forever.

PSALM 119 a

א Aleph

1 Blessed are they whose ways are
　blameless,
　who walk according to the law of
　the LORD.
2 Blessed are they who keep his statutes
　and seek him with all their heart.
3 They do nothing wrong;
　they walk in his ways.
4 You have laid down precepts
　that are to be fully obeyed.
5 Oh, that my ways were steadfast
　in obeying your decrees!
6 Then I would not be put to shame
　when I consider all your commands.
7 I will praise you with an upright heart
　as I learn your righteous laws.
8 I will obey your decrees;
　do not utterly forsake me.

ב Beth

9 How can a young man keep his way
　pure?
　By living according to your word.
10 I seek you with all my heart;
　do not let me stray from your
　commands.
11 I have hidden your word in my heart
　that I might not sin against you.
12 Praise be to you, O LORD;
　teach me your decrees.
13 With my lips I recount
　all the laws that come from your
　mouth.
14 I rejoice in following your statutes
　as one rejoices in great riches.
15 I meditate on your precepts
　and consider your ways.
16 I delight in your decrees;
　I will not neglect your word.

ג Gimel

17 Do good to your servant, and I will
　live;
　I will obey your word.
18 Open my eyes that I may see
　wonderful things in your law.
19 I am a stranger on earth;
　do not hide your commands from
　me.
20 My soul is consumed with longing
　for your laws at all times.

21 You rebuke the arrogant, who are
　cursed
　and who stray from your
　commands.
22 Remove from me scorn and contempt,
　for I keep your statutes.
23 Though rulers sit together and slander
　me,
　your servant will meditate on your
　decrees.
24 Your statutes are my delight;
　they are my counselors.

ד Daleth

25 I am laid low in the dust;
　preserve my life according to your
　word.
26 I recounted my ways and you
　answered me;
　teach me your decrees.
27 Let me understand the teaching of
　your precepts;
　then I will meditate on your
　wonders.
28 My soul is weary with sorrow;
　strengthen me according to your
　word.
29 Keep me from deceitful ways;
　be gracious to me through your law.
30 I have chosen the way of truth;
　I have set my heart on your laws.
31 I hold fast to your statutes, O LORD;
　do not let me be put to shame.
32 I run in the path of your commands,
　for you have set my heart free.

ה He

33 Teach me, O LORD, to follow your
　decrees;
　then I will keep them to the end.
34 Give me understanding, and I will keep
　your law
　and obey it with all my heart.
35 Direct me in the path of your
　commands,
　for there I find delight.
36 Turn my heart toward your statutes
　and not toward selfish gain.
37 Turn my eyes away from worthless
　things;
　preserve my life according to your
　word. b

---

a This psalm is an acrostic poem; the verses of each stanza
begin with the same letter of the Hebrew alphabet.
b 37 Two manuscripts of the Masoretic Text and Dead Sea
Scrolls; most manuscripts of the Masoretic Text life in your
way

38 Fulfill your promise to your servant,
   so that you may be feared.
39 Take away the disgrace I dread,
   for your laws are good.
40 How I long for your precepts!
   Preserve my life in your
      righteousness.

ו Waw

41 May your unfailing love come to me,
      O LORD,
   your salvation according to your
      promise;
42 then I will answer the one who taunts
      me,
   for I trust in your word.
43 Do not snatch the word of truth from
      my mouth,
   for I have put my hope in your laws.
44 I will always obey your law,
   for ever and ever.
45 I will walk about in freedom,
   for I have sought out your precepts.
46 I will speak of your statutes before
      kings
   and will not be put to shame,
47 for I delight in your commands

because I love them.
48 I lift up my hands to*a* your commands,
      which I love,
   and I meditate on your decrees.

ז Zayin

49 Remember your word to your servant,
   for you have given me hope.
50 My comfort in my suffering is this:
   Your promise preserves my life.
51 The arrogant mock me without
      restraint,
   but I do not turn from your law.
52 I remember your ancient laws, O LORD,
   and I find comfort in them.
53 Indignation grips me because of the
      wicked,
   who have forsaken your law.
54 Your decrees are the theme of my song
   wherever I lodge.
55 In the night I remember your name,
      O LORD,
   and I will keep your law.
56 This has been my practice:
   I obey your precepts.

a 48 Or *for*

100% Pure

READ PSALM 119:1–16

Keeping pure in today's world can be a tough job, especially for a
man. It seems like temptations are everywhere: billboards, magazines,
TV, you name it. And it's only getting worse. But there is a way out.
"How can a young man keep his way pure? By living according to
your word" (verse 9). Here's how it works: (1) *Decide* to live
according to God's Word. (Make your mind up to please him.)
(2) *Fill* yourself with God's Word. "I have hidden your word in
my heart that I might not sin against you" (verse 11). (3)
Seek God in prayer each day and allow him to live and work
in your life. As you rely on God, he will help you live the
way you're supposed to. So if you want to be pure,
follow these three simple steps. You may still
stumble, but God will pick you up, dust you off
and set you back on your way.

Your next reading is on page 767.

ח Heth

57 You are my portion, O LORD;
  I have promised to obey your words.
58 I have sought your face with all my
    heart;
  be gracious to me according to your
    promise.
59 I have considered my ways
  and have turned my steps to your
    statutes.
60 I will hasten and not delay
  to obey your commands.
61 Though the wicked bind me with ropes,
  I will not forget your law.
62 At midnight I rise to give you thanks
  for your righteous laws.
63 I am a friend to all who fear you,
  to all who follow your precepts.
64 The earth is filled with your love,
    O LORD;
  teach me your decrees.

ט Teth

65 Do good to your servant
  according to your word, O LORD.
66 Teach me knowledge and good
    judgment,
  for I believe in your commands.
67 Before I was afflicted I went astray,
  but now I obey your word.
68 You are good, and what you do is good;
  teach me your decrees.
69 Though the arrogant have smeared me
    with lies,
  I keep your precepts with all my
    heart.
70 Their hearts are callous and unfeeling,
  but I delight in your law.
71 It was good for me to be afflicted
  so that I might learn your decrees.
72 The law from your mouth is more
    precious to me
  than thousands of pieces of silver
    and gold.

י Yodh

73 Your hands made me and formed me;
  give me understanding to learn your
    commands.
74 May those who fear you rejoice when
    they see me,
  for I have put my hope in your word.
75 I know, O LORD, that your laws are
    righteous,
  and in faithfulness you have afflicted
    me.

76 May your unfailing love be my comfort,
  according to your promise to your
    servant.
77 Let your compassion come to me that I
    may live,
  for your law is my delight.
78 May the arrogant be put to shame for
    wronging me without cause;
  but I will meditate on your precepts.
79 May those who fear you turn to me,
  those who understand your statutes.
80 May my heart be blameless toward
    your decrees,
  that I may not be put to shame.

כ Kaph

81 My soul faints with longing for your
    salvation,
  but I have put my hope in your word.
82 My eyes fail, looking for your promise;
  I say, "When will you comfort me?"
83 Though I am like a wineskin in the
    smoke,
  I do not forget your decrees.
84 How long must your servant wait?
  When will you punish my
    persecutors?
85 The arrogant dig pitfalls for me,
  contrary to your law.
86 All your commands are trustworthy;
  help me, for men persecute me
    without cause.
87 They almost wiped me from the earth,
  but I have not forsaken your
    precepts.
88 Preserve my life according to your love,
  and I will obey the statutes of your
    mouth.

ל Lamedh

89 Your word, O LORD, is eternal;
  it stands firm in the heavens.
90 Your faithfulness continues through all
    generations;
  you established the earth, and it
    endures.
91 Your laws endure to this day,
  for all things serve you.
92 If your law had not been my delight,
  I would have perished in my
    affliction.
93 I will never forget your precepts,
  for by them you have preserved my
    life.
94 Save me, for I am yours;
  I have sought out your precepts.

95 The wicked are waiting to destroy me,
  but I will ponder your statutes.
96 To all perfection I see a limit;
  but your commands are boundless.

מ Mem

97 Oh, how I love your law!
  I meditate on it all day long.
98 Your commands make me wiser than
    my enemies,
  for they are ever with me.
99 I have more insight than all my
    teachers,
  for I meditate on your statutes.
100 I have more understanding than the
    elders,
  for I obey your precepts.
101 I have kept my feet from every evil path
  so that I might obey your word.
102 I have not departed from your laws,
  for you yourself have taught me.
103 How sweet are your words to my taste,
  sweeter than honey to my mouth!
104 I gain understanding from your
    precepts;
  therefore I hate every wrong path.

נ Nun

105 Your word is a lamp to my feet
  and a light for my path.
106 I have taken an oath and confirmed it,
  that I will follow your righteous laws.
107 I have suffered much;
  preserve my life, O Lord, according
    to your word.
108 Accept, O Lord, the willing praise of
    my mouth,
  and teach me your laws.
109 Though I constantly take my life in my
    hands,
  I will not forget your law.
110 The wicked have set a snare for me,
  but I have not strayed from your
    precepts.
111 Your statutes are my heritage forever;
  they are the joy of my heart.
112 My heart is set on keeping your decrees
  to the very end.

ס Samekh

113 I hate double-minded men,
  but I love your law.
114 You are my refuge and my shield;

Strike It Rich!

READ PSALM 119:89–104, 127

In the late 1800s, people raced out West in the great "Gold Rush." Gold had been discovered, and everyone hoped to strike it rich. God's Word is like a river full of gold nuggets. It contains the most valuable insights and principles in the world—more valuable than all of the knowledge and information in all the libraries on earth. Many people, such as professors and scientists, have great knowledge, but they don't believe the Bible and don't understand what life is *really* about. Mind you, education and learning is not bad. But the foundation of all knowledge has to be God. Without him, nothing else matters or makes sense. You can have four Ph.D.'s, but if you don't know God, you're like a prospector walking right past the Mother Lode. So why not join the gold rush and dig into God's Word? You're guaranteed to strike it rich!

Your next reading is on page 772.

I have put my hope in your word.

115Away from me, you evildoers,
  that I may keep the commands of
    my God!
116Sustain me according to your promise,
    and I will live;
  do not let my hopes be dashed.
117Uphold me, and I will be delivered;
  I will always have regard for your
    decrees.
118You reject all who stray from your
    decrees,
  for their deceitfulness is in vain.
119All the wicked of the earth you discard
    like dross;
  therefore I love your statutes.
120My flesh trembles in fear of you;
  I stand in awe of your laws.

ע Ayin

121I have done what is righteous and just;
  do not leave me to my oppressors.
122Ensure your servant's well-being;
  let not the arrogant oppress me.
123My eyes fail, looking for your salvation,
  looking for your righteous promise.
124Deal with your servant according to
    your love
  and teach me your decrees.
125I am your servant; give me discernment
  that I may understand your statutes.
126It is time for you to act, O Lord;
  your law is being broken.
127Because I love your commands
    more than gold, more than pure
      gold,
128and because I consider all your
    precepts right,
  I hate every wrong path.

פ Pe

129Your statutes are wonderful;
  therefore I obey them.
130The unfolding of your words gives
    light;
  it gives understanding to the simple.
131I open my mouth and pant,
  longing for your commands.
132Turn to me and have mercy on me,
  as you always do to those who love
    your name.
133Direct my footsteps according to your
    word;
  let no sin rule over me.
134Redeem me from the oppression of
    men,
  that I may obey your precepts.

135Make your face shine upon your
    servant
  and teach me your decrees.
136Streams of tears flow from my eyes,
  for your law is not obeyed.

צ Tsadhe

137Righteous are you, O Lord,
  and your laws are right.
138The statutes you have laid down are
    righteous;
  they are fully trustworthy.
139My zeal wears me out,
  for my enemies ignore your words.
140Your promises have been thoroughly
    tested,
  and your servant loves them.
141Though I am lowly and despised,
  I do not forget your precepts.
142Your righteousness is everlasting
  and your law is true.
143Trouble and distress have come
    upon me,
  but your commands are my delight.
144Your statutes are forever right;
  give me understanding that I may
    live.

ק Qoph

145I call with all my heart; answer me,
    O Lord,
  and I will obey your decrees.
146I call out to you; save me
  and I will keep your statutes.
147I rise before dawn and cry for help;
  I have put my hope in your word.
148My eyes stay open through the
    watches of the night,
  that I may meditate on your
    promises.
149Hear my voice in accordance with your
    love;
  preserve my life, O Lord, according
    to your laws.
150Those who devise wicked schemes are
    near,
  but they are far from your law.
151Yet you are near, O Lord,
  and all your commands are true.
152Long ago I learned from your statutes
  that you established them to last
    forever.

ר Resh

153Look upon my suffering and
    deliver me,
  for I have not forgotten your law.

¹⁵⁴Defend my cause and redeem me;
　　preserve my life according to your
　　　promise.
¹⁵⁵Salvation is far from the wicked,
　　for they do not seek out your
　　　decrees.
¹⁵⁶Your compassion is great, O Lord;
　　preserve my life according to your
　　　laws.
¹⁵⁷Many are the foes who persecute me,
　　but I have not turned from your
　　　statutes.
¹⁵⁸I look on the faithless with loathing,
　　for they do not obey your word.
¹⁵⁹See how I love your precepts;
　　preserve my life, O Lord, according
　　　to your love.
¹⁶⁰All your words are true;
　　all your righteous laws are eternal.

ש Sin and Shin
¹⁶¹Rulers persecute me without cause,
　　but my heart trembles at your word.
¹⁶²I rejoice in your promise
　　like one who finds great spoil.
¹⁶³I hate and abhor falsehood
　　but I love your law.
¹⁶⁴Seven times a day I praise you
　　for your righteous laws.
¹⁶⁵Great peace have they who love your
　　law,
　　and nothing can make them stumble.
¹⁶⁶I wait for your salvation, O Lord,
　　and I follow your commands.
¹⁶⁷I obey your statutes,
　　for I love them greatly.
¹⁶⁸I obey your precepts and your
　　statutes,
　　for all my ways are known to you.

ת Taw
¹⁶⁹May my cry come before you, O Lord;
　　give me understanding according to
　　　your word.
¹⁷⁰May my supplication come before you;
　　deliver me according to your
　　　promise.
¹⁷¹May my lips overflow with praise,
　　for you teach me your decrees.
¹⁷²May my tongue sing of your word,
　　for all your commands are righteous.
¹⁷³May your hand be ready to help me,
　　for I have chosen your precepts.
¹⁷⁴I long for your salvation, O Lord,
　　and your law is my delight.
¹⁷⁵Let me live that I may praise you,
　　and may your laws sustain me.

¹⁷⁶I have strayed like a lost sheep.
　　Seek your servant,
　　for I have not forgotten your
　　　commands.

PSALM 120

A song of ascents.

¹I call on the Lord in my distress,
　　and he answers me.
²Save me, O Lord, from lying lips
　　and from deceitful tongues.

³What will he do to you,
　　and what more besides, O deceitful
　　　tongue?
⁴He will punish you with a warrior's
　　sharp arrows,
　　with burning coals of the broom
　　　tree.

⁵Woe to me that I dwell in Meshech,
　　that I live among the tents of Kedar!
⁶Too long have I lived
　　among those who hate peace.
⁷I am a man of peace;
　　but when I speak, they are for war.

PSALM 121

A song of ascents.

¹I lift up my eyes to the hills—
　　where does my help come from?
²My help comes from the Lord,
　　the Maker of heaven and earth.

³He will not let your foot slip—
　　he who watches over you will not
　　　slumber;
⁴indeed, he who watches over Israel
　　will neither slumber nor sleep.

⁵The Lord watches over you—
　　the Lord is your shade at your right
　　　hand;
⁶the sun will not harm you by day,
　　nor the moon by night.

⁷The Lord will keep you from all harm—
　　he will watch over your life;
⁸the Lord will watch over your coming
　　and going
　　both now and forevermore.

PSALM 122

A song of ascents. Of David.

¹I rejoiced with those who said to me,
　　"Let us go to the house of the Lord."
²Our feet are standing
　　in your gates, O Jerusalem.

³Jerusalem is built like a city
  that is closely compacted together.
⁴That is where the tribes go up,
  the tribes of the Lord,
to praise the name of the Lord
  according to the statute given to
    Israel.
⁵There the thrones for judgment stand,
  the thrones of the house of David.

⁶Pray for the peace of Jerusalem:
  "May those who love you be secure.
⁷May there be peace within your walls
  and security within your citadels."
⁸For the sake of my brothers and friends,
  I will say, "Peace be within you."
⁹For the sake of the house of the Lord
  our God,
  I will seek your prosperity.

PSALM 123

A song of ascents.

¹I lift up my eyes to you,
  to you whose throne is in heaven.
²As the eyes of slaves look to the hand
  of their master,
  as the eyes of a maid look to the
    hand of her mistress,
so our eyes look to the Lord our God,
  till he shows us his mercy.

³Have mercy on us, O Lord, have mercy
  on us,
  for we have endured much contempt.
⁴We have endured much ridicule from
  the proud,
  much contempt from the arrogant.

PSALM 124

A song of ascents. Of David.

¹If the Lord had not been on our side—
  let Israel say—
²if the Lord had not been on our side
  when men attacked us,
³when their anger flared against us,
  they would have swallowed us alive;
⁴the flood would have engulfed us,
  the torrent would have swept over us,
⁵the raging waters
  would have swept us away.

⁶Praise be to the Lord,
  who has not let us be torn by their
    teeth.
⁷We have escaped like a bird
  out of the fowler's snare;
  the snare has been broken,

and we have escaped.
⁸Our help is in the name of the Lord,
  the Maker of heaven and earth.

PSALM 125

A song of ascents.

¹Those who trust in the Lord are like
  Mount Zion,
  which cannot be shaken but endures
    forever.
²As the mountains surround Jerusalem,
  so the Lord surrounds his people
  both now and forevermore.

³The scepter of the wicked will not
  remain
  over the land allotted to the righteous,
for then the righteous might use
  their hands to do evil.

⁴Do good, O Lord, to those who are
  good,
  to those who are upright in heart.
⁵But those who turn to crooked ways
  the Lord will banish with the
    evildoers.

Peace be upon Israel.

PSALM 126

A song of ascents.

¹When the Lord brought back the
  captives toᵃ Zion,
  we were like men who dreamed. ᵇ
²Our mouths were filled with laughter,
  our tongues with songs of joy.
Then it was said among the nations,
  "The Lord has done great things for
    them."
³The Lord has done great things for us,
  and we are filled with joy.

⁴Restore our fortunes, ᶜ O Lord,
  like streams in the Negev.
⁵Those who sow in tears
  will reap with songs of joy.
⁶He who goes out weeping,
  carrying seed to sow,
will return with songs of joy,
  carrying sheaves with him.

PSALM 127

A song of ascents. Of Solomon.

¹Unless the Lord builds the house,
  its builders labor in vain.

ᵃ 1 Or Lord restored the fortunes of   ᵇ 1 Or men restored
to health   ᶜ 4 Or Bring back our captives

Unless the LORD watches over the city,
the watchmen stand guard in vain.
2 In vain you rise early
and stay up late,
toiling for food to eat—
for he grants sleep to[a] those he loves.

3 Sons are a heritage from the LORD,
children a reward from him.
4 Like arrows in the hands of a warrior
are sons born in one's youth.
5 Blessed is the man
whose quiver is full of them.
They will not be put to shame
when they contend with their
enemies in the gate.

PSALM 128

A song of ascents.

1 Blessed are all who fear the LORD,
who walk in his ways.
2 You will eat the fruit of your labor;
blessings and prosperity will be yours.
3 Your wife will be like a fruitful vine

within your house;
your sons will be like olive shoots
around your table.
4 Thus is the man blessed
who fears the LORD.

5 May the LORD bless you from Zion
all the days of your life;
may you see the prosperity of Jerusalem,
6   and may you live to see your
children's children.

Peace be upon Israel.

PSALM 129

A song of ascents.

1 They have greatly oppressed me from
my youth—
let Israel say—
2 they have greatly oppressed me from
my youth,
but they have not gained the victory
over me.

a 2 Or eat— / for while they sleep he provides for

Make It Stick

READ PSALM 126:2–3

Have you ever laughed so hard that you cried? Laughter is God's gift to us to help take our cares away (see verse 2). Write down your favorite joke on a sticky note and turn to it whenever you need a good chuckle.

³ Plowmen have plowed my back
  and made their furrows long.
⁴ But the LORD is righteous;
  he has cut me free from the cords of
    the wicked.

⁵ May all who hate Zion
  be turned back in shame.
⁶ May they be like grass on the roof,
  which withers before it can grow;
⁷ with it the reaper cannot fill his hands,
  nor the one who gathers fill his arms.
⁸ May those who pass by not say,
  "The blessing of the LORD be upon you;
  we bless you in the name of the LORD."

PSALM 130

A song of ascents.

¹ Out of the depths I cry to you, O LORD;
² O Lord, hear my voice.
  Let your ears be attentive
  to my cry for mercy.

³ If you, O LORD, kept a record of sins,
  O Lord, who could stand?

⁴ But with you there is forgiveness;
  therefore you are feared.

⁵ I wait for the LORD, my soul waits,
  and in his word I put my hope.
⁶ My soul waits for the Lord
  more than watchmen wait for the
    morning,
  more than watchmen wait for the
    morning.

⁷ O Israel, put your hope in the LORD,
  for with the LORD is unfailing love
  and with him is full redemption.
⁸ He himself will redeem Israel
  from all their sins.

PSALM 131

A song of ascents. Of David.

¹ My heart is not proud, O LORD,
  my eyes are not haughty;
  I do not concern myself with great
    matters
  or things too wonderful for me.

GET STRONGER

Life Is a Balancing Act

READ PSALM 127

Ever heard the saying "burning the candle at both ends"? It describes someone who is pushing things to the max, to the point where his or her health might be in danger. People like that are living out of balance. They've taken one thing and focus on it so much that everything else suffers. God has *not* called us to live this way. When you trust God, you don't need to push yourself until your eyes are bloodshot and your face looks like a rubber Halloween mask. God wants you to strive for excellence. But you need to know when to call it quits. "In vain you rise early and stay up late, toiling for food to eat—for [God] grants sleep to those he loves" (verse 2). Work hard, trust God to bless your work and leave the rest in his hands. Too much of anything—even a good thing—is no good.

Your next reading is on page 776.

2 But I have stilled and quieted my soul;
    like a weaned child with its mother,
    like a weaned child is my soul within
      me.
3 O Israel, put your hope in the LORD
    both now and forevermore.

PSALM 132

A song of ascents.

1 O LORD, remember David
    and all the hardships he endured.

2 He swore an oath to the LORD
    and made a vow to the Mighty One
      of Jacob:
3 "I will not enter my house
    or go to my bed—
4 I will allow no sleep to my eyes,
    no slumber to my eyelids,
5 till I find a place for the LORD,
    a dwelling for the Mighty One of
      Jacob."

6 We heard it in Ephrathah,
    we came upon it in the fields of
      Jaar[a: b]
7 "Let us go to his dwelling place;
    let us worship at his footstool—
8 arise, O LORD, and come to your resting
      place,
    you and the ark of your might.
9 May your priests be clothed with
      righteousness;
    may your saints sing for joy."

10 For the sake of David your servant,
    do not reject your anointed one.

11 The LORD swore an oath to David,
    a sure oath that he will not revoke:
  "One of your own descendants
    I will place on your throne—
12 if your sons keep my covenant
    and the statutes I teach them,
  then their sons will sit
    on your throne for ever and ever."

13 For the LORD has chosen Zion,
    he has desired it for his dwelling:
14 "This is my resting place for ever and
      ever;
    here I will sit enthroned, for I have
      desired it—
15 I will bless her with abundant
      provisions;
    her poor will I satisfy with food.
16 I will clothe her priests with salvation,
    and her saints will ever sing for joy.

17 "Here I will make a horn[c] grow for
      David
    and set up a lamp for my anointed
      one.
18 I will clothe his enemies with shame,
    but the crown on his head will be
      resplendent."

PSALM 133

A song of ascents. Of David.

1 How good and pleasant it is
    when brothers live together in unity!
2 It is like precious oil poured on the
      head,
    running down on the beard,
  running down on Aaron's beard,
    down upon the collar of his robes.
3 It is as if the dew of Hermon
    were falling on Mount Zion.
  For there the LORD bestows his
      blessing,
    even life forevermore.

PSALM 134

A song of ascents.

1 Praise the LORD, all you servants of the
      LORD
    who minister by night in the house
      of the LORD.
2 Lift up your hands in the sanctuary
    and praise the LORD.

3 May the LORD, the Maker of heaven
      and earth,
    bless you from Zion.

PSALM 135

1 Praise the LORD.[d]

Praise the name of the LORD;
    praise him, you servants of the LORD,
2 you who minister in the house of the
      LORD,
    in the courts of the house of our
      God.

3 Praise the LORD, for the LORD is good;
    sing praise to his name, for that is
      pleasant.
4 For the LORD has chosen Jacob to be his
      own,
    Israel to be his treasured possession.

5 I know that the LORD is great,

[a] 6 That is, Kiriath Jearim   [b] 6 Or heard it in Ephrathah, /
we found it in the fields of Jaar. (And no quotes around verses
7–9)   [c] 17 Horn here symbolizes strong one, that is, king.
[d] 1 Hebrew Hallelu Yah; also in verses 3 and 21

Get a Load of This...

It's good for brothers to get along (Psalm 133:1), but this verse doesn't just apply to boys. It's also great when sisters, friends, parents, neighbors, computer programmers, dogsledders, cake decorators, dolphin trainers, football players, violinists and professional wrestlers live in unity. Well, maybe not professional wrestlers. But definitely everyone else!

that our Lord is greater than all gods.
6 The LORD does whatever pleases him,
    in the heavens and on the earth,
    in the seas and all their depths.
7 He makes clouds rise from the ends of the earth;
    he sends lightning with the rain
    and brings out the wind from his storehouses.

8 He struck down the firstborn of Egypt,
    the firstborn of men and animals.
9 He sent his signs and wonders into your midst,
        O Egypt,
    against Pharaoh and all his servants.
10 He struck down many nations
    and killed mighty kings—
11 Sihon king of the Amorites,
    Og king of Bashan
    and all the kings of Canaan—
12 and he gave their land as an inheritance,
    an inheritance to his people Israel.

13 Your name, O LORD, endures forever,
    your renown, O LORD, through all generations.
14 For the LORD will vindicate his people
    and have compassion on his servants.

15 The idols of the nations are silver and gold,
    made by the hands of men.
16 They have mouths, but cannot speak,
    eyes, but they cannot see;
17 they have ears, but cannot hear,
    nor is there breath in their mouths.
18 Those who make them will be like them,
    and so will all who trust in them.

19 O house of Israel, praise the LORD;
    O house of Aaron, praise the LORD;
20 O house of Levi, praise the LORD;
    you who fear him, praise the LORD.
21 Praise be to the LORD from Zion,
    to him who dwells in Jerusalem.

    Praise the LORD.

PSALM 136

1 Give thanks to the LORD, for he is good.
        His love endures forever.
2 Give thanks to the God of gods.
        His love endures forever.
3 Give thanks to the Lord of lords:
        His love endures forever.

4 to him who alone does great wonders,
        His love endures forever.
5 who by his understanding made the heavens,
        His love endures forever.
6 who spread out the earth upon the waters,
        His love endures forever.
7 who made the great lights—
        His love endures forever.

8 the sun to govern the day,
   His love endures forever.
9 the moon and stars to govern the
   night;
   His love endures forever.
10 to him who struck down the firstborn
   of Egypt
   His love endures forever.
11 and brought Israel out from among
   them
   His love endures forever.
12 with a mighty hand and outstretched
   arm;
   His love endures forever.
13 to him who divided the Red Sea[a]
   asunder
   His love endures forever.
14 and brought Israel through the midst
   of it,
   His love endures forever.
15 but swept Pharaoh and his army into
   the Red Sea;
   His love endures forever.
16 to him who led his people through the
   desert,
   His love endures forever.
17 who struck down great kings,
   His love endures forever.
18 and killed mighty kings—
   His love endures forever.
19 Sihon king of the Amorites
   His love endures forever.
20 and Og king of Bashan—
   His love endures forever.
21 and gave their land as an inheritance,
   His love endures forever.
22 an inheritance to his servant Israel;
   His love endures forever.
23 to the One who remembered us in our
   low estate
   His love endures forever.
24 and freed us from our enemies,
   His love endures forever.
25 and who gives food to every creature.
   His love endures forever.
26 Give thanks to the God of heaven.
   His love endures forever.

PSALM 137

1 By the rivers of Babylon we sat and
   wept
   when we remembered Zion.
2 There on the poplars
   we hung our harps,

3 for there our captors asked us for
   songs,
   our tormentors demanded songs of
   joy;
   they said, "Sing us one of the songs
   of Zion!"
4 How can we sing the songs of the LORD
   while in a foreign land?
5 If I forget you, O Jerusalem,
   may my right hand forget ⌊its skill⌋.
6 May my tongue cling to the roof of my
   mouth
   if I do not remember you,
if I do not consider Jerusalem
   my highest joy.

7 Remember, O LORD, what the Edomites
   did
   on the day Jerusalem fell.
"Tear it down," they cried,
   "tear it down to its foundations!"
8 O Daughter of Babylon, doomed to
   destruction,
   happy is he who repays you
   for what you have done to us—
9 he who seizes your infants
   and dashes them against the rocks.

PSALM 138

Of David.

1 I will praise you, O LORD, with all my
   heart;
   before the "gods" I will sing your
   praise.
2 I will bow down toward your holy
   temple
   and will praise your name
   for your love and your faithfulness,
for you have exalted above all things
   your name and your word.
3 When I called, you answered me;
   you made me bold and stouthearted.

4 May all the kings of the earth praise
   you, O LORD,
   when they hear the words of your
   mouth.
5 May they sing of the ways of the LORD,
   for the glory of the LORD is great.
6 Though the LORD is on high, he looks
   upon the lowly,
   but the proud he knows from afar.
7 Though I walk in the midst of trouble,
   you preserve my life;

---

[a] 13 Hebrew *Yam Suph*; that is, Sea of Reeds; also in verse 15

you stretch out your hand against the
    anger of my foes,
  with your right hand you save me.
8 The LORD will fulfill his purpose for me;
  your love, O LORD, endures forever—
    do not abandon the works of your
    hands.

PSALM 139

For the director of music. Of David. A psalm.

1 O LORD, you have searched me
  and you know me.
2 You know when I sit and when I rise;
  you perceive my thoughts from afar.
3 You discern my going out and my lying
    down;
  you are familiar with all my ways.
4 Before a word is on my tongue
  you know it completely, O LORD.

5 You hem me in—behind and before;
  you have laid your hand upon me.
6 Such knowledge is too wonderful for
    me,
  too lofty for me to attain.

7 Where can I go from your Spirit?
  Where can I flee from your presence?
8 If I go up to the heavens, you are there;
  if I make my bed in the depths,[a] you
    are there.
9 If I rise on the wings of the dawn,
  if I settle on the far side of the sea,
10 even there your hand will guide me,
  your right hand will hold me fast.
11 If I say, "Surely the darkness will hide me
  and the light become night around
    me,"
12 even the darkness will not be dark to
    you;
  the night will shine like the day,
  for darkness is as light to you.

13 For you created my inmost being;
  you knit me together in my mother's
    womb.
14 I praise you because I am fearfully and
    wonderfully made;
  your works are wonderful,
  I know that full well.

[a] 8 Hebrew Sheol

GET STRONGER

Right Down to Your DNA

READ PSALM 139:13–18

When Lamborghini creates a new sports car, they design every little detail to perfection, right from the tiniest nuts and bolts. God designed you in much the same way—only you're *way* more complicated than a sports car! When you were conceived, God watched over every detail. David said, "Your eyes saw my unformed body. All the days ordained for me were written in your book before one of them came to be" (verse 16). God saw your entire life, he knew every opportunity you would have, and he gave you the DNA, the talents and the personality to match it. He didn't create you one way but intend you to be something different. Every part of you—your desires, your body, your abilities—was created for a purpose. If you seek God and follow him, your life will match his purpose, and you'll have a blast being who he created you to be.

Your next reading is on page 781.

15 My frame was not hidden from you
    when I was made in the secret
        place.
When I was woven together in the
        depths of the earth,
16   your eyes saw my unformed body.
All the days ordained for me
    were written in your book
    before one of them came to be.

17 How precious to[a] me are your
        thoughts, O God!
How vast is the sum of them!
18 Were I to count them,
    they would outnumber the grains of
        sand.
When I awake,
    I am still with you.

19 If only you would slay the wicked,
        O God!
Away from me, you bloodthirsty
        men!
20 They speak of you with evil intent;
    your adversaries misuse your name.

21 Do I not hate those who hate you,
        O Lord,
    and abhor those who rise up against
        you?
22 I have nothing but hatred for them;
    I count them my enemies.

23 Search me, O God, and know my
        heart;
    test me and know my anxious
        thoughts.
24 See if there is any offensive way in me,
    and lead me in the way everlasting.

PSALM 140

For the director of music. A psalm of David.

1 Rescue me, O Lord, from evil men;
    protect me from men of violence,
2 who devise evil plans in their hearts
    and stir up war every day.
3 They make their tongues as sharp as a
        serpent's;

[a] 17 Or concerning

Make It Stick

READ PSALM 139:23–24

Have you ever wanted something even though it wasn't right? Ask God to check your motives
before you make a decision (see Psalm 139:23–24). Ask yourself, in this order of importance:
1) What's in it for God? 2) What's in it for others? 3) What's in it for me?
That way your desires won't get the best of you.

the poison of vipers is on their lips.
Selah

⁴ Keep me, O Lᴏʀᴅ, from the hands of
the wicked;
protect me from men of violence
who plan to trip my feet.
⁵ Proud men have hidden a snare for
me;
they have spread out the cords of
their net
and have set traps for me along my
path. *Selah*

⁶ O Lᴏʀᴅ, I say to you, "You are my
God."
Hear, O Lᴏʀᴅ, my cry for mercy.
⁷ O Sovereign Lᴏʀᴅ, my strong deliverer,
who shields my head in the day of
battle—
⁸ do not grant the wicked their desires,
O Lᴏʀᴅ;
do not let their plans succeed,
or they will become proud. *Selah*

⁹ Let the heads of those who surround
me
be covered with the trouble their lips
have caused.
¹⁰ Let burning coals fall upon them;
may they be thrown into the fire,
into miry pits, never to rise.
¹¹ Let slanderers not be established in the
land;
may disaster hunt down men of
violence.

¹² I know that the Lᴏʀᴅ secures justice for
the poor
and upholds the cause of the needy.
¹³ Surely the righteous will praise your
name
and the upright will live before you.

PSALM 141

A psalm of David.

¹ O Lᴏʀᴅ, I call to you; come quickly to
me.
Hear my voice when I call to you.
² May my prayer be set before you like
incense;
may the lifting up of my hands be
like the evening sacrifice.

³ Set a guard over my mouth, O Lᴏʀᴅ;
keep watch over the door of my lips.
⁴ Let not my heart be drawn to what is
evil,
to take part in wicked deeds

with men who are evildoers;
let me not eat of their delicacies.

⁵ Let a righteous manᵃ strike me—it is a
kindness;
let him rebuke me—it is oil on my
head.
My head will not refuse it.

Yet my prayer is ever against the deeds
of evildoers;
⁶ their rulers will be thrown down
from the cliffs,
and the wicked will learn that my
words were well spoken.
⁷ ⌊They will say,⌋ "As one plows and
breaks up the earth,
so our bones have been scattered at
the mouth of the grave. ᵇ"

⁸ But my eyes are fixed on you,
O Sovereign Lᴏʀᴅ;
in you I take refuge—do not give me
over to death.
⁹ Keep me from the snares they have
laid for me,
from the traps set by evildoers.
¹⁰ Let the wicked fall into their own nets,
while I pass by in safety.

PSALM 142

A *maskil*ᶜ of David. When he was in the cave.
A prayer.

¹ I cry aloud to the Lᴏʀᴅ;
I lift up my voice to the Lᴏʀᴅ for
mercy.
² I pour out my complaint before him;
before him I tell my trouble.

³ When my spirit grows faint within me,
it is you who know my way.
In the path where I walk
men have hidden a snare for me.
⁴ Look to my right and see;
no one is concerned for me.
I have no refuge;
no one cares for my life.

⁵ I cry to you, O Lᴏʀᴅ;
I say, "You are my refuge,
my portion in the land of the living."
⁶ Listen to my cry,
for I am in desperate need;
rescue me from those who pursue me,
for they are too strong for me.
⁷ Set me free from my prison,
that I may praise your name.

ᵃ 5 Or *Let the Righteous One*　　ᵇ 7 Hebrew *Sheol*　　ᶜ Title:
Probably a literary or musical term

Then the righteous will gather about me
    because of your goodness to me.

PSALM 143

A psalm of David.

¹ O LORD, hear my prayer,
    listen to my cry for mercy;
in your faithfulness and righteousness
    come to my relief.
² Do not bring your servant into
        judgment,
    for no one living is righteous before
        you.

³ The enemy pursues me,
    he crushes me to the ground;
he makes me dwell in darkness
    like those long dead.
⁴ So my spirit grows faint within me;
    my heart within me is dismayed.
⁵ I remember the days of long ago;
    I meditate on all your works
    and consider what your hands have
        done.
⁶ I spread out my hands to you;
    my soul thirsts for you like a parched
        land.   *Selah*

Make It Stick

READ PSALM 142–143
Ever felt like everyone was against you? That's how David felt when he wrote Psalms 142 and 143. But David realized that no matter how bad he felt, the Lord still cared for him. On a sticky note, write the verses from these psalms that describe how you feel when you're down. Then write down how God can help.

Get a Load of This...

God trained David's hands for war (Psalm 144:1), because that's what God called David to do. God hasn't called you to war (at least not yet), but you can still ask him to "train your hands" for whatever he wants you to be, from a computer whiz to a basketball star to a Mozart wonder.

7 Answer me quickly, O Lord;
    my spirit fails.
Do not hide your face from me
    or I will be like those who go down to the pit.
8 Let the morning bring me word of your unfailing
       love,
    for I have put my trust in you.
Show me the way I should go,
    for to you I lift up my soul.
9 Rescue me from my enemies, O Lord,
    for I hide myself in you.
10 Teach me to do your will,
    for you are my God;
may your good Spirit
    lead me on level ground.

11 For your name's sake, O Lord, preserve my life;
    in your righteousness, bring me out of trouble.
12 In your unfailing love, silence my enemies;
    destroy all my foes,
    for I am your servant.

PSALM 144

Of David.

1 Praise be to the Lord my Rock,
    who trains my hands for war,
    my fingers for battle.
2 He is my loving God and my fortress,
    my stronghold and my deliverer,
my shield, in whom I take refuge,
    who subdues peoples[a] under me.

3 O Lord, what is man that you care for him,
    the son of man that you think of him?
4 Man is like a breath;
    his days are like a fleeting shadow.

5 Part your heavens, O Lord, and come down;
    touch the mountains, so that they smoke.
6 Send forth lightning and scatter ⌊the enemies⌋;
    shoot your arrows and rout them.
7 Reach down your hand from on high;
    deliver me and rescue me
from the mighty waters,
    from the hands of foreigners
8 whose mouths are full of lies,
    whose right hands are deceitful.

9 I will sing a new song to you, O God;
    on the ten-stringed lyre I will make music to you,
10 to the One who gives victory to kings,
    who delivers his servant David from the deadly
       sword.

11 Deliver me and rescue me
    from the hands of foreigners

---

a 2 Many manuscripts of the Masoretic Text, Dead Sea Scrolls, Aquila, Jerome and Syriac; most manuscripts of the Masoretic Text *subdues my people*

whose mouths are full of lies,
  whose right hands are deceitful.

12 Then our sons in their youth
    will be like well-nurtured plants,
  and our daughters will be like pillars
    carved to adorn a palace.
13 Our barns will be filled
    with every kind of provision.
  Our sheep will increase by thousands,
    by tens of thousands in our fields;
14   our oxen will draw heavy loads. *a*
  There will be no breaching of walls,
    no going into captivity,
    no cry of distress in our streets.
15 Blessed are the people of whom this is
      true;
  blessed are the people whose God is
    the LORD.

PSALM 145 *b*

A psalm of praise. Of David.

1 I will exalt you, my God the King;
  I will praise your name for ever and
    ever.
2 Every day I will praise you

and extol your name for ever and
    ever.

3 Great is the LORD and most worthy of
    praise;
  his greatness no one can fathom.
4 One generation will commend your
      works to another;
  they will tell of your mighty acts.
5 They will speak of the glorious
      splendor of your majesty,
  and I will meditate on your
    wonderful works. *c*
6 They will tell of the power of your
    awesome works,
  and I will proclaim your great
    deeds.
7 They will celebrate your abundant
    goodness
  and joyfully sing of your
    righteousness.

a 14 Or *our chieftains will be firmly established*   *b* This
psalm is an acrostic poem, the verses of which (including
verse 13b) begin with the successive letters of the Hebrew
alphabet.   *c 5* Dead Sea Scrolls and Syriac (see also
Septuagint); Masoretic Text *On the glorious splendor of your
majesty / and on your wonderful works I will meditate*

Who Is God?

READ PSALM 145

Read this psalm! Memorize it. Write it on a poster. Write it in chalk on your driveway. Whatever it takes so you won't forget it. It describes God's character. And, believe it or not, what you believe about God's character shapes nearly everything else in your life, including how you treat others, how you feel about yourself and how you think God feels about you. For example, if you believe God is good and loving, you yourself will become more good and loving. But if you believe God is ready to pounce on you for every little mistake, you will either reject God or become a people pouncer yourself. As a man of God, it's important to have a clear understanding of God's character so you can become like that yourself. So read this psalm. Then read it again, and again . . .

Your next reading is on page 787.

8 The LORD is gracious and compassionate,
    slow to anger and rich in love.
9 The LORD is good to all;
    he has compassion on all he has
      made.
10 All you have made will praise you,
    O LORD;
    your saints will extol you.
11 They will tell of the glory of your
      kingdom
    and speak of your might,
12 so that all men may know of your
      mighty acts
    and the glorious splendor of your
      kingdom.
13 Your kingdom is an everlasting kingdom,
    and your dominion endures through
      all generations.

    The LORD is faithful to all his promises
    and loving toward all he has made. [a]
14 The LORD upholds all those who fall
    and lifts up all who are bowed down.
15 The eyes of all look to you,
    and you give them their food at the
      proper time.
16 You open your hand
    and satisfy the desires of every living
      thing.

17 The LORD is righteous in all his ways
    and loving toward all he has made.
18 The LORD is near to all who call on him,
    to all who call on him in truth.
19 He fulfills the desires of those who fear
      him;
    he hears their cry and saves them.
20 The LORD watches over all who love
      him,
    but all the wicked he will destroy.

21 My mouth will speak in praise of the
    LORD.
    Let every creature praise his holy
      name
    for ever and ever.

PSALM 146

1 Praise the LORD. [b]

    Praise the LORD, O my soul.
2   I will praise the LORD all my life;
    I will sing praise to my God as long
      as I live.

3 Do not put your trust in princes,
    in mortal men, who cannot save.
4 When their spirit departs, they return
    to the ground;

    on that very day their plans come to
      nothing.

5 Blessed is he whose help is the God of
      Jacob,
    whose hope is in the LORD his God,
6 the Maker of heaven and earth,
    the sea, and everything in them—
    the LORD, who remains faithful
      forever.
7 He upholds the cause of the oppressed
    and gives food to the hungry.
    The LORD sets prisoners free,
8   the LORD gives sight to the blind,
    the LORD lifts up those who are bowed
      down,
    the LORD loves the righteous.
9 The LORD watches over the alien
    and sustains the fatherless and the
      widow,
    but he frustrates the ways of the
      wicked.

10 The LORD reigns forever,
    your God, O Zion, for all generations.

    Praise the LORD.

PSALM 147

1 Praise the LORD. [c]

    How good it is to sing praises to our
      God,
    how pleasant and fitting to praise
      him!

2 The LORD builds up Jerusalem;
    he gathers the exiles of Israel.
3 He heals the brokenhearted
    and binds up their wounds.
4 He determines the number of the stars
    and calls them each by name.
5 Great is our Lord and mighty in power;
    his understanding has no limit.
6 The LORD sustains the humble
    but casts the wicked to the ground.

7 Sing to the LORD with thanksgiving;
    make music to our God on the harp.
8 He covers the sky with clouds;
    he supplies the earth with rain
    and makes grass grow on the hills.
9 He provides food for the cattle
    and for the young ravens when they
      call.

[a] 13 One manuscript of the Masoretic Text, Dead Sea Scrolls
and Syriac (see also Septuagint); most manuscripts of the
Masoretic Text do not have the last two lines of verse 13.
[b] 1 Hebrew Hallelu Yah; also in verse 10   [c] 1 Hebrew
Hallelu Yah; also in verse 20

10 His pleasure is not in the strength of the horse,
   nor his delight in the legs of a man;
11 the LORD delights in those who fear him,
   who put their hope in his unfailing love.

12 Extol the LORD, O Jerusalem;
   praise your God, O Zion,
13 for he strengthens the bars of your gates
   and blesses your people within you.
14 He grants peace to your borders
   and satisfies you with the finest of wheat.

15 He sends his command to the earth;
   his word runs swiftly.
16 He spreads the snow like wool
   and scatters the frost like ashes.
17 He hurls down his hail like pebbles.
   Who can withstand his icy blast?
18 He sends his word and melts them;
   he stirs up his breezes, and the waters flow.

19 He has revealed his word to Jacob,
   his laws and decrees to Israel.
20 He has done this for no other nation;
   they do not know his laws.

   Praise the LORD.

PSALM 148

1 Praise the LORD. [a]

Praise the LORD from the heavens,
   praise him in the heights above.
2 Praise him, all his angels,
   praise him, all his heavenly hosts.
3 Praise him, sun and moon,
   praise him, all you shining stars.
4 Praise him, you highest heavens
   and you waters above the skies.
5 Let them praise the name of the LORD,
   for he commanded and they were created.
6 He set them in place for ever and ever;
   he gave a decree that will never pass away.

7 Praise the LORD from the earth,
   you great sea creatures and all ocean depths,
8 lightning and hail, snow and clouds,
   stormy winds that do his bidding,
9 you mountains and all hills,
   fruit trees and all cedars,
10 wild animals and all cattle,
   small creatures and flying birds,
11 kings of the earth and all nations,
   you princes and all rulers on earth,
12 young men and maidens,
   old men and children.

13 Let them praise the name of the LORD,
   for his name alone is exalted;

Get a Load of This...

How do birds praise God (Psalm 148:10)? Just by being, by flying around, eating stuff and chirping. By just doing what God made them to do, they show how creative and powerful God is. Live God's way, and your life will show God's greatness, too.

---

his splendor is above the earth and
   the heavens.
14 He has raised up for his people a
       horn,[a]
   the praise of all his saints,
   of Israel, the people close to his
       heart.

Praise the LORD.

PSALM 149

1 Praise the LORD.[b]

Sing to the LORD a new song,
   his praise in the assembly of the
       saints.

2 Let Israel rejoice in their Maker;
   let the people of Zion be glad in
       their King.
3 Let them praise his name with dancing
   and make music to him with
       tambourine and harp.
4 For the LORD takes delight in his
       people;
   he crowns the humble with
       salvation.
5 Let the saints rejoice in this honor
   and sing for joy on their beds.

6 May the praise of God be in their
       mouths
   and a double-edged sword in their
       hands,

7 to inflict vengeance on the nations
   and punishment on the peoples,
8 to bind their kings with fetters,
   their nobles with shackles of iron,
9 to carry out the sentence written
       against them.
   This is the glory of all his saints.

Praise the LORD.

PSALM 150

1 Praise the LORD.[c]

Praise God in his sanctuary;
   praise him in his mighty heavens.
2 Praise him for his acts of power;
   praise him for his surpassing
       greatness.
3 Praise him with the sounding of the
       trumpet,
   praise him with the harp and lyre,
4 praise him with tambourine and
       dancing,
   praise him with the strings and flute,
5 praise him with the clash of cymbals,
   praise him with resounding cymbals.

6 Let everything that has breath praise
       the LORD.

Praise the LORD.

---

[a] 14 *Horn* here symbolizes strong one, that is, king.
[b] 1 Hebrew *Hallelu Yah*; also in verse 9   [c] 1 Hebrew *Hallelu Yah*; also in verse 6

PROVERBS

Who wrote this book?
Solomon wrote many of the proverbs. Other wise men added others.

Why was this book written?
This book was written to help people make wise choices.

For whom was this book written?
This book was written for everyone. Even people who do not believe in God can use its good advice.

What kind of advice is found in Proverbs?
This book gives advice on making friends, living in a family, handling money, doing right, caring about poor people, and many other important things.

When was this book written?
The proverbs in this book were probably written between 970 and 686 B.C.

What are some proverbs for children in this book?

Advice about trusting God	Proverbs 3:5–6
Advice about working hard	Proverbs 6:6–11
Advice about insults	Proverbs 12:16
Advice about gossip	Proverbs 17:9
Advice about revenge	Proverbs 20:22
Advice about discipline	Proverbs 22:15

Prologue: Purpose and Theme

1 The proverbs of Solomon son of David, king of Israel:

² for attaining wisdom and discipline;
 for understanding words of insight;
³ for acquiring a disciplined and prudent life,
 doing what is right and just and fair;
⁴ for giving prudence to the simple,
 knowledge and discretion to the young—
⁵ let the wise listen and add to their learning,
 and let the discerning get guidance—
⁶ for understanding proverbs and parables,
 the sayings and riddles of the wise.

⁷ The fear of the Lord is the beginning of knowledge,
 but fools*a* despise wisdom and discipline.

Exhortations to Embrace Wisdom

Warning Against Enticement

⁸ Listen, my son, to your father's instruction
 and do not forsake your mother's teaching.
⁹ They will be a garland to grace your head
 and a chain to adorn your neck.

¹⁰ My son, if sinners entice you,
 do not give in to them.
¹¹ If they say, "Come along with us;
 let's lie in wait for someone's blood,
 let's waylay some harmless soul;
¹² let's swallow them alive, like the grave,*b*
 and whole, like those who go down to the pit;
¹³ we will get all sorts of valuable things
 and fill our houses with plunder;

a 7 The Hebrew words rendered *fool* in Proverbs, and often elsewhere in the Old Testament, denote one who is morally deficient.   *b 12* Hebrew *Sheol*

Make It Stick

READ PROVERBS 1:8

Think your parents are too ancient to give you good advice? Think again. One of the main ways God teaches you wisdom is through your parents (Proverbs 1:8). They have been at this thing called "life" for a while, and you can learn a lot from them. Write down three things you have learned from your parents or grandparents.

14 throw in your lot with us,
  and we will share a common purse"—
15 my son, do not go along with them,
  do not set foot on their paths;
16 for their feet rush into sin,
  they are swift to shed blood.
17 How useless to spread a net
  in full view of all the birds!
18 These men lie in wait for their own
      blood;
  they waylay only themselves!
19 Such is the end of all who go after ill-
      gotten gain;
  it takes away the lives of those who
      get it.

Warning Against Rejecting Wisdom

20 Wisdom calls aloud in the street,
  she raises her voice in the public
      squares;
21 at the head of the noisy streets*a* she
      cries out,
  in the gateways of the city she
      makes her speech:

22 "How long will you simple ones*b* love
  your simple ways?

How long will mockers delight in
      mockery
  and fools hate knowledge?
23 If you had responded to my rebuke,
  I would have poured out my heart
      to you
  and made my thoughts known to
      you.
24 But since you rejected me when I
      called
  and no one gave heed when I
      stretched out my hand,
25 since you ignored all my advice
  and would not accept my rebuke,
26 I in turn will laugh at your disaster;
  I will mock when calamity overtakes
      you—
27 when calamity overtakes you like a
      storm,
  when disaster sweeps over you like a
      whirlwind,
  when distress and trouble
      overwhelm you.

a 21 Hebrew; Septuagint / *on the tops of the walls*
b 22 The Hebrew word rendered *simple* in Proverbs generally
denotes one without moral direction and inclined to evil.

GET SMARTER.

God's Foundation for Learning

READ PROVERBS 1:1–7

Check out Proverbs 1:7: "The fear of the LORD is the beginning of knowledge." To *fear* God means to respect him and be in awe of him. And you *should*. God not only created the universe, but made possible every bit of learning in existence—science, mathematics, art, music, language and technology. "His understanding has no limit" (Psalm 147:5). Want to be smart? Start by fearing and obeying God. Read what he says in the Bible, get to know him, and he'll open up the mysteries of life to you. Unbelievers who don't start by knowing God "despise wisdom" (Proverbs 1:7) and get confused. Don't let that be you. When reading a science magazine, for example, ask yourself, "Does the Bible agree with this scientific theory?" As a man of God, you need to be in total awe of God's greatness and recognize his Word as the foundation of all knowledge.

Your next reading is on page 789.

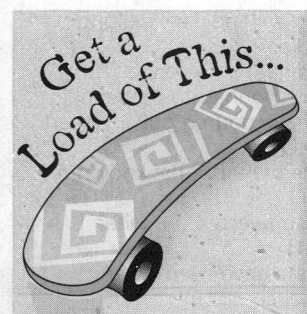

Get a Load of This...

Ignore God's Word and you're headed for a face-plant (see Proverbs 1:22–27). Imagine someone who tried water skiing, but refused to learn the right way to do it. They would wipe out big-time. Don't wait till it's too late to listen to God. Seek wisdom every day.

In other words...

28 "Then they will call to me but I will not answer;
   they will look for me but will not find me.
29 Since they hated knowledge
   and did not choose to fear the LORD,
30 since they would not accept my advice
   and spurned my rebuke,
31 they will eat the fruit of their ways
   and be filled with the fruit of their schemes.
32 For the waywardness of the simple will kill them,
   and the complacency of fools will destroy them;
33 but whoever listens to me will live in safety
   and be at ease, without fear of harm."

Moral Benefits of Wisdom

2 My son, if you accept my words
   and store up my commands within you,
2 turning your ear to wisdom
   and applying your heart to understanding,
3 and if you call out for insight
   and cry aloud for understanding,
4 and if you look for it as for silver
   and search for it as for hidden treasure,
5 then you will understand the fear of the LORD
   and find the knowledge of God.
6 For the LORD gives wisdom,
   and from his mouth come knowledge and
      understanding.
7 He holds victory in store for the upright,
   he is a shield to those whose walk is blameless,
8 for he guards the course of the just
   and protects the way of his faithful ones.

9 Then you will understand what is right and just
   and fair—every good path.
10 For wisdom will enter your heart,
   and knowledge will be pleasant to your soul.
11 Discretion will protect you,
   and understanding will guard you.

12 Wisdom will save you from the ways of wicked men,
   from men whose words are perverse,
13 who leave the straight paths
   to walk in dark ways,
14 who delight in doing wrong
   and rejoice in the perverseness of evil,
15 whose paths are crooked
   and who are devious in their ways.

16 It will save you also from the adulteress,
   from the wayward wife with her seductive words,
17 who has left the partner of her youth
   and ignored the covenant she made before God. a
18 For her house leads down to death
   and her paths to the spirits of the dead.
19 None who go to her return
   or attain the paths of life.

a 17 Or covenant of her God

20 Thus you will walk in the ways of good
        men
     and keep to the paths of the
        righteous.
21 For the upright will live in the land,
     and the blameless will remain in it;
22 but the wicked will be cut off from the
        land,
     and the unfaithful will be torn from
        it.

Further Benefits of Wisdom

3 My son, do not forget my teaching,
     but keep my commands in your
        heart,
 2 for they will prolong your life
        many years
 and bring you prosperity.

3 Let love and faithfulness never leave
        you;
     bind them around your neck,
     write them on the tablet of your
        heart.
4 Then you will win favor and a good
        name
     in the sight of God and man.

5 Trust in the LORD with all your heart
     and lean not on your own
        understanding;
6 in all your ways acknowledge him,
     and he will make your paths
        straight.*a*

7 Do not be wise in your own eyes;
     fear the LORD and shun evil.
8 This will bring health to your body
     and nourishment to your bones.

9 Honor the LORD with your wealth,
     with the firstfruits of all your crops;
10 then your barns will be filled to
        overflowing,
     and your vats will brim over with
        new wine.

11 My son, do not despise the LORD's
        discipline
     and do not resent his rebuke,
12 because the LORD disciplines those he
        loves,
     as a father*b* the son he delights in.

a 6 Or *will direct your paths*   *b 12* Hebrew; Septuagint
/ *and he punishes*

GET

SMARTER

Use Your Gray Matter
READ PROVERBS 2:1–11

"OK, OK, I know I need wisdom," you may be thinking. "But how do I get it?" Getting wisdom is like making the football team. You won't get anywhere just standing around. First, you must *want* to learn how to play. Then you need to practice your throwing, catching, tackling and blocking skills. Only then are you ready to try out for the team. It's the same with wisdom. First, you must *want* to learn and grow. Then you must "turn your ear to wisdom" and "apply your heart to understanding" (see Proverbs 2:2). You have to work at it, not just loaf around. That's why Proverbs 2:3–4 says you need to search for wisdom like hidden treasure. This means exercising your "gray matter" (brain) every day by reading books (especially the Bible), going to church and learning from older, wiser Christians. Keep at it and you'll become wise.

Your next reading is on page 791.

Get a Load of This...

Check out Proverbs 3:3–4. Cars have air filters to let the air in and keep dust, twigs, and other junk out. If you want to find favor with God and others, get an "air" filter for your heart that lets love and faithfulness in, but keeps junk stuff out.

In other words...

13 Blessed is the man who finds wisdom,
    the man who gains understanding,
14 for she is more profitable than silver
    and yields better returns than gold.
15 She is more precious than rubies;
    nothing you desire can compare with her.
16 Long life is in her right hand;
    in her left hand are riches and honor.
17 Her ways are pleasant ways,
    and all her paths are peace.
18 She is a tree of life to those who embrace her;
    those who lay hold of her will be blessed.

19 By wisdom the LORD laid the earth's foundations,
    by understanding he set the heavens in place;
20 by his knowledge the deeps were divided,
    and the clouds let drop the dew.

21 My son, preserve sound judgment and discernment,
    do not let them out of your sight;
22 they will be life for you,
    an ornament to grace your neck.
23 Then you will go on your way in safety,
    and your foot will not stumble;
24 when you lie down, you will not be afraid;
    when you lie down, your sleep will be sweet.
25 Have no fear of sudden disaster
    or of the ruin that overtakes the wicked,
26 for the LORD will be your confidence
    and will keep your foot from being snared.

27 Do not withhold good from those who deserve it,
    when it is in your power to act.
28 Do not say to your neighbor,
    "Come back later; I'll give it tomorrow"—
    when you now have it with you.

29 Do not plot harm against your neighbor,
    who lives trustfully near you.
30 Do not accuse a man for no reason—
    when he has done you no harm.

31 Do not envy a violent man
    or choose any of his ways,
32 for the LORD detests a perverse man
    but takes the upright into his confidence.

33 The LORD's curse is on the house of the wicked,
    but he blesses the home of the righteous.
34 He mocks proud mockers
    but gives grace to the humble.
35 The wise inherit honor,
    but fools he holds up to shame.

Wisdom Is Supreme

Listen, my sons, to a father's instruction;
    pay attention and gain understanding.
2 I give you sound learning,
    so do not forsake my teaching.
3 When I was a boy in my father's house,

still tender, and an only child of my
    mother,
⁴ he taught me and said,
    "Lay hold of my words with all your
        heart;
    keep my commands and you will live.
⁵ Get wisdom, get understanding;
    do not forget my words or swerve
        from them.
⁶ Do not forsake wisdom, and she will
        protect you;
    love her, and she will watch over you.
⁷ Wisdom is supreme; therefore get
    wisdom.
    Though it cost all you have,[a] get
        understanding.
⁸ Esteem her, and she will exalt you;
    embrace her, and she will honor you.
⁹ She will set a garland of grace on your
    head
    and present you with a crown of
        splendor."
¹⁰ Listen, my son, accept what I say,
    and the years of your life will be
        many.
¹¹ I guide you in the way of wisdom

and lead you along straight paths.
¹² When you walk, your steps will not be
    hampered;
    when you run, you will not stumble.
¹³ Hold on to instruction, do not let it go;
    guard it well, for it is your life.
¹⁴ Do not set foot on the path of the
    wicked
    or walk in the way of evil men.
¹⁵ Avoid it, do not travel on it;
    turn from it and go on your way.
¹⁶ For they cannot sleep till they do evil;
    they are robbed of slumber till they
        make someone fall.
¹⁷ They eat the bread of wickedness
    and drink the wine of violence.
¹⁸ The path of the righteous is like the
    first gleam of dawn,
    shining ever brighter till the full light
        of day.
¹⁹ But the way of the wicked is like deep
    darkness;
    they do not know what makes them
        stumble.

[a] 7 Or *Whatever else you get*

The Light Is Always On

READ PROVERBS 3:5–6

Lighthouses warn sailors of reefs or shallow water so they don't accidentally ram their ships into the rocks. But if the light in a lighthouse ever goes out, everyone's in a real mess. God is like a lighthouse whose light *never* goes out. No matter how bad the seas of life get, you can always trust him to guide you to safety. When you give God your life, you trust him like a sailor trusts a lighthouse. You put your life in God's hands and you trust him with everything. If you do this, you won't get all worried and fret about things or about what will happen next. So go to God and put your concerns in his hands. Don't try to figure things out all by yourself. Trust him to give you the wisdom you need to get out of tough situations. Remember, he is the light and nothing is hidden from him.

Your next reading is on page 793.

Get a Load of This...

Check out Proverbs 3:28. Don't hold out on your neighbor! If you've got it and they really need it, you don't need to be a brain surgeon to know what you should do. Be generous with your things. You never know when *you'll* be the one needing help.

In Other Words...

20 My son, pay attention to what I say;
     listen closely to my words.
21 Do not let them out of your sight,
     keep them within your heart;
22 for they are life to those who find them
     and health to a man's whole body.
23 Above all else, guard your heart,
     for it is the wellspring of life.
24 Put away perversity from your mouth;
     keep corrupt talk far from your lips.
25 Let your eyes look straight ahead,
     fix your gaze directly before you.
26 Make level[a] paths for your feet
     and take only ways that are firm.
27 Do not swerve to the right or the left;
     keep your foot from evil.

Warning Against Adultery

5 My son, pay attention to my wisdom,
     listen well to my words of insight,
2 that you may maintain discretion
     and your lips may preserve knowledge.
3 For the lips of an adulteress drip honey,
     and her speech is smoother than oil;
4 but in the end she is bitter as gall,
     sharp as a double-edged sword.
5 Her feet go down to death;
     her steps lead straight to the grave.[b]
6 She gives no thought to the way of life;
     her paths are crooked, but she knows it not.

7 Now then, my sons, listen to me;
     do not turn aside from what I say.
8 Keep to a path far from her,
     do not go near the door of her house,
9 lest you give your best strength to others
     and your years to one who is cruel,
10 lest strangers feast on your wealth
     and your toil enrich another man's house.
11 At the end of your life you will groan,
     when your flesh and body are spent.
12 You will say, "How I hated discipline!
     How my heart spurned correction!
13 I would not obey my teachers
     or listen to my instructors.
14 I have come to the brink of utter ruin
     in the midst of the whole assembly."

15 Drink water from your own cistern,
     running water from your own well.
16 Should your springs overflow in the streets,
     your streams of water in the public squares?
17 Let them be yours alone,
     never to be shared with strangers.
18 May your fountain be blessed,
     and may you rejoice in the wife of your youth.

a 26 Or *Consider the*   *b 5* Hebrew *Sheol*

19 A loving doe, a graceful deer—
   may her breasts satisfy you always,
   may you ever be captivated by her
      love.
20 Why be captivated, my son, by an
      adulteress?
   Why embrace the bosom of another
      man's wife?

21 For a man's ways are in full view of the
      LORD,
   and he examines all his paths.
22 The evil deeds of a wicked man
      ensnare him;
   the cords of his sin hold him fast.
23 He will die for lack of discipline,
   led astray by his own great folly.

Warnings Against Folly

6 My son, if you have put up security
      for your neighbor,
   if you have struck hands in pledge
      for another,
2 if you have been trapped by what you
      said,
   ensnared by the words of your
      mouth,

3 then do this, my son, to free yourself,
   since you have fallen into your
      neighbor's hands:
   Go and humble yourself;
   press your plea with your
      neighbor!
4 Allow no sleep to your eyes,
   no slumber to your eyelids.
5 Free yourself, like a gazelle from the
      hand of the hunter,
   like a bird from the snare of the
      fowler.

6 Go to the ant, you sluggard;
   consider its ways and be wise!
7 It has no commander,
   no overseer or ruler,
8 yet it stores its provisions in summer
   and gathers its food at harvest.

9 How long will you lie there, you
      sluggard?
   When will you get up from your
      sleep?
10 A little sleep, a little slumber,
   a little folding of the hands to
      rest—

GET SMARTER

Frog in Hot Water

READ PROVERBS 4:23–27

The number one rule of the mind is this: What goes in must come out. That is why Proverbs 4:23 says, "Above all else, guard your heart, for it is the wellspring of life." You can't dump sewage into a spring, right? You'd end up drinking polluted water. You also can't dump spiritual sewage into your heart (mind); otherwise nasty words and actions will come out. Proverbs 4:24–27 tells you how to stay unpolluted: Keep your mouth clean, keep your eyes on the truth and follow God. Another way to look at it is the boiled frog syndrome: Drop a frog into hot water, and he'll jump out. But put him in warm water and slowly increase the heat, and he won't realize he's getting cooked until ... well ... he's *cooked*. Don't be a frog. Be careful what you allow into your mind and don't get cooked in hot water.

Your next reading is on page 794.

¹¹ and poverty will come on you like a
        bandit
    and scarcity like an armed man.^a

¹² A scoundrel and villain,
    who goes about with a corrupt
        mouth,
¹³ who winks with his eye,
    signals with his feet
    and motions with his fingers,
¹⁴ who plots evil with deceit in his
        heart—
    he always stirs up dissension.
¹⁵ Therefore disaster will overtake him in
        an instant;
    he will suddenly be destroyed—
        without remedy.

¹⁶ There are six things the Lord hates,
    seven that are detestable to him:
¹⁷   haughty eyes,
        a lying tongue,
        hands that shed innocent blood,
¹⁸   a heart that devises wicked
            schemes,

        feet that are quick to rush into evil,
¹⁹   a false witness who pours out lies
        and a man who stirs up dissension
            among brothers.

Warning Against Adultery

²⁰ My son, keep your father's commands
    and do not forsake your mother's
        teaching.
²¹ Bind them upon your heart forever;
    fasten them around your neck.
²² When you walk, they will guide you;
    when you sleep, they will watch over
        you;
    when you awake, they will speak to
        you.
²³ For these commands are a lamp,
    this teaching is a light,
    and the corrections of discipline
    are the way to life,
²⁴ keeping you from the immoral woman,
    from the smooth tongue of the
        wayward wife.

^a 11 Or like a vagrant / and scarcity like a beggar

Fire in the Fireplace

READ PROVERBS 5

If you were going to build a fire in your house, where would you build it? In the middle of the living room? No, you would build it in the fireplace (if you have one). If you built it anywhere else, your house would burn down. You should think about sex the same way. Sex belongs in one place only: marriage (see verses 17–19). Sex is a wonderful thing, but God created it to be shared only between a husband and wife. It helps make their relationship deeper and more wonderful. Today, our culture accepts the idea of sex outside of marriage, but that's like burning embers exploding out of the fireplace and landing on the rug and burning it up. It becomes a destructive force that wrecks everything, causing jealousy, mistrust, divorce, broken homes and pain. The same goes for sex *before* marriage. Wait until marriage to enjoy sex. Then it'll be better than anything the world offers.

Your next reading is on page 799.

²⁵ Do not lust in your heart after her beauty
    or let her captivate you with her eyes,
²⁶ for the prostitute reduces you to a loaf of bread,
    and the adulteress preys upon your very life.
²⁷ Can a man scoop fire into his lap
    without his clothes being burned?
²⁸ Can a man walk on hot coals
    without his feet being scorched?
²⁹ So is he who sleeps with another man's wife;
    no one who touches her will go unpunished.

³⁰ Men do not despise a thief if he steals
    to satisfy his hunger when he is starving.
³¹ Yet if he is caught, he must pay sevenfold,
    though it costs him all the wealth of his house.
³² But a man who commits adultery lacks judgment;
    whoever does so destroys himself.
³³ Blows and disgrace are his lot,
    and his shame will never be wiped away;
³⁴ for jealousy arouses a husband's fury,
    and he will show no mercy when he takes revenge.
³⁵ He will not accept any compensation;
    he will refuse the bribe, however great it is.

Warning Against the Adulteress

7 My son, keep my words
    and store up my commands within you.
² Keep my commands and you will live;
    guard my teachings as the apple of your eye.
³ Bind them on your fingers;
    write them on the tablet of your heart.
⁴ Say to wisdom, "You are my sister,"
    and call understanding your kinsman;
⁵ they will keep you from the adulteress,
    from the wayward wife with her seductive words.

⁶ At the window of my house
    I looked out through the lattice.
⁷ I saw among the simple,
    I noticed among the young men,
    a youth who lacked judgment.
⁸ He was going down the street near her corner,
    walking along in the direction of her house
⁹ at twilight, as the day was fading,
    as the dark of night set in.

¹⁰ Then out came a woman to meet him,
    dressed like a prostitute and with crafty intent.
¹¹ (She is loud and defiant,
    her feet never stay at home;
¹² now in the street, now in the squares,
    at every corner she lurks.)
¹³ She took hold of him and kissed him
    and with a brazen face she said:

¹⁴ "I have fellowship offerings ᵃ at home;
    today I fulfilled my vows.

ᵃ *14* Traditionally *peace offerings*

Get a Load of This...

Check out Proverbs 6:6. Look at the ant. Not your *aunt,* but the little bugs on your sidewalk. No one tells them to do their chores, yet they work hard and diligently all day long. Want a good life? Hard work will move you forward. Laziness only moves you backward.

In Other Words...

¹⁵ So I came out to meet you;
 I looked for you and have found you!
¹⁶ I have covered my bed
 with colored linens from Egypt.
¹⁷ I have perfumed my bed
 with myrrh, aloes and cinnamon.
¹⁸ Come, let's drink deep of love till
 morning;
 let's enjoy ourselves with love!
¹⁹ My husband is not at home;
 he has gone on a long journey.
²⁰ He took his purse filled with money
 and will not be home till full moon."

²¹ With persuasive words she led him
 astray;
 she seduced him with her smooth
 talk.
²² All at once he followed her
 like an ox going to the slaughter,
 like a deer^a stepping into a noose^b
²³ till an arrow pierces his liver,
 like a bird darting into a snare,
 little knowing it will cost him his life.

²⁴ Now then, my sons, listen to me;
 pay attention to what I say.
²⁵ Do not let your heart turn to her ways
 or stray into her paths.
²⁶ Many are the victims she has brought
 down;
 her slain are a mighty throng.
²⁷ Her house is a highway to the grave,^c
 leading down to the chambers of
 death.

Wisdom's Call

8 Does not wisdom call out?
 Does not understanding raise her
 voice?
² On the heights along the way,
 where the paths meet, she takes her
 stand;
³ beside the gates leading into the city,
 at the entrances, she cries aloud:
⁴ "To you, O men, I call out;

^a 22 Syriac (see also Septuagint); Hebrew *fool*
^b 22 The meaning of the Hebrew for this line is uncertain.
^c 27 Hebrew *Sheol*

Make It Stick

READ PROVERBS 7:25–26

Sex appeal is used to sell everything these days, from cars to vacations to video games. With women in bikinis staring at you from the TV, magazines, and the Internet, it's tough not to get sucked in. But beware! This is a trap that can ruin your life. Look up Job 31:1 (page 662) and write it out.

I raise my voice to all mankind.
⁵You who are simple, gain prudence;
  you who are foolish, gain understanding.
⁶Listen, for I have worthy things to say;
  I open my lips to speak what is right.
⁷My mouth speaks what is true,
  for my lips detest wickedness.
⁸All the words of my mouth are just;
  none of them is crooked or perverse.
⁹To the discerning all of them are right;
  they are faultless to those who have knowledge.
¹⁰Choose my instruction instead of silver,
  knowledge rather than choice gold,
¹¹for wisdom is more precious than rubies,
  and nothing you desire can compare with her.

¹²"I, wisdom, dwell together with prudence;
  I possess knowledge and discretion.
¹³To fear the LORD is to hate evil;
  I hate pride and arrogance,
  evil behavior and perverse speech.
¹⁴Counsel and sound judgment are mine;
  I have understanding and power.
¹⁵By me kings reign
  and rulers make laws that are just;
¹⁶by me princes govern,
  and all nobles who rule on earth. ᵃ
¹⁷I love those who love me,
  and those who seek me find me.
¹⁸With me are riches and honor,
  enduring wealth and prosperity.
¹⁹My fruit is better than fine gold;
  what I yield surpasses choice silver.
²⁰I walk in the way of righteousness,
  along the paths of justice,
²¹bestowing wealth on those who love me
  and making their treasuries full.

²²"The LORD brought me forth as the first of his
      works, ᵇʼ ᶜ
  before his deeds of old;
²³I was appointed ᵈ from eternity,
  from the beginning, before the world began.
²⁴When there were no oceans, I was given birth,
  when there were no springs abounding with water;
²⁵before the mountains were settled in place,
  before the hills, I was given birth,
²⁶before he made the earth or its fields
  or any of the dust of the world.
²⁷I was there when he set the heavens in place,
  when he marked out the horizon on the face of
      the deep,
²⁸when he established the clouds above
  and fixed securely the fountains of the deep,

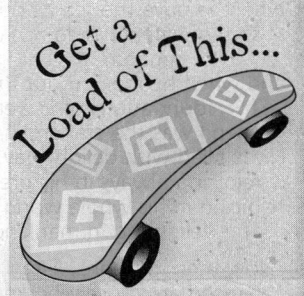

Get a Load of This...

Check out Proverbs 8:12–21. (Rap:) If you want to get knowledge, you don't need to go to college. Get wisdom. If you want prudence and discretion, don't just sit there guessin', get wisdom. Want counsel? Get wisdom. Sound judgment? No problem. Understanding? They're yours if you get wisdom. Power by the hour, riches by the ton, and prosperity you will find when you get wisdom.

In Other Words...

ᵃ 16 Many Hebrew manuscripts and Septuagint; most Hebrew manuscripts *and nobles—all righteous rulers*   ᵇ 22 Or *way; or dominion*   ᶜ 22 Or *The LORD possessed me at the beginning of his work; or The LORD brought me forth at the beginning of his work*   ᵈ 23 Or *fashioned*

29 when he gave the sea its boundary
    so the waters would not overstep his
        command,
and when he marked out the
    foundations of the earth.
30   Then I was the craftsman at his side.
I was filled with delight day after day,
    rejoicing always in his presence,
31 rejoicing in his whole world
    and delighting in mankind.

32 "Now then, my sons, listen to me;
    blessed are those who keep my
        ways.
33 Listen to my instruction and be wise;
    do not ignore it.
34 Blessed is the man who listens to me,
    watching daily at my doors,
    waiting at my doorway.
35 For whoever finds me finds life
    and receives favor from the LORD.
36 But whoever fails to find me harms
        himself;
    all who hate me love death."

Invitations of Wisdom and of Folly

9 Wisdom has built her house;
    she has hewn out its seven pillars.
2 She has prepared her meat and
    mixed her wine;
    she has also set her table.
3 She has sent out her maids, and she
    calls
    from the highest point of the city.
4 "Let all who are simple come in here!"
    she says to those who lack judgment.
5 "Come, eat my food
    and drink the wine I have mixed.
6 Leave your simple ways and you will live;
    walk in the way of understanding.

7 "Whoever corrects a mocker invites
    insult;
    whoever rebukes a wicked man
        incurs abuse.
8 Do not rebuke a mocker or he will hate
    you;
    rebuke a wise man and he will love
    you.

Make It Stick

READ PROVERBS 9:7–9

Smart alecks all have one thing in common: Instead of listening to people who correct them, they make fun of them. Don't be a smart aleck. When someone tries to teach you, listen up. Write down three people who are wise, and make a commitment to listen and learn from them.

⁹Instruct a wise man and he will be
     wiser still;
  teach a righteous man and he will
     add to his learning.

¹⁰"The fear of the LORD is the beginning
     of wisdom,
  and knowledge of the Holy One is
     understanding.
¹¹For through me your days will be many,
  and years will be added to your life.
¹²If you are wise, your wisdom will
     reward you;
  if you are a mocker, you alone will
     suffer."

¹³The woman Folly is loud;
  she is undisciplined and without
     knowledge.
¹⁴She sits at the door of her house,
  on a seat at the highest point of the
     city,
¹⁵calling out to those who pass by,
  who go straight on their way.
¹⁶"Let all who are simple come in here!"
  she says to those who lack judgment.
¹⁷"Stolen water is sweet;

food eaten in secret is delicious!"
¹⁸But little do they know that the dead
     are there,
  that her guests are in the depths of
     the grave. ª

Proverbs of Solomon

The proverbs of Solomon:

A wise son brings joy to his
     father,
  but a foolish son grief to his mother.

²Ill-gotten treasures are of no value,
  but righteousness delivers from
     death.

³The LORD does not let the righteous go
     hungry
  but he thwarts the craving of the
     wicked.

⁴Lazy hands make a man poor,
  but diligent hands bring wealth.

⁵He who gathers crops in summer is a
     wise son,

ª 18 Hebrew *Sheol*

Turn off the Adrenaline!

READ PROVERBS 9:13–18

Lady Folly calls out, "Stolen water is sweet" (verse 17). Some kids get a "rush" from ripping off or deceiving others, by shoplifting, or by breaking and entering. The truth is that people who do this sort of thing get a rush all right—rushed right off to jail (without passing Go, without collecting $200). People who feel good about doing bad things are mixed up. Their brain pumps adrenaline into their blood and that makes them feel good, so they think that that bad activity *is* good. We're meant to get excited about accomplishing positive things. But when we get excited about doing evil, we're in for a major fall. Pretty soon we don't know good from evil anymore. And then we're in trouble, because the Bible says, "Woe to those who call evil good and good evil" (Isaiah 5:20). As Proverbs 10:23 says, only "a fool finds pleasure in evil conduct." Don't be a fool.

Your next reading is on page 800.

but he who sleeps during harvest is
a disgraceful son.

6 Blessings crown the head of the
righteous,
but violence overwhelms the mouth
of the wicked. [a]

7 The memory of the righteous will be a
blessing,
but the name of the wicked will rot.

8 The wise in heart accept commands,
but a chattering fool comes to ruin.

9 The man of integrity walks securely,
but he who takes crooked paths will
be found out.

10 He who winks maliciously causes grief,
and a chattering fool comes to ruin.

11 The mouth of the righteous is a
fountain of life,
but violence overwhelms the mouth
of the wicked.

12 Hatred stirs up dissension,
but love covers over all wrongs.

13 Wisdom is found on the lips of the
discerning,
but a rod is for the back of him who
lacks judgment.

14 Wise men store up knowledge,
but the mouth of a fool invites ruin.

15 The wealth of the rich is their fortified
city,
but poverty is the ruin of the poor.

16 The wages of the righteous bring them
life,
but the income of the wicked brings
them punishment.

17 He who heeds discipline shows the
way to life,
but whoever ignores correction leads
others astray.

[a] 6 Or but the mouth of the wicked conceals violence; also in
verse 11

GET STRONGER

Time to Work

READ PROVERBS 10:3-5

There's nothing like hitting the snooze button on Saturday morning,
then hitting it again, and again, and again, and ... hey, why even set
the alarm on Saturday! However, if you treat *every* day like a Saturday, one morning you're going to wake up on the street. Why? "Lazy
hands make a man poor, but diligent hands bring wealth"
(verse 4). In life, there's a time for everything: sleep, family,
friends, play, you name it. But there's also a time for work.
Being a man of God means discovering what God has called
you to do, then rolling up your sleeves and *doing* it. Be a
good worker by (a) concentrating on your job and working hard, (b) getting better at it, (c) always going
the extra mile. But remember: Don't work super
hard *all* the time. Having fun is important, too.
Find a balance between the two.

Your next reading is on page 805.

¹⁸He who conceals his hatred has lying lips,
   and whoever spreads slander is a fool.

¹⁹When words are many, sin is not absent,
   but he who holds his tongue is wise.

²⁰The tongue of the righteous is choice silver,
   but the heart of the wicked is of little value.

²¹The lips of the righteous nourish many,
   but fools die for lack of judgment.

²²The blessing of the LORD brings wealth,
   and he adds no trouble to it.

²³A fool finds pleasure in evil conduct,
   but a man of understanding delights in wisdom.

²⁴What the wicked dreads will overtake him;
   what the righteous desire will be granted.

²⁵When the storm has swept by, the wicked are gone,
   but the righteous stand firm forever.

²⁶As vinegar to the teeth and smoke to the eyes,
   so is a sluggard to those who send him.

²⁷The fear of the LORD adds length to life,
   but the years of the wicked are cut short.

²⁸The prospect of the righteous is joy,
   but the hopes of the wicked come to nothing.

²⁹The way of the LORD is a refuge for the righteous,
   but it is the ruin of those who do evil.

³⁰The righteous will never be uprooted,
   but the wicked will not remain in the land.

³¹The mouth of the righteous brings forth wisdom,
   but a perverse tongue will be cut out.

³²The lips of the righteous know what is fitting,
   but the mouth of the wicked only what is perverse.

11 The LORD abhors dishonest scales,
   but accurate weights are his delight.

²When pride comes, then comes disgrace,
   but with humility comes wisdom.

³The integrity of the upright guides them,
   but the unfaithful are destroyed by their duplicity.

⁴Wealth is worthless in the day of wrath,
   but righteousness delivers from death.

⁵The righteousness of the blameless makes a straight
      way for them,
   but the wicked are brought down by their own
      wickedness.

⁶The righteousness of the upright delivers them,
   but the unfaithful are trapped by evil desires.

⁷When a wicked man dies, his hope perishes;
   all he expected from his power comes to nothing.

Get a Load of This...

Check out Proverbs 10:26. If you want a sure-fire way to lose your job, here's how: Be a slug. Show up late, work slowly and go overtime on your breaks. But, if you don't want to leave a trail of slime behind you, do yourself and your boss a favor and work hard instead.

In Other Words...

8 The righteous man is rescued from
trouble,
and it comes on the wicked instead.

9 With his mouth the godless destroys
his neighbor,
but through knowledge the
righteous escape.

10 When the righteous prosper, the city
rejoices;
when the wicked perish, there are
shouts of joy.

11 Through the blessing of the upright a
city is exalted,
but by the mouth of the wicked it is
destroyed.

12 A man who lacks judgment derides his
neighbor,
but a man of understanding holds
his tongue.

13 A gossip betrays a confidence,
but a trustworthy man keeps a secret.

14 For lack of guidance a nation falls,
but many advisers make victory sure.

15 He who puts up security for another
will surely suffer,
but whoever refuses to strike hands
in pledge is safe.

16 A kindhearted woman gains respect,
but ruthless men gain only wealth.

17 A kind man benefits himself,
but a cruel man brings trouble on
himself.

18 The wicked man earns deceptive
wages,
but he who sows righteousness
reaps a sure reward.

19 The truly righteous man attains life,
but he who pursues evil goes to his
death.

20 The LORD detests men of perverse heart
but he delights in those whose ways
are blameless.

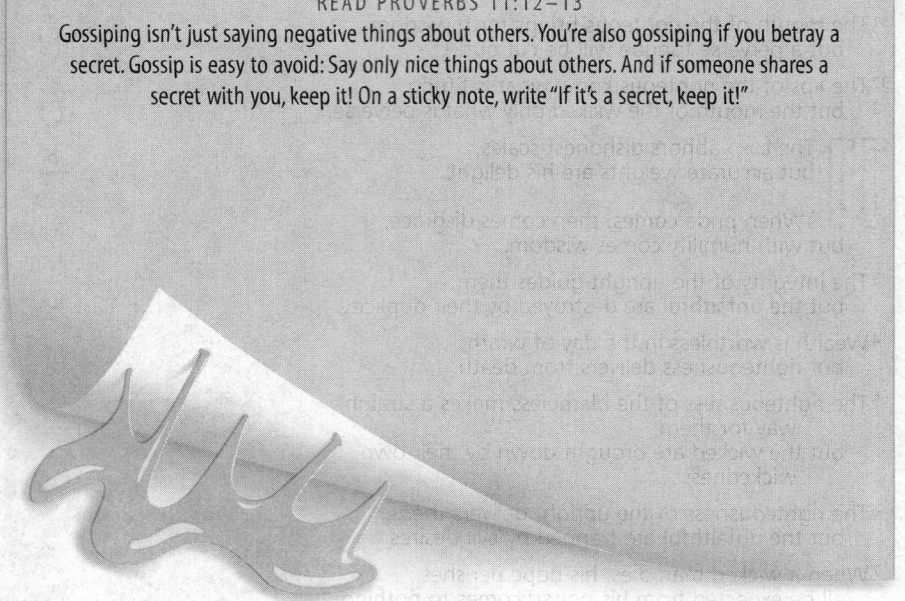

Make It Stick

READ PROVERBS 11:12–13

Gossiping isn't just saying negative things about others. You're also gossiping if you betray a
secret. Gossip is easy to avoid: Say only nice things about others. And if someone shares a
secret with you, keep it! On a sticky note, write "If it's a secret, keep it!"

21 Be sure of this: The wicked will not go
  unpunished,
   but those who are righteous will go
   free.

22 Like a gold ring in a pig's snout
   is a beautiful woman who shows no
   discretion.

23 The desire of the righteous ends only
   in good,
   but the hope of the wicked only in
   wrath.

24 One man gives freely, yet gains even
   more;

another withholds unduly, but
comes to poverty.

25 A generous man will prosper;
   he who refreshes others will himself
   be refreshed.

26 People curse the man who hoards
   grain,
   but blessing crowns him who is
   willing to sell.

27 He who seeks good finds
   goodwill,
   but evil comes to him who searches
   for it.

Make It Stick

_____

_____

_____

_____

_____

_____

**READ PROVERBS
11:24–26**

Go figure—the more you
give, the more you will have.
But if you only try to hold
on to what you have, you'll
wind up with nothing. God
really is amazing. Read Proverbs 11:24–26 and write
down what you think these
verses are specifically telling
you to be generous about.

Get a Load of This...

Check out Proverbs 12:10. It's 4 a.m. and the tomcat outside just won't be quiet! You bury your head under your pillow and vow to kick that cat to the moon next time you see it. Hey! It's OK to be upset, but cruelty to animals is *not cool* with God.

28 Whoever trusts in his riches will fall,
   but the righteous will thrive like a green leaf.

29 He who brings trouble on his family will inherit only
     wind,
   and the fool will be servant to the wise.

30 The fruit of the righteous is a tree of life,
   and he who wins souls is wise.

31 If the righteous receive their due on earth,
   how much more the ungodly and the sinner!

12 Whoever loves discipline loves knowledge,
   but he who hates correction is stupid.

2 A good man obtains favor from the LORD,
   but the LORD condemns a crafty man.

3 A man cannot be established through wickedness,
   but the righteous cannot be uprooted.

4 A wife of noble character is her husband's crown,
   but a disgraceful wife is like decay in his bones.

5 The plans of the righteous are just,
   but the advice of the wicked is deceitful.

6 The words of the wicked lie in wait for blood,
   but the speech of the upright rescues them.

7 Wicked men are overthrown and are no more,
   but the house of the righteous stands firm.

8 A man is praised according to his wisdom,
   but men with warped minds are despised.

9 Better to be a nobody and yet have a servant
   than pretend to be somebody and have no food.

10 A righteous man cares for the needs of his animal,
   but the kindest acts of the wicked are cruel.

11 He who works his land will have abundant food,
   but he who chases fantasies lacks judgment.

12 The wicked desire the plunder of evil men,
   but the root of the righteous flourishes.

13 An evil man is trapped by his sinful talk,
   but a righteous man escapes trouble.

14 From the fruit of his lips a man is filled with good
     things
   as surely as the work of his hands rewards him.

15 The way of a fool seems right to him,
   but a wise man listens to advice.

16 A fool shows his annoyance at once,
   but a prudent man overlooks an insult.

17 A truthful witness gives honest testimony,
   but a false witness tells lies.

18 Reckless words pierce like a sword,
   but the tongue of the wise brings healing.

19 Truthful lips endure forever,
  but a lying tongue lasts only a
    moment.

20 There is deceit in the hearts of those
    who plot evil,
  but joy for those who promote
    peace.

21 No harm befalls the righteous,
  but the wicked have their fill of
    trouble.

22 The LORD detests lying lips,
  but he delights in men who are
    truthful.

23 A prudent man keeps his knowledge to
    himself,
  but the heart of fools blurts out folly.

24 Diligent hands will rule,
  but laziness ends in slave labor.

25 An anxious heart weighs a man down,
  but a kind word cheers him up.

26 A righteous man is cautious in
    friendship,[a]
  but the way of the wicked leads
    them astray.

27 The lazy man does not roast[b] his
    game,
  but the diligent man prizes his
    possessions.

28 In the way of righteousness there is
    life;
  along that path is immortality.

13 A wise son heeds his father's
    instruction,
  but a mocker does not listen to
    rebuke.

2 From the fruit of his lips a man enjoys
    good things,
  but the unfaithful have a craving for
    violence.

---

[a] 26 Or man is a guide to his neighbor   [b] 27 The meaning
of the Hebrew for this word is uncertain.

Learning to Communicate

READ PROVERBS 12:13–23

If you're looking for an instruction manual on how to use your tongue, you've come to the right place. Proverbs 12:13–23 tells you how to use it and not to abuse it. Here are a few tidbits: Sinful talk? Don't even go there. People know you by what you say, so control your speech. "Turn on" your ears. Know when to listen. And take good advice, especially from someone with experience. Never overreact. Don't set your mouth on autopilot and start spewing out foolishness. Slow down, think and respond correctly. Avoid lies like you avoid head lice. Make sure everything you say is the truth. Build people up with your words; don't beat them down. Use your brain before you use your mouth. Don't fire out words that you know could hurt others. Speak truth. If you want people to consider what you say important, say things that last. (Hint: Lies never last.) Promote peace, not fights. Listen first; speak second. Don't bore people by saying everything you know, and don't annoy people by talking about things you know nothing about. Finally, be kind in how you say things.

Your next reading is on page 808.

Get a Load of This...

Proverbs 13:24 says, "He who spares the rod hates his son." We all need discipline—whether our name is Rod or not—because discipline helps keep us from destructive behavior. Mind you, "the rod" is probably a figure of speech meaning punishment of any kind.

In Other Words...

3 He who guards his lips guards his life,
     but he who speaks rashly will come to ruin.

4 The sluggard craves and gets nothing,
     but the desires of the diligent are fully satisfied.

5 The righteous hate what is false,
     but the wicked bring shame and disgrace.

6 Righteousness guards the man of integrity,
     but wickedness overthrows the sinner.

7 One man pretends to be rich, yet has nothing;
     another pretends to be poor, yet has great wealth.

8 A man's riches may ransom his life,
     but a poor man hears no threat.

9 The light of the righteous shines brightly,
     but the lamp of the wicked is snuffed out.

10 Pride only breeds quarrels,
     but wisdom is found in those who take advice.

11 Dishonest money dwindles away,
     but he who gathers money little by little makes it grow.

12 Hope deferred makes the heart sick,
     but a longing fulfilled is a tree of life.

13 He who scorns instruction will pay for it,
     but he who respects a command is rewarded.

14 The teaching of the wise is a fountain of life,
     turning a man from the snares of death.

15 Good understanding wins favor,
     but the way of the unfaithful is hard. [a]

16 Every prudent man acts out of knowledge,
     but a fool exposes his folly.

17 A wicked messenger falls into trouble,
     but a trustworthy envoy brings healing.

18 He who ignores discipline comes to poverty and shame,
     but whoever heeds correction is honored.

19 A longing fulfilled is sweet to the soul,
     but fools detest turning from evil.

20 He who walks with the wise grows wise,
     but a companion of fools suffers harm.

21 Misfortune pursues the sinner,
     but prosperity is the reward of the righteous.

22 A good man leaves an inheritance for his children's children,
     but a sinner's wealth is stored up for the righteous.

23 A poor man's field may produce abundant food,
     but injustice sweeps it away.

[a] 15 Or unfaithful does not endure

²⁴He who spares the rod hates his son,
   but he who loves him is careful to discipline him.

²⁵The righteous eat to their hearts' content,
   but the stomach of the wicked goes hungry.

14 The wise woman builds her house,
   but with her own hands the foolish one tears
   hers down.

²He whose walk is upright fears the Lord,
   but he whose ways are devious despises him.

³A fool's talk brings a rod to his back,
   but the lips of the wise protect them.

⁴Where there are no oxen, the manger is empty,
   but from the strength of an ox comes an
      abundant harvest.

⁵A truthful witness does not deceive,
   but a false witness pours out lies.

⁶The mocker seeks wisdom and finds none,
   but knowledge comes easily to the discerning.

⁷Stay away from a foolish man,
   for you will not find knowledge on his lips.

⁸The wisdom of the prudent is to give thought to
      their ways,
   but the folly of fools is deception.

⁹Fools mock at making amends for sin,
   but goodwill is found among the upright.

¹⁰Each heart knows its own bitterness,
   and no one else can share its joy.

¹¹The house of the wicked will be destroyed,
   but the tent of the upright will flourish.

¹²There is a way that seems right to a man,
   but in the end it leads to death.

¹³Even in laughter the heart may ache,
   and joy may end in grief.

¹⁴The faithless will be fully repaid for their ways,
   and the good man rewarded for his.

¹⁵A simple man believes anything,
   but a prudent man gives thought to his steps.

¹⁶A wise man fears the Lord and shuns evil,
   but a fool is hotheaded and reckless.

¹⁷A quick-tempered man does foolish things,
   and a crafty man is hated.

¹⁸The simple inherit folly,
   but the prudent are crowned with knowledge.

¹⁹Evil men will bow down in the presence of the
      good,
   and the wicked at the gates of the righteous.

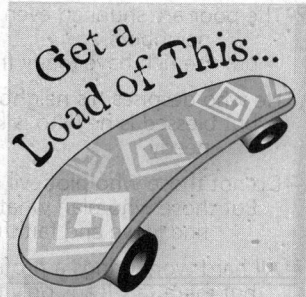

Get a Load of This...

Check out Proverbs 14:12. If you want the lead role in the school play, is it OK to threaten your competitors until they drop out? Not! Some people stop at nothing to get what they want. It may look like they're winning now, but they'll lose out in the end!

In Other Words...

²⁰ The poor are shunned even by their
     neighbors,
     but the rich have many friends.

²¹ He who despises his neighbor sins,
     but blessed is he who is kind to the
     needy.

²² Do not those who plot evil go astray?
     But those who plan what is good
     find^a love and faithfulness.

²³ All hard work brings a profit,
     but mere talk leads only to poverty.

²⁴ The wealth of the wise is their crown,
     but the folly of fools yields folly.

²⁵ A truthful witness saves lives,
     but a false witness is deceitful.

²⁶ He who fears the LORD has a secure
     fortress,
     and for his children it will be a
     refuge.

²⁷ The fear of the LORD is a fountain of life,
     turning a man from the snares of
     death.

²⁸ A large population is a king's glory,

but without subjects a prince is
     ruined.

²⁹ A patient man has great understanding,
     but a quick-tempered man displays
     folly.

³⁰ A heart at peace gives life to the body,
     but envy rots the bones.

³¹ He who oppresses the poor shows
     contempt for their Maker,
     but whoever is kind to the needy
     honors God.

³² When calamity comes, the wicked are
     brought down,
     but even in death the righteous have
     a refuge.

³³ Wisdom reposes in the heart of the
     discerning
     and even among fools she lets
     herself be known. ^b

³⁴ Righteousness exalts a nation,
     but sin is a disgrace to any people.

^a 22 Or show   ^b 33 Hebrew; Septuagint and Syriac / but in
the heart of fools she is not known

Don't Blow up Bridges

READ PROVERBS 14:16–17

During a war, armies often blow up bridges to prevent the enemy
from entering their territory. This works well except for one thing: If
your enemy can't use the bridge, um … neither can you, and you may
wind up trapping yourself. In life, we form "bridges" to other people,
called "relationships." But when we're hot-headed, we run the
risk of blowing these bridges up. The emotion of anger in and
of itself isn't wrong; but if someone offends you and your first
response is to blow up in anger, you're a bomb waiting to go
off. To prevent a blow-up, instead of just thinking how upset
you are, or how someone offended you, take a moment
to imagine how your anger will affect others (see
Proverbs 15:18). Instead of blowing up bridges,
think about a calm way to communicate and try
to fix the problem.

Your next reading is on page 813.

35 A king delights in a wise servant,
   but a shameful servant incurs his
   wrath.

15 A gentle answer turns away
      wrath,
      but a harsh word stirs up anger.

2 The tongue of the wise commends
   knowledge,
   but the mouth of the fool gushes
   folly.

3 The eyes of the LORD are everywhere,
   keeping watch on the wicked and
   the good.

4 The tongue that brings healing is a
   tree of life,
   but a deceitful tongue crushes the
   spirit.

5 A fool spurns his father's discipline,
   but whoever heeds correction shows
   prudence.

6 The house of the righteous contains
   great treasure,

Make It Stick

READ PROVERBS 15:1
Many boys, when they are insulted, shout insults back. But Proverbs 15:1 says that when someone calls you names, it's better to respond calmly. Ask them what's bothering them. When was the last time someone blew up at you? How did you respond? How can you respond better next time?

Get a Load of This...

Is Proverbs 15:17 trying to say vegetarians are more loving than meat-eaters? Not at all. It's saying that it's better to not have much and live in harmony than to have everything and live with anger and hatred. Remember: Good relationships are important!

In Other Words...

but the income of the wicked brings them trouble.

7 The lips of the wise spread knowledge;
  not so the hearts of fools.

8 The LORD detests the sacrifice of the wicked,
  but the prayer of the upright pleases him.

9 The LORD detests the way of the wicked
  but he loves those who pursue righteousness.

10 Stern discipline awaits him who leaves the path;
  he who hates correction will die.

11 Death and Destruction[a] lie open before the LORD—
  how much more the hearts of men!

12 A mocker resents correction;
  he will not consult the wise.

13 A happy heart makes the face cheerful,
  but heartache crushes the spirit.

14 The discerning heart seeks knowledge,
  but the mouth of a fool feeds on folly.

15 All the days of the oppressed are wretched,
  but the cheerful heart has a continual feast.

16 Better a little with the fear of the LORD
  than great wealth with turmoil.

17 Better a meal of vegetables where there is love
  than a fattened calf with hatred.

18 A hot-tempered man stirs up dissension,
  but a patient man calms a quarrel.

19 The way of the sluggard is blocked with thorns,
  but the path of the upright is a highway.

20 A wise son brings joy to his father,
  but a foolish man despises his mother.

21 Folly delights a man who lacks judgment,
  but a man of understanding keeps a straight course.

22 Plans fail for lack of counsel,
  but with many advisers they succeed.

23 A man finds joy in giving an apt reply—
  and how good is a timely word!

24 The path of life leads upward for the wise
  to keep him from going down to the grave.[b]

25 The LORD tears down the proud man's house
  but he keeps the widow's boundaries intact.

26 The LORD detests the thoughts of the wicked,
  but those of the pure are pleasing to him.

27 A greedy man brings trouble to his family,
  but he who hates bribes will live.

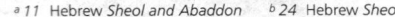

[a] 11 Hebrew *Sheol* and *Abaddon*   [b] 24 Hebrew *Sheol*

28 The heart of the righteous weighs its answers,
　　but the mouth of the wicked gushes evil.

29 The LORD is far from the wicked
　　but he hears the prayer of the righteous.

30 A cheerful look brings joy to the heart,
　　and good news gives health to the bones.

31 He who listens to a life-giving rebuke
　　will be at home among the wise.

32 He who ignores discipline despises himself,
　　but whoever heeds correction gains understanding.

33 The fear of the LORD teaches a man wisdom,[a]
　　and humility comes before honor.

16 To man belong the plans of the heart,
　　but from the LORD comes the reply of the
　　tongue.

2 All a man's ways seem innocent to him,
　　but motives are weighed by the LORD.

3 Commit to the LORD whatever you do,
　　and your plans will succeed.

4 The LORD works out everything for his own ends—
　　even the wicked for a day of disaster.

5 The LORD detests all the proud of heart.
　　Be sure of this: They will not go unpunished.

6 Through love and faithfulness sin is atoned for;
　　through the fear of the LORD a man avoids evil.

7 When a man's ways are pleasing to the LORD,
　　he makes even his enemies live at peace with him.

8 Better a little with righteousness
　　than much gain with injustice.

9 In his heart a man plans his course,
　　but the LORD determines his steps.

10 The lips of a king speak as an oracle,
　　and his mouth should not betray justice.

11 Honest scales and balances are from the LORD;
　　all the weights in the bag are of his making.

12 Kings detest wrongdoing,
　　for a throne is established through righteousness.

13 Kings take pleasure in honest lips;
　　they value a man who speaks the truth.

14 A king's wrath is a messenger of death,
　　but a wise man will appease it.

15 When a king's face brightens, it means life;
　　his favor is like a rain cloud in spring.

16 How much better to get wisdom than gold,
　　to choose understanding rather than silver!

a 33 Or Wisdom teaches the fear of the LORD

Get a Load of This...

Check out Proverbs 15:26. What thoughts fill your mind when you daydream? God gave you the freedom to think about anything you want, but he wants you to keep your thoughts pure and clean. Keep your mind clean—cleaner than your bedroom!

In other Words...

Get a Load of This...

Check out Proverbs 16:18. You may have heard the saying "pride comes before a fall." But did you know that saying comes from the Bible? What it means is, if you spend too much time looking down your nose, you'll soon fall flat on your face. Youch!

In Other Words...

17 The highway of the upright avoids evil;
    he who guards his way guards his life.

18 Pride goes before destruction,
    a haughty spirit before a fall.

19 Better to be lowly in spirit and among the oppressed
    than to share plunder with the proud.

20 Whoever gives heed to instruction prospers,
    and blessed is he who trusts in the LORD.

21 The wise in heart are called discerning,
    and pleasant words promote instruction.^a

22 Understanding is a fountain of life to those who have it,
    but folly brings punishment to fools.

23 A wise man's heart guides his mouth,
    and his lips promote instruction.^b

24 Pleasant words are a honeycomb,
    sweet to the soul and healing to the bones.

25 There is a way that seems right to a man,
    but in the end it leads to death.

26 The laborer's appetite works for him;
    his hunger drives him on.

27 A scoundrel plots evil,
    and his speech is like a scorching fire.

28 A perverse man stirs up dissension,
    and a gossip separates close friends.

29 A violent man entices his neighbor
    and leads him down a path that is not good.

30 He who winks with his eye is plotting perversity;
    he who purses his lips is bent on evil.

31 Gray hair is a crown of splendor;
    it is attained by a righteous life.

32 Better a patient man than a warrior,
    a man who controls his temper than one who takes a city.

33 The lot is cast into the lap,
    but its every decision is from the LORD.

17   Better a dry crust with peace and quiet
    than a house full of feasting,^c with strife.

2 A wise servant will rule over a disgraceful son,
    and will share the inheritance as one of the brothers.

3 The crucible for silver and the furnace for gold,
    but the LORD tests the heart.

4 A wicked man listens to evil lips;
    a liar pays attention to a malicious tongue.

^a 21 Or *words make a man persuasive*   ^b 23 Or *mouth / and makes his lips persuasive*   ^c 1 Hebrew *sacrifices*

⁵ He who mocks the poor shows
      contempt for their Maker;
   whoever gloats over disaster will not
      go unpunished.

⁶ Children's children are a crown to the
      aged,
   and parents are the pride of their
      children.

⁷ Arrogant*a* lips are unsuited to a fool—
   how much worse lying lips to a ruler!

⁸ A bribe is a charm to the one who
      gives it;
   wherever he turns, he succeeds.

⁹ He who covers over an offense
      promotes love,
   but whoever repeats the matter
      separates close friends.

¹⁰ A rebuke impresses a man of
      discernment
   more than a hundred lashes a fool.

¹¹ An evil man is bent only on rebellion;
   a merciless official will be sent
      against him.

¹² Better to meet a bear robbed of her cubs
   than a fool in his folly.

¹³ If a man pays back evil for good,
   evil will never leave his house.

¹⁴ Starting a quarrel is like breaching a
      dam;
   so drop the matter before a dispute
      breaks out.

¹⁵ Acquitting the guilty and condemning
      the innocent—
   the LORD detests them both.

¹⁶ Of what use is money in the hand of a
      fool,
   since he has no desire to get
      wisdom?

¹⁷ A friend loves at all times,
   and a brother is born for adversity.

¹⁸ A man lacking in judgment strikes
      hands in pledge
   and puts up security for his
      neighbor.

a 7 Or *Eloquent*

Mind Over Muscle

READ PROVERBS 16:32

A key way to becoming successful at judo, karate and other martial arts is to learn how to use your opponent's strength against him. In other words, learn to fight smarter, not harder. You can defeat someone much larger and stronger than yourself if you use your brains first and your brawn second. On the other hand, one of the quickest ways to lose a fight is to lose your temper, because anger causes you to be hasty and make mistakes. The same is true for the rest of life. More can be accomplished through wisdom and patience than through anger and conflict. Just as a wise fighter can defeat a stronger fighter, so a man who thinks before he acts will accomplish more than the man who just bulldozes his way through life. Remember: Brains first, brawn second and you'll rarely lose.

Your next reading is on page 817.

¹⁹ He who loves a quarrel loves sin;
    he who builds a high gate invites
        destruction.

²⁰ A man of perverse heart does not
        prosper;
    he whose tongue is deceitful falls
        into trouble.

²¹ To have a fool for a son brings grief;
    there is no joy for the father of a fool.

²² A cheerful heart is good medicine,
    but a crushed spirit dries up the
        bones.

²³ A wicked man accepts a bribe in secret
    to pervert the course of justice.

²⁴ A discerning man keeps wisdom in
        view,
    but a fool's eyes wander to the ends
        of the earth.

²⁵ A foolish son brings grief to his father
    and bitterness to the one who bore
        him.

²⁶ It is not good to punish an innocent
        man,
    or to flog officials for their integrity.

²⁷ A man of knowledge uses words with
        restraint,
    and a man of understanding is even-
        tempered.

²⁸ Even a fool is thought wise if he keeps
        silent,
    and discerning if he holds his
        tongue.

 An unfriendly man pursues
    selfish ends;
    he defies all sound judgment.

² A fool finds no pleasure in
        understanding
    but delights in airing his own
        opinions.

³ When wickedness comes, so does
        contempt,
    and with shame comes disgrace.

Make It Stick

READ PROVERBS 17:9

What are two things that someone has done to you that still bother you? Write them on a sticky
note and then scribble them out until you can't see them anymore. Feel better? If not, perhaps
you need to work things out with that person. If you need help, talk to an adult about it.

⁴The words of a man's mouth are deep waters,
   but the fountain of wisdom is a bubbling brook.

⁵It is not good to be partial to the wicked
   or to deprive the innocent of justice.

⁶A fool's lips bring him strife,
   and his mouth invites a beating.

⁷A fool's mouth is his undoing,
   and his lips are a snare to his soul.

⁸The words of a gossip are like choice morsels;
   they go down to a man's inmost parts.

⁹One who is slack in his work
   is brother to one who destroys.

¹⁰The name of the LORD is a strong tower;
   the righteous run to it and are safe.

¹¹The wealth of the rich is their fortified city;
   they imagine it an unscalable wall.

¹²Before his downfall a man's heart is proud,
   but humility comes before honor.

¹³He who answers before listening—
   that is his folly and his shame.

¹⁴A man's spirit sustains him in sickness,
   but a crushed spirit who can bear?

¹⁵The heart of the discerning acquires knowledge;
   the ears of the wise seek it out.

¹⁶A gift opens the way for the giver
   and ushers him into the presence of the great.

¹⁷The first to present his case seems right,
   till another comes forward and questions him.

¹⁸Casting the lot settles disputes
   and keeps strong opponents apart.

¹⁹An offended brother is more unyielding than a
      fortified city,
   and disputes are like the barred gates of a citadel.

²⁰From the fruit of his mouth a man's stomach is
      filled;
   with the harvest from his lips he is satisfied.

²¹The tongue has the power of life and death,
   and those who love it will eat its fruit.

²²He who finds a wife finds what is good
   and receives favor from the LORD.

²³A poor man pleads for mercy,
   but a rich man answers harshly.

²⁴A man of many companions may come to ruin,
   but there is a friend who sticks closer than a
      brother.

Family members should be able to count on you. The verse, "A brother is born for adversity" (Proverbs 17:17) does *not* mean, "You can't help but fight with your brother." It means, "A brother is there for you when times *really* get tough." Are you that kind of brother (or friend)?

Get a Load of This...

Check out Proverbs 18:13. Ever start blabbing away before a friend even finished a sentence? Here's a tip: If you want others to listen to you, listen to them first and *then* answer. Otherwise, "he who listens by the inch and talks by the yard will be kicked by the foot."

In Other Words...

19 Better a poor man whose walk is blameless
than a fool whose lips are perverse.

2 It is not good to have zeal without
knowledge,
nor to be hasty and miss the way.

3 A man's own folly ruins his life,
yet his heart rages against the Lord.

4 Wealth brings many friends,
but a poor man's friend deserts him.

5 A false witness will not go unpunished,
and he who pours out lies will not go free.

6 Many curry favor with a ruler,
and everyone is the friend of a man who gives
gifts.

7 A poor man is shunned by all his relatives—
how much more do his friends avoid him!
Though he pursues them with pleading,
they are nowhere to be found.*a*

8 He who gets wisdom loves his own soul;
he who cherishes understanding prospers.

9 A false witness will not go unpunished,
and he who pours out lies will perish.

10 It is not fitting for a fool to live in luxury—
how much worse for a slave to rule over princes!

11 A man's wisdom gives him patience;
it is to his glory to overlook an offense.

12 A king's rage is like the roar of a lion,
but his favor is like dew on the grass.

13 A foolish son is his father's ruin,
and a quarrelsome wife is like a constant dripping.

14 Houses and wealth are inherited from parents,
but a prudent wife is from the Lord.

15 Laziness brings on deep sleep,
and the shiftless man goes hungry.

16 He who obeys instructions guards his life,
but he who is contemptuous of his ways will die.

17 He who is kind to the poor lends to the Lord,
and he will reward him for what he has done.

18 Discipline your son, for in that there is hope;
do not be a willing party to his death.

19 A hot-tempered man must pay the penalty;
if you rescue him, you will have to do it again.

20 Listen to advice and accept instruction,
and in the end you will be wise.

---

a 7 The meaning of the Hebrew for this sentence is uncertain.

21 Many are the plans in a man's heart,
    but it is the LORD's purpose that
        prevails.

22 What a man desires is unfailing love^a;
    better to be poor than a liar.

23 The fear of the LORD leads to life:
    Then one rests content, untouched
        by trouble.

24 The sluggard buries his hand in the
        dish;
    he will not even bring it back to his
        mouth!

25 Flog a mocker, and the simple will
        learn prudence;
    rebuke a discerning man, and he will
        gain knowledge.

26 He who robs his father and drives out
        his mother
    is a son who brings shame and
        disgrace.

27 Stop listening to instruction, my son,
    and you will stray from the words of
        knowledge.

28 A corrupt witness mocks at justice,
    and the mouth of the wicked gulps
        down evil.

29 Penalties are prepared for mockers,
    and beatings for the backs of fools.

 Wine is a mocker and beer a
    brawler;
    whoever is led astray by them
        is not wise.

2 A king's wrath is like the roar of a
        lion;
    he who angers him forfeits his life.

3 It is to a man's honor to avoid strife,
    but every fool is quick to quarrel.

4 A sluggard does not plow in season;
    so at harvest time he looks but finds
        nothing.

5 The purposes of a man's heart are
        deep waters,
    but a man of understanding draws
        them out.

^a 22 Or A man's greed is his shame

Melon Patch or Weeds?

READ PROVERBS 18:21

GET SMARTER

When people think of war, they usually picture guns, bombs and other weapons. But almost every battle is started by words. No wonder Proverbs 18:21 says, "The tongue has the power of life and death." The book of James compares the power of the tongue to a fire: A great forest can be burned to the ground with a small spark. This is serious business. Jesus said we will be held accountable for every careless word we speak (Matthew 12:36). However, Proverbs 18:21 also says those who use their tongue properly will "eat its fruit." You can grow good stuff with your tongue by being uplifting and positive. If you speak loving words, it's like you're walking around in a garden, spitting out watermelon seeds. Every time you spit a seed out, you grow a watermelon. Will you grow a melon patch or just weeds? It depends on what you plant.

Your next reading is on page 820.

6 Many a man claims to have unfailing
love,
　but a faithful man who can find?

7 The righteous man leads a blameless
life;
　blessed are his children after him.

8 When a king sits on his throne to
judge,
　he winnows out all evil with his
eyes.

9 Who can say, "I have kept my heart
pure;
　I am clean and without sin"?

10 Differing weights and differing
measures—
　the LORD detests them both.

11 Even a child is known by his actions,
　by whether his conduct is pure and
right.

12 Ears that hear and eyes that see—
　the LORD has made them both.

13 Do not love sleep or you will grow poor;
　stay awake and you will have food
to spare.

14 "It's no good, it's no good!" says the
buyer;
　then off he goes and boasts about
his purchase.

15 Gold there is, and rubies in
abundance,
　but lips that speak knowledge are a
rare jewel.

16 Take the garment of one who puts up
security for a stranger;
　hold it in pledge if he does it for a
wayward woman.

17 Food gained by fraud tastes sweet to a
man,
　but he ends up with a mouth full of
gravel.

18 Make plans by seeking advice;
　if you wage war, obtain guidance.

Make It Stick

READ PROVERBS 19:21

With all of the ideas you have for your life, how can you know which are from God and
which aren't? By praying over them. Write on a sticky note: "Dear God, please give me peace
about the plan that lines up with your will for me. Take the other plans away."

¹⁹ A gossip betrays a confidence;
   so avoid a man who talks too much.

²⁰ If a man curses his father or mother,
   his lamp will be snuffed out in pitch darkness.

²¹ An inheritance quickly gained at the beginning
   will not be blessed at the end.

²² Do not say, "I'll pay you back for this wrong!"
   Wait for the LORD, and he will deliver you.

²³ The LORD detests differing weights,
   and dishonest scales do not please him.

²⁴ A man's steps are directed by the LORD.
   How then can anyone understand his own way?

²⁵ It is a trap for a man to dedicate something rashly
   and only later to consider his vows.

²⁶ A wise king winnows out the wicked;
   he drives the threshing wheel over them.

²⁷ The lamp of the LORD searches the spirit of a man ᵃ;
   it searches out his inmost being.

²⁸ Love and faithfulness keep a king safe;
   through love his throne is made secure.

²⁹ The glory of young men is their strength,
   gray hair the splendor of the old.

³⁰ Blows and wounds cleanse away evil,
   and beatings purge the inmost being.

21 The king's heart is in the hand of the LORD;
   he directs it like a watercourse wherever he
   pleases.
   ²All a man's ways seem right to him,
   but the LORD weighs the heart.

³ To do what is right and just
   is more acceptable to the LORD than sacrifice.

⁴ Haughty eyes and a proud heart,
   the lamp of the wicked, are sin!

⁵ The plans of the diligent lead to profit
   as surely as haste leads to poverty.

⁶ A fortune made by a lying tongue
   is a fleeting vapor and a deadly snare. ᵇ

⁷ The violence of the wicked will drag them away,
   for they refuse to do what is right.

⁸ The way of the guilty is devious,
   but the conduct of the innocent is upright.

⁹ Better to live on a corner of the roof
   than share a house with a quarrelsome wife.

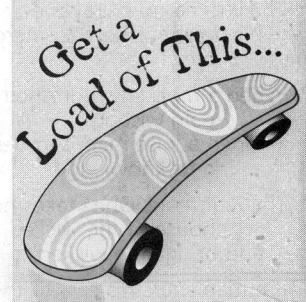

Get a Load of This...

Check out Proverbs 20:13. (Rap:) If all you do is lay in bed, your bank account will sink like lead. But if you work and stay awake, you'll stuff your face with yummy cake. If you like food and want to chew, get out of bed; there's work to do.

ᵃ *27* Or *The spirit of man is the* LORD's *lamp*   ᵇ *6* Some Hebrew manuscripts,
Septuagint and Vulgate; most Hebrew manuscripts *vapor for those who seek death*

¹⁰ The wicked man craves evil;
   his neighbor gets no mercy from
      him.

¹¹ When a mocker is punished, the simple
      gain wisdom;
   when a wise man is instructed, he
      gets knowledge.

¹² The Righteous One*ᵃ* takes note of the
      house of the wicked
   and brings the wicked to ruin.

¹³ If a man shuts his ears to the cry of the
      poor,
   he too will cry out and not be
      answered.

¹⁴ A gift given in secret soothes anger,
   and a bribe concealed in the cloak
      pacifies great wrath.

¹⁵ When justice is done, it brings joy to
      the righteous
   but terror to evildoers.

¹⁶ A man who strays from the path of
      understanding
   comes to rest in the company of the
      dead.

¹⁷ He who loves pleasure will become
      poor;
   whoever loves wine and oil will
      never be rich.

¹⁸ The wicked become a ransom for the
      righteous,
   and the unfaithful for the upright.

¹⁹ Better to live in a desert
   than with a quarrelsome and
      ill-tempered wife.

²⁰ In the house of the wise are stores of
      choice food and oil,
   but a foolish man devours all he
      has.

²¹ He who pursues righteousness and
      love
   finds life, prosperity*ᵇ* and honor.

²² A wise man attacks the city of the
      mighty
   and pulls down the stronghold in
      which they trust.

ᵃ 12 Or *The righteous man*   *ᵇ 21* Or *righteousness*

Eye-for-eye Attitudes

READ PROVERBS 20:22; 24:29

Many action movies exalt "getting revenge" as the ultimate satisfaction. They teach that a real man takes the law into his own hands. But these kind of eye-for-eye attitudes create gangs and gang wars, with rival gangs continually taking revenge on each other. This is sometimes true even with cliques at your school. Stay away from this attitude in yourself and in others. It's better to stop revenge before it starts. If someone does something bad to you, turn the other cheek (see Matthew 5:39) and trust God to sort things out. This doesn't mean you should stand around waiting to get smacked. It means you should love and forgive others and not punish them for their sins. So work to resolve a quarrel, not make it worse. Refusing to seek revenge is not a wimpy thing to do. It takes a real man with real guts.

Your next reading is on page 821.

23 He who guards his mouth and his
tongue
  keeps himself from calamity.

24 The proud and arrogant man—
  "Mocker" is his name;
  he behaves with overweening pride.

25 The sluggard's craving will be the
death of him,
  because his hands refuse to work.

26 All day long he craves for more,
  but the righteous give without
sparing.

27 The sacrifice of the wicked is
detestable—
  how much more so when brought
with evil intent!

28 A false witness will perish,
  and whoever listens to him will be
destroyed forever. [a]

29 A wicked man puts up a bold front,
  but an upright man gives thought to
his ways.

30 There is no wisdom, no insight, no plan
  that can succeed against the LORD.

31 The horse is made ready for the day of
battle,
  but victory rests with the LORD.

22 A good name is more
desirable than great riches;
  to be esteemed is better than
silver or gold.

2 Rich and poor have this in common:
  The LORD is the Maker of them all.

3 A prudent man sees danger and takes
refuge,
  but the simple keep going and suffer
for it.

4 Humility and the fear of the LORD
  bring wealth and honor and life.

5 In the paths of the wicked lie thorns
and snares,
  but he who guards his soul stays far
from them.

6 Train [b] a child in the way he should go,
  and when he is old he will not turn
from it.

a 28 Or / but the words of an obedient man will live on
b 6 Or Start

What's Your Name Worth?

READ PROVERBS 22:1

Companies do everything possible to build a good name for themselves so people will buy their products. The best way to build their
brand name is to make good products. The surest way to get a bad
name is to produce junk. The same is true for us. A good name is
more desirable than riches, because a good name is the *key*
to riches—and *all* kinds of success. If you have a reputation
for being honest, respectful and hard-working, people will
come to you when they have a job that needs to get done.
But the quickest way to ruin your name is to be sassy, or to
lie, cheat or steal to get ahead. Wreck your name with
that sort of behavior and it's hard to repair the
damage. So protect your name with your life.
Work at building up a good name and success
will surely come.

Your next reading is on page 824.

⁷The rich rule over the poor,
  and the borrower is servant to the
    lender.

⁸He who sows wickedness reaps trouble,
  and the rod of his fury will be
    destroyed.

⁹A generous man will himself be blessed,
  for he shares his food with the poor.

¹⁰Drive out the mocker, and out goes
    strife;
  quarrels and insults are ended.

¹¹He who loves a pure heart and whose
    speech is gracious
  will have the king for his friend.

¹²The eyes of the LORD keep watch over
    knowledge,
  but he frustrates the words of the
    unfaithful.

¹³The sluggard says, "There is a lion
    outside!"
  or, "I will be murdered in the streets!"

¹⁴The mouth of an adulteress is a deep
    pit;
  he who is under the LORD's wrath
    will fall into it.

¹⁵Folly is bound up in the heart of a child,
  but the rod of discipline will drive it
    far from him.

¹⁶He who oppresses the poor to increase
    his wealth
  and he who gives gifts to the rich—
    both come to poverty.

Sayings of the Wise

¹⁷Pay attention and listen to the sayings
    of the wise;
  apply your heart to what I teach,
¹⁸for it is pleasing when you keep them
    in your heart
  and have all of them ready on your
    lips.
¹⁹So that your trust may be in the LORD,
  I teach you today, even you.
²⁰Have I not written thirty[a] sayings for
    you,
  sayings of counsel and knowledge,
²¹teaching you true and reliable words,
  so that you can give sound answers
    to him who sent you?

²²Do not exploit the poor because they
    are poor
  and do not crush the needy in court,
²³for the LORD will take up their case
  and will plunder those who plunder
    them.

²⁴Do not make friends with a
    hot-tempered man,
  do not associate with one easily
    angered,
²⁵or you may learn his ways
  and get yourself ensnared.

²⁶Do not be a man who strikes hands in
    pledge
  or puts up security for debts;
²⁷if you lack the means to pay,
  your very bed will be snatched from
    under you.

²⁸Do not move an ancient boundary
    stone
  set up by your forefathers.

²⁹Do you see a man skilled in his work?
  He will serve before kings;
  he will not serve before obscure men.

23 When you sit to dine with a
    ruler,
  note well what[b] is before you,
  ²and put a knife to your throat
  if you are given to gluttony.
³Do not crave his delicacies,
  for that food is deceptive.

⁴Do not wear yourself out to get rich;
  have the wisdom to show restraint.
⁵Cast but a glance at riches, and they
    are gone,
  for they will surely sprout wings
  and fly off to the sky like an eagle.

⁶Do not eat the food of a stingy man,
  do not crave his delicacies;
⁷for he is the kind of man
  who is always thinking about the
    cost.[c]
  "Eat and drink," he says to you,
  but his heart is not with you.
⁸You will vomit up the little you have
    eaten
  and will have wasted your
    compliments.

⁹Do not speak to a fool,
  for he will scorn the wisdom of your
    words.

---

[a] 20 Or not formerly written; or not written excellent
[b] 1 Or who   [c] 7 Or for as he thinks within himself, / so he
is; or for as he puts on a feast, / so he is

10 Do not move an ancient boundary stone
    or encroach on the fields of the fatherless,
11 for their Defender is strong;
    he will take up their case against you.

12 Apply your heart to instruction
    and your ears to words of knowledge.

13 Do not withhold discipline from a child;
    if you punish him with the rod, he will not die.
14 Punish him with the rod
    and save his soul from death.[a]

15 My son, if your heart is wise,
    then my heart will be glad;
16 my inmost being will rejoice
    when your lips speak what is right.

17 Do not let your heart envy sinners,
    but always be zealous for the fear of the LORD.
18 There is surely a future hope for you,
    and your hope will not be cut off.

19 Listen, my son, and be wise,
    and keep your heart on the right path.
20 Do not join those who drink too much wine
    or gorge themselves on meat,
21 for drunkards and gluttons become poor,
    and drowsiness clothes them in rags.

22 Listen to your father, who gave you life,
    and do not despise your mother when she is old.
23 Buy the truth and do not sell it;
    get wisdom, discipline and understanding.
24 The father of a righteous man has great joy;
    he who has a wise son delights in him.
25 May your father and mother be glad;
    may she who gave you birth rejoice!

26 My son, give me your heart
    and let your eyes keep to my ways,
27 for a prostitute is a deep pit
    and a wayward wife is a narrow well.
28 Like a bandit she lies in wait,
    and multiplies the unfaithful among men.

29 Who has woe? Who has sorrow?
    Who has strife? Who has complaints?
    Who has needless bruises? Who has bloodshot
        eyes?
30 Those who linger over wine,
    who go to sample bowls of mixed wine.
31 Do not gaze at wine when it is red,
    when it sparkles in the cup,
    when it goes down smoothly!
32 In the end it bites like a snake
    and poisons like a viper.
33 Your eyes will see strange sights
    and your mind imagine confusing things.

Gross!

Check out Proverbs
23:8. Want to learn to
say "vomit" in Hebrew?
Qayah (kaw-yaw).
Use that word the
next time you're lean-
ing over the toilet
heaving your guts out
and your mom asks
you what's wrong.

[a] 14 Hebrew *Sheol*

34 You will be like one sleeping on the
    high seas,
    lying on top of the rigging.
35 "They hit me," you will say, "but I'm
    not hurt!
    They beat me, but I don't feel it!
When will I wake up
    so I can find another drink?"

24 Do not envy wicked men,
    do not desire their company;
2 for their hearts plot violence,
    and their lips talk about
    making trouble.

3 By wisdom a house is built,
    and through understanding it is
    established;
4 through knowledge its rooms are
    filled
    with rare and beautiful treasures.

5 A wise man has great power,
    and a man of knowledge increases
    strength;
6 for waging war you need guidance,
    and for victory many advisers.

7 Wisdom is too high for a fool;
    in the assembly at the gate he has
    nothing to say.

8 He who plots evil
    will be known as a schemer.
9 The schemes of folly are sin,
    and men detest a mocker.

10 If you falter in times of trouble,
    how small is your strength!

11 Rescue those being led away to death;
    hold back those staggering toward
    slaughter.
12 If you say, "But we knew nothing
    about this,"
    does not he who weighs the heart
    perceive it?
Does not he who guards your life
    know it?
    Will he not repay each person
    according to what he has done?

13 Eat honey, my son, for it is good;
    honey from the comb is sweet to
    your taste.
14 Know also that wisdom is sweet to
    your soul;

Do Us Proud!

PROVERBS 23:22–25

For some guys, hardly anything is more embarrassing than getting a
hug from Mom in public—unless it's having their mom give them a
kiss. Yeech! But moms don't hug and kiss their sons to embarrass
them. They do it because they love them. Rather than be embarrassed when your mom hugs you, you should be proud, because it means you have a good relationship with her. Some
people think children and parents are *supposed* to have bad
relationships. *Bwaaaaap!* Wrong answer. Nothing is further
from the truth. God calls kids to love, honor and respect their
parents. If you do, you will bring joy and happiness to
both you and your parents. That's how God meant
things to be. So if your mom ever hugs you and
tells you how proud she is of you, don't moan,
"*Moommm . . .*" Thank God that she's proud of
you and loves you.

Your next reading is on page 826.

if you find it, there is a future hope
  for you,
and your hope will not be cut off.

15 Do not lie in wait like an outlaw against
    a righteous man's house,
  do not raid his dwelling place;
16 for though a righteous man falls seven
    times, he rises again,
  but the wicked are brought down by
    calamity.

17 Do not gloat when your enemy falls;
  when he stumbles, do not let your
    heart rejoice,
18 or the LORD will see and disapprove
  and turn his wrath away from him.

19 Do not fret because of evil men
  or be envious of the wicked,
20 for the evil man has no future hope,
  and the lamp of the wicked will be
    snuffed out.

21 Fear the LORD and the king, my son,
  and do not join with the rebellious,
22 for those two will send sudden
    destruction upon them,
  and who knows what calamities
    they can bring?

Further Sayings of the Wise

23 These also are sayings of the wise:

To show partiality in judging is not
  good:
24 Whoever says to the guilty, "You are
    innocent"—
  peoples will curse him and nations
    denounce him.
25 But it will go well with those who
    convict the guilty,
  and rich blessing will come upon
    them.

26 An honest answer
  is like a kiss on the lips.

27 Finish your outdoor work
  and get your fields ready;
  after that, build your house.

28 Do not testify against your neighbor
    without cause,
  or use your lips to deceive.
29 Do not say, "I'll do to him as he has
    done to me;
  I'll pay that man back for what he
    did."

30 I went past the field of the sluggard,
  past the vineyard of the man who
    lacks judgment;
31 thorns had come up everywhere,
  the ground was covered with weeds,
  and the stone wall was in ruins.
32 I applied my heart to what I observed
  and learned a lesson from what I saw:
33 A little sleep, a little slumber,
  a little folding of the hands to rest—
34 and poverty will come on you like a
    bandit
  and scarcity like an armed man. [a]

More Proverbs of Solomon

25 These are more proverbs of
Solomon, copied by the men
of Hezekiah king of Judah:

2 It is the glory of God to conceal a matter;
  to search out a matter is the glory of
    kings.

3 As the heavens are high and the earth
    is deep,
  so the hearts of kings are
    unsearchable.

4 Remove the dross from the silver,
  and out comes material for [b] the
    silversmith;
5 remove the wicked from the king's
    presence,
  and his throne will be established
    through righteousness.

6 Do not exalt yourself in the king's
    presence,
  and do not claim a place among
    great men;
7 it is better for him to say to you,
    "Come up here,"
  than for him to humiliate you before
    a nobleman.

What you have seen with your eyes
8   do not bring [c] hastily to court,
  for what will you do in the end
    if your neighbor puts you to shame?

9 If you argue your case with a neighbor,
  do not betray another man's
    confidence,
10 or he who hears it may shame you
  and you will never lose your bad
    reputation.

---

[a] 34 Or like a vagrant / and scarcity like a beggar
[b] 4 Or comes a vessel from   [c] 7,8 Or nobleman / on whom
you had set your eyes. / [8] Do not go

[11] A word aptly spoken
  is like apples of gold in settings of
    silver.

[12] Like an earring of gold or an ornament
    of fine gold
  is a wise man's rebuke to a listening
    ear.

[13] Like the coolness of snow at harvest
    time
  is a trustworthy messenger to those
    who send him;
  he refreshes the spirit of his masters.

[14] Like clouds and wind without rain
  is a man who boasts of gifts he does
    not give.

[15] Through patience a ruler can be
    persuaded,
  and a gentle tongue can break a
    bone.

[16] If you find honey, eat just enough—
  too much of it, and you will vomit.

[17] Seldom set foot in your neighbor's
    house—
  too much of you, and he will hate
    you.

[18] Like a club or a sword or a sharp arrow
  is the man who gives false testimony
    against his neighbor.

[19] Like a bad tooth or a lame foot
  is reliance on the unfaithful in times
    of trouble.

[20] Like one who takes away a garment on
    a cold day,
  or like vinegar poured on soda,
  is one who sings songs to a heavy
    heart.

[21] If your enemy is hungry, give him food
    to eat;
  if he is thirsty, give him water to
    drink.

[22] In doing this, you will heap burning
    coals on his head,
  and the LORD will reward you.

GET STRONGER.

Men at Work

READ PROVERBS 24:30–34

Instead of "I went past the field of a sluggard ...", this passage could begin, "I went past the bedroom of my son ..." That's because the same fate awaits all lazy people, whether they're farmers or kids. Laziness is an attitude—a *bad* attitude. It makes you see work as something to avoid rather than something that gives you happiness and fulfillment. Worst of all, laziness creates more laziness. You can end up so bad off you don't even want to lift your hand to feed yourself (Proverbs 26:15). That's pretty bad. Why not adopt a positive attitude toward work instead? Instead of whining about household chores, see them as a way to contribute to your family. And always strive to do your best. Hard work will give you a sense of achievement and even more energy. Tell yourself, "I enjoy my work!"

Your next reading is on page 831.

²³ As a north wind brings rain,
    so a sly tongue brings angry looks.

²⁴ Better to live on a corner of the roof
    than share a house with a quarrelsome wife.

²⁵ Like cold water to a weary soul
    is good news from a distant land.

²⁶ Like a muddied spring or a polluted well
    is a righteous man who gives way to the wicked.

²⁷ It is not good to eat too much honey,
    nor is it honorable to seek one's own honor.

²⁸ Like a city whose walls are broken down
    is a man who lacks self-control.

26 Like snow in summer or rain in harvest,
    honor is not fitting for a fool.

² Like a fluttering sparrow or a darting swallow,
    an undeserved curse does not come to rest.

³ A whip for the horse, a halter for the donkey,
    and a rod for the backs of fools!

⁴ Do not answer a fool according to his folly,
    or you will be like him yourself.

⁵ Answer a fool according to his folly,
    or he will be wise in his own eyes.

⁶ Like cutting off one's feet or drinking violence
    is the sending of a message by the hand of a fool.

⁷ Like a lame man's legs that hang limp
    is a proverb in the mouth of a fool.

⁸ Like tying a stone in a sling
    is the giving of honor to a fool.

⁹ Like a thornbush in a drunkard's hand
    is a proverb in the mouth of a fool.

¹⁰ Like an archer who wounds at random
    is he who hires a fool or any passer-by.

¹¹ As a dog returns to its vomit,
    so a fool repeats his folly.

¹² Do you see a man wise in his own eyes?
    There is more hope for a fool than for him.

¹³ The sluggard says, "There is a lion in the road,
    a fierce lion roaming the streets!"

¹⁴ As a door turns on its hinges,
    so a sluggard turns on his bed.

¹⁵ The sluggard buries his hand in the dish;
    he is too lazy to bring it back to his mouth.

¹⁶ The sluggard is wiser in his own eyes
    than seven men who answer discreetly.

Get a Load of This...

Check out Proverbs 25:19. What if you sprained your ankle an hour before the big race? An unreliable person is like a bad ankle. Guys who can't be depended on when they're needed won't be trusted to do cool and important things.

In other Words...

17 Like one who seizes a dog by the ears
　　is a passer-by who meddles in a
　　　quarrel not his own.

18 Like a madman shooting
　　firebrands or deadly arrows
19 is a man who deceives his neighbor
　　and says, "I was only joking!"

20 Without wood a fire goes out;
　　without gossip a quarrel dies down.

21 As charcoal to embers and as wood to
　　fire,
　　so is a quarrelsome man for kindling
　　　strife.

22 The words of a gossip are like choice
　　morsels;
　　they go down to a man's inmost
　　　parts.

23 Like a coating of glaze[a] over
　　earthenware
　　are fervent lips with an evil heart.

24 A malicious man disguises himself with
　　his lips,
　　but in his heart he harbors deceit.
25 Though his speech is charming, do not
　　believe him,
　　for seven abominations fill his heart.
26 His malice may be concealed by
　　deception,
　　but his wickedness will be exposed
　　　in the assembly.

27 If a man digs a pit, he will fall into it;
　　if a man rolls a stone, it will roll back
　　　on him.

28 A lying tongue hates those it hurts,
　　and a flattering mouth works ruin.

Do not boast about tomorrow,
for you do not know what a
day may bring forth.

a 23 With a different word division of the Hebrew; Masoretic Text of silver dross

Make It Stick

READ PROVERBS 25:28

Without self-control, you're wide open for the enemy's attack. Self-control protects you by giving you the strength to say "no" to anything stupid or sinful. Ask God to help you build self-control like a wall around your life so you can keep his blessing in and the damage out.

2 Let another praise you, and not your own mouth;
 someone else, and not your own lips.

3 Stone is heavy and sand a burden,
 but provocation by a fool is heavier than both.

4 Anger is cruel and fury overwhelming,
 but who can stand before jealousy?

5 Better is open rebuke
 than hidden love.

6 Wounds from a friend can be trusted,
 but an enemy multiplies kisses.

7 He who is full loathes honey,
 but to the hungry even what is bitter tastes sweet.

8 Like a bird that strays from its nest
 is a man who strays from his home.

9 Perfume and incense bring joy to the heart,
 and the pleasantness of one's friend springs from
   his earnest counsel.

10 Do not forsake your friend and the friend of your
    father,
 and do not go to your brother's house when
   disaster strikes you—
 better a neighbor nearby than a brother far away.

11 Be wise, my son, and bring joy to my heart;
 then I can answer anyone who treats me with
   contempt.

12 The prudent see danger and take refuge,
 but the simple keep going and suffer for it.

13 Take the garment of one who puts up security for a
    stranger;
 hold it in pledge if he does it for a wayward
   woman.

14 If a man loudly blesses his neighbor early in the
    morning,
 it will be taken as a curse.

15 A quarrelsome wife is like
 a constant dripping on a rainy day;
16 restraining her is like restraining the wind
 or grasping oil with the hand.

17 As iron sharpens iron,
 so one man sharpens another.

18 He who tends a fig tree will eat its fruit,
 and he who looks after his master will be
   honored.

19 As water reflects a face,
 so a man's heart reflects the man.

20 Death and Destruction*a* are never satisfied,
 and neither are the eyes of man.

a 20 Hebrew Sheol and Abaddon

Get a Load of This...

Check out Proverbs
26:13. Ever notice how
much effort lazy people
put into making incredi-
ble excuses to avoid
doing work? If they put
that same energy into
working and getting the
job done, they'd be
rich! A diligent per-
son doesn't avoid
work. He finds ways
to get the job done.

In other words...

Get a Load of This...

Check out Proverbs 26:21. It's usually not good to be called a "wet blanket"—someone who discourages everyone else's dreams and plans. But when it comes to quarrels, a sopping wet blanket is exactly what you want to be so you can put out the spark of a problem before it ignites.

In Other Words...

21 The crucible for silver and the furnace for gold,
  but man is tested by the praise he receives.

22 Though you grind a fool in a mortar,
  grinding him like grain with a pestle,
  you will not remove his folly from him.

23 Be sure you know the condition of your flocks,
  give careful attention to your herds;
24 for riches do not endure forever,
  and a crown is not secure for all generations.
25 When the hay is removed and new growth appears
  and the grass from the hills is gathered in,
26 the lambs will provide you with clothing,
  and the goats with the price of a field.
27 You will have plenty of goats' milk
  to feed you and your family
  and to nourish your servant girls.

28 The wicked man flees though no one pursues,
  but the righteous are as bold as a lion.

2 When a country is rebellious, it has many rulers,
  but a man of understanding and knowledge
    maintains order.

3 A ruler[a] who oppresses the poor
  is like a driving rain that leaves no crops.

4 Those who forsake the law praise the wicked,
  but those who keep the law resist them.

5 Evil men do not understand justice,
  but those who seek the LORD understand it fully.

6 Better a poor man whose walk is blameless
  than a rich man whose ways are perverse.

7 He who keeps the law is a discerning son,
  but a companion of gluttons disgraces his father.

8 He who increases his wealth by exorbitant interest
  amasses it for another, who will be kind to the
    poor.

9 If anyone turns a deaf ear to the law,
  even his prayers are detestable.

10 He who leads the upright along an evil path
  will fall into his own trap,
  but the blameless will receive a good inheritance.

11 A rich man may be wise in his own eyes,
  but a poor man who has discernment sees
    through him.

12 When the righteous triumph, there is great elation;
  but when the wicked rise to power, men go into
    hiding.

---

a 3 Or A poor man

13 He who conceals his sins does not
    prosper,
  but whoever confesses and
    renounces them finds mercy.

14 Blessed is the man who always fears
    the LORD,
  but he who hardens his heart falls
    into trouble.

15 Like a roaring lion or a charging bear
  is a wicked man ruling over a
    helpless people.

16 A tyrannical ruler lacks judgment,
  but he who hates ill-gotten gain will
    enjoy a long life.

17 A man tormented by the guilt of murder
  will be a fugitive till death;
  let no one support him.

18 He whose walk is blameless is kept safe,
  but he whose ways are perverse will
    suddenly fall.

19 He who works his land will have
    abundant food,
  but the one who chases fantasies
    will have his fill of poverty.

20 A faithful man will be richly blessed,
  but one eager to get rich will not go
    unpunished.

21 To show partiality is not good—
  yet a man will do wrong for a piece
    of bread.

22 A stingy man is eager to get rich
  and is unaware that poverty awaits
    him.

23 He who rebukes a man will in the end
    gain more favor
  than he who has a flattering tongue.

24 He who robs his father or mother
  and says, "It's not wrong"—
  he is partner to him who destroys.

25 A greedy man stirs up dissension,
  but he who trusts in the LORD will
    prosper.

26 He who trusts in himself is a fool,
  but he who walks in wisdom is kept
    safe.

27 He who gives to the poor will lack
    nothing,

Pointing Out Pimples
READ PROVERBS 27:5–6, 9–10, 17

If your friend has a zit on his nose that desperately needs to be popped before it explodes, tell him about it. But don't announce it over your school's PA system; take him aside and tell him in private. And don't get angry if he's the one who points out *your* zits. Apart from pointing out zits, friends should also encourage and motivate each other to do good. When choosing friends, pick people who know right from wrong. Avoid troublemakers. Good friends will help each other stay on track. Another thing: Don't make friends one day and then throw them out like bathroom trash the next day, just because of a small mistake. Friendship is a commitment you make to someone. A true friend is a friend always. You wouldn't want to get "dumped" by your friends just because of a zit on your nose, would you?

Your next reading is on page 833.

Get a Load of This...

Check out Proverbs 28:13. Concealing your sins is like locking yourself in a closet. No one may find you, but it's kind of cramped and you'll run out of air. Why not open the door and confess your mistakes? God is more forgiving than you think!

In Other Words...

but he who closes his eyes to them receives many
   curses.

28 When the wicked rise to power, people go into hiding;
   but when the wicked perish, the righteous thrive.

 A man who remains
stiff-necked after many rebukes
will suddenly be destroyed—without
remedy.

2 When the righteous thrive, the people rejoice;
   when the wicked rule, the people groan.

3 A man who loves wisdom brings joy to his father,
   but a companion of prostitutes squanders his
      wealth.

4 By justice a king gives a country stability,
   but one who is greedy for bribes tears it down.

5 Whoever flatters his neighbor
   is spreading a net for his feet.

6 An evil man is snared by his own sin,
   but a righteous one can sing and be glad.

7 The righteous care about justice for the poor,
   but the wicked have no such concern.

8 Mockers stir up a city,
   but wise men turn away anger.

9 If a wise man goes to court with a fool,
   the fool rages and scoffs, and there is no peace.

10 Bloodthirsty men hate a man of integrity
   and seek to kill the upright.

11 A fool gives full vent to his anger,
   but a wise man keeps himself under control.

12 If a ruler listens to lies,
   all his officials become wicked.

13 The poor man and the oppressor have this in
      common:
   The LORD gives sight to the eyes of both.

14 If a king judges the poor with fairness,
   his throne will always be secure.

15 The rod of correction imparts wisdom,
   but a child left to himself disgraces his mother.

16 When the wicked thrive, so does sin,
   but the righteous will see their downfall.

17 Discipline your son, and he will give you peace;
   he will bring delight to your soul.

18 Where there is no revelation, the people cast off
      restraint;
   but blessed is he who keeps the law.

19 A servant cannot be corrected by mere words;
   though he understands, he will not respond.

20 Do you see a man who speaks in haste?
   There is more hope for a fool than
      for him.

21 If a man pampers his servant from
      youth,
   he will bring grief[a] in the end.

22 An angry man stirs up dissension,
   and a hot-tempered one commits
      many sins.

23 A man's pride brings him low,
   but a man of lowly spirit gains honor.

24 The accomplice of a thief is his own
      enemy;
   he is put under oath and dare not
      testify.

25 Fear of man will prove to be a snare,
   but whoever trusts in the LORD is
      kept safe.

26 Many seek an audience with a ruler,
   but it is from the LORD that man gets
      justice.

27 The righteous detest the dishonest;
   the wicked detest the upright.

Sayings of Agur

The sayings of Agur son of Jakeh—an oracle[b]:

   This man declared to Ithiel,
   to Ithiel and to Ucal:[c]

2 "I am the most ignorant of men;
   I do not have a man's understanding.
3 I have not learned wisdom,
   nor have I knowledge of the Holy
      One.
4 Who has gone up to heaven and come
      down?
   Who has gathered up the wind in
      the hollow of his hands?
   Who has wrapped up the waters in his
      cloak?
   Who has established all the ends of
      the earth?
   What is his name, and the name of his
      son?
   Tell me if you know!

a 21 The meaning of the Hebrew for this word is uncertain.
b 1 Or Jakeh of Massa   c 1 Masoretic Text; with a different
word division of the Hebrew declared, "I am weary, O God; / I
am weary, O God, and faint.

Be There for the Poor

READ PROVERBS 28:27

If you have two sandwiches for lunch and the kid next to you at school doesn't even have one, what should you do? Share a sandwich, of course. When God gives to you in abundance, he *expects* you to help others not as fortunate. It is your *duty* as a man of God to help others. There's nothing wrong with saving money to buy yourself cool stuff, but just how *much* stuff do you need? If you've been blessed big-time, then share with those in need.

Ways to do this include sponsoring a poor child in another country, helping when a disaster hits, or helping poor families in your community. On the other hand, some people might not need *things*—they simply need a friend when they're sick or lonely. Whenever someone is needy or downtrodden, God is there; and he wants you to be there, too (see also Proverbs 21:13; 22:9,16).

Your next reading is on page 837.

Get a Load of This...

Check out Proverbs 29:20. No meal tastes worse than a feast of your own words, especially after you've just spewed them out without thinking. It's like eating your own vomit. Even a fool isn't *that* stupid! Make a habit of using your brain before opening your mouth.

In other words...

5 "Every word of God is flawless;
  he is a shield to those who take refuge in him.
6 Do not add to his words,
  or he will rebuke you and prove you a liar.

7 "Two things I ask of you, O LORD;
  do not refuse me before I die:
8 Keep falsehood and lies far from me;
  give me neither poverty nor riches,
  but give me only my daily bread.
9 Otherwise, I may have too much and disown you
  and say, 'Who is the LORD?'
Or I may become poor and steal,
  and so dishonor the name of my God.

10 "Do not slander a servant to his master,
  or he will curse you, and you will pay for it.

11 "There are those who curse their fathers
  and do not bless their mothers;
12 those who are pure in their own eyes
  and yet are not cleansed of their filth;
13 those whose eyes are ever so haughty,
  whose glances are so disdainful;
14 those whose teeth are swords
  and whose jaws are set with knives
to devour the poor from the earth,
  the needy from among mankind.

15 "The leech has two daughters.
  'Give! Give!' they cry.

"There are three things that are never satisfied,
  four that never say, 'Enough!':
16 the grave,ᵃ the barren womb,
  land, which is never satisfied with water,
  and fire, which never says, 'Enough!'

17 "The eye that mocks a father,
  that scorns obedience to a mother,
will be pecked out by the ravens of the valley,
  will be eaten by the vultures.

18 "There are three things that are too amazing for me,
  four that I do not understand:
19 the way of an eagle in the sky,
  the way of a snake on a rock,
the way of a ship on the high seas,
  and the way of a man with a maiden.

20 "This is the way of an adulteress:
  She eats and wipes her mouth
  and says, 'I've done nothing wrong.'

21 "Under three things the earth trembles,
  under four it cannot bear up:
22 a servant who becomes king,
  a fool who is full of food,
23 an unloved woman who is married,
  and a maidservant who displaces her mistress.

ᵃ 16 Hebrew *Sheol*

24 "Four things on earth are small,
    yet they are extremely wise:
25 Ants are creatures of little strength,
    yet they store up their food in the summer;
26 coneys*a* are creatures of little power,
    yet they make their home in the crags;
27 locusts have no king,
    yet they advance together in ranks;
28 a lizard can be caught with the hand,
    yet it is found in kings' palaces.

29 "There are three things that are stately in their stride,
    four that move with stately bearing:
30 a lion, mighty among beasts,
    who retreats before nothing;
31 a strutting rooster, a he-goat,
    and a king with his army around him.*b*

32 "If you have played the fool and exalted yourself,
    or if you have planned evil,
    clap your hand over your mouth!
33 For as churning the milk produces butter,
    and as twisting the nose produces blood,
    so stirring up anger produces strife."

Sayings of King Lemuel

31 The sayings of King Lemuel—an oracle*c* his mother taught him:

2 "O my son, O son of my womb,
O son of my vows,*d*
3 do not spend your strength on women,
    your vigor on those who ruin kings.

4 "It is not for kings, O Lemuel—
    not for kings to drink wine,
    not for rulers to crave beer,
5 lest they drink and forget what the law decrees,
    and deprive all the oppressed of their rights.
6 Give beer to those who are perishing,
    wine to those who are in anguish;
7 let them drink and forget their poverty
    and remember their misery no more.

8 "Speak up for those who cannot speak for
      themselves,
    for the rights of all who are destitute.
9 Speak up and judge fairly;
    defend the rights of the poor and needy."

Epilogue: The Wife of Noble Character

10 *e* A wife of noble character who can find?
    She is worth far more than rubies.
11 Her husband has full confidence in her
    and lacks nothing of value.

Gross!

Ever given your dad a "dirty look" after he disciplined you? Proverbs 30:17 talks about the carcass of a disobedient, disgraceful son being dumped like dead meat on the ground for ravens and vultures to eat. The birds started by pecking out the eyeballs! Yummy!

a 26 That is, the hyrax or rock badger   *b 31* Or *king secure against revolt*
c 1 Or *of Lemuel king of Massa, which*   *d 2* Or / *the answer to my prayers*
e 10 Verses 10–31 are an acrostic, each verse beginning with a successive letter of the Hebrew alphabet.

¹²She brings him good, not harm,
   all the days of her life.
¹³She selects wool and flax
   and works with eager hands.
¹⁴She is like the merchant ships,
   bringing her food from afar.
¹⁵She gets up while it is still dark;
   she provides food for her family
   and portions for her servant girls.
¹⁶She considers a field and buys it;
   out of her earnings she plants a
     vineyard.
¹⁷She sets about her work vigorously;
   her arms are strong for her tasks.
¹⁸She sees that her trading is profitable,
   and her lamp does not go out at
     night.
¹⁹In her hand she holds the distaff
   and grasps the spindle with her
     fingers.
²⁰She opens her arms to the poor
   and extends her hands to the needy.
²¹When it snows, she has no fear for her
   household;

for all of them are clothed in scarlet.
²²She makes coverings for her bed;
   she is clothed in fine linen and
     purple.
²³Her husband is respected at the city
     gate,
   where he takes his seat among the
     elders of the land.
²⁴She makes linen garments and sells
     them,
   and supplies the merchants with
     sashes.
²⁵She is clothed with strength and
     dignity;
   she can laugh at the days to come.
²⁶She speaks with wisdom,
   and faithful instruction is on her
     tongue.
²⁷She watches over the affairs of her
     household
   and does not eat the bread of
     idleness.
²⁸Her children arise and call her
     blessed;

Make It Stick

READ PROVERBS 30:24–25

Think ants have nothing to teach you? Think again. Ants save up food for winter, right? Well, you should also save up money for your future. Start small and watch your savings grow (see Proverbs 13:11). Why not start today? Talk to your parents about opening a savings account.

her husband also, and he praises her:

29 "Many women do noble things,
   but you surpass them all."
30 Charm is deceptive, and beauty is
   fleeting;

but a woman who fears the LORD is
   to be praised.
31 Give her the reward she has earned,
   and let her works bring her praise at
   the city gate.

More Than Skin-deep

READ PROVERBS 31:10, 25–31

Tummy tucks, facelifts, super-thick makeup—some women will do anything to be beautiful. But as Proverbs 11:22 says, "Like a gold ring in a pig's snout is a beautiful woman who shows no discretion." Beauty is wonderful. But if a woman doesn't have the character to go with it, well . . . just remember that ring covered with pig slime. Looks are just a small part of who a girl is. Unfortunately, many guys aren't interested in a girl who isn't gorgeous. But you have to hold onto your hormones and look for more than just beauty; otherwise you'll forget to ask important questions such as, "Does she love God?" "Is she wise, generous and considerate?" If she's a godly woman, she'll be asking these questions about *you*. So don't get caught up on her looks—or on your own looks either. Build godly character in yourself, and look for it in others.

Your next reading is on page 839.

ECCLESIASTES

Who wrote this book?
Solomon.

Why was this book written?
Ecclesiastes shows that no one can have a happy life without God.

For whom was this book written?
Ecclesiastes was written for anyone who thinks that God is not important.

What do we learn about God in this book?
God is more important than money, pleasure, work or anything else in life.

When was this book written?
This book was written between 970 and 930 B.C.

What are some important passages in this book?

Pleasure can't make people happy	Ecclesiastes 2:1–11
Success can't make people happy	Ecclesiastes 2:17–26
Riches can't make people happy	Ecclesiastes 5:8—6:2

Everything Is Meaningless

1 The words of the Teacher,[a] son of David, king in Jerusalem:

2 "Meaningless! Meaningless!"
says the Teacher.
"Utterly meaningless!
Everything is meaningless."

3 What does man gain from all his labor
at which he toils under the sun?
4 Generations come and generations go,
but the earth remains forever.
5 The sun rises and the sun sets,
and hurries back to where it rises.
6 The wind blows to the south
and turns to the north;
round and round it goes,
ever returning on its course.
7 All streams flow into the sea,
yet the sea is never full.
To the place the streams come from,
there they return again.
8 All things are wearisome,
more than one can say.
The eye never has enough of seeing,
nor the ear its fill of hearing.

9 What has been will be again,
what has been done will be done
again;
there is nothing new under the sun.
10 Is there anything of which one can say,
"Look! This is something new"?
It was here already, long ago;
it was here before our time.
11 There is no remembrance of men of
old,
and even those who are yet to come
will not be remembered
by those who follow.

Wisdom Is Meaningless

12 I, the Teacher, was king over Israel in Jerusalem. 13 I devoted myself to study and to explore by wisdom all that is done under heaven. What a heavy burden God has laid on men! 14 I have seen all the things that are done under the sun; all of them are meaningless, a chasing after the wind.

15 What is twisted cannot be straightened;
what is lacking cannot be counted.

a 1 Or leader of the assembly; also in verses 2 and 12

What's the Point?

READ ECCLESIASTES 1

You name it and Solomon had it—power, wisdom, wealth, women and respect. So what's he saying about all this? "Meaningless! Meaningless! … Everything is meaningless" (verse 2). Whoa! Hold on a minute. He has it all and he's saying "having it all" means nothing? Right! Without God, life *is* meaningless. Life is an empty candy wrapper if all you live for is things and pleasure. For example: There are things you *like* to do—hanging out, skateboarding, playing on the computer—and there are things you *don't* like to do— cleaning your room, washing the dishes, homework, etc. What if you *only* wanted to do the entertainment stuff? Fun things are only a *part* of the picture. Life isn't com- plete without all the other stuff. Get the point? So find a balance between work and play and do your best to follow God's plan for your life. Do that and you'll have a meaningful—*and* fun—life.

Your next reading is on page 841.

16I thought to myself, "Look, I have grown and increased in wisdom more than anyone who has ruled over Jerusalem before me; I have experienced much of wisdom and knowledge." 17Then I applied myself to the understanding of wisdom, and also of madness and folly, but I learned that this, too, is a chasing after the wind.

18For with much wisdom comes much
　　sorrow;
　the more knowledge, the more grief.

Pleasures Are Meaningless

I thought in my heart, "Come now, I will test you with pleasure to find out what is good." But that also proved to be meaningless. 2"Laughter," I said, "is foolish. And what does pleasure accomplish?" 3I tried cheering myself with wine, and embracing folly— my mind still guiding me with wisdom. I wanted to see what was worthwhile for men to do under heaven during the few days of their lives.

4I undertook great projects: I built houses for myself and planted vineyards. 5I made gardens and parks and planted all kinds of fruit trees in them. 6I made reservoirs to water groves of flourishing trees. 7I bought male and female slaves and had other slaves who were born in my house. I also owned more herds and flocks than anyone in Jerusalem before me. 8I amassed silver and gold for myself, and the treasure of kings and provinces. I acquired men and women singers, and a harema as well—the delights of the heart of man. 9I became greater by far than anyone in Jerusalem before me. In all this my wisdom stayed with me.

10I denied myself nothing my eyes desired;
　I refused my heart no pleasure.
My heart took delight in all my work,
　and this was the reward for all my
　　labor.
11Yet when I surveyed all that my hands
　　had done
　and what I had toiled to achieve,
everything was meaningless, a chasing
　　after the wind;
　nothing was gained under the sun.

Wisdom and Folly Are Meaningless

12Then I turned my thoughts to consider
　　wisdom,
　and also madness and folly.

What more can the king's successor do
　than what has already been done?
13I saw that wisdom is better than folly,
　just as light is better than darkness.
14The wise man has eyes in his head,
　while the fool walks in the darkness;
but I came to realize
　that the same fate overtakes them
　　both.

15Then I thought in my heart,

"The fate of the fool will overtake me
　　also.
　What then do I gain by being wise?"
I said in my heart,
　"This too is meaningless."
16For the wise man, like the fool, will not
　　be long remembered;
　in days to come both will be
　　forgotten.
Like the fool, the wise man too must
　　die!

Toil Is Meaningless

17So I hated life, because the work that is done under the sun was grievous to me. All of it is meaningless, a chasing after the wind. 18I hated all the things I had toiled for under the sun, because I must leave them to the one who comes after me. 19And who knows whether he will be a wise man or a fool? Yet he will have control over all the work into which I have poured my effort and skill under the sun. This too is meaningless. 20So my heart began to despair over all my toilsome labor under the sun. 21For a man may do his work with wisdom, knowledge and skill, and then he must leave all he owns to someone who has not worked for it. This too is meaningless and a great misfortune. 22What does a man get for all the toil and anxious striving with which he labors under the sun? 23All his days his work is pain and grief; even at night his mind does not rest. This too is meaningless.

24A man can do nothing better than to eat and drink and find satisfaction in his work. This too, I see, is from the hand of God, 25for without him, who can eat or find enjoyment? 26To the man who pleases him, God gives wisdom, knowledge and happiness, but to the sinner he gives the task of gathering and storing up wealth to hand it over to the one who

a 8 The meaning of the Hebrew for this phrase is uncertain.

pleases God. This too is meaningless, a chasing after the wind.

A Time for Everything

3 There is a time for everything, and a season for every activity under heaven:

2 a time to be born and a time to die,
a time to plant and a time to uproot,
3 a time to kill and a time to heal,
a time to tear down and a time to build,
4 a time to weep and a time to laugh,
a time to mourn and a time to dance,
5 a time to scatter stones and a time to gather them,
a time to embrace and a time to refrain,
6 a time to search and a time to give up,
a time to keep and a time to throw away,
7 a time to tear and a time to mend,
a time to be silent and a time to speak,
8 a time to love and a time to hate,
a time for war and a time for peace.

9What does the worker gain from his toil? 10I have seen the burden God has laid on men. 11He has made everything beautiful in its time. He has also set eternity in the hearts of men; yet they cannot fathom what God has done from beginning to end. 12I know that there is nothing better for men than to be happy and do good while they live. 13That everyone may eat and drink, and find satisfaction in all his toil—this is the gift of God. 14I know that everything God does will endure forever; nothing can be added to it and nothing taken from it. God does it so that men will revere him.

15Whatever is has already been,
and what will be has been before;
and God will call the past to account. a

a 15 Or God calls back the past

A Slice of Life

GET SMARTER

READ ECCLESIASTES 3:1–15

"There is a time for everything ... for every activity" (Ecclesiastes 3:1). Think of your life as a pie chart, only made out of *real* pie. Each different activity is a slice of a different flavor—apple for sports, cherry for your relationship with God, mincemeat for homework, etc. Some pieces will be bigger, others smaller, but you'll need them all. You need school (rhubarb pie) because you need an education to get ready for the rest of your life. Rhubarb may not be your fave, but it still belongs in your pie. Hanging out with your friends (chocolate!) is fun, but if that's all you eat you'll miss out on the cherry. All the priorities in your life require balance. Make time for each. Tell yourself, "I need to do *this*, then my homework, then devotions, then have time for me." A planned, organized life is a balanced pie.

Your next reading is on page 849.

16And I saw something else under the sun:

In the place of judgment—wickedness was there,
  in the place of justice—wickedness was there.

17I thought in my heart,

"God will bring to judgment
  both the righteous and the wicked,
for there will be a time for every activity,
  a time for every deed."

18I also thought, "As for men, God tests them so that they may see that they are like the animals. 19Man's fate is like that of the animals; the same fate awaits them both: As one dies, so dies the other. All have the same breath[a]; man has no advantage over the animal. Everything is meaningless. 20All go to the same place; all come from dust, and to dust all return. 21Who knows if the spirit of man rises upward and if the spirit of the animal[b] goes down into the earth?"

22So I saw that there is nothing better

Make It Stick

_____

_____

_____

_____

_____

_____

_____

READ ECCLESIASTES 3:17
OK, so your life is a pie. Start with today (see Ecclesiastes 3:17). What do you have to do today? Jot it all down. Then draw a circle and divide it like pie slices. Label each slice with something you're planning to do today. Try doing this every morning or evening for the next few weeks.

for a man than to enjoy his work, because that is his lot. For who can bring him to see what will happen after him?

Oppression, Toil, Friendlessness

4 Again I looked and saw all the oppression that was taking place under the sun:

I saw the tears of the oppressed—
    and they have no comforter;
power was on the side of their oppressors—
    and they have no comforter.
2 And I declared that the dead,
    who had already died,
are happier than the living,
    who are still alive.
3 But better than both
    is he who has not yet been,
who has not seen the evil
    that is done under the sun.

4 And I saw that all labor and all achievement spring from man's envy of his neighbor. This too is meaningless, a chasing after the wind.

5 The fool folds his hands
    and ruins himself.
6 Better one handful with tranquillity
    than two handfuls with toil
    and chasing after the wind.

7 Again I saw something meaningless under the sun:

8 There was a man all alone;
    he had neither son nor brother.
There was no end to his toil,
    yet his eyes were not content with his wealth.
"For whom am I toiling," he asked,
    "and why am I depriving myself of enjoyment?"
This too is meaningless—
    a miserable business!

9 Two are better than one,
    because they have a good return for their work:
10 If one falls down,
    his friend can help him up.
But pity the man who falls
    and has no one to help him up!
11 Also, if two lie down together, they will keep warm.
    But how can one keep warm alone?
12 Though one may be overpowered,
    two can defend themselves.
A cord of three strands is not quickly broken.

Advancement Is Meaningless

13 Better a poor but wise youth than an old but foolish king who no longer knows how to take warning. 14 The youth may have come from prison to the kingship, or he may have been born in poverty within his kingdom. 15 I

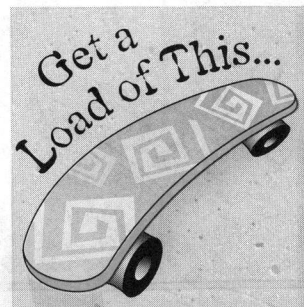

Get a Load of This...

Some traps are obvious—like an alligator with a sign around his neck that says "I'm hungry. Come pet me." Other traps are trickier. Like envying people (Ecclesiastes 4:4), for example—wanting stuff just because they have it, or wanting to go places just because they've gone there.

In Other Words...

saw that all who lived and walked under the sun followed the youth, the king's successor. [16]There was no end to all the people who were before them. But those who came later were not pleased with the successor. This too is meaningless, a chasing after the wind.

Stand in Awe of God

Guard your steps when you go to the house of God. Go near to listen rather than to offer the sacrifice of fools, who do not know that they do wrong.

[2]Do not be quick with your mouth,
　do not be hasty in your heart
　to utter anything before God.
God is in heaven
　and you are on earth,
　so let your words be few.
[3]As a dream comes when there are many cares,
　so the speech of a fool when there are many
　　words.

[4]When you make a vow to God, do not delay in fulfilling it. He has no pleasure in fools; fulfill your vow. [5]It is better not to vow than to make a vow and not fulfill it. [6]Do not let your mouth lead you into sin. And do not protest to the ⌊temple⌋ messenger, "My vow was a mistake." Why should God be angry at what you say and destroy the work of your hands? [7]Much dreaming and many words are meaningless. Therefore stand in awe of God.

Riches Are Meaningless

[8]If you see the poor oppressed in a district, and justice and rights denied, do not be surprised at such things; for one official is eyed by a higher one, and over them both are others higher still. [9]The increase from the land is taken by all; the king himself profits from the fields.

[10]Whoever loves money never has money enough;
　whoever loves wealth is never satisfied with his
　　income.
This too is meaningless.

[11]As goods increase,
　so do those who consume them.
And what benefit are they to the owner
　except to feast his eyes on them?

[12]The sleep of a laborer is sweet,
　whether he eats little or much,
but the abundance of a rich man
　permits him no sleep.

[13]I have seen a grievous evil under the sun:

wealth hoarded to the harm of its owner,
[14]　or wealth lost through some misfortune,
so that when he has a son
　there is nothing left for him.

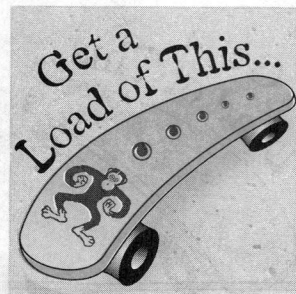

Get a Load of This...

Society says, "Bigger and more is best." Not true. You came into the world with nothing and you won't take any stuff out when you leave (see Ecclesiastes 5:10–15). So what's important in life? What *can* you take with you?—Only your relationship with God and the people you love.

In Other Words...

15 Naked a man comes from his mother's
        womb,
    and as he comes, so he departs.
He takes nothing from his labor
        that he can carry in his hand.

16 This too is a grievous evil:

As a man comes, so he departs,
    and what does he gain,
        since he toils for the wind?
17 All his days he eats in darkness,
        with great frustration, affliction and
        anger.

18 Then I realized that it is good and
proper for a man to eat and drink, and to
find satisfaction in his toilsome labor under the sun during the few days of life
God has given him—for this is his lot.
19 Moreover, when God gives any man
wealth and possessions, and enables him
to enjoy them, to accept his lot and be
happy in his work—this is a gift of God.
20 He seldom reflects on the days of his
life, because God keeps him occupied
with gladness of heart.

6 I have seen another evil under the
sun, and it weighs heavily on men:
2 God gives a man wealth, possessions and honor, so that he lacks
nothing his heart desires, but God does
not enable him to enjoy them, and a
stranger enjoys them instead. This is
meaningless, a grievous evil.

3 A man may have a hundred children
and live many years; yet no matter how
long he lives, if he cannot enjoy his prosperity and does not receive proper burial, I
say that a stillborn child is better off than
he. 4 It comes without meaning, it departs
in darkness, and in darkness its name is
shrouded. 5 Though it never saw the sun or
knew anything, it has more rest than does
that man— 6 even if he lives a thousand
years twice over but fails to enjoy his prosperity. Do not all go to the same place?

7 All man's efforts are for his mouth,
    yet his appetite is never satisfied.
8 What advantage has a wise man
    over a fool?
What does a poor man gain
    by knowing how to conduct himself
        before others?
9 Better what the eye sees
    than the roving of the appetite.
This too is meaningless,
    a chasing after the wind.

10 Whatever exists has already been
        named,
    and what man is has been known;
no man can contend
    with one who is stronger than he.
11 The more the words,
    the less the meaning,
    and how does that profit anyone?

12 For who knows what is good for a
man in life, during the few and meaningless days he passes through like a shadow? Who can tell him what will happen
under the sun after he is gone?

Wisdom

7 A good name is better than fine
        perfume,
    and the day of death better than
        the day of birth.
2 It is better to go to a house of
        mourning
    than to go to a house of feasting,
for death is the destiny of every man;
    the living should take this to heart.
3 Sorrow is better than laughter,
    because a sad face is good for the
        heart.
4 The heart of the wise is in the house of
        mourning,
    but the heart of fools is in the house
        of pleasure.
5 It is better to heed a wise man's rebuke
    than to listen to the song of fools.
6 Like the crackling of thorns under the
        pot,
    so is the laughter of fools.
    This too is meaningless.

7 Extortion turns a wise man into a fool,
    and a bribe corrupts the heart.

8 The end of a matter is better than its
        beginning,
    and patience is better than pride.
9 Do not be quickly provoked in your
        spirit,
    for anger resides in the lap of fools.

10 Do not say, "Why were the old days
        better than these?"
    For it is not wise to ask such
        questions.

11 Wisdom, like an inheritance, is a good
        thing
    and benefits those who see the sun.
12 Wisdom is a shelter
    as money is a shelter,

but the advantage of knowledge is
this:
that wisdom preserves the life of its
possessor.

¹³Consider what God has done:

Who can straighten
what he has made crooked?
¹⁴When times are good, be happy;
but when times are bad, consider:
God has made the one
as well as the other.
Therefore, a man cannot discover
anything about his future.

¹⁵In this meaningless life of mine I have
seen both of these:

a righteous man perishing in his
righteousness,
and a wicked man living long in his
wickedness.
¹⁶Do not be overrighteous,
neither be overwise—
why destroy yourself?
¹⁷Do not be overwicked,
and do not be a fool—
why die before your time?
¹⁸It is good to grasp the one
and not let go of the other.
The man who fears God will avoid
all ⌊extremes⌋.^a

¹⁹Wisdom makes one wise man more
powerful
than ten rulers in a city.

²⁰There is not a righteous man on earth
who does what is right and never
sins.

²¹Do not pay attention to every word
people say,
or you may hear your servant cursing
you—
²²for you know in your heart
that many times you yourself have
cursed others.

²³All this I tested by wisdom and I said,

"I am determined to be wise"—
but this was beyond me.
²⁴Whatever wisdom may be,
it is far off and most profound—
who can discover it?
²⁵So I turned my mind to understand,
to investigate and to search out
wisdom and the scheme of
things

and to understand the stupidity of
wickedness
and the madness of folly.

²⁶I find more bitter than death
the woman who is a snare,
whose heart is a trap
and whose hands are chains.
The man who pleases God will escape
her,
but the sinner she will ensnare.

²⁷"Look," says the Teacher,^b "this is
what I have discovered:

"Adding one thing to another to
discover the scheme of things—
²⁸   while I was still searching
but not finding—
I found one ⌊upright⌋ man among a
thousand,
but not one ⌊upright⌋ woman
among them all.
²⁹This only have I found:
God made mankind upright,
but men have gone in search of
many schemes."

Who is like the wise man?
Who knows the explanation of
things?
Wisdom brightens a man's face
and changes its hard appearance.

Obey the King

²Obey the king's command, I say, be-
cause you took an oath before God. ³Do
not be in a hurry to leave the king's presence. Do not stand up for a bad cause, for
he will do whatever he pleases. ⁴Since a
king's word is supreme, who can say to
him, "What are you doing?"

⁵Whoever obeys his command will
come to no harm,
and the wise heart will know the
proper time and procedure.
⁶For there is a proper time and
procedure for every matter,
though a man's misery weighs
heavily upon him.

⁷Since no man knows the future,
who can tell him what is to come?
⁸No man has power over the wind to
contain it^c;

a 18 Or *will follow them both*   *b 27* Or *leader of the
assembly*   *c 8* Or *over his spirit to retain it*

so no one has power over the day of his death.
As no one is discharged in time of war,
so wickedness will not release those who practice it.

⁹All this I saw, as I applied my mind to everything done under the sun. There is a time when a man lords it over others to his own*a* hurt. ¹⁰Then too, I saw the wicked buried—those who used to come and go from the holy place and receive praise*b* in the city where they did this. This too is meaningless.

¹¹When the sentence for a crime is not quickly carried out, the hearts of the people are filled with schemes to do wrong. ¹²Although a wicked man commits a hundred crimes and still lives a long time, I know that it will go better with God-fearing men, who are reverent before God. ¹³Yet because the wicked do not fear God, it will not go well with them, and their days will not lengthen like a shadow.

¹⁴There is something else meaningless that occurs on earth: righteous men who get what the wicked deserve, and wicked men who get what the righteous deserve. This too, I say, is meaningless. ¹⁵So I commend the enjoyment of life, because nothing is better for a man under the sun than to eat and drink and be glad. Then joy will accompany him in his work all the days of the life God has given him under the sun.

¹⁶When I applied my mind to know wisdom and to observe man's labor on earth—his eyes not seeing sleep day or night— ¹⁷then I saw all that God has done. No one can comprehend what goes on under the sun. Despite all his efforts to search it out, man cannot discover its meaning. Even if a wise man claims he knows, he cannot really comprehend it.

A Common Destiny for All

9 So I reflected on all this and concluded that the righteous and the wise and what they do are in God's hands, but no man knows whether love or hate awaits him. ²All share a common destiny—the righteous and the wicked, the good and the bad,*c* the clean and the unclean, those who offer sacrifices and those who do not.

As it is with the good man,
so with the sinner;
as it is with those who take oaths,
so with those who are afraid to take them.

³This is the evil in everything that happens under the sun: The same destiny overtakes all. The hearts of men, moreover, are full of evil and there is madness in their hearts while they live, and afterward they join the dead. ⁴Anyone who is among the living has hope*d*—even a live dog is better off than a dead lion!

a 9 Or *to their*   *b 10* Some Hebrew manuscripts and Septuagint (Aquila); most Hebrew manuscripts *and are forgotten*   *c 2* Septuagint (Aquila), Vulgate and Syriac; Hebrew does not have *and the bad.*   *d 4* Or *What then is to be chosen? With all who live, there is hope*

Get a Load of This...

Rules exist to protect us. Just because lightning doesn't strike your house immediately after you do something wrong doesn't mean God didn't notice. Even though the wicked sometimes seem to have all the fun, in the long run it will go better with the righteous (see Ecclesiastes 8:11–13).

In Other Words...

5For the living know that they will die,
   but the dead know nothing;
they have no further reward,
   and even the memory of them is
      forgotten.
6Their love, their hate
   and their jealousy have long since
      vanished;
never again will they have a part
   in anything that happens under the
      sun.

7Go, eat your food with gladness, and drink your wine with a joyful heart, for it is now that God favors what you do. 8Always be clothed in white, and always anoint your head with oil. 9Enjoy life with your wife, whom you love, all the days of this meaningless life that God has given you under the sun—all your meaningless days. For this is your lot in life and in your toilsome labor under the sun. 10Whatever your hand finds to do, do it with all your might, for in the grave,a where you are going, there is neither working nor planning nor knowledge nor wisdom.

11I have seen something else under the sun:

The race is not to the swift
   or the battle to the strong,
nor does food come to the wise
   or wealth to the brilliant
   or favor to the learned;
but time and chance happen to them
   all.

12Moreover, no man knows when his hour will come:

As fish are caught in a cruel net,
   or birds are taken in a snare,
so men are trapped by evil times
   that fall unexpectedly upon them.

Wisdom Better Than Folly

13I also saw under the sun this example of wisdom that greatly impressed me: 14There was once a small city with only a few people in it. And a powerful king came against it, surrounded it and built huge siegeworks against it. 15Now there lived in that city a man poor but wise, and he saved the city by his wisdom. But nobody remembered that poor man. 16So I said, "Wisdom is better than strength." But the poor man's wisdom is despised, and his words are no longer heeded.

17The quiet words of the wise are more
   to be heeded
than the shouts of a ruler of fools.
18Wisdom is better than weapons of
      war,
   but one sinner destroys much good.

As dead flies give perfume a
   bad smell,
so a little folly outweighs
   wisdom and honor.
2The heart of the wise inclines to the
      right,
   but the heart of the fool to the left.
3Even as he walks along the road,
   the fool lacks sense
   and shows everyone how stupid he
      is.
4If a ruler's anger rises against you,
   do not leave your post;
   calmness can lay great errors to rest.

5There is an evil I have seen under the
      sun,
   the sort of error that arises from a
      ruler:
6Fools are put in many high positions,
   while the rich occupy the low ones.
7I have seen slaves on horseback,
   while princes go on foot like slaves.

8Whoever digs a pit may fall into it;
   whoever breaks through a wall may
      be bitten by a snake.
9Whoever quarries stones may be
      injured by them;
   whoever splits logs may be
      endangered by them.

10If the ax is dull
   and its edge unsharpened,
more strength is needed
   but skill will bring success.

11If a snake bites before it is charmed,
   there is no profit for the charmer.

12Words from a wise man's mouth are
      gracious,
   but a fool is consumed by his own
      lips.
13At the beginning his words are folly;
   at the end they are wicked
      madness—
14   and the fool multiplies words.

No one knows what is coming—
   who can tell him what will happen
      after him?

a 10 Hebrew Sheol

15 A fool's work wearies him;
   he does not know the way to town.

16 Woe to you, O land whose king was a
     servant[a]
   and whose princes feast in the
     morning.
17 Blessed are you, O land whose king is
     of noble birth
   and whose princes eat at a proper
     time—
   for strength and not for drunkenness.

18 If a man is lazy, the rafters sag;
   if his hands are idle, the house leaks.

19 A feast is made for laughter,
   and wine makes life merry,
   but money is the answer for
     everything.

20 Do not revile the king even in your
     thoughts,
   or curse the rich in your bedroom,
   because a bird of the air may carry
     your words,
   and a bird on the wing may report
     what you say.

Bread Upon the Waters

11 Cast your bread upon the waters,
   for after many days you will find it
     again.
2 Give portions to seven, yes to
     eight,
   for you do not know what disaster
     may come upon the land.

3 If clouds are full of water,
   they pour rain upon the earth.
   Whether a tree falls to the south or to
     the north,
   in the place where it falls, there will
     it lie.
4 Whoever watches the wind will not
     plant;
   whoever looks at the clouds will not
     reap.

5 As you do not know the path of the
     wind,
   or how the body is formed[b] in a
     mother's womb,

a 16 Or king is a child   b 5 Or know how life (or the spirit) /
enters the body being formed

Life Is This Moment

READ ECCLESIASTES 11:7–10

GET SMARTER

Life is wonderful when you want to please God and unselfishly help others. The great news is, God will reward you in heaven for that! But don't get so caught up with "doing more for God" that you don't take time to enjoy life. You'll burn out. Imagine you want to be the first astronaut on Mars, so for 20 years you spend every waking moment training for the mission. When you finally land on Mars, you meet an alien skating along the Martian canals (OK, that's a stretch) and he asks you what earthlings do for fun. And you have no idea! So take time out to enjoy life now! Life is this moment. "For it is now that God favors what you do" (Ecclesiastes 9:7). Enjoy your work, enjoy serving God, enjoy relaxing. And hey, if you get to Mars, that's a bonus.

Your next reading is on page 853.

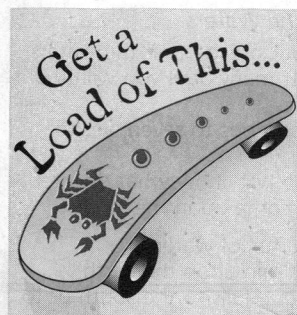

Get a Load of This...

Solomon did and saw it all, and this is what he learned: Be happy, but obey God (see Ecclesiastes 12:13). Work hard and enjoy life, but keep your faith strong. Life is God's gift to you. For your safety and happiness, live it the right way.

In other words...

so you cannot understand the work of God,
    the Maker of all things.

6 Sow your seed in the morning,
    and at evening let not your hands be idle,
for you do not know which will succeed,
    whether this or that,
    or whether both will do equally well.

Remember Your Creator While Young

7 Light is sweet,
    and it pleases the eyes to see the sun.
8 However many years a man may live,
    let him enjoy them all.
But let him remember the days of darkness,
    for they will be many.
Everything to come is meaningless.

9 Be happy, young man, while you are young,
    and let your heart give you joy in the days of your
        youth.
Follow the ways of your heart
    and whatever your eyes see,
but know that for all these things
    God will bring you to judgment.
10 So then, banish anxiety from your heart
    and cast off the troubles of your body,
for youth and vigor are meaningless.

12 Remember your Creator
    in the days of your youth,
    before the days of trouble come
    and the years approach when you will say,
    "I find no pleasure in them"—
2 before the sun and the light
    and the moon and the stars grow dark,
    and the clouds return after the rain;
3 when the keepers of the house tremble,
    and the strong men stoop,
when the grinders cease because they are few,
    and those looking through the windows grow dim;
4 when the doors to the street are closed
    and the sound of grinding fades;
when men rise up at the sound of birds,
    but all their songs grow faint;
5 when men are afraid of heights
    and of dangers in the streets;
when the almond tree blossoms
    and the grasshopper drags himself along
    and desire no longer is stirred.
Then man goes to his eternal home
    and mourners go about the streets.

6 Remember him—before the silver cord is severed,
    or the golden bowl is broken;
before the pitcher is shattered at the spring,
    or the wheel broken at the well,
7 and the dust returns to the ground it came from,
    and the spirit returns to God who gave it.

8 "Meaningless! Meaningless!" says the
    Teacher. [a]
  "Everything is meaningless!"

The Conclusion of the Matter

9Not only was the Teacher wise, but
also he imparted knowledge to the people. He pondered and searched out and
set in order many proverbs. 10The Teacher
searched to find just the right words, and
what he wrote was upright and true.
11The words of the wise are like goads,
their collected sayings like firmly embed-
ded nails—given by one Shepherd. 12Be
warned, my son, of anything in addition
to them.
  Of making many books there is no end,
and much study wearies the body.

13Now all has been heard;
    here is the conclusion of the matter:
  Fear God and keep his commandments,
    for this is the whole ⌊duty⌋ of man.
14For God will bring every deed into
      judgment,
    including every hidden thing,
    whether it is good or evil.

---

[a] 8 Or the leader of the assembly; also in verses 9 and 10

SONG OF SONGS

Who wrote this book?

This book was probably written by Solomon.

What is this book about?

This book is a collection of poems about grown-up love between a man and a woman.

For whom was this book written?

The book was written for grown-ups to help them understand love and marriage.

When was this book written?

If Solomon wrote Song of Songs, it was written sometime during the tenth century B.C. If it was written by someone else, the date is unknown.

1

Solomon's Song of Songs.

Beloved[a]

[2] Let him kiss me with the kisses of
his mouth—
for your love is more delightful than
wine.
[3] Pleasing is the fragrance of your
perfumes;
your name is like perfume poured
out.
No wonder the maidens love you!
[4] Take me away with you—let us hurry!
Let the king bring me into his
chambers.

Friends

We rejoice and delight in you[b];
we will praise your love more than
wine.

Beloved

How right they are to adore you!

[5] Dark am I, yet lovely,
O daughters of Jerusalem,
dark like the tents of Kedar,
like the tent curtains of Solomon.[c]
[6] Do not stare at me because I am
dark,
because I am darkened by the sun.
My mother's sons were angry with me
and made me take care of the
vineyards;
my own vineyard I have neglected.
[7] Tell me, you whom I love, where you
graze your flock
and where you rest your sheep at
midday.
Why should I be like a veiled woman
beside the flocks of your friends?

Friends

[8] If you do not know, most beautiful of
women,
follow the tracks of the sheep
and graze your young goats
by the tents of the shepherds.

[a] Primarily on the basis of the gender of the Hebrew pronouns
used, male and female speakers are indicated in the margins
by the captions *Lover* and *Beloved* respectively. The words of
others are marked *Friends*. In some instances the divisions and
their captions are debatable.   [b] 4 The Hebrew is masculine
singular.   [c] 5 Or *Salma*

Pretty Cool Aliens

SONG OF SONGS

Are you surrounded by aliens at school, at church and at the mall?
Sometimes it seems like girls really *are* from a different planet.
Sometimes they really *do* think differently. When a girl looks at a field
of flowers, she thinks it's beautiful; you're wondering how you could
cut a trail through it on your dirt bike. But consider this: Even
though your guy friends have different hobbies, or different
ways of dressing or talking—or a different sense of humor—
you accept them because it's cool to have their own style.
Right? Well, girls are different in cool ways, too. You don't
have to make fun of *girl stuff* to be a real guy. Sure, making jewelry or watching ballet might only happen in
your nightmares, but it's not dumb for *girls* to like
those things. Show respect for them. Girls are different, but they're pretty cool in their own way.

Your next reading is on page 856.

Lover

9 I liken you, my darling, to a mare
   harnessed to one of the chariots of
      Pharaoh.
10 Your cheeks are beautiful with earrings,
   your neck with strings of jewels.
11 We will make you earrings of gold,
   studded with silver.

Beloved

12 While the king was at his table,
   my perfume spread its fragrance.
13 My lover is to me a sachet of myrrh
   resting between my breasts.
14 My lover is to me a cluster of henna
      blossoms
   from the vineyards of En Gedi.

Lover

15 How beautiful you are, my darling!
   Oh, how beautiful!
   Your eyes are doves.

Beloved

16 How handsome you are, my lover!
   Oh, how charming!
   And our bed is verdant.

Lover

17 The beams of our house are cedars;
   our rafters are firs.

Beloved [a]

I am a rose [b] of Sharon,
   a lily of the valleys.

Lover

2 Like a lily among thorns
   is my darling among the maidens.

Beloved

3 Like an apple tree among the trees of
      the forest
   is my lover among the young men.
 I delight to sit in his shade,
   and his fruit is sweet to my taste.
4 He has taken me to the banquet hall,
   and his banner over me is love.
5 Strengthen me with raisins,
   refresh me with apples,
   for I am faint with love.
6 His left arm is under my head,
   and his right arm embraces me.
7 Daughters of Jerusalem, I charge you
   by the gazelles and by the does of
      the field:

Do not arouse or awaken love
   until it so desires.

8 Listen! My lover!
   Look! Here he comes,
   leaping across the mountains,
   bounding over the hills.
9 My lover is like a gazelle or a young
      stag.
   Look! There he stands behind our
      wall,
   gazing through the windows,
   peering through the lattice.
10 My lover spoke and said to me,
   "Arise, my darling,
   my beautiful one, and come with me.
11 See! The winter is past;
   the rains are over and gone.
12 Flowers appear on the earth;
   the season of singing has come,
   the cooing of doves
   is heard in our land.
13 The fig tree forms its early fruit;
   the blossoming vines spread their
      fragrance.
   Arise, come, my darling;
   my beautiful one, come with me."

Lover

14 My dove in the clefts of the rock,
   in the hiding places on the
      mountainside,
   show me your face,
   let me hear your voice;
   for your voice is sweet,
   and your face is lovely.
15 Catch for us the foxes,
   the little foxes
   that ruin the vineyards,
   our vineyards that are in bloom.

Beloved

16 My lover is mine and I am his;
   he browses among the lilies.
17 Until the day breaks
   and the shadows flee,
   turn, my lover,
   and be like a gazelle
   or like a young stag
   on the rugged hills. [c]

All night long on my bed
I looked for the one my heart loves;
I looked for him but did not find
   him.

---

[a] 1 Or *Lover*   [b] 1 Possibly a member of the crocus family
[c] 17 Or *the hills of Bether*

2 I will get up now and go about the city,
    through its streets and squares;
 I will search for the one my heart loves.
    So I looked for him but did not find
    him.
3 The watchmen found me
    as they made their rounds in the city.
 "Have you seen the one my heart
    loves?"
4 Scarcely had I passed them
    when I found the one my heart
    loves.
 I held him and would not let him go
    till I had brought him to my
    mother's house,
 to the room of the one who
    conceived me.
5 Daughters of Jerusalem, I charge you
    by the gazelles and by the does of
    the field:
 Do not arouse or awaken love
    until it so desires.

6 Who is this coming up from the desert
    like a column of smoke,
 perfumed with myrrh and incense
    made from all the spices of the
    merchant?
7 Look! It is Solomon's carriage,
    escorted by sixty warriors,
    the noblest of Israel,
8 all of them wearing the sword,
    all experienced in battle,
 each with his sword at his side,
    prepared for the terrors of the night.
9 King Solomon made for himself the
    carriage;
 he made it of wood from Lebanon.
10 Its posts he made of silver,
    its base of gold.
 Its seat was upholstered with purple,
    its interior lovingly inlaid
    by*a* the daughters of Jerusalem.
11 Come out, you daughters of Zion,
    and look at King Solomon wearing
    the crown,
 the crown with which his mother
    crowned him
 on the day of his wedding,
    the day his heart rejoiced.

Lover

4 How beautiful you are, my darling!
    Oh, how beautiful!
 Your eyes behind your veil are
    doves.
 Your hair is like a flock of goats

descending from Mount Gilead.
2 Your teeth are like a flock of sheep just
    shorn,
 coming up from the washing.
 Each has its twin;
    not one of them is alone.
3 Your lips are like a scarlet ribbon;
    your mouth is lovely.
 Your temples behind your veil
    are like the halves of a pomegranate.
4 Your neck is like the tower of David,
    built with elegance*b*;
 on it hang a thousand shields,
    all of them shields of warriors.
5 Your two breasts are like two fawns,
    like twin fawns of a gazelle
    that browse among the lilies.
6 Until the day breaks
    and the shadows flee,
 I will go to the mountain of myrrh
    and to the hill of incense.
7 All beautiful you are, my darling;
    there is no flaw in you.

8 Come with me from Lebanon, my bride,
    come with me from Lebanon.
 Descend from the crest of Amana,
    from the top of Senir, the summit of
    Hermon,
 from the lions' dens
    and the mountain haunts of the
    leopards.
9 You have stolen my heart, my sister, my
    bride;
 you have stolen my heart
 with one glance of your eyes,
    with one jewel of your necklace.
10 How delightful is your love, my sister,
    my bride!
 How much more pleasing is your
    love than wine,
 and the fragrance of your perfume
    than any spice!
11 Your lips drop sweetness as the
    honeycomb, my bride;
 milk and honey are under your
    tongue.
 The fragrance of your garments is
    like that of Lebanon.
12 You are a garden locked up, my sister,
    my bride;
 you are a spring enclosed, a sealed
    fountain.
13 Your plants are an orchard of
    pomegranates

a 10 Or *its inlaid interior a gift of love / from*
b 4 The meaning of the Hebrew for this word is uncertain.

with choice fruits,
with henna and nard,
14 nard and saffron,
    calamus and cinnamon,
with every kind of incense tree,
with myrrh and aloes
    and all the finest spices.
15 You are[a] a garden fountain,
    a well of flowing water
    streaming down from Lebanon.

Beloved

16 Awake, north wind,
    and come, south wind!
Blow on my garden,
    that its fragrance may spread abroad.
Let my lover come into his garden
    and taste its choice fruits.

Lover

5 I have come into my garden, my
    sister, my bride;
I have gathered my myrrh with my
    spice.
I have eaten my honeycomb and my
    honey;
I have drunk my wine and my milk.

Friends

Eat, O friends, and drink;
    drink your fill, O lovers.

Beloved

2 I slept but my heart was awake.
    Listen! My lover is knocking:
"Open to me, my sister, my darling,
    my dove, my flawless one.
My head is drenched with dew,
    my hair with the dampness of the
        night."
3 I have taken off my robe—
    must I put it on again?
I have washed my feet—
    must I soil them again?
4 My lover thrust his hand through the
        latch-opening;
    my heart began to pound for him.
5 I arose to open for my lover,
    and my hands dripped with myrrh,
    my fingers with flowing myrrh,
    on the handles of the lock.
6 I opened for my lover,
    but my lover had left; he was gone.

[a] 15 Or *I am* (spoken by the *Beloved*)

Learning to Compliment

READ SONG OF SONGS 4:1–3

You'd better have your football helmet on if you tell the girl sitting next to you, "Your hair is like a flock of goats . . . your teeth are like a flock of sheep just shorn" (verses 1–2). That would've been a great compliment if she was a shepherd girl in Israel 3,000 years ago and thought sheep and goats were cute. But times have changed. That compliment just doesn't work anymore. So think a bit and come up with something she can relate to. And remember, a few kind words really *can* make someone's day. If she's just aced a math quiz or won a track event, tell her you think that's great. If she's fun to be around, *tell* her. Don't worry if it seems a little awkward the first time; giving compliments is a skill that takes practice. Just avoid the "shorn sheep" line. It's old. *Really* old.

Your next reading is on page 857.

My heart sank at his departure.[a]
I looked for him but did not find him.
I called him but he did not answer.
7 The watchmen found me
  as they made their rounds in the city.
They beat me, they bruised me;
  they took away my cloak,
  those watchmen of the walls!
8 O daughters of Jerusalem, I charge
        you—
  if you find my lover,
what will you tell him?
  Tell him I am faint with love.

Friends

9 How is your beloved better than others,
  most beautiful of women?
How is your beloved better than others,
  that you charge us so?

Beloved

10 My lover is radiant and ruddy,
  outstanding among ten thousand.
11 His head is purest gold;

his hair is wavy
  and black as a raven.
12 His eyes are like doves
  by the water streams,
washed in milk,
  mounted like jewels.
13 His cheeks are like beds of spice
  yielding perfume.
His lips are like lilies
  dripping with myrrh.
14 His arms are rods of gold
  set with chrysolite.
His body is like polished ivory
  decorated with sapphires. [b]
15 His legs are pillars of marble
  set on bases of pure gold.
His appearance is like Lebanon,
  choice as its cedars.
16 His mouth is sweetness itself;
  he is altogether lovely.
This is my lover, this my friend,
  O daughters of Jerusalem.

[a] 6 Or *heart had gone out to him when he spoke*
[b] 14 Or *lapis lazuli*

Looking Like a Hunk

READ SONG OF SONGS 5:10–16

Ever fall asleep in English class? Stay awake for *this* little poetry lesson; it could change your life. This poem gives you the inside scoop: It says that girls like it when a guy looks after himself. And it's not just girls who notice; everyone sees when someone cares about how they look. When you were a little kid you could crawl around in the dirt all day, playing with toy dump trucks. You'd probably have worn the same clothes for a month straight if your mom hadn't cornered you and ordered you into the bathtub. As you get older, you need to learn how to look after your body on your own. Taking care of your appearance means learning how to wear clothes that match, wearing deodorant and brushing your teeth. A real man cares about his appearance because he knows it will affect the rest of his life.

Your next reading is on page 863.

Friends

6 Where has your lover gone,
   most beautiful of women?
   Which way did your lover turn,
   that we may look for him with you?

Beloved

2 My lover has gone down to his garden,
   to the beds of spices,
to browse in the gardens
   and to gather lilies.
3 I am my lover's and my lover is mine;
   he browses among the lilies.

Lover

4 You are beautiful, my darling, as
   Tirzah,
   lovely as Jerusalem,
   majestic as troops with banners.
5 Turn your eyes from me;
   they overwhelm me.
 Your hair is like a flock of goats
   descending from Gilead.
6 Your teeth are like a flock of sheep
   coming up from the washing.
 Each has its twin,
   not one of them is alone.
7 Your temples behind your veil
   are like the halves of a pomegranate.
8 Sixty queens there may be,
   and eighty concubines,
   and virgins beyond number;
9 but my dove, my perfect one, is
   unique,
   the only daughter of her mother,
   the favorite of the one who bore
   her.
 The maidens saw her and called her
   blessed;
   the queens and concubines praised
   her.

Friends

10 Who is this that appears like the dawn,
   fair as the moon, bright as the sun,
   majestic as the stars in procession?

Lover

11 I went down to the grove of nut trees
   to look at the new growth in the
   valley,
 to see if the vines had budded
   or the pomegranates were in bloom.
12 Before I realized it,
   my desire set me among the royal
   chariots of my people. *a*

Friends

13 Come back, come back,
   O Shulammite;
 come back, come back, that we may
   gaze on you!

Lover

 Why would you gaze on the
   Shulammite
 as on the dance of Mahanaim?

7 How beautiful your sandaled feet,
   O prince's daughter!
   Your graceful legs are like jewels,
   the work of a craftsman's hands.
2 Your navel is a rounded goblet
   that never lacks blended wine.
 Your waist is a mound of wheat
   encircled by lilies.
3 Your breasts are like two fawns,
   twins of a gazelle.
4 Your neck is like an ivory tower.
 Your eyes are the pools of Heshbon
   by the gate of Bath Rabbim.
 Your nose is like the tower of Lebanon
   looking toward Damascus.
5 Your head crowns you like Mount
   Carmel.
 Your hair is like royal tapestry;
   the king is held captive by its tresses.
6 How beautiful you are and how
   pleasing,
   O love, with your delights!
7 Your stature is like that of the palm,
   and your breasts like clusters of fruit.
8 I said, "I will climb the palm tree;
   I will take hold of its fruit."
 May your breasts be like the clusters of
   the vine,
   the fragrance of your breath like
   apples,
9   and your mouth like the best wine.

Beloved

 May the wine go straight to my lover,
   flowing gently over lips and teeth. *b*
10 I belong to my lover,
   and his desire is for me.
11 Come, my lover, let us go to the
   countryside,
   let us spend the night in the
   villages. *c*
12 Let us go early to the vineyards

---

a 12 Or *among the chariots of Amminadab; or among the
chariots of the people of the prince*   *b 9* Septuagint, Aquila,
Vulgate and Syriac; Hebrew *lips of sleepers*   *c 11* Or *henna
bushes*

to see if the vines have budded,
if their blossoms have opened,
    and if the pomegranates are in bloom—
    there I will give you my love.
13 The mandrakes send out their fragrance,
    and at our door is every delicacy,
both new and old,
    that I have stored up for you, my lover.

8 If only you were to me like a brother,
    who was nursed at my mother's breasts!
Then, if I found you outside,
    I would kiss you,
    and no one would despise me.
2 I would lead you
    and bring you to my mother's house—
    she who has taught me.
I would give you spiced wine to drink,
    the nectar of my pomegranates.
3 His left arm is under my head
    and his right arm embraces me.
4 Daughters of Jerusalem, I charge you:
    Do not arouse or awaken love
    until it so desires.

Friends

5 Who is this coming up from the desert
    leaning on her lover?

Beloved

Under the apple tree I roused you;
    there your mother conceived you,
    there she who was in labor gave you birth.
6 Place me like a seal over your heart,
    like a seal on your arm;
for love is as strong as death,
    its jealousy^a unyielding as the grave.^b
It burns like blazing fire,
    like a mighty flame.^c
7 Many waters cannot quench love;
    rivers cannot wash it away.
If one were to give
    all the wealth of his house for love,
    it^d would be utterly scorned.

Friends

8 We have a young sister,
    and her breasts are not yet grown.
What shall we do for our sister
    for the day she is spoken for?
9 If she is a wall,
    we will build towers of silver on her.
If she is a door,
    we will enclose her with panels of cedar.

Get a Load of This...

Song of Songs 8:4 says, "Do not arouse or awaken love until it so desires"—meaning before it's time. Okaaaaay, we have *definitely* read this before! (Yup! Back in Song of Songs 3:5 AND 2:7.) God obviously wants to make sure we put education and other important stuff before romance.

In other words...

---

^a 6 Or *ardor*   ^b 6 Hebrew *Sheol*   ^c 6 Or / *like the very flame of the* LORD
^d 7 Or *he*

Beloved

¹⁰I am a wall,
　　and my breasts are like towers.
　Thus I have become in his eyes
　　like one bringing contentment.
¹¹Solomon had a vineyard in Baal Hamon;
　　he let out his vineyard to tenants.
　Each was to bring for its fruit
　　a thousand shekels^a of silver.
¹²But my own vineyard is mine to give;
　　the thousand shekels are for you,
　　　O Solomon,
　and two hundred^b are for those
　　who tend its fruit.

Lover

¹³You who dwell in the gardens
　　with friends in attendance,
　　let me hear your voice!

Beloved

¹⁴Come away, my lover,
　　and be like a gazelle
　or like a young stag
　　on the spice-laden mountains.

---

^a 11 That is, about 25 pounds (about 11.5 kilograms); also in
verse 12　^b 12 That is, about 5 pounds (about 2.3
kilograms)

Who wrote this book?

The prophet Isaiah.

Why was this book written?

Isaiah warns the people of Judah that God will punish them just as he is punishing Israel, if they keep on doing wicked things. Isaiah also promises that God will comfort his people after punishing them and that he will make their nation strong again.

What do we learn about God in this book?

Isaiah uses many special names for God. These names show that God is holy, God is judge, and God is our salvation.

What is special about this book?

Isaiah gives many wonderful prophecies about Jesus, the coming Savior.

When was this book written?

Isaiah was written between 739 and 680 B.C. During this time the Assyrian armies that took Israel captive were driven out of Judah by God.

What are some important chapters in this book?

1 The vision concerning Judah and Jerusalem that Isaiah son of Amoz saw during the reigns of Uzziah, Jotham, Ahaz and Hezekiah, kings of Judah.

A Rebellious Nation

2 Hear, O heavens! Listen, O earth!
    For the LORD has spoken:
"I reared children and brought them
        up,
    but they have rebelled against me.
3 The ox knows his master,
    the donkey his owner's manger,
but Israel does not know,
    my people do not understand."

4 Ah, sinful nation,
    a people loaded with guilt,
a brood of evildoers,
    children given to corruption!
They have forsaken the LORD;
    they have spurned the Holy One of
        Israel
    and turned their backs on him.

5 Why should you be beaten anymore?
    Why do you persist in rebellion?
Your whole head is injured,
    your whole heart afflicted.
6 From the sole of your foot to the top
        of your head
    there is no soundness—
only wounds and welts
    and open sores,
not cleansed or bandaged
    or soothed with oil.

7 Your country is desolate,
    your cities burned with fire;
your fields are being stripped by
        foreigners
    right before you,
    laid waste as when overthrown by
        strangers.
8 The Daughter of Zion is left
    like a shelter in a vineyard,
like a hut in a field of melons,
    like a city under siege.
9 Unless the LORD Almighty
    had left us some survivors,
we would have become like Sodom,
    we would have been like Gomorrah.

10 Hear the word of the LORD,
    you rulers of Sodom;
listen to the law of our God,
    you people of Gomorrah!
11 "The multitude of your sacrifices—
    what are they to me?" says the LORD.

"I have more than enough of burnt
        offerings,
    of rams and the fat of fattened
        animals;
I have no pleasure
    in the blood of bulls and lambs and
        goats.
12 When you come to appear before me,
    who has asked this of you,
    this trampling of my courts?
13 Stop bringing meaningless offerings!
    Your incense is detestable to me.
New Moons, Sabbaths and
        convocations—
    I cannot bear your evil assemblies.
14 Your New Moon festivals and your
        appointed feasts
    my soul hates.
They have become a burden to me;
    I am weary of bearing them.
15 When you spread out your hands in
        prayer,
    I will hide my eyes from you;
even if you offer many prayers,
    I will not listen.
Your hands are full of blood;
16   wash and make yourselves clean.
Take your evil deeds
    out of my sight!
Stop doing wrong,
17   learn to do right!
Seek justice,
    encourage the oppressed. a
Defend the cause of the fatherless,
    plead the case of the widow.

18 "Come now, let us reason together,"
    says the LORD.
"Though your sins are like scarlet,
    they shall be as white as snow;
though they are red as crimson,
    they shall be like wool.
19 If you are willing and obedient,
    you will eat the best from the land;
20 but if you resist and rebel,
    you will be devoured by the sword."
                For the mouth of the LORD
                        has spoken.

21 See how the faithful city
    has become a harlot!
She once was full of justice;
    righteousness used to dwell in her—
    but now murderers!
22 Your silver has become dross,
    your choice wine is diluted with water.

a 17 Or / rebuke the oppressor

23 Your rulers are rebels,
    companions of thieves;
  they all love bribes
    and chase after gifts.
  They do not defend the cause of the
      fatherless;
    the widow's case does not come
        before them.
24 Therefore the Lord, the LORD Almighty,
    the Mighty One of Israel, declares:
  "Ah, I will get relief from my foes
    and avenge myself on my enemies.
25 I will turn my hand against you;
    I will thoroughly purge away your
        dross
    and remove all your impurities.
26 I will restore your judges as in days of
        old,
    your counselors as at the beginning.
  Afterward you will be called
    the City of Righteousness,
    the Faithful City."

27 Zion will be redeemed with justice,
    her penitent ones with righteousness.
28 But rebels and sinners will both be
        broken,

  and those who forsake the LORD will
      perish.

29 "You will be ashamed because of the
        sacred oaks
    in which you have delighted;
  you will be disgraced because of the
        gardens
    that you have chosen.
30 You will be like an oak with fading
        leaves,
    like a garden without water.
31 The mighty man will become tinder
    and his work a spark;
  both will burn together,
    with no one to quench the fire."

The Mountain of the LORD

2 This is what Isaiah son of Amoz saw
  concerning Judah and Jerusalem:

2 In the last days

  the mountain of the LORD's temple will
      be established
    as chief among the mountains;
  it will be raised above the hills,
    and all nations will stream to it.

Extreme Faith

READ ISAIAH 1:10–20

The Israelites were going to the temple, keeping the feasts on the
right dates, but ... they were just going through the motions. These
days, many people talk God stuff, but don't live the way he wants
them to live. They say, "Sure, I'm a Christian, I try to be nice, but I live
my life the way *I* want to." *Come again?* It's not enough to go
to church, say the right words, sing the songs, and drop some
dimes into the collection plate. You need to give God your
whole life. Have extreme faith! Do some spiritual sky-diving.
Have *you* made the jump? Believing Christian stuff is like
having a parachute on your back. That's a start, but it's
not enough. You need to leap out of the plane, yank
the ripcord, and trust that the parachute will
open.

Your next reading is on page 867.

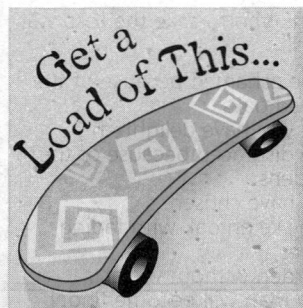

Get a Load of This...

Check out Isaiah 2:19-20. When God judges the land, the rich idolaters run from their mansions and hide out in caves and holes in the ground. Can't you just picture them looking over at the moles and saying, "Here! You can have my gold idols! They didn't do me any good."

³Many peoples will come and say,

"Come, let us go up to the mountain of the LORD,
　　to the house of the God of Jacob.
He will teach us his ways,
　　so that we may walk in his paths."
The law will go out from Zion,
　　the word of the LORD from Jerusalem.
⁴He will judge between the nations
　　and will settle disputes for many peoples.
They will beat their swords into plowshares
　　and their spears into pruning hooks.
Nation will not take up sword against nation,
　　nor will they train for war anymore.

⁵Come, O house of Jacob,
　　let us walk in the light of the LORD.

The Day of the LORD

⁶You have abandoned your people,
　　the house of Jacob.
They are full of superstitions from the East;
　　they practice divination like the Philistines
　　and clasp hands with pagans.
⁷Their land is full of silver and gold;
　　there is no end to their treasures.
Their land is full of horses;
　　there is no end to their chariots.
⁸Their land is full of idols;
　　they bow down to the work of their hands,
　　to what their fingers have made.
⁹So man will be brought low
　　and mankind humbled—
　　do not forgive them. ᵃ

¹⁰Go into the rocks,
　　hide in the ground
from dread of the LORD
　　and the splendor of his majesty!
¹¹The eyes of the arrogant man will be humbled
　　and the pride of men brought low;
the LORD alone will be exalted in that day.

¹²The LORD Almighty has a day in store
　　for all the proud and lofty,
　　for all that is exalted
　　（and they will be humbled），
¹³for all the cedars of Lebanon, tall and lofty,
　　and all the oaks of Bashan,
¹⁴for all the towering mountains
　　and all the high hills,
¹⁵for every lofty tower
　　and every fortified wall,
¹⁶for every trading ship ᵇ
　　and every stately vessel.
¹⁷The arrogance of man will be brought low
　　and the pride of men humbled;

ᵃ9 Or *not raise them up*　　ᵇ16 Hebrew *every ship of Tarshish*

the Lord alone will be exalted in that
        day,
18   and the idols will totally disappear.

19 Men will flee to caves in the rocks
        and to holes in the ground
from dread of the Lord
        and the splendor of his majesty,
        when he rises to shake the earth.
20 In that day men will throw away
        to the rodents and bats
their idols of silver and idols of gold,
        which they made to worship.
21 They will flee to caverns in the rocks
        and to the overhanging crags
from dread of the Lord
        and the splendor of his majesty,
        when he rises to shake the earth.

22 Stop trusting in man,
        who has but a breath in his nostrils.
Of what account is he?

Judgment on Jerusalem and Judah

3 See now, the Lord,
        the Lord Almighty,
        is about to take from Jerusalem
                and Judah
        both supply and support:
all supplies of food and all supplies of
                water,
2   the hero and warrior,
        the judge and prophet,
        the soothsayer and elder,
3 the captain of fifty and man of rank,
        the counselor, skilled craftsman and
                clever enchanter.

4 I will make boys their officials;
        mere children will govern them.
5 People will oppress each other—
        man against man, neighbor against
                neighbor.
The young will rise up against the old,
        the base against the honorable.

6 A man will seize one of his brothers
        at his father's home, and say,
"You have a cloak, you be our leader;
        take charge of this heap of ruins!"
7 But in that day he will cry out,
        "I have no remedy.
I have no food or clothing in my
                house;
        do not make me the leader of the
                people."

8 Jerusalem staggers,
        Judah is falling;

their words and deeds are against the
        Lord,
        defying his glorious presence.
9 The look on their faces testifies against
        them;
        they parade their sin like Sodom;
        they do not hide it.
Woe to them!
        They have brought disaster upon
                themselves.

10 Tell the righteous it will be well with
        them,
        for they will enjoy the fruit of their
                deeds.
11 Woe to the wicked! Disaster is upon
        them!
They will be paid back for what their
        hands have done.

12 Youths oppress my people,
        women rule over them.
O my people, your guides lead you
        astray;
        they turn you from the path.

13 The Lord takes his place in court;
        he rises to judge the people.
14 The Lord enters into judgment
        against the elders and leaders of his
                people:
"It is you who have ruined my
                vineyard;
        the plunder from the poor is in your
                houses.
15 What do you mean by crushing my
                people
        and grinding the faces of the poor?"
                declares the Lord,
                        the Lord Almighty.

16 The Lord says,
        "The women of Zion are haughty,
walking along with outstretched necks,
        flirting with their eyes,
tripping along with mincing steps,
        with ornaments jingling on their
                ankles.
17 Therefore the Lord will bring sores on
        the heads of the women of Zion;
        the Lord will make their scalps bald."

18 In that day the Lord will snatch away
their finery: the bangles and headbands
and crescent necklaces, 19 the earrings and
bracelets and veils, 20 the headdresses and
ankle chains and sashes, the perfume bot-
tles and charms, 21 the signet rings and
nose rings, 22 the fine robes and the capes

and cloaks, the purses 23and mirrors, and the linen garments and tiaras and shawls.

24Instead of fragrance there will be a
    stench;
  instead of a sash, a rope;
instead of well-dressed hair, baldness;
  instead of fine clothing, sackcloth;
  instead of beauty, branding.
25Your men will fall by the sword,
  your warriors in battle.
26The gates of Zion will lament and
    mourn;
  destitute, she will sit on the ground.

In that day seven women
will take hold of one man
and say, "We will eat our own food
and provide our own clothes;
only let us be called by your name.
Take away our disgrace!"

The Branch of the LORD

2In that day the Branch of the LORD will be beautiful and glorious, and the fruit of the land will be the pride and glory of the survivors in Israel. 3Those who are left in Zion, who remain in Jerusalem, will be called holy, all who are recorded among the living in Jerusalem. 4The Lord will wash away the filth of the women of Zion; he will cleanse the bloodstains from Jerusalem by a spirit*a* of judgment and a spirit*a* of fire. 5Then the LORD will create over all of Mount Zion and over those who assemble there a cloud of smoke by day and a glow of flaming fire by night; over all the glory will be a canopy. 6It will be a shelter and shade from the heat of the day, and a refuge and hiding place from the storm and rain.

The Song of the Vineyard

I will sing for the one I love
  a song about his vineyard:
My loved one had a vineyard
  on a fertile hillside.
2He dug it up and cleared it of stones
  and planted it with the choicest
    vines.
He built a watchtower in it
  and cut out a winepress as well.
Then he looked for a crop of good
    grapes,
  but it yielded only bad fruit.

3"Now you dwellers in Jerusalem and
    men of Judah,
  judge between me and my vineyard.

4What more could have been done for
    my vineyard
  than I have done for it?
When I looked for good grapes,
  why did it yield only bad?
5Now I will tell you
  what I am going to do to my
    vineyard:
I will take away its hedge,
  and it will be destroyed;
I will break down its wall,
  and it will be trampled.
6I will make it a wasteland,
  neither pruned nor cultivated,
  and briers and thorns will grow there.
I will command the clouds
  not to rain on it."

7The vineyard of the LORD Almighty
  is the house of Israel,
and the men of Judah
  are the garden of his delight.
And he looked for justice, but saw
    bloodshed;
  for righteousness, but heard cries of
    distress.

Woes and Judgments

8Woe to you who add house to house
  and join field to field
till no space is left
  and you live alone in the land.

9The LORD Almighty has declared in my hearing:

"Surely the great houses will become
    desolate,
  the fine mansions left without
    occupants.
10A ten-acre*b* vineyard will produce only
    a bath*c* of wine,
  a homer*d* of seed only an ephah*e* of
    grain."

11Woe to those who rise early in the
    morning
  to run after their drinks,
who stay up late at night
  till they are inflamed with wine.
12They have harps and lyres at their
    banquets,
  tambourines and flutes and wine,

---

a 4 Or *the Spirit*   *b 10* Hebrew *ten-yoke,* that is, the land plowed by 10 yoke of oxen in one day   *c 10* That is, probably about 6 gallons (about 22 liters)   *d 10* That is, probably about 6 bushels (about 220 liters)   *e 10* That is, probably about 3/5 bushel (about 22 liters)

but they have no regard for the deeds
   of the LORD,
no respect for the work of his hands.
¹³Therefore my people will go into exile
   for lack of understanding;
their men of rank will die of hunger
   and their masses will be parched
      with thirst.
¹⁴Therefore the grave[a] enlarges its appetite
   and opens its mouth without limit;
into it will descend their nobles and
      masses
   with all their brawlers and revelers.
¹⁵So man will be brought low
   and mankind humbled,
   the eyes of the arrogant humbled.
¹⁶But the LORD Almighty will be exalted
   by his justice,
and the holy God will show himself
   holy by his righteousness.
¹⁷Then sheep will graze as in their own
      pasture;
   lambs will feed[b] among the ruins of
      the rich.

¹⁸Woe to those who draw sin along with
   cords of deceit,

and wickedness as with cart ropes,
¹⁹to those who say, "Let God hurry,
   let him hasten his work
   so we may see it.
Let it approach,
   let the plan of the Holy One of Israel
      come,
   so we may know it."

²⁰Woe to those who call evil good
   and good evil,
who put darkness for light
   and light for darkness,
who put bitter for sweet
   and sweet for bitter.

²¹Woe to those who are wise in their
      own eyes
   and clever in their own sight.

²²Woe to those who are heroes at
      drinking wine
   and champions at mixing drinks,
²³who acquit the guilty for a bribe,
   but deny justice to the innocent.

---

[a] 14 Hebrew Sheol   [b] 17 Septuagint; Hebrew / strangers
will eat

Woe! Woe! Woe!

READ ISAIAH 5:20–25

"Maaaan, that's wicked!" "Hey, that's bad!" "Ooooo, sick!" Isn't it strange how many negative words people use to describe something *good*? Talking like that isn't evil, though it is kind of dumb. The problem comes if you *really* start thinking bad things are good and good things are bad. Do that and bad things ("woe") will happen to you. "Woe to those who call evil good and good evil" (verse 20). Count all the woes in Isaiah 5:20–25. There are so many "woes" it sounds like someone trying to stop a runaway stagecoach. This is serious stuff! When God says something is bad, it *is*. If you do bad things, expecting good to result, well . . . Duh! . . . you're in for a surprise. Focus on God and his Word, learn what he calls "good" and go after it. Learn what he calls "bad" and steer clear.

Your next reading is on page 873.

²⁴Therefore, as tongues of fire lick up
straw
and as dry grass sinks down in the
flames,
so their roots will decay
and their flowers blow away like dust;
for they have rejected the law of the
LORD Almighty
and spurned the word of the Holy
One of Israel.
²⁵Therefore the LORD's anger burns
against his people;
his hand is raised and he strikes
them down.
The mountains shake,
and the dead bodies are like refuse
in the streets.

Yet for all this, his anger is not turned
away,
his hand is still upraised.

²⁶He lifts up a banner for the distant
nations,
he whistles for those at the ends of
the earth.
Here they come,
swiftly and speedily!
²⁷Not one of them grows tired or
stumbles,
not one slumbers or sleeps;
not a belt is loosened at the waist,
not a sandal thong is broken.
²⁸Their arrows are sharp,
all their bows are strung;
their horses' hoofs seem like flint,
their chariot wheels like a whirlwind.
²⁹Their roar is like that of the lion,
they roar like young lions;
they growl as they seize their prey
and carry it off with no one to rescue.
³⁰In that day they will roar over it
like the roaring of the sea.
And if one looks at the land,
he will see darkness and distress;
even the light will be darkened by
the clouds.

Isaiah's Commission

6 In the year that King Uzziah died, I
saw the Lord seated on a throne,
high and exalted, and the train of
his robe filled the temple. ²Above
him were seraphs, each with six wings:
With two wings they covered their faces,
with two they covered their feet, and with
two they were flying. ³And they were calling to one another:

"Holy, holy, holy is the LORD Almighty;
the whole earth is full of his glory."

⁴At the sound of their voices the doorposts and thresholds shook and the temple was filled with smoke.

⁵"Woe to me!" I cried. "I am ruined!
For I am a man of unclean lips, and I live
among a people of unclean lips, and my
eyes have seen the King, the LORD Almighty."

⁶Then one of the seraphs flew to me
with a live coal in his hand, which he had
taken with tongs from the altar. ⁷With it
he touched my mouth and said, "See, this
has touched your lips; your guilt is taken
away and your sin atoned for."

⁸Then I heard the voice of the Lord saying, "Whom shall I send? And who will go
for us?"

And I said, "Here am I. Send me!"

⁹He said, "Go and tell this people:

" 'Be ever hearing, but never
understanding;
be ever seeing, but never
perceiving.'
¹⁰Make the heart of this people calloused;
make their ears dull
and close their eyes.ᵃ
Otherwise they might see with their
eyes,
hear with their ears,
understand with their hearts,
and turn and be healed."

¹¹Then I said, "For how long, O Lord?"
And he answered:

"Until the cities lie ruined
and without inhabitant,
until the houses are left deserted
and the fields ruined and ravaged,
¹²until the LORD has sent everyone far
away
and the land is utterly forsaken.
¹³And though a tenth remains in the
land,
it will again be laid waste.
But as the terebinth and oak
leave stumps when they are cut
down,
so the holy seed will be the stump in
the land."

ᵃ 9,10 Hebrew; Septuagint 'You will be ever hearing, but
never understanding; / you will be ever seeing, but never
perceiving.' / ¹⁰This people's heart has become calloused; /
they hardly hear with their ears, / and they have closed their
eyes

The Sign of Immanuel

7 When Ahaz son of Jotham, the son of Uzziah, was king of Judah, King Rezin of Aram and Pekah son of Remaliah king of Israel marched up to fight against Jerusalem, but they could not overpower it.

2 Now the house of David was told, "Aram has allied itself with[a] Ephraim"; so the hearts of Ahaz and his people were shaken, as the trees of the forest are shaken by the wind.

3 Then the LORD said to Isaiah, "Go out, you and your son Shear-Jashub,[b] to meet Ahaz at the end of the aqueduct of the Upper Pool, on the road to the Washerman's Field. 4 Say to him, 'Be careful, keep calm and don't be afraid. Do not lose heart because of these two smoldering stubs of firewood—because of the fierce anger of Rezin and Aram and of the son of Remaliah. 5 Aram, Ephraim and Remaliah's son have plotted your ruin, saying, 6 "Let us invade Judah; let us tear it apart and divide it among ourselves, and make the son of Tabeel king over it." 7 Yet this is what the Sovereign LORD says:

" 'It will not take place,
    it will not happen,
8 for the head of Aram is Damascus,
    and the head of Damascus is only Rezin.
Within sixty-five years
    Ephraim will be too shattered to be a people.
9 The head of Ephraim is Samaria,
    and the head of Samaria is only Remaliah's son.
If you do not stand firm in your faith,
    you will not stand at all.' "

10 Again the LORD spoke to Ahaz, 11 "Ask the LORD your God for a sign, whether in the deepest depths or in the highest heights."

---

a 2 Or has set up camp in   b 3 Shear-Jashub means a remnant will return.

Make It Stick

READ ISAIAH 6:8

When God needed something done, Isaiah was first in line. Can *you* say, "Do what you want with my life, Lord!"? Don't let the thought worry you. God has your best interests in mind. When you're ready to pray these words, write them on a sticky note along with the date you prayed them.

Get a Load of This...

Check out Isaiah 7:9. You can't stand solid if you're like a jellyfish with no backbone. When your faith gets tested and you moan, "God isn't there, because he's not doing what I *want* him to do," you have flop-on-the-floor jellyfish faith.

In other words...

¹²But Ahaz said, "I will not ask; I will not put the Lᴏʀᴅ to the test."

¹³Then Isaiah said, "Hear now, you house of David! Is it not enough to try the patience of men? Will you try the patience of my God also? ¹⁴Therefore the Lord himself will give you*ᵃ* a sign: The virgin will be with child and will give birth to a son, and*ᵇ* will call him Immanuel.*ᶜ* ¹⁵He will eat curds and honey when he knows enough to reject the wrong and choose the right. ¹⁶But before the boy knows enough to reject the wrong and choose the right, the land of the two kings you dread will be laid waste. ¹⁷The Lᴏʀᴅ will bring on you and on your people and on the house of your father a time unlike any since Ephraim broke away from Judah—he will bring the king of Assyria."

¹⁸In that day the Lᴏʀᴅ will whistle for flies from the distant streams of Egypt and for bees from the land of Assyria. ¹⁹They will all come and settle in the steep ravines and in the crevices in the rocks, on all the thornbushes and at all the water holes. ²⁰In that day the Lord will use a razor hired from beyond the River*ᵈ*—the king of Assyria—to shave your head and the hair of your legs, and to take off your beards also. ²¹In that day, a man will keep alive a young cow and two goats. ²²And because of the abundance of the milk they give, he will have curds to eat. All who remain in the land will eat curds and honey. ²³In that day, in every place where there were a thousand vines worth a thousand silver shekels,*ᵉ* there will be only briers and thorns. ²⁴Men will go there with bow and arrow, for the land will be covered with briers and thorns. ²⁵As for all the hills once cultivated by the hoe, you will no longer go there for fear of the briers and thorns; they will become places where cattle are turned loose and where sheep run.

Assyria, the Lᴏʀᴅ's Instrument

8 The Lᴏʀᴅ said to me, "Take a large scroll and write on it with an ordinary pen: Maher-Shalal-Hash-Baz.*ᶠ* ²And I will call in Uriah the priest and Zechariah son of Jeberekiah as reliable witnesses for me."

³Then I went to the prophetess, and she conceived and gave birth to a son. And the Lᴏʀᴅ said to me, "Name him Maher-Shalal-Hash-Baz. ⁴Before the boy knows how to say 'My father' or 'My mother,' the wealth of Damascus and the plunder of Samaria will be carried off by the king of Assyria."

⁵The Lᴏʀᴅ spoke to me again:

⁶ "Because this people has rejected
    the gently flowing waters of Shiloah
  and rejoices over Rezin
    and the son of Remaliah,
⁷therefore the Lord is about to bring against them

ᵃ 14 The Hebrew is plural.   *ᵇ 14* Masoretic Text; Dead Sea Scrolls *and he* or *and they*   *ᶜ 14 Immanuel* means *God with us.*   *ᵈ 20* That is, the Euphrates   *ᵉ 23* That is, about 25 pounds (about 11.5 kilograms)   *ᶠ 1 Maher-Shalal-Hash-Baz* means *quick to the plunder, swift to the spoil*; also in verse 3.

the mighty floodwaters of the River[a]—
the king of Assyria with all his pomp.
It will overflow all its channels,
run over all its banks
8 and sweep on into Judah, swirling over it,
passing through it and reaching up to the neck.
Its outspread wings will cover the breadth of your
land,
O Immanuel[b]!"

9 Raise the war cry,[c] you nations, and be shattered!
Listen, all you distant lands.
Prepare for battle, and be shattered!
Prepare for battle, and be shattered!
10 Devise your strategy, but it will be thwarted;
propose your plan, but it will not stand,
for God is with us.[d]

Fear God

11 The LORD spoke to me with his strong hand upon me, warning me not to follow the way of this people. He said:

12 "Do not call conspiracy
everything that these people call conspiracy[e];
do not fear what they fear,
and do not dread it.
13 The LORD Almighty is the one you are to regard as
holy,
he is the one you are to fear,
he is the one you are to dread,
14 and he will be a sanctuary;
but for both houses of Israel he will be
a stone that causes men to stumble
and a rock that makes them fall.
And for the people of Jerusalem he will be
a trap and a snare.
15 Many of them will stumble;
they will fall and be broken,
they will be snared and captured."

16 Bind up the testimony
and seal up the law among my disciples.
17 I will wait for the LORD,
who is hiding his face from the house of Jacob.
I will put my trust in him.

18 Here am I, and the children the LORD has given me. We are signs and symbols in Israel from the LORD Almighty, who dwells on Mount Zion.
19 When men tell you to consult mediums and spiritists, who whisper and mutter, should not a people inquire of their God? Why consult the dead on behalf of the living? 20 To the law and to the testimony! If they do not speak according to this word, they have no light of dawn. 21 Distressed and hungry, they will roam through

Gross!

Cool! God can whistle for swarms of flies, and they come! He's even got a special whistle to make the bees come humming (see Isaiah 7:18). And how long did it take you to even get your *dog* to answer to a whistle?

---

[a] 7 That is, the Euphrates   [b] 8 Immanuel means God with us.   [c] 9 Or Do your worst   [d] 10 Hebrew Immanuel   [e] 12 Or Do not call for a treaty / every time these people call for a treaty

Get a Load of This...

"Name him Maher-Shal-al-Hash-Baz" (Isaiah 8:3). Ho! See if you can even *pronounce* this name! (When you get it down, then try saying it really fast.) Aren't you glad your parents didn't name you something like that?

the land; when they are famished, they will become enraged and, looking upward, will curse their king and their God. 22 Then they will look toward the earth and see only distress and darkness and fearful gloom, and they will be thrust into utter darkness.

To Us a Child Is Born

9 Nevertheless, there will be no more gloom for those who were in distress. In the past he humbled the land of Zebulun and the land of Naphtali, but in the future he will honor Galilee of the Gentiles, by the way of the sea, along the Jordan—

2 The people walking in darkness
　　have seen a great light;
on those living in the land of the shadow of death[a]
　　a light has dawned.
3 You have enlarged the nation
　　and increased their joy;
they rejoice before you
　　as people rejoice at the harvest,
as men rejoice
　　when dividing the plunder.
4 For as in the day of Midian's defeat,
　　you have shattered
the yoke that burdens them,
　　the bar across their shoulders,
　　the rod of their oppressor.
5 Every warrior's boot used in battle
　　and every garment rolled in blood
will be destined for burning,
　　will be fuel for the fire.
6 For to us a child is born,
　　to us a son is given,
　　and the government will be on his shoulders.
And he will be called
　　Wonderful Counselor,[b] Mighty God,
　　Everlasting Father, Prince of Peace.
7 Of the increase of his government and peace
　　there will be no end.
He will reign on David's throne
　　and over his kingdom,
establishing and upholding it
　　with justice and righteousness
　　from that time on and forever.
The zeal of the LORD Almighty
　　will accomplish this.

The LORD's Anger Against Israel

8 The Lord has sent a message against Jacob;
　　it will fall on Israel.
9 All the people will know it—
　　Ephraim and the inhabitants of Samaria—
who say with pride
　　and arrogance of heart,
10 "The bricks have fallen down,

---

[a] 2 Or *land of darkness*　　[b] 6 Or *Wonderful, Counselor*

but we will rebuild with dressed stone;
the fig trees have been felled,
but we will replace them with cedars."

11 But the LORD has strengthened Rezin's foes against them
and has spurred their enemies on.
12 Arameans from the east and Philistines from the west
have devoured Israel with open mouth.

Yet for all this, his anger is not turned away,
his hand is still upraised.

13 But the people have not returned to him who struck them,
nor have they sought the LORD Almighty.
14 So the LORD will cut off from Israel both head and tail,
both palm branch and reed in a single day;
15 the elders and prominent men are the head,

the prophets who teach lies are the tail.
16 Those who guide this people mislead them,
and those who are guided are led astray.
17 Therefore the Lord will take no pleasure in the young men,
nor will he pity the fatherless and widows,
for everyone is ungodly and wicked, every mouth speaks vileness.

Yet for all this, his anger is not turned away,
his hand is still upraised.

18 Surely wickedness burns like a fire;
it consumes briers and thorns,
it sets the forest thickets ablaze,
so that it rolls upward in a column of smoke.
19 By the wrath of the LORD Almighty the land will be scorched
and the people will be fuel for the fire;
no one will spare his brother.
20 On the right they will devour,
but still be hungry;

Psycho Psychic Stuff

READ ISAIAH 8:19–20

People want to know what their future holds, so astrology, palm-reading, tarot cards, fortune-tellers and mediums have become very popular. Even some Christians think "psychic stuff" is OK. Think again. God's Word says it's foolishness and off limits. God has a plan for your life, and he wants you to commit your life to him, pray and find out his will. But a lot of people want to take shortcuts. They want to pay a few bucks to find out their future, not pay the *full* price and give their life to God. Doesn't work. Your future isn't decided by the stars or "fate" or by little wrinkles in your hand. God has a plan for your life, so ask him.

Also, a lot of what happens to you depends on the choices you make. Choose wrong things, and you'll have trouble. Choose good, and good will come to you (see Galatians 6:7–8).

Your next reading is on page 874.

on the left they will eat,
  but not be satisfied.
Each will feed on the flesh of his own
    offspring[a]:
21 Manasseh will feed on Ephraim, and
    Ephraim on Manasseh;
  together they will turn against
    Judah.

Yet for all this, his anger is not turned
    away,
  his hand is still upraised.

10 Woe to those who make unjust
    laws,
  to those who issue oppressive
    decrees,
2 to deprive the poor of their rights
  and withhold justice from the
    oppressed of my people,
making widows their prey
  and robbing the fatherless.
3 What will you do on the day of
    reckoning,
  when disaster comes from afar?
To whom will you run for help?
  Where will you leave your riches?

4 Nothing will remain but to cringe
    among the captives
  or fall among the slain.

Yet for all this, his anger is not turned
    away,
  his hand is still upraised.

God's Judgment on Assyria

5 "Woe to the Assyrian, the rod of my
    anger,
  in whose hand is the club of my
    wrath!
6 I send him against a godless nation,
  I dispatch him against a people who
    anger me,
to seize loot and snatch plunder,
  and to trample them down like mud
    in the streets.
7 But this is not what he intends,
  this is not what he has in mind;
his purpose is to destroy,
  to put an end to many nations.
8 'Are not my commanders all kings?' he
    says.

a 20 Or arm

A Child Is Born

READ ISAIAH 9:6–7

"To us a child is born" (verse 6). What child is this? Jesus! These verses
prophesied his birth 700 years before it ever happened! In the
comics, there's a nothing-special dude called Clark Kent, but unknown
to anybody, he's *really* ... ta da! ... Superman! Well, Jesus has Clark all
beat. This little "child," as it turns out, is actually the "Mighty
God." You can't top *that!* So why did the Son of God come to
earth as a man? Because when Adam and Eve disobeyed the
Lord, sin and death entered the world. God knew this would
happen, so he had a plan right from el beginning-o to fix the
problem: Jesus would die for our sins so we could come
back into relationship with him. People blew it, but
God didn't write us off. Instead, he sent his Son to
give us another chance. How good is *that* (see
also John 1:1–10; 3:16)?

Your next reading is on page 877.

9   'Has not Calno fared like Carchemish?
Is not Hamath like Arpad,
        and Samaria like Damascus?
10 As my hand seized the kingdoms of the idols,
        kingdoms whose images excelled those of
                Jerusalem and Samaria—
11 shall I not deal with Jerusalem and her images
        as I dealt with Samaria and her idols?' "

12 When the Lord has finished all his work against
Mount Zion and Jerusalem, he will say, "I will punish the
king of Assyria for the willful pride of his heart and the
haughty look in his eyes. 13 For he says:

" 'By the strength of my hand I have done this,
        and by my wisdom, because I have understanding.
I removed the boundaries of nations,
        I plundered their treasures;
        like a mighty one I subdued[a] their kings.
14 As one reaches into a nest,
        so my hand reached for the wealth of the nations;
as men gather abandoned eggs,
        so I gathered all the countries;
not one flapped a wing,
        or opened its mouth to chirp.' "

15 Does the ax raise itself above him who swings it,
        or the saw boast against him who uses it?
As if a rod were to wield him who lifts it up,
        or a club brandish him who is not wood!
16 Therefore, the Lord, the LORD Almighty,
        will send a wasting disease upon his sturdy
                warriors;
under his pomp a fire will be kindled
        like a blazing flame.
17 The Light of Israel will become a fire,
        their Holy One a flame;
in a single day it will burn and consume
        his thorns and his briers.
18 The splendor of his forests and fertile fields
        it will completely destroy,
        as when a sick man wastes away.
19 And the remaining trees of his forests will be so few
        that a child could write them down.

The Remnant of Israel

20 In that day the remnant of Israel,
        the survivors of the house of Jacob,
will no longer rely on him
        who struck them down
but will truly rely on the LORD,
        the Holy One of Israel.
21 A remnant will return,[b] a remnant of Jacob
        will return to the Mighty God.
22 Though your people, O Israel, be like the sand by the
                sea,
        only a remnant will return.

Get a Load of This...

Check out Isaiah 10:15. Can your skateboard boast that it does a great job? Nope. Can your basketball bounce itself across the court without getting intercepted, then hurl itself through the hoop without you? Nope. Can you live God's way and do things for him without *his* help? Nope.

In Other Words...

---

a 13 Or / I subdued the mighty,   b 21 Hebrew shear-jashub; also in verse 22

Destruction has been decreed,
overwhelming and righteous.
23 The Lord, the LORD Almighty, will carry
out
the destruction decreed upon the
whole land.

24 Therefore, this is what the Lord, the
LORD Almighty, says:

"O my people who live in Zion,
do not be afraid of the Assyrians,
who beat you with a rod
and lift up a club against you, as
Egypt did.
25 Very soon my anger against you will
end
and my wrath will be directed to
their destruction."

26 The LORD Almighty will lash them with
a whip,
as when he struck down Midian at
the rock of Oreb;
and he will raise his staff over the
waters,
as he did in Egypt.
27 In that day their burden will be lifted
from your shoulders,
their yoke from your neck;
the yoke will be broken
because you have grown so fat. a

28 They enter Aiath;
they pass through Migron;
they store supplies at Micmash.
29 They go over the pass, and say,
"We will camp overnight at Geba."
Ramah trembles;
Gibeah of Saul flees.
30 Cry out, O Daughter of Gallim!
Listen, O Laishah!
Poor Anathoth!
31 Madmenah is in flight;
the people of Gebim take cover.
32 This day they will halt at Nob;
they will shake their fist
at the mount of the Daughter of Zion,
at the hill of Jerusalem.

33 See, the Lord, the LORD Almighty,
will lop off the boughs with great
power.
The lofty trees will be felled,
the tall ones will be brought low.
34 He will cut down the forest thickets
with an ax;
Lebanon will fall before the Mighty
One.

The Branch From Jesse

11 A shoot will come up from the
stump of Jesse;
from his roots a Branch will bear
fruit.
2 The Spirit of the LORD will rest on
him—
the Spirit of wisdom and of
understanding,
the Spirit of counsel and of power,
the Spirit of knowledge and of the
fear of the LORD—
3 and he will delight in the fear of the
LORD.

He will not judge by what he sees with
his eyes,
or decide by what he hears with his
ears;
4 but with righteousness he will judge
the needy,
with justice he will give decisions for
the poor of the earth.
He will strike the earth with the rod of
his mouth;
with the breath of his lips he will
slay the wicked.
5 Righteousness will be his belt
and faithfulness the sash around his
waist.

6 The wolf will live with the lamb,
the leopard will lie down with the
goat,
the calf and the lion and the yearling b
together;
and a little child will lead them.
7 The cow will feed with the bear,
their young will lie down together,
and the lion will eat straw like the
ox.
8 The infant will play near the hole of
the cobra,
and the young child put his hand
into the viper's nest.
9 They will neither harm nor destroy
on all my holy mountain,
for the earth will be full of the
knowledge of the LORD
as the waters cover the sea.

10 In that day the Root of Jesse will
stand as a banner for the peoples; the nations will rally to him, and his place of rest
will be glorious. 11 In that day the Lord will
reach out his hand a second time to re-

a 27 Hebrew; Septuagint broken / from your shoulders
b 6 Hebrew; Septuagint lion will feed

claim the remnant that is left of his people from Assyria, from Lower Egypt, from Upper Egypt,[a] from Cush,[b] from Elam, from Babylonia,[c] from Hamath and from the islands of the sea.

12 He will raise a banner for the nations
and gather the exiles of Israel;
he will assemble the scattered people
of Judah
from the four quarters of the earth.
13 Ephraim's jealousy will vanish,
and Judah's enemies[d] will be cut
off;
Ephraim will not be jealous of Judah,
nor Judah hostile toward Ephraim.
14 They will swoop down on the slopes of
Philistia to the west;
together they will plunder the
people to the east.
They will lay hands on Edom and
Moab,
and the Ammonites will be subject
to them.
15 The Lord will dry up
the gulf of the Egyptian sea;

with a scorching wind he will sweep
his hand
over the Euphrates River.[e]
He will break it up into seven streams
so that men can cross over in
sandals.
16 There will be a highway for the
remnant of his people
that is left from Assyria,
as there was for Israel
when they came up from Egypt.

Songs of Praise

12 In that day you will say:

"I will praise you, O Lord.
Although you were angry with
me,
your anger has turned away
and you have comforted me.
2 Surely God is my salvation;
I will trust and not be afraid.

---

[a] 11 Hebrew from Pathros   [b] 11 That is, the upper Nile region   [c] 11 Hebrew Shinar   [d] 13 Or hostility   [e] 15 Hebrew the River

---

GET SMARTER: Equipped for the Job

READ ISAIAH 11:1–5

Ever imagined what it would be like to be a knight in armor, riding a warhorse full gallop, battling with swords and lances? We are talking major excitement! This passage talks about the gifts and abilities that God gave Jesus when he sent him to earth to do a job. God also gives us tasks and equips us to do them. Now, chances are that God hasn't called you to be a knight so you can probably cancel your order for that broadsword. But God has equipped you with the talents and abilities you need to do whatever he's called you to. You may not know every talent God has placed inside you. They may be hidden like the "sword in the stone" right now, but they are there. Whether God leads you to become a policeman, an astronaut, a carpenter or a pastor, God has equipped you with the talents to do that job.

Your next reading is on page 887.

The LORD, the LORD, is my strength and
   my song;
  he has become my salvation."
³With joy you will draw water
  from the wells of salvation.

⁴In that day you will say:

"Give thanks to the LORD, call on his
   name;
  make known among the nations
   what he has done,
  and proclaim that his name is exalted.
⁵Sing to the LORD, for he has done
   glorious things;
  let this be known to all the world.
⁶Shout aloud and sing for joy, people of
   Zion,
  for great is the Holy One of Israel
   among you."

A Prophecy Against Babylon

13 An oracle concerning Babylon
    that Isaiah son of Amoz saw:

²Raise a banner on a bare
   hilltop,
  shout to them;
beckon to them
  to enter the gates of the nobles.
³I have commanded my holy ones;
  I have summoned my warriors to
   carry out my wrath—
  those who rejoice in my triumph.

⁴Listen, a noise on the mountains,
  like that of a great multitude!
Listen, an uproar among the
   kingdoms,
  like nations massing together!
The LORD Almighty is mustering
  an army for war.
⁵They come from faraway lands,
  from the ends of the heavens—
the LORD and the weapons of his
   wrath—
  to destroy the whole country.

⁶Wail, for the day of the LORD is near;
  it will come like destruction from the
   Almighty.ᵃ
⁷Because of this, all hands will go limp,
  every man's heart will melt.
⁸Terror will seize them,
  pain and anguish will grip them;
  they will writhe like a woman in
   labor.
They will look aghast at each other,
  their faces aflame.

⁹See, the day of the LORD is coming
  —a cruel day, with wrath and fierce
   anger—
to make the land desolate
  and destroy the sinners within it.
¹⁰The stars of heaven and their
   constellations
  will not show their light.
The rising sun will be darkened
  and the moon will not give its light.
¹¹I will punish the world for its evil,
  the wicked for their sins.
I will put an end to the arrogance of
   the haughty
  and will humble the pride of the
   ruthless.
¹²I will make man scarcer than pure gold,
  more rare than the gold of Ophir.
¹³Therefore I will make the heavens
   tremble;
  and the earth will shake from its place
at the wrath of the LORD Almighty,
  in the day of his burning anger.

¹⁴Like a hunted gazelle,
  like sheep without a shepherd,
each will return to his own people,
  each will flee to his native land.
¹⁵Whoever is captured will be thrust
   through;
  all who are caught will fall by the
   sword.
¹⁶Their infants will be dashed to pieces
   before their eyes;
  their houses will be looted and their
   wives ravished.

¹⁷See, I will stir up against them the
   Medes,
  who do not care for silver
  and have no delight in gold.
¹⁸Their bows will strike down the young
   men;
  they will have no mercy on infants
  nor will they look with compassion
   on children.
¹⁹Babylon, the jewel of kingdoms,
  the glory of the Babylonians'ᵇ pride,
will be overthrown by God
  like Sodom and Gomorrah.
²⁰She will never be inhabited
  or lived in through all generations;
no Arab will pitch his tent there,
  no shepherd will rest his flocks there.
²¹But desert creatures will lie there,
  jackals will fill her houses;

ᵃ 6 Hebrew *Shaddai*   ᵇ 19 Or *Chaldeans'*

there the owls will dwell,
    and there the wild goats will leap about.
22 Hyenas will howl in her strongholds,
    jackals in her luxurious palaces.
Her time is at hand,
    and her days will not be prolonged.

14 The LORD will have compassion on Jacob;
    once again he will choose Israel
    and will settle them in their own land.
    Aliens will join them
and unite with the house of Jacob.
2 Nations will take them
    and bring them to their own place.
And the house of Israel will possess the nations
    as menservants and maidservants in the LORD's
    land.
They will make captives of their captors
    and rule over their oppressors.

3 On the day the LORD gives you relief from suffering
and turmoil and cruel bondage, 4 you will take up this
taunt against the king of Babylon:

How the oppressor has come to an end!
    How his fury[a] has ended!
5 The LORD has broken the rod of the wicked,
    the scepter of the rulers,
6 which in anger struck down peoples
    with unceasing blows,
and in fury subdued nations
    with relentless aggression.
7 All the lands are at rest and at peace;
    they break into singing.
8 Even the pine trees and the cedars of Lebanon
    exult over you and say,
"Now that you have been laid low,
    no woodsman comes to cut us down."

9 The grave[b] below is all astir
    to meet you at your coming;
it rouses the spirits of the departed to greet you—
    all those who were leaders in the world;
it makes them rise from their thrones—
    all those who were kings over the nations.
10 They will all respond,
    they will say to you,
"You also have become weak, as we are;
    you have become like us."
11 All your pomp has been brought down to the grave,
    along with the noise of your harps;
maggots are spread out beneath you
    and worms cover you.

12 How you have fallen from heaven,
    O morning star, son of the dawn!

a 4 Dead Sea Scrolls, Septuagint and Syriac; the meaning of the word in the
Masoretic Text is uncertain.   b 9 Hebrew *Sheol*; also in verses 11 and 15

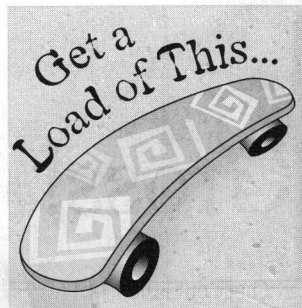

Get a Load of This...

God prophesied through Isaiah that the Medes would conquer Babylon (Isaiah 13:17–21), and 200 years later that's exactly what they did. God said Babylon would be empty ruins, and that's what happened—it's still a rock dump today. Does God know his stuff, or what?

Gross!

Check out Isaiah 14:11. Imagine if your mattress was maggots and your blanket was worms. Hmmm ... but maybe it's best not to imagine this just before you go to sleep.

You have been cast down to the earth,
    you who once laid low the nations!
13 You said in your heart,
    "I will ascend to heaven;
    I will raise my throne
        above the stars of God;
    I will sit enthroned on the mount of assembly,
        on the utmost heights of the sacred mountain. [a]
14 I will ascend above the tops of the clouds;
        I will make myself like the Most High."
15 But you are brought down to the grave,
        to the depths of the pit.

16 Those who see you stare at you,
        they ponder your fate:
    "Is this the man who shook the earth
        and made kingdoms tremble,
17 the man who made the world a desert,
        who overthrew its cities
        and would not let his captives go home?"

18 All the kings of the nations lie in state,
        each in his own tomb.
19 But you are cast out of your tomb
        like a rejected branch;
    you are covered with the slain,
        with those pierced by the sword,
        those who descend to the stones of the pit.
    Like a corpse trampled underfoot,
20   you will not join them in burial,
    for you have destroyed your land
        and killed your people.

    The offspring of the wicked
        will never be mentioned again.
21 Prepare a place to slaughter his sons
        for the sins of their forefathers;
    they are not to rise to inherit the land
        and cover the earth with their cities.

22 "I will rise up against them,"
        declares the LORD Almighty.
    "I will cut off from Babylon her name and survivors,
        her offspring and descendants,"
                                declares the LORD.
23 "I will turn her into a place for owls
        and into swampland;
    I will sweep her with the broom of destruction,"
        declares the LORD Almighty.

A Prophecy Against Assyria
24 The LORD Almighty has sworn,

    "Surely, as I have planned, so it will be,
        and as I have purposed, so it will stand.
25 I will crush the Assyrian in my land;
        on my mountains I will trample him down.

a 13 Or the north; Hebrew Zaphon

His yoke will be taken from my people,
and his burden removed from their
shoulders."

26 This is the plan determined for the
whole world;
this is the hand stretched out over
all nations.
27 For the LORD Almighty has purposed,
and who can thwart him?
His hand is stretched out, and who
can turn it back?

A Prophecy Against the Philistines

28 This oracle came in the year King
Ahaz died:

29 Do not rejoice, all you Philistines,
that the rod that struck you is
broken;
from the root of that snake will spring
up a viper,
its fruit will be a darting, venomous
serpent.
30 The poorest of the poor will find
pasture,
and the needy will lie down in safety.
But your root I will destroy by famine;
it will slay your survivors.

31 Wail, O gate! Howl, O city!
Melt away, all you Philistines!
A cloud of smoke comes from the north,
and there is not a straggler in its
ranks.
32 What answer shall be given
to the envoys of that nation?
"The LORD has established Zion,
and in her his afflicted people will
find refuge."

A Prophecy Against Moab

15 An oracle concerning Moab:

Ar in Moab is ruined,
destroyed in a night!
Kir in Moab is ruined,
destroyed in a night!
2 Dibon goes up to its temple,
to its high places to weep;
Moab wails over Nebo and Medeba.
Every head is shaved
and every beard cut off.
3 In the streets they wear sackcloth;
on the roofs and in the public squares
they all wail,
prostrate with weeping.
4 Heshbon and Elealeh cry out,

their voices are heard all the way to
Jahaz.
Therefore the armed men of Moab cry
out,
and their hearts are faint.

5 My heart cries out over Moab;
her fugitives flee as far as Zoar,
as far as Eglath Shelishiyah.
They go up the way to Luhith,
weeping as they go;
on the road to Horonaim
they lament their destruction.
6 The waters of Nimrim are dried up
and the grass is withered;
the vegetation is gone
and nothing green is left.
7 So the wealth they have acquired and
stored up
they carry away over the Ravine of
the Poplars.
8 Their outcry echoes along the border
of Moab;
their wailing reaches as far as Eglaim,
their lamentation as far as Beer Elim.
9 Dimon's[a] waters are full of blood,
but I will bring still more upon
Dimon[a]—
a lion upon the fugitives of Moab
and upon those who remain in the
land.

16 Send lambs as tribute
to the ruler of the land,
from Sela, across the desert,
to the mount of the Daughter
of Zion.
2 Like fluttering birds
pushed from the nest,
so are the women of Moab
at the fords of the Arnon.

3 "Give us counsel,
render a decision.
Make your shadow like night—
at high noon.
Hide the fugitives,
do not betray the refugees.
4 Let the Moabite fugitives stay with you;
be their shelter from the destroyer."

The oppressor will come to an end,
and destruction will cease;
the aggressor will vanish from the
land.
5 In love a throne will be established;

---

a 9 Masoretic Text; Dead Sea Scrolls, some Septuagint
manuscripts and Vulgate *Dibon*

in faithfulness a man will sit on it—
one from the house[a] of David—
one who in judging seeks justice
and speeds the cause of
righteousness.

6 We have heard of Moab's pride—
her overweening pride and conceit,
her pride and her insolence—
but her boasts are empty.
7 Therefore the Moabites wail,
they wail together for Moab.
Lament and grieve
for the men[b] of Kir Hareseth.
8 The fields of Heshbon wither,
the vines of Sibmah also.
The rulers of the nations
have trampled down the choicest
vines,
which once reached Jazer
and spread toward the desert.
Their shoots spread out
and went as far as the sea.
9 So I weep, as Jazer weeps,
for the vines of Sibmah.
O Heshbon, O Elealeh,
I drench you with tears!
The shouts of joy over your ripened fruit
and over your harvests have been
stilled.
10 Joy and gladness are taken away from
the orchards;
no one sings or shouts in the
vineyards;
no one treads out wine at the presses,
for I have put an end to the
shouting.
11 My heart laments for Moab like a harp,
my inmost being for Kir Hareseth.
12 When Moab appears at her high place,
she only wears herself out;
when she goes to her shrine to pray,
it is to no avail.

13 This is the word the LORD has already
spoken concerning Moab. 14 But now the
LORD says: "Within three years, as a servant bound by contract would count
them, Moab's splendor and all her many
people will be despised, and her survivors
will be very few and feeble."

An Oracle Against Damascus

17 An oracle concerning Damascus:

"See, Damascus will no longer
be a city
but will become a heap of ruins.

2 The cities of Aroer will be deserted
and left to flocks, which will lie
down,
with no one to make them afraid.
3 The fortified city will disappear from
Ephraim,
and royal power from Damascus;
the remnant of Aram will be
like the glory of the Israelites,"
declares the LORD Almighty.

4 "In that day the glory of Jacob will fade;
the fat of his body will waste away.
5 It will be as when a reaper gathers the
standing grain
and harvests the grain with his arm—
as when a man gleans heads of grain
in the Valley of Rephaim.
6 Yet some gleanings will remain,
as when an olive tree is beaten,
leaving two or three olives on the
topmost branches,
four or five on the fruitful boughs,"
declares the LORD, the God
of Israel.

7 In that day men will look to their Maker
and turn their eyes to the Holy One
of Israel.
8 They will not look to the altars,
the work of their hands,
and they will have no regard for the
Asherah poles[c]
and the incense altars their fingers
have made.

9 In that day their strong cities, which
they left because of the Israelites, will be
like places abandoned to thickets and un-
dergrowth. And all will be desolation.

10 You have forgotten God your Savior;
you have not remembered the Rock,
your fortress.
Therefore, though you set out the
finest plants
and plant imported vines,
11 though on the day you set them out,
you make them grow,
and on the morning when you plant
them, you bring them to bud,
yet the harvest will be as nothing
in the day of disease and incurable
pain.

12 Oh, the raging of many nations—
they rage like the raging sea!

---

a 5 Hebrew tent   b 7 Or "raisin cakes," a wordplay
c 8 That is, symbols of the goddess Asherah

Oh, the uproar of the peoples—
    they roar like the roaring of great waters!
13 Although the peoples roar like the roar of surging
        waters,
    when he rebukes them they flee far away,
driven before the wind like chaff on the hills,
    like tumbleweed before a gale.
14 In the evening, sudden terror!
    Before the morning, they are gone!
This is the portion of those who loot us,
    the lot of those who plunder us.

A Prophecy Against Cush

18 Woe to the land of whirring wings[a]
    along the rivers of Cush,[b]
    2 which sends envoys by sea
    in papyrus boats over the water.

Go, swift messengers,
    to a people tall and smooth-skinned,
      to a people feared far and wide,
    an aggressive nation of strange speech,
      whose land is divided by rivers.

3 All you people of the world,
    you who live on the earth,
when a banner is raised on the mountains,
    you will see it,
and when a trumpet sounds,
    you will hear it.
4 This is what the LORD says to me:
    "I will remain quiet and will look on from my
        dwelling place,
    like shimmering heat in the sunshine,
    like a cloud of dew in the heat of harvest."
5 For, before the harvest, when the blossom is gone
    and the flower becomes a ripening grape,
he will cut off the shoots with pruning knives,
    and cut down and take away the spreading
        branches.
6 They will all be left to the mountain birds of prey
    and to the wild animals;
the birds will feed on them all summer,
    the wild animals all winter.

7 At that time gifts will be brought to the LORD Almighty

from a people tall and smooth-skinned,
    from a people feared far and wide,
an aggressive nation of strange speech,
    whose land is divided by rivers—

the gifts will be brought to Mount Zion, the place of the
Name of the LORD Almighty.

---

a 1 Or of locusts   b 1 That is, the upper Nile region

Get a Load of This...

Check out Isaiah 18:1–2. The ancient kingdom of Cush (in modern-day Sudan) was home "to a people tall." And the further south you went, the bigger these guys got! The Sudd Swamp is home to the tallest people on this planet, the Dinkas. Manute Bol, NBA record holder for the most blocked shots, is a Dinka.

A Prophecy About Egypt

19 An oracle concerning Egypt:

See, the LORD rides on a swift
   cloud
and is coming to Egypt.
The idols of Egypt tremble before him,
   and the hearts of the Egyptians melt
      within them.

2 "I will stir up Egyptian against
      Egyptian—
   brother will fight against brother,
   neighbor against neighbor,
   city against city,
   kingdom against kingdom.
3 The Egyptians will lose heart,
   and I will bring their plans to
      nothing;
they will consult the idols and the
      spirits of the dead,
   the mediums and the spiritists.
4 I will hand the Egyptians over
   to the power of a cruel master,
and a fierce king will rule over them,"
   declares the Lord, the LORD Almighty.

5 The waters of the river will dry up,
   and the riverbed will be parched and
      dry.
6 The canals will stink;
   the streams of Egypt will dwindle
      and dry up.
The reeds and rushes will wither,
7   also the plants along the Nile,
   at the mouth of the river.
Every sown field along the Nile
   will become parched, will blow away
      and be no more.
8 The fishermen will groan and lament,
   all who cast hooks into the Nile;
those who throw nets on the water
   will pine away.
9 Those who work with combed flax will
      despair,
   the weavers of fine linen will lose
      hope.
10 The workers in cloth will be dejected,
   and all the wage earners will be sick
      at heart.

11 The officials of Zoan are nothing but
      fools;
   the wise counselors of Pharaoh give
      senseless advice.
How can you say to Pharaoh,
   "I am one of the wise men,
   a disciple of the ancient kings"?

12 Where are your wise men now?
   Let them show you and make known
what the LORD Almighty
   has planned against Egypt.
13 The officials of Zoan have become fools,
   the leaders of Memphis[a] are deceived;
the cornerstones of her peoples
   have led Egypt astray.
14 The LORD has poured into them
   a spirit of dizziness;
they make Egypt stagger in all that she
      does,
   as a drunkard staggers around in his
      vomit.
15 There is nothing Egypt can do—
   head or tail, palm branch or reed.

16 In that day the Egyptians will be like
women. They will shudder with fear at the
uplifted hand that the LORD Almighty raises against them. 17 And the land of Judah
will bring terror to the Egyptians; everyone to whom Judah is mentioned will be
terrified, because of what the LORD Almighty is planning against them.

18 In that day five cities in Egypt will
speak the language of Canaan and swear
allegiance to the LORD Almighty. One of
them will be called the City of Destruction.[b]

19 In that day there will be an altar to
the LORD in the heart of Egypt, and a monument to the LORD at its border. 20 It will be
a sign and witness to the LORD Almighty in
the land of Egypt. When they cry out to
the LORD because of their oppressors, he
will send them a savior and defender, and
he will rescue them. 21 So the LORD will
make himself known to the Egyptians,
and in that day they will acknowledge the
LORD. They will worship with sacrifices and
grain offerings; they will make vows to
the LORD and keep them. 22 The LORD will
strike Egypt with a plague; he will strike
them and heal them. They will turn to the
LORD, and he will respond to their pleas
and heal them.

23 In that day there will be a highway
from Egypt to Assyria. The Assyrians will
go to Egypt and the Egyptians to Assyria.
The Egyptians and Assyrians will worship
together. 24 In that day Israel will be the
third, along with Egypt and Assyria, a
blessing on the earth. 25 The LORD Almighty

---

a 13 Hebrew *Noph*   b 18 Most manuscripts of the
Masoretic Text; some manuscripts of the Masoretic Text, Dead
Sea Scrolls and Vulgate *City of the Sun* (that is, Heliopolis)

will bless them, saying, "Blessed be Egypt my people, Assyria my handiwork, and Israel my inheritance."

A Prophecy Against Egypt and Cush

20 In the year that the supreme commander, sent by Sargon king of Assyria, came to Ashdod and attacked and captured it— [2]at that time the LORD spoke through Isaiah son of Amoz. He said to him, "Take off the sackcloth from your body and the sandals from your feet." And he did so, going around stripped and barefoot.

[3]Then the LORD said, "Just as my servant Isaiah has gone stripped and barefoot for three years, as a sign and portent against Egypt and Cush,[a] [4]so the king of Assyria will lead away stripped and barefoot the Egyptian captives and Cushite exiles, young and old, with buttocks bared—to Egypt's shame. [5]Those who trusted in Cush and boasted in Egypt will be afraid and put to shame. [6]In that day the people who live on this coast will say, 'See what has happened to those we relied on, those we fled to for help and deliverance from the king of Assyria! How then can we escape?' "

A Prophecy Against Babylon

21 An oracle concerning the Desert by the Sea:

Like whirlwinds sweeping through the
   southland,
an invader comes from the desert,
   from a land of terror.

[2]A dire vision has been shown to me:
   The traitor betrays, the looter takes loot.
Elam, attack! Media, lay siege!
   I will bring to an end all the groaning she caused.

[3]At this my body is racked with pain,
   pangs seize me, like those of a woman in labor;
I am staggered by what I hear,
   I am bewildered by what I see.
[4]My heart falters,
   fear makes me tremble;
the twilight I longed for
   has become a horror to me.

[5]They set the tables,
   they spread the rugs,
   they eat, they drink!
Get up, you officers,
   oil the shields!

[6]This is what the Lord says to me:

"Go, post a lookout
   and have him report what he sees.
[7]When he sees chariots
   with teams of horses,
riders on donkeys

[a] 3 That is, the upper Nile region; also in verse 5

Get a Load of This...

Check out Isaiah 20:1–4. God told Isaiah to run around stripped of his sackcloth (a garment prophets wore) for three years, probably wearing nothing but his loincloth. Isaiah might've protested, "But ... but ..." but God wanted to warn Judah of what would soon happen to the Egyptians and what could happen to Judah as well: In those days, it was a custom to tie prisoners of war together and march them away naked.

In Other Words...

or riders on camels,
let him be alert,
   fully alert."

8 And the lookout[a] shouted,

"Day after day, my lord, I stand on the
   watchtower;
   every night I stay at my post.
9 Look, here comes a man in a chariot
   with a team of horses.
And he gives back the answer:
   'Babylon has fallen, has fallen!
All the images of its gods
   lie shattered on the ground!' "

10 O my people, crushed on the threshing
   floor,
   I tell you what I have heard
from the LORD Almighty,
   from the God of Israel.

A Prophecy Against Edom

11 An oracle concerning Dumah[b]:

Someone calls to me from Seir,
   "Watchman, what is left of the night?
   Watchman, what is left of the night?"
12 The watchman replies,
   "Morning is coming, but also the
   night.
If you would ask, then ask;
   and come back yet again."

A Prophecy Against Arabia

13 An oracle concerning Arabia:

You caravans of Dedanites,
   who camp in the thickets of Arabia,
14   bring water for the thirsty;
you who live in Tema,
   bring food for the fugitives.
15 They flee from the sword,
   from the drawn sword,
from the bent bow
   and from the heat of battle.

16 This is what the Lord says to me:
"Within one year, as a servant bound by
contract would count it, all the pomp of
Kedar will come to an end. 17 The survivors
of the bowmen, the warriors of Kedar, will
be few." The LORD, the God of Israel, has
spoken.

A Prophecy About Jerusalem

An oracle concerning the Valley of Vision:

What troubles you now,
that you have all gone up on the
   roofs,
2 O town full of commotion,
   O city of tumult and revelry?
Your slain were not killed by the sword,
   nor did they die in battle.
3 All your leaders have fled together;
   they have been captured without
   using the bow.
All you who were caught were taken
   prisoner together,
   having fled while the enemy was still
   far away.
4 Therefore I said, "Turn away from me;
   let me weep bitterly.
Do not try to console me
   over the destruction of my people."

5 The Lord, the LORD Almighty, has a day
   of tumult and trampling and terror
   in the Valley of Vision,
a day of battering down walls
   and of crying out to the mountains.
6 Elam takes up the quiver,
   with her charioteers and horses;
Kir uncovers the shield.
7 Your choicest valleys are full of chariots,
   and horsemen are posted at the city
   gates;
8   the defenses of Judah are stripped
   away.

And you looked in that day
   to the weapons in the Palace of the
   Forest;
9 you saw that the City of David
   had many breaches in its defenses;
you stored up water
   in the Lower Pool.
10 You counted the buildings in Jerusalem
   and tore down houses to strengthen
   the wall.
11 You built a reservoir between the two
   walls
   for the water of the Old Pool,
but you did not look to the One who
   made it,
   or have regard for the One who
   planned it long ago.

12 The Lord, the LORD Almighty,
   called you on that day
to weep and to wail,
   to tear out your hair and put on
   sackcloth.
13 But see, there is joy and revelry,

---

[a] 8 Dead Sea Scrolls and Syriac; Masoretic Text *A lion*
[b] 11 *Dumah* means *silence* or *stillness,* a wordplay on *Edom.*

slaughtering of cattle and killing of
    sheep,
    eating of meat and drinking of wine!
"Let us eat and drink," you say,
    "for tomorrow we die!"

14The LORD Almighty has revealed this in
my hearing: "Till your dying day this sin
will not be atoned for," says the Lord, the
LORD Almighty.

15This is what the Lord, the LORD Almighty, says:

"Go, say to this steward,
    to Shebna, who is in charge of the
        palace:
16What are you doing here and who
        gave you permission
    to cut out a grave for yourself here,
hewing your grave on the height
    and chiseling your resting place in
        the rock?

17"Beware, the LORD is about to take firm
    hold of you

and hurl you away, O you mighty
    man.
18He will roll you up tightly like a ball
    and throw you into a large country.
There you will die
    and there your splendid chariots will
        remain—
    you disgrace to your master's house!
19I will depose you from your office,
    and you will be ousted from your
        position.

20"In that day I will summon my servant, Eliakim son of Hilkiah. 21I will clothe
him with your robe and fasten your sash
around him and hand your authority over
to him. He will be a father to those who
live in Jerusalem and to the house of Judah. 22I will place on his shoulder the key
to the house of David; what he opens no
one can shut, and what he shuts no one
can open. 23I will drive him like a peg into
a firm place; he will be a seat a of honor

a 23 Or throne

Help in an Alien Invasion

READ ISAIAH 22:7-11

GET STRONGER

What preparations would you make if your town was going to be invaded by Martians in one week? Stock up on ray guns? Buy UFO re-
pellent? When Jerusalem was about to be besieged by enemy armies,
they counted all the weapons in their armory (verse 8), made their
city walls thicker and stronger (verses 9–10) and built up
their water supply (verses 9, 11). But oops . . . they forgot to do
the most important thing of all: ask *God* for help (verse 11).
God is not against preparation and hard work. He's all for it.
But doing it without his help can be useless and even a
disaster. God wants to work hand-in-hand with you. He'll
provide wisdom and counsel so that all your plans
and hard work actually accomplish something. Do
you have plans or projects that you haven't asked
God to help you with? Talk to him about them
right now.

Your next reading is on page 892.

How would you like to be God's bowling ball like Shebna was (see Isaiah 22:15–18)? You might say Shebna was "on a roll," but he ended up in the gutter.

In Other Words...

for the house of his father. [24]All the glory of his family will hang on him: its offspring and offshoots—all its lesser vessels, from the bowls to all the jars.

[25]"In that day," declares the LORD Almighty, "the peg driven into the firm place will give way; it will be sheared off and will fall, and the load hanging on it will be cut down." The LORD has spoken.

A Prophecy About Tyre

23 An oracle concerning Tyre:

Wail, O ships of Tarshish!
    For Tyre is destroyed
and left without house or harbor.
From the land of Cyprus[a]
    word has come to them.

[2] Be silent, you people of the island
    and you merchants of Sidon,
    whom the seafarers have enriched.
[3] On the great waters
    came the grain of the Shihor;
the harvest of the Nile[b] was the revenue of Tyre,
    and she became the marketplace of the nations.

[4] Be ashamed, O Sidon, and you, O fortress of the sea,
    for the sea has spoken:
"I have neither been in labor nor given birth;
    I have neither reared sons nor brought up
        daughters."
[5] When word comes to Egypt,
    they will be in anguish at the report from Tyre.

[6] Cross over to Tarshish;
    wail, you people of the island.
[7] Is this your city of revelry,
    the old, old city,
whose feet have taken her
    to settle in far-off lands?
[8] Who planned this against Tyre,
    the bestower of crowns,
whose merchants are princes,
    whose traders are renowned in the earth?
[9] The LORD Almighty planned it,
    to bring low the pride of all glory
    and to humble all who are renowned on the earth.

[10] Till[c] your land as along the Nile,
    O Daughter of Tarshish,
    for you no longer have a harbor.
[11] The LORD has stretched out his hand over the sea
    and made its kingdoms tremble.
He has given an order concerning Phoenicia[d]
    that her fortresses be destroyed.

---

[a] 1 Hebrew *Kittim*   [b] 2,3 Masoretic Text; one Dead Sea Scroll *Sidon, / who cross over the sea; / your envoys* [3]*are on the great waters. / The grain of the Shihor, / the harvest of the Nile,*   [c] 10 Dead Sea Scrolls and some Septuagint manuscripts; Masoretic Text *Go through*   [d] 11 Hebrew *Canaan*

¹²He said, "No more of your reveling,
  O Virgin Daughter of Sidon, now
    crushed!

"Up, cross over to Cyprus^a;
  even there you will find no rest."
¹³Look at the land of the Babylonians,^b
  this people that is now of no
    account!
The Assyrians have made it
  a place for desert creatures;
they raised up their siege towers,
  they stripped its fortresses bare
  and turned it into a ruin.

¹⁴Wail, you ships of Tarshish;
  your fortress is destroyed!

¹⁵At that time Tyre will be forgotten for
seventy years, the span of a king's life. But
at the end of these seventy years, it will
happen to Tyre as in the song of the prostitute:

¹⁶"Take up a harp, walk through the city,
  O prostitute forgotten;
play the harp well, sing many a song,
  so that you will be remembered."

¹⁷At the end of seventy years, the LORD
will deal with Tyre. She will return to her
hire as a prostitute and will ply her trade
with all the kingdoms on the face of the
earth. ¹⁸Yet her profit and her earnings
will be set apart for the LORD; they will not
be stored up or hoarded. Her profits will
go to those who live before the LORD, for
abundant food and fine clothes.

The LORD's Devastation of the Earth

See, the LORD is going to lay
waste the earth
and devastate it;
he will ruin its face
  and scatter its inhabitants—
²it will be the same
  for priest as for people,
  for master as for servant,
  for mistress as for maid,
  for seller as for buyer,
  for borrower as for lender,
  for debtor as for creditor.
³The earth will be completely laid waste
  and totally plundered.
      The LORD has spoken this word.

⁴The earth dries up and withers,
  the world languishes and withers,
  the exalted of the earth languish.
⁵The earth is defiled by its people;

they have disobeyed the laws,
  violated the statutes
  and broken the everlasting covenant.
⁶Therefore a curse consumes the earth;
  its people must bear their guilt.
Therefore earth's inhabitants are
    burned up,
  and very few are left.
⁷The new wine dries up and the vine
    withers;
  all the merrymakers groan.
⁸The gaiety of the tambourines is stilled,
  the noise of the revelers has stopped,
  the joyful harp is silent.
⁹No longer do they drink wine with a
    song;
  the beer is bitter to its drinkers.
¹⁰The ruined city lies desolate;
  the entrance to every house is barred.
¹¹In the streets they cry out for wine;
  all joy turns to gloom,
  all gaiety is banished from the earth.
¹²The city is left in ruins,
  its gate is battered to pieces.
¹³So will it be on the earth
  and among the nations,
as when an olive tree is beaten,
  or as when gleanings are left after
    the grape harvest.

¹⁴They raise their voices, they shout for
    joy;
  from the west they acclaim the
    LORD's majesty.
¹⁵Therefore in the east give glory to the
    LORD;
  exalt the name of the LORD, the God
    of Israel,
  in the islands of the sea.
¹⁶From the ends of the earth we hear
    singing:
  "Glory to the Righteous One."

But I said, "I waste away, I waste away!
    Woe to me!
The treacherous betray!
  With treachery the treacherous
    betray!"
¹⁷Terror and pit and snare await you,
  O people of the earth.
¹⁸Whoever flees at the sound of terror
  will fall into a pit;
whoever climbs out of the pit
  will be caught in a snare.

The floodgates of the heavens are
    opened,

^a 12 Hebrew Kittim   ^b 13 Or Chaldeans

the foundations of the earth shake.
¹⁹ The earth is broken up,
   the earth is split asunder,
   the earth is thoroughly shaken.
²⁰ The earth reels like a drunkard,
   it sways like a hut in the wind;
   so heavy upon it is the guilt of its
      rebellion
   that it falls—never to rise again.

²¹ In that day the LORD will punish
   the powers in the heavens above
   and the kings on the earth below.
²² They will be herded together
   like prisoners bound in a dungeon;

they will be shut up in prison
   and be punished ᵃ after many days.
²³ The moon will be abashed, the sun
      ashamed;
   for the LORD Almighty will reign
on Mount Zion and in Jerusalem,
   and before its elders, gloriously.

Praise to the LORD

O LORD, you are my God;
I will exalt you and praise your
   name,
   for in perfect faithfulness

ᵃ 22 Or *released*

Make It Stick

_____

_____

_____

_____

_____

_____

READ ISAIAH 24:5–6
Pollution. Extinctions. Natural disasters. People aren't the only ones suffering from the curse of sin. The earth itself is decaying (see Isaiah 24:4–6 and Romans 8:18–22). One reason is that people don't understand God's principles and end up trashing the earth. Write on a sticky note three things you can do to care for God's creation. Then work with your parents on how to make them happen.

you have done marvelous things,
things planned long ago.
2 You have made the city a heap of
rubble,
the fortified town a ruin,
the foreigners' stronghold a city no
more;
it will never be rebuilt.
3 Therefore strong peoples will honor
you;
cities of ruthless nations will revere
you.
4 You have been a refuge for the poor,
a refuge for the needy in his distress,
a shelter from the storm
and a shade from the heat.
For the breath of the ruthless
is like a storm driving against a wall
5   and like the heat of the desert.
You silence the uproar of foreigners;
as heat is reduced by the shadow of
a cloud,
so the song of the ruthless is stilled.

6 On this mountain the LORD Almighty
will prepare
a feast of rich food for all peoples,
a banquet of aged wine—
the best of meats and the finest of
wines.
7 On this mountain he will destroy
the shroud that enfolds all peoples,
the sheet that covers all nations;
8   he will swallow up death forever.
The Sovereign LORD will wipe away the
tears
from all faces;
he will remove the disgrace of his
people
from all the earth.
            The LORD has spoken.

9 In that day they will say,

"Surely this is our God;
we trusted in him, and he saved us.
This is the LORD, we trusted in him;
let us rejoice and be glad in his
salvation."

10 The hand of the LORD will rest on this
mountain;
but Moab will be trampled under
him
as straw is trampled down in the
manure.
11 They will spread out their hands in it,
as a swimmer spreads out his hands
to swim.

God will bring down their pride
despite the cleverness[a] of their hands.
12 He will bring down your high fortified
walls
and lay them low;
he will bring them down to the ground,
to the very dust.

A Song of Praise

26 In that day this song will be
sung in the land of Judah:

We have a strong city;
God makes salvation
its walls and ramparts.
2 Open the gates
that the righteous nation may enter,
the nation that keeps faith.
3 You will keep in perfect peace
him whose mind is steadfast,
because he trusts in you.
4 Trust in the LORD forever,
for the LORD, the LORD, is the Rock
eternal.
5 He humbles those who dwell on high,
he lays the lofty city low;
he levels it to the ground
and casts it down to the dust.
6 Feet trample it down—
the feet of the oppressed,
the footsteps of the poor.

7 The path of the righteous is level;
O upright One, you make the way of
the righteous smooth.
8 Yes, LORD, walking in the way of your
laws,[b]
we wait for you;
your name and renown
are the desire of our hearts.
9 My soul yearns for you in the night;
in the morning my spirit longs for
you.
When your judgments come upon the
earth,
the people of the world learn
righteousness.
10 Though grace is shown to the wicked,
they do not learn righteousness;
even in a land of uprightness they go
on doing evil
and regard not the majesty of the
LORD.
11 O LORD, your hand is lifted high,
but they do not see it.

a 11 The meaning of the Hebrew for this word is uncertain.
b 8 Or judgments

Let them see your zeal for your people
and be put to shame;
let the fire reserved for your enemies
consume them.

¹² Lord, you establish peace for us;
all that we have accomplished you
have done for us.
¹³ O Lord, our God, other lords besides
you have ruled over us,
but your name alone do we honor.
¹⁴ They are now dead, they live no more;
those departed spirits do not rise.
You punished them and brought them
to ruin;
you wiped out all memory of them.
¹⁵ You have enlarged the nation, O Lord;
you have enlarged the nation.
You have gained glory for yourself;
you have extended all the borders of
the land.

¹⁶ Lord, they came to you in their distress;
when you disciplined them,
they could barely whisper a prayer. ᵃ
¹⁷ As a woman with child and about to
give birth

writhes and cries out in her pain,
so were we in your presence, O Lord.
¹⁸ We were with child, we writhed in
pain,
but we gave birth to wind.
We have not brought salvation to the
earth;
we have not given birth to people of
the world.

¹⁹ But your dead will live;
their bodies will rise.
You who dwell in the dust,
wake up and shout for joy.
Your dew is like the dew of the
morning;
the earth will give birth to her dead.

²⁰ Go, my people, enter your rooms
and shut the doors behind you;
hide yourselves for a little while
until his wrath has passed by.
²¹ See, the Lord is coming out of his
dwelling
to punish the people of the earth for
their sins.

ᵃ 16 The meaning of the Hebrew for this clause is uncertain.

Muscular Brains

READ ISAIAH 26:3–12

If you want muscles like Arnold Schwarzeneggar, you've got to spend a *lot* of time in the gym, pumping iron. The same goes for your mind. If you want it to be strong, you've got to keep working it out. Otherwise, your thoughts will go all over the place like a flopping fish. Then you'll be stuck lying awake in bed worrying about things you shouldn't even be thinking about. God can help stop this from happening. He "will keep in perfect peace him whose mind is steadfast, because he trusts in [God]" (verse 3). Here's the deal: You need to *choose* to believe in God and trust him to take care of you. When you do this, your mind gets stronger—just like pumping iron makes your muscles big. But you have to do this every day. Like a muscle, if you don't use your mind, you'll lose it.

Your next reading is on page 897.

The earth will disclose the blood shed
upon her;
she will conceal her slain no longer.

Deliverance of Israel

27 In that day,

the LORD will punish with his
sword,
his fierce, great and powerful sword,
Leviathan the gliding serpent,
Leviathan the coiling serpent;
he will slay the monster of the sea.

2 In that day—

"Sing about a fruitful vineyard:
3 I, the LORD, watch over it;
I water it continually.
I guard it day and night
so that no one may harm it.
4 I am not angry.
If only there were briers and thorns
confronting me!
I would march against them in battle;
I would set them all on fire.
5 Or else let them come to me for refuge;
let them make peace with me,
yes, let them make peace with me."

6 In days to come Jacob will take root,
Israel will bud and blossom
and fill all the world with fruit.

7 Has ᴌthe LORDᴊ struck her
as he struck down those who struck
her?
Has she been killed
as those were killed who killed her?
8 By warfareᵃ and exile you contend
with her—
with his fierce blast he drives her
out,
as on a day the east wind blows.
9 By this, then, will Jacob's guilt be
atoned for,
and this will be the full fruitage of
the removal of his sin:
When he makes all the altar stones
to be like chalk stones crushed to
pieces,
no Asherah polesᵇ or incense altars
will be left standing.
10 The fortified city stands desolate,
an abandoned settlement, forsaken
like the desert;
there the calves graze,
there they lie down;
they strip its branches bare.

11 When its twigs are dry, they are broken
off
and women come and make fires
with them.
For this is a people without
understanding;
so their Maker has no compassion
on them,
and their Creator shows them no
favor.

12 In that day the LORD will thresh from
the flowing Euphratesᶜ to the Wadi of
Egypt, and you, O Israelites, will be gathered up one by one. 13 And in that day a
great trumpet will sound. Those who were
perishing in Assyria and those who were
exiled in Egypt will come and worship the
LORD on the holy mountain in Jerusalem.

Woe to Ephraim

28 Woe to that wreath, the pride
of Ephraim's drunkards,
to the fading flower, his
glorious beauty,
set on the head of a fertile valley—
to that city, the pride of those laid
low by wine!
2 See, the Lord has one who is powerful
and strong.
Like a hailstorm and a destructive
wind,
like a driving rain and a flooding
downpour,
he will throw it forcefully to the
ground.
3 That wreath, the pride of Ephraim's
drunkards,
will be trampled underfoot.
4 That fading flower, his glorious beauty,
set on the head of a fertile valley,
will be like a fig ripe before harvest—
as soon as someone sees it and
takes it in his hand,
he swallows it.

5 In that day the LORD Almighty
will be a glorious crown,
a beautiful wreath
for the remnant of his people.
6 He will be a spirit of justice
to him who sits in judgment,
a source of strength
to those who turn back the battle at
the gate.

ᵃ 8 See Septuagint; the meaning of the Hebrew for this word
is uncertain.   ᵇ 9 That is, symbols of the goddess Asherah
ᶜ 12 Hebrew River

Gross!

"All the tables are covered with vomit" (Isaiah 28:8). How would you like to be a bus boy cleaning tables in *this* restaurant?

7 And these also stagger from wine
    and reel from beer:
Priests and prophets stagger from beer
    and are befuddled with wine;
they reel from beer,
    they stagger when seeing visions,
    they stumble when rendering decisions.
8 All the tables are covered with vomit
    and there is not a spot without filth.

9 "Who is it he is trying to teach?
    To whom is he explaining his message?
To children weaned from their milk,
    to those just taken from the breast?
10 For it is:
    Do and do, do and do,
    rule on rule, rule on rule*a*;
    a little here, a little there."

11 Very well then, with foreign lips and strange tongues
    God will speak to this people,
12 to whom he said,
    "This is the resting place, let the weary rest";
and, "This is the place of repose"—
    but they would not listen.
13 So then, the word of the LORD to them will become:
    Do and do, do and do,
    rule on rule, rule on rule;
    a little here, a little there—
so that they will go and fall backward,
    be injured and snared and captured.

14 Therefore hear the word of the LORD, you scoffers
    who rule this people in Jerusalem.
15 You boast, "We have entered into a covenant with death,
    with the grave*b* we have made an agreement.
When an overwhelming scourge sweeps by,
    it cannot touch us,
for we have made a lie our refuge
    and falsehood*c* our hiding place."

16 So this is what the Sovereign LORD says:

"See, I lay a stone in Zion,
    a tested stone,
a precious cornerstone for a sure foundation;
    the one who trusts will never be dismayed.
17 I will make justice the measuring line
    and righteousness the plumb line;
hail will sweep away your refuge, the lie,
    and water will overflow your hiding place.
18 Your covenant with death will be annulled;
    your agreement with the grave will not stand.
When the overwhelming scourge sweeps by,
    you will be beaten down by it.

a 10 Hebrew / *sav lasav sav lasav* / *kav lakav kav lakav* (possibly meaningless
sounds; perhaps a mimicking of the prophet's words); also in verse 13
b 15 Hebrew *Sheol*; also in verse 18   *c 15* Or *false gods*

19 As often as it comes it will carry you away;
    morning after morning, by day and by night,
    it will sweep through."

The understanding of this message
    will bring sheer terror.
20 The bed is too short to stretch out on,
    the blanket too narrow to wrap around you.
21 The LORD will rise up as he did at Mount Perazim,
    he will rouse himself as in the Valley of Gibeon—
to do his work, his strange work,
    and perform his task, his alien task.
22 Now stop your mocking,
    or your chains will become heavier;
the Lord, the LORD Almighty, has told me
    of the destruction decreed against the whole land.

23 Listen and hear my voice;
    pay attention and hear what I say.
24 When a farmer plows for planting, does he plow
        continually?
    Does he keep on breaking up and harrowing the
        soil?
25 When he has leveled the surface,
    does he not sow caraway and scatter cummin?
Does he not plant wheat in its place, a
    barley in its plot, b
    and spelt in its field?
26 His God instructs him
    and teaches him the right way.

27 Caraway is not threshed with a sledge,
    nor is a cartwheel rolled over cummin;
caraway is beaten out with a rod,
    and cummin with a stick.
28 Grain must be ground to make bread;
    so one does not go on threshing it forever.
Though he drives the wheels of his threshing cart
        over it,
    his horses do not grind it.
29 All this also comes from the LORD Almighty,
    wonderful in counsel and magnificent in wisdom.

Woe to David's City

29 Woe to you, Ariel, Ariel,
    the city where David settled!
Add year to year
    and let your cycle of festivals go on.
2 Yet I will besiege Ariel;
    she will mourn and lament,
    she will be to me like an altar hearth. c
3 I will encamp against you all around;
    I will encircle you with towers
    and set up my siege works against you.
4 Brought low, you will speak from the ground;

Get a Load of This...

God will do his "strange work" and perform his "alien task" (Isaiah 28:21). This does *not* mean that he's working with little green men in flying saucers. In this case "alien" means "out of the ordinary"—because, due to their rebellion, God was going to fight *against* his people Israel.

---

a 25 The meaning of the Hebrew for this word is uncertain.   b 25 The meaning
of the Hebrew for this word is uncertain.   c 2 The Hebrew for *altar hearth*
sounds like the Hebrew for *Ariel*.

your speech will mumble out of the
dust.
Your voice will come ghostlike from
the earth;
out of the dust your speech will
whisper.

5 But your many enemies will become
like fine dust,
the ruthless hordes like blown chaff.
Suddenly, in an instant,
6 the LORD Almighty will come
with thunder and earthquake and
great noise,
with windstorm and tempest and
flames of a devouring fire.
7 Then the hordes of all the nations that
fight against Ariel,
that attack her and her fortress and
besiege her,
will be as it is with a dream,
with a vision in the night—
8 as when a hungry man dreams that he
is eating,
but he awakens, and his hunger
remains;
as when a thirsty man dreams that he
is drinking,
but he awakens faint, with his thirst
unquenched.
So will it be with the hordes of all the
nations
that fight against Mount Zion.

9 Be stunned and amazed,
blind yourselves and be sightless;
be drunk, but not from wine,
stagger, but not from beer.
10 The LORD has brought over you a deep
sleep:
He has sealed your eyes (the
prophets);
he has covered your heads (the
seers).

11 For you this whole vision is nothing
but words sealed in a scroll. And if you
give the scroll to someone who can read,
and say to him, "Read this, please," he
will answer, "I can't; it is sealed." 12 Or if
you give the scroll to someone who cannot read, and say, "Read this, please," he
will answer, "I don't know how to read."

13 The Lord says:

"These people come near to me with
their mouth
and honor me with their lips,

but their hearts are far from me.
Their worship of me
is made up only of rules taught by
men. ª
14 Therefore once more I will astound
these people
with wonder upon wonder;
the wisdom of the wise will perish,
the intelligence of the intelligent will
vanish."
15 Woe to those who go to great depths
to hide their plans from the LORD,
who do their work in darkness and
think,
"Who sees us? Who will know?"
16 You turn things upside down,
as if the potter were thought to be
like the clay!
Shall what is formed say to him who
formed it,
"He did not make me"?
Can the pot say of the potter,
"He knows nothing"?

17 In a very short time, will not Lebanon
be turned into a fertile field
and the fertile field seem like a
forest?
18 In that day the deaf will hear the
words of the scroll,
and out of gloom and darkness
the eyes of the blind will see.
19 Once more the humble will rejoice in
the LORD;
the needy will rejoice in the Holy
One of Israel.
20 The ruthless will vanish,
the mockers will disappear,
and all who have an eye for evil will
be cut down—
21 those who with a word make a man
out to be guilty,
who ensnare the defender in court
and with false testimony deprive the
innocent of justice.

22 Therefore this is what the LORD, who
redeemed Abraham, says to the house of
Jacob:

"No longer will Jacob be ashamed;
no longer will their faces grow pale.
23 When they see among them their
children,
the work of my hands,
they will keep my name holy;

ª 13 Hebrew; Septuagint *They worship me in vain, / their
teachings are but rules taught by men*

they will acknowledge the holiness
  of the Holy One of Jacob,
and will stand in awe of the God of
  Israel.
24 Those who are wayward in spirit will
  gain understanding;
those who complain will accept
  instruction."

Woe to the Obstinate Nation

30 "Woe to the obstinate
  children,"
declares the LORD,
"to those who carry out plans
  that are not mine,
forming an alliance, but not by my
  Spirit,
heaping sin upon sin;
2 who go down to Egypt
  without consulting me;
who look for help to Pharaoh's
  protection,
to Egypt's shade for refuge.
3 But Pharaoh's protection will be to
  your shame,
Egypt's shade will bring you disgrace.
4 Though they have officials in Zoan

and their envoys have arrived in
  Hanes,
5 everyone will be put to shame
  because of a people useless to them,
who bring neither help nor advantage,
  but only shame and disgrace."

6 An oracle concerning the animals of
the Negev:

Through a land of hardship and distress,
  of lions and lionesses,
  of adders and darting snakes,
the envoys carry their riches on
  donkeys' backs,
  their treasures on the humps of
  camels,
to that unprofitable nation,
7   to Egypt, whose help is utterly useless.
Therefore I call her
  Rahab the Do-Nothing.

8 Go now, write it on a tablet for them,
  inscribe it on a scroll,
that for the days to come
  it may be an everlasting witness.
9 These are rebellious people, deceitful
  children,

The Entertainment Generation

READ ISAIAH 30:8–11

Five hundred channels and people still complain there's nothing on TV. We live in the "Entertainment Age," and too many kids spend hours burning out their eyeballs so they can rack up points on video games. Yet they don't have a minute to tune in to what God says in the Bible. Sound familiar? It should. The prophet Isaiah talked about people like that: "They say to the … prophets, 'Give us no more visions of what is right! Tell us pleasant things, prophesy illusions.'" (Isaiah 30:10). Too many people today just want to be entertained, laugh and treat life like one big party. They ignore God but still expect to have a good life. But things don't work that way. Without God, life is empty and meaningless. But if you have God, and you keep fun and entertainment in second place, you can have a blast!

Your next reading is on page 905.

Get a Load of This...

If you trust God to direct your life, God promises that he will guide you—through his Word and his voice in your heart—telling you the way to go (Isaiah 30:21). So wherever you go, keep your ears, like satellite dishes, tuned in to God.

In other words...

children unwilling to listen to the LORD's
instruction.
¹⁰ They say to the seers,
     "See no more visions!"
and to the prophets,
     "Give us no more visions of what is right!
Tell us pleasant things,
     prophesy illusions.
¹¹ Leave this way,
     get off this path,
and stop confronting us
     with the Holy One of Israel!"

¹² Therefore, this is what the Holy One of Israel says:

"Because you have rejected this message,
     relied on oppression
     and depended on deceit,
¹³ this sin will become for you
     like a high wall, cracked and bulging,
     that collapses suddenly, in an instant.
¹⁴ It will break in pieces like pottery,
     shattered so mercilessly
that among its pieces not a fragment will be found
     for taking coals from a hearth
     or scooping water out of a cistern."

¹⁵ This is what the Sovereign LORD, the Holy One of Israel, says:

"In repentance and rest is your salvation,
     in quietness and trust is your strength,
     but you would have none of it.
¹⁶ You said, 'No, we will flee on horses.'
     Therefore you will flee!
You said, 'We will ride off on swift horses.'
     Therefore your pursuers will be swift!
¹⁷ A thousand will flee
     at the threat of one;
at the threat of five
     you will all flee away,
till you are left
     like a flagstaff on a mountaintop,
     like a banner on a hill."

¹⁸ Yet the LORD longs to be gracious to you;
     he rises to show you compassion.
For the LORD is a God of justice.
     Blessed are all who wait for him!

¹⁹ O people of Zion, who live in Jerusalem, you will weep no more. How gracious he will be when you cry for help! As soon as he hears, he will answer you. ²⁰ Although the Lord gives you the bread of adversity and the water of affliction, your teachers will be hidden no more; with your own eyes you will see them. ²¹ Whether you turn to the right or to the left, your ears will hear a voice behind you, saying, "This is the way; walk in it." ²² Then you will defile your idols overlaid with silver and your images covered with gold; you will throw them

away like a menstrual cloth and say to them, "Away with you!"

23He will also send you rain for the seed you sow in the ground, and the food that comes from the land will be rich and plentiful. In that day your cattle will graze in broad meadows. 24The oxen and donkeys that work the soil will eat fodder and mash, spread out with fork and shovel. 25In the day of great slaughter, when the towers fall, streams of water will flow on every high mountain and every lofty hill. 26The moon will shine like the sun, and the sunlight will be seven times brighter, like the light of seven full days, when the LORD binds up the bruises of his people and heals the wounds he inflicted.

27See, the Name of the LORD comes from
  afar,
    with burning anger and dense
      clouds of smoke;
  his lips are full of wrath,
    and his tongue is a consuming fire.
28His breath is like a rushing torrent,
    rising up to the neck.
  He shakes the nations in the sieve of
      destruction;
    he places in the jaws of the peoples
    a bit that leads them astray.
29And you will sing
    as on the night you celebrate a holy
      festival;
  your hearts will rejoice
    as when people go up with flutes
  to the mountain of the LORD,
    to the Rock of Israel.
30The LORD will cause men to hear his
      majestic voice
    and will make them see his arm
      coming down
  with raging anger and consuming fire,
    with cloudburst, thunderstorm and
      hail.
31The voice of the LORD will shatter Assyria;
    with his scepter he will strike them
      down.
32Every stroke the LORD lays on them
    with his punishing rod
  will be to the music of tambourines
      and harps,
    as he fights them in battle with the
      blows of his arm.
33Topheth has long been prepared;
    it has been made ready for the king.
  Its fire pit has been made deep and
      wide,

with an abundance of fire and wood;
  the breath of the LORD,
    like a stream of burning sulfur,
      sets it ablaze.

Woe to Those Who Rely on Egypt

31 Woe to those who go down to
  Egypt for help,
  who rely on horses,
  who trust in the multitude of
      their chariots
  and in the great strength of their
      horsemen,
  but do not look to the Holy One of
      Israel,
    or seek help from the LORD.
2Yet he too is wise and can bring disaster;
    he does not take back his words.
  He will rise up against the house of the
      wicked,
    against those who help evildoers.
3But the Egyptians are men and not
      God;
    their horses are flesh and not spirit.
  When the LORD stretches out his hand,
    he who helps will stumble,
    he who is helped will fall;
    both will perish together.

4This is what the LORD says to me:

"As a lion growls,
    a great lion over his prey—
  and though a whole band of shepherds
    is called together against him,
  he is not frightened by their shouts
    or disturbed by their clamor—
  so the LORD Almighty will come down
    to do battle on Mount Zion and on
      its heights.
5Like birds hovering overhead,
    the LORD Almighty will shield
      Jerusalem;
  he will shield it and deliver it,
    he will 'pass over' it and will rescue
      it."

6Return to him you have so greatly revolted against, O Israelites. 7For in that day every one of you will reject the idols of silver and gold your sinful hands have made.

8"Assyria will fall by a sword that is not
      of man;
    a sword, not of mortals, will devour
      them.
  They will flee before the sword
    and their young men will be put to
      forced labor.

⁹Their stronghold will fall because of
   terror;
   at sight of the battle standard their
      commanders will panic,"
declares the LORD,
   whose fire is in Zion,
   whose furnace is in Jerusalem.

The Kingdom of Righteousness

32 See, a king will reign in
   righteousness
   and rulers will rule with
   justice.
²Each man will be like a shelter from
   the wind
   and a refuge from the storm,
like streams of water in the desert
   and the shadow of a great rock in a
      thirsty land.

³Then the eyes of those who see will no
   longer be closed,
   and the ears of those who hear will
   listen.

⁴The mind of the rash will know and
   understand,
   and the stammering tongue will be
   fluent and clear.
⁵No longer will the fool be called noble
   nor the scoundrel be highly respected.
⁶For the fool speaks folly,
   his mind is busy with evil:
He practices ungodliness
   and spreads error concerning the LORD;
the hungry he leaves empty
   and from the thirsty he withholds
      water.
⁷The scoundrel's methods are wicked,
   he makes up evil schemes
to destroy the poor with lies,
   even when the plea of the needy is
      just.
⁸But the noble man makes noble plans,
   and by noble deeds he stands.

The Women of Jerusalem

⁹You women who are so complacent,
   rise up and listen to me;

Make It Stick

READ ISAIAH 32:5–6

Can you think of someone famous who is highly respected by many people, but who is really a scoundrel (see Isaiah 32:5)? It shouldn't be difficult. Write the name of some celebrity like that as a reminder to pray for them to change.

you daughters who feel secure,
  hear what I have to say!
[10] In little more than a year
  you who feel secure will tremble;
  the grape harvest will fail,
    and the harvest of fruit will not come.
[11] Tremble, you complacent women;
    shudder, you daughters who feel
      secure!
  Strip off your clothes,
    put sackcloth around your waists.
[12] Beat your breasts for the pleasant fields,
    for the fruitful vines
[13] and for the land of my people,
    a land overgrown with thorns and
      briers—
  yes, mourn for all houses of merriment
    and for this city of revelry.
[14] The fortress will be abandoned,
    the noisy city deserted;
  citadel and watchtower will become a
      wasteland forever,
  the delight of donkeys, a pasture for
      flocks,
[15] till the Spirit is poured upon us from
      on high,
  and the desert becomes a fertile field,
  and the fertile field seems like a
      forest.
[16] Justice will dwell in the desert
    and righteousness live in the fertile
      field.
[17] The fruit of righteousness will be peace;
    the effect of righteousness will be
      quietness and confidence
      forever.
[18] My people will live in peaceful dwelling
      places,
  in secure homes,
  in undisturbed places of rest.
[19] Though hail flattens the forest
    and the city is leveled completely,
[20] how blessed you will be,
    sowing your seed by every stream,
    and letting your cattle and donkeys
      range free.

Distress and Help

33 Woe to you, O destroyer,
    you who have not been
    destroyed!
  Woe to you, O traitor,
    you who have not been betrayed!
  When you stop destroying,
    you will be destroyed;
  when you stop betraying,
    you will be betrayed.

[2] O LORD, be gracious to us;
    we long for you.
  Be our strength every morning,
    our salvation in time of distress.
[3] At the thunder of your voice, the
      peoples flee;
    when you rise up, the nations scatter.
[4] Your plunder, O nations, is harvested
      as by young locusts;
    like a swarm of locusts men pounce
      on it.

[5] The LORD is exalted, for he dwells on
      high;
    he will fill Zion with justice and
      righteousness.
[6] He will be the sure foundation for your
      times,
    a rich store of salvation and wisdom
      and knowledge;
    the fear of the LORD is the key to this
      treasure. [a]

[7] Look, their brave men cry aloud in the
      streets;
    the envoys of peace weep bitterly.
[8] The highways are deserted,
    no travelers are on the roads.
  The treaty is broken,
    its witnesses [b] are despised,
    no one is respected.
[9] The land mourns [c] and wastes away,
    Lebanon is ashamed and withers;
  Sharon is like the Arabah,
    and Bashan and Carmel drop their
      leaves.

[10] "Now will I arise," says the LORD.
    "Now will I be exalted;
    now will I be lifted up.
[11] You conceive chaff,
    you give birth to straw;
    your breath is a fire that consumes
      you.
[12] The peoples will be burned as if to lime;
    like cut thornbushes they will be set
      ablaze."

[13] You who are far away, hear what I
      have done;
    you who are near, acknowledge my
      power!
[14] The sinners in Zion are terrified;
    trembling grips the godless:
  "Who of us can dwell with the
      consuming fire?

---

[a] 6 Or *is a treasure from him*   [b] 8 Dead Sea Scrolls;
Masoretic Text / *the cities*   [c] 9 Or *dries up*

Who of us can dwell with everlasting
burning?"
¹⁵ He who walks righteously
and speaks what is right,
who rejects gain from extortion
and keeps his hand from accepting
bribes,
who stops his ears against plots of
murder
and shuts his eyes against
contemplating evil—
¹⁶ this is the man who will dwell on the
heights,
whose refuge will be the mountain
fortress.
His bread will be supplied,
and water will not fail him.

¹⁷ Your eyes will see the king in his
beauty
and view a land that stretches afar.
¹⁸ In your thoughts you will ponder the
former terror:
"Where is that chief officer?
Where is the one who took the
revenue?
Where is the officer in charge of the
towers?"
¹⁹ You will see those arrogant people no
more,
those people of an obscure speech,
with their strange, incomprehensible
tongue.

²⁰ Look upon Zion, the city of our
festivals;
your eyes will see Jerusalem,
a peaceful abode, a tent that will
not be moved;
its stakes will never be pulled up,
nor any of its ropes broken.
²¹ There the LORD will be our Mighty One.
It will be like a place of broad rivers
and streams.
No galley with oars will ride them,
no mighty ship will sail them.
²² For the LORD is our judge,
the LORD is our lawgiver,
the LORD is our king;
it is he who will save us.

²³ Your rigging hangs loose:
The mast is not held secure,
the sail is not spread.
Then an abundance of spoils will be
divided
and even the lame will carry off
plunder.

²⁴ No one living in Zion will say, "I am ill";
and the sins of those who dwell
there will be forgiven.

Judgment Against the Nations

34 Come near, you nations, and
listen;
pay attention, you peoples!
Let the earth hear, and all that
is in it,
the world, and all that comes out of
it!
² The LORD is angry with all nations;
his wrath is upon all their armies.
He will totally destroy[a] them,
he will give them over to slaughter.
³ Their slain will be thrown out,
their dead bodies will send up a
stench;
the mountains will be soaked with
their blood.
⁴ All the stars of the heavens will be
dissolved
and the sky rolled up like a scroll;
all the starry host will fall
like withered leaves from the vine,
like shriveled figs from the fig tree.

⁵ My sword has drunk its fill in the
heavens;
see, it descends in judgment on
Edom,
the people I have totally destroyed.
⁶ The sword of the LORD is bathed in
blood,
it is covered with fat—
the blood of lambs and goats,
fat from the kidneys of rams.
For the LORD has a sacrifice in Bozrah
and a great slaughter in Edom.
⁷ And the wild oxen will fall with them,
the bull calves and the great bulls.
Their land will be drenched with blood,
and the dust will be soaked with fat.

⁸ For the LORD has a day of vengeance,
a year of retribution, to uphold
Zion's cause.
⁹ Edom's streams will be turned into
pitch,
her dust into burning sulfur;
her land will become blazing pitch!
¹⁰ It will not be quenched night and day;
its smoke will rise forever.

ᵃ 2 The Hebrew term refers to the irrevocable giving over of
things or persons to the LORD, often by totally destroying
them; also in verse 5.

From generation to generation it will lie desolate;
 no one will ever pass through it again.
11 The desert owl[a] and screech owl[a] will possess it;
 the great owl[a] and the raven will nest there.
God will stretch out over Edom
 the measuring line of chaos
 and the plumb line of desolation.
12 Her nobles will have nothing there to be called a
 kingdom,
 all her princes will vanish away.
13 Thorns will overrun her citadels,
 nettles and brambles her strongholds.
She will become a haunt for jackals,
 a home for owls.
14 Desert creatures will meet with hyenas,
 and wild goats will bleat to each other;
there the night creatures will also repose
 and find for themselves places of rest.
15 The owl will nest there and lay eggs,
 she will hatch them, and care for her young under
 the shadow of her wings;
there also the falcons will gather,
 each with its mate.

16 Look in the scroll of the LORD and read:

None of these will be missing,
 not one will lack her mate.
For it is his mouth that has given the order,
 and his Spirit will gather them together.
17 He allots their portions;
 his hand distributes them by measure.
They will possess it forever
 and dwell there from generation to generation.

Joy of the Redeemed

35 The desert and the parched land will be glad;
 the wilderness will rejoice and blossom.
Like the crocus, 2 it will burst into bloom;
 it will rejoice greatly and shout for joy.
The glory of Lebanon will be given to it,
 the splendor of Carmel and Sharon;
they will see the glory of the LORD,
 the splendor of our God.

3 Strengthen the feeble hands,
 steady the knees that give way;
4 say to those with fearful hearts,
 "Be strong, do not fear;
your God will come,
 he will come with vengeance;
with divine retribution
 he will come to save you."

5 Then will the eyes of the blind be opened
 and the ears of the deaf unstopped.
6 Then will the lame leap like a deer,

Get a Load of This...

When someone is feeling weak, sick, lonely or in need of encouragement, don't just sit there and tell them how sorry you feel. Get up and do something! The best way to show that *God* cares is to show them *you* care (see Isaiah 35:3–4).

In Other Words...

---

a 11 The precise identification of these birds is uncertain.

and the mute tongue shout for joy.
Water will gush forth in the wilderness
and streams in the desert.
⁷The burning sand will become a pool,
the thirsty ground bubbling springs.
In the haunts where jackals once lay,
grass and reeds and papyrus will
grow.

⁸And a highway will be there;
it will be called the Way of Holiness.
The unclean will not journey on it;
it will be for those who walk in that
Way;
wicked fools will not go about on it.ᵃ
⁹No lion will be there,
nor will any ferocious beast get up
on it;
they will not be found there.
But only the redeemed will walk there,
10   and the ransomed of the LORD will
return.
They will enter Zion with singing;
everlasting joy will crown their heads.
Gladness and joy will overtake them,
and sorrow and sighing will flee away.

Sennacherib Threatens Jerusalem

36 In the fourteenth year of King Hezekiah's reign, Sennacherib king of Assyria attacked all the fortified cities of Judah and captured them. ²Then the king of Assyria sent his field commander with a large army from Lachish to King Hezekiah at Jerusalem. When the commander stopped at the aqueduct of the Upper Pool, on the road to the Washerman's Field, ³Eliakim son of Hilkiah the palace administrator, Shebna the secretary, and Joah son of Asaph the recorder went out to him.

⁴The field commander said to them, "Tell Hezekiah,

" 'This is what the great king, the king of Assyria, says: On what are you basing this confidence of yours? ⁵You say you have strategy and military strength—but you speak only empty words. On whom are you depending, that you rebel against me? ⁶Look now, you are depending on Egypt, that splintered reed of a staff, which pierces a man's hand and wounds him if he leans on it! Such is Pharaoh king of Egypt to all who depend on him. ⁷And if you say to me, "We are depending on the LORD our

God"—isn't he the one whose high places and altars Hezekiah removed, saying to Judah and Jerusalem, "You must worship before this altar"?

⁸" 'Come now, make a bargain with my master, the king of Assyria: I will give you two thousand horses—if you can put riders on them! ⁹How then can you repulse one officer of the least of my master's officials, even though you are depending on Egypt for chariots and horsemen? ¹⁰Furthermore, have I come to attack and destroy this land without the LORD? The LORD himself told me to march against this country and destroy it.' "

¹¹Then Eliakim, Shebna and Joah said to the field commander, "Please speak to your servants in Aramaic, since we understand it. Don't speak to us in Hebrew in the hearing of the people on the wall."

¹²But the commander replied, "Was it only to your master and you that my master sent me to say these things, and not to the men sitting on the wall—who, like you, will have to eat their own filth and drink their own urine?"

¹³Then the commander stood and called out in Hebrew, "Hear the words of the great king, the king of Assyria! ¹⁴This is what the king says: Do not let Hezekiah deceive you. He cannot deliver you! ¹⁵Do not let Hezekiah persuade you to trust in the LORD when he says, 'The LORD will surely deliver us; this city will not be given into the hand of the king of Assyria.'

¹⁶"Do not listen to Hezekiah. This is what the king of Assyria says: Make peace with me and come out to me. Then every one of you will eat from his own vine and fig tree and drink water from his own cistern, ¹⁷until I come and take you to a land like your own—a land of grain and new wine, a land of bread and vineyards.

¹⁸"Do not let Hezekiah mislead you when he says, 'The LORD will deliver us.' Has the god of any nation ever delivered his land from the hand of the king of Assyria? ¹⁹Where are the gods of Hamath and Arpad? Where are the gods of Sepharvaim? Have they rescued Samaria from my hand? ²⁰Who of all the gods of these countries has been able to save his land from me? How then can the LORD deliver Jerusalem from my hand?"

ᵃ 8 Or / the simple will not stray from it

²¹But the people remained silent and said nothing in reply, because the king had commanded, "Do not answer him."

²²Then Eliakim son of Hilkiah the palace administrator, Shebna the secretary, and Joah son of Asaph the recorder went to Hezekiah, with their clothes torn, and told him what the field commander had said.

Jerusalem's Deliverance Foretold

37 When King Hezekiah heard this, he tore his clothes and put on sackcloth and went into the temple of the LORD. ²He sent Eliakim the palace administrator, Shebna the secretary, and the leading priests, all wearing sackcloth, to the prophet Isaiah son of Amoz. ³They told him, "This is what Hezekiah says: This day is a day of distress and rebuke and disgrace, as when children come to the point of birth and there is no strength to deliver them. ⁴It may be that the LORD your God will hear the words of the field commander, whom

his master, the king of Assyria, has sent to ridicule the living God, and that he will rebuke him for the words the LORD your God has heard. Therefore pray for the remnant that still survives."

⁵When King Hezekiah's officials came to Isaiah, ⁶Isaiah said to them, "Tell your master, 'This is what the LORD says: Do not be afraid of what you have heard—those words with which the underlings of the king of Assyria have blasphemed me. ⁷Listen! I am going to put a spirit in him so that when he hears a certain report, he will return to his own country, and there I will have him cut down with the sword.' "

⁸When the field commander heard that the king of Assyria had left Lachish, he withdrew and found the king fighting against Libnah.

⁹Now Sennacherib received a report that Tirhakah, the Cushiteᵃ king ₍of Egyptᵤ, was marching out to fight against him. When he heard it, he sent messen-

ᵃ 9 That is, from the upper Nile region

gers to Hezekiah with this word: ¹⁰"Say to Hezekiah king of Judah: Do not let the god you depend on deceive you when he says, 'Jerusalem will not be handed over to the king of Assyria.' ¹¹Surely you have heard what the kings of Assyria have done to all the countries, destroying them completely. And will you be delivered? ¹²Did the gods of the nations that were destroyed by my forefathers deliver them— the gods of Gozan, Haran, Rezeph and the people of Eden who were in Tel Assar? ¹³Where is the king of Hamath, the king of Arpad, the king of the city of Sepharvaim, or of Hena or Ivvah?"

Hezekiah's Prayer

¹⁴Hezekiah received the letter from the messengers and read it. Then he went up to the temple of the Lord and spread it out before the Lord. ¹⁵And Hezekiah prayed to the Lord: ¹⁶"O Lord Almighty, God of Israel, enthroned between the cherubim, you alone are God over all the kingdoms of the earth. You have made heaven and earth. ¹⁷Give ear, O Lord, and hear; open your eyes, O Lord, and see; listen to all the words Sennacherib has sent to insult the living God.

¹⁸"It is true, O Lord, that the Assyrian kings have laid waste all these peoples and their lands. ¹⁹They have thrown their gods into the fire and destroyed them, for they were not gods but only wood and stone, fashioned by human hands. ²⁰Now, O Lord our God, deliver us from his hand, so that all kingdoms on earth may know that you alone, O Lord, are God.[a]"

Sennacherib's Fall

²¹Then Isaiah son of Amoz sent a message to Hezekiah: "This is what the Lord, the God of Israel, says: Because you have prayed to me concerning Sennacherib king of Assyria, ²²this is the word the Lord has spoken against him:

"The Virgin Daughter of Zion
  despises and mocks you.
The Daughter of Jerusalem
  tosses her head as you flee.
²³Who is it you have insulted and
    blasphemed?
  Against whom have you raised your
    voice
and lifted your eyes in pride?
  Against the Holy One of Israel!

²⁴By your messengers
  you have heaped insults on the Lord.
And you have said,
  'With my many chariots
I have ascended the heights of the
    mountains,
  the utmost heights of Lebanon.
I have cut down its tallest cedars,
  the choicest of its pines.
I have reached its remotest heights,
  the finest of its forests.
²⁵I have dug wells in foreign lands[b]
  and drunk the water there.
With the soles of my feet
  I have dried up all the streams of
    Egypt.'

²⁶"Have you not heard?
  Long ago I ordained it.
In days of old I planned it;
  now I have brought it to pass,
that you have turned fortified cities
  into piles of stone.
²⁷Their people, drained of power,
  are dismayed and put to shame.
They are like plants in the field,
  like tender green shoots,
like grass sprouting on the roof,
  scorched[c] before it grows up.

²⁸"But I know where you stay
  and when you come and go
  and how you rage against me.
²⁹Because you rage against me
  and because your insolence has
    reached my ears,
I will put my hook in your nose
  and my bit in your mouth,
and I will make you return
  by the way you came.

³⁰"This will be the sign for you, O Hezekiah:

"This year you will eat what grows by
    itself,
  and the second year what springs
    from that.
But in the third year sow and reap,
  plant vineyards and eat their fruit.
³¹Once more a remnant of the house of
    Judah

^a 20 Dead Sea Scrolls (see also 2 Kings 19:19); Masoretic Text alone are the Lord   ^b 25 Dead Sea Scrolls (see also 2 Kings 19:24); Masoretic Text does not have *in foreign lands.*
^c 27 Some manuscripts of the Masoretic Text, Dead Sea Scrolls and some Septuagint manuscripts (see also 2 Kings 19:26); most manuscripts of the Masoretic Text *roof / and terraced fields*

will take root below and bear fruit above.
32 For out of Jerusalem will come a remnant,
    and out of Mount Zion a band of survivors.
The zeal of the Lord Almighty
    will accomplish this.

33 "Therefore this is what the Lord says concerning the king of Assyria:

"He will not enter this city
    or shoot an arrow here.
He will not come before it with shield
    or build a siege ramp against it.
34 By the way that he came he will return;
    he will not enter this city,"
                                        declares the Lord.
35 "I will defend this city and save it,
    for my sake and for the sake of David my servant!"

36 Then the angel of the Lord went out and put to death a hundred and eighty-five thousand men in the Assyrian camp. When the people got up the next morning—there were all the dead bodies! 37 So Sennacherib king of Assyria broke camp and withdrew. He returned to Nineveh and stayed there.

38 One day, while he was worshiping in the temple of his god Nisroch, his sons Adrammelech and Sharezer cut him down with the sword, and they escaped to the land of Ararat. And Esarhaddon his son succeeded him as king.

Hezekiah's Illness

38 In those days Hezekiah became ill and was at the point of death. The prophet Isaiah son of Amoz went to him and said, "This is what the Lord says: Put your house in order, because you are going to die; you will not recover."

2 Hezekiah turned his face to the wall and prayed to the Lord, 3 "Remember, O Lord, how I have walked before you faithfully and with wholehearted devotion and have done what is good in your eyes." And Hezekiah wept bitterly.

4 Then the word of the Lord came to Isaiah: 5 "Go and tell Hezekiah, 'This is what the Lord, the God of your father David, says: I have heard your prayer and seen your tears; I will add fifteen years to your life. 6 And I will deliver you and this city from the hand of the king of Assyria. I will defend this city.

7 " 'This is the Lord's sign to you that the Lord will do what he has promised: 8 I will make the shadow cast by the sun go back the ten steps it has gone down on the stairway of Ahaz.' " So the sunlight went back the ten steps it had gone down.

9 A writing of Hezekiah king of Judah after his illness and recovery:

10 I said, "In the prime of my life
    must I go through the gates of death[a]

---
a 10 Hebrew *Sheol*

and be robbed of the rest of my
    years?"
11 I said, "I will not again see the Lord,
    the Lord, in the land of the living;
no longer will I look on mankind,
    or be with those who now dwell in
      this world. *a*
12 Like a shepherd's tent my house
    has been pulled down and taken
      from me.
Like a weaver I have rolled up my life,
    and he has cut me off from the loom;
    day and night you made an end of
      me.
13 I waited patiently till dawn,
    but like a lion he broke all my bones;
    day and night you made an end of
      me.
14 I cried like a swift or thrush,
    I moaned like a mourning dove.
My eyes grew weak as I looked to the
    heavens.
    I am troubled; O Lord, come to my
      aid!"

15 But what can I say?
    He has spoken to me, and he
      himself has done this.
I will walk humbly all my years
    because of this anguish of my
      soul.
16 Lord, by such things men live;
    and my spirit finds life in them too.
You restored me to health
    and let me live.
17 Surely it was for my benefit
    that I suffered such anguish.
In your love you kept me
    from the pit of destruction;
you have put all my sins
    behind your back.
18 For the grave *b* cannot praise you,
    death cannot sing your praise;
those who go down to the pit
    cannot hope for your faithfulness.
19 The living, the living—they praise you,

a 11 A few Hebrew manuscripts; most Hebrew manuscripts *in
the place of cessation*   *b 18* Hebrew *Sheol*

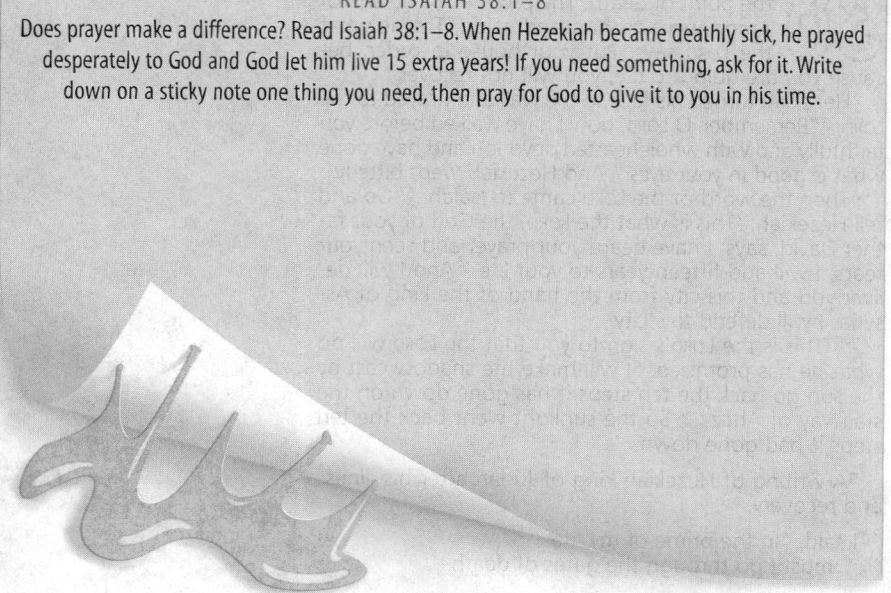

Make It Stick

READ ISAIAH 38:1–8

Does prayer make a difference? Read Isaiah 38:1–8. When Hezekiah became deathly sick, he prayed
desperately to God and God let him live 15 extra years! If you need something, ask for it. Write
down on a sticky note one thing you need, then pray for God to give it to you in his time.

as I am doing today;
  fathers tell their children
    about your faithfulness.

20 The LORD will save me,
    and we will sing with stringed instruments
all the days of our lives
    in the temple of the LORD.

21 Isaiah had said, "Prepare a poultice of figs and apply it to the boil, and he will recover." 22 Hezekiah had asked, "What will be the sign that I will go up to the temple of the LORD?"

Envoys From Babylon

39 At that time Merodach-Baladan son of Baladan king of Babylon sent Hezekiah letters and a gift, because he had heard of his illness and recovery. 2 Hezekiah received the envoys gladly and showed them what was in his storehouses—the silver, the gold, the spices, the fine oil, his entire armory and everything found among his treasures. There was nothing in his palace or in all his kingdom that Hezekiah did not show them.

3 Then Isaiah the prophet went to King Hezekiah and asked, "What did those men say, and where did they come from?"

"From a distant land," Hezekiah replied. "They came to me from Babylon."

4 The prophet asked, "What did they see in your palace?"

"They saw everything in my palace," Hezekiah said. "There is nothing among my treasures that I did not show them."

5 Then Isaiah said to Hezekiah, "Hear the word of the LORD Almighty: 6 The time will surely come when everything in your palace, and all that your fathers have stored up until this day, will be carried off to Babylon. Nothing will be left, says the LORD. 7 And some of your descendants, your own flesh and blood who will be born to you, will be taken away, and they will become eunuchs in the palace of the king of Babylon."

8 "The word of the LORD you have spoken is good," Hezekiah replied. For he thought, "There will be peace and security in my lifetime."

Comfort for God's People

40 Comfort, comfort my people,
    says your God.
2 Speak tenderly to Jerusalem,
    and proclaim to her
that her hard service has been completed,
    that her sin has been paid for,
that she has received from the LORD's hand
    double for all her sins.

3 A voice of one calling:
  "In the desert prepare

Gross!

They cut open figs, laid them on Hezekiah's boil, and let them soak up the infection (Isaiah 38:21). Imagine those puss-filled figs. Hope they threw them out afterwards. Ewww.

the way for the LORD[a];
make straight in the wilderness
  a highway for our God. [b]
⁴ Every valley shall be raised up,
  every mountain and hill made low;
the rough ground shall become level,
  the rugged places a plain.
⁵ And the glory of the LORD will be
       revealed,
  and all mankind together will see it.
        For the mouth of the LORD
           has spoken."

⁶ A voice says, "Cry out."
  And I said, "What shall I cry?"

"All men are like grass,
  and all their glory is like the flowers
    of the field.
⁷ The grass withers and the flowers fall,
  because the breath of the LORD
    blows on them.
  Surely the people are grass.
⁸ The grass withers and the flowers fall,
  but the word of our God stands
    forever."

⁹ You who bring good tidings to Zion,
  go up on a high mountain.
You who bring good tidings to
    Jerusalem,[c]
  lift up your voice with a shout,
lift it up, do not be afraid;
  say to the towns of Judah,
  "Here is your God!"
¹⁰ See, the Sovereign LORD comes with
    power,
  and his arm rules for him.
See, his reward is with him,
  and his recompense accompanies
    him.
¹¹ He tends his flock like a shepherd:
  He gathers the lambs in his arms
and carries them close to his heart;
  he gently leads those that have
    young.

¹² Who has measured the waters in the
    hollow of his hand,
  or with the breadth of his hand
    marked off the heavens?
Who has held the dust of the earth in
    a basket,
  or weighed the mountains on the
    scales
  and the hills in a balance?
¹³ Who has understood the mind[d] of the
    LORD,
  or instructed him as his counselor?

¹⁴ Whom did the LORD consult to
    enlighten him,
  and who taught him the right way?
Who was it that taught him knowledge
  or showed him the path of
    understanding?

¹⁵ Surely the nations are like a drop in a
    bucket;
  they are regarded as dust on the
    scales;
  he weighs the islands as though
    they were fine dust.
¹⁶ Lebanon is not sufficient for altar fires,
  nor its animals enough for burnt
    offerings.
¹⁷ Before him all the nations are as
    nothing;
  they are regarded by him as
    worthless
  and less than nothing.

¹⁸ To whom, then, will you compare God?
  What image will you compare him
    to?
¹⁹ As for an idol, a craftsman casts it,
  and a goldsmith overlays it with gold
  and fashions silver chains for it.
²⁰ A man too poor to present such an
    offering
  selects wood that will not rot.
He looks for a skilled craftsman
  to set up an idol that will not topple.

²¹ Do you not know?
  Have you not heard?
Has it not been told you from the
    beginning?
  Have you not understood since the
    earth was founded?
²² He sits enthroned above the circle of
    the earth,
  and its people are like grasshoppers.
He stretches out the heavens like a
    canopy,
  and spreads them out like a tent to
    live in.
²³ He brings princes to naught
  and reduces the rulers of this world
    to nothing.
²⁴ No sooner are they planted,
  no sooner are they sown,
  no sooner do they take root in the
    ground,

---

[a] 3 Or *A voice of one calling in the desert: / "Prepare the way
for the LORD*   [b] 3 Hebrew; Septuagint *make straight the
paths of our God*   [c] 9 Or *O Zion, bringer of good tidings, /
go up on a high mountain. / O Jerusalem, bringer of good
tidings*   [d] 13 Or *Spirit; or spirit*

than he blows on them and they wither,
and a whirlwind sweeps them away
like chaff.
25 "To whom will you compare me?
Or who is my equal?" says the Holy
One.
26 Lift your eyes and look to the heavens:
Who created all these?
He who brings out the starry host one
by one,
and calls them each by name.
Because of his great power and mighty
strength,
not one of them is missing.
27 Why do you say, O Jacob,
and complain, O Israel,
"My way is hidden from the LORD;
my cause is disregarded by my God"?
28 Do you not know?
Have you not heard?
The LORD is the everlasting God,
the Creator of the ends of the earth.
He will not grow tired or weary,
and his understanding no one can
fathom.
29 He gives strength to the weary

and increases the power of the
weak.
30 Even youths grow tired and weary,
and young men stumble and fall;
31 but those who hope in the LORD
will renew their strength.
They will soar on wings like eagles;
they will run and not grow weary,
they will walk and not be faint.

The Helper of Israel

41 "Be silent before me, you
islands!
Let the nations renew their
strength!
Let them come forward and speak;
let us meet together at the place of
judgment.

2 "Who has stirred up one from the east,
calling him in righteousness to his
service[a]?
He hands nations over to him
and subdues kings before him.
He turns them to dust with his sword,
to windblown chaff with his bow.

[a] 2 Or / whom victory meets at every step

The One, the Only!

READ ISAIAH 40:12–15, 25–31

When you look up at the stars at night, you might wonder if anyone has ever been there before. The answer is no, unless you're eyeballing the moon. And since there probably are *no* aliens, then *no* one has been out there. But guess what? God has covered every cubic inch of it because he made it all and he's everywhere. He knows every star, every planet, every meteorite, by name. He also knows every shark, every snail and every speck of dust on planet Earth. That means God also knows exactly what is going on in your life. He's not sitting off somewhere deep in space ignoring what's happening down here. Don't ever think, "My life is hidden from the LORD; my cause is disregarded by my God" (verse 27). He is here with us, totally involved in our lives, and he cares for you.

Your next reading is on page 913.

³He pursues them and moves on
    unscathed,
  by a path his feet have not traveled
    before.
⁴Who has done this and carried it
    through,
  calling forth the generations from
    the beginning?
I, the LORD—with the first of them
  and with the last—I am he."

⁵The islands have seen it and fear;
  the ends of the earth tremble.
They approach and come forward;
⁶ each helps the other
  and says to his brother, "Be strong!"
⁷The craftsman encourages the
    goldsmith,
  and he who smooths with the
    hammer
  spurs on him who strikes the anvil.
He says of the welding, "It is good."
  He nails down the idol so it will not
    topple.

⁸"But you, O Israel, my servant,
  Jacob, whom I have chosen,
  you descendants of Abraham my
    friend,
⁹I took you from the ends of the earth,
  from its farthest corners I called you.
I said, 'You are my servant';
  I have chosen you and have not
    rejected you.
¹⁰So do not fear, for I am with you;
  do not be dismayed, for I am your
    God.
I will strengthen you and help you;
  I will uphold you with my righteous
    right hand.

¹¹"All who rage against you
  will surely be ashamed and
    disgraced;
those who oppose you
  will be as nothing and perish.
¹²Though you search for your enemies,
  you will not find them.
Those who wage war against you
  will be as nothing at all.
¹³For I am the LORD, your God,
  who takes hold of your right hand
and says to you, Do not fear;
  I will help you.
¹⁴Do not be afraid, O worm Jacob,
  O little Israel,
for I myself will help you," declares the
  LORD,

your Redeemer, the Holy One of Israel.
¹⁵"See, I will make you into a threshing
    sledge,
  new and sharp, with many teeth.
You will thresh the mountains and
    crush them,
  and reduce the hills to chaff.
¹⁶You will winnow them, the wind will
    pick them up,
  and a gale will blow them away.
But you will rejoice in the LORD
  and glory in the Holy One of Israel.

¹⁷"The poor and needy search for water,
  but there is none;
  their tongues are parched with thirst.
But I the LORD will answer them;
  I, the God of Israel, will not forsake
    them.
¹⁸I will make rivers flow on barren
    heights,
  and springs within the valleys.
I will turn the desert into pools of water,
  and the parched ground into springs.
¹⁹I will put in the desert
  the cedar and the acacia, the myrtle
    and the olive.
I will set pines in the wasteland,
  the fir and the cypress together,
²⁰so that people may see and know,
  may consider and understand,
that the hand of the LORD has done
    this,
  that the Holy One of Israel has
    created it.

²¹"Present your case," says the LORD.
  "Set forth your arguments," says
    Jacob's King.
²²"Bring in ⌊your idols⌋ to tell us
  what is going to happen.
Tell us what the former things were,
  so that we may consider them
  and know their final outcome.
Or declare to us the things to come,
²³ tell us what the future holds,
  so we may know that you are gods.
Do something, whether good or bad,
  so that we will be dismayed and
    filled with fear.
²⁴But you are less than nothing
  and your works are utterly worthless;
  he who chooses you is detestable.

²⁵"I have stirred up one from the north,
  and he comes—
  one from the rising sun who calls on
    my name.

He treads on rulers as if they were
mortar,
as if he were a potter treading the
clay.
26 Who told of this from the beginning,
so we could know,
or beforehand, so we could say, 'He
was right'?
No one told of this,
no one foretold it,
no one heard any words from you.
27 I was the first to tell Zion, 'Look, here
they are!'
I gave to Jerusalem a messenger of
good tidings.
28 I look but there is no one—
no one among them to give counsel,
no one to give answer when I ask
them.
29 See, they are all false!
Their deeds amount to nothing;
their images are but wind and
confusion.

The Servant of the Lord

42 "Here is my servant, whom I
uphold,
my chosen one in whom I
delight;
I will put my Spirit on him
and he will bring justice to the
nations.
2 He will not shout or cry out,
or raise his voice in the streets.
3 A bruised reed he will not break,
and a smoldering wick he will not
snuff out.
In faithfulness he will bring forth justice;
4 he will not falter or be discouraged
till he establishes justice on earth.
In his law the islands will put their
hope."

5 This is what God the Lord says—
he who created the heavens and
stretched them out,
who spread out the earth and all
that comes out of it,

Stopping for Refreshments

GET STRONGER

READ ISAIAH 40:28–31

Ever gone for a long, long hike over difficult wilderness terrain? At first you're full of energy, but somewhere around halfway you're exhausted, out of breath and sweating like a pig. What do you do? You flop down on the grass, wondering if you'll even make it to the end of the trail. This can also happen when you're going through a difficult time with friends or family, or if you're troubled about something, or frustrated over a tough job. You just want to flop down on the grass and give up. But if you know God is beside you and will help you, that hope will give you the strength to carry on. "Even youths grow tired and weary . . . but those who hope in the Lord will renew their strength" (verse 31). Ask God to help you, then trust that he's heard and *will* help. And he will.

Your next reading is on page 922.

who gives breath to its people,
   and life to those who walk on it:
⁶ "I, the LORD, have called you in
      righteousness;
   I will take hold of your hand.
I will keep you and will make you
      to be a covenant for the people
      and a light for the Gentiles,
⁷ to open eyes that are blind,
   to free captives from prison
   and to release from the dungeon
      those who sit in darkness.

⁸ "I am the LORD; that is my name!
   I will not give my glory to another
   or my praise to idols.
⁹ See, the former things have taken place,
   and new things I declare;
before they spring into being
   I announce them to you."

Song of Praise to the LORD

¹⁰ Sing to the LORD a new song,
      his praise from the ends of the earth,
you who go down to the sea, and all
      that is in it,
   you islands, and all who live in them.
¹¹ Let the desert and its towns raise their
      voices;
   let the settlements where Kedar lives
      rejoice.
Let the people of Sela sing for joy;
   let them shout from the
      mountaintops.
¹² Let them give glory to the LORD
   and proclaim his praise in the islands.
¹³ The LORD will march out like a mighty
      man,
   like a warrior he will stir up his zeal;
with a shout he will raise the battle cry
   and will triumph over his enemies.

¹⁴ "For a long time I have kept silent,
   I have been quiet and held myself
      back.
But now, like a woman in childbirth,
   I cry out, I gasp and pant.
¹⁵ I will lay waste the mountains and hills
   and dry up all their vegetation;
I will turn rivers into islands
   and dry up the pools.
¹⁶ I will lead the blind by ways they have
      not known,
   along unfamiliar paths I will guide
      them;
I will turn the darkness into light
      before them
and make the rough places smooth.

These are the things I will do;
   I will not forsake them.
¹⁷ But those who trust in idols,
   who say to images, 'You are our
      gods,'
   will be turned back in utter shame.

Israel Blind and Deaf

¹⁸ "Hear, you deaf;
   look, you blind, and see!
¹⁹ Who is blind but my servant,
   and deaf like the messenger I send?
Who is blind like the one committed to
      me,
   blind like the servant of the LORD?
²⁰ You have seen many things, but have
      paid no attention;
   your ears are open, but you hear
      nothing."
²¹ It pleased the LORD
   for the sake of his righteousness
   to make his law great and glorious.
²² But this is a people plundered and
      looted,
   all of them trapped in pits
   or hidden away in prisons.
They have become plunder,
   with no one to rescue them;
they have been made loot,
   with no one to say, "Send them
      back."

²³ Which of you will listen to this
   or pay close attention in time to
      come?
²⁴ Who handed Jacob over to become
      loot,
   and Israel to the plunderers?
Was it not the LORD,
   against whom we have sinned?
For they would not follow his ways;
   they did not obey his law.
²⁵ So he poured out on them his burning
      anger,
   the violence of war.
It enveloped them in flames, yet they
      did not understand;
   it consumed them, but they did not
      take it to heart.

Israel's Only Savior

43 But now, this is what the LORD
      says—
he who created you, O Jacob,
he who formed you, O Israel:
"Fear not, for I have redeemed you;

I have summoned you by name; you are mine.
2 When you pass through the waters,
    I will be with you;
and when you pass through the rivers,
    they will not sweep over you.
When you walk through the fire,
    you will not be burned;
    the flames will not set you ablaze.
3 For I am the LORD, your God,
    the Holy One of Israel, your Savior;
I give Egypt for your ransom,
    Cush[a] and Seba in your stead.
4 Since you are precious and honored in my sight,
    and because I love you,
I will give men in exchange for you,
    and people in exchange for your life.
5 Do not be afraid, for I am with you;
    I will bring your children from the east
    and gather you from the west.
6 I will say to the north, 'Give them up!'
    and to the south, 'Do not hold them back.'
Bring my sons from afar
    and my daughters from the ends of the earth—
7 everyone who is called by my name,
    whom I created for my glory,
    whom I formed and made."

8 Lead out those who have eyes but are blind,
    who have ears but are deaf.
9 All the nations gather together
    and the peoples assemble.
Which of them foretold this
    and proclaimed to us the former things?
Let them bring in their witnesses to prove they were
        right,
    so that others may hear and say, "It is true."
10 "You are my witnesses," declares the LORD,
    "and my servant whom I have chosen,
so that you may know and believe me
    and understand that I am he.
Before me no god was formed,
    nor will there be one after me.
11 I, even I, am the LORD,
    and apart from me there is no savior.
12 I have revealed and saved and proclaimed—
    I, and not some foreign god among you.
You are my witnesses," declares the LORD, "that I am
        God.
13   Yes, and from ancient days I am he.
No one can deliver out of my hand.
    When I act, who can reverse it?"

God's Mercy and Israel's Unfaithfulness

14 This is what the LORD says—
    your Redeemer, the Holy One of Israel:
"For your sake I will send to Babylon

Get a Load of This...

Make sure you focus on God's Word and tune in to—and do—what it says to do (see Isaiah 42:20). Otherwise you'll be like the cat who just sits there with a blank look on his face and doesn't clue into a single word you say.

In Other Words...

---

and bring down as fugitives all the
    Babylonians, *a*
in the ships in which they took pride.
15 I am the LORD, your Holy One,
    Israel's Creator, your King."

16 This is what the LORD says—
    he who made a way through the sea,
    a path through the mighty waters,
17 who drew out the chariots and horses,
    the army and reinforcements
      together,
and they lay there, never to rise again,
    extinguished, snuffed out like a wick:
18 "Forget the former things;
    do not dwell on the past.
19 See, I am doing a new thing!
    Now it springs up; do you not
      perceive it?
I am making a way in the desert
    and streams in the wasteland.
20 The wild animals honor me,
    the jackals and the owls,
because I provide water in the desert
    and streams in the wasteland,
to give drink to my people, my chosen,
21   the people I formed for myself
    that they may proclaim my praise.

22 "Yet you have not called upon me,
    O Jacob,
    you have not wearied yourselves for
      me, O Israel.
23 You have not brought me sheep for
      burnt offerings,
    nor honored me with your sacrifices.
I have not burdened you with grain
      offerings
    nor wearied you with demands for
      incense.
24 You have not bought any fragrant
      calamus for me,
    or lavished on me the fat of your
      sacrifices.
But you have burdened me with your
      sins
    and wearied me with your offenses.

25 "I, even I, am he who blots out
    your transgressions, for my own sake,
    and remembers your sins no more.
26 Review the past for me,
    let us argue the matter together;
    state the case for your innocence.
27 Your first father sinned;
    your spokesmen rebelled against me.
28 So I will disgrace the dignitaries of
    your temple,

and I will consign Jacob to
    destruction *b*
and Israel to scorn.

Israel the Chosen

44 "But now listen, O Jacob, my
    servant,
    Israel, whom I have chosen.
2 This is what the LORD says—
he who made you, who formed you
    in the womb,
    and who will help you:
Do not be afraid, O Jacob, my servant,
    Jeshurun, whom I have chosen.
3 For I will pour water on the thirsty land,
    and streams on the dry ground;
I will pour out my Spirit on your
      offspring,
    and my blessing on your descendants.
4 They will spring up like grass in a
      meadow,
    like poplar trees by flowing streams.
5 One will say, 'I belong to the LORD';
    another will call himself by the name
      of Jacob;
still another will write on his hand,
    'The LORD's,'
    and will take the name Israel.

The LORD, Not Idols

6 "This is what the LORD says—
    Israel's King and Redeemer, the LORD
      Almighty:
I am the first and I am the last;
    apart from me there is no God.
7 Who then is like me? Let him proclaim
    it.
Let him declare and lay out before
      me
what has happened since I established
    my ancient people,
    and what is yet to come—
    yes, let him foretell what will come.
8 Do not tremble, do not be afraid.
    Did I not proclaim this and foretell it
      long ago?
You are my witnesses. Is there any God
      besides me?
    No, there is no other Rock; I know
      not one."

9 All who make idols are nothing,
    and the things they treasure are
      worthless.

a 14 Or *Chaldeans*   *b 28* The Hebrew term refers to the
irrevocable giving over of things or persons to the LORD, often
by totally destroying them.

Those who would speak up for them
are blind;
they are ignorant, to their own
shame.
10 Who shapes a god and casts an idol,
which can profit him nothing?
11 He and his kind will be put to shame;
craftsmen are nothing but men.
Let them all come together and take
their stand;
they will be brought down to terror
and infamy.

12 The blacksmith takes a tool
and works with it in the coals;
he shapes an idol with hammers,
he forges it with the might of his
arm.
He gets hungry and loses his strength;
he drinks no water and grows faint.
13 The carpenter measures with a line
and makes an outline with a marker;
he roughs it out with chisels
and marks it with compasses.

He shapes it in the form of man,
of man in all his glory,
that it may dwell in a shrine.
14 He cut down cedars,
or perhaps took a cypress or oak.
He let it grow among the trees of the
forest,
or planted a pine, and the rain made
it grow.
15 It is man's fuel for burning;
some of it he takes and warms
himself,
he kindles a fire and bakes bread.
But he also fashions a god and
worships it;
he makes an idol and bows down to
it.
16 Half of the wood he burns in the fire;
over it he prepares his meal,
he roasts his meat and eats his fill.
He also warms himself and says,
"Ah! I am warm; I see the fire."
17 From the rest he makes a god, his idol;
he bows down to it and worships.

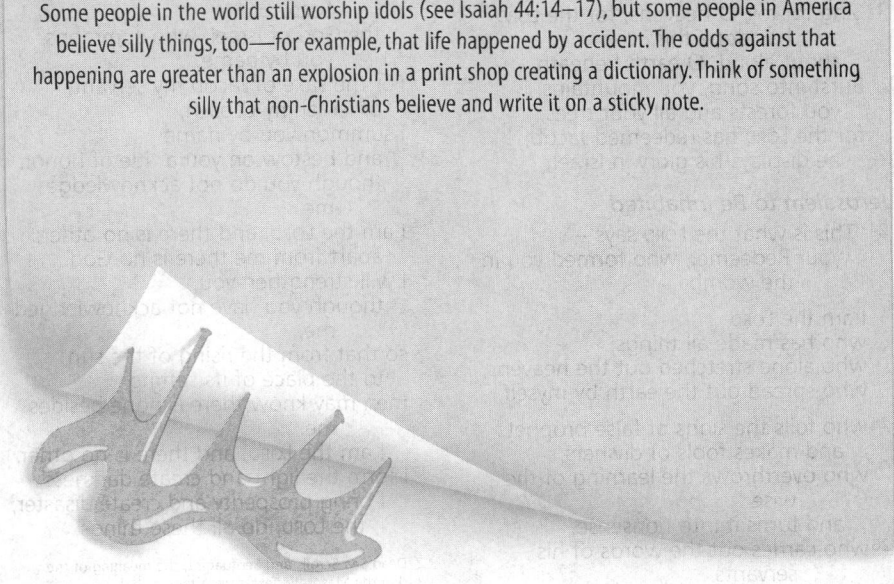

Make It Stick

READ ISAIAH 44:14–17

Some people in the world still worship idols (see Isaiah 44:14–17), but some people in America believe silly things, too—for example, that life happened by accident. The odds against that happening are greater than an explosion in a print shop creating a dictionary. Think of something silly that non-Christians believe and write it on a sticky note.

He prays to it and says,
  "Save me; you are my god."
¹⁸They know nothing, they understand
    nothing;
  their eyes are plastered over so they
    cannot see,
  and their minds closed so they
    cannot understand.
¹⁹No one stops to think,
  no one has the knowledge or
    understanding to say,
  "Half of it I used for fuel;
  I even baked bread over its coals,
  I roasted meat and I ate.
  Shall I make a detestable thing from
    what is left?
  Shall I bow down to a block of
    wood?"
²⁰He feeds on ashes, a deluded heart
    misleads him;
  he cannot save himself, or say,
  "Is not this thing in my right hand a
    lie?"

²¹"Remember these things, O Jacob,
  for you are my servant, O Israel.
  I have made you, you are my servant;
  O Israel, I will not forget you.
²²I have swept away your offenses like a
    cloud,
  your sins like the morning mist.
  Return to me,
  for I have redeemed you."

²³Sing for joy, O heavens, for the LORD
    has done this;
  shout aloud, O earth beneath.
  Burst into song, you mountains,
  you forests and all your trees,
  for the LORD has redeemed Jacob,
  he displays his glory in Israel.

Jerusalem to Be Inhabited

²⁴"This is what the LORD says—
  your Redeemer, who formed you in
    the womb:

  I am the LORD,
  who has made all things,
  who alone stretched out the heavens,
  who spread out the earth by myself,

²⁵who foils the signs of false prophets
  and makes fools of diviners,
  who overthrows the learning of the
    wise
  and turns it into nonsense,
²⁶who carries out the words of his
    servants

and fulfills the predictions of his
    messengers,

who says of Jerusalem, 'It shall be
    inhabited,'
  of the towns of Judah, 'They shall be
    built,'
  and of their ruins, 'I will restore
    them,'
²⁷who says to the watery deep, 'Be dry,
  and I will dry up your streams,'
²⁸who says of Cyrus, 'He is my shepherd
  and will accomplish all that I please;
  he will say of Jerusalem, "Let it be
    rebuilt,"
  and of the temple, "Let its
    foundations be laid." '

45 "This is what the LORD says to
    his anointed,
    to Cyrus, whose right hand I
      take hold of
to subdue nations before him
  and to strip kings of their armor,
to open doors before him
  so that gates will not be shut:
²I will go before you
  and will level the mountains^a;
  I will break down gates of bronze
  and cut through bars of iron.
³I will give you the treasures of darkness,
  riches stored in secret places,
so that you may know that I am the
    LORD,
  the God of Israel, who summons
    you by name.
⁴For the sake of Jacob my servant,
  of Israel my chosen,
I summon you by name
  and bestow on you a title of honor,
  though you do not acknowledge
    me.
⁵I am the LORD, and there is no other;
  apart from me there is no God.
I will strengthen you,
  though you have not acknowledged
    me,
⁶so that from the rising of the sun
  to the place of its setting
men may know there is none besides
    me.
  I am the LORD, and there is no other.
⁷I form the light and create darkness,
  I bring prosperity and create disaster;
  I, the LORD, do all these things.

---

^a 2 Dead Sea Scrolls and Septuagint; the meaning of the
word in the Masoretic Text is uncertain.

8 "You heavens above, rain down
      righteousness;
   let the clouds shower it down.
Let the earth open wide,
   let salvation spring up,
let righteousness grow with it;
   I, the LORD, have created it.

9 "Woe to him who quarrels with his
      Maker,
   to him who is but a potsherd among
      the potsherds on the ground.
Does the clay say to the potter,
   'What are you making?'
Does your work say,
   'He has no hands'?
10 Woe to him who says to his father,
   'What have you begotten?'
or to his mother,
   'What have you brought to birth?'

11 "This is what the LORD says—
   the Holy One of Israel, and its
      Maker:
Concerning things to come,

do you question me about my
   children,
or give me orders about the work of
   my hands?
12 It is I who made the earth
   and created mankind upon it.
My own hands stretched out the
   heavens;
   I marshaled their starry hosts.
13 I will raise up Cyrus[a] in my
   righteousness:
   I will make all his ways straight.
He will rebuild my city
   and set my exiles free,
but not for a price or reward,
   says the LORD Almighty."

14 This is what the LORD says:

"The products of Egypt and the
   merchandise of Cush,[b]
   and those tall Sabeans—
they will come over to you

---

a 13 Hebrew *him*   b 14 That is, the upper Nile region

Make It Stick

READ ISAIAH 45:1

Cyrus the Great, king of Persia, wasn't even a believer, but God used him big-time! Read
Isaiah 44:28, 45:1–4, 13. These prophecies were given 100 years before Cyrus was born,
yet Cyrus did *all* of these things! Pray for the leaders of your land, so that when you're
old enough to vote, there will be somebody worth voting for.

and will be yours;
they will trudge behind you,
   coming over to you in chains.
They will bow down before you
   and plead with you, saying,
'Surely God is with you, and there is
      no other;
   there is no other god.' "

¹⁵ Truly you are a God who hides himself,
   O God and Savior of Israel.
¹⁶ All the makers of idols will be put to
      shame and disgraced;
   they will go off into disgrace
      together.
¹⁷ But Israel will be saved by the LORD
   with an everlasting salvation;
you will never be put to shame or
      disgraced,
   to ages everlasting.

¹⁸ For this is what the LORD says—
he who created the heavens,
   he is God;
he who fashioned and made the earth,
   he founded it;
he did not create it to be empty,
   but formed it to be inhabited—
he says:
"I am the LORD,
   and there is no other.
¹⁹ I have not spoken in secret,
   from somewhere in a land of
      darkness;
I have not said to Jacob's descendants,
   'Seek me in vain.'
I, the LORD, speak the truth;
   I declare what is right.

²⁰ "Gather together and come;
   assemble, you fugitives from the
      nations.
Ignorant are those who carry about
      idols of wood,
   who pray to gods that cannot save.
²¹ Declare what is to be, present it—
   let them take counsel together.
Who foretold this long ago,
   who declared it from the distant past?
Was it not I, the LORD?
   And there is no God apart from me,
a righteous God and a Savior;
   there is none but me.

²² "Turn to me and be saved,
   all you ends of the earth;
   for I am God, and there is no other.
²³ By myself I have sworn,
   my mouth has uttered in all integrity

a word that will not be revoked:
Before me every knee will bow;
   by me every tongue will swear.
²⁴ They will say of me, 'In the LORD alone
   are righteousness and strength.' "
All who have raged against him
   will come to him and be put to
      shame.
²⁵ But in the LORD all the descendants of
      Israel
   will be found righteous and will exult.

Gods of Babylon

46 Bel bows down, Nebo stoops
   low;
   their idols are borne by
   beasts of burden.ᵃ
The images that are carried about are
      burdensome,
   a burden for the weary.
² They stoop and bow down together;
   unable to rescue the burden,
   they themselves go off into captivity.

³ "Listen to me, O house of Jacob,
   all you who remain of the house of
      Israel,
you whom I have upheld since you
      were conceived,
   and have carried since your birth.
⁴ Even to your old age and gray hairs
   I am he, I am he who will sustain
      you.
I have made you and I will carry you;
   I will sustain you and I will rescue
      you.

⁵ "To whom will you compare me or
      count me equal?
   To whom will you liken me that we
      may be compared?
⁶ Some pour out gold from their bags
   and weigh out silver on the scales;
they hire a goldsmith to make it into a
      god,
   and they bow down and worship it.
⁷ They lift it to their shoulders and carry
      it;
   they set it up in its place, and there
      it stands.
   From that spot it cannot move.
Though one cries out to it, it does not
      answer;
   it cannot save him from his troubles.

⁸ "Remember this, fix it in mind,
   take it to heart, you rebels.

ᵃ 1 Or are but beasts and cattle

9 Remember the former things, those of
  long ago;
  I am God, and there is no other;
  I am God, and there is none like me.
10 I make known the end from the
  beginning,
  from ancient times, what is still to
  come.
  I say: My purpose will stand,
  and I will do all that I please.
11 From the east I summon a bird of prey;
  from a far-off land, a man to fulfill
  my purpose.
  What I have said, that will I bring
  about;
  what I have planned, that will I do.
12 Listen to me, you stubborn-hearted,
  you who are far from righteousness.
13 I am bringing my righteousness near,
  it is not far away;
  and my salvation will not be
  delayed.
  I will grant salvation to Zion,
  my splendor to Israel.

The Fall of Babylon

47 "Go down, sit in the dust,
  Virgin Daughter of Babylon;
  sit on the ground without a
  throne,
  Daughter of the Babylonians.ᵃ
  No more will you be called
  tender or delicate.
2 Take millstones and grind flour;
  take off your veil.
  Lift up your skirts, bare your legs,
  and wade through the streams.
3 Your nakedness will be exposed
  and your shame uncovered.
  I will take vengeance;
  I will spare no one."

4 Our Redeemer—the Lord Almighty is
  his name—
  is the Holy One of Israel.

5 "Sit in silence, go into darkness,
  Daughter of the Babylonians;
  no more will you be called
  queen of kingdoms.
6 I was angry with my people
  and desecrated my inheritance;
  I gave them into your hand,
  and you showed them no mercy.
  Even on the aged
  you laid a very heavy yoke.
7 You said, 'I will continue forever—
  the eternal queen!'

But you did not consider these things
  or reflect on what might happen.
8 "Now then, listen, you wanton
  creature,
  lounging in your security
  and saying to yourself,
  'I am, and there is none besides me.
  I will never be a widow
  or suffer the loss of children.'
9 Both of these will overtake you
  in a moment, on a single day:
  loss of children and widowhood.
  They will come upon you in full
  measure,
  in spite of your many sorceries
  and all your potent spells.
10 You have trusted in your wickedness
  and have said, 'No one sees me.'
  Your wisdom and knowledge mislead
  you
  when you say to yourself,
  'I am, and there is none besides me.'
11 Disaster will come upon you,
  and you will not know how to
  conjure it away.
  A calamity will fall upon you
  that you cannot ward off with a
  ransom;
  a catastrophe you cannot foresee
  will suddenly come upon you.

12 "Keep on, then, with your magic spells
  and with your many sorceries,
  which you have labored at since
  childhood.
  Perhaps you will succeed,
  perhaps you will cause terror.
13 All the counsel you have received has
  only worn you out!
  Let your astrologers come forward,
  those stargazers who make predictions
  month by month,
  let them save you from what is
  coming upon you.
14 Surely they are like stubble;
  the fire will burn them up.
  They cannot even save themselves
  from the power of the flame.
  Here are no coals to warm anyone;
  here is no fire to sit by.
15 That is all they can do for you—
  these you have labored with
  and trafficked with since childhood.
  Each of them goes on in his error;
  there is not one that can save you.

ᵃ 1 Or *Chaldeans*; also in verse 5

Stubborn Israel

48 "Listen to this, O house of Jacob,
you who are called by the name of Israel
and come from the line of Judah,
you who take oaths in the name of the LORD
and invoke the God of Israel—
but not in truth or righteousness—
² you who call yourselves citizens of the holy city
and rely on the God of Israel—
the LORD Almighty is his name:
³ I foretold the former things long ago,
my mouth announced them and I made them known;
then suddenly I acted, and they came to pass.
⁴ For I knew how stubborn you were;
the sinews of your neck were iron,
your forehead was bronze,
⁵ Therefore I told you these things long ago;
before they happened I announced them to you

so that you could not say,
'My idols did them;
my wooden image and metal god ordained them.'
⁶ You have heard these things; look at them all.
Will you not admit them?

"From now on I will tell you of new things,
of hidden things unknown to you.
⁷ They are created now, and not long ago;
you have not heard of them before today.
So you cannot say,
'Yes, I knew of them.'
⁸ You have neither heard nor understood;
from of old your ear has not been open.
Well do I know how treacherous you are;
you were called a rebel from birth.
⁹ For my own name's sake I delay my wrath;
for the sake of my praise I hold it back from you,
so as not to cut you off.

GET SMARTER

Horror Scopes

READ ISAIAH 47:11–15

Ever had a friend ask you when your birthday is, then say, "Oh, your sign is Virgo!" or, "You're a Libra"? This is astrology, guys. Astrologers believe that your personality is designed by the position of the stars and planets at your birth. Then some planet supposedly "rules" over you. That makes up your so-called *horoscope*. (What they don't say is that the stars have completely changed position in the past 4,000 years, throwing all "horoscopes" off.) The day-by-day, monthly prediction stuff ("November 8 is a bad day for Scorpios. Stay in the house.") is even hokier. God is in charge, not the stars. Your "fate" is determined by God's plan for your life and the choices you make—not the planets. Obey God and things go great. Disobey him and things get rotten. Are you being led by balls of burning gases out in space or by the living God?

Your next reading is on page 929.

¹⁰ See, I have refined you, though not as
    silver;
  I have tested you in the furnace of
    affliction.
¹¹ For my own sake, for my own sake, I
    do this.
  How can I let myself be defamed?
  I will not yield my glory to another.

Israel Freed

¹² "Listen to me, O Jacob,
  Israel, whom I have called:
  I am he;
  I am the first and I am the last.
¹³ My own hand laid the foundations of
    the earth,
  and my right hand spread out the
    heavens;
  when I summon them,
  they all stand up together.

¹⁴ "Come together, all of you, and listen:
  Which of ⌊the idols⌋ has foretold
    these things?

The Lord's chosen ally
  will carry out his purpose against
    Babylon;
  his arm will be against the
    Babylonians. ^a
¹⁵ I, even I, have spoken;
  yes, I have called him.
  I will bring him,
  and he will succeed in his mission.

¹⁶ "Come near me and listen to this:

"From the first announcement I have
  not spoken in secret;
  at the time it happens, I am there."

And now the Sovereign Lord has sent
  me,
  with his Spirit.

¹⁷ This is what the Lord says—
  your Redeemer, the Holy One of Israel:
  "I am the Lord your God,
  who teaches you what is best for you,

---

^a 14 Or *Chaldeans*; also in verse 20

Make It Stick

READ ISAIAH 48:17–18

After you read through Isaiah 48:17–18, write your own "In Other Words . . ." on a sticky note.
Explain what you think these verses mean. Then stick it here in your Bible. Try doing this for other
passages you find interesting or difficult to understand.

who directs you in the way you should go.
¹⁸ If only you had paid attention to my commands,
    your peace would have been like a river,
    your righteousness like the waves of the sea.
¹⁹ Your descendants would have been like the sand,
    your children like its numberless grains;
their name would never be cut off
    nor destroyed from before me."

²⁰ Leave Babylon,
    flee from the Babylonians!
Announce this with shouts of joy
    and proclaim it.
Send it out to the ends of the earth;
    say, "The LORD has redeemed his servant Jacob."
²¹ They did not thirst when he led them through the deserts;
    he made water flow for them from the rock;
he split the rock
    and water gushed out.

²² "There is no peace," says the LORD, "for the wicked."

The Servant of the LORD

49 Listen to me, you islands;
    hear this, you distant nations:
Before I was born the LORD called me;
    from my birth he has made mention of my name.
² He made my mouth like a sharpened sword,
    in the shadow of his hand he hid me;
he made me into a polished arrow
    and concealed me in his quiver.
³ He said to me, "You are my servant,
    Israel, in whom I will display my splendor."
⁴ But I said, "I have labored to no purpose;
    I have spent my strength in vain and for nothing.
Yet what is due me is in the LORD's hand,
    and my reward is with my God."

⁵ And now the LORD says—
    he who formed me in the womb to be his servant
to bring Jacob back to him
    and gather Israel to himself,
for I am honored in the eyes of the LORD
    and my God has been my strength—
⁶ he says:
"It is too small a thing for you to be my servant
    to restore the tribes of Jacob
    and bring back those of Israel I have kept.
I will also make you a light for the Gentiles,
    that you may bring my salvation to the ends of the earth."

⁷ This is what the LORD says—
    the Redeemer and Holy One of Israel—
to him who was despised and abhorred by the nation,
    to the servant of rulers:

"Kings will see you and rise up,
    princes will see and bow down,
because of the LORD, who is faithful,
    the Holy One of Israel, who has
        chosen you."

Restoration of Israel

8This is what the LORD says:

"In the time of my favor I will answer
        you,
    and in the day of salvation I will help
        you;
I will keep you and will make you
    to be a covenant for the people,
to restore the land
    and to reassign its desolate
        inheritances,
9to say to the captives, 'Come out,'
    and to those in darkness, 'Be free!'

"They will feed beside the roads
    and find pasture on every barren hill.
10They will neither hunger nor thirst,
    nor will the desert heat or the sun
        beat upon them.
He who has compassion on them will
        guide them
    and lead them beside springs of
        water.
11I will turn all my mountains into roads,
    and my highways will be raised up.
12See, they will come from afar—
    some from the north, some from the
        west,
    some from the region of Aswan.a"

13Shout for joy, O heavens;
    rejoice, O earth;
    burst into song, O mountains!
For the LORD comforts his people
    and will have compassion on his
        afflicted ones.

14But Zion said, "The LORD has forsaken
        me,
    the Lord has forgotten me."

15"Can a mother forget the baby at her
        breast
    and have no compassion on the
        child she has borne?
Though she may forget,
    I will not forget you!
16See, I have engraved you on the palms
        of my hands;
    your walls are ever before me.
17Your sons hasten back,

and those who laid you waste
        depart from you.
18Lift up your eyes and look around;
    all your sons gather and come to you.
As surely as I live," declares the LORD,
    "you will wear them all as
        ornaments;
    you will put them on, like a bride.

19"Though you were ruined and made
        desolate
    and your land laid waste,
now you will be too small for your
        people,
    and those who devoured you will be
        far away.
20The children born during your
        bereavement
    will yet say in your hearing,
'This place is too small for us;
    give us more space to live in.'
21Then you will say in your heart,
    'Who bore me these?
I was bereaved and barren;
    I was exiled and rejected.
Who brought these up?
    I was left all alone,
    but these—where have they come
        from?' "

22This is what the Sovereign LORD says:

"See, I will beckon to the Gentiles,
    I will lift up my banner to the
        peoples;
they will bring your sons in their arms
    and carry your daughters on their
        shoulders.
23Kings will be your foster fathers,
    and their queens your nursing
        mothers.
They will bow down before you with
        their faces to the ground;
    they will lick the dust at your feet.
Then you will know that I am the LORD;
    those who hope in me will not be
        disappointed."

24Can plunder be taken from warriors,
    or captives rescued from the fierceb?

25But this is what the LORD says:

"Yes, captives will be taken from
        warriors,
    and plunder retrieved from the fierce;

---

a 12 Dead Sea Scrolls; Masoretic Text Sinim   b 24 Dead Sea
Scrolls, Vulgate and Syriac (see also Septuagint and verse 25);
Masoretic Text righteous

I will contend with those who contend with you,
　　and your children I will save.
26 I will make your oppressors eat their own flesh;
　　they will be drunk on their own blood, as with
　　　wine.
Then all mankind will know
　　that I, the LORD, am your Savior,
　　your Redeemer, the Mighty One of Jacob."

Israel's Sin and the Servant's Obedience

50 This is what the LORD says:

"Where is your mother's certificate of divorce
　　with which I sent her away?
Or to which of my creditors
　　did I sell you?
Because of your sins you were sold;
　　because of your transgressions your mother was
　　　sent away.
2 When I came, why was there no one?
　　When I called, why was there no one to answer?
Was my arm too short to ransom you?
　　Do I lack the strength to rescue you?
By a mere rebuke I dry up the sea,
　　I turn rivers into a desert;
their fish rot for lack of water
　　and die of thirst.
3 I clothe the sky with darkness
　　and make sackcloth its covering."

4 The Sovereign LORD has given me an instructed
　　　tongue,
　　to know the word that sustains the weary.
He wakens me morning by morning,
　　wakens my ear to listen like one being taught.
5 The Sovereign LORD has opened my ears,
　　and I have not been rebellious;
　　I have not drawn back.
6 I offered my back to those who beat me,
　　my cheeks to those who pulled out my beard;
I did not hide my face
　　from mocking and spitting.
7 Because the Sovereign LORD helps me,
　　I will not be disgraced.
Therefore have I set my face like flint,
　　and I know I will not be put to shame.
8 He who vindicates me is near.
　　Who then will bring charges against me?
　　Let us face each other!
Who is my accuser?
　　Let him confront me!
9 It is the Sovereign LORD who helps me.
　　Who is he that will condemn me?
They will all wear out like a garment;
　　the moths will eat them up.

10 Who among you fears the LORD
　　and obeys the word of his servant?

Gross!

"Eat their own flesh"
and "drunk on their
own blood." Isaiah has
quite a way with
words, doesn't he?
But read all of Isaiah
49:24–26 and you'll
see that he's saying
that God will fight for
his people, and their
enemies will be over-
come with hunger and
thirst.

Let him who walks in the dark,
   who has no light,
trust in the name of the LORD
   and rely on his God.
¹¹ But now, all you who light fires
   and provide yourselves with flaming torches,
go, walk in the light of your fires
   and of the torches you have set ablaze.
This is what you shall receive from my hand:
   You will lie down in torment.

Everlasting Salvation for Zion

51 "Listen to me, you who pursue righteousness
   and who seek the LORD:
Look to the rock from which you were cut
   and to the quarry from which you were hewn;
² look to Abraham, your father,
   and to Sarah, who gave you birth.
When I called him he was but one,
   and I blessed him and made him many.
³ The LORD will surely comfort Zion
   and will look with compassion on all her ruins;
he will make her deserts like Eden,
   her wastelands like the garden of the LORD.
Joy and gladness will be found in her,
   thanksgiving and the sound of singing.

⁴ "Listen to me, my people;
   hear me, my nation:
The law will go out from me;
   my justice will become a light to the nations.
⁵ My righteousness draws near speedily,
   my salvation is on the way,
   and my arm will bring justice to the nations.
The islands will look to me
   and wait in hope for my arm.
⁶ Lift up your eyes to the heavens,
   look at the earth beneath;
the heavens will vanish like smoke,
   the earth will wear out like a garment
   and its inhabitants die like flies.
But my salvation will last forever,
   my righteousness will never fail.

⁷ "Hear me, you who know what is right,
   you people who have my law in your hearts:
Do not fear the reproach of men
   or be terrified by their insults.
⁸ For the moth will eat them up like a garment;
   the worm will devour them like wool.
But my righteousness will last forever,
   my salvation through all generations."

⁹ Awake, awake! Clothe yourself with strength,
   O arm of the LORD;
awake, as in days gone by,
   as in generations of old.
Was it not you who cut Rahab to pieces,

Get a Load of This...

Ever been referred to as a "chip off the old block"? That saying is similar to Isaiah 51:1–2. You're not only a chip off your parents' block. As a Christian, you are also cut from the same stone as Abraham, the father of all who have faith.

who pierced that monster through?
10 Was it not you who dried up the sea,
　　the waters of the great deep,
who made a road in the depths of the sea
　　so that the redeemed might cross over?
11 The ransomed of the LORD will return.
　　They will enter Zion with singing;
　　everlasting joy will crown their heads.
Gladness and joy will overtake them,
　　and sorrow and sighing will flee away.

12 "I, even I, am he who comforts you.
　　Who are you that you fear mortal men,
　　the sons of men, who are but grass,
13 that you forget the LORD your Maker,
　　who stretched out the heavens
　　and laid the foundations of the earth,
that you live in constant terror every day
　　because of the wrath of the oppressor,
　　who is bent on destruction?
For where is the wrath of the oppressor?
14 　The cowering prisoners will soon be set free;
　　they will not die in their dungeon,
　　nor will they lack bread.
15 For I am the LORD your God,
　　who churns up the sea so that its waves roar—
　　the LORD Almighty is his name.
16 I have put my words in your mouth
　　and covered you with the shadow of my hand—
　　I who set the heavens in place,
　　who laid the foundations of the earth,
　　and who say to Zion, 'You are my people.' "

The Cup of the LORD's Wrath

17 Awake, awake!
　　Rise up, O Jerusalem,
you who have drunk from the hand of the LORD
　　the cup of his wrath,
you who have drained to its dregs
　　the goblet that makes men stagger.
18 Of all the sons she bore
　　there was none to guide her;
of all the sons she reared
　　there was none to take her by the hand.
19 These double calamities have come upon you—
　　who can comfort you?—
ruin and destruction, famine and sword—
　　who can[a] console you?
20 Your sons have fainted;
　　they lie at the head of every street,
　　like antelope caught in a net.
They are filled with the wrath of the LORD
　　and the rebuke of your God.

21 Therefore hear this, you afflicted one,
　　made drunk, but not with wine.

a 19 Dead Sea Scrolls, Septuagint, Vulgate and Syriac; Masoretic Text / how can I

Gross!

Check out Isaiah 51:6. The wicked will "die like flies" during God's judgment at the end of the world. How would *you* like to die? At a good old age? Or like a fly, being ker-splatted by a giant fly-swatter? Hmmm. That's not a tough choice . . .

22 This is what your Sovereign LORD says,
    your God, who defends his people:
"See, I have taken out of your hand
    the cup that made you stagger;
from that cup, the goblet of my wrath,
    you will never drink again.
23 I will put it into the hands of your
        tormentors,
    who said to you,
    'Fall prostrate that we may walk over
        you.'
And you made your back like the
        ground,
    like a street to be walked over."

52 Awake, awake, O Zion,
    clothe yourself with strength.
    Put on your garments of
        splendor,
O Jerusalem, the holy city.
The uncircumcised and defiled
    will not enter you again.
2 Shake off your dust;
    rise up, sit enthroned, O Jerusalem.
Free yourself from the chains on your
        neck,
O captive Daughter of Zion.

3 For this is what the LORD says:

"You were sold for nothing,
    and without money you will be
        redeemed."

4 For this is what the Sovereign LORD
says:

"At first my people went down to
        Egypt to live;
    lately, Assyria has oppressed them.

5 "And now what do I have here?" declares the LORD.

"For my people have been taken away
        for nothing,
    and those who rule them mock,[a]"
                    declares the LORD.
"And all day long
    my name is constantly blasphemed.
6 Therefore my people will know my
        name;
    therefore in that day they will know
    that it is I who foretold it.
    Yes, it is I."

a 5 Dead Sea Scrolls and Vulgate; Masoretic Text wail

Fear God, Not Grass

READ ISAIAH 51:12–13

Ever had a bully pick on you at school? No matter how big or pushy or loudmouthed a bully is, you don't need to be afraid of him. Remember, bullies are like grass—just cow chow. "Who are you that you fear mortal men, the sons of men, who are but grass" (Isaiah 51:12)? Bullies will come and they will go. The best part is when they go. In the meantime, try to live at peace with others, as long as that doesn't mean compromising your faith. And never return evil for evil (see Romans 12:17). Take your fears to God, and don't hesitate to tell an adult if you're being shoved around. Keep on obeying God no matter what some pushy kid says. And you know, this is true even with people you love. Don't let their opinions wreck your day. Put God first, and don't be afraid to stand up for the truth.

Your next reading is on page 930.

7 How beautiful on the mountains
  are the feet of those who bring
    good news,
who proclaim peace,
  who bring good tidings,
  who proclaim salvation,
who say to Zion,
  "Your God reigns!"
8 Listen! Your watchmen lift up their
    voices;
  together they shout for joy.
When the LORD returns to Zion,
  they will see it with their own eyes.
9 Burst into songs of joy together,
  you ruins of Jerusalem,
for the LORD has comforted his people,
  he has redeemed Jerusalem.
10 The LORD will lay bare his holy arm
  in the sight of all the nations,
and all the ends of the earth will see
  the salvation of our God.

11 Depart, depart, go out from there!
  Touch no unclean thing!

Come out from it and be pure,
  you who carry the vessels of the LORD.
12 But you will not leave in haste
  or go in flight;
for the LORD will go before you,
  the God of Israel will be your rear
    guard.

The Suffering and Glory of the Servant

13 See, my servant will act wisely[a];
  he will be raised and lifted up and
    highly exalted.
14 Just as there were many who were
    appalled at him[b]—
  his appearance was so disfigured
    beyond that of any man
  and his form marred beyond human
    likeness—
15 so will he sprinkle many nations,[c]

---

[a] 13 Or will prosper   [b] 14 Hebrew you   [c] 15 Hebrew;
Septuagint so will many nations marvel at him

Death of the Messiah

READ ISAIAH 52:13—53:12

It's sometimes hard—even for the experts—to predict whether to-morrow will be a good beach day or not. But that's nothing! Try predicting what the Messiah, the Savior, will be like 700 years before he's born! Isaiah did it with the Holy Spirit's help. A few highlights: the Messiah would be "despised and rejected by men" (Isaiah 53:3). Jesus *was* (see Mark 15:29–32). He would be "pierced for our transgressions [sins]" (Isaiah 53:5). Jesus *was* pierced—when a Roman soldier pierced his side with a spear after he died on the cross (see John 19:34). He would heal us "by his wounds" (Isaiah 53:5). Jesus did *exactly* that (see 1 Peter 2:24). There are many more prophecies here, but the main point is that Jesus "bore [our] sin" when he died (Isaiah 53:12). We sin because that's unfortunately what imperfect, messed-up human beings do. Even though the penalty for sin is spiritual death, we can "get out of jail free." How? By accepting that Jesus took our punishment for us, and letting God rule in our lives. Sound like a good deal? Then go for it!

Your next reading is on page 932.

and kings will shut their mouths
　　because of him.
For what they were not told, they will
　　see,
　and what they have not heard, they
　　will understand.

53

Who has believed our message
and to whom has the arm of
the LORD been revealed?
2 He grew up before him like a
tender shoot,
　and like a root out of dry ground.
He had no beauty or majesty to attract
　　us to him,
　nothing in his appearance that we
　　should desire him.
3 He was despised and rejected by men,
　a man of sorrows, and familiar with
　　suffering.
Like one from whom men hide their
　　faces
　he was despised, and we esteemed
　　him not.

4 Surely he took up our infirmities
　and carried our sorrows,
yet we considered him stricken by God,
　smitten by him, and afflicted.
5 But he was pierced for our
　　transgressions,
　he was crushed for our iniquities;
the punishment that brought us peace
　　was upon him,
　and by his wounds we are healed.
6 We all, like sheep, have gone astray,
　each of us has turned to his own
　　way;
and the LORD has laid on him
　the iniquity of us all.

7 He was oppressed and afflicted,
　yet he did not open his mouth;
he was led like a lamb to the slaughter,
　and as a sheep before her shearers is
　　silent,
　so he did not open his mouth.
8 By oppression[a] and judgment he was
　　taken away.
　And who can speak of his
　　descendants?
For he was cut off from the land of the
　　living;
　for the transgression of my people
　　he was stricken.[b]
9 He was assigned a grave with the
　　wicked,
　and with the rich in his death,

though he had done no violence,
　nor was any deceit in his mouth.
10 Yet it was the LORD's will to crush him
　　and cause him to suffer,
　and though the LORD makes[c] his life
　　a guilt offering,
he will see his offspring and prolong
　　his days,
　and the will of the LORD will prosper
　　in his hand.
11 After the suffering of his soul,
　he will see the light ⌊of life⌋[d] and be
　　satisfied[e];
by his knowledge[f] my righteous
　　servant will justify many,
　and he will bear their iniquities.
12 Therefore I will give him a portion
　　among the great,[g]
　and he will divide the spoils with the
　　strong,[h]
because he poured out his life unto
　　death,
　and was numbered with the
　　transgressors.
For he bore the sin of many,
　and made intercession for the
　　transgressors.

The Future Glory of Zion

54

"Sing, O barren woman,
you who never bore a child;
burst into song, shout for joy,
you who were never in labor;
because more are the children of the
　　desolate woman
　than of her who has a husband,"
　　　　　　　　　　says the LORD.
2 "Enlarge the place of your tent,
　stretch your tent curtains wide,
　do not hold back;
lengthen your cords,
　strengthen your stakes.
3 For you will spread out to the right
　　and to the left;
　your descendants will dispossess
　　nations
　and settle in their desolate cities.

---

a 8 Or From arrest　b 8 Or away. / Yet who of his
generation considered / that he was cut off from the land of
the living / for the transgression of my people, / to whom the
blow was due?　c 10 Hebrew though you make
d 11 Dead Sea Scrolls (see also Septuagint); Masoretic Text
does not have the light ⌊of life⌋.　e 11 Or (with Masoretic
Text) 11 He will see the result of the suffering of his soul / and
be satisfied　f 11 Or by knowledge of him　g 12 Or many
h 12 Or numerous

4 "Do not be afraid; you will not suffer
　　shame.
　Do not fear disgrace; you will not be
　　humiliated.
You will forget the shame of your youth
　and remember no more the
　　reproach of your widowhood.
5 For your Maker is your husband—
　the LORD Almighty is his name—
the Holy One of Israel is your
　　Redeemer;
　he is called the God of all the earth.
6 The LORD will call you back
　as if you were a wife deserted and
　　distressed in spirit—
a wife who married young,
　only to be rejected," says your God.
7 "For a brief moment I abandoned you,
　but with deep compassion I will
　　bring you back.
8 In a surge of anger
　I hid my face from you for a
　　moment,
but with everlasting kindness
　I will have compassion on you,"
　says the LORD your Redeemer.

9 "To me this is like the days of Noah,
　when I swore that the waters of
　　Noah would never again cover
　　the earth.
So now I have sworn not to be angry
　with you,
　never to rebuke you again.
10 Though the mountains be shaken
　and the hills be removed,
yet my unfailing love for you will not
　　be shaken
　nor my covenant of peace be
　　removed,"
　says the LORD, who has compassion
　on you.

11 "O afflicted city, lashed by storms and
　not comforted,
　I will build you with stones of
　　turquoise, a
　your foundations with sapphires. b
12 I will make your battlements of rubies,
　your gates of sparkling jewels,
　and all your walls of precious stones.
13 All your sons will be taught by the LORD,

a 11 The meaning of the Hebrew for this word is uncertain.
b 11 Or lapis lazuli

No Lightning Bolts

READ ISAIAH 54:9–10

Many people picture God as a cranky, old, bearded guy sitting on a cloud, lightning bolt in hand, ready to toast anyone who ticks him off. That's probably because the Old Testament has many stories where God did a job on the wicked. However, if you're a Christian, you shouldn't fear God's judgment. As God said, "I have sworn not to be angry with you, never to rebuke you again" (Isaiah 54:9). God is a kind and loving Father whom you can always turn to for help. His wrath is not for you. No lightning bolts will ever come your way. Even when you make mistakes, if you ask God's forgiveness, he always accepts you where you're at. He may discipline you to keep you on track (see Hebrews 12:4–11), but he always does it out of love, not anger.

Your next reading is on page 933.

and great will be your children's
  peace.
14 In righteousness you will be
  established:
Tyranny will be far from you;
  you will have nothing to fear.
Terror will be far removed;
  it will not come near you.
15 If anyone does attack you, it will not
  be my doing;
whoever attacks you will surrender
  to you.

16 "See, it is I who created the blacksmith
  who fans the coals into flame
and forges a weapon fit for its work.
And it is I who have created the
  destroyer to work havoc;
17   no weapon forged against you will
  prevail,
and you will refute every tongue
  that accuses you.
This is the heritage of the servants of
  the LORD,
and this is their vindication from
  me,"
                    declares the LORD.

Invitation to the Thirsty

55 "Come, all you who are thirsty,
  come to the waters;
and you who have no money,
  come, buy and eat!
Come, buy wine and milk
  without money and without cost.
2 Why spend money on what is not
  bread,
and your labor on what does not
  satisfy?
Listen, listen to me, and eat what is
  good,
and your soul will delight in the
  richest of fare.
3 Give ear and come to me;
  hear me, that your soul may live.
I will make an everlasting covenant
  with you,
my faithful love promised to David.
4 See, I have made him a witness to the
  peoples,
a leader and commander of the
  peoples.
5 Surely you will summon nations you
  know not,

Nations You Know Not

READ ISAIAH 55:1–5

For the first time in history you can visit all the cultures of the world
while sitting in your living room. Watch a news program and you'll
find out what's happening all over the world, within hours—sometimes even minutes—after it happens. You can see amazing rescues,
typhoons, earthquakes or far out situations in far off nations
you never heard of before. It's a good reminder that there are
millions of people out there—people God created and
loves—who need to hear the gospel. If your church has
missionaries, get involved. Pray for them, give money or write
them letters of encouragement. By helping Christians
who are preaching the gospel, you too will be "a
witness to the peoples" (verse 4). You might not
know a lot about some of these countries, but
hey—that's half the fun! "Surely you will summon nations you know not" (verse 5).

Your next reading is on page 934.

and nations that do not know you
   will hasten to you,
because of the LORD your God,
   the Holy One of Israel,
   for he has endowed you with
     splendor."

6 Seek the LORD while he may be
   found;
   call on him while he is near.
7 Let the wicked forsake his way
   and the evil man his thoughts.
Let him turn to the LORD, and he will
   have mercy on him,
   and to our God, for he will freely
     pardon.

8 "For my thoughts are not your
   thoughts,
   neither are your ways my ways,"
                declares the LORD.
9 "As the heavens are higher than the
   earth,
   so are my ways higher than your
   ways
   and my thoughts than your
   thoughts.

10 As the rain and the snow
   come down from heaven,
   and do not return to it
   without watering the earth
   and making it bud and flourish,
   so that it yields seed for the sower
     and bread for the eater,
11 so is my word that goes out from my
   mouth:
   It will not return to me empty,
   but will accomplish what I desire
   and achieve the purpose for which I
     sent it.
12 You will go out in joy
   and be led forth in peace;
the mountains and hills
   will burst into song before you,
and all the trees of the field
   will clap their hands.
13 Instead of the thornbush will grow the
   pine tree,
   and instead of briers the myrtle will
   grow.
This will be for the LORD's renown,
   for an everlasting sign,
   which will not be destroyed."

GET SMARTER

High Ways, High Thoughts

READ ISAIAH 55:6–11

What would you think if an ant walked up and said you were doing things all wrong? Probably, "What do *you* know? Your brain is even smaller than a pea!" Compared to God, we have pea-brains, too. His ways and thoughts are far, *far* higher than ours (see verse 9). Sure, we're surrounded by the world and its "natural" way of thinking, so we can be tempted to think the world's ways make more sense than God's ways. But, as men of God, we should follow God's Word rather than trying to figure things out in our little ant-like brains. We may not always understand what God is up to, because God's ways are far higher than our ways—just as our ways are far higher than those of an ant—but we just need to trust that God has our best interests in mind.

Your next reading is on page 937.

Salvation for Others

56

This is what the LORD says:

"Maintain justice
  and do what is right,
for my salvation is close at hand
  and my righteousness will soon be
    revealed.
2 Blessed is the man who does this,
  the man who holds it fast,
who keeps the Sabbath without
    desecrating it,
  and keeps his hand from doing any
    evil."

3 Let no foreigner who has bound
    himself to the LORD say,
  "The LORD will surely exclude me
    from his people."
And let not any eunuch complain,
  "I am only a dry tree."

4 For this is what the LORD says:

"To the eunuchs who keep my
    Sabbaths,
  who choose what pleases me
  and hold fast to my covenant—
5 to them I will give within my temple
    and its walls
  a memorial and a name
  better than sons and daughters;
I will give them an everlasting name
  that will not be cut off.
6 And foreigners who bind themselves to
    the LORD
  to serve him,
to love the name of the LORD,
  and to worship him,
all who keep the Sabbath without
    desecrating it
  and who hold fast to my covenant—
7 these I will bring to my holy mountain
  and give them joy in my house of
    prayer.
Their burnt offerings and sacrifices
  will be accepted on my altar;
for my house will be called
  a house of prayer for all nations."
8 The Sovereign LORD declares—
  he who gathers the exiles of Israel:
"I will gather still others to them
  besides those already gathered."

God's Accusation Against the Wicked

9 Come, all you beasts of the field,
  come and devour, all you beasts of
    the forest!
10 Israel's watchmen are blind,
  they all lack knowledge;
they are all mute dogs,
  they cannot bark;
they lie around and dream,
  they love to sleep.
11 They are dogs with mighty appetites;
  they never have enough.
They are shepherds who lack
    understanding;
  they all turn to their own way,
  each seeks his own gain.
12 "Come," each one cries, "let me get
    wine!
Let us drink our fill of beer!
And tomorrow will be like today,
  or even far better."

57

The righteous perish,
  and no one ponders it in his
    heart;
  devout men are taken away,
and no one understands
that the righteous are taken away
  to be spared from evil.
2 Those who walk uprightly
  enter into peace;
  they find rest as they lie in death.

3 "But you—come here, you sons of a
    sorceress,
  you offspring of adulterers and
    prostitutes!
4 Whom are you mocking?
  At whom do you sneer
  and stick out your tongue?
Are you not a brood of rebels,
  the offspring of liars?
5 You burn with lust among the oaks
  and under every spreading tree;
you sacrifice your children in the ravines
  and under the overhanging crags.
6 ⌞The idols⌟ among the smooth stones
    of the ravines are your portion;
  they, they are your lot.
Yes, to them you have poured out
    drink offerings
  and offered grain offerings.
In the light of these things, should I
    relent?
7 You have made your bed on a high
    and lofty hill;
  there you went up to offer your
    sacrifices.
8 Behind your doors and your doorposts
  you have put your pagan symbols.
Forsaking me, you uncovered your bed,

you climbed into it and opened it
wide;
you made a pact with those whose
beds you love,
and you looked on their nakedness.
⁹You went to Molech[a] with olive oil
and increased your perfumes.
You sent your ambassadors[b] far away;
you descended to the grave[c] itself!
¹⁰You were wearied by all your ways,
but you would not say, 'It is
hopeless.'
You found renewal of your strength,
and so you did not faint.

¹¹ "Whom have you so dreaded and
feared
that you have been false to me,
and have neither remembered me
nor pondered this in your hearts?
Is it not because I have long been silent
that you do not fear me?
¹²I will expose your righteousness and
your works,
and they will not benefit you.
¹³When you cry out for help,
let your collection ₍of idols₎ save you!
The wind will carry all of them off,
a mere breath will blow them away.
But the man who makes me his refuge
will inherit the land
and possess my holy mountain."

Comfort for the Contrite

¹⁴And it will be said:

"Build up, build up, prepare the road!
Remove the obstacles out of the way
of my people."
¹⁵For this is what the high and lofty One
says—
he who lives forever, whose name is
holy:
"I live in a high and holy place,
but also with him who is contrite
and lowly in spirit,
to revive the spirit of the lowly
and to revive the heart of the contrite.
¹⁶I will not accuse forever,
nor will I always be angry,
for then the spirit of man would grow
faint before me—
the breath of man that I have
created.
¹⁷I was enraged by his sinful greed;
I punished him, and hid my face in
anger,
yet he kept on in his willful ways.

¹⁸I have seen his ways, but I will heal him;
I will guide him and restore comfort
to him,
¹⁹ creating praise on the lips of the
mourners in Israel.
Peace, peace, to those far and near,"
says the LORD. "And I will heal them."
²⁰But the wicked are like the tossing sea,
which cannot rest,
whose waves cast up mire and mud.
²¹ "There is no peace," says my God, "for
the wicked."

True Fasting

58 "Shout it aloud, do not hold
back.
Raise your voice like a
trumpet.
Declare to my people their rebellion
and to the house of Jacob their sins.
²For day after day they seek me out;
they seem eager to know my ways,
as if they were a nation that does what
is right
and has not forsaken the commands
of its God.
They ask me for just decisions
and seem eager for God to come
near them.
³'Why have we fasted,' they say,
'and you have not seen it?
Why have we humbled ourselves,
and you have not noticed?'

"Yet on the day of your fasting, you do
as you please
and exploit all your workers.
⁴Your fasting ends in quarreling and
strife,
and in striking each other with
wicked fists.
You cannot fast as you do today
and expect your voice to be heard
on high.
⁵Is this the kind of fast I have chosen,
only a day for a man to humble
himself?
Is it only for bowing one's head like a
reed
and for lying on sackcloth and ashes?
Is that what you call a fast,
a day acceptable to the LORD?

⁶"Is not this the kind of fasting I have
chosen:
to loose the chains of injustice

---

[a] 9 Or to the king   [b] 9 Or idols   [c] 9 Hebrew Sheol

and untie the cords of the yoke,
  to set the oppressed free
  and break every yoke?
7 Is it not to share your food with the
    hungry
  and to provide the poor wanderer
    with shelter—
  when you see the naked, to clothe
    him,
  and not to turn away from your own
    flesh and blood?
8 Then your light will break forth like the
    dawn,
  and your healing will quickly appear;
  then your righteousness[a] will go
    before you,
  and the glory of the LORD will be
    your rear guard.
9 Then you will call, and the LORD will
    answer;
  you will cry for help, and he will say:
    Here am I.

"If you do away with the yoke of
    oppression,
  with the pointing finger and
    malicious talk,

10 and if you spend yourselves in behalf
    of the hungry
  and satisfy the needs of the
    oppressed,
  then your light will rise in the darkness,
  and your night will become like the
    noonday.
11 The LORD will guide you always;
  he will satisfy your needs in a sun-
    scorched land
  and will strengthen your frame.
  You will be like a well-watered garden,
  like a spring whose waters never fail.
12 Your people will rebuild the ancient
    ruins
  and will raise up the age-old
    foundations;
  you will be called Repairer of Broken
    Walls,
  Restorer of Streets with Dwellings.

13 "If you keep your feet from breaking
    the Sabbath
  and from doing as you please on my
    holy day,
  if you call the Sabbath a delight

a 8 Or your righteous One

In God's "Fast" Lane

READ ISAIAH 58:3–11

Have you ever been accused of "going through the motions"? Hopefully not. That means you're just doing something to keep up appearances but your heart really isn't in it. It's like going to church every weekend but not obeying God the rest of the week. This is what God accused the Jews of doing. They appeared to be obeying God by fasting, but they weren't really in the fast lane: loosening "the chains of injustice" and setting "the oppressed free" (verse 6). They expected God to answer their prayers because they were doing the right religious things, but they didn't want to obey him with the rest of their lives— like treating the needy the right way. What they didn't realize is that God isn't pleased by a bunch of religious mumbo jumbo. What matters to him is seeing us respond to each other with grace, mercy and love—just as God responds to us.

Your next reading is on page 949.

and the Lord's holy day honorable,
and if you honor it by not going your
own way
and not doing as you please or
speaking idle words,
¹⁴ then you will find your joy in the Lord,
and I will cause you to ride on the
heights of the land
and to feast on the inheritance of
your father Jacob."
The mouth of the Lord
has spoken.

Sin, Confession and Redemption

59 Surely the arm of the Lord is
not too short to save,
nor his ear too dull to hear.
² But your iniquities have
separated
you from your God;
your sins have hidden his face from you,
so that he will not hear.
³ For your hands are stained with blood,
your fingers with guilt.
Your lips have spoken lies,
and your tongue mutters wicked
things.
⁴ No one calls for justice;
no one pleads his case with integrity.
They rely on empty arguments and
speak lies;
they conceive trouble and give birth
to evil.
⁵ They hatch the eggs of vipers
and spin a spider's web.
Whoever eats their eggs will die,
and when one is broken, an adder is
hatched.
⁶ Their cobwebs are useless for clothing;
they cannot cover themselves with
what they make.
Their deeds are evil deeds,
and acts of violence are in their hands.
⁷ Their feet rush into sin;
they are swift to shed innocent
blood.
Their thoughts are evil thoughts;
ruin and destruction mark their ways.
⁸ The way of peace they do not know;
there is no justice in their paths.
They have turned them into crooked
roads;
no one who walks in them will know
peace.

⁹ So justice is far from us,
and righteousness does not reach us.

We look for light, but all is darkness;
for brightness, but we walk in deep
shadows.
¹⁰ Like the blind we grope along the wall,
feeling our way like men without
eyes.
At midday we stumble as if it were
twilight;
among the strong, we are like the
dead.
¹¹ We all growl like bears;
we moan mournfully like doves.
We look for justice, but find none;
for deliverance, but it is far away.

¹² For our offenses are many in your sight,
and our sins testify against us.
Our offenses are ever with us,
and we acknowledge our iniquities:
¹³ rebellion and treachery against the Lord,
turning our backs on our God,
fomenting oppression and revolt,
uttering lies our hearts have
conceived.
¹⁴ So justice is driven back,
and righteousness stands at a
distance;
truth has stumbled in the streets,
honesty cannot enter.
¹⁵ Truth is nowhere to be found,
and whoever shuns evil becomes a
prey.

The Lord looked and was displeased
that there was no justice.
¹⁶ He saw that there was no one,
he was appalled that there was no
one to intervene;
so his own arm worked salvation for
him,
and his own righteousness sustained
him.
¹⁷ He put on righteousness as his
breastplate,
and the helmet of salvation on his
head;
he put on the garments of vengeance
and wrapped himself in zeal as in a
cloak.
¹⁸ According to what they have done,
so will he repay
wrath to his enemies
and retribution to his foes;
he will repay the islands their due.
¹⁹ From the west, men will fear the name
of the Lord,
and from the rising of the sun, they
will revere his glory.

For he will come like a pent-up flood
  that the breath of the LORD drives
    along. *a*

20 "The Redeemer will come to Zion,
  to those in Jacob who repent of
    their sins,"
                       declares the LORD.

21 "As for me, this is my covenant with
them," says the LORD. "My Spirit, who is on
you, and my words that I have put in your
mouth will not depart from your mouth, or
from the mouths of your children, or from
the mouths of their descendants from this
time on and forever," says the LORD.

The Glory of Zion

60 "Arise, shine, for your light
  has come,
  and the glory of the LORD rises
    upon you.
2 See, darkness covers the earth
  and thick darkness is over the
    peoples,
but the LORD rises upon you
  and his glory appears over you.
3 Nations will come to your light,
  and kings to the brightness of your
    dawn.

4 "Lift up your eyes and look about you:
  All assemble and come to you;
your sons come from afar,
  and your daughters are carried on
    the arm.
5 Then you will look and be radiant,
  your heart will throb and swell with
    joy;
the wealth on the seas will be brought
    to you,
  to you the riches of the nations will
    come.
6 Herds of camels will cover your land,
  young camels of Midian and Ephah.
And all from Sheba will come,
  bearing gold and incense
  and proclaiming the praise of the
    LORD.
7 All Kedar's flocks will be gathered to
    you,
  the rams of Nebaioth will serve you;
they will be accepted as offerings on
    my altar,
  and I will adorn my glorious temple.

8 "Who are these that fly along like
    clouds,
  like doves to their nests?

9 Surely the islands look to me;
  in the lead are the ships of Tarshish, *b*
bringing your sons from afar,
  with their silver and gold,
to the honor of the LORD your God,
  the Holy One of Israel,
  for he has endowed you with
    splendor.

10 "Foreigners will rebuild your walls,
  and their kings will serve you.
Though in anger I struck you,
  in favor I will show you compassion.
11 Your gates will always stand open,
  they will never be shut, day or night,
so that men may bring you the wealth
    of the nations—
  their kings led in triumphal
    procession.
12 For the nation or kingdom that will not
    serve you will perish;
  it will be utterly ruined.

13 "The glory of Lebanon will come to
    you,
  the pine, the fir and the cypress
    together,
to adorn the place of my sanctuary;
  and I will glorify the place of my feet.
14 The sons of your oppressors will come
    bowing before you;
  all who despise you will bow down
    at your feet
and will call you the City of the LORD,
  Zion of the Holy One of Israel.

15 "Although you have been forsaken and
    hated,
  with no one traveling through,
I will make you the everlasting pride
  and the joy of all generations.
16 You will drink the milk of nations
  and be nursed at royal breasts.
Then you will know that I, the LORD,
  am your Savior,
  your Redeemer, the Mighty One of
    Jacob.
17 Instead of bronze I will bring you gold,
  and silver in place of iron.
Instead of wood I will bring you bronze,
  and iron in place of stones.
I will make peace your governor
  and righteousness your ruler.
18 No longer will violence be heard in
    your land,

---

*a 19 Or When the enemy comes in like a flood, / the Spirit of
the LORD will put him to flight*   *b 9 Or the trading ships*

nor ruin or destruction within your
    borders,
but you will call your walls Salvation
    and your gates Praise.
19 The sun will no more be your light by
    day,
    nor will the brightness of the moon
        shine on you,
for the LORD will be your everlasting light,
    and your God will be your glory.
20 Your sun will never set again,
    and your moon will wane no more;
the LORD will be your everlasting light,
    and your days of sorrow will end.
21 Then will all your people be righteous
    and they will possess the land forever.
They are the shoot I have planted,
    the work of my hands,
    for the display of my splendor.
22 The least of you will become a
    thousand,
    the smallest a mighty nation.
I am the LORD;
    in its time I will do this swiftly."

The Year of the LORD's Favor

 The Spirit of the Sovereign LORD
        is on me,
        because the LORD has anointed
        me
to preach good news to the poor.
He has sent me to bind up the
        brokenhearted,
    to proclaim freedom for the captives
    and release from darkness for the
        prisoners, a
2 to proclaim the year of the LORD's favor
    and the day of vengeance of our God,
to comfort all who mourn,
3   and provide for those who grieve in
        Zion—
    to bestow on them a crown of beauty
        instead of ashes,
    the oil of gladness
        instead of mourning,
    and a garment of praise
        instead of a spirit of despair.

a 1 Hebrew; Septuagint the blind

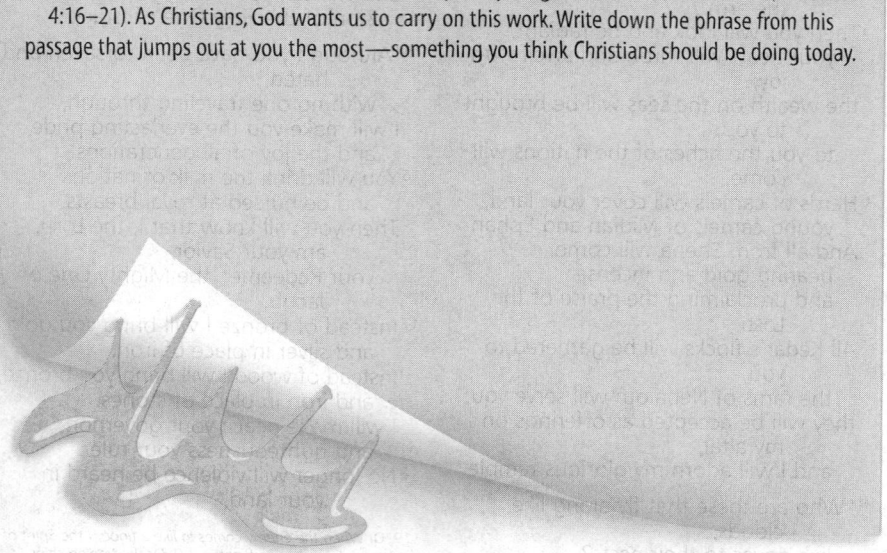

Make It Stick

READ ISAIAH 61:1–3

What a list of tasks! Isaiah 61:1–3 includes nearly everything Jesus did while on earth (see Luke 4:16–21). As Christians, God wants us to carry on this work. Write down the phrase from this passage that jumps out at you the most—something you think Christians should be doing today.

They will be called oaks of righteousness,
a planting of the Lord
for the display of his splendor.

4 They will rebuild the ancient ruins
and restore the places long devastated;
they will renew the ruined cities
that have been devastated for generations.
5 Aliens will shepherd your flocks;
foreigners will work your fields and vineyards.
6 And you will be called priests of the Lord,
you will be named ministers of our God.
You will feed on the wealth of nations,
and in their riches you will boast.

7 Instead of their shame
my people will receive a double portion,
and instead of disgrace
they will rejoice in their inheritance;
and so they will inherit a double portion in their
land,
and everlasting joy will be theirs.

8 "For I, the Lord, love justice;
I hate robbery and iniquity.
In my faithfulness I will reward them
and make an everlasting covenant with them.
9 Their descendants will be known among the
nations
and their offspring among the peoples.
All who see them will acknowledge
that they are a people the Lord has blessed."

10 I delight greatly in the Lord;
my soul rejoices in my God.
For he has clothed me with garments of salvation
and arrayed me in a robe of righteousness,
as a bridegroom adorns his head like a priest,
and as a bride adorns herself with her jewels.
11 For as the soil makes the sprout come up
and a garden causes seeds to grow,
so the Sovereign Lord will make righteousness and
praise
spring up before all nations.

Zion's New Name

62 For Zion's sake I will not keep silent,
for Jerusalem's sake I will not remain quiet,
till her righteousness shines out like the
dawn,
her salvation like a blazing torch.
2 The nations will see your righteousness,
and all kings your glory;
you will be called by a new name
that the mouth of the Lord will bestow.
3 You will be a crown of splendor in the Lord's hand,
a royal diadem in the hand of your God.
4 No longer will they call you Deserted,
or name your land Desolate.

Get a Load of This...

These "aliens" in Isaiah 61:5 were not creatures from a sci-fi TV show. *Aliens* here simply means "foreigners."

But you will be called Hephzibah,[a]
  and your land Beulah[b];
for the LORD will take delight in you,
  and your land will be married.
5 As a young man marries a maiden,
  so will your sons[c] marry you;
as a bridegroom rejoices over his bride,
  so will your God rejoice over you.

6 I have posted watchmen on your walls,
  O Jerusalem;
they will never be silent day or night.
You who call on the LORD,
  give yourselves no rest,
7 and give him no rest till he establishes
  Jerusalem
and makes her the praise of the
  earth.

8 The LORD has sworn by his right hand
  and by his mighty arm:
"Never again will I give your grain
  as food for your enemies,
and never again will foreigners drink
  the new wine
for which you have toiled;
9 but those who harvest it will eat it
  and praise the LORD,
and those who gather the grapes will
  drink it
in the courts of my sanctuary."

10 Pass through, pass through the gates!
  Prepare the way for the people.
Build up, build up the highway!
  Remove the stones.
Raise a banner for the nations.

11 The LORD has made proclamation
  to the ends of the earth:
"Say to the Daughter of Zion,
  'See, your Savior comes!
See, his reward is with him,
  and his recompense accompanies
  him.' "
12 They will be called the Holy People,
  the Redeemed of the LORD;
and you will be called Sought After,
  the City No Longer Deserted.

God's Day of Vengeance and Redemption

63 Who is this coming from
  Edom,
from Bozrah, with his
  garments stained crimson?
Who is this, robed in splendor,
  striding forward in the greatness of
  his strength?

"It is I, speaking in righteousness,
  mighty to save."

2 Why are your garments red,
  like those of one treading the
  winepress?

3 "I have trodden the winepress alone;
  from the nations no one was with
  me.
I trampled them in my anger
  and trod them down in my wrath;
their blood spattered my garments,
  and I stained all my clothing.
4 For the day of vengeance was in my
  heart,
and the year of my redemption has
  come.
5 I looked, but there was no one to help,
  I was appalled that no one gave
  support;
so my own arm worked salvation for
  me,
and my own wrath sustained me.
6 I trampled the nations in my anger;
  in my wrath I made them drunk
and poured their blood on the
  ground."

Praise and Prayer

7 I will tell of the kindnesses of the LORD,
  the deeds for which he is to be
  praised,
according to all the LORD has done
  for us—
yes, the many good things he has
  done
for the house of Israel,
  according to his compassion and
  many kindnesses.
8 He said, "Surely they are my people,
  sons who will not be false to me";
and so he became their Savior.
9 In all their distress he too was
  distressed,
and the angel of his presence saved
  them.
In his love and mercy he redeemed
  them;
he lifted them up and carried them
  all the days of old.
10 Yet they rebelled
  and grieved his Holy Spirit.
So he turned and became their enemy
  and he himself fought against them.

---

[a] 4 *Hephzibah* means *my delight is in her.* [b] 4 *Beulah* means *married.* [c] 5 Or *Builder*

11 Then his people recalled[a] the days of
  old,
    the days of Moses and his people—
  where is he who brought them
      through the sea,
    with the shepherd of his flock?
  Where is he who set
    his Holy Spirit among them,
12 who sent his glorious arm of power
    to be at Moses' right hand,
  who divided the waters before them,
    to gain for himself everlasting
      renown,
13 who led them through the depths?
  Like a horse in open country,
    they did not stumble;
14 like cattle that go down to the plain,
    they were given rest by the Spirit of
      the LORD.
  This is how you guided your people
    to make for yourself a glorious
      name.

15 Look down from heaven and see
    from your lofty throne, holy and
      glorious.
  Where are your zeal and your might?
    Your tenderness and compassion are
      withheld from us.
16 But you are our Father,
    though Abraham does not know us
      or Israel acknowledge us;
  you, O LORD, are our Father,
    our Redeemer from of old is your
      name.
17 Why, O LORD, do you make us wander
    from your ways
  and harden our hearts so we do not
      revere you?
  Return for the sake of your servants,
    the tribes that are your inheritance.
18 For a little while your people possessed
    your holy place,
  but now our enemies have trampled
    down your sanctuary.
19 We are yours from of old;
    but you have not ruled over them,
  they have not been called by your
    name.[b]

64 Oh, that you would rend the
  heavens and come down,
  that the mountains would
  tremble before you!
2 As when fire sets twigs ablaze
  and causes water to boil,

  come down to make your name
    known to your enemies
  and cause the nations to quake
    before you!
3 For when you did awesome things that
    we did not expect,
  you came down, and the mountains
    trembled before you.
4 Since ancient times no one has heard,
    no ear has perceived,
  no eye has seen any God besides you,
    who acts on behalf of those who
      wait for him.
5 You come to the help of those who
    gladly do right,
  who remember your ways.
  But when we continued to sin against
    them,
    you were angry.
  How then can we be saved?
6 All of us have become like one who is
    unclean,
  and all our righteous acts are like
    filthy rags;
  we all shrivel up like a leaf,
    and like the wind our sins sweep us
      away.
7 No one calls on your name
    or strives to lay hold of you;
  for you have hidden your face from us
    and made us waste away because of
      our sins.

8 Yet, O LORD, you are our Father.
  We are the clay, you are the potter;
    we are all the work of your hand.
9 Do not be angry beyond measure,
    O LORD;
  do not remember our sins forever.
  Oh, look upon us, we pray,
    for we are all your people.
10 Your sacred cities have become a
    desert;
  even Zion is a desert, Jerusalem a
    desolation.
11 Our holy and glorious temple, where
    our fathers praised you,
  has been burned with fire,
    and all that we treasured lies in
      ruins.
12 After all this, O LORD, will you hold
    yourself back?
  Will you keep silent and punish us
    beyond measure?

a 11 Or But may he recall   b 19 Or We are like those you
have never ruled, / like those never called by your name

Judgment and Salvation

65 "I revealed myself to those
who did not ask for me;
I was found by those who did
not seek me.
To a nation that did not call on my
name,
I said, 'Here am I, here am I.'
2 All day long I have held out my hands
to an obstinate people,
who walk in ways not good,
pursuing their own imaginations—
3 a people who continually provoke me
to my very face,
offering sacrifices in gardens
and burning incense on altars of
brick;
4 who sit among the graves
and spend their nights keeping
secret vigil;
who eat the flesh of pigs,
and whose pots hold broth of
unclean meat;
5 who say, 'Keep away; don't come near
me,
for I am too sacred for you!'
Such people are smoke in my nostrils,
a fire that keeps burning all day.

6 "See, it stands written before me:
I will not keep silent but will pay
back in full;
I will pay it back into their laps—
7 both your sins and the sins of your
fathers,"
says the LORD.
"Because they burned sacrifices on the
mountains
and defied me on the hills,
I will measure into their laps
the full payment for their former
deeds."

8 This is what the LORD says:

"As when juice is still found in a cluster
of grapes
and men say, 'Don't destroy it,
there is yet some good in it,'
so will I do in behalf of my servants;
I will not destroy them all.
9 I will bring forth descendants from
Jacob,
and from Judah those who will
possess my mountains;
my chosen people will inherit them,
and there will my servants live.
10 Sharon will become a pasture for flocks,

and the Valley of Achor a resting
place for herds,
for my people who seek me.

11 "But as for you who forsake the LORD
and forget my holy mountain,
who spread a table for Fortune
and fill bowls of mixed wine for
Destiny,
12 I will destine you for the sword,
and you will all bend down for the
slaughter;
for I called but you did not answer,
I spoke but you did not listen.
You did evil in my sight
and chose what displeases me."

13 Therefore this is what the Sovereign
LORD says:

"My servants will eat,
but you will go hungry;
my servants will drink,
but you will go thirsty;
my servants will rejoice,
but you will be put to shame.
14 My servants will sing
out of the joy of their hearts,
but you will cry out
from anguish of heart
and wail in brokenness of spirit.
15 You will leave your name
to my chosen ones as a curse;
the Sovereign LORD will put you to
death,
but to his servants he will give
another name.
16 Whoever invokes a blessing in the land
will do so by the God of truth;
he who takes an oath in the land
will swear by the God of truth.
For the past troubles will be forgotten
and hidden from my eyes.

New Heavens and a New Earth

17 "Behold, I will create
new heavens and a new earth.
The former things will not be
remembered,
nor will they come to mind.
18 But be glad and rejoice forever
in what I will create,
for I will create Jerusalem to be a delight
and its people a joy.
19 I will rejoice over Jerusalem
and take delight in my people;
the sound of weeping and of crying
will be heard in it no more.

20 "Never again will there be in it
    an infant who lives but a few days,
    or an old man who does not live out
       his years;
  he who dies at a hundred
    will be thought a mere youth;
  he who fails to reach[a] a hundred
    will be considered accursed.
21 They will build houses and dwell in
       them;
  they will plant vineyards and eat
     their fruit.
22 No longer will they build houses and
     others live in them,

or plant and others eat.
For as the days of a tree,
  so will be the days of my people;
my chosen ones will long enjoy
  the works of their hands.
23 They will not toil in vain
    or bear children doomed to
       misfortune;
for they will be a people blessed by the
  LORD,
  they and their descendants with
     them.
24 Before they call I will answer;

a 20 Or / the sinner who reaches

Make It Stick

READ ISAIAH 65:17–25

Can you imagine people who are 100 years old being considered young? That's what Isaiah 65:20 says life will be like when God creates new heavens and a new earth, a place without sin and evil. After you read through Isaiah 65:17–25, write down your favorite part about the age to come.

while they are still speaking I will
hear.
25 The wolf and the lamb will feed
together,
and the lion will eat straw like the
ox,
but dust will be the serpent's food.
They will neither harm nor destroy
on all my holy mountain,"
says the LORD.

Judgment and Hope

66 This is what the LORD says:

"Heaven is my throne,
and the earth is my footstool.
Where is the house you will build for
me?
Where will my resting place be?
2 Has not my hand made all these
things,
and so they came into being?"
declares the LORD.

"This is the one I esteem:
he who is humble and contrite in
spirit,
and trembles at my word.
3 But whoever sacrifices a bull
is like one who kills a man,
and whoever offers a lamb,
like one who breaks a dog's neck;
whoever makes a grain offering
is like one who presents pig's blood,
and whoever burns memorial incense,
like one who worships an idol.
They have chosen their own ways,
and their souls delight in their
abominations;
4 so I also will choose harsh treatment
for them
and will bring upon them what they
dread.
For when I called, no one answered,
when I spoke, no one listened.
They did evil in my sight
and chose what displeases me."

5 Hear the word of the LORD,
you who tremble at his word:
"Your brothers who hate you,
and exclude you because of my
name, have said,
'Let the LORD be glorified,
that we may see your joy!'
Yet they will be put to shame.
6 Hear that uproar from the city,
hear that noise from the temple!

It is the sound of the LORD
repaying his enemies all they deserve.

7 "Before she goes into labor,
she gives birth;
before the pains come upon her,
she delivers a son.
8 Who has ever heard of such a thing?
Who has ever seen such things?
Can a country be born in a day
or a nation be brought forth in a
moment?
Yet no sooner is Zion in labor
than she gives birth to her children.
9 Do I bring to the moment of birth
and not give delivery?" says the LORD.
"Do I close up the womb
when I bring to delivery?" says your
God.
10 "Rejoice with Jerusalem and be glad
for her,
all you who love her;
rejoice greatly with her,
all you who mourn over her.
11 For you will nurse and be satisfied
at her comforting breasts;
you will drink deeply
and delight in her overflowing
abundance."

12 For this is what the LORD says:

"I will extend peace to her like a river,
and the wealth of nations like a
flooding stream;
you will nurse and be carried on her
arm
and dandled on her knees.
13 As a mother comforts her child,
so will I comfort you;
and you will be comforted over
Jerusalem."

14 When you see this, your heart will
rejoice
and you will flourish like grass;
the hand of the LORD will be made
known to his servants,
but his fury will be shown to his
foes.
15 See, the LORD is coming with fire,
and his chariots are like a whirlwind;
he will bring down his anger with fury,
and his rebuke with flames of fire.
16 For with fire and with his sword
the LORD will execute judgment upon
all men,
and many will be those slain by the
LORD.

¹⁷"Those who consecrate and purify themselves to go into the gardens, following the one in the midst of[a] those who eat the flesh of pigs and rats and other abominable things—they will meet their end together," declares the LORD.

¹⁸"And I, because of their actions and their imaginations, am about to come[b] and gather all nations and tongues, and they will come and see my glory.

¹⁹"I will set a sign among them, and I will send some of those who survive to the nations—to Tarshish, to the Libyans[c] and Lydians (famous as archers), to Tubal and Greece, and to the distant islands that have not heard of my fame or seen my glory. They will proclaim my glory among the nations. ²⁰And they will bring all your brothers, from all the nations, to my holy mountain in Jerusalem as an offering to the LORD—on horses, in chariots and wagons, and on mules and camels," says the LORD. "They will bring them, as the Israelites bring their grain offerings, to the temple of the LORD in ceremonially clean vessels. ²¹And I will select some of them also to be priests and Levites," says the LORD.

²²"As the new heavens and the new earth that I make will endure before me," declares the LORD, "so will your name and descendants endure. ²³From one New Moon to another and from one Sabbath to another, all mankind will come and bow down before me," says the LORD. ²⁴"And they will go out and look upon the dead bodies of those who rebelled against me; their worm will not die, nor will their fire be quenched, and they will be loathsome to all mankind."

---

a 17 Or gardens behind one of your temples, and
b 18 The meaning of the Hebrew for this clause is uncertain.
c 19 Some Septuagint manuscripts Put (Libyans); Hebrew Pul

JEREMIAH

Who wrote this book?

The prophet Jeremiah.

Why was this book written?

God intended to use Babylon to punish Judah's sin. Jeremiah urged the king and people to surrender to Babylon.

What is special about this book?

Jeremiah is faithful to God even though the people of Judah mock and hate him. Jeremiah prophesies that one day God will forgive and restore his people.

When was this book written?

Jeremiah was written between 627 B.C. and the destruction of Jerusalem in 586 B.C.

What chapters tell about Jeremiah's experiences?

God calls Jeremiah	Jeremiah 1
Jeremiah is beaten	Jeremiah 20
Jeremiah is threatened	Jeremiah 26
Jeremiah and a false prophet	Jeremiah 28
Jeremiah buys a field	Jeremiah 32
Jeremiah in a cistern	Jeremiah 38
Jeremiah is set free	Jeremiah 40

What are some important chapters in this book?

The wickedness of Judah	Jeremiah 5
God and idols	Jeremiah 10
False prophets	Jeremiah 23
God's lasting love	Jeremiah 31
A family that obeyed God	Jeremiah 35
God's future punishment	Jeremiah 51

The words of Jeremiah son of Hilkiah, one of the priests at Anathoth in the territory of Benjamin. ²The word of the LORD came to him in the thirteenth year of the reign of Josiah son of Amon king of Judah, ³and through the reign of Jehoiakim son of Josiah king of Judah, down to the fifth month of the eleventh year of Zedekiah son of Josiah king of Judah, when the people of Jerusalem went into exile.

The Call of Jeremiah

⁴The word of the LORD came to me, saying,

⁵ "Before I formed you in the womb I
knew*a* you,
   before you were born I set you
      apart;
   I appointed you as a prophet to the
      nations."

⁶"Ah, Sovereign LORD," I said, "I do not know how to speak; I am only a child."

⁷But the LORD said to me, "Do not say, 'I am only a child.' You must go to everyone I send you to and say whatever I command you. ⁸Do not be afraid of them, for I am with you and will rescue you," declares the LORD.

⁹Then the LORD reached out his hand and touched my mouth and said to me, "Now, I have put my words in your mouth. ¹⁰See, today I appoint you over nations and kingdoms to uproot and tear down, to destroy and overthrow, to build and to plant."

¹¹The word of the LORD came to me: "What do you see, Jeremiah?"

"I see the branch of an almond tree," I replied.

¹²The LORD said to me, "You have seen correctly, for I am watching*b* to see that my word is fulfilled."

¹³The word of the LORD came to me again: "What do you see?"

a 5 Or *chose*   *b 12* The Hebrew for *watching* sounds like the Hebrew for *almond tree.*

Not Ready? Try it!

READ JEREMIAH 1:4–10

Remember the first time you bailed big-time on your bike? You weren't quite ready for that big jump and BAM! Skinned-knee city. What did you do? Quit? Or try again? When God has a job for you to do, he already knows your story. He knows you're capable of much more than you think. "Do not say, 'I am only a child'" (verse 7). Young–shmung. God doesn't expect you to know everything or do everything, but when he calls, he does expect you to obey. So even if you make mistakes, go for it. God will be with you. Whatever he's calling you to do, you *can* do it. God knew Jeremiah was ready. Jeremiah had spent time learning about God and growing close to him. Same with you: If you learn and mature and prepare yourself, when God wants you to do something, you'll be ready.

Your next reading is on page 952.

"I see a boiling pot, tilting away from the north," I answered.

[14] The LORD said to me, "From the north disaster will be poured out on all who live in the land. [15] I am about to summon all the peoples of the northern kingdoms," declares the LORD.

"Their kings will come and set up their
thrones
in the entrance of the gates of
Jerusalem;
they will come against all her
surrounding walls
and against all the towns of Judah.
[16] I will pronounce my judgments on my
people
because of their wickedness in
forsaking me,
in burning incense to other gods
and in worshiping what their hands
have made.

[17] "Get yourself ready! Stand up and say to them whatever I command you. Do not be terrified by them, or I will terrify you before them. [18] Today I have made you a fortified city, an iron pillar and a bronze wall to stand against the whole land— against the kings of Judah, its officials, its priests and the people of the land. [19] They will fight against you but will not overcome you, for I am with you and will rescue you," declares the LORD.

Israel Forsakes God

2 The word of the LORD came to me: [2] "Go and proclaim in the hearing of Jerusalem:

" 'I remember the devotion of your
youth,
how as a bride you loved me
and followed me through the desert,
through a land not sown.
[3] Israel was holy to the LORD,
the firstfruits of his harvest;
all who devoured her were held guilty,
and disaster overtook them,' "
declares the LORD.

[4] Hear the word of the LORD, O house of
Jacob,
all you clans of the house of Israel.

[5] This is what the LORD says:

"What fault did your fathers find in me,
that they strayed so far from me?

They followed worthless idols
and became worthless themselves.
[6] They did not ask, 'Where is the LORD,
who brought us up out of Egypt
and led us through the barren
wilderness,
through a land of deserts and rifts,
a land of drought and darkness,[a]
a land where no one travels and no
one lives?'
[7] I brought you into a fertile land
to eat its fruit and rich produce.
But you came and defiled my land
and made my inheritance detestable.
[8] The priests did not ask,
'Where is the LORD?'
Those who deal with the law did not
know me;
the leaders rebelled against me.
The prophets prophesied by Baal,
following worthless idols.

[9] "Therefore I bring charges against you
again,"
declares the LORD.
"And I will bring charges against
your children's children.
[10] Cross over to the coasts of Kittim[b] and
look,
send to Kedar[c] and observe closely;
see if there has ever been anything
like this:
[11] Has a nation ever changed its gods?
(Yet they are not gods at all.)
But my people have exchanged their[d]
Glory
for worthless idols.
[12] Be appalled at this, O heavens,
and shudder with great horror,"
declares the LORD.
[13] "My people have committed two sins:
They have forsaken me,
the spring of living water,
and have dug their own cisterns,
broken cisterns that cannot hold
water.
[14] Is Israel a servant, a slave by birth?
Why then has he become plunder?
[15] Lions have roared;
they have growled at him.
They have laid waste his land;
his towns are burned and deserted.

---

[a] 6 Or and the shadow of death   [b] 10 That is, Cyprus and
western coastlands   [c] 10 The home of Bedouin tribes in the
Syro-Arabian desert   [d] 11 Masoretic Text; an ancient
Hebrew scribal tradition my

¹⁶ Also, the men of Memphis*ᵃ* and Tahpanhes
    have shaved the crown of your head.*ᵇ*
¹⁷ Have you not brought this on yourselves
    by forsaking the Lᴏʀᴅ your God
    when he led you in the way?
¹⁸ Now why go to Egypt
    to drink water from the Shihor*ᶜ*?
    And why go to Assyria
    to drink water from the River*ᵈ*?
¹⁹ Your wickedness will punish you;
    your backsliding will rebuke you.
    Consider then and realize
    how evil and bitter it is for you
    when you forsake the Lᴏʀᴅ your God
    and have no awe of me,"
                declares the Lord,
                the Lᴏʀᴅ Almighty.

²⁰ "Long ago you broke off your yoke
    and tore off your bonds;
    you said, 'I will not serve you!'
    Indeed, on every high hill
and under every spreading tree
    you lay down as a prostitute.
²¹ I had planted you like a choice vine
    of sound and reliable stock.
    How then did you turn against me
    into a corrupt, wild vine?
²² Although you wash yourself with soda
    and use an abundance of soap,
    the stain of your guilt is still before me,"
            declares the Sovereign Lᴏʀᴅ.
²³ "How can you say, 'I am not defiled;
    I have not run after the Baals'?
    See how you behaved in the valley;
    consider what you have done.
    You are a swift she-camel
    running here and there,
²⁴ a wild donkey accustomed to the desert,
    sniffing the wind in her craving—
    in her heat who can restrain her?

ᵃ 16 Hebrew *Noph*   *ᵇ 16* Or *have cracked your skull*
ᶜ 18 That is, a branch of the Nile   *ᵈ 18* That is, the Euphrates

Make It Stick

READ JEREMIAH 2:5

Lots of people follow "worthless" things and they themselves end up being "worthless" (verse 5). Want your life to count for something? Want to be respected and loved? Help others. How valuable your life ends up *being* depends on what you spend your life *doing*. Write down two worthless things people waste time on.

Any males that pursue her need not
    tire themselves;
  at mating time they will find her.
25 Do not run until your feet are bare
    and your throat is dry.
But you said, 'It's no use!
  I love foreign gods,
  and I must go after them.'

26 "As a thief is disgraced when he is
    caught,
  so the house of Israel is disgraced—
they, their kings and their officials,
  their priests and their prophets.
27 They say to wood, 'You are my father,'
  and to stone, 'You gave me birth.'
They have turned their backs to me
  and not their faces;
yet when they are in trouble, they say,
  'Come and save us!'
28 Where then are the gods you made for
    yourselves?
  Let them come if they can save you
  when you are in trouble!
For you have as many gods
  as you have towns, O Judah.

29 "Why do you bring charges against me?
  You have all rebelled against me,"
                declares the LORD.
30 "In vain I punished your people;
  they did not respond to correction.
Your sword has devoured your prophets
  like a ravening lion.

31 "You of this generation, consider the
word of the LORD:

"Have I been a desert to Israel
  or a land of great darkness?
Why do my people say, 'We are free to
    roam;
  we will come to you no more'?
32 Does a maiden forget her jewelry,
  a bride her wedding ornaments?
Yet my people have forgotten me,
  days without number.
33 How skilled you are at pursuing love!
  Even the worst of women can learn
    from your ways.
34 On your clothes men find
  the lifeblood of the innocent poor,
  though you did not catch them
    breaking in.

"I Can't Help It"

READ JEREMIAH 2:25

You've seen it happen to the pros—a famous athlete with great skills and accomplishments is brought low by the one desire he can't control. You wonder, "What's with that guy? He has it all! Why is he throwing his life away over that thing?" A man of God must not put desire over will. If you say, "It's no use ... I must go after them" (verse 25), you're saying that your desires control you instead of your will and decisions controlling you. Here's the test: If there is one thing in your life that you will do *anything* to get, you're addicted. Doesn't matter if it's chocolate *cake*. For the Israelites, it was false gods. They went to extremes to do something they knew was evil. Who's in charge of your life—you or God? Why waste your time chasing wrong things when they ruin your life?

Your next reading is on page 958.

Yet in spite of all this
35   you say, 'I am innocent;
     he is not angry with me.'
But I will pass judgment on you
     because you say, 'I have not sinned.'
36 Why do you go about so much,
     changing your ways?
You will be disappointed by Egypt
     as you were by Assyria.
37 You will also leave that place
     with your hands on your head,
for the LORD has rejected those you
     trust;
     you will not be helped by them.

3 "If a man divorces his wife
     and she leaves him and marries
     another man,
     should he return to her again?
Would not the land be completely
     defiled?
But you have lived as a prostitute with
     many lovers—
     would you now return to me?"
                    declares the LORD.
2 "Look up to the barren heights and see.
     Is there any place where you have
     not been ravished?
By the roadside you sat waiting for
     lovers,
     sat like a nomad^a in the desert.
You have defiled the land
     with your prostitution and
     wickedness.
3 Therefore the showers have been
     withheld,
     and no spring rains have fallen.
Yet you have the brazen look of a
     prostitute;
     you refuse to blush with shame.
4 Have you not just called to me:
     'My Father, my friend from my youth,
5 will you always be angry?
     Will your wrath continue forever?'
This is how you talk,
     but you do all the evil you can."

Unfaithful Israel

6 During the reign of King Josiah, the
LORD said to me, "Have you seen what
faithless Israel has done? She has gone up
on every high hill and under every spreading tree and has committed adultery
there. 7 I thought that after she had done
all this she would return to me but she did
not, and her unfaithful sister Judah saw it.
8 I gave faithless Israel her certificate of divorce and sent her away because of all her
adulteries. Yet I saw that her unfaithful
sister Judah had no fear; she also went
out and committed adultery. 9 Because Israel's immorality mattered so little to her,
she defiled the land and committed adultery with stone and wood. 10 In spite of all
this, her unfaithful sister Judah did not return to me with all her heart, but only in
pretense," declares the LORD.

11 The LORD said to me, "Faithless Israel
is more righteous than unfaithful Judah.
12 Go, proclaim this message toward the
north:

" 'Return, faithless Israel,' declares the
          LORD,
     'I will frown on you no longer,
for I am merciful,' declares the LORD,
     'I will not be angry forever.
13 Only acknowledge your guilt—
     you have rebelled against the LORD
          your God,
you have scattered your favors to
     foreign gods
     under every spreading tree,
     and have not obeyed me,' "
                    declares the LORD.

14 "Return, faithless people," declares
the LORD, "for I am your husband. I will
choose you—one from a town and two
from a clan—and bring you to Zion.
15 Then I will give you shepherds after my
own heart, who will lead you with knowledge and understanding. 16 In those days,
when your numbers have increased greatly in the land," declares the LORD, "men
will no longer say, 'The ark of the covenant of the LORD.' It will never enter their
minds or be remembered; it will not be
missed, nor will another one be made.
17 At that time they will call Jerusalem The
Throne of the LORD, and all nations will
gather in Jerusalem to honor the name of
the LORD. No longer will they follow the
stubbornness of their evil hearts. 18 In
those days the house of Judah will join the
house of Israel, and together they will
come from a northern land to the land I
gave your forefathers as an inheritance.
19 "I myself said,

" 'How gladly would I treat you like sons
     and give you a desirable land,
     the most beautiful inheritance of any
          nation.'

---

^a 2 Or an Arab

I thought you would call me 'Father'
and not turn away from following
me.
20 But like a woman unfaithful to her
husband,
so you have been unfaithful to me,
O house of Israel,"
declares the LORD.

21 A cry is heard on the barren heights,
the weeping and pleading of the
people of Israel,
because they have perverted their ways
and have forgotten the LORD their
God.

22 "Return, faithless people;
I will cure you of backsliding."

"Yes, we will come to you,
for you are the LORD our God.
23 Surely the ⌊idolatrous⌋ commotion on
the hills
and mountains is a deception;
surely in the LORD our God

is the salvation of Israel.
24 From our youth shameful gods have
consumed
the fruits of our fathers' labor—
their flocks and herds,
their sons and daughters.
25 Let us lie down in our shame,
and let our disgrace cover us.
We have sinned against the LORD our
God,
both we and our fathers;
from our youth till this day
we have not obeyed the LORD our
God."

4 "If you will return, O Israel,
return to me,"
declares the LORD.
"If you put your detestable idols
out of my sight
and no longer go astray,
2 and if in a truthful, just and righteous
way
you swear, 'As surely as the LORD lives,'

Make It Stick

READ JEREMIAH 3:15

Men can be shepherds in many ways—by pastoring a church, running a business or being
a father. The key is to lead with "knowledge and understanding" (Jeremiah 3:15). And
remember, leaders must first of all be servants (Matthew 20:27). Write the name of
a man you think is a good leader, and why you think he is.

then the nations will be blessed by him
  and in him they will glory."

³This is what the LORD says to the men
of Judah and to Jerusalem:

"Break up your unplowed ground
  and do not sow among thorns.
⁴Circumcise yourselves to the LORD,
  circumcise your hearts,
  you men of Judah and people of
    Jerusalem,
or my wrath will break out and burn
    like fire
  because of the evil you have done—
  burn with no one to quench it.

Disaster From the North

⁵"Announce in Judah and proclaim in
    Jerusalem and say:
  'Sound the trumpet throughout the
    land!'
Cry aloud and say:
  'Gather together!
  Let us flee to the fortified cities!'
⁶Raise the signal to go to Zion!
  Flee for safety without delay!
For I am bringing disaster from the
    north,
  even terrible destruction."

⁷A lion has come out of his lair;
  a destroyer of nations has set out.
He has left his place
  to lay waste your land.
Your towns will lie in ruins
  without inhabitant.
⁸So put on sackcloth,
  lament and wail,
for the fierce anger of the LORD
  has not turned away from us.

⁹"In that day," declares the LORD,
  "the king and the officials will lose
    heart,
the priests will be horrified,
  and the prophets will be appalled."

¹⁰Then I said, "Ah, Sovereign LORD, how
completely you have deceived this people
and Jerusalem by saying, 'You will have
peace,' when the sword is at our throats."

¹¹At that time this people and Jerusalem will be told, "A scorching wind from
the barren heights in the desert blows toward my people, but not to winnow or
cleanse; ¹²a wind too strong for that
comes from me.ᵃ Now I pronounce my
judgments against them."

¹³Look! He advances like the clouds,
  his chariots come like a whirlwind,
his horses are swifter than eagles.
  Woe to us! We are ruined!
¹⁴O Jerusalem, wash the evil from your
    heart and be saved.
  How long will you harbor wicked
    thoughts?
¹⁵A voice is announcing from Dan,
  proclaiming disaster from the hills of
    Ephraim.
¹⁶"Tell this to the nations,
  proclaim it to Jerusalem:
  'A besieging army is coming from a
    distant land,
  raising a war cry against the cities of
    Judah.
¹⁷They surround her like men guarding a
    field,
  because she has rebelled against
    me,' "
                    declares the LORD.
¹⁸"Your own conduct and actions
  have brought this upon you.
This is your punishment.
  How bitter it is!
  How it pierces to the heart!"

¹⁹Oh, my anguish, my anguish!
  I writhe in pain.
Oh, the agony of my heart!
  My heart pounds within me,
  I cannot keep silent.
For I have heard the sound of the
    trumpet;
  I have heard the battle cry.
²⁰Disaster follows disaster;
  the whole land lies in ruins.
In an instant my tents are destroyed,
  my shelter in a moment.
²¹How long must I see the battle standard
  and hear the sound of the trumpet?

²²"My people are fools;
  they do not know me.
They are senseless children;
  they have no understanding.
They are skilled in doing evil;
  they know not how to do good."

²³I looked at the earth,
  and it was formless and empty;
and at the heavens,
  and their light was gone.
²⁴I looked at the mountains,
  and they were quaking;
  all the hills were swaying.

ᵃ 12 Or comes at my command

25I looked, and there were no people;
    every bird in the sky had flown away.
26I looked, and the fruitful land was a
        desert;
    all its towns lay in ruins
    before the LORD, before his fierce
        anger.

27This is what the LORD says:

"The whole land will be ruined,
    though I will not destroy it
        completely.
28Therefore the earth will mourn
    and the heavens above grow dark,
because I have spoken and will not
        relent,
    I have decided and will not turn
        back."

29At the sound of horsemen and archers
    every town takes to flight.
Some go into the thickets;
    some climb up among the rocks.
All the towns are deserted;
    no one lives in them.

30What are you doing, O devastated one?
    Why dress yourself in scarlet
    and put on jewels of gold?
Why shade your eyes with paint?
    You adorn yourself in vain.
Your lovers despise you;
    they seek your life.

31I hear a cry as of a woman in labor,
    a groan as of one bearing her first
        child—
the cry of the Daughter of Zion
        gasping for breath,
    stretching out her hands and saying,
"Alas! I am fainting;
    my life is given over to murderers."

Not One Is Upright

5 "Go up and down the streets of
    Jerusalem,
    look around and consider,
    search through her squares.
If you can find but one person
    who deals honestly and seeks the
        truth,
    I will forgive this city.
2Although they say, 'As surely as the
        LORD lives,'
    still they are swearing falsely."

3O LORD, do not your eyes look for truth?
    You struck them, but they felt no
        pain;

you crushed them, but they refused
        correction.
They made their faces harder than stone
    and refused to repent.
4I thought, "These are only the poor;
    they are foolish,
for they do not know the way of the
        LORD,
    the requirements of their God.
5So I will go to the leaders
    and speak to them;
surely they know the way of the LORD,
    the requirements of their God."
But with one accord they too had
        broken off the yoke
    and torn off the bonds.
6Therefore a lion from the forest will
        attack them,
    a wolf from the desert will ravage
        them,
a leopard will lie in wait near their
        towns
    to tear to pieces any who venture
        out,
for their rebellion is great
    and their backslidings many.

7"Why should I forgive you?
    Your children have forsaken me
    and sworn by gods that are not gods.
I supplied all their needs,
    yet they committed adultery
    and thronged to the houses of
        prostitutes.
8They are well-fed, lusty stallions,
    each neighing for another man's
        wife.
9Should I not punish them for this?"
        declares the LORD.
"Should I not avenge myself
    on such a nation as this?

10"Go through her vineyards and ravage
        them,
    but do not destroy them completely.
Strip off her branches,
    for these people do not belong to
        the LORD.
11The house of Israel and the house of
        Judah
    have been utterly unfaithful to me,"
                        declares the LORD.

12They have lied about the LORD;
    they said, "He will do nothing!
No harm will come to us;
    we will never see sword or famine.
13The prophets are but wind

and the word is not in them;
so let what they say be done to
them."

¹⁴Therefore this is what the Lᴏʀᴅ God Almighty says:

"Because the people have spoken
these words,
I will make my words in your mouth
a fire
and these people the wood it
consumes.
¹⁵O house of Israel," declares the Lᴏʀᴅ,
"I am bringing a distant nation
against you—
an ancient and enduring nation,
a people whose language you do
not know,
whose speech you do not
understand.
¹⁶Their quivers are like an open grave;
all of them are mighty warriors.
¹⁷They will devour your harvests and
food,
devour your sons and daughters;
they will devour your flocks and herds,
devour your vines and fig trees.
With the sword they will destroy
the fortified cities in which you trust.

¹⁸"Yet even in those days," declares the Lᴏʀᴅ, "I will not destroy you completely. ¹⁹And when the people ask, 'Why has the Lᴏʀᴅ our God done all this to us?' you will tell them, 'As you have forsaken me and served foreign gods in your own land, so now you will serve foreigners in a land not your own.'

²⁰"Announce this to the house of Jacob
and proclaim it in Judah:
²¹Hear this, you foolish and senseless
people,
who have eyes but do not see,
who have ears but do not hear:
²²Should you not fear me?" declares the
Lᴏʀᴅ.
"Should you not tremble in my
presence?
I made the sand a boundary for the
sea,
an everlasting barrier it cannot cross.
The waves may roll, but they cannot
prevail;
they may roar, but they cannot cross
it.
²³But these people have stubborn and
rebellious hearts;

they have turned aside and gone
away.
²⁴They do not say to themselves,
'Let us fear the Lᴏʀᴅ our God,
who gives autumn and spring rains in
season,
who assures us of the regular weeks
of harvest.'
²⁵Your wrongdoings have kept these
away;
your sins have deprived you of good.

²⁶"Among my people are wicked men
who lie in wait like men who snare
birds
and like those who set traps to catch
men.
²⁷Like cages full of birds,
their houses are full of deceit;
they have become rich and powerful
²⁸   and have grown fat and sleek.
Their evil deeds have no limit;
they do not plead the case of the
fatherless to win it,
they do not defend the rights of the
poor.
²⁹Should I not punish them for this?"
declares the Lᴏʀᴅ.
"Should I not avenge myself
on such a nation as this?

³⁰"A horrible and shocking thing
has happened in the land:
³¹The prophets prophesy lies,
the priests rule by their own authority,
and my people love it this way.
But what will you do in the end?

Jerusalem Under Siege

6 "Flee for safety, people of
Benjamin!
Flee from Jerusalem!
Sound the trumpet in Tekoa!
Raise the signal over Beth Hakkerem!
For disaster looms out of the north,
even terrible destruction.
²I will destroy the Daughter of Zion,
so beautiful and delicate.
³Shepherds with their flocks will come
against her;
they will pitch their tents around her,
each tending his own portion."

⁴"Prepare for battle against her!
Arise, let us attack at noon!
But, alas, the daylight is fading,
and the shadows of evening grow
long.

5 So arise, let us attack at night
  and destroy her fortresses!"

6 This is what the LORD Almighty says:

"Cut down the trees
  and build siege ramps against
    Jerusalem.
This city must be punished;
  it is filled with oppression.
7 As a well pours out its water,
  so she pours out her wickedness.
Violence and destruction resound in her;
  her sickness and wounds are ever
    before me.
8 Take warning, O Jerusalem,
  or I will turn away from you
and make your land desolate
  so no one can live in it."

9 This is what the LORD Almighty says:

"Let them glean the remnant of Israel
  as thoroughly as a vine;
pass your hand over the branches
    again,
  like one gathering grapes."

10 To whom can I speak and give warning?

Who will listen to me?
Their ears are closed[a]
  so they cannot hear.
The word of the LORD is offensive to
    them;
  they find no pleasure in it.
11 But I am full of the wrath of the LORD,
  and I cannot hold it in.

"Pour it out on the children in the street
  and on the young men gathered
    together;
both husband and wife will be caught
    in it,
  and the old, those weighed down
    with years.
12 Their houses will be turned over to
    others,
  together with their fields and their
    wives,
when I stretch out my hand
  against those who live in the land,"
    declares the LORD.
13 "From the least to the greatest,
  all are greedy for gain;

---

[a] 10 Hebrew uncircumcised

Are You Deprived?

READ JEREMIAH 5:24–25

We might feel "deprived" sometimes—like, if our parents don't buy us the coolest new clothes—but most Americans are *not* deprived. Far from it! We've got it so good that it's easy to forget about God. We're provided for. Life seems to go along well even when we don't stay close to God. Result? We can feel like we don't even need to obey God and that sinning is no big deal. We feel we can just cruise along, and if God's on board, cool, but if he's not … no big deal because nothing bad will ever happen. Whoa! That's the surest way to *really* be deprived, because it's a law of God: If we sin, our sins *will* deprive us of good things (Jeremiah 5:25; see also Isaiah 59:1–2). It may take years before we see the result of not living God's way, but one day, ohhh yeaahh, we'll reap what we sow (Galatians 6:7).

Your next reading is on page 963.

prophets and priests alike,
  all practice deceit.
14 They dress the wound of my people
  as though it were not serious.
'Peace, peace,' they say,
  when there is no peace.
15 Are they ashamed of their loathsome
    conduct?
  No, they have no shame at all;
  they do not even know how to blush.
So they will fall among the fallen;
  they will be brought down when I
    punish them,"
                          says the LORD.

16 This is what the LORD says:

"Stand at the crossroads and look;
  ask for the ancient paths,
ask where the good way is, and walk
    in it,
  and you will find rest for your souls.
  But you said, 'We will not walk in it.'
17 I appointed watchmen over you and
    said,
  'Listen to the sound of the trumpet!'
  But you said, 'We will not listen.'
18 Therefore hear, O nations;
  observe, O witnesses,
  what will happen to them.
19 Hear, O earth:
I am bringing disaster on this people,
  the fruit of their schemes,
because they have not listened to my
    words
  and have rejected my law.
20 What do I care about incense from
    Sheba
  or sweet calamus from a distant
    land?
Your burnt offerings are not acceptable;
  your sacrifices do not please me."

21 Therefore this is what the LORD says:

"I will put obstacles before this people.
  Fathers and sons alike will stumble
    over them;
  neighbors and friends will perish."

22 This is what the LORD says:

"Look, an army is coming
  from the land of the north;
a great nation is being stirred up
  from the ends of the earth.
23 They are armed with bow and spear;
  they are cruel and show no mercy.
They sound like the roaring sea
  as they ride on their horses;

they come like men in battle formation
  to attack you, O Daughter of Zion."

24 We have heard reports about them,
  and our hands hang limp.
Anguish has gripped us,
  pain like that of a woman in labor.
25 Do not go out to the fields
  or walk on the roads,
for the enemy has a sword,
  and there is terror on every side.
26 O my people, put on sackcloth
  and roll in ashes;
mourn with bitter wailing
  as for an only son,
for suddenly the destroyer
  will come upon us.

27 "I have made you a tester of metals
  and my people the ore,
that you may observe
  and test their ways.
28 They are all hardened rebels,
  going about to slander.
They are bronze and iron;
  they all act corruptly.
29 The bellows blow fiercely
  to burn away the lead with fire,
but the refining goes on in vain;
  the wicked are not purged out.
30 They are called rejected silver,
  because the LORD has rejected them."

False Religion Worthless

7 This is the word that came to Jeremiah from the LORD: 2 "Stand at the gate of the LORD's house and there proclaim this message:

" 'Hear the word of the LORD, all you people of Judah who come through these gates to worship the LORD. 3 This is what the LORD Almighty, the God of Israel, says: Reform your ways and your actions, and I will let you live in this place. 4 Do not trust in deceptive words and say, "This is the temple of the LORD, the temple of the LORD, the temple of the LORD!" 5 If you really change your ways and your actions and deal with each other justly, 6 if you do not oppress the alien, the fatherless or the widow and do not shed innocent blood in this place, and if you do not follow other gods to your own harm, 7 then I will let you live in this place, in the land I gave your forefathers for ever and ever. 8 But look, you are trusting in deceptive words that are worthless.

9 " 'Will you steal and murder, commit

Don't be like the people in Jeremiah 7:9–10 and think, "As long as I go to church, I'm covered. It doesn't matter what I do." Don't kid yourself. It *does* matter what you do. You need to not only hear God's Word, but live it as well.

In Other Words...

adultery and perjury,[a] burn incense to Baal and follow other gods you have not known, 10and then come and stand before me in this house, which bears my Name, and say, "We are safe"—safe to do all these detestable things? 11Has this house, which bears my Name, become a den of robbers to you? But I have been watching! declares the LORD.

12" 'Go now to the place in Shiloh where I first made a dwelling for my Name, and see what I did to it because of the wickedness of my people Israel. 13While you were doing all these things, declares the LORD, I spoke to you again and again, but you did not listen; I called you, but you did not answer. 14Therefore, what I did to Shiloh I will now do to the house that bears my Name, the temple you trust in, the place I gave to you and your fathers. 15I will thrust you from my presence, just as I did all your brothers, the people of Ephraim.'

16"So do not pray for this people nor offer any plea or petition for them; do not plead with me, for I will not listen to you. 17Do you not see what they are doing in the towns of Judah and in the streets of Jerusalem? 18The children gather wood, the fathers light the fire, and the women knead the dough and make cakes of bread for the Queen of Heaven. They pour out drink offerings to other gods to provoke me to anger. 19But am I the one they are provoking? declares the LORD. Are they not rather harming themselves, to their own shame?

20" 'Therefore this is what the Sovereign LORD says: My anger and my wrath will be poured out on this place, on man and beast, on the trees of the field and on the fruit of the ground, and it will burn and not be quenched.

21" 'This is what the LORD Almighty, the God of Israel, says: Go ahead, add your burnt offerings to your other sacrifices and eat the meat yourselves! 22For when I brought your forefathers out of Egypt and spoke to them, I did not just give them commands about burnt offerings and sacrifices, 23but I gave them this command: Obey me, and I will be your God and you will be my people. Walk in all the ways I command you, that it may go well with you. 24But they did not listen or pay attention; instead, they followed the stubborn inclinations of their evil hearts. They went backward and not forward. 25From the time your forefathers left Egypt until now, day after day, again and again I sent you my servants the prophets. 26But they did not listen to me or pay attention. They were stiff-necked and did more evil than their forefathers.'

27"When you tell them all this, they will not listen to you; when you call to them, they will not answer. 28Therefore say to them, 'This is the nation that has not obeyed the LORD its God or responded to correction. Truth has perished; it has vanished from their lips. 29Cut off your hair and throw it away; take up a lament on the barren heights, for the LORD has rejected and abandoned this generation that is under his wrath.

a 9 Or and swear by false gods

The Valley of Slaughter

30 " 'The people of Judah have done evil in my eyes, declares the LORD. They have set up their detestable idols in the house that bears my Name and have defiled it. 31 They have built the high places of Topheth in the Valley of Ben Hinnom to burn their sons and daughters in the fire—something I did not command, nor did it enter my mind. 32 So beware, the days are coming, declares the LORD, when people will no longer call it Topheth or the Valley of Ben Hinnom, but the Valley of Slaughter, for they will bury the dead in Topheth until there is no more room. 33 Then the carcasses of this people will become food for the birds of the air and the beasts of the earth, and there will be no one to frighten them away. 34 I will bring an end to the sounds of joy and gladness and to the voices of bride and bridegroom in the towns of Judah and the streets of Jerusalem, for the land will become desolate.

8 " 'At that time, declares the LORD, the bones of the kings and officials of Judah, the bones of the priests and prophets, and the bones of the people of Jerusalem will be removed from their graves. 2 They will be exposed to the sun and the moon and all the stars of the heavens, which they have loved and served and which they have followed and consulted and worshiped. They will not be gathered up or buried, but will be like refuse lying on the ground. 3 Wherever I banish them, all the survivors of this evil nation will prefer death to life, declares the LORD Almighty.'

Sin and Punishment

4 "Say to them, 'This is what the LORD says:

" 'When men fall down, do they not get up?
    When a man turns away, does he not return?
5 Why then have these people turned away?
    Why does Jerusalem always turn away?
They cling to deceit;
    they refuse to return.
6 I have listened attentively,
    but they do not say what is right.
No one repents of his wickedness,
    saying, "What have I done?"
Each pursues his own course
    like a horse charging into battle.
7 Even the stork in the sky
    knows her appointed seasons,
and the dove, the swift and the thrush
    observe the time of their migration.
But my people do not know
    the requirements of the LORD.

8 " 'How can you say, "We are wise,
    for we have the law of the LORD,"
when actually the lying pen of the scribes
    has handled it falsely?
9 The wise will be put to shame;

Ever try chasing a chicken into a barn? It runs *every* direction *except* into the barn. You can read Jeremiah 7:23–24 and think, "Wow! Did those guys ever have things backwards!" But sometimes when your parents tell you to do things, do *you* act just like that chicken?

they will be dismayed and trapped.
Since they have rejected the word of the LORD,
    what kind of wisdom do they have?
¹⁰ Therefore I will give their wives to other men
    and their fields to new owners.
From the least to the greatest,
    all are greedy for gain;
prophets and priests alike,
    all practice deceit.
¹¹ They dress the wound of my people
    as though it were not serious.
"Peace, peace," they say,
    when there is no peace.
¹² Are they ashamed of their loathsome conduct?
    No, they have no shame at all;
    they do not even know how to blush.
So they will fall among the fallen;
    they will be brought down when they are
        punished,
                                    says the LORD.
¹³ " 'I will take away their harvest,
                                    declares the LORD.
There will be no grapes on the vine.
There will be no figs on the tree,
    and their leaves will wither.
What I have given them
    will be taken from them.ᵃ' "
¹⁴ "Why are we sitting here?
    Gather together!
Let us flee to the fortified cities
    and perish there!
For the LORD our God has doomed us to perish
    and given us poisoned water to drink,
    because we have sinned against him.
¹⁵ We hoped for peace
    but no good has come,
for a time of healing
    but there was only terror.
¹⁶ The snorting of the enemy's horses
    is heard from Dan;
at the neighing of their stallions
    the whole land trembles.
They have come to devour
    the land and everything in it,
    the city and all who live there."
¹⁷ "See, I will send venomous snakes among you,
    vipers that cannot be charmed,
    and they will bite you,"
                                    declares the LORD.
¹⁸ O my Comforterᵇ in sorrow,
    my heart is faint within me.
¹⁹ Listen to the cry of my people

ᵃ 13 The meaning of the Hebrew for this sentence is uncertain.
ᵇ 18 The meaning of the Hebrew for this word is uncertain.

Gross!

Imagine walking through a graveyard at night and every single skeleton had been dug up and dumped on the ground. Jeremiah 8:1–2 says that the bones of the priests, prophets and princes would be piled up like so much garbage. (Wanna go for a walk?)

from a land far away:
"Is the LORD not in Zion?
    Is her King no longer there?"

"Why have they provoked me to anger
        with their images,
    with their worthless foreign idols?"

20 "The harvest is past,
    the summer has ended,
    and we are not saved."

21 Since my people are crushed, I am
        crushed;
    I mourn, and horror grips me.
22 Is there no balm in Gilead?
    Is there no physician there?
Why then is there no healing
    for the wound of my people?
    1 Oh, that my head were a spring
        of water
    and my eyes a fountain of tears!
    I would weep day and night
    for the slain of my people.
2 Oh, that I had in the desert
    a lodging place for travelers,
so that I might leave my people
    and go away from them;

for they are all adulterers,
    a crowd of unfaithful people.

3 "They make ready their tongue
    like a bow, to shoot lies;
it is not by truth
    that they triumph*a* in the land.
They go from one sin to another;
    they do not acknowledge me,"
                    declares the LORD.
4 "Beware of your friends;
    do not trust your brothers.
For every brother is a deceiver,*b*
    and every friend a slanderer.
5 Friend deceives friend,
    and no one speaks the truth.
They have taught their tongues to lie;
    they weary themselves with sinning.
6 You*c* live in the midst of deception;
    in their deceit they refuse to
        acknowledge me,"
                    declares the LORD.

7 Therefore this is what the LORD Almighty says:

a 3 Or lies; / they are not valiant for truth   *b 4 Or a deceiving Jacob*   *c 6 That is, Jeremiah (the Hebrew is singular)*

Hold the Line

READ JEREMIAH 8:11–12

It starts innocently enough. You say, "I'll just watch this show for a minute ... even though I know I shouldn't." Then it's, "That wasn't so bad. Maybe I'll check out that *other* show." Next it's games: Things you wouldn't even *look* at last year don't seem so bad now. That line in the back of your mind—the one that says "Acceptable"— keeps moving, an inch at a time. After a while you say, "Huh? What line?" It's like treating a shotgun wound with a band-aid—it doesn't work. "They dress the wound of my people as though it were not serious" (verse 11). It's like people who think sin is no big deal. Even when you make small decisions, ask yourself, "Would God be happy with this? Would Jesus do this?" Not, "Am I comfortable doing this?" Not, "But other people are doing it." Think for yourself. Hold the line.

Your next reading is on page 964.

"See, I will refine and test them,
    for what else can I do
    because of the sin of my people?
8 Their tongue is a deadly arrow;
    it speaks with deceit.
With his mouth each speaks cordially
      to his neighbor,
    but in his heart he sets a trap for him.
9 Should I not punish them for this?"
    declares the LORD.
"Should I not avenge myself
    on such a nation as this?"

10 I will weep and wail for the mountains
    and take up a lament concerning
      the desert pastures.
They are desolate and untraveled,
    and the lowing of cattle is not heard.
The birds of the air have fled
    and the animals are gone.

11 "I will make Jerusalem a heap of ruins,
    a haunt of jackals;
and I will lay waste the towns of Judah
    so no one can live there."

12 What man is wise enough to understand this? Who has been instructed by the LORD and can explain it? Why has the land been ruined and laid waste like a desert that no one can cross?

13 The LORD said, "It is because they have forsaken my law, which I set before them; they have not obeyed me or followed my law. 14 Instead, they have followed the stubbornness of their hearts; they have followed the Baals, as their fathers taught them." 15 Therefore, this is what the LORD Almighty, the God of Israel, says: "See, I will make this people eat bitter food and drink poisoned water. 16 I will scatter them among nations that neither they nor their fathers have known, and I will pursue them with the sword until I have destroyed them."

17 This is what the LORD Almighty says:

"Consider now! Call for the wailing
      women to come;
    send for the most skillful of them.
18 Let them come quickly
    and wail over us
till our eyes overflow with tears
    and water streams from our eyelids.
19 The sound of wailing is heard from Zion:

'How ruined we are!
How great is our shame!
We must leave our land
because our houses are in ruins.' "

20 Now, O women, hear the word of the
LORD;
open your ears to the words of his
mouth.
Teach your daughters how to wail;
teach one another a lament.
21 Death has climbed in through our
windows
and has entered our fortresses;
it has cut off the children from the
streets
and the young men from the public
squares.

22 Say, "This is what the LORD declares:

" 'The dead bodies of men will lie
like refuse on the open field,
like cut grain behind the reaper,
with no one to gather them.' "

23 This is what the LORD says:

"Let not the wise man boast of his
wisdom
or the strong man boast of his
strength
or the rich man boast of his riches,
24 but let him who boasts boast about this:
that he understands and knows me,
that I am the LORD, who exercises
kindness,
justice and righteousness on earth,
for in these I delight,"
declares the LORD.

25 "The days are coming," declares the
LORD, "when I will punish all who are circumcised only in the flesh— 26 Egypt, Judah, Edom, Ammon, Moab and all who
live in the desert in distant places.ᵃ For all
these nations are really uncircumcised,
and even the whole house of Israel is uncircumcised in heart."

ᵃ 26 Or desert and who clip the hair by their foreheads

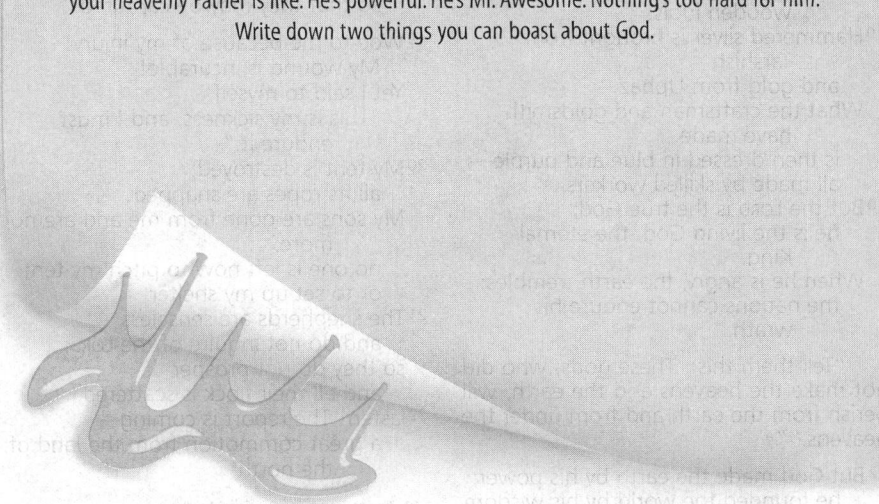

Make It Stick

READ JEREMIAH 9:23–24

Next time you want to crow like a rooster, boast about God! If you had the greatest dad on
the planet, you'd go around saying, "My dad's great. He can do such-and-such." That's what
your heavenly Father is like. He's powerful. He's Mr. Awesome. Nothing's too hard for him.
Write down two things you can boast about God.

God and Idols

10 Hear what the LORD says to you,
O house of Israel. ²This is what
the LORD says:

"Do not learn the ways of the nations
or be terrified by signs in the sky,
though the nations are terrified by
them.
³ For the customs of the peoples are
worthless;
they cut a tree out of the forest,
and a craftsman shapes it with his
chisel.
⁴ They adorn it with silver and gold;
they fasten it with hammer and nails
so it will not totter.
⁵ Like a scarecrow in a melon patch,
their idols cannot speak;
they must be carried
because they cannot walk.
Do not fear them;
they can do no harm
nor can they do any good."

⁶ No one is like you, O LORD;
you are great,
and your name is mighty in power.
⁷ Who should not revere you,
O King of the nations?
This is your due.
Among all the wise men of the nations
and in all their kingdoms,
there is no one like you.
⁸ They are all senseless and foolish;
they are taught by worthless
wooden idols.
⁹ Hammered silver is brought from
Tarshish
and gold from Uphaz.
What the craftsman and goldsmith
have made
is then dressed in blue and purple—
all made by skilled workers.
¹⁰ But the LORD is the true God;
he is the living God, the eternal
King.
When he is angry, the earth trembles;
the nations cannot endure his
wrath.

¹¹ "Tell them this: 'These gods, who did
not make the heavens and the earth, will
perish from the earth and from under the
heavens.' " ª

¹² But God made the earth by his power;
he founded the world by his wisdom
and stretched out the heavens by his
understanding.
¹³ When he thunders, the waters in the
heavens roar;
he makes clouds rise from the ends
of the earth.
He sends lightning with the rain
and brings out the wind from his
storehouses.

¹⁴ Everyone is senseless and without
knowledge;
every goldsmith is shamed by his
idols.
His images are a fraud;
they have no breath in them.
¹⁵ They are worthless, the objects of
mockery;
when their judgment comes, they
will perish.
¹⁶ He who is the Portion of Jacob is not
like these,
for he is the Maker of all things,
including Israel, the tribe of his
inheritance—
the LORD Almighty is his name.

Coming Destruction

¹⁷ Gather up your belongings to leave the
land,
you who live under siege.
¹⁸ For this is what the LORD says:
"At this time I will hurl out
those who live in this land;
I will bring distress on them
so that they may be captured."

¹⁹ Woe to me because of my injury!
My wound is incurable!
Yet I said to myself,
"This is my sickness, and I must
endure it."
²⁰ My tent is destroyed;
all its ropes are snapped.
My sons are gone from me and are no
more;
no one is left now to pitch my tent
or to set up my shelter.
²¹ The shepherds are senseless
and do not inquire of the LORD;
so they do not prosper
and all their flock is scattered.
²² Listen! The report is coming—
a great commotion from the land of
the north!

ª 11 The text of this verse is in Aramaic.

It will make the towns of Judah desolate,
    a haunt of jackals.

Jeremiah's Prayer

23 I know, O LORD, that a man's life is not his own;
    it is not for man to direct his steps.
24 Correct me, LORD, but only with justice—
    not in your anger,
    lest you reduce me to nothing.
25 Pour out your wrath on the nations
    that do not acknowledge you,
    on the peoples who do not call on your name.
For they have devoured Jacob;
    they have devoured him completely
    and destroyed his homeland.

The Covenant Is Broken

11 This is the word that came to Jeremiah from the LORD: 2 "Listen to the terms of this covenant and tell them to the people of Judah and to those who live in Jerusalem. 3 Tell them that this is what the LORD, the God of Israel, says: 'Cursed is the man who does not obey the terms of this covenant— 4 the terms I commanded your forefathers when I brought them out of Egypt, out of the iron-smelting furnace.' I said, 'Obey me and do everything I command you, and you will be my people, and I will be your God. 5 Then I will fulfill the oath I swore to your forefathers, to give them a land flowing with milk and honey'—the land you possess today."

I answered, "Amen, LORD."

6 The LORD said to me, "Proclaim all these words in the towns of Judah and in the streets of Jerusalem: 'Listen to the terms of this covenant and follow them. 7 From the time I brought your forefathers up from Egypt until today, I warned them again and again, saying, "Obey me." 8 But they did not listen or pay attention; instead, they followed the stubbornness of their evil hearts. So I brought on them all the curses of the covenant I had commanded them to follow but that they did not keep.' "

9 Then the LORD said to me, "There is a conspiracy among the people of Judah and those who live in Jerusalem. 10 They have returned to the sins of their forefathers, who refused to listen to my words. They have followed other gods to serve them. Both the house of Israel and the house of Judah have broken the covenant I made with their forefathers. 11 Therefore this is what the LORD says: 'I will bring on them a disaster they cannot escape. Although they cry out to me, I will not listen to them. 12 The towns of Judah and the people of Jerusalem will go and cry out to the gods to whom they burn incense, but they will not help them at all when disaster strikes. 13 You have as many gods as you have towns, O Judah; and the altars you have set up to burn incense to that shameful god Baal are as many as the streets of Jerusalem.'

Get a Load of This...

Check out Jeremiah 10:23. Who would you rather have in charge of your life? Someone who can answer any question, made the universe and loves you incredibly? Or somebody who is stumped on a trivia game, can't drive a car (at least legally) and is still learning how to take care of himself? (You)

14"Do not pray for this people nor offer any plea or petition for them, because I will not listen when they call to me in the time of their distress.

15"What is my beloved doing in my
      temple
  as she works out her evil schemes
      with many?
Can consecrated meat avert ⌊your
      punishment⌋?
When you engage in your wickedness,
      then you rejoice.ᵃ"

16The LORD called you a thriving olive tree
    with fruit beautiful in form.
But with the roar of a mighty storm
    he will set it on fire,
    and its branches will be broken.

17The LORD Almighty, who planted you, has decreed disaster for you, because the house of Israel and the house of Judah have done evil and provoked me to anger by burning incense to Baal.

Plot Against Jeremiah

18Because the LORD revealed their plot to me, I knew it, for at that time he showed me what they were doing. 19I had been like a gentle lamb led to the slaughter; I did not realize that they had plotted against me, saying,

  "Let us destroy the tree and its fruit;
    let us cut him off from the land of
      the living,
  that his name be remembered no
      more."
20But, O LORD Almighty, you who judge
      righteously
  and test the heart and mind,
let me see your vengeance upon them,
  for to you I have committed my
      cause.

21"Therefore this is what the LORD says about the men of Anathoth who are seeking your life and saying, 'Do not prophesy in the name of the LORD or you will die by our hands'— 22therefore this is what the LORD Almighty says: 'I will punish them. Their young men will die by the sword, their sons and daughters by famine. 23Not even a remnant will be left to them, because I will bring disaster on the men of Anathoth in the year of their punishment.' "

Jeremiah's Complaint

12 You are always righteous, O LORD,
    when I bring a case before you.
  Yet I would speak with you
    about your justice:
Why does the way of the wicked
    prosper?
Why do all the faithless live at ease?
2You have planted them, and they have
    taken root;
  they grow and bear fruit.
You are always on their lips
  but far from their hearts.
3Yet you know me, O LORD;
  you see me and test my thoughts
    about you.
Drag them off like sheep to be
    butchered!
Set them apart for the day of
    slaughter!
4How long will the land lie parchedᵇ
  and the grass in every field be
    withered?
Because those who live in it are wicked,
  the animals and birds have perished.
Moreover, the people are saying,
  "He will not see what happens to us."

God's Answer

5"If you have raced with men on foot
  and they have worn you out,
  how can you compete with horses?
If you stumble in safe country,ᶜ
  how will you manage in the thickets
    byᵈ the Jordan?
6Your brothers, your own family—
  even they have betrayed you;
  they have raised a loud cry against
    you.
Do not trust them,
  though they speak well of you.

7"I will forsake my house,
  abandon my inheritance;
I will give the one I love
  into the hands of her enemies.
8My inheritance has become to me
  like a lion in the forest.
She roars at me;
  therefore I hate her.
9Has not my inheritance become to me
  like a speckled bird of prey
  that other birds of prey surround
    and attack?

ᵃ 15 Or Could consecrated meat avert your punishment? / Then you would rejoice   ᵇ 4 Or land mourn   ᶜ 5 Or If you put your trust in a land of safety   ᵈ 5 Or the flooding of

Go and gather all the wild beasts;
  bring them to devour.
10 Many shepherds will ruin my vineyard
    and trample down my field;
  they will turn my pleasant field
    into a desolate wasteland.
11 It will be made a wasteland,
    parched and desolate before me;
  the whole land will be laid waste
    because there is no one who cares.
12 Over all the barren heights in the
      desert
    destroyers will swarm,
  for the sword of the LORD will devour
    from one end of the land to the
        other;
  no one will be safe.
13 They will sow wheat but reap thorns;
    they will wear themselves out but
        gain nothing.
  So bear the shame of your harvest
    because of the LORD's fierce anger."

14 This is what the LORD says: "As for all
my wicked neighbors who seize the inheritance I gave my people Israel, I will uproot them from their lands and I will uproot the house of Judah from among
them. 15 But after I uproot them, I will
again have compassion and will bring
each of them back to his own inheritance
and his own country. 16 And if they learn
well the ways of my people and swear by
my name, saying, 'As surely as the LORD
lives'—even as they once taught my people to swear by Baal—then they will be established among my people. 17 But if any
nation does not listen, I will completely
uproot and destroy it," declares the LORD.

A Linen Belt

13 This is what the LORD said to me:
"Go and buy a linen belt and put
it around your waist, but do not
let it touch water." 2 So I bought
a belt, as the LORD directed, and put it
around my waist.

3 Then the word of the LORD came to me
a second time: 4 "Take the belt you bought
and are wearing around your waist, and
go now to Perath[a] and hide it there in a
crevice in the rocks." 5 So I went and hid it
at Perath, as the LORD told me.

6 Many days later the LORD said to me,
"Go now to Perath and get the belt I told
you to hide there." 7 So I went to Perath
and dug up the belt and took it from the

place where I had hidden it, but now it
was ruined and completely useless.

8 Then the word of the LORD came to
me: 9 "This is what the LORD says: 'In the
same way I will ruin the pride of Judah
and the great pride of Jerusalem. 10 These
wicked people, who refuse to listen to my
words, who follow the stubbornness of
their hearts and go after other gods to
serve and worship them, will be like this
belt—completely useless! 11 For as a belt is
bound around a man's waist, so I bound
the whole house of Israel and the whole
house of Judah to me,' declares the LORD,
'to be my people for my renown and
praise and honor. But they have not listened.'

Wineskins

12 "Say to them: 'This is what the LORD,
the God of Israel, says: Every wineskin
should be filled with wine.' And if they say
to you, 'Don't we know that every wineskin should be filled with wine?' 13 then
tell them, 'This is what the LORD says: I am
going to fill with drunkenness all who live
in this land, including the kings who sit on
David's throne, the priests, the prophets
and all those living in Jerusalem. 14 I will
smash them one against the other, fathers
and sons alike, declares the LORD. I will allow no pity or mercy or compassion to
keep me from destroying them.' "

Threat of Captivity

15 Hear and pay attention,
    do not be arrogant,
  for the LORD has spoken.
16 Give glory to the LORD your God
    before he brings the darkness,
  before your feet stumble
    on the darkening hills.
  You hope for light,
    but he will turn it to thick darkness
    and change it to deep gloom.
17 But if you do not listen,
    I will weep in secret
    because of your pride;
  my eyes will weep bitterly,
    overflowing with tears,
    because the LORD's flock will be
      taken captive.

18 Say to the king and to the queen
      mother,
  "Come down from your thrones,

---

a 4 Or possibly the Euphrates; also in verses 5–7

Get a Load of This...

You may think, "It's OK to tell a small lie if it keeps me out of trouble" or "It's OK to cheat in small things." Really? Read Jeremiah 13:23. Get in the habit of doing wrong and you'll end up with habits you won't be able to change later—at least without a ton of blood, sweat and tears.

for your glorious crowns
    will fall from your heads."
¹⁹ The cities in the Negev will be shut up,
    and there will be no one to open them.
All Judah will be carried into exile,
    carried completely away.

²⁰ Lift up your eyes and see
    those who are coming from the north.
Where is the flock that was entrusted to you,
    the sheep of which you boasted?
²¹ What will you say when ⌞the LORD⌟ sets over you
    those you cultivated as your special allies?
Will not pain grip you
    like that of a woman in labor?
²² And if you ask yourself,
    "Why has this happened to me?"—
it is because of your many sins
    that your skirts have been torn off
    and your body mistreated.
²³ Can the Ethiopian[a] change his skin
    or the leopard its spots?
Neither can you do good
    who are accustomed to doing evil.

²⁴ "I will scatter you like chaff
    driven by the desert wind.
²⁵ This is your lot,
    the portion I have decreed for you,"

               declares the LORD,

"because you have forgotten me
    and trusted in false gods.
²⁶ I will pull up your skirts over your face
    that your shame may be seen—
²⁷ your adulteries and lustful neighings,
    your shameless prostitution!
I have seen your detestable acts
    on the hills and in the fields.
Woe to you, O Jerusalem!
    How long will you be unclean?"

Drought, Famine, Sword

14 This is the word of the LORD to Jeremiah concerning the drought:

² "Judah mourns,
    her cities languish;
they wail for the land,
    and a cry goes up from Jerusalem.
³ The nobles send their servants for water;
    they go to the cisterns
    but find no water.
They return with their jars unfilled;
    dismayed and despairing,
    they cover their heads.
⁴ The ground is cracked

ᵃ 23 Hebrew *Cushite* (probably a person from the upper Nile region)

because there is no rain in the land;
the farmers are dismayed
    and cover their heads.
⁵Even the doe in the field
    deserts her newborn fawn
because there is no grass.
⁶Wild donkeys stand on the barren
        heights
    and pant like jackals;
their eyesight fails
    for lack of pasture."

⁷Although our sins testify against us,
    O LORD, do something for the sake
        of your name.
For our backsliding is great;
    we have sinned against you.
⁸O Hope of Israel,
    its Savior in times of distress,
why are you like a stranger in the land,
    like a traveler who stays only a night?
⁹Why are you like a man taken by
        surprise,
    like a warrior powerless to save?
You are among us, O LORD,
    and we bear your name;
    do not forsake us!

¹⁰This is what the LORD says about this
people:

"They greatly love to wander;
    they do not restrain their feet.
So the LORD does not accept them;
    he will now remember their
        wickedness
    and punish them for their sins."

¹¹Then the LORD said to me, "Do not
pray for the well-being of this people.
¹²Although they fast, I will not listen to
their cry; though they offer burnt offerings and grain offerings, I will not accept
them. Instead, I will destroy them with the
sword, famine and plague."

¹³But I said, "Ah, Sovereign LORD, the
prophets keep telling them, 'You will not
see the sword or suffer famine. Indeed, I
will give you lasting peace in this place.' "

¹⁴Then the LORD said to me, "The
prophets are prophesying lies in my name.
I have not sent them or appointed them
or spoken to them. They are prophesying
to you false visions, divinations, idolatries[a]

---

[a] 14 Or visions, worthless divinations

How Dumb Is This?

READ JEREMIAH 14:7–12

Imagine a driver and his pit crew never put oil in the engine of their race car, and it burns up. When the driver asks his sponsor for a new car, the sponsor will probably *only* give him one if he promises to be faithful to put oil in the engine. If he won't, what would be the point of helping him? Same with the people in Jeremiah's day: They wanted God's help, but they wouldn't stop sinning big-time (verse 7). They kept bringing destruction on themselves. Instead of tuning in to Station Jeremiah, they were listening to the false prophets who said, "Do whatever you want. You'll never suffer" (see verse 15). If you want God's help, you've got to come clean and admit that you're doing wrong things. Then you need to change and live God's way. Then—and *only* then—will he bless you.

Your next reading is on page 973.

and the delusions of their own minds. ¹⁵Therefore, this is what the LORD says about the prophets who are prophesying in my name: I did not send them, yet they are saying, 'No sword or famine will touch this land.' Those same prophets will perish by sword and famine. ¹⁶And the people they are prophesying to will be thrown out into the streets of Jerusalem because of the famine and sword. There will be no one to bury them or their wives, their sons or their daughters. I will pour out on them the calamity they deserve.

¹⁷"Speak this word to them:

" 'Let my eyes overflow with tears
    night and day without ceasing;
for my virgin daughter—my people—
    has suffered a grievous wound,
    a crushing blow.
¹⁸If I go into the country,
    I see those slain by the sword;
if I go into the city,
    I see the ravages of famine.
Both prophet and priest
    have gone to a land they know not.' "

¹⁹Have you rejected Judah completely?
    Do you despise Zion?
Why have you afflicted us
    so that we cannot be healed?
We hoped for peace
    but no good has come,
for a time of healing
    but there is only terror.
²⁰O LORD, we acknowledge our
    wickedness
    and the guilt of our fathers;
we have indeed sinned against you.
²¹For the sake of your name do not
    despise us;
    do not dishonor your glorious throne.
Remember your covenant with us
    and do not break it.
²²Do any of the worthless idols of the
    nations bring rain?
    Do the skies themselves send down
      showers?
No, it is you, O LORD our God.
    Therefore our hope is in you,
    for you are the one who does all this.

15 Then the LORD said to me: "Even if Moses and Samuel were to stand before me, my heart would not go out to this people. Send them away from my presence! Let them go! ²And if they ask you, 'Where

shall we go?' tell them, 'This is what the LORD says:

" 'Those destined for death, to death;
    those for the sword, to the sword;
those for starvation, to starvation;
    those for captivity, to captivity.'

³"I will send four kinds of destroyers against them," declares the LORD, "the sword to kill and the dogs to drag away and the birds of the air and the beasts of the earth to devour and destroy. ⁴I will make them abhorrent to all the kingdoms of the earth because of what Manasseh son of Hezekiah king of Judah did in Jerusalem.

⁵"Who will have pity on you,
    O Jerusalem?
Who will mourn for you?
    Who will stop to ask how you are?
⁶You have rejected me," declares the
    LORD.
    "You keep on backsliding.
So I will lay hands on you and destroy
    you;
    I can no longer show compassion.
⁷I will winnow them with a winnowing
    fork
    at the city gates of the land.
I will bring bereavement and
      destruction on my people,
    for they have not changed their ways.
⁸I will make their widows more
    numerous
    than the sand of the sea.
At midday I will bring a destroyer
    against the mothers of their young
    men;
suddenly I will bring down on them
    anguish and terror.
⁹The mother of seven will grow faint
    and breathe her last.
Her sun will set while it is still day;
    she will be disgraced and humiliated.
I will put the survivors to the sword
    before their enemies,"
                  declares the LORD.
¹⁰Alas, my mother, that you gave me
    birth,
    a man with whom the whole land
      strives and contends!
I have neither lent nor borrowed,
    yet everyone curses me.

¹¹The LORD said,

"Surely I will deliver you for a good
    purpose;

surely I will make your enemies
    plead with you
in times of disaster and times of
    distress.
12 "Can a man break iron—
    iron from the north—or bronze?
13 Your wealth and your treasures
    I will give as plunder, without charge,
because of all your sins
    throughout your country.
14 I will enslave you to your enemies
    in[a] a land you do not know,
for my anger will kindle a fire
    that will burn against you."

15 You understand, O LORD;
    remember me and care for me.
    Avenge me on my persecutors.
You are long-suffering—do not take
    me away;
    think of how I suffer reproach for
    your sake.
16 When your words came, I ate them;
    they were my joy and my heart's
    delight,
for I bear your name,

O LORD God Almighty.
17 I never sat in the company of revelers,
    never made merry with them;
I sat alone because your hand was on
    me
and you had filled me with
    indignation.
18 Why is my pain unending
    and my wound grievous and
    incurable?
Will you be to me like a deceptive
    brook,
    like a spring that fails?

19 Therefore this is what the LORD says:

"If you repent, I will restore you
    that you may serve me;
if you utter worthy, not worthless,
    words,
    you will be my spokesman.
Let this people turn to you,
    but you must not turn to them.
20 I will make you a wall to this people,

a 14 Some Hebrew manuscripts, Septuagint and Syriac (see also Jer. 17:4); most Hebrew manuscripts *I will cause your enemies to bring you* / *into*

GET SMARTER

Hurting and Blurting

READ JEREMIAH 15:16–19

Jeremiah was obedient and faithful, but he still had his moments. He blurted out that he thought God was about as helpful as a dry watering hole (verse 18). Ever had a moment like that? You think, "I'm upset and angry, so it's OK to say something mean to people around me or even God." Oops—better to bite your tongue. Part of being a man is learning to be careful not to say something you'll regret. There's no excuse for blurting out unkind words. "For by your words you will be acquitted, and by your words you will be condemned" (Matthew 12:37). You're responsible for what you say. Next time you're upset, count to ten or say to someone, "I can't talk now. I need to calm down." Get yourself under control. Pray for wisdom to handle the situation and *then* go speak calmly and kindly.

Your next reading is on page 977.

a fortified wall of bronze;
they will fight against you
    but will not overcome you,
for I am with you
    to rescue and save you,"
                  declares the LORD.
21 "I will save you from the hands of the
    wicked
    and redeem you from the grasp of
    the cruel."

Day of Disaster

16 Then the word of the LORD came to me: 2 "You must not marry and have sons or daughters in this place." 3 For this is what the LORD says about the sons and daughters born in this land and about the women who are their mothers and the men who are their fathers: 4 "They will die of deadly diseases. They will not be mourned or buried but will be like refuse lying on the ground. They will perish by sword and famine, and their dead bodies will become food for the birds of the air and the beasts of the earth."

5 For this is what the LORD says: "Do not enter a house where there is a funeral meal; do not go to mourn or show sympathy, because I have withdrawn my blessing, my love and my pity from this people," declares the LORD. 6 "Both high and low will die in this land. They will not be buried or mourned, and no one will cut himself or shave his head for them. 7 No one will offer food to comfort those who mourn for the dead—not even for a father or a mother—nor will anyone give them a drink to console them.

8 "And do not enter a house where there is feasting and sit down to eat and drink. 9 For this is what the LORD Almighty, the God of Israel, says: Before your eyes and in your days I will bring an end to the sounds of joy and gladness and to the voices of bride and bridegroom in this place.

10 "When you tell these people all this and they ask you, 'Why has the LORD decreed such a great disaster against us? What wrong have we done? What sin have we committed against the LORD our God?' 11 then say to them, 'It is because your fathers forsook me,' declares the LORD, 'and followed other gods and served and worshiped them. They forsook me and did not keep my law. 12 But you have behaved more wickedly than your fathers.

See how each of you is following the stubbornness of his evil heart instead of obeying me. 13 So I will throw you out of this land into a land neither you nor your fathers have known, and there you will serve other gods day and night, for I will show you no favor.'

14 "However, the days are coming," declares the LORD, "when men will no longer say, 'As surely as the LORD lives, who brought the Israelites up out of Egypt,' 15 but they will say, 'As surely as the LORD lives, who brought the Israelites up out of the land of the north and out of all the countries where he had banished them.' For I will restore them to the land I gave their forefathers.

16 "But now I will send for many fishermen," declares the LORD, "and they will catch them. After that I will send for many hunters, and they will hunt them down on every mountain and hill and from the crevices of the rocks. 17 My eyes are on all their ways; they are not hidden from me, nor is their sin concealed from my eyes. 18 I will repay them double for their wickedness and their sin, because they have defiled my land with the lifeless forms of their vile images and have filled my inheritance with their detestable idols."

19 O LORD, my strength and my fortress,
    my refuge in time of distress,
to you the nations will come
    from the ends of the earth and say,
"Our fathers possessed nothing but
        false gods,
    worthless idols that did them no
        good.
20 Do men make their own gods?
    Yes, but they are not gods!"

21 "Therefore I will teach them—
    this time I will teach them
    my power and might.
Then they will know
    that my name is the LORD.

17 "Judah's sin is engraved with an iron tool,
    inscribed with a flint point,
    on the tablets of their hearts
and on the horns of their altars.
2 Even their children remember
    their altars and Asherah poles[a]
beside the spreading trees
    and on the high hills.

[a] 2 That is, symbols of the goddess Asherah

³ My mountain in the land
    and your ᵃ wealth and all your treasures
I will give away as plunder,
    together with your high places,
    because of sin throughout your country.
⁴ Through your own fault you will lose
    the inheritance I gave you.
I will enslave you to your enemies
    in a land you do not know,
for you have kindled my anger,
    and it will burn forever."

⁵ This is what the LORD says:

"Cursed is the one who trusts in man,
    who depends on flesh for his strength
    and whose heart turns away from the LORD.
⁶ He will be like a bush in the wastelands;
    he will not see prosperity when it comes.
He will dwell in the parched places of the desert,
    in a salt land where no one lives.

⁷ "But blessed is the man who trusts in the LORD,
    whose confidence is in him.
⁸ He will be like a tree planted by the water
    that sends out its roots by the stream.
It does not fear when heat comes;
    its leaves are always green.
It has no worries in a year of drought
    and never fails to bear fruit."

⁹ The heart is deceitful above all things
    and beyond cure.
    Who can understand it?

¹⁰ "I the LORD search the heart
    and examine the mind,
to reward a man according to his conduct,
    according to what his deeds deserve."

¹¹ Like a partridge that hatches eggs it did not lay
    is the man who gains riches by unjust means.
When his life is half gone, they will desert him,
    and in the end he will prove to be a fool.

¹² A glorious throne, exalted from the beginning,
    is the place of our sanctuary.
¹³ O LORD, the hope of Israel,
    all who forsake you will be put to shame.
Those who turn away from you will be written in the
        dust
    because they have forsaken the LORD,
    the spring of living water.

¹⁴ Heal me, O LORD, and I will be healed;
    save me and I will be saved,
    for you are the one I praise.
¹⁵ They keep saying to me,
    "Where is the word of the LORD?

Get a Load of This...

Check out Jeremiah 17:5–8. Your choice: You can either be a withered scrub bush in a bone-dry salt desert, or an apple tree stretching out your roots and slurping up the H₂0 in a well-watered valley.

ᵃ 2,3 Or hills / ³and the mountains of the land. / Your

Let it now be fulfilled!"
¹⁶I have not run away from being your
　　shepherd;
　　you know I have not desired the day
　　　of despair.
　　What passes my lips is open before
　　　you.
¹⁷Do not be a terror to me;
　　you are my refuge in the day of
　　　disaster.
¹⁸Let my persecutors be put to shame,
　　but keep me from shame;
　let them be terrified,
　　but keep me from terror.
　Bring on them the day of disaster;
　　destroy them with double destruction.

Keeping the Sabbath Holy

¹⁹This is what the LORD said to me: "Go
and stand at the gate of the people,
through which the kings of Judah go in
and out; stand also at all the other gates
of Jerusalem. ²⁰Say to them, 'Hear the
word of the LORD, O kings of Judah and all
people of Judah and everyone living in Jerusalem who come through these gates.
²¹This is what the LORD says: Be careful not
to carry a load on the Sabbath day or
bring it through the gates of Jerusalem.
²²Do not bring a load out of your houses
or do any work on the Sabbath, but keep
the Sabbath day holy, as I commanded
your forefathers. ²³Yet they did not listen
or pay attention; they were stiff-necked
and would not listen or respond to discipline. ²⁴But if you are careful to obey me,
declares the LORD, and bring no load
through the gates of this city on the Sabbath, but keep the Sabbath day holy by
not doing any work on it, ²⁵then kings
who sit on David's throne will come
through the gates of this city with their
officials. They and their officials will come
riding in chariots and on horses, accompanied by the men of Judah and those living in Jerusalem, and this city will be inhabited forever. ²⁶People will come from
the towns of Judah and the villages

Make It Stick

READ JEREMIAH 17:9–10

God looks at what you do and at *why* you do it. So when you do the right thing, do it with
your whole heart. Your motives drive your deeds like a motor drives a car. On a sticky note,
draw a picture of a really cool car as a reminder of this.

around Jerusalem, from the territory of Benjamin and the western foothills, from the hill country and the Negev, bringing burnt offerings and sacrifices, grain offerings, incense and thank offerings to the house of the LORD. 27But if you do not obey me to keep the Sabbath day holy by not carrying any load as you come through the gates of Jerusalem on the Sabbath day, then I will kindle an unquenchable fire in the gates of Jerusalem that will consume her fortresses.' "

At the Potter's House

18 This is the word that came to Jeremiah from the LORD: 2"Go down to the potter's house, and there I will give you my message." 3So I went down to the potter's house, and I saw him working at the wheel. 4But the pot he was shaping from the clay was marred in his hands; so the potter formed it into another pot, shaping it as seemed best to him.

5Then the word of the LORD came to me: 6"O house of Israel, can I not do with you as this potter does?" declares the LORD.

"Like clay in the hand of the potter, so are you in my hand, O house of Israel. 7If at any time I announce that a nation or kingdom is to be uprooted, torn down and destroyed, 8and if that nation I warned repents of its evil, then I will relent and not inflict on it the disaster I had planned. 9And if at another time I announce that a nation or kingdom is to be built up and planted, 10and if it does evil in my sight and does not obey me, then I will reconsider the good I had intended to do for it.

11"Now therefore say to the people of Judah and those living in Jerusalem, 'This is what the LORD says: Look! I am preparing a disaster for you and devising a plan against you. So turn from your evil ways, each one of you, and reform your ways and your actions.' 12But they will reply, 'It's no use. We will continue with our own plans; each of us will follow the stubbornness of his evil heart.' "

13Therefore this is what the LORD says:

"Inquire among the nations:
    Who has ever heard anything like
        this?

The Clay Is Still Wet

READ JEREMIAH 18:1–12

Your life's not set in stone. As long as the potter's clay is still wet, God can change plans. God says, "I know the plans I have for you … plans to prosper you and not to harm you" (Jeremiah 29:11). But … if you refuse to yield to God, he will change his plans for you into some not-quite-so-fun stuff. Hey, but bad little pots can repent and have a great future. So get alongside of God to find out what wonderful things he has for you. Then, do your part to bring those plans to pass. Example: If you tell everyone you have this huge desire to be a world-class chef, but years pass and you never bother to crack open a cookbook, guess what?— You aren't going to be making any gourmet meals any time soon! You'll probably be stuck with tuna fish on toast or mac-n-cheese. But if you walk with God and work hard to cook up a storm, people will come to your first-class restaurant.

Your next reading is on page 985.

A most horrible thing has been done
    by Virgin Israel.
14 Does the snow of Lebanon
    ever vanish from its rocky slopes?
Do its cool waters from distant sources
    ever cease to flow? *a*
15 Yet my people have forgotten me;
    they burn incense to worthless idols,
which made them stumble in their ways
    and in the ancient paths.
They made them walk in bypaths
    and on roads not built up.
16 Their land will be laid waste,
    an object of lasting scorn;
all who pass by will be appalled
    and will shake their heads.
17 Like a wind from the east,
    I will scatter them before their
      enemies;
I will show them my back and not my
      face
in the day of their disaster."

18 They said, "Come, let's make plans against Jeremiah; for the teaching of the law by the priest will not be lost, nor will counsel from the wise, nor the word from the prophets. So come, let's attack him with our tongues and pay no attention to anything he says."

19 Listen to me, O LORD;
    hear what my accusers are saying!
20 Should good be repaid with evil?
    Yet they have dug a pit for me.
Remember that I stood before you
    and spoke in their behalf
    to turn your wrath away from them.
21 So give their children over to famine;
    hand them over to the power of the
      sword.
Let their wives be made childless and
      widows;
    let their men be put to death,
    their young men slain by the sword
      in battle.
22 Let a cry be heard from their houses
    when you suddenly bring invaders
      against them,
for they have dug a pit to capture me
    and have hidden snares for my feet.
23 But you know, O LORD,
    all their plots to kill me.
Do not forgive their crimes
    or blot out their sins from your sight.
Let them be overthrown before you;
    deal with them in the time of your
      anger.

19 This is what the LORD says: "Go and buy a clay jar from a potter. Take along some of the elders of the people and of the priests ²and go out to the Valley of Ben Hinnom, near the entrance of the Potsherd Gate. There proclaim the words I tell you, ³and say, 'Hear the word of the LORD, O kings of Judah and people of Jerusalem. This is what the LORD Almighty, the God of Israel, says: Listen! I am going to bring a disaster on this place that will make the ears of everyone who hears of it tingle. ⁴For they have forsaken me and made this a place of foreign gods; they have burned sacrifices in it to gods that neither they nor their fathers nor the kings of Judah ever knew, and they have filled this place with the blood of the innocent. ⁵They have built the high places of Baal to burn their sons in the fire as offerings to Baal—something I did not command or mention, nor did it enter my mind. ⁶So beware, the days are coming, declares the LORD, when people will no longer call this place Topheth or the Valley of Ben Hinnom, but the Valley of Slaughter.

7 " 'In this place I will ruin *b* the plans of Judah and Jerusalem. I will make them fall by the sword before their enemies, at the hands of those who seek their lives, and I will give their carcasses as food to the birds of the air and the beasts of the earth. ⁸I will devastate this city and make it an object of scorn; all who pass by will be appalled and will scoff because of all its wounds. ⁹I will make them eat the flesh of their sons and daughters, and they will eat one another's flesh during the stress of the siege imposed on them by the enemies who seek their lives.'

10 "Then break the jar while those who go with you are watching, ¹¹and say to them, 'This is what the LORD Almighty says: I will smash this nation and this city just as this potter's jar is smashed and cannot be repaired. They will bury the dead in Topheth until there is no more room. ¹²This is what I will do to this place and to those who live here, declares the LORD. I will make this city like Topheth. ¹³The houses in Jerusalem and those of the kings of Judah will be defiled like this place, Topheth—all the houses where

---

a 14 The meaning of the Hebrew for this sentence is uncertain.   *b 7* The Hebrew for *ruin* sounds like the Hebrew for *jar* (see verses 1 and 10).

they burned incense on the roofs to all the starry hosts and poured out drink offerings to other gods.' "

¹⁴Jeremiah then returned from Topheth, where the LORD had sent him to prophesy, and stood in the court of the LORD's temple and said to all the people, ¹⁵"This is what the LORD Almighty, the God of Israel, says: 'Listen! I am going to bring on this city and the villages around it every disaster I pronounced against them, because they were stiff-necked and would not listen to my words.' "

Jeremiah and Pashhur

20 When the priest Pashhur son of Immer, the chief officer in the temple of the LORD, heard Jeremiah prophesying these things, ²he had Jeremiah the prophet beaten and put in the stocks at the Upper Gate of Benjamin at the LORD's temple. ³The next day, when Pashhur released him from the stocks, Jeremiah said to him, "The LORD's name for you is not Pashhur, but Magor-Missabib.ᵃ ⁴For this is what the LORD says: 'I will make you a terror to yourself and to all your friends; with your own eyes you will see them fall by the sword of their enemies. I will hand all Judah over to the king of Babylon, who will carry them away to Babylon or put them to the sword. ⁵I will hand over to their enemies all the wealth of this city—all its products, all its valuables and all the treasures of the kings of Judah. They will take it away as plunder and carry it off to Babylon. ⁶And you, Pashhur, and all who live in your house will go into exile to Babylon. There you will die and be buried, you and all your friends to whom you have prophesied lies.' "

Jeremiah's Complaint

⁷O LORD, you deceivedᵇ me, and I was deceivedᶜ;
    you overpowered me and prevailed.
I am ridiculed all day long;
    everyone mocks me.
⁸Whenever I speak, I cry out
    proclaiming violence and destruction.
So the word of the LORD has brought me
    insult and reproach all day long.
⁹But if I say, "I will not mention him
    or speak any more in his name,"
his word is in my heart like a fire,
    a fire shut up in my bones.
I am weary of holding it in;
    indeed, I cannot.
¹⁰I hear many whispering,
    "Terror on every side!
    Report him! Let's report him!"
All my friends
    are waiting for me to slip, saying,
    "Perhaps he will be deceived;

Gross!

In Jeremiah's day, if you got the authorities mad, they locked your hands, feet and head inside a wooden frame called stocks (Jeremiah 20:2). Uncomfortable! Try going to sleep in *that*. At least food wasn't a problem—it is said that people often threw rotten fruit at folks in stocks. Eww.

ᵃ 3 Magor-Missabib means *terror on every side.*   ᵇ 7 Or persuaded
ᶜ 7 Or persuaded

then we will prevail over him
and take our revenge on him."

¹¹ But the LORD is with me like a mighty
warrior;
so my persecutors will stumble and
not prevail.
They will fail and be thoroughly
disgraced;
their dishonor will never be
forgotten.
¹² O LORD Almighty, you who examine the
righteous
and probe the heart and mind,
let me see your vengeance upon them,
for to you I have committed my
cause.

¹³ Sing to the LORD!
Give praise to the LORD!
He rescues the life of the needy
from the hands of the wicked.

¹⁴ Cursed be the day I was born!
May the day my mother bore me
not be blessed!
¹⁵ Cursed be the man who brought my
father the news,
who made him very glad, saying,
"A child is born to you—a son!"
¹⁶ May that man be like the towns
the LORD overthrew without pity.
May he hear wailing in the morning,
a battle cry at noon.
¹⁷ For he did not kill me in the womb,
with my mother as my grave,
her womb enlarged forever.
¹⁸ Why did I ever come out of the womb
to see trouble and sorrow
and to end my days in shame?

God Rejects Zedekiah's Request

21 The word came to Jeremiah from
the LORD when King Zedekiah
sent to him Pashhur son of Malkijah and the priest Zephaniah
son of Maaseiah. They said: ²"Inquire now
of the LORD for us because Nebuchadnezzar[a] king of Babylon is attacking us. Perhaps the LORD will perform wonders for us
as in times past so that he will withdraw
from us."

³ But Jeremiah answered them, "Tell
Zedekiah, ⁴'This is what the LORD, the God
of Israel, says: I am about to turn against
you the weapons of war that are in your
hands, which you are using to fight the
king of Babylon and the Babylonians[b]

who are outside the wall besieging you.
And I will gather them inside this city. ⁵ I
myself will fight against you with an outstretched hand and a mighty arm in anger
and fury and great wrath. ⁶ I will strike
down those who live in this city—both
men and animals—and they will die of a
terrible plague. ⁷ After that, declares the
LORD, I will hand over Zedekiah king of Judah, his officials and the people in this city
who survive the plague, sword and famine, to Nebuchadnezzar king of Babylon
and to their enemies who seek their lives.
He will put them to the sword; he will
show them no mercy or pity or compassion.'

⁸ "Furthermore, tell the people, 'This is
what the LORD says: See, I am setting before you the way of life and the way of
death. ⁹ Whoever stays in this city will die
by the sword, famine or plague. But whoever goes out and surrenders to the Babylonians who are besieging you will live;
he will escape with his life. ¹⁰ I have determined to do this city harm and not good,
declares the LORD. It will be given into the
hands of the king of Babylon, and he will
destroy it with fire.'

¹¹ "Moreover, say to the royal house of
Judah, 'Hear the word of the LORD;
¹² O house of David, this is what the LORD
says:

" 'Administer justice every morning;
rescue from the hand of his
oppressor
the one who has been robbed,
or my wrath will break out and burn
like fire
because of the evil you have done—
burn with no one to quench it.
¹³ I am against you, Jerusalem,
you who live above this valley
on the rocky plateau,
declares the LORD—
you who say, "Who can come against
us?
Who can enter our refuge?"
¹⁴ I will punish you as your deeds
deserve,
declares the LORD.
I will kindle a fire in your forests
that will consume everything around
you.' "

---

[a] 2 Hebrew *Nebuchadrezzar*, of which *Nebuchadnezzar* is a
variant; here and often in Jeremiah and Ezekiel
[b] 4 Or *Chaldeans*; also in verse 9

Judgment Against Evil Kings

22 This is what the LORD says: "Go down to the palace of the king of Judah and proclaim this message there: ²'Hear the word of the LORD, O king of Judah, you who sit on David's throne—you, your officials and your people who come through these gates. ³This is what the LORD says: Do what is just and right. Rescue from the hand of his oppressor the one who has been robbed. Do no wrong or violence to the alien, the fatherless or the widow, and do not shed innocent blood in this place. ⁴For if you are careful to carry out these commands, then kings who sit on David's throne will come through the gates of this palace, riding in chariots and on horses, accompanied by their officials and their people. ⁵But if you do not obey these commands, declares the LORD, I swear by myself that this palace will become a ruin.' "

⁶For this is what the LORD says about the palace of the king of Judah:

"Though you are like Gilead to me,
    like the summit of Lebanon,
I will surely make you like a desert,
    like towns not inhabited.
⁷I will send destroyers against you,
    each man with his weapons,
and they will cut up your fine cedar
        beams
    and throw them into the fire.

⁸"People from many nations will pass by this city and will ask one another, 'Why has the LORD done such a thing to this great city?' ⁹And the answer will be: 'Because they have forsaken the covenant of the LORD their God and have worshiped and served other gods.' "

¹⁰Do not weep for the dead ⌊king⌋ or
        mourn his loss;
rather, weep bitterly for him who is
        exiled,
    because he will never return
        nor see his native land again.

¹¹For this is what the LORD says about Shallum^a son of Josiah, who succeeded his father as king of Judah but has gone from this place: "He will never return. ¹²He will die in the place where they have led him captive; he will not see this land again."

¹³"Woe to him who builds his palace by
        unrighteousness,
    his upper rooms by injustice,
making his countrymen work for
        nothing,
    not paying them for their labor.
¹⁴He says, 'I will build myself a great
        palace
    with spacious upper rooms.'
So he makes large windows in it,
    panels it with cedar
    and decorates it in red.

¹⁵"Does it make you a king
    to have more and more cedar?
Did not your father have food and
        drink?
    He did what was right and just,
    so all went well with him.
¹⁶He defended the cause of the poor
        and needy,
    and so all went well.
Is that not what it means to know me?"
    declares the LORD.
¹⁷"But your eyes and your heart
    are set only on dishonest gain,
on shedding innocent blood
    and on oppression and extortion."

¹⁸Therefore this is what the LORD says about Jehoiakim son of Josiah king of Judah:

"They will not mourn for him:
    'Alas, my brother! Alas, my sister!'
They will not mourn for him:
    'Alas, my master! Alas, his splendor!'
¹⁹He will have the burial of a donkey—
    dragged away and thrown
    outside the gates of Jerusalem."

²⁰"Go up to Lebanon and cry out,
    let your voice be heard in Bashan,
cry out from Abarim,
    for all your allies are crushed.
²¹I warned you when you felt secure,
    but you said, 'I will not listen!'
This has been your way from your
        youth;
    you have not obeyed me.
²²The wind will drive all your shepherds
        away,
    and your allies will go into exile.
Then you will be ashamed and disgraced
    because of all your wickedness.
²³You who live in 'Lebanon,^b'
    who are nestled in cedar buildings,

---

^a 11 Also called *Jehoahaz*   ^b 23 That is, the palace in Jerusalem (see 1 Kings 7:2)

how you will groan when pangs come
      upon you,
   pain like that of a woman in labor!

24"As surely as I live," declares the LORD,
"even if you, Jehoiachin*a* son of Jehoiakim
king of Judah, were a signet ring on my
right hand, I would still pull you off. 25I
will hand you over to those who seek your
life, those you fear—to Nebuchadnezzar
king of Babylon and to the Babylonians.*b*
26I will hurl you and the mother who gave
you birth into another country, where neither of you was born, and there you both
will die. 27You will never come back to the
land you long to return to."

28Is this man Jehoiachin a despised,
      broken pot,
   an object no one wants?
   Why will he and his children be hurled
      out,
   cast into a land they do not know?
29O land, land, land,
   hear the word of the LORD!

30This is what the LORD says:
   "Record this man as if childless,
      a man who will not prosper in his
      lifetime,
   for none of his offspring will prosper,
      none will sit on the throne of David
      or rule anymore in Judah."

The Righteous Branch

23 "Woe to the shepherds who
are destroying and scattering
the sheep of my pasture!" declares the LORD. 2Therefore this
is what the LORD, the God of Israel, says to
the shepherds who tend my people: "Because you have scattered my flock and
driven them away and have not bestowed
care on them, I will bestow punishment
on you for the evil you have done," declares the LORD. 3"I myself will gather the
remnant of my flock out of all the coun-

a 24 Hebrew *Coniah,* a variant of *Jehoiachin;* also in verse 28
b 25 Or *Chaldeans*

Make It Stick

READ JEREMIAH 22:15–16

To know God is to know what he's *like.* To become like God is to do what he loves. God is all
about righteousness, mercy, justice and love. Are you? Write on a sticky note an example of
how you have (a) done right, (b) shown mercy, (c) been just and (d) been loving.

tries where I have driven them and will bring them back to their pasture, where they will be fruitful and increase in number. ⁴I will place shepherds over them who will tend them, and they will no longer be afraid or terrified, nor will any be missing," declares the LORD.

⁵ "The days are coming," declares the LORD,
"when I will raise up to David*a* a
     righteous Branch,
a King who will reign wisely
     and do what is just and right in the
     land.
⁶ In his days Judah will be saved
     and Israel will live in safety.
This is the name by which he will be
     called:
The LORD Our Righteousness.

⁷ "So then, the days are coming," declares the LORD, "when people will no longer say, 'As surely as the LORD lives, who brought the Israelites up out of Egypt,' ⁸but they will say, 'As surely as the LORD lives, who brought the descendants of Israel up out of the land of the north and out of all the countries where he had banished them.' Then they will live in their own land."

Lying Prophets

⁹ Concerning the prophets:

My heart is broken within me;
     all my bones tremble.
I am like a drunken man,
     like a man overcome by wine,
because of the LORD
     and his holy words.
¹⁰ The land is full of adulterers;
     because of the curse*b* the land lies
     parched*c*
and the pastures in the desert are
     withered.
The ⌐prophets⌐ follow an evil course
     and use their power unjustly.

¹¹ "Both prophet and priest are godless;
     even in my temple I find their
     wickedness,"
                         declares the LORD.
¹² "Therefore their path will become
     slippery;
they will be banished to darkness
     and there they will fall.
I will bring disaster on them
     in the year they are punished,"
                         declares the LORD.

¹³ "Among the prophets of Samaria
     I saw this repulsive thing:
They prophesied by Baal
     and led my people Israel astray.
¹⁴ And among the prophets of Jerusalem
     I have seen something horrible:
They commit adultery and live a lie.
They strengthen the hands of evildoers,
     so that no one turns from his
     wickedness.
They are all like Sodom to me;
     the people of Jerusalem are like
     Gomorrah."

¹⁵ Therefore, this is what the LORD Almighty says concerning the prophets:

"I will make them eat bitter food
     and drink poisoned water,
because from the prophets of
     Jerusalem
ungodliness has spread throughout
     the land."

¹⁶ This is what the LORD Almighty says:

"Do not listen to what the prophets
     are prophesying to you;
     they fill you with false hopes.
They speak visions from their own
     minds,
     not from the mouth of the LORD.
¹⁷ They keep saying to those who despise
     me,
     'The LORD says: You will have peace.'
And to all who follow the
     stubbornness of their hearts
     they say, 'No harm will come to you.'
¹⁸ But which of them has stood in the
     council of the LORD
to see or to hear his word?
Who has listened and heard his
     word?
¹⁹ See, the storm of the LORD
     will burst out in wrath,
a whirlwind swirling down
     on the heads of the wicked.
²⁰ The anger of the LORD will not turn back
     until he fully accomplishes
     the purposes of his heart.
In days to come
     you will understand it clearly.
²¹ I did not send these prophets,
     yet they have run with their message;
I did not speak to them,
     yet they have prophesied.

---

*a 5 Or up from David's line   b 10 Or because of these
things   c 10 Or land mourns*

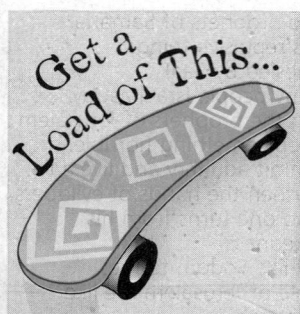

Get a Load of This...

All Points Bulletin— Watch out for false prophets (see Jeremiah 23:21–22)! These people will tell you it's OK to do the wrong things, that God doesn't care what you do. Huh! Compare that with *true* prophets who tell you the truth, even if it hurts.

In other words...

22 But if they had stood in my council,
    they would have proclaimed my words to my
      people
and would have turned them from their evil ways
    and from their evil deeds.
23 "Am I only a God nearby,"
                    declares the LORD,
    "and not a God far away?
24 Can anyone hide in secret places
    so that I cannot see him?"
                    declares the LORD.
    "Do not I fill heaven and earth?"
                    declares the LORD.

25 "I have heard what the prophets say who prophesy lies in my name. They say, 'I had a dream! I had a dream!' 26 How long will this continue in the hearts of these lying prophets, who prophesy the delusions of their own minds? 27 They think the dreams they tell one another will make my people forget my name, just as their fathers forgot my name through Baal worship. 28 Let the prophet who has a dream tell his dream, but let the one who has my word speak it faithfully. For what has straw to do with grain?" declares the LORD. 29 "Is not my word like fire," declares the LORD, "and like a hammer that breaks a rock in pieces?

30 "Therefore," declares the LORD, "I am against the prophets who steal from one another words supposedly from me. 31 Yes," declares the LORD, "I am against the prophets who wag their own tongues and yet declare, 'The LORD declares.' 32 Indeed, I am against those who prophesy false dreams," declares the LORD. "They tell them and lead my people astray with their reckless lies, yet I did not send or appoint them. They do not benefit these people in the least," declares the LORD.

False Oracles and False Prophets

33 "When these people, or a prophet or a priest, ask you, 'What is the oracle[a] of the LORD?' say to them, 'What oracle?[b] I will forsake you, declares the LORD.' 34 If a prophet or a priest or anyone else claims, 'This is the oracle of the LORD,' I will punish that man and his household. 35 This is what each of you keeps on saying to his friend or relative: 'What is the LORD's answer?' or 'What has the LORD spoken?' 36 But you must not mention 'the oracle of the LORD' again, because every man's own word becomes his oracle and so you distort the words of the living God, the LORD Almighty, our God. 37 This is what you keep saying to a prophet: 'What is the LORD's answer to you?' or 'What has the LORD spoken?' 38 Although you claim, 'This is the oracle of the LORD,' this is what the LORD says: You used the words, 'This is the oracle of the LORD,' even though I told you that you must not claim, 'This is the oracle of the LORD.'

[a] 33 Or *burden* (see Septuagint and Vulgate)   [b] 33 Hebrew; Septuagint and Vulgate *'You are the burden.* (The Hebrew for *oracle* and *burden* is the same.)

³⁹Therefore, I will surely forget you and cast you out of my presence along with the city I gave to you and your fathers. ⁴⁰I will bring upon you everlasting disgrace—everlasting shame that will not be forgotten."

Two Baskets of Figs

24 After Jehoiachin^a son of Jehoiakim king of Judah and the officials, the craftsmen and the artisans of Judah were carried into exile from Jerusalem to Babylon by Nebuchadnezzar king of Babylon, the LORD showed me two baskets of figs placed in front of the temple of the LORD. ²One basket had very good figs, like those that ripen early; the other basket had very poor figs, so bad they could not be eaten.

³Then the LORD asked me, "What do you see, Jeremiah?"

"Figs," I answered. "The good ones are very good, but the poor ones are so bad they cannot be eaten."

⁴Then the word of the LORD came to me: ⁵"This is what the LORD, the God of Israel, says: 'Like these good figs, I regard as good the exiles from Judah, whom I sent away from this place to the land of the Babylonians.^b ⁶My eyes will watch over them for their good, and I will bring them back to this land. I will build them up and not tear them down; I will plant them and not uproot them. ⁷I will give them a heart to know me, that I am the LORD. They will be my people, and I will be their God, for they will return to me with all their heart.

⁸" 'But like the poor figs, which are so bad they cannot be eaten,' says the LORD, 'so will I deal with Zedekiah king of Judah, his officials and the survivors from Jerusalem, whether they remain in this land or live in Egypt. ⁹I will make them abhorrent and an offense to all the kingdoms of the earth, a reproach and a byword, an object of ridicule and cursing, wherever I banish them. ¹⁰I will send the sword, famine and plague against them until they are destroyed from the land I gave to them and their fathers.' "

^a 1 Hebrew *Jeconiah*, a variant of *Jehoiachin*
^b 5 Or *Chaldeans*

We Are the People!

READ JEREMIAH 24:4–8; 25:12; 29:10–11

Ever think you were the hottest thing since sliced bread? The Jews in Judah had a blown up idea of how important they were. Jerusalem was the holy city. God's temple was there. They figured they were the chosen people living in the Promised Land, and God *had* to look out for them, even if they were totally disobedient. Not. God *was* watching out for the Jews, sure, the Jewish prisoners in Babylon, not those rotters in Judah (Jeremiah 24:4–8). God kept the Jews in Babylon out of harm's way for seventy years, then brought them back to Judah and blessed the socks off them. But the people remaining in Judah were trying to make God line up with their will when what they *needed* to do was line themselves up with God's will. It's the same with us: Instead of assuming we're God's gift to the world, or that God just *has* to bless us, we need to be humble, seek God and follow him.

Your next reading is on page 988.

Seventy Years of Captivity

25 The word came to Jeremiah concerning all the people of Judah in the fourth year of Jehoiakim son of Josiah king of Judah, which was the first year of Nebuchadnezzar king of Babylon. ²So Jeremiah the prophet said to all the people of Judah and to all those living in Jerusalem: ³For twenty-three years—from the thirteenth year of Josiah son of Amon king of Judah until this very day—the word of the LORD has come to me and I have spoken to you again and again, but you have not listened.

⁴And though the LORD has sent all his servants the prophets to you again and again, you have not listened or paid any attention. ⁵They said, "Turn now, each of you, from your evil ways and your evil practices, and you can stay in the land the LORD gave to you and your fathers for ever and ever. ⁶Do not follow other gods to serve and worship them; do not provoke me to anger with what your hands have made. Then I will not harm you."

⁷"But you did not listen to me," declares the LORD, "and you have provoked me with what your hands have made, and you have brought harm to yourselves."

⁸Therefore the LORD Almighty says this: "Because you have not listened to my words, ⁹I will summon all the peoples of the north and my servant Nebuchadnezzar king of Babylon," declares the LORD, "and I will bring them against this land and its inhabitants and against all the surrounding nations. I will completely destroyᵃ them and make them an object of horror and scorn, and an everlasting ruin. ¹⁰I will banish from them the sounds of joy and gladness, the voices of bride and bridegroom, the sound of millstones and the light of the lamp. ¹¹This whole country will become a desolate wasteland, and these nations will serve the king of Babylon seventy years.

¹²"But when the seventy years are fulfilled, I will punish the king of Babylon and his nation, the land of the Babylonians,ᵇ for their guilt," declares the LORD, "and will make it desolate forever. ¹³I will bring upon that land all the things I have spoken against it, all that are written in this book and prophesied by Jeremiah against all the nations. ¹⁴They themselves will be enslaved by many nations and great kings; I will repay them according to their deeds and the work of their hands."

The Cup of God's Wrath

¹⁵This is what the LORD, the God of Israel, said to me: "Take from my hand this cup filled with the wine of my wrath and make all the nations to whom I send you drink it. ¹⁶When they drink it, they will stagger and go mad because of the sword I will send among them."

¹⁷So I took the cup from the LORD's hand and made all the nations to whom he sent me drink it: ¹⁸Jerusalem and the towns of Judah, its kings and officials, to make them a ruin and an object of horror and scorn and cursing, as they are today; ¹⁹Pharaoh king of Egypt, his attendants, his officials and all his people, ²⁰and all the foreign people there; all the kings of Uz; all the kings of the Philistines (those of Ashkelon, Gaza, Ekron, and the people left at Ashdod); ²¹Edom, Moab and Ammon; ²²all the kings of Tyre and Sidon; the kings of the coastlands across the sea; ²³Dedan, Tema, Buz and all who are in distant placesᶜ; ²⁴all the kings of Arabia and all the kings of the foreign people who live in the desert; ²⁵all the kings of Zimri, Elam and Media; ²⁶and all the kings of the north, near and far, one after the other—all the kingdoms on the face of the earth. And after all of them, the king of Sheshachᵈ will drink it too.

²⁷"Then tell them, 'This is what the LORD Almighty, the God of Israel, says: Drink, get drunk and vomit, and fall to rise no more because of the sword I will send among you.' ²⁸But if they refuse to take the cup from your hand and drink, tell them, 'This is what the LORD Almighty says: You must drink it! ²⁹See, I am beginning to bring disaster on the city that bears my Name, and will you indeed go unpunished? You will not go unpunished, for I am calling down a sword upon all who live on the earth, declares the LORD Almighty.'

³⁰"Now prophesy all these words against them and say to them:

" 'The LORD will roar from on high;
    he will thunder from his holy dwelling

ᵃ9 The Hebrew term refers to the irrevocable giving over of things or persons to the LORD, often by totally destroying them.   ᵇ12 Or Chaldeans   ᶜ23 Or who clip the hair by their foreheads   ᵈ26 Sheshach is a cryptogram for Babylon.

and roar mightily against his land.
He will shout like those who tread the
grapes,
shout against all who live on the
earth.
[31] The tumult will resound to the ends of
the earth,
for the LORD will bring charges
against the nations;
he will bring judgment on all mankind
and put the wicked to the sword,' "
declares the LORD.

[32] This is what the LORD Almighty says:

"Look! Disaster is spreading
from nation to nation;
a mighty storm is rising
from the ends of the earth."

[33] At that time those slain by the LORD will
be everywhere—from one end of the
earth to the other. They will not be
mourned or gathered up or buried, but
will be like refuse lying on the ground.

[34] Weep and wail, you shepherds;
roll in the dust, you leaders of the
flock.
For your time to be slaughtered has
come;
you will fall and be shattered like
fine pottery.
[35] The shepherds will have nowhere to
flee,
the leaders of the flock no place to
escape.
[36] Hear the cry of the shepherds,
the wailing of the leaders of the
flock,
for the LORD is destroying their
pasture.
[37] The peaceful meadows will be laid
waste
because of the fierce anger of the
LORD.
[38] Like a lion he will leave his lair,
and their land will become desolate
because of the sword[a] of the oppressor
and because of the LORD's fierce
anger.

Jeremiah Threatened With Death

26 Early in the reign of Jehoiakim
son of Josiah king of Judah,
this word came from the LORD:
[2] "This is what the LORD says:
Stand in the courtyard of the LORD's house
and speak to all the people of the towns
of Judah who come to worship in the
house of the LORD. Tell them everything I
command you; do not omit a word. [3] Perhaps they will listen and each will turn
from his evil way. Then I will relent and
not bring on them the disaster I was planning because of the evil they have done.
[4] Say to them, 'This is what the LORD says:
If you do not listen to me and follow my
law, which I have set before you, [5] and if
you do not listen to the words of my servants the prophets, whom I have sent to
you again and again (though you have
not listened), [6] then I will make this house
like Shiloh and this city an object of cursing among all the nations of the earth.' "

[7] The priests, the prophets and all the
people heard Jeremiah speak these words
in the house of the LORD. [8] But as soon as
Jeremiah finished telling all the people everything the LORD had commanded him to
say, the priests, the prophets and all the
people seized him and said, "You must
die! [9] Why do you prophesy in the LORD's
name that this house will be like Shiloh
and this city will be desolate and deserted?" And all the people crowded around
Jeremiah in the house of the LORD.

[10] When the officials of Judah heard
about these things, they went up from
the royal palace to the house of the LORD
and took their places at the entrance of
the New Gate of the LORD's house. [11] Then
the priests and the prophets said to the
officials and all the people, "This man
should be sentenced to death because he
has prophesied against this city. You have
heard it with your own ears!"

[12] Then Jeremiah said to all the officials
and all the people: "The LORD sent me to
prophesy against this house and this city
all the things you have heard. [13] Now reform your ways and your actions and
obey the LORD your God. Then the LORD
will relent and not bring the disaster he
has pronounced against you. [14] As for me,
I am in your hands; do with me whatever
you think is good and right. [15] Be assured,
however, that if you put me to death, you
will bring the guilt of innocent blood on
yourselves and on this city and on those
who live in it, for in truth the LORD has sent
me to you to speak all these words in your
hearing."

[a] 38 Some Hebrew manuscripts and Septuagint (see also Jer.
46:16 and 50:16); most Hebrew manuscripts *anger*

¹⁶Then the officials and all the people said to the priests and the prophets, "This man should not be sentenced to death! He has spoken to us in the name of the LORD our God."

¹⁷Some of the elders of the land stepped forward and said to the entire assembly of people, ¹⁸"Micah of Moresheth prophesied in the days of Hezekiah king of Judah. He told all the people of Judah, 'This is what the LORD Almighty says:

" 'Zion will be plowed like a field,
 Jerusalem will become a heap of
  rubble,
 the temple hill a mound overgrown
  with thickets.'ᵃ

¹⁹"Did Hezekiah king of Judah or anyone else in Judah put him to death? Did not Hezekiah fear the LORD and seek his favor? And did not the LORD relent, so that he did not bring the disaster he pronounced against them? We are about to bring a terrible disaster on ourselves!"

²⁰(Now Uriah son of Shemaiah from Kiriath Jearim was another man who prophesied in the name of the LORD; he prophesied the same things against this city and this land as Jeremiah did. ²¹When King Jehoiakim and all his officers and officials heard his words, the king sought to put him to death. But Uriah heard of it and fled in fear to Egypt. ²²King Jehoiakim, however, sent Elnathan son of Acbor to Egypt, along with some other men. ²³They brought Uriah out of Egypt and took him to King Jehoiakim, who had him struck down with a sword and his body thrown into the burial place of the common people.)

²⁴Furthermore, Ahikam son of Shaphan supported Jeremiah, and so he was not handed over to the people to be put to death.

Judah to Serve Nebuchadnezzar

27 Early in the reign of Zedekiahᵇ son of Josiah king of Judah, this word came to Jeremiah from the LORD: ²This is what the

---

ᵃ 18 Micah 3:12 ᵇ 1 A few Hebrew manuscripts and Syriac (see also Jer. 27:3, 12 and 28:1); most Hebrew manuscripts *Jehoiakim* (Most Septuagint manuscripts do not have this verse.)

A Few Faithful Friends

READ JEREMIAH 26

Do you get the idea that most people just didn't like what Jeremiah was saying? But he still had a small handful of friends. When all the priests, prophets and people wanted to kill Jeremiah, a few white-bearded elders "stepped forward" (verse 17) and spoke out for him. And don't forget Ahikam. He "supported Jeremiah" (verse 24). You've got to understand: Jeremiah had a lynch mob after him. It wasn't exactly a good time to say, "I'm Jeremiah's buddy. You touch him over my dead body." But these were true friends and they stood up. You can be a true friend, too. When others are gossiping or saying bad things about a bud of yours, stand up and say, "That's not true." Or even if it *might* be true, tell them, "I want to hear *his* side." A true friend stands up for his friends—even when times are tough.

Your next reading is on page 990.

LORD said to me: "Make a yoke out of straps and cross-bars and put it on your neck. ³Then send word to the kings of Edom, Moab, Ammon, Tyre and Sidon through the envoys who have come to Jerusalem to Zedekiah king of Judah. ⁴Give them a message for their masters and say, 'This is what the LORD Almighty, the God of Israel, says: "Tell this to your masters: ⁵With my great power and outstretched arm I made the earth and its people and the animals that are on it, and I give it to anyone I please. ⁶Now I will hand all your countries over to my servant Nebuchadnezzar king of Babylon; I will make even the wild animals subject to him. ⁷All nations will serve him and his son and his grandson until the time for his land comes; then many nations and great kings will subjugate him.

⁸" ' "If, however, any nation or kingdom will not serve Nebuchadnezzar king of Babylon or bow its neck under his yoke, I will punish that nation with the sword, famine and plague, declares the LORD, until I destroy it by his hand. ⁹So do not listen to your prophets, your diviners, your interpreters of dreams, your mediums or your sorcerers who tell you, 'You will not serve the king of Babylon.' ¹⁰They prophesy lies to you that will only serve to remove you far from your lands; I will banish you and you will perish. ¹¹But if any nation will bow its neck under the yoke of the king of Babylon and serve him, I will let that nation remain in its own land to till it and to live there, declares the LORD." ' "

¹²I gave the same message to Zedekiah king of Judah. I said, "Bow your neck under the yoke of the king of Babylon; serve him and his people, and you will live. ¹³Why will you and your people die by the sword, famine and plague with which the LORD has threatened any nation that will not serve the king of Babylon? ¹⁴Do not listen to the words of the prophets who say to you, 'You will not serve the king of Babylon,' for they are prophesying lies to you. ¹⁵'I have not sent them,' declares the LORD. 'They are prophesying lies in my name. Therefore, I will banish you and you will perish, both you and the prophets who prophesy to you.' "

¹⁶Then I said to the priests and all these people, "This is what the LORD says: Do not listen to the prophets who say, 'Very soon now the articles from the LORD's house will be brought back from Babylon.' They are prophesying lies to you. ¹⁷Do not listen to them. Serve the king of Babylon, and you will live. Why should this city become a ruin? ¹⁸If they are prophets and have the word of the LORD, let them plead with the LORD Almighty that the furnishings remaining in the house of the LORD and in the palace of the king of Judah and in Jerusalem not be taken to Babylon. ¹⁹For this is what the LORD Almighty says about the pillars, the Sea, the movable stands and the other furnishings that are left in this city, ²⁰which Nebuchadnezzar king of Babylon did not take away when he carried Jehoiachin*ᵃ* son of Jehoiakim

Get a Load of This...

Oh, so you don't think God's in control of *everything*? To make the point absolutely clear that he is in control of all people and all nations, God said that he would make even the wild animals subject to his "servant," King Nebuchadnezzar (Jeremiah 27:5–7). Talk about being "king of the beasts"!

ᵃ 20 Hebrew *Jeconiah*, a variant of *Jehoiachin*

king of Judah into exile from Jerusalem to Babylon, along with all the nobles of Judah and Jerusalem— 21yes, this is what the LORD Almighty, the God of Israel, says about the things that are left in the house of the LORD and in the palace of the king of Judah and in Jerusalem: 22'They will be taken to Babylon and there they will remain until the day I come for them,' declares the LORD. 'Then I will bring them back and restore them to this place.' "

The False Prophet Hananiah

In the fifth month of that same year, the fourth year, early in the reign of Zedekiah king of Judah, the prophet Hananiah son of Azzur, who was from Gibeon, said to me in the house of the LORD in the presence of the priests and all the people: 2"This is what the LORD Almighty, the God of Israel, says: 'I will break the yoke of the king of Babylon. 3Within two years I will bring back to this place all the articles of the LORD's house that Nebuchadnezzar king of Babylon removed from here and took to Babylon. 4I will also bring back to this place Jehoiachin[a] son of Jehoiakim king of Judah and all the other exiles from Judah who went to Babylon,' declares the LORD, 'for I will break the yoke of the king of Babylon.' "

5Then the prophet Jeremiah replied to the prophet Hananiah before the priests and all the people who were standing in the house of the LORD. 6He said, "Amen! May the LORD do so! May the LORD fulfill the words you have prophesied by bringing the articles of the LORD's house and all the exiles back to this place from Babylon. 7Nevertheless, listen to what I have to say in your hearing and in the hearing of all the people: 8From early times the prophets who preceded you and me have prophesied war, disaster and plague against many countries and great kingdoms. 9But the prophet who prophesies peace will be recognized as one truly sent by the LORD only if his prediction comes true."

10Then the prophet Hananiah took the yoke off the neck of the prophet Jeremiah

[a] 4 Hebrew *Jeconiah,* a variant of *Jehoiachin*

GET SMARTER

Limits of Positive Thinking

READ JEREMIAH 28

Your team is losing 8-0 and time is running out. You grit your teeth, snarl, and decide that *nothing* can stop you from running the football the entire length of the field. Hut! Hut! Hike! Suddenly you have the pigskin and you're running. You zig, you zag, you leap, you dodge, you ... OK, OK, stop daydreaming. Ten guys at the five-yard line took you down. Just like the prophet Hananiah, it doesn't matter *how* positive a mental attitude you have; if you're not going God's way, things just won't work. You can't get so confident in the power of your will that you think you can just push and *make* things happen. If God has another plan, or what you're pushing for is against God's plan, forget it! The real power of willpower only comes into play when you line up your will with God's will. *Then* things happen.

Your next reading is on page 994.

and broke it, [11]and he said before all the people, "This is what the LORD says: 'In the same way will I break the yoke of Nebuchadnezzar king of Babylon off the neck of all the nations within two years.' " At this, the prophet Jeremiah went on his way.

[12]Shortly after the prophet Hananiah had broken the yoke off the neck of the prophet Jeremiah, the word of the LORD came to Jeremiah: [13]"Go and tell Hananiah, 'This is what the LORD says: You have broken a wooden yoke, but in its place you will get a yoke of iron. [14]This is what the LORD Almighty, the God of Israel, says: I will put an iron yoke on the necks of all these nations to make them serve Nebuchadnezzar king of Babylon, and they will serve him. I will even give him control over the wild animals.' "

[15]Then the prophet Jeremiah said to Hananiah the prophet, "Listen, Hananiah! The LORD has not sent you, yet you have persuaded this nation to trust in lies. [16]Therefore, this is what the LORD says: 'I am about to remove you from the face of the earth. This very year you are going to die, because you have preached rebellion against the LORD.' "

[17]In the seventh month of that same year, Hananiah the prophet died.

A Letter to the Exiles

29 This is the text of the letter that the prophet Jeremiah sent from Jerusalem to the surviving elders among the exiles and to the priests, the prophets and all the other people Nebuchadnezzar had carried into exile from Jerusalem to Babylon. [2](This was after King Jehoiachin[a] and the queen mother, the court officials and the leaders of Judah and Jerusalem, the craftsmen and the artisans had gone into exile from Jerusalem.) [3]He entrusted the letter to Elasah son of Shaphan and to Gemariah son of Hilkiah, whom Zedekiah king of Judah sent to King Nebuchadnezzar in Babylon. It said:

[4]This is what the LORD Almighty, the God of Israel, says to all those I carried into exile from Jerusalem to Babylon: [5]"Build houses and settle down; plant gardens and eat what they produce. [6]Marry and have sons and daughters; find wives for your sons and give your daughters in marriage, so that they too may have sons and daughters. Increase in number there; do not decrease. [7]Also, seek the peace and prosperity of the city to which I have carried you into exile. Pray to the LORD for it, because if it prospers, you too will prosper." [8]Yes, this is what the LORD Almighty, the God of Israel, says: "Do not let the prophets and diviners among you deceive you. Do not listen to the dreams you encourage them to have. [9]They are prophesying lies to you in my name. I have not sent them," declares the LORD.

[10]This is what the LORD says: "When seventy years are completed for Babylon, I will come to you and fulfill my gracious promise to bring you back to this place. [11]For I know the plans I have for you," declares the LORD, "plans to prosper you and not to harm you, plans to give you hope and a future. [12]Then you will call upon me and come and pray to me, and I will listen to you. [13]You will seek me and find me when you seek me with all your heart. [14]I will be found by you," declares the LORD, "and will bring you back from captivity.[b] I will gather you from all the nations and places where I have banished you," declares the LORD, "and will bring you back to the place from which I carried you into exile."

[15]You may say, "The LORD has raised up prophets for us in Babylon," [16]but this is what the LORD says about the king who sits on David's throne and all the people who remain in this city, your countrymen who did not go with you into exile— [17]yes, this is what the LORD Almighty says: "I will send the sword, famine and plague against them and I will make them like poor figs that are so bad they cannot be eaten. [18]I will pursue them with the sword, famine and plague and will make them abhorrent to all the kingdoms of the earth and an object of cursing and horror, of scorn and reproach, among all the nations where I drive them. [19]For they have not listened to

[a] 2 Hebrew *Jeconiah*, a variant of *Jehoiachin*   [b] 14 Or will restore your fortunes

my words," declares the LORD, "words that I sent to them again and again by my servants the prophets. And you exiles have not listened either," declares the LORD.

²⁰Therefore, hear the word of the LORD, all you exiles whom I have sent away from Jerusalem to Babylon. ²¹This is what the LORD Almighty, the God of Israel, says about Ahab son of Kolaiah and Zedekiah son of Maaseiah, who are prophesying lies to you in my name: "I will hand them over to Nebuchadnezzar king of Babylon, and he will put them to death before your very eyes. ²²Because of them, all the exiles from Judah who are in Babylon will use this curse: 'The LORD treat you like Zedekiah and Ahab, whom the king of Babylon burned in the fire.' ²³For they have done outrageous things in Israel; they have committed adultery with their neighbors' wives and in my name have spoken lies, which I did not tell them to do. I know it and am a witness to it," declares the LORD.

Message to Shemaiah

²⁴Tell Shemaiah the Nehelamite, ²⁵"This is what the LORD Almighty, the God of Israel, says: You sent letters in your own name to all the people in Jerusalem, to Zephaniah son of Maaseiah the priest, and to all the other priests. You said to Zephaniah, ²⁶'The LORD has appointed you priest in place of Jehoiada to be in charge of the house of the LORD; you should put any madman who acts like a prophet into the stocks and neck-irons. ²⁷So why have you not reprimanded Jeremiah from Anathoth, who poses as a prophet among you? ²⁸He has sent this message to us in Babylon: It will be a long time. Therefore build houses and settle down; plant gardens and eat what they produce.' "

²⁹Zephaniah the priest, however, read the letter to Jeremiah the prophet. ³⁰Then

Make It Stick

READ JEREMIAH 29:11

Want a great future? Then Jeremiah 29:11 is a verse that needs to travel with you. Write it on a sticky note, and make it into a sign and tape it to your wall, inside your locker—wherever you might need a reminder that God has an awesome plan for your life.

the word of the LORD came to Jeremiah: 31"Send this message to all the exiles: 'This is what the LORD says about Shemaiah the Nehelamite: Because Shemaiah has prophesied to you, even though I did not send him, and has led you to believe a lie, 32this is what the LORD says: I will surely punish Shemaiah the Nehelamite and his descendants. He will have no one left among this people, nor will he see the good things I will do for my people, declares the LORD, because he has preached rebellion against me.' "

Restoration of Israel

This is the word that came to Jeremiah from the LORD: 2"This is what the LORD, the God of Israel, says: 'Write in a book all the words I have spoken to you. 3The days are coming,' declares the LORD, 'when I will bring my people Israel and Judah back from captivity[a] and restore them to the land I gave their forefathers to possess,' says the LORD."

4These are the words the LORD spoke concerning Israel and Judah: 5"This is what the LORD says:

" 'Cries of fear are heard—
    terror, not peace.
6Ask and see:
    Can a man bear children?
Then why do I see every strong man
    with his hands on his stomach like a
        woman in labor,
    every face turned deathly pale?
7How awful that day will be!
    None will be like it.
It will be a time of trouble for Jacob,
    but he will be saved out of it.

8" 'In that day,' declares the LORD
        Almighty,
    'I will break the yoke off their necks
and will tear off their bonds;
    no longer will foreigners enslave
        them.
9Instead, they will serve the LORD their
        God
    and David their king,
    whom I will raise up for them.

10" 'So do not fear, O Jacob my servant;
    do not be dismayed, O Israel,'
                        declares the LORD.
'I will surely save you out of a distant
    place,

your descendants from the land of
    their exile.
Jacob will again have peace and security,
    and no one will make him afraid.
11I am with you and will save you,'
    declares the LORD.
'Though I completely destroy all the
        nations
    among which I scatter you,
    I will not completely destroy you.
I will discipline you but only with
        justice;
    I will not let you go entirely
        unpunished.'

12"This is what the LORD says:

" 'Your wound is incurable,
    your injury beyond healing.
13There is no one to plead your cause,
    no remedy for your sore,
    no healing for you.
14All your allies have forgotten you;
    they care nothing for you.
I have struck you as an enemy would
    and punished you as would the cruel,
because your guilt is so great
    and your sins so many.
15Why do you cry out over your wound,
    your pain that has no cure?
Because of your great guilt and many
        sins
    I have done these things to you.

16" 'But all who devour you will be
        devoured;
    all your enemies will go into exile.
Those who plunder you will be
        plundered;
    all who make spoil of you I will
        despoil.
17But I will restore you to health
    and heal your wounds,'
                        declares the LORD,
'because you are called an outcast,
    Zion for whom no one cares.'

18"This is what the LORD says:

" 'I will restore the fortunes of Jacob's
        tents
    and have compassion on his
        dwellings;
the city will be rebuilt on her ruins,
    and the palace will stand in its
        proper place.
19From them will come songs of
        thanksgiving

---

a 3 Or will restore the fortunes of my people Israel and Judah

and the sound of rejoicing.
I will add to their numbers,
  and they will not be decreased;
I will bring them honor,
  and they will not be disdained.
20 Their children will be as in days of old,
  and their community will be
    established before me;
I will punish all who oppress them.
21 Their leader will be one of their own;
  their ruler will arise from among
    them.
I will bring him near and he will come
  close to me,
  for who is he who will devote
    himself
  to be close to me?'
          declares the LORD.
22 " 'So you will be my people,
  and I will be your God.' "

23 See, the storm of the LORD
  will burst out in wrath,
a driving wind swirling down
  on the heads of the wicked.
24 The fierce anger of the LORD will not
  turn back

until he fully accomplishes
  the purposes of his heart.
In days to come
  you will understand this.

31 "At that time," declares the LORD, "I will be the God of all the clans of Israel, and they will be my people."

2 This is what the LORD says:

"The people who survive the sword
  will find favor in the desert;
  I will come to give rest to Israel."

3 The LORD appeared to us in the past,[a] saying:

"I have loved you with an everlasting
  love;
I have drawn you with
  loving-kindness.
4 I will build you up again
  and you will be rebuilt, O Virgin Israel.
Again you will take up your tambourines
  and go out to dance with the joyful.

a 3 Or LORD *has appeared to us from afar*

Banging Into Walls

READ JEREMIAH 30:11

When you give your life to God, he takes you like an apprentice and teaches and trains you in his ways. He's also like a dad: When you step out of line and make bad decisions, he'll probably let you deal with the results, to teach you. Then he helps you through those difficult times. He turns them into good and you end up smarter and better. He does this because you're his child. But when unbelievers break God's laws, watch out!—They don't learn a thing. They *keep* banging into walls and they don't have a clue why. Finally they hit one too many walls and down they go. (May Day! May Day! One horizontal pedestrian!) Sure, God puts up walls to stop *you* from going bad places, too, but he only lets you take bumps because he loves you. "Those whom I love I rebuke and discipline" (Revelation 3:19).

Your next reading is on page 997.

5 Again you will plant vineyards
on the hills of Samaria;
the farmers will plant them
and enjoy their fruit.
6 There will be a day when watchmen
cry out
on the hills of Ephraim,
'Come, let us go up to Zion,
to the LORD our God.' "

7 This is what the LORD says:

"Sing with joy for Jacob;
shout for the foremost of the nations.
Make your praises heard, and say,
'O LORD, save your people,
the remnant of Israel.'
8 See, I will bring them from the land of
the north
and gather them from the ends of
the earth.
Among them will be the blind and the
lame,
expectant mothers and women in
labor;
a great throng will return.
9 They will come with weeping;
they will pray as I bring them back.
I will lead them beside streams of water
on a level path where they will not
stumble,
because I am Israel's father,
and Ephraim is my firstborn son.

10 "Hear the word of the LORD, O nations;
proclaim it in distant coastlands:
'He who scattered Israel will gather
them
and will watch over his flock like a
shepherd.'
11 For the LORD will ransom Jacob
and redeem them from the hand of
those stronger than they.
12 They will come and shout for joy on
the heights of Zion;
they will rejoice in the bounty of the
LORD—
the grain, the new wine and the oil,
the young of the flocks and herds.
They will be like a well-watered
garden,
and they will sorrow no more.
13 Then maidens will dance and be glad,
young men and old as well.
I will turn their mourning into
gladness;
I will give them comfort and joy
instead of sorrow.

14 I will satisfy the priests with abundance,
and my people will be filled with my
bounty,"
declares the LORD.

15 This is what the LORD says:

"A voice is heard in Ramah,
mourning and great weeping,
Rachel weeping for her children
and refusing to be comforted,
because her children are no more."

16 This is what the LORD says:

"Restrain your voice from weeping
and your eyes from tears,
for your work will be rewarded,"
declares the LORD.
"They will return from the land of
the enemy.
17 So there is hope for your future,"
declares the LORD.
"Your children will return to their
own land.

18 "I have surely heard Ephraim's moaning:
'You disciplined me like an unruly
calf,
and I have been disciplined.
Restore me, and I will return,
because you are the LORD my God.
19 After I strayed,
I repented;
after I came to understand,
I beat my breast.
I was ashamed and humiliated
because I bore the disgrace of my
youth.'
20 Is not Ephraim my dear son,
the child in whom I delight?
Though I often speak against him,
I still remember him.
Therefore my heart yearns for him;
I have great compassion for him,"
declares the LORD.

21 "Set up road signs;
put up guideposts.
Take note of the highway,
the road that you take.
Return, O Virgin Israel,
return to your towns.
22 How long will you wander,
O unfaithful daughter?
The LORD will create a new thing on
earth—
a woman will surround[a] a man."

a 22 Or will go about ⸤seeking⸥; or will protect

23This is what the LORD Almighty, the God of Israel, says: "When I bring them back from captivity,a the people in the land of Judah and in its towns will once again use these words: 'The LORD bless you, O righteous dwelling, O sacred mountain.' 24People will live together in Judah and all its towns—farmers and those who move about with their flocks. 25I will refresh the weary and satisfy the faint."

26At this I awoke and looked around. My sleep had been pleasant to me.

27"The days are coming," declares the LORD, "when I will plant the house of Israel and the house of Judah with the offspring of men and of animals. 28Just as I watched over them to uproot and tear down, and to overthrow, destroy and bring disaster, so I will watch over them to build and to plant," declares the LORD. 29"In those days people will no longer say,

'The fathers have eaten sour grapes,
    and the children's teeth are set on
       edge.'

30Instead, everyone will die for his own

a 23 Or I restore their fortunes

Make It Stick

READ JEREMIAH 31:29–30

Ever heard about those talk shows where people blame their mom and dad for how they turned out? "Yeah, dude, my dad always eats old cheese, but I'm the one who gets bad breath!" Write on a sticky note what *you* think Jeremiah 31:29–30 means.

sin; whoever eats sour grapes—his own teeth will be set on edge.

31 "The time is coming," declares the LORD,
   "when I will make a new covenant
with the house of Israel
   and with the house of Judah.
32 It will not be like the covenant
   I made with their forefathers
when I took them by the hand
   to lead them out of Egypt,
because they broke my covenant,
   though I was a husband to*a*
      them,*b*"
               declares the LORD.
33 "This is the covenant I will make with
      the house of Israel
   after that time," declares the LORD.
"I will put my law in their minds
   and write it on their hearts.
I will be their God,
   and they will be my people.
34 No longer will a man teach his
      neighbor,
   or a man his brother, saying, 'Know
      the LORD,'
because they will all know me,

from the least of them to the
   greatest,"
               declares the LORD.
"For I will forgive their wickedness
   and will remember their sins no
      more."

35 This is what the LORD says,

he who appoints the sun
   to shine by day,
who decrees the moon and stars
   to shine by night,
who stirs up the sea
   so that its waves roar—
   the LORD Almighty is his name:
36 "Only if these decrees vanish from my
      sight,"
   declares the LORD,
"will the descendants of Israel ever cease
   to be a nation before me."

37 This is what the LORD says:

"Only if the heavens above can be
   measured

a 32 Hebrew; Septuagint and Syriac / *and I turned away from*
b 32 Or *was their master*

God Didn't Forget

READ JEREMIAH 31:31–34

Ever watch the news on TV and think, "Man, this world is messed up! People get away with all kinds of junk! Did God forget about us?" Truth is, it was no different in Jeremiah's day. Even then, in the middle of the long string of wicked kings and disobedient people, God's whole plan was to send Jesus Christ. God knew that without changing people's hearts, they'd constantly give him the cold shoulder. In the middle of a lot of gloom and judgment, Jeremiah reminded the people that God planned to meet their biggest need. "I will forgive their wickedness and will remember their sins no more" (verse 34). Jesus came to forgive us and God will give us a new heart that's soft toward him and wants to follow him. God knew ever since the Garden of Eden that he had to send his Son to bring us back into relationship with him again. God didn't forget.

Your next reading is on page 998.

and the foundations of the earth
    below be searched out
will I reject all the descendants of Israel
    because of all they have done,"
                    declares the LORD.

38"The days are coming," declares the LORD, "when this city will be rebuilt for me from the Tower of Hananel to the Corner Gate. 39The measuring line will stretch from there straight to the hill of Gareb and then turn to Goah. 40The whole valley where dead bodies and ashes are thrown, and all the terraces out to the Kidron Valley on the east as far as the corner of the Horse Gate, will be holy to the LORD. The city will never again be uprooted or demolished."

Jeremiah Buys a Field

32 This is the word that came to Jeremiah from the LORD in the tenth year of Zedekiah king of Judah, which was the eighteenth year of Nebuchadnezzar. 2The army of the king of Babylon was then besieging Jerusalem, and Jeremiah the prophet was confined in the courtyard of the guard in the royal palace of Judah.

3Now Zedekiah king of Judah had imprisoned him there, saying, "Why do you prophesy as you do? You say, 'This is what the LORD says: I am about to hand this city over to the king of Babylon, and he will capture it. 4Zedekiah king of Judah will not escape out of the hands of the Babylonians[a] but will certainly be handed over to the king of Babylon, and will speak with him face to face and see him with his own eyes. 5He will take Zedekiah to Babylon, where he will remain until I deal with him, declares the LORD. If you fight against the Babylonians, you will not succeed.' "

6Jeremiah said, "The word of the LORD came to me: 7Hanamel son of Shallum your uncle is going to come to you and say, 'Buy my field at Anathoth, because as

[a] 4 Or *Chaldeans*; also in verses 5, 24, 25, 28, 29 and 43

Can You Believe It?

GET STRONGER

READ JEREMIAH 32:1–2, 6–17, 24–27, 36–44

Talk about hope in a baaaad time. The Babylonian army had been camped around Jerusalem for over a year. They had built siege ramps against the city walls. Their battering rams were pounding on the gates. The Jews inside began starving. And Jeremiah? Not only was he trapped in the city, he was in *prison*! Then along comes Jeremiah's uncle like a used-car salesman and wants to sell him a field—outside the city, of course, where it won't do him a bit of good. Guess what? Jeremiah slapped down seventeen shekels, signed the deed and laughed, "Now I own an apple orchard!" Jeremiah believed God's message to him that good times would come again. He knew he'd live to enjoy his field. When life deals *you* hard blows, hold onto God's Word and don't stop hoping. Nothing is too hard for God. He can do miracles.

Your next reading is on page 1004.

nearest relative it is your right and duty to buy it.'

8"Then, just as the LORD had said, my cousin Hanamel came to me in the courtyard of the guard and said, 'Buy my field at Anathoth in the territory of Benjamin. Since it is your right to redeem it and possess it, buy it for yourself.'

"I knew that this was the word of the LORD; 9so I bought the field at Anathoth from my cousin Hanamel and weighed out for him seventeen shekels^a of silver. 10I signed and sealed the deed, had it witnessed, and weighed out the silver on the scales. 11I took the deed of purchase—the sealed copy containing the terms and conditions, as well as the unsealed copy— 12and I gave this deed to Baruch son of Neriah, the son of Mahseiah, in the presence of my cousin Hanamel and of the witnesses who had signed the deed and of all the Jews sitting in the courtyard of the guard.

13"In their presence I gave Baruch these instructions: 14'This is what the LORD Almighty, the God of Israel, says: Take these documents, both the sealed and unsealed copies of the deed of purchase, and put them in a clay jar so they will last a long time. 15For this is what the LORD Almighty, the God of Israel, says: Houses, fields and vineyards will again be bought in this land.'

16"After I had given the deed of purchase to Baruch son of Neriah, I prayed to the LORD:

17"Ah, Sovereign LORD, you have made the heavens and the earth by your great power and outstretched arm. Nothing is too hard for you. 18You show love to thousands but bring the punishment for the fathers' sins into the laps of their children after them. O great and powerful God, whose name is the LORD Almighty, 19great are your purposes and mighty are your deeds. Your eyes are open to all the ways of men; you reward everyone according to his conduct and as his deeds deserve. 20You performed miraculous signs and wonders in Egypt and have continued them to this day, both in Israel and among all mankind, and have gained the renown that is still yours. 21You brought your people Israel out of Egypt with signs and wonders, by a mighty hand and an outstretched arm and with great terror. 22You gave them this land you had sworn to give their forefathers, a land flowing with milk and honey. 23They came in and took possession of it, but they did not obey you or follow your law; they did not do what you commanded them to do. So you brought all this disaster upon them.

24"See how the siege ramps are built up to take the city. Because of the sword, famine and plague, the city will be handed over to the Babylonians who are attacking it. What you said has happened, as you now see. 25And though the city will be handed over to the Babylonians, you, O Sovereign LORD, say to me, 'Buy the field with silver and have the transaction witnessed.' "

26Then the word of the LORD came to Jeremiah: 27"I am the LORD, the God of all mankind. Is anything too hard for me? 28Therefore, this is what the LORD says: I am about to hand this city over to the Babylonians and to Nebuchadnezzar king of Babylon, who will capture it. 29The Babylonians who are attacking this city will come in and set it on fire; they will burn it down, along with the houses where the people provoked me to anger by burning incense on the roofs to Baal and by pouring out drink offerings to other gods.

30"The people of Israel and Judah have done nothing but evil in my sight from their youth; indeed, the people of Israel have done nothing but provoke me with what their hands have made, declares the LORD. 31From the day it was built until now, this city has so aroused my anger and wrath that I must remove it from my sight. 32The people of Israel and Judah have provoked me by all the evil they have done—they, their kings and officials, their priests and prophets, the men of Judah and the people of Jerusalem. 33They turned their backs to me and not their faces; though I taught them again and again, they would not listen or respond to discipline. 34They set up their abominable idols in the house that bears my Name and defiled it. 35They built high places for Baal in the Valley of Ben Hinnom to sacri-

^{a} 9 That is, about 7 ounces (about 200 grams)

fice their sons and daughters*a* to Molech, though I never commanded, nor did it enter my mind, that they should do such a detestable thing and so make Judah sin.

36"You are saying about this city, 'By the sword, famine and plague it will be handed over to the king of Babylon'; but this is what the LORD, the God of Israel, says: 37I will surely gather them from all the lands where I banish them in my furious anger and great wrath; I will bring them back to this place and let them live in safety. 38They will be my people, and I will be their God. 39I will give them singleness of heart and action, so that they will always fear me for their own good and the good of their children after them. 40I will make an everlasting covenant with them: I will never stop doing good to them, and I will inspire them to fear me, so that they will never turn away from me. 41I will rejoice in doing them good and will assuredly plant them in this land with all my heart and soul.

42"This is what the LORD says: As I have brought all this great calamity on this people, so I will give them all the prosperity I have promised them. 43Once more fields will be bought in this land of which you say, 'It is a desolate waste, without men or animals, for it has been handed over to the Babylonians.' 44Fields will be bought for silver, and deeds will be signed, sealed and witnessed in the territory of Benjamin, in the villages around Jerusalem, in the towns of Judah and in the towns of the hill country, of the western foothills and of the Negev, because I will restore their fortunes,*b* declares the LORD."

Promise of Restoration

33 While Jeremiah was still confined in the courtyard of the guard, the word of the LORD came to him a second time:

a 35 Or to make their sons and daughters pass through the fire;   b 44 Or will bring them back from captivity

Make It Stick

READ JEREMIAH 32:38–41

In Jeremiah 32:38–41, God made some awesome promises to the Jews. They apply to us, too. When we receive Jesus, we become one of God's people and receive his promises. Write on a sticky note your favorite part of these verses as a reminder of what God wants to do for you.

2 "This is what the LORD says, he who made the earth, the LORD who formed it and established it—the LORD is his name: 3 'Call to me and I will answer you and tell you great and unsearchable things you do not know.' 4 For this is what the LORD, the God of Israel, says about the houses in this city and the royal palaces of Judah that have been torn down to be used against the siege ramps and the sword 5 in the fight with the Babylonians[a]: 'They will be filled with the dead bodies of the men I will slay in my anger and wrath. I will hide my face from this city because of all its wickedness.

6 " 'Nevertheless, I will bring health and healing to it; I will heal my people and will let them enjoy abundant peace and security. 7 I will bring Judah and Israel back from captivity[b] and will rebuild them as they were before. 8 I will cleanse them from all the sin they have committed against me and will forgive all their sins of rebellion against me. 9 Then this city will bring me renown, joy, praise and honor before all nations on earth that hear of all the good things I do for it; and they will be in awe and will tremble at the abundant prosperity and peace I provide for it.'

10 "This is what the LORD says: 'You say about this place, "It is a desolate waste, without men or animals." Yet in the towns of Judah and the streets of Jerusalem that are deserted, inhabited by neither men nor animals, there will be heard once more 11 the sounds of joy and gladness, the voices of bride and bridegroom, and the voices of those who bring thank offerings to the house of the LORD, saying,

"Give thanks to the LORD Almighty,
    for the LORD is good;
    his love endures forever."

For I will restore the fortunes of the land as they were before,' says the LORD.

12 "This is what the LORD Almighty says: 'In this place, desolate and without men or animals—in all its towns there will again be pastures for shepherds to rest their flocks. 13 In the towns of the hill country, of the western foothills and of the Negev, in the territory of Benjamin, in the villages around Jerusalem and in the towns of Judah, flocks will again pass under the hand of the one who counts them,' says the LORD.

14 " 'The days are coming,' declares the LORD, 'when I will fulfill the gracious promise I made to the house of Israel and to the house of Judah.

15 " 'In those days and at that time
    I will make a righteous Branch
        sprout from David's line;
    he will do what is just and right in
        the land.
16 In those days Judah will be saved
    and Jerusalem will live in safety.
This is the name by which it[c] will be
    called:
    The LORD Our Righteousness.'

17 For this is what the LORD says: 'David will never fail to have a man to sit on the throne of the house of Israel, 18 nor will the priests, who are Levites, ever fail to have a man to stand before me continually to offer burnt offerings, to burn grain offerings and to present sacrifices.' "

19 The word of the LORD came to Jeremiah: 20 "This is what the LORD says: 'If you can break my covenant with the day and my covenant with the night, so that day and night no longer come at their appointed time, 21 then my covenant with David my servant—and my covenant with the Levites who are priests ministering before me—can be broken and David will no longer have a descendant to reign on his throne. 22 I will make the descendants of David my servant and the Levites who minister before me as countless as the stars of the sky and as measureless as the sand on the seashore.' "

23 The word of the LORD came to Jeremiah: 24 "Have you not noticed that these people are saying, 'The LORD has rejected the two kingdoms[d] he chose'? So they despise my people and no longer regard them as a nation. 25 This is what the LORD says: 'If I have not established my covenant with day and night and the fixed laws of heaven and earth, 26 then I will reject the descendants of Jacob and David my servant and will not choose one of his sons to rule over the descendants of Abraham, Isaac and Jacob. For I will restore their fortunes[e] and have compassion on them.' "

a 5 Or Chaldeans   b 7 Or will restore the fortunes of Judah and Israel   c 16 Or he   d 24 Or families   e 26 Or will bring them back from captivity

Warning to Zedekiah

34 While Nebuchadnezzar king of Babylon and all his army and all the kingdoms and peoples in the empire he ruled were fighting against Jerusalem and all its surrounding towns, this word came to Jeremiah from the LORD: ²"This is what the LORD, the God of Israel, says: Go to Zedekiah king of Judah and tell him, 'This is what the LORD says: I am about to hand this city over to the king of Babylon, and he will burn it down. ³You will not escape from his grasp but will surely be captured and handed over to him. You will see the king of Babylon with your own eyes, and he will speak with you face to face. And you will go to Babylon.

⁴"'Yet hear the promise of the LORD, O Zedekiah king of Judah. This is what the LORD says concerning you: You will not die by the sword; ⁵you will die peacefully. As people made a funeral fire in honor of your fathers, the former kings who preceded you, so they will make a fire in your honor and lament, "Alas, O master!" I myself make this promise, declares the LORD.' "

⁶Then Jeremiah the prophet told all this to Zedekiah king of Judah, in Jerusalem, ⁷while the army of the king of Babylon was fighting against Jerusalem and the other cities of Judah that were still holding out—Lachish and Azekah. These were the only fortified cities left in Judah.

Freedom for Slaves

⁸The word came to Jeremiah from the LORD after King Zedekiah had made a covenant with all the people in Jerusalem to proclaim freedom for the slaves. ⁹Everyone was to free his Hebrew slaves, both male and female; no one was to hold a fellow Jew in bondage. ¹⁰So all the officials and people who entered into this covenant agreed that they would free their male and female slaves and no longer hold them in bondage. They agreed, and set them free. ¹¹But afterward they changed their minds and took back the slaves they had freed and enslaved them again.

¹²Then the word of the LORD came to Jeremiah: ¹³"This is what the LORD, the God of Israel, says: I made a covenant with your forefathers when I brought them out of Egypt, out of the land of slavery. I said, ¹⁴'Every seventh year each of you must free any fellow Hebrew who has sold himself to you. After he has served you six years, you must let him go free.'ᵃ Your fathers, however, did not listen to me or pay attention to me. ¹⁵Recently you repented and did what is right in my sight: Each of you proclaimed freedom to his countrymen. You even made a covenant before me in the house that bears my Name. ¹⁶But now you have turned around and profaned my name; each of you has taken back the male and female slaves you had set free to go where they wished. You have forced them to become your slaves again.

¹⁷"Therefore, this is what the LORD says: You have not obeyed me; you have not proclaimed freedom for your fellow countrymen. So I now proclaim 'freedom' for you, declares the LORD—'freedom' to fall by the sword, plague and famine. I will make you abhorrent to all the kingdoms of the earth. ¹⁸The men who have violated my covenant and have not fulfilled the terms of the covenant they made before me, I will treat like the calf they cut in two and then walked between its pieces. ¹⁹The leaders of Judah and Jerusalem, the court officials, the priests and all the people of the land who walked between the pieces of the calf, ²⁰I will hand over to their enemies who seek their lives. Their dead bodies will become food for the birds of the air and the beasts of the earth.

²¹"I will hand Zedekiah king of Judah and his officials over to their enemies who seek their lives, to the army of the king of Babylon, which has withdrawn from you. ²²I am going to give the order, declares the LORD, and I will bring them back to this city. They will fight against it, take it and burn it down. And I will lay waste the towns of Judah so no one can live there."

The Recabites

35 This is the word that came to Jeremiah from the LORD during the reign of Jehoiakim son of Josiah king of Judah: ²"Go to the Recabite family and invite them to come to one of the side rooms of the house of the LORD and give them wine to drink."

³So I went to get Jaazaniah son of Jere-

ᵃ *14* Deut. 15:12

miah, the son of Habazziniah, and his brothers and all his sons—the whole family of the Recabites. 4I brought them into the house of the LORD, into the room of the sons of Hanan son of Igdaliah the man of God. It was next to the room of the officials, which was over that of Maaseiah son of Shallum the doorkeeper. 5Then I set bowls full of wine and some cups before the men of the Recabite family and said to them, "Drink some wine."

6But they replied, "We do not drink wine, because our forefather Jonadab son of Recab gave us this command: 'Neither you nor your descendants must ever drink wine. 7Also you must never build houses, sow seed or plant vineyards; you must never have any of these things, but must always live in tents. Then you will live a long time in the land where you are nomads.' 8We have obeyed everything our forefather Jonadab son of Recab commanded us. Neither we nor our wives nor our sons and daughters have ever drunk wine 9or built houses to live in or had vineyards, fields or crops. 10We have lived in tents and have fully obeyed everything our forefather Jonadab commanded us. 11But when Nebuchadnezzar king of Babylon invaded this land, we said, 'Come, we must go to Jerusalem to escape the Babylonian[a] and Aramean armies.' So we have remained in Jerusalem."

12Then the word of the LORD came to Jeremiah, saying: 13"This is what the LORD Almighty, the God of Israel, says: Go and tell the men of Judah and the people of Jerusalem, 'Will you not learn a lesson and obey my words?' declares the LORD. 14'Jonadab son of Recab ordered his sons not to drink wine and this command has been kept. To this day they do not drink wine, because they obey their forefather's command. But I have spoken to you again and again, yet you have not obeyed me. 15Again and again I sent all my servants the prophets to you. They said, "Each of you must turn from your wicked ways and reform your actions; do not follow other gods to serve them. Then you will live in the land I have given to you and your fathers." But you have not paid attention or listened to me. 16The descendants of Jonadab son of Recab have carried out the command their forefather gave them, but these people have not obeyed me.'

17"Therefore, this is what the LORD God Almighty, the God of Israel, says: 'Listen! I am going to bring on Judah and on everyone living in Jerusalem every disaster I pronounced against them. I spoke to them, but they did not listen; I called to them, but they did not answer.' "

18Then Jeremiah said to the family of the Recabites, "This is what the LORD Almighty, the God of Israel, says: 'You have obeyed the command of your forefather Jonadab and have followed all his instructions and have done everything he ordered.' 19Therefore, this is what the LORD Almighty, the God of Israel, says: 'Jonadab son of Recab will never fail to have a man to serve me.' "

Jehoiakim Burns Jeremiah's Scroll

36 In the fourth year of Jehoiakim son of Josiah king of Judah, this word came to Jeremiah from the LORD: 2"Take a scroll and write on it all the words I have spoken to you concerning Israel, Judah and all the other nations from the time I began speaking to you in the reign of Josiah till now. 3Perhaps when the people of Judah hear about every disaster I plan to inflict on them, each of them will turn from his wicked way; then I will forgive their wickedness and their sin."

4So Jeremiah called Baruch son of Neriah, and while Jeremiah dictated all the words the LORD had spoken to him, Baruch wrote them on the scroll. 5Then Jeremiah told Baruch, "I am restricted; I cannot go to the LORD's temple. 6So you go to the house of the LORD on a day of fasting and read to the people from the scroll the words of the LORD that you wrote as I dictated. Read them to all the people of Judah who come in from their towns. 7Perhaps they will bring their petition before the LORD, and each will turn from his wicked ways, for the anger and wrath pronounced against this people by the LORD are great."

8Baruch son of Neriah did everything Jeremiah the prophet told him to do; at the LORD's temple he read the words of the LORD from the scroll. 9In the ninth month of the fifth year of Jehoiakim son of Josiah king of Judah, a time of fasting before the LORD was proclaimed for all the people in Jerusalem and those who had

a 11 Or Chaldean

come from the towns of Judah. ¹⁰From the room of Gemariah son of Shaphan the secretary, which was in the upper courtyard at the entrance of the New Gate of the temple, Baruch read to all the people at the LORD's temple the words of Jeremiah from the scroll.

¹¹When Micaiah son of Gemariah, the son of Shaphan, heard all the words of the LORD from the scroll, ¹²he went down to the secretary's room in the royal palace, where all the officials were sitting: Elishama the secretary, Delaiah son of Shemaiah, Elnathan son of Acbor, Gemariah son of Shaphan, Zedekiah son of Hananiah, and all the other officials. ¹³After Micaiah told them everything he had heard Baruch read to the people from the scroll, ¹⁴all the officials sent Jehudi son of Nethaniah, the son of Shelemiah, the son of Cushi, to say to Baruch, "Bring the scroll from which you have read to the people and come." So Baruch son of Neriah went to them with the scroll in his hand. ¹⁵They said to him, "Sit down, please, and read it to us."

So Baruch read it to them. ¹⁶When they heard all these words, they looked at each other in fear and said to Baruch, "We must report all these words to the king." ¹⁷Then they asked Baruch, "Tell us, how did you come to write all this? Did Jeremiah dictate it?"

¹⁸"Yes," Baruch replied, "he dictated all these words to me, and I wrote them in ink on the scroll."

¹⁹Then the officials said to Baruch, "You and Jeremiah, go and hide. Don't let anyone know where you are."

²⁰After they put the scroll in the room of Elishama the secretary, they went to the king in the courtyard and reported everything to him. ²¹The king sent Jehudi to get the scroll, and Jehudi brought it from the room of Elishama the secretary and read it to the king and all the officials standing beside him. ²²It was the ninth month and the king was sitting in the winter apartment, with a fire burning in the firepot in front of him. ²³Whenever Jehudi had read three or four columns of the scroll, the king cut them off with a scribe's knife and threw them into the

---

GET SMARTER

Copy It All Out Again?

READ JEREMIAH 36:1–8, 19–32

Ever drag yourself into class, your homework assignment uncompleted, and tell the teacher, "I actually *did* my homework, but then the dog *ate* it"? Something like that sort of happened to Jeremiah. Baruch wrote out twenty years' worth of Jeremiah's prophecies, but then (Aaaggh!) King Jehoiakim burned the only copy! *The end?* No way! Jeremiah "took another scroll" (verse 32), and wrote everything out *all over again.* Talk about bulldog persistence! Talk about booorrring work. Hey! It *had* to be done. Doing stuff for God is not all flash and dash and roller-coaster excitement. A lot of it is doing what's right, day after day after day, like being faithful to do your chores and school work. In the end, all that hard work adds up and makes a *big* difference. So don't just look for whopper-sized, earth-saving opportunities to serve God. You can be faithful in the piddly, ho-hum details, too.

Your next reading is on page 1006.

firepot, until the entire scroll was burned in the fire. 24The king and all his attendants who heard all these words showed no fear, nor did they tear their clothes. 25Even though Elnathan, Delaiah and Gemariah urged the king not to burn the scroll, he would not listen to them. 26Instead, the king commanded Jerahmeel, a son of the king, Seraiah son of Azriel and Shelemiah son of Abdeel to arrest Baruch the scribe and Jeremiah the prophet. But the LORD had hidden them.

27After the king burned the scroll containing the words that Baruch had written at Jeremiah's dictation, the word of the LORD came to Jeremiah: 28"Take another scroll and write on it all the words that were on the first scroll, which Jehoiakim king of Judah burned up. 29Also tell Jehoiakim king of Judah, 'This is what the LORD says: You burned that scroll and said, "Why did you write on it that the king of Babylon would certainly come and destroy this land and cut off both men and animals from it?" 30Therefore, this is what the LORD says about Jehoiakim king of Judah: He will have no one to sit on the throne of David; his body will be thrown out and exposed to the heat by day and the frost by night. 31I will punish him and his children and his attendants for their wickedness; I will bring on them and those living in Jerusalem and the people of Judah every disaster I pronounced against them, because they have not listened.' "

32So Jeremiah took another scroll and gave it to the scribe Baruch son of Neriah, and as Jeremiah dictated, Baruch wrote on it all the words of the scroll that Jehoiakim king of Judah had burned in the fire. And many similar words were added to them.

Jeremiah in Prison

37 Zedekiah son of Josiah was made king of Judah by Nebuchadnezzar king of Babylon; he reigned in place of Jehoiachin*a* son of Jehoiakim. 2Neither he nor his attendants nor the people of the land paid any attention to the words the LORD had spoken through Jeremiah the prophet.

3King Zedekiah, however, sent Jehucal son of Shelemiah with the priest Zephaniah son of Maaseiah to Jeremiah the prophet with this message: "Please pray to the LORD our God for us."

4Now Jeremiah was free to come and go among the people, for he had not yet been put in prison. 5Pharaoh's army had marched out of Egypt, and when the Babylonians*b* who were besieging Jerusalem heard the report about them, they withdrew from Jerusalem.

6Then the word of the LORD came to Jeremiah the prophet: 7"This is what the LORD, the God of Israel, says: Tell the king of Judah, who sent you to inquire of me, 'Pharaoh's army, which has marched out to support you, will go back to its own land, to Egypt. 8Then the Babylonians will return and attack this city; they will capture it and burn it down.'

9"This is what the LORD says: Do not deceive yourselves, thinking, 'The Babylonians will surely leave us.' They will not! 10Even if you were to defeat the entire Babylonian*c* army that is attacking you and only wounded men were left in their tents, they would come out and burn this city down."

11After the Babylonian army had withdrawn from Jerusalem because of Pharaoh's army, 12Jeremiah started to leave the city to go to the territory of Benjamin to get his share of the property among the people there. 13But when he reached the Benjamin Gate, the captain of the guard, whose name was Irijah son of Shelemiah, the son of Hananiah, arrested him and said, "You are deserting to the Babylonians!"

14"That's not true!" Jeremiah said. "I am not deserting to the Babylonians." But Irijah would not listen to him; instead, he arrested Jeremiah and brought him to the officials. 15They were angry with Jeremiah and had him beaten and imprisoned in the house of Jonathan the secretary, which they had made into a prison.

16Jeremiah was put into a vaulted cell in a dungeon, where he remained a long time. 17Then King Zedekiah sent for him and had him brought to the palace, where he asked him privately, "Is there any word from the LORD?"

"Yes," Jeremiah replied, "you will be handed over to the king of Babylon."

18Then Jeremiah said to King Zedekiah, "What crime have I committed against you or your officials or this people, that

---

a 1 Hebrew *Coniah*, a variant of *Jehoiachin*
b 5 Or *Chaldeans*; also in verses 8, 9, 13 and 14
c 10 Or *Chaldean*; also in verse 11

you have put me in prison? ¹⁹Where are your prophets who prophesied to you, 'The king of Babylon will not attack you or this land'? ²⁰But now, my lord the king, please listen. Let me bring my petition before you: Do not send me back to the house of Jonathan the secretary, or I will die there."

²¹King Zedekiah then gave orders for Jeremiah to be placed in the courtyard of the guard and given bread from the street of the bakers each day until all the bread in the city was gone. So Jeremiah remained in the courtyard of the guard.

Jeremiah Thrown Into a Cistern

38 Shephatiah son of Mattan, Gedaliah son of Pashhur, Jehucal[a] son of Shelemiah, and Pashhur son of Malkijah heard what Jeremiah was telling all the people when he said, ²"This is what the LORD says: 'Whoever stays in this city will die by the sword, famine or plague, but whoever goes over to the Babylonians[b] will live. He will escape with his life; he will live.' ³And this is what the LORD says: 'This city will

certainly be handed over to the army of the king of Babylon, who will capture it.' "

⁴Then the officials said to the king, "This man should be put to death. He is discouraging the soldiers who are left in this city, as well as all the people, by the things he is saying to them. This man is not seeking the good of these people but their ruin."

⁵"He is in your hands," King Zedekiah answered. "The king can do nothing to oppose you."

⁶So they took Jeremiah and put him into the cistern of Malkijah, the king's son, which was in the courtyard of the guard. They lowered Jeremiah by ropes into the cistern; it had no water in it, only mud, and Jeremiah sank down into the mud.

⁷But Ebed-Melech, a Cushite,[c] an official[d] in the royal palace, heard that they had put Jeremiah into the cistern. While the king was sitting in the Benjamin Gate, ⁸Ebed-Melech went out of the palace and said to him, ⁹"My lord the king, these

---

ª1 Hebrew *Jucal,* a variant of *Jehucal*   ᵇ2 Or *Chaldeans;* also in verses 18, 19 and 23   ᶜ7 Probably from the upper Nile region   ᵈ7 Or a *eunuch*

It's Not All Politics

READ JEREMIAH 37:4–10

The Jews made a deal with Egypt: "Drive off the Babylonians and we'll be your pals." When the Babylonians stopped sieging Jerusalem to face the Egyptians, the Jews cheered, "Yay! It worked!" Jeremiah said, "Nuh-uh. God's still going to use the Babylonians to fight you and *they're* going to win." The Jews thought that everything was "just politics," with maybe a bit of chance and luck thrown in. They just did not *get* it—God had sent the Babylonians to punish them for their sins. The more people get away from God, the more they find "logical" reasons to explain bad stuff. But Jeremiah reminded them that what they were seeing in the evening news was God's principles in action—"A man reaps what he sows" (Galatians 6:7). Politics-schmolitics. God Almighty had rolled up his sleeves. God was involved. The same holds true today: We need to recognize when God is involved in stuff around us.

Your next reading is on page 1007.

men have acted wickedly in all they have done to Jeremiah the prophet. They have thrown him into a cistern, where he will starve to death when there is no longer any bread in the city."

¹⁰Then the king commanded Ebed-Melech the Cushite, "Take thirty men from here with you and lift Jeremiah the prophet out of the cistern before he dies."

¹¹So Ebed-Melech took the men with him and went to a room under the treasury in the palace. He took some old rags and worn-out clothes from there and let them down with ropes to Jeremiah in the cistern. ¹²Ebed-Melech the Cushite said to Jeremiah, "Put these old rags and worn-out clothes under your arms to pad the ropes." Jeremiah did so, ¹³and they pulled him up with the ropes and lifted him out of the cistern. And Jeremiah remained in the courtyard of the guard.

Zedekiah Questions Jeremiah Again

¹⁴Then King Zedekiah sent for Jeremiah the prophet and had him brought to the third entrance to the temple of the LORD. "I am going to ask you something," the king said to Jeremiah. "Do not hide anything from me."

¹⁵Jeremiah said to Zedekiah, "If I give you an answer, will you not kill me? Even if I did give you counsel, you would not listen to me."

¹⁶But King Zedekiah swore this oath secretly to Jeremiah: "As surely as the LORD lives, who has given us breath, I will neither kill you nor hand you over to those who are seeking your life."

¹⁷Then Jeremiah said to Zedekiah, "This is what the LORD God Almighty, the God of Israel, says: 'If you surrender to the officers of the king of Babylon, your life will be spared and this city will not be burned down; you and your family will live. ¹⁸But if you will not surrender to the officers of the king of Babylon, this city will be handed over to the Babylonians and they will burn it down; you yourself will not escape from their hands.' "

¹⁹King Zedekiah said to Jeremiah, "I am afraid of the Jews who have gone over to the Babylonians, for the Babylonians may hand me over to them and they will mistreat me."

Who Will Help Me?

READ JEREMIAH 37:11–16; 38:4–13

It's amazing how Jeremiah's friends popped out of nowhere. God sent them! Can you see him sitting in the muddy well, thinking, "OK. Been in the stocks, had lynch mobs after me and done jail time. Had my journal burned and now I'm sinking in the mud. God, *HELLLP!*" Then suddenly this dude named Ebed-Melech throws down a rope. Cool. When you're in trouble you want to rely on people to help you. People can let you down, but God won't. God wants you to look to *him* for help and assistance. Then, if he pleases, he can send people to do the actual hands-on, here-let-me-pull-you-out-of-the-mud type stuff. Looking at it this way keeps you from getting bitter. If a certain person doesn't help you, you just say, "That wasn't God's way of meeting my need." But you see those who *do* as proof of God's kindness.

Your next reading is on page 1009.

20"They will not hand you over," Jeremiah replied. "Obey the LORD by doing what I tell you. Then it will go well with you, and your life will be spared. 21But if you refuse to surrender, this is what the LORD has revealed to me: 22All the women left in the palace of the king of Judah will be brought out to the officials of the king of Babylon. Those women will say to you:

" 'They misled you and overcame you—
    those trusted friends of yours.
Your feet are sunk in the mud;
    your friends have deserted you.'

23"All your wives and children will be brought out to the Babylonians. You yourself will not escape from their hands but will be captured by the king of Babylon; and this city will*a* be burned down."

24Then Zedekiah said to Jeremiah, "Do not let anyone know about this conversation, or you may die. 25If the officials hear that I talked with you, and they come to you and say, 'Tell us what you said to the king and what the king said to you; do not hide it from us or we will kill you,' 26then tell them, 'I was pleading with the king not to send me back to Jonathan's house to die there.' "

27All the officials did come to Jeremiah and question him, and he told them everything the king had ordered him to say. So they said no more to him, for no one had heard his conversation with the king.

28And Jeremiah remained in the courtyard of the guard until the day Jerusalem was captured.

The Fall of Jerusalem

39 This is how Jerusalem was taken: 1In the ninth year of Zedekiah king of Judah, in the tenth month, Nebuchadnezzar king of Babylon marched against Jerusalem with his whole army and laid siege to it. 2And on the ninth day of the fourth month of Zedekiah's eleventh year, the city wall was broken through. 3Then all the officials of the king of Babylon came and took seats in the Middle Gate: Nergal-Sharezer of Samgar, Nebo-Sarsekim*b* a chief officer, Nergal-Sharezer a high official and all the other officials of the king of Babylon. 4When Zedekiah king of Judah and all the soldiers saw them, they fled; they left the city at night by way of the king's garden, through the gate between the two walls, and headed toward the Arabah.*c*

5But the Babylonian*d* army pursued them and overtook Zedekiah in the plains of Jericho. They captured him and took him to Nebuchadnezzar king of Babylon at Riblah in the land of Hamath, where he pronounced sentence on him. 6There at Riblah the king of Babylon slaughtered the sons of Zedekiah before his eyes and also killed all the nobles of Judah. 7Then he put out Zedekiah's eyes and bound him with bronze shackles to take him to Babylon.

8The Babylonians*e* set fire to the royal palace and the houses of the people and broke down the walls of Jerusalem. 9Nebuzaradan commander of the imperial guard carried into exile to Babylon the people who remained in the city, along with those who had gone over to him, and the rest of the people. 10But Nebuzaradan the commander of the guard left behind in the land of Judah some of the poor people, who owned nothing; and at that time he gave them vineyards and fields.

11Now Nebuchadnezzar king of Babylon had given these orders about Jeremiah through Nebuzaradan commander of the imperial guard: 12"Take him and look after him; don't harm him but do for him whatever he asks." 13So Nebuzaradan the commander of the guard, Nebushazban a chief officer, Nergal-Sharezer a high official and all the other officers of the king of Babylon 14sent and had Jeremiah taken out of the courtyard of the guard. They turned him over to Gedaliah son of Ahikam, the son of Shaphan, to take him back to his home. So he remained among his own people.

15While Jeremiah had been confined in the courtyard of the guard, the word of the LORD came to him: 16"Go and tell Ebed-Melech the Cushite, 'This is what the LORD Almighty, the God of Israel, says: I am about to fulfill my words against this city through disaster, not prosperity. At that time they will be fulfilled before your eyes. 17But I will rescue you on that day, declares the LORD; you will not be handed over to those you fear. 18I will save you; you will not fall by the sword but will escape with your life, because you trust in me, declares the LORD.' "

---

a 23 Or *and you will cause this city to*   *b 3* Or *Nergal-Sharezer, Samgar-Nebo, Sarsekim*   *c 4* Or *the Jordan Valley*   *d 5* Or *Chaldean*   *e 8* Or *Chaldeans*

Jeremiah Freed

40 The word came to Jeremiah from the Lord after Nebuzaradan commander of the imperial guard had released him at Ramah. He had found Jeremiah bound in chains among all the captives from Jerusalem and Judah who were being carried into exile to Babylon. ²When the commander of the guard found Jeremiah, he said to him, "The Lord your God decreed this disaster for this place. ³And now the Lord has brought it about; he has done just as he said he would. All this happened because you people sinned against the Lord and did not obey him. ⁴But today I am freeing you from the chains on your wrists. Come with me to Babylon, if you like, and I will look after you; but if you do not want to, then don't come. Look, the whole country lies before you; go wherever you please." ⁵However, before Jeremiah turned to go,ᵃ Nebuzaradan added, "Go back to Gedaliah son of Ahikam, the son of Shaphan, whom the king of Babylon has appointed over the towns of Judah, and live with him among the people, or go anywhere else you please."

Then the commander gave him provisions and a present and let him go. ⁶So Jeremiah went to Gedaliah son of Ahikam at Mizpah and stayed with him among the people who were left behind in the land.

Gedaliah Assassinated

⁷When all the army officers and their men who were still in the open country heard that the king of Babylon had appointed Gedaliah son of Ahikam as governor over the land and had put him in charge of the men, women and children who were the poorest in the land and who had not been carried into exile to Babylon, ⁸they came to Gedaliah at Mizpah—Ishmael son of Nethaniah, Johanan and Jonathan the sons of Kareah, Seraiah son of Tanhumeth, the sons of Ephai the Netophathite, and Jaazaniahᵇ the son of

ᵃ5 Or *Jeremiah answered*   ᵇ8 Hebrew *Jezaniah,* a variant of *Jaazaniah*

Trust Me on This One

READ JEREMIAH 39:1—40:6

Jeremiah passed the prophet test with flying colors—what he predicted *would* happen, *did* happen. The Jews would have saved themselves a lot of trouble if they had listened. Jeremiah was willing to let the Babylonians take over. He cooperated with them because he knew God had sent them to judge his people. Result? He ended up set free and honored. Compare that with Zedekiah: Not only *didn't* he listen to God, but he ran from the Babylonians like a scared rabbit, was caught, blinded, humiliated and chucked into prison. All because Zedekiah didn't have the guts to buck peer pressure (Jeremiah 38:4–5) and do what was right. A lot of times it's pride that keeps people from doing the right thing. Sometimes God asks us to do things that don't seem cool, where we don't come out on top, or where we have to "compromise." Not fun. But sometimes God can only bring the victory after we humbly step aside.

Your next reading is on page 1011.

the Maacathite, and their men. ⁹Gedaliah son of Ahikam, the son of Shaphan, took an oath to reassure them and their men. "Do not be afraid to serve the Babylonians,ᵃ" he said. "Settle down in the land and serve the king of Babylon, and it will go well with you. ¹⁰I myself will stay at Mizpah to represent you before the Babylonians who come to us, but you are to harvest the wine, summer fruit and oil, and put them in your storage jars, and live in the towns you have taken over."

¹¹When all the Jews in Moab, Ammon, Edom and all the other countries heard that the king of Babylon had left a remnant in Judah and had appointed Gedaliah son of Ahikam, the son of Shaphan, as governor over them, ¹²they all came back to the land of Judah, to Gedaliah at Mizpah, from all the countries where they had been scattered. And they harvested an abundance of wine and summer fruit.

¹³Johanan son of Kareah and all the army officers still in the open country came to Gedaliah at Mizpah ¹⁴and said to him, "Don't you know that Baalis king of the Ammonites has sent Ishmael son of Nethaniah to take your life?" But Gedaliah son of Ahikam did not believe them.

¹⁵Then Johanan son of Kareah said privately to Gedaliah in Mizpah, "Let me go and kill Ishmael son of Nethaniah, and no one will know it. Why should he take your life and cause all the Jews who are gathered around you to be scattered and the remnant of Judah to perish?"

¹⁶But Gedaliah son of Ahikam said to Johanan son of Kareah, "Don't do such a thing! What you are saying about Ishmael is not true."

41 In the seventh month Ishmael son of Nethaniah, the son of Elishama, who was of royal blood and had been one of the king's officers, came with ten men to Gedaliah son of Ahikam at Mizpah. While they were eating together there, ²Ishmael son of Nethaniah and the ten men who were with him got up and struck down Gedaliah son of Ahikam, the son of Shaphan, with the sword, killing the one whom the king of Babylon had appointed as governor over the land. ³Ishmael also killed all the Jews who were with Gedaliah at Mizpah, as well as the Babylonianᵇ soldiers who were there.

⁴The day after Gedaliah's assassination,

before anyone knew about it, ⁵eighty men who had shaved off their beards, torn their clothes and cut themselves came from Shechem, Shiloh and Samaria, bringing grain offerings and incense with them to the house of the LORD. ⁶Ishmael son of Nethaniah went out from Mizpah to meet them, weeping as he went. When he met them, he said, "Come to Gedaliah son of Ahikam." ⁷When they went into the city, Ishmael son of Nethaniah and the men who were with him slaughtered them and threw them into a cistern. ⁸But ten of them said to Ishmael, "Don't kill us! We have wheat and barley, oil and honey, hidden in a field." So he let them alone and did not kill them with the others. ⁹Now the cistern where he threw all the bodies of the men he had killed along with Gedaliah was the one King Asa had made as part of his defense against Baasha king of Israel. Ishmael son of Nethaniah filled it with the dead.

¹⁰Ishmael made captives of all the rest of the people who were in Mizpah—the king's daughters along with all the others who were left there, over whom Nebuzaradan commander of the imperial guard had appointed Gedaliah son of Ahikam. Ishmael son of Nethaniah took them captive and set out to cross over to the Ammonites.

¹¹When Johanan son of Kareah and all the army officers who were with him heard about all the crimes Ishmael son of Nethaniah had committed, ¹²they took all their men and went to fight Ishmael son of Nethaniah. They caught up with him near the great pool in Gibeon. ¹³When all the people Ishmael had with him saw Johanan son of Kareah and the army officers who were with him, they were glad. ¹⁴All the people Ishmael had taken captive at Mizpah turned and went over to Johanan son of Kareah. ¹⁵But Ishmael son of Nethaniah and eight of his men escaped from Johanan and fled to the Ammonites.

Flight to Egypt

¹⁶Then Johanan son of Kareah and all the army officers who were with him led away all the survivors from Mizpah whom he had recovered from Ishmael son of Nethaniah after he had assassinated Gedaliah son of Ahikam: the soldiers, women,

ᵃ 9 Or Chaldeans; also in verse 10   ᶜ 3 Or Chaldean

children and court officials he had brought from Gibeon. ¹⁷And they went on, stopping at Geruth Kimham near Bethlehem on their way to Egypt ¹⁸to escape the Babylonians.ᵃ They were afraid of them because Ishmael son of Nethaniah had killed Gedaliah son of Ahikam, whom the king of Babylon had appointed as governor over the land.

42 Then all the army officers, including Johanan son of Kareah and Jezaniahᵇ son of Hoshaiah, and all the people from the least to the greatest approached ²Jeremiah the prophet and said to him, "Please hear our petition and pray to the LORD your God for this entire remnant. For as you now see, though we were once many, now only a few are left. ³Pray that the LORD your God will tell us where we should go and what we should do."

⁴"I have heard you," replied Jeremiah the prophet. "I will certainly pray to the LORD your God as you have requested; I will tell you everything the LORD says and will keep nothing back from you."

⁵Then they said to Jeremiah, "May the LORD be a true and faithful witness against us if we do not act in accordance with everything the LORD your God sends you to tell us. ⁶Whether it is favorable or unfavorable, we will obey the LORD our God, to whom we are sending you, so that it will go well with us, for we will obey the LORD our God."

⁷Ten days later the word of the LORD came to Jeremiah. ⁸So he called together Johanan son of Kareah and all the army officers who were with him and all the people from the least to the greatest. ⁹He said to them, "This is what the LORD, the God of Israel, to whom you sent me to present your petition, says: ¹⁰'If you stay in this land, I will build you up and not tear you down; I will plant you and not uproot you, for I am grieved over the di-

ᵃ 18 Or *Chaldeans*   ᵇ 1 Hebrew; Septuagint (see also 43:2) *Azariah*

We Promise to Obey

READ JEREMIAH 42:1–16; 43:1–4, 7

You'd think at this point that the Jews would just listen to Jeremiah. He hadn't been wrong yet. But Egypt looked so good to them that they figured God would give them the thumbs-up to go there. When God didn't, they rebelled. Oh yeah, it's easy to say, "I'll do what God wants me to do," when things look easy, and you figure you *know* what God's answer will be. But the test comes when God says, "Do the tough thing." If you were playing baseball and someone shattered a grumpy neighbor's window, and everyone wanted to run, would you have the guts to say, "Guys! Let's stay and face the music"? Hmmm? It's easy to be honest and obey God when his will is easy, but are you still willing when things are hard? Here's a clue: Do the right thing and let God take care of the results.

Your next reading is on page 1015.

saster I have inflicted on you. ¹¹Do not be afraid of the king of Babylon, whom you now fear. Do not be afraid of him, declares the LORD, for I am with you and will save you and deliver you from his hands. ¹²I will show you compassion so that he will have compassion on you and restore you to your land.'

¹³"However, if you say, 'We will not stay in this land,' and so disobey the LORD your God, ¹⁴and if you say, 'No, we will go and live in Egypt, where we will not see war or hear the trumpet or be hungry for bread,' ¹⁵then hear the word of the LORD, O remnant of Judah. This is what the LORD Almighty, the God of Israel, says: 'If you are determined to go to Egypt and you do go to settle there, ¹⁶then the sword you fear will overtake you there, and the famine you dread will follow you into Egypt, and there you will die. ¹⁷Indeed, all who are determined to go to Egypt to settle there will die by the sword, famine and plague; not one of them will survive or escape the disaster I will bring on them.' ¹⁸This is what the LORD Almighty, the God of Israel, says: 'As my anger and wrath have been poured out on those who lived in Jerusalem, so will my wrath be poured out on you when you go to Egypt. You will be an object of cursing and horror, of condemnation and reproach; you will never see this place again.'

¹⁹"O remnant of Judah, the LORD has told you, 'Do not go to Egypt.' Be sure of this: I warn you today ²⁰that you made a fatal mistake ᵃ when you sent me to the LORD your God and said, 'Pray to the LORD our God for us; tell us everything he says and we will do it.' ²¹I have told you today, but you still have not obeyed the LORD your God in all he sent me to tell you. ²²So now, be sure of this: You will die by the sword, famine and plague in the place where you want to go to settle."

43 When Jeremiah finished telling the people all the words of the LORD their God—everything the LORD had sent him to tell them— ²Azariah son of Hoshaiah and Johanan son of Kareah and all the arrogant men said to Jeremiah, "You are lying! The LORD our God has not sent you to say, 'You must not go to Egypt to settle there.' ³But Baruch son of Neriah is inciting you against us to hand us over to the Babylo-

nians, ᵇ so they may kill us or carry us into exile to Babylon."

⁴So Johanan son of Kareah and all the army officers and all the people disobeyed the LORD's command to stay in the land of Judah. ⁵Instead, Johanan son of Kareah and all the army officers led away all the remnant of Judah who had come back to live in the land of Judah from all the nations where they had been scattered. ⁶They also led away all the men, women and children and the king's daughters whom Nebuzaradan commander of the imperial guard had left with Gedaliah son of Ahikam, the son of Shaphan, and Jeremiah the prophet and Baruch son of Neriah. ⁷So they entered Egypt in disobedience to the LORD and went as far as Tahpanhes.

⁸In Tahpanhes the word of the LORD came to Jeremiah: ⁹"While the Jews are watching, take some large stones with you and bury them in clay in the brick pavement at the entrance to Pharaoh's palace in Tahpanhes. ¹⁰Then say to them, 'This is what the LORD Almighty, the God of Israel, says: I will send for my servant Nebuchadnezzar king of Babylon, and I will set his throne over these stones I have buried here; he will spread his royal canopy above them. ¹¹He will come and attack Egypt, bringing death to those destined for death, captivity to those destined for captivity, and the sword to those destined for the sword. ¹²Heᶜ will set fire to the temples of the gods of Egypt; he will burn their temples and take their gods captive. As a shepherd wraps his garment around him, so will he wrap Egypt around himself and depart from there unscathed. ¹³There in the temple of the sun ᵈ in Egypt he will demolish the sacred pillars and will burn down the temples of the gods of Egypt.' "

Disaster Because of Idolatry

44 This word came to Jeremiah concerning all the Jews living in Lower Egypt—in Migdol, Tahpanhes and Memphis ᵉ— and in Upper Egypt ᶠ: ²"This is what the LORD Almighty, the God of Israel, says: You saw the great disaster I brought on Jerusalem and on all the towns of Judah. Today they lie deserted and in ruins ³because of the evil they have done. They

---

ᵃ 20 Or you erred in your hearts   ᵇ 3 Or Chaldeans
ᶜ 12 Or I   ᵈ 13 Or in Heliopolis   ᵉ 1 Hebrew Noph
ᶠ 1 Hebrew in Pathros

provoked me to anger by burning incense and by worshiping other gods that neither they nor you nor your fathers ever knew. 4Again and again I sent my servants the prophets, who said, 'Do not do this detestable thing that I hate!' 5But they did not listen or pay attention; they did not turn from their wickedness or stop burning incense to other gods. 6Therefore, my fierce anger was poured out; it raged against the towns of Judah and the streets of Jerusalem and made them the desolate ruins they are today.

7"Now this is what the LORD God Almighty, the God of Israel, says: Why bring such great disaster on yourselves by cutting off from Judah the men and women, the children and infants, and so leave yourselves without a remnant? 8Why provoke me to anger with what your hands have made, burning incense to other gods in Egypt, where you have come to live? You will destroy yourselves and make yourselves an object of cursing and reproach among all the nations on earth. 9Have you forgotten the wickedness committed by your fathers and by the kings and queens of Judah and the wickedness committed by you and your wives in the land of Judah and the streets of Jerusalem? 10To this day they have not humbled themselves or shown reverence, nor have they followed my law and the decrees I set before you and your fathers.

11"Therefore, this is what the LORD Almighty, the God of Israel, says: I am determined to bring disaster on you and to destroy all Judah. 12I will take away the remnant of Judah who were determined to go to Egypt to settle there. They will all perish in Egypt; they will fall by the sword or die from famine. From the least to the greatest, they will die by sword or famine. They will become an object of cursing and horror, of condemnation and reproach. 13I will punish those who live in Egypt with the sword, famine and plague, as I punished Jerusalem. 14None of the remnant of Judah who have gone to live in Egypt will escape or survive to return to the land of Judah, to which they long to return and live; none will return except a few fugitives."

15Then all the men who knew that their wives were burning incense to other gods, along with all the women who were present—a large assembly—and all the people living in Lower and Upper Egypt,ᵃ said to Jeremiah, 16"We will not listen to the message you have spoken to us in the name of the LORD! 17We will certainly do everything we said we would: We will burn incense to the Queen of Heaven and will pour out drink offerings to her just as we and our fathers, our kings and our officials did in the towns of Judah and in the streets of Jerusalem. At that time we had plenty of food and were well off and suffered no harm. 18But ever since we stopped burning incense to the Queen of Heaven and pouring out drink offerings to her, we have had nothing and have been perishing by sword and famine."

19The women added, "When we burned incense to the Queen of Heaven and poured out drink offerings to her, did not our husbands know that we were making cakes like her image and pouring out drink offerings to her?"

20Then Jeremiah said to all the people, both men and women, who were answering him, 21"Did not the LORD remember and think about the incense burned in the towns of Judah and the streets of Jerusalem by you and your fathers, your kings and your officials and the people of the land? 22When the LORD could no longer endure your wicked actions and the detestable things you did, your land became an object of cursing and a desolate waste without inhabitants, as it is today. 23Because you have burned incense and have sinned against the LORD and have not obeyed him or followed his law or his decrees or his stipulations, this disaster has come upon you, as you now see."

24Then Jeremiah said to all the people, including the women, "Hear the word of the LORD, all you people of Judah in Egypt. 25This is what the LORD Almighty, the God of Israel, says: You and your wives have shown by your actions what you promised when you said, 'We will certainly carry out the vows we made to burn incense and pour out drink offerings to the Queen of Heaven.'

"Go ahead then, do what you promised! Keep your vows! 26But hear the word of the LORD, all Jews living in Egypt: 'I swear by my great name,' says the LORD, 'that no one from Judah living anywhere in Egypt will ever again invoke my name

---

ᵃ 15 Hebrew in Egypt and Pathros

or swear, "As surely as the Sovereign LORD lives." 27For I am watching over them for harm, not for good; the Jews in Egypt will perish by sword and famine until they are all destroyed. 28Those who escape the sword and return to the land of Judah from Egypt will be very few. Then the whole remnant of Judah who came to live in Egypt will know whose word will stand—mine or theirs.

29" 'This will be the sign to you that I will punish you in this place,' declares the LORD, 'so that you will know that my threats of harm against you will surely stand.' 30This is what the LORD says: 'I am going to hand Pharaoh Hophra king of Egypt over to his enemies who seek his life, just as I handed Zedekiah king of Judah over to Nebuchadnezzar king of Babylon, the enemy who was seeking his life.' "

A Message to Baruch

45 This is what Jeremiah the prophet told Baruch son of Neriah in the fourth year of Jehoiakim son of Josiah king of Judah, after Baruch had written on a scroll the words Jeremiah was then dictating: 2"This is what the LORD, the God of Israel, says to you, Baruch: 3You said, 'Woe to me! The LORD has added sorrow to my pain; I am worn out with groaning and find no rest.' "

4The LORD said, "Say this to him: 'This is what the LORD says: I will overthrow what I have built and uproot what I have planted, throughout the land. 5Should you then seek great things for yourself? Seek them not. For I will bring disaster on all people, declares the LORD, but wherever you go I will let you escape with your life.' "

A Message About Egypt

46 This is the word of the LORD that came to Jeremiah the prophet concerning the nations:

2Concerning Egypt:

This is the message against the army of Pharaoh Neco king of Egypt, which was defeated at Carchemish on the Euphrates River by Nebuchadnezzar king of Babylon in the fourth year of Jehoiakim son of Josiah king of Judah:

3"Prepare your shields, both large and small,
 and march out for battle!
4Harness the horses,
 mount the steeds!
Take your positions
 with helmets on!
Polish your spears,
 put on your armor!
5What do I see?
 They are terrified,
they are retreating,
 their warriors are defeated.
They flee in haste
 without looking back,
 and there is terror on every side,"
                declares the LORD.
6"The swift cannot flee
 nor the strong escape.
In the north by the River Euphrates
 they stumble and fall.

7"Who is this that rises like the Nile,
 like rivers of surging waters?
8Egypt rises like the Nile,
 like rivers of surging waters.
She says, 'I will rise and cover the earth;
 I will destroy cities and their people.'
9Charge, O horses!
 Drive furiously, O charioteers!
March on, O warriors—
 men of Cush[a] and Put who carry
   shields,
 men of Lydia who draw the bow.
10But that day belongs to the Lord, the
   LORD Almighty—
 a day of vengeance, for vengeance
   on his foes.
The sword will devour till it is satisfied,
 till it has quenched its thirst with
   blood.
For the Lord, the LORD Almighty, will
   offer sacrifice
 in the land of the north by the River
   Euphrates.

11"Go up to Gilead and get balm,
 O Virgin Daughter of Egypt.
But you multiply remedies in vain;
 there is no healing for you.
12The nations will hear of your shame;
 your cries will fill the earth.
One warrior will stumble over another;
 both will fall down together."

13This is the message the LORD spoke to Jeremiah the prophet about the coming

---

a 9 That is, the upper Nile region

of Nebuchadnezzar king of Babylon to attack Egypt:

14 "Announce this in Egypt, and proclaim
it in Migdol;
proclaim it also in Memphis*a* and
Tahpanhes:
'Take your positions and get ready,
for the sword devours those around
you.'
15 Why will your warriors be laid low?
They cannot stand, for the LORD will
push them down.
16 They will stumble repeatedly;
they will fall over each other.
They will say, 'Get up, let us go back
to our own people and our native
lands,
away from the sword of the
oppressor.'
17 There they will exclaim,
'Pharaoh king of Egypt is only a loud
noise;
he has missed his opportunity.'

18 "As surely as I live," declares the King,
whose name is the LORD Almighty,

"one will come who is like Tabor
among the mountains,
like Carmel by the sea.
19 Pack your belongings for exile,
you who live in Egypt,
for Memphis will be laid waste
and lie in ruins without inhabitant.

20 "Egypt is a beautiful heifer,
but a gadfly is coming
against her from the north.
21 The mercenaries in her ranks
are like fattened calves.
They too will turn and flee together,
they will not stand their ground,
for the day of disaster is coming upon
them,
the time for them to be punished.
22 Egypt will hiss like a fleeing serpent
as the enemy advances in force;
they will come against her with axes,
like men who cut down trees.
23 They will chop down her forest,"
declares the LORD.
"dense though it be.
They are more numerous than locusts,

b 14 Hebrew *Noph*; also in verse 19

Pharaoh the Do-Nothing

READ JEREMIAH 46:17

A friend has to give up his super-easy paper route. Head to the newspaper office now and the job's yours. Three days later you go. Surprise, surprise. The route is taken. Lesson? Don't sit on your duff and wait for things to happen. When an opportunity comes, grab it. God said that Pharaoh was a "loud noise" (a big talker) but that he was a "do-nothing" (see also Isaiah 30:7). When Nebuchadnezzar's dad died and he returned to Babylon, Pharaoh had a chance to take over. Instead, he missed his opportunity by doing ... *nothing*. Men of God don't talk about what they'll do. They just do it. If it's important to prove that you're trustworthy or a hard worker, and the opportunity comes, seize it! Even do things that are outside your comfort zone if they help you grow as a man. Whatever you do, don't be a do-nothing.

Your next reading is on page 1019.

they cannot be counted.
24 The Daughter of Egypt will be put to shame,
    handed over to the people of the north."

25 The LORD Almighty, the God of Israel, says: "I am about to bring punishment on Amon god of Thebes,[a] on Pharaoh, on Egypt and her gods and her kings, and on those who rely on Pharaoh. 26 I will hand them over to those who seek their lives, to Nebuchadnezzar king of Babylon and his officers. Later, however, Egypt will be inhabited as in times past," declares the LORD.

27 "Do not fear, O Jacob my servant;
    do not be dismayed, O Israel.
I will surely save you out of a distant place,
    your descendants from the land of their exile.
Jacob will again have peace and security,
    and no one will make him afraid.
28 Do not fear, O Jacob my servant,
    for I am with you," declares the LORD.
"Though I completely destroy all the nations
    among which I scatter you,
    I will not completely destroy you.
I will discipline you but only with justice;
    I will not let you go entirely unpunished."

A Message About the Philistines

47 This is the word of the LORD that came to Jeremiah the prophet concerning the Philistines before Pharaoh attacked Gaza:

2 This is what the LORD says:

"See how the waters are rising in the north;
    they will become an overflowing torrent.
They will overflow the land and everything in it,
    the towns and those who live in them.
The people will cry out;
    all who dwell in the land will wail
3 at the sound of the hoofs of galloping steeds,
    at the noise of enemy chariots
    and the rumble of their wheels.
Fathers will not turn to help their children;
    their hands will hang limp.
4 For the day has come
    to destroy all the Philistines
and to cut off all survivors
    who could help Tyre and Sidon.
The LORD is about to destroy the Philistines,
    the remnant from the coasts of Caphtor.[b]
5 Gaza will shave her head in mourning;
    Ashkelon will be silenced.
O remnant on the plain,
    how long will you cut yourselves?
6 " 'Ah, sword of the LORD,' ⌊you cry,⌋
    'how long till you rest?

a 25 Hebrew No   b 4 That is, Crete

Get a Load of This...

There are some 2500 species of snakes and about 500 of them are poisonous. In Sri Lanka, over 900 people die each year from snake bites! There would be more, but apparently the *really* venomous snakes flee from humans—sort of like Egypt does in Jeremiah 46:22.

Return to your scabbard;
  cease and be still.'
7 But how can it rest
  when the LORD has commanded it,
when he has ordered it
  to attack Ashkelon and the coast?"

A Message About Moab

48 Concerning Moab:

This is what the LORD Almighty,
the God of Israel, says:

"Woe to Nebo, for it will be ruined.
  Kiriathaim will be disgraced and
    captured;
  the stronghold[a] will be disgraced
    and shattered.
2 Moab will be praised no more;
  in Heshbon[b] men will plot her
    downfall:
  'Come, let us put an end to that
    nation.'
You too, O Madmen,[c] will be silenced;
  the sword will pursue you.
3 Listen to the cries from Horonaim,
  cries of great havoc and destruction.
4 Moab will be broken;
  her little ones will cry out.[d]
5 They go up the way to Luhith,
  weeping bitterly as they go;
on the road down to Horonaim
  anguished cries over the destruction
    are heard.
6 Flee! Run for your lives;
  become like a bush[e] in the desert.
7 Since you trust in your deeds and riches,
  you too will be taken captive,
and Chemosh will go into exile,
  together with his priests and
    officials.
8 The destroyer will come against every
    town,
  and not a town will escape.
The valley will be ruined
  and the plateau destroyed,
  because the LORD has spoken.
9 Put salt on Moab,
  for she will be laid waste[f];
her towns will become desolate,
  with no one to live in them.

10 "A curse on him who is lax in doing
    the LORD's work!
  A curse on him who keeps his sword
    from bloodshed!

11 "Moab has been at rest from youth,

like wine left on its dregs,
  not poured from one jar to another—
  she has not gone into exile.
So she tastes as she did,
  and her aroma is unchanged.
12 But days are coming,"
  declares the LORD,
"when I will send men who pour from
    jars,
  and they will pour her out;
they will empty her jars
  and smash her jugs.
13 Then Moab will be ashamed of
    Chemosh,
  as the house of Israel was ashamed
  when they trusted in Bethel.

14 "How can you say, 'We are warriors,
  men valiant in battle'?
15 Moab will be destroyed and her towns
    invaded;
  her finest young men will go down
    in the slaughter,"
  declares the King, whose name is
    the LORD Almighty.
16 "The fall of Moab is at hand;
  her calamity will come quickly.
17 Mourn for her, all who live around her,
  all who know her fame;
say, 'How broken is the mighty scepter,
  how broken the glorious staff!'

18 "Come down from your glory
  and sit on the parched ground,
  O inhabitants of the Daughter of
    Dibon,
for he who destroys Moab
  will come up against you
  and ruin your fortified cities.
19 Stand by the road and watch,
  you who live in Aroer.
Ask the man fleeing and the woman
    escaping,
  ask them, 'What has happened?'
20 Moab is disgraced, for she is shattered.
  Wail and cry out!
Announce by the Arnon
  that Moab is destroyed.
21 Judgment has come to the plateau—
  to Holon, Jahzah and Mephaath,
22   to Dibon, Nebo and Beth Diblathaim,
23   to Kiriathaim, Beth Gamul and Beth
    Meon,

---

a 1 Or / *Misgab*   *b 2* The Hebrew for *Heshbon* sounds like
the Hebrew for *plot*.   *c 2* The name of the Moabite town
Madmen sounds like the Hebrew for *be silenced*.
d 4 Hebrew; Septuagint / *proclaim it to Zoar*   *e 6* Or like
Aroer   *f 9* Or *Give wings to Moab,* / *for she will fly away*

24 to Kerioth and Bozrah—
    to all the towns of Moab, far and
        near.
25 Moab's horn[a] is cut off;
    her arm is broken,"
                        declares the LORD.

26 "Make her drunk,
    for she has defied the LORD.
Let Moab wallow in her vomit;
    let her be an object of ridicule.
27 Was not Israel the object of your
        ridicule?
    Was she caught among thieves,
that you shake your head in scorn
    whenever you speak of her?
28 Abandon your towns and dwell among
        the rocks,
    you who live in Moab.
Be like a dove that makes its nest
    at the mouth of a cave.

29 "We have heard of Moab's pride—
    her overweening pride and conceit,
her pride and arrogance
    and the haughtiness of her heart.
30 I know her insolence but it is futile,"
                        declares the LORD,
    "and her boasts accomplish nothing.
31 Therefore I wail over Moab,
    for all Moab I cry out,
    I moan for the men of Kir Hareseth.
32 I weep for you, as Jazer weeps,
    O vines of Sibmah.
Your branches spread as far as the sea;
    they reached as far as the sea of
        Jazer.
The destroyer has fallen
    on your ripened fruit and grapes.
33 Joy and gladness are gone
    from the orchards and fields of
        Moab.
I have stopped the flow of wine from
        the presses;
    no one treads them with shouts of
        joy.
Although there are shouts,
    they are not shouts of joy.

34 "The sound of their cry rises
    from Heshbon to Elealeh and Jahaz,
from Zoar as far as Horonaim and
        Eglath Shelishiyah,
    for even the waters of Nimrim are
        dried up.
35 In Moab I will put an end
    to those who make offerings on the
        high places

and burn incense to their gods,"
                        declares the LORD.
36 "So my heart laments for Moab like a
        flute;
    it laments like a flute for the men of
        Kir Hareseth.
The wealth they acquired is gone.
37 Every head is shaved
    and every beard cut off;
every hand is slashed
    and every waist is covered with
        sackcloth.
38 On all the roofs in Moab
    and in the public squares
there is nothing but mourning,
    for I have broken Moab
    like a jar that no one wants,"
                        declares the LORD.
39 "How shattered she is! How they wail!
    How Moab turns her back in shame!
Moab has become an object of
        ridicule,
    an object of horror to all those
        around her."

40 This is what the LORD says:

"Look! An eagle is swooping down,
    spreading its wings over Moab.
41 Kerioth[b] will be captured
    and the strongholds taken.
In that day the hearts of Moab's
        warriors
    will be like the heart of a woman in
        labor.
42 Moab will be destroyed as a nation
    because she defied the LORD.
43 Terror and pit and snare await you,
    O people of Moab,"
                        declares the LORD.
44 "Whoever flees from the terror
    will fall into a pit,
whoever climbs out of the pit
    will be caught in a snare;
for I will bring upon Moab
    the year of her punishment,"
                        declares the LORD.
45 "In the shadow of Heshbon
    the fugitives stand helpless,
for a fire has gone out from Heshbon,
    a blaze from the midst of Sihon;
it burns the foreheads of Moab,
    the skulls of the noisy boasters.
46 Woe to you, O Moab!
    The people of Chemosh are
        destroyed;

---

a 25 *Horn* here symbolizes strength.   b 41 Or *The cities*

your sons are taken into exile
  and your daughters into captivity.
47 "Yet I will restore the fortunes of Moab
  in days to come,"
                                    declares the LORD.

Here ends the judgment on Moab.

A Message About Ammon

49 Concerning the Ammonites:

This is what the LORD says:

"Has Israel no sons?
  Has she no heirs?
Why then has Molech[a] taken
  possession of Gad?
  Why do his people live in its towns?
2 But the days are coming,"
  declares the LORD,
"when I will sound the battle cry
  against Rabbah of the Ammonites;
it will become a mound of ruins,

and its surrounding villages will be
  set on fire.
Then Israel will drive out
  those who drove her out,"
                                    says the LORD.
3 "Wail, O Heshbon, for Ai is destroyed!
  Cry out, O inhabitants of Rabbah!
Put on sackcloth and mourn;
  rush here and there inside the walls,
for Molech will go into exile,
  together with his priests and officials.
4 Why do you boast of your valleys,
  boast of your valleys so fruitful?
O unfaithful daughter,
  you trust in your riches and say,
  'Who will attack me?'
5 I will bring terror on you
  from all those around you,"
                                    declares the Lord,
                                the LORD Almighty.
"Every one of you will be driven away,
  and no one will gather the fugitives.

a 1 Or their king; Hebrew malcam; also in verse 3

Big God, Big Possibilities

READ JEREMIAH 49:1–2, 7–8, 23–24, 28–29, 34–35

Some prophets were only prophets to Israel, but God called Jeremiah to give a message to *all* the nations. God told Jeremiah when he was a kid that he'd end up preaching God's judgment against other kingdoms, too (Jeremiah 1:10), and in Jeremiah 46–51 Jeremiah fulfilled that role. He went way beyond belting it out to just Judah. You too can fulfill all that God meant you to do. Nine out of ten people never leave the social or economic circle they're born into, but if God has *big* plans for your life, and you're willing to jump, he can help you get there. Be faithful and develop your talents. Be open to new experiences. Why be one of the nine when you can be the one?

Your next reading is on page 1024.

6 "Yet afterward, I will restore the
   fortunes of the Ammonites,"
          declares the LORD.

A Message About Edom

7 Concerning Edom:

This is what the LORD Almighty says:

"Is there no longer wisdom in Teman?
   Has counsel perished from the
      prudent?
   Has their wisdom decayed?
8 Turn and flee, hide in deep caves,
   you who live in Dedan,
for I will bring disaster on Esau
   at the time I punish him.
9 If grape pickers came to you,
   would they not leave a few grapes?
If thieves came during the night,
   would they not steal only as much
      as they wanted?
10 But I will strip Esau bare;
   I will uncover his hiding places,
   so that he cannot conceal himself.
His children, relatives and neighbors
      will perish,
   and he will be no more.
11 Leave your orphans; I will protect their
      lives.
   Your widows too can trust in me."

12 This is what the LORD says: "If those
who do not deserve to drink the cup must
drink it, why should you go unpunished?
You will not go unpunished, but must drink
it. 13 I swear by myself," declares the LORD,
"that Bozrah will become a ruin and an object of horror, of reproach and of cursing;
and all its towns will be in ruins forever."

14 I have heard a message from the LORD:
   An envoy was sent to the nations to
      say,
   "Assemble yourselves to attack it!
   Rise up for battle!"

15 "Now I will make you small among the
      nations,
   despised among men.
16 The terror you inspire
   and the pride of your heart have
      deceived you,
you who live in the clefts of the rocks,
   who occupy the heights of the hill.
Though you build your nest as high as
      the eagle's,
   from there I will bring you down,"
          declares the LORD.

17 "Edom will become an object of horror;
   all who pass by will be appalled and
      will scoff
   because of all its wounds.
18 As Sodom and Gomorrah were
      overthrown,
   along with their neighboring towns,"
          says the LORD,
   "so no one will live there;
   no man will dwell in it.

19 "Like a lion coming up from Jordan's
      thickets
   to a rich pastureland,
I will chase Edom from its land in an
      instant.
   Who is the chosen one I will appoint
      for this?
   Who is like me and who can challenge
      me?
   And what shepherd can stand
      against me?"
20 Therefore, hear what the LORD has
      planned against Edom,
   what he has purposed against those
      who live in Teman:
The young of the flock will be dragged
      away;
   he will completely destroy their
      pasture because of them.
21 At the sound of their fall the earth will
      tremble;
   their cry will resound to the Red Sea.[a]
22 Look! An eagle will soar and swoop
      down,
   spreading its wings over Bozrah.
In that day the hearts of Edom's
      warriors
   will be like the heart of a woman in
      labor.

A Message About Damascus

23 Concerning Damascus:

"Hamath and Arpad are dismayed,
   for they have heard bad news.
They are disheartened,
   troubled like[b] the restless sea.
24 Damascus has become feeble,
   she has turned to flee
   and panic has gripped her;
anguish and pain have seized her,
   pain like that of a woman in labor.
25 Why has the city of renown not been
      abandoned,

[a] 21 Hebrew *Yam Suph*; that is, Sea of Reeds   [b] 23 Hebrew
on or *by*

the town in which I delight?
26 Surely, her young men will fall in the
streets;
all her soldiers will be silenced in
that day,"
declares the LORD Almighty.
27 "I will set fire to the walls of Damascus;
it will consume the fortresses of
Ben-Hadad."

A Message About Kedar and Hazor

28 Concerning Kedar and the kingdoms
of Hazor, which Nebuchadnezzar king of
Babylon attacked:

This is what the LORD says:

"Arise, and attack Kedar
and destroy the people of the East.
29 Their tents and their flocks will be taken;
their shelters will be carried off
with all their goods and camels.
Men will shout to them,
'Terror on every side!'

30 "Flee quickly away!
Stay in deep caves, you who live in
Hazor,"
declares the LORD.
"Nebuchadnezzar king of Babylon has
plotted against you;
he has devised a plan against you.

31 "Arise and attack a nation at ease,
which lives in confidence,"
declares the LORD,
"a nation that has neither gates nor
bars;
its people live alone.
32 Their camels will become plunder,
and their large herds will be booty.
I will scatter to the winds those who
are in distant places[a]
and will bring disaster on them from
every side,"
declares the LORD.
33 "Hazor will become a haunt of jackals,
a desolate place forever.
No one will live there;
no man will dwell in it."

A Message About Elam

34 This is the word of the LORD that came
to Jeremiah the prophet concerning Elam,
early in the reign of Zedekiah king of Judah:

35 This is what the LORD Almighty says:

"See, I will break the bow of Elam,
the mainstay of their might.
36 I will bring against Elam the four
winds
from the four quarters of the
heavens;
I will scatter them to the four winds,
and there will not be a nation
where Elam's exiles do not go.
37 I will shatter Elam before their foes,
before those who seek their lives;
I will bring disaster upon them,
even my fierce anger,"
declares the LORD.
"I will pursue them with the sword
until I have made an end of them.
38 I will set my throne in Elam
and destroy her king and officials,"
declares the LORD.

39 "Yet I will restore the fortunes of Elam
in days to come,"
declares the LORD.

A Message About Babylon

 This is the word the LORD spoke
through Jeremiah the prophet
concerning Babylon and the
land of the Babylonians[b]:

2 "Announce and proclaim among the
nations,
lift up a banner and proclaim it;
keep nothing back, but say,
'Babylon will be captured;
Bel will be put to shame,
Marduk filled with terror.
Her images will be put to shame
and her idols filled with terror.'
3 A nation from the north will attack her
and lay waste her land.
No one will live in it;
both men and animals will flee
away.

4 "In those days, at that time,"
declares the LORD,
"the people of Israel and the people of
Judah together
will go in tears to seek the LORD their
God.
5 They will ask the way to Zion
and turn their faces toward it.
They will come and bind themselves to
the LORD
in an everlasting covenant
that will not be forgotten.

---

a 32 Or *who clip the hair by their foreheads*
b 1 Or *Chaldeans; also in verses 8, 25, 35 and 45*

6 "My people have been lost sheep;
  their shepherds have led them astray
  and caused them to roam on the
    mountains.
They wandered over mountain and hill
  and forgot their own resting place.
7 Whoever found them devoured them;
  their enemies said, 'We are not guilty,
for they sinned against the LORD, their
    true pasture,
  the LORD, the hope of their fathers.'

8 "Flee out of Babylon;
  leave the land of the Babylonians,
  and be like the goats that lead the
    flock.
9 For I will stir up and bring against
    Babylon
  an alliance of great nations from the
    land of the north.
They will take up their positions
    against her,
  and from the north she will be
    captured.
Their arrows will be like skilled warriors
  who do not return empty-handed.
10 So Babylonia[a] will be plundered;
  all who plunder her will have their
    fill,"
                    declares the LORD.

11 "Because you rejoice and are glad,
  you who pillage my inheritance,
because you frolic like a heifer
    threshing grain
  and neigh like stallions,
12 your mother will be greatly ashamed;
  she who gave you birth will be
    disgraced.
She will be the least of the nations—
  a wilderness, a dry land, a desert.
13 Because of the LORD's anger she will
    not be inhabited
  but will be completely desolate.
All who pass Babylon will be horrified
    and scoff
  because of all her wounds.

14 "Take up your positions around
    Babylon,
  all you who draw the bow.
Shoot at her! Spare no arrows,
  for she has sinned against the LORD.
15 Shout against her on every side!
  She surrenders, her towers fall,
  her walls are torn down.
Since this is the vengeance of the LORD,
  take vengeance on her;

do to her as she has done to others.
16 Cut off from Babylon the sower,
  and the reaper with his sickle at
    harvest.
Because of the sword of the oppressor
  let everyone return to his own
    people,
  let everyone flee to his own land.

17 "Israel is a scattered flock
  that lions have chased away.
The first to devour him
  was the king of Assyria;
the last to crush his bones
  was Nebuchadnezzar king of
    Babylon."

18 Therefore this is what the LORD Almighty, the God of Israel, says:

"I will punish the king of Babylon and
    his land
  as I punished the king of Assyria.
19 But I will bring Israel back to his own
    pasture
  and he will graze on Carmel and
    Bashan;
his appetite will be satisfied
  on the hills of Ephraim and Gilead.
20 In those days, at that time,"
    declares the LORD,
"search will be made for Israel's guilt,
  but there will be none,
and for the sins of Judah,
  but none will be found,
  for I will forgive the remnant I spare.

21 "Attack the land of Merathaim
  and those who live in Pekod.
Pursue, kill and completely destroy[b]
    them,"
                    declares the LORD.
"Do everything I have commanded
    you.
22 The noise of battle is in the land,
  the noise of great destruction!
23 How broken and shattered
  is the hammer of the whole earth!
How desolate is Babylon
  among the nations!
24 I set a trap for you, O Babylon,
  and you were caught before you
    knew it;
you were found and captured
  because you opposed the LORD.
25 The LORD has opened his arsenal

---

a 10 Or *Chaldea*   *b 21* The Hebrew term refers to the irrevocable giving over of things or persons to the LORD, often by totally destroying them; also in verse 26.

and brought out the weapons of his wrath,
for the Sovereign LORD Almighty has work to do
  in the land of the Babylonians.
26 Come against her from afar.
    Break open her granaries;
      pile her up like heaps of grain.
  Completely destroy her
      and leave her no remnant.
27 Kill all her young bulls;
    let them go down to the slaughter!
  Woe to them! For their day has come,
    the time for them to be punished.
28 Listen to the fugitives and refugees from Babylon
    declaring in Zion
  how the LORD our God has taken vengeance,
    vengeance for his temple.

29 "Summon archers against Babylon,
    all those who draw the bow.
  Encamp all around her;
    let no one escape.
  Repay her for her deeds;
    do to her as she has done.
  For she has defied the LORD,
    the Holy One of Israel.
30 Therefore, her young men will fall in the streets;
    all her soldiers will be silenced in that day,"
                        declares the LORD.
31 "See, I am against you, O arrogant one,"
    declares the Lord, the LORD Almighty,
  "for your day has come,
    the time for you to be punished.
32 The arrogant one will stumble and fall
    and no one will help her up;
  I will kindle a fire in her towns
    that will consume all who are around her."

33 This is what the LORD Almighty says:

"The people of Israel are oppressed,
    and the people of Judah as well.
  All their captors hold them fast,
    refusing to let them go.
34 Yet their Redeemer is strong;
    the LORD Almighty is his name.
  He will vigorously defend their cause
    so that he may bring rest to their land,
    but unrest to those who live in Babylon.

35 "A sword against the Babylonians!"
    declares the LORD—
  "against those who live in Babylon
    and against her officials and wise men!
36 A sword against her false prophets!
    They will become fools.
  A sword against her warriors!
    They will be filled with terror.
37 A sword against her horses and chariots
    and all the foreigners in her ranks!

Get a Load of This...

If people have made nuclear weapons that can fry the planet, what kind of stuff has God got in *his* armory (see Jeremiah 50:25)? With an arsenal that size, aren't you glad that you're on God's side?

They will become women.
A sword against her treasures!
They will be plundered.
38 A drought on[a] her waters!
They will dry up.
For it is a land of idols,
idols that will go mad with terror.

39 "So desert creatures and hyenas will
live there,
and there the owl will dwell.
It will never again be inhabited
or lived in from generation to
generation.
40 As God overthrew Sodom and
Gomorrah
along with their neighboring towns,"
      declares the LORD,
"so no one will live there;
no man will dwell in it.

41 "Look! An army is coming from the
north;
a great nation and many kings
are being stirred up from the ends
of the earth.

42 They are armed with bows and spears;
they are cruel and without mercy.
They sound like the roaring sea
as they ride on their horses;
they come like men in battle formation
to attack you, O Daughter of Babylon.
43 The king of Babylon has heard reports
about them,
and his hands hang limp.
Anguish has gripped him,
pain like that of a woman in labor.
44 Like a lion coming up from Jordan's
thickets
to a rich pastureland,
I will chase Babylon from its land in an
instant.
Who is the chosen one I will appoint
for this?
Who is like me and who can challenge
me?
And what shepherd can stand
against me?"
45 Therefore, hear what the LORD has
planned against Babylon,

[a] 38 Or A sword against

Stop Hammering!

READ JEREMIAH 50:14–17, 41–43; 51:6–12

Babylon was the hammer God used to pound his disobedient people. It would be like you letting your kid brother nail a few boards up in your tree fort. But what if he started laughing and began smashing the boards? Well, that's what happened with God's hammer: Nebuchadnezzar kept at it when God had said, "Enough." He was crushing Israel's bones (see verse 17). So God punished Nebuchadnezzar by sending the Medes to pound *his* kingdom. The Babylonians started off doing what God wanted, but when they went beyond what he intended, they set themselves up for judgment. When you start serving God and become successful, be careful to *keep* doing what God wants. Don't start off doing God's will, then figure you know the ropes so well you can do things your way. Never forget the importance of obeying God. (Important mental note: This is a decision you're making for your lifetime.)

Your next reading is on page 1029.

what he has purposed against the
   land of the Babylonians:
The young of the flock will be dragged
   away;
he will completely destroy their
   pasture because of them.
46 At the sound of Babylon's capture the
   earth will tremble;
its cry will resound among the
   nations.

51 This is what the LORD says:

"See, I will stir up the spirit of a
   destroyer
against Babylon and the people of
   Leb Kamai. *a*
2 I will send foreigners to Babylon
   to winnow her and to devastate her
   land;
they will oppose her on every side
   in the day of her disaster.
3 Let not the archer string his bow,
   nor let him put on his armor.
Do not spare her young men;
   completely destroy *b* her army.
4 They will fall down slain in Babylon, *c*
   fatally wounded in her streets.
5 For Israel and Judah have not been
   forsaken
   by their God, the LORD Almighty,
though their land *d* is full of guilt
   before the Holy One of Israel.

6 "Flee from Babylon!
   Run for your lives!
   Do not be destroyed because of her
   sins.
It is time for the LORD's vengeance;
   he will pay her what she deserves.
7 Babylon was a gold cup in the LORD's
   hand;
   she made the whole earth drunk.
The nations drank her wine;
   therefore they have now gone mad.
8 Babylon will suddenly fall and be
   broken.
   Wail over her!
Get balm for her pain;
   perhaps she can be healed.

9 " 'We would have healed Babylon,
   but she cannot be healed;
let us leave her and each go to his own
   land,
for her judgment reaches to the
   skies,
it rises as high as the clouds.'

10 " 'The LORD has vindicated us;
   come, let us tell in Zion
   what the LORD our God has done.'

11 "Sharpen the arrows,
   take up the shields!
The LORD has stirred up the kings of the
   Medes,
because his purpose is to destroy
   Babylon.
The LORD will take vengeance,
   vengeance for his temple.
12 Lift up a banner against the walls of
   Babylon!
Reinforce the guard,
station the watchmen,
   prepare an ambush!
The LORD will carry out his purpose,
   his decree against the people of
   Babylon.
13 You who live by many waters
   and are rich in treasures,
your end has come,
   the time for you to be cut off.
14 The LORD Almighty has sworn by himself:
   I will surely fill you with men, as
   with a swarm of locusts,
   and they will shout in triumph over
   you.

15 "He made the earth by his power;
   he founded the world by his wisdom
   and stretched out the heavens by his
   understanding.
16 When he thunders, the waters in the
   heavens roar;
he makes clouds rise from the ends
   of the earth.
He sends lightning with the rain
   and brings out the wind from his
   storehouses.

17 "Every man is senseless and without
   knowledge;
every goldsmith is shamed by his
   idols.
His images are a fraud;
   they have no breath in them.
18 They are worthless, the objects of
   mockery;
when their judgment comes, they
   will perish.
19 He who is the Portion of Jacob is not
   like these,

---

a 1 Leb Kamai is a cryptogram for Chaldea, that is, Babylonia.
b 3 The Hebrew term refers to the irrevocable giving over of
things or persons to the LORD, often by totally destroying
them.   *c 4* Or *Chaldea*   *d 5* Or *I and the land of the
Babylonians*

Get a Load of This...

Are you a war club (Jeremiah 51:20)? Will you stand up for God and do what's right? Or are you a wet noodle—all slippery and soft, trying to conform to the plate you're on? It's not about personality, but attitude.

for he is the Maker of all things,
   including the tribe of his inheritance—
   the LORD Almighty is his name.

20 "You are my war club,
      my weapon for battle—
   with you I shatter nations,
      with you I destroy kingdoms,
21 with you I shatter horse and rider,
      with you I shatter chariot and driver,
22 with you I shatter man and woman,
      with you I shatter old man and youth,
      with you I shatter young man and maiden,
23 with you I shatter shepherd and flock,
      with you I shatter farmer and oxen,
      with you I shatter governors and officials.

24 "Before your eyes I will repay Babylon and all who live in Babylonia[a] for all the wrong they have done in Zion," declares the LORD.

25 "I am against you, O destroying mountain,
      you who destroy the whole earth,"
                              declares the LORD.
   "I will stretch out my hand against you,
      roll you off the cliffs,
      and make you a burned-out mountain.
26 No rock will be taken from you for a cornerstone,
      nor any stone for a foundation,
      for you will be desolate forever,"
                              declares the LORD.

27 "Lift up a banner in the land!
      Blow the trumpet among the nations!
   Prepare the nations for battle against her;
      summon against her these kingdoms:
      Ararat, Minni and Ashkenaz.
   Appoint a commander against her;
      send up horses like a swarm of locusts.
28 Prepare the nations for battle against her—
      the kings of the Medes,
   their governors and all their officials,
      and all the countries they rule.
29 The land trembles and writhes,
      for the LORD's purposes against Babylon stand—
   to lay waste the land of Babylon
      so that no one will live there.
30 Babylon's warriors have stopped fighting;
      they remain in their strongholds.
   Their strength is exhausted;
      they have become like women.
   Her dwellings are set on fire;
      the bars of her gates are broken.
31 One courier follows another
      and messenger follows messenger
   to announce to the king of Babylon
      that his entire city is captured,

a 24 Or Chaldea; also in verse 35

32 the river crossings seized,
 the marshes set on fire,
 and the soldiers terrified."

33 This is what the LORD Almighty, the God of Israel, says:

"The Daughter of Babylon is like a threshing floor
 at the time it is trampled;
 the time to harvest her will soon come."

34 "Nebuchadnezzar king of Babylon has devoured us,
 he has thrown us into confusion,
 he has made us an empty jar.
Like a serpent he has swallowed us
 and filled his stomach with our delicacies,
 and then has spewed us out.
35 May the violence done to our flesh*a* be upon
 Babylon,"
 say the inhabitants of Zion.
"May our blood be on those who live in Babylonia,"
 says Jerusalem.

36 Therefore, this is what the LORD says:

"See, I will defend your cause
 and avenge you;
I will dry up her sea
 and make her springs dry.
37 Babylon will be a heap of ruins,
 a haunt of jackals,
an object of horror and scorn,
 a place where no one lives.
38 Her people all roar like young lions,
 they growl like lion cubs.
39 But while they are aroused,
 I will set out a feast for them
 and make them drunk,
so that they shout with laughter—
 then sleep forever and not awake,"
 declares the LORD.
40 "I will bring them down
 like lambs to the slaughter,
 like rams and goats.

41 "How Sheshach*b* will be captured,
 the boast of the whole earth seized!
What a horror Babylon will be
 among the nations!
42 The sea will rise over Babylon;
 its roaring waves will cover her.
43 Her towns will be desolate,
 a dry and desert land,
a land where no one lives,
 through which no man travels.
44 I will punish Bel in Babylon
 and make him spew out what he has swallowed.
The nations will no longer stream to him.

Gross!

What's worse?—That you're a pig and an anaconda just swallowed you, or that you're so disgusting that it hurls you back up? King Nebbie bit off more than he could chew when he messed with God's people. (see Jeremiah 51:34).

---

a 35 Or *done to us and to our children*   *b 41 Sheshach* is a cryptogram for Babylon.

And the wall of Babylon will fall.

45 "Come out of her, my people!
　　Run for your lives!
　　Run from the fierce anger of the LORD.
46 Do not lose heart or be afraid
　　　when rumors are heard in the land;
　one rumor comes this year, another
　　　the next,
　　rumors of violence in the land
　　and of ruler against ruler.
47 For the time will surely come
　　　when I will punish the idols of
　　　　Babylon;
　her whole land will be disgraced
　　and her slain will all lie fallen within
　　　her.
48 Then heaven and earth and all that is
　　　in them
　　will shout for joy over Babylon,
　for out of the north
　　destroyers will attack her,"
　　　　　　　　　　　declares the LORD.

49 "Babylon must fall because of Israel's
　　　slain,
　　just as the slain in all the earth
　　have fallen because of Babylon.
50 You who have escaped the sword,
　　leave and do not linger!
　Remember the LORD in a distant land,
　　and think on Jerusalem."

51 "We are disgraced,
　　　for we have been insulted
　　and shame covers our faces,
　because foreigners have entered
　　the holy places of the LORD's house."

52 "But days are coming," declares the
　　　LORD,
　　"when I will punish her idols,
　and throughout her land
　　the wounded will groan.
53 Even if Babylon reaches the sky
　　and fortifies her lofty stronghold,
　I will send destroyers against her,"
　　　　　　　　　　　declares the LORD.

54 "The sound of a cry comes from
　　　Babylon,
　　the sound of great destruction
　　from the land of the Babylonians.ᵃ
55 The LORD will destroy Babylon;
　　he will silence her noisy din.
　Waves ˻of enemies˼ will rage like great
　　　waters;
　　the roar of their voices will resound.
56 A destroyer will come against Babylon;

　　her warriors will be captured,
　　and their bows will be broken.
For the LORD is a God of retribution;
　　he will repay in full.
57 I will make her officials and wise men
　　　drunk,
　　her governors, officers and warriors
　　　as well;
　they will sleep forever and not awake,"
　　declares the King, whose name is
　　　the LORD Almighty.

58 This is what the LORD Almighty says:

"Babylon's thick wall will be leveled
　　and her high gates set on fire;
　the peoples exhaust themselves for
　　　nothing,
　　the nations' labor is only fuel for the
　　　flames."

59 This is the message Jeremiah gave to the staff officer Seraiah son of Neriah, the son of Mahseiah, when he went to Babylon with Zedekiah king of Judah in the fourth year of his reign. 60 Jeremiah had written on a scroll about all the disasters that would come upon Babylon—all that had been recorded concerning Babylon. 61 He said to Seraiah, "When you get to Babylon, see that you read all these words aloud. 62 Then say, 'O LORD, you have said you will destroy this place, so that neither man nor animal will live in it; it will be desolate forever.' 63 When you finish reading this scroll, tie a stone to it and throw it into the Euphrates. 64 Then say, 'So will Babylon sink to rise no more because of the disaster I will bring upon her. And her people will fall.' "

The words of Jeremiah end here.

The Fall of Jerusalem

52 Zedekiah was twenty-one years old when he became king, and he reigned in Jerusalem eleven years. His mother's name was Hamutal daughter of Jeremiah; she was from Libnah. 2 He did evil in the eyes of the LORD, just as Jehoiakim had done. 3 It was because of the LORD's anger that all this happened to Jerusalem and Judah, and in the end he thrust them from his presence.

Now Zedekiah rebelled against the king of Babylon.

4 So in the ninth year of Zedekiah's reign, on the tenth day of the tenth

ᵃ 54 Or Chaldeans

month, Nebuchadnezzar king of Babylon marched against Jerusalem with his whole army. They camped outside the city and built siege works all around it. ⁵The city was kept under siege until the eleventh year of King Zedekiah.

⁶By the ninth day of the fourth month the famine in the city had become so severe that there was no food for the people to eat. ⁷Then the city wall was broken through, and the whole army fled. They left the city at night through the gate between the two walls near the king's garden, though the Babylonians*ᵃ* were surrounding the city. They fled toward the Arabah,*ᵇ* ⁸but the Babylonian*ᶜ* army pursued King Zedekiah and overtook him in the plains of Jericho. All his soldiers were separated from him and scattered, ⁹and he was captured.

He was taken to the king of Babylon at Riblah in the land of Hamath, where he pronounced sentence on him. ¹⁰There at Riblah the king of Babylon slaughtered the sons of Zedekiah before his eyes; he also killed all the officials of Judah. ¹¹Then he put out Zedekiah's eyes, bound him

with bronze shackles and took him to Babylon, where he put him in prison till the day of his death.

¹²On the tenth day of the fifth month, in the nineteenth year of Nebuchadnezzar king of Babylon, Nebuzaradan commander of the imperial guard, who served the king of Babylon, came to Jerusalem. ¹³He set fire to the temple of the Lᴏʀᴅ, the royal palace and all the houses of Jerusalem. Every important building he burned down. ¹⁴The whole Babylonian army under the commander of the imperial guard broke down all the walls around Jerusalem. ¹⁵Nebuzaradan the commander of the guard carried into exile some of the poorest people and those who remained in the city, along with the rest of the craftsmen*ᵈ* and those who had gone over to the king of Babylon. ¹⁶But Nebuzaradan left behind the rest of the poorest people of the land to work the vineyards and fields.

¹⁷The Babylonians broke up the bronze pillars, the movable stands and the bronze

ᵃ 7 Or *Chaldeans*; also in verse 17   ᵇ 7 Or *the Jordan Valley*
ᶜ 8 Or *Chaldean*; also in verse 14   ᵈ 15 Or *populace*

A Siege Attitude

READ JEREMIAH 52:4–6

The Babylonian army laid siege to Jerusalem. They didn't let anyone in or out. They just sat around and waited for the Jews to run out of food and water and give up. People suffered big-time—they sold all their belongings for a few crusts of bread. It wasn't a pretty picture. Guess what? We do this sometimes in smaller ways: We get upset with people so we stop talking to them. We stop being nice to them. We cut off the food of friendship and the water of communication. We settle down for a personal siege, just camping out till they surrender and come crawling to us on our terms. A "siege attitude" is not cool. Jesus said to forgive people who sin against us. Instead of laying siege to people, God wants us to take them aside, forgive them and work things out (see Matthew 18:15, 21–22).

Your next reading is on page 1035.

Get a Load of This...

Have you ever thought about the word "pome-granate" (Jeremiah 52:23)? It's such a cool-sounding word—(PAH muh GRAN it). You can say "pomegranate" whenever you have nothing else to say.

Sea that were at the temple of the LORD and they carried all the bronze to Babylon. ¹⁸They also took away the pots, shovels, wick trimmers, sprinkling bowls, dishes and all the bronze articles used in the temple service. ¹⁹The commander of the imperial guard took away the basins, censers, sprinkling bowls, pots, lampstands, dishes and bowls used for drink offerings—all that were made of pure gold or silver.

²⁰The bronze from the two pillars, the Sea and the twelve bronze bulls under it, and the movable stands, which King Solomon had made for the temple of the LORD, was more than could be weighed. ²¹Each of the pillars was eighteen cubits high and twelve cubits in circumference*a*; each was four fingers thick, and hollow. ²²The bronze capital on top of the one pillar was five cubits*b* high and was decorated with a network and pomegranates of bronze all around. The other pillar, with its pomegranates, was similar. ²³There were ninety-six pomegranates on the sides; the total number of pomegranates above the surrounding network was a hundred.

²⁴The commander of the guard took as prisoners Seraiah the chief priest, Zephaniah the priest next in rank and the three doorkeepers. ²⁵Of those still in the city, he took the officer in charge of the fighting men, and seven royal advisers. He also took the secretary who was chief officer in charge of conscripting the people of the land and sixty of his men who were found in the city. ²⁶Nebuzaradan the commander took them all and brought them to the king of Babylon at Riblah. ²⁷There at Riblah, in the land of Hamath, the king had them executed.

So Judah went into captivity, away from her land. ²⁸This is the number of the people Nebuchadnezzar carried into exile:

in the seventh year, 3,023 Jews;
²⁹in Nebuchadnezzar's eighteenth year,
832 people from Jerusalem;
³⁰in his twenty-third year,
745 Jews taken into exile by Nebuzaradan the commander of the imperial guard.
There were 4,600 people in all.

Jehoiachin Released

³¹In the thirty-seventh year of the exile of Jehoiachin king of Judah, in the year Evil-Merodach*c* became king of Babylon, he released Jehoiachin king of Judah and freed him from prison on the twenty-fifth day of the twelfth month. ³²He spoke kindly to him and gave him a seat of honor higher than those of the other kings who were with him in Babylon. ³³So Jehoiachin put aside his prison clothes and for the rest of his life ate regularly at the king's table. ³⁴Day by day the king of Babylon gave Jehoiachin a regular allowance as long as he lived, till the day of his death.

a 21 That is, about 27 feet (about 8.1 meters) high and 18 feet (about 5.4 meters) in circumference   *b 22* That is, about 7 1/2 feet (about 2.3 meters)   *c 31* Also called *Amel-Marduk*

LAMENTATIONS

Who wrote this book?

The writer is unknown. Many people think Jeremiah is the author.

Why was this book written?

Lamentations shows how sad the captives in Babylon were, and it shows that they finally realized that they were being punished because of their sin.

What is special about this book?

Lamentations is "dirge poetry." This is very sad poetry, like sadness over a person's death.

When was this book written?

This book was written after Jerusalem was destroyed by the Babylonians in 586 B.C.

Where was this book written?

Lamentations was written in Babylon, where the Jewish people were taken as captives.

¹ ᵃHow deserted lies the city,
    once so full of people!
How like a widow is she,
    who once was great among the
        nations!
She who was queen among the
        provinces
    has now become a slave.

² Bitterly she weeps at night,
    tears are upon her cheeks.
Among all her lovers
    there is none to comfort her.
All her friends have betrayed her;
    they have become her enemies.

³ After affliction and harsh labor,
    Judah has gone into exile.
She dwells among the nations;
    she finds no resting place.
All who pursue her have overtaken her
    in the midst of her distress.

⁴ The roads to Zion mourn,
    for no one comes to her appointed
        feasts.
All her gateways are desolate,
    her priests groan,
her maidens grieve,
    and she is in bitter anguish.

⁵ Her foes have become her masters;
    her enemies are at ease.
The LORD has brought her grief
    because of her many sins.
Her children have gone into exile,
    captive before the foe.

⁶ All the splendor has departed
    from the Daughter of Zion.
Her princes are like deer
    that find no pasture;
in weakness they have fled
    before the pursuer.

⁷ In the days of her affliction and
        wandering
    Jerusalem remembers all the treasures
    that were hers in days of old.
When her people fell into enemy hands,
    there was no one to help her.
Her enemies looked at her
    and laughed at her destruction.

⁸ Jerusalem has sinned greatly
    and so has become unclean.
All who honored her despise her,
    for they have seen her nakedness;
she herself groans
    and turns away.

⁹ Her filthiness clung to her skirts;
    she did not consider her future.
Her fall was astounding;
    there was none to comfort her.
"Look, O LORD, on my affliction,
    for the enemy has triumphed."

¹⁰ The enemy laid hands
    on all her treasures;
she saw pagan nations
    enter her sanctuary—
those you had forbidden
    to enter your assembly.

¹¹ All her people groan
    as they search for bread;
they barter their treasures for food
    to keep themselves alive.
"Look, O LORD, and consider,
    for I am despised."

¹² "Is it nothing to you, all you who pass
        by?
Look around and see.
Is any suffering like my suffering
    that was inflicted on me,
that the LORD brought on me
    in the day of his fierce anger?

¹³ "From on high he sent fire,
    sent it down into my bones.
He spread a net for my feet
    and turned me back.
He made me desolate,
    faint all the day long.

¹⁴ "My sins have been bound into a yokeᵇ;
    by his hands they were woven
        together.
They have come upon my neck
    and the Lord has sapped my
        strength.
He has handed me over
    to those I cannot withstand.

¹⁵ "The Lord has rejected
    all the warriors in my midst;
he has summoned an army against me
    toᶜ crush my young men.
In his winepress the Lord has trampled
    the Virgin Daughter of Judah.

¹⁶ "This is why I weep
    and my eyes overflow with tears.
No one is near to comfort me,
    no one to restore my spirit.

ᵃ This chapter is an acrostic poem, the verses of which begin
with the successive letters of the Hebrew alphabet.
ᵇ 14 Most Hebrew manuscripts; Septuagint *He kept watch
over my sins*   ᶜ 15 Or *has set a time for me / when he will*

My children are destitute
because the enemy has prevailed."

¹⁷Zion stretches out her hands,
but there is no one to comfort her.
The LORD has decreed for Jacob
that his neighbors become his foes;
Jerusalem has become
an unclean thing among them.

¹⁸"The LORD is righteous,
yet I rebelled against his command.
Listen, all you peoples;
look upon my suffering.
My young men and maidens
have gone into exile.

¹⁹"I called to my allies
but they betrayed me.
My priests and my elders
perished in the city
while they searched for food
to keep themselves alive.

²⁰"See, O LORD, how distressed I am!
I am in torment within,
and in my heart I am disturbed,
for I have been most rebellious.
Outside, the sword bereaves;
inside, there is only death.

²¹"People have heard my groaning,
but there is no one to comfort me.
All my enemies have heard of my
distress;
they rejoice at what you have done.
May you bring the day you have
announced
so they may become like me.

²²"Let all their wickedness come before
you;
deal with them
as you have dealt with me
because of all my sins.
My groans are many
and my heart is faint."

Make It Stick

READ LAMENTATION 1:11

Under siege, you find out quickly what really matters. You can't eat gold and jewels, so unless
you can trade them for food, they're pretty, sure—but useless. What do you value? Things like
godly values, family and friends have lasting worth. Write out a few of the things in your life
that you value most.

2 [a]How the Lord has covered the
　　　Daughter of Zion
　　with the cloud of his anger[b]!
　　He has hurled down the splendor
　　　of Israel
　　from heaven to earth;
　he has not remembered his footstool
　　in the day of his anger.

2 Without pity the Lord has swallowed up
　　all the dwellings of Jacob;
　in his wrath he has torn down
　　　the strongholds of the Daughter of
　　　Judah.
　He has brought her kingdom and its
　　　princes
　　down to the ground in dishonor.

3 In fierce anger he has cut off
　　every horn[c] of Israel.
　He has withdrawn his right hand
　　at the approach of the enemy.
　He has burned in Jacob like a flaming
　　　fire
　　that consumes everything around it.

4 Like an enemy he has strung his bow;
　　his right hand is ready.
　Like a foe he has slain
　　all who were pleasing to the eye;
　he has poured out his wrath like fire
　　on the tent of the Daughter of Zion.

5 The Lord is like an enemy;
　　he has swallowed up Israel.
　He has swallowed up all her palaces
　　and destroyed her strongholds.
　He has multiplied mourning and
　　　lamentation
　　for the Daughter of Judah.

6 He has laid waste his dwelling like a
　　　garden;
　　he has destroyed his place of
　　　meeting.
　The LORD has made Zion forget
　　　her appointed feasts and her
　　　Sabbaths;
　in his fierce anger he has spurned
　　both king and priest.

7 The Lord has rejected his altar
　　and abandoned his sanctuary.
　He has handed over to the enemy
　　　the walls of her palaces;
　they have raised a shout in the house
　　　of the LORD
　　as on the day of an appointed feast.

8 The LORD determined to tear down
　　　the wall around the Daughter of Zion.
　He stretched out a measuring line
　　and did not withhold his hand from
　　　destroying.
　He made ramparts and walls lament;
　　together they wasted away.

9 Her gates have sunk into the ground;
　　their bars he has broken and
　　　destroyed.
　Her king and her princes are exiled
　　　among the nations,
　　the law is no more,
　and her prophets no longer find
　　visions from the LORD.

10 The elders of the Daughter of Zion
　　sit on the ground in silence;
　they have sprinkled dust on their heads
　　and put on sackcloth.
　The young women of Jerusalem
　　have bowed their heads to the
　　　ground.

11 My eyes fail from weeping,
　　I am in torment within,
　my heart is poured out on the ground
　　because my people are destroyed,
　because children and infants faint
　　in the streets of the city.

12 They say to their mothers,
　　"Where is bread and wine?"
　as they faint like wounded men
　　in the streets of the city,
　as their lives ebb away
　　in their mothers' arms.

13 What can I say for you?
　　With what can I compare you,
　　O Daughter of Jerusalem?
　To what can I liken you,
　　that I may comfort you,
　　O Virgin Daughter of Zion?
　Your wound is as deep as the sea.
　　Who can heal you?

14 The visions of your prophets
　　were false and worthless;
　they did not expose your sin
　　to ward off your captivity.
　The oracles they gave you
　　were false and misleading.

15 All who pass your way
　　clap their hands at you;

---

[a] This chapter is an acrostic poem, the verses of which begin
with the successive letters of the Hebrew alphabet.
[b] 1 Or How the Lord in his anger / has treated the Daughter
of Zion with contempt　　[c] 3 Or / all the strength; or every
king; horn here symbolizes strength.

they scoff and shake their heads
  at the Daughter of Jerusalem:
"Is this the city that was called
  the perfection of beauty,
  the joy of the whole earth?"

16 All your enemies open their mouths
  wide against you;
they scoff and gnash their teeth
  and say, "We have swallowed her up.
This is the day we have waited for;
  we have lived to see it."

17 The LORD has done what he planned;
  he has fulfilled his word,
  which he decreed long ago.
He has overthrown you without pity,
  he has let the enemy gloat over you,
  he has exalted the horn^a of your
    foes.

18 The hearts of the people
  cry out to the Lord.
O wall of the Daughter of Zion,
  let your tears flow like a river
  day and night;

give yourself no relief,
  your eyes no rest.

19 Arise, cry out in the night,
  as the watches of the night begin;
pour out your heart like water
  in the presence of the Lord.
Lift up your hands to him
  for the lives of your children,
who faint from hunger
  at the head of every street.

20 "Look, O LORD, and consider:
  Whom have you ever treated like
    this?
Should women eat their offspring,
  the children they have cared for?
Should priest and prophet be killed
  in the sanctuary of the Lord?

21 "Young and old lie together
  in the dust of the streets;
my young men and maidens
  have fallen by the sword.

---

^a 17 *Horn* here symbolizes strength.

Don't Just "Take It"

READ LAMENTATIONS 2:11, 19

Jeremiah wept at the destruction of his people and their starving children. "My eyes fail from weeping [and] I am in torment within" (verse 11). Whoa! Wasn't Jeremiah a tough prophet? Sure he was. But he felt pain. We all experience things that hurt. Don't let anyone fool you into thinking that, as a man, you have to "take" all your pain and not show it. *Not true.* We can rely on God to get us through emotional and physical pain. God promised to be there for us and give us strength (see Hebrews 13:5; 2 Corinthians 1:3–5). But we also need to be able to let others know: "It hurts." Even Jesus wept (see John 11:35). So there's nothing wrong with crying, as long as you're not just crying because you can't get your own way. Feeling sorrow is not weakness, friend—it's strength.

Your next reading is on page 1037.

You have slain them in the day of your
   anger;
   you have slaughtered them without
      pity.
22 "As you summon to a feast day,
   so you summoned against me
      terrors on every side.
In the day of the Lord's anger
   no one escaped or survived;
those I cared for and reared,
   my enemy has destroyed."

3

a I am the man who has seen
   affliction
   by the rod of his wrath.
2 He has driven me away and made
   me walk
in darkness rather than light;
3 indeed, he has turned his hand against
   me
again and again, all day long.

4 He has made my skin and my flesh
   grow old
and has broken my bones.
5 He has besieged me and surrounded me
   with bitterness and hardship.
6 He has made me dwell in darkness
   like those long dead.

7 He has walled me in so I cannot escape;
   he has weighed me down with
      chains.
8 Even when I call out or cry for help,
   he shuts out my prayer.
9 He has barred my way with blocks of
   stone;
   he has made my paths crooked.

10 Like a bear lying in wait,
   like a lion in hiding,
11 he dragged me from the path and
   mangled me
and left me without help.
12 He drew his bow
   and made me the target for his
      arrows.

13 He pierced my heart
   with arrows from his quiver.
14 I became the laughingstock of all my
   people;
   they mock me in song all day long.
15 He has filled me with bitter herbs
   and sated me with gall.

16 He has broken my teeth with gravel;
   he has trampled me in the dust.
17 I have been deprived of peace;

I have forgotten what prosperity is.
18 So I say, "My splendor is gone
   and all that I had hoped from the
      Lord."

19 I remember my affliction and my
   wandering,
   the bitterness and the gall.
20 I well remember them,
   and my soul is downcast within me.
21 Yet this I call to mind
   and therefore I have hope:

22 Because of the Lord's great love we are
   not consumed,
   for his compassions never fail.
23 They are new every morning;
   great is your faithfulness.
24 I say to myself, "The Lord is my portion;
   therefore I will wait for him."

25 The Lord is good to those whose hope
   is in him,
   to the one who seeks him;
26 it is good to wait quietly
   for the salvation of the Lord.
27 It is good for a man to bear the yoke
   while he is young.

28 Let him sit alone in silence,
   for the Lord has laid it on him.
29 Let him bury his face in the dust—
   there may yet be hope.
30 Let him offer his cheek to one who
   would strike him,
   and let him be filled with disgrace.

31 For men are not cast off
   by the Lord forever.
32 Though he brings grief, he will show
   compassion,
   so great is his unfailing love.
33 For he does not willingly bring affliction
   or grief to the children of men.

34 To crush underfoot
   all prisoners in the land,
35 to deny a man his rights
   before the Most High,
36 to deprive a man of justice—
   would not the Lord see such things?

37 Who can speak and have it happen
   if the Lord has not decreed it?
38 Is it not from the mouth of the Most
   High

a This chapter is an acrostic poem; the verses of each stanza
begin with the successive letters of the Hebrew alphabet, and
the verses within each stanza begin with the same letter.

that both calamities and good
things come?
³⁹ Why should any living man complain
when punished for his sins?

⁴⁰ Let us examine our ways and test them,
and let us return to the LORD.
⁴¹ Let us lift up our hearts and our hands
to God in heaven, and say:
⁴² "We have sinned and rebelled
and you have not forgiven.

⁴³ "You have covered yourself with anger
and pursued us;
you have slain without pity.
⁴⁴ You have covered yourself with a cloud
so that no prayer can get through.
⁴⁵ You have made us scum and refuse
among the nations.

⁴⁶ "All our enemies have opened their
mouths
wide against us.
⁴⁷ We have suffered terror and pitfalls,
ruin and destruction."

⁴⁸ Streams of tears flow from my eyes
because my people are destroyed.
⁴⁹ My eyes will flow unceasingly,
without relief,
⁵⁰ until the LORD looks down
from heaven and sees.
⁵¹ What I see brings grief to my soul
because of all the women of my city.

⁵² Those who were my enemies without
cause
hunted me like a bird.
⁵³ They tried to end my life in a pit
and threw stones at me;
⁵⁴ the waters closed over my head,
and I thought I was about to be cut
off.

⁵⁵ I called on your name, O LORD,
from the depths of the pit.
⁵⁶ You heard my plea: "Do not close your
ears
to my cry for relief."
⁵⁷ You came near when I called you,
and you said, "Do not fear."

⁵⁸ O Lord, you took up my case;
you redeemed my life.
⁵⁹ You have seen, O LORD, the wrong
done to me.
Uphold my cause!

Hope and Your Dog

READ LAMENTATIONS 3:19–26

Things had bottomed out for the Jews, but Jeremiah knew that God
would keep his promises and bless them. The same is true for you.
When everything's bad—even your *dog* won't look at you!—God is
still there for you and loves you. First Corinthians 13:13 says the top
three things are faith, love and hope. This kind of hope is
when you *know* things will work out because you serve a loving God. *Hope* doesn't mean "sure would be nice." Hope in
God is a "for sure" thing. No matter how hard today was,
hold on to the hope that God is good and that he loves you.
God will carry you through a rough, tough day, and his
compassions are "new every morning" (Lamentations 3:23). When you wake up and your feet hit
the floor, pet your dog and start the new day
with hope.

Your next reading is on page 1038.

⁶⁰ You have seen the depth of their
     vengeance,
   all their plots against me.
⁶¹ O Lᴏʀᴅ, you have heard their insults,
   all their plots against me—
⁶² what my enemies whisper and mutter
   against me all day long.
⁶³ Look at them! Sitting or standing,
   they mock me in their songs.

⁶⁴ Pay them back what they deserve,
     O Lᴏʀᴅ,
   for what their hands have done.
⁶⁵ Put a veil over their hearts,
   and may your curse be on them!
⁶⁶ Pursue them in anger and destroy them
   from under the heavens of the Lᴏʀᴅ.

4 ᵃ How the gold has lost its luster,
   the fine gold become dull!
   The sacred gems are scattered
   at the head of every street.

² How the precious sons of Zion,
   once worth their weight in gold,
are now considered as pots of clay,
   the work of a potter's hands!

³ Even jackals offer their breasts
   to nurse their young,
but my people have become
     heartless
   like ostriches in the desert.

⁴ Because of thirst the infant's tongue
   sticks to the roof of its mouth;
the children beg for bread,
   but no one gives it to them.

⁵ Those who once ate delicacies
   are destitute in the streets.
Those nurtured in purple
   now lie on ash heaps.

⁶ The punishment of my people
   is greater than that of Sodom,
which was overthrown in a moment
   without a hand turned to help her.

⁷ Their princes were brighter than snow
   and whiter than milk,
their bodies more ruddy than rubies,
   their appearance like sapphires. ᵇ

ᵃ This chapter is an acrostic poem, the verses of which begin
with the successive letters of the Hebrew alphabet.
ᵇ 7 Or *lapis lazuli*

People Die Daily

READ LAMENTATIONS 4:4–9

People were starving, and their skin was shrivelling up on their bones. Starvation is a horrible thing, and it's real in the world today. When you hear about a famine, pray about what you can do to help. It might not be much but "if the willingness is there, the gift is acceptable according to what one has, not according to what he does not have" (2 Corinthians 8:12). No way can you solve the whole world's hunger problems, but you can do a little bit to help one person. The need is real and you *can* make a difference. Read Lamentations 4:4 again: "The children beg for bread, but no one gives it to them." Over 12 million children live in poverty in the United States alone. Around the world, eight babies die every minute before reaching one month of age. There's no food or care for them or their mothers. People die daily. That's why, if sometimes you even give a few dollars, it will help.

Your next reading is on page 1040.

8 But now they are blacker than soot;
  they are not recognized in the
  streets.
Their skin has shriveled on their bones;
  it has become as dry as a stick.

9 Those killed by the sword are better off
  than those who die of famine;
racked with hunger, they waste away
  for lack of food from the field.

10 With their own hands compassionate
  women
  have cooked their own children,
who became their food
  when my people were destroyed.

11 The LORD has given full vent to his
  wrath;
  he has poured out his fierce anger.
He kindled a fire in Zion
  that consumed her foundations.

12 The kings of the earth did not believe,
  nor did any of the world's people,
that enemies and foes could enter
  the gates of Jerusalem.

13 But it happened because of the sins of
  her prophets
  and the iniquities of her priests,
who shed within her
  the blood of the righteous.

14 Now they grope through the streets
  like men who are blind.
They are so defiled with blood
  that no one dares to touch their
  garments.

15 "Go away! You are unclean!" men cry
  to them.
  "Away! Away! Don't touch us!"
When they flee and wander about,
  people among the nations say,
  "They can stay here no longer."

16 The LORD himself has scattered them;
  he no longer watches over them.
The priests are shown no honor,
  the elders no favor.

17 Moreover, our eyes failed,
  looking in vain for help;
from our towers we watched
  for a nation that could not save us.

18 Men stalked us at every step,
  so we could not walk in our streets.
Our end was near, our days were
  numbered,
  for our end had come.

19 Our pursuers were swifter
  than eagles in the sky;
they chased us over the mountains
  and lay in wait for us in the desert.

20 The LORD's anointed, our very life
  breath,
  was caught in their traps.
We thought that under his shadow
  we would live among the nations.

21 Rejoice and be glad, O Daughter of
  Edom,
  you who live in the land of Uz.
But to you also the cup will be passed;
  you will be drunk and stripped
  naked.

22 O Daughter of Zion, your punishment
  will end;
  he will not prolong your exile.
But, O Daughter of Edom, he will
  punish your sin
  and expose your wickedness.

5 Remember, O LORD, what has
  happened to us;
  look, and see our disgrace.
2 Our inheritance has been turned
  over to aliens,
  our homes to foreigners.
3 We have become orphans and
  fatherless,
  our mothers like widows.
4 We must buy the water we drink;
  our wood can be had only at a
  price.
5 Those who pursue us are at our heels;
  we are weary and find no rest.
6 We submitted to Egypt and Assyria
  to get enough bread.
7 Our fathers sinned and are no more,
  and we bear their punishment.
8 Slaves rule over us,
  and there is none to free us from
  their hands.
9 We get our bread at the risk of our
  lives
  because of the sword in the desert.
10 Our skin is hot as an oven,
  feverish from hunger.
11 Women have been ravished in Zion,
  and virgins in the towns of Judah.
12 Princes have been hung up by their
  hands;
  elders are shown no respect.
13 Young men toil at the millstones;
  boys stagger under loads of wood.

¹⁴The elders are gone from the city gate;
    the young men have stopped their
       music.
¹⁵Joy is gone from our hearts;
    our dancing has turned to mourning.
¹⁶The crown has fallen from our head.
    Woe to us, for we have sinned!
¹⁷Because of this our hearts are faint,
    because of these things our eyes
      grow dim
¹⁸for Mount Zion, which lies desolate,
    with jackals prowling over it.

¹⁹You, O LORD, reign forever;
    your throne endures from
      generation to generation.
²⁰Why do you always forget us?
    Why do you forsake us so long?
²¹Restore us to yourself, O LORD, that we
    may return;
    renew our days as of old
²²unless you have utterly rejected us
    and are angry with us beyond
      measure.

GET SMARTER

Sin Is Not Cool

Jeremiah painted a grim picture when he wrote Lamentations. We've read about people who starved to death, had their homes taken away and saw their nation crushed. Jeremiah bawled his eyes out over his people, not only because of their sufferings but also because he knew its cause: sin. Why does God hate sin? Because he knows it results in pain and suffering. A *lot* of pain and suffering. When the Jews sinned and stopped listening to God, they opened the Horror Door. It's no different today. That's why we need to hate sin like God does. When you see evil in the world today—death, violence, hatred—you see sin with its mask off. The mask looks like a lot of things—a good time, a harmless prank, selfishness and rebellion—but in the end, the mask comes off and there's nothing left but sin. Sin is not cool.

Your next reading is on page 1042.

EZEKIEL

Who wrote this book?
The prophet Ezekiel.

Why was this book written?
The first part of Ezekiel shows why God must punish the wicked people still in Judah. The second part shows that God will bring his people back to their land and that their faith and position before God will be restored.

What do we learn about God in this book?
God is holy. He will not live among a wicked people.

What is special about this book?
Ezekiel acts out many of his prophecies. Ezekiel vividly pictures both Judah's punishment and restoration.

When was this book written?
Ezekiel was written between 593 and 571 B.C.

Where was this book written?
Ezekiel was a captive in Babylon when he wrote this book.

What chapters tell about Ezekiel's experiences?

Ezekiel's vision	Ezekiel 1; 10
Ezekiel acts out the attack on Jerusalem	Ezekiel 4
Ezekiel, God's watchman	Ezekiel 33

The Living Creatures and the Glory of the LORD

In the[a] thirtieth year, in the fourth month on the fifth day, while I was among the exiles by the Kebar River, the heavens were opened and I saw visions of God.

2On the fifth of the month—it was the fifth year of the exile of King Jehoiachin—3the word of the LORD came to Ezekiel the priest, the son of Buzi,[b] by the Kebar River in the land of the Babylonians.[c] There the hand of the LORD was upon him.

4I looked, and I saw a windstorm coming out of the north—an immense cloud with flashing lightning and surrounded by brilliant light. The center of the fire looked like glowing metal, 5and in the fire was what looked like four living creatures. In appearance their form was that of a man, 6but each of them had four faces and four wings. 7Their legs were straight; their feet were like those of a calf and gleamed like burnished bronze. 8Under their wings on their four sides they had the hands of a man. All four of them had faces and wings, 9and their wings touched one another. Each one went straight ahead; they did not turn as they moved.

10Their faces looked like this: Each of the four had the face of a man, and on the right side each had the face of a lion, and on the left the face of an ox; each also had the face of an eagle. 11Such were their faces. Their wings were spread out upward; each had two wings, one touching the wing of another creature on either side, and two wings covering its body. 12Each one went straight ahead. Wherever the spirit would go, they would go, without turning as they went. 13The appearance of the living creatures was like burning coals of fire or like torches. Fire moved back and forth among the creatures; it was bright, and lightning flashed out of it. 14The creatures sped back and forth like flashes of lightning.

15As I looked at the living creatures, I saw a wheel on the ground beside each creature with its four faces. 16This was the

a 1 Or ,my, b 3 Or Ezekiel son of Buzi the priest
c 3 Or Chaldeans

Imagination

READ EZEKIEL 1:1–28

GET SMARTER.

Moviemakers today create amazing worlds where creatures live under water, speak to each other in weird-sounding languages and move on strangely shaped claws and legs. The reason writers can dream up such fantastic worlds and invent such bizarre beings is because God gave humans an incredible gift of imagination. God himself has awesome imagination and incredible creativity. Look at the creatures *he* created, not only in this world, but in the heavenly world—like the four living creatures Ezekiel saw in his vision! Think of a recent sci-fi or fantasy movie you've seen, or seen the ads for. Cool special effects? Ho! Imagine multi-million dollar special effects showing Ezekiel's vision! What an extravaganza *that* would be! And these living creatures are just the beginning! There's no telling how many *more* amazing things you'll see in heaven. God has given you a wonderful gift of imagination.

Your next reading is on page 1044.

appearance and structure of the wheels: They sparkled like chrysolite, and all four looked alike. Each appeared to be made like a wheel intersecting a wheel. ¹⁷As they moved, they would go in any one of the four directions the creatures faced; the wheels did not turn about*a* as the creatures went. ¹⁸Their rims were high and awesome, and all four rims were full of eyes all around.

¹⁹When the living creatures moved, the wheels beside them moved; and when the living creatures rose from the ground, the wheels also rose. ²⁰Wherever the spirit would go, they would go, and the wheels would rise along with them, because the spirit of the living creatures was in the wheels. ²¹When the creatures moved, they also moved; when the creatures stood still, they also stood still; and when the creatures rose from the ground, the wheels rose along with them, because the spirit of the living creatures was in the wheels.

²²Spread out above the heads of the living creatures was what looked like an expanse, sparkling like ice, and awesome. ²³Under the expanse their wings were stretched out one toward the other, and each had two wings covering its body. ²⁴When the creatures moved, I heard the sound of their wings, like the roar of rushing waters, like the voice of the Almighty,*b* like the tumult of an army. When they stood still, they lowered their wings.

²⁵Then there came a voice from above the expanse over their heads as they stood with lowered wings. ²⁶Above the expanse over their heads was what looked like a throne of sapphire,*c* and high above on the throne was a figure like that of a man. ²⁷I saw that from what appeared to be his waist up he looked like glowing metal, as if full of fire, and that from there down he looked like fire; and brilliant light surrounded him. ²⁸Like the appearance of a

a 17 Or *aside*   *b 24* Hebrew *Shaddai*   *c 26* Or *lapis lazuli*

Make It Stick

READ CHAPTER 1

You can make your "visions of God" real. Imagine what God's throne—or the living creatures— looks like, then draw it on a sticky note. Try building it with Legos® or write a story about it and read it to your buddies or your parents. You can even post it on the Internet!

rainbow in the clouds on a rainy day, so was the radiance around him.

This was the appearance of the likeness of the glory of the LORD. When I saw it, I fell facedown, and I heard the voice of one speaking.

Ezekiel's Call

He said to me, "Son of man, stand up on your feet and I will speak to you." ²As he spoke, the Spirit came into me and raised me to my feet, and I heard him speaking to me.

³He said: "Son of man, I am sending you to the Israelites, to a rebellious nation that has rebelled against me; they and their fathers have been in revolt against me to this very day. ⁴The people to whom I am sending you are obstinate and stubborn. Say to them, 'This is what the Sovereign LORD says.' ⁵And whether they listen or fail to listen—for they are a rebellious house—they will know that a prophet has been among them. ⁶And you, son of man, do not be afraid of them or their words. Do not be afraid, though briers and thorns are all around you and you live among scorpions. Do not be afraid of what they say or terrified by them, though they are a rebellious house. ⁷You must speak my words to them, whether they listen or fail to listen, for they are rebellious. ⁸But you, son of man, listen to what I say to you. Do not rebel like that rebellious house; open your mouth and eat what I give you."

⁹Then I looked, and I saw a hand stretched out to me. In it was a scroll, ¹⁰which he unrolled before me. On both sides of it were written words of lament and mourning and woe.

And he said to me, "Son of man, eat what is before you, eat this scroll; then go and speak to the house of Israel." ²So I opened my mouth, and he gave me the scroll to eat.

³Then he said to me, "Son of man, eat this scroll I am giving you and fill your stomach with it." So I ate it, and it tasted as sweet as honey in my mouth.

⁴He then said to me: "Son of man, go now to the house of Israel and speak my

---

GET SMARTER

Down the Hatch

READ EZEKIEL 3:1–3

If you want muscles—bulging biceps that make your little brother run for cover—you have to eat good food that gives you energy. The same goes for spiritual muscles. If you "eat" God's Word, it gets inside you and gives energy and strength to your spirit. For real! As part of the spiritual vision God gave them, some prophets in the Bible (Ezekiel, Jeremiah and the Apostle John) "ate" God's Word. Like Ezekiel found out (verse 3), God's words and ways are sweet, even when their message is bitter. And when life is hard or unfair, God's Word will be sweet by giving you strength and hope. Want strength? Don't just breeze through the Bible like it's some kind of homework assignment. Chew, swallow and digest what you read. Make it *part* of you. Thinking about a Bible verse is like digesting it. Remember: you *are* what you eat.

Your next reading is on page 1050.

words to them. ⁵You are not being sent to a people of obscure speech and difficult language, but to the house of Israel— ⁶not to many peoples of obscure speech and difficult language, whose words you cannot understand. Surely if I had sent you to them, they would have listened to you. ⁷But the house of Israel is not willing to listen to you because they are not willing to listen to me, for the whole house of Israel is hardened and obstinate. ⁸But I will make you as unyielding and hardened as they are. ⁹I will make your forehead like the hardest stone, harder than flint. Do not be afraid of them or terrified by them, though they are a rebellious house."

¹⁰And he said to me, "Son of man, listen carefully and take to heart all the words I speak to you. ¹¹Go now to your countrymen in exile and speak to them. Say to them, 'This is what the Sovereign LORD says,' whether they listen or fail to listen."

¹²Then the Spirit lifted me up, and I heard behind me a loud rumbling sound—May the glory of the LORD be praised in his dwelling place!— ¹³the sound of the wings of the living creatures brushing against each other and the sound of the wheels beside them, a loud rumbling sound. ¹⁴The Spirit then lifted me up and took me away, and I went in bitterness and in the anger of my spirit, with the strong hand of the LORD upon me. ¹⁵I came to the exiles who lived at Tel Abib near the Kebar River. And there, where they were living, I sat among them for seven days—overwhelmed.

Warning to Israel

¹⁶At the end of seven days the word of the LORD came to me: ¹⁷"Son of man, I have made you a watchman for the house of Israel; so hear the word I speak and give them warning from me. ¹⁸When I say to a wicked man, 'You will surely die,' and you do not warn him or speak out to dissuade him from his evil ways in order to save his life, that wicked man will die for*ᵃ* his sin, and I will hold you accountable for his blood. ¹⁹But if you do warn the wicked man and he does not turn from his wickedness or from his evil ways, he will die for his sin; but you will have saved yourself.

²⁰"Again, when a righteous man turns from his righteousness and does evil, and I put a stumbling block before him, he will die. Since you did not warn him, he will die for his sin. The righteous things he did will not be remembered, and I will hold you accountable for his blood. ²¹But if you do warn the righteous man not to sin and he does not sin, he will surely live because he took warning, and you will have saved yourself."

²²The hand of the LORD was upon me there, and he said to me, "Get up and go out to the plain, and there I will speak to you." ²³So I got up and went out to the plain. And the glory of the LORD was standing there, like the glory I had seen by the Kebar River, and I fell facedown.

ᵃ 18 Or *in*; also in verses 19 and 20

Get a Load of This...

If God made your forehead hard as a rock (Ezekiel 3:9), you could break a stack of six bricks like some guy in a strongman show. Of course, what God's talking about here is having the strength to stand up against ungodly peer pressure and rebellious people.

Get a Load of This...

Check out Ezekiel 4:4–6. Ezekiel lay down on his left side for 390 days, then lay down on his right side for another 40 days! Talk about being unbalanced! Ezekiel probably walked around with a crick in his neck after this was done, looking for a chiropractor.

24Then the Spirit came into me and raised me to my feet. He spoke to me and said: "Go, shut yourself inside your house. 25And you, son of man, they will tie with ropes; you will be bound so that you cannot go out among the people. 26I will make your tongue stick to the roof of your mouth so that you will be silent and unable to rebuke them, though they are a rebellious house. 27But when I speak to you, I will open your mouth and you shall say to them, 'This is what the Sovereign Lord says.' Whoever will listen let him listen, and whoever will refuse let him refuse; for they are a rebellious house.

Siege of Jerusalem Symbolized

"Now, son of man, take a clay tablet, put it in front of you and draw the city of Jerusalem on it. 2Then lay siege to it: Erect siege works against it, build a ramp up to it, set up camps against it and put battering rams around it. 3Then take an iron pan, place it as an iron wall between you and the city and turn your face toward it. It will be under siege, and you shall besiege it. This will be a sign to the house of Israel.

4"Then lie on your left side and put the sin of the house of Israel upon yourself.[a] You are to bear their sin for the number of days you lie on your side. 5I have assigned you the same number of days as the years of their sin. So for 390 days you will bear the sin of the house of Israel.

6"After you have finished this, lie down again, this time on your right side, and bear the sin of the house of Judah. I have assigned you 40 days, a day for each year. 7Turn your face toward the siege of Jerusalem and with bared arm prophesy against her. 8I will tie you up with ropes so that you cannot turn from one side to the other until you have finished the days of your siege.

9"Take wheat and barley, beans and lentils, millet and spelt; put them in a storage jar and use them to make bread for yourself. You are to eat it during the 390 days you lie on your side. 10Weigh out twenty shekels[b] of food to eat each day and eat it at set times. 11Also measure out a sixth of a hin[c] of water and drink it at set times. 12Eat the food as you would a barley cake; bake it in the sight of the people, using human excrement for fuel." 13The Lord said, "In this way the people of Israel will eat defiled food among the nations where I will drive them."

14Then I said, "Not so, Sovereign Lord! I have never defiled myself. From my youth until now I have never eaten anything found dead or torn by wild animals. No unclean meat has ever entered my mouth."

15"Very well," he said, "I will let you bake your bread over cow manure instead of human excrement."

16He then said to me: "Son of man, I will cut off the supply of food in Jerusalem. The people will eat rationed food in anxiety and drink rationed water in despair, 17for food and water will be scarce. They will be

---

a 4 Or your side   b 10 That is, about 8 ounces (about 0.2 kilogram)
c 11 That is, about 2/3 quart (about 0.6 liter)

appalled at the sight of each other and will waste away because of^a their sin.

5 "Now, son of man, take a sharp sword and use it as a barber's razor to shave your head and your beard. Then take a set of scales and divide up the hair. ²When the days of your siege come to an end, burn a third of the hair with fire inside the city. Take a third and strike it with the sword all around the city. And scatter a third to the wind. For I will pursue them with drawn sword. ³But take a few strands of hair and tuck them away in the folds of your garment. ⁴Again, take a few of these and throw them into the fire and burn them up. A fire will spread from there to the whole house of Israel.

⁵"This is what the Sovereign LORD says: This is Jerusalem, which I have set in the center of the nations, with countries all around her. ⁶Yet in her wickedness she has rebelled against my laws and decrees more than the nations and countries around her. She has rejected my laws and has not followed my decrees.

⁷"Therefore this is what the Sovereign LORD says: You have been more unruly than the nations around you and have not followed my decrees or kept my laws. You have not even^b conformed to the standards of the nations around you.

⁸"Therefore this is what the Sovereign LORD says: I myself am against you, Jerusalem, and I will inflict punishment on you in the sight of the nations. ⁹Because of all your detestable idols, I will do to you what I have never done before and will never do again. ¹⁰Therefore in your midst fathers will eat their children, and children will eat their fathers. I will inflict punishment on you and will scatter all your survivors to the winds. ¹¹Therefore as surely as I live, declares the Sovereign LORD, because you have defiled my sanctuary with all your vile images and detestable practices, I myself will withdraw my favor; I will not look on you with pity or spare you. ¹²A third of your people will die of the plague or perish by famine inside you; a third will fall by the sword outside your walls; and a third I will scatter to the winds and pursue with drawn sword.

¹³"Then my anger will cease and my wrath against them will subside, and I will be avenged. And when I have spent my wrath upon them, they will know that I the LORD have spoken in my zeal.

¹⁴"I will make you a ruin and a reproach among the nations around you, in the sight of all who pass by. ¹⁵You will be a reproach and a taunt, a warning and an object of horror to the nations around you when I inflict punishment on you in anger and in wrath and with stinging rebuke. I the LORD have spoken. ¹⁶When I shoot at you with my deadly and destructive arrows of famine, I will shoot to destroy you. I will bring more and more famine upon you and cut off your supply of food. ¹⁷I

Gross!

Check out Ezekiel 4:12–15. Ezekiel didn't want to cook his food over human dung—like, would *you* want to?—so God said, "OK, fine. Burn cow dung instead." It was like a camping trip gone bad. Did you even know this stuff could burn?

---

^a 17 Or *away in*   ^b 7 Most Hebrew manuscripts; some Hebrew manuscripts and Syriac *You have*

will send famine and wild beasts against you, and they will leave you childless. Plague and bloodshed will sweep through you, and I will bring the sword against you. I the LORD have spoken."

A Prophecy Against the Mountains of Israel

6 The word of the LORD came to me: ²"Son of man, set your face against the mountains of Israel; prophesy against them ³and say: 'O mountains of Israel, hear the word of the Sovereign LORD. This is what the Sovereign LORD says to the mountains and hills, to the ravines and valleys: I am about to bring a sword against you, and I will destroy your high places. ⁴Your altars will be demolished and your incense altars will be smashed; and I will slay your people in front of your idols. ⁵I will lay the dead bodies of the Israelites in front of their idols, and I will scatter your bones around your altars. ⁶Wherever you live, the towns will be laid waste and the high places demolished, so that your altars will be laid waste and devastated, your idols smashed and ruined, your incense altars broken down, and what you have made wiped out. ⁷Your people will fall slain among you, and you will know that I am the LORD.

⁸" 'But I will spare some, for some of you will escape the sword when you are scattered among the lands and nations. ⁹Then in the nations where they have been carried captive, those who escape will remember me—how I have been grieved by their adulterous hearts, which have turned away from me, and by their eyes, which have lusted after their idols. They will loathe themselves for the evil they have done and for all their detestable practices. ¹⁰And they will know that I am the LORD; I did not threaten in vain to bring this calamity on them.

¹¹" 'This is what the Sovereign LORD says: Strike your hands together and stamp your feet and cry out "Alas!" because of all the wicked and detestable practices of the house of Israel, for they will fall by the sword, famine and plague. ¹²He that is far away will die of the plague, and he that is near will fall by the sword, and he that survives and is spared will die of famine. So will I spend my wrath upon them. ¹³And they will know that I am the LORD, when their people lie slain among their idols

around their altars, on every high hill and on all the mountaintops, under every spreading tree and every leafy oak—places where they offered fragrant incense to all their idols. ¹⁴And I will stretch out my hand against them and make the land a desolate waste from the desert to Diblahᵃ—wherever they live. Then they will know that I am the LORD.' "

The End Has Come

7 The word of the LORD came to me: ²"Son of man, this is what the Sovereign LORD says to the land of Israel: The end! The end has come upon the four corners of the land. ³The end is now upon you and I will unleash my anger against you. I will judge you according to your conduct and repay you for all your detestable practices. ⁴I will not look on you with pity or spare you; I will surely repay you for your conduct and the detestable practices among you. Then you will know that I am the LORD.

⁵"This is what the Sovereign LORD says: Disaster! An unheard-ofᵇ disaster is coming. ⁶The end has come! The end has come! It has roused itself against you. It has come! ⁷Doom has come upon you— you who dwell in the land. The time has come, the day is near; there is panic, not joy, upon the mountains. ⁸I am about to pour out my wrath on you and spend my anger against you; I will judge you according to your conduct and repay you for all your detestable practices. ⁹I will not look on you with pity or spare you; I will repay you in accordance with your conduct and the detestable practices among you. Then you will know that it is I the LORD who strikes the blow.

¹⁰"The day is here! It has come! Doom has burst forth, the rod has budded, arrogance has blossomed! ¹¹Violence has grown intoᶜ a rod to punish wickedness; none of the people will be left, none of that crowd—no wealth, nothing of value. ¹²The time has come, the day has arrived. Let not the buyer rejoice nor the seller grieve, for wrath is upon the whole crowd. ¹³The seller will not recover the land he has sold as long as both of them live, for the vision concerning the whole crowd will

ᵃ 14 Most Hebrew manuscripts; a few Hebrew manuscripts Riblah   ᵇ 5 Most Hebrew manuscripts; some Hebrew manuscripts and Syriac Disaster after   ᶜ 11 Or The violent one has become not be reversed. Because of their sins, not one of them will preserve his life. [14]Though they blow the trumpet and get everything ready, no one will go into battle, for my wrath is upon the whole crowd.

[15]"Outside is the sword, inside are plague and famine; those in the country will die by the sword, and those in the city will be devoured by famine and plague. [16]All who survive and escape will be in the mountains, moaning like doves of the valleys, each because of his sins. [17]Every hand will go limp, and every knee will become as weak as water. [18]They will put on sackcloth and be clothed with terror. Their faces will be covered with shame and their heads will be shaved. [19]They will throw their silver into the streets, and their gold will be an unclean thing. Their silver and gold will not be able to save them in the day of the LORD's wrath. They will not satisfy their hunger or fill their stomachs with it, for it has made them stumble into sin. [20]They were proud of their beautiful jewelry and used it to make their detestable idols and vile images. Therefore I will turn these into an unclean thing for them. [21]I will hand it all over as plunder to foreigners and as loot to the wicked of the earth, and they will defile it. [22]I will turn my face away from them, and they will desecrate my treasured place; robbers will enter it and desecrate it.

[23]"Prepare chains, because the land is full of bloodshed and the city is full of violence. [24]I will bring the most wicked of the nations to take possession of their houses; I will put an end to the pride of the mighty, and their sanctuaries will be desecrated. [25]When terror comes, they will seek peace, but there will be none. [26]Calamity upon calamity will come, and rumor upon rumor. They will try to get a vision from the prophet; the teaching of the law by the priest will be lost, as will the counsel of the elders. [27]The king will mourn, the prince will be clothed with despair, and the hands of the people of the land will tremble. I will deal with them according to their conduct, and by their own standards I will judge them. Then they will know that I am the LORD."

Idolatry in the Temple

In the sixth year, in the sixth month on the fifth day, while I was sitting in my house and the elders of Judah were sitting before me, the hand of the Sovereign LORD came upon me there. [2]I looked, and I saw a figure like that of a man.[a] From what appeared to be his waist down he was like fire, and from there up his appearance was as bright as glowing metal. [3]He stretched out what looked like a hand and took me by the hair of my head. The Spirit lifted me up between earth and heaven and in visions of God he took me to Jerusalem, to the entrance to the north gate of the inner court, where the idol that provokes to jealousy stood. [4]And there before me was the glory of the God of Israel, as in the vision I had seen in the plain.

[5]Then he said to me, "Son of man, look toward the north." So I looked, and in the entrance north of the gate of the altar I saw this idol of jealousy.

[6]And he said to me, "Son of man, do you see what they are doing—the utterly detestable things the house of Israel is doing here, things that will drive me far from my sanctuary? But you will see things that are even more detestable."

[7]Then he brought me to the entrance to the court. I looked, and I saw a hole in the wall. [8]He said to me, "Son of man, now dig into the wall." So I dug into the wall and saw a doorway there.

[9]And he said to me, "Go in and see the wicked and detestable things they are doing here." [10]So I went in and looked, and I saw portrayed all over the walls all kinds of crawling things and detestable animals and all the idols of the house of Israel. [11]In front of them stood seventy elders of the house of Israel, and Jaazaniah son of Shaphan was standing among them. Each had a censer in his hand, and a fragrant cloud of incense was rising.

[12]He said to me, "Son of man, have you seen what the elders of the house of Israel are doing in the darkness, each at the shrine of his own idol? They say, 'The LORD does not see us; the LORD has forsaken the land.'" [13]Again, he said, "You will see them doing things that are even more detestable."

[14]Then he brought me to the entrance to the north gate of the house of the LORD, and I saw women sitting there, mourning for Tammuz. [15]He said to me, "Do you see this, son of man? You will see things that are even more detestable than this."

---

[a] 2 Or saw a fiery figure

¹⁶He then brought me into the inner court of the house of the Lᴏʀᴅ, and there at the entrance to the temple, between the portico and the altar, were about twenty-five men. With their backs toward the temple of the Lᴏʀᴅ and their faces toward the east, they were bowing down to the sun in the east.

¹⁷He said to me, "Have you seen this, son of man? Is it a trivial matter for the house of Judah to do the detestable things they are doing here? Must they also fill the land with violence and continually provoke me to anger? Look at them putting the branch to their nose! ¹⁸Therefore I will deal with them in anger; I will not look on them with pity or spare them. Although they shout in my ears, I will not listen to them."

Idolaters Killed

Then I heard him call out in a loud voice, "Bring the guards of the city here, each with a weapon in his hand." ²And I saw six men coming from the direction of the upper gate, which faces north, each with a deadly weapon in his hand. With them was a man clothed in linen who had a writing kit at his side. They came in and stood beside the bronze altar.

³Now the glory of the God of Israel went up from above the cherubim, where it had been, and moved to the threshold of the temple. Then the Lᴏʀᴅ called to the man clothed in linen who had the writing kit at his side ⁴and said to him, "Go throughout the city of Jerusalem and put a mark on the foreheads of those who grieve and lament over all the detestable things that are done in it."

⁵As I listened, he said to the others, "Follow him through the city and kill, without showing pity or compassion. ⁶Slaughter old men, young men and maidens, women and children, but do not touch anyone who has the mark. Begin at my sanctuary." So they began with the elders who were in front of the temple.

⁷Then he said to them, "Defile the temple and fill the courts with the slain. Go!" So they went out and began killing throughout the city. ⁸While they were killing and I was left alone, I fell facedown,

Fly on the Wall

READ EZEKIEL 8

Zing! One minute you're in your room, the next minute you're across the world, spying on men plotting behind closed doors. You're like a fly on the wall. They don't even know you're there. We don't know whether Ezekiel was actually transported from Babylon to Jerusalem, or whether he saw this incredible stuff in a vision. Whatever happened, he didn't need state-of-the-art listening devices or infrared goggles to spy with. Imagine if you had this gift. The CIA and the FBI would be begging you to work for them. God is not a spy, but he knows exactly what you do—even if you're getting ready to do something wrong behind closed doors. The good news is that he still loves you. He's your heavenly Father and you can talk to him about anything. God's there to help you. He'll give you a hand, so you can say "no way" to temptation.

Your next reading is on page 1052.

crying out, "Ah, Sovereign LORD! Are you going to destroy the entire remnant of Israel in this outpouring of your wrath on Jerusalem?"

⁹He answered me, "The sin of the house of Israel and Judah is exceedingly great; the land is full of bloodshed and the city is full of injustice. They say, 'The LORD has forsaken the land; the LORD does not see.' ¹⁰So I will not look on them with pity or spare them, but I will bring down on their own heads what they have done."

¹¹Then the man in linen with the writing kit at his side brought back word, saying, "I have done as you commanded."

The Glory Departs From the Temple

10 I looked, and I saw the likeness of a throne of sapphire[a] above the expanse that was over the heads of the cherubim. ²The LORD said to the man clothed in linen, "Go in among the wheels beneath the cherubim. Fill your hands with burning coals from among the cherubim and scatter them over the city." And as I watched, he went in.

³Now the cherubim were standing on the south side of the temple when the man went in, and a cloud filled the inner court. ⁴Then the glory of the LORD rose from above the cherubim and moved to the threshold of the temple. The cloud filled the temple, and the court was full of the radiance of the glory of the LORD. ⁵The sound of the wings of the cherubim could be heard as far away as the outer court, like the voice of God Almighty[b] when he speaks.

⁶When the LORD commanded the man in linen, "Take fire from among the wheels, from among the cherubim," the man went in and stood beside a wheel. ⁷Then one of the cherubim reached out his hand to the fire that was among them. He took up some of it and put it into the hands of the man in linen, who took it and went out. ⁸(Under the wings of the

---

[a] 1 Or lapis lazuli   [b] 5 Hebrew El-Shaddai

Make It Stick

READ EZEKIEL 8

In Ezekiel's vision, someone had drawn creepy, crawling creatures all over the temple walls, and other people were worshiping his doodles (see verses 10–11). Creepy crawlers can be cool, but it's pretty brainless to think they're gods. What kind of gross crawling thing can you invent? Draw one on your sticky note.

cherubim could be seen what looked like the hands of a man.)

⁹I looked, and I saw beside the cherubim four wheels, one beside each of the cherubim; the wheels sparkled like chrysolite. ¹⁰As for their appearance, the four of them looked alike; each was like a wheel intersecting a wheel. ¹¹As they moved, they would go in any one of the four directions the cherubim faced; the wheels did not turn aboutᵃ as the cherubim went. The cherubim went in whatever direction the head faced, without turning as they went. ¹²Their entire bodies, including their backs, their hands and their wings, were completely full of eyes, as were their four wheels. ¹³I heard the wheels being called "the whirling wheels." ¹⁴Each of the cherubim had four faces: One face was that of a cherub, the second the face of a man, the third the face of a lion, and the fourth the face of an eagle.

¹⁵Then the cherubim rose upward. These were the living creatures I had seen by the Kebar River. ¹⁶When the cherubim moved, the wheels beside them moved; and when the cherubim spread their wings to rise from the ground, the wheels did not leave their side. ¹⁷When the cherubim stood still, they also stood still; and when the cherubim rose, they rose with them, because the spirit of the living creatures was in them.

¹⁸Then the glory of the LORD departed from over the threshold of the temple and stopped above the cherubim. ¹⁹While I watched, the cherubim spread their wings and rose from the ground, and as they went, the wheels went with them. They stopped at the entrance to the east gate of the LORD's house, and the glory of the God of Israel was above them.

²⁰These were the living creatures I had seen beneath the God of Israel by the Kebar River, and I realized that they were cherubim. ²¹Each had four faces and four wings, and under their wings was what looked like the hands of a man. ²²Their faces had the same appearance as those I had seen by the Kebar River. Each one went straight ahead.

ᵃ 11 Or aside

Cherubim, Angels and People

READ EZEKIEL 10:1–14

What if you heard the beating of incredibly loud wings, looked up and saw a *cherubim* landing on your front lawn? Can you imagine a monstrous flying beast with four different faces (see verses 5 and 14)? You might have guessed: Cherubim are different from regular angels. Angels often look like people, don't have wings, and go for the one-head look. Cherubim and angels are powerful, glorious, beautiful beings. God doesn't make junk. And remember, humans are the crown of God's creation (see Psalm 8:5–6; 1 Corinthians 6:3). God does such cool stuff for people that "even angels long to look into these things" (1 Peter 1:12). Don't feel special? The cherubim think you are! They would *love* to have the relationship with God that you can have. So go look in the mirror. Thank God for how he made you, and how special you are to him.

Your next reading is on page 1056.

Judgment on Israel's Leaders

11 Then the Spirit lifted me up and brought me to the gate of the house of the LORD that faces east. There at the entrance to the gate were twenty-five men, and I saw among them Jaazaniah son of Azzur and Pelatiah son of Benaiah, leaders of the people. ²The LORD said to me, "Son of man, these are the men who are plotting evil and giving wicked advice in this city. ³They say, 'Will it not soon be time to build houses?ᵃ This city is a cooking pot, and we are the meat.' ⁴Therefore prophesy against them; prophesy, son of man."

⁵Then the Spirit of the LORD came upon me, and he told me to say: "This is what the LORD says: That is what you are saying, O house of Israel, but I know what is going through your mind. ⁶You have killed many people in this city and filled its streets with the dead.

⁷"Therefore this is what the Sovereign LORD says: The bodies you have thrown there are the meat and this city is the pot, but I will drive you out of it. ⁸You fear the sword, and the sword is what I will bring against you, declares the Sovereign LORD. ⁹I will drive you out of the city and hand you over to foreigners and inflict punishment on you. ¹⁰You will fall by the sword, and I will execute judgment on you at the borders of Israel. Then you will know that I am the LORD. ¹¹This city will not be a pot for you, nor will you be the meat in it; I will execute judgment on you at the borders of Israel. ¹²And you will know that I am the LORD, for you have not followed my decrees or kept my laws but have conformed to the standards of the nations around you."

¹³Now as I was prophesying, Pelatiah son of Benaiah died. Then I fell facedown and cried out in a loud voice, "Ah, Sovereign LORD! Will you completely destroy the remnant of Israel?"

¹⁴The word of the LORD came to me: ¹⁵"Son of man, your brothers—your brothers who are your blood relativesᵇ and the whole house of Israel—are those of whom the people of Jerusalem have said, 'Theyᶜ are far away from the LORD; this land was given to us as our possession.'

Promised Return of Israel

¹⁶"Therefore say: 'This is what the Sovereign LORD says: Although I sent them far away among the nations and scattered them among the countries, yet for a little while I have been a sanctuary for them in the countries where they have gone.'

¹⁷"Therefore say: 'This is what the Sovereign LORD says: I will gather you from the nations and bring you back from the countries where you have been scattered, and I will give you back the land of Israel again.'

¹⁸"They will return to it and remove all its vile images and detestable idols. ¹⁹I will give them an undivided heart and put a new spirit in them; I will remove from them their heart of stone and give them a heart of flesh. ²⁰Then they will follow my decrees and be careful to keep my laws. They will be my people, and I will be their God. ²¹But as for those whose hearts are devoted to their vile images and detestable idols, I will bring down on their own heads what they have done, declares the Sovereign LORD."

²²Then the cherubim, with the wheels beside them, spread their wings, and the glory of the God of Israel was above them. ²³The glory of the LORD went up from within the city and stopped above the mountain east of it. ²⁴The Spirit lifted me up and brought me to the exiles in Babyloniaᵈ in the vision given by the Spirit of God.

Then the vision I had seen went up from me, ²⁵and I told the exiles everything the LORD had shown me.

The Exile Symbolized

12 The word of the LORD came to me: ²"Son of man, you are living among a rebellious people. They have eyes to see but do not see and ears to hear but do not hear, for they are a rebellious people.

³"Therefore, son of man, pack your belongings for exile and in the daytime, as they watch, set out and go from where you are to another place. Perhaps they will understand, though they are a rebellious house. ⁴During the daytime, while they watch, bring out your belongings packed for exile. Then in the evening, while they are watching, go out like those who go into exile. ⁵While they watch, dig through the wall and take your belongings out through it. ⁶Put them on your shoulder as

---

ᵃ 3 Or This is not the time to build houses.　　ᵇ 15 Or are in exile with you (see Septuagint and Syriac)　　ᶜ 15 Or those to whom the people of Jerusalem have said, 'Stay　　ᵈ 24 Or Chaldea they are watching and carry them out at dusk. Cover your face so that you cannot see the land, for I have made you a sign to the house of Israel."

⁷So I did as I was commanded. During the day I brought out my things packed for exile. Then in the evening I dug through the wall with my hands. I took my belongings out at dusk, carrying them on my shoulders while they watched.

⁸In the morning the word of the LORD came to me: ⁹"Son of man, did not that rebellious house of Israel ask you, 'What are you doing?'

¹⁰"Say to them, 'This is what the Sovereign LORD says: This oracle concerns the prince in Jerusalem and the whole house of Israel who are there.' ¹¹Say to them, 'I am a sign to you.'

"As I have done, so it will be done to them. They will go into exile as captives.

¹²"The prince among them will put his things on his shoulder at dusk and leave, and a hole will be dug in the wall for him

to go through. He will cover his face so that he cannot see the land. ¹³I will spread my net for him, and he will be caught in my snare; I will bring him to Babylonia, the land of the Chaldeans, but he will not see it, and there he will die. ¹⁴I will scatter to the winds all those around him—his staff and all his troops—and I will pursue them with drawn sword.

¹⁵"They will know that I am the LORD, when I disperse them among the nations and scatter them through the countries. ¹⁶But I will spare a few of them from the sword, famine and plague, so that in the nations where they go they may acknowledge all their detestable practices. Then they will know that I am the LORD."

¹⁷The word of the LORD came to me: ¹⁸Son of man, tremble as you eat your food, and shudder in fear as you drink your water. ¹⁹Say to the people of the land: 'This is what the Sovereign LORD says about those living in Jerusalem and in the land of Israel: They will eat their food in

Make It Stick

READ EZEKIEL 11:19

Ezekiel 11:19 sounds like God giving people heart transplants—and he *is*! When Jesus forgives our sins, he changes our hearts and they become open to God, soft and compassionate. But we need to *keep* our hearts soft to God by obeying his Spirit. Draw a picture of what you think your heart looks like (sponge, rock, etc.).

anxiety and drink their water in despair, for their land will be stripped of everything in it because of the violence of all who live there. 20The inhabited towns will be laid waste and the land will be desolate. Then you will know that I am the LORD.' "

21The word of the LORD came to me: 22"Son of man, what is this proverb you have in the land of Israel: 'The days go by and every vision comes to nothing'? 23Say to them, 'This is what the Sovereign LORD says: I am going to put an end to this proverb, and they will no longer quote it in Israel.' Say to them, 'The days are near when every vision will be fulfilled. 24For there will be no more false visions or flattering divinations among the people of Israel. 25But I the LORD will speak what I will, and it shall be fulfilled without delay. For in your days, you rebellious house, I will fulfill whatever I say, declares the Sovereign LORD.' "

26The word of the LORD came to me: 27"Son of man, the house of Israel is saying, 'The vision he sees is for many years from now, and he prophesies about the distant future.'

28"Therefore say to them, 'This is what the Sovereign LORD says: None of my words will be delayed any longer; whatever I say will be fulfilled, declares the Sovereign LORD.' "

False Prophets Condemned

13 The word of the LORD came to me: 2"Son of man, prophesy against the prophets of Israel who are now prophesying. Say to those who prophesy out of their own imagination: 'Hear the word of the LORD! 3This is what the Sovereign LORD says: Woe to the foolisha prophets who follow their own spirit and have seen nothing! 4Your prophets, O Israel, are like jackals among ruins. 5You have not gone up to the breaks in the wall to repair it for the house of Israel so that it will stand firm in the battle on the day of the LORD. 6Their visions are false and their divinations a lie. They say, "The LORD declares," when the LORD has not sent them; yet they expect their words to be fulfilled. 7Have you not seen false visions and uttered lying divinations when you say, "The LORD declares," though I have not spoken?

8" 'Therefore this is what the Sovereign LORD says: Because of your false words and

lying visions, I am against you, declares the Sovereign LORD. 9My hand will be against the prophets who see false visions and utter lying divinations. They will not belong to the council of my people or be listed in the records of the house of Israel, nor will they enter the land of Israel. Then you will know that I am the Sovereign LORD.

10" 'Because they lead my people astray, saying, "Peace," when there is no peace, and because, when a flimsy wall is built, they cover it with whitewash, 11therefore tell those who cover it with whitewash that it is going to fall. Rain will come in torrents, and I will send hailstones hurtling down, and violent winds will burst forth. 12When the wall collapses, will people not ask you, "Where is the whitewash you covered it with?"

13" 'Therefore this is what the Sovereign LORD says: In my wrath I will unleash a violent wind, and in my anger hailstones and torrents of rain will fall with destructive fury. 14I will tear down the wall you have covered with whitewash and will level it to the ground so that its foundation will be laid bare. When itb falls, you will be destroyed in it; and you will know that I am the LORD. 15So I will spend my wrath against the wall and against those who covered it with whitewash. I will say to you, "The wall is gone and so are those who whitewashed it, 16those prophets of Israel who prophesied to Jerusalem and saw visions of peace for her when there was no peace, declares the Sovereign LORD." '

17"Now, son of man, set your face against the daughters of your people who prophesy out of their own imagination. Prophesy against them 18and say, 'This is what the Sovereign LORD says: Woe to the women who sew magic charms on all their wrists and make veils of various lengths for their heads in order to ensnare people. Will you ensnare the lives of my people but preserve your own? 19You have profaned me among my people for a few handfuls of barley and scraps of bread. By lying to my people, who listen to lies, you have killed those who should not have died and have spared those who should not live.

20" 'Therefore this is what the Sovereign LORD says: I am against your magic charms with which you ensnare people

a 3 Or wicked   b 14 Or the city

like birds and I will tear them from your arms; I will set free the people that you ensnare like birds. ²¹I will tear off your veils and save my people from your hands, and they will no longer fall prey to your power. Then you will know that I am the Lord. ²²Because you disheartened the righteous with your lies, when I had brought them no grief, and because you encouraged the wicked not to turn from their evil ways and so save their lives, ²³therefore you will no longer see false visions or practice divination. I will save my people from your hands. And then you will know that I am the Lord.' "

Idolaters Condemned

14 Some of the elders of Israel came to me and sat down in front of me. ²Then the word of the Lord came to me: ³"Son of man, these men have set up idols in their hearts and put wicked stumbling blocks before their faces. Should I let them inquire of me at all? ⁴Therefore speak to them and tell them, 'This is what the Sovereign Lord says: When any Israelite sets up idols in his

heart and puts a wicked stumbling block before his face and then goes to a prophet, I the Lord will answer him myself in keeping with his great idolatry. ⁵I will do this to recapture the hearts of the people of Israel, who have all deserted me for their idols.'

⁶"Therefore say to the house of Israel, 'This is what the Sovereign Lord says: Repent! Turn from your idols and renounce all your detestable practices!

⁷" 'When any Israelite or any alien living in Israel separates himself from me and sets up idols in his heart and puts a wicked stumbling block before his face and then goes to a prophet to inquire of me, I the Lord will answer him myself. ⁸I will set my face against that man and make him an example and a byword. I will cut him off from my people. Then you will know that I am the Lord.

⁹" 'And if the prophet is enticed to utter a prophecy, I the Lord have enticed that prophet, and I will stretch out my hand against him and destroy him from among my people Israel. ¹⁰They will bear their guilt—the prophet will be as guilty as the

Weak Walls

READ EZEKIEL 13:10–16

Ever seen a rotting, weather-beaten plywood fort? You could probably kick a hole right through the walls. What would happen if you painted the walls white? They'd *look* better, but they'd still be the same, wimpy walls. Ezekiel wrote about painting whitewash on weak walls, too. He compared it to people who look good on the outside, but are bad news on the inside. Some guys are good actors: They go to church and act like a nice solid wall. But man, are they rotten when adults aren't looking. Building strong walls doesn't mean you have to be perfect. Sometimes your mind and your desires will try to take you the wrong way, but as long as you use your willpower to resist them, you'll be solid. Saying, "I'm tempted, but I'm going to do the right thing" will make you into a wall that nobody can push over!

Your next reading is on page 1057.

one who consults him. ¹¹Then the people of Israel will no longer stray from me, nor will they defile themselves anymore with all their sins. They will be my people, and I will be their God, declares the Sovereign LORD.' "

Judgment Inescapable

¹²The word of the LORD came to me: ¹³"Son of man, if a country sins against me by being unfaithful and I stretch out my hand against it to cut off its food supply and send famine upon it and kill its men and their animals, ¹⁴even if these three men—Noah, Daniel[a] and Job— were in it, they could save only themselves by their righteousness, declares the Sovereign LORD.

¹⁵"Or if I send wild beasts through that country and they leave it childless and it becomes desolate so that no one can pass through it because of the beasts, ¹⁶as surely as I live, declares the Sovereign LORD, even if these three men were in it, they could not save their own sons or daughters. They alone would be saved, but the land would be desolate.

¹⁷"Or if I bring a sword against that country and say, 'Let the sword pass throughout the land,' and I kill its men and their animals, ¹⁸as surely as I live, declares the Sovereign LORD, even if these three men were in it, they could not save their own sons or daughters. They alone would be saved.

¹⁹"Or if I send a plague into that land and pour out my wrath upon it through bloodshed, killing its men and their animals, ²⁰as surely as I live, declares the Sovereign LORD, even if Noah, Daniel and Job were in it, they could save neither son nor daughter. They would save only themselves by their righteousness.

²¹"For this is what the Sovereign LORD says: How much worse will it be when I send against Jerusalem my four dreadful judgments—sword and famine and wild beasts and plague—to kill its men and their animals! ²²Yet there will be some survivors—sons and daughters who will be brought out of it. They will come to you,

a 14 Or *Danel*; the Hebrew spelling may suggest a person other than the prophet Daniel; also in verse 20.

Toboggan Ride

READ EZEKIEL 14:12–20

You know your country's pretty far gone when even Noah, Daniel and Job can't save it from being judged. If you're trying to grow with God, but you slip up once in a while, you can ask him to forgive you and you're back on track. But if you're stubbornly doing your own thing *all* the time, you can't just hope to say a quick "sorry" and make things perfect. That's like hitting the slopes on a toboggan: You start off slow, but soon you're jetting down the hill. Once you reach warp speed, jumping off is going to leave some big-time bumps. There's just too much momentum for you to escape without consequences. The same is true if you get godly momentum. If you're listening to God, you pick up righteous speed. Instead of a runaway accident, your life will be a great ride.

Your next reading is on page 1066.

and when you see their conduct and their actions, you will be consoled regarding the disaster I have brought upon Jerusalem—every disaster I have brought upon it. [23]You will be consoled when you see their conduct and their actions, for you will know that I have done nothing in it without cause, declares the Sovereign LORD."

Jerusalem, A Useless Vine

The word of the LORD came to me: [2]"Son of man, how is the wood of a vine better than that of a branch on any of the trees in the forest? [3]Is wood ever taken from it to make anything useful? Do they make pegs from it to hang things on? [4]And after it is thrown on the fire as fuel and the fire burns both ends and chars the middle, is it then useful for anything? [5]If it was not useful for anything when it was whole, how much less can it be made into something useful when the fire has burned it and it is charred?

[6]"Therefore this is what the Sovereign LORD says: As I have given the wood of the vine among the trees of the forest as fuel for the fire, so will I treat the people living in Jerusalem. [7]I will set my face against them. Although they have come out of the fire, the fire will yet consume them. And when I set my face against them, you will know that I am the LORD. [8]I will make the land desolate because they have been unfaithful, declares the Sovereign LORD."

An Allegory of Unfaithful Jerusalem

The word of the LORD came to me: [2]"Son of man, confront Jerusalem with her detestable practices [3]and say, 'This is what the Sovereign LORD says to Jerusalem: Your ancestry and birth were in the land of the Canaanites; your father was an Amorite and your mother a Hittite. [4]On the day you were born your cord was not cut, nor were you washed with water to make you clean, nor were you rubbed with salt or wrapped in cloths. [5]No one looked on you with pity or had compassion enough to do any of these things for you. Rather, you were thrown out into the open field, for on the day you were born you were despised.

[6]"'Then I passed by and saw you kicking about in your blood, and as you lay there in your blood I said to you, "Live!" [a] [7]I made you grow like a plant of the field.

You grew up and developed and became the most beautiful of jewels. [b] Your breasts were formed and your hair grew, you who were naked and bare.

[8]"'Later I passed by, and when I looked at you and saw that you were old enough for love, I spread the corner of my garment over you and covered your nakedness. I gave you my solemn oath and entered into a covenant with you, declares the Sovereign LORD, and you became mine.

[9]"'I bathed [c] you with water and washed the blood from you and put ointments on you. [10]I clothed you with an embroidered dress and put leather sandals on you. I dressed you in fine linen and covered you with costly garments. [11]I adorned you with jewelry: I put bracelets on your arms and a necklace around your neck, [12]and I put a ring on your nose, earrings on your ears and a beautiful crown on your head. [13]So you were adorned with gold and silver; your clothes were of fine linen and costly fabric and embroidered cloth. Your food was fine flour, honey and olive oil. You became very beautiful and rose to be a queen. [14]And your fame spread among the nations on account of your beauty, because the splendor I had given you made your beauty perfect, declares the Sovereign LORD.

[15]"'But you trusted in your beauty and used your fame to become a prostitute. You lavished your favors on anyone who passed by and your beauty became his. [d] [16]You took some of your garments to make gaudy high places, where you carried on your prostitution. Such things should not happen, nor should they ever occur. [17]You also took the fine jewelry I gave you, the jewelry made of my gold and silver, and you made for yourself male idols and engaged in prostitution with them. [18]And you took your embroidered clothes to put on them, and you offered my oil and incense before them. [19]Also the food I provided for you—the fine flour, olive oil and honey I gave you to eat—you offered as fragrant incense before them. That is what happened, declares the Sovereign LORD.

a 6 A few Hebrew manuscripts, Septuagint and Syriac; most Hebrew manuscripts *"Live!" And as you lay there in your blood I said to you, "Live!"*   b 7 Or *became mature*   c 9 Or *I had bathed*   d 15 Most Hebrew manuscripts; one Hebrew manuscript (see some Septuagint manuscripts) *by. Such a thing should not happen*

20" 'And you took your sons and daughters whom you bore to me and sacrificed them as food to the idols. Was your prostitution not enough? 21You slaughtered my children and sacrificed them*a* to the idols. 22In all your detestable practices and your prostitution you did not remember the days of your youth, when you were naked and bare, kicking about in your blood.

23" 'Woe! Woe to you, declares the Sovereign Lord. In addition to all your other wickedness, 24you built a mound for yourself and made a lofty shrine in every public square. 25At the head of every street you built your lofty shrines and degraded your beauty, offering your body with increasing promiscuity to anyone who passed by. 26You engaged in prostitution with the Egyptians, your lustful neighbors, and provoked me to anger with your increasing promiscuity. 27So I stretched out my hand against you and reduced your territory; I gave you over to the greed of your enemies, the daughters of the Philistines, who were shocked by your lewd conduct. 28You engaged in prostitution with the Assyrians too, because you were insatiable; and even after that, you still were not satisfied. 29Then you increased your promiscuity to include Babylonia,*b* a land of merchants, but even with this you were not satisfied.

30" 'How weak-willed you are, declares the Sovereign Lord, when you do all these things, acting like a brazen prostitute! 31When you built your mounds at the head of every street and made your lofty shrines in every public square, you were unlike a prostitute, because you scorned payment.

32" 'You adulterous wife! You prefer strangers to your own husband! 33Every prostitute receives a fee, but you give gifts to all your lovers, bribing them to come to you from everywhere for your illicit favors. 34So in your prostitution you are the opposite of others; no one runs after you for your favors. You are the very opposite, for you give payment and none is given to you.

35" 'Therefore, you prostitute, hear the word of the Lord! 36This is what the Sovereign Lord says: Because you poured out your wealth*c* and exposed your nakedness in your promiscuity with your lovers, and because of all your detestable idols, and because you gave them your children's blood, 37therefore I am going to gather all your lovers, with whom you found pleasure, those you loved as well as those you hated. I will gather them against you from all around and will strip you in front of them, and they will see all your nakedness. 38I will sentence you to the punishment of women who commit adultery and who shed blood; I will bring upon you the blood vengeance of my wrath and jealous anger. 39Then I will hand you over to your lovers, and they will tear down your mounds and destroy your lofty shrines. They will strip you of your clothes and take your fine jewelry and leave you naked and bare. 40They will bring a mob against you, who will stone you and hack you to pieces with their swords. 41They will burn down your houses and inflict punishment on you in the sight of many women. I will put a stop to your prostitution, and you will no longer pay your lovers. 42Then my wrath against you will subside and my jealous anger will turn away from you; I will be calm and no longer angry.

43" 'Because you did not remember the days of your youth but enraged me with all these things, I will surely bring down on your head what you have done, declares the Sovereign Lord. Did you not add lewdness to all your other detestable practices?

44" 'Everyone who quotes proverbs will quote this proverb about you: "Like mother, like daughter." 45You are a true daughter of your mother, who despised her husband and her children; and you are a true sister of your sisters, who despised their husbands and their children. Your mother was a Hittite and your father an Amorite. 46Your older sister was Samaria, who lived to the north of you with her daughters; and your younger sister, who lived to the south of you with her daughters, was Sodom. 47You not only walked in their ways and copied their detestable practices, but in all your ways you soon became more depraved than they. 48As surely as I live, declares the Sovereign Lord, your sister Sodom and her daughters never did what you and your daughters have done.

49" 'Now this was the sin of your sister Sodom: She and her daughters were arrogant, overfed and unconcerned; they did

a 21 Or and made them pass through ⌊the fire⌋
b 29 Or Chaldea   c 36 Or lust

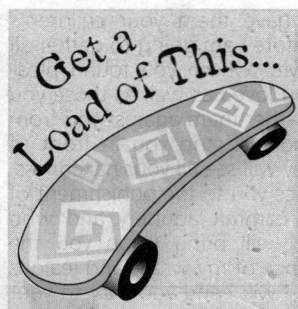

Eagles have always been symbols of courage and power (see Ezekiel 17:3, 7). Why?—Because they are awesome hunters and strike fear into their prey. Armies in Rome, Russia, Germany and Austria all painted pictures of eagles on their flags as symbols of their power.

not help the poor and needy. 50They were haughty and did detestable things before me. Therefore I did away with them as you have seen. 51Samaria did not commit half the sins you did. You have done more detestable things than they, and have made your sisters seem righteous by all these things you have done. 52Bear your disgrace, for you have furnished some justification for your sisters. Because your sins were more vile than theirs, they appear more righteous than you. So then, be ashamed and bear your disgrace, for you have made your sisters appear righteous.

53" 'However, I will restore the fortunes of Sodom and her daughters and of Samaria and her daughters, and your fortunes along with them, 54so that you may bear your disgrace and be ashamed of all you have done in giving them comfort. 55And your sisters, Sodom with her daughters and Samaria with her daughters, will return to what they were before; and you and your daughters will return to what you were before. 56You would not even mention your sister Sodom in the day of your pride, 57before your wickedness was uncovered. Even so, you are now scorned by the daughters of Edom[a] and all her neighbors and the daughters of the Philistines—all those around you who despise you. 58You will bear the consequences of your lewdness and your detestable practices, declares the LORD.

59" 'This is what the Sovereign LORD says: I will deal with you as you deserve, because you have despised my oath by breaking the covenant. 60Yet I will remember the covenant I made with you in the days of your youth, and I will establish an everlasting covenant with you. 61Then you will remember your ways and be ashamed when you receive your sisters, both those who are older than you and those who are younger. I will give them to you as daughters, but not on the basis of my covenant with you. 62So I will establish my covenant with you, and you will know that I am the LORD. 63Then, when I make atonement for you for all you have done, you will remember and be ashamed and never again open your mouth because of your humiliation, declares the Sovereign LORD.' "

Two Eagles and a Vine

17 The word of the LORD came to me: 2"Son of man, set forth an allegory and tell the house of Israel a parable. 3Say to them, 'This is what the Sovereign LORD says: A great eagle with powerful wings, long feathers and full plumage of varied colors came to Lebanon. Taking hold of the top of a cedar, 4he broke off its topmost shoot and carried it away to a land of merchants, where he planted it in a city of traders.

5" 'He took some of the seed of your land and put it in fertile soil. He planted it like a willow by abundant water, 6and it sprouted and became a low, spreading vine. Its branches turned toward him, but its roots remained

---

[a] 57 Many Hebrew manuscripts and Syriac; most Hebrew manuscripts, Septuagint and Vulgate *Aram*

under it. So it became a vine and produced branches and put out leafy boughs.

7 " 'But there was another great eagle with powerful wings and full plumage. The vine now sent out its roots toward him from the plot where it was planted and stretched out its branches to him for water. 8 It had been planted in good soil by abundant water so that it would produce branches, bear fruit and become a splendid vine.'

9 "Say to them, 'This is what the Sovereign LORD says: Will it thrive? Will it not be uprooted and stripped of its fruit so that it withers? All its new growth will wither. It will not take a strong arm or many people to pull it up by the roots. 10 Even if it is transplanted, will it thrive? Will it not wither completely when the east wind strikes it—wither away in the plot where it grew?' "

11 Then the word of the LORD came to me: 12 "Say to this rebellious house, 'Do you not know what these things mean?' Say to them: 'The king of Babylon went to Jerusalem and carried off her king and her nobles, bringing them back with him to Babylon. 13 Then he took a member of the royal family and made a treaty with him, putting him under oath. He also carried away the leading men of the land, 14 so that the kingdom would be brought low, unable to rise again, surviving only by keeping his treaty. 15 But the king rebelled against him by sending his envoys to Egypt to get horses and a large army. Will he succeed? Will he who does such things escape? Will he break the treaty and yet escape?

16 " 'As surely as I live, declares the Sovereign LORD, he shall die in Babylon, in the land of the king who put him on the throne, whose oath he despised and whose treaty he broke. 17 Pharaoh with his mighty army and great horde will be of no help to him in war, when ramps are built and siege works erected to destroy many lives. 18 He despised the oath by breaking the covenant. Because he had given his hand in pledge and yet did all these things, he shall not escape.

19 " 'Therefore this is what the Sovereign LORD says: As surely as I live, I will bring down on his head my oath that he despised and my covenant that he broke. 20 I will spread my net for him, and he will be caught in my snare. I will bring him to Babylon and execute judgment upon him there because he was unfaithful to me. 21 All his fleeing troops will fall by the sword, and the survivors will be scattered to the winds. Then you will know that I the LORD have spoken.

22 " 'This is what the Sovereign LORD says: I myself will take a shoot from the very top of a cedar and plant it; I will break off a tender sprig from its topmost shoots and plant it on a high and lofty mountain. 23 On the mountain heights of Israel I will plant it; it will produce branches and bear fruit and become a splendid cedar. Birds of every kind will nest in it; they will find shelter in the shade of its branches. 24 All the trees of the field will know that I the LORD bring down the tall tree and make the low tree grow tall. I dry up the green tree and make the dry tree flourish.

" 'I the LORD have spoken, and I will do it.' "

The Soul Who Sins Will Die

18 The word of the LORD came to me: 2 "What do you people mean by quoting this proverb about the land of Israel:

" 'The fathers eat sour grapes,
    and the children's teeth are set on
        edge'?

3 "As surely as I live, declares the Sovereign LORD, you will no longer quote this proverb in Israel. 4 For every living soul belongs to me, the father as well as the son—both alike belong to me. The soul who sins is the one who will die.

5 "Suppose there is a righteous man
    who does what is just and right.
6 He does not eat at the mountain
        shrines
    or look to the idols of the house of
        Israel.
He does not defile his neighbor's wife
    or lie with a woman during her
        period.
7 He does not oppress anyone,
    but returns what he took in pledge
        for a loan.
He does not commit robbery
    but gives his food to the hungry
    and provides clothing for the naked.
8 He does not lend at usury
    or take excessive interest.ᵃ

ᵃ 8 Or take interest; similarly in verses 13 and 17

He withholds his hand from doing
    wrong
  and judges fairly between man and
    man.
⁹He follows my decrees
  and faithfully keeps my laws.
That man is righteous;
  he will surely live,
         declares the Sovereign LORD.

¹⁰"Suppose he has a violent son, who
sheds blood or does any of these other
things*ᵃ* ¹¹(though the father has done
none of them):

"He eats at the mountain shrines.
He defiles his neighbor's wife.
¹²He oppresses the poor and needy.
He commits robbery.
He does not return what he took in
    pledge.
He looks to the idols.
He does detestable things.
¹³He lends at usury and takes excessive
    interest.

Will such a man live? He will not! Because
he has done all these detestable things,
he will surely be put to death and his
blood will be on his own head.

¹⁴"But suppose this son has a son who
sees all the sins his father commits, and
though he sees them, he does not do
such things:

¹⁵"He does not eat at the mountain
    shrines
  or look to the idols of the house of
    Israel.
He does not defile his neighbor's wife.
¹⁶He does not oppress anyone
  or require a pledge for a loan.
He does not commit robbery
  but gives his food to the hungry
  and provides clothing for the naked.
¹⁷He withholds his hand from sin*ᵇ*
  and takes no usury or excessive
    interest.
He keeps my laws and follows my
    decrees.

He will not die for his father's sin; he will
surely live. ¹⁸But his father will die for his
own sin, because he practiced extortion,
robbed his brother and did what was
wrong among his people.

¹⁹"Yet you ask, 'Why does the son not
share the guilt of his father?' Since the
son has done what is just and right and

has been careful to keep all my decrees,
he will surely live. ²⁰The soul who sins is
the one who will die. The son will not
share the guilt of the father, nor will the
father share the guilt of the son. The righteousness of the righteous man will be
credited to him, and the wickedness of
the wicked will be charged against him.

²¹"But if a wicked man turns away from
all the sins he has committed and keeps
all my decrees and does what is just and
right, he will surely live; he will not die.
²²None of the offenses he has committed
will be remembered against him. Because
of the righteous things he has done, he
will live. ²³Do I take any pleasure in the
death of the wicked? declares the Sovereign LORD. Rather, am I not pleased when
they turn from their ways and live?

²⁴"But if a righteous man turns from his
righteousness and commits sin and does
the same detestable things the wicked
man does, will he live? None of the righteous things he has done will be remembered. Because of the unfaithfulness he is
guilty of and because of the sins he has
committed, he will die.

²⁵"Yet you say, 'The way of the Lord is
not just.' Hear, O house of Israel: Is my
way unjust? Is it not your ways that are
unjust? ²⁶If a righteous man turns from
his righteousness and commits sin, he will
die for it; because of the sin he has committed he will die. ²⁷But if a wicked man
turns away from the wickedness he has
committed and does what is just and
right, he will save his life. ²⁸Because he
considers all the offenses he has committed and turns away from them, he will
surely live; he will not die. ²⁹Yet the house
of Israel says, 'The way of the Lord is not
just.' Are my ways unjust, O house of Israel? Is it not your ways that are unjust?

³⁰"Therefore, O house of Israel, I will
judge you, each one according to his
ways, declares the Sovereign LORD. Repent! Turn away from all your offenses;
then sin will not be your downfall. ³¹Rid
yourselves of all the offenses you have
committed, and get a new heart and a
new spirit. Why will you die, O house of
Israel? ³²For I take no pleasure in the
death of anyone, declares the Sovereign
LORD. Repent and live!

ᵃ 10 Or *things to a brother*   *ᵇ 17* Septuagint (see also
verse 8); Hebrew *from the poor*

A Lament for Israel's Princes

19 "Take up a lament concerning the princes of Israel ²and say:

" 'What a lioness was your mother
among the lions!
She lay down among the young lions
and reared her cubs.
³ She brought up one of her cubs,
and he became a strong lion.
He learned to tear the prey
and he devoured men.
⁴ The nations heard about him,
and he was trapped in their pit.
They led him with hooks
to the land of Egypt.

⁵ " 'When she saw her hope unfulfilled,
her expectation gone,
she took another of her cubs
and made him a strong lion.
⁶ He prowled among the lions,
for he was now a strong lion.

He learned to tear the prey
and he devoured men.
⁷ He broke down*a* their strongholds
and devastated their towns.
The land and all who were in it
were terrified by his roaring.
⁸ Then the nations came against him,
those from regions round about.
They spread their net for him,
and he was trapped in their pit.
⁹ With hooks they pulled him into a cage
and brought him to the king of
Babylon.
They put him in prison,
so his roar was heard no longer
on the mountains of Israel.

¹⁰ " 'Your mother was like a vine in your
vineyard*b*
planted by the water;
it was fruitful and full of branches

a 7 Targum (see Septuagint); Hebrew *He knew*
b 10 Two Hebrew manuscripts; most Hebrew manuscripts
your blood

Make It Stick

READ EZEKIEL 19:1–9

When God wants to describe people's negative or positive behavior, sometimes he compares them to animals. What animal would describe you? Are you are a bear in the morning? Are you a night owl? Write down (or draw) an animal that you would like God to compare you to.

because of abundant water.
¹¹ Its branches were strong,
　　fit for a ruler's scepter.
It towered high
　　above the thick foliage,
conspicuous for its height
　　and for its many branches.
¹² But it was uprooted in fury
　　and thrown to the ground.
The east wind made it shrivel,
　　it was stripped of its fruit;
its strong branches withered
　　and fire consumed them.
¹³ Now it is planted in the desert,
　　in a dry and thirsty land.
¹⁴ Fire spread from one of its main^a
　　　branches
　　and consumed its fruit.
No strong branch is left on it
　　fit for a ruler's scepter.'

This is a lament and is to be used as a lament."

Rebellious Israel

20 In the seventh year, in the fifth month on the tenth day, some of the elders of Israel came to inquire of the LORD, and they sat down in front of me.

² Then the word of the LORD came to me: ³"Son of man, speak to the elders of Israel and say to them, 'This is what the Sovereign LORD says: Have you come to inquire of me? As surely as I live, I will not let you inquire of me, declares the Sovereign LORD.'

⁴"Will you judge them? Will you judge them, son of man? Then confront them with the detestable practices of their fathers ⁵and say to them: 'This is what the Sovereign LORD says: On the day I chose Israel, I swore with uplifted hand to the descendants of the house of Jacob and revealed myself to them in Egypt. With uplifted hand I said to them, "I am the LORD your God." ⁶On that day I swore to them that I would bring them out of Egypt into a land I had searched out for them, a land flowing with milk and honey, the most beautiful of all lands. ⁷And I said to them, "Each of you, get rid of the vile images you have set your eyes on, and do not defile yourselves with the idols of Egypt. I am the LORD your God."

⁸ 'But they rebelled against me and would not listen to me; they did not get rid of the vile images they had set their eyes on, nor did they forsake the idols of Egypt. So I said I would pour out my wrath on them and spend my anger against them in Egypt. ⁹But for the sake of my name I did what would keep it from being profaned in the eyes of the nations they lived among and in whose sight I had revealed myself to the Israelites by bringing them out of Egypt. ¹⁰Therefore I led them out of Egypt and brought them into the desert. ¹¹I gave them my decrees and made known to them my laws, for the man who obeys them will live by them. ¹²Also I gave them my Sabbaths as a sign between us, so they would know that I the LORD made them holy.

¹³" 'Yet the people of Israel rebelled against me in the desert. They did not follow my decrees but rejected my laws—although the man who obeys them will live by them—and they utterly desecrated my Sabbaths. So I said I would pour out my wrath on them and destroy them in the desert. ¹⁴But for the sake of my name I did what would keep it from being profaned in the eyes of the nations in whose sight I had brought them out. ¹⁵Also with uplifted hand I swore to them in the desert that I would not bring them into the land I had given them—a land flowing with milk and honey, most beautiful of all lands— ¹⁶because they rejected my laws and did not follow my decrees and desecrated my Sabbaths. For their hearts were devoted to their idols. ¹⁷Yet I looked on them with pity and did not destroy them or put an end to them in the desert. ¹⁸I said to their children in the desert, "Do not follow the statutes of your fathers or keep their laws or defile yourselves with their idols. ¹⁹I am the LORD your God; follow my decrees and be careful to keep my laws. ²⁰Keep my Sabbaths holy, that they may be a sign between us. Then you will know that I am the LORD your God."

²¹" 'But the children rebelled against me: They did not follow my decrees, they were not careful to keep my laws—although the man who obeys them will live by them—and they desecrated my Sabbaths. So I said I would pour out my wrath on them and spend my anger against them in the desert. ²²But I withheld my hand, and for the sake of my name I did

---

^a 14 Or from under its

what would keep it from being profaned in the eyes of the nations in whose sight I had brought them out. 23 Also with uplifted hand I swore to them in the desert that I would disperse them among the nations and scatter them through the countries, 24 because they had not obeyed my laws but had rejected my decrees and desecrated my Sabbaths, and their eyes lusted after their fathers' idols. 25 I also gave them over to statutes that were not good and laws they could not live by; 26 I let them become defiled through their gifts—the sacrifice of every firstborn*a*—that I might fill them with horror so they would know that I am the LORD.'

27 "Therefore, son of man, speak to the people of Israel and say to them, 'This is what the Sovereign LORD says: In this also your fathers blasphemed me by forsaking me: 28 When I brought them into the land I had sworn to give them and they saw any high hill or any leafy tree, there they offered their sacrifices, made offerings that provoked me to anger, presented their fragrant incense and poured out their drink offerings. 29 Then I said to them: What is this high place you go to?' " (It is called Bamah*b* to this day.)

Judgment and Restoration

30 "Therefore say to the house of Israel: 'This is what the Sovereign LORD says: Will you defile yourselves the way your fathers did and lust after their vile images? 31 When you offer your gifts—the sacrifice of your sons in*c* the fire—you continue to defile yourselves with all your idols to this day. Am I to let you inquire of me, O house of Israel? As surely as I live, declares the Sovereign LORD, I will not let you inquire of me.

32 " 'You say, "We want to be like the nations, like the peoples of the world, who serve wood and stone." But what you have in mind will never happen. 33 As surely as I live, declares the Sovereign LORD, I will rule over you with a mighty hand and an outstretched arm and with outpoured wrath. 34 I will bring you from the nations and gather you from the countries where you have been scattered—with a mighty hand and an outstretched arm and with outpoured wrath. 35 I will bring you into the desert of the nations and there, face to face, I will execute judgment upon you. 36 As I judged your

fathers in the desert of the land of Egypt, so I will judge you, declares the Sovereign LORD. 37 I will take note of you as you pass under my rod, and I will bring you into the bond of the covenant. 38 I will purge you of those who revolt and rebel against me. Although I will bring them out of the land where they are living, yet they will not enter the land of Israel. Then you will know that I am the LORD.

39 " 'As for you, O house of Israel, this is what the Sovereign LORD says: Go and serve your idols, every one of you! But afterward you will surely listen to me and no longer profane my holy name with your gifts and idols. 40 For on my holy mountain, the high mountain of Israel, declares the Sovereign LORD, there in the land the entire house of Israel will serve me, and there I will accept them. There I will require your offerings and your choice gifts,*d* along with all your holy sacrifices. 41 I will accept you as fragrant incense when I bring you out from the nations and gather you from the countries where you have been scattered, and I will show myself holy among you in the sight of the nations. 42 Then you will know that I am the LORD, when I bring you into the land of Israel, the land I had sworn with uplifted hand to give to your fathers. 43 There you will remember your conduct and all the actions by which you have defiled yourselves, and you will loathe yourselves for all the evil you have done. 44 You will know that I am the LORD, when I deal with you for my name's sake and not according to your evil ways and your corrupt practices, O house of Israel, declares the Sovereign LORD.' "

Prophecy Against the South

45 The word of the LORD came to me: 46 "Son of man, set your face toward the south; preach against the south and prophesy against the forest of the southland. 47 Say to the southern forest: 'Hear the word of the LORD. This is what the Sovereign LORD says: I am about to set fire to you, and it will consume all your trees, both green and dry. The blazing flame will not be quenched, and every face from south to north will be scorched by it. 48 Everyone will see that I the LORD have kindled it; it will not be quenched.' "

---

a 26 Or *—making every firstborn pass through ⸤the fire⸥*
b 29 *Bamah* means high place.   *c 31* Or *—making your sons pass through*   *d 40* Or *and the gifts of your firstfruits*

⁴⁹Then I said, "Ah, Sovereign LORD! They are saying of me, 'Isn't he just telling parables?'"

Babylon, God's Sword of Judgment

21 The word of the LORD came to me: ²"Son of man, set your face against Jerusalem and preach against the sanctuary. Prophesy against the land of Israel ³and say to her: 'This is what the LORD says: I am against you. I will draw my sword from its scabbard and cut off from you both the righteous and the wicked. ⁴Because I am going to cut off the righteous and the wicked, my sword will be unsheathed against everyone from south to north. ⁵Then all people will know that I the LORD have drawn my sword from its scabbard; it will not return again.'

⁶"Therefore groan, son of man! Groan before them with broken heart and bitter grief. ⁷And when they ask you, 'Why are you groaning?' you shall say, 'Because of the news that is coming. Every heart will melt and every hand go limp; every spirit will become faint and every knee become as weak as water.' It is coming! It will surely take place, declares the Sovereign LORD."

⁸The word of the LORD came to me: ⁹"Son of man, prophesy and say, 'This is what the Lord says:

" 'A sword, a sword,
   sharpened and polished—
¹⁰sharpened for the slaughter,
   polished to flash like lightning!

" 'Shall we rejoice in the scepter of my son ⌊Judah⌋? The sword despises every such stick.

¹¹ " 'The sword is appointed to be
     polished,
  to be grasped with the hand;
it is sharpened and polished,
  made ready for the hand of the
     slayer.
¹²Cry out and wail, son of man,
  for it is against my people;
  it is against all the princes of Israel.
They are thrown to the sword
  along with my people.
Therefore beat your breast.

The Ultimate Sword Show

READ EZEKIEL 21:1–17

Ever watch an electrical storm? Bright bolts of lightning flash across the sky at unimaginable speeds. God's judgment is like a sharp sword, and he swings it like lightning slicing through the sky. He's an awesome swordsman; think of the best samurai, then multiply his skill by a million. Too bad Israel had to see this skill first-hand. That's why God tells you to judge yourself, and get things right, so you don't need him to judge you later (see 1 Corinthians 11:31). Let the sword of God's Word judge your heart (Hebrews 4:12) and make changes in your life now. This way you're not sitting back, waiting for the real sword show. In the end, you have two choices: do your own thing, ignore the warning and feel the sting of judgment; or get busy now, sort things out and become better friends with God. If you want to watch swordplay, stick to the movies or the Olympics.

Your next reading is on page 1069.

GET DEEPER

13 " 'Testing will surely come. And what if the scepter ⌊of Judah⌋, which the sword despises, does not continue? declares the Sovereign LORD.'

14 "So then, son of man, prophesy
        and strike your hands together.
Let the sword strike twice,
        even three times.
It is a sword for slaughter—
        a sword for great slaughter,
        closing in on them from every side.
15 So that hearts may melt
        and the fallen be many,
I have stationed the sword for slaughter[a]
        at all their gates.
Oh! It is made to flash like lightning,
        it is grasped for slaughter.
16 O sword, slash to the right,
        then to the left,
        wherever your blade is turned.
17 I too will strike my hands together,
        and my wrath will subside.
I the LORD have spoken."

18 The word of the LORD came to me: 19 "Son of man, mark out two roads for the sword of the king of Babylon to take, both starting from the same country. Make a signpost where the road branches off to the city. 20 Mark out one road for the sword to come against Rabbah of the Ammonites and another against Judah and fortified Jerusalem. 21 For the king of Babylon will stop at the fork in the road, at the junction of the two roads, to seek an omen: He will cast lots with arrows, he will consult his idols, he will examine the liver. 22 Into his right hand will come the lot for Jerusalem, where he is to set up battering rams, to give the command to slaughter, to sound the battle cry, to set battering rams against the gates, to build a ramp and to erect siege works. 23 It will seem like a false omen to those who have sworn allegiance to him, but he will remind them of their guilt and take them captive.

24 "Therefore this is what the Sovereign LORD says: 'Because you people have brought to mind your guilt by your open rebellion, revealing your sins in all that you do—because you have done this, you will be taken captive.

25 " 'O profane and wicked prince of Israel, whose day has come, whose time of punishment has reached its climax, 26 this is what the Sovereign LORD says: Take off the turban, remove the crown. It will not be as it was: The lowly will be exalted and the exalted will be brought low. 27 A ruin! A ruin! I will make it a ruin! It will not be restored until he comes to whom it rightfully belongs; to him I will give it.'

28 "And you, son of man, prophesy and say, 'This is what the Sovereign LORD says about the Ammonites and their insults:

Gross!

Oh fun! The king of Babylon is holding a big, bloody, slippery sheep's liver and studying it so close that his nose is practically sticking in it (Ezekiel 21:21). Why? He's trying to figure out the future. Doesn't it make you want to hurl? Praying to God is a much better option. Highly recommend it.

---

[a] 15 Septuagint; the meaning of the Hebrew for this word is uncertain.

" 'A sword, a sword,
    drawn for the slaughter,
polished to consume
    and to flash like lightning!
29 Despite false visions concerning you
    and lying divinations about you,
it will be laid on the necks
    of the wicked who are to be slain,
whose day has come,
    whose time of punishment has
        reached its climax.
30 Return the sword to its scabbard.
    In the place where you were created,
in the land of your ancestry,
    I will judge you.
31 I will pour out my wrath upon you
    and breathe out my fiery anger
        against you;
I will hand you over to brutal men,
    men skilled in destruction.
32 You will be fuel for the fire,
    your blood will be shed in your land,
you will be remembered no more;
    for I the LORD have spoken.' "

Jerusalem's Sins

22 The word of the LORD came to me: 2 "Son of man, will you judge her? Will you judge this city of bloodshed? Then confront her with all her detestable practices 3 and say: 'This is what the Sovereign LORD says: O city that brings on herself doom by shedding blood in her midst and defiles herself by making idols, 4 you have become guilty because of the blood you have shed and have become defiled by the idols you have made. You have brought your days to a close, and the end of your years has come. Therefore I will make you an object of scorn to the nations and a laughingstock to all the countries. 5 Those who are near and those who are far away will mock you, O infamous city, full of turmoil.

6 " 'See how each of the princes of Israel who are in you uses his power to shed blood. 7 In you they have treated father and mother with contempt; in you they have oppressed the alien and mistreated the fatherless and the widow. 8 You have despised my holy things and desecrated my Sabbaths. 9 In you are slanderous men bent on shedding blood; in you are those who eat at the mountain shrines and commit lewd acts. 10 In you are those who dishonor their fathers' bed; in you are those

who violate women during their period, when they are ceremonially unclean. 11 In you one man commits a detestable offense with his neighbor's wife, another shamefully defiles his daughter-in-law, and another violates his sister, his own father's daughter. 12 In you men accept bribes to shed blood; you take usury and excessive interest[a] and make unjust gain from your neighbors by extortion. And you have forgotten me, declares the Sovereign LORD.

13 " 'I will surely strike my hands together at the unjust gain you have made and at the blood you have shed in your midst. 14 Will your courage endure or your hands be strong in the day I deal with you? I the LORD have spoken, and I will do it. 15 I will disperse you among the nations and scatter you through the countries; and I will put an end to your uncleanness. 16 When you have been defiled[b] in the eyes of the nations, you will know that I am the LORD.' "

17 Then the word of the LORD came to me: 18 "Son of man, the house of Israel has become dross to me; all of them are the copper, tin, iron and lead left inside a furnace. They are but the dross of silver. 19 Therefore this is what the Sovereign LORD says: 'Because you have all become dross, I will gather you into Jerusalem. 20 As men gather silver, copper, iron, lead and tin into a furnace to melt it with a fiery blast, so will I gather you in my anger and my wrath and put you inside the city and melt you. 21 I will gather you and I will blow on you with my fiery wrath, and you will be melted inside her. 22 As silver is melted in a furnace, so you will be melted inside her, and you will know that I the LORD have poured out my wrath upon you.' "

23 Again the word of the LORD came to me: 24 "Son of man, say to the land, 'You are a land that has had no rain or showers[c] in the day of wrath.' 25 There is a conspiracy of her princes[d] within her like a roaring lion tearing its prey; they devour people, take treasures and precious things and make many widows within her. 26 Her priests do violence to my law and profane my holy things; they do not distinguish between the holy and the common; they teach that there is no difference between the unclean and the clean; and they shut

---

[a] 12 Or usury and interest   [b] 16 Or When I have allotted you your inheritance   [c] 24 Septuagint; Hebrew has not been cleansed or rained on   [d] 25 Septuagint; Hebrew prophets

their eyes to the keeping of my Sabbaths, so that I am profaned among them. ²⁷Her officials within her are like wolves tearing their prey; they shed blood and kill people to make unjust gain. ²⁸Her prophets whitewash these deeds for them by false visions and lying divinations. They say, 'This is what the Sovereign LORD says'—when the LORD has not spoken. ²⁹The people of the land practice extortion and commit robbery; they oppress the poor and needy and mistreat the alien, denying them justice.

³⁰"I looked for a man among them who would build up the wall and stand before me in the gap on behalf of the land so I would not have to destroy it, but I found none. ³¹So I will pour out my wrath on them and consume them with my fiery anger, bringing down on their own heads all they have done, declares the Sovereign LORD."

Two Adulterous Sisters

23 The word of the LORD came to me: ²"Son of man, there were two women, daughters of the same mother. ³They became prostitutes in Egypt, engaging in prostitution from their youth. In that land their breasts were fondled and their virgin bosoms caressed. ⁴The older was named Oholah, and her sister was Oholibah. They were mine and gave birth to sons and daughters. Oholah is Samaria, and Oholibah is Jerusalem.

⁵"Oholah engaged in prostitution while she was still mine; and she lusted after her lovers, the Assyrians—warriors ⁶clothed in blue, governors and commanders, all of them handsome young men, and mounted horsemen. ⁷She gave herself as a prostitute to all the elite of the Assyrians and defiled herself with all the idols of everyone she lusted after. ⁸She did not give up the prostitution she began in Egypt, when during her youth men slept with her, caressed her virgin bosom and poured out their lust upon her.

⁹"Therefore I handed her over to her lovers, the Assyrians, for whom she lusted. ¹⁰They stripped her naked, took away her sons and daughters and killed her with the sword. She became a byword among women, and punishment was inflicted on her.

Standing Alone
READ EZEKIEL 22:30

Just like the Army, God's always looking for "a few good men." Sometimes even one will do. Before the Flood, Noah was the only one God could count on. When Sodom was about to be destroyed, Abraham was the only one praying. Elijah was the only one to stand boldly and publicly against Israel's evil king and the prophets of Baal. Standing up for what's right can be pretty lonely, but God's looking for men who stand up for him and don't look to see who's standing with them. The devil will try to tell you to "go with the flow," but in the Bible, people who did the right thing, no matter what, were the ones who made a difference. Ezekiel 22:30 shows the nation being crushed because no one would step up to the plate and lead the wayward Israelites back to God. You can be the one to make a difference in your country. It only takes an army of one. After all, you have an undefeated General on your side.

Your next reading is on page 1072.

11"Her sister Oholibah saw this, yet in her lust and prostitution she was more depraved than her sister. 12She too lusted after the Assyrians—governors and commanders, warriors in full dress, mounted horsemen, all handsome young men. 13I saw that she too defiled herself; both of them went the same way.

14"But she carried her prostitution still further. She saw men portrayed on a wall, figures of Chaldeans[a] portrayed in red, 15with belts around their waists and flowing turbans on their heads; all of them looked like Babylonian chariot officers, natives of Chaldea.[b] 16As soon as she saw them, she lusted after them and sent messengers to them in Chaldea. 17Then the Babylonians came to her, to the bed of love, and in their lust they defiled her. After she had been defiled by them, she turned away from them in disgust. 18When she carried on her prostitution openly and exposed her nakedness, I turned away from her in disgust, just as I had turned away from her sister. 19Yet she became more and more promiscuous as she recalled the days of her youth, when she was a prostitute in Egypt. 20There she lusted after her lovers, whose genitals were like those of donkeys and whose emission was like that of horses. 21So you longed for the lewdness of your youth, when in Egypt your bosom was caressed and your young breasts fondled.[c]

22"Therefore, Oholibah, this is what the Sovereign LORD says: I will stir up your lovers against you, those you turned away from in disgust, and I will bring them against you from every side— 23the Babylonians and all the Chaldeans, the men of Pekod and Shoa and Koa, and all the Assyrians with them, handsome young men, all of them governors and commanders, chariot officers and men of high rank, all mounted on horses. 24They will come against you with weapons,[d] chariots and wagons and with a throng of people; they will take up positions against you on every side with large and small shields and with helmets. I will turn you over to them for punishment, and they will punish you according to their standards. 25I will direct my jealous anger against you, and they will deal with you in fury. They will cut off your noses and your ears, and those of you who are left will fall by the sword. They will take away your

sons and daughters, and those of you who are left will be consumed by fire. 26They will also strip you of your clothes and take your fine jewelry. 27So I will put a stop to the lewdness and prostitution you began in Egypt. You will not look on these things with longing or remember Egypt anymore.

28"For this is what the Sovereign LORD says: I am about to hand you over to those you hate, to those you turned away from in disgust. 29They will deal with you in hatred and take away everything you have worked for. They will leave you naked and bare, and the shame of your prostitution will be exposed. Your lewdness and promiscuity 30have brought this upon you, because you lusted after the nations and defiled yourself with their idols. 31You have gone the way of your sister; so I will put her cup into your hand.

32"This is what the Sovereign LORD says:

"You will drink your sister's cup,
    a cup large and deep;
it will bring scorn and derision,
    for it holds so much.
33 You will be filled with drunkenness and
        sorrow,
    the cup of ruin and desolation,
    the cup of your sister Samaria.
34 You will drink it and drain it dry;
    you will dash it to pieces
    and tear your breasts.

I have spoken, declares the Sovereign LORD.

35"Therefore this is what the Sovereign LORD says: Since you have forgotten me and thrust me behind your back, you must bear the consequences of your lewdness and prostitution."

36The LORD said to me: "Son of man, will you judge Oholah and Oholibah? Then confront them with their detestable practices, 37for they have committed adultery and blood is on their hands. They committed adultery with their idols; they even sacrificed their children, whom they bore to me,[e] as food for them. 38They have also done this to me: At that same time they defiled my sanctuary and desecrated my Sabbaths. 39On the very day they sacrificed

---

[a] 14 Or Babylonians   [b] 15 Or Babylonia; also in verse 16
[c] 21 Syriac (see also verse 3); Hebrew caressed because of your young breasts   [d] 24 The meaning of the Hebrew for this word is uncertain.   [e] 37 Or even made the children they bore to me pass through the fire.

their children to their idols, they entered my sanctuary and desecrated it. That is what they did in my house.

40 "They even sent messengers for men who came from far away, and when they arrived you bathed yourself for them, painted your eyes and put on your jewelry. 41 You sat on an elegant couch, with a table spread before it on which you had placed the incense and oil that belonged to me.

42 "The noise of a carefree crowd was around her; Sabeans*a* were brought from the desert along with men from the rabble, and they put bracelets on the arms of the woman and her sister and beautiful crowns on their heads. 43 Then I said about the one worn out by adultery, 'Now let them use her as a prostitute, for that is all she is.' 44 And they slept with her. As men sleep with a prostitute, so they slept with those lewd women, Oholah and Oholibah. 45 But righteous men will sentence them to the punishment of women who commit adultery and shed blood, because they are adulterous and blood is on their hands.

46 "This is what the Sovereign LORD says: Bring a mob against them and give them over to terror and plunder. 47 The mob will stone them and cut them down with their swords; they will kill their sons and daughters and burn down their houses.

48 "So I will put an end to lewdness in the land, that all women may take warning and not imitate you. 49 You will suffer the penalty for your lewdness and bear the consequences of your sins of idolatry. Then you will know that I am the Sovereign LORD."

The Cooking Pot

24 In the ninth year, in the tenth month on the tenth day, the word of the LORD came to me: 2 "Son of man, record this date, this very date, because the king of Babylon has laid siege to Jerusalem this very day. 3 Tell this rebellious house a parable and say to them: 'This is what the Sovereign LORD says:

" 'Put on the cooking pot; put it on
    and pour water into it.
4 Put into it the pieces of meat,
    all the choice pieces—the leg and
        the shoulder.

Fill it with the best of these bones;
5   take the pick of the flock.
Pile wood beneath it for the bones;
    bring it to a boil
    and cook the bones in it.

6 " 'For this is what the Sovereign LORD says:

" 'Woe to the city of bloodshed,
    to the pot now encrusted,
    whose deposit will not go away!
Empty it piece by piece
    without casting lots for them.

7 " 'For the blood she shed is in her
        midst:
    She poured it on the bare rock;
    she did not pour it on the ground,
    where the dust would cover it.
8 To stir up wrath and take revenge
    I put her blood on the bare rock,
    so that it would not be covered.

9 " 'Therefore this is what the Sovereign LORD says:

" 'Woe to the city of bloodshed!
    I, too, will pile the wood high.
10 So heap on the wood
    and kindle the fire.
Cook the meat well,
    mixing in the spices;
    and let the bones be charred.
11 Then set the empty pot on the coals
    till it becomes hot and its copper
        glows
so its impurities may be melted
    and its deposit burned away.
12 It has frustrated all efforts;
    its heavy deposit has not been
        removed,
    not even by fire.

13 " 'Now your impurity is lewdness. Because I tried to cleanse you but you would not be cleansed from your impurity, you will not be clean again until my wrath against you has subsided.

14 " 'I the LORD have spoken. The time has come for me to act. I will not hold back; I will not have pity, nor will I relent. You will be judged according to your conduct and your actions, declares the Sovereign LORD.' "

Ezekiel's Wife Dies

15 The word of the LORD came to me:

a 42 Or drunkards

16"Son of man, with one blow I am about to take away from you the delight of your eyes. Yet do not lament or weep or shed any tears. 17Groan quietly; do not mourn for the dead. Keep your turban fastened and your sandals on your feet; do not cover the lower part of your face or eat the customary food ⌊of mourners⌋."

18So I spoke to the people in the morning, and in the evening my wife died. The next morning I did as I had been commanded.

19Then the people asked me, "Won't you tell us what these things have to do with us?"

20So I said to them, "The word of the LORD came to me: 21Say to the house of Israel, 'This is what the Sovereign LORD says: I am about to desecrate my sanctuary— the stronghold in which you take pride, the delight of your eyes, the object of your affection. The sons and daughters you left behind will fall by the sword. 22And you

will do as I have done. You will not cover the lower part of your face or eat the customary food ⌊of mourners⌋. 23You will keep your turbans on your heads and your sandals on your feet. You will not mourn or weep but will waste away because of[a] your sins and groan among yourselves. 24Ezekiel will be a sign to you; you will do just as he has done. When this happens, you will know that I am the Sovereign LORD.'

25"And you, son of man, on the day I take away their stronghold, their joy and glory, the delight of their eyes, their heart's desire, and their sons and daughters as well— 26on that day a fugitive will come to tell you the news. 27At that time your mouth will be opened; you will speak with him and will no longer be silent. So you will be a sign to them, and they will know that I am the LORD."

[a] 23 Or *away in*

Personality Types

READ EZEKIEL 24:1

Look at that date in verse 1. Ezekiel was totally organized and constantly gave exact dates for his revelations. Jeremiah ... well, *he* was another matter. He barely dated anything. In fact, most of his book is *totally* out of order. Why? Jeremiah's personality was different than Ezekiel's. He was far more emotional. Yet God loved both men and they were both prophets. God created each of us and loves us, too. We're all different, yes, but God has created four major personality types. First of all, there are Lions—born leaders who always have the goal in mind. Then there are practical, organized Beavers who always do things "the right way." Golden Retrievers are people persons—emotional and concerned about others. Otters are fun-loving individuals. We weren't there and we don't know for sure, but a good guess is that Ezekiel was a Beaver. Jeremiah, yeah, he was a Golden Retriever. Isaiah was a Lion and Daniel was an Otter. If you're going to understand others and work together with them, it helps to realize what "animal" they are. And hey! What are *you*?

Your next reading is on page 1074.

GET COOLER

A Prophecy Against Ammon

25 The word of the LORD came to me: 2"Son of man, set your face against the Ammonites and prophesy against them. 3Say to them, 'Hear the word of the Sovereign LORD. This is what the Sovereign LORD says: Because you said "Aha!" over my sanctuary when it was desecrated and over the land of Israel when it was laid waste and over the people of Judah when they went into exile, 4therefore I am going to give you to the people of the East as a possession. They will set up their camps and pitch their tents among you; they will eat your fruit and drink your milk. 5I will turn Rabbah into a pasture for camels and Ammon into a resting place for sheep. Then you will know that I am the LORD. 6For this is what the Sovereign LORD says: Because you have clapped your hands and stamped your feet, rejoicing with all the malice of your heart against the land of Israel, 7therefore I will stretch out my hand against you and give you as plunder to the nations. I will cut you off from the nations and exterminate you from the countries. I will destroy you, and you will know that I am the LORD.' "

A Prophecy Against Moab

8"This is what the Sovereign LORD says: 'Because Moab and Seir said, "Look, the house of Judah has become like all the other nations," 9therefore I will expose the flank of Moab, beginning at its frontier towns—Beth Jeshimoth, Baal Meon and Kiriathaim—the glory of that land. 10I will give Moab along with the Ammonites to the people of the East as a possession, so that the Ammonites will not be remembered among the nations; 11and I will inflict punishment on Moab. Then they will know that I am the LORD.' "

A Prophecy Against Edom

12"This is what the Sovereign LORD says: 'Because Edom took revenge on the house of Judah and became very guilty by doing so, 13therefore this is what the Sovereign LORD says: I will stretch out my hand against Edom and kill its men and their animals. I will lay it waste, and from Teman to Dedan they will fall by the sword. 14I will take vengeance on Edom by the hand of my people Israel, and they will deal with Edom in accordance with my anger and my wrath; they will know my vengeance, declares the Sovereign LORD.' "

A Prophecy Against Philistia

15"This is what the Sovereign LORD says: 'Because the Philistines acted in vengeance and took revenge with malice in their hearts, and with ancient hostility sought to destroy Judah, 16therefore this is what the Sovereign LORD says: I am about to stretch out my hand against the Philistines, and I will cut off the Kerethites and destroy those remaining along the coast. 17I will carry out great vengeance on them and punish them in my wrath. Then they will know that I am the LORD, when I take vengeance on them.' "

A Prophecy Against Tyre

26 In the eleventh year, on the first day of the month, the word of the LORD came to me: 2"Son of man, because Tyre has said of Jerusalem, 'Aha! The gate to the nations is broken, and its doors have swung open to me; now that she lies in ruins I will prosper,' 3therefore this is what the Sovereign LORD says: I am against you, O Tyre, and I will bring many nations against you, like the sea casting up its waves. 4They will destroy the walls of Tyre and pull down her towers; I will scrape away her rubble and make her a bare rock. 5Out in the sea she will become a place to spread fishnets, for I have spoken, declares the Sovereign LORD. She will become plunder for the nations, 6and her settlements on the mainland will be ravaged by the sword. Then they will know that I am the LORD.

7"For this is what the Sovereign LORD says: From the north I am going to bring against Tyre Nebuchadnezzar[a] king of Babylon, king of kings, with horses and chariots, with horsemen and a great army. 8He will ravage your settlements on the mainland with the sword; he will set up siege works against you, build a ramp up to your walls and raise his shields against you. 9He will direct the blows of his battering rams against your walls and demolish your towers with his weapons. 10His horses will be so many that they will cover you with dust. Your walls will tremble

---

a 7 Hebrew *Nebuchadrezzar*, of which *Nebuchadnezzar* is a variant; here and often in Ezekiel and Jeremiah at the noise of the war horses, wagons and chariots when he enters your gates as men enter a city whose walls have been broken through. ¹¹The hoofs of his horses will trample all your streets; he will kill your people with the sword, and your strong pillars will fall to the ground. ¹²They will plunder your wealth and loot your merchandise; they will break down your walls and demolish your fine houses and throw your stones, timber and rubble into the sea. ¹³I will put an end to your noisy songs, and the music of your harps will be heard no more. ¹⁴I will make you a bare rock, and you will become a place to spread fishnets. You will never be rebuilt, for I the Lord have spoken, declares the Sovereign Lord.

¹⁵"This is what the Sovereign Lord says to Tyre: Will not the coastlands tremble at the sound of your fall, when the wounded groan and the slaughter takes place in you? ¹⁶Then all the princes of the coast will step down from their thrones and lay aside their robes and take off their embroidered garments. Clothed with terror, they will sit on the ground, trembling every moment, appalled at you. ¹⁷Then they will take up a lament concerning you and say to you:

" 'How you are destroyed, O city of
        renown,
    peopled by men of the sea!
You were a power on the seas,
    you and your citizens;
you put your terror
    on all who lived there.
¹⁸Now the coastlands tremble
    on the day of your fall;
the islands in the sea
    are terrified at your collapse.'

¹⁹This is what the Sovereign Lord says: When I make you a desolate city, like cities no longer inhabited, and when I bring the ocean depths over you and its vast waters cover you, ²⁰then I will bring you down with those who go down to the pit, to the

A Flat Tyre

READ EZEKIEL 26:1–14

Tyre was a rich city in Ezekiel's day, and its people laughed out loud when Jerusalem fell. Part of the city was built on the coast of the Mediterranean Sea and part of it was built on two rocky islands about half a mile from the shore. God said, "I am going to bring against Tyre Nebuchadnezzar king of Babylon ... He will ravage your settlements on the mainland" (verses 7–8). Right after Ezekiel prophesied this judgment, Nebuchadnezzar laid siege to the coastal city. It took 15 years, but the city was eventually sacked and destroyed. Nebuchadnezzar didn't conquer the island city, but about 250 years later along came Alexander the Great. God had said that an army would "throw your stones, timber and rubble into the sea" (verse 12). Alexander's army chucked the ruins of the old mainland city into the water, created a bridge out to the island (smart idea!), besieged it and plundered its wealth. To this day, fishermen spread their nets out on the bridge, just like God said they would (verse 14). Cool!

Your next reading is on page 1077.

people of long ago. I will make you dwell in the earth below, as in ancient ruins, with those who go down to the pit, and you will not return or take your place[a] in the land of the living. 21I will bring you to a horrible end and you will be no more. You will be sought, but you will never again be found, declares the Sovereign LORD."

A Lament for Tyre

27 The word of the LORD came to me: 2"Son of man, take up a lament concerning Tyre. 3Say to Tyre, situated at the gateway to the sea, merchant of peoples on many coasts, 'This is what the Sovereign LORD says:

" 'You say, O Tyre,
  "I am perfect in beauty."
4Your domain was on the high seas;
  your builders brought your beauty to perfection.
5They made all your timbers
  of pine trees from Senir[b];
they took a cedar from Lebanon
  to make a mast for you.
6Of oaks from Bashan
  they made your oars;
of cypress wood[c] from the coasts of Cyprus[d]
  they made your deck, inlaid with ivory.
7Fine embroidered linen from Egypt was your sail
  and served as your banner;
your awnings were of blue and purple
  from the coasts of Elishah.
8Men of Sidon and Arvad were your oarsmen;
  your skilled men, O Tyre, were aboard as your
    seamen.
9Veteran craftsmen of Gebal[e] were on board
  as shipwrights to caulk your seams.
All the ships of the sea and their sailors
  came alongside to trade for your wares.

10" 'Men of Persia, Lydia and Put
  served as soldiers in your army.
They hung their shields and helmets on your walls,
  bringing you splendor.
11Men of Arvad and Helech
  manned your walls on every side;
men of Gammad
  were in your towers.
They hung their shields around your walls;
  they brought your beauty to perfection.

12" 'Tarshish did business with you because of your great wealth of goods; they exchanged silver, iron, tin and lead for your merchandise.
13" 'Greece, Tubal and Meshech traded with you; they exchanged slaves and articles of bronze for your wares.
14" 'Men of Beth Togarmah exchanged work horses,

Get a Load of This...

Check out Ezekiel 27. Even thousands of years ago, nations all around the Mediterranean Sea were getting rich trading their products. All kinds of amazing treasure have been found in an ancient shipwreck off the coast of Turkey. (See *The National Geographic*, December 1987.)

---

a 20 Septuagint; Hebrew *return, and I will give glory*   b 5 That is, Hermon
c 6 Targum; the Masoretic Text has a different division of the consonants.
d 6 Hebrew *Kittim*   e 9 That is, Byblos

war horses and mules for your merchandise.

15 " 'The men of Rhodes[a] traded with you, and many coastlands were your customers; they paid you with ivory tusks and ebony.

16 " 'Aram[b] did business with you because of your many products; they exchanged turquoise, purple fabric, embroidered work, fine linen, coral and rubies for your merchandise.

17 " 'Judah and Israel traded with you; they exchanged wheat from Minnith and confections,[c] honey, oil and balm for your wares.

18 " 'Damascus, because of your many products and great wealth of goods, did business with you in wine from Helbon and wool from Zahar.

19 " 'Danites and Greeks from Uzal bought your merchandise; they exchanged wrought iron, cassia and calamus for your wares.

20 " 'Dedan traded in saddle blankets with you.

21 " 'Arabia and all the princes of Kedar were your customers; they did business with you in lambs, rams and goats.

22 " 'The merchants of Sheba and Raamah traded with you; for your merchandise they exchanged the finest of all kinds of spices and precious stones, and gold.

23 " 'Haran, Canneh and Eden and merchants of Sheba, Asshur and Kilmad traded with you. 24 In your marketplace they traded with you beautiful garments, blue fabric, embroidered work and multicolored rugs with cords twisted and tightly knotted.

25 " 'The ships of Tarshish serve
    as carriers for your wares.
You are filled with heavy cargo
    in the heart of the sea.
26 Your oarsmen take you
    out to the high seas.
But the east wind will break you to
        pieces
    in the heart of the sea.
27 Your wealth, merchandise and wares,
    your mariners, seamen and
        shipwrights,
your merchants and all your soldiers,
    and everyone else on board
will sink into the heart of the sea
    on the day of your shipwreck.
28 The shorelands will quake

when your seamen cry out.
29 All who handle the oars
    will abandon their ships;
the mariners and all the seamen
    will stand on the shore.
30 They will raise their voice
    and cry bitterly over you;
they will sprinkle dust on their heads
    and roll in ashes.
31 They will shave their heads because of
        you
    and will put on sackcloth.
They will weep over you with anguish
        of soul
    and with bitter mourning.
32 As they wail and mourn over you,
    they will take up a lament
        concerning you:
"Who was ever silenced like Tyre,
    surrounded by the sea?"
33 When your merchandise went out on
        the seas,
    you satisfied many nations;
with your great wealth and your wares
    you enriched the kings of the earth.
34 Now you are shattered by the sea
    in the depths of the waters;
your wares and all your company
    have gone down with you.
35 All who live in the coastlands
    are appalled at you;
their kings shudder with horror
    and their faces are distorted with fear.
36 The merchants among the nations hiss
        at you;
    you have come to a horrible end
    and will be no more.' "

A Prophecy Against the King of Tyre

28 The word of the LORD came to me: 2 "Son of man, say to the ruler of Tyre, 'This is what the Sovereign LORD says:

" 'In the pride of your heart
    you say, "I am a god;
I sit on the throne of a god
    in the heart of the seas."
But you are a man and not a god,
    though you think you are as wise as
        a god.
3 Are you wiser than Daniel[d]?
    Is no secret hidden from you?

---

a 15 Septuagint; Hebrew Dedan   b 16 Most Hebrew
manuscripts; some Hebrew manuscripts and Syriac Edom
c 17 The meaning of the Hebrew for this word is uncertain.
d 3 Or Danel; the Hebrew spelling may suggest a person
other than the prophet Daniel.

4 By your wisdom and understanding
   you have gained wealth for yourself
and amassed gold and silver
   in your treasuries.
5 By your great skill in trading
   you have increased your wealth,
and because of your wealth
   your heart has grown proud.

6 " 'Therefore this is what the Sovereign
LORD says:

" 'Because you think you are wise,
   as wise as a god,
7 I am going to bring foreigners against
      you,
   the most ruthless of nations;
they will draw their swords against
      your beauty and wisdom
   and pierce your shining splendor.
8 They will bring you down to the pit,
   and you will die a violent death
   in the heart of the seas.
9 Will you then say, "I am a god,"
   in the presence of those who kill
      you?
You will be but a man, not a god,

in the hands of those who slay you.
10 You will die the death of the
      uncircumcised
   at the hands of foreigners.

I have spoken, declares the Sovereign
LORD.' "

11 The word of the LORD came to me:
12 "Son of man, take up a lament concerning the king of Tyre and say to him: 'This is
what the Sovereign LORD says:

" 'You were the model of perfection,
   full of wisdom and perfect in beauty.
13 You were in Eden,
   the garden of God;
every precious stone adorned you:
   ruby, topaz and emerald,
   chrysolite, onyx and jasper,
   sapphire,[a] turquoise and beryl.[b]
Your settings and mountings[c] were
      made of gold;
   on the day you were created they
      were prepared.

[a] 13 Or lapis lazuli   [b] 13 The precise identification of some
of these precious stones is uncertain.   [c] 13 The meaning of
the Hebrew for this phrase is uncertain.

GET SMARTER

Satan's Fall

READ EZEKIEL 28:1–2, 11–17

Being proud can get you into a *lot* of trouble. In these verses, Ezekiel
was referring to the king of Tyre, but when you look deeper, it might
be describing Satan as well. Satan once hung out with God, but rebelled in pride and had to be thrown out of heaven. Satan was wise,
rich and very good-looking. The problem was that he fell in
love with what he saw in the mirror. Pride sets you up for a
big fall (Isaiah 2:11). Satan thought he could do things his
way and things would turn out better than God's way of
doing things, so God had to let Satan see how wrong he
really was. Satan was "cut from the team" even though he
was one of God's captains. Someday Satan will
come to "a horrible end" and the nations of the
world will be "appalled" at him (verse 19).

Your next reading is on page 1080.

¹⁴You were anointed as a guardian
　　cherub,
　　for so I ordained you.
You were on the holy mount of God;
　　you walked among the fiery stones.
¹⁵You were blameless in your ways
　　from the day you were created
　　till wickedness was found in you.
¹⁶Through your widespread trade
　　you were filled with violence,
　　and you sinned.
So I drove you in disgrace from the
　　mount of God,
　　and I expelled you, O guardian
　　cherub,
　　from among the fiery stones.
¹⁷Your heart became proud
　　on account of your beauty,
　　and you corrupted your wisdom
　　because of your splendor.
So I threw you to the earth;
　　I made a spectacle of you before
　　kings.
¹⁸By your many sins and dishonest trade
　　you have desecrated your sanctuaries.
So I made a fire come out from you,
　　and it consumed you,
　　and I reduced you to ashes on the
　　ground
　　in the sight of all who were watching.
¹⁹All the nations who knew you
　　are appalled at you;
　　you have come to a horrible end
　　and will be no more.' "

A Prophecy Against Sidon

²⁰The word of the LORD came to me:
²¹"Son of man, set your face against Sidon; prophesy against her ²²and say: 'This
is what the Sovereign LORD says:

" 'I am against you, O Sidon,
　　and I will gain glory within you.
They will know that I am the LORD,
　　when I inflict punishment on her
　　and show myself holy within her.
²³I will send a plague upon her
　　and make blood flow in her streets.
The slain will fall within her,
　　with the sword against her on every
　　side.
Then they will know that I am the LORD.

²⁴" 'No longer will the people of Israel
have malicious neighbors who are painful
briers and sharp thorns. Then they will
know that I am the Sovereign LORD.
²⁵" 'This is what the Sovereign LORD

says: When I gather the people of Israel
from the nations where they have been
scattered, I will show myself holy among
them in the sight of the nations. Then
they will live in their own land, which I
gave to my servant Jacob. ²⁶They will live
there in safety and will build houses and
plant vineyards; they will live in safety
when I inflict punishment on all their
neighbors who maligned them. Then they
will know that I am the LORD their God.' "

A Prophecy Against Egypt

29 In the tenth year, in the tenth
month on the twelfth day, the
word of the LORD came to me:
²"Son of man, set your face
against Pharaoh king of Egypt and prophesy against him and against all Egypt.
³Speak to him and say: 'This is what the
Sovereign LORD says:

" 'I am against you, Pharaoh king of
　　Egypt,
　　you great monster lying among your
　　streams.
You say, "The Nile is mine;
　　I made it for myself."
⁴But I will put hooks in your jaws
　　and make the fish of your streams
　　stick to your scales.
I will pull you out from among your
　　streams,
　　with all the fish sticking to your scales.
⁵I will leave you in the desert,
　　you and all the fish of your streams.
You will fall on the open field
　　and not be gathered or picked up.
I will give you as food
　　to the beasts of the earth and the
　　birds of the air.

⁶Then all who live in Egypt will know that
I am the LORD.

" 'You have been a staff of reed for the
house of Israel. ⁷When they grasped you
with their hands, you splintered and you
tore open their shoulders; when they
leaned on you, you broke and their backs
were wrenched.ᵃ

⁸" 'Therefore this is what the Sovereign
LORD says: I will bring a sword against you
and kill your men and their animals.
⁹Egypt will become a desolate wasteland.
Then they will know that I am the LORD.

ᵃ 7 Syriac (see also Septuagint and Vulgate); Hebrew *and you
caused their backs to stand*

" 'Because you said, "The Nile is mine; I made it," ¹⁰therefore I am against you and against your streams, and I will make the land of Egypt a ruin and a desolate waste from Migdol to Aswan, as far as the border of Cush.ᵃ ¹¹No foot of man or animal will pass through it; no one will live there for forty years. ¹²I will make the land of Egypt desolate among devastated lands, and her cities will lie desolate forty years among ruined cities. And I will disperse the Egyptians among the nations and scatter them through the countries.

¹³" 'Yet this is what the Sovereign LORD says: At the end of forty years I will gather the Egyptians from the nations where they were scattered. ¹⁴I will bring them back from captivity and return them to Upper Egypt,ᵇ the land of their ancestry. There they will be a lowly kingdom. ¹⁵It will be the lowliest of kingdoms and will never again exalt itself above the other nations. I will make it so weak that it will never again rule over the nations. ¹⁶Egypt will no longer be a source of confidence for the people of Israel but will be a reminder of their sin in turning to her for help. Then they will know that I am the Sovereign LORD.' "

¹⁷In the twenty-seventh year, in the first month on the first day, the word of the LORD came to me: ¹⁸"Son of man, Nebuchadnezzar king of Babylon drove his army in a hard campaign against Tyre; every head was rubbed bare and every shoulder made raw. Yet he and his army got no reward from the campaign he led against Tyre. ¹⁹Therefore this is what the Sovereign LORD says: I am going to give Egypt to Nebuchadnezzar king of Babylon, and he will carry off its wealth. He will loot and plunder the land as pay for his army. ²⁰I have given him Egypt as a reward for his efforts because he and his army did it for me, declares the Sovereign LORD.

²¹"On that day I will make a hornᶜ grow for the house of Israel, and I will open your mouth among them. Then they will know that I am the LORD."

A Lament for Egypt

30 The word of the LORD came to me: ²"Son of man, prophesy and say: 'This is what the Sovereign LORD says:

" 'Wail and say,
    "Alas for that day!"
³ For the day is near,
    the day of the LORD is near—
a day of clouds,
    a time of doom for the nations.
⁴ A sword will come against Egypt,
    and anguish will come upon Cush.ᵈ
When the slain fall in Egypt,
    her wealth will be carried away
    and her foundations torn down.

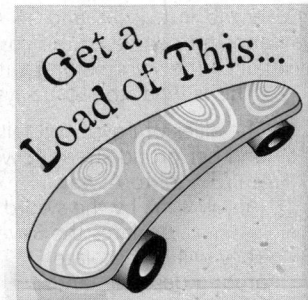

Get a Load of This...

Check out Ezekiel 29:3–5. Can you imagine pulling *this* critter over the side of your boat? God said he'd go fishing in the Nile River and reel in a monster (Pharaoh), then dump him in the desert. This was a cool way of saying he would judge Egypt.

ᵃ 10 That is, the upper Nile region   ᵇ 14 Hebrew to Pathros   ᶜ 21 Horn here symbolizes strength.   ᵈ 4 That is, the upper Nile region; also in verses 5 and 9

⁵Cush and Put, Lydia and all Arabia, Libya[a] and the people of the covenant land will fall by the sword along with Egypt.

⁶ 'This is what the LORD says:

" 'The allies of Egypt will fall
    and her proud strength will fail.
From Migdol to Aswan
    they will fall by the sword within her,
            declares the Sovereign LORD.

⁷ " 'They will be desolate
    among desolate lands,
and their cities will lie
    among ruined cities.

⁸Then they will know that I am the LORD,
    when I set fire to Egypt
    and all her helpers are crushed.

⁹ " 'On that day messengers will go out from me in ships to frighten Cush out of her complacency. Anguish will take hold of them on the day of Egypt's doom, for it is sure to come.

¹⁰" 'This is what the Sovereign LORD says:

" 'I will put an end to the hordes of Egypt
    by the hand of Nebuchadnezzar
        king of Babylon.

¹¹He and his army—the most ruthless of nations—
    will be brought in to destroy the land.
They will draw their swords against Egypt
    and fill the land with the slain.

¹²I will dry up the streams of the Nile
    and sell the land to evil men;
by the hand of foreigners
    I will lay waste the land and
        everything in it.

I the LORD have spoken.

¹³ 'This is what the Sovereign LORD says:

" 'I will destroy the idols
    and put an end to the images in Memphis.[b]

ᵃ 5 Hebrew *Cub*   ᵇ 13 Hebrew *Noph*; also in verse 16

Flexing God's Muscles

READ EZEKIEL 30:6–12

Just like that huge linebacker on your football team, Egypt was stronger than anyone else around. But physical strength doesn't last forever. There's always someone stronger waiting for the chance to outdo today's champ. In this case, the challenger was Babylon. For a long time, Egypt had a really tough army that couldn't be beaten. But, like hot sports cars that eventually get rusty and fall apart, armies can lose their shine, too. *You'll* fall apart if you try to get by on your own strength. You need to let God flex his muscles *for* you. The way you build physical muscles is by working out, playing sports (and by eating your broccoli). It's tough at first, but you get results by sticking with it. It's the same with your spiritual strength: Trusting God is like working out your soul. Unlike the muscles you can see, spiritual biceps last forever.

Your next reading is on page 1084.

No longer will there be a prince in
  Egypt,
  and I will spread fear throughout
    the land.
¹⁴I will lay waste Upper Egypt, *a*
  set fire to Zoan
  and inflict punishment on Thebes. *b*
¹⁵I will pour out my wrath on Pelusium, *c*
  the stronghold of Egypt,
  and cut off the hordes of Thebes.
¹⁶I will set fire to Egypt;
  Pelusium will writhe in agony.
  Thebes will be taken by storm;
    Memphis will be in constant distress.
¹⁷The young men of Heliopolis *d* and
    Bubastis *e*
  will fall by the sword,
  and the cities themselves will go into
    captivity.
¹⁸Dark will be the day at Tahpanhes
  when I break the yoke of Egypt;
  there her proud strength will come
    to an end.
  She will be covered with clouds,
  and her villages will go into captivity.
¹⁹So I will inflict punishment on Egypt,
  and they will know that I am the
    LORD.' "

²⁰In the eleventh year, in the first month
on the seventh day, the word of the LORD
came to me: ²¹"Son of man, I have broken
the arm of Pharaoh king of Egypt. It has
not been bound up for healing or put in a
splint so as to become strong enough to
hold a sword. ²²Therefore this is what the
Sovereign LORD says: I am against Pharaoh
king of Egypt. I will break both his arms,
the good arm as well as the broken one,
and make the sword fall from his hand.
²³I will disperse the Egyptians among the
nations and scatter them through the
countries. ²⁴I will strengthen the arms of
the king of Babylon and put my sword in
his hand, but I will break the arms of Pharaoh, and he will groan before him like a
mortally wounded man. ²⁵I will strength-
en the arms of the king of Babylon, but
the arms of Pharaoh will fall limp. Then
they will know that I am the LORD, when I
put my sword into the hand of the king of
Babylon and he brandishes it against
Egypt. ²⁶I will disperse the Egyptians
among the nations and scatter them
through the countries. Then they will
know that I am the LORD."

A Cedar in Lebanon

31 In the eleventh year, in the third
month on the first day, the word
of the LORD came to me: ²"Son of
man, say to Pharaoh king of
Egypt and to his hordes:

" 'Who can be compared with you in
  majesty?
³Consider Assyria, once a cedar in
    Lebanon,
  with beautiful branches
    overshadowing the forest;
  it towered on high,
  its top above the thick foliage.
⁴The waters nourished it,
  deep springs made it grow tall;
  their streams flowed
    all around its base
  and sent their channels
    to all the trees of the field.
⁵So it towered higher
  than all the trees of the field;
  its boughs increased
  and its branches grew long,
  spreading because of abundant
    waters.
⁶All the birds of the air
  nested in its boughs,
  all the beasts of the field
  gave birth under its branches;
  all the great nations
  lived in its shade.
⁷It was majestic in beauty,
  with its spreading boughs,
  for its roots went down
  to abundant waters.
⁸The cedars in the garden of God
  could not rival it,
  nor could the pine trees
  equal its boughs,
  nor could the plane trees
  compare with its branches—
  no tree in the garden of God
  could match its beauty.
⁹I made it beautiful
  with abundant branches,
  the envy of all the trees of Eden
  in the garden of God.

¹⁰" 'Therefore this is what the Sovereign LORD says: Because it towered on
high, lifting its top above the thick foliage,
and because it was proud of its height, ¹¹I

---

a 14 Hebrew *waste Pathros*   *b 14* Hebrew *No*; also in
verses 15 and 16   *c 15* Hebrew *Sin*; also in verse 16
d 17 Hebrew *Awen* (or *On*)   *e 17* Hebrew *Pi Beseth*

handed it over to the ruler of the nations, for him to deal with according to its wickedness. I cast it aside, ¹²and the most ruthless of foreign nations cut it down and left it. Its boughs fell on the mountains and in all the valleys; its branches lay broken in all the ravines of the land. All the nations of the earth came out from under its shade and left it. ¹³All the birds of the air settled on the fallen tree, and all the beasts of the field were among its branches. ¹⁴Therefore no other trees by the waters are ever to tower proudly on high, lifting their tops above the thick foliage. No other trees so well-watered are ever to reach such a height; they are all destined for death, for the earth below, among mortal men, with those who go down to the pit.

¹⁵" 'This is what the Sovereign Lord says: On the day it was brought down to the grave*a* I covered the deep springs with mourning for it; I held back its streams, and its abundant waters were restrained. Because of it I clothed Lebanon with gloom, and all the trees of the field withered away. ¹⁶I made the nations tremble at the sound of its fall when I brought it down to the grave with those who go down to the pit. Then all the trees of Eden, the choicest and best of Lebanon, all the trees that were well-watered, were consoled in the earth below. ¹⁷Those who lived in its shade, its allies among the nations, had also gone down to the grave with it, joining those killed by the sword.

¹⁸" 'Which of the trees of Eden can be compared with you in splendor and majesty? Yet you, too, will be brought down with the trees of Eden to the earth below; you will lie among the uncircumcised, with those killed by the sword.

" 'This is Pharaoh and all his hordes, declares the Sovereign Lord.' "

A Lament for Pharaoh

32 In the twelfth year, in the twelfth month on the first day, the word of the Lord came to me: ²"Son of man, take up a lament concerning Pharaoh king of Egypt and say to him:

" 'You are like a lion among the
    nations;
you are like a monster in the seas
    thrashing about in your streams,

churning the water with your feet
    and muddying the streams.

³" 'This is what the Sovereign Lord says:

" 'With a great throng of people
    I will cast my net over you,
    and they will haul you up in my net.
⁴I will throw you on the land
    and hurl you on the open field.
I will let all the birds of the air settle on
    you
    and all the beasts of the earth gorge
      themselves on you.
⁵I will spread your flesh on the mountains
    and fill the valleys with your remains.
⁶I will drench the land with your
      flowing blood
    all the way to the mountains,
    and the ravines will be filled with
      your flesh.
⁷When I snuff you out, I will cover the
      heavens
    and darken their stars;
I will cover the sun with a cloud,
    and the moon will not give its light.
⁸All the shining lights in the heavens
    I will darken over you;
    I will bring darkness over your land,
      declares the Sovereign Lord.
⁹I will trouble the hearts of many peoples
    when I bring about your destruction
      among the nations,
    among*b* lands you have not known.
¹⁰I will cause many peoples to be
      appalled at you,
    and their kings will shudder with
      horror because of you
    when I brandish my sword before
      them.
On the day of your downfall
    each of them will tremble
    every moment for his life.

¹¹" 'For this is what the Sovereign Lord says:

" 'The sword of the king of Babylon
    will come against you.
¹²I will cause your hordes to fall
    by the swords of mighty men—
    the most ruthless of all nations.
They will shatter the pride of Egypt,
    and all her hordes will be
      overthrown.
¹³I will destroy all her cattle

---

a 15 Hebrew *Sheol*; also in verses 16 and 17   *b 9* Hebrew; Septuagint *bring you into captivity among the nations, / to*

from beside abundant waters
no longer to be stirred by the foot of
    man
    or muddied by the hoofs of cattle.
¹⁴Then I will let her waters settle
    and make her streams flow like oil,
            declares the Sovereign LORD.
¹⁵When I make Egypt desolate
    and strip the land of everything in it,
when I strike down all who live there,
    then they will know that I am the
    LORD.'

¹⁶"This is the lament they will chant for her. The daughters of the nations will chant it; for Egypt and all her hordes they will chant it, declares the Sovereign LORD."

¹⁷In the twelfth year, on the fifteenth day of the month, the word of the LORD came to me: ¹⁸"Son of man, wail for the hordes of Egypt and consign to the earth below both her and the daughters of mighty nations, with those who go down to the pit. ¹⁹Say to them, 'Are you more favored than others? Go down and be laid among the uncircumcised.' ²⁰They will fall among those killed by the sword. The sword is drawn; let her be dragged off with all her hordes. ²¹From within the grave[a] the mighty leaders will say of Egypt and her allies, 'They have come down and they lie with the uncircumcised, with those killed by the sword.'

²²"Assyria is there with her whole army; she is surrounded by the graves of all her slain, all who have fallen by the sword. ²³Their graves are in the depths of the pit and her army lies around her grave. All who had spread terror in the land of the living are slain, fallen by the sword.

²⁴"Elam is there, with all her hordes around her grave. All of them are slain, fallen by the sword. All who had spread terror in the land of the living went down uncircumcised to the earth below. They bear their shame with those who go down to the pit. ²⁵A bed is made for her among the slain, with all her hordes around her grave. All of them are uncircumcised, killed by the sword. Because their terror had spread in the land of the living, they bear their shame with those who go down to the pit; they are laid among the slain.

²⁶"Meshech and Tubal are there, with all their hordes around their graves. All of them are uncircumcised, killed by the sword because they spread their terror in the land of the living. ²⁷Do they not lie with the other uncircumcised warriors who have fallen, who went down to the grave with their weapons of war, whose swords were placed under their heads? The punishment for their sins rested on their bones, though the terror of these warriors had stalked through the land of the living.

²⁸"You too, O Pharaoh, will be broken and will lie among the uncircumcised, with those killed by the sword.

²⁹"Edom is there, her kings and all her princes; despite their power, they are laid with those killed by the sword. They lie with the uncircumcised, with those who go down to the pit.

³⁰"All the princes of the north and all the Sidonians are there; they went down with the slain in disgrace despite the terror caused by their power. They lie uncircumcised with those killed by the sword and bear their shame with those who go down to the pit.

³¹"Pharaoh—he and all his army—will see them and he will be consoled for all his hordes that were killed by the sword, declares the Sovereign LORD. ³²Although I had him spread terror in the land of the living, Pharaoh and all his hordes will be laid among the uncircumcised, with those killed by the sword, declares the Sovereign LORD."

Ezekiel a Watchman

33 The word of the LORD came to me: ²"Son of man, speak to your countrymen and say to them: 'When I bring the sword against a land, and the people of the land choose one of their men and make him their watchman, ³and he sees the sword coming against the land and blows the trumpet to warn the people, ⁴then if anyone hears the trumpet but does not take warning and the sword comes and takes his life, his blood will be on his own head. ⁵Since he heard the sound of the trumpet but did not take warning, his blood will be on his own head. If he had taken warning, he would have saved himself. ⁶But if the watchman sees the sword coming and does not blow the trumpet to warn the people and the sword comes and

---

[a] *21* Hebrew *Sheol*; also in verse 27

takes the life of one of them, that man will be taken away because of his sin, but I will hold the watchman accountable for his blood.'

7"Son of man, I have made you a watchman for the house of Israel; so hear the word I speak and give them warning from me. 8When I say to the wicked, 'O wicked man, you will surely die,' and you do not speak out to dissuade him from his ways, that wicked man will die for*a* his sin, and I will hold you accountable for his blood. 9But if you do warn the wicked man to turn from his ways and he does not do so, he will die for his sin, but you will have saved yourself.

10"Son of man, say to the house of Israel, 'This is what you are saying: "Our offenses and sins weigh us down, and we are wasting away because of*b* them. How then can we live?" ' 11Say to them, 'As surely as I live, declares the Sovereign LORD, I take no pleasure in the death of the wicked, but rather that they turn from their ways and live. Turn! Turn from your evil ways! Why will you die, O house of Israel?'

12"Therefore, son of man, say to your countrymen, 'The righteousness of the righteous man will not save him when he disobeys, and the wickedness of the wicked man will not cause him to fall when he turns from it. The righteous man, if he sins, will not be allowed to live because of his former righteousness.' 13If I tell the righteous man that he will surely live, but then he trusts in his righteousness and does evil, none of the righteous things he has done will be remembered; he will die for the evil he has done. 14And if I say to the wicked man, 'You will surely die,' but he then turns away from his sin and does what is just and right— 15if he gives back what he took in pledge for a loan, returns what he has stolen, follows the decrees that give life, and does no evil, he will surely live; he will not die. 16None of the sins he has committed will be remembered against him. He has done what is just and right; he will surely live.

17"Yet your countrymen say, 'The way of the Lord is not just.' But it is their way that is not just. 18If a righteous man turns

a 8 Or in; also in verse 9   *b 10 Or away in*

Watchman on the Lookout

READ EZEKIEL 33:1–11

Ezekiel wasn't called a "watchman" because he invented a sundial to strap to people's wrists. A watchman was someone who looked out for danger and warned people about it. Today, you can be a watchman when you see one of your buddies about to get into some bad stuff. That doesn't mean you should be a know-it-all or judge him. You can "speak the truth in love" (Ephesians 4:15). On the other hand, you might not want him to get mad at you for saying something, so . . . you mind your own business. But sitting silent won't help him get back on the right track. Being a watchman means you encourage a friend not to do wrong and you tell it to him straight without getting preachy. Pray for wisdom, then tell him you're concerned. Let him know you're looking out for him.

Your next reading is on page 1086.

from his righteousness and does evil, he will die for it. ¹⁹And if a wicked man turns away from his wickedness and does what is just and right, he will live by doing so. ²⁰Yet, O house of Israel, you say, 'The way of the Lord is not just.' But I will judge each of you according to his own ways."

Jerusalem's Fall Explained

²¹In the twelfth year of our exile, in the tenth month on the fifth day, a man who had escaped from Jerusalem came to me and said, "The city has fallen!" ²²Now the evening before the man arrived, the hand of the LORD was upon me, and he opened my mouth before the man came to me in the morning. So my mouth was opened and I was no longer silent.

²³Then the word of the LORD came to me: ²⁴"Son of man, the people living in those ruins in the land of Israel are saying, 'Abraham was only one man, yet he possessed the land. But we are many; surely the land has been given to us as our possession.' ²⁵Therefore say to them, 'This is what the Sovereign LORD says: Since you eat meat with the blood still in it and look to your idols and shed blood, should you then possess the land? ²⁶You rely on your sword, you do detestable things, and each of you defiles his neighbor's wife. Should you then possess the land?'

²⁷"Say this to them: 'This is what the Sovereign LORD says: As surely as I live, those who are left in the ruins will fall by the sword, those out in the country I will give to the wild animals to be devoured, and those in strongholds and caves will die of a plague. ²⁸I will make the land a desolate waste, and her proud strength will come to an end, and the mountains of Israel will become desolate so that no one will cross them. ²⁹Then they will know that I am the LORD, when I have made the land a desolate waste because of all the detestable things they have done.'

³⁰"As for you, son of man, your countrymen are talking together about you by the walls and at the doors of the houses, saying to each other, 'Come and hear the message that has come from the LORD.' ³¹My people come to you, as they usually do, and sit before you to listen to your words, but they do not put them into practice. With their mouths they express devotion, but their hearts are greedy for unjust gain. ³²Indeed, to them you are nothing more than one who sings love songs with a beautiful voice and plays an instrument well, for they hear your words but do not put them into practice.

³³"When all this comes true—and it surely will—then they will know that a prophet has been among them."

Shepherds and Sheep

34 The word of the LORD came to me: ²"Son of man, prophesy against the shepherds of Israel; prophesy and say to them: 'This is what the Sovereign LORD says: Woe to the shepherds of Israel who only take care of themselves! Should

Get a Load of This...

Check out Ezekiel 33:30–32. When you listen to a sermon in church, do you *really* listen? When your parents tell you to listen, they don't just mean, "Let the sound waves enter your ears." They mean, "Soak the truth into your heart like a sponge soaking up water."

In other words...

not shepherds take care of the flock? ³You eat the curds, clothe yourselves with the wool and slaughter the choice animals, but you do not take care of the flock. ⁴You have not strengthened the weak or healed the sick or bound up the injured. You have not brought back the strays or searched for the lost. You have ruled them harshly and brutally. ⁵So they were scattered because there was no shepherd, and when they were scattered they became food for all the wild animals. ⁶My sheep wandered over all the mountains and on every high hill. They were scattered over the whole earth, and no one searched or looked for them.

⁷" 'Therefore, you shepherds, hear the word of the LORD: ⁸As surely as I live, declares the Sovereign LORD, because my flock lacks a shepherd and so has been plundered and has become food for all the wild animals, and because my shepherds did not search for my flock but cared for themselves rather than for my flock, ⁹therefore, O shepherds, hear the word of the LORD: ¹⁰This is what the Sovereign LORD says: I am against the shepherds and will hold them accountable for my flock. I will remove them from tending the flock so that the shepherds can no longer feed themselves. I will rescue my flock from their mouths, and it will no longer be food for them.

¹¹" 'For this is what the Sovereign LORD says: I myself will search for my sheep and look after them. ¹²As a shepherd looks after his scattered flock when he is with them, so will I look after my sheep. I will rescue them from all the places where they were scattered on a day of clouds and darkness. ¹³I will bring them out from the nations and gather them from the countries, and I will bring them into their own land. I will pasture them on the mountains of Israel, in the ravines and in all the settlements in the land. ¹⁴I will tend them in a good pasture, and the mountain heights of Israel will be their grazing land. There they will lie down in good grazing land, and there they will feed in a rich pasture on the mountains of Israel. ¹⁵I myself will tend my sheep and have them lie down, declares the Sovereign LORD. ¹⁶I will search for the lost and

Shoving and Butting In

READ EZEKIEL 34:17–24

Do your brothers and sisters groan when you sit down at the dinner table? Are you known as Mr. Me First, or the pushy prince of pasta? God's not happy with guys who always use their shoulders—or any other part of their body—to get what they want (verse 21). A man of God looks out for others, especially little kids and older people, and lets them go ahead of him. People who are always pushing to be first in line tick people off and lose friends. But if you let other people go first, you gain friends and get on God's to-be-blessed list. Next time you have dessert, try letting your sister have the last piece of pie. Your mom will be so surprised she might bake another one just to see if you'll do it again.

Your next reading is on page 1090.

bring back the strays. I will bind up the injured and strengthen the weak, but the sleek and the strong I will destroy. I will shepherd the flock with justice.

17 " 'As for you, my flock, this is what the Sovereign LORD says: I will judge between one sheep and another, and between rams and goats. 18Is it not enough for you to feed on the good pasture? Must you also trample the rest of your pasture with your feet? Is it not enough for you to drink clear water? Must you also muddy the rest with your feet? 19Must my flock feed on what you have trampled and drink what you have muddied with your feet?

20 " 'Therefore this is what the Sovereign LORD says to them: See, I myself will judge between the fat sheep and the lean sheep. 21Because you shove with flank and shoulder, butting all the weak sheep with your horns until you have driven them away, 22I will save my flock, and they will no longer be plundered. I will judge between one sheep and another. 23I will place over them one shepherd, my servant David, and he will tend them; he will tend them and be their shepherd. 24I

Make It Stick

READ EZEKIEL 34:21
Write down a few ways you can give others a break. Next time you go to the mall, you could hold a door open for someone instead of charging into the arcade. You might want to give some of the smaller kids a turn on the skateboard ramp first. Thinking about other people before yourself is called *courtesy*.

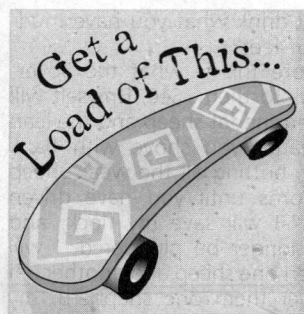

Get a Load of This...

When God said his people could safely "sleep in the forests" (Ezekiel 34:25), he wasn't saying, "Set up your tent in grizzly bear country." The Lord was talking about a future time of peace brought about by Christ that will give God's people complete security.

the LORD will be their God, and my servant David will be prince among them. I the LORD have spoken.

²⁵ " 'I will make a covenant of peace with them and rid the land of wild beasts so that they may live in the desert and sleep in the forests in safety. ²⁶I will bless them and the places surrounding my hill.ᵃ I will send down showers in season; there will be showers of blessing. ²⁷The trees of the field will yield their fruit and the ground will yield its crops; the people will be secure in their land. They will know that I am the LORD, when I break the bars of their yoke and rescue them from the hands of those who enslaved them. ²⁸They will no longer be plundered by the nations, nor will wild animals devour them. They will live in safety, and no one will make them afraid. ²⁹I will provide for them a land renowned for its crops, and they will no longer be victims of famine in the land or bear the scorn of the nations. ³⁰Then they will know that I, the LORD their God, am with them and that they, the house of Israel, are my people, declares the Sovereign LORD. ³¹You my sheep, the sheep of my pasture, are people, and I am your God, declares the Sovereign LORD.' "

A Prophecy Against Edom

35 The word of the LORD came to me: ²"Son of man, set your face against Mount Seir; prophesy against it ³and say: 'This is what the Sovereign LORD says: I am against you, Mount Seir, and I will stretch out my hand against you and make you a desolate waste. ⁴I will turn your towns into ruins and you will be desolate. Then you will know that I am the LORD.

⁵ " 'Because you harbored an ancient hostility and delivered the Israelites over to the sword at the time of their calamity, the time their punishment reached its climax, ⁶therefore as surely as I live, declares the Sovereign LORD, I will give you over to bloodshed and it will pursue you. Since you did not hate bloodshed, bloodshed will pursue you. ⁷I will make Mount Seir a desolate waste and cut off from it all who come and go. ⁸I will fill your mountains with the slain; those killed by the sword will fall on your hills and in your valleys and in all your ravines. ⁹I will make you desolate forever; your towns will not be inhabited. Then you will know that I am the LORD.

¹⁰ " 'Because you have said, "These two nations and countries will be ours and we will take possession of them," even though I the LORD was there, ¹¹therefore as surely as I live, declares the Sovereign LORD, I will treat you in accordance with the anger and jealousy you showed in your hatred of them and I will make myself known among them when I judge you. ¹²Then you will know that I the LORD have heard all the contemptible things you have said against the mountains of Israel. You said, "They have been laid waste and have been given over to us to devour." ¹³You boasted against me and

---

ᵃ 26 Or I will make them and the places surrounding my hill a blessing spoke against me without restraint, and I heard it. 14This is what the Sovereign Lord says: While the whole earth rejoices, I will make you desolate. 15Because you rejoiced when the inheritance of the house of Israel became desolate, that is how I will treat you. You will be desolate, O Mount Seir, you and all of Edom. Then they will know that I am the Lord.' "

A Prophecy to the Mountains of Israel

3️⃣6️⃣ "Son of man, prophesy to the mountains of Israel and say, 'O mountains of Israel, hear the word of the Lord. 2This is what the Sovereign Lord says: The enemy said of you, "Aha! The ancient heights have become our possession." ' 3Therefore prophesy and say, 'This is what the Sovereign Lord says: Because they ravaged and hounded you from every side so that you became the possession of the rest of the nations and the object of people's malicious talk and slander, 4therefore, O mountains of Israel, hear the word of the Sovereign Lord: This is what the Sovereign Lord says to the mountains and hills, to the ravines and valleys, to the desolate ruins and the deserted towns that have been plundered and ridiculed by the rest of the nations around you— 5this is what the Sovereign Lord says: In my burning zeal I have spoken against the rest of the nations, and against all Edom, for with glee and with malice in their hearts they made my land their own possession so that they might plunder its pastureland.' 6Therefore prophesy concerning the land of Israel and say to the mountains and hills, to the ravines and valleys: 'This is what the Sovereign Lord says: I speak in my jealous wrath because you have suffered the scorn of the nations. 7Therefore this is what the Sovereign Lord says: I swear with uplifted hand that the nations around you will also suffer scorn.

8" 'But you, O mountains of Israel, will produce branches and fruit for my people Israel, for they will soon come home. 9I am concerned for you and will look on you with favor; you will be plowed and sown, 10and I will multiply the number of people upon you, even the whole house of Israel. The towns will be inhabited and the ruins rebuilt. 11I will increase the number of men and animals upon you, and they will be fruitful and become numer-

ous. I will settle people on you as in the past and will make you prosper more than before. Then you will know that I am the Lord. 12I will cause people, my people Israel, to walk upon you. They will possess you, and you will be their inheritance; you will never again deprive them of their children.

13" 'This is what the Sovereign Lord says: Because people say to you, "You devour men and deprive your nation of its children," 14therefore you will no longer devour men or make your nation childless, declares the Sovereign Lord. 15No longer will I make you hear the taunts of the nations, and no longer will you suffer the scorn of the peoples or cause your nation to fall, declares the Sovereign Lord.' "

16Again the word of the Lord came to me: 17"Son of man, when the people of Israel were living in their own land, they defiled it by their conduct and their actions. Their conduct was like a woman's monthly uncleanness in my sight. 18So I poured out my wrath on them because they had shed blood in the land and because they had defiled it with their idols. 19I dispersed them among the nations, and they were scattered through the countries; I judged them according to their conduct and their actions. 20And wherever they went among the nations they profaned my holy name, for it was said of them, 'These are the Lord's people, and yet they had to leave his land.' 21I had concern for my holy name, which the house of Israel profaned among the nations where they had gone.

22"Therefore say to the house of Israel, 'This is what the Sovereign Lord says: It is not for your sake, O house of Israel, that I am going to do these things, but for the sake of my holy name, which you have profaned among the nations where you have gone. 23I will show the holiness of my great name, which has been profaned among the nations, the name you have profaned among them. Then the nations will know that I am the Lord, declares the Sovereign Lord, when I show myself holy through you before their eyes.

24" 'For I will take you out of the nations; I will gather you from all the countries and bring you back into your own land. 25I will sprinkle clean water on you, and you will be clean; I will cleanse you from all your impurities and from all your idols. ²⁶I will give you a new heart and put a new spirit in you; I will remove from you your heart of stone and give you a heart of flesh. ²⁷And I will put my Spirit in you and move you to follow my decrees and be careful to keep my laws. ²⁸You will live in the land I gave your forefathers; you will be my people, and I will be your God. ²⁹I will save you from all your uncleanness. I will call for the grain and make it plentiful and will not bring famine upon you. ³⁰I will increase the fruit of the trees and the crops of the field, so that you will no longer suffer disgrace among the nations because of famine. ³¹Then you will remember your evil ways and wicked deeds, and you will loathe yourselves for your sins and detestable practices. ³²I want you to know that I am not doing this for your sake, declares the Sovereign LORD. Be ashamed and disgraced for your conduct, O house of Israel!

³³" 'This is what the Sovereign LORD says: On the day I cleanse you from all your sins, I will resettle your towns, and the ruins will be rebuilt. ³⁴The desolate land will be cultivated instead of lying desolate in the sight of all who pass through it. ³⁵They will say, "This land that was laid waste has become like the garden of Eden; the cities that were lying in ruins, desolate and destroyed, are now fortified and inhabited." ³⁶Then the nations around you that remain will know that I the LORD have rebuilt what was destroyed and have replanted what was desolate. I the LORD have spoken, and I will do it.'

³⁷"This is what the Sovereign LORD says: Once again I will yield to the plea of the house of Israel and do this for them: I will make their people as numerous as sheep, ³⁸as numerous as the flocks for offerings at Jerusalem during her appointed feasts. So will the ruined cities be filled with flocks of people. Then they will know that I am the LORD."

The Valley of Dry Bones

37 The hand of the LORD was upon me, and he brought me out by the Spirit of the LORD and set me in the middle of a valley; it was full of bones. ²He led me back and

I Want to Want To

READ EZEKIEL 36:25–27

God says he wants to "move you" (verse 27). This doesn't mean he wants to fly you to outer Mongolia. He wants to move you to obey and trust him and help you grow. Then you'll get so close that you'll start doing stuff that makes him happy. It's more than just following a bunch of rules because you have to. It means doing the right thing because you *want* to, and because you know how cool things turn out when you do. When you ask Jesus into your heart, he gives you the Holy Spirit. Then you have a helper to keep you out of trouble. When you're really close to messing up, pray: "God, I want to do the right thing." He'll move you, change your direction, so you can turn your back on the bad stuff. Jesus says anything is possible if you choose to believe (see Mark 9:23; 11:23).

Your next reading is on page 1091.

forth among them, and I saw a great many bones on the floor of the valley, bones that were very dry. ³He asked me, "Son of man, can these bones live?"

I said, "O Sovereign LORD, you alone know."

⁴Then he said to me, "Prophesy to these bones and say to them, 'Dry bones, hear the word of the LORD! ⁵This is what the Sovereign LORD says to these bones: I will make breathᵃ enter you, and you will come to life. ⁶I will attach tendons to you and make flesh come upon you and cover you with skin; I will put breath in you, and you will come to life. Then you will know that I am the LORD.' "

⁷So I prophesied as I was commanded. And as I was prophesying, there was a noise, a rattling sound, and the bones came together, bone to bone. ⁸I looked, and tendons and flesh appeared on them and skin covered them, but there was no breath in them.

⁹Then he said to me, "Prophesy to the breath; prophesy, son of man, and say to it, 'This is what the Sovereign LORD says: Come from the four winds, O breath, and breathe into these slain, that they may live.' " ¹⁰So I prophesied as he commanded me, and breath entered them; they came to life and stood up on their feet—a vast army.

¹¹Then he said to me: "Son of man, these bones are the whole house of Israel. They say, 'Our bones are dried up and our hope is gone; we are cut off.' ¹²Therefore prophesy and say to them: 'This is what the Sovereign LORD says: O my people, I am going to open your graves and bring you up from them; I will bring you back to the land of Israel. ¹³Then you, my people, will know that I am the LORD, when I open your graves and bring you up from them. ¹⁴I will put my Spirit in you and you will live, and I will settle you in your own land. Then you will know that I the LORD have spoken, and I have done it, declares the LORD.' "

ᵃ 5 The Hebrew for this word can also mean *wind* or *spirit* (see verses 6–14).

GET STRONGER

Dry Bones

READ EZEKIEL 37:1–14

Israel's hope had dried up. It was as dry as a bone, like they'd hiked into a dead-end valley and been cut off from the rest of the world, left to die. But, just when things looked totally harsh, God got them out of trouble. You may feel dead, just like the skeletons that littered the valley. You figure you're going to fail math no matter how hard you study. Or maybe you're down because your best pal is really sick. Whatever's worrying you, don't do the dry bone moan. Talk to the One who even makes nature obey him. There are tons of stories in the Bible where God got people out of a jam. With him, everything is possible (see Mark 10:27). You can't tell him how to answer your prayers—like ordering from a menu in a restaurant—but trust him to make things right, even when you can't see a way out.

Your next reading is on page 1101.

One Nation Under One King

15The word of the LORD came to me: **16**"Son of man, take a stick of wood and write on it, 'Belonging to Judah and the Israelites associated with him.' Then take another stick of wood, and write on it, 'Ephraim's stick, belonging to Joseph and all the house of Israel associated with him.' **17**Join them together into one stick so that they will become one in your hand.

18"When your countrymen ask you, 'Won't you tell us what you mean by this?' **19**say to them, 'This is what the Sovereign LORD says: I am going to take the stick of Joseph—which is in Ephraim's hand—and of the Israelite tribes associated with him, and join it to Judah's stick, making them a single stick of wood, and they will become one in my hand.' **20**Hold before their eyes the sticks you have written on **21**and say to them, 'This is what the Sovereign LORD says: I will take the Israelites out of the nations where they have gone. I will gather them from all around and bring them back into their own land. **22**I will make them one nation in the land, on the mountains of Israel. There will be one king over all of them and they will never again be two nations or be divided into two kingdoms. **23**They will no longer defile themselves with their idols and vile images or with any of their offenses, for I will save them from all their sinful backsliding,*a* and I will cleanse them. They will be my people, and I will be their God.

24" 'My servant David will be king over them, and they will all have one shepherd. They will follow my laws and be careful to keep my decrees. **25**They will live in the land I gave to my servant Jacob, the land where your fathers lived. They and their children and their children's children will live there forever, and David my servant will be their prince forever. **26**I will make a covenant of peace with them; it will be an everlasting covenant. I will establish them and increase their numbers, and I will put my sanctuary among them forever. **27**My dwelling place will be with them; I will be their God, and they will be my people. **28**Then the nations will know that I the LORD make Israel holy, when my sanctuary is among them forever.' "

A Prophecy Against Gog

38 The word of the LORD came to me: **2**"Son of man, set your face against Gog, of the land of Magog, the chief prince of*b* Meshech and Tubal; prophesy against him **3**and say: 'This is what the Sovereign LORD says: I am against you, O Gog, chief prince of*c* Meshech and Tubal. **4**I will turn you around, put hooks in your jaws and bring you out with your whole army—your horses, your horsemen fully armed, and a great horde with large and small shields, all of them brandishing their swords. **5**Persia, Cush*d* and Put will be with them, all with shields and helmets, **6**also Gomer with all its troops, and Beth Togarmah from the far north with all its troops—the many nations with you.

7" 'Get ready; be prepared, you and all the hordes gathered about you, and take command of them. **8**After many days you will be called to arms. In future years you will invade a land that has recovered from war, whose people were gathered from many nations to the mountains of Israel, which had long been desolate. They had been brought out from the nations, and now all of them live in safety. **9**You and all your troops and the many nations with you will go up, advancing like a storm; you will be like a cloud covering the land.

10" 'This is what the Sovereign LORD says: On that day thoughts will come into your mind and you will devise an evil scheme. **11**You will say, "I will invade a land of unwalled villages; I will attack a peaceful and unsuspecting people—all of them living without walls and without gates and bars. **12**I will plunder and loot and turn my hand against the resettled ruins and the people gathered from the nations, rich in livestock and goods, living at the center of the land." **13**Sheba and Dedan and the merchants of Tarshish and all her villages*e* will say to you, "Have you come to plunder? Have you gathered your hordes to loot, to carry off silver and gold, to take away livestock and goods and to seize much plunder?" '

14"Therefore, son of man, prophesy and say to Gog: 'This is what the Sover-

---

a 23   Many Hebrew manuscripts (see also Septuagint); most Hebrew manuscripts *all their dwelling places where they sinned*   *b 2*   Or *the prince of Rosh,*   *c 3*   Or *Gog, prince of Rosh,*   *d 5*   That is, the upper Nile region   *e 13*   Or *her strong lions* eign LORD says: In that day, when my people Israel are living in safety, will you not take notice of it? 15You will come from your place in the far north, you and many nations with you, all of them riding on horses, a great horde, a mighty army. 16You will advance against my people Israel like a cloud that covers the land. In days to come, O Gog, I will bring you against my land, so that the nations may know me when I show myself holy through you before their eyes.

17" 'This is what the Sovereign LORD says: Are you not the one I spoke of in former days by my servants the prophets of Israel? At that time they prophesied for years that I would bring you against them. 18This is what will happen in that day: When Gog attacks the land of Israel, my hot anger will be aroused, declares the Sovereign LORD. 19In my zeal and fiery wrath I declare that at that time there shall be a great earthquake in the land of Israel. 20The fish of the sea, the birds of the air, the beasts of the field, every creature that moves along the ground, and all the people on the face of the earth will tremble at my presence. The mountains will be overturned, the cliffs will crumble and every wall will fall to the ground. 21I will summon a sword against Gog on all my mountains, declares the Sovereign LORD. Every man's sword will be against his brother. 22I will execute judgment upon him with plague and bloodshed; I will pour down torrents of rain, hailstones and burning sulfur on him and on his troops and on the many nations with him. 23And so I will show my greatness and my holiness, and I will make myself known in the sight of many nations. Then they will know that I am the LORD.'

39 "Son of man, prophesy against Gog and say: 'This is what the Sovereign LORD says: I am against you, O Gog, chief prince ofᵃ Meshech and Tubal. 2I will turn you around and drag you along. I will bring you from the far north and send you against the mountains of Israel. 3Then I will strike your bow from your left hand and make your arrows drop from your right hand. 4On the mountains of Israel you will fall, you and all your troops and the nations with you. I will give you as food to all kinds of carrion birds and to the wild animals. 5You will fall in the open

field, for I have spoken, declares the Sovereign LORD. 6I will send fire on Magog and on those who live in safety in the coastlands, and they will know that I am the LORD.

7" 'I will make known my holy name among my people Israel. I will no longer let my holy name be profaned, and the nations will know that I the LORD am the Holy One in Israel. 8It is coming! It will surely take place, declares the Sovereign LORD. This is the day I have spoken of.

9" 'Then those who live in the towns of Israel will go out and use the weapons for fuel and burn them up—the small and large shields, the bows and arrows, the war clubs and spears. For seven years they will use them for fuel. 10They will not need to gather wood from the fields or cut it from the forests, because they will use the weapons for fuel. And they will plunder those who plundered them and loot those who looted them, declares the Sovereign LORD.

11" 'On that day I will give Gog a burial place in Israel, in the valley of those who travel east towardᵇ the Sea.ᶜ It will block the way of travelers, because Gog and all his hordes will be buried there. So it will be called the Valley of Hamon Gog.ᵈ

12" 'For seven months the house of Israel will be burying them in order to cleanse the land. 13All the people of the land will bury them, and the day I am glorified will be a memorable day for them, declares the Sovereign LORD.

14" 'Men will be regularly employed to cleanse the land. Some will go throughout the land and, in addition to them, others will bury those that remain on the ground. At the end of the seven months they will begin their search. 15As they go through the land and one of them sees a human bone, he will set up a marker beside it until the gravediggers have buried it in the Valley of Hamon Gog. 16(Also a town called Hamonahᵉ will be there.) And so they will cleanse the land.'

17"Son of man, this is what the Sovereign LORD says: Call out to every kind of bird and all the wild animals: 'Assemble and come together from all around to the sacrifice I am preparing for you, the great sacrifice on the mountains of Israel. There

ᵃ 1 Or Gog, prince of Rosh,   ᵇ 11 Or of   ᶜ 11 That is, the Dead Sea   ᵈ 11 Hamon Gog means hordes of Gog.
ᵉ 16 Hamonah means horde.

Gross!

Imagine being "employed" to walk along through a battlefield seven months after a massive battle, looking for bones and tying little markers on them (see Ezekiel 39:14–15). This is not exactly anyone's idea of a dream job—unless you're an archaeologist!

you will eat flesh and drink blood. 18You will eat the flesh of mighty men and drink the blood of the princes of the earth as if they were rams and lambs, goats and bulls—all of them fattened animals from Bashan. 19At the sacrifice I am preparing for you, you will eat fat till you are glutted and drink blood till you are drunk. 20At my table you will eat your fill of horses and riders, mighty men and soldiers of every kind,' declares the Sovereign LORD.

21"I will display my glory among the nations, and all the nations will see the punishment I inflict and the hand I lay upon them. 22From that day forward the house of Israel will know that I am the LORD their God. 23And the nations will know that the people of Israel went into exile for their sin, because they were unfaithful to me. So I hid my face from them and handed them over to their enemies, and they all fell by the sword. 24I dealt with them according to their uncleanness and their offenses, and I hid my face from them.

25"Therefore this is what the Sovereign LORD says: I will now bring Jacob back from captivity^a and will have compassion on all the people of Israel, and I will be zealous for my holy name. 26They will forget their shame and all the unfaithfulness they showed toward me when they lived in safety in their land with no one to make them afraid. 27When I have brought them back from the nations and have gathered them from the countries of their enemies, I will show myself holy through them in the sight of many nations. 28Then they will know that I am the LORD their God, for though I sent them into exile among the nations, I will gather them to their own land, not leaving any behind. 29I will no longer hide my face from them, for I will pour out my Spirit on the house of Israel, declares the Sovereign LORD."

The New Temple Area

40 In the twenty-fifth year of our exile, at the beginning of the year, on the tenth of the month, in the fourteenth year after the fall of the city—on that very day the hand of the LORD was upon me and he took me there. 2In visions of God he took me to the land of Israel and set me on a very high mountain, on whose south side were some buildings that looked like a city. 3He took me there, and I saw a man whose appearance was like bronze; he was standing in the gateway with a linen cord and a measuring rod in his hand. 4The man said to me, "Son of man, look with your eyes and hear with your ears and pay attention to everything I am going to show you, for that is why you have been brought here. Tell the house of Israel everything you see."

The East Gate to the Outer Court

5I saw a wall completely surrounding the temple area. The length of the measuring rod in the man's

^a 25 Or now restore the fortunes of Jacob

hand was six long cubits, each of which was a cubit[a] and a handbreadth.[b] He measured the wall; it was one measuring rod thick and one rod high.

⁶Then he went to the gate facing east. He climbed its steps and measured the threshold of the gate; it was one rod deep.[c] ⁷The alcoves for the guards were one rod long and one rod wide, and the projecting walls between the alcoves were five cubits thick. And the threshold of the gate next to the portico facing the temple was one rod deep.

⁸Then he measured the portico of the gateway; ⁹it[d] was eight cubits deep and its jambs were two cubits thick. The portico of the gateway faced the temple.

¹⁰Inside the east gate were three alcoves on each side; the three had the same measurements, and the faces of the projecting walls on each side had the same measurements. ¹¹Then he measured the width of the entrance to the gateway; it was ten cubits and its length was thirteen cubits. ¹²In front of each alcove was a wall one cubit high, and the alcoves were six cubits square. ¹³Then he measured the gateway from the top of the rear wall of one alcove to the top of the opposite one; the distance was twenty-five cubits from one parapet opening to the opposite one. ¹⁴He measured along the faces of the projecting walls all around the inside of the gateway—sixty cubits. The measurement was up to the portico[e] facing the courtyard.[f] ¹⁵The distance from the entrance of the gateway to the far end of its portico was fifty cubits. ¹⁶The alcoves and the projecting walls inside the gateway were surmounted by narrow parapet openings all around, as was the portico; the openings all around faced inward. The faces of the projecting walls were decorated with palm trees.

The Outer Court

¹⁷Then he brought me into the outer court. There I saw some rooms and a pavement that had been constructed all around the court; there were thirty rooms along the pavement. ¹⁸It abutted the sides of the gateways and was as wide as they were long; this was the lower pavement. ¹⁹Then he measured the distance from the inside of the lower gateway to the outside of the inner court; it was a hundred cubits on the east side as well as on the north.

The North Gate

²⁰Then he measured the length and width of the gate facing north, leading into the outer court. ²¹Its alcoves—three on each side—its projecting walls and its portico had the same measurements as those of the first gateway. It was fifty cubits long and twenty-five cubits

Get a Load of This...

Check out Ezekiel 40:1. The temple described in these chapters was *never* built. This wasn't the temple that Solomon built (1 Kings 6:1), and it wasn't the temple that Zerubbabel built (Ezra 6:14–15), and it wasn't the temple that Herod built (John 2:20). Some people believe that Ezekiel's temple will be built when Christ returns to the earth; other people believe that Ezekiel's temple is a symbolic description of God's future plan of blessing and perfection for the church.

---

a 5 The common cubit was about 1 1/2 feet (about 0.5 meter).   *b 5* That is, about 3 inches (about 8 centimeters)   *c 6* Septuagint; Hebrew *deep, the first threshold, one rod deep*   *d 8,9* Many Hebrew manuscripts, Septuagint, Vulgate and Syriac; most Hebrew manuscripts *gateway facing the temple; it was one rod deep. 9Then he measured the portico of the gateway; it*   *e 14* Septuagint; Hebrew *projecting wall*   *f 14* The meaning of the Hebrew for this verse is uncertain.

wide. ²²Its openings, its portico and its palm tree decorations had the same measurements as those of the gate facing east. Seven steps led up to it, with its portico opposite them. ²³There was a gate to the inner court facing the north gate, just as there was on the east. He measured from one gate to the opposite one; it was a hundred cubits.

The South Gate

²⁴Then he led me to the south side and I saw a gate facing south. He measured its jambs and its portico, and they had the same measurements as the others. ²⁵The gateway and its portico had narrow openings all around, like the openings of the others. It was fifty cubits long and twenty-five cubits wide. ²⁶Seven steps led up to it, with its portico opposite them; it had palm tree decorations on the faces of the projecting walls on each side. ²⁷The inner court also had a gate facing south, and he measured from this gate to the outer gate on the south side; it was a hundred cubits.

Gates to the Inner Court

²⁸Then he brought me into the inner court through the south gate, and he measured the south gate; it had the same measurements as the others. ²⁹Its alcoves, its projecting walls and its portico had the same measurements as the others. The gateway and its portico had openings all around. It was fifty cubits long and twenty-five cubits wide. ³⁰(The porticoes of the gateways around the inner court were twenty-five cubits wide and five cubits deep.) ³¹Its portico faced the outer court; palm trees decorated its jambs, and eight steps led up to it.

³²Then he brought me to the inner court on the east side, and he measured the gateway; it had the same measurements as the others. ³³Its alcoves, its projecting walls and its portico had the same measurements as the others. The gateway and its portico had openings all around. It was fifty cubits long and twenty-five cubits wide. ³⁴Its portico faced the outer court; palm trees decorated the jambs on either side, and eight steps led up to it.

³⁵Then he brought me to the north gate and measured it. It had the same measurements as the others, ³⁶as did its alcoves, its projecting walls and its portico, and it had openings all around. It was

fifty cubits long and twenty-five cubits wide. ³⁷Its portico^a faced the outer court; palm trees decorated the jambs on either side, and eight steps led up to it.

The Rooms for Preparing Sacrifices

³⁸A room with a doorway was by the portico in each of the inner gateways, where the burnt offerings were washed. ³⁹In the portico of the gateway were two tables on each side, on which the burnt offerings, sin offerings and guilt offerings were slaughtered. ⁴⁰By the outside wall of the portico of the gateway, near the steps at the entrance to the north gateway were two tables, and on the other side of the steps were two tables. ⁴¹So there were four tables on one side of the gateway and four on the other—eight tables in all—on which the sacrifices were slaughtered. ⁴²There were also four tables of dressed stone for the burnt offerings, each a cubit and a half long, a cubit and a half wide and a cubit high. On them were placed the utensils for slaughtering the burnt offerings and the other sacrifices. ⁴³And double-pronged hooks, each a handbreadth long, were attached to the wall all around. The tables were for the flesh of the offerings.

Rooms for the Priests

⁴⁴Outside the inner gate, within the inner court, were two rooms, one^b at the side of the north gate and facing south, and another at the side of the south^c gate and facing north. ⁴⁵He said to me, "The room facing south is for the priests who have charge of the temple, ⁴⁶and the room facing north is for the priests who have charge of the altar. These are the sons of Zadok, who are the only Levites who may draw near to the Lord to minister before him."

⁴⁷Then he measured the court: It was square—a hundred cubits long and a hundred cubits wide. And the altar was in front of the temple.

The Temple

⁴⁸He brought me to the portico of the temple and measured the jambs of the portico; they were five cubits wide on either side. The width of the entrance was fourteen cubits and its projecting walls

---

^a 37 Septuagint (see also verses 31 and 34); Hebrew *jambs*
^b 44 Septuagint; Hebrew *were rooms for singers, which were*
^c 44 Septuagint; Hebrew *east*

were[a] three cubits wide on either side. [49]The portico was twenty cubits wide, and twelve[b] cubits from front to back. It was reached by a flight of stairs,[c] and there were pillars on each side of the jambs.

Then the man brought me to the outer sanctuary and measured the jambs; the width of the jambs was six cubits[d] on each side.[e] [2]The entrance was ten cubits wide, and the projecting walls on each side of it were five cubits wide. He also measured the outer sanctuary; it was forty cubits long and twenty cubits wide.

[3]Then he went into the inner sanctuary and measured the jambs of the entrance; each was two cubits wide. The entrance was six cubits wide, and the projecting walls on each side of it were seven cubits wide. [4]And he measured the length of the inner sanctuary; it was twenty cubits, and its width was twenty cubits across the end of the outer sanctuary. He said to me, "This is the Most Holy Place."

[5]Then he measured the wall of the temple; it was six cubits thick, and each side room around the temple was four cubits wide. [6]The side rooms were on three levels, one above another, thirty on each level. There were ledges all around the wall of the temple to serve as supports for the side rooms, so that the supports were not inserted into the wall of the temple. [7]The side rooms all around the temple were wider at each successive level. The structure surrounding the temple was built in ascending stages, so that the rooms widened as one went upward. A stairway went up from the lowest floor to the top floor through the middle floor.

[8]I saw that the temple had a raised base all around it, forming the foundation of the side rooms. It was the length of the rod, six long cubits. [9]The outer wall of the side rooms was five cubits thick. The open area between the side rooms of the temple [10]and the ⌊priests'⌋ rooms was twenty cubits wide all around the temple. [11]There were entrances to the side rooms from the open area, one on the north and another on the south; and the base adjoining the open area was five cubits wide all around.

[12]The building facing the temple courtyard on the west side was seventy cubits wide. The wall of the building was five cubits thick all around, and its length was ninety cubits.

[13]Then he measured the temple; it was a hundred cubits long, and the temple courtyard and the building with its walls were also a hundred cubits long. [14]The width of the temple courtyard on the east, including the front of the temple, was a hundred cubits.

[15]Then he measured the length of the building facing the courtyard at the rear of the temple, including its galleries on each side; it was a hundred cubits.

The outer sanctuary, the inner sanctuary and the portico facing the court, [16]as well as the thresholds and the narrow windows and galleries around the three of them—everything beyond and including the threshold was covered with wood. The floor, the wall up to the windows, and the windows were covered. [17]In the space above the outside of the entrance to the inner sanctuary and on the walls at regular intervals all around the inner and outer sanctuary [18]were carved cherubim and palm trees. Palm trees alternated with cherubim. Each cherub had two faces: [19]the face of a man toward the palm tree on one side and the face of a lion toward the palm tree on the other. They were carved all around the whole temple. [20]From the floor to the area above the entrance, cherubim and palm trees were carved on the wall of the outer sanctuary.

[21]The outer sanctuary had a rectangular doorframe, and the one at the front of the Most Holy Place was similar. [22]There was a wooden altar three cubits high and two cubits square[f]; its corners, its base[g] and its sides were of wood. The man said to me, "This is the table that is before the LORD." [23]Both the outer sanctuary and the Most Holy Place had double doors. [24]Each door had two leaves—two hinged leaves for each door. [25]And on the doors of the outer sanctuary were carved cherubim and palm trees like those carved on the walls, and there was a wooden overhang on the front of the portico. [26]On the sidewalls of the portico were narrow windows with palm trees carved on each side. The side rooms of the temple also had overhangs.

a 48 Septuagint; Hebrew entrance was   b 49 Septuagint; Hebrew eleven   c 49 Hebrew; Septuagint Ten steps led up to it   d 1 The common cubit was about 1 1/2 feet (about 0.5 meter).   e 1 One Hebrew manuscript and Septuagint; most Hebrew manuscripts side, the width of the tent   f 22 Septuagint; Hebrew long   g 22 Septuagint; Hebrew length

Rooms for the Priests

42 Then the man led me north-ward into the outer court and brought me to the rooms op-posite the temple courtyard and opposite the outer wall on the north side. ²The building whose door faced north was a hundred cubits*a* long and fif-ty cubits wide. ³Both in the section twen-ty cubits from the inner court and in the section opposite the pavement of the out-er court, gallery faced gallery at the three levels. ⁴In front of the rooms was an inner passageway ten cubits wide and a hun-dred cubits*b* long. Their doors were on the north. ⁵Now the upper rooms were narrower, for the galleries took more space from them than from the rooms on the lower and middle floors of the build-ing. ⁶The rooms on the third floor had no pillars, as the courts had; so they were smaller in floor space than those on the lower and middle floors. ⁷There was an outer wall parallel to the rooms and the outer court; it extended in front of the rooms for fifty cubits. ⁸While the row of rooms on the side next to the outer court was fifty cubits long, the row on the side nearest the sanctuary was a hundred cu-bits long. ⁹The lower rooms had an en-trance on the east side as one enters them from the outer court.

¹⁰On the south side*c* along the length of the wall of the outer court, adjoining the temple courtyard and opposite the outer wall, were rooms ¹¹with a passageway in front of them. These were like the rooms on the north; they had the same length and width, with similar exits and dimen-sions. Similar to the doorways on the north ¹²were the doorways of the rooms on the south. There was a doorway at the begin-ning of the passageway that was parallel to the corresponding wall extending east-ward, by which one enters the rooms.

¹³Then he said to me, "The north and south rooms facing the temple courtyard are the priests' rooms, where the priests who approach the LORD will eat the most holy offerings. There they will put the most holy offerings—the grain offerings, the sin offerings and the guilt offerings—for the place is holy. ¹⁴Once the priests en-ter the holy precincts, they are not to go into the outer court until they leave be-hind the garments in which they minister,

for these are holy. They are to put on oth-er clothes before they go near the places that are for the people."

¹⁵When he had finished measuring what was inside the temple area, he led me out by the east gate and measured the area all around: ¹⁶He measured the east side with the measuring rod; it was five hundred cubits.*d* ¹⁷He measured the north side; it was five hundred cubits*e* by the measuring rod. ¹⁸He measured the south side; it was five hundred cubits by the measuring rod. ¹⁹Then he turned to the west side and measured; it was five hundred cubits by the measuring rod. ²⁰So he measured the area on all four sides. It had a wall around it, five hundred cubits long and five hundred cubits wide, to separate the holy from the common.

The Glory Returns to the Temple

43 Then the man brought me to the gate facing east, ²and I saw the glory of the God of Is-rael coming from the east. His voice was like the roar of rushing waters, and the land was radiant with his glory. ³The vision I saw was like the vision I had seen when he*f* came to destroy the city and like the visions I had seen by the Ke-bar River, and I fell facedown. ⁴The glory of the LORD entered the temple through the gate facing east. ⁵Then the Spirit lifted me up and brought me into the inner court, and the glory of the LORD filled the temple.

⁶While the man was standing beside me, I heard someone speaking to me from inside the temple. ⁷He said: "Son of man, this is the place of my throne and the place for the soles of my feet. This is where I will live among the Israelites for-ever. The house of Israel will never again defile my holy name—neither they nor their kings—by their prostitution*g* and the lifeless idols*h* of their kings at their high places. ⁸When they placed their threshold next to my threshold and their doorposts beside my doorposts, with only a wall be-tween me and them, they defiled my holy

---

a 2 The common cubit was about 1 1/2 feet (about 0.5 meter).　　*b 4* Septuagint and Syriac; Hebrew *and one cubit*　　*c 10* Septuagint; Hebrew *Eastward*
d 16 See Septuagint of verse 17; Hebrew *rods*; also in verses 18 and 19.　　*e 17* Septuagint; Hebrew *rods*　　*f 3* Some Hebrew manuscripts and Vulgate; most Hebrew manuscripts *I*
g 7 Or *their spiritual adultery*; also in verse 9　　*h 7* Or *the corpses*; also in verse 9

name by their detestable practices. So I destroyed them in my anger. ⁹Now let them put away from me their prostitution and the lifeless idols of their kings, and I will live among them forever.

¹⁰"Son of man, describe the temple to the people of Israel, that they may be ashamed of their sins. Let them consider the plan, ¹¹and if they are ashamed of all they have done, make known to them the design of the temple—its arrangement, its exits and entrances—its whole design and all its regulationsᵃ and laws. Write these down before them so that they may be faithful to its design and follow all its regulations.

¹²"This is the law of the temple: All the surrounding area on top of the mountain will be most holy. Such is the law of the temple.

The Altar

¹³"These are the measurements of the altar in long cubits, that cubit being a cubitᵇ and a handbreadthᶜ: Its gutter is a cubit deep and a cubit wide, with a rim of one spanᵈ around the edge. And this is the height of the altar: ¹⁴From the gutter on the ground up to the lower ledge it is two cubits high and a cubit wide, and from the smaller ledge up to the larger ledge it is four cubits high and a cubit wide. ¹⁵The altar hearth is four cubits high, and four horns project upward from the hearth. ¹⁶The altar hearth is square, twelve cubits long and twelve cubits wide. ¹⁷The upper ledge also is square, fourteen cubits long and fourteen cubits wide, with a rim of half a cubit and a gutter of a cubit all around. The steps of the altar face east."

¹⁸Then he said to me, "Son of man, this is what the Sovereign LORD says: These will be the regulations for sacrificing burnt offerings and sprinkling blood upon the altar when it is built: ¹⁹You are to give a young bull as a sin offering to the priests, who are Levites, of the family of Zadok, who come near to minister before me, declares the Sovereign LORD. ²⁰You are to take some of its blood and put it on the four horns of the altar and on the four corners of the upper ledge and all around the rim, and so purify the altar and make atonement for it. ²¹You are to take the bull for the sin offering and burn it in the designated part of the temple area outside the sanctuary.

²²"On the second day you are to offer a male goat without defect for a sin offering, and the altar is to be purified as it was purified with the bull. ²³When you have finished purifying it, you are to offer a young bull and a ram from the flock, both without defect. ²⁴You are to offer them before the LORD, and the priests are to sprinkle salt on them and sacrifice them as a burnt offering to the LORD.

²⁵"For seven days you are to provide a male goat daily for a sin offering; you are also to provide a young bull and a ram from the flock, both without defect. ²⁶For seven days they are to make atonement for the altar and cleanse it; thus they will dedicate it. ²⁷At the end of these days, from the eighth day on, the priests are to present your burnt offerings and fellowship offeringsᵉ on the altar. Then I will accept you, declares the Sovereign LORD."

The Prince, the Levites, the Priests

44 Then the man brought me back to the outer gate of the sanctuary, the one facing east, and it was shut. ²The LORD said to me, "This gate is to remain shut. It must not be opened; no one may enter through it. It is to remain shut because the LORD, the God of Israel, has entered through it. ³The prince himself is the only one who may sit inside the gateway to eat in the presence of the LORD. He is to enter by way of the portico of the gateway and go out the same way."

⁴Then the man brought me by way of the north gate to the front of the temple. I looked and saw the glory of the LORD filling the temple of the LORD, and I fell facedown.

⁵The LORD said to me, "Son of man, look carefully, listen closely and give attention to everything I tell you concerning all the regulations regarding the temple of the LORD. Give attention to the entrance of the temple and all the exits of the sanctuary. ⁶Say to the rebellious house of Israel, 'This is what the Sovereign LORD says: Enough of your detestable practices, O house of Israel! ⁷In addition to all your other de-

---

ᵃ 11 Some Hebrew manuscripts and Septuagint; most Hebrew manuscripts *regulations and its whole design*
ᵇ 13 The common cubit was about 1 1/2 feet (about 0.5 meter).   ᶜ 13 That is, about 3 inches (about 8 centimeters)
ᵈ 13 That is, about 9 inches (about 22 centimeters)
ᵉ 27 Traditionally *peace offerings*

Get a Load of This...

Ezekiel 44:1–2 said that the east gate of the outer court of the temple would be shut "because the LORD ... has entered through it." In Ezekiel's vision, God entered through this gate—making it holy. So it was to remain shut. A Muslim mosque now sits at the temple site; and the east gate has been permanently sealed shut!

testable practices, you brought foreigners uncircumcised in heart and flesh into my sanctuary, desecrating my temple while you offered me food, fat and blood, and you broke my covenant. 8Instead of carrying out your duty in regard to my holy things, you put others in charge of my sanctuary. 9This is what the Sovereign LORD says: No foreigner uncircumcised in heart and flesh is to enter my sanctuary, not even the foreigners who live among the Israelites.

10" 'The Levites who went far from me when Israel went astray and who wandered from me after their idols must bear the consequences of their sin. 11They may serve in my sanctuary, having charge of the gates of the temple and serving in it; they may slaughter the burnt offerings and sacrifices for the people and stand before the people and serve them. 12But because they served them in the presence of their idols and made the house of Israel fall into sin, therefore I have sworn with uplifted hand that they must bear the consequences of their sin, declares the Sovereign LORD. 13They are not to come near to serve me as priests or come near any of my holy things or my most holy offerings; they must bear the shame of their detestable practices. 14Yet I will put them in charge of the duties of the temple and all the work that is to be done in it.

15" 'But the priests, who are Levites and descendants of Zadok and who faithfully carried out the duties of my sanctuary when the Israelites went astray from me, are to come near to minister before me; they are to stand before me to offer sacrifices of fat and blood, declares the Sovereign LORD. 16They alone are to enter my sanctuary; they alone are to come near my table to minister before me and perform my service.

17" 'When they enter the gates of the inner court, they are to wear linen clothes; they must not wear any woolen garment while ministering at the gates of the inner court or inside the temple. 18They are to wear linen turbans on their heads and linen undergarments around their waists. They must not wear anything that makes them perspire. 19When they go out into the outer court where the people are, they are to take off the clothes they have been ministering in and are to leave them in the sacred rooms, and put on other clothes, so that they do not consecrate the people by means of their garments.

20" 'They must not shave their heads or let their hair grow long, but they are to keep the hair of their heads trimmed. 21No priest is to drink wine when he enters the inner court. 22They must not marry widows or divorced women; they may marry only virgins of Israelite descent or widows of priests. 23They are to teach my people the difference between the holy and the common and show them how to distinguish between the unclean and the clean.

24" 'In any dispute, the priests are to serve as judges and decide it according to my ordinances. They are to keep my laws and my decrees for all my appointed feasts, and they are to keep my Sabbaths holy.

25" 'A priest must not defile himself by going near a dead person; however, if the dead person was his father or mother, son or daughter, brother or unmarried sister, then he may defile himself. 26After he is cleansed, he must wait seven days. 27On the day he goes into the inner court of the sanctuary to minister in the sanctuary, he is to offer a sin offering for himself, declares the Sovereign LORD.

28" 'I am to be the only inheritance the priests have. You are to give them no possession in Israel; I will be their possession. 29They will eat the grain offerings, the sin offerings and the guilt offerings; and everything in Israel devoted*a* to the LORD will belong to them. 30The best of all the firstfruits and of all your special gifts will belong to the priests. You are to give them the first portion of your ground meal so that a blessing may rest on your household. 31The priests must not eat anything, bird or animal, found dead or torn by wild animals.

Division of the Land

45 " 'When you allot the land as an inheritance, you are to present to the LORD a portion of the land as a sacred district, 25,000 cubits long and 20,000*b* cubits wide; the entire area will be holy. 2Of this, a section 500 cubits square is to be for the sanctuary, with 50 cubits around it for open land. 3In the sacred district, measure off a section 25,000 cubits*c* long and 10,000 cubits*d* wide. In it will be the sanctuary, the Most Holy Place. 4It will be the sacred portion of the land for the priests, who minister in the sanctuary and who draw near to minister before the LORD. It will be a place for their houses as well as a holy place for the sanctuary. 5An area 25,000 cubits long and 10,000 cubits

a 29 The Hebrew term refers to the irrevocable giving over of things or persons to the LORD.　　*b 1* Septuagint (see also verses 3 and 5 and 48:9); Hebrew *10,000*　　*c 3* That is, about 7 miles (about 12 kilometers)　　*d 3* That is, about 3 miles (about 5 kilometers)

Sweat, BO and Germs

READ EZEKIEL 44:18

The priests were not supposed to wear clothes that made them sweat. Hey! Like, can we *learn* something from that? Ever watch a documentary where they show germs—magnified a zillion times—that look like space aliens? They didn't have microscopes in Moses' and Ezekiel's day and they didn't know germs existed, so God just told the Israelites to stay clean. He told them to wash themselves and clean their clothes (Leviticus 15:4–18). He even told them to keep their paws off dead bodies. You probably won't be touching any corpses, but be sure you wash after getting into the mud at the park or playing street hockey. When you're a man, you'll sweat more, and your sweat will stink, so get used to taking showers and changing your clothes now. Your buddies shouldn't be able to smell you before they see you. God wants you to look after your body, so keep it clean.

Your next reading is on page 1103.

wide will belong to the Levites, who serve in the temple, as their possession for towns to live in.[a]

6" 'You are to give the city as its property an area 5,000 cubits wide and 25,000 cubits long, adjoining the sacred portion; it will belong to the whole house of Israel. 7" 'The prince will have the land bordering each side of the area formed by the sacred district and the property of the city. It will extend westward from the west side and eastward from the east side, running lengthwise from the western to the eastern border parallel to one of the tribal portions. 8This land will be his possession in Israel. And my princes will no longer oppress my people but will allow the house of Israel to possess the land according to their tribes.

9" 'This is what the Sovereign LORD says: You have gone far enough, O princes of Israel! Give up your violence and oppression and do what is just and right. Stop dispossessing my people, declares the Sovereign LORD. 10You are to use accurate scales, an accurate ephah[b] and an accurate bath.[c] 11The ephah and the bath are to be the same size, the bath containing a tenth of a homer[d] and the ephah a tenth of a homer; the homer is to be the standard measure for both. 12The shekel[e] is to consist of twenty gerahs. Twenty shekels plus twenty-five shekels plus fifteen shekels equal one mina.[f]

Offerings and Holy Days

13" 'This is the special gift you are to offer: a sixth of an ephah from each homer of wheat and a sixth of an ephah from each homer of barley. 14The prescribed portion of oil, measured by the bath, is a tenth of a bath from each cor (which consists of ten baths or one homer, for ten baths are equivalent to a homer). 15Also one sheep is to be taken from every flock of two hundred from the well-watered pastures of Israel. These will be used for the grain offerings, burnt offerings and fellowship offerings[g] to make atonement for the people, declares the Sovereign LORD. 16All the people of the land will participate in this special gift for the use of the prince in Israel. 17It will be the duty of the prince to provide the burnt offerings, grain offerings and drink offerings at the festivals, the New Moons and the Sabbaths—at all the appointed feasts of the

house of Israel. He will provide the sin offerings, grain offerings, burnt offerings and fellowship offerings to make atonement for the house of Israel.

18" 'This is what the Sovereign LORD says: In the first month on the first day you are to take a young bull without defect and purify the sanctuary. 19The priest is to take some of the blood of the sin offering and put it on the doorposts of the temple, on the four corners of the upper ledge of the altar and on the gateposts of the inner court. 20You are to do the same on the seventh day of the month for anyone who sins unintentionally or through ignorance; so you are to make atonement for the temple.

21" 'In the first month on the fourteenth day you are to observe the Passover, a feast lasting seven days, during which you shall eat bread made without yeast. 22On that day the prince is to provide a bull as a sin offering for himself and for all the people of the land. 23Every day during the seven days of the Feast he is to provide seven bulls and seven rams without defect as a burnt offering to the LORD, and a male goat for a sin offering. 24He is to provide as a grain offering an ephah for each bull and an ephah for each ram, along with a hin[h] of oil for each ephah.

25" 'During the seven days of the Feast, which begins in the seventh month on the fifteenth day, he is to make the same provision for sin offerings, burnt offerings, grain offerings and oil.

46 " 'This is what the Sovereign LORD says: The gate of the inner court facing east is to be shut on the six working days, but on the Sabbath day and on the day of the New Moon it is to be opened. 2The prince is to enter from the outside through the portico of the gateway and stand by the gatepost. The priests are to sacrifice his burnt offering and his fellowship offerings.[i] He is to worship at the threshold of the gateway and then go out, but the gate will not be shut until evening. 3On the Sabbaths and New Moons the people of

---

[a] 5 Septuagint; Hebrew *temple; they will have as their possession 20 rooms*   [b] 10 An ephah was a dry measure.   [c] 10 A bath was a liquid measure.   [d] 11 A homer was a dry measure.   [e] 12 A shekel weighed about 2/5 ounce (about 11.5 grams).   [f] 12 That is, 60 shekels; the common mina was 50 shekels.   [g] 15 Traditionally *peace offerings*; also in verse 17   [h] 24 That is, probably about 4 quarts (about 4 liters)   [i] 2 Traditionally *peace offerings*; also in verse 12

the land are to worship in the presence of the Lord at the entrance to that gateway. ⁴The burnt offering the prince brings to the Lord on the Sabbath day is to be six male lambs and a ram, all without defect. ⁵The grain offering given with the ram is to be an ephah,ᵃ and the grain offering with the lambs is to be as much as he pleases, along with a hinᵇ of oil for each ephah. ⁶On the day of the New Moon he is to offer a young bull, six lambs and a ram, all without defect. ⁷He is to provide as a grain offering one ephah with the bull, one ephah with the ram, and with the lambs as much as he wants to give, along with a hin of oil with each ephah. ⁸When the prince enters, he is to go in through the portico of the gateway, and he is to come out the same way.

⁹" 'When the people of the land come before the Lord at the appointed feasts, whoever enters by the north gate to worship is to go out the south gate; and whoever enters by the south gate is to go out the north gate. No one is to return through the gate by which he entered, but each is to go out the opposite gate. ¹⁰The prince is to be among them, going in when they go in and going out when they go out.

¹¹" 'At the festivals and the appointed feasts, the grain offering is to be an ephah with a bull, an ephah with a ram, and with the lambs as much as one pleases, along with a hin of oil for each ephah. ¹²When the prince provides a freewill offering to the Lord—whether a burnt offering or fellowship offerings—the gate facing east is to be opened for him. He shall offer his burnt offering or his fellowship offerings as he does on the Sabbath day. Then he shall go out, and after he has gone out, the gate will be shut.

¹³" 'Every day you are to provide a year-old lamb without defect for a burnt offering to the Lord; morning by morning you shall provide it. ¹⁴You are also to provide with it morning by morning a grain offering, consisting of a sixth of an ephah with a third of a hin of oil to moisten the flour. The presenting of this grain offering to the Lord

ᵃ 5 That is, probably about 3/5 bushel (about 22 liters)
ᵇ 5 That is, probably about 4 quarts (about 4 liters)

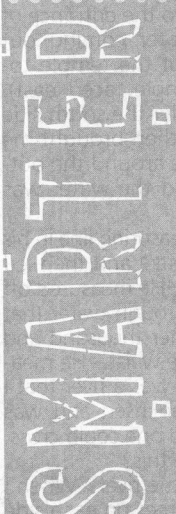

GET SMARTER

In This Way, Out That

READ EZEKIEL 46:9–10

Who knows why God told the Jews to go in one door and come out another. Maybe it was like in hockey, where you go onto the ice through one door and get off the ice through the other, so you don't skate on your teammates' toes. The Israelites probably needed a way to get around without bumping into each other. Even if they didn't know *why* they had to do it, they still had to obey God, because he knows what's best. It's fun to try to figure out why God wants you to do some things. But even if you don't understand why, you still need to obey. Remember Adam and Eve? They couldn't figure out why God told them to stay away from one tree. So, after being coaxed by the devil, they decided to do their own thing. *That* worked out well ... *Not*. Be wise. Obey God even when you don't understand the whys.

Your next reading is on page 1109.

Get a Load of This...

Ezekiel 47 talks about a very broad, shallow river, perfect for wading in (verses 3–4). Since it was full of "swarms of living creatures" and fish (verse 9), it sounds like a great place to catch frogs and lay on a raft, fishing like Huckleberry Finn.

is a lasting ordinance. ¹⁵So the lamb and the grain offering and the oil shall be provided morning by morning for a regular burnt offering.

¹⁶" 'This is what the Sovereign Lᴏʀᴅ says: If the prince makes a gift from his inheritance to one of his sons, it will also belong to his descendants; it is to be their property by inheritance. ¹⁷If, however, he makes a gift from his inheritance to one of his servants, the servant may keep it until the year of freedom; then it will revert to the prince. His inheritance belongs to his sons only; it is theirs. ¹⁸The prince must not take any of the inheritance of the people, driving them off their property. He is to give his sons their inheritance out of his own property, so that none of my people will be separated from his property.' "

¹⁹Then the man brought me through the entrance at the side of the gate to the sacred rooms facing north, which belonged to the priests, and showed me a place at the western end. ²⁰He said to me, "This is the place where the priests will cook the guilt offering and the sin offering and bake the grain offering, to avoid bringing them into the outer court and consecrating the people."

²¹He then brought me to the outer court and led me around to its four corners, and I saw in each corner another court. ²²In the four corners of the outer court were enclosed*a* courts, forty cubits long and thirty cubits wide; each of the courts in the four corners was the same size. ²³Around the inside of each of the four courts was a ledge of stone, with places for fire built all around under the ledge. ²⁴He said to me, "These are the kitchens where those who minister at the temple will cook the sacrifices of the people."

The River From the Temple

47 The man brought me back to the entrance of the temple, and I saw water coming out from under the threshold of the temple toward the east (for the temple faced east). The water was coming down from under the south side of the temple, south of the altar. ²He then brought me out through the north gate and led me around the outside to the outer gate facing east, and the water was flowing from the south side.

³As the man went eastward with a measuring line in his hand, he measured off a thousand cubits*b* and then led me through water that was ankle-deep. ⁴He measured off another thousand cubits and led me through water that was knee-deep. He measured off another thousand and led me through water that was up to the waist. ⁵He measured off another thousand, but now it was a river that I could not cross, because the water had risen and was deep enough to swim in—a river that no one could cross. ⁶He asked me, "Son of man, do you see this?"

Then he led me back to the bank of the river. ⁷When I arrived there, I saw a great number of trees on each side

a 22 The meaning of the Hebrew for this word is uncertain.   *b 3* That is, about 1,500 feet (about 450 meters) of the river. [8]He said to me, "This water flows toward the eastern region and goes down into the Arabah,[a] where it enters the Sea.[b] When it empties into the Sea,[b] the water there becomes fresh. [9]Swarms of living creatures will live wherever the river flows. There will be large numbers of fish, because this water flows there and makes the salt water fresh; so where the river flows everything will live. [10]Fishermen will stand along the shore; from En Gedi to En Eglaim there will be places for spreading nets. The fish will be of many kinds— like the fish of the Great Sea.[c] [11]But the swamps and marshes will not become fresh; they will be left for salt. [12]Fruit trees of all kinds will grow on both banks of the river. Their leaves will not wither, nor will their fruit fail. Every month they will bear, because the water from the sanctuary flows to them. Their fruit will serve for food and their leaves for healing."

The Boundaries of the Land

[13]This is what the Sovereign LORD says: "These are the boundaries by which you are to divide the land for an inheritance among the twelve tribes of Israel, with two portions for Joseph. [14]You are to divide it equally among them. Because I swore with uplifted hand to give it to your forefathers, this land will become your inheritance.

[15]"This is to be the boundary of the land:

"On the north side it will run from the Great Sea by the Hethlon road past Lebo[d] Hamath to Zedad, [16]Berothah[e] and Sibraim (which lies on the border between Damascus and Hamath), as far as Hazer Hatticon, which is on the border of Hauran. [17]The boundary will extend from the sea to Hazar Enan,[f] along the northern border of Damascus, with the border of Hamath to the north. This will be the north boundary.

[18]"On the east side the boundary will run between Hauran and Damascus, along the Jordan between Gilead and the land of Israel, to the eastern sea and as far as Tamar.[g] This will be the east boundary.

[19]"On the south side it will run from Tamar as far as the waters of Meribah Kadesh, then along the Wadi [of Egypt] to the Great Sea. This will be the south boundary.

[20]"On the west side, the Great Sea will be the boundary to a point opposite Lebo[h] Hamath. This will be the west boundary.

[21]"You are to distribute this land among yourselves according to the tribes of Israel. [22]You are to allot it as an inheritance for yourselves and for the aliens who have settled among you and who have children. You are to consider them as native-born Israelites; along with you they are to be allotted an inheritance among the tribes of Israel. [23]In whatever tribe the alien settles, there you are to give him his inheritance," declares the Sovereign LORD.

The Division of the Land

48 "These are the tribes, listed by name: At the northern frontier, Dan will have one portion; it will follow the Hethlon road to Lebo[i] Hamath; Hazar Enan and the northern border of Damascus next to Hamath will be part of its border from the east side to the west side.

[2]"Asher will have one portion; it will border the territory of Dan from east to west.

[3]"Naphtali will have one portion; it will border the territory of Asher from east to west.

[4]"Manasseh will have one portion; it will border the territory of Naphtali from east to west.

[5]"Ephraim will have one portion; it will border the territory of Manasseh from east to west.

[6]"Reuben will have one portion; it will border the territory of Ephraim from east to west.

[7]"Judah will have one portion; it will border the territory of Reuben from east to west.

[8]"Bordering the territory of Judah from east to west will be the portion you are to present as a special gift. It will be 25,000 cubits[j] wide, and its length from east to west will equal one of the tribal portions; the sanctuary will be in the center of it.

[9]"The special portion you are to offer to

---

[a] 8 Or the Jordan Valley   [b] 8 That is, the Dead Sea
[c] 10 That is, the Mediterranean; also in verses 15, 19 and 20
[d] 15 Or past the entrance to   [e] 15,16 See Septuagint and Ezekiel 48:1; Hebrew road to go into Zedad, [16]Hamath, Berothah   [f] 17 Hebrew Enon, a variant of Enan
[g] 18 Septuagint and Syriac; Hebrew Israel. You will measure to the eastern sea   [h] 20 Or opposite the entrance to
[i] 1 Or to the entrance to   [j] 8 That is, about 7 miles (about 12 kilometers)

the LORD will be 25,000 cubits long and 10,000 cubits[a] wide. ¹⁰This will be the sacred portion for the priests. It will be 25,000 cubits long on the north side, 10,000 cubits wide on the west side, 10,000 cubits wide on the east side and 25,000 cubits long on the south side. In the center of it will be the sanctuary of the LORD. ¹¹This will be for the consecrated priests, the Zadokites, who were faithful in serving me and did not go astray as the Levites did when the Israelites went astray. ¹²It will be a special gift to them from the sacred portion of the land, a most holy portion, bordering the territory of the Levites.

¹³"Alongside the territory of the priests, the Levites will have an allotment 25,000 cubits long and 10,000 cubits wide. Its total length will be 25,000 cubits and its width 10,000 cubits. ¹⁴They must not sell or exchange any of it. This is the best of the land and must not pass into other hands, because it is holy to the LORD.

¹⁵"The remaining area, 5,000 cubits wide and 25,000 cubits long, will be for the common use of the city, for houses and for pastureland. The city will be in the center of it ¹⁶and will have these measurements: the north side 4,500 cubits, the south side 4,500 cubits, the east side 4,500 cubits, and the west side 4,500 cubits. ¹⁷The pastureland for the city will be 250 cubits on the north, 250 cubits on the south, 250 cubits on the east, and 250 cubits on the west. ¹⁸What remains of the area, bordering on the sacred portion and running the length of it, will be 10,000 cubits on the east side and 10,000 cubits on the west side. Its produce will supply food for the workers of the city. ¹⁹The workers from the city who farm it will come from all the tribes of Israel. ²⁰The entire portion will be a square, 25,000 cubits on each side. As a special gift you will set aside the sacred portion, along with the property of the city.

²¹"What remains on both sides of the area formed by the sacred portion and the city property will belong to the prince. It will extend eastward from the 25,000 cubits of the sacred portion to the eastern border, and westward from the 25,000 cubits to the western border. Both these areas running the length of the tribal portions will belong to the prince, and the sacred portion with the temple sanctuary will be in the center of them. ²²So the property of

the Levites and the property of the city will lie in the center of the area that belongs to the prince. The area belonging to the prince will lie between the border of Judah and the border of Benjamin.

²³"As for the rest of the tribes: Benjamin will have one portion; it will extend from the east side to the west side.

²⁴"Simeon will have one portion; it will border the territory of Benjamin from east to west.

²⁵"Issachar will have one portion; it will border the territory of Simeon from east to west.

²⁶"Zebulun will have one portion; it will border the territory of Issachar from east to west.

²⁷"Gad will have one portion; it will border the territory of Zebulun from east to west.

²⁸"The southern boundary of Gad will run south from Tamar to the waters of Meribah Kadesh, then along the Wadi ⌊of Egypt⌋ to the Great Sea. [b]

²⁹"This is the land you are to allot as an inheritance to the tribes of Israel, and these will be their portions," declares the Sovereign LORD.

The Gates of the City

³⁰"These will be the exits of the city: Beginning on the north side, which is 4,500 cubits long, ³¹the gates of the city will be named after the tribes of Israel. The three gates on the north side will be the gate of Reuben, the gate of Judah and the gate of Levi.

³²"On the east side, which is 4,500 cubits long, will be three gates: the gate of Joseph, the gate of Benjamin and the gate of Dan.

³³"On the south side, which measures 4,500 cubits, will be three gates: the gate of Simeon, the gate of Issachar and the gate of Zebulun.

³⁴"On the west side, which is 4,500 cubits long, will be three gates: the gate of Gad, the gate of Asher and the gate of Naphtali.

³⁵"The distance all around will be 18,000 cubits.

"And the name of the city from that time on will be:

THE LORD IS THERE."

---

[a] 9 That is, about 3 miles (about 5 kilometers)   [b] 28 That is, the Mediterranean

DANIEL

Who wrote this book?

Daniel, a Jew who became an important government official in Babylon and Persia, wrote this book.

Why was this book written?

Daniel shows the Jewish people that foreign nations will have power over their homeland until God sends the promised Savior.

What do we learn about God in this book?

God is in charge of history. He knows ahead of time what will happen in our world.

What is special about this book?

The first part of the book tells stories of Daniel's life. The second part of the book tells about future governments that will have power over the Holy Land.

When was this book written?

Daniel was written near the end of Daniel's life, probably about 535 B.C.

What are some of the stories in this book?

Daniel obeys God	Daniel 1
Daniel explains a dream	Daniel 2
The fiery furnace	Daniel 3
Another dream	Daniel 4
The writing on the wall	Daniel 5
The lions' den	Daniel 6

Daniel's Training in Babylon

In the third year of the reign of Jehoiakim king of Judah, Nebuchadnezzar king of Babylon came to Jerusalem and besieged it. ²And the Lord delivered Jehoiakim king of Judah into his hand, along with some of the articles from the temple of God. These he carried off to the temple of his god in Babylonia*a* and put in the treasure house of his god.

³Then the king ordered Ashpenaz, chief of his court officials, to bring in some of the Israelites from the royal family and the nobility— ⁴young men without any physical defect, handsome, showing aptitude for every kind of learning, well informed, quick to understand, and qualified to serve in the king's palace. He was to teach them the language and literature of the Babylonians.*b* ⁵The king assigned them a daily amount of food and wine from the king's table. They were to be trained for three years, and after that they were to enter the king's service.

⁶Among these were some from Judah: Daniel, Hananiah, Mishael and Azariah. ⁷The chief official gave them new names: to Daniel, the name Belteshazzar; to Hananiah, Shadrach; to Mishael, Meshach; and to Azariah, Abednego.

⁸But Daniel resolved not to defile himself with the royal food and wine, and he asked the chief official for permission not to defile himself this way. ⁹Now God had caused the official to show favor and sympathy to Daniel, ¹⁰but the official told Daniel, "I am afraid of my lord the king, who has assigned your*c* food and drink. Why should he see you looking worse than the other young men your age? The king would then have my head because of you."

¹¹Daniel then said to the guard whom

a 2 Hebrew *Shinar*   *b 4* Or *Chaldeans*   *c 10* The Hebrew for *your* and *you* in this verse is plural.

Make It Stick

READ DANIEL 1:4

Daniel and his friends believed God's Word and knew it well, so when they had to study the literature of Babylon, they knew what was true and what wasn't. Have you been taught anything in school that contradicts the Bible? Write it on a sticky note, then draw an "X" through it.

GET

Four "252 Men"

READ DANIEL 1

Daniel and his three young friends, Hananiah, Mishael and Azariah (better known as Shadrach, Meshach and Abednego), were from upper-class families in Jerusalem. Suddenly the Babylonians dragged them from their homes and forced them to walk 500 miles to Babylon. But Daniel and his friends were "252 men," way above the rest, and soon they were trained to serve in King Nebuchadnezzar's palace.

DEEPER:

Daniel and his friends were determined to obey God. According to the Law of Moses, they couldn't eat certain foods. It would have been disobeying God to eat the kind of junk food that King Nebuchadnezzar was eating. This wasn't just about "healthy food." It was about right or wrong, about obeying God. You also need to stay true to God. Cultures around the world are different today, true, but being obedient to God on basic issues is the same in every culture.

SMARTER:

Aptitude means "quick to understand," and Daniel and his friends definitely had it (see verse 4). They quickly learned to speak Babylonian, and when they could read it, Nebuchadnezzar had them plowing through thick books of Babylonian literature. A lot of their ability to learn was *attitude*: They were humble and willing to listen, plus they stayed true to God, so he poured it on. "God gave knowledge and understanding" to them (verse 17). Are you willing to listen and learn, like them?

STRONGER:

These four youths took care of themselves physically. They made a decision to eat nothing but good, wholesome food. No deep-fried food for these boys! They "looked healthier and better nourished than any of the young men who ate the royal food" (verse 15). They were also handsome. Do the Daniel thing: Make a commitment to be stronger; take care of yourself physically.

COOLER:

They were "qualified to serve in the king's palace" (verse 4). That means they had proper manners and knew how to serve—and *that* means they were on the job when it came time to take out the garbage and do dishes. Whew! These guys changed cultures overnight to fit in to their new country: They learned new customs, dressed differently, had different haircuts, and even had their *names* changed! The only thing they refused to change was their faith in God. You can fit in with the people around you, too, as long as you don't compromise your faith.

Your next reading is on page 1110.

the chief official had appointed over Daniel, Hananiah, Mishael and Azariah, [12]"Please test your servants for ten days: Give us nothing but vegetables to eat and water to drink. [13]Then compare our appearance with that of the young men who eat the royal food, and treat your servants in accordance with what you see." [14]So he agreed to this and tested them for ten days.

[15]At the end of the ten days they looked healthier and better nourished than any of the young men who ate the royal food. [16]So the guard took away their choice food and the wine they were to drink and gave them vegetables instead.

[17]To these four young men God gave knowledge and understanding of all kinds of literature and learning. And Daniel could understand visions and dreams of all kinds.

[18]At the end of the time set by the king to bring them in, the chief official presented them to Nebuchadnezzar. [19]The king talked with them, and he found none equal to Daniel, Hananiah, Mishael and Azariah; so they entered the king's service. [20]In every matter of wisdom and understanding about which the king questioned them, he found them ten times better than all the magicians and enchanters in his whole kingdom.

[21]And Daniel remained there until the first year of King Cyrus.

Nebuchadnezzar's Dream

2 In the second year of his reign, Nebuchadnezzar had dreams; his mind was troubled and he could not sleep. [2]So the king summoned the magicians, enchanters, sorcerers and astrologers[a] to tell him what he had dreamed. When they came in and stood before the king, [3]he said to them, "I have had a dream that troubles me and I want to know what it means.[b]"

[4]Then the astrologers answered the king in Aramaic,[c] "O king, live forever! Tell your servants the dream, and we will interpret it."

[5]The king replied to the astrologers,

---

[a]2 Or *Chaldeans*; also in verses 4, 5 and 10   [b]3 Or *was*
[c]4 The text from here through chapter 7 is in Aramaic.

Daniel's Special Gift

READ DANIEL 2:1–30

God gave Daniel "knowledge and understanding of all kinds of literature and learning," including the ability to "understand vision and dreams" (Daniel 1:17). This was *very* cool. Some talents are given to you before birth. They're part of who you are. Daniel was gifted in learning literature. Your strength may be in music or you might have mechanical abilities or be good in sports. But God often gives *extra* talents to people later on in life. These talents are over and beyond the normal talents—like when God supernaturally drops a big chunk of knowledge into your brain. In Daniel's case this was a spiritual gift to understand dreams. Joseph had this gift, too. Daniel knew this gift was not a natural ability. Each and every time a vision or dream was interpreted, it was *God* revealing what it meant. That's why Daniel gave God the credit and refused to take credit himself (Daniel 2:27–30).

Your next reading is on page 1114.

"This is what I have firmly decided: If you do not tell me what my dream was and interpret it, I will have you cut into pieces and your houses turned into piles of rubble. 6But if you tell me the dream and explain it, you will receive from me gifts and rewards and great honor. So tell me the dream and interpret it for me."

7Once more they replied, "Let the king tell his servants the dream, and we will interpret it."

8Then the king answered, "I am certain that you are trying to gain time, because you realize that this is what I have firmly decided: 9If you do not tell me the dream, there is just one penalty for you. You have conspired to tell me misleading and wicked things, hoping the situation will change. So then, tell me the dream, and I will know that you can interpret it for me."

10The astrologers answered the king, "There is not a man on earth who can do what the king asks! No king, however great and mighty, has ever asked such a thing of any magician or enchanter or astrologer. 11What the king asks is too difficult. No one can reveal it to the king except the gods, and they do not live among men."

12This made the king so angry and furious that he ordered the execution of all the wise men of Babylon. 13So the decree was issued to put the wise men to death, and men were sent to look for Daniel and his friends to put them to death.

14When Arioch, the commander of the king's guard, had gone out to put to death the wise men of Babylon, Daniel spoke to him with wisdom and tact. 15He asked the king's officer, "Why did the king issue such a harsh decree?" Arioch then explained the matter to Daniel. 16At this, Daniel went in to the king and asked for time, so that he might interpret the dream for him.

17Then Daniel returned to his house and explained the matter to his friends Hananiah, Mishael and Azariah. 18He urged them to plead for mercy from the God of heaven concerning this mystery, so that he and his friends might not be executed with the rest of the wise men of Babylon. 19During the night the mystery was revealed to Daniel in a vision. Then Daniel praised the God of heaven 20and said:

"Praise be to the name of God for ever and ever;
    wisdom and power are his.
21 He changes times and seasons;
    he sets up kings and deposes them.
He gives wisdom to the wise
    and knowledge to the discerning.
22 He reveals deep and hidden things;
    he knows what lies in darkness,
    and light dwells with him.
23 I thank and praise you, O God of my fathers:
    You have given me wisdom and power,
you have made known to me what we asked of you,
    you have made known to us the dream of the
        king."

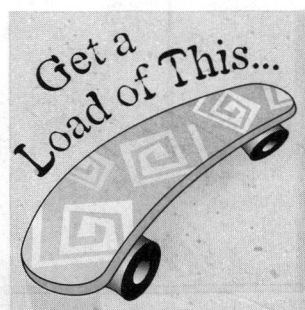

Get a Load of This...

The astrologers wanted to hear the dream. They needed information to work with so they could make up a halfway believable interpretation (see Daniel 2:7–9). Nebuchadnezzar had a point: "If you're so supernatural, you should be able to *tell* me the dream." He knew that they didn't have a clue.

In Other Words...

Get a Load of This...

Check out Daniel 2. Bible teachers agree that the kingdoms in Nebuchadnezzar's vision were Babylon (gold), Medo-Persia (silver), Greece (bronze), Rome (iron), and the eternal kingdom of God (established by Christ, the rock). Isn't it great that God knows the big picture from the beginning right up until the end of time?

Daniel Interprets the Dream

24Then Daniel went to Arioch, whom the king had appointed to execute the wise men of Babylon, and said to him, "Do not execute the wise men of Babylon. Take me to the king, and I will interpret his dream for him."

25Arioch took Daniel to the king at once and said, "I have found a man among the exiles from Judah who can tell the king what his dream means."

26The king asked Daniel (also called Belteshazzar), "Are you able to tell me what I saw in my dream and interpret it?"

27Daniel replied, "No wise man, enchanter, magician or diviner can explain to the king the mystery he has asked about, 28but there is a God in heaven who reveals mysteries. He has shown King Nebuchadnezzar what will happen in days to come. Your dream and the visions that passed through your mind as you lay on your bed are these:

29"As you were lying there, O king, your mind turned to things to come, and the revealer of mysteries showed you what is going to happen. 30As for me, this mystery has been revealed to me, not because I have greater wisdom than other living men, but so that you, O king, may know the interpretation and that you may understand what went through your mind.

31"You looked, O king, and there before you stood a large statue—an enormous, dazzling statue, awesome in appearance. 32The head of the statue was made of pure gold, its chest and arms of silver, its belly and thighs of bronze, 33its legs of iron, its feet partly of iron and partly of baked clay. 34While you were watching, a rock was cut out, but not by human hands. It struck the statue on its feet of iron and clay and smashed them. 35Then the iron, the clay, the bronze, the silver and the gold were broken to pieces at the same time and became like chaff on a threshing floor in the summer. The wind swept them away without leaving a trace. But the rock that struck the statue became a huge mountain and filled the whole earth.

36"This was the dream, and now we will interpret it to the king. 37You, O king, are the king of kings. The God of heaven has given you dominion and power and might and glory; 38in your hands he has placed mankind and the beasts of the field and the birds of the air. Wherever they live, he has made you ruler over them all. You are that head of gold.

39"After you, another kingdom will rise, inferior to yours. Next, a third kingdom, one of bronze, will rule over the whole earth. 40Finally, there will be a fourth kingdom, strong as iron—for iron breaks and smashes everything—and as iron breaks things to pieces, so it will crush and break all the others. 41Just as you saw that the feet and toes were partly of baked clay and partly of iron, so this will be a divided kingdom; yet it will have some of the strength of iron in it, even as you saw iron mixed with clay. 42As the toes were partly iron and partly clay, so this kingdom will be partly strong and partly brittle. 43And just as you saw the iron mixed with baked clay, so the people will be a mixture and will not remain united, any more than iron mixes with clay.

44"In the time of those kings, the God of heaven will set up a kingdom that will never be destroyed, nor will it be left to another people. It will crush all those kingdoms and bring them to an end, but it will itself endure forever. 45This is the meaning of the vision of the rock cut out of a mountain, but not by human hands—a rock that broke the iron, the bronze, the clay, the silver and the gold to pieces.

"The great God has shown the king what will take place in the future. The dream is true and the interpretation is trustworthy."

46Then King Nebuchadnezzar fell prostrate before Daniel and paid him honor and ordered that an offering and incense be presented to him. 47The king said to Daniel, "Surely your God is the God of gods and the Lord of kings and a revealer of mysteries, for you were able to reveal this mystery."

48Then the king placed Daniel in a high position and lavished many gifts on him. He made him ruler over the entire province of Babylon and placed him in charge of all its wise men. 49Moreover, at Daniel's request the king appointed Shadrach, Meshach and Abednego administrators over the province of Babylon, while Daniel himself remained at the royal court.

The Image of Gold and the Fiery Furnace

3 King Nebuchadnezzar made an image of gold, ninety feet high and nine feet[a] wide, and set it up on the plain of Dura in the province of Babylon. 2He then summoned the satraps, prefects, governors, advisers, treasurers, judges, magistrates and all the other provincial officials to come to the dedication of the image he had set up. 3So the satraps, prefects, governors, advisers, treasurers, judges, magistrates and all the other provincial officials assembled for the dedication of the image that King Nebuchadnezzar had set up, and they stood before it.

4Then the herald loudly proclaimed, "This is what you are commanded to do, O peoples, nations and men of every language: 5As soon as you hear the sound of the horn, flute, zither, lyre, harp, pipes and all kinds of music, you must fall down and worship the image of gold that King Nebuchadnezzar has set up. 6Whoever does not fall down and worship will immediately be thrown into a blazing furnace."

7Therefore, as soon as they heard the sound of the horn, flute, zither, lyre, harp and all kinds of music, all the peoples, nations and men of every language fell down and worshiped the image of gold that King Nebuchadnezzar had set up.

8At this time some astrologers[b] came forward and denounced the Jews. 9They said to King Nebuchadnezzar, "O king, live forever! 10You have issued a decree, O king, that everyone who hears the sound of the horn, flute, zither, lyre, harp, pipes and all kinds of music must fall down and worship the image of gold, 11and that whoever does not fall down and worship will be thrown into a blazing furnace. 12But there are some Jews whom you have set over the affairs of the province of Babylon—Shadrach, Meshach and Abednego—who pay no attention to you, O king. They neither serve your gods nor worship the image of gold you have set up."

13Furious with rage, Nebuchadnezzar summoned Shadrach, Meshach and Abednego. So these men were brought before the king, 14and Nebuchadnezzar said to them, "Is it true, Shadrach, Meshach and Abednego, that you do not serve my gods or worship the image of gold I have set up? 15Now when you hear the sound of the horn, flute, zither, lyre, harp, pipes and all kinds of music, if you are ready to fall down and worship the image I made, very good. But if you do not worship it, you will be thrown immediately into a blazing furnace. Then what god will be able to rescue you from my hand?"

16Shadrach, Meshach and Abednego replied to the king, "O Nebuchadnezzar, we do not need to defend ourselves before you in this matter. 17If we are thrown into the blazing furnace, the God we serve is able to save us from it, and he will rescue us from your hand, O king. 18But even if he does not, we want you to

---

a 1 Aramaic sixty cubits high and six cubits wide (about 27 meters high and 2.7 meters wide)   b 8 Or Chaldeans know, O king, that we will not serve your gods or worship the image of gold you have set up."

19Then Nebuchadnezzar was furious with Shadrach, Meshach and Abednego, and his attitude toward them changed. He ordered the furnace heated seven times hotter than usual 20and commanded some of the strongest soldiers in his army to tie up Shadrach, Meshach and Abednego and throw them into the blazing furnace. 21So these men, wearing their robes, trousers, turbans and other clothes, were bound and thrown into the blazing furnace. 22The king's command was so urgent and the furnace so hot that the flames of the fire killed the soldiers who took up Shadrach, Meshach and Abednego, 23and these three men, firmly tied, fell into the blazing furnace.

24Then King Nebuchadnezzar leaped to his feet in amazement and asked his advisers, "Weren't there three men that we tied up and threw into the fire?"

They replied, "Certainly, O king."

25He said, "Look! I see four men walking around in the fire, unbound and unharmed, and the fourth looks like a son of the gods."

26Nebuchadnezzar then approached the opening of the blazing furnace and shouted, "Shadrach, Meshach and Abednego, servants of the Most High God, come out! Come here!"

So Shadrach, Meshach and Abednego came out of the fire, 27and the satraps, prefects, governors and royal advisers crowded around them. They saw that the fire had not harmed their bodies, nor was a hair of their heads singed; their robes were not scorched, and there was no smell of fire on them.

28Then Nebuchadnezzar said, "Praise be to the God of Shadrach, Meshach and Abednego, who has sent his angel and rescued his servants! They trusted in him and defied the king's command and were willing to give up their lives rather than serve

GET STRONGER

Heavenly Heat Shields

READ DANIEL 3

This is the story of three very "cool" young men who didn't burn to a crisp inside a roaring furnace. Heat shields? No way! They had God. Shadrach, Meshach and Abednego had strong faith in God. They knew God was completely *able* to save them. The catch was, they didn't know for sure that was his will in this case. Gulp! Just the same, they determined to stand strong in their faith no matter what it cost them (see verses 16–18). They knew that God loved them and it was likely that he would protect them, but they also said, "Even if he doesn't save us, we'll still trust him and be obedient to him." It's the same with us today: We trust God to protect us, but even if we get sick or have accidents, we need to remain true to him and trust that he didn't fail us.

Your next reading is on page 1115.

or worship any god except their own God. 29Therefore I decree that the people of any nation or language who say anything against the God of Shadrach, Meshach and Abednego be cut into pieces and their houses be turned into piles of rubble, for no other god can save in this way."

30Then the king promoted Shadrach, Meshach and Abednego in the province of Babylon.

Nebuchadnezzar's Dream of a Tree

King Nebuchadnezzar,

To the peoples, nations and men of every language, who live in all the world:

May you prosper greatly!

2It is my pleasure to tell you about the miraculous signs and wonders that the Most High God has performed for me.

3 How great are his signs,
    how mighty his wonders!
His kingdom is an eternal kingdom;
    his dominion endures from
        generation to generation.

4I, Nebuchadnezzar, was at home in my palace, contented and prosperous. 5I had a dream that made me afraid. As I was lying in my bed, the images and visions that passed through my mind terrified me. 6So I commanded that all the wise men of Babylon be brought before me to interpret the dream for me. 7When the magicians, enchanters, astrologers[a] and diviners came, I told them the dream, but they could not interpret it for me. 8Finally, Daniel came into my presence and I told him the dream. (He is called Belteshazzar, after the name of my god, and the spirit of the holy gods is in him.)

9I said, "Belteshazzar, chief of the magicians, I know that the spirit of the holy gods is in you, and no mystery is too difficult for you. Here is my dream; interpret it for me. 10These are the visions I saw while lying in my

a 7 Or Chaldeans

Praying for Leaders

READ DANIEL 4:1–9, 24–37

Nebuchadnezzar had a mammoth ego and had to get his face in the dirt—literally—before he learned that he wasn't in control of all the kingdoms of earth. God was (see verse 25). When leaders are proud they plow ahead and follow their own plans and programs. Not good. Daniel surely prayed for Nebuchadnezzar, and you need to pray for your leaders and your land, too. Ask God to heal it (2 Chronicles 7:14). The good news is, Nebuchadnezzar ended up writing a confession to the citizens of his empire—*this* chapter, in fact. Paul says to pray for leaders so we can live quiet and peaceful lives (1 Timothy 2:1–2). You can influence political events by praying. Pray that the right people get into power and that your government does the right thing. Who are the leaders of your city, state or country?

Your next reading is on page 1118.

bed: I looked, and there before me stood a tree in the middle of the land. Its height was enormous. ¹¹The tree grew large and strong and its top touched the sky; it was visible to the ends of the earth. ¹²Its leaves were beautiful, its fruit abundant, and on it was food for all. Under it the beasts of the field found shelter, and the birds of the air lived in its branches; from it every creature was fed.

¹³"In the visions I saw while lying in my bed, I looked, and there before me was a messenger,ᵃ a holy one, coming down from heaven. ¹⁴He called in a loud voice: 'Cut down the tree and trim off its branches; strip off its leaves and scatter its fruit. Let the animals flee from under it and the birds from its branches. ¹⁵But let the stump and its roots, bound with iron and bronze, remain in the ground, in the grass of the field.

" 'Let him be drenched with the dew of heaven, and let him live with the animals among the plants of the earth. ¹⁶Let his mind be changed from that of a man and let him be given the mind of an animal, till seven timesᵇ pass by for him.

¹⁷" 'The decision is announced by messengers, the holy ones declare the verdict, so that the living may know that the Most High is sovereign over the kingdoms of men and gives them to anyone he wishes and sets over them the lowliest of men.'

¹⁸"This is the dream that I, King Nebuchadnezzar, had. Now, Belteshazzar, tell me what it means, for none of the wise men in my kingdom can interpret it for me. But you can, because the spirit of the holy gods is in you."

Daniel Interprets the Dream

¹⁹Then Daniel (also called Belteshazzar) was greatly perplexed for a time, and his thoughts terrified him. So the king said, "Belteshazzar, do not let the dream or its meaning alarm you."

Belteshazzar answered, "My lord, if only the dream applied to your enemies and its meaning to your adversaries! ²⁰The tree you saw, which grew large and strong, with its top

touching the sky, visible to the whole earth, ²¹with beautiful leaves and abundant fruit, providing food for all, giving shelter to the beasts of the field, and having nesting places in its branches for the birds of the air— ²²you, O king, are that tree! You have become great and strong; your greatness has grown until it reaches the sky, and your dominion extends to distant parts of the earth.

²³"You, O king, saw a messenger, a holy one, coming down from heaven and saying, 'Cut down the tree and destroy it, but leave the stump, bound with iron and bronze, in the grass of the field, while its roots remain in the ground. Let him be drenched with the dew of heaven; let him live like the wild animals, until seven times pass by for him.'

²⁴"This is the interpretation, O king, and this is the decree the Most High has issued against my lord the king: ²⁵You will be driven away from people and will live with the wild animals; you will eat grass like cattle and be drenched with the dew of heaven. Seven times will pass by for you until you acknowledge that the Most High is sovereign over the kingdoms of men and gives them to anyone he wishes. ²⁶The command to leave the stump of the tree with its roots means that your kingdom will be restored to you when you acknowledge that Heaven rules. ²⁷Therefore, O king, be pleased to accept my advice: Renounce your sins by doing what is right, and your wickedness by being kind to the oppressed. It may be that then your prosperity will continue."

The Dream Is Fulfilled

²⁸All this happened to King Nebuchadnezzar. ²⁹Twelve months later, as the king was walking on the roof of the royal palace of Babylon, ³⁰he said, "Is not this the great Babylon I have built as the royal residence, by my mighty power and for the glory of my majesty?"

³¹The words were still on his lips

ᵃ 13 Or *watchman*; also in verses 17 and 23   ᵇ 16 Or *years*; also in verses 23, 25 and 32 when a voice came from heaven, "This is what is decreed for you, King Nebuchadnezzar: Your royal authority has been taken from you. 32You will be driven away from people and will live with the wild animals; you will eat grass like cattle. Seven times will pass by for you until you acknowledge that the Most High is sovereign over the kingdoms of men and gives them to anyone he wishes."

33Immediately what had been said about Nebuchadnezzar was fulfilled. He was driven away from people and ate grass like cattle. His body was drenched with the dew of heaven until his hair grew like the feathers of an eagle and his nails like the claws of a bird.

34At the end of that time, I, Nebuchadnezzar, raised my eyes toward heaven, and my sanity was restored. Then I praised the Most High; I honored and glorified him who lives forever.

His dominion is an eternal dominion;
　　his kingdom endures from
　　　　generation to generation.
35All the peoples of the earth
　　are regarded as nothing.
He does as he pleases
　　with the powers of heaven
　　and the peoples of the earth.
No one can hold back his hand
　　or say to him: "What have you
　　　　done?"

36At the same time that my sanity was restored, my honor and splendor were returned to me for the glory of my kingdom. My advisers and nobles sought me out, and I was restored to my throne and became even greater than before. 37Now I, Nebuchadnezzar, praise and exalt and glorify the King of heaven, because everything he does is right and all his ways are just. And those who walk in pride he is able to humble.

The Writing on the Wall

5 King Belshazzar gave a great banquet for a thousand of his nobles and drank wine with them. 2While Belshazzar was drinking his wine, he gave orders to bring in the gold and silver goblets that Nebuchadnezzar his father*a* had taken from the temple in Jerusalem, so that the king and his nobles, his wives and his concubines might drink from them. 3So they brought in the gold goblets that had been taken from the temple of God in Jerusalem, and the king and his nobles, his wives and his concubines drank from them. 4As they drank the wine, they praised the gods of gold and silver, of bronze, iron, wood and stone.

5Suddenly the fingers of a human hand appeared and wrote on the plaster of the wall, near the lampstand in the royal palace. The king watched the hand as it wrote. 6His face turned pale and he was so frightened that his knees knocked together and his legs gave way.

7The king called out for the enchanters, astrologers*b* and diviners to be brought and said to these wise men of Babylon, "Whoever reads this writing and tells me what it means will be clothed in purple and have a gold chain placed around his neck, and he will be made the third highest ruler in the kingdom."

8Then all the king's wise men came in, but they could not read the writing or tell the king what it meant. 9So King Belshazzar became even more terrified and his face grew more pale. His nobles were baffled.

10The queen,*c* hearing the voices of the king and his nobles, came into the banquet hall. "O king, live forever!" she said. "Don't be alarmed! Don't look so pale! 11There is a man in your kingdom who has the spirit of the holy gods in him. In the time of your father he was found to have insight and intelligence and wisdom like that of the gods. King Nebuchadnezzar your father—your father the king, I say—appointed him chief of the magicians, enchanters, astrologers and diviners. 12This man Daniel, whom the king called Belteshazzar, was found to have a keen mind and knowledge and understanding, and also the ability to interpret dreams, explain riddles and solve difficult problems. Call for Daniel, and he will tell you what the writing means."

13So Daniel was brought before the king, and the king said to him, "Are you Daniel, one of the exiles my father the king brought from Judah? 14I have heard

a 2 Or ancestor; or predecessor; also in verses 11, 13 and 18
b 7 Or Chaldeans; also in verse 11　*c 10 Or queen mother*

that the spirit of the gods is in you and that you have insight, intelligence and outstanding wisdom. 15The wise men and enchanters were brought before me to read this writing and tell me what it means, but they could not explain it. 16Now I have heard that you are able to give interpretations and to solve difficult problems. If you can read this writing and tell me what it means, you will be clothed in purple and have a gold chain placed around your neck, and you will be made the third highest ruler in the kingdom."

17Then Daniel answered the king, "You may keep your gifts for yourself and give your rewards to someone else. Nevertheless, I will read the writing for the king and tell him what it means.

18"O king, the Most High God gave your father Nebuchadnezzar sovereignty and greatness and glory and splendor. 19Because of the high position he gave him, all the peoples and nations and men of every language dreaded and feared

him. Those the king wanted to put to death, he put to death; those he wanted to spare, he spared; those he wanted to promote, he promoted; and those he wanted to humble, he humbled. 20But when his heart became arrogant and hardened with pride, he was deposed from his royal throne and stripped of his glory. 21He was driven away from people and given the mind of an animal; he lived with the wild donkeys and ate grass like cattle; and his body was drenched with the dew of heaven, until he acknowledged that the Most High God is sovereign over the kingdoms of men and sets over them anyone he wishes.

22"But you his son,[a] O Belshazzar, have not humbled yourself, though you knew all this. 23Instead, you have set yourself up against the Lord of heaven. You had the goblets from his temple brought to you, and you and your nobles, your wives and your concubines drank wine from them.

[a] 22 Or *descendant;* or *successor*

GET STRONGER.

False Sense of Security

READ DANIEL 5

When God says something's going to fall, it *will* take the dive, sooner or later, one way or the other. God had said way back in the prophecies of Isaiah and Jeremiah that Babylon would go down. Now it happened. Belshazzar *knew* that armies of the Medes had surrounded the city, and he *knew* that God had humbled Nebuchadnezzar when *he* had been proud. But Belshazzar just couldn't stop oozing with cocky pride. Medes-schmedes. He was safe inside Babylon with its high, thick walls. *Guess what?* He lost his kingdom that very night (verse 30). These days people think if they won the lottery they'd be secure. If they were famous and people worshiped them, they'd have it made. *That* kind of "security" is ... well ... worthless. Only God can be our security. If we look to him and trust him, he will take care of us.

Your next reading is on page 1120.

You praised the gods of silver and gold, of bronze, iron, wood and stone, which cannot see or hear or understand. But you did not honor the God who holds in his hand your life and all your ways. ²⁴Therefore he sent the hand that wrote the inscription.

²⁵"This is the inscription that was written:

MENE, MENE, TEKEL, PARSIN ᵃ

²⁶"This is what these words mean:

Mene ᵇ: God has numbered the days of your reign and brought it to an end.

²⁷ Tekel ᶜ: You have been weighed on the scales and found wanting.

²⁸Peres ᵈ: Your kingdom is divided and given to the Medes and Persians."

²⁹Then at Belshazzar's command, Daniel was clothed in purple, a gold chain was placed around his neck, and he was proclaimed the third highest ruler in the kingdom.

³⁰That very night Belshazzar, king of the Babylonians, ᵉ was slain, ³¹and Darius the Mede took over the kingdom, at the age of sixty-two.

Daniel in the Den of Lions

It pleased Darius to appoint 120 satraps to rule throughout the kingdom, ²with three administrators over them, one of whom was Daniel. The satraps were made accountable to them so that the king might not suffer loss. ³Now Daniel so distinguished himself among the administrators and the satraps by his exceptional qualities that the king planned to set him over the whole kingdom. ⁴At this, the administrators and the satraps tried to find grounds for charges against Daniel in his conduct of government affairs, but they were unable to do so. They could find no corruption in him, because he was trustworthy and neither corrupt nor negligent. ⁵Finally these men said, "We will never find any basis for charges against this man Daniel unless it has something to do with the law of his God."

⁶So the administrators and the satraps went as a group to the king and said: "O King Darius, live forever! ⁷The royal administrators, prefects, satraps, advisers and governors have all agreed that the king should issue an edict and enforce the decree that anyone who prays to any god or man during the next thirty days, except to you, O king, shall be thrown into the lions' den. ⁸Now, O king, issue the decree and put it in writing so that it cannot be altered—in accordance with the laws of the Medes and Persians, which cannot be repealed." ⁹So King Darius put the decree in writing.

¹⁰Now when Daniel learned that the decree had been published, he went home to his upstairs room where the windows opened toward Jerusalem. Three times a day

Get a Load of This...

The Babylonians knew what these Aramaic words meant (Daniel 5:25), but they made no sense together. Belshazzar didn't have enough clues to understand them. Can you just picture him asking, "Can I buy a vowel?" But it was Daniel who said, "I'd like to solve the puzzle now." And it wasn't a pleasant puzzle . . .

ᵃ 25 Aramaic UPARSIN (that is, AND PARSIN)   ᵇ 26 Mene can mean numbered or mina (a unit of money).   ᶜ 27 Tekel can mean weighed or shekel.
ᵈ 28 Peres (the singular of Parsin) can mean divided or Persia or a half mina or a half shekel.   ᵉ 30 Or Chaldeans

he got down on his knees and prayed, giving thanks to his God, just as he had done before. ¹¹Then these men went as a group and found Daniel praying and asking God for help. ¹²So they went to the king and spoke to him about his royal decree: "Did you not publish a decree that during the next thirty days anyone who prays to any god or man except to you, O king, would be thrown into the lions' den?"

The king answered, "The decree stands—in accordance with the laws of the Medes and Persians, which cannot be repealed."

¹³Then they said to the king, "Daniel, who is one of the exiles from Judah, pays no attention to you, O king, or to the decree you put in writing. He still prays three times a day." ¹⁴When the king heard this, he was greatly distressed; he was determined to rescue Daniel and made every effort until sundown to save him.

¹⁵Then the men went as a group to the king and said to him, "Remember, O king, that according to the law of the Medes and Persians no decree or edict that the king issues can be changed."

¹⁶So the king gave the order, and they brought Daniel and threw him into the lions' den. The king said to Daniel, "May your God, whom you serve continually, rescue you!"

¹⁷A stone was brought and placed over the mouth of the den, and the king sealed it with his own signet ring and with the rings of his nobles, so that Daniel's situation might not be changed. ¹⁸Then the king returned to his palace and spent the night without eating and without any entertainment being brought to him. And he could not sleep.

¹⁹At the first light of dawn, the king got up and hurried to the lions' den. ²⁰When he came near the den, he called to Daniel in an anguished voice, "Daniel, servant of the living God, has your God, whom you serve continually, been able to rescue you from the lions?"

²¹Daniel answered, "O king, live forever! ²²My God sent his angel, and he shut the mouths of the lions. They have not hurt me, because I was found innocent in his sight. Nor have I ever done any wrong before you, O king."

Not Lyin' Around

READ DANIEL 6:1–24

Daniel was probably in his eighties when he spent the night with starving lions. He had served God faithfully all his life. He knew Babylonian wisdom, sure, but he had majored in studying God's Word—and in *living* what he believed. The kings and rulers came and went, but Daniel remained, because he had political skills and was good at what he did. He was hardworking and honest. When Darius took over, he recognized Daniel's abilities and appointed him a ruler. Daniel was "trustworthy and neither corrupt nor negligent" (verse 4). He wasn't lying around ... well, except for the one night he was lying with the lions—no fault of his own. God may call *you* to a high position and bless you, but it will be because you first learned to be God's man. You can't compromise the truth, do so-so work and still keep your fingers on the blessing. You have to follow God's ways and live according to his principles.

GET COOLER

Your next reading is on page 1122.

23The king was overjoyed and gave orders to lift Daniel out of the den. And when Daniel was lifted from the den, no wound was found on him, because he had trusted in his God.

24At the king's command, the men who had falsely accused Daniel were brought in and thrown into the lions' den, along with their wives and children. And before they reached the floor of the den, the lions overpowered them and crushed all their bones.

25Then King Darius wrote to all the peoples, nations and men of every language throughout the land:

"May you prosper greatly!

26"I issue a decree that in every part of my kingdom people must fear and reverence the God of Daniel.

"For he is the living God
and he endures forever;
his kingdom will not be destroyed,
his dominion will never end.
27He rescues and he saves;
he performs signs and wonders
in the heavens and on the earth.
He has rescued Daniel
from the power of the lions."

28So Daniel prospered during the reign of Darius and the reign of Cyrus[a] the Persian.

Daniel's Dream of Four Beasts

7 In the first year of Belshazzar king of Babylon, Daniel had a dream, and visions passed through his mind as he was lying on his bed. He wrote down the substance of his dream.

2Daniel said: "In my vision at night I looked, and there before me were the four winds of heaven churning up the great sea. 3Four great beasts, each different from the others, came up out of the sea.

4"The first was like a lion, and it had the wings of an eagle. I watched until its wings were torn off and it was lifted from the ground so that it stood on two feet like a man, and the heart of a man was given to it.

5"And there before me was a second beast, which looked like a bear. It was raised up on one of its sides, and it had three ribs in its mouth between its teeth. It was told, 'Get up and eat your fill of flesh!'

6"After that, I looked, and there before me was another beast, one that looked like a leopard. And on its back it had four wings like those of a bird. This beast had four heads, and it was given authority to rule.

7"After that, in my vision at night I looked, and there before me was a fourth beast—terrifying and frightening and very powerful. It had large iron teeth; it crushed and devoured its victims and trampled underfoot what-

Get a Load of This...

Check out Daniel 6. In Babylon, lions were used as executioners. They thought of humans as food and when they saw people, it was dinnertime. You wouldn't want to be out for an evening stroll just before "dinner" if the lions escaped from their den, right?!

---

a 28 Or Darius, that is, the reign of Cyrus

ever was left. It was different from all the former beasts, and it had ten horns.

8 "While I was thinking about the horns, there before me was another horn, a little one, which came up among them; and three of the first horns were uprooted before it. This horn had eyes like the eyes of a man and a mouth that spoke boastfully.

9 "As I looked,

"thrones were set in place,
    and the Ancient of Days took his
        seat.
His clothing was as white as snow;
    the hair of his head was white like
        wool.
His throne was flaming with fire,
    and its wheels were all ablaze.
10 A river of fire was flowing,
    coming out from before him.
Thousands upon thousands attended
        him;
    ten thousand times ten thousand
        stood before him.
The court was seated,
    and the books were opened.

11 "Then I continued to watch because of the boastful words the horn was speaking. I kept looking until the beast was slain and its body destroyed and thrown into the blazing fire. 12 (The other beasts had been stripped of their authority, but were allowed to live for a period of time.)

13 "In my vision at night I looked, and there before me was one like a son of man, coming with the clouds of heaven. He approached the Ancient of Days and was led into his presence. 14 He was given authority, glory and sovereign power; all peoples, nations and men of every language worshiped him. His dominion is an everlasting dominion that will not pass away, and his kingdom is one that will never be destroyed.

The Interpretation of the Dream

15 "I, Daniel, was troubled in spirit, and the visions that passed through my mind disturbed me. 16 I approached one of those standing there and asked him the true meaning of all this.

"So he told me and gave me the inter-

Whence Dreams?

READ DANIEL 7:1–3, 15–18

In the Bible, when God sent a dream, three things happened: (a) As soon as the person woke up, they knew that God was giving them a message, (b) they usually knew what the message was (Job 33:14–18), or someone was around to interpret it (Genesis 40), (c) they understood what they needed to do (Matthew 2:13–14). Most dreams, however, are simply your own thoughts (Ecclesiastes 5:3). Hmmm. So why have *those* dreams? It seems to be the way God created for you to file things away: Your mind goes over things you've experienced and dream, dream, dream, file, file, file. If you have a weird dream but don't know what it means, it was most likely the pizza you ate or the TV show you watched. Your brain is trying to sort troubling images out. Solution: If you want peaceful dreams, watch peaceful images. Another thing: The better you know God's Word, the more easily you can sort things out.

Your next reading is on page 1124.

pretation of these things: 17'The four great beasts are four kingdoms that will rise from the earth. 18But the saints of the Most High will receive the kingdom and will possess it forever—yes, for ever and ever.'

19"Then I wanted to know the true meaning of the fourth beast, which was different from all the others and most terrifying, with its iron teeth and bronze claws—the beast that crushed and devoured its victims and trampled underfoot whatever was left. 20I also wanted to know about the ten horns on its head and about the other horn that came up, before which three of them fell—the horn that looked more imposing than the others and that had eyes and a mouth that spoke boastfully. 21As I watched, this horn was waging war against the saints and defeating them, 22until the Ancient of Days came and pronounced judgment in favor of the saints of the Most High, and the time came when they possessed the kingdom.

23"He gave me this explanation: 'The fourth beast is a fourth kingdom that will appear on earth. It will be different from all the other kingdoms and will devour the whole earth, trampling it down and crushing it. 24The ten horns are ten kings who will come from this kingdom. After them another king will arise, different from the earlier ones; he will subdue three kings. 25He will speak against the Most High and oppress his saints and try to change the set times and the laws. The saints will be handed over to him for a time, times and half a time.ª

26" 'But the court will sit, and his power will be taken away and completely destroyed forever. 27Then the sovereignty, power and greatness of the kingdoms under the whole heaven will be handed over to the saints, the people of the Most High. His kingdom will be an everlasting kingdom, and all rulers will worship and obey him.'

28"This is the end of the matter. I, Daniel, was deeply troubled by my thoughts, and my face turned pale, but I kept the matter to myself."

Daniel's Vision of a Ram and a Goat

8 In the third year of King Belshazzar's reign, I, Daniel, had a vision, after the one that had already appeared to me. 2In my vision I saw myself in the citadel of Susa in the province of Elam; in the vision I was beside the Ulai Canal. 3I looked up, and there before me was a ram with two horns, standing beside the canal, and the horns were long. One of the horns was longer than the other but grew up later. 4I watched the ram as he charged toward the west and the north and the south. No animal could stand against him, and none could rescue from his power. He did as he pleased and became great.

5As I was thinking about this, suddenly a goat with a prominent horn between his eyes came from the west,

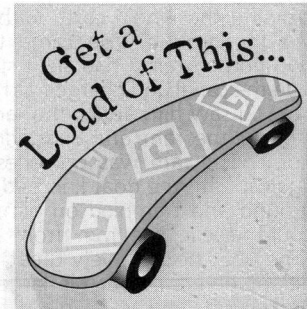

Get a Load of This...

Daniel 7:9–14 is some vision! Have you figured out who's who? The "Ancient of Days" is God the Father, and Jesus is the "son of man" who was given "authority, glory and ... power." (Jesus often called himself the Son of Man.) This vision happened over 500 years before Jesus was *born.*

ª 25 Or for a year, two years and half a year

crossing the whole earth without touching the ground. 6He came toward the two-horned ram I had seen standing beside the canal and charged at him in great rage. 7I saw him attack the ram furiously, striking the ram and shattering his two horns. The ram was powerless to stand against him; the goat knocked him to the ground and trampled on him, and none could rescue the ram from his power. 8The goat became very great, but at the height of his power his large horn was broken off, and in its place four prominent horns grew up toward the four winds of heaven.

9Out of one of them came another horn, which started small but grew in power to the south and to the east and toward the Beautiful Land. 10It grew until it reached the host of the heavens, and it threw some of the starry host down to the earth and trampled on them. 11It set itself up to be as great as the Prince of the host; it took away the daily sacrifice from him, and the place of his sanctuary was brought low. 12Because of rebellion, the host ⌊of the saints⌋ᵃ and the daily sacrifice were giv-

en over to it. It prospered in everything it did, and truth was thrown to the ground.

13Then I heard a holy one speaking, and another holy one said to him, "How long will it take for the vision to be fulfilled— the vision concerning the daily sacrifice, the rebellion that causes desolation, and the surrender of the sanctuary and of the host that will be trampled underfoot?"

14He said to me, "It will take 2,300 evenings and mornings; then the sanctuary will be reconsecrated."

The Interpretation of the Vision

15While I, Daniel, was watching the vision and trying to understand it, there before me stood one who looked like a man. 16And I heard a man's voice from the Ulai calling, "Gabriel, tell this man the meaning of the vision."

17As he came near the place where I was standing, I was terrified and fell prostrate. "Son of man," he said to me, "understand that the vision concerns the time of the end."

ᵃ 12 Or rebellion, the armies

Visions—Awake or Asleep

READ DANIEL 8:1–4

In the Bible, visions usually came when a person was awake, and dreams came when they were under the sheets, asleep. Sometimes people had visions while they were sleeping. Either way, having a vision is seeing something supernaturally. It's similar to seeing a holographic movie, like putting on the fancy goggles and—stepping into virtual reality. It's like you've suddenly been taken to another place. God usually gave his prophets visions when their eyes were wide open. Peter had a vision at noon about a sheet full of creepy, crawling animals (see Acts 10:9–12). (If Peter had been asleep at the time, he would've been *inside* the sheet, not looking at it!) Peter knew that it was God showing him this vision, because God spoke, and the message was clear. One last thing: A person receiving a true vision always sensed the presence of God.

Your next reading is on page 1126.

¹⁸While he was speaking to me, I was in a deep sleep, with my face to the ground. Then he touched me and raised me to my feet.

¹⁹He said: "I am going to tell you what will happen later in the time of wrath, because the vision concerns the appointed time of the end.[a] ²⁰The two-horned ram that you saw represents the kings of Media and Persia. ²¹The shaggy goat is the king of Greece, and the large horn between his eyes is the first king. ²²The four horns that replaced the one that was broken off represent four kingdoms that will emerge from his nation but will not have the same power.

²³"In the latter part of their reign, when rebels have become completely wicked, a stern-faced king, a master of intrigue, will arise. ²⁴He will become very strong, but not by his own power. He will cause astounding devastation and will succeed in whatever he does. He will destroy the mighty men and the holy people. ²⁵He will cause deceit to prosper, and he will consider himself superior. When they feel secure, he will destroy many and take his stand against the Prince of princes. Yet he will be destroyed, but not by human power.

²⁶"The vision of the evenings and mornings that has been given you is true, but seal up the vision, for it concerns the distant future."

²⁷I, Daniel, was exhausted and lay ill for several days. Then I got up and went about the king's business. I was appalled by the vision; it was beyond understanding.

Daniel's Prayer

In the first year of Darius son of Xerxes[b] (a Mede by descent), who was made ruler over the Babylonian[c] kingdom— ²in the first year of his reign, I, Daniel, understood from the Scriptures, according to the word of the LORD given to Jeremiah the prophet, that the desolation of Jerusalem would last seventy years. ³So I turned to the Lord God and pleaded with him in prayer and petition, in fasting, and in sackcloth and ashes.

⁴I prayed to the LORD my God and confessed:

"O Lord, the great and awesome God, who keeps his covenant of love with all who love him and obey his commands, ⁵we have sinned and done wrong. We have been wicked and have rebelled; we have turned away from your commands and laws. ⁶We have not listened to your servants the prophets, who spoke in your name to our kings, our princes and our fathers, and to all the people of the land.

⁷"Lord, you are righteous, but this day we are covered with shame—the men of Judah and people of Jerusalem and all Israel, both near and far, in all the countries where you have scattered us because of our unfaithfulness to you. ⁸O LORD, we

Get a Load of This...

Check out Daniel 8:5. What is Daniel seeing? A unicorn goat? Yes, but this creature didn't really exist. Daniel was seeing it in a vision. The goat symbolized the Greek empire and the great horn symbolized Alexander the Great.

---

a 19 Or *because the end will be at the appointed time*   *b 1* Hebrew *Ahasuerus*
c 1 Or *Chaldean*

and our kings, our princes and our fathers are covered with shame because we have sinned against you. ⁹The Lord our God is merciful and forgiving, even though we have rebelled against him; ¹⁰we have not obeyed the LORD our God or kept the laws he gave us through his servants the prophets. ¹¹All Israel has transgressed your law and turned away, refusing to obey you.

"Therefore the curses and sworn judgments written in the Law of Moses, the servant of God, have been poured out on us, because we have sinned against you. ¹²You have fulfilled the words spoken against us and against our rulers by bringing upon us great disaster. Under the whole heaven nothing has ever been done like what has been done to Jerusalem. ¹³Just as it is written in the Law of Moses, all this disaster has come upon us, yet we have not sought the favor of the LORD our God by turning from our sins and giving attention to your truth. ¹⁴The LORD did not hesitate to bring the disaster upon us, for the LORD our God is righteous in everything he does; yet we have not obeyed him.

¹⁵"Now, O Lord our God, who brought your people out of Egypt with a mighty hand and who made for yourself a name that endures to this day, we have sinned, we have done wrong. ¹⁶O Lord, in keeping with all your righteous acts, turn away your anger and your wrath from Jerusalem, your city, your holy hill. Our sins and the iniquities of our fathers have made Jerusalem and your people an object of scorn to all those around us.

¹⁷"Now, our God, hear the prayers and petitions of your servant. For your sake, O Lord, look with favor on your desolate sanctuary. ¹⁸Give ear, O God, and hear; open your eyes and see the desolation of the city that bears your Name. We do not make requests of you because we are righteous, but because of your great mercy. ¹⁹O Lord, listen! O Lord, for-

---

Praying God's Will

READ DANIEL 9:1–19

When Daniel prayed, he knew exactly what to pray for, because he knew what God's will was. How'd he know? Easy. He studied Scripture. He studied the Law of Moses as well as the writings of Jeremiah. One day when Daniel was studying Jeremiah's prophecies— Wham!—God hit him with truth right between the eyes. Daniel discovered that, lo and behold, the seventy years of captivity (Jeremiah 29:10–14) were just about up. It was now time for God to restore and forgive his people, and send them jogging back to Judah. So Daniel prayed God's will for his country. We should pray for our country too. We pray, "Your will be done" (Matthew 6:10), and if we want to make a difference, it helps to know what God's will is, and what's *supposed* to happen. Then we can pray accordingly (1 John 5:14–15). Find out God's will, then pray that he will make it happen.

Your next reading is on page 1133.

give! O Lord, hear and act! For your sake, O my God, do not delay, because your city and your people bear your Name."

The Seventy "Sevens"

²⁰While I was speaking and praying, confessing my sin and the sin of my people Israel and making my request to the LORD my God for his holy hill— ²¹while I was still in prayer, Gabriel, the man I had seen in the earlier vision, came to me in swift flight about the time of the evening sacrifice. ²²He instructed me and said to me, "Daniel, I have now come to give you insight and understanding. ²³As soon as you began to pray, an answer was given, which I have come to tell you, for you are highly esteemed. Therefore, consider the message and understand the vision:

²⁴"Seventy 'sevens'ᵃ are decreed for your people and your holy city to finishᵇ transgression, to put an end to sin, to atone for wickedness, to bring in everlasting righteousness, to seal up vision and prophecy and to anoint the most holy.ᶜ

²⁵"Know and understand this: From the issuing of the decreeᵈ to restore and rebuild Jerusalem until the Anointed One,ᵉ the ruler, comes, there will be seven 'sevens,' and sixty-two 'sevens.' It will be rebuilt with streets and a trench, but in times of trouble. ²⁶After the sixty-two 'sevens,' the Anointed One will be cut off and will have nothing.ᶠ The people of the ruler who will come will destroy the city and the sanctuary. The end will come like a flood: War will continue until the end, and desolations have been decreed. ²⁷He will confirm a covenant with many for one 'seven.'ᵍ In the middle of the 'seven'ᵍ he will put an end to sacrifice and offering. And on a wing ⌊of the temple⌋ he will set up an abomination that causes desolation, until the end that is decreed is poured out on him.ʰ"ⁱ

Daniel's Vision of a Man

10 In the third year of Cyrus king of Persia, a revelation was given to Daniel (who was called Belteshazzar). Its message was true and it concerned a great war.ʲ The understanding of the message came to him in a vision.

²At that time I, Daniel, mourned for three weeks. ³I ate no choice food; no meat or wine touched my lips; and I used no lotions at all until the three weeks were over.

⁴On the twenty-fourth day of the first month, as I was standing on the bank of the great river, the Tigris, ⁵I looked up and there before me was a man dressed in linen, with a belt of the finest gold around his waist. ⁶His body was like chrysolite, his face like lightning, his eyes like flaming torches, his arms and legs like the gleam of burnished bronze, and his voice like the sound of a multitude.

⁷I, Daniel, was the only one who saw the vision; the men with me did not see it, but such terror overwhelmed them that they fled and hid themselves. ⁸So I was left alone, gazing at this great vision; I had no strength left, my face turned deathly pale and I was helpless. ⁹Then I heard him speaking, and as I listened to him, I fell into a deep sleep, my face to the ground.

¹⁰A hand touched me and set me trembling on my hands and knees. ¹¹He said, "Daniel, you who are highly esteemed, consider carefully the words I am about to speak to you, and stand up, for I have now been sent to you." And when he said this to me, I stood up trembling.

¹²Then he continued, "Do not be afraid, Daniel. Since the first day that you set your mind to gain understanding and to humble yourself before your God, your words were heard, and I have come in response to them. ¹³But the prince of the Persian kingdom resisted me twenty-one days. Then Michael, one of the chief princes, came to help me, because I was detained there with the king of Persia. ¹⁴Now I have come to explain to you what will happen to your people in the future, for the vision concerns a time yet to come."

¹⁵While he was saying this to me, I bowed with my face toward the ground and was speechless. ¹⁶Then one who looked like a manᵏ touched my lips, and I opened my mouth and began to speak. I said to the one standing before me, "I am

---

ᵃ 24 Or 'weeks'; also in verses 25 and 26   ᵇ 24 Or restrain   ᶜ 24 Or Most Holy Place; or most holy One   ᵈ 25 Or word   ᵉ 25 Or an anointed one; also in verse 26   ᶠ 26 Or off and will have no one; or off, but not for himself   ᵍ 27 Or 'week'   ʰ 27 Or it   ⁱ 27 Or And one who causes desolation will come upon the pinnacle of the abominable ⌊temple⌋, until the end that is decreed is poured out on the desolated ⌊city⌋   ʲ 1 Or true and burdensome   ᵏ 16 Most manuscripts of the Masoretic Text; one manuscript of the Masoretic Text, Dead Sea Scrolls and Septuagint Then something that looked like a man's hand

Get a Load of This...

In *this* corner ... the angel Gabriel! In *that* corner ... the demon prince of Persia (Daniel 10:12–13)! The prince is throwing his weight around! Watch out, Gabriel! Ouch! *That* had to hurt! Looks like the prince is getting the upper hand and ... Wait! Here comes Gabriel's partner, Michael! The crowd is going wild!

overcome with anguish because of the vision, my lord, and I am helpless. [17]How can I, your servant, talk with you, my lord? My strength is gone and I can hardly breathe."

[18]Again the one who looked like a man touched me and gave me strength. [19]"Do not be afraid, O man highly esteemed," he said. "Peace! Be strong now; be strong."

When he spoke to me, I was strengthened and said, "Speak, my lord, since you have given me strength."

[20]So he said, "Do you know why I have come to you? Soon I will return to fight against the prince of Persia, and when I go, the prince of Greece will come; [21]but first I will tell you what is written in the Book of Truth. (No one supports me against them except Michael, your prince.) [1]And in the first year of Darius the Mede, I took my stand to support and protect him.)

The Kings of the South and the North

[2]"Now then, I tell you the truth: Three more kings will appear in Persia, and then a fourth, who will be far richer than all the others. When he has gained power by his wealth, he will stir up everyone against the kingdom of Greece. [3]Then a mighty king will appear, who will rule with great power and do as he pleases. [4]After he has appeared, his empire will be broken up and parceled out toward the four winds of heaven. It will not go to his descendants, nor will it have the power he exercised, because his empire will be uprooted and given to others.

[5]"The king of the South will become strong, but one of his commanders will become even stronger than he and will rule his own kingdom with great power. [6]After some years, they will become allies. The daughter of the king of the South will go to the king of the North to make an alliance, but she will not retain her power, and he and his power[a] will not last. In those days she will be handed over, together with her royal escort and her father[b] and the one who supported her.

[7]"One from her family line will arise to take her place. He will attack the forces of the king of the North and enter his fortress; he will fight against them and be victorious. [8]He will also seize their gods, their metal images and their valuable articles of silver and gold and carry them off to Egypt. For some years he will leave the king of the North alone. [9]Then the king of the North will invade the realm of the king of the South but will retreat to his own country. [10]His sons will prepare for war and assemble a great army, which will sweep on like an irresistible flood and carry the battle as far as his fortress.

[11]"Then the king of the South will march out in a rage and fight against the king of the North, who will raise a large army, but it will be defeated. [12]When the army is carried off, the king of the South will be filled with pride and will slaughter many thousands, yet he will not remain triumphant. [13]For the king of the North

[a] 6 Or *offspring*　　[b] 6 Or *child* (see Vulgate and Syriac)

will muster another army, larger than the first; and after several years, he will advance with a huge army fully equipped.

¹⁴"In those times many will rise against the king of the South. The violent men among your own people will rebel in fulfillment of the vision, but without success. ¹⁵Then the king of the North will come and build up siege ramps and will capture a fortified city. The forces of the South will be powerless to resist; even their best troops will not have the strength to stand. ¹⁶The invader will do as he pleases; no one will be able to stand against him. He will establish himself in the Beautiful Land and will have the power to destroy it. ¹⁷He will determine to come with the might of his entire kingdom and will make an alliance with the king of the South. And he will give him a daughter in marriage in order to overthrow the kingdom, but his plans[a] will not succeed or help him. ¹⁸Then he will turn his attention to the coastlands and will take many of them, but a commander will put an end to his insolence and will turn his insolence back upon him. ¹⁹After this, he will turn back toward the fortresses of his own country but will stumble and fall, to be seen no more.

²⁰"His successor will send out a tax collector to maintain the royal splendor. In a few years, however, he will be destroyed, yet not in anger or in battle.

²¹"He will be succeeded by a contemptible person who has not been given the honor of royalty. He will invade the kingdom when its people feel secure, and he will seize it through intrigue. ²²Then an overwhelming army will be swept away before him; both it and a prince of the covenant will be destroyed. ²³After coming to an agreement with him, he will act deceitfully, and with only a few people he will rise to power. ²⁴When the richest provinces feel secure, he will invade them and will achieve what neither his fathers nor his forefathers did. He will distribute plunder, loot and wealth among his followers. He will plot the overthrow of fortresses—but only for a time.

²⁵"With a large army he will stir up his strength and courage against the king of the South. The king of the South will wage war with a large and very powerful army, but he will not be able to stand because of the plots devised against him.

²⁶Those who eat from the king's provisions will try to destroy him; his army will be swept away, and many will fall in battle. ²⁷The two kings, with their hearts bent on evil, will sit at the same table and lie to each other, but to no avail, because an end will still come at the appointed time. ²⁸The king of the North will return to his own country with great wealth, but his heart will be set against the holy covenant. He will take action against it and then return to his own country.

²⁹"At the appointed time he will invade the South again, but this time the outcome will be different from what it was before. ³⁰Ships of the western coastlands[b] will oppose him, and he will lose heart. Then he will turn back and vent his fury against the holy covenant. He will return and show favor to those who forsake the holy covenant.

³¹"His armed forces will rise up to desecrate the temple fortress and will abolish the daily sacrifice. Then they will set up the abomination that causes desolation. ³²With flattery he will corrupt those who have violated the covenant, but the people who know their God will firmly resist him.

³³"Those who are wise will instruct many, though for a time they will fall by the sword or be burned or captured or plundered. ³⁴When they fall, they will receive a little help, and many who are not sincere will join them. ³⁵Some of the wise will stumble, so that they may be refined, purified and made spotless until the time of the end, for it will still come at the appointed time.

The King Who Exalts Himself

³⁶"The king will do as he pleases. He will exalt and magnify himself above every god and will say unheard-of things against the God of gods. He will be successful until the time of wrath is completed, for what has been determined must take place. ³⁷He will show no regard for the gods of his fathers or for the one desired by women, nor will he regard any god, but will exalt himself above them all. ³⁸Instead of them, he will honor a god of fortresses; a god unknown to his fathers he will honor with gold and silver, with precious stones and costly gifts. ³⁹He will

---

a 17 Or *but she*   *b 30* Hebrew of *Kittim*

attack the mightiest fortresses with the help of a foreign god and will greatly honor those who acknowledge him. He will make them rulers over many people and will distribute the land at a price. [a]

40 "At the time of the end the king of the South will engage him in battle, and the king of the North will storm out against him with chariots and cavalry and a great fleet of ships. He will invade many countries and sweep through them like a flood. 41 He will also invade the Beautiful Land. Many countries will fall, but Edom, Moab and the leaders of Ammon will be delivered from his hand. 42 He will extend his power over many countries; Egypt will not escape. 43 He will gain control of the treasures of gold and silver and all the riches of Egypt, with the Libyans and Nubians in submission. 44 But reports from the east and the north will alarm him, and he will set out in a great rage to destroy and annihilate many. 45 He will pitch his royal tents between the seas at [b] the beau-

tiful holy mountain. Yet he will come to his end, and no one will help him.

The End Times

12 "At that time Michael, the great prince who protects your people, will arise. There will be a time of distress such as has not happened from the beginning of nations until then. But at that time your people—everyone whose name is found written in the book—will be delivered. 2 Multitudes who sleep in the dust of the earth will awake: some to everlasting life, others to shame and everlasting contempt. 3 Those who are wise [c] will shine like the brightness of the heavens, and those who lead many to righteousness, like the stars for ever and ever. 4 But you, Daniel, close up and seal the words of the scroll until the time of the end. Many will go here and there to increase knowledge."

[a] 39 Or land for a reward   [b] 45 Or the sea and
[c] 3 Or who impart wisdom

Make It Stick

READ DANIEL 12:1–4

God says that in heaven we will have new resurrection bodies. The greater our reward, the greater our shine (see Daniel 12:2–3). What will your resurrection body be like?—A fizzled-out red dwarf star or a super nova? Draw a picture that shows how brightly you hope you'll shine. If you're not into drawing you could plot your "shine" on a chart or a Richter scale (like what they use to measure earthquakes).

⁵Then I, Daniel, looked, and there before me stood two others, one on this bank of the river and one on the opposite bank. ⁶One of them said to the man clothed in linen, who was above the waters of the river, "How long will it be before these astonishing things are fulfilled?"

⁷The man clothed in linen, who was above the waters of the river, lifted his right hand and his left hand toward heaven, and I heard him swear by him who lives forever, saying, "It will be for a time, times and half a time.ᵃ When the power of the holy people has been finally broken, all these things will be completed."

⁸I heard, but I did not understand. So I asked, "My lord, what will the outcome of all this be?"

⁹He replied, "Go your way, Daniel, because the words are closed up and sealed until the time of the end. ¹⁰Many will be purified, made spotless and refined, but the wicked will continue to be wicked. None of the wicked will understand, but those who are wise will understand.

¹¹"From the time that the daily sacrifice is abolished and the abomination that causes desolation is set up, there will be 1,290 days. ¹²Blessed is the one who waits for and reaches the end of the 1,335 days.

¹³"As for you, go your way till the end. You will rest, and then at the end of the days you will rise to receive your allotted inheritance."

ᵃ 7 Or *a year, two years and half a year*

HOSEA

Who wrote this book?
The prophet Hosea.

Why was this book written?
Hosea warns the people of Israel about their unfaithfulness to God.

What do we learn about God in this book?
God keeps on loving us even if we are unfaithful. Punishment does not mean that God has stopped loving us.

What is special about this book?
Hosea's wife is not faithful to him, but Hosea keeps on loving her. Even though the people of Israel are unfaithful to God, God keeps on loving them.

When was this book written?
The sermons in Hosea were preached between 753 and 723 B.C. This was just before the Assyrians destroyed Israel and took all its people captive.

What are some important chapters in this book?
Israel's unfaithfulness	Hosea 4
God's love for Israel	Hosea 11

1 The word of the LORD that came to Hosea son of Beeri during the reigns of Uzziah, Jotham, Ahaz and Hezekiah, kings of Judah, and during the reign of Jeroboam son of Jehoash[a] king of Israel:

Hosea's Wife and Children

2When the LORD began to speak through Hosea, the LORD said to him, "Go, take to yourself an adulterous wife and children of unfaithfulness, because the land is guilty of the vilest adultery in departing from the LORD." 3So he married Gomer daughter of Diblaim, and she conceived and bore him a son.

4Then the LORD said to Hosea, "Call him Jezreel, because I will soon punish the house of Jehu for the massacre at Jezreel, and I will put an end to the kingdom of Israel. 5In that day I will break Israel's bow in the Valley of Jezreel."

6Gomer conceived again and gave birth to a daughter. Then the LORD said to Hosea, "Call her Lo-Ruhamah,[b] for I will no longer show love to the house of Israel, that I should at all forgive them. 7Yet I will show love to the house of Judah; and I will save them—not by bow, sword or battle, or by horses and horsemen, but by the LORD their God."

8After she had weaned Lo-Ruhamah, Gomer had another son. 9Then the LORD said, "Call him Lo-Ammi,[c] for you are not my people, and I am not your God.

10"Yet the Israelites will be like the sand on the seashore, which cannot be measured or counted. In the place where it was said to them, 'You are not my people,' they will be called 'sons of the living God.' 11The people of Judah and the people of Israel will be reunited, and they will appoint one leader and will come up out of the land, for great will be the day of Jezreel.

a 1 Hebrew *Joash,* a variant of *Jehoash*   b 6 *Lo-Ruhamah* means *not loved.*   c 9 *Lo-Ammi* means *not my people.*

Adultery Is Not for Me

READ HOSEA 1; 3:1–3

The marriage relationship between a husband and a wife is the most sacred relationship on the earth. It's one of the closest illustrations of a Christian's relationship to God. That's why God told Hosea to marry Gomer—a woman he *knew* would be unfaithful in marriage. God wanted Hosea to understand the pain *he* felt when the people of Israel were unfaithful to him. Big number seven of the Ten Commandments says, "You shall not commit adultery" (Exodus 20:14). Adultery is when a married person has sexual relations with someone other than their husband or wife. God strongly warned against adultery in many other places in the Bible. Why? Because it destroys relationships and families. That's why God wants us to honor the marriage relationship and stay faithful. As a man of God you should already be committing in your heart to be a faithful partner to your future wife.

Your next reading is on page 1139.

2 "Say of your brothers, 'My people,'
and of your sisters, 'My loved one.'

Israel Punished and Restored

2 "Rebuke your mother, rebuke her,
  for she is not my wife,
  and I am not her husband.
Let her remove the adulterous look
    from her face
  and the unfaithfulness from
    between her breasts.
3 Otherwise I will strip her naked
  and make her as bare as on the day
    she was born;
  I will make her like a desert,
  turn her into a parched land,
  and slay her with thirst.
4 I will not show my love to her children,
  because they are the children of
    adultery.
5 Their mother has been unfaithful
  and has conceived them in disgrace.
  She said, 'I will go after my lovers,
    who give me my food and my water,
    my wool and my linen, my oil and
    my drink.'
6 Therefore I will block her path with
    thornbushes;
  I will wall her in so that she cannot
    find her way.
7 She will chase after her lovers but not
    catch them;
  she will look for them but not find
    them.
  Then she will say,
  'I will go back to my husband as at
    first,
  for then I was better off than now.'
8 She has not acknowledged that I was
    the one
  who gave her the grain, the new
    wine and oil,
  who lavished on her the silver and
    gold—
  which they used for Baal.

9 "Therefore I will take away my grain
    when it ripens,
  and my new wine when it is ready.
  I will take back my wool and my linen,
    intended to cover her nakedness.
10 So now I will expose her lewdness
  before the eyes of her lovers;
  no one will take her out of my
    hands.
11 I will stop all her celebrations:
  her yearly festivals, her New Moons,
  her Sabbath days—all her appointed
    feasts.
12 I will ruin her vines and her fig trees,
  which she said were her pay from
    her lovers;
  I will make them a thicket,
  and wild animals will devour them.
13 I will punish her for the days
  she burned incense to the Baals;
  she decked herself with rings and
    jewelry,
  and went after her lovers,
  but me she forgot,"
              declares the LORD.

14 "Therefore I am now going to allure
    her;
  I will lead her into the desert
  and speak tenderly to her.
15 There I will give her back her vineyards,
  and will make the Valley of Achor[a] a
    door of hope.
  There she will sing[b] as in the days of
    her youth,
  as in the day she came up out of
    Egypt.

16 "In that day," declares the LORD,
  "you will call me 'my husband';
  you will no longer call me 'my
    master.'[c]
17 I will remove the names of the Baals
    from her lips;
  no longer will their names be invoked.
18 In that day I will make a covenant for
    them
  with the beasts of the field and the
    birds of the air
  and the creatures that move along
    the ground.
  Bow and sword and battle
  I will abolish from the land,
  so that all may lie down in safety.
19 I will betroth you to me forever;
  I will betroth you in[d] righteousness
    and justice,
  in[e] love and compassion.
20 I will betroth you in faithfulness,
  and you will acknowledge the LORD.

21 "In that day I will respond,"
  declares the LORD—
  "I will respond to the skies,
  and they will respond to the earth;
22 and the earth will respond to the grain,

---

[a] 15 Achor means trouble.　　[b] 15 Or respond
[c] 16 Hebrew baal　　[d] 19 Or with; also in verse 20
[e] 19 Or with

the new wine and oil,
and they will respond to Jezreel.*a*
23 I will plant her for myself in the land;
I will show my love to the one I
called 'Not my loved one.*b*'
I will say to those called 'Not my
people,*c*' 'You are my people';
and they will say, 'You are my God.' "

Hosea's Reconciliation With His Wife

3 The LORD said to me, "Go, show
your love to your wife again,
though she is loved by another and
is an adulteress. Love her as the
LORD loves the Israelites, though they turn
to other gods and love the sacred raisin
cakes."

2 So I bought her for fifteen shekels*d* of
silver and about a homer and a lethek*e* of
barley. 3 Then I told her, "You are to live
with*f* me many days; you must not be a
prostitute or be intimate with any man,
and I will live with*f* you."

4 For the Israelites will live many days
without king or prince, without sacrifice
or sacred stones, without ephod or idol.
5 Afterward the Israelites will return and
seek the LORD their God and David their
king. They will come trembling to the LORD
and to his blessings in the last days.

The Charge Against Israel

4 Hear the word of the LORD, you
Israelites,
because the LORD has a charge to
bring
against you who live in the land:
"There is no faithfulness, no love,
no acknowledgment of God in the
land.
2 There is only cursing,*g* lying and murder,
stealing and adultery;
they break all bounds,
and bloodshed follows bloodshed.
3 Because of this the land mourns,*h*
and all who live in it waste away;
the beasts of the field and the birds of
the air
and the fish of the sea are dying.

4 "But let no man bring a charge,
let no man accuse another,
for your people are like those
who bring charges against a priest.
5 You stumble day and night,
and the prophets stumble with you.
So I will destroy your mother—

6 my people are destroyed from lack
of knowledge.

"Because you have rejected knowledge,
I also reject you as my priests;
because you have ignored the law of
your God,
I also will ignore your children.
7 The more the priests increased,
the more they sinned against me;
they exchanged*i* their*j* Glory for
something disgraceful.
8 They feed on the sins of my people
and relish their wickedness.
9 And it will be: Like people, like priests.
I will punish both of them for their
ways
and repay them for their deeds.

10 "They will eat but not have enough;
they will engage in prostitution but
not increase,
because they have deserted the LORD
to give themselves 11 to prostitution,
to old wine and new,
which take away the understanding
12 of my people.
They consult a wooden idol
and are answered by a stick of wood.
A spirit of prostitution leads them
astray;
they are unfaithful to their God.
13 They sacrifice on the mountaintops
and burn offerings on the hills,
under oak, poplar and terebinth,
where the shade is pleasant.
Therefore your daughters turn to
prostitution
and your daughters-in-law to adultery.

14 "I will not punish your daughters
when they turn to prostitution,
nor your daughters-in-law
when they commit adultery,
because the men themselves consort
with harlots
and sacrifice with shrine
prostitutes—
a people without understanding will
come to ruin!

15 "Though you commit adultery, O Israel,
let not Judah become guilty.

a 22 Jezreel means God plants.   *b 23* Hebrew Lo-Ruhamah
c 23 Hebrew Lo-Ammi   *d 2* That is, about 6 ounces (about
170 grams)   *e 2* That is, probably about 10 bushels (about
330 liters)   *f 3* Or wait for   *g 2* That is, to pronounce a
curse upon   *h 3* Or dries up   *i 7* Syriac and an ancient
Hebrew scribal tradition; Masoretic Text I will exchange
j 7 Masoretic Text; an ancient Hebrew scribal tradition my

"Do not go to Gilgal;
  do not go up to Beth Aven.ᵃ
And do not swear, 'As surely as the
  LORD lives!'
¹⁶ The Israelites are stubborn,
  like a stubborn heifer.
How then can the LORD pasture them
  like lambs in a meadow?
¹⁷ Ephraim is joined to idols;
  leave him alone!
¹⁸ Even when their drinks are gone,
  they continue their prostitution;
  their rulers dearly love shameful ways.
¹⁹ A whirlwind will sweep them away,
  and their sacrifices will bring them
    shame.

Judgment Against Israel

5 "Hear this, you priests!
  Pay attention, you Israelites!
  Listen, O royal house!
  This judgment is against you:
You have been a snare at Mizpah,
  a net spread out on Tabor.

² The rebels are deep in slaughter.
  I will discipline all of them.
³ I know all about Ephraim;
  Israel is not hidden from me.
Ephraim, you have now turned to
    prostitution;
  Israel is corrupt.

⁴ "Their deeds do not permit them
  to return to their God.
A spirit of prostitution is in their heart;
  they do not acknowledge the LORD.
⁵ Israel's arrogance testifies against them;
  the Israelites, even Ephraim, stumble
    in their sin;
  Judah also stumbles with them.
⁶ When they go with their flocks and
    herds
  to seek the LORD,
they will not find him;
  he has withdrawn himself from
    them.

ᵃ 15 *Beth Aven* means *house of wickedness* (a name for
Bethel, which means *house of God*).

Make It Stick

READ HOSEA 4:6

Imagine a boy who says, "I *love* baseball!" but he knows nearly nothing about how the game is played. *Huh?* That's like a Christian who's clueless about Christianity and living his faith. People like that are set on auto-destruct. Write on a sticky note something you don't understand about Christianity, then determine to learn about it.

7 They are unfaithful to the LORD;
  they give birth to illegitimate children.
Now their New Moon festivals
  will devour them and their fields.

8 "Sound the trumpet in Gibeah,
  the horn in Ramah.
Raise the battle cry in Beth Aven*a*;
  lead on, O Benjamin.
9 Ephraim will be laid waste
  on the day of reckoning.
Among the tribes of Israel
  I proclaim what is certain.
10 Judah's leaders are like those
  who move boundary stones.
I will pour out my wrath on them
  like a flood of water.
11 Ephraim is oppressed,
  trampled in judgment,
  intent on pursuing idols.*b*
12 I am like a moth to Ephraim,
  like rot to the people of Judah.

13 "When Ephraim saw his sickness,
  and Judah his sores,
then Ephraim turned to Assyria,
  and sent to the great king for help.
But he is not able to cure you,
  not able to heal your sores.
14 For I will be like a lion to Ephraim,
  like a great lion to Judah.
I will tear them to pieces and go away;
  I will carry them off, with no one to rescue them.
15 Then I will go back to my place
  until they admit their guilt.
And they will seek my face;
  in their misery they will earnestly seek me."

Israel Unrepentant

6 "Come, let us return to the LORD.
He has torn us to pieces
  but he will heal us;
he has injured us
  but he will bind up our wounds.
2 After two days he will revive us;
  on the third day he will restore us,
  that we may live in his presence.
3 Let us acknowledge the LORD;
  let us press on to acknowledge him.
As surely as the sun rises,
  he will appear;
he will come to us like the winter rains,
  like the spring rains that water the earth."

4 "What can I do with you, Ephraim?
  What can I do with you, Judah?

Check out Hosea 5:12, 14. It's better to have God as a Father and a Provider and a Guide to you, than a moth who eats your favorite clothes, a rot that destroys your house and a lion that tears you in pieces. Um ... yes. That *would* be better.

---

a 8 Beth Aven means *house of wickedness* (a name for Bethel, which means *house of God*).   *b 11* The meaning of the Hebrew for this word is uncertain.

Get a Load of This...

"Ephraim is a flat cake not turned over" (Hosea 7:8). This is like a pancake burned on one side and doughy on the other. Can you imagine your mom serving you *that* for breakfast? You'd sure hope the dog was under the table.

Your love is like the morning mist,
    like the early dew that disappears.
5 Therefore I cut you in pieces with my prophets,
    I killed you with the words of my mouth;
    my judgments flashed like lightning upon you.
6 For I desire mercy, not sacrifice,
    and acknowledgment of God rather than burnt
       offerings.
7 Like Adam,[a] they have broken the covenant—
    they were unfaithful to me there.
8 Gilead is a city of wicked men,
    stained with footprints of blood.
9 As marauders lie in ambush for a man,
    so do bands of priests;
they murder on the road to Shechem,
    committing shameful crimes.
10 I have seen a horrible thing
    in the house of Israel.
There Ephraim is given to prostitution
    and Israel is defiled.

11 "Also for you, Judah,
    a harvest is appointed.

"Whenever I would restore the fortunes of my
       people,
7 1 whenever I would heal Israel,
    the sins of Ephraim are exposed
    and the crimes of Samaria revealed.
    They practice deceit,
    thieves break into houses,
    bandits rob in the streets;
2 but they do not realize
    that I remember all their evil deeds.
Their sins engulf them;
    they are always before me.

3 "They delight the king with their wickedness,
    the princes with their lies.
4 They are all adulterers,
    burning like an oven
whose fire the baker need not stir
    from the kneading of the dough till it rises.
5 On the day of the festival of our king
    the princes become inflamed with wine,
    and he joins hands with the mockers.
6 Their hearts are like an oven;
    they approach him with intrigue.
Their passion smolders all night;
    in the morning it blazes like a flaming fire.
7 All of them are hot as an oven;
    they devour their rulers.
All their kings fall,
    and none of them calls on me.

8 "Ephraim mixes with the nations;
    Ephraim is a flat cake not turned over.

a 7 Or *As at Adam;* or *Like men*

9 Foreigners sap his strength,
    but he does not realize it.
  His hair is sprinkled with gray,
    but he does not notice.
10 Israel's arrogance testifies against him,
    but despite all this
  he does not return to the LORD his God
    or search for him.

11 "Ephraim is like a dove,
    easily deceived and senseless—
  now calling to Egypt,
    now turning to Assyria.
12 When they go, I will throw my net over
      them;
    I will pull them down like birds of
      the air.
  When I hear them flocking together,
    I will catch them.
13 Woe to them,
    because they have strayed from me!
  Destruction to them,
    because they have rebelled against
      me!
  I long to redeem them
    but they speak lies against me.

14 They do not cry out to me from their
      hearts
    but wail upon their beds.
  They gather together[a] for grain and
      new wine
    but turn away from me.
15 I trained them and strengthened them,
    but they plot evil against me.
16 They do not turn to the Most High;
    they are like a faulty bow.
  Their leaders will fall by the sword
    because of their insolent words.
  For this they will be ridiculed
    in the land of Egypt.

Israel to Reap the Whirlwind

8 "Put the trumpet to your lips!
  An eagle is over the house of the
      LORD
  because the people have broken
    my covenant
  and rebelled against my law.
2 Israel cries out to me,
    'O our God, we acknowledge you!'

[a] 14 Most Hebrew manuscripts; some Hebrew manuscripts
and Septuagint *They slash themselves*

Going Through the Motions

READ HOSEA 8

Imagine someone who came to your birthday party, brought you a nice gift, then told all your friends that you were a loser, and bullied your kid brother. Say hello to the Israelites, back in Hosea's day. They gave gifts to God, but they were just going through religious motions without truly loving God or their fellow people. God blew the whistle on this kind of behavior. "They offer sacrifices ... but the LORD ... will remember their wickedness and punish their sins" (verse 13). God doesn't like people playing games, pretending to serve him. He didn't like it then, and he doesn't like it now. It's important to pray, read your Bible and go to church, but don't just go through the motions. Being a Christian is not repeating a bunch of religious mumbo jumbo. It's about having a relationship with God, loving him and loving the people around you.

Your next reading is on page 1149.

³But Israel has rejected what is good;
   an enemy will pursue him.
⁴They set up kings without my consent;
   they choose princes without my
     approval.
With their silver and gold
   they make idols for themselves
   to their own destruction.
⁵Throw out your calf-idol, O Samaria!
   My anger burns against them.
How long will they be incapable of
     purity?
⁶   They are from Israel!
This calf—a craftsman has made it;
   it is not God.
It will be broken in pieces,
   that calf of Samaria.

⁷"They sow the wind
   and reap the whirlwind.
The stalk has no head;
   it will produce no flour.
Were it to yield grain,
   foreigners would swallow it up.
⁸Israel is swallowed up;
   now she is among the nations
   like a worthless thing.
⁹For they have gone up to Assyria
   like a wild donkey wandering alone.
   Ephraim has sold herself to lovers.
¹⁰Although they have sold themselves
   among the nations,
   I will now gather them together.
They will begin to waste away
   under the oppression of the mighty
     king.

¹¹"Though Ephraim built many altars for
     sin offerings,
   these have become altars for
     sinning.
¹²I wrote for them the many things of
     my law,
   but they regarded them as
     something alien.
¹³They offer sacrifices given to me
   and they eat the meat,
   but the LORD is not pleased with
     them.
Now he will remember their
     wickedness
   and punish their sins:
They will return to Egypt.
¹⁴Israel has forgotten his Maker
   and built palaces;
   Judah has fortified many towns.
But I will send fire upon their cities
   that will consume their fortresses."

Punishment for Israel

9 Do not rejoice, O Israel;
   do not be jubilant like the other
     nations.
For you have been unfaithful to
     your God;
   you love the wages of a prostitute
   at every threshing floor.
²Threshing floors and winepresses will
     not feed the people;
   the new wine will fail them.
³They will not remain in the LORD's land;
   Ephraim will return to Egypt
   and eat unclean ᵃ food in Assyria.
⁴They will not pour out wine offerings
     to the LORD,
   nor will their sacrifices please him.
Such sacrifices will be to them like the
     bread of mourners;
   all who eat them will be unclean.
This food will be for themselves;
   it will not come into the temple of
     the LORD.

⁵What will you do on the day of your
     appointed feasts,
   on the festival days of the LORD?
⁶Even if they escape from destruction,
   Egypt will gather them,
   and Memphis will bury them.
Their treasures of silver will be taken
     over by briers,
   and thorns will overrun their tents.
⁷The days of punishment are coming,
   the days of reckoning are at hand.
   Let Israel know this.
Because your sins are so many
   and your hostility so great,
   the prophet is considered a fool,
   the inspired man a maniac.
⁸The prophet, along with my God,
   is the watchman over Ephraim, ᵇ
yet snares await him on all his paths,
   and hostility in the house of his God.
⁹They have sunk deep into corruption,
   as in the days of Gibeah.
God will remember their wickedness
   and punish them for their sins.

¹⁰"When I found Israel,
   it was like finding grapes in the
     desert;
when I saw your fathers,
   it was like seeing the early fruit on
     the fig tree.

ᵃ 3 That is, ceremonially unclean   ᵇ 8 Or The prophet is the
watchman over Ephraim, / the people of my God

But when they came to Baal Peor,
  they consecrated themselves to that
    shameful idol
  and became as vile as the thing they
    loved.
11 Ephraim's glory will fly away like a
    bird—
  no birth, no pregnancy, no
    conception.
12 Even if they rear children,
  I will bereave them of every one.
Woe to them
  when I turn away from them!
13 I have seen Ephraim, like Tyre,
  planted in a pleasant place.
But Ephraim will bring out
  their children to the slayer."

14 Give them, O Lord—
  what will you give them?
Give them wombs that miscarry
  and breasts that are dry.

15 "Because of all their wickedness in
    Gilgal,
  I hated them there.
Because of their sinful deeds,
  I will drive them out of my house.
I will no longer love them;
  all their leaders are rebellious.
16 Ephraim is blighted,
  their root is withered,
  they yield no fruit.
Even if they bear children,
  I will slay their cherished offspring."

17 My God will reject them
  because they have not obeyed him;
  they will be wanderers among the
    nations.

10 Israel was a spreading vine;
  he brought forth fruit for himself.
As his fruit increased,
  he built more altars;
as his land prospered,
  he adorned his sacred stones.
2 Their heart is deceitful,
  and now they must bear their guilt.
The Lord will demolish their altars
  and destroy their sacred stones.

3 Then they will say, "We have no king
  because we did not revere the Lord.
But even if we had a king,
  what could he do for us?"
4 They make many promises,
  take false oaths
  and make agreements;

therefore lawsuits spring up
  like poisonous weeds in a plowed
    field.
5 The people who live in Samaria fear
  for the calf-idol of Beth Aven.ᵃ
Its people will mourn over it,
  and so will its idolatrous priests,
those who had rejoiced over its
    splendor,
because it is taken from them into
    exile.
6 It will be carried to Assyria
  as tribute for the great king.
Ephraim will be disgraced;
  Israel will be ashamed of its wooden
    idols.ᵇ
7 Samaria and its king will float away
  like a twig on the surface of the
    waters.
8 The high places of wickednessᶜ will be
    destroyed—
  it is the sin of Israel.
Thorns and thistles will grow up
  and cover their altars.
Then they will say to the mountains,
    "Cover us!"
  and to the hills, "Fall on us!"

9 "Since the days of Gibeah, you have
    sinned, O Israel,
  and there you have remained.ᵈ
Did not war overtake
  the evildoers in Gibeah?
10 When I please, I will punish them;
  nations will be gathered against them
  to put them in bonds for their
    double sin.
11 Ephraim is a trained heifer
  that loves to thresh;
so I will put a yoke
  on her fair neck.
I will drive Ephraim,
  Judah must plow,
  and Jacob must break up the
    ground.
12 Sow for yourselves righteousness,
  reap the fruit of unfailing love,
and break up your unplowed ground;
  for it is time to seek the Lord,
until he comes
  and showers righteousness on you.
13 But you have planted wickedness,
  you have reaped evil,

ᵃ 5 *Beth Aven* means *house of wickedness* (a name for Bethel,
which means *house of God*).   ᵇ 6 Or *its counsel*
ᶜ 8 Hebrew *aven,* a reference to Beth Aven (a derogatory
name for Bethel)   ᵈ 9 Or *there a stand was taken*

Get a Load of This...

Ever told a riddle that made sense on one level but made even more sense on a deeper level? God said, "Out of Egypt I called my son" (Hosea 11:1). He was not only talking about when the Israelites left Egypt at the time of Moses, but giving a future prophecy about Jesus (see Matthew 2:15).

you have eaten the fruit of deception.
Because you have depended on your own strength
and on your many warriors,
14 the roar of battle will rise against your people,
so that all your fortresses will be devastated—
as Shalman devastated Beth Arbel on the day of
battle,
when mothers were dashed to the ground with
their children.
15 Thus will it happen to you, O Bethel,
because your wickedness is great.
When that day dawns,
the king of Israel will be completely destroyed.

God's Love for Israel

11 "When Israel was a child, I loved him,
and out of Egypt I called my son.
2 But the more I a called Israel,
the further they went from me. b
They sacrificed to the Baals
and they burned incense to images.
3 It was I who taught Ephraim to walk,
taking them by the arms;
but they did not realize
it was I who healed them.
4 I led them with cords of human kindness,
with ties of love;
I lifted the yoke from their neck
and bent down to feed them.

5 "Will they not return to Egypt
and will not Assyria rule over them
because they refuse to repent?
6 Swords will flash in their cities,
will destroy the bars of their gates
and put an end to their plans.
7 My people are determined to turn from me.
Even if they call to the Most High,
he will by no means exalt them.

8 "How can I give you up, Ephraim?
How can I hand you over, Israel?
How can I treat you like Admah?
How can I make you like Zeboiim?
My heart is changed within me;
all my compassion is aroused.
9 I will not carry out my fierce anger,
nor will I turn and devastate Ephraim.
For I am God, and not man—
the Holy One among you.
I will not come in wrath. c
10 They will follow the LORD;
he will roar like a lion.
When he roars,
his children will come trembling from the west.

a 2 Some Septuagint manuscripts; Hebrew they   b 2 Septuagint; Hebrew them
c 9 Or come against any city

¹¹ They will come trembling
    like birds from Egypt,
    like doves from Assyria.
I will settle them in their homes,"
    declares the LORD.

Israel's Sin

¹² Ephraim has surrounded me with lies,
    the house of Israel with deceit.
And Judah is unruly against God,
    even against the faithful Holy One.

12 ¹ Ephraim feeds on the wind;
    he pursues the east wind all day
    and multiplies lies and violence.
He makes a treaty with Assyria
    and sends olive oil to Egypt.
² The LORD has a charge to bring against
    Judah;
he will punish Jacob*ᵃ* according to
    his ways
and repay him according to his deeds.
³ In the womb he grasped his brother's
    heel;
    as a man he struggled with God.
⁴ He struggled with the angel and
    overcame him;
    he wept and begged for his favor.
He found him at Bethel
    and talked with him there—
⁵ the LORD God Almighty,
    the LORD is his name of renown!
⁶ But you must return to your God;
    maintain love and justice,
    and wait for your God always.

⁷ The merchant uses dishonest scales;
    he loves to defraud.
⁸ Ephraim boasts,
    "I am very rich; I have become
        wealthy.
With all my wealth they will not find in
    me
    any iniquity or sin."

⁹ "I am the LORD your God,
    ⌊who brought you⌋ out of*ᵇ* Egypt;
I will make you live in tents again,
    as in the days of your appointed
        feasts.
¹⁰ I spoke to the prophets,
    gave them many visions
    and told parables through them."

¹¹ Is Gilead wicked?
    Its people are worthless!
Do they sacrifice bulls in Gilgal?
    Their altars will be like piles of stones
    on a plowed field.

¹² Jacob fled to the country of Aram*ᶜ*;
    Israel served to get a wife,
    and to pay for her he tended sheep.
¹³ The LORD used a prophet to bring Israel
    up from Egypt,
    by a prophet he cared for him.
¹⁴ But Ephraim has bitterly provoked him
    to anger;
    his Lord will leave upon him the
        guilt of his bloodshed
    and will repay him for his contempt.

The LORD's Anger Against Israel

13 When Ephraim spoke, men
    trembled;
    he was exalted in Israel.
But he became guilty of Baal
    worship and died.
² Now they sin more and more;
    they make idols for themselves from
        their silver,
cleverly fashioned images,
    all of them the work of craftsmen.
It is said of these people,
    "They offer human sacrifice
    and kiss*ᵈ* the calf-idols."
³ Therefore they will be like the morning
    mist,
    like the early dew that disappears,
    like chaff swirling from a threshing
        floor,
    like smoke escaping through a
        window.

⁴ "But I am the LORD your God,
    ⌊who brought you⌋ out of*ᵉ* Egypt.
You shall acknowledge no God but me,
    no Savior except me.
⁵ I cared for you in the desert,
    in the land of burning heat.
⁶ When I fed them, they were satisfied;
    when they were satisfied, they
        became proud;
    then they forgot me.
⁷ So I will come upon them like a lion,
    like a leopard I will lurk by the path.
⁸ Like a bear robbed of her cubs,
    I will attack them and rip them open.
Like a lion I will devour them;
    a wild animal will tear them apart.

⁹ "You are destroyed, O Israel,
    because you are against me, against
        your helper.

ᵃ 2 Jacob means *he grasps the heel* (figuratively, *he deceives*).
ᵇ 9 Or *God / ever since you were in*   *ᶜ 12* That is,
Northwest Mesopotamia   *ᵈ 2* Or *"Men who sacrifice / kiss*
ᵉ 4 Or *God / ever since you were in*

10 Where is your king, that he may save
  you?
 Where are your rulers in all your
  towns,
 of whom you said,
  'Give me a king and princes'?
11 So in my anger I gave you a king,
  and in my wrath I took him away.
12 The guilt of Ephraim is stored up,
  his sins are kept on record.
13 Pains as of a woman in childbirth
  come to him,
 but he is a child without wisdom;
 when the time arrives,

he does not come to the opening of
  the womb.
14 "I will ransom them from the power of
  the grave[a];
 I will redeem them from death.
 Where, O death, are your plagues?
 Where, O grave,[b] is your
  destruction?

"I will have no compassion,
15 even though he thrives among his
  brothers.
 An east wind from the LORD will come,

---

[a] 14 Hebrew *Sheol*   [b] 14 Hebrew *Sheol*

Make It Stick

READ HOSEA 14:5–7

A garden full of fruit and vegetables symbolizes rich blessings. That's why God said Israel would be like olives, grapes and grain if they obeyed him. Take a walk in your garden (or down the fruit and veggie aisles of a supermarket) and think about God's promise of blessing if you obey him. What are two of your favorite blessings? What are two of your favorite fruits and veggies?

blowing in from the desert;
his spring will fail
  and his well dry up.
His storehouse will be plundered
  of all its treasures.
16 The people of Samaria must bear their
      guilt,
  because they have rebelled against
      their God.
They will fall by the sword;
  their little ones will be dashed to the
      ground,
  their pregnant women ripped
      open."

Repentance to Bring Blessing

14 Return, O Israel, to the Lord
    your God.
  Your sins have been your
    downfall!
2 Take words with you
  and return to the Lord.
Say to him:
  "Forgive all our sins
and receive us graciously,
  that we may offer the fruit of our
      lips. *a*
3 Assyria cannot save us;
  we will not mount war-horses.
We will never again say 'Our gods'
  to what our own hands have made,
  for in you the fatherless find
      compassion."

4 "I will heal their waywardness
  and love them freely,
  for my anger has turned away from
      them.
5 I will be like the dew to Israel;
  he will blossom like a lily.
Like a cedar of Lebanon
  he will send down his roots;
6   his young shoots will grow.
His splendor will be like an olive tree,
  his fragrance like a cedar of
      Lebanon.
7 Men will dwell again in his shade.
  He will flourish like the grain.
He will blossom like a vine,
  and his fame will be like the wine
      from Lebanon.
8 O Ephraim, what more have I *b* to do
      with idols?
  I will answer him and care for him.
I am like a green pine tree;
  your fruitfulness comes from me."
9 Who is wise? He will realize these
      things.
  Who is discerning? He will
      understand them.
The ways of the Lord are right;
  the righteous walk in them,
  but the rebellious stumble in them.

---

*a 2 Or offer our lips as sacrifices of bulls   b 8 Or What more
has Ephraim*

JOEL

Who wrote this book?
The prophet Joel.

Why was this book written?
Joel wants the people of Judah to repent and stop sinning.

What do we learn about God in this book?
God is judge. He will punish people who sin.

What is special about this book?
Joel realizes that the swarm of locusts is like the great enemy army God will use someday to punish his people for their sins. Joel promises that God will save and bless his people after he punishes them.

When was this book written?
Joel was written just after a terrible swarm of locusts destroyed crops in Judah. This was before the Babylonians destroyed Judah in 586 B.C.

What are some important passages in this book?
How to repent   Joel 2:12–14
How God will bless   Joel 2:18–27

The word of the Lord that came to Joel son of Pethuel.

An Invasion of Locusts

2 Hear this, you elders;
  listen, all who live in the land.
Has anything like this ever happened in
    your days
  or in the days of your forefathers?
3 Tell it to your children,
    and let your children tell it to their
      children,
    and their children to the next
      generation.
4 What the locust swarm has left
    the great locusts have eaten;
  what the great locusts have left
    the young locusts have eaten;
  what the young locusts have left
    other locusts*a* have eaten.

5 Wake up, you drunkards, and weep!
    Wail, all you drinkers of wine;
  wail because of the new wine,
    for it has been snatched from your
      lips.
6 A nation has invaded my land,
    powerful and without number;
  it has the teeth of a lion,
    the fangs of a lioness.
7 It has laid waste my vines
    and ruined my fig trees.
  It has stripped off their bark
    and thrown it away,
    leaving their branches white.

8 Mourn like a virgin*b* in sackcloth
    grieving for the husband*c* of her
      youth.
9 Grain offerings and drink offerings
    are cut off from the house of the
      Lord.
  The priests are in mourning,
    those who minister before the Lord.
10 The fields are ruined,
    the ground is dried up*d*;
  the grain is destroyed,
    the new wine is dried up,
    the oil fails.
11 Despair, you farmers,
    wail, you vine growers;
  grieve for the wheat and the barley,
    because the harvest of the field is
      destroyed.
12 The vine is dried up
    and the fig tree is withered;

the pomegranate, the palm and the
      apple tree—
  all the trees of the field—are dried
    up.
Surely the joy of mankind
  is withered away.

A Call to Repentance

13 Put on sackcloth, O priests, and mourn;
    wail, you who minister before the
      altar.
  Come, spend the night in sackcloth,
    you who minister before my God;
  for the grain offerings and drink
      offerings
    are withheld from the house of your
      God.
14 Declare a holy fast;
    call a sacred assembly.
  Summon the elders
    and all who live in the land
  to the house of the Lord your God,
    and cry out to the Lord.

15 Alas for that day!
  For the day of the Lord is near;
    it will come like destruction from the
      Almighty.*e*

16 Has not the food been cut off
    before our very eyes—
  joy and gladness
    from the house of our God?
17 The seeds are shriveled
    beneath the clods.*f*
  The storehouses are in ruins,
    the granaries have been broken
      down,
  for the grain has dried up.
18 How the cattle moan!
    The herds mill about
  because they have no pasture;
    even the flocks of sheep are
      suffering.

19 To you, O Lord, I call,
    for fire has devoured the open
      pastures
  and flames have burned up all the
      trees of the field.
20 Even the wild animals pant for you;
    the streams of water have dried up
  and fire has devoured the open
      pastures.

---

a 4 The precise meaning of the four Hebrew words used here
for locusts is uncertain.   *b 8* Or *young woman*
c 8 Or *betrothed*   *d 10* Or *ground mourns*   *e 15* Hebrew
Shaddai   *f 17* The meaning of the Hebrew for this word is
uncertain.

An Army of Locusts

2 Blow the trumpet in Zion;
    sound the alarm on my holy hill.

Let all who live in the land tremble,
    for the day of the LORD is coming.
It is close at hand—
2 a day of darkness and gloom,
    a day of clouds and blackness.
Like dawn spreading across the
    mountains
    a large and mighty army comes,
such as never was of old
    nor ever will be in ages to come.

3 Before them fire devours,
    behind them a flame blazes.
Before them the land is like the garden
    of Eden,
    behind them, a desert waste—
nothing escapes them.
4 They have the appearance of horses;
    they gallop along like cavalry.
5 With a noise like that of chariots
    they leap over the mountaintops,
like a crackling fire consuming stubble,
    like a mighty army drawn up for
    battle.

6 At the sight of them, nations are in
    anguish;
    every face turns pale.
7 They charge like warriors;
    they scale walls like soldiers.
They all march in line,
    not swerving from their course.
8 They do not jostle each other;
    each marches straight ahead.
They plunge through defenses
    without breaking ranks.
9 They rush upon the city;
    they run along the wall.
They climb into the houses;
    like thieves they enter through the
    windows.

10 Before them the earth shakes,
    the sky trembles,
the sun and moon are darkened,
    and the stars no longer shine.
11 The LORD thunders
    at the head of his army;
his forces are beyond number,
    and mighty are those who obey his
    command.
The day of the LORD is great;
    it is dreadful.
    Who can endure it?

Rend Your Heart

12 "Even now," declares the LORD,
    "return to me with all your heart,
    with fasting and weeping and
    mourning."

13 Rend your heart
    and not your garments.
Return to the LORD your God,
    for he is gracious and
    compassionate,
slow to anger and abounding in love,
    and he relents from sending
    calamity.
14 Who knows? He may turn and have
    pity
    and leave behind a blessing—
grain offerings and drink offerings
    for the LORD your God.

15 Blow the trumpet in Zion,
    declare a holy fast,
    call a sacred assembly.
16 Gather the people,
    consecrate the assembly;
bring together the elders,
    gather the children,
    those nursing at the breast.
Let the bridegroom leave his room
    and the bride her chamber.
17 Let the priests, who minister before the
    LORD,
    weep between the temple porch
    and the altar.
Let them say, "Spare your people,
    O LORD.
Do not make your inheritance an
    object of scorn,
    a byword among the nations.
Why should they say among the
    peoples,
    'Where is their God?' "

The LORD's Answer

18 Then the LORD will be jealous for his
    land
    and take pity on his people.

19 The LORD will reply[a] to them:

"I am sending you grain, new wine
    and oil,
    enough to satisfy you fully;
never again will I make you
    an object of scorn to the nations.

---

a 18,19 Or LORD was jealous . . . / and took pity . . . / 19The
LORD replied

20 "I will drive the northern army far from you,
  pushing it into a parched and barren land,
with its front columns going into the eastern sea[a]
and those in the rear into the western sea.[b]
And its stench will go up;
  its smell will rise."

Surely he has done great things.[c]
21 Be not afraid, O land;
  be glad and rejoice.
Surely the LORD has done great things.
22 Be not afraid, O wild animals,
  for the open pastures are becoming green.
The trees are bearing their fruit;
  the fig tree and the vine yield their riches.
23 Be glad, O people of Zion,
  rejoice in the LORD your God,
for he has given you
  the autumn rains in righteousness.[d]
He sends you abundant showers,
  both autumn and spring rains, as before.
24 The threshing floors will be filled with grain;
  the vats will overflow with new wine and oil.

25 "I will repay you for the years the locusts have eaten—
  the great locust and the young locust,
  the other locusts and the locust swarm[e]—
my great army that I sent among you.
26 You will have plenty to eat, until you are full,
  and you will praise the name of the LORD your God,
  who has worked wonders for you;
never again will my people be shamed.
27 Then you will know that I am in Israel,
  that I am the LORD your God,
  and that there is no other;
never again will my people be shamed.

---

a 20 That is, the Dead Sea   *b 20* That is, the Mediterranean
c 20 Or rise. / Surely it has done great things."   *d 23* Or /
the teacher for righteousness: *e 25* The precise meaning of
the four Hebrew words used here for locusts is uncertain.

Repent in the Middle

READ JOEL 2:12–13

When you're losing a big game and the referee is looking the other way, it's tempting to cheat. A guy at school says he'll sell you a brand new CD player for way less than the store price. Even though you suspect he stole it, you may be tempted to buy it. The number one weapon against sin is repentance. Even when you're right in the *middle* of messing up, you can say "sorry" and ask God to get you out of your mess. You don't have to wait until after the fact, when you have that sick-to-your-stomach feeling. Repent in the middle and turn back right away. Ask God to help you and forgive you. Even if you fall and do a faceplant this time, getting used to relying on God's forgiveness will give you the spiritual muscles to help you the next time around.

Your next reading is on page 1159.

The Day of the Lord

28 "And afterward,
    I will pour out my Spirit on all
      people.
  Your sons and daughters will prophesy,
    your old men will dream dreams,
    your young men will see visions.
29 Even on my servants, both men and
      women,
  I will pour out my Spirit in those
    days.
30 I will show wonders in the heavens
    and on the earth,
    blood and fire and billows of smoke.
31 The sun will be turned to darkness
    and the moon to blood
    before the coming of the great and
      dreadful day of the Lord.
32 And everyone who calls
    on the name of the Lord will be
      saved;
  for on Mount Zion and in Jerusalem
    there will be deliverance,
    as the Lord has said,
  among the survivors
    whom the Lord calls.

The Nations Judged

3 "In those days and at that time,
    when I restore the fortunes of
      Judah and Jerusalem,
  2 I will gather all nations
  and bring them down to the Valley
    of Jehoshaphat.ᵃ
  There I will enter into judgment
    against them
  concerning my inheritance, my
    people Israel,
  for they scattered my people among
    the nations
  and divided up my land.
3 They cast lots for my people
  and traded boys for prostitutes;
  they sold girls for wine
    that they might drink.

4 "Now what have you against me,
O Tyre and Sidon and all you regions of
Philistia? Are you repaying me for something I have done? If you are paying me
back, I will swiftly and speedily return on
your own heads what you have done. 5 For
you took my silver and my gold and carried off my finest treasures to your temples. 6 You sold the people of Judah and
Jerusalem to the Greeks, that you might
send them far from their homeland.

7 "See, I am going to rouse them out of
the places to which you sold them, and I
will return on your own heads what you
have done. 8 I will sell your sons and
daughters to the people of Judah, and
they will sell them to the Sabeans, a nation far away." The Lord has spoken.

9 Proclaim this among the nations:
    Prepare for war!
  Rouse the warriors!
    Let all the fighting men draw near
      and attack.
10 Beat your plowshares into swords
    and your pruning hooks into spears.
  Let the weakling say,
    "I am strong!"
11 Come quickly, all you nations from
      every side,
  and assemble there.

  Bring down your warriors, O Lord!

12 "Let the nations be roused;
    let them advance into the Valley of
      Jehoshaphat,
  for there I will sit
    to judge all the nations on every
      side.
13 Swing the sickle,
    for the harvest is ripe.
  Come, trample the grapes,
    for the winepress is full
    and the vats overflow—
  so great is their wickedness!"

14 Multitudes, multitudes
    in the valley of decision!
  For the day of the Lord is near
    in the valley of decision.
15 The sun and moon will be darkened,
    and the stars no longer shine.
16 The Lord will roar from Zion
    and thunder from Jerusalem;
    the earth and the sky will tremble.
  But the Lord will be a refuge for his
    people,
    a stronghold for the people of Israel.

Blessings for God's People

17 "Then you will know that I, the Lord
    your God,
    dwell in Zion, my holy hill.
  Jerusalem will be holy;
    never again will foreigners invade
      her.

ᵃ 2 *Jehoshaphat* means *the Lord judges*; also in verse 12.

18 "In that day the mountains will drip
    new wine,
  and the hills will flow with milk;
  all the ravines of Judah will run with
    water.
  A fountain will flow out of the LORD's
    house
  and will water the valley of acacias. [a]
19 But Egypt will be desolate,
  Edom a desert waste,
  because of violence done to the people
    of Judah,
in whose land they shed innocent
    blood.
20 Judah will be inhabited forever
  and Jerusalem through all
    generations.
21 Their bloodguilt, which I have not
    pardoned,
  I will pardon."

  The LORD dwells in Zion!

---

[a] 18 Or *Valley of Shittim*

AMOS

Who wrote this book?
Amos wrote this book. He was a shepherd whom God sent from Judah to preach to the people of Israel.

Why was this book written?
Amos preaches against rich people who are cruel to the poor. He warns the Israelites that God is angry and tells them that they must begin doing right.

What do we learn about God in this book?
God cares very much about people who are poor and helpless. He wants fair treatment for everyone.

What is special about this book?
Amos shows us that sins bring a nation under God's judgment. He also shows us how important it is to see that everyone in a nation is treated fairly.

When was this book written?
Amos preached his sermons about 760 B.C.

What are some important passages in this book?

Doing justice	Amos 5:7–15
Rich people who don't care about the poor	Amos 6:1–7
What God will do to people who oppress the poor	Amos 8:4–14

1 The words of Amos, one of the shepherds of Tekoa—what he saw concerning Israel two years before the earthquake, when Uzziah was king of Judah and Jeroboam son of Jehoash[a] was king of Israel.

²He said:

"The Lord roars from Zion
and thunders from Jerusalem;
the pastures of the shepherds dry up,[b]
and the top of Carmel withers."

Judgment on Israel's Neighbors

³This is what the Lord says:

"For three sins of Damascus,
even for four, I will not turn back
⌞my wrath⌟.
Because she threshed Gilead
with sledges having iron teeth,
⁴I will send fire upon the house of
Hazael
that will consume the fortresses of
Ben-Hadad.
⁵I will break down the gate of Damascus;
I will destroy the king who is in[c] the
Valley of Aven[d]
and the one who holds the scepter in
Beth Eden.
The people of Aram will go into exile
to Kir,"
says the Lord.

⁶This is what the Lord says:

"For three sins of Gaza,
even for four, I will not turn back
⌞my wrath⌟.
Because she took captive whole
communities
and sold them to Edom,
⁷I will send fire upon the walls of Gaza
that will consume her fortresses.
⁸I will destroy the king[e] of Ashdod
and the one who holds the scepter
in Ashkelon.
I will turn my hand against Ekron,
till the last of the Philistines is dead,"
says the Sovereign Lord.

⁹This is what the Lord says:

"For three sins of Tyre,
even for four, I will not turn back
⌞my wrath⌟.
Because she sold whole communities
of captives to Edom,
disregarding a treaty of
brotherhood,

¹⁰I will send fire upon the walls of Tyre
that will consume her fortresses."

¹¹This is what the Lord says:

"For three sins of Edom,
even for four, I will not turn back
⌞my wrath⌟.
Because he pursued his brother with a
sword,
stifling all compassion,[f]
because his anger raged continually
and his fury flamed unchecked,
¹²I will send fire upon Teman
that will consume the fortresses of
Bozrah."

¹³This is what the Lord says:

"For three sins of Ammon,
even for four, I will not turn back
⌞my wrath⌟.
Because he ripped open the pregnant
women of Gilead
in order to extend his borders,
¹⁴I will set fire to the walls of Rabbah
that will consume her fortresses
amid war cries on the day of battle,
amid violent winds on a stormy day.
¹⁵Her king[g] will go into exile,
he and his officials together,"
says the Lord.

2 This is what the Lord says:

"For three sins of Moab,
even for four, I will not turn back
⌞my wrath⌟.
Because he burned, as if to lime,
the bones of Edom's king,
²I will send fire upon Moab
that will consume the fortresses of
Kerioth.[h]
Moab will go down in great tumult
amid war cries and the blast of the
trumpet.
³I will destroy her ruler
and kill all her officials with him,"
says the Lord.

⁴This is what the Lord says:

"For three sins of Judah,
even for four, I will not turn back
⌞my wrath⌟.

---

a 1 Hebrew Joash, a variant of Jehoash   b 2 Or shepherds
mourn   c 5 Or the inhabitants of   d 5 Aven means
wickedness.   e 8 Or inhabitants   f 11 Or sword / and
destroyed his allies   g 15 Or / Molech; Hebrew malcam
h 2 Or of her cities

Because they have rejected the law of
   the LORD
  and have not kept his decrees,
because they have been led astray by
   false gods,[a]
  the gods[b] their ancestors followed,
⁵I will send fire upon Judah
  that will consume the fortresses of
   Jerusalem."

Judgment on Israel

⁶This is what the LORD says:

"For three sins of Israel,
  even for four, I will not turn back
   ⌊my wrath⌋.
They sell the righteous for silver,
  and the needy for a pair of sandals.
⁷They trample on the heads of the poor
  as upon the dust of the ground
  and deny justice to the oppressed.
Father and son use the same girl
  and so profane my holy name.
⁸They lie down beside every altar
  on garments taken in pledge.
In the house of their god
  they drink wine taken as fines.

⁹"I destroyed the Amorite before them,
  though he was tall as the cedars
  and strong as the oaks.
I destroyed his fruit above
  and his roots below.

¹⁰"I brought you up out of Egypt,
  and I led you forty years in the desert
  to give you the land of the Amorites.
¹¹I also raised up prophets from among
   your sons
  and Nazirites from among your
   young men.
Is this not true, people of Israel?"
           declares the LORD.
¹²"But you made the Nazirites drink wine
  and commanded the prophets not
   to prophesy.

¹³"Now then, I will crush you
  as a cart crushes when loaded with
   grain.
¹⁴The swift will not escape,
  the strong will not muster their
   strength,
  and the warrior will not save his life.
¹⁵The archer will not stand his ground,
  the fleet-footed soldier will not get
   away,
  and the horseman will not save his
   life.

¹⁶Even the bravest warriors
  will flee naked on that day,"
           declares the LORD.

Witnesses Summoned Against Israel

3 Hear this word the LORD has spoken
against you, O people of Israel—
against the whole family I brought
up out of Egypt:

²"You only have I chosen
  of all the families of the earth;
therefore I will punish you
  for all your sins."

³Do two walk together
  unless they have agreed to do so?
⁴Does a lion roar in the thicket
  when he has no prey?
Does he growl in his den
  when he has caught nothing?
⁵Does a bird fall into a trap on the
   ground
  where no snare has been set?
Does a trap spring up from the earth
  when there is nothing to catch?
⁶When a trumpet sounds in a city,
  do not the people tremble?
When disaster comes to a city,
  has not the LORD caused it?

⁷Surely the Sovereign LORD does nothing
  without revealing his plan
  to his servants the prophets.

⁸The lion has roared—
  who will not fear?
The Sovereign LORD has spoken—
  who can but prophesy?

⁹Proclaim to the fortresses of Ashdod
  and to the fortresses of Egypt:
"Assemble yourselves on the
   mountains of Samaria;
  see the great unrest within her
  and the oppression among her
   people."

¹⁰"They do not know how to do right,"
     declares the LORD,
  "who hoard plunder and loot in
   their fortresses."

¹¹Therefore this is what the Sovereign
LORD says:

"An enemy will overrun the land;
  he will pull down your strongholds
  and plunder your fortresses."

---

[a] 4 Or by lies   [b] 4 Or lies

12This is what the LORD says:

"As a shepherd saves from the lion's mouth
only two leg bones or a piece of an ear,
so will the Israelites be saved,
those who sit in Samaria
on the edge of their beds
and in Damascus on their couches.*a*"

13"Hear this and testify against the house of Jacob," declares the Lord, the LORD God Almighty.

14"On the day I punish Israel for her sins,
I will destroy the altars of Bethel;
the horns of the altar will be cut off
and fall to the ground.
15I will tear down the winter house
along with the summer house;
the houses adorned with ivory will be destroyed
and the mansions will be demolished,"
declares the LORD.

Israel Has Not Returned to God

Hear this word, you cows of
Bashan on Mount Samaria,
you women who oppress the poor
and crush the needy
and say to your husbands, "Bring us some drinks!"
2The Sovereign LORD has sworn by his holiness:
"The time will surely come
when you will be taken away with hooks,
the last of you with fishhooks.
3You will each go straight out
through breaks in the wall,
and you will be cast out toward Harmon,*b*"
declares the LORD.
4"Go to Bethel and sin;
go to Gilgal and sin yet more.

a 12 The meaning of the Hebrew for this line is uncertain.
b 3 Masoretic Text; with a different word division of the Hebrew (see Septuagint) *out, O mountain of oppression*

Make It Stick

READ AMOS 3:3

Have you ever run a three-legged race? The key to winning is not running as fast as you can, but getting in step with your partner. Otherwise you'll both do a face-plant. This is like walking with God and keeping in step with him. Draw two legs tied together as a reminder to keep in step with God.

Bring your sacrifices every morning,
  your tithes every three years. *a*
5 Burn leavened bread as a thank offering
  and brag about your freewill
    offerings—
boast about them, you Israelites,
  for this is what you love to do,"
        declares the Sovereign LORD.

6 "I gave you empty stomachs *b* in every
    city
  and lack of bread in every town,
  yet you have not returned to me,"
        declares the LORD.

7 "I also withheld rain from you
  when the harvest was still three
    months away.
I sent rain on one town,
  but withheld it from another.
One field had rain;
  another had none and dried up.
8 People staggered from town to town
    for water
  but did not get enough to drink,
  yet you have not returned to me,"
        declares the LORD.

9 "Many times I struck your gardens and
    vineyards,
  I struck them with blight and mildew.
Locusts devoured your fig and olive
    trees,
  yet you have not returned to me,"
        declares the LORD.

10 "I sent plagues among you
  as I did to Egypt.
I killed your young men with the sword,
  along with your captured horses.
I filled your nostrils with the stench of
    your camps,
  yet you have not returned to me,"
        declares the LORD.

11 "I overthrew some of you
  as I *c* overthrew Sodom and
    Gomorrah.
You were like a burning stick snatched
    from the fire,
  yet you have not returned to me,"
        declares the LORD.

12 "Therefore this is what I will do to you,
    Israel,
  and because I will do this to you,
  prepare to meet your God, O Israel."

13 He who forms the mountains,
  creates the wind,

and reveals his thoughts to man,
he who turns dawn to darkness,
  and treads the high places of the
    earth—
  the LORD God Almighty is his name.

A Lament and Call to Repentance

5 Hear this word, O house of Israel,
  this lament I take up concerning
  you:

2 "Fallen is Virgin Israel,
  never to rise again,
deserted in her own land,
  with no one to lift her up."

3 This is what the Sovereign LORD says:

"The city that marches out a thousand
    strong for Israel
  will have only a hundred left;
the town that marches out a hundred
    strong
  will have only ten left."

4 This is what the LORD says to the house
of Israel:

"Seek me and live;
5   do not seek Bethel,
do not go to Gilgal,
  do not journey to Beersheba.
For Gilgal will surely go into exile,
  and Bethel will be reduced to
    nothing. *d*"
6 Seek the LORD and live,
  or he will sweep through the house
    of Joseph like a fire;
it will devour,
  and Bethel will have no one to
    quench it.

7 You who turn justice into bitterness
  and cast righteousness to the
    ground
8 (he who made the Pleiades and Orion,
  who turns blackness into dawn
  and darkens day into night,
who calls for the waters of the sea
  and pours them out over the face of
    the land—
  the LORD is his name—
9 he flashes destruction on the
    stronghold
  and brings the fortified city to ruin),

---

a 4 Or *tithes on the third day*   *b 6* Hebrew *you cleanness of
teeth*   *c 11* Hebrew *God*   *d 5* Or *grief;* or *wickedness;*
Hebrew *aven,* a reference to Beth Aven (a derogatory name
for Bethel)

10 you hate the one who reproves in court
    and despise him who tells the truth.

11 You trample on the poor
    and force him to give you grain.
Therefore, though you have built stone
      mansions,
    you will not live in them;
  though you have planted lush
      vineyards,
    you will not drink their wine.
12 For I know how many are your offenses
    and how great your sins.

  You oppress the righteous and take
      bribes
    and you deprive the poor of justice
      in the courts.
13 Therefore the prudent man keeps quiet
      in such times,
    for the times are evil.

14 Seek good, not evil,
    that you may live.
  Then the LORD God Almighty will be
      with you,
    just as you say he is.
15 Hate evil, love good;
    maintain justice in the courts.
  Perhaps the LORD God Almighty will
      have mercy
    on the remnant of Joseph.

16 Therefore this is what the Lord, the
  LORD God Almighty, says:

  "There will be wailing in all the streets
    and cries of anguish in every public
      square.
  The farmers will be summoned to weep
    and the mourners to wail.
17 There will be wailing in all the vineyards,
    for I will pass through your midst,"
                              says the LORD.

The Day of the LORD

18 Woe to you who long
    for the day of the LORD!
  Why do you long for the day of the
      LORD?
    That day will be darkness, not light.
19 It will be as though a man fled from a
      lion
    only to meet a bear,
  as though he entered his house
    and rested his hand on the wall
    only to have a snake bite him.
20 Will not the day of the LORD be
    darkness, not light—

  pitch-dark, without a ray of
      brightness?

21 "I hate, I despise your religious feasts;
    I cannot stand your assemblies.
22 Even though you bring me burnt
      offerings and grain offerings,
    I will not accept them.
  Though you bring choice fellowship
      offerings, a
    I will have no regard for them.
23 Away with the noise of your songs!
    I will not listen to the music of your
      harps.
24 But let justice roll on like a river,
    righteousness like a never-failing
      stream!

25 "Did you bring me sacrifices and
      offerings
    forty years in the desert, O house of
      Israel?
26 You have lifted up the shrine of your
      king,
    the pedestal of your idols,
    the star of your god b—
    which you made for yourselves.
27 Therefore I will send you into exile
      beyond Damascus,"
    says the LORD, whose name is God
      Almighty.

Woe to the Complacent

6 Woe to you who are complacent in
      Zion,
  and to you who feel secure on
      Mount Samaria,
  you notable men of the foremost
      nation,
    to whom the people of Israel come!
2 Go to Calneh and look at it;
    go from there to great Hamath,
  and then go down to Gath in
      Philistia.
  Are they better off than your two
      kingdoms?
    Is their land larger than yours?
3 You put off the evil day
    and bring near a reign of terror.
4 You lie on beds inlaid with ivory
    and lounge on your couches.
  You dine on choice lambs
    and fattened calves.

─────────────────
a 22 Traditionally peace offerings   b 26 Or lifted up Sakkuth
your king / and Kaiwan your idols, / your star-gods; Septuagint
lifted up the shrine of Molech / and the star of your god
Rephan, / their idols

⁵You strum away on your harps like
David
and improvise on musical
instruments.
⁶You drink wine by the bowlful
and use the finest lotions,
but you do not grieve over the ruin
of Joseph.
⁷Therefore you will be among the first
to go into exile;
your feasting and lounging will end.

The LORD Abhors the Pride of Israel

⁸The Sovereign LORD has sworn by himself—the LORD God Almighty declares:

"I abhor the pride of Jacob
and detest his fortresses;
I will deliver up the city
and everything in it."

⁹If ten men are left in one house, they too will die. ¹⁰And if a relative who is to burn the bodies comes to carry them out of the house and asks anyone still hiding there, "Is anyone with you?" and he says, "No," then he will say, "Hush! We must not mention the name of the LORD."

¹¹For the LORD has given the command,
and he will smash the great house
into pieces
and the small house into bits.

¹²Do horses run on the rocky crags?
Does one plow there with oxen?
But you have turned justice into poison
and the fruit of righteousness into
bitterness—
¹³you who rejoice in the conquest of Lo
Debar*a*
and say, "Did we not take Karnaim*b*
by our own strength?"

¹⁴For the LORD God Almighty declares,
"I will stir up a nation against you,
O house of Israel,
that will oppress you all the way
from Lebo*c* Hamath to the valley of
the Arabah."

Locusts, Fire and a Plumb Line

7 This is what the Sovereign LORD showed me: He was preparing swarms of locusts after the king's share had been harvested and just as the second crop was coming up. ²When they had stripped the land clean, I

cried out, "Sovereign LORD, forgive! How can Jacob survive? He is so small!"
³So the LORD relented.
"This will not happen," the LORD said.

⁴This is what the Sovereign LORD showed me: The Sovereign LORD was calling for judgment by fire; it dried up the great deep and devoured the land. ⁵Then I cried out, "Sovereign LORD, I beg you, stop! How can Jacob survive? He is so small!"
⁶So the LORD relented.
"This will not happen either," the Sovereign LORD said.

⁷This is what he showed me: The Lord was standing by a wall that had been built true to plumb, with a plumb line in his hand. ⁸And the LORD asked me, "What do you see, Amos?"
"A plumb line," I replied.
Then the Lord said, "Look, I am setting a plumb line among my people Israel; I will spare them no longer.

⁹"The high places of Isaac will be
destroyed
and the sanctuaries of Israel will be
ruined;
with my sword I will rise against the
house of Jeroboam."

Amos and Amaziah

¹⁰Then Amaziah the priest of Bethel sent a message to Jeroboam king of Israel: "Amos is raising a conspiracy against you in the very heart of Israel. The land cannot bear all his words. ¹¹For this is what Amos is saying:

" 'Jeroboam will die by the sword,
and Israel will surely go into exile,
away from their native land.' "

¹²Then Amaziah said to Amos, "Get out, you seer! Go back to the land of Judah. Earn your bread there and do your prophesying there. ¹³Don't prophesy anymore at Bethel, because this is the king's sanctuary and the temple of the kingdom."
¹⁴Amos answered Amaziah, "I was neither a prophet nor a prophet's son, but I was a shepherd, and I also took care of sycamore-fig trees. ¹⁵But the LORD took me from tending the flock and said to me, 'Go, prophesy to my people Israel.' ¹⁶Now then, hear the word of the LORD. You say,

---

a 13 Lo Debar means nothing.   *b 13* Karnaim means horns; horn here symbolizes strength.   *c 14* Or from the entrance to

" 'Do not prophesy against Israel,
and stop preaching against the
house of Isaac.'

17"Therefore this is what the Lord says:

" 'Your wife will become a prostitute in
the city,
and your sons and daughters will fall
by the sword.
Your land will be measured and
divided up,
and you yourself will die in a pagan[a]
country.
And Israel will certainly go into exile,
away from their native land.' "

A Basket of Ripe Fruit

This is what the Sovereign Lord
showed me: a basket of ripe fruit.
2"What do you see, Amos?" he
asked.

"A basket of ripe fruit," I answered.

Then the Lord said to me, "The time is
ripe for my people Israel; I will spare them
no longer.

3"In that day," declares the Sovereign
Lord, "the songs in the temple will turn to
wailing.[b] Many, many bodies—flung everywhere! Silence!"

4Hear this, you who trample the needy
and do away with the poor of the
land,

5saying,

"When will the New Moon be over
that we may sell grain,
and the Sabbath be ended
that we may market wheat?"—
skimping the measure,
boosting the price
and cheating with dishonest scales,
6buying the poor with silver
and the needy for a pair of sandals,
selling even the sweepings with the
wheat.

7The Lord has sworn by the Pride of Jacob: "I will never forget anything they
have done.

8"Will not the land tremble for this,
and all who live in it mourn?

---

[a] 17 Hebrew *an unclean*   [b] 3 Or *"the temple singers will wail*

The Fig-picker Prophet

READ AMOS 7:10–17

Amaziah was trying to put Amos in his place, but Amos wasn't proud.
He freely admitted he was no big shot: "I was neither a prophet nor a
prophet's son, but I was a shepherd, and I also took care of sycamore-
fig trees" (verse 14). He didn't brag about his bank account to prove
he was someone important. He worked with fig trees. Oh
yeah, and he watched some sheep. Sometimes you may think
you have to be rich or talented to do something great for God.
But all that really matters is your heart. God can use your
talents and wealth if you have them, sure, but he's looking for
more than that. He's looking for willing hearts: "For the
eyes of the Lord range throughout the earth to
strengthen those whose hearts are fully committed to him" (2 Chronicles 16:9).

Your next reading is on page 1160.

The whole land will rise like the Nile;
  it will be stirred up and then sink
  like the river of Egypt.

⁹"In that day," declares the Sovereign
LORD,

"I will make the sun go down at noon
  and darken the earth in broad
    daylight.
¹⁰I will turn your religious feasts into
    mourning
  and all your singing into weeping.
I will make all of you wear sackcloth
  and shave your heads.
I will make that time like mourning for
    an only son
  and the end of it like a bitter day.

¹¹"The days are coming," declares the
    Sovereign LORD,
  "when I will send a famine through
    the land—
not a famine of food or a thirst for
    water,
  but a famine of hearing the words
    of the LORD.
¹²Men will stagger from sea to sea

and wander from north to east,
  searching for the word of the LORD,
  but they will not find it.

¹³"In that day

"the lovely young women and strong
    young men
  will faint because of thirst.
¹⁴They who swear by the shame[a] of
    Samaria,
  or say, 'As surely as your god lives,
    O Dan,'
  or, 'As surely as the god[b] of
    Beersheba lives'—
they will fall,
  never to rise again."

Israel to Be Destroyed

9 I saw the Lord standing by the altar,
  and he said:

"Strike the tops of the pillars
  so that the thresholds shake.
Bring them down on the heads of all
    the people;

ᵃ 14 Or by Ashima; or by the idol   ᵇ 14 Or power

How Not to "Get Ahead"

READ AMOS 8:4–7

Getting ahead in life shouldn't involve stepping on other people's heads (or toes or fingers, for that matter). "God is love" (1 John 4:16), and he cares about everyone. But there is one thing he hates: when we are unjust or unmerciful to others. That's why he was so angry at the Israelites: "Hear this, you who trample the needy and do away with the poor of the land" (Amos 8:4). As men of God, we need to follow God's example and love everyone. When we take advantage of those who are poor or ignore their cries for help, we fail to be the men that God has called us to be. The same goes for when we cheat or try to get ahead at the expense of someone else. God wants us to look out for others, especially those who can't help themselves. That's the real way to get ahead.

Your next reading is on page 1163.

those who are left I will kill with the
    sword.
Not one will get away,
    none will escape.
2 Though they dig down to the depths
    of the grave,[a]
from there my hand will take them.
Though they climb up to the heavens,
    from there I will bring them down.
3 Though they hide themselves on the
    top of Carmel,
there I will hunt them down and
    seize them.
Though they hide from me at the
    bottom of the sea,
there I will command the serpent to
    bite them.
4 Though they are driven into exile by
    their enemies,
there I will command the sword to
    slay them.
I will fix my eyes upon them
    for evil and not for good."

5 The Lord, the LORD Almighty,
    he who touches the earth and it
    melts,
    and all who live in it mourn—
the whole land rises like the Nile,
    then sinks like the river of Egypt—
6 he who builds his lofty palace[b] in the
    heavens
    and sets its foundation[c] on the
    earth,
who calls for the waters of the sea
    and pours them out over the face of
    the land—
    the LORD is his name.

7 "Are not you Israelites
    the same to me as the Cushites[d]?"
                declares the LORD.
"Did I not bring Israel up from Egypt,
    the Philistines from Caphtor[e]
    and the Arameans from Kir?

8 "Surely the eyes of the Sovereign LORD
    are on the sinful kingdom.
I will destroy it
    from the face of the earth—
yet I will not totally destroy
    the house of Jacob,"
                declares the LORD.

9 "For I will give the command,
    and I will shake the house of Israel
    among all the nations
as grain is shaken in a sieve,
    and not a pebble will reach the
    ground.
10 All the sinners among my people
    will die by the sword,
all those who say,
    'Disaster will not overtake or meet
    us.'

Israel's Restoration

11 "In that day I will restore
    David's fallen tent.
I will repair its broken places,
    restore its ruins,
    and build it as it used to be,
12 so that they may possess the remnant
    of Edom
    and all the nations that bear my
    name,[f]"
                declares the LORD,
         who will do these things.

13 "The days are coming," declares the
LORD,

    "when the reaper will be overtaken by
    the plowman
    and the planter by the one treading
    grapes.
New wine will drip from the mountains
    and flow from all the hills.
14 I will bring back my exiled[g] people
    Israel;
    they will rebuild the ruined cities and
    live in them.
They will plant vineyards and drink
    their wine;
    they will make gardens and eat their
    fruit.
15 I will plant Israel in their own land,
    never again to be uprooted
    from the land I have given them,"
        says the LORD your God.

a 2 Hebrew to Sheol   b 6 The meaning of the Hebrew for
this phrase is uncertain.   c 6 The meaning of the Hebrew
for this word is uncertain.   d 7 That is, people from the
upper Nile region   e 7 That is, Crete   f 12 Hebrew;
Septuagint so that the remnant of men / and all the nations
that bear my name may seek ِthe Lord٫   g 14 Or will restore
the fortunes of my

OBADIAH

Who wrote this book?

Obadiah. Nothing more is known about this prophet.

Why was this book written?

Obadiah speaks of the punishment God will bring on the Edomites, who have invaded Judah and plundered Jerusalem.

What do we learn about God in this book?

God is faithful. He will keep his promise to Abraham: "Whoever curses you I will curse" (Genesis 12:3).

When was this book written?

No one knows for sure when Obadiah was written.

¹The vision of Obadiah.

This is what the Sovereign LORD says about Edom—

We have heard a message from the
   LORD:
  An envoy was sent to the nations to
    say,
"Rise, and let us go against her for
    battle"—

²"See, I will make you small among the
    nations;
  you will be utterly despised.
³The pride of your heart has deceived
    you,
  you who live in the clefts of the
    rocksª
  and make your home on the
    heights,
you who say to yourself,
  'Who can bring me down to the
    ground?'
⁴Though you soar like the eagle

and make your nest among the
    stars,
  from there I will bring you down,"
             declares the LORD.
⁵"If thieves came to you,
  if robbers in the night—
Oh, what a disaster awaits you—
  would they not steal only as much
    as they wanted?
If grape pickers came to you,
  would they not leave a few
    grapes?
⁶But how Esau will be ransacked,
  his hidden treasures pillaged!
⁷All your allies will force you to the
    border;
  your friends will deceive and
    overpower you;
those who eat your bread will set a
    trap for you, ᵇ
  but you will not detect it.

ª 3 Or of Sela   ᵇ 7 The meaning of the Hebrew for this clause is uncertain.

The Edom Attitude

READ OBADIAH 1–7

The people of Edom thought they were IT. Sometimes we feel that way because we're great at sports or get good grades. Know what that is? Pride. And guess what—God hates pride. A *lot*. Why? It messes up our mind. God said, "The pride of your heart has deceived you" (verse 3). We start thinking we are Number One, that we are the greatest, and that keeps us from loving God and others the way God wants us to. It also makes us treat people badly. When you are tempted to think you are hot stuff, stay cool—and be humble. That's what God loves. Remember, your talents are a gift from God. Make the best of them, enjoy them, but don't get puffed up about them. While you're at it, encourage others to make the most of their gifts, too.

Your next reading is on page 1166.

8 "In that day," declares the LORD,
    "will I not destroy the wise men of
        Edom,
    men of understanding in the
        mountains of Esau?
9 Your warriors, O Teman, will be terrified,
    and everyone in Esau's mountains
    will be cut down in the slaughter.
10 Because of the violence against your
        brother Jacob,
    you will be covered with shame;
    you will be destroyed forever.
11 On the day you stood aloof
        while strangers carried off his wealth
    and foreigners entered his gates
        and cast lots for Jerusalem,
    you were like one of them.
12 You should not look down on your
        brother
    in the day of his misfortune,
    nor rejoice over the people of Judah
        in the day of their destruction,
    nor boast so much
        in the day of their trouble.
13 You should not march through the
        gates of my people
    in the day of their disaster,
    nor look down on them in their calamity
        in the day of their disaster,
    nor seize their wealth
        in the day of their disaster.
14 You should not wait at the crossroads
        to cut down their fugitives,
    nor hand over their survivors
        in the day of their trouble.
15 "The day of the LORD is near
        for all nations.
    As you have done, it will be done to
        you;

your deeds will return upon your
    own head.
16 Just as you drank on my holy hill,
    so all the nations will drink
        continually;
    they will drink and drink
    and be as if they had never been.
17 But on Mount Zion will be deliverance;
    it will be holy,
    and the house of Jacob
    will possess its inheritance.
18 The house of Jacob will be a fire
    and the house of Joseph a flame;
    the house of Esau will be stubble,
        and they will set it on fire and
            consume it.
    There will be no survivors
        from the house of Esau."
                        The LORD has spoken.

19 People from the Negev will occupy
        the mountains of Esau,
    and people from the foothills will
        possess
        the land of the Philistines.
    They will occupy the fields of Ephraim
        and Samaria,
    and Benjamin will possess Gilead.
20 This company of Israelite exiles who
        are in Canaan
    will possess ˻the land˼ as far as
        Zarephath;
    the exiles from Jerusalem who are in
        Sepharad
    will possess the towns of the Negev.
21 Deliverers will go up on[a] Mount Zion
    to govern the mountains of Esau.
    And the kingdom will be the LORD's.

[a] 21 Or from

JONAH

Who wrote this book?
The prophet Jonah.

Why was this book written?
Jonah shows Israel that God does not punish if people repent and are sorry for their sins.

What do we learn about God in this book?
God forgives his disobedient prophet and gives Jonah a second chance. God also forgives the people of Nineveh. God does not punish people who repent.

What is special about this book?
God shows love for the foreign people in Nineveh as well as for his own Hebrew people.

When was this book written?
Jonah was written about 760 B.C.

What are some of the stories of this book?
Jonah is swallowed by a fish	Jonah 1
The people of Nineveh repent	Jonah 3
God teaches Jonah to care about all people	Jonah 4

Jonah Flees From the LORD

1 The word of the LORD came to Jonah son of Amittai: 2"Go to the great city of Nineveh and preach against it, because its wickedness has come up before me."

3But Jonah ran away from the LORD and headed for Tarshish. He went down to Joppa, where he found a ship bound for that port. After paying the fare, he went aboard and sailed for Tarshish to flee from the LORD.

4Then the LORD sent a great wind on the sea, and such a violent storm arose that the ship threatened to break up. 5All the sailors were afraid and each cried out to his own god. And they threw the cargo into the sea to lighten the ship.

But Jonah had gone below deck, where he lay down and fell into a deep sleep. 6The captain went to him and said, "How can you sleep? Get up and call on your god! Maybe he will take notice of us, and we will not perish."

7Then the sailors said to each other, "Come, let us cast lots to find out who is responsible for this calamity." They cast lots and the lot fell on Jonah.

8So they asked him, "Tell us, who is responsible for making all this trouble for us? What do you do? Where do you come from? What is your country? From what people are you?"

9He answered, "I am a Hebrew and I worship the LORD, the God of heaven, who made the sea and the land."

10This terrified them and they asked, "What have you done?" (They knew he was running away from the LORD, because he had already told them so.)

11The sea was getting rougher and rougher. So they asked him, "What should we do to you to make the sea calm down for us?"

12"Pick me up and throw me into the sea," he replied, "and it will become calm. I know that it is my fault that this great storm has come upon you."

13Instead, the men did their best to row back to land. But they could not, for the sea grew even wilder than before. 14Then they cried to the LORD, "O LORD, please do not let us die for taking this man's life. Do

Prophet on the Run

READ JONAH 1; 2:10—3:6

When God told Jonah to warn Nineveh, Jonah "sailed for Tarshish to flee from the LORD" (Jonah 1:3). God decided Jonah needed to think some more about his response, so he put him in a stink tank ... er ... *think* tank. Jonah spent three days in the smelly belly of a great fish, and then God had the critter vomit Jonah onto the beach. Now, when the Lord commanded Jonah a second time to go to Nineveh, he obeyed. Like Jonah, we often have our own ideas on how we will serve God. Jonah just wanted to preach to Israel, but God wanted Jonah to be obedient in *every*thing, even if that meant preaching to Israel's enemies. It's the same thing if you're a Christian: Let God call the shots. That means trusting him and not limiting what you will or will not do.

Your next reading is on page 1168.

not hold us accountable for killing an innocent man, for you, O LORD, have done as you pleased." [15]Then they took Jonah and threw him overboard, and the raging sea grew calm. [16]At this the men greatly feared the LORD, and they offered a sacrifice to the LORD and made vows to him.

[17]But the LORD provided a great fish to swallow Jonah, and Jonah was inside the fish three days and three nights.

Jonah's Prayer

From inside the fish Jonah prayed to the LORD his God. [2]He said:

> "In my distress I called to the LORD,
>   and he answered me.
> From the depths of the grave[a] I called for help,
>   and you listened to my cry.
> [3]You hurled me into the deep,
>   into the very heart of the seas,
>   and the currents swirled about me;
> all your waves and breakers
>   swept over me.
> [4]I said, 'I have been banished
>   from your sight;
> yet I will look again
>   toward your holy temple.'
> [5]The engulfing waters threatened me,[b]
>   the deep surrounded me;
>   seaweed was wrapped around my head.
> [6]To the roots of the mountains I sank down;
>   the earth beneath barred me in forever.
> But you brought my life up from the pit,
>   O LORD my God.
>
> [7]"When my life was ebbing away,
>   I remembered you, LORD,
> and my prayer rose to you,
>   to your holy temple.
>
> [8]"Those who cling to worthless idols
>   forfeit the grace that could be theirs.
> [9]But I, with a song of thanksgiving,
>   will sacrifice to you.
> What I have vowed I will make good.
>   Salvation comes from the LORD."

[10]And the LORD commanded the fish, and it vomited Jonah onto dry land.

Jonah Goes to Nineveh

Then the word of the LORD came to Jonah a second time: [2]"Go to the great city of Nineveh and proclaim to it the message I give you."

[3]Jonah obeyed the word of the LORD and went to Nineveh. Now Nineveh was a very important city—a visit required three days. [4]On the first day, Jonah started

Get a Load of This...

Check out Jonah 1:17. Jonah was swallowed by a "great fish," but we really don't know what kind of fish or creature it was. It could have been a whale, a whale shark (which can grow up to 49 feet), or some other monster of the depths that—fortunately for you—is now extinct.

a 2 Hebrew *Sheol*   b 5 Or *waters were at my throat*

into the city. He proclaimed: "Forty more days and Nineveh will be overturned." ⁵The Ninevites believed God. They declared a fast, and all of them, from the greatest to the least, put on sackcloth.

⁶When the news reached the king of Nineveh, he rose from his throne, took off his royal robes, covered himself with sackcloth and sat down in the dust. ⁷Then he issued a proclamation in Nineveh:

"By the decree of the king and his nobles:

Do not let any man or beast, herd or flock, taste anything; do not let them eat or drink. ⁸But let man and beast be covered with sackcloth. Let everyone call urgently on God. Let them give up their evil ways and their violence. ⁹Who knows? God may yet relent and with compassion turn from his fierce anger so that we will not perish."

¹⁰When God saw what they did and how they turned from their evil ways, he had compassion and did not bring upon them the destruction he had threatened.

Jonah's Anger at the LORD's Compassion

But Jonah was greatly displeased and became angry. ²He prayed to the LORD, "O LORD, is this not what I said when I was still at home? That is why I was so quick to flee to Tarshish. I knew that you are a gracious and compassionate God, slow to anger and abounding in love, a God who relents from sending calamity. ³Now, O LORD, take away my life, for it is better for me to die than to live."

⁴But the LORD replied, "Have you any right to be angry?"

⁵Jonah went out and sat down at a place east of the city. There he made himself a shelter, sat in its shade and waited to see what would happen to the city. ⁶Then the LORD God provided a vine and made it grow up over Jonah to give shade for his head to ease his discomfort, and Jonah was very happy about the vine. ⁷But at dawn the next day God provided a worm, which chewed the vine so that it withered. ⁸When the sun rose, God provided a scorching east wind, and the sun blazed

But ... They're Different!

READ JONAH 3:10—4:11

"Why should God care about the Ninevites?" Jonah wondered. They didn't even worship God. But God loved the Ninevites, because he created them, and he wanted to steer them in the right direction. "Nineveh has more than a hundred and twenty thousand people who cannot tell their right hand from their left ... Should I not be concerned about that great city?" (Jonah 4:11). As Christians, sometimes we can become snooty like Jonah was—as if it were up to *us* whom God accepted or not. But God loves everyone, no matter what they believe. And he wants the gospel to go to every person on earth. Just because people are different than us doesn't mean God doesn't love them. God doesn't require that they become like us—as if we were the best thing going—only that they accept Jesus as their Savior, and worship him.

Your next reading is on page 1177.

on Jonah's head so that he grew faint. He wanted to die, and said, "It would be better for me to die than to live."

9But God said to Jonah, "Do you have a right to be angry about the vine?"

"I do," he said. "I am angry enough to die."

10But the Lord said, "You have been concerned about this vine, though you did not tend it or make it grow. It sprang up overnight and died overnight. 11But Nineveh has more than a hundred and twenty thousand people who cannot tell their right hand from their left, and many cattle as well. Should I not be concerned about that great city?"

MICAH

Who wrote this book?
The prophet Micah.

Why was this book written?
Micah reveals God's concern for justice in Judah as well as in Israel.

What do we learn about God in this book?
God cares for the poor and helpless. God will judge the rich who mistreat them.

What is special about this book?
Micah tells people to turn to God. Only love for God will move people to do what is right, and so save Judah from judgment.

When was this book written?
Micah preached in Judah between 742 and 687 B.C.

What are some important passages in this book?

Punishment for the wicked	Micah 2:1–5
A ruler from Bethlehem	Micah 5:1–5
Our forgiving God	Micah 7:18–20

1 The word of the LORD that came to Micah of Moresheth during the reigns of Jotham, Ahaz and Hezekiah, kings of Judah—the vision he saw concerning Samaria and Jerusalem.

2 Hear, O peoples, all of you,
    listen, O earth and all who are in it,
that the Sovereign LORD may witness against you,
    the Lord from his holy temple.

Judgment Against Samaria and Jerusalem

3 Look! The LORD is coming from his dwelling place;
    he comes down and treads the high places of the earth.
4 The mountains melt beneath him
    and the valleys split apart,
like wax before the fire,
    like water rushing down a slope.
5 All this is because of Jacob's transgression,
    because of the sins of the house of Israel.
What is Jacob's transgression?
    Is it not Samaria?
What is Judah's high place?
    Is it not Jerusalem?

6 "Therefore I will make Samaria a heap of rubble,
    a place for planting vineyards.
I will pour her stones into the valley
    and lay bare her foundations.
7 All her idols will be broken to pieces;
    all her temple gifts will be burned with fire;
    I will destroy all her images.
Since she gathered her gifts from the wages of prostitutes,
    as the wages of prostitutes they will again be used."

Weeping and Mourning

8 Because of this I will weep and wail;
    I will go about barefoot and naked.
I will howl like a jackal
    and moan like an owl.
9 For her wound is incurable;
    it has come to Judah.
It*a* has reached the very gate of my people,
    even to Jerusalem itself.
10 Tell it not in Gath*b*;
    weep not at all. *c*
In Beth Ophrah*d*
    roll in the dust.
11 Pass on in nakedness and shame,
    you who live in Shaphir. *e*
Those who live in Zaanan*f*
    will not come out.

Get a Load of This...

Check out Micah 1:8. Jackals howl at night and owls moan then. Creepy! Micah said he was so sad about God's coming judgment on his rebellious people that he was going to run around naked, howling like a jackal and moaning like an owl. Now, if *that* doesn't sound like your two-year-old kid brother in the middle of the night, nothing does!

---

a 9 Or *He*   *b* 10 *Gath* sounds like the Hebrew for *tell*.   *c* 10 Hebrew; Septuagint may suggest *not in Acco*. The Hebrew for *in Acco* sounds like the Hebrew for *weep*.   *d* 10 *Beth Ophrah* means *house of dust*.   *e* 11 *Shaphir* means *pleasant*.   *f* 11 *Zaanan* sounds like the Hebrew for *come out*.

Beth Ezel is in mourning;
     its protection is taken from you.
12 Those who live in Maroth*a* writhe in
       pain,
     waiting for relief,
because disaster has come from the
     LORD,
     even to the gate of Jerusalem.
13 You who live in Lachish,*b*
     harness the team to the chariot.
You were the beginning of sin
     to the Daughter of Zion,
for the transgressions of Israel
     were found in you.
14 Therefore you will give parting gifts
     to Moresheth Gath.
The town of Aczib*c* will prove deceptive
     to the kings of Israel.
15 I will bring a conqueror against you
     who live in Mareshah.*d*
He who is the glory of Israel
     will come to Adullam.
16 Shave your heads in mourning
     for the children in whom you delight;
make yourselves as bald as the vulture,
     for they will go from you into exile.

Man's Plans and God's

2 Woe to those who plan iniquity,
     to those who plot evil on their
       beds!
At morning's light they carry it out
     because it is in their power to do it.
2 They covet fields and seize them,
     and houses, and take them.
They defraud a man of his home,
     a fellowman of his inheritance.

3 Therefore, the LORD says:

"I am planning disaster against this
     people,
     from which you cannot save
       yourselves.
You will no longer walk proudly,
     for it will be a time of calamity.
4 In that day men will ridicule you;
     they will taunt you with this
       mournful song:
'We are utterly ruined;
     my people's possession is divided
       up.
He takes it from me!
     He assigns our fields to traitors.' "

5 Therefore you will have no one in the
       assembly of the LORD
     to divide the land by lot.

False Prophets

6 "Do not prophesy," their prophets say.
     "Do not prophesy about these things;
     disgrace will not overtake us."
7 Should it be said, O house of Jacob:
     "Is the Spirit of the LORD angry?
     Does he do such things?"

"Do not my words do good
     to him whose ways are upright?
8 Lately my people have risen up
     like an enemy.
You strip off the rich robe
     from those who pass by without a
       care,
     like men returning from battle.
9 You drive the women of my people
     from their pleasant homes.
You take away my blessing
     from their children forever.
10 Get up, go away!
     For this is not your resting place,
because it is defiled,
     it is ruined, beyond all remedy.
11 If a liar and deceiver comes and says,
     'I will prophesy for you plenty of
       wine and beer,'
     he would be just the prophet for this
       people!

Deliverance Promised

12 "I will surely gather all of you, O Jacob;
     I will surely bring together the
       remnant of Israel.
I will bring them together like sheep in
       a pen,
     like a flock in its pasture;
     the place will throng with people.
13 One who breaks open the way will go
       up before them;
they will break through the gate and
       go out.
Their king will pass through before
       them,
     the LORD at their head."

Leaders and Prophets Rebuked

3 Then I said,

"Listen, you leaders of Jacob,
     you rulers of the house of Israel.
Should you not know justice,
2   you who hate good and love evil;

a 12 Maroth sounds like the Hebrew for bitter.
b 13 Lachish sounds like the Hebrew for team.   *c 14 Aczib*
means deception.   *d 15 Mareshah sounds like the Hebrew*
for conqueror.

who tear the skin from my people
and the flesh from their bones;
3 who eat my people's flesh,
strip off their skin
and break their bones in pieces;
who chop them up like meat for the
pan,
like flesh for the pot?"

4 Then they will cry out to the LORD,
but he will not answer them.
At that time he will hide his face from
them
because of the evil they have done.

5 This is what the LORD says:

"As for the prophets
who lead my people astray,
if one feeds them,
they proclaim 'peace';
if he does not,
they prepare to wage war against
him.
6 Therefore night will come over you,
without visions,
and darkness, without divination.
The sun will set for the prophets,
and the day will go dark for them.
7 The seers will be ashamed
and the diviners disgraced.
They will all cover their faces
because there is no answer from
God."

8 But as for me, I am filled with power,
with the Spirit of the LORD,
and with justice and might,
to declare to Jacob his transgression,
to Israel his sin.
9 Hear this, you leaders of the house of
Jacob,
you rulers of the house of Israel,
who despise justice
and distort all that is right;
10 who build Zion with bloodshed,
and Jerusalem with wickedness.
11 Her leaders judge for a bribe,
her priests teach for a price,
and her prophets tell fortunes for
money.
Yet they lean upon the LORD and say,
"Is not the LORD among us?
No disaster will come upon us."
12 Therefore because of you,
Zion will be plowed like a field,
Jerusalem will become a heap of rubble,
the temple hill a mound overgrown
with thickets.

The Mountain of the LORD

4 In the last days

the mountain of the LORD's temple
will be established
as chief among the mountains;
it will be raised above the hills,
and peoples will stream to it.

2 Many nations will come and say,

"Come, let us go up to the mountain
of the LORD,
to the house of the God of Jacob.
He will teach us his ways,
so that we may walk in his paths."
The law will go out from Zion,
the word of the LORD from Jerusalem.
3 He will judge between many peoples
and will settle disputes for strong
nations far and wide.
They will beat their swords into
plowshares
and their spears into pruning hooks.
Nation will not take up sword against
nation,
nor will they train for war anymore.
4 Every man will sit under his own vine
and under his own fig tree,
and no one will make them afraid,
for the LORD Almighty has spoken.
5 All the nations may walk
in the name of their gods;
we will walk in the name of the LORD
our God for ever and ever.

The LORD's Plan

6 "In that day," declares the LORD,

"I will gather the lame;
I will assemble the exiles
and those I have brought to grief.
7 I will make the lame a remnant,
those driven away a strong nation.
The LORD will rule over them in Mount
Zion
from that day and forever.
8 As for you, O watchtower of the flock,
O stronghold[a] of the Daughter of
Zion,
the former dominion will be restored
to you;
kingship will come to the Daughter
of Jerusalem."

9 Why do you now cry aloud—
have you no king?

a 8 Or hill

Has your counselor perished,
  that pain seizes you like that of a
    woman in labor?
10 Writhe in agony, O Daughter of Zion,
  like a woman in labor,
for now you must leave the city
  to camp in the open field.
You will go to Babylon;
  there you will be rescued.
There the LORD will redeem you
  out of the hand of your enemies.

11 But now many nations
  are gathered against you.

They say, "Let her be defiled,
  let our eyes gloat over Zion!"
12 But they do not know
  the thoughts of the LORD;
they do not understand his plan,
  he who gathers them like sheaves to
    the threshing floor.

13 "Rise and thresh, O Daughter of Zion,
  for I will give you horns of iron;
I will give you hoofs of bronze
  and you will break to pieces many
    nations."

Make It Stick

_____

_____

_____

_____

_____

_____

READ MICAH 4:1–4
Micah was looking forward to sitting under his own fig tree in God's kingdom on earth. What would you rather do? Spend all day enjoying endless bike trails and skateboard parks, water slides, horse rides and tree forts? Write down a few things you'd like to enjoy.

You will devote their ill-gotten gains to the Lord,
    their wealth to the Lord of all the earth.

A Promised Ruler From Bethlehem

5 Marshal your troops, O city of troops,[a]
    for a siege is laid against us.
    They will strike Israel's ruler
    on the cheek with a rod.

2 "But you, Bethlehem Ephrathah,
    though you are small among the clans[b] of Judah,
out of you will come for me
    one who will be ruler over Israel,
whose origins[c] are from of old,
    from ancient times.[d]"

3 Therefore Israel will be abandoned
    until the time when she who is in labor gives birth
and the rest of his brothers return
    to join the Israelites.

4 He will stand and shepherd his flock
    in the strength of the Lord,
    in the majesty of the name of the Lord his God.
And they will live securely, for then his greatness
    will reach to the ends of the earth.
5   And he will be their peace.

Deliverance and Destruction

When the Assyrian invades our land
    and marches through our fortresses,
we will raise against him seven shepherds,
    even eight leaders of men.
6 They will rule[e] the land of Assyria with the sword,
    the land of Nimrod with drawn sword.[f]
He will deliver us from the Assyrian
    when he invades our land
    and marches into our borders.

7 The remnant of Jacob will be
    in the midst of many peoples
like dew from the Lord,
    like showers on the grass,
which do not wait for man
    or linger for mankind.
8 The remnant of Jacob will be among the nations,
    in the midst of many peoples,
like a lion among the beasts of the forest,
    like a young lion among flocks of sheep,
which mauls and mangles as it goes,
    and no one can rescue.
9 Your hand will be lifted up in triumph over your
        enemies,
    and all your foes will be destroyed.

10 "In that day," declares the Lord,

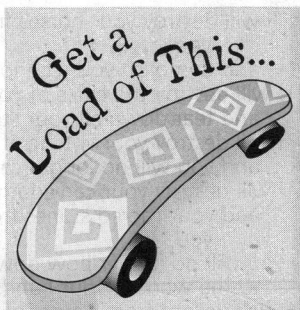

Get a Load of This...

Check out Micah 5:2. Micah didn't just close his eyes and point at the map to guess where the Messiah would be born. Seven hundred years before the first Christmas, he pegged Bethlehem as the exact spot. His detailed prophecy was just one of hundreds of prophecies in the Old Testament that came true about Jesus' birth, life and death.

---

a 1 Or Strengthen your walls, O walled city   b 2 Or rulers   c 2 Hebrew goings out   d 2 Or from days of eternity   e 6 Or crush   f 6 Or Nimrod in its gates

"I will destroy your horses from among
  you
  and demolish your chariots.
11 I will destroy the cities of your land
  and tear down all your strongholds.
12 I will destroy your witchcraft
  and you will no longer cast spells.
13 I will destroy your carved images
  and your sacred stones from among
  you;
  you will no longer bow down
  to the work of your hands.
14 I will uproot from among you your
  Asherah poles[a]
  and demolish your cities.
15 I will take vengeance in anger and
  wrath
  upon the nations that have not
  obeyed me."

The LORD's Case Against Israel

6 Listen to what the LORD says:

  "Stand up, plead your case before
  the mountains;
  let the hills hear what you have to
  say.
2 Hear, O mountains, the LORD's
  accusation;
  listen, you everlasting foundations of
  the earth.
  For the LORD has a case against his
  people;
  he is lodging a charge against Israel.

3 "My people, what have I done to you?
  How have I burdened you? Answer
  me.
4 I brought you up out of Egypt
  and redeemed you from the land of
  slavery.
  I sent Moses to lead you,
  also Aaron and Miriam.
5 My people, remember
  what Balak king of Moab counseled
  and what Balaam son of Beor
  answered.
  Remember ⌊your journey⌋ from Shittim
  to Gilgal,
  that you may know the righteous
  acts of the LORD."

6 With what shall I come before the LORD
  and bow down before the exalted
  God?
  Shall I come before him with burnt
  offerings,
  with calves a year old?

7 Will the LORD be pleased with
  thousands of rams,
  with ten thousand rivers of oil?
  Shall I offer my firstborn for my
  transgression,
  the fruit of my body for the sin of
  my soul?
8 He has showed you, O man, what is
  good.
  And what does the LORD require of
  you?
  To act justly and to love mercy
  and to walk humbly with your God.

Israel's Guilt and Punishment

9 Listen! The LORD is calling to the city—
  and to fear your name is wisdom—
  "Heed the rod and the One who
  appointed it.[b]
10 Am I still to forget, O wicked house,
  your ill-gotten treasures
  and the short ephah,[c] which is
  accursed?
11 Shall I acquit a man with dishonest
  scales,
  with a bag of false weights?
12 Her rich men are violent;
  her people are liars
  and their tongues speak deceitfully.
13 Therefore, I have begun to destroy
  you,
  to ruin you because of your sins.
14 You will eat but not be satisfied;
  your stomach will still be empty.[d]
  You will store up but save nothing,
  because what you save I will give to
  the sword.
15 You will plant but not harvest;
  you will press olives but not use the
  oil on yourselves,
  you will crush grapes but not drink
  the wine.
16 You have observed the statutes of
  Omri
  and all the practices of Ahab's
  house,
  and you have followed their
  traditions.
  Therefore I will give you over to ruin
  and your people to derision;
  you will bear the scorn of the
  nations.[e]"

---

a 14 That is, symbols of the goddess Asherah
b 9 The meaning of the Hebrew for this line is uncertain.
c 10 An ephah was a dry measure.   d 14 The meaning of
the Hebrew for this word is uncertain.   e 16 Septuagint;
Hebrew *scorn due my people*

Israel's Misery

7 What misery is mine!
I am like one who gathers summer
fruit
at the gleaning of the vineyard;
there is no cluster of grapes to eat,
none of the early figs that I crave.
2 The godly have been swept from the
land;
not one upright man remains.
All men lie in wait to shed blood;
each hunts his brother with a net.
3 Both hands are skilled in doing evil;
the ruler demands gifts,
the judge accepts bribes,
the powerful dictate what they
desire—
they all conspire together.
4 The best of them is like a brier,
the most upright worse than a thorn
hedge.
The day of your watchmen has come,
the day God visits you.
Now is the time of their confusion.
5 Do not trust a neighbor;
put no confidence in a friend.
Even with her who lies in your embrace
be careful of your words.
6 For a son dishonors his father,
a daughter rises up against her
mother,
a daughter-in-law against her mother-
in-law—
a man's enemies are the members of
his own household.

7 But as for me, I watch in hope for the
LORD,
I wait for God my Savior;
my God will hear me.

Israel Will Rise

8 Do not gloat over me, my enemy!
Though I have fallen, I will rise.
Though I sit in darkness,
the LORD will be my light.
9 Because I have sinned against him,
I will bear the LORD's wrath,
until he pleads my case
and establishes my right.
He will bring me out into the light;
I will see his righteousness.
10 Then my enemy will see it

Mercy Is Cool

READ MICAH 6:6–8

God calls men to show mercy to one another. Think about baseball:
Not just Little League, but many high school programs, have a "mercy
rule." If one team is creaming another, the mismatch is recognized
and the game is ended before the score gets *really* embarrassing. It
hurts to be humiliated on the playing field—or in life. You
can show mercy in all kinds of ways. Sometimes it means
sticking up for the underdog: helping a classmate who's being
pushed around, or giving part of your lawn-mowing money
to a food bank. Mercy isn't about showing off how good you
can be when you go to church, then walking past
scraped-up kids laying on crashed, bent bikes the
rest of the week. Mercy is about helping others,
even stopping to help the least popular kid in
your school. A true man of God doesn't look out
for "number one" all the time. He shows mercy.

Your next reading is on page 1181.

and will be covered with shame,
she who said to me,
   "Where is the LORD your God?"
My eyes will see her downfall;
   even now she will be trampled
      underfoot
   like mire in the streets.

11 The day for building your walls will
      come,
   the day for extending your
      boundaries.
12 In that day people will come to you
   from Assyria and the cities of Egypt,
even from Egypt to the Euphrates
   and from sea to sea
   and from mountain to mountain.
13 The earth will become desolate
      because of its inhabitants,
   as the result of their deeds.

Prayer and Praise

14 Shepherd your people with your staff,
   the flock of your inheritance,
which lives by itself in a forest,
   in fertile pasturelands. a
Let them feed in Bashan and Gilead
   as in days long ago.

15 "As in the days when you came out of
      Egypt,

I will show them my wonders."
16 Nations will see and be ashamed,
   deprived of all their power.
They will lay their hands on their
      mouths
   and their ears will become deaf.
17 They will lick dust like a snake,
   like creatures that crawl on the
      ground.
They will come trembling out of their
      dens;
   they will turn in fear to the LORD our
      God
   and will be afraid of you.
18 Who is a God like you,
   who pardons sin and forgives the
      transgression
   of the remnant of his inheritance?
You do not stay angry forever
   but delight to show mercy.
19 You will again have compassion on us;
   you will tread our sins underfoot
   and hurl all our iniquities into the
      depths of the sea.
20 You will be true to Jacob,
   and show mercy to Abraham,
as you pledged on oath to our fathers
   in days long ago.

a 14 Or in the middle of Carmel

NAHUM

Who wrote this book?
The prophet Nahum.

Why was this book written?
Nahum assures the people of Judah that God will destroy Nineveh, the capital city of their great enemy, Assyria.

What do we learn about God in this book?
God will punish the enemies of the people he loves.

What is special about this book?
The city of Nineveh is captured, just as Nahum says, by using a river (Nahum 2:5–10).

When was this book written?
Nahum was written sometime between 663 and 612 B.C.

An oracle concerning Nineveh. The book of the vision of Nahum the Elkoshite.

The LORD's Anger Against Nineveh

2 The LORD is a jealous and avenging God;
  the LORD takes vengeance and is
    filled with wrath.
The LORD takes vengeance on his foes
  and maintains his wrath against his
    enemies.
3 The LORD is slow to anger and great in
    power;
  the LORD will not leave the guilty
    unpunished.
His way is in the whirlwind and the
    storm,
  and clouds are the dust of his feet.
4 He rebukes the sea and dries it up;
  he makes all the rivers run dry.
Bashan and Carmel wither
  and the blossoms of Lebanon fade.
5 The mountains quake before him
  and the hills melt away.
The earth trembles at his presence,
  the world and all who live in it.
6 Who can withstand his indignation?
  Who can endure his fierce anger?
His wrath is poured out like fire;
  the rocks are shattered before him.

7 The LORD is good,
  a refuge in times of trouble.
He cares for those who trust in him,
8   but with an overwhelming flood
he will make an end of ⌐Nineveh⌐;
  he will pursue his foes into darkness.

9 Whatever they plot against the LORD
  he[a] will bring to an end;
  trouble will not come a second time.
10 They will be entangled among thorns
  and drunk from their wine;
  they will be consumed like dry
    stubble. [b]
11 From you, ⌐O Nineveh,⌐ has one come
    forth
  who plots evil against the LORD
  and counsels wickedness.

12 This is what the LORD says:

"Although they have allies and are
    numerous,
  they will be cut off and pass away.
Although I have afflicted you,
  ⌐O Judah,⌐
  I will afflict you no more.

13 Now I will break their yoke from your
    neck
  and tear your shackles away."

14 The LORD has given a command
  concerning you, ⌐Nineveh⌐:
"You will have no descendants to
    bear your name.
I will destroy the carved images and
    cast idols
  that are in the temple of your gods.
I will prepare your grave,
  for you are vile."

15 Look, there on the mountains,
  the feet of one who brings good
    news,
  who proclaims peace!
Celebrate your festivals, O Judah,
  and fulfill your vows.
No more will the wicked invade you;
  they will be completely destroyed.

Nineveh to Fall

An attacker advances against you,
  ⌐Nineveh⌐.
  Guard the fortress,
  watch the road,
brace yourselves,
  marshal all your strength!

2 The LORD will restore the splendor of
    Jacob
  like the splendor of Israel,
though destroyers have laid them
    waste
  and have ruined their vines.

3 The shields of his soldiers are red;
  the warriors are clad in scarlet.
The metal on the chariots flashes
  on the day they are made ready;
  the spears of pine are brandished. [c]
4 The chariots storm through the streets,
  rushing back and forth through the
    squares.
They look like flaming torches;
  they dart about like lightning.

5 He summons his picked troops,
  yet they stumble on their way.
They dash to the city wall;
  the protective shield is put in place.
6 The river gates are thrown open
  and the palace collapses.

a 9 Or What do you foes plot against the LORD? / He
b 10 The meaning of the Hebrew for this verse is uncertain.
c 3 Hebrew; Septuagint and Syriac / the horsemen rush to
and fro

⁷ It is decreed *a* that ⌊the city⌋
    be exiled and carried away.
Its slave girls moan like doves
    and beat upon their breasts.
⁸ Nineveh is like a pool,
    and its water is draining away.
"Stop! Stop!" they cry,
    but no one turns back.
⁹ Plunder the silver!
    Plunder the gold!
The supply is endless,
    the wealth from all its treasures!
¹⁰ She is pillaged, plundered, stripped!
    Hearts melt, knees give way,
    bodies tremble, every face grows pale.

¹¹ Where now is the lions' den,
    the place where they fed their
        young,
where the lion and lioness went,
    and the cubs, with nothing to fear?
¹² The lion killed enough for his cubs
    and strangled the prey for his mate,
filling his lairs with the kill
    and his dens with the prey.

¹³ "I am against you,"
    declares the LORD Almighty.

"I will burn up your chariots in smoke,
    and the sword will devour your
        young lions.
I will leave you no prey on the earth.
The voices of your messengers
    will no longer be heard."

Woe to Nineveh

3 Woe to the city of blood,
    full of lies,
    full of plunder,
    never without victims!
² The crack of whips,
    the clatter of wheels,
galloping horses
    and jolting chariots!
³ Charging cavalry,
    flashing swords
    and glittering spears!
Many casualties,
    piles of dead,
bodies without number,
    people stumbling over the corpses—
⁴ all because of the wanton lust of a
        harlot,

a 7 The meaning of the Hebrew for this word is uncertain.

Back to the Black Hole

READ NAHUM 1:1–2, 7–8; 2:1–6; 3:1–7

The Assyrians were notoriously cruel. They were so wicked that if you could go back in time and video them in action, your footage wouldn't be allowed on public television. God loved them enough to warn them, but Nineveh (Assyria's capital) had its last chance with Jonah. They temporarily repented, but pretty soon they went back to the black hole they'd been in. By Nahum's day there was no more Jonah ... just judgment. Nahum gave prophecies of exactly how Nineveh would fall with a flood that opened the walls for an attacking army (see Nahum 1:8; 2:6)—and that's how it happened! If you've mucked up, repent like Nineveh did, yes, but then go *on* from there and make a commitment to change your life. Repentance is just the first step. The rest is showing *proof* of the repentance and changing your life around.

Your next reading is on page 1184.

alluring, the mistress of sorceries,
who enslaved nations by her
    prostitution
and peoples by her witchcraft.

⁵ "I am against you," declares the LORD
    Almighty.
    "I will lift your skirts over your face.
I will show the nations your nakedness
    and the kingdoms your shame.
⁶ I will pelt you with filth,
    I will treat you with contempt
    and make you a spectacle.
⁷ All who see you will flee from you and
    say,
    'Nineveh is in ruins—who will mourn
    for her?'
    Where can I find anyone to comfort
    you?"

⁸ Are you better than Thebes,ᵃ
    situated on the Nile,
    with water around her?
The river was her defense,
    the waters her wall.
⁹ Cushᵇ and Egypt were her boundless
    strength;
    Put and Libya were among her allies.
¹⁰ Yet she was taken captive
    and went into exile.
Her infants were dashed to pieces
    at the head of every street.
Lots were cast for her nobles,
    and all her great men were put in
    chains.
¹¹ You too will become drunk;
    you will go into hiding
    and seek refuge from the enemy.

¹² All your fortresses are like fig trees
    with their first ripe fruit;
when they are shaken,
    the figs fall into the mouth of the
    eater.
¹³ Look at your troops—

they are all women!
The gates of your land
    are wide open to your enemies;
    fire has consumed their bars.

¹⁴ Draw water for the siege,
    strengthen your defenses!
Work the clay,
    tread the mortar,
    repair the brickwork!
¹⁵ There the fire will devour you;
    the sword will cut you down
    and, like grasshoppers, consume you.
Multiply like grasshoppers,
    multiply like locusts!
¹⁶ You have increased the number of your
    merchants
    till they are more than the stars of
    the sky,
but like locusts they strip the land
    and then fly away.
¹⁷ Your guards are like locusts,
    your officials like swarms of locusts
    that settle in the walls on a cold
    day—
but when the sun appears they fly
    away,
    and no one knows where.

¹⁸ O king of Assyria, your shepherdsᶜ
    slumber;
    your nobles lie down to rest.
Your people are scattered on the
    mountains
    with no one to gather them.
¹⁹ Nothing can heal your wound;
    your injury is fatal.
Everyone who hears the news about
    you
    claps his hands at your fall,
for who has not felt
    your endless cruelty?

ᵃ 8 Hebrew *No Amon*   ᵇ 9 That is, the upper Nile region
ᶜ 18 Or *rulers*

HABAKKUK

Who wrote this book?

The prophet Habakkuk.

Why was this book written?

Habakkuk shows that people never get away with being wicked and that God will punish the wicked.

What do we learn about God in this book?

God is too holy to let people get away with sin. He punishes everyone who sins, even people like the Babylonians, who seemed to get rich by being wicked.

What is special about this book?

Habakkuk is afraid when he learns that God will send the Babylonians against Judah. But in the end Habakkuk decides to trust God anyway.

When was this book written?

Habakkuk was written about 605 B.C., during the reign of good King Josiah, who ruled Judah from 639 to 597 B.C.

1 The oracle that Habakkuk the prophet received.

Habakkuk's Complaint

2 How long, O Lᴏʀᴅ, must I call for help,
  but you do not listen?
 Or cry out to you, "Violence!"
  but you do not save?
3 Why do you make me look at injustice?
  Why do you tolerate wrong?
 Destruction and violence are before me;
  there is strife, and conflict abounds.
4 Therefore the law is paralyzed,
  and justice never prevails.
 The wicked hem in the righteous,
  so that justice is perverted.

The Lᴏʀᴅ's Answer

5 "Look at the nations and watch—
  and be utterly amazed.
 For I am going to do something in
   your days
  that you would not believe,
  even if you were told.
6 I am raising up the Babylonians,ᵃ
  that ruthless and impetuous people,

 who sweep across the whole earth
  to seize dwelling places not their
    own.
7 They are a feared and dreaded people;
  they are a law to themselves
  and promote their own honor.
8 Their horses are swifter than leopards,
  fiercer than wolves at dusk.
 Their cavalry gallops headlong;
  their horsemen come from afar.
 They fly like a vulture swooping to
    devour;
9 they all come bent on violence.
 Their hordesᵇ advance like a desert wind
  and gather prisoners like sand.
10 They deride kings
  and scoff at rulers.
 They laugh at all fortified cities;
  they build earthen ramps and
    capture them.
11 Then they sweep past like the wind
  and go on—
 guilty men, whose own strength is
  their god."

ᵃ 6 Or *Chaldeans*   ᵇ 9 The meaning of the Hebrew for this
word is uncertain.

Questions and Answers

READ HABAKKUK 1:1—2:3

Habakkuk wasn't afraid to ask serious questions like, "Why doesn't God seem to punish evil people?" or "Why doesn't God answer my prayer?" People ask questions. That's how they get answers. So ask God questions. Being a Christian doesn't mean not using your brain. Having a relationship with God means being able to talk seriously to him—so talk to him. Tell him you wonder about this or that. Don't be afraid to ask questions like, "Why does that bully at school get away with stuff?" Seeking answers is a key to deepening your faith. There's a difference between a scoffer or skeptic who says, "I don't believe God is in control. God isn't doing the right thing. I know more than God," and honest questions. If you're asking honest questions because you want to understand, more power to you.

Your next reading is on page 1186.

Habakkuk's Second Complaint

12 O LORD, are you not from everlasting?
My God, my Holy One, we will not
die.

O LORD, you have appointed them to
execute judgment;
O Rock, you have ordained them to
punish.
13 Your eyes are too pure to look on evil;
you cannot tolerate wrong.
Why then do you tolerate the
treacherous?
Why are you silent while the wicked
swallow up those more righteous
than themselves?
14 You have made men like fish in the
sea,
like sea creatures that have no ruler.
15 The wicked foe pulls all of them up
with hooks,
he catches them in his net,
he gathers them up in his dragnet;
and so he rejoices and is glad.
16 Therefore he sacrifices to his net
and burns incense to his dragnet,
for by his net he lives in luxury
and enjoys the choicest food.
17 Is he to keep on emptying his net,
destroying nations without mercy?

2 I will stand at my watch
and station myself on the ramparts;
I will look to see what he will say to
me,
and what answer I am to give to this
complaint.[a]

The LORD's Answer

2 Then the LORD replied:

"Write down the revelation
and make it plain on tablets
so that a herald[b] may run with it.
3 For the revelation awaits an appointed
time;
it speaks of the end
and will not prove false.
Though it linger, wait for it;
it[c] will certainly come and will not
delay.

4 "See, he is puffed up;
his desires are not upright—
but the righteous will live by his
faith[d]—
5 indeed, wine betrays him;
he is arrogant and never at rest.

Because he is as greedy as the grave[e]
and like death is never satisfied,
he gathers to himself all the nations
and takes captive all the peoples.

6 "Will not all of them taunt him with
ridicule and scorn, saying,

" 'Woe to him who piles up stolen
goods
and makes himself wealthy by
extortion!
How long must this go on?'
7 Will not your debtors[f] suddenly arise?
Will they not wake up and make you
tremble?
Then you will become their victim.
8 Because you have plundered many
nations,
the peoples who are left will plunder
you.
For you have shed man's blood;
you have destroyed lands and cities
and everyone in them.

9 "Woe to him who builds his realm by
unjust gain
to set his nest on high,
to escape the clutches of ruin!
10 You have plotted the ruin of many
peoples,
shaming your own house and
forfeiting your life.
11 The stones of the wall will cry out,
and the beams of the woodwork will
echo it.

12 "Woe to him who builds a city with
bloodshed
and establishes a town by crime!
13 Has not the LORD Almighty determined
that the people's labor is only fuel
for the fire,
that the nations exhaust themselves
for nothing?
14 For the earth will be filled with the
knowledge of the glory of the
LORD,
as the waters cover the sea.

15 "Woe to him who gives drink to his
neighbors,
pouring it from the wineskin till they
are drunk,

---

a 1 Or and what to answer when I am rebuked   b 2 Or so
that whoever reads it   c 3 Or Though he linger, wait for
him; / he   d 4 Or faithfulness   e 5 Hebrew Sheol
f 7 Or creditors

so that he can gaze on their naked
bodies.
16 You will be filled with shame instead of
glory.
Now it is your turn! Drink and be
exposed[a]!
The cup from the LORD's right hand is
coming around to you,
and disgrace will cover your glory.
17 The violence you have done to
Lebanon will overwhelm you,
and your destruction of animals will
terrify you.
For you have shed man's blood;
you have destroyed lands and cities
and everyone in them.

18 "Of what value is an idol, since a man
has carved it?
Or an image that teaches lies?
For he who makes it trusts in his own
creation;
he makes idols that cannot speak.
19 Woe to him who says to wood, 'Come
to life!'
Or to lifeless stone, 'Wake up!'
Can it give guidance?

It is covered with gold and silver;
there is no breath in it.
20 But the LORD is in his holy temple;
let all the earth be silent before him.'"

Habakkuk's Prayer

3 A prayer of Habakkuk the prophet.
On *shigionoth*.[b]

2 LORD, I have heard of your fame;
I stand in awe of your deeds,
O LORD.
Renew them in our day,
in our time make them known;
in wrath remember mercy.

3 God came from Teman,
the Holy One from Mount Paran.
Selah[c]
His glory covered the heavens
and his praise filled the earth.
4 His splendor was like the sunrise;
rays flashed from his hand,

a 16 Masoretic Text; Dead Sea Scrolls, Aquila, Vulgate and
Syriac (see also Septuagint) *and stagger   b 1* Probably a
literary or musical term   *c 3* A word of uncertain meaning;
possibly a musical term; also in verses 9 and 13

One of Those Days!

READ HABAKKUK 3:16–19

When things go wrong, it's OK to question God. Maybe you were
headed to summer camp, but then your dad loses his job, and you
can't go. It's OK to ask God why. Just don't grumble that God is unlov-
ing or unfair. Don't accuse him of dumping you. Even if you break
your leg just before baseball season starts, you still need to
trust that God loves you and is not snoozing at the controls.
And hey!—if you trust that God loves you, if you trust that
he's looking out for you, you can praise him and be happy,
right? Right! Habakkuk said that even if all his crops failed
and his fridge was empty, "yet I will rejoice in the LORD"
(verse 18). Now *that* is trust! Habakkuk started out
asking God questions, but when the dust settled,
he was still trusting God. Two thumbs up—way
up!—for Habakkuk.

Your next reading is on page 1192.

where his power was hidden.
5 Plague went before him;
  pestilence followed his steps.
6 He stood, and shook the earth;
  he looked, and made the nations
    tremble.
The ancient mountains crumbled
and the age-old hills collapsed.
His ways are eternal.
7 I saw the tents of Cushan in distress,
  the dwellings of Midian in anguish.

8 Were you angry with the rivers,
    O LORD?
  Was your wrath against the
    streams?
Did you rage against the sea
  when you rode with your horses
  and your victorious chariots?
9 You uncovered your bow,
  you called for many arrows.   *Selah*
You split the earth with rivers;
10   the mountains saw you and writhed.
  Torrents of water swept by;
    the deep roared
    and lifted its waves on high.

11 Sun and moon stood still in the
    heavens
  at the glint of your flying arrows,
  at the lightning of your flashing
    spear.
12 In wrath you strode through the earth
  and in anger you threshed the
    nations.
13 You came out to deliver your people,
  to save your anointed one.

You crushed the leader of the land of
    wickedness,
  you stripped him from head to foot.
                                Selah
14 With his own spear you pierced his
    head
  when his warriors stormed out to
    scatter us,
  gloating as though about to devour
    the wretched who were in hiding.
15 You trampled the sea with your horses,
  churning the great waters.

16 I heard and my heart pounded,
  my lips quivered at the sound;
decay crept into my bones,
  and my legs trembled.
Yet I will wait patiently for the day of
    calamity
  to come on the nation invading us.
17 Though the fig tree does not bud
  and there are no grapes on the
    vines,
though the olive crop fails
  and the fields produce no food,
though there are no sheep in the pen
  and no cattle in the stalls,
18 yet I will rejoice in the LORD,
  I will be joyful in God my Savior.

19 The Sovereign LORD is my strength;
  he makes my feet like the feet of a
    deer,
  he enables me to go on the heights.

For the director of music. On my
    stringed instruments.

ZEPHANIAH

Who wrote this book?

The prophet Zephaniah, a descendant of good King Hezekiah, wrote this book.

Why was this book written?

Zephaniah prepares Judah for Josiah's revival of 621 B.C. Zephaniah warns Judah that God will judge a sinful people.

What do we learn about God in this book?

God is a God of judgment. He will punish sin when history comes to an end. But God does not wait. He also punishes sinful nations now.

What is special about this book?

Zephaniah's preaching may have helped to turn people to God during Josiah's revival.

When was this book written?

Zephaniah was written during the reign of Josiah, probably about 620 B.C.

1 The word of the LORD that came to Zephaniah son of Cushi, the son of Gedaliah, the son of Amariah, the son of Hezekiah, during the reign of Josiah son of Amon king of Judah:

Warning of Coming Destruction

2 "I will sweep away everything
    from the face of the earth,"
                declares the LORD.
3 "I will sweep away both men and
        animals;
    I will sweep away the birds of the air
        and the fish of the sea.
The wicked will have only heaps of
        rubble[a]
    when I cut off man from the face of
        the earth,"
                declares the LORD.

Against Judah

4 "I will stretch out my hand against
        Judah
    and against all who live in Jerusalem.
I will cut off from this place every
        remnant of Baal,
    the names of the pagan and the
        idolatrous priests—
5 those who bow down on the roofs
        to worship the starry host,
    those who bow down and swear by
        the LORD
    and who also swear by Molech,[b]
6 those who turn back from following
        the LORD
    and neither seek the LORD nor inquire
        of him.
7 Be silent before the Sovereign LORD,
    for the day of the LORD is near.
The LORD has prepared a sacrifice;
    he has consecrated those he has
        invited.
8 On the day of the LORD's sacrifice
    I will punish the princes
    and the king's sons
and all those clad
    in foreign clothes.
9 On that day I will punish
    all who avoid stepping on the
        threshold,[c]
who fill the temple of their gods
    with violence and deceit.
10 "On that day," declares the LORD,
    "a cry will go up from the Fish Gate,
    wailing from the New Quarter,
    and a loud crash from the hills.

11 Wail, you who live in the market
        district[d];
    all your merchants will be wiped
        out,
    all who trade with[e] silver will be
        ruined.
12 At that time I will search Jerusalem
        with lamps
    and punish those who are
        complacent,
    who are like wine left on its dregs,
who think, 'The LORD will do nothing,
    either good or bad.'
13 Their wealth will be plundered,
    their houses demolished.
They will build houses
    but not live in them;
they will plant vineyards
    but not drink the wine.

The Great Day of the LORD

14 "The great day of the LORD is near—
        near and coming quickly.
    Listen! The cry on the day of the LORD
        will be bitter,
    the shouting of the warrior there.
15 That day will be a day of wrath,
    a day of distress and anguish,
    a day of trouble and ruin,
    a day of darkness and gloom,
    a day of clouds and blackness,
16 a day of trumpet and battle cry
    against the fortified cities
    and against the corner towers.
17 I will bring distress on the people
    and they will walk like blind men,
    because they have sinned against
        the LORD.
Their blood will be poured out like
        dust
    and their entrails like filth.
18 Neither their silver nor their gold
    will be able to save them
    on the day of the LORD's wrath.
In the fire of his jealousy
    the whole world will be consumed,
for he will make a sudden end
    of all who live in the earth."

2 Gather together, gather together,
    O shameful nation,
2 before the appointed time arrives
    and that day sweeps on like chaff,

---

[a] 3 The meaning of the Hebrew for this line is uncertain.
[b] 5 Hebrew *Malcam*, that is, Milcom   [c] 9 See 1 Samuel 5:5.
[d] 11 Or *the Mortar*   [e] 11 Or *in*

before the fierce anger of the LORD
　　comes upon you,
　before the day of the LORD's wrath
　　comes upon you.
³ Seek the LORD, all you humble of the
　　land,
　you who do what he commands.
　Seek righteousness, seek humility;
　　perhaps you will be sheltered
　on the day of the LORD's anger.

Against Philistia

⁴ Gaza will be abandoned
　　and Ashkelon left in ruins.
　At midday Ashdod will be emptied
　　and Ekron uprooted.
⁵ Woe to you who live by the sea,
　　O Kerethite people;
　the word of the LORD is against you,
　　O Canaan, land of the Philistines.

　"I will destroy you,
　　and none will be left."

⁶ The land by the sea, where the
　　Kerethites^a dwell,
　will be a place for shepherds and
　　sheep pens.
⁷ It will belong to the remnant of the
　　house of Judah;
　there they will find pasture.
　In the evening they will lie down
　　in the houses of Ashkelon.
　The LORD their God will care for them;
　　he will restore their fortunes. ^b

Against Moab and Ammon

⁸ "I have heard the insults of Moab
　　and the taunts of the Ammonites,
　who insulted my people
　　and made threats against their land.
⁹ Therefore, as surely as I live,"
　　declares the LORD Almighty, the God
　　　of Israel,
　"surely Moab will become like Sodom,

---

^a 6   The meaning of the Hebrew for this word is uncertain.
^b 7   Or *will bring back their captives*

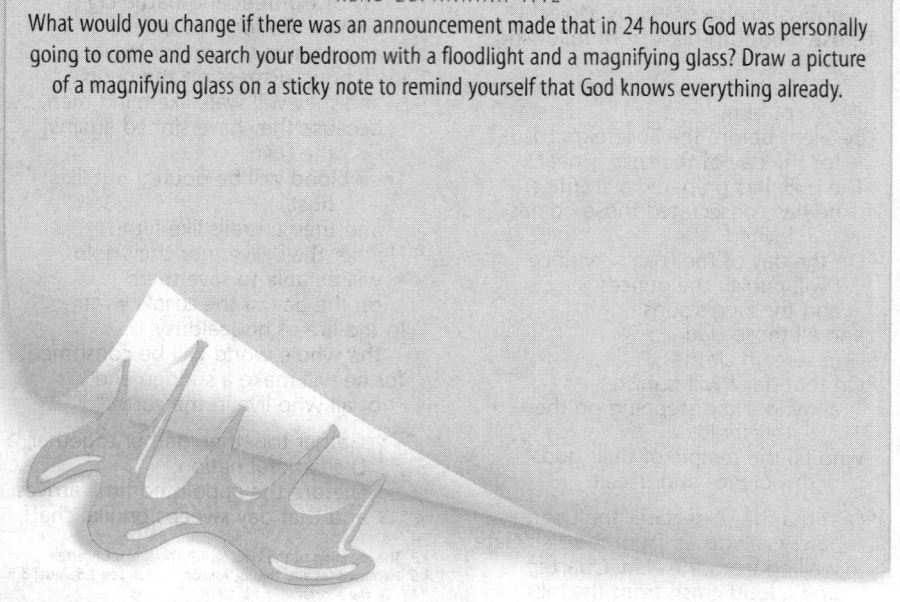

Make It Stick

READ ZEPHANIAH 1:12

What would you change if there was an announcement made that in 24 hours God was personally going to come and search your bedroom with a floodlight and a magnifying glass? Draw a picture of a magnifying glass on a sticky note to remind yourself that God knows everything already.

the Ammonites like Gomorrah—
a place of weeds and salt pits,
a wasteland forever.
The remnant of my people will plunder
them;
the survivors of my nation will
inherit their land."

10 This is what they will get in return for
their pride,
for insulting and mocking the
people of the LORD Almighty.
11 The LORD will be awesome to them
when he destroys all the gods of the
land.
The nations on every shore will
worship him,
every one in its own land.

Against Cush

12 "You too, O Cushites,*a*
will be slain by my sword."

Against Assyria

13 He will stretch out his hand against the
north
and destroy Assyria,
leaving Nineveh utterly desolate
and dry as the desert.
14 Flocks and herds will lie down there,
creatures of every kind.
The desert owl and the screech owl
will roost on her columns.
Their calls will echo through the
windows,
rubble will be in the doorways,
the beams of cedar will be exposed.
15 This is the carefree city
that lived in safety.
She said to herself,
"I am, and there is none besides
me."
What a ruin she has become,
a lair for wild beasts!
All who pass by her scoff
and shake their fists.

The Future of Jerusalem

3 Woe to the city of oppressors,
rebellious and defiled!
2 She obeys no one,
she accepts no correction.
She does not trust in the LORD,
she does not draw near to her God.
3 Her officials are roaring lions,
her rulers are evening wolves,
who leave nothing for the morning.

4 Her prophets are arrogant;
they are treacherous men.
Her priests profane the sanctuary
and do violence to the law.
5 The LORD within her is righteous;
he does no wrong.
Morning by morning he dispenses his
justice,
and every new day he does not fail,
yet the unrighteous know no shame.

6 "I have cut off nations;
their strongholds are demolished.
I have left their streets deserted,
with no one passing through.
Their cities are destroyed;
no one will be left—no one at all.
7 I said to the city,
'Surely you will fear me
and accept correction!'
Then her dwelling would not be cut
off,
nor all my punishments come upon
her.
But they were still eager
to act corruptly in all they did.
8 Therefore wait for me," declares the
LORD,
"for the day I will stand up to
testify.*b*
I have decided to assemble the
nations,
to gather the kingdoms
and to pour out my wrath on them—
all my fierce anger.
The whole world will be consumed
by the fire of my jealous anger.

9 "Then will I purify the lips of the
peoples,
that all of them may call on the
name of the LORD
and serve him shoulder to shoulder.
10 From beyond the rivers of Cush*c*
my worshipers, my scattered people,
will bring me offerings.
11 On that day you will not be put to
shame
for all the wrongs you have done to
me,
because I will remove from this city
those who rejoice in their pride.
Never again will you be haughty
on my holy hill.
12 But I will leave within you

a 12 That is, people from the upper Nile region
b 8 Septuagint and Syriac; Hebrew *will rise up to plunder*
c 10 That is, the upper Nile region

the meek and humble,
who trust in the name of the LORD.
¹³ The remnant of Israel will do no
　　wrong;
they will speak no lies,
nor will deceit be found in their
　　mouths.
They will eat and lie down
and no one will make them afraid."

¹⁴ Sing, O Daughter of Zion;
shout aloud, O Israel!
Be glad and rejoice with all your heart,
O Daughter of Jerusalem!
¹⁵ The LORD has taken away your
　　punishment,
he has turned back your enemy.
The LORD, the King of Israel, is with you;
never again will you fear any harm.
¹⁶ On that day they will say to Jerusalem,
"Do not fear, O Zion;
do not let your hands hang limp.
¹⁷ The LORD your God is with you,
he is mighty to save.
He will take great delight in you,

he will quiet you with his love,
he will rejoice over you with singing."

¹⁸ "The sorrows for the appointed feasts
I will remove from you;
they are a burden and a reproach to
　　you. ᵃ
¹⁹ At that time I will deal
with all who oppressed you;
I will rescue the lame
and gather those who have been
　　scattered.
I will give them praise and honor
in every land where they were put to
　　shame.
²⁰ At that time I will gather you;
at that time I will bring you home.
I will give you honor and praise
among all the peoples of the earth
when I restore your fortunes ᵇ
before your very eyes,"
　　　　　　　　　　　　says the LORD.

ᵃ 18 Or "I will gather you who mourn for the appointed
feasts; / your reproach is a burden to you   ᵇ 20 Or I bring
back your captives

Timing Is Everything

READ ZEPHANIAH 3:14–20

God can hear the seconds ticking by. He's aware of the time. It may seem like people get away with bad stuff, but God will deal with them when the time is right. You may wonder, "OK, but what's he *waiting* for?" Don't worry. God has a big book and he's checking it twice. He knows who's naughty or nice. But unlike Santa, God *does* take care of business. There were rebellious oppressors In Zephaniah's day, too, and God called them on it. "At that time I will deal with all who oppressed you" (verse 19). And he did. He still deals in the life of every person on earth. If people re-fuse to feel any twinge of conscience but instead harden their hearts, God will bring judgment against them. If they respond to their conscience and repent, he will draw them closer to himself.

Your next reading is on page 1194.

HAGGAI

Who wrote this book?
The prophet Haggai.

Why was this book written?
The people had stopped rebuilding God's temple. Haggai tells them the temple
must be rebuilt—now.

What do we learn about God in this book?
God will bless people when they put him first.

What is special about this book?
The people listen to Haggai's preaching. They go to work and finish rebuilding the
temple.

When was this book written?
Haggai was written after some of the Jews returned to Judah from captivity in
Babylon. Haggai preached in 520 B.C.

What are some important passages in this book?
The people are poor because they have not put God first   Haggai 1:2–11
The people have obeyed and from now on God will bless them   Haggai 2:15–19

A Call to Build the House of the LORD

1 In the second year of King Darius, on the first day of the sixth month, the word of the LORD came through the prophet Haggai to Zerubbabel son of Shealtiel, governor of Judah, and to Joshua[a] son of Jehozadak, the high priest:

² This is what the LORD Almighty says: "These people say, 'The time has not yet come for the LORD's house to be built.' "

³ Then the word of the LORD came through the prophet Haggai: ⁴ "Is it a time for you yourselves to be living in your paneled houses, while this house remains a ruin?"

⁵ Now this is what the LORD Almighty says: "Give careful thought to your ways. ⁶ You have planted much, but have harvested little. You eat, but never have enough. You drink, but never have your fill. You put on clothes, but are not warm. You earn wages, only to put them in a purse with holes in it."

⁷ This is what the LORD Almighty says: "Give careful thought to your ways. ⁸ Go up into the mountains and bring down timber and build the house, so that I may take pleasure in it and be honored," says the LORD. ⁹ "You expected much, but see, it turned out to be little. What you brought home, I blew away. Why?" declares the LORD Almighty. "Because of my house, which remains a ruin, while each of you is busy with his own house. ¹⁰ Therefore, because of you the heavens have withheld their dew and the earth its crops. ¹¹ I called for a drought on the fields and the mountains, on the grain, the new wine, the oil and whatever the ground produces, on men and cattle, and on the labor of your hands."

¹² Then Zerubbabel son of Shealtiel, Joshua son of Jehozadak, the high priest, and the whole remnant of the people obeyed the voice of the LORD their God and the message of the prophet Haggai, because the LORD their God had sent him. And the people feared the LORD.

¹³ Then Haggai, the LORD's messenger, gave this message of the LORD to the peo-

---

a 1 A variant of Jeshua; here and elsewhere in Haggai

Looking Out for Number One

READ HAGGAI 1; 2:15–19

When Jesus told us to seek God's kingdom before anything else (Matthew 6:33), there was a good reason for it. Just look at what happens if you don't: When the Jews returned to Jerusalem, they were *supposed* to focus on rebuilding God's ruined temple. But they got caught up in building their own homes instead. So rather than bless them, God huffed and he puffed and he "blew" their blessings away (Haggai 1:9). It was only after the Jews went back to building the temple that God began blessing them again (Haggai 2:19). God's work needs to be first in our lives as well (yep, even before soccer and video games). But Jesus promised that if we *do* seek him first and spend our time, talents and resources on God, he'll give us more blessings than we could ask for or imagine.

Your next reading is on page 1198.

ple: "I am with you," declares the LORD. ¹⁴So the LORD stirred up the spirit of Zerubbabel son of Shealtiel, governor of Judah, and the spirit of Joshua son of Jehozadak, the high priest, and the spirit of the whole remnant of the people. They came and began to work on the house of the LORD Almighty, their God, ¹⁵on the twenty-fourth day of the sixth month in the second year of King Darius.

The Promised Glory of the New House

On the twenty-first day of the seventh month, the word of the LORD came through the prophet Haggai: ²"Speak to Zerubbabel son of Shealtiel, governor of Judah, to Joshua son of Jehozadak, the high priest, and to the remnant of the people. Ask them, ³'Who of you is left who saw this house in its former glory? How does it look to you now? Does it not seem to you like nothing? ⁴But now be strong, O Zerubbabel,' declares the LORD. 'Be strong, O Joshua son of Jehozadak, the high priest. Be strong, all you people of the land,' declares the LORD, 'and work. For I am with you,' declares the LORD Almighty. ⁵'This is what I covenanted with you when you came out of Egypt. And my Spirit remains among you. Do not fear.'

⁶"This is what the LORD Almighty says: 'In a little while I will once more shake the heavens and the earth, the sea and the dry land. ⁷I will shake all nations, and the desired of all nations will come, and I will fill this house with glory,' says the LORD Almighty. ⁸'The silver is mine and the gold is mine,' declares the LORD Almighty. ⁹'The glory of this present house will be greater than the glory of the former house,' says the LORD Almighty. 'And in this place I will grant peace,' declares the LORD Almighty."

Blessings for a Defiled People

¹⁰On the twenty-fourth day of the ninth month, in the second year of Darius, the word of the LORD came to the prophet Haggai: ¹¹"This is what the LORD Almighty says: 'Ask the priests what the law says: ¹²If a person carries consecrated meat in the fold of his garment, and that fold touches some bread or stew, some wine, oil or other food, does it become consecrated?' "

The priests answered, "No."

¹³Then Haggai said, "If a person defiled by contact with a dead body touches one of these things, does it become defiled?"

"Yes," the priests replied, "it becomes defiled."

¹⁴Then Haggai said, " 'So it is with this people and this nation in my sight,' declares the LORD. 'Whatever they do and whatever they offer there is defiled.

¹⁵" 'Now give careful thought to this from this day on[a]—consider how things were before one stone was laid on another in the LORD's temple. ¹⁶When anyone came to a heap of twenty measures, there were only

---

a 15 Or to the days past

Get a Load of This...

God owns everything, and here in Haggai 2:6–8 he causes a m-m-major sh-sh-shakeup so that all the gold and silver ends up in his house. It's like he's holding thieves upside down by the ankles and shaking them so all his loot falls out of their pockets.

This "signet ring" in Haggai 2:23 was a king's ring with a design etched in it like a stamp. It was a symbol of his authority. When a law was made, a spot of wax was dropped on the document and the king stamped the wax with his ring to make the law official (see Esther 8:8).

ten. When anyone went to a wine vat to draw fifty measures, there were only twenty. [17]I struck all the work of your hands with blight, mildew and hail, yet you did not turn to me,' declares the LORD. [18]'From this day on, from this twenty-fourth day of the ninth month, give careful thought to the day when the foundation of the LORD's temple was laid. Give careful thought: [19]Is there yet any seed left in the barn? Until now, the vine and the fig tree, the pomegranate and the olive tree have not borne fruit.

" 'From this day on I will bless you.' "

Zerubbabel the LORD's Signet Ring

[20]The word of the LORD came to Haggai a second time on the twenty-fourth day of the month: [21]"Tell Zerubbabel governor of Judah that I will shake the heavens and the earth. [22]I will overturn royal thrones and shatter the power of the foreign kingdoms. I will overthrow chariots and their drivers; horses and their riders will fall, each by the sword of his brother.

[23]" 'On that day,' declares the LORD Almighty, 'I will take you, my servant Zerubbabel son of Shealtiel,' declares the LORD, 'and I will make you like my signet ring, for I have chosen you,' declares the LORD Almighty."

ZECHARIAH

Who wrote this book?

The prophet Zechariah.

Why was this book written?

Zechariah encourages the people of Judah to finish rebuilding the temple.

What do we learn about God in this book?

God will cleanse the sin of his people. God will come and rule the earth.

What is special about this book?

Zechariah uses many symbols that are hard to understand, like a flying scroll and a woman in a basket.

When was this book written?

Most of Zechariah's preaching and writing was done about 520 B.C. The vision of chapters 9–14 probably occurred about 480 B.C.

What are some important chapters in this book?

God wants his people to love justice and mercy   Zechariah 7–8
God will come to earth and rule as King   Zechariah 14

A Call to Return to the LORD

In the eighth month of the second year of Darius, the word of the LORD came to the prophet Zechariah son of Berekiah, the son of Iddo:

2 "The LORD was very angry with your forefathers. 3Therefore tell the people: This is what the LORD Almighty says: 'Return to me,' declares the LORD Almighty, 'and I will return to you,' says the LORD Almighty. 4Do not be like your forefathers, to whom the earlier prophets proclaimed: This is what the LORD Almighty says: 'Turn from your evil ways and your evil practices.' But they would not listen or pay attention to me, declares the LORD. 5Where are your forefathers now? And the prophets, do they live forever? 6But did not my words and my decrees, which I commanded my servants the prophets, overtake your forefathers?

"Then they repented and said, 'The LORD Almighty has done to us what our ways and practices deserve, just as he determined to do.' "

The Man Among the Myrtle Trees

7On the twenty-fourth day of the eleventh month, the month of Shebat, in the second year of Darius, the word of the LORD came to the prophet Zechariah son of Berekiah, the son of Iddo.

8During the night I had a vision—and there before me was a man riding a red horse! He was standing among the myrtle trees in a ravine. Behind him were red, brown and white horses.

9I asked, "What are these, my lord?"

The angel who was talking with me answered, "I will show you what they are."

10Then the man standing among the myrtle trees explained, "They are the ones the LORD has sent to go throughout the earth."

11And they reported to the angel of the LORD, who was standing among the myrtle trees, "We have gone throughout the earth and found the whole world at rest and in peace."

12Then the angel of the LORD said, "LORD Almighty, how long will you withhold

---

No Shortcuts

READ ZECHARIAH 1:1–6

Imagine biking with someone who insists they know a shortcut, only to discover their "shortcut" means pushing your bikes through a garbage dump. That's a trick Satan pulls all the time. He makes sin look like the right way to go. But when we follow him, we wind up *way* off track and it's a long way back to God. The people of Judah insisted on worshiping idols even though God warned them against it, so God punished them by allowing the Babylonians to carry them away as prisoners. When the Jews returned 70 years later, the *last* thing they wanted to look at was another idol. They had learned how worthless it was to go down that path. There would have been no need for that if they'd simply listened to God in the first place. So don't let Satan tempt you with a shortcut. Go God's way.

Your next reading is on page 1201.

mercy from Jerusalem and from the towns of Judah, which you have been angry with these seventy years?" ¹³So the LORD spoke kind and comforting words to the angel who talked with me.

¹⁴Then the angel who was speaking to me said, "Proclaim this word: This is what the LORD Almighty says: 'I am very jealous for Jerusalem and Zion, ¹⁵but I am very angry with the nations that feel secure. I was only a little angry, but they added to the calamity.'

¹⁶"Therefore, this is what the LORD says: 'I will return to Jerusalem with mercy, and there my house will be rebuilt. And the measuring line will be stretched out over Jerusalem,' declares the LORD Almighty.

¹⁷"Proclaim further: This is what the LORD Almighty says: 'My towns will again overflow with prosperity, and the LORD will again comfort Zion and choose Jerusalem.' "

Four Horns and Four Craftsmen

¹⁸Then I looked up—and there before me were four horns! ¹⁹I asked the angel who was speaking to me, "What are these?"

He answered me, "These are the horns that scattered Judah, Israel and Jerusalem."

²⁰Then the LORD showed me four craftsmen. ²¹I asked, "What are these coming to do?"

He answered, "These are the horns that scattered Judah so that no one could raise his head, but the craftsmen have come to terrify them and throw down these horns of the nations who lifted up their horns against the land of Judah to scatter its people."

A Man With a Measuring Line

Then I looked up—and there before me was a man with a measuring line in his hand! ²I asked, "Where are you going?"

He answered me, "To measure Jerusalem, to find out how wide and how long it is."

³Then the angel who was speaking to me left, and another angel came to meet him ⁴and said to him: "Run, tell that young man, 'Jerusalem will be a city without walls because of the great number of men and livestock in it. ⁵And I myself will be a wall of fire around it,' declares the LORD, 'and I will be its glory within.'

⁶"Come! Come! Flee from the land of the north," declares the LORD, "for I have scattered you to the four winds of heaven," declares the LORD.

⁷"Come, O Zion! Escape, you who live in the Daughter of Babylon!" ⁸For this is what the LORD Almighty says: "After he has honored me and has sent me against the nations that have plundered you—for whoever touches you touches the apple of his eye— ⁹I will surely raise my hand against them so that their slaves will plunder them.ᵃ Then you will know that the LORD Almighty has sent me.

¹⁰"Shout and be glad, O Daughter of Zion. For I am

ᵃ 8,9 Or says after . . . eye: ⁹"I . . . plunder them."

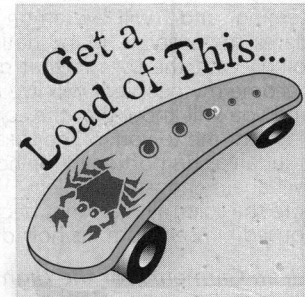

Get a Load of This...

God said he'd be a "wall of fire" around his people to protect them (Zechariah 2:5). This is like what he did when he put a wall of fire between the Hebrews and the Egyptian army (see Exodus 14:15–25). Was this actual fire? Who knows!

coming, and I will live among you," declares the LORD. 11"Many nations will be joined with the LORD in that day and will become my people. I will live among you and you will know that the LORD Almighty has sent me to you. 12The LORD will inherit Judah as his portion in the holy land and will again choose Jerusalem. 13Be still before the LORD, all mankind, because he has roused himself from his holy dwelling."

Clean Garments for the High Priest

Then he showed me Joshua[a] the high priest standing before the angel of the LORD, and Satan[b] standing at his right side to accuse him. 2The LORD said to Satan, "The LORD rebuke you, Satan! The LORD, who has chosen Jerusalem, rebuke you! Is not this man a burning stick snatched from the fire?"

3Now Joshua was dressed in filthy clothes as he stood before the angel. 4The angel said to those who were standing before him, "Take off his filthy clothes."

Then he said to Joshua, "See, I have taken away your sin, and I will put rich garments on you."

5Then I said, "Put a clean turban on his head." So they put a clean turban on his head and clothed him, while the angel of the LORD stood by.

6The angel of the LORD gave this charge to Joshua: 7"This is what the LORD Almighty says: 'If you will walk in my ways and keep my requirements, then you will govern my house and have charge of my courts, and I will give you a place among these standing here.

8" 'Listen, O high priest Joshua and your associates seated before you, who are men symbolic of things to come: I am going to bring my servant, the Branch. 9See, the stone I have set in front of Joshua! There are seven eyes[c] on that one stone, and I will engrave an inscription on it,' says the LORD Almighty, 'and I will remove the sin of this land in a single day.

10" 'In that day each of you will invite his neighbor to sit under his vine and fig tree,' declares the LORD Almighty."

The Gold Lampstand and the Two Olive Trees

Then the angel who talked with me returned and wakened me, as a man is wakened from his sleep. 2He asked me, "What do you see?"

I answered, "I see a solid gold lampstand with a bowl at the top and seven lights on it, with seven channels to the lights. 3Also there are two olive trees by it, one on the right of the bowl and the other on its left."

4I asked the angel who talked with me, "What are these, my lord?"

5He answered, "Do you not know what these are?"

"No, my lord," I replied.

6So he said to me, "This is the word of the LORD to Zerubbabel: 'Not by might nor by power, but by my Spirit,' says the LORD Almighty.

7"What[d] are you, O mighty mountain? Before Zerubbabel you will become level ground. Then he will bring out the capstone to shouts of 'God bless it! God bless it!' "

8Then the word of the LORD came to me: 9"The hands of Zerubbabel have laid the foundation of this temple; his hands will also complete it. Then you will know that the LORD Almighty has sent me to you.

10"Who despises the day of small things? Men will rejoice when they see the plumb line in the hand of Zerubbabel.

"(These seven are the eyes of the LORD, which range throughout the earth.)"

11Then I asked the angel, "What are these two olive trees on the right and the left of the lampstand?"

12Again I asked him, "What are these two olive branches beside the two gold pipes that pour out golden oil?"

13He replied, "Do you not know what these are?"

"No, my lord," I said.

14So he said, "These are the two who are anointed to[e] serve the Lord of all the earth."

The Flying Scroll

I looked again—and there before me was a flying scroll!

2He asked me, "What do you see?"

I answered, "I see a flying scroll, thirty feet long and fifteen feet wide.[f]"

3And he said to me, "This is the curse that is going out over the whole land; for according to what it says on one side, ev-

---

[a] 1 A variant of Jeshua; here and elsewhere in Zechariah
[b] 1 Satan means accuser.   [c] 9 Or facets   [d] 7 Or Who
[e] 14 Or two who bring oil and   [f] 2 Hebrew twenty cubits long and ten cubits wide (about 9 meters long and 4.5 meters wide)

ery thief will be banished, and according to what it says on the other, everyone who swears falsely will be banished. 4The LORD Almighty declares, 'I will send it out, and it will enter the house of the thief and the house of him who swears falsely by my name. It will remain in his house and destroy it, both its timbers and its stones.' "

The Woman in a Basket

5Then the angel who was speaking to me came forward and said to me, "Look up and see what this is that is appearing."

6I asked, "What is it?"

He replied, "It is a measuring basket.a" And he added, "This is the iniquityb of the people throughout the land."

7Then the cover of lead was raised, and there in the basket sat a woman! 8He said, "This is wickedness," and he pushed her back into the basket and pushed the lead cover down over its mouth.

9Then I looked up—and there before me were two women, with the wind in their wings! They had wings like those of a stork, and they lifted up the basket between heaven and earth.

10"Where are they taking the basket?" I asked the angel who was speaking to me.

11He replied, "To the country of Babyloniac to build a house for it. When it is ready, the basket will be set there in its place."

Four Chariots

6 I looked up again—and there before me were four chariots coming out from between two mountains—mountains of bronze! 2The first chariot had red horses, the second black, 3the third white, and the fourth dappled—all of them powerful. 4I asked the angel who was speaking to me, "What are these, my lord?"

5The angel answered me, "These are the four spiritsd of heaven, going out from standing in the presence of the Lord

a 6 Hebrew an ephah; also in verses 7–11   b 6 Or appearance
c 11 Hebrew Shinar   d 5 Or winds

GET STRONGER

Might and Power

READ ZECHARIAH 4

Okay, so you can't snatch a 400-pound barbell and hoist it over your head. Hey, maybe you can't walk 1,000 miles during a dust storm to witness to nomads in the Sahara desert. In fact, when you're young, you might not be able to picture yourself doing anything big for God's kingdom. You may think you're not big enough, strong enough, smart enough, or talented enough to do anything that counts. But don't look down on yourself. Just plug in to God. He has no end of might and power and can do mighty things through you no matter how small you are. It's like you're the pair of work gloves on God's hands but he's the one lifting the ten-ton weights. " 'Not by [your] might nor by [your] power, but by my Spirit,' says the LORD Almighty" (verse 6). You may be small, but God is big—really big!

Your next reading is on page 1205.

of the whole world. ⁶The one with the black horses is going toward the north country, the one with the white horses toward the west,^a and the one with the dappled horses toward the south."

⁷When the powerful horses went out, they were straining to go throughout the earth. And he said, "Go throughout the earth!" So they went throughout the earth.

⁸Then he called to me, "Look, those going toward the north country have given my Spirit^b rest in the land of the north."

A Crown for Joshua

⁹The word of the Lord came to me: ¹⁰"Take ⌊silver and gold⌋ from the exiles Heldai, Tobijah and Jedaiah, who have arrived from Babylon. Go the same day to the house of Josiah son of Zephaniah. ¹¹Take the silver and gold and make a crown, and set it on the head of the high priest, Joshua son of Jehozadak. ¹²Tell him this is what the Lord Almighty says: 'Here is the man whose name is the Branch, and

he will branch out from his place and build the temple of the Lord. ¹³It is he who will build the temple of the Lord, and he will be clothed with majesty and will sit and rule on his throne. And he will be a priest on his throne. And there will be harmony between the two.' ¹⁴The crown will be given to Heldai,^c Tobijah, Jedaiah and Hen^d son of Zephaniah as a memorial in the temple of the Lord. ¹⁵Those who are far away will come and help to build the temple of the Lord, and you will know that the Lord Almighty has sent me to you. This will happen if you diligently obey the Lord your God."

Justice and Mercy, Not Fasting

7 In the fourth year of King Darius, the word of the Lord came to Zechariah on the fourth day of the ninth month, the month of Kislev. ²The

---

^a 6 Or horses after them   ^b 8 Or spirit   ^c 14 Syriac; Hebrew Helem   ^d 14 Or and the gracious one, the

Make It Stick

READ ZECHARIAH 5:1

Read Zechariah 5:1–4. This scroll, which was a symbol for God's Word, was thirty feet long and fifteen feet wide, and could *fly!* No ordinary scroll!—It entered and demolished thieves' houses. Puts a whole new twist on "Bible thumpers," huh? Imagine a gang of thieves plotting a robbery when *"Super Scroll"* comes flying in the window! Draw a *"Super Scroll"* on a sticky note.

people of Bethel had sent Sharezer and Regem-Melech, together with their men, to entreat the LORD ³by asking the priests of the house of the LORD Almighty and the prophets, "Should I mourn and fast in the fifth month, as I have done for so many years?"

⁴Then the word of the LORD Almighty came to me: ⁵"Ask all the people of the land and the priests, 'When you fasted and mourned in the fifth and seventh months for the past seventy years, was it really for me that you fasted? ⁶And when you were eating and drinking, were you not just feasting for yourselves? ⁷Are these not the words the LORD proclaimed through the earlier prophets when Jerusalem and its surrounding towns were at rest and prosperous, and the Negev and the western foothills were settled?' "

⁸And the word of the LORD came again to Zechariah: ⁹"This is what the LORD Almighty says: 'Administer true justice; show mercy and compassion to one another. ¹⁰Do not oppress the widow or the fatherless, the alien or the poor. In your hearts do not think evil of each other.'

¹¹"But they refused to pay attention; stubbornly they turned their backs and stopped up their ears. ¹²They made their hearts as hard as flint and would not listen to the law or to the words that the LORD Almighty had sent by his Spirit through the earlier prophets. So the LORD Almighty was very angry.

¹³" 'When I called, they did not listen; so when they called, I would not listen,' says the LORD Almighty. ¹⁴'I scattered them with a whirlwind among all the nations, where they were strangers. The land was left so desolate behind them that no one could come or go. This is how they made the pleasant land desolate.' "

The LORD Promises to Bless Jerusalem

Again the word of the LORD Almighty came to me. ²This is what the LORD Almighty says: "I am very jealous for Zion; I am burning with jealousy for her."

³This is what the LORD says: "I will return to Zion and dwell in Jerusalem. Then Jerusalem will be called the City of Truth, and the mountain of the LORD Almighty will be called the Holy Mountain."

⁴This is what the LORD Almighty says: "Once again men and women of ripe old age will sit in the streets of Jerusalem, each with cane in hand because of his age. ⁵The city streets will be filled with boys and girls playing there."

⁶This is what the LORD Almighty says: "It may seem marvelous to the remnant of this people at that time, but will it seem marvelous to me?" declares the LORD Almighty.

⁷This is what the LORD Almighty says: "I will save my people from the countries of the east and the west. ⁸I will bring them back to live in Jerusalem; they will be my people, and I will be faithful and righteous to them as their God."

⁹This is what the LORD Almighty says: "You who now

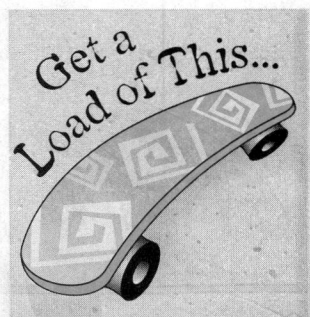

Get a Load of This...

In Zechariah 5:5–11 an evil woman is stuffed into a basket. The basket has a *lead cover* to keep the evil in—just like lead protects Superman from Kryptonite. The lesson? When evil pokes its head out, slam that lead covering down before it sucks away all your strength.

Get a Load of This...

Check out Zechariah 8:5. Past or present, some things never change, like kids playing in the streets. Imagine kids in Zechariah's day playing street hockey, and suddenly the goalie yells, "*Donkey* coming!" and everyone waits by the side of the road until it passes.

hear these words spoken by the prophets who were there when the foundation was laid for the house of the LORD Almighty, let your hands be strong so that the temple may be built. [10]Before that time there were no wages for man or beast. No one could go about his business safely because of his enemy, for I had turned every man against his neighbor. [11]But now I will not deal with the remnant of this people as I did in the past," declares the LORD Almighty.

[12]"The seed will grow well, the vine will yield its fruit, the ground will produce its crops, and the heavens will drop their dew. I will give all these things as an inheritance to the remnant of this people. [13]As you have been an object of cursing among the nations, O Judah and Israel, so will I save you, and you will be a blessing. Do not be afraid, but let your hands be strong."

[14]This is what the LORD Almighty says: "Just as I had determined to bring disaster upon you and showed no pity when your fathers angered me," says the LORD Almighty, [15]"so now I have determined to do good again to Jerusalem and Judah. Do not be afraid. [16]These are the things you are to do: Speak the truth to each other, and render true and sound judgment in your courts; [17]do not plot evil against your neighbor, and do not love to swear falsely. I hate all this," declares the LORD.

[18]Again the word of the LORD Almighty came to me. [19]This is what the LORD Almighty says: "The fasts of the fourth, fifth, seventh and tenth months will become joyful and glad occasions and happy festivals for Judah. Therefore love truth and peace."

[20]This is what the LORD Almighty says: "Many peoples and the inhabitants of many cities will yet come, [21]and the inhabitants of one city will go to another and say, 'Let us go at once to entreat the LORD and seek the LORD Almighty. I myself am going.' [22]And many peoples and powerful nations will come to Jerusalem to seek the LORD Almighty and to entreat him."

[23]This is what the LORD Almighty says: "In those days ten men from all languages and nations will take firm hold of one Jew by the hem of his robe and say, 'Let us go with you, because we have heard that God is with you.' "

Judgment on Israel's Enemies

An Oracle

9 The word of the LORD is against the land of Hadrach
and will rest upon Damascus—
for the eyes of men and all the tribes of Israel
are on the LORD—[a]
[2]and upon Hamath too, which borders on it,
and upon Tyre and Sidon, though they are very skillful.
[3]Tyre has built herself a stronghold;

[a] 1 Or Damascus. / For the eye of the LORD is on all mankind, / as well as on the tribes of Israel,

she has heaped up silver like dust,
and gold like the dirt of the streets.
⁴But the Lord will take away her
possessions
and destroy her power on the sea,
and she will be consumed by fire.
⁵Ashkelon will see it and fear;
Gaza will writhe in agony,
and Ekron too, for her hope will
wither.
Gaza will lose her king
and Ashkelon will be deserted.
⁶Foreigners will occupy Ashdod,
and I will cut off the pride of the
Philistines.
⁷I will take the blood from their
mouths,
the forbidden food from between
their teeth.
Those who are left will belong to our
God
and become leaders in Judah,
and Ekron will be like the Jebusites.
⁸But I will defend my house

against marauding forces.
Never again will an oppressor overrun
my people,
for now I am keeping watch.

The Coming of Zion's King

⁹Rejoice greatly, O Daughter of Zion!
Shout, Daughter of Jerusalem!
See, your king*a* comes to you,
righteous and having salvation,
gentle and riding on a donkey,
on a colt, the foal of a donkey.
¹⁰I will take away the chariots from
Ephraim
and the war-horses from Jerusalem,
and the battle bow will be broken.
He will proclaim peace to the nations.
His rule will extend from sea to sea
and from the River*b* to the ends of
the earth.*c*
¹¹As for you, because of the blood of my
covenant with you,

a 9 Or *King*   *b 10* That is, the Euphrates   *c 10* Or *the end*
of the land

Strong Heart, Strong Hands

READ ZECHARIAH 8:9–13

When the Jews saw what a mess Jerusalem was in after being in
ruins for 70 years, they must have been pretty depressed. How were
they ever going to rebuild that dump? But God encouraged them
through Zechariah. Twice he told them, "Let your hands be strong"
(Zechariah 8:9, 13). The job may have seemed impossible, but
they just had to *decide* to give it their best shot and let God
handle the rest. Have you ever been given a job that seemed
impossible to complete? Maybe you had to clean out the
garage on the hottest day of summer when you'd rather have
gone swimming. What's true for the Jews is true for you.
The job may seem impossible. But if you *let* your
hands be strong, God will bless whatever you do
with them. Who knows? If you work quickly, there
may be time for swimming later on!

Your next reading is on page 1212.

I will free your prisoners from the waterless pit.
¹² Return to your fortress, O prisoners of hope;
　　even now I announce that I will restore twice as
　　　　much to you.
¹³ I will bend Judah as I bend my bow
　　and fill it with Ephraim.
　I will rouse your sons, O Zion,
　　against your sons, O Greece,
　　and make you like a warrior's sword.

The LORD Will Appear

¹⁴ Then the LORD will appear over them;
　　his arrow will flash like lightning.
　The Sovereign LORD will sound the trumpet;
　　he will march in the storms of the south,
¹⁵ 　and the LORD Almighty will shield them.
　They will destroy
　　and overcome with slingstones.
　They will drink and roar as with wine;
　　they will be full like a bowl
　　used for sprinkling*ᵃ* the corners of the altar.
¹⁶ The LORD their God will save them on that day
　　as the flock of his people.
　They will sparkle in his land
　　like jewels in a crown.
¹⁷ How attractive and beautiful they will be!
　　Grain will make the young men thrive,
　　and new wine the young women.

The LORD Will Care for Judah

10 Ask the LORD for rain in the springtime;
　　it is the LORD who makes the storm clouds.
　　He gives showers of rain to men,
　　　and plants of the field to everyone.
² The idols speak deceit,
　　diviners see visions that lie;
　they tell dreams that are false,
　　they give comfort in vain.
　Therefore the people wander like sheep
　　oppressed for lack of a shepherd.

³ "My anger burns against the shepherds,
　　and I will punish the leaders;
　for the LORD Almighty will care
　　for his flock, the house of Judah,
　　and make them like a proud horse in battle.
⁴ From Judah will come the cornerstone,
　　from him the tent peg,
　　from him the battle bow,
　　from him every ruler.
⁵ Together they*ᵇ* will be like mighty men
　　trampling the muddy streets in battle.
　Because the LORD is with them,
　　they will fight and overthrow the horsemen.

ᵃ 15 Or bowl, / like　　ᵇ 4,5 Or ruler, all of them together. / ⁵They

Gross!

God forbade his people
to drink the blood of
sacrificial animals
　(Zechariah 9:7). Like,
why would anyone
want to disobey this
commandment? An-
other thing: When God
yanks "forbidden food
from between their
teeth," people better let
go or they'll lose teeth.

6 "I will strengthen the house of Judah
   and save the house of Joseph.
I will restore them
   because I have compassion on them.
They will be as though
   I had not rejected them,
for I am the LORD their God
   and I will answer them.
7 The Ephraimites will become like mighty men,
   and their hearts will be glad as with wine.
Their children will see it and be joyful;
   their hearts will rejoice in the LORD.
8 I will signal for them
   and gather them in.
Surely I will redeem them;
   they will be as numerous as before.
9 Though I scatter them among the peoples,
   yet in distant lands they will remember me.
They and their children will survive,
   and they will return.
10 I will bring them back from Egypt
   and gather them from Assyria.
I will bring them to Gilead and Lebanon,
   and there will not be room enough for them.
11 They will pass through the sea of trouble;
   the surging sea will be subdued
   and all the depths of the Nile will dry up.
Assyria's pride will be brought down
   and Egypt's scepter will pass away.
12 I will strengthen them in the LORD
   and in his name they will walk,"

declares the LORD.

11 Open your doors, O Lebanon,
   so that fire may devour your cedars!
2 Wail, O pine tree, for the cedar has fallen;
   the stately trees are ruined!
Wail, oaks of Bashan;
   the dense forest has been cut down!
3 Listen to the wail of the shepherds;
   their rich pastures are destroyed!
Listen to the roar of the lions;
   the lush thicket of the Jordan is ruined!

Two Shepherds

4 This is what the LORD my God says: "Pasture the flock marked for slaughter. 5 Their buyers slaughter them and go unpunished. Those who sell them say, 'Praise the LORD, I am rich!' Their own shepherds do not spare them. 6 For I will no longer have pity on the people of the land," declares the LORD. "I will hand everyone over to his neighbor and his king. They will oppress the land, and I will not rescue them from their hands."

7 So I pastured the flock marked for slaughter, particularly the oppressed of the flock. Then I took two staffs and called one Favor and the other Union, and I pastured the flock. 8 In one month I got rid of the three shepherds.

Get a Load of This...

Ever want to skip breakfast and not eat your cereal, and your mom says, "You need to eat so you can do your best in school"? She's *right!* Zechariah 9:17 says, "Grain will make the young men thrive."

Get a Load of This...

Zechariah 11:12–13 includes the "blood money" prophecy. These words were fulfilled by Judas Iscariot, who betrayed Jesus (see Matthew 27:3–10). It goes to show, God is never taken by surprise when bad stuff happens.

The flock detested me, and I grew weary of them ⁹and said, "I will not be your shepherd. Let the dying die, and the perishing perish. Let those who are left eat one another's flesh."

¹⁰Then I took my staff called Favor and broke it, revoking the covenant I had made with all the nations. ¹¹It was revoked on that day, and so the afflicted of the flock who were watching me knew it was the word of the LORD.

¹²I told them, "If you think it best, give me my pay; but if not, keep it." So they paid me thirty pieces of silver.

¹³And the LORD said to me, "Throw it to the potter"— the handsome price at which they priced me! So I took the thirty pieces of silver and threw them into the house of the LORD to the potter.

¹⁴Then I broke my second staff called Union, breaking the brotherhood between Judah and Israel.

¹⁵Then the LORD said to me, "Take again the equipment of a foolish shepherd. ¹⁶For I am going to raise up a shepherd over the land who will not care for the lost, or seek the young, or heal the injured, or feed the healthy, but will eat the meat of the choice sheep, tearing off their hoofs.

¹⁷"Woe to the worthless shepherd,
    who deserts the flock!
May the sword strike his arm and his right eye!
    May his arm be completely withered,
    his right eye totally blinded!"

Jerusalem's Enemies to Be Destroyed
An Oracle

12 This is the word of the LORD concerning Israel. The LORD, who stretches out the heavens, who lays the foundation of the earth, and who forms the spirit of man within him, declares: ²"I am going to make Jerusalem a cup that sends all the surrounding peoples reeling. Judah will be besieged as well as Jerusalem. ³On that day, when all the nations of the earth are gathered against her, I will make Jerusalem an immovable rock for all the nations. All who try to move it will injure themselves. ⁴On that day I will strike every horse with panic and its rider with madness," declares the LORD. "I will keep a watchful eye over the house of Judah, but I will blind all the horses of the nations. ⁵Then the leaders of Judah will say in their hearts, 'The people of Jerusalem are strong, because the LORD Almighty is their God.'

⁶"On that day I will make the leaders of Judah like a firepot in a woodpile, like a flaming torch among sheaves. They will consume right and left all the surrounding peoples, but Jerusalem will remain intact in her place.

⁷"The LORD will save the dwellings of Judah first, so that the honor of the house of David and of Jerusalem's inhabitants may not be greater than that of Judah. ⁸On that day the LORD will shield those who live in Jerusalem,

so that the feeblest among them will be like David, and the house of David will be like God, like the Angel of the LORD going before them. ⁹On that day I will set out to destroy all the nations that attack Jerusalem.

Mourning for the One They Pierced

¹⁰"And I will pour out on the house of David and the inhabitants of Jerusalem a spirit[a] of grace and supplication. They will look on[b] me, the one they have pierced, and they will mourn for him as one mourns for an only child, and grieve bitterly for him as one grieves for a firstborn son. ¹¹On that day the weeping in Jerusalem will be great, like the weeping of Hadad Rimmon in the plain of Megiddo. ¹²The land will mourn, each clan by itself, with their wives by themselves: the clan of the house of David and their wives, the clan of the house of Nathan and their wives, ¹³the clan of the house of Levi and their wives, the clan of Shimei and their wives, ¹⁴and all the rest of the clans and their wives.

Cleansing From Sin

13 "On that day a fountain will be opened to the house of David and the inhabitants of Jerusalem, to cleanse them from sin and impurity.

²"On that day, I will banish the names of the idols from the land, and they will be remembered no more," declares the LORD Almighty. "I will remove both the prophets and the spirit of impurity from the land. ³And if anyone still prophesies, his father and mother, to whom he was born, will say to him, 'You must die, because you have told lies in the LORD's name.' When he prophesies, his own parents will stab him.

⁴"On that day every prophet will be ashamed of his prophetic vision. He will not put on a prophet's garment of hair in order to deceive. ⁵He will say, 'I am not a prophet. I am a farmer; the land has been my livelihood since my youth.[c]' ⁶If someone asks him, 'What are these wounds on your body[d]?' he will answer, 'The wounds I was given at the house of my friends.'

The Shepherd Struck, the Sheep Scattered

⁷"Awake, O sword, against my shepherd, against the man who is close to me!"

declares the LORD Almighty.
"Strike the shepherd,
    and the sheep will be scattered,
    and I will turn my hand against the
        little ones.
⁸In the whole land," declares the LORD,
"two-thirds will be struck down and
        perish;
    yet one-third will be left in it.
⁹This third I will bring into the fire;
    I will refine them like silver
    and test them like gold.
They will call on my name
    and I will answer them;
I will say, 'They are my people,'
    and they will say, 'The LORD is our
        God.' "

The LORD Comes and Reigns

14 A day of the LORD is coming when your plunder will be divided among you.

²I will gather all the nations to Jerusalem to fight against it; the city will be captured, the houses ransacked, and the women raped. Half of the city will go into exile, but the rest of the people will not be taken from the city.

³Then the LORD will go out and fight against those nations, as he fights in the day of battle. ⁴On that day his feet will stand on the Mount of Olives, east of Jerusalem, and the Mount of Olives will be split in two from east to west, forming a great valley, with half of the mountain moving north and half moving south. ⁵You will flee by my mountain valley, for it will extend to Azel. You will flee as you fled from the earthquake[e] in the days of Uzziah king of Judah. Then the LORD my God will come, and all the holy ones with him.

⁶On that day there will be no light, no cold or frost. ⁷It will be a unique day, without daytime or nighttime—a day known to the LORD. When evening comes, there will be light.

⁸On that day living water will flow out from Jerusalem, half to the eastern sea[f] and half to the western sea,[g] in summer and in winter.

<hr>

a 10 Or the Spirit   b 10 Or to   c 5 Or farmer; a man sold me in my youth   d 6 Or wounds between your hands
e 5 Or ⁵My mountain valley will be blocked and will extend to Azel. It will be blocked as it was blocked because of the earthquake   f 8 That is, the Dead Sea   g 8 That is, the Mediterranean

Gross!

This is *some* plague! "Their flesh will rot while they are standing on their feet, their eyes will rot in their sockets, and their tongues will rot in their mouths" (Zechariah 14:12). Bet you'd like to see the special effects for *that* in a movie!

⁹The LORD will be king over the whole earth. On that day there will be one LORD, and his name the only name. ¹⁰The whole land, from Geba to Rimmon, south of Jerusalem, will become like the Arabah. But Jerusalem will be raised up and remain in its place, from the Benjamin Gate to the site of the First Gate, to the Corner Gate, and from the Tower of Hananel to the royal winepresses. ¹¹It will be inhabited; never again will it be destroyed. Jerusalem will be secure.

¹²This is the plague with which the LORD will strike all the nations that fought against Jerusalem: Their flesh will rot while they are still standing on their feet, their eyes will rot in their sockets, and their tongues will rot in their mouths. ¹³On that day men will be stricken by the LORD with great panic. Each man will seize the hand of another, and they will attack each other. ¹⁴Judah too will fight at Jerusalem. The wealth of all the surrounding nations will be collected—great quantities of gold and silver and clothing. ¹⁵A similar plague will strike the horses and mules, the camels and donkeys, and all the animals in those camps.

¹⁶Then the survivors from all the nations that have attacked Jerusalem will go up year after year to worship the King, the LORD Almighty, and to celebrate the Feast of Tabernacles. ¹⁷If any of the peoples of the earth do not go up to Jerusalem to worship the King, the LORD Almighty, they will have no rain. ¹⁸If the Egyptian people do not go up and take part, they will have no rain. The LORDᵃ will bring on them the plague he inflicts on the nations that do not go up to celebrate the Feast of Tabernacles. ¹⁹This will be the punishment of Egypt and the punishment of all the nations that do not go up to celebrate the Feast of Tabernacles.

²⁰On that day HOLY TO THE LORD will be inscribed on the bells of the horses, and the cooking pots in the LORD's house will be like the sacred bowls in front of the altar. ²¹Every pot in Jerusalem and Judah will be holy to the LORD Almighty, and all who come to sacrifice will take some of the pots and cook in them. And on that day there will no longer be a Canaaniteᵇ in the house of the LORD Almighty.

MALACHI

Who wrote this book?
The prophet Malachi.

Why was this book written?
Malachi shows how the children of the people who returned to Judah from Babylon have strayed from God.

What do we learn about God in this book?
God deserves our best. God will remember those who love him and talk about him.

What is special about this book?
The prophet answers foolish questions the people ask. His answers teach us how to show love for God.

When was this book written?
Malachi was written between 465 and 430 B.C.

What are some important passages in this book?

Honoring God	Malachi 1:6–11
Robbing God	Malachi 3:6–12
God's treasured possession	Malachi 3:16–18

An oracle: The word of the Lord to Israel through Malachi.ᵃ

Jacob Loved, Esau Hated

2"I have loved you," says the Lord.

"But you ask, 'How have you loved us?'

"Was not Esau Jacob's brother?" the Lord says. "Yet I have loved Jacob, 3but Esau I have hated, and I have turned his mountains into a wasteland and left his inheritance to the desert jackals."

4Edom may say, "Though we have been crushed, we will rebuild the ruins."

But this is what the Lord Almighty says: "They may build, but I will demolish. They will be called the Wicked Land, a people always under the wrath of the Lord. 5You will see it with your own eyes and say, 'Great is the Lord—even beyond the borders of Israel!'

Blemished Sacrifices

6"A son honors his father, and a servant his master. If I am a father, where is the honor due me? If I am a master, where is the respect due me?" says the Lord Almighty. "It is you, O priests, who show contempt for my name.

"But you ask, 'How have we shown contempt for your name?'

7"You place defiled food on my altar.

"But you ask, 'How have we defiled you?'

"By saying that the Lord's table is contemptible. 8When you bring blind animals for sacrifice, is that not wrong? When you sacrifice crippled or diseased animals, is that not wrong? Try offering them to your governor! Would he be pleased with you? Would he accept you?" says the Lord Almighty.

9"Now implore God to be gracious to us. With such offerings from your hands, will he accept you?"—says the Lord Almighty.

10"Oh, that one of you would shut the temple doors, so that you would not light useless fires on my altar! I am not pleased with you," says the Lord Almighty, "and I will accept no offering from your hands. 11My name will be great among the nations, from the rising to the setting of the sun. In every place incense and pure offer-

ᵃ 1 Malachi means my messenger.

Just Don't Get It?

READ MALACHI 1:6–7; 2:17; 3:7–8, 13

Ever tried pointing out a mistake to someone with an attitude? All they do is justify themselves. Listen to how God's people answered back when he pointed out their problems. They said: "How do we rob you?" "How have we shown contempt for your name?" "How have we defiled you?" "What have we said against you?" You can imagine how mad Malachi was and how red his face was by the time he told them, "You have wearied the Lord with your words." Then they had the gall to reply, "How have we wearied him?" Ho! Now that is some attitude! Bet steam was blowing out of Malachi's ears by that point. Well, that kind of attitude didn't become extinct 2,500 years ago. Some kids today think having an attitude proves that they're tough. Actually . . . real toughness is being able to face your mistakes, learn from them and change.

Your next reading is on page 1221.

ings will be brought to my name, because my name will be great among the nations," says the LORD Almighty.

¹²"But you profane it by saying of the Lord's table, 'It is defiled,' and of its food, 'It is contemptible.' ¹³And you say, 'What a burden!' and you sniff at it contemptuously," says the LORD Almighty.

"When you bring injured, crippled or diseased animals and offer them as sacrifices, should I accept them from your hands?" says the LORD. ¹⁴"Cursed is the cheat who has an acceptable male in his flock and vows to give it, but then sacrifices a blemished animal to the Lord. For I am a great king," says the LORD Almighty, "and my name is to be feared among the nations.

Admonition for the Priests

2 "And now this admonition is for you, O priests. ²If you do not listen, and if you do not set your heart to honor my name," says the LORD Almighty, "I will send a curse upon you, and I will curse your blessings. Yes, I have already cursed them, because you have not set your heart to honor me.

³"Because of you I will rebukeᵃ your descendantsᵇ; I will spread on your faces the offal from your festival sacrifices, and you will be carried off with it. ⁴And you will know that I have sent you this admonition so that my covenant with Levi may continue," says the LORD Almighty. ⁵"My covenant was with him, a covenant of life and peace, and I gave them to him; this called for reverence and he revered me and stood in awe of my name. ⁶True instruction was in his mouth and nothing false was found on his lips. He walked with me in peace and uprightness, and turned many from sin.

⁷"For the lips of a priest ought to preserve knowledge, and from his mouth men should seek instruction—because he is the messenger of the LORD Almighty.

ᵃ 3 Or cut off (see Septuagint)   ᵇ 3 Or will blight your grain

Make It Stick

READ MALACHI 1:8

When the Jews brought blind, crippled and diseased animals to sacrifice to God, he was *not* pleased (Malachi 1:8). God didn't give *us* leftovers—he gave us his own Son (Romans 8:32)—so don't just toss God your leftover pennies. Give him the good stuff. Decide right now what you'll put in the offering next time you go to church.

⁸But you have turned from the way and by your teaching have caused many to stumble; you have violated the covenant with Levi," says the LORD Almighty. ⁹"So I have caused you to be despised and humiliated before all the people, because you have not followed my ways but have shown partiality in matters of the law."

Judah Unfaithful

¹⁰Have we not all one Father*ᵃ*? Did not one God create us? Why do we profane the covenant of our fathers by breaking faith with one another?

¹¹Judah has broken faith. A detestable thing has been committed in Israel and in Jerusalem: Judah has desecrated the sanctuary the LORD loves, by marrying the daughter of a foreign god. ¹²As for the man who does this, whoever he may be, may the LORD cut him off from the tents of Jacob *ᵇ*—even though he brings offerings to the LORD Almighty.

¹³Another thing you do: You flood the LORD's altar with tears. You weep and wail

ᵃ 10 Or *father*   *ᵇ 12* Or *¹²May the LORD cut off from the tents of Jacob anyone who gives testimony in behalf of the man who does this*

Make It Stick

READ MALACHI 2:3

God told his people, "I will spread on your faces the offal" (Malachi 2:3). Now, offal is dung. When a puppy "goes" on the rug, it gets its nose rubbed in the awful offal to teach it not to do that again. Ever been disobedient and then suffered the consequences? Write about it on a sticky note.

because he no longer pays attention to your offerings or accepts them with pleasure from your hands. [14]You ask, "Why?" It is because the LORD is acting as the witness between you and the wife of your youth, because you have broken faith with her, though she is your partner, the wife of your marriage covenant.

[15]Has not ʟthe LORDʜ made them one? In flesh and spirit they are his. And why one? Because he was seeking godly offspring.ᵃ So guard yourself in your spirit, and do not break faith with the wife of your youth. [16]"I hate divorce," says the LORD God of Israel, "and I hate a man's covering himselfᵇ with violence as well as with his garment," says the LORD Almighty.

So guard yourself in your spirit, and do not break faith.

The Day of Judgment

[17]You have wearied the LORD with your words.

"How have we wearied him?" you ask.

By saying, "All who do evil are good in the eyes of the LORD, and he is pleased with them" or "Where is the God of justice?"

3 "See, I will send my messenger, who will prepare the way before me. Then suddenly the Lord you are seeking will come to his temple; the messenger of the covenant, whom you desire, will come," says the LORD Almighty.

[2]But who can endure the day of his coming? Who can stand when he appears? For he will be like a refiner's fire or a launderer's soap. [3]He will sit as a refiner and purifier of silver; he will purify the Levites and refine them like gold and silver. Then the LORD will have men who will bring offerings in righteousness, [4]and the offerings of Judah and Jerusalem will be acceptable to the LORD, as in days gone by, as in former years.

[5]"So I will come near to you for judgment. I will be quick to testify against sorcerers, adulterers and perjurers, against those who defraud laborers of their wages, who oppress the widows and the fatherless, and deprive aliens of justice, but do not fear me," says the LORD Almighty.

Robbing God

[6]"I the LORD do not change. So you, O descendants of Jacob, are not destroyed. [7]Ever since the time of your forefathers you have turned away from my

decrees and have not kept them. Return to me, and I will return to you," says the LORD Almighty.

"But you ask, 'How are we to return?'

[8]"Will a man rob God? Yet you rob me.

"But you ask, 'How do we rob you?'

"In tithes and offerings. [9]You are under a curse—the whole nation of you—because you are robbing me. [10]Bring the whole tithe into the storehouse, that there may be food in my house. Test me in this," says the LORD Almighty, "and see if I will not throw open the floodgates of heaven and pour out so much blessing that you will not have room enough for it. [11]I will prevent pests from devouring your crops, and the vines in your fields will not cast their fruit," says the LORD Almighty. [12]"Then all the nations will call you blessed, for yours will be a delightful land," says the LORD Almighty.

[13]"You have said harsh things against me," says the LORD.

"Yet you ask, 'What have we said against you?'

[14]"You have said, 'It is futile to serve God. What did we gain by carrying out his requirements and going about like mourners before the LORD Almighty? [15]But now we call the arrogant blessed. Certainly the evildoers prosper, and even those who challenge God escape.' "

[16]Then those who feared the LORD talked with each other, and the LORD listened and heard. A scroll of remembrance was written in his presence concerning those who feared the LORD and honored his name.

[17]"They will be mine," says the LORD Almighty, "in the day when I make up my treasured possession.ᶜ I will spare them, just as in compassion a man spares his son who serves him. [18]And you will again see the distinction between the righteous and the wicked, between those who serve God and those who do not.

The Day of the LORD

4 "Surely the day is coming; it will burn like a furnace. All the arrogant and every evildoer will be stubble, and that day that is coming will set them on fire," says the LORD Almighty.

ᵃ 15 Or ¹⁵But the one ʟwho is our fatherʜ did not do this, not as long as life remained in him. And what was he seeking? An offspring from God   ᵇ 16 Or his wife   ᶜ 17 Or Almighty, "my treasured possession, in the day when I act

"Not a root or a branch will be left to them. ²But for you who revere my name, the sun of righteousness will rise with healing in its wings. And you will go out and leap like calves released from the stall. ³Then you will trample down the wicked; they will be ashes under the soles of your feet on the day when I do these things," says the LORD Almighty.

⁴"Remember the law of my servant Moses, the decrees and laws I gave him at Horeb for all Israel.

⁵"See, I will send you the prophet Elijah before that great and dreadful day of the LORD comes. ⁶He will turn the hearts of the fathers to their children, and the hearts of the children to their fathers; or else I will come and strike the land with a curse."

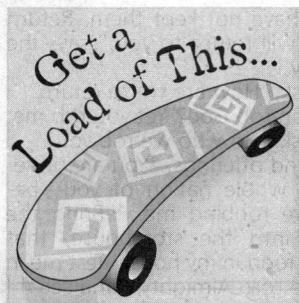

Get a Load of This...

This prophecy about Elijah coming back (Malachi 4:5–6), was not talking about him "swinging low on his sweet chariot" on a return run. This is talking about John the Baptist, New Testament wild man, coming in the power and spirit of Elijah (see Matthew 17:10–13).

NEW TESTAMENT

MATTHEW

Who wrote this book?
Matthew, one of Jesus' 12 disciples, wrote this book.

Why was this book written?
Matthew shows the Jews that Jesus is the Messiah promised in the Old Testament.

For whom was this book written?
Matthew was written for the Jewish people.

What happens in this book?
This book tells about Jesus' birth, his life as an adult, his teaching, death and resurrection.

Who is important in this book?
Jesus is the important person in this book.

When did this happen?
These events took place between 6 B.C. and A.D. 30.

Where did this happen?
Most events took placed in towns in Galilee.

What are some of the stories in this book?

Wise men visit Jesus	Matthew 2:1–23
How to be blessed	Matthew 5:1–12
The Lord's Prayer	Matthew 6:9–13
Jesus feeds 5,000 people	Matthew 14:13–21
Jesus walks on water	Matthew 14:22–33
Lost sheep	Matthew 18:10–14
Jesus enters Jerusalem	Matthew 21:1–11
Jesus is crucified	Matthew 27:32–56
Jesus returns to life	Matthew 28:1–10
Jesus' Great Commission	Matthew 28:16–20

Get a Load of This...

Check out Matthew 1:6. Look at these names: Abraham, Jacob, Boaz, Rahab, King David ... We've met all these people in the Old Testament, now here they are again. Wow! It turns out they were all ancestors of Jesus, the Messiah. So *that's* what the Old Testament was about!

The Genealogy of Jesus

A record of the genealogy of Jesus Christ the son of David, the son of Abraham:

2 Abraham was the father of Isaac,
Isaac the father of Jacob,
Jacob the father of Judah and his brothers,
3 Judah the father of Perez and Zerah, whose mother was Tamar,
Perez the father of Hezron,
Hezron the father of Ram,
4 Ram the father of Amminadab,
Amminadab the father of Nahshon,
Nahshon the father of Salmon,
5 Salmon the father of Boaz, whose mother was Rahab,
Boaz the father of Obed, whose mother was Ruth,
Obed the father of Jesse,
6 and Jesse the father of King David.

David was the father of Solomon, whose mother had been Uriah's wife,
7 Solomon the father of Rehoboam,
Rehoboam the father of Abijah,
Abijah the father of Asa,
8 Asa the father of Jehoshaphat,
Jehoshaphat the father of Jehoram,
Jehoram the father of Uzziah,
9 Uzziah the father of Jotham,
Jotham the father of Ahaz,
Ahaz the father of Hezekiah,
10 Hezekiah the father of Manasseh,
Manasseh the father of Amon,
Amon the father of Josiah,
11 and Josiah the father of Jeconiah[a] and his brothers at the time of the exile to Babylon.

12 After the exile to Babylon:
Jeconiah was the father of Shealtiel,
Shealtiel the father of Zerubbabel,
13 Zerubbabel the father of Abiud,
Abiud the father of Eliakim,
Eliakim the father of Azor,
14 Azor the father of Zadok,
Zadok the father of Akim,
Akim the father of Eliud,
15 Eliud the father of Eleazar,
Eleazar the father of Matthan,
Matthan the father of Jacob,
16 and Jacob the father of Joseph, the husband of Mary, of whom was born Jesus, who is called Christ.

17 Thus there were fourteen generations in all from Abraham to David, fourteen from David to the exile to Babylon, and fourteen from the exile to the Christ.[b]

a 11 That is, Jehoiachin; also in verse 12   b 17 Or Messiah. "The Christ" (Greek) and "the Messiah" (Hebrew) both mean "the Anointed One."

The Birth of Jesus Christ

18This is how the birth of Jesus Christ came about: His mother Mary was pledged to be married to Joseph, but before they came together, she was found to be with child through the Holy Spirit. 19Because Joseph her husband was a righteous man and did not want to expose her to public disgrace, he had in mind to divorce her quietly.

20But after he had considered this, an angel of the Lord appeared to him in a dream and said, "Joseph son of David, do not be afraid to take Mary home as your wife, because what is conceived in her is from the Holy Spirit. 21She will give birth to a son, and you are to give him the name Jesus,a because he will save his people from their sins."

22All this took place to fulfill what the Lord had said through the prophet: 23"The virgin will be with child and will give birth to a son, and they will call him Immanuel"b—which means, "God with us."

24When Joseph woke up, he did what the angel of the Lord had commanded him and took Mary home as his wife. 25But he had no union with her until she gave birth to a son. And he gave him the name Jesus.

The Visit of the Magi

After Jesus was born in Bethlehem in Judea, during the time of King Herod, Magic from the east came to Jerusalem 2and asked, "Where is the one who has been born king of the Jews? We saw his star in the eastd and have come to worship him."

3When King Herod heard this he was disturbed, and all Jerusalem with him. 4When he had called together all the people's chief priests and teachers of the law, he asked them where the Christe was to be born. 5"In Bethlehem in Judea," they replied, "for this is what the prophet has written:

6" 'But you, Bethlehem, in the land of Judah,

a 21 *Jesus* is the Greek form of *Joshua*, which means *the LORD saves.*   b 23 Isaiah 7:14   c 1 Traditionally *Wise Men*   d 2 Or *star when it rose*   e 4 Or *Messiah*

GET SMARTER

Joseph's Dilemma

READ MATTHEW 1:18–24

Ever get that look from your dad—the "I honestly don't know what to *do* with you" look? It's usually after you do something crazy and stupid. Joseph had it tough. His fiancée was pregnant, and not by him. Joseph didn't know the best and most godly way to react. It was a long, painful decision. He considered breaking up with Mary, but while he thought and prayed, God told him what to do. Just like Joseph needed to trust God to help him do the right thing, you need to trust God when you don't know what you're supposed to do. Pray, give your problem to God, then accept his answer. "Joseph ... did what the angel of the Lord had commanded him" (Matthew 1:24). He was a real man of God. He stopped worrying about what was "expected" and just did what was right. Smart guy.

Your next reading is on page 1224.

are by no means least among the
rulers of Judah;
for out of you will come a ruler
who will be the shepherd of my
people Israel.'ᵃ"

7Then Herod called the Magi secretly and found out from them the exact time the star had appeared. 8He sent them to Bethlehem and said, "Go and make a careful search for the child. As soon as you find him, report to me, so that I too may go and worship him."

9After they had heard the king, they went on their way, and the star they had seen in the eastᵇ went ahead of them until it stopped over the place where the child was. 10When they saw the star, they were overjoyed. 11On coming to the house, they saw the child with his mother Mary, and they bowed down and worshiped him. Then they opened their treasures and presented him with gifts of gold and of incense and of myrrh. 12And hav-

ing been warned in a dream not to go back to Herod, they returned to their country by another route.

The Escape to Egypt

13When they had gone, an angel of the Lord appeared to Joseph in a dream. "Get up," he said, "take the child and his mother and escape to Egypt. Stay there until I tell you, for Herod is going to search for the child to kill him."

14So he got up, took the child and his mother during the night and left for Egypt, 15where he stayed until the death of Herod. And so was fulfilled what the Lord had said through the prophet: "Out of Egypt I called my son."ᶜ

16When Herod realized that he had been outwitted by the Magi, he was furious, and he gave orders to kill all the boys in Bethlehem and its vicinity who were

ᵃ 6 Micah 5:2   ᵇ 9 Or seen when it rose
ᶜ 15 Hosea 11:1

Make It Stick

READ MATTHEW 2:1–12

This star could move! People have guessed that it was a migrating dwarf star, a comet or Jupiter lining up with Saturn. Whatever it was, it got the Magi's attention and brought them to Jesus. God still does miracles to bring people to Jesus. Draw what you think the star looked like.

two years old and under, in accordance with the time he had learned from the Magi. ¹⁷Then what was said through the prophet Jeremiah was fulfilled:

¹⁸ "A voice is heard in Ramah,
　　weeping and great mourning,
　Rachel weeping for her children
　　and refusing to be comforted,
　because they are no more." ᵃ

The Return to Nazareth

¹⁹After Herod died, an angel of the Lord appeared in a dream to Joseph in Egypt ²⁰and said, "Get up, take the child and his mother and go to the land of Israel, for those who were trying to take the child's life are dead."

²¹So he got up, took the child and his mother and went to the land of Israel. ²²But when he heard that Archelaus was reigning in Judea in place of his father Herod, he was afraid to go there. Having been warned in a dream, he withdrew to the district of Galilee, ²³and he went and lived in a town called Nazareth. So was fulfilled what was said through the prophets: "He will be called a Nazarene."

John the Baptist Prepares the Way

In those days John the Baptist came, preaching in the Desert of Judea ²and saying, "Repent, for the kingdom of heaven is near." ³This is he who was spoken of through the prophet Isaiah:

"A voice of one calling in the desert,
'Prepare the way for the Lord,
　make straight paths for him.' " ᵇ

⁴John's clothes were made of camel's hair, and he had a leather belt around his waist. His food was locusts and wild honey. ⁵People went out to him from Jerusalem and all Judea and the whole region of the Jordan. ⁶Confessing their sins, they were baptized by him in the Jordan River.

⁷But when he saw many of the Pharisees and Sadducees coming to where he was baptizing, he said to them: "You brood of vipers! Who warned you to flee from the coming wrath? ⁸Produce fruit in keeping with repentance. ⁹And do not think you can say to yourselves, 'We have Abraham as our father.' I tell you that out of these stones God can raise up children for Abraham. ¹⁰The ax is already at the root of the trees, and every tree that does not produce good fruit will be cut down and thrown into the fire.

¹¹ "I baptize you withᶜ water for repentance. But after me will come one who is more powerful than I, whose sandals I am not fit to carry. He will baptize you with the Holy Spirit and with fire. ¹²His winnowing fork is in his hand, and he will clear his threshing floor, gathering his wheat into the barn and burning up the chaff with unquenchable fire."

ᵃ 18 Jer. 31:15　　ᵇ 3 Isaiah 40:3　　ᶜ 11 Or in

Get a Load of This...

Check out Matthew 2:4–6, 14–15, 17–18, 23. Bull's-eye! All these Old Testament prophecies came true! They were fulfilled in Jesus' life. It goes to show, God knew *exactly* what would happen, hundreds of years before Jesus was even born.

The Baptism of Jesus

13Then Jesus came from Galilee to the Jordan to be baptized by John. 14But John tried to deter him, saying, "I need to be baptized by you, and do you come to me?"

15Jesus replied, "Let it be so now; it is proper for us to do this to fulfill all righteousness." Then John consented.

16As soon as Jesus was baptized, he went up out of the water. At that moment heaven was opened, and he saw the Spirit of God descending like a dove and lighting on him. 17And a voice from heaven said, "This is my Son, whom I love; with him I am well pleased."

The Temptation of Jesus

4 Then Jesus was led by the Spirit into the desert to be tempted by the devil. 2After fasting forty days and forty nights, he was hungry. 3The tempter came to him and said, "If you are the Son of God, tell these stones to become bread."

4Jesus answered, "It is written: 'Man does not live on bread alone, but on every word that comes from the mouth of God.'a"

5Then the devil took him to the holy city and had him stand on the highest point of the temple. 6"If you are the Son of God," he said, "throw yourself down. For it is written:

" 'He will command his angels
        concerning you,
and they will lift you up in their
        hands,
so that you will not strike your foot
        against a stone.'b"

7Jesus answered him, "It is also written: 'Do not put the Lord your God to the test.'c"

8Again, the devil took him to a very high mountain and showed him all the kingdoms of the world and their splendor. 9"All this I will give you," he said, "if you will bow down and worship me."

a 4 Deut. 8:3   b 6 Psalm 91:11,12   c 7 Deut. 6:16

John the Baptist

READ MATTHEW 3:1–12

John the Baptist was *different*, to say the least. His clothes were made from camel's hair. He chased down locusts and ate them for lunch. He battled with wild bees for honey. What if a kid that strange came to your school? People would say, "Have you seen the new kid?" "Did you see his clothes? He's wearing camel's hair." "Oh, that's nothing! At lunch today, he was munching on grasshopper heads!" Nowadays people dress all different ways, and we assume things about them because of the way they wear their clothes or hair. "Man looks at the outward appearance, but the LORD looks at the heart" (1 Samuel 16:7). Be a man of God. When you see someone who looks different, go introduce yourself. Stereotype people and you might never get to know what they're *really* like. There's no room for friendship inside a box, so why put a potential friend there?

Your next reading is on page 1225.

10Jesus said to him, "Away from me, Satan! For it is written: 'Worship the Lord your God, and serve him only.'[a]"

11Then the devil left him, and angels came and attended him.

Jesus Begins to Preach

12When Jesus heard that John had been put in prison, he returned to Galilee. 13Leaving Nazareth, he went and lived in Capernaum, which was by the lake in the area of Zebulun and Naphtali— 14to fulfill what was said through the prophet Isaiah:

15"Land of Zebulun and land of Naphtali,
　　the way to the sea, along the Jordan,
　　Galilee of the Gentiles—
16the people living in darkness
　　have seen a great light;
on those living in the land of the
　　　shadow of death
　　a light has dawned."[b]

17From that time on Jesus began to preach, "Repent, for the kingdom of heaven is near."

The Calling of the First Disciples

18As Jesus was walking beside the Sea of Galilee, he saw two brothers, Simon called Peter and his brother Andrew. They were casting a net into the lake, for they were fishermen. 19"Come, follow me," Jesus said, "and I will make you fishers of men." 20At once they left their nets and followed him.

21Going on from there, he saw two other brothers, James son of Zebedee and his brother John. They were in a boat with their father Zebedee, preparing their nets. Jesus called them, 22and immediately they left the boat and their father and followed him.

Jesus Heals the Sick

23Jesus went throughout Galilee, teaching in their synagogues, preaching the good news of the kingdom, and healing every disease and sickness among the people. 24News about him spread all over Syria, and people brought to him all who

[a] 10 Deut. 6:13   [b] 16 Isaiah 9:1,2

It Is Written
READ MATTHEW 4:1–11

Battle in the wilderness! The Son of God against the Prince of Lies in a battle of wills! When Satan tempted him, did Jesus call down heavenly fire to singe Satan? Nope. Jesus stuck with what God had said. How different from Eve way back in the beginning of the Bible. When Satan tempted her, she doubted God's Word and caved in. Use your Bible to fight against lies. Hide God's Word in your heart (see Psalm 119:11). When you memorize Scriptures, you have a defense system against temptation. Then, when your little brother messes with your stuff for the 142nd time and you're tempted to feed him to the bears at the zoo, you remember something Jesus said about forgiveness. You forgive, your brother lives—everybody's happy. Jesus promised his disciples that the Holy Spirit would remind them of everything he said to them (John 14:26); so if you want to be a 252 man, dig into God's Word and stand on it. Satan can't touch that.

Your next reading is on page 1226.

were ill with various diseases, those suffering severe pain, the demon-possessed, those having seizures, and the paralyzed, and he healed them. 25 Large crowds from Galilee, the Decapolis, a Jerusalem, Judea and the region across the Jordan followed him.

The Beatitudes

Now when he saw the crowds, he went up on a mountainside and sat down. His disciples came to him, 2 and he began to teach them, saying:

3 "Blessed are the poor in spirit,
    for theirs is the kingdom of heaven.
4 Blessed are those who mourn,
    for they will be comforted.
5 Blessed are the meek,
    for they will inherit the earth.
6 Blessed are those who hunger and
        thirst for righteousness,
    for they will be filled.
7 Blessed are the merciful,
    for they will be shown mercy.
8 Blessed are the pure in heart,
    for they will see God.
9 Blessed are the peacemakers,
    for they will be called sons of God.
10 Blessed are those who are persecuted
        because of righteousness,
    for theirs is the kingdom of heaven.

11 "Blessed are you when people insult you, persecute you and falsely say all kinds of evil against you because of me. 12 Rejoice and be glad, because great is your reward in heaven, for in the same way they persecuted the prophets who were before you.

Salt and Light

13 "You are the salt of the earth. But if the salt loses its saltiness, how can it be made salty again? It is no longer good for anything, except to be thrown out and trampled by men.

14 "You are the light of the world. A city on a hill cannot be hidden. 15 Neither do people light a lamp and put it under a bowl. Instead they put it on its stand, and it gives light to everyone in the house. 16 In

a 25 That is, the Ten Cities

GET SMARTER

The Be Attitude Blocks

READ MATTHEW 5:1–12

These are the "Be Attitudes"—the attitudes you need to *be* a man of God. These attitudes are not like lunch in a school cafeteria where you can pick what you like and leave the rest. Nuh-uh. They all work together. If you start poor in spirit, you'll grow. If you hunger and thirst for righteousness, you'll be filled and you'll recognize that you only get by through God's mercy. God shows you mercy, then you *become* merciful. As you grow in God and his Word, you grow purer in heart. Then, as a peacemaker, you want to tell other people about God. Finally there's persecution: People either respect your stand or they mock you and persecute you. It's important to try to obey everything Jesus taught here. Living for God isn't pick-and-choose. It's like eating *all* your veggies, but with a much bigger bonus—"great is your reward in heaven" (verse 12).

Your next reading is on page 1229.

the same way, let your light shine before men, that they may see your good deeds and praise your Father in heaven.

The Fulfillment of the Law

17 "Do not think that I have come to abolish the Law or the Prophets; I have not come to abolish them but to fulfill them. 18 I tell you the truth, until heaven and earth disappear, not the smallest letter, not the least stroke of a pen, will by any means disappear from the Law until everything is accomplished. 19 Anyone who breaks one of the least of these commandments and teaches others to do the same will be called least in the kingdom of heaven, but whoever practices and teaches these commands will be called great in the kingdom of heaven. 20 For I tell you that unless your righteousness surpasses that of the Pharisees and the teachers of the law, you will certainly not enter the kingdom of heaven.

Murder

21 "You have heard that it was said to the people long ago, 'Do not murder,[a] and anyone who murders will be subject to judgment.' 22 But I tell you that anyone who is angry with his brother[b] will be subject to judgment. Again, anyone who says to his brother, 'Raca,[c]' is answerable to the Sanhedrin. But anyone who says, 'You fool!' will be in danger of the fire of hell.

23 "Therefore, if you are offering your gift at the altar and there remember that your brother has something against you, 24 leave your gift there in front of the altar. First go and be reconciled to your brother; then come and offer your gift.

25 "Settle matters quickly with your adversary who is taking you to court. Do it while you are still with him on the way, or he may hand you over to the judge, and the judge may hand you over to the officer, and you may be thrown into prison. 26 I tell you the truth, you will not get out until you have paid the last penny.[d]

Adultery

27 "You have heard that it was said, 'Do not commit adultery.'[e] 28 But I tell you that anyone who looks at a woman lustfully has already committed adultery with her in his heart. 29 If your right eye causes you to sin, gouge it out and throw it away. It is better for you to lose one part of your body than for your whole body to be thrown into hell. 30 And if your right hand causes you to sin, cut it off and throw it away. It is better for you to lose one part of your body than for your whole body to go into hell.

Divorce

31 "It has been said, 'Anyone who divorces his wife must give her a certificate of divorce.'[f] 32 But I tell you

Get a Load of This...

Check out Matthew 5:13. What does the world need? *Salt!* Um . . . in the spiritual sense! You need to be "salty," and sprinkle the world with 252-man godliness. OK, ready for a saltshaker tongue twister? How many souls does a saltshaker save if a saltshaker surely salts souls?

---

a 21 Exodus 20:13   b 22 Some manuscripts *brother without cause*
c 22 An Aramaic term of contempt   d 26 Greek *kodrantes*
e 27 Exodus 20:14   f 31 Deut. 24:1

that anyone who divorces his wife, except for marital unfaithfulness, causes her to become an adulteress, and anyone who marries the divorced woman commits adultery.

Oaths

33"Again, you have heard that it was said to the people long ago, 'Do not break your oath, but keep the oaths you have made to the Lord.' 34But I tell you, Do not swear at all: either by heaven, for it is God's throne; 35or by the earth, for it is his footstool; or by Jerusalem, for it is the city of the Great King. 36And do not swear by your head, for you cannot make even one hair white or black. 37Simply let your 'Yes' be 'Yes,' and your 'No,' 'No'; anything beyond this comes from the evil one.

An Eye for an Eye

38"You have heard that it was said, 'Eye for eye, and tooth for tooth.' ª 39But I tell you, Do not resist an evil person. If someone strikes you on the right cheek, turn to him the other also. 40And if someone wants to sue you and take your tunic, let him have your cloak as well. 41If someone forces you to go one mile, go with him two miles. 42Give to the one who asks you, and do not turn away from the one who wants to borrow from you.

Love for Enemies

43"You have heard that it was said, 'Love your neighbor ᵇ and hate your enemy.' 44But I tell you: Love your enemies ᶜ and pray for those who persecute you, 45that you may be sons of your Father in heaven. He causes his sun to rise on the evil and the good, and sends rain on the righteous and the unrighteous. 46If you love those who love you, what reward will you get? Are not even the tax collectors

ª 38 Exodus 21:24; Lev. 24:20; Deut. 19:21
ᵇ 43 Lev. 19:18   ᶜ 44 Some late manuscripts enemies, bless those who curse you, do good to those who hate you

Make It Stick

READ MATTHEW 5:21–22

Matthew 5:21–22 isn't about teasing and harmless name-calling. It's about hurting others. *Raca* means "empty-head." If you call someone "Raca," you're calling him an idiot. We know that murder is wrong. Well, angry thoughts and verbal attacks are the beginning of murder. They head you in that direction. Write on a sticky note, "I will not call anyone Raca."

doing that? 47And if you greet only your brothers, what are you doing more than others? Do not even pagans do that? 48Be perfect, therefore, as your heavenly Father is perfect.

Giving to the Needy

6 "Be careful not to do your 'acts of righteousness' before men, to be seen by them. If you do, you will have no reward from your Father in heaven.

2"So when you give to the needy, do not announce it with trumpets, as the hypocrites do in the synagogues and on the streets, to be honored by men. I tell you the truth, they have received their reward in full. 3But when you give to the needy, do not let your left hand know what your right hand is doing, 4so that your giving may be in secret. Then your Father, who sees what is done in secret, will reward you.

Prayer

5"And when you pray, do not be like the hypocrites, for they love to pray standing in the synagogues and on the street corners to be seen by men. I tell you the truth, they have received their reward in full. 6But when you pray, go into your room, close the door and pray to your Father, who is unseen. Then your Father, who sees what is done in secret, will reward you. 7And when you pray, do not keep on babbling like pagans, for they think they will be heard because of their many words. 8Do not be like them, for your Father knows what you need before you ask him.

9"This, then, is how you should pray:

" 'Our Father in heaven,
    hallowed be your name,
10your kingdom come,
    your will be done
        on earth as it is in heaven.
11Give us today our daily bread.

Cheek-striking Stuff

READ MATTHEW 5:38–48

If someone gives you a good old punch and you say, "Slug my other cheek, too," they'll think you're being a wise guy and *will* hit you. You'll get a matching set of bruises. That's not what Jesus meant. Jesus was not saying, "Let someone break all your teeth." He was trying to teach you to love others, to not hold a grudge or strike back in revenge. When someone hurts you, it's natural to want to hate them and hurt them back. Instead, Jesus said to "turn the other cheek"—keep a loving attitude and keep an open heart toward them. You may need to defend yourself *while* you're loving them, or take a step backwards so they can't smash your braces. That's common sense. But you need to keep a loving attitude and not hate them. God can help anyone change, grow up and become a better person—so don't write them off.

Your next reading is on page 1230.

¹²Forgive us our debts,
  as we also have forgiven our
    debtors.
¹³And lead us not into temptation,
  but deliver us from the evil one.ᵃ'

¹⁴For if you forgive men when they sin against you, your heavenly Father will also forgive you. ¹⁵But if you do not forgive men their sins, your Father will not forgive your sins.

Fasting

¹⁶"When you fast, do not look somber as the hypocrites do, for they disfigure their faces to show men they are fasting. I tell you the truth, they have received their reward in full. ¹⁷But when you fast, put oil on your head and wash your face, ¹⁸so that it will not be obvious to men that you are fasting, but only to your Father, who is unseen; and your Father, who sees what is done in secret, will reward you.

Treasures in Heaven

¹⁹"Do not store up for yourselves treasures on earth, where moth and rust de-stroy, and where thieves break in and steal. ²⁰But store up for yourselves trea-sures in heaven, where moth and rust do not destroy, and where thieves do not break in and steal. ²¹For where your trea-sure is, there your heart will be also.

²²"The eye is the lamp of the body. If your eyes are good, your whole body will be full of light. ²³But if your eyes are bad, your whole body will be full of darkness. If then the light within you is darkness, how great is that darkness!

²⁴"No one can serve two masters. Ei-ther he will hate the one and love the oth-er, or he will be devoted to the one and despise the other. You cannot serve both God and Money.

Do Not Worry

²⁵"Therefore I tell you, do not worry about your life, what you will eat or drink; or about your body, what you will wear. Is not life more important than food, and the body more important than clothes?

ᵃ 13 Or from evil; some late manuscripts one, / for yours is the kingdom and the power and the glory forever. Amen.

The Lord's Prayer From A to G

READ MATTHEW 6:5–15

How many times have you mumbled through the Lord's Prayer with-out thinking about what it means? Guess what? It's not meant to just be repeated over and over again. It's actually a guideline or an *out-line* for chunkier prayers. Check this out. You should begin every prayer by (a) addressing God personally. (It's cool to have a personal relationship with him, after all.) (b) Next, you should praise him. Then (c) you should pray for God's church and Christians all around the world to grow. (d) After that, pray for God's will to be done everywhere—especially in *your* life. (e) Next, ask God to provide for your needs, desires and concerns. (f) Ask God to forgive your sins and help you forgive others. (g) Finally, ask God to help you obey him and resist temptation. Don't know what to pray? Stick to this A–G outline and you can't go wrong!

Your next reading is on page 1231.

26Look at the birds of the air; they do not sow or reap or store away in barns, and yet your heavenly Father feeds them. Are you not much more valuable than they? 27Who of you by worrying can add a single hour to his life*a*?

28"And why do you worry about clothes? See how the lilies of the field grow. They do not labor or spin. 29Yet I tell you that not even Solomon in all his splendor was dressed like one of these. 30If that is how God clothes the grass of the field, which is here today and tomorrow is thrown into the fire, will he not much more clothe you, O you of little faith? 31So do not worry, saying, 'What shall we eat?' or 'What shall we drink?' or 'What shall we wear?' 32For the pagans run after all these things, and your heavenly Father knows that you need them. 33But seek first his kingdom and his righteousness, and all these things will be given to you as well. 34Therefore do not worry about tomorrow, for tomorrow will worry about itself. Each day has enough trouble of its own.

Judging Others

7 "Do not judge, or you too will be judged. 2For in the same way you judge others, you will be judged, and with the measure you use, it will be measured to you.

3"Why do you look at the speck of sawdust in your brother's eye and pay no attention to the plank in your own eye? 4How can you say to your brother, 'Let me take the speck out of your eye,' when all the time there is a plank in your own eye? 5You hypocrite, first take the plank out of your own eye, and then you will see clearly to remove the speck from your brother's eye.

6"Do not give dogs what is sacred; do not throw your pearls to pigs. If you do, they may trample them under their feet, and then turn and tear you to pieces.

Ask, Seek, Knock

7"Ask and it will be given to you; seek and you will find; knock and the door will be opened to you. 8For everyone who asks

a 27 Or single cubit to his height

Treasure in Heaven

READ MATTHEW 6:19–34

Food, drink, clothes, sports, getting stuff, hanging out—these are all a *part* of life, but they shouldn't be your reason for being alive. God wants your heart. Is *your* treasure just having fun or is it knowing and pleasing God? Put first things first. OK, example: What if you got a model airplane, grabbed the glue and started glomming pieces together? Do that and your model plane wouldn't be anything you'd want your friends to see. The smart thing is to read the instructions first and see how it goes together, right? Well, the Bible is your instruction manual for life. And what's instruction number one? Put God first in your life. Do that, and he'll help you get the most out of life *and* give you everything you need—including fun.

Your next reading is on page 1233.

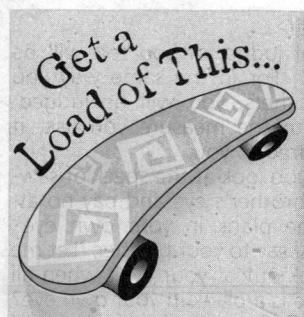

receives; he who seeks finds; and to him who knocks, the door will be opened.

9"Which of you, if his son asks for bread, will give him a stone? 10Or if he asks for a fish, will give him a snake? 11If you, then, though you are evil, know how to give good gifts to your children, how much more will your Father in heaven give good gifts to those who ask him! 12So in everything, do to others what you would have them do to you, for this sums up the Law and the Prophets.

The Narrow and Wide Gates

13"Enter through the narrow gate. For wide is the gate and broad is the road that leads to destruction, and many enter through it. 14But small is the gate and narrow the road that leads to life, and only a few find it.

A Tree and Its Fruit

15"Watch out for false prophets. They come to you in sheep's clothing, but inwardly they are ferocious wolves. 16By their fruit you will recognize them. Do people pick grapes from thornbushes, or figs from thistles? 17Likewise every good tree bears good fruit, but a bad tree bears bad fruit. 18A good tree cannot bear bad fruit, and a bad tree cannot bear good fruit. 19Every tree that does not bear good fruit is cut down and thrown into the fire. 20Thus, by their fruit you will recognize them.

21"Not everyone who says to me, 'Lord, Lord,' will enter the kingdom of heaven, but only he who does the will of my Father who is in heaven. 22Many will say to me on that day, 'Lord, Lord, did we not prophesy in your name, and in your name drive out demons and perform many miracles?' 23Then I will tell them plainly, 'I never knew you. Away from me, you evildoers!'

The Wise and Foolish Builders

24"Therefore everyone who hears these words of mine and puts them into practice is like a wise man who built his house on the rock. 25The rain came down, the streams rose, and the winds blew and beat against that house; yet it did not fall, because it had its foundation on the rock. 26But everyone who hears these words of mine and does not put them into practice is like a foolish man who built his house on sand. 27The rain came down, the streams rose, and the winds blew and beat against that house, and it fell with a great crash."

28When Jesus had finished saying these things, the crowds were amazed at his teaching, 29because he taught as one who had authority, and not as their teachers of the law.

The Man With Leprosy

When he came down from the mountainside, large crowds followed him. ²A man with leprosy[a] came and knelt before him and said, "Lord, if you are willing, you can make me clean."

³Jesus reached out his hand and touched the man. "I am willing," he said. "Be clean!" Immediately he was cured[b] of his leprosy. ⁴Then Jesus said to him, "See that you don't tell anyone. But go, show yourself to the priest and offer the gift Moses commanded, as a testimony to them."

The Faith of the Centurion

⁵When Jesus had entered Capernaum, a centurion came to him, asking for help. ⁶"Lord," he said, "my servant lies at home paralyzed and in terrible suffering."

⁷Jesus said to him, "I will go and heal him."

⁸The centurion replied, "Lord, I do not deserve to have you come under my roof. But just say the word, and my servant will be healed. ⁹For I myself am a man under authority, with soldiers under me. I tell this one, 'Go,' and he goes; and that one, 'Come,' and he comes. I say to my servant, 'Do this,' and he does it."

¹⁰When Jesus heard this, he was astonished and said to those following him, "I tell you the truth, I have not found anyone in Israel with such great faith. ¹¹I say to you that many will come from the east and the west, and will take their places at the feast with Abraham, Isaac and Jacob in the kingdom of heaven. ¹²But the subjects of the kingdom will be thrown outside, into the darkness, where there will be weeping and gnashing of teeth."

¹³Then Jesus said to the centurion, "Go! It will be done just as you believed it would." And his servant was healed at that very hour.

Jesus Heals Many

¹⁴When Jesus came into Peter's house, he saw Peter's mother-in-law lying in bed with a fever. ¹⁵He touched her hand and

---

a 2 The Greek word was used for various diseases affecting the skin—not necessarily leprosy.   *b 3* Greek *made clean*

False Prophets

READ MATTHEW 7:15–23

You're visiting a petting zoo. You buy some sheep feed and walk up to a cute, fluffy sheep. Suddenly, there's a low growl and Fluffy's head snaps up, revealing the fangs of a wolf! Run! Young church "wolves" are just as dangerous—they talk like Christians and act like Christians, but when adults aren't around, their "fangs" come out. Watch out for kids who say, "Praise *God*, Pastor," but as soon as he leaves, they whisper to you, "Let's do *this* ..." Here's Jesus' wolf-detector test: "By their fruit you will recognize them" (verse 16). Good trees don't bear bad fruit. Sheepy trees don't bear wolfy fruit. It's that simple. If some kid goes church-wolf on you, clear out. Now, you shouldn't think some kid's a false prophet just because he's not perfect or gets into trouble sometimes. If he loves God, give him time; he'll grow up into a 252 man. It's important to tell the difference.

Your next reading is on page 1237.

the fever left her, and she got up and began to wait on him.

16When evening came, many who were demon-possessed were brought to him, and he drove out the spirits with a word and healed all the sick. 17This was to fulfill what was spoken through the prophet Isaiah:

"He took up our infirmities
　and carried our diseases." *a*

The Cost of Following Jesus

18When Jesus saw the crowd around him, he gave orders to cross to the other side of the lake. 19Then a teacher of the law came to him and said, "Teacher, I will follow you wherever you go."

20Jesus replied, "Foxes have holes and birds of the air have nests, but the Son of Man has no place to lay his head."

21Another disciple said to him, "Lord, first let me go and bury my father."

22But Jesus told him, "Follow me, and let the dead bury their own dead."

Jesus Calms the Storm

23Then he got into the boat and his disciples followed him. 24Without warning, a furious storm came up on the lake, so that the waves swept over the boat. But Jesus was sleeping. 25The disciples went and woke him, saying, "Lord, save us! We're going to drown!"

26He replied, "You of little faith, why are you so afraid?" Then he got up and rebuked the winds and the waves, and it was completely calm.

27The men were amazed and asked, "What kind of man is this? Even the winds and the waves obey him!"

The Healing of Two Demon-possessed Men

28When he arrived at the other side in the region of the Gadarenes, *b* two demon-possessed men coming from the

---

a 17 Isaiah 53:4　　*b 28* Some manuscripts *Gergesenes*; others *Gerasenes*

Make It Stick

READ MATTHEW 8:1–3

Jesus said, "I am willing" (see Matthew 8:1–3). God is *able* to do anything and he's *willing* to answer your prayers, because he loves you. But he also knows what's best for you. On a sticky note, write something that you're praying for, then write: "Lord, I know you're able and willing. Please give this to me if it's good for me."

tombs met him. They were so violent that no one could pass that way. ²⁹"What do you want with us, Son of God?" they shouted. "Have you come here to torture us before the appointed time?"

³⁰Some distance from them a large herd of pigs was feeding. ³¹The demons begged Jesus, "If you drive us out, send us into the herd of pigs."

³²He said to them, "Go!" So they came out and went into the pigs, and the whole herd rushed down the steep bank into the lake and died in the water. ³³Those tending the pigs ran off, went into the town and reported all this, including what had happened to the demon-possessed men. ³⁴Then the whole town went out to meet Jesus. And when they saw him, they pleaded with him to leave their region.

Jesus Heals a Paralytic

Jesus stepped into a boat, crossed over and came to his own town. ²Some men brought to him a paralytic, lying on a mat. When Jesus saw their faith, he said to the paralytic, "Take heart, son; your sins are forgiven."

³At this, some of the teachers of the law said to themselves, "This fellow is blaspheming!"

⁴Knowing their thoughts, Jesus said, "Why do you entertain evil thoughts in your hearts? ⁵Which is easier: to say, 'Your sins are forgiven,' or to say, 'Get up and walk'? ⁶But so that you may know that the Son of Man has authority on earth to forgive sins . . ." Then he said to the paralytic, "Get up, take your mat and go home." ⁷And the man got up and went home. ⁸When the crowd saw this, they were filled with awe; and they praised God, who had given such authority to men.

The Calling of Matthew

⁹As Jesus went on from there, he saw a man named Matthew sitting at the tax collector's booth. "Follow me," he told him, and Matthew got up and followed him.

¹⁰While Jesus was having dinner at Matthew's house, many tax collectors and "sinners" came and ate with him and his disciples. ¹¹When the Pharisees saw this, they asked his disciples, "Why does your teacher eat with tax collectors and 'sinners'?"

¹²On hearing this, Jesus said, "It is not the healthy who need a doctor, but the sick. ¹³But go and learn what this means: 'I desire mercy, not sacrifice.'ᵃ For I have not come to call the righteous, but sinners."

Jesus Questioned About Fasting

¹⁴Then John's disciples came and asked him, "How is it that we and the Pharisees fast, but your disciples do not fast?"

¹⁵Jesus answered, "How can the guests of the bride-groom mourn while he is with them? The time will

ᵃ 13 Hosea 6:6

Get a Load of This...

Check out Matthew 8:28–29. A frantic demon shrieked at Jesus, "Have you come to *destroy* us?" (see Mark 1:23–24). The demons were terrified of Jesus. They knew that he had the power to destroy them. Isn't it great to have Jesus on your side?

Get a Load of This...

"Let the dead bury their own dead" (Matthew 8:22). This is not talking about zombies. Or *is* it? OK, in a sense, it is. Some people actually *do* walk around like zombies with no spiritual life. Pray for the spiritual "zombies" you know.

come when the bridegroom will be taken from them; then they will fast.

16"No one sews a patch of unshrunk cloth on an old garment, for the patch will pull away from the garment, making the tear worse. 17Neither do men pour new wine into old wineskins. If they do, the skins will burst, the wine will run out and the wineskins will be ruined. No, they pour new wine into new wineskins, and both are preserved."

A Dead Girl and a Sick Woman

18While he was saying this, a ruler came and knelt before him and said, "My daughter has just died. But come and put your hand on her, and she will live." 19Jesus got up and went with him, and so did his disciples.

20Just then a woman who had been subject to bleeding for twelve years came up behind him and touched the edge of his cloak. 21She said to herself, "If I only touch his cloak, I will be healed."

22Jesus turned and saw her. "Take heart, daughter," he said, "your faith has healed you." And the woman was healed from that moment.

23When Jesus entered the ruler's house and saw the flute players and the noisy crowd, 24he said, "Go away. The girl is not dead but asleep." But they laughed at him. 25After the crowd had been put outside, he went in and took the girl by the hand, and she got up. 26News of this spread through all that region.

Jesus Heals the Blind and Mute

27As Jesus went on from there, two blind men followed him, calling out, "Have mercy on us, Son of David!"

28When he had gone indoors, the blind men came to him, and he asked them, "Do you believe that I am able to do this?"

"Yes, Lord," they replied.

29Then he touched their eyes and said, "According to your faith will it be done to you"; 30and their sight was restored. Jesus warned them sternly, "See that no one knows about this." 31But they went out and spread the news about him all over that region.

32While they were going out, a man who was demon-possessed and could not talk was brought to Jesus. 33And when the demon was driven out, the man who had been mute spoke. The crowd was amazed and said, "Nothing like this has ever been seen in Israel."

34But the Pharisees said, "It is by the prince of demons that he drives out demons."

The Workers Are Few

35Jesus went through all the towns and villages, teaching in their synagogues, preaching the good news of the kingdom and healing every disease and sickness. 36When he saw the crowds, he had compassion on them, because they were harassed and helpless, like sheep without a shepherd. 37Then he said to his disciples, "The harvest is plentiful but the workers are few. 38Ask the Lord of the harvest, therefore, to send out workers into his harvest field."

Jesus Sends Out the Twelve

10 He called his twelve disciples to him and gave them authority to drive out evil[a] spirits and to heal every disease and sickness.

2These are the names of the twelve apostles: first, Simon (who is called Peter) and his brother Andrew; James son of Zebedee, and his brother John; 3Philip and Bartholomew; Thomas and Matthew the tax collector; James son of Alphaeus, and Thaddaeus; 4Simon the Zealot and Judas Iscariot, who betrayed him.

5These twelve Jesus sent out with the following instructions: "Do not go among the Gentiles or enter any town of the Samaritans. 6Go rather to the lost sheep of Israel. 7As you go, preach this message: 'The kingdom of heaven is near.' 8Heal the sick, raise the dead, cleanse those who have leprosy,[b] drive out demons. Freely you have received, freely give. 9Do not take along any gold or silver or copper in your belts; 10take no bag for the journey, or extra tunic, or sandals or a staff; for the worker is worth his keep.

11"Whatever town or village you enter, search for some worthy person there and stay at his house until you leave. 12As you enter the home, give it your greeting. 13If the home is deserving, let your peace rest on it; if it is not, let your peace return to you. 14If anyone will not welcome you or listen to your words, shake the dust off your feet when you leave that home or town. 15I tell you the truth, it will be more bearable for Sodom and Gomorrah on the day of judgment than for that town. 16I am sending you out like sheep among wolves. Therefore be as shrewd as snakes and as innocent as doves.

[a] 1 Greek unclean   [b] 8 The Greek word was used for various diseases affecting the skin—not necessarily leprosy.

GET STRONGER

Big Job and Understaffed

READ MATTHEW 9:35—10:20

Ever taken on the Monster Leaf Raking Job of All Time? It's usually at some old guy's house, with all these huge trees, each with about 5,000 leaves—and they're not on the trees anymore. And if you skip them this year, there'll just be more next year. Leaves and lost souls are alike. When Jesus sent out the apostles, he told them, "The harvest is plentiful but the workers are few" (Matthew 9:37). Jesus saw people who were harassed, helpless and needy and his heart went out to them. So much so, he was willing to die on the cross to save them. You too can work for Jesus. Open your eyes and look! People around you need help and you've got the goods: truth, direction, hope and love. Jesus could've done everything himself but he chose to send us out. Will you go? Pray, "God, I'm here. Send me into the harvest."

Your next reading is on page 1241.

17"Be on your guard against men; they will hand you over to the local councils and flog you in their synagogues. 18On my account you will be brought before governors and kings as witnesses to them and to the Gentiles. 19But when they arrest you, do not worry about what to say or how to say it. At that time you will be given what to say, 20for it will not be you speaking, but the Spirit of your Father speaking through you.

21"Brother will betray brother to death, and a father his child; children will rebel against their parents and have them put to death. 22All men will hate you because of me, but he who stands firm to the end will be saved. 23When you are persecuted in one place, flee to another. I tell you the truth, you will not finish going through the cities of Israel before the Son of Man comes.

24"A student is not above his teacher, nor a servant above his master. 25It is enough for the student to be like his teacher, and the servant like his master. If the head of the house has been called Beelzebub,[a] how much more the members of his household!

26"So do not be afraid of them. There is nothing concealed that will not be disclosed, or hidden that will not be made known. 27What I tell you in the dark, speak in the daylight; what is whispered in your ear, proclaim from the roofs. 28Do not be afraid of those who kill the body but cannot kill the soul. Rather, be afraid of the One who can destroy both soul and body in hell. 29Are not two sparrows sold for a penny[b]? Yet not one of them will fall to the ground apart from the will of your Father. 30And even the very hairs of your head are all numbered. 31So don't be afraid; you are worth more than many sparrows.

32"Whoever acknowledges me before men, I will also acknowledge him before my Father in heaven. 33But whoever disowns me before men, I will disown him before my Father in heaven.

34"Do not suppose that I have come to bring peace to the earth. I did not come to bring peace, but a sword. 35For I have come to turn

" 'a man against his father,
a daughter against her mother,
a daughter-in-law against her
mother-in-law—

36   a man's enemies will be the members
of his own household.'[c]

37"Anyone who loves his father or mother more than me is not worthy of me; anyone who loves his son or daughter more than me is not worthy of me; 38and anyone who does not take his cross and follow me is not worthy of me. 39Whoever finds his life will lose it, and whoever loses his life for my sake will find it.

40"He who receives you receives me, and he who receives me receives the one who sent me. 41Anyone who receives a prophet because he is a prophet will receive a prophet's reward, and anyone who receives a righteous man because he is a righteous man will receive a righteous man's reward. 42And if anyone gives even a cup of cold water to one of these little ones because he is my disciple, I tell you the truth, he will certainly not lose his reward."

Jesus and John the Baptist

After Jesus had finished instructing his twelve disciples, he went on from there to teach and preach in the towns of Galilee.[d]

2When John heard in prison what Christ was doing, he sent his disciples 3to ask him, "Are you the one who was to come, or should we expect someone else?"

4Jesus replied, "Go back and report to John what you hear and see: 5The blind receive sight, the lame walk, those who have leprosy[e] are cured, the deaf hear, the dead are raised, and the good news is preached to the poor. 6Blessed is the man who does not fall away on account of me."

7As John's disciples were leaving, Jesus began to speak to the crowd about John: "What did you go out into the desert to see? A reed swayed by the wind? 8If not, what did you go out to see? A man dressed in fine clothes? No, those who wear fine clothes are in kings' palaces. 9Then what did you go out to see? A prophet? Yes, I tell you, and more than a prophet. 10This is the one about whom it is written:

" 'I will send my messenger ahead of
you,
who will prepare your way before
you.'[f]

---

[a] 25 Greek Beezeboul or Beelzeboul   [b] 29 Greek an
assarion   [c] 36 Micah 7:6   [d] 1 Greek in their towns
[e] 5 The Greek word was used for various diseases affecting
the skin—not necessarily leprosy.   [f] 10 Mal. 3:1

11I tell you the truth: Among those born of women there has not risen anyone greater than John the Baptist; yet he who is least in the kingdom of heaven is greater than he. 12From the days of John the Baptist until now, the kingdom of heaven has been forcefully advancing, and forceful men lay hold of it. 13For all the Prophets and the Law prophesied until John. 14And if you are willing to accept it, he is the Elijah who was to come. 15He who has ears, let him hear.

16"To what can I compare this generation? They are like children sitting in the marketplaces and calling out to others:

17" 'We played the flute for you,
　　and you did not dance;
　we sang a dirge,
　　and you did not mourn.'

18For John came neither eating nor drinking, and they say, 'He has a demon.' 19The Son of Man came eating and drinking, and they say, 'Here is a glutton and a drunkard, a friend of tax collectors and "sinners." ' But wisdom is proved right by her actions."

Woe on Unrepentant Cities

20Then Jesus began to denounce the cities in which most of his miracles had been performed, because they did not repent. 21"Woe to you, Korazin! Woe to you, Bethsaida! If the miracles that were performed in you had been performed in Tyre and Sidon, they would have repented long ago in sackcloth and ashes. 22But I tell you, it will be more bearable for Tyre and Sidon on the day of judgment than for you. 23And you, Capernaum, will you be lifted up to the skies? No, you will go down to the depths.ª If the miracles that were performed in you had been performed in Sodom, it would have remained to this day. 24But I tell you that it will be more bearable for Sodom on the day of judgment than for you."

ª 23 Greek Hades

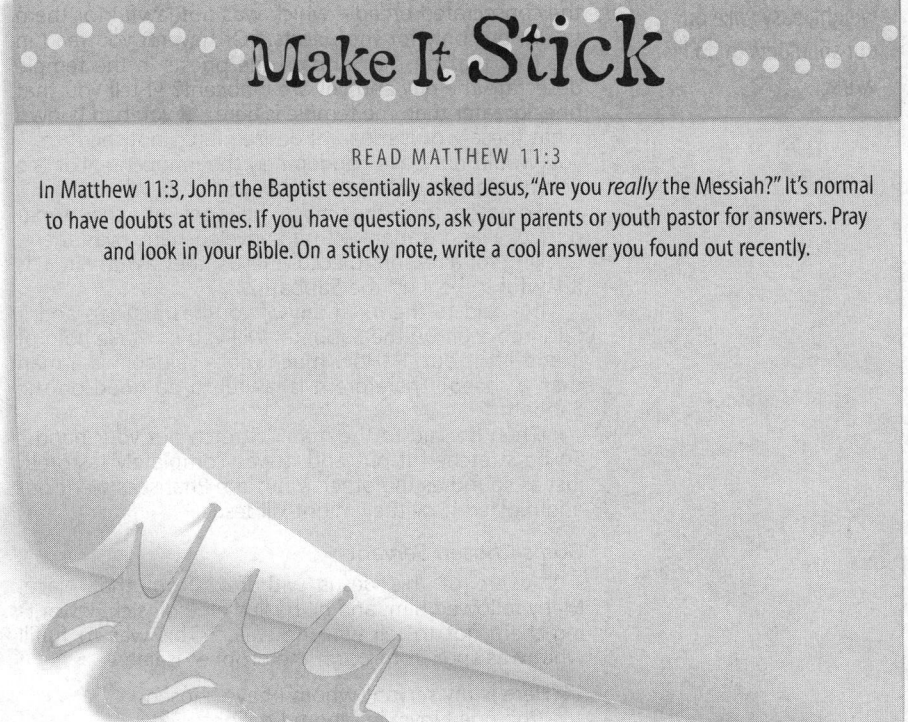

Make It Stick

READ MATTHEW 11:3

In Matthew 11:3, John the Baptist essentially asked Jesus, "Are you *really* the Messiah?" It's normal to have doubts at times. If you have questions, ask your parents or youth pastor for answers. Pray and look in your Bible. On a sticky note, write a cool answer you found out recently.

Get a Load of This...

When Jesus said, "Take my yoke upon you" (Matthew 11:29), he was not talking about being egged. Oxen wore a yoke on their shoulders to pull a plow, and Jesus was telling us to take *his* super-light-weight, easy yoke on our shoulders to do his work.

Rest for the Weary

25 At that time Jesus said, "I praise you, Father, Lord of heaven and earth, because you have hidden these things from the wise and learned, and revealed them to little children. 26 Yes, Father, for this was your good pleasure.

27 "All things have been committed to me by my Father. No one knows the Son except the Father, and no one knows the Father except the Son and those to whom the Son chooses to reveal him.

28 "Come to me, all you who are weary and burdened, and I will give you rest. 29 Take my yoke upon you and learn from me, for I am gentle and humble in heart, and you will find rest for your souls. 30 For my yoke is easy and my burden is light."

Lord of the Sabbath

12 At that time Jesus went through the grainfields on the Sabbath. His disciples were hungry and began to pick some heads of grain and eat them. 2 When the Pharisees saw this, they said to him, "Look! Your disciples are doing what is unlawful on the Sabbath."

3 He answered, "Haven't you read what David did when he and his companions were hungry? 4 He entered the house of God, and he and his companions ate the consecrated bread—which was not lawful for them to do, but only for the priests. 5 Or haven't you read in the Law that on the Sabbath the priests in the temple desecrate the day and yet are innocent? 6 I tell you that one*a* greater than the temple is here. 7 If you had known what these words mean, 'I desire mercy, not sacrifice,'*b* you would not have condemned the innocent. 8 For the Son of Man is Lord of the Sabbath."

9 Going on from that place, he went into their synagogue, 10 and a man with a shriveled hand was there. Looking for a reason to accuse Jesus, they asked him, "Is it lawful to heal on the Sabbath?"

11 He said to them, "If any of you has a sheep and it falls into a pit on the Sabbath, will you not take hold of it and lift it out? 12 How much more valuable is a man than a sheep! Therefore it is lawful to do good on the Sabbath."

13 Then he said to the man, "Stretch out your hand." So he stretched it out and it was completely restored, just as sound as the other. 14 But the Pharisees went out and plotted how they might kill Jesus.

God's Chosen Servant

15 Aware of this, Jesus withdrew from that place. Many followed him, and he healed all their sick, 16 warning them not to tell who he was. 17 This was to fulfill what was spoken through the prophet Isaiah:

18 "Here is my servant whom I have chosen,
     the one I love, in whom I delight;

a 6 Or *something*; also in verses 41 and 42   *b 7* Hosea 6:6

I will put my Spirit on him,
and he will proclaim justice to the
nations.
19 He will not quarrel or cry out;
no one will hear his voice in the
streets.
20 A bruised reed he will not break,
and a smoldering wick he will not
snuff out,
till he leads justice to victory.
21   In his name the nations will put their
hope." *a*

Jesus and Beelzebub

22 Then they brought him a demon-possessed man who was blind and mute, and
Jesus healed him, so that he could both
talk and see. 23 All the people were astonished and said, "Could this be the Son of
David?"

24 But when the Pharisees heard this,
they said, "It is only by Beelzebub, *b* the
prince of demons, that this fellow drives
out demons."

25 Jesus knew their thoughts and said to
them, "Every kingdom divided against itself will be ruined, and every city or household divided against itself will not stand.
26 If Satan drives out Satan, he is divided
against himself. How then can his kingdom stand? 27 And if I drive out demons
by Beelzebub, by whom do your people
drive them out? So then, they will be your
judges. 28 But if I drive out demons by the
Spirit of God, then the kingdom of God
has come upon you.

29 "Or again, how can anyone enter a
strong man's house and carry off his possessions unless he first ties up the strong
man? Then he can rob his house.

30 "He who is not with me is against me,
and he who does not gather with me
scatters. 31 And so I tell you, every sin and
blasphemy will be forgiven men, but the
blasphemy against the Spirit will not be
forgiven. 32 Anyone who speaks a word
against the Son of Man will be forgiven,
but anyone who speaks against the Holy

a 21 Isaiah 42:1–4   *b 24* Greek *Beezeboul* or *Beelzeboul*;
also in verse 27

Kingdoms Divided

READ MATTHEW 12:25

If you and your friends decided to make a movie, what would it be
like if one guy wanted sci-fi, another wanted a war flick, the third
wanted car chases and you wanted some good laughs? Unless you
agree on just one approach, your movie would never work. You'd end
up with *Space Clowns in Corvettes Vs. the Kamikazes*! It's
the same when you go about God's business—kingdom business. Even well-meaning people have disagreements. Why?
They have different styles and personalities. Well, that's life. As
Christians, we *don't* have to pretend our differences don't
exist. Sure we can disagree, but not to the point that it tears
apart your family and friendships. Since "every kingdom divided against itself will be ruined" (verse
25), men of God *do* need to work through their
disagreements and work together for one goal.
Keep in mind the ultimate goal—to serve God
together.

Your next reading is on page 1243.

Spirit will not be forgiven, either in this age or in the age to come.

³³"Make a tree good and its fruit will be good, or make a tree bad and its fruit will be bad, for a tree is recognized by its fruit. ³⁴You brood of vipers, how can you who are evil say anything good? For out of the overflow of the heart the mouth speaks. ³⁵The good man brings good things out of the good stored up in him, and the evil man brings evil things out of the evil stored up in him. ³⁶But I tell you that men will have to give account on the day of judgment for every careless word they have spoken. ³⁷For by your words you will be acquitted, and by your words you will be condemned."

The Sign of Jonah

³⁸Then some of the Pharisees and teachers of the law said to him, "Teacher, we want to see a miraculous sign from you."

³⁹He answered, "A wicked and adulterous generation asks for a miraculous sign! But none will be given it except the sign of the prophet Jonah. ⁴⁰For as Jonah was three days and three nights in the belly of a huge fish, so the Son of Man will be three days and three nights in the heart of the earth. ⁴¹The men of Nineveh will stand up at the judgment with this generation and condemn it; for they repented at the preaching of Jonah, and now one*ᵃ* greater than Jonah is here. ⁴²The Queen of the South will rise at the judgment with this generation and condemn it; for she came from the ends of the earth to listen to Solomon's wisdom, and now one greater than Solomon is here.

⁴³"When an evil*ᵇ* spirit comes out of a man, it goes through arid places seeking rest and does not find it. ⁴⁴Then it says, 'I will return to the house I left.' When it arrives, it finds the house unoccupied, swept clean and put in order. ⁴⁵Then it goes and takes with it seven other spirits more wicked than itself, and they go in and live there. And the final condition of that man is worse than the first. That is how it will be with this wicked generation."

Jesus' Mother and Brothers

⁴⁶While Jesus was still talking to the crowd, his mother and brothers stood outside, wanting to speak to him. ⁴⁷Someone told him, "Your mother and brothers are standing outside, wanting to speak to you."*ᶜ*

⁴⁸He replied to him, "Who is my mother, and who are my brothers?" ⁴⁹Pointing to his disciples, he said, "Here are my mother and my brothers. ⁵⁰For whoever does the will of my Father in heaven is my brother and sister and mother."

The Parable of the Sower

13 That same day Jesus went out of the house and sat by the lake. ²Such large crowds gathered around him that he got into a boat and sat in it, while all the people stood on the shore. ³Then he told them many things in parables, saying: "A farmer went out to sow his seed. ⁴As he was scattering the seed, some fell along the path, and the birds came and ate it up. ⁵Some fell on rocky places, where it did not have much soil. It sprang up quickly, because the soil was shallow. ⁶But when the sun came up, the plants were scorched, and they withered because they had no root. ⁷Other seed fell among thorns, which grew up and choked the plants. ⁸Still other seed fell on good soil, where it produced a crop—a hundred, sixty or thirty times what was sown. ⁹He who has ears, let him hear."

¹⁰The disciples came to him and asked, "Why do you speak to the people in parables?"

¹¹He replied, "The knowledge of the secrets of the kingdom of heaven has been given to you, but not to them. ¹²Whoever has will be given more, and he will have an abundance. Whoever does not have, even what he has will be taken from him. ¹³This is why I speak to them in parables:

"Though seeing, they do not see;
    though hearing, they do not hear or
        understand.

¹⁴In them is fulfilled the prophecy of Isaiah:

" 'You will be ever hearing but never
        understanding;
    you will be ever seeing but never
        perceiving.
¹⁵For this people's heart has become
        calloused;
    they hardly hear with their ears,
    and they have closed their eyes.

ᵃ 41 Or *something*; also in verse 42   *ᵇ 43* Greek *unclean*
ᶜ 47 Some manuscripts do not have verse 47.

Otherwise they might see with their
    eyes,
  hear with their ears,
  understand with their hearts
and turn, and I would heal them.' [a]

[16] But blessed are your eyes because they see, and your ears because they hear. [17] For I tell you the truth, many prophets and righteous men longed to see what you see but did not see it, and to hear what you hear but did not hear it.

[18] "Listen then to what the parable of the sower means: [19] When anyone hears the message about the kingdom and does not understand it, the evil one comes and snatches away what was sown in his heart. This is the seed sown along the path. [20] The one who received the seed that fell on rocky places is the man who hears the word and at once receives it with joy. [21] But since he has no root, he lasts only a short time. When trouble or persecution comes because of the word, he quickly falls away. [22] The one who received the seed that fell among the thorns is the man who hears the word, but the worries of this life and the deceitfulness of wealth choke it, making it unfruitful. [23] But the one who received the seed that fell on good soil is the man who hears the word and understands it. He produces a crop, yielding a hundred, sixty or thirty times what was sown."

The Parable of the Weeds

[24] Jesus told them another parable: "The kingdom of heaven is like a man who sowed good seed in his field. [25] But while everyone was sleeping, his enemy came and sowed weeds among the wheat, and went away. [26] When the wheat sprouted and formed heads, then the weeds also appeared.

[27] "The owner's servants came to him and said, 'Sir, didn't you sow good seed in your field? Where then did the weeds come from?'

[28] " 'An enemy did this,' he replied.

[a] 15 Isaiah 6:9,10

Farmer Brown's Crop

READ MATTHEW 13:1-9, 18-23

OK, Farmer Brown, it's time to choose your soil. Let's check your options. The path? Throwing your seed there is like planting on pavement. The wind just blows it away. Next. The rock pile? Sure, there's hardly any dirt, but aren't those rocks pretty? Some little plants came up, but the sun roasted them like popcorn. Nope. The thorn patch? Yeah, you got a few plants but you haven't weeded in ages—which plants are which? What's left? "Still other seed fell on good soil, where it produced a crop—a hundred ... times what was sown" (verse 8). Pavement, rocks, thorn bushes—have you tried *soil*, Farmer Brown? Yeah—good, rich dirt. A little fertilizer, sunshine and enough water, and you got yourself a crop. And don't forget to weed it. What's this mean to Christians? It means ground yourself in God's Word, water with prayer and get enough "Son"shine. Pull out your sin-weeds regularly. Then grow, man, grow.

Your next reading is on page 1248.

"The servants asked him, 'Do you want us to go and pull them up?'

29 " 'No,' he answered, 'because while you are pulling the weeds, you may root up the wheat with them. 30Let both grow together until the harvest. At that time I will tell the harvesters: First collect the weeds and tie them in bundles to be burned; then gather the wheat and bring it into my barn.' "

The Parables of the Mustard Seed and the Yeast

31He told them another parable: "The kingdom of heaven is like a mustard seed, which a man took and planted in his field. 32Though it is the smallest of all your seeds, yet when it grows, it is the largest of garden plants and becomes a tree, so that the birds of the air come and perch in its branches."

33He told them still another parable: "The kingdom of heaven is like yeast that a woman took and mixed into a large amount*a* of flour until it worked all through the dough."

34Jesus spoke all these things to the crowd in parables; he did not say anything to them without using a parable. 35So was fulfilled what was spoken through the prophet:

"I will open my mouth in parables,
    I will utter things hidden since the
        creation of the world." *b*

The Parable of the Weeds Explained

36Then he left the crowd and went into the house. His disciples came to him and said, "Explain to us the parable of the weeds in the field."

37He answered, "The one who sowed the good seed is the Son of Man. 38The field is the world, and the good seed stands for the sons of the kingdom. The weeds are the sons of the evil one, 39and the enemy who sows them is the devil. The harvest is the end of the age, and the harvesters are angels.

40"As the weeds are pulled up and burned in the fire, so it will be at the end of the age. 41The Son of Man will send out his angels, and they will weed out of his kingdom everything that causes sin and all who do evil. 42They will throw them into the fiery furnace, where there will be weeping and gnashing of teeth. 43Then the righteous will shine like the sun in the kingdom of their Father. He who has ears, let him hear.

The Parables of the Hidden Treasure and the Pearl

44"The kingdom of heaven is like treasure hidden in a field. When a man found it, he hid it again, and then in his joy went and sold all he had and bought that field.

45"Again, the kingdom of heaven is like a merchant looking for fine pearls. 46When he found one of great value, he went away and sold everything he had and bought it.

The Parable of the Net

47"Once again, the kingdom of heaven is like a net that was let down into the lake and caught all kinds of fish. 48When it was full, the fishermen pulled it up on the shore. Then they sat down and collected the good fish in baskets, but threw the bad away. 49This is how it will be at the end of the age. The angels will come and separate the wicked from the righteous 50and throw them into the fiery furnace, where there will be weeping and gnashing of teeth.

51"Have you understood all these things?" Jesus asked.

"Yes," they replied.

52He said to them, "Therefore every teacher of the law who has been instructed about the kingdom of heaven is like the owner of a house who brings out of his storeroom new treasures as well as old."

A Prophet Without Honor

53When Jesus had finished these parables, he moved on from there. 54Coming to his hometown, he began teaching the people in their synagogue, and they were amazed. "Where did this man get this wisdom and these miraculous powers?" they asked. 55"Isn't this the carpenter's son? Isn't his mother's name Mary, and aren't his brothers James, Joseph, Simon and Judas? 56Aren't all his sisters with us? Where then did this man get all these things?" 57And they took offense at him.

But Jesus said to them, "Only in his hometown and in his own house is a prophet without honor."

58And he did not do many miracles there because of their lack of faith.

---

a 33 Greek three *satas* (probably about 1/2 bushel or 22 liters)
b 35 Psalm 78:2

John the Baptist Beheaded

14 At that time Herod the tetrarch heard the reports about Jesus, ²and he said to his attendants, "This is John the Baptist; he has risen from the dead! That is why miraculous powers are at work in him."

³Now Herod had arrested John and bound him and put him in prison because of Herodias, his brother Philip's wife, ⁴for John had been saying to him: "It is not lawful for you to have her." ⁵Herod wanted to kill John, but he was afraid of the people, because they considered him a prophet.

⁶On Herod's birthday the daughter of Herodias danced for them and pleased Herod so much ⁷that he promised with an oath to give her whatever she asked. ⁸Prompted by her mother, she said, "Give me here on a platter the head of John the Baptist." ⁹The king was distressed, but because of his oaths and his dinner guests, he ordered that her request be granted

¹⁰and had John beheaded in the prison. ¹¹His head was brought in on a platter and given to the girl, who carried it to her mother. ¹²John's disciples came and took his body and buried it. Then they went and told Jesus.

Jesus Feeds the Five Thousand

¹³When Jesus heard what had happened, he withdrew by boat privately to a solitary place. Hearing of this, the crowds followed him on foot from the towns. ¹⁴When Jesus landed and saw a large crowd, he had compassion on them and healed their sick.

¹⁵As evening approached, the disciples came to him and said, "This is a remote place, and it's already getting late. Send the crowds away, so they can go to the villages and buy themselves some food."

¹⁶Jesus replied, "They do not need to go away. You give them something to eat."

¹⁷"We have here only five loaves of bread and two fish," they answered.

Make It Stick

READ MATTHEW 13:44

Imagine building a sand castle when suddenly your shovel goes "clunk" and you dig up a treasure chest (see Matthew 13:44)! You should desire salvation and heaven and all the things of God as much as a chest of pirate treasure. Draw a treasure chest on a sticky note or describe what would be inside of it.

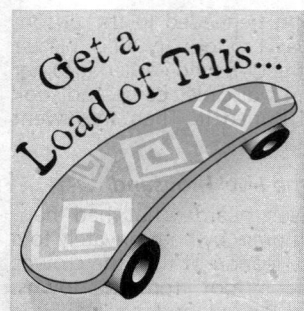

Get a Load of This...

Jesus talked about a net that scooped up all kinds of fish. Some were so disgusting nobody would eat them, so they got tossed (see Matthew 13:47–50). Did you ever catch a bottom-feeder and wanted to keep it, but your dad made you throw it back?

18"Bring them here to me," he said. 19And he directed the people to sit down on the grass. Taking the five loaves and the two fish and looking up to heaven, he gave thanks and broke the loaves. Then he gave them to the disciples, and the disciples gave them to the people. 20They all ate and were satisfied, and the disciples picked up twelve basketfuls of broken pieces that were left over. 21The number of those who ate was about five thousand men, besides women and children.

Jesus Walks on the Water

22Immediately Jesus made the disciples get into the boat and go on ahead of him to the other side, while he dismissed the crowd. 23After he had dismissed them, he went up on a mountainside by himself to pray. When evening came, he was there alone, 24but the boat was already a considerable distance*a* from land, buffeted by the waves because the wind was against it.

25During the fourth watch of the night Jesus went out to them, walking on the lake. 26When the disciples saw him walking on the lake, they were terrified. "It's a ghost," they said, and cried out in fear.

27But Jesus immediately said to them: "Take courage! It is I. Don't be afraid."

28"Lord, if it's you," Peter replied, "tell me to come to you on the water."

29"Come," he said.

Then Peter got down out of the boat, walked on the water and came toward Jesus. 30But when he saw the wind, he was afraid and, beginning to sink, cried out, "Lord, save me!"

31Immediately Jesus reached out his hand and caught him. "You of little faith," he said, "why did you doubt?"

32And when they climbed into the boat, the wind died down. 33Then those who were in the boat worshiped him, saying, "Truly you are the Son of God."

34When they had crossed over, they landed at Gennesaret. 35And when the men of that place recognized Jesus, they sent word to all the surrounding country. People brought all their sick to him 36and begged him to let the sick just touch the edge of his cloak, and all who touched him were healed.

Clean and Unclean

15 Then some Pharisees and teachers of the law came to Jesus from Jerusalem and asked, 2"Why do your disciples break the tradition of the elders? They don't wash their hands before they eat!"

3Jesus replied, "And why do you break the command of God for the sake of your tradition? 4For God said, 'Honor your father and mother'*b* and 'Anyone who curses his father or mother must be put to death.'*c* 5But

a 24 Greek *many stadia*　　*b 4* Exodus 20:12; Deut. 5:16　　*c 4* Exodus 21:17; Lev. 20:9

you say that if a man says to his father or mother, 'Whatever help you might otherwise have received from me is a gift devoted to God,' 6he is not to 'honor his father*a*' with it. Thus you nullify the word of God for the sake of your tradition. 7You hypocrites! Isaiah was right when he prophesied about you:

8" 'These people honor me with their lips,
  but their hearts are far from me.
9They worship me in vain;
  their teachings are but rules taught by men.'*b*"

10Jesus called the crowd to him and said, "Listen and understand. 11What goes into a man's mouth does not make him 'unclean,' but what comes out of his mouth, that is what makes him 'unclean.' "

12Then the disciples came to him and asked, "Do you know that the Pharisees were offended when they heard this?"

13He replied, "Every plant that my heavenly Father has not planted will be pulled up by the roots. 14Leave them; they are blind guides.*c* If a blind man leads a blind man, both will fall into a pit."

15Peter said, "Explain the parable to us."

16"Are you still so dull?" Jesus asked them. 17"Don't you see that whatever enters the mouth goes into the stomach and then out of the body? 18But the things that come out of the mouth come from the heart, and these make a man 'unclean.' 19For out of the heart come evil thoughts, murder, adultery, sexual immorality, theft, false testimony, slander. 20These are what make a man 'unclean'; but eating with unwashed hands does not make him 'unclean.' "

The Faith of the Canaanite Woman

21Leaving that place, Jesus withdrew to the region of Tyre and Sidon. 22A Canaanite woman from that vicinity came to him, crying out, "Lord, Son of David, have mercy on me! My daughter is suffering terribly from demon-possession."

23Jesus did not answer a word. So his disciples came to him and urged him, "Send her away, for she keeps crying out after us."

24He answered, "I was sent only to the lost sheep of Israel."

25The woman came and knelt before him. "Lord, help me!" she said.

26He replied, "It is not right to take the children's bread and toss it to their dogs."

27"Yes, Lord," she said, "but even the dogs eat the crumbs that fall from their masters' table."

28Then Jesus answered, "Woman, you have great faith! Your request is granted." And her daughter was healed from that very hour.

a 6 Some manuscripts *father or his mother*   *b 9* Isaiah 29:13   *c 14* Some manuscripts *guides of the blind*

Gross!

Herod's promise got John beheaded (see Matthew 14:1–12). Be very careful what you promise someone. If a friend asks you, "If I tell you something, will you promise not to tell anyone else?" *don't* always say "yes." It could be something lowlife, dangerous or wrong. Never make a promise without knowing what you're agreeing to.

Jesus Feeds the Four Thousand

²⁹Jesus left there and went along the Sea of Galilee. Then he went up on a mountainside and sat down. ³⁰Great crowds came to him, bringing the lame, the blind, the crippled, the mute and many others, and laid them at his feet; and he healed them. ³¹The people were amazed when they saw the mute speaking, the crippled made well, the lame walking and the blind seeing. And they praised the God of Israel.

³²Jesus called his disciples to him and said, "I have compassion for these people; they have already been with me three days and have nothing to eat. I do not want to send them away hungry, or they may collapse on the way."

³³His disciples answered, "Where could we get enough bread in this remote place to feed such a crowd?"

³⁴"How many loaves do you have?" Jesus asked.

"Seven," they replied, "and a few small fish."

³⁵He told the crowd to sit down on the ground. ³⁶Then he took the seven loaves and the fish, and when he had given thanks, he broke them and gave them to the disciples, and they in turn to the people. ³⁷They all ate and were satisfied. Afterward the disciples picked up seven basketfuls of broken pieces that were left over. ³⁸The number of those who ate was four thousand, besides women and children. ³⁹After Jesus had sent the crowd away, he got into the boat and went to the vicinity of Magadan.

The Demand for a Sign

16 The Pharisees and Sadducees came to Jesus and tested him by asking him to show them a sign from heaven.

²He replied,ᵃ "When evening comes, you say, 'It will be fair weather, for the sky is red,' ³and in the morning, 'Today it will be stormy, for the sky is red and overcast.' You know how to interpret the appearance of the sky, but you cannot interpret

---

ᵃ *2* Some early manuscripts do not have the rest of verse 2 and all of verse 3.

Walking on Waves

READ MATTHEW 14:22–34

Got the picture? The disciples are in a boat, it's dark, the wind blows furiously and waves pound the boat. They're already scared when suddenly—they see Jesus walking along the waves! Peter thought, "That's cool. Can I do it, too?" Jesus said, "Sure." Pete stepped out and did his water-walk until *Bloop!*—down he went. Later, Jesus told Peter that he had little faith. But look what Peter *did* with "little" faith! When the disciples saw this miracle, they confessed that Jesus was the Son of God! But the cool thing is that this miracle helped Jesus with a basic problem: He needed to get from the beach to the boat. So he walked!

God's willing to help with little things we think we shouldn't even bother him about—not just the big stuff. God will even give you strength for a job or wisdom in your science class. There's nothing too small for him.

Your next reading is on page 1250.

the signs of the times. ⁴A wicked and adulterous generation looks for a miraculous sign, but none will be given it except the sign of Jonah." Jesus then left them and went away.

The Yeast of the Pharisees and Sadducees

⁵When they went across the lake, the disciples forgot to take bread. ⁶"Be careful," Jesus said to them. "Be on your guard against the yeast of the Pharisees and Sadducees."

⁷They discussed this among themselves and said, "It is because we didn't bring any bread."

⁸Aware of their discussion, Jesus asked, "You of little faith, why are you talking among yourselves about having no bread? ⁹Do you still not understand? Don't you remember the five loaves for the five thousand, and how many basketfuls you gathered? ¹⁰Or the seven loaves for the four thousand, and how many basketfuls you gathered? ¹¹How is it you don't understand that I was not talking to you about bread? But be on your guard against the yeast of the Pharisees and Sadducees." ¹²Then they understood that he was not telling them to guard against the yeast used in bread, but against the teaching of the Pharisees and Sadducees.

Peter's Confession of Christ

¹³When Jesus came to the region of Caesarea Philippi, he asked his disciples, "Who do people say the Son of Man is?"

¹⁴They replied, "Some say John the Baptist; others say Elijah; and still others, Jeremiah or one of the prophets."

¹⁵"But what about you?" he asked. "Who do you say I am?"

¹⁶Simon Peter answered, "You are the Christ,ᵃ the Son of the living God."

¹⁷Jesus replied, "Blessed are you, Simon son of Jonah, for this was not revealed to you by man, but by my Father in heaven. ¹⁸And I tell you that you are Peter,ᵇ and on this rock I will build my church, and the gates of Hadesᶜ will not overcome it.ᵈ ¹⁹I will give you the keys of the kingdom of heaven; whatever you bind on earth will beᵉ bound in heaven, and whatever you loose on earth will beᵉ loosed in heaven." ²⁰Then he warned his disciples not to tell anyone that he was the Christ.

Jesus Predicts His Death

²¹From that time on Jesus began to explain to his disciples that he must go to Jerusalem and suffer many things at the hands of the elders, chief priests and teachers of the law, and that he must be killed and on the third day be raised to life.

²²Peter took him aside and began to rebuke him. "Never, Lord!" he said. "This shall never happen to you!"

Get a Load of This...

There's a saying: "Red sky tonight, sailor's delight. Red sky in the morning, sailor's warning." That may sound like a weather report from Mars, but it's actually talking about a red sunrise or sunset on Earth. Know where that saying came from? From Matthew 16:2–3.

ᵃ 16 Or Messiah; also in verse 20   ᵇ 18 Peter means rock.   ᶜ 18 Or hell
ᵈ 18 Or not prove stronger than it   ᵉ 19 Or have been

²³Jesus turned and said to Peter, "Get behind me, Satan! You are a stumbling block to me; you do not have in mind the things of God, but the things of men."

²⁴Then Jesus said to his disciples, "If anyone would come after me, he must deny himself and take up his cross and follow me. ²⁵For whoever wants to save his life[a] will lose it, but whoever loses his life for me will find it. ²⁶What good will it be for a man if he gains the whole world, yet forfeits his soul? Or what can a man give in exchange for his soul? ²⁷For the Son of Man is going to come in his Father's glory with his angels, and then he will reward each person according to what he has done. ²⁸I tell you the truth, some who are standing here will not taste death before they see the Son of Man coming in his kingdom."

The Transfiguration

17 After six days Jesus took with him Peter, James and John the brother of James, and led them up a high mountain by themselves. ²There he was transfigured before them. His face shone like the sun, and his clothes became as white as the light. ³Just then there appeared before them Moses and Elijah, talking with Jesus.

⁴Peter said to Jesus, "Lord, it is good for us to be here. If you wish, I will put up three shelters—one for you, one for Moses and one for Elijah."

⁵While he was still speaking, a bright cloud enveloped them, and a voice from the cloud said, "This is my Son, whom I love; with him I am well pleased. Listen to him!"

⁶When the disciples heard this, they fell facedown to the ground, terrified. ⁷But Jesus came and touched them. "Get up," he said. "Don't be afraid." ⁸When they looked up, they saw no one except Jesus.

⁹As they were coming down the mountain, Jesus instructed them, "Don't tell anyone what you have seen, until the Son of Man has been raised from the dead."

¹⁰The disciples asked him, "Why then

---

[a] *25* The Greek word means either *life* or *soul*; also in verse 26.

Peter Speaks Up

READ MATTHEW 16:13–23

First, Peter says that Jesus is the Messiah, and Jesus calls Peter the Rock. Then after Jesus predicts his death, Peter blurts out, "No way that'll happen to *you*, Lord!" Then Jesus tells him, "Get behind me, Satan!" Um ... quite a contrast here. Peter gets it really right then really wrong. That's OK. We all make mistakes. We just need to learn from them. Over time we'll get it more right than wrong.

Your next reading is on page 1251.

do the teachers of the law say that Elijah must come first?"

¹¹Jesus replied, "To be sure, Elijah comes and will restore all things. ¹²But I tell you, Elijah has already come, and they did not recognize him, but have done to him everything they wished. In the same way the Son of Man is going to suffer at their hands." ¹³Then the disciples understood that he was talking to them about John the Baptist.

The Healing of a Boy With a Demon

¹⁴When they came to the crowd, a man approached Jesus and knelt before him. ¹⁵"Lord, have mercy on my son," he said. "He has seizures and is suffering greatly. He often falls into the fire or into the water. ¹⁶I brought him to your disciples, but they could not heal him."

¹⁷"O unbelieving and perverse generation," Jesus replied, "how long shall I stay with you? How long shall I put up with you? Bring the boy here to me." ¹⁸Jesus rebuked the demon, and it came out of the boy, and he was healed from that moment.

¹⁹Then the disciples came to Jesus in private and asked, "Why couldn't we drive it out?"

²⁰He replied, "Because you have so little faith. I tell you the truth, if you have faith as small as a mustard seed, you can say to this mountain, 'Move from here to there' and it will move. Nothing will be impossible for you. *a*"

²²When they came together in Galilee, he said to them, "The Son of Man is going to be betrayed into the hands of men. ²³They will kill him, and on the third day he will be raised to life." And the disciples were filled with grief.

The Temple Tax

²⁴After Jesus and his disciples arrived in Capernaum, the collectors of the two-drachma tax came to Peter and asked, "Doesn't your teacher pay the temple tax *b*?"

²⁵"Yes, he does," he replied.

When Peter came into the house, Jesus

a 20 Some manuscripts *you.* ²¹But this kind does not go out except by prayer and fasting.   *b 24* Greek *the two drachmas*

Take Up Your Cross
READ MATTHEW 16:24–26

Jesus obeyed God even though that meant getting nailed to the cross. Chances are good we won't be crucified, but Jesus said a Christian must "deny himself and take up his cross and follow [him]" (verse 24). To "take up your cross" means fulfilling God's plan for your life. God wants you to give him the steering wheel. Why? So he can park you and leave you to rust on a boring back street? Not. Because he loves you so much that he wants the *best* for you. He can't take you to all those good places unless he's in the driver's seat. If you try to "save" your life by keeping control, you'll miss out on all the good stuff. You want life— *real* life? Get God behind the steering wheel. Scoot over, buckle up and take the ride. *Now* you're going places!

Your next reading is on page 1254.

was the first to speak. "What do you think, Simon?" he asked. "From whom do the kings of the earth collect duty and taxes—from their own sons or from others?"

26"From others," Peter answered.

"Then the sons are exempt," Jesus said to him. 27"But so that we may not offend them, go to the lake and throw out your line. Take the first fish you catch; open its mouth and you will find a four-drachma coin. Take it and give it to them for my tax and yours."

The Greatest in the Kingdom of Heaven

18 At that time the disciples came to Jesus and asked, "Who is the greatest in the kingdom of heaven?"

2He called a little child and had him stand among them. 3And he said: "I tell you the truth, unless you change and become like little children, you will never enter the kingdom of heaven. 4Therefore, whoever humbles himself like this child is the greatest in the kingdom of heaven. 5"And whoever welcomes a little child like this in my name welcomes me. 6But if anyone causes one of these little ones who believe in me to sin, it would be better for him to have a large millstone hung around his neck and to be drowned in the depths of the sea.

7"Woe to the world because of the things that cause people to sin! Such things must come, but woe to the man through whom they come! 8If your hand or your foot causes you to sin, cut it off and throw it away. It is better for you to enter life maimed or crippled than to have two hands or two feet and be thrown into eternal fire. 9And if your eye causes you to sin, gouge it out and throw it away. It is better for you to enter life with one eye than to have two eyes and be thrown into the fire of hell.

Make It Stick

READ MATTHEW 17:1–9

Moses and Elijah showed up, buddies now—even though they had lived five hundred years apart—and were visiting and chatting with Jesus (see Matthew 17:3). This is a lot like how it will be in heaven. If you could get a chance to sit down and talk with Elijah or Moses, what would you ask them? Write your question on a sticky note.

The Parable of the Lost Sheep

10"See that you do not look down on one of these little ones. For I tell you that their angels in heaven always see the face of my Father in heaven. [a]

12"What do you think? If a man owns a hundred sheep, and one of them wanders away, will he not leave the ninety-nine on the hills and go to look for the one that wandered off? 13And if he finds it, I tell you the truth, he is happier about that one sheep than about the ninety-nine that did not wander off. 14In the same way your Father in heaven is not willing that any of these little ones should be lost.

A Brother Who Sins Against You

15"If your brother sins against you, [b] go and show him his fault, just between the two of you. If he listens to you, you have won your brother over. 16But if he will not listen, take one or two others along, so that 'every matter may be established by the testimony of two or three witnesses.' [c] 17If he refuses to listen to them, tell it to the church; and if he refuses to listen even to the church, treat him as you would a pagan or a tax collector.

18"I tell you the truth, whatever you bind on earth will be [d] bound in heaven, and whatever you loose on earth will be [d] loosed in heaven.

19"Again, I tell you that if two of you on earth agree about anything you ask for, it will be done for you by my Father in heaven. 20For where two or three come together in my name, there am I with them."

The Parable of the Unmerciful Servant

21Then Peter came to Jesus and asked, "Lord, how many times shall I forgive my brother when he sins against me? Up to seven times?"

22Jesus answered, "I tell you, not seven times, but seventy-seven times. [e]

23"Therefore, the kingdom of heaven is like a king who wanted to settle accounts with his servants. 24As he began the settlement, a man who owed him ten thousand talents [f] was brought to him. 25Since he was not able to pay, the master ordered that he and his wife and his children and all that he had be sold to repay the debt.

26"The servant fell on his knees before him. 'Be patient with me,' he begged, 'and I will pay back everything.' 27The servant's master took pity on him, canceled the debt and let him go.

28"But when that servant went out, he found one of his fellow servants who owed him a hundred denarii. [g] He grabbed him and began to choke him. 'Pay back what you owe me!' he demanded.

29"His fellow servant fell to his knees and begged him, 'Be patient with me, and I will pay you back.'

30"But he refused. Instead, he went off and had the

Gross!

Check out Matthew 18:9. What would your eyeball look like if you gouged it out and tossed it away? We're talking major pain. OK, Jesus didn't *really* intend you to do this! This is an example of hyperbole, going over the top to get a point across, like if you saw a $50 baseball card and said, "That must be worth a million bucks!"

a 10 Some manuscripts *heaven*. 11*The Son of Man came to save what was lost.*
b 15 Some manuscripts do not have *against you.*   c 16 Deut. 19:15
d 18 Or *have been*   e 22 Or *seventy times seven*   f 24 That is, millions of dollars   g 28 That is, a few dollars

man thrown into prison until he could pay the debt. ³¹When the other servants saw what had happened, they were greatly distressed and went and told their master everything that had happened.

³²"Then the master called the servant in. 'You wicked servant,' he said, 'I canceled all that debt of yours because you begged me to. ³³Shouldn't you have had mercy on your fellow servant just as I had on you?' ³⁴In anger his master turned him over to the jailers to be tortured, until he should pay back all he owed.

³⁵"This is how my heavenly Father will treat each of you unless you forgive your brother from your heart."

Divorce

19 When Jesus had finished saying these things, he left Galilee and went into the region of Judea to the other side of the Jordan. ²Large crowds followed him, and he healed them there.

³Some Pharisees came to him to test him. They asked, "Is it lawful for a man to divorce his wife for any and every reason?"

⁴"Haven't you read," he replied, "that at the beginning the Creator 'made them male and female,'ᵃ ⁵and said, 'For this reason a man will leave his father and mother and be united to his wife, and the two will become one flesh'ᵇ? ⁶So they are no longer two, but one. Therefore what God has joined together, let man not separate."

⁷"Why then," they asked, "did Moses command that a man give his wife a certificate of divorce and send her away?"

⁸Jesus replied, "Moses permitted you to divorce your wives because your hearts were hard. But it was not this way from the beginning. ⁹I tell you that anyone who divorces his wife, except for marital unfaithfulness, and marries another woman commits adultery."

¹⁰The disciples said to him, "If this is the situation between a husband and wife, it is better not to marry."

¹¹Jesus replied, "Not everyone can accept this word, but only those to whom it has been given. ¹²For some are eunuchs

ᵃ4 Gen. 1:27   ᵇ5 Gen. 2:24

Payback Time? Nope

READ MATTHEW 18:15–17, 21–35

When people do things that bug you, you can give them the cold shoulder, get mad and yell at them, or mouth off to everyone else about what bad things they've done. Not. These "solutions" just lead to bigger problems. Jesus says to go *talk* with the person, tell him or her how you feel and try to sort things out. Peter brought up a good point: "That's fine. But what if the guy *keeps* bugging me?" Jesus said to forgive "seventy-seven times" (verse 22). That's how much God keeps forgiving you—more times than you can count. We all need to be forgiven, but if we do payback to others—Look out!—God will pay us back, too. He gets *verrrrry* unhappy when we don't forgive each other. *How* unhappy? Read verses 34–35 again. The point here is, if a person doesn't forgive others, they are setting themselves above God's plan of mercy and outside his kingdom of love.

Your next reading is on page 1255.

because they were born that way; others were made that way by men; and others have renounced marriage[a] because of the kingdom of heaven. The one who can accept this should accept it."

The Little Children and Jesus

[13]Then little children were brought to Jesus for him to place his hands on them and pray for them. But the disciples rebuked those who brought them.

[14]Jesus said, "Let the little children come to me, and do not hinder them, for the kingdom of heaven belongs to such as these." [15]When he had placed his hands on them, he went on from there.

The Rich Young Man

[16]Now a man came up to Jesus and asked, "Teacher, what good thing must I do to get eternal life?"

[17]"Why do you ask me about what is good?" Jesus replied. "There is only One who is good. If you want to enter life, obey the commandments."

[18]"Which ones?" the man inquired.

Jesus replied, " 'Do not murder, do not commit adultery, do not steal, do not give false testimony, [19]honor your father and mother,'[b] and 'love your neighbor as yourself.'[c]"

[20]"All these I have kept," the young man said. "What do I still lack?"

[21]Jesus answered, "If you want to be perfect, go, sell your possessions and give to the poor, and you will have treasure in heaven. Then come, follow me."

[22]When the young man heard this, he went away sad, because he had great wealth.

[23]Then Jesus said to his disciples, "I tell you the truth, it is hard for a rich man to enter the kingdom of heaven. [24]Again I tell you, it is easier for a camel to go through the eye of a needle than for a rich man to enter the kingdom of God."

[25]When the disciples heard this, they were greatly astonished and asked, "Who then can be saved?"

[26]Jesus looked at them and said, "With

---

[a] 12 Or *have made themselves eunuchs*
[b] 19 Exodus 20:12–16; Deut. 5:16–20   [c] 19 Lev. 19:18

The Rich Young Ruler

READ MATTHEW 19:16–30

Here was a rich, powerful guy who seemed to have it made. In Jesus' day, a lot of people believed that if you were godly and kept every tiny little rule, that God would bless you with riches. Not quite. This young man was living by godly principles and was rich, but something big was missing. He asked Jesus, "What *good* thing must I do to get eternal life?" What he didn't have was a relationship with God. If you have ever been into stamp collecting, you know how easy it is to get totally preoccupied collecting stamps. At the end of the day though, when you lift your head up out of your stamp book, you realize that life is *so* much more than just collecting stamps. It's the same with rules: Don't just follow God's principles of hard work to try to get rich. Make sure you're plugged into God for real adventure.

Your next reading is on page 1256.

man this is impossible, but with God all things are possible."

²⁷Peter answered him, "We have left everything to follow you! What then will there be for us?"

²⁸Jesus said to them, "I tell you the truth, at the renewal of all things, when the Son of Man sits on his glorious throne, you who have followed me will also sit on twelve thrones, judging the twelve tribes of Israel. ²⁹And everyone who has left houses or brothers or sisters or father or mother*a* or children or fields for my sake will receive a hundred times as much and will inherit eternal life. ³⁰But many who are first will be last, and many who are last will be first.

The Parable of the Workers in the Vineyard

20 "For the kingdom of heaven is like a landowner who went out early in the morning to hire men to work in his vineyard. ²He agreed to pay them a denarius for the day and sent them into his vineyard.

³"About the third hour he went out and saw others standing in the marketplace doing nothing. ⁴He told them, 'You also go and work in my vineyard, and I will pay you whatever is right.' ⁵So they went.

"He went out again about the sixth hour and the ninth hour and did the same thing. ⁶About the eleventh hour he went out and found still others standing around. He asked them, 'Why have you been standing here all day long doing nothing?'

⁷" 'Because no one has hired us,' they answered.

"He said to them, 'You also go and work in my vineyard.'

⁸"When evening came, the owner of the vineyard said to his foreman, 'Call the workers and pay them their wages, beginning with the last ones hired and going on to the first.'

⁹"The workers who were hired about the eleventh hour came and each received a denarius. ¹⁰So when those came who were hired first, they expected to receive more. But each one of them also received a denarius. ¹¹When they received it, they

a 29 Some manuscripts mother or wife

Arm Wrestling

READ MATTHEW 20:1–16

Just because some boy boasts that he has the biggest muscles of all and can beat anyone else in arm wrestling, doesn't make him the top athlete. Some "weaker" boy could be a better gymnast or baseball player, right?—or better on a skateboard. So don't compare yourself with others. Life isn't about being the best. In Jesus' story, a landowner paid all his workers the same flat rate no matter how little or much they worked. Doesn't seem fair? Hey, there's an important point here: God will reward you according to how well you do with the talent *you* were given. Don't go looking at others and think they're not doing much. The problem with comparing yourself with others is that you end up doing *only* enough to be "better" than other people. If you're talented at something, then do the best *you* can do.

Your next reading is on page 1258.

began to grumble against the landowner. ¹²'These men who were hired last worked only one hour,' they said, 'and you have made them equal to us who have borne the burden of the work and the heat of the day.'

¹³"But he answered one of them, 'Friend, I am not being unfair to you. Didn't you agree to work for a denarius? ¹⁴Take your pay and go. I want to give the man who was hired last the same as I gave you. ¹⁵Don't I have the right to do what I want with my own money? Or are you envious because I am generous?'

¹⁶"So the last will be first, and the first will be last."

Jesus Again Predicts His Death

¹⁷Now as Jesus was going up to Jerusalem, he took the twelve disciples aside and said to them, ¹⁸"We are going up to Jerusalem, and the Son of Man will be betrayed to the chief priests and the teachers of the law. They will condemn him to death ¹⁹and will turn him over to the Gentiles to be mocked and flogged and crucified. On the third day he will be raised to life!"

A Mother's Request

²⁰Then the mother of Zebedee's sons came to Jesus with her sons and, kneeling down, asked a favor of him.

²¹"What is it you want?" he asked.

She said, "Grant that one of these two sons of mine may sit at your right and the other at your left in your kingdom."

²²"You don't know what you are asking," Jesus said to them. "Can you drink the cup I am going to drink?"

"We can," they answered.

²³Jesus said to them, "You will indeed drink from my cup, but to sit at my right or left is not for me to grant. These places belong to those for whom they have been prepared by my Father."

²⁴When the ten heard about this, they were indignant with the two brothers. ²⁵Jesus called them together and said, "You know that the rulers of the Gentiles lord it over them, and their high officials exercise authority over them. ²⁶Not so with you. Instead, whoever wants to become great among you must be your servant, ²⁷and whoever wants to be first must be your slave— ²⁸just as the Son of Man did not come to be served, but to serve, and to give his life as a ransom for many."

Two Blind Men Receive Sight

²⁹As Jesus and his disciples were leaving Jericho, a large crowd followed him. ³⁰Two blind men were sitting by the roadside, and when they heard that Jesus was going by, they shouted, "Lord, Son of David, have mercy on us!"

³¹The crowd rebuked them and told them to be quiet, but they shouted all the louder, "Lord, Son of David, have mercy on us!"

³²Jesus stopped and called them. "What do you want me to do for you?" he asked.

³³"Lord," they answered, "we want our sight."

³⁴Jesus had compassion on them and touched their eyes. Immediately they received their sight and followed him.

The Triumphal Entry

21 As they approached Jerusalem and came to Bethphage on the Mount of Olives, Jesus sent two disciples, ²saying to them, "Go to the village ahead of you, and at once you will find a donkey tied there, with her colt by her. Untie them and bring them to me. ³If anyone says anything to you, tell him that the Lord needs them, and he will send them right away."

⁴This took place to fulfill what was spoken through the prophet:

⁵"Say to the Daughter of Zion,
  'See, your king comes to you,
gentle and riding on a donkey,
  on a colt, the foal of a donkey.' "ᵃ

⁶The disciples went and did as Jesus had instructed them. ⁷They brought the donkey and the colt, placed their cloaks on them, and Jesus sat on them. ⁸A very large crowd spread their cloaks on the road, while others cut branches from the trees and spread them on the road. ⁹The crowds that went ahead of him and those that followed shouted,

"Hosannaᵇ to the Son of David!"

"Blessed is he who comes in the name of the Lord!"ᶜ

"Hosannaᵇ in the highest!"

ᵃ 5 Zech. 9:9   ᵇ 9 A Hebrew expression meaning "Save!" which became an exclamation of praise; also in verse 15
ᶜ 9 Psalm 118:26

¹⁰When Jesus entered Jerusalem, the whole city was stirred and asked, "Who is this?"

¹¹The crowds answered, "This is Jesus, the prophet from Nazareth in Galilee."

Jesus at the Temple

¹²Jesus entered the temple area and drove out all who were buying and selling there. He overturned the tables of the money changers and the benches of those selling doves. ¹³"It is written," he said to them, " 'My house will be called a house of prayer,'ᵃ but you are making it a 'den of robbers.'ᵇ"

¹⁴The blind and the lame came to him at the temple, and he healed them. ¹⁵But when the chief priests and the teachers of the law saw the wonderful things he did and the children shouting in the temple area, "Hosanna to the Son of David," they were indignant.

¹⁶"Do you hear what these children are saying?" they asked him.

"Yes," replied Jesus, "have you never read,

" 'From the lips of children and infants you have ordained praise'ᶜ?"

¹⁷And he left them and went out of the city to Bethany, where he spent the night.

The Fig Tree Withers

¹⁸Early in the morning, as he was on his way back to the city, he was hungry. ¹⁹Seeing a fig tree by the road, he went up to it but found nothing on it except leaves. Then he said to it, "May you never bear fruit again!" Immediately the tree withered.

²⁰When the disciples saw this, they were amazed. "How did the fig tree wither so quickly?" they asked.

²¹Jesus replied, "I tell you the truth, if you have faith and do not doubt, not only can you do what was done to the fig tree, but also you can say to this mountain, 'Go, throw yourself into the sea,' and it will be done. ²²If you believe, you will receive whatever you ask for in prayer."

The Authority of Jesus Questioned

²³Jesus entered the temple courts, and,

ᵃ 13 Isaiah 56:7   ᵇ 13 Jer. 7:11   ᶜ 16 Psalm 8:2

Son of David

READ MATTHEW 21:1–16

Talk about a double standard: The religious leaders criticized the children for shouting *praises* in the temple, yet they were overcharging and cheating the people who bought sacrifices to worship in the temple! Un-be-liev-able. They were especially mad that the kids called Jesus the "Son of David." That was a title for the Messiah, and the men in control of the temple weren't about to believe that Jesus was the Messiah. But God had given the children eyes to see the truth: Jesus absolutely was the promised Son of David, the Messiah the Jews had been awaiting for centuries. God often uses small things instead of big things. Case in point: the way he used the kids in this story to teach the adults an important lesson.

Your next reading is on page 1262.

while he was teaching, the chief priests and the elders of the people came to him. "By what authority are you doing these things?" they asked. "And who gave you this authority?"

^{24}Jesus replied, "I will also ask you one question. If you answer me, I will tell you by what authority I am doing these things. ^{25}John's baptism—where did it come from? Was it from heaven, or from men?"

They discussed it among themselves and said, "If we say, 'From heaven,' he will ask, 'Then why didn't you believe him?' ^{26}But if we say, 'From men'—we are afraid of the people, for they all hold that John was a prophet."

^{27}So they answered Jesus, "We don't know."

Then he said, "Neither will I tell you by what authority I am doing these things.

The Parable of the Two Sons

^{28}"What do you think? There was a man who had two sons. He went to the first and said, 'Son, go and work today in the vineyard.'

^{29}" 'I will not,' he answered, but later he changed his mind and went.

^{30}"Then the father went to the other son and said the same thing. He answered, 'I will, sir,' but he did not go.

^{31}"Which of the two did what his father wanted?"

"The first," they answered.

Jesus said to them, "I tell you the truth, the tax collectors and the prostitutes are entering the kingdom of God ahead of you. ^{32}For John came to you to show you the way of righteousness, and you did not believe him, but the tax collectors and the prostitutes did. And even after you saw this, you did not repent and believe him.

The Parable of the Tenants

^{33}"Listen to another parable: There was a landowner who planted a vineyard. He put a wall around it, dug a winepress in it and built a watchtower. Then he rented the vineyard to some farmers and went away on a journey. ^{34}When the harvest time approached, he sent his servants to the tenants to collect his fruit.

^{35}"The tenants seized his servants; they beat one, killed another, and stoned a third. ^{36}Then he sent other servants to them, more than the first time, and the tenants treated them the same way. ^{37}Last of all, he sent his son to them. 'They will respect my son,' he said.

^{38}"But when the tenants saw the son, they said to each other, 'This is the heir. Come, let's kill him and take his inheritance.' ^{39}So they took him and threw him out of the vineyard and killed him.

^{40}"Therefore, when the owner of the vineyard comes, what will he do to those tenants?"

^{41}"He will bring those wretches to a wretched end," they replied, "and he will rent the vineyard to other tenants, who will give him his share of the crop at harvest time."

^{42}Jesus said to them, "Have you never read in the Scriptures:

Get a Load of This...

It's often wise to answer a question by asking a question, like Jesus did (see Matthew 21:23–25). But do *not* try this with your parents. For example, don't answer them: "Well, let me ask you: Is *your* bedroom clean?"

" 'The stone the builders rejected
  has become the capstone[a];
the Lord has done this,
  and it is marvelous in our eyes'[b]?

43"Therefore I tell you that the kingdom of God will be taken away from you and given to a people who will produce its fruit. 44He who falls on this stone will be broken to pieces, but he on whom it falls will be crushed."[c]

45When the chief priests and the Pharisees heard Jesus' parables, they knew he was talking about them. 46They looked for a way to arrest him, but they were afraid of the crowd because the people held that he was a prophet.

The Parable of the Wedding Banquet

22 Jesus spoke to them again in parables, saying: 2"The kingdom of heaven is like a king who prepared a wedding banquet for his son. 3He sent his servants to those who had been invited to the banquet to tell them to come, but they refused to come.

4"Then he sent some more servants and said, 'Tell those who have been invited that I have prepared my dinner: My oxen and fattened cattle have been butchered, and everything is ready. Come to the wedding banquet.'

5"But they paid no attention and went off—one to his field, another to his business. 6The rest seized his servants, mistreated them and killed them. 7The king was enraged. He sent his army and destroyed those murderers and burned their city.

8"Then he said to his servants, 'The wedding banquet is ready, but those I invited did not deserve to come. 9Go to the street corners and invite to the banquet anyone you find.' 10So the servants went out into the streets and gathered all the

a 42 Or cornerstone   b 42 Psalm 118:22,23   c 44 Some manuscripts do not have verse 44.

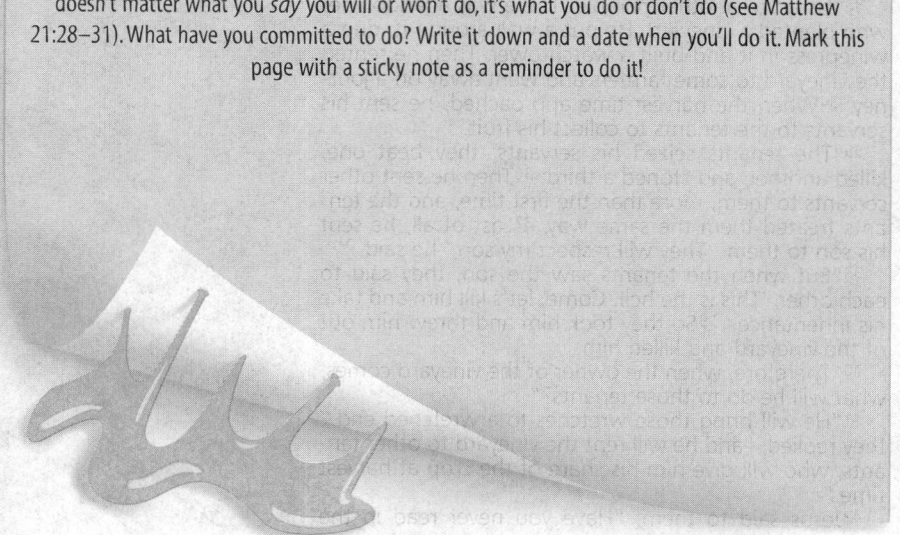

Make It Stick

READ MATTHEW 21:28–31

Do you say you'll do something, but then can't be bothered, or "forget" to do it? In the end it really doesn't matter what you *say* you will or won't do, it's what you do or don't do (see Matthew 21:28–31). What have you committed to do? Write it down and a date when you'll do it. Mark this page with a sticky note as a reminder to do it!

people they could find, both good and bad, and the wedding hall was filled with guests.

11 "But when the king came in to see the guests, he noticed a man there who was not wearing wedding clothes. 12 'Friend,' he asked, 'how did you get in here without wedding clothes?' The man was speechless.

13 "Then the king told the attendants, 'Tie him hand and foot, and throw him outside, into the darkness, where there will be weeping and gnashing of teeth.'

14 "For many are invited, but few are chosen."

Paying Taxes to Caesar

15 Then the Pharisees went out and laid plans to trap him in his words. 16 They sent their disciples to him along with the Herodians. "Teacher," they said, "we know you are a man of integrity and that you teach the way of God in accordance with the truth. You aren't swayed by men, because you pay no attention to who they are. 17 Tell us then, what is your opinion? Is it right to pay taxes to Caesar or not?"

18 But Jesus, knowing their evil intent, said, "You hypocrites, why are you trying to trap me? 19 Show me the coin used for paying the tax." They brought him a denarius, 20 and he asked them, "Whose portrait is this? And whose inscription?"

21 "Caesar's," they replied.

Then he said to them, "Give to Caesar what is Caesar's, and to God what is God's."

22 When they heard this, they were amazed. So they left him and went away.

Marriage at the Resurrection

23 That same day the Sadducees, who say there is no resurrection, came to him with a question. 24 "Teacher," they said, "Moses told us that if a man dies without having children, his brother must marry the widow and have children for him. 25 Now there were seven brothers among us. The first one married and died, and since he had no children, he left his wife to his brother. 26 The same thing happened to the second and third brother, right on down to the seventh. 27 Finally, the woman died. 28 Now then, at the resurrection, whose wife will she be of the seven, since all of them were married to her?"

29 Jesus replied, "You are in error because you do not know the Scriptures or the power of God. 30 At the resurrection people will neither marry nor be given in marriage; they will be like the angels in heaven. 31 But about the resurrection of the dead— have you not read what God said to you, 32 'I am the God of Abraham, the God of Isaac, and the God of Jacob'[a]? He is not the God of the dead but of the living."

33 When the crowds heard this, they were astonished at his teaching.

The Greatest Commandment

34 Hearing that Jesus had silenced the Sadducees, the Pharisees got together. 35 One of them, an expert in the law, tested him with this question: 36 "Teacher, which is the greatest commandment in the Law?"

37 Jesus replied: " 'Love the Lord your God with all your heart and with all your soul and with all your mind.'[b] 38 This is the first and greatest commandment. 39 And the second is like it: 'Love your neighbor as yourself.'[c] 40 All the Law and the Prophets hang on these two commandments."

Whose Son Is the Christ?

41 While the Pharisees were gathered together, Jesus asked them, 42 "What do you think about the Christ[d]? Whose son is he?"

"The son of David," they replied.

43 He said to them, "How is it then that David, speaking by the Spirit, calls him 'Lord'? For he says,

44 " 'The Lord said to my Lord:
   "Sit at my right hand
until I put your enemies
   under your feet." '[e]

45 If then David calls him 'Lord,' how can he be his son?" 46 No one could say a word in reply, and from that day on no one dared to ask him any more questions.

Seven Woes

23 Then Jesus said to the crowds and to his disciples: 2 "The teachers of the law and the Pharisees sit in Moses' seat. 3 So you must obey them and do everything they tell you. But do not do what they do, for they do not practice what they preach. 4 They tie up heavy loads and put them on

a 32 Exodus 3:6   b 37 Deut. 6:5   c 39 Lev. 19:18
d 42 Or Messiah   e 44 Psalm 110:1

men's shoulders, but they themselves are not willing to lift a finger to move them.

5 "Everything they do is done for men to see: They make their phylacteries*a* wide and the tassels on their garments long; 6they love the place of honor at banquets and the most important seats in the synagogues; 7they love to be greeted in the marketplaces and to have men call them 'Rabbi.'

8 "But you are not to be called 'Rabbi,' for you have only one Master and you are all brothers. 9And do not call anyone on earth 'father,' for you have one Father, and he is in heaven. 10Nor are you to be called 'teacher,' for you have one Teacher, the Christ.*b* 11The greatest among you will be your servant. 12For whoever exalts himself will be humbled, and whoever humbles himself will be exalted.

13 "Woe to you, teachers of the law and Pharisees, you hypocrites! You shut the kingdom of heaven in men's faces. You yourselves do not enter, nor will you let those enter who are trying to.*c*

15 "Woe to you, teachers of the law and Pharisees, you hypocrites! You travel over land and sea to win a single convert, and when he becomes one, you make him twice as much a son of hell as you are.

16 "Woe to you, blind guides! You say, 'If anyone swears by the temple, it means nothing; but if anyone swears by the gold of the temple, he is bound by his oath.' 17You blind fools! Which is greater: the gold, or the temple that makes the gold sacred? 18You also say, 'If anyone swears by the altar, it means nothing; but if anyone swears by the gift on it, he is bound by his oath.' 19You blind men! Which is greater: the gift, or the altar that makes the gift sacred? 20Therefore, he who swears by the altar swears by it and by everything on it. 21And he who swears by the temple swears by it and by the one who dwells in it. 22And he who swears by heaven swears by God's throne and by the one who sits on it.

a 5 That is, boxes containing Scripture verses, worn on forehead and arm   *b 10* Or *Messiah*   *c 13* Some manuscripts to. *14Woe to you, teachers of the law and Pharisees, you hypocrites! You devour widows' houses and for a show make lengthy prayers. Therefore you will be punished more severely.*

The Greatest Commandments

READ MATTHEW 22:34–40

Imagine Academy Awards for movie props. "In the category of best-looking fake cactus, the winner is …" Sounds pretty dumb, doesn't it? Props are not the focus of movies. Actors are. When it comes to the focus of life, that's found in verses 37–39: Love God and love your neighbor as yourself. Life isn't about things; it's about people and relationships. When God commands us to do something, he's doing it for our own good. Jesus narrowed things down to the two most important commandments in life so we could have better relationships with people and with him. Don't get so distracted by physical things around you. Focus on obeying these two commands—loving God and loving others—and you'll have a great life. Everything else is secondary. "Cut! Who told the rocks they could take a break?"

Your next reading is on page 1263.

23"Woe to you, teachers of the law and Pharisees, you hypocrites! You give a tenth of your spices—mint, dill and cummin. But you have neglected the more important matters of the law—justice, mercy and faithfulness. You should have practiced the latter, without neglecting the former. 24You blind guides! You strain out a gnat but swallow a camel.

25"Woe to you, teachers of the law and Pharisees, you hypocrites! You clean the outside of the cup and dish, but inside they are full of greed and self-indulgence. 26Blind Pharisee! First clean the inside of the cup and dish, and then the outside also will be clean.

27"Woe to you, teachers of the law and Pharisees, you hypocrites! You are like whitewashed tombs, which look beautiful on the outside but on the inside are full of dead men's bones and everything unclean. 28In the same way, on the outside you appear to people as righteous but on the inside you are full of hypocrisy and wickedness.

29"Woe to you, teachers of the law and Pharisees, you hypocrites! You build tombs for the prophets and decorate the graves of the righteous. 30And you say, 'If we had lived in the days of our forefathers, we would not have taken part with them in shedding the blood of the prophets.' 31So you testify against yourselves that you are the descendants of those who murdered the prophets. 32Fill up, then, the measure of the sin of your forefathers!

33"You snakes! You brood of vipers! How will you escape being condemned to hell? 34Therefore I am sending you prophets and wise men and teachers. Some of them you will kill and crucify; others you will flog in your synagogues and pursue from town to town. 35And so upon you will come all the righteous blood that has been shed on earth, from the blood of righteous Abel to the blood of Zechariah son of Berekiah, whom you murdered between the temple and the altar. 36I tell you the truth, all this will come upon this generation.

37"O Jerusalem, Jerusalem, you who kill the prophets and stone those sent to you,

GET SMARTER

Scripture Sun Shades

READ MATTHEW 23:5

You can read all you want about performing brain surgery; *doing* it is a little trickier. In the same way, it's easier to memorize Bible verses than it is to live them. You might win a prize for quoting the Ten Commandments, but if you lie and steal, what good is the prize? The Pharisees made large, showy phylacteries (boxes with Scriptures inside) and tied them to their forehead and hands. Now, Moses did talk about binding God's laws to your forehead in Deuteronomy 6:8, but he *meant* "Get the Word in your minds and hearts." The Pharisees thought it meant, "Decorate your foreheads." Their phylacteries were so big they were like sun shades. God meant for you to focus on his Word and live by it, but the Pharisees wore passages of Scripture literally and ignored the One who gave the rules. Bottom line? Learn and memorize Bible verses, yes, but more importantly, live them out.

Your next reading is on page 1265.

Get a
Load of This...

Check out Matthew 23:24. And for his *next* act, Pharisee Phil will swallow this camel! Whole! Ladies and gentlemen, move back. Please move back. Give him space. Take any small children from the room. This is not going to be a pretty sight. (Hey, this was figurative, or symbolic, way of Jesus telling the Pharisees to pay more attention to the bigger, more important matters of the law, not just the little stuff.)

how often I have longed to gather your children together, as a hen gathers her chicks under her wings, but you were not willing. ³⁸Look, your house is left to you desolate. ³⁹For I tell you, you will not see me again until you say, 'Blessed is he who comes in the name of the Lord.'ᵃ"

Signs of the End of the Age

24 Jesus left the temple and was walking away when his disciples came up to him to call his attention to its buildings. ²"Do you see all these things?" he asked. "I tell you the truth, not one stone here will be left on another; every one will be thrown down."

³As Jesus was sitting on the Mount of Olives, the disciples came to him privately. "Tell us," they said, "when will this happen, and what will be the sign of your coming and of the end of the age?"

⁴Jesus answered: "Watch out that no one deceives you. ⁵For many will come in my name, claiming, 'I am the Christ,ᵇ' and will deceive many. ⁶You will hear of wars and rumors of wars, but see to it that you are not alarmed. Such things must happen, but the end is still to come. ⁷Nation will rise against nation, and kingdom against kingdom. There will be famines and earthquakes in various places. ⁸All these are the beginning of birth pains.

⁹"Then you will be handed over to be persecuted and put to death, and you will be hated by all nations because of me. ¹⁰At that time many will turn away from the faith and will betray and hate each other, ¹¹and many false prophets will appear and deceive many people. ¹²Because of the increase of wickedness, the love of most will grow cold, ¹³but he who stands firm to the end will be saved. ¹⁴And this gospel of the kingdom will be preached in the whole world as a testimony to all nations, and then the end will come.

¹⁵"So when you see standing in the holy place 'the abomination that causes desolation,'ᶜ spoken of through the prophet Daniel—let the reader understand— ¹⁶then let those who are in Judea flee to the mountains. ¹⁷Let no one on the roof of his house go down to take anything out of the house. ¹⁸Let no one in the field go back to get his cloak. ¹⁹How dreadful it will be in those days for pregnant women and nursing mothers! ²⁰Pray that your flight will not take place in winter or on the Sabbath. ²¹For then there will be great distress, unequaled from the beginning of the world until now—and never to be equaled again. ²²If those days had not been cut short, no one would survive, but for the sake of the elect those days will be shortened. ²³At that time if anyone says to you, 'Look, here is the Christ!' or, 'There he is!' do not believe it. ²⁴For false Christs and false prophets will appear and perform

ᵃ 39 Psalm 118:26   ᵇ 5 Or *Messiah*; also in verse 23   ᶜ 15 Daniel 9:27; 11:31; 12:11

great signs and miracles to deceive even the elect—if that were possible. 25See, I have told you ahead of time.

26"So if anyone tells you, 'There he is, out in the desert,' do not go out; or, 'Here he is, in the inner rooms,' do not believe it. 27For as lightning that comes from the east is visible even in the west, so will be the coming of the Son of Man. 28Wherever there is a carcass, there the vultures will gather.

29"Immediately after the distress of those days

" 'the sun will be darkened,
    and the moon will not give its light;
the stars will fall from the sky,
    and the heavenly bodies will be
        shaken.'a

30"At that time the sign of the Son of Man will appear in the sky, and all the nations of the earth will mourn. They will see the Son of Man coming on the clouds of the sky, with power and great glory. 31And he will send his angels with a loud trumpet call, and they will gather his elect from the four winds, from one end of the heavens to the other.

32"Now learn this lesson from the fig tree: As soon as its twigs get tender and its leaves come out, you know that summer is near. 33Even so, when you see all these things, you know that itb is near, right at the door. 34I tell you the truth, this generationc will certainly not pass away until all these things have happened. 35Heaven and earth will pass away, but my words will never pass away.

The Day and Hour Unknown

36"No one knows about that day or hour, not even the angels in heaven, nor the Son,d but only the Father. 37As it was in the days of Noah, so it will be at the coming of the Son of Man. 38For in the days before the flood, people were eating and drinking, marrying and giving in marriage, up to the day Noah entered the ark; 39and they knew nothing about what would happen until the flood came and took them all

a 29 Isaiah 13:10; 34:4   b 33 Or he   c 34 Or race
d 36 Some manuscripts do not have nor the Son.

The End Time

READ MATTHEW 24:1–21, 29–31

Verses 4–14 describe things that show us we're living in the end time. Earthquakes, wars, famines, false prophets? Sure, "such things must happen, but the end is still to come" (verse 6). The key is verse 14: "And this gospel of the kingdom will be preached . . . to all nations, and then the end will come." That has *not* happened yet. A lot of people read Daniel and Revelation and Matthew 24 and go bananas trying to figure out how soon Jesus will return. Bible prophecy is interesting, and God *wants* us to read it, but we're not supposed to get tunnel vision over it. Before Jesus returned to heaven, the disciples were all hyped asking how soon everything would happen. Jesus said, "It is not for you to know the times or dates." Then he told them what they *should* do: get going and preach the gospel (see Acts 1:7–8).

Your next reading is on page 1267.

Get a Load of This...

Check out Matthew 24:28. *Carcass* is such an interesting word. Say "kar-cuss." Say it five times. Think of ways to use this word, like, "Move your carcass."

away. That is how it will be at the coming of the Son of Man. 40Two men will be in the field; one will be taken and the other left. 41Two women will be grinding with a hand mill; one will be taken and the other left.

42"Therefore keep watch, because you do not know on what day your Lord will come. 43But understand this: If the owner of the house had known at what time of night the thief was coming, he would have kept watch and would not have let his house be broken into. 44So you also must be ready, because the Son of Man will come at an hour when you do not expect him.

45"Who then is the faithful and wise servant, whom the master has put in charge of the servants in his household to give them their food at the proper time? 46It will be good for that servant whose master finds him doing so when he returns. 47I tell you the truth, he will put him in charge of all his possessions. 48But suppose that servant is wicked and says to himself, 'My master is staying away a long time,' 49and he then begins to beat his fellow servants and to eat and drink with drunkards. 50The master of that servant will come on a day when he does not expect him and at an hour he is not aware of. 51He will cut him to pieces and assign him a place with the hypocrites, where there will be weeping and gnashing of teeth.

The Parable of the Ten Virgins

25 "At that time the kingdom of heaven will be like ten virgins who took their lamps and went out to meet the bridegroom. 2Five of them were foolish and five were wise. 3The foolish ones took their lamps but did not take any oil with them. 4The wise, however, took oil in jars along with their lamps. 5The bridegroom was a long time in coming, and they all became drowsy and fell asleep.

6"At midnight the cry rang out: 'Here's the bridegroom! Come out to meet him!'

7"Then all the virgins woke up and trimmed their lamps. 8The foolish ones said to the wise, 'Give us some of your oil; our lamps are going out.'

9"'No,' they replied, 'there may not be enough for both us and you. Instead, go to those who sell oil and buy some for yourselves.'

10"But while they were on their way to buy the oil, the bridegroom arrived. The virgins who were ready went in with him to the wedding banquet. And the door was shut.

11"Later the others also came. 'Sir! Sir!' they said. 'Open the door for us!'

12"But he replied, 'I tell you the truth, I don't know you.'

13"Therefore keep watch, because you do not know the day or the hour.

The Parable of the Talents

14"Again, it will be like a man going on a journey, who called his servants and entrusted his property to them. ¹⁵To one he gave five talents*ᵃ* of money, to another two talents, and to another one talent, each according to his ability. Then he went on his journey. ¹⁶The man who had received the five talents went at once and put his money to work and gained five more. ¹⁷So also, the one with the two talents gained two more. ¹⁸But the man who had received the one talent went off, dug a hole in the ground and hid his master's money.

¹⁹"After a long time the master of those servants returned and settled accounts with them. ²⁰The man who had received the five talents brought the other five. 'Master,' he said, 'you entrusted me with five talents. See, I have gained five more.'

²¹"His master replied, 'Well done, good and faithful servant! You have been faithful with a few things; I will put you in charge of many things. Come and share your master's happiness!'

²²"The man with the two talents also came. 'Master,' he said, 'you entrusted me with two talents; see, I have gained two more.'

²³"His master replied, 'Well done, good and faithful servant! You have been faithful with a few things; I will put you in charge of many things. Come and share your master's happiness!'

²⁴"Then the man who had received the one talent came. 'Master,' he said, 'I knew that you are a hard man, harvesting where you have not sown and gathering where you have not scattered seed. ²⁵So I was afraid and went out and hid your talent in the ground. See, here is what belongs to you.'

²⁶"His master replied, 'You wicked, lazy servant! So you knew that I harvest where I have not sown and gather where I have not scattered seed? ²⁷Well then, you should have put my money on deposit with the bankers, so that when I returned I would have received it back with interest.

²⁸" 'Take the talent from him and give it to the one who has the ten talents. ²⁹For everyone who has will be given more, and he will have an abundance. Whoever does not have, even what he has will be taken

ᵃ 15 A talent was worth more than a thousand dollars.

GET SMARTER

Talents and Treasure Chests

READ MATTHEW 25:14–30

After attacking a ship on the high seas, pirates often buried their treasure in a deserted place so no one would find it. But because pirates were generally a bunch of brawny dunderheads, and their treasure maps were so bad, they often forgot where the booty was buried. Thus, the pirates never got to enjoy it, and neither did the people they took it from. Blimey, what a waste! Someone who receives a gift from God but doesn't use it is just like those pirates. What they have is extremely valuable, but if they don't use it, no one benefits. When God gives us something, he expects us to use it to help his kingdom, not just bury it and forget about it. And, best of all, when we use our gifts, he gives us more (Matthew 25:21). Are you using the talents God has given you?

Your next reading is on page 1269.

from him. 30And throw that worthless servant outside, into the darkness, where there will be weeping and gnashing of teeth.'

The Sheep and the Goats

31"When the Son of Man comes in his glory, and all the angels with him, he will sit on his throne in heavenly glory. 32All the nations will be gathered before him, and he will separate the people one from another as a shepherd separates the sheep from the goats. 33He will put the sheep on his right and the goats on his left.

34"Then the King will say to those on his right, 'Come, you who are blessed by my Father; take your inheritance, the kingdom prepared for you since the creation of the world. 35For I was hungry and you gave me something to eat, I was thirsty and you gave me something to drink, I was a stranger and you invited me in, 36I needed clothes and you clothed me, I was sick and you looked after me, I was in prison and you came to visit me.'

37"Then the righteous will answer him, 'Lord, when did we see you hungry and feed you, or thirsty and give you something to drink? 38When did we see you a stranger and invite you in, or needing clothes and clothe you? 39When did we see you sick or in prison and go to visit you?'

40"The King will reply, 'I tell you the truth, whatever you did for one of the least of these brothers of mine, you did for me.'

41"Then he will say to those on his left, 'Depart from me, you who are cursed, into the eternal fire prepared for the devil and his angels. 42For I was hungry and you gave me nothing to eat, I was thirsty and you gave me nothing to drink, 43I was a stranger and you did not invite me in, I needed clothes and you did not clothe me, I was sick and in prison and you did not look after me.'

44"They also will answer, 'Lord, when did we see you hungry or thirsty or a stranger or needing clothes or sick or in prison, and did not help you?'

45"He will reply, 'I tell you the truth, whatever you did not do for one of the least of these, you did not do for me.'

46"Then they will go away to eternal punishment, but the righteous to eternal life."

The Plot Against Jesus

26 When Jesus had finished saying all these things, he said to his disciples, 2"As you know, the Passover is two days away—and the Son of Man will be handed over to be crucified."

3Then the chief priests and the elders of the people assembled in the palace of the high priest, whose name was Caiaphas, 4and they plotted to arrest Jesus in some sly way and kill him. 5"But not during the Feast," they said, "or there may be a riot among the people."

Jesus Anointed at Bethany

6While Jesus was in Bethany in the home of a man known as Simon the Leper, 7a woman came to him with an alabaster jar of very expensive perfume, which she poured on his head as he was reclining at the table.

8When the disciples saw this, they were indignant. "Why this waste?" they asked. 9"This perfume could have been sold at a high price and the money given to the poor."

10Aware of this, Jesus said to them, "Why are you bothering this woman? She has done a beautiful thing to me. 11The poor you will always have with you, but you will not always have me. 12When she poured this perfume on my body, she did it to prepare me for burial. 13I tell you the truth, wherever this gospel is preached throughout the world, what she has done will also be told, in memory of her."

Judas Agrees to Betray Jesus

14Then one of the Twelve—the one called Judas Iscariot—went to the chief priests 15and asked, "What are you willing to give me if I hand him over to you?" So they counted out for him thirty silver coins. 16From then on Judas watched for an opportunity to hand him over.

The Lord's Supper

17On the first day of the Feast of Unleavened Bread, the disciples came to Jesus and asked, "Where do you want us to make preparations for you to eat the Passover?"

18He replied, "Go into the city to a certain man and tell him, 'The Teacher says: My appointed time is near. I am going to celebrate the Passover with my disciples at your house.' " ¹⁹So the disciples did as Jesus had directed them and prepared the Passover.

²⁰When evening came, Jesus was reclining at the table with the Twelve. ²¹And while they were eating, he said, "I tell you the truth, one of you will betray me."

²²They were very sad and began to say to him one after the other, "Surely not I, Lord?"

²³Jesus replied, "The one who has dipped his hand into the bowl with me will betray me. ²⁴The Son of Man will go just as it is written about him. But woe to that man who betrays the Son of Man! It would be better for him if he had not been born."

²⁵Then Judas, the one who would betray him, said, "Surely not I, Rabbi?"

Jesus answered, "Yes, it is you."ᵃ

²⁶While they were eating, Jesus took bread, gave thanks and broke it, and gave it to his disciples, saying, "Take and eat; this is my body."

²⁷Then he took the cup, gave thanks and offered it to them, saying, "Drink from it, all of you. ²⁸This is my blood of theᵇ covenant, which is poured out for many for the forgiveness of sins. ²⁹I tell you, I will not drink of this fruit of the vine from now on until that day when I drink it anew with you in my Father's kingdom."

³⁰When they had sung a hymn, they went out to the Mount of Olives.

Jesus Predicts Peter's Denial

³¹Then Jesus told them, "This very night you will all fall away on account of me, for it is written:

" 'I will strike the shepherd,
    and the sheep of the flock will be
        scattered.'ᶜ

³²But after I have risen, I will go ahead of you into Galilee."

³³Peter replied, "Even if all fall away on account of you, I never will."

³⁴"I tell you the truth," Jesus answered, "this very night, before the rooster crows, you will disown me three times."

ᵃ 25 Or "You yourself have said it"   ᵇ 28 Some manuscripts the new   ᶜ 31 Zech. 13:7

Real Life and Sit-coms

READ MATTHEW 26:17–30, 47–50

Every week, sit-com actors try to get ahead by lying, cheating or stealing in the hope that something good will come out of it. But their plans always seem to blow up in their face. When Satan filled Judas' heart and he betrayed Jesus, Judas could've been doing evil just to do evil. However, some think that Judas did it hoping that it would force Jesus to *prove* that he was the Messiah. Judas' plan backfired on him as well. It may be funny to watch people mess up on TV, but when it comes to real life, there's *no* canned laughter or commercial break to save you. If you do something wrong, guaranteed something bad will come out of it. Apply this principle to your life: When you're tempted to tell a "white lie" or compromise to get what you want, do the opposite. After all, your life is not a sit-com.

Your next reading is on page 1270.

³⁵But Peter declared, "Even if I have to die with you, I will never disown you." And all the other disciples said the same.

Gethsemane

³⁶Then Jesus went with his disciples to a place called Gethsemane, and he said to them, "Sit here while I go over there and pray." ³⁷He took Peter and the two sons of Zebedee along with him, and he began to be sorrowful and troubled. ³⁸Then he said to them, "My soul is overwhelmed with sorrow to the point of death. Stay here and keep watch with me."

³⁹Going a little farther, he fell with his face to the ground and prayed, "My Father, if it is possible, may this cup be taken from me. Yet not as I will, but as you will."

⁴⁰Then he returned to his disciples and found them sleeping. "Could you men not keep watch with me for one hour?" he asked Peter. ⁴¹"Watch and pray so that you will not fall into temptation. The spirit is willing, but the body is weak."

⁴²He went away a second time and prayed, "My Father, if it is not possible for this cup to be taken away unless I drink it, may your will be done."

⁴³When he came back, he again found them sleeping, because their eyes were heavy. ⁴⁴So he left them and went away once more and prayed the third time, saying the same thing.

⁴⁵Then he returned to the disciples and said to them, "Are you still sleeping and resting? Look, the hour is near, and the Son of Man is betrayed into the hands of sinners. ⁴⁶Rise, let us go! Here comes my betrayer!"

Jesus Arrested

⁴⁷While he was still speaking, Judas, one of the Twelve, arrived. With him was a large crowd armed with swords and clubs, sent from the chief priests and the elders of the people. ⁴⁸Now the betrayer had arranged a signal with them: "The one I kiss is the man; arrest him." ⁴⁹Going

GET STRONGER.

Peter's Denials

MATTHEW 26:31–35, 69–75

If a heat wave baked your town and you were asked to take over for a paperboy who literally keeled over halfway through his route, you would be foolish to boast, "*I can do it!*" (Unless you found a way to put air conditioning on your bike!) In the same way, right after Jesus warned Peter that everyone would desert him, Peter was foolish to say, "Even if all fall away on account of you, I never will" (Matthew 26:33). Peter's intentions were good, but he didn't really have the strength to make good his boast. As a 252 man, you need to hold onto your faith. But you need to realize that your ability to *do* this comes not from yourself, but from God. So when your faith is weak, call out to God. Pray this prayer: "God, I will always stay true to you, because I trust *you* to keep me true to you."

Your next reading is on page 1271.

at once to Jesus, Judas said, "Greetings, Rabbi!" and kissed him.

50 Jesus replied, "Friend, do what you came for."[a]

Then the men stepped forward, seized Jesus and arrested him. 51 With that, one of Jesus' companions reached for his sword, drew it out and struck the servant of the high priest, cutting off his ear.

52 "Put your sword back in its place," Jesus said to him, "for all who draw the sword will die by the sword. 53 Do you think I cannot call on my Father, and he will at once put at my disposal more than twelve legions of angels? 54 But how then would the Scriptures be fulfilled that say it must happen in this way?"

55 At that time Jesus said to the crowd, "Am I leading a rebellion, that you have come out with swords and clubs to capture me? Every day I sat in the temple courts teaching, and you did not arrest me. 56 But this has all taken place that the writings of the prophets might be fulfilled." Then all the disciples deserted him and fled.

Before the Sanhedrin

57 Those who had arrested Jesus took him to Caiaphas, the high priest, where the teachers of the law and the elders had assembled. 58 But Peter followed him at a distance, right up to the courtyard of the high priest. He entered and sat down with the guards to see the outcome.

59 The chief priests and the whole Sanhedrin were looking for false evidence against Jesus so that they could put him to death. 60 But they did not find any, though many false witnesses came forward.

Finally two came forward 61 and declared, "This fellow said, 'I am able to destroy the temple of God and rebuild it in three days.' "

62 Then the high priest stood up and said to Jesus, "Are you not going to answer? What is this testimony that these men are bringing against you?" 63 But Jesus remained silent.

[a] 50 Or "Friend, why have you come?"

God? Or Moral Good Guy?

READ MATTHEW 26:57–68

Maybe you've seen this on TV or in real life: Some adult says, "Jesus was a kind man who did good and taught good morals, but he wasn't God." *Helllloooo!* Jesus did not get tortured and killed for teaching good morals. He was murdered because he claimed he was *God*. On an earlier occasion, his religious enemies said, "We are not stoning you for any of these, but for blasphemy, because you . . . claim to be God" (John 10:31–33). And when Jesus flat out told them that he *was* God's Son (Matthew 26:63–65; see also Luke 22:67–71), it was Exhibit A in his trial. What's more, he said he was crucified for everyone's sins and that he was the *only* way to heaven. Well? *Was* Jesus who he *said* he was? You betcha! He wasn't just mixed up, and he sure wasn't lying. Make no mistake about it: Jesus was more than a good man who did and taught good things. Much more. He's our Savior. He suffered and died for us so we could have eternal life.

Your next reading is on page 1273.

The high priest said to him, "I charge you under oath by the living God: Tell us if you are the Christ,[a] the Son of God."

64"Yes, it is as you say," Jesus replied. "But I say to all of you: In the future you will see the Son of Man sitting at the right hand of the Mighty One and coming on the clouds of heaven."

65Then the high priest tore his clothes and said, "He has spoken blasphemy! Why do we need any more witnesses? Look, now you have heard the blasphemy. 66What do you think?"

"He is worthy of death," they answered.

67Then they spit in his face and struck him with their fists. Others slapped him 68and said, "Prophesy to us, Christ. Who hit you?"

Peter Disowns Jesus

69Now Peter was sitting out in the courtyard, and a servant girl came to him. "You also were with Jesus of Galilee," she said.

70But he denied it before them all. "I don't know what you're talking about," he said.

71Then he went out to the gateway, where another girl saw him and said to the people there, "This fellow was with Jesus of Nazareth."

72He denied it again, with an oath: "I don't know the man!"

73After a little while, those standing there went up to Peter and said, "Surely you are one of them, for your accent gives you away."

74Then he began to call down curses on himself and he swore to them, "I don't know the man!"

Immediately a rooster crowed. 75Then Peter remembered the word Jesus had spoken: "Before the rooster crows, you will disown me three times." And he went outside and wept bitterly.

Judas Hangs Himself

27 Early in the morning, all the chief priests and the elders of the people came to the decision to put Jesus to death. 2They bound him, led him away and handed him over to Pilate, the governor.

3When Judas, who had betrayed him, saw that Jesus was condemned, he was seized with remorse and returned the thirty silver coins to the chief priests and the elders. 4"I have sinned," he said, "for I have betrayed innocent blood."

"What is that to us?" they replied. "That's your responsibility."

5So Judas threw the money into the temple and left. Then he went away and hanged himself.

6The chief priests picked up the coins and said, "It is against the law to put this into the treasury, since it is blood money." 7So they decided to use the money to buy the potter's field as a burial place for foreigners. 8That is why it has been called the Field of Blood to this day. 9Then what was spoken by Jeremiah the prophet was fulfilled: "They took the thirty silver coins, the price set on him by the people of Israel, 10and they used them to buy the potter's field, as the Lord commanded me."[b]

Jesus Before Pilate

11Meanwhile Jesus stood before the governor, and the governor asked him, "Are you the king of the Jews?"

"Yes, it is as you say," Jesus replied.

12When he was accused by the chief priests and the elders, he gave no answer. 13Then Pilate asked him, "Don't you hear the testimony they are bringing against you?" 14But Jesus made no reply, not even to a single charge—to the great amazement of the governor.

15Now it was the governor's custom at the Feast to release a prisoner chosen by the crowd. 16At that time they had a notorious prisoner, called Barabbas. 17So when the crowd had gathered, Pilate asked them, "Which one do you want me to release to you: Barabbas, or Jesus who is called Christ?" 18For he knew it was out of envy that they had handed Jesus over to him.

19While Pilate was sitting on the judge's seat, his wife sent him this message: "Don't have anything to do with that innocent man, for I have suffered a great deal today in a dream because of him."

20But the chief priests and the elders persuaded the crowd to ask for Barabbas and to have Jesus executed.

21"Which of the two do you want me to release to you?" asked the governor.

"Barabbas," they answered.

a 63 Or Messiah; also in verse 68　　b 10 See Zech. 11:12,13; Jer. 19:1–13; 32:6–9.

22"What shall I do, then, with Jesus who is called Christ?" Pilate asked.

They all answered, "Crucify him!"

23"Why? What crime has he committed?" asked Pilate.

But they shouted all the louder, "Crucify him!"

24When Pilate saw that he was getting nowhere, but that instead an uproar was starting, he took water and washed his hands in front of the crowd. "I am innocent of this man's blood," he said. "It is your responsibility!"

25All the people answered, "Let his blood be on us and on our children!"

26Then he released Barabbas to them. But he had Jesus flogged, and handed him over to be crucified.

The Soldiers Mock Jesus

27Then the governor's soldiers took Jesus into the Praetorium and gathered the whole company of soldiers around him. 28They stripped him and put a scarlet robe on him, 29and then twisted together a crown of thorns and set it on his head. They put a staff in his right hand and knelt in front of him and mocked him. "Hail, king of the Jews!" they said. 30They spit on him, and took the staff and struck him on the head again and again. 31After they had mocked him, they took off the robe and put his own clothes on him. Then they led him away to crucify him.

The Crucifixion

32As they were going out, they met a man from Cyrene, named Simon, and they forced him to carry the cross. 33They came to a place called Golgotha (which means The Place of the Skull). 34There they offered Jesus wine to drink, mixed with gall; but after tasting it, he refused to drink it. 35When they had crucified him, they divided up his clothes by casting lots.[a] 36And

[a] 35 A few late manuscripts lots that the word spoken by the prophet might be fulfilled: "They divided my garments among themselves and cast lots for my clothing" (Psalm 22:18)

Jesus Before Pilate

READ MATTHEW 27:11–26

Which would you rather eat—a bowl of macaroni and cheese that's ready in two minutes or a sumptuous wedding feast that takes twelve hours to prepare? Chances are you'd choose the second option. The religious leaders, however, were like a bunch of microwaved macaroni eaters. They were into taking shortcuts. God's big picture was for Jesus to solve the problems of all humankind, but the Jewish leaders only wanted an independent Judea. They wanted answers just for them. They weren't willing to wait around and do things God's way. Their idea of a Messiah was a sword-swinging military leader like Samson or Gideon. Barabbas was just that sort of man, so they "persuaded the crowd to ask for Barabbas and to have Jesus executed" (verse 20). Sometimes we also try to take shortcuts around God's plan. But God isn't into shortcuts. He's into doing things right, and that usually takes a little longer. So have patience!

Your next reading is on page 1275.

GET STRONGER

Get a Load of This...

Check out Matthew 27:52. When Jesus was raised from the dead, other departed saints came back to life also. It was part of the huge miracle of Jesus' resurrection. "Look, Mom! I'm telling you, it's Aunt Martha at the door!" "No way! She died twenty years ago."

sitting down, they kept watch over him there. 37Above his head they placed the written charge against him: THIS IS JESUS, THE KING OF THE JEWS. 38Two robbers were crucified with him, one on his right and one on his left. 39Those who passed by hurled insults at him, shaking their heads 40and saying, "You who are going to destroy the temple and build it in three days, save yourself! Come down from the cross, if you are the Son of God!"

41In the same way the chief priests, the teachers of the law and the elders mocked him. 42"He saved others," they said, "but he can't save himself! He's the King of Israel! Let him come down now from the cross, and we will believe in him. 43He trusts in God. Let God rescue him now if he wants him, for he said, 'I am the Son of God.' " 44In the same way the robbers who were crucified with him also heaped insults on him.

The Death of Jesus

45From the sixth hour until the ninth hour darkness came over all the land. 46About the ninth hour Jesus cried out in a loud voice, *"Eloi, Eloi,ª lama sabachthani?"*—which means, "My God, my God, why have you forsaken me?"b

47When some of those standing there heard this, they said, "He's calling Elijah."

48Immediately one of them ran and got a sponge. He filled it with wine vinegar, put it on a stick, and offered it to Jesus to drink. 49The rest said, "Now leave him alone. Let's see if Elijah comes to save him."

50And when Jesus had cried out again in a loud voice, he gave up his spirit.

51At that moment the curtain of the temple was torn in two from top to bottom. The earth shook and the rocks split. 52The tombs broke open and the bodies of many holy people who had died were raised to life. 53They came out of the tombs, and after Jesus' resurrection they went into the holy city and appeared to many people.

54When the centurion and those with him who were guarding Jesus saw the earthquake and all that had happened, they were terrified, and exclaimed, "Surely he was the Sonc of God!"

55Many women were there, watching from a distance. They had followed Jesus from Galilee to care for his needs. 56Among them were Mary Magdalene, Mary the mother of James and Joses, and the mother of Zebedee's sons.

The Burial of Jesus

57As evening approached, there came a rich man from Arimathea, named Joseph, who had himself become a disciple of Jesus. 58Going to Pilate, he asked for Jesus' body, and Pilate ordered that it be given to him. 59Joseph took the body, wrapped it in a clean linen cloth, 60and placed it in his own new tomb that he had

ª46 Some manuscripts *Eli, Eli*   b46 Psalm 22:1   c54 Or *a son* cut out of the rock. He rolled a big stone in front of the entrance to the tomb and went away. 61Mary Magdalene and the other Mary were sitting there opposite the tomb.

The Guard at the Tomb

62The next day, the one after Preparation Day, the chief priests and the Pharisees went to Pilate. 63"Sir," they said, "we remember that while he was still alive that deceiver said, 'After three days I will rise again.' 64So give the order for the tomb to be made secure until the third day. Otherwise, his disciples may come and steal the body and tell the people that he has been raised from the dead. This last deception will be worse than the first."

65"Take a guard," Pilate answered. "Go, make the tomb as secure as you know how." 66So they went and made the tomb secure by putting a seal on the stone and posting the guard.

The Resurrection

28 After the Sabbath, at dawn on the first day of the week, Mary Magdalene and the other Mary went to look at the tomb.

2There was a violent earthquake, for an angel of the Lord came down from heaven and, going to the tomb, rolled back the stone and sat on it. 3His appearance was like lightning, and his clothes were white as snow. 4The guards were so afraid of him that they shook and became like dead men.

5The angel said to the women, "Do not be afraid, for I know that you are looking for Jesus, who was crucified. 6He is not here; he has risen, just as he said. Come and see the place where he lay. 7Then go quickly and tell his disciples: 'He has risen from the dead and is going ahead of you into Galilee. There you will see him.' Now I have told you."

8So the women hurried away from the tomb, afraid yet filled with joy, and ran to

Phase One, Two, Three
READ MATTHEW 28:1–20

Some people think all Jesus did was die on the cross for our sins. Wrong. That was only phase one of God's plan. Jesus didn't just *die* for our sins; he was also raised back to life and taken up into heaven where he lives forever at the right hand of God (Ephesians 1:20). Wow! Don't bother trying to find his tomb. There's no body there. The angels at his tomb said, "He is not here; he has risen, just as he said" (Matthew 28:6). That was phase two. But the best part of all is phase three: Because Jesus was able to rise from the dead, one day *we'll* all be able to rise from the dead and go up into heaven, too (see 1 Corinthians 15:3–5, 12–20)! Jesus died, but death couldn't hold him. And, if you put your faith in Jesus, it won't be able to hold you either!

Your next reading is on page 1278.

tell his disciples. [9]Suddenly Jesus met them. "Greetings," he said. They came to him, clasped his feet and worshiped him. [10]Then Jesus said to them, "Do not be afraid. Go and tell my brothers to go to Galilee; there they will see me."

The Guards' Report

[11]While the women were on their way, some of the guards went into the city and reported to the chief priests everything that had happened. [12]When the chief priests had met with the elders and devised a plan, they gave the soldiers a large sum of money, [13]telling them, "You are to say, 'His disciples came during the night and stole him away while we were asleep.' [14]If this report gets to the governor, we will satisfy him and keep you out of trouble." [15]So the soldiers took the money and did as they were instructed. And this story has been widely circulated among the Jews to this very day.

The Great Commission

[16]Then the eleven disciples went to Galilee, to the mountain where Jesus had told them to go. [17]When they saw him, they worshiped him; but some doubted. [18]Then Jesus came to them and said, "All authority in heaven and on earth has been given to me. [19]Therefore go and make disciples of all nations, baptizing them in[a] the name of the Father and of the Son and of the Holy Spirit, [20]and teaching them to obey everything I have commanded you. And surely I am with you always, to the very end of the age."

[a] 19 Or into; see Acts 8:16; 19:5; Romans 6:3; 1 Cor. 1:13; 10:2 and Gal. 3:27.

MARK

Who wrote this book?
A young man named John Mark wrote down stories Peter told about Jesus.

Why was this book written?
Mark shows people who Jesus is by telling what Jesus did.

For whom was this book written?
Mark wrote this book for Gentiles (people who were not Jews).

What happens in this book?
Jesus shows his power by performing miracles that help people, and he teaches his disciples.

Who is important in this book?
Jesus is the important person in this book.

When did this happen?
Jesus worked miracles and taught from A.D. 26 to 30.

Where did this happen?
Most events in Mark 1–9 happened in Galilee. Most events in Mark 10–16 took place in or near Jerusalem.

What are some of the stories in this book?

Jesus heals a paralyzed man	Mark 2:1–12
Jesus calms a storm	Mark 4:35–41
Jesus raises a dead girl	Mark 5:21–43
Jesus walks on water	Mark 6:45–56
Jesus feeds four thousand people	Mark 8:1–10
Jesus heals a young boy	Mark 9:14–32
Jesus holds the Lord's Supper	Mark 14:12–26
Jesus dies and is buried	Mark 15:21–47
Jesus is raised again	Mark 16:1–8

John the Baptist Prepares the Way

1 The beginning of the gospel about Jesus Christ, the Son of God. [a]

2It is written in Isaiah the prophet:

"I will send my messenger ahead of you,
who will prepare your way" [b]—
3 "a voice of one calling in the desert,
'Prepare the way for the Lord,
make straight paths for him.' " [c]

4And so John came, baptizing in the desert region and preaching a baptism of repentance for the forgiveness of sins. 5The whole Judean countryside and all the people of Jerusalem went out to him. Confessing their sins, they were baptized by him in the Jordan River. 6John wore clothing made of camel's hair, with a leather belt around his waist, and he ate locusts and wild honey. 7And this was his message: "After me will come one more powerful than I, the thongs of whose sandals I am not worthy to stoop down and untie. 8I baptize you with[d] water, but he will baptize you with the Holy Spirit."

The Baptism and Temptation of Jesus

9At that time Jesus came from Nazareth in Galilee and was baptized by John in the Jordan. 10As Jesus was coming up out of the water, he saw heaven being torn open and the Spirit descending on him like a dove. 11And a voice came from heaven: "You are my Son, whom I love; with you I am well pleased."

12At once the Spirit sent him out into the desert, 13and he was in the desert forty days, being tempted by Satan. He was with the wild animals, and angels attended him.

The Calling of the First Disciples

14After John was put in prison, Jesus went into Galilee, proclaiming the good news of God. 15"The time has come," he said. "The kingdom of God is near. Repent and believe the good news!"

16As Jesus walked beside the Sea of Galilee, he saw Simon and his brother Andrew casting a net into the lake, for they

---

[a] 1 Some manuscripts do not have the Son of God.
[b] 2 Mal. 3:1   [c] 3 Isaiah 40:3   [d] 8 Or in

John's Message

READ MARK 1:1–8

Ever felt like you had an "in" with someone famous? He autographed a ball for you, even wrote your name on it, and ever since then, you've watched all his games, read every box score and collected all his cards and posters. You may know all *about* him, but you don't *know* him, like his best friend does. There's a big difference. A lot of Jewish people felt they had an "in" with God. But John said, "Uh-uh. Not good enough. You've got to repent." Is your family Christian? Not good enough. You live in a Christian nation? Doesn't cut it, bud. You believe in God? Not enough. "Even the demons believe that—and shudder" (James 2:19). Just believing in God isn't enough. You need to get right with God *yourself*. You need to truly follow and obey Jesus. Jesus made it possible to really have an "in" with God, so let him take you in.

Your next reading is on page 1280.

were fishermen. [17]"Come, follow me," Jesus said, "and I will make you fishers of men." [18]At once they left their nets and followed him.

[19]When he had gone a little farther, he saw James son of Zebedee and his brother John in a boat, preparing their nets. [20]Without delay he called them, and they left their father Zebedee in the boat with the hired men and followed him.

Jesus Drives Out an Evil Spirit

[21]They went to Capernaum, and when the Sabbath came, Jesus went into the synagogue and began to teach. [22]The people were amazed at his teaching, because he taught them as one who had authority, not as the teachers of the law. [23]Just then a man in their synagogue who was possessed by an evil[a] spirit cried out, [24]"What do you want with us, Jesus of Nazareth? Have you come to destroy us? I know who you are—the Holy One of God!"

[25]"Be quiet!" said Jesus sternly. "Come out of him!" [26]The evil spirit shook the man violently and came out of him with a shriek.

[27]The people were all so amazed that they asked each other, "What is this? A new teaching—and with authority! He even gives orders to evil spirits and they obey him." [28]News about him spread quickly over the whole region of Galilee.

Jesus Heals Many

[29]As soon as they left the synagogue, they went with James and John to the home of Simon and Andrew. [30]Simon's mother-in-law was in bed with a fever, and they told Jesus about her. [31]So he went to her, took her hand and helped her up. The fever left her and she began to wait on them.

[32]That evening after sunset the people brought to Jesus all the sick and demon-possessed. [33]The whole town gathered at the door, [34]and Jesus healed many who had various diseases. He also drove out many demons, but he would not let the demons speak because they knew who he was.

Jesus Prays in a Solitary Place

[35]Very early in the morning, while it was still dark, Jesus got up, left the house and went off to a solitary place, where he prayed. [36]Simon and his companions went to look for him, [37]and when they found him, they exclaimed: "Everyone is looking for you!"

[38]Jesus replied, "Let us go somewhere else—to the nearby villages—so I can preach there also. That is why I have come." [39]So he traveled throughout Galilee, preaching in their synagogues and driving out demons.

A Man With Leprosy

[40]A man with leprosy[b] came to him and begged him

Get a Load of This...

In Mark 1:9–11 when Jesus is baptized, God the Father, the Son of God (Jesus) and the Holy Spirit each play a role. All three of them are God, but they're separate personalities. Don't understand that? Don't worry. It's like the theory of relativity: It works, even if *you* can't explain it.

---

[a] 23 Greek unclean; also in verses 26 and 27   [b] 40 The Greek word was used for various diseases affecting the skin—not necessarily leprosy.

on his knees, "If you are willing, you can make me clean."

41 Filled with compassion, Jesus reached out his hand and touched the man. "I am willing," he said. "Be clean!" 42 Immediately the leprosy left him and he was cured.

43 Jesus sent him away at once with a strong warning: 44 "See that you don't tell this to anyone. But go, show yourself to the priest and offer the sacrifices that Moses commanded for your cleansing, as a testimony to them." 45 Instead he went out and began to talk freely, spreading the news. As a result, Jesus could no longer enter a town openly but stayed outside in lonely places. Yet the people still came to him from everywhere.

Jesus Heals a Paralytic

2 A few days later, when Jesus again entered Capernaum, the people heard that he had come home. 2 So many gathered that there was no room left, not even outside the door, and he preached the word to them. 3 Some men came, bringing to him a paralytic, carried by four of them. 4 Since they could not get him to Jesus because of the crowd, they made an opening in the roof above Jesus and, after digging through it, lowered the mat the paralyzed man was lying on. 5 When Jesus saw their faith, he said to the paralytic, "Son, your sins are forgiven."

6 Now some teachers of the law were sitting there, thinking to themselves, 7 "Why does this fellow talk like that? He's blaspheming! Who can forgive sins but God alone?"

8 Immediately Jesus knew in his spirit that this was what they were thinking in their hearts, and he said to them, "Why are you thinking these things? 9 Which is easier: to say to the paralytic, 'Your sins are forgiven,' or to say, 'Get up, take your mat and walk'? 10 But that you may know that the Son of Man has authority on earth to forgive sins . . ." He said to the paralytic, 11 "I tell you, get up, take your mat and go home." 12 He got up, took his mat and walked out in full view of them all. This amazed everyone and they praised God, saying, "We have never seen anything like this!"

Skylight to Heaven

READ MARK 2:1–12

These guys knew Jesus could heal their buddy, so they busted a hole in the roof to get their friend to him … and the skylight was invented! Seriously now, "When Jesus saw their faith, he said to the paralytic, 'Son, your sins are forgiven'" (verse 5). Notice: "Jesus *saw* their faith." Faith isn't like a bag of chips where you've got to eat a ton of them to get filled up. All you need is a mustard seed's worth (see Matthew 17:20), and then *act* on it. Also, get this part: "Jesus saw *their* faith." He saw the faith of this guy's friends. When one of your friends is having a tough time, ask yourself, "What can I do that will show God my faith?" Take your friend to church, pray for him, go skating, hang out—whatever says that you're there and that you care. Open a skylight to heaven—God won't let either of you down.

Your next reading is on page 1282.

The Calling of Levi

13Once again Jesus went out beside the lake. A large crowd came to him, and he began to teach them. 14As he walked along, he saw Levi son of Alphaeus sitting at the tax collector's booth. "Follow me," Jesus told him, and Levi got up and followed him.

15While Jesus was having dinner at Levi's house, many tax collectors and "sinners" were eating with him and his disciples, for there were many who followed him. 16When the teachers of the law who were Pharisees saw him eating with the "sinners" and tax collectors, they asked his disciples: "Why does he eat with tax collectors and 'sinners'?"

17On hearing this, Jesus said to them, "It is not the healthy who need a doctor, but the sick. I have not come to call the righteous, but sinners."

Jesus Questioned About Fasting

18Now John's disciples and the Pharisees were fasting. Some people came and asked Jesus, "How is it that John's disciples and the disciples of the Pharisees are fasting, but yours are not?"

19Jesus answered, "How can the guests of the bridegroom fast while he is with them? They cannot, so long as they have him with them. 20But the time will come when the bridegroom will be taken from them, and on that day they will fast.

21"No one sews a patch of unshrunk cloth on an old garment. If he does, the new piece will pull away from the old, making the tear worse. 22And no one pours new wine into old wineskins. If he does, the wine will burst the skins, and both the wine and the wineskins will be ruined. No, he pours new wine into new wineskins."

Lord of the Sabbath

23One Sabbath Jesus was going through the grainfields, and as his disciples walked along, they began to pick some heads of grain. 24The Pharisees said to him, "Look, why are they doing what is unlawful on the Sabbath?"

25He answered, "Have you never read what David did when he and his companions were hungry and in need? 26In the days of Abiathar the high priest, he entered the house of God and ate the consecrated bread, which is lawful only for priests to eat. And he also gave some to his companions."

27Then he said to them, "The Sabbath was made for man, not man for the Sabbath. 28So the Son of Man is Lord even of the Sabbath."

3 Another time he went into the synagogue, and a man with a shriveled hand was there. 2Some of them were looking for a reason to accuse Jesus, so they watched him closely to see if he would heal him on the Sabbath. 3Jesus said to the man with the shriveled hand, "Stand up in front of everyone."

4Then Jesus asked them, "Which is lawful on the Sabbath: to do good or to do evil, to save life or to kill?" But they remained silent.

5He looked around at them in anger and, deeply distressed at their stubborn hearts, said to the man, "Stretch out your hand." He stretched it out, and his hand was completely restored. 6Then the Pharisees went out and began to plot with the Herodians how they might kill Jesus.

Crowds Follow Jesus

7Jesus withdrew with his disciples to the lake, and a large crowd from Galilee followed. 8When they heard all he was doing, many people came to him from Judea, Jerusalem, Idumea, and the regions across the Jordan and around Tyre and Sidon. 9Because of the crowd he told his disciples to have a small boat ready for him, to keep the people from crowding him. 10For he had healed many, so that those with diseases were pushing forward to touch him. 11Whenever the evila spirits saw him, they fell down before him and cried out, "You are the Son of God." 12But he gave them strict orders not to tell who he was.

The Appointing of the Twelve Apostles

13Jesus went up on a mountainside and called to him those he wanted, and they came to him. 14He appointed twelve—designating them apostlesb—that they might be with him and that he might send them out to preach 15and to have authority to drive out demons. 16These are the twelve he appointed: Simon (to

a 11 Greek unclean; also in verse 30   b 14 Some manuscripts do not have designating them apostles.

whom he gave the name Peter); [17]James son of Zebedee and his brother John (to them he gave the name Boanerges, which means Sons of Thunder); [18]Andrew, Philip, Bartholomew, Matthew, Thomas, James son of Alphaeus, Thaddaeus, Simon the Zealot [19]and Judas Iscariot, who betrayed him.

Jesus and Beelzebub

[20]Then Jesus entered a house, and again a crowd gathered, so that he and his disciples were not even able to eat. [21]When his family heard about this, they went to take charge of him, for they said, "He is out of his mind."

[22]And the teachers of the law who came down from Jerusalem said, "He is possessed by Beelzebub[a]! By the prince of demons he is driving out demons."

[23]So Jesus called them and spoke to them in parables: "How can Satan drive out Satan? [24]If a kingdom is divided against itself, that kingdom cannot stand. [25]If a house is divided against itself, that house cannot stand. [26]And if Satan opposes himself and is divided, he cannot stand; his end has come. [27]In fact, no one can enter a strong man's house and carry off his possessions unless he first ties up the strong man. Then he can rob his house. [28]I tell you the truth, all the sins and blasphemies of men will be forgiven them. [29]But whoever blasphemes against the Holy Spirit will never be forgiven; he is guilty of an eternal sin."

[30]He said this because they were saying, "He has an evil spirit."

Jesus' Mother and Brothers

[31]Then Jesus' mother and brothers arrived. Standing outside, they sent someone in to call him. [32]A crowd was sitting around him, and they told him, "Your mother and brothers are outside looking for you."

[33]"Who are my mother and my brothers?" he asked.

[34]Then he looked at those seated in a circle around him and said, "Here are my

[a] 22 Greek *Beezeboul* or *Beelzeboul*

The Sabbath Mix-up

READ MARK 2:23—3:6

God made a day for people to rest and focus on him—the Sabbath. Jesus said, "The Sabbath was made for man, not man for the Sabbath" (Mark 2:27), but the Pharisees were so focused on every detail of the law that they missed the point. The law said no eating unclean animals, so they strained their drinking water for gnats! The law said no work on the Sabbath, so they didn't even allow you to cut your fingernails! You get the picture. God never said, "To follow me, leave your brains at the door." God *wants* you to think! Jesus used common sense. The Pharisees said, "Look! He's harvesting grain on the Sabbath. Bad teacher!" Jesus addressed the bottom line—the need to eat. Think things through. Even Christians can get caught up in the Shoulds and Should-nots. Know your Bible so you'll know which ideas come from people and which ideas come from God.

Your next reading is on page 1285.

mother and my brothers! 35Whoever does God's will is my brother and sister and mother."

The Parable of the Sower

4 Again Jesus began to teach by the lake. The crowd that gathered around him was so large that he got into a boat and sat in it out on the lake, while all the people were along the shore at the water's edge. 2He taught them many things by parables, and in his teaching said: 3"Listen! A farmer went out to sow his seed. 4As he was scattering the seed, some fell along the path, and the birds came and ate it up. 5Some fell on rocky places, where it did not have much soil. It sprang up quickly, because the soil was shallow. 6But when the sun came up, the plants were scorched, and they withered because they had no root. 7Other seed fell among thorns, which grew up and choked the plants, so that they did not bear grain. 8Still other seed fell on good soil. It came up, grew and produced a crop, multiplying thirty, sixty, or even a hundred times."

9Then Jesus said, "He who has ears to hear, let him hear."

10When he was alone, the Twelve and the others around him asked him about the parables. 11He told them, "The secret of the kingdom of God has been given to you. But to those on the outside everything is said in parables 12so that,

" 'they may be ever seeing but never perceiving,
    and ever hearing but never understanding;
otherwise they might turn and be forgiven!'ᵃ"

13Then Jesus said to them, "Don't you understand this parable? How then will you understand any parable? 14The farmer sows the word. 15Some people are like seed along the path, where the word is sown. As soon as they hear it, Satan comes and takes away the word that was sown in them. 16Others, like seed sown on rocky places, hear the word and at once receive it with joy. 17But since they have no root, they last only a short time. When trouble or persecution comes because of the word, they quickly fall away. 18Still others, like seed sown among thorns, hear the word; 19but the worries of this life, the deceitfulness of wealth and the desires for other things come in and choke the word, making it unfruitful. 20Others, like seed sown on good soil, hear the word, accept it, and produce a crop—thirty, sixty or even a hundred times what was sown."

A Lamp on a Stand

21He said to them, "Do you bring in a lamp to put it under a bowl or a bed? Instead, don't you put it on its stand? 22For whatever is hidden is meant to be disclosed, and whatever is concealed is meant to be brought out into the open. 23If anyone has ears to hear, let him hear."

Get a Load of This...

Jesus called James and John the "Sons of Thunder" (Mark 3:17). You get the impression these two boys were *loud*. On top of it, they had violent tempers. Know any kids like that in your school?

ᵃ 12 Isaiah 6:9,10

Gross!

"Beelzebub" (Mark 3:22) was the name of a pagan Philistine god. This was *not* a complimentary title. *Beelzebub* means "lord of the flies." Think of flies buzzing around dung, eating it, having it stick to their hairy legs. Wheeeee! His kingdom stinks!

²⁴"Consider carefully what you hear," he continued. "With the measure you use, it will be measured to you—and even more. ²⁵Whoever has will be given more; whoever does not have, even what he has will be taken from him."

The Parable of the Growing Seed

²⁶He also said, "This is what the kingdom of God is like. A man scatters seed on the ground. ²⁷Night and day, whether he sleeps or gets up, the seed sprouts and grows, though he does not know how. ²⁸All by itself the soil produces grain—first the stalk, then the head, then the full kernel in the head. ²⁹As soon as the grain is ripe, he puts the sickle to it, because the harvest has come."

The Parable of the Mustard Seed

³⁰Again he said, "What shall we say the kingdom of God is like, or what parable shall we use to describe it? ³¹It is like a mustard seed, which is the smallest seed you plant in the ground. ³²Yet when planted, it grows and becomes the largest of all garden plants, with such big branches that the birds of the air can perch in its shade."

³³With many similar parables Jesus spoke the word to them, as much as they could understand. ³⁴He did not say anything to them without using a parable. But when he was alone with his own disciples, he explained everything.

Jesus Calms the Storm

³⁵That day when evening came, he said to his disciples, "Let us go over to the other side." ³⁶Leaving the crowd behind, they took him along, just as he was, in the boat. There were also other boats with him. ³⁷A furious squall came up, and the waves broke over the boat, so that it was nearly swamped. ³⁸Jesus was in the stern, sleeping on a cushion. The disciples woke him and said to him, "Teacher, don't you care if we drown?"

³⁹He got up, rebuked the wind and said to the waves, "Quiet! Be still!" Then the wind died down and it was completely calm.

⁴⁰He said to his disciples, "Why are you so afraid? Do you still have no faith?"

⁴¹They were terrified and asked each other, "Who is this? Even the wind and the waves obey him!"

The Healing of a Demon-possessed Man

5 They went across the lake to the region of the Gerasenes.ᵃ ²When Jesus got out of the boat, a man with an evilᵇ spirit came from the tombs to meet him. ³This man lived in the tombs, and no one could bind him any more, not even with a chain. ⁴For he had often been chained hand and foot, but he tore the chains apart and broke the irons on his feet. No one was strong enough to subdue him. ⁵Night and day among

---

ᵃ 1 Some manuscripts *Gadarenes*; other manuscripts *Gergesenes* ᵇ 2 Greek *unclean*; also in verses 8 and 13 the tombs and in the hills he would cry out and cut himself with stones.

⁶When he saw Jesus from a distance, he ran and fell on his knees in front of him. ⁷He shouted at the top of his voice, "What do you want with me, Jesus, Son of the Most High God? Swear to God that you won't torture me!" ⁸For Jesus had said to him, "Come out of this man, you evil spirit!"

⁹Then Jesus asked him, "What is your name?"

"My name is Legion," he replied, "for we are many." ¹⁰And he begged Jesus again and again not to send them out of the area.

¹¹A large herd of pigs was feeding on the nearby hillside. ¹²The demons begged Jesus, "Send us among the pigs; allow us to go into them." ¹³He gave them permission, and the evil spirits came out and went into the pigs. The herd, about two thousand in number, rushed down the steep bank into the lake and were drowned.

¹⁴Those tending the pigs ran off and reported this in the town and countryside, and the people went out to see what had happened. ¹⁵When they came to Jesus, they saw the man who had been possessed by the legion of demons, sitting there, dressed and in his right mind; and they were afraid. ¹⁶Those who had seen it told the people what had happened to the demon-possessed man—and told about the pigs as well. ¹⁷Then the people began to plead with Jesus to leave their region.

¹⁸As Jesus was getting into the boat, the man who had been demon-possessed begged to go with him. ¹⁹Jesus did not let him, but said, "Go home to your family and tell them how much the Lord has done for you, and how he has had mercy on you." ²⁰So the man went away and began to tell in the Decapolis*ᵃ* how much Jesus had done for him. And all the people were amazed.

A Dead Girl and a Sick Woman

²¹When Jesus had again crossed over by boat to the other side of the lake, a large

ᵃ 20 That is, the Ten Cities

No Secrets

READ MARK 4:21–25

What's your darkest secret? The time you swiped the bubble gum at the supermarket? The time you slipped your broccoli to the dog under the table? Something more serious? Yeah, every man has that serious one, the one they hope will stay hidden. Ho! Read this headline: God Knows Everything! Whatever is hidden will eventually be brought out into the open (see Mark 4:22). We're all part of a community and everything we do affects someone else, somehow. Politicians are easy proof of that. How often is their dirty laundry aired out in public? When people's bad deeds come out, their careers and reputations are sometimes destroyed. Even if nobody finds out in *this* life, it'll all be revealed eventually. Ask yourself, "If everyone on earth heard me say this, or knew I was doing this, would I still go for it? If the answer is "yes," great. If it's "no," better think twice.

Your next reading is on page 1286.

crowd gathered around him while he was by the lake. ²²Then one of the synagogue rulers, named Jairus, came there. Seeing Jesus, he fell at his feet ²³and pleaded earnestly with him, "My little daughter is dying. Please come and put your hands on her so that she will be healed and live." ²⁴So Jesus went with him.

A large crowd followed and pressed around him. ²⁵And a woman was there who had been subject to bleeding for twelve years. ²⁶She had suffered a great deal under the care of many doctors and had spent all she had, yet instead of getting better she grew worse. ²⁷When she heard about Jesus, she came up behind him in the crowd and touched his cloak, ²⁸because she thought, "If I just touch his clothes, I will be healed." ²⁹Immediately her bleeding stopped and she felt in her body that she was freed from her suffering.

³⁰At once Jesus realized that power had gone out from him. He turned around in the crowd and asked, "Who touched my clothes?"

³¹"You see the people crowding against you," his disciples answered, "and yet you can ask, 'Who touched me?' "

³²But Jesus kept looking around to see who had done it. ³³Then the woman, knowing what had happened to her, came and fell at his feet and, trembling with fear, told him the whole truth. ³⁴He said to her, "Daughter, your faith has healed you. Go in peace and be freed from your suffering."

³⁵While Jesus was still speaking, some men came from the house of Jairus, the synagogue ruler. "Your daughter is dead," they said. "Why bother the teacher any more?"

³⁶Ignoring what they said, Jesus told the synagogue ruler, "Don't be afraid; just believe."

³⁷He did not let anyone follow him except Peter, James and John the brother of James. ³⁸When they came to the home of the synagogue ruler, Jesus saw a commotion, with people crying and wailing loudly. ³⁹He went in and said to them, "Why all this commotion and wailing? The child is not dead but asleep." ⁴⁰But they laughed at him.

Stronger Than Demons

READ MARK 5:1–20

Did you *read* this Bible story? Whew! It's like the final scene out of some horror movie. This demon-possessed lunatic terrorized the countryside. He lived—get this—in the *tombs* and wandered through the hills at night, howling. Creepy. And he was unstoppable. Many times the villagers tied him up with iron chains and he snapped them apart! When he saw Jesus, he came running toward him. Jesus rebuked the demons and the man collapsed on his knees, shouting, "What do you want with me, Jesus? Swear to God that you won't torture me!" (verse 7). The demons could see God's power in Jesus, and they begged for mercy. They have no power against Jesus. When he died on the cross, he stripped them of power (see Colossians 2:15). We have the power of Jesus in us; and if we pray in his name, the enemy has no power over us.

Your next reading is on page 1287.

After he put them all out, he took the child's father and mother and the disciples who were with him, and went in where the child was. ⁴¹He took her by the hand and said to her, *"Talitha koum!"* (which means, "Little girl, I say to you, get up!"). ⁴²Immediately the girl stood up and walked around (she was twelve years old). At this they were completely astonished. ⁴³He gave strict orders not to let anyone know about this, and told them to give her something to eat.

A Prophet Without Honor

Jesus left there and went to his hometown, accompanied by his disciples. ²When the Sabbath came, he began to teach in the synagogue, and many who heard him were amazed.

"Where did this man get these things?" they asked. "What's this wisdom that has been given him, that he even does miracles! ³Isn't this the carpenter? Isn't this Mary's son and the brother of James, Joseph,ᵃ Judas and Simon? Aren't his sisters here with us?" And they took offense at him.

⁴Jesus said to them, "Only in his hometown, among his relatives and in his own house is a prophet without honor." ⁵He could not do any miracles there, except lay his hands on a few sick people and heal them. ⁶And he was amazed at their lack of faith.

Jesus Sends Out the Twelve

Then Jesus went around teaching from village to village. ⁷Calling the Twelve to him, he sent them out two by two and gave them authority over evilᵇ spirits.

⁸These were his instructions: "Take nothing for the journey except a staff—no bread, no bag, no money in your belts. ⁹Wear sandals but not an extra tunic. ¹⁰Whenever you enter a house, stay there until you leave that town. ¹¹And if any place will not welcome you or listen to you, shake the dust off your feet when you leave, as a testimony against them."

¹²They went out and preached that people should repent. ¹³They drove out many demons and anointed many sick people with oil and healed them.

ᵃ 3 Greek *Joses,* a variant of *Joseph*   ᵇ 7 Greek *unclean*

Who Do You Think You Are?

READ MARK 6:1–6

" 'Isn't this the carpenter? Isn't this Mary's son?'...And they took offense at him" (verse 3). What a crazy scene! Jesus was out telling amazing truths, healing people left and right, even raising folks from the dead—and what welcome does he get in his hometown? "Jesus? Yeah, we know him. He's nobody special." Jesus did what he could in Nazareth, then left. As a man of God, you'll face that kind of rejection. Sometimes it's from those closest to you—friends and family who don't respect your choice to be a Christian. Don't let them grind you down. God didn't make junk. You're special and God has awesome things for you to do. Follow him and, day by day, you'll accomplish great things. They asked about Jesus, "Who does this guy think he is?" The answer is, "God's Son." When they ask, "Who do you think *you* are?" the answer is almost the same. "God's follower and his son."

Your next reading is on page 1289.

John the Baptist Beheaded

¹⁴King Herod heard about this, for Jesus' name had become well known. Some were saying,ᵃ "John the Baptist has been raised from the dead, and that is why miraculous powers are at work in him."

¹⁵Others said, "He is Elijah."

And still others claimed, "He is a prophet, like one of the prophets of long ago."

¹⁶But when Herod heard this, he said, "John, the man I beheaded, has been raised from the dead!"

¹⁷For Herod himself had given orders to have John arrested, and he had him bound and put in prison. He did this because of Herodias, his brother Philip's wife, whom he had married. ¹⁸For John had been saying to Herod, "It is not lawful for you to have your brother's wife." ¹⁹So Herodias nursed a grudge against John and wanted to kill him. But she was not able to, ²⁰because Herod feared John and protected him, knowing him to be a righteous and holy man. When Herod heard John, he was greatly puzzledᵇ; yet he liked to listen to him.

²¹Finally the opportune time came. On his birthday Herod gave a banquet for his high officials and military commanders and the leading men of Galilee. ²²When the daughter of Herodias came in and danced, she pleased Herod and his dinner guests.

The king said to the girl, "Ask me for anything you want, and I'll give it to you." ²³And he promised her with an oath, "Whatever you ask I will give you, up to half my kingdom."

²⁴She went out and said to her mother, "What shall I ask for?"

"The head of John the Baptist," she answered.

²⁵At once the girl hurried in to the king with the request: "I want you to give me right now the head of John the Baptist on a platter."

²⁶The king was greatly distressed, but because of his oaths and his dinner guests, he did not want to refuse her. ²⁷So he immediately sent an executioner with orders to bring John's head. The man went, beheaded John in the prison, ²⁸and brought back his head on a platter. He presented it to the girl, and she gave it to her mother. ²⁹On hearing of this, John's disciples came and took his body and laid it in a tomb.

Jesus Feeds the Five Thousand

³⁰The apostles gathered around Jesus and reported to him all they had done and taught. ³¹Then, because so many people were coming and going that they did not even have a chance to eat, he said to them, "Come with me by yourselves to a quiet place and get some rest."

³²So they went away by themselves in a boat to a solitary place. ³³But many who saw them leaving recognized them and ran on foot from all the towns and got there ahead of them. ³⁴When Jesus landed and saw a large crowd, he had compassion on them, because they were like sheep without a shepherd. So he began teaching them many things.

³⁵By this time it was late in the day, so his disciples came to him. "This is a remote place," they said, "and it's already very late. ³⁶Send the people away so they can go to the surrounding countryside and villages and buy themselves something to eat."

³⁷But he answered, "You give them something to eat."

They said to him, "That would take eight months of a man's wagesᶜ! Are we to go and spend that much on bread and give it to them to eat?"

³⁸"How many loaves do you have?" he asked. "Go and see."

When they found out, they said, "Five—and two fish."

³⁹Then Jesus directed them to have all the people sit down in groups on the green grass. ⁴⁰So they sat down in groups of hundreds and fifties. ⁴¹Taking the five loaves and the two fish and looking up to heaven, he gave thanks and broke the loaves. Then he gave them to his disciples to set before the people. He also divided the two fish among them all. ⁴²They all ate and were satisfied, ⁴³and the disciples picked up twelve basketfuls of broken pieces of bread and fish. ⁴⁴The number of the men who had eaten was five thousand.

Jesus Walks on the Water

⁴⁵Immediately Jesus made his disciples get into the boat and go on ahead of him to Bethsaida, while he dismissed the

---

ᵃ 14 Some early manuscripts *He was saying*   ᵇ 20 Some early manuscripts *he did many things*   ᶜ 37 Greek *take two hundred denarii* crowd. 46After leaving them, he went up on a mountainside to pray.

47When evening came, the boat was in the middle of the lake, and he was alone on land. 48He saw the disciples straining at the oars, because the wind was against them. About the fourth watch of the night he went out to them, walking on the lake. He was about to pass by them, 49but when they saw him walking on the lake, they thought he was a ghost. They cried out, 50because they all saw him and were terrified.

Immediately he spoke to them and said, "Take courage! It is I. Don't be afraid." 51Then he climbed into the boat with them, and the wind died down. They were completely amazed, 52for they had not understood about the loaves; their hearts were hardened.

53When they had crossed over, they landed at Gennesaret and anchored there. 54As soon as they got out of the boat,

people recognized Jesus. 55They ran throughout that whole region and carried the sick on mats to wherever they heard he was. 56And wherever he went—into villages, towns or countryside—they placed the sick in the marketplaces. They begged him to let them touch even the edge of his cloak, and all who touched him were healed.

Clean and Unclean

7 The Pharisees and some of the teachers of the law who had come from Jerusalem gathered around Jesus and 2saw some of his disciples eating food with hands that were "unclean," that is, unwashed. 3(The Pharisees and all the Jews do not eat unless they give their hands a ceremonial washing, holding to the tradition of the elders. 4When they come from the marketplace they do not eat unless they wash. And they observe many other traditions, such

Washing Your Elbows

READ MARK 7:1–23

Washing your hands is a good habit, right? Keeps the germ level low, keeps you from eating dirt, makes your mom happy. That's all good stuff. But what if you started thinking that you had to wash your hands up to your elbows all the time as a way to purify yourself from the religious "uncleanness" that comes with everyday life—like the possibility of coming into contact with religiously "unclean" people or objects? And what if you got to the place where you paid more attention to cleaning your hands with a special little ceremony than to obeying the Bible? Sounds goofy but that's what the Pharisees did. Jesus' disciples probably *did* wash their hands. They just didn't do it according to "the tradition of the elders," meaning the elbow thing. Jesus told them, "You have let go of the commands of God and are holding on to the traditions of men" (verse 8). Hey, if you *want* to wash your hands all the way up to your elbows, go for it. Just make sure that, more importantly, you clean your heart by turning from your sins and asking Jesus to forgive you.

Your next reading is on page 1291.

as the washing of cups, pitchers and kettles.[a])

5So the Pharisees and teachers of the law asked Jesus, "Why don't your disciples live according to the tradition of the elders instead of eating their food with 'unclean' hands?"

6He replied, "Isaiah was right when he prophesied about you hypocrites; as it is written:

" 'These people honor me with their lips,
but their hearts are far from me.
7They worship me in vain;
their teachings are but rules taught by men.'[b]

8You have let go of the commands of God and are holding on to the traditions of men."

9And he said to them: "You have a fine way of setting aside the commands of God in order to observe[c] your own traditions! 10For Moses said, 'Honor your father and your mother,'[d] and, 'Anyone who curses his father or mother must be put to death.'[e] 11But you say that if a man says to his father or mother: 'Whatever help you might otherwise have received from me is Corban' (that is, a gift devoted to God), 12then you no longer let him do anything for his father or mother. 13Thus you nullify the word of God by your tradition that you have handed down. And you do many things like that."

14Again Jesus called the crowd to him and said, "Listen to me, everyone, and understand this. 15Nothing outside a man can make him 'unclean' by going into him. Rather, it is what comes out of a man that makes him 'unclean.'[f]"

17After he had left the crowd and entered the house, his disciples asked him about this parable. 18"Are you so dull?" he asked. "Don't you see that nothing that enters a man from the outside can make him 'unclean'? 19For it doesn't go into his heart but into his stomach, and then out of his body." (In saying this, Jesus declared all foods "clean.")

20He went on: "What comes out of a man is what makes him 'unclean.' 21For from within, out of men's hearts, come evil thoughts, sexual immorality, theft, murder, adultery, 22greed, malice, deceit, lewdness, envy, slander, arrogance and folly. 23All these evils come from inside and make a man 'unclean.' "

The Faith of a Syrophoenician Woman

24Jesus left that place and went to the vicinity of Tyre.[g] He entered a house and did not want anyone to know it; yet he could not keep his presence secret. 25In fact, as soon as she heard about him, a woman whose little daughter was possessed by an evil[h] spirit came and fell at his feet. 26The woman was a Greek, born in Syrian Phoenicia. She begged Jesus to drive the demon out of her daughter.

27"First let the children eat all they want," he told her, "for it is not right to take the children's bread and toss it to their dogs."

28"Yes, Lord," she replied, "but even the dogs under the table eat the children's crumbs."

29Then he told her, "For such a reply, you may go; the demon has left your daughter."

30She went home and found her child lying on the bed, and the demon gone.

The Healing of a Deaf and Mute Man

31Then Jesus left the vicinity of Tyre and went through Sidon, down to the Sea of Galilee and into the region of the Decapolis.[i] 32There some people brought to him a man who was deaf and could hardly talk, and they begged him to place his hand on the man.

33After he took him aside, away from the crowd, Jesus put his fingers into the man's ears. Then he spit and touched the man's tongue. 34He looked up to heaven and with a deep sigh said to him, "Ephphatha!" (which means, "Be opened!"). 35At this, the man's ears were opened, his tongue was loosened and he began to speak plainly.

36Jesus commanded them not to tell anyone. But the more he did so, the more they kept talking about it. 37People were overwhelmed with amazement. "He has done everything well," they said. "He even makes the deaf hear and the mute speak."

---

[a] 4 Some early manuscripts *pitchers, kettles and dining couches* [b] 6,7 Isaiah 29:13 [c] 9 Some manuscripts *set up* [d] 10 Exodus 20:12; Deut. 5:16 [e] 10 Exodus 21:17; Lev. 20:9 [f] 15 Some early manuscripts *'unclean.'* 16*If anyone has ears to hear, let him hear.* [g] 24 Many early manuscripts *Tyre and Sidon* [h] 25 Greek *unclean* [i] 31 That is, the Ten Cities

Jesus Feeds the Four Thousand

During those days another large crowd gathered. Since they had nothing to eat, Jesus called his disciples to him and said, 2"I have compassion for these people; they have already been with me three days and have nothing to eat. 3If I send them home hungry, they will collapse on the way, because some of them have come a long distance."

4His disciples answered, "But where in this remote place can anyone get enough bread to feed them?"

5"How many loaves do you have?" Jesus asked.

"Seven," they replied.

6He told the crowd to sit down on the ground. When he had taken the seven loaves and given thanks, he broke them and gave them to his disciples to set before the people, and they did so. 7They had a few small fish as well; he gave thanks for them also and told the disciples to distribute them. 8The people ate and were satisfied. Afterward the disciples picked up seven basketfuls of broken pieces that were left over. 9About four thousand men were present. And having sent them away, 10he got into the boat with his disciples and went to the region of Dalmanutha.

11The Pharisees came and began to question Jesus. To test him, they asked him for a sign from heaven. 12He sighed deeply and said, "Why does this generation ask for a miraculous sign? I tell you the truth, no sign will be given to it." 13Then he left them, got back into the boat and crossed to the other side.

The Yeast of the Pharisees and Herod

14The disciples had forgotten to bring bread, except for one loaf they had with them in the boat. 15"Be careful," Jesus warned them. "Watch out for the yeast of the Pharisees and that of Herod."

Jesus Feeds Thousands

READ MARK 6:30–44; 8:1–13

Jesus fed a crowd of 5,000, then another crowd of 4,000—and that's just counting *men*, not the women and children! Talk about a mountain of loaves and fishes! That was like feeding an entire crowd at a packed baseball stadium! It was comparable to taking two hot dogs and five bags of popcorn and feeding everyone on the bleachers! Jesus actually *did* a miracle that big. Whew! Then, after everyone had eaten, the critics wanted to know if Jesus would do a *miracle* for them. He just *did* the whole fish-loaves extravaganza and they're asking for a *sign*? Hellooo? Jesus didn't humor them—he knew their doubting attitude and said, "You're not seeing anything" (see Mark 8:12). What would *you* expect if you went to God and defiantly said, "Prove yourself"? Trust God. He can do miracles, sure, but not on demand.

Your next reading is on page 1294.

STRONGER

Gross!

Jesus spat (*Hhkkk!*) and put his spit on a deaf and mute man's tongue (Mark 7:33). Jesus (*Hhkkk!*) spat again and put his spit on a blind man's eyes (Mark 8:23). Jesus did this to heal people, but unless you're called to a healing ministry, keep your spit where it belongs.

16They discussed this with one another and said, "It is because we have no bread."

17Aware of their discussion, Jesus asked them: "Why are you talking about having no bread? Do you still not see or understand? Are your hearts hardened? 18Do you have eyes but fail to see, and ears but fail to hear? And don't you remember? 19When I broke the five loaves for the five thousand, how many basketfuls of pieces did you pick up?"

"Twelve," they replied.

20"And when I broke the seven loaves for the four thousand, how many basketfuls of pieces did you pick up?"

They answered, "Seven."

21He said to them, "Do you still not understand?"

The Healing of a Blind Man at Bethsaida

22They came to Bethsaida, and some people brought a blind man and begged Jesus to touch him. 23He took the blind man by the hand and led him outside the village. When he had spit on the man's eyes and put his hands on him, Jesus asked, "Do you see anything?"

24He looked up and said, "I see people; they look like trees walking around."

25Once more Jesus put his hands on the man's eyes. Then his eyes were opened, his sight was restored, and he saw everything clearly. 26Jesus sent him home, saying, "Don't go into the village. *a*"

Peter's Confession of Christ

27Jesus and his disciples went on to the villages around Caesarea Philippi. On the way he asked them, "Who do people say I am?"

28They replied, "Some say John the Baptist; others say Elijah; and still others, one of the prophets."

29"But what about you?" he asked. "Who do you say I am?"

Peter answered, "You are the Christ. *b*"

30Jesus warned them not to tell anyone about him.

Jesus Predicts His Death

31He then began to teach them that the Son of Man must suffer many things and be rejected by the elders, chief priests and teachers of the law, and that he must be killed and after three days rise again. 32He spoke plainly about this, and Peter took him aside and began to rebuke him.

33But when Jesus turned and looked at his disciples, he rebuked Peter. "Get behind me, Satan!" he said. "You do not have in mind the things of God, but the things of men."

34Then he called the crowd to him along with his disciples and said: "If anyone would come after me, he must deny himself and take up his cross and follow me.

a 26 Some manuscripts *Don't go and tell anyone in the village*
b 29 Or *Messiah.* "The Christ" (Greek) and "the Messiah" (Hebrew) both mean "the Anointed One."

35 For whoever wants to save his life*a* will lose it, but whoever loses his life for me and for the gospel will save it. 36 What good is it for a man to gain the whole world, yet forfeit his soul? 37 Or what can a man give in exchange for his soul? 38 If anyone is ashamed of me and my words in this adulterous and sinful generation, the Son of Man will be ashamed of him when he comes in his Father's glory with the holy angels."

9 And he said to them, "I tell you the truth, some who are standing here will not taste death before they see the kingdom of God come with power."

The Transfiguration

2 After six days Jesus took Peter, James and John with him and led them up a high mountain, where they were all alone. There he was transfigured before them. 3 His clothes became dazzling white, whiter than anyone in the world could bleach them. 4 And there appeared before them Elijah and Moses, who were talking with Jesus.

5 Peter said to Jesus, "Rabbi, it is good for us to be here. Let us put up three shelters—one for you, one for Moses and one for Elijah." 6 (He did not know what to say, they were so frightened.)

7 Then a cloud appeared and enveloped them, and a voice came from the cloud: "This is my Son, whom I love. Listen to him!"

8 Suddenly, when they looked around, they no longer saw anyone with them except Jesus.

9 As they were coming down the mountain, Jesus gave them orders not to tell anyone what they had seen until the Son of Man had risen from the dead. 10 They kept the matter to themselves, discussing what "rising from the dead" meant.

11 And they asked him, "Why do the teachers of the law say that Elijah must come first?"

12 Jesus replied, "To be sure, Elijah does come first, and restores all things. Why then is it written that the Son of Man must suffer much and be rejected? 13 But I tell you, Elijah has come, and they have done to him everything they wished, just as it is written about him."

The Healing of a Boy With an Evil Spirit

14 When they came to the other disciples, they saw a large crowd around them and the teachers of the law arguing with them. 15 As soon as all the people saw Jesus, they were overwhelmed with wonder and ran to greet him.

16 "What are you arguing with them about?" he asked.

17 A man in the crowd answered, "Teacher, I brought you my son, who is possessed by a spirit that has robbed him of speech. 18 Whenever it seizes him, it throws him to the ground. He foams at the mouth, gnashes his teeth and becomes rigid. I asked your disciples to drive out the spirit, but they could not."

19 "O unbelieving generation," Jesus replied, "how long shall I stay with you? How long shall I put up with you? Bring the boy to me."

20 So they brought him. When the spirit saw Jesus, it immediately threw the boy into a convulsion. He fell to the ground and rolled around, foaming at the mouth.

21 Jesus asked the boy's father, "How long has he been like this?"

"From childhood," he answered. 22 "It has often thrown him into fire or water to kill him. But if you can do anything, take pity on us and help us."

23 " 'If you can'?" said Jesus. "Everything is possible for him who believes."

24 Immediately the boy's father exclaimed, "I do believe; help me overcome my unbelief!"

25 When Jesus saw that a crowd was running to the scene, he rebuked the evil*b* spirit. "You deaf and mute spirit," he said, "I command you, come out of him and never enter him again."

26 The spirit shrieked, convulsed him violently and came out. The boy looked so much like a corpse that many said, "He's dead." 27 But Jesus took him by the hand and lifted him to his feet, and he stood up.

28 After Jesus had gone indoors, his disciples asked him privately, "Why couldn't we drive it out?"

29 He replied, "This kind can come out only by prayer.*c*"

30 They left that place and passed

a 35 The Greek word means either *life* or *soul*; also in verse 36.   *b 25* Greek *unclean*   *c 29* Some manuscripts *prayer and fasting* through Galilee. Jesus did not want anyone to know where they were, 31because he was teaching his disciples. He said to them, "The Son of Man is going to be betrayed into the hands of men. They will kill him, and after three days he will rise." 32But they did not understand what he meant and were afraid to ask him about it.

Who Is the Greatest?

33They came to Capernaum. When he was in the house, he asked them, "What were you arguing about on the road?" 34But they kept quiet because on the way they had argued about who was the greatest.

35Sitting down, Jesus called the Twelve and said, "If anyone wants to be first, he must be the very last, and the servant of all."

36He took a little child and had him stand among them. Taking him in his arms, he said to them, 37"Whoever welcomes one of these little children in my name welcomes me; and whoever welcomes me does not welcome me but the one who sent me."

Whoever Is Not Against Us Is for Us

38"Teacher," said John, "we saw a man driving out demons in your name and we told him to stop, because he was not one of us."

39"Do not stop him," Jesus said. "No one who does a miracle in my name can in the next moment say anything bad about me, 40for whoever is not against us is for us. 41I tell you the truth, anyone who gives you a cup of water in my name because you belong to Christ will certainly not lose his reward.

Causing to Sin

42"And if anyone causes one of these little ones who believe in me to sin, it would be better for him to be thrown into the sea with a large millstone tied around his neck. 43If your hand causes you to sin, cut it off. It is better for you to enter life maimed than with two hands to go into hell, where the fire never goes out.[a] 45And if your foot causes you to sin, cut it

[a] 43 Some manuscripts out, 44where / " 'their worm does not die, / and the fire is not quenched.'

Use What You Have

READ MARK 9:14–29

After watching a Hollywood stunt man jump out of a fifty-storey window, you probably wonder how anybody could be so fearless—or so crazy! But no stunt man *starts* at fifty storeys. They begin by falling a few feet and then gradually work their way up. Literally. Growing in faith is no different. The father of the demon-possessed boy in this story didn't start out with a lot of faith. But when Jesus said, "Everything is possible for him who believes," Dad begged Jesus to help his small faith (Mark 9:23–24). Jesus responded by driving the demons out of the boy. That's a sure-fire way to increase someone's faith! To move a mountain, all it takes is faith the size of a mustard seed (Matthew 17:20). You don't need to have great faith for God to use you. You just have to choose to put whatever faith you *do* have into action. Only then will it grow.

Your next reading is on page 1296.

off. It is better for you to enter life crippled than to have two feet and be thrown into hell.ᵃ ⁴⁷And if your eye causes you to sin, pluck it out. It is better for you to enter the kingdom of God with one eye than to have two eyes and be thrown into hell, ⁴⁸where

" 'their worm does not die,
　and the fire is not quenched.'ᵇ

⁴⁹Everyone will be salted with fire.

⁵⁰"Salt is good, but if it loses its saltiness, how can you make it salty again? Have salt in yourselves, and be at peace with each other."

Divorce

10 Jesus then left that place and went into the region of Judea and across the Jordan. Again crowds of people came to him, and as was his custom, he taught them.

²Some Pharisees came and tested him by asking, "Is it lawful for a man to divorce his wife?"

³"What did Moses command you?" he replied.

⁴They said, "Moses permitted a man to write a certificate of divorce and send her away."

⁵"It was because your hearts were hard that Moses wrote you this law," Jesus replied. ⁶"But at the beginning of creation God 'made them male and female.'ᶜ ⁷'For this reason a man will leave his father and mother and be united to his wife,ᵈ ⁸and the two will become one flesh.'ᵉ So they are no longer two, but one. ⁹Therefore what God has joined together, let man not separate."

¹⁰When they were in the house again, the disciples asked Jesus about this. ¹¹He answered, "Anyone who divorces his wife and marries another woman commits adultery against her. ¹²And if she divorces her husband and marries another man, she commits adultery."

The Little Children and Jesus

¹³People were bringing little children to Jesus to have him touch them, but the disciples rebuked them. ¹⁴When Jesus saw this, he was indignant. He said to them, "Let the little children come to me, and do not hinder them, for the kingdom of God belongs to such as these. ¹⁵I tell you the truth, anyone who will not receive the kingdom of God like a little child will never enter it." ¹⁶And he took the children in his arms, put his hands on them and blessed them.

The Rich Young Man

¹⁷As Jesus started on his way, a man ran up to him and fell on his knees before him. "Good teacher," he asked, "what must I do to inherit eternal life?"

¹⁸"Why do you call me good?" Jesus answered. "No one is good—except God alone. ¹⁹You know the commandments: 'Do not murder, do not commit adultery, do not steal, do not give false testimony, do not defraud, honor your father and mother.'ᶠ"

²⁰"Teacher," he declared, "all these I have kept since I was a boy."

²¹Jesus looked at him and loved him. "One thing you lack," he said. "Go, sell everything you have and give to the poor, and you will have treasure in heaven. Then come, follow me."

²²At this the man's face fell. He went away sad, because he had great wealth.

²³Jesus looked around and said to his disciples, "How hard it is for the rich to enter the kingdom of God!"

²⁴The disciples were amazed at his words. But Jesus said again, "Children, how hard it isᵍ to enter the kingdom of God! ²⁵It is easier for a camel to go through the eye of a needle than for a rich man to enter the kingdom of God."

²⁶The disciples were even more amazed, and said to each other, "Who then can be saved?"

²⁷Jesus looked at them and said, "With man this is impossible, but not with God; all things are possible with God."

²⁸Peter said to him, "We have left everything to follow you!"

²⁹"I tell you the truth," Jesus replied, "no one who has left home or brothers or sisters or mother or father or children or fields for me and the gospel ³⁰will fail to receive a hundred times as much in this present age (homes, brothers, sisters, mothers, children and fields—and with them, persecutions) and in the age to

---

ᵃ 45 Some manuscripts hell, ⁴⁶where / " 'their worm does not die, / and the fire is not quenched.'　ᵇ 48 Isaiah 66:24
ᶜ 6 Gen. 1:27　ᵈ 7 Some early manuscripts do not have and be united to his wife.　ᵉ 8 Gen. 2:24
ᶠ 19 Exodus 20:12–16; Deut. 5:16–20　ᵍ 24 Some manuscripts is for those who trust in riches

come, eternal life. ³¹But many who are first will be last, and the last first."

Jesus Again Predicts His Death

³²They were on their way up to Jerusalem, with Jesus leading the way, and the disciples were astonished, while those who followed were afraid. Again he took the Twelve aside and told them what was going to happen to him. ³³"We are going up to Jerusalem," he said, "and the Son of Man will be betrayed to the chief priests and teachers of the law. They will condemn him to death and will hand him over to the Gentiles, ³⁴who will mock him and spit on him, flog him and kill him. Three days later he will rise."

The Request of James and John

³⁵Then James and John, the sons of Zebedee, came to him. "Teacher," they said, "we want you to do for us whatever we ask."

³⁶"What do you want me to do for you?" he asked.

³⁷They replied, "Let one of us sit at your right and the other at your left in your glory."

³⁸"You don't know what you are asking," Jesus said. "Can you drink the cup I drink or be baptized with the baptism I am baptized with?"

³⁹"We can," they answered.

Jesus said to them, "You will drink the cup I drink and be baptized with the baptism I am baptized with, ⁴⁰but to sit at my right or left is not for me to grant. These places belong to those for whom they have been prepared."

⁴¹When the ten heard about this, they became indignant with James and John. ⁴²Jesus called them together and said, "You know that those who are regarded as rulers of the Gentiles lord it over them, and their high officials exercise authority over them. ⁴³Not so with you. Instead, whoever wants to become great among you must be your servant, ⁴⁴and whoever wants to be first must be slave of all. ⁴⁵For even the Son of Man did not come to be served, but to serve, and to give his life as a ransom for many."

Jesus Loves Kids

READ MARK 10:13–16

"You're just a kid!" usually means, "You, small human being, are not old enough to make important decisions or do big stuff." That might be OK if it means you can't go to war, but it's *nuts* to think that a kid can't truly love God and understand who he is. There are no age limits to that. Being a kid doesn't mean you can't have a relationship with God. Just the opposite! Jesus said that unless people were willing to accept him like children, they couldn't get into the kingdom of God. (Uh oh. Sounds like some grouchy, old, stuck up adults are in trouble.) Think about it. If Adam and Eve hadn't sinned, kids would have grown up walking and talking with God—right from day one! So who says kids can't know God? It's a wonderful time in your life to get to know and love him.

Your next reading is on page 1297.

Blind Bartimaeus Receives His Sight

46Then they came to Jericho. As Jesus and his disciples, together with a large crowd, were leaving the city, a blind man, Bartimaeus (that is, the Son of Timaeus), was sitting by the roadside begging. 47When he heard that it was Jesus of Nazareth, he began to shout, "Jesus, Son of David, have mercy on me!"

48Many rebuked him and told him to be quiet, but he shouted all the more, "Son of David, have mercy on me!"

49Jesus stopped and said, "Call him."

So they called to the blind man, "Cheer up! On your feet! He's calling you." 50Throwing his cloak aside, he jumped to his feet and came to Jesus.

51"What do you want me to do for you?" Jesus asked him.

The blind man said, "Rabbi, I want to see."

52"Go," said Jesus, "your faith has healed you." Immediately he received his sight and followed Jesus along the road.

The Triumphal Entry

11 As they approached Jerusalem and came to Bethphage and Bethany at the Mount of Olives, Jesus sent two of his disciples, 2saying to them, "Go to the village ahead of you, and just as you enter it, you will find a colt tied there, which no one has ever ridden. Untie it and bring it here. 3If anyone asks you, 'Why are you doing this?' tell him, 'The Lord needs it and will send it back here shortly.' "

4They went and found a colt outside in the street, tied at a doorway. As they untied it, 5some people standing there asked, "What are you doing, untying that colt?" 6They answered as Jesus had told them to, and the people let them go. 7When they brought the colt to Jesus and threw their cloaks over it, he sat on it. 8Many people spread their cloaks on the road, while others spread branches they had cut in the fields. 9Those who went ahead and those who followed shouted,

King of the Castle

READ MARK 10:35–45

James and John wanted to be the "kings of the castle." They asked Jesus to do one tiny little favor for them. "Give us the two most powerful positions in God's kingdom." (Oh, is *that* all you wanted?) Jesus said that if we want to be powerful, we need to learn to serve others. Normally we want to use our strength to get what *we* want, like the last piece of pizza or the best seat on the bus. Jesus said that we need to use our strength to help other people get what *they* need. *Come again?* Oh yeah, you read that right. The more you serve, the more you move up. You want to be the king of the castle? Start scrubbing the drawbridge and cleaning out the stables. Being a man of God is all about helping others.

Your next reading is on page 1300.

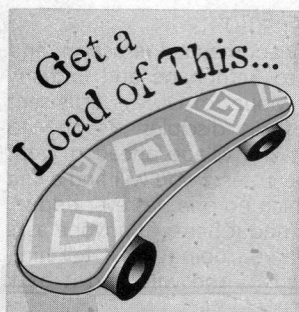

Get a Load of This...

Read Mark 11:15–19 about how Jesus kicked out some hypocrites and kicked over their tables. But don't get any ideas about knocking over tables during a bake sale or a fund-raiser in your church. Jesus was laying into the religious leaders because they were short-changing and cheating the people who were buying sacrifices to worship in the temple.

"Hosanna!ᵃ"

"Blessed is he who comes in the name of the Lord!"ᵇ

10 "Blessed is the coming kingdom of our father David!"

"Hosanna in the highest!"

11 Jesus entered Jerusalem and went to the temple. He looked around at everything, but since it was already late, he went out to Bethany with the Twelve.

Jesus Clears the Temple

12 The next day as they were leaving Bethany, Jesus was hungry. 13 Seeing in the distance a fig tree in leaf, he went to find out if it had any fruit. When he reached it, he found nothing but leaves, because it was not the season for figs. 14 Then he said to the tree, "May no one ever eat fruit from you again." And his disciples heard him say it.

15 On reaching Jerusalem, Jesus entered the temple area and began driving out those who were buying and selling there. He overturned the tables of the money changers and the benches of those selling doves, 16 and would not allow anyone to carry merchandise through the temple courts. 17 And as he taught them, he said, "Is it not written:

" 'My house will be called
a house of prayer for all nations'ᶜ?

But you have made it 'a den of robbers.'ᵈ"

18 The chief priests and the teachers of the law heard this and began looking for a way to kill him, for they feared him, because the whole crowd was amazed at his teaching.

19 When evening came, theyᵉ went out of the city.

The Withered Fig Tree

20 In the morning, as they went along, they saw the fig tree withered from the roots. 21 Peter remembered and said to Jesus, "Rabbi, look! The fig tree you cursed has withered!"

22 "Haveᶠ faith in God," Jesus answered. 23 "I tell you the truth, if anyone says to this mountain, 'Go, throw yourself into the sea,' and does not doubt in his heart but believes that what he says will happen, it will be done for him. 24 Therefore I tell you, whatever you ask for in prayer, believe that you have received it, and it will be yours. 25 And when you stand praying, if you hold anything against anyone, forgive him, so that your Father in heaven may forgive you your sins.ᵍ"

ᵃ 9 A Hebrew expression meaning "Save!" which became an exclamation of praise; also in verse 10   ᵇ 9 Psalm 118:25,26   ᶜ 17 Isaiah 56:7   ᵈ 17 Jer. 7:11   ᵉ 19 Some early manuscripts he   ᶠ 22 Some early manuscripts If you have   ᵍ 25 Some manuscripts sins. 26 But if you do not forgive, neither will your Father who is in heaven forgive your sins.

The Authority of Jesus Questioned

27They arrived again in Jerusalem, and while Jesus was walking in the temple courts, the chief priests, the teachers of the law and the elders came to him. 28"By what authority are you doing these things?" they asked. "And who gave you authority to do this?"

29Jesus replied, "I will ask you one question. Answer me, and I will tell you by what authority I am doing these things. 30John's baptism—was it from heaven, or from men? Tell me!"

31They discussed it among themselves and said, "If we say, 'From heaven,' he will ask, 'Then why didn't you believe him?' 32But if we say, 'From men' . . ." (They feared the people, for everyone held that John really was a prophet.)

33So they answered Jesus, "We don't know."

Jesus said, "Neither will I tell you by what authority I am doing these things."

The Parable of the Tenants

12 He then began to speak to them in parables: "A man planted a vineyard. He put a wall around it, dug a pit for the winepress and built a watchtower. Then he rented the vineyard to some farmers and went away on a journey. 2At harvest time he sent a servant to the tenants to collect from them some of the fruit of the vineyard. 3But they seized him, beat him and sent him away empty-handed. 4Then he sent another servant to them; they struck this man on the head and treated him shamefully. 5He sent still another, and that one they killed. He sent many others; some of them they beat, others they killed.

6"He had one left to send, a son, whom he loved. He sent him last of all, saying, 'They will respect my son.'

7"But the tenants said to one another, 'This is the heir. Come, let's kill him, and the inheritance will be ours.' 8So they took him and killed him, and threw him out of the vineyard.

9"What then will the owner of the vineyard do? He will come and kill those tenants and give the vineyard to others. 10Haven't you read this scripture:

" 'The stone the builders rejected
    has become the capstone[a];
11 the Lord has done this,
    and it is marvelous in our eyes'[b]?"

12Then they looked for a way to arrest him because they knew he had spoken the parable against them. But they were afraid of the crowd; so they left him and went away.

Paying Taxes to Caesar

13Later they sent some of the Pharisees and Herodians to Jesus to catch him in his words. 14They came to him and said, "Teacher, we know you are a man of in-

Get a Load of This...

Check out Mark 11:23. Having the faith to move a mountain is cool. The bad news is that if you have that much faith but you don't love others, you are nothin', Mister (1 Corinthians 13:2). Now the good news: If faith can move a mountain, and love is *more* important, what can love do?

---

a 10 Or cornerstone   b 11 Psalm 118:22,23

tegrity. You aren't swayed by men, because you pay no attention to who they are; but you teach the way of God in accordance with the truth. Is it right to pay taxes to Caesar or not? [15]Should we pay or shouldn't we?"

But Jesus knew their hypocrisy. "Why are you trying to trap me?" he asked. "Bring me a denarius and let me look at it." [16]They brought the coin, and he asked them, "Whose portrait is this? And whose inscription?"

"Caesar's," they replied.

[17]Then Jesus said to them, "Give to Caesar what is Caesar's and to God what is God's."

And they were amazed at him.

Marriage at the Resurrection

[18]Then the Sadducees, who say there is no resurrection, came to him with a question. [19]"Teacher," they said, "Moses wrote for us that if a man's brother dies and leaves a wife but no children, the man must marry the widow and have children for his brother. [20]Now there were seven brothers. The first one married and died without leaving any children. [21]The second one married the widow, but he also died, leaving no child. It was the same with the third. [22]In fact, none of the seven left any children. Last of all, the woman died too. [23]At the resurrection[a] whose wife will she be, since the seven were married to her?"

[24]Jesus replied, "Are you not in error because you do not know the Scriptures or the power of God? [25]When the dead rise, they will neither marry nor be given in marriage; they will be like the angels in heaven. [26]Now about the dead rising— have you not read in the book of Moses, in the account of the bush, how God said to him, 'I am the God of Abraham, the God of Isaac, and the God of Jacob'[b]? [27]He is not the God of the dead, but of the living. You are badly mistaken!"

The Greatest Commandment

[28]One of the teachers of the law came and heard them debating. Noticing that

---

[a] 23 Some manuscripts resurrection, when men rise from the dead,   [b] 26 Exodus 3:6

The Unteachable Teachers

READ MARK 12:1–12

Do you *love* to be told that you're wrong? Obviously, no. You wouldn't be smiling if you saw your mom talking to your teacher on the phone, hang up, then walk your way frowning. But the news is, no one's perfect and we all need to be told at times that we're wrong.

    Just don't come unglued over it. The Jewish religious leaders realized that Jesus was rebuking them in this parable and— HoooEEEE!—they did *not* like that one bit. See, they thought they were nearly perfect and didn't need any correction. (Well, in this case, Jesus' talked about God *killing* them, so you can't blame them for becoming a *little* bit unglued.) If your parents correct you, don't get your nose out of joint. Think of correction as a chance to learn and a chance to make sure you don't make the same mistake again.

Your next reading is on page 1302.

Jesus had given them a good answer, he asked him, "Of all the commandments, which is the most important?"

29"The most important one," answered Jesus, "is this: 'Hear, O Israel, the Lord our God, the Lord is one.ᵃ 30Love the Lord your God with all your heart and with all your soul and with all your mind and with all your strength.'ᵇ 31The second is this: 'Love your neighbor as yourself.'ᶜ There is no commandment greater than these."

32"Well said, teacher," the man replied. "You are right in saying that God is one and there is no other but him. 33To love him with all your heart, with all your understanding and with all your strength, and to love your neighbor as yourself is more important than all burnt offerings and sacrifices."

34When Jesus saw that he had answered wisely, he said to him, "You are not far from the kingdom of God." And from then on no one dared ask him any more questions.

Whose Son Is the Christ?

35While Jesus was teaching in the temple courts, he asked, "How is it that the teachers of the law say that the Christᵈ is the son of David? 36David himself, speaking by the Holy Spirit, declared:

" 'The Lord said to my Lord:
   "Sit at my right hand
until I put your enemies
   under your feet." 'ᵉ

37David himself calls him 'Lord.' How then can he be his son?"

The large crowd listened to him with delight.

38As he taught, Jesus said, "Watch out for the teachers of the law. They like to walk around in flowing robes and be greeted in the marketplaces, 39and have the most important seats in the synagogues and the places of honor at banquets. 40They devour widows' houses and for a show make lengthy prayers. Such men will be punished most severely."

The Widow's Offering

41Jesus sat down opposite the place where the offerings were put and watched the crowd putting their money into the temple treasury. Many rich people threw in large amounts. 42But a poor widow came and put in two very small copper coins,ᶠ worth only a fraction of a penny.ᵍ

43Calling his disciples to him, Jesus said, "I tell you the truth, this poor widow has put more into the treasury than all the others. 44They all gave out of their wealth; but she, out of her poverty, put in everything—all she had to live on."

Get a Load of This...

This is *some* story!— the story some guys made up about a woman whose seven husbands all died (Mark 12:20–22). By brother number five, you'd think these guys would've started getting a little nervous about marrying her. If she lived today, the FBI would say, "Ma'am, we'd like to ask you some questions."

ᵃ 29 Or the Lord our God is one Lord   ᵇ 30 Deut. 6:4,5   ᶜ 31 Lev. 19:18
ᵈ 35 Or Messiah   ᵉ 36 Psalm 110:1   ᶠ 42 Greek two lepta   ᵍ 42 Greek kodrantes

Signs of the End of the Age

13 As he was leaving the temple, one of his disciples said to him, "Look, Teacher! What massive stones! What magnificent buildings!"

[2] "Do you see all these great buildings?" replied Jesus. "Not one stone here will be left on another; every one will be thrown down."

[3] As Jesus was sitting on the Mount of Olives opposite the temple, Peter, James, John and Andrew asked him privately, [4] "Tell us, when will these things happen? And what will be the sign that they are all about to be fulfilled?"

[5] Jesus said to them: "Watch out that no one deceives you. [6] Many will come in my name, claiming, 'I am he,' and will deceive many. [7] When you hear of wars and rumors of wars, do not be alarmed. Such things must happen, but the end is still to come. [8] Nation will rise against nation, and kingdom against kingdom. There will be earthquakes in various places, and famines. These are the beginning of birth pains.

[9] "You must be on your guard. You will be handed over to the local councils and flogged in the synagogues. On account of me you will stand before governors and kings as witnesses to them. [10] And the gospel must first be preached to all nations. [11] Whenever you are arrested and brought to trial, do not worry beforehand about what to say. Just say whatever is given you at the time, for it is not you speaking, but the Holy Spirit.

[12] "Brother will betray brother to death, and a father his child. Children will rebel against their parents and have them put to death. [13] All men will hate you because of me, but he who stands firm to the end will be saved.

[14] "When you see 'the abomination that causes desolation'[a] standing where it[b] does not belong—let the reader under-

[a] 14 Daniel 9:27; 11:31; 12:11   [b] 14 Or he; also in verse 29

stand—then let those who are in Judea flee to the mountains. [15]Let no one on the roof of his house go down or enter the house to take anything out. [16]Let no one in the field go back to get his cloak. [17]How dreadful it will be in those days for pregnant women and nursing mothers! [18]Pray that this will not take place in winter, [19]because those will be days of distress unequaled from the beginning, when God created the world, until now—and never to be equaled again. [20]If the Lord had not cut short those days, no one would survive. But for the sake of the elect, whom he has chosen, he has shortened them. [21]At that time if anyone says to you, 'Look, here is the Christ[a]!' or, 'Look, there he is!' do not believe it. [22]For false Christs and false prophets will appear and perform signs and miracles to deceive the elect—if that were possible. [23]So be on your guard; I have told you everything ahead of time.

[24]"But in those days, following that distress,

" 'the sun will be darkened,
    and the moon will not give its light;
[25]the stars will fall from the sky,
    and the heavenly bodies will be shaken.'[b]

[26]"At that time men will see the Son of Man coming in clouds with great power and glory. [27]And he will send his angels and gather his elect from the four winds, from the ends of the earth to the ends of the heavens.

[28]"Now learn this lesson from the fig tree: As soon as its twigs get tender and its leaves come out, you know that summer is near. [29]Even so, when you see these things happening, you know that it is near, right at the door. [30]I tell you the truth, this generation[c] will certainly not pass away until all these things have happened. [31]Heaven and earth will pass away, but my words will never pass away.

The Day and Hour Unknown

[32]"No one knows about that day or hour, not even the angels in heaven, nor the Son, but only the Father. [33]Be on guard! Be alert[d]! You do not know when that time will come. [34]It's like a man going away: He leaves his house and puts his servants in charge, each with his assigned task, and tells the one at the door to keep watch.

[35]"Therefore keep watch because you do not know when the owner of the house will come back—whether in the evening, or at midnight, or when the rooster crows, or at dawn. [36]If he comes suddenly, do not let him find you sleeping. [37]What I say to you, I say to everyone: 'Watch!' "

Jesus Anointed at Bethany

14 Now the Passover and the Feast of Unleavened Bread were only two days away, and the chief priests and the teachers of the law were looking for some sly way to arrest Jesus and kill

Get a Load of This...

What would people be doing up on the roof of their house (Mark 13:15)? Well, they had flat roofs back then, so they could sit or walk up there. Even today they have flat roofs in Israel. If a chicken lays an egg on a roof in Jerusalem, it doesn't roll anywhere. Question is, what would the *chicken* be doing up there?

[a] 21 Or *Messiah*   [b] 25 Isaiah 13:10; 34:4   [c] 30 Or *race*   [d] 33 Some manuscripts *alert and pray*

him. ²"But not during the Feast," they said, "or the people may riot."

³While he was in Bethany, reclining at the table in the home of a man known as Simon the Leper, a woman came with an alabaster jar of very expensive perfume, made of pure nard. She broke the jar and poured the perfume on his head.

⁴Some of those present were saying indignantly to one another, "Why this waste of perfume? ⁵It could have been sold for more than a year's wages[a] and the money given to the poor." And they rebuked her harshly.

⁶"Leave her alone," said Jesus. "Why are you bothering her? She has done a beautiful thing to me. ⁷The poor you will always have with you, and you can help them any time you want. But you will not always have me. ⁸She did what she could. She poured perfume on my body beforehand to prepare for my burial. ⁹I tell you the truth, wherever the gospel is preached

throughout the world, what she has done will also be told, in memory of her."

¹⁰Then Judas Iscariot, one of the Twelve, went to the chief priests to betray Jesus to them. ¹¹They were delighted to hear this and promised to give him money. So he watched for an opportunity to hand him over.

The Lord's Supper

¹²On the first day of the Feast of Unleavened Bread, when it was customary to sacrifice the Passover lamb, Jesus' disciples asked him, "Where do you want us to go and make preparations for you to eat the Passover?"

¹³So he sent two of his disciples, telling them, "Go into the city, and a man carrying a jar of water will meet you. Follow him. ¹⁴Say to the owner of the house he enters, 'The Teacher asks: Where is my guest room, where I may eat the Passover

ª 5 Greek than three hundred denarii

Make It Stick

READ MARK 14:1–11

When Mary poured perfume on Jesus, some disciples just about lost it. "Are you nuts? It would take a year's wages to pay for a bottle of that stuff!" But Mary knew it was important to give her time and valued possessions to God. What is one special thing can you give to God this week?

with my disciples?' [15]He will show you a large upper room, furnished and ready. Make preparations for us there."

[16]The disciples left, went into the city and found things just as Jesus had told them. So they prepared the Passover.

[17]When evening came, Jesus arrived with the Twelve. [18]While they were reclining at the table eating, he said, "I tell you the truth, one of you will betray me—one who is eating with me."

[19]They were saddened, and one by one they said to him, "Surely not I?"

[20]"It is one of the Twelve," he replied, "one who dips bread into the bowl with me. [21]The Son of Man will go just as it is written about him. But woe to that man who betrays the Son of Man! It would be better for him if he had not been born."

[22]While they were eating, Jesus took bread, gave thanks and broke it, and gave it to his disciples, saying, "Take it; this is my body."

[23]Then he took the cup, gave thanks and offered it to them, and they all drank from it.

[24]"This is my blood of the[a] covenant, which is poured out for many," he said to them. [25]"I tell you the truth, I will not drink again of the fruit of the vine until that day when I drink it anew in the kingdom of God."

[26]When they had sung a hymn, they went out to the Mount of Olives.

Jesus Predicts Peter's Denial

[27]"You will all fall away," Jesus told them, "for it is written:

" 'I will strike the shepherd,
    and the sheep will be scattered.'[b]

[28]But after I have risen, I will go ahead of you into Galilee."

[29]Peter declared, "Even if all fall away, I will not."

[30]"I tell you the truth," Jesus answered, "today—yes, tonight—before the rooster crows twice[c] you yourself will disown me three times."

[31]But Peter insisted emphatically, "Even if I have to die with you, I will never disown you." And all the others said the same.

Gethsemane

[32]They went to a place called Gethsemane, and Jesus said to his disciples, "Sit here while I pray." [33]He took Peter, James and John along with him, and he began to be deeply distressed and troubled. [34]"My soul is overwhelmed with sorrow to the point of death," he said to them. "Stay here and keep watch."

[35]Going a little farther, he fell to the ground and prayed that if possible the hour might pass from him. [36]"Abba,[d] Father," he said, "everything is possible for you. Take this cup from me. Yet not what I will, but what you will."

[37]Then he returned to his disciples and found them sleeping. "Simon," he said to Peter, "are you asleep? Could you not keep watch for one hour? [38]Watch and pray so that you will not fall into temptation. The spirit is willing, but the body is weak."

[39]Once more he went away and prayed the same thing. [40]When he came back, he again found them sleeping, because their eyes were heavy. They did not know what to say to him.

[41]Returning the third time, he said to them, "Are you still sleeping and resting? Enough! The hour has come. Look, the Son of Man is betrayed into the hands of sinners. [42]Rise! Let us go! Here comes my betrayer!"

Jesus Arrested

[43]Just as he was speaking, Judas, one of the Twelve, appeared. With him was a crowd armed with swords and clubs, sent from the chief priests, the teachers of the law, and the elders.

[44]Now the betrayer had arranged a signal with them: "The one I kiss is the man; arrest him and lead him away under guard." [45]Going at once to Jesus, Judas said, "Rabbi!" and kissed him. [46]The men seized Jesus and arrested him. [47]Then one of those standing near drew his sword and struck the servant of the high priest, cutting off his ear.

[48]"Am I leading a rebellion," said Jesus, "that you have come out with swords and clubs to capture me? [49]Every day I was with you, teaching in the temple courts, and you did not arrest me. But the Scriptures must be fulfilled." [50]Then everyone deserted him and fled.

[51]A young man, wearing nothing but a linen garment, was following Jesus. When

---

[a] 24 Some manuscripts the new   [b] 27 Zech. 13:7
[c] 30 Some early manuscripts do not have twice.
[d] 36 Aramaic for Father

they seized him, ⁵²he fled naked, leaving his garment behind.

Before the Sanhedrin

⁵³They took Jesus to the high priest, and all the chief priests, elders and teachers of the law came together. ⁵⁴Peter followed him at a distance, right into the courtyard of the high priest. There he sat with the guards and warmed himself at the fire.

⁵⁵The chief priests and the whole Sanhedrin were looking for evidence against Jesus so that they could put him to death, but they did not find any. ⁵⁶Many testified falsely against him, but their statements did not agree.

⁵⁷Then some stood up and gave this false testimony against him: ⁵⁸"We heard him say, 'I will destroy this man-made temple and in three days will build another, not made by man.' " ⁵⁹Yet even then their testimony did not agree.

⁶⁰Then the high priest stood up before them and asked Jesus, "Are you not going to answer? What is this testimony that these men are bringing against you?" ⁶¹But Jesus remained silent and gave no answer.

Again the high priest asked him, "Are you the Christ,ᵃ the Son of the Blessed One?"

⁶²"I am," said Jesus. "And you will see the Son of Man sitting at the right hand of the Mighty One and coming on the clouds of heaven."

⁶³The high priest tore his clothes. "Why do we need any more witnesses?" he asked. ⁶⁴"You have heard the blasphemy. What do you think?"

They all condemned him as worthy of death. ⁶⁵Then some began to spit at him; they blindfolded him, struck him with their fists, and said, "Prophesy!" And the guards took him and beat him.

Peter Disowns Jesus

⁶⁶While Peter was below in the courtyard, one of the servant girls of the high priest came by. ⁶⁷When she saw Peter warming himself, she looked closely at him.

"You also were with that Nazarene, Jesus," she said.

⁶⁸But he denied it. "I don't know or un-

ᵃ 61 Or *Messiah*

Sooooo Sleepy

READ MARK 14:32–42

Imagine: you've just had the greatest meal of roast turkey, mashed potatoes, thick, brown gravy, loads of stuffing and pumpkin pie for dessert. You loosen your belt, lie on the couch and (yawn) drift off to dreamland. This is how the disciples felt when they went out with Jesus to pray, after a huge Passover feast. When Jesus found them sleeping, he warned them, "Watch and pray so that you will not fall into temptation" (verse 38). What do you think he meant—that you should "watch and pray" every minute, look for the devil behind every door and spend every spare minute in church? No. On the other hand, he wasn't telling you to just have a "once-a-week, go-to-church faith" either. Jesus was saying you need to stick close to God and grow closer to him each day. Otherwise you won't be able to withstand the temptations life throws your way.

Your next reading is on page 1308.

derstand what you're talking about," he said, and went out into the entryway. *a*

69When the servant girl saw him there, she said again to those standing around, "This fellow is one of them." 70Again he denied it.

After a little while, those standing near said to Peter, "Surely you are one of them, for you are a Galilean."

71He began to call down curses on himself, and he swore to them, "I don't know this man you're talking about."

72Immediately the rooster crowed the second time. *b* Then Peter remembered the word Jesus had spoken to him: "Before the rooster crows twice *c* you will disown me three times." And he broke down and wept.

Jesus Before Pilate

15 Very early in the morning, the chief priests, with the elders, the teachers of the law and the whole Sanhedrin, reached a decision. They bound Jesus, led him away and handed him over to Pilate.

2"Are you the king of the Jews?" asked Pilate.

"Yes, it is as you say," Jesus replied.

3The chief priests accused him of many things. 4So again Pilate asked him, "Aren't you going to answer? See how many things they are accusing you of."

5But Jesus still made no reply, and Pilate was amazed.

6Now it was the custom at the Feast to release a prisoner whom the people requested. 7A man called Barabbas was in prison with the insurrectionists who had committed murder in the uprising. 8The crowd came up and asked Pilate to do for them what he usually did.

9"Do you want me to release to you the king of the Jews?" asked Pilate, 10knowing it was out of envy that the chief priests had handed Jesus over to him. 11But the chief priests stirred up the crowd to have Pilate release Barabbas instead.

12"What shall I do, then, with the one you call the king of the Jews?" Pilate asked them.

13"Crucify him!" they shouted.

14"Why? What crime has he committed?" asked Pilate.

But they shouted all the louder, "Crucify him!"

15Wanting to satisfy the crowd, Pilate released Barabbas to them. He had Jesus flogged, and handed him over to be crucified.

The Soldiers Mock Jesus

16The soldiers led Jesus away into the palace (that is, the Praetorium) and called together the whole company of soldiers. 17They put a purple robe on him, then twisted together a crown of thorns and set it on him. 18And they began to call out to him, "Hail, king of the Jews!" 19Again and again they struck him on the head with a staff and spit on him. Falling on their knees, they paid homage to him. 20And when they had mocked him, they took off the purple robe and put his own clothes on him. Then they led him out to crucify him.

The Crucifixion

21A certain man from Cyrene, Simon, the father of Alexander and Rufus, was passing by on his way in from the country, and they forced him to carry the cross. 22They brought Jesus to the place called Golgotha (which means The Place of the Skull). 23Then they offered him wine mixed with myrrh, but he did not take it. 24And they crucified him. Dividing up his clothes, they cast lots to see what each would get.

25It was the third hour when they crucified him. 26The written notice of the charge against him read: THE KING OF THE JEWS. 27They crucified two robbers with him, one on his right and one on his left. *d* 29Those who passed by hurled insults at him, shaking their heads and saying, "So! You who are going to destroy the temple and build it in three days, 30come down from the cross and save yourself!"

31In the same way the chief priests and the teachers of the law mocked him among themselves. "He saved others," they said, "but he can't save himself! 32Let this Christ, *e* this King of Israel, come down now from the cross, that we may see and believe." Those crucified with him also heaped insults on him.

The Death of Jesus

33At the sixth hour darkness came over

---

a 68 Some early manuscripts *entryway and the rooster crowed*　　*b 72* Some early manuscripts do not have *the second time.*　　*c 72* Some early manuscripts do not have *twice.*　　*d 27* Some manuscripts *left,* 28*and the scripture was fulfilled which says, "He was counted with the lawless ones"* (Isaiah 53:12)　　*e 32* Or *Messiah* the whole land until the ninth hour. [34] And at the ninth hour Jesus cried out in a loud voice, *"Eloi, Eloi, lama sabachthani?"*— which means, "My God, my God, why have you forsaken me?" [a]

[35] When some of those standing near heard this, they said, "Listen, he's calling Elijah."

[36] One man ran, filled a sponge with wine vinegar, put it on a stick, and offered it to Jesus to drink. "Now leave him alone. Let's see if Elijah comes to take him down," he said.

[37] With a loud cry, Jesus breathed his last.

[38] The curtain of the temple was torn in two from top to bottom. [39] And when the centurion, who stood there in front of Jesus, heard his cry and [b] saw how he died, he said, "Surely this man was the Son [c] of God!"

[40] Some women were watching from a distance. Among them were Mary Magdalene, Mary the mother of James the younger and of Joses, and Salome. [41] In Galilee these women had followed him and cared for his needs. Many other women who had come up with him to Jerusalem were also there.

The Burial of Jesus

[42] It was Preparation Day (that is, the day before the Sabbath). So as evening approached, [43] Joseph of Arimathea, a prominent member of the Council, who was himself waiting for the kingdom of God, went boldly to Pilate and asked for Jesus' body. [44] Pilate was surprised to hear that he was already dead. Summoning the centurion, he asked him if Jesus had already died. [45] When he learned from the centurion that it was so, he gave the body to Joseph. [46] So Joseph bought some linen cloth, took down the body, wrapped it in the linen, and placed it in a tomb cut out of rock. Then he rolled a stone against the entrance of the tomb. [47] Mary Magdalene

[a] 34 Psalm 22:1   *[b] 39* Some manuscripts do not have *heard his cry and*   *[c] 39* Or *a son*

A Gory Death

READ MARK 15:16–39

What did Jesus go through when he died to save you? First, the Romans lashed Jesus' back with a "cat-o-nine tails," a whip with metal and bones attached to many strips of leather. His entire back and shoulders and sides were sliced and bleeding, perhaps even exposing his ribs. Sometimes a victim of flogging didn't even survive. This kind of pain you simply *never* want to experience. Then the Roman soldiers mocked Jesus, spit on him and repeatedly punched him. When they shoved the "crown of thorns" onto Jesus' head, long thorns sliced his skin open. Then huge iron nails were driven through his wrists and ankles and he was hung on a cross to die an extremely painful death. However, the strength of Jesus' loud cry in Mark 15:37 shows that he *voluntarily* gave up his life as a sacrifice for the sins of the world. Talk about love! Next time you think of Jesus dying to save you, remember the incredible price he paid.

Your next reading is on page 1311.

STRONGER

GET

and Mary the mother of Joses saw where he was laid.

The Resurrection

16 When the Sabbath was over, Mary Magdalene, Mary the mother of James, and Salome bought spices so that they might go to anoint Jesus' body. 2Very early on the first day of the week, just after sunrise, they were on their way to the tomb 3and they asked each other, "Who will roll the stone away from the entrance of the tomb?"

4But when they looked up, they saw that the stone, which was very large, had been rolled away. 5As they entered the tomb, they saw a young man dressed in a white robe sitting on the right side, and they were alarmed.

6"Don't be alarmed," he said. "You are looking for Jesus the Nazarene, who was crucified. He has risen! He is not here. See the place where they laid him. 7But go, tell his disciples and Peter, 'He is going ahead of you into Galilee. There you will see him, just as he told you.' "

8Trembling and bewildered, the women went out and fled from the tomb. They said nothing to anyone, because they were afraid.

[The earliest manuscripts and some other ancient witnesses do not have Mark 16:9–20.]

9When Jesus rose early on the first day of the week, he appeared first to Mary Magdalene, out of whom he had driven seven demons. 10She went and told those who had been with him and who were mourning and weeping. 11When they heard that Jesus was alive and that she had seen him, they did not believe it.

12Afterward Jesus appeared in a different form to two of them while they were walking in the country. 13These returned and reported it to the rest; but they did not believe them either.

14Later Jesus appeared to the Eleven as they were eating; he rebuked them for their lack of faith and their stubborn refusal to believe those who had seen him after he had risen.

15He said to them, "Go into all the world and preach the good news to all creation. 16Whoever believes and is baptized will be saved, but whoever does not believe will be condemned. 17And these signs will accompany those who believe: In my name they will drive out demons; they will speak in new tongues; 18they will pick up snakes with their hands; and when they drink deadly poison, it will not hurt them at all; they will place their hands on sick people, and they will get well."

19After the Lord Jesus had spoken to them, he was taken up into heaven and he sat at the right hand of God. 20Then the disciples went out and preached everywhere, and the Lord worked with them and confirmed his word by the signs that accompanied it.

LUKE

Who wrote this book?
Luke, a physician who often traveled with Paul, wrote this book.

Why was this book written?
Luke tells what many people who knew Jesus remembered of his life and teaching.

For whom was this book written?
Luke wrote for people who wanted to know the kind of person Jesus was.

What happens in this book?
Jesus meets, teaches, and helps many different kinds of people.

Who is important in this book?
Jesus is the important person in this book.

When did this happen?
The events in this book took place between 6 B.C. and A.D. 30.

Where did this happen?
Most of the events in this book happened in Galilee and Judea.

What are some stories found only in this book?

The birth of John the Baptist	Luke 1:57–80
The shepherds and the angels	Luke 2:8–20
Jesus raises a widow's son	Luke 7:11–17
The good Samaritan	Luke 10:25–37
The rich fool	Luke 12:13–21
The lost son	Luke 15:11–32
The rich man and Lazarus	Luke 16:19–31
Jesus heals ten lepers	Luke 17:11–19
The Pharisee and the tax collector	Luke 18:9–14
Zacchaeus	Luke 19:1–10

Introduction

1 Many have undertaken to draw up an account of the things that have been fulfilled[a] among us, 2just as they were handed down to us by those who from the first were eyewitnesses and servants of the word. 3Therefore, since I myself have carefully investigated everything from the beginning, it seemed good also to me to write an orderly account for you, most excellent Theophilus, 4so that you may know the certainty of the things you have been taught.

The Birth of John the Baptist Foretold

5In the time of Herod king of Judea there was a priest named Zechariah, who belonged to the priestly division of Abijah; his wife Elizabeth was also a descendant of Aaron. 6Both of them were upright in the sight of God, observing all the Lord's commandments and regulations blamelessly. 7But they had no children, because Elizabeth was barren; and they were both well along in years.

8Once when Zechariah's division was on duty and he was serving as priest before God, 9he was chosen by lot, according to the custom of the priesthood, to go into the temple of the Lord and burn incense. 10And when the time for the burning of incense came, all the assembled worshipers were praying outside.

11Then an angel of the Lord appeared to him, standing at the right side of the altar of incense. 12When Zechariah saw him, he was startled and was gripped with fear. 13But the angel said to him: "Do not be afraid, Zechariah; your prayer has been heard. Your wife Elizabeth will bear you a son, and you are to give him the name John. 14He will be a joy and delight to you, and many will rejoice because of his birth, 15for he will be great in the sight of the Lord. He is never to take wine or other fermented drink, and he will be filled with the Holy Spirit even from birth.[b] 16Many of the people of Israel will he bring back to the Lord their God. 17And he will go on before the Lord, in

a 1 Or been surely believed   b 15 Or from his mother's womb

These Things Are Certain

READ LUKE 1:1–4

Luke knew he had a good story when he started talking to people about Jesus' life. Luke wanted to get the facts straight, so he didn't base his gospel on rumors; he interviewed the people who had seen Jesus do all that very cool stuff. He investigated; he went right to the sources "so that you may know the certainty of the things you have been taught" (verse 4). After all, his editor, God, wanted the story to be accurate. God and Luke worked together to get this story. As a man of God, *you* need to take the truth seriously, too, and get your facts straight. When you're talking with your buddies, you should be building a reputation as a reliable and trustworthy guy. Don't be known as the neighborhood Pinocchio. Only talk about things you've checked out and that you know are true.

Your next reading is on page 1312.

the spirit and power of Elijah, to turn the hearts of the fathers to their children and the disobedient to the wisdom of the righteous—to make ready a people prepared for the Lord."

18Zechariah asked the angel, "How can I be sure of this? I am an old man and my wife is well along in years."

19The angel answered, "I am Gabriel. I stand in the presence of God, and I have been sent to speak to you and to tell you this good news. 20And now you will be silent and not able to speak until the day this happens, because you did not believe my words, which will come true at their proper time."

21Meanwhile, the people were waiting for Zechariah and wondering why he stayed so long in the temple. 22When he came out, he could not speak to them. They realized he had seen a vision in the temple, for he kept making signs to them but remained unable to speak.

23When his time of service was completed, he returned home. 24After this his wife Elizabeth became pregnant and for five months remained in seclusion. 25"The Lord has done this for me," she said. "In these days he has shown his favor and taken away my disgrace among the people."

The Birth of Jesus Foretold

26In the sixth month, God sent the angel Gabriel to Nazareth, a town in Galilee, 27to a virgin pledged to be married to a man named Joseph, a descendant of David. The virgin's name was Mary. 28The angel went to her and said, "Greetings, you who are highly favored! The Lord is with you."

29Mary was greatly troubled at his words and wondered what kind of greeting this might be. 30But the angel said to her, "Do not be afraid, Mary, you have found favor with God. 31You will be with child and give birth to a son, and you are to give him the name Jesus. 32He will be great and will be called the Son of the Most High. The Lord God will give him the throne of his father David, 33and he will reign over the house of Jacob forever; his kingdom will never end."

34"How will this be," Mary asked the angel, "since I am a virgin?"

It's All in the Attitude

READ LUKE 1:5–7, 11–20, 26–38

Think of what Zechariah's face looked like when the angel Gabriel told him he was about to become a dad. "Huh ... say what?!" Zechariah thought the angel had his facts mixed up. He must've knocked himself silly against a meteorite flying down through the stratosphere. Zechariah's questions were full of doubt, so because he didn't believe Gabriel's words (verses 19–20), Gabriel struck him speechless for the next nine months. (Where's Gabriel when your little brother is singing nursery songs?) Look at the huge difference in Mary's attitude! Same angel, similar kind of incredible news, but Mary reacted completely differently. She asked a few questions about how these things would happen, but she believed the angel right from the start. Right on! God likes to answer our questions. But a man of God asks God questions with the understanding that God is right, and that he's telling the truth.

Your next reading is on page 1318.

35The angel answered, "The Holy Spirit will come upon you, and the power of the Most High will overshadow you. So the holy one to be born will be called*a* the Son of God. 36Even Elizabeth your relative is going to have a child in her old age, and she who was said to be barren is in her sixth month. 37For nothing is impossible with God."

38"I am the Lord's servant," Mary answered. "May it be to me as you have said." Then the angel left her.

Mary Visits Elizabeth

39At that time Mary got ready and hurried to a town in the hill country of Judea, 40where she entered Zechariah's home and greeted Elizabeth. 41When Elizabeth heard Mary's greeting, the baby leaped in her womb, and Elizabeth was filled with the Holy Spirit. 42In a loud voice she exclaimed: "Blessed are you among women, and blessed is the child you will bear! 43But why am I so favored, that the mother of my Lord should come to me? 44As soon as the sound of your greeting reached my ears, the baby in my womb leaped for joy. 45Blessed is she who has believed that what the Lord has said to her will be accomplished!"

Mary's Song

46And Mary said:

"My soul glorifies the Lord
47   and my spirit rejoices in God my Savior,
48for he has been mindful
        of the humble state of his servant.
    From now on all generations will call me blessed,
49   for the Mighty One has done great things for me—
        holy is his name.
50His mercy extends to those who fear him,
        from generation to generation.
51He has performed mighty deeds with his arm;
        he has scattered those who are proud in their inmost thoughts.
52He has brought down rulers from their thrones
        but has lifted up the humble.
53He has filled the hungry with good things
        but has sent the rich away empty.

54He has helped his servant Israel,
        remembering to be merciful
55to Abraham and his descendants forever,
        even as he said to our fathers."

56Mary stayed with Elizabeth for about three months and then returned home.

The Birth of John the Baptist

57When it was time for Elizabeth to have her baby, she gave birth to a son. 58Her neighbors and relatives heard that the Lord had shown her great mercy, and they shared her joy.

59On the eighth day they came to circumcise the child, and they were going to name him after his father Zechariah, 60but his mother spoke up and said, "No! He is to be called John."

61They said to her, "There is no one among your relatives who has that name."

62Then they made signs to his father, to find out what he would like to name the child. 63He asked for a writing tablet, and to everyone's astonishment he wrote, "His name is John." 64Immediately his mouth was opened and his tongue was loosed, and he began to speak, praising God. 65The neighbors were all filled with awe, and throughout the hill country of Judea people were talking about all these things. 66Everyone who heard this wondered about it, asking, "What then is this child going to be?" For the Lord's hand was with him.

Zechariah's Song

67His father Zechariah was filled with the Holy Spirit and prophesied:

68"Praise be to the Lord, the God of Israel,
        because he has come and has redeemed his people.
69He has raised up a horn*b* of salvation for us
        in the house of his servant David
70(as he said through his holy prophets of long ago),
71salvation from our enemies
        and from the hand of all who hate us—
72to show mercy to our fathers
        and to remember his holy covenant,

---

a 35 Or *So the child to be born will be called holy,*
b 69 Horn here symbolizes strength.

73 the oath he swore to our father
  Abraham:
74 to rescue us from the hand of our
  enemies,
  and to enable us to serve him
  without fear
75 in holiness and righteousness before
  him all our days.

76 And you, my child, will be called a
  prophet of the Most High;
  for you will go on before the Lord to
  prepare the way for him,
77 to give his people the knowledge of
  salvation
  through the forgiveness of their sins,
78 because of the tender mercy of our
  God,
  by which the rising sun will come to
  us from heaven
79 to shine on those living in darkness
  and in the shadow of death,
  to guide our feet into the path of
  peace."

80 And the child grew and became strong in spirit; and he lived in the desert until he appeared publicly to Israel.

The Birth of Jesus

2 In those days Caesar Augustus issued a decree that a census should be taken of the entire Roman world. 2 (This was the first census that took place while Quirinius was governor of Syria.) 3 And everyone went to his own town to register.

4 So Joseph also went up from the town of Nazareth in Galilee to Judea, to Bethlehem the town of David, because he belonged to the house and line of David. 5 He went there to register with Mary, who was pledged to be married to him and was expecting a child. 6 While they were there, the time came for the baby to be born, 7 and she gave birth to her firstborn, a son. She wrapped him in cloths and placed him in a manger, because there was no room for them in the inn.

Make It Stick

READ LUKE 2:1–21

Read the amazing story of Jesus' birth in Luke 2:1–21. Jesus would have been born and lived and died even if you were the *only* person on earth. He did all this for you. Which part of the story of Jesus' birth do you like the best? Write it down or draw it on a sticky note.

The Shepherds and the Angels

8And there were shepherds living out in the fields nearby, keeping watch over their flocks at night. 9An angel of the Lord appeared to them, and the glory of the Lord shone around them, and they were terrified. 10But the angel said to them, "Do not be afraid. I bring you good news of great joy that will be for all the people. 11Today in the town of David a Savior has been born to you; he is Christ[a] the Lord. 12This will be a sign to you: You will find a baby wrapped in cloths and lying in a manger."

13Suddenly a great company of the heavenly host appeared with the angel, praising God and saying,

14"Glory to God in the highest,
    and on earth peace to men on
        whom his favor rests."

15When the angels had left them and gone into heaven, the shepherds said to one another, "Let's go to Bethlehem and see this thing that has happened, which the Lord has told us about."

16So they hurried off and found Mary and Joseph, and the baby, who was lying in the manger. 17When they had seen him, they spread the word concerning what had been told them about this child, 18and all who heard it were amazed at what the shepherds said to them. 19But Mary treasured up all these things and pondered them in her heart. 20The shepherds returned, glorifying and praising God for all the things they had heard and seen, which were just as they had been told.

Jesus Presented in the Temple

21On the eighth day, when it was time to circumcise him, he was named Jesus, the name the angel had given him before he had been conceived.

22When the time of their purification according to the Law of Moses had been completed, Joseph and Mary took him to Jerusalem to present him to the Lord 23(as it is written in the Law of the Lord, "Every firstborn male is to be consecrated to the Lord"[b]), 24and to offer a sacrifice in keeping with what is said in the Law of the Lord: "a pair of doves or two young pigeons."[c]

25Now there was a man in Jerusalem called Simeon, who was righteous and devout. He was waiting for the consolation of Israel, and the Holy Spirit was upon him. 26It had been revealed to him by the Holy Spirit that he would not die before he had seen the Lord's Christ. 27Moved by the Spirit, he went into the temple courts. When the parents brought in the child Jesus to do for him what the custom of the Law required, 28Simeon took him in his arms and praised God, saying:

29"Sovereign Lord, as you have promised,
    you now dismiss[d] your servant in
        peace.
30For my eyes have seen your salvation,
31   which you have prepared in the
        sight of all people,
32a light for revelation to the Gentiles
    and for glory to your people Israel."

33The child's father and mother marveled at what was said about him. 34Then Simeon blessed them and said to Mary, his mother: "This child is destined to cause the falling and rising of many in Israel, and to be a sign that will be spoken against, 35so that the thoughts of many hearts will be revealed. And a sword will pierce your own soul too."

36There was also a prophetess, Anna, the daughter of Phanuel, of the tribe of Asher. She was very old; she had lived with her husband seven years after her marriage, 37and then was a widow until she was eighty-four.[e] She never left the temple but worshiped night and day, fasting and praying. 38Coming up to them at that very moment, she gave thanks to God and spoke about the child to all who were looking forward to the redemption of Jerusalem.

39When Joseph and Mary had done everything required by the Law of the Lord, they returned to Galilee to their own town of Nazareth. 40And the child grew and became strong; he was filled with wisdom, and the grace of God was upon him.

The Boy Jesus at the Temple

41Every year his parents went to Jerusalem for the Feast of the Passover. 42When he was twelve years old, they went up to the Feast, according to the custom. 43After the Feast was over, while his parents were returning home, the boy Jesus

a 11 Or *Messiah.* "The Christ" (Greek) and "the Messiah" (Hebrew) both mean "the Anointed One"; also in verse 26. *b 23* Exodus 13:2,12   *c 24* Lev. 12:8   *d 29* Or *promised, / now dismiss*   *e 37* Or *widow for eighty-four years* stayed behind in Jerusalem, but they were unaware of it. 44Thinking he was in their company, they traveled on for a day. Then they began looking for him among their relatives and friends. 45When they did not find him, they went back to Jerusalem to look for him. 46After three days they found him in the temple courts, sitting among the teachers, listening to them and asking them questions. 47Everyone who heard him was amazed at his understanding and his answers. 48When his parents saw him, they were astonished. His mother said to him, "Son, why have you treated us like this? Your father and I have been anxiously searching for you."

49"Why were you searching for me?" he asked. "Didn't you know I had to be in my Father's house?" 50But they did not understand what he was saying to them.

51Then he went down to Nazareth with them and was obedient to them. But his mother treasured all these things in her heart. 52And Jesus grew in wisdom and stature, and in favor with God and men.

John the Baptist Prepares the Way

3 In the fifteenth year of the reign of Tiberius Caesar—when Pontius Pilate was governor of Judea, Herod tetrarch of Galilee, his brother Philip tetrarch of Iturea and Traconitis, and Lysanias tetrarch of Abilene— 2during the high priesthood of Annas and Caiaphas, the word of God came to John son of Zechariah in the desert. 3He went into all the country around the Jordan, preaching a baptism of repentance for the forgiveness of sins. 4As is written in the book of the words of Isaiah the prophet:

"A voice of one calling in the desert,
'Prepare the way for the Lord,
　make straight paths for him.
5Every valley shall be filled in,
　every mountain and hill made low.
The crooked roads shall become
　　straight,
　the rough ways smooth.
6And all mankind will see God's
　　salvation.' "a

7John said to the crowds coming out to be baptized by him, "You brood of vipers! Who warned you to flee from the coming wrath? 8Produce fruit in keeping with repentance. And do not begin to say to yourselves, 'We have Abraham as our father.'

For I tell you that out of these stones God can raise up children for Abraham. 9The ax is already at the root of the trees, and every tree that does not produce good fruit will be cut down and thrown into the fire."

10"What should we do then?" the crowd asked.

11John answered, "The man with two tunics should share with him who has none, and the one who has food should do the same."

12Tax collectors also came to be baptized. "Teacher," they asked, "what should we do?"

13"Don't collect any more than you are required to," he told them.

14Then some soldiers asked him, "And what should we do?"

He replied, "Don't extort money and don't accuse people falsely—be content with your pay."

15The people were waiting expectantly and were all wondering in their hearts if John might possibly be the Christ.b 16John answered them all, "I baptize you withc water. But one more powerful than I will come, the thongs of whose sandals I am not worthy to untie. He will baptize you with the Holy Spirit and with fire. 17His winnowing fork is in his hand to clear his threshing floor and to gather the wheat into his barn, but he will burn up the chaff with unquenchable fire." 18And with many other words John exhorted the people and preached the good news to them.

19But when John rebuked Herod the tetrarch because of Herodias, his brother's wife, and all the other evil things he had done, 20Herod added this to them all: He locked John up in prison.

The Baptism and Genealogy of Jesus

21When all the people were being baptized, Jesus was baptized too. And as he was praying, heaven was opened 22and the Holy Spirit descended on him in bodily form like a dove. And a voice came from heaven: "You are my Son, whom I love; with you I am well pleased."

23Now Jesus himself was about thirty years old when he began his ministry. He was the son, so it was thought, of Joseph,

the son of Heli, 24the son of Matthat,
　the son of Levi, the son of Melki,
　the son of Jannai, the son of Joseph,

a 6 Isaiah 40:3–5　　b 15 Or Messiah　　c 16 Or in

25the son of Mattathias, the son of Amos,
the son of Nahum, the son of Esli,
the son of Naggai, 26the son of Maath,
the son of Mattathias, the son of Semein,
the son of Josech, the son of Joda,
27the son of Joanan, the son of Rhesa,
the son of Zerubbabel, the son of Shealtiel,
the son of Neri, 28the son of Melki,
the son of Addi, the son of Cosam,
the son of Elmadam, the son of Er,
29the son of Joshua, the son of Eliezer,
the son of Jorim, the son of Matthat,
the son of Levi, 30the son of Simeon,
the son of Judah, the son of Joseph,
the son of Jonam, the son of Eliakim,
31the son of Melea, the son of Menna,
the son of Mattatha, the son of Nathan,
the son of David, 32the son of Jesse,
the son of Obed, the son of Boaz,

the son of Salmon,a the son of Nahshon,
33the son of Amminadab, the son of Ram,b
the son of Hezron, the son of Perez,
the son of Judah, 34the son of Jacob,
the son of Isaac, the son of Abraham,
the son of Terah, the son of Nahor,
35the son of Serug, the son of Reu,
the son of Peleg, the son of Eber,
the son of Shelah, 36the son of Cainan,
the son of Arphaxad, the son of Shem,
the son of Noah, the son of Lamech,
37the son of Methuselah, the son of Enoch,
the son of Jared, the son of Mahalalel,
the son of Kenan, 38the son of Enosh,
the son of Seth, the son of Adam,
the son of God.

a 32 Some early manuscripts *Sala*   b 33 Some manuscripts
Amminadab, the son of Admin, the son of Arni; other
manuscripts vary widely.

Make It Stick

READ LUKE 3:21–22

God said to Jesus, "You are my Son, whom I love; with you I am well pleased." God's attitude toward us is very similar, since Jesus' righteousness—not our own—is what saves us. Write on a sticky note: "I am God's son. He loves me. I can please him."

The Temptation of Jesus

Jesus, full of the Holy Spirit, returned from the Jordan and was led by the Spirit in the desert, ²where for forty days he was tempted by the devil. He ate nothing during those days, and at the end of them he was hungry.

³The devil said to him, "If you are the Son of God, tell this stone to become bread."

⁴Jesus answered, "It is written: 'Man does not live on bread alone.'*ᵃ*"

⁵The devil led him up to a high place and showed him in an instant all the kingdoms of the world. ⁶And he said to him, "I will give you all their authority and splendor, for it has been given to me, and I can give it to anyone I want to. ⁷So if you worship me, it will all be yours."

⁸Jesus answered, "It is written: 'Worship the Lord your God and serve him only.'*ᵇ*"

⁹The devil led him to Jerusalem and had him stand on the highest point of the temple. "If you are the Son of God," he said, "throw yourself down from here. ¹⁰For it is written:

" 'He will command his angels
  concerning you
to guard you carefully;
¹¹ they will lift you up in their hands,
  so that you will not strike your foot
    against a stone.'*ᶜ*"

¹²Jesus answered, "It says: 'Do not put the Lord your God to the test.'*ᵈ*"

¹³When the devil had finished all this tempting, he left him until an opportune time.

Jesus Rejected at Nazareth

¹⁴Jesus returned to Galilee in the power of the Spirit, and news about him spread through the whole countryside. ¹⁵He taught in their synagogues, and everyone praised him.

¹⁶He went to Nazareth, where he had been brought up, and on the Sabbath day he went into the synagogue, as was his custom. And he stood up to read. ¹⁷The

ᵃ 4 Deut. 8:3   *ᵇ 8* Deut. 6:13   *ᶜ 11* Psalm 91:11,12
ᵈ 12 Deut. 6:16

Dealing With Rejection

READ LUKE 4:14–30

Have you ever been picked on, bullied or had a group of kids laugh at you? Then you know how rejection feels. The key is not to take it personally when kids shut you out. Getting rejected doesn't mean that you're not worthy of love. It's just the way the world acts. Jesus was rejected, too: When he went to his hometown, the people threw him out of the synagogue, "drove him out of the town" (verse 29) and tried to chuck him over the cliff. Caramba! Now THAT'S rejection! They could hardly have made it plainer that they didn't want him around. Isaiah 53:3 says, "He was despised and rejected by men." Jesus was later abandoned by his closest friends and crucified by his own nation. Does he understand rejection? Oh yeah. More than anyone else, Jesus understands. He can comfort you and help you through it.

Your next reading is on page 1320.

scroll of the prophet Isaiah was handed to him. Unrolling it, he found the place where it is written:

18 "The Spirit of the Lord is on me,
     because he has anointed me
     to preach good news to the poor.
   He has sent me to proclaim freedom for the prisoners
     and recovery of sight for the blind,
   to release the oppressed,
19   to proclaim the year of the Lord's favor."[a]

20Then he rolled up the scroll, gave it back to the attendant and sat down. The eyes of everyone in the synagogue were fastened on him, 21and he began by saying to them, "Today this scripture is fulfilled in your hearing."

22All spoke well of him and were amazed at the gracious words that came from his lips. "Isn't this Joseph's son?" they asked.

23Jesus said to them, "Surely you will quote this proverb to me: 'Physician, heal yourself! Do here in your hometown what we have heard that you did in Capernaum.' "

24"I tell you the truth," he continued, "no prophet is accepted in his hometown. 25I assure you that there were many widows in Israel in Elijah's time, when the sky was shut for three and a half years and there was a severe famine throughout the land. 26Yet Elijah was not sent to any of them, but to a widow in Zarephath in the region of Sidon. 27And there were many in Israel with leprosy[b] in the time of Elisha the prophet, yet not one of them was cleansed—only Naaman the Syrian."

28All the people in the synagogue were furious when they heard this. 29They got up, drove him out of the town, and took him to the brow of the hill on which the town was built, in order to throw him down the cliff. 30But he walked right through the crowd and went on his way.

Jesus Drives Out an Evil Spirit

31Then he went down to Capernaum, a town in Galilee, and on the Sabbath began to teach the people. 32They were amazed at his teaching, because his message had authority.

33In the synagogue there was a man possessed by a demon, an evil[c] spirit. He cried out at the top of his voice, 34"Ha! What do you want with us, Jesus of Nazareth? Have you come to destroy us? I know who you are—the Holy One of God!"

35"Be quiet!" Jesus said sternly. "Come out of him!" Then the demon threw the man down before them all and came out without injuring him.

36All the people were amazed and said to each other, "What is this teaching? With authority and power he gives orders to evil spirits and they come out!" 37And the news about him spread throughout the surrounding area.

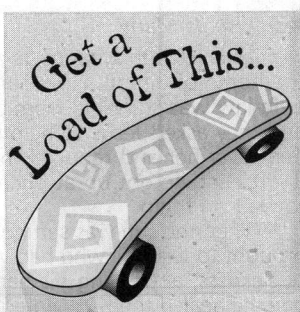

Get a Load of This...

You never see Jesus being rude and telling other people to put a lid on it. The only time he ever bluntly told someone to hush up was when he was talking to the demons from hell. He commanded them sternly, "Be quiet!" (Luke 4:33–35).

---

a 19 Isaiah 61:1,2   *b 27* The Greek word was used for various diseases affecting the skin—not necessarily leprosy.   *c 33* Greek *unclean*; also in verse 36

Jesus Heals Many

38Jesus left the synagogue and went to the home of Simon. Now Simon's mother-in-law was suffering from a high fever, and they asked Jesus to help her. **39**So he bent over her and rebuked the fever, and it left her. She got up at once and began to wait on them.

40When the sun was setting, the people brought to Jesus all who had various kinds of sickness, and laying his hands on each one, he healed them. **41**Moreover, demons came out of many people, shouting, "You are the Son of God!" But he rebuked them and would not allow them to speak, because they knew he was the Christ.*a*

42At daybreak Jesus went out to a solitary place. The people were looking for him and when they came to where he was, they tried to keep him from leaving them. **43**But he said, "I must preach the good news of the kingdom of God to the other towns also, because that is why I was sent." **44**And he kept on preaching in the synagogues of Judea.*b*

The Calling of the First Disciples

5 One day as Jesus was standing by the Lake of Gennesaret,*c* with the people crowding around him and listening to the word of God, **2**he saw at the water's edge two boats, left there by the fishermen, who were washing their nets. **3**He got into one of the boats, the one belonging to Simon, and asked him to put out a little from shore. Then he sat down and taught the people from the boat.

4When he had finished speaking, he said to Simon, "Put out into deep water, and let down*d* the nets for a catch."

5Simon answered, "Master, we've worked hard all night and haven't caught anything. But because you say so, I will let down the nets."

6When they had done so, they caught such a large number of fish that their nets began to break. **7**So they signaled their

a 41 Or *Messiah*   *b 44* Or *the land of the Jews;* some manuscripts *Galilee*   *c 1* That is, Sea of Galilee
d 4 The Greek verb is plural.

Talk About Personalities!

READ LUKE 5:1–11, 27–32; 6:12–16

When Jesus picked his disciples, he picked men with really different personalities. Just like on a football team, guys have different jobs that match who they are. Obviously Jesus was the coach. Peter was loud and all over you, like a confident middle linebacker. Matthew, who wrote one of the Gospels, paid attention to details, like a quarterback. James and John were hot-headed and zealous. These guys also had lots of faults, too, but God used them (and their goof-ups) to spread his Word anyway. Matthew was a tax collector and several of the others were fishermen—who even …well …smelled unique. God can work with anyone. He'll take whoever loves him, and he'll use him. Jesus wasn't looking for a bunch of men that fell off an assembly line like a bunch of identical plastic action figures. He wanted a mix. He calls us to be his disciples, too. No matter what your personality is like, you can be part of God's team.

Your next reading is on page 1323.

partners in the other boat to come and help them, and they came and filled both boats so full that they began to sink.

8When Simon Peter saw this, he fell at Jesus' knees and said, "Go away from me, Lord; I am a sinful man!" 9For he and all his companions were astonished at the catch of fish they had taken, 10and so were James and John, the sons of Zebedee, Simon's partners.

Then Jesus said to Simon, "Don't be afraid; from now on you will catch men." 11So they pulled their boats up on shore, left everything and followed him.

The Man With Leprosy

12While Jesus was in one of the towns, a man came along who was covered with leprosy.*a* When he saw Jesus, he fell with his face to the ground and begged him, "Lord, if you are willing, you can make me clean."

13Jesus reached out his hand and touched the man. "I am willing," he said. "Be clean!" And immediately the leprosy left him.

14Then Jesus ordered him, "Don't tell anyone, but go, show yourself to the priest and offer the sacrifices that Moses commanded for your cleansing, as a testimony to them."

15Yet the news about him spread all the more, so that crowds of people came to hear him and to be healed of their sicknesses. 16But Jesus often withdrew to lonely places and prayed.

Jesus Heals a Paralytic

17One day as he was teaching, Pharisees and teachers of the law, who had come from every village of Galilee and from Judea and Jerusalem, were sitting there. And the power of the Lord was present for him to heal the sick. 18Some men came carrying a paralytic on a mat and tried to take him into the house to lay him before Jesus. 19When they could not find a way to do this because of the crowd, they went up on the roof and lowered him on his mat through the tiles into the middle of the crowd, right in front of Jesus.

20When Jesus saw their faith, he said, "Friend, your sins are forgiven."

21The Pharisees and the teachers of the law began thinking to themselves, "Who is this fellow who speaks blasphemy? Who can forgive sins but God alone?"

22Jesus knew what they were thinking and asked, "Why are you thinking these things in your hearts? 23Which is easier: to say, 'Your sins are forgiven,' or to say, 'Get up and walk'? 24But that you may know that the Son of Man has authority on earth to forgive sins . . ." He said to the paralyzed man, "I tell you, get up, take your mat and go home." 25Immediately he stood up in front of them, took what he had been lying on and went home praising God. 26Everyone was amazed and gave praise to God. They were filled with awe and said, "We have seen remarkable things today."

The Calling of Levi

27After this, Jesus went out and saw a tax collector by the name of Levi sitting at his tax booth. "Follow me," Jesus said to him, 28and Levi got up, left everything and followed him.

29Then Levi held a great banquet for Jesus at his house, and a large crowd of tax collectors and others were eating with them. 30But the Pharisees and the teachers of the law who belonged to their sect complained to his disciples, "Why do you eat and drink with tax collectors and 'sinners'?"

31Jesus answered them, "It is not the healthy who need a doctor, but the sick. 32I have not come to call the righteous, but sinners to repentance."

Jesus Questioned About Fasting

33They said to him, "John's disciples often fast and pray, and so do the disciples of the Pharisees, but yours go on eating and drinking."

34Jesus answered, "Can you make the guests of the bridegroom fast while he is with them? 35But the time will come when the bridegroom will be taken from them; in those days they will fast."

36He told them this parable: "No one tears a patch from a new garment and sews it on an old one. If he does, he will have torn the new garment, and the patch from the new will not match the old. 37And no one pours new wine into old wineskins. If he does, the new wine will burst the skins, the wine will run out and the wineskins will be ruined. 38No, new wine must be poured into new wine-

---

a 12 The Greek word was used for various diseases affecting the skin—not necessarily leprosy.

Get a Load of This...

In Luke 6:1 Jesus' disciples yanked off the heads of wheat, rubbed away the chaff in their hands and chowed down on the juicy grains. Sound like a fun snack? This was "Wheaties" in the real sense of the word: wheat straight out of the wheatfield.

skins. ³⁹And no one after drinking old wine wants the new, for he says, 'The old is better.' "

Lord of the Sabbath

6 One Sabbath Jesus was going through the grainfields, and his disciples began to pick some heads of grain, rub them in their hands and eat the kernels. ²Some of the Pharisees asked, "Why are you doing what is unlawful on the Sabbath?"

³Jesus answered them, "Have you never read what David did when he and his companions were hungry? ⁴He entered the house of God, and taking the consecrated bread, he ate what is lawful only for priests to eat. And he also gave some to his companions." ⁵Then Jesus said to them, "The Son of Man is Lord of the Sabbath."

⁶On another Sabbath he went into the synagogue and was teaching, and a man was there whose right hand was shriveled. ⁷The Pharisees and the teachers of the law were looking for a reason to accuse Jesus, so they watched him closely to see if he would heal on the Sabbath. ⁸But Jesus knew what they were thinking and said to the man with the shriveled hand, "Get up and stand in front of everyone." So he got up and stood there.

⁹Then Jesus said to them, "I ask you, which is lawful on the Sabbath: to do good or to do evil, to save life or to destroy it?"

¹⁰He looked around at them all, and then said to the man, "Stretch out your hand." He did so, and his hand was completely restored. ¹¹But they were furious and began to discuss with one another what they might do to Jesus.

The Twelve Apostles

¹²One of those days Jesus went out to a mountainside to pray, and spent the night praying to God. ¹³When morning came, he called his disciples to him and chose twelve of them, whom he also designated apostles: ¹⁴Simon (whom he named Peter), his brother Andrew, James, John, Philip, Bartholomew, ¹⁵Matthew, Thomas, James son of Alphaeus, Simon who was called the Zealot, ¹⁶Judas son of James, and Judas Iscariot, who became a traitor.

Blessings and Woes

¹⁷He went down with them and stood on a level place. A large crowd of his disciples was there and a great number of people from all over Judea, from Jerusalem, and from the coast of Tyre and Sidon, ¹⁸who had come to hear him and to be healed of their diseases. Those troubled by evil^a spirits were cured, ¹⁹and the people all tried to touch him, because power was coming from him and healing them all.

²⁰Looking at his disciples, he said:

"Blessed are you who are poor,
   for yours is the kingdom of God.

^a 18 Greek *unclean*

21 Blessed are you who hunger now,
for you will be satisfied.
Blessed are you who weep now,
for you will laugh.
22 Blessed are you when men hate you,
when they exclude you and insult you
and reject your name as evil,
because of the Son of Man.

23 "Rejoice in that day and leap for joy, because great is your reward in heaven. For that is how their fathers treated the prophets.

24 "But woe to you who are rich,
for you have already received your
comfort.
25 Woe to you who are well fed now,
for you will go hungry.
Woe to you who laugh now,
for you will mourn and weep.
26 Woe to you when all men speak well
of you,
for that is how their fathers treated
the false prophets.

Love for Enemies

27 "But I tell you who hear me: Love your enemies, do good to those who hate you, 28 bless those who curse you, pray for those who mistreat you. 29 If someone strikes you on one cheek, turn to him the other also. If someone takes your cloak, do not stop him from taking your tunic. 30 Give to everyone who asks you, and if anyone takes what belongs to you, do not demand it back. 31 Do to others as you would have them do to you.

32 "If you love those who love you, what credit is that to you? Even 'sinners' love those who love them. 33 And if you do good to those who are good to you, what credit is that to you? Even 'sinners' do that. 34 And if you lend to those from whom you expect repayment, what credit is that to you? Even 'sinners' lend to 'sinners,' expecting to be repaid in full. 35 But love your enemies, do good to them, and lend to them without expecting to get anything back. Then your reward will be

GET STRONGER

Using Reasonable Force

READ LUKE 6:27–31

If someone's trying to slug you, get out of the way. HELLO! This is common sense, guys. If you need to put up your fists to defend yourself, do it. When Jesus said, "If someone strikes you on one cheek, turn to him the other also" (verse 29), he was not talking about letting someone turn you into a toothless, broken-nosed punching bag. What he meant was don't respond in hate and try to hurt those people back. Use "reasonable force" to get them away from you—or from other kids they're hurting—then leave. (By the way, it's against the law for them to be striking people. You should report them to adults or even to the authorities.) "Turn the other cheek" means loving your enemies and not seeking revenge, but hey, when a Luke 252 man is being attacked, it's OK to square his chin and use reasonable force to defend himself.

Your next reading is on page 1324.

great, and you will be sons of the Most High, because he is kind to the ungrateful and wicked. 36Be merciful, just as your Father is merciful.

Judging Others

37"Do not judge, and you will not be judged. Do not condemn, and you will not be condemned. Forgive, and you will be forgiven. 38Give, and it will be given to you. A good measure, pressed down, shaken together and running over, will be poured into your lap. For with the measure you use, it will be measured to you."

39He also told them this parable: "Can a blind man lead a blind man? Will they not both fall into a pit? 40A student is not above his teacher, but everyone who is fully trained will be like his teacher.

41"Why do you look at the speck of sawdust in your brother's eye and pay no attention to the plank in your own eye? 42How can you say to your brother, 'Brother, let me take the speck out of your eye,' when you yourself fail to see the plank in your own eye? You hypocrite, first take the plank out of your eye, and then you will see clearly to remove the speck from your brother's eye.

A Tree and Its Fruit

43"No good tree bears bad fruit, nor does a bad tree bear good fruit. 44Each tree is recognized by its own fruit. People do not pick figs from thornbushes, or grapes from briers. 45The good man brings good things out of the good stored up in his heart, and the evil man brings evil things out of the evil stored up in his heart. For out of the overflow of his heart his mouth speaks.

The Wise and Foolish Builders

46"Why do you call me, 'Lord, Lord,' and do not do what I say? 47I will show you what he is like who comes to me and hears my words and puts them into practice. 48He is like a man building a house, who dug down deep and laid the foundation on rock. When a flood came, the torrent struck that house but could not shake it, because it was well built. 49But the one

GET SMARTER

Judgment and Sawdust

READ LUKE 6:37, 41–42

Jesus said, "Do not judge, and you will not be judged" (verse 37). Some people use this to say, "Don't judge others at *all*." What it gets down to is, "Don't ever say that anything anyone is doing is ever wrong." But Jesus constantly judged matters. When something was wrong he SAID it was wrong. It isn't "judging" if you point out that someone shouldn't be shoplifting. Judging is when you look down on them and say, "They're doing wrong. They must be evil," and give them no hope of ever changing—and don't even lift a pinkie to help them change. THAT is judging. Instead, you should love them, pray for them and believe God can change them. But before you go to someone and try to help them with a problem in their life, make sure that you've taken care of things in your own life. Take care of any "plank in your own eye" before you try to remove the "speck of sawdust" in somebody else's eye (verses 41–42).

Your next reading is on page 1326.

who hears my words and does not put them into practice is like a man who built a house on the ground without a foundation. The moment the torrent struck that house, it collapsed and its destruction was complete."

The Faith of the Centurion

7 When Jesus had finished saying all this in the hearing of the people, he entered Capernaum. ²There a centurion's servant, whom his master valued highly, was sick and about to die. ³The centurion heard of Jesus and sent some elders of the Jews to him, asking him to come and heal his servant. ⁴When they came to Jesus, they pleaded earnestly with him, "This man deserves to have you do this, ⁵because he loves our nation and has built our synagogue." ⁶So Jesus went with them.

He was not far from the house when the centurion sent friends to say to him: "Lord, don't trouble yourself, for I do not deserve to have you come under my roof. ⁷That is why I did not even consider myself worthy to come to you. But say the word, and my servant will be healed. ⁸For I myself am a man under authority, with soldiers under me. I tell this one, 'Go,' and he goes; and that one, 'Come,' and he comes. I say to my servant, 'Do this,' and he does it."

⁹When Jesus heard this, he was amazed at him, and turning to the crowd following him, he said, "I tell you, I have not found such great faith even in Israel." ¹⁰Then the men who had been sent returned to the house and found the servant well.

Jesus Raises a Widow's Son

¹¹Soon afterward, Jesus went to a town called Nain, and his disciples and a large crowd went along with him. ¹²As he approached the town gate, a dead person was being carried out—the only son of his mother, and she was a widow. And a large crowd from the town was with her.

Make It Stick

READ LUKE 6:46–49

When you read this passage, it's hard not to think about the three little pigs, especially the one building a straw house and the one building a brick house. Are you building your life out of "wood, hay and straw" (1 Corinthians 3:10–15) or something solid? Draw a picture of your building materials.

¹³When the Lord saw her, his heart went out to her and he said, "Don't cry."

¹⁴Then he went up and touched the coffin, and those carrying it stood still. He said, "Young man, I say to you, get up!" ¹⁵The dead man sat up and began to talk, and Jesus gave him back to his mother.

¹⁶They were all filled with awe and praised God. "A great prophet has appeared among us," they said. "God has come to help his people." ¹⁷This news about Jesus spread throughout Judea*ᵃ* and the surrounding country.

Jesus and John the Baptist

¹⁸John's disciples told him about all these things. Calling two of them, ¹⁹he sent them to the Lord to ask, "Are you the one who was to come, or should we expect someone else?"

²⁰When the men came to Jesus, they said, "John the Baptist sent us to you to ask, 'Are you the one who was to come, or should we expect someone else?' "

²¹At that very time Jesus cured many who had diseases, sicknesses and evil spirits, and gave sight to many who were blind. ²²So he replied to the messengers, "Go back and report to John what you have seen and heard: The blind receive sight, the lame walk, those who have leprosy*ᵇ* are cured, the deaf hear, the dead are raised, and the good news is preached to the poor. ²³Blessed is the man who does not fall away on account of me."

²⁴After John's messengers left, Jesus began to speak to the crowd about John: "What did you go out into the desert to see? A reed swayed by the wind? ²⁵If not, what did you go out to see? A man dressed in fine clothes? No, those who wear expensive clothes and indulge in luxury are in palaces. ²⁶But what did you go out to see? A prophet? Yes, I tell you, and

ᵃ 17 Or *the land of the Jews*　　*ᵇ 22* The Greek word was used for various diseases affecting the skin—not necessarily leprosy.

Just Say the Word

READ LUKE 7:1–10

The Roman centurion knew that if he asked Jesus to heal his servant, it was a done deal. He didn't even need to ask Jesus in person. That's the kind of faith that got Jesus pumped! If that happened today, he'd probably give high-fives all around. God loves it when we have the faith that he'll answer prayer. See, the centurion understood authority. He was used to having his troops—100 men—obey his slightest command. If he wanted a snack at midnight, he just had to say the word and one of his men would cook steak, even if he had to kill an animal right then to get it. The centurion knew that Jesus was sent from God and that he had TOTAL authority. The man snaps his fingers and angels jump into action. And he was right. Like the centurion, we need to have faith that God can help us.

Your next reading is on page 1333.

more than a prophet. 27This is the one about whom it is written:

" 'I will send my messenger ahead of you,
    who will prepare your way before you.'[a]

28I tell you, among those born of women there is no one greater than John; yet the one who is least in the kingdom of God is greater than he."

29(All the people, even the tax collectors, when they heard Jesus' words, acknowledged that God's way was right, because they had been baptized by John. 30But the Pharisees and experts in the law rejected God's purpose for themselves, because they had not been baptized by John.)

31"To what, then, can I compare the people of this generation? What are they like? 32They are like children sitting in the marketplace and calling out to each other:

" 'We played the flute for you,
    and you did not dance;
  we sang a dirge,
    and you did not cry.'

33For John the Baptist came neither eating bread nor drinking wine, and you say, 'He has a demon.' 34The Son of Man came eating and drinking, and you say, 'Here is a glutton and a drunkard, a friend of tax collectors and "sinners." ' 35But wisdom is proved right by all her children."

Jesus Anointed by a Sinful Woman

36Now one of the Pharisees invited Jesus to have dinner with him, so he went to the Pharisee's house and reclined at the table. 37When a woman who had lived a sinful life in that town learned that Jesus was eating at the Pharisee's house, she brought an alabaster jar of perfume, 38and as she stood behind him at his feet weeping, she began to wet his feet with

a 27 Mal. 3:1

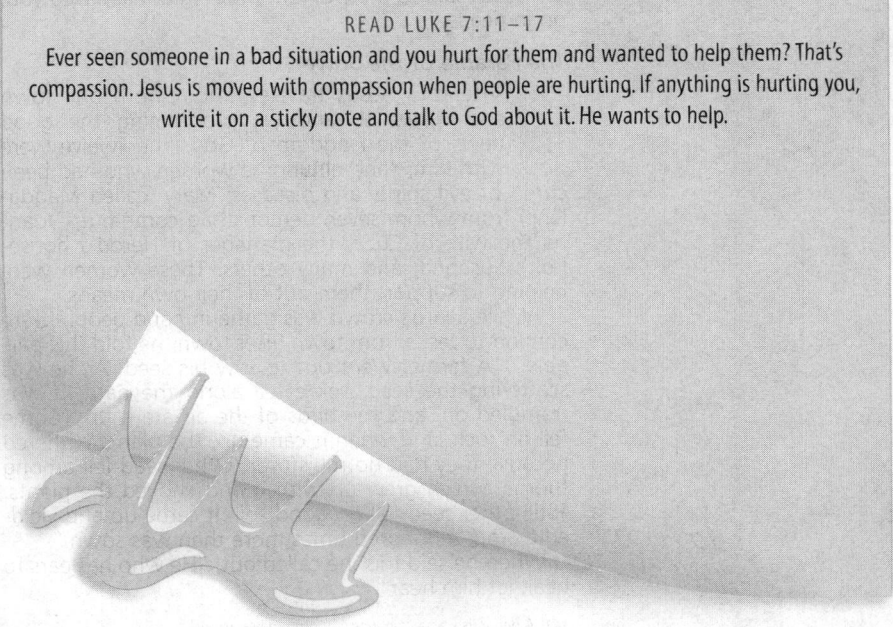

Make It Stick

READ LUKE 7:11–17

Ever seen someone in a bad situation and you hurt for them and wanted to help them? That's compassion. Jesus is moved with compassion when people are hurting. If anything is hurting you, write it on a sticky note and talk to God about it. He wants to help.

Get a Load of This...

"We sang a dirge, and you did not cry" (Luke 7:32). Dirges were slow, mournful, sad songs, and were often sung at funerals. It was sort of like "singing the blues" in Bible times.

her tears. Then she wiped them with her hair, kissed them and poured perfume on them.

³⁹When the Pharisee who had invited him saw this, he said to himself, "If this man were a prophet, he would know who is touching him and what kind of woman she is—that she is a sinner."

⁴⁰Jesus answered him, "Simon, I have something to tell you."

"Tell me, teacher," he said.

⁴¹"Two men owed money to a certain moneylender. One owed him five hundred denarii,ᵃ and the other fifty. ⁴²Neither of them had the money to pay him back, so he canceled the debts of both. Now which of them will love him more?"

⁴³Simon replied, "I suppose the one who had the bigger debt canceled."

"You have judged correctly," Jesus said.

⁴⁴Then he turned toward the woman and said to Simon, "Do you see this woman? I came into your house. You did not give me any water for my feet, but she wet my feet with her tears and wiped them with her hair. ⁴⁵You did not give me a kiss, but this woman, from the time I entered, has not stopped kissing my feet. ⁴⁶You did not put oil on my head, but she has poured perfume on my feet. ⁴⁷Therefore, I tell you, her many sins have been forgiven—for she loved much. But he who has been forgiven little loves little."

⁴⁸Then Jesus said to her, "Your sins are forgiven."

⁴⁹The other guests began to say among themselves, "Who is this who even forgives sins?"

⁵⁰Jesus said to the woman, "Your faith has saved you; go in peace."

The Parable of the Sower

After this, Jesus traveled about from one town and village to another, proclaiming the good news of the kingdom of God. The Twelve were with him, ²and also some women who had been cured of evil spirits and diseases: Mary (called Magdalene) from whom seven demons had come out; ³Joanna the wife of Cuza, the manager of Herod's household; Susanna; and many others. These women were helping to support them out of their own means.

⁴While a large crowd was gathering and people were coming to Jesus from town after town, he told this parable: ⁵"A farmer went out to sow his seed. As he was scattering the seed, some fell along the path; it was trampled on, and the birds of the air ate it up. ⁶Some fell on rock, and when it came up, the plants withered because they had no moisture. ⁷Other seed fell among thorns, which grew up with it and choked the plants. ⁸Still other seed fell on good soil. It came up and yielded a crop, a hundred times more than was sown."

When he said this, he called out, "He who has ears to hear, let him hear."

ᵃ 41 A denarius was a coin worth about a day's wages.

9His disciples asked him what this parable meant. 10He said, "The knowledge of the secrets of the kingdom of God has been given to you, but to others I speak in parables, so that,

" 'though seeing, they may not see;
  though hearing, they may not
  understand.'[a]

11"This is the meaning of the parable: The seed is the word of God. 12Those along the path are the ones who hear, and then the devil comes and takes away the word from their hearts, so that they may not believe and be saved. 13Those on the rock are the ones who receive the word with joy when they hear it, but they have no root. They believe for a while, but in the time of testing they fall away. 14The seed that fell among thorns stands for those who hear, but as they go on their way they are choked by life's worries, riches and pleasures, and they do not mature. 15But the seed on good soil stands for those with a noble and good heart, who hear the word, retain it, and by persevering produce a crop.

A Lamp on a Stand

16"No one lights a lamp and hides it in a jar or puts it under a bed. Instead, he puts it on a stand, so that those who come in can see the light. 17For there is nothing hidden that will not be disclosed, and nothing concealed that will not be known or brought out into the open. 18Therefore consider carefully how you listen. Whoever has will be given more; whoever does not have, even what he thinks he has will be taken from him."

Jesus' Mother and Brothers

19Now Jesus' mother and brothers came to see him, but they were not able to get near him because of the crowd. 20Someone told him, "Your mother and brothers are standing outside, wanting to see you."

21He replied, "My mother and brothers are those who hear God's word and put it into practice."

Jesus Calms the Storm

22One day Jesus said to his disciples, "Let's go over to the other side of the lake." So they got into a boat and set out. 23As they sailed, he fell asleep. A squall came down on the lake, so that the boat was being swamped, and they were in great danger.

24The disciples went and woke him, saying, "Master, Master, we're going to drown!"

He got up and rebuked the wind and the raging waters; the storm subsided, and all was calm. 25"Where is your faith?" he asked his disciples.

In fear and amazement they asked one another, "Who is this? He commands even the winds and the water, and they obey him."

The Healing of a Demon-possessed Man

26They sailed to the region of the Gerasenes,[b] which is across the lake from Galilee. 27When Jesus stepped ashore, he was met by a demon-possessed man from the town. For a long time this man had not worn clothes or lived in a house, but had lived in the tombs. 28When he saw Jesus, he cried out and fell at his feet, shouting at the top of his voice, "What do you want with me, Jesus, Son of the Most High God? I beg you, don't torture me!" 29For Jesus had commanded the evil[c] spirit to come out of the man. Many times it had seized him, and though he was chained hand and foot and kept under guard, he had broken his chains and had been driven by the demon into solitary places.

30Jesus asked him, "What is your name?"

"Legion," he replied, because many demons had gone into him. 31And they begged him repeatedly not to order them to go into the Abyss.

32A large herd of pigs was feeding there on the hillside. The demons begged Jesus to let them go into them, and he gave them permission. 33When the demons came out of the man, they went into the pigs, and the herd rushed down the steep bank into the lake and was drowned.

34When those tending the pigs saw what had happened, they ran off and reported this in the town and countryside, 35and the people went out to see what had happened. When they came to Jesus, they found the man from whom the demons had gone out, sitting at Jesus' feet,

[a] 10 Isaiah 6:9   [b] 26 Some manuscripts Gadarenes; other manuscripts Gergesenes; also in verse 37   [c] 29 Greek unclean

dressed and in his right mind; and they were afraid. 36Those who had seen it told the people how the demon-possessed man had been cured. 37Then all the people of the region of the Gerasenes asked Jesus to leave them, because they were overcome with fear. So he got into the boat and left.

38The man from whom the demons had gone out begged to go with him, but Jesus sent him away, saying, 39"Return home and tell how much God has done for you." So the man went away and told all over town how much Jesus had done for him.

A Dead Girl and a Sick Woman

40Now when Jesus returned, a crowd welcomed him, for they were all expecting him. 41Then a man named Jairus, a ruler of the synagogue, came and fell at Jesus' feet, pleading with him to come to his house 42because his only daughter, a girl of about twelve, was dying.

As Jesus was on his way, the crowds almost crushed him. 43And a woman was there who had been subject to bleeding for twelve years,[a] but no one could heal her. 44She came up behind him and touched the edge of his cloak, and immediately her bleeding stopped.

45"Who touched me?" Jesus asked.

When they all denied it, Peter said, "Master, the people are crowding and pressing against you."

46But Jesus said, "Someone touched me; I know that power has gone out from me."

47Then the woman, seeing that she could not go unnoticed, came trembling and fell at his feet. In the presence of all the people, she told why she had touched him and how she had been instantly healed. 48Then he said to her, "Daughter, your faith has healed you. Go in peace."

49While Jesus was still speaking, some-

[a] 43 Many manuscripts *years, and she had spent all she had on doctors*

Make It Stick

READ LUKE 8:22–25

When the disciples wailed, "We're going to drown!" they were saying, "Probably even you can't save us now, Lord!" We should go to Jesus with faith saying, "You have the power. Please help us." On a sticky note, draw a boat in a storm. Underneath, write what problem is a "storm" in your life.

one came from the house of Jairus, the synagogue ruler. "Your daughter is dead," he said. "Don't bother the teacher any more."

50 Hearing this, Jesus said to Jairus, "Don't be afraid; just believe, and she will be healed."

51 When he arrived at the house of Jairus, he did not let anyone go in with him except Peter, John and James, and the child's father and mother. 52 Meanwhile, all the people were wailing and mourning for her. "Stop wailing," Jesus said. "She is not dead but asleep."

53 They laughed at him, knowing that she was dead. 54 But he took her by the hand and said, "My child, get up!" 55 Her spirit returned, and at once she stood up. Then Jesus told them to give her something to eat. 56 Her parents were astonished, but he ordered them not to tell anyone what had happened.

Jesus Sends Out the Twelve

9 When Jesus had called the Twelve together, he gave them power and authority to drive out all demons and to cure diseases, 2 and he sent them out to preach the kingdom of God and to heal the sick. 3 He told them: "Take nothing for the journey—no staff, no bag, no bread, no money, no extra tunic. 4 Whatever house you enter, stay there until you leave that town. 5 If people do not welcome you, shake the dust off your feet when you leave their town, as a testimony against them." 6 So they set out and went from village to village, preaching the gospel and healing people everywhere.

7 Now Herod the tetrarch heard about all that was going on. And he was perplexed, because some were saying that John had been raised from the dead, 8 others that Elijah had appeared, and still others that one of the prophets of long ago had come back to life. 9 But Herod said, "I beheaded John. Who, then, is this I hear such things about?" And he tried to see him.

Jesus Feeds the Five Thousand

10 When the apostles returned, they reported to Jesus what they had done. Then he took them with him and they withdrew by themselves to a town called Bethsaida, 11 but the crowds learned about it and followed him. He welcomed them and spoke to them about the kingdom of God, and healed those who needed healing.

12 Late in the afternoon the Twelve came to him and said, "Send the crowd away so they can go to the surrounding villages and countryside and find food and lodging, because we are in a remote place here."

13 He replied, "You give them something to eat."

They answered, "We have only five loaves of bread and two fish—unless we go and buy food for all this crowd." 14 (About five thousand men were there.)

But he said to his disciples, "Have them sit down in groups of about fifty each." 15 The disciples did so, and everybody sat down. 16 Taking the five loaves and the two fish and looking up to heaven, he gave thanks and

Gross!

Check out Luke 8:30–33. Legion turns pigs into lemmings. Stand back! It's a ham-pede! The lake must have been filled with floating pig corpses. Do you suppose the townspeople fished any of the demon-possessed pork out of the sea? Er ... maybe not. Yeah, for sure not. Who'd want to eat a possessed pig?!

broke them. Then he gave them to the disciples to set before the people. [17]They all ate and were satisfied, and the disciples picked up twelve basketfuls of broken pieces that were left over.

Peter's Confession of Christ

[18]Once when Jesus was praying in private and his disciples were with him, he asked them, "Who do the crowds say I am?"

[19]They replied, "Some say John the Baptist; others say Elijah; and still others, that one of the prophets of long ago has come back to life."

[20]"But what about you?" he asked. "Who do you say I am?"

Peter answered, "The Christ[a] of God."

[21]Jesus strictly warned them not to tell this to anyone. [22]And he said, "The Son of Man must suffer many things and be rejected by the elders, chief priests and teachers of the law, and he must be killed and on the third day be raised to life."

[23]Then he said to them all: "If anyone would come after me, he must deny himself and take up his cross daily and follow me. [24]For whoever wants to save his life will lose it, but whoever loses his life for me will save it. [25]What good is it for a man to gain the whole world, and yet lose or forfeit his very self? [26]If anyone is ashamed of me and my words, the Son of Man will be ashamed of him when he comes in his glory and in the glory of the Father and of the holy angels. [27]I tell you the truth, some who are standing here will not taste death before they see the kingdom of God."

The Transfiguration

[28]About eight days after Jesus said this, he took Peter, John and James with him and went up onto a mountain to pray. [29]As he was praying, the appearance of his face changed, and his clothes became

a 20 Or *Messiah*

Make It Stick

READ LUKE 8:38–39

One of the best ways we can show others how good God is by telling them how God answered one of our prayers. Write down one big thing God has done for you that you can tell others about. Ask God to do more in your life so you'll have even more to tell others.

as bright as a flash of lightning. ³⁰Two men, Moses and Elijah, ³¹appeared in glorious splendor, talking with Jesus. They spoke about his departure, which he was about to bring to fulfillment at Jerusalem. ³²Peter and his companions were very sleepy, but when they became fully awake, they saw his glory and the two men standing with him. ³³As the men were leaving Jesus, Peter said to him, "Master, it is good for us to be here. Let us put up three shelters—one for you, one for Moses and one for Elijah." (He did not know what he was saying.)

³⁴While he was speaking, a cloud appeared and enveloped them, and they were afraid as they entered the cloud. ³⁵A voice came from the cloud, saying, "This is my Son, whom I have chosen; listen to him." ³⁶When the voice had spoken, they found that Jesus was alone. The disciples kept this to themselves, and told no one at that time what they had seen.

The Healing of a Boy With an Evil Spirit

³⁷The next day, when they came down from the mountain, a large crowd met him. ³⁸A man in the crowd called out, "Teacher, I beg you to look at my son, for he is my only child. ³⁹A spirit seizes him and he suddenly screams; it throws him into convulsions so that he foams at the mouth. It scarcely ever leaves him and is destroying him. ⁴⁰I begged your disciples to drive it out, but they could not."

⁴¹"O unbelieving and perverse generation," Jesus replied, "how long shall I stay with you and put up with you? Bring your son here."

⁴²Even while the boy was coming, the demon threw him to the ground in a convulsion. But Jesus rebuked the evil^a spirit, healed the boy and gave him back to his father. ⁴³And they were all amazed at the greatness of God.

While everyone was marveling at all that Jesus did, he said to his disciples, ⁴⁴"Listen carefully to what I am about to tell you: The Son of Man is going to be betrayed into the hands of men." ⁴⁵But they did not understand what this meant.

^a 42 Greek unclean

GET SMARTER

Who Do You Say That I Am?

READ LUKE 9:18–22

Jesus asked the Twelve who the crowds were saying he was. They told him the popular rumors: John the Baptist, Elijah or one of the other prophets. Then Jesus asked the big question: "Who do you say I am?" (Luke 9:20). It doesn't matter what the crowds say. The crowds back then thought the Christ, or Messiah, would be a military general, so Jesus had to tell the disciples to keep their knowledge to themselves for the time being (verse 21). The crowds today usually agree that Jesus lived about 2,000 years ago, did miracles and taught people to love one another. But many people don't think Jesus was God's one and only Son. "Who do you say I am?" Could Jesus be "Mr. Always-love Always-honest Guy" and then LIE about being God's Son? It doesn't add up. Jesus was God's Son, just like he said he was.

Your next reading is on page 1336.

It was hidden from them, so that they did not grasp it, and they were afraid to ask him about it.

Who Will Be the Greatest?

46An argument started among the disciples as to which of them would be the greatest. 47Jesus, knowing their thoughts, took a little child and had him stand beside him. 48Then he said to them, "Whoever welcomes this little child in my name welcomes me; and whoever welcomes me welcomes the one who sent me. For he who is least among you all—he is the greatest."

49"Master," said John, "we saw a man driving out demons in your name and we tried to stop him, because he is not one of us."

50"Do not stop him," Jesus said, "for whoever is not against you is for you."

Samaritan Opposition

51As the time approached for him to be taken up to heaven, Jesus resolutely set out for Jerusalem. 52And he sent messengers on ahead, who went into a Samaritan village to get things ready for him; 53but the people there did not welcome him, because he was heading for Jerusalem. 54When the disciples James and John saw this, they asked, "Lord, do you want us to call fire down from heaven to destroy them[a]?" 55But Jesus turned and rebuked them, 56and[b] they went to another village.

The Cost of Following Jesus

57As they were walking along the road, a man said to him, "I will follow you wherever you go."

58Jesus replied, "Foxes have holes and birds of the air have nests, but the Son of Man has no place to lay his head."

59He said to another man, "Follow me." But the man replied, "Lord, first let me go and bury my father."

60Jesus said to him, "Let the dead bury their own dead, but you go and proclaim the kingdom of God."

61Still another said, "I will follow you, Lord; but first let me go back and say good-by to my family."

62Jesus replied, "No one who puts his hand to the plow and looks back is fit for service in the kingdom of God."

Jesus Sends Out the Seventy-two

10 After this the Lord appointed seventy-two[c] others and sent them two by two ahead of him to every town and place where he was about to go. 2He told them, "The harvest is plentiful, but the workers are few. Ask the Lord of the harvest, therefore, to send out workers into his harvest field. 3Go! I am sending you out like lambs among wolves. 4Do not take a purse or bag or sandals; and do not greet anyone on the road.

5"When you enter a house, first say, 'Peace to this house.' 6If a man of peace is there, your peace will rest on him; if not, it will return to you. 7Stay in that house, eating and drinking whatever they give you, for the worker deserves his wages. Do not move around from house to house.

8"When you enter a town and are welcomed, eat what is set before you. 9Heal the sick who are there and tell them, 'The kingdom of God is near you.' 10But when you enter a town and are not welcomed, go into its streets and say, 11'Even the dust of your town that sticks to our feet we wipe off against you. Yet be sure of this: The kingdom of God is near.' 12I tell you, it will be more bearable on that day for Sodom than for that town.

13"Woe to you, Korazin! Woe to you, Bethsaida! For if the miracles that were performed in you had been performed in Tyre and Sidon, they would have repented long ago, sitting in sackcloth and ashes. 14But it will be more bearable for Tyre and Sidon at the judgment than for you. 15And you, Capernaum, will you be lifted up to the skies? No, you will go down to the depths.[d]

16"He who listens to you listens to me; he who rejects you rejects me; but he who rejects me rejects him who sent me."

17The seventy-two returned with joy and said, "Lord, even the demons submit to us in your name."

18He replied, "I saw Satan fall like lightning from heaven. 19I have given you authority to trample on snakes and scorpi-

---

a 54 Some manuscripts them, even as Elijah did
b 55,56 Some manuscripts them. And he said, "You do not know what kind of spirit you are of, for the Son of Man did not come to destroy men's lives, but to save them." 56And
c 1 Some manuscripts seventy; also in verse 17   d 15 Greek Hades

ons and to overcome all the power of the enemy; nothing will harm you. 20However-er, do not rejoice that the spirits submit to you, but rejoice that your names are written in heaven."

21At that time Jesus, full of joy through the Holy Spirit, said, "I praise you, Father, Lord of heaven and earth, because you have hidden these things from the wise and learned, and revealed them to little children. Yes, Father, for this was your good pleasure.

22"All things have been committed to me by my Father. No one knows who the Son is except the Father, and no one knows who the Father is except the Son and those to whom the Son chooses to reveal him."

23Then he turned to his disciples and said privately, "Blessed are the eyes that see what you see. 24For I tell you that many prophets and kings wanted to see what you see but did not see it, and to hear what you hear but did not hear it."

The Parable of the Good Samaritan

25On one occasion an expert in the law stood up to test Jesus. "Teacher," he asked, "what must I do to inherit eternal life?"

26"What is written in the Law?" he replied. "How do you read it?"

27He answered: " 'Love the Lord your God with all your heart and with all your soul and with all your strength and with all your mind'ᵃ; and, 'Love your neighbor as yourself.' ᵇ"

28"You have answered correctly," Jesus replied. "Do this and you will live."

29But he wanted to justify himself, so he asked Jesus, "And who is my neighbor?"

30In reply Jesus said: "A man was going down from Jerusalem to Jericho, when he fell into the hands of robbers. They stripped him of his clothes, beat him and went away, leaving him half dead. 31A priest happened to be going down the same road, and when he saw the man, he

a 27 Deut. 6:5   b 27 Lev. 19:18

READ LUKE 10:17–20

Compared with the thrills God has planned for you in heaven, demon-bashing is nothing. God can and does give you power now, but the best thing of all is that, if you are a Christian, your name is written in heaven in the book of life (Luke 10:20; Revelation 21:27). On a sticky note, draw the book of life ... with your name in it.

passed by on the other side. ³²So too, a Levite, when he came to the place and saw him, passed by on the other side. ³³But a Samaritan, as he traveled, came where the man was; and when he saw him, he took pity on him. ³⁴He went to him and bandaged his wounds, pouring on oil and wine. Then he put the man on his own donkey, took him to an inn and took care of him. ³⁵The next day he took out two silver coins[a] and gave them to the innkeeper. 'Look after him,' he said, 'and when I return, I will reimburse you for any extra expense you may have.'

³⁶"Which of these three do you think was a neighbor to the man who fell into the hands of robbers?"

³⁷The expert in the law replied, "The one who had mercy on him."

Jesus told him, "Go and do likewise."

At the Home of Martha and Mary

³⁸As Jesus and his disciples were on their way, he came to a village where a woman named Martha opened her home to him. ³⁹She had a sister called Mary, who sat at the Lord's feet listening to what he said. ⁴⁰But Martha was distracted by all the preparations that had to be made. She came to him and asked, "Lord, don't you care that my sister has left me to do the work by myself? Tell her to help me!"

⁴¹"Martha, Martha," the Lord answered, "you are worried and upset about many things, ⁴²but only one thing is needed.[b] Mary has chosen what is better, and it will not be taken away from her."

Jesus' Teaching on Prayer

11 One day Jesus was praying in a certain place. When he finished, one of his disciples said to him, "Lord, teach us to pray, just as John taught his disciples."

²He said to them, "When you pray, say:

" 'Father,[c]
hallowed be your name,
    your kingdom come.[d]
³Give us each day our daily bread.

---

[a] 35 Greek *two denarii*   [b] 42 Some manuscripts *but few things are needed—or only one*   [c] 2 Some manuscripts *Our Father in heaven*   [d] 2 Some manuscripts *come. May your will be done on earth as it is in heaven.*

The Good Samaritan

READ LUKE 10:25–37

It's too easy to find a reason not to help others. The people who ignored the beat-up, half-dead man were supposedly the "good guys"—a priest and a Levite (an assistant to the priests). But they both found reasons not to help. Along comes the Samaritan (there was bad blood between Samaritans and Jews back then) and he helped the guy. When can *you* be a "Good Samaritan"? When a little kid is getting picked on. When washing a few cars brings in money for a good cause. Being too important to help may seem "cool," but it's not. Throwing snowballs with your friends may seem like fun—and right on! It sure is! Duck! But what's more important? Knocking a friend's stocking cap off or caring enough to help someone who's hurting? "A Samaritan . . . when he saw him, he took pity on him" (Luke 10:33) and helped. When there's a need, be a Good Samaritan.

Your next reading is on page 1338.

4 Forgive us our sins,
    for we also forgive everyone who
       sins against us.*a*
   And lead us not into temptation.*b*' "

5 Then he said to them, "Suppose one of you has a friend, and he goes to him at midnight and says, 'Friend, lend me three loaves of bread, 6 because a friend of mine on a journey has come to me, and I have nothing to set before him.'

7 "Then the one inside answers, 'Don't bother me. The door is already locked, and my children are with me in bed. I can't get up and give you anything.' 8 I tell you, though he will not get up and give him the bread because he is his friend, yet because of the man's boldness*c* he will get up and give him as much as he needs.

9 "So I say to you: Ask and it will be given to you; seek and you will find; knock and the door will be opened to you. 10 For everyone who asks receives; he who seeks

finds; and to him who knocks, the door will be opened.

11 "Which of you fathers, if your son asks for*d* a fish, will give him a snake instead? 12 Or if he asks for an egg, will give him a scorpion? 13 If you then, though you are evil, know how to give good gifts to your children, how much more will your Father in heaven give the Holy Spirit to those who ask him!"

Jesus and Beelzebub

14 Jesus was driving out a demon that was mute. When the demon left, the man who had been mute spoke, and the crowd was amazed. 15 But some of them said, "By Beelzebub,*e* the prince of demons, he is driving out demons." 16 Others tested him by asking for a sign from heaven.

a 4 Greek *everyone who is indebted to us*   *b 4* Some manuscripts *temptation but deliver us from the ev'*, one   *c 8* Or *persistence*   *d 11* Some manuscripts *for bread, will give him a stone; or if he asks for*   *e 15* Greek *Beezeboul* or *Beelzeboul*; also in verses 18 and 19

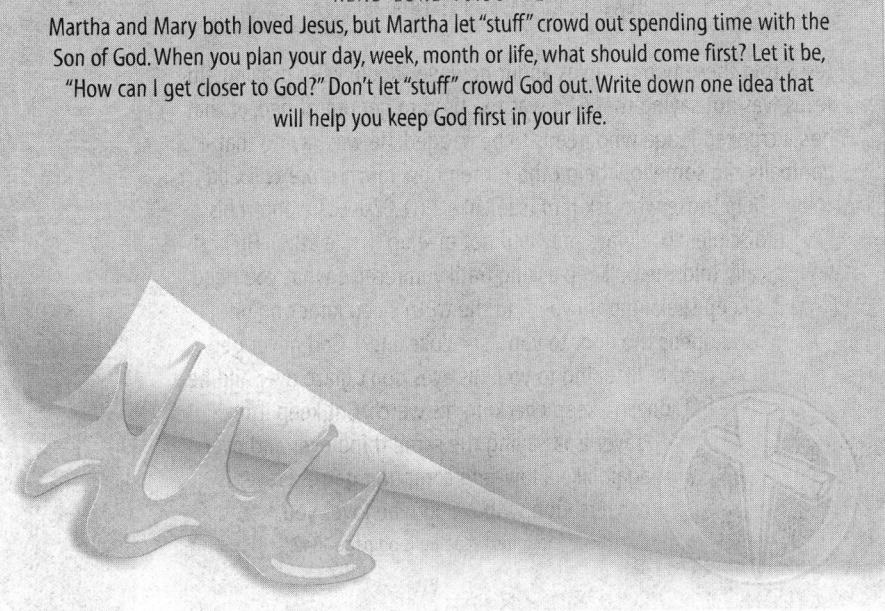

Make It Stick

READ LUKE 10:38–42

Martha and Mary both loved Jesus, but Martha let "stuff" crowd out spending time with the Son of God. When you plan your day, week, month or life, what should come first? Let it be, "How can I get closer to God?" Don't let "stuff" crowd God out. Write down one idea that will help you keep God first in your life.

¹⁷Jesus knew their thoughts and said to them: "Any kingdom divided against itself will be ruined, and a house divided against itself will fall. ¹⁸If Satan is divided against himself, how can his kingdom stand? I say this because you claim that I drive out demons by Beelzebub. ¹⁹Now if I drive out demons by Beelzebub, by whom do your followers drive them out? So then, they will be your judges. ²⁰But if I drive out demons by the finger of God, then the kingdom of God has come to you.

²¹"When a strong man, fully armed, guards his own house, his possessions are safe. ²²But when someone stronger attacks and overpowers him, he takes away the armor in which the man trusted and divides up the spoils.

²³"He who is not with me is against me, and he who does not gather with me, scatters.

²⁴"When an evil^a spirit comes out of a man, it goes through arid places seeking rest and does not find it. Then it says, 'I will return to the house I left.' ²⁵When it arrives, it finds the house swept clean and put in order. ²⁶Then it goes and takes seven other spirits more wicked than itself, and they go in and live there. And the final condition of that man is worse than the first."

²⁷As Jesus was saying these things, a woman in the crowd called out, "Blessed is the mother who gave you birth and nursed you."

²⁸He replied, "Blessed rather are those who hear the word of God and obey it."

The Sign of Jonah

²⁹As the crowds increased, Jesus said, "This is a wicked generation. It asks for a miraculous sign, but none will be given it except the sign of Jonah. ³⁰For as Jonah was a sign to the Ninevites, so also will the Son of Man be to this generation. ³¹The Queen of the South will rise at the judgment with the men of this generation and condemn them; for she came from the ends of the earth to listen to Solomon's wisdom, and now one^b greater than Solomon is here. ³²The men of Nineveh will stand up at the judgment with this generation and condemn it; for they

---

^a 24 Greek *unclean*   ^b 31 Or *something*; also in verse 32

Keep Praying

READ LUKE 11:5–13; 18:1–8

Jesus told these two parables about how we should keep praying. No, Jesus was not saying that God was too tired to get out of bed, or that he's a crooked judge who needs to be nagged. He was saying that if goofballs can somehow help others, then how much more will God help those who ask him (see Luke 11:13)? Jesus wanted his disciples to "always pray and not give up" (Luke 18:1). He basically told them, "Keep asking until you receive what you need. Keep seeking until you find the truth. Keep knocking until God opens the door to you" (see Luke 11:9). God never gets tired of listening to you. His eyes don't glaze over and he doesn't keep checking his watch. But keep it real. Prayer isn't saying the same thing over and over again like a low-end computer game. Prayer is conversation with a God who loves you.

Your next reading is on page 1342.

repented at the preaching of Jonah, and now one greater than Jonah is here.

The Lamp of the Body

33 "No one lights a lamp and puts it in a place where it will be hidden, or under a bowl. Instead he puts it on its stand, so that those who come in may see the light. 34 Your eye is the lamp of your body. When your eyes are good, your whole body also is full of light. But when they are bad, your body also is full of darkness. 35 See to it, then, that the light within you is not darkness. 36 Therefore, if your whole body is full of light, and no part of it dark, it will be completely lighted, as when the light of a lamp shines on you."

Six Woes

37 When Jesus had finished speaking, a Pharisee invited him to eat with him; so he went in and reclined at the table. 38 But the Pharisee, noticing that Jesus did not first wash before the meal, was surprised.

39 Then the Lord said to him, "Now then, you Pharisees clean the outside of the cup and dish, but inside you are full of greed and wickedness. 40 You foolish people! Did not the one who made the outside make the inside also? 41 But give what is inside ⌊the dish⌋ᵃ to the poor, and everything will be clean for you.

42 "Woe to you Pharisees, because you give God a tenth of your mint, rue and all other kinds of garden herbs, but you neglect justice and the love of God. You should have practiced the latter without leaving the former undone.

43 "Woe to you Pharisees, because you love the most important seats in the synagogues and greetings in the marketplaces.

44 "Woe to you, because you are like unmarked graves, which men walk over without knowing it."

45 One of the experts in the law an-

a 41 Or *what you have*

Make It Stick

READ LUKE 11:42

The Pharisees tithed teeny little spices, but let more important things slide, like justice and loving God. That's just … well … flaky! Tape a tiny flake of some spice (basil, parsley, etc.) to your sticky note as a reminder that your faith isn't just for little things—it's for everything.

Get a Load of This...

Scary thought!—The words you whisper in private in your bedroom will one day be shouted from the roof (see Luke 12:3). It's like a movie where the villain is bugged and his boasts of how he's planning to seize power are broadcast over public radio.

swered him, "Teacher, when you say these things, you insult us also."

46Jesus replied, "And you experts in the law, woe to you, because you load people down with burdens they can hardly carry, and you yourselves will not lift one finger to help them.

47"Woe to you, because you build tombs for the prophets, and it was your forefathers who killed them. 48So you testify that you approve of what your forefathers did; they killed the prophets, and you build their tombs. 49Because of this, God in his wisdom said, 'I will send them prophets and apostles, some of whom they will kill and others they will persecute.' 50Therefore this generation will be held responsible for the blood of all the prophets that has been shed since the beginning of the world, 51from the blood of Abel to the blood of Zechariah, who was killed between the altar and the sanctuary. Yes, I tell you, this generation will be held responsible for it all.

52"Woe to you experts in the law, because you have taken away the key to knowledge. You yourselves have not entered, and you have hindered those who were entering."

53When Jesus left there, the Pharisees and the teachers of the law began to oppose him fiercely and to besiege him with questions, 54waiting to catch him in something he might say.

Warnings and Encouragements

12 Meanwhile, when a crowd of many thousands had gathered, so that they were trampling on one another, Jesus began to speak first to his disciples, saying: "Be on your guard against the yeast of the Pharisees, which is hypocrisy. 2There is nothing concealed that will not be disclosed, or hidden that will not be made known. 3What you have said in the dark will be heard in the daylight, and what you have whispered in the ear in the inner rooms will be proclaimed from the roofs.

4"I tell you, my friends, do not be afraid of those who kill the body and after that can do no more. 5But I will show you whom you should fear: Fear him who, after the killing of the body, has power to throw you into hell. Yes, I tell you, fear him. 6Are not five sparrows sold for two pennies[a]? Yet not one of them is forgotten by God. 7Indeed, the very hairs of your head are all numbered. Don't be afraid; you are worth more than many sparrows.

8"I tell you, whoever acknowledges me before men, the Son of Man will also acknowledge him before the angels of God. 9But he who disowns me before men will be disowned before the angels of God. 10And everyone who speaks a word against the Son of Man will be forgiven, but anyone who blasphemes against the Holy Spirit will not be forgiven.

11"When you are brought before synagogues, rulers

a 6 Greek two assaria

and authorities, do not worry about how you will defend yourselves or what you will say, ¹²for the Holy Spirit will teach you at that time what you should say."

The Parable of the Rich Fool

¹³Someone in the crowd said to him, "Teacher, tell my brother to divide the inheritance with me."

¹⁴Jesus replied, "Man, who appointed me a judge or an arbiter between you?" ¹⁵Then he said to them, "Watch out! Be on your guard against all kinds of greed; a man's life does not consist in the abundance of his possessions."

¹⁶And he told them this parable: "The ground of a certain rich man produced a good crop. ¹⁷He thought to himself, 'What shall I do? I have no place to store my crops.'

¹⁸"Then he said, 'This is what I'll do. I will tear down my barns and build bigger ones, and there I will store all my grain and my goods. ¹⁹And I'll say to myself, "You have plenty of good things laid up for many years. Take life easy; eat, drink and be merry." '

²⁰"But God said to him, 'You fool! This very night your life will be demanded from you. Then who will get what you have prepared for yourself?'

²¹"This is how it will be with anyone who stores up things for himself but is not rich toward God."

Do Not Worry

²²Then Jesus said to his disciples: "Therefore I tell you, do not worry about your life, what you will eat; or about your body, what you will wear. ²³Life is more than food, and the body more than clothes. ²⁴Consider the ravens: They do not sow or reap, they have no storeroom or barn; yet God feeds them. And how much more valuable you are than birds! ²⁵Who of you by worrying can add a single hour to his life*a*? ²⁶Since you cannot do this very little thing, why do you worry about the rest?

²⁷"Consider how the lilies grow. They do not labor or spin. Yet I tell you, not even Solomon in all his splendor was dressed like one of these. ²⁸If that is how God clothes the grass of the field, which is here today, and tomorrow is thrown into the fire, how much more will he clothe you, O you of little faith! ²⁹And do not set your heart on what you will eat or drink; do not worry about it. ³⁰For the pagan world runs after all such things, and your Father knows that you need them. ³¹But seek his kingdom, and these things will be given to you as well.

³²"Do not be afraid, little flock, for your Father has been pleased to give you the kingdom. ³³Sell your possessions and give to the poor. Provide purses for yourselves that will not wear out, a treasure in heaven that will not be exhausted, where no thief comes near and no moth destroys. ³⁴For where your treasure is, there your heart will be also.

a 25 Or single cubit to his height

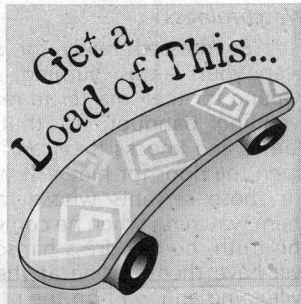

Get a Load of This...

In Jesus' day, five sparrows were sold for ten cents (Luke 12:6). Know why they sold them?—because they ate them for food. They ate sparrows? You betcha! How? On a stick? Chocolate-dipped sparrows? In a bun? "Hey buddy, could you spare a sparrow?"

Watchfulness

35 "Be dressed ready for service and keep your lamps burning, 36like men waiting for their master to return from a wedding banquet, so that when he comes and knocks they can immediately open the door for him. 37It will be good for those servants whose master finds them watching when he comes. I tell you the truth, he will dress himself to serve, will have them recline at the table and will come and wait on them. 38It will be good for those servants whose master finds them ready, even if he comes in the second or third watch of the night. 39But understand this: If the owner of the house had known at what hour the thief was coming, he would not have let his house be broken into. 40You also must be ready, because the Son of Man will come at an hour when you do not expect him."

41 Peter asked, "Lord, are you telling this parable to us, or to everyone?"

42 The Lord answered, "Who then is the faithful and wise manager, whom the master puts in charge of his servants to give them their food allowance at the proper time? 43It will be good for that servant whom the master finds doing so when he returns. 44I tell you the truth, he will put him in charge of all his possessions. 45But suppose the servant says to himself, 'My master is taking a long time in coming,' and he then begins to beat the menservants and maidservants and to eat and drink and get drunk. 46The master of that servant will come on a day when he does not expect him and at an hour he is not aware of. He will cut him to pieces and assign him a place with the unbelievers.

47 "That servant who knows his master's will and does not get ready or does not do what his master wants will be beaten with many blows. 48But the one who does not know and does things deserving punishment will be beaten with few blows. From everyone who has been given much, much will be demanded; and from the one who has been entrusted with much, much more will be asked.

The Rich Fool

READ LUKE 12:13–21

What if you had three wishes? Would one be, "I wish for unlimited wishes"? You think you're beating the system, but what if you get hit by a bus before you make another wish? "This is how it will be with anyone who stores up things for himself but is not rich toward God" (verse 21). (Not so much the bus thing, but it's definitely important to give to God, in part by helping others.) Being rich isn't necessarily a bad thing. It is a problem when you're *only* looking for ways to take care of yourself with not a thought for others. Strike a balance. You don't have to give away your skateboard and computer and all your games and always, only think of others. God wants to bless you, too. Of course, but that's so you can bless others in turn. When you see someone in need and you have more than enough, pray about giving to others.

Your next reading is on page 1345.

Not Peace but Division

⁴⁹"I have come to bring fire on the earth, and how I wish it were already kindled! ⁵⁰But I have a baptism to undergo, and how distressed I am until it is completed! ⁵¹Do you think I came to bring peace on earth? No, I tell you, but division. ⁵²From now on there will be five in one family divided against each other, three against two and two against three. ⁵³They will be divided, father against son and son against father, mother against daughter and daughter against mother, mother-in-law against daughter-in-law and daughter-in-law against mother-in-law."

Interpreting the Times

⁵⁴He said to the crowd: "When you see a cloud rising in the west, immediately you say, 'It's going to rain,' and it does. ⁵⁵And when the south wind blows, you say, 'It's going to be hot,' and it is. ⁵⁶Hypocrites! You know how to interpret the appearance of the earth and the sky. How is it that you don't know how to interpret this present time?

⁵⁷"Why don't you judge for yourselves

Make It Stick

_____

_____

_____

_____

_____

_____

_____

READ LUKE 12:32–34
God owns everything. Not that he wants your gym socks, but he does expect you to be faithful and responsible with what you have. If God has given you a lot, you should give in return. On a sticky note, write three ways you can use what you have to help those around you.

Gross!

In Luke 13:8 they placed fertilizer around plants to make them grow. This fertilizer wasn't the stuff that came in nice clean sacks from the store either. It came out of a farm animal and had to be moved with a shovel. Aren't you glad you're not a plant?

what is right? 58As you are going with your adversary to the magistrate, try hard to be reconciled to him on the way, or he may drag you off to the judge, and the judge turn you over to the officer, and the officer throw you into prison. 59I tell you, you will not get out until you have paid the last penny.ᵃ"

Repent or Perish

13 Now there were some present at that time who told Jesus about the Galileans whose blood Pilate had mixed with their sacrifices. 2Jesus answered, "Do you think that these Galileans were worse sinners than all the other Galileans because they suffered this way? 3I tell you, no! But unless you repent, you too will all perish. 4Or those eighteen who died when the tower in Siloam fell on them— do you think they were more guilty than all the others living in Jerusalem? 5I tell you, no! But unless you repent, you too will all perish."

6Then he told this parable: "A man had a fig tree, planted in his vineyard, and he went to look for fruit on it, but did not find any. 7So he said to the man who took care of the vineyard, 'For three years now I've been coming to look for fruit on this fig tree and haven't found any. Cut it down! Why should it use up the soil?'

8" 'Sir,' the man replied, 'leave it alone for one more year, and I'll dig around it and fertilize it. 9If it bears fruit next year, fine! If not, then cut it down.' "

A Crippled Woman Healed on the Sabbath

10On a Sabbath Jesus was teaching in one of the synagogues, 11and a woman was there who had been crippled by a spirit for eighteen years. She was bent over and could not straighten up at all. 12When Jesus saw her, he called her forward and said to her, "Woman, you are set free from your infirmity." 13Then he put his hands on her, and immediately she straightened up and praised God.

14Indignant because Jesus had healed on the Sabbath, the synagogue ruler said to the people, "There are six days for work. So come and be healed on those days, not on the Sabbath."

15The Lord answered him, "You hypocrites! Doesn't each of you on the Sabbath untie his ox or donkey from the stall and lead it out to give it water? 16Then should not this woman, a daughter of Abraham, whom Satan has kept bound for eighteen long years, be set free on the Sabbath day from what bound her?"

17When he said this, all his opponents were humiliated, but the people were delighted with all the wonderful things he was doing.

The Parables of the Mustard Seed and the Yeast

18Then Jesus asked, "What is the kingdom of God like? What shall I compare it to? 19It is like a mustard seed,

ᵃ 59 Greek lepton

which a man took and planted in his garden. It grew and became a tree, and the birds of the air perched in its branches."

20Again he asked, "What shall I compare the kingdom of God to? 21It is like yeast that a woman took and mixed into a large amount*a* of flour until it worked all through the dough."

The Narrow Door

22Then Jesus went through the towns and villages, teaching as he made his way to Jerusalem. 23Someone asked him, "Lord, are only a few people going to be saved?"

He said to them, 24"Make every effort to enter through the narrow door, because many, I tell you, will try to enter and will not be able to. 25Once the owner of the house gets up and closes the door, you will stand outside knocking and pleading, 'Sir, open the door for us.'

"But he will answer, 'I don't know you or where you come from.'

26"Then you will say, 'We ate and drank with you, and you taught in our streets.'

27"But he will reply, 'I don't know you or where you come from. Away from me, all you evildoers!'

28"There will be weeping there, and gnashing of teeth, when you see Abraham, Isaac and Jacob and all the prophets in the kingdom of God, but you yourselves thrown out. 29People will come from east and west and north and south, and will take their places at the feast in the kingdom of God. 30Indeed there are those who are last who will be first, and first who will be last."

Jesus' Sorrow for Jerusalem

31At that time some Pharisees came to Jesus and said to him, "Leave this place and go somewhere else. Herod wants to kill you."

32He replied, "Go tell that fox, 'I will drive out demons and heal people today and tomorrow, and on the third day I will reach my goal.' 33In any case, I must keep going today and tomorrow and the next day—for surely no prophet can die outside Jerusalem!

a 21 Greek *three satas* (probably about 1/2 bushel or 22 liters)

Hot Mustard!

READ LUKE 13:18–21

Do you "relish" hot mustard? And do you find you're always trying to "catch up"? OK, ENOUGH bad condiment jokes. Jesus' stories about the mustard seed and yeast are talking about spiritual growth, where the kingdom of God gets inside your heart and then grows. A mustard seed is tiny but it becomes a big tree, so big that birds perch there (verse 19), and it gives seeds that can be used to make mustard. But it takes time for that seed to grow into a tree. When you become a Christian, God puts his Spirit in you; and as you learn and grow, that seed grows in you, changing you and making you more like Jesus. Do your best to grow, but remember: Jack's overnight beanstalk was a fairy tale. You do NOT become a mustard tree Christian in a flash. Growing spiritually takes patience and time.

Your next reading is on page 1348.

³⁴"O Jerusalem, Jerusalem, you who kill the prophets and stone those sent to you, how often I have longed to gather your children together, as a hen gathers her chicks under her wings, but you were not willing! ³⁵Look, your house is left to you desolate. I tell you, you will not see me again until you say, 'Blessed is he who comes in the name of the Lord.'ᵃ"

Jesus at a Pharisee's House

One Sabbath, when Jesus went to eat in the house of a prominent Pharisee, he was being carefully watched. ²There in front of him was a man suffering from dropsy. ³Jesus asked the Pharisees and experts in the law, "Is it lawful to heal on the Sabbath or not?" ⁴But they remained silent. So taking hold of the man, he healed him and sent him away.

⁵Then he asked them, "If one of you has a sonᵇ or an ox that falls into a well on the Sabbath day, will you not immedi-

ately pull him out?" ⁶And they had nothing to say.

⁷When he noticed how the guests picked the places of honor at the table, he told them this parable: ⁸"When someone invites you to a wedding feast, do not take the place of honor, for a person more distinguished than you may have been invited. ⁹If so, the host who invited both of you will come and say to you, 'Give this man your seat.' Then, humiliated, you will have to take the least important place. ¹⁰But when you are invited, take the lowest place, so that when your host comes, he will say to you, 'Friend, move up to a better place.' Then you will be honored in the presence of all your fellow guests. ¹¹For everyone who exalts himself will be humbled, and he who humbles himself will be exalted."

¹²Then Jesus said to his host, "When you give a luncheon or dinner, do not in-

ᵃ 35 Psalm 118:26   ᵇ 5 Some manuscripts *donkey*

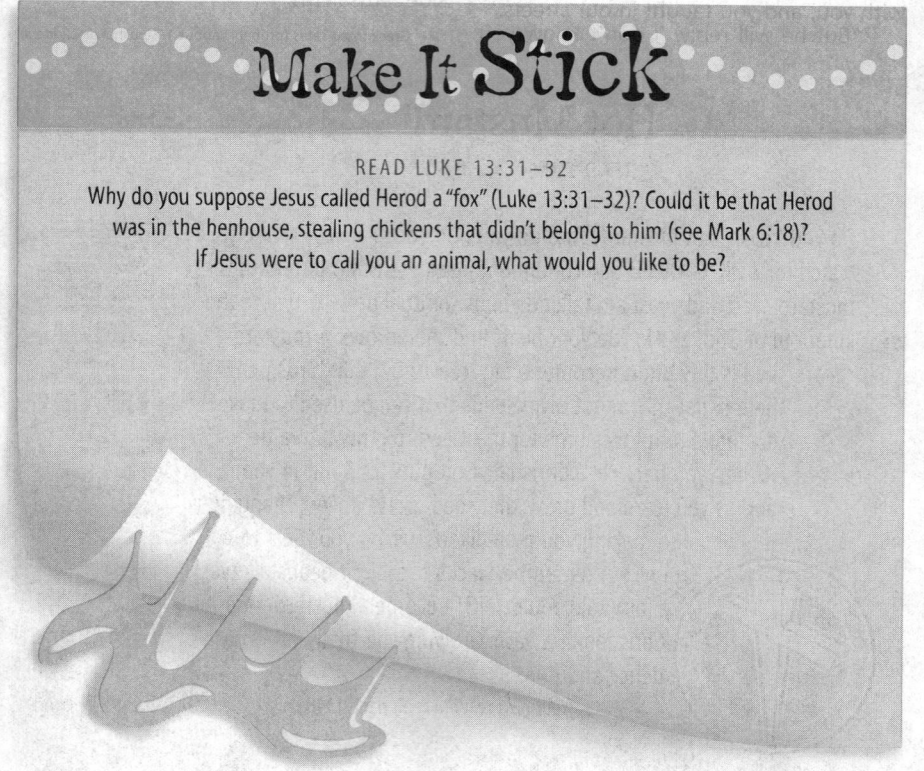

Make It Stick

READ LUKE 13:31–32

Why do you suppose Jesus called Herod a "fox" (Luke 13:31–32)? Could it be that Herod was in the henhouse, stealing chickens that didn't belong to him (see Mark 6:18)? If Jesus were to call you an animal, what would you like to be?

vite your friends, your brothers or relatives, or your rich neighbors; if you do, they may invite you back and so you will be repaid. ¹³But when you give a banquet, invite the poor, the crippled, the lame, the blind, ¹⁴and you will be blessed. Although they cannot repay you, you will be repaid at the resurrection of the righteous."

The Parable of the Great Banquet

¹⁵When one of those at the table with him heard this, he said to Jesus, "Blessed is the man who will eat at the feast in the kingdom of God."

¹⁶Jesus replied: "A certain man was preparing a great banquet and invited many guests. ¹⁷At the time of the banquet he sent his servant to tell those who had been invited, 'Come, for everything is now ready.'

¹⁸"But they all alike began to make excuses. The first said, 'I have just bought a field, and I must go and see it. Please excuse me.'

¹⁹"Another said, 'I have just bought five yoke of oxen, and I'm on my way to try them out. Please excuse me.'

²⁰"Still another said, 'I just got married, so I can't come.'

²¹"The servant came back and reported this to his master. Then the owner of the house became angry and ordered his servant, 'Go out quickly into the streets and alleys of the town and bring in the poor, the crippled, the blind and the lame.'

²²" 'Sir,' the servant said, 'what you ordered has been done, but there is still room.'

²³"Then the master told his servant, 'Go out to the roads and country lanes and make them come in, so that my house will be full. ²⁴I tell you, not one of those men who were invited will get a taste of my banquet.' "

The Cost of Being a Disciple

²⁵Large crowds were traveling with Jesus, and turning to them he said: ²⁶"If anyone comes to me and does not hate his father and mother, his wife and children, his brothers and sisters—yes, even his own life—he cannot be my disciple. ²⁷And anyone who does not carry his cross and follow me cannot be my disciple.

²⁸"Suppose one of you wants to build a tower. Will he not first sit down and estimate the cost to see if he has enough money to complete it? ²⁹For if he lays the foundation and is not able to finish it, everyone who sees it will ridicule him, ³⁰saying, 'This fellow began to build and was not able to finish.'

³¹"Or suppose a king is about to go to war against another king. Will he not first sit down and consider whether he is able with ten thousand men to oppose the one coming against him with twenty thousand? ³²If he is not able, he will send a delegation while the other is still a long way off and will ask for terms of peace. ³³In the same way, any of you who does not give up everything he has cannot be my disciple.

³⁴"Salt is good, but if it loses its saltiness, how can it

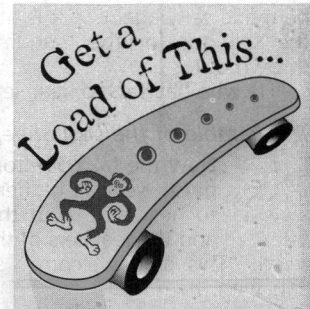

Get a Load of This...

"If one of you has ... an ox that falls into a well on the Sabbath day, will you not immediately pull him out?" (Luke 14:5). Ha! TRY it! It may not be as easy as you think. ("All right, wise guys! Who put the ox in the well again?" "Not me, Dad." "I don't know, Dad, but I don't want any water for a couple days.")

be made salty again? ³⁵It is fit neither for the soil nor for the manure pile; it is thrown out.

"He who has ears to hear, let him hear."

The Parable of the Lost Sheep

15 Now the tax collectors and "sinners" were all gathering around to hear him. ²But the Pharisees and the teachers of the law muttered, "This man welcomes sinners and eats with them."

³Then Jesus told them this parable: ⁴"Suppose one of you has a hundred sheep and loses one of them. Does he not leave the ninety-nine in the open country and go after the lost sheep until he finds it? ⁵And when he finds it, he joyfully puts it on his shoulders ⁶and goes home. Then he calls his friends and neighbors together and says, 'Rejoice with me; I have found my lost sheep.' ⁷I tell you that in the same way there will be more rejoicing in heaven over one sinner who repents than over ninety-nine righteous persons who do not need to repent.

The Parable of the Lost Coin

⁸"Or suppose a woman has ten silver coinsᵃ and loses one. Does she not light a lamp, sweep the house and search carefully until she finds it? ⁹And when she finds it, she calls her friends and neighbors together and says, 'Rejoice with me; I have found my lost coin.' ¹⁰In the same way, I tell you, there is rejoicing in the presence of the angels of God over one sinner who repents."

The Parable of the Lost Son

¹¹Jesus continued: "There was a man who had two sons. ¹²The younger one said to his father, 'Father, give me my share of the estate.' So he divided his property between them.

¹³"Not long after that, the younger son got together all he had, set off for a dis-

ᵃ 8 Greek *ten drachmas*, each worth about a day's wages

Check the Price Tag

READ LUKE 14:28–33

Suppose you want to build a skate park. Wouldn't you first sit down and estimate the cost to see if you've got everything you need to finish it? "Welcome to the grand opening of Skate Central!" "Hey! Where's the concrete?" ("Uh … that's when we ran out of cash.") When you hear that kind of answer, you know someone didn't do their math first. Being a Christian isn't just believing. It's a complete commitment to get to know God and let him guide every part of your life, every day. You'll be blessed and you'll be challenged to keep growing and learning. It's a big-time commitment. Imagine being a king's son. He's raised and groomed to be the next king—very educated, high standards—a totally different life. Guess what? You are God's son, and that makes you royalty. That makes you different. Commit yourself and your life now to being the King's son, and he'll make the cost worthwhile.

Your next reading is on page 1350.

tant country and there squandered his wealth in wild living. ¹⁴After he had spent everything, there was a severe famine in that whole country, and he began to be in need. ¹⁵So he went and hired himself out to a citizen of that country, who sent him to his fields to feed pigs. ¹⁶He longed to fill his stomach with the pods that the pigs were eating, but no one gave him anything.

¹⁷"When he came to his senses, he said, 'How many of my father's hired men have food to spare, and here I am starving to death! ¹⁸I will set out and go back to my father and say to him: Father, I have sinned against heaven and against you. ¹⁹I am no longer worthy to be called your son; make me like one of your hired men.' ²⁰So he got up and went to his father.

"But while he was still a long way off, his father saw him and was filled with compassion for him; he ran to his son, threw his arms around him and kissed him.

²¹"The son said to him, 'Father, I have sinned against heaven and against you. I am no longer worthy to be called your son.ᵃ'

²²"But the father said to his servants, 'Quick! Bring the best robe and put it on him. Put a ring on his finger and sandals on his feet. ²³Bring the fattened calf and kill it. Let's have a feast and celebrate. ²⁴For this son of mine was dead and is alive again; he was lost and is found.' So they began to celebrate.

²⁵"Meanwhile, the older son was in the field. When he came near the house, he heard music and dancing. ²⁶So he called one of the servants and asked him what was going on. ²⁷'Your brother has come,' he replied, 'and your father has killed the fattened calf because he has him back safe and sound.'

²⁸"The older brother became angry and refused to go in. So his father went out and pleaded with him. ²⁹But he answered his father, 'Look! All these years I've been slaving for you and never disobeyed your orders. Yet you never gave me even a young goat so I could celebrate with my friends. ³⁰But when this son of yours who has squandered your property with prostitutes comes home, you kill the fattened calf for him!'

³¹"'My son,' the father said, 'you are always with me, and everything I have is yours. ³²But we had to celebrate and be glad, because this brother of yours was dead and is alive again; he was lost and is found.'"

The Parable of the Shrewd Manager

16 Jesus told his disciples: "There was a rich man whose manager was accused of wasting his possessions. ²So he called him in and asked him, 'What is this I hear about you? Give an account of your management, because you cannot be manager any longer.'

³"The manager said to himself, 'What shall I do now? My master is taking away my job. I'm not strong enough to dig, and I'm ashamed to beg— ⁴I know what I'll do

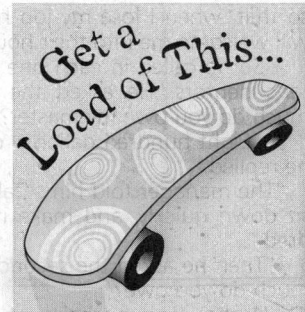

Get a Load of This...

Read Luke 15:1–10. Lost sheep? Lost coin? Lost son? Someone needs to remember where they PUT stuff! Does this sound like you?

ᵃ 21 Some early manuscripts son. Make me like one of your hired men.

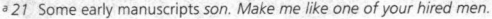

so that, when I lose my job here, people will welcome me into their houses.'

5 "So he called in each one of his master's debtors. He asked the first, 'How much do you owe my master?'

6 " 'Eight hundred gallons*a* of olive oil,' he replied.

"The manager told him, 'Take your bill, sit down quickly, and make it four hundred.'

7 "Then he asked the second, 'And how much do you owe?'

" 'A thousand bushels*b* of wheat,' he replied.

"He told him, 'Take your bill and make it eight hundred.'

8 "The master commended the dishonest manager because he had acted shrewdly. For the people of this world are more shrewd in dealing with their own kind than are the people of the light. 9 I tell you, use worldly wealth to gain friends for yourselves, so that when it is gone, you will be welcomed into eternal dwellings.

10 "Whoever can be trusted with very little can also be trusted with much, and whoever is dishonest with very little will also be dishonest with much. 11 So if you have not been trustworthy in handling worldly wealth, who will trust you with true riches? 12 And if you have not been trustworthy with someone else's property, who will give you property of your own?

13 "No servant can serve two masters. Either he will hate the one and love the other, or he will be devoted to the one and despise the other. You cannot serve both God and Money."

14 The Pharisees, who loved money, heard all this and were sneering at Jesus. 15 He said to them, "You are the ones who justify yourselves in the eyes of men, but God knows your hearts. What is highly valued among men is detestable in God's sight.

Additional Teachings

16 "The Law and the Prophets were proclaimed until John. Since that time, the good news of the kingdom of God is be-

a 6 Greek *one hundred batous* (probably about 3 kiloliters)
b 7 Greek *one hundred korous* (probably about 35 kiloliters)

God Invented Fun

READ LUKE 15:11–32

One kid figured that in order to have fun he had to scrap the rules, leave home and get a taste of the wild life. He ended up wasting his whole inheritance and begging scraps while sitting in a pig pen. The other brother was the exact opposite. He didn't spend his money and complained he didn't get even a roast goat for a party. (OK, some people like pizza, some like goats. Whatever.) The older son didn't get it. He could have partied any time (see verses 29, 31). Remember, God invented celebrations and fun. Good friends, food, laughter, music, beauty, a sense of humor, adventure, even goat barbecues—those are all HIS ideas. In fact, the people having the best time are the ones who appreciate God's gifts. So don't buy the world's line that "fun" has to be illegal, immoral or intoxicated. Work hard, but take time to celebrate and enjoy life.

Your next reading is on page 1352.

ing preached, and everyone is forcing his way into it. 17It is easier for heaven and earth to disappear than for the least stroke of a pen to drop out of the Law.

18"Anyone who divorces his wife and marries another woman commits adultery, and the man who marries a divorced woman commits adultery.

The Rich Man and Lazarus

19"There was a rich man who was dressed in purple and fine linen and lived in luxury every day. 20At his gate was laid a beggar named Lazarus, covered with sores 21and longing to eat what fell from the rich man's table. Even the dogs came and licked his sores.

22"The time came when the beggar died and the angels carried him to Abraham's side. The rich man also died and was buried. 23In hell,a where he was in torment, he looked up and saw Abraham far away, with Lazarus by his side. 24So he called to him, 'Father Abraham, have pity on me and send Lazarus to dip the tip of his finger in water and cool my tongue, because I am in agony in this fire.'

25"But Abraham replied, 'Son, remember that in your lifetime you received your good things, while Lazarus received bad things, but now he is comforted here and you are in agony. 26And besides all this, between us and you a great chasm has been fixed, so that those who want to go from here to you cannot, nor can anyone cross over from there to us.'

27"He answered, 'Then I beg you, father, send Lazarus to my father's house, 28for I have five brothers. Let him warn them, so that they will not also come to this place of torment.'

29"Abraham replied, 'They have Moses and the Prophets; let them listen to them.'

30" 'No, father Abraham,' he said, 'but if someone from the dead goes to them, they will repent.'

a 23 Greek Hades

Make It Stick

READ LUKE 16:19–31

Hell's a one-way ticket. Ask the rich man. He wanted relief. There was none. He wanted out. No exit. He wanted to let his family know. Too late. This guy learned the hard way that only living for pleasure was a dead end. On a sticky note, list some people who don't know Jesus, and start praying for them.

31 "He said to him, 'If they do not listen to Moses and the Prophets, they will not be convinced even if someone rises from the dead.' "

Sin, Faith, Duty

17 Jesus said to his disciples: "Things that cause people to sin are bound to come, but woe to that person through whom they come. 2 It would be better for him to be thrown into the sea with a millstone tied around his neck than for him to cause one of these little ones to sin. 3 So watch yourselves.

"If your brother sins, rebuke him, and if he repents, forgive him. 4 If he sins against you seven times in a day, and seven times comes back to you and says, 'I repent,' forgive him."

5 The apostles said to the Lord, "Increase our faith!"

6 He replied, "If you have faith as small as a mustard seed, you can say to this mulberry tree, 'Be uprooted and planted in the sea,' and it will obey you.

7 "Suppose one of you had a servant plowing or looking after the sheep. Would he say to the servant when he comes in from the field, 'Come along now and sit down to eat'? 8 Would he not rather say, 'Prepare my supper, get yourself ready and wait on me while I eat and drink; after that you may eat and drink'? 9 Would he thank the servant because he did what he was told to do? 10 So you also, when you have done everything you were told to do, should say, 'We are unworthy servants; we have only done our duty.' "

Ten Healed of Leprosy

11 Now on his way to Jerusalem, Jesus traveled along the border between Samaria and Galilee. 12 As he was going into a village, ten men who had leprosy[a] met him. They stood at a distance 13 and called out in a loud voice, "Jesus, Master, have pity on us!"

14 When he saw them, he said, "Go, show yourselves to the priests." And as they went, they were cleansed.

[a] 12 The Greek word was used for various diseases affecting the skin—not necessarily leprosy.

Don't Be a Gorilla

READ LUKE 17:1–3

"Things that cause people to sin are bound to come, but woe to that person through whom they come" (verse 1). Everything you do has an effect on somebody. That's true whether you're doing the right thing or the wrong thing. You may think something is a joke, but it could be a nine hundred pound gorilla on someone's back—not fun. Even if you wouldn't deliberately cause somebody to do something bad, you still have to be careful. Those little brothers or sisters or friends who look up to you are influenced by what you do and say. If you say that doing just a little bit of wrong stuff is fine, man oh man, who knows how far they'll take it? Make sure your words and deeds reflect your beliefs in God. Ask yourself, "Is what I'm doing or saying inspiring others to greatness and godliness, or am I setting a bad example?" Don't be that gorilla on someone's back.

GET COOLER

Your next reading is on page 1356.

¹⁵One of them, when he saw he was healed, came back, praising God in a loud voice. ¹⁶He threw himself at Jesus' feet and thanked him—and he was a Samaritan.

¹⁷Jesus asked, "Were not all ten cleansed? Where are the other nine? ¹⁸Was no one found to return and give praise to God except this foreigner?" ¹⁹Then he said to him, "Rise and go; your faith has made you well."

The Coming of the Kingdom of God

²⁰Once, having been asked by the Pharisees when the kingdom of God would come, Jesus replied, "The kingdom of God does not come with your careful observation, ²¹nor will people say, 'Here it is,' or 'There it is,' because the kingdom of God is within*a* you."

²²Then he said to his disciples, "The time is coming when you will long to see one of the days of the Son of Man, but you will not see it. ²³Men will tell you, 'There he is!' or 'Here he is!' Do not go running off after them. ²⁴For the Son of Man in his day*b* will be like the lightning, which flashes and lights up the sky from one end to the other. ²⁵But first he must suffer many things and be rejected by this generation.

²⁶"Just as it was in the days of Noah, so also will it be in the days of the Son of Man. ²⁷People were eating, drinking, marrying and being given in marriage up to the day Noah entered the ark. Then the flood came and destroyed them all.

²⁸"It was the same in the days of Lot. People were eating and drinking, buying and selling, planting and building. ²⁹But the day Lot left Sodom, fire and sulfur rained down from heaven and destroyed them all.

³⁰"It will be just like this on the day the Son of Man is revealed. ³¹On that day no one who is on the roof of his house, with his goods inside, should go down to get them. Likewise, no one in the field should go back for anything. ³²Remember Lot's wife! ³³Whoever tries to keep his life will lose it, and whoever loses his life will preserve it. ³⁴I tell you, on that night two people will be in one bed; one will be taken and the other left. ³⁵Two women will be grinding grain together; one will be taken and the other left.*c*

³⁷"Where, Lord?" they asked.

He replied, "Where there is a dead body, there the vultures will gather."

The Parable of the Persistent Widow

18 Then Jesus told his disciples a parable to show them that they should always pray and not give up. ²He said: "In a certain town there was a judge who neither feared God nor cared about men. ³And there was a widow in that town who kept coming to him with the plea, 'Grant me justice against my adversary.'

Get a Load of This...

How does a mulberry tree uproot itself and plant itself in the sea (Luke 17:6)? Pull itself up, walk on its roots and jump in the sea? Can you picture a mulberry tree walking along, muttering, "On my way to the ocean"? People would see it coming and get out of its way. Don't try this at home—Jesus wasn't promising that this actual prayer request would be answered. He was exaggerating in order to make a point.

---

a 21 Or *among*   *b 24* Some manuscripts do not have *in his day.*   *c 35* Some manuscripts *left. 36Two men will be in the field; one will be taken and the other left.*

⁴"For some time he refused. But finally he said to himself, 'Even though I don't fear God or care about men, ⁵yet because this widow keeps bothering me, I will see that she gets justice, so that she won't eventually wear me out with her coming!' "

⁶And the Lord said, "Listen to what the unjust judge says. ⁷And will not God bring about justice for his chosen ones, who cry out to him day and night? Will he keep putting them off? ⁸I tell you, he will see that they get justice, and quickly. However, when the Son of Man comes, will he find faith on the earth?"

The Parable of the Pharisee and the Tax Collector

⁹To some who were confident of their own righteousness and looked down on everybody else, Jesus told this parable: ¹⁰"Two men went up to the temple to pray, one a Pharisee and the other a tax collector. ¹¹The Pharisee stood up and prayed about*ᵃ* himself: 'God, I thank you that I am not like other men—robbers, evildoers, adulterers—or even like this tax collector. ¹²I fast twice a week and give a tenth of all I get.'

¹³"But the tax collector stood at a distance. He would not even look up to heaven, but beat his breast and said, 'God, have mercy on me, a sinner.'

¹⁴"I tell you that this man, rather than the other, went home justified before God. For everyone who exalts himself will be humbled, and he who humbles himself will be exalted."

The Little Children and Jesus

¹⁵People were also bringing babies to Jesus to have him touch them. When the disciples saw this, they rebuked them. ¹⁶But Jesus called the children to him and said, "Let the little children come to me, and do not hinder them, for the kingdom of God belongs to such as these. ¹⁷I tell

ᵃ 11 Or to

Make It Stick

READ LUKE 17:11–19

Only one cleansed leper, a Samaritan (who wasn't even a Jew), returned to thank Jesus. Instead of "ask-ask-ask," take a moment to count the blessings you already have and thank God for them. Fill up a sticky note with good stuff—from Jesus to a new video game and everything in between.

you the truth, anyone who will not receive the kingdom of God like a little child will never enter it."

The Rich Ruler

18A certain ruler asked him, "Good teacher, what must I do to inherit eternal life?"

19"Why do you call me good?" Jesus answered. "No one is good—except God alone. 20You know the commandments: 'Do not commit adultery, do not murder, do not steal, do not give false testimony, honor your father and mother.'a"

21"All these I have kept since I was a boy," he said.

22When Jesus heard this, he said to him, "You still lack one thing. Sell everything you have and give to the poor, and you will have treasure in heaven. Then come, follow me."

23When he heard this, he became very sad, because he was a man of great wealth. 24Jesus looked at him and said, "How hard it is for the rich to enter the kingdom of God! 25Indeed, it is easier for a camel to go through the eye of a needle than for a rich man to enter the kingdom of God."

26Those who heard this asked, "Who then can be saved?"

27Jesus replied, "What is impossible with men is possible with God."

28Peter said to him, "We have left all we had to follow you!"

29"I tell you the truth," Jesus said to them, "no one who has left home or wife or brothers or parents or children for the sake of the kingdom of God 30will fail to receive many times as much in this age and, in the age to come, eternal life."

Jesus Again Predicts His Death

31Jesus took the Twelve aside and told them, "We are going up to Jerusalem, and everything that is written by the prophets about the Son of Man will be fulfilled. 32He will be handed over to the Gentiles. They will mock him, insult him, spit on him, flog him and kill him. 33On the third day he will rise again."

34The disciples did not understand any of this. Its meaning was hidden from them, and they did not know what he was talking about.

A Blind Beggar Receives His Sight

35As Jesus approached Jericho, a blind man was sitting by the roadside begging. 36When he heard the crowd going by, he asked what was happening. 37They told him, "Jesus of Nazareth is passing by."

38He called out, "Jesus, Son of David, have mercy on me!"

39Those who led the way rebuked him and told him to be quiet, but he shouted all the more, "Son of David, have mercy on me!"

a 20 Exodus 20:12–16; Deut. 5:16–20

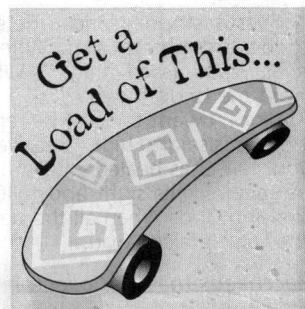

Get a Load of This...

Read Luke 18:9–14 and take a tip: Don't measure other people against some kind of list. Don't have a "Who's cool and who's not" list—not even in your MIND—that says how others should behave, what brand names they should wear, cool phrases they should use, etc.

⁴⁰Jesus stopped and ordered the man to be brought to him. When he came near, Jesus asked him, ⁴¹"What do you want me to do for you?"

"Lord, I want to see," he replied.

⁴²Jesus said to him, "Receive your sight; your faith has healed you." ⁴³Immediately he received his sight and followed Jesus, praising God. When all the people saw it, they also praised God.

Zacchaeus the Tax Collector

19 Jesus entered Jericho and was passing through. ²A man was there by the name of Zacchaeus; he was a chief tax collector and was wealthy. ³He wanted to see who Jesus was, but being a short man he could not, because of the crowd. ⁴So he ran ahead and climbed a sycamore-fig tree to see him, since Jesus was coming that way.

⁵When Jesus reached the spot, he looked up and said to him, "Zacchaeus, come down immediately. I must stay at your house today." ⁶So he came down at once and welcomed him gladly.

⁷All the people saw this and began to mutter, "He has gone to be the guest of a 'sinner.' "

⁸But Zacchaeus stood up and said to the Lord, "Look, Lord! Here and now I give half of my possessions to the poor, and if I have cheated anybody out of anything, I will pay back four times the amount."

⁹Jesus said to him, "Today salvation has come to this house, because this man, too, is a son of Abraham. ¹⁰For the Son of Man came to seek and to save what was lost."

The Parable of the Ten Minas

¹¹While they were listening to this, he went on to tell them a parable, because he was near Jerusalem and the people thought that the kingdom of God was going to appear at once. ¹²He said: "A man of noble birth went to a distant country to have himself appointed king and then to return. ¹³So he called ten of his servants and gave them ten minas.ᵃ 'Put this money to work,' he said, 'until I come back.'

¹⁴"But his subjects hated him and sent

ᵃ 13 A mina was about three months' wages.

Believing Is Seeing

READ LUKE 18:35–43

Persistence pays off. Struggling with math? Try that killer problem one more time. Miss that free throw again? C'mon—one more shot. Is someone you love still sick? Pray—again. The blind man didn't need to see Jesus to know he was there. That's a wonderful picture of prayer. This guy knew Jesus was nearby, and he got excited and simply would not quit babbling until Jesus answered. Ever wonder why God doesn't just show himself to you? Remember, your eyes are for seeing physical things. God isn't a physical being; he's spirit (John 4:24). So close your eyes. Talk to God. He said he'll never leave or forsake you (Hebrews 13:5). He's there listening, just like Jesus was there even though the blind man couldn't see him. Get the picture? The more you pray and get used to talking to God from your heart, the more you will sense him nearby.

Your next reading is on page 1357.

a delegation after him to say, 'We don't want this man to be our king.'

15 "He was made king, however, and returned home. Then he sent for the servants to whom he had given the money, in order to find out what they had gained with it.

16 "The first one came and said, 'Sir, your mina has earned ten more.'

17 " 'Well done, my good servant!' his master replied. 'Because you have been trustworthy in a very small matter, take charge of ten cities.'

18 "The second came and said, 'Sir, your mina has earned five more.'

19 "His master answered, 'You take charge of five cities.'

20 "Then another servant came and said, 'Sir, here is your mina; I have kept it laid away in a piece of cloth. 21 I was afraid of you, because you are a hard man. You take out what you did not put in and reap what you did not sow.'

22 "His master replied, 'I will judge you by your own words, you wicked servant! You knew, did you, that I am a hard man,

taking out what I did not put in, and reaping what I did not sow? 23 Why then didn't you put my money on deposit, so that when I came back, I could have collected it with interest?'

24 "Then he said to those standing by, 'Take his mina away from him and give it to the one who has ten minas.'

25 " 'Sir,' they said, 'he already has ten!'

26 "He replied, 'I tell you that to everyone who has, more will be given, but as for the one who has nothing, even what he has will be taken away. 27 But those enemies of mine who did not want me to be king over them—bring them here and kill them in front of me.' "

The Triumphal Entry

28 After Jesus had said this, he went on ahead, going up to Jerusalem. 29 As he approached Bethphage and Bethany at the hill called the Mount of Olives, he sent two of his disciples, saying to them, 30 "Go to the village ahead of you, and as you enter it, you will find a colt tied there, which no one has ever ridden. Untie it and bring

Are You Really Sorry?

READ LUKE 19:1-10

GET SMARTER:

C'mon, what's better than a good old climbing tree? We're talking about a GOOD one, one you've just GOT to climb, the kind no boy on earth could resist climbing. The only thing better is maybe having a tree fort. When Zacchaeus shinnied up that sycamore, he must've been recalling the good old days—only he wanted better days ahead. It's one thing to say, "I was wrong. I'm sorry for my sin." But Zacchaeus wanted to make things right. He promised to pay back FOUR times the amount he cheated people (Luke 19:8). Talk about restitution! Restitution is repaying what you took or broke. As you're growing up, show you're sorry when you make a mistake. First, change your habits—don't do it again. If you broke something, tell people you're sorry. Then, if you really mean it, fix or replace what you broke. That's really making things right.

Your next reading is on page 1358.

it here. ³¹If anyone asks you, 'Why are you untying it?' tell him, 'The Lord needs it.' "

³²Those who were sent ahead went and found it just as he had told them. ³³As they were untying the colt, its owners asked them, "Why are you untying the colt?"

³⁴They replied, "The Lord needs it."

³⁵They brought it to Jesus, threw their cloaks on the colt and put Jesus on it. ³⁶As he went along, people spread their cloaks on the road.

³⁷When he came near the place where the road goes down the Mount of Olives, the whole crowd of disciples began joyfully to praise God in loud voices for all the miracles they had seen:

³⁸"Blessed is the king who comes in the
name of the Lord!"ᵃ

"Peace in heaven and glory in the
highest!"

³⁹Some of the Pharisees in the crowd said to Jesus, "Teacher, rebuke your disciples!"

⁴⁰"I tell you," he replied, "if they keep quiet, the stones will cry out."

⁴¹As he approached Jerusalem and saw the city, he wept over it ⁴²and said, "If you, even you, had only known on this day what would bring you peace—but now it is hidden from your eyes. ⁴³The days will come upon you when your enemies will build an embankment against you and encircle you and hem you in on every side. ⁴⁴They will dash you to the ground, you and the children within your walls. They will not leave one stone on another, because you did not recognize the time of God's coming to you."

Jesus at the Temple

⁴⁵Then he entered the temple area and began driving out those who were selling. ⁴⁶"It is written," he said to them, " 'My house will be a house of prayer'ᵇ; but you have made it 'a den of robbers.'ᶜ"

⁴⁷Every day he was teaching at the temple. But the chief priests, the teachers of the law and the leaders among the people were trying to kill him. ⁴⁸Yet they could not find any way to do it, because all the people hung on his words.

ᵃ 38 Psalm 118:26   ᵇ 46 Isaiah 56:7   ᶜ 46 Jer. 7:11

GET SMARTER

God Knows What's Up

READ LUKE 19:28–44

Jesus was all OVER the situation with the colt. He knew where to go to find it, the shape it would be in, what people would ask and how to respond. Naturally, he was right. Every detail. Jesus knows us better than we know ourselves. He knows what we'll do in any situation; that's why he can give us the wisdom we need to face any situation the right way. Think about the whole colt thing—would you stop and pray and think first, or would you just charge off and do it your way? Your approach might lead you to a hyena chained to a fire hydrant. Not what God had in mind. Make a habit of thinking before you speak or do something. Ask yourself, "What would I normally blurt out?" Then, "What would God want me to say?" No excuses, please—Jesus knows the difference between the colt and the hyena.

Your next reading is on page 1360.

The Authority of Jesus Questioned

20 One day as he was teaching the people in the temple courts and preaching the gospel, the chief priests and the teachers of the law, together with the elders, came up to him. ²"Tell us by what authority you are doing these things," they said. "Who gave you this authority?"

³He replied, "I will also ask you a question. Tell me, ⁴John's baptism—was it from heaven, or from men?"

⁵They discussed it among themselves and said, "If we say, 'From heaven,' he will ask, 'Why didn't you believe him?' ⁶But if we say, 'From men,' all the people will stone us, because they are persuaded that John was a prophet."

⁷So they answered, "We don't know where it was from."

⁸Jesus said, "Neither will I tell you by what authority I am doing these things."

The Parable of the Tenants

⁹He went on to tell the people this parable: "A man planted a vineyard, rented it to some farmers and went away for a long time. ¹⁰At harvest time he sent a servant to the tenants so they would give him some of the fruit of the vineyard. But the tenants beat him and sent him away empty-handed. ¹¹He sent another servant, but that one also they beat and treated shamefully and sent away empty-handed. ¹²He sent still a third, and they wounded him and threw him out.

¹³"Then the owner of the vineyard said, 'What shall I do? I will send my son, whom I love; perhaps they will respect him.'

¹⁴"But when the tenants saw him, they talked the matter over. 'This is the heir,' they said. 'Let's kill him, and the inheritance will be ours.' ¹⁵So they threw him out of the vineyard and killed him.

"What then will the owner of the vineyard do to them? ¹⁶He will come and kill those tenants and give the vineyard to others."

When the people heard this, they said, "May this never be!"

¹⁷Jesus looked directly at them and asked, "Then what is the meaning of that which is written:

" 'The stone the builders rejected
has become the capstone*a' b*?

¹⁸Everyone who falls on that stone will be broken to pieces, but he on whom it falls will be crushed."

¹⁹The teachers of the law and the chief priests looked for a way to arrest him immediately, because they knew he had spoken this parable against them. But they were afraid of the people.

Paying Taxes to Caesar

²⁰Keeping a close watch on him, they sent spies, who pretended to be honest. They hoped to catch Jesus in

Get a Load of This...

Check out Luke 19:45–46. Jesus really laid into people for turning God's temple into a den of thieves. But in 1 Corinthians 6:19, we're told our bodies are now the temple of the Holy Spirit. Think about it: What does Jesus see when he takes a walk through your temple?

---

a 17 Or *cornerstone*   *b 17* Psalm 118:22

something he said so that they might hand him over to the power and authority of the governor. ²¹So the spies questioned him: "Teacher, we know that you speak and teach what is right, and that you do not show partiality but teach the way of God in accordance with the truth. ²²Is it right for us to pay taxes to Caesar or not?"

²³He saw through their duplicity and said to them, ²⁴"Show me a denarius. Whose portrait and inscription are on it?"

²⁵"Caesar's," they replied.

He said to them, "Then give to Caesar what is Caesar's, and to God what is God's."

²⁶They were unable to trap him in what he had said there in public. And astonished by his answer, they became silent.

The Resurrection and Marriage

²⁷Some of the Sadducees, who say there is no resurrection, came to Jesus with a question. ²⁸"Teacher," they said, "Moses wrote for us that if a man's brother dies and leaves a wife but no children,

the man must marry the widow and have children for his brother. ²⁹Now there were seven brothers. The first one married a woman and died childless. ³⁰The second ³¹and then the third married her, and in the same way the seven died, leaving no children. ³²Finally, the woman died too. ³³Now then, at the resurrection whose wife will she be, since the seven were married to her?"

³⁴Jesus replied, "The people of this age marry and are given in marriage. ³⁵But those who are considered worthy of taking part in that age and in the resurrection from the dead will neither marry nor be given in marriage, ³⁶and they can no longer die; for they are like the angels. They are God's children, since they are children of the resurrection. ³⁷But in the account of the bush, even Moses showed that the dead rise, for he calls the Lord 'the God of Abraham, and the God of Isaac, and the God of Jacob.'^a ³⁸He is not the God of the dead, but of the living, for to him all are alive."

^a 37 Exodus 3:6

Three Trick Questions

READ LUKE 20:1–8, 20–40

A man of God should try to always be respectful to others and speak in love. But that does not mean turning your brains down to "dim" or just walking away grinning if kids are ridiculing your faith and voicing ungodly opinions. No way! Being loving does not mean losing every argument and scoring zero in every debate. HELLO! If some kids are challenging the truth, ask God for wisdom. Don't take the doormat position and let them wipe their feet all over your faith. If you don't know what to say, go find the answers and come back with them another time. Study and learn God's Word so you know answers to give (see Luke 21:15). Then give those answers with respect and love, not mocking people or making them feel like idiots. That way you'll leave people like Jesus left them—thinking, not feeling put down.

Your next reading is on page 1363.

39Some of the teachers of the law responded, "Well said, teacher!" 40And no one dared to ask him any more questions.

Whose Son Is the Christ?

41Then Jesus said to them, "How is it that they say the Christ[a] is the Son of David? 42David himself declares in the Book of Psalms:

" 'The Lord said to my Lord:
    "Sit at my right hand
43 until I make your enemies
    a footstool for your feet." ' [b]

44David calls him 'Lord.' How then can he be his son?"

45While all the people were listening, Jesus said to his disciples, 46"Beware of the teachers of the law. They like to walk around in flowing robes and love to be greeted in the marketplaces and have the most important seats in the synagogues and the places of honor at banquets. 47They devour widows' houses and for a show make lengthy prayers. Such men will be punished most severely."

The Widow's Offering

As he looked up, Jesus saw the rich putting their gifts into the temple treasury. 2He also saw a poor widow put in two very small copper coins.[c] 3"I tell you the truth," he said, "this poor widow has put in more than all the others. 4All these people gave their gifts out of their wealth; but she out of her poverty put in all she had to live on."

Signs of the End of the Age

5Some of his disciples were remarking about how the temple was adorned with beautiful stones and with gifts dedicated to God. But Jesus said, 6"As for what you see here, the time will come when not one stone will be left on another; every one of them will be thrown down."

7"Teacher," they asked, "when will these things happen? And what will be the sign that they are about to take place?"

8He replied: "Watch out that you are not deceived. For many will come in my name, claiming, 'I am he,' and, 'The time is near.' Do not follow them. 9When you hear of wars and revolutions, do not be frightened. These things must happen first, but the end will not come right away."

10Then he said to them: "Nation will rise against nation, and kingdom against kingdom. 11There will be great earthquakes, famines and pestilences in various places, and fearful events and great signs from heaven.

12"But before all this, they will lay hands on you and persecute you. They will deliver you to synagogues and prisons, and you will be brought before kings and governors, and all on account of my name. 13This will result in

Get a Load of This...

Jesus said, "Show me a denarius" (Luke 20:24). Then he showed them something with that denarius: Whether he likes the government or not, a man of God should obey its laws and pay his taxes (Luke 20:25). OK, so you don't pay taxes . . . YET. But obey its laws.

a 41 Or Messiah   b 43 Psalm 110:1   c 2 Greek two lepta

your being witnesses to them. ¹⁴But make up your mind not to worry beforehand how you will defend yourselves. ¹⁵For I will give you words and wisdom that none of your adversaries will be able to resist or contradict. ¹⁶You will be betrayed even by parents, brothers, relatives and friends, and they will put some of you to death. ¹⁷All men will hate you because of me. ¹⁸But not a hair of your head will perish. ¹⁹By standing firm you will gain life.

²⁰"When you see Jerusalem being surrounded by armies, you will know that its desolation is near. ²¹Then let those who are in Judea flee to the mountains, let those in the city get out, and let those in the country not enter the city. ²²For this is the time of punishment in fulfillment of all that has been written. ²³How dreadful it will be in those days for pregnant women and nursing mothers! There will be great distress in the land and wrath against this people. ²⁴They will fall by the sword and will be taken as prisoners to all the nations. Jerusalem will be trampled on by the Gentiles until the times of the Gentiles are fulfilled.

²⁵"There will be signs in the sun, moon and stars. On the earth, nations will be in anguish and perplexity at the roaring and tossing of the sea. ²⁶Men will faint from terror, apprehensive of what is coming on the world, for the heavenly bodies will be shaken. ²⁷At that time they will see the Son of Man coming in a cloud with power and great glory. ²⁸When these things begin to take place, stand up and lift up your heads, because your redemption is drawing near."

²⁹He told them this parable: "Look at the fig tree and all the trees. ³⁰When they sprout leaves, you can see for yourselves and know that summer is near. ³¹Even so, when you see these things happening, you know that the kingdom of God is near.

³²"I tell you the truth, this generation*a* will certainly not pass away until all these things have happened. ³³Heaven and earth will pass away, but my words will never pass away.

³⁴"Be careful, or your hearts will be weighed down with dissipation, drunkenness and the anxieties of life, and that day will close on you unexpectedly like a trap. ³⁵For it will come upon all those who live on the face of the whole earth. ³⁶Be always on the watch, and pray that you

may be able to escape all that is about to happen, and that you may be able to stand before the Son of Man."

³⁷Each day Jesus was teaching at the temple, and each evening he went out to spend the night on the hill called the Mount of Olives, ³⁸and all the people came early in the morning to hear him at the temple.

Judas Agrees to Betray Jesus

22 Now the Feast of Unleavened Bread, called the Passover, was approaching, ²and the chief priests and the teachers of the law were looking for some way to get rid of Jesus, for they were afraid of the people. ³Then Satan entered Judas, called Iscariot, one of the Twelve. ⁴And Judas went to the chief priests and the officers of the temple guard and discussed with them how he might betray Jesus. ⁵They were delighted and agreed to give him money. ⁶He consented, and watched for an opportunity to hand Jesus over to them when no crowd was present.

The Last Supper

⁷Then came the day of Unleavened Bread on which the Passover lamb had to be sacrificed. ⁸Jesus sent Peter and John, saying, "Go and make preparations for us to eat the Passover."

⁹"Where do you want us to prepare for it?" they asked.

¹⁰He replied, "As you enter the city, a man carrying a jar of water will meet you. Follow him to the house that he enters, ¹¹and say to the owner of the house, 'The Teacher asks: Where is the guest room, where I may eat the Passover with my disciples?' ¹²He will show you a large upper room, all furnished. Make preparations there."

¹³They left and found things just as Jesus had told them. So they prepared the Passover.

¹⁴When the hour came, Jesus and his apostles reclined at the table. ¹⁵And he said to them, "I have eagerly desired to eat this Passover with you before I suffer. ¹⁶For I tell you, I will not eat it again until it finds fulfillment in the kingdom of God."

¹⁷After taking the cup, he gave thanks and said, "Take this and divide it among

a 32 Or *race*

you. 18For I tell you I will not drink again of the fruit of the vine until the kingdom of God comes."

19And he took bread, gave thanks and broke it, and gave it to them, saying, "This is my body given for you; do this in remembrance of me."

20In the same way, after the supper he took the cup, saying, "This cup is the new covenant in my blood, which is poured out for you. 21But the hand of him who is going to betray me is with mine on the table. 22The Son of Man will go as it has been decreed, but woe to that man who betrays him." 23They began to question among themselves which of them it might be who would do this.

24Also a dispute arose among them as to which of them was considered to be greatest. 25Jesus said to them, "The kings of the Gentiles lord it over them; and those who exercise authority over them call themselves Benefactors. 26But you are not to be like that. Instead, the greatest among you should be like the youngest, and the one who rules like the one who serves. 27For who is greater, the one who is at the table or the one who serves? Is it not the one who is at the table? But I am among you as one who serves. 28You are those who have stood by me in my trials. 29And I confer on you a kingdom, just as my Father conferred one on me, 30so that you may eat and drink at my table in my kingdom and sit on thrones, judging the twelve tribes of Israel.

31"Simon, Simon, Satan has asked to sift you*a* as wheat. 32But I have prayed for you, Simon, that your faith may not fail. And when you have turned back, strengthen your brothers."

33But he replied, "Lord, I am ready to go with you to prison and to death."

34Jesus answered, "I tell you, Peter, before the rooster crows today, you will deny three times that you know me."

35Then Jesus asked them, "When I sent you without purse, bag or sandals, did you lack anything?"

"Nothing," they answered.

36He said to them, "But now if you have a purse, take it, and also a bag; and if you

a 31 The Greek is plural.

Servant or Leader?

READ LUKE 22:24–30

Man! It seems like the disciples were constantly involved in a giant game of "king of the castle." Everyone was fighting to reach the top of the pile and Jesus kept telling them that wasn't the way he did things. Jesus said, "The greatest among you should be like the youngest, and the one who rules like the one who serves" (Luke 22:26). Jesus lived that. He could have had his disciples bow down and wait on him hand and foot all day long. He didn't. We *do* worship Jesus, but it's because he put his needs last, put us first and even gave his life to save us. He's got the scars to prove that he put us first—before his own comfort. We should be the same toward others when we're put in charge. Instead of saying, "Now I can boss everyone around," we should say, "I'll serve others and pull everyone together."

Your next reading is on page 1364.

don't have a sword, sell your cloak and buy one. ³⁷It is written: 'And he was numbered with the transgressors'ᵃ; and I tell you that this must be fulfilled in me. Yes, what is written about me is reaching its fulfillment."

³⁸The disciples said, "See, Lord, here are two swords."

"That is enough," he replied.

Jesus Prays on the Mount of Olives

³⁹Jesus went out as usual to the Mount of Olives, and his disciples followed him. ⁴⁰On reaching the place, he said to them, "Pray that you will not fall into temptation." ⁴¹He withdrew about a stone's throw beyond them, knelt down and prayed, ⁴²"Father, if you are willing, take this cup from me; yet not my will, but yours be done." ⁴³An angel from heaven appeared to him and strengthened him. ⁴⁴And being in anguish, he prayed more earnestly, and his sweat was like drops of blood falling to the ground.ᵇ

⁴⁵When he rose from prayer and went back to the disciples, he found them asleep, exhausted from sorrow. ⁴⁶"Why

are you sleeping?" he asked them. "Get up and pray so that you will not fall into temptation."

Jesus Arrested

⁴⁷While he was still speaking a crowd came up, and the man who was called Judas, one of the Twelve, was leading them. He approached Jesus to kiss him, ⁴⁸but Jesus asked him, "Judas, are you betraying the Son of Man with a kiss?"

⁴⁹When Jesus' followers saw what was going to happen, they said, "Lord, should we strike with our swords?" ⁵⁰And one of them struck the servant of the high priest, cutting off his right ear.

⁵¹But Jesus answered, "No more of this!" And he touched the man's ear and healed him.

⁵²Then Jesus said to the chief priests, the officers of the temple guard, and the elders, who had come for him, "Am I leading a rebellion, that you have come with swords and clubs? ⁵³Every day I was with

ᵃ 37 Isaiah 53:12   ᵇ 44 Some early manuscripts do not have verses 43 and 44.

No Can Do

READ LUKE 22:39–54

Ever been asked to do a super-difficult job, like stopping aliens from invading your town (armed with a slingshot) or shoveling five tons of manure behind your grandfather's barn? Did you automatically moan, "I can't do that!"? Or did you say, "I don't want that job, but if I have to, I'll do it"? Jesus prayed, "Father, if you are willing, take this cup from me; yet not my will, but yours be done" (verse 42). Look at Moses: When God told him to go to Egypt, Moses argued that he wasn't the right man, couldn't speak well, etc. Although Moses' excuses displeased God, God graciously provided support for Moses in the person of Moses' brother Aaron (see Exodus 3:11–14; 4:1–17). When you have a tough job, tell God how you feel, then trust him to help you, and say, "I'll do whatever you want. Your will be done. You know what's best."

Your next reading is on page 1367.

you in the temple courts, and you did not lay a hand on me. But this is your hour—when darkness reigns."

Peter Disowns Jesus

54Then seizing him, they led him away and took him into the house of the high priest. Peter followed at a distance. 55But when they had kindled a fire in the middle of the courtyard and had sat down together, Peter sat down with them. 56A servant girl saw him seated there in the firelight. She looked closely at him and said, "This man was with him."

57But he denied it. "Woman, I don't know him," he said.

58A little later someone else saw him and said, "You also are one of them."

"Man, I am not!" Peter replied.

59About an hour later another asserted, "Certainly this fellow was with him, for he is a Galilean."

60Peter replied, "Man, I don't know what you're talking about!" Just as he was speaking, the rooster crowed. 61The Lord turned and looked straight at Peter. Then Peter remembered the word the Lord had spoken to him: "Before the rooster crows today, you will disown me three times." 62And he went outside and wept bitterly.

The Guards Mock Jesus

63The men who were guarding Jesus began mocking and beating him. 64They blindfolded him and demanded, "Prophesy! Who hit you?" 65And they said many other insulting things to him.

Jesus Before Pilate and Herod

66At daybreak the council of the elders of the people, both the chief priests and teachers of the law, met together, and Jesus was led before them. 67"If you are the Christ,a" they said, "tell us."

Jesus answered, "If I tell you, you will not believe me, 68and if I asked you, you would not answer. 69But from now on, the Son of Man will be seated at the right hand of the mighty God."

70They all asked, "Are you then the Son of God?"

He replied, "You are right in saying I am."

71Then they said, "Why do we need any more testimony? We have heard it from his own lips."

23

Then the whole assembly rose and led him off to Pilate. 2And they began to accuse him, saying, "We have found this man subverting our nation. He opposes payment of taxes to Caesar and claims to be Christ,b a king."

3So Pilate asked Jesus, "Are you the king of the Jews?"

"Yes, it is as you say," Jesus replied.

4Then Pilate announced to the chief priests and the crowd, "I find no basis for a charge against this man."

5But they insisted, "He stirs up the people all over Judeac by his teaching. He started in Galilee and has come all the way here."

6On hearing this, Pilate asked if the man was a Galilean. 7When he learned that Jesus was under Herod's jurisdiction, he sent him to Herod, who was also in Jerusalem at that time.

8When Herod saw Jesus, he was greatly pleased, because for a long time he had been wanting to see him. From what he had heard about him, he hoped to see him perform some miracle. 9He plied him with many questions, but Jesus gave him no answer. 10The chief priests and the teachers of the law were standing there, vehemently accusing him. 11Then Herod and his soldiers ridiculed and mocked him. Dressing him in an elegant robe, they sent him back to Pilate. 12That day Herod and Pilate became friends—before this they had been enemies.

13Pilate called together the chief priests, the rulers and the people, 14and said to them, "You brought me this man as one who was inciting the people to rebellion. I have examined him in your presence and have found no basis for your charges against him. 15Neither has Herod, for he sent him back to us; as you can see, he has done nothing to deserve death. 16Therefore, I will punish him and then release him.d"

18With one voice they cried out, "Away with this man! Release Barabbas to us!" 19(Barabbas had been thrown into prison for an insurrection in the city, and for murder.)

20Wanting to release Jesus, Pilate ap-

---

a 67 Or Messiah   b 2 Or Messiah; also in verses 35 and 39   c 5 Or over the land of the Jews   d 16 Some manuscripts him." 17Now he was obliged to release one man to them at the Feast.

Get a Load of This...

Herod expected Jesus to perform a miracle on demand, just for his entertainment (see Luke 23:8). This was the same Herod who had John the Baptist's head cut off at his birthday party. Now he expected Jesus to act like a magician at a birthday party.

pealed to them again. [21] But they kept shouting, "Crucify him! Crucify him!"

[22] For the third time he spoke to them: "Why? What crime has this man committed? I have found in him no grounds for the death penalty. Therefore I will have him punished and then release him."

[23] But with loud shouts they insistently demanded that he be crucified, and their shouts prevailed. [24] So Pilate decided to grant their demand. [25] He released the man who had been thrown into prison for insurrection and murder, the one they asked for, and surrendered Jesus to their will.

The Crucifixion

[26] As they led him away, they seized Simon from Cyrene, who was on his way in from the country, and put the cross on him and made him carry it behind Jesus. [27] A large number of people followed him, including women who mourned and wailed for him. [28] Jesus turned and said to them, "Daughters of Jerusalem, do not weep for me; weep for yourselves and for your children. [29] For the time will come when you will say, 'Blessed are the barren women, the wombs that never bore and the breasts that never nursed!' [30] Then

" 'they will say to the mountains, "Fall on us!"
    and to the hills, "Cover us!" ' [a]

[31] For if men do these things when the tree is green, what will happen when it is dry?"

[32] Two other men, both criminals, were also led out with him to be executed. [33] When they came to the place called the Skull, there they crucified him, along with the criminals—one on his right, the other on his left. [34] Jesus said, "Father, forgive them, for they do not know what they are doing." [b] And they divided up his clothes by casting lots.

[35] The people stood watching, and the rulers even sneered at him. They said, "He saved others; let him save himself if he is the Christ of God, the Chosen One."

[36] The soldiers also came up and mocked him. They offered him wine vinegar [37] and said, "If you are the king of the Jews, save yourself."

[38] There was a written notice above him, which read: THIS IS THE KING OF THE JEWS.

[39] One of the criminals who hung there hurled insults at him: "Aren't you the Christ? Save yourself and us!"

[40] But the other criminal rebuked him. "Don't you fear God," he said, "since you are under the same sentence? [41] We are punished justly, for we are getting what our deeds deserve. But this man has done nothing wrong."

[42] Then he said, "Jesus, remember me when you come into your kingdom. [c]"

[43] Jesus answered him, "I tell you the truth, today you will be with me in paradise."

[a] 30 Hosea 10:8   [b] 34 Some early manuscripts do not have this sentence.
[c] 42 Some manuscripts come with your kingly power

Jesus' Death

44It was now about the sixth hour, and darkness came over the whole land until the ninth hour, 45for the sun stopped shining. And the curtain of the temple was torn in two. 46Jesus called out with a loud voice, "Father, into your hands I commit my spirit." When he had said this, he breathed his last.

47The centurion, seeing what had happened, praised God and said, "Surely this was a righteous man." 48When all the people who had gathered to witness this sight saw what took place, they beat their breasts and went away. 49But all those who knew him, including the women who had followed him from Galilee, stood at a distance, watching these things.

Jesus' Burial

50Now there was a man named Joseph, a member of the Council, a good and upright man, 51who had not consented to their decision and action. He came from the Judean town of Arimathea and he was waiting for the kingdom of God. 52Going to Pilate, he asked for Jesus' body. 53Then he took it down, wrapped it in linen cloth and placed it in a tomb cut in the rock, one in which no one had yet been laid. 54It was Preparation Day, and the Sabbath was about to begin.

55The women who had come with Jesus from Galilee followed Joseph and saw the tomb and how his body was laid in it. 56Then they went home and prepared spices and perfumes. But they rested on the Sabbath in obedience to the commandment.

The Resurrection

24 On the first day of the week, very early in the morning, the women took the spices they had prepared and went to the tomb. 2They found the stone rolled away from the tomb, 3but when they entered, they did not find the body of the Lord Jesus. 4While they were wondering about this, suddenly two men in clothes that gleamed like lightning stood beside them.

GET SMARTER

When God's at Work

READ LUKE 23:26, 32–47

Darkness covered the land from noon until 3 p.m., the huge, thick curtain in the temple was shredded from top to bottom, an earthquake struck and people kicked up out of their graves and later walked into the city (Luke 23:44–45; Matthew 27:50–53). It didn't take long before all Jerusalem heard about these amazing signs. When the centurion saw Jesus forgive those who killed him, then saw the darkness and the way Jesus died, he said, "Surely this was a righteous man" (verse 47). The religious leaders saw all the same things but ... ah! ... they shrugged them off as coincidence. Maybe they tried to explain away the darkness as an eclipse. They just didn't want to believe. When Jesus later rose from the dead, they still chose not to believe. Take a lesson: When God works in your life and some "coincidence" happens—recognize it for what it is: God at work.

Your next reading is on page 1368.

5In their fright the women bowed down with their faces to the ground, but the men said to them, "Why do you look for the living among the dead? 6He is not here; he has risen! Remember how he told you, while he was still with you in Galilee: 7'The Son of Man must be delivered into the hands of sinful men, be crucified and on the third day be raised again.' " 8Then they remembered his words.

9When they came back from the tomb, they told all these things to the Eleven and to all the others. 10It was Mary Magdalene, Joanna, Mary the mother of James, and the others with them who told this to the apostles. 11But they did not believe the women, because their words seemed to them like nonsense. 12Peter, however, got up and ran to the tomb. Bending over, he saw the strips of linen lying by themselves, and he went away, wondering to himself what had happened.

On the Road to Emmaus

13Now that same day two of them were going to a village called Emmaus, about seven miles*a* from Jerusalem. 14They were talking with each other about everything that had happened. 15As they talked and discussed these things with each other, Jesus himself came up and walked along with them; 16but they were kept from recognizing him.

17He asked them, "What are you discussing together as you walk along?"

They stood still, their faces downcast. 18One of them, named Cleopas, asked him, "Are you only a visitor to Jerusalem and do not know the things that have happened there in these days?"

19"What things?" he asked.

"About Jesus of Nazareth," they replied. "He was a prophet, powerful in word and deed before God and all the people. 20The chief priests and our rulers handed him over to be sentenced to death, and they crucified him; 21but we had hoped that he was the one who was going to redeem Israel. And what is more, it is the third day since all this took place. 22In addition, some of our women amazed us. They went to the tomb early this morning 23but

a 13 Greek *sixty stadia* (about 11 kilometers)

Mystery Man

READ LUKE 24:13–35

If a bum on the street said he could give you anything you wanted in the world, you'd probably warn him that you're going to call the police. But what if, after the bum was gone, you discovered he was a rich man dressed up in disguise? Would you ever stop kicking yourself?

This sort of thing happens more than you think. Only it isn't a rich man in disguise, it's God. The two disciples didn't recognize Jesus on the road to Emmaus (Luke 24:16), and some people "have entertained angels without knowing it" (Hebrews 13:2). Plus, in Matthew 25:40 and 25:45, Jesus says that how we treat others is the same as how we treat him. We need to always treat others kindly, whether they're angels in disguise or not, because everyone was created by God and deserves respect. How would you treat an angel or Jesus if you met one of them? That's how you should treat everyone.

Your next reading is on page 1371.

didn't find his body. They came and told us that they had seen a vision of angels, who said he was alive. 24Then some of our companions went to the tomb and found it just as the women had said, but him they did not see."

25He said to them, "How foolish you are, and how slow of heart to believe all that the prophets have spoken! 26Did not the Christ[a] have to suffer these things and then enter his glory?" 27And beginning with Moses and all the Prophets, he explained to them what was said in all the Scriptures concerning himself.

28As they approached the village to which they were going, Jesus acted as if he were going farther. 29But they urged him strongly, "Stay with us, for it is nearly evening; the day is almost over." So he went in to stay with them.

30When he was at the table with them, he took bread, gave thanks, broke it and began to give it to them. 31Then their eyes were opened and they recognized him, and he disappeared from their sight. 32They asked each other, "Were not our hearts burning within us while he talked with us on the road and opened the Scriptures to us?"

33They got up and returned at once to Jerusalem. There they found the Eleven and those with them, assembled together 34and saying, "It is true! The Lord has risen and has appeared to Simon." 35Then the two told what had happened on the way, and how Jesus was recognized by them when he broke the bread.

Jesus Appears to the Disciples

36While they were still talking about this, Jesus himself stood among them and said to them, "Peace be with you."

37They were startled and frightened, thinking they saw a ghost. 38He said to them, "Why are you troubled, and why do doubts rise in your minds? 39Look at my hands and my feet. It is I myself! Touch me and see; a ghost does not have flesh and bones, as you see I have."

40When he had said this, he showed them his hands and feet. 41And while they still did not believe it because of joy and amazement, he asked them, "Do you have anything here to eat?" 42They gave him a piece of broiled fish, 43and he took it and ate it in their presence.

44He said to them, "This is what I told you while I was still with you: Everything must be fulfilled that is written about me in the Law of Moses, the Prophets and the Psalms."

45Then he opened their minds so they could understand the Scriptures. 46He told them, "This is what is written: The Christ will suffer and rise from the dead on the third day, 47and repentance and forgiveness of sins will be preached in his name to all nations, beginning at Jerusalem. 48You are witnesses of these things. 49I am going to send you what my Father has promised; but stay in the city until you have been clothed with power from on high."

The Ascension

50When he had led them out to the vicinity of Bethany, he lifted up his hands and blessed them. 51While he was blessing them, he left them and was taken up into heaven. 52Then they worshiped him and returned to Jerusalem with great joy. 53And they stayed continually at the temple, praising God.

---

[a] 26 Or Messiah; also in verse 46

JOHN

Who wrote this book?
John, the disciple of Jesus, wrote this book.

Why was this book written?
The Gospel of John shows that Jesus is the Son of God and helps people believe in him.

For whom was this book written?
John was written for everyone who wants to understand who Jesus really is.

What happens in this book?
John reports miracles and teachings that show that Jesus is the Son of God.

Who is important in this book?
Jesus is the important person in this book.

When did this happen?
Jesus taught and performed miracles from A.D. 26 to 30.

Where did this happen?
Most of the events in this book happened in Judea.

What are some of the stories in this book?

Jesus chooses disciples	John 1:35–51
Jesus teaches Nicodemus	John 3:1–21
Jesus and a Samaritan woman	John 4:1–26
Jesus walks on water	John 6:16–24
Jesus says he is God's Son	John 8:31–59
Jesus heals a blind man	John 9:1–41
The good shepherd	John 10:1–21
Jesus raises Lazarus	John 11:1–44
Jesus rides into Jerusalem	John 12:12–19
Washing the disciples' feet	John 13:1–17
Praying for the disciples	John 17:6–19
Jesus is crucified	John 19:1–42
Jesus is raised to life	John 20:1–31
Jesus forgives Peter	John 21:15–25

The Word Became Flesh

1 In the beginning was the Word, and the Word was with God, and the Word was God. ²He was with God in the beginning.

³Through him all things were made; without him nothing was made that has been made. ⁴In him was life, and that life was the light of men. ⁵The light shines in the darkness, but the darkness has not understood*a* it.

⁶There came a man who was sent from God; his name was John. ⁷He came as a witness to testify concerning that light, so that through him all men might believe. ⁸He himself was not the light; he came only as a witness to the light. ⁹The true light that gives light to every man was coming into the world.*b*

¹⁰He was in the world, and though the world was made through him, the world did not recognize him. ¹¹He came to that which was his own, but his own did not receive him. ¹²Yet to all who received him, to those who believed in his name, he gave the right to become children of God— ¹³children born not of natural descent,*c* nor of human decision or a husband's will, but born of God.

¹⁴The Word became flesh and made his dwelling among us. We have seen his glory, the glory of the One and Only,*d* who came from the Father, full of grace and truth.

¹⁵John testifies concerning him. He cries out, saying, "This was he of whom I said, 'He who comes after me has surpassed me because he was before me.'" ¹⁶From the fullness of his grace we have all received one blessing after another. ¹⁷For the law was given through Moses; grace and truth came through Jesus Christ. ¹⁸No one has ever seen God, but God the One and Only,*d, e* who is at the Father's side, has made him known.

a 5 Or *darkness, and the darkness has not overcome*
b 9 Or *This was the true light that gives light to every man who comes into the world*   *c 13* Greek *of bloods*
d 14, 18 Or *the Only Begotten*   *e 18* Some manuscripts *but the only* (or *only begotten*) *Son*

Undercover Agent

READ JOHN 1:1–14

God had a big mission: rescue hundreds of millions of people on planet Earth. To get the job done, he went undercover. He didn't come down in a blaze of glory, thundering through the atmosphere. He was born a baby, then quietly grew up as a carpenter, working amongst the sawdust in dusty old Galilee. Talk about the perfect cover! "The world did not recognize him" (verse 10). But what would you have chosen?—to live on Earth or spend 33 years in heaven where you could be having a blast, doing the most incredible, mind-boggling things imaginable? "The Word" gave up A LOT to take on his long, tough undercover assignment on Earth. And then he willingly gave up his life so that he could rescue us! While most undercover men sneak around trying NOT to get caught, Jesus' master plan INCLUDED being captured. He allowed himself to be arrested and crucified to save us. And he wanted everyone to know that their sins could be forgiven if they believed he was their Lord and Savior.

Your next reading is on page 1373.

John the Baptist Denies Being the Christ

¹⁹Now this was John's testimony when the Jews of Jerusalem sent priests and Levites to ask him who he was. ²⁰He did not fail to confess, but confessed freely, "I am not the Christ.ᵃ"

²¹They asked him, "Then who are you? Are you Elijah?"

He said, "I am not."

"Are you the Prophet?"

He answered, "No."

²²Finally they said, "Who are you? Give us an answer to take back to those who sent us. What do you say about yourself?"

²³John replied in the words of Isaiah the prophet, "I am the voice of one calling in the desert, 'Make straight the way for the Lord.' "ᵇ

²⁴Now some Pharisees who had been sent ²⁵questioned him, "Why then do you baptize if you are not the Christ, nor Elijah, nor the Prophet?"

²⁶"I baptize withᶜ water," John replied, "but among you stands one you do not know. ²⁷He is the one who comes after me, the thongs of whose sandals I am not worthy to untie."

²⁸This all happened at Bethany on the other side of the Jordan, where John was baptizing.

Jesus the Lamb of God

²⁹The next day John saw Jesus coming toward him and said, "Look, the Lamb of God, who takes away the sin of the world! ³⁰This is the one I meant when I said, 'A man who comes after me has surpassed me because he was before me.' ³¹I myself did not know him, but the reason I came baptizing with water was that he might be revealed to Israel."

³²Then John gave this testimony: "I saw the Spirit come down from heaven as a dove and remain on him. ³³I would not have known him, except that the one who sent me to baptize with water told me, 'The man on whom you see the Spirit come down and remain is he who will baptize with the Holy Spirit.' ³⁴I have seen and I testify that this is the Son of God."

Jesus' First Disciples

³⁵The next day John was there again with two of his disciples. ³⁶When he saw Jesus passing by, he said, "Look, the Lamb of God!"

³⁷When the two disciples heard him say this, they followed Jesus. ³⁸Turning around, Jesus saw them following and asked, "What do you want?"

They said, "Rabbi" (which means Teacher), "where are you staying?"

³⁹"Come," he replied, "and you will see."

So they went and saw where he was staying, and spent that day with him. It was about the tenth hour.

⁴⁰Andrew, Simon Peter's brother, was one of the two who heard what John had said and who had followed Jesus. ⁴¹The first thing Andrew did was to find his brother Simon and tell him, "We have found the Messiah" (that is, the Christ). ⁴²And he brought him to Jesus.

Jesus looked at him and said, "You are Simon son of John. You will be called Cephas" (which, when translated, is Peterᵈ).

Jesus Calls Philip and Nathanael

⁴³The next day Jesus decided to leave for Galilee. Finding Philip, he said to him, "Follow me."

⁴⁴Philip, like Andrew and Peter, was from the town of Bethsaida. ⁴⁵Philip found Nathanael and told him, "We have found the one Moses wrote about in the Law, and about whom the prophets also wrote—Jesus of Nazareth, the son of Joseph."

⁴⁶"Nazareth! Can anything good come from there?" Nathanael asked.

"Come and see," said Philip.

⁴⁷When Jesus saw Nathanael approaching, he said of him, "Here is a true Israelite, in whom there is nothing false."

⁴⁸"How do you know me?" Nathanael asked.

Jesus answered, "I saw you while you were still under the fig tree before Philip called you."

⁴⁹Then Nathanael declared, "Rabbi, you are the Son of God; you are the King of Israel."

⁵⁰Jesus said, "You believeᵉ because I told you I saw you under the fig tree. You shall see greater things than that." ⁵¹He then added, "I tell youᶠ the truth, youᶠ shall see heaven open, and the angels of God ascending and descending on the Son of Man."

ᵃ 20 Or Messiah. "The Christ" (Greek) and "the Messiah" (Hebrew) both mean "the Anointed One"; also in verse 25.
ᵇ 23 Isaiah 40:3   ᶜ 26 Or in; also in verses 31 and 33
ᵈ 42 Both Cephas (Aramaic) and Peter (Greek) mean rock.
ᵉ 50 Or Do you believe . . . ?   ᶠ 51 The Greek is plural.

The Incredible Water Boy

READ LUKE 3:7–17; JOHN 1:19–36

John introduced Jesus to the world; he prepared the way and got a lot of people ready for Jesus. When he said, "Look, the Lamb of God! . . . 'A man who comes after me has surpassed me . . .'" (John 1:29–30), it was like a huge awards show where a famous person introduces an even more famous star, the guy who wins the award. But hey, John himself was a pretty phenomenal man. Let's have a look:

STRONGER: The Bible says, "And the child grew and . . . he lived in the desert" (Luke 1:80). Living in the desert is tough. If you want to really grow hair on your chest, live in the desert. It's blazing hot by day and deep-freeze cold at night. But John was tough—and hairy (since he wore clothes made of camel's hair). This guy was disciplined to really rough it. He dressed rough and even *ate* rough (see Matthew 3:4).

DEEPER: John "became strong in spirit" (Luke 1:80) and had a deep relationship with God. This man was so committed and given over to God, he was off the Richter scale. That's why he could turn around and shout to Israel, "REPENT!" Talk about being devoted to God.

COOLER: Sure, John was in your face big-time, but he genuinely cared about people. He put up with incredible hardships so he could know God and then belt out God's message. He bellowed, "The Messiah is coming!" and people RAN to hear him! They mobbed him to hear what he had to say and do what he said to do.

SMARTER: John's advice was nitty-gritty practical. He told people to share their clothes and food with the poor, he told tax collectors to be honest, and he told soldiers not to give people the shake down (see Luke 3:10–14). Want to be smart? Take John's advice: truly please God with your life.

Your next reading is on page 1375.

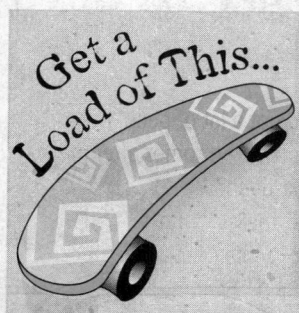

Get a Load of This...

"Nazareth! Can anything good come from there?" (John 1:44–46). Nazareth was a little nowhere town. In Jesus' day calling someone a "Nazarene" was about the same as calling him "despised." There were probably lots of Nazareth jokes going around.

Jesus Changes Water to Wine

On the third day a wedding took place at Cana in Galilee. Jesus' mother was there, ²and Jesus and his disciples had also been invited to the wedding. ³When the wine was gone, Jesus' mother said to him, "They have no more wine."

⁴"Dear woman, why do you involve me?" Jesus replied. "My time has not yet come."

⁵His mother said to the servants, "Do whatever he tells you."

⁶Nearby stood six stone water jars, the kind used by the Jews for ceremonial washing, each holding from twenty to thirty gallons.ᵃ

⁷Jesus said to the servants, "Fill the jars with water"; so they filled them to the brim.

⁸Then he told them, "Now draw some out and take it to the master of the banquet."

They did so, ⁹and the master of the banquet tasted the water that had been turned into wine. He did not realize where it had come from, though the servants who had drawn the water knew. Then he called the bridegroom aside ¹⁰and said, "Everyone brings out the choice wine first and then the cheaper wine after the guests have had too much to drink; but you have saved the best till now."

¹¹This, the first of his miraculous signs, Jesus performed at Cana in Galilee. He thus revealed his glory, and his disciples put their faith in him.

Jesus Clears the Temple

¹²After this he went down to Capernaum with his mother and brothers and his disciples. There they stayed for a few days.

¹³When it was almost time for the Jewish Passover, Jesus went up to Jerusalem. ¹⁴In the temple courts he found men selling cattle, sheep and doves, and others sitting at tables exchanging money. ¹⁵So he made a whip out of cords, and drove all from the temple area, both sheep and cattle; he scattered the coins of the money changers and overturned their tables. ¹⁶To those who sold doves he said, "Get these out of here! How dare you turn my Father's house into a market!"

¹⁷His disciples remembered that it is written: "Zeal for your house will consume me."ᵇ

¹⁸Then the Jews demanded of him, "What miraculous sign can you show us to prove your authority to do all this?"

¹⁹Jesus answered them, "Destroy this temple, and I will raise it again in three days."

²⁰The Jews replied, "It has taken forty-six years to build this temple, and you are going to raise it in three days?" ²¹But the temple he had spoken of was his body. ²²After he was raised from the dead, his disciples re-

ᵃ 6 Greek *two to three metretes* (probably about 75 to 115 liters)
ᵇ 17 Psalm 69:9

called what he had said. Then they believed the Scripture and the words that Jesus had spoken.

23Now while he was in Jerusalem at the Passover Feast, many people saw the miraculous signs he was doing and believed in his name.[a] 24But Jesus would not entrust himself to them, for he knew all men. 25He did not need man's testimony about man, for he knew what was in a man.

Jesus Teaches Nicodemus

Now there was a man of the Pharisees named Nicodemus, a member of the Jewish ruling council. 2He came to Jesus at night and said, "Rabbi, we know you are a teacher who has come from God. For no one could perform the miraculous signs you are doing if God were not with him."

3In reply Jesus declared, "I tell you the truth, no one can see the kingdom of God unless he is born again.[b]"

4"How can a man be born when he is old?" Nicodemus asked. "Surely he cannot enter a second time into his mother's womb to be born!"

5Jesus answered, "I tell you the truth, no one can enter the kingdom of God unless he is born of water and the Spirit. 6Flesh gives birth to flesh, but the Spirit[c] gives birth to spirit. 7You should not be surprised at my saying, 'You[d] must be born again.' 8The wind blows wherever it pleases. You hear its sound, but you cannot tell where it comes from or where it is going. So it is with everyone born of the Spirit."

9"How can this be?" Nicodemus asked.

10"You are Israel's teacher," said Jesus, "and do you not understand these things? 11I tell you the truth, we speak of what we know, and we testify to what we have seen, but still you people do not accept our testimony. 12I have spoken to you of earthly things and you do not believe; how then will you believe if I speak of heavenly things? 13No one has ever gone into heaven except the one who came from heaven—the Son of Man.[e] 14Just as Moses lifted up the snake in the desert, so

---

[a] 23 Or and believed in him   [b] 3 Or born from above; also in verse 7   [c] 6 Or but spirit   [d] 7 The Greek is plural.
[e] 13 Some manuscripts Man, who is in heaven

What? Born Twice?

READ JOHN 3:1–17

Have you ever said something and the other person, like, totally doesn't get what you were talking about? You tell your three-year-old sister her shoes are on the wrong feet and she looks down and says, "What do you mean? These are MY feet." When Jesus told Nicodemus he had to be "born again," Nicodemus was thinking, "I don't have a CLUE what you're talking about." He thought Jesus meant, "Climb back in your mother's womb and do the 'get born' thing one more time." Not. Jesus meant, "Be born as God's son." (Check out Romans 10:9–10 about how this works.) When Adam and Eve sinned and broke their relationship with God, God told them they would die. Sure enough, they died spiritually and later physically. The good news is that Jesus died in our place to restore our relationship with God. Accept his gift and you have spiritual life—you're born again!

Your next reading is on page 1377.

the Son of Man must be lifted up, [15]that everyone who believes in him may have eternal life.[a]

[16]"For God so loved the world that he gave his one and only Son,[b] that whoever believes in him shall not perish but have eternal life. [17]For God did not send his Son into the world to condemn the world, but to save the world through him. [18]Whoever believes in him is not condemned, but whoever does not believe stands condemned already because he has not believed in the name of God's one and only Son.[c] [19]This is the verdict: Light has come into the world, but men loved darkness instead of light because their deeds were evil. [20]Everyone who does evil hates the light, and will not come into the light for fear that his deeds will be exposed. [21]But whoever lives by the truth comes into the light, so that it may be seen plainly that what he has done has been done through God."[d]

John the Baptist's Testimony About Jesus

[22]After this, Jesus and his disciples went out into the Judean countryside, where he spent some time with them, and baptized. [23]Now John also was baptizing at Aenon near Salim, because there was plenty of water, and people were constantly coming to be baptized. [24](This was before John was put in prison.) [25]An argument developed between some of John's disciples and a certain Jew[e] over the matter of ceremonial washing. [26]They came to John and said to him, "Rabbi, that man who was with you on the other side of the Jordan—the one you testified about—well, he is baptizing, and everyone is going to him."

[27]To this John replied, "A man can receive only what is given him from heaven. [28]You yourselves can testify that I said, 'I am not the Christ[f] but am sent ahead of him.' [29]The bride belongs to the bridegroom. The friend who attends the bridegroom waits and listens for him, and is full of joy when he hears the bridegroom's voice. That joy is mine, and it is now complete. [30]He must become greater; I must become less.

[31]"The one who comes from above is above all; the one who is from the earth belongs to the earth, and speaks as one from the earth. The one who comes from

heaven is above all. [32]He testifies to what he has seen and heard, but no one accepts his testimony. [33]The man who has accepted it has certified that God is truthful. [34]For the one whom God has sent speaks the words of God, for God[g] gives the Spirit without limit. [35]The Father loves the Son and has placed everything in his hands. [36]Whoever believes in the Son has eternal life, but whoever rejects the Son will not see life, for God's wrath remains on him."[h]

Jesus Talks With a Samaritan Woman

4 The Pharisees heard that Jesus was gaining and baptizing more disciples than John, [2]although in fact it was not Jesus who baptized, but his disciples. [3]When the Lord learned of this, he left Judea and went back once more to Galilee.

[4]Now he had to go through Samaria. [5]So he came to a town in Samaria called Sychar, near the plot of ground Jacob had given to his son Joseph. [6]Jacob's well was there, and Jesus, tired as he was from the journey, sat down by the well. It was about the sixth hour.

[7]When a Samaritan woman came to draw water, Jesus said to her, "Will you give me a drink?" [8](His disciples had gone into the town to buy food.)

[9]The Samaritan woman said to him, "You are a Jew and I am a Samaritan woman. How can you ask me for a drink?" (For Jews do not associate with Samaritans.[i])

[10]Jesus answered her, "If you knew the gift of God and who it is that asks you for a drink, you would have asked him and he would have given you living water."

[11]"Sir," the woman said, "you have nothing to draw with and the well is deep. Where can you get this living water? [12]Are you greater than our father Jacob, who gave us the well and drank from it himself, as did also his sons and his flocks and herds?"

[13]Jesus answered, "Everyone who drinks this water will be thirsty again, [14]but whoever drinks the water I give him will never thirst. Indeed, the water I give

---

[a] 15 Or believes may have eternal life in him   [b] 16 Or his only begotten Son   [c] 18 Or God's only begotten Son
[d] 21 Some interpreters end the quotation after verse 15.
[e] 25 Some manuscripts and certain Jews   [f] 28 Or Messiah
[g] 34 Greek he   [h] 36 Some interpreters end the quotation after verse 30.   [i] 9 Or do not use dishes Samaritans have used

him will become in him a spring of water welling up to eternal life."

15The woman said to him, "Sir, give me this water so that I won't get thirsty and have to keep coming here to draw water." 16He told her, "Go, call your husband and come back."

17"I have no husband," she replied.

Jesus said to her, "You are right when you say you have no husband. 18The fact is, you have had five husbands, and the man you now have is not your husband. What you have just said is quite true."

19"Sir," the woman said, "I can see that you are a prophet. 20Our fathers worshiped on this mountain, but you Jews claim that the place where we must worship is in Jerusalem."

21Jesus declared, "Believe me, woman, a time is coming when you will worship the Father neither on this mountain nor in Jerusalem. 22You Samaritans worship what you do not know; we worship what we do know, for salvation is from the Jews. 23Yet a time is coming and has now come when the true worshipers will worship the Father in spirit and truth, for they are the kind of worshipers the Father seeks. 24God is spirit, and his worshipers must worship in spirit and in truth."

25The woman said, "I know that Messiah" (called Christ) "is coming. When he comes, he will explain everything to us."

26Then Jesus declared, "I who speak to you am he."

The Disciples Rejoin Jesus

27Just then his disciples returned and were surprised to find him talking with a woman. But no one asked, "What do you want?" or "Why are you talking with her?"

28Then, leaving her water jar, the woman went back to the town and said to the people, 29"Come, see a man who told me everything I ever did. Could this be the Christ*a*?" 30They came out of the town and made their way toward him.

31Meanwhile his disciples urged him, "Rabbi, eat something."

32But he said to them, "I have food to eat that you know nothing about."

a 29 Or Messiah

Which Church Is Best?

READ JOHN 4:1–26, 39–42

What kind of church is the best? One where you rock out on fast worship songs or the kind where you slowly sing one thousand-year-old hymns? Where you dance in the aisles or where you stay glued to a pew? The Samaritan woman was trying to make a big deal about who worshiped God the right way, when there's no best way to worship God. You just need to worship him "in spirit and in truth" (verse 24). That means praising God sincerely and honestly and thinking about him, not things around you. Do *that* and the rest are details. Whether you rock for the kingdom or quietly sing about the Rock, having Jesus in your heart and living his truth is what counts. Maybe God didn't give us an exhaustive how-to guide on worship because he knew we would come up with lots of good heartfelt ways to praise him on our own.

Your next reading is on page 1382.

GET COOLER

³³Then his disciples said to each other, "Could someone have brought him food?"

³⁴"My food," said Jesus, "is to do the will of him who sent me and to finish his work. ³⁵Do you not say, 'Four months more and then the harvest'? I tell you, open your eyes and look at the fields! They are ripe for harvest. ³⁶Even now the reaper draws his wages, even now he harvests the crop for eternal life, so that the sower and the reaper may be glad together. ³⁷Thus the saying 'One sows and another reaps' is true. ³⁸I sent you to reap what you have not worked for. Others have done the hard work, and you have reaped the benefits of their labor."

Many Samaritans Believe

³⁹Many of the Samaritans from that town believed in him because of the woman's testimony, "He told me everything I ever did." ⁴⁰So when the Samaritans came to him, they urged him to stay with them, and he stayed two days.

⁴¹And because of his words many more became believers.

⁴²They said to the woman, "We no longer believe just because of what you said; now we have heard for ourselves, and we know that this man really is the Savior of the world."

Jesus Heals the Official's Son

⁴³After the two days he left for Galilee. ⁴⁴(Now Jesus himself had pointed out that a prophet has no honor in his own country.) ⁴⁵When he arrived in Galilee, the Galileans welcomed him. They had seen all that he had done in Jerusalem at the Passover Feast, for they also had been there.

⁴⁶Once more he visited Cana in Galilee, where he had turned the water into wine. And there was a certain royal official whose son lay sick at Capernaum. ⁴⁷When this man heard that Jesus had arrived in Galilee from Judea, he went to him and begged him to come and heal his son, who was close to death.

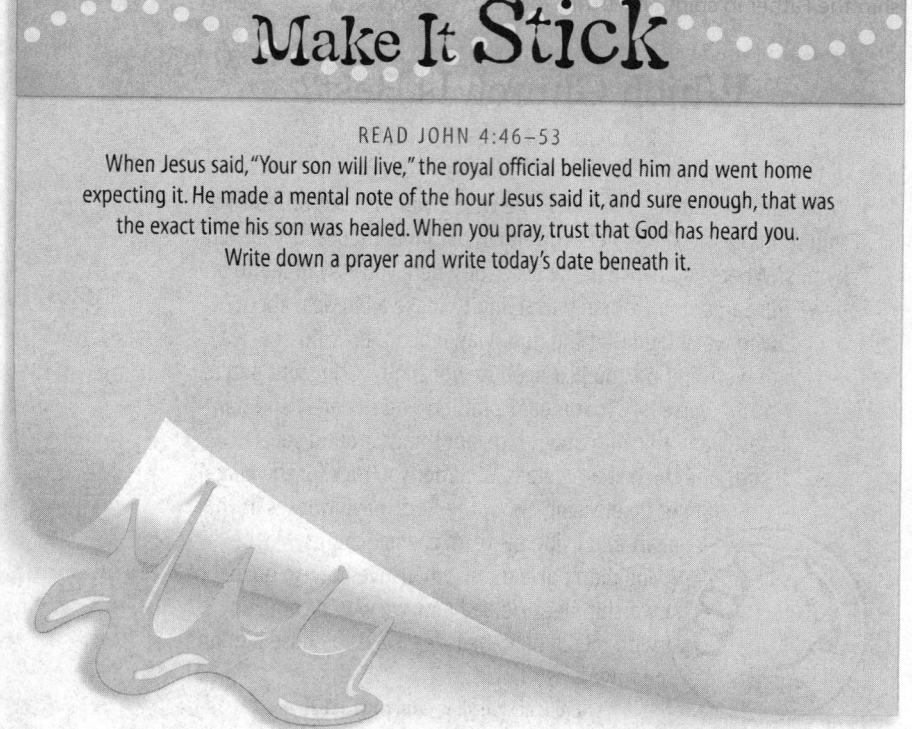

Make It Stick

READ JOHN 4:46–53

When Jesus said, "Your son will live," the royal official believed him and went home expecting it. He made a mental note of the hour Jesus said it, and sure enough, that was the exact time his son was healed. When you pray, trust that God has heard you. Write down a prayer and write today's date beneath it.

⁴⁸"Unless you people see miraculous signs and wonders," Jesus told him, "you will never believe."

⁴⁹The royal official said, "Sir, come down before my child dies."

⁵⁰Jesus replied, "You may go. Your son will live."

The man took Jesus at his word and departed. ⁵¹While he was still on the way, his servants met him with the news that his boy was living. ⁵²When he inquired as to the time when his son got better, they said to him, "The fever left him yesterday at the seventh hour."

⁵³Then the father realized that this was the exact time at which Jesus had said to him, "Your son will live." So he and all his household believed.

⁵⁴This was the second miraculous sign that Jesus performed, having come from Judea to Galilee.

The Healing at the Pool

5 Some time later, Jesus went up to Jerusalem for a feast of the Jews. ²Now there is in Jerusalem near the Sheep Gate a pool, which in Aramaic is called Bethesda*a* and which is surrounded by five covered colonnades. ³Here a great number of disabled people used to lie—the blind, the lame, the paralyzed.*b* ⁵One who was there had been an invalid for thirty-eight years. ⁶When Jesus saw him lying there and learned that he had been in this condition for a long time, he asked him, "Do you want to get well?"

⁷"Sir," the invalid replied, "I have no one to help me into the pool when the water is stirred. While I am trying to get in, someone else goes down ahead of me."

⁸Then Jesus said to him, "Get up! Pick up your mat and walk." ⁹At once the man was cured; he picked up his mat and walked.

The day on which this took place was a Sabbath, ¹⁰and so the Jews said to the man who had been healed, "It is the Sabbath; the law forbids you to carry your mat."

¹¹But he replied, "The man who made me well said to me, 'Pick up your mat and walk.' "

¹²So they asked him, "Who is this fellow who told you to pick it up and walk?"

¹³The man who was healed had no idea who it was, for Jesus had slipped away into the crowd that was there.

¹⁴Later Jesus found him at the temple and said to him, "See, you are well again. Stop sinning or something worse may happen to you." ¹⁵The man went away and told the Jews that it was Jesus who had made him well.

Life Through the Son

¹⁶So, because Jesus was doing these things on the Sabbath, the Jews persecuted him. ¹⁷Jesus said to them, "My Father is always at his work to this very day, and I, too, am working." ¹⁸For this reason the Jews tried all the harder to kill him; not only was he breaking the Sabbath, but he was even calling God his own Father, making himself equal with God.

¹⁹Jesus gave them this answer: "I tell you the truth, the Son can do nothing by himself; he can do only what he sees his Father doing, because whatever the Father does the Son also does. ²⁰For the Father loves the Son and shows him all he does. Yes, to your amazement he will show him even greater things than these. ²¹For just as the Father raises the dead and gives them life, even so the Son gives life to whom he is pleased to give it. ²²Moreover, the Father judges no one, but has entrusted all judgment to the Son, ²³that all may honor the Son just as they honor the Father. He who does not honor the Son does not honor the Father, who sent him.

²⁴"I tell you the truth, whoever hears my word and believes him who sent me has eternal life and will not be condemned; he has crossed over from death to life. ²⁵I tell you the truth, a time is coming and has now come when the dead will hear the voice of the Son of God and those who hear will live. ²⁶For as the Father has life in himself, so he has granted the Son to have life in himself. ²⁷And he has given him authority to judge because he is the Son of Man.

²⁸"Do not be amazed at this, for a time is coming when all who are in their graves will hear his voice ²⁹and come out—those who have done good will rise to live, and those who have done evil will rise to be condemned. ³⁰By myself I can do nothing;

a 2 Some manuscripts Bethzatha; other manuscripts Bethsaida
b 3 Some less important manuscripts paralyzed—and they waited for the moving of the waters. ⁴From time to time an angel of the Lord would come down and stir up the waters. The first one into the pool after each such disturbance would be cured of whatever disease he had.

I judge only as I hear, and my judgment is just, for I seek not to please myself but him who sent me.

Testimonies About Jesus

31"If I testify about myself, my testimony is not valid. 32There is another who testifies in my favor, and I know that his testimony about me is valid.

33"You have sent to John and he has testified to the truth. 34Not that I accept human testimony; but I mention it that you may be saved. 35John was a lamp that burned and gave light, and you chose for a time to enjoy his light.

36"I have testimony weightier than that of John. For the very work that the Father has given me to finish, and which I am doing, testifies that the Father has sent me. 37And the Father who sent me has himself testified concerning me. You have never heard his voice nor seen his form, 38nor does his word dwell in you, for you do not believe the one he sent. 39You diligently study*a* the Scriptures because you think that by them you possess eternal life. These are the Scriptures that testify about me, 40yet you refuse to come to me to have life.

41"I do not accept praise from men, 42but I know you. I know that you do not have the love of God in your hearts. 43I have come in my Father's name, and you do not accept me; but if someone else comes in his own name, you will accept him. 44How can you believe if you accept praise from one another, yet make no effort to obtain the praise that comes from the only God*b*?

45"But do not think I will accuse you before the Father. Your accuser is Moses, on whom your hopes are set. 46If you believed Moses, you would believe me, for he wrote about me. 47But since you do not believe what he wrote, how are you going to believe what I say?"

Jesus Feeds the Five Thousand

6 Some time after this, Jesus crossed to the far shore of the Sea of Galilee (that is, the Sea of Tiberias), 2and a great crowd of people followed him because they saw the miraculous signs he had performed on the sick. 3Then Jesus went up on a mountainside and sat down with his disciples. 4The Jewish Passover Feast was near.

5When Jesus looked up and saw a great crowd coming toward him, he said to Philip, "Where shall we buy bread for these people to eat?" 6He asked this only to test him, for he already had in mind what he was going to do.

7Philip answered him, "Eight months' wages*c* would not buy enough bread for each one to have a bite!"

8Another of his disciples, Andrew, Simon Peter's brother, spoke up, 9"Here is a boy with five small barley loaves and two small fish, but how far will they go among so many?"

10Jesus said, "Have the people sit down." There was plenty of grass in that place, and the men sat down, about five thousand of them. 11Jesus then took the loaves, gave thanks, and distributed to those who were seated as much as they wanted. He did the same with the fish.

12When they had all had enough to eat, he said to his disciples, "Gather the pieces that are left over. Let nothing be wasted." 13So they gathered them and filled twelve baskets with the pieces of the five barley loaves left over by those who had eaten.

14After the people saw the miraculous sign that Jesus did, they began to say, "Surely this is the Prophet who is to come into the world." 15Jesus, knowing that they intended to come and make him king by force, withdrew again to a mountain by himself.

Jesus Walks on the Water

16When evening came, his disciples went down to the lake, 17where they got into a boat and set off across the lake for Capernaum. By now it was dark, and Jesus had not yet joined them. 18A strong wind was blowing and the waters grew rough. 19When they had rowed three or three and a half miles,*d* they saw Jesus approaching the boat, walking on the water; and they were terrified. 20But he said to them, "It is I; don't be afraid." 21Then they were willing to take him into the boat, and immediately the boat reached the shore where they were heading.

22The next day the crowd that had stayed on the opposite shore of the lake realized that only one boat had been

a 39 Or *Study diligently* (the imperative)   *b 44* Some early manuscripts *the Only One*   *c 7* Greek *two hundred denarii*   *d 19* Greek *rowed twenty-five or thirty stadia* (about 5 or 6 kilometers) there, and that Jesus had not entered it with his disciples, but that they had gone away alone. 23Then some boats from Tiberias landed near the place where the people had eaten the bread after the Lord had given thanks. 24Once the crowd realized that neither Jesus nor his disciples were there, they got into the boats and went to Capernaum in search of Jesus.

Jesus the Bread of Life

25When they found him on the other side of the lake, they asked him, "Rabbi, when did you get here?"

26Jesus answered, "I tell you the truth, you are looking for me, not because you saw miraculous signs but because you ate the loaves and had your fill. 27Do not work for food that spoils, but for food that endures to eternal life, which the Son of Man will give you. On him God the Father has placed his seal of approval."

28Then they asked him, "What must we do to do the works God requires?"

29Jesus answered, "The work of God is this: to believe in the one he has sent."

30So they asked him, "What miraculous sign then will you give that we may see it and believe you? What will you do? 31Our forefathers ate the manna in the desert; as it is written: 'He gave them bread from heaven to eat.'ᵃ"

32Jesus said to them, "I tell you the truth, it is not Moses who has given you the bread from heaven, but it is my Father who gives you the true bread from heaven. 33For the bread of God is he who comes down from heaven and gives life to the world."

34"Sir," they said, "from now on give us this bread."

35Then Jesus declared, "I am the bread of life. He who comes to me will never go hungry, and he who believes in me will never be thirsty. 36But as I told you, you have seen me and still you do not believe.

a 31 Exodus 16:4; Neh. 9:15; Psalm 78:24,25

Make It Stick

READ JOHN 6:1–15

In John 6:1–15, a boy volunteered the food he had. It wasn't much, but it helped a lot of people. You may say, "I have nothing to give." Hey, give some old clothes to charity. Put a quarter in the offering. Give a frog to a kid who has no pet. It doesn't have to be a big expensive gift. Just put some thought into it. On a sticky note, write one thing you can give.

37All that the Father gives me will come to me, and whoever comes to me I will never drive away. 38For I have come down from heaven not to do my will but to do the will of him who sent me. 39And this is the will of him who sent me, that I shall lose none of all that he has given me, but raise them up at the last day. 40For my Father's will is that everyone who looks to the Son and believes in him shall have eternal life, and I will raise him up at the last day."

41At this the Jews began to grumble about him because he said, "I am the bread that came down from heaven." 42They said, "Is this not Jesus, the son of Joseph, whose father and mother we know? How can he now say, 'I came down from heaven'?"

43"Stop grumbling among yourselves," Jesus answered. 44"No one can come to me unless the Father who sent me draws him, and I will raise him up at the last day. 45It is written in the Prophets: 'They will all be taught by God.'a Everyone who listens to the Father and learns from him comes to me. 46No one has seen the Father except the one who is from God; only he has seen the Father. 47I tell you the truth, he who believes has everlasting life. 48I am the bread of life. 49Your forefathers ate the manna in the desert, yet they died. 50But here is the bread that comes down from heaven, which a man may eat and not die. 51I am the living bread that came down from heaven. If anyone eats of this bread, he will live forever. This bread is my flesh, which I will give for the life of the world."

52Then the Jews began to argue sharply among themselves, "How can this man give us his flesh to eat?"

53Jesus said to them, "I tell you the truth, unless you eat the flesh of the Son of Man and drink his blood, you have no life in you. 54Whoever eats my flesh and drinks my blood has eternal life, and I will raise him up at the last day. 55For my flesh is real food and my blood is real drink. 56Whoever eats my flesh and drinks my blood remains in me, and I in him. 57Just as the living Father sent me and I live because of the Father, so the one who feeds on me will live because of me. 58This is the

a 45 Isaiah 54:13

Bread of Life

READ JOHN 6:26–40

As you build a relationship with God, he supplies all of your needs (Matthew 6:33). He'll be there when you hit a tough trail on your mountain bike or when you need help studying to pass a test or when you're sick. He'll make sure you have enough to eat—your "daily bread" (Matthew 6:11)—and a warm place to sleep. But living a happy life and having all your needs met isn't the number one goal for a man of God. Jesus died and gave himself as the "bread from heaven" so that you could feast on him and have spiritual life. Is that cool or what? Don't be a kid who treats his Father like the owner of a toy store, always asking for stuff. Jesus tells you to pray for your "daily bread"—which in some cases could be pizza—but he also said that "heavenly bread" (spiritual things) is even better.

Your next reading is on page 1384.

bread that came down from heaven. Your forefathers ate manna and died, but he who feeds on this bread will live forever." [59]He said this while teaching in the synagogue in Capernaum.

Many Disciples Desert Jesus

[60]On hearing it, many of his disciples said, "This is a hard teaching. Who can accept it?"

[61]Aware that his disciples were grumbling about this, Jesus said to them, "Does this offend you? [62]What if you see the Son of Man ascend to where he was before! [63]The Spirit gives life; the flesh counts for nothing. The words I have spoken to you are spirit[a] and they are life. [64]Yet there are some of you who do not believe." For Jesus had known from the beginning which of them did not believe and who would betray him. [65]He went on to say, "This is why I told you that no one can come to me unless the Father has enabled him."

[66]From this time many of his disciples turned back and no longer followed him.

[67]"You do not want to leave too, do you?" Jesus asked the Twelve.

[68]Simon Peter answered him, "Lord, to whom shall we go? You have the words of eternal life. [69]We believe and know that you are the Holy One of God."

[70]Then Jesus replied, "Have I not chosen you, the Twelve? Yet one of you is a devil!" [71](He meant Judas, the son of Simon Iscariot, who, though one of the Twelve, was later to betray him.)

Jesus Goes to the Feast of Tabernacles

After this, Jesus went around in Galilee, purposely staying away from Judea because the Jews there were waiting to take his life. [2]But when the Jewish Feast of Tabernacles was near, [3]Jesus' brothers said to him, "You ought to leave here and go to Judea, so that

[a] 63 Or Spirit

Make It Stick

READ JOHN 6:53–66

When Jesus told the crowd that they had to eat his flesh and drink his blood (John 6:53–66), a lot of them were grossed out and offended. They didn't clue in that he was talking about his body being killed and his blood spilling to give them life. On a sticky note, draw a disciple with a shocked expression on his face.

your disciples may see the miracles you do. ⁴No one who wants to become a public figure acts in secret. Since you are doing these things, show yourself to the world." ⁵For even his own brothers did not believe in him.

⁶Therefore Jesus told them, "The right time for me has not yet come; for you any time is right. ⁷The world cannot hate you, but it hates me because I testify that what it does is evil. ⁸You go to the Feast. I am not yet*ᵃ* going up to this Feast, because for me the right time has not yet come." ⁹Having said this, he stayed in Galilee.

¹⁰However, after his brothers had left for the Feast, he went also, not publicly, but in secret. ¹¹Now at the Feast the Jews were watching for him and asking, "Where is that man?"

¹²Among the crowds there was widespread whispering about him. Some said, "He is a good man."

Others replied, "No, he deceives the people." ¹³But no one would say anything publicly about him for fear of the Jews.

Jesus Teaches at the Feast

¹⁴Not until halfway through the Feast did Jesus go up to the temple courts and begin to teach. ¹⁵The Jews were amazed and asked, "How did this man get such learning without having studied?"

¹⁶Jesus answered, "My teaching is not my own. It comes from him who sent me. ¹⁷If anyone chooses to do God's will, he will find out whether my teaching comes from God or whether I speak on my own. ¹⁸He who speaks on his own does so to gain honor for himself, but he who works for the honor of the one who sent him is a man of truth; there is nothing false about him. ¹⁹Has not Moses given you the law? Yet not one of you keeps the law. Why are you trying to kill me?"

²⁰"You are demon-possessed," the crowd answered. "Who is trying to kill you?"

²¹Jesus said to them, "I did one miracle, and you are all astonished. ²²Yet, because Moses gave you circumcision (though actually it did not come from Moses, but from

ᵃ 8 Some early manuscripts do not have *yet*.

Hanging in There

READ JOHN 6:53–69

"Fish and loaves? Great! Flesh and blood? That's hard, man. We're outta here." Maybe something has made you question God—something didn't go your way or life dealt you a tough blow. In skateboarding, you get lots of skinned knees and elbows. In following Jesus, sometimes your faith gets skinned. Everyone gets knocked down. The problem is when they don't get back up. God allows things for a reason, so when you take a blow, tell yourself, "God is real. Jesus is God's Son. So even when I don't understand what's happening, I'm going to trust him. I'm going to hang in there and keep following Jesus." That's how you grow. When those other disciples bailed, Jesus asked the Twelve if they were going to stick around. Peter answered, "Lord, to whom shall we go? You have the words of eternal life" (John 6:68). Peter chose to trust Jesus no matter what. Way to go, Pete!

Your next reading is on page 1387.

the patriarchs), you circumcise a child on the Sabbath. 23Now if a child can be circumcised on the Sabbath so that the law of Moses may not be broken, why are you angry with me for healing the whole man on the Sabbath? 24Stop judging by mere appearances, and make a right judgment."

Is Jesus the Christ?

25At that point some of the people of Jerusalem began to ask, "Isn't this the man they are trying to kill? 26Here he is, speaking publicly, and they are not saying a word to him. Have the authorities really concluded that he is the Christ*a*? 27But we know where this man is from; when the Christ comes, no one will know where he is from."

28Then Jesus, still teaching in the temple courts, cried out, "Yes, you know me, and you know where I am from. I am not here on my own, but he who sent me is true. You do not know him, 29but I know him because I am from him and he sent me."

30At this they tried to seize him, but no one laid a hand on him, because his time had not yet come. 31Still, many in the crowd put their faith in him. They said, "When the Christ comes, will he do more miraculous signs than this man?"

32The Pharisees heard the crowd whispering such things about him. Then the chief priests and the Pharisees sent temple guards to arrest him.

33Jesus said, "I am with you for only a short time, and then I go to the one who sent me. 34You will look for me, but you will not find me; and where I am, you cannot come."

35The Jews said to one another, "Where does this man intend to go that we cannot find him? Will he go where our people live scattered among the Greeks, and teach the Greeks? 36What did he mean when he said, 'You will look for me, but you will not find me,' and 'Where I am, you cannot come'?"

37On the last and greatest day of the Feast, Jesus stood and said in a loud voice, "If anyone is thirsty, let him come to me and drink. 38Whoever believes in me, as*b* the Scripture has said, streams of living water will flow from within him." 39By this he meant the Spirit, whom those who believed in him were later to receive. Up to that time the Spirit had not been given, since Jesus had not yet been glorified.

40On hearing his words, some of the people said, "Surely this man is the Prophet."

41Others said, "He is the Christ."

Still others asked, "How can the Christ come from Galilee? 42Does not the Scripture say that the Christ will come from David's family*c* and from Bethlehem, the town where David lived?" 43Thus the people were divided because of Jesus. 44Some wanted to seize him, but no one laid a hand on him.

Unbelief of the Jewish Leaders

45Finally the temple guards went back to the chief priests and Pharisees, who asked them, "Why didn't you bring him in?"

46"No one ever spoke the way this man does," the guards declared.

47"You mean he has deceived you also?" the Pharisees retorted. 48"Has any of the rulers or of the Pharisees believed in him? 49No! But this mob that knows nothing of the law—there is a curse on them."

50Nicodemus, who had gone to Jesus earlier and who was one of their own number, asked, 51"Does our law condemn anyone without first hearing him to find out what he is doing?"

52They replied, "Are you from Galilee, too? Look into it, and you will find that a prophet*d* does not come out of Galilee."

[The earliest manuscripts and many other ancient witnesses do not have John 7:53–8:11.]

53Then each went to his own home.

But Jesus went to the Mount of Olives. 2At dawn he appeared again in the temple courts, where all the people gathered around him, and he sat down to teach them. 3The teachers of the law and the Pharisees brought in a woman caught in adultery. They made her stand before the group 4and said to Jesus, "Teacher, this woman was caught in the act of adultery. 5In the Law Moses commanded us to stone such women. Now what do you say?" 6They were using this question as a trap, in order to have a basis for accusing him.

a 26 Or *Messiah*; also in verses 27, 31, 41 and 42
b 37,38 Or / If anyone is thirsty, let him come to me. / And let him drink, *38who believes in me. / As   c 42* Greek *seed*
d 52 Two early manuscripts *the Prophet*

But Jesus bent down and started to write on the ground with his finger. 7When they kept on questioning him, he straightened up and said to them, "If any one of you is without sin, let him be the first to throw a stone at her." 8Again he stooped down and wrote on the ground.

9At this, those who heard began to go away one at a time, the older ones first, until only Jesus was left, with the woman still standing there. 10Jesus straightened up and asked her, "Woman, where are they? Has no one condemned you?"

11"No one, sir," she said.

"Then neither do I condemn you," Jesus declared. "Go now and leave your life of sin."

The Validity of Jesus' Testimony

12When Jesus spoke again to the people, he said, "I am the light of the world. Whoever follows me will never walk in darkness, but will have the light of life."

13The Pharisees challenged him, "Here you are, appearing as your own witness; your testimony is not valid."

14Jesus answered, "Even if I testify on my own behalf, my testimony is valid, for I know where I came from and where I am going. But you have no idea where I come from or where I am going. 15You judge by human standards; I pass judgment on no one. 16But if I do judge, my decisions are right, because I am not alone. I stand with the Father, who sent me. 17In your own Law it is written that the testimony of two men is valid. 18I am one who testifies for myself; my other witness is the Father, who sent me."

19Then they asked him, "Where is your father?"

"You do not know me or my Father," Jesus replied. "If you knew me, you would know my Father also." 20He spoke these words while teaching in the temple area

Make It Stick

READ JOHN 8:7

Read Jesus' "stone-throwing rule" in John 8:7. When someone stumbles, help them. Simply judging them is like kicking them when they're down. Find and keep a stone to remind you that for every rock you "throw," one could be chucked at you. Trace your stone on a sticky note.

near the place where the offerings were put. Yet no one seized him, because his time had not yet come.

21Once more Jesus said to them, "I am going away, and you will look for me, and you will die in your sin. Where I go, you cannot come."

22This made the Jews ask, "Will he kill himself? Is that why he says, 'Where I go, you cannot come'?"

23But he continued, "You are from below; I am from above. You are of this world; I am not of this world. 24I told you that you would die in your sins; if you do not believe that I am ˻the one I claim to be˼,ᵃ you will indeed die in your sins."

25"Who are you?" they asked.

"Just what I have been claiming all along," Jesus replied. 26"I have much to say in judgment of you. But he who sent me is reliable, and what I have heard from him I tell the world."

27They did not understand that he was telling them about his Father. 28So Jesus said, "When you have lifted up the Son of Man, then you will know that I am ˻the

one I claim to be˼, and that I do nothing on my own but speak just what the Father has taught me. 29The one who sent me is with me; he has not left me alone, for I always do what pleases him." 30Even as he spoke, many put their faith in him.

The Children of Abraham

31To the Jews who had believed him, Jesus said, "If you hold to my teaching, you are really my disciples. 32Then you will know the truth, and the truth will set you free."

33They answered him, "We are Abraham's descendantsᵇ and have never been slaves of anyone. How can you say that we shall be set free?"

34Jesus replied, "I tell you the truth, everyone who sins is a slave to sin. 35Now a slave has no permanent place in the family, but a son belongs to it forever. 36So if the Son sets you free, you will be free indeed. 37I know you are Abraham's descendants. Yet you are ready to kill me,

ᵃ 24 Or I am he; also in verse 28   ᵇ 33 Greek seed; also in verse 37

GET SMARTER

Truth Sets You Free

READ JOHN 8:31–36

Once you've learned to ride a bike, chances are good you'll always remember how. Even if you haven't ridden a bike for years, it's something you never quite forget. Ask your grandpa. It's different with truth. If you don't hang on to truth and obey it daily, it becomes foggy in your mind. When it's foggy, you start to cave in on important things and the truth gets even blurrier. Eventually you even argue against the truth. Hold tight to Jesus' teaching—*that's* the truth. "If you hold to my teaching ... Then you will know the truth, and the truth will set you free" (verses 31–32). Truth frees you from all of the trouble that sin gets you into. But if you keep forgetting the truth, then coming back to it, it's like learning to ride a bike from scratch (literally)—upside down in the ditch. So stick to the truth and ditch the ditch.

Your next reading is on page 1389.

because you have no room for my word. [38]I am telling you what I have seen in the Father's presence, and you do what you have heard from your father.[a]"

[39]"Abraham is our father," they answered.

"If you were Abraham's children," said Jesus, "then you would[b] do the things Abraham did. [40]As it is, you are determined to kill me, a man who has told you the truth that I heard from God. Abraham did not do such things. [41]You are doing the things your own father does."

"We are not illegitimate children," they protested. "The only Father we have is God himself."

The Children of the Devil

[42]Jesus said to them, "If God were your Father, you would love me, for I came from God and now am here. I have not come on my own; but he sent me. [43]Why is my language not clear to you? Because you are unable to hear what I say. [44]You belong to your father, the devil, and you want to carry out your father's desire. He was a murderer from the beginning, not holding to the truth, for there is no truth in him. When he lies, he speaks his native language, for he is a liar and the father of lies. [45]Yet because I tell the truth, you do not believe me! [46]Can any of you prove me guilty of sin? If I am telling the truth, why don't you believe me? [47]He who belongs to God hears what God says. The reason you do not hear is that you do not belong to God."

The Claims of Jesus About Himself

[48]The Jews answered him, "Aren't we right in saying that you are a Samaritan and demon-possessed?"

[49]"I am not possessed by a demon," said Jesus, "but I honor my Father and you dishonor me. [50]I am not seeking glory for myself; but there is one who seeks it, and he is the judge. [51]I tell you the truth, if anyone keeps my word, he will never see death."

[52]At this the Jews exclaimed, "Now we know that you are demon-possessed! Abraham died and so did the prophets, yet you say that if anyone keeps your word, he will never taste death. [53]Are you greater than our father Abraham? He died, and so did the prophets. Who do you think you are?"

[54]Jesus replied, "If I glorify myself, my glory means nothing. My Father, whom you claim as your God, is the one who glorifies me. [55]Though you do not know him, I know him. If I said I did not, I would be a liar like you, but I do know him and keep his word. [56]Your father Abraham rejoiced at the thought of seeing my day; he saw it and was glad."

[57]"You are not yet fifty years old," the Jews said to him, "and you have seen Abraham!"

[58]"I tell you the truth," Jesus answered, "before Abraham was born, I am!" [59]At this, they picked up stones to stone him, but Jesus hid himself, slipping away from the temple grounds.

Jesus Heals a Man Born Blind

As he went along, he saw a man blind from birth. [2]His disciples asked him, "Rabbi, who sinned, this man or his parents, that he was born blind?"

[3]"Neither this man nor his parents sinned," said Jesus, "but this happened so that the work of God might be displayed in his life. [4]As long as it is day, we must do the work of him who sent me. Night is coming, when no one can work. [5]While I am in the world, I am the light of the world."

[6]Having said this, he spit on the ground, made some mud with the saliva, and put it on the man's eyes. [7]"Go," he told him, "wash in the Pool of Siloam" (this word means Sent). So the man went and washed, and came home seeing.

[8]His neighbors and those who had formerly seen him begging asked, "Isn't this the same man who used to sit and beg?" [9]Some claimed that he was.

Others said, "No, he only looks like him."

But he himself insisted, "I am the man."

[10]"How then were your eyes opened?" they demanded.

[11]He replied, "The man they call Jesus made some mud and put it on my eyes. He told me to go to Siloam and wash. So I went and washed, and then I could see."

[12]"Where is this man?" they asked him.

"I don't know," he said.

The Pharisees Investigate the Healing

[13]They brought to the Pharisees the man who had been blind. [14]Now the day

---

[a] 38 Or presence. Therefore do what you have heard from the Father.   [b] 39 Some early manuscripts "If you are Abraham's children," said Jesus, "then

on which Jesus had made the mud and opened the man's eyes was a Sabbath. [15]Therefore the Pharisees also asked him how he had received his sight. "He put mud on my eyes," the man replied, "and I washed, and now I see."

[16]Some of the Pharisees said, "This man is not from God, for he does not keep the Sabbath."

But others asked, "How can a sinner do such miraculous signs?" So they were divided.

[17]Finally they turned again to the blind man, "What have you to say about him? It was your eyes he opened."

The man replied, "He is a prophet."

[18]The Jews still did not believe that he had been blind and had received his sight until they sent for the man's parents. [19]"Is this your son?" they asked. "Is this the one you say was born blind? How is it that now he can see?"

[20]"We know he is our son," the parents answered, "and we know he was born blind. [21]But how he can see now, or who opened his eyes, we don't know. Ask him. He is of age; he will speak for himself." [22]His parents said this because they were afraid of the Jews, for already the Jews had decided that anyone who acknowledged that Jesus was the Christ[a] would be put out of the synagogue. [23]That was why his parents said, "He is of age; ask him."

[24]A second time they summoned the man who had been blind. "Give glory to God,[b]" they said. "We know this man is a sinner."

[25]He replied, "Whether he is a sinner or not, I don't know. One thing I do know. I was blind but now I see!"

[26]Then they asked him, "What did he do to you? How did he open your eyes?"

[27]He answered, "I have told you already and you did not listen. Why do you want to hear it again? Do you want to become his disciples, too?"

[a] 22 Or *Messiah*   [b] 24 A solemn charge to tell the truth (see Joshua 7:19)

Short of Perfect

READ JOHN 9:1–7

Ever feel like your body is less than perfect? No one's is really perfect, but maybe your legs don't work, or you have diabetes or asthma and it gets you down. Maybe none of this describes you. Maybe it's someone you know. In John 9, this guy was born blind. He couldn't see from day one. Then Jesus healed him. God may not choose to heal you, but you WILL be made perfect and whole in heaven (1 Corinthians 15:42–43). Accidents, scars, diseases, disabilities—these things happen in our fallen world. You may not understand why, but know this: It's not because God loves you less than other kids. "'Neither this man nor his parents sinned,' said Jesus, 'but this happened so that the work of God might be displayed in his life'" (John 9:3). Remember, no matter who you are or how less-than-perfect you think you are, God has plans for your life.

Your next reading is on page 1392.

28Then they hurled insults at him and said, "You are this fellow's disciple! We are disciples of Moses! 29We know that God spoke to Moses, but as for this fellow, we don't even know where he comes from."

30The man answered, "Now that is remarkable! You don't know where he comes from, yet he opened my eyes. 31We know that God does not listen to sinners. He listens to the godly man who does his will. 32Nobody has ever heard of opening the eyes of a man born blind. 33If this man were not from God, he could do nothing."

34To this they replied, "You were steeped in sin at birth; how dare you lecture us!" And they threw him out.

Spiritual Blindness

35Jesus heard that they had thrown him out, and when he found him, he said, "Do you believe in the Son of Man?"

36"Who is he, sir?" the man asked. "Tell me so that I may believe in him."

37Jesus said, "You have now seen him; in fact, he is the one speaking with you."

38Then the man said, "Lord, I believe," and he worshiped him.

39Jesus said, "For judgment I have come into this world, so that the blind will see and those who see will become blind."

40Some Pharisees who were with him heard him say this and asked, "What? Are we blind too?"

41Jesus said, "If you were blind, you would not be guilty of sin; but now that you claim you can see, your guilt remains.

The Shepherd and His Flock

10 "I tell you the truth, the man who does not enter the sheep pen by the gate, but climbs in by some other way, is a thief and a robber. 2The man who enters by the gate is the shepherd of his sheep. 3The watchman opens the gate for him, and the sheep listen to his voice. He calls his own sheep by name and leads them out. 4When he has brought out all his own, he goes on ahead of them, and his sheep follow him because they know his voice. 5But they will never follow a stranger; in fact, they will run away from him because they do not recognize a stranger's voice." 6Jesus used this figure of speech, but they did not understand what he was telling them.

7Therefore Jesus said again, "I tell you the truth, I am the gate for the sheep. 8All

who ever came before me were thieves and robbers, but the sheep did not listen to them. 9I am the gate; whoever enters through me will be saved.*a* He will come in and go out, and find pasture. 10The thief comes only to steal and kill and destroy; I have come that they may have life, and have it to the full.

11"I am the good shepherd. The good shepherd lays down his life for the sheep. 12The hired hand is not the shepherd who owns the sheep. So when he sees the wolf coming, he abandons the sheep and runs away. Then the wolf attacks the flock and scatters it. 13The man runs away because he is a hired hand and cares nothing for the sheep.

14"I am the good shepherd; I know my sheep and my sheep know me— 15just as the Father knows me and I know the Father—and I lay down my life for the sheep. 16I have other sheep that are not of this sheep pen. I must bring them also. They too will listen to my voice, and there shall be one flock and one shepherd. 17The reason my Father loves me is that I lay down my life—only to take it up again. 18No one takes it from me, but I lay it down of my own accord. I have authority to lay it down and authority to take it up again. This command I received from my Father."

19At these words the Jews were again divided. 20Many of them said, "He is demon-possessed and raving mad. Why listen to him?"

21But others said, "These are not the sayings of a man possessed by a demon. Can a demon open the eyes of the blind?"

The Unbelief of the Jews

22Then came the Feast of Dedication*b* at Jerusalem. It was winter, 23and Jesus was in the temple area walking in Solomon's Colonnade. 24The Jews gathered around him, saying, "How long will you keep us in suspense? If you are the Christ,*c* tell us plainly."

25Jesus answered, "I did tell you, but you do not believe. The miracles I do in my Father's name speak for me, 26but you do not believe because you are not my sheep. 27My sheep listen to my voice; I know them, and they follow me. 28I give them eternal life, and they shall never per-

---

a 9 Or *kept safe*　*b 22* That is, Hanukkah
c 24 Or *Messiah*

ish; no one can snatch them out of my hand. 29My Father, who has given them to me, is greater than all[a]; no one can snatch them out of my Father's hand. 30I and the Father are one."

31Again the Jews picked up stones to stone him, 32but Jesus said to them, "I have shown you many great miracles from the Father. For which of these do you stone me?"

33"We are not stoning you for any of these," replied the Jews, "but for blasphemy, because you, a mere man, claim to be God."

34Jesus answered them, "Is it not written in your Law, 'I have said you are gods'[b]? 35If he called them 'gods,' to whom the word of God came—and the Scripture cannot be broken— 36what about the one whom the Father set apart as his very own and sent into the world? Why then do you accuse me of blasphemy because I said, 'I am God's Son'? 37Do not believe me unless I do what my Father does. 38But if I do it, even though you do not believe me, believe the miracles, that you may know and understand that the Father is in me, and I in the Father." 39Again they tried to seize him, but he escaped their grasp.

40Then Jesus went back across the Jordan to the place where John had been baptizing in the early days. Here he stayed 41and many people came to him. They said, "Though John never performed a miraculous sign, all that John said about this man was true." 42And in that place many believed in Jesus.

The Death of Lazarus

11 Now a man named Lazarus was sick. He was from Bethany, the village of Mary and her sister Martha. 2This Mary, whose brother Lazarus now lay sick, was the same one who

---

[a] 29 Many early manuscripts *What my Father has given me is greater than all*   [b] 34 Psalm 82:6

Make It Stick

READ JOHN 10:7–16, 27–29

The devil, because of the sin he draws people into, is a thief, murderer and destroyer. But Jesus made it possible to plug into life—life to the MAXIMUM. Life RIGHT NOW. And when you get to heaven, things will be *really* great! On a sticky note, list at least two life-destroying things you're giving up to follow Jesus in this life (examples: swearing, lying).

poured perfume on the Lord and wiped his feet with her hair. ³So the sisters sent word to Jesus, "Lord, the one you love is sick."

⁴When he heard this, Jesus said, "This sickness will not end in death. No, it is for God's glory so that God's Son may be glorified through it." ⁵Jesus loved Martha and her sister and Lazarus. ⁶Yet when he heard that Lazarus was sick, he stayed where he was two more days.

⁷Then he said to his disciples, "Let us go back to Judea."

⁸"But Rabbi," they said, "a short while ago the Jews tried to stone you, and yet you are going back there?"

⁹Jesus answered, "Are there not twelve hours of daylight? A man who walks by day will not stumble, for he sees by this world's light. ¹⁰It is when he walks by night that he stumbles, for he has no light."

¹¹After he had said this, he went on to tell them, "Our friend Lazarus has fallen asleep; but I am going there to wake him up."

¹²His disciples replied, "Lord, if he sleeps, he will get better." ¹³Jesus had been speaking of his death, but his disciples thought he meant natural sleep.

¹⁴So then he told them plainly, "Lazarus is dead, ¹⁵and for your sake I am glad I was not there, so that you may believe. But let us go to him."

¹⁶Then Thomas (called Didymus) said to the rest of the disciples, "Let us also go, that we may die with him."

Jesus Comforts the Sisters

¹⁷On his arrival, Jesus found that Lazarus had already been in the tomb for four days. ¹⁸Bethany was less than two miles*a* from Jerusalem, ¹⁹and many Jews had come to Martha and Mary to comfort them in the loss of their brother. ²⁰When Martha heard that Jesus was coming, she went out to meet him, but Mary stayed at home.

²¹"Lord," Martha said to Jesus, "if you had been here, my brother would not have died. ²²But I know that even now God will give you whatever you ask."

---

a 18 Greek *fifteen stadia* (about 3 kilometers)

Lazarus Dies and Then . . .

READ JOHN 11:1–7, 17–44

What tops your list of worst smells? Sweaty feet? Stinky pits? Sour milk? Well, a dead body tops 'em all. Martha was thinking about the stink when Jesus told them to remove the stone from Lazarus's tomb. "But, Lord . . . he has been there four days" (verse 39). Besides the smell, Mary and Martha were wondering about Jesus' timing. "Lord, if you had been here, my brother would not have died" (verse 32). After all, Jesus was going around healing everyone else, why not his good friend? They thought their hope died with Lazarus. Not so. When you pray for things, God understands the situation. But sometimes he answers in a different way and in a different time. You say, "Now." God says, "Wait." It's hard to wait. But God is in control and you can trust him. You won't always understand his timing, but that doesn't mean it stinks. When Jesus is your hope, hope never dies.

Your next reading is on page 1398.

23 Jesus said to her, "Your brother will rise again."

24 Martha answered, "I know he will rise again in the resurrection at the last day."

25 Jesus said to her, "I am the resurrection and the life. He who believes in me will live, even though he dies; 26 and whoever lives and believes in me will never die. Do you believe this?"

27 "Yes, Lord," she told him, "I believe that you are the Christ,a the Son of God, who was to come into the world."

28 And after she had said this, she went back and called her sister Mary aside. "The Teacher is here," she said, "and is asking for you." 29 When Mary heard this, she got up quickly and went to him. 30 Now Jesus had not yet entered the village, but was still at the place where Martha had met him. 31 When the Jews who had been with Mary in the house, comforting her, noticed how quickly she got up and went out, they followed her, supposing she was going to the tomb to mourn there.

32 When Mary reached the place where Jesus was and saw him, she fell at his feet and said, "Lord, if you had been here, my brother would not have died."

33 When Jesus saw her weeping, and the Jews who had come along with her also weeping, he was deeply moved in spirit and troubled. 34 "Where have you laid him?" he asked.

"Come and see, Lord," they replied.

35 Jesus wept.

36 Then the Jews said, "See how he loved him!"

37 But some of them said, "Could not he who opened the eyes of the blind man have kept this man from dying?"

Jesus Raises Lazarus From the Dead

38 Jesus, once more deeply moved, came to the tomb. It was a cave with a stone laid across the entrance. 39 "Take away the stone," he said.

"But, Lord," said Martha, the sister of the dead man, "by this time there is a bad odor, for he has been there four days."

40 Then Jesus said, "Did I not tell you that if you believed, you would see the glory of God?"

41 So they took away the stone. Then Jesus looked up and said, "Father, I thank you that you have heard me. 42 I knew that you always hear me, but I said this for the benefit of the people standing here, that they may believe that you sent me."

43 When he had said this, Jesus called in a loud voice, "Lazarus, come out!" 44 The dead man came out, his hands and feet wrapped with strips of linen, and a cloth around his face.

Jesus said to them, "Take off the grave clothes and let him go."

The Plot to Kill Jesus

45 Therefore many of the Jews who had come to visit Mary, and had seen what Jesus did, put their faith in him. 46 But some of them went to the Pharisees and told them what Jesus had done. 47 Then the chief priests and the Pharisees called a meeting of the Sanhedrin.

"What are we accomplishing?" they asked. "Here is this man performing many miraculous signs. 48 If we let him go on like this, everyone will believe in him, and then the Romans will come and take away both our placeb and our nation."

49 Then one of them, named Caiaphas, who was high priest that year, spoke up, "You know nothing at all! 50 You do not realize that it is better for you that one man die for the people than that the whole nation perish."

51 He did not say this on his own, but as high priest that year he prophesied that Jesus would die for the Jewish nation, 52 and not only for that nation but also for the scattered children of God, to bring them together and make them one. 53 So from that day on they plotted to take his life.

54 Therefore Jesus no longer moved about publicly among the Jews. Instead he withdrew to a region near the desert, to a village called Ephraim, where he stayed with his disciples.

55 When it was almost time for the Jewish Passover, many went up from the country to Jerusalem for their ceremonial cleansing before the Passover. 56 They kept looking for Jesus, and as they stood in the temple area they asked one another, "What do you think? Isn't he coming to the Feast at all?" 57 But the chief priests and Pharisees had given orders that if anyone found out where Jesus was, he should report it so that they might arrest him.

a 27 Or Messiah   b 48 Or temple

Gross!

Check out John 12:9–11. The religious leaders plotted to kill Lazarus. Hey, come on you guys! Give the poor man a break! He just WAS dead for four days.

Jesus Anointed at Bethany

12 Six days before the Passover, Jesus arrived at Bethany, where Lazarus lived, whom Jesus had raised from the dead. ²Here a dinner was given in Jesus' honor. Martha served, while Lazarus was among those reclining at the table with him. ³Then Mary took about a pint*ᵃ* of pure nard, an expensive perfume; she poured it on Jesus' feet and wiped his feet with her hair. And the house was filled with the fragrance of the perfume.

⁴But one of his disciples, Judas Iscariot, who was later to betray him, objected, ⁵"Why wasn't this perfume sold and the money given to the poor? It was worth a year's wages.*ᵇ*" ⁶He did not say this because he cared about the poor but because he was a thief; as keeper of the money bag, he used to help himself to what was put into it.

⁷"Leave her alone," Jesus replied. ⌊It was intended⌋ that she should save this perfume for the day of my burial. ⁸You will always have the poor among you, but you will not always have me."

⁹Meanwhile a large crowd of Jews found out that Jesus was there and came, not only because of him but also to see Lazarus, whom he had raised from the dead. ¹⁰So the chief priests made plans to kill Lazarus as well, ¹¹for on account of him many of the Jews were going over to Jesus and putting their faith in him.

The Triumphal Entry

¹²The next day the great crowd that had come for the Feast heard that Jesus was on his way to Jerusalem. ¹³They took palm branches and went out to meet him, shouting,

"Hosanna!*ᶜ*"

"Blessed is he who comes in the name of the Lord!"*ᵈ*

"Blessed is the King of Israel!"

¹⁴Jesus found a young donkey and sat upon it, as it is written,

¹⁵"Do not be afraid, O Daughter of Zion;
    see, your king is coming,
    seated on a donkey's colt."*ᵉ*

¹⁶At first his disciples did not understand all this. Only after Jesus was glorified did they realize that these things had been written about him and that they had done these things to him.

¹⁷Now the crowd that was with him when he called Lazarus from the tomb and raised him from the dead continued to spread the word. ¹⁸Many people, because they had heard that he had given this miraculous sign, went out to meet him. ¹⁹So the Pharisees said to one

ᵃ 3 Greek *a litra* (probably about 0.5 liter)   *ᵇ 5* Greek *three hundred denarii*
ᶜ 13 A Hebrew expression meaning "Save!" which became an exclamation of praise   *ᵈ 13* Psalm 118:25,26   *ᵉ 15* Zech. 9:9

another, "See, this is getting us nowhere. Look how the whole world has gone after him!"

Jesus Predicts His Death

20 Now there were some Greeks among those who went up to worship at the Feast. 21 They came to Philip, who was from Bethsaida in Galilee, with a request. "Sir," they said, "we would like to see Jesus." 22 Philip went to tell Andrew; Andrew and Philip in turn told Jesus.

23 Jesus replied, "The hour has come for the Son of Man to be glorified. 24 I tell you the truth, unless a kernel of wheat falls to the ground and dies, it remains only a single seed. But if it dies, it produces many seeds. 25 The man who loves his life will lose it, while the man who hates his life in this world will keep it for eternal life. 26 Whoever serves me must follow me; and where I am, my servant also will be. My Father will honor the one who serves me.

27 "Now my heart is troubled, and what shall I say? 'Father, save me from this hour'? No, it was for this very reason I came to this hour. 28 Father, glorify your name!"

Then a voice came from heaven, "I have glorified it, and will glorify it again." 29 The crowd that was there and heard it said it had thundered; others said an angel had spoken to him.

30 Jesus said, "This voice was for your benefit, not mine. 31 Now is the time for judgment on this world; now the prince of this world will be driven out. 32 But I, when I am lifted up from the earth, will draw all men to myself." 33 He said this to show the kind of death he was going to die.

34 The crowd spoke up, "We have heard from the Law that the Christ a will remain forever, so how can you say, 'The Son of Man must be lifted up'? Who is this 'Son of Man'?"

35 Then Jesus told them, "You are going to have the light just a little while longer. Walk while you have the light, before darkness overtakes you. The man who walks in the dark does not know where he is going. 36 Put your trust in the light while you have it, so that you may become sons of light." When he had finished speaking, Jesus left and hid himself from them.

The Jews Continue in Their Unbelief

37 Even after Jesus had done all these miraculous signs in their presence, they still would not believe in him. 38 This was to fulfill the word of Isaiah the prophet:

"Lord, who has believed our message
    and to whom has the arm of the
        Lord been revealed?" b

39 For this reason they could not believe, because, as Isaiah says elsewhere:

40 "He has blinded their eyes
    and deadened their hearts,
so they can neither see with their eyes,
    nor understand with their hearts,
    nor turn—and I would heal them." c

41 Isaiah said this because he saw Jesus' glory and spoke about him.

42 Yet at the same time many even among the leaders believed in him. But because of the Pharisees they would not confess their faith for fear they would be put out of the synagogue; 43 for they loved praise from men more than praise from God.

44 Then Jesus cried out, "When a man believes in me, he does not believe in me only, but in the one who sent me. 45 When he looks at me, he sees the one who sent me. 46 I have come into the world as a light, so that no one who believes in me should stay in darkness.

47 "As for the person who hears my words but does not keep them, I do not judge him. For I did not come to judge the world, but to save it. 48 There is a judge for the one who rejects me and does not accept my words; that very word which I spoke will condemn him at the last day. 49 For I did not speak of my own accord, but the Father who sent me commanded me what to say and how to say it. 50 I know that his command leads to eternal life. So whatever I say is just what the Father has told me to say."

Jesus Washes His Disciples' Feet

13 It was just before the Passover Feast. Jesus knew that the time had come for him to leave this world and go to the Father. Having loved his own who were in the world, he now showed them the full extent of his love. d

2 The evening meal was being served, and the devil had already prompted Judas

a 34 Or Messiah   b 38 Isaiah 53:1   c 40 Isaiah 6:10
d 1 Or he loved them to the last

Iscariot, son of Simon, to betray Jesus. ³Jesus knew that the Father had put all things under his power, and that he had come from God and was returning to God; ⁴so he got up from the meal, took off his outer clothing, and wrapped a towel around his waist. ⁵After that, he poured water into a basin and began to wash his disciples' feet, drying them with the towel that was wrapped around him.

⁶He came to Simon Peter, who said to him, "Lord, are you going to wash my feet?"

⁷Jesus replied, "You do not realize now what I am doing, but later you will understand."

⁸"No," said Peter, "you shall never wash my feet."

Jesus answered, "Unless I wash you, you have no part with me."

⁹"Then, Lord," Simon Peter replied, "not just my feet but my hands and my head as well!"

¹⁰Jesus answered, "A person who has had a bath needs only to wash his feet; his whole body is clean. And you are clean, though not every one of you." ¹¹For he knew who was going to betray him, and that was why he said not every one was clean.

¹²When he had finished washing their feet, he put on his clothes and returned to his place. "Do you understand what I have done for you?" he asked them. ¹³"You call me 'Teacher' and 'Lord,' and rightly so, for that is what I am. ¹⁴Now that I, your Lord and Teacher, have washed your feet, you also should wash one another's feet. ¹⁵I have set you an example that you should do as I have done for you. ¹⁶I tell you the truth, no servant is greater than his master, nor is a messenger greater than the one who sent him. ¹⁷Now that you know these things, you will be blessed if you do them.

Jesus Predicts His Betrayal

¹⁸"I am not referring to all of you; I know those I have chosen. But this is to fulfill the scripture: 'He who shares my bread has lifted up his heel against me.'[a]

¹⁹"I am telling you now before it happens, so that when it does happen you will believe that I am He. ²⁰I tell you the truth, whoever accepts anyone I send accepts me; and whoever accepts me accepts the one who sent me."

²¹After he had said this, Jesus was troubled in spirit and testified, "I tell you the truth, one of you is going to betray me."

²²His disciples stared at one another, at a loss to know which of them he meant. ²³One of them, the disciple whom Jesus loved, was reclining next to him. ²⁴Simon Peter motioned to this disciple and said, "Ask him which one he means."

²⁵Leaning back against Jesus, he asked him, "Lord, who is it?"

²⁶Jesus answered, "It is the one to whom I will give this piece of bread when I have dipped it in the dish." Then, dipping the piece of bread, he gave it to Judas Iscariot, son of Simon. ²⁷As soon as Judas took the bread, Satan entered into him.

"What you are about to do, do quickly," Jesus told him, ²⁸but no one at the meal understood why Jesus said this to him. ²⁹Since Judas had charge of the money, some thought Jesus was telling him to buy what was needed for the Feast, or to give something to the poor. ³⁰As soon as Judas had taken the bread, he went out. And it was night.

Jesus Predicts Peter's Denial

³¹When he was gone, Jesus said, "Now is the Son of Man glorified and God is glorified in him. ³²If God is glorified in him,[b] God will glorify the Son in himself, and will glorify him at once.

³³"My children, I will be with you only a little longer. You will look for me, and just as I told the Jews, so I tell you now: Where I am going, you cannot come.

³⁴"A new command I give you: Love one another. As I have loved you, so you must love one another. ³⁵By this all men will know that you are my disciples, if you love one another."

³⁶Simon Peter asked him, "Lord, where are you going?"

Jesus replied, "Where I am going, you cannot follow now, but you will follow later."

³⁷Peter asked, "Lord, why can't I follow you now? I will lay down my life for you."

³⁸Then Jesus answered, "Will you really lay down your life for me? I tell you the truth, before the rooster crows, you will disown me three times!

---

[a] 18 Psalm 41:9   [b] 32 Many early manuscripts do not have *If God is glorified in him.*

Jesus Comforts His Disciples

14 "Do not let your hearts be troubled. Trust in God*a*; trust also in me. ²In my Father's house are many rooms; if it were not so, I would have told you. I am going there to prepare a place for you. ³And if I go and prepare a place for you, I will come back and take you to be with me that you also may be where I am. ⁴You know the way to the place where I am going."

Jesus the Way to the Father

⁵Thomas said to him, "Lord, we don't know where you are going, so how can we know the way?"

⁶Jesus answered, "I am the way and the truth and the life. No one comes to the Father except through me. ⁷If you really knew me, you would know*b* my Father as well. From now on, you do know him and have seen him."

⁸Philip said, "Lord, show us the Father and that will be enough for us."

⁹Jesus answered: "Don't you know me, Philip, even after I have been among you such a long time? Anyone who has seen me has seen the Father. How can you say, 'Show us the Father'? ¹⁰Don't you believe that I am in the Father, and that the Father is in me? The words I say to you are not just my own. Rather, it is the Father, living in me, who is doing his work. ¹¹Believe me when I say that I am in the Father and the Father is in me; or at least believe on the evidence of the miracles themselves. ¹²I tell you the truth, anyone who has faith in me will do what I have been doing. He will do even greater things than these, because I am going to the Father. ¹³And I will do whatever you ask in my name, so that the Son may bring glory to the Father. ¹⁴You may ask me for anything in my name, and I will do it.

Jesus Promises the Holy Spirit

¹⁵"If you love me, you will obey what I command. ¹⁶And I will ask the Father, and he will give you another Counselor to be with you forever— ¹⁷the Spirit of truth. The world cannot accept him, because it neither sees him nor knows him. But you know him, for he lives with you and will be*c* in you. ¹⁸I will not leave you as orphans; I will come to you. ¹⁹Before long, the world will not see me anymore, but you will see me. Because I live, you also will live. ²⁰On that day you will realize that I am in my Father, and you are in me, and I am in you. ²¹Whoever has my commands and obeys them, he is the one who loves me. He who loves me will be loved by my Father, and I too will love him and show myself to him."

²²Then Judas (not Judas Iscariot) said, "But, Lord, why do you intend to show yourself to us and not to the world?"

²³Jesus replied, "If anyone loves me, he will obey my teaching. My Father will love him, and we will come to him

Get a Load of This...

Jesus is "the way and the truth and the life" (John 14:6). When he died, that was the WAY for us to have our sins forgiven and become God's children. Everything Jesus taught was the TRUTH, and what he wants to give us is LIFE, now and for all eternity.

---

a 1 Or *You trust in God*   *b 7* Some early manuscripts *If you really have known me, you will know*   *c 17* Some early manuscripts *and is* and make our home with him. 24He who does not love me will not obey my teaching. These words you hear are not my own; they belong to the Father who sent me.

25"All this I have spoken while still with you. 26But the Counselor, the Holy Spirit, whom the Father will send in my name, will teach you all things and will remind you of everything I have said to you. 27Peace I leave with you; my peace I give you. I do not give to you as the world gives. Do not let your hearts be troubled and do not be afraid.

28"You heard me say, 'I am going away and I am coming back to you.' If you loved me, you would be glad that I am going to the Father, for the Father is greater than I. 29I have told you now before it happens, so that when it does happen you will believe. 30I will not speak with you much longer, for the prince of this world is coming. He has no hold on me, 31but the world must learn that I love the Father and that I do exactly what my Father has commanded me.

"Come now; let us leave.

The Vine and the Branches

"I am the true vine, and my Father is the gardener. 2He cuts off every branch in me that bears no fruit, while every branch that does bear fruit he prunes[a] so that it will be even more fruitful. 3You are already clean because of the word I have spoken to you. 4Remain in me, and I will remain in you. No branch can bear fruit by itself; it must remain in the vine. Neither can you bear fruit unless you remain in me.

5"I am the vine; you are the branches. If a man remains in me and I in him, he will bear much fruit; apart from me you can do nothing. 6If anyone does not remain in me, he is like a branch that is thrown away and withers; such branches are picked up, thrown into the fire and burned. 7If you remain in me and my words remain in you, ask whatever you wish, and it will be given you. 8This is to my Father's glory, that you bear much fruit, showing yourselves to be my disciples.

9"As the Father has loved me, so have I

---

a 2 The Greek for *prunes* also means *cleans*.

Choose Not to Worry

READ JOHN 14:1, 27

GET SMARTER

Ever watched one of those rescue shows where someone is stranded on top of a car in the middle of a flash flood? Usually a helicopter will try to rescue the person with a rope. But sometimes the person is so scared that he won't let go of the car to grab it! "How could he be so stupid?" you wonder. Know what? When you worry, you act just *like* that guy. Jesus offers peace, but you have to grab it. "Do not let your hearts be troubled," Jesus said. Easy enough when things are going well, but try it on for size when you're on top of that car. When the rope ladder swings your way, *grab* it and hold on for dear life! You want peace and not worry? Keep your mind focused on God (Isaiah 26:3) like a hand that grabs a rope and just won't let go.

Your next reading is on page 1400.

loved you. Now remain in my love. [10]If you obey my commands, you will remain in my love, just as I have obeyed my Father's commands and remain in his love. [11]I have told you this so that my joy may be in you and that your joy may be complete. [12]My command is this: Love each other as I have loved you. [13]Greater love has no one than this, that he lay down his life for his friends. [14]You are my friends if you do what I command. [15]I no longer call you servants, because a servant does not know his master's business. Instead, I have called you friends, for everything that I learned from my Father I have made known to you. [16]You did not choose me, but I chose you and appointed you to go and bear fruit—fruit that will last. Then the Father will give you whatever you ask in my name. [17]This is my command: Love each other.

The World Hates the Disciples

[18]"If the world hates you, keep in mind that it hated me first. [19]If you belonged to the world, it would love you as its own. As it is, you do not belong to the world, but I have chosen you out of the world. That is why the world hates you. [20]Remember the words I spoke to you: 'No servant is greater than his master.'[a] If they persecuted me, they will persecute you also. If they obeyed my teaching, they will obey yours also. [21]They will treat you this way because of my name, for they do not know the One who sent me. [22]If I had not come and spoken to them, they would not be guilty of sin. Now, however, they have no excuse for their sin. [23]He who hates me hates my Father as well. [24]If I had not done among them what no one else did, they would not be guilty of sin. But now they have seen these miracles, and yet they have hated both me and my Father. [25]But this is to fulfill what is written in their Law: 'They hated me without reason.'[b]

[26]"When the Counselor comes, whom I

[a] 20 John 13:16   [b] 25 Psalms 35:19; 69:4

READ JOHN 14:21–24

Some people are good at making Christianity sound REALLY complicated. Jesus was a pro at keeping it simple. In John 14:21–24, Jesus repeats the same message three times. Read these verses again. It's clear: If you love God, you'll obey Jesus' teachings. If you don't, you won't. Write down this simple formula so you won't forget it.

will send to you from the Father, the Spirit of truth who goes out from the Father, he will testify about me. 27And you also must testify, for you have been with me from the beginning.

16 "All this I have told you so that you will not go astray. 2They will put you out of the synagogue; in fact, a time is coming when anyone who kills you will think he is offering a service to God. 3They will do such things because they have not known the Father or me. 4I have told you this, so that when the time comes you will remember that I warned you. I did not tell you this at first because I was with you.

The Work of the Holy Spirit

5"Now I am going to him who sent me, yet none of you asks me, 'Where are you going?' 6Because I have said these things, you are filled with grief. 7But I tell you the truth: It is for your good that I am going away. Unless I go away, the Counselor will not come to you; but if I go, I will send him to you. 8When he comes, he will convict the world of guilt*a* in regard to sin and righteousness and judgment: 9in regard to sin, because men do not believe in me; 10in regard to righteousness, because I am going to the Father, where you can see me no longer; 11and in regard to judgment, because the prince of this world now stands condemned.

12"I have much more to say to you, more than you can now bear. 13But when he, the Spirit of truth, comes, he will guide you into all truth. He will not speak on his own; he will speak only what he hears, and he will tell you what is yet to come. 14He will bring glory to me by taking from what is mine and making it known to you. 15All that belongs to the Father is mine. That is why I said the Spirit will take from what is mine and make it known to you.

16"In a little while you will see me no more, and then after a little while you will see me."

The Disciples' Grief Will Turn to Joy

17Some of his disciples said to one another, "What does he mean by saying, 'In

a 8 Or will expose the guilt of the world

The Vine and Branches

READ JOHN 15:1–17

Think of a branch of a grape vine with a cluster of really delicious grapes hanging from it. How can that branch produce such great grapes? It's connected to the vine! The roots suck the nutrients out of the soil and slurp it up into the vine, and from there it's pumped to the branches. Jesus said, "I am the vine; you are the branches. If a man remains in me and I in him, he will bear much fruit" (verse 5). If a branch is cut off from the vine, it's finished. The secret is to stay connected to Jesus, spend time praying, reading God's Word and doing what it says. The great pianist, Jan Paderewski, said, "If I miss one day's practice, I notice it. If I miss two days, the critics notice it. (They would.) If I miss three days, the whole WORLD notices it." If you want to be the best you can be, spend time with God every day.

GET DEEPER

Your next reading is on page 1401.

a little while you will see me no more, and then after a little while you will see me,' and 'Because I am going to the Father'?" [18]They kept asking, "What does he mean by 'a little while'? We don't understand what he is saying."

[19]Jesus saw that they wanted to ask him about this, so he said to them, "Are you asking one another what I meant when I said, 'In a little while you will see me no more, and then after a little while you will see me'? [20]I tell you the truth, you will weep and mourn while the world rejoices. You will grieve, but your grief will turn to joy. [21]A woman giving birth to a child has pain because her time has come; but when her baby is born she forgets the anguish because of her joy that a child is born into the world. [22]So with you: Now is your time of grief, but I will see you again and you will rejoice, and no one will take away your joy. [23]In that day you will no longer ask me anything. I tell you the truth, my Father will give you whatever you ask in my name. [24]Until now you have not asked for anything in my name. Ask and you will receive, and your joy will be complete.

[25]"Though I have been speaking figuratively, a time is coming when I will no longer use this kind of language but will tell you plainly about my Father. [26]In that day you will ask in my name. I am not saying that I will ask the Father on your behalf. [27]No, the Father himself loves you because you have loved me and have believed that I came from God. [28]I came from the Father and entered the world; now I am leaving the world and going back to the Father."

[29]Then Jesus' disciples said, "Now you are speaking clearly and without figures of speech. [30]Now we can see that you know all things and that you do not even need to have anyone ask you questions. This makes us believe that you came from God."

[31]"You believe at last!"[a] Jesus answered. [32]"But a time is coming, and has come, when you will be scattered, each to his own home. You will leave me all alone. Yet I am not alone, for my Father is with me.

[a] 31 Or *"Do you now believe?"*

Fantastic Holy Spirit

READ JOHN 14:15–18, 25–26; 15:26–27; 16:7–16

For centuries people have referred to the Holy Spirit as the "Holy Ghost." Woooo! Scary, right? Not exactly someone you'd turn to for help——unless you were trying to come up with an award-winning Halloween costume! Actually, the meaning of words changes over time. The word "ghost" used to simply mean "spirit." The Holy Spirit is not a ghost in the way we think of that word today; he's God. Jesus, who is also God, sent the Holy Spirit to help us after he left. "When … the Spirit of truth, comes, he will guide you into all truth" (John 16:13). Like Jesus, the Holy Spirit teaches, guides and counsels us and helps us grow spiritually. He gives us the boldness and knowledge we need to talk to others about Christ (Acts 1:8). How do we get his help? Easy——asking God for it! "How much more will God give the Holy Spirit to those who ask him?" (see Luke 11:13). And the bonus is, when we obey God, we get even *more* of his Spirit!

Your next reading is on page 1402.

33 "I have told you these things, so that in me you may have peace. In this world you will have trouble. But take heart! I have overcome the world."

Jesus Prays for Himself

17 After Jesus said this, he looked toward heaven and prayed:

"Father, the time has come. Glorify your Son, that your Son may glorify you. 2 For you granted him authority over all people that he might give eternal life to all those you have given him. 3 Now this is eternal life: that they may know you, the only true God, and Jesus Christ, whom you have sent. 4 I have brought you glory on earth by completing the work you gave me to do. 5 And now, Father, glorify me in your presence with the glory I had with you before the world began.

Jesus Prays for His Disciples

6 "I have revealed you[a] to those whom you gave me out of the world.

They were yours; you gave them to me and they have obeyed your word. 7 Now they know that everything you have given me comes from you. 8 For I gave them the words you gave me and they accepted them. They knew with certainty that I came from you, and they believed that you sent me. 9 I pray for them. I am not praying for the world, but for those you have given me, for they are yours. 10 All I have is yours, and all you have is mine. And glory has come to me through them. 11 I will remain in the world no longer, but they are still in the world, and I am coming to you. Holy Father, protect them by the power of your name— the name you gave me—so that they may be one as we are one. 12 While I was with them, I protected them and kept them safe by that name you gave me. None has been lost except the one doomed to destruction so that Scripture would be fulfilled.

13 "I am coming to you now, but I

a 6 Greek *your name*; also in verse 26

Ask for Anything

READ JOHN 14:12–14; 15:7, 16; 16:23–26

Jesus said over and over again that the Father would do anything we asked. He would "graciously give us all things" (Romans 8:32). But … God is not some genie just waiting for you to rub his lamp with your hands. Jesus also said that if you loved the Father, you'd be obedient to anything he asked. Get the connection?—If you live God's way and desire the things he desires, then you won't be drooling over garbage. You won't be just trying to selfishly collect as many toys as you can. You'll want things that he wants you to want. (Check out 1 John 5:14–15 and you'll see!) When you ask him for things he already wants to give you, it's a no-brainer that he's going to say "yes." The "anything you ask for" promises are true. But first you need to have an understanding with God that you'll do anything *he* asks.

Your next reading is on page 1403.

say these things while I am still in the world, so that they may have the full measure of my joy within them. [14]I have given them your word and the world has hated them, for they are not of the world any more than I am of the world. [15]My prayer is not that you take them out of the world but that you protect them from the evil one. [16]They are not of the world, even as I am not of it. [17]Sanctify[a] them by the truth; your word is truth. [18]As you sent me into the world, I have sent them into the world. [19]For them I sanctify myself, that they too may be truly sanctified.

Jesus Prays for All Believers

[20]"My prayer is not for them alone. I pray also for those who will believe in me through their message, [21]that all of them may be one, Father, just as you are in me and I am in you. May they also be in us so that the world may believe that you have sent me. [22]I have given them the glory that you gave me, that they may be one as we are one: [23]I in them and you in me. May they be brought to complete unity to let the world know that you sent me and have loved them even as you have loved me.

[24]"Father, I want those you have given me to be with me where I am, and to see my glory, the glory you have given me because you loved me before the creation of the world.

[25]"Righteous Father, though the world does not know you, I know you, and they know that you have sent me. [26]I have made you known to them, and will continue to make you known in order that the love you have for me may be in them and that I myself may be in them."

Jesus Arrested

18 When he had finished praying, Jesus left with his disciples and crossed the Kidron Valley. On the other side there was an olive

[a] 17 Greek *hagiazo* (set apart for sacred use or make holy); also in verse 19

A New Command
READ JOHN 13:34–35; 17:20–23

Some Christians act like the two greatest commandments are to memorize Scripture and to tell everyone else how sinful they are. But according to Jesus, the two greatest commands are to love God and to love others (Matthew 22:37–39). "By this all men will know that you are my disciples, if you love one another" (John 13:35). Bible knowledge may impress some people, but most kids want a friend who understands where they're at and cares, not a Bible-thumping, Scripture-pumping session in a spiritual boxing ring. The best way for Christians to prove God exists is by loving, accepting and forgiving one another, even when it hurts—especially when it hurts! As a man of God, you need to make a commitment to love others so the world will know that we have the truth and that the God we serve loves and cares for them as well. So love others, no matter what the cost!

Your next reading is on page 1404.

grove, and he and his disciples went into it.

²Now Judas, who betrayed him, knew the place, because Jesus had often met there with his disciples. ³So Judas came to the grove, guiding a detachment of soldiers and some officials from the chief priests and Pharisees. They were carrying torches, lanterns and weapons.

⁴Jesus, knowing all that was going to happen to him, went out and asked them, "Who is it you want?"

⁵"Jesus of Nazareth," they replied.

"I am he," Jesus said. (And Judas the traitor was standing there with them.) ⁶When Jesus said, "I am he," they drew back and fell to the ground.

⁷Again he asked them, "Who is it you want?"

And they said, "Jesus of Nazareth."

⁸"I told you that I am he," Jesus answered. "If you are looking for me, then let these men go." ⁹This happened so that the words he had spoken would be ful-filled: "I have not lost one of those you gave me." ᵃ

¹⁰Then Simon Peter, who had a sword, drew it and struck the high priest's servant, cutting off his right ear. (The servant's name was Malchus.)

¹¹Jesus commanded Peter, "Put your sword away! Shall I not drink the cup the Father has given me?"

Jesus Taken to Annas

¹²Then the detachment of soldiers with its commander and the Jewish officials arrested Jesus. They bound him ¹³and brought him first to Annas, who was the father-in-law of Caiaphas, the high priest that year. ¹⁴Caiaphas was the one who had advised the Jews that it would be good if one man died for the people.

Peter's First Denial

¹⁵Simon Peter and another disciple were following Jesus. Because this disciple was

ᵃ 9 John 6:39

Ear-hacking Time!

READ JOHN 18:1–13

When the soldiers came to arrest Jesus, "Peter, who had a sword, drew it and struck the high priest's servant, cutting off his right ear" (verse 10). So much for Peter's fancy swordplay. He probably tried to cut off Malchus' head, not just his ear. Jesus said that if his kingdom was of this world, his servants would fight (John 18:36), and that's what Peter thought: "This is it! The time has come to fight! Charge!" But Pete's war was over in three seconds. Casualty: one ear. This was not the time for head chopping. Angels who were *good* with swords could've fought (Matthew 26:52–54), and it would've been cool to see, but it wasn't time. God had once been with Israel in military battles, but in the New Testament God's emphasis was on preaching salvation through Christ's death. There's still a battle, but now it's with the powers of evil in the spirit realm (Ephesians 6:11–12).

Your next reading is on page 1405.

GET STRONGER.

known to the high priest, he went with Jesus into the high priest's courtyard, [16]but Peter had to wait outside at the door. The other disciple, who was known to the high priest, came back, spoke to the girl on duty there and brought Peter in.

[17]"You are not one of his disciples, are you?" the girl at the door asked Peter.

He replied, "I am not."

[18]It was cold, and the servants and officials stood around a fire they had made to keep warm. Peter also was standing with them, warming himself.

The High Priest Questions Jesus

[19]Meanwhile, the high priest questioned Jesus about his disciples and his teaching.

[20]"I have spoken openly to the world," Jesus replied. "I always taught in synagogues or at the temple, where all the Jews come together. I said nothing in secret. [21]Why question me? Ask those who heard me. Surely they know what I said."

[22]When Jesus said this, one of the officials nearby struck him in the face. "Is this the way you answer the high priest?" he demanded.

[23]"If I said something wrong," Jesus replied, "testify as to what is wrong. But if I spoke the truth, why did you strike me?" [24]Then Annas sent him, still bound, to Caiaphas the high priest.[a]

Peter's Second and Third Denials

[25]As Simon Peter stood warming himself, he was asked, "You are not one of his disciples, are you?"

He denied it, saying, "I am not."

[26]One of the high priest's servants, a relative of the man whose ear Peter had cut off, challenged him, "Didn't I see you with him in the olive grove?" [27]Again Peter denied it, and at that moment a rooster began to crow.

[a] 24 Or (Now Annas had sent him, still bound, to Caiaphas the high priest.)

When You Fall

READ JOHN 18:15–18, 25–27; 21:1–17

Peter had proudly boasted to Jesus, "I will lay down my life for you!" Jesus said, "Will you really? . . . You will disown me three times" (John 13:37–38). Jesus wasn't permanently condemning Peter. Jesus knew Peter and how he would react. The Gospel of Luke tells us that Jesus also encouraged Peter that he'd later strengthen the other disciples (Luke 22:31–32). After Peter did disown Jesus, he was really beating himself up. That's probably why, after his resurrection, Jesus made a point of appearing to Peter privately (see Luke 24:34). Jesus later let Peter affirm his love for Jesus three times, just like he'd denied him three times (John 21:15–17). Christianity isn't about being perfect. God understands your weaknesses. He's there to help you grow, not to condemn you. God is not a prison guard waiting to blow the whistle on you. He's a friend waiting to help and heal you and teach you how to not fall the next time.

Your next reading is on page 1407.

Jesus Before Pilate

28Then the Jews led Jesus from Caiaphas to the palace of the Roman governor. By now it was early morning, and to avoid ceremonial uncleanness the Jews did not enter the palace; they wanted to be able to eat the Passover. 29So Pilate came out to them and asked, "What charges are you bringing against this man?"

30"If he were not a criminal," they replied, "we would not have handed him over to you."

31Pilate said, "Take him yourselves and judge him by your own law."

"But we have no right to execute anyone," the Jews objected. 32This happened so that the words Jesus had spoken indicating the kind of death he was going to die would be fulfilled.

33Pilate then went back inside the palace, summoned Jesus and asked him, "Are you the king of the Jews?"

34"Is that your own idea," Jesus asked, "or did others talk to you about me?"

35"Am I a Jew?" Pilate replied. "It was your people and your chief priests who handed you over to me. What is it you have done?"

36Jesus said, "My kingdom is not of this world. If it were, my servants would fight to prevent my arrest by the Jews. But now my kingdom is from another place."

37"You are a king, then!" said Pilate.

Jesus answered, "You are right in saying I am a king. In fact, for this reason I was born, and for this I came into the world, to testify to the truth. Everyone on the side of truth listens to me."

38"What is truth?" Pilate asked. With this he went out again to the Jews and said, "I find no basis for a charge against him. 39But it is your custom for me to release to you one prisoner at the time of the Passover. Do you want me to release 'the king of the Jews'?"

40They shouted back, "No, not him! Give us Barabbas!" Now Barabbas had taken part in a rebellion.

Jesus Sentenced to Be Crucified

19 Then Pilate took Jesus and had him flogged. 2The soldiers twisted together a crown of thorns and put it on his head. They clothed him in a purple robe 3and went up to him again and again, saying, "Hail, king of the Jews!" And they struck him in the face.

4Once more Pilate came out and said to the Jews, "Look, I am bringing him out to you to let you know that I find no basis for a charge against him." 5When Jesus came out wearing the crown of thorns and the purple robe, Pilate said to them, "Here is the man!"

6As soon as the chief priests and their officials saw him, they shouted, "Crucify! Crucify!"

But Pilate answered, "You take him and crucify him. As for me, I find no basis for a charge against him."

7The Jews insisted, "We have a law, and according to that law he must die, because he claimed to be the Son of God."

8When Pilate heard this, he was even more afraid, 9and he went back inside the palace. "Where do you come from?" he asked Jesus, but Jesus gave him no answer. 10"Do you refuse to speak to me?" Pilate said. "Don't you realize I have power either to free you or to crucify you?"

11Jesus answered, "You would have no power over me if it were not given to you from above. Therefore the one who handed me over to you is guilty of a greater sin."

12From then on, Pilate tried to set Jesus free, but the Jews kept shouting, "If you let this man go, you are no friend of Caesar. Anyone who claims to be a king opposes Caesar."

13When Pilate heard this, he brought Jesus out and sat down on the judge's seat at a place known as the Stone Pavement (which in Aramaic is Gabbatha). 14It was the day of Preparation of Passover Week, about the sixth hour.

"Here is your king," Pilate said to the Jews.

15But they shouted, "Take him away! Take him away! Crucify him!"

"Shall I crucify your king?" Pilate asked.

"We have no king but Caesar," the chief priests answered.

16Finally Pilate handed him over to them to be crucified.

The Crucifixion

So the soldiers took charge of Jesus. 17Carrying his own cross, he went out to the place of the Skull (which in Aramaic is called Golgotha). 18Here they crucified him, and with him two others—one on each side and Jesus in the middle.

19Pilate had a notice prepared and fastened to the cross. It read: JESUS OF NAZARETH, THE KING OF THE JEWS. 20Many of the Jews read this sign, for the place where Jesus was crucified was near the city, and the sign was written in Aramaic, Latin and Greek. 21The chief priests of the Jews protested to Pilate, "Do not write 'The King of the Jews,' but that this man claimed to be king of the Jews."

22Pilate answered, "What I have written, I have written."

23When the soldiers crucified Jesus, they took his clothes, dividing them into four shares, one for each of them, with the undergarment remaining. This garment was seamless, woven in one piece from top to bottom.

24"Let's not tear it," they said to one another. "Let's decide by lot who will get it."

This happened that the scripture might be fulfilled which said,

"They divided my garments among them
    and cast lots for my clothing."[a]

So this is what the soldiers did.

25Near the cross of Jesus stood his mother, his mother's sister, Mary the wife of Clopas, and Mary Magdalene. 26When Jesus saw his mother there, and the disciple whom he loved standing nearby, he said to his mother, "Dear woman, here is your son," 27and to the disciple, "Here is your mother." From that time on, this disciple took her into his home.

The Death of Jesus

28Later, knowing that all was now completed, and so that the Scripture would be fulfilled, Jesus said, "I am thirsty." 29A jar of wine vinegar was there, so they soaked a sponge in it, put the sponge on a stalk of the hyssop plant, and lifted it to Jesus' lips. 30When he had received the drink, Jesus said, "It is finished." With that, he bowed his head and gave up his spirit.

a 24 Psalm 22:18

Everyone Chooses Sides

READ JOHN 18:28—19:16

When the heat was on, everyone chose sides—for or against Jesus. Judas chose to betray him. Pilate tried to set Jesus free, but finally caved in to the pressure of Jesus' accusers and gave the order for him to be crucified (John 19:12, 16). King Herod? "Herod . . . ridiculed and mocked him" (Luke 23:11) and dressed him in a fancy robe as a joke. The Jewish religious leaders shouted for Jesus to be crucified, but one of them, Joseph of Arimathea, "had not consented to their decision and action" (Luke 23:51) and took a stand for Jesus. The Roman soldiers? They mocked and beat Jesus. But one of them said, "Surely this man was the Son of God!" (Mark 15:39). Even the two thieves made different decisions: one insulted Jesus, the other stood up for him (Luke 23:39–43). People were totally divided over Jesus. The way that each person responded to Jesus said who they were as a person, and determined their eternal destination. How do you respond to Jesus?

Your next reading is on page 1410.

³¹Now it was the day of Preparation, and the next day was to be a special Sabbath. Because the Jews did not want the bodies left on the crosses during the Sabbath, they asked Pilate to have the legs broken and the bodies taken down. ³²The soldiers therefore came and broke the legs of the first man who had been crucified with Jesus, and then those of the other. ³³But when they came to Jesus and found that he was already dead, they did not break his legs. ³⁴Instead, one of the soldiers pierced Jesus' side with a spear, bringing a sudden flow of blood and water. ³⁵The man who saw it has given testimony, and his testimony is true. He knows that he tells the truth, and he testifies so that you also may believe. ³⁶These things happened so that the scripture would be fulfilled: "Not one of his bones will be broken,"ᵃ ³⁷and, as another scripture says, "They will look on the one they have pierced."ᵇ

The Burial of Jesus

³⁸Later, Joseph of Arimathea asked Pilate for the body of Jesus. Now Joseph was a disciple of Jesus, but secretly because he feared the Jews. With Pilate's permission, he came and took the body away. ³⁹He was accompanied by Nicodemus, the man who earlier had visited Jesus at night. Nicodemus brought a mixture of myrrh and aloes, about seventy-five pounds.ᶜ ⁴⁰Taking Jesus' body, the two of them wrapped it, with the spices, in strips of linen. This was in accordance with Jewish burial customs. ⁴¹At the place where Jesus was crucified, there was a garden, and in the garden a new tomb, in which no one had ever been laid. ⁴²Because it was the Jewish day of Preparation and since the tomb was nearby, they laid Jesus there.

ᵃ 36 Exodus 12:46; Num. 9:12; Psalm 34:20
ᵇ 37 Zech. 12:10   ᶜ 39 Greek a hundred litrai (about 34 kilograms)

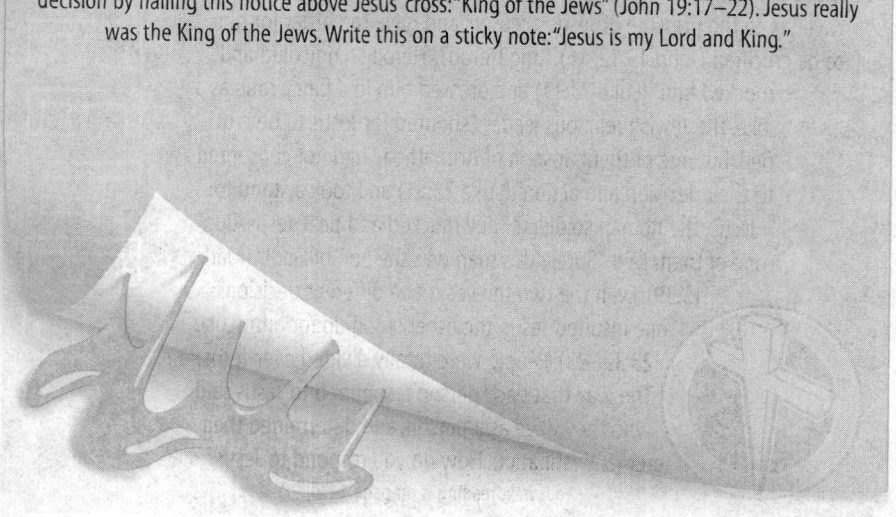

Make It Stick

READ JOHN 19:17–22

Pilate knew that Jesus was innocent. But there had to be an official charge against Jesus, so Pilate took advantage of an opportunity to get back at the Jewish leaders for forcing him into this decision by nailing this notice above Jesus' cross: "King of the Jews" (John 19:17–22). Jesus really was the King of the Jews. Write this on a sticky note: "Jesus is my Lord and King."

The Empty Tomb

20 Early on the first day of the week, while it was still dark, Mary Magdalene went to the tomb and saw that the stone had been removed from the entrance. ²So she came running to Simon Peter and the other disciple, the one Jesus loved, and said, "They have taken the Lord out of the tomb, and we don't know where they have put him!"

³So Peter and the other disciple started for the tomb. ⁴Both were running, but the other disciple outran Peter and reached the tomb first. ⁵He bent over and looked in at the strips of linen lying there but did not go in. ⁶Then Simon Peter, who was behind him, arrived and went into the tomb. He saw the strips of linen lying there, ⁷as well as the burial cloth that had been around Jesus' head. The cloth was folded up by itself, separate from the linen. ⁸Finally the other disciple, who had reached the tomb first, also went inside. He saw and believed. ⁹(They still did not understand from Scripture that Jesus had to rise from the dead.)

Jesus Appears to Mary Magdalene

¹⁰Then the disciples went back to their homes, ¹¹but Mary stood outside the tomb crying. As she wept, she bent over to look into the tomb ¹²and saw two angels in white, seated where Jesus' body had been, one at the head and the other at the foot.

¹³They asked her, "Woman, why are you crying?"

"They have taken my Lord away," she said, "and I don't know where they have put him." ¹⁴At this, she turned around and saw Jesus standing there, but she did not realize that it was Jesus.

¹⁵"Woman," he said, "why are you crying? Who is it you are looking for?"

Thinking he was the gardener, she said, "Sir, if you have carried him away, tell me where you have put him, and I will get him."

¹⁶Jesus said to her, "Mary."

She turned toward him and cried out in Aramaic, "Rabboni!" (which means Teacher).

¹⁷Jesus said, "Do not hold on to me, for I have not yet returned to the Father. Go instead to my brothers and tell them, 'I am returning to my Father and your Father, to my God and your God.' "

¹⁸Mary Magdalene went to the disciples with the news: "I have seen the Lord!" And she told them that he had said these things to her.

Jesus Appears to His Disciples

¹⁹On the evening of that first day of the week, when the disciples were together, with the doors locked for fear of the Jews, Jesus came and stood among them and said, "Peace be with you!" ²⁰After he said this, he showed them his hands and side. The disciples were overjoyed when they saw the Lord.

Gross!

Check out John 19:23–24. Can you imagine sitting in an execution chamber gambling to get the victim's clothes while he's waiting to get fried? That's basically what the Roman soldiers did while Jesus was on the cross. It fulfilled a prophecy (Psalm 22:18) and was the ultimate insult, as if what Jesus was going through didn't even matter.

²¹Again Jesus said, "Peace be with you! As the Father has sent me, I am sending you." ²²And with that he breathed on them and said, "Receive the Holy Spirit. ²³If you forgive anyone his sins, they are forgiven; if you do not forgive them, they are not forgiven."

Jesus Appears to Thomas

²⁴Now Thomas (called Didymus), one of the Twelve, was not with the disciples when Jesus came. ²⁵So the other disciples told him, "We have seen the Lord!"

But he said to them, "Unless I see the nail marks in his hands and put my finger where the nails were, and put my hand into his side, I will not believe it."

²⁶A week later his disciples were in the house again, and Thomas was with them. Though the doors were locked, Jesus came and stood among them and said, "Peace be with you!" ²⁷Then he said to Thomas, "Put your finger here; see my hands. Reach out your hand and put it into my side. Stop doubting and believe."

²⁸Thomas said to him, "My Lord and my God!"

²⁹Then Jesus told him, "Because you have seen me, you have believed; blessed are those who have not seen and yet have believed."

³⁰Jesus did many other miraculous signs in the presence of his disciples, which are not recorded in this book. ³¹But these are written that you may*ᵃ* believe that Jesus is the Christ, the Son of God, and that by believing you may have life in his name.

Jesus and the Miraculous Catch of Fish

Afterward Jesus appeared again to his disciples, by the Sea of Tiberias.*ᵇ* It happened this way: ²Simon Peter, Thomas (called Didymus), Nathanael from Cana in Galilee, the sons of Zebedee, and two other disciples were together. ³"I'm going out to fish," Simon Peter told them, and they said, "We'll go with you." So they went out and got into the boat, but that night they caught nothing.

ᵃ 31 Some manuscripts *may continue to*   *ᵇ 1* That is, Sea of Galilee

---

Jesus Is Back

READ JOHN 20:1–31

After Jesus' death, the eleven apostles—Jesus' closest friends—were emotionally smashed. Jesus understood their grief and he slowly prepared them before revealing himself fully. After he raised up from the dead, he didn't just appear and say, "Hey guys, I'm back!" First he told them through the angels, then he told the women, then he appeared to two men on the road to Emmaus. Finally "Jesus came and stood among the apostles and said, 'Peace be with you!'" (John 20:19). It still scared them (see Luke 24:37), but not like if he had just shown up without warning. In the same way, when you ask God to help you grow, he doesn't give you a short, sharp shock and take you the limit overnight. So don't be afraid to ask God to make you into a better person. He won't strap you to a rocket to make you more heavenly. He'll get you there at a speed you can handle.

Your next reading is on page 1413.

4Early in the morning, Jesus stood on the shore, but the disciples did not realize that it was Jesus.

5He called out to them, "Friends, haven't you any fish?"

"No," they answered.

6He said, "Throw your net on the right side of the boat and you will find some." When they did, they were unable to haul the net in because of the large number of fish.

7Then the disciple whom Jesus loved said to Peter, "It is the Lord!" As soon as Simon Peter heard him say, "It is the Lord," he wrapped his outer garment around him (for he had taken it off) and jumped into the water. 8The other disciples followed in the boat, towing the net full of fish, for they were not far from shore, about a hundred yards.ᵃ 9When they landed, they saw a fire of burning coals there with fish on it, and some bread.

10Jesus said to them, "Bring some of the fish you have just caught."

11Simon Peter climbed aboard and dragged the net ashore. It was full of large fish, 153, but even with so many the net was not torn. 12Jesus said to them, "Come and have breakfast." None of the disciples dared ask him, "Who are you?" They knew it was the Lord. 13Jesus came, took the bread and gave it to them, and did the same with the fish. 14This was now the third time Jesus appeared to his disciples after he was raised from the dead.

Jesus Reinstates Peter

15When they had finished eating, Jesus said to Simon Peter, "Simon son of John, do you truly love me more than these?"

"Yes, Lord," he said, "you know that I love you."

Jesus said, "Feed my lambs."

16Again Jesus said, "Simon son of John, do you truly love me?"

He answered, "Yes, Lord, you know that I love you."

Jesus said, "Take care of my sheep."

17The third time he said to him, "Simon son of John, do you love me?"

Peter was hurt because Jesus asked him the third time, "Do you love me?" He said, "Lord, you know all things; you know that I love you."

Jesus said, "Feed my sheep. 18I tell you the truth, when you were younger you dressed yourself and went where you wanted; but when you are old you will stretch out your hands, and someone else will dress you and lead you where you do not want to go." 19Jesus said this to indicate the kind of death by which Peter would glorify God. Then he said to him, "Follow me!"

20Peter turned and saw that the disciple whom Jesus loved was following them. (This was the one who had leaned back against Jesus at the supper and had said, "Lord, who is going to betray you?") 21When Peter saw him, he asked, "Lord, what about him?"

22Jesus answered, "If I want him to remain alive until I return, what is that to you? You must follow me." 23Because of this, the rumor spread among the brothers that this disciple would not die. But Jesus did not say that he would not die; he only said, "If I want him to remain alive until I return, what is that to you?"

24This is the disciple who testifies to these things and who wrote them down. We know that his testimony is true.

25Jesus did many other things as well. If every one of them were written down, I suppose that even the whole world would not have room for the books that would be written.

ᵃ 8 Greek about two hundred cubits (about 90 meters)

ACTS

Who wrote this book?

Luke, the physician who traveled as a missionary with Paul, wrote this book.

Why was this book written?

Acts tells how the Christian faith spread to the whole world.

For whom was this book written?

Acts was written for everyone who wants to know what happened after Jesus returned to heaven.

What people are important in this book?

The most important people in this book are Peter and Paul.

When did this happen?

This book tells what happened from about A.D. 30 to 61.

Where did this happen?

The events in this book happened in many important cities in the Roman Empire.

What are some of the stories in this book?

Jesus goes to heaven	Acts 1:1–11
The Holy Spirit comes	Acts 2:1–13
Peter heals a beggar	Acts 3:1–10
Peter and John are arrested	Acts 4:1–31
Ananias and Sapphira lie	Acts 5:1–11
Stephen, the first martyr	Acts 6:8—7:60
Saul is converted	Acts 9:1–31
Peter has a vision	Acts 10:1–48
Peter escapes from prison	Acts 12:1–19
Prisoners are freed	Acts 16:16–40
A riot in Ephesus	Acts 19:23–41
Paul goes on trial	Acts 24:1–27
Paul is shipwrecked	Acts 27:1–44
Paul goes to Rome	Acts 28:1–31

Jesus Taken Up Into Heaven

1 In my former book, Theophilus, I wrote about all that Jesus began to do and to teach ²until the day he was taken up to heaven, after giving instructions through the Holy Spirit to the apostles he had chosen. ³After his suffering, he showed himself to these men and gave many convincing proofs that he was alive. He appeared to them over a period of forty days and spoke about the kingdom of God. ⁴On one occasion, while he was eating with them, he gave them this command: "Do not leave Jerusalem, but wait for the gift my Father promised, which you have heard me speak about. ⁵For John baptized with*ᵃ* water, but in a few days you will be baptized with the Holy Spirit."

⁶So when they met together, they asked him, "Lord, are you at this time going to restore the kingdom to Israel?"

⁷He said to them: "It is not for you to know the times or dates the Father has set by his own authority. ⁸But you will receive power when the Holy Spirit comes on you; and you will be my witnesses in Jerusalem, and in all Judea and Samaria, and to the ends of the earth."

⁹After he said this, he was taken up before their very eyes, and a cloud hid him from their sight.

¹⁰They were looking intently up into the sky as he was going, when suddenly two men dressed in white stood beside them. ¹¹"Men of Galilee," they said, "why do you stand here looking into the sky? This same Jesus, who has been taken from you into heaven, will come back in the same way you have seen him go into heaven."

Matthias Chosen to Replace Judas

¹²Then they returned to Jerusalem from the hill called the Mount of Olives, a Sabbath day's walk*ᵇ* from the city. ¹³When they arrived, they went upstairs to the room where they were staying. Those present were Peter, John, James and Andrew; Philip and Thomas, Bartholomew and Matthew; James son of Alphaeus and

ᵃ 5 Or *in*   *ᵇ 12* That is, about 3/4 mile (about 1,100 meters)

Convincing Proofs

READ ACTS 1:1–11

"After his suffering, [Jesus] showed himself to these men and gave many convincing proofs that he was alive" (verse 3). Wow! Wouldn't you have liked to have seen those proofs? They sure convinced the disciples, who went from hiding like chickens behind locked doors to boldly confronting the chief priests! If Jesus' resurrection was a hoax like some sceptics say, the apostles would've been risking their lives for nothing. Worse, they would have been liars and hypocrites if they'd said, "We *know* Jesus is alive! We've seen him!" but were just pretending. Their enemies were right there listening, too. If Jesus' body *was* still around, they would have dragged it out and shown it to everybody. But even they had to admit that the body was gone (see Matthew 28:2–3, 11–15). Conclusion? Jesus *did* rise from the dead, the apostles *saw* him, and he *proved* to them that he was the real article!

Your next reading is on page 1416.

Simon the Zealot, and Judas son of James. ¹⁴They all joined together constantly in prayer, along with the women and Mary the mother of Jesus, and with his brothers.

¹⁵In those days Peter stood up among the believers[a] (a group numbering about a hundred and twenty) ¹⁶and said, "Brothers, the Scripture had to be fulfilled which the Holy Spirit spoke long ago through the mouth of David concerning Judas, who served as guide for those who arrested Jesus— ¹⁷he was one of our number and shared in this ministry."

¹⁸(With the reward he got for his wickedness, Judas bought a field; there he fell headlong, his body burst open and all his intestines spilled out. ¹⁹Everyone in Jerusalem heard about this, so they called that field in their language Akeldama, that is, Field of Blood.)

²⁰"For," said Peter, "it is written in the book of Psalms,

" 'May his place be deserted;
    let there be no one to dwell in it,'[b]

and,

" 'May another take his place of
    leadership.'[c]

²¹Therefore it is necessary to choose one of the men who have been with us the whole time the Lord Jesus went in and out among us, ²²beginning from John's baptism to the time when Jesus was taken up from us. For one of these must become a witness with us of his resurrection."

²³So they proposed two men: Joseph called Barsabbas (also known as Justus) and Matthias. ²⁴Then they prayed, "Lord, you know everyone's heart. Show us which of these two you have chosen ²⁵to take over this apostolic ministry, which Judas left to go where he belongs." ²⁶Then they cast lots, and the lot fell to Matthias; so he was added to the eleven apostles.

The Holy Spirit Comes at Pentecost

When the day of Pentecost came, they were all together in one place. ²Suddenly a sound like the blowing of a violent wind came from heaven and filled the whole house where they were sitting. ³They saw what seemed to be tongues of fire that separated and came to rest on each of them. ⁴All of them were filled with the Holy Spirit and began to speak in other tongues[d] as the Spirit enabled them.

⁵Now there were staying in Jerusalem God-fearing Jews from every nation under heaven. ⁶When they heard this sound, a crowd came together in bewilderment, because each one heard them speaking in his own language. ⁷Utterly amazed, they asked: "Are not all these men who are speaking Galileans? ⁸Then how is it that each of us hears them in his own native language? ⁹Parthians, Medes and Elamites; residents of Mesopotamia, Judea and Cappadocia, Pontus and Asia, ¹⁰Phrygia and Pamphylia, Egypt and the parts of Libya near Cyrene; visitors from Rome ¹¹(both Jews and converts to Judaism); Cretans and Arabs—we hear them declaring the wonders of God in our own tongues!" ¹²Amazed and perplexed, they asked one another, "What does this mean?"

¹³Some, however, made fun of them and said, "They have had too much wine.[e]"

Peter Addresses the Crowd

¹⁴Then Peter stood up with the Eleven, raised his voice and addressed the crowd: "Fellow Jews and all of you who live in Jerusalem, let me explain this to you; listen carefully to what I say. ¹⁵These men are not drunk, as you suppose. It's only nine in the morning! ¹⁶No, this is what was spoken by the prophet Joel:

¹⁷" 'In the last days, God says,
    I will pour out my Spirit on all people.
  Your sons and daughters will prophesy,
    your young men will see visions,
    your old men will dream dreams.
¹⁸Even on my servants, both men and
        women,
    I will pour out my Spirit in those days,
    and they will prophesy.
¹⁹I will show wonders in the heaven above
    and signs on the earth below,
    blood and fire and billows of smoke.
²⁰The sun will be turned to darkness
    and the moon to blood
    before the coming of the great and
        glorious day of the Lord.
²¹ And everyone who calls
    on the name of the Lord will be
        saved.'[f]

---

a 15 Greek brothers   b 20 Psalm 69:25
c 20 Psalm 109:8   d 4 Or languages; also in verse 11
e 13 Or sweet wine   f 21 Joel 2:28–32

22"Men of Israel, listen to this: Jesus of Nazareth was a man accredited by God to you by miracles, wonders and signs, which God did among you through him, as you yourselves know. 23This man was handed over to you by God's set purpose and foreknowledge; and you, with the help of wicked men,ᵃ put him to death by nailing him to the cross. 24But God raised him from the dead, freeing him from the agony of death, because it was impossible for death to keep its hold on him. 25David said about him:

" 'I saw the Lord always before me.
    Because he is at my right hand,
    I will not be shaken.
26Therefore my heart is glad and my
        tongue rejoices;
    my body also will live in hope,
27because you will not abandon me to
        the grave,
    nor will you let your Holy One see
        decay.

28You have made known to me the
        paths of life;
    you will fill me with joy in your
        presence.' ᵇ

29"Brothers, I can tell you confidently that the patriarch David died and was buried, and his tomb is here to this day. 30But he was a prophet and knew that God had promised him on oath that he would place one of his descendants on his throne. 31Seeing what was ahead, he spoke of the resurrection of the Christ,ᶜ that he was not abandoned to the grave, nor did his body see decay. 32God has raised this Jesus to life, and we are all witnesses of the fact. 33Exalted to the right hand of God, he has received from the Father the promised Holy Spirit and has poured out what you now see and hear.

ᵃ 23 Or of those not having the law (that is, Gentiles)
ᵇ 28 Psalm 16:8–11   ᶜ 31 Or Messiah. "The Christ" (Greek) and "the Messiah" (Hebrew) both mean "the Anointed One"; also in verse 36.

Make It Stick

READ ACTS 2:4–11

In Acts 2:4–11, the disciples spoke languages they'd never learned, and all the people who heard them—no matter what languages those people spoke—understood them! The disciples didn't even need a fancy Star Trek translator device. On a sticky note, write a word from a foreign language (example: taco).

³⁴For David did not ascend to heaven, and yet he said,

" 'The Lord said to my Lord:
  "Sit at my right hand
³⁵until I make your enemies
  a footstool for your feet." '^a

³⁶"Therefore let all Israel be assured of this: God has made this Jesus, whom you crucified, both Lord and Christ."

³⁷When the people heard this, they were cut to the heart and said to Peter and the other apostles, "Brothers, what shall we do?"

³⁸Peter replied, "Repent and be baptized, every one of you, in the name of Jesus Christ for the forgiveness of your sins. And you will receive the gift of the Holy Spirit. ³⁹The promise is for you and your children and for all who are far off—for all whom the Lord our God will call."

⁴⁰With many other words he warned them; and he pleaded with them, "Save yourselves from this corrupt generation." ⁴¹Those who accepted his message were baptized, and about three thousand were added to their number that day.

The Fellowship of the Believers

⁴²They devoted themselves to the apostles' teaching and to the fellowship, to the breaking of bread and to prayer. ⁴³Everyone was filled with awe, and many wonders and miraculous signs were done by the apostles. ⁴⁴All the believers were together and had everything in common. ⁴⁵Selling their possessions and goods, they gave to anyone as he had need. ⁴⁶Every day they continued to meet together in the temple courts. They broke bread in their homes and ate together with glad and sincere hearts, ⁴⁷praising God and enjoying the favor of all the people. And the Lord added to their number daily those who were being saved.

Peter Heals the Crippled Beggar

3 One day Peter and John were going up to the temple at the time of prayer—at three in the afternoon. ²Now a man crippled from birth was being carried to the temple gate called Beautiful, where he was put every

^a 35 Psalm 110:1

Everybody Gets Zapped

READ ACTS 2:1–21, 37–41

When you were two years old, you couldn't go on *any* of the fun rides at the fair. They were only for *big* boys. You probably bawled your eyes out. But cheer up. *Now* you can do lots of cool rides! Long ago, it was similar with God's Holy Spirit—only kings and prophets got zapped with the Spirit. But Joel prophesied, "In the last days, God says, I will pour out my Spirit on all people" (Acts 2:17). Now the anointing of the Holy Spirit is upon all believers! Everybody gets zapped (see Romans 8:9)! Not necessarily to part the Jordan River or call down fire from heaven, but for God to work in our lives. When we became Christians, "God sent the Spirit of his Son into our hearts" (Galatians 4:6). The Holy Spirit gives us power to live a Christian life and to share the gospel with others (Acts 1:8).

Your next reading is on page 1422.

day to beg from those going into the temple courts. ³When he saw Peter and John about to enter, he asked them for money. ⁴Peter looked straight at him, as did John. Then Peter said, "Look at us!" ⁵So the man gave them his attention, expecting to get something from them.

⁶Then Peter said, "Silver or gold I do not have, but what I have I give you. In the name of Jesus Christ of Nazareth, walk." ⁷Taking him by the right hand, he helped him up, and instantly the man's feet and ankles became strong. ⁸He jumped to his feet and began to walk. Then he went with them into the temple courts, walking and jumping, and praising God. ⁹When all the people saw him walking and praising God, ¹⁰they recognized him as the same man who used to sit begging at the temple gate called Beautiful, and they were filled with wonder and amazement at what had happened to him.

Peter Speaks to the Onlookers

¹¹While the beggar held on to Peter and John, all the people were astonished and came running to them in the place called Solomon's Colonnade. ¹²When Peter saw this, he said to them: "Men of Israel, why does this surprise you? Why do you stare at us as if by our own power or godliness we had made this man walk? ¹³The God of Abraham, Isaac and Jacob, the God of our fathers, has glorified his servant Jesus. You handed him over to be killed, and you disowned him before Pilate, though he had decided to let him go. ¹⁴You disowned the Holy and Righteous One and asked that a murderer be released to you. ¹⁵You killed the author of life, but God raised him from the dead. We are witnesses of this. ¹⁶By faith in the name of Jesus, this man whom you see and know was made strong. It is Jesus' name and the faith that comes through

Make It Stick

READ ACTS 2:42–47

The early Christians were super united! They spent every spare minute with other believers—learning, witnessing, praying, praising God and talking to their new friends about their faith. What do you like about getting together with your Christian friends? Write it on a sticky note.

him that has given this complete healing to him, as you can all see.

¹⁷"Now, brothers, I know that you acted in ignorance, as did your leaders. ¹⁸But this is how God fulfilled what he had foretold through all the prophets, saying that his Christ^a would suffer. ¹⁹Repent, then, and turn to God, so that your sins may be wiped out, that times of refreshing may come from the Lord, ²⁰and that he may send the Christ, who has been appointed for you—even Jesus. ²¹He must remain in heaven until the time comes for God to restore everything, as he promised long ago through his holy prophets. ²²For Moses said, 'The Lord your God will raise up for you a prophet like me from among your own people; you must listen to everything he tells you. ²³Anyone who does not listen to him will be completely cut off from among his people.'^b

²⁴"Indeed, all the prophets from Samuel on, as many as have spoken, have foretold these days. ²⁵And you are heirs of the prophets and of the covenant God made with your fathers. He said to Abraham, 'Through your offspring all peoples on earth will be blessed.'^c ²⁶When God raised up his servant, he sent him first to you to bless you by turning each of you from your wicked ways."

Peter and John Before the Sanhedrin

The priests and the captain of the temple guard and the Sadducees came up to Peter and John while they were speaking to the people. ²They were greatly disturbed because the apostles were teaching the people and proclaiming in Jesus the resurrection of the dead. ³They seized Peter and John, and because it was evening, they put them in jail until the next day. ⁴But many who heard the message believed, and the number of men grew to about five thousand.

⁵The next day the rulers, elders and teachers of the law met in Jerusalem. ⁶Annas the high priest was there, and so were Caiaphas, John, Alexander and the other men of the high priest's family. ⁷They had Peter and John brought before them and began to question them: "By what power or what name did you do this?"

⁸Then Peter, filled with the Holy Spirit, said to them: "Rulers and elders of the people! ⁹If we are being called to account today for an act of kindness shown to a cripple and are asked how he was healed, ¹⁰then know this, you and all the people of Israel: It is by the name of Jesus Christ of Nazareth, whom you crucified but whom God raised from the dead, that this man stands before you healed. ¹¹He is

" 'the stone you builders rejected,
which has become the capstone.^{d' e}

¹²Salvation is found in no one else, for there is no other name under heaven given to men by which we must be saved."

¹³When they saw the courage of Peter and John and realized that they were unschooled, ordinary men, they were astonished and they took note that these men had been with Jesus. ¹⁴But since they could see the man who had been healed standing there with them, there was nothing they could say. ¹⁵So they ordered them to withdraw from the Sanhedrin and then conferred together. ¹⁶"What are we going to do with these men?" they asked. "Everybody living in Jerusalem knows they have done an outstanding miracle, and we cannot deny it. ¹⁷But to stop this thing from spreading any further among the people, we must warn these men to speak no longer to anyone in this name."

¹⁸Then they called them in again and commanded them not to speak or teach at all in the name of Jesus. ¹⁹But Peter and John replied, "Judge for yourselves whether it is right in God's sight to obey you rather than God. ²⁰For we cannot help speaking about what we have seen and heard."

²¹After further threats they let them go. They could not decide how to punish them, because all the people were praising God for what had happened. ²²For the man who was miraculously healed was over forty years old.

The Believers' Prayer

²³On their release, Peter and John went back to their own people and reported all that the chief priests and elders had said to them. ²⁴When they heard this, they raised their voices together in prayer to God. "Sovereign Lord," they said, "you made the heaven and the earth and the sea, and everything in them. ²⁵You spoke by the Holy Spirit through the mouth of your servant, our father David:

---

^a 18 Or Messiah; also in verse 20   ^b 23 Deut. 18:15,18,19   ^c 25 Gen. 22:18; 26:4   ^d 11 Or cornerstone   ^e 11 Psalm 118:22

" 'Why do the nations rage
   and the peoples plot in vain?
²⁶The kings of the earth take their stand
   and the rulers gather together
against the Lord
   and against his Anointed One.ª'ᵇ

²⁷Indeed Herod and Pontius Pilate met together with the Gentiles and the peopleᶜ of Israel in this city to conspire against your holy servant Jesus, whom you anointed. ²⁸They did what your power and will had decided beforehand should happen. ²⁹Now, Lord, consider their threats and enable your servants to speak your word with great boldness. ³⁰Stretch out your hand to heal and perform miraculous signs and wonders through the name of your holy servant Jesus."

³¹After they prayed, the place where they were meeting was shaken. And they were all filled with the Holy Spirit and spoke the word of God boldly.

The Believers Share Their Possessions

³²All the believers were one in heart and mind. No one claimed that any of his possessions was his own, but they shared everything they had. ³³With great power the apostles continued to testify to the resurrection of the Lord Jesus, and much grace was upon them all. ³⁴There were no needy persons among them. For from time to time those who owned lands or houses sold them, brought the money from the sales ³⁵and put it at the apostles' feet, and it was distributed to anyone as he had need.

³⁶Joseph, a Levite from Cyprus, whom the apostles called Barnabas (which means Son of Encouragement), ³⁷sold a field he owned and brought the money and put it at the apostles' feet.

Ananias and Sapphira

5 Now a man named Ananias, together with his wife Sapphira, also sold a piece of property. ²With his wife's full knowledge he kept back part of the money for himself, but brought the rest and put it at the apostles' feet.

³Then Peter said, "Ananias, how is it that Satan has so filled your heart that you have lied to the Holy Spirit and have kept for yourself some of the money you received for the land? ⁴Didn't it belong to you before it was sold? And after it was sold, wasn't the money at your disposal? What made you think of doing such a thing? You have not lied to men but to God."

⁵When Ananias heard this, he fell down and died. And great fear seized all who heard what had happened. ⁶Then the young men came forward, wrapped up his body, and carried him out and buried him.

⁷About three hours later his wife came in, not knowing what had happened. ⁸Peter asked her, "Tell me, is this the price you and Ananias got for the land?"

"Yes," she said, "that is the price."

In Acts 4:29, the Christians prayed for boldness to witness their faith to others. "After they prayed, the place were they were meeting was shaken" (verse 31). Whoa! God hit the house with a Holy Spirit earthquake.

ª 26 That is, Christ or Messiah   ᵇ 26 Psalm 2:1,2   ᶜ 27 The Greek is plural.

Get a Load of This...

Ananias and Sapphira lied to God's Spirit, and they dropped down *dead* (see Acts 5:1–11)! Talk about a face plant! Now, you probably won't die on the spot if you tell a lie, but there's a mega-lesson here: show respect to the Spirit of God.

⁹Peter said to her, "How could you agree to test the Spirit of the Lord? Look! The feet of the men who buried your husband are at the door, and they will carry you out also."

¹⁰At that moment she fell down at his feet and died. Then the young men came in and, finding her dead, carried her out and buried her beside her husband. ¹¹Great fear seized the whole church and all who heard about these events.

The Apostles Heal Many

¹²The apostles performed many miraculous signs and wonders among the people. And all the believers used to meet together in Solomon's Colonnade. ¹³No one else dared join them, even though they were highly regarded by the people. ¹⁴Nevertheless, more and more men and women believed in the Lord and were added to their number. ¹⁵As a result, people brought the sick into the streets and laid them on beds and mats so that at least Peter's shadow might fall on some of them as he passed by. ¹⁶Crowds gathered also from the towns around Jerusalem, bringing their sick and those tormented by evil[a] spirits, and all of them were healed.

The Apostles Persecuted

¹⁷Then the high priest and all his associates, who were members of the party of the Sadducees, were filled with jealousy. ¹⁸They arrested the apostles and put them in the public jail. ¹⁹But during the night an angel of the Lord opened the doors of the jail and brought them out. ²⁰"Go, stand in the temple courts," he said, "and tell the people the full message of this new life."

²¹At daybreak they entered the temple courts, as they had been told, and began to teach the people.

When the high priest and his associates arrived, they called together the Sanhedrin—the full assembly of the elders of Israel—and sent to the jail for the apostles. ²²But on arriving at the jail, the officers did not find them there. So they went back and reported, ²³"We found the jail securely locked, with the guards standing at the doors; but when we opened them, we found no one inside." ²⁴On hearing this report, the captain of the temple guard and the chief priests were puzzled, wondering what would come of this.

²⁵Then someone came and said, "Look! The men you put in jail are standing in the temple courts teaching the people." ²⁶At that, the captain went with his officers and brought the apostles. They did not use force, because they feared that the people would stone them.

²⁷Having brought the apostles, they made them appear before the Sanhedrin to be questioned by the high priest. ²⁸"We gave you strict orders not to teach in this name," he said. "Yet you have filled Jerusalem with your teaching and are determined to make us guilty of this man's blood."

---

a 16 Greek *unclean*

²⁹Peter and the other apostles replied: "We must obey God rather than men! ³⁰The God of our fathers raised Jesus from the dead—whom you had killed by hanging him on a tree. ³¹God exalted him to his own right hand as Prince and Savior that he might give repentance and forgiveness of sins to Israel. ³²We are witnesses of these things, and so is the Holy Spirit, whom God has given to those who obey him."

³³When they heard this, they were furious and wanted to put them to death. ³⁴But a Pharisee named Gamaliel, a teacher of the law, who was honored by all the people, stood up in the Sanhedrin and ordered that the men be put outside for a little while. ³⁵Then he addressed them: "Men of Israel, consider carefully what you intend to do to these men. ³⁶Some time ago Theudas appeared, claiming to be somebody, and about four hundred men rallied to him. He was killed, all his followers were dispersed, and it all came to nothing. ³⁷After him, Judas the Galilean appeared in the days of the census and led a band of people in revolt. He too was killed, and all his followers were scattered. ³⁸Therefore, in the present case I advise you: Leave these men alone! Let them go! For if their purpose or activity is of human origin, it will fail. ³⁹But if it is from God, you will not be able to stop these men; you will only find yourselves fighting against God."

⁴⁰His speech persuaded them. They called the apostles in and had them flogged. Then they ordered them not to speak in the name of Jesus, and let them go.

⁴¹The apostles left the Sanhedrin, rejoicing because they had been counted worthy of suffering disgrace for the Name. ⁴²Day after day, in the temple courts and from house to house, they never stopped teaching and proclaiming the good news that Jesus is the Christ.ᵃ

The Choosing of the Seven

In those days when the number of disciples was increasing, the Grecian Jews among them complained against the Hebraic Jews because their widows were being overlooked in the daily distribution of food. ²So the Twelve gathered all the disciples together and said, "It would not be right for us to neglect the ministry of the word of God in order to wait on tables. ³Brothers, choose seven men from among you who are known to be full of the Spirit and wisdom. We will turn this responsibility over to them ⁴and will give our attention to prayer and the ministry of the word."

⁵This proposal pleased the whole group. They chose Stephen, a man full of faith and of the Holy Spirit; also Philip, Procorus, Nicanor, Timon, Parmenas, and Nicolas from Antioch, a convert to Judaism. ⁶They presented these men to the apostles, who prayed and laid their hands on them.

⁷So the word of God spread. The number of disciples

ᵃ 42 Or Messiah

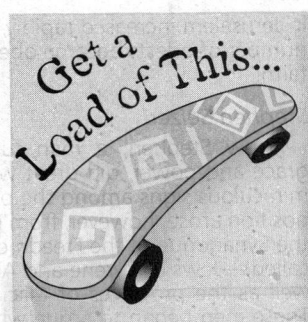

Jailbreak! Whoopie! "An angel of the Lord opened the doors of the jail" and let the apostles out (Acts 5:19). Was it hard for the angel to pick the lock? Ab-so-lute-ly not. He was a pro. He didn't even need the secret pass key.

in Jerusalem increased rapidly, and a large number of priests became obedient to the faith.

Stephen Seized

8Now Stephen, a man full of God's grace and power, did great wonders and miraculous signs among the people. 9Opposition arose, however, from members of the Synagogue of the Freedmen (as it was called)—Jews of Cyrene and Alexandria as well as the provinces of Cilicia and Asia. These men began to argue with Stephen, 10but they could not stand up against his wisdom or the Spirit by whom he spoke. 11Then they secretly persuaded some men to say, "We have heard Stephen speak words of blasphemy against Moses and against God."

12So they stirred up the people and the elders and the teachers of the law. They seized Stephen and brought him before the Sanhedrin. 13They produced false witnesses, who testified, "This fellow never stops speaking against this holy place and against the law. 14For we have heard him say that this Jesus of Nazareth will destroy this place and change the customs Moses handed down to us."

15All who were sitting in the Sanhedrin looked intently at Stephen, and they saw that his face was like the face of an angel.

Stephen's Speech to the Sanhedrin

7 Then the high priest asked him, "Are these charges true?"

2To this he replied: "Brothers and fathers, listen to me! The God of glory appeared to our father Abraham while he was still in Mesopotamia, before he lived in Haran. 3'Leave your country and your people,' God said, 'and go to the land I will show you.'*a*

4"So he left the land of the Chaldeans and settled in Haran. After the death of his father, God sent him to this land where you are now living. 5He gave him no inheritance here, not even a foot of ground. But God promised him that he and his descendants after him would possess the land, even though at that time Abraham had no child. 6God spoke to

a 3 Gen. 12:1

Obeying God First

READ ACTS 5:27–42

Some kids think they're "cool" or "tough" if they cross a busy street dodging cars. But if you want to live to grow up and be a man, play it safe and use the crosswalks. There are reasons for laws, and God said to obey them for your own good and for the good of others (Romans 13:1–7). There are a few times, however, when society's laws really *are* out to lunch. If the authorities order you to do something wrong—or if the law forbids you to tell others about Jesus—then you need to disobey that law. "We must obey God rather than men" (Acts 5:29). If unbelievers choose to obey ungodly laws, well, *let them.* Don't be surprised if they reject you and call you a goodie-goodie and persecute you for not going along with them. If they do, have the attitude the disciples had: Count it a privilege to suffer for Jesus (verse 41).

Your next reading is on page 1427.

him in this way: 'Your descendants will be strangers in a country not their own, and they will be enslaved and mistreated four hundred years. [7]But I will punish the nation they serve as slaves,' God said, 'and afterward they will come out of that country and worship me in this place.'[a] [8]Then he gave Abraham the covenant of circumcision. And Abraham became the father of Isaac and circumcised him eight days after his birth. Later Isaac became the father of Jacob, and Jacob became the father of the twelve patriarchs.

[9]"Because the patriarchs were jealous of Joseph, they sold him as a slave into Egypt. But God was with him [10]and rescued him from all his troubles. He gave Joseph wisdom and enabled him to gain the goodwill of Pharaoh king of Egypt; so he made him ruler over Egypt and all his palace.

[11]"Then a famine struck all Egypt and Canaan, bringing great suffering, and our fathers could not find food. [12]When Jacob heard that there was grain in Egypt, he sent our fathers on their first visit. [13]On their second visit, Joseph told his brothers who he was, and Pharaoh learned about Joseph's family. [14]After this, Joseph sent for his father Jacob and his whole family, seventy-five in all. [15]Then Jacob went down to Egypt, where he and our fathers died. [16]Their bodies were brought back to Shechem and placed in the tomb that Abraham had bought from the sons of Hamor at Shechem for a certain sum of money.

[17]"As the time drew near for God to fulfill his promise to Abraham, the number of our people in Egypt greatly increased. [18]Then another king, who knew nothing about Joseph, became ruler of Egypt. [19]He dealt treacherously with our people and oppressed our forefathers by forcing them to throw out their newborn babies so that they would die.

[20]"At that time Moses was born, and he was no ordinary child.[b] For three months he was cared for in his father's house. [21]When he was placed outside, Pharaoh's daughter took him and brought him up as her own son. [22]Moses was educated in all the wisdom of the Egyptians and was powerful in speech and action.

[23]"When Moses was forty years old, he decided to visit his fellow Israelites. [24]He saw one of them being mistreated by an Egyptian, so he went to his defense and avenged him by killing the Egyptian.

[25]Moses thought that his own people would realize that God was using him to rescue them, but they did not. [26]The next day Moses came upon two Israelites who were fighting. He tried to reconcile them by saying, 'Men, you are brothers; why do you want to hurt each other?'

[27]"But the man who was mistreating the other pushed Moses aside and said, 'Who made you ruler and judge over us? [28]Do you want to kill me as you killed the Egyptian yesterday?'[c] [29]When Moses heard this, he fled to Midian, where he settled as a foreigner and had two sons.

[30]"After forty years had passed, an angel appeared to Moses in the flames of a burning bush in the desert near Mount Sinai. [31]When he saw this, he was amazed at the sight. As he went over to look more closely, he heard the Lord's voice: [32]'I am the God of your fathers, the God of Abraham, Isaac and Jacob.'[d] Moses trembled with fear and did not dare to look.

[33]"Then the Lord said to him, 'Take off your sandals; the place where you are standing is holy ground. [34]I have indeed seen the oppression of my people in Egypt. I have heard their groaning and have come down to set them free. Now come, I will send you back to Egypt.'[e]

[35]"This is the same Moses whom they had rejected with the words, 'Who made you ruler and judge?' He was sent to be their ruler and deliverer by God himself, through the angel who appeared to him in the bush. [36]He led them out of Egypt and did wonders and miraculous signs in Egypt, at the Red Sea[f] and for forty years in the desert.

[37]"This is that Moses who told the Israelites, 'God will send you a prophet like me from your own people.'[g] [38]He was in the assembly in the desert, with the angel who spoke to him on Mount Sinai, and with our fathers; and he received living words to pass on to us.

[39]"But our fathers refused to obey him. Instead, they rejected him and in their hearts turned back to Egypt. [40]They told Aaron, 'Make us gods who will go before us. As for this fellow Moses who led us out of Egypt—we don't know what has happened to him!'[h] [41]That was the time

---

[a] 7 Gen. 15:13,14   [b] 20 Or was fair in the sight of God
[c] 28 Exodus 2:14   [d] 32 Exodus 3:6
[e] 34 Exodus 3:5,7,8,10   [f] 36 That is, Sea of Reeds
[g] 37 Deut. 18:15   [h] 40 Exodus 32:1

they made an idol in the form of a calf. They brought sacrifices to it and held a celebration in honor of what their hands had made. 42But God turned away and gave them over to the worship of the heavenly bodies. This agrees with what is written in the book of the prophets:

" 'Did you bring me sacrifices and
        offerings
    forty years in the desert, O house of
        Israel?
43 You have lifted up the shrine of Molech
        and the star of your god Rephan,
    the idols you made to worship.
    Therefore I will send you into exile'a
        beyond Babylon.

44"Our forefathers had the tabernacle of the Testimony with them in the desert. It had been made as God directed Moses, according to the pattern he had seen. 45Having received the tabernacle, our fathers under Joshua brought it with them when they took the land from the nations God drove out before them. It remained in the land until the time of David, 46who enjoyed God's favor and asked that he might provide a dwelling place for the God of Jacob.b 47But it was Solomon who built the house for him.

48"However, the Most High does not live in houses made by men. As the prophet says:

49 " 'Heaven is my throne,
        and the earth is my footstool.
    What kind of house will you build for
        me?
            says the Lord.
    Or where will my resting place be?
50 Has not my hand made all these
            things?'c

51"You stiff-necked people, with uncircumcised hearts and ears! You are just like your fathers: You always resist the Holy Spirit! 52Was there ever a prophet your fathers did not persecute? They even killed those who predicted the coming of the Righteous One. And now you have betrayed and murdered him— 53you who have received the law that was put into effect through angels but have not obeyed it."

The Stoning of Stephen

54When they heard this, they were furious and gnashed their teeth at him. 55But

Stephen, full of the Holy Spirit, looked up to heaven and saw the glory of God, and Jesus standing at the right hand of God. 56"Look," he said, "I see heaven open and the Son of Man standing at the right hand of God."

57At this they covered their ears and, yelling at the top of their voices, they all rushed at him, 58dragged him out of the city and began to stone him. Meanwhile, the witnesses laid their clothes at the feet of a young man named Saul.

59While they were stoning him, Stephen prayed, "Lord Jesus, receive my spirit." 60Then he fell on his knees and cried out, "Lord, do not hold this sin against them." When he had said this, he fell asleep.

8 And Saul was there, giving approval to his death.

The Church Persecuted and Scattered

On that day a great persecution broke out against the church at Jerusalem, and all except the apostles were scattered throughout Judea and Samaria. 2Godly men buried Stephen and mourned deeply for him. 3But Saul began to destroy the church. Going from house to house, he dragged off men and women and put them in prison.

Philip in Samaria

4Those who had been scattered preached the word wherever they went. 5Philip went down to a city in Samaria and proclaimed the Christd there. 6When the crowds heard Philip and saw the miraculous signs he did, they all paid close attention to what he said. 7With shrieks, evile spirits came out of many, and many paralytics and cripples were healed. 8So there was great joy in that city.

Simon the Sorcerer

9Now for some time a man named Simon had practiced sorcery in the city and amazed all the people of Samaria. He boasted that he was someone great, 10and all the people, both high and low, gave him their attention and exclaimed, "This man is the divine power known as the Great Power." 11They followed him be-

---

a 43 Amos 5:25–27   b 46 Some early manuscripts the house of Jacob   c 50 Isaiah 66:1,2   d 5 Or Messiah
e 7 Greek unclean

cause he had amazed them for a long time with his magic. 12But when they believed Philip as he preached the good news of the kingdom of God and the name of Jesus Christ, they were baptized, both men and women. 13Simon himself believed and was baptized. And he followed Philip everywhere, astonished by the great signs and miracles he saw.

14When the apostles in Jerusalem heard that Samaria had accepted the word of God, they sent Peter and John to them. 15When they arrived, they prayed for them that they might receive the Holy Spirit, 16because the Holy Spirit had not yet come upon any of them; they had simply been baptized into*a* the name of the Lord Jesus. 17Then Peter and John placed their hands on them, and they received the Holy Spirit.

18When Simon saw that the Spirit was given at the laying on of the apostles' hands, he offered them money 19and said, "Give me also this ability so that everyone on whom I lay my hands may receive the Holy Spirit."

20Peter answered: "May your money perish with you, because you thought you could buy the gift of God with money! 21You have no part or share in this ministry, because your heart is not right before God. 22Repent of this wickedness and pray to the Lord. Perhaps he will forgive you for having such a thought in your heart. 23For I see that you are full of bitterness and captive to sin."

24Then Simon answered, "Pray to the Lord for me so that nothing you have said may happen to me."

25When they had testified and proclaimed the word of the Lord, Peter and John returned to Jerusalem, preaching the gospel in many Samaritan villages.

Philip and the Ethiopian

26Now an angel of the Lord said to Philip, "Go south to the road—the desert road—that goes down from Jerusalem to Gaza." 27So he started out, and on his way he met an Ethiopian*b* eunuch, an important official in charge of all the treasury of Candace, queen of the Ethiopians. This man had gone to Jerusalem to worship, 28and on his way home was sitting in his chariot reading the book of Isaiah the prophet. 29The Spirit told Philip, "Go to that chariot and stay near it."

30Then Philip ran up to the chariot and heard the man reading Isaiah the prophet. "Do you understand what you are reading?" Philip asked.

31"How can I," he said, "unless someone explains it to me?" So he invited Philip to come up and sit with him.

32The eunuch was reading this passage of Scripture:

"He was led like a sheep to the
     slaughter,
  and as a lamb before the shearer is
     silent,
  so he did not open his mouth.
33 In his humiliation he was deprived of
     justice.
  Who can speak of his descendants?
  For his life was taken from the
     earth."*c*

34The eunuch asked Philip, "Tell me, please, who is the prophet talking about, himself or someone else?" 35Then Philip began with that very passage of Scripture and told him the good news about Jesus.

36As they traveled along the road, they came to some water and the eunuch said, "Look, here is water. Why shouldn't I be baptized?"*d* 38And he gave orders to stop the chariot. Then both Philip and the eunuch went down into the water and Philip baptized him. 39When they came up out of the water, the Spirit of the Lord suddenly took Philip away, and the eunuch did not see him again, but went on his way rejoicing. 40Philip, however, appeared at Azotus and traveled about, preaching the gospel in all the towns until he reached Caesarea.

Saul's Conversion

Meanwhile, Saul was still breathing out murderous threats against the Lord's disciples. He went to the high priest 2and asked him for letters to the synagogues in Damascus, so that if he found any there who belonged to the Way, whether men or women, he might take them as prisoners to Jerusalem. 3As he neared Damascus on his journey, suddenly a light from heaven flashed around him. 4He fell to the ground and heard a

*a 16 Or in   b 27 That is, from the upper Nile region
c 33 Isaiah 53:7,8   d 36 Some late manuscripts baptized?"
37Philip said, "If you believe with all your heart, you may." The eunuch answered, "I believe that Jesus Christ is the Son of God."*

Get a Load of This...

"The Spirit of the Lord suddenly took Philip away" (Acts 8:39). One minute he was there, the next minute he was in the town of Azotus! Ho! How did God do *that*? You think Philip got motion sickness being "transported" like that?

voice say to him, "Saul, Saul, why do you persecute me?"

⁵"Who are you, Lord?" Saul asked.

"I am Jesus, whom you are persecuting," he replied. ⁶"Now get up and go into the city, and you will be told what you must do."

⁷The men traveling with Saul stood there speechless; they heard the sound but did not see anyone. ⁸Saul got up from the ground, but when he opened his eyes he could see nothing. So they led him by the hand into Damascus. ⁹For three days he was blind, and did not eat or drink anything.

¹⁰In Damascus there was a disciple named Ananias. The Lord called to him in a vision, "Ananias!"

"Yes, Lord," he answered.

¹¹The Lord told him, "Go to the house of Judas on Straight Street and ask for a man from Tarsus named Saul, for he is praying. ¹²In a vision he has seen a man named Ananias come and place his hands on him to restore his sight."

¹³"Lord," Ananias answered, "I have heard many reports about this man and all the harm he has done to your saints in Jerusalem. ¹⁴And he has come here with authority from the chief priests to arrest all who call on your name."

¹⁵But the Lord said to Ananias, "Go! This man is my chosen instrument to carry my name before the Gentiles and their kings and before the people of Israel. ¹⁶I will show him how much he must suffer for my name."

¹⁷Then Ananias went to the house and entered it. Placing his hands on Saul, he said, "Brother Saul, the Lord—Jesus, who appeared to you on the road as you were coming here—has sent me so that you may see again and be filled with the Holy Spirit." ¹⁸Immediately, something like scales fell from Saul's eyes, and he could see again. He got up and was baptized, ¹⁹and after taking some food, he regained his strength.

Saul in Damascus and Jerusalem

Saul spent several days with the disciples in Damascus. ²⁰At once he began to preach in the synagogues that Jesus is the Son of God. ²¹All those who heard him were astonished and asked, "Isn't he the man who raised havoc in Jerusalem among those who call on this name? And hasn't he come here to take them as prisoners to the chief priests?" ²²Yet Saul grew more and more powerful and baffled the Jews living in Damascus by proving that Jesus is the Christ.[a]

²³After many days had gone by, the Jews conspired to kill him, ²⁴but Saul learned of their plan. Day and night they kept close watch on the city gates in order to kill him. ²⁵But his followers took him by night and lowered him in a basket through an opening in the wall.

²⁶When he came to Jerusalem, he tried to join the disciples, but they were all afraid of him, not believing that

a 22 Or Messiah

he really was a disciple. 27But Barnabas took him and brought him to the apostles. He told them how Saul on his journey had seen the Lord and that the Lord had spoken to him, and how in Damascus he had preached fearlessly in the name of Jesus. 28So Saul stayed with them and moved about freely in Jerusalem, speaking boldly in the name of the Lord. 29He talked and debated with the Grecian Jews, but they tried to kill him. 30When the brothers learned of this, they took him down to Caesarea and sent him off to Tarsus.

31Then the church throughout Judea, Galilee and Samaria enjoyed a time of peace. It was strengthened; and encouraged by the Holy Spirit, it grew in numbers, living in the fear of the Lord.

Aeneas and Dorcas

32As Peter traveled about the country, he went to visit the saints in Lydda. 33There he found a man named Aeneas, a paralytic who had been bedridden for eight years. 34"Aeneas," Peter said to him, "Jesus Christ heals you. Get up and take care of your mat." Immediately Aeneas got up. 35All those who lived in Lydda and Sharon saw him and turned to the Lord.

36In Joppa there was a disciple named Tabitha (which, when translated, is Dorcasa), who was always doing good and helping the poor. 37About that time she became sick and died, and her body was washed and placed in an upstairs room. 38Lydda was near Joppa; so when the disciples heard that Peter was in Lydda, they sent two men to him and urged him, "Please come at once!"

39Peter went with them, and when he arrived he was taken upstairs to the room. All the widows stood around him, crying and showing him the robes and other clothing that Dorcas had made while she was still with them.

40Peter sent them all out of the room; then he got down on his knees and prayed. Turning toward the dead woman, he said, "Tabitha, get up." She opened her eyes, and seeing Peter she sat up. 41He took her by the hand and helped her to her feet. Then he called the believers and

a 36 Both *Tabitha* (Aramaic) and *Dorcas* (Greek) mean *gazelle.*

A Totally Changed Man

READ ACTS 9:1–19

Paul was one of these kids who had grown up in church all his life. He knew what the Bible said; he knew what was right and wrong; he could talk the talk. Only one thing was missing: Paul didn't know God. Sure he knew *about* God—his head was stuffed with "God information." But what he *didn't* realize was that he needed God's forgiveness—he needed God's Son, Jesus, to save him. Let's apply this to today: If you offend a friend, it's not enough just to realize, "Oh yeah. I hurt him." You need to *go* to him and say, "I'm really sorry." You ask him to forgive you and he does. It's the same with God. It's not enough to simply know that Jesus died for everybody. You must come to God personally and *ask* his forgiveness, and accept Jesus as Lord of your life.

Your next reading is on page 1431.

Get a Load of This...

When Paul was trapped in Damascus, he was a real basket case. Why? He escaped by being lowered over the city wall in a basket (Acts 9:25). Maybe a laundry basket. You've got to have a lot of confidence in the basket-weaver to try *this* trick.

the widows and presented her to them alive. ⁴²This became known all over Joppa, and many people believed in the Lord. ⁴³Peter stayed in Joppa for some time with a tanner named Simon.

Cornelius Calls for Peter

At Caesarea there was a man named Cornelius, a centurion in what was known as the Italian Regiment. ²He and all his family were devout and God-fearing; he gave generously to those in need and prayed to God regularly. ³One day at about three in the afternoon he had a vision. He distinctly saw an angel of God, who came to him and said, "Cornelius!"

⁴Cornelius stared at him in fear. "What is it, Lord?" he asked.

The angel answered, "Your prayers and gifts to the poor have come up as a memorial offering before God. ⁵Now send men to Joppa to bring back a man named Simon who is called Peter. ⁶He is staying with Simon the tanner, whose house is by the sea."

⁷When the angel who spoke to him had gone, Cornelius called two of his servants and a devout soldier who was one of his attendants. ⁸He told them everything that had happened and sent them to Joppa.

Peter's Vision

⁹About noon the following day as they were on their journey and approaching the city, Peter went up on the roof to pray. ¹⁰He became hungry and wanted something to eat, and while the meal was being prepared, he fell into a trance. ¹¹He saw heaven opened and something like a large sheet being let down to earth by its four corners. ¹²It contained all kinds of four-footed animals, as well as reptiles of the earth and birds of the air. ¹³Then a voice told him, "Get up, Peter. Kill and eat."

¹⁴"Surely not, Lord!" Peter replied. "I have never eaten anything impure or unclean."

¹⁵The voice spoke to him a second time, "Do not call anything impure that God has made clean."

¹⁶This happened three times, and immediately the sheet was taken back to heaven.

¹⁷While Peter was wondering about the meaning of the vision, the men sent by Cornelius found out where Simon's house was and stopped at the gate. ¹⁸They called out, asking if Simon who was known as Peter was staying there.

¹⁹While Peter was still thinking about the vision, the Spirit said to him, "Simon, three*ᵃ* men are looking for you. ²⁰So get up and go downstairs. Do not hesitate to go with them, for I have sent them."

²¹Peter went down and said to the men, "I'm the one you're looking for. Why have you come?"

²²The men replied, "We have come from Cornelius the centurion. He is a righteous and God-fearing man,

---

ᵃ 19 One early manuscript *two*; other manuscripts do not have the number.

who is respected by all the Jewish people. A holy angel told him to have you come to his house so that he could hear what you have to say." 23Then Peter invited the men into the house to be his guests.

Peter at Cornelius's House

The next day Peter started out with them, and some of the brothers from Joppa went along. 24The following day he arrived in Caesarea. Cornelius was expecting them and had called together his relatives and close friends. 25As Peter entered the house, Cornelius met him and fell at his feet in reverence. 26But Peter made him get up. "Stand up," he said, "I am only a man myself."

27Talking with him, Peter went inside and found a large gathering of people. 28He said to them: "You are well aware that it is against our law for a Jew to associate with a Gentile or visit him. But God has shown me that I should not call any man impure or unclean. 29So when I was

sent for, I came without raising any objection. May I ask why you sent for me?"

30Cornelius answered: "Four days ago I was in my house praying at this hour, at three in the afternoon. Suddenly a man in shining clothes stood before me 31and said, 'Cornelius, God has heard your prayer and remembered your gifts to the poor. 32Send to Joppa for Simon who is called Peter. He is a guest in the home of Simon the tanner, who lives by the sea.' 33So I sent for you immediately, and it was good of you to come. Now we are all here in the presence of God to listen to everything the Lord has commanded you to tell us."

34Then Peter began to speak: "I now realize how true it is that God does not show favoritism 35but accepts men from every nation who fear him and do what is right. 36You know the message God sent to the people of Israel, telling the good news of peace through Jesus Christ, who is Lord of all. 37You know what has happened throughout Judea, beginning in

Make It Stick

READ ACTS 10:28

It was a huge deal for Peter to preach the gospel in Cornelius' house. Up until then, Peter didn't even think Gentiles could *get* saved (unless they became Jews first). If you want an idea of how Peter felt, picture going to an alien planet to witness. Would you think the aliens there *needed* to be saved? Or *could* be? On a sticky note, draw a picture of an alien.

Galilee after the baptism that John preached— 38how God anointed Jesus of Nazareth with the Holy Spirit and power, and how he went around doing good and healing all who were under the power of the devil, because God was with him.

39"We are witnesses of everything he did in the country of the Jews and in Jerusalem. They killed him by hanging him on a tree, 40but God raised him from the dead on the third day and caused him to be seen. 41He was not seen by all the people, but by witnesses whom God had already chosen—by us who ate and drank with him after he rose from the dead. 42He commanded us to preach to the people and to testify that he is the one whom God appointed as judge of the living and the dead. 43All the prophets testify about him that everyone who believes in him receives forgiveness of sins through his name."

44While Peter was still speaking these words, the Holy Spirit came on all who heard the message. 45The circumcised believers who had come with Peter were astonished that the gift of the Holy Spirit had been poured out even on the Gentiles. 46For they heard them speaking in tongues*a* and praising God.

Then Peter said, 47"Can anyone keep these people from being baptized with water? They have received the Holy Spirit just as we have." 48So he ordered that they be baptized in the name of Jesus Christ. Then they asked Peter to stay with them for a few days.

Peter Explains His Actions

11 The apostles and the brothers throughout Judea heard that the Gentiles also had received the word of God. 2So when Peter went up to Jerusalem, the circumcised believers criticized him 3and said, "You went into the house of uncircumcised men and ate with them."

4Peter began and explained everything to them precisely as it had happened: 5"I was in the city of Joppa praying, and in a trance I saw a vision. I saw something like a large sheet being let down from heaven by its four corners, and it came down to where I was. 6I looked into it and saw four-footed animals of the earth, wild beasts, reptiles, and birds of the air. 7Then I heard a voice telling me, 'Get up, Peter. Kill and eat.'

8"I replied, 'Surely not, Lord! Nothing impure or unclean has ever entered my mouth.'

9"The voice spoke from heaven a second time, 'Do not call anything impure that God has made clean.' 10This happened three times, and then it was all pulled up to heaven again.

11"Right then three men who had been sent to me from Caesarea stopped at the house where I was staying. 12The Spirit told me to have no hesitation about going with them. These six brothers also went with me, and we entered the man's house. 13He told us how he had seen an angel appear in his house and say, 'Send to Joppa for Simon who is called Peter. 14He will bring you a message through which you and all your household will be saved.'

15"As I began to speak, the Holy Spirit came on them as he had come on us at the beginning. 16Then I remembered what the Lord had said: 'John baptized with*b* water, but you will be baptized with the Holy Spirit.' 17So if God gave them the same gift as he gave us, who believed in the Lord Jesus Christ, who was I to think that I could oppose God?"

18When they heard this, they had no further objections and praised God, saying, "So then, God has granted even the Gentiles repentance unto life."

The Church in Antioch

19Now those who had been scattered by the persecution in connection with Stephen traveled as far as Phoenicia, Cyprus and Antioch, telling the message only to Jews. 20Some of them, however, men from Cyprus and Cyrene, went to Antioch and began to speak to Greeks also, telling them the good news about the Lord Jesus. 21The Lord's hand was with them, and a great number of people believed and turned to the Lord.

22News of this reached the ears of the church at Jerusalem, and they sent Barnabas to Antioch. 23When he arrived and saw the evidence of the grace of God, he was glad and encouraged them all to remain true to the Lord with all their hearts. 24He was a good man, full of the Holy Spirit and faith, and a great number of people were brought to the Lord.

25Then Barnabas went to Tarsus to look

---

a 46 Or *other languages*　　*b 16* Or *in*

for Saul, 26and when he found him, he brought him to Antioch. So for a whole year Barnabas and Saul met with the church and taught great numbers of people. The disciples were called Christians first at Antioch.

27During this time some prophets came down from Jerusalem to Antioch. 28One of them, named Agabus, stood up and through the Spirit predicted that a severe famine would spread over the entire Roman world. (This happened during the reign of Claudius.) 29The disciples, each according to his ability, decided to provide help for the brothers living in Judea. 30This they did, sending their gift to the elders by Barnabas and Saul.

Peter's Miraculous Escape From Prison

12 It was about this time that King Herod arrested some who belonged to the church, intending to persecute them. 2He had James, the brother of John, put to death with the sword. 3When he saw that this pleased the Jews, he proceeded to seize Peter also. This happened during the Feast of Unleavened Bread. 4After arresting him, he put him in prison, handing him over to be guarded by four squads of four soldiers each. Herod intended to bring him out for public trial after the Passover.

5So Peter was kept in prison, but the church was earnestly praying to God for him.

6The night before Herod was to bring him to trial, Peter was sleeping between two soldiers, bound with two chains, and sentries stood guard at the entrance. 7Suddenly an angel of the Lord appeared and a light shone in the cell. He struck Peter on the side and woke him up. "Quick, get up!" he said, and the chains fell off Peter's wrists.

8Then the angel said to him, "Put on your clothes and sandals." And Peter did so. "Wrap your cloak around you and follow me," the angel told him. 9Peter followed him out of the prison, but he had no idea that what the angel was doing was really happening; he thought he was seeing a vision. 10They passed the first and second guards and came to the iron gate leading to the city. It opened for them by

It's Really Happening!
READ ACTS 12:1–12

Ever seen a movie or video that was both scary and funny at the same time? Acts 12 was one of those mixed-emotion moments. Peter was arrested and about to be killed so the Christian leaders met and prayed like crazy for him. Result? An angel none-too-gently "struck Peter on the side" to wake him up. Peter's chains (*Clunk!*) fell off and the angel walked him straight out of prison. Finally Peter realized, "This is really *happening*!" He ran to Mary's house and knocked on the door, but the servant girl was so excited that she forgot to open the door. Ha! She ran inside where everyone was praying for Peter to get out of prison and told them Peter *was* out of prison and . . . nobody *believed* her. Helllooo! What were you praying for, folks? Finally Peter knocked *so* loud that they opened the door for him. Lesson: When you pray, expect that God will *answer*.

Your next reading is on page 1434.

Gross!

When King Herod was eaten by worms (Acts 12:23), they were probably intestinal roundworms— *Ascaris Lumericoides*—which grow 10-16 inches long and feed on fluids in the intestines. Bunches of roundworms can block up a guy's intestines, making him vomit up mouthfuls of worms and die!

itself, and they went through it. When they had walked the length of one street, suddenly the angel left him.

11 Then Peter came to himself and said, "Now I know without a doubt that the Lord sent his angel and rescued me from Herod's clutches and from everything the Jewish people were anticipating."

12 When this had dawned on him, he went to the house of Mary the mother of John, also called Mark, where many people had gathered and were praying. 13 Peter knocked at the outer entrance, and a servant girl named Rhoda came to answer the door. 14 When she recognized Peter's voice, she was so overjoyed she ran back without opening it and exclaimed, "Peter is at the door!"

15 "You're out of your mind," they told her. When she kept insisting that it was so, they said, "It must be his angel."

16 But Peter kept on knocking, and when they opened the door and saw him, they were astonished. 17 Peter motioned with his hand for them to be quiet and described how the Lord had brought him out of prison. "Tell James and the brothers about this," he said, and then he left for another place.

18 In the morning, there was no small commotion among the soldiers as to what had become of Peter. 19 After Herod had a thorough search made for him and did not find him, he cross-examined the guards and ordered that they be executed.

Herod's Death

Then Herod went from Judea to Caesarea and stayed there a while. 20 He had been quarreling with the people of Tyre and Sidon; they now joined together and sought an audience with him. Having secured the support of Blastus, a trusted personal servant of the king, they asked for peace, because they depended on the king's country for their food supply.

21 On the appointed day Herod, wearing his royal robes, sat on his throne and delivered a public address to the people. 22 They shouted, "This is the voice of a god, not of a man." 23 Immediately, because Herod did not give praise to God, an angel of the Lord struck him down, and he was eaten by worms and died.

24 But the word of God continued to increase and spread.

25 When Barnabas and Saul had finished their mission, they returned from^a Jerusalem, taking with them John, also called Mark.

Barnabas and Saul Sent Off

13 In the church at Antioch there were prophets and teachers: Barnabas, Simeon called Niger, Lucius of Cyrene, Manaen (who had been brought up with Herod the tetrarch) and Saul. 2 While they were worshiping the Lord and fasting, the Holy Spirit said, "Set apart for me Barnabas and Saul for

^a 25 Some manuscripts to

the work to which I have called them." ³So after they had fasted and prayed, they placed their hands on them and sent them off.

On Cyprus

⁴The two of them, sent on their way by the Holy Spirit, went down to Seleucia and sailed from there to Cyprus. ⁵When they arrived at Salamis, they proclaimed the word of God in the Jewish synagogues. John was with them as their helper.

⁶They traveled through the whole island until they came to Paphos. There they met a Jewish sorcerer and false prophet named Bar-Jesus, ⁷who was an attendant of the proconsul, Sergius Paulus. The proconsul, an intelligent man, sent for Barnabas and Saul because he wanted to hear the word of God. ⁸But Elymas the sorcerer (for that is what his name means) opposed them and tried to turn the proconsul from the faith. ⁹Then Saul, who was also called Paul, filled with the Holy Spirit, looked straight at Elymas and said, ¹⁰"You are a child of the devil and an enemy of everything that is right! You are full of all kinds of deceit and trickery. Will you never stop perverting the right ways of the Lord? ¹¹Now the hand of the Lord is against you. You are going to be blind, and for a time you will be unable to see the light of the sun."

Immediately mist and darkness came over him, and he groped about, seeking someone to lead him by the hand. ¹²When the proconsul saw what had happened, he believed, for he was amazed at the teaching about the Lord.

In Pisidian Antioch

¹³From Paphos, Paul and his companions sailed to Perga in Pamphylia, where John left them to return to Jerusalem. ¹⁴From Perga they went on to Pisidian Antioch. On the Sabbath they entered the synagogue and sat down. ¹⁵After the reading from the Law and the Prophets, the synagogue rulers sent word to them, saying, "Brothers, if you have a message of encouragement for the people, please speak."

¹⁶Standing up, Paul motioned with his hand and said: "Men of Israel and you Gentiles who worship God, listen to me! ¹⁷The God of the people of Israel chose our fathers; he made the people prosper during their stay in Egypt, with mighty power he led them out of that country, ¹⁸he endured their conductᵃ for about forty years in the desert, ¹⁹he overthrew seven nations in Canaan and gave their land to his people as their inheritance. ²⁰All this took about 450 years.

"After this, God gave them judges until the time of Samuel the prophet. ²¹Then the people asked for a king, and he gave them Saul son of Kish, of the tribe of Benjamin, who ruled forty years. ²²After removing Saul, he made David their king. He testified concerning him:

ᵃ 18 Some manuscripts *and cared for them*

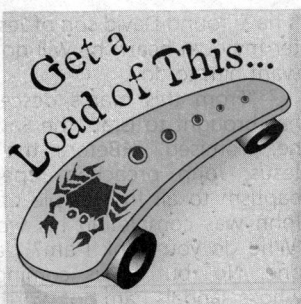

Get a Load of This...

Manaen was a leader of the church, and he was also the foster brother of Herod Antipas (Acts 13:1), who had beheaded John the Baptist and mocked Jesus. Hmmm . . . must have been *very* interesting listening to Manaen tell the inside scoop about Herod.

'I have found David son of Jesse a man after my own heart; he will do everything I want him to do.'

23 "From this man's descendants God has brought to Israel the Savior Jesus, as he promised. 24 Before the coming of Jesus, John preached repentance and baptism to all the people of Israel. 25 As John was completing his work, he said: 'Who do you think I am? I am not that one. No, but he is coming after me, whose sandals I am not worthy to untie.'

26 "Brothers, children of Abraham, and you God-fearing Gentiles, it is to us that this message of salvation has been sent. 27 The people of Jerusalem and their rulers did not recognize Jesus, yet in condemning him they fulfilled the words of the prophets that are read every Sabbath. 28 Though they found no proper ground for a death sentence, they asked Pilate to have him executed. 29 When they had carried out all that was written about him, they took him down from the tree and laid him in a tomb. 30 But God raised him

from the dead, 31 and for many days he was seen by those who had traveled with him from Galilee to Jerusalem. They are now his witnesses to our people.

32 "We tell you the good news: What God promised our fathers 33 he has fulfilled for us, their children, by raising up Jesus. As it is written in the second Psalm:

" 'You are my Son;
     today I have become your Father.[a][b]

34 The fact that God raised him from the dead, never to decay, is stated in these words:

" 'I will give you the holy and sure
     blessings promised to David.'[c]

35 So it is stated elsewhere:

" 'You will not let your Holy One see
     decay.'[d]

36 "For when David had served God's purpose in his own generation, he fell asleep;

---

[a] 33 Or have begotten you   [b] 33 Psalm 2:7
[c] 34 Isaiah 55:3   [d] 35 Psalm 16:10

The Gospel's Power

READ ACTS 13:13–16, 38–52

Remember your first book report in front of the class? Sweaty palms, butterfly-filled stomach, a fight to get the words out. With God, *what* you say is more important than *how* you say it. Paul knew that even though many would consider his preaching foolish, God would use it because of the *message* being preached (1 Corinthians 1:20–25). The gospel is full of God's power and truth (Romans 1:16). That's why, all through Acts, when people heard the gospel, those who were ready for salvation received Paul warmly (Acts 13:42–43). Those who weren't ready reacted by fighting the truth (Acts 13:45, 49–50). When Paul preached, it was a "demonstration of the Spirit's power" (1 Corinthians 2:4). God was doing the persuading through the message. When you speak the gospel with respect and at the proper time, it's not just words (unlike your book report). You're speaking God's power. Nothing on earth is more powerful.

Your next reading is on page 1436.

he was buried with his fathers and his body decayed. 37But the one whom God raised from the dead did not see decay.

38"Therefore, my brothers, I want you to know that through Jesus the forgiveness of sins is proclaimed to you. 39Through him everyone who believes is justified from everything you could not be justified from by the law of Moses. 40Take care that what the prophets have said does not happen to you:

41 " 'Look, you scoffers,
        wonder and perish,
    for I am going to do something in your
        days
      that you would never believe,
      even if someone told you.' a "

42As Paul and Barnabas were leaving the synagogue, the people invited them to speak further about these things on the next Sabbath. 43When the congregation was dismissed, many of the Jews and devout converts to Judaism followed Paul and Barnabas, who talked with them and urged them to continue in the grace of God.

44On the next Sabbath almost the whole city gathered to hear the word of the Lord. 45When the Jews saw the crowds, they were filled with jealousy and talked abusively against what Paul was saying.

46Then Paul and Barnabas answered them boldly: "We had to speak the word of God to you first. Since you reject it and do not consider yourselves worthy of eternal life, we now turn to the Gentiles. 47For this is what the Lord has commanded us:

    " 'I have made you b a light for the
        Gentiles,
      that you b may bring salvation to the
        ends of the earth.' c "

48When the Gentiles heard this, they were glad and honored the word of the Lord; and all who were appointed for eternal life believed.

49The word of the Lord spread through the whole region. 50But the Jews incited the God-fearing women of high standing and the leading men of the city. They stirred up persecution against Paul and Barnabas, and expelled them from their region. 51So they shook the dust from their feet in protest against them and went to Iconium. 52And the disciples were filled with joy and with the Holy Spirit.

In Iconium

14 At Iconium Paul and Barnabas went as usual into the Jewish synagogue. There they spoke so effectively that a great number of Jews and Gentiles believed. 2But the Jews who refused to believe stirred up the Gentiles and poisoned their minds against the brothers. 3So Paul and Barnabas spent considerable time there, speaking boldly for the Lord, who confirmed the message of his grace by enabling them to do miraculous signs and wonders. 4The people of the city were divided; some sided with the Jews, others with the apostles. 5There was a plot afoot among the Gentiles and Jews, together with their leaders, to mistreat them and stone them. 6But they found out about it and fled to the Lycaonian cities of Lystra and Derbe and to the surrounding country, 7where they continued to preach the good news.

In Lystra and Derbe

8In Lystra there sat a man crippled in his feet, who was lame from birth and had never walked. 9He listened to Paul as he was speaking. Paul looked directly at him, saw that he had faith to be healed 10and called out, "Stand up on your feet!" At that, the man jumped up and began to walk.

11When the crowd saw what Paul had done, they shouted in the Lycaonian language, "The gods have come down to us in human form!" 12Barnabas they called Zeus, and Paul they called Hermes because he was the chief speaker. 13The priest of Zeus, whose temple was just outside the city, brought bulls and wreaths to the city gates because he and the crowd wanted to offer sacrifices to them.

14But when the apostles Barnabas and Paul heard of this, they tore their clothes and rushed out into the crowd, shouting: 15"Men, why are you doing this? We too are only men, human like you. We are bringing you good news, telling you to turn from these worthless things to the living God, who made heaven and earth and sea and everything in them. 16In the past, he let all nations go their own way. 17Yet he has not left himself without testimony: He has shown kindness by giving you rain

a 41 Hab. 1:5   b 47 The Greek is singular.
c 47 Isaiah 49:6

from heaven and crops in their seasons; he provides you with plenty of food and fills your hearts with joy." 18Even with these words, they had difficulty keeping the crowd from sacrificing to them.

19Then some Jews came from Antioch and Iconium and won the crowd over. They stoned Paul and dragged him outside the city, thinking he was dead. 20But after the disciples had gathered around him, he got up and went back into the city. The next day he and Barnabas left for Derbe.

The Return to Antioch in Syria

21They preached the good news in that city and won a large number of disciples. Then they returned to Lystra, Iconium and Antioch, 22strengthening the disciples and encouraging them to remain true to the faith. "We must go through many hardships to enter the kingdom of God," they said. 23Paul and Barnabas appointed elders[a] for them in each church and, with prayer and fasting, committed them to the Lord, in whom they had put their trust. 24After going through Pisidia, they came into Pamphylia, 25and when they

had preached the word in Perga, they went down to Attalia.

26From Attalia they sailed back to Antioch, where they had been committed to the grace of God for the work they had now completed. 27On arriving there, they gathered the church together and reported all that God had done through them and how he had opened the door of faith to the Gentiles. 28And they stayed there a long time with the disciples.

The Council at Jerusalem

15 Some men came down from Judea to Antioch and were teaching the brothers: "Unless you are circumcised, according to the custom taught by Moses, you cannot be saved." 2This brought Paul and Barnabas into sharp dispute and debate with them. So Paul and Barnabas were appointed, along with some other believers, to go up to Jerusalem to see the apostles and elders about this question. 3The church sent

a 23 Or Barnabas ordained elders; or Barnabas had elders elected

---

them on their way, and as they traveled through Phoenicia and Samaria, they told how the Gentiles had been converted. This news made all the brothers very glad. [4]When they came to Jerusalem, they were welcomed by the church and the apostles and elders, to whom they reported everything God had done through them.

[5]Then some of the believers who belonged to the party of the Pharisees stood up and said, "The Gentiles must be circumcised and required to obey the law of Moses."

[6]The apostles and elders met to consider this question. [7]After much discussion, Peter got up and addressed them: "Brothers, you know that some time ago God made a choice among you that the Gentiles might hear from my lips the message of the gospel and believe. [8]God, who knows the heart, showed that he accepted them by giving the Holy Spirit to them, just as he did to us. [9]He made no distinction between us and them, for he purified their hearts by faith. [10]Now then, why do you try to test God by putting on the necks of the disciples a yoke that neither we nor our fathers have been able to bear? [11]No! We believe it is through the grace of our Lord Jesus that we are saved, just as they are."

[12]The whole assembly became silent as they listened to Barnabas and Paul telling about the miraculous signs and wonders God had done among the Gentiles through them. [13]When they finished, James spoke up: "Brothers, listen to me. [14]Simon[a] has described to us how God at first showed his concern by taking from the Gentiles a people for himself. [15]The words of the prophets are in agreement with this, as it is written:

[16]" 'After this I will return
        and rebuild David's fallen tent.
    Its ruins I will rebuild,
        and I will restore it,

[a] 14 Greek *Simeon*, a variant of *Simon*; that is, Peter

Make It Stick

READ ACTS 14:21–23

Church is not just a social club or a good place to hang out. We go there because it strengthens us and encourages us to remain true to God (see Acts 14:22). What things at *your* church do that for you? Friends? The sermon? Singing? Write it here on a sticky note.

[17] that the remnant of men may seek the
Lord,
     and all the Gentiles who bear my
name,
   says the Lord, who does these things'[a]
[18]   that have been known for ages.[b]

[19] "It is my judgment, therefore, that we should not make it difficult for the Gentiles who are turning to God. [20] Instead we should write to them, telling them to abstain from food polluted by idols, from sexual immorality, from the meat of strangled animals and from blood. [21] For Moses has been preached in every city from the earliest times and is read in the synagogues on every Sabbath."

The Council's Letter to Gentile Believers

[22] Then the apostles and elders, with the whole church, decided to choose some of their own men and send them to Antioch with Paul and Barnabas. They chose Judas (called Barsabbas) and Silas, two men who were leaders among the brothers. [23] With them they sent the following letter:

The apostles and elders, your brothers,

To the Gentile believers in Antioch, Syria and Cilicia:

Greetings.

[24] We have heard that some went out from us without our authorization and disturbed you, troubling your minds by what they said. [25] So we all agreed to choose some men and send them to you with our dear friends Barnabas and Paul— [26] men who have risked their lives for the name of our Lord Jesus Christ. [27] Therefore we are sending Judas and Silas to confirm by word of mouth what we are writing. [28] It seemed good to the Holy Spirit and to us not to burden you with anything beyond the following requirements: [29] You are to abstain from food sacrificed to idols, from blood, from the meat of strangled animals

[a] 17 Amos 9:11,12   [b] 17,18 Some manuscripts things'— /
[18] known to the Lord for ages is his work

Stone Laws, Stone Hearts

READ ACTS 15:1–21

What if people had to be circumcised to be saved? Well, that's what some people taught (see Acts 15:1). Peter, Paul and Barnabas quickly set the record straight: Obeying Jewish laws doesn't save us; grace does. Before Jesus came, the Jewish people had the Law of Moses. The Law said lying, cheating, stealing, sex outside of marriage—those things are sin. Problem was, people didn't have God's Spirit inside them, changing their hearts and helping them obey. Then Jesus came, and when people believed in him he took their stony hearts and replaced them with hearts of flesh (Ezekiel 36:26)—soft hearts, not stone hearts. Then he wrote his law on their hearts (Hebrews 8:10). God's Spirit made them *want* to obey God. Now that we have God's Spirit, we don't need all the ceremonial details people needed in Moses' day. And being circumcised? Hey, if you are, you are; if you're not, you're not. No big deal.

Your next reading is on page 1439.

and from sexual immorality. You will do well to avoid these things.

Farewell.

30The men were sent off and went down to Antioch, where they gathered the church together and delivered the letter. 31The people read it and were glad for its encouraging message. 32Judas and Silas, who themselves were prophets, said much to encourage and strengthen the brothers. 33After spending some time there, they were sent off by the brothers with the blessing of peace to return to those who had sent them.ª 35But Paul and Barnabas remained in Antioch, where they and many others taught and preached the word of the Lord.

Disagreement Between Paul and Barnabas

36Some time later Paul said to Barnabas, "Let us go back and visit the brothers in all the towns where we preached the word of the Lord and see how they are

doing." 37Barnabas wanted to take John, also called Mark, with them, 38but Paul did not think it wise to take him, because he had deserted them in Pamphylia and had not continued with them in the work. 39They had such a sharp disagreement that they parted company. Barnabas took Mark and sailed for Cyprus, 40but Paul chose Silas and left, commended by the brothers to the grace of the Lord. 41He went through Syria and Cilicia, strengthening the churches.

Timothy Joins Paul and Silas

He came to Derbe and then to Lystra, where a disciple named Timothy lived, whose mother was a Jewess and a believer, but whose father was a Greek. 2The brothers at Lystra and Iconium spoke well of him. 3Paul wanted to take him along on the journey, so he circumcised him because of the Jews who lived in that area, for they all

ª 33 Some manuscripts them, 34but Silas decided to remain there

We're Both Right!

READ ACTS 15:36–41

When two men of God disagree, it's not always that one is right and the other is wrong. Both could be wrong or both could be right. Each may have a point of view worth considering. Paul was right: Mark had deserted their last mission and there was no guarantee that he was strong enough now to go with them on a tough trip. But Barnabas thought that, with some encouragement, Mark would make it. Paul was right, but Barnabas was right, too. Later on, Mark proved to be very helpful to Paul (see 2 Timothy 4:11). It was probably God's will that Paul and Barnabas separated into two teams so that more people could be reached with the gospel, but they should have done it with respect for one another's opinions. When you disagree with someone, don't just repeat your point. Listen to their point of view. Say, "Why don't we talk this out? Maybe we're both right." Most heated arguments are about two people not listening to each other.

Your next reading is on page 1440.

knew that his father was a Greek. 4As they traveled from town to town, they delivered the decisions reached by the apostles and elders in Jerusalem for the people to obey. 5So the churches were strengthened in the faith and grew daily in numbers.

Paul's Vision of the Man of Macedonia

6Paul and his companions traveled throughout the region of Phrygia and Galatia, having been kept by the Holy Spirit from preaching the word in the province of Asia. 7When they came to the border of Mysia, they tried to enter Bithynia, but the Spirit of Jesus would not allow them to. 8So they passed by Mysia and went down to Troas. 9During the night Paul had a vision of a man of Macedonia standing and begging him, "Come over to Macedonia and help us." 10After Paul had seen the vision, we got ready at once to leave for Macedonia, concluding that God had called us to preach the gospel to them.

Lydia's Conversion in Philippi

11From Troas we put out to sea and sailed straight for Samothrace, and the next day on to Neapolis. 12From there we traveled to Philippi, a Roman colony and the leading city of that district of Macedonia. And we stayed there several days.

13On the Sabbath we went outside the city gate to the river, where we expected to find a place of prayer. We sat down and began to speak to the women who had gathered there. 14One of those listening was a woman named Lydia, a dealer in purple cloth from the city of Thyatira, who was a worshiper of God. The Lord opened her heart to respond to Paul's message. 15When she and the members of her household were baptized, she invited us to her home. "If you consider me a believer in the Lord," she said, "come and stay at my house." And she persuaded us.

Paul and Silas in Prison

16Once when we were going to the place of prayer, we were met by a slave girl who had a spirit by which she predicted the future. She earned a great deal of money for her owners by fortune-telling.

GET SMARTER

Miss Fortune Telling

READ ACTS 16:16–19

Don't fool around and don't be fooled! The Bible is clear: Divination and fortune telling are off limits (Leviticus 20:6,27; Deuteronomy 18:10–11). Trust God for your future. Your future is in his hands. You've seen people on TV promising that they can "tell your future." For a sizeable fee, of course. Psychics, fortune-tellers and tarot card readers all memorize formulas that help them sound like they know all about you. They cleverly guess what you're worried about, or what you want to hear, and predict generalized mumbo-jumbo that could mean, well ... *anything*. They cheat people out of their money. At best, this psychic stuff is a moneymaking scheme and a fraud. At worst, these people are empowered by evil spirits. Either way, avoid this whole scene like a pile of elephant dung. Don't fear it—just realize that it stinks and you need to stay clear of it.

Your next reading is on page 1441.

17This girl followed Paul and the rest of us, shouting, "These men are servants of the Most High God, who are telling you the way to be saved." 18She kept this up for many days. Finally Paul became so troubled that he turned around and said to the spirit, "In the name of Jesus Christ I command you to come out of her!" At that moment the spirit left her.

19When the owners of the slave girl realized that their hope of making money was gone, they seized Paul and Silas and dragged them into the marketplace to face the authorities. 20They brought them before the magistrates and said, "These men are Jews, and are throwing our city into an uproar 21by advocating customs unlawful for us Romans to accept or practice."

22The crowd joined in the attack against Paul and Silas, and the magistrates ordered them to be stripped and beaten. 23After they had been severely flogged, they were thrown into prison, and the jailer was commanded to guard them carefully. 24Upon receiving such orders, he put them in the inner cell and fastened their feet in the stocks.

25About midnight Paul and Silas were praying and singing hymns to God, and the other prisoners were listening to them. 26Suddenly there was such a violent earthquake that the foundations of the prison were shaken. At once all the prison doors flew open, and everybody's chains came loose. 27The jailer woke up, and when he saw the prison doors open, he drew his sword and was about to kill himself because he thought the prisoners had escaped. 28But Paul shouted, "Don't harm yourself! We are all here!"

29The jailer called for lights, rushed in and fell trembling before Paul and Silas. 30He then brought them out and asked, "Sirs, what must I do to be saved?"

31They replied, "Believe in the Lord Jesus, and you will be saved—you and your household." 32Then they spoke the word of the Lord to him and to all the others in his house. 33At that hour of the night the jailer took them and washed their wounds; then immediately he and all his family were

Focus on Good Stuff

READ ACTS 16:19–40

Paul and Silas spoke the truth and got whipped and thrown in jail for it. Their reaction? "About midnight Paul and Silas were praying and singing hymns to God" (verse 25). A 252 man chooses to trust God even when the situation is rough and he feels lousy. Sometimes the best thing to do is to get together with others to pray and give your problems to God. Thank him for all the great things he's done in the past, for happy times and answered prayers, and all your blessings. It'll encourage you to know that God will help you again. Paul and Silas didn't focus on their wounds or the prison bars—they tuned in to God's goodness. Then God shook things up and sprung them from prison. Strong faith triggers God's power (Matthew 17:20). When you're focused on God, he can do great things.

Your next reading is on page 1457.

baptized. 34The jailer brought them into his house and set a meal before them; he was filled with joy because he had come to believe in God—he and his whole family.

35When it was daylight, the magistrates sent their officers to the jailer with the order: "Release those men." 36The jailer told Paul, "The magistrates have ordered that you and Silas be released. Now you can leave. Go in peace."

37But Paul said to the officers: "They beat us publicly without a trial, even though we are Roman citizens, and threw us into prison. And now do they want to get rid of us quietly? No! Let them come themselves and escort us out."

38The officers reported this to the magistrates, and when they heard that Paul and Silas were Roman citizens, they were alarmed. 39They came to appease them and escorted them from the prison, requesting them to leave the city. 40After Paul and Silas came out of the prison, they went to Lydia's house, where they met with the brothers and encouraged them. Then they left.

In Thessalonica

17 When they had passed through Amphipolis and Apollonia, they came to Thessalonica, where there was a Jewish synagogue. 2As his custom was, Paul went into the synagogue, and on three Sabbath days he reasoned with them from the Scriptures, 3explaining and proving that the Christ[a] had to suffer and rise from the dead. "This Jesus I am proclaiming to you is the Christ,[a]" he said. 4Some of the Jews were persuaded and joined Paul and Silas, as did a large number of God-fearing Greeks and not a few prominent women.

5But the Jews were jealous; so they rounded up some bad characters from the marketplace, formed a mob and started a riot in the city. They rushed to Jason's house in search of Paul and Silas in order to bring them out to the crowd.[b] 6But when they did not find them, they dragged Jason and some other brothers before the city officials, shouting: "These men who have caused trouble all over the world have now come here, 7and Jason has welcomed them into his house. They are all defying Caesar's decrees, saying that there is another king, one called Jesus." 8When

they heard this, the crowd and the city officials were thrown into turmoil. 9Then they made Jason and the others post bond and let them go.

In Berea

10As soon as it was night, the brothers sent Paul and Silas away to Berea. On arriving there, they went to the Jewish synagogue. 11Now the Bereans were of more noble character than the Thessalonians, for they received the message with great eagerness and examined the Scriptures every day to see if what Paul said was true. 12Many of the Jews believed, as did also a number of prominent Greek women and many Greek men.

13When the Jews in Thessalonica learned that Paul was preaching the word of God at Berea, they went there too, agitating the crowds and stirring them up. 14The brothers immediately sent Paul to the coast, but Silas and Timothy stayed at Berea. 15The men who escorted Paul brought him to Athens and then left with instructions for Silas and Timothy to join him as soon as possible.

In Athens

16While Paul was waiting for them in Athens, he was greatly distressed to see that the city was full of idols. 17So he reasoned in the synagogue with the Jews and the God-fearing Greeks, as well as in the marketplace day by day with those who happened to be there. 18A group of Epicurean and Stoic philosophers began to dispute with him. Some of them asked, "What is this babbler trying to say?" Others remarked, "He seems to be advocating foreign gods." They said this because Paul was preaching the good news about Jesus and the resurrection. 19Then they took him and brought him to a meeting of the Areopagus, where they said to him, "May we know what this new teaching is that you are presenting? 20You are bringing some strange ideas to our ears, and we want to know what they mean." 21(All the Athenians and the foreigners who lived there spent their time doing nothing but talking about and listening to the latest ideas.)

22Paul then stood up in the meeting of the Areopagus and said: "Men of Athens!

a 3 Or Messiah   b 5 Or the assembly of the people

I see that in every way you are very religious. 23For as I walked around and looked carefully at your objects of worship, I even found an altar with this inscription: TO AN UNKNOWN GOD. Now what you worship as something unknown I am going to proclaim to you.

24"The God who made the world and everything in it is the Lord of heaven and earth and does not live in temples built by hands. 25And he is not served by human hands, as if he needed anything, because he himself gives all men life and breath and everything else. 26From one man he made every nation of men, that they should inhabit the whole earth; and he determined the times set for them and the exact places where they should live. 27God did this so that men would seek him and perhaps reach out for him and find him, though he is not far from each one of us. 28'For in him we live and move and have our being.' As some of your own poets have said, 'We are his offspring.'

29"Therefore since we are God's offspring, we should not think that the divine being is like gold or silver or stone—an image made by man's design and skill. 30In the past God overlooked such ignorance, but now he commands all people everywhere to repent. 31For he has set a day when he will judge the world with justice by the man he has appointed. He has given proof of this to all men by raising him from the dead."

32When they heard about the resurrection of the dead, some of them sneered, but others said, "We want to hear you again on this subject." 33At that, Paul left the Council. 34A few men became followers of Paul and believed. Among them was Dionysius, a member of the Areopagus, also a woman named Damaris, and a number of others.

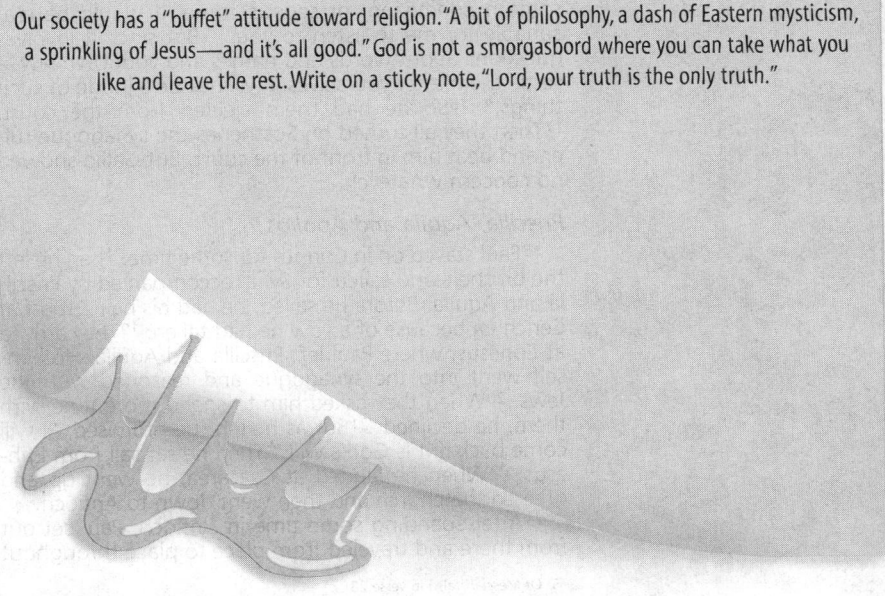

Make It Stick

READ ACTS 17:15–21

Our society has a "buffet" attitude toward religion. "A bit of philosophy, a dash of Eastern mysticism, a sprinkling of Jesus—and it's all good." God is not a smorgasbord where you can take what you like and leave the rest. Write on a sticky note, "Lord, your truth is the only truth."

Get a Load of This...

Even though Paul worked hard at preaching the gospel, he also held down a job to support himself (see Acts 18:3). He didn't have to, but he wanted to give more than he took. A man of God should work so that he's a blessing, not a mooch.

In Corinth

18 After this, Paul left Athens and went to Corinth. ²There he met a Jew named Aquila, a native of Pontus, who had recently come from Italy with his wife Priscilla, because Claudius had ordered all the Jews to leave Rome. Paul went to see them, ³and because he was a tentmaker as they were, he stayed and worked with them. ⁴Every Sabbath he reasoned in the synagogue, trying to persuade Jews and Greeks.

⁵When Silas and Timothy came from Macedonia, Paul devoted himself exclusively to preaching, testifying to the Jews that Jesus was the Christ.ᵃ ⁶But when the Jews opposed Paul and became abusive, he shook out his clothes in protest and said to them, "Your blood be on your own heads! I am clear of my responsibility. From now on I will go to the Gentiles."

⁷Then Paul left the synagogue and went next door to the house of Titius Justus, a worshiper of God. ⁸Crispus, the synagogue ruler, and his entire household believed in the Lord; and many of the Corinthians who heard him believed and were baptized.

⁹One night the Lord spoke to Paul in a vision: "Do not be afraid; keep on speaking, do not be silent. ¹⁰For I am with you, and no one is going to attack and harm you, because I have many people in this city." ¹¹So Paul stayed for a year and a half, teaching them the word of God.

¹²While Gallio was proconsul of Achaia, the Jews made a united attack on Paul and brought him into court. ¹³"This man," they charged, "is persuading the people to worship God in ways contrary to the law."

¹⁴Just as Paul was about to speak, Gallio said to the Jews, "If you Jews were making a complaint about some misdemeanor or serious crime, it would be reasonable for me to listen to you. ¹⁵But since it involves questions about words and names and your own law—settle the matter yourselves. I will not be a judge of such things." ¹⁶So he had them ejected from the court. ¹⁷Then they all turned on Sosthenes the synagogue ruler and beat him in front of the court. But Gallio showed no concern whatever.

Priscilla, Aquila and Apollos

¹⁸Paul stayed on in Corinth for some time. Then he left the brothers and sailed for Syria, accompanied by Priscilla and Aquila. Before he sailed, he had his hair cut off at Cenchrea because of a vow he had taken. ¹⁹They arrived at Ephesus, where Paul left Priscilla and Aquila. He himself went into the synagogue and reasoned with the Jews. ²⁰When they asked him to spend more time with them, he declined. ²¹But as he left, he promised, "I will come back if it is God's will." Then he set sail from Ephesus. ²²When he landed at Caesarea, he went up and greeted the church and then went down to Antioch.

²³After spending some time in Antioch, Paul set out from there and traveled from place to place throughout

ᵃ 5 Or Messiah; also in verse 28

the region of Galatia and Phrygia, strengthening all the disciples.

24Meanwhile a Jew named Apollos, a native of Alexandria, came to Ephesus. He was a learned man, with a thorough knowledge of the Scriptures. 25He had been instructed in the way of the Lord, and he spoke with great fervor[a] and taught about Jesus accurately, though he knew only the baptism of John. 26He began to speak boldly in the synagogue. When Priscilla and Aquila heard him, they invited him to their home and explained to him the way of God more adequately.

27When Apollos wanted to go to Achaia, the brothers encouraged him and wrote to the disciples there to welcome him. On arriving, he was a great help to those who by grace had believed. 28For he vigorously refuted the Jews in public debate, proving from the Scriptures that Jesus was the Christ.

Paul in Ephesus

19 While Apollos was at Corinth, Paul took the road through the interior and arrived at Ephesus. There he found some disciples 2and asked them, "Did you receive the Holy Spirit when[b] you believed?"

They answered, "No, we have not even heard that there is a Holy Spirit."

3So Paul asked, "Then what baptism did you receive?"

"John's baptism," they replied.

4Paul said, "John's baptism was a baptism of repentance. He told the people to believe in the one coming after him, that is, in Jesus." 5On hearing this, they were baptized into[c] the name of the Lord Jesus. 6When Paul placed his hands on them, the Holy Spirit came on them, and they spoke in tongues[d] and prophesied. 7There were about twelve men in all.

8Paul entered the synagogue and spoke boldly there for three months, arguing persuasively about the kingdom of God. 9But some of them became obstinate; they refused to believe and publicly maligned the Way. So Paul left them. He took the disciples with him and had discussions daily in the lecture hall of Tyrannus. 10This went on for two years, so that all the Jews and Greeks who lived in the province of Asia heard the word of the Lord.

11God did extraordinary miracles through Paul, 12so that even handkerchiefs and aprons that had touched him were taken to the sick, and their illnesses were cured and the evil spirits left them.

13Some Jews who went around driving out evil spirits tried to invoke the name of the Lord Jesus over those who were demon-possessed. They would say, "In the name of Jesus, whom Paul preaches, I command you to come out." 14Seven sons of Sceva, a Jewish chief priest, were doing this. 15One day, the evil spirit answered them, "Jesus I know, and I know about Paul, but who are you?"

Get a Load of This...

"Hey! Where'd my hankies go?" These handkerchiefs that they took from Paul to sick people (Acts 19:11–12) were cloths Paul tied around his head to keep the hair and sweat out of his eyes while he was stitching up tents (see Acts 18:3). Of course God was doing the healing, and he sure was doing plenty of that!

Get a Load of This...

The Christian converts in Ephesus burned their occult books worth millions of dollars by today's standards (Acts 19:18–20). Right, but that *doesn't* mean you need to have a marshmallow roast over all your westerns and sci-fi novels. Those books they torched were evil, occult, demonic books used to cast spells on people.

16Then the man who had the evil spirit jumped on them and overpowered them all. He gave them such a beating that they ran out of the house naked and bleeding. 17When this became known to the Jews and Greeks living in Ephesus, they were all seized with fear, and the name of the Lord Jesus was held in high honor. 18Many of those who believed now came and openly confessed their evil deeds. 19A number who had practiced sorcery brought their scrolls together and burned them publicly. When they calculated the value of the scrolls, the total came to fifty thousand drachmas.*a* 20In this way the word of the Lord spread widely and grew in power.

21After all this had happened, Paul decided to go to Jerusalem, passing through Macedonia and Achaia. "After I have been there," he said, "I must visit Rome also." 22He sent two of his helpers, Timothy and Erastus, to Macedonia, while he stayed in the province of Asia a little longer.

The Riot in Ephesus

23About that time there arose a great disturbance about the Way. 24A silversmith named Demetrius, who made silver shrines of Artemis, brought in no little business for the craftsmen. 25He called them together, along with the workmen in related trades, and said: "Men, you know we receive a good income from this business. 26And you see and hear how this fellow Paul has convinced and led astray large numbers of people here in Ephesus and in practically the whole province of Asia. He says that man-made gods are no gods at all. 27There is danger not only that our trade will lose its good name, but also that the temple of the great goddess Artemis will be discredited, and the goddess herself, who is worshiped throughout the province of Asia and the world, will be robbed of her divine majesty."

28When they heard this, they were furious and began shouting: "Great is Artemis of the Ephesians!" 29Soon the whole city was in an uproar. The people seized Gaius and Aristarchus, Paul's traveling companions from Macedonia, and rushed as one man into the theater. 30Paul wanted to appear before the crowd, but the disciples would not let him. 31Even some of the officials of the province, friends of Paul, sent him a message begging him not to venture into the theater.

32The assembly was in confusion: Some were shouting one thing, some another. Most of the people did not even know why they were there. 33The Jews pushed Alexander to the front, and some of the crowd shouted instructions to him. He motioned for silence in order to make a defense before the people. 34But when they realized he was a Jew, they all shouted in unison for about two hours: "Great is Artemis of the Ephesians!"

35The city clerk quieted the crowd and said: "Men of Ephesus, doesn't all the world know that the city of Ephesus is the guardian of the temple of the great Artemis and of her image, which fell from heaven? 36Therefore,

---

a 19 A drachma was a silver coin worth about a day's wages.

since these facts are undeniable, you ought to be quiet and not do anything rash. ³⁷You have brought these men here, though they have neither robbed temples nor blasphemed our goddess. ³⁸If, then, Demetrius and his fellow craftsmen have a grievance against anybody, the courts are open and there are proconsuls. They can press charges. ³⁹If there is anything further you want to bring up, it must be settled in a legal assembly. ⁴⁰As it is, we are in danger of being charged with rioting because of today's events. In that case we would not be able to account for this commotion, since there is no reason for it." ⁴¹After he had said this, he dismissed the assembly.

Through Macedonia and Greece

When the uproar had ended, Paul sent for the disciples and, after encouraging them, said good-by and set out for Macedonia. ²He traveled through that area, speaking many words of encouragement to the people, and finally arrived in Greece, ³where he stayed three months. Because the Jews made a plot against him just as he was about to sail for Syria, he decided to go back through Macedonia. ⁴He was accompanied by Sopater son of Pyrrhus from Berea, Aristarchus and Secundus from Thessalonica, Gaius from Derbe, Timothy also, and Tychicus and Trophimus from the province of Asia. ⁵These men went on ahead and waited for us at Troas. ⁶But we sailed from Philippi after the Feast of Unleavened Bread, and five days later joined the others at Troas, where we stayed seven days.

Eutychus Raised From the Dead at Troas

⁷On the first day of the week we came together to break bread. Paul spoke to the people and, because he intended to leave the next day, kept on talking until midnight. ⁸There were many lamps in the upstairs room where we were meeting. ⁹Seated in a window was a young man named Eutychus, who was sinking into a deep sleep as Paul talked on and on. When he was sound asleep, he fell to the ground from the third story and was picked up dead. ¹⁰Paul went down, threw himself on the young man and put his arms around him. "Don't be alarmed," he said. "He's alive!" ¹¹Then he went upstairs again and broke bread and ate. After talking until daylight, he left. ¹²The people took the young man home alive and were greatly comforted.

Paul's Farewell to the Ephesian Elders

¹³We went on ahead to the ship and sailed for Assos, where we were going to take Paul aboard. He had made this arrangement because he was going there on foot. ¹⁴When he met us at Assos, we took him aboard and went on to Mitylene. ¹⁵The next day we set sail from there and arrived off Kios. The day after that we crossed over to Samos, and on the following day arrived at Miletus. ¹⁶Paul had decided to sail past Ephesus to avoid spending time in the province of Asia, for he was

Get a Load of This...

Acts 20:7–9 is a warning about what can happen if you fall asleep in church. (Just kidding.) If you're going to sit in the balcony at church and fall asleep, make sure you're wearing a seat belt. Or better yet, don't let those eyelids slide down over your eyeballs.

in a hurry to reach Jerusalem, if possible, by the day of Pentecost.

¹⁷From Miletus, Paul sent to Ephesus for the elders of the church. ¹⁸When they arrived, he said to them: "You know how I lived the whole time I was with you, from the first day I came into the province of Asia. ¹⁹I served the Lord with great humility and with tears, although I was severely tested by the plots of the Jews. ²⁰You know that I have not hesitated to preach anything that would be helpful to you but have taught you publicly and from house to house. ²¹I have declared to both Jews and Greeks that they must turn to God in repentance and have faith in our Lord Jesus.

²²"And now, compelled by the Spirit, I am going to Jerusalem, not knowing what will happen to me there. ²³I only know that in every city the Holy Spirit warns me that prison and hardships are facing me. ²⁴However, I consider my life worth nothing to me, if only I may finish the race and complete the task the Lord

Jesus has given me—the task of testifying to the gospel of God's grace.

²⁵"Now I know that none of you among whom I have gone about preaching the kingdom will ever see me again. ²⁶Therefore, I declare to you today that I am innocent of the blood of all men. ²⁷For I have not hesitated to proclaim to you the whole will of God. ²⁸Keep watch over yourselves and all the flock of which the Holy Spirit has made you overseers.ᵃ Be shepherds of the church of God,ᵇ which he bought with his own blood. ²⁹I know that after I leave, savage wolves will come in among you and will not spare the flock. ³⁰Even from your own number men will arise and distort the truth in order to draw away disciples after them. ³¹So be on your guard! Remember that for three years I never stopped warning each of you night and day with tears.

ᵃ 28 Traditionally *bishops*   ᵇ 28 Many manuscripts *of the Lord*

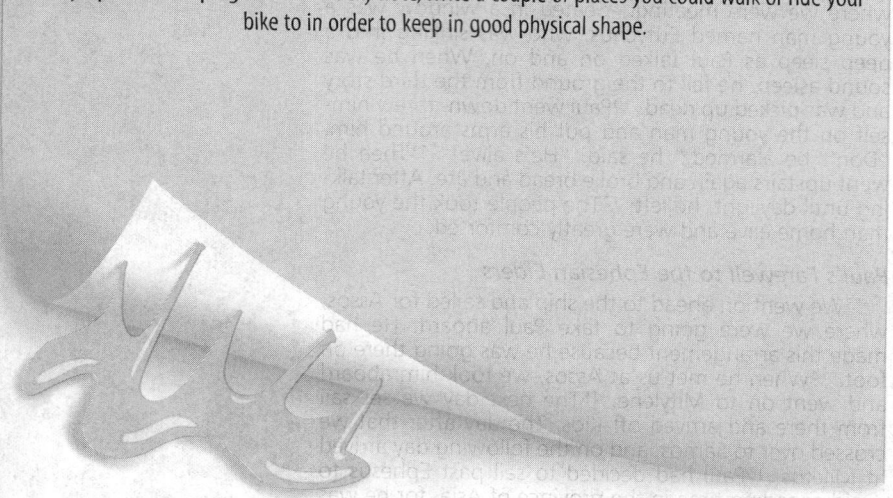

Make It Stick

READ ACTS 20:13–14

Paul walked across the peninsula instead of taking the boat. If you can walk or ride your bike, do that instead of begging your parents to drive you everywhere. Staying in shape doesn't have to be an Olympic exercise program. On a sticky note, write a couple of places you could walk or ride your bike to in order to keep in good physical shape.

³²"Now I commit you to God and to the word of his grace, which can build you up and give you an inheritance among all those who are sanctified. ³³I have not coveted anyone's silver or gold or clothing. ³⁴You yourselves know that these hands of mine have supplied my own needs and the needs of my companions. ³⁵In everything I did, I showed you that by this kind of hard work we must help the weak, remembering the words the Lord Jesus himself said: 'It is more blessed to give than to receive.' "

³⁶When he had said this, he knelt down with all of them and prayed. ³⁷They all wept as they embraced him and kissed him. ³⁸What grieved them most was his statement that they would never see his face again. Then they accompanied him to the ship.

On to Jerusalem

21 After we had torn ourselves away from them, we put out to sea and sailed straight to Cos. The next day we went to Rhodes and from there to Patara. ²We found a ship crossing over to Phoenicia, went on board and set sail. ³After sighting Cyprus and passing to the south of it, we sailed on to Syria. We landed at Tyre, where our ship was to unload its cargo. ⁴Finding the disciples there, we stayed with them seven days. Through the Spirit they urged Paul not to go on to Jerusalem. ⁵But when our time was up, we left and continued on our way. All the disciples and their wives and children accompanied us out of the city, and there on the beach we knelt to pray. ⁶After saying goodbye to each other, we went aboard the ship, and they returned home.

⁷We continued our voyage from Tyre and landed at Ptolemais, where we greeted the brothers and stayed with them for a day. ⁸Leaving the next day, we reached Caesarea and stayed at the house of Philip the evangelist, one of the Seven. ⁹He had four unmarried daughters who prophesied.

¹⁰After we had been there a number of days, a prophet named Agabus came down from Judea. ¹¹Coming over to us, he took Paul's belt, tied his own hands and feet with it and said, "The Holy Spirit says, 'In this way the Jews of Jerusalem will bind the owner of this belt and will hand him over to the Gentiles.' "

¹²When we heard this, we and the people there pleaded with Paul not to go up to Jerusalem. ¹³Then Paul answered, "Why are you weeping and breaking my heart? I am ready not only to be bound, but also to die in Jerusalem for the name of the Lord Jesus." ¹⁴When he would not be dissuaded, we gave up and said, "The Lord's will be done."

¹⁵After this, we got ready and went up to Jerusalem. ¹⁶Some of the disciples from Caesarea accompanied us and brought us to the home of Mnason, where we were to stay. He was a man from Cyprus and one of the early disciples.

Paul's Arrival at Jerusalem

¹⁷When we arrived at Jerusalem, the brothers received us warmly. ¹⁸The next day Paul and the rest of us went to see James, and all the elders were present. ¹⁹Paul greeted them and reported in detail what God had done among the Gentiles through his ministry.

²⁰When they heard this, they praised God. Then they said to Paul: "You see, brother, how many thousands of Jews have believed, and all of them are zealous for the law. ²¹They have been informed that you teach all the Jews who live among the Gentiles to turn away from Moses, telling them not to circumcise their children or live according to our customs. ²²What shall we do? They will certainly hear that you have come, ²³so do what we tell you. There are four men with us who have made a vow. ²⁴Take these men, join in their purification rites and pay their expenses, so that they can have their heads shaved. Then everybody will know there is no truth in these reports about you, but that you yourself are living in obedience to the law. ²⁵As for the Gentile believers, we have written to them our decision that they should abstain from food sacrificed to idols, from blood, from the meat of strangled animals and from sexual immorality."

²⁶The next day Paul took the men and purified himself along with them. Then he went to the temple to give notice of the date when the days of purification would end and the offering would be made for each of them.

Paul Arrested

²⁷When the seven days were nearly over, some Jews from the province of Asia

Check out Acts 21:35. A mob was attacking Paul—*again*! This wasn't because he was so popular, like a Hollywood star; quite the opposite. Once Paul was led out of the chaos (in chains, no less), he was able to explain who he was and got permission to speak to the people. This was his chance to tell his testimony of how he turned from being a Christian-hater to a Christian himself. How cool is that?!

saw Paul at the temple. They stirred up the whole crowd and seized him, 28shouting, "Men of Israel, help us! This is the man who teaches all men everywhere against our people and our law and this place. And besides, he has brought Greeks into the temple area and defiled this holy place." 29(They had previously seen Trophimus the Ephesian in the city with Paul and assumed that Paul had brought him into the temple area.)

30The whole city was aroused, and the people came running from all directions. Seizing Paul, they dragged him from the temple, and immediately the gates were shut. 31While they were trying to kill him, news reached the commander of the Roman troops that the whole city of Jerusalem was in an uproar. 32He at once took some officers and soldiers and ran down to the crowd. When the rioters saw the commander and his soldiers, they stopped beating Paul.

33The commander came up and arrested him and ordered him to be bound with two chains. Then he asked who he was and what he had done. 34Some in the crowd shouted one thing and some another, and since the commander could not get at the truth because of the uproar, he ordered that Paul be taken into the barracks. 35When Paul reached the steps, the violence of the mob was so great he had to be carried by the soldiers. 36The crowd that followed kept shouting, "Away with him!"

Paul Speaks to the Crowd

37As the soldiers were about to take Paul into the barracks, he asked the commander, "May I say something to you?"

"Do you speak Greek?" he replied. 38"Aren't you the Egyptian who started a revolt and led four thousand terrorists out into the desert some time ago?"

39Paul answered, "I am a Jew, from Tarsus in Cilicia, a citizen of no ordinary city. Please let me speak to the people."

40Having received the commander's permission, Paul stood on the steps and motioned to the crowd. When they were all silent, he said to them in Aramaic*a*:

22 1"Brothers and fathers, listen now to my defense."

2When they heard him speak to them in Aramaic, they became very quiet.

Then Paul said: 3"I am a Jew, born in Tarsus of Cilicia, but brought up in this city. Under Gamaliel I was thoroughly trained in the law of our fathers and was just as zealous for God as any of you are today. 4I persecuted the followers of this Way to their death, arresting both men and women and throwing them into prison, 5as also the high priest and all the Council can testify. I even obtained letters from them to their brothers in Damascus, and went there to bring these people as prisoners to Jerusalem to be punished.

6"About noon as I came near Damascus, suddenly a

a 40 Or possibly *Hebrew*; also in 22:2

bright light from heaven flashed around me. 7I fell to the ground and heard a voice say to me, 'Saul! Saul! Why do you persecute me?'

8" 'Who are you, Lord?' I asked.

" 'I am Jesus of Nazareth, whom you are persecuting,' he replied. 9My companions saw the light, but they did not understand the voice of him who was speaking to me.

10" 'What shall I do, Lord?' I asked.

" 'Get up,' the Lord said, 'and go into Damascus. There you will be told all that you have been assigned to do.' 11My companions led me by the hand into Damascus, because the brilliance of the light had blinded me.

12"A man named Ananias came to see me. He was a devout observer of the law and highly respected by all the Jews living there. 13He stood beside me and said, 'Brother Saul, receive your sight!' And at that very moment I was able to see him.

14"Then he said: 'The God of our fathers has chosen you to know his will and to see the Righteous One and to hear words from his mouth. 15You will be his witness to all men of what you have seen and heard. 16And now what are you waiting for? Get up, be baptized and wash your sins away, calling on his name.'

17"When I returned to Jerusalem and was praying at the temple, I fell into a trance 18and saw the Lord speaking. 'Quick!' he said to me. 'Leave Jerusalem immediately, because they will not accept your testimony about me.'

19" 'Lord,' I replied, 'these men know that I went from one synagogue to another to imprison and beat those who believe in you. 20And when the blood of your martyr*a* Stephen was shed, I stood there giving my approval and guarding the clothes of those who were killing him.'

21"Then the Lord said to me, 'Go; I will send you far away to the Gentiles.' "

Paul the Roman Citizen

22The crowd listened to Paul until he said this. Then they raised their voices and shouted, "Rid the earth of him! He's not fit to live!"

23As they were shouting and throwing off their cloaks and flinging dust into the air, 24the commander ordered Paul to be taken into the barracks. He directed that he be flogged and questioned in order to find out why the people were shouting at him like this. 25As they stretched him out to flog him, Paul said to the centurion standing there, "Is it legal for you to flog a Roman citizen who hasn't even been found guilty?"

26When the centurion heard this, he went to the commander and reported it. "What are you going to do?" he asked. "This man is a Roman citizen."

27The commander went to Paul and asked, "Tell me, are you a Roman citizen?"

a 20 Or witness

Get a Load of This...

Check out Acts 22:22–23. These people were hoppin' mad at Paul. They threw off their coats to show that they were ready to tear into him, and flinging dust in the air was a sign of their rage. Imagine if your friends did this when they got upset! What would they look like?!

Get a Load of This...

Check out Acts 23:12–24. Forty-plus men swore not to eat or drink until they'd killed Paul. *Did* they ever eat and drink?—because they never did do Paul in. Do you think they broke their oath, or did they keep chasing Paul until they collapsed from dehydration and hunger and died?

"Yes, I am," he answered.

²⁸Then the commander said, "I had to pay a big price for my citizenship."

"But I was born a citizen," Paul replied.

²⁹Those who were about to question him withdrew immediately. The commander himself was alarmed when he realized that he had put Paul, a Roman citizen, in chains.

Before the Sanhedrin

³⁰The next day, since the commander wanted to find out exactly why Paul was being accused by the Jews, he released him and ordered the chief priests and all the Sanhedrin to assemble. Then he brought Paul and had him stand before them.

23 Paul looked straight at the Sanhedrin and said, "My brothers, I have fulfilled my duty to God in all good conscience to this day." ²At this the high priest Ananias ordered those standing near Paul to strike him on the mouth. ³Then Paul said to him, "God will strike you, you whitewashed wall! You sit there to judge me according to the law, yet you yourself violate the law by commanding that I be struck!"

⁴Those who were standing near Paul said, "You dare to insult God's high priest?"

⁵Paul replied, "Brothers, I did not realize that he was the high priest; for it is written: 'Do not speak evil about the ruler of your people.'ᵃ"

⁶Then Paul, knowing that some of them were Sadducees and the others Pharisees, called out in the Sanhedrin, "My brothers, I am a Pharisee, the son of a Pharisee. I stand on trial because of my hope in the resurrection of the dead." ⁷When he said this, a dispute broke out between the Pharisees and the Sadducees, and the assembly was divided. ⁸(The Sadducees say that there is no resurrection, and that there are neither angels nor spirits, but the Pharisees acknowledge them all.)

⁹There was a great uproar, and some of the teachers of the law who were Pharisees stood up and argued vigorously. "We find nothing wrong with this man," they said. "What if a spirit or an angel has spoken to him?" ¹⁰The dispute became so violent that the commander was afraid Paul would be torn to pieces by them. He ordered the troops to go down and take him away from them by force and bring him into the barracks.

¹¹The following night the Lord stood near Paul and said, "Take courage! As you have testified about me in Jerusalem, so you must also testify in Rome."

The Plot to Kill Paul

¹²The next morning the Jews formed a conspiracy and bound themselves with an oath not to eat or drink until they had killed Paul. ¹³More than forty men were involved in this plot. ¹⁴They went to the chief priests and elders and said, "We have taken a solemn oath not

---

ᵃ 5 Exodus 22:28

to eat anything until we have killed Paul. [15]Now then, you and the Sanhedrin petition the commander to bring him before you on the pretext of wanting more accurate information about his case. We are ready to kill him before he gets here."

[16]But when the son of Paul's sister heard of this plot, he went into the barracks and told Paul.

[17]Then Paul called one of the centurions and said, "Take this young man to the commander; he has something to tell him." [18]So he took him to the commander.

The centurion said, "Paul, the prisoner, sent for me and asked me to bring this young man to you because he has something to tell you."

[19]The commander took the young man by the hand, drew him aside and asked, "What is it you want to tell me?"

[20]He said: "The Jews have agreed to ask you to bring Paul before the Sanhedrin tomorrow on the pretext of wanting more accurate information about him. [21]Don't give in to them, because more than forty of them are waiting in ambush for him. They have taken an oath not to eat or drink until they have killed him. They are ready now, waiting for your consent to their request."

[22]The commander dismissed the young man and cautioned him, "Don't tell anyone that you have reported this to me."

Paul Transferred to Caesarea

[23]Then he called two of his centurions and ordered them, "Get ready a detachment of two hundred soldiers, seventy horsemen and two hundred spearmen[a] to go to Caesarea at nine tonight. [24]Provide mounts for Paul so that he may be taken safely to Governor Felix."

[25]He wrote a letter as follows:

[26]Claudius Lysias,

To His Excellency, Governor Felix:

Greetings.

[27]This man was seized by the Jews and they were about to kill him, but I came with my troops and rescued him, for I had learned that he is a Roman citizen. [28]I wanted to know why they were accusing him, so I brought him to their Sanhedrin. [29]I found that the accusation had to do with questions about their law, but there was

no charge against him that deserved death or imprisonment. [30]When I was informed of a plot to be carried out against the man, I sent him to you at once. I also ordered his accusers to present to you their case against him.

[31]So the soldiers, carrying out their orders, took Paul with them during the night and brought him as far as Antipatris. [32]The next day they let the cavalry go on with him, while they returned to the barracks. [33]When the cavalry arrived in Caesarea, they delivered the letter to the governor and handed Paul over to him. [34]The governor read the letter and asked what province he was from. Learning that he was from Cilicia, [35]he said, "I will hear your case when your accusers get here." Then he ordered that Paul be kept under guard in Herod's palace.

The Trial Before Felix

24 Five days later the high priest Ananias went down to Caesarea with some of the elders and a lawyer named Tertullus, and they brought their charges against Paul before the governor. [2]When Paul was called in, Tertullus presented his case before Felix: "We have enjoyed a long period of peace under you, and your foresight has brought about reforms in this nation. [3]Everywhere and in every way, most excellent Felix, we acknowledge this with profound gratitude. [4]But in order not to weary you further, I would request that you be kind enough to hear us briefly.

[5]"We have found this man to be a troublemaker, stirring up riots among the Jews all over the world. He is a ringleader of the Nazarene sect [6]and even tried to desecrate the temple; so we seized him. [8b]By examining him yourself you will be able to learn the truth about all these charges we are bringing against him."

[9]The Jews joined in the accusation, asserting that these things were true.

[10]When the governor motioned for him to speak, Paul replied: "I know that for a number of years you have been a judge over this nation; so I gladly make my de-

---

[a] 23 The meaning of the Greek for this word is uncertain.
[b] 6–8 Some manuscripts him and wanted to judge him according to our law. [7]But the commander, Lysias, came and with the use of much force snatched him from our hands [8]and ordered his accusers to come before you. By

fense. [11]You can easily verify that no more than twelve days ago I went up to Jerusalem to worship. [12]My accusers did not find me arguing with anyone at the temple, or stirring up a crowd in the synagogues or anywhere else in the city. [13]And they cannot prove to you the charges they are now making against me. [14]However, I admit that I worship the God of our fathers as a follower of the Way, which they call a sect. I believe everything that agrees with the Law and that is written in the Prophets, [15]and I have the same hope in God as these men, that there will be a resurrection of both the righteous and the wicked. [16]So I strive always to keep my conscience clear before God and man.

[17]"After an absence of several years, I came to Jerusalem to bring my people gifts for the poor and to present offerings. [18]I was ceremonially clean when they found me in the temple courts doing this. There was no crowd with me, nor was I involved in any disturbance. [19]But there are some Jews from the province of Asia, who ought to be here before you and bring charges if they have anything against me. [20]Or these who are here should state what crime they found in me when I stood before the Sanhedrin— [21]unless it was this one thing I shouted as I stood in their presence: 'It is concerning the resurrection of the dead that I am on trial before you today.' "

[22]Then Felix, who was well acquainted with the Way, adjourned the proceedings. "When Lysias the commander comes," he said, "I will decide your case." [23]He ordered the centurion to keep Paul under guard but to give him some freedom and permit his friends to take care of his needs.

[24]Several days later Felix came with his wife Drusilla, who was a Jewess. He sent for Paul and listened to him as he spoke about faith in Christ Jesus. [25]As Paul discoursed on righteousness, self-control and the judgment to come, Felix was afraid and said, "That's enough for now! You may leave. When I find it convenient, I will send for you." [26]At the same time he was hoping that Paul would offer him a bribe, so he sent for him frequently and talked with him.

[27]When two years had passed, Felix was succeeded by Porcius Festus, but because Felix wanted to grant a favor to the Jews, he left Paul in prison.

The Trial Before Festus

25 Three days after arriving in the province, Festus went up from Caesarea to Jerusalem, [2]where the chief priests and Jewish leaders appeared before him and presented the charges against Paul. [3]They urgently requested Festus, as a favor to them, to have Paul transferred to Jerusalem, for they were preparing an ambush to kill him along the way. [4]Festus answered, "Paul is being held at Caesarea, and I myself am going there soon. [5]Let some of your leaders come with me and press charges against the man there, if he has done anything wrong."

[6]After spending eight or ten days with them, he went down to Caesarea, and the next day he convened the court and ordered that Paul be brought before him. [7]When Paul appeared, the Jews who had come down from Jerusalem stood around him, bringing many serious charges against him, which they could not prove.

[8]Then Paul made his defense: "I have done nothing wrong against the law of the Jews or against the temple or against Caesar."

[9]Festus, wishing to do the Jews a favor, said to Paul, "Are you willing to go up to Jerusalem and stand trial before me there on these charges?"

[10]Paul answered: "I am now standing before Caesar's court, where I ought to be tried. I have not done any wrong to the Jews, as you yourself know very well. [11]If, however, I am guilty of doing anything deserving death, I do not refuse to die. But if the charges brought against me by these Jews are not true, no one has the right to hand me over to them. I appeal to Caesar!"

[12]After Festus had conferred with his council, he declared: "You have appealed to Caesar. To Caesar you will go!"

Festus Consults King Agrippa

[13]A few days later King Agrippa and Bernice arrived at Caesarea to pay their respects to Festus. [14]Since they were spending many days there, Festus discussed Paul's case with the king. He said: "There is a man here whom Felix left as a prisoner. [15]When I went to Jerusalem, the chief priests and elders of the Jews brought charges against him and asked that he be condemned.

16"I told them that it is not the Roman custom to hand over any man before he has faced his accusers and has had an opportunity to defend himself against their charges. 17When they came here with me, I did not delay the case, but convened the court the next day and ordered the man to be brought in. 18When his accusers got up to speak, they did not charge him with any of the crimes I had expected. 19Instead, they had some points of dispute with him about their own religion and about a dead man named Jesus who Paul claimed was alive. 20I was at a loss how to investigate such matters; so I asked if he would be willing to go to Jerusalem and stand trial there on these charges. 21When Paul made his appeal to be held over for the Emperor's decision, I ordered him held until I could send him to Caesar."

22Then Agrippa said to Festus, "I would like to hear this man myself."

He replied, "Tomorrow you will hear him."

Paul Before Agrippa

23The next day Agrippa and Bernice came with great pomp and entered the audience room with the high ranking officers and the leading men of the city. At the command of Festus, Paul was brought in. 24Festus said: "King Agrippa, and all who are present with us, you see this man! The whole Jewish community has petitioned me about him in Jerusalem and here in Caesarea, shouting that he ought not to live any longer. 25I found he had done nothing deserving of death, but because he made his appeal to the Emperor I decided to send him to Rome. 26But I have nothing definite to write to His Majesty about him. Therefore I have brought him before all of you, and especially before you, King Agrippa, so that as a result of this investigation I may have something to write. 27For I think it is unreasonable to send on a prisoner without specifying the charges against him."

26 Then Agrippa said to Paul, "You have permission to speak for yourself."

So Paul motioned with his hand and began his defense: 2"King Agrippa, I consider myself fortunate to stand before you today as I make my defense against all the accusations of the Jews, 3and especially so because you are well acquainted with all the Jewish customs and controversies. Therefore, I beg you to listen to me patiently.

4"The Jews all know the way I have lived ever since I was a child, from the beginning of my life in my own country, and also in Jerusalem. 5They have known me for a long time and can testify, if they are willing, that according to the strictest sect of our religion, I lived as a Pharisee. 6And now it is because of my hope in what God has promised our fathers that I am on trial today. 7This is the promise our twelve tribes are hoping to see fulfilled as they earnestly serve God day and night. O king, it is because of this hope that the Jews are accusing me. 8Why should any of you consider it incredible that God raises the dead?

9"I too was convinced that I ought to do all that was possible to oppose the name of Jesus of Nazareth. 10And that is just what I did in Jerusalem. On the authority of the chief priests I put many of the saints in prison, and when they were put to death, I cast my vote against them. 11Many a time I went from one synagogue to another to have them punished, and I tried to force them to blaspheme. In my obsession against them, I even went to foreign cities to persecute them.

12"On one of these journeys I was going to Damascus with the authority and commission of the chief priests. 13About noon, O king, as I was on the road, I saw a light from heaven, brighter than the sun, blazing around me and my companions. 14We all fell to the ground, and I heard a voice saying to me in Aramaic,a 'Saul, Saul, why do you persecute me? It is hard for you to kick against the goads.'

15"Then I asked, 'Who are you, Lord?'

" 'I am Jesus, whom you are persecuting,' the Lord replied. 16'Now get up and stand on your feet. I have appeared to you to appoint you as a servant and as a witness of what you have seen of me and what I will show you. 17I will rescue you from your own people and from the Gentiles. I am sending you to them 18to open their eyes and turn them from darkness to light, and from the power of Satan to God, so that they may receive forgiveness of sins and a place among those who are sanctified by faith in me.'

a 14 Or Hebrew

Get a Load of This...

There is no proof that "great learning" drives you insane—contrary to what Festus said here (Acts 26:24). So, *no*, you can't use this as an excuse to not do your homework.

¹⁹"So then, King Agrippa, I was not disobedient to the vision from heaven. ²⁰First to those in Damascus, then to those in Jerusalem and in all Judea, and to the Gentiles also, I preached that they should repent and turn to God and prove their repentance by their deeds. ²¹That is why the Jews seized me in the temple courts and tried to kill me. ²²But I have had God's help to this very day, and so I stand here and testify to small and great alike. I am saying nothing beyond what the prophets and Moses said would happen— ²³that the Christᵃ would suffer and, as the first to rise from the dead, would proclaim light to his own people and to the Gentiles."

²⁴At this point Festus interrupted Paul's defense. "You are out of your mind, Paul!" he shouted. "Your great learning is driving you insane."

²⁵"I am not insane, most excellent Festus," Paul replied. "What I am saying is true and reasonable. ²⁶The king is familiar with these things, and I can speak freely to him. I am convinced that none of this has escaped his notice, because it was not done in a corner. ²⁷King Agrippa, do you believe the prophets? I know you do."

²⁸Then Agrippa said to Paul, "Do you think that in such a short time you can persuade me to be a Christian?"

²⁹Paul replied, "Short time or long—I pray God that not only you but all who are listening to me today may become what I am, except for these chains."

³⁰The king rose, and with him the governor and Bernice and those sitting with them. ³¹They left the room, and while talking with one another, they said, "This man is not doing anything that deserves death or imprisonment."

³²Agrippa said to Festus, "This man could have been set free if he had not appealed to Caesar."

Paul Sails for Rome

27 When it was decided that we would sail for Italy, Paul and some other prisoners were handed over to a centurion named Julius, who belonged to the Imperial Regiment. ²We boarded a ship from Adramyttium about to sail for ports along the coast of the province of Asia, and we put out to sea. Aristarchus, a Macedonian from Thessalonica, was with us.

³The next day we landed at Sidon; and Julius, in kindness to Paul, allowed him to go to his friends so they might provide for his needs. ⁴From there we put out to sea again and passed to the lee of Cyprus because the winds were against us. ⁵When we had sailed across the open sea off the coast of Cilicia and Pamphylia, we landed at Myra in Lycia. ⁶There the centurion found an Alexandrian ship sailing for Italy and put us on board. ⁷We made slow headway for many days and had difficulty arriving off Cnidus. When the wind did not allow us to hold our course, we sailed to the lee of Crete, opposite Salmone. ⁸We moved along the coast with diffi-

ᵃ 23 Or *Messiah*

culty and came to a place called Fair Havens, near the town of Lasea.

⁹Much time had been lost, and sailing had already become dangerous because by now it was after the Fast.ᵃ So Paul warned them, ¹⁰"Men, I can see that our voyage is going to be disastrous and bring great loss to ship and cargo, and to our own lives also." ¹¹But the centurion, instead of listening to what Paul said, followed the advice of the pilot and of the owner of the ship. ¹²Since the harbor was unsuitable to winter in, the majority decided that we should sail on, hoping to reach Phoenix and winter there. This was a harbor in Crete, facing both southwest and northwest.

The Storm

¹³When a gentle south wind began to blow, they thought they had obtained what they wanted; so they weighed anchor and sailed along the shore of Crete. ¹⁴Before very long, a wind of hurricane force, called the "northeaster," swept down from the island. ¹⁵The ship was caught by the storm and could not head into the wind; so we gave way to it and were driven along. ¹⁶As we passed to the lee of a small island called Cauda, we were hardly able to make the lifeboat secure. ¹⁷When the men had hoisted it aboard, they passed ropes under the ship itself to hold it together. Fearing that they would run aground on the sandbars of Syrtis, they lowered the sea anchor and let the ship be driven along. ¹⁸We took such a violent battering from the storm that the next day they began to throw the cargo overboard. ¹⁹On the third day, they threw the ship's tackle overboard with their own hands. ²⁰When neither sun nor stars appeared for many days and the storm continued raging, we finally gave up all hope of being saved.

²¹After the men had gone a long time without food, Paul stood up before them and said: "Men, you should have taken my advice not to sail from Crete; then you would have spared yourselves this damage and loss. ²²But now I urge you to keep up your courage, because not one of

ᵃ 9 That is, the Day of Atonement (Yom Kippur)

275 Plus One

READ ACTS 27

On this voyage to Rome, Paul was just a prisoner in chains. (You aren't going nowhere, buddy.) But from God's perspective, Paul was the most important person on that ship, and he was *definitely* going places! The Roman soldiers were basically his taxi service, and the "taxi" sank to the bottom of the sea with all the cargo. *The number one priority was Paul's need to get to Rome.* When the ship was in danger, an angel told Paul, "God has graciously given you the lives of all who sail with you" (verse 24). Paul was going to live—*that* was a done deal. The bonus was that, because he prayed, God kept the other 275 passengers safe. If some so-called tough kids pick on you and call you a "loser," remember: it's what God thinks that's important. And in God's eyes, you count big-time.

Your next reading is on page 1459.

you will be lost; only the ship will be destroyed. ²³Last night an angel of the God whose I am and whom I serve stood beside me ²⁴and said, 'Do not be afraid, Paul. You must stand trial before Caesar; and God has graciously given you the lives of all who sail with you.' ²⁵So keep up your courage, men, for I have faith in God that it will happen just as he told me. ²⁶Nevertheless, we must run aground on some island."

The Shipwreck

²⁷On the fourteenth night we were still being driven across the Adriatic[a] Sea, when about midnight the sailors sensed they were approaching land. ²⁸They took soundings and found that the water was a hundred and twenty feet[b] deep. A short time later they took soundings again and found it was ninety feet[c] deep. ²⁹Fearing that we would be dashed against the rocks, they dropped four anchors from the stern and prayed for daylight. ³⁰In an attempt to escape from the ship, the sailors let the lifeboat down into the sea, pretending they were going to lower some anchors from the bow. ³¹Then Paul said to the centurion and the soldiers, "Unless these men stay with the ship, you cannot be saved." ³²So the soldiers cut the ropes that held the lifeboat and let it fall away.

³³Just before dawn Paul urged them all to eat. "For the last fourteen days," he said, "you have been in constant suspense and have gone without food—you haven't eaten anything. ³⁴Now I urge you to take some food. You need it to survive. Not one of you will lose a single hair from his head." ³⁵After he said this, he took some bread and gave thanks to God in front of them all. Then he broke it and began to eat. ³⁶They were all encouraged and ate some food themselves. ³⁷Altogether there were 276 of us on board. ³⁸When they had eaten as much as they wanted, they lightened the ship by throwing the grain into the sea.

³⁹When daylight came, they did not recognize the land, but they saw a bay with a sandy beach, where they decided to run the ship aground if they could. ⁴⁰Cutting loose the anchors, they left them in the sea and at the same time untied the ropes that held the rudders. Then they hoisted the foresail to the wind and made for the beach. ⁴¹But the ship struck a sandbar and ran aground. The bow stuck fast and would not move, and the stern was broken to pieces by the pounding of the surf.

⁴²The soldiers planned to kill the prisoners to prevent any of them from swimming away and escaping. ⁴³But the centurion wanted to spare Paul's life and kept them from carrying out their plan. He ordered those who could swim to jump overboard first and get to land. ⁴⁴The rest were to get there on planks or on pieces of the ship. In this way everyone reached land in safety.

Ashore on Malta

28 Once safely on shore, we found out that the island was called Malta. ²The islanders showed us unusual kindness. They built a fire and welcomed us all because it was raining and cold. ³Paul gathered a pile of brushwood and, as he put it on the fire, a viper, driven out by the heat, fastened itself on his hand. ⁴When the islanders saw the snake hanging from his hand, they said to each other, "This man must be a murderer; for though he escaped from the sea, Justice has not allowed him to live." ⁵But Paul shook the snake off into the fire and suffered no ill effects. ⁶The people expected him to swell up or suddenly fall dead, but after waiting a long time and seeing nothing unusual happen to him, they changed their minds and said he was a god.

⁷There was an estate nearby that belonged to Publius, the chief official of the island. He welcomed us to his home and for three days entertained us hospitably. ⁸His father was sick in bed, suffering from fever and dysentery. Paul went in to see him and, after prayer, placed his hands on him and healed him. ⁹When this had happened, the rest of the sick on the island came and were cured. ¹⁰They honored us in many ways and when we were ready to sail, they furnished us with the supplies we needed.

Arrival at Rome

¹¹After three months we put out to sea in a ship that had wintered in the island. It was an Alexandrian ship with the figure-

---

[a] 27 In ancient times the name referred to an area extending well south of Italy.　[b] 28 Greek twenty orguias (about 37 meters)　[c] 28 Greek fifteen orguias (about 27 meters)

head of the twin gods Castor and Pollux. [12]We put in at Syracuse and stayed there three days. [13]From there we set sail and arrived at Rhegium. The next day the south wind came up, and on the following day we reached Puteoli. [14]There we found some brothers who invited us to spend a week with them. And so we came to Rome. [15]The brothers there had heard that we were coming, and they traveled as far as the Forum of Appius and the Three Taverns to meet us. At the sight of these men Paul thanked God and was encouraged. [16]When we got to Rome, Paul was allowed to live by himself, with a soldier to guard him.

Paul Preaches at Rome Under Guard

[17]Three days later he called together the leaders of the Jews. When they had assembled, Paul said to them: "My brothers, although I have done nothing against our people or against the customs of our ancestors, I was arrested in Jerusalem and handed over to the Romans. [18]They examined me and wanted to release me, because I was not guilty of any crime deserving death. [19]But when the Jews objected, I was compelled to appeal to Caesar—not that I had any charge to bring against my own people. [20]For this reason I have asked to see you and talk with you. It is because of the hope of Israel that I am bound with this chain."

[21]They replied, "We have not received any letters from Judea concerning you, and none of the brothers who have come from there has reported or said anything bad about you. [22]But we want to hear what your views are, for we know that people everywhere are talking against this sect."

[23]They arranged to meet Paul on a certain day, and came in even larger numbers to the place where he was staying. From morning till evening he explained and declared to them the kingdom of God and tried to convince them about Jesus from the Law of Moses and from the Prophets. [24]Some were convinced by what he said, but others would not believe. [25]They disagreed among themselves and began to leave after Paul had made this final statement: "The Holy Spirit spoke the truth to

Malta Gets the Message

READ ACTS 28:1–10

Ever made a horrible mistake?—like running through the living room in a bath towel, screaming, "Mom! I don't have even one clean pair of underwear!" then notice that she's leading ladies from your church in a Bible study? Everyone makes mistakes. God showed Paul that there was a storm coming and that they shouldn't set sail (Acts 27:10–11), but since they wouldn't listen to the warning—and Paul trusted God—God still worked things out. Sure, they lost the ship in the storm, but God brought something good out of it: Malta was evangelized. Wow! Does God *rule* or what? So even when you make mistakes, ask for forgiveness and trust that God will turn the situation around and make good come out of it (Romans 8:28). God can work things out for good from that point forward, no matter how you goofed up to get into that situation.

Your next reading is on page 1460.

Paul the Apostle

READ ACTS 28:16–24, 30–31

Paul (formerly known as Saul) went bonkers persecuting Christians, but once God turned him around, he used Paul to do more than perhaps any other guy in the New Testament church (see Acts 9:1–16).

SMARTER: Paul was highly educated. He studied under Gamaliel, *the* top Jewish teacher of the day (see Acts 22:3). Paul applied himself so zealously to studying that he was top of the class (see Galatians 1:14). He not only knew the books of the Old Testament inside out, but he was familiar with Greek literature. Paul could debate with the most intelligent philosophers of his day (see Acts 17:18) and had "great learning" (Acts 26:24). But when he became a Christian, Paul counted all his accomplishments as "rubbish" compared to knowing Jesus (see Philippians 3:8). God had Paul write letters to the church—thirteen *new* Bible books, in fact—which established much of the teaching of the New Testament.

DEEPER: Paul realized that the most important thing in life was his relationship with God. For starters, that meant his prayer life. Paul told Christians to "pray continually" (1 Thessalonians 5:17). Paul talked to God anytime and anywhere about anything. Reading God's Word was high on Paul's list, too. He paid close attention to reading and studying the Word (see 1 Timothy 4:13).

STRONGER: Paul wrote, "Physical training is of some value" (1 Timothy 4:8). You bet it is! Paul was strong enough to survive incredible beatings (see 2 Corinthians 11:23–27), and traveled the known world—which meant a *lot* of walking. Style? When he talked to intellectuals in the Areopagus (Acts 17:19–22), you can bet he was presentable. Being in shape and presentable was part of his being a godly man.

COOLER: Paul was a great conversationalist. This guy adapted quickly to different cultures and languages and could chat with workers on the street or present himself to world leaders. He strongly believed in getting along with others. He told the Corinthians that jealousy and quarreling was proof that they weren't mature Christians (see 1 Corinthians 3:3). Paul explained how to relate to others, how to get along, how to deal with problems in the church, and constantly told Christians to love one another.

Your next reading is on page 1467.

your forefathers when he said through Isaiah the prophet:

26 " 'Go to this people and say,
    "You will be ever hearing but never
        understanding;
    you will be ever seeing but never
        perceiving."
27 For this people's heart has become
        calloused;
    they hardly hear with their ears,
    and they have closed their eyes.
    Otherwise they might see with their
        eyes,
    hear with their ears,

understand with their hearts
    and turn, and I would heal them.' [a]

28 "Therefore I want you to know that God's salvation has been sent to the Gentiles, and they will listen!" [b]

30 For two whole years Paul stayed there in his own rented house and welcomed all who came to see him. 31 Boldly and without hindrance he preached the kingdom of God and taught about the Lord Jesus Christ.

---

[a] 27 Isaiah 6:9,10   [b] 28 Some manuscripts listen!" 29 After he said this, the Jews left, arguing vigorously among themselves.

ROMANS

Who wrote this book?
Paul wrote this book to the church in Rome.

Why was this book written?
Romans shows how Jesus' death makes us right with God and how Jesus will help us live a good life.

For whom was this book written?
This book is a letter Paul sent to Christians in Rome.

When was this book written?
This book was written about A.D. 57 from the city of Corinth.

What are some important teachings in this book?

Everyone sins	Romans 3:9–20
God saves people who believe	Romans 4:1–25
Jesus died for us	Romans 5:1–11
God's Spirit helps us to do right	Romans 8:1–11
God loves us forever	Romans 8:28–39
God shows us how to love	Romans 12:9–21

Paul, a servant of Christ Jesus, called to be an apostle and set apart for the gospel of God— ²the gospel he promised beforehand through his prophets in the Holy Scriptures ³regarding his Son, who as to his human nature was a descendant of David, ⁴and who through the Spirit^a of holiness was declared with power to be the Son of God^b by his resurrection from the dead: Jesus Christ our Lord. ⁵Through him and for his name's sake, we received grace and apostleship to call people from among all the Gentiles to the obedience that comes from faith. ⁶And you also are among those who are called to belong to Jesus Christ.

⁷To all in Rome who are loved by God and called to be saints:

Grace and peace to you from God our Father and from the Lord Jesus Christ.

Paul's Longing to Visit Rome

⁸First, I thank my God through Jesus Christ for all of you, because your faith is being reported all over the world. ⁹God, whom I serve with my whole heart in preaching the gospel of his Son, is my witness how constantly I remember you ¹⁰in my prayers at all times; and I pray that now at last by God's will the way may be opened for me to come to you.

¹¹I long to see you so that I may impart to you some spiritual gift to make you strong— ¹²that is, that you and I may be mutually encouraged by each other's faith. ¹³I do not want you to be unaware, brothers, that I planned many times to come to you (but have been prevented from doing so until now) in order that I might have a harvest among you, just as I have had among the other Gentiles.

¹⁴I am obligated both to Greeks and non-Greeks, both to the wise and the foolish. ¹⁵That is why I am so eager to preach the gospel also to you who are at Rome.

¹⁶I am not ashamed of the gospel, because it is the power of God for the salvation of everyone who believes: first for the Jew, then for the Gentile. ¹⁷For in the gospel a righteousness from God is revealed, a righteousness that is by faith from first to last,^{c} just as it is written: "The righteous will live by faith."^{d}

God's Wrath Against Mankind

¹⁸The wrath of God is being revealed from heaven against all the godlessness and wickedness of men who suppress the truth by their wickedness, ¹⁹since what may be known about God is plain to them, because God has made it plain to them. ²⁰For since the creation of the world God's invisible qualities—his eternal power and divine nature—have been clearly seen, being understood from what has been made, so that men are without excuse.

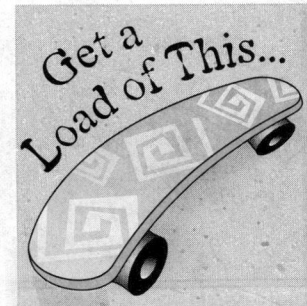

Get a Load of This...

It's obvious that somebody with incredible power created the world. When you study everything from DNA to bees to the Milky Way galaxy, you *know* it was made by a super-intelligent Being. Creation shows us God's "eternal power and divine nature" (Romans 1:20).

---

^{a} 4 Or who as to his spirit ^{b} 4 Or was appointed to be the Son of God with power ^{c} 17 Or is from faith to faith ^{d} 17 Hab. 2:4

Get a Load of This...

The culture we live in tells us that a homosexual lifestyle is acceptable. The Bible tells us clearly that it is sin (Romans 1:26–28). A man of God does not do such things. God loves homosexuals, but that does *not* mean he approves of their lifestyle.

In Other Words...

²¹For although they knew God, they neither glorified him as God nor gave thanks to him, but their thinking became futile and their foolish hearts were darkened. ²²Although they claimed to be wise, they became fools ²³and exchanged the glory of the immortal God for images made to look like mortal man and birds and animals and reptiles.

²⁴Therefore God gave them over in the sinful desires of their hearts to sexual impurity for the degrading of their bodies with one another. ²⁵They exchanged the truth of God for a lie, and worshiped and served created things rather than the Creator—who is forever praised. Amen.

²⁶Because of this, God gave them over to shameful lusts. Even their women exchanged natural relations for unnatural ones. ²⁷In the same way the men also abandoned natural relations with women and were inflamed with lust for one another. Men committed indecent acts with other men, and received in themselves the due penalty for their perversion.

²⁸Furthermore, since they did not think it worthwhile to retain the knowledge of God, he gave them over to a depraved mind, to do what ought not to be done. ²⁹They have become filled with every kind of wickedness, evil, greed and depravity. They are full of envy, murder, strife, deceit and malice. They are gossips, ³⁰slanderers, God-haters, insolent, arrogant and boastful; they invent ways of doing evil; they disobey their parents; ³¹they are senseless, faithless, heartless, ruthless. ³²Although they know God's righteous decree that those who do such things deserve death, they not only continue to do these very things but also approve of those who practice them.

God's Righteous Judgment

2 You, therefore, have no excuse, you who pass judgment on someone else, for at whatever point you judge the other, you are condemning yourself, because you who pass judgment do the same things. ²Now we know that God's judgment against those who do such things is based on truth. ³So when you, a mere man, pass judgment on them and yet do the same things, do you think you will escape God's judgment? ⁴Or do you show contempt for the riches of his kindness, tolerance and patience, not realizing that God's kindness leads you toward repentance?

⁵But because of your stubbornness and your unrepentant heart, you are storing up wrath against yourself for the day of God's wrath, when his righteous judgment will be revealed. ⁶God "will give to each person according to what he has done."ᵃ ⁷To those who by persistence in doing good seek glory, honor and immortality, he will give eternal life. ⁸But for those who are self-seeking and who reject the truth and follow evil, there will be wrath and anger. ⁹There will be trouble

ᵃ 6 Psalm 62:12; Prov. 24:12

and distress for every human being who does evil: first for the Jew, then for the Gentile; 10but glory, honor and peace for everyone who does good: first for the Jew, then for the Gentile. 11For God does not show favoritism.

12All who sin apart from the law will also perish apart from the law, and all who sin under the law will be judged by the law. 13For it is not those who hear the law who are righteous in God's sight, but it is those who obey the law who will be declared righteous. 14(Indeed, when Gentiles, who do not have the law, do by nature things required by the law, they are a law for themselves, even though they do not have the law, 15since they show that the requirements of the law are written on their hearts, their consciences also bearing witness, and their thoughts now accusing, now even defending them.) 16This will take place on the day when God will judge men's secrets through Jesus Christ, as my gospel declares.

The Jews and the Law

17Now you, if you call yourself a Jew; if you rely on the law and brag about your relationship to God; 18if you know his will and approve of what is superior because you are instructed by the law; 19if you are convinced that you are a guide for the blind, a light for those who are in the dark, 20an instructor of the foolish, a teacher of infants, because you have in the law the embodiment of knowledge and truth— 21you, then, who teach others, do you not teach yourself? You who preach against stealing, do you steal? 22You who say that people should not commit adultery, do you commit adultery? You who abhor idols, do you rob temples? 23You who brag about the law, do you dishonor God by breaking the law? 24As it is written: "God's name is blasphemed among the Gentiles because of you."[a]

a 24 Isaiah 52:5; Ezek. 36:22

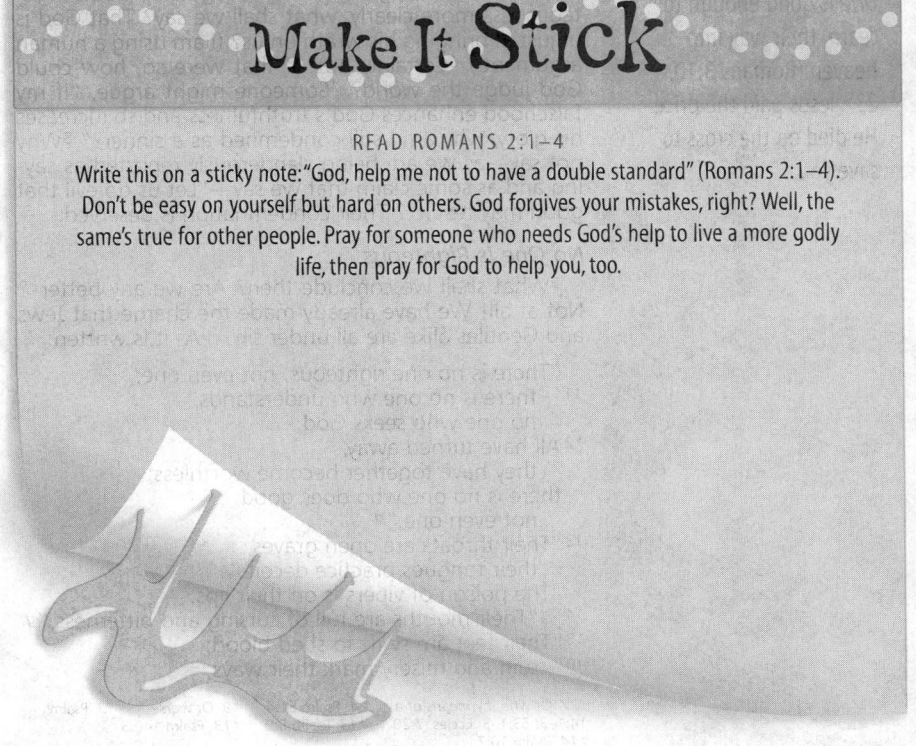

Make It Stick

READ ROMANS 2:1–4

Write this on a sticky note: "God, help me not to have a double standard" (Romans 2:1–4). Don't be easy on yourself but hard on others. God forgives your mistakes, right? Well, the same's true for other people. Pray for someone who needs God's help to live a more godly life, then pray for God to help you, too.

Get a Load of This...

You may have heard someone say, "He's a *good* person. I'll bet my boots he makes it to heaven." Well, unless that "good" person also knows Christ, the guy who said that is about to lose his boots! *No one* is good enough to "earn" their way into heaven (Romans 3:10, 23). Jesus paid the price. He died on the cross to save you.

²⁵Circumcision has value if you observe the law, but if you break the law, you have become as though you had not been circumcised. ²⁶If those who are not circumcised keep the law's requirements, will they not be regarded as though they were circumcised? ²⁷The one who is not circumcised physically and yet obeys the law will condemn you who, even though you have the*ᵃ* written code and circumcision, are a lawbreaker.

²⁸A man is not a Jew if he is only one outwardly, nor is circumcision merely outward and physical. ²⁹No, a man is a Jew if he is one inwardly; and circumcision is circumcision of the heart, by the Spirit, not by the written code. Such a man's praise is not from men, but from God.

God's Faithfulness

3 What advantage, then, is there in being a Jew, or what value is there in circumcision? ²Much in every way! First of all, they have been entrusted with the very words of God.

³What if some did not have faith? Will their lack of faith nullify God's faithfulness? ⁴Not at all! Let God be true, and every man a liar. As it is written:

> "So that you may be proved right when you speak
>   and prevail when you judge."*ᵇ*

⁵But if our unrighteousness brings out God's righteousness more clearly, what shall we say? That God is unjust in bringing his wrath on us? (I am using a human argument.) ⁶Certainly not! If that were so, how could God judge the world? ⁷Someone might argue, "If my falsehood enhances God's truthfulness and so increases his glory, why am I still condemned as a sinner?" ⁸Why not say—as we are being slanderously reported as saying and as some claim that we say—"Let us do evil that good may result"? Their condemnation is deserved.

No One Is Righteous

⁹What shall we conclude then? Are we any better*ᶜ*? Not at all! We have already made the charge that Jews and Gentiles alike are all under sin. ¹⁰As it is written:

> "There is no one righteous, not even one;
> ¹¹   there is no one who understands,
>   no one who seeks God.
> ¹²All have turned away,
>   they have together become worthless;
>   there is no one who does good,
>   not even one."*ᵈ*
> ¹³"Their throats are open graves;
>   their tongues practice deceit."*ᵉ*
>   "The poison of vipers is on their lips."*ᶠ*
> ¹⁴   "Their mouths are full of cursing and bitterness."*ᵍ*
> ¹⁵"Their feet are swift to shed blood;
> ¹⁶   ruin and misery mark their ways,

ᵃ 27 Or *who, by means of a*   *ᵇ 4* Psalm 51:4   *ᶜ 9* Or *worse*   *ᵈ 12* Psalms 14:1–3; 53:1–3; Eccles. 7:20   *ᵉ 13* Psalm 5:9   *ᶠ 13* Psalm 140:3   *ᵍ 14* Psalm 10:7

17and the way of peace they do not
know."ᵃ

18   "There is no fear of God before their
eyes."ᵇ

19Now we know that whatever the law
says, it says to those who are under the
law, so that every mouth may be silenced
and the whole world held accountable to
God. 20Therefore no one will be declared
righteous in his sight by observing the
law; rather, through the law we become
conscious of sin.

Righteousness Through Faith

21But now a righteousness from God,
apart from law, has been made known, to
which the Law and the Prophets testify.
22This righteousness from God comes
through faith in Jesus Christ to all who believe. There is no difference, 23for all have
sinned and fall short of the glory of God,
24and are justified freely by his grace
through the redemption that came by
Christ Jesus. 25God presented him as a
sacrifice of atonement,ᶜ through faith in
his blood. He did this to demonstrate his

justice, because in his forbearance he had
left the sins committed beforehand unpunished— 26he did it to demonstrate his
justice at the present time, so as to be just
and the one who justifies those who have
faith in Jesus.

27Where, then, is boasting? It is excluded. On what principle? On that of observing the law? No, but on that of faith. 28For
we maintain that a man is justified by faith
apart from observing the law. 29Is God the
God of Jews only? Is he not the God of
Gentiles too? Yes, of Gentiles too, 30since
there is only one God, who will justify the
circumcised by faith and the uncircumcised through that same faith. 31Do we,
then, nullify the law by this faith? Not at
all! Rather, we uphold the law.

Abraham Justified by Faith

What then shall we say that Abraham, our forefather, discovered in
this matter? 2If, in fact, Abraham
was justified by works, he had

ᵃ 17 Isaiah 59:7,8   ᵇ 18 Psalm 36:1   ᶜ 25 Or as the one
who would turn aside his wrath, taking away sin

Trusting God

READ ROMANS 4:1–3, 18–25

Imagine if your teacher sent you to the principal to pick up your track-
and-field award, and you answered, "But . . . but . . . I don't believe the
principal *exists*." Think you'll collect that award? Nope. Hebrews 11:6
says, "Without faith it is impossible to please God, because anyone who
comes to him must believe that he exists and that he rewards
those who earnestly seek him." No faith in God = no rewards. It
doesn't get a whole lot simpler than that. To receive salvation,
you need to believe that God exists and that he sent his Son
Jesus to die for your sins. After you're a Christian, you need to
continue to believe that God rewards you, now and for all
eternity. When you feel like you're *not* being rewarded, or that God is *not* answering your prayers, remember how Abraham prayed and believed and
hung in there—and get a grip. Does God have the
power to do what he promised? *Oh yeah.*

Your next reading is on page 1471.

something to boast about—but not before God. [3]What does the Scripture say? "Abraham believed God, and it was credited to him as righteousness."[a]

[4]Now when a man works, his wages are not credited to him as a gift, but as an obligation. [5]However, to the man who does not work but trusts God who justifies the wicked, his faith is credited as righteousness. [6]David says the same thing when he speaks of the blessedness of the man to whom God credits righteousness apart from works:

[7]"Blessed are they
    whose transgressions are forgiven,
    whose sins are covered.
[8]Blessed is the man
    whose sin the Lord will never count
        against him."[b]

[9]Is this blessedness only for the circumcised, or also for the uncircumcised? We have been saying that Abraham's faith was credited to him as righteousness. [10]Under what circumstances was it credited? Was it after he was circumcised, or before? It was not after, but before! [11]And he received the sign of circumcision, a seal of the righteousness that he had by faith while he was still uncircumcised. So then, he is the father of all who believe but have not been circumcised, in order that righteousness might be credited to them. [12]And he is also the father of the circumcised who not only are circumcised but who also walk in the footsteps of the faith that our father Abraham had before he was circumcised.

[13]It was not through law that Abraham and his offspring received the promise that he would be heir of the world, but through the righteousness that comes by faith. [14]For if those who live by law are heirs, faith has no value and the promise is worthless, [15]because law brings wrath. And where there is no law there is no transgression.

[16]Therefore, the promise comes by faith, so that it may be by grace and may be guaranteed to all Abraham's offspring—not only to those who are of the law but also to those who are of the faith of Abraham. He is the father of us all. [17]As it is written: "I have made you a father of many nations."[c] He is our father in the sight of God, in whom he believed—the God who gives life to the dead and

calls things that are not as though they were.

[18]Against all hope, Abraham in hope believed and so became the father of many nations, just as it had been said to him, "So shall your offspring be."[d] [19]Without weakening in his faith, he faced the fact that his body was as good as dead—since he was about a hundred years old—and that Sarah's womb was also dead. [20]Yet he did not waver through unbelief regarding the promise of God, but was strengthened in his faith and gave glory to God, [21]being fully persuaded that God had power to do what he had promised. [22]This is why "it was credited to him as righteousness." [23]The words "it was credited to him" were written not for him alone, [24]but also for us, to whom God will credit righteousness—for us who believe in him who raised Jesus our Lord from the dead. [25]He was delivered over to death for our sins and was raised to life for our justification.

Peace and Joy

5 Therefore, since we have been justified through faith, we[e] have peace with God through our Lord Jesus Christ, [2]through whom we have gained access by faith into this grace in which we now stand. And we[e] rejoice in the hope of the glory of God. [3]Not only so, but we[e] also rejoice in our sufferings, because we know that suffering produces perseverance; [4]perseverance, character; and character, hope. [5]And hope does not disappoint us, because God has poured out his love into our hearts by the Holy Spirit, whom he has given us.

[6]You see, at just the right time, when we were still powerless, Christ died for the ungodly. [7]Very rarely will anyone die for a righteous man, though for a good man someone might possibly dare to die. [8]But God demonstrates his own love for us in this: While we were still sinners, Christ died for us.

[9]Since we have now been justified by his blood, how much more shall we be saved from God's wrath through him! [10]For if, when we were God's enemies, we were reconciled to him through the death of his Son, how much more, having been

---

[a] 3 Gen. 15:6; also in verse 22   [b] 8 Psalm 32:1,2
[c] 17 Gen. 17:5   [d] 18 Gen. 15:5   [e] 1,2,3 Or let us

reconciled, shall we be saved through his life! ¹¹Not only is this so, but we also rejoice in God through our Lord Jesus Christ, through whom we have now received reconciliation.

Death Through Adam, Life Through Christ

¹²Therefore, just as sin entered the world through one man, and death through sin, and in this way death came to all men, because all sinned— ¹³for before the law was given, sin was in the world. But sin is not taken into account when there is no law. ¹⁴Nevertheless, death reigned from the time of Adam to the time of Moses, even over those who did not sin by breaking a command, as did Adam, who was a pattern of the one to come.

¹⁵But the gift is not like the trespass. For if the many died by the trespass of the one man, how much more did God's grace and the gift that came by the grace of the one man, Jesus Christ, overflow to the many! ¹⁶Again, the gift of God is not like the result of the one man's sin: The judgment followed one sin and brought condemnation, but the gift followed many trespasses and brought justification. ¹⁷For if, by the trespass of the one man, death reigned through that one man, how much more will those who receive God's abundant provision of grace and of the gift of righteousness reign in life through the one man, Jesus Christ.

¹⁸Consequently, just as the result of one trespass was condemnation for all men, so also the result of one act of righteousness was justification that brings life for all men. ¹⁹For just as through the disobedience of the one man the many were made sinners, so also through the obedience of the one man the many will be made righteous.

²⁰The law was added so that the trespass might increase. But where sin increased, grace increased all the more, ²¹so that, just as sin reigned in death, so also grace might reign through righteousness to bring eternal life through Jesus Christ our Lord.

Dead to Sin, Alive in Christ

6 What shall we say, then? Shall we go on sinning so that grace may increase? ²By no means! We died to sin; how can we live in it any longer? ³Or don't you know that all of us who were baptized into Christ Jesus were baptized into his death? ⁴We were therefore buried with him through baptism into death in order that, just as Christ was raised from the dead through the glory of the Father, we too may live a new life.

⁵If we have been united with him like this in his death, we will certainly also be united with him in his resurrection. ⁶For we know that our old self was crucified with him so that the body of sin might be done away with,ª that we should no longer be slaves to sin— ⁷because anyone who has died has been freed from sin. ⁸Now if we died with Christ, we believe that we will

Get a Load of This...

Check out Romans 5:3–4. No one *likes* to suffer, but suffering produces perseverance. When you persevere, you continue to trust God during hard times. That builds character. When you have strength of character and believe God, that builds hope.

ª 6 Or be rendered powerless

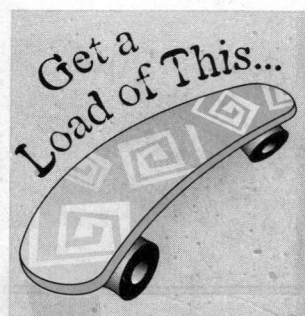

When Adam sinned, we all became sinners. When we get to heaven, you might think there will be a huge line of people waiting to ask Adam the same question over and over: "Why'd you *do* it?" But actually, we will all be lined up to thank Jesus for dying for us so that we could *be in* heaven (Romans 5:19).

also live with him. 9For we know that since Christ was raised from the dead, he cannot die again; death no longer has mastery over him. 10The death he died, he died to sin once for all; but the life he lives, he lives to God.

11In the same way, count yourselves dead to sin but alive to God in Christ Jesus. 12Therefore do not let sin reign in your mortal body so that you obey its evil desires. 13Do not offer the parts of your body to sin, as instruments of wickedness, but rather offer yourselves to God, as those who have been brought from death to life; and offer the parts of your body to him as instruments of righteousness. 14For sin shall not be your master, because you are not under law, but under grace.

Slaves to Righteousness

15What then? Shall we sin because we are not under law but under grace? By no means! 16Don't you know that when you offer yourselves to someone to obey him as slaves, you are slaves to the one whom you obey—whether you are slaves to sin, which leads to death, or to obedience, which leads to righteousness? 17But thanks be to God that, though you used to be slaves to sin, you wholeheartedly obeyed the form of teaching to which you were entrusted. 18You have been set free from sin and have become slaves to righteousness.

19I put this in human terms because you are weak in your natural selves. Just as you used to offer the parts of your body in slavery to impurity and to ever-increasing wickedness, so now offer them in slavery to righteousness leading to holiness. 20When you were slaves to sin, you were free from the control of righteousness. 21What benefit did you reap at that time from the things you are now ashamed of? Those things result in death! 22But now that you have been set free from sin and have become slaves to God, the benefit you reap leads to holiness, and the result is eternal life. 23For the wages of sin is death, but the gift of God is eternal life in*a* Christ Jesus our Lord.

An Illustration From Marriage

7 Do you not know, brothers—for I am speaking to men who know the law—that the law has authority over a man only as long as he lives? 2For example, by law a married woman is bound to her husband as long as he is alive, but if her husband dies, she is released from the law of marriage. 3So then, if she marries another man while her husband is still alive, she is called an adulteress. But if her husband dies, she is released from that law and is not an adulteress, even though she marries another man.

4So, my brothers, you also died to the law through the body of Christ, that you might belong to another, to him who was raised from the dead, in order that we might bear fruit to God. 5For when we were controlled by the sinful nature,*b* the sinful passions aroused by the

a 23 Or *through*   *b 5* Or *the flesh; also in verse 25* law were at work in our bodies, so that we bore fruit for death. 6But now, by dying to what once bound us, we have been released from the law so that we serve in the new way of the Spirit, and not in the old way of the written code.

Struggling With Sin

7What shall we say, then? Is the law sin? Certainly not! Indeed I would not have known what sin was except through the law. For I would not have known what coveting really was if the law had not said, "Do not covet."*a* 8But sin, seizing the opportunity afforded by the commandment, produced in me every kind of covetous desire. For apart from law, sin is dead. 9Once I was alive apart from law; but when the commandment came, sin sprang to life and I died. 10I found that the very commandment that was intended to bring life actually brought death. 11For sin, seizing the opportunity afforded by the commandment, deceived me, and through the commandment put me to death. 12So then, the law is holy, and the commandment is holy, righteous and good.

13Did that which is good, then, become death to me? By no means! But in order that sin might be recognized as sin, it produced death in me through what was good, so that through the commandment sin might become utterly sinful.

14We know that the law is spiritual; but I am unspiritual, sold as a slave to sin. 15I do not understand what I do. For what I want to do I do not do, but what I hate I do. 16And if I do what I do not want to do, I agree that the law is good. 17As it is, it is no longer I myself who do it, but it is sin living in me. 18I know that nothing good lives in me, that is, in my sinful nature.*b* For I have the desire to do what is good, but I cannot carry it out. 19For what I do is not the good I want to do; no, the evil I do not want to do—this I keep on doing. 20Now if I do what I do not want to do, it is no longer I who do it, but it is sin living in me that does it.

21So I find this law at work: When I want to do good, evil is right there with me. 22For in my inner being I delight in

---

a 7 Exodus 20:17; Deut. 5:21   *b 18* Or *my flesh*

Just Say No

READ ROMANS 6:1–2, 8–14

The only way to heaven and God is to accept that Jesus died for your sins. You can't be good enough. *But,* once you've accepted Jesus, realize that he's not just some real great pal who died to save you, but he's also your Lord. You don't just say, "Whoopee! I've been forgiven for my sins! I'll be forgiven no matter *what* I do, so why not keep on sinning?" Bad idea—really, *really* bad idea. You've been forgiven, but you also need to *stop* deliberately sinning. Just say no. As you grow with God and become like Jesus, you need to make a choice to say "no" to sin. Once you're saved, God's Holy Spirit inspires you to do good things, so listen to the Spirit. Sure, you'll stumble from time to time, but when it comes to deliberately disobeying God and sinning, there's only one word you have to remember: *Don't.*

Your next reading is on page 1474.

Check out Romans 6:23. The penalty for sin is death. It's not just a detention. You don't just get grounded. The penalty is *death*. D-e-a-t-h. Now, want to hear a *real* problem? We all sin. That means we all die. The solution? Jesus took our punishment for us.

God's law; 23but I see another law at work in the members of my body, waging war against the law of my mind and making me a prisoner of the law of sin at work within my members. 24What a wretched man I am! Who will rescue me from this body of death? 25Thanks be to God—through Jesus Christ our Lord!

So then, I myself in my mind am a slave to God's law, but in the sinful nature a slave to the law of sin.

Life Through the Spirit

Therefore, there is now no condemnation for those who are in Christ Jesus,[a] 2because through Christ Jesus the law of the Spirit of life set me free from the law of sin and death. 3For what the law was powerless to do in that it was weakened by the sinful nature,[b] God did by sending his own Son in the likeness of sinful man to be a sin offering.[c] And so he condemned sin in sinful man,[d] 4in order that the righteous requirements of the law might be fully met in us, who do not live according to the sinful nature but according to the Spirit.

5Those who live according to the sinful nature have their minds set on what that nature desires; but those who live in accordance with the Spirit have their minds set on what the Spirit desires. 6The mind of sinful man[e] is death, but the mind controlled by the Spirit is life and peace; 7the sinful mind[f] is hostile to God. It does not submit to God's law, nor can it do so. 8Those controlled by the sinful nature cannot please God.

9You, however, are controlled not by the sinful nature but by the Spirit, if the Spirit of God lives in you. And if anyone does not have the Spirit of Christ, he does not belong to Christ. 10But if Christ is in you, your body is dead because of sin, yet your spirit is alive because of righteousness. 11And if the Spirit of him who raised Jesus from the dead is living in you, he who raised Christ from the dead will also give life to your mortal bodies through his Spirit, who lives in you.

12Therefore, brothers, we have an obligation—but it is not to the sinful nature, to live according to it. 13For if you live according to the sinful nature, you will die; but if by the Spirit you put to death the misdeeds of the body, you will live, 14because those who are led by the Spirit of God are sons of God. 15For you did not receive a spirit that makes you a slave again to fear, but you received the Spirit of sonship.[g] And by him we cry, "Abba,[h] Father." 16The Spirit himself testifies with our spirit that we are God's children. 17Now if we are children, then we are heirs—heirs of God and co-heirs with Christ, if indeed we share in his sufferings in order that we may also share in his glory.

Future Glory

18I consider that our present sufferings are not worth

---

[a] 1 Some later manuscripts *Jesus, who do not live according to the sinful nature but according to the Spirit,*   [b] 3 Or *the flesh; also in verses 4, 5, 8, 9, 12 and 13*   [c] 3 Or *man, for sin*   [d] 3 Or *in the flesh*   [e] 6 Or *mind set on the flesh*   [f] 7 Or *the mind set on the flesh*   [g] 15 Or *adoption*   [h] 15 Aramaic for *Father*

comparing with the glory that will be revealed in us. [19]The creation waits in eager expectation for the sons of God to be revealed. [20]For the creation was subjected to frustration, not by its own choice, but by the will of the one who subjected it, in hope [21]that[a] the creation itself will be liberated from its bondage to decay and brought into the glorious freedom of the children of God.

[22]We know that the whole creation has been groaning as in the pains of childbirth right up to the present time. [23]Not only so, but we ourselves, who have the firstfruits of the Spirit, groan inwardly as we wait eagerly for our adoption as sons, the redemption of our bodies. [24]For in this hope we were saved. But hope that is seen is no hope at all. Who hopes for what he already has? [25]But if we hope for what we do not yet have, we wait for it patiently.

[26]In the same way, the Spirit helps us in our weakness. We do not know what we ought to pray for, but the Spirit himself intercedes for us with groans that words cannot express. [27]And he who searches our hearts knows the mind of the Spirit, because the Spirit intercedes for the saints in accordance with God's will.

More Than Conquerors

[28]And we know that in all things God works for the good of those who love him,[b] who[c] have been called according to his purpose. [29]For those God foreknew he also predestined to be conformed to the likeness of his Son, that he might be the firstborn among many brothers. [30]And those he predestined, he also called; those he called, he also justified; those he justified, he also glorified.

[31]What, then, shall we say in response to this? If God is for us, who can be against us? [32]He who did not spare his own Son, but gave him up for us all—how will he not also, along with him, graciously give us all things? [33]Who will bring any charge against those whom God has chosen? It is God who justifies. [34]Who is he that condemns? Christ Jesus, who died—more than that, who was raised to life—is at the right hand of God and is also interceding for us. [35]Who shall separate us from the love of Christ? Shall trouble or hardship or persecution or famine or nakedness or danger or sword? [36]As it is written:

"For your sake we face death all day long;
we are considered as sheep to be slaughtered."[d]

[37]No, in all these things we are more than conquerors through him who loved us. [38]For I am convinced that neither death nor life, neither angels nor demons,[e] neither the present nor the future, nor any powers, [39]neither height nor depth, nor anything else in all creation, will be able to separate us from the love of God that is in Christ Jesus our Lord.

Get a Load of This...

Even the great apostle Paul struggled against sin and groaned, "What a wretched man I am!" (Romans 7:15, 24–25). Caramba! Where does that leave us? Thank God that Jesus died for us and his Holy Spirit works in our hearts to help us win this struggle.

In Other Words...

---

[a] 20,21 Or subjected it in hope. [21]For   [b] 28 Some manuscripts And we know that all things work together for good to those who love God   [c] 28 Or works together with those who love him to bring about what is good—with those who   [d] 36 Psalm 44:22   [e] 38 Or nor heavenly rulers

God's Sovereign Choice

9 I speak the truth in Christ—I am not lying, my conscience confirms it in the Holy Spirit— ²I have great sorrow and unceasing anguish in my heart. ³For I could wish that I myself were cursed and cut off from Christ for the sake of my brothers, those of my own race, ⁴the people of Israel. Theirs is the adoption as sons; theirs the divine glory, the covenants, the receiving of the law, the temple worship and the promises. ⁵Theirs are the patriarchs, and from them is traced the human ancestry of Christ, who is God over all, forever praised!ᵃ Amen.

⁶It is not as though God's word had failed. For not all who are descended from Israel are Israel. ⁷Nor because they are his descendants are they all Abraham's children. On the contrary, "It is through Isaac that your offspring will be reckoned."ᵇ ⁸In other words, it is not the natural children who are God's children, but it is the children of the promise who are regarded as Abraham's offspring. ⁹For this was how the promise was stated: "At the appointed time I will return, and Sarah will have a son."ᶜ

¹⁰Not only that, but Rebekah's children had one and the same father, our father Isaac. ¹¹Yet, before the twins were born or had done anything good or bad—in order that God's purpose in election might stand: ¹²not by works but by him who calls—she was told, "The older will serve the younger."ᵈ ¹³Just as it is written: "Jacob I loved, but Esau I hated."ᵉ

¹⁴What then shall we say? Is God unjust? Not at all! ¹⁵For he says to Moses,

"I will have mercy on whom I have mercy,
and I will have compassion on whom I have compassion."ᶠ

¹⁶It does not, therefore, depend on man's desire or effort, but on God's mercy. ¹⁷For the Scripture says to Pharaoh: "I raised you up for this very purpose, that I might display my power in you and that my

---

ᵃ 5 Or Christ, who is over all. God be forever praised! Or Christ. God who is over all be forever praised!
ᵇ 7 Gen. 21:12   ᶜ 9 Gen. 18:10,14   ᵈ 12 Gen. 25:23
ᵉ 13 Mal. 1:2,3   ᶠ 15 Exodus 33:19

GET SMARTER

Changing Mindsets

READ ROMANS 8:5–16

The world's mindset is all about selfishness and sin—*not* a good place for one's mind, since it leads to death. Garbage thoughts lead to garbage life. You're growing into a man of God, but you probably have to deal a lot with sinful thoughts and selfish desires, right? Ever try getting control of your thoughts when your mind is out of control? You feel like a cowboy, flopping like a rag doll all over the back of a two-ton bull, trying to just hang on. Not easy. The good news is that you don't have to fight sin by yourself. God's Spirit can not only help you *control* your desires, thoughts and actions but can *change* your whole mindset! Over time, you'll start thinking the way Jesus thinks. That is *so* cool! Your brain won't think the old way. Sure, wrong thoughts will still enter your head, but you can say, "No, I'm not going that way."

Your next reading is on page 1476.

name might be proclaimed in all the earth."[a] [18]There-
fore God has mercy on whom he wants to have mercy,
and he hardens whom he wants to harden.

[19]One of you will say to me: "Then why does God still
blame us? For who resists his will?" [20]But who are you,
O man, to talk back to God? "Shall what is formed say
to him who formed it, 'Why did you make me like
this?' "[b] [21]Does not the potter have the right to make
out of the same lump of clay some pottery for noble
purposes and some for common use?

[22]What if God, choosing to show his wrath and make
his power known, bore with great patience the objects
of his wrath—prepared for destruction? [23]What if he
did this to make the riches of his glory known to the objects of his mercy, whom he prepared in advance for
glory— [24]even us, whom he also called, not only from
the Jews but also from the Gentiles? [25]As he says in Hosea:

"I will call them 'my people' who are not my people;
    and I will call her 'my loved one' who is not my
        loved one,"[c]

[26]and,

"It will happen that in the very place where it was
        said to them,
    'You are not my people,'
they will be called 'sons of the living God.' "[d]

[27]Isaiah cries out concerning Israel:

"Though the number of the Israelites be like the
        sand by the sea,
    only the remnant will be saved.
[28]For the Lord will carry out
    his sentence on earth with speed and finality."[e]

[29]It is just as Isaiah said previously:

"Unless the Lord Almighty
    had left us descendants,
we would have become like Sodom,
    we would have been like Gomorrah."[f]

Israel's Unbelief

[30]What then shall we say? That the Gentiles, who did
not pursue righteousness, have obtained it, a righteousness that is by faith; [31]but Israel, who pursued a law of
righteousness, has not attained it. [32]Why not? Because
they pursued it not by faith but as if it were by works.
They stumbled over the "stumbling stone." [33]As it is
written:

"See, I lay in Zion a stone that causes men to stumble
    and a rock that makes them fall,
and the one who trusts in him will never be put to
        shame."[g]

---

[a] 17 Exodus 9:16   [b] 20 Isaiah 29:16; 45:9   [c] 25 Hosea 2:23
[d] 26 Hosea 1:10   [e] 28 Isaiah 10:22,23   [f] 29 Isaiah 1:9   [g] 33 Isaiah 8:14;
28:16

10 Brothers, my heart's desire and prayer to God for the Israelites is that they may be saved. ²For I can testify about them that they are zealous for God, but their zeal is not based on knowledge. ³Since they did not know the righteousness that comes from God and sought to establish their own, they did not submit to God's righteousness. ⁴Christ is the end of the law so that there may be righteousness for everyone who believes.

⁵Moses describes in this way the righteousness that is by the law: "The man who does these things will live by them."*ᵃ* ⁶But the righteousness that is by faith says: "Do not say in your heart, 'Who will ascend into heaven?'*ᵇ*" (that is, to bring Christ down) ⁷or 'Who will descend into the deep?'*ᶜ* (that is, to bring Christ up from the dead). ⁸But what does it say? "The word is near you; it is in your mouth and in your heart,"*ᵈ* that is, the word of faith we are proclaiming: ⁹That if you confess with your mouth, "Jesus is Lord," and believe in your heart that God raised him from the dead, you will be saved. ¹⁰For it is with your

heart that you believe and are justified, and it is with your mouth that you confess and are saved. ¹¹As the Scripture says, "Anyone who trusts in him will never be put to shame."*ᵉ* ¹²For there is no difference between Jew and Gentile—the same Lord is Lord of all and richly blesses all who call on him, ¹³for, "Everyone who calls on the name of the Lord will be saved."*ᶠ*

¹⁴How, then, can they call on the one they have not believed in? And how can they believe in the one of whom they have not heard? And how can they hear without someone preaching to them? ¹⁵And how can they preach unless they are sent? As it is written, "How beautiful are the feet of those who bring good news!"*ᵍ*

¹⁶But not all the Israelites accepted the good news. For Isaiah says, "Lord, who has believed our message?"*ʰ* ¹⁷Consequently, faith comes from hearing the message, and the message is heard through the word of Christ. ¹⁸But I ask: Did they not hear? Of course they did:

ᵃ 5 Lev. 18:5   *ᵇ 6* Deut. 30:12   *ᶜ 7* Deut. 30:13
ᵈ 8 Deut. 30:14   *ᵉ 11* Isaiah 28:16   *ᶠ 13* Joel 2:32
ᵍ 15 Isaiah 52:7   *ʰ 16* Isaiah 53:1

Tell It to God

READ ROMANS 10:9–10

If you did something wrong against someone else, you make it right by going to them and apologizing. You have your sins forgiven the same way: You go to God, confess your sins and ask God to forgive you. Romans 10:9–10 spells it out: If you believe that Jesus died for you and was raised from the dead to pay for your sins and you're willing to say that Jesus is the Lord of your life, say that directly to God. You can pray a prayer something like this from your heart: "Dear God, I know I've done bad and selfish things. I'm sorry. Please forgive me. I know your Son Jesus died for me, and raised up from the dead. I believe in him. Please make me your son. Please help me to love and obey you, and learn more about you. In Jesus' name, amen." If you prayed this prayer sincerely, you are now God's son!

Your next reading is on page 1479.

"Their voice has gone out into all the
    earth,
  their words to the ends of the
    world."[a]

19Again I ask: Did Israel not understand?
First, Moses says,

"I will make you envious by those who
    are not a nation;
  I will make you angry by a nation
    that has no understanding."[b]

20And Isaiah boldly says,

"I was found by those who did not
    seek me;
  I revealed myself to those who did
    not ask for me."[c]

21But concerning Israel he says,

"All day long I have held out my hands
  to a disobedient and obstinate
    people."[d]

The Remnant of Israel

11 I ask then: Did God reject his people? By no means! I am an Israelite
myself, a descendant of Abraham,
from the tribe of Benjamin. 2God
did not reject his people, whom he foreknew. Don't you know what the Scripture
says in the passage about Elijah—how he
appealed to God against Israel: 3"Lord,
they have killed your prophets and torn
down your altars; I am the only one left,
and they are trying to kill me"[e]? 4And
what was God's answer to him? "I have
reserved for myself seven thousand who
have not bowed the knee to Baal."[f] 5So
too, at the present time there is a remnant
chosen by grace. 6And if by grace, then it
is no longer by works; if it were, grace
would no longer be grace.[g]

7What then? What Israel sought so
earnestly it did not obtain, but the elect
did. The others were hardened, 8as it is
written:

"God gave them a spirit of stupor,
  eyes so that they could not see
  and ears so that they could not hear,
  to this very day."[h]

9And David says:

"May their table become a snare and a
    trap,
  a stumbling block and a retribution
    for them.

10May their eyes be darkened so they
    cannot see,
  and their backs be bent forever."[i]

Ingrafted Branches

11Again I ask: Did they stumble so as to
fall beyond recovery? Not at all! Rather,
because of their transgression, salvation
has come to the Gentiles to make Israel
envious. 12But if their transgression means
riches for the world, and their loss means
riches for the Gentiles, how much greater
riches will their fullness bring!

13I am talking to you Gentiles. Inas-
much as I am the apostle to the Gentiles,
I make much of my ministry, 14in the hope
that I may somehow arouse my own people to envy and save some of them. 15For
if their rejection is the reconciliation of the
world, what will their acceptance be but
life from the dead? 16If the part of the
dough offered as firstfruits is holy, then
the whole batch is holy; if the root is holy,
so are the branches.

17If some of the branches have been
broken off, and you, though a wild olive
shoot, have been grafted in among the
others and now share in the nourishing
sap from the olive root, 18do not boast
over those branches. If you do, consider
this: You do not support the root, but the
root supports you. 19You will say then,
"Branches were broken off so that I could
be grafted in." 20Granted. But they were
broken off because of unbelief, and you
stand by faith. Do not be arrogant, but be
afraid. 21For if God did not spare the natural branches, he will not spare you either.

22Consider therefore the kindness and
sternness of God: sternness to those who
fell, but kindness to you, provided that
you continue in his kindness. Otherwise,
you also will be cut off. 23And if they do
not persist in unbelief, they will be grafted
in, for God is able to graft them in again.
24After all, if you were cut out of an olive
tree that is wild by nature, and contrary to
nature were grafted into a cultivated olive
tree, how much more readily will these,
the natural branches, be grafted into their
own olive tree!

---

a 18 Psalm 19:4   b 19 Deut. 32:21   c 20 Isaiah 65:1
d 21 Isaiah 65:2   e 3 1 Kings 19:10,14
f 4 1 Kings 19:18   g 6 Some manuscripts be grace. But if
by works, then it is no longer grace; if it were, work would no
longer be work.   h 8 Deut. 29:4; Isaiah 29:10
i 10 Psalm 69:22,23

All Israel Will Be Saved

25I do not want you to be ignorant of this mystery, brothers, so that you may not be conceited: Israel has experienced a hardening in part until the full number of the Gentiles has come in. 26And so all Israel will be saved, as it is written:

"The deliverer will come from Zion;
  he will turn godlessness away from Jacob.
27 And this is*a* my covenant with them
  when I take away their sins."*b*

28As far as the gospel is concerned, they are enemies on your account; but as far as election is concerned, they are loved on account of the patriarchs, 29for God's gifts and his call are irrevocable. 30Just as you who were at one time disobedient to God have now received mercy as a result of their disobedience, 31so they too have now become disobedient in order that they too may now*c* receive mercy as a result of God's mercy to you. 32For God has bound all men over to disobedience so that he may have mercy on them all.

Doxology

33Oh, the depth of the riches of the wisdom and*d* knowledge of God!
  How unsearchable his judgments,
  and his paths beyond tracing out!
34"Who has known the mind of the Lord?
  Or who has been his counselor?"*e*
35"Who has ever given to God,
  that God should repay him?"*f*
36For from him and through him and to him are all things.
  To him be the glory forever! Amen.

Living Sacrifices

12 Therefore, I urge you, brothers, in view of God's mercy, to offer your bodies as living sacrifices, holy and pleasing to God—this is your spiritual*g* act of worship. 2Do not conform any longer to the pattern of this world, but be transformed by the renewing of your mind. Then you will be able to test and approve what God's will is—his good, pleasing and perfect will.

3For by the grace given me I say to every one of you: Do not think of yourself more highly than you ought, but rather think of yourself with sober judgment, in accordance with the measure of faith God has given you. 4Just as each of us has one body with many members, and these members do not all have the same function, 5so in Christ we who are many form one body, and each member belongs to all the others. 6We have different gifts, according to the grace given us. If a man's gift is prophesying, let him use it in proportion to his*h* faith. 7If it is serving, let him serve; if it is teaching, let him teach; 8if it is encouraging, let him encourage; if it is contributing to the needs of others, let him give generously; if it is leadership, let him govern diligently; if it is showing mercy, let him do it cheerfully.

Love

9Love must be sincere. Hate what is evil; cling to what is good. 10Be devoted to one another in brotherly love. Honor one another above yourselves. 11Never be lacking in zeal, but keep your spiritual fervor, serving the Lord. 12Be joyful in hope, patient in affliction, faithful in prayer. 13Share with God's people who are in need. Practice hospitality.

14Bless those who persecute you; bless and do not curse. 15Rejoice with those who rejoice; mourn with those who mourn. 16Live in harmony with one another. Do not be proud, but be willing to associate with people of low position.*i* Do not be conceited.

17Do not repay anyone evil for evil. Be careful to do what is right in the eyes of everybody. 18If it is possible, as far as it depends on you, live at peace with everyone. 19Do not take revenge, my friends, but leave room for God's wrath, for it is written: "It is mine to avenge; I will repay,"*j* says the Lord. 20On the contrary:

"If your enemy is hungry, feed him;
  if he is thirsty, give him something to drink.
In doing this, you will heap burning coals on his head."*k*

21Do not be overcome by evil, but overcome evil with good.

---

a 27 Or will be   *b* 27 Isaiah 59:20,21; 27:9; Jer. 31:33,34
c 31 Some manuscripts do not have now.   *d* 33 Or riches and the wisdom and the   *e* 34 Isaiah 40:13
f 35 Job 41:11   *g* 1 Or reasonable   *h* 6 Or in agreement with the   *i* 16 Or willing to do menial work
j 19 Deut. 32:35   *k* 20 Prov. 25:21,22

Submission to the Authorities

13 Everyone must submit himself to the governing authorities, for there is no authority except that which God has established. The authorities that exist have been established by God. 2Consequently, he who rebels against the authority is rebelling against what God has instituted, and those who do so will bring judgment on themselves. 3For rulers hold no terror for those who do right, but for those who do wrong. Do you want to be free from fear of the one in authority? Then do what is right and he will commend you. 4For he is God's servant to do you good. But if you do wrong, be afraid, for he does not bear the sword for nothing. He is God's servant, an agent of wrath to bring punishment on the wrongdoer. 5Therefore, it is necessary to submit to the authorities, not only because of possible punishment but also because of conscience.

6This is also why you pay taxes, for the authorities are God's servants, who give their full time to governing. 7Give everyone what you owe him: If you owe taxes, pay taxes; if revenue, then revenue; if respect, then respect; if honor, then honor.

Love, for the Day Is Near

8Let no debt remain outstanding, except the continuing debt to love one another, for he who loves his fellowman has fulfilled the law. 9The commandments, "Do not commit adultery," "Do not murder," "Do not steal," "Do not covet,"*a* and whatever other commandment there may be, are summed up in this one rule: "Love your neighbor as yourself."*b* 10Love does no harm to its neighbor. Therefore love is the fulfillment of the law.

11And do this, understanding the present time. The hour has come for you to wake up from your slumber, because our salvation is nearer now than when we first believed. 12The night is nearly over; the

a 9 Exodus 20:13–15,17; Deut. 5:17–19,21   *b* 9 Lev. 19:18

GET STRONGER

Living Sacrifice

READ ROMANS 12:1–2

"Offer your bodies as living sacrifices" (verse 1). Whoa! What is *this*? No, God isn't saying tie yourself down to an altar. You're not about to be thrown into a volcano or fed to King Kong. The Old Testament called for sacrificing animals to clean people's lives from sin, true, but when Paul says to present *your* body as a living sacrifice he means don't deliberately sin or chase after wrong things any more, but totally commit yourself to use your body and strength to serve God. *That* is a very cool act of worship. So how do you find out what God *wants* you to do with your body? Simple. Let him transform the way your mind thinks. *Okaaaay* ... and how do you do *that*? Easy. Read God's Word. You'll find out what God's will is, then you'll think the way God thinks, and use your body to serve God and please him.

Your next reading is on page 1480.

day is almost here. So let us put aside the deeds of darkness and put on the armor of light. ¹³Let us behave decently, as in the daytime, not in orgies and drunkenness, not in sexual immorality and debauchery, not in dissension and jealousy. ¹⁴Rather, clothe yourselves with the Lord Jesus Christ, and do not think about how to gratify the desires of the sinful nature.ᵃ

The Weak and the Strong

14 Accept him whose faith is weak, without passing judgment on disputable matters. ²One man's faith allows him to eat everything, but another man, whose faith is weak, eats only vegetables. ³The man who eats everything must not look down on him who does not, and the man who does not eat everything must not condemn the man who does, for God has accepted him. ⁴Who are you to judge someone else's servant? To his own master he stands or falls. And he will stand, for the Lord is able to make him stand.

⁵One man considers one day more sacred than another; another man considers every day alike. Each one should be fully convinced in his own mind. ⁶He who regards one day as special, does so to the Lord. He who eats meat, eats to the Lord, for he gives thanks to God; and he who abstains, does so to the Lord and gives thanks to God. ⁷For none of us lives to himself alone and none of us dies to himself alone. ⁸If we live, we live to the Lord; and if we die, we die to the Lord. So, whether we live or die, we belong to the Lord.

⁹For this very reason, Christ died and returned to life so that he might be the Lord of both the dead and the living. ¹⁰You, then, why do you judge your brother? Or why do you look down on your brother? For we will all stand before God's judgment seat. ¹¹It is written:

ᵃ 14 Or the flesh

Gifts and Abilities

READ ROMANS 12:3–8

GET STRONGER

God created each one of us and gave us different gifts. Of course, the gifts don't come fully developed already. If, for example, you have a talent for music, you can't just pick up a violin and play in the symphony. You need to practice in order to develop that gift. What is *your* gift? Well, think about what you're naturally good at and what others compliment you on. If you can say, "I know I'm good at this and others say I'm good," that's very likely a gift. Develop that gift, just like practicing the violin. Learn from others who've been doing that kind of thing for years——whether your gift is music, math, drama, sports, drawing, encouraging others or *whatever*. You learn by listening to others, then by just stepping out and starting to do it.

Your next reading is on page 1482.

" 'As surely as I live,' says the Lord,
'every knee will bow before me;
   every tongue will confess to God.' "[a]

[12]So then, each of us will give an account of himself to God.

[13]Therefore let us stop passing judgment on one another. Instead, make up your mind not to put any stumbling block or obstacle in your brother's way. [14]As one who is in the Lord Jesus, I am fully convinced that no food[b] is unclean in itself. But if anyone regards something as unclean, then for him it is unclean. [15]If your brother is distressed because of what you eat, you are no longer acting in love. Do not by your eating destroy your brother for whom Christ died. [16]Do not allow what you consider good to be spoken of as evil. [17]For the kingdom of God is not a matter of eating and drinking, but of righteousness, peace and joy in the Holy Spirit, [18]because anyone who serves Christ in this way is pleasing to God and approved by men.

[19]Let us therefore make every effort to do what leads to peace and to mutual edification. [20]Do not destroy the work of God for the sake of food. All food is clean, but it is wrong for a man to eat anything that causes someone else to stumble. [21]It is better not to eat meat or drink wine or to do anything else that will cause your brother to fall.

[22]So whatever you believe about these things keep between yourself and God. Blessed is the man who does not condemn himself by what he approves. [23]But the man who has doubts is condemned if he eats, because his eating is not from faith; and everything that does not come from faith is sin.

We who are strong ought to bear with the failings of the weak and not to please ourselves. [2]Each of us should please his neighbor for his good, to build him

a 11 Isaiah 45:23   *b 14* Or *that nothing*

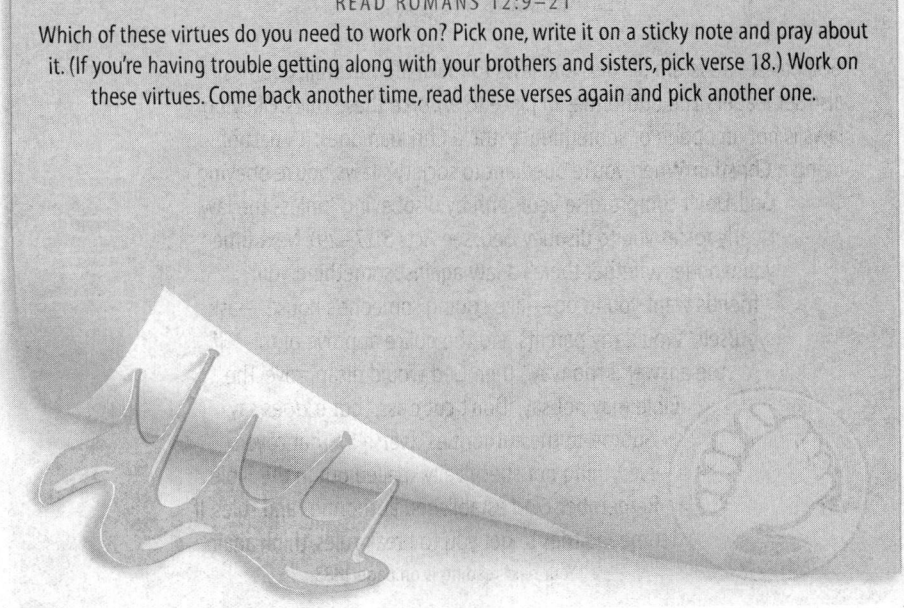

Make It Stick

READ ROMANS 12:9–21
Which of these virtues do you need to work on? Pick one, write it on a sticky note and pray about it. (If you're having trouble getting along with your brothers and sisters, pick verse 18.) Work on these virtues. Come back another time, read these verses again and pick another one.

up. ³For even Christ did not please himself but, as it is written: "The insults of those who insult you have fallen on me."ᵃ ⁴For everything that was written in the past was written to teach us, so that through endurance and the encouragement of the Scriptures we might have hope.

⁵May the God who gives endurance and encouragement give you a spirit of unity among yourselves as you follow Christ Jesus, ⁶so that with one heart and mouth you may glorify the God and Father of our Lord Jesus Christ.

⁷Accept one another, then, just as Christ accepted you, in order to bring praise to God. ⁸For I tell you that Christ has become a servant of the Jewsᵇ on behalf of God's truth, to confirm the promises made to the patriarchs ⁹so that the Gentiles may glorify God for his mercy, as it is written:

"Therefore I will praise you among the
    Gentiles;
 I will sing hymns to your name."ᶜ

¹⁰Again, it says,

"Rejoice, O Gentiles, with his people."ᵈ

¹¹And again,

"Praise the Lord, all you Gentiles,
    and sing praises to him, all you
    peoples."ᵉ

¹²And again, Isaiah says,

"The Root of Jesse will spring up,
    one who will arise to rule over the
    nations;
 the Gentiles will hope in him."ᶠ

¹³May the God of hope fill you with all joy and peace as you trust in him, so that you may overflow with hope by the power of the Holy Spirit.

Paul the Minister to the Gentiles

¹⁴I myself am convinced, my brothers, that you yourselves are full of goodness, complete in knowledge and competent to instruct one another. ¹⁵I have written you quite boldly on some points, as if to remind you of them again, because of the grace God gave me ¹⁶to be a minister of

ᵃ 3 Psalm 69:9   ᵇ 8 Greek circumcision
ᶜ 9 2 Samuel 22:50; Psalm 18:49   ᵈ 10 Deut. 32:43
ᵉ 11 Psalm 117:1   ᶠ 12 Isaiah 11:10

Rules and Enforcement

READ ROMANS 13:1–7

God has set a system of rules and laws to make life run well. God has also set leaders and authorities in place to *enforce* these rules. Obeying laws is not an option or something "extra" a Christian does. It's part of being a Christian. When you're obedient to society's laws, you're obeying God. Don't compromise your faith by disobeying (unless the law clearly forces you to disobey God; see Acts 5:27–29). Next time you wonder whether there's a law against something your friends want you to do—like egging someone's house—ask yourself, "Would my parents and the police approve of this?" If the answer is "no way," then God would disapprove. The Bible may not say, "Don't cut class," but it *does* say, "Submit to the authorities" (verse 5). That covers everything not specifically spelled out in the Bible. Remember, *God* established authorities and rules. If someone tries to get you to break rules, think again.

Your next reading is on page 1483.

Christ Jesus to the Gentiles with the priestly duty of proclaiming the gospel of God, so that the Gentiles might become an offering acceptable to God, sanctified by the Holy Spirit.

17Therefore I glory in Christ Jesus in my service to God. 18I will not venture to speak of anything except what Christ has accomplished through me in leading the Gentiles to obey God by what I have said and done— 19by the power of signs and miracles, through the power of the Spirit. So from Jerusalem all the way around to Illyricum, I have fully proclaimed the gospel of Christ. 20It has always been my ambition to preach the gospel where Christ was not known, so that I would not be building on someone else's foundation. 21Rather, as it is written:

"Those who were not told about him
    will see,
  and those who have not heard will
    understand."a

22This is why I have often been hindered from coming to you.

Paul's Plan to Visit Rome

23But now that there is no more place for me to work in these regions, and since I have been longing for many years to see you, 24I plan to do so when I go to Spain. I hope to visit you while passing through and to have you assist me on my journey there, after I have enjoyed your company for a while. 25Now, however, I am on my way to Jerusalem in the service of the saints there. 26For Macedonia and Achaia were pleased to make a contribution for the poor among the saints in Jerusalem. 27They were pleased to do it, and indeed they owe it to them. For if the Gentiles have shared in the Jews' spiritual blessings, they owe it to the Jews to share with them their material blessings. 28So after I have completed this task and have made sure that they have received this fruit, I will go to Spain and visit you on the way. 29I know that when I come to you, I will come in the full measure of the blessing of Christ.

30I urge you, brothers, by our Lord Jesus

a 21 Isaiah 52:15

What Movies Are OK?

READ ROMANS 14:1–4, 12–23

GET SMARTER

They didn't have movies in New Testament times, but they did have theatres. Did Paul go to the theatre? We don't know, but this guy could rattle off lines from about five Greek poets and in 1 Corinthians 15:33 Paul quotes a line from the comedy, *Thais*, by the Greek writer, Menander. (Paul quoting a *comedy play*? Yup!) So we know good clean movies and comedies are in. What else is in? What's off-limits? The Bible doesn't specifically *say*, although it does tell us to absolutely avoid the raunchy humor of lots of today's movies (Ephesians 5:4). Other than that, if the Bible doesn't say flat-out if something is right or wrong, there's room for Christians to come to different conclusions (verse 2). If you're having trouble deciding if a movie would be good for you to watch, ask your parents or youth pastor. They can give you some good advice.

Your next reading is on page 1487.

Get a Load of This...

Check out all the "greetings" in Romans 16. A man of God should be friendly. It isn't being "cool" to slide into a room, say nothing and merely nod. Go into a room and greet people, shake hands, smile. Let others know that you're *glad* that they're there. Don't just grunt to acknowledge that they're alive.

Christ and by the love of the Spirit, to join me in my struggle by praying to God for me. ³¹Pray that I may be rescued from the unbelievers in Judea and that my service in Jerusalem may be acceptable to the saints there, ³²so that by God's will I may come to you with joy and together with you be refreshed. ³³The God of peace be with you all. Amen.

Personal Greetings

16 I commend to you our sister Phoebe, a servant[a] of the church in Cenchrea. ²I ask you to receive her in the Lord in a way worthy of the saints and to give her any help she may need from you, for she has been a great help to many people, including me.

³Greet Priscilla[b] and Aquila, my fellow workers in Christ Jesus. ⁴They risked their lives for me. Not only I but all the churches of the Gentiles are grateful to them.

⁵Greet also the church that meets at their house.
Greet my dear friend Epenetus, who was the first convert to Christ in the province of Asia.

⁶Greet Mary, who worked very hard for you.

⁷Greet Andronicus and Junias, my relatives who have been in prison with me. They are outstanding among the apostles, and they were in Christ before I was.

⁸Greet Ampliatus, whom I love in the Lord.

⁹Greet Urbanus, our fellow worker in Christ, and my dear friend Stachys.

¹⁰Greet Apelles, tested and approved in Christ.
Greet those who belong to the household of Aristobulus.

¹¹Greet Herodion, my relative.
Greet those in the household of Narcissus who are in the Lord.

¹²Greet Tryphena and Tryphosa, those women who work hard in the Lord.
Greet my dear friend Persis, another woman who has worked very hard in the Lord.

¹³Greet Rufus, chosen in the Lord, and his mother, who has been a mother to me, too.

¹⁴Greet Asyncritus, Phlegon, Hermes, Patrobas, Hermas and the brothers with them.

¹⁵Greet Philologus, Julia, Nereus and his sister, and Olympas and all the saints with them.

¹⁶Greet one another with a holy kiss.
All the churches of Christ send greetings.

¹⁷I urge you, brothers, to watch out for those who cause divisions and put obstacles in your way that are contrary to the teaching you have learned. Keep away from them. ¹⁸For such people are not serving our Lord Christ, but their own appetites. By smooth talk and flattery they deceive the minds of naive people. ¹⁹Everyone

a 1 Or deaconess   *b 3 Greek* Prisca, *a variant of* Priscilla has heard about your obedience, so I am full of joy over you; but I want you to be wise about what is good, and innocent about what is evil.

20The God of peace will soon crush Satan under your feet.

The grace of our Lord Jesus be with you.

21Timothy, my fellow worker, sends his greetings to you, as do Lucius, Jason and Sosipater, my relatives.

22I, Tertius, who wrote down this letter, greet you in the Lord.

23Gaius, whose hospitality I and the whole church here enjoy, sends you his greetings.

Erastus, who is the city's director of public works, and our brother Quartus send you their greetings. [a]

25Now to him who is able to establish you by my gospel and the proclamation of Jesus Christ, according to the revelation of the mystery hidden for long ages past, 26but now revealed and made known through the prophetic writings by the command of the eternal God, so that all nations might believe and obey him— 27to the only wise God be glory forever through Jesus Christ! Amen.

---

[a] 23 Some manuscripts *their greetings.* 24*May the grace of our Lord Jesus Christ be with all of you. Amen.*

1 CORINTHIANS

Who wrote this book?
Paul.

Why was this book written?
Paul wrote 1 Corinthians to help the Corinthians solve problems in their church.

For whom was this book written?
This book is a letter that Paul sent to Christians in Corinth.

When was this book written?
This book was written about A.D. 55 from the city of Ephesus.

What are some important teachings in this book?

Believers must stop sinning	1 Corinthians 6:9–11
Each of us is important	1 Corinthians 12:14–31
What love is really like	1 Corinthians 13:1–13
Jesus is alive	1 Corinthians 15:3–8
We will be resurrected too	1 Corinthians 15:35–58

1 Paul, called to be an apostle of Christ Jesus by the will of God, and our brother Sosthenes,

2To the church of God in Corinth, to those sanctified in Christ Jesus and called to be holy, together with all those everywhere who call on the name of our Lord Jesus Christ—their Lord and ours:

3Grace and peace to you from God our Father and the Lord Jesus Christ.

Thanksgiving

4I always thank God for you because of his grace given you in Christ Jesus. 5For in him you have been enriched in every way— in all your speaking and in all your knowledge— 6because our testimony about Christ was confirmed in you. 7Therefore you do not lack any spiritual gift as you eagerly wait for our Lord Jesus Christ to be revealed. 8He will keep you strong to the end, so that you will be blameless on the day of our Lord Jesus Christ. 9God, who has called you into fellowship with his Son Jesus Christ our Lord, is faithful.

Divisions in the Church

10I appeal to you, brothers, in the name of our Lord Jesus Christ, that all of you agree with one another so that there may be no divisions among you and that you may be perfectly united in mind and thought. 11My brothers, some from Chloe's household have informed me that there are quarrels among you. 12What I mean is this: One of you says, "I follow Paul"; another, "I follow Apollos"; another, "I follow Cephas*a*"; still another, "I follow Christ."

13Is Christ divided? Was Paul crucified for you? Were you baptized into*b* the name of Paul? 14I am thankful that I did not baptize any of you except Crispus and Gaius, 15so no one can say that you were baptized into my name. 16(Yes, I also baptized the household of Stephanas; beyond that, I don't remember if I baptized anyone else.) 17For Christ did not send me to baptize, but to preach the gospel—not with words of human wisdom, lest the cross of Christ be emptied of its power.

a 12 That is, Peter   *b 13* Or *in;* also in verse 15

Amazing Apollos
READ 1 CORINTHIANS 1:10–13

GET SMARTER

Ever heard of a Bible character named Apollos? He was *some* guy! He was born in Alexandria, Egypt, *the* Jewish intellectual center on planet earth, and he was so educated in the Scriptures and such an excellent speaker that he usually won hands-down in public debates. When Priscilla and Aquila heard him in Ephesus, they knew he was a winner. He just needed to know more about Jesus (see Acts 18:24–28). After Ephesus, Apollos set sail for Corinth, where he was so popular that he contributed to a split in the church, with some of the believers joining an Apollos fan club (1 Corinthians 1:11–13; 3:1–8). But Apollos didn't let this go to his head. He even refused to return to Corinth, probably because the problem hadn't been solved (1 Corinthians 16:12). Apollos was a man of God: intelligent, hardworking and gifted, and still humble enough to learn from others.

Your next reading is on page 1489.

Christ the Wisdom and Power of God

18For the message of the cross is foolishness to those who are perishing, but to us who are being saved it is the power of God. 19For it is written:

"I will destroy the wisdom of the wise;
    the intelligence of the intelligent I
    will frustrate."[a]

20Where is the wise man? Where is the scholar? Where is the philosopher of this age? Has not God made foolish the wisdom of the world? 21For since in the wisdom of God the world through its wisdom did not know him, God was pleased through the foolishness of what was preached to save those who believe. 22Jews demand miraculous signs and Greeks look for wisdom, 23but we preach Christ crucified: a stumbling block to Jews and foolishness to Gentiles, 24but to those whom God has called, both Jews and Greeks, Christ the power of God and the wisdom of God. 25For the foolishness of God is wiser than man's wisdom, and the weakness of God is stronger than man's strength.

26Brothers, think of what you were when you were called. Not many of you were wise by human standards; not many were influential; not many were of noble birth. 27But God chose the foolish things of the world to shame the wise; God chose the weak things of the world to shame the strong. 28He chose the lowly things of this world and the despised things—and the things that are not—to nullify the things that are, 29so that no one may boast before him. 30It is because of him that you are in Christ Jesus, who has become for us wisdom from God—that is, our righteousness, holiness and redemption. 31Therefore, as it is written: "Let him who boasts boast in the Lord."[b]

When I came to you, brothers, I did not come with eloquence or superior wisdom as I proclaimed to you the testimony about God.[c] 2For I resolved to know nothing while I was with you except Jesus Christ and him crucified. 3I came to you in weakness and fear, and with much trembling. 4My message and my preaching were not with wise and persuasive words, but with a demonstration of the Spirit's power, 5so that your faith might not rest on men's wisdom, but on God's power.

Wisdom From the Spirit

6We do, however, speak a message of wisdom among the mature, but not the wisdom of this age or of the rulers of this age, who are coming to nothing. 7No, we speak of God's secret wisdom, a wisdom that has been hidden and that God destined for our glory before time began. 8None of the rulers of this age understood it, for if they had, they would not have crucified the Lord of glory. 9However, as it is written:

"No eye has seen,
    no ear has heard,
    no mind has conceived
    what God has prepared for those
        who love him"[d]—

10but God has revealed it to us by his Spirit.

The Spirit searches all things, even the deep things of God. 11For who among men knows the thoughts of a man except the man's spirit within him? In the same way no one knows the thoughts of God except the Spirit of God. 12We have not received the spirit of the world but the Spirit who is from God, that we may understand what God has freely given us. 13This is what we speak, not in words taught us by human wisdom but in words taught by the Spirit, expressing spiritual truths in spiritual words.[e] 14The man without the Spirit does not accept the things that come from the Spirit of God, for they are foolishness to him, and he cannot understand them, because they are spiritually discerned. 15The spiritual man makes judgments about all things, but he himself is not subject to any man's judgment:

16"For who has known the mind of the
        Lord
    that he may instruct him?"[f]

But we have the mind of Christ.

On Divisions in the Church

Brothers, I could not address you as spiritual but as worldly—mere infants in Christ. 2I gave you milk, not solid food, for you were not yet ready for it. Indeed, you are still not ready. 3You are still worldly. For since there is jealousy and quarreling among you, are

---

a 19 Isaiah 29:14   b 31 Jer. 9:24   c 1 Some manuscripts as I proclaimed to you God's mystery   d 9 Isaiah 64:4
e 13 Or Spirit, interpreting spiritual truths to spiritual men
f 16 Isaiah 40:13

you not worldly? Are you not acting like mere men? [4]For when one says, "I follow Paul," and another, "I follow Apollos," are you not mere men?

[5]What, after all, is Apollos? And what is Paul? Only servants, through whom you came to believe—as the Lord has assigned to each his task. [6]I planted the seed, Apollos watered it, but God made it grow. [7]So neither he who plants nor he who waters is anything, but only God, who makes things grow. [8]The man who plants and the man who waters have one purpose, and each will be rewarded according to his own labor. [9]For we are God's fellow workers; you are God's field, God's building.

[10]By the grace God has given me, I laid a foundation as an expert builder, and someone else is building on it. But each one should be careful how he builds. [11]For no one can lay any foundation other than the one already laid, which is Jesus Christ. [12]If any man builds on this foundation using gold, silver, costly stones, wood, hay or straw, [13]his work will be shown for what it is, because the Day will bring it to light. It will be revealed with fire, and the fire will test the quality of each man's work. [14]If what he has built survives, he will receive his reward. [15]If it is burned up, he will suffer loss; he himself will be saved, but only as one escaping through the flames.

[16]Don't you know that you yourselves are God's temple and that God's Spirit lives in you? [17]If anyone destroys God's temple, God will destroy him; for God's temple is sacred, and you are that temple.

[18]Do not deceive yourselves. If any one of you thinks he is wise by the standards of this age, he should become a "fool" so that he may become wise. [19]For the wisdom of this world is foolishness in God's sight. As it is written: "He catches the wise in their craftiness"[a]; [20]and again, "The Lord knows that the thoughts of the wise are futile."[b] [21]So then, no more boasting about men! All things are yours, [22]whether Paul or Apollos or Cephas[c] or the world or life or death or the present or the future—all are yours, [23]and you are of Christ, and Christ is of God.

[a]19 Job 5:13   [b]20 Psalm 94:11   [c]22 That is, Peter

Tacos, Sushi, Pizza—It's All Food

READ 1 CORINTHIANS 3:1–9

If someone said you were less spiritual than they were because they liked sushi and you liked tacos—or, horror of horrors, you enjoyed pizza!—you'd think they were joking. But is this any more ridiculous than people who think their denomination is more "spiritual" than other denominations? Whether you're Lutheran, Baptist, Pentecostal or Anglican, you're still a *Christian*. And all Christians agree on the basics of the faith. Many of the "extra" things that make churches different—such as what kind of music they like and the way they pray—are matters of taste only, not doctrine. It's fine for churches to do things their own way, but that doesn't make everyone else wrong or less spiritual. You wouldn't fight over which foods taste the best, would you? So why argue about tastes in music and worship? Just focus on what's common to all denominations: loving and worshiping Jesus.

Your next reading is on page 1492.

Gross!

When Paul said he was treated like "the scum of the earth" (1 Corinthians 4:13), the Greek word he used was *soooo* nasty that it never appears again in the New Testament. Some believe it referred to the ashes of low life criminals who were sacrificed to please pagan gods. Yuck!

Apostles of Christ

So then, men ought to regard us as servants of Christ and as those entrusted with the secret things of God. ²Now it is required that those who have been given a trust must prove faithful. ³I care very little if I am judged by you or by any human court; indeed, I do not even judge myself. ⁴My conscience is clear, but that does not make me innocent. It is the Lord who judges me. ⁵Therefore judge nothing before the appointed time; wait till the Lord comes. He will bring to light what is hidden in darkness and will expose the motives of men's hearts. At that time each will receive his praise from God.

⁶Now, brothers, I have applied these things to myself and Apollos for your benefit, so that you may learn from us the meaning of the saying, "Do not go beyond what is written." Then you will not take pride in one man over against another. ⁷For who makes you different from anyone else? What do you have that you did not receive? And if you did receive it, why do you boast as though you did not?

⁸Already you have all you want! Already you have become rich! You have become kings—and that without us! How I wish that you really had become kings so that we might be kings with you! ⁹For it seems to me that God has put us apostles on display at the end of the procession, like men condemned to die in the arena. We have been made a spectacle to the whole universe, to angels as well as to men. ¹⁰We are fools for Christ, but you are so wise in Christ! We are weak, but you are strong! You are honored, we are dishonored! ¹¹To this very hour we go hungry and thirsty, we are in rags, we are brutally treated, we are homeless. ¹²We work hard with our own hands. When we are cursed, we bless; when we are persecuted, we endure it; ¹³when we are slandered, we answer kindly. Up to this moment we have become the scum of the earth, the refuse of the world.

¹⁴I am not writing this to shame you, but to warn you, as my dear children. ¹⁵Even though you have ten thousand guardians in Christ, you do not have many fathers, for in Christ Jesus I became your father through the gospel. ¹⁶Therefore I urge you to imitate me. ¹⁷For this reason I am sending to you Timothy, my son whom I love, who is faithful in the Lord. He will remind you of my way of life in Christ Jesus, which agrees with what I teach everywhere in every church.

¹⁸Some of you have become arrogant, as if I were not coming to you. ¹⁹But I will come to you very soon, if the Lord is willing, and then I will find out not only how these arrogant people are talking, but what power they have. ²⁰For the kingdom of God is not a matter of talk but of power. ²¹What do you prefer? Shall I come to you with a whip, or in love and with a gentle spirit?

Expel the Immoral Brother!

It is actually reported that there is sexual immorality among you, and of a kind that does not occur even among pagans: A man has his father's wife. ²And you are proud! Shouldn't you rather have been filled with grief and have put out of your fellowship the man who did this? ³Even though I am not physically present, I am with you in spirit. And I have already passed judgment on the one who did this, just as if I were present. ⁴When you are assembled in the name of our Lord Jesus and I am with you in spirit, and the power of our Lord Jesus is present, ⁵hand this man over to Satan, so that the sinful nature*ª* may be destroyed and his spirit saved on the day of the Lord.

⁶Your boasting is not good. Don't you know that a little yeast works through the whole batch of dough? ⁷Get rid of the old yeast that you may be a new batch without yeast—as you really are. For Christ, our Passover lamb, has been sacrificed. ⁸Therefore let us keep the Festival, not with the old yeast, the yeast of malice and wickedness, but with bread without yeast, the bread of sincerity and truth.

⁹I have written you in my letter not to associate with sexually immoral people— ¹⁰not at all meaning the people of this world who are immoral, or the greedy and swindlers, or idolaters. In that case you would have to leave this world. ¹¹But now I am writing you that you must not associate with anyone who calls himself a brother but is sexually immoral or greedy, an idolater or a slanderer, a drunkard or a swindler. With such a man do not even eat.

¹²What business is it of mine to judge those outside the church? Are you not to judge those inside? ¹³God will judge those outside. "Expel the wicked man from among you."*ᵇ*

ª 5 Or that *his body;* or that the *flesh*   *ᵇ 13* Deut. 17:7; 19:19; 21:21; 22:21,24; 24:7

Make It Stick

READ 1 CORINTHIANS 5:6–7

Imagine a taco as thick as a bread loaf. Oops! *Somebody* dumped yeast in the dough and it rose when baked. Sin acts like yeast. Sometimes we think a little bit is okay, but, like yeast, it soon spreads throughout our life. Write: "Up with tacos! Down with sin!" on a sticky note.

Lawsuits Among Believers

6 If any of you has a dispute with another, dare he take it before the ungodly for judgment instead of before the saints? ²Do you not know that the saints will judge the world? And if you are to judge the world, are you not competent to judge trivial cases? ³Do you not know that we will judge angels? How much more the things of this life! ⁴Therefore, if you have disputes about such matters, appoint as judges even men of little account in the church!ᵃ ⁵I say this to shame you. Is it possible that there is nobody among you wise enough to judge a dispute between believers? ⁶But instead, one brother goes to law against another—and this in front of unbelievers!

⁷The very fact that you have lawsuits among you means you have been completely defeated already. Why not rather be wronged? Why not rather be cheated? ⁸Instead, you yourselves cheat and do wrong, and you do this to your brothers.

⁹Do you not know that the wicked will not inherit the kingdom of God? Do not be deceived: Neither the sexually immoral nor idolaters nor adulterers nor male prostitutes nor homosexual offenders ¹⁰nor thieves nor the greedy nor drunkards nor slanderers nor swindlers will inherit the kingdom of God. ¹¹And that is what some of you were. But you were washed, you were sanctified, you were justified in the name of the Lord Jesus Christ and by the Spirit of our God.

Sexual Immorality

¹²"Everything is permissible for me"—but not everything is beneficial. "Everything is permissible for me"—but I will not be mastered by anything. ¹³"Food for the stomach and the stomach for food"—but God will destroy them both. The body is not meant for sexual immorality, but for the Lord, and the Lord for the body. ¹⁴By

ᵃ 4 Or matters, do you appoint as judges men of little account in the church?

GET STRONGER.

Hormones Kicking In

READ 1 CORINTHIANS 6:12–20

A lot of people say they have faith in God. Only thing is, they think they can have Jesus Christ in their heart, yet do whatever they please with their bodies and their lives. When you become a Christian, you give your *entire* self to God—body, mind and spirit. As you grow older, you'll notice your hormones kicking in. Next thing you know, you're thinking about sex. Just remember, God made sex and it's a wonderful thing, but it's to be enjoyed within marriage *only*.

Your next reading is on page 1494.

his power God raised the Lord from the dead, and he will raise us also. 15Do you not know that your bodies are members of Christ himself? Shall I then take the members of Christ and unite them with a prostitute? Never! 16Do you not know that he who unites himself with a prostitute is one with her in body? For it is said, "The two will become one flesh."a 17But he who unites himself with the Lord is one with him in spirit.

18Flee from sexual immorality. All other sins a man commits are outside his body, but he who sins sexually sins against his own body. 19Do you not know that your body is a temple of the Holy Spirit, who is in you, whom you have received from God? You are not your own; 20you were bought at a price. Therefore honor God with your body.

Marriage

Now for the matters you wrote about: It is good for a man not to marry.b 2But since there is so much immorality, each man should have his own wife, and each woman her own husband. 3The husband should fulfill his marital duty to his wife, and likewise the wife to her husband. 4The wife's body does not belong to her alone but also to her husband. In the same way, the husband's body does not belong to him alone but also to his wife. 5Do not deprive each other except by mutual consent and for a time, so that you may devote yourselves to prayer. Then come together again so that Satan will not tempt you because of your lack of self-control. 6I say this as a concession, not as a command. 7I wish that all men were as I am. But each man has his own gift from God; one has this gift, another has that.

8Now to the unmarried and the widows I say: It is good for them to stay unmarried, as I am. 9But if they cannot control themselves, they should marry, for it is better to marry than to burn with passion.

10To the married I give this command (not I, but the Lord): A wife must not separate from her husband. 11But if she does, she must remain unmarried or else be reconciled to her husband. And a husband must not divorce his wife.

12To the rest I say this (I, not the Lord): If any brother has a wife who is not a believer and she is willing to live with him, he must not divorce her. 13And if a woman has a husband who is not a believer and he is willing to live with her, she must not divorce him. 14For the unbelieving husband has been sanctified through his wife, and the unbelieving wife has been sanctified through her believing husband. Otherwise your children would be unclean, but as it is, they are holy.

15But if the unbeliever leaves, let him do so. A believing man or woman is not bound in such circumstances; God has called us to live in peace. 16How do you know,

a 16 Gen. 2:24   b 1 Or "It is good for a man not to have sexual relations with a woman."

Gross!

Having your computer's hard drive infected by a virus is a major pain! But that's nothing compared to having your body infected by a sexually transmitted disease (STD). When people have sex outside of marriage, they not only sin against God, they sin against their own bodies (1 Corinthians 6:18) and run the risk of getting such a disease.

wife, whether you will save your husband? Or, how do you know, husband, whether you will save your wife?

17Nevertheless, each one should retain the place in life that the Lord assigned to him and to which God has called him. This is the rule I lay down in all the churches. 18Was a man already circumcised when he was called? He should not become uncircumcised. Was a man uncircumcised when he was called? He should not be circumcised. 19Circumcision is nothing and uncircumcision is nothing. Keeping God's commands is what counts. 20Each one should remain in the situation which he was in when God called him. 21Were you a slave when you were called? Don't let it trouble you—although if you can gain your freedom, do so. 22For he who was a slave when he was called by the Lord is the Lord's freedman; similarly, he who was a free man when he was called is Christ's slave. 23You were bought at a price; do not become slaves of men. 24Brothers, each man, as responsible to God, should remain in the situation God called him to.

25Now about virgins: I have no command from the Lord, but I give a judgment as one who by the Lord's mercy is trustworthy. 26Because of the present crisis, I think that it is good for you to remain as you are. 27Are you married? Do not seek a divorce. Are you unmarried? Do not look for a wife. 28But if you do marry, you have not sinned; and if a virgin marries, she has not sinned. But those who marry will face many troubles in this life, and I want to spare you this.

29What I mean, brothers, is that the time is short. From now on those who have wives should live as if they had none; 30those who mourn, as if they did not; those who are happy, as if they were not; those who buy something, as if it were not theirs to keep; 31those who use the things of the world, as if not engrossed in them. For this world in its present form is passing away.

32I would like you to be free from concern. An unmarried man is concerned

Preparing for Marriage

READ 1 CORINTHIANS 7:10–15

Ever think about marriage? It probably seems a long way off—and hopefully it is! But here are some tips to help you think straight when you do meet "Miss Right": First, don't let other kids push you into dating. Focus on friendships and God instead. Second, you'll need a stable job, so plan to get your career in place before getting married. As Proverbs 24:27 says, "Get your fields ready; after that, build your house." Third, read up on marriage and get advice from your pastor and other mature Christians. Finally, don't just marry a pretty face. Your wife's looks will fade to some degree one day—so will *yours*—so you'd better have more than looks holding your relationship together. You and your wife should also value the same things (especially a relationship with God), share similar interests, and support each other's dreams and goals. If you follow this advice, it can help avoid divorce and other problems Paul talks about here.

Your next reading is on page 1497.

about the Lord's affairs—how he can please the Lord. ³³But a married man is concerned about the affairs of this world—how he can please his wife—³⁴and his interests are divided. An unmarried woman or virgin is concerned about the Lord's affairs: Her aim is to be devoted to the Lord in both body and spirit. But a married woman is concerned about the affairs of this world—how she can please her husband. ³⁵I am saying this for your own good, not to restrict you, but that you may live in a right way in undivided devotion to the Lord.

³⁶If anyone thinks he is acting improperly toward the virgin he is engaged to, and if she is getting along in years and he feels he ought to marry, he should do as he wants. He is not sinning. They should get married. ³⁷But the man who has settled the matter in his own mind, who is under no compulsion but has control over his own will, and who has made up his mind not to marry the virgin—this man also does the right thing. ³⁸So then, he who marries the virgin does right, but he who does not marry her does even better.ᵃ

³⁹A woman is bound to her husband as long as she lives. But if her husband dies, she is free to marry anyone she wishes, but he must belong to the Lord. ⁴⁰In my judgment, she is happier if she stays as she is—and I think that I too have the Spirit of God.

Food Sacrificed to Idols

Now about food sacrificed to idols: We know that we all possess knowledge.ᵇ Knowledge puffs up, but love builds up. ²The man who thinks he knows something does not yet know as he ought to know. ³But the man who loves God is known by God.

⁴So then, about eating food sacrificed to idols: We know that an idol is nothing at all in the world and that there is no God but one. ⁵For even if there are so-called gods, whether in heaven or on earth (as indeed there are many "gods" and many "lords"), ⁶yet for us there is but one God, the Father, from whom all things came and for whom we live; and there is but one Lord, Jesus Christ, through whom all things came and through whom we live.

⁷But not everyone knows this. Some people are still so accustomed to idols

that when they eat such food they think of it as having been sacrificed to an idol, and since their conscience is weak, it is defiled. ⁸But food does not bring us near to God; we are no worse if we do not eat, and no better if we do.

⁹Be careful, however, that the exercise of your freedom does not become a stumbling block to the weak. ¹⁰For if anyone with a weak conscience sees you who have this knowledge eating in an idol's temple, won't he be emboldened to eat what has been sacrificed to idols? ¹¹So this weak brother, for whom Christ died, is destroyed by your knowledge. ¹²When you sin against your brothers in this way and wound their weak conscience, you sin against Christ. ¹³Therefore, if what I eat causes my brother to fall into sin, I will never eat meat again, so that I will not cause him to fall.

The Rights of an Apostle

Am I not free? Am I not an apostle? Have I not seen Jesus our Lord? Are you not the result of my work in the Lord? ²Even though I may not be an apostle to others, surely I am to you! For you are the seal of my apostleship in the Lord.

³This is my defense to those who sit in judgment on me. ⁴Don't we have the right to food and drink? ⁵Don't we have the right to take a believing wife along with us, as do the other apostles and the Lord's brothers and Cephasᶜ? ⁶Or is it only I and Barnabas who must work for a living?

⁷Who serves as a soldier at his own expense? Who plants a vineyard and does not eat of its grapes? Who tends a flock and does not drink of the milk? ⁸Do I say this merely from a human point of view? Doesn't the Law say the same thing? ⁹For it is written in the Law of Moses: "Do not muzzle an ox while it is treading out the grain."ᵈ Is it about oxen that God is concerned? ¹⁰Surely he says this for us, doesn't he? Yes, this was written for us,

---

ᵃ 36–38 Or ³⁶If anyone thinks he is not treating his daughter properly, and if she is getting along in years, and he feels she ought to marry, he should do as he wants. He is not sinning. He should let her get married. ³⁷But the man who has settled the matter in his own mind, who is under no compulsion but has control over his own will, and who has made up his mind to keep the virgin unmarried—this man also does the right thing. ³⁸So then, he who gives his virgin in marriage does right, but he who does not give her in marriage does even better. ᵇ 1 Or "We all possess knowledge," as you say ᶜ 5 That is, Peter ᵈ 9 Deut. 25:4

because when the plowman plows and the thresher threshes, they ought to do so in the hope of sharing in the harvest. ¹¹If we have sown spiritual seed among you, is it too much if we reap a material harvest from you? ¹²If others have this right of support from you, shouldn't we have it all the more?

But we did not use this right. On the contrary, we put up with anything rather than hinder the gospel of Christ. ¹³Don't you know that those who work in the temple get their food from the temple, and those who serve at the altar share in what is offered on the altar? ¹⁴In the same way, the Lord has commanded that those who preach the gospel should receive their living from the gospel.

¹⁵But I have not used any of these rights. And I am not writing this in the hope that you will do such things for me. I would rather die than have anyone deprive me of this boast. ¹⁶Yet when I preach the gospel, I cannot boast, for I am compelled to preach. Woe to me if I do not preach the gospel! ¹⁷If I preach voluntarily, I have a reward; if not voluntarily, I am simply discharging the trust committed to me. ¹⁸What then is my reward? Just this: that in preaching the gospel I may offer it free of charge, and so not make use of my rights in preaching it.

¹⁹Though I am free and belong to no man, I make myself a slave to everyone, to win as many as possible. ²⁰To the Jews I became like a Jew, to win the Jews. To those under the law I became like one under the law (though I myself am not under the law), so as to win those under the law. ²¹To those not having the law I became like one not having the law (though I am not free from God's law but am under Christ's law), so as to win those not having the law. ²²To the weak I became weak, to win the weak. I have become all things to all men so that by all possible means I might save some. ²³I do all this for the sake of the gospel, that I may share in its blessings.

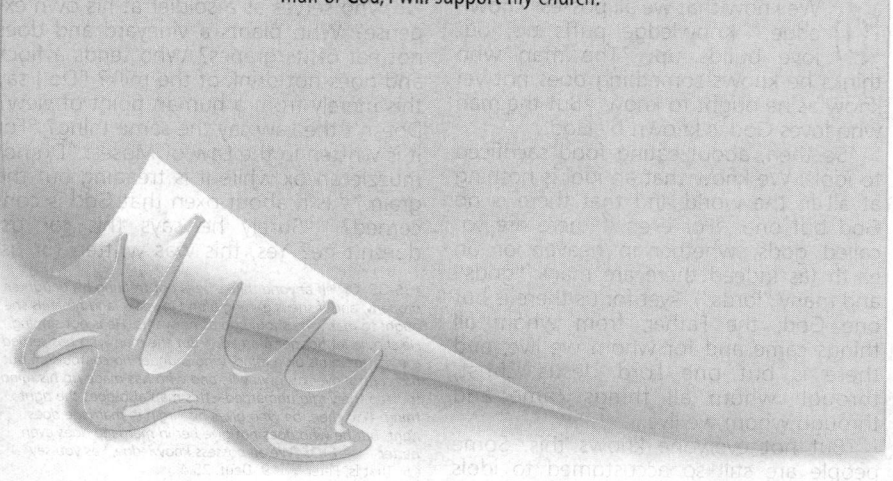

Make It Stick

READ 1 CORINTHIANS 9:9–10

If you just read this passage, you might think that God is saying *we're* oxen. But read the verses around it and you'll see God isn't calling us cattle. He's saying we should help support our church and pastors, by giving money and encouragement. On a sticky note write, "As a man of God, I will support my church."

24Do you not know that in a race all the runners run, but only one gets the prize? Run in such a way as to get the prize. 25Everyone who competes in the games goes into strict training. They do it to get a crown that will not last; but we do it to get a crown that will last forever. 26Therefore I do not run like a man running aimlessly; I do not fight like a man beating the air. 27No, I beat my body and make it my slave so that after I have preached to others, I myself will not be disqualified for the prize.

Warnings From Israel's History

10 For I do not want you to be ignorant of the fact, brothers, that our forefathers were all under the cloud and that they all passed through the sea. 2They were all baptized into Moses in the cloud and in the sea. 3They all ate the same spiritual food 4and drank the same spiritual drink; for they drank from the spiritual rock that accompanied them, and that rock was

Christ. 5Nevertheless, God was not pleased with most of them; their bodies were scattered over the desert.

6Now these things occurred as examples[a] to keep us from setting our hearts on evil things as they did. 7Do not be idolaters, as some of them were; as it is written: "The people sat down to eat and drink and got up to indulge in pagan revelry."[b] 8We should not commit sexual immorality, as some of them did—and in one day twenty-three thousand of them died. 9We should not test the Lord, as some of them did—and were killed by snakes. 10And do not grumble, as some of them did—and were killed by the destroying angel.

11These things happened to them as examples and were written down as warnings for us, on whom the fulfillment of the ages has come. 12So, if you think you are standing firm, be careful that you don't fall! 13No temptation has seized you except what is common to man. And God

a 6 Or types; also in verse 11   b 7 Exodus 32:6

Training and Discipline

READ 1 CORINTHIANS 9:24–27

GET STRONGER

New Year's resolutions are usually a waste of time. Few people keep them! How many times have people resolved to stop smoking or quit their nasty nose-picking habit, only to be caught just a few hours—or even minutes—later? Setting a goal to become smarter, stronger, deeper, cooler is pointless unless you have an actual plan to make it happen. Good intentions, sure, but you'll be "like a man running aimlessly" (1 Corinthians 9:26). At the same time, don't set a goal that is too big that you set yourself up to fail. Be realistic. Take one step at a time. For example, if you want to become fit, do some exercise today—walk instead of ride, join a sports team, change your diet. The same goes if you want to become smarter, cooler, or more spiritual. Create a step-by-step plan, then put it into action.

Your next reading is on page 1499.

is faithful; he will not let you be tempted beyond what you can bear. But when you are tempted, he will also provide a way out so that you can stand up under it.

Idol Feasts and the Lord's Supper

[14]Therefore, my dear friends, flee from idolatry. [15]I speak to sensible people; judge for yourselves what I say. [16]Is not the cup of thanksgiving for which we give thanks a participation in the blood of Christ? And is not the bread that we break a participation in the body of Christ? [17]Because there is one loaf, we, who are many, are one body, for we all partake of the one loaf.

[18]Consider the people of Israel: Do not those who eat the sacrifices participate in the altar? [19]Do I mean then that a sacrifice offered to an idol is anything, or that an idol is anything? [20]No, but the sacrifices of pagans are offered to demons, not to God, and I do not want you to be participants with demons. [21]You cannot drink the cup of the Lord and the cup of demons too; you cannot have a part in both the Lord's table and the table of demons. [22]Are we trying to arouse the Lord's jealousy? Are we stronger than he?

The Believer's Freedom

[23]"Everything is permissible"—but not everything is beneficial. "Everything is permissible"—but not everything is constructive. [24]Nobody should seek his own good, but the good of others.

[25]Eat anything sold in the meat market without raising questions of conscience, [26]for, "The earth is the Lord's, and everything in it."[a]

[27]If some unbeliever invites you to a meal and you want to go, eat whatever is put before you without raising questions of conscience. [28]But if anyone says to you, "This has been offered in sacrifice," then do not eat it, both for the sake of the man who told you and for conscience' sake[b]— [29]the other man's conscience, I mean, not yours. For why should my freedom be judged by another's conscience? [30]If I take part in the meal with thankfulness, why am I denounced because of something I thank God for?

[31]So whether you eat or drink or whatever you do, do it all for the glory of God. [32]Do not cause anyone to stumble, whether Jews, Greeks or the church of God— [33]even as I try to please everybody in every way. For I am not seeking my own good but the good of many, so that they may be saved. [1]Follow my example, as I follow the example of Christ.

Propriety in Worship

[2]I praise you for remembering me in everything and for holding to the teachings,[c] just as I passed them on to you.

[3]Now I want you to realize that the head of every man is Christ, and the head of the woman is man, and the head of Christ is God. [4]Every man who prays or prophesies with his head covered dishonors his head. [5]And every woman who prays or prophesies with her head uncovered dishonors her head—it is just as though her head were shaved. [6]If a woman does not cover her head, she should have her hair cut off; and if it is a disgrace for a woman to have her hair cut or shaved off, she should cover her head. [7]A man ought not to cover his head,[d] since he is the image and glory of God; but the woman is the glory of man. [8]For man did not come from woman, but woman from man; [9]neither was man created for woman, but woman for man. [10]For this reason, and because of the angels, the woman ought to have a sign of authority on her head.

[11]In the Lord, however, woman is not independent of man, nor is man independent of woman. [12]For as woman came from man, so also man is born of woman. But everything comes from God. [13]Judge for yourselves: Is it proper for a woman to pray to God with her head uncovered? [14]Does not the very nature of things teach you that if a man has long hair, it is a disgrace to him, [15]but that if a woman has long hair, it is her glory? For long hair is given to her as a covering. [16]If anyone wants to be contentious about this, we have no other practice—nor do the churches of God.

---

a 26 Psalm 24:1　　*b 28* Some manuscripts *conscience' sake, for "the earth is the Lord's and everything in it"*
c 2 Or *traditions*　　*d 4–7* Or *4Every man who prays or prophesies with long hair dishonors his head. 5And every woman who prays or prophesies with no covering of hair, on her head dishonors her head—she is just like one of the "shorn women." 6If a woman has no covering, let her be for now with short hair, but since it is a disgrace for a woman to have her hair shorn or shaved, she should grow it again. 7A man ought not to have long hair*

The Lord's Supper

17In the following directives I have no praise for you, for your meetings do more harm than good. 18In the first place, I hear that when you come together as a church, there are divisions among you, and to some extent I believe it. 19No doubt there have to be differences among you to show which of you have God's approval. 20When you come together, it is not the Lord's Supper you eat, 21for as you eat, each of you goes ahead without waiting for anybody else. One remains hungry, another gets drunk. 22Don't you have homes to eat and drink in? Or do you despise the church of God and humiliate those who have nothing? What shall I say to you? Shall I praise you for this? Certainly not!

23For I received from the Lord what I also passed on to you: The Lord Jesus, on the night he was betrayed, took bread, 24and when he had given thanks, he broke it and said, "This is my body, which is for you; do this in remembrance of me." 25In the same way, after supper he took the cup, saying, "This cup is the new covenant in my blood; do this, whenever you drink it, in remembrance of me." 26For whenever you eat this bread and drink this cup, you proclaim the Lord's death until he comes.

27Therefore, whoever eats the bread or drinks the cup of the Lord in an unworthy manner will be guilty of sinning against the body and blood of the Lord. 28A man ought to examine himself before he eats of the bread and drinks of the cup. 29For anyone who eats and drinks without recognizing the body of the Lord eats and drinks judgment on himself. 30That is why many among you are weak and sick, and a number of you have fallen asleep. 31But if we judged ourselves, we would not come under judgment. 32When we are judged by the Lord, we are being disciplined so that we will not be condemned with the world.

33So then, my brothers, when you come together to eat, wait for each other. 34If anyone is hungry, he should eat at home, so that when you meet together it may not result in judgment.

And when I come I will give further directions.

Checking Yourself Out

READ 1 CORINTHIANS 11:23–32

Different churches do communion differently, but no matter how they do it—or how often—it's always a good time to reflect on the fact that Jesus died to save us. That's why we should never take communion lightly. As Paul says, "A man ought to examine himself before he eats of the bread and drinks of the cup" (verse 28). This doesn't mean you should fall down on your knees wailing, "I'm not worthy!" Examining yourself doesn't mean condemning yourself for your problems, then refusing to take communion. It means reflecting on your relationship with God. Is your relationship growing? Are you receiving his grace, love and power? If God shows you an area of sin in your life, you need to confess that sin. But you should never *refuse* to take communion simply because you think you're not worthy. None of us are worthy—that's the whole point!

Your next reading is on page 1500.

Spiritual Gifts

12 Now about spiritual gifts, brothers, I do not want you to be ignorant. ²You know that when you were pagans, somehow or other you were influenced and led astray to mute idols. ³Therefore I tell you that no one who is speaking by the Spirit of God says, "Jesus be cursed," and no one can say, "Jesus is Lord," except by the Holy Spirit.

⁴There are different kinds of gifts, but the same Spirit. ⁵There are different kinds of service, but the same Lord. ⁶There are different kinds of working, but the same God works all of them in all men.

⁷Now to each one the manifestation of the Spirit is given for the common good. ⁸To one there is given through the Spirit the message of wisdom, to another the message of knowledge by means of the same Spirit, ⁹to another faith by the same Spirit, to another gifts of healing by that one Spirit, ¹⁰to another miraculous powers, to another prophecy, to another distinguishing between spirits, to another speaking in different kinds of tongues,ᵃ and to still another the interpretation of tongues.ᵃ ¹¹All these are the work of one and the same Spirit, and he gives them to each one, just as he determines.

One Body, Many Parts

¹²The body is a unit, though it is made up of many parts; and though all its parts are many, they form one body. So it is with Christ. ¹³For we were all baptized byᵇ one Spirit into one body—whether Jews or Greeks, slave or free—and we were all given the one Spirit to drink.

¹⁴Now the body is not made up of one part but of many. ¹⁵If the foot should say, "Because I am not a hand, I do not belong to the body," it would not for that reason cease to be part of the body. ¹⁶And if the ear should say, "Because I am not an eye, I do not belong to the body," it would not for that reason cease to be part of the body. ¹⁷If the whole body were an eye, where would the sense of hearing be? If the whole body were an ear, where would

ᵃ 10 Or languages; also in verse 28   ᵇ 13 Or with; or in

No Independent Eyeballs

READ 1 CORINTHIANS 12:12–27

When it comes to church, sometimes the leaders get all the credit. Meanwhile, you're just the "Joe Schmoe" who sweeps up after youth group. On the other hand, you may be one of the leaders wishing that slacker with the broom would get a move on! We often think some jobs—and some people—are more important than others. But as Paul reminds us, the church is like a body and every part is important. "The eye cannot say to the hand, 'I don't need you!' And the head cannot say to the feet, 'I don't need you!' " (verse 21). So rather than argue about who is more important, just work at being the best "you" you can be, whether you're a leader, a follower or a broom pusher! Then you won't waste time wishing you were like someone else or wondering why everyone else isn't like you.

Your next reading is on page 1502.

the sense of smell be? [18]But in fact God has arranged the parts in the body, every one of them, just as he wanted them to be. [19]If they were all one part, where would the body be? [20]As it is, there are many parts, but one body.

[21]The eye cannot say to the hand, "I don't need you!" And the head cannot say to the feet, "I don't need you!" [22]On the contrary, those parts of the body that seem to be weaker are indispensable, [23]and the parts that we think are less honorable we treat with special honor. And the parts that are unpresentable are treated with special modesty, [24]while our presentable parts need no special treatment. But God has combined the members of the body and has given greater honor to the parts that lacked it, [25]so that there should be no division in the body, but that its parts should have equal concern for each other. [26]If one part suffers, every part suffers with it; if one part is honored, every part rejoices with it.

[27]Now you are the body of Christ, and each one of you is a part of it. [28]And in the church God has appointed first of all apostles, second prophets, third teachers, then workers of miracles, also those having gifts of healing, those able to help others, those with gifts of administration, and those speaking in different kinds of tongues. [29]Are all apostles? Are all prophets? Are all teachers? Do all work miracles? [30]Do all have gifts of healing? Do all speak in tongues[a]? Do all interpret? [31]But eagerly desire[b] the greater gifts.

Love

And now I will show you the most excellent way.

13 If I speak in the tongues[c] of men and of angels, but have not love, I am only a resounding gong or a clanging cymbal. [2]If I have the gift of prophecy and can fathom all mysteries and all knowledge, and if I have a faith that can move mountains, but have not love, I am nothing. [3]If I give all I possess to the poor and surrender my body to the flames,[d] but have not love, I gain nothing.

[4]Love is patient, love is kind. It does not envy, it does not boast, it is not proud. [5]It is not rude, it is not self-seeking, it is not easily angered, it keeps no record of wrongs. [6]Love does not delight in evil but rejoices with the truth. [7]It always protects, always trusts, always hopes, always perseveres.

[8]Love never fails. But where there are prophecies, they will cease; where there are tongues, they will be stilled; where there is knowledge, it will pass away. [9]For we know in part and we prophesy in part, [10]but when perfection comes, the imperfect disappears. [11]When I was a child, I talked like a child, I thought like a child, I reasoned like a child. When I became a man, I put childish ways behind me. [12]Now we see but a poor reflection as in a mirror; then we shall see face to face. Now I

Get a Load of This...

During the reign of Augustus, there was a religious fanatic who "protested" by throwing himself into the fire and setting his body on fire (see 1 Corinthians 13:3). If you were going to protest, wouldn't you rather carry a sign?

---

[a] 30 Or other languages   [b] 31 Or But you are eagerly desiring
[c] 1 Or languages   [d] 3 Some early manuscripts body that I may boast

The ABC's of Love

READ 1 CORINTHIANS 13

Some people talk about "Christian love" as if it were something so poetic and perfect and ideal that no normal human being could expect to live it. But 1 Corinthians 13 shows that love is not gushy, poetic nonsense. It's the how-to manual on love that shows how *practical* Christian love works in pairs.

"Love is patient, love is kind." Patience expresses itself by being kind. If you're being unkind, chances are you need to work on being more patient. When you get all impatient, that's when you start tromping on other people's feelings.

"Love does not envy and does not boast." No one likes a bragger. A bragger is usually trying to look better than he is because he's feeling inferior to someone else and envies them. If you catch yourself bragging, work on focusing less on yourself and more on others.

"It is not proud, it is not rude." Proud people are rude people. They think they're the best and have the right to treat everyone else like dirt. Don't be a fool by thinking you're cool. Instead, "consider others better than yourself" (Philippians 2:3). God loves everyone the same, and so should you.

"Is not self-seeking. Is not easily angered." There's nothing worse than a whiny little brat throwing a tantrum because he didn't get his way. Well, maybe there is something worse: a whiny *big* brat doing the same. Anger is usually a sign things aren't going your way. Rather than whine, it's better to chill out and let someone *else* have their way.

"Keeps no record of wrongs. Does not delight in evil but rejoices with the truth." Some people never forgive or forget other people's mistakes. It's like they have a secret scoreboard of life—and you're losing big-time! Now turn this around: If *you're* happy when bad things happen to others or feel bad when something good happens to them, sounds like you're holding a grudge against them. Let it go.

"It always protects, always trusts, always hopes, always perseveres. Love never fails." Love isn't some gushy emotion you fall into—or out of. It's something that grows between two people who respect and admire one another. If your love for someone starts failing, it's time to do an attitude check. Do you have their best interests at heart or are you just looking out for number one? In God's mathematics, you should be more like number two or three (after God and others). If you don't get hung up on yourself but put God and others first, you'll have real love.

Your next reading is on page 1511.

know in part; then I shall know fully, even as I am fully known.

¹³And now these three remain: faith, hope and love. But the greatest of these is love.

Gifts of Prophecy and Tongues

14 Follow the way of love and eagerly desire spiritual gifts, especially the gift of prophecy. ²For anyone who speaks in a tongue[a] does not speak to men but to God. Indeed, no one understands him; he utters mysteries with his spirit.[b] ³But everyone who prophesies speaks to men for their strengthening, encouragement and comfort. ⁴He who speaks in a tongue edifies himself, but he who prophesies edifies the church. ⁵I would like every one of you to speak in tongues,[c] but I would rather have you prophesy. He who prophesies is greater than one who speaks in tongues,[c] unless he interprets, so that the church may be edified.

⁶Now, brothers, if I come to you and speak in tongues, what good will I be to you, unless I bring you some revelation or knowledge or prophecy or word of instruction? ⁷Even in the case of lifeless things that make sounds, such as the flute or harp, how will anyone know what tune is being played unless there is a distinction in the notes? ⁸Again, if the trumpet does not sound a clear call, who will get ready for battle? ⁹So it is with you. Unless you speak intelligible words with your tongue, how will anyone know what you are saying? You will just be speaking into the air. ¹⁰Undoubtedly there are all sorts of languages in the world, yet none of them is without meaning. ¹¹If then I do not grasp the meaning of what someone is saying, I am a foreigner to the speaker, and he is a foreigner to me. ¹²So it is with you. Since you are eager to have spiritual gifts, try to excel in gifts that build up the church.

¹³For this reason anyone who speaks in a tongue should pray that he may interpret what he says. ¹⁴For if I pray in a tongue, my spirit prays, but my mind is unfruitful. ¹⁵So what shall I do? I will pray with my spirit, but I will also pray with my mind; I will sing with my spirit, but I will also sing with my mind. ¹⁶If you are praising God with your spirit, how can one who finds himself among those who do not understand[d] say "Amen" to your thanksgiving, since he does not know what you are saying? ¹⁷You may be giving thanks well enough, but the other man is not edified.

¹⁸I thank God that I speak in tongues more than all of you. ¹⁹But in the church I would rather speak five intelligible words to instruct others than ten thousand words in a tongue.

²⁰Brothers, stop thinking like children. In regard to evil be infants, but in your thinking be adults. ²¹In the Law it is written:

"Through men of strange tongues
    and through the lips of foreigners
I will speak to this people,
    but even then they will not listen to me,"[e]

says the Lord.

²²Tongues, then, are a sign, not for believers but for unbelievers; prophecy, however, is for believers, not for unbelievers. ²³So if the whole church comes together and everyone speaks in tongues, and some who do not understand[f] or some unbelievers come in, will they not say that you are out of your mind? ²⁴But if an unbeliever or someone who does not understand[g] comes in while everybody is prophesying, he will be convinced by all that he is a sinner and will be judged by all, ²⁵and the secrets of his heart will be laid bare. So he will fall down and worship God, exclaiming, "God is really among you!"

Orderly Worship

²⁶What then shall we say, brothers? When you come together, everyone has a hymn, or a word of instruction, a revelation, a tongue or an interpretation. All of these must be done for the strengthening of the church. ²⁷If anyone speaks in a tongue, two—or at the most three—should speak, one at a time, and someone must interpret. ²⁸If there is no interpreter, the speaker should keep quiet in the church and speak to himself and God.

²⁹Two or three prophets should speak, and the others should weigh carefully what is said. ³⁰And if a revelation comes to someone who is sitting down, the first

---

a 2 Or another language; also in verses 4, 13, 14, 19, 26 and 27   b 2 Or by the Spirit   c 5 Or other languages; also in verses 6, 18, 22, 23 and 39   d 16 Or among the inquirers   e 21 Isaiah 28:11,12   f 23 Or some inquirers   g 24 Or or some inquirer speaker should stop. 31For you can all prophesy in turn so that everyone may be instructed and encouraged. 32The spirits of prophets are subject to the control of prophets. 33For God is not a God of disorder but of peace.

As in all the congregations of the saints, 34women should remain silent in the churches. They are not allowed to speak, but must be in submission, as the Law says. 35If they want to inquire about something, they should ask their own husbands at home; for it is disgraceful for a woman to speak in the church.

36Did the word of God originate with you? Or are you the only people it has reached? 37If anybody thinks he is a prophet or spiritually gifted, let him acknowledge that what I am writing to you is the Lord's command. 38If he ignores this, he himself will be ignored.*a*

39Therefore, my brothers, be eager to prophesy, and do not forbid speaking in tongues. 40But everything should be done in a fitting and orderly way.

The Resurrection of Christ

15 Now, brothers, I want to remind you of the gospel I preached to you, which you received and on which you have taken your stand. 2By this gospel you are saved, if you hold firmly to the word I preached to you. Otherwise, you have believed in vain.

3For what I received I passed on to you as of first importance*b*: that Christ died for our sins according to the Scriptures, 4that he was buried, that he was raised on the third day according to the Scriptures, 5and that he appeared to Peter,*c* and then to the Twelve. 6After that, he appeared to more than five hundred of the brothers at the same time, most of whom are still living, though some have fallen asleep. 7Then he appeared to James, then to all the apostles, 8and last of all he appeared to me also, as to one abnormally born.

9For I am the least of the apostles and do not even deserve to be called an apostle, because I persecuted the church of God. 10But by the grace of God I am what I am, and his grace to me was not without effect. No, I worked harder than all of them—yet not I, but the grace of God that was with me. 11Whether, then, it was I or they, this is what we preach, and this is what you believed.

The Resurrection of the Dead

12But if it is preached that Christ has been raised from the dead, how can some of you say that there is no resurrection of the dead? 13If there is no resurrection of the dead, then not even Christ has been raised. 14And if Christ has not been raised, our preaching is useless and so is your faith. 15More than that, we are then found to be false witnesses about God, for we have testified about God that he raised Christ from the dead. But he did not raise him if in fact the dead are not raised. 16For if the dead are not raised, then Christ has not been raised either. 17And if Christ has not been raised, your faith is futile; you are still in your sins. 18Then those also who have fallen asleep in Christ are lost. 19If only for this life we have hope in Christ, we are to be pitied more than all men.

20But Christ has indeed been raised from the dead, the firstfruits of those who have fallen asleep. 21For since death came through a man, the resurrection of the dead comes also through a man. 22For as in Adam all die, so in Christ all will be made alive. 23But each in his own turn: Christ, the firstfruits; then, when he comes, those who belong to him. 24Then the end will come, when he hands over the kingdom to God the Father after he has destroyed all dominion, authority and power. 25For he must reign until he has put all his enemies under his feet. 26The last enemy to be destroyed is death. 27For he "has put everything under his feet."*d* Now when it says that "everything" has been put under him, it is clear that this does not include God himself, who put everything under Christ. 28When he has done this, then the Son himself will be made subject to him who put everything under him, so that God may be all in all.

29Now if there is no resurrection, what will those do who are baptized for the dead? If the dead are not raised at all, why are people baptized for them? 30And as for us, why do we endanger ourselves every hour? 31I die every day—I mean that, brothers—just as surely as I glory over you in Christ Jesus our Lord. 32If I fought wild beasts in Ephesus for merely

a 38 Some manuscripts If he is ignorant of this, let him be ignorant   b 3 Or you at the first   c 5 Greek Cephas   d 27 Psalm 8:6 human reasons, what have I gained? If the dead are not raised,

"Let us eat and drink,
    for tomorrow we die."[a]

33Do not be misled: "Bad company corrupts good character." 34Come back to your senses as you ought, and stop sinning; for there are some who are ignorant of God—I say this to your shame.

The Resurrection Body

35But someone may ask, "How are the dead raised? With what kind of body will they come?" 36How foolish! What you sow does not come to life unless it dies. 37When you sow, you do not plant the body that will be, but just a seed, perhaps of wheat or of something else. 38But God gives it a body as he has determined, and to each kind of seed he gives its own body. 39All flesh is not the same: Men have one kind of flesh, animals have another, birds another and fish another.

40There are also heavenly bodies and there are earthly bodies; but the splendor of the heavenly bodies is one kind, and the splendor of the earthly bodies is another. 41The sun has one kind of splendor, the moon another and the stars another; and star differs from star in splendor.

42So will it be with the resurrection of the dead. The body that is sown is perishable, it is raised imperishable; 43it is sown in dishonor, it is raised in glory; it is sown in weakness, it is raised in power; 44it is sown a natural body, it is raised a spiritual body.

If there is a natural body, there is also a spiritual body. 45So it is written: "The first man Adam became a living being"[b]; the last Adam, a life-giving spirit. 46The spiritual did not come first, but the natural, and after that the spiritual. 47The first man was of the dust of the earth, the second man from heaven. 48As was the

a 32 Isaiah 22:13   b 45 Gen. 2:7

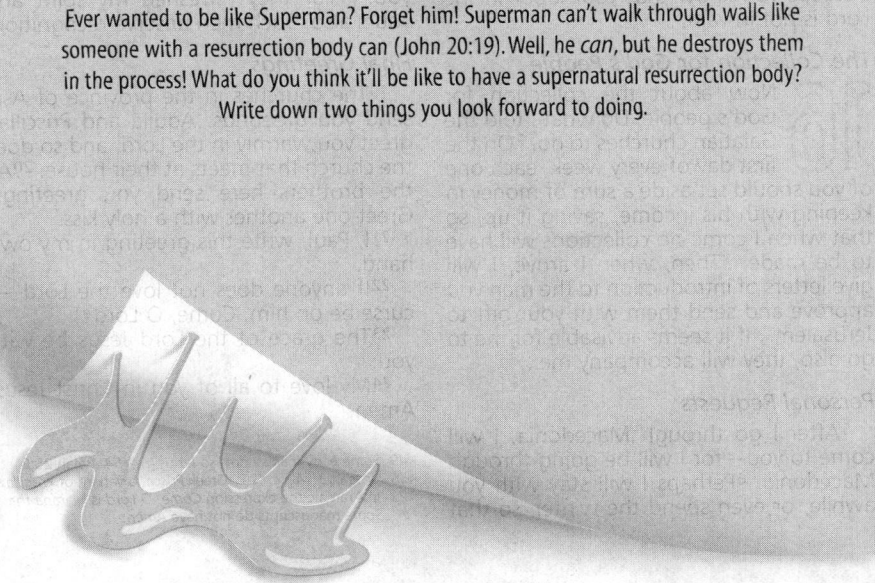

Make It Stick

READ 1 CORINTHIANS 15:42–44, 49

Ever wanted to be like Superman? Forget him! Superman can't walk through walls like someone with a resurrection body can (John 20:19). Well, he *can*, but he destroys them in the process! What do you think it'll be like to have a supernatural resurrection body? Write down two things you look forward to doing.

earthly man, so are those who are of the earth; and as is the man from heaven, so also are those who are of heaven. [49]And just as we have borne the likeness of the earthly man, so shall we[a] bear the likeness of the man from heaven.

[50]I declare to you, brothers, that flesh and blood cannot inherit the kingdom of God, nor does the perishable inherit the imperishable. [51]Listen, I tell you a mystery: We will not all sleep, but we will all be changed— [52]in a flash, in the twinkling of an eye, at the last trumpet. For the trumpet will sound, the dead will be raised imperishable, and we will be changed. [53]For the perishable must clothe itself with the imperishable, and the mortal with immortality. [54]When the perishable has been clothed with the imperishable, and the mortal with immortality, then the saying that is written will come true: "Death has been swallowed up in victory."[b]

[55] "Where, O death, is your victory?
   Where, O death, is your sting?"[c]

[56]The sting of death is sin, and the power of sin is the law. [57]But thanks be to God! He gives us the victory through our Lord Jesus Christ.

[58]Therefore, my dear brothers, stand firm. Let nothing move you. Always give yourselves fully to the work of the Lord, because you know that your labor in the Lord is not in vain.

The Collection for God's People

16 Now about the collection for God's people: Do what I told the Galatian churches to do. [2]On the first day of every week, each one of you should set aside a sum of money in keeping with his income, saving it up, so that when I come no collections will have to be made. [3]Then, when I arrive, I will give letters of introduction to the men you approve and send them with your gift to Jerusalem. [4]If it seems advisable for me to go also, they will accompany me.

Personal Requests

[5]After I go through Macedonia, I will come to you—for I will be going through Macedonia. [6]Perhaps I will stay with you awhile, or even spend the winter, so that you can help me on my journey, wherever I go. [7]I do not want to see you now and make only a passing visit; I hope to spend some time with you, if the Lord permits. [8]But I will stay on at Ephesus until Pentecost, [9]because a great door for effective work has opened to me, and there are many who oppose me.

[10]If Timothy comes, see to it that he has nothing to fear while he is with you, for he is carrying on the work of the Lord, just as I am. [11]No one, then, should refuse to accept him. Send him on his way in peace so that he may return to me. I am expecting him along with the brothers.

[12]Now about our brother Apollos: I strongly urged him to go to you with the brothers. He was quite unwilling to go now, but he will go when he has the opportunity.

[13]Be on your guard; stand firm in the faith; be men of courage; be strong. [14]Do everything in love.

[15]You know that the household of Stephanas were the first converts in Achaia, and they have devoted themselves to the service of the saints. I urge you, brothers, [16]to submit to such as these and to everyone who joins in the work, and labors at it. [17]I was glad when Stephanas, Fortunatus and Achaicus arrived, because they have supplied what was lacking from you. [18]For they refreshed my spirit and yours also. Such men deserve recognition.

Final Greetings

[19]The churches in the province of Asia send you greetings. Aquila and Priscilla[d] greet you warmly in the Lord, and so does the church that meets at their house. [20]All the brothers here send you greetings. Greet one another with a holy kiss.

[21]I, Paul, write this greeting in my own hand.

[22]If anyone does not love the Lord—a curse be on him. Come, O Lord[e]!

[23]The grace of the Lord Jesus be with you.

[24]My love to all of you in Christ Jesus. Amen.[f]

---

[a] 49 Some early manuscripts so let us   [b] 54 Isaiah 25:8
[c] 55 Hosea 13:14   [d] 19 Greek Prisca, a variant of Priscilla
[e] 22 In Aramaic the expression Come, O Lord is Marana tha.
[f] 24 Some manuscripts do not have Amen.

2 CORINTHIANS

Who wrote this book?
Paul.

Why was this book written?
The book of 2 Corinthians lets the Corinthians know that Paul loves them even if their church does have many problems.

For whom was this book written?
This book is a letter that was sent to Christians in Corinth.

When was this book written?
This book was written about A.D. 55 from Macedonia.

What are some important teachings in this book?

Our prayers help leaders	2 Corinthians 1:8–11
Forgive those who repent	2 Corinthians 2:5–11
We are God's ministers	2 Corinthians 5:11–21
Give generously	2 Corinthians 9:6–15
Strength in weakness	2 Corinthians 12:7–10

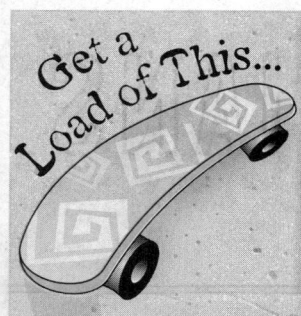

Get a Load of This...

It's important to pray for missionaries. Can your prayers help? Sure, you're just one person, but even *one* person's prayers help—and "the prayers of many" help a lot! (see 2 Corinthians 1:11). Picture a tug-of-war team losing ... until one last person jumps in and pulls! Then they win!

1 Paul, an apostle of Christ Jesus by the will of God, and Timothy our brother,

To the church of God in Corinth, together with all the saints throughout Achaia:

2 Grace and peace to you from God our Father and the Lord Jesus Christ.

The God of All Comfort

3 Praise be to the God and Father of our Lord Jesus Christ, the Father of compassion and the God of all comfort, 4 who comforts us in all our troubles, so that we can comfort those in any trouble with the comfort we ourselves have received from God. 5 For just as the sufferings of Christ flow over into our lives, so also through Christ our comfort overflows. 6 If we are distressed, it is for your comfort and salvation; if we are comforted, it is for your comfort, which produces in you patient endurance of the same sufferings we suffer. 7 And our hope for you is firm, because we know that just as you share in our sufferings, so also you share in our comfort.

8 We do not want you to be uninformed, brothers, about the hardships we suffered in the province of Asia. We were under great pressure, far beyond our ability to endure, so that we despaired even of life. 9 Indeed, in our hearts we felt the sentence of death. But this happened that we might not rely on ourselves but on God, who raises the dead. 10 He has delivered us from such a deadly peril, and he will deliver us. On him we have set our hope that he will continue to deliver us, 11 as you help us by your prayers. Then many will give thanks on our *a* behalf for the gracious favor granted us in answer to the prayers of many.

Paul's Change of Plans

12 Now this is our boast: Our conscience testifies that we have conducted ourselves in the world, and especially in our relations with you, in the holiness and sincerity that are from God. We have done so not according to worldly wisdom but according to God's grace. 13 For we do not write you anything you cannot read or understand. And I hope that, 14 as you have understood us in part, you will come to understand fully that you can boast of us just as we will boast of you in the day of the Lord Jesus.

15 Because I was confident of this, I planned to visit you first so that you might benefit twice. 16 I planned to visit you on my way to Macedonia and to come back to you from Macedonia, and then to have you send me on my way to Judea. 17 When I planned this, did I do it lightly? Or do I make my plans in a worldly manner so that in the same breath I say, "Yes, yes" and "No, no"?

18 But as surely as God is faithful, our message to you is not "Yes" and "No." 19 For the Son of God, Jesus Christ, who was preached among you by me and Silas *b* and Timothy, was not "Yes" and "No," but in him it has

a 11 Many manuscripts *your*   *b 19* Greek *Silvanus*, a variant of *Silas* always been "Yes." 20For no matter how many promises God has made, they are "Yes" in Christ. And so through him the "Amen" is spoken by us to the glory of God. 21Now it is God who makes both us and you stand firm in Christ. He anointed us, 22set his seal of ownership on us, and put his Spirit in our hearts as a deposit, guaranteeing what is to come.

23I call God as my witness that it was in order to spare you that I did not return to Corinth. 24Not that we lord it over your faith, but we work with you for your joy, because it is by faith you stand firm. 1So I made up my mind that I would not make another painful visit to you. 2For if I grieve you, who is left to make me glad but you whom I have grieved? 3I wrote as I did so that when I came I should not be distressed by those who ought to make me rejoice. I had confidence in all of you, that you would all share my joy. 4For I wrote you out of great distress and anguish of heart and with many tears, not to grieve you but to let you know the depth of my love for you.

Forgiveness for the Sinner

5If anyone has caused grief, he has not so much grieved me as he has grieved all of you, to some extent—not to put it too severely. 6The punishment inflicted on him by the majority is sufficient for him. 7Now instead, you ought to forgive and comfort him, so that he will not be overwhelmed by excessive sorrow. 8I urge you, therefore, to reaffirm your love for him. 9The reason I wrote you was to see if you would stand the test and be obedient in everything. 10If you forgive anyone, I also forgive him. And what I have forgiven—if there was anything to forgive—I have forgiven in the sight of Christ for your sake, 11in order that Satan might not outwit us. For we are not unaware of his schemes.

Ministers of the New Covenant

12Now when I went to Troas to preach the gospel of Christ and found that the Lord had opened a door for me, 13I still had no peace of mind, because I did not find my brother Titus there. So I said good-by to them and went on to Macedonia.

14But thanks be to God, who always leads us in triumphal procession in Christ and through us spreads everywhere the fragrance of the knowledge of him. 15For we are to God the aroma of Christ among those who are being saved and those who are perishing. 16To the one we are the smell of death; to the other, the fragrance of life. And who is equal to such a task? 17Unlike so many, we do not peddle the word of God for profit. On the contrary, in Christ we speak before God with sincerity, like men sent from God.

Are we beginning to commend ourselves again? Or do we need, like some people, letters of recommendation to you or from you? 2You yourselves are our letter, written on our hearts, known and read by everybody. 3You show that you are a letter

Gross!

Check out 2 Corinthians 2:16. Do you smell like *death*? Need some mouthwash? A shower? Maybe, but this "smell of death" stuff is more serious than B.O. It describes how people who reject God's grace and salvation are choosing *death* for themselves. And death stinks!

from Christ, the result of our ministry, written not with ink but with the Spirit of the living God, not on tablets of stone but on tablets of human hearts.

4Such confidence as this is ours through Christ before God. 5Not that we are competent in ourselves to claim anything for ourselves, but our competence comes from God. 6He has made us competent as ministers of a new covenant—not of the letter but of the Spirit; for the letter kills, but the Spirit gives life.

The Glory of the New Covenant

7Now if the ministry that brought death, which was engraved in letters on stone, came with glory, so that the Israelites could not look steadily at the face of Moses because of its glory, fading though it was, 8will not the ministry of the Spirit be even more glorious? 9If the ministry that condemns men is glorious, how much more glorious is the ministry that brings righteousness! 10For what was glorious has no glory now in comparison with the surpassing glory. 11And if what was fading away came with glory, how much greater is the glory of that which lasts!

12Therefore, since we have such a hope, we are very bold. 13We are not like Moses, who would put a veil over his face to keep the Israelites from gazing at it while the radiance was fading away. 14But their minds were made dull, for to this day the same veil remains when the old covenant is read. It has not been removed, because only in Christ is it taken away. 15Even to this day when Moses is read, a veil covers their hearts. 16But whenever anyone turns to the Lord, the veil is taken away. 17Now the Lord is the Spirit, and where the Spirit of the Lord is, there is freedom. 18And we, who with unveiled faces all reflect[a] the Lord's glory, are being transformed into his likeness with ever-increasing glory, which comes from the Lord, who is the Spirit.

Treasures in Jars of Clay

Therefore, since through God's mercy we have this ministry, we do not lose heart. 2Rather, we have renounced secret and shameful ways; we do not use deception, nor do we distort the word of God. On the contrary, by setting forth the truth plainly we commend ourselves to every man's conscience in the sight of God. 3And even if our gos-

pel is veiled, it is veiled to those who are perishing. 4The god of this age has blinded the minds of unbelievers, so that they cannot see the light of the gospel of the glory of Christ, who is the image of God. 5For we do not preach ourselves, but Jesus Christ as Lord, and ourselves as your servants for Jesus' sake. 6For God, who said, "Let light shine out of darkness,"[b] made his light shine in our hearts to give us the light of the knowledge of the glory of God in the face of Christ.

7But we have this treasure in jars of clay to show that this all-surpassing power is from God and not from us. 8We are hard pressed on every side, but not crushed; perplexed, but not in despair; 9persecuted, but not abandoned; struck down, but not destroyed. 10We always carry around in our body the death of Jesus, so that the life of Jesus may also be revealed in our body. 11For we who are alive are always being given over to death for Jesus' sake, so that his life may be revealed in our mortal body. 12So then, death is at work in us, but life is at work in you.

13It is written: "I believed; therefore I have spoken."[c] With that same spirit of faith we also believe and therefore speak, 14because we know that the one who raised the Lord Jesus from the dead will also raise us with Jesus and present us with you in his presence. 15All this is for your benefit, so that the grace that is reaching more and more people may cause thanksgiving to overflow to the glory of God.

16Therefore we do not lose heart. Though outwardly we are wasting away, yet inwardly we are being renewed day by day. 17For our light and momentary troubles are achieving for us an eternal glory that far outweighs them all. 18So we fix our eyes not on what is seen, but on what is unseen. For what is seen is temporary, but what is unseen is eternal.

Our Heavenly Dwelling

Now we know that if the earthly tent we live in is destroyed, we have a building from God, an eternal house in heaven, not built by human hands. 2Meanwhile we groan, longing to be clothed with our heavenly dwelling, 3because when we are clothed, we will not be found naked. 4For while we

---

a 18 Or contemplate   b 6 Gen. 1:3   c 13 Psalm 116:10

are in this tent, we groan and are burdened, because we do not wish to be unclothed but to be clothed with our heavenly dwelling, so that what is mortal may be swallowed up by life. ⁵Now it is God who has made us for this very purpose and has given us the Spirit as a deposit, guaranteeing what is to come.

⁶Therefore we are always confident and know that as long as we are at home in the body we are away from the Lord. ⁷We live by faith, not by sight. ⁸We are confident, I say, and would prefer to be away from the body and at home with the Lord. ⁹So we make it our goal to please him, whether we are at home in the body or away from it. ¹⁰For we must all appear before the judgment seat of Christ, that each one may receive what is due him for the things done while in the body, whether good or bad.

The Ministry of Reconciliation

¹¹Since, then, we know what it is to fear the Lord, we try to persuade men. What we are is plain to God, and I hope it is also plain to your conscience. ¹²We are not trying to commend ourselves to you again, but are giving you an opportunity to take pride in us, so that you can answer those who take pride in what is seen rather than in what is in the heart. ¹³If we are out of our mind, it is for the sake of God; if we are in our right mind, it is for you. ¹⁴For Christ's love compels us, because we are convinced that one died for all, and therefore all died. ¹⁵And he died for all, that those who live should no longer live for themselves but for him who died for them and was raised again.

¹⁶So from now on we regard no one from a worldly point of view. Though we once regarded Christ in this way, we do so no longer. ¹⁷Therefore, if anyone is in Christ, he is a new creation; the old has gone, the new has come! ¹⁸All this is from God, who reconciled us to himself through Christ and gave us the ministry of reconciliation: ¹⁹that God was reconciling the world to himself in Christ, not counting men's sins against them. And he has committed to us the message of reconciliation. ²⁰We are therefore Christ's ambassadors, as though God were making his

Blindness and Light

READ 2 CORINTHIANS 4:3–6

If you owned a computer game with ultra-cool graphics but refused to plug in your monitor, think you'd enjoy the game? *Not* likely. Unbelievers have a similar problem. They can't see the light because their minds are blinded. We as Christians *can* see the light because our mental monitors are plugged into the gospel. The gospel message is the power and the light of God that cut through our darkness to let us see the truth. Now one of our main jobs as men of God is to battle blindness with light by telling others about Jesus. Ask God, "Who can I bring the light to? How can I help tell others about Jesus?" If you don't know how to explain the gospel well, you can *learn* how. Remember, you don't need to know everything. Share what you believe and what God has done in your life. There's power in that. John 3:16 is a good summary of faith to know (page 1376).

Your next reading is on page 1514.

appeal through us. We implore you on Christ's behalf: Be reconciled to God. [21]God made him who had no sin to be sin[a] for us, so that in him we might become the righteousness of God.

6 As God's fellow workers we urge you not to receive God's grace in vain. [2]For he says,

"In the time of my favor I heard you,
   and in the day of salvation I helped
    you."[b]

I tell you, now is the time of God's favor, now is the day of salvation.

Paul's Hardships

[3]We put no stumbling block in anyone's path, so that our ministry will not be discredited. [4]Rather, as servants of God we commend ourselves in every way: in great endurance; in troubles, hardships and distresses; [5]in beatings, imprisonments and riots; in hard work, sleepless nights and hunger; [6]in purity, understanding, patience and kindness; in the Holy Spirit and in sincere love; [7]in truthful speech and in the power of God; with

[a] 21 Or be a sin offering   [b] 2 Isaiah 49:8

Make It Stick

_____

_____

_____

_____

_____

_____

_____

READ 2 CORINTHIANS 5:10

Once you're a Christian, you have eternal life! But you'll still "appear before the judgment seat of Christ" to give an account for everything you've said and done (2 Corinthians 5:9–10). This is Awards Night when you receive what you deserve. How pleased would Jesus be by your life? On a sticky note, write down some things you'd like to be given an award for when you appear before Christ.

weapons of righteousness in the right hand and in the left; [8]through glory and dishonor, bad report and good report; genuine, yet regarded as impostors; [9]known, yet regarded as unknown; dying, and yet we live on; beaten, and yet not killed; [10]sorrowful, yet always rejoicing; poor, yet making many rich; having nothing, and yet possessing everything.

[11]We have spoken freely to you, Corinthians, and opened wide our hearts to you. [12]We are not withholding our affection from you, but you are withholding yours from us. [13]As a fair exchange—I speak as to my children—open wide your hearts also.

Do Not Be Yoked With Unbelievers

[14]Do not be yoked together with unbelievers. For what do righteousness and wickedness have in common? Or what fellowship can light have with darkness? [15]What harmony is there between Christ and Belial[a]? What does a believer have in common with an unbeliever? [16]What agreement is there between the temple of God and idols? For we are the temple of the living God. As God has said: "I will live with them and walk among them, and I will be their God, and they will be my people."[b]

[17]"Therefore come out from them
    and be separate,
                    says the Lord.
Touch no unclean thing,
    and I will receive you."[c]
[18]"I will be a Father to you,
    and you will be my sons and
        daughters,
            says the Lord Almighty."[d]

Since we have these promises, dear friends, let us purify ourselves from everything that contaminates body and spirit, perfecting holiness out of reverence for God.

[a] 15 Greek *Beliar*, a variant of *Belial*   [b] 16 Lev. 26:12; Jer. 32:38; Ezek. 37:27   [c] 17 Isaiah 52:11; Ezek. 20:34,41   [d] 18 2 Samuel 7:14; 7:8

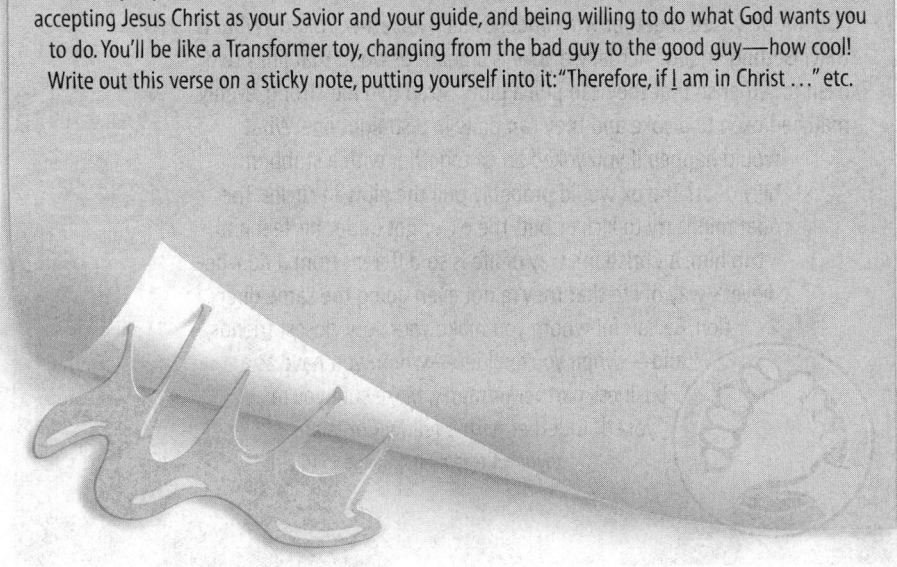

Make It Stick

READ 2 CORINTHIANS 5:17

Some people think that becoming a Christian just means deciding to "be good." Not so. It's accepting Jesus Christ as your Savior and your guide, and being willing to do what God wants you to do. You'll be like a Transformer toy, changing from the bad guy to the good guy—how cool! Write out this verse on a sticky note, putting yourself into it: "Therefore, if I am in Christ ..." etc.

Paul's Joy

[2] Make room for us in your hearts. We have wronged no one, we have corrupted no one, we have exploited no one. [3] I do not say this to condemn you; I have said before that you have such a place in our hearts that we would live or die with you. [4] I have great confidence in you; I take great pride in you. I am greatly encouraged; in all our troubles my joy knows no bounds.

[5] For when we came into Macedonia, this body of ours had no rest, but we were harassed at every turn—conflicts on the outside, fears within. [6] But God, who comforts the downcast, comforted us by the coming of Titus, [7] and not only by his coming but also by the comfort you had given him. He told us about your longing for me, your deep sorrow, your ardent concern for me, so that my joy was greater than ever.

[8] Even if I caused you sorrow by my letter, I do not regret it. Though I did regret it—I see that my letter hurt you, but only for a little while— [9] yet now I am happy, not because you were made sorry, but because your sorrow led you to repentance. For you became sorrowful as God intended and so were not harmed in any way by us. [10] Godly sorrow brings repentance that leads to salvation and leaves no regret, but worldly sorrow brings death. [11] See what this godly sorrow has produced in you: what earnestness, what eagerness to clear yourselves, what indignation, what alarm, what longing, what concern, what readiness to see justice done. At every point you have proved yourselves to be innocent in this matter. [12] So even though I wrote to you, it was not on account of the one who did the wrong or of the injured party, but rather that before God you could see for yourselves how devoted to us you are. [13] By all this we are encouraged.

In addition to our own encouragement, we were especially delighted to see how happy Titus was, because his spirit has been refreshed by all of you. [14] I had boasted to him about you, and you have not embarrassed me. But just as everything we said to you was true, so our boasting about you to Titus has proved to be true as well. [15] And his affection for you

Yoked Together

READ 2 CORINTHIANS 6:14–18

"Do not be yoked together with unbelievers" (verse 14). *Yoked?* What is that? Getting egged? Actually, a yoke is a beam of wood that links two oxen together so that they can pull a plow. Strap two big strong, evenly matched oxen to a yoke and they can plow in a straight line. What would happen if you yoked an ox together with a stubborn billy goat? The ox would probably pull the plow in circles. The goat might try to kick or butt the ox, or get under his feet and trip him. A Christian's way of life is so different from a non-believer's way of life that they're not even going the same direction. Be careful whom you make your very closest friends, and—when you're older—whom you have as a business partner or marry. Make sure you're "yoked" together with a fellow Christian.

Your next reading is on page 1516.

is all the greater when he remembers that you were all obedient, receiving him with fear and trembling. [16]I am glad I can have complete confidence in you.

Generosity Encouraged

And now, brothers, we want you to know about the grace that God has given the Macedonian churches. [2]Out of the most severe trial, their overflowing joy and their extreme poverty welled up in rich generosity. [3]For I testify that they gave as much as they were able, and even beyond their ability. Entirely on their own, [4]they urgently pleaded with us for the privilege of sharing in this service to the saints. [5]And they did not do as we expected, but they gave themselves first to the Lord and then to us in keeping with God's will. [6]So we urged Titus, since he had earlier made a beginning, to bring also to completion this act of grace on your part. [7]But just as you excel in everything—in faith, in speech, in knowledge, in complete earnestness and in your love for us[a]—see that you also excel in this grace of giving.

[8]I am not commanding you, but I want to test the sincerity of your love by comparing it with the earnestness of others. [9]For you know the grace of our Lord Jesus Christ, that though he was rich, yet for your sakes he became poor, so that you through his poverty might become rich.

[10]And here is my advice about what is best for you in this matter: Last year you were the first not only to give but also to have the desire to do so. [11]Now finish the work, so that your eager willingness to do it may be matched by your completion of it, according to your means. [12]For if the willingness is there, the gift is acceptable according to what one has, not according to what he does not have.

[13]Our desire is not that others might be relieved while you are hard pressed, but that there might be equality. [14]At the present time your plenty will supply what they need, so that in turn their plenty will supply what you need. Then there will be equality, [15]as it is written: "He who gathered much did not have too much, and he who gathered little did not have too little."[b]

Titus Sent to Corinth

[16]I thank God, who put into the heart of Titus the same concern I have for you.

[17]For Titus not only welcomed our appeal, but he is coming to you with much enthusiasm and on his own initiative. [18]And we are sending along with him the brother who is praised by all the churches for his service to the gospel. [19]What is more, he was chosen by the churches to accompany us as we carry the offering, which we administer in order to honor the Lord himself and to show our eagerness to help. [20]We want to avoid any criticism of the way we administer this liberal gift. [21]For we are taking pains to do what is right, not only in the eyes of the Lord but also in the eyes of men.

[22]In addition, we are sending with them our brother who has often proved to us in many ways that he is zealous, and now even more so because of his great confidence in you. [23]As for Titus, he is my partner and fellow worker among you; as for our brothers, they are representatives of the churches and an honor to Christ. [24]Therefore show these men the proof of your love and the reason for our pride in you, so that the churches can see it.

There is no need for me to write to you about this service to the saints. [2]For I know your eagerness to help, and I have been boasting about it to the Macedonians, telling them that since last year you in Achaia were ready to give; and your enthusiasm has stirred most of them to action. [3]But I am sending the brothers in order that our boasting about you in this matter should not prove hollow, but that you may be ready, as I said you would be. [4]For if any Macedonians come with me and find you unprepared, we—not to say anything about you— would be ashamed of having been so confident. [5]So I thought it necessary to urge the brothers to visit you in advance and finish the arrangements for the generous gift you had promised. Then it will be ready as a generous gift, not as one grudgingly given.

Sowing Generously

[6]Remember this: Whoever sows sparingly will also reap sparingly, and whoever sows generously will also reap generously. [7]Each man should give what he has decided in his heart to give, not reluctantly

---

[a] 7 Some manuscripts *in our love for you*
[b] 15 Exodus 16:18

or under compulsion, for God loves a cheerful giver. 8And God is able to make all grace abound to you, so that in all things at all times, having all that you need, you will abound in every good work. 9As it is written:

"He has scattered abroad his gifts to
   the poor;
  his righteousness endures forever." a

10Now he who supplies seed to the sower and bread for food will also supply and increase your store of seed and will enlarge the harvest of your righteousness. 11You will be made rich in every way so that you can be generous on every occasion, and through us your generosity will result in thanksgiving to God.

12This service that you perform is not only supplying the needs of God's people but is also overflowing in many expressions of thanks to God. 13Because of the service by which you have proved yourselves, men will praise God for the obedience that accompanies your confession of the gospel of Christ, and for your generosity in sharing with them and with every-

one else. 14And in their prayers for you their hearts will go out to you, because of the surpassing grace God has given you. 15Thanks be to God for his indescribable gift!

Paul's Defense of His Ministry

10 By the meekness and gentleness of Christ, I appeal to you—I, Paul, who am "timid" when face to face with you, but "bold" when away! 2I beg you that when I come I may not have to be as bold as I expect to be toward some people who think that we live by the standards of this world. 3For though we live in the world, we do not wage war as the world does. 4The weapons we fight with are not the weapons of the world. On the contrary, they have divine power to demolish strongholds. 5We demolish arguments and every pretension that sets itself up against the knowledge of God, and we take captive every thought to make it obedient to Christ. 6And we will be ready to punish

a 9 Psalm 112:9

Generous Giving
READ 2 CORINTHIANS 9:6–15

God doesn't let you have money just so you can keep stocked up on slurpies and chocolate bars, or buy the meanest-looking velociraptor in the dollar store. Sure, enjoy those things, but God is generous to you "so that you can be generous on every occasion" to others (verse 11). Try it! Give some money to help get out the gospel. Give some to help the poor. You may not have a lot, but you can still give some of it to the church. Or if some kid at school forgot his lunch, share yours with him. The key is to have a generous attitude. As you share, God will be able to trust you with more. The more you get, the more you can give to help. Remember, life isn't about how many goodies you can collect; it's about how much you can help spread Christianity and help others.

Your next reading is on page 1518.

every act of disobedience, once your obedience is complete.

[7]You are looking only on the surface of things.[a] If anyone is confident that he belongs to Christ, he should consider again that we belong to Christ just as much as he. [8]For even if I boast somewhat freely about the authority the Lord gave us for building you up rather than pulling you down, I will not be ashamed of it. [9]I do not want to seem to be trying to frighten you with my letters. [10]For some say, "His letters are weighty and forceful, but in person he is unimpressive and his speaking amounts to nothing." [11]Such people should realize that what we are in our letters when we are absent, we will be in our actions when we are present.

[12]We do not dare to classify or compare ourselves with some who commend themselves. When they measure themselves by themselves and compare themselves with themselves, they are not wise. [13]We, however, will not boast beyond proper limits, but will confine our boasting to the field God has assigned to us, a field that reaches even to you. [14]We are not going too far in our boasting, as would be the case if we had not come to you, for we did get as far as you with the gospel of Christ. [15]Neither do we go beyond our limits by boasting of work done by others.[b] Our hope is that, as your faith continues to grow, our area of activity among you will greatly expand, [16]so that we can preach the gospel in the regions beyond you. For we do not want to boast about work already done in another man's territory. [17]But, "Let him who boasts boast in the Lord."[c] [18]For it is not the one who commends himself who is approved, but the one whom the Lord commends.

[a] 7 Or Look at the obvious facts　　[b] 13–15 Or [13]We, however, will not boast about things that cannot be measured, but we will boast according to the standard of measurement that the God of measure has assigned us—a measurement that relates even to you. [14] . . . [15]Neither do we boast about things that cannot be measured in regard to the work done by others.　　[c] 17 Jer. 9:24

Make It Stick

READ 2 CORINTHIANS 10:3–5

Today's battles aren't like Old Testament battles with swords, axes and heaps of dead Philistines. Today it's a battle of good versus evil. Our sword?—the Word, the truth of Jesus Christ! It demolishes the lies that take people as prisoners to evil. On a sticky note, draw a really cool sword of truth.

Paul and the False Apostles

11 I hope you will put up with a little of my foolishness; but you are already doing that. ²I am jealous for you with a godly jealousy. I promised you to one husband, to Christ, so that I might present you as a pure virgin to him. ³But I am afraid that just as Eve was deceived by the serpent's cunning, your minds may somehow be led astray from your sincere and pure devotion to Christ. ⁴For if someone comes to you and preaches a Jesus other than the Jesus we preached, or if you receive a different spirit from the one you received, or a different gospel from the one you accepted, you put up with it easily enough. ⁵But I do not think I am in the least inferior to those "super-apostles." ⁶I may not be a trained speaker, but I do have knowledge. We have made this perfectly clear to you in every way.

⁷Was it a sin for me to lower myself in order to elevate you by preaching the gospel of God to you free of charge? ⁸I robbed other churches by receiving support from them so as to serve you. ⁹And when I was with you and needed something, I was not a burden to anyone, for the brothers who came from Macedonia supplied what I needed. I have kept myself from being a burden to you in any way, and will continue to do so. ¹⁰As surely as the truth of Christ is in me, nobody in the regions of Achaia will stop this boasting of mine. ¹¹Why? Because I do not love you? God knows I do! ¹²And I will keep on doing what I am doing in order to cut the ground from under those who want an opportunity to be considered equal with us in the things they boast about.

¹³For such men are false apostles, deceitful workmen, masquerading as apostles of Christ. ¹⁴And no wonder, for Satan himself masquerades as an angel of light. ¹⁵It is not surprising, then, if his servants masquerade as servants of righteousness. Their end will be what their actions deserve.

Paul Boasts About His Sufferings

¹⁶I repeat: Let no one take me for a

GET SMARTER

Outsmart the Devil

READ 2 CORINTHIANS 11:13–15

Satan dresses like an angel of light because he knows it doesn't work to say, "Yo! Why don't you do some big, terrible sin that you know is wrong?" Instead, he works his way in when you make small compromises, letting the devil have a "foothold" (Ephesians 4:27). If he can get you to disobey in small ways, then he takes you further. Suddenly you realize you're 200 yards out from the shore in heavy surf and the sharks are hungry! Don't be scared of the devil, but don't kid yourself and say, "Hey, I'm strong enough. This little sin won't hurt." It *will* hurt. Bible passages like this warn us not to be unaware of the devil's schemes (see 2 Corinthians 2:11 and Ephesians 6:11). Stay completely away from his tricks. When you sin, even if it's small, quickly ask God for forgiveness, and he'll erase the devil's toehold. Then keep strong by staying close to God, learning his Word, and plug your ears to temptation.

Your next reading is on page 1523.

fool. But if you do, then receive me just as you would a fool, so that I may do a little boasting. ¹⁷In this self-confident boasting I am not talking as the Lord would, but as a fool. ¹⁸Since many are boasting in the way the world does, I too will boast. ¹⁹You gladly put up with fools since you are so wise! ²⁰In fact, you even put up with anyone who enslaves you or exploits you or takes advantage of you or pushes himself forward or slaps you in the face. ²¹To my shame I admit that we were too weak for that!

What anyone else dares to boast about—I am speaking as a fool—I also dare to boast about. ²²Are they Hebrews? So am I. Are they Israelites? So am I. Are they Abraham's descendants? So am I. ²³Are they servants of Christ? (I am out of my mind to talk like this.) I am more. I have worked much harder, been in prison more frequently, been flogged more severely, and been exposed to death again and again. ²⁴Five times I received from the Jews the forty lashes minus one. ²⁵Three times I was beaten with rods, once I was stoned, three times I was shipwrecked, I spent a night and a day in the open sea, ²⁶I have been constantly on the move. I have been in danger from rivers, in danger from bandits, in danger from my own countrymen, in danger from Gentiles; in danger in the city, in danger in the country, in danger at sea; and in danger from false brothers. ²⁷I have labored and toiled and have often gone without sleep; I have known hunger and thirst and have often gone without food; I have been cold and naked. ²⁸Besides everything else, I face daily the pressure of my concern for all the churches. ²⁹Who is weak, and I do not feel weak? Who is led into sin, and I do not inwardly burn?

³⁰If I must boast, I will boast of the things that show my weakness. ³¹The God and Father of the Lord Jesus, who is to be praised forever, knows that I am not lying. ³²In Damascus the governor under King Aretas had the city of the Damascenes guarded in order to arrest me. ³³But I was lowered in a basket from a window in the wall and slipped through his hands.

Paul's Vision and His Thorn

12 I must go on boasting. Although there is nothing to be gained, I will go on to visions and revelations from the Lord. ²I know a man in Christ who fourteen years ago was caught up to the third heaven. Whether it was in the body or out of the body I do not know—God knows. ³And I know that this man—whether in the body or apart from the body I do not know, but God knows— ⁴was caught up to paradise. He heard inexpressible things, things that man is not permitted to tell. ⁵I will boast about a man like that, but I will not boast about myself, except about my weaknesses. ⁶Even if I should choose to boast, I would not be a fool, because I would be speaking the truth. But I refrain, so no one will think more of me than is warranted by what I do or say.

⁷To keep me from becoming conceited because of

Get a Load of This...

Back in Acts 9:16, God told Ananias to tell Paul how much he would suffer. Look at 2 Corinthians 11:23–29! This was not just a bad day of Capture the Flag. This was serious grief. Did Ananias tell Paul all *this* would happen?

these surpassingly great revelations, there was given me a thorn in my flesh, a messenger of Satan, to torment me. ⁸Three times I pleaded with the Lord to take it away from me. ⁹But he said to me, "My grace is sufficient for you, for my power is made perfect in weakness." Therefore I will boast all the more gladly about my weaknesses, so that Christ's power may rest on me. ¹⁰That is why, for Christ's sake, I delight in weaknesses, in insults, in hardships, in persecutions, in difficulties. For when I am weak, then I am strong.

Paul's Concern for the Corinthians

¹¹I have made a fool of myself, but you drove me to it. I ought to have been commended by you, for I am not in the least inferior to the "super-apostles," even though I am nothing. ¹²The things that mark an apostle—signs, wonders and miracles—were done among you with great perseverance. ¹³How were you inferior to the other churches, except that I was nev-

er a burden to you? Forgive me this wrong!

¹⁴Now I am ready to visit you for the third time, and I will not be a burden to you, because what I want is not your possessions but you. After all, children should not have to save up for their parents, but parents for their children. ¹⁵So I will very gladly spend for you everything I have and expend myself as well. If I love you more, will you love me less? ¹⁶Be that as it may, I have not been a burden to you. Yet, crafty fellow that I am, I caught you by trickery! ¹⁷Did I exploit you through any of the men I sent you? ¹⁸I urged Titus to go to you and I sent our brother with him. Titus did not exploit you, did he? Did we not act in the same spirit and follow the same course?

¹⁹Have you been thinking all along that we have been defending ourselves to you? We have been speaking in the sight of God as those in Christ; and everything we do, dear friends, is for your strength-

READ 2 CORINTHIANS 12:2–4

In 2 Corinthians 12:2–4, Paul writes about being caught up into the third heaven where he listened in on the most incredible stuff imaginable. You can't ask God for those kinds of experiences; he either gives them or he doesn't. But if this *did* happen to you, what would you like to see or hear? Write it on a sticky note.

ening. ²⁰For I am afraid that when I come I may not find you as I want you to be, and you may not find me as you want me to be. I fear that there may be quarreling, jealousy, outbursts of anger, factions, slander, gossip, arrogance and disorder. ²¹I am afraid that when I come again my God will humble me before you, and I will be grieved over many who have sinned earlier and have not repented of the impurity, sexual sin and debauchery in which they have indulged.

Final Warnings

13 This will be my third visit to you. "Every matter must be established by the testimony of two or three witnesses." ^a ²I already gave you a warning when I was with you the second time. I now repeat it while absent: On my return I will not spare those who sinned earlier or any of the others, ³since you are demanding proof that Christ is speaking through me. He is not weak in dealing with you, but is powerful among you. ⁴For to be sure, he was crucified in weakness, yet he lives by God's power. Likewise, we are weak in him, yet by God's power we will live with him to serve you.

⁵Examine yourselves to see whether you are in the faith; test yourselves. Do you not realize that Christ Jesus is in you—unless, of course, you fail the test? ⁶And I trust that you will discover that we have not failed the test. ⁷Now we pray to God that you will not do anything wrong. Not that people will see that we have stood the test but that you will do what is right even though we may seem to have failed. ⁸For we cannot do anything against the truth, but only for the truth. ⁹We are glad whenever we are weak but you are strong; and our prayer is for your perfection. ¹⁰This is why I write these things when I am absent, that when I come I may not have to be harsh in my use of authority—the authority the Lord gave me for building you up, not for tearing you down.

Final Greetings

¹¹Finally, brothers, good-by. Aim for perfection, listen to my appeal, be of one mind, live in peace. And the God of love and peace will be with you.

¹²Greet one another with a holy kiss. ¹³All the saints send their greetings.

¹⁴May the grace of the Lord Jesus Christ, and the love of God, and the fellowship of the Holy Spirit be with you all.

Get a Load of This...

What's a "super-apostle" (2 Corinthians 12:11)? Do they wear capes? Masks? Blue tights? Maybe a big red "SA" symbol on their chests? Nope. Paul had his tongue in his cheek when he said this. Paul ... you *joker*.

---

^a *1* Deut. 19:15

GALATIANS

Who wrote this book?
Paul.

Why was this book written?
The book of Galatians helps the Galatian believers rely on Jesus rather than on trying to keep God's law.

For whom was this book written?
This book is a letter sent to several churches in the province of Galatia.

When was this book written?
Galatians was written about A.D. 49 from Antioch.

What are some important teachings in this book?

Jesus died for our sins	Galatians 1:3–5
Jesus saves us	Galatians 3:6–14
We belong to Christ	Galatians 3:26–29
Serve others in love	Galatians 5:13–14
The Spirit makes us good	Galatians 5:22–25
Do good to all people	Galatians 6:7–10

Paul, an apostle—sent not from men nor by man, but by Jesus Christ and God the Father, who raised him from the dead— ²and all the brothers with me,

To the churches in Galatia:

³Grace and peace to you from God our Father and the Lord Jesus Christ, ⁴who gave himself for our sins to rescue us from the present evil age, according to the will of our God and Father, ⁵to whom be glory for ever and ever. Amen.

No Other Gospel

⁶I am astonished that you are so quickly deserting the one who called you by the grace of Christ and are turning to a different gospel— ⁷which is really no gospel at all. Evidently some people are throwing you into confusion and are trying to pervert the gospel of Christ. ⁸But even if we or an angel from heaven should preach a gospel other than the one we preached to you, let him be eternally condemned! ⁹As

we have already said, so now I say again: If anybody is preaching to you a gospel other than what you accepted, let him be eternally condemned!

¹⁰Am I now trying to win the approval of men, or of God? Or am I trying to please men? If I were still trying to please men, I would not be a servant of Christ.

Paul Called by God

¹¹I want you to know, brothers, that the gospel I preached is not something that man made up. ¹²I did not receive it from any man, nor was I taught it; rather, I received it by revelation from Jesus Christ.

¹³For you have heard of my previous way of life in Judaism, how intensely I persecuted the church of God and tried to destroy it. ¹⁴I was advancing in Judaism beyond many Jews of my own age and was extremely zealous for the traditions of my fathers. ¹⁵But when God, who set me apart from birth*a* and called me by his grace, was pleased ¹⁶to reveal his Son in

a 15 Or from my mother's womb

The Right Church?

READ GALATIANS 1:6-9

How do you recognize the animals at the zoo? First, you know them by sight. Zebras have stripes, cheetahs have spots. Second, if you don't recognize one, you *read the sign*. For example, the sign over a sheep pen reads "Sheep." In real life, however, some "churches" say they're Christian, and at first glance, they *seem* like they're Christian— but look closer. They're actually a *cult*. How can you tell? Because they preach a "different gospel" (see Galatians 1:6). They claim that (A) only they have the truth and are saved and they tell you that to leave their group is leaving God, (B) they insist on obedience to their leaders and warn you not to ask questions and (C) they teach heresy: They say that Jesus wasn't God, or didn't rise from the dead. They say the Bible has mistakes or has been "misunderstood," and that the writings of their group are more important than the Bible. True gospel? No way! They're playing with fire (Galatians 1:9).

Your next reading is on page 1525.

me so that I might preach him among the Gentiles, I did not consult any man, [17]nor did I go up to Jerusalem to see those who were apostles before I was, but I went immediately into Arabia and later returned to Damascus.

[18]Then after three years, I went up to Jerusalem to get acquainted with Peter[a] and stayed with him fifteen days. [19]I saw none of the other apostles—only James, the Lord's brother. [20]I assure you before God that what I am writing you is no lie. [21]Later I went to Syria and Cilicia. [22]I was personally unknown to the churches of Judea that are in Christ. [23]They only heard the report: "The man who formerly persecuted us is now preaching the faith he once tried to destroy." [24]And they praised God because of me.

Paul Accepted by the Apostles

Fourteen years later I went up again to Jerusalem, this time with Barnabas. I took Titus along also. [2]I went in response to a revelation and set before them the gospel that I preach among the Gentiles. But I did this privately to those who seemed to be leaders, for fear that I was running or had run my race in vain. [3]Yet not even Titus, who was with me, was compelled to be circumcised, even though he was a Greek. [4]This matter arose⌋ because some false brothers had infiltrated our ranks to spy on the freedom we have in Christ Jesus and to make us slaves. [5]We did not give in to them for a moment, so that the truth of the gospel might remain with you.

[6]As for those who seemed to be important—whatever they were makes no difference to me; God does not judge by external appearance—those men added nothing to my message. [7]On the contrary, they saw that I had been entrusted with the task of preaching the gospel to the Gentiles,[b] just as Peter had been to the Jews.[c] [8]For God, who was at work in the ministry of Peter as an apostle to the Jews, was also at work in my ministry as an apostle to the Gentiles. [9]James, Peter[d] and John, those reputed to be pillars, gave me and Barnabas the right hand of fellowship when they recognized the grace given to me. They agreed that we should go to the Gentiles, and they to the Jews. [10]All they asked was that we should

continue to remember the poor, the very thing I was eager to do.

Paul Opposes Peter

[11]When Peter came to Antioch, I opposed him to his face, because he was clearly in the wrong. [12]Before certain men came from James, he used to eat with the Gentiles. But when they arrived, he began to draw back and separate himself from the Gentiles because he was afraid of those who belonged to the circumcision group. [13]The other Jews joined him in his hypocrisy, so that by their hypocrisy even Barnabas was led astray.

[14]When I saw that they were not acting in line with the truth of the gospel, I said to Peter in front of them all, "You are a Jew, yet you live like a Gentile and not like a Jew. How is it, then, that you force Gentiles to follow Jewish customs?

[15]"We who are Jews by birth and not 'Gentile sinners' [16]know that a man is not justified by observing the law, but by faith in Jesus Christ. So we, too, have put our faith in Christ Jesus that we may be justified by faith in Christ and not by observing the law, because by observing the law no one will be justified.

[17]"If, while we seek to be justified in Christ, it becomes evident that we ourselves are sinners, does that mean that Christ promotes sin? Absolutely not! [18]If I rebuild what I destroyed, I prove that I am a lawbreaker. [19]For through the law I died to the law so that I might live for God. [20]I have been crucified with Christ and I no longer live, but Christ lives in me. The life I live in the body, I live by faith in the Son of God, who loved me and gave himself for me. [21]I do not set aside the grace of God, for if righteousness could be gained through the law, Christ died for nothing!"[e]

Faith or Observance of the Law

You foolish Galatians! Who has bewitched you? Before your very eyes Jesus Christ was clearly portrayed as crucified. [2]I would like to learn just one thing from you: Did you receive the Spirit by observing the law, or by believing what you heard? [3]Are you so foolish? After beginning with the Spirit, are you now

[a] 18 Greek Cephas   [b] 7 Greek uncircumcised   [c] 7 Greek circumcised; also in verses 8 and 9   [d] 9 Greek Cephas; also in verses 11 and 14   [e] 21 Some interpreters end the quotation after verse 14.

trying to attain your goal by human effort? [4]Have you suffered so much for nothing—if it really was for nothing? [5]Does God give you his Spirit and work miracles among you because you observe the law, or because you believe what you heard?

[6]Consider Abraham: "He believed God, and it was credited to him as righteousness."[a] [7]Understand, then, that those who believe are children of Abraham. [8]The Scripture foresaw that God would justify the Gentiles by faith, and announced the gospel in advance to Abraham: "All nations will be blessed through you."[b] [9]So those who have faith are blessed along with Abraham, the man of faith.

[10]All who rely on observing the law are under a curse, for it is written: "Cursed is everyone who does not continue to do everything written in the Book of the Law."[c] [11]Clearly no one is justified before God by the law, because, "The righteous will live by faith."[d] [12]The law is not based on faith; on the contrary, "The man who does these things will live by them."[e] [13]Christ redeemed us from the curse of the law by becoming a curse for us, for it is written: "Cursed is everyone who is hung on a tree."[f] [14]He redeemed us in order that the blessing given to Abraham might come to the Gentiles through Christ Jesus, so that by faith we might receive the promise of the Spirit.

The Law and the Promise

[15]Brothers, let me take an example from everyday life. Just as no one can set aside or add to a human covenant that has been duly established, so it is in this case. [16]The promises were spoken to Abraham and to his seed. The Scripture does not say "and to seeds," meaning many people, but "and to your seed,"[g] meaning one person, who is Christ.

[a] 6 Gen. 15:6   [b] 8 Gen. 12:3; 18:18; 22:18
[c] 10 Deut. 27:26   [d] 11 Hab. 2:4   [e] 12 Lev. 18:5
[f] 13 Deut. 21:23   [g] 16 Gen. 12:7; 13:15; 24:7

Acting Differently

READ GALATIANS 2:11–21

"Hey Peter, weren't you sitting over here with the Gentiles a minute ago? So why'd you move?" Do *you* behave a certain way with one group of friends, but when you're with another group, you act differently? That's normal—some people bring out your funny side, for instance, while others draw out your serious side. No sweat there—God treats us all as individuals and acts differently with each of us. God's *character*, however, never changes. He's always loving and fair with each of us. Right is right and wrong is wrong for everyone. He's consistent. But Peter wasn't being consistent.

Being a Jew himself, Peter wanted to be accepted by the "circumcision group," legalistic Jews who believed it was wrong to hang out with Gentiles (non-Jews). So he ditched the Gentile Christians (Galatians 2:11–14). It's cool to behave a certain way when you're with a certain group, but it is not cool to compromise the truth to be accepted by a group. Godly men don't change the way they act just to fit in.

Your next reading is on page 1527.

17What I mean is this: The law, introduced 430 years later, does not set aside the covenant previously established by God and thus do away with the promise. 18For if the inheritance depends on the law, then it no longer depends on a promise; but God in his grace gave it to Abraham through a promise.

19What, then, was the purpose of the law? It was added because of transgressions until the Seed to whom the promise referred had come. The law was put into effect through angels by a mediator. 20A mediator, however, does not represent just one party; but God is one.

21Is the law, therefore, opposed to the promises of God? Absolutely not! For if a law had been given that could impart life, then righteousness would certainly have come by the law. 22But the Scripture declares that the whole world is a prisoner of sin, so that what was promised, being given through faith in Jesus Christ, might be given to those who believe.

23Before this faith came, we were held prisoners by the law, locked up until faith should be revealed. 24So the law was put in charge to lead us to Christ*a* that we might be justified by faith. 25Now that faith has come, we are no longer under the supervision of the law.

Sons of God

26You are all sons of God through faith in Christ Jesus, 27for all of you who were baptized into Christ have clothed yourselves with Christ. 28There is neither Jew nor Greek, slave nor free, male nor female, for you are all one in Christ Jesus. 29If you belong to Christ, then you are Abraham's seed, and heirs according to the promise.

What I am saying is that as long as the heir is a child, he is no different from a slave, although he owns the whole estate. 2He is subject to

a 24 Or charge until Christ came

Make It Stick

READ GALATIANS 3:1

Chapter 3 begins with these tough words: "You foolish Galatians!" Paul was saying that these people, when they entertained the thought that they could be saved by their own actions rather than the death and resurrection of Christ, simply weren't using their heads. Write on a sticky note, "God, help me not to get fooled about your gift of salvation."

guardians and trustees until the time set by his father. ³So also, when we were children, we were in slavery under the basic principles of the world. ⁴But when the time had fully come, God sent his Son, born of a woman, born under law, ⁵to redeem those under law, that we might receive the full rights of sons. ⁶Because you are sons, God sent the Spirit of his Son into our hearts, the Spirit who calls out, *"Abba,ᵃ* Father." ⁷So you are no longer a slave, but a son; and since you are a son, God has made you also an heir.

Paul's Concern for the Galatians

⁸Formerly, when you did not know God, you were slaves to those who by nature are not gods. ⁹But now that you know God—or rather are known by God—how is it that you are turning back to those weak and miserable principles? Do you wish to be enslaved by them all over again? ¹⁰You are observing special days and months and seasons and years! ¹¹I fear for you, that somehow I have wasted my efforts on you.

¹²I plead with you, brothers, become like me, for I became like you. You have done me no wrong. ¹³As you know, it was because of an illness that I first preached the gospel to you. ¹⁴Even though my illness was a trial to you, you did not treat me with contempt or scorn. Instead, you welcomed me as if I were an angel of God, as if I were Christ Jesus himself. ¹⁵What has happened to all your joy? I can testify that, if you could have done so, you would have torn out your eyes and given them to me. ¹⁶Have I now become your enemy by telling you the truth?

¹⁷Those people are zealous to win you over, but for no good. What they want is to alienate you ⌊from us⌋, so that you may be zealous for them. ¹⁸It is fine to be zealous, provided the purpose is good, and to be so always and not just when I am with you. ¹⁹My dear children, for whom I am again in the pains of childbirth until Christ is formed in you, ²⁰how I wish I could be with you now and change my tone, because I am perplexed about you!

ᵃ 6 Aramaic for *Father*

Male and Female
READ GALATIANS 3:28

Some Jewish men thanked God every morning that they were not Gentiles, slaves or women. Pretty pompous and self-righteous, huh? Jesus put an end to that when he died to save *everyone.* "There is neither ... male nor female, for you are all one in Christ Jesus" (verse 28). Every single Christian has a relationship with Jesus. That puts us all on the same level. As a man of God, have a godly attitude toward women. Make sure you treat them like Jesus did—with kindness and respect. Men aren't better than women, just different. You should always stand up for the rights of others, and make sure they're treated with respect. Remember, God loves everybody and everybody deserves to be treated with honor and respect. That's true regardless of their skin color, how they dress and whether they're male or female.

GET COOLER

Your next reading is on page 1530.

Gross!

Check out Galatians 4:15. Imagine the Galatians plucking out their eyeballs and giving them to Paul ("Thank you, thank you. I have five eyeballs now. That's enough.") Many Bible experts believe Paul's eyesight was so bad that he either needed new eyeballs—or glasses.

Hagar and Sarah

21 Tell me, you who want to be under the law, are you not aware of what the law says? 22 For it is written that Abraham had two sons, one by the slave woman and the other by the free woman. 23 His son by the slave woman was born in the ordinary way; but his son by the free woman was born as the result of a promise.

24 These things may be taken figuratively, for the women represent two covenants. One covenant is from Mount Sinai and bears children who are to be slaves: This is Hagar. 25 Now Hagar stands for Mount Sinai in Arabia and corresponds to the present city of Jerusalem, because she is in slavery with her children. 26 But the Jerusalem that is above is free, and she is our mother. 27 For it is written:

"Be glad, O barren woman,
   who bears no children;
break forth and cry aloud,
   you who have no labor pains;
because more are the children of the desolate
     woman
   than of her who has a husband."[a]

28 Now you, brothers, like Isaac, are children of promise. 29 At that time the son born in the ordinary way persecuted the son born by the power of the Spirit. It is the same now. 30 But what does the Scripture say? "Get rid of the slave woman and her son, for the slave woman's son will never share in the inheritance with the free woman's son."[b] 31 Therefore, brothers, we are not children of the slave woman, but of the free woman.

Freedom in Christ

5 It is for freedom that Christ has set us free. Stand firm, then, and do not let yourselves be burdened again by a yoke of slavery.

2 Mark my words! I, Paul, tell you that if you let yourselves be circumcised, Christ will be of no value to you at all. 3 Again I declare to every man who lets himself be circumcised that he is obligated to obey the whole law. 4 You who are trying to be justified by law have been alienated from Christ; you have fallen away from grace. 5 But by faith we eagerly await through the Spirit the righteousness for which we hope. 6 For in Christ Jesus neither circumcision nor uncircumcision has any value. The only thing that counts is faith expressing itself through love.

7 You were running a good race. Who cut in on you and kept you from obeying the truth? 8 That kind of persuasion does not come from the one who calls you. 9 "A little yeast works through the whole batch of dough." 10 I am confident in the Lord that you will take no other view. The one who is throwing you into confusion will pay the penalty, whoever he may be. 11 Brothers, if I am still preaching circumcision, why am I still being perse-

a 27 Isaiah 54:1   *b* 30 Gen. 21:10

cuted? In that case the offense of the cross has been abolished. ¹²As for those agitators, I wish they would go the whole way and emasculate themselves!

¹³You, my brothers, were called to be free. But do not use your freedom to indulge the sinful nature[a]; rather, serve one another in love. ¹⁴The entire law is summed up in a single command: "Love your neighbor as yourself."[b] ¹⁵If you keep on biting and devouring each other, watch out or you will be destroyed by each other.

Life by the Spirit

¹⁶So I say, live by the Spirit, and you will not gratify the desires of the sinful nature. ¹⁷For the sinful nature desires what is contrary to the Spirit, and the Spirit what is contrary to the sinful nature. They are in conflict with each other, so that you do not do what you want. ¹⁸But if you are led by the Spirit, you are not under law.

¹⁹The acts of the sinful nature are obvious: sexual immorality, impurity and debauchery; ²⁰idolatry and witchcraft; hatred, discord, jealousy, fits of rage, selfish ambition, dissensions, factions ²¹and envy; drunkenness, orgies, and the like. I warn you, as I did before, that those who live like this will not inherit the kingdom of God.

²²But the fruit of the Spirit is love, joy, peace, patience, kindness, goodness, faithfulness, ²³gentleness and self-control. Against such things there is no law. ²⁴Those who belong to Christ Jesus have crucified the sinful nature with its passions and desires. ²⁵Since we live by the Spirit, let us keep in step with the Spirit. ²⁶Let us not become conceited, provoking and envying each other.

Doing Good to All

Brothers, if someone is caught in a sin, you who are spiritual should restore him gently. But watch yourself, or you also may be tempted. ²Carry each other's burdens, and in this way you will fulfill the law of Christ. ³If anyone thinks he is something when he is nothing, he deceives himself. ⁴Each one should test his own actions. Then he can take pride in himself, without comparing himself to somebody else, ⁵for each one should carry his own load.

⁶Anyone who receives instruction in the word must share all good things with his instructor.

⁷Do not be deceived: God cannot be mocked. A man reaps what he sows. ⁸The one who sows to please his sinful nature, from that nature[c] will reap destruction; the one who sows to please the Spirit, from the Spirit will reap eternal life. ⁹Let us not become weary in doing good, for at the proper time we will reap a harvest if we do not give up. ¹⁰Therefore, as we have opportunity, let us do good to all people, especially to those who belong to the family of believers.

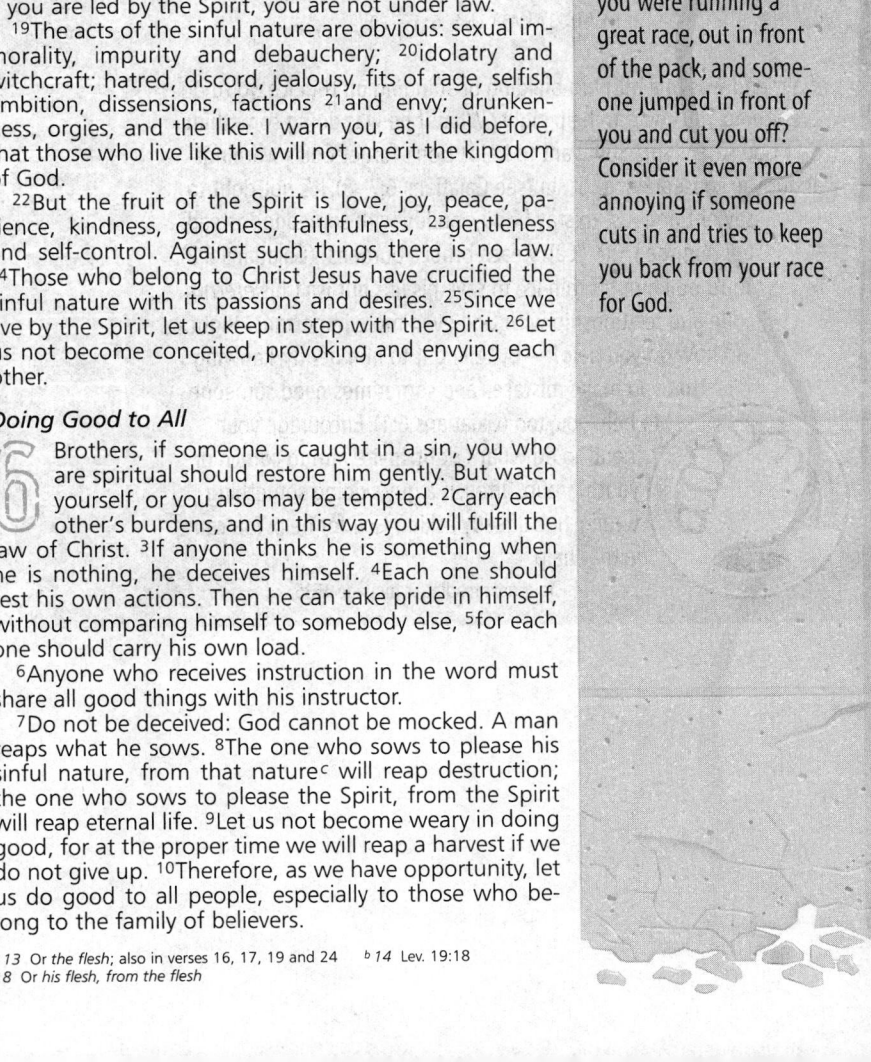

Get a Load of This...

Check out Galatians 5:7. How would you feel if you were running a great race, out in front of the pack, and someone jumped in front of you and cut you off? Consider it even more annoying if someone cuts in and tries to keep you back from your race for God.

---

a 13 Or the flesh; also in verses 16, 17, 19 and 24   b 14 Lev. 19:18
c 8 Or his flesh, from the flesh

Not Circumcision but a New Creation

11 See what large letters I use as I write to you with my own hand!

12 Those who want to make a good impression outwardly are trying to compel you to be circumcised. The only reason they do this is to avoid being persecuted for the cross of Christ. 13 Not even those who are circumcised obey the law, yet they want you to be circumcised that they may boast about your flesh. 14 May I never boast except in the cross of our Lord Jesus Christ, through which[a] the world has been crucified to me, and I to the world. 15 Neither circumcision nor uncircumcision means anything; what counts is a new creation. 16 Peace and mercy to all who follow this rule, even to the Israel of God.

17 Finally, let no one cause me trouble, for I bear on my body the marks of Jesus.

18 The grace of our Lord Jesus Christ be with your spirit, brothers. Amen.

a 14 Or whom

Godly Man, Good Advice

READ GALATIANS 6:1–10

If a friend was in a burning building or standing on thin ice, you'd do everything you could to help, right? What if he was doing something that God says is sin? Still want to help? Don't forget God's warnings about the consequences of sin (see Galatians 6:7–8). It's not right to say nothing just to stay buddy-buddy with someone. Instead, tell him the truth. "Carry each other's burdens" (Galatians 6:2). You'd pull him off thin ice to save his life, but isn't his *eternal* life and relationship with God even more important? Right. So how do you help?—By telling it to him gently, knowing that you make mistakes and sometimes need someone to help you, too (Galatians 6:1). Encourage your friend to do what's right. Invite him to church or youth group. Often, if a guy's doing something wrong, he's already asking God for help. You can *be* that help.

Your next reading is on page 1535.

EPHESIANS

Who wrote this book?
Paul.

Why was this book written?
Ephesians shows that the church is not a building but people who love and obey Jesus.

For whom was this book written?
This book is a letter Paul sent to the Christians in Ephesus.

When was this book written?
Ephesians was written about A.D. 60 from Rome, where Paul was in prison.

What are some important teachings in this book?

What God did to save us	Ephesians 1:3–14
God gives life in Christ	Ephesians 2:1–10
Jesus gives peace	Ephesians 2:11–18
How to live a holy life	Ephesians 4:20–32
Children and parents	Ephesians 6:1–4

1 Paul, an apostle of Christ Jesus by the will of God,

To the saints in Ephesus,[a] the faithful[b] in Christ Jesus:

2Grace and peace to you from God our Father and the Lord Jesus Christ.

Spiritual Blessings in Christ

3Praise be to the God and Father of our Lord Jesus Christ, who has blessed us in the heavenly realms with every spiritual blessing in Christ. 4For he chose us in him before the creation of the world to be holy and blameless in his sight. In love 5he[c] predestined us to be adopted as his sons through Jesus Christ, in accordance with his pleasure and will— 6to the praise of his glorious grace, which he has freely given us in the One he loves. 7In him we have redemption through his blood, the forgiveness of sins, in accordance with the riches of God's grace 8that he lavished on us with all wisdom and understanding. 9And he[d] made known to us the mystery of his will according to his good pleasure, which he purposed in Christ, 10to be put into effect when the times will have reached their fulfillment—to bring all things in heaven and on earth together under one head, even Christ.

11In him we were also chosen,[e] having been predestined according to the plan of him who works out everything in conformity with the purpose of his will, 12in order that we, who were the first to hope in Christ, might be for the praise of his glory. 13And you also were included in Christ when you heard the word of truth, the gospel of your salvation. Having believed, you were marked in him with a seal, the promised Holy Spirit, 14who is a deposit guaranteeing our inheritance until the re-

---

[a] 1 Some early manuscripts do not have *in Ephesus*.
[b] 1 Or *believers who are*　[c] 4,5 Or *sight in love. 5He*
[d] 8,9 Or *us. With all wisdom and understanding, 9he*
[e] 11 Or *were made heirs*

Make It Stick

READ EPHESIANS 1:15–23

In Ephesians 1:15–19, Paul prayed that God would open Christians' eyes of the heart—their *spiritual* eyes—so they could receive wisdom and a deeper understanding of who God is and how powerful he is. On a sticky note, draw a picture of a heart with two wide-open eyes.

demption of those who are God's possession—to the praise of his glory.

Thanksgiving and Prayer

¹⁵For this reason, ever since I heard about your faith in the Lord Jesus and your love for all the saints, ¹⁶I have not stopped giving thanks for you, remembering you in my prayers. ¹⁷I keep asking that the God of our Lord Jesus Christ, the glorious Father, may give you the Spirit[a] of wisdom and revelation, so that you may know him better. ¹⁸I pray also that the eyes of your heart may be enlightened in order that you may know the hope to which he has called you, the riches of his glorious inheritance in the saints, ¹⁹and his incomparably great power for us who believe. That power is like the working of his mighty strength, ²⁰which he exerted in Christ when he raised him from the dead and seated him at his right hand in the heavenly realms, ²¹far above all rule and authority, power and dominion, and every title that can be given, not only in the present age but also in the one to come. ²²And God placed all things under his feet and appointed him to be head over everything for the church, ²³which is his body, the fullness of him who fills everything in every way.

Made Alive in Christ

As for you, you were dead in your transgressions and sins, ²in which you used to live when you followed the ways of this world and of the ruler of the kingdom of the air, the spirit who is now at work in those who are disobedient. ³All of us also lived among them at one time, gratifying the cravings of our sinful nature[b] and following its desires and thoughts. Like the rest, we were by nature objects of wrath. ⁴But because of his great love for us, God, who is rich in mercy, ⁵made us alive with Christ even when we were dead in transgressions—it is by grace you have been saved. ⁶And God raised us up with Christ and seated us with him in the heavenly realms in Christ Jesus, ⁷in order that in the coming ages he might show the incomparable riches of his grace, expressed in his kindness to us in Christ Jesus. ⁸For it is by grace you have been saved, through faith—and this not from yourselves, it is the gift of God— ⁹not by works, so that no one can boast. ¹⁰For we are God's workmanship, created in Christ Jesus to do good works, which God prepared in advance for us to do.

One in Christ

¹¹Therefore, remember that formerly you who are Gentiles by birth and called "uncircumcised" by those who call themselves "the circumcision" (that done in the body by the hands of men)— ¹²remember that at that time you were separate from Christ, excluded from citizenship in Israel and foreigners to the covenants of the promise, without hope and without God in the world.

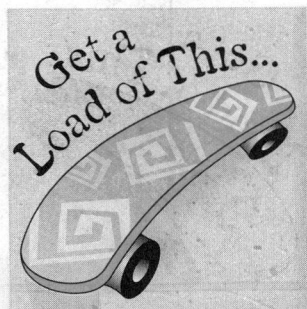

Get a Load of This...

Ephesians 2:8–10 spells things out *really* clear: Our good works don't save us—accepting Christ's death as payment for our sins does that job. But once we are saved, we'll be motivated to do good works from then on.

---

a 17 Or *a spirit*   *b 3* Or *our flesh*

13But now in Christ Jesus you who once were far away have been brought near through the blood of Christ.

14For he himself is our peace, who has made the two one and has destroyed the barrier, the dividing wall of hostility, 15by abolishing in his flesh the law with its commandments and regulations. His purpose was to create in himself one new man out of the two, thus making peace, 16and in this one body to reconcile both of them to God through the cross, by which he put to death their hostility. 17He came and preached peace to you who were far away and peace to those who were near. 18For through him we both have access to the Father by one Spirit.

19Consequently, you are no longer foreigners and aliens, but fellow citizens with God's people and members of God's household, 20built on the foundation of the apostles and prophets, with Christ Jesus himself as the chief cornerstone. 21In him the whole building is joined together and rises to become a holy temple in the Lord. 22And in him you too are being built together to become a dwelling in which God lives by his Spirit.

Paul the Preacher to the Gentiles

3 For this reason I, Paul, the prisoner of Christ Jesus for the sake of you Gentiles—

2Surely you have heard about the administration of God's grace that was given to me for you, 3that is, the mystery made known to me by revelation, as I have already written briefly. 4In reading this, then, you will be able to understand my insight into the mystery of Christ, 5which was not made known to men in other generations as it has now been revealed by the Spirit to God's holy apostles and prophets. 6This mystery is that through the gospel the Gentiles are heirs together with Israel, members together of one body, and sharers together in the promise in Christ Jesus.

7I became a servant of this gospel by the gift of God's grace given me through the working of his power. 8Although I am less than the least of all God's people, this grace was given me: to preach to the Gentiles the unsearchable riches of Christ, 9and to make plain to everyone the administration of this mystery, which for ages past was kept hidden in God, who created all things. 10His intent was that now, through the church, the manifold wisdom of God should be made known to the rulers and authorities in the heavenly realms, 11according to his eternal purpose which he accomplished in Christ Jesus our Lord. 12In him and through faith in him we may approach God with freedom and confidence. 13I ask you, therefore, not to be discouraged because of my sufferings for you, which are your glory.

A Prayer for the Ephesians

14For this reason I kneel before the Father, 15from whom his whole family*a* in heaven and on earth derives

a 15 Or whom all fatherhood

its name. ¹⁶I pray that out of his glorious riches he may strengthen you with power through his Spirit in your inner being, ¹⁷so that Christ may dwell in your hearts through faith. And I pray that you, being rooted and established in love, ¹⁸may have power, together with all the saints, to grasp how wide and long and high and deep is the love of Christ, ¹⁹and to know this love that surpasses knowledge—that you may be filled to the measure of all the fullness of God.

²⁰Now to him who is able to do immeasurably more than all we ask or imagine, according to his power that is at work within us, ²¹to him be glory in the church and in Christ Jesus throughout all generations, for ever and ever! Amen.

Unity in the Body of Christ

As a prisoner for the Lord, then, I urge you to live a life worthy of the calling you have received. ²Be completely humble and gentle; be patient, bearing with one another in love. ³Make every effort to keep the unity of the Spirit through the bond of peace.

⁴There is one body and one Spirit—just as you were called to one hope when you were called— ⁵one Lord, one faith, one baptism; ⁶one God and Father of all, who is over all and through all and in all.

⁷But to each one of us grace has been given as Christ apportioned it. ⁸This is why it[a] says:

"When he ascended on high,
    he led captives in his train
    and gave gifts to men."[b]

⁹(What does "he ascended" mean except that he also descended to the lower, earthly regions[c]? ¹⁰He who descended is the very one who ascended higher than all the heavens, in order to fill the whole universe.) ¹¹It was he who gave some to be apostles, some to be prophets, some to be evangelists, and some to be pastors and teachers, ¹²to prepare God's people for works of service, so that the body of Christ may be built up ¹³until we all reach unity in the faith and in the knowledge of

[a] 8 Or God   [b] 8 Psalm 68:18   [c] 9 Or the depths of the earth

The Deep Dimension

READ EPHESIANS 3:14–21

Wouldn't it be awesome if you could step into another dimension, more exciting than anything on earth? You can!—and it's not sci-fi! Paul said, "I pray . . . that Christ may dwell in your hearts through faith" (verse 17). That's the door to this incredible world: believing. And power (*power* is good) "to grasp how wide and long and high and deep is the love of Christ" (verse 18). Wide! Long! High! Deep! Sounds vast! "And to know this love that surpasses knowledge" (verse 19). Way past human knowledge on this little dust ball planet. Then get filled with "all the fullness of God" (verse 19). How? By being "rooted and established in love" (verse 17). God tells you to seek him so that he can *pour* out his love on you and do "more than all [you] ask or imagine" (verse 20). See? You start with faith, gain speed with love, and end up shooting beyond the borders of your imagination.

Your next reading is on page 1537.

Get a Load of This...

Why are there leaders and teachers in the church (Ephesians 4:11–12)? To take care of everybody's needs *and* get the gospel to the world? Only *half* right. Their job is to prepare and teach us, so that *we* can go out and witness and serve God.

the Son of God and become mature, attaining to the whole measure of the fullness of Christ. ¹⁴Then we will no longer be infants, tossed back and forth by the waves, and blown here and there by every wind of teaching and by the cunning and craftiness of men in their deceitful scheming. ¹⁵Instead, speaking the truth in love, we will in all things grow up into him who is the Head, that is, Christ. ¹⁶From him the whole body, joined and held together by every supporting ligament, grows and builds itself up in love, as each part does its work.

Living as Children of Light

¹⁷So I tell you this, and insist on it in the Lord, that you must no longer live as the Gentiles do, in the futility of their thinking. ¹⁸They are darkened in their understanding and separated from the life of God because of the ignorance that is in them due to the hardening of their hearts. ¹⁹Having lost all sensitivity, they have given themselves over to sensuality so as to indulge in every kind of impurity, with a continual lust for more.

²⁰You, however, did not come to know Christ that way. ²¹Surely you heard of him and were taught in him in accordance with the truth that is in Jesus. ²²You were taught, with regard to your former way of life, to put off your old self, which is being corrupted by its deceitful desires; ²³to be made new in the attitude of your minds; ²⁴and to put on the new self, created to be like God in true righteousness and holiness.

²⁵Therefore each of you must put off falsehood and speak truthfully to his neighbor, for we are all members of one body. ²⁶"In your anger do not sin"ᵃ: Do not let the sun go down while you are still angry, ²⁷and do not give the devil a foothold. ²⁸He who has been stealing must steal no longer, but must work, doing something useful with his own hands, that he may have something to share with those in need.

²⁹Do not let any unwholesome talk come out of your mouths, but only what is helpful for building others up according to their needs, that it may benefit those who listen. ³⁰And do not grieve the Holy Spirit of God, with whom you were sealed for the day of redemption. ³¹Get rid of all bitterness, rage and anger, brawling and slander, along with every form of malice. ³²Be kind and compassionate to one another, forgiving each other, just as in Christ God forgave you.

Be imitators of God, therefore, as dearly loved children ²and live a life of love, just as Christ loved us and gave himself up for us as a fragrant offering and sacrifice to God.

³But among you there must not be even a hint of sexual immorality, or of any kind of impurity, or of greed, because these are improper for God's holy people. ⁴Nor should there be obscenity, foolish talk or coarse joking, which are out of place, but rather thanksgiving. ⁵For of

ᵃ 26 Psalm 4:4

this you can be sure: No immoral, impure or greedy person—such a man is an idolater—has any inheritance in the kingdom of Christ and of God.ᵃ ⁶Let no one deceive you with empty words, for because of such things God's wrath comes on those who are disobedient. ⁷Therefore do not be partners with them.

⁸For you were once darkness, but now you are light in the Lord. Live as children of light ⁹(for the fruit of the light consists in all goodness, righteousness and truth) ¹⁰and find out what pleases the Lord. ¹¹Have nothing to do with the fruitless deeds of darkness, but rather expose them. ¹²For it is shameful even to mention what the disobedient do in secret. ¹³But everything exposed by the light becomes visible, ¹⁴for it is light that makes everything visible. This is why it is said:

"Wake up, O sleeper,
    rise from the dead,
and Christ will shine on you."

¹⁵Be very careful, then, how you live—not as unwise but as wise, ¹⁶making the most of every opportunity, because the days are evil. ¹⁷Therefore do not be foolish, but understand what the Lord's will is. ¹⁸Do not get drunk on wine, which leads to debauchery. Instead, be filled with the Spirit. ¹⁹Speak to one another with psalms, hymns and spiritual songs. Sing and make music in your heart to the Lord, ²⁰always giving thanks to God the Father for everything, in the name of our Lord Jesus Christ.

²¹Submit to one another out of reverence for Christ.

Wives and Husbands

²²Wives, submit to your husbands as to the Lord. ²³For the husband is the head of the wife as Christ is the head of the church, his body, of which he is the Savior. ²⁴Now as the church submits to Christ, so also wives should submit to their husbands in everything.

²⁵Husbands, love your wives, just as Christ loved the church and gave himself up for her ²⁶to make her holy, cleansingᵇ

ᵃ 5 Or kingdom of the Christ and God   ᵇ 26 Or having cleansed

GET SMARTER

Christian Camping List
READ EPHESIANS 4:22—5:4

Paul said that once you're a Christian, you are to "put off your old self ... and to put on the new self" (verses 22, 24) Huh? He then gives a whole list of practical advice. When you're preparing to go camping, you write down everything you need to take, right? That way, when you're out in the wilderness you have everything and you haven't forgotten the toilet paper. Well, this is sort of like that camping list but much more important—it's your Being a Christian list. You won't build up all these "supplies" overnight, but *do* read this list once in a while and ask yourself what's missing so you can become a stronger Christian. *Christian* means "Christlike," *not* "a sinner like anyone else, only forgiven."

Your next reading is on page 1539.

Get a Load of This...

"Wake up, O sleeper, rise from the dead" (Ephesians 5:14). What is *this*? A Christian alarm clock? No. It means now that the light of Jesus is shining on you, don't live in the darkness anymore (see verses 11–16).

her by the washing with water through the word, ²⁷and to present her to himself as a radiant church, without stain or wrinkle or any other blemish, but holy and blameless. ²⁸In this same way, husbands ought to love their wives as their own bodies. He who loves his wife loves himself. ²⁹After all, no one ever hated his own body, but he feeds and cares for it, just as Christ does the church— ³⁰for we are members of his body. ³¹"For this reason a man will leave his father and mother and be united to his wife, and the two will become one flesh."ᵃ ³²This is a profound mystery—but I am talking about Christ and the church. ³³However, each one of you also must love his wife as he loves himself, and the wife must respect her husband.

Children and Parents

6 Children, obey your parents in the Lord, for this is right. ²"Honor your father and mother"—which is the first commandment with a promise— ³"that it may go well with you and that you may enjoy long life on the earth."ᵇ

⁴Fathers, do not exasperate your children; instead, bring them up in the training and instruction of the Lord.

Slaves and Masters

⁵Slaves, obey your earthly masters with respect and fear, and with sincerity of heart, just as you would obey Christ. ⁶Obey them not only to win their favor when their eye is on you, but like slaves of Christ, doing the will of God from your heart. ⁷Serve wholeheartedly, as if you were serving the Lord, not men, ⁸because you know that the Lord will reward everyone for whatever good he does, whether he is slave or free.

⁹And masters, treat your slaves in the same way. Do not threaten them, since you know that he who is both their Master and yours is in heaven, and there is no favoritism with him.

The Armor of God

¹⁰Finally, be strong in the Lord and in his mighty power. ¹¹Put on the full armor of God so that you can take your stand against the devil's schemes. ¹²For our struggle is not against flesh and blood, but against the rulers, against the authorities, against the powers of this dark world and against the spiritual forces of evil in the heavenly realms. ¹³Therefore put on the full armor of God, so that when the day of evil comes, you may be able to stand your ground, and after you have done everything, to stand. ¹⁴Stand firm then, with the belt of truth buckled around your waist, with the breastplate of righteousness in place, ¹⁵and with your feet fitted with the readiness that comes from the gospel of peace. ¹⁶In addition to all this, take up the shield of faith, with which you can extinguish all the flaming arrows of the evil

ᵃ31 Gen. 2:24　　ᵇ3 Deut. 5:16

one. [17]Take the helmet of salvation and the sword of the Spirit, which is the word of God. [18]And pray in the Spirit on all occasions with all kinds of prayers and requests. With this in mind, be alert and always keep on praying for all the saints.

[19]Pray also for me, that whenever I open my mouth, words may be given me so that I will fearlessly make known the mystery of the gospel, [20]for which I am an ambassador in chains. Pray that I may declare it fearlessly, as I should.

Final Greetings

[21]Tychicus, the dear brother and faithful servant in the Lord, will tell you everything, so that you also may know how I am and what I am doing. [22]I am sending him to you for this very purpose, that you may know how we are, and that he may encourage you.

[23]Peace to the brothers, and love with faith from God the Father and the Lord Jesus Christ. [24]Grace to all who love our Lord Jesus Christ with an undying love.

Going for the Big Blessings

READ EPHESIANS 6:1–3

God wants you to obey your parents and *hey*, you can keep out of trouble and learn good stuff by doing what they say. But is Ephesians 6:1–3 saying that if you obey your mom and dad you'll be blessed and live a long life? No. This promise Paul quotes comes from the Ten Commandments in Deuteronomy 5:16. And guess what! In the very next chapter, God told the Israelite *parents* three times that if *they* obeyed his law, they would be blessed and live long in the land he was giving them. Then he told them three times to teach their kids to love and obey him. Why? You guessed it! So *they* too could be blessed and live long in the land. Obeying your parents is a good thing—so *go* for it—but to get the *really* big blessings, make sure you obey *God*!

Your next reading is on page 1545.

PHILIPPIANS

Who wrote this book?
Paul.

Why was this book written?
Philippians thanks the people for their love and gifts and gives them instructions on how to live good Christian lives.

For whom was this book written?
This book is a letter Paul sent to Christians at Philippi.

When was the book written?
This book was written about A.D. 61 from Rome, where Paul was in prison.

What are some important teachings in this book?

Live as good Christians	Philippians 1:27–30
Live a humble life	Philippians 2:1–4
How Jesus was humble	Philippians 2:5–11
The Christian's goal	Philippians 3:12–16
How to be at peace	Philippians 4:4–7
Think about good things	Philippians 4:8–9

Paul and Timothy, servants of Christ Jesus,

To all the saints in Christ Jesus at Philippi, together with the overseers[a] and deacons:

2Grace and peace to you from God our Father and the Lord Jesus Christ.

Thanksgiving and Prayer

3I thank my God every time I remember you. 4In all my prayers for all of you, I always pray with joy 5because of your partnership in the gospel from the first day until now, 6being confident of this, that he who began a good work in you will carry it on to completion until the day of Christ Jesus.

7It is right for me to feel this way about all of you, since I have you in my heart; for whether I am in chains or defending and confirming the gospel, all of you share in God's grace with me. 8God can testify how I long for all of you with the affection of Christ Jesus.

9And this is my prayer: that your love may abound more and more in knowledge and depth of insight, 10so that you may be able to discern what is best and may be pure and blameless until the day of Christ, 11filled with the fruit of righteousness that comes through Jesus Christ—to the glory and praise of God.

Paul's Chains Advance the Gospel

12Now I want you to know, brothers, that what has happened to me has really served to advance the gospel. 13As a result, it has become clear throughout the whole palace guard[b] and to everyone else that I am in chains for Christ. 14Because of my chains, most of the brothers in the Lord have been encouraged to speak the word of God more courageously and fearlessly.

15It is true that some preach Christ out of envy and rivalry, but others out of goodwill. 16The latter do so in love, knowing that I am put here for the defense of the gospel. 17The former preach Christ out of selfish ambition, not sincerely, supposing that they can stir up trouble for me while I am in chains.[c] 18But what does it matter? The important thing is that in every way, whether from false motives or true, Christ is preached. And because of this I rejoice.

Yes, and I will continue to rejoice, 19for I know that through your prayers and the help given by the Spirit of Jesus Christ, what has happened to me will turn out for my deliverance.[d] 20I eagerly expect and hope that I will in no way be ashamed, but will have sufficient courage so that now as always Christ will be exalted in my body, whether by life or by death. 21For to me, to live is Christ and to die is gain. 22If I am to go on living in the body, this will mean fruitful labor for me. Yet what shall I choose? I do not know! 23I am torn between the two: I desire to depart and be with Christ, which is better by

Get a Load of This...

There's no hiding from God—even in Emperor Nero's palace! Chains of imprisonment didn't keep Paul from helping others become Christians (Philippians 1:12–13; 4:22). Can you hear the guards humming praise songs at their posts, while Paul chuckles, "Ner-o far, God knows where you are!"

---

a 1 Traditionally *bishops*   b 13 Or *whole palace*   c 16,17 Some late manuscripts have verses 16 and 17 in reverse order.   d 19 Or *salvation* far; [24]but it is more necessary for you that I remain in the body. [25]Convinced of this, I know that I will remain, and I will continue with all of you for your progress and joy in the faith, [26]so that through my being with you again your joy in Christ Jesus will overflow on account of me.

[27]Whatever happens, conduct yourselves in a manner worthy of the gospel of Christ. Then, whether I come and see you or only hear about you in my absence, I will know that you stand firm in one spirit, contending as one man for the faith of the gospel [28]without being frightened in any way by those who oppose you. This is a sign to them that they will be destroyed, but that you will be saved—and that by God. [29]For it has been granted to you on behalf of Christ not only to believe on him, but also to suffer for him, [30]since you are going through the same struggle you saw I had, and now hear that I still have.

Imitating Christ's Humility

If you have any encouragement from being united with Christ, if any comfort from his love, if any fellowship with the Spirit, if any tenderness and compassion, [2]then make my joy complete by being like-minded, having the same love, being one in spirit and purpose. [3]Do nothing out of selfish ambition or vain conceit, but in humility consider others better than yourselves. [4]Each of you should look not only to your own interests, but also to the interests of others.

[5]Your attitude should be the same as that of Christ Jesus:

[6]Who, being in very nature[a] God,
    did not consider equality with God
        something to be grasped,
[7]but made himself nothing,
    taking the very nature[b] of a servant,
    being made in human likeness.

[a] 6 Or in the form of   [b] 7 Or the form

Make It Stick

READ PHILIPPIANS 2:1–4

Worldly man says, "I've got mine! Good luck getting yours." Godly man says, "What can I do to help you?" Be aware of others' needs, even above your own (see Philippians 2:1–4). Who can you help today? How? Write it down on a sticky note. (Hey, even sending an email could do the trick. It doesn't have to be super complicated or take a ton of time.)

8 And being found in appearance as a man,
  he humbled himself
  and became obedient to death—
    even death on a cross!
9 Therefore God exalted him to the highest place
  and gave him the name that is above every name,
10 that at the name of Jesus every knee should bow,
  in heaven and on earth and under the earth,
11 and every tongue confess that Jesus Christ is Lord,
    to the glory of God the Father.

Shining as Stars

12 Therefore, my dear friends, as you have always obeyed—not only in my presence, but now much more in my absence—continue to work out your salvation with fear and trembling, 13 for it is God who works in you to will and to act according to his good purpose.

14 Do everything without complaining or arguing, 15 so that you may become blameless and pure, children of God without fault in a crooked and depraved generation, in which you shine like stars in the universe 16 as you hold out[a] the word of life—in order that I may boast on the day of Christ that I did not run or labor for nothing. 17 But even if I am being poured out like a drink offering on the sacrifice and service coming from your faith, I am glad and rejoice with all of you. 18 So you too should be glad and rejoice with me.

Timothy and Epaphroditus

19 I hope in the Lord Jesus to send Timothy to you soon, that I also may be cheered when I receive news about you. 20 I have no one else like him, who takes a genuine interest in your welfare. 21 For everyone looks out for his own interests, not those of Jesus Christ. 22 But you know that Timothy has proved himself, because as a son with his father he has served with me in the work of the gospel. 23 I hope, therefore, to send him as soon as I see how things go with me. 24 And I am confident in the Lord that I myself will come soon.

25 But I think it is necessary to send back to you Epaphroditus, my brother, fellow worker and fellow soldier, who is also your messenger, whom you sent to take care of my needs. 26 For he longs for all of you and is distressed because you heard he was ill. 27 Indeed he was ill, and almost died. But God had mercy on him, and not on him only but also on me, to spare me sorrow upon sorrow. 28 Therefore I am all the more eager to send him, so that when you see him again you may be glad and I may have less anxiety. 29 Welcome him in the Lord with great joy, and honor men like him, 30 because he almost died for the work of Christ, risking his life to make up for the help you could not give me.

a 16 Or hold on to

Get a Load of This...

Living Water (see John 7:37–39) is better than the ultimate sports drink. It works deep inside you, pumping up your heart toward holiness, energizing your mind to love and do right. It'll never leave you high and dry! You'll not only *do* God's will, you'll *want* to (see Philippians 2:13)!

In Other Words...

No Confidence in the Flesh

Finally, my brothers, rejoice in the Lord! It is no trouble for me to write the same things to you again, and it is a safeguard for you.

²Watch out for those dogs, those men who do evil, those mutilators of the flesh. ³For it is we who are the circumcision, we who worship by the Spirit of God, who glory in Christ Jesus, and who put no confidence in the flesh— ⁴though I myself have reasons for such confidence.

If anyone else thinks he has reasons to put confidence in the flesh, I have more: ⁵circumcised on the eighth day, of the people of Israel, of the tribe of Benjamin, a Hebrew of Hebrews; in regard to the law, a Pharisee; ⁶as for zeal, persecuting the church; as for legalistic righteousness, faultless.

⁷But whatever was to my profit I now consider loss for the sake of Christ. ⁸What is more, I consider everything a loss compared to the surpassing greatness of knowing Christ Jesus my Lord, for whose sake I have lost all things. I consider them rubbish, that I may gain Christ ⁹and be found in him, not having a righteousness of my own that comes from the law, but that which is through faith in Christ—the righteousness that comes from God and is by faith. ¹⁰I want to know Christ and the power of his resurrection and the fellowship of sharing in his sufferings, becoming like him in his death, ¹¹and so, somehow, to attain to the resurrection from the dead.

Pressing on Toward the Goal

¹²Not that I have already obtained all this, or have already been made perfect, but I press on to take hold of that for which Christ Jesus took hold of me. ¹³Brothers, I do not consider myself yet to have taken hold of it. But one thing I do: Forgetting what is behind and straining toward what is ahead, ¹⁴I press on toward

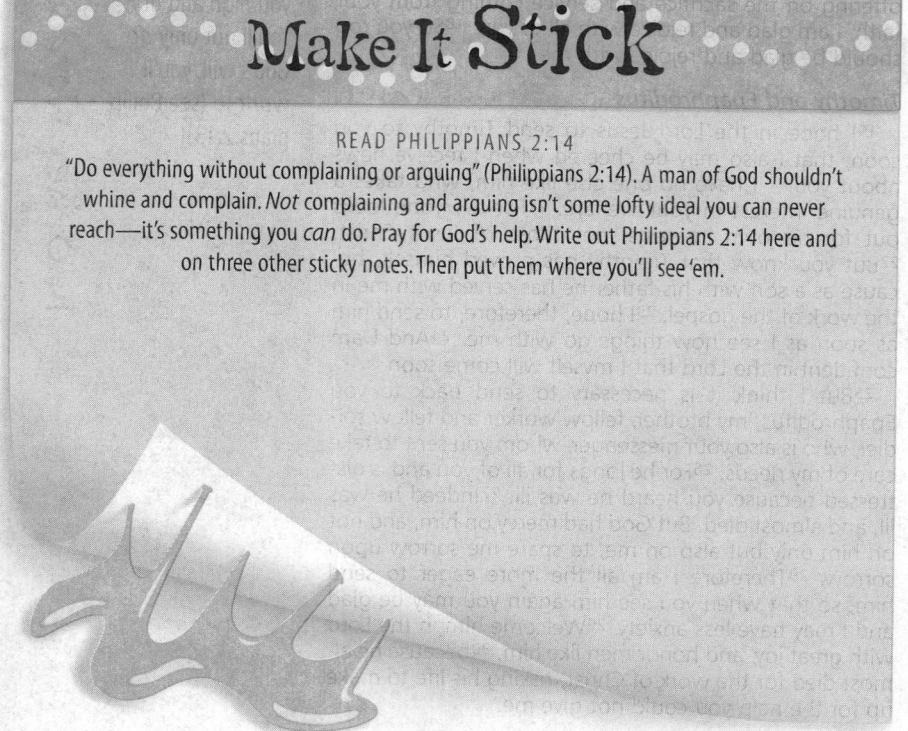

Make It Stick

READ PHILIPPIANS 2:14

"Do everything without complaining or arguing" (Philippians 2:14). A man of God shouldn't whine and complain. *Not* complaining and arguing isn't some lofty ideal you can never reach—it's something you *can* do. Pray for God's help. Write out Philippians 2:14 here and on three other sticky notes. Then put them where you'll see 'em.

the goal to win the prize for which God has called me heavenward in Christ Jesus.

15All of us who are mature should take such a view of things. And if on some point you think differently, that too God will make clear to you. 16Only let us live up to what we have already attained.

17Join with others in following my example, brothers, and take note of those who live according to the pattern we gave you. 18For, as I have often told you before and now say again even with tears, many live as enemies of the cross of Christ. 19Their destiny is destruction, their god is their stomach, and their glory is in their shame. Their mind is on earthly things. 20But our citizenship is in heaven. And we eagerly await a Savior from there, the Lord Jesus Christ, 21who, by the power that enables him to bring everything under his control, will transform our lowly bodies so that they will be like his glorious body.

4 Therefore, my brothers, you whom I love and long for, my joy and crown, that is how you should stand firm in the Lord, dear friends!

Exhortations

2I plead with Euodia and I plead with Syntyche to agree with each other in the Lord. 3Yes, and I ask you, loyal yokefellow,[a] help these women who have contended at my side in the cause of the gospel, along with Clement and the rest of my fellow workers, whose names are in the book of life.

4Rejoice in the Lord always. I will say it again: Rejoice! 5Let your gentleness be evident to all. The Lord is near. 6Do not be anxious about anything, but in everything, by prayer and petition, with thanksgiving, present your requests to God. 7And the peace of God, which transcends all understanding, will guard your hearts and your minds in Christ Jesus.

8Finally, brothers, whatever is true, whatever is noble, whatever is right, whatever is pure, whatever is lovely, whatever is admirable—if anything is excellent or praiseworthy—think about such things. 9Whatever you have learned or received or heard from me, or seen in me—

a 3 Or loyal Syzygus

Pressing to the Goal

READ PHILIPPIANS 3:12–14

Ever watch the 4x100 relays at the Olympics? Those guys practice and practice to get it right. What if, each time a guy tripped or fumbled the baton handoff in practice, he had to wear a weight around his neck the next race? Uh … maybe not. What's your attitude about the race you're running as a Christian? If you carried every sin and mistake you've ever made, you'd be a statue. Want to keep on going—keep moving toward the goal of being more like Jesus? Then "forget what is behind and strain toward what is ahead" (Philippians 3:13). When you go to God for help, he doesn't look back on what you did wrong. Instead he says, "The past is behind and you're my child. Let's press on together."

Your next reading is on page 1551.

put it into practice. And the God of peace will be with you.

Thanks for Their Gifts

[10] I rejoice greatly in the Lord that at last you have renewed your concern for me. Indeed, you have been concerned, but you had no opportunity to show it. [11] I am not saying this because I am in need, for I have learned to be content whatever the circumstances. [12] I know what it is to be in need, and I know what it is to have plenty. I have learned the secret of being content in any and every situation, whether well fed or hungry, whether living in plenty or in want. [13] I can do everything through him who gives me strength.

[14] Yet it was good of you to share in my troubles. [15] Moreover, as you Philippians know, in the early days of your acquaintance with the gospel, when I set out from Macedonia, not one church shared with me in the matter of giving and receiving, except you only; [16] for even when I was in Thessalonica, you sent me aid again and again when I was in need. [17] Not that I am looking for a gift, but I am looking for what may be credited to your

Make It Stick

_____

_____

_____

_____

_____

_____

READ PHILIPPIANS 4:8
You have to filter dirty water to make it drinkable. Need a thought-filter? Philippians 4:8 has you covered with eight standards for pure thinking. Write all eight down on a sticky note and pass your thoughts through each. What has the "water" in your mind been like lately? Drinkable? Toxic waste? Or somewhere in between? Keep working on it.

account. [18]I have received full payment and even more; I am amply supplied, now that I have received from Epaphroditus the gifts you sent. They are a fragrant offering, an acceptable sacrifice, pleasing to God. [19]And my God will meet all your needs according to his glorious riches in Christ Jesus.

[20]To our God and Father be glory for ever and ever. Amen.

Final Greetings

[21]Greet all the saints in Christ Jesus. The brothers who are with me send greetings. [22]All the saints send you greetings, especially those who belong to Caesar's household.

[23]The grace of the Lord Jesus Christ be with your spirit. Amen.[a]

Get a Load of This...

Hey, you want to be let in on a really cool *secret*? In Philippians 4:11 –12, Paul said that he had discovered one of the secrets to having a great, fun life. Check it out.

COLOSSIANS

Who wrote this book?
Paul.

Why was this book written?
Colossians shows that Jesus is supreme and that he saves us completely.

For whom was this book written?
This book is a letter written to Christians at Colosse.

When was this book written?
Colossians was written about A.D. 60, when Paul was in prison in Rome.

What are some important teachings in this book?

Jesus is supreme   Colossians 1:15–20
Jesus forgives our sins   Colossians 2:13–15
How to live a holy life   Colossians 3:12–17

Paul, an apostle of Christ Jesus by the will of God, and Timothy our brother,

2To the holy and faithful*a* brothers in Christ at Colosse:

Grace and peace to you from God our Father.*b*

Thanksgiving and Prayer

3We always thank God, the Father of our Lord Jesus Christ, when we pray for you, 4because we have heard of your faith in Christ Jesus and of the love you have for all the saints— 5the faith and love that spring from the hope that is stored up for you in heaven and that you have already heard about in the word of truth, the gospel 6that has come to you. All over the world this gospel is bearing fruit and growing, just as it has been doing among you since the day you heard it and understood God's grace in all its truth. 7You learned it from Epaphras, our dear fellow servant, who is a faithful minister of Christ on our*c* behalf, 8and who also told us of your love in the Spirit.

9For this reason, since the day we heard about you, we have not stopped praying for you and asking God to fill you with the knowledge of his will through all spiritual wisdom and understanding. 10And we pray this in order that you may live a life worthy of the Lord and may please him in every way: bearing fruit in every good work, growing in the knowledge of God, 11being strengthened with all power according to his glorious might so that you may have great endurance and patience, and joyfully 12giving thanks to the Father, who has qualified you*d* to share in the inheritance of the saints in the kingdom of light. 13For he has rescued us from the dominion of darkness and brought us into the kingdom of the Son he loves, 14in whom we have redemption,*e* the forgiveness of sins.

The Supremacy of Christ

15He is the image of the invisible God, the firstborn over all creation. 16For by him all things were created: things in heaven and on earth, visible and invisible, whether thrones or powers or rulers or authorities; all things were created by him and for him. 17He is before all things, and in him all things hold together. 18And he is the head of the body, the church; he is the beginning and the firstborn from among the dead, so that in everything he might have the supremacy. 19For God was pleased to have all his fullness dwell in him, 20and through him to reconcile to himself all things, whether things on earth or things in heaven, by making peace through his blood, shed on the cross.

21Once you were alienated from God and were enemies in your minds because of*f* your evil behavior. 22But now he has reconciled you by Christ's physical body through death to present you holy in his sight, without blemish and free from accusation— 23if you continue in your faith, established and firm, not moved from the hope held out in the gospel. This is the gospel that you heard and that has been proclaimed to every creature under heaven, and of which I, Paul, have become a servant.

Paul's Labor for the Church

24Now I rejoice in what was suffered for you, and I fill up in my flesh what is still lacking in regard to Christ's afflictions, for the sake of his body, which is the church. 25I have become its servant by the commission God gave me to present to you the word of God in its fullness— 26the mystery that has been kept hidden for ages and generations, but is now disclosed to the saints. 27To them God has chosen to make known among the Gentiles the glorious riches of this mystery, which is Christ in you, the hope of glory.

28We proclaim him, admonishing and teaching everyone with all wisdom, so that we may present everyone perfect in Christ. 29To this end I labor, struggling with all his energy, which so powerfully works in me.

I want you to know how much I am struggling for you and for those at Laodicea, and for all who have not met me personally. 2My purpose is that they may be encouraged in heart and united in love, so that they may have the full riches of complete understanding, in order that they may know the mystery of God, namely, Christ, 3in whom are hidden all the treasures of wisdom and knowl-

a 2 Or *believing*   *b 2* Some manuscripts *Father and the Lord Jesus Christ*   *c 7* Some manuscripts *your*   *d 12* Some manuscripts *us*   *e 14* A few late manuscripts *redemption through his blood*   *f 21* Or *minds, as shown by*

Get a Load of This...

Jesus took away the power of the devil and his cronies. Through his death and resurrection he had a victory parade, like a Roman general leading captives through the streets (Colossians 2:15), throwing treats to the crowds. What did Jesus give? Galilee gumdrops? Jerusalem jelly beans? No way! His gift was grace!

edge. 4I tell you this so that no one may deceive you by fine-sounding arguments. 5For though I am absent from you in body, I am present with you in spirit and delight to see how orderly you are and how firm your faith in Christ is.

Freedom From Human Regulations Through Life With Christ

6So then, just as you received Christ Jesus as Lord, continue to live in him, 7rooted and built up in him, strengthened in the faith as you were taught, and overflowing with thankfulness.

8See to it that no one takes you captive through hollow and deceptive philosophy, which depends on human tradition and the basic principles of this world rather than on Christ.

9For in Christ all the fullness of the Deity lives in bodily form, 10and you have been given fullness in Christ, who is the head over every power and authority. 11In him you were also circumcised, in the putting off of the sinful nature,*a* not with a circumcision done by the hands of men but with the circumcision done by Christ, 12having been buried with him in baptism and raised with him through your faith in the power of God, who raised him from the dead.

13When you were dead in your sins and in the uncircumcision of your sinful nature,*b* God made you*c* alive with Christ. He forgave us all our sins, 14having canceled the written code, with its regulations, that was against us and that stood opposed to us; he took it away, nailing it to the cross. 15And having disarmed the powers and authorities, he made a public spectacle of them, triumphing over them by the cross.*d*

16Therefore do not let anyone judge you by what you eat or drink, or with regard to a religious festival, a New Moon celebration or a Sabbath day. 17These are a shadow of the things that were to come; the reality, however, is found in Christ. 18Do not let anyone who delights in false humility and the worship of angels disqualify you for the prize. Such a person goes into great detail about what he has seen, and his unspiritual mind puffs him up with idle notions. 19He has lost connection with the Head, from whom the whole body, supported and held together by its ligaments and sinews, grows as God causes it to grow.

20Since you died with Christ to the basic principles of this world, why, as though you still belonged to it, do you submit to its rules: 21"Do not handle! Do not taste! Do not touch!"? 22These are all destined to perish with use, because they are based on human commands and teachings. 23Such regulations indeed have an appearance of wisdom, with their self-imposed worship, their false humility and their harsh treatment of the body, but they lack any value in restraining sensual indulgence.

a 11 Or the flesh   *b 13* Or your flesh   *c 13* Some manuscripts us   *d 15* Or them in him

Rules for Holy Living

3 Since, then, you have been raised with Christ, set your hearts on things above, where Christ is seated at the right hand of God. ²Set your minds on things above, not on earthly things. ³For you died, and your life is now hidden with Christ in God. ⁴When Christ, who is your*ᵃ* life, appears, then you also will appear with him in glory.

⁵Put to death, therefore, whatever belongs to your earthly nature: sexual immorality, impurity, lust, evil desires and greed, which is idolatry. ⁶Because of these, the wrath of God is coming.*ᵇ* ⁷You used to walk in these ways, in the life you once lived. ⁸But now you must rid yourselves of all such things as these: anger, rage, malice, slander, and filthy language from your lips. ⁹Do not lie to each other, since you have taken off your old self with its practices ¹⁰and have put on the new self, which is being renewed in knowledge in the image of its Creator. ¹¹Here there is no Greek or Jew, circumcised or uncircum-cised, barbarian, Scythian, slave or free, but Christ is all, and is in all.

¹²Therefore, as God's chosen people, holy and dearly loved, clothe yourselves with compassion, kindness, humility, gentleness and patience. ¹³Bear with each other and forgive whatever grievances you may have against one another. Forgive as the Lord forgave you. ¹⁴And over all these virtues put on love, which binds them all together in perfect unity.

¹⁵Let the peace of Christ rule in your hearts, since as members of one body you were called to peace. And be thankful. ¹⁶Let the word of Christ dwell in you richly as you teach and admonish one another with all wisdom, and as you sing psalms, hymns and spiritual songs with gratitude in your hearts to God. ¹⁷And whatever you do, whether in word or deed, do it all in the name of the Lord Jesus, giving thanks to God the Father through him.

ᵃ 4 Some manuscripts our   ᵇ 6 Some early manuscripts coming on those who are disobedient

Filthy Language

READ COLOSSIANS 3:1–10

The Bible says that filthy language (verse 8), obscenity and coarse joking (Ephesians 5:4) are wrong. Why? Because they don't line up with being a Christian and it's *sure* not part of who God is. Profanity and dirty jokes usually lead to thinking sinful things; they cut people down and cheapen beautiful things God has made, such as sex. Swearing when talking to friends is not cool. Filthy language makes clean things filthy. It's as dumb as smearing dog doo-doo all over your clothes, then wearing them to school. Like, why would you even *do* it? "Rid yourselves of all such things" (verse 8). You may think, "Ahhh ... what's so bad about that word or joke?" But swearing and using filthy language promotes things that are wrong and messes up things that are good. A man of God should use words to build people up, not use words for low purposes.

Your next reading is on page 1557.

Rules for Christian Households

¹⁸Wives, submit to your husbands, as is fitting in the Lord.

¹⁹Husbands, love your wives and do not be harsh with them.

²⁰Children, obey your parents in everything, for this pleases the Lord.

²¹Fathers, do not embitter your children, or they will become discouraged.

²²Slaves, obey your earthly masters in everything; and do it, not only when their eye is on you and to win their favor, but with sincerity of heart and reverence for the Lord. ²³Whatever you do, work at it with all your heart, as working for the Lord, not for men, ²⁴since you know that you will receive an inheritance from the Lord as a reward. It is the Lord Christ you are serving. ²⁵Anyone who does wrong will be repaid for his wrong, and there is no favoritism.

 Masters, provide your slaves with what is right and fair, because you know that you also have a Master in heaven.

Further Instructions

²Devote yourselves to prayer, being watchful and thankful. ³And pray for us, too, that God may open a door for our message, so that we may proclaim the mystery of Christ, for which I am in chains. ⁴Pray that I may proclaim it clearly, as I should. ⁵Be wise in the way you act toward outsiders; make the most of every opportunity. ⁶Let your conversation be always full of grace, seasoned with salt, so that you may know how to answer everyone.

Final Greetings

⁷Tychicus will tell you all the news about me. He is a dear brother, a faithful

Make It Stick

READ COLOSSIANS 3:12–14

This passage gives God's fashion tips. Here's how you should clothe yourself. Read down the list. Are you fully clothed or um …more like in your swimming suit? On two sticky notes, write a godly attitude you need to have. Stick one note here and the other on your dresser so you'll remember to put on that attitude when you're clothing yourself.

minister and fellow servant in the Lord. [8]I am sending him to you for the express purpose that you may know about our[a] circumstances and that he may encourage your hearts. [9]He is coming with Onesimus, our faithful and dear brother, who is one of you. They will tell you everything that is happening here.

[10]My fellow prisoner Aristarchus sends you his greetings, as does Mark, the cousin of Barnabas. (You have received instructions about him; if he comes to you, welcome him.) [11]Jesus, who is called Justus, also sends greetings. These are the only Jews among my fellow workers for the kingdom of God, and they have proved a comfort to me. [12]Epaphras, who is one of you and a servant of Christ Jesus, sends greetings. He is always wrestling in prayer for you, that you may stand firm in all the will of God, mature and fully assured. [13]I vouch for him that he is working hard for you and for those at Laodicea and Hierapolis. [14]Our dear friend Luke, the doctor, and Demas send greetings. [15]Give my greetings to the brothers at Laodicea, and to Nympha and the church in her house.

[16]After this letter has been read to you, see that it is also read in the church of the Laodiceans and that you in turn read the letter from Laodicea.

[17]Tell Archippus: "See to it that you complete the work you have received in the Lord."

[18]I, Paul, write this greeting in my own hand. Remember my chains. Grace be with you.

---

[a] 8 Some manuscripts *that he may know about your*

1 THESSALONIANS

Who wrote this book?
Paul.

Why was this book written?
The book of 1 Thessalonians teaches the Christians in Thessalonica how to please God.

For whom was this book written?
This book is a letter Paul sent to Christians at Thessalonica.

When was this book written?
This book was written about A.D. 51 from Corinth.

What are some important teachings in this book?

Being Christian examples	1 Thessalonians 1:4–10
Living to please God	1 Thessalonians 4:3–12
Jesus will come again	1 Thessalonians 4:13–18

Paul, Silas[a] and Timothy,

To the church of the Thessalonians in God the Father and the Lord Jesus Christ:

Grace and peace to you.[b]

Thanksgiving for the Thessalonians' Faith

2We always thank God for all of you, mentioning you in our prayers. 3We continually remember before our God and Father your work produced by faith, your labor prompted by love, and your endurance inspired by hope in our Lord Jesus Christ.

4For we know, brothers loved by God, that he has chosen you, 5because our gospel came to you not simply with words, but also with power, with the Holy Spirit and with deep conviction. You know how we lived among you for your sake. 6You became imitators of us and of the Lord; in spite of severe suffering, you welcomed the message with the joy given by the Holy Spirit. 7And so you became a model to all the believers in Macedonia and Achaia. 8The Lord's message rang out from you not only in Macedonia and Achaia—your faith in God has become known everywhere. Therefore we do not need to say anything about it, 9for they themselves report what kind of reception you gave us. They tell how you turned to God from idols to serve the living and true God, 10and to wait for his Son from heaven, whom he raised from the dead—Jesus, who rescues us from the coming wrath.

Paul's Ministry in Thessalonica

You know, brothers, that our visit to you was not a failure. 2We had previously suffered and been insulted in Philippi, as you know, but with the help of our God we dared to tell you his gospel in spite of strong opposition. 3For the appeal we make does not spring from error or impure motives, nor are we trying to trick you. 4On the contrary, we speak as men approved by God to be entrusted with the gospel. We are not trying to please men but God, who tests our hearts. 5You know we never used flattery, nor did we put on a mask to cover up greed—God is our witness. 6We were not looking for praise from men, not from you or anyone else.

As apostles of Christ we could have been a burden to you, 7but we were gentle among you, like a mother caring for her little children. 8We loved you so much that we were delighted to share with you not only the gospel of God but our lives as well, because you had become so dear to us. 9Surely you remember, brothers, our toil and hardship; we worked night and day in order not to be a burden to anyone while we preached the gospel of God to you.

10You are witnesses, and so is God, of how holy, righteous and blameless we were among you who believed. 11For you know that we dealt with each of you as a father deals with his own children, 12encouraging, comforting and urging you to live lives worthy of God, who calls you into his kingdom and glory.

13And we also thank God continually because, when you received the word of God, which you heard from us, you accepted it not as the word of men, but as it actually is, the word of God, which is at work in you who believe. 14For you, brothers, became imitators of God's churches in Judea, which are in Christ Jesus: You suffered from your own countrymen the same things those churches suffered from the Jews, 15who killed the Lord Jesus and the prophets and also drove us out. They displease God and are hostile to all men 16in their effort to keep us from speaking to the Gentiles so that they may be saved. In this way they always heap up their sins to the limit. The wrath of God has come upon them at last.[c]

Paul's Longing to See the Thessalonians

17But, brothers, when we were torn away from you for a short time (in person, not in thought), out of our intense longing we made every effort to see you. 18For we wanted to come to you—certainly I, Paul, did, again and again—but Satan stopped us. 19For what is our hope, our joy, or the crown in which we will glory in the presence of our Lord Jesus when he comes? Is it not you? 20Indeed, you are our glory and joy.

[a] 1 Greek *Silvanus*, a variant of *Silas*   [b] 1 Some early manuscripts *you from God our Father and the Lord Jesus Christ*   [c] 16 Or *them fully*

So when we could stand it no longer, we thought it best to be left by ourselves in Athens. [2]We sent Timothy, who is our brother and God's fellow worker[a] in spreading the gospel of Christ, to strengthen and encourage you in your faith, [3]so that no one would be unsettled by these trials. You know quite well that we were destined for them. [4]In fact, when we were with you, we kept telling you that we would be persecuted. And it turned out that way, as you well know. [5]For this reason, when I could stand it no longer, I sent to find out about your faith. I was afraid that in some way the tempter might have tempted you and our efforts might have been useless.

Timothy's Encouraging Report

[6]But Timothy has just now come to us from you and has brought good news about your faith and love. He has told us that you always have pleasant memories of us and that you long to see us, just as we also long to see you. [7]Therefore, brothers, in all our distress and persecution we were encouraged about you because of your faith. [8]For now we really live, since you are standing firm in the Lord. [9]How can we thank God enough for you in return for all the joy we have in the presence of our God because of you? [10]Night and day we pray most earnestly that we may see you again and supply what is lacking in your faith.

[11]Now may our God and Father himself and our Lord Jesus clear the way for us to come to you. [12]May the Lord make your love increase and overflow for each other and for everyone else, just as ours does for you. [13]May he strengthen your hearts so that you will be blameless and holy in the presence of our God and Father when our Lord Jesus comes with all his holy ones.

[a] 2 Some manuscripts brother and fellow worker; other manuscripts brother and God's servant

Make It Stick

READ 1 THESSALONIANS 2:5

Ever tried to flatter someone by saying they looked great despite the glaring red zit on their nose? Were you buttering them up for a favor? It's good to encourage others, but it's got to be *real*. On a sticky note, write the name of someone and how you can encourage that person today.

Living to Please God

Finally, brothers, we instructed you how to live in order to please God, as in fact you are living. Now we ask you and urge you in the Lord Jesus to do this more and more. [2]For you know what instructions we gave you by the authority of the Lord Jesus.

[3]It is God's will that you should be sanctified: that you should avoid sexual immorality; [4]that each of you should learn to control his own body[a] in a way that is holy and honorable, [5]not in passionate lust like the heathen, who do not know God; [6]and that in this matter no one should wrong his brother or take advantage of him. The Lord will punish men for all such sins, as we have already told you and warned you. [7]For God did not call us to be impure, but to live a holy life. [8]Therefore, he who rejects this instruction does not reject man but God, who gives you his Holy Spirit.

[9]Now about brotherly love we do not need to write to you, for you yourselves have been taught by God to love each other. [10]And in fact, you do love all the brothers throughout Macedonia. Yet we urge you, brothers, to do so more and more.

[11]Make it your ambition to lead a quiet life, to mind your own business and to work with your hands, just as we told you, [12]so that your daily life may win the respect of outsiders and so that you will not be dependent on anybody.

The Coming of the Lord

[13]Brothers, we do not want you to be ignorant about those who fall asleep, or to grieve like the rest of men, who have no hope. [14]We believe that Jesus died and rose again and so we believe that God will bring with Jesus those who have fallen

a 4 Or learn to live with his own wife; or learn to acquire a wife

Control Your Body

READ 1 THESSALONIANS 4:3–8

STRONGER

GET

After a skydiver jumps out of an airplane, it's too late to realize that a parachute would've helped him avoid smashing into the ground. In the same way, the time you're faced with sexual temptation is the wrong moment to be thinking about how you're going to "control your body" (verse 4). In both cases, you'd better plan ahead. Sex stirs up a man's deepest emotional and physical desires. And once those desires get stirred up, it's like jumping out of a plane—there's no turning back! To avoid disaster, decide beforehand to control your thoughts. Also, avoid anything that may stir up your desires, such as bad-news movies, web sites or magazines. Sex is God-created, and when a man enjoys it God's way (with his wife) it can be as thrilling as skydiving. But if you go outside God's boundaries, things can only end one way—disaster. So plan ahead.

Your next reading is on page 1558.

asleep in him. [15]According to the Lord's own word, we tell you that we who are still alive, who are left till the coming of the Lord, will certainly not precede those who have fallen asleep. [16]For the Lord himself will come down from heaven, with a loud command, with the voice of the archangel and with the trumpet call of God, and the dead in Christ will rise first. [17]After that, we who are still alive and are left will be caught up together with them in the clouds to meet the Lord in the air. And so we will be with the Lord forever. [18]Therefore encourage each other with these words.

Now, brothers, about times and dates we do not need to write to you, [2]for you know very well that the day of the Lord will come like a thief in the night. [3]While people are saying, "Peace and safety," destruction will come on them suddenly, as labor pains on a pregnant woman, and they will not escape.

[4]But you, brothers, are not in darkness so that this day should surprise you like a thief. [5]You are all sons of the light and sons of the day. We do not belong to the night or to the darkness. [6]So then, let us not be like others, who are asleep, but let us be alert and self-controlled. [7]For those who sleep, sleep at night, and those who get drunk, get drunk at night. [8]But since we belong to the day, let us be self-controlled, putting on faith and love as a breastplate, and the hope of salvation as a helmet. [9]For God did not appoint us to suffer wrath but to receive salvation through our Lord Jesus Christ. [10]He died for us so that, whether we are awake or asleep, we may live together with him. [11]Therefore encourage one another and build each other up, just as in fact you are doing.

Final Instructions

[12]Now we ask you, brothers, to respect those who work hard among you, who are over you in the Lord and who admonish you. [13]Hold them in the highest regard in love because of their work. Live in peace with each other. [14]And we urge

Even God Laughs

READ 1 THESSALONIANS 5:16–18

It's hard to "be joyful always" (verse 16) if you're living in the armpit of life. But we all need a sense of humor to cheer us up. God invented serious rules about right and wrong, yes, but he also invented happiness, laughter and humor. But how do you stay joyful when times are *tough*? Simple. Make the decision to be thankful and positive no matter what's happening (verse 18). You have to *concentrate* on it, choose to look on the bright side of things. It doesn't mean you ignore negative bad stuff. It's just that when you see bad situations, you choose to believe God can change negatives into positives. A bonus is that as you develop a "joyful always" attitude and a sense of humor, you'll become a 252 man that others want to be around, because you'll always leave them with a smile.

Your next reading is on page 1563.

you, brothers, warn those who are idle, encourage the timid, help the weak, be patient with everyone. 15Make sure that nobody pays back wrong for wrong, but always try to be kind to each other and to everyone else.

16Be joyful always; 17pray continually; 18give thanks in all circumstances, for this is God's will for you in Christ Jesus.

19Do not put out the Spirit's fire; 20do not treat prophecies with contempt. 21Test everything. Hold on to the good. 22Avoid every kind of evil.

23May God himself, the God of peace, sanctify you through and through. May your whole spirit, soul and body be kept blameless at the coming of our Lord Jesus Christ. 24The one who calls you is faithful and he will do it.

25Brothers, pray for us. 26Greet all the brothers with a holy kiss. 27I charge you before the Lord to have this letter read to all the brothers.

28The grace of our Lord Jesus Christ be with you.

Get a Load of This...

Read 1 Thessalonians 4:13–18. This is what will happen when Christ returns to the earth. Angel shouts! Trumpet blasts! Dead people resurrected! Living mortals morphing into supernatural immortals and getting beamed up into heaven! You will *like* this!

2 THESSALONIANS

Who wrote this book?
Paul.

Why was this book written?
The book of 2 Thessalonians tells these Christians to work hard until Jesus comes again.

For whom was this book written?
The book of 2 Thessalonians is a letter Paul sent to Christians at Thessalonica.

When was this book written?
This book was written about A.D. 52 from Corinth.

What are some important teachings in this book?

God will punish the wicked   2 Thessalonians 1:5–10

Everyone should work   2 Thessalonians 3:6–15

Paul, Silas[a] and Timothy,

To the church of the Thessalonians in God our Father and the Lord Jesus Christ:

[2]Grace and peace to you from God the Father and the Lord Jesus Christ.

Thanksgiving and Prayer

[3]We ought always to thank God for you, brothers, and rightly so, because your faith is growing more and more, and the love every one of you has for each other is increasing. [4]Therefore, among God's churches we boast about your perseverance and faith in all the persecutions and trials you are enduring.

[5]All this is evidence that God's judgment is right, and as a result you will be counted worthy of the kingdom of God, for which you are suffering. [6]God is just: He will pay back trouble to those who trouble you [7]and give relief to you who are troubled, and to us as well. This will happen when the Lord Jesus is revealed from heaven in blazing fire with his powerful angels. [8]He will punish those who do not know God and do not obey the gospel of our Lord Jesus. [9]They will be punished with everlasting destruction and shut out from the presence of the Lord and from the majesty of his power [10]on the day he comes to be glorified in his holy people and to be marveled at among all those who have believed. This includes you, because you believed our testimony to you.

[11]With this in mind, we constantly pray for you, that our God may count you worthy of his calling, and that by his power he may fulfill every good purpose of yours and every act prompted by your faith. [12]We pray this so that the name of our Lord Jesus may be glorified in you, and you in him, according to the grace of our God and the Lord Jesus Christ.[b]

The Man of Lawlessness

Concerning the coming of our Lord Jesus Christ and our being gathered to him, we ask you, brothers, [2]not to become easily unsettled or alarmed by some prophecy, report or letter supposed to have come from us, saying that the day of the Lord has already come. [3]Don't let anyone deceive you in any way, for ⌊that day will not come⌋ until the rebellion occurs and the man of lawlessness[c] is revealed, the man doomed to destruction. [4]He will oppose and will exalt himself over everything that is called God or is worshiped, so that he sets himself up in God's temple, proclaiming himself to be God.

[5]Don't you remember that when I was with you I used to tell you these things? [6]And now you know what is holding him back, so that he may be revealed at the proper time. [7]For the secret power of lawlessness is al-

Get a Load of This...

Check out 2 Thessalonians 1:6–10. Pay back time! But remember: God is judging people who refuse to accept the gospel of Jesus Christ. This is *not* talking about kids who tease you or cut in front of you in a line.

---

[a] 1 Greek *Silvanus*, a variant of *Silas*   [b] 12 Or *God and Lord, Jesus Christ*
[a] 3 Some manuscripts *sin*

Get a Load of This...

Check out 2 Thessalonians 2:3–4. "Exalt himself"? "Proclaim himself to be God"? Wow, sounds like the Antichrist has a big *ego* problem. Don't worry: God will grab him, drag him in front of a mirror and show him who's *really* God and who's the phony.

ready at work; but the one who now holds it back will continue to do so till he is taken out of the way. ⁸And then the lawless one will be revealed, whom the Lord Jesus will overthrow with the breath of his mouth and destroy by the splendor of his coming. ⁹The coming of the lawless one will be in accordance with the work of Satan displayed in all kinds of counterfeit miracles, signs and wonders, ¹⁰and in every sort of evil that deceives those who are perishing. They perish because they refused to love the truth and so be saved. ¹¹For this reason God sends them a powerful delusion so that they will believe the lie ¹²and so that all will be condemned who have not believed the truth but have delighted in wickedness.

Stand Firm

¹³But we ought always to thank God for you, brothers loved by the Lord, because from the beginning God chose you *a* to be saved through the sanctifying work of the Spirit and through belief in the truth. ¹⁴He called you to this through our gospel, that you might share in the glory of our Lord Jesus Christ. ¹⁵So then, brothers, stand firm and hold to the teachings *b* we passed on to you, whether by word of mouth or by letter.

¹⁶May our Lord Jesus Christ himself and God our Father, who loved us and by his grace gave us eternal encouragement and good hope, ¹⁷encourage your hearts and strengthen you in every good deed and word.

Request for Prayer

Finally, brothers, pray for us that the message of the Lord may spread rapidly and be honored, just as it was with you. ²And pray that we may be delivered from wicked and evil men, for not everyone has faith. ³But the Lord is faithful, and he will strengthen and protect you from the evil one. ⁴We have confidence in the Lord that you are doing and will continue to do the things we command. ⁵May the Lord direct your hearts into God's love and Christ's perseverance.

Warning Against Idleness

⁶In the name of the Lord Jesus Christ, we command you, brothers, to keep away from every brother who is idle and does not live according to the teaching *c* you received from us. ⁷For you yourselves know how you ought to follow our example. We were not idle when we were with you, ⁸nor did we eat anyone's food without paying for it. On the contrary, we worked night and day, laboring and toiling so that we would not be a burden to any of you. ⁹We did this, not because we do not have the right to such help, but in order to make ourselves a model for you to follow. ¹⁰For even when we

---

a 13 Some manuscripts *because God chose you as his firstfruits*
b 15 Or *traditions* *c 6* Or *tradition*

were with you, we gave you this rule: "If a man will not work, he shall not eat."

¹¹We hear that some among you are idle. They are not busy; they are busybodies. ¹²Such people we command and urge in the Lord Jesus Christ to settle down and earn the bread they eat. ¹³And as for you, brothers, never tire of doing what is right.

¹⁴If anyone does not obey our instruction in this letter, take special note of him. Do not associate with him, in order that he may feel ashamed. ¹⁵Yet do not regard him as an enemy, but warn him as a brother.

Final Greetings

¹⁶Now may the Lord of peace himself give you peace at all times and in every way. The Lord be with all of you.

¹⁷I, Paul, write this greeting in my own hand, which is the distinguishing mark in all my letters. This is how I write.

¹⁸The grace of our Lord Jesus Christ be with you all.

GET STRONGER

Be a Hard Worker

READ 2 THESSALONIANS 3:6–15

A lot of people talk about winning the lottery so they can quit their job and spend their time on some sunny beach, doing *nothing*. God didn't create life to be that way. Verse 10 says, "If a man will not work, he shall not eat." In order for families and communities to function, people need to work. Go figure. Work isn't just to keep you busy. Work lets you create value and helps make your community and church and world (and bedroom!) a better place to live. Steer clear of lazy loafers who don't want to do anything. A man of God works hard. He doesn't look at work as some awful thing he "has" to do. As you get older, find out what your talents are, what you enjoy doing and what makes you feel valuable, then aim yourself toward a career that matches those gifts. That's how God created things to work.

Your next reading is on page 1569.

1 TIMOTHY

Who wrote this book?

Paul.

Why was this book written?

The book of 1 Timothy gives Timothy advice on how to do his important work.

For whom was this book written?

This book is a letter Paul sent to his young helper Timothy.

When was this book written?

This book was written about A.D. 65 from Macedonia.

What are some important teachings in this book?

Beware of false teachers	1 Timothy 1:3–11
Choosing leaders	1 Timothy 3:1–16
Be an example	1 Timothy 4:11–16
The Christian family	1 Timothy 5:1–2
Don't love money	1 Timothy 6:3–10
Advice to the rich	1 Timothy 6:17–21

Paul, an apostle of Christ Jesus by the command of God our Savior and of Christ Jesus our hope,

2To Timothy my true son in the faith:

Grace, mercy and peace from God the Father and Christ Jesus our Lord.

Warning Against False Teachers of the Law

3As I urged you when I went into Macedonia, stay there in Ephesus so that you may command certain men not to teach false doctrines any longer 4nor to devote themselves to myths and endless genealogies. These promote controversies rather than God's work—which is by faith. 5The goal of this command is love, which comes from a pure heart and a good conscience and a sincere faith. 6Some have wandered away from these and turned to meaningless talk. 7They want to be teachers of the law, but they do not know what they are talking about or what they so confidently affirm.

8We know that the law is good if one uses it properly. 9We also know that law*a* is made not for the righteous but for lawbreakers and rebels, the ungodly and sinful, the unholy and irreligious; for those who kill their fathers or mothers, for murderers, 10for adulterers and perverts, for slave traders and liars and perjurers—and for whatever else is contrary to the sound doctrine 11that conforms to the glorious gospel of the blessed God, which he entrusted to me.

The Lord's Grace to Paul

12I thank Christ Jesus our Lord, who has given me strength, that he considered me faithful, appointing me to his service. 13Even though I was once a blasphemer and a persecutor and a violent man, I was shown mercy because I acted in ignorance

a 9 Or that the law

Make It Stick

READ 1 TIMOTHY 1:19

God gave you a conscience and the Holy Spirit works *with* it to keep your ship on course. Ignore your conscience too much and too long and suddenly *CRUNCH!*—You could end up with "shipwrecked . . . faith" (1 Timothy 1:19). On a sticky note, write down the last thing your conscience bugged you about. If you need to ask God (and/or some person) for forgiveness, do that—and then tear up the note.

and unbelief. ¹⁴The grace of our Lord was poured out on me abundantly, along with the faith and love that are in Christ Jesus.

¹⁵Here is a trustworthy saying that deserves full acceptance: Christ Jesus came into the world to save sinners—of whom I am the worst. ¹⁶But for that very reason I was shown mercy so that in me, the worst of sinners, Christ Jesus might display his unlimited patience as an example for those who would believe on him and receive eternal life. ¹⁷Now to the King eternal, immortal, invisible, the only God, be honor and glory for ever and ever. Amen.

¹⁸Timothy, my son, I give you this instruction in keeping with the prophecies once made about you, so that by following them you may fight the good fight, ¹⁹holding on to faith and a good conscience. Some have rejected these and so have shipwrecked their faith. ²⁰Among them are Hymenaeus and Alexander, whom I have handed over to Satan to be taught not to blaspheme.

Instructions on Worship

2 I urge, then, first of all, that requests, prayers, intercession and thanksgiving be made for everyone— ²for kings and all those in authority, that we may live peaceful and quiet lives in all godliness and holiness. ³This is good, and pleases God our Savior, ⁴who wants all men to be saved and to come to a knowledge of the truth. ⁵For there is one God and one mediator between God and men, the man Christ Jesus, ⁶who gave himself as a ransom for all men—the testimony given in its proper time. ⁷And for this purpose I was appointed a herald and an apostle—I am telling the truth, I am not lying—and a teacher of the true faith to the Gentiles.

⁸I want men everywhere to lift up holy hands in prayer, without anger or disputing.

⁹I also want women to dress modestly, with decency and propriety, not with

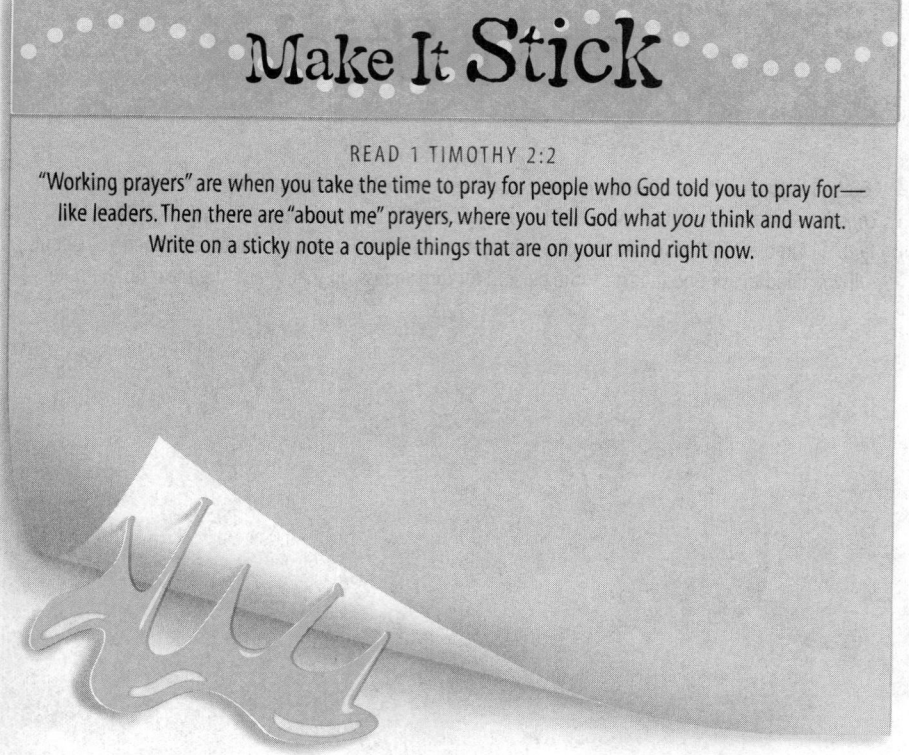

Make It Stick

READ 1 TIMOTHY 2:2

"Working prayers" are when you take the time to pray for people who God told you to pray for— like leaders. Then there are "about me" prayers, where you tell God what *you* think and want. Write on a sticky note a couple things that are on your mind right now.

braided hair or gold or pearls or expensive clothes, ¹⁰but with good deeds, appropriate for women who profess to worship God.

¹¹A woman should learn in quietness and full submission. ¹²I do not permit a woman to teach or to have authority over a man; she must be silent. ¹³For Adam was formed first, then Eve. ¹⁴And Adam was not the one deceived; it was the woman who was deceived and became a sinner. ¹⁵But women*a* will be saved*b* through childbearing—if they continue in faith, love and holiness with propriety.

Overseers and Deacons

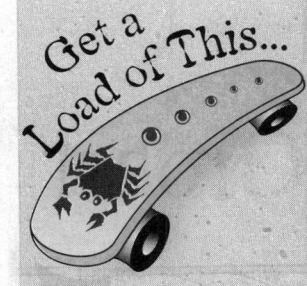

Here is a trustworthy saying: If anyone sets his heart on being an overseer,*c* he desires a noble task. ²Now the overseer must be above reproach, the husband of but one wife, temperate, self-controlled, respectable, hospitable, able to teach, ³not given to drunkenness, not violent but gentle, not quarrelsome, not a lover of money. ⁴He must manage his own family well and see that his children obey him with proper respect. ⁵(If anyone does not know how to manage his own family, how can he take care of God's church?) ⁶He must not be a recent convert, or he may become conceited and fall under the same judgment as the devil. ⁷He must also have a good reputation with outsiders, so that he will not fall into disgrace and into the devil's trap.

⁸Deacons, likewise, are to be men worthy of respect, sincere, not indulging in much wine, and not pursuing dishonest gain. ⁹They must keep hold of the deep truths of the faith with a clear conscience. ¹⁰They must first be tested; and then if there is nothing against them, let them serve as deacons.

¹¹In the same way, their wives*d* are to be women worthy of respect, not malicious talkers but temperate and trustworthy in everything.

¹²A deacon must be the husband of but one wife and must manage his children and his household well. ¹³Those who have served well gain an excellent standing and great assurance in their faith in Christ Jesus.

¹⁴Although I hope to come to you soon, I am writing you these instructions so that, ¹⁵if I am delayed, you will know how people ought to conduct themselves in God's household, which is the church of the living God, the pillar and foundation of the truth. ¹⁶Beyond all question, the mystery of godliness is great:

He*e* appeared in a body,*f*
  was vindicated by the Spirit,
was seen by angels,
  was preached among the nations,
was believed on in the world,
  was taken up in glory.

a 15 Greek *she*   *b 15* Or *restored*   *c 1* Traditionally *bishop;* also in verse 2   *d 11* Or *way, deaconesses*   *e 16* Some manuscripts *God*   *f 16* Or *in the flesh*

Get a Load of This...

Want to have a great reputation (1 Timothy 3:7)? If you're becoming the 252 man that God wants you to be and growing smarter, stronger, deeper and cooler, then even unsaved people will notice the change and give you a thumbs up.

In Other Words...

Gross!

When a steer is branded with a red-hot iron, its hide is *seared*. That spot becomes a huge callous with no feeling left. A conscience can be "seared as with a hot iron," too (1 Timothy 4:2). A "branded" conscience can't feel God's Spirit anymore.

Instructions to Timothy

4 The Spirit clearly says that in later times some will abandon the faith and follow deceiving spirits and things taught by demons. ²Such teachings come through hypocritical liars, whose consciences have been seared as with a hot iron. ³They forbid people to marry and order them to abstain from certain foods, which God created to be received with thanksgiving by those who believe and who know the truth. ⁴For everything God created is good, and nothing is to be rejected if it is received with thanksgiving, ⁵because it is consecrated by the word of God and prayer.

⁶If you point these things out to the brothers, you will be a good minister of Christ Jesus, brought up in the truths of the faith and of the good teaching that you have followed. ⁷Have nothing to do with godless myths and old wives' tales; rather, train yourself to be godly. ⁸For physical training is of some value, but godliness has value for all things, holding promise for both the present life and the life to come. ⁹This is a trustworthy saying that deserves full acceptance ¹⁰(and for this we labor and strive), that we have put our hope in the living God, who is the Savior of all men, and especially of those who believe.

¹¹Command and teach these things. ¹²Don't let anyone look down on you because you are young, but set an example for the believers in speech, in life, in love, in faith and in purity. ¹³Until I come, devote yourself to the public reading of Scripture, to preaching and to teaching. ¹⁴Do not neglect your gift, which was given you through a prophetic message when the body of elders laid their hands on you.

¹⁵Be diligent in these matters; give yourself wholly to them, so that everyone may see your progress. ¹⁶Watch your life and doctrine closely. Persevere in them, because if you do, you will save both yourself and your hearers.

Advice About Widows, Elders and Slaves

5 Do not rebuke an older man harshly, but exhort him as if he were your father. Treat younger men as brothers, ²older women as mothers, and younger women as sisters, with absolute purity.

³Give proper recognition to those widows who are really in need. ⁴But if a widow has children or grandchildren, these should learn first of all to put their religion into practice by caring for their own family and so repaying their parents and grandparents, for this is pleasing to God. ⁵The widow who is really in need and left all alone puts her hope in God and continues night and day to pray and to ask God for help. ⁶But the widow who lives for pleasure is dead even while she lives. ⁷Give the people these instructions, too, so that no one may be open to blame. ⁸If anyone does not provide for his relatives, and especially for his immediate family, he has

denied the faith and is worse than an unbeliever.

9No widow may be put on the list of widows unless she is over sixty, has been faithful to her husband,a 10and is well known for her good deeds, such as bringing up children, showing hospitality, washing the feet of the saints, helping those in trouble and devoting herself to all kinds of good deeds.

11As for younger widows, do not put them on such a list. For when their sensual desires overcome their dedication to Christ, they want to marry. 12Thus they bring judgment on themselves, because they have broken their first pledge. 13Besides, they get into the habit of being idle and going about from house to house. And not only do they become idlers, but also gossips and busybodies, saying things they ought not to. 14So I counsel younger widows to marry, to have children, to manage their homes and to give the enemy no opportunity for slander.

15Some have in fact already turned away to follow Satan.

16If any woman who is a believer has widows in her family, she should help them and not let the church be burdened with them, so that the church can help those widows who are really in need.

17The elders who direct the affairs of the church well are worthy of double honor, especially those whose work is preaching and teaching. 18For the Scripture says, "Do not muzzle the ox while it is treading out the grain,"b and "The worker deserves his wages."c 19Do not entertain an accusation against an elder unless it is brought by two or three witnesses. 20Those who sin are to be rebuked publicly, so that the others may take warning.

21I charge you, in the sight of God and Christ Jesus and the elect angels, to keep these instructions without partiality, and to do nothing out of favoritism.

a 9 Or has had but one husband   b 18 Deut. 25:4
c 18 Luke 10:7

GET STRONGER

Exercise Is Important

READ 1 TIMOTHY 4:7-8

Paul was a fan. He knew a lot about running races and other athletic events, and he understood the value of physical conditioning. He even compared training your spirit to training your body. Athletes that shoot hard, score big and whiz past opposing teams didn't get that way by accident. They worked at it. Same with godliness: When you hang out with godly people, read your Bible and pray, you're "working out" your spirit. Staying in shape physically means exercising regularly, not taking a month off and being lazy. In the same way, skipping devotions or prayer time can turn you into a wimpy Christian. A godly man sticks to his workout program. You can't become strong—physically or spiritually—by vegging out in front of the TV for hours at a time. What are you doing this week to build your spirit and your muscles? Turn off the TV and think about it.

Your next reading is on page 1571.

22Do not be hasty in the laying on of hands, and do not share in the sins of others. Keep yourself pure.

23Stop drinking only water, and use a little wine because of your stomach and your frequent illnesses.

24The sins of some men are obvious, reaching the place of judgment ahead of them; the sins of others trail behind them. 25In the same way, good deeds are obvious, and even those that are not cannot be hidden.

All who are under the yoke of slavery should consider their masters worthy of full respect, so that God's name and our teaching may not be slandered. 2Those who have believing masters are not to show less respect for them because they are brothers. Instead, they are to serve them even better, because those who benefit from their service are believers, and dear to them. These are the things you are to teach and urge on them.

Make It Stick

_____

_____

_____

_____

_____

_____

_____

READ 1 TIMOTHY 5:4

Moms and dads are supposed to provide for their kids (2 Corinthians 12:14), and when kids grow up, they're supposed to turn around and help care for their parents (1 Timothy 5:4). On a sticky note, write down some different ways you can help your parents even now. (Example: mow the lawn, rake leaves, give a compliment, etc.)

Love of Money

3If anyone teaches false doctrines and does not agree to the sound instruction of our Lord Jesus Christ and to godly teaching, 4he is conceited and understands nothing. He has an unhealthy interest in controversies and quarrels about words that result in envy, strife, malicious talk, evil suspicions 5and constant friction between men of corrupt mind, who have been robbed of the truth and who think that godliness is a means to financial gain.

6But godliness with contentment is great gain. 7For we brought nothing into the world, and we can take nothing out of it. 8But if we have food and clothing, we will be content with that. 9People who want to get rich fall into temptation and a trap and into many foolish and harmful desires that plunge men into ruin and destruction. 10For the love of money is a root of all kinds of evil. Some people, eager for money, have wandered from the faith and pierced themselves with many griefs.

Paul's Charge to Timothy

11But you, man of God, flee from all this, and pursue righteousness, godliness, faith, love, endurance and gentleness. 12Fight the good fight of the faith. Take hold of the eternal life to which you were called when you made your good confession in the presence of many witnesses. 13In the sight of God, who gives life to everything, and of Christ Jesus, who while testifying before Pontius Pilate made the good confession, I charge you 14to keep this command without spot or blame until the appearing of our Lord Jesus Christ, 15which God will bring about in his own time—God, the blessed and only Ruler, the King of kings and Lord of lords, 16who alone is immortal and who lives in unapproachable light, whom no one has seen or can see. To him be honor and might forever. Amen.

17Command those who are rich in this present world not to be arrogant nor to put their hope in wealth, which is so uncertain, but to put their hope in God, who

GET SMARTER.

The Love of Money

READ 1 TIMOTHY 6:6–10, 17–18

Paul never said it's a bad thing to have enough money to buy cool stuff and go to fun places. But he did warn that "the *love* of money is a root of all kinds of evil" (verse 10). Guess what? It's not necessarily even wrong to be rich. The mistake is when people spend all their energy trying to pile up money and think that being filthy rich will give them peace and a good life. Whoa! Wrong turn! Even American dollar bills tell you where to put your trust. They say: "In *God* we trust." Live a godly life, work hard, then use your Ben Franklins to help yourself and others. There's nothing wrong with buying some nice things—but having toys is only a bonus. Godly men know there's more to life than that.

Your next reading is on page 1574.

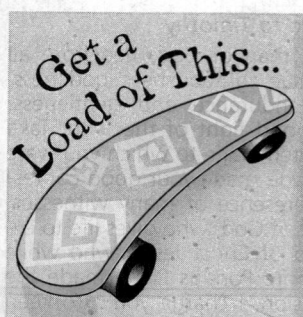

Get a Load of This...

Stay clear of guys who argue that only *they* know what the Bible really says!—as if God has been throwing airballs for 2,000 years trying to get the truth out, until finally he found a slam dunk with them (1 Timothy 6:3–5). Not!

richly provides us with everything for our enjoyment. [18]Command them to do good, to be rich in good deeds, and to be generous and willing to share. [19]In this way they will lay up treasure for themselves as a firm foundation for the coming age, so that they may take hold of the life that is truly life.

[20]Timothy, guard what has been entrusted to your care. Turn away from godless chatter and the opposing ideas of what is falsely called knowledge, [21]which some have professed and in so doing have wandered from the faith.

Grace be with you.

2 TIMOTHY

Who wrote this book?
Paul.

Why was this book written?
This letter encourages Timothy to keep on working hard after Paul dies.

For whom was this book written?
This book is a letter Paul sent to his young helper, Timothy.

When was this book written?
This book was written about A.D. 67, when Paul was in prison a second time.

What are some important teachings in this book?

Teach God's truth	2 Timothy 1:8–15
Teach gently	2 Timothy 2:22–26
Teach faithfully	2 Timothy 4:1–5

Paul, an apostle of Christ Jesus by the will of God, according to the promise of life that is in Christ Jesus,

2To Timothy, my dear son:

Grace, mercy and peace from God the Father and Christ Jesus our Lord.

Encouragement to Be Faithful

3I thank God, whom I serve, as my forefathers did, with a clear conscience, as night and day I constantly remember you in my prayers. 4Recalling your tears, I long to see you, so that I may be filled with joy. 5I have been reminded of your sincere faith, which first lived in your grandmother Lois and in your mother Eunice and, I am persuaded, now lives in you also. 6For this reason I remind you to fan into flame the gift of God, which is in you through the laying on of my hands. 7For God did not give us a spirit of timidity, but a spirit of power, of love and of self-discipline.

8So do not be ashamed to testify about our Lord, or ashamed of me his prisoner. But join with me in suffering for the gospel, by the power of God, 9who has saved us and called us to a holy life—not because of anything we have done but because of his own purpose and grace. This grace was given us in Christ Jesus before the beginning of time, 10but it has now been revealed through the appearing of our Savior, Christ Jesus, who has destroyed death and has brought life and immortality to light through the gospel. 11And of this gospel I was appointed a herald and an apostle and a teacher. 12That is why I am suffering as I am. Yet I am not ashamed, because I know whom I have believed, and am convinced that he is able to guard what I have entrusted to him for that day.

13What you heard from me, keep as the pattern of sound teaching, with faith and love in Christ Jesus. 14Guard the good deposit that was entrusted to you—guard it with the help of the Holy Spirit who lives in us.

15You know that everyone in the province of Asia has deserted me, including Phygelus and Hermogenes.

Setting Goals

READ 2 TIMOTHY 2:3–7

When you've set a goal—like building some muscles, getting an "A" in math or disciplining yourself to pray and read your Bible every day—don't be discouraged when the going gets tough. Keep at it (verse 3). Don't get distracted by less important interests and activities (verse 4). Don't cut corners or cheat (verse 5). Sticking to your goal is hard work (verse 6), but if you cheat and don't stick to the program, you're only cheating yourself. No perseverance means no "A's" and no muscles. When little things distract you from reaching your goal, you're not just getting "distracted," you're setting a *new* goal. The new goal is the distraction. You might tell yourself, "I can still make it, but for *now* I'll do this." Don't. Once you've set yourself a goal, stick to it. Remind yourself how important it is to build those muscles or read that Bible. Focus on the goal; ditch the distractions.

Your next reading is on page 1577.

16May the Lord show mercy to the household of Onesiphorus, because he often refreshed me and was not ashamed of my chains. 17On the contrary, when he was in Rome, he searched hard for me until he found me. 18May the Lord grant that he will find mercy from the Lord on that day! You know very well in how many ways he helped me in Ephesus.

You then, my son, be strong in the grace that is in Christ Jesus. 2And the things you have heard me say in the presence of many witnesses entrust to reliable men who will also be qualified to teach others. 3Endure hardship with us like a good soldier of Christ Jesus. 4No one serving as a soldier gets involved in civilian affairs—he wants to please his commanding officer. 5Similarly, if anyone competes as an athlete, he does not receive the victor's crown unless he competes according to the rules. 6The hardworking farmer should be the first to receive a share of the crops. 7Reflect on what I am saying, for the Lord will give you insight into all this.

8Remember Jesus Christ, raised from the dead, descended from David. This is my gospel, 9for which I am suffering even to the point of being chained like a criminal. But God's word is not chained. 10Therefore I endure everything for the sake of the elect, that they too may obtain the salvation that is in Christ Jesus, with eternal glory.

11Here is a trustworthy saying:

If we died with him,
we will also live with him;
12if we endure,
we will also reign with him.
If we disown him,
he will also disown us;
13if we are faithless,
he will remain faithful,
for he cannot disown himself.

A Workman Approved by God

14Keep reminding them of these things. Warn them before God against quarreling about words; it is of no value, and only ruins those who listen. 15Do your best to present yourself to God as one approved, a workman who does not need to be ashamed and who correctly handles the word of truth. 16Avoid godless chatter, because those who indulge in it will become more and more ungodly. 17Their teaching will spread like gangrene. Among them are Hymenaeus and Philetus, 18who have wandered away from the truth. They say that the resurrection has already taken place, and they destroy the faith of some. 19Nevertheless, God's solid foundation stands firm, sealed with this inscription: "The Lord knows those who are his,"a and, "Everyone who confesses the name of the Lord must turn away from wickedness."

a 19 Num. 16:5 (see Septuagint)

Gross!

Paul warned Timothy that false teaching could "spread like gangrene" (2 Timothy 2:17). Gangrene occurs when blood is cut off from a body part and that part *rots!* Ever seen a dark, oozy, rotten potato? That's what gangrene looks and smells like.

It seems like temptations are everywhere when you're young (2 Timothy 2:22). You know when you run into them. It's like running into a spider's web. The minute it happens, brush the cobwebs from your face, look for that spider on your shirt and squash it!

In other words...

20In a large house there are articles not only of gold and silver, but also of wood and clay; some are for noble purposes and some for ignoble. 21If a man cleanses himself from the latter, he will be an instrument for noble purposes, made holy, useful to the Master and prepared to do any good work.

22Flee the evil desires of youth, and pursue righteousness, faith, love and peace, along with those who call on the Lord out of a pure heart. 23Don't have anything to do with foolish and stupid arguments, because you know they produce quarrels. 24And the Lord's servant must not quarrel; instead, he must be kind to everyone, able to teach, not resentful. 25Those who oppose him he must gently instruct, in the hope that God will grant them repentance leading them to a knowledge of the truth, 26and that they will come to their senses and escape from the trap of the devil, who has taken them captive to do his will.

Godlessness in the Last Days

But mark this: There will be terrible times in the last days. 2People will be lovers of themselves, lovers of money, boastful, proud, abusive, disobedient to their parents, ungrateful, unholy, 3without love, unforgiving, slanderous, without self-control, brutal, not lovers of the good, 4treacherous, rash, conceited, lovers of pleasure rather than lovers of God— 5having a form of godliness but denying its power. Have nothing to do with them.

6They are the kind who worm their way into homes and gain control over weak-willed women, who are loaded down with sins and are swayed by all kinds of evil desires, 7always learning but never able to acknowledge the truth. 8Just as Jannes and Jambres opposed Moses, so also these men oppose the truth—men of depraved minds, who, as far as the faith is concerned, are rejected. 9But they will not get very far because, as in the case of those men, their folly will be clear to everyone.

Paul's Charge to Timothy

10You, however, know all about my teaching, my way of life, my purpose, faith, patience, love, endurance, 11persecutions, sufferings—what kinds of things happened to me in Antioch, Iconium and Lystra, the persecutions I endured. Yet the Lord rescued me from all of them. 12In fact, everyone who wants to live a godly life in Christ Jesus will be persecuted, 13while evil men and impostors will go from bad to worse, deceiving and being deceived. 14But as for you, continue in what you have learned and have become convinced of, because you know those from whom you learned it, 15and how from infancy you have known the holy Scriptures, which are able to make you wise for salvation through faith in Christ Jesus. 16All Scripture is God-breathed and is useful for teaching, rebuking, correcting and training in righteousness, [17]so that the man of God may be thoroughly equipped for every good work.

In the presence of God and of Christ Jesus, who will judge the living and the dead, and in view of his appearing and his kingdom, I give you this charge: [2]Preach the Word; be prepared in season and out of season; correct, rebuke and encourage—with great patience and careful instruction. [3]For the time will come when men will not put up with sound doctrine. Instead, to suit their own desires, they will gather around them a great number of teachers to say what their itching ears want to hear. [4]They will turn their ears away from the truth and turn aside to myths. [5]But you, keep your head in all situations, endure hardship, do the work of an evangelist, discharge all the duties of your ministry.

[6]For I am already being poured out like a drink offering, and the time has come for my departure. [7]I have fought the good fight, I have finished the race, I have kept the faith. [8]Now there is in store for me the crown of righteousness, which the Lord, the righteous Judge, will award to me on that day—and not only to me, but also to all who have longed for his appearing.

Personal Remarks

[9]Do your best to come to me quickly, [10]for Demas, because he loved this world, has deserted me and has gone to Thessalonica. Crescens has gone to Galatia, and Titus to Dalmatia. [11]Only Luke is with me. Get Mark and bring him with you, because he is helpful to me in my ministry. [12]I sent Tychicus to Ephesus. [13]When you come, bring the cloak that I left with Carpus at Troas, and my scrolls, especially the parchments.

[14]Alexander the metalworker did me a great deal of harm. The Lord will repay him for what he has done. [15]You too should be on your guard against him, because he strongly opposed our message.

[16]At my first defense, no one came to my support, but everyone deserted me. May it not be held against them. [17]But the Lord stood at my side and gave me strength, so that through me the message might be fully proclaimed and all the Gen-

---

The Manufacturer's MANual

READ 2 TIMOTHY 3:14–17

A good auto mechanic wouldn't repair a fancy new car without studying the book from the company who made the car. This book is called the manufacturer's manual: It tells him or her how the car was put together and how it's supposed to work. That's what the Bible does: It's your ultimate MANual—a man's guide for life. It teaches you how to live, how to act, what to believe and who to be. It gets right down to the "nuts and bolts" of what it means to be a Christian. If you start to get some funny ideas—like a few loose screws—it'll tell you how to tighten up your act. Want to be a spiritual grease monkey? Stay in the Word of God and read it daily. It doesn't just tell you "Be this," but will give you step-by-step instruction on how to keep your life well oiled and running smoothly.

Your next reading is on page 1580.

tiles might hear it. And I was delivered from the lion's mouth. [18]The Lord will rescue me from every evil attack and will bring me safely to his heavenly kingdom. To him be glory for ever and ever. Amen.

Final Greetings

[19]Greet Priscilla[a] and Aquila and the household of Onesiphorus. [20]Erastus stayed in Corinth, and I left Trophimus sick in Miletus. [21]Do your best to get here before winter. Eubulus greets you, and so do Pudens, Linus, Claudia and all the brothers.

[22]The Lord be with your spirit. Grace be with you.

[a] 19 Greek *Prisca*, a variant of *Priscilla*

TITUS

Who wrote this book?

Paul.

Why was this book written?

The book of Titus shows Titus how to be a good teacher and leader.

For whom was this book written?

This book is a letter Paul sent to a young helper named Titus.

When was this book written?

Paul wrote this letter to Titus about A.D. 65 from Corinth.

What are some important teachings in this book?

How to live a Christian life   Titus 2:1–15

Christians are to do good   Titus 3:3–8

Paul, a servant of God and an apostle of Jesus Christ for the faith of God's elect and the knowledge of the truth that leads to godliness— ²a faith and knowledge resting on the hope of eternal life, which God, who does not lie, promised before the beginning of time, ³and at his appointed season he brought his word to light through the preaching entrusted to me by the command of God our Savior,

⁴To Titus, my true son in our common faith:

Grace and peace from God the Father and Christ Jesus our Savior.

Titus's Task on Crete

⁵The reason I left you in Crete was that you might straighten out what was left unfinished and appoint[a] elders in every town, as I directed you. ⁶An elder must be blameless, the husband of but one wife, a man whose children believe and are not open to the charge of being wild and disobedient. ⁷Since an overseer[b] is entrusted with God's work, he must be blameless—

not overbearing, not quick-tempered, not given to drunkenness, not violent, not pursuing dishonest gain. ⁸Rather he must be hospitable, one who loves what is good, who is self-controlled, upright, holy and disciplined. ⁹He must hold firmly to the trustworthy message as it has been taught, so that he can encourage others by sound doctrine and refute those who oppose it.

¹⁰For there are many rebellious people, mere talkers and deceivers, especially those of the circumcision group. ¹¹They must be silenced, because they are ruining whole households by teaching things they ought not to teach—and that for the sake of dishonest gain. ¹²Even one of their own prophets has said, "Cretans are always liars, evil brutes, lazy gluttons." ¹³This testimony is true. Therefore, rebuke them sharply, so that they will be sound in the faith ¹⁴and will pay no attention to Jewish myths or to the commands of those who reject the truth. ¹⁵To the pure, all things are pure, but to those who are

[a] 5 Or ordain   [b] 7 Traditionally bishop

Getting More Daily

READ TITUS 1:1–3

Want to play football the *dumb* way? Here it is: As soon as you get the ball, try to run it the entire length of the field yourself—without running a play or following your blockers. (Yeah. And get carried off in a stretcher.) The *smart* way is to study the game and learn the do's and don'ts. Knowledge of the game will lead to victory. Get out there and *WIN!* In the same way, "the knowledge of the truth ... leads to godliness" (verse 1). Knowing the truth isn't just understanding that Jesus died to save you. That's the beginning. As a man of God, you need to *continue* to learn about the truth. Learn how to live a more godly life, how to get free from the garbage of the world and become more like God. Knowing the truth in God's Word, living by it—and changing as a result—is the greatest, most powerful secret of life and eternity.

Your next reading is on page 1584.

corrupted and do not believe, nothing is pure. In fact, both their minds and consciences are corrupted. 16They claim to know God, but by their actions they deny him. They are detestable, disobedient and unfit for doing anything good.

What Must Be Taught to Various Groups

2 You must teach what is in accord with sound doctrine. 2Teach the older men to be temperate, worthy of respect, self-controlled, and sound in faith, in love and in endurance.

3Likewise, teach the older women to be reverent in the way they live, not to be slanderers or addicted to much wine, but to teach what is good. 4Then they can train the younger women to love their husbands and children, 5to be self-controlled and pure, to be busy at home, to be kind, and to be subject to their husbands, so that no one will malign the word of God.

6Similarly, encourage the young men to be self-controlled. 7In everything set them an example by doing what is good. In your teaching show integrity, seriousness 8and soundness of speech that cannot be condemned, so that those who oppose you may be ashamed because they have nothing bad to say about us.

9Teach slaves to be subject to their masters in everything, to try to please them, not to talk back to them, 10and not to steal from them, but to show that they can be fully trusted, so that in every way they will make the teaching about God our Savior attractive.

11For the grace of God that brings salvation has appeared to all men. 12It teaches us to say "No" to ungodliness and worldly passions, and to live self-controlled, upright and godly lives in this present age, 13while we wait for the blessed hope—the glorious appearing of our great God and Savior, Jesus Christ, 14who gave himself for us to redeem us from all wickedness and to purify for himself a people that are his very own, eager to do what is good.

15These, then, are the things you should teach. Encourage and rebuke with all authority. Do not let anyone despise you.

Doing What Is Good

3 Remind the people to be subject to rulers and authorities, to be obedient, to be ready to do whatever is good, 2to slander no one, to be peaceable and considerate, and to show true humility toward all men.

3At one time we too were foolish, disobedient, deceived and enslaved by all kinds of passions and pleasures. We lived in malice and envy, being hated and hating one another. 4But when the kindness and love of God our Savior appeared, 5he saved us, not because of righteous things we had done, but because of his mercy. He saved us through the washing of rebirth and renewal by the Holy Spirit, 6whom he poured out on us

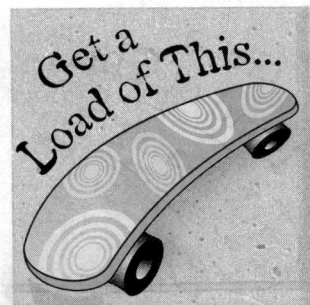

Get a Load of This...

A poet named Epimenides said, "Cretans are always liars, evil brutes, lazy gluttons" (Titus 1:12). Of course, Epimenides was Cretan *himself,* which would mean ... (Seriously though, do your best to avoid being an evil, lazy, lying, brutal glutton.)

Get a Load of This...

When Titus 3:2 says to be "considerate," the original Greek means "yielding." In other words, consider other people and yield to their wishes sometimes. That means stop at the Yield sign. Don't push your weight around and smash through the other cars in the intersection.

generously through Jesus Christ our Savior, ⁷so that, having been justified by his grace, we might become heirs having the hope of eternal life. ⁸This is a trustworthy saying. And I want you to stress these things, so that those who have trusted in God may be careful to devote themselves to doing what is good. These things are excellent and profitable for everyone.

⁹But avoid foolish controversies and genealogies and arguments and quarrels about the law, because these are unprofitable and useless. ¹⁰Warn a divisive person once, and then warn him a second time. After that, have nothing to do with him. ¹¹You may be sure that such a man is warped and sinful; he is self-condemned.

Final Remarks

¹²As soon as I send Artemas or Tychicus to you, do your best to come to me at Nicopolis, because I have decided to winter there. ¹³Do everything you can to help Zenas the lawyer and Apollos on their way and see that they have everything they need. ¹⁴Our people must learn to devote themselves to doing what is good, in order that they may provide for daily necessities and not live unproductive lives.

¹⁵Everyone with me sends you greetings. Greet those who love us in the faith.

Grace be with you all.

PHILEMON

Who wrote this book?
Paul.

Why was this book written?
This book asks Philemon to welcome back a runaway slave named Onesimus, who had become a Christian.

To whom was this book written?
This book is a personal letter sent to a Christian named Philemon.

When was this book written?
Philemon was written about A.D. 60 while Paul was in prison in Rome.

¹Paul, a prisoner of Christ Jesus, and Timothy our brother,

To Philemon our dear friend and fellow worker, ²to Apphia our sister, to Archippus our fellow soldier and to the church that meets in your home:

³Grace to you and peace from God our Father and the Lord Jesus Christ.

Thanksgiving and Prayer

⁴I always thank my God as I remember you in my prayers, ⁵because I hear about your faith in the Lord Jesus and your love for all the saints. ⁶I pray that you may be active in sharing your faith, so that you will have a full understanding of every good thing we have in Christ. ⁷Your love has given me great joy and encouragement, because you, brother, have refreshed the hearts of the saints.

Paul's Plea for Onesimus

⁸Therefore, although in Christ I could be bold and order you to do what you ought to do, ⁹yet I appeal to you on the basis of love. I then, as Paul—an old man and now also a prisoner of Christ Jesus— ¹⁰I appeal to you for my son Onesimus,ᵃ who became my son while I was in chains. ¹¹Formerly he was useless to you, but now he has become useful both to you and to me.

¹²I am sending him—who is my very heart—back to you. ¹³I would have liked to keep him with me so that he could take your place in helping me while I am in chains for the gospel. ¹⁴But I did not want to do anything without your consent, so that any favor you do will be spontaneous and not forced. ¹⁵Perhaps the reason he was separated from you for a little while was that you might have him back for good— ¹⁶no longer as a slave, but better than a slave, as a dear brother. He is very dear to me but even dearer to you, both as a man and as a brother in the Lord.

¹⁷So if you consider me a partner, welcome him as you would welcome me. ¹⁸If

ᵃ 10 Onesimus means useful.

Godly Influence

READ PHILEMON 1–25

Having influence means you can persuade others to do things, either good or bad. If a friend tries to get you to lie for him ("Pleaaaase. Do it because we're *friends*.") and you *do*, that's a *bad* use of influence. The apostle Paul had helped a lot of people, including Philemon, and they looked up to him and respected him. Paul had influence over people—he said something, they tried to do it. When Onesimus, Philemon's slave, stole from him and then ran away, Onesimus could have been sentenced to death. But when Onesimus met Paul, he became a Christian. So Paul went to bat for Onesimus and likely saved his life. Proverbs 22:1 says, "A good name is more desirable than great riches." Paul had a good name and he used that name and that influence to persuade Philemon to forgive Onesimus. Think of people *you* influence—like friends or younger brothers or sisters. Do you influence them in a good way?

Your next reading is on page 1588.

he has done you any wrong or owes you anything, charge it to me. ¹⁹I, Paul, am writing this with my own hand. I will pay it back—not to mention that you owe me your very self. ²⁰I do wish, brother, that I may have some benefit from you in the Lord; refresh my heart in Christ. ²¹Confident of your obedience, I write to you, knowing that you will do even more than I ask.

²²And one thing more: Prepare a guest room for me, because I hope to be restored to you in answer to your prayers.

²³Epaphras, my fellow prisoner in Christ Jesus, sends you greetings. ²⁴And so do Mark, Aristarchus, Demas and Luke, my fellow workers.

²⁵The grace of the Lord Jesus Christ be with your spirit.

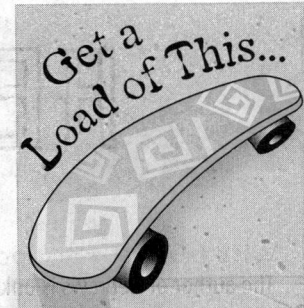

Get a Load of This...

Philemon 6 shows that when you witness, you begin to understand more about Jesus. It is like a sponge that has soaked up something and now needs to be squeezed out. Go ahead and be squeezed and you'll be ready to soak up more of Jesus.

HEBREWS

Who wrote this book?
The author of Hebrews is unknown.

Why was this book written?
Hebrews shows how the Christian faith is superior to the faith of Old Testament times.

For whom was this book written?
This book is a letter sent to Jewish Christians.

When was this book written?
The book of Hebrews was probably written about A.D. 68.

What are some important teachings in this book?

Superior to angels	Hebrews 1:1–24
A real human being	Hebrews 2:5–18
We must believe	Hebrews 3:7–19
Jesus understands	Hebrews 4:14–16
God keeps his promises	Hebrews 6:13–20
The blood of Christ	Hebrews 9:11–28
Heroes of the faith	Hebrews 11:1–40
God disciplines us	Hebrews 12:1–13

The Son Superior to Angels

In the past God spoke to our forefathers through the prophets at many times and in various ways, ²but in these last days he has spoken to us by his Son, whom he appointed heir of all things, and through whom he made the universe. ³The Son is the radiance of God's glory and the exact representation of his being, sustaining all things by his powerful word. After he had provided purification for sins, he sat down at the right hand of the Majesty in heaven. ⁴So he became as much superior to the angels as the name he has inherited is superior to theirs.

⁵For to which of the angels did God ever say,

"You are my Son;
today I have become your Father*a*"*b*?

Or again,

"I will be his Father,
and he will be my Son"*c*?

⁶And again, when God brings his firstborn into the world, he says,

"Let all God's angels worship him."*d*

⁷In speaking of the angels he says,

"He makes his angels winds,
his servants flames of fire."*e*

⁸But about the Son he says,

"Your throne, O God, will last for ever and ever,
and righteousness will be the scepter of your kingdom.
⁹You have loved righteousness and hated wickedness;
therefore God, your God, has set you above your companions
by anointing you with the oil of joy."*f*

¹⁰He also says,

"In the beginning, O Lord, you laid the foundations of the earth,
and the heavens are the work of your hands.
¹¹They will perish, but you remain;
they will all wear out like a garment.
¹²You will roll them up like a robe;
like a garment they will be changed.
But you remain the same,
and your years will never end."*g*

¹³To which of the angels did God ever say,

"Sit at my right hand
until I make your enemies
a footstool for your feet"*h*?

¹⁴Are not all angels ministering spirits sent to serve those who will inherit salvation?

Warning to Pay Attention

We must pay more careful attention, therefore, to what we have heard, so that we do not drift away. ²For if the message spoken by angels was binding, and every violation and disobedience received its just punishment, ³how shall we escape if we ignore such a great salvation? This salvation, which was first announced by the Lord, was confirmed to us by those who heard him. ⁴God also testified to it by signs, wonders and various miracles, and gifts of the Holy Spirit distributed according to his will.

Jesus Made Like His Brothers

⁵It is not to angels that he has subjected the world to come, about which we are speaking. ⁶But there is a place where someone has testified:

"What is man that you are mindful of him,
the son of man that you care for him?
⁷You made him a little*i* lower than the angels;
you crowned him with glory and honor
⁸ and put everything under his feet."*j*

In putting everything under him, God left nothing that is not subject to him. Yet at present we do not see everything subject to him. ⁹But we see Jesus, who was made a little lower than the angels, now crowned with glory and honor because he suffered death, so that by the grace of God he might taste death for everyone.

¹⁰In bringing many sons to glory, it was fitting that God, for whom and through whom everything exists, should make the author of their salvation perfect through suffering. ¹¹Both the one who makes men

a 5 Or *have begotten you*   *b 5* Psalm 2:7
c 5 2 Samuel 7:14; 1 Chron. 17:13   *d 6* Deut. 32:43 (see Dead Sea Scrolls and Septuagint)   *e 7* Psalm 104:4
f 9 Psalm 45:6,7   *g 12* Psalm 102:25–27
h 13 Psalm 110:1   *i 7* Or *him for a little while;* also in verse 9   *j 8* Psalm 8:4–6

holy and those who are made holy are of the same family. So Jesus is not ashamed to call them brothers. [12]He says,

"I will declare your name to my brothers;
in the presence of the congregation I will sing your praises."[a]

[13]And again,

"I will put my trust in him."[b]

And again he says,

"Here am I, and the children God has given me."[c]

[14]Since the children have flesh and blood, he too shared in their humanity so that by his death he might destroy him who holds the power of death—that is, the devil— [15]and free those who all their lives were held in slavery by their fear of death. [16]For surely it is not angels he helps, but Abraham's descendants. [17]For this reason he had to be made like his

brothers in every way, in order that he might become a merciful and faithful high priest in service to God, and that he might make atonement for[d] the sins of the people. [18]Because he himself suffered when he was tempted, he is able to help those who are being tempted.

Jesus Greater Than Moses

3 Therefore, holy brothers, who share in the heavenly calling, fix your thoughts on Jesus, the apostle and high priest whom we confess. [2]He was faithful to the one who appointed him, just as Moses was faithful in all God's house. [3]Jesus has been found worthy of greater honor than Moses, just as the builder of a house has greater honor than the house itself. [4]For every house is built by someone, but God is the builder of everything. [5]Moses was faithful as a

[a] 12 Psalm 22:22   [b] 13 Isaiah 8:17   [c] 13 Isaiah 8:18
[d] 17 Or and that he might turn aside God's wrath, taking away

---

All About Angels

READ HEBREWS 1:14

Do angels really have halos over their heads and big white wings sprouting out of their shoulder blades? No, they *don't*. Only cherubim have wings, and *those* creatures have four different faces and four wings! (see Ezekiel 1:4–14). But even minus the wings, angels *are* powerful supernatural beings. They have blazing faces, eyes like torches and legs and arms gleaming like polished, burning bronze (Daniel 10:5–6; Revelation 10:1). It's a good thing they're on *our* side. Angels fight pitched battles against demons (Daniel 10:13), carry messages to humans (Daniel 10:12,14; Luke 1:11–38; Acts 27:23–24), and are "ministering spirits" who comfort and strengthen God's people (Matthew 4:11; Luke 22:43). They sometimes appear to people in *human* form—minus the blazing eyes and shining skin so people won't know they're an angel (Hebrews 13:2). Oh yeah, one last thing: People do not *become* angels when they die. Angels are a totally separate type of being.

Your next reading is on page 1591.

servant in all God's house, testifying to what would be said in the future. ⁶But Christ is faithful as a son over God's house. And we are his house, if we hold on to our courage and the hope of which we boast.

Warning Against Unbelief

⁷So, as the Holy Spirit says:

"Today, if you hear his voice,
8   do not harden your hearts
as you did in the rebellion,
      during the time of testing in the desert,
⁹where your fathers tested and tried me
      and for forty years saw what I did.
¹⁰That is why I was angry with that generation,
      and I said, 'Their hearts are always going astray,
      and they have not known my ways.'
¹¹So I declared on oath in my anger,
      'They shall never enter my rest.' " ^a

¹²See to it, brothers, that none of you has a sinful, unbelieving heart that turns away from the living God. ¹³But encourage one another daily, as long as it is called Today, so that none of you may be hardened by sin's deceitfulness. ¹⁴We have come to share in Christ if we hold firmly till the end the confidence we had at first. ¹⁵As has just been said:

"Today, if you hear his voice,
      do not harden your hearts
as you did in the rebellion." ^b

¹⁶Who were they who heard and rebelled? Were they not all those Moses led out of Egypt? ¹⁷And with whom was he angry for forty years? Was it not with those who sinned, whose bodies fell in the desert? ¹⁸And to whom did God swear that they would never enter his rest if not to those who disobeyed^c? ¹⁹So we see that they were not able to enter, because of their unbelief.

A Sabbath-Rest for the People of God

Therefore, since the promise of entering his rest still stands, let us be careful that none of you be found to have fallen short of it. ²For we also have had the gospel preached to us, just as they did; but the message they heard was of no value to them, because those who heard did not combine it with faith.^d ³Now we who have believed enter that rest, just as God has said,

"So I declared on oath in my anger,
      'They shall never enter my rest.' " ^e

And yet his work has been finished since the creation of the world. ⁴For somewhere he has spoken about the seventh day in these words: "And on the seventh day

Check out Hebrews 2:14–15. Jesus *destroyed* the devil! How? He smashed the power in Satan's biggest weapon—death. When Jesus brought eternal life to believers, he made it possible for Christians to live forever with him in heaven.

^a 11 Psalm 95:7–11   ^b 15 Psalm 95:7,8   ^c 18 Or *disbelieved*   ^d 2 Many manuscripts *because they did not share in the faith of those who obeyed*
^e 3 Psalm 95:11; also in verse 5

Get a Load of This...

Check out Hebrews 4:12–13. As you read God's Word, God's Word and Spirit work in powerful ways deep inside you, more than you can imagine. Don't think it's just *you* trying to change your life and make you a better person. Be obedient to God's Word, yes, then trust God to do the rest.

God rested from all his work."[a] 5And again in the passage above he says, "They shall never enter my rest."

6It still remains that some will enter that rest, and those who formerly had the gospel preached to them did not go in, because of their disobedience. 7Therefore God again set a certain day, calling it Today, when a long time later he spoke through David, as was said before:

"Today, if you hear his voice,
    do not harden your hearts."[b]

8For if Joshua had given them rest, God would not have spoken later about another day. 9There remains, then, a Sabbath-rest for the people of God; 10for anyone who enters God's rest also rests from his own work, just as God did from his. 11Let us, therefore, make every effort to enter that rest, so that no one will fall by following their example of disobedience.

12For the word of God is living and active. Sharper than any double-edged sword, it penetrates even to dividing soul and spirit, joints and marrow; it judges the thoughts and attitudes of the heart. 13Nothing in all creation is hidden from God's sight. Everything is uncovered and laid bare before the eyes of him to whom we must give account.

Jesus the Great High Priest

14Therefore, since we have a great high priest who has gone through the heavens,[c] Jesus the Son of God, let us hold firmly to the faith we profess. 15For we do not have a high priest who is unable to sympathize with our weaknesses, but we have one who has been tempted in every way, just as we are—yet was without sin. 16Let us then approach the throne of grace with confidence, so that we may receive mercy and find grace to help us in our time of need.

5 Every high priest is selected from among men and is appointed to represent them in matters related to God, to offer gifts and sacrifices for sins. 2He is able to deal gently with those who are ignorant and are going astray, since he himself is subject to weakness. 3This is why he has to offer sacrifices for his own sins, as well as for the sins of the people.

4No one takes this honor upon himself; he must be called by God, just as Aaron was. 5So Christ also did not take upon himself the glory of becoming a high priest. But God said to him,

"You are my Son;
    today I have become your Father.[d]"[e]

6And he says in another place,

"You are a priest forever,
    in the order of Melchizedek."[f]

[a]4 Gen. 2:2   [b]7 Psalm 95:7,8   [c]14 Or gone into heaven   [d]5 Or have begotten you   [e]5 Psalm 2:7   [f]6 Psalm 110:4

7During the days of Jesus' life on earth, he offered up prayers and petitions with loud cries and tears to the one who could save him from death, and he was heard because of his reverent submission. 8Although he was a son, he learned obedience from what he suffered 9and, once made perfect, he became the source of eternal salvation for all who obey him 10and was designated by God to be high priest in the order of Melchizedek.

Warning Against Falling Away

11We have much to say about this, but it is hard to explain because you are slow to learn. 12In fact, though by this time you ought to be teachers, you need someone to teach you the elementary truths of God's word all over again. You need milk, not solid food! 13Anyone who lives on milk, being still an infant, is not acquainted with the teaching about righteousness. 14But solid food is for the mature, who by constant use have trained themselves to distinguish good from evil.

6 Therefore let us leave the elementary teachings about Christ and go on to maturity, not laying again the foundation of repentance from acts that lead to death,a and of faith in God, 2instruction about baptisms, the laying on of hands, the resurrection of the dead, and eternal judgment. 3And God permitting, we will do so.

4It is impossible for those who have once been enlightened, who have tasted the heavenly gift, who have shared in the Holy Spirit, 5who have tasted the goodness of the word of God and the powers of the coming age, 6if they fall away, to be brought back to repentance, becauseb to their loss they are crucifying the Son of God all over again and subjecting him to public disgrace.

7Land that drinks in the rain often falling on it and that produces a crop useful to those for whom it is farmed receives the blessing of God. 8But land that produces thorns and thistles is worthless and

a 1 Or from useless rituals   b 6 Or repentance while

Been There, Done That

READ HEBREWS 4:14–16

Jesus wore long robes, lived 2,000 years ago, *always* told the truth and *always* did the right thing. He was *perfect!* Hmmm ... so can he possibly relate to *you*? You bet he can! He was once a boy who was "tempted in every way, just as [you] are" (verse 15). Jesus grew up as a regular kid with all the temptations to do wrong that you're faced with—and he had to obey his parents, learn to look after himself, do his chores and study and learn. As the Son of God, he remembers *every* eensy, tiny detail of what he experienced at your age. So he can relate to everything you face and can "sympathize with [your] weaknesses" (verse 15). That means you can go to him and talk to him without any hesitation, because you *know* he will understand and will have mercy on you and help you.

Your next reading is on page 1592.

is in danger of being cursed. In the end it will be burned.

⁹Even though we speak like this, dear friends, we are confident of better things in your case—things that accompany salvation. ¹⁰God is not unjust; he will not forget your work and the love you have shown him as you have helped his people and continue to help them. ¹¹We want each of you to show this same diligence to the very end, in order to make your hope sure. ¹²We do not want you to become lazy, but to imitate those who through faith and patience inherit what has been promised.

The Certainty of God's Promise

¹³When God made his promise to Abraham, since there was no one greater for him to swear by, he swore by himself, ¹⁴saying, "I will surely bless you and give you many descendants."ᵃ ¹⁵And so after waiting patiently, Abraham received what was promised.

¹⁶Men swear by someone greater than themselves, and the oath confirms what is said and puts an end to all argument. ¹⁷Because God wanted to make the unchanging nature of his purpose very clear to the heirs of what was promised, he confirmed it with an oath. ¹⁸God did this so that, by two unchangeable things in which it is impossible for God to lie, we who have fled to take hold of the hope offered to us may be greatly encouraged. ¹⁹We have this hope as an anchor for the soul, firm and secure. It enters the inner sanctuary behind the curtain, ²⁰where Jesus, who went before us, has entered on our behalf. He has become a high priest forever, in the order of Melchizedek.

Melchizedek the Priest

7 This Melchizedek was king of Salem and priest of God Most High. He met Abraham returning from the defeat of the kings and blessed him, ²and Abraham gave him a tenth of everything. First, his name means "king of righteousness"; then also, "king of Salem" means "king of peace." ³Without father or mother, without genealogy, without beginning of days or end of life, like the Son of God he remains a priest forever.

⁴Just think how great he was: Even the patriarch Abraham gave him a tenth of the plunder! ⁵Now the law requires the descendants of Levi who become priests to

ᵃ 14 Gen. 22:17

From Basics to Advanced

READ HEBREWS 5:11—6:3

Imagine a kid who owned the absolute best video game in existence—it had 100 playing levels, each one more challenging and fun than the next. But this kid had zero interest in even going to level two. For him, playing around in level one was enough. Sound like a cool kid? Not. Well, becoming a Christian and just learning a little bit about the basic Bible stories is not enough either. Once you learn the basics, you'll want to grow and learn more. Just like you grow physically and mature mentally as you grow up into a strong man, you also need to grow and get more mature in your faith.

Your next reading is on page 1597.

collect a tenth from the people—that is, their brothers—even though their brothers are descended from Abraham. ⁶This man, however, did not trace his descent from Levi, yet he collected a tenth from Abraham and blessed him who had the promises. ⁷And without doubt the lesser person is blessed by the greater. ⁸In the one case, the tenth is collected by men who die; but in the other case, by him who is declared to be living. ⁹One might even say that Levi, who collects the tenth, paid the tenth through Abraham, ¹⁰because when Melchizedek met Abraham, Levi was still in the body of his ancestor.

Jesus Like Melchizedek

¹¹If perfection could have been attained through the Levitical priesthood (for on the basis of it the law was given to the people), why was there still need for another priest to come—one in the order of Melchizedek, not in the order of Aaron? ¹²For when there is a change of the priesthood, there must also be a change of the law. ¹³He of whom these things are said belonged to a different tribe, and no one from that tribe has ever served at the altar. ¹⁴For it is clear that our Lord descended from Judah, and in regard to that tribe Moses said nothing about priests. ¹⁵And what we have said is even more clear if another priest like Melchizedek appears, ¹⁶one who has become a priest not on the basis of a regulation as to his ancestry but on the basis of the power of an indestructible life. ¹⁷For it is declared:

"You are a priest forever,
  in the order of Melchizedek." ᵃ

¹⁸The former regulation is set aside because it was weak and useless ¹⁹(for the law made nothing perfect), and a better hope is introduced, by which we draw near to God.

²⁰And it was not without an oath! Others became priests without any oath, ²¹but he became a priest with an oath when God said to him:

"The Lord has sworn
  and will not change his mind:
  'You are a priest forever.' " ᵃ

²²Because of this oath, Jesus has become the guarantee of a better covenant.

²³Now there have been many of those priests, since death prevented them from continuing in office; ²⁴but because Jesus lives forever, he has a permanent priesthood. ²⁵Therefore he is able to save completely ᵇ those who come to God through him, because he always lives to intercede for them.

²⁶Such a high priest meets our need—one who is holy, blameless, pure, set apart from sinners, exalted above the heavens. ²⁷Unlike the other high priests, he does not need to offer sacrifices day after day, first for his own sins, and then for the sins of the people. He sacrificed for their

Get a Load of This...

We have "an anchor for the soul, firm and secure" that "enters the inner sanctuary" (Hebrews 6:19). Imagine a big boat chain tied to your belt reaching all the way up to heaven and anchored to the throne of God!

ᵃ 17 Psalm 110:4   ᵇ 25 Or forever

sins once for all when he offered himself. ²⁸For the law appoints as high priests men who are weak; but the oath, which came after the law, appointed the Son, who has been made perfect forever.

The High Priest of a New Covenant

The point of what we are saying is this: We do have such a high priest, who sat down at the right hand of the throne of the Majesty in heaven, ²and who serves in the sanctuary, the true tabernacle set up by the Lord, not by man.

³Every high priest is appointed to offer both gifts and sacrifices, and so it was necessary for this one also to have something to offer. ⁴If he were on earth, he would not be a priest, for there are already men who offer the gifts prescribed by the law. ⁵They serve at a sanctuary that is a copy and shadow of what is in heaven. This is why Moses was warned when he was about to build the tabernacle: "See to it that you make everything according to the pattern shown you on the mountain."ᵃ ⁶But the ministry Jesus has received is as superior to theirs as the covenant of which he is mediator is superior to the old one, and it is founded on better promises.

⁷For if there had been nothing wrong with that first covenant, no place would have been sought for another. ⁸But God found fault with the people and said ᵇ:

"The time is coming, declares the Lord,
   when I will make a new covenant
with the house of Israel
   and with the house of Judah.
⁹It will not be like the covenant
   I made with their forefathers
when I took them by the hand
   to lead them out of Egypt,
because they did not remain faithful to
   my covenant,
   and I turned away from them,
         declares the Lord.
¹⁰This is the covenant I will make with
   the house of Israel
after that time, declares the Lord.
I will put my laws in their minds
   and write them on their hearts.
I will be their God,
   and they will be my people.
¹¹No longer will a man teach his neighbor,
   or a man his brother, saying, 'Know
      the Lord,'
because they will all know me,

from the least of them to the
   greatest.
¹²For I will forgive their wickedness
   and will remember their sins no
     more."ᶜ

¹³By calling this covenant "new," he has made the first one obsolete; and what is obsolete and aging will soon disappear.

Worship in the Earthly Tabernacle

Now the first covenant had regulations for worship and also an earthly sanctuary. ²A tabernacle was set up. In its first room were the lampstand, the table and the consecrated bread; this was called the Holy Place. ³Behind the second curtain was a room called the Most Holy Place, ⁴which had the golden altar of incense and the gold-covered ark of the covenant. This ark contained the gold jar of manna, Aaron's staff that had budded, and the stone tablets of the covenant. ⁵Above the ark were the cherubim of the Glory, overshadowing the atonement cover.ᵈ But we cannot discuss these things in detail now.

⁶When everything had been arranged like this, the priests entered regularly into the outer room to carry on their ministry. ⁷But only the high priest entered the inner room, and that only once a year, and never without blood, which he offered for himself and for the sins the people had committed in ignorance. ⁸The Holy Spirit was showing by this that the way into the Most Holy Place had not yet been disclosed as long as the first tabernacle was still standing. ⁹This is an illustration for the present time, indicating that the gifts and sacrifices being offered were not able to clear the conscience of the worshiper. ¹⁰They are only a matter of food and drink and various ceremonial washings—external regulations applying until the time of the new order.

The Blood of Christ

¹¹When Christ came as high priest of the good things that are already here,ᵉ he went through the greater and more perfect tabernacle that is not man-made, that is to say, not a part of this creation. ¹²He did not

---

ᵃ 5 Exodus 25:40   ᵇ 8 Some manuscripts may be translated *fault and said to the people.*   ᶜ 12 Jer. 31:31–34   ᵈ 5 Traditionally *the mercy seat*   ᵉ 11 Some early manuscripts *are to come* enter by means of the blood of goats and calves; but he entered the Most Holy Place once for all by his own blood, having obtained eternal redemption. ¹³The blood of goats and bulls and the ashes of a heifer sprinkled on those who are ceremonially unclean sanctify them so that they are outwardly clean. ¹⁴How much more, then, will the blood of Christ, who through the eternal Spirit offered himself unblemished to God, cleanse our consciences from acts that lead to death,ᵃ so that we may serve the living God!

¹⁵For this reason Christ is the mediator of a new covenant, that those who are called may receive the promised eternal inheritance—now that he has died as a ransom to set them free from the sins committed under the first covenant.

¹⁶In the case of a will,ᵇ it is necessary to prove the death of the one who made it, ¹⁷because a will is in force only when somebody has died; it never takes effect while the one who made it is living. ¹⁸This is why even the first covenant was not put into effect without blood. ¹⁹When Moses had proclaimed every commandment of the law to all the people, he took the blood of calves, together with water, scarlet wool and branches of hyssop, and sprinkled the scroll and all the people. ²⁰He said, "This is the blood of the covenant, which God has commanded you to keep."ᶜ ²¹In the same way, he sprinkled with the blood both the tabernacle and everything used in its ceremonies. ²²In fact, the law requires that nearly everything be cleansed with blood, and without the shedding of blood there is no forgiveness.

²³It was necessary, then, for the copies of the heavenly things to be purified with these sacrifices, but the heavenly things themselves with better sacrifices than these. ²⁴For Christ did not enter a man-made sanctuary that was only a copy of the true one; he entered heaven itself, now to appear for us in God's presence. ²⁵Nor did he enter heaven to offer himself again and again, the way the high priest enters the Most Holy Place every year with blood that is not his own. ²⁶Then Christ would have had to suffer many times since the creation of the world. But now he has appeared once for all at the end of the ages to do away with sin by the sacrifice of himself. ²⁷Just as man is destined to die once, and after that to face judgment, ²⁸so Christ was sacrificed once to take away the sins of many people; and he will appear a second time, not to bear sin, but to bring salvation to those who are waiting for him.

Christ's Sacrifice Once for All

10 The law is only a shadow of the good things that are coming—not the realities themselves. For this reason it can never, by the same sacrifices repeated endlessly year after year, make perfect those who draw near to worship. ²If it could,

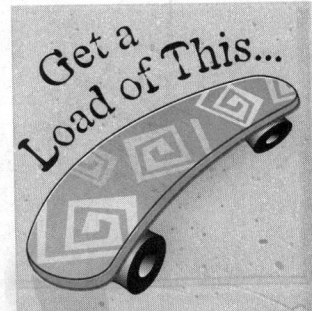

Get a Load of This...

Check out Hebrews 9:12–14. Up until Jesus' day, the Jewish people had been sacrificing all kinds of animals—oxen, goats, sheep and doves—to temporarily pay the price for their sins. Jesus was the perfect sacrifice. He came along and gave his own life and blood to *permanently* save us from sin.

ᵃ 14 Or *from useless rituals*   ᵇ 16 Same Greek word as *covenant*; also in verse 17   ᶜ 20 Exodus 24:8

Get a Load of This...

Check out Hebrews 9:27. Some people believe in reincarnation. They think, "Maybe I was a prince in a past life." The *Bible* says people die *once*, then go into eternity and are judged by God for how they lived. They don't come back. Not even as a bug.

would they not have stopped being offered? For the worshipers would have been cleansed once for all, and would no longer have felt guilty for their sins. ³But those sacrifices are an annual reminder of sins, ⁴because it is impossible for the blood of bulls and goats to take away sins.

⁵Therefore, when Christ came into the world, he said:

"Sacrifice and offering you did not desire,
　　but a body you prepared for me;
⁶with burnt offerings and sin offerings
　　you were not pleased.
⁷Then I said, 'Here I am—it is written about me in the
　　scroll—
　　I have come to do your will, O God.' "*a*

⁸First he said, "Sacrifices and offerings, burnt offerings and sin offerings you did not desire, nor were you pleased with them" (although the law required them to be made). ⁹Then he said, "Here I am, I have come to do your will." He sets aside the first to establish the second. ¹⁰And by that will, we have been made holy through the sacrifice of the body of Jesus Christ once for all.

¹¹Day after day every priest stands and performs his religious duties; again and again he offers the same sacrifices, which can never take away sins. ¹²But when this priest had offered for all time one sacrifice for sins, he sat down at the right hand of God. ¹³Since that time he waits for his enemies to be made his footstool, ¹⁴because by one sacrifice he has made perfect forever those who are being made holy.

¹⁵The Holy Spirit also testifies to us about this. First he says:

¹⁶"This is the covenant I will make with them
　　after that time, says the Lord.
I will put my laws in their hearts,
　　and I will write them on their minds."*b*

¹⁷Then he adds:

"Their sins and lawless acts
　　I will remember no more."*c*

¹⁸And where these have been forgiven, there is no longer any sacrifice for sin.

A Call to Persevere

¹⁹Therefore, brothers, since we have confidence to enter the Most Holy Place by the blood of Jesus, ²⁰by a new and living way opened for us through the curtain, that is, his body, ²¹and since we have a great priest over the house of God, ²²let us draw near to God with a sincere heart in full assurance of faith, having our hearts sprinkled to cleanse us from a guilty conscience and having our bodies washed with pure water. ²³Let us hold unswervingly to the hope we profess, for he who promised is faithful. ²⁴And let us consider how we may spur one

a 7 Psalm 40:6–8 (see Septuagint)　　*b 16* Jer. 31:33　　*c 17* Jer. 31:34

another on toward love and good deeds. 25Let us not give up meeting together, as some are in the habit of doing, but let us encourage one another—and all the more as you see the Day approaching.

26If we deliberately keep on sinning after we have received the knowledge of the truth, no sacrifice for sins is left, 27but only a fearful expectation of judgment and of raging fire that will consume the enemies of God. 28Anyone who rejected the law of Moses died without mercy on the testimony of two or three witnesses. 29How much more severely do you think a man deserves to be punished who has trampled the Son of God under foot, who has treated as an unholy thing the blood of the covenant that sanctified him, and who has insulted the Spirit of grace? 30For we know him who said, "It is mine to avenge; I will repay,"a and again, "The Lord will judge his people."b 31It is a dreadful thing to fall into the hands of the living God.

32Remember those earlier days after you had received the light, when you stood your ground in a great contest in the face of suffering. 33Sometimes you were publicly exposed to insult and persecution; at other times you stood side by side with those who were so treated. 34You sympathized with those in prison and joyfully accepted the confiscation of your property, because you knew that you yourselves had better and lasting possessions.

35So do not throw away your confidence; it will be richly rewarded. 36You need to persevere so that when you have done the will of God, you will receive what he has promised. 37For in just a very little while,

"He who is coming will come and will not delay.

38   But my righteous onec will live by faith.
  And if he shrinks back,
     I will not be pleased with him."d

39But we are not of those who shrink back and are destroyed, but of those who believe and are saved.

a 30 Deut. 32:35   b 30 Deut. 32:36; Psalm 135:14
c 38 One early manuscript But the righteous   d 38 Hab. 2:3,4

Why Church?

READ HEBREWS 10:23–25

If you were a Boy Scout, it would be kind of dumb if you never went to a meeting, never went to camp and never learned to start a fire, tie a knot or pitch a tent. It's the same if you're a Christian but don't go to church. There are *good* reasons for going. You need to (1) meet with other Christians and encourage each other, (2) learn life skills from the pastor and your teachers and (3) work together with other Christians to preach the gospel. Church was *God's* idea, and ever since the book of Acts, Christians have been meeting together regularly, once a week. We're *still* supposed to meet together. Who you hang out with is who you become, so if you want to become a smarter, stronger, deeper, cooler man of God, put down roots in a local church and go there on a regular basis.

Your next reading is on page 1601.

By Faith

11 Now faith is being sure of what we hope for and certain of what we do not see. ²This is what the ancients were commended for.

³By faith we understand that the universe was formed at God's command, so that what is seen was not made out of what was visible.

⁴By faith Abel offered God a better sacrifice than Cain did. By faith he was commended as a righteous man, when God spoke well of his offerings. And by faith he still speaks, even though he is dead.

⁵By faith Enoch was taken from this life, so that he did not experience death; he could not be found, because God had taken him away. For before he was taken, he was commended as one who pleased God. ⁶And without faith it is impossible to please God, because anyone who comes to him must believe that he exists and that he rewards those who earnestly seek him.

⁷By faith Noah, when warned about things not yet seen, in holy fear built an ark to save his family. By his faith he condemned the world and became heir of the righteousness that comes by faith.

⁸By faith Abraham, when called to go to a place he would later receive as his inheritance, obeyed and went, even though he did not know where he was going. ⁹By faith he made his home in the promised land like a stranger in a foreign country; he lived in tents, as did Isaac and Jacob, who were heirs with him of the same promise. ¹⁰For he was looking forward to the city with foundations, whose architect and builder is God.

¹¹By faith Abraham, even though he was past age—and Sarah herself was barren—was enabled to become a father because he*a* considered him faithful who had made the promise. ¹²And so from

a 11 Or By faith even Sarah, who was past age, was enabled to bear children because she

Make It Stick

READ HEBREWS 11

This passage is the Faith Hall of Fame. It doesn't take faith to see a fact, but it *does* take faith to believe God's promises. Faith in God's power causes us to live for him. What would you like to be famous for, that would get you added to the Faith Hall of Fame? Write it on a sticky note.

this one man, and he as good as dead, came descendants as numerous as the stars in the sky and as countless as the sand on the seashore.

13All these people were still living by faith when they died. They did not receive the things promised; they only saw them and welcomed them from a distance. And they admitted that they were aliens and strangers on earth. 14People who say such things show that they are looking for a country of their own. 15If they had been thinking of the country they had left, they would have had opportunity to return. 16Instead, they were longing for a better country—a heavenly one. Therefore God is not ashamed to be called their God, for he has prepared a city for them.

17By faith Abraham, when God tested him, offered Isaac as a sacrifice. He who had received the promises was about to sacrifice his one and only son, 18even though God had said to him, "It is through Isaac that your offspring*a* will be reckoned."*b* 19Abraham reasoned that God could raise the dead, and figuratively speaking, he did receive Isaac back from death.

20By faith Isaac blessed Jacob and Esau in regard to their future.

21By faith Jacob, when he was dying, blessed each of Joseph's sons, and worshiped as he leaned on the top of his staff.

22By faith Joseph, when his end was near, spoke about the exodus of the Israelites from Egypt and gave instructions about his bones.

23By faith Moses' parents hid him for three months after he was born, because they saw he was no ordinary child, and they were not afraid of the king's edict.

24By faith Moses, when he had grown up, refused to be known as the son of Pharaoh's daughter. 25He chose to be mistreated along with the people of God rather than to enjoy the pleasures of sin for a short time. 26He regarded disgrace for the sake of Christ as of greater value than the treasures of Egypt, because he was looking ahead to his reward. 27By faith he left Egypt, not fearing the king's anger; he persevered because he saw him who is invisible. 28By faith he kept the Passover and the sprinkling of blood, so that the destroyer of the firstborn would not touch the firstborn of Israel.

29By faith the people passed through the Red Sea*c* as on dry land; but when the Egyptians tried to do so, they were drowned.

30By faith the walls of Jericho fell, after the people had marched around them for seven days.

31By faith the prostitute Rahab, because she welcomed the spies, was not killed with those who were disobedient.*d*

32And what more shall I say? I do not have time to tell about Gideon, Barak, Samson, Jephthah, David, Samuel and the prophets, 33who through faith conquered kingdoms, administered justice, and gained what was promised; who shut the mouths of lions, 34quenched the fury of the flames, and escaped the edge of the sword; whose weakness was turned to strength; and who became powerful in battle and routed foreign armies. 35Women received back their dead, raised to life again. Others were tortured and refused to be released, so that they might gain a better resurrection. 36Some faced jeers and flogging, while still others were chained and put in prison. 37They were stoned*e*; they were sawed in two; they were put to death by the sword. They went about in sheepskins and goatskins, destitute, persecuted and mistreated— 38the world was not worthy of them. They wandered in deserts and mountains, and in caves and holes in the ground.

39These were all commended for their faith, yet none of them received what had been promised. 40God had planned something better for us so that only together with us would they be made perfect.

God Disciplines His Sons

12 Therefore, since we are surrounded by such a great cloud of witnesses, let us throw off everything that hinders and the sin that so easily entangles, and let us run with perseverance the race marked out for us. 2Let us fix our eyes on Jesus, the author and perfecter of our faith, who for the joy set before him endured the cross, scorning its shame, and sat down at the right hand of the throne of God. 3Consider him who endured such opposition from sinful men, so that you will not grow weary and lose heart.

4In your struggle against sin, you have

a 18 Greek *seed*   *b 18* Gen. 21:12   *c 29* That is, Sea of Reeds   *d 31* Or *unbelieving*   *e 37* Some early manuscripts *stoned; they were put to the test;*

Gross!

"They were sawed in two" (Hebrews 11:37). This was no stage trick! This was the real thing! According to tradition, Isaiah was the man of God who was martyred by being sawed in half—orders of wicked king Manasseh.

not yet resisted to the point of shedding your blood. [5]And you have forgotten that word of encouragement that addresses you as sons:

> "My son, do not make light of the Lord's discipline,
>   and do not lose heart when he rebukes you,
> [6]because the Lord disciplines those he loves,
>   and he punishes everyone he accepts as a son." [a]

[7]Endure hardship as discipline; God is treating you as sons. For what son is not disciplined by his father? [8]If you are not disciplined (and everyone undergoes discipline), then you are illegitimate children and not true sons. [9]Moreover, we have all had human fathers who disciplined us and we respected them for it. How much more should we submit to the Father of our spirits and live! [10]Our fathers disciplined us for a little while as they thought best; but God disciplines us for our good, that we may share in his holiness. [11]No discipline seems pleasant at the time, but painful. Later on, however, it produces a harvest of righteousness and peace for those who have been trained by it.

[12]Therefore, strengthen your feeble arms and weak knees. [13]"Make level paths for your feet," [b] so that the lame may not be disabled, but rather healed.

Warning Against Refusing God

[14]Make every effort to live in peace with all men and to be holy; without holiness no one will see the Lord. [15]See to it that no one misses the grace of God and that no bitter root grows up to cause trouble and defile many. [16]See that no one is sexually immoral, or is godless like Esau, who for a single meal sold his inheritance rights as the oldest son. [17]Afterward, as you know, when he wanted to inherit this blessing, he was rejected. He could bring about no change of mind, though he sought the blessing with tears.

[18]You have not come to a mountain that can be touched and that is burning with fire; to darkness, gloom and storm; [19]to a trumpet blast or to such a voice speaking words that those who heard it begged that no further word be spoken to them, [20]because they could not bear what was commanded: "If even an animal touches the mountain, it must be stoned." [c] [21]The sight was so terrifying that Moses said, "I am trembling with fear." [d]

[22]But you have come to Mount Zion, to the heavenly Jerusalem, the city of the living God. You have come to thousands upon thousands of angels in joyful assembly, [23]to the church of the firstborn, whose names are written in heaven. You have come to God, the judge of all men, to the spirits of righteous men made perfect, [24]to Jesus the mediator of a new covenant, and to the sprinkled blood that speaks a better word than the blood of Abel.

[25]See to it that you do not refuse him who speaks. If

[a]6 Prov. 3:11,12　[b]13 Prov. 4:26　[c]20 Exodus 19:12,13　[d]21 Deut. 9:19

they did not escape when they refused him who warned them on earth, how much less will we, if we turn away from him who warns us from heaven? 26At that time his voice shook the earth, but now he has promised, "Once more I will shake not only the earth but also the heavens."*a* 27The words "once more" indicate the removing of what can be shaken—that is, created things—so that what cannot be shaken may remain.

28Therefore, since we are receiving a kingdom that cannot be shaken, let us be thankful, and so worship God acceptably with reverence and awe, 29for our "God is a consuming fire."*b*

Concluding Exhortations

13 Keep on loving each other as brothers. 2Do not forget to entertain strangers, for by so doing some people have entertained angels without knowing it. 3Remember those in prison as if you were their fellow prisoners, and those who are mistreated as if you yourselves were suffering.

4Marriage should be honored by all, and the marriage bed kept pure, for God will judge the adulterer and all the sexually immoral. 5Keep your lives free from the love of money and be content with what you have, because God has said,

"Never will I leave you;
    never will I forsake you."*c*

6So we say with confidence,

"The Lord is my helper; I will not be
    afraid.
What can man do to me?"*d*

7Remember your leaders, who spoke the word of God to you. Consider the outcome of their way of life and imitate their faith. 8Jesus Christ is the same yesterday and today and forever.

9Do not be carried away by all kinds of strange teachings. It is good for our hearts to be strengthened by grace, not by ceremonial foods, which are of no value to those who eat them. 10We have an altar

a 26 Haggai 2:6   *b 29* Deut. 4:24   *c 5* Deut. 31:6
d 6 Psalm 118:6,7

Discipline Is Training

READ HEBREWS 12:4–13

Your parents' job is to raise you and help you to learn and grow, so that by the time you leave their home and are out on your own, you're ready for life. That's why they teach you how to take care of yourself, know right from wrong, clean up your messes, handle money and eat right. They discipline and train you, not to make you miserable, but because they *care* about you. So don't sulk and say, "*Whatever* ..." if they remind you about something. In the same way, God also trains you and helps you grow. So "do not make light of the Lord's discipline ... because the Lord disciplines those he loves" (verses 5–6). The Greek word for "discipline" also can be translated as "training." It's not always comfortable to be trained in new responsibilities, but if you accept the process and don't whine about it, you'll become a true man of God.

Your next reading is on page 1605.

from which those who minister at the tabernacle have no right to eat.

¹¹The high priest carries the blood of animals into the Most Holy Place as a sin offering, but the bodies are burned outside the camp. ¹²And so Jesus also suffered outside the city gate to make the people holy through his own blood. ¹³Let us, then, go to him outside the camp, bearing the disgrace he bore. ¹⁴For here we do not have an enduring city, but we are looking for the city that is to come.

¹⁵Through Jesus, therefore, let us continually offer to God a sacrifice of praise— the fruit of lips that confess his name. ¹⁶And do not forget to do good and to share with others, for with such sacrifices God is pleased.

¹⁷Obey your leaders and submit to their authority. They keep watch over you as men who must give an account. Obey them so that their work will be a joy, not a burden, for that would be of no advantage to you.

¹⁸Pray for us. We are sure that we have a clear conscience and desire to live honorably in every way. ¹⁹I particularly urge you to pray so that I may be restored to you soon.

²⁰May the God of peace, who through the blood of the eternal covenant brought back from the dead our Lord Jesus, that great Shepherd of the sheep, ²¹equip you with everything good for doing his will, and may he work in us what is pleasing to him, through Jesus Christ, to whom be glory for ever and ever. Amen.

²²Brothers, I urge you to bear with my word of exhortation, for I have written you only a short letter.

²³I want you to know that our brother Timothy has been released. If he arrives soon, I will come with him to see you.

²⁴Greet all your leaders and all God's people. Those from Italy send you their greetings.

²⁵Grace be with you all.

Make It Stick

READ HEBREWS 13:7, 17

"Remember your leaders, who spoke the Word of God to you ... and submit to their authority" (Hebrews 13:7, 17). Church leaders can see what you need, and God uses them to tell you stuff you need to hear. On a sticky note, write down the names of pastors and church teachers whom you know and respect.

JAMES

Who wrote this book?

James, the brother of Jesus, wrote this book.

Why was this book written?

James shows Christians how to practice their faith in Jesus.

For whom was this book written?

This book was written to Christians everywhere.

When was this book written?

James was probably written about A.D. 48.

What are some important teachings in this book?

God does not tempt us	James 1:12–18
We are to do what God says	James 1:22–25
Don't show favoritism	James 2:1–13
Be careful what you say	James 3:1–12
Don't criticize others	James 4:11–12
Be patient when you suffer	James 5:7–11
Pray when you are sick	James 5:13–16

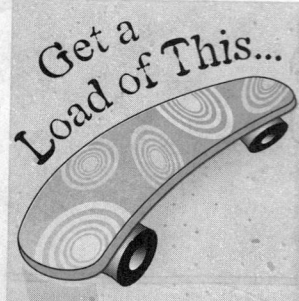

James, a servant of God and of the Lord Jesus Christ,

To the twelve tribes scattered among the nations:

Greetings.

Trials and Temptations

²Consider it pure joy, my brothers, whenever you face trials of many kinds, ³because you know that the testing of your faith develops perseverance. ⁴Perseverance must finish its work so that you may be mature and complete, not lacking anything. ⁵If any of you lacks wisdom, he should ask God, who gives generously to all without finding fault, and it will be given to him. ⁶But when he asks, he must believe and not doubt, because he who doubts is like a wave of the sea, blown and tossed by the wind. ⁷That man should not think he will receive anything from the Lord; ⁸he is a double-minded man, unstable in all he does.

⁹The brother in humble circumstances ought to take pride in his high position. ¹⁰But the one who is rich should take pride in his low position, because he will pass away like a wild flower. ¹¹For the sun rises with scorching heat and withers the plant; its blossom falls and its beauty is destroyed. In the same way, the rich man will fade away even while he goes about his business.

¹²Blessed is the man who perseveres under trial, because when he has stood the test, he will receive the crown of life that God has promised to those who love him.

¹³When tempted, no one should say, "God is tempting me." For God cannot be tempted by evil, nor does he tempt anyone; ¹⁴but each one is tempted when, by his own evil desire, he is dragged away and enticed. ¹⁵Then, after desire has conceived, it gives birth to sin; and sin, when it is full-grown, gives birth to death.

¹⁶Don't be deceived, my dear brothers. ¹⁷Every good and perfect gift is from above, coming down from the Father of the heavenly lights, who does not change like shifting shadows. ¹⁸He chose to give us birth through the word of truth, that we might be a kind of firstfruits of all he created.

Listening and Doing

¹⁹My dear brothers, take note of this: Everyone should be quick to listen, slow to speak and slow to become angry, ²⁰for man's anger does not bring about the righteous life that God desires. ²¹Therefore, get rid of all moral filth and the evil that is so prevalent and humbly accept the word planted in you, which can save you.

²²Do not merely listen to the word, and so deceive yourselves. Do what it says. ²³Anyone who listens to the word but does not do what it says is like a man who looks at his face in a mirror ²⁴and, after looking at him-

Knowing the Enemy

READ JAMES 1:13–15

In an NFL training room, you'd see players studying their own team's moves but also watching films of the *opposing* team. A winning tactic is knowing your opponent. If you know what the devil is up to, you can avoid temptation and sin. Call out to God to block him and take him down.

TRICK NUMBER 1: When you're tempted to sin, does *God* sometimes say it's OK? Does he shrug and say, "Ahhhh, why not?" *Warning!* God does *not* lead you into sin or ever approve of it. That's the devil's voice. "When tempted, no one should say, 'God is tempting me.'" (verse 13).

TRICK NUMBER 2: If Satan knows you have a weakness in a certain area, he'll keep dangling that thing in front of you to tempt you. You may think, "I *can't* do that, but it sure would be *good* if I could." *Warning!* Sin is never good. "Each one is tempted when, by his own evil desire, he is dragged away and enticed" (verse 14).

TRICK NUMBER 3: "No temptation has seized you except what is common to man," but "God is faithful; he will . . . provide a way out" (1 Corinthians 10:13). Once you *start* to give in, the devil will tell you: "It's too late. You're going to do it. Might as well get it over with." *Warning!* Don't tell yourself, "I *can't* stop." You *can.*

TRICK NUMBER 4: Another lie of the devil is, "Go ahead. It's not hurting anyone *else*, right?" Or he'll tell you, "Nothing will happen if you do this." *Warning!* "A man reaps what he sows" (Galatians 6:7). Sin hurts someone every single time.

TRICK NUMBER 5: The devil tries to draw you closer to the temptation. "It won't hurt if you're just *around* it." You might tell yourself, "I'm strong enough." *Warning!* "Do not set foot on their paths" (Proverbs 1:15). Don't even start down that road.

TRICK NUMBER 6: First Satan tempts you to sin, then he lays a huge guilt trip on you if you sin (see 1 John 1:9). (Wrong. God is still there. He's waiting to pick you up again.) "Submit yourselves, then, to God. Resist the devil, and he will *flee* from you" (James 4:7).

Your next reading is on page 1606.

self, goes away and immediately forgets what he looks like. 25But the man who looks intently into the perfect law that gives freedom, and continues to do this, not forgetting what he has heard, but doing it—he will be blessed in what he does.

26If anyone considers himself religious and yet does not keep a tight rein on his tongue, he deceives himself and his religion is worthless. 27Religion that God our Father accepts as pure and faultless is this: to look after orphans and widows in their distress and to keep oneself from being polluted by the world.

Favoritism Forbidden

My brothers, as believers in our glorious Lord Jesus Christ, don't show favoritism. 2Suppose a man comes into your meeting wearing a gold ring and fine clothes, and a poor man in shabby clothes also comes in. 3If you show special attention to the man wearing fine clothes and say, "Here's a good seat for you," but say to the poor man, "You stand there" or "Sit on the floor by my feet," 4have you not discriminated among yourselves and become judges with evil thoughts?

5Listen, my dear brothers: Has not God chosen those who are poor in the eyes of the world to be rich in faith and to inherit the kingdom he promised those who love him? 6But you have insulted the poor. Is it not the rich who are exploiting you? Are they not the ones who are dragging you into court? 7Are they not the ones who are slandering the noble name of him to whom you belong?

8If you really keep the royal law found in Scripture, "Love your neighbor as yourself,"a you are doing right. 9But if you show favoritism, you sin and are convicted by the law as lawbreakers. 10For whoever keeps the whole law and yet stumbles at just one point is guilty of breaking all of it. 11For he who said, "Do not commit adultery,"b also said, "Do not murder."c If you

a 8 Lev. 19:18   b 11 Exodus 20:14; Deut. 5:18
c 11 Exodus 20:13; Deut. 5:17

Men and Emotions

READ JAMES 1:19–20

Men and boys are sometimes given the message, "Be a man. Men don't show emotion." *False.* God gave you emotions; you shouldn't ignore them or pretend you don't have them. You feel the way you do for a reason. Just deal with your emotions wisely. For example, don't just mope around sad and moan, "This is the way I am. These are my honest feelings." Instead, ask yourself, "*Why* am I sad?" If you can't figure out why, then just make a choice to be happy. If you've been wronged, don't explode in anger. Calmly explain your feelings and try to work things out. You *can* control your emotions. James 1:19 says that men of God "should be . . . slow to become angry." Emotions are from God, so be honest with your emotions; just control them and go slow. Don't let them loose like a river overflowing its banks.

Your next reading is on page 1607.

do not commit adultery but do commit murder, you have become a lawbreaker. ¹²Speak and act as those who are going to be judged by the law that gives freedom, ¹³because judgment without mercy will be shown to anyone who has not been merciful. Mercy triumphs over judgment!

Faith and Deeds

¹⁴What good is it, my brothers, if a man claims to have faith but has no deeds? Can such faith save him? ¹⁵Suppose a brother or sister is without clothes and daily food. ¹⁶If one of you says to him, "Go, I wish you well; keep warm and well fed," but does nothing about his physical needs, what good is it? ¹⁷In the same way, faith by itself, if it is not accompanied by action, is dead.

¹⁸But someone will say, "You have faith; I have deeds."

Show me your faith without deeds, and I will show you my faith by what I do. ¹⁹You believe that there is one God.

Good! Even the demons believe that—and shudder.

²⁰You foolish man, do you want evidence that faith without deeds is useless[a]? ²¹Was not our ancestor Abraham considered righteous for what he did when he offered his son Isaac on the altar? ²²You see that his faith and his actions were working together, and his faith was made complete by what he did. ²³And the scripture was fulfilled that says, "Abraham believed God, and it was credited to him as righteousness,"[b] and he was called God's friend. ²⁴You see that a person is justified by what he does and not by faith alone.

²⁵In the same way, was not even Rahab the prostitute considered righteous for what she did when she gave lodging to the spies and sent them off in a different direction? ²⁶As the body without the spirit is dead, so faith without deeds is dead.

[a] 20 Some early manuscripts *dead*   [b] 23 Gen. 15:6

Cliques & Clothes

READ JAMES 2:1–7

Prejudice means to *pre-judge* someone—to judge them before you get to know them. It's no headline that disliking someone because of skin color or nationality is majorly uncool. But being prejudiced sometimes takes *other* forms. You size up a guy's looks—clothes, haircut, glasses—and . . . maybe you don't feel comfortable hanging out with him. Maybe he's in such-and-such a club or listens to music that "cool" kids don't like. Judging people based on whether they're rich or cool or what they look like is wrong (James 2:1–7). What if Jesus had said, "Yuck! Sin offends me. I'm not going to hang out with sinners. Only angels are good enough company for me." We'd all be in serious trouble! Try to approach other kids—especially the ones who don't seem to fit in—with the same acceptance and openness that Jesus showed us.

Your next reading is on page 1608.

Taming the Tongue

Not many of you should presume to be teachers, my brothers, because you know that we who teach will be judged more strictly. ²We all stumble in many ways. If anyone is never at fault in what he says, he is a perfect man, able to keep his whole body in check.

³When we put bits into the mouths of horses to make them obey us, we can turn the whole animal. ⁴Or take ships as an example. Although they are so large and are driven by strong winds, they are steered by a very small rudder wherever the pilot wants to go. ⁵Likewise the tongue is a small part of the body, but it makes great boasts. Consider what a great forest is set on fire by a small spark. ⁶The tongue also is a fire, a world of evil among the parts of the body. It corrupts the whole person, sets the whole course of his life on fire, and is itself set on fire by hell.

⁷All kinds of animals, birds, reptiles and creatures of the sea are being tamed and have been tamed by man, ⁸but no man can tame the tongue. It is a restless evil, full of deadly poison.

⁹With the tongue we praise our Lord and Father, and with it we curse men, who have been made in God's likeness. ¹⁰Out of the same mouth come praise and cursing. My brothers, this should not be. ¹¹Can both fresh water and salt^a water flow from the same spring? ¹²My brothers, can a fig tree bear olives, or a grapevine bear figs? Neither can a salt spring produce fresh water.

Two Kinds of Wisdom

¹³Who is wise and understanding among you? Let him show it by his good life, by deeds done in the humility that comes from wisdom. ¹⁴But if you harbor bitter envy and selfish ambition in your hearts, do not boast about it or deny the truth. ¹⁵Such "wisdom" does not come down from heaven but is earthly, unspiritual, of the devil. ¹⁶For where you have envy and selfish ambition, there you find disorder and every evil practice.

^{a} 11 Greek bitter (see also verse 14)

Taming the Tongue

READ JAMES 3:1–12

One thing you learn watching a three-ring circus is that humankind has tamed almost every animal out there: lions, elephants, tigers and bears. Meanwhile, there's this little three-ounce slab of meat in people's mouths that no one's *ever* managed to fully tame——the tongue! "With the tongue we praise our Lord ... and with it we curse men, who have been made in God's likeness" (verse 9). No wonder James says it's like fire (verse 6), hard to control and always dangerous. Ask God for big-time help as you try to tackle your tongue. Otherwise, you're praising God at church in the morning and cursing (or complaining or gossiping or putting people down) that same afternoon. Praising God continually doesn't mean humming worship songs all day until people scream for you to stop. Hum if you want, but remember: Praising God continually also means constantly saying good things about God and others.

Your next reading is on page 1610.

17But the wisdom that comes from heaven is first of all pure; then peace-loving, considerate, submissive, full of mercy and good fruit, impartial and sincere. 18Peacemakers who sow in peace raise a harvest of righteousness.

Submit Yourselves to God

4 What causes fights and quarrels among you? Don't they come from your desires that battle within you? 2You want something but don't get it. You kill and covet, but you cannot have what you want. You quarrel and fight. You do not have, because you do not ask God. 3When you ask, you do not receive, because you ask with wrong motives, that you may spend what you get on your pleasures.

4You adulterous people, don't you know that friendship with the world is hatred toward God? Anyone who chooses to be a friend of the world becomes an enemy of God. 5Or do you think Scripture says without reason that the spirit he caused to live in us envies intensely?a 6But he gives us more grace. That is why Scripture says:

"God opposes the proud
    but gives grace to the humble."b

7Submit yourselves, then, to God. Resist the devil, and he will flee from you. 8Come near to God and he will come near to you. Wash your hands, you sinners, and purify your hearts, you double-minded. 9Grieve, mourn and wail. Change your laughter to mourning and your joy to gloom. 10Humble yourselves before the Lord, and he will lift you up.

11Brothers, do not slander one another. Anyone who speaks against his brother or judges him speaks against the law and judges it. When you judge the law, you are not keeping it, but sitting in judgment on it. 12There is only one Lawgiver and Judge, the one who is able to save and destroy. But you—who are you to judge your neighbor?

Boasting About Tomorrow

13Now listen, you who say, "Today or tomorrow we will go to this or that city, spend a year there, carry on business and make money." 14Why, you do not even know what will happen tomorrow. What is your life? You are a mist that appears for a little while and then vanishes. 15Instead, you ought to say, "If it is the Lord's will, we will live and do this or that." 16As it is, you boast and brag. All such boasting is evil. 17Anyone, then, who knows the good he ought to do and doesn't do it, sins.

a 5 Or that God jealously longs for the spirit that he made to live in us; or that the Spirit he caused to live in us longs jealously   b 6 Prov. 3:34

Get a Load of This...

When you're making decisions or giving out advice, what's the source of your wisdom? TV? A music or sports celebrity? Your*self*? Get hooked up to the only source of *true* wisdom—God. Check your attitude against James 3:17–18. If it doesn't match up, quit winging it and look to God.

Warning to Rich Oppressors

5 Now listen, you rich people, weep and wail because of the misery that is coming upon you. ²Your wealth has rotted, and moths have eaten your clothes. ³Your gold and silver are corroded. Their corrosion will testify against you and eat your flesh like fire. You have hoarded wealth in the last days. ⁴Look! The wages you failed to pay the workmen who mowed your fields are crying out against you. The cries of the harvesters have reached the ears of the Lord Almighty. ⁵You have lived on earth in luxury and self-indulgence. You have fattened yourselves in the day of slaughter.ᵃ ⁶You have condemned and murdered innocent men, who were not opposing you.

Patience in Suffering

⁷Be patient, then, brothers, until the Lord's coming. See how the farmer waits for the land to yield its valuable crop and how patient he is for the autumn and spring rains. ⁸You too, be patient and stand firm, because the Lord's coming is near. ⁹Don't grumble against each other, brothers, or you will be judged. The Judge is standing at the door!

¹⁰Brothers, as an example of patience in the face of suffering, take the prophets who spoke in the name of the Lord. ¹¹As you know, we consider blessed those who have persevered. You have heard of Job's perseverance and have seen what the Lord finally brought about. The Lord is full of compassion and mercy.

¹²Above all, my brothers, do not swear—not by heaven or by earth or by anything else. Let your "Yes" be yes, and your "No," no, or you will be condemned.

The Prayer of Faith

¹³Is any one of you in trouble? He should pray. Is anyone happy? Let him sing songs of praise. ¹⁴Is any one of you sick? He should call the elders of the church to pray over him and anoint him with oil in the name of the Lord. ¹⁵And the prayer offered in faith will make the

---

ᵃ 5 Or yourselves as in a day of feasting

Life Planning

READ JAMES 4:13–16

GET SMARTER.

We don't know the future, and we must leave our plans open to any changes God might want to make. But does that mean, "Don't plan *anything*"? Don't give any thought before going to college or choosing your life's career or even deciding whom you'll marry? No. You need to plan. Jesus himself talked about how important it is to give very serious thought and preparation before building something (see Luke 14:28). Planning is important, and long term life planning is very important. The point James is making is this: "Bring God into your plans for your life." And while you're at it, counsel with your counselors, parents and mentors. Get information, write down your dreams and plans and check things out. Having zero goals might sound good, but God has much more for you, and he'll show you what he has if you pray and seek his wisdom while you plan.

Your next reading is on page 1611.

sick person well; the Lord will raise him up. If he has sinned, he will be forgiven. [16]Therefore confess your sins to each other and pray for each other so that you may be healed. The prayer of a righteous man is powerful and effective.

[17]Elijah was a man just like us. He prayed earnestly that it would not rain, and it did not rain on the land for three and a half years. [18]Again he prayed, and the heavens gave rain, and the earth produced its crops.

[19]My brothers, if one of you should wander from the truth and someone should bring him back, [20]remember this: Whoever turns a sinner from the error of his way will save him from death and cover over a multitude of sins.

GET SMARTER

Keep On Keepin' On

READ JAMES 5:10–11

It's important to face hardship with a good attitude—to stick with it and never give up. Sometimes the only difference between winners and losers is that, although winners lose just as many times as losers, winners *never quit*. If life were all sodas and pizza, trouble would swallow you up like a T-rex inhaling a sardine. Hanging tough means realizing that God is still in control—even when things seem out of control. Remember Job? He had it all, lost it all, then had it all again. Job's secret was he trusted God and kept on keepin' on—he persevered. "We consider blessed those who have persevered" (verse 11). When you find yourself ready to quit or to run or looking for a shortcut, remember that you'd cheat yourself in the long run. Instead, ask God for strength and keep going. God uses tough times to build your character (see James 1:2–4). So keep on keepin' on.

Your next reading is on page 1618.

1 PETER

Who wrote this book?

Peter, the disciple of Jesus, wrote this book.

Why was this book written?

The book of 1 Peter encourages Christians to live holy lives in spite of suffering.

For whom was this book written?

This book is a letter sent to Christians everywhere.

When was this book written?

This book was written about A.D. 64.

What are some important teachings in this book?

Faith is precious	1 Peter 1:3–9
God chose us	1 Peter 2:9–12
Love as brothers	1 Peter 3:8–12
Suffering as Christians	1 Peter 4:12–19
Be humble	1 Peter 5:6–11

Peter, an apostle of Jesus Christ,

To God's elect, strangers in the world, scattered throughout Pontus, Galatia, Cappadocia, Asia and Bithynia, ²who have been chosen according to the foreknowledge of God the Father, through the sanctifying work of the Spirit, for obedience to Jesus Christ and sprinkling by his blood:

Grace and peace be yours in abundance.

Praise to God for a Living Hope

³Praise be to the God and Father of our Lord Jesus Christ! In his great mercy he has given us new birth into a living hope through the resurrection of Jesus Christ from the dead, ⁴and into an inheritance that can never perish, spoil or fade—kept in heaven for you, ⁵who through faith are shielded by God's power until the coming of the salvation that is ready to be revealed in the last time. ⁶In this you greatly rejoice, though now for a little while you may have had to suffer grief in all kinds of trials. ⁷These have come so that your faith—of greater worth than gold, which perishes even though refined by fire—may be proved genuine and may result in praise, glory and honor when Jesus Christ is revealed. ⁸Though you have not seen him, you love him; and even though you do not see him now, you believe in him and are filled with an inexpressible and glorious joy, ⁹for you are receiving the goal of your faith, the salvation of your souls.

¹⁰Concerning this salvation, the prophets, who spoke of the grace that was to come to you, searched intently and with the greatest care, ¹¹trying to find out the time and circumstances to which the Spirit of Christ in them was pointing when he predicted the sufferings of Christ and the glories that would follow. ¹²It was revealed to them that they were not serving themselves but you, when they spoke of the things that have now been told you by those who have preached the gospel to you by the Holy Spirit sent from heaven. Even angels long to look into these things.

Be Holy

¹³Therefore, prepare your minds for action; be self-controlled; set your hope fully on the grace to be given you when Jesus Christ is revealed. ¹⁴As obedient children, do not conform to the evil desires you had when you lived in ignorance. ¹⁵But just as he who called you is holy, so be holy in all you do; ¹⁶for it is written: "Be holy, because I am holy."ᵃ

¹⁷Since you call on a Father who judges each man's work impartially, live your lives as strangers here in reverent fear. ¹⁸For you know that it was not with perishable things such as silver or gold that you were redeemed from the empty way of life handed down to you from your forefathers, ¹⁹but with the precious

ᵃ *16* Lev. 11:44,45; 19:2

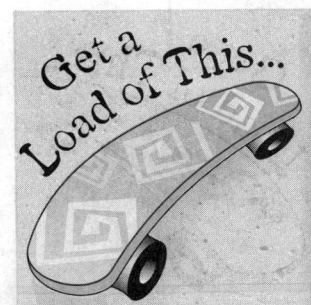

Get a Load of This...

"Even angels long to look into these things..." (1 Peter 1:12). Angels are obviously into learning about God's plan of salvation for humans. Do they have libraries and books and debates on the subject? Have some angels made a hobby out of trying to figure things out?

blood of Christ, a lamb without blemish or defect. 20He was chosen before the creation of the world, but was revealed in these last times for your sake. 21Through him you believe in God, who raised him from the dead and glorified him, and so your faith and hope are in God.

22Now that you have purified yourselves by obeying the truth so that you have sincere love for your brothers, love one another deeply, from the heart.ª 23For you have been born again, not of perishable seed, but of imperishable, through the living and enduring word of God. 24For,

> "All men are like grass,
>   and all their glory is like the flowers of the field;
> the grass withers and the flowers fall,
> 25   but the word of the Lord stands forever."ᵇ

And this is the word that was preached to you.

Therefore, rid yourselves of all malice and all deceit, hypocrisy, envy, and slander of every kind. 2Like newborn babies, crave pure spiritual milk, so that by it you may grow up in your salvation, 3now that you have tasted that the Lord is good.

The Living Stone and a Chosen People

4As you come to him, the living Stone—rejected by men but chosen by God and precious to him— 5you also, like living stones, are being built into a spiritual house to be a holy priesthood, offering spiritual sacrifices acceptable to God through Jesus Christ. 6For in Scripture it says:

> "See, I lay a stone in Zion,
>   a chosen and precious cornerstone,
> and the one who trusts in him
>   will never be put to shame."ᶜ

7Now to you who believe, this stone is precious. But to those who do not believe,

> "The stone the builders rejected
>   has become the capstone,ᵈ"ᵉ

8and,

> "A stone that causes men to stumble
>   and a rock that makes them fall."ᶠ

They stumble because they disobey the message— which is also what they were destined for.

9But you are a chosen people, a royal priesthood, a holy nation, a people belonging to God, that you may declare the praises of him who called you out of darkness into his wonderful light. 10Once you were not a people, but now you are the people of God; once you had not received mercy, but now you have received mercy.

ª 22 Some early manuscripts *from a pure heart*   ᵇ 25 Isaiah 40:6–8   ᶜ 6 Isaiah 28:16   ᵈ 7 Or *cornerstone*   ᵉ 7 Psalm 118:22   ᶠ 8 Isaiah 8:14

¹¹Dear friends, I urge you, as aliens and strangers in the world, to abstain from sinful desires, which war against your soul. ¹²Live such good lives among the pagans that, though they accuse you of doing wrong, they may see your good deeds and glorify God on the day he visits us.

Submission to Rulers and Masters

¹³Submit yourselves for the Lord's sake to every authority instituted among men: whether to the king, as the supreme authority, ¹⁴or to governors, who are sent by him to punish those who do wrong and to commend those who do right. ¹⁵For it is God's will that by doing good you should silence the ignorant talk of foolish men. ¹⁶Live as free men, but do not use your freedom as a cover-up for evil; live as servants of God. ¹⁷Show proper respect to everyone: Love the brotherhood of believers, fear God, honor the king.

¹⁸Slaves, submit yourselves to your masters with all respect, not only to those who are good and considerate, but also to those who are harsh. ¹⁹For it is commendable if a man bears up under the pain of unjust suffering because he is conscious of God. ²⁰But how is it to your credit if you receive a beating for doing wrong and endure it? But if you suffer for doing good and you endure it, this is commendable before God. ²¹To this you were called, because Christ suffered for you, leaving you an example, that you should follow in his steps.

²²"He committed no sin,
and no deceit was found in his
mouth."ᵃ

²³When they hurled their insults at him, he did not retaliate; when he suffered, he made no threats. Instead, he entrusted himself to him who judges justly. ²⁴He himself bore our sins in his body on the tree, so that we might die to sins and live

ᵃ 22 Isaiah 53:9

Make It Stick

READ 1 PETER 2:17

Your respect should come out in the way you talk to people and act toward them. This includes showing respect to authorities—for instance, even when your team is playing for a championship and the official makes a call you don't like. On a sticky note, write down two ways to respect authority (you know, like stopping at stop signs, crossing on crosswalks, etc.).

"You brainless baboon!"
"That was dumb!"
"Good move, clumsy!"
Sometimes we joke like this with our friends and no one's hurt because they know we don't mean it. But 1 Peter 3:9–10 tells us to never try to deliberately hurt others or even to repay "insult with insult."

In other Words...

for righteousness; by his wounds you have been healed. ²⁵For you were like sheep going astray, but now you have returned to the Shepherd and Overseer of your souls.

Wives and Husbands

Wives, in the same way be submissive to your husbands so that, if any of them do not believe the word, they may be won over without words by the behavior of their wives, ²when they see the purity and reverence of your lives. ³Your beauty should not come from outward adornment, such as braided hair and the wearing of gold jewelry and fine clothes. ⁴Instead, it should be that of your inner self, the unfading beauty of a gentle and quiet spirit, which is of great worth in God's sight. ⁵For this is the way the holy women of the past who put their hope in God used to make themselves beautiful. They were submissive to their own husbands, ⁶like Sarah, who obeyed Abraham and called him her master. You are her daughters if you do what is right and do not give way to fear.

⁷Husbands, in the same way be considerate as you live with your wives, and treat them with respect as the weaker partner and as heirs with you of the gracious gift of life, so that nothing will hinder your prayers.

Suffering for Doing Good

⁸Finally, all of you, live in harmony with one another; be sympathetic, love as brothers, be compassionate and humble. ⁹Do not repay evil with evil or insult with insult, but with blessing, because to this you were called so that you may inherit a blessing. ¹⁰For,

"Whoever would love life
    and see good days
must keep his tongue from evil
    and his lips from deceitful speech.
¹¹He must turn from evil and do good;
    he must seek peace and pursue it.
¹²For the eyes of the Lord are on the righteous
    and his ears are attentive to their prayer,
but the face of the Lord is against those who do
        evil."ᵃ

¹³Who is going to harm you if you are eager to do good? ¹⁴But even if you should suffer for what is right, you are blessed. "Do not fear what they fearᵇ; do not be frightened."ᶜ ¹⁵But in your hearts set apart Christ as Lord. Always be prepared to give an answer to everyone who asks you to give the reason for the hope that you have. But do this with gentleness and respect, ¹⁶keeping a clear conscience, so that those who speak maliciously against your good behavior in Christ may be ashamed of their slander. ¹⁷It is better, if it is God's will, to suffer for doing good than for doing evil. ¹⁸For Christ died for sins once for all, the righteous for the unrigh-

---

ᵃ 12 Psalm 34:12–16   ᵇ 14 Or *not fear their threats*   ᶜ 14 Isaiah 8:12

teous, to bring you to God. He was put to death in the body but made alive by the Spirit, [19]through whom[a] also he went and preached to the spirits in prison [20]who disobeyed long ago when God waited patiently in the days of Noah while the ark was being built. In it only a few people, eight in all, were saved through water, [21]and this water symbolizes baptism that now saves you also—not the removal of dirt from the body but the pledge[b] of a good conscience toward God. It saves you by the resurrection of Jesus Christ, [22]who has gone into heaven and is at God's right hand—with angels, authorities and powers in submission to him.

Living for God

Therefore, since Christ suffered in his body, arm yourselves also with the same attitude, because he who has suffered in his body is done with sin. [2]As a result, he does not live the rest of his earthly life for evil human desires, but rather for the will of God. [3]For you have spent enough time in the past doing what pagans choose to do—living in debauchery, lust, drunkenness, orgies, carousing and detestable idolatry. [4]They think it strange that you do not plunge with them into the same flood of dissipation, and they heap abuse on you. [5]But they will have to give account to him who is ready to judge the living and the dead. [6]For this is the reason the gospel was preached even to those who are now dead, so that they might be judged according to men in regard to the body, but live according to God in regard to the spirit.

[7]The end of all things is near. Therefore be clear minded and self-controlled so that you can pray. [8]Above all, love each other deeply, because love covers over a

[a] 18,19 Or alive in the spirit, [19]through which
[b] 21 Or response

Make It Stick

READ 1 PETER 4:9

"Offer hospitality to one another without grumbling" (1 Peter 4:9). What's "hospitality"? (It *doesn't* mean "little hospital.") It means showing kindness towards guests. If you're generous and cheerful—not grumbling—then you'll make people feel welcome. On a sticky note, write down these three things you can do to be hospitable to others:

1. Smile
2. Talk to Them
3. Accept Them

multitude of sins. ⁹Offer hospitality to one another without grumbling. ¹⁰Each one should use whatever gift he has received to serve others, faithfully administering God's grace in its various forms. ¹¹If anyone speaks, he should do it as one speaking the very words of God. If anyone serves, he should do it with the strength God provides, so that in all things God may be praised through Jesus Christ. To him be the glory and the power for ever and ever. Amen.

Suffering for Being a Christian

¹²Dear friends, do not be surprised at the painful trial you are suffering, as though something strange were happening to you. ¹³But rejoice that you participate in the sufferings of Christ, so that you may be overjoyed when his glory is revealed. ¹⁴If you are insulted because of the name of Christ, you are blessed, for the Spirit of glory and of God rests on you. ¹⁵If you suffer, it should not be as a murderer or thief or any other kind of criminal, or even as a meddler. ¹⁶However, if you suffer as a Christian, do not be

ashamed, but praise God that you bear that name. ¹⁷For it is time for judgment to begin with the family of God; and if it begins with us, what will the outcome be for those who do not obey the gospel of God? ¹⁸And,

"If it is hard for the righteous to be
saved,
what will become of the ungodly
and the sinner?" ᵃ

¹⁹So then, those who suffer according to God's will should commit themselves to their faithful Creator and continue to do good.

To Elders and Young Men

5 To the elders among you, I appeal as a fellow elder, a witness of Christ's sufferings and one who also will share in the glory to be revealed: ²Be shepherds of God's flock that is under your care, serving as overseers—not because you must, but because you are willing, as God wants you to be; not greedy

ᵃ 18 Prov. 11:31

It's Called Persecution

READ 1 PETER 4:12–16; 5:8–9

When people are razzing you or making fun of you because they think you're a wimp for believing in God, or the devil actually stirs them up to attack you, that's called persecution. You're "suffering as a Christian" (1 Peter 4:16). But hey, if you're doing things *against* God's Word and things go wrong and you suffer for it, you can't say you're "being persecuted." Another kind of suffering (like cancer or what happened in New York and Washington D.C. on September 11, 2001) happens because we live in a fallen world. There's a lot of suffering in life because of sin in the world. But through it all, God said he'd be with you and help you. Jesus declared that his followers would be persecuted (Luke 6:22–23; John 15:18–20); but even when that happens, keep on going and continue to share your faith. Your reward will be great in heaven.

Your next reading is on page 1623.

for money, but eager to serve; ³not lording it over those entrusted to you, but being examples to the flock. ⁴And when the Chief Shepherd appears, you will receive the crown of glory that will never fade away.

⁵Young men, in the same way be submissive to those who are older. All of you, clothe yourselves with humility toward one another, because,

"God opposes the proud
   but gives grace to the humble." ᵃ

⁶Humble yourselves, therefore, under God's mighty hand, that he may lift you up in due time. ⁷Cast all your anxiety on him because he cares for you.

⁸Be self-controlled and alert. Your enemy the devil prowls around like a roaring lion looking for someone to devour. ⁹Resist him, standing firm in the faith, because you know that your brothers throughout the world are undergoing the same kind of sufferings.

¹⁰And the God of all grace, who called you to his eternal glory in Christ, after you have suffered a little while, will himself restore you and make you strong, firm and steadfast. ¹¹To him be the power for ever and ever. Amen.

Final Greetings

¹²With the help of Silas, ᵇ whom I regard as a faithful brother, I have written to you briefly, encouraging you and testifying that this is the true grace of God. Stand fast in it.

¹³She who is in Babylon, chosen together with you, sends you her greetings, and so does my son Mark. ¹⁴Greet one another with a kiss of love.

Peace to all of you who are in Christ.

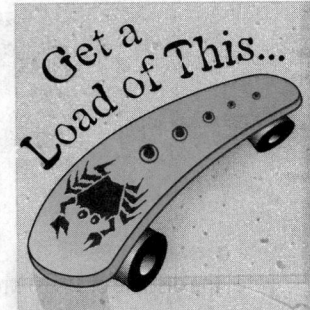

Get a Load of This...

"Greet one another with a kiss of love" (1 Peter 5:14). Don't worry. This was a custom they did back then. *You* don't have to pucker up your lips and kiss people in church.

ᵃ 5 Prov. 3:34   ᵇ 12 Greek *Silvanus*, a variant of *Silas*

2 PETER

Who wrote this book?
Peter, the disciple of Jesus, wrote this book.

Why was this book written?
The book of 2 Peter warns Christians against false teachers.

For whom was this book written?
This book is a letter sent to Christians everywhere.

When was this book written?
This book was written about A.D. 67.

What are some important teachings in this book?

What false teachers are like   2 Peter 2:1–22
How the world will end   2 Peter 3:1–13

Simon Peter, a servant and apostle of Jesus Christ,

To those who through the righteousness of our God and Savior Jesus Christ have received a faith as precious as ours:

²Grace and peace be yours in abundance through the knowledge of God and of Jesus our Lord.

Making One's Calling and Election Sure

³His divine power has given us everything we need for life and godliness through our knowledge of him who called us by his own glory and goodness. ⁴Through these he has given us his very great and precious promises, so that through them you may participate in the divine nature and escape the corruption in the world caused by evil desires.

⁵For this very reason, make every effort to add to your faith goodness; and to goodness, knowledge; ⁶and to knowledge, self-control; and to self-control, perseverance; and to perseverance, godliness; ⁷and to godliness, brotherly kindness; and to brotherly kindness, love. ⁸For if you possess these qualities in increasing measure, they will keep you from being ineffective and unproductive in your knowledge of our Lord Jesus Christ. ⁹But if anyone does not have them, he is nearsighted and blind, and has forgotten that he has been cleansed from his past sins.

¹⁰Therefore, my brothers, be all the more eager to make your calling and election sure. For if you do these things, you will never fall, ¹¹and you will receive a rich welcome into the eternal kingdom of our Lord and Savior Jesus Christ.

Prophecy of Scripture

¹²So I will always remind you of these things, even though you know them and are firmly established in the truth you now have. ¹³I think it is right to refresh your memory as long as I live in the tent of this body, ¹⁴because I know that I will soon put it aside, as our Lord Jesus Christ has made clear to me. ¹⁵And I will make every effort to see that after my departure you will always be able to remember these things.

¹⁶We did not follow cleverly invented stories when we told you about the power and coming of our Lord Jesus Christ, but we were eyewitnesses of his majesty. ¹⁷For he received honor and glory from God the Father when the voice came to him from the Majestic Glory, saying, "This is my Son, whom I love; with him I am well pleased."ᵃ ¹⁸We ourselves heard this voice that came from heaven when we were with him on the sacred mountain.

¹⁹And we have the word of the prophets made more certain, and you will do well to pay attention to it, as to a light shining in a dark place, until the day dawns and the morning star rises in your hearts. ²⁰Above all, you

Get a Load of This...

The dictionary defines *corrupt* as "putrid" or "rotten." Sin may be fun but along with sin comes corruption. Blech! The best way to "escape the corruption in the world" (2 Peter 1:4) is to deliberately choose to obey God and avoid wallowing around in the garbage dump of sin.

must understand that no prophecy of Scripture came about by the prophet's own interpretation. ²¹For prophecy never had its origin in the will of man, but men spoke from God as they were carried along by the Holy Spirit.

False Teachers and Their Destruction

But there were also false prophets among the people, just as there will be false teachers among you. They will secretly introduce destructive heresies, even denying the sovereign Lord who bought them—bringing swift destruction on themselves. ²Many will follow their shameful ways and will bring the way of truth into disrepute. ³In their greed these teachers will exploit you with stories they have made up. Their condemnation has long been hanging over them, and their destruction has not been sleeping.

⁴For if God did not spare angels when they sinned, but sent them to hell,ᵃ putting them into gloomy dungeonsᵇ to be held for judgment; ⁵if he did not spare the ancient world when he brought the flood on its ungodly people, but protected Noah, a preacher of righteousness, and seven others; ⁶if he condemned the cities of Sodom and Gomorrah by burning them to ashes, and made them an example of what is going to happen to the ungodly; ⁷and if he rescued Lot, a righteous man, who was distressed by the filthy lives of lawless men ⁸(for that righteous man, living among them day after day, was tormented in his righteous soul by the lawless deeds he saw and heard)— ⁹if this is so, then the Lord knows how to rescue godly men from trials and to hold the unrighteous for the day of judgment, while continuing their punishment.ᶜ ¹⁰This is especially true of those who follow the corrupt desire of the sinful natureᵈ and despise authority.

ᵃ 4 Greek *Tartarus*   ᵇ 4 Some manuscripts *into chains of darkness*   ᶜ 9 Or *unrighteous for punishment until the day of judgment*   ᵈ 10 Or *the flesh*

Make It Stick

READ 2 PETER 1:5–9

Here's Peter's math lesson. It focuses on adding up what it takes to be a Christian who makes a difference. Write on a sticky note: "Faith + goodness + knowledge + self-control + perseverance + godliness + brotherly kindness + love = THE GOAL." That's one looong math problem!

Bold and arrogant, these men are not afraid to slander celestial beings; [11]yet even angels, although they are stronger and more powerful, do not bring slanderous accusations against such beings in the presence of the Lord. [12]But these men blaspheme in matters they do not understand. They are like brute beasts, creatures of instinct, born only to be caught and destroyed, and like beasts they too will perish.

[13]They will be paid back with harm for the harm they have done. Their idea of pleasure is to carouse in broad daylight. They are blots and blemishes, reveling in their pleasures while they feast with you.[a] [14]With eyes full of adultery, they never stop sinning; they seduce the unstable; they are experts in greed—an accursed brood! [15]They have left the straight way and wandered off to follow the way of Balaam son of Beor, who loved the wages of wickedness. [16]But he was rebuked for his wrongdoing by a donkey—a beast without speech—who spoke with a man's voice and restrained the prophet's madness.

[17]These men are springs without water and mists driven by a storm. Blackest darkness is reserved for them. [18]For they mouth empty, boastful words and, by appealing to the lustful desires of sinful human nature, they entice people who are just escaping from those who live in error. [19]They promise them freedom, while they themselves are slaves of depravity—for a man is a slave to whatever has mastered him. [20]If they have escaped the corruption of the world by knowing our Lord and Savior Jesus Christ and are again entangled in it and overcome, they are worse off at the end than they were at the beginning. [21]It would have been better for them not to have known the way of righteousness, than to have known it and then to turn their backs on the sacred command that was passed on to them. [22]Of them the proverbs are true: "A dog returns to its vomit,"[b] and, "A sow that is washed goes back to her wallowing in the mud."

[a] 13 Some manuscripts *in their love feasts*
[b] 22 Prov. 26:11

Up to the Next Level

READ 2 PETER 1:12–15

Say you're into being tops at skate boarding. Do you arrive at a certain level, stop learning new tricks and just *coast* from then on? No, you keep pushing yourself and trying new stuff. You step it up, learn more and get to the next level. It's the same with church: After you've been going for a while, it might seem like the same old thing. You may moan, "I've already heard this." Peter said that although he was confident the believers he was writing to already knew the truth about living as a Christian, it was important to tell them again (verse 12). You can have so many experiences in just one week—that if you don't stay focused on the truth, it's easy for your focus to change. But if you keep listening to the truth, keep looking deeper, you'll keep focused. Best of all, you'll learn cool new stuff on the "same old" skateboard of faith and go up to the next level with God.

Your next reading is on page 1625.

Gross!

Check out 2 Peter 2:4.
The Greek word for
"hell" here is *Tartarus*.
The fallen angels
mentioned in 2 Peter
2:4 weren't allowed to
help Satan influence
the world for evil, but
were locked up in
"gloomy dungeons" in
Tartarus, considered the
worst, deepest part of
hell.

The Day of the Lord

3 Dear friends, this is now my second letter to you. I have written both of them as reminders to stimulate you to wholesome thinking. ²I want you to recall the words spoken in the past by the holy prophets and the command given by our Lord and Savior through your apostles.

³First of all, you must understand that in the last days scoffers will come, scoffing and following their own evil desires. ⁴They will say, "Where is this 'coming' he promised? Ever since our fathers died, everything goes on as it has since the beginning of creation." ⁵But they deliberately forget that long ago by God's word the heavens existed and the earth was formed out of water and by water. ⁶By these waters also the world of that time was deluged and destroyed. ⁷By the same word the present heavens and earth are reserved for fire, being kept for the day of judgment and destruction of ungodly men.

⁸But do not forget this one thing, dear friends: With the Lord a day is like a thousand years, and a thousand years are like a day. ⁹The Lord is not slow in keeping his promise, as some understand slowness. He is patient with you, not wanting anyone to perish, but everyone to come to repentance.

¹⁰But the day of the Lord will come like a thief. The heavens will disappear with a roar; the elements will be destroyed by fire, and the earth and everything in it will be laid bare. *a*

¹¹Since everything will be destroyed in this way, what kind of people ought you to be? You ought to live holy and godly lives ¹²as you look forward to the day of God and speed its coming. *b* That day will bring about the destruction of the heavens by fire, and the elements will melt in the heat. ¹³But in keeping with his promise we are looking forward to a new heaven and a new earth, the home of righteousness.

¹⁴So then, dear friends, since you are looking forward to this, make every effort to be found spotless, blameless and at peace with him. ¹⁵Bear in mind that our Lord's patience means salvation, just as our dear brother Paul also wrote you with the wisdom that God gave him. ¹⁶He writes the same way in all his letters, speaking in them of these matters. His letters contain some things that are hard to understand, which ignorant and unstable people distort, as they do the other Scriptures, to their own destruction.

¹⁷Therefore, dear friends, since you already know this, be on your guard so that you may not be carried away by the error of lawless men and fall from your secure position. ¹⁸But grow in the grace and knowledge of our Lord and Savior Jesus Christ. To him be glory both now and forever! Amen.

a 10 Some manuscripts *be burned up*   *b 12* Or *as you wait eagerly for the day of God to come*

GET

Peter's Bio

2 PETER

Peter went from being a rough-around-the-edges fisherman to a man of God who was deeper, smarter, stronger and cooler. Let's have a look at his life:

SMARTER: Peter went to school in the synagogue where he learned his three R's: reading, writing and religion (OK, he probably learned "arithmetic" too!). The priests called him "unschooled and ordinary" (Acts 4:13). Yeah, but Peter had spoken such a powerful sermon that 3,000 people got saved (Acts 2:40–41), and even the priests had to admit that he spoke with authority and "took note that [he] had been with Jesus" (Acts 4:13). Peter went from being a simple fisherman to a man who helped shake the foundations of the world with the gospel. He helped organize the church and wrote books of the New Testament.

STRONGER: Peter was an outdoorsman, a well-built, strong, burly man. They didn't have power-winches with scoops back then to pull nets full of fish from the sea, so Peter was Mr. Bulging Biceps. After leaving fishing, Peter walked all over Judea and Galilee with Jesus. That kept him in shape! Swimming was also something Peter was good at! We are talking "Peter the Otter." Check out John 21:7.

COOLER: Peter was a very social, outgoing, talkative person. He loved to be with people, and he was excellent at motivating others. That made him a natural leader. Mixing and mingling and motivating came very naturally to Peter. What he had to *work* on, however, was his (ahem!) people-handling skills. In the beginning, Peter was a bit rough: He was sometimes pushy, and had quarrels with the other disciples over who would be leader. Over time, however, he grew to be very humble and learned how to serve others (see 1 Peter 1:22; 5:1–3). Peter went from "cool" to "*way* cool."

DEEPER: Peter had a lot of zeal and was excited about serving God! But sometimes he flip-flopped like a fish. Peter declared, "I'll never deny you," then denied Jesus three times. The thing about Peter, though, was that he loved God and *never gave up*. Sure, he compromised at times (see Galatians 2:11–14), but when he knew he was wrong, he changed and served God with even more effort.

Your next reading is on page 1627.

1 JOHN

Who wrote this book?
John, the disciple of Jesus, wrote this book.

Why was this book written?
This book shows Christians how to live close to God and other people.

For whom was this book written?
The book of 1 John is a letter John sent to Christians everywhere.

When was this book written?
John probably wrote this book about A.D. 90.

What are some important teachings in this book?

God forgives sins	1 John 1:5–10
God's children love others	1 John 2:7–11
God's children do right	1 John 3:7–11
Jesus shows us what love is	1 John 3:16–20
Love comes from God	1 John 4:7–11
God gives us eternal life	1 John 5:10–12

The Word of Life

1 That which was from the beginning, which we have heard, which we have seen with our eyes, which we have looked at and our hands have touched—this we proclaim concerning the Word of life. ²The life appeared; we have seen it and testify to it, and we proclaim to you the eternal life, which was with the Father and has appeared to us. ³We proclaim to you what we have seen and heard, so that you also may have fellowship with us. And our fellowship is with the Father and with his Son, Jesus Christ. ⁴We write this to make our[a] joy complete.

Walking in the Light

⁵This is the message we have heard from him and declare to you: God is light; in him there is no darkness at all. ⁶If we claim to have fellowship with him yet walk in the darkness, we lie and do not live by the truth. ⁷But if we walk in the light, as he is in the light, we have fellowship with one another, and the blood of Jesus, his Son, purifies us from all[b] sin.

⁸If we claim to be without sin, we deceive ourselves and the truth is not in us. ⁹If we confess our sins, he is faithful and just and will forgive us our sins and purify us from all unrighteousness. ¹⁰If we claim we have not sinned, we make him out to be a liar and his word has no place in our lives.

2 My dear children, I write this to you so that you will not sin. But if anybody does sin, we have one who speaks to the Father in our defense—Jesus Christ, the Righteous One. ²He is the atoning sacrifice for our sins, and not only for ours but also for[c] the sins of the whole world.

³We know that we have come to know him if we obey his commands. ⁴The man who says, "I know him," but does not do what he commands is a liar, and the truth is not in him. ⁵But if anyone obeys his word, God's love[d] is truly made complete in him. This is how we know we are in him: ⁶Whoever claims to live in him must walk as Jesus did.

a 4 Some manuscripts *your*   *b 7* Or *every*   *c 2* Or *He is the one who turns aside God's wrath, taking away our sins, and not only ours but also*   *d 5* Or *word, love for God*

Rock Climbing—252 Style

READ 1 JOHN 1:5—2:1

Imagine a pro is teaching you rock-climbing and now he's taking you up *the Crag*. He says, "Grab hold exactly where I do. It's *important* not to fool around and slip up. But if you do, call for help *immediately*." Living Christianity is like rock-climbing: A man of God does not deliberately sin and do things he shouldn't. If you play fast and easy, yet say, "I'm following Jesus," you're lying. But hey, you *will* slip up sometimes. You just need to call out to God, then re-grip the solid truth—quickly! "If we claim to be without sin, we deceive ourselves ... If we confess our sins, he ... will forgive us" (verses 8–9). Ask God to forgive you and help you not to sin again, and he'll "purify [you] from all unrighteousness" (verse 9), help get your feet back on the rock and say, "C'mon bud! We're not at the top yet."

Your next reading is on page 1628.

7Dear friends, I am not writing you a new command but an old one, which you have had since the beginning. This old command is the message you have heard. 8Yet I am writing you a new command; its truth is seen in him and you, because the darkness is passing and the true light is already shining.

9Anyone who claims to be in the light but hates his brother is still in the darkness. 10Whoever loves his brother lives in the light, and there is nothing in him*a* to make him stumble. 11But whoever hates his brother is in the darkness and walks around in the darkness; he does not know where he is going, because the darkness has blinded him.

12I write to you, dear children,
    because your sins have been forgiven
        on account of his name.
13I write to you, fathers,
    because you have known him who is
        from the beginning.
I write to you, young men,
    because you have overcome the evil
        one.

I write to you, dear children,
    because you have known the Father.
14I write to you, fathers,
    because you have known him who is
        from the beginning.
I write to you, young men,
    because you are strong,
    and the word of God lives in you,
    and you have overcome the evil one.

Do Not Love the World

15Do not love the world or anything in the world. If anyone loves the world, the love of the Father is not in him. 16For everything in the world—the cravings of sinful man, the lust of his eyes and the boasting of what he has and does—comes not from the Father but from the world. 17The world and its desires pass away, but the man who does the will of God lives forever.

Warning Against Antichrists

18Dear children, this is the last hour; and as you have heard that the antichrist

a 10 Or *it*

Loving the World

READ 1 JOHN 2:15–17

"Do not love the world or anything in the world" (verse 15). Does that mean you can't love baseball? You can't have fun rollerblading, or enjoy a video? You can't love fishing? Slow down. John was *not* talking about the world God made. God created the earth and said that it was *good*. He created cool stuff and fun and friends and family. No, by "world" John is talking about the sinful world ruled by the devil, the corrupt world system that came about as a result of human sin. If we love God, we'll love the good things *he* created, but hate the things in the world that draw people away from God—that are full of sin and selfishness and destruction. Remember, Jesus said, "I have come that they may have life, and have it to the full" (John 10:10). You can't hate *that*, can you?

Your next reading is on page 1632.

is coming, even now many antichrists have come. This is how we know it is the last hour. ¹⁹They went out from us, but they did not really belong to us. For if they had belonged to us, they would have remained with us; but their going showed that none of them belonged to us.

²⁰But you have an anointing from the Holy One, and all of you know the truth. *ᵃ* ²¹I do not write to you because you do not know the truth, but because you do know it and because no lie comes from the truth. ²²Who is the liar? It is the man who denies that Jesus is the Christ. Such a man is the antichrist—he denies the Father and the Son. ²³No one who denies the Son has the Father; whoever acknowledges the Son has the Father also.

²⁴See that what you have heard from the beginning remains in you. If it does, you also will remain in the Son and in the Father. ²⁵And this is what he promised us— even eternal life.

²⁶I am writing these things to you about those who are trying to lead you astray. ²⁷As for you, the anointing you received from him remains in you, and you do not need anyone to teach you. But as his anointing teaches you about all things and as that anointing is real, not counterfeit—just as it has taught you, remain in him.

Children of God

²⁸And now, dear children, continue in him, so that when he appears we may be confident and unashamed before him at his coming.

²⁹If you know that he is righteous, you know that everyone who does what is right has been born of him.

3 How great is the love the Father has lavished on us, that we should be called children of God! And that is what we are! The reason the world does not know us is that it did not know him. ²Dear friends, now we are children of God, and what we will be has not yet been made known. But we know that when he appears, *ᵇ* we shall be like him, for we shall see him as he is. ³Everyone who has this hope in him purifies himself, just as he is pure.

⁴Everyone who sins breaks the law; in fact, sin is lawlessness. ⁵But you know that he appeared so that he might take away our sins. And in him is no sin. ⁶No one who lives in him keeps on sinning. No one who continues to sin has either seen him or known him.

⁷Dear children, do not let anyone lead you astray. He who does what is right is righteous, just as he is righteous. ⁸He who does what is sinful is of the devil, because the devil has been sinning from the beginning. The reason the Son of God appeared was to destroy the devil's work. ⁹No one who is born of God will continue to sin, because God's seed remains in him; he cannot go on sinning, because he has been born of God. ¹⁰This is how we know who the children of God are and who the children of the devil are: Anyone who does not do

Get a Load of This...

We don't know *exactly* what we'll look and be like when we're with Jesus, but "we shall be like him" (1 John 3:2), and that's pretty phenomenal. Will we be able to walk through walls like him? Maybe! And do other stuff beyond our wildest imagination.

ᵃ 20 Some manuscripts *and you know all things*   *ᵇ 2* Or *when it is made known*

Get a Load of This...

If someone desperately needs help and you don't help, you've got problems. You can't just *believe* in doing good; you have to actually *do* it (1 John 3:16–18). Otherwise it's like watching water-skiing and thinking you're a pro even though you've never put on skis in your life.

In Other Words...

what is right is not a child of God; nor is anyone who does not love his brother.

Love One Another

¹¹This is the message you heard from the beginning: We should love one another. ¹²Do not be like Cain, who belonged to the evil one and murdered his brother. And why did he murder him? Because his own actions were evil and his brother's were righteous. ¹³Do not be surprised, my brothers, if the world hates you. ¹⁴We know that we have passed from death to life, because we love our brothers. Anyone who does not love remains in death. ¹⁵Anyone who hates his brother is a murderer, and you know that no murderer has eternal life in him.

¹⁶This is how we know what love is: Jesus Christ laid down his life for us. And we ought to lay down our lives for our brothers. ¹⁷If anyone has material possessions and sees his brother in need but has no pity on him, how can the love of God be in him? ¹⁸Dear children, let us not love with words or tongue but with actions and in truth. ¹⁹This then is how we know that we belong to the truth, and how we set our hearts at rest in his presence ²⁰whenever our hearts condemn us. For God is greater than our hearts, and he knows everything.

²¹Dear friends, if our hearts do not condemn us, we have confidence before God ²²and receive from him anything we ask, because we obey his commands and do what pleases him. ²³And this is his command: to believe in the name of his Son, Jesus Christ, and to love one another as he commanded us. ²⁴Those who obey his commands live in him, and he in them. And this is how we know that he lives in us: We know it by the Spirit he gave us.

Test the Spirits

Dear friends, do not believe every spirit, but test the spirits to see whether they are from God, because many false prophets have gone out into the world. ²This is how you can recognize the Spirit of God: Every spirit that acknowledges that Jesus Christ has come in the flesh is from God, ³but every spirit that does not acknowledge Jesus is not from God. This is the spirit of the antichrist, which you have heard is coming and even now is already in the world.

⁴You, dear children, are from God and have overcome them, because the one who is in you is greater than the one who is in the world. ⁵They are from the world and therefore speak from the viewpoint of the world, and the world listens to them. ⁶We are from God, and whoever knows God listens to us; but whoever is not from God does not listen to us. This is how we recognize the Spirit[a] of truth and the spirit of falsehood.

God's Love and Ours

⁷Dear friends, let us love one another, for love comes

---

[a] 6 Or *spirit*

from God. Everyone who loves has been born of God and knows God. ⁸Whoever does not love does not know God, because God is love. ⁹This is how God showed his love among us: He sent his one and only Son*a* into the world that we might live through him. ¹⁰This is love: not that we loved God, but that he loved us and sent his Son as an atoning sacrifice for*b* our sins. ¹¹Dear friends, since God so loved us, we also ought to love one another. ¹²No one has ever seen God; but if we love one another, God lives in us and his love is made complete in us.

¹³We know that we live in him and he in us, because he has given us of his Spirit. ¹⁴And we have seen and testify that the Father has sent his Son to be the Savior of the world. ¹⁵If anyone acknowledges that Jesus is the Son of God, God lives in him and he in God. ¹⁶And so we know and rely on the love God has for us.

God is love. Whoever lives in love lives in God, and God in him. ¹⁷In this way, love is made complete among us so that we will have confidence on the day of judgment, because in this world we are like him. ¹⁸There is no fear in love. But perfect love drives out fear, because fear has to do with punishment. The one who fears is not made perfect in love.

¹⁹We love because he first loved us. ²⁰If anyone says, "I love God," yet hates his brother, he is a liar. For anyone who does not love his brother, whom he has seen, cannot love God, whom he has not seen. ²¹And he has given us this command: Whoever loves God must also love his brother.

Faith in the Son of God

5 Everyone who believes that Jesus is the Christ is born of God, and everyone who loves the father loves his child as well. ²This is how we know that we love the children of God: by lov-

---

a 9 Or his only begotten Son 　 *b 10 Or as the one who would turn aside his wrath, taking away*

Make It Stick

READ 1 JOHN 3:21–22

If your conscience is bothering you about some rotten thing you've done, stop right now and ask for God's forgiveness. He'll forgive you. Now that the slate is clean, you'll have the faith to ask God to give you something you need. Write your prayer request on a sticky note.

ing God and carrying out his commands. ³This is love for God: to obey his commands. And his commands are not burdensome, ⁴for everyone born of God overcomes the world. This is the victory that has overcome the world, even our faith. ⁵Who is it that overcomes the world? Only he who believes that Jesus is the Son of God.

⁶This is the one who came by water and blood—Jesus Christ. He did not come by water only, but by water and blood. And it is the Spirit who testifies, because the Spirit is the truth. ⁷For there are three that testify: ⁸theᵃ Spirit, the water and the blood; and the three are in agreement. ⁹We accept man's testimony, but God's testimony is greater because it is the testimony of God, which he has given about his Son. ¹⁰Anyone who believes in the Son of God has this testimony in his heart. Anyone who does not believe God has made him out to be a liar, because he has not believed the testimony God has given about his Son. ¹¹And this is the testimony: God has given us eternal life, and this life is in his Son. ¹²He who has the Son has life; he who does not have the Son of God does not have life.

Concluding Remarks

¹³I write these things to you who believe in the name of the Son of God so that you may know that you have eternal life. ¹⁴This is the confidence we have in approaching God: that if we ask anything according to his will, he hears us. ¹⁵And if we know that he hears us—whatever we ask—we know that we have what we asked of him.

¹⁶If anyone sees his brother commit a sin that does not lead to death, he should pray and God will give him life. I refer to those whose sin does not lead to death. There is a sin that leads to death. I am not saying that he should pray about that. ¹⁷All wrongdoing is sin, and there is sin that does not lead to death.

¹⁸We know that anyone born of God does not continue to sin; the one who

ᵃ 7,8 Late manuscripts of the Vulgate *testify in heaven: the Father, the Word and the Holy Spirit, and these three are one.* ⁸*And there are three that testify on earth: the* (not found in any Greek manuscript before the fourteenth century)

Love Your Brothers

READ 1 JOHN 4:16–21

You've probably heard of an "armchair quarterback"—someone who watches football but doesn't ever play the game. But have you ever heard of an "armchair Christian"? That's someone who says they love God but doesn't demonstrate it by loving others. They "talk the talk" but they don't "walk the walk." God doesn't want us to just talk about loving him; he wants us to get into the game and demonstrate our love by how we treat others. For, "Anyone who does not love his brother, whom he has seen, cannot love God, whom he has not seen" (verse 20). Let's put that a little blunter: "Whoever loves God must also love his brother" (verse 21). Loving others is not an *option*, it's not just good advice, it's not something that only certain Christians do. This is a *commandment*. All Christians *must* get up out of the armchair and love others.

Your next reading is on page 1635.

was born of God keeps him safe, and the evil one cannot harm him. ¹⁹We know that we are children of God, and that the whole world is under the control of the evil one. ²⁰We know also that the Son of God has come and has given us under-standing, so that we may know him who is true. And we are in him who is true—even in his Son Jesus Christ. He is the true God and eternal life.

²¹Dear children, keep yourselves from idols.

2 JOHN

Who wrote this book?
John, the disciple of Jesus, wrote this book.

Why was this book written?
The book of 2 John shows Christians how to live close to God and other people.

For whom was this book written?
This book is a letter John sent to Christians everywhere.

When was this book written?
John probably wrote this book about A.D. 90.

¹The elder,

To the chosen lady and her children, whom I love in the truth—and not I only, but also all who know the truth— ²because of the truth, which lives in us and will be with us forever:

³Grace, mercy and peace from God the Father and from Jesus Christ, the Father's Son, will be with us in truth and love.

⁴It has given me great joy to find some of your children walking in the truth, just as the Father commanded us. ⁵And now, dear lady, I am not writing you a new command but one we have had from the beginning. I ask that we love one another. ⁶And this is love: that we walk in obedience to his commands. As you have heard from the beginning, his command is that you walk in love. ⁷Many deceivers, who do not acknowledge Jesus Christ as coming in the flesh, have gone out into the world. Any such person is the deceiver and the antichrist. ⁸Watch out that you do not lose what you have worked for, but that you may be rewarded fully. ⁹Anyone who runs ahead and does not continue in the teaching of Christ does not have God; whoever continues in the teaching has both the Father and the Son. ¹⁰If anyone comes to you and does not bring this teaching, do not take him into your house or welcome him. ¹¹Anyone who welcomes him shares in his wicked work.

¹²I have much to write to you, but I do not want to use paper and ink. Instead, I hope to visit you and talk with you face to face, so that our joy may be complete.

¹³The children of your chosen sister send their greetings.

Don't Be a Dead Fish

READ 2 JOHN 7–11

Being a Christian is like swimming upstream against the current. If you keep paddling, you'll keep moving ahead. But if you stop even for a second, you'll be pulled back. John encourages you to keep swimming so that "you do not lose what you have worked for" (verse 8). If anyone tries to distract you from God's teaching, "do not take him into your house or welcome him" (verse 10). John was telling Christians not to provide lodging for traveling false teachers. He wasn't condemning hospitality to unbelievers in general. So this doesn't mean you shouldn't let your cousin into your house if he has strange religious ideas. It's good to reach out to others. But if you spend *too* much time with him, you'll end up compromising. Soon you'll stop swimming, and the current will drag you back downriver . . . like a dead fish! That's why *close* friendship should be only with genuine believers. As Proverbs 13:20 says, "He who walks with the wise grows wise, but a companion of fools suffers harm."

Your next reading is on page 1637.

3 JOHN

Who wrote this book?

John, the disciple of Jesus, wrote this book.

Why was this book written?

The book of 3 John shows Christians how to live close to God and other people.

For whom was this book written?

This book is a letter John sent to Christians everywhere.

When was this book written?

John probably wrote this book about A.D. 90.

¹The elder,

To my dear friend Gaius, whom I love in the truth.

²Dear friend, I pray that you may enjoy good health and that all may go well with you, even as your soul is getting along well. ³It gave me great joy to have some brothers come and tell about your faithfulness to the truth and how you continue to walk in the truth. ⁴I have no greater joy than to hear that my children are walking in the truth.

⁵Dear friend, you are faithful in what you are doing for the brothers, even though they are strangers to you. ⁶They have told the church about your love. You will do well to send them on their way in a manner worthy of God. ⁷It was for the sake of the Name that they went out, receiving no help from the pagans. ⁸We ought therefore to show hospitality to such men so that we may work together for the truth.

⁹I wrote to the church, but Diotrephes, who loves to be first, will have nothing to do with us. ¹⁰So if I come, I will call attention to what he is doing, gossiping maliciously about us. Not satisfied with that, he refuses to welcome the brothers. He also stops those who want to do so and puts them out of the church.

¹¹Dear friend, do not imitate what is evil but what is good. Anyone who does what is good is from God. Anyone who does what is evil has not seen God. ¹²Demetrius is well spoken of by everyone—and even by the truth itself. We also speak well of him, and you know that our testimony is true.

¹³I have much to write you, but I do not want to do so with pen and ink. ¹⁴I hope to see you soon, and we will talk face to face.

Peace to you. The friends here send their greetings. Greet the friends there by name.

Loving to Be First

READ 3 JOHN 9–10

In games and competition, there's nothing wrong with wanting to do your best and lead the pack. Go for it! The rush of winning is great. But if you feed on that *so* much that you *have* to be first—and if someone else wins, your whole week is ruined—then you're not *feeding* any more. You're pigging out. And if you're always shouting and shoving and bullying your way to the front of the cake line or movie line or line to get in the pool, what you're saying is, "Step aside! I am *the* most important person." God condemns that piggy attitude. Look at Diotrephes. The core of his problem was that "he loved to be first" (verse 9). Sure, you're important, but everyone around you is important, too. They need a chance to be first sometimes. Try thinking of the happiness of others, step aside and give them a turn.

Your next reading is on page 1638.

The Apostle John

GET

The Apostle John is one of the most amazing disciples in the New Testament. He went from being a hot-tempered, impulsive young social climber to a 252 man who was as deep and cool as an ocean. It had *everything* to do with his relationship with Jesus.

COOLER: At first, Jesus called John and his brother James "Sons of Thunder" because of their tempers. Once these firebrands wanted to ask God to burn down an entire village. And they were always pushing to be *the* top leaders in the kingdom of God. They simply did not get Jesus' message about serving others—*until* they were filled with the Holy Spirit. Then they grew up quick. John ended up writing the Gospel of John and three epistles, which, more than any other books of the Bible, emphasized loving other people. John went from being a son of thunder to a disciple of love—serving others and laying down his life for people.

DEEPER: John was "the disciple whom Jesus loved" (John 13:23) and one of the three apostles closest to Jesus. John stayed right beside Jesus till the end (see John 19:25–27). John loved God's Word, and his writings strongly emphasize relationship with God—how we need to be close to him, love him and receive his love.

STRONGER: John, like Peter, had been a fisherman. He was an outdoors guy working at a very physical job. John also did a lot of walking from town to town, following Jesus. This guy could lay some serious sandal rubber. When he and Peter ran to Jesus' tomb, John left Pete inhaling dust (see John 20:2–4). If John went to your school, he'd probably be on the track team.

SMARTER: Like other Jewish boys, John learned the basics in a synagogue school. The priests knew that he and Peter were "unschooled, ordinary men" (Acts 4:13), but studying under Jesus taught John cool stuff the Pharisees knew nothing about. John went from knowing mostly fishing to graduating at the top of the class as a 252 man. When John wrote five books of the New Testament, he didn't just throw words down on paper. Our man John had become a scholar, and he commented on philosophies and heresies and ... *you know* ... deep, theological stuff.

John was far from perfect, but he worked hard to be smarter, stronger, deeper and cooler.

Your next reading is on page 1640.

JUDE

Who wrote this book?
Jude, the brother of Jesus, wrote this book.

Why was this book written?
Jude warns Christians about false teachers.

For whom was this book written?
This book is a letter written to Christians everywhere.

When was this book written?
Jude was written about A.D. 65.

¹Jude, a servant of Jesus Christ and a brother of James,

To those who have been called, who are loved by God the Father and kept by[a] Jesus Christ:

²Mercy, peace and love be yours in abundance.

The Sin and Doom of Godless Men

³Dear friends, although I was very eager to write to you about the salvation we share, I felt I had to write and urge you to contend for the faith that was once for all entrusted to the saints. ⁴For certain men whose condemnation was written about[b] long ago have secretly slipped in among you. They are godless men, who change the grace of our God into a license for immorality and deny Jesus Christ our only Sovereign and Lord.

⁵Though you already know all this, I want to remind you that the Lord[c] delivered his people out of Egypt, but later destroyed those who did not believe. ⁶And the angels who did not keep their positions of authority but abandoned their own home—these he has kept in darkness, bound with everlasting chains for judgment on the great Day. ⁷In a similar way, Sodom and Gomorrah and the surrounding towns gave themselves up to sexual immorality and perversion. They serve as an example of those who suffer the punishment of eternal fire.

⁸In the very same way, these dreamers pollute their own bodies, reject authority and slander celestial beings. ⁹But even the archangel Michael, when he was disputing with the devil about the body of Moses, did not dare to bring a slanderous accusation against him, but said, "The Lord rebuke you!" ¹⁰Yet these men speak abusively against whatever they do not understand; and what things they do understand by instinct, like unreasoning animals—these are the very things that destroy them.

¹¹Woe to them! They have taken the way of Cain; they have rushed for profit into Balaam's error; they have been destroyed in Korah's rebellion.

---

[a] 1 Or for; or in   [b] 4 Or men who were marked out for condemnation   [c] 5 Some early manuscripts Jesus

Power of the Gospel

READ JUDE 3

Most people only use 10 percent of their brainpower. (You probably know people who use even less!) You *need* brains to "contend for the faith" intelligently (verse 3). This not only means correcting other Christians who spout wacky doctrines, but we "contend for the faith" by sharing Christ with non-Christians. The gospel gives us power to change people's lives, so we should pray for them to get saved. But guess what? *Most* of the time, God tells us to pray that Christians (including us!) will get off our duffs, get out there and share the gospel. God prepares people's hearts, but it's up to us to deliver the goods. Otherwise, "how can they believe in the one of whom they have not heard? And how can they hear without someone preaching to them?" (Romans 10:14). God's power through the gospel can change lives. Let's share it with others.

Your next reading is on page 1645.

12These men are blemishes at your love feasts, eating with you without the slightest qualm—shepherds who feed only themselves. They are clouds without rain, blown along by the wind; autumn trees, without fruit and uprooted—twice dead. 13They are wild waves of the sea, foaming up their shame; wandering stars, for whom blackest darkness has been reserved forever.

14Enoch, the seventh from Adam, prophesied about these men: "See, the Lord is coming with thousands upon thousands of his holy ones 15to judge everyone, and to convict all the ungodly of all the ungodly acts they have done in the ungodly way, and of all the harsh words ungodly sinners have spoken against him." 16These men are grumblers and faultfinders; they follow their own evil desires; they boast about themselves and flatter others for their own advantage.

A Call to Persevere

17But, dear friends, remember what the apostles of our Lord Jesus Christ foretold. 18They said to you, "In the last times there will be scoffers who will follow their own ungodly desires." 19These are the men who divide you, who follow mere natural instincts and do not have the Spirit.

20But you, dear friends, build yourselves up in your most holy faith and pray in the Holy Spirit. 21Keep yourselves in God's love as you wait for the mercy of our Lord Jesus Christ to bring you to eternal life.

22Be merciful to those who doubt; 23snatch others from the fire and save them; to others show mercy, mixed with fear—hating even the clothing stained by corrupted flesh.

Doxology

24To him who is able to keep you from falling and to present you before his glorious presence without fault and with great joy— 25to the only God our Savior be glory, majesty, power and authority, through Jesus Christ our Lord, before all ages, now and forevermore! Amen.

Gross!

Exile in the "blackest darkness" of hell (Jude 13) is worse than just being in the darkness of outer space. "*Blackest* darkness" is like being exiled inside a black hole, where *no* light escapes. Black holes suck up entire stars like solar slurpies.

REVELATION

Who wrote this book?
John, the disciple of Jesus, wrote this book.

Why was this book written?
John wrote this book to tell people about a vision he had of Jesus and about "what must soon take place."

For whom was this book written?
This book was written for all Christians everywhere.

When was this book written?
John wrote this book about A.D. 90.

What are some important teachings in this book?

Jesus is God — Revelation 1:9–18
Letters to seven churches — Revelation 2–3
God is on his throne — Revelation 4:1–11
God will judge Satan — Revelation 20:7–10
God will judge the dead — Revelation 20:11–15
A new world — Revelation 21:1—22:6

Prologue

1 The revelation of Jesus Christ, which God gave him to show his servants what must soon take place. He made it known by sending his angel to his servant John, ²who testifies to everything he saw—that is, the word of God and the testimony of Jesus Christ. ³Blessed is the one who reads the words of this prophecy, and blessed are those who hear it and take to heart what is written in it, because the time is near.

Greetings and Doxology

⁴John,

To the seven churches in the province of Asia:

Grace and peace to you from him who is, and who was, and who is to come, and from the seven spirits*ᵃ* before his throne, ⁵and from Jesus Christ, who is the faithful witness, the firstborn from the dead, and the ruler of the kings of the earth.

To him who loves us and has freed us from our sins by his blood, ⁶and has made us to be a kingdom and priests to serve his God and Father—to him be glory and power for ever and ever! Amen.

⁷ Look, he is coming with the clouds,
  and every eye will see him,
even those who pierced him;
  and all the peoples of the earth will mourn
    because of him.
                    So shall it be! Amen.

⁸"I am the Alpha and the Omega," says the Lord God, "who is, and who was, and who is to come, the Almighty."

One Like a Son of Man

⁹I, John, your brother and companion in the suffering and kingdom and patient endurance that are ours in Jesus, was on the island of Patmos because of the word of God and the testimony of Jesus. ¹⁰On the Lord's Day I was in the Spirit, and I heard behind me a loud voice like a trumpet, ¹¹which said: "Write on a scroll what you see and send it to the seven churches: to Ephesus, Smyrna, Pergamum, Thyatira, Sardis, Philadelphia and Laodicea."

¹²I turned around to see the voice that was speaking to me. And when I turned I saw seven golden lampstands, ¹³and among the lampstands was someone "like a son of man,"*ᵇ* dressed in a robe reaching down to his feet and with a golden sash around his chest. ¹⁴His head and hair were white like wool, as white as snow, and his eyes were like blazing fire. ¹⁵His feet were like bronze glowing in a furnace, and his voice was like the sound of rushing waters. ¹⁶In his right hand he held seven stars, and out of his mouth came a sharp double-

ᵃ 4 Or the sevenfold Spirit   *ᵇ 13 Daniel 7:13*

Get a Load of This...

When Jesus went to heaven in the clouds, the angels told his disciples, "Jesus ... will come back in the same way" (Acts 1:9–11). Sure enough, that's what he'll do (see Revelation 1:7). This is the key point of the book of Revelation: Jesus is coming back!

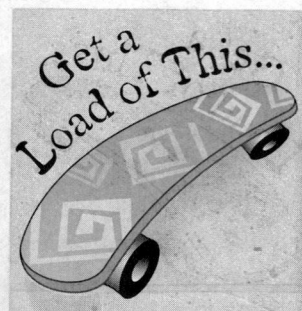

Check out Revelation 1:9. When John was an old man in Ephesus, the crazy Roman Emperor Domitian persecuted the church. John was arrested and shipped (literally) off to the tiny prison island of Patmos. When Domitian died, John was released and sailed back to Ephesus.

edged sword. His face was like the sun shining in all its brilliance.

¹⁷When I saw him, I fell at his feet as though dead. Then he placed his right hand on me and said: "Do not be afraid. I am the First and the Last. ¹⁸I am the Living One; I was dead, and behold I am alive for ever and ever! And I hold the keys of death and Hades.

¹⁹"Write, therefore, what you have seen, what is now and what will take place later. ²⁰The mystery of the seven stars that you saw in my right hand and of the seven golden lampstands is this: The seven stars are the angels*a* of the seven churches, and the seven lampstands are the seven churches.

To the Church in Ephesus

"To the angel*b* of the church in Ephesus write:

These are the words of him who holds the seven stars in his right hand and walks among the seven golden lampstands: ²I know your deeds, your hard work and your perseverance. I know that you cannot tolerate wicked men, that you have tested those who claim to be apostles but are not, and have found them false. ³You have persevered and have endured hardships for my name, and have not grown weary.

⁴Yet I hold this against you: You have forsaken your first love. ⁵Remember the height from which you have fallen! Repent and do the things you did at first. If you do not repent, I will come to you and remove your lampstand from its place. ⁶But you have this in your favor: You hate the practices of the Nicolaitans, which I also hate.

⁷He who has an ear, let him hear what the Spirit says to the churches. To him who overcomes, I will give the right to eat from the tree of life, which is in the paradise of God.

To the Church in Smyrna

⁸"To the angel of the church in Smyrna write:

These are the words of him who is the First and the Last, who died and came to life again. ⁹I know your afflictions and your poverty—yet you are rich! I know the slander of those who say they are Jews and are not, but are a synagogue of Satan. ¹⁰Do not be afraid of what you are about to suffer. I tell you, the devil will put some of you in prison to test you, and you will suffer persecution for ten days. Be faithful, even to the point of death, and I will give you the crown of life.

¹¹He who has an ear, let him hear what the Spirit says to the churches. He who overcomes will not be hurt at all by the second death.

a 20 Or *messengers*   *b 1* Or *messenger; also in verses 8, 12 and 18*

To the Church in Pergamum

12"To the angel of the church in Pergamum write:

These are the words of him who has the sharp, double-edged sword. 13I know where you live—where Satan has his throne. Yet you remain true to my name. You did not renounce your faith in me, even in the days of Antipas, my faithful witness, who was put to death in your city—where Satan lives.

14Nevertheless, I have a few things against you: You have people there who hold to the teaching of Balaam, who taught Balak to entice the Israelites to sin by eating food sacrificed to idols and by committing sexual immorality. 15Likewise you also have those who hold to the teaching of the Nicolaitans. 16Repent therefore! Otherwise, I will soon come to you and will fight against them with the sword of my mouth.

17He who has an ear, let him hear what the Spirit says to the churches.

To him who overcomes, I will give some of the hidden manna. I will also give him a white stone with a new name written on it, known only to him who receives it.

To the Church in Thyatira

18"To the angel of the church in Thyatira write:

These are the words of the Son of God, whose eyes are like blazing fire and whose feet are like burnished bronze. 19I know your deeds, your love and faith, your service and perseverance, and that you are now doing more than you did at first.

20Nevertheless, I have this against you: You tolerate that woman Jezebel, who calls herself a prophetess. By her teaching she misleads my servants into sexual immorality and the eating of food sacrificed to idols. 21I have given her time to repent of her immorality, but she is unwilling. 22So I will cast her on a bed of suffering, and I will make those who commit

Jesus' Resurrection Body

READ REVELATION 1:12–18

When Jesus was on earth he was loving—and he *still* is. Jesus is still the same loving Son of God, even though his eyes are now like blazing fire and his face shines like the sun. It's like this: You see your dad at home in the morning wearing a robe, and he gives you a hug as you head to school. That evening you flip on the TV and there's your dad, the NFL football player, wearing helmet and shoulder pads, black paint under his eyes, teeth gritted, grunting as he plows through the opposition. Hey, he's still your *dad!* He's still huggable—though the other team might not think so. Well, it's the same with Jesus: Now in his resurrected state, he appears full force with his divine power and glory. The double-edged sword coming out of his mouth symbolizes judgment. And one day Christ will return on a white horse as the Warrior-King who will punish sin and evil (Revelation 19:11–16).

Your next reading is on page 1653.

adultery with her suffer intensely, unless they repent of her ways. 23I will strike her children dead. Then all the churches will know that I am he who searches hearts and minds, and I will repay each of you according to your deeds. 24Now I say to the rest of you in Thyatira, to you who do not hold to her teaching and have not learned Satan's so-called deep secrets (I will not impose any other burden on you): 25Only hold on to what you have until I come.

26To him who overcomes and does my will to the end, I will give authority over the nations—

27 'He will rule them with an iron scepter;
  he will dash them to pieces like pottery' a—

just as I have received authority from my Father. 28I will also give him the morning star. 29He who has an ear, let him hear what the Spirit says to the churches.

a 27 Psalm 2:9

Make It Stick

_____

_____

_____

_____

_____

_____

READ REVELATION 2
There are some really cool rewards for obeying God and overcoming: You get to eat from the tree of life (2:7); you'll get manna and a white stone with a special name written on it (2:17); you'll have authority over the nations (2:26); God will write his name on you (3:12); you'll sit on Jesus' throne with him (3:21). Write on a sticky note which one of these rewards is your favorite—and why.

To the Church in Sardis

"To the angel[a] of the church in Sardis write:

These are the words of him who holds the seven spirits[b] of God and the seven stars. I know your deeds; you have a reputation of being alive, but you are dead. ²Wake up! Strengthen what remains and is about to die, for I have not found your deeds complete in the sight of my God. ³Remember, therefore, what you have received and heard; obey it, and repent. But if you do not wake up, I will come like a thief, and you will not know at what time I will come to you.

⁴Yet you have a few people in Sardis who have not soiled their clothes. They will walk with me, dressed in white, for they are worthy. ⁵He who overcomes will, like them, be dressed in white. I will never blot out his name from the book of life, but will acknowledge his name before my Father and his angels. ⁶He who has an ear, let him hear what the Spirit says to the churches.

To the Church in Philadelphia

⁷"To the angel of the church in Philadelphia write:

These are the words of him who is holy and true, who holds the key of David. What he opens no one can shut, and what he shuts no one can open. ⁸I know your deeds. See, I have placed before you an open door that no one can shut. I know that you have little strength, yet you have kept my word and have not denied my name. ⁹I will make those who are of the synagogue of Satan, who claim to be Jews though they are not, but are liars—I will make them come and fall down at your feet and acknowledge that I have loved you. ¹⁰Since you have kept my command to endure patiently, I will also keep you from the hour of trial that is going to come upon the whole world to test those who live on the earth.

¹¹I am coming soon. Hold on to what you have, so that no one will take your crown. ¹²Him who overcomes I will make a pillar in the temple of my God. Never again will he leave it. I will write on him the name of my God and the name of the city of my God, the new Jerusalem, which is coming down out of heaven from my God; and I will also write on him my new name. ¹³He who has an ear, let him hear what the Spirit says to the churches.

To the Church in Laodicea

¹⁴"To the angel of the church in Laodicea write:

These are the words of the Amen, the faithful and true witness, the ruler of God's creation. ¹⁵I know your deeds, that you are neither cold nor

Get a Load of This...

Whoa! Check out Revelation 3:15–16. If you want to avoid being a big old gob of spit on the ground, don't be lukewarm. You're only fooling yourself if you think you can have one foot in sin and the other foot in God's kingdom. There's no middle ground! Serve God with your *whole* heart!

In other Words...

---

[a] 1 Or *messenger;* also in verses 7 and 14   [b] 1 Or *the sevenfold Spirit*

Get a Load of This...

Check out Revelation 3:20. Jesus wants to spend time with you. Do you think, "I don't have *time*"? Well, how about praying for even *five* minutes? Jesus, the creator of the universe, is knocking at the door of your heart every day. Are you too busy? Hey! You'd answer the door for anyone else—especially if they were bringing pizza.

hot. I wish you were either one or the other! ¹⁶So, because you are lukewarm—neither hot nor cold—I am about to spit you out of my mouth. ¹⁷You say, 'I am rich; I have acquired wealth and do not need a thing.' But you do not realize that you are wretched, pitiful, poor, blind and naked. ¹⁸I counsel you to buy from me gold refined in the fire, so you can become rich; and white clothes to wear, so you can cover your shameful nakedness; and salve to put on your eyes, so you can see.

¹⁹Those whom I love I rebuke and discipline. So be earnest, and repent. ²⁰Here I am! I stand at the door and knock. If anyone hears my voice and opens the door, I will come in and eat with him, and he with me.

²¹To him who overcomes, I will give the right to sit with me on my throne, just as I overcame and sat down with my Father on his throne. ²²He who has an ear, let him hear what the Spirit says to the churches."

The Throne in Heaven

After this I looked, and there before me was a door standing open in heaven. And the voice I had first heard speaking to me like a trumpet said, "Come up here, and I will show you what must take place after this." ²At once I was in the Spirit, and there before me was a throne in heaven with someone sitting on it. ³And the one who sat there had the appearance of jasper and carnelian. A rainbow, resembling an emerald, encircled the throne. ⁴Surrounding the throne were twenty-four other thrones, and seated on them were twenty-four elders. They were dressed in white and had crowns of gold on their heads. ⁵From the throne came flashes of lightning, rumblings and peals of thunder. Before the throne, seven lamps were blazing. These are the seven spirits*a* of God. ⁶Also before the throne there was what looked like a sea of glass, clear as crystal.

In the center, around the throne, were four living creatures, and they were covered with eyes, in front and in back. ⁷The first living creature was like a lion, the second was like an ox, the third had a face like a man, the fourth was like a flying eagle. ⁸Each of the four living creatures had six wings and was covered with eyes all around, even under his wings. Day and night they never stop saying:

> "Holy, holy, holy
> is the Lord God Almighty,
> who was, and is, and is to come."

⁹Whenever the living creatures give glory, honor and thanks to him who sits on the throne and who lives for ever and ever, ¹⁰the twenty-four elders fall down before

a 5 Or the sevenfold Spirit

him who sits on the throne, and worship him who lives for ever and ever. They lay their crowns before the throne and say:

11 "You are worthy, our Lord and God,
    to receive glory and honor and power,
  for you created all things,
    and by your will they were created
    and have their being."

The Scroll and the Lamb

Then I saw in the right hand of him who sat on the throne a scroll with writing on both sides and sealed with seven seals. 2And I saw a mighty angel proclaiming in a loud voice, "Who is worthy to break the seals and open the scroll?" 3But no one in heaven or on earth or under the earth could open the scroll or even look inside it. 4I wept and wept because no one was found who was worthy to open the scroll or look inside. 5Then one of the elders said to me, "Do not weep! See, the Lion of the tribe of Judah, the Root of David, has triumphed. He is able to open the scroll and its seven seals."

6Then I saw a Lamb, looking as if it had been slain, standing in the center of the throne, encircled by the four living creatures and the elders. He had seven horns and seven eyes, which are the seven spiritsª of God sent out into all the earth. 7He came and took the scroll from the right hand of him who sat on the throne. 8And when he had taken it, the four living creatures and the twenty-four elders fell down before the Lamb. Each one had a harp and they were holding golden bowls full of incense, which are the prayers of the saints. 9And they sang a new song:

  "You are worthy to take the scroll
    and to open its seals,
  because you were slain,
    and with your blood you purchased men for God
    from every tribe and language and people and
      nation.
10 You have made them to be a kingdom and priests to
      serve our God,
    and they will reign on the earth."

11Then I looked and heard the voice of many angels, numbering thousands upon thousands, and ten thousand times ten thousand. They encircled the throne and the living creatures and the elders. 12In a loud voice they sang:

  "Worthy is the Lamb, who was slain,
    to receive power and wealth and wisdom and strength
    and honor and glory and praise!"

13Then I heard every creature in heaven and on earth and under the earth and on the sea, and all that is in them, singing:

ª 6 Or the sevenfold Spirit

Get a Load of This...

Check out the "four living creatures" hovering over God's throne in Revelation 4:6–8. The creatures and alien beings of science fiction are peanuts compared to the *real* ones God created! When we see the world to come and God's throne, we're going to be blown away!

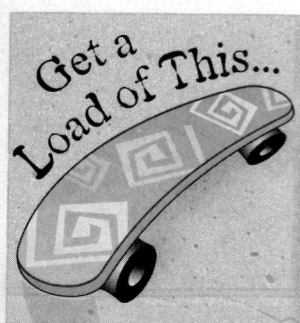

Get a Load of This...

Count these angels in Revelation 5:11. *How many are there?* This has got to be one of the world's hardest math problems. Actually, this number simply means gobs of angels, more than you can count.

"To him who sits on the throne and to the Lamb
be praise and honor and glory and power,
for ever and ever!"

[14]The four living creatures said, "Amen," and the elders fell down and worshiped.

The Seals

6 I watched as the Lamb opened the first of the seven seals. Then I heard one of the four living creatures say in a voice like thunder, "Come!" [2]I looked, and there before me was a white horse! Its rider held a bow, and he was given a crown, and he rode out as a conqueror bent on conquest.

[3]When the Lamb opened the second seal, I heard the second living creature say, "Come!" [4]Then another horse came out, a fiery red one. Its rider was given power to take peace from the earth and to make men slay each other. To him was given a large sword.

[5]When the Lamb opened the third seal, I heard the third living creature say, "Come!" I looked, and there before me was a black horse! Its rider was holding a pair of scales in his hand. [6]Then I heard what sounded like a voice among the four living creatures, saying, "A quart[a] of wheat for a day's wages,[b] and three quarts of barley for a day's wages,[b] and do not damage the oil and the wine!"

[7]When the Lamb opened the fourth seal, I heard the voice of the fourth living creature say, "Come!" [8]I looked, and there before me was a pale horse! Its rider was named Death, and Hades was following close behind him. They were given power over a fourth of the earth to kill by sword, famine and plague, and by the wild beasts of the earth.

[9]When he opened the fifth seal, I saw under the altar the souls of those who had been slain because of the word of God and the testimony they had maintained. [10]They called out in a loud voice, "How long, Sovereign Lord, holy and true, until you judge the inhabitants of the earth and avenge our blood?" [11]Then each of them was given a white robe, and they were told to wait a little longer, until the number of their fellow servants and brothers who were to be killed as they had been was completed.

[12]I watched as he opened the sixth seal. There was a great earthquake. The sun turned black like sackcloth made of goat hair, the whole moon turned blood red, [13]and the stars in the sky fell to earth, as late figs drop from a fig tree when shaken by a strong wind. [14]The sky receded like a scroll, rolling up, and every mountain and island was removed from its place.

[15]Then the kings of the earth, the princes, the generals, the rich, the mighty, and every slave and every free man hid in caves and among the rocks of the mountains. [16]They called to the mountains and the rocks, "Fall on us and hide us from the face of him who sits on the throne

[a] 6 Greek a *choinix* (probably about a liter)   [b] 6 Greek a *denarius*

and from the wrath of the Lamb! ¹⁷For the great day of their wrath has come, and who can stand?"

144,000 Sealed

7 After this I saw four angels standing at the four corners of the earth, holding back the four winds of the earth to prevent any wind from blowing on the land or on the sea or on any tree. ²Then I saw another angel coming up from the east, having the seal of the living God. He called out in a loud voice to the four angels who had been given power to harm the land and the sea: ³"Do not harm the land or the sea or the trees until we put a seal on the foreheads of the servants of our God." ⁴Then I heard the number of those who were sealed: 144,000 from all the tribes of Israel.

⁵From the tribe of Judah 12,000 were sealed,
from the tribe of Reuben 12,000,
from the tribe of Gad 12,000,
⁶from the tribe of Asher 12,000,
from the tribe of Naphtali 12,000,
from the tribe of Manasseh 12,000,
⁷from the tribe of Simeon 12,000,
from the tribe of Levi 12,000,
from the tribe of Issachar 12,000,
⁸from the tribe of Zebulun 12,000,
from the tribe of Joseph 12,000,
from the tribe of Benjamin 12,000.

The Great Multitude in White Robes

⁹After this I looked and there before me was a great multitude that no one could count, from every nation, tribe, people and language, standing before the throne and in front of the Lamb. They were wearing white robes and were holding palm branches in their hands. ¹⁰And they cried out in a loud voice:

"Salvation belongs to our God,
who sits on the throne,
and to the Lamb."

¹¹All the angels were standing around the throne and around the elders and the four living creatures. They fell down on their faces before the throne and worshiped God, ¹²saying:

"Amen!
Praise and glory
and wisdom and thanks and honor
and power and strength
be to our God for ever and ever.
Amen!"

¹³Then one of the elders asked me, "These in white robes—who are they, and where did they come from?"
¹⁴I answered, "Sir, you know."
And he said, "These are they who have come out of the great tribulation; they have washed their robes and

Get a Load of This...

Have you ever heard of the Four Horsemen of the Apocalypse—conquest, bloodshed, famine and death? Ever wonder where the account of those horsemen came from? From right here: Revelation 6:2, 4, 5, 8.

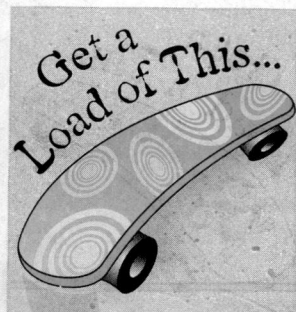

Get a Load of This...

Check out Revelation 8:13. What do we have here, a talking eagle? Get out of here! Is this for *real*? Actually, it's probably symbolic, like a parable. Then again, Balaam's donkey could talk (see Numbers 22:28). So who knows?

made them white in the blood of the Lamb. [15]Therefore,

"they are before the throne of God
  and serve him day and night in his temple;
and he who sits on the throne will spread his tent
    over them.
[16]Never again will they hunger;
  never again will they thirst.
The sun will not beat upon them,
  nor any scorching heat.
[17]For the Lamb at the center of the throne will be their
    shepherd;
  he will lead them to springs of living water.
And God will wipe away every tear from their eyes."

The Seventh Seal and the Golden Censer

When he opened the seventh seal, there was silence in heaven for about half an hour.
[2]And I saw the seven angels who stand before God, and to them were given seven trumpets.

[3]Another angel, who had a golden censer, came and stood at the altar. He was given much incense to offer, with the prayers of all the saints, on the golden altar before the throne. [4]The smoke of the incense, together with the prayers of the saints, went up before God from the angel's hand. [5]Then the angel took the censer, filled it with fire from the altar, and hurled it on the earth; and there came peals of thunder, rumblings, flashes of lightning and an earthquake.

The Trumpets

[6]Then the seven angels who had the seven trumpets prepared to sound them.

[7]The first angel sounded his trumpet, and there came hail and fire mixed with blood, and it was hurled down upon the earth. A third of the earth was burned up, a third of the trees were burned up, and all the green grass was burned up.

[8]The second angel sounded his trumpet, and something like a huge mountain, all ablaze, was thrown into the sea. A third of the sea turned into blood, [9]a third of the living creatures in the sea died, and a third of the ships were destroyed.

[10]The third angel sounded his trumpet, and a great star, blazing like a torch, fell from the sky on a third of the rivers and on the springs of water— [11]the name of the star is Wormwood.[a] A third of the waters turned bitter, and many people died from the waters that had become bitter.

[12]The fourth angel sounded his trumpet, and a third of the sun was struck, a third of the moon, and a third of the stars, so that a third of them turned dark. A third of the day was without light, and also a third of the night.

[13]As I watched, I heard an eagle that was flying in

[a] 11 That is, Bitterness

midair call out in a loud voice: "Woe! Woe! Woe to the inhabitants of the earth, because of the trumpet blasts about to be sounded by the other three angels!"

9 The fifth angel sounded his trumpet, and I saw a star that had fallen from the sky to the earth. The star was given the key to the shaft of the Abyss. ²When he opened the Abyss, smoke rose from it like the smoke from a gigantic furnace. The sun and sky were darkened by the smoke from the Abyss. ³And out of the smoke locusts came down upon the earth and were given power like that of scorpions of the earth. ⁴They were told not to harm the grass of the earth or any plant or tree, but only those people who did not have the seal of God on their foreheads. ⁵They were not given power to kill them, but only to torture them for five months. And the agony they suffered was like that of the sting of a scorpion when it strikes a man. ⁶During those days men will seek death, but will not find it; they will long to die, but death will elude them.

⁷The locusts looked like horses prepared for battle. On their heads they wore something like crowns of gold, and their faces resembled human faces. ⁸Their hair was like women's hair, and their teeth were like lions' teeth. ⁹They had breastplates like breastplates of iron, and the sound of their wings was like the thundering of many horses and chariots rushing into battle. ¹⁰They had tails and stings like scorpions, and in their tails they had power to torment people for five months. ¹¹They had as king over them the angel of the Abyss, whose name in Hebrew is Abaddon, and in Greek, Apollyon.ᵃ

¹²The first woe is past; two other woes are yet to come.

¹³The sixth angel sounded his trumpet, and I heard a voice coming from the hornsᵇ of the golden altar that is before God. ¹⁴It said to the sixth angel who had the trumpet, "Release the four angels who are bound at the great river Euphrates." ¹⁵And the four angels who had been

ᵃ 11 *Abaddon* and *Apollyon* mean *Destroyer.* ᵇ 13 That is, projections

---

Visions and Symbols

READ REVELATION 9:1–19

Remember when Peter had a vision of all kinds of creepy crawly critters slithering in the sheet, and God said, "Eat up, Peter"? (see Acts 10:9–13). Later, Peter found out that the vision meant (whew!) that Gentiles were "clean" and the gospel could be preached to them. God does use symbolism to get his message across. Well, the book of Revelation was one *huge* symbolic vision full of even stranger, more bizarre beasts! Peter's vision had a clear interpretation, but very few interpretations are given for visions in the book of Revelation, so we really don't know *what* some of this stuff means. Just the same, God gave these heavenly visions to John to share with us, so we should read them and be inspired by their message. We just shouldn't get detailed interpretations for what we think each vision means. The time will come when God will make everything clear.

Your next reading is on page 1664.

kept ready for this very hour and day and month and year were released to kill a third of mankind. ¹⁶The number of the mounted troops was two hundred million. I heard their number.

¹⁷The horses and riders I saw in my vision looked like this: Their breastplates were fiery red, dark blue, and yellow as sulfur. The heads of the horses resembled the heads of lions, and out of their mouths came fire, smoke and sulfur. ¹⁸A third of mankind was killed by the three plagues of fire, smoke and sulfur that came out of their mouths. ¹⁹The power of the horses was in their mouths and in their tails; for their tails were like snakes, having heads with which they inflict injury.

²⁰The rest of mankind that were not killed by these plagues still did not repent of the work of their hands; they did not stop worshiping demons, and idols of gold, silver, bronze, stone and wood— idols that cannot see or hear or walk. ²¹Nor did they repent of their murders, their magic arts, their sexual immorality or their thefts.

The Angel and the Little Scroll

10 Then I saw another mighty angel coming down from heaven. He was robed in a cloud, with a rainbow above his head; his face was like the sun, and his legs were like fiery pillars. ²He was holding a little scroll, which lay open in his hand. He planted his right foot on the sea and his left foot on the land, ³and he gave a loud shout like the roar of a lion. When he shouted, the voices of the seven thunders spoke. ⁴And when the seven thunders spoke, I was about to write; but I heard a voice from heaven say, "Seal up what the seven thunders have said and do not write it down."

⁵Then the angel I had seen standing on the sea and on the land raised his right hand to heaven. ⁶And he swore by him who lives for ever and ever, who created the heavens and all that is in them, the earth and all that is in it, and the sea and all that is in it, and said, "There will be no more delay! ⁷But in the days when the seventh angel is about to sound his trumpet, the mystery of God will be accomplished, just as he announced to his servants the prophets."

⁸Then the voice that I had heard from heaven spoke to me once more: "Go, take the scroll that lies open in the hand of the angel who is standing on the sea and on the land."

⁹So I went to the angel and asked him to give me the little scroll. He said to me, "Take it and eat it. It will turn your stomach sour, but in your mouth it will be as sweet as honey." ¹⁰I took the little scroll from the angel's hand and ate it. It tasted as sweet as honey in my mouth, but when I had eaten it, my stomach turned sour. ¹¹Then I was told, "You must prophesy again about many peoples, nations, languages and kings."

The Two Witnesses

11 I was given a reed like a measuring rod and was told, "Go and measure the temple of God and the altar, and count the worshipers there. ²But exclude the outer court; do not measure it, because it has been given to the Gentiles. They will trample on the holy city for 42 months. ³And I will give power to my two witnesses, and they will prophesy for 1,260 days, clothed in sackcloth." ⁴These are the two olive trees and the two lampstands that stand before the Lord of the earth. ⁵If anyone tries to harm them, fire comes from their mouths and devours their enemies. This is how anyone who wants to harm them must die. ⁶These men have power to shut up the sky so that it will not rain during the time they are prophesying; and they have power to turn the waters into blood and to strike the earth with every kind of plague as often as they want.

⁷Now when they have finished their testimony, the beast that comes up from the Abyss will attack them, and overpower and kill them. ⁸Their bodies will lie in the street of the great city, which is figuratively called Sodom and Egypt, where also their Lord was crucified. ⁹For three and a half days men from every people, tribe, language and nation will gaze on their bodies and refuse them burial. ¹⁰The inhabitants of the earth will gloat over them and will celebrate by sending each other gifts, because these two prophets had tormented those who live on the earth.

¹¹But after the three and a half days a breath of life from God entered them, and they stood on their feet, and terror struck those who saw them. ¹²Then they heard a loud voice from heaven saying to them,

"Come up here." And they went up to heaven in a cloud, while their enemies looked on.

[13]At that very hour there was a severe earthquake and a tenth of the city collapsed. Seven thousand people were killed in the earthquake, and the survivors were terrified and gave glory to the God of heaven.

[14]The second woe has passed; the third woe is coming soon.

The Seventh Trumpet

[15]The seventh angel sounded his trumpet, and there were loud voices in heaven, which said:

"The kingdom of the world has become the
      kingdom of our Lord and of his Christ,
   and he will reign for ever and ever."

[16]And the twenty-four elders, who were seated on their thrones before God, fell on their faces and worshiped God, [17]saying:

"We give thanks to you, Lord God Almighty,
   the One who is and who was,
because you have taken your great power
   and have begun to reign.
[18]The nations were angry;
   and your wrath has come.
The time has come for judging the dead,
   and for rewarding your servants the prophets
and your saints and those who reverence your name,
   both small and great—
and for destroying those who destroy the earth."

[19]Then God's temple in heaven was opened, and within his temple was seen the ark of his covenant. And there came flashes of lightning, rumblings, peals of thunder, an earthquake and a great hailstorm.

The Woman and the Dragon

12 A great and wondrous sign appeared in heaven: a woman clothed with the sun, with the moon under her feet and a crown of twelve stars on her head. [2]She was pregnant and cried out in pain as she was about to give birth. [3]Then another sign appeared in heaven: an enormous red dragon with seven heads and ten horns and seven crowns on his heads. [4]His tail swept a third of the stars out of the sky and flung them to the earth. The dragon stood in front of the woman who was about to give birth, so that he might devour her child the moment it was born. [5]She gave birth to a son, a male child, who will rule all the nations with an iron scepter. And her child was snatched up to God and to his throne. [6]The woman fled into the desert to a place prepared for her by God, where she might be taken care of for 1,260 days.

[7]And there was war in heaven. Michael and his angels fought against the dragon, and the dragon and his angels fought back. [8]But he was not strong enough,

Get a Load of This...

Check out Revelation 11:15. And now, an important announcement from the seventh angel! Ta da! Jesus has just taken over the kingdoms of the world and has made the whole world his kingdom.

In Other Words...

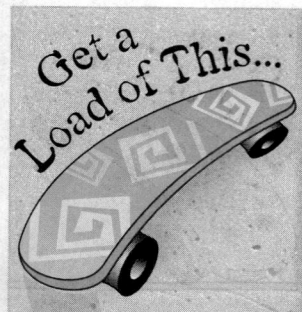

Get a Load of This...

This gigantic, flaming red, seven-headed dragon in Revelation 12:3 is not real. It's a mythological creature. And this is no cutesy "good" dragon from a kiddie movie either. This monster symbolizes Satan, the devil himself, the enemy of God, who is persecuting Christians.

and they lost their place in heaven. [9]The great dragon was hurled down—that ancient serpent called the devil, or Satan, who leads the whole world astray. He was hurled to the earth, and his angels with him. [10]Then I heard a loud voice in heaven say:

"Now have come the salvation and the power and
    the kingdom of our God,
and the authority of his Christ.
For the accuser of our brothers,
    who accuses them before our God day and night,
    has been hurled down.
[11]They overcame him
    by the blood of the Lamb
    and by the word of their testimony;
they did not love their lives so much
    as to shrink from death.
[12]Therefore rejoice, you heavens
    and you who dwell in them!
But woe to the earth and the sea,
    because the devil has gone down to you!
He is filled with fury,
    because he knows that his time is short."

[13]When the dragon saw that he had been hurled to the earth, he pursued the woman who had given birth to the male child. [14]The woman was given the two wings of a great eagle, so that she might fly to the place prepared for her in the desert, where she would be taken care of for a time, times and half a time, out of the serpent's reach. [15]Then from his mouth the serpent spewed water like a river, to overtake the woman and sweep her away with the torrent. [16]But the earth helped the woman by opening its mouth and swallowing the river that the dragon had spewed out of his mouth. [17]Then the dragon was enraged at the woman and went off to make war against the rest of her offspring— those who obey God's commandments and hold to the testimony of Jesus. [1]And the dragon[a] stood on the shore of the sea.

The Beast out of the Sea

And I saw a beast coming out of the sea. He had ten horns and seven heads, with ten crowns on his horns, and on each head a blasphemous name. [2]The beast I saw resembled a leopard, but had feet like those of a bear and a mouth like that of a lion. The dragon gave the beast his power and his throne and great authority. [3]One of the heads of the beast seemed to have had a fatal wound, but the fatal wound had been healed. The whole world was astonished and followed the beast. [4]Men worshiped the dragon because he had given authority to the beast, and they also worshiped the beast and asked, "Who is like the beast? Who can make war against him?"
[5]The beast was given a mouth to utter proud words

a 1 Some late manuscripts And I

and blasphemies and to exercise his authority for forty-two months. 6He opened his mouth to blaspheme God, and to slander his name and his dwelling place and those who live in heaven. 7He was given power to make war against the saints and to conquer them. And he was given authority over every tribe, people, language and nation. 8All inhabitants of the earth will worship the beast—all whose names have not been written in the book of life belonging to the Lamb that was slain from the creation of the world.*a*

9He who has an ear, let him hear.

10If anyone is to go into captivity,
    into captivity he will go.
  If anyone is to be killed*b* with the sword,
    with the sword he will be killed.

This calls for patient endurance and faithfulness on the part of the saints.

The Beast out of the Earth

11Then I saw another beast, coming out of the earth. He had two horns like a lamb, but he spoke like a dragon. 12He exercised all the authority of the first beast on his behalf, and made the earth and its inhabitants worship the first beast, whose fatal wound had been healed. 13And he performed great and miraculous signs, even causing fire to come down from heaven to earth in full view of men. 14Because of the signs he was given power to do on behalf of the first beast, he deceived the inhabitants of the earth. He ordered them to set up an image in honor of the beast who was wounded by the sword and yet lived. 15He was given power to give breath to the image of the first beast, so that it could speak and cause all who refused to worship the image to be killed. 16He also forced everyone, small and great, rich and poor, free and slave, to receive a mark on his right hand or on his forehead, 17so that no one could buy or sell unless he had the mark, which is the name of the beast or the number of his name.

18This calls for wisdom. If anyone has insight, let him calculate the number of the beast, for it is man's number. His number is 666.

The Lamb and the 144,000

14 Then I looked, and there before me was the Lamb, standing on Mount Zion, and with him 144,000 who had his name and his Father's name written on their foreheads. 2And I heard a sound from heaven like the roar of rushing waters and like a loud peal of thunder. The sound I heard was like that of harpists playing their harps. 3And they sang a new song before the throne and before the four living creatures and the elders. No one could learn the song except the 144,000 who had been redeemed from the

Get a Load of This...

Check out Revelation 13:16–18 and 14:11–12. You've probably heard about the mark of the beast, the number 666 imprinted on people's right hand or forehead. Christians have lots of different ideas as to what this might be. What do *you* think it is?

---

a 8 Or written from the creation of the world in the book of life belonging to the Lamb that was slain   b 10 Some manuscripts anyone kills earth. [4]These are those who did not defile themselves with women, for they kept themselves pure. They follow the Lamb wherever he goes. They were purchased from among men and offered as firstfruits to God and the Lamb. [5]No lie was found in their mouths; they are blameless.

The Three Angels

[6]Then I saw another angel flying in mid-air, and he had the eternal gospel to proclaim to those who live on the earth—to every nation, tribe, language and people. [7]He said in a loud voice, "Fear God and give him glory, because the hour of his judgment has come. Worship him who made the heavens, the earth, the sea and the springs of water."

[8]A second angel followed and said, "Fallen! Fallen is Babylon the Great, which made all the nations drink the maddening wine of her adulteries."

[9]A third angel followed them and said in a loud voice: "If anyone worships the beast and his image and receives his mark on the forehead or on the hand, [10]he, too, will drink of the wine of God's fury, which has been poured full strength into the cup of his wrath. He will be tormented with burning sulfur in the presence of the holy angels and of the Lamb. [11]And the smoke of their torment rises for ever and ever. There is no rest day or night for those who worship the beast and his image, or for anyone who receives the mark of his name." [12]This calls for patient endurance on the part of the saints who obey God's commandments and remain faithful to Jesus.

[13]Then I heard a voice from heaven say, "Write: Blessed are the dead who die in the Lord from now on."

"Yes," says the Spirit, "they will rest from their labor, for their deeds will follow them."

The Harvest of the Earth

[14]I looked, and there before me was a white cloud, and seated on the cloud was one "like a son of man"[a] with a crown of gold on his head and a sharp sickle in his hand. [15]Then another angel came out of the temple and called in a loud voice to him who was sitting on the cloud, "Take your sickle and reap, because the time to reap has come, for the harvest of the earth is ripe." [16]So he who was seated on the cloud swung his sickle over the earth, and the earth was harvested.

[17]Another angel came out of the temple in heaven, and he too had a sharp sickle. [18]Still another angel, who had charge of the fire, came from the altar and called in a loud voice to him who had the sharp sickle, "Take your sharp sickle and gather the clusters of grapes from the earth's vine, because its grapes are ripe." [19]The angel swung his sickle on the earth, gathered its grapes and threw them into the great winepress of God's wrath. [20]They were trampled in the winepress outside the city, and blood flowed out of the press, rising as high as the horses' bridles for a distance of 1,600 stadia.[b]

Seven Angels With Seven Plagues

15 I saw in heaven another great and marvelous sign: seven angels with the seven last plagues—last, because with them God's wrath is completed. [2]And I saw what looked like a sea of glass mixed with fire and, standing beside the sea, those who had been victorious over the beast and his image and over the number of his name. They held harps given them by God [3]and sang the song of Moses the servant of God and the song of the Lamb:

"Great and marvelous are your deeds,
    Lord God Almighty.
Just and true are your ways,
    King of the ages.
[4]Who will not fear you, O Lord,
    and bring glory to your name?
For you alone are holy.
All nations will come
    and worship before you,
for your righteous acts have been
    revealed."

[5]After this I looked and in heaven the temple, that is, the tabernacle of the Testimony, was opened. [6]Out of the temple came the seven angels with the seven plagues. They were dressed in clean, shining linen and wore golden sashes around their chests. [7]Then one of the four living creatures gave to the seven angels seven golden bowls filled with the wrath of God, who lives for ever and ever. [8]And the temple was filled with smoke from the

---

[a] 14 Daniel 7:13 [b] 20 That is, about 180 miles (about 300 kilometers)

glory of God and from his power, and no one could enter the temple until the seven plagues of the seven angels were completed.

The Seven Bowls of God's Wrath

16 Then I heard a loud voice from the temple saying to the seven angels, "Go, pour out the seven bowls of God's wrath on the earth." ²The first angel went and poured out his bowl on the land, and ugly and painful sores broke out on the people who had the mark of the beast and worshiped his image.

³The second angel poured out his bowl on the sea, and it turned into blood like that of a dead man, and every living thing in the sea died.

⁴The third angel poured out his bowl on the rivers and springs of water, and they became blood. ⁵Then I heard the angel in charge of the waters say:

"You are just in these judgments,
    you who are and who were, the Holy One,
    because you have so judged;
⁶ for they have shed the blood of your saints and
        prophets,
    and you have given them blood to drink as they
        deserve."

⁷And I heard the altar respond:

"Yes, Lord God Almighty,
    true and just are your judgments."

⁸The fourth angel poured out his bowl on the sun, and the sun was given power to scorch people with fire. ⁹They were seared by the intense heat and they cursed the name of God, who had control over these plagues, but they refused to repent and glorify him.

¹⁰The fifth angel poured out his bowl on the throne of the beast, and his kingdom was plunged into darkness. Men gnawed their tongues in agony ¹¹and cursed the God of heaven because of their pains and their sores, but they refused to repent of what they had done.

¹²The sixth angel poured out his bowl on the great river Euphrates, and its water was dried up to prepare the way for the kings from the East. ¹³Then I saw three evilᵃ spirits that looked like frogs; they came out of the mouth of the dragon, out of the mouth of the beast and out of the mouth of the false prophet. ¹⁴They are spirits of demons performing miraculous signs, and they go out to the kings of the whole world, to gather them for the battle on the great day of God Almighty.

¹⁵"Behold, I come like a thief! Blessed is he who stays awake and keeps his clothes with him, so that he may not go naked and be shamefully exposed."

¹⁶Then they gathered the kings together to the place that in Hebrew is called Armageddon.

¹⁷The seventh angel poured out his bowl into the air,

ᵃ 13 Greek unclean

Gross!

Why do these demons look like *frogs* (see Revelation 16:13)? Maybe because this fits disgusting evil spirits— cold, clammy, green skin with bumps all over. These plagues in verses 1–14 (sores, darkness, waters into blood, frogs, etc.) are *very* similar to the plagues God sent to judge Egypt. Just like Pharaoh and the Egyptians hardened their hearts, the Antichrist and his followers refuse to repent.

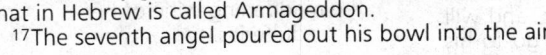

and out of the temple came a loud voice from the throne, saying, "It is done!" 18Then there came flashes of lightning, rumblings, peals of thunder and a severe earthquake. No earthquake like it has ever occurred since man has been on earth, so tremendous was the quake. 19The great city split into three parts, and the cities of the nations collapsed. God remembered Babylon the Great and gave her the cup filled with the wine of the fury of his wrath. 20Every island fled away and the mountains could not be found. 21From the sky huge hailstones of about a hundred pounds each fell upon men. And they cursed God on account of the plague of hail, because the plague was so terrible.

The Woman on the Beast

17 One of the seven angels who had the seven bowls came and said to me, "Come, I will show you the punishment of the great prostitute, who sits on many waters. 2With her the kings of the earth committed adultery and the inhabitants of the earth were intoxicated with the wine of her adulteries."

3Then the angel carried me away in the Spirit into a desert. There I saw a woman sitting on a scarlet beast that was covered with blasphemous names and had seven heads and ten horns. 4The woman was dressed in purple and scarlet, and was glittering with gold, precious stones and pearls. She held a golden cup in her hand, filled with abominable things and the filth of her adulteries. 5This title was written on her forehead:

MYSTERY
BABYLON THE GREAT
THE MOTHER OF PROSTITUTES
AND OF THE ABOMINATIONS OF THE EARTH.

6I saw that the woman was drunk with the blood of the saints, the blood of those who bore testimony to Jesus.

When I saw her, I was greatly astonished. 7Then the angel said to me: "Why are you astonished? I will explain to you the mystery of the woman and of the beast she rides, which has the seven heads and ten horns. 8The beast, which you saw, once was, now is not, and will come up out of the Abyss and go to his destruction. The inhabitants of the earth whose names have not been written in the book of life from the creation of the world will be astonished when they see the beast, because he once was, now is not, and yet will come.

9"This calls for a mind with wisdom. The seven heads are seven hills on which the woman sits. 10They are also seven kings. Five have fallen, one is, the other has not yet come; but when he does come, he must remain for a little while. 11The beast who once was, and now is not, is an eighth king. He belongs to the seven and is going to his destruction.

12"The ten horns you saw are ten kings who have not yet received a kingdom, but who for one hour will receive authority as kings along with the beast. 13They have one purpose and will give their power and authority to the beast. 14They will make war against the Lamb, but the Lamb will overcome them because he is Lord of lords and King of kings—and with him will be his called, chosen and faithful followers."

15Then the angel said to me, "The waters you saw, where the prostitute sits, are peoples, multitudes, nations and languages. 16The beast and the ten horns you saw will hate the prostitute. They will bring her to ruin and leave her naked; they will eat her flesh and burn her with fire. 17For God has put it into their hearts to accomplish his purpose by agreeing to give the beast their power to rule, until God's words are fulfilled. 18The woman you saw is the great city that rules over the kings of the earth."

The Fall of Babylon

18 After this I saw another angel coming down from heaven. He had great authority, and the earth was illuminated by his splendor. 2With a mighty voice he shouted:

"Fallen! Fallen is Babylon the Great!
　She has become a home for demons
and a haunt for every evil*a* spirit,
　a haunt for every unclean and
　　detestable bird.
3For all the nations have drunk
　the maddening wine of her
　adulteries.

a 2 Greek unclean

The kings of the earth committed
adultery with her,
and the merchants of the earth grew
rich from her excessive
luxuries."

4Then I heard another voice from heaven say:

"Come out of her, my people,
so that you will not share in her sins,
so that you will not receive any of
her plagues;
5for her sins are piled up to heaven,
and God has remembered her
crimes.
6Give back to her as she has given;
pay her back double for what she
has done.
Mix her a double portion from her
own cup.
7Give her as much torture and grief
as the glory and luxury she gave
herself.
In her heart she boasts,
'I sit as queen; I am not a widow,
and I will never mourn.'
8Therefore in one day her plagues will
overtake her:
death, mourning and famine.
She will be consumed by fire,
for mighty is the Lord God who
judges her.

9"When the kings of the earth who
committed adultery with her and shared
her luxury see the smoke of her burning,
they will weep and mourn over her. 10Terrified at her torment, they will stand far
off and cry:

" 'Woe! Woe, O great city,
O Babylon, city of power!
In one hour your doom has come!'

11"The merchants of the earth will
weep and mourn over her because no one
buys their cargoes any more— 12cargoes
of gold, silver, precious stones and pearls;
fine linen, purple, silk and scarlet cloth;
every sort of citron wood, and articles of
every kind made of ivory, costly wood,
bronze, iron and marble; 13cargoes of cinnamon and spice, of incense, myrrh and
frankincense, of wine and olive oil, of fine
flour and wheat; cattle and sheep; horses
and carriages; and bodies and souls of
men.
14"They will say, 'The fruit you longed

for is gone from you. All your riches and
splendor have vanished, never to be recovered.' 15The merchants who sold these
things and gained their wealth from her
will stand far off, terrified at her torment.
They will weep and mourn 16and cry out:

" 'Woe! Woe, O great city,
dressed in fine linen, purple and
scarlet,
and glittering with gold, precious
stones and pearls!
17In one hour such great wealth has
been brought to ruin!'

"Every sea captain, and all who travel
by ship, the sailors, and all who earn their
living from the sea, will stand far off.
18When they see the smoke of her burning, they will exclaim, 'Was there ever a
city like this great city?' 19They will throw
dust on their heads, and with weeping
and mourning cry out:

" 'Woe! Woe, O great city,
where all who had ships on the sea
became rich through her wealth!
In one hour she has been brought to
ruin!
20Rejoice over her, O heaven!
Rejoice, saints and apostles and
prophets!
God has judged her for the way she
treated you.' "

21Then a mighty angel picked up a
boulder the size of a large millstone and
threw it into the sea, and said:

"With such violence
the great city of Babylon will be
thrown down,
never to be found again.
22The music of harpists and musicians,
flute players and trumpeters,
will never be heard in you again.
No workman of any trade
will ever be found in you again.
The sound of a millstone
will never be heard in you again.
23The light of a lamp
will never shine in you again.
The voice of bridegroom and bride
will never be heard in you again.
Your merchants were the world's great
men.
By your magic spell all the nations
were led astray.

Get a Load of This...

Hallelujah means "Praise Yah"—that is, "Praise the Lord." (*Yah* is an abbreviation for God's name, Yahweh.) God just finished judging the wicked—*finally!*—and these people in Revelation 19:1, 3, 4, 6 are so jazzed about it they just can't stop saying "Hallelujah!"

²⁴ In her was found the blood of prophets and of the saints,
    and of all who have been killed on the earth."

Hallelujah!

19 After this I heard what sounded like the roar of a great multitude in heaven shouting:

"Hallelujah!
Salvation and glory and power belong to our God,
²   for true and just are his judgments.
He has condemned the great prostitute
    who corrupted the earth by her adulteries.
He has avenged on her the blood of his servants."

³ And again they shouted:

"Hallelujah!
The smoke from her goes up for ever and ever."

⁴ The twenty-four elders and the four living creatures fell down and worshiped God, who was seated on the throne. And they cried:

"Amen, Hallelujah!"

⁵ Then a voice came from the throne, saying:

"Praise our God,
    all you his servants,
you who fear him,
    both small and great!"

⁶ Then I heard what sounded like a great multitude, like the roar of rushing waters and like loud peals of thunder, shouting:

"Hallelujah!
    For our Lord God Almighty reigns.
⁷ Let us rejoice and be glad
    and give him glory!
For the wedding of the Lamb has come,
    and his bride has made herself ready.
⁸ Fine linen, bright and clean,
    was given her to wear."
(Fine linen stands for the righteous acts of the saints.)

⁹ Then the angel said to me, "Write: 'Blessed are those who are invited to the wedding supper of the Lamb!'" And he added, "These are the true words of God."

¹⁰ At this I fell at his feet to worship him. But he said to me, "Do not do it! I am a fellow servant with you and with your brothers who hold to the testimony of Jesus. Worship God! For the testimony of Jesus is the spirit of prophecy."

The Rider on the White Horse

¹¹ I saw heaven standing open and there before me was a white horse, whose rider is called Faithful and True. With justice he judges and makes war. ¹² His eyes

are like blazing fire, and on his head are many crowns. He has a name written on him that no one knows but he himself. ¹³He is dressed in a robe dipped in blood, and his name is the Word of God. ¹⁴The armies of heaven were following him, riding on white horses and dressed in fine linen, white and clean. ¹⁵Out of his mouth comes a sharp sword with which to strike down the nations. "He will rule them with an iron scepter."ᵃ He treads the winepress of the fury of the wrath of God Almighty. ¹⁶On his robe and on his thigh he has this name written:

KING OF KINGS AND LORD OF LORDS.

¹⁷And I saw an angel standing in the sun, who cried in a loud voice to all the birds flying in midair, "Come, gather together for the great supper of God, ¹⁸so that you may eat the flesh of kings, generals, and mighty men, of horses and their riders, and the flesh of all people, free and slave, small and great."

¹⁹Then I saw the beast and the kings of the earth and their armies gathered together to make war against the rider on the horse and his army. ²⁰But the beast was captured, and with him the false prophet who had performed the miraculous signs on his behalf. With these signs he had deluded those who had received the mark of the beast and worshiped his image. The two of them were thrown alive into the fiery lake of burning sulfur. ²¹The rest of them were killed with the sword that came out of the mouth of the rider on the horse, and all the birds gorged themselves on their flesh.

The Thousand Years

20 And I saw an angel coming down out of heaven, having the key to the Abyss and holding in his hand a great chain. ²He seized the dragon, that ancient serpent, who is the devil, or Satan, and bound him for a thousand years. ³He threw him into the Abyss, and locked and sealed it over him, to keep him from deceiving the nations anymore until the thousand years were ended. After that, he must be set free for a short time.

⁴I saw thrones on which were seated those who had been given authority to judge. And I saw the souls of those who had been beheaded because of their testimony for Jesus and because of the word of God. They had not worshiped the beast or his image and had not received his mark on their foreheads or their hands. They came to life and reigned with Christ a thousand years. ⁵(The rest of the dead did not come to life until the thousand years were ended.) This is the first resurrection. ⁶Blessed and holy are those who have part in the first resurrection. The second death has no power over them, but they will be priests of God and of Christ and will reign with him for a thousand years.

ᵃ 15 Psalm 2:9

Gross!

"The devil ... was thrown into the lake of burning sulfur" (Revelation 20:10). Remember all those times you were discouraged because you felt the devil was getting the upper hand? Well, in the end, he gets his.

Satan's Doom

⁷When the thousand years are over, Satan will be released from his prison ⁸and will go out to deceive the nations in the four corners of the earth—Gog and Magog—to gather them for battle. In number they are like the sand on the seashore. ⁹They marched across the breadth of the earth and surrounded the camp of God's people, the city he loves. But fire came down from heaven and devoured them. ¹⁰And the devil, who deceived them, was thrown into the lake of burning sulfur, where the beast and the false prophet had been thrown. They will be tormented day and night for ever and ever.

The Dead Are Judged

¹¹Then I saw a great white throne and him who was seated on it. Earth and sky fled from his presence, and there was no place for them. ¹²And I saw the dead, great and small, standing before the throne, and books were opened. Another book was opened, which is the book of life. The dead were judged according to what they had done as recorded in the books. ¹³The sea gave up the dead that were in it, and death and Hades gave up the dead that were in them, and each person was judged according to what he had done. ¹⁴Then death and Hades were thrown into the lake of fire. The lake of fire is the second death. ¹⁵If anyone's name was not found written in the book of life, he was thrown into the lake of fire.

The New Jerusalem

21 Then I saw a new heaven and a new earth, for the first heaven and the first earth had passed away, and there was no longer any sea. ²I saw the Holy City, the new Jerusalem, coming down out of heaven from God, prepared as a bride beautifully dressed for her husband. ³And I heard a loud voice from the throne saying, "Now the dwelling of God is with men, and he will live with them. They will be his people, and God himself will be with them and be their God. ⁴He will wipe every tear from their eyes. There will be no more

GET SMARTER:

Red Hot Choices

READ REVELATION 20:11–15

If a dad pleads and warns his son not to smoke, and *especially* not to smoke in the firecracker factory next door—but the kid keeps on puffing near the pyros—who's going to be surprised if the Fourth of July comes early? We tend to focus a lot on God's love and forgiveness, and he *is* all that, but God has clearly let us know what will happen in the end of the world to those who refuse to be obedient to the truth. Those who know the truth and were warned, but rebel (Revelation 16:8–11), will deal with the consequences: punishment for eternity. Those who obey God and have received eternal life will live forever in heaven. We obey God because we love him and know that his way is best; but we *also* obey him because he is *God*, and we know that there are consequences for living in rebellion.

Your next reading is on page 1665.

death or mourning or crying or pain, for the old order of things has passed away."

⁵He who was seated on the throne said, "I am making everything new!" Then he said, "Write this down, for these words are trustworthy and true."

⁶He said to me: "It is done. I am the Alpha and the Omega, the Beginning and the End. To him who is thirsty I will give to drink without cost from the spring of the water of life. ⁷He who overcomes will inherit all this, and I will be his God and he will be my son. ⁸But the cowardly, the unbelieving, the vile, the murderers, the sexually immoral, those who practice magic arts, the idolaters and all liars—their place will be in the fiery lake of burning sulfur. This is the second death."

⁹One of the seven angels who had the seven bowls full of the seven last plagues came and said to me, "Come, I will show you the bride, the wife of the Lamb." ¹⁰And he carried me away in the Spirit to a mountain great and high, and showed me the Holy City, Jerusalem, coming down out of heaven from God. ¹¹It shone with the glory of God, and its brilliance was like that of a very precious jewel, like a jasper, clear as crystal. ¹²It had a great, high wall with twelve gates, and with twelve angels at the gates. On the gates were written the names of the twelve tribes of Israel. ¹³There were three gates on the east, three on the north, three on the south and three on the west. ¹⁴The wall of the city had twelve foundations, and on them were the names of the twelve apostles of the Lamb.

¹⁵The angel who talked with me had a measuring rod of gold to measure the city, its gates and its walls. ¹⁶The city was laid out like a square, as long as it was wide. He measured the city with the rod and found it to be 12,000 stadia*a* in length, and as wide and high as it is long. ¹⁷He measured its wall and it was 144 cubits*b* thick,*c* by man's measurement, which the angel was using. ¹⁸The wall was made of jasper, and the city of pure gold, as pure as glass. ¹⁹The foundations of the city walls were decorated with ev-

a 16 That is, about 1,400 miles (about 2,200 kilometers)
b 17 That is, about 200 feet (about 65 meters)
c 17 Or *high*

Family Reunion

READ REVELATION 21:1–5

When a friend or someone in your family dies, it can be rough dealing with the loss. You miss them so bad it hurts, and life just doesn't seem the same. If you loved them a lot, it's natural to cry. You need to mourn them, to take time to express all your emotions and sadness.

Jesus knows what it's like. But he wants you to know something *else*: If your loved ones were Christians, then they are in an unimaginably wonderful paradise *right now*, with no more pain or death—only eternal life forever! And the day you join them there, God will "wipe every tear from [your] eyes. There will be no more death or mourning or crying or pain" (verse 4). Can you imagine how wonderful it'll be to race through the streets of heaven and hug your loved ones?—never to be separated from them again!

Your next reading is on page 1667.

In Revelation 21:6, God says, "I am the Alpha and the Omega." These were the first and last letters of the Greek alphabet. God is not trying to say that he likes alphabet soup. By calling himself Mr. A-to-Z, he's letting us know that he's got all the bases covered.

ery kind of precious stone. The first foundation was jasper, the second sapphire, the third chalcedony, the fourth emerald, 20the fifth sardonyx, the sixth carnelian, the seventh chrysolite, the eighth beryl, the ninth topaz, the tenth chrysoprase, the eleventh jacinth, and the twelfth amethyst.[a] 21The twelve gates were twelve pearls, each gate made of a single pearl. The great street of the city was of pure gold, like transparent glass.

22I did not see a temple in the city, because the Lord God Almighty and the Lamb are its temple. 23The city does not need the sun or the moon to shine on it, for the glory of God gives it light, and the Lamb is its lamp. 24The nations will walk by its light, and the kings of the earth will bring their splendor into it. 25On no day will its gates ever be shut, for there will be no night there. 26The glory and honor of the nations will be brought into it. 27Nothing impure will ever enter it, nor will anyone who does what is shameful or deceitful, but only those whose names are written in the Lamb's book of life.

The River of Life

Then the angel showed me the river of the water of life, as clear as crystal, flowing from the throne of God and of the Lamb 2down the middle of the great street of the city. On each side of the river stood the tree of life, bearing twelve crops of fruit, yielding its fruit every month. And the leaves of the tree are for the healing of the nations. 3No longer will there be any curse. The throne of God and of the Lamb will be in the city, and his servants will serve him. 4They will see his face, and his name will be on their foreheads. 5There will be no more night. They will not need the light of a lamp or the light of the sun, for the Lord God will give them light. And they will reign for ever and ever.

6The angel said to me, "These words are trustworthy and true. The Lord, the God of the spirits of the prophets, sent his angel to show his servants the things that must soon take place."

Jesus Is Coming

7"Behold, I am coming soon! Blessed is he who keeps the words of the prophecy in this book."

8I, John, am the one who heard and saw these things. And when I had heard and seen them, I fell down to worship at the feet of the angel who had been showing them to me. 9But he said to me, "Do not do it! I am a fellow servant with you and with your brothers the prophets and of all who keep the words of this book. Worship God!"

10Then he told me, "Do not seal up the words of the prophecy of this book, because the time is near. 11Let him who does wrong continue to do wrong; let him

---

[a] 20 The precise identification of some of these precious stones is uncertain.

who is vile continue to be vile; let him who does right continue to do right; and let him who is holy continue to be holy."

12"Behold, I am coming soon! My reward is with me, and I will give to everyone according to what he has done. 13I am the Alpha and the Omega, the First and the Last, the Beginning and the End.

14"Blessed are those who wash their robes, that they may have the right to the tree of life and may go through the gates into the city. 15Outside are the dogs, those who practice magic arts, the sexually immoral, the murderers, the idolaters and everyone who loves and practices falsehood.

16"I, Jesus, have sent my angel to give you*a* this testimony for the churches. I am the Root and the Offspring of David, and the bright Morning Star."

17The Spirit and the bride say, "Come!" And let him who hears say, "Come!" Whoever is thirsty, let him come; and whoever wishes, let him take the free gift of the water of life.

18I warn everyone who hears the words of the prophecy of this book: If anyone adds anything to them, God will add to him the plagues described in this book. 19And if anyone takes words away from this book of prophecy, God will take away from him his share in the tree of life and in the holy city, which are described in this book.

20He who testifies to these things says, "Yes, I am coming soon."

Amen. Come, Lord Jesus.

21The grace of the Lord Jesus be with God's people. Amen.

a 16 The Greek is plural.

Wonderful Stuff!

READ REVELATION 22:12–17, 20–21

In verse 12, Jesus says, "Behold, I am coming soon! My reward is with me." If you're growing as a man of God—smarter, stronger, deeper and cooler—you'll be ready when Jesus returns. Once this world ends it'll be the beginning of a fabulous eternity. Think of standing before the throne of God, singing and shouting praises as part of a vast multitude of millions upon millions of people from every nation, tribe and language. Think of all the rewards Jesus has waiting for you. Think of all of the wonder that God created in paradise before sin came. God *meant* for you to enjoy those things, and enjoy fantastic times with him. One day you'll live in a paradise that's beyond your wildest imagination—minus any pain or sorrow or disease or poverty. Just endless fun with no bad times ...*ever!* Is that incredible to think about? Hard to imagine? Well, it's true! It's like the best day that you ever had, multiplied by ten or even ten thousand." 'I am coming soon.' Amen. Come, Lord Jesus" (verse 20).

Your next reading is ...Wait! There *are* no more *next* readings! This is the last one!

Weights & Measures

	BIBLICAL UNIT	APPROXIMATE AMERICAN EQUIVALENT	APPROXIMATE METRIC EQUIVALENT
WEIGHTS	talent (60 minas)	75 pounds	34 kilograms
	mina (50 shekels)	1 1/4 pounds	0.6 kilogram
	shekel (2 bekas)	2/5 ounce	11.5 grams
	pim (2/3 shekel)	1/3 ounce	7.6 grams
	beka (10 gerahs)	1/5 ounce	5.5 grams
	gerah	1/50 ounce	0.6 gram
LENGTH	cubit	18 inches	0.5 meter
	span	9 inches	23 centimeters
	handbreadth	3 inches	8 centimeters
CAPACITY			
Dry Measure	cor [homer] (10 ephahs)	6 bushels	220 liters
	lethek (5 ephahs)	3 bushels	110 liters
	ephah (10 omers)	3/5 bushel	22 liters
	seah (1/3 ephah)	7 quarts	7.3 liters
	omer (1/10 ephah)	2 quarts	2 liters
	cab (1/18 ephah)	1 quart	1 liter
Liquid Measure	bath (1 ephah)	6 gallons	22 liters
	hin (1/6 bath)	4 quarts	4 liters
	log (1/72 bath)	1/3 quart	0.3 liter

The figures of the table are calculated on the basis of a shekel equaling 11.5 grams, a cubit equaling 18 inches and an ephah equaling 22 liters. The quart referred to is either a dry quart (slightly larger than a liter) or a liquid quart (slightly smaller than a liter), whichever is applicable. The ton referred to in the footnotes is the American ton of 2,000 pounds.

This table is based upon the best available information, but it is not intended to be mathematically precise; like the measurement equivalents in the footnotes, it merely gives approximate amounts and distances. Weights and measures differed somewhat at various times and places in the ancient world. There is uncertainty particularly about the ephah and the bath; further discoveries may shed more light on these units of capacity.

Index to Deeper, Smarter, Stronger, Cooler

Do you want to read about one of the 252 Tracks all the way through the Bible? Check out this index. It shows you the page number for each reading under each track.

Old Testament

SMARTER

STRONGER

Index to Deeper, Smarter, Stronger, Cooler

Index to Deeper, Smarter, Stronger, Cooler

Index to Deeper, Smarter, Stronger, Cooler

New Testament

1230, 1231, 1243, 1248, 1251, 1255,
1258, 1262, 1278, 1286, 1287, 1289,
1294, 1306, 1312, 1338, 1345, 1348,
1356, 1368, 1371, 1375, 1382, 1392,
1400, 1401, 1402, 1407, 1416, 1422,
1427, 1431, 1434, 1438, 1457, 1459,
1471, 1476, 1499, 1511, 1535, 1539,
1577, 1588, 1591, 1592, 1601, 1608,
1623, 1627, 1640, 1645, 1668

1233, 1241, 1254, 1256, 1280, 1297,
1300, 1318, 1320, 1336, 1342, 1352,
1363, 1364, 1377, 1403, 1410, 1439,
1482, 1489, 1494, 1500, 1514, 1516,
1523, 1525, 1527, 1530, 1551, 1584,
1597, 1606, 1607, 1618, 1628, 1632,
1635, 1637, 1665

New Testament
Full-page biographies

Here's what I think...

Here's what I think...

Here's what **I** think...